wwnorton.com/naal

The StudySpace site that accompanies *The Norton Anthology of American Literature* is FREE, but you will need the code below to register for a password that will allow you to access the copyrighted materials on the site.

AMER-ICAN

THE NORTON ANTHOLOGY OF

AMERICAN LITERATURE

EIGHTH EDITION

VOLUME B: 1820–1865

VOLUME A

Beginnings to 1700 • FRANKLIN

American Literature 1700–1820 • GURA

Native American Literatures • KRUPAT

VOLUME B

American Literature 1820–1865 • LEVINE • KRUPAT

VOLUME C

American Literature 1865–1914 • BAYM • LEVINE • KRUPAT • REESMAN

VOLUME D

American Literature 1914–1945

LOEFFELHOLZ

VOLUME E

American Literature since 1945

KLINKOWITZ • WALLACE

Wayne Franklin
PROFESSOR AND HEAD, ENGLISH
UNIVERSITY OF CONNECTICUT

Philip F. Gura
WILLIAM S. NEWMAN DISTINGUISHED PROFESSOR OF AMERICAN LITERATURE AND CULTURE
UNIVERSITY OF NORTH CAROLINA, CHAPEL HILL

Jerome Klinkowitz
UNIVERSITY DISTINGUISHED SCHOLAR AND PROFESSOR OF ENGLISH
UNIVERSITY OF NORTHERN IOWA

Arnold Krupat
PROFESSOR OF LITERATURE
SARAH LAWRENCE COLLEGE

Robert S. Levine
PROFESSOR OF ENGLISH AND DISTINGUISHED SCHOLAR-TEACHER
UNIVERSITY OF MARYLAND, COLLEGE PARK

Mary Loeffelholz
PROFESSOR OF ENGLISH
NORTHEASTERN UNIVERSITY

Jeanne Campbell Reesman
PROFESSOR OF ENGLISH
UNIVERSITY OF TEXAS AT SAN ANTONIO

Patricia B. Wallace
MARY AUGUSTA SCOTT PROFESSOR OF ENGLISH
VASSAR COLLEGE

THE NORTON ANTHOLOGY OF AMERICAN LITERATURE

EIGHTH EDITION

Nina Baym, *General Editor*

SWANLUND CHAIR AND CENTER FOR ADVANCED STUDY PROFESSOR EMERITA OF ENGLISH
JUBILEE PROFESSOR OF LIBERAL ARTS AND SCIENCES
University of Illinois at Urbana-Champaign

Robert S. Levine, *Associate General Editor*

PROFESSOR OF ENGLISH AND DISTINGUISHED SCHOLAR-TEACHER
University of Maryland, College Park

VOLUME B: 1820–1865

W · W · NORTON & COMPANY
NEW YORK · LONDON

W. W. Norton & Company has been independent since its founding in 1923, when William Warder Norton and Mary D. Herter Norton first published lectures delivered at the People's Institute, the adult education division of New York City's Cooper Union. The firm soon expanded its program beyond the Institute, publishing books by celebrated academics from America and abroad. By midcentury, the two major pillars of Norton's publishing program—trade books and college texts—were firmly established. In the 1950s, the Norton family transferred control of the company to its employees, and today—with a staff of four hundred and a comparable number of trade, college, and professional titles published each year—W. W. Norton & Company stands as the largest and oldest publishing house owned wholly by its employees.

Editor: Julia Reidhead
Associate Editor: Carly Fraser Doria
Managing Editor, College: Marian Johnson
Manuscript Editors: Michael Fleming, Katharine Ings, Candace Levy, Susan Joseph, Pam Lawson
Electronic Media Editor: Eileen Connell
Production Manager: Benjamin Reynolds
Marketing Manager, Literature: Kimberly Bowers
Photo Editor: Stephanie Romeo
Photo Research: Jane Sanders Miller
Permissions Manager: Megan Jackson
Permissions Clearing: Margaret Gorenstein
Text Design: Jo Anne Metsch
Art Director: Rubina Yeh

The text of this book is composed in Fairfield Medium with the display set in Aperto.

Composition: The Westchester Book Group
Manufacturing: R. R. Donnelley & Sons—Crawfordsville, IN

Library of Congress Cataloging-in-Publication Data has been applied for.

ISBN 978-0-393-93477-9

W. W. Norton & Company, Inc., 500 Fifth Avenue, New York, NY 10110-0017
wwnorton.com

W. W. Norton & Company Ltd., Castle House, 75/76 Wells Street, London W1T 3QT

1 2 3 4 5 6 7 8 9 0

Contents

Preface to the Eighth Edition

This edition of *The Norton Anthology of American Literature* is the last for me as General Editor, and I am delighted to announce that Robert S. Levine, the editor of Volume B, will take over as General Editor for the next and subsequent editions. Here he joins me as Associate Editor; together we have continued the work for which Norton has achieved its leading position among American literature anthologies. It has been a great pleasure to work on this anthology, to make contact with teachers and students around the country—indeed around the world. I know I leave *The Norton Anthology of American Literature* in immensely capable hands.

From the anthology's inception in 1979, the editors have had three main aims: first, to present a rich and substantial enough variety of works to enable teachers to build courses according to their own ideals (thus, teachers are offered more authors and more selections than they will probably use in any one course); second, to make the anthology self-sufficient by featuring many works in their entirety along with extensive selections for individual authors; third, to balance traditional interests with developing critical concerns in a way that points to a coherent American literary history. As early as 1979, we anthologized work by Anne Bradstreet, Mary Rowlandson, Sarah Kemble Knight, Phillis Wheatley, Margaret Fuller, Harriet Beecher Stowe, Frederick Douglass, Sarah Orne Jewett, Kate Chopin, Mary E. Wilkins Freeman, Booker T. Washington, Charles Chesnutt, Edith Wharton, W. E. B. Du Bois, and other writers who were not yet part of a standard canon. Yet we never short-changed writers like Franklin, Emerson, Whitman, Hawthorne, Melville, Dickinson, Hemingway, Fitzgerald, and Faulkner, whose work students expected to read in their American literature courses, and whom teachers then and now would not think of doing without.

Although the so-called canon wars of the 1980s and 1990s have subsided, they initiated a review of our understanding of American literature that has enlarged the number and diversity of authors now recognized as contributors to the totality of American literature. The traditional writers, who look different in this expanded context, also appear different according to which of their works are selected. Teachers and students remain committed to the idea of the literary—that writers strive to produce artifacts that are both intellectually serious and formally skillful—but believe more than ever that writers should also be understood in relation to their cultural and historical situations. In endeavoring to do justice to these complex realities, we have worked, as in previous editions, with detailed suggestions from many teachers and, through those teachers, the students who use the anthology. Thanks to questionnaires, comment cards, face-to-face and phone discussions, letters, and email, we have been able to listen to those for whom this book is intended. For this Eighth Edition, we have drawn on the careful commentary of over 200 reviewers.

Our new materials continue the work of broadening the canon by representing 13 new writers in depth, without sacrificing widely assigned writers, many of whose selections have been reconsidered, reselected, and expanded. Our aim is always to provide extensive enough selections to do the writers justice, including complete works wherever possible. To the 34 complete longer texts already in the anthology—among them Hawthorne's *The Scarlet Letter* and Kate Chopin's *The Awakening*—we have added Margaret Fuller's "The Great Lawsuit," August Wilson's *Fences,* and Katherine Anne Porter's *Pale Horse, Pale Rider.* Two complete works—Eugene O'Neill's *Long Day's Journey into Night* and Tennessee Williams's *A Streetcar Named Desire*—are exclusive to *The Norton Anthology of American Literature.* Charles Brockden Brown, Louisa May Alcott, Upton Sinclair, Mourning Dove, Martin Luther King Jr., and Junot Díaz are among more than a dozen writers new to the Eighth Edition, which has expanded and in some cases reconfigured such central figures as Emerson, Hawthorne, Melville, Dickinson, and Twain, offering new approaches in the headnotes and section introductions. In fact, over the last two editions, the headnotes and, in many cases, selections for such frequently assigned authors as Benjamin Franklin, Washington Irving, James Fenimore Cooper, William Cullen Bryant, Lydia Maria Child, Henry Wadsworth Longfellow, Ralph Waldo Emerson, Harriet Beecher Stowe, Mark Twain, William Dean Howells, Henry James, Kate Chopin, W. E. B. Du Bois, Edith Wharton, Willa Cather, and William Faulkner have been revised, updated, and in some cases entirely rewritten in light of recent scholarship. The Eighth Edition further expands its selections of women writers and writers from diverse ethnic, racial, and regional backgrounds—always with attention to the critical acclaim that recognizes their contributions to the American literary record. New and recently added writers such as Sarah Winnemucca and Jane Johnston Schoolcraft, more selections from writers such as Zitkala Ša, and a cluster on "The Ghost Dance and Wounded Knee," all introduced and annotated by Native American specialist Arnold Krupat, enable teachers to bring early Native American writing and oratory into their syllabuses, or should they prefer, to focus on these selections as a free-standing unit leading toward the moment after 1945 when Native writers fully entered the mainstream of literary activity.

We are pleased to continue our popular innovation of topical gatherings of short texts that illuminate the cultural, historical, intellectual, and literary concerns of their respective periods. Designed to be taught in a class period or two, or used as background, each of the 14 clusters consists of brief, carefully excerpted primary and (in one case) secondary texts, about 6–10 per cluster, and an introduction. Diverse voices—many new to the anthology—highlight a range of views current when writers of a particular time period were active, and thus allow students better to understand some of the large issues that were being debated at particular historical moments. For example, in "Slavery, Race, and the Making of American Literature," texts by David Walker, William Lloyd Garrison, Angelina Grimké, Sojourner Truth, and Martin R. Delany speak to the great paradox of pre–Civil War

America, addressed by numerous authors of the period: the contradictory rupture between the realities of slavery and the nation's ideals of freedom.

The Eighth Edition strengthens this feature with six new and revised clusters attuned to the requests of teachers. To help students address the controversy over race and aesthetics in *Adventures of Huckleberry Finn,* we introduce a cluster in Volume C that shows what some of the leading critics of the past few decades have thought was at stake in reading and interpreting Twain's canonical novel. Entitled "Critical Controversy: Race and the Ending of *Adventures of Huckleberry Finn,*" the cluster brings together selections by Toni Morrison, Jane Smiley, Leo Marx, Justin Kaplan, Julius Lester, Shelley Fisher Fishkin, and David L. Smith. For the contemporary period in Volume E, we print for the first time "Creative Nonfiction," a much-requested topic showcasing a newly important (and highly popular) literary genre, with selections by Edward Abbey, Barry Lopez, Jamaica Kincaid, Joan Didion, and Edwidge Danticat, among others. New to Volume A is a cluster on "First Encounters: Early European Accounts of Native Americans," while Volume B has a revised cluster, "Section, Region, Nation, Hemisphere," which puts new emphasis on U.S. imperial ambitions in the western hemisphere. Volume C also includes "Debates over 'Americanization,'" with selections by Theodore Roosevelt and others, and a new cluster on "The Ghost Dance and Wounded Knee."

The Eighth Edition of *The Norton Anthology of American Literature* features a dramatic expansion of our illustrations, including not only the color plates so popular in the last edition, but also over 120 black-and-white illustrations added throughout the volumes. In selecting color plates—from Juan de la Cosa's world map at the start of the sixteenth century to *The Gates* by Christo and Jeanne-Claude at the beginning of the twenty-first—the editors aimed to provide images relevant to literary works in the anthology while depicting arts and artifacts representative of each era. Throughout the five volumes of the Eighth Edition, we have similarly added visually striking black-and-white images that will provoke discussion. In addition, graphic works—segments from Art Spiegelman's canonical graphic novel *Maus* and from the colonial children's classic *The New-England Primer,* a facsimile page of Emily Dickinson manuscript, and an original illustration from Twain's *Roughing It,* along with the many new illustrations—open possibilities for teaching visual texts.

Period-by-Period Revisions

Volume A, Beginnings to 1820. "Beginnings to 1700," edited by Wayne Franklin, continues to feature narratives by early European explorers of the North American continent as they encountered and attempted to make sense of the diverse cultures they met, and as they attempted to justify their aim of claiming the territory for Europeans. These are precisely the issues foregrounded by the new cluster on "First Encounters," which gathers writings by Hernán Cortés, Samuel de Champlain, Robert Juet, and others. In addition to the recently added material from *The Bay Psalm Book,* Roger Williams, Edward Taylor, and *The New-England Primer,* we have added for this edition a contemporary telling by Navajo Irvin Morris of the Navajo Creation Story and Cotton Mather's "Bonifacius." We continue to offer the complete text of

Rowlandson's enormously influential *A Narrative of the Captivity and Restoration of Mrs. Mary Rowlandson.* The heightened attention in this section to the combined religious and territorial aspirations of the Anglo settlers, which fail to take account of the perspectives of the Native American writers featured in Volume A, gives students a fuller sense of the inevitable conflicts ensuing from the European perception that North America was a "New World" rather than a long-settled world with its own history and traditions. We note, too, the important role of the experiences of, and narratives by, women in the early European settlement of the future United States.

In "American Literature 1700–1820," edited by Philip Gura, we approach the eighteenth century as a period of consolidation and development in an emergent American literature. The inclusion of a long excerpt from one of Charles Brockden Brown's major novels, *Edgar Huntly*, new to the Eighth Edition, calls attention to the Americanization of such important literary developments as the gothic. We have also added new selections by Benjamin Franklin and Thomas Jefferson. Understanding of the emergence of an "American" self is augmented by Franklin's *Autobiography*, included complete by teacher request, and Royall Tyler's popular play *The Contrast.* Recently added is the complete text of Hannah Foster's novel *The Coquette*, which uses a real-life tragedy to meditate on the proper role of well-bred women in the new republic and testifies to the existence of a female audience for the popular novels of the period. The cluster "Women's Poetry: From Manuscript to Print," with verse by six poets—among them Mercy Otis Warren, Sarah Wentworth Morton, and Annis Boudinot Stockton—indicates the importance of female literacy and the new sense among women that their writing could have political effect. A second cluster, edited by Arnold Krupat, "Native Americans: Contact and Conflict," collects speeches and accounts by Pontiac, Samson Occom, Chief Logan (as cited by Thomas Jefferson), Red Jacket, and Tecumseh, which, as a group, underscore a centuries-long pattern of initial friendly contact mutating into bitter and violent conflict between Native Americans and whites. This cluster, which focuses on Native Americans' points of view, wonderfully complements the new cluster on "First Encounters," which focuses on European colonizers' points of view.

Volume B, American Literature 1820–1865. Under the editorship of Robert S. Levine, this volume is now much more diverse. Emerson's *Nature*, Hawthorne's *Scarlet Letter*, Thoreau's *Walden*, Douglass's *Narrative*, and Whitman's *Song of Myself* are still complete in this volume, as well as novellas by Melville, Davis's *Life in the Iron Mills,* and other frequently assigned works. Aware of the important role of African American writers in the period, the omnipresence of race and slavery as literary and political themes, and the recognition of literary value in a previously ignored population, we have recently added two major African American writers, William Wells Brown and Frances E. W. Harper, as well as Douglass's complete novella, "The Heroic Slave." Thoreau's "Plea for Captain John Brown," more chapters from Stowe's *Uncle Tom's Cabin* (including a new chapter for the Eighth Edition), and the cluster "Slavery, Race, and the Making of American Literature" also help to remind students of how central slavery was to the literary and political life of the nation during this period. The volume also includes the newly revised cluster "Section, Region, Nation, Hemisphere," in which writers from various regions—such as the northerner Daniel Webster, the southerner William Gilmore Simms, and the Mexican Lorenzo de Zavala—convey their differing perspectives on a "national" literature while reflecting on the extraordinary enlargement of U.S. territory following the war with Mexico in 1846–48—land stretching to the Pacific Ocean that more than doubled the nation's size. The writings by Zavala, James Whitfield, and Julia Ward Howe in particular, added for this edition, offer new perspectives on expansionism and nation in a hemispheric context. "Native Americans: Resistance and Removal," edited by Arnold Krupat, gathers oratory and writings—by Native Americans such as Black Hawk, Petelasharo, Elias Boudinot, and the collective authors of the Cherokee Memorials as well as by whites such as Ralph Waldo Emerson—protesting Andrew Jackson's ruthless national policy of Indian removal. Political themes, far from diluting the literary imagination of American authors, served to inspire some of the most memorable writing of the day.

Women writers recently added to Volume B include Lydia Huntley Sigourney and the Native American writer Jane Johnston Schoolcraft. Recently added prose fiction includes chapters from Cooper's *Last of the Mohicans*, Sedgwick's *Hope Leslie*, and Melville's *Moby-Dick*, along with Poe's "The Black Cat" and Hawthorne's "Wakefield." By instructors' request, we increased the representation of poems by Longfellow and Whittier; poetry by Emily Dickinson is now presented in the texts recently established by R. W. Franklin (we retain the traditional Thomas Johnson numbers in brackets for reference) and includes a facsimile page from Fascicle 10. For the Eighth Edition there are a number of substantial additions: new poems and letters by Dickinson; the complete text of Margaret Fuller's important feminist essay "The Great Lawsuit"; a new section on Louisa May Alcott featuring her Civil War story "My Contraband" and a chapter from her best-selling *Little Women*. Other selections added to this edition include Washington Irving's "The Author's Account of Himself," a key chapter from Harriet Beecher Stowe's *Uncle Tom's Cabin* (on the death of Little Eva), Longfellow's poem "Hawthorne," Emerson's "Circles," Lydia Maria Child's influential antislavery story "The Quadroons," Fanny Fern's review of Whitman's *Leaves of Grass*, and Frances Harper's "Learning to Read."

Volume C, American Literature 1865–1914. Edited by Nina Baym, Robert S. Levine, and Jeanne Campbell Reesman, this volume over the last two editions has taken on a striking new look. To our well-received complete longer works—Twain's *Adventures of Huckleberry Finn*, Chopin's *The Awakening*, and James's *Daisy Miller*—we have added complete texts of Stephen Crane's *Maggie: A Girl of the Streets* and Abraham Cahan's *The Imported Bridegroom*, as well as chapters from Theodore Dreiser's *Sister Carrie* and Twain's *Roughing It*. Also recently added are selections from Twain's *Letters from the Earth*, Edith Wharton's "The Other Two" and "Roman Fever," and works by Sui Sin Far, Zitkala Ša, Joel Chandler Harris, and Ambrose Bierce. Along with additional writings by Walt Whitman and Emily Dickinson to help students bridge the years between the Civil War and the industrializing 1890s, we include James Weldon Johnson, Paul Laurence Dunbar, and Emma Lazarus. The recent additions of Maria Ruíz de Burton, Pauline Hopkins, Sarah Winnemucca, Mourning Dove, and Ida Wells-Barnett underscore the emergence of a literary culture in which women from diverse ethnic, racial, and regional backgrounds became part of American literary culture. Two clusters take up key political and literary disputes from the era: "Debates over 'Americanization,'" which has been newly revised for the Eighth Edition, addresses the sense of crisis engendered by the huge influx of immigrants in the century's last two decades, the relentless effort to deny Native Americans their rights unless they entirely abandoned their traditions, the debates over African American citizenship, and the question of national boundaries in an age of imperialist expansion that took the United States to far-flung places around the globe. Texts by Frederick Jackson Turner, Theodore Roosevelt, José Martí, Jane Addams, and Senator Albert Beveridge ask repeatedly, Who is an American? Literary movements attuned to these divisions are considered in "Realism and Naturalism," where critical writings by William Dean Howells, Henry James, Frank Norris, Theodore Dreiser, and Jack London illuminate the turn to realism and naturalism, styles developed to represent and deal with the rapidly changing character of the American nation as it entered the industrial era with a markedly more diverse and larger population.

We have added a number of new selections. For the first time, we include a chapter from Upton Sinclair's influential reformist novel *The Jungle* (a novel that continues to have a profound influence on how we think about the production and consumption of meat). We now include a complete short story by Pauline Hopkins, "A Dash for Liberty," which is based on the same slave rebellion that Frederick Douglass wrote about in "The Heroic Slave." By request of instructors and students, we have added two new stories by Kate Chopin, "Desiree's Baby" and "The Story of an Hour," and the volume also includes new selections by Sarah Orne Jewett, Sui Sin Far, Mary Austin, and Mourning Dove.

Volume D, American Literature 1914–1945. Edited by Mary Loeffelholz, Volume D offers a number of complete longer works—Eugene O'Neill's *Long Day's Journey into Night* (exclusive to the Norton Anthology), Nella Larsen's eminently teachable *Quicksand*, William Faulkner's *As I Lay Dying*, and Willa Cather's *My Ántonia*, which was returned by instructor request to the Seventh Edition and remains a popular work with instructors and students alike. The poet Mina Loy's experimental work and reconsidered selections by Ezra Pound, T. S. Eliot, Marianne Moore, Hart Crane, and Langston Hughes encourage students and teachers to contemplate the interrelation of modernist aesthetics with ethnic, regional, and popular writing. Two illuminating clusters address central events of the modern period. In "World War I and Its Aftermath," writings by Ernest Hemingway, Gertrude Stein, Jessie Redmon Fauset, and others explore sharply divided views on the U.S. role in World War I, as well as the radicalizing effect of modern warfare—with 365,000 American casualties—on contemporary writing. And in "Modernist Manifestos," F. T. Marinetti, Mina Loy, Ezra Pound, Willa Cather, William Carlos Williams, and Langston Hughes show how the manifesto as a form exerted a powerful influence on international modernism in all the arts. Additions to the Eighth Edition include Faulkner's popular "A Rose for Emily," Katherine Anne Porter's novella *Pale Horse, Pale Rider*, Gertrude

Stein's "Objects," and Jean Toomer's "Blood Burning Man." We also print for the first time Pietro Di Donato's "Christ in Concrete," one of the most popular works of the period, which helps to bring a new ethnic and class perspective into Volume D.

Volume E, American Literature since 1945. Volume E, jointly edited by Jerome Klinkowitz and Patricia B. Wallace, features a period introduction in which prose and poetry intermingle and for which "Postwar" no longer explains a period that grows longer with every edition. The result is a rich representation of the period's literary activity, and a more accurate presentation of the writers themselves, many of whom write in multiple genres. The volume continues to offer the complete texts of Tennessee Williams's *A Streetcar Named Desire* (exclusive to this anthology), Arthur Miller's *Death of a Salesman*, David Mamet's *Glengarry Glen Ross*, Allen Ginsberg's *Howl*, Sam Shepard's *True West*, and Louise Glück's long poem *October*, and we have added the complete text of August Wilson's play *Fences*. Introduced in the Seventh Edition, Art Spiegelman's prize-winning *Maus* opens possibilities for teaching the graphic novel. Another innovation from the Seventh Edition was the inclusion of teachable stand-alone segments from important novels by Saul Bellow (*The Adventures of Augie March*), Kurt Vonnegut (*Slaughterhouse-Five*), Rudolfo Anaya (*Bless Me, Ultima*), and Jack Kerouac (*Big Sur*), and we continue to print those chapters. Newly anthologized writers include Stephen Dixon, Martin Luther King, Jr., Thomas McGuane, Kay Ryan, and the Dominican-American fiction writer Junot Díaz, whose 2008 novel, *The Brief Wondrous Life of Oscar Wao*, won the Pulitzer Prize and was an international sensation. We have also added new selections for Elizabeth Bishop, Richard Powers, Grace Paley, Robert Haas, and a number of other writers. Two clusters, one entirely new, add literary and topical context to this diverse volume. "Postmodernist Manifestos," with texts by Ronald Sukenick, William H. Gass, Hunter S. Thompson, Charles Olson, Frank O'Hara, Elizabeth Bishop, A. R. Ammons, and Audre Lorde, shows how many literary artists saw experimentation in poetry and fiction as the best way to register politics and culture in the postwar era. The cluster pairs nicely with "Modernist Manifestos" in Volume D. New to the Eighth Edition is a cluster on "Creative Nonfiction." Here students are introduced to writers such as Joan Didion and Edward Abbey who self-consciously blend fiction and nonfiction, creating works that over the past few decades have become enormously popular and influential.

In all, we are delighted to offer this revised Eighth Edition to teachers and students, and we welcome your comments.

Additional Resources from the Publisher

The Eighth Edition retains the paperback splits format that has been welcomed by instructors and students for its flexibility and portability. This format accommodates the many instructors who use the anthology in a two-semester survey, but allows for mixing and matching the five volumes in a variety of courses organized by period or topic, at levels from introductory to advanced. To give instructors even more flexibility, the publisher is making available the full list of 220 Norton Critical Editions, including such frequently assigned novels as Harriet Beecher Stowe's *Uncle Tom's Cabin*, Herman Melville's *Moby-Dick*, Edith Wharton's *The House of Mirth*, and William Faulkner's *The Sound and the Fury*, among many others. A Norton Critical Edition can be included with either package or any individual paperback-split volume for free. Each Norton Critical Edition gives students an authoritative, carefully annotated text accompanied by rich contextual and critical materials prepared by an expert in the subject.

For students using *The Norton Anthology of American Literature*, the publisher provides a wealth of resources on the free StudySpace website (wwnorton.com/naal). Students who activate the password included in each new copy of the anthology gain access to more than 70 reading-comprehension quizzes with extensive feedback; bulleted period summaries and period review quizzes with feedback; timelines; maps; audio readings of public domain texts; Literary Workshops that show students step-by-step how to read, analyze, and respond in writing to a work of literature; and a new "Literary Places" feature that uses Google Tours tools to let students (virtually) visit Thoreau's Walden Pond, Faulkner's Oxford, Mississippi, home, Cather's Nebraska plains, and other literary places. The rich gathering of content on StudySpace is designed to help students understand individual works and appreciate the places, sounds, and sights of literature.

The publisher also provides extensive instructor-support materials. Designed to enhance large or small lecture environments, the Instructor Resource Disc, expanded for the Eighth Edition, features more than 300 images with explanatory captions; lecture PowerPoint slides for each period introduction and for most topic clusters°d audio recordings (MP3). Much praised by both new and experienced instructors, *Teaching with The Norton Anthology of American Literature: A Guide for Instructors* by Edward Whitley, Lehigh University, and Bruce Michelson, University of Illinois at Urbana-Champaign, provides detailed reading lists for a variety of approaches—the historical approach, the "major authors" approach, the literary traditions approach, and the approach by genre or theme. Each author/work entry offers teaching suggestions, discussion questions, and suggestions for incorporating multimedia from the Instructor Resource Disc, the *American Passages* website, as well as other outside resources. The Guide is available both in print and in a searchable online format. Finally, Norton Coursepacks bring high-quality digital media into a new or existing online course. The Coursepacks include all content from the StudySpace website, short-answer questions with suggested answers, and a bank of discussion questions adapted from the Guide. Norton's Coursepacks are available in a variety of formats, including Blackboard/WebCT, Desire2Learn, Angel, and Moodle, at no cost to instructors or students.

Instructors who adopt *The Norton Anthology of American Literature* have access to an extensive array of films and videos. In addition to videos of the plays by O'Neill, Williams, Miller, Mamet, and Shepard in the anthology, segments of the award-winning video series *American Passages: A Literary Survey* are available without charge on orders of specified quantities of the Norton Anthology. Funded by Annenberg/CPB, produced by Oregon Public

Broadcasting, and developed with the Norton Anthology as its exclusive companion anthology, *American Passages* contains sixteen segments, each covering a literary movement or period by exploring two or three authors in depth. The videos are supported by the *American Passages* Archive, a searchable online archive of over 3,000 items, including visual art, audio files, primary-source materials, and additional texts, which may be accessed through the link on the StudySpace student website. A print instructor's guide and student guide are also available. For information about the videos, contact your Norton representative.

Editorial Procedures

As in past editions, editorial features—period introductions, headnotes, annotations, and bibliographies—are designed to be concise yet full and to give students necessary information without imposing an interpretation. The editors have updated all apparatus in response to new scholarship: period introductions have been substantially rewritten, as have many headnotes. All Selected Bibliographies and each period's general-resources bibliographies categorized by Reference Works, Histories, and Literary Criticism have been thoroughly updated. The Eighth Edition retains three editorial features that help students place their reading in historical and cultural context—a Texts/Contexts timeline following each period introduction, a map on the front endpaper of each volume, and a chronological chart, on the back endpaper, showing the lifespans of many of the writers anthologized.

Our policy has been to reprint each text in the form that accords, as far as it is possible to determine, to the intention of its author. There is one exception: we have modernized most spellings and (very sparingly) the punctuation in Volume A on the principle that archaic spellings and typography pose unnecessary problems for beginning students. We have used square brackets to indicate titles supplied by the editors for the convenience of students. Whenever a portion of a text has been omitted, we have indicated that omission with three asterisks. If the omitted portion is important for following the plot or argument, we give a brief summary within the text or in a footnote. After each work, we cite (when known) the date of composition on the left and the date of first publication on the right; in some instances, the latter is followed by the date of a revised edition for which the author was responsible.

The editors have benefited from commentary offered by hundreds of teachers throughout the country. Those teachers who prepared detailed critiques, or who offered special help in preparing texts, are listed under Acknowledgments, on a separate page. We also thank the many people at Norton who contributed to the Eighth Edition: Julia Reidhead, who supervised the Eighth Edition; Marian Johnson, managing editor, college; Carly Fraser Doria, associate editor; Eileen Connell, electronic media editor; Michael Fleming, Candace Levy, Katharine Ings, and Susan Joseph, manuscript editors; Pam Lawson, Jack Borrebach, Sophie Hagen, Diane Cipollone, project editors; Hannah Blaisdell, editorial assistant; Benjamin Reynolds, production manager; Jo Anne Metsch, designer; Trish Marx, manager, photo department; Stephanie Romeo, photo editor; Jane Sanders Miller, photo researcher. Debra Morton Hoyt, art director; Megan Jackson, permissions manager; and Margaret Gorenstein, who cleared permissions. We also wish to acknowledge our debt to the late George P. Brockway, former president and chairman at Norton, who invented this anthology, and to M. H. Abrams, Norton's advisor on English texts. All have helped us to create an anthology that, more than ever, is testimony to the continuing richness of American literary traditions.

NINA BAYM, General Editor
ROBERT S. LEVINE, Associate General Editor

Acknowledgments

Among our many critics, advisors, and friends, the following were of especial help toward the preparation of the Eighth Edition, either with advice or by providing critiques of particular periods of the anthology: David L. Anderson (Butler County Community College); Booker T. Anthony (Fayetteville State University); George Bailey (Northern Essex Community College); Anne Baker (North Carolina State University); Jack Barbera (University of Mississippi); Philip Barnard (University of Kansas); Brian Bartlett (Saint Mary's University); Richard Baskin (Gordon College); John Battenburg (California Polytechnic State University); Geraldine Cannon Becker (University of Maine–Fort Kent); Carolyn Bergonzo; Laura Bloxham (Whitworth College Spokane); Hester Blum (Penn State); Andrew Bodenrader (Manhattanville College); Constance Bracewell (University of Arizona); Norton Bradley Christie (Erskine College); David Brottman (Iowa State University); Adam Burkey (Miami University Oxford); Jill Hunter Burrill (Bunker Hill Community College); Dan Butcher (University of Alabama); Gina Caison (University of Alabama at Birmingham); Linda Camarasana (Queens College); Pat Campbell (Lake Sumter Community College); Marci Carrasquillo (Simpson College); Vincent Casaregola (Saint Louis University); Karen Chandler (University of Louisville); Wayne Chandler (Northwest Missouri State University); Chiung-huei Chang (National Taiwan Normal University); Kathryn Chittick (Trent University); Deborah Christie (University of Miama); Paul Colby (North Carolina State University); Brian Condrey (Yuba Community College); Ken Cox (Florence-Darlington Technical College); Kristine Dassinger (Genesee Community College); Clark David (University of Denver); Cynthia Davis (UCSB); Marybeth Davis (Liberty University). Laura Dawkins (Murray State University); Bruce Degi (Metropolitan State College of Denver); Regina Dilgen (Palm Beach Community College); Christine Doyle (Central Connecticut State University); Michael Drexler (Bucknell University); Robert Dunne (Central Connecticut State University); Gregory Eiselein (Kansas State University); Monika Elbert (Montclair State University); Hilary Emmett (University of Queensland, Australia); Lise Esch (Trident Technical College); Duncan Flaherty (Queens College); Seth Frechie (Cabrini College); Paul Gallipeo (Adirondack Community College); Granville Ganter (St. John's University); Jared Gardner (Ohio State University); Sarah Garland (University of East Anglia); Jerry Gibbens (Williams Baptist College); Marivel Gonzales-Herna (Del Mar College); Mary Goodwin (National Taiwan Normal University); Carey Goyette (Clinton Community College); Paul Grant (Sir Wilfred Grenfell College); Mark Graves (Morehead

State University); Beth Gray (Gadsden State Community College); Lashun Griffin (North Harris College); George Griffith (Chadron State College); Susan Hagen (Riverland Community College); Heidi Hanrahan (Shepherd University); Rabiul Hasan (Southern University of Baton Rouge); Thomas Heise (McGill University); Charles Hernandez (Gordon College); Carmine Hernwood (Gordon College); Avis Hewitt (Grand Valley State University); Elizabeth Hewitt (Ohio State University); Trent Hickman (Brigham Young University); Kathleen Hicks (Arizona State University); Marianna Hofer (University of Findlay); Melissa Homestead (University of Nebraska, Lincoln); Carl Horner (Flagler College); Brad Johnson (Palm Beach Community College); Gwendolyn Jones (Clayton State University); Daniel Kane (University of Sussex); Virginia M. Kennedy; Catherine Keohane (Bergen Community College); James Kirkpatrick (Central Piedmont Community College); Denise Knight (SUNY Cortland); Peter Kvidera (John Carroll University); Michael Latza (College of Lake County); William Lawton (James Madison University); Heidi Lee (Messiah College); Paul Lewis (Boston College); Gretchen Lieb (Vassar College); Sarah Locke (Weatherford College); Paul Long (Baltimore City Community College); Trish Loughran (University of Illinois); Scott Richard Lyons (University of Michigan); Jim Machor (Kansas State University); Paul Madachy (Prince George's Community College); D'Ann Madewell (North Lake College); Ursula McTaggart (Wilmington College); Phil Metres (John Carroll University); Shellie Michael (Volunteer State Community College); Bruce Michelson (University of Illinois at Urbana-Champaign); Wendy Pearce Miller (Marian College); Bob Morace (Daemen College); Thomas Morgan (University of Dayton); Irvin Morris; David Murdock (Gadsden State Community College); Axel Nissen (University of Oslo); John O'Brien (University of Virginia); Patrick O'Connell (Gannon University); Louis Oldani (Rockhurst University); Emily Orlando (Fairfield University); Amanda Page (University of North Carolina, Chapel Hill); Daniel Payne (SUNY Oneonta); H. Daniel Peck (Vassar College); Caesar Perkowski (Gordon College); Jeanne Phoenix Laurel (Niagara University); Albert Pionke (University of Alabama); Stephen Powers (Gordon College); Colin Ramsey (Appalachian State University); Elizabeth Renker (Ohio State University); John Ribar (Palm Beach Community College); Julien Rice; Sian Silyn Roberts (Queens College); Debra Rosenthal (John Carroll University); Dave Rota (University of Missouri St. Louis); Susan Ryan (University of Louisville); Charles Scarborough (Northern Virginia Community College); Jennifer Schell (Wichita State University); Carl Sederholm (Brigham Young University); Jessica Sellountos (Emory University); Linda Furg Selzer (Penn State University); Hal Shows (Keiser University); Cristobal Silva (Florida State University); Merrill Maguire Skaggs (Drew University); Derrick Spradlin (Freed Hardeman College); Roy Stamper (North Carolina State University); Jeffrey Steele (University of Wisconsin); Julia Stern (Northwestern University); Paul Strong (Alfred University); Brian Sweeney (Saint Joseph's University); Marcy Tanter (Tarleton State University); Erin Templeton (Converse College); Annette Trefzner (University of Mississippi); William Tucker (Olney Central College); April Van Camp (Indian River Community College); Adam Vines (University of Alabama at Birmingham); Pierre Walker (Salem State College); Laura Wallmenich (Alma College); Rick Walters (White Mountains Community College); Bill Ward (Appalachian State University); Robert West

(Mississippi State University); Stephen Whited (Piedmont College); Edward Whitelock (Gordon College); Edward Whitley (Lehigh University); Steve Whitton (Jacksonville State University); Lea Williamson (Blinn College); Kelly Wisecup (University of North Texas); Wesley Xi (National Taiwan University); Tamara Yohannes (University of Louisville); Elizabeth Young; Francis Zauhar (University of Pittsburgh at Johnstown).

THE NORTON ANTHOLOGY OF AMERICAN LITERATURE

EIGHTH EDITION

VOLUME B: 1820–1865

American Literature 1820–1865

AN AMERICAN RENAISSANCE?

This volume of *The Norton Anthology of American Literature* presents works by Ralph Waldo Emerson, Edgar Allan Poe, Frederick Douglass, Nathaniel Hawthorne, Herman Melville, Walt Whitman, Emily Dickinson, Henry David Thoreau, Harriet Beecher Stowe, and their contemporaries—the writers generally regarded as central to our understanding of American literary traditions from the nineteenth century to the present day. The writers in this volume, particularly those who began publishing after 1830, are often celebrated as a group for having sparked a literary renaissance that helped American writing to achieve its first significant maturity. But the authors of this period were not always valued so highly by literary historians. In the early decades of the twentieth century, American literature was generally not taught in American universities, or else it was taught in subordinate relation to English literature, which was viewed as having an infinitely superior literary tradition. Among the important critical books that helped change this situation was F. O. Matthiessen's *American Renaissance: Art and Expression in the Age of Emerson and Whitman* (1941). Matthiessen gave American literature what had always been integral to the study of English literature: a Renaissance. England may have had Spenser, Shakespeare, and Donne, but America, Matthiessen argued, had Emerson, Thoreau, Hawthorne, Melville, and Whitman. According to the critics who helped to establish American literature as a field of study, the "Renaissance" was inspired during the 1830s by the writings of

George Innes, ***The Lackawanna Valley*** (detail), 1855. For more information about this painting, see the color insert in this volume.

Emerson and came into its own in the 1850s with such major works as Hawthorne's *The Scarlet Letter* (1850), Melville's *Moby-Dick* (1851), Thoreau's *Walden* (1854), and Whitman's *Leaves of Grass* (1855). These and other key texts have an important place in this anthology, which owes a large debt to mid-twentieth-century formulations of the literary significance of the antebellum period.

Nevertheless, over the past several decades, the idea of an American Renaissance has come under considerable challenge. For instance, critics have noted that Matthiessen and others tended to exclude the significant contributions of women and minority writers, especially African Americans, and consequently closed off considerations of the wide range of writing developing in the United States during this time. Up to the 1970s and 1980s, critics working in the field of American literary studies generally had little interest in popular authors of the period, such as the poets Lydia Sigourney and Henry Wadsworth Longfellow or the novelists Fanny Fern and Harriet Beecher Stowe, and little interest in publications outside of Massachusetts and New York. Critics have also faulted exponents of an American Renaissance for failing to attend to slavery, immigration, and other political and social contexts, all of which had a significant influence on the writing of the time, and for overemphasizing the separateness of English and American literary traditions, given that writers on both sides of the Atlantic were working in the same language and reading each other's works.

And yet, granting all of the shortcomings of the concept of an American Renaissance, one could say about the term what Benjamin Franklin in his *Autobiography* says about his efforts to subdue his pride: "Disguise it, struggle with it, beat it down, stifle it, mortify it as much as one pleases, it is still alive, and will every now and then peep out and show itself." For better or worse, the notion of an American Renaissance has continued to exert an enormous influence on the way that the literature of this period is understood, even though the idea of a literal renaissance (or rebirth) makes little sense in relation to a national literary tradition that was still in the process of coming into being.

The idea of an American Renaissance has been so influential in part because the literature of this period truly was crucial to the development of American literary traditions, at once building on writings that had preceded it and pointing to future possibilities. When this literature is viewed in much broader contexts and appreciated in its full complexity, its centrality to American literary history becomes even more evident. But the literature of the 1830s through the 1850s, and especially that of the 1850s, cannot be disconnected from the decades immediately preceding it, a time when many U.S. cultural commentators were calling on Americans to produce literary texts worthy of a great nation. The American literary renaissance could be viewed retrospectively as a fulfillment of the repeated calls, from the 1770s on, for such an exemplary literature, though it may also be said that early expressions of American literary nationalism reveal the conflicts and concerns attending the development of U.S. nationalism from the 1790s to the 1820s—conflicts and concerns that would continue to engage writers of the antebellum period. In fact, it was in the decade of the 1820s rather than the 1850s that critics of the time generally agreed that the United States *had* produced writers worthy of a great nation and agreed as well on the identity of the most important writers—namely, Washington Irving, William Cullen Bryant, James Fenimore Cooper, and Catharine Maria Sedgwick. No such consensus existed in the 1850s, as writers like Melville, Thoreau, and Whitman had very small readerships; Dickinson, who would publish just a small number of poems in newspapers and miscellanies, was basically unknown; and Hawthorne's most enthusiastic readers were limited to a relatively small number of people in the Northeast. The 1820s can be seen as the first great culmination of American literary nationalism, a decade that helped spawn the "Renaissance" to come.

AMERICAN LITERARY NATIONALISM AND THE 1820s

From the moment of the successful outcome of the American Revolution, literary nationalism had an important place in the emergent culture of the new nation. Convinced that a sign of a great nation was the existence of a great national literature, patriotic writers of the early republic attempted to produce "American" works as quickly as possible; such epic poems as Timothy Dwight's *The Conquest of Canaan* (1785) and Joel Barlow's *The Columbiad* (1807) can be regarded as simultaneously bombastic and impressive achievements along these lines. From a different but still highly nationalistic perspective, Charles Brockden Brown proclaimed in the preface to his 1799 novel *Edgar Huntly* that he would make use of native materials—"incidents of Indian hostility, and the perils of the western wilderness"—to show how the United States offers "themes to the moral painter" that "differ essentially from those which exist in Europe." But even as writers of the time boldly sought to produce distinctively American works, there was a sense during the 1790s and early 1800s—a period haunted by the French Revolution's Reign of Terror and the subsequent Napoleonic Wars—that American nationality was provisional, vulnerable, fragile. The War of 1812, which emerged from ongoing conflicts with England, can therefore be seen as a war that, at least in part, spoke to Americans' desires to put an end to national anxiety by in effect reenacting the American Revolution against England and winning a victory once and for all. In its own time, this war was labeled "The Second War with England." When English troops stormed the District of Columbia in 1814 and burned the Capitol and the White House, Americans' grim sense of vulnerability was underscored. But all that changed when Andrew Jackson's outnumbered troops defeated the English army at New Orleans in 1815, shortly after a peace treaty had officially ended the second major war between the two nations. From New Orleans there emerged a national mythology of the republican hero—the antiaristocratic, antimonarchical person from an obscure background—who incarnated the strengths and virtues of the U.S. nation. The immediate beneficiary of that mythology, Andrew Jackson, would achieve further acclaim among his white compatriots for fighting the Indians in the Floridas. When he was eventually elected president in 1828, he was regarded as the incarnation of the democratic spirit of the age. Jacksonian democratic energies and ideals would have an enormous impact on the writing that would emerge in the United States over the next several decades, both in its celebration of the capacities of ordinary people and its hostility to unearned social distinction and inherited wealth.

Well before 1828, however, the optimistic nationalism that found expression after the War of 1812 led to renewed efforts to develop a distinctively American literature worthy of a democratic republic that fully expected to take its place among the great nations of the world. Calls for a new American literature appeared regularly in the pages of the *North American Review*, an influential journal founded in Boston shortly after the war ended in 1815. In the journal's November 1815 issue, for instance, the critic Walter Channing urged his countrymen to produce "a literature of our own," even as he worried over the difficulties of developing such a literature in relation to English literary traditions. As the critic Edward Tyrell Channing remarked in an 1816 issue of the journal, a national literature "will have but feeble claims to excellence and distinction, when it stoops to put on foreign ornament and manner, and to adopt from other nations, images, allusions, and a metaphorical language, which are perfectly unmeaning and sickly out of their birth-place." Similarly, in his 1818 book, *An Essay on American Poetry*, the critic Solyman Brown asserted that Americans could not claim to have won the War of 1812 until that victory manifested itself in the production of a distinctively American literature: "The proudest freedom to which a nation can aspire, not excepting even political independence, is found in complete emancipation from literary thralldom." From the perspective of British literary nationalists, such emancipation would be slow in coming, given that, as they regularly maintained, American literature would always be overshadowed and subsumed by the long literary tradition of the parent country. Making just such an argument, the English critic Sydney Smith, in an oft-quoted attack on American literary nationalists, sarcastically demanded in an 1820 issue of the *Edinburgh Review*: "In the four quarters of the globe, who reads an American book?" As it turned out, Smith posed his question at an inopportune moment, for Americans could gloatingly respond that thousands of people in the United States and England were beginning to read American books. Not only were Charles Brockden Brown's novels of the 1790s achieving a new popularity in England but, right around the time of Smith's attack, the publication of Irving's *The Sketch Book* (1819–20), Bryant's *Poems* (1821), and Cooper's *The Spy* (1821) and *The Pioneers* (1823) suggested to many in the United States, England, and elsewhere that a worthy American literature *had* begun to take its place among the literatures of the more established nations.

It is worth underscoring, however, that during the 1820s Americans took pride in a literature that they regarded not necessarily as distinct from but rather in conversation with English literary traditions. Given the language that the countries shared, most American literary nationalists simply hoped that American writers could take their places alongside their British siblings or cousins. After all, literate Americans delighted in Spenser's *The Faerie Queen*, Shakespeare's plays, Milton's *Paradise Lost*, the essays of Joseph Addison and Richard Steele, and the poetry of Alexander Pope; and in the early decades of the nineteenth century they were reading the romantic poets Wordsworth and Byron (among others) and, beginning in 1814 with the publication of *Waverley*, the historical novels of Walter Scott. Moreover, Irving's *The Sketch Book* had important sources in the essays of Addison and Steele; Bryant's poetry had important sources in Wordsworth; and Cooper's novels had important sources in Scott. Cooper objected to being termed the "American Scott," but the label would ultimately have been viewed as testimony to his novelistic mastery. For the most part, American writers of this time had a sophisticated understanding of their relationship to British and other literary traditions and would have regarded as nonsense the idea that they were expected to create a completely separate American literature.

They would have also regarded as nonsense the idea that American literature should be uncritically patriotic. One of the more notable features of the acclaimed 1820s writings of Irving, Bryant, and Cooper (along with the writings of their contemporaries such as Sedgwick, Sigourney, and Lydia Maria Child) was just how critical these writings could be of early national culture. Much of Irving's *The Sketch Book* is set in Europe, and though an often playfully ironic narrative voice of the American traveler holds the volume together, that persona is generally reverential toward the European historical past while casting a skeptical eye on a boastful U.S. culture that seems to have little interest in art and history. In his historical fictions of that decade, Cooper is similarly skeptical of U.S. claims to progress, presenting a demythified vision of the American Revolution in *The Spy*, and in *The Pioneers* depicting democratic energies as sometimes a threat to orderly government and the natural environment. In Cooper, as in Bryant, Sedgwick, and other writers of the period, visions of historical progress are tempered by the notion, widely disseminated during the Enlightenment and beyond, that all mighty nations must eventually fall. At a time when Indian removal was becoming national policy on the basis that, as many Americans believed, the day of the Indian was over, Cooper and Bryant suggested in works like *The Last of the Mohicans* and "The Prairies" that the U.S. nation was equally subject to the historical cycle of rise and decline.

Adding to uncertainty about the future was the fact that the very shape, size, and demographic character of the nation were in flux. Jefferson's acquisition of the Louisiana Territory from France in 1803 doubled the size of the nation's total acreage, but its borders remained ill-defined, and the purchase soon raised difficult questions about how to balance the admission of new free states and new slave states in the expanding republic. The Missouri Compromises of 1820–21 appeared to resolve the political question by admitting Missouri as a slave state, Maine as a free state, and banning slavery in the northern reaches of the Louisiana Territory, but sectional conflict on slavery, states' rights, internal improvements, national tariffs, and other matters would continue to intensify in the wake of a compromise that was supposed to put an end to such conflicts. The assertion by South Carolina's legislature in 1832 of its right to "nullify" federal policies was one among many signs of the lack of national consensus during the two decades (1815–35) that have been celebrated by some historians as the era of good feelings.

Still, in the wake of the War of 1812, there was a shared belief among the major writers of the time that, as Brockden Brown had suggested back in the 1790s, the United States did have distinct materials with which to develop a distinctive (though not separate) national literature. Authors such as Irving, Cooper, and Bryant placed a special emphasis on the importance of the natural landscape for the development of national character, finding in the relatively unspoiled vast lands of the continent a nurturing ground for

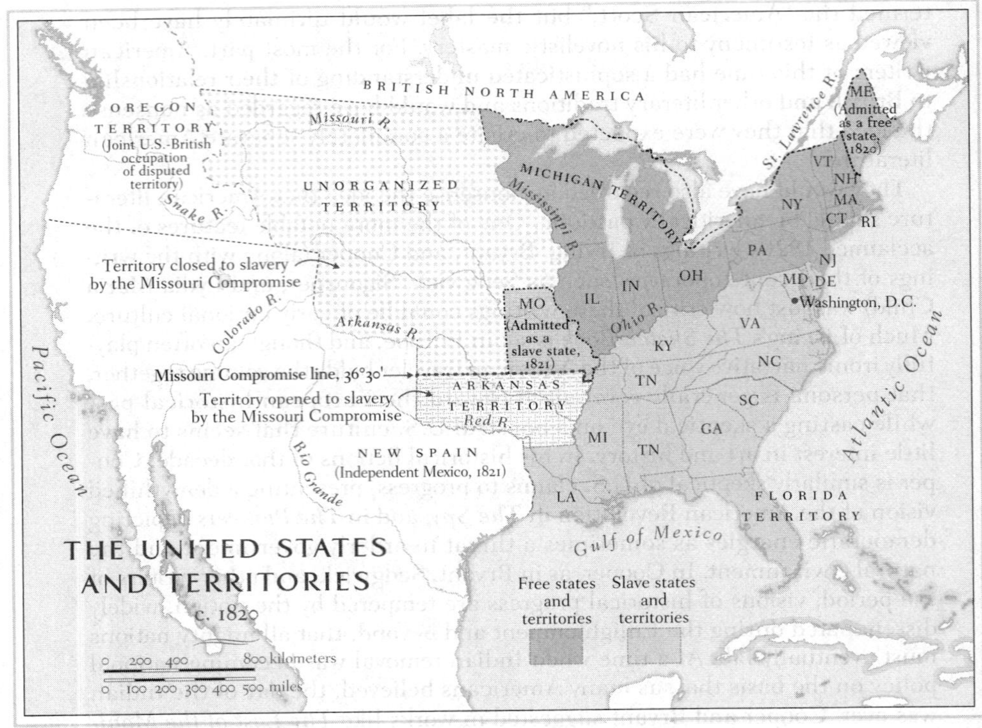

the spiritual growth of a nation that, they sometimes suggested, could possibly emerge as "better" than any of those of long-settled Europe. These writers shared the vision of the popular Hudson River landscape painters of the antebellum period, New Yorkers like Thomas Cole and Asher Durand, who regularly portrayed individuals dwarfed by mountains and forests in a vast and unsettled nature where God's spirit could be apprehended. Cole may have identified republican decline as the ultimate historical reality (see his 1836 "The Course of Empire: Desolation," in the color insert to this volume), but most writers and artists of the period, including Cole, imagined that decline as hundreds, if not thousands, of years away. The American literary nationalism of the 1820s, like the American literary nationalism of the 1790s, explored difficult questions about the nation's future, about its strengths and vulnerabilities, and about its character and potential as a democratic republic. But the emergence of internationally acclaimed writers like Irving, Bryant, and Cooper also helped open up new literary opportunities for American writers, even as they would continue to have to compete with English writers for markets and prestige.

THE LITERARY MARKETPLACE IN AN EXPANDING NATION

By the second decade of the nineteenth century, Americans had easy access to contemporary British literature and criticism. Crossing the Atlantic on sailing ships and by the late 1830s on steamers, books or magazines first published in London could be distributed or republished almost immediately in the larger coastal cities—Boston, New York, Philadelphia, and Charleston. Volumes of poetry by the Scottish poet Robert Burns and by the English Romantics (Wordsworth, Coleridge, Byron, Shelley, Keats, and others), then Tennyson, and a little later Elizabeth Barrett Browning and Robert Browning were reprinted in the United States within months of their initial publication. Sir Walter Scott's historical novels were immensely popular in the United States (as a young man Hawthorne dreamed of becoming an American Scott), and during the 1840s and 1850s crowds of Charles Dickens fans would congregate at the docks to greet steamships arriving in New York City with the latest installment of one of his serialized novels.

Geography and modes of transportation bore directly on publishing practices in the United States during this period. In 1800 there were few publishing firms; writers who wanted to publish a book generally took the handwritten manuscript to a local printer. They paid job rates to have it printed and made their own arrangements for distribution and sales, frequently having signed up committed purchasers beforehand in what was then called the "subscription" system. By around 1820 publishing centers began to develop in the major seaports, which could receive the latest British books by the fastest ships; these publishers shipped hastily reprinted copies inland by river traffic. The leading publishing towns were New York and Philadelphia; the Erie Canal, completed in 1825, gave New York an advantage in distributing books west to Ohio. Boston remained peripheral to the publishing industry until railroad connections to the West developed during the 1840s. Despite the aggressive merchandizing techniques of a few firms, a national market for American literature was slow to develop.

Besides the technical problems of book distribution across the nation's huge expanse, economic interests of American publishers and booksellers were sometimes (but not always) antithetical to the interests of American writers. A national copyright law became effective in the United States in 1790, but not until 1891 did U.S. writers get international copyright protection and foreign writers receive similar protection in the United States. For most of the century, American publishers routinely pirated English writers, paying nothing to Scott, Dickens, and other popular writers for works sold widely in inexpensive editions throughout the United States. American readers benefited from the situation, but the availability to publishers of texts that they did not have to purchase or pay royalties on made it perpetually difficult for U.S. writers to be paid for their work in their home country. As a result, there were relatively few professional authors in the United States before the Civil War. Bryant supported himself as a newspaper editor; Hawthorne received various political appointments over his lifetime; Emerson lived on a legacy from his first wife and on his well-compensated lectures; the financially struggling Melville was forced to spend the last several decades of his life working in the New York custom house; for most of his career, Longfellow taught languages at Harvard.

To survive economically, some American writers attempted to line up contracts with British publishers. But Irving's apparent conquest of the British publishing system, by which he received large sums for *The Sketch Book* and succeeding volumes, proved to be a short-term solution that worked mostly for Irving. Cooper and others followed in Irving's path for a time and were paid by magnanimous British publishers under a system whereby works first printed in Great Britain were presumed to hold a British copyright. But this practice was ruled illegal by a British judge in 1849, making it even harder for American writers to stake a claim to the British market, though Melville and other writers continued to make the effort and occasionally met with success. Some of the American authors who did best in England were antislavery writers, for the English apparently could not get enough of works that held their former colony up to shame. Frederick Douglass and William Wells Brown found a significant audience in Great Britain (the first African American novel, Brown's *Clotel* [1853], was published *only* in England), and there were few writers more admired and widely read in England than Harriet Beecher Stowe.

Nevertheless, authorship and publishing were far from moribund in the antebellum United States. The period from 1820 to 1865 saw a dizzying growth in the nation's population and territorial reach; dramatic technological developments that would allow publishers to bring out works in ever-greater numbers at ever-greater profits; increasing urbanization (which helped enlarge readership in key profitable markets); and the expansion of railroads, canals, and other forms of transportation that would allow for more extensive and economical forms of distribution. The nation's population of approximately four million in 1790 jumped to thirty million by 1860, in part because of the massive emigration from Ireland and elsewhere in Europe that occurred during the 1840s and 1850s. Territorial space available to this burgeoning population dramatically increased following the war with Mexico (1846–48), which, as a result of the 1848 Treaty of Guadalupe Hidalgo, added 1.2 million square miles of land to the 1.8 million square miles that the nation held before the war; this is the area that would become Texas, California, Arizona, Nevada, and Utah, and parts of New Mexico, Colorado, and Wyoming. Beginning in the 1820s and continuing through the nineteenth century, there were ongoing efforts to connect and extend U.S. territory through the development of roads, canals, and railroads. Travel literature to the West (or what we now call the Midwest), such as Caroline Kirkland's *A New Home—Who'll Follow?* (1839) and Margaret Fuller's *Summer on the Lakes* (1843), became an increasingly popular genre. Richard Henry Dana in *Two Years before the Mast* (1840) and Francis Parkman in *The Oregon Trail* (1849) would write popular accounts of their respective travels to the Pacific Northwest. Dana's and Parkman's writings especially resonated with readers during the 1850s, the heyday of California immigration following the discovery of gold in California in the late 1840s.

There was also an increasing interest in urban writings, in large part because of the tremendous rise in the populations of Boston, Philadelphia, and New York brought about mostly by Irish immigration but also by an influx of native-born rural people to the cities from the farms, which suffered massive failures during the economic depression of the 1850s. Taken together, the growth of U.S. cities and the ongoing expansion of the nation's territorial reach contributed to one of the most significant developments of the time for those writers aspiring to professional authorship: the dramatic growth of newspaper and magazine publishing from the early years of the nineteenth century to the 1860s. Between 1800 and 1825, approximately four hundred newspapers were founded, and that number went into the thousands by 1860. Before 1825 there were approximately a hundred magazines published in the United States; by 1850 there were about six hundred. More than the typical U.S. book publisher, the proliferating newspapers and magazines provided writers with forums for their poetry and fiction, along with personal essays, travel writing, political reportage, and other writings suitable for daily, weekly, and monthly presses. Poe, Sigourney, Fuller, Hawthorne, Fern, and many other writers worked on their craft and developed their reputations with the help of their periodical publications.

Among the most popular magazines of the time were the mass-market *Graham's* and *Godey's Lady's Book*, both published in Philadelphia. Poe published stories and sketches in these journals, as did many women writers. The *Lady's Book*, in fact, though published by Louis A. Godey, was edited

"A Reading Party." Plate from *Godey's Lady's Book*, 1846.

for some forty years by the novelist and essayist Sarah J. Hale, whose editorial role in one of the major journals of the day points to the key place of women in the antebellum literary marketplace. Despite traditional notions that imaginative literature and creative writing could be especially harmful to women by inflaming their imaginations and undermining their moral place in the private domain of the home, women found ways to enter the literary marketplace. For example, they could write at home and mail their manuscripts to magazines, thus retaining their status as domestic beings. Much writing by women of the antebellum period addressed questions of domesticity head-on, sometimes, as with Fuller, criticizing the idea of separate cultural spheres for men and women; but more often, as with Stowe, showing how women could have an effect on the culture from within the home. But even with her emphasis on the cultural power of domesticity, Stowe, like Fuller, fully embraced the public sphere of authorship. Just about all of the women writers represented in this anthology made an important mark in the periodical culture of the time, and some used their connections to magazines and newspapers to develop as professional authors who were able to live on earnings from their writings. Child, Fuller, Fern, and Rebecca Harding Davis all had newspaper columns, and Fern was paid lavishly for hers. Kirkland edited the New York *Union* and wrote for other magazines; Child and Fuller also served as editors of journals; Stowe and Louisa May Alcott got their starts writing sketches and short stories for regional newspapers. In this context, the refusal of Emily Dickinson to follow any of the norms of female authorship, while remaining firmly enclosed in the home space and writing some of the great lyrics of the century, points to her recognition of and resistance to cultural ideals of female authorship in her day.

"RENAISSANCE," REFORM, CONFLICT

Various reform movements, such as antislavery, temperance, women's rights, and even nativist anti-Catholicism (an extreme manifestation of Protestant evangelical reform), contributed to the proliferation of print during the antebellum period. As a theme and focus of cultural debate, reform emerged as a crucial constituent of the antebellum writings traditionally associated with the American Renaissance. Recognizing the centrality of reform to his cultural moment, Emerson declared in "Man the Reformer" (1841) that "the doctrine of Reform had never such scope as at the present hour." Though the Transcendentalism for which he stood emphasized self-culture and personal reform rather than public initiatives, by the 1840s Emerson had begun to link himself to activist reform movements. In "Emancipation in the West Indies" (1844), for example, he called on the "great masses of men" to take a larger role in opposing slavery, and he would remain firmly committed to antislavery reform up to the time of the Civil War. He also offered occasional remarks on the value of temperance (one of the most popular reform movements of the antebellum period); in the spirit of Protestant reformers going back to the Reformation (when Protestant meant quite specifically a protest against Catholicism), he drew on anti-Catholic rhetoric in some essays attacking the hierarchies and deadness of established institutions; and in 1855 he addressed a women's rights convention in support of women's suffrage, which he would continue to endorse.

Emersonian reform also had a literary aspect to it, rejecting the American literary nationalism of the 1820s as imitative and timid. Emerson's "The American Scholar" (1837) is often referred to as the nation's "declaration of cultural independence," the essay that helped inspire many authors who have come to be associated with both traditional and more multicultural notions of an American Renaissance. First delivered as a lecture to Harvard's Phi Beta Kappa Society, "The American Scholar" called on those Americans with a "love of letters" to "lead in a new age" of men "inspired by the Divine Soul which also inspires all men." Trained as a Unitarian minister, Emerson had broken with the church by the time he began to deliver and publish his lectures, and in *Nature*, a short book of 1836, made it clear that he had absorbed some of the major ideas of the European romantics on the creative powers of the individual mind, the regenerative value of nature, the limits of historical associations and traditions, the stultifying effects of established institutions, and the mystical glories of a presocialized infancy. Ironically, in *Nature*, "The American Scholar," and his other writings of the time, Emerson drew on major philosophical and aesthetic ideas circulating in Europe to write as a literary reformer exhorting Americans to break their dependency on the "courtly muses of Europe." In this lecture and other writings of the 1830s and 1840s, Emerson underscored the parallels between Romantic ideas of infancy and the infancy of the new nation, invoked the regenerative and spiritual powers of the American landscape ("America is a poem in our eyes," he declared in "The Poet" [1844]), drew connections between self-reliance and Jacksonian democratic energies, and linked his celebration of nonconformity and resistance to the reform agenda of many Americans of the period.

Emerson's attacks on the Unitarian and other established churches for what he described as their refusal to honor the possibility of the miraculous in the here and now, and his affirmations of the near god-like powers of the creative imagination, helped popularize what many literary historians have termed the Transcendentalist movement. In various ways, Emersonian Transcendentalism (which was never really a formalized movement) inspired the writings of Fuller, Thoreau, and Whitman. Even more skeptical authors like Poe, Hawthorne, Melville, and Dickinson, through their resistance to Emerson's proclamations on the individual's ability to break from institutions and traditional Christian beliefs to become a kind of god, arguably exhibited the influence of Emerson, who himself could be skeptical of transcendental extremism (for the dark side of the ecstasies of *Nature*, see his "Experience" [1844], which presents the individual as forever skating on surfaces). In the wake of Emerson's important essays of the 1830s and 1840s, much writing of the antebellum period grappled with questions about the value of history, the ability of the individual to apprehend the godhead directly, the capacity of language to achieve and convey knowledge, and the difficulties of making sense of a universe in which meaning derives from individual creative insights rather than received authority. The fictional worlds of *The Scarlet Letter* and *Moby-Dick*, works that are obsessed with the problematics of interpretation, whether of the letter *A* or a whale, have a profoundly different feel from the more consensual, commonsensical fictional worlds of Irving, Sedgwick, and Cooper.

Antebellum writing taken as a whole is much too various and conflicted to be viewed simply through the lens of Emerson's New England–based reformism. (For instance, see the selections in the cluster on "Section, Region, Nation, Hemisphere.") But as Emerson himself helps us to understand, one of the impulses that holds together many of the writings of the period, including Emerson's, is reformism—the conviction that American literature and culture were not living up to their Revolutionary or democratic promises. But during this time there were also a variety of notions about what constituted reform. Proslavery, not just antislavery, could be regarded in a reform context; many southerners, for instance, looked back to the founding of the nation and believed that the Constitution favored states' rights over what they regarded as the encroaching authoritarianism of the federal government. Reformism, particularly in the context of an expanding nation with its multiple constituencies and agendas, could be as much a source of conflict as consensus.

Many of the antebellum reform movements based in the North were actively directed by Protestant elites concerned with maintaining their social power and authority during a time of increasing class and ethnic diversity. Desires to hold on to such power could be taken to an unattractive extreme in the period's pervasive anti-Catholic nativism. But concerns about the poor and working-class immigrants also had an important place in antebellum urban reform movements, as writers sought to expose readers to the plight of the impoverished in order to prompt philanthropic interventions; see, for example, the urban-based reformist journalism of Lydia Maria Child. The fact that women had such a significant place in urban reform movements is not surprising, given that urban reform often centered on creating homelike, domestically attractive conditions for the poor, and that another major reform effort of the antebellum period centered on women's rights. In "The Great Lawsuit" (1843), Margaret Fuller drew on the Declaration of Independence and Emersonian transcendental reform, among numerous other sources, to make the case that women should have greater opportunities for education and participation in the public sphere, including the right to "represent themselves"—that is, to vote. In 1848, at the first women's rights convention in Seneca Falls, New York, Elizabeth Cady Stanton's resounding "Declaration of Sentiments" invoked Jefferson's Declaration, substituting male for British tyrannical authority to show how the nation's social institutions and legal codes mainly served the interests of America's white male citizenry. That same year, the New York State Legislature, in response to critics like Stanton, passed the nation's most liberalized married women's property act, which made it legal for women to maintain control over the property they brought to their marriages. But throughout the nineteenth century, in most states married women remained without any legal rights to property or earnings within marriage.

For good reason, then, a number of women writers of the period addressed questions of power: how to use power from within the domestic sphere, how to gain power in the public sphere, how to fend off the dangers of unchecked patriarchal power. The danger posed by patriarchal power was a central theme of both antislavery and temperance reform. Sigourney and Stowe were two of the most prominent antislavery writers who supported the temperance movement, as they saw drinking as a male activity that lured men away from their homes into the saloons and transformed them into drunken hooligans. In temperance writings of the period, women authors regularly depicted drunken husbands or fathers as men who became driven by their animal passions, to the point where these "slaves to the bottle" became slaves to their own bodies. Such imagery and cultural concerns informed Child's antislavery story "The Quadroons" (1842); Stowe's antislavery novels *Uncle Tom's Cabin* (1852) and *Dred* (1856), whose villains were drunkards; and the antislavery writer Frances Harper's short story "The Two Offers" (1859).

A number of writers of the antebellum period, male and female, took as one of their main subjects the anguishing paradox that the nation that boastfully presented itself as the most idealistic in the world—the bastion of freedom and equality—was implicated in ongoing national crimes: the near-genocide of the American Indians, the enslavement of black people, and an expansionism that ignored other national sovereignties, especially that of Mexico. Because the war with Mexico of 1846–48 came to be understood by many Americans as consistent with the nation's "Manifest Destiny" to expand across the continent, only a small minority of American writers voiced more than perfunctory opposition; the best known of these dissenters was Thoreau, who spent a night in the Concord jail in symbolic protest against being taxed to support a war that he believed was mainly intended to enlarge the domain of slavery. Emerson and Child were dissenters earlier, during the 1830s, when most writers were silent about the forced removal of southeastern Indian tribes from their homelands to territory west of the Mississippi River, as permitted by the Indian Removal Act of 1830. American destiny plainly required a little practical callousness, most whites felt, or if not callousness, then the worst kind of sympathy: a lament for "vanishing" Indians who were being killed off all the more quickly or at least without remorse because of such sentimental acquiescence. Native American spokespersons and authors like Black Hawk and William Apess questioned whites' constant interventions into Indian affairs. They were particularly critical of whites' deceptive treaties and land-grabbing policies, as were those grouped in the section in this anthology titled "Native Americans: Removal and Resistance." Of the major antebellum writers who were not Native American, only Child kept a critical eye over the decades on the white power, as opposed to the presumed providential inevitability, that was relentlessly working to shrink Indian lands and confuse extinction with extermination.

Most white Americans accepted what they thought of as the destined "extinction" of the Native Americans. There was much more conflict over the practice of slavery, which Melville called "man's foulest crime." The antislavery campaign stirred the consciences of a number of white writers, and, unsurprisingly, resistance to slavery and critiques of whites' antiblack racism were among the principal topics of antebellum African American writing. Describing his own enslavement, the fugitive Frederick Douglass displayed a powerful capacity to stir both readers and audiences in lecture halls, in large part through his ability to make whites sympathize with the situation of blacks. The reformist potential of sympathy is the crucial theme of his novella, "The Heroic Slave" (1853), and of Frances Harper's antislavery poetry. Harper and Douglass were both inspired by Stowe's *Uncle Tom's Cabin*, the best-selling novel of the antebellum period. Twentieth-century attacks on this novel for its supposed bad faith would have made little sense to Harper and Douglass. William Wells Brown may have been more skeptical of Stowe, as his ironically conceived novel *Clotel* suggests, but even he praised Stowe in the pages of William Lloyd Garrison's antislavery newspaper, the *Liberator*.

A politics of antislavery had an important place in the careers of a number of the writers represented in this anthology, ranging from Sigourney to Longfellow, Child to Stowe, Emerson to Melville. (For further commentary on slavery, along with selections from some of the other most important antislavery writers of the period, see the section on "Slavery, Race, and the Making of American Literature.") When the Fugitive Slave Law of 1850 was enforced in Boston in 1851 (by Melville's father-in-law, Chief Justice Lemuel Shaw), Thoreau in his journals expressed his outrage that Massachusetts citizens were being compelled to return escaping slaves to their Southern masters; after another famous case in 1854, he wrote his most scathing speech, "Slavery in Massachusetts," for delivery at a Fourth of July counter-ceremony at which a copy of the Constitution was burned. In that speech he summed up the disillusionment that many of his generation shared, presenting Massachusetts as a type of hell. More obliquely than Thoreau, Melville explored slavery in "Benito Cereno" as an index to the white supremacism that he regarded as a stain on the national character. At his bitterest, he felt in the mid-1850s that "free Ameriky" was "intrepid, unprincipled, reckless, predatory, with boundless ambition, civilized in externals but a savage at heart." In response to antislavery criticism, Southerners passionately defended the institution of slavery in such works as George Fitzhugh's *Sociology for the South* (1854) and Caroline Lee Hentz's *The Planter's Northern Bride* (1854), one of several anti–*Uncle Tom's Cabin* novels published during the 1850s.

John Brown's violent raid on Harpers Ferry in 1859, a failed effort to initiate a slave rebellion in the South, drew eloquent defenses from Emerson, Thoreau, Douglass, Stowe, and Child, though most in the North and across the country condemned Brown as a radical who threatened to bring the nation into a bloody civil war. With the outbreak of the Civil War, Douglass, Wells Brown, Child, Stowe, and other major writers of the period sought to present the war as, in the spirit of John Brown, a holy war against slavery that might redeem the millennial promise of the nation, which is to say, as the fulfillment of the promise of reform going back to Emerson and, as Lincoln himself suggested in his "Address Delivered at the Dedication of the Cemetery at Gettysburg" (1863), to the principles of the Declaration of Independence itself. The idea of the United States as an exceptional nation because it had been set aside for an exceptional destiny proved almost impossible to overcome, even in moments when the country marched into bloody internal conflict. When the war began on April 12, 1861, with Confederate guns opening fire on Fort Sumter, in South Carolina's Charleston Harbor, few understood what lay ahead; Northerners and Southerners alike erroneously expected the war to last only a few months. Visiting Boston and Concord in 1862, fresh from the newly formed West Virginia (the portion of the slave state Virginia that had chosen to stay with the Union), Rebecca Harding

Davis saw that Emerson had little notion of the suffering involved in the war. Shortly before he died, Hawthorne, who had remained committed to the Democrats' vision of Union even at the price of retaining slavery for the foreseeable future, published a negative account of the war, "Chiefly about War Matters," in the 1862 *Atlantic*; while mocking Lincoln as a leader, the essay nonetheless raised pointed questions about Americans' failure to anticipate that a war of this nature would bring unimagined bloodshed, eventually killing over six hundred thousand Americans before Robert E. Lee's surrender to Ulysses S. Grant at Appomattox, Virginia, on April 9, 1865.

Among the most notable literary responses to the Civil War from writers who had published during the antebellum period were two poetry collections: Whitman's *Drum-Taps* (1865) and Melville's *Battle-Pieces* (1866). (More privately at home, Dickinson was spurred to tragic lyricism by the deaths of young Amherst students she had known.) After a small run of his *Drum-Taps* had been sold, Whitman held back the edition for a sequel mainly consisting of newly written poems on the just-assassinated Lincoln, among them his great elegy, "When Lilacs Last in the Dooryard Bloom'd." Both Whitman and Melville looked ahead as well as backward, Whitman calling "reconciliation" the "word over all," and Melville urging in his "Supplement" to *Battle-Pieces* that the victorious North "be Christians toward our fellow-whites, as well as philanthropic toward the blacks, our fellow-men." But Melville's emphasis on Northern whites' responsibility to show charity and "kindliness" toward Southern whites, who he remarked "stand nearer to us in nature," was problematic, for it pointed to the racism that contributed to the nation's larger failure to follow through on the reformist potential of the Civil War. By the time she died, Child was lamenting Reconstruction's failure to educate and offer economic uplift to the the former slaves. In

"Burial Trench at Gettysburg." Photograph by Timothy H. O'Sullivan (1840–1882).

Democratic Vistas (1870), Whitman railed against the political corruption and materialism on display in the immediate wake of the Civil War. Though he worked for several Republican administrations, Douglass became disillusioned by the resurgence of segregationist practices and antiblack violence, most notably lynching, after the end of Reconstruction in 1877. A year before his death, in one of his greatest speeches, "The Lessons of the Hour" (1894), he called on the nation, as he had in "What to the Slave Is the Fourth of July?" (1852), to live up to its founding ideals of "human brotherhood and the self-evident truths of liberty and equality," proclaiming that if Americans were only willing to do that, "your problem will be solved" and "your Republic will stand and flourish forever." With his insistence on the unbounded potential of every individual and his critique of the racist and materialistic nation of the 1890s, Douglass re-articulated some of the same arguments that he had made in 1845 and that Emerson had made in the 1830s and 1840s. Viewed from this reformist perspective, the cultural work of the American Renaissance continues to remain in process.

THE SMALL AND LARGE WORLD OF AMERICAN WRITERS, 1820–1865

An anthology organized by a national literature, a specific time period, and an array of major authors presented in the chronological order of their birthdates might seem artificially closed off from literature of other eras and nations. But close attention to nation and chronology by no means cuts off conversations among the writers included here and those of other periods and nations. On the contrary, it provides a foundation for developing such complex conversations. Nevertheless, it is important to underscore that the era has a real existence of its own in literary terms: the authors in this anthology often *were* in conversation with one another; their world was relatively small and the number of instances of direct and indirect influences, counterinfluences, productive friendships, productive rejections of influences and friendships, and so on, are stunning. Sedgwick read Cooper's *Last of the Mohicans* and wrote a "response" in *Hope Leslie*, emphasizing the domestic and cross-racial possibilities in ways she thought Cooper did not. Whitman and Bryant were on friendly terms in New York City, even as Whitman was turning against the studied meditative verse of his compatriot; Child and John Greenleaf Whittier were long-time friends in the antislavery cause. Emerson was friends with Fuller and Thoreau, both of whom were influenced by his writings, and though he did not meet Whitman until after the publication of the first edition of *Leaves of Grass* (1855), Emerson's theorizing on poetry in "The Poet," which implicitly attacked Poe's ideas on poetry, had a pronounced influence not only on Whitman but also on Dickinson and a number of other American poets. While in Massachusetts during the early 1840s, Douglass imbibed the spirit of Emersonian self-reliance, and his *Narrative* presented his own variations on Emerson's notion of the divinity of self. Douglass inspired Stowe, who, while working on *Uncle Tom's Cabin*, wrote Douglass asking for more precise descriptions of a slave plantation and, after the publication of *Uncle Tom's Cabin*, met with him at her home in Andover and took pleasure in the fact that Douglass was one of her greatest champions.

As much as Douglass admired *Uncle Tom's Cabin*, however, he pointed to problems with Stowe's conception of race in his novella of slave rebellion, "The Heroic Slave," which may have had an influence on Melville's novella of slave rebellion, "Benito Cereno." There is evidence that Douglass influenced Melville's conception of black music and dance in *Moby-Dick*; and it is worth noting that Douglass printed an excerpt from Melville's first novel, *Typee* (1846), in his newspaper the *North Star*.

Melville admired a number of American writers, championing Cooper in the late 1840s, writing several sketches in the mode of Irving, parodying Sedgwick, and responding both positively and negatively to Emerson. He called Emerson a "deep diver" and yet at times found him naively optimistic; in *Moby-Dick* he posits the specter of an indifferent and even hostile nature in which it would be next to impossible, even suicidal, for an individual to become what Emerson termed a "transparent eyeball." Melville dedicated *Moby-Dick* to Nathaniel Hawthorne, whom he met at a picnic in 1850 and idolized in the early 1850s, writing an essay on American literary nationalism in his honor, "Hawthorne and His Mosses" (1850); Hawthorne and Melville mutually influenced one another during the early 1850s. At around the same time, the African American writer William Wells Brown was reading the short stories of Lydia Maria Child and almost word for word used one of those stories, "The Quadroons," to establish the plot of his novel *Clotel*. Frances Harper knew Wells Brown and his work and also took inspiration from such popular poets as Sigourney, Longfellow, and Whittier, who wrote a number of powerful antislavery poems. Poe, who admired Sigourney, knew and attacked many of the celebrated writers of the day, such as Longfellow and Hawthorne, even as his poetry and criticism inspired some of Whitman's poetry, most notably "Out of the Cradle Endlessly Rocking" (1859), and his short stories influenced Hawthorne, whose fiction, much as Poe would have wanted to deny it, influenced his own: there are close connections between Hawthorne's "Young Goodman Brown" (1835), Poe's "The Fall of the House of Usher" (1839), and Hawthorne's *The House of the Seven Gables* (1851). Stowe thought highly of Hawthorne; and Harriet Jacobs, who may have known of Hawthorne's work, esteemed *Uncle Tom's Cabin* and wrote directly to Stowe asking for help in editing her autobiographical *Incidents in the Life of a Slave Girl* (1861). When Stowe refused, Jacobs got the editorial support of Child, whose fiction earlier had had an impact on Wells Brown. After escaping from slavery, Jacobs lived in New York City in the household of the brother of the best-selling writer Fanny Fern, Nathaniel Parker Willis, whom Fern satirized as "Hyacinth" in her most popular novel, *Ruth Hall*. Fern admired Whitman, Irving, and Hawthorne; and Hawthorne praised Fern in a letter to his editor and friend William Ticknor. Hawthorne also praised Rebecca Harding Davis, who claimed Hawthorne as one of her most important influences. After reading Davis's "Life in the Iron Mills" (1861), Hawthorne considered traveling to Wheeling, Virginia, to meet her, but was happy when she chose to visit him at his home in Concord, Massachusetts. Louisa May Alcott borrowed books from Emerson, got nature lessons from Thoreau, and read (and was influenced by) the fiction of her neighbor Nathaniel Hawthorne. Dickinson, whose family subscribed to numerous newspapers and magazines, and who ordered books by mail from Boston, read just about all of these authors and argued with them in many of her poems.

Most of the writers represented in this anthology also ranged beyond the borders of the United States. Washington Irving was in England when *The Sketch Book* was published, and he remained abroad for over a decade, serving as a U.S. diplomat in Spain; at the height of his early career, Cooper traveled to France in 1826 and remained in Europe for the next seven years. Two decades later, Margaret Fuller traveled to Italy and participated in the Roman Revolution of the late 1840s; and in the early 1850s Hawthorne became consul in Liverpool and remained in Europe for nearly eight years. Travel abroad was central to Poe's, Emerson's, and Longfellow's educations; Stowe made a grand tour of Europe during the 1850s; and Douglass, Wells Brown, Jacobs, and many other African Americans spent significant time in England. Melville toured England and later the Holy Land. All of these writers had friends abroad, regarded the literature of the United States as part of a larger world literature, and, accordingly, read widely, particularly in English and other European literatures.

A number of the U.S. authors from this period also had significant interests in the literatures of the southern Americas. Because of his fascination with Christopher Columbus, which culminated in his best-selling biography of 1828 and several other works about Spanish America, Irving was perhaps the most celebrated U.S. author to read widely in writings south of the national borders, but authors ranging from Hawthorne to Melville, Douglass to Whitman, Child to Wells Brown, exhibited a curiosity about the Caribbean and Central and South America. Douglass's "The Heroic Slave" and Melville's "Benito Cereno" are two compelling examples of works that look beyond the southern borders of the United States. Whitman also had a capacious hemispheric perspective on the Americas, and in the twentieth century he would find some of his most enthusiastic readers in Chile, Argentina, and Mexico.

As far as literary matters are concerned, all of the writers in this anthology were interested in much more than the contemporary. A glance at the footnotes in this volume will reveal the enormous influence of classics from ancient Greece and Rome, Greek and Roman myth, Indian and Asian religions (which is especially true for Thoreau), the English Renaissance (especially Shakespeare), Milton, English and German Romantics, the Bible, and a range of popular and classic literature from Scandinavian and numerous other countries. And yet even as many of these writers had a capacious vision that took them beyond national borders and the limits of any period chronology, they were aware that they resided in a relatively new nation lacking literary traditions, and that there was a burden on them to establish such traditions. Melville's essay "Hawthorne and His Mosses" is among the period's notable examples of such literary nationalist ambition, which was neither insular nor separatist. As Melville remarks when comparing Hawthorne to Shakespeare: "I do not say that Nathaniel of Salem is a greater than William of Avon, or as great. But the difference between the two men is by no means immeasurable." Melville, who resented British condescension toward American writers, aspired for parity between English and American literary traditions rather than a separation of American from English literature. With his emphasis on the democratic individual, Whitman was capable of a more hyperbolic American literary nationalism than any of the other writers in this volume, so it is ironic that the great majority of his most enthusiastic nineteenth-century readers lived in England.

In addition to making claims for an American literary nationalism, the writers in this anthology sought to *create* American literary traditions. They did so by looking back to earlier colonial literatures and claiming them as "American." Many of the colonial texts that we now read as canonical, such as works by John Winthrop and William Bradford, were first republished in the nineteenth century and owe some of their current status to their recovery by early national and antebellum writers. Linking their nineteenth-century writings to the colonial past, Sedgwick, Cooper, Hawthorne, Whittier, and many others created a sense of a continuously unfolding national history and literature that came to a fruition of sorts in the nineteenth century.

Crucial to this period of American literary history, then, was a pronounced sense among a number of its authors about their role not just in consolidating traditions but also in creating the traditions that would develop from their writings. Such an orientation is most pronounced in Whitman, whose poetry regularly imagines future readers and writers, but it is arguably a central impulse behind much of the literature of the period. In this respect, it should be kept in mind that a number of the writers represented in this anthology were somewhat neglected when they first began publishing, and that their greatest impact was not on writing of their own time but on writing to come. In addition to Whitman, who was generally neglected until the turn into the twentieth century, authors such as Thoreau, Melville, and Dickinson found their most enthusiastic readers in the twentieth century. Melville and Dickinson, for instance, weren't really "discovered" until the 1920s and 1930s, when they had an immediate impact on writers living then. Even those who were fairly well known during the antebellum period—Poe, Hawthorne, Douglass, and others—came to be much better known in the twentieth century (Douglass's 1845 *Narrative*, for instance, was not republished after the early 1850s until 1960) and in some ways exerted an influence on twentieth-century literature and culture more significant than what they exerted on their nineteenth-century contemporaries. The point that should be emphasized is that the diverse writings of the 1820–65 period continue to remain foundational to the study of American literature not only because of what they accomplished within their own antebellum moment but also because, as Whitman would say about himself, they ultimately cannot be contained within that moment and even within a national frame. The literature of this period encompasses multitudes and continues to write its (and our) literary futures.

AMERICAN LITERATURE 1820–1865

TEXTS	CONTEXTS
1815 Founding of the *North American Review*	**1815** Treaty of Ghent, ending the second war with England. Before news of the treaty reaches Andrew Jackson, he leads American troops to victory over the British at the Battle of New Orleans.
1817 William Cullen Bryant, **"Thanatopsis"**	
1820 Washington Irving, ***The Sketch Book***	**1820** Missouri Compromise admits Missouri as a slave state, Maine as a free state, and excludes slavery in the Louisiana Territory north of latitude 36° 30'
1821 Bryant, ***Poems***	**1821** Sequoyah (George Guess) invents syllabary in which Cherokee language can be written
1823 James Fenimore Cooper, ***The Pioneers***	**1823** Monroe Doctrine warns all European powers not to establish new colonies on either American continent
	1825 Erie Canal opens, connecting Great Lakes region with the Atlantic
1826 Cooper, ***The Last of the Mohicans***	
1827 David Cusick, *Sketches Of Ancient History of the Six Nations* • Lydia Sigourney, ***Poems*** • Catharine Sedgwick, ***Hope Leslie***	**1827** Baltimore & Ohio, first U.S. railroad
	1827–28 Cherokee Nation ratifies its new constitution • The newspaper *The Cherokee Phoenix* founded
1828–30 Cherokee Council composes **Memorials** to Congress	
1829 William Apess, ***A Son of the Forest*** • David Walker, **Appeal**	**1829–37** President Andrew Jackson encourages westward migration of white population
	1830 Congress passes Indian Removal Act, allowing Jackson to negotiate treaties with the eastern tribes for their relocation west of the Mississippi
	1831 William Lloyd Garrison starts *The Liberator*, antislavery journal • Nat Turner leads a slave rebellion in Southampton County, Virginia; approximately sixty whites are killed and two hundred blacks are killed in retaliation
1833 Black Hawk, ***Life***	
1835 William Glmore Simms, *The Yemassee: A Romance of Carolina*	
1836 Ralph Waldo Emerson, ***Nature***	
1837 Nathaniel Hawthorne, ***Twice-Told Tales***	**1837** Financial panic: failures of numerous banks lead to severe unemployment that persists into the early 1840s

Boldface titles indicate works in the anthology.

TEXTS	CONTEXTS
	1838 Around this time, Underground Railroad begins aiding slaves escaping north, often to Canada
	1838–39 "Trail of Tears": Cherokees forced from their homelands by federal troops
1839 Caroline Stansbury Kirkland, *A New Home—Who'll Follow?*	
1840 Richard Henry Dana Jr., ***Two Years before the Mast***	**1840** Founding of the Washingtonian Temperance Society; temperance quickly emerges as one of the most popular social reform movements of the period
1843 Margaret Fuller, **"The Great Lawsuit"** • Lydia Maria Child, ***Letters from New-York***	
	1844 Samuel Morse invents telegraph
1845 Edgar Allan Poe, **"The Raven"** • Frederick Douglass, ***Narrative of the Life of Frederick Douglass***	**1845** United States annexes Texas
	1846 David Wilmot, a congressman from Pennsylvania, proposes in Congress that slavery be banned in territories gained from the Mexican War; his proviso is defeated
	1846–48 United States wages war against Mexico; Treaty of Guadalupe Hidalgo cedes entire Southwest to United States
1847 Henry Wadsworth Longfellow, ***Evangeline***	**1847** Brigham Young leads Mormons from Nauvoo, Illinois, to Salt Lake, Utah Territory
	1848 Seneca Falls Convention inaugurates campaign for women's rights
	1848–49 Beginning years of the California Gold Rush, which brings hundreds of thousands of new settlers to California
1850 Nathaniel Hawthorne, ***The Scarlet Letter***	**1850** Fugitive Slave Act of the Compromise of 1850 obliges free states to return escaped slaves to slaveholders
1851 Herman Melville, ***Moby-Dick***	
1852 Harriet Beecher Stowe, ***Uncle Tom's Cabin***	
1853 William Wells Brown, ***Clotel***	
1854 Henry David Thoreau, ***Walden*** • Frances Ellen Watkins Harper, ***Poems on Miscellaneous Subjects***	**1854** Republican Party formed, consolidating antislavery factions • Kansas-Nebraska Act approved by Congress; the act repeals the Missouri Compromise, making it legal for the white voting residents of a territory to determine whether it should be admitted as a slave or free state

TEXTS	CONTEXTS
1855 Walt Whitman, *Leaves of Grass* • P. T. Barnum, *The Life of P.T. Barnum, Written by Himself*	
1857 Fanny Fern (Sarah Willis Parton), *Fresh Leaves*	**1857** Supreme Court *Dred Scott* decision denies citizenship to African Americans
1858 Abraham Lincoln, "A House Divided"	
1859 E.D.E.N. Southworth, *The Hidden Hand*	**1859** First successful U.S. oil well drilled, in Pennsylvania
1860–65 Emily Dickinson writes several hundred poems	**1860** Short-Lived Pony Express runs from Missouri to California
1861 Harriet Jacobs, *Incidents in the Life of a Slave Girl* • Rebecca Harding Davis, *Life in the Iron-Mills*	**1861** South Carolina batteries fire on U.S. fort, initiating the Civil War; Southern states secede from the Union and found the Confederate States of America
	1861–65 Civil War
1862 Elizabeth Stoddard, *The Morgesons*	
	1863 Emancipation Proclamation • Battle of Gettysburg
	1865 Thirteenth Amendment abolishes slavery in the United States
1866 John Greenleaf Whittier, *Snow-Bound: A Winter Idyl*	**1866** Completion of two successful transatlantic cables • Civil Rights Act
	1868 Fourteenth Amendment grants citizenship to those born or naturalized in the United States
1868–69 Louisa May Alcott, *Little Women*	
	1869 First transcontinental railroad completed; Central Pacific construction crews composed largely of Chinese laborers

WASHINGTON IRVING
1783–1859

Washington Irving had an unusually long and varied career, publishing his first satirical essays in 1802, when he was nineteen, and his last book, a five-volume life of George Washington, just a few months before he died at age seventy-six. Celebrated by Americans for his contributions to a burgeoning national literature, Irving also became the first American writer of the nineteenth century to achieve an international literary reputation. Although he was regarded as a genial and comic writer, Irving regularly addressed darker and more complex themes of historical transformation and personal dislocation. His innovative travel sketches blurred the line between the personal essay and fiction, and he is considered one of the "inventors" of the modern short story. During a time in which there were no international copyright agreements, he managed to secure simultaneous British and American copyrights for his work. His canny understanding of the literary marketplace helped him to become the first American who was able to support himself solely through his writing.

Irving was born in New York City on April 3, 1783, the last of eleven children of a Scottish-born father and English-born mother. He read widely in English literature at home, modeling his early prose on the *Spectator* papers by Joseph Addison and delighting in many other writers, including Shakespeare, Oliver Goldsmith, and Laurence Sterne. His brothers enjoyed writing poems and essays as companionable recreation, and, inspired by their example, he wrote a series of satirical essays on the theater and New York society under the pseudonym of Jonathan Oldstyle. Nine of these essays were published in his brother Peter's newspaper, the *Morning Chronicle*, during 1802–3.

When Irving showed signs of tuberculosis in 1804, his brothers sent him abroad for a two-year tour of Europe. On his return in 1806, he studied law with Judge Josiah Hoffman, and he was admitted to the bar shortly thereafter. More important for his literary career, he and his brother William (along with William's brother-in-law, James Kirke Paulding) started a satirical magazine, *Salmagundi* (the name of a spicy hash), which ran from 1807 to 1808 with poems, sketches, and essays on a range of topics. In 1808 Irving began work on *A History of New-York from the Beginning of the World to the End of the Dutch Dynasty*, at first conceiving it as a parody of Samuel Lathem Mitchell's *The Picture of New-York* (1807), then taking on a variety of satiric targets, including President Jefferson, whom he portrayed as an early Dutch governor of New Amsterdam, William the Testy. Narrated by the comical invented character Diedrich Knickerbocker, who dabbles in historical research, *A History of New-York* appeared in 1809 and brought Irving his first literary celebrity. That same year Judge Hoffman's daughter Matilda, to whom he had become engaged, died suddenly from consumption; Irving would remain a lifelong bachelor. Most biographers attribute Irving's bachelorhood to his grief at the death of Matilda. But her death did free him from the commitment he had made to her father to devote himself to the law, which he hated; and in the figure of his most famous fictional persona, the genial bachelor Geoffrey Crayon, and even in his most famous fictional creation, Rip Van Winkle, there are hints that the single life suited Irving just fine.

During the War of 1812 Irving was editor of the *Analectic Magazine*, which he filled mainly with writings from British periodicals, while also including his own timely series of patriotic biographical sketches of American naval heroes. Toward the end of the war he was made a colonel in the New York State militia. In May 1815, a major change occurred in his life: he left for Europe and stayed away for seventeen years. At first he worked in Liverpool with his brother Peter, an importer of English hardware, but in 1818, shortly after their mother died in New York, Peter went bankrupt. Grief-stricken, and yet grateful to be freed from the responsibilities of working for the family firm, Irving once again took up writing. He met Sir Walter Scott, an admirer of the Knickerbocker *History*, who directed him to the wealth of unused literary material in German folktales. There, as scholars have shown, Irving found the source for "Rip Van Winkle," some passages of which are close paraphrases of the original, J.C.C.N. Otmar's "Peter Klaus" (1800), which also depicts a protagonist sleeping for twenty years. Irving began sending sections of *The Sketch Book* to the United States for publication in what would turn out to be seven installments published from 1819 to 1820. When the two-volume complete *Sketch Book* was printed in England in 1820, it made Irving famous and brought him the friendship of many of the leading British writers of the time. As Irving knew, part of his success derived from British reviewers' pleasure that a book by an American, as Frances Jeffrey wrote in the *Edinburgh Review*, "should be written throughout with the greatest care and accuracy, and worked up to great purity and beauty of diction, on the model of the most elegant and polished of our native writers." Addison lay behind Irving's depiction of English country life, and Oliver Goldsmith influenced his sketch of Westminster Abbey. But among *The Sketch Book*'s graceful tributes to English scenes and characters were two immensely popular tales set in rural New York, "Rip Van Winkle" and "The Legend of Sleepy Hollow."

Irving's next two books, *Bracebridge Hall* (1822) and *Tales of a Traveller* (1824), were less successful, and in 1824 he accepted an invitation from the American minister to Spain to work with original manuscripts in Madrid to produce an account of Columbus's voyages. In 1828 he published *The Life and Voyages of Christopher Columbus*, which became the basis for standard schoolroom accounts of Columbus during the nineteenth and early twentieth century. Out of Irving's Spanish years came also *The Conquest of Granada* (1829), *Voyages and Discoveries of the Companions of Columbus* (1831), and *The Alhambra* (1832), which was soon known as "the Spanish *Sketch Book*."

In 1829 Irving was appointed secretary to the American legation in London. When he finally returned to the United States in 1832 after his long absence, critics wondered openly about whether this much admired "native" writer had become Europeanized. Setting out to reclaim his Americanness, Irving proclaimed his love for his country and headed west, taking a horseback journey into what is now Oklahoma. His travels and research resulted in three major works on the American West: *A Tour of the Prairies* (1835); *Astoria* (1836), an account of John Jacob Astor's fur-trading colony in Oregon; and *The Adventures of Captain Bonneville, U.S.A.* (1837), a narrative of explorations in the Rockies and the Far West.

In the late 1830s Irving bought and began refurbishing a house near Tarrytown, along the Hudson north of New York City. But before settling down, in 1842 he accepted an appointment as minister to Spain and returned to Europe, spending four years in Madrid. After his return to the United States in 1846, he arranged with G.P. Putnam to publish a collected edition of his writings; he also prepared a biography of Oliver Goldsmith (1849). Irving's main work after 1850 was his long-contemplated life of George Washington, which he himself regarded as his greatest literary accomplishment. He collapsed just after finishing the last of its five volumes, and he died a few months later, on November 28, 1859.

Cooper, Hawthorne, and many other American writers were inspired by the success of *The Sketch Book*. Although Melville, in his essay on Hawthorne's *Mosses from an Old Manse*, declared his preference for creative geniuses over adept imitators like Irving, he could not escape Irving's influence, which emerges both in his short stories and in a late poem, "Rip Van Winkle's Lilacs." From the beginning, many readers identified with Rip as a counterhero, an anti-Franklinian who made a success of failure; and subsequent generations have responded profoundly to Irving's pervasive theme of mutability, especially as localized in his portrayal of the bewildering rapidity of change in American life.

The Author's Account of *Himself*[1]

> I am of this mind with Homer, that as the snaile that crept out of her shel was turned eftsoones into a toad, and thereby was forced to make a stoole to sit on; so the traveller that stragleth from his owne country is in a short time transformed into so monstrous a shape, that he is faine to alter his mansion with his manners, and to live where he can, not where he would.
>
> Lyly's *Euphues*.[2]

I was always fond of visiting new scenes, and observing strange characters and manners. Even when a mere child I began my travels, and made many tours of discovery into foreign parts and unknown regions of my native city, to the frequent alarm of my parents, and the emolument of the town-crier. As I grew into boyhood, I extended the range of my observations. My holiday afternoons were spent in rambles about the surrounding country. I made myself familiar with all its places famous in history or fable. I knew every spot where a murder or robbery had been committed, or a ghost been seen. I visited the neighbouring villages, and added greatly to my stock of knowledge, by noting their habits and customs, and conversing with their sages and great men. I even journeyed one long summer's day to the summit of the most distant hill, from whence I stretched my eye over many a mile of terra incognita,[3] and was astonished to find how vast a globe I inhabited.

This rambling propensity strengthened with my years. Books of voyages and travels became my passion, and in devouring their contents, I neglected the regular exercises of the school. How wistfully would I wander about the pier heads in fine weather, and watch the parting ships, bound to distant climes—with what longing eyes would I gaze after their lessening sails, and waft myself in imagination to the ends of the earth.

Farther reading and thinking, though they brought this vague inclination into more reasonable bounds, only served to make it more decided. I visited various parts of my own country; and had I been merely a lover of fine scenery, I should have felt little desire to seek elsewhere for its gratification: for on no country have the charms of nature been more prodigally lavished. Her mighty lakes, like oceans of liquid silver; her mountains, with their bright aerial tints; her valleys, teeming with wild fertility; her tremendous cataracts, thundering in their solitudes; her boundless plains, waving with spontaneous verdure; her broad deep rivers, rolling in solemn silence to the ocean; her trackless forests, where vegetation puts forth all its magnificence; her

1. The text is taken from the May 1819 first installment of *The Sketch Book of Geoffrey Crayon, Gent.* (For *The Sketch Book* and some of his subsequent essays and books, Irving adopted the pseudonym of Geoffrey Crayon.)
2. From *Euphues and His England* (1580), by the English writer John Lyly (1554–1606).
3. Unknown land (Latin).

skies, kindling with the magic of summer clouds and glorious sunshine:—no, never need an American look beyond his own country for the sublime and beautiful of natural scenery.

But Europe held forth all the charms of storied and poetical association. There were to be seen the masterpieces of art, the refinements of highly cultivated society, the quaint peculiarities of ancient and local custom. My native country was full of youthful promise; Europe was rich in the accumulated treasures of age. Her very ruins told the history of times gone by, and every mouldering stone was a chronicle. I longed to wander over the scenes of renowned achievement—to tread, as it were, in the footsteps of antiquity—to loiter about the ruined castle—to meditate on the falling tower—to escape, in short, from the commonplace realities of the present, and lose myself among the shadowy grandeurs of the past.

I had, beside all this, an earnest desire to see the great men of the earth. We have, it is true, our great men in America: not a city but has an ample share of them. I have mingled among them in my time, and been almost withered by the shade into which they cast me; for there is nothing so baleful to a small man as the shade of a great one, particularly the great man of a city. But I was anxious to see the great men of Europe; for I had read in the works of various philosophers, that all animals degenerated in America, and man among the number.[4] A great man of Europe, therefore, thought I, must be as superior to a great man of America, as a peak of the Alps to a highland of the Hudson; and in this idea I was confirmed, by observing the comparative importance and swelling magnitude of many English travellers among us; who, I was assured, were very little people in their own country. I will visit this land of wonders, therefore, thought I, and see the gigantic race from which I am degenerated.

It has been either my good or evil lot to have my roving passion gratified. I have wandered through different countries, and witnessed many of the shifting scenes of life. I cannot say that I have studied them with the eye of a philosopher, but rather with the sauntering gaze with which humble lovers of the picturesque stroll from the window of one print shop to another; caught sometimes by the delineations of beauty, sometimes by the distortions of caricature, and sometimes by the loveliness of landscape. As it is the fashion for modern tourists to travel pencil in hand, and bring home their port folios filled with sketches, I am disposed to get up a few for the entertainment of my friends. When I look over, however, the hints and memorandums I have taken down for the purpose, my heart almost fails me to find how my idle humour has led me aside from the great objects studied by every regular traveller who would make a book. I fear I shall give equal disappointment with an unlucky landscape painter, who had travelled on the continent, but following the bent of his vagrant inclination, had sketched in nooks, and corners, and by-places. His sketch book was accordingly crowded with cottages, and landscapes, and obscure ruins; but he had neglected to paint St. Peter's, or the

4. In the late 18th century, some Europeans argued that the North American environment caused humans to degenerate physically. These arguments were made most forcefully by the French naturalist Georges-Louis Leclerc, Comte de Buffon (1707–1788). Thomas Jefferson refuted de Buffon in his 1787 *Notes on the State of Virginia*.

Coliseum; the cascade of Terni,[5] or the bay of Naples; and had not a single glacier or volcano in his whole collection.

1819

Rip Van Winkle[1]

The following Tale was found among the papers of the late Diedrich Knickerbocker, an old gentleman of New-York, who was very curious in the Dutch history of the province, and the manners of the descendants from its primitive settlers. His historical researches, however, did not lay so much among books, as among men; for the former are lamentably scanty on his favourite topics; whereas he found the old burghers, and still more, their wives, rich in that legendary lore, so invaluable to true history. Whenever, therefore, he happened upon a genuine Dutch family, snugly shut up in its low-roofed farm house, under a spreading sycamore, he looked upon it as a little clasped volume of black-letter,[2] and studied it with the zeal of a book-worm.

The result of all these researches was a history of the province, during the reign of the Dutch governors, which he published some years since. There have been various opinions as to the literary character of his work, and, to tell the truth, it is not a whit better than it should be. Its chief merit is its scrupulous accuracy, which, indeed, was a little questioned, on its first appearance, but has since been completely established;[3] and it is now admitted into all historical collections, as a book of unquestionable authority.

The old gentleman died shortly after the publication of his work, and now, that he is dead and gone, it cannot do much harm to his memory, to say, that his time might have been much better employed in weightier labours. He, however, was apt to ride his hobby his own way; and though it did now and then kick up the dust a little in the eyes of his neighbours, and grieve the spirit of some friends, for whom he felt the truest deference and affection; yet his errors and follies are remembered "more in sorrow than in anger,"[4] and it begins to be suspected, that he never intended to injure or offend. But however his memory may be appreciated by critics, it is still held dear among many folk, whose good opinion is well worth having; particularly certain biscuit bakers, who have gone so far as to imprint his likeness on their new year cakes, and have thus given him a chance for immortality,

5. The locale of Mount Vesuvius and the ruins of Pompeii. Other popular tourist sites listed here are St. Peter's Basilica (built 1506–1626) in Vatican City; the Roman Colosseum (built c. 70–86 C.E.); and the Cascata della Mamore, a man-made waterfall built near Terni (60 miles north of Rome) in 271 B.C.E.

1. "Rip Van Winkle" was the last of the sketches printed in the May 1819 first installment of *The Sketch Book*, the source of the present text.

2. Typeface in early printed books, resembling medieval script; such books, because of their value, were often equipped with clasps so they could be shut tightly and even locked.

3. A comical allusion to the deliberate inaccuracies of his 1809 Knickerbocker's *History of New-York*.

4. Shakespeare's *Hamlet* 1.2.231. To this quotation Irving appended the following footnote: "Vide [see] the excellent discourse of G. C. Verplanck, Esq. before the New-York Historical Society." If Irving's friend Gulian C. Verplanck ever made such an address about a fictional character, it would have been in fun.

almost equal to being stamped on a Waterloo medal, or a Queen Anne's farthing.[5]

Rip Van Winkle
A Posthumous Writing of Diedrich Knickerbocker

> By Woden, God of Saxons,
> From whence comes Wensday, that is Wodensday,
> Truth is a thing that ever I will keep
> Unto thylke day in which I creep into
> My sepulchre—
> —CARTWRIGHT[6]

Whoever has made a voyage up the Hudson, must remember the Kaatskill mountains.[7] They are a dismembered branch of the great Appalachian family, and are seen away to the west of the river, swelling up to a noble height, and lording it over the surrounding country. Every change of season, every change of weather, indeed, every hour of the day, produces some change in the magical hues and shapes of these mountains, and they are regarded by all the good wives, far and near, as perfect barometers. When the weather is fair and settled, they are clothed in blue and purple, and print their bold outlines on the clear evening sky; but some times, when the rest of the landscape is cloudless, they will gather a hood of gray vapours about their summits, which, in the last rays of the setting sun, will glow and light up like a crown of glory.

At the foot of these fairy mountains, the voyager may have descried the light smoke curling up from a village, whose shingle roofs gleam among the trees, just where the blue tints of the upland melt away into the fresh green of the nearer landscape. It is a little village of great antiquity, having been founded by some of the Dutch colonists, in the early times of the province, just about the beginning of the government of the good Peter Stuyvesant,[8] (may he rest in peace!) and there were some of the houses of the original settlers standing within a few years, with lattice windows, gable fronts surmounted with weathercocks, and built of small yellow bricks brought from Holland.

In that same village, and in one of these very houses, (which, to tell the precise truth, was sadly time worn and weather beaten,) there lived many years since, while the country was yet a province of Great Britain, a simple good natured fellow, of the name of Rip Van Winkle. He was a descendant of the Van Winkles who figured so gallantly in the chivalrous days of Peter Stuyvesant, and accompanied him to the siege of Fort Christina. He inherited, however, but little of the martial character of his ancestors. I have observed that he was a simple good natured man; he was moreover a kind neighbour, and an obedient, henpecked husband. Indeed, to the latter cir-

5. Waterloo medals were minted liberally after the defeat of Napoleon in 1815, whereas farthings (tiny coins) from the reign of Queen Anne of England (1702–14) were commonly, though wrongly, considered rare.
6. In this quotation from *The Ordinary*, 3.1.1050–54, a play by the English writer William Cartwright (1611–1643), the speaker is a pedant named Moth. "Woden": Old English for "Odin," the chief Norse god.
7. Catskill Mountains, a range in southeastern New York.
8. Last governor of the Dutch province of New Netherlands (1592–1672); in 1655 (as mentioned in the next paragraph), his troops defeated Swedish colonists at Fort Christina, near what is now Wilmington, Delaware.

cumstance might be owing that meekness of spirit which gained him such universal popularity; for those men are most apt to be obsequious and conciliating abroad, who are under the discipline of shrews at home. Their tempers, doubtless, are rendered pliant and malleable in the fiery furnace of domestic tribulation, and a curtain lecture[9] is worth all the sermons in the world for teaching the virtues of patience and long suffering. A termagant wife may, therefore, in some respects, be considered a tolerable blessing; and if so, Rip Van Winkle was thrice blessed.

Certain it is, that he was a great favourite among all the good wives of the village, who, as usual with the amiable sex, took his part in all family squabbles, and never failed, whenever they talked those matters over in their evening gossippings, to lay all the blame on Dame Van Winkle. The children of the village, too, would shout with joy whenever he approached. He assisted at their sports, made their playthings, taught them to fly kites and shoot marbles, and told them long stories of ghosts, witches, and Indians. Whenever he went dodging about the village, he was surrounded by a troop of them, hanging on his skirts, clambering on his back, and playing a thousand tricks on him with impunity; and not a dog would bark at him throughout the neighbourhood.

The great error in Rip's composition was an insuperable aversion to all kinds of profitable labour. It could not be for the want of assiduity or perseverance; for he would sit on a wet rock, with a rod as long and heavy as a Tartar's lance, and fish all day without a murmur, even though he should not be encouraged by a single nibble. He would carry a fowling piece on his shoulder, for hours together, trudging through woods and swamps, and up hill and down dale, to shoot a few squirrels or wild pigeons. He would never even refuse to assist a neighbour in the roughest toil, and was a foremost man at all country frolicks for husking Indian corn, or building stone fences; the women of the village, too, used to employ him to run their errands, and to do such little odd jobs as their less obliging husbands would not do for them;—in a word, Rip was ready to attend to any body's business but his own; but as to doing family duty, and keeping his farm in order, it was impossible.

In fact, he declared it was no use to work on his farm; it was the most pestilent little piece of ground in the whole country; every thing about it went wrong, and would go wrong, in spite of him. His fences were continually falling to pieces; his cow would either go astray, or get among the cabbages; weeds were sure to grow quicker in his fields than any where else; the rain always made a point of setting in just as he had some out-door work to do. So that though his patrimonial estate had dwindled away under his management, acre by acre, until there was little more left than a mere patch of Indian corn and potatoes, yet it was the worst conditioned farm in the neighbourhood.

His children, too, were as ragged and wild as if they belonged to nobody. His son Rip, an urchin begotten in his own likeness, promised to inherit the habits, with the old clothes of his father. He was generally seen trooping like a colt at his mother's heels, equipped in a pair of his father's cast-off

9. Archaic term for when a wife says no to her husband's sexual entreaties after the curtains around the four-poster bed have been drawn for the night.

galligaskins,[1] which he had much ado to hold up with one hand, as a fine lady does her train in bad weather.

Rip Van Winkle, however, was one of those happy mortals, of foolish, well-oiled dispositions, who take the world easy, eat white bread or brown, which ever can be got with least thought or trouble, and would rather starve on a penny than work for a pound. If left to himself, he would have whistled life away, in perfect contentment; but his wife kept continually dinning in his ears about his idleness, his carelessness, and the ruin he was bringing on his family. Morning, noon, and night, her tongue was incessantly going, and every thing he said or did was sure to produce a torrent of household eloquence. Rip had but one way of replying to all lectures of the kind, and that, by frequent use, had grown into a habit. He shrugged his shoulders, shook his head, cast up his eyes, but said nothing. This, however, always provoked a fresh volley from his wife, so that he was fain to draw off his forces, and take to the outside of the house—the only side which, in truth, belongs to a henpecked husband.

Rip's sole domestic adherent was his dog Wolf, who was as much henpecked as his master; for Dame Van Winkle regarded them as companions in idleness, and even looked upon Wolf with an evil eye, as the cause of his master's so often going astray. True it is, in all points of spirit befitting an honourable dog, he was as courageous an animal as ever scoured the woods—but what courage can withstand the ever-during and all-besetting terrors of a woman's tongue? The moment Wolf entered the house, his crest fell, his tail drooped to the ground, or curled between his legs, he sneaked about with a gallows air, casting many a sidelong glance at Dame Van Winkle, and at the least flourish of a broomstick or ladle, would fly to the door with yelping precipitation.

Times grew worse and worse with Rip Van Winkle as years of matrimony rolled on; a tart temper never mellows with age, and a sharp tongue is the only edge tool that grows keener by constant use. For a long while he used to console himself, when driven from home, by frequenting a kind of perpetual club of the sages, philosophers, and other idle personages of the village, that held its sessions on a bench before a small inn, designated by a rubicund portrait of his majesty George the Third. Here they used to sit in the shade, of a long lazy summer's day, talk listlessly over village gossip, or tell endless sleepy stories about nothing. But it would have been worth any statesman's money to have heard the profound discussions that sometimes took place, when by chance an old newspaper fell into their hands, from some passing traveller. How solemnly they would listen to the contents, as drawled out by Derrick Van Bummel, the schoolmaster, a dapper learned little man, who was not to be daunted by the most gigantic word in the dictionary; and how sagely they would deliberate upon public events some months after they had taken place.

The opinions of this junto[2] were completely controlled by Nicholas Vedder, a patriarch of the village, and landlord of the inn, at the door of which he took his seat from morning till night, just moving sufficiently to avoid the sun, and keep in the shade of a large tree; so that the neighbours could tell the hour by his movements as accurately as by a sun dial. It is true, he was

1. Loose, wide trousers.

2. Ruling committee (Spanish).

rarely heard to speak, but smoked his pipe incessantly. His adherents, however, (for every great man has his adherents,) perfectly understood him, and knew how to gather his opinions. When any thing that was read or related displeased him, he was observed to smoke his pipe vehemently, and send forth short, frequent, and angry puffs; but when pleased, he would inhale the smoke slowly and tranquilly, and emit it in light and placid clouds, and sometimes taking the pipe from his mouth, and letting the fragrant vapour curl about his nose, would gravely nod his head in token of perfect approbation.

From even this strong hold the unlucky Rip was at length routed by his termagant wife, who would suddenly break in upon the tranquillity of the assemblage, call the members all to nought, nor was that august personage, Nicholas Vedder himself, sacred from the daring tongue of this terrible virago, who charged him outright with encouraging her husband in habits of idleness.

Poor Rip was at last reduced almost to despair; and his only alternative to escape from the labour of the farm and the clamour of his wife, was to take gun in hand, and stroll away into the woods. Here he would sometimes seat himself at the foot of a tree, and share the contents of his wallet[3] with Wolf, with whom he sympathised as a fellow sufferer in persecution. "Poor Wolf," he would say, "thy mistress leads thee a dogs' life of it; but never mind, my lad, while I live thou shalt never want a friend to stand by thee!" Wolf would wag his tail, look wistfully in his master's face, and if dogs can feel pity, I verily believe he reciprocated the sentiment with all his heart.

In a long ramble of the kind on a fine autumnal day, Rip had unconsciously scrambled to one of the highest parts of the Kaatskill mountains. He was after his favourite sport of squirrel shooting, and the still solitudes had echoed and re-echoed with the reports of his gun. Panting and fatigued, he threw himself, late in the afternoon, on a green knoll, covered with mountain herbage, that crowned the brow of a precipice. From an opening between the trees, he could overlook all the lower country for many a mile of rich woodland. He saw at a distance the lordly Hudson, far, far below him, moving on its silent but majestic course, the reflection of a purple cloud, or the sail of a lagging bark, here and there sleeping on its glassy bosom, and at last losing itself in the blue highlands.

On the other side he looked down into a deep mountain glen, wild, lonely, and shagged, the bottom filled with fragments from the impending cliffs, and scarcely lighted by the reflected rays of the setting sun. For some time Rip lay musing on this scene, evening was gradually advancing, the mountains began to throw their long blue shadows over the valleys, he saw that it would be dark long before he could reach the village, and he heaved a heavy sigh when he thought of encountering the terrors of Dame Van Winkle.

As he was about to descend, he heard a voice from a distance, hallooing, "Rip Van Winkle! Rip Van Winkle!" He looked around, but could see nothing but a crow winging its solitary flight across the mountain. He thought his fancy must have deceived him, and turned again to descend, when he heard the same cry ring through the still evening air; "Rip Van Winkle! Rip Van Winkle!"—at the same time Wolf bristled up his back, and giving a low growl,

3. Knapsack.

skulked to his master's side, looking fearfully down into the glen. Rip now felt a vague apprehension stealing over him; he looked anxiously in the same direction, and perceived a strange figure slowly toiling up the rocks, and bending under the weight of something he carried on his back. He was surprised to see any human being in this lonely and unfrequented place, but supposing it to be some one of the neighbourhood in need of his assistance, he hastened down to yield it.

On nearer approach, he was still more surprised at the singularity of the stranger's appearance. He was a short square built old fellow, with thick bushy hair, and a grizzled beard. His dress was of the antique Dutch fashion—a cloth jerkin[4] strapped round the waist—several pair of breeches, the outer one of ample volume, decorated with rows of buttons down the sides, and bunches at the knees. He bore on his shoulder a stout keg, that seemed full of liquor, and made signs for Rip to approach and assist him with the load. Though rather shy and distrustful of this new acquaintance, Rip complied with his usual alacrity, and mutually relieving each other, they clambered up a narrow gully, apparently the dry bed of a mountain torrent. As they ascended, Rip every now and then heard long rolling peals, like distant thunder, that seemed to issue out of a deep ravine, or rather cleft between lofty rocks, toward which their rugged path conducted. He paused for an instant, but supposing it to be the muttering of one of those transient thunder showers which often take place in mountain heights, he proceeded. Passing through the ravine, they came to a hollow, like a small amphitheatre, surrounded by perpendicular precipices, over the brinks of which impending trees shot their branches, so that you only caught glimpses of the azure sky, and the bright evening cloud. During the whole time, Rip and his companion had laboured on in silence; for though the former marvelled greatly what could be the object of carrying a keg of liquor up this wild mountain, yet there was something strange and incomprehensible about the unknown, that inspired awe, and checked familiarity.

On entering the amphitheatre, new objects of wonder presented themselves. On a level spot in the centre was a company of odd-looking personages playing at nine-pins. They were dressed in a quaint, outlandish fashion: some wore short doublets,[5] others jerkins, with long knives in their belts, and most had enormous breeches, of similar style with that of the guide's. Their visages, too, were peculiar: one had a large head, broad face, and small piggish eyes; the face of another seemed to consist entirely of nose, and was surmounted by a white sugarloaf hat, set off with a little red cockstail. They all had beards, of various shapes and colours. There was one who seemed to be the commander. He was a stout old gentleman, with a weather-beaten countenance; he wore a laced doublet, broad belt and hanger,[6] high crowned hat and feather, red stockings, and high heeled shoes, with roses in them. The whole group reminded Rip of the figures in an old Flemish painting, in the parlour of Dominie[7] Van Schaick, the village parson, and which had been brought over from Holland at the time of the settlement.

What seemed particularly odd to Rip, was, that though these folks were evidently amusing themselves, yet they maintained the gravest faces, the

4. Jacket fitted tightly at the waist.
5. Male jacket covering from neck to upper thighs, where it hooked to hose.
6. Short, curved sword.
7. Minister.

most mysterious silence, and were, withal, the most melancholy party of pleasure he had ever witnessed. Nothing interrupted the stillness of the scene, but the noise of the balls, which, whenever they were rolled, echoed along the mountains like rumbling peals of thunder.

As Rip and his companion approached them, they suddenly desisted from their play, and stared at him with such fixed statue-like gaze, and such strange, uncouth, lack lustre countenances, that his heart turned within him, and his knees smote together. His companion now emptied the contents of the keg into large flagons, and made signs to him to wait upon the company. He obeyed with fear and trembling; they quaffed the liquor in profound silence, and then returned to their game.

By degrees, Rip's awe and apprehension subsided. He even ventured, when no eye was fixed upon him, to taste the beverage, which he found had much of the flavour of excellent Hollands.[8] He was naturally a thirsty soul, and was soon tempted to repeat the draught. One taste provoked another, and he reiterated his visits to the flagon so often, that at length his senses were overpowered, his eyes swam in his head, his head gradually declined, and he fell into a deep sleep.

On awaking, he found himself on the green knoll from whence he had first seen the old man of the glen. He rubbed his eyes—it was a bright sunny morning. The birds were hopping and twittering among the bushes, and the eagle was wheeling aloft, and breasting the pure mountain breeze. "Surely," thought Rip, "I have not slept here all night." He recalled the occurrences before he fell asleep. The strange man with the keg of liquor—the mountain ravine—the wild retreat among the rocks—the wo-begone party at nine-pins—the flagon—"Oh! that flagon! that wicked flagon!" thought Rip—"what excuse shall I make to Dame Van Winkle?"

He looked round for his gun, but in place of the clean well-oiled fowling-piece, he found an old firelock lying by him, the barrel encrusted with rust, the lock falling off, and the stock worm-eaten. He now suspected that the grave roysters[9] of the mountain had put a trick upon him, and having dosed him with liquor, had robbed him of his gun. Wolf, too, had disappeared, but he might have strayed away after a squirrel or partridge. He whistled after him, shouted his name, but all in vain; the echoes repeated his whistle and shout, but no dog was to be seen.

He determined to revisit the scene of the last evening's gambol, and if he met with any of the party, to demand his dog and gun. As he arose to walk he found himself stiff in the joints, and wanting in his usual activity. "These mountain beds do not agree with me," thought Rip, "and if this frolick should lay me up with a fit of the rheumatism, I shall have a blessed time with Dame Van Winkle." With some difficulty he got down into the glen: he found the gully up which he and his companion had ascended the preceding evening, but to his astonishment a mountain stream was now foaming down it, leaping from rock to rock, and filling the glen with babbling murmurs. He, however, made shift to scramble up its sides, working his toilsome way through thickets of birch, sassafras, and witch hazle, and sometimes tripped up or

8. Gin made in Holland.

9. Revelers.

entangled by the wild grape vines that twisted their coils and tendrils from tree to tree, and spread a kind of network in his path.

At length he reached to where the ravine had opened through the cliffs, to the amphitheatre; but no traces of such opening remained. The rocks presented a high impenetrable wall, over which the torrent came tumbling in a sheet of feathery foam, and fell into a broad deep basin, black from the shadows of the surrounding forest. Here, then, poor Rip was brought to a stand. He again called and whistled after his dog; he was only answered by the cawing of a flock of idle crows, sporting high in air about a dry tree that overhung a sunny precipice; and who, secure in their elevation, seemed to look down and scoff at the poor man's perplexities. What was to be done? the morning was passing away, and Rip felt famished for his breakfast. He grieved to give up his dog and gun; he dreaded to meet his wife; but it would not do to starve among the mountains. He shook his head, shouldered the rusty firelock, and, with a heart full of trouble and anxiety, turned his steps homeward.

As he approached the village, he met a number of people, but none that he knew, which somewhat surprised him, for he had thought himself acquainted with every one in the country round. Their dress, too, was of a different fashion from that to which he was accustomed. They all stared at him with equal marks of surprise, and whenever they cast eyes upon him, invariably stroked their chins. The constant recurrence of this gesture, induced Rip, involuntarily, to do the same, when, to his astonishment, he found his beard had grown a foot long!

He had now entered the skirts of the village. A troop of strange children ran at his heels, hooting after him, and pointing at his gray beard. The dogs, too, not one of which he recognized for his old acquaintances, barked at him as he passed. The very village seemed altered: it was larger and more populous. There were rows of houses which he had never seen before, and those which had been his familiar haunts had disappeared. Strange names were over the doors—strange faces at the windows—every thing was strange. His mind now began to misgive him, that both he and the world around him were bewitched. Surely this was his native village, which he had left but the day before. There stood the Kaatskill mountains—there ran the silver Hudson at a distance—there was every hill and dale precisely as it had always been—Rip was sorely perplexed—"That flagon last night," thought he, "has addled my poor head sadly!"

It was with some difficulty he found the way to his own house, which he approached with silent awe, expecting every moment to hear the shrill voice of Dame Van Winkle. He found the house gone to decay—the roof fallen in, the windows shattered, and the doors off the hinges. A half starved dog, that looked like Wolf, was skulking about it. Rip called him by name, but the cur snarled, showed his teeth, and passed on. This was an unkind cut indeed—"My very dog," sighed poor Rip, "has forgotten me!"

He entered the house, which, to tell the truth, Dame Van Winkle had always kept in neat order. It was empty, forlorn, and apparently abandoned. This desolateness overcame all his connubial fears—he called loudly for his wife and children—the lonely chambers rung for a moment with his voice, and then all again was silence.

He now hurried forth, and hastened to his old resort, the little village inn—but it too was gone. A large rickety wooden building stood in its place, with great gaping windows, some of them broken, and mended with old hats and petticoats, and over the door was painted, "The Union Hotel, by Jonathan Doolittle." Instead of the great tree that used to shelter the quiet little Dutch inn of yore, there now was reared a tall naked pole, with something on top that looked like a red night cap,[1] and from it was fluttering a flag, on which was a singular assemblage of stars and stripes—all this was strange and incomprehensible. He recognised on the sign, however, the ruby face of King George, under which he had smoked so many a peaceful pipe, but even this was singularly metamorphosed. The red coat was changed for one of blue and buff,[2] a sword was stuck in the hand instead of a sceptre, the head was decorated with a cocked hat, and underneath was painted in large characters, GENERAL WASHINGTON.

There was, as usual, a crowd of folk about the door, but none that Rip recollected. The very character of the people seemed changed. There was a busy, bustling, disputatious tone about it, instead of the accustomed phlegm and drowsy tranquillity. He looked in vain for the sage Nicholas Vedder, with his broad face, double chin, and fair long pipe, uttering clouds of tobacco smoke instead of idle speeches; or Van Bummel, the schoolmaster, doling forth the contents of an ancient newspaper. In place of these, a lean bilious looking fellow, with his pockets full of handbills, was haranguing vehemently about rights of citizens—election—members of congress—liberty—Bunker's hill—heroes of seventy-six—and other words, that were a perfect Babylonish jargon[3] to the bewildered Van Winkle.

The appearance of Rip, with his long grizzled beard, his rusty fowling piece, his uncouth dress, and the army of women and children that had gathered at his heels, soon attracted the attention of the tavern politicians. They crowded around him, eyeing him from head to foot, with great curiosity.[4] The orator bustled up to him, and drawing him partly aside, inquired "which side he voted?" Rip stared in vacant stupidity. Another short but busy little fellow pulled him by the arm, and raising on tiptoe, inquired in his ear, "whether he was Federal or Democrat."[5] Rip was equally at a loss to comprehend the question; when a knowing, self-important old gentleman, in a sharp cocked hat, made his way through the crowd, putting them to the right and left with his elbows as he passed, and planting himself before Van Winkle, with one arm akimbo, the other resting on his cane, his keen eyes and sharp hat penetrating, as it were, into his very soul, demanded, in an austere tone, "what brought him to the election with a gun on his shoulder, and a mob at his heels, and whether he meant to breed a riot in the village?" "Alas! gentlemen," cried Rip, somewhat dismayed, "I am a poor quiet man, a native of the place, and a loyal subject of the King, God bless him!"

Here a general shout burst from the bystanders—"A tory! a tory! a spy! a refugee! hustle him! away with him!" It was with great difficulty that the

1. Limp, close-fitting cap adopted during the French Revolution as a symbol of liberty (such caps were worn by freed slaves in ancient Rome). The pole is a "liberty pole"—i.e., a tall flagstaff topped by a liberty cap.
2. Colors of the Revolutionary uniform.
3. Cf. Genesis 11.1–9, Babel being confused with Babylon.
4. For a contemporary painting depicting Rip Van Winkle's appearance in his village, see John Quidor's *The Return of Rip Van Winkle* (1829) in the color plates section of this volume.
5. Political parties that developed in the Washington administration (1789–97), with Alexander Hamilton (1755–1804) leading the Federalists and Thomas Jefferson (1743–1826), the Democrats.

self-important man in the cocked hat restored order; and having assumed a tenfold austerity of brow, demanded again of the unknown culprit, what he came there for, and whom he was seeking. The poor man humbly assured them that he meant no harm; but merely came there in search of some of his neighbours, who used to keep about the tavern.

"Well—who are they?—name them."

Rip bethought himself a moment, and inquired, "where's Nicholas Vedder?"

There was a silence for a little while, when an old man replied, in a thin piping voice, "Nicholas Vedder? why he is dead and gone these eighteen years! There was a wooden tombstone in the church yard that used to tell all about him, but that's rotted and gone too."

"Where's Brom Dutcher?"

"Oh he went off to the army in the beginning of the war; some say he was killed at the battle of Stoney-Point—others say he was drowned in a squall, at the foot of Antony's Nose.[6] I don't know—he never came back again."

"Where's Van Bummel, the schoolmaster?"

"He went off to the wars too, was a great militia general, and is now in Congress."

Rip's heart died away, at hearing of these sad changes in his home and friends, and finding himself thus alone in the world. Every answer puzzled him, too, by treating of such enormous lapses of time, and of matters which he could not understand: war—congress—Stoney-Point;—he had no courage to ask after any more friends, but cried out in despair, "does nobody here know Rip Van Winkle?"

"Oh, Rip Van Winkle!" exclaimed two or three, "Oh, to be sure! that's Rip Van Winkle yonder, leaning against the tree."

Rip looked, and beheld a precise counterpart of himself, as he went up the mountain: apparently as lazy, and certainly as ragged. The poor fellow was now completely confounded. He doubted his own identity, and whether he was himself or another man. In the midst of his bewilderment, the man in the cocked hat demanded who he was, and what was his name?

"God knows," exclaimed he, at his wit's end; "I'm not myself—I'm somebody else—that's me yonder—no—that's somebody else, got into my shoes—I was myself last night, but I fell asleep on the mountain, and they've changed my gun, and every thing's changed, and I'm changed, and I can't tell what's my name, or who I am!"

The bystanders began now to look at each other, nod, wink significantly, and tap their fingers against their foreheads. There was a whisper, also, about securing the gun, and keeping the old fellow from doing mischief. At the very suggestion of which, the self-important man in the cocked hat retired with some precipitation. At this critical moment a fresh likely woman pressed through the throng to get a peep at the graybearded man. She had a chubby child in her arms, which, frightened at his looks, began to cry. "Hush, Rip," cried she, "hush, you little fool, the old man wont hurt you." The name of the child, the air of the mother, the tone of her voice, all awakened a train of recollections in his mind.

6. A mountain near West Point. Stoney Point, a British fort, was captured by General Anthony Wayne (1745–1796) during the Revolution.

"What is your name, my good woman?" asked he.

"Judith Gardenier."

"And your father's name?"

"Ah, poor man, his name was Rip Van Winkle; it's twenty years since he went away from home with his gun, and never has been heard of since—his dog came home without him; but whether he shot himself, or was carried away by the Indians, nobody can tell. I was then but a little girl."

Rip had but one question more to ask; but he put it with a faltering voice: "Where's your mother?"

Oh, she too had died but a short time since; she broke a blood vessel in a fit of passion at a New-England pedlar.

There was a drop of comfort, at least, in this intelligence. The honest man could contain himself no longer.—He caught his daughter and her child in his arms.—"I am your father!" cried he—"Young Rip Van Winkle once—old Rip Van Winkle now!—Does nobody know poor Rip Van Winkle!"

All stood amazed, until an old woman, tottering out from among the crowd, put her hand to her brow, and peering under it in his face for a moment, exclaimed, "Sure enough! it is Rip Van Winkle—it is himself. Welcome home again, old neighbour—Why, where have you been these twenty long years?"

Rip's story was soon told, for the whole twenty years had been to him but as one night. The neighbours stared when they heard it; some were seen to wink at each other, and put their tongues in their cheeks; and the self-important man in the cocked hat, who, when the alarm was over, had returned to the field, screwed down the corners of his mouth, and shook his head—upon which there was a general shaking of the head throughout the assemblage.

It was determined, however, to take the opinion of old Peter Vanderdonk, who was seen slowly advancing up the road. He was a descendant of the historian of that name,[7] who wrote one of the earliest accounts of the province. Peter was the most ancient inhabitant of the village, and well versed in all the wonderful events and traditions of the neighbourhood. He recollected Rip at once, and corroborated his story in the most satisfactory manner. He assured the company that it was a fact, handed down from his ancestor the historian, that the Kaatskill mountains had always been haunted by strange beings. That it was affirmed that the great Hendrick Hudson, the first discoverer of the river and country, kept a kind of vigil there every twenty years, with his crew of the Half-moon, being permitted in this way to revisit the scenes of his enterprize, and keep a guardian eye upon the river, and the great city[8] called by his name. That his father had once seen them in their old Dutch dresses playing at nine pins in a hollow of the mountain; and that he himself had heard, one summer afternoon, the sound of their balls, like long peals of thunder.

To make a long story short, the company broke up, and returned to the more important concerns of the election. Rip's daughter took him home to live with her; she had a snug, well-furnished house, and a stout cheery farmer

7. Adriaen Van der Donck (1620–1655?) wrote a history of New Netherlands (1655).

8. Henry Hudson (d. 1611), English navigator in the service of the Dutch. The "great city" is actually a small town on the east bank of the Hudson River.

for a husband, whom Rip recollected for one of the urchins that used to climb upon his back. As to Rip's son and heir, who was the ditto of himself, seen leaning against the tree, he was employed to work on the farm; but evinced an hereditary disposition to attend to any thing else but his business.

Rip now resumed his old walks and habits; he soon found many of his former cronies, though all rather the worse for the wear and tear of time; and preferred making friends among the rising generation, with whom he soon grew into great favour.

Having nothing to do at home, and being arrived at that happy age when a man can do nothing with impunity, he took his place once more on the bench, at the inn door, and was reverenced as one of the patriarchs of the village, and a chronicle of the old times "before the war." It was some time before he could get into the regular track of gossip, or could be made to comprehend the strange events that had taken place during his torpor. How that there had been a revolutionary war—that the country had thrown off the yoke of old England—and that, instead of being a subject of his Majesty George the Third, he was now a free citizen of the United States. Rip, in fact, was no politician; the changes of states and empires made but little impression on him. But there was one species of despotism under which he had long groaned, and that was—petticoat government. Happily, that was at an end; he had got his neck out of the yoke of matrimony, and could go in and out whenever he pleased, without dreading the tyranny of Dame Van Winkle. Whenever her name was mentioned, however, he shook his head, shrugged his shoulders, and cast up his eyes; which might pass either for an expression of resignation to his fate, or joy at his deliverance.

He used to tell his story to every stranger that arrived at Mr. Doolittle's hotel. He was observed, at first, to vary on some points every time he told it, which was, doubtless, owing to his having so recently awaked. It at last settled down precisely to the tale I have related, and not a man, woman, or child in the neighbourhood, but knew it by heart. Some always pretended to doubt the reality of it, and insisted that Rip had been out of his head, and that this was one point on which he always remained flighty. The old Dutch inhabitants, however, almost universally gave it full credit. Even to this day they never hear a thunder storm of a summer afternoon, about the Kaatskill, but they say Hendrick Hudson and his crew are at their game of nine pins; and it is a common wish of all henpecked husbands in the neighbourhood, when life hangs heavy on their hands, that they might have a quieting draught out of Rip Van Winkle's flagon.

NOTE

The foregoing tale, one would suspect, had been suggested to Mr. Knickerbocker by a little German superstition about Charles V.[9] and the Kypphauser mountain; the subjoined note, however, which he had appended to the tale, shows that it is an absolute fact, narrated with his usual fidelity:

9. Later Irving changed "Charles V." (Holy Roman emperor, 1519–56) to "The Emperor Frederick *der Rothbart*" (i.e., Frederick Barbarossa; Holy Roman emperor, 1152–90). ("Rothbart" and "Barbarossa" both mean "redbeard.") In either form, the allusion is to a source other than the actual one, the story of Peter Klaus in the folktales of J.C.C.N. Otmar (1800).

"The story of Rip Van Winkle may seem incredible to many, but nevertheless I give it my full belief, for I know the vicinity of our old Dutch settlements to have been very subject to marvellous events and appearances. Indeed, I have heard many stranger stories than this, in the villages along the Hudson; all of which were too well authenticated to admit of a doubt. I have even talked with Rip Van Winkle myself, who, when last I saw him, was a very venerable old man, and so perfectly rational and consistent on every other point, that I think no conscientious person could refuse to take this into the bargain; nay, I have seen a certificate on the subject taken before a country justice, and signed with a cross, in the justice's own hand writing. The story, therefore, is beyond the possibility of doubt. D.K."

1819

The Legend of Sleepy Hollow

(Found among the Papers of the Late Diedrich Knickerbocker)[1]

> A pleasing land of drowsy head it was,
> Of dreams that wave before the half-shut eye;
> And of gay castles in the clouds that pass,
> Forever flushing round a summer sky.
> —*Castle of Indolence*[2]

In the bosom of one of the spacious coves which indent the eastern shore of the Hudson, at that broad expansion of the river denominated by the ancient Dutch navigators the Tappaan Zee,[3] and where they always prudently shortened sail, and implored the protection of St. Nicholas when they crossed, there lies a small market town or rural port, which by some is called Greensburgh, but which is more universally and properly known by the name of Tarry Town. This name was given it, we are told, in former days, by the good housewives of the adjacent country, from the inveterate propensity of their husbands to linger about the village tavern on market days. Be that as it may, I do not vouch for the fact, but merely advert to it, for the sake of being precise and authentic. Not far from this village, perhaps about three miles, there is a little valley, or rather lap of land among high hills, which is one of the quietest places in the whole world. A small brook glides through it, with just murmur enough to lull you to repose, and the occasional whistle of a quail, or tapping of a woodpecker, is almost the only sound that ever breaks in upon the uniform tranquillity.

I recollect that when a stripling, my first exploit in squirrel shooting was in a grove of tall walnut trees that shades one side of the valley. I had wandered into it at noon time, when all nature is peculiarly quiet, and was startled by the roar of my own gun, as it broke the sabbath stillness around, and was prolonged and reverberated by the angry echoes. If ever I should wish for a retreat, whither I might steal from the world and its distractions, and dream

1. "The Legend of Sleepy Hollow" was the last of three pieces printed in February 1820 as the sixth installment of *The Sketch Book*, the source of the present text.

2. By the Scottish poet James Thomson (1700–1748), lines 46–49.

3. Wide "sea" in the Hudson near Tarrytown.

quietly away the remnant of a troubled life, I know of none more promising than this little valley.

From the listless repose of the place, and the peculiar character of its inhabitants, who are descendants from the original Dutch settlers, this sequestered glen has long been known by the name of SLEEPY HOLLOW, and its rustic lads are called the Sleepy Hollow Boys throughout all the neighbouring country. A drowsy, dreamy influence seems to hang over the land, and pervade the very atmosphere. Some say that the place was bewitched by a high German[4] doctor during the early days of the settlement; others, that an old Indian chief, the prophet or wizard of his tribe, held his powwows there before the country was discovered by Master Hendrick Hudson.[5] Certain it is, the place still continues under the sway of some witching power, that holds a spell over the minds of the good people, causing them to walk in a continual reverie. They are given to all kinds of marvellous beliefs; have trances and visions, and see strange sights, and hear music and voices in the air. The whole neighbourhood abounds with local tales, haunted spots, and twilight superstitions; stars shoot and meteors glare oftener across the valley than in any other part of the country, and the night-mare, with her whole nine fold,[6] seems to make it the favourite scene of her gambols.

The dominant spirit, however, that haunts this enchanted region, and seems to be commander of all the powers of the air, is the apparition of a figure on horseback without a head. It is said by some to be the ghost of a Hessian[7] trooper, whose head had been carried away by a cannon-ball, in some nameless battle during the revolutionary war, and who is ever and anon seen by various of the country people, hurrying along in the gloom of night, as if on the wings of the wind. His haunts are not confined to the valley, but extend at times to the adjacent roads, and especially to the vicinity of a church that is at no great distance. Indeed, certain of the most authentic historians of those parts, who have been careful in collecting and collating the floating facts concerning this spectre, allege, that the body of the trooper having been buried in the church-yard, the ghost rides forth to the scene of battle in nightly quest of his head, and the rushing speed with which he sometimes passes along the hollow, like a midnight blast, is owing to his being belated, and in a hurry to get back to the church-yard before day-break.

Such is the general purport of this legendary superstition, which has furnished materials for many a wild story in that region of shadows; and the spectre is known, at all the country firesides, by the name of The Headless Horseman of Sleepy Hollow.

It is remarkable, that the visionary turn I have mentioned is not confined to the native inhabitants of the valley, but is imperceptibly acquired by every one who resides there for a time. However wide awake they may have been before they entered that sleepy region, they are sure, in a little time, to imbibe the witching influence of the air, and begin to grow imaginative—to dream dreams, and see apparitions.

4. I.e., from southern Germany.
5. Henry Hudson (d. 1611), English navigator in the service of the Dutch.
6. The nine foals of the demonic nightmare who "rides" her sleeping victims. Cf. Shakespeare's *King Lear* 3.4.128.
7. German mercenaries from Hesse were hired by the British to fight against the colonists in the American Revolution.

I mention this peaceful spot with all possible laud; for it is in such little retired Dutch valleys, found here and there embosomed in the great state of New-York, that populations, manners, and customs, remain fixed, while the great torrent of emigration and improvement, which is making such incessant changes in other parts of this restless country, sweeps by them unobserved. They are like those little nooks of still water, which border a rapid stream, where we may see the straw and bubble riding quietly at anchor, or slowly revolving in their mimic harbour, undisturbed by the rushing of the passing current. Though many years have elapsed since I trod the drowsy shades of Sleepy Hollow, yet I question whether I should not still find the same trees and the same families vegetating in its sheltered bosom.

In this by-place of nature there abode, in a remote period of American history, that is to say, some thirty years since, a worthy wight of the name of Ichabod Crane, who sojourned, or, as he expressed it, "tarried," in Sleepy Hollow, for the purpose of instructing the children of the vicinity. He was a native of Connecticut, a state which supplies the Union with pioneers for the mind as well as the forest, and sends forth yearly its legions of frontier woodmen and country schoolmasters. The cognomen of Crane was not inapplicable to his person. He was tall, but exceedingly lank, with narrow shoulders, long arms and legs, hands that dangled a mile out of his sleeves, feet that might have served for shovels, and his whole frame most loosely hung together. His head was small, and flat at top, with huge ears, large green glassy eyes, and a long snipe nose, so that it might have been mistaken for a weathercock perched upon his spindle neck, to tell which way the wind blew. To see him striding along the profile of a hill on a windy day, with his clothes bagging and fluttering about him, one might have mistaken him for the genius[8] of famine descending upon the earth, or some scarecrow eloped from a cornfield.

His school-house was a low building of one large room, rudely constructed of logs; the windows partly glazed, and partly patched with leaves of old copy books. It was most ingeniously secured at vacant hours, by a withe[9] twisted in the handle of the door, and stakes set against the window shutters; so that though a thief might get in with perfect ease, he would find some embarrassment in getting out; an idea most probably borrowed by the architect, Yost Van Houten, from the mystery of an eelpot.[1] The school-house stood in rather a lonely but a pleasant situation, just at the foot of a woody hill, with a brook running close by, and a formidable birch tree growing at one end of it. From hence the low murmur of his pupils' voices conning over their lessons, might be heard of a drowsy summer's day, like the hum of a bee-hive; interrupted now and then by the authoritative voice of the master, giving menace or command, or, peradventure, the appalling sound of the birch, as he urged some tardy loiterer along the flowery path of knowledge. Truth to say, he was a conscientious man, that ever bore in mind the golden maxim, "spare the rod and spoil the child."[2]—Ichabod Crane's scholars certainly were not spoiled.

8. Spirit; an echo of Shakespeare's 2 *Henry IV* 3.2, Falstaff's description of the youthful Justice Shallow.

9. Slender, flexible branch (usually from a willow), used in place of rope.

1. Eel trap.

2. From *Hudibras* 2.843 (1664), by the English poet Samuel Butler (1612–1680), ultimately from Proverbs 13.24.

I would not have it imagined, however, that he was one of those cruel potentates of the school, who joy in the smart[3] of their subjects; on the contrary, he administered justice with discrimination rather than severity; taking the burthen off the backs of the weak, and laying it on those of the strong. Your mere puny stripling, that winced at the least flourish of the rod, was passed by with indulgence; but the claims of justice were satisfied, by giving a double portion to some little, tough, wrong-headed, broad-skirted Dutch urchin, who sulked and swelled and grew dogged and sullen beneath the birch. All this he called "doing his duty by their parents;" and he never inflicted a chastisement without following it by the assurance, so consolatory to the smarting urchin, that he would remember it and thank him for it the longest day he had to live.

When school hours were over, he was even the companion and playmate of his larger boys; and would convoy some of the smaller ones home of a holyday, who happened to have pretty sisters, or good housewives for mothers, noted for the comforts of the cupboard. Indeed, it behooved him to keep on good terms with his pupils. The revenue arising from his school was small, and would have been scarcely sufficient to furnish him with daily bread, for he was a huge feeder, and though lank, had the dilating powers of an Anaconda;[4] but to help out his maintenance, he was, according to country custom in those parts, boarded and lodged at the houses of the farmers, whose children he instructed. With these he lived alternately a week at a time, thus going the rounds of the neighbourhood, with all his worldly effects tied up in a cotton handkerchief.

That all this might not be too onerous on the purses of his rustic patrons, who are apt to consider the costs of schooling a grievous burthen, and schoolmasters mere drones, he had various ways of rendering himself both useful and agreeable. He assisted the farmers occasionally in the light labours of their farms, helped to make hay, mended the fences, took the horses to water, drove the cows from pasture, and cut wood for the winter fire. He laid aside, too, all the dominant dignity and absolute sway, with which he lorded it in his little empire, the school, and became wonderfully gentle and ingratiating. He found favour in the eyes of the mothers, by petting the children, particularly the youngest, and like the lion bold, which whilome so magnanimously the lamb did hold,[5] he would sit with a child on one knee, and rock a cradle with his foot, for whole hours together.

In addition to his other vocations, he was the singing-master of the neighbourhood, and picked up many bright shillings by instructing the young folks in psalmody.[6] It was a matter of no little vanity to him on Sundays, to take his station in front of the church gallery, with a band of chosen singers; where, in his own mind, he completely carried away the palm from the parson. Certain it is, his voice resounded far above all the rest of the congregation, and there are peculiar quavers still to be heard in that church, and which may even be heard half-a-mile off, quite to the opposite side of the mill-pond, of a still Sunday morning, which are said to be legitimately descended from the nose of Ichabod Crane. Thus, by diverse little make shifts, in that ingenious way

3. Pain, sting.
4. Tropical boa constrictor.
5. In the *New England Primer*, a widely used school text, the letter *L* consists of an illustration depicting Isaiah 11.6–9 and the rhyme "The lion bold / The lamb doth hold." "Whilome": formerly.
6. Singing of rhymed versions of the Psalms.

which is commonly denominated "by hook and by crook,"[7] the worthy pedagogue got on tolerably enough, and was thought, by all those who understood nothing of the labour of headwork, to have a wonderful easy life of it.

The schoolmaster is generally a man of some importance in the female circle of a rural neighbourhood, being considered a kind of idle gentleman-like personage, of vastly superior taste and accomplishments to the rough country swains, and, indeed, inferior in learning only to the parson. His appearance, therefore, is apt to occasion some little stir at the tea-table of a farm-house, and the addition of a supernumerary dish of cakes or sweet-meats, or, peradventure, the parade of a silver tea-pot. Our man of letters, therefore, was peculiarly happy in the smiles of all the country damsels. How he would figure among them in the church-yard, between services on Sundays; gathering grapes for them from the wild vines that overrun the surrounding trees; reciting for them all the epitaphs on the tomb-stones, or sauntering, with a whole bevy of them, along the banks of the adjacent mill-pond; while the more bashful country bumpkins hung sheepishly back, envying his superior elegance and address.

From his half itinerant life, also, he was a kind of travelling gazette, carrying the whole budget of local gossip from house to house; so that his appearance was always greeted with satisfaction. He was, moreover, esteemed by the women as a man of great erudition, for he had read several books quite through, and was a perfect master of Cotton Mather's History of New-England Witchcraft,[8] in which, by the way, he most firmly and potently believed.

He was, in fact, an odd mixture of small shrewdness and simple credulity. His appetite for the marvellous, and his powers of digesting it, were equally extraordinary; and both had been increased by his residence in this spell-bound region. No tale was too gross or monstrous for his capacious swallow. It was often his delight, after his school was dismissed of an afternoon, to stretch himself on the rich bed of clover, bordering the little brook that whimpered past his school-house, and there con over old Mather's direful tales, until the gathering dusk of evening made the printed page a mere mist before his eyes. Then, as he wended his way, by swamp and stream and awful[9] woodland, to the farm-house where he happened to be quartered, every sound of nature, at that witching hour, fluttered his excited imagination: the moan of the whip-poor-will from the hill side; the boding cry of the tree-toad, that harbinger of storm; the dreary hooting of the screech-owl; or the sudden rustling in the thicket, of birds frightened from their roost. The fire-flies, too, which sparkled most vividly in the darkest places, now and then startled him, as one of uncommon brightness would stream across his path; and if, by chance, a huge blockhead of a beetle came winging his blundering flight against him, the poor varlet was ready to give up the ghost, with the idea that he was struck with a witch's token. His only resource on such occasions, either to drown thought, or drive away evil spirits, was to sing psalm tunes;—and the good people of Sleepy Hollow, as they sat by their doors of an evening, were often filled with awe, at hearing his nasal melody, "in linked

7. From *Colin Clout* (1523), by the English poet John Skelton (1460?–1529).

8. Mather (1663–1728), a Puritan minister, wrote *Memorable Providences, Relating to Witchcrafts and Possessions* (1689) and *The Wonders of the Invisible World* (1693).

9. Terrifying.

sweetness long drawn out,"[1] floating from the distant hill, or along the dusky road.

Another of his sources of fearful pleasure was, to pass long winter evenings with the old Dutch wives, as they sat spinning by the fire, with a row of apples roasting and sputtering along the hearth, and listen to their marvellous tales of ghosts and goblins, and haunted fields and haunted brooks, and haunted bridges and haunted houses, and particularly of the headless horseman, or galloping Hessian of the Hollow, as they sometimes called him. He would delight them equally by his anecdotes of witchcraft, and of the direful omens and portentous sights and sounds in the air, which prevailed in the earlier times of Connecticut; and would frighten them wofully with speculations upon comets and shooting stars, and with the alarming fact that the world did absolutely turn round, and that they were half the time topsy-turvy!

But if there was a pleasure in all this, while snugly cuddling in the chimney corner of a chamber that was all of a ruddy glow from the crackling wood fire, and where, of course, no spectre dare to show its face, it was dearly purchased by the terrors of his subsequent walk homewards. What fearful shapes and shadows beset his path, amidst the dim and ghostly glare of a snowy night!—With what wistful look did he eye every trembling ray of light streaming across the waste fields from some distant window!—How often was he appalled by some shrub covered with snow, which like sheeted spectre beset his very path!—How often did he shrink with curdling awe at the sound of his own steps on the frosty crust beneath his feet; and dread to look over his shoulder, lest he should behold some uncouth being tramping close behind him!—and how often was he thrown into complete dismay by some rushing blast, howling among the trees, in the idea that it was the gallopping Hessian on one of his nightly scourings.

All these, however, were mere terrors of the night, phantoms of the mind, that walk in darkness; and though he had seen many spectres in his time, and been more than once beset by Satan in diverse shapes, in his lonely perambulations, yet day-light put an end to all these evils; and he would have passed a pleasant life of it, in despite of the Devil and all his works, if his path had not been crossed by a being that causes more perplexity to mortal man, than ghosts, goblins, and the whole race of witches put together, and that was—a woman.

Among the musical disciples who assembled, one evening in each week, to receive his instructions in psalmody, was Katrina Van Tassel, the daughter and only child of a substantial Dutch farmer. She was a blooming lass of fresh eighteen; plump as a partridge; ripe and melting and rosy-cheeked as one of her father's peaches, and universally famed, not merely for her beauty, but her vast expectations. She was withal a little of a coquette, as might be perceived even in her dress, which was a mixture of ancient and modern fashions, as most suited to set off her charms. She wore the ornaments of pure yellow gold, which her great-great-grandmother had brought over from Saardam; the tempting stomacher[2] of the olden time, and withal a provok-

1. "L'Allegro," line 140, by the English poet John Milton (1608–1674).

2. Wide, ornamental waistband worn over a dress. "Saardam": now Zaandam, town near Amsterdam.

ingly short petticoat, to display the prettiest foot and ankle in the country round.

Ichabod Crane had a soft and foolish heart toward the sex; and it is not to be wondered at, that so tempting a morsel soon found favour in his eyes, more especially after he had visited her in her paternal mansion. Old Baltus Van Tassel was a perfect picture of a thriving, contented, liberal-hearted farmer. He seldom, it is true, sent either his eyes or his thoughts beyond the boundaries of his own farm; but within those every thing was snug, happy, and well-conditioned. He was satisfied with his wealth, but not proud of it, and piqued himself upon the hearty abundance, rather than the style in which he lived. His strong hold was situated on the banks of the Hudson, in one of those green, sheltered, fertile nooks, into which the Dutch farmers are so fond of nestling. A great elm tree spread its broad branches over it, at the foot of which bubbled up a spring of the softest and sweetest water, in a little kind of well, formed of a barrel, and then stole sparkling away through the grass, to a neighbouring brook, that babbled along among elders and dwarf willows. Hard by the farm-house was a vast barn, that might have served for a church; every window and crevice of which seemed bursting forth with the treasures of the farm; the flail was busily resounding within it; swallows and martins skimmed twittering about the eaves, and rows of pigeons, some with one eye turned up, as if watching the weather, some with their heads under their wings, or buried in their bosoms, and others, swelling, and cooing, and bowing about their dames, were enjoying the sunshine on the roof. Sleek unwieldy porkers were grunting in the repose and abundance of their pens, from whence sallied forth, now and then, troops of sucking pigs, as if to snuff the air. A stately squadron of snowy geese were riding in an adjoining pond, convoying whole fleets of ducks; regiments of turkeys were gobbling about the farm yard, and guinea fowls fretting like ill-tempered housewives, with their peevish discontented cry. Before the barn door strutted the gallant cock, that pattern of a husband, a warrior, and a fine gentleman, clapping his burnished wings, and crowing in the pride and gladness of his heart—sometimes tearing up the earth with his feet, and then generously calling his ever-hungry family of wives and children to enjoy the rich morsel he had discovered.

The pedagogue's mouth watered, as he looked upon this sumptuous promise of luxurious winter fare. In his devouring mind's eye, he pictured to himself every roasting pig running about with a pudding in its belly,[3] and an apple in its mouth; the pigeons were snugly put to bed in a comfortable pie, and tucked in with a coverlet of crust; the geese were swimming in their own gravy; and the ducks pairing cosily in dishes, like snug married couples, with a decent competency of onion sauce; in the porkers he saw carved out the future sleek side of bacon, and juicy relishing ham; not a turkey, but he beheld daintily trussed up, with its gizzard under its wing, and, peradventure, a necklace of savoury sausages; and even bright chanticleer himself lay sprawling on his back, in a side dish, with uplifted claws, as if craving that quarter,[4] which his chivalrous spirit disdained to ask while living.

3. Cf. "that roasted Manningtree ox with the pudding in his belly" (Shakespeare's *1 Henry IV* 2.4).

4. Clemency. "Chanticleer": rooster.

As the enraptured Ichabod fancied all this, and as he rolled his great green eyes over the fat meadow lands, the rich fields of wheat, of rye, of buckwheat, and Indian corn, and the orchards burthened with ruddy fruit, which surrounded the warm tenement[5] of Van Tassel, his heart yearned after the damsel who was to inherit these domains, and his imagination expanded with the idea, how they might be readily turned into cash, and the money invested in immense tracts of wild land, and shingle palaces in the wilderness. Nay, his busy fancy already put him in possession of his hopes, and presented to him the blooming Katrina, with a whole family of children, mounted on the top of a waggon loaded with household trumpery, with pots and kettles dangling beneath; and he beheld himself bestriding a pacing mare, with a colt at her heels, setting out for Kentucky, Tennessee, or the Lord knows where!

When he entered the house, the conquest of his heart was complete. It was one of those spacious farm-houses, with high-ridged, but lowly-sloping roofs, built in the style handed down from the first Dutch settlers. The low, projecting eaves formed a piazza along the front, capable of being closed up in bad weather. Under this were hung flails, harness, various utensils of husbandry, and nets for fishing in the neighbouring river. Benches were built along the sides for summer use; and a great spinning wheel at one end, and a churn at the other, showed the various uses to which this important porch might be devoted. From this piazza the wondering Ichabod entered the hall, which formed the centre of the mansion, and the place of usual residence. Here, rows of resplendent pewter, ranged on a long dresser, dazzled his eyes. In one corner stood a huge bag of wool ready to be spun; in another a quantity of linsey-woolsey just from the loom; ears of Indian corn, and strings of dried apples and peaches, hung in gay festoons along the walls, mingled with the gaud of red peppers; and a door left ajar, gave him a peep into the best parlour, where the claw-footed chairs, and dark mahogany tables, shone like mirrors; andirons, with their accompanying shovel and tongs, glistened from their covert of asparagus tops; mock oranges[6] and conch shells decorated the mantlepiece; strings of various coloured birds' eggs were suspended above it; a great ostrich egg was hung from the centre of the room, and a corner cupboard, knowingly left open, displayed immense treasures of old silver and well-mended china.

From the moment Ichabod laid his eyes upon these regions of delight, the peace of his mind was at an end, and his only study was how to gain the affections of the peerless daughter of Van Tassel. In this enterprize, however, he had more real difficulties than generally fell to the lot of a knight-errant of yore, who seldom had any thing but giants, enchanters, fiery dragons, and such like easily conquered adversaries, to contend with; and had to make his way merely through gates of iron and brass, and walls of adamant,[7] to the castle keep, where the lady of his heart was confined; all which he achieved as easily as a man would carve his way to the centre of a Christmas pie, and then the lady gave him her hand as a matter of course. Ichabod, on the contrary, had to win his way to the heart of a country coquette, beset with a labyrinth of whims and caprices, which were for ever presenting new difficul-

5. Residence.
6. Probably gourds in the size and shape of oranges.
7. Fabled stone of impenetrable hardness.

ties and impediments, and he had to encounter a host of fearful adversaries of real flesh and blood, the numerous rustic admirers, who beset every portal to her heart, keeping a watchful and angry eye upon each other, but ready to fly out in the common cause against any new competitor.

Among these, the most formidable, was a burley, roaring, roystering blade, of the name of Abraham, or, according to the Dutch abbreviation, Brom Van Brunt, the hero of the country round, which rung with his feats of strength and hardihood. He was broad shouldered and double jointed, with short curly black hair, and a bluff, but not unpleasant countenance, having a mingled air of fun and arrogance. From his Herculean frame and great powers of limb, he had received the nick-name of BROM BONES, by which he was universally known. He was famed for great knowledge and skill in horsemanship, being as dexterous on horseback as a Tartar. He was foremost at all races and cock-fights, and with the ascendancy which bodily strength always acquires in rustic life, was the umpire in all disputes, setting his hat on one side, and giving his decisions with an air and tone that admitted of no gainsay or appeal. He was always ready for either a fight or a frolick; had more mischief than ill-will in his composition; and with all his overbearing roughness, there was a strong dash of waggish good humour at bottom. He had three or four boon companions of his own stamp, who regarded him as their model, and at the head of whom he scoured the country, attending every scene of feud or merriment for miles round. In cold weather he was distinguished by a fur cap, surmounted with a flaunting fox's tail, and when the folks at a country gathering descried this well-known crest at a distance, whisking about among a squad of hard riders, they always stood by for a squall. Sometimes his crew would be heard dashing along past the farm-houses at midnight, with whoop and halloo, like a troop of Don Cossacks,[8] and the old dames, startled out of their sleep, would listen for a moment till the hurry scurry had clattered by, and then exclaim, "aye, there goes Brom Bones and his gang!" The neighbours looked upon him with a mixture of awe, admiration, and good-will; and when any mad-cap prank, or rustic brawl, occurred in the vicinity, always shook their heads, and warranted Brom Bones was at the bottom of it.

This rantipole[9] hero had for some time singled out the blooming Katrina for the object of his uncouth gallantries, and though his amorous toyings were something like the gentle caresses and endearments of a bear, yet it was whispered that she did not altogether discourage his hopes. Certain it is, his advances were signals for rival candidates to retire, who felt no inclination to cross a lion in his amours; insomuch, that when his horse was seen tied to Van Tassel's paling,[1] of a Sunday night, (a sure sign that his master was courting, or, as it is termed, "sparking," within,) all other suitors passed by in despair, and carried the war into other quarters.

Such was the formidable rival with whom Ichabod Crane had to contend, and, considering all things, a stouter man than he would have shrunk from the competition, and a wiser man would have despaired. He had, however, a happy mixture of pliability and perseverance in his nature; he was in form and spirit like a supple jack[2]—yielding, but tough; though he bent, he never

8. Russian cavalry ranging the area around the Don River.
9. Wild, unruly.
1. Fence.
2. Cane made from a climbing plant with tough, pliant stems.

broke; and though he bowed beneath the slightest pressure, yet, the moment it was away—jerk!—he was as erect, and carried his head as high as ever.

To have taken the field openly against his rival, would have been madness; for he was not a man to be thwarted in his amours, any more than that stormy lover, Achilles.[3] Ichabod, therefore, made his advances in a quiet and gently-insinuating manner. Under cover of his character of singing master, he made frequent visits at the farm-house; not that he had any thing to apprehend from the meddlesome interference of parents, which is so often a stumbling block in the path of lovers. Balt Van Tassel was an easy indulgent soul; he loved his daughter better even than his pipe, and like a reasonable man, and an excellent father, let her have her way in every thing. His notable little wife too, had enough to do to attend to her housekeeping and manage the poultry, for, as she sagely observed, ducks and geese are foolish things, and must be looked after, but girls can take care of themselves. Thus while the busy dame bustled about the house, or plied her spinning wheel at one end of the piazza, honest Balt would sit smoking his evening pipe at the other, watching the achievements of a little wooden warrior, who, armed with a sword in each hand, was most valiantly fighting the wind on the pinnacle of the barn. In the mean time, Ichabod would carry on his suit with the daughter by the side of the spring under the great elm, or sauntering along in the twilight, that hour so favourable to the lover's eloquence.

I profess not to know how women's hearts are wooed and won. To me they have always been matters of riddle and admiration. Some seem to have but one vulnerable point, or door of access; while others have a thousand avenues, and may be captured a thousand different ways. It is a great triumph of skill to gain the former, but a still greater proof of generalship to maintain possession of the latter, for a man must battle for his fortress at every door and window. He that wins a thousand common hearts, is therefore entitled to some renown; but he who keeps undisputed sway over the heart of a coquette, is indeed a hero. Certain it is, this was not the case with the redoutable Brom Bones; and from the moment Ichabod Crane made his advances, the interests of the former evidently declined; his horse was no longer seen tied at the palings on Sunday nights, and a deadly feud gradually arose between him and the preceptor of Sleepy Hollow.

Brom, who had a degree of rough chivalry in his nature, would fain have carried matters to open warfare, and settled their pretensions to the lady, according to the mode of those most concise and simple reasoners, the knights-errant of yore—by single combat: but Ichabod was too conscious of the superior might of his adversary to enter the lists against him; he had overheard the boast of Bones, that he would "double the schoolmaster up, and put him on a shelf;" and he was too wary to give him an opportunity. There was something extremely provoking in this obstinately pacific system; it left Brom no alternative but to draw upon the funds of rustic waggery in his disposition, and play off boorish practical jokes upon his rival. Ichabod became the object of whimsical persecution to Bones, and his gang of rough riders. They harried his hitherto peaceful domains; smoked out his singing school,

3. In book 1 of Homer's *Iliad*, King Agamemnon takes the captive maiden Briseis from the warrior Achilles, who thereupon sulks in his tent during the Trojan War until he is roused to avenge the death of his favorite comrade, Patroclus.

by stopping up the chimney; broke into the school-house at night, in spite of its formidable fastenings of withe and window stakes, and turned every thing topsy-turvy, so that the poor schoolmaster began to think all the witches in the country held their meetings there. But what was still more annoying, Brom took all opportunities of turning him into ridicule in presence of his mistress, and had a scoundrel dog, whom he taught to whine in the most ludicrous manner, and introduced as a rival of Ichabod's, to instruct her in psalmody.

In this way, matters went on for some time, without producing any material effect on the relative situations of the contending powers. On a fine autumnal afternoon, Ichabod, in pensive mood, sat enthroned on the lofty stool from whence he usually watched all the concerns of his little literary realm. In his hand he swayed a ferule, that sceptre of despotic power; the birch of justice reposed on three nails, behind the throne, a constant terror to evil doers; while on the desk before him might be seen sundry contraband articles and prohibited weapons, detected upon the persons of idle urchins, such as half-munched apples, popguns, whirligigs,[4] fly-cages, and whole legions of rampant little paper game cocks. Apparently there had been some appalling act of justice recently inflicted, for his scholars were all busily intent upon their books, or slyly whispering behind them with one eye kept upon the master; and a kind of buzzing stillness reigned throughout the school-room. It was suddenly interrupted by the appearance of a negro in tow-cloth jacket and trowsers, a round crowned fragment of a hat, like the cap of Mercury,[5] and mounted on the back of a ragged, wild, half-broken colt, which he managed with a rope by way of halter. He came clattering up to the school door with an invitation to Ichabod to attend a merry-making, or "quilting frolick," to be held that evening at Mynheer Van Tassel's, and having delivered his message with that air of importance, and effort at fine language, which a negro is apt to display on petty embassies of the kind, he dashed over the brook, and was seen scampering away up the hollow, full of the importance and hurry of his mission.

All was now bustle and hubbub in the late quiet school room. The scholars were hurried through their lessons, without stopping at trifles; those who were nimble, skipped over half with impunity, and those who were tardy, had a smart application now and then in the rear, to quicken their speed, or help them over a tall word. Books were flung aside, without being put away on the shelves; inkstands were overturned, benches thrown down, and the whole school turned loose an hour before the usual time; bursting forth like a legion of young imps, yelping and racketing about the green, in joy at their early emancipation.

The gallant Ichabod now spent at least an extra half hour at his toilet, brushing and furbishing up his best, and indeed only suit of rusty black, and arranging his looks by a bit of broken looking glass, that hung up in the school house. That he might make his appearance before his mistress in the true style of a cavalier, he borrowed a horse from the farmer with whom he was domiciliated, a choleric old Dutchman, of the name of Hans Van Ripper, and thus gallantly mounted, issued forth like a knight-errant in quest of

4. Child's toys, spun like a top.
5. A winged cap symbolized the speed of Mercury, messenger of the gods. Slavery was legal in New York until 1827.

adventures. But it is meet[6] I should, in the true spirit of romantic story, give some account of the looks and equipments of my hero and his steed. The animal he bestrode was a broken-down plough horse, that had outlived almost every thing but his viciousness. He was gaunt and shagged, with a ewe neck and hammer head; his rusty mane and tail were tangled and knotted with burrs; one eye had lost its pupil, and was glaring and spectral, but the other had the gleam of a genuine devil in it. Still he must have had fire and mettle in his day, if we may judge from his name, which was Gunpowder. He had, in fact, been a favourite steed of his master's, the cholerick Van Ripper, who was a furious rider, and had infused, very probably, some of his own spirit into the animal, for, old and broken-down as he looked, there was more lurking deviltry in him than in any young filly in the country.

Ichabod was a suitable figure for such a steed. He rode with short stirrups, which brought his knees nearly up to the pommel of the saddle; his sharp elbows stuck out like grasshoppers'; he carried his whip perpendicularly in his hand, like a sceptre, and as the horse jogged on, the motion of his arms was not unlike the flapping of a pair of wings. A small wool hat rested on the top of his nose, for so his scanty strip of forehead might be called, and the skirts of his black coat fluttered out almost to the horse's tail. Such was the appearance of Ichabod and his steed, as they shambled out of the gate of Hans Van Ripper, and it was altogether such an apparition as is seldom to be met with in broad day light.

It was, as I have said, a fine autumnal day, the sky was clear and serene, and nature wore that rich and golden livery which we always associate with the idea of abundance. The forests had put on their sober brown and yellow, while some trees of the tenderer kind had been nipped by the frosts into brilliant dyes of orange, purple, and scarlet. Streaming files of wild ducks began to make their appearance high in the air; the bark of the squirrel might be heard from the groves of beech and hickory nuts, and the pensive whistle of the quail at intervals from the neighbouring stubble field.

The small birds were taking their farewell banquets. In the fullness of their revelry, they fluttered, chirping and frolicking, from bush to bush, and tree to tree, capricious from the very profusion and variety around them. There was the honest cock-robin, the favourite game of stripling sportsmen, with its loud querulous note; and the twittering blackbirds flying in sable clouds; and the golden winged woodpecker, with his crimson crest, his broad black gorget,[7] and splendid plumage; and the cedar bird, with its red tipt wings and yellow tipt tail, and its little monteiro cap[8] of feathers; and the blue jay, that noisy coxcomb, in his gay light blue coat and white under clothes, screaming and chattering, nodding, and bobbing, and bowing, and pretending to be on good terms with every songster of the grove.

As Ichabod jogged slowly on his way, his eye, ever open to every symptom of culinary abundance, ranged with delight over the treasures of jolly autumn. On all sides he beheld vast store of apples, some hanging in oppressive opulence on the trees, some gathered into baskets and barrels for the market, others heaped up in rich piles for the cider-press. Further on he beheld great fields of Indian corn, with its golden ears peeping from their leafy coverts,

6. Fitting, appropriate.
7. Throat.
8. Hunting cap with a flap at the front.

and holding out the promise of cakes and hasty pudding; and the yellow pumpkins lying beneath them, turning up their fair round bellies to the sun, and giving ample prospects of the most luxurious of pies; and anon he passed the fragrant buckwheat fields, breathing the odour of the bee-hive, and as he beheld them, soft anticipations stole over his mind of dainty slap-jacks, well buttered, and garnished with honey or treacle,[9] by the delicate little dimpled hand of Katrina Van Tassel.

Thus feeding his mind with many sweet thoughts and "sugared suppositions," he journeyed along the sides of a range of hills which look out upon some of the goodliest scenes of the mighty Hudson. The sun gradually wheeled his broad disk down into the west. The wide bosom of the Tappaan Zee lay motionless and glassy, excepting that here and there a gentle undulation waved and prolonged the blue shadow of the distant mountain: a few amber clouds floated in the sky, without a breath of air to move them. The horizon was of a fine golden tint, changing gradually into a pure apple green, and from that into a deep blue of the mid-heaven. A slanting ray lingered on the woody crests of the precipices that overhung some parts of the river, giving greater depth to the dark grey and purple of their rocky sides. A sloop was loitering in the distance, dropping slowly down with the tide, her sail hanging uselessly against the mast, and as the reflection of the sky gleamed along the still water, it seemed as if the vessel was suspended in the air.

It was toward evening that Ichabod arrived at the castle of the Heer Van Tassel, which he found thronged with the pride and flower of the adjacent country. Old farmers, a spare, leathern-faced race, in homespun coats and small clothes, blue stockings, huge shoes and magnificent pewter buckles. Their brisk withered little dames in close crimped caps, long waisted short gowns, homespun petticoats, with scissors and pincushions, and gay calico pockets, hanging on the outside. Buxom lasses, almost as antiquated as their mothers, excepting where a straw hat, a fine ribband, or perhaps a white frock, gave symptoms of city innovations. The sons, in short square-skirted coats with rows of stupendous brass buttons, and their hair generally queued in the fashion of the times, especially if they could procure an eel-skin for the purpose, it being esteemed throughout the country as a potent nourisher and strengthener of the hair.

Brom Bones, however, was the hero of the scene, having come to the gathering on his favourite steed Daredevil, a creature, like himself, full of mettle and mischief, and which no one but himself could manage. He was in fact noted for preferring vicious animals, given to all kinds of tricks, which kept the rider in constant risk of his neck, and held a tractable well-broken horse as unworthy a lad of spirit.

Fain would I pause to dwell upon the world of charms that burst upon the enraptured gaze of my hero, as he entered the state parlour of Van Tassel's mansion. Not those of the bevy of buxom lasses, with their luxurious display of red and white: but the ample charms of a genuine Dutch country tea-table, in the sumptuous time of autumn. Such heaped up platters of cakes of various and almost indescribable kinds, known only to experienced Dutch housewives. There was the doughty dough-nut, the tenderer oly koek,[1] and

9. Molasses.

1. Kind of cruller or doughnut.

the crisp and crumbling cruller; sweet cakes and short cakes, ginger cakes and honey cakes, and the whole family of cakes. And then there were apple pies and peach pies and pumpkin pies; not to mention slices of ham and smoked beef, together with broiled shad and roasted chickens; besides delectable dishes of preserved plums, and peaches, and pears, and quinces; with bowls of milk and cream, all mingled higgledy-piggledy, pretty much as I have enumerated them, with the motherly tea-pot sending up its clouds of vapour from the midst—Heaven bless the mark! I want[2] breath and time to discuss this banquet as it deserves, and am too eager to get on with my story. Happily, Ichabod Crane was not in so great a hurry as his historian, but did ample justice to every dainty.

He was a kind and thankful toad, whose heart dilated in proportion as his skin was filled with good cheer, and whose spirits rose with eating, as some men's do with drink. He could not help, too, rolling his large eyes round him as he eat, and chuckling with the possibility that he might one day be lord of all this scene of almost unimaginable luxury and splendour. Then, he thought, how soon he'd turn his back upon the old school house; snap his fingers in the face of Hans Van Ripper, and every other niggardly patron, and kick any itinerant pedagogue out of doors that dared to call him comrade!

Old Baltus Van Tassel moved about among his guests with a face dilated with content and good humour, round and jolly as the harvest moon. His hospitable attentions were brief, but expressive, being confined to a shake of the hand, a slap on the shoulder, a loud laugh, and a pressing invitation to "reach to, and help themselves."

And now the sound of the music from the common room or hall, summoned to the dance. The musician was an old grey-headed negro, who had been the itinerant orchestra of the neighbourhood for more than half a century. His instrument was as old and battered as himself. The greater part of the time he scraped away on two or three strings, accompanying every movement of the bow with a motion of the head; bowing almost to the ground, and stamping with his foot whenever a fresh couple were to start.

Ichabod prided himself upon his dancing as much as upon his vocal powers. Not a limb, not a fibre about him was idle, and to have seen his loosely hung frame in full motion, and clattering about the room, you would have thought Saint Vitus[3] himself, that blessed patron of the dance, was figuring before you in person. He was the admiration of all the negroes, who, having gathered, of all ages and sizes, from the farm and the neighbourhood, stood forming a pyramid of shining black faces at every door and window, gazing with delight at the scene, rolling their white eye-balls, and showing grinning rows of ivory from ear to ear. How could the flogger of urchins be otherwise than animated and joyous; the lady of his heart was his partner in the dance; she smiled graciously in reply to all his amorous oglings, while Brom Bones, sorely smitten with love and jealousy, sat brooding by himself in one corner.

When the dance was at an end, Ichabod was attracted to a knot of the sager folks, who, with old Van Tassel, sat smoking at one end of the piazza, gossipping over former times, and drawling out long stories about the war.

2. Lack.
3. Early Christian martyr prayed to by Catholics suffering from chorea, epilepsy, or other nervous disorders.

This neighbourhood, at the time of which I am speaking, was one of those highly favoured places which abound with chronicle and great men. The British and American line had run near it during the war; it had, therefore, been the scene of marauding, and been infested with refugees, cow boys,[4] and all kind of border chivalry. Just sufficient time had elapsed to enable each story teller to dress up his tale with a little becoming fiction, and in the indistinctness of his recollection, to make himself the hero of every exploit.

There was the story of Doffue Martling, a large, blue-bearded Dutchman, who had nearly taken a British frigate with an old iron nine-pounder from a mud breastwork,[5] only that his gun burst at the sixth discharge. And there was an old gentleman who shall be nameless, being too rich a mynheer to be lightly mentioned, who in the battle of Whiteplains,[6] being an excellent master of defence, parried a musket ball with a small sword, insomuch that he absolutely felt it whiz round the blade, and glance off at the hilt; in proof of which, he was ready at any time to show the sword, with the hilt a little bent. There were several more who had been equally great in the field, not one of whom but was persuaded that he had a considerable hand in bringing the war to a happy termination.

But all these were nothing to the tales of ghosts and apparitions that succeeded. The neighbourhood is rich in legendary treasures of the kind. Local tales and superstitions thrive best in these sheltered, long settled retreats; but they are trampled under foot, by the shifting throng that forms the population of most of our country places. Besides, there is no encouragement for ghosts in the generality of our villages, for they have scarce had time to take their first nap, and turn themselves in their graves, before their surviving friends have travelled away from the neighbourhood, so that when they turn out of a night to walk the rounds, they have no acquaintance left to call upon. This is perhaps the reason why we so seldom hear of ghosts excepting in our long-established Dutch communities.

The immediate cause, however, of the prevalence of supernatural stories in these parts, was doubtless owing to the vicinity of Sleepy Hollow. There was a contagion in the very air that blew from that haunted region; it breathed forth an atmosphere of dreams and fancies infecting all the land. Several of the Sleepy Hollow people were present at Van Tassel's, and, as usual, were doling out their wild and wonderful legends. Many dismal tales were told about funeral trains, and mournful cries and wailings heard and seen about the great tree where the unfortunate Major André[7] was taken, and which stood in the neighbourhood. Some mention was made also of the woman in white, that haunted the dark glen at Raven Rock, and was often heard to shriek on winter nights before a storm, having perished there in the snow. The chief part of the stories, however, turned upon the favourite spectre of Sleepy Hollow, the headless horseman, who had been heard several times of late, patroling the country; and it was said, tethered his horse nightly among the graves in the church-yard.

4. Tory guerrillas (i.e., British partisans) who raided the Tarrytown area during the Revolution.
5. Hastily erected fortification. "Nine-pounder": small cannon firing nine-pound balls.
6. The British general William Howe defeated George Washington at the battle of White Plains, near New York City, in 1776.
7. John André (1751–1780), British spy arrested at Tarrytown and executed at Tappan, across the Hudson; he carried documents proving that Benedict Arnold had betrayed the colonial army.

The sequestered situation of this church seems always to have made it a favourite haunt of troubled spirits. It stands on a knoll, surrounded by locust trees and lofty elms, from among which its decent, whitewashed walls shine modestly forth, like Christian purity, beaming through the shades of retirement. A gentle slope descends from it to a silver sheet of water, bordered by high trees, between which, peeps may be caught at the blue hills of the Hudson. To look upon its grass-grown yard, where the sunbeams seem to sleep so quietly, one would think that here at least the dead might rest in peace. On one side of the church extends a wide woody dell, along which raves a large brook among broken rocks and trunks of fallen trees. Over a deep black part of the stream, not far from the church, was formerly thrown a wooden bridge; the road that led to it, and the bridge itself, were thickly shaded by overhanging trees, which cast a gloom about it, even in the day time; but occasioned a fearful darkness at night. Such was one of the favourite haunts of the headless horseman, and the place where he was most frequently encountered. The tale was told of old Brouwer, a most heretical disbeliever in ghosts, that he met the horseman returning from his foray into Sleepy Hollow, and was obliged to get up behind him; that they gallopped over bush and brake, over hill and swamp, until they reached the bridge, when the horseman suddenly turned into a skeleton, threw old Brouwer into the brook, and sprang away over the tree-tops with a clap of thunder.

This story was immediately matched by a thrice marvellous adventure of Brom Bones, who made light of the gallopping Hessian as an errant jockey.[8] He affirmed, that on returning one night from the neighbouring village of Sing-Sing,[9] he had been overtaken by this midnight trooper; that he had offered to race with him for a bowl of punch, and would have won it too, for Daredevil beat the goblin horse all hollow, but just as they came to the church bridge, the Hessian bolted, and vanished in a flash of fire.

All these tales, told in that drowsy under tone with which men talk in the dark, the countenances of the listeners only now and then receiving a casual gleam from the glare of a pipe, sunk deep in the mind of Ichabod. He repaid them in kind with large extracts from his invaluable author, Cotton Mather, and added many very marvellous events that had taken place in his native state of Connecticut, and fearful sights which he had seen in his nightly walks about Sleepy Hollow.

The revel now gradually broke up. The old farmers gathered together their families in their wagons, and were heard for some time rattling along the hollow roads, and over the distant hills. Some of the damsels, mounted on pillions[1] behind their favourite swains, and their light-hearted laughter mingling with the clatter of hoofs, echoed along the silent woodlands, sounding fainter and fainter until they gradually died away—and the late scene of noise and frolick was all silent and deserted. Ichabod only lingered behind, according to the custom of country lovers, to have a tête-a-tête[2] with the heiress; fully convinced that he was now on the high road to success. What passed at this interview I will not pretend to say, for in fact I do not know. Something, however, I fear me, must have gone wrong, for he certainly sallied forth, after

8. Horseman who had lost his way.
9. Ossining.
1. Pads behind a saddle for a second rider.
2. Head to head (French); i.e., a confidential conversation.

no very great interval, with an air quite desolate and chopfallen—Oh these women! these women! Could that girl have been playing off any of her coquettish tricks?—Was her encouragement of the poor pedagogue all a mere sham to secure her conquest of his rival?—Heaven only knows, not I!—Let it suffice to say, Ichabod stole forth with the air of one who had been sacking a hen roost, rather than a fair lady's heart. Without looking to the right or left to notice the scene of rural wealth, on which he had so often gloated, he went straight to the stable, and with several hearty cuffs and kicks, roused his steed most uncourteously from the comfortable quarters in which he was soundly sleeping, dreaming of mountains of corn and oats, and whole valleys of timothy and clover.

It was the very witching time of night[3] that Ichabod, heavyhearted and bedrooped, pursued his travel homewards, along the sides of the lofty hills which rise above Tarry Town, and which he had traversed so cheerily in the afternoon. The hour was as dismal as himself. Far below him the Tappaan Zee spread its dusky and indistinct waste of waters, with here and there the tall mast of a sloop, riding quietly at anchor under the land. In the dead hush of midnight, he could even hear the barking of the watch-dog from the opposite shore of the Hudson; but it was so vague and faint as only to give an idea of his distance from this faithful companion of man. Now and then, too, the long-drawn crowing of a cock, accidentally awakened, would sound far, far off, from some farm house away among the hills—but it was like a dreaming sound in his ear. No signs of life occurred near him, but occasionally the melancholy chirp of a cricket, or perhaps the guttural twang of a bull frog, from a neighbouring marsh, as if sleeping uncomfortably, and turning suddenly in his bed.

All the stories of ghosts and goblins that Ichabod had heard in the afternoon, now came crowding upon his recollection. The night grew darker and darker; the stars seemed to sink deeper in the sky, and driving clouds occasionally hid them from his sight. He had never felt so lonely and dismal. He was, moreover, approaching the very place where many of the scenes of the ghost stories had been laid. In the centre of the road stood an enormous tulip tree, which towered like a giant above all the other trees of the neighbourhood, and formed a kind of land-mark. Its limbs were vast, gnarled, and fantastic, twisting down almost to the earth, and rising again into the air, and they would have formed trunks for ordinary trees. It was connected with the tragical story of the unfortunate André, who had been taken prisoner hard by it, and it was universally known by the name of Major André's tree. The common people regarded it with a mixture of respect and superstition, partly out of sympathy for the memory of its ill-starred namesake, and partly from the tales, strange sights, and doleful lamentations, told concerning it.

As Ichabod approached this fearful tree, he began to whistle; he thought his whistle was answered: it was but a blast sweeping sharply through the dry branches. As he approached a little nearer, he thought he saw something white, hanging in the midst of the tree: he paused and ceased whistling; but on looking more narrowly, perceived that it was a place where the tree had been scathed by lightning, and the white wood laid bare. Suddenly he heard

3. Cf. Shakespeare's *Hamlet* 3.2.406.

a groan—his teeth chattered, and his knees smote against the saddle: it was but the rubbing of one huge bough upon another, as they were swayed about by the breeze. He passed the tree in safety, but new perils lay still before him.

About two hundred yards from the tree, a small brook crossed the road, and ran into a marshy and thickly wooded glen, known by the name of Wiley's Swamp. A few rough logs, laid side by side, served for a bridge over this stream. On that side of the road where the brook entered the wood, a group of oaks and chestnuts, matted thick with wild grape vines, threw a cavernous gloom over it. To pass this bridge, was the severest trial. It was at this identical spot that the unfortunate André was captured, and under the covert of those chestnuts and vines were the sturdy yeomen concealed who surprised him. This has ever since been considered a haunted stream, and fearful are the feelings of the schoolboy who has to pass it alone after dark.

As he approached the stream, his heart began to thump; he, however, summoned up all his resolution, gave his horse half a score of kicks in the ribs, and attempted to dash briskly across the bridge; but instead of starting forward, the perverse old animal made a lateral movement, and ran broadside against the fence. Ichabod, whose fears increased with the delay, jerked the reins on the other side, and kicked lustily with the contrary foot: it was all in vain; his steed started, it is true, but it was only to plunge to the opposite side of the road into a thicket of brambles and alder bushes. The schoolmaster now bestowed both whip and heel upon the starvelling ribs of old Gunpowder, who dashed forward, snuffling and snorting, but came to a stand just by the bridge with a suddenness that had nearly sent his rider sprawling over his head. Just at this moment a plashy tramp by the side of the bridge caught the sensitive ear of Ichabod. In the dark shadow of the grove, on the margin of the brook, he beheld something huge, misshapen, black and towering. It stirred not, but seemed gathered up in the gloom, like some gigantic monster ready to spring upon the traveller.

The hair of the affrighted pedagogue rose upon his head with terror. What was to be done? To turn and fly was now too late; and besides, what chance was there of escaping ghost or goblin, if such it was, which can ride upon the wings of the wind? Summoning up, therefore, a show of courage, he demanded in stammering accents—"who are you?" He received no reply. He repeated his demand in a still more agitated voice.—Still there was no answer. Once more he cudgelled the sides of the inflexible Gunpowder, and shutting his eyes, broke forth with involuntary fervour into a psalm tune. Just then the shadowy object of alarm put itself in motion, and with a scramble and a bound, stood at once in the middle of the road. Though the night was dark and dismal, yet the form of the unknown might now in some degree be ascertained. He appeared to be a horseman of large dimensions, and mounted on a black horse of powerful frame. He made no offer of molestation or sociability, but kept aloof on one side of the road, jogging along on the blind side of old Gunpowder, who had now got over his fright and waywardness.

Ichabod, who had no relish for this strange midnight companion, and bethought himself of the adventure of Brom Bones with the gallopping Hessian, now quickened his steed, in hopes of leaving him behind. The stranger, however, quickened his horse to an equal pace; Ichabod pulled up, and fell into a walk, thinking to lag behind—the other did the same. His heart began to sink within him; he endeavoured to resume his psalm tune, but his parched tongue clove to the roof of his mouth, and he could not utter a stave.[4] There was something in the moody and dogged silence of this pertinacious companion, that was mysterious and appalling. It was soon fearfully accounted for. On mounting a rising ground, which brought the figure of his fellow traveller in relief against the sky, gigantic in height, and muffled in a cloak, Ichabod was horror-struck, on perceiving that he was headless! but his horror was still more increased, on observing, that the head, which should have rested on his shoulders, was carried before him on the pommel of the saddle! His terror rose to desperation; he rained a shower of kicks and blows upon Gunpowder, hoping, by a sudden movement, to give his companion the slip—but the spectre started full jump with him. Away, then, they dashed, through thick and thin; stones flying, and sparks flashing, at every bound. Ichabod's flimsy garments fluttered in the air, as he stretched his long lank body away over his horse's head, in the eagerness of his flight.

They had now reached the road which turns off to Sleepy Hollow; but Gunpowder, who seemed possessed with a demon, instead of keeping up it, made an opposite turn, and plunged headlong down hill to the left. This road leads through a sandy hollow shaded by trees for about a quarter of a mile, where it crosses the bridge famous in goblin story, and just beyond swells the green knoll on which stands the whitewashed church.

As yet the panic of the steed had given his unskilful rider an apparent advantage in the chase, but just as he had got half way through the hollow, the girths of the saddle gave way, and he felt it slipping from under him; he seized it by the pommel, and endeavoured to hold it firm, but in vain; and had just time to save himself by clasping old Gunpowder round the neck, when the saddle fell to the earth, and he heard it trampled under foot by his pursuer. For a moment the terror of Hans Van Ripper's wrath passed across his mind—for it was his Sunday saddle; but this was no time for petty fears: the goblin was hard on his haunches; and, unskilful rider that he was! he had much-ado to maintain his seat; sometimes slipping on one side, sometimes on another, and sometimes jolted on the high ridge of his horse's back bone, with a violence that he verily feared would cleave him asunder.

An opening in the trees now cheered him with the hopes that the Church Bridge was at hand. The wavering reflection of a silver star in the bosom of the brook told him that he was not mistaken. He saw the walls of the church dimly glaring under the trees beyond. He recollected the place where Brom Bones' ghostly competitor had disappeared. "If I can but reach that bridge," thought Ichabod, "I am safe."[5] Just then he heard the black steed panting and blowing close behind him; he fancied he felt his hot breath. Another convulsive kick in the ribs, and old Gunpowder sprung upon the bridge; he thundered over the resounding planks; he gained the opposite side, and now Ichabod cast a look behind to see if his pursuer should vanish, according to rule, in a flash of fire and brimstone. Just then he saw the goblin rising in his stirrups, and in the very act of hurling his head at him. Ichabod endeavoured to dodge the horrible missile, but too late. It encountered his cranium with a tremendous crash—he was tumbled

4. Verse.
5. Superstition held that spirits could not cross water.

headlong into the dust, and Gunpowder, the black steed, and the goblin rider, passed by like a whirlwind.——

The next morning the old horse was found without his saddle, and the bridle under his feet, soberly cropping the grass at his master's gate. Ichabod did not make his appearance at breakfast—dinner-hour came, but no Ichabod. The boys assembled at the schoolhouse, and strolled idly about the banks of the brook; but no schoolmaster. Hans Van Ripper now began to feel some uneasiness about the fate of poor Ichabod, and his saddle. An inquiry was set on foot, and after diligent investigation they came upon his traces. In one part of the road leading to the church, was found the saddle trampled in the dirt; the tracks of horses' hoofs deeply dented in the road, and evidently at furious speed, were traced to the bridge, beyond which, on the bank of a broad part of the brook, where the water ran deep and black, was found the hat of the unfortunate Ichabod, and close beside it a shattered pumpkin.

The brook was searched, but the body of the schoolmaster was not to be discovered. Hans Van Ripper, as executor of his estate, examined the bundle which contained all his worldly effects. They consisted of two old shirts and a half; two stocks[6] for the neck; a pair of worsted stockings with holes in them; an old pair of corduroy small-clothes; a book of psalm tunes full of dog's ears; a pitch pipe out of order; a rusty razor; a small pot of bear's grease for the hair, and a cast-iron comb. As to the books and furniture of the schoolhouse, they belonged to the community, excepting Cotton Mather's History of Witchcraft, a New-England Almanack, and a book of dreams and fortune telling, in which last was a sheet of foolscap much scribbled and blotted, by several fruitless attempts to make a copy of verses in honour of the heiress of Van Tassel. These magic books and the poetic scrawl were forthwith consigned to the flames by Hans Van Ripper, who from that time forward determined to send his children no more to school, observing, that he never knew any good come of this same reading and writing. Whatever money the schoolmaster possessed, and he had received his quarter's pay but a day or two before, he must have had about his person at the time of his disappearance.

The mysterious event caused much speculation at the Church on the following Sunday. Knots of gazers and gossips were collected in the churchyard, at the bridge, and at the spot where the hat and pumpkin had been found. The stories of Brouwer, of Bones, and a whole budget of others, were called to mind; and when they had diligently considered them all, and compared them with the symptoms of the present case, they shook their heads, and came to the conclusion, that Ichabod had been carried off by the galloping Hessian. As he was a bachelor, and in nobody's debt, nobody troubled his head any more about him, the school was removed to a different quarter of the hollow, and another pedagogue reigned in his stead.

It is true, an old farmer, who had been down to New-York on a visit several years after, and from whom this account of the ghostly adventure was received, brought home the intelligence that Ichabod Crane was still alive; that he had left the neighbourhood partly through fear of the goblin and Hans Van

6. Wide bands or cravats.

Ripper, and partly in mortification at having been suddenly dismissed by the heiress; that he had changed his quarters to a distant part of the country; had kept school and studied law at the same time; had been admitted to the bar, turned politician, electioneered, written for the newspapers, and finally had been made a Justice of the Ten Pound Court.[7] Brom Bones too, who, shortly after his rival's disappearance, conducted the blooming Katrina in triumph to the altar, was observed to look exceedingly knowing whenever the story of Ichabod was related, and always burst into a hearty laugh at the mention of the pumpkin; which led some to suspect that he knew more about the matter than he chose to tell.

The old country wives, however, who are the best judges of these matters, maintain to this day, that Ichabod was spirited away by supernatural means; and it is a favourite story often told about the neighbourhood round the winter evening fire. The bridge became more than ever an object of superstitious awe, and that may be the reason why the road has been altered of late years, so as to approach the church by the border of the millpond. The schoolhouse being deserted, soon fell to decay, and was reported to be haunted by the ghost of the unfortunate pedagogue; and the plough boy, loitering homeward of a still summer evening, has often fancied his voice at a distance, chanting a melancholy psalm tune among the tranquil solitudes of Sleepy Hollow.

POSTSCRIPT, FOUND IN THE HANDWRITING OF MR. KNICKERBOCKER

The preceding Tale is given, almost in the precise words in which I heard it related at the corporation meeting of the ancient city of the Manhattoes, at which were present many of its sagest and most illustrious burghers. The narrator was a pleasant, shabby, gentlemanly old fellow, in pepper and salt clothes, with a sadly humourous face, and one whom I strongly suspected of being poor, he made such efforts to be entertaining. When his story was concluded, there was much laughter and approbation, particularly from two or three deputy aldermen, who had been asleep the greater part of the time. There was, however, one tall, dry-looking old gentleman, with beetling eyebrows, who maintained a grave and rather severe face throughout; now and then folding his arms, inclining his head, and looking down upon the floor, as if turning a doubt over in his mind. He was one of your wary men, who never laugh but upon good grounds—when they have reason and the law on their side. When the mirth of the rest of the company had subsided, and silence was restored, he leaned one arm on the elbow of his chair, and sticking the other a-kimbo, demanded, with a slight, but exceedingly sage motion of the head, and contraction of the brow, what was the moral of the story, and what it went to prove.

The story-teller, who was just putting a glass of wine to his lips, as a refreshment after his toils, paused for a moment, looked at his inquirer with an air of infinite deference, and lowering the glass slowly to the table, observed, that the story was intended most logically to prove,

"That there is no situation in life but has its advantages and pleasures, provided we will but take a joke as we find it:

7. Small-claims court.

"That, therefore, he that runs races with goblin troopers, is likely to have rough riding of it:

"Ergo, for a country schoolmaster to be refused the hand of a Dutch heiress, is a certain step to high preferment in the state."

The cautious old gentleman knit his brows tenfold closer after this explanation, being sorely puzzled by the ratiocination of the syllogism; while methought the one in pepper and salt eyed him with something of a triumphant leer. At length he observed, that all this was very well, but still he thought the story a little on the extravagant—there were one or two points on which he had his doubts.

"Faith, sir," replied the story-teller, "as to that matter, I don't believe one half of it myself." D.K.

1820

JAMES FENIMORE COOPER
1789–1851

The author of thirty-two novels, a history of the American navy, five travel books, and two major works of social criticism, James Fenimore Cooper was among the most important writers of his time—a writer who helped chart the future course of American fiction. He wrote novels of manners, transatlantic and European fiction, and several historical novels on the American Revolution. A pioneering author of sea fiction, he had a significant influence on Herman Melville. But Cooper remains best known for the five historical novels of the Leatherstocking series, which are set between 1740 and the early 1800s. These novels—*The Pioneers* (1823), *The Last of the Mohicans* (1826), *The Prairie* (1827), *The Pathfinder* (1840), and *The Deerslayer* (1841)—explore the imperial, racial, and social conflicts central to the emergence of the United States; and their evocative portrayals of the frontiersman Natty Bumppo and his Indian friend Chingachgook helped to develop what the British novelist and critic D. H. Lawrence influentially called "the myth of America." Central to that myth is the image of a nation founded through conflict and dispossession that nonetheless managed to sustain belief in its youthful innocence.

Cooper was born on September 15, 1789, in Burlington, New Jersey, and in 1790 moved with his parents to Cooperstown, on Otsego Lake in central New York, a town founded and developed by his father, Judge William Cooper. A two-term member of Congress known for his energetic entrepreneurship and ardent Federalism, the judge hoped to educate his son to manage the family settlements, sending him first to an academy in Albany and then to Yale, where the thirteen-year-old Cooper became known as a prankster. Expelled from Yale because of misconduct in 1805, Cooper (at his father's insistence) became a sailor in 1806 and was commissioned as a midshipman in the U.S. Navy in 1808. One year later, when Judge Cooper unexpectedly died, leaving behind an apparently large fortune for his heirs, the twenty-year-old Cooper seemed set for life. He resigned from the navy and, in 1811, married Susan DeLancey, whose prominent New York State family had lost considerable possessions by siding with the British during the Revolution but still owned lands in Westchester County.

For several years Cooper oversaw properties in Westchester County and Cooperstown. But the family fortunes steadily diminished. In 1819, with the death of an older brother, Cooper became the person primarily responsible for the debt-ridden Cooper estate. A failure at managing the "real" Cooperstown, Cooper through his authorship of the Leatherstocking novels may well have sought to take imaginative possession of the New York lands he could never oversee with the skill of his father.

Cooper began his writing career in 1820, in large part in an effort to earn enough money to pay his debts. According to family lore, he bet his wife that he could write a better novel than the British novel of manners the two had been reading together. The result was *Precaution* (1820), a leaden novel of British high society modeled on Jane Austen's *Persuasion* (1818). Following that insignificant start, Cooper turned to the historical romance as popularized by the Scottish writer Sir Walter Scott, and produced *The Spy* (1821), the first important novel about the American Revolution. Its success led him to move to New York City and embark on a successful literary career. He founded a literary society there, the Bread and Cheese Club, and became the center of a circle that included notable painters of the Hudson River School as well as writers (William Cullen Bryant among them) and professionals. In 1823 he published *The Pioneers*, the first of the Leatherstocking novels featuring Natty Bumppo. Cooper had not written *The Pioneers* with the intention of inaugurating a series, but response to Natty Bumppo was so positive that he returned to him three years later with *The Last of the Mohicans*, consolidating his creation of one of the most popular characters in world literature. With his previous novels, Cooper had assumed the financial risk of paying printers and doing the bulk of the promotion. *Mohicans* was the first of his novels published by the Philadelphia firm of Carey and Lea, which paid him $5,000 (around $85,000 in today's value) for the novel. Although Cooper was never financially secure, this new arrangement helped him to pay off his family's debts.

In 1826, at the height of his fame, Cooper sailed for Europe with his wife and their five children. In Paris, where he became intimate with the aged Lafayette, he wrote *The Prairie* (1827) and *Notions of the Americans* (1828), a defense of the United States against criticism by European travelers. Smarting under the half-complimentary, half-patronizing epithet of "The American Scott," he wrote three historical novels set in medieval Europe—*The Bravo* (1831), *The Heidenmauer* (1832), and *The Headsman* (1833)—as a realistic corrective to what he regarded as Sir Walter Scott's glorifications of the past. On his return to the United States in 1833, Cooper was so angered by the negative reception of these novels that he renounced novel writing in *Letter to His Countrymen* (1834). Subsequently, at Cooperstown he gave notice that a point of land on Otsego Lake where the townspeople had been picnicking was private property and not to be used without his permission. Newspapers began attacking him as a would-be aristocrat poisoned by his residence abroad, and for years Cooper embroiled himself in lawsuits designed not to gain damages for libels but to tame the vitriolic press. Even while pursuing these legal efforts, Cooper continued to write book after book—social and political satires growing out of his experiences with the press, a political primer on the dangers of an unchecked, demagogic democracy (*The American Democrat* [1838]), and (silently retracting his 1834 renunciation of fiction writing) a series of sociopolitical novels and two additional Leatherstocking novels: *The Pathfinder* (1840) and *The Deerslayer* (1841). His monumental *History of the Navy of the United States of America* (1839) became the focus of new quarrels and a new lawsuit, and controversy continued to surround Cooper when he published his "Littlepage" novels—*Satanstoe* (1845), *The Chainbearer* (1845), and *The Redskins* (1846)—which supported landowners over tenants in the controversy known as the Anti-Rent War, and his anti-utopian novel *The Crater* (1847), which imagined the demise of the American republic as a result of demagogues' assaults on the Constitution. When Herman Melville reviewed Cooper's last great sea novel, *The*

Sea Lions (1849), in the April 1849 issue of the *Literary World*, he lambasted "those who more for fashion's sake than anything else, have of late joined in decrying our national novelist" and concluded by warmly recommending what he termed one of Cooper's "happiest" novels.

A lifelong defender of American democracy against European aristocracy and home-grown demagoguery, Cooper had become out of step with some of his countrypeople. When Cooper died on September 14, 1851, a day before his sixty-second birthday, his detractors—who spoke of him as a reactionary prig—were vastly outnumbered by his admirers. At a memorial commemoration on February 25, 1852, Washington Irving declared that the death of Cooper "left a space in our literature which will not be easily supplied"; Emerson spoke of "an old debt to him of happy days, on the first appearance of the *Pioneers*"; and the historian Francis Parkman proclaimed that of "all American writers, Cooper is the most original and the most thoroughly national." Throughout the century and into the next, Cooper's Leatherstocking novels had an incalculable vogue in the United States and abroad. Major European writers as diverse as Honoré de Balzac and Leo Tolstoy were profoundly moved by *The Pioneers* and the subsequent Natty Bumppo novels, while the novelist Joseph Conrad proclaimed that Cooper "wrote as well as any novelist of the time." Dissenting from such adulation, Mark Twain asserted in his classic essay "Fenimore Cooper's Literary Offenses" (1895; included in Volume C of the *Norton Anthology of American Literature*) that Cooper's English is "a crime against the language." Nevertheless, the Leatherstocking novels are probably the books that most influenced Twain's own *Huckleberry Finn* and many other frontier and western novels published after the appearance of *Mohicans* in 1826. Twain's account of Huck's flight from society and his friendship with the runaway slave Jim drew on what continues to appeal to modern readers of Cooper: the profound dramatizations of such key American conflicts as natural rights versus legal rights, order versus change, wilderness versus established society, and—especially—the possibilities of democratic freedom and interracial friendship as exemplified by the enduring image of Natty Bumppo and Chingachgook on the vanishing frontier.

The Pioneers

The Pioneers; or, The Sources of the Susquehanna; A Descriptive Tale (1823) is the first of five Cooper novels that came to be known collectively as the Leatherstocking Tales because they center on Natty Bumppo, whose hunting clothes are made of leather. Natty's popularity with readers of *The Pioneers* surprised Cooper, who had intended him in this novel to be merely one of an ensemble of characters covering the range of types who lived on the early frontier.

The Pioneers begins in December 1793 at the settlement of Templeton (modeled on Cooperstown, founded by Cooper's father) at Otsego Lake in central New York, some fifty miles west of Albany. The episodes reprinted here occur in the spring of 1794. Besides Natty Bumppo—a hunter who is among the earliest white settlers on the frontier and is already a kind of relic at the start of the novel—other characters are the Quaker and chief landowner in the region, Judge Marmaduke Temple; Temple's only child, Elizabeth (Bess), just back from "finishing school"; Temple's cousin Richard (Dickon) Jones, the local sheriff; Temple's steward, Benjamin Penquillan (called Ben Pump), a former seaman from the Cornwall district in England; the Frenchman Monsieur Le Quoi, once a West Indian planter but now a refugee; Louisa Grant, daughter of the town's one minister, an Episcopalian; and Oliver Edwards, a stranger living in Natty's hut on the outskirts of town and thought by many to be a Native American because Natty's other housemate is Chingachgook, the only remaining Mohican Indian in the district. The second episode introduces Billy Kirby, a woodchopper whose work of leveling the forests is vital to the advancing pioneers and whose attitude regarding natural resources is opposed to Natty's. The two chapters juxtapose images from past and present, putting the book's main action in the context of successful white settlement of the territory, with "wilderness" giving way to "civilization." Through this juxtaposition, Cooper presciently raises environmentalist questions for a democratic polity about how best to manage and respect natural resources.

The text is from the first edition, volume 2, chapters 2 and 3 (chapters 21 and 22 in later one-volume editions).

From The Pioneers

From Volume II

Chapter II

[THE JUDGE'S HISTORY OF THE SETTLEMENT; A SUDDEN STORM]

"Speed! Malise, speed! such cause of haste
Thine active sinews never brac'd."

—SCOTT[1]

The roads of Otsego, if we except the more principal highways, were, at the early day of our tale, but little better than wood-paths of unusual width. The high trees that were growing on the very verge of the wheel-tracks, excluded the sun's rays, except when at meridian, and the slowness of the evaporation, united with the rich mould of vegetable decomposition, that covered the whole county, to the depth of several inches, occasioned but an indifferent foundation for the footing of travellers. Added to these, there were the ups and downs of natural surface, and the constant recurrence of enormous and slippery roots, laid bare by the removal of the light soil, together with stumps of trees, to make a passage not only difficult, but dangerous. Yet the riders, among these numerous obstructions, which were such as would terrify an unpractised eye, gave no demonstrations of uneasiness, as their horses toiled through the sloughs, or trotted with uncertain paces along their dark route. In many places, the marks on the trees were the only indications of a road, with, perhaps, an occasional remnant of a pine, that, by being cut close to the earth, so as to leave nothing visible but its base of roots, spreading for twenty feet in every direction, was apparently placed there as a beacon, to warn the traveller that it was the centre of the highway.

Into one of these roads the active Sheriff led the way, first striking out of the footpath, by which they had descended from the sugar-bush, across a little bridge, formed of round logs laid loosely on sleepers[2] of pine, in which large openings were frequent, and, in one instance, of a formidable width. The nag of Richard, when it reached this barrier, laid its nose along the logs, and stepped across the difficult passage with the sagacity of a man; but the

1. From the poem *The Lady of the Lake* (1810), by the Scottish writer Sir Walter Scott (1771–1832).

2. Heavy beams. "Sugar-bush": grove of sugar maples.

blooded filly[3] which Miss Temple rode disdained so humble a movement. She made a step or two with an unusual caution, and then, on reaching the broadest opening, obedient to the curb and whip of her fearless mistress, she bounded across the dangerous pass, with the activity of a squirrel.

"Gently, gently, my child," said Marmaduke, who was following in the manner of Richard—"this is not a country for equestrian feats. Much prudence is requisite, to journey through our rough paths with safety. Thou mayst practise thy skill in horsemanship on the plains of New Jersey, with safety, but in the hills of Otsego, they must be suspended for a time."

"I may as well, then, relinquish my saddle at once, dear sir," returned his daughter; "for if it is to be laid aside until this wild country be improved, old age will overtake me, and put an end to what you term by equestrian feats."

"Say not so, my child," returned her father; "but if thou venturest again, as in crossing this bridge, old age will never overtake thee, but I shall be left to mourn thee, cut off in thy pride, my Elizabeth. If thou hadst seen this district of country, as I did, when it lay in the sleep of nature, and witnessed its rapid changes, as it awoke to supply the wants of man, thou wouldst curb thy impatience for a little time, though thou should not curb thy steed."

"I have a remembrance of hearing you speak, sir, of your first visit to these woods, but the recollection of it is faint, and blended with the confused images of childhood. Wild and unsettled as it may yet seem, it must have been a thousand times more dreary then. Will you repeat, dear sir, what you then thought of your enterprise, and what you felt?"

During this speech of Elizabeth, which was uttered with the interested fervour of affection, young Edwards rode more closely to the side of the Judge, and bent his dark eyes on his countenance, with an expression that seemed to read his thoughts.

"Thou wast then young, my child, but must remember when I left thee and thy mother, to take my first survey of these uninhabited mountains," said Marmaduke. "But thou dost not feel all the secret motives that can urge a man to endure privations in order to accumulate wealth. In my case they have not been trifling, and God has been pleased to smile on my efforts. If I have encountered pain, famine, and disease, in accomplishing the settlement of this rough territory, I have not the misery of failure to add to the grievances."

"Famine!" echoed Elizabeth; "I thought this was the land of abundance! had you famine to contend with?"

"Even so, my child," said her father. "Those who look around them now, and see the loads of produce that issue out of every wild path in these mountains, during the season of travelling, will hardly credit that no more than five years have elapsed, since the tenants of these woods were compelled to eat the scanty fruits of the forest to sustain life, and, with their unpractised skill, to hunt the beasts as food for their starving families."

"Ay!" cried Richard, who happened to overhear the last of this speech, between the notes of the wood-chopper's song, which he was endeavoring to breathe aloud; "that was the starvingtime, cousin Bess. I grew as lank as a

3. Thoroughbred young mare. "Nag": older, nondescript horse.

weasel that fall, and my face was as pale as one of your fever-and-ague visages. Monsieur Le Quoi, there, fell away like a pumpkin in drying; nor do I think you have got fairly over it yet, Monsieur. Benjamin, I thought, bore it with a worse grace than any of the family, for he swore it was harder to endure than a short allowance in the calm latitudes.[4] Benjamin is a sad fellow to swear, if you starve him ever so little. I had half a mind to quit you then, 'duke,[5] and go into Pennsylvania to fatten; but, damn it, thinks I, we are sisters' children, and I will live or die with him, after all."

"I do not forget thy kindness," said Marmaduke, "nor that we are of one blood."

"But, my dear father," cried the wondering Elizabeth, "was there actual suffering? where were the beautiful and fertile vales of the Mohawk? could not they furnish food for your wants?"

"It was a season of scarcity; the necessities of life commanded a high price in Europe, and were greedily sought after by the speculators. The emigrants, from the east to the west, invariably passed along the valley of the Mohawk, and swept away the means of subsistence, like a swarm of locusts. Nor were the people on the Flats in a much better condition. They were in want themselves, but they spared the little excess of provisions, that nature did not absolutely require, with the justice of the German character. There was no grinding of the poor. The word speculator was then unknown to them. I have seen many a stout man, bending under the load of the bag of meal, which he was carrying from the mills of the Mohawk, through the rugged passes of these mountains, to feed his half-famished children, with a heart so light, as he approached his hut, that the thirty miles he had passed seemed nothing. Remember, my child, it was in our very infancy: we had neither mills, nor grain, nor roads, nor often clearings;—we had nothing of increase, but the mouths that were to be fed; for, even at that inauspicious moment, the restless spirit of emigration was not idle; nay, the general scarcity, which extended to the east, tended to increase the number of adventurers."

"And how, dearest father, didst thou encounter this dreadful evil?" said Elizabeth, unconsciously adopting the dialect of her parent,[6] in the warmth of her sympathy. "Upon thee must have fallen all the responsibility, if not the suffering."

"It did, Elizabeth," returned the Judge, pausing for a single moment, as if musing on his former feelings. "I had hundreds, at that dreadful time, daily looking up to me for bread. The sufferings of their families, and the gloomy prospect before them, had paralysed the enterprise and efforts of my settlers; hunger drove them to the woods for food, but despair sent them, at night, enfeebled and wan, to a sleepless pillow. It was not a moment for inaction. I purchased cargoes of wheat from the granaries of Pennsylvania; they were landed at Albany, and brought up the Mohawk in boats; from thence it was transported on pack-horses into the wilderness, and distributed amongst my people. Seines[7] were made, and the lakes and rivers were dragged for fish. Something like a miracle was wrought in our favour, for enormous schools of herring were discovered to have wandered five hundred miles, through the windings of the impetuous Susquehanna, and the lake was alive with their

4. Short supplies of food on a becalmed ship.
5. Nickname for Marmaduke.
6. I.e., the Quaker use of "thee" and "thou."
7. Large nets.

numbers. These were at length caught, and dealt out to the people, with proper portions of salt; and from that moment, we again began to prosper."

"Yes," cried Richard, "and I was the man who served out both the fish and the salt; and when the poor devils came to receive their rations, Benjamin, who was my deputy, was obliged to keep them off by stretching ropes around me, for they smelt so of garlic, from eating nothing but the wild onion, that the fumes put me out, often, in my measurement. You were a child then, Bess, and knew nothing of the matter, for great care was observed to keep both you and your mother from suffering. That year put me back, dreadfully, both in the breed of my hogs, and of my turkeys."

"No, Bess," cried the Judge, in a more cheerful tone, utterly disregarding the interruption of his cousin, "he who hears of the settlement of a country, knows but little of the actual toil and suffering by which it is accomplished. Unimproved and wild as this district now seems to your eyes, what was it when I first entered the hills! I left my party, the morning of my arrival, back near the farms of the Cherry Valley, and, following a deer-path, rode to the summit of the mountain, that I have since called Mount Vision; for the sight that there met my eyes seemed to me as the deceptions of a dream. The fire[8] had run over the pinnacle, and, in a great measure, laid open the view. The leaves were fallen, and I mounted a tree, and sat for an hour looking on the silent wilderness. Not an opening was to be seen in the boundless forest, except where the lake lay, like a mirror of glass. The water was covered by myriads of the wild-fowl that migrate with the changes in the season; and, while in my situation on the branch of the beech, I saw a bear, with her cubs, descend to the shore to drink. I had met many deer, gliding through the woods, in my journey; but not the vestige of a man could I trace, during my progress, nor from my elevated observatory. No clearing, no hut, none of the winding roads that are now to be seen, were there; nothing but mountains rising back of mountains, and the valley, with its surface of branches, enlivened here and there with the faded foliage of some tree, that parted from its leaves with more than ordinary reluctance. Even the little Susquehanna was then hid, by the height and density of the forest."

"And were you there alone?" asked Elizabeth;—"passed you the night in that solitary state?"

"Not so, my child," returned her father. "After musing on the view for an hour, with a mingled feeling of pleasure and desolation, I left my perch, and descended the mountain. My horse was left to browse on the twigs that grew within his reach, while I explored the shores of the lake, and the spot where Templeton stands. A pine of more than ordinary growth stood where my dwelling is now placed, and a wind-row had been opened through the trees from thence to the lake, so that my view was but little impeded. Under the branches of that tree I made my solitary dinner; and I had just finished my repast as I saw a smoke curling from under the mountain, near the east bank of the lake. It was the only indication of the vicinity of man that I had then seen. After much toil, I made my way to the spot, and found a rough cabin of logs, built against the foot of a rock, and bearing the marks of a tenant, though I found none within it.—"

"It was the hut of Leather-stocking," said Edwards, quickly.

8. Started by lightning in a dry season.

"It was; though I had, at first, supposed it to be a habitation of the Indians. But while I was lingering around the spot, Natty made his appearance, staggering under the load of the carcass of a buck that he had slain. Our acquaintance commenced at that time; before, I had never heard that such a being tenanted the woods. He launched his bark canoe, and set me across the foot of the lake, to the place where I had fastened my horse, and pointed out a spot where he might get a scanty browsing until the morning; and I returned and passed the night in the cabin of the hunter."

Miss Temple was so much struck by the deep attention of young Edwards, during this speech, that she forgot to resume her interrogatories; but the youth himself continued the discourse, by asking, with something like a smile lurking around his features—

"And how did the Leather-stocking discharge the duties of a host, sir?"

"Why, simply but kindly, until late in the evening, when he discovered my name and object, and the cordiality of his manner very sensibly diminished, or, I might better say, disappeared. He considered the introduction of the settlers as an innovation[9] on his rights, I believe; for he expressed much dissatisfaction at the measure, though in his confused and ambiguous manner. I hardly understood his objections myself, but suppose they referred chiefly to an interruption of the hunting."

"Had you then purchased the estate, or were you examining it with an intent to buy?" asked Edwards, a little abruptly.

"It had been mine for several years. It was with a view to people the land that I visited the lake. Natty treated me hospitably, but coldly, I thought, after he learnt the nature of my journey. I slept on his own bear-skin, however, and in the morning joined my surveyors again."

"Said he nothing of the Indian rights, sir?" continued Edwards. "The Leather-stocking is much given to impeach the justice of the tenure by which the whites hold the country."

"I remember that he spoke of them, but I did not clearly comprehend him, and may have forgotten what he then said; for the Indian title was extinguished so far back as the close of the old war; and if it had not been at all, I hold under the patents of the Royal Governors, confirmed by an act of our own State Legislature, so that no court in our country can affect my title."

"Doubtless, sir, your title is both legal and equitable," returned the youth, coldly, reining his horse back, and remaining silent till the subject was changed.

It was seldom that Mr. Jones suffered any conversation to continue, for a great length of time, without his participation. It seems that he was of the party that Judge Temple had designated as his surveyors; and he embraced the opportunity of the pause that succeeded the retreat of young Edwards, to take up the discourse, and with it a narration of their further proceedings, after his own manner. As it wanted, however, the deep interest that had accompanied the description of the Judge, we must decline the task of committing his sentences to paper.

They soon reached the point where the promised view was to be seen. It was one of those picturesque and peculiar scenes, that belong to the Otsego, but which required the absence of the ice, and the softness of a summer's

9. Imposition.

landscape, to be enjoyed in all its beauty. Marmaduke had early forewarned his daughter of the season, and of its effect on the prospect, so that after casting a cursory glance at its capabilities, the party returned homeward, perfectly satisfied that its beauties would repay them for the toil of a second ride, at a more propitious season.

"The spring is the gloomy time of the American year," said the Judge; "and it is more peculiarly the case in these mountains. The winter seems to retreat to the fastnesses of the hills, as to the citadel of its dominion, and is only expelled, after a tedious siege, in which either party, at times, would seem to be gaining the victory."

"A very just and apposite figure, Judge Temple," observed the Sheriff; "and the garrison under the command of Jack Frost make formidable sorties—you understand what I mean by sorties, Monsieur; sallies, in English—and sometimes drive General Spring and his troops back again into the low countries."

"Yes, sair," returned the Frenchman, whose prominent eyes were watching the precarious footsteps of the beast he rode, as it picked its dangerous way among the roots of trees, holes, logbridges, and sloughs, that formed the aggregate of the highway. "Je vous entend;[1] de low countrie, it ees freeze up for half de year."

The error[2] of Mr. Le Quoi was not noticed by the Sheriff; and the rest of the party were yielding to the influence of the changeful season, that was already teaching the equestrians that a continuance of its mildness was not to be expected for any length of time. Silence and thoughtfulness succeeded the gayety and conversation that had prevailed during the commencement of their ride, as clouds began to gather about the heavens, apparently collecting from every quarter, in quick motion, without the agency of a breath of air.

While riding over one of the cleared eminences that occurred in their route, the watchful eye of Judge Temple pointed out to his daughter the approach of a tempest. Flurries of snow already obscured the mountain that formed the northern boundary of the lake, and the genial sensation which had quickened the blood through their veins, was already succeeded by the deadening influence of an approaching *north-wester*.[3]

All of the party were now busily engaged in making the best of their way to the village, though the badness of the roads frequently compelled them to check the impatience of their animals, which often carried them over places that would not admit of any gait faster than a walk.

Richard continued in advance, and was followed by Mr. Le Quoi; next to whom rode Elizabeth, who seemed to have imbibed the distance which pervaded the manner of young Edwards, since the termination of the discourse between the latter and her father. Marmaduke followed his daughter, giving her frequent and tender warnings, as to her safety, and the management of her horse. It was, possibly, the evident dependence that Louisa Grant placed on his assistance, which induced the youth to continue by her side, as they pursued their way through a dreary and dark wood, where the rays of the sun could but rarely penetrate, and where even the daylight was obscured and rendered gloomy by the deep forests that surrounded them. No wind had yet

1. I understand you (French).
2. Le Quoi mistakes Jones's reference to low-lying terrain for a specific allusion to the so-called Low Countries (such as the Netherlands).
3. Storm blowing from the northwest.

reached the spot where the equestrians were in motion, but that dead stillness that often precedes a storm, contributed to render their situation more irksome than if they were already subjected to the fury of the tempest. Suddenly the voice of young Edwards was heard shouting, in those appalling tones that carry alarm to the very soul, and which curdle the blood of him who hears them—

"A tree! a tree! whip—spur for your lives! a tree! a tree!"

"A tree! a tree!" echoed Richard, giving his horse a blow, that caused the alarmed beast to jump nearly a rod, throwing the mud and water into the air, like a hurricane.

"Von tree! von tree!" shouted the Frenchman, bending his body on the neck of his charger, shutting his eyes, and playing on the ribs of his beast with his heels, at a rate that caused him to be conveyed, on the crupper[4] of the Sheriff, with a marvellous speed.

Elizabeth checked her filly, and looked up, with an unconscious but alarmed air, at the very cause of their danger, as she listened to the crackling sounds that awoke the stillness of the forest; but, at the next instant, her bridle was seized by her father, who cried—

"God protect my child!" and she felt herself hurried onward, impelled by the vigour of his nervous arm.

Each one of the party bowed to their saddlebows,[5] as the tearing of branches was succeeded by a sound like the rushing of the winds, which was followed by a thundering report, and a shock that caused the very earth to tremble, as one of the noblest ruins in the forest fell directly across their path.

One glance was enough to assure Judge Temple that his daughter, and those in front of him, were safe, and he turned his eyes, in dreadful anxiety, to learn the fate of the others. Young Edwards was on the opposite side of the tree, with his form thrown back in his saddle to its utmost distance, his left hand drawing up his bridle with its greatest force, while the right grasped that of Miss Grant, so as to draw the head of her horse under its body. Both the animals stood shaking in every joint with terror, and snorting fearfully. The maiden herself had relinquished her reins, and with her hands pressed on her face, sat bending forward in her saddle, in an attitude of despair mingled strangely with resignation.

"Are you safe?" cried the Judge, first breaking the awful silence of the moment.

"By God's blessing," returned the youth; "but if there had been branches to the tree we must have been lost———"

He was interrupted by the figure of Louisa, slowly yielding in her saddle; and but for his arm, she would have sunken to the earth. Terror, however, was the only injury that the clergyman's daughter had sustained, and, with the aid of Elizabeth, she was soon restored to her senses. After some little time was lost in recovering her strength, the young lady was replaced in her saddle, and, supported on either side, by Judge Temple and Mr. Edwards, she was enabled to follow the party in their slow progress.

4. Strap on the back of the horse's saddle.

5. Arched upper front of a saddle.

"The sudden falling of the trees," said Marmaduke, "are the most dangerous of our accidents in the forest, for they are not to be foreseen, being impelled by no winds, nor any extraneous or visible cause, against which we can guard."

"The reason of their falling, Judge Temple, is very obvious," said the Sheriff. "The tree is old and decayed, and it is gradually weakened by the frosts, until a line drawn from the centre of gravity falls without its base, and the tree comes of a certainty; and I should like to know, what greater compulsion there can be for any thing, than a mathematical certainty. I studied mathe———"

"Very true, Richard," interrupted Marmaduke; "thy reasoning is true, and, if my memory be not over treacherous, was furnished by myself, on a former occasion. But how is one to guard against the danger? canst thou go through the forests, measuring the bases, and calculating the centres of the oaks? answer me that, friend Jones, and I will say thou wilt do the country a service."

"Answer thee that, friend Temple!" returned Richard; "a well-educated man can answer thee any thing, sir. Do any trees fall in this manner, but such as are decayed? Take care not to approach the roots of any rotten trees, and you will be safe enough."

"That would be excluding us entirely from the forests," said Marmaduke. "But, happily, the winds usually force down most of these dangerous ruins, as their currents are admitted into the woods by the surrounding clearings, and such a fall as this has been is very rare."

Louisa, by this time, had recovered so much of her strength, as to allow the party to proceed at a quicker pace; but long before they were safely housed, they were overtaken by the storm; and when they dismounted at the door of the Mansionhouse, the black plumes in Miss Temple's hat were drooping with the weight of a load of damp snow, and the coats of the gentlemen were powdered with the same material.

While Edwards was assisting Louisa from her horse, the warm-hearted girl caught his hand with fervour, and whispered—

"Now, Mr. Edwards, both father and daughter owe their lives to you."

A driving, north-westerly storm succeeded; and before the sun was set, every vestige of spring had vanished; the lake, the mountains, the village, and the fields, being again hid under one dazzling coat of snow.

Chapter III

[THE SLAUGHTER OF THE PIGEONS]

"Men, boys, and girls.
Desert th' unpeopled village; and wild crowds
Spread o'er the plain, by the sweet frenzy driven."[6]
—SOMERVILLE

From this time to the close of April, the weather continued to be a succession of great and rapid changes. One day, the soft airs of spring would seem to be stealing along the valley, and, in unison with an invigorating sun,

6. From *The Chace* (1735), by the English poet William Somerville (1675–1742).

attempting, covertly, to rouse the dormant powers of the vegetable world; while on the next, the surly blasts from the north would sweep across the lake, and erase every impression left by their gentle adversaries. The snow, however, finally disappeared, and the green wheat fields were seen in every direction, spotted with the dark and charred stumps that had, the preceding season, supported some of the proudest trees of the forest.[7] Ploughs were in motion, wherever those useful implements could be used, and the smokes of the sugar-camps[8] were no longer seen issuing from the summits of the woods of maple. The lake had lost all the characteristic beauty of a field of ice, but still a dark and gloomy covering concealed its waters, for the absence of currents left them yet hid under a porous crust, which, saturated with the fluid, barely retained enough of its strength to preserve the contiguity of its parts. Large flocks of wild geese were seen passing over the country, which would hover, for a time, around the hidden sheet of water, apparently searching for an opening, where they might obtain a resting-place; and then, on finding themselves excluded by the chill covering, would soar away to the north, filling the air with their discordant screams, as if venting their complaints at the tardy operations of nature.

For a week, the dark covering of the Otsego was left to the undisturbed possession of two eagles, who alighted on the centre of its field, and sat proudly eyeing the extent of their undisputed territory. During the presence of these monarchs of the air, the flocks of migrating birds avoided crossing the plain of ice, by turning into the hills, and apparently seeking the protection of the forests, while the white and bald heads of the tenants of the lake were turned upward, with a look of majestic contempt, as if penetrating to the very heavens, with the acuteness of their vision. But the time had come, when even these kings of birds were to be dispossessed. An opening had been gradually increasing, at the lower extremity of the lake, and around the dark spot where the current of the river had prevented the formation of ice, during even the coldest weather; and the fresh southerly winds, that now breathed freely up the valley, obtained an impression on the waters. Mimic waves begun to curl over the margin of the frozen field, which exhibited an outline of crystallizations, that slowly receded towards the north. At each step the power of the winds and the waves increased, until, after a struggle of a few hours, the turbulent little billows succeeded in setting the whole field in an undulating motion, when it was driven beyond the reach of the eye, with a rapidity, that was as magical as the change produced in the scene by this expulsion of the lingering remnant of winter. Just as the last sheet of agitated ice was disappearing in the distance, the eagles rose over the border of crystals, and soared with a wide sweep far above the clouds, while the waves tossed their little caps of snow into the air, as if rioting in their release from a thraldom of five months duration.

The following morning Elizabeth was awakened by the exhilarating sounds of the martins, who were quarrelling and chattering around the little boxes which were suspended above her windows, and the cries of Richard, who was calling, in tones as animating as the signs of the season itself—

7. Trees were cut down in the spring and left to dry in the summer; the cleared areas were then burned over, leaving only blackened logs and stumps.

8. Where sugar was made from maple sap.

"Awake! awake! my lady fair! the gulls are hovering over the lake already, and the heavens are alive with the pigeons. You may look an hour before you can find a hole, through which, to get a peep at the sun. Awake! awake! lazy ones! Benjamin is overhauling the ammunition, and we only wait for our breakfasts, and away for the mountains and pigeon-shooting."

There was no resisting this animated appeal, and in a few minutes Miss Temple and her friend descended to the parlour. The doors of the hall were thrown open, and the mild, balmy air of a clear spring morning was ventilating the apartment, where the vigilance of the ex-steward had been so long maintaining an artificial heat, with such unremitted diligence. All of the gentlemen, we do not include Monsieur Le Quoi, were impatiently waiting their morning's repast, each being equipt in the garb of a sportsman. Mr. Jones made many visits to the southern door, and would cry—

"See, cousin Bess! see, 'duke! the pigeon-roosts of the south have broken up! They are growing more thick every instant. Here is a flock that the eye cannot see the end of. There is food enough in it to keep the army of Xerxes[9] for a month, and feathers enough to make beds for the whole county. Xerxes, Mr. Edwards, was a Grecian king, who—no, he was a Turk, or a Persian, who wanted to conquer Greece, just the same as these rascals will overrun our wheat-fields, when they come back in the fall.—Away! away! Bess; I long to pepper them from the mountain."

In this wish both Marmaduke and young Edwards seemed equally to participate, for really the sight was most exhilarating to a sportsman; and the ladies soon dismissed the party, after a hasty breakfast.

If the heavens were alive with pigeons, the whole village seemed equally in motion, with men, women, and children. Every species of fire-arms, from the French ducking-gun, with its barrel of near six feet in length, to the common horseman's pistol, was to be seen in the hands of the men and boys; while bows and arrows, some made of the simple stick of a walnut sapling, and others in a rude imitation of the ancient cross-bows, were carried by many of the latter.

The houses, and the signs of life apparent in the village, drove the alarmed birds from the direct line of their flight, towards the mountains, along the sides and near the bases of which they were glancing in dense masses, that were equally wonderful by the rapidity of their motion, as by their incredible numbers.

We have already said, that across the inclined plane which fell from the steep ascent of the mountain to the banks of the Susquehanna, ran the highway, on either side of which a clearing of many acres had been made, at a very early day. Over those clearings, and up the eastern mountain, and along the dangerous path that was cut into its side, the different individuals posted themselves, as suited their inclinations; and in a few moments the attack commenced.

Amongst the sportsmen was to be seen the tall, gaunt form of Leather-stocking, who was walking over the field, with his rifle hanging on his arm, his dogs following close at his heels, now scenting the dead or wounded birds, that were beginning to tumble from the flocks, and then crouching

9. Xerxes the Great (519?–465 B.C.E.) was king of Persia (486–465 B.C.E.).

under the legs of their master, as if they participated in his feelings, at this wasteful and unsportsmanlike execution.

The reports of the fire-arms became rapid, whole volleys rising from the plain, as flocks of more than ordinary numbers darted over the opening, covering the field with darkness, like an interposing cloud; and then the light smoke of a single piece would issue from among the leafless bushes on the mountain, as death was hurled on the retreat of the affrighted birds, who would rise from a volley, for many feet into the air, in a vain effort to escape the attacks of man. Arrows, and missiles of every kind, were seen in the midst of the flocks; and so numerous were the birds, and so low did they take their flight, that even long poles, in the hands of those on the sides of the mountain, were used to strike them to the earth.

During all this time, Mr. Jones, who disdained the humble and ordinary means of destruction used by his companions, was busily occupied, aided by Benjamin, in making arrangements for an assault of a more than ordinarily fatal character. Among the relics of the old military excursions, that occasionally are discovered throughout the different districts of the western part of New-York, there had been found in Templeton, at its settlement, a small swivel,[1] which would carry a ball of a pound weight. It was thought to have been deserted by a war-party of the whites, in one of their inroads into the Indian settlements, when, perhaps, their convenience or their necessities induced them to leave such an encumbrance to the rapidity of their march, behind them in the woods. This miniature cannon had been released from the rust, and mounted on little wheels, in a state for actual service. For several years, it was the sole organ for extraordinary rejoicings that was used in those mountains. On the mornings of the Fourth of July, it would be heard, with its echoes ringing among the hills, and telling forth its sounds, for thirteen times, with all the dignity of a two-and-thirty pounder; and even Captain Hollister,[2] who was the highest authority in that part of the country on all such occasions, affirmed that, considering its dimensions, it was no despicable gun for a salute. It was somewhat the worse for the service it had performed, it is true, there being but a trifling difference in size between the touch-hole and the muzzle.[3] Still, the grand conceptions of Richard had suggested the importance of such an instrument, in hurling death at his nimble enemies. The swivel was dragged by a horse into a part of the open space, that the sheriff thought most eligible for planting a battery of the kind, and Mr. Pump[4] proceeded to load it. Several handfuls of duck-shot were placed on top of the powder, and the Major-domo soon announced that his piece was ready for service.

The sight of such an implement collected all the idle spectators to the spot, who, being mostly boys, filled the air with their cries of exultation and delight. The gun was pointed on high, and Richard, holding a coal of fire in a pair of tongs, patiently took his seat on a stump, awaiting the appearance of a flock that was worthy of his notice.

1. Small cannon capable of being swung higher or lower.
2. The landlord of the major village inn, The Bold Dragoon; his rank comes from his having been a commander of local militia.
3. Ordinarily the muzzle (or mouth) would be considerably larger than the touchhole, the vent by which fire is conveyed to the powder.
4. "Pump" is the nickname of Benjamin Penguillan, a servant to Judge Temple and a former seaman who doesn't know how to swim.

So prodigious was the number of the birds, that the scattering fire of the guns, with the hurling of missiles, and the cries of the boys, had no other effect than to break off small flocks from the immense masses that continued to dart along the valley, as if the whole creation of the feathered tribe were pouring through that one pass. None pretended to collect the game, which lay scattered over the fields in such profusion, as to cover the very ground with the fluttering victims.

Leather-stocking was a silent, but uneasy spectator of all these proceedings, but was able to keep his sentiments to himself until he saw the introduction of the swivel into the sports.

"This comes of settling a country" he said—"here have I known the pigeons to fly for forty long years, and, till you made your clearings, there was nobody to scare or to hurt them. I loved to see them come into the woods, for they were company to a body; hurting nothing; being, as it was, as harmless as a garter-snake. But now it gives me sore thoughts when I hear the frighty things whizzing through the air, for I know it's only a motion to bring out all the brats in the village at them. Well! the Lord won't see the waste of his creaters for nothing, and right will be done to the pigeons, as well as others, by-and-by.—There's Mr. Oliver, as bad as the rest of them, firing into the flocks as if he was shooting down nothing but the Mingo[5] warriors."

Among the sportsmen was Billy Kirby, who, armed with an old musket, was loading, and, without even looking into the air, was firing, and shouting as his victims fell even on his own person. He heard the speech of Natty, and took upon himself to reply—

"What's that, old Leather-stocking!" he cried; "grumbling at the loss of a few pigeons! If you had to sow your wheat twice, and three times, as I have done, you wouldn't be so massyfully[6] feeling'd to'ards the divils.—Hurrah, boys! scatter the feathers. This is better than shooting at a turkey's head and neck, old fellow."

"It's better for you, maybe, Billy Kirby," returned the indignant old hunter, "and all them as don't know how to put a ball down a rifle-barrel, or how to bring it up ag'in with a true aim; but it's wicked to be shooting into flocks in this wastey manner; and none do it, who know how to knock over a single bird. If a body has a craving for pigeon's flesh, why! it's made the same as all other creaters, for man's eating, but not to kill twenty and eat one. When I want such a thing, I go into the woods till I find one to my liking, and then I shoot him off the branches without touching a feather of another, though there might be a hundred on the same tree. But you couldn't do such a thing, Billy Kirby—you couldn't do it if you tried."

"What's that you say, you old, dried cornstalk! you sapless stub!" cried the wood-chopper. "You've grown mighty boasting, sin[7] you killed the turkey; but if you're for a single shot, here goes at that bird which comes on by himself."

The fire from the distant part of the field had driven a single pigeon below the flock to which it had belonged, and, frightened with the constant reports of the muskets, it was approaching the spot where the disputants stood, darting first from one side, and then to the other, cutting the air with the swift-

5. As conceived by Cooper in the Leatherstocking novels, the "Mingos" are Iroquois Indians who fought with the English during the Revolution and are hostile to the American territorial advance; the Delawares, by contrast, are favorably inclined toward the Americans.

6. Mercifully.

7. Since.

ness of lightning, and making a noise with its wings, not unlike the rushing of a bullet. Unfortunately for the wood-chopper, notwithstanding his vaunt, he did not see his bird until it was too late for him to fire as it approached, and he pulled his trigger at the unlucky moment when it was darting immediately over his head. The bird continued its course with incredible velocity.

Natty had dropped his piece from his arm, when the challenge was made, and, waiting a moment, until the terrified victim had got in a line with his eyes, and had dropped near the bank of the lake, he raised his rifle with uncommon rapidity, and fired. It might have been chance, or it might have been skill, that produced the result; it was probably a union of both; but the pigeon whirled over in the air, and fell into the lake, with a broken wing. At the sound of his rifle, both his dogs started from his feet, and in a few minutes the "slut"[8] brought out the bird, still alive.

The wonderful exploit of Leather-stocking was noised through the field with great rapidity, and the sportsmen gathered in to learn the truth of the report.

"What," said young Edwards, "have you really killed a pigeon on the wing, Natty, with a single ball?"

"Haven't I killed loons before now, lad, that dive at the flash?" returned the hunter. "It's much better to kill only such as you want, without wasting your powder and lead, than to be firing into God's creaters in such a wicked manner. But I come out for a bird, and you know the reason why I like small game, Mr. Oliver, and now I have got one I will go home, for I don't like to see these wasty ways that you are all practysing, as if the least thing was not made for use, and not to destroy."

"Thou sayest well, Leather-stocking," cried Marmaduke, "and I begin to think it time to put an end to this work of destruction."

"Put an ind, Judge, to your clearings. An't the woods his work as well as the pigeons? Use, but don't waste. Wasn't the woods made for the beasts and birds to harbour in? and when man wanted their flesh, their skins, or their feathers, there's the place to seek them. But I'll go to the hut with my own game, for I wouldn't touch one of the harmless things that kiver the ground here, looking up with their eyes at me, as if they only wanted tongues to say their thoughts."

With this sentiment in his mouth, Leather-stocking threw his rifle over his arm, and, followed by his dogs, stepped across the clearing with great caution, taking care not to tread on one, of the hundreds of the wounded birds that lay in his path. He soon entered the bushes on the margin of the lake, and was hid from view.

Whatever might be the impression the morality of Natty made on the Judge, it was utterly lost on Richard. He availed himself of the gathering of the sportsmen, to lay a plan for one "fell swoop"[9] of destruction. The musketmen were drawn up in battle array, in a line extending on each side of his artillery, with orders to await the signal of firing from himself.

"Stand by, my lads," said Benjamin, who acted as an aid-de-camp on this momentous occasion, "stand by, my hearties, and when Squire Dickens heaves out the signal for to begin the firing, d'ye see, you may open upon

8. Bitch, female dog.

9. Shakespeare's *Macbeth* 4.3.219, from Macduff's lament for his dead wife and children.

them in a broadside. Take care and fire low, boys, and you'll be sure to hull the flock."

"Fire low!" shouted Kirby—"hear the old fool! If we fire low, we may hit the stumps, but not ruffle a pigeon."

"How should you know, you lubber?"[1] cried Benjamin, with a very unbecoming heat, for an officer on the eve of battle—"how should you know, you grampus? Havn't I sailed aboard of the Boadishy[2] for five years? and wasn't it a standing order to fire low, and to hull your enemy? Keep silence at your guns, boys, and mind the order that is passed."

The loud laughs of the musketmen were silenced by the authoritative voice of Richard, who called to them for attention and obedience to his signals.

Some millions of pigeons were supposed to have already passed, that morning, over the valley of Templeton; but nothing like the flock that was now approaching had been seen before. It extended from mountain to mountain in one solid blue mass, and the eye looked in vain over the southern hills to find its termination. The front of this living column was distinctly marked by a line, but very slightly indented, so regular and even was the flight. Even Marmaduke forgot the morality of Leather-stocking as it approached, and, in common with the rest, brought his musket to his shoulder.

"Fire!" cried the Sheriff, clapping his coal to the priming of the cannon. As half of Benjamin's charge escaped through the touch-hole, the whole volley of the musketry preceded the report of the swivel. On receiving this united discharge of small-arms, the front of the flock darted upward, while, at the same instant, myriads of those in their rear rushed with amazing rapidity into their places, so that when the column of white smoke gushed from the mouth of the little cannon, an accumulated mass of objects was gliding over its point of direction. The roar of the gun echoed along the mountains, and died away to the north, like distant thunder, while the whole flock of alarmed birds seemed, for a moment, thrown into one disorderly and agitated mass. The air was filled with their irregular flights, layer rising over layer, far above the tops of the highest pines, none daring to advance beyond the dangerous pass; when, suddenly, some of the leaders of the feathered tribe shot across the valley, taking their flight directly over the village, and the hundreds of thousands in their rear followed their example, deserting the eastern side of the plain to their persecutors and the fallen.

"Victory!" shouted Richard, "victory! we have driven the enemy from the field."

"Not so, Dickon," said Marmaduke; "the field is covered with them; and, like the Leather-stocking, I see nothing but eyes, in every direction, as the innocent sufferers turn their heads in terror, to examine my movements. Full one half of those that have fallen are yet alive: and I think it is time to end the sport; if sport it be."

"Sport!" cried the Sheriff; "it is princely sport. There are some thousands of the blue-coated boys on the ground, so that every old woman in the village may have a pot-pie for the asking."

"Well, we have happily frightened the birds from this pass," said Marmaduke, "and our carnage must of necessity end, for the present.—Boys,

1. Landlubber, clumsy fellow.
2. The *Boadicea*, a ship named for the British queen who led a rebellion against the Roman rulers in 62 C.E. "Grampus": variety of small whale, used here as a term of contempt.

I will give thee sixpence a hundred for the pigeons' heads only; so go to work, and bring them into the village, when I will pay thee."

This expedient produced the desired effect, for every urchin on the ground went industriously to work to wring the necks of the wounded birds. Judge Temple retired towards his dwelling with that kind of feeling, that many a man has experienced before him, who discovers, after the excitement of the moment has passed, that he has purchased pleasure at the price of misery to others. Horses were loaded with the dead; and, after this first burst of sporting, the shooting of pigeons became a business, for the remainder of the season, more in proportion to the wants of the people.[3] Richard, however, boasted for many a year, of his shot with the "cricket;"[4] and Benjamin gravely asserted, that he thought that they killed nearly as many pigeons on that day, as there were Frenchmen destroyed on the memorable occasion of Rodney's victory.[5]

1823

The Last of the Mohicans

The second novel in the Leatherstocking series, *The Last of the Mohicans; A Narrative of 1757* (1826), depicts Natty Bumppo, also known as Hawk-eye, as a wilderness scout in the British colony of New York at the time of the French and Indian War (1754–63). At the center of the novel is a fictionalized account of the August 10, 1757, massacre at Fort William Henry, in which perhaps hundreds of British colonists were killed or injured by the Huron Indians and other tribes allied with the French general Montcalm. According to Cooper, the ineptness of the British general Webb left the colonists vulnerable to the retaliatory violence of the Indians. By drawing on this historical incident, Cooper suggests that the colonists' progress toward independence required the departure from North America of both the French and the British military as well as any other European power aspiring to rule the continent. Published a few years before President Andrew Jackson initiated his Indian removal policies, the novel at first glance seems to reinforce the idea that progress required the "extinction" or expulsion of the Indians. But

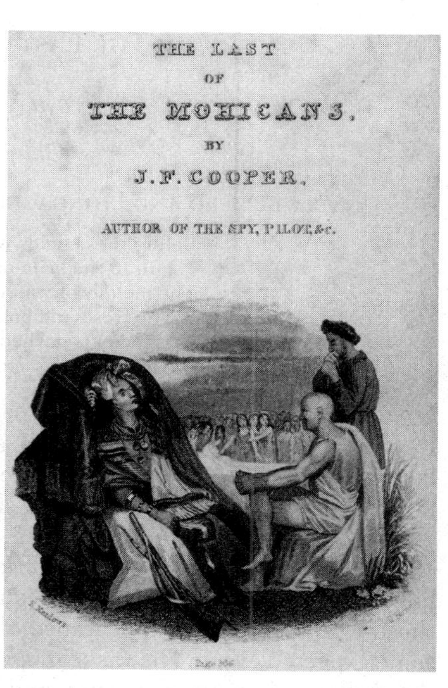

The cover of an 1836 British printing of ***The Last of the Mohicans*** (1826).

3. The pigeons described in this chapter—the passenger pigeons—are extinct, the last known specimen dying in 1914 at the Cincinnati Zoological Garden.
4. I.e., the little cannon.
5. The British admiral George Brydges, Baron Rodney (1719–1792), defeated the French off Dominica, in the West Indies, in April 1782. Penguillan's nickname "Pump" comes from his tall tale about manning the pumps to keep the ship from sinking after Rodney's victory.

at the heart of the novel is a poignant interracial friendship between the white man, Natty Bumppo, and the Mohican, Chingachgook, suggestive of Cooper's unhappiness with the brutalities that would eventually result in the death of Chingachgook's heroic son Uncas, "the last of the Mohicans." In Cooper's complex historical vision, progress always comes at a price, and the overall novel laments the sufferings of the Mohicans, whom Cooper presents as committed to the highest moral and ethical standards.

The chapter reprinted here comes from the beginning of the novel. Major Duncan Hayward is escorting the daughters of the British Lieutenant Colonel Munro, Alice and Cora, to Fort William Henry, which at the time is under the command of Munro himself. Unbeknownst to Hayward and the daughters, the Huron Magua, who offers himself as a guide in the wilderness, had once been flogged by Munro, and now vengefully wishes to capture the daughters. Natty, Chingachgook, and Uncas will eventually help the daughters reunite with their father. At this early point in the novel, however, before they have even met the Munro party, the friends Natty and Chingachgook discuss the colonial history of the Americas and convey the differing historical perspectives of the English and the Native Americans.

From The Last of the Mohicans

From Volume I

Chapter III

[NATTY BUMPPO AND CHINGACHGOOK; STORIES OF THE FATHERS]

Before these fields were shorn and tilled,
  Full to the brim our rivers flowed;
The melody of waters filled
  The fresh and boundless wood;
And torrents dashed, and rivulets played,
  And fountains spouted in the shade.
Bryant[1]

Leaving the unsuspecting Heyward, and his confiding companions, to penetrate still deeper into a forest that contained such treacherous inmates, we must use an author's privilege, and shift the scene a few miles to the westward of the place where we have last seen them.

On that day, two men might be observed, lingering on the banks of a small but rapid stream, within an hour's journey of the encampment of Webb, like those who awaited the appearance of an absent person, or the approach of some expected event. The vast canopy of woods spread itself to the margin of the river, overhanging the water, and shadowing its dark glassy current with a deeper hue. The rays of the sun were beginning to grow less fierce, and the intense heat of the day was lessened, as the cooler vapours of the springs and fountains rose above their leafy beds, and rested in the atmosphere. Still that breathing silence, which marks the drowsy sultriness of an American land-

1. From "An Indian at the Burial-Place of His Fathers" (1824), by William Cullen Bryant (1794–1878).

scape in July, pervaded the secluded spot, interrupted, only, by the low voices of the men in question, an occasional and lazy tap of a reviving wood-pecker, the discordant cry of some gaudy jay, or a swelling on the ear, from the dull roar of a distant water-fall.

These feeble and broken sounds were, however, too familiar to the foresters, to draw their attention from the more interesting matter of their dialogue. While one of these loiterers showed the red skin and wild accoutrements of a native of the woods, the other exhibited, through the mask of his rude and nearly savage equipments, the brighter, though sun-burnt and long-faded complexion of one who might claim descent from an European parentage. The former was seated on the end of a mossy log, in a posture that permitted him to heighten the effect of his earnest language, by the calm but expressive gestures of an Indian, engaged in debate. His body, which was nearly naked, presented a terrific emblem of death, drawn in intermingled colours of white and black. His closely shaved head, on which no other hair than the well known and chivalrous scalping tuft was preserved, was without ornament of any kind, with the exception of a solitary Eagle's plume, that crossed his crown, and depended[2] over the left shoulder. A tomahawk and scalping-knife, of English manufacture, were in his girdle; while a short military rifle, of that sort with which the policy of the whites armed their savage allies, lay carelessly across his bare and sinewy knee. The expanded chest, full-formed limbs, and grave countenance of this warrior, would denote that he had reached the vigour of his days, though no symptoms of decay appeared to have yet weakened his manhood.

The frame of the white man, judging by such parts as were not concealed by his clothes, was like that of one who had known hardships and exertion from his earliest youth. His person, though muscular, was rather attenuated than full; but every nerve and muscle appeared strung and indurated,[3] by unremitted exposure and toil. He wore a hunting-shirt of forest-green, fringed with faded yellow, and a summer cap, of skins which had been shorn of their fur. He also bore a knife in a girdle of wampum, like that which confined the scanty garments of the Indian, but no tomahawk. His moccasins were ornamented after the gay fashion of the natives, while the only part of his under dress which appeared below the hunting-frock, was a pair of buckskin leggings, that laced at the sides, and were gartered above the knees, with the sinews of a deer. A pouch and horn completed his personal accoutrements, though a rifle of a great length, which the theory of the more ingenious whites had taught them, was the most dangerous of all fire-arms, leaned against a neighbouring sapling. The eye of the hunter, or scout, whichever he might be, was small, quick, keen, and restless, roving while he spoke, on every side of him, as if in quest of game, or distrusting the sudden approach of some lurking enemy. Notwithstanding these symptoms of habitual suspicion, his

2. Hung down. "Scalping tuft": Cooper supplied the following note to the 1831 edition of *Mohicans*: "The North American warrior caused the hair to be plucked from his whole body; a small tuft, only, was left on the crown of his head, in order that his enemy might avail himself of it, in wrenching the scalp in the event of his fall. The scalp was the only admissible trophy of victory. Thus, it was deemed more important to obtain the scalp than to kill the man. . . ."

3. Hardened.

countenance was not only without guile, but at the moment at which he is introduced was charged with an expression of sturdy honesty.

"Even your traditions make the case in my favour, Chingachgook," he said, speaking in the tongue which was known to all the natives who formerly inhabited the country between the Hudson and the Potomack,[4] and of which we shall give a free translation for the benefit of the reader; endeavouring, at the same time, to preserve some of the peculiarities, both of the individual and of the language. "Your fathers came from the setting sun, crossed the big river,[5] fought the people of the country, and took the land; and mine came from the red sky of the morning, over the salt lake, and did their work much after the fashion that had been set them by yours; then let God judge the matter between us, and friends, spare their words!"

"My fathers fought with the naked red-man!" returned the Indian, sternly, in the same language. "Is there no difference, Hawk-eye, between the stone-headed arrow of the warrior, and the leaden bullet with which you kill?"

"There is reason in an Indian, though nature has made him with a red skin!" said the white man, shaking his head, like one on whom such an appeal to his justice was not thrown away. For a moment he appeared to be conscious of having the worst of the argument, then rallying again, he answered to the objection of his antagonist in the best manner his limited information would allow: "I am no scholar, and I care not who knows it; but judging from what I have seen at deer chaces, and squirrel hunts, of the sparks below, I should think a rifle in the hands of their grandfathers, was not so dangerous as a hickory bow, and a good flint-head might be, if drawn with Indian judgment, and sent by an Indian eye."

"You have the story told by your fathers," returned the other, coldly waving his hand, in proud disdain. "What say your old men? do they tell the young warriors, that the pale-faces met the red-men, painted for war and armed with the stone hatchet or wooden gun?"

"I am not a prejudiced man, nor one who vaunts himself on his natural privileges, though the worst enemy I have on earth, and he is an Iroquois, daren't deny that I am genuine white," the scout replied, surveying, with secret satisfaction, the faded colour of his bony and sinewy hand; "and I am willing to own that my people have many ways, of which, as an honest man, I can't approve. It is one of their customs to write in books what they have done and seen, instead of telling them in their villages, where the lie can be given to the face of a cowardly boaster, and the brave soldier can call on his comrades to witness for the truth of his words. In consequence of this bad fashion, a man who is too conscientious to misspend his days among the women, in learning the names of black marks, may never hear of the deeds of his fathers, nor feel a pride in striving to outdo them. For myself, I conclude all the Bumppos could shoot; for I have a natural turn with a rifle, which must have been handed down from generation to generation, as our

4. Potomac; river flowing from the Alleghenies to the Chesapeake Bay.

5. Cooper supplied the following note to the 1831 edition of *Mohicans*: "The Mississippi. The scout alludes to a tradition which is very popular among the tribes of the Atlantic states. Evidence of their Asiatic origin is deduced from the circumstance, though great uncertainty hangs over the whole history of the Indians."

holy commandments tell us, all good and evil gifts are bestowed; though I should be loth to answer for other people in such a matter. But every story has its two sides; so I ask you, Chingachgook, what passed when our fathers first met?"

A silence of a minute succeeded, during which the Indian sat mute; then, full of the dignity of his office, he commenced his brief tale, with a solemnity that served to heighten its appearance of truth.

"Listen, Hawk-eye, and your ears shall drink no lies. 'Tis what my fathers have said, and what the Mohicans have done." He hesitated a single instant, and bending a cautious glance towards his companion, he continued in a manner that was divided between interrogation and assertion—"does not this stream at our feet, run towards the summer, until its waters grow salt, and the current flows upward!"

"It can't be denied, that your traditions tell you true in both these matters," said the white man; "for I have been there, and have seen them; though, why water, which is so sweet in the shade, should become bitter in the sun, is an alteration for which I have never been able to account."

"And the current!" demanded the Indian, who expected his reply with that sort of interest that a man feels in the confirmation of testimony, at which he marvels even while he respects it; "the fathers of Chingachgook have not lied!"

"The Holy Bible is not more true, and that is the truest thing in nature. They call this up-stream current the tide, which is a thing soon explained, and clear enough. Six hours the waters run in, and six hours they run out, and the reason is this; when there is higher water in the sea than in the river, it runs in, until the river gets to be highest, and then it runs out again."

"The waters in the woods, and on the great lakes, run downward until they lie like my hand," said the Indian, stretching the limb horizontally before him, "and then they run no more."

"No honest man will deny it," said the scout, a little nettled at the implied distrust of his explanation of the mystery of the tides; "and I grant that it is true on the small scale, and where the land is level. But every thing depends on what scale you look at things. Now, on the small scale, the 'arth is level; but on the large scale it is round. In this manner, pools and ponds, and even the great fresh water lakes, may be stagnant, as you and I both know they are, having seen them; but when you come to spread water over a great tract, like the sea, where the earth is round, how in reason can the water be quiet? You might as well expect the river to lie still on the brink of those black rocks a mile above us, though your own ears tell you that it is tumbling over them at this very moment!"

If unsatisfied by the philosophy of his companion, the Indian was far too dignified to betray his unbelief. He listened like one who was convinced, and resumed his narrative in his former solemn manner.

"We came from the place where the sun is hid at night, over great plains where the buffaloes live, until we reached the big river. There we fought the Alligewi,[6] till the ground was red with their blood. From the banks of

6. Alleghanys, who, according to the Mohicans' tradition, were identical with the Cherokees.

the big river to the shores of the salt lake, there were none to meet us. The Maquas[7] followed at a distance. We said the country should be ours from the place where the water runs up no longer, on this stream, to a river, twenty suns' journey toward the summer. The land we had taken like warriors, we kept like men. We drove the Maquas into the woods with the bears. They only tasted salt at the licks; they drew no fish from the great lake: we threw them the bones."

"All this I have heard and believe," said the white man, observing that the Indian paused; "but it was long before the English came into the country."

"A pine grew then, where this chestnut now stands. The first pale faces who came among us spoke no English. They came in a large canoe, when my fathers had buried the tomahawk with the red men around them. Then, Hawk-eye," he continued, betraying his deep emotion, only by permitting his voice to fall to those low, guttural tones, which render his language, as spoken at times, so very musical; "then, Hawk-eye, we were one people, and we were happy. The salt lake gave us its fish, the wood its deer, and the air its birds. We took wives who bore us children; we worshipped the Great Spirit; and we kept the Maquas beyond the sound of our songs of triumph!"

"Know you any thing of your own family, at that time?" demanded the white. "But you are a just man for an Indian! and as I suppose you hold their gifts, your fathers must have been brave warriors, and wise men at the council fire."

"My tribe is the grandfather of nations," said the native, "but I am an unmixed man. The blood of chiefs is in my veins, where it must stay for ever. The Dutch landed, and gave my people the fire-water;[8] they drank until the heavens and the earth seemed to meet, and they foolishly thought they had found the Great Spirit. Then they parted with their land. Foot by foot, they were driven back from the shores, until I, that am a chief and a Sagamore,[9] have never seen the sun shine but through the trees, and have never visited the graves of my fathers."

"Graves bring solemn feelings over the mind," returned the scout, a good deal touched at the calm suffering of his companion; "and often aid a man in his good intentions, though, for myself, I expect to leave my own bones unburied, to bleach in the woods, or to be torn asunder by the wolves. But where are to be found your race, which came to their kin in the Delaware country, so many summers since?"

"Where are the blossoms of those summers!—fallen, one by one: so all of my family departed, each in his turn, to the land of spirits. I am on the hill-top, and must go down into the valley; and when Uncas follows in my footsteps, there will no longer be any of the blood of the Sagamores, for my boy is the last of the Mohicans."

"Uncas is here!" said another voice, in the same soft, guttural tones, near his elbow; "who wishes Uncas?"

The white man loosened his knife in its leathern sheath, and made an involuntary movement of the hand towards his rifle, at this sudden interruption, but the Indian sat composed, and without turning his head at the unexpected sounds.

7. Iroquois.
8. Alcoholic beverages.
9. Leader among chiefs.

At the next instant, a youthful warrior passed between them, with a noiseless step, and seated himself on the bank of the rapid stream. No exclamation of surprise escaped the father, nor was any question made or reply given for several minutes, each appearing to await the moment, when he might speak, without betraying a womanish curiosity or childish impatience. The white man seemed to take counsel from their customs, and relinquishing his grasp of the rifle, he also remained silent and reserved. At length Chingachgook turned his eyes slowly towards his son, and demanded—

"Do the Maquas dare to leave the print of their moccasins in these woods?"

"I have been on their trail," replied the young Indian, "and know that they number as many as the fingers of my two hands; but they lie hid like cowards."

"The thieves are outlying for scalps and plunder!" said the white man, whom we shall call Hawk-eye, after the manner of his companions. "That busy Frenchman, Montcalm, will send his spies into our very camp, but he will know what road we travel!"

"'Tis enough!" returned the father, glancing his eye towards the setting sun; "they shall be driven like deer from their bushes. Hawk-eye, let us eat to-night, and show the Maquas that we are men tomorrow."

"I am as ready to do the one as the other," replied the scout; "but to fight the Iroquois,'tis necessary to find the skulkers; and to eat,'tis necessary to get the game—talk of the devil and he will come; there is a pair of the biggest antlers I have seen this season, moving the bushes below the hill! Now, Uncas," he continued in a half whisper, and laughing with a kind of inward sound, like one who had learnt to be watchful, "I will bet my charger three times full of powder, against a foot of wampum,[1] that I take him atwixt the eyes, and nearer to the right than to the left."

"It cannot be!" said the young Indian, springing to his feet with youthful eagerness; "all but the tips of his horns are hid!"

"He's a boy!" said the white man, shaking his head while he spoke, and addressing the father. "Does he think when a hunter sees a part of the creatur, he can't tell where the rest of him should be!"

Adjusting his rifle, he was about to make an exhibition of that skill, on which he so much valued himself, when the warrior struck up the piece with his hand, saying,

"Hawk-eye! will you fight the Maquas?"

"These Indians know the nature of the woods, as it might be by instinct!" returned the scout, dropping his rifle, and turning away like a man who was convinced of his error. "I must leave the buck to your arrow, Uncas, or we may kill a deer for them thieves, the Iroquois, to eat."

The instant the father seconded this intimation by an expressive gesture of the hand, Uncas threw himself on the ground, and approached the animal with wary movements. When, within a few yards of the cover, he fitted an arrow to his bow with the utmost care, while the antlers moved, as if their owner snuffed an enemy in the tainted air. In another moment the twang of the bow was heard, a white streak was seen glancing into the bushes, and the wounded buck plunged from the cover, to the very feet of his hidden enemy. Avoiding the horns of the infuriated animal, Uncas darted to his side, and

1. Beads or other articles used as currency.

passed his knife across the throat, when bounding to the edge of the river, it fell, dying the waters with its blood to a great distance.

"'Twas done with Indian skill," said the scout, laughing inwardly, but with vast satisfaction; "and was a pretty sight to behold! Though an arrow is a near shot, and needs a knife to finish the work."

"Hugh!" ejaculated his companion, turning quickly, like a hound who scented his game.

"By the Lord, there is a drove of them!" exclaimed the hunting scout, whose eyes began to glisten with the ardour of his usual occupation; "if they come within range of a bullet, I will drop one, though the whole Six Nations[2] should be lurking within sound! What do you hear, Chingachgook? for to my ears the woods are dumb."

"There is but one deer, and he is dead," said the Indian, bending his body, till his ear nearly touched the earth. "I hear the sounds of feet!"

"Perhaps the wolves have driven that buck to shelter, and are following in his trail."

"No. The horses of white men are coming!" returned the other, raising himself with dignity, and resuming his seat on the log with all his former composure. "Hawk-eye, they are your brothers; speak to them."

"That will I, and in English that the king needn't be ashamed to answer," returned the hunter, speaking in the language of which he boasted; "but I see nothing, nor do I hear the sounds of man or beast; 'tis strange that an Indian should understand white sounds better than a man, who, his very enemies will own, has no cross[3] in his blood, although he may have lived with the red skins long enough to be suspected! Ha! there goes something like the cracking of a dry stick, too—now I hear the bushes move—yes, yes, there is a tramping that I mistook for the falls—and—but here they come themselves; God keep them from the Iroquois!"

1826

2. A formal tribal alliance, also known as the Iroquois Confederacy, of the Mohawks, Oneidas, Onondagas, Cayugas, Senecas, and Tuscaroras in the area of what is now upstate New York.

3. In this and other novels of the Leatherstocking series, Natty Bumppo insists on his pure whiteness.

CATHARINE MARIA SEDGWICK
1789–1867

Catharine Maria Sedgwick was among the most popular and critically respected antebellum writers, publishing six novels, a highly regarded travel volume, religious tracts, domestic and reform literature, dozens of short stories, and eight volumes of children's writings. Sedgwick was admired by James Fenimore Cooper (who celebrated her "fine power of imagination"), Edgar Allan Poe (who stated that she had "few rivals near the throne"), and numerous other readers of the time. By the end of the nineteenth century, however, her reputation had diminished. Interest in Sedgwick revived as a result of the critical reassessment of neglected women writers during the 1980s, which led to the republication of her 1827 novel *Hope Leslie* in 1987. Since then, critics have been paying increasing attention to her not only as an author of historical novels that rival those of Cooper but also as a social reformer and novelist of manners with a strong interest in the role of women in U.S. culture.

Catharine M. Sedgwick. Plate accompanying the chapter on Sedgwick in *The National Portrait Gallery of Distinguished Americans* (1836), edited by James B. Longacre and James Herring.

Sedgwick was born on December 28, 1789, in Stockbridge, Massachusetts, the ninth of ten children of a prominent Federalist family. Her father became Speaker of the U.S. House of Representatives, and some of her brothers were successful in business and law. Her early education was spotty, partly because of the illness of her mother, who died in 1807, partly because good schools for girls were rare in an era before women's colleges existed. She attended various schools on a short-term basis between 1798 and 1804. At home she had few books, although her father read aloud when he was home (as she recalled) from Shakespeare, Cervantes's *Don Quixote*, Samuel Butler's *Hudibras*, and the philosopher David Hume. Later, she read great quantities of novels and histories on her own, but always regretted that she had not had a more systematic education.

In 1813, Sedgwick's father died shortly after converting from Congregationalism to Unitarianism. Sedgwick eventually followed his lead in rejecting the Congregationalists' Calvinistic emphasis on eternal damnation in favor of the liberal rationalism of Unitarianism. In 1821 she became a member of the Unitarian Society in New York City, and owed much of her early reputation to the interest of Unitarians in her fiction. She began her first novel, *A New-England Tale* (1822), as a Unitarian tract, but inspired by the historical novels of Sir Walter Scott and the literary nationalism of the time, she then determined, as she said in the preface, to add to "the scanty stock of native American literature" by portraying the moral trials of an orphan girl in New England. The novel was well received, and Sedgwick secured her reputation with her second novel, *Redwood* (1824), which set out "to denote the passing character and manners of the present time and place." She returned to historical fiction with *Hope Leslie*, set in New England during the 1630s and 1640s and featuring both a noble Native American woman, along the lines of the legendary Pocahontas, and a marriage between an Indian man and a white woman. Sedgwick's next historical novel, *The Linwoods* (1835), was set during the American Revolution and had a supporting cast of characters that included George Washington and the Marquis de Lafayette. In all her novels, female agency is crucial to plot and theme. In *Clarence* (1830) she depicted a strong female character, Gertrude Clarence, who rejects the materialism of her time and emerges as the very embodiment of republican ideals; and in her late novel *Married or Single?* (1857), Sedgwick, who herself did not marry, disputed the prevalent idea that women were useless except as wives and mothers.

Sedgwick could at times seem remote from the various reform movements that engaged Lydia Maria Child, Harriet Beecher Stowe, and other women writers of the period. In 1872 Child complained that Sedgwick's failure to "contend" for the African American cause "or for anything else" showed a lack of moral courage. In fact, Sedgwick wrote against slavery (her father had fought for its abolition in Massachusetts), challenged the racist ideologies that informed Andrew Jackson's Indian removal policies, and advocated education and prison reforms as well as women's rights. She also wrote powerfully about matters of social class, though she was ultimately most sympathetic to the aspirations and insecurities of the rising middle class. In such best-selling didactic books as *Home* (1835), *The Poor Rich Man and the Rich Poor Man* (1836), and *Live and Let Live* (1837), Sedgwick anticipated the literary domesticity of Stowe and many other American women writers of the mid-nineteenth century. Like Stowe, Sedgwick believed women could best reform the culture by keeping their distance from the hurly-burly of partisan politics and instead exerting their influence from within the home. Writing for Sedgwick was the appropriately female strategy to challenge settled ways of thinking and promote social reform.

Recognizing her own exceptional good fortune in having the support of a loving and prosperous family, Sedgwick for several decades spent winters with her brother Theodore and his family in New York City, and summers with her brother Charles and his family in Lenox, Massachusetts, amid the Berkshire mountains. The visits of the famous woman writer became a special attraction of the school for girls that Charles's wife, Elizabeth, ran at home. Sedgwick's celebrity also brought other famous people to Lenox, among them the British actress Fanny Kemble. After her brothers died, Sedgwick lived with a beloved niece, Kate Minot (Charles's daughter), in West Roxbury, Massachusetts, until her own death in 1867.

Hope Leslie

Sedgwick's third novel, *Hope Leslie; or, Early Times in the Massachusetts* (1827), portrays the historical conflicts between the Puritans and Native Americans in seventeenth-century New England. It provides a revisionary perspective on what the Puritans called the Pequod War of 1637, which Sedgwick represents as a brutal conquest (the Puritans killed several hundred women and children in their assault on a Pequod village along the Mystic River in what is now southeastern Connecticut). Self-consciously positioning *Hope Leslie* against James Fenimore Cooper's *The Last of the Mohicans* (1826), Sedgwick focuses on the crucial role of women in early American history; and despite her horrific account of massacre and retaliation, she imagines the possibility of love and friendship developing across racial and cultural boundaries. Though she challenges Puritan histories that ignore the issue of the Puritans' unprovoked violence against Native American women and children, she also extols the Puritans as heroic founders and progenitors of the new nation.

The plot of *Hope Leslie* is intricate and complex. The chapters reprinted here center on Everell Fletcher, Magawisca, and Hope Leslie. Everell is the son of the Puritan William Fletcher, who, when living in England, was thwarted in his desire to marry his distant relative Alice Fletcher; he instead married an orphan woman named Martha and emigrated to Massachusetts. Hope Leslie is the older daughter of Alice Fletcher and Charles Leslie, the husband forced on Alice by her father. When Charles Leslie dies, Alice starts for New England with her daughters, but dies onboard ship. The Fletchers adopt Hope and her sister, Faith, into their home at Springfield, Massachusetts, in the settlement they call Bethel. To help them with their added responsibilities, the Puritan authorities give the Fletchers two Indian "servants," the Pequods Magawisca and her brother Oneco, whose mother, Monoco, had recently died in captivity. Their father, Mononotto, who had defied the rival Pequod chief Sassacus in attempting to develop alliances with the English, now seeks revenge for the Puritans' killing of his people, and especially for their brutal act of beheading his son Samoset. The selections begin with Magawisca sneaking off at night to visit with the Indian woman Nelema, while William Fletcher's domestic servant, Digby, remains suspicious that Magawisca, Nelema, and Mononotto are plotting to attack the Fletcher household. At the time, Hope Leslie is in Boston with William Fletcher.

The text is taken from the first edition, published in New York in 1827.

From Hope Leslie

From Volume I

Chapter IV

[Magawisca's History of "The Pequod War"]

"It would have been happy if they had converted some before they had killed any."

—Robinson[1]

The house at Bethel had, both in front and in rear, a portico, or, as it was more humbly, and therefore more appropriately named, a shed; that in the rear, was a sort of adjunct to the kitchen, and one end of it was enclosed for the purpose of a bed-room, and occupied by Magawisca. Everell found Digby sitting at the other extremity of this portico; his position was prudently chosen. The moon was high, and the heavens clear, and there concealed and sheltered by the shadow of the roof, he could, without being seen, command the whole extent of cleared ground that bordered on the forest, whence the foe would come, if he came at all.

Everell, like a good knight, had carefully inspected his arms and just taken his position beside Digby, when they heard Magawisca's window cautiously opened, and saw her spring through it. Everell would have spoken to her, but Digby made a signal of silence, and she, without observing them, hastened with a quick and light step towards the wood, and entered it, taking the path that led to Nelema's hut.

"Confound her!" exclaimed Digby; "she is in a plot with the old woman."

"No—no. On my life she is not, Digby."

"Some mischief—some mischief," said Digby, shaking his head. "They are a treacherous race. Let's follow her. No, we had best keep clear of the wood. Do you call after her; she will hearken to you."

1. From a letter by the Puritan minister John Robinson (c. 1576–1625) to the founder and governor of Plymouth colony, William Bradford (1590–1657), which was included in the appendix to Bradford's *Of Plymouth Plantation* (1630–50). Robinson was critical of the Puritans' violence against the Indians.

Everell hesitated. "Speak quickly, Mr. Everell," urged Digby; "she will be beyond the reach of your voice. It is no light matter that could take her to Nelema's hut at this time of the night."

"She has good reason for going, Digby. I am sure of it; and I will not call her back."

"Reason," muttered Digby; "reason is but a jack-o'-lantern light in most people's minds. You trust her too far, Mr. Everell; but there, she is returning! See how she looks all around her, like a frightened bird that hears an enemy in every rustling leaf. Stand close—observe her—see, she lays her ear to the earth—it is their crafty way of listening—there, she is gone again!" he exclaimed, as Magawisca darted away into the wood. "It is past doubt she holds communication with some one. God send us a safe deliverance. I had rather meet a legion of Frenchmen than a company of these savages. They are a kind of beast we don't comprehend—out of the range of God's creatures—neither angel, man, nor yet quite devil. I would have sent to the fort for a guard to-night, but I liked not being driven hither and yon by that old hag's tokens; nor yet quite to take counsel from your good mother's fears, she being but a woman."

"I think you have caught the fear, Digby, without taking its counsel," said Everell, "which does little credit to your wisdom; the only use of fear, being to provide against danger."

"That is true, Mr. Everell; but don't think I am afraid. It is one thing to know what danger is, and wish to shun it; and another thing to feel like you, fear-nought lads, that have never felt a twinge of pain, and have scarce a sense of your own mortality. You would be the boldest at an attack, Mr. Everell, and I should stand a siege best. A boy's courage is a keen weapon that wants temper."

"Apt to break at the first stroke from the enemy, you mean, Digby?" Digby nodded assent. "Well, I should like, at any rate, to prove it," added Everell.

"Time enough this half-dozen years yet, my young master. I should be loath to see that fair skin of thine stained with blood; and, besides, you have yet to get a little more worldly prudence than to trust a young Indian girl, just because she takes your fancy."

"And why does she take my fancy, Digby? because she is true and noble-minded. I am certain, that if she knows of any danger approaching us, she is seeking to avert it."

"I don't know that, Mr. Everell; she'll be first true to her own people. The old proverb holds fast with these savages, as well as with the rest of the world—'hawks won't pick out hawks' eyes.' Like to like, throughout all nature. I grant you, she hath truly a fair seeming."

"And all that's foul is our own suspicion, is it not, Digby?"

"Not exactly; there's plainly some mystery between Magawisca and the old woman, and we know these Pequods were famed above all the Indian tribes for their cunning."

"And what is superior cunning among savages but superior sense?"

"You may out-talk me, Mr. Everell," replied Digby, with the impatience that a man feels when he is sure he is right, without being able to make it appear. "You may out-talk me, but you will never convince me. Was not I in the Pequod war? I ought to know, I think."

"Yes, and I think you have told me they shewed more resolution than cunning there; in particular, that the brother of Magawisca, whom she so piteously bemoans to this day, fought like a young lion."

"Yes, he did, poor dog!—and he was afterwards cruelly cut off; and it is this that makes me think they will take some terrible revenge for his death. I often hear Magawisca talking to Oneco of her brother, and I think it is to stir his spirit; but this boy is no more like to him than a spaniel to a blood-hound."

Nothing Digby said had any tendency to weaken Everell's confidence in Magawisca.

The subject of the Pequod war once started, Digby and Everell were in no danger of sleeping at their post. Digby loved, as well as another man, and particularly those who have had brief military experience, to fight his battles o'er again; and Everell was at an age to listen with delight to tales of adventure, and danger. They thus wore away the time till the imaginations of both relater and listener were at that pitch, when every shadow is embodied, and every passing sound bears a voice to the quickened sense. "Hark!" said Digby, "did you not hear footsteps?"

"I hear them now," replied Everell; "they seem not very near. Is it not Magawisca returning?"

"No; there is more than one; and it is the heavy, though cautious, tread of men. Ha! Argus scents them." The old house-dog now sprang from his rest on a mat at the door-stone, and gave one of those loud inquiring barks, by which this animal first hails the approach of a strange footstep. "Hush, Argus, hush," cried Everell; and the old dog, having obeyed his instinct, seemed satisfied to submit to his master's voice, and crept lazily back to his place of repose.

"You have hushed Argus, and the footsteps too," said Digby; "but it is well, perhaps, if there really is an enemy near, that he should know we are on guard."

"If there really is, Digby!" said Everell, who, terrific as the apprehended danger was, felt the irrepressible thirst of youth for adventure; "do you think we could both have been deceived?"

"Nothing easier, Mr. Everell, than to deceive senses on the watch for alarm. We heard something, but it might have been the wolves that even now prowl about the very clearing here at night. Ha!" he exclaimed, "there they are"—and starting forward he levelled his musket towards the wood.

"You are mad," said Everell, striking down Digby's musket with the butt end of his own. "It is Magawisca." Magawisca at that moment emerged from the wood.

Digby appeared confounded. "Could I have been so deceived?" he said; "could it have been her shadow—I thought I saw an Indian beyond that birch tree; you see the white bark? well, just beyond in the shade. It could not have been Magawisca, nor her shadow, for you see there are trees between the foot-path and that place; and yet, how should he have vanished without motion or sound?"

"Our senses deceive us, Digby," said Everell, reciprocating Digby's own argument.

"In this tormenting moonlight they do; but my senses have been well schooled in their time, and should have learned to know a man from a woman, and a shadow from a substance."

Digby had not a very strong conviction of the actual presence of an enemy, as was evident from his giving no alarm to his auxiliaries in the house; and he believed that if there were hostile Indians prowling about them, they were few in number, and fearful; still he deemed it prudent to persevere in their precautionary measures. "I will remain here," he said, "Mr. Everell, and do you follow Magawisca; sift what you can from her. Depend on't, there's something wrong. Why should she have turned away on seeing us? and did you not observe her hide something beneath her mantle?"

Everell acceded to Digby's proposition; not with the expectation of confirming his suspicions, but in the hope that Magawisca would shew they were groundless. He followed her to the front of the house, to which she seemed involuntarily to have bent her steps on perceiving him.

"You have taken the most difficult part of our duty on yourself, Magawisca," he said, on coming up to her. "You have acted as vidette,[2] while I have been quiet at my post."

Perhaps Magawisca did not understand him, at any rate she made no reply.

"Have you met an enemy in your reconnoitring? Digby and I fancied that we both heard and saw the foe."

"When and where?" exclaimed Magawisca, in a hurried, alarmed tone.

"Not many minutes since, and just at the very edge of the wood."

"What! when Digby raised his gun? I thought that had been in sport to startle me."

"No—Magawisca. Sporting does not suit our present case. My mother and her little ones are in peril, and Digby is a faithful servant."

"Faithful!" echoed Magawisca, as if there were more in Everell's expression than met the ear; "he surely may walk straight who hath nothing to draw him aside. Digby hath but one path, and that is plain before him—but one voice from his heart, and why should he not obey it?" The girl's voice faltered as she spoke, and as she concluded she burst into tears. Everell had never before witnessed this expression of feeling from her. She had an habitual self-command that hid the motions of her heart from common observers, and veiled them even from those who most narrowly watched her. Everell's confidence in Magawisca had not been in the least degree weakened by all the appearances against her. He did not mean to imply suspicion by his commendation of Digby, but merely to throw out a leading observation which she might follow if she would.

He felt reproached and touched by her distress, but struck by the clew, which, as he thought, her language afforded to the mystery of her conduct, and confident that she would in no way aid or abet any mischief that her own people might be contriving against them, he followed the natural bent of his generous temper, and assured her again, and again, of his entire trust in her. This seemed rather to aggravate than abate her distress. She threw herself on the ground, drew her mantle over her face, and wept convulsively. He found

2. A sentry.

he could not allay the storm he had raised, and he seated himself beside her. After a little while, either exhausted by the violence of her emotion, or comforted by Everell's silent sympathy, she became composed; and raised her face from her mantle, and as she did so, something fell from beneath its folds. She hastily recovered and replaced it, but not till Everell had perceived it was an eagle's feather. He knew this was the badge of her tribe, and he had heard her say, that "a tuft from the wing of the monarch-bird was her father's crest." A suspicion flashed through his mind, and was conveyed to Magawisca's, by one bright glance of inquiry. She said nothing, but her responding look was rather sorrowful than confused, and Everell, anxious to believe what he wished to be true, came, after a little consideration, to the conclusion, that the feather had been dropped in her path by a passing bird. He did not scrutinise her motive in concealing it; he could not think her capable of evil, and anxious to efface from her mind the distrust his countenance might have expressed—"This beautiful moon and her train of stars," he said, "look as if they were keeping their watch over our dwelling. There are those, Magawisca, who believe the stars have a mysterious influence on human destiny. I know nothing of the grounds of their faith, and my imagination is none of the brightest, but I can almost fancy they are stationed there as guardian angels, and I feel quite sure that nothing evil could walk abroad in their light."

"They do look peaceful," she replied mournfully; "but ah! Everell, man is ever breaking the peace of nature. It was such a night as this—so bright and still, when your English came upon our quiet homes."

"You have never spoken to me of that night Magawisca."

"No—Everell, for our hands have taken hold of the chain of friendship, and I feared to break it by speaking of the wrongs your people laid on mine."

"You need not fear it; I can honour noble deeds though done by our enemies, and see that cruelty is cruelty, though inflicted by our friends."

"Then listen to me; and when the hour of vengeance comes, if it should come, remember it was provoked."

She paused for a few moments, sighed deeply, and then began the recital of the last acts in the tragedy of her people; the principal circumstances of which are detailed in the chronicles of the times, by the witnesses of the bloody scenes. "You know," she said, "our fortress-homes were on the level summit of a hill. Thence we could see as far as the eye could stretch, our hunting-grounds, and our gardens, which lay beneath us on the borders of a stream that glided around our hill, and so near to it, that in the still nights we could hear its gentle voice. Our fort and wigwams were encompassed with a palisade,[3] formed of young trees, and branches interwoven and sharply pointed. No enemy's foot had ever approached this nest, which the eagles of the tribe had built for their mates and their young. Sassacus and my father were both away on that dreadful night. They had called a council of our chiefs, and old men; our young men had been out in their canoes, and when they returned they had danced and feasted, and were now in deep sleep. My mother was in her hut with her children, not sleeping, for my brother Samoset had lingered behind his companions, and had not yet returned from the

3. A defensive wall or enclosure.

water-sport. The warning spirit, that ever keeps its station at a mother's pillow, whispered that some evil was near; and my mother, bidding me lie still with the little ones, went forth in quest of my brother. All the servants of the Great Spirit spoke to my mother's ear and eye of danger and death. The moon, as she sunk behind the hills, appeared a ball of fire; strange lights darted through the air; to my mother's eye they seemed fiery arrows; to her ear the air was filled with death-sighs.

'She had passed the palisade, and was descending the hill, when she met old Cushmakin. 'Do you know aught of my boy?' she asked.

'Your boy is safe, and sleeps with his companions; he returned by the Sassafras[4] knoll; that way can only be trodden by the strong-limbed, and light-footed.' 'My boy is safe,' said my mother; 'then tell me, for thou art wise, and canst see quite through the dark future, tell me, what evil is coming to our tribe?' She then described the omens she had seen. 'I know not,' said Cushmakin, 'of late darkness hath spread over my soul, and all is black there, as before these eyes, that the arrows of death have pierced; but tell me, Monoco, what see you now in the fields of heaven?'

'Oh, now,' said my mother, 'I see nothing but the blue depths, and the watching stars. The spirits of the air have ceased their moaning, and steal over my cheek like an infant's breath. The water-spirits are rising, and will soon spread their soft wings around the nest of our tribe.'

'The boy sleeps safely,' muttered the old man, 'and I have listened to the idle fear of a doating mother.'

'I come not of a fearful race,' said my mother.

'Nay, that I did not mean,' replied Cushmakin, 'but the panther watching her young is fearful as a doe.' The night was far spent, and my mother bade him go home with her, for our pow-wows have always a mat in the wigwam of their chief. 'Nay,' he said, 'the day is near, and I am always abroad at the rising of the sun.' It seemed that the first warm touch of the sun opened the eye of the old man's soul, and he saw again the flushed hills, and the shaded vallies, the sparkling waters, the green maize, and the gray old rocks of our home. They were just passing the little gate of the palisade, when the old man's dog sprang from him with a fearful bark. A rushing sound was heard. 'Owanox! Owanox! (the English! the English!)' cried Cushmakin. My mother joined her voice to his, and in an instant the cry of alarm spread through the wigwams. The enemy were indeed upon us. They had surrounded the palisade, and opened their fire."

"Was it so sudden? Did they so rush on sleeping women and children?" asked Everell, who was unconsciously lending all his interest to the party of the narrator.

"Even so; they were guided to us by the traitor Wequash; he from whose bloody hand my mother had shielded the captive English maidens—he who had eaten from my father's dish, and slept on his mat. They were flanked by the cowardly Narragansetts, who shrunk from the sight of our tribe—who were pale as white men at the thought of Sassacus, and so feared him, that when his name was spoken, they were like an unstrung bow, and they said, 'He is all one God—no man can kill him.' These cowardly allies waited for the prey they dared not attack."

4. The bark of the sassafras tree was sometimes used medicinally and for flavoring beverages.

"Then," said Everell, "as I have heard, our people had all the honour of the fight."

"Honour! was it, Everell—ye shall hear. Our warriors rushed forth to meet the foe; they surrounded the huts of their mothers, wives, sisters, children; they fought as if each man had a hundred lives, and would give each, and all, to redeem their homes. Oh! the dreadful fray, even now, rings in my ears! Those fearful guns that we had never heard before—the shouts of your people—our own battle yell—the piteous cries of the little children—the groans of our mothers, and, oh! worse—worse than all—the silence of those that could not speak——The English fell back; they were driven to the palisade; some beyond it, when their leader gave the cry to fire our huts, and led the way to my mother's. Samoset, the noble boy, defended the entrance with a prince-like courage, till they struck him down; prostrate and bleeding he again bent his bow, and had taken deadly aim at the English leader, when a sabre-blow severed his bowstring. Then was taken from our hearth-stone, where the English had been so often warmed and cherished, the brand to consume our dwellings. They were covered with mats, and burnt like dried straw. The enemy retreated without the palisade. In vain did our warriors fight for a path by which we might escape from the consuming fire; they were beaten back; the fierce element gained on us; the Narragansetts pressed on the English, howling like wolves for their prey. Some of our people threw themselves into the midst of the crackling flames, and their courageous souls parted with one shout of triumph; others mounted the palisade, but they were shot and dropped like a flock of birds smitten by the hunter's arrows. Thus did the strangers destroy, in our own homes, hundreds of our tribe."

"And how did you escape in that dreadful hour, Magawisca—you were not then taken prisoners?"

"No; there was a rock at one extremity of our hut, and beneath it a cavity into which my mother crept, with Oneco, myself, and the two little ones that afterwards perished. Our simple habitations were soon consumed; we heard the foe retiring, and when the last sound had died away, we came forth to a sight that made us lament to be among the living. The sun was scarce an hour from his rising, and yet in this brief space our homes had vanished. The bodies of our people were strewn about the smouldering ruin; and all around the palisade lay the strong and valiant warriors—cold—silent—powerless as the unformed clay."

Magawisca paused; she was overcome with the recollection of this scene of desolation. She looked upward with an intent gaze, as if she held communion with an invisible being. "Spirit of my mother!" burst from her lips. "Oh! that I could follow thee to that blessed land where I should no more dread the war-cry, nor the death-knife." Everell dashed the gathering tears from his eyes, and Magawisca proceeded in her narrative.

"While we all stood silent and motionless, we heard footsteps and cheerful voices. They came from my father and Sassacus, and their band, returning from the friendly council. They approached on the side of the hill that was covered with a thicket of oaks, and their ruined homes at once burst upon their view. Oh! what horrid sounds then pealed on the air! shouts of wailing, and cries for vengeance. Every eye was turned with suspicion and hatred on my father. *He* had been the friend of the English; *he* had counselled peace and alliance with them; *he* had protected their traders; delivered the captives taken from them, and restored them to their people: now *his* wife and children alone were living, and they called him traitor. I heard an angry murmur, and many hands were lifted to strike the death-blow. He moved not—'Nay, nay,' cried Sassacus, beating them off. 'Touch him not; his soul is bright as the sun; sooner shall you darken that, than find treason in his breast. If he hath shown the dove's heart to the English when he believed them friends, he will show himself the fierce eagle now he knows them enemies. Touch him not, warriors; remember my blood runneth in his veins.'

"From that moment my father was a changed man. He neither spoke nor looked at his wife, or children; but placing himself at the head of one band of the young men he shouted his war-cry, and then silently pursued the enemy. Sassacus went forth to assemble the tribe, and we followed my mother to one of our villages."

"You did not tell me, Magawisca," said Everell, "how Samoset perished; was he consumed in the flames, or shot from the palisade?"

"Neither—neither. He was reserved to whet my father's revenge to a still keener edge. He had forced a passage through the English, and hastily collecting a few warriors, they pursued the enemy, sprung upon them from a covert, and did so annoy them that the English turned and gave them battle. All fled save my brother, and him they took prisoner. They told him they would spare his life if he would guide them to our strong holds; he refused.[5] He had, Everell, lived but sixteen summers; he loved the light of the sun even as we love it; his manly spirit was tamed by wounds and weariness; his limbs were like a bending reed, and his heart beat like a woman's; but the fire of his soul burnt clear. Again they pressed him with offers of life and reward; he faithfully refused, and with one sabre-stroke they severed his head from his body."

Magawisca paused—she looked at Everell and said with a bitter smile—"You English tell us, Everell, that the book of your law is better than that written on our hearts,[6] for ye say it teaches mercy, compassion, forgiveness—if ye had such a law and believed it, would ye thus have treated a captive boy?"

Magawisca's reflecting mind suggested the most serious obstacle to the progress of the christian religion, in all ages and under all circumstances; the contrariety between its divine principles and the conduct of its professors; which, instead of always being a medium for the light that emanates from our holy law, is too often the darkest cloud that obstructs the passage of its rays to the hearts of heathen men. Everell had been carefully instructed

5. Sedgwick supplied the following note: "'But finding that the sachems whom they had spared, would give them no information, they beheaded them on their march at a place called Mekunkatuck, since Guilford.'—*Ibid*." (Her note is from Benjamin Trumbull's *A Complete History of Connecticut, Civil and Ecclesiastical* [1797].)

6. Sedgwick provided this note: "The language of the Indians, as reported by Heckwelder, verifies so strongly the sentiment in our text, and is so powerful an admonition to Christians, that we here quote it for those who may not have met with the interesting work of this excellent Moravian missionary—'"And yet," say those injured people, "these white men would always be telling us of their great Book which God had given to them. They would persuade us that every man was good who believed in what the Book said, and every man was bad who did not believe in it. They told us a great many things, which they said were written in the good Book, and wanted us to believe it all. We would probably have done so, if we had seen them practise what they pretended to believe, and act according to the *good words* which they told us. But no! while they held their big Book in one hand, in the other they had murderous weapons, guns, and swords wherewith to kill us poor Indians. Ah! and they did so too!"'" (Her note is from John Gottlieb Ernestus Heckewelder's *Account of the History, Manners, and Customs of the Indian Nations* [1819].)

in the principles of his religion, and he felt Magawisca's relation to be an awkward comment on them, and her inquiry natural; but though he knew not what answer to make, he was sure there must be a good one, and mentally resolving to refer the case to his mother, he begged Magawisca to proceed with her narrative.

"The fragments of our broken tribe," she said, "were collected, and some other small dependent tribes persuaded to join us. We were obliged to flee from the open grounds, and shelter ourselves in a dismal swamp. The English surrounded us; they sent in to us a messenger and offered life and pardon to all who had not shed the blood of Englishmen. Our allies listened, and fled from us, as frightened birds fly from a falling tree. My father looked upon his warriors; they answered that look with their battle-shout. 'Tell your people,' said my father to the messenger, 'that we have shed and drank English blood, and that we will take nothing from them but death.'

"The messenger departed and again returned with offers of pardon, if we would come forth and lay our arrows and our tomahawks at the feet of the English. 'What say you, warriors,' cried my father—'shall we take *pardon* from those who have burned your wives and children, and given your homes to the beasts of prey—who have robbed you of your hunting-grounds, and driven your canoes from their waters?' A hundred arrows were pointed to the messenger. 'English—you have your answer,' said my father, and the messenger returned to announce the fate we had chosen."

"Where was Sassacus?—had he abandoned his people?" asked Everell.

"Abandoned them! No—his life was in theirs; but accustomed to attack and victory, he could not bear to be thus driven, like a fox to his hole. His soul was sick within him, and he was silent and left all to my father. All day we heard the strokes of the English axes felling the trees that defended us, and when night came, they had approached so near that we could see the glimmering of their watch-lights through the branches of the trees. All night they were pouring in their bullets, alike on warriors, women, and children. Old Cushmakin was lying at my mother's feet, when he received a death-wound. Gasping for breath he called on Sassacus and my father—'Stay not here,' he said; 'look not on your wives and children, but burst your prison bound; sound through the nations the cry of revenge! Linked together, ye shall drive the English into the sea. I speak the word of the Great Spirit—obey it!' While he was yet speaking he stiffened in death. 'Obey him, warriors,' cried my mother; 'see,' she said, pointing to the mist that was now wrapping itself around the wood like a thick curtain—'see, our friends have come from the spirit-land to shelter you. Nay, look not on us—our hearts have been tender in the wigwam, but we can die before our enemies without a groan. Go forth and avenge us.'

"'Have we come to the counsel of old men and old women!' said Sassacus, in the bitterness of his spirit.

"'When women put down their womanish thoughts and counsel like men, they should be obeyed,' said my father. 'Follow me, warriors.'

"They burst through the enclosure. We saw nothing more, but we heard the shout from the foe, as they issued from the wood—the momentary fierce encounter—and the cry, 'they have escaped!' Then it was that my mother, who had listened with breathless silence, threw herself down on the mossy stones, and laying her hot cheek to mine—'Oh, my children—my children!'

she said, 'would that I could die for you! But fear, not death—the blood of a hundred chieftains, that never knew fear, runneth in your veins. Hark, the enemy comes nearer and nearer. Now lift up your heads, my children, and show them that even the weak ones of our tribe are strong in soul.'

"We rose from the ground—all about sat women and children in family clusters, awaiting unmoved their fate. The English had penetrated the forest-screen, and were already on the little rising-ground where we had been entrenched. Death was dealt freely. None resisted—not a movement was made—not a voice lifted—not a sound escaped, save the wailings of the dying children.

"One of your soldiers knew my mother, and a command was given that her life and that of her children should be spared. A guard was stationed round us.

"You know that, after our tribe was thus cut off, we were taken, with a few other captives, to Boston. Some were sent to the Islands of the Sun,[7] to bend their free limbs to bondage like your beasts of burden. There are among your people those who have not put out the light of the Great Spirit; they can remember a kindness, albeit done by an Indian; and when it was known to your Sachems[8] that the wife of Mononotto, once the protector and friend of your people, was a prisoner, they treated her with honour and gentleness. But her people were extinguished—her husband driven to distant forests—forced on earth to the misery of wicked souls—to wander without a home; her children were captives—and her heart was broken. You know the rest."

This war, so fatal to the Pequods, had transpired the preceding year. It was an important event to the infant colonies, and its magnitude probably somewhat heightened to the imaginations of the English, by the terror this resolute tribe had inspired. All the circumstances attending it were still fresh in men's minds, and Everell had heard them detailed with the interest and particularity that belongs to recent adventures; but he had heard them in the language of the enemies and conquerors of the Pequods; and from Magawisca's lips they took a new form and hue; she seemed, to him, to embody nature's best gifts, and her feelings to be the inspiration of heaven. This new version of an old story reminded him of the man and the lion in the fable.[9] But here it was not merely changing sculptors to give the advantage to one or the other of the artist's subjects; but it was putting the chisel into the hands of truth, and giving it to whom it belonged.

He had heard this destruction of the original possessors of the soil described, as we find it in the history of the times, where, we are told, "the number destroyed was about four hundred;" and "it was a fearful sight to see them thus frying in the fire, and the streams of blood quenching the same, and the horrible scent thereof; but the victory seemed a sweet sacrifice, and they gave the praise thereof to God."[1]

In the relations of their enemies, the courage of the Pequods was distorted into ferocity, and their fortitude, in their last extremity, thus set forth: "many

7. The West Indies, which depended on slave labor.
8. Leaders.
9. In the Aesop fable "The Man and the Lion," the lion asserts that a different history of the encounters between people and lions will emerge when lions can tell their own histories and erect their own monuments.
1. From William Bradford's *Of Plymouth Plantation*, chap. 28.

were killed in the swamp, like sullen dogs, that would rather, in their self-willedness and madness, sit still to be shot or cut in pieces, than receive their lives for asking, at the hands of those into whose power they had now fallen."[2]

Everell's imagination, touched by the wand of feeling, presented a very different picture of those defenceless families of savages, pent in the recesses of their native forests, and there exterminated, not by superior natural force, but by the adventitious circumstances of arms, skill, and knowledge; from that offered by those who "then living and worthy of credit did affirm, that in the morning entering into the swamp, they saw several heaps of them [the Pequods] sitting close together, upon whom they discharged their pieces, laden with ten or twelve pistol bullets at a time, putting the muzzles of their pieces under the boughs, within a few yards of them."[3]

Everell did not fail to express to Magawisca, with all the eloquence of a heated imagination, his sympathy and admiration of her heroic and suffering people. She listened with a mournful pleasure, as one listens to the praise of a departed friend. Both seemed to have forgotten the purpose of their vigil, which they had marvellously kept without apprehension, or heaviness, when they were roused from their romantic abstraction by Digby's voice: "Now to your beds, children," he said; "the family is stirring, and the day is at hand. See the morning star hanging just over those trees, like a single watch-light in all the wide canopy. As you have not to look in a prayer-book for it, master Everell, don't forget to thank the Lord for keeping us safe, as your mother, God bless her, would say, through the night-watches. Stop one moment," added Digby, lowering his voice to Everell as he rose to follow Magawisca, "did she tell you?"

"Tell me! what?"

"What! Heaven's mercy! what ails the boy! Why, did she tell you what brought her out tonight? Did she explain all the mysterious actions we have seen? Are you crazy? Did not you ask her?"

Everell hesitated—fortunately for him the light was too dim to expose to Digby's eye the blushes that betrayed his consciousness that he had forgotten his duty. "Magawisca did not tell me," he said, "but I am sure Digby that"——

"That she can do no wrong—hey, Master Everell, well, that may be very satisfactory to you—but it does not content me. I like not her secret ways—'it's bad ware that needs a dark store.'"[4]

Everell had tried the force of his own convictions on Digby, and knew it to be unavailing, therefore having no reply to make, he very discreetly retreated without attempting any.

Magawisca crept to her bed, but not to repose—neither watching nor weariness procured sleep for her. Her mind was racked with apprehensions, and conflicting duties, the cruellest rack to an honourable mind.

Nelema had communicated to her the preceding day, the fact which she had darkly intimated to Mrs. Fletcher, that Mononotto, with one or two associates was lurking in the forest, and watching an opportunity to make an attack on Bethel. How far his purpose extended, whether simply to the

2. From the Puritan William Hubbard's *The Present State of New-England, Being a Narrative of the Troubles with the Indians in New-England* (1677), which had been republished in 1814 as *Narrative of the Indian Wars in New-England*.

3. From Hubbard's *The Present State of New-England*.

4. Proverb with obscure French sources. "Ware": merchandise.

recovery of his children, or to the destruction of the family, she knew not. The latter was most probable, for hostile Indians always left blood on their trail. In reply to Magawisca's eager inquiries, Nelema said she had again, and again, assured her father of the kind treatment his children had received at the hands of Mrs. Fletcher; but he seemed scarcely to hear what she said, and precipitately left her, telling her that she would not again see him, till his work was done.

Magawisca's first impulse had been to reveal all to Mrs. Fletcher; but by doing this, she would jeopard her father's life. Her natural sympathies—her strong affections—her pride, were all enlisted on the side of her people; but she shrunk, as if her own life were menaced, from the blow that was about to fall on her friends. She would have done or suffered any thing to avert it—any thing but betray her father. The hope of meeting him, explains all that seemed mysterious to Digby. She did go to Nelema's hut—but all was quiet there. In returning she found an eagle's feather in the path,—she believed it must have just been dropped there by her father, and this circumstance determined her to remain watching through the night, that if her father should appear, she might avert his vengeance.

She did not doubt that Digby had really seen and heard him; and believing that her father would not shrink from a single armed man, she hoped against hope, that his sole object was to recover his children; hoped against hope, we say, for her reason told her, that if that were his only purpose, it might easily have been accomplished by the intervention of Nelema.

Magawisca had said truly to Everell, that her father's nature had been changed by the wrongs he received. When the Pequods were proud and prosperous, he was more noted for his humane virtues, than his warlike spirit. The supremacy of his tribe was acknowledged, and it seemed to be his noble nature, as it is sometimes the instinct of the most powerful animals, to protect and defend, rather than attack and oppress. The ambitious spirit of his brother chieftain Sassacus, had ever aspired to dominion over the allied tribes; and immediately after the appearance of the English, the same temper was manifest in a jealousy of their encroachments. He employed all his art and influence and authority, to unite the tribes for the extirpation of the dangerous invaders. Mononotto, on the contrary, averse to all hostility, and foreseeing no danger from them, was the advocate of a hospitable reception, and pacific conduct.

This difference of feeling between the two chiefs, may account for the apparent treachery of the Pequods, who, as the influence of one or the other prevailed, received the English traders with favour and hospitality, or, violating their treaties of friendship, inflicted on them cruelties and death.

The stories of the murders of Stone, Norton, and Oldham, are familiar to every reader of our early annals; and the anecdote of the two English girls, who were captured at Wethersfield, and protected and restored to their friends by the wife of Mononotto, has already been illustrated by a sister labourer;[5]

5. The incident is described in Harriet Vaughan Cheney's *A Peep at the Pilgrims in Sixteen Hundred Thirty-Six* (1824). "Stone, Norton, and Oldham": as recounted in Hubbard's *The Present State of New-England* and other works of colonial history, John Stone, John Norton, and John Oldham were English traders who were killed by the Pequods. The Puritans used the killings to legitimate their attacks on the Indians.

and is precious to all those who would accumulate proofs, that the image of God is never quite effaced from the souls of his creatures; and that in their darkest ignorance, and deepest degradation, there are still to be found traits of mercy and benevolence. These will be gathered and treasured in the memory, with that fond feeling with which Mungo Park[6] describes himself to have culled and cherished in his bosom, the single flower that bloomed in his melancholy track over the African desert.

The chieftain of a savage race, is the depository of the honour of his tribe; and their defeat is a disgrace to him, that can only be effaced by the blood of his conquerors. It is a common case with the unfortunate, to be compelled to endure the reproach of inevitable evils; and Mononotto was often reminded by the remnant of his tribe, in the bitterness of their spirit, of his former kindness for the English. This reproach sharpened too keenly the edge of his adversity.

He had seen his people slaughtered, or driven from their homes and hunting-grounds, into shameful exile; his wife had died in captivity, and his children lived in servile dependence in the house of his enemies.

Sassacus perished by treachery, and Mononotto alone remained to endure this accumulated misery. In this extremity, he determined on the rescue of his children, and the infliction of some signal deed of vengeance, by which he hoped to revive the spirit of the natives, and reinstate himself as the head of his broken and dispersed people: in his most sanguine moments, he meditated a unity and combination that should eventually expel the invaders.[7]

From Volume II

Summary After Magawisca's rescue of Everell Fletcher, the novel jumps forward seven years. Marriage and seduction plots dominate the novel's second half. Hope Leslie and Everell fall in love, but Hope impetuously forces Everell to become engaged to Esther Downing, while the corrupt seducer Sir Philip Gardiner (based on an obscure historical figure of the same name) attempts to marry Hope. (The engagement between Esther and Everell is eventually broken off, and Gardiner will be exposed as a royalist attempting to subvert the Puritans' community.) Meanwhile, Hope's efforts to communicate with her sister, Faith, who lives with the Indians, result in the imprisonment of Magawisca, who then escapes with the help of Hope and Everell. In this chapter from near the end of the novel, Magawisca says goodbye to her liberators while defending the interracial marriage of her brother and Faith Leslie as a union based on love.

6. Scottish surgeon (1771–1806) who recounted his explorations of the Niger in *Travels in the Interior Districts of Africa* (1799).

7. In the next chapter Mononotto leads a retaliatory attack on Bethel, which results in the deaths of Everell's mother and siblings and the capture of Hope Leslie's sister, Faith, and Everell himself. Magawisca rescues Everell when, just as her father is about to behead him, she interposes her body and loses an arm. Several years later, Faith Leslie marries Magawisca's brother Oneco. Having become integrated into Native culture, she elects to stay with her Indian husband when she has a chance to return to the English settlements.

Chapter XIV

[MAGAWISCA'S FAREWELL]

"Basta cosi t'intendo
Già ti spiegasti a pieno;
E mi diresti meno
Se mi dicessi più."
METASTASIO.[1]

We trust we have not exhausted the patience of our readers, and that they will vouchsafe to go forth with us once more, on the eventful evening on which we have fallen, to watch the safe conduct of the released prisoner.

The fugitives had not proceeded many yards from the jail, when Everell joined them. This was the first occasion on which Magawisca and Everell had had an opportunity freely to interchange their feelings. Everell's tongue faltered when he would have expressed what he had felt for her: his manly, generous nature, disdained vulgar professions, and he feared that his ineffectual efforts in her behalf had left him without any other testimony of the constancy of his friendship, and the warmth of his gratitude.

Magawisca comprehended his feelings, and anticipated their expression. She related the scene with Sir Philip,[2] in the prison; and dwelt long on her knowledge of the attempt Everell then made to rescue her. "That bad man," she said, "made me, for the first time, lament for my lost limb. He darkened the clouds that were gathering over my soul; and, for a little while, Everell, I did deem thee like most of thy race, on whom kindness falls like drops of rain on the lake, dimpling its surface for a moment, but leaving no mark there—but when I found thou wert true," she continued in a swelling, exulting voice—"when I heard thee in my prison, and saw thee on my trail, I again rejoiced that I had sacrificed my precious limb for thee; that I had worn away the days and nights in the solitudes of the forest musing on the memory of thee, and counting the moons till the Great Spirit shall bid us to those regions where there will be no more gulfs between us, and I may hail thee as my brother."

"And why not now, Magawisca, regard me as your brother? True, neither time nor distance can sever the bonds by which our souls are united, but why not enjoy this friendship while youth, and as long as life lasts? Nay, hear me, Magawisca—the present difference of the English with the Indians, is but a vapour that has, even now, nearly passed away. Go, for a short time, where you may be concealed from those who are not yet prepared to do you justice, and then—I will answer for it—every heart and every voice will unite to recall you; you shall be welcomed with the honour due to you from all, and always cherished with the devotion due from us."

"Oh! do not hesitate, Magawisca," cried Hope, who had, till now, been only a listener to the conversation in which she took a deep interest. "Promise us that you will return and dwell with us—as you would say, Magawisca, we will

1. Mary Kelley, the editor of the 1987 edition of *Hope Leslie*, identifies the passage as written by the Italian poet and librettist Metastasio (1698–1792). Kelley translates as follows: "Enough, I understand you / You have already explained yourself; / And would say less to me / Were you to say more."

2. Sir Philip Gardiner had offered to help Magawisca escape from prison if she would take Rosa, a young woman enamored of Gardiner, to a convent in Canada. Rosa eventually detonates explosives that kill herself, Gardiner, and his plotting associates.

walk in the same path, the same joys shall shine on us, and, if need be that sorrows come over us, why, we will all sit under their shadow together."

"It cannot be—it cannot be," replied Magawisca, the persuasions of those she loved, not, for a moment, overcoming her deep invincible sense of the wrongs her injured race had sustained. "My people have been spoiled—we cannot take as a gift that which is our own—the law of vengeance is written on our hearts—you say you have a written rule of forgiveness—it may be better—if ye would be guided by it—it is not for us—the Indian and the white man can no more mingle, and become one, than day and night."

Everell and Hope would have interrupted her with further entreaties and arguments: "Touch no more on that," she said, "we must part—and for ever." Her voice faltered for the first time, and, turning from her own fate to what appeared to her the bright destiny of her companions, "my spirit will joy in the thought," she said, "that you are dwelling in love and happiness together. Nelema told me your souls were mated—she said your affections mingled like streams from the same fountain. Oh! may the chains by which He, who sent you from the spirit land, bound you together, grow brighter and stronger till you return thither again."

She paused—neither of her companions spoke—neither could speak—and, naturally, misinterpreting their silence, "have I passed your bound of modesty," she said, "in speaking to the maiden as if she were a wife?"[3]

"Oh, no, Magawisca," said Everell, feeling a strange and undefinable pleasure in an illusion, which, though he could not for an instant participate, he would not for the world have dissipated—"oh, no, do not check one expression, one word, they are your last to us." 'And may not the last words of a friend, be, like the sayings of a death-bed, prophetic?' he would have added, but his lips refused to utter what he felt was the treachery of his heart.

To Hope it seemed that too much had already been spoken. She could be prudent when any thing but her own safety depended on her discretion. Before Magawisca could reply to Everell, she gave a turn to the conversation: "Ere we part, Magawisca," she said, "cannot you give me some charm, by which I may win my sister's affections? she is wasting away with grief and pining."

"Ask your own heart, Hope Leslie, if any charm could win your affections from Everell Fletcher?"

She paused for a reply. The gulf from which Hope had retreated, seemed to be widening before her, but, summoning all her courage, she answered with a tolerably firm voice, "yes—yes, Magawisca, if virtue, if duty to others required it, I trust in heaven I could command and direct my affections."

We hope Everell may be forgiven, for the joy that gushed through his heart when Hope expressed a confidence in her own strength, which at least implied a consciousness that she needed it. Nature will rejoice in reciprocated love, under whatever adversities it comes.

Magawisca replied to Hope's apparent meaning: "Both virtue and duty," she said, "bind your sister to Oneco. She hath been married according to our simple modes, and persuaded by a Romish father,[4] as she came from Christian blood, to observe the rites of their law. When she flies from you,

3. At this point in the novel, Everell is still engaged to Esther Downing.

4. Roman Catholic priest.

as she will, mourn not over her, Hope Leslie—the wild flower would perish in your gardens—the forest is like a native home to her—and she will sing as gaily again as the bird that hath found its mate."

They now approached the place where Digby, with a trusty friend, was awaiting them. A light canoe had been provided, and Digby had his instructions from Everell to convey Magawisca to any place she might herself select. The good fellow had entered into the confederacy with hearty good will, giving, as a reason for his obedience to the impulse of his heart, 'that the poor Indian girl could not commit sins enough against the English to weigh down her good deed to Mr. Everell.'

Everell now inquired of Magawisca whither he should direct the boat: "To Moscutusett,"[5] she said; "I shall there get tidings, at least, of my father."

"And must we now part, Magawisca? must we live without you?"

"Oh! no, no" cried Hope, joining her entreaties, "your noble mind must not be wasted in those hideous solitudes."

"Solitudes!" echoed Magawisca, in a voice in which some pride mingled with her parting sadness. "Hope Leslie, there is no solitude to me; the Great Spirit, and his ministers, are every where present and visible to the eye of the soul that loves him; nature is but his interpreter; her forms are but bodies for his spirit. I hear him in the rushing winds—in the summer breeze—in the gushing fountains—in the softly running streams. I see him in the bursting life of spring—in the ripening maize—in the falling leaf. Those beautiful lights," and she pointed upward, "that shine alike on your stately domes and our forest homes, speak to me of his love to all,—think you I go to a solitude, Hope Leslie?"

"No, Magawisca; there is no solitude, nor privation, nor sorrow, to a soul that thus feels the presence of God," replied Hope. She paused—it was not a time for calm reflection or protracted solicitation; but the thought that a mind so disposed to religious impressions and affections, might enjoy the brighter light of Christian revelation—a revelation so much higher, nobler, and fuller, than that which proceeds from the voice of nature—made Hope feel a more intense desire than ever to retain Magawisca; but this was a motive Magawisca could not now appreciate, and she could not, therefore, urge: "I cannot ask you," she said, "I do not ask you, for your sake, but for ours, to return to us."

"Oh! yes, Magawisca," urged Everell, "come back to us and teach us to be happy, as you are, without human help or agency."

"Ah!" she replied, with a faint smile, "ye need not the lesson, ye will each be to the other a full stream of happiness. May it be fed from the fountain of love, and grow broader and deeper through all the passage of life."

The picture Magawisca presented, was, in the minds of the lovers, too painfully contrasted with the real state of their affairs. Both felt their emotions were beyond their control; both silently appealed to heaven to aid them in repressing feelings that might not be expressed.

Hope naturally sought relief in action: she took a morocco case from her pocket, and drew from it a rich gold chain, with a clasp containing hair, and set round with precious stones: "Magawisca," she said, with as much steadi-

5. Probably in Connecticut or elsewhere in southern New England.

ness of voice as she could assume, "take this token with you, it will serve as a memorial of us both, for I have put in the clasp a lock of Everell's hair, taken from his head when he was a boy, at Bethel—it will remind you of your happiest days there."

Magawisca took the chain, and held it in her hand a moment, as if deliberating. "This is beautiful," she said, "and would, when I am far away from thee, speak sweetly to me of thy kindness, Hope Leslie. But I would rather—if I could demean myself to be a beggar"—she hesitated, and then added, "I wrong thy generous nature in fearing thus to speak; I know thou wilt freely give me the image when thou hast the living form."

Before she had finished, Hope's quick apprehension had comprehended her meaning. Immediately after Everell's arrival in England, he had, at his father's desire, had a small miniature of himself painted, and sent to Hope. She attached it to a ribbon, and had always worn it. Soon after Everell's engagement to Miss Downing, she took it off to put it aside, but feeling, at the moment, that this action implied a consciousness of weakness, she, with a mixed feeling of pride, and reluctance to part with it, restored it to her bosom. While she was adjusting Magawisca's disguise in the prison, the miniature slid from beneath her dress, and she, at the time, observed that Magawisca's eye rested intently on it. She must not now hesitate—Everell must not see her reluctance, and yet, such are the strange contrarieties of human feeling, the severest pang she felt in parting with it, was the fear that Everell would think it was a willing gift. Hoping to shelter all her feelings in the haste of the action, she took the miniature from her own neck, and tied it around Magawisca's. "You have but reminded me of my duty," she said; "nay, keep them both, Magawisca, do not stint the little kindness I can show you."

Digby had at this moment come up to urge no more delay; and we leave to others to adjust the proportions of emotion that were indicated by Hope's faltering voice, and an irrepressible burst of tears, between her grief at parting, and other and secret feelings.

All stood as if they were rivetted to the ground, till Digby again spoke, and suggested the danger to which Magawisca was exposed by this delay. All felt the necessity of immediate separation, and all shrunk from it as from witnessing the last gasp of life. They moved to the water's edge, and, once more prompted by Digby, Everell and Hope, in broken voices, expressed their last wishes and prayers. Magawisca joined their hands, and bowing her head on them,—"The Great Spirit guide ye," she said, and then turning away, leaped into the boat, muffled her face in her mantle, and in a few brief moments disappeared for ever from their sight.

Everell and Hope remained immoveable, gazing on the little boat till it faded in the dim distance; for a few moments, every feeling for themselves was lost in the grief of parting for ever from the admirable being, who seemed to her enthusiastic young friends, one of the noblest of the works of God—a bright witness to the beauty, the independence, and the immortality of virtue. They breathed their silent prayers for her; and when their thoughts returned to themselves, though they gave them no expression, there was a consciousness of perfect unity of feeling, a joy in the sympathy that was consecrated by its object, and might be innocently indulged, that was a delicious spell to their troubled hearts.

Strong as the temptation was, they both felt the impropriety of lingering where they were, and they bent their slow, unwilling footsteps homeward. Not one word during the long protracted walk was spoken by either; but no language could have been so expressive of their mutual love and mutual resolution, as this silence. They both afterwards confessed, that though they had never felt so deeply as at that moment, the bitterness of their divided destiny, yet neither had they before known the worth of those principles of virtue, that can subdue the strongest passions to their obedience. An experience worth a tenfold suffering.

As they approached Governor Winthrop's[6] they observed that instead of the profound darkness and silence that usually reigned in that exemplary mansion at eleven o'clock, the house seemed to be in great bustle. The doors were open, and they heard loud voices, and lights were swiftly passing from room to room. Hope inferred, that notwithstanding her precautions, the apprehensions of the family had probably been excited in regard to her untimely absence, and she passed the little distance that remained with dutiful haste. Everell attended her to the gate of the court, and pressing her hand to his lips, with an emotion that he felt he might indulge for the last time, he left her and went, according to a previous determination, to Barnaby Tuttle's, where, by a surrender of himself to the jailer's custody, he expected to relieve poor Cradock from his involuntary confinement.[7]

1827

6. John Winthrop (1588–1649), the governor of Massachusetts Bay Colony.

7. Hope had successfully managed Magawisca's escape from the trustful watchman Barnaby by disguising Magawisca as her tutor, Cradock, and leaving Cradock wrapped in a blanket in Magawisca's former cell. At the novel's conclusion, Hope and Everell marry, while their friend Esther Downing chooses not to marry, deciding instead to devote herself to serving the Puritan community. In the closing paragraph, Sedgwick writes that Esther's choice "illustrated a truth, which, if more generally received by her sex, might save a vast deal of misery: that marriage is not *essential* to the contentment, the dignity, or the happiness of woman."

LYDIA HOWARD HUNTLEY SIGOURNEY

1791–1865

Lydia Sigourney was the most popular woman poet of the early national and ante-bellum period. She was a prolific author whose more than fifty published volumes in prose and poetry included travel narratives, education manuals, autobiographies, and volumes of thematically connected poems on such topics as temperance, westward expansion, and the plight of the Indians in the United States. She wrote elegies and epics, odes and lyrics, varying the verse patterns and mood to fit the particular poem's subject matter and ambition. She aspired to convey religious and moral truths based on something larger than individual subjectivity, emphasizing the spiritual truths of Christianity and the political truths of classical republicanism. But she was also capable of the ironic twists and turns that anticipate the work of Emily Dickinson, who may well have been significantly influenced by Sigourney's poems of nature and death.

Sigourney was born in Norwich, Connecticut, on September 1, 1791, the only child of Zerviah Wentworth Huntley and Ezekiel Huntley, a gardener and handyman. She was encouraged in her educational interests by her parents and by her father's wealthy employer, Jerusha Lathrop, who died when Sigourney was fourteen. The subsequent financial support of Lathrop's acquaintance Daniel Wadsworth enabled Sigourney to begin her career as an educator and poet. In 1814, three years after the failure of her initial effort to start up a school for girls, Wadsworth provided her with the funds to establish a similar school in Hartford; one year later, he financed the publication of her first book of poems, *Moral Pieces, in Prose and Verse* (1815). Throughout her career, Sigourney saw the roles of educator and poet as interchangeable. In 1819 she married Charles Sigourney, a widower with three children. Her husband disapproved of her writing, but when his hardware business collapsed in the late 1820s, it became apparent that they needed the income from her work to support their growing family (just two of the Sigourneys' children survived to adulthood). Sigourney's early volumes and periodical writings had been published anonymously, but when her identity as author became widely known in the early 1830s, she traded on her name. Her domestic manual *Letters to Young Ladies* (1833) and her *Poems* (1834) sold thousands of copies. Celebrated for their moral virtue, religious vision, pathos, and wit, her poems, sketches, and essays appeared in numerous periodicals, newspapers, and gift books; such was the extent of her popularity that by the 1840s *Godey's Lady's Book*, one of the most popular magazines of the time—edited by another culturally influential woman, Sarah J. Hale (1788–1879), who was always on the lookout for female talent—offered her $500 annually (around $10,000 in today's value) for the privilege of listing her as a contributing editor. Sigourney used her earnings to support her parents and her family; and after her husband died in 1854, she continued as the mainstay of her family until her death on June 10, 1865. Among her most popular books were her volumes focusing on Native American history and culture, *Traits of the Aborigines* (1822), *Zinzendorff and Other Poems* (1833), and *Pocahantas and Other Poems* (1841); her European travelog *Memories of Pleasant Lands* (1842); and her many collections of poems, especially *Illustrated Poems* (1849), with drawings by the noted artist Felix Darley (1822–1888).

Crucially, Sigourney hoped that her writings would prompt the nation to live up to its republican and spiritual ideals, especially with respect to the treatment of the disenfranchised, whether slaves, the poor, or Indians. At some risk to her career, she wrote antislavery poetry well before abolitionism became a popular reform in New England. Though she respected difference, she thought that by teaching her readers about Indian history in particular, they would come to understand the Indians' claims to their native land and thus, rather than removing them from that land, would choose to make them into U.S. citizens by instructing them in what Sigourney regarded as the superior values of Christian republicanism. She also wrote temperance poems, poems on historical subjects, poems on the plight of the emigrant, poems on environmental concerns, along with poems on poetry itself and occasional poems that simply told a good story or addressed small domestic matters. In her posthumously published autobiography, *Letters of Life* (1866), she proclaimed that she wrote out of "womanly duty" and with the hope of "being an instrument of good." She was not an advocate of women's suffrage, holding that women who used their influence wisely could make a substantial impact on the culture. Her own remarkable career as a writer demonstrated the influence one woman could have on the moral and political life of the nation.

Death of an Infant[1]

Death found strange beauty on that cherub brow,
And dash'd it out.—There was a tint of rose
On cheek and lip;—he touch'd the veins with ice,
And the rose faded.—Forth from those blue eyes
There spake a wishful tenderness,—a doubt
Whether to grieve or sleep, which Innocence
Alone can wear.—With ruthless haste he bound
The silken fringes of their curtaining lids
Forever.—There had been a murmuring sound
With which the babe would claim its mother's ear,
Charming her even to tears.—The spoiler set
His seal of silence.—But there beam'd a smile
So fix'd and holy from that marble brow,—
Death gazed and left it there;—he dared not steal
The signet-ring[2] of Heaven.

1827

The Suttee[1]

She sat upon the pile by her dead lord,
And in her full, dark eye, and shining hair
Youth revell'd.—The glad murmur of the crowd
Applauding her consent to the dread doom,
And the hoarse chanting of infuriate priests
She heeded not, for her quick ear had caught
An infant's wail.—Feeble and low that moan,
Yet it was answer'd in her heaving heart,
For the Mimosa in its shrinking fold
From the rude pressure, is not half so true,
So tremulous, as is a mother's soul
Unto her wailing babe.—There was such wo
In her imploring aspect,—in her tones
Such thrilling agony, that even the hearts
Of the flame-kindlers soften'd, and they laid
The famish'd infant on her yearning breast.
There with his tear-wet cheek he lay and drew
Plentiful nourishment from that full fount
Of infant happiness,—and long he prest
With eager lip the chalice of his joy.—
And then his little hands he stretch'd to grasp
His mother's flower-wove tresses, and with smile
And gay caress embraced his bloated sire—

1. The text is from *Poems* (1827).
2. In the Bible, a sign of salvation (Haggai 2:23).
1. The text is from *Poems* (1827). "Suttee": practice in India, banned by the British in 1829, of burning widows alive on their husbands' funeral pyres.

As if kind Nature taught that innocent one
With fond delay to cheat the hour which seal'd
His hopeless orphanage.—But those were near
Who mock'd such dalliance, as that Spirit malign
Who twined his serpent length mid Eden's bowers
Frown'd on our parents' bliss.—The victim mark'd
Their harsh intent, and clasp'd the unconscious babe
With such convulsive force, that when they tore
His writhing form away, the very nerves
Whose deep-sown fibres rack the inmost soul
Uprooted seem'd.—
With voice of high command
Tossing her arms, she bade them bring her son,—
And then in maniac rashness sought to leap
Among the astonish'd throng.—But the rough cord
Compress'd her slender limbs, and bound her fast
Down to her loathsome partner.—Quick the fire
In showers was hurl'd upon the reeking pile;—
But yet amid the wild, demoniac shout
Of priest and people, mid the thundering yell
Of the infernal gong,—was heard to rise
Thrice a dire death-shriek.—And the men who stood
Near the red pile and heard that fearful cry,
Call'd on their idol-gods, and stopp'd their ears,
And oft amid their nightly dream would start
As frighted Fancy echoed in her cell
That burning mother's scream.

1827

To the First Slave Ship[1]

First of that train which cursed the wave,
And from the rifled cabin bore,
Inheritor of wo,—*the slave*
To bless his palm-tree's shade no more,

Dire engine!—o'er the troubled main
Borne on in unresisted state,—
Know'st thou within thy dark domain
The secrets of thy prison'd freight?—

Hear'st thou *their* moans whom hope hath fled?—
Wild cries, in agonizing starts?—
Know'st thou thy humid sails are spread
With ceaseless sighs from broken hearts?—

1. The text is from *Poems* (1827).

The fetter'd chieftain's burning tear,—
  The parted lover's mute despair,—
The childless mother's pang severe,—
  The orphan's misery, are there.

Ah!—could'st thou from the scroll of fate
  The annal read of future years,
Stripes,—tortures,—unrelenting hate,
  And death-gasps drown'd in slavery's tears,

Down,—down,—beneath the cleaving main
  Thou fain would'st plunge where monsters lie,
Rather than ope the gates of pain
  For time and for Eternity.—

Oh Afric!—what has been thy crime?—
  That thus like Eden's fratricide,
A mark[2] is set upon thy clime,
  And every brother shuns thy side.—

Yet are thy wrongs, thou long-distrest!—
  Thy burdens, by the world unweigh'd,
Safe in that *Unforgetful Breast*
  Where all the sins of earth are laid.—

Poor outcast slave!—Our guilty land
  Should tremble while she drinks thy tears,
Or sees in vengeful silence stand,
  The beacon of thy shorten'd years;—

Should shrink to hear her sons proclaim
  The sacred truth that heaven is just,—
Shrink even at her Judge's name,—
  "Jehovah,—Saviour of the opprest."

The Sun upon thy forehead frown'd,
  But Man more cruel far than he,
Dark fetters on thy spirit bound:—
  Look to the mansions of the free!

Look to that realm where chains unbind,—
  Where the pale tyrant drops his rod,
And where the patient sufferers find
  A friend,—a father in their God.

1827

2. Allusion to the curse (the mark of Cain) that God placed on the firstborn son of Adam and Eve for killing his brother Abel (Genesis 4).

Columbus before the University of Salamanca[1]

"Columbus found that in advocating the spherical figure of the earth, he was in danger of being convicted not merely of, *error*, but even of *heterodoxy*."
Washington Irving[2]

St. Stephen's[3] cloistered hall was proud
  In learning's pomp that day,
For there a robed and stately crowd
  Pressed on in long array.
A mariner with simple chart
  Confronts that conclave high,
While strong ambition stirs his heart,
And burning thoughts of wonder part
  From lip and sparkling eye.

What hath he said? With frowning face,
  In whispered tones they speak,
And lines upon their tablets trace,
  Which flush each ashen cheek;
The Inquisition's mystic doom
  Sits on their brows severe,
And bursting forth in visioned gloom,
Sad heresy from burning tomb
  Groans on the startled ear.

Courage, thou Genoese![4] Old Time
  Thy splendid dream shall crown,
Yon Western hemisphere sublime,
  Where unshorn forests frown,
The awful Andes' cloud-wrapt brow,
  The Indian hunter's bow,
Bold streams untamed by helm or prow,
And rocks of gold and diamonds thou
  To thankless Spain shalt show.

Courage, World-finder! Thou hast need!
  In Fates' unfolding scroll,
Dark woes,[5] and ingrate wrongs I read,
  That rack the noble soul.
On! On! Creation's secrets probe,
  Then drink thy cup of scorn,
And wrapped in fallen Cesar's robe,[6]

1. The text is from *Poems* (1834).
2. In *The Life and Voyages of Christopher Columbus* (1828), Irving invents a moment in 1486 when Columbus was supposedly criticized by Catholic clerics of Spain's University of Salamanca for asserting that the world is round.
3. A college of the University of Salamanca.
4. Columbus, who was from Genoa, Italy.
5. After his third voyage (1498–1500), Columbus was brought back to Spain in chains and temporarily imprisoned.
6. The Roman general Julius Caesar (c. 102–44 B.C.E.), who was assassinated in the Roman senate house.

Sleep like that master of the globe,
All glorious,—yet forlorn.

1834

Indian Names[1]

"How can the red men be forgotten, while so many of our states and territories, bays, lakes and rivers, are indelibly stamped by names of their giving?"

Ye say they all have passed away,
That noble race and brave,
That their light canoes have vanished
From off the crested wave;
That 'mid the forests where they roamed
There rings no hunter shout,
But their name is on your waters,
Ye may not wash it out.

'Tis where Ontario's billow
Like Ocean's surge is curled,
Where strong Niagara's thunders wake
The echo of the world.
Where red Missouri bringeth
Rich tribute from the west,
And Rappahannock sweetly sleeps
On green Virginia's breast.

Ye say their cone-like cabins,
That clustered o'er the vale,
Have fled away like withered leaves
Before the autumn gale,
But their memory liveth on your hills,
Their baptism on your shore,
Your everlasting rivers speak
Their dialect of yore.

Old Massachusetts wears it,
Within her lordly crown,
And broad Ohio bears it,
Amid his young renown;
Connecticut hath wreathed it
Where her quiet foliage waves,
And bold Kentucky breathed it hoarse
Through all her ancient caves.

Wachuset[2] hides its lingering voice
Within his rocky heart,

1. The text is from *Poems* (1834).

2. Mountain in Massachusetts.

And Alleghany graves its tone
  Throughout his lofty chart;
Monadnock[3] on his forehead hoar
  Doth seal the sacred trust,
Your mountains build their monument,
  Though ye destroy their dust.

Ye call these red-browed brethren
  The insects of an hour,
Crushed like the noteless worm amid
  The regions of their power;
Ye drive them from their father's lands,
  Ye break of faith the seal,
But can ye from the court of Heaven
  Exclude their last appeal?

Ye see their unresisting tribes,
  With toilsome step and slow,
On through the trackless desert pass,
  A caravan of woe;
Think ye the Eternal's ear is deaf?
  His sleepless vision dim?
Think ye the *soul's blood* may not cry
  From that far land to him?

1834

Slavery[1]

"Slavery is a dark shade on the Map of the United States."
La Fayette.[2]

Written for the Celebration of the Fourth of July

We have a goodly clime,
  Broad vales and streams we boast,
Our mountain frontiers frown sublime,
  Old Ocean guards our coast;
Suns bless our harvest fair,
  With fervid smile serene,
But a dark shade is gathering there—
  What can its blackness mean?

We have a birth-right proud,
  For our young sons to claim,
An eagle soaring o'er the cloud,

3. Mountain in New Hampshire.
1. The text is from *Poems* (1834).
2. The French aristocrat Marquis de Lafayette (1757–1834) served under General George Washington during the American Revolution, and in 1824–25 he made a triumphal return to the United States. Lafayette opposed slavery, but the source of this passage is unclear.

In freedom and in fame;
We have a scutcheon[3] bright,
By our dead fathers bought,
A fearful blot distains its white—
Who hath such evil wrought?

Our banner o'er the sea
Looks forth with starry eye,
Emblazoned glorious, bold and free,
A letter on the sky,
What hand with shameful stain
Hath marred its heavenly blue?
The yoke, the fasces[4] and the chain,
Say, are these emblems true?

This day doth music rare
Swell through our nation's bound,
But Afric's wailing mingles there,
And Heaven doth hear the sound:
O God of power!—we turn
In penitence to thee,
Bid our loved land the lesson learn—
To bid the slave be free.

1834

To a Shred of Linen[1]

Would they swept cleaner!—
Here's a littering shred
Of linen left behind—a vile reproach
To all good housewifery. Right glad am I,
That no neat lady, train'd in ancient times
Of pudding-making, and sampler-work,
And speckless sanctity of household care,
Hath happened here, to spy thee. She, no doubt,
Keen looking through her spectacles, would say,
"*This comes of reading books*:—or some spruce beau,
Essenc'd and lilly-handed, had he chanc'd
To scan thy slight superfices, 'twould be
"*This comes of writing poetry.*"—Well—well—
Come forth—offender!—hast thou aught to say?
Canst thou by merry thought, or quaint conceit,
Repay this risk, that I have run for thee?
———Begin at alpha, and resolve thyself
Into thine elements. I see the stalk
And bright, blue flower of flax, which erst o'erspread

3. Escutcheon; shield with coat of arms.
4. Bundle of sticks with a projecting ax; in ancient Rome a symbol of power and authority.
1. The text is from *Select Poems* (1838).

That fertile land, where mighty Moses stretch'd
His rod[2] miraculous. I see thy bloom
Tinging, too scantly, these New England vales.
But, lo! the sturdy farmer lifts his flail,[3]
To crush thy bones unpitying, and his wife
With 'kerchief'd head, and eyes brimful of dust,
Thy fibrous nerves, with hatchel-tooth[4] divides.
———I hear a voice of music—and behold!
The ruddy damsel singeth at her wheel,[5]
While by her side the rustic lover sits.
Perchance, his shrewd eye secretly doth count
The mass of skeins, which, hanging on the wall,
Increaseth day by day. Perchance his thought,
(For men have deeper minds than women—sure!)
Is calculating what a thrifty wife
The maid will make; and how his dairy shelves
Shall groan beneath the weight of golden cheese,
Made by her dexterous hand, while many a keg
And pot of butter, to the market borne,
May, transmigrated, on his back appear,
In new thanksgiving coats.
Fain would I ask,
Mine own New England, for thy once loved wheel,
By sofa and piano quite displac'd.
Why dost thou banish from thy parlor-hearth
That old Hygeian[6] harp, whose magic rul'd
Dyspepsia,[7] as the minstrel-shepherd's skill
Exorcis'd Saul's ennui?[8] There was no need,
In those good times, of trim callisthenics,
And there was less of gadding, and far more
Of home-born, heart-felt comfort, rooted strong
In industry, and bearing such rare fruit,
As wealth might never purchase.
But come back,
Thou shred of linen. I did let thee drop,
In my harangue, as wiser ones have lost
The thread of their discourse. What was thy lot
When the rough battery of the loom had stretch'd
And knit thy sinews, and the chemist sun
Thy blown complexion bleach'd?
Methinks I scan
Some idiosyncrasy, that marks thee out
A defunct pillow-case.—Did the trim guest,
To the best chamber usher'd, e'er admire
The snowy whiteness of thy freshn'd youth
Feeding thy vanity? or some sweet babe
Pour its pure dream of innocence on thee?

2. God empowered Moses by turning his rod into a serpent when he threw it to the ground (Exodus 4).
3. Tool for separating seed from a harvested plant.
4. Tool for combing flax.
5. Spinning wheel.
6. Hygeia was the Greek goddess of health.
7. Indigestion.
8. In 1 Samuel 16, David's harp playing helped Saul rid himself of an evil spirit.

Say, hast thou listen'd to the sick one's moan,
When there was none to comfort?—or shrunk back
From the dire tossings of the proud man's brow?
Or gather'd from young beauty's restless sigh
A tale of untold love?
Still, close and mute!—
Will tell no secrets, ha?—Well then, go down,
With all thy churl-kept hoard of curious lore,
In majesty and mystery, go down
Into the paper-mill, and from its jaws,
Stainless and smooth, emerge.—Happy shall be
The renovation, if on thy fair page
Wisdom and truth, their hallow'd lineaments
Trace for posterity. So shall thine end
Be better than thy birth, and worthier bard
Thine apotheosis immortalise.

1838

Our Aborigines[1]

I heard the forests as they cried
Unto the valleys green,
"Where is the red-brow'd hunter-race,
Who lov'd our leafy screen?
Who humbled 'mid these dewy glades
The red deer's antler'd crown,
Or soaring at his highest noon,
Struck the strong eagle down."

Then in the zephyr's[2] voice replied
Those vales, so meekly blest,
"They rear'd their dwellings on our side,
Their corn upon our breast;
A blight came down, a blast swept by,
The cone-roof'd cabins fell,
And where that exil'd people fled,
It is not ours to tell."

Niagara, of the mountains gray,
Demanded, from his throne,
And old Ontario's billowy lake
Prolong'd the thunder tone,
"The chieftains at our side who stood
Upon our christening day,
Who gave the glorious names we bear,
Our sponsors, where are they?"

1. The text is from *Select Poems* (1838).
2. Gentle breeze, from "Zephyrus," ancient Greek god of the west wind.

And then the fair Ohio charg'd
Her many sisters dear,
"Show me once more, those stately forms
Within my mirror clear;"
But they replied, "tall barks of pride
Do cleave our waters blue,
And strong keels ride our farthest tide,
But where's their light canoe?"

The farmer drove his plough-share deep
"Whose bones are these?" said he,
"I find them where my browsing sheep
Roam o'er the upland lea."
But starting sudden to his path
A phantom seem'd to glide,
A plume of feathers on his head,
A quiver at his side.

He pointed to the rifled grave
Then rais'd his hand on high,
And with a hollow groan invok'd
The vengeance of the sky.
O'er the broad realm so long his own
Gaz'd with despairing ray,
Then on the mist that slowly curl'd,
Fled mournfully away.

1838

The Two Draughts[1]

There's a draught that causeth sadness,
Though of mirth it seems the friend;
To the brain it mounts in madness,
And in misery hath its end.

To the household hearth it creepeth,
And the fire in winter dies;
There a lonely woman weepeth,
While the famished infant cries.

Bloated form and brow it bringeth,
Limbs that totter to and fro,
And at last, like scorpion, stingeth
To an agony of woe.

Round the victim's feet it weaveth
Snares, that blind his eyes in gloom;

1. The text is from *Water-Drops* (1848), a collection of poems, stories, and sketches devoted to temperance reform.

Sin it sows, and shame receiveth,
Frowns of hate, and deeds of doom.

Bitter words of strife it teacheth,
Striketh kind affections dead;
Even beyond the grave it reacheth,
To the judgment bar of dread.

Hath not life enough of sorrow,
Sickness, mourning, and decay,
That we needs must madly borrow
Thorns to strew its shortening way?

There's a draught that heaven distilleth,
Pure as crystal, from the skies;
Freely, whosoever willeth,
May partake it, and be wise.

1848

Fallen Forests[1]

Man's warfare on the trees is terrible.
He lifts his rude hut in the wilderness,
And, lo! the loftiest trunks, that age on age
Were nurtured to nobility, and bore
Their summer coronets so gloriously,
Fall with a thunder sound to rise no more.
He toucheth flame unto them, and they lie
A blackened wreck, their tracery and wealth
Of sky-fed emerald, madly spent, to feed
An arch of brilliance for a single night,
And searing thence the wild deer, and the fox,
And the lithe squirrel from the nut-strewn home,
So long enjoyed.
He lifts his puny arm,
And every echo of the axe doth hew
The iron heart of centuries away.
He entereth boldly to the solemn groves
On whose green altar tops, since time was young
The wingéd birds have poured their incense stream
Of praise and love, within whose mighty nave
The wearied cattle from a thousand hills
Have found their shelter mid the heat of day;
Perchance in their mute worship pleasing Him
Who careth for the meanest He hath made.
I said, he entereth to the sacred groves
Where nature in her beauty bows to God,

1. The text is from *The Western Home, and Other Poems* (1854).

And, lo! their temple arch is desecrate.
Sinks the sweet hymn, the ancient ritual fades,
And uptorn roots and prostrate columns mark
The invader's footsteps.
Silent years roll on,
His babes are men. His ant-heap dwelling grows
Too narrow—for his hand hath gotten wealth.
He builds a stately mansion, but it stands
Unblessed by trees. He smote them recklessly
When their green arms were round him, as a guard
Of tutelary deities, and feels
Their maledictions, now the burning noon
Maketh his spirit faint. With anxious care,
He casteth acorns in the earth, and woos
Sunbeam and rain; he planteth the young shoot,
And props it from the storm; but neither he,
Nor yet his children's children, shall behold
What he hath swept away.
Methinks, 'twere well
Not as a spoiler or a thief to prey
On Nature's bosom, that sweet, gentle nurse
Who loveth us, and spreads a sheltering couch
When our brief task is o'er. O'er that green mound
Affection's hand may set the willow tree,
Or train the cypress, and let none profane
Her pious care.
Oh, Father! grant us grace
In all life's toils, so, with a steadfast hand
Evil and good to poise, as not to pave
Our way with wrecks, nor leave our blackened name
A beacon to the way-worn mariner.

1854

Erin's Daughter[1]

Poor Erin's daughter cross'd the main
In youth's unfolding prime,
A lot of servitude to bear
In this our western clime.

And when the drear heart-sickness came
Beneath a stranger sky,
Tears on her nightly pillow lay,
But morning saw them dry.

For still with earnest hope she strove
Her distant home to cheer,

1. The text is from *The Western Home, and Other Poems* (1854). "Erin": Ireland.

And from her parents lift the load
  Of poverty severe.

To them with liberal hand she sent
  Her all—her hard-earn'd store—
A rapture thrilling through her soul,
  She ne'er had felt before.

E'en mid her quiet slumbers gleam'd
  A cabin's lighted pane,
A board with simple plenty crown'd,
  A loved and loving train.

And so her life of earnest toil
  With secret joy was blest,
For the sweet warmth of filial love
  Made sunshine in her breast.

But bitter tidings o'er the wave
  With fearful echo sped;
Gaunt famine[2] o'er her home had strode,
  And all were with the dead!

All gone!—her brothers in their glee,
  Her sisters young and fair;
And Erin's daughter bow'd her down
  In desolate despair.

1854

Two Old Women[1]

Two neighboring crones, antique and gray,
Together talk'd at close of day.

One said, with brow of wrinkled care,
"Life's cup, *at first*, was sweet and fair,

On our young lips, with laughter gay,
Its cream of brimming nectar lay,

But vapid then it grew, and stale,
And tiresome as a twice-told tale,

And so in weary age and pain
Its bitter dregs alone remain."

2. Ireland had a disastrous potato famine in the mid-1840s.

1. The text is from *Gleanings* (1860).

The other with contented eye,
Laid down her work and made reply:

"Yes, Life was sweet at morning tide,
Yet when the foam and sparkle died,

More rich, methought, and purer too
Its well-concocted essence grew,

Even now, though low its spirit drains,
And little in the cup remains,

There's sugar at the bottom still,
And we may taste it, if we will."

1860

WILLIAM CULLEN BRYANT
1794–1878

William Cullen Bryant made his mark on American poetry in 1821 with the publication of a slim volume, *Poems*, whose lyrical meditations on nature and death brought him international recognition as a poet worthy of being considered alongside William Wordsworth. He continued to publish poetry in miscellanies and newspapers, while bringing out volumes of his new and collected poems throughout his long lifetime. Though he never again received the critical acclaim that he had in 1821, he became increasingly popular and had many admirers. In an 1846 issue of the *Brooklyn Eagle*, for instance, Walt Whitman criticized the "literary quacks" who failed to appreciate "this beautiful poet," describing him as "a poet who, to our mind, stands among the first in the world." That same year, Poe proclaimed in the widely read *Godey's Lady's Book* that "Mr. Bryant has genius, and that of a marked character" and lamented that his talent "has been overlooked by modern schools." In part Bryant was overlooked because he refused to promote himself. Unlike Poe, Emerson, and Whitman, who all wrote poetic manifestos celebrating their own approaches to poetry, Bryant quietly published his work without making large claims for its importance. For much of his adult life he worked as a newspaper editor committed first to the Jacksonian Democratic party and then to the Free Soil and Republican parties. The poetry he continued to write and publish took on an increasingly public aspect, adding political topics of the day to his subject matter.

Bryant was born in the rural town of Cummington, Massachusetts. Encouraged by his parents, he learned Greek and Latin as a child. In 1807, when he was twelve, he published his first poem in the *Hampshire Gazette* in Northampton, Massachusetts; in 1808, he wrote a long anti-Jefferson poem, *The Embargo; or, Sketches of the Times: A Satire by a Youth of Thirteen*, which his Federalist father printed as a pamphlet. Bryant entered Williams College in 1810, but left after seven months with the hope of transferring to Yale. When his father revealed that he could no longer afford Bryant's college expenses, he continued to write poetry while preparing for a legal career by working in the law office of a family friend. He was admitted to the bar in 1815.

In July 1815, Bryant wrote "To a Waterfowl" and soon after wrote the first, shorter version of "Thanatopsis," the poem that established his reputation. Bryant's mother had taught him a harsh Calvinism, emphasizing that with Adam and Eve's sin, God withdrew from nature as He withdrew from humankind. "Thanatopsis," however, conveys a pantheistic view of God in nature indicative of the increasing influence of liberal Protestantism, particularly Unitarianism, on Bryant's imagination. In his early teens Bryant was attracted to the pensive gloom of such eighteenth-century British graveyard poets as Robert Blair ("The Grave" [1743]) and Thomas Gray ("Elegy Written in a Country Churchyard" [1750]). His reading of Wordsworth's *Lyrical Ballads* (1798) influenced his prosody and inspired his own continuing development from a neoclassical to a Romantic poet who discerned moral lessons and a divine presence in the American landscape. Bryant's ever-supportive father sponsored the publication of the early version of "Thanatopsis" in the 1817 *North American Review*; the 1821 version concludes with a fervent injunction to trust in self and nature, thereby anticipating (and perhaps helping to inspire) Emerson's writings of the 1830s and 1840s.

Bryant would have liked to support himself as a poet, but this was impossible at the time, so in 1816 he opened a law partnership; he worked as a lawyer into the mid-1820s. In 1821 he married Frances Fairchild; the couple had two daughters. That same year he was invited to deliver the Phi Beta Kappa poem at Harvard College's commencement. He read a long poem on the progress of liberty, "The Ages," whose favorable reception induced him to publish his *Poems* later that year. Buoyed by the book's success, Bryant, who found the practice of law uncongenial, embarked on a practical kind of literary career by moving to New York City to edit the *New-York Review and Atheneum Magazine*. Welcomed as a celebrity, he embraced metropolitan life, becoming an early member of James Fenimore Cooper's Bread and Cheese Club and developing a close friendship with Catharine Sedgwick. She dedicated her second novel, *Redwood* (1823), to him and he favorably reviewed it in the April 1825 *North American Review*. Though the *New-York Review* failed, Bryant stayed in New York as an editorial assistant on the New York *Evening Post*. By 1829 he was the newspaper's part owner and editor-in-chief, a position he would keep for nearly fifty years. Over the decades he made the *Evening Post* one of the most respected, widely read, and profitable newspapers in the country. By then a deeply committed Jacksonian Democrat, he championed the rights of labor unions, the virtues of free trade, prison reform, the importance of international copyright protection for authors, and antislavery. Bryant's loathing of slavery eventually prompted him to lead the antislavery Free-Soil movement within the Democratic Party, and then leave the party altogether. In the mid-1850s he helped form the Republican Party and in 1860 was an influential supporter of Abraham Lincoln.

As he and his newspaper prospered, Bryant traveled widely in the United States and abroad. In 1834, on his first trip to Europe, he sent back travel essays that were published in his newspaper. After continuing to publish similar essays during the 1830s and 1840s, in 1850 he brought out *Letters of a Traveller*, the first of three collections of his travel writings. He also published more than ten volumes of poetry between 1832 and 1876. His best known public poem was "The Death of Lincoln," which he wrote shortly after the assassination; it was read to thousands gathered at New York City's Union Square the day before Lincoln's body arrived for a viewing. Bryant's wife, Frances, died in 1866, but he held on to his editorship at the *Evening Post*. In his seventies he began the remarkably ambitious project of translating Homer. His blank-verse version of the *Iliad* appeared in 1870 and his *Odyssey* followed in 1872. The 1876 publication of his collected *Poems* crowned his career. Two years later, he died of the consequences of a fall after he gave a speech at the unveiling of a statue of the Italian patriot and revolutionary Giuseppe Mazzini in Central Park. In New York City flags were lowered to half-staff, and Bryant was mourned as a great poet and editor.

Thanatopsis[1]

To him who in the love of Nature holds
Communion with her visible forms, she speaks
A various language; for his gayer hours
She has a voice of gladness, and a smile
And eloquence of beauty, and she glides
Into his darker musings, with a mild
And gentle sympathy, that steals away
Their sharpness, ere he is aware. When thoughts
Of the last bitter hour come like a blight
Over thy spirit, and sad images
Of the stern agony, and shroud, and pall,
And breathless darkness, and the narrow house,
Make thee to shudder, and grow sick at heart;—
Go forth under the open sky, and list[2]
To Nature's teachings, while from all around—
Earth and her waters, and the depths of air,—
Comes a still voice—Yet a few days, and thee
The all-beholding sun shall see no more
In all his course; nor yet in the cold ground,
Where thy pale form was laid, with many tears,
Nor in the embrace of ocean shall exist
Thy image. Earth, that nourished thee, shall claim
Thy growth, to be resolv'd to earth again;
And, lost each human trace, surrend'ring up
Thine individual being, shalt thou go
To mix forever with the elements,
To be a brother to th' insensible rock
And to the sluggish clod, which the rude swain
Turns with his share,[3] and treads upon. The oak
Shall send his roots abroad, and pierce thy mould.
Yet not to thy eternal resting place
Shalt thou retire alone—nor couldst thou wish
Couch more magnificent. Thou shalt lie down
With patriarchs of the infant world—with kings,
The powerful of the earth—the wise, the good,
Fair forms, and hoary seers of ages past,
All in one mighty sepulchre.—The hills
Rock-ribb'd and ancient as the sun,—the vales
Stretching in pensive quietness between;
The venerable woods—rivers that move
In majesty, and the complaining brooks

1. From *Poems* (1821); a shorter version appeared in the September 1817 issue of the *North American Review.*

2. Listen.

3. Plowshare. "Swain": farmer.

That make the meadows green; and pour'd round all,
Old ocean's grey and melancholy waste,—
Are but the solemn decorations all
Of the great tomb of man. The golden sun,
The planets, all the infinite host of heaven,
Are shining on the sad abodes of death,
Through the still lapse of ages. All that tread
The globe are but a handful to the tribes
That slumber in its bosom.—Take the wings
Of morning—and the Barcan desert[4] pierce,
Or lose thyself in the continuous woods
Where rolls the Oregan,[5] and hears no sound,
Save his own dashings—yet—the dead are there,
And millions in those solitudes, since first
The flight of years began, have laid them down
In their last sleep—the dead reign there alone.—
So shalt thou rest—and what if thou shalt fall
Unnoticed by the living—and no friend
Take note of thy departure? All that breathe
Will share thy destiny. The gay will laugh
When thou art gone, the solemn brood of care
Plod on, and each one as before will chase
His favourite phantom; yet all these shall leave
Their mirth and their employments, and shall come,
And make their bed with thee. As the long train
Of ages glide away, the sons of men,
The youth in life's green spring, and he who goes
In the full strength of years, matron, and maid,
The bow'd with age, the infant in the smiles
And beauty of its innocent age cut off,—
Shall one by one be gathered to thy side,
By those, who in their turn shall follow them.
So live, that when thy summons comes to join
The innumerable caravan, that moves
To the pale realms of shade, where each shall take
His chamber in the silent halls of death,
Thou go not, like the quarry-slave at night,
Scourged to his dungeon, but sustain'd and sooth'd
By an unfaltering trust, approach thy grave,
Like one who wraps the drapery of his couch
About him, and lies down to pleasant dreams.

1817 1821

4. In Barca (northeast Libya).
5. An early variant spelling of Oregon; now the Columbia River.

To a Waterfowl[1]

Whither, 'midst falling dew,
While glow the heavens with the last steps of day,
Far, through their rosy depths, dost thou pursue
Thy solitary way?

Vainly the fowler's eye
Might mark thy distant flight to do thee wrong,
As, darkly painted on the crimson sky,
Thy figure floats along.

Seek'st thou the plashy[2] brink
Of weedy lake, or marge of river wide,
Or where the rocking billows rise and sink
On the chafed ocean side?

There is a Power whose care
Teaches thy way along that pathless coast,—
The desert and illimitable air,—
Lone wandering, but not lost.

All day thy wings have fann'd
At that far height, the cold thin atmosphere:
Yet stoop not, weary, to the welcome land,
Though the dark night is near.

And soon that toil shall end,
Soon shalt thou find a summer home, and rest,
And scream among thy fellows; reeds shall bend
Soon o'er thy sheltered nest.

Thou'rt gone, the abyss of heaven
Hath swallowed up thy form; yet, on my heart
Deeply hath sunk the lesson thou hast given,
And shall not soon depart.

He, who, from zone to zone,
Guides through the boundless sky thy certain flight,
In the long way that I must tread alone,
Will lead my steps aright.

1818 1821

1. From *Poems* (1821); an earlier version appeared in the May 1818 issue of the *North American Review*.
2. Marshy.

Sonnet—To an American Painter Departing for Europe[1]

Thine eyes shall see the light of distant skies:
Yet, Cole![2] thy heart shall bear to Europe's strand
A living image of thy native land,
Such as on thy own glorious canvass lies.
Lone lakes—savannahs where the bison roves—
Rocks rich with summer garlands—solemn streams—
Skies, where the desert eagle wheels and screams—
Spring bloom and autumn blaze of boundless groves.
Fair scenes shall greet thee where thou goest—fair,
But different—every where the trace of men,
Paths, homes, graves, ruins, from the lowest glen
To where life shrinks from the fierce Alpine air.
Gaze on them, till the tears shall dim thy sight,
But keep that earlier, wilder image bright.

1829 1832

The Prairies[1]

These are the Gardens of the Desert, these
The unshorn fields, boundless and beautiful,
And fresh as the young earth, ere man had sinned—
The Prairies. I behold them for the first,
And my heart swells, while the dilated sight
Takes in the encircling vastness. Lo! they stretch
In airy undulations, far away,
As if the ocean, in his gentlest swell,
Stood still, with all his rounded billows fixed,
And motionless for ever.—Motionless?—
No—they are all unchained again. The clouds
Sweep over with their shadows, and beneath
The surface rolls and fluctuates to the eye;
Dark hollows seem to glide along and chase
The sunny ridges. Breezes of the South!
Who toss the golden and the flame-like flowers,
And pass the prairie-hawk that, poised on high,
Flaps his broad wings, yet moves not—ye have played
Among the palms of Mexico and vines
Of Texas, and have crisped the limpid brooks
That from the fountains of Sonora[2] glide

1. The text is that of the first book printing in *Poems* (1832). Bryant drafted the poem in 1829 and eventually retitled it "To Cole, the Painter, Departing for Europe."
2. The Hudson River School painter Thomas Cole (1801–1848) traveled in 1829 to Italy, where he would remain for three years. (For examples of Cole's art, see the reproductions from his "Course of Empire" [1836] series in the color insert to this volume.) In 1849, the year after Cole's death, Asher B. Durand painted a landscape image of Cole and Bryant in New York's Catskill Mountains.

1. From the first printing in *Poems* (1834). Bryant wrote the poem over a year after visiting his brothers in Illinois during 1832.
2. River in northwest Mexico.

Into the calm Pacific—have ye fanned
A nobler or a lovelier scene than this?
Man hath no part in all this glorious work:
The hand that built the firmament hath heaved
And smoothed these verdant swells, and sown their slopes
With herbage, planted them with island groves,
And hedged them round with forests. Fitting floor
For this magnificent temple of the sky—
With flowers whose glory and whose multitude
Rival the constellations! The great heavens
Seem to stoop down upon the scene in love,—
A nearer vault, and of a tenderer blue,
Than that which bends above the eastern hills.
   As o'er the verdant waste I guide my steed,
Among the high rank grass that sweeps his sides,
The hollow beating of his footstep seems
A sacrilegious sound. I think of those
Upon whose rest he tramples. Are they here—
The dead of other days!—and did the dust
Of these fair solitudes once stir with life
And burn with passion? Let the mighty mounds[3]
That overlook the rivers, or that rise
In the dim forest crowded with old oaks,
Answer. A race, that long has passed away,
Built them;—a disciplined and populous race
Heaped, with long toil, the earth, while yet the Greek
Was hewing the Pentelicus[4] to forms
Of symmetry, and rearing on its rock
The glittering Parthenon. These ample fields
Nourished their harvests, here their herds were fed,
When haply by their stalls the bison lowed,
And bowed his maned shoulder to the yoke.
All day this desert murmured with their toils,
Till twilight blushed and lovers walked, and wooed
In a forgotten language, and old tunes,
From instruments of unremembered form,
Gave the soft winds a voice. The red man came—
The roaming hunter tribes, warlike and fierce,
And the mound-builders vanished from the earth.
The solitude of centuries untold
Has settled where they dwelt. The prairie wolf
Hunts in their meadows, and his fresh dug den
Yawns by my path. The gopher mines the ground
Where stood their swarming cities. All is gone—
All—save the piles of earth that hold their bones—
The platforms where they worshipped unknown gods—
The barriers which they builded from the soil
To keep the foe at bay—till o'er the walls

3. The burial mounds common in Illinois. Bryant follows a contemporary theory that they were built by a culture older than the American Indians.
4. Greek mountain from which a fine white marble was quarried, including that used in building the Parthenon, the temple of Athena on the Acropolis in Athens.

The wild beleaguerers broke, and, one by one,
The strong holds of the plain were forced, and heaped
With corpses. The brown vultures of the wood
Flocked to those vast uncovered sepulchres,
And sat, unscared and silent, at their feast.
Haply some solitary fugitive,
Lurking in marsh and forest, till the sense
Of desolation and of fear became
Bitterer than death, yielded himself to die.
Man's better nature triumphed. Kindly words
Welcomed and soothed him; the rude conquerors
Seated the captive with their chiefs. He chose
A bride among their maidens. And at length
Seemed to forget,—yet ne'er forgot,—the wife
Of his first love, and her sweet little ones
Butchered, amid their shrieks, with all his race.
  Thus change the forms of being. Thus arise
Races of living things, glorious in strength,
And perish, as the quickening breath of God
Fills them, or is withdrawn. The red man too—
Has left the blooming wilds he ranged so long,
And, nearer to the Rocky Mountains, sought
A wider hunting ground. The beaver builds
No longer by these streams, but far away,
On waters whose blue surface ne'er gave back
The white man's face—among Missouri's springs,
And pools whose issues swell the Oregan,[5]
He rears his little Venice.[6] In these plains
The bison feeds no more. Twice twenty leagues
Beyond remotest smoke of hunter's camp,
Roams the majestic brute, in herds that shake
The earth with thundering steps—yet here I meet
His ancient footprints stamped beside the pool.
  Still this great solitude is quick with life.
Myriads of insects, gaudy as the flowers
They flutter over, gentle quadrupeds,
And birds, that scarce have learned the fear of man
Are here, and sliding reptiles of the ground,
Startlingly beautiful. The graceful deer
Bounds to the wood at my approach. The bee,
A more adventurous colonist than man,
With whom he came across the eastern deep,
Fills the savannas with his murmurings,
And hides his sweets, as in the golden age,
Within the hollow oak. I listen long
To his domestic hum, and think I hear
The sound of that advancing multitude
Which soon shall fill these deserts. From the ground
Comes up the laugh of children, the soft voice
Of maidens, and the sweet and solemn hymn

5. The Columbia River.

6. I.e., builds a city in the water.

Of Sabbath worshippers. The low of herds
Blends with the rustling of the heavy grain
Over the dark-brown furrows. All at once
A fresher wind sweeps by, and breaks my dream,
And I am in the wilderness alone.

1834

The Death of Lincoln[1]

Oh, slow to smite and swift to spare,
   Gentle and merciful and just!
Who, in the fear of God, didst bear
   The sword of power, a nation's trust!
In sorrow by thy bier we stand,
   Amid the awe that hushes all,
And speak the anguish of a land
   That shook with horror at thy fall.

Thy task is done; the bond are free;
   We bear thee to an honored grave,
Whose proudest monument shall be
   The broken fetters of the slave.

Pure was thy life; its bloody close
   Hath placed thee with the sons of light,
Among the noble host of those
   Who perished in the cause of Right.[2]

1865

1. Lincoln was assassinated by John Wilkes Booth on April 15, 1865. This poem first appeared in the April 20, 1865, issue of the New York *Evening Post*, the source of the text printed here. The Unitarian minister Samuel Osgood read the poem to thousands of mourners at New York City's Cooper Union on the evening of April 24, the day before Lincoln's body arrived for a viewing in New York.

2. In his famous Cooper Union speech of February 27, 1860, delivered at a campaign event that Bryant had helped to organize, Lincoln declared: "Let us have faith that right makes might, and in that faith, let us, to the end, dare to do our duty as we understand it."

WILLIAM APESS

1798–1839

Little is known of William Apess's life other than what he tells us in *A Son of the Forest* (1829), the first extensive autobiography published by a Native American. His grandfather, says Apess, was a white man who married the granddaughter of the Wampanoag leader King Philip, or Metacom, the loser, in 1676, of King Philip's

War. Philip increasingly occupied Apess's thoughts during his lifetime, serving as the subject of his last published work. Apess's father, although of mixed blood, joined the Pequot tribe and married an Indian woman who may have been part African American. Born in Colrain, Massachusetts, Apess drops from public record after 1838. He died in New York on April 10, 1839, of what was described as "apoplexy."

In *A Son of the Forest*, Apess details the pains of his early life: at three he was taken into the home of his poor, alcoholic maternal grandparents; he was severely beaten and, at four or five, sold as an indentured laborer. His first master allowed him to attend school for six years, which constituted his entire formal education; he also introduced Apess to Christianity. Apess served as a soldier in the abortive American attack on Montreal in the War of 1812 and converted to evangelical Methodism after leaving the army. At the conclusion of *A Son of the Forest*, Apess writes that he achieved an "exhorter's" license from his church, enabling him to earn a living as an itinerant preacher; only later would he realize his goal of ordination as a Methodist minister.

A fervent Christian, Apess early understood Christianity as incompatible with any form of race prejudice, sounding a note that presages Christian abolitionists later in the nineteenth century. In 1833, Apess went to preach at Mashpee, the only remaining Indian town in Massachusetts. There he became involved in the Mashpees' struggle to preserve their resources and rights, which were threatened by the overseers imposed on them by the Commonwealth of Massachusetts. The Mashpee eventually drew up petitions, probably composed by Apess, requiring that no whites cut wood or hay on Mashpee lands without the Indians' consent for "we, as a tribe, will rule ourselves, and have the right to do so; for all men are born free and equal, says the Constitution of the Country." Such unprecedented assertiveness on the part of the Indians alarmed the governor of Massachusetts, who announced his readiness to put down the unrest with troops. Apess's version of the controversy appears in his *Indian Nullification of the Unconstitutional Laws of Massachusetts, Relative to the Marshpee* [sic] *Tribe; or, The Pretended Riot Explained* (1835). A year before the book appeared, its case was won when the state legislature granted the Mashpee the same rights of self-governance that other Massachusetts townships possessed.

Apess's career as a preacher and an author comes to a close with his "Eulogy on King Philip," delivered in 1836 at the Odeon in Boston, one of the city's largest public lecture halls, and published that same year. In the "Eulogy" Apess meditates on his distant relation, naming Philip the foremost man that America had thus far produced. He reminds his audience, descendants of the Pilgrims, of the crimes of their ancestors, although "you and I have to rejoice that we have not to answer for our fathers' crimes; neither shall we do right to charge them one to another." Nonetheless, he notes, "in vain have I looked for the Christian to take me by the hand and bid me welcome to his cabin, as my fathers did them [the Christians], before we were born." Apess concludes that a "different course must be pursued. . . . And while you ask yourselves, 'What do they, the Indians, want?' you have only to look at the unjust laws made for them and say, 'They want what I want'": justice and Christian fellowship.

We begin with chapters 1, 2, and 3 of the first edition of Apess's *A Son of the Forest* (1829). As the title page makes clear, he published it under the name of "Apes," although for other of his works he uses the spelling "Apess." The latter has become standard since Barry O'Connell's 1992 publication of *On Our Own Ground: The Complete Writings of William Apess, a Pequot*.

Also included is the final chapter of *The Experiences of Five Christian Indians of the Pequot Tribe*, published in 1833, the year Apess came to Mashpee. The first of these "experiences" is Apess's own, an account of his life and conversion that repeats some of the material in *A Son of the Forest* but intensifies considerably the condemnation of Euro-American treatment of Native peoples. Apess concludes this book with the text included here, "An Indian's Looking-Glass for the White Man," a searing indictment of race prejudice against people of color generally and Native Americans particularly. Apess's probing, ironic voice, with its direct address to the reader, may well have influenced that later speaker on behalf of racial justice, Henry David Thoreau. There is also a good deal of evidence suggesting that Apess's work may have been known to Herman Melville and Frederick Douglass.

From A Son of the Forest

Chapter 1

William Apes, the author of the following narrative is a native of the American soil, and a descendant of one of the principal chiefs of the Pequod Tribe, so well known in that part of American history called King Philip's Wars.[1] This tribe inhabited a part of Connecticut, and lived in comparative peace on the river Thames, in the town of Groton or Pacatonic, and was commanded by King Philip. As the story of King Philip is perhaps generally known, it will be sufficient for our purpose to say that he was overcome by treachery. Betrayed to their avowed enemies, the nation was completely routed and the way thereby opened for the whites to possess themselves of the goodly heritage occupied by this once peaceable and happy tribe. But this was not the only act of injustice which this oppressed nation suffered at the hands of their white neighbors. They were subject to a more intense and heart corroding affliction—that of having their daughters claimed by the conquerors, and however much subsequent efforts were made to soothe their sorrows in this particular, they considered the glory of their nation as departed.

My grandfather was a white, and married a female attached to the royal family: she was fair and beautiful. How nearly she was connected with the king I cannot tell; but without doubt some degree of affinity subsisted between them. I have frequently heard my grandmother talk about it, and as nearly as I can tell, she was his grand or great-grand daughter. I do not make this statement in order to boast of my origin, or to appear great in the estimation of others, when, in fact of myself, I am nothing but a worm of the earth, but with the simple view of giving the reader the truth as I have received it, and more especially as I must render an account to the Sovereign Judge of all men for every thing contained in this little book. From what I have already stated, it will appear that my father was of mixed blood—his father being a white man, and his mother, a native of the soil, or in other words a red woman; but when he attained sufficient age to act for himself, he joined the tribe to which he was connected maternally, shortly after which he married a female of the tribe, in whose veins, not a single drop of the white man's blood

1. Philip was not a Pequot but a Wampanoag of the Pokanoket band; his people's traditional lands were not in Connecticut but in the area of Mount Hope, Rhode Island. It isn't clear whether this is simply an error on Apess's part or whether he changed Philip's tribal allegiance for some purpose. Drawn into war with the Puritans in 1675, Philip and his people were defeated in 1676. Apess's use of the word "betrayed" below probably refers to the fact that Native people antagonistic to Philip (some Pequots, in fact) aided the Puritans and it was an Indian who actually killed him. His body was drawn and quartered, his head displayed on a pike, and his wife and children sold into Caribbean slavery.

William Apess. A portrait of Apess from the second, 1831 edition of *A Son of the Forest.*

had ever flowed.[2] He then removed to the back settlements, directing his course to the west and afterwards to the north-east, and pitched his tent in the woods of a town called Colereign, near the Connecticut river, in the state of Massachusetts, where he continued for some time. During the time of their sojourning here I was born—January 31st, 1798. Our next remove was to Colchester Conn., near the sea-board; where my father lived between two and three years, with his little family in comparative comfort. Circumstances however changed. I then lived with my grand-father and his family, in which dwelt my uncle. My grandfather and his companion were not the best people in the world,—like all other people who are wedded to the beastly vice of intemperance they would drink to intoxication whenever they could procure rum, and as usual in such cases when under the influence of liquor, they would not only fight and quarrel with each other, but would frequently turn upon their unoffending grand children, five in number, and beat them in a most cruel manner. My two brothers and two sisters also lived with them, and we were always kept in continual dread or torment. My father and mother made baskets which they would sell to the whites, or exchange for

2. Apess's mother, Candace, may not have had "a single drop of the white man's blood," but it is possible that she possessed some African "blood."

those articles only, which were absolutely necessary to keep soul and body in a state of unity. Our fare was of the poorest kind, and even of this we had not enough, and our clothing also was of the poorest description. literally speaking we were clothed with rags, so far as rags would suffice to cover our nakedness. We were always happy to get a cold potatoe for our dinner, and many a night have we gone supperless to rest, if stretching our wearied limbs on a bundle of straw without any covering against the weather, may be called rest. We were in a most distressing situation. Too young to obtain subsistence for ourselves by the labor of our hands, and our wants disregarded by those who should have made exertions to supply them. Some of our white neighbors however taking pity on us, frequently brought us frozen milk, which my mother would make into porridge, and we would all lap it down like so many hungry dogs, and thought ourselves well off when the calls of hunger were thus satisfied. And we lived in this way suffering from cold and hunger for some time. Once in particular, I remember, that when it rained my grandmother put us all down cellar, and when we complained of being cold and hungry, she told us to dance and keep ourselves warm: but we had no food of any kind, and my sister almost died of hunger. Poor girl she was quite overcome. Think not dear reader that I have exagerated—I assure you that I have not—I merely relate this circumstance to show you how intense our sufferings were. We did not, however, continue in this most deplorable situation a very great while. Providence smiled on us—but it was in a particular way. My father and mother fell out, that is, they quarrelled, parted, went off a great distance, leaving us with grandfather and mother to shift for ourselves. We lived at this time in an old house divided into two apar[t]ments. My uncle lived in one part, and the old folks in another.

My grandmother went out one day; she got too much rum from the whites, and on returning she not only began to scold me, but to beat me shamefully with a club: (the reason of her doing so I never could tell.) She asked me if I hated her, and I very innocently said, yes, for I did not then know what the word hate meant, and thought I was answering aright. And so she kept asking me the same question, and I always answered the same way, and then she would commence beating me again, and so she continued until she had broken my arm in three places. I was only four years of age, and of course could not take care of [myself]. But my uncle, who lived in the other part of the house, came down to take me away, when my grandfather made towards him with a fire-brand; but he succeeded in rescuing me, and thus saved my life, for had he not come at the time he did to my relief, I would certainly have been killed. My grand-parents who acted so were by my mother's side, those by my father's side were Christians, lived and died happy in God, and if I live faithful to that grace with which God has already blessed me, I expect to meet them in glory, and praise Him with them to all eternity. I will now return: My uncle took and hid me away from them, and secreted me until the next day. When they found me, and discovered how dangerously I had been injured, they were compelled to have recourse to the whites. My uncle went to the person who had often sent us milk, and as soon as he learned what had happened, he came straight off to see me—and when he reached the place he found a poor little Indian boy, all b[r]uised and mangled to pieces. He was anxious that something should be done for us, and especially for me. He therefore applied in our behalf to the selectmen of the town, who after considering the application, adjudged that we should be taken and bound out.[3] As for my part, I was a town charge for about a year, as the wounds inflicted by my grandmother entirely disabled me for that length of time. I was then put among good Christian people, called the Close Order, who used me as tenderly as though I had been one of the elect, or one of their sons.[4] The surgeon was sent for, who called in another doctor, and down they came to Mr. Furman's house, where the selectmen had ordered me to be carried. Now this dear man and family were sad on my account. Mrs. Furman was a tender-hearted lady, and nursed me, and had it not been that they took the best possible care of me, I think I should have died. But it pleased God to support me, and you know my dear reader, from what I have related, that my situation must have been dreadful. If I remember right, it was four or five days before the doctor set my arm, which was consequently very sore. I was afterwards told that during the painful operation I never murmured. I attributed this to the improvement in my situation. Before this I was almost naked, cold, and hungry—now I was comfortable, (with the exception of my wounds.) Before, in order to satisfy the cravings of nature, I would frequently run away to the whites and beg food, who invariably supplied my wants in that respect, as they looked upon me with pity, considering me a poor helpless and neglected child.

I recollect that on one occasion I had been out begging for food, and in returning home lost my way. After the darkness of night had closed upon me, I came to a large brook surrounded by woods, where I sat down and began to cry; at last some persons heard my lamentations, and came to my assistance. By them I was directed in the right way, so that I reached home in safety, to catch a little more trouble, that is, to get a sound flagellation for begging for victuals to keep me alive. Hence, I call my deliverance from such a scene of suffering, the Providence of God.

I suppose that the reader will naturally say, "What savage creatures my grandparents were to treat unoffending or helpless children in this manner." But this treatment was the effect of some cause. I attribute it in part to the whites, because they introduced among my countrymen ardent spirits; seduced them into a love for it, and when under its baleful influence, wronged them out of their lawful possessions—that land where reposed the ashes of their sires—and not only so, but they committed violence of the most revolting and basest kind upon the persons of the female portion of the tribe, who until the arts, and vices, and debauchery of the whites were introduced among them, were as happy, and peaceable, and cheerful, as they roamed over their goodly possessions, as any people on whom the sun of heaven hath ever shone. The consequence was, that they were scattered abroad. Now, many of them were seen reeling about intoxicated with liquor, neglecting to provide for themselves or families, who before were

3. Debtors or poor people with no means of support were frequently "bound out" as indentured servants for a term of years. Apess, only five at the time, was a bit young for indentured servitude, although young children were sometimes bound out. It's been noted that in the eighteenth and early nineteenth centuries, nearly all Indians in southern New England were affected by indentured servitude in one degree or another with not only material but also cultural effects, including loss of their Native languages and exposure to corporal punishment.

4. These are the Furmans. The "Close Order" Christians are thought to have been a dissident Methodist group, although Mrs. Furman is later (p. 135) called a Baptist.

assiduously engaged in supplying the necessities of those depending upon them.

But to return—After I had been nursed up about a year, I had so far recovered, that it was thought proper to bind me out, until I should attain the age of twenty-one years. As I was then only five years old, Mr. Furman thought he could not keep me, as he was a poor man, and obtained his living by the work of his hands. He was a cooper[5] by trade, and employed himself in his business when he was not engaged in working on his farm. They had become very fond of me, and as I could not be satisfied to leave them, as I loved them with the strength of filial love, he at last concluded to keep me until I was of age. According to the spirit of the indentures, if I mistake not, I was to have so much instruction as to be able to read and write, and at the expiration of the term of my apprenticeship they were to furnish me with two suits of clothes. They used me with the utmost kindness—I had enough to eat and to wear—and every thing in short to make me comfortable. According to their agreement, when I had reached my sixth year, they sent me to school—this they continued to do for six successive winters, in which time I learned to read and write, so that I might be understood. This was all the instruction of the kind I ever received. But I desire to be truly thankful to God for this—I cannot make you sensible of the amount of benefit I have received from it.

Chapter II

Since I have "entered upon the stage of action," I have heard much said about infants feeling as it were the operations of the Holy Spirit, or convictions, on their little minds, relative to a future state. But were I called upon for my opinion on this, I should say in the first place that it is owing mainly to the manner in which children are brought up. If proper and constant means are used to impress upon their young and susceptible minds, sentiments of truth, virtue, morality, and religion, and these efforts are sustained by a corresponding practice on the part of parents or those who essay to make these early impressions, we may rationally trust that as their young minds expand, they will be led to act upon the wholesome principles they have received—and that at a very early period these good impressions will be more indelibly engraved on their hearts by the co-operating influences of that Spirit, who in the days of his glorious incarnation, said, "Suffer little children to come unto me, and forbid them not, for of such is the kingdom of heaven."[6]

But to my experience, and the reader knows full well that experience is the best schoolmaster: for, what we have experienced, that we know, and all the world cannot possibly beat it out of us. I well remember the conversation that took place between Mrs. Furman and myself when I was about six years of age. She was attached to the Baptist church, and was esteemed as a very pious woman. Of this I have not the shadow of a doubt, as her whole course of conduct was upright and exemplary. On this occasion she spoke to me respecting a future state of existence, and told me that I might die, and enter upon it, to which I replied that I was too young—that old people only died.

5. Coopers were craftsmen who constructed and repaired wood barrels, buckets, and casks.

6. Jesus is said to have spoken these words (Luke 18.16, Mark 10.13–14, and Matthew 19.14).

But she assured me that I was not too young, and in order to convince me of the truth of the observation, she referred me to the grave yard, where many younger and smaller persons than myself were laid to moulder in the earth. I had of course nothing to say—but, notwithstanding, I could not fully comprehend the nature of death, the meaning of a future state, yet I felt an indescribable sensation pass through my frame, I trembled and was sore afraid, and for sometime endeavoured to hide myself from the destroying monster, but I could find no place of refuge. The conversation and pious admonitions of this godly lady made a lasting impression on my mind. At times, however, this impression appeared to be wearing away—then again I would become thoughtful, make serious enquiries, and seem anxious to know something more certain respecting myself, and that state of existence beyond the grave, in which I was instructed to believe. About this time I was taken to [church] in order to hear the word of God, and receive instruction in divine things. This was the first time I had ever entered a house of worship, and instead of attending to what the minister said, I was employed in gazing about the house, or playing with the unruly boys, with whom I was seated in the gallery. On my return home, Mr. Furman, who had been apprised of my conduct, told me that I had acted very wrong. He did not however stop here. He went on to tell me how I ought to behave in church, and to this very day I bless God for such wholesome and timely instruction, and the man who taught me these things. In this particular I was not slow to learn, as I do not remember that I have from that day to this, misbehaved in the house of God.

It may not be improper to remark in this place, that a vast proportion of the misconduct of young people in church, is chargeable to their parents and guardians. It is to be feared that there are too many professing Christians who feel satisfied if their children or those under their care enter on a sabbath day within the walls of the sanctuary, without reference to their conduct while there. I would have such persons seriously ask themselves whether they think they discharge the duties obligatory on them by the relation in which they stand to their Maker, as well as those committed to their care, by so much negligence on their part. The Christian feels it a duty imposed on him to conduct his children to the house of God. But he rests not here. He must have an eye over them, and if they act well, approve and encourage them; if otherwise, point out to them their error, and persuade them to observe a discreet and exemplary course of conduct while in church.

After a while I became very fond of attending on the word of God—then again I would meet the enemy of my soul, who would strive to lead me away, and in many instances he was but too successful, and to this day I remember that nothing scarcely grieved me so much, when my mind had been thus petted, than to be called by a nick name. If I was spoken to in the spirit of kindness, I would be instantly disarmed of my stubbornness, and ready to perform any thing required of me. I know of nothing so disgusting to a child as to be repeatedly called by an improper name. I thought it disgraceful to be called an Indian; it was considered as a slur upon an oppressed and scattered nation, and I have often been led to inquire where the whites received this word, which they so often threw as an opprobrious epithet at the sons of the forest. I could not find it in the bible, and therefore come to the conclusion that it was a word imported for the special purpose of degrading us.

At other times I thought it was derived from the term in-genuity. The proper term which ought to be applied to our nation, to distinguish it from the rest of the human family, is that of "*Natives*"—and I humbly conceive that the natives of this country are the only people under heaven who have a just title to the name, inasmuch as we are the only people who retain the original complexion of our father Adam.[7] Notwithstanding my thoughts on this matter, so completely was I weaned from the interests and affections of my brethren, that a mere threat of being sent away among the [I]ndians into the dreary woods, had a much better effect in making me obedient to the commands of my superiors, than any corporeal punishment that they ever inflicted. I had received a lesson in the unnatural treatment of my own relations, which could not be effaced; and I thought that if those who should have loved and protected me, treated me with such unkindness, surely I had no reason to expect mercy or favour at the hands of those who knew me in no other relation than that of a cast off member of the tribe. A threat, of the kind alluded to, invariably produced obedience on my part, so far as I understood the nature of the command.

I cannot perhaps give a better idea of the dread which pervaded my mind on seeing any of my brethren of the forest, than by relating the following occurrence. One day several of the family went into the woods to gather berries, taking me with them. We had not been out long before we fell in with a company of females, on the same errand—their complexion was, to say the least, as dark as that of the natives. This circumstance filled my mind with terror, and I broke from the party with my utmost speed, and I could not muster courage enough to look back until I had reached home. By this time my imagination had pictured out a tale of blood, and as soon as I regained breath sufficient to answer the questions which my master asked, I informed him that we had met a body of the natives in the woods, but what had become of the party I could not tell. Notwithstanding the manifest incredibility of my tale of terror, Mr. Furman was agitated; my very appearance was sufficient to convince him that I had been terrified by something, and summoning the remainder of the family, we sallied out in quest of the absent party, whom we found searching for me among the bushes. The whole mystery was soon unravelled. It may be proper for me here to remark, that the great fear I entertained of my brethren, was occasioned by the many stories I had heard of their cruelty towards the whites—how they were in the habit of killing and scalping men, women and children. But the whites did not tell me that they were in a great majority of instances the aggressors—that they had imbrued their hands in the life blood of my brethren, driven them from their once peaceful and happy homes—that they introduced among them the fatal and exterminating diseases of civilized life. If the whites had told me how cruel they had been to the "poor indian," I should have apprehended as much harm from them.

Shortly after this occurrence I relapsed into my former bad habits—was fond of the company of the boys, and in a short time lost in a great measure that spirit of obedience which had made me the favourite of my mistress. I was easily led astray, and once in particular, I was induced by a boy, (my

7. Like many others in his day, Apess thought that indigenous people were descendants of the Ten Lost Tribes of Israel, who would, as Semites, have had a skin color, derived from Adam, which was more like that of the American Natives than the European invader-settlers.

senior by five or six years) to assist him in his depredations on a water melon patch belonging to one of the neighbors. But we were found out, and my companion in wickedness led me deeper in sin, by persuading me to deny the crime laid to our charge. I obeyed him to the very letter, and when accused, flatly denied knowing any thing of the matter. The boasted courage of the boy, however, began to fail as soon as he saw danger thicken, and he confessed it as strongly as he had denied it. The man from whom we had pillaged the melons threatened to send us to Newgate,[8] but he relented. The story shortly afterward reached the ears of the good Mrs. Furman, who talked seriously to me about it. She told me that I could be sent to prison for it—that I had done wrong, and gave me a great deal of wholesome advice. This had a much better effect than forty floggings—it sunk so deep into my mind that the impression can never be effaced.

I now went on without difficulty for a few months, when I was assailed by fresh and unexpected troubles. One of the girls belonging to the house had taken some offence at me, and declared she would be revenged. The better to effect this end, she told Mr. Furman that I had not only threatened to kill her, but had actually pursued her with a knife, whereupon he came to the place where I was working and began to whip me severely. I could not tell for what. I told him I had done no harm, to which he replied, "I will learn you, you Indian dog, how to chase people with a knife." I told him I had not, but he would not believe me, as he knew that I had denied taking the melons, and continued to whip me for a long while. But the poor man soon found out his error, as *after* he had flogged me, he undertook to investigate the matter, when to his amazement he discovered it was nothing but fiction, as all the children assured him that I did no such thing. He regretted being so hasty—but I saw wherein the great difficulty consisted, if I had not denied the melon affair, he would have believed me, but as I had uttered an untruth about that, it was natural for him to think that the person who will tell one lie, will not scruple at two. For a long while after this circumstance transpired, I did not associate with my companions.

About this time the Christians came in our neighbourhood,[9] and as their hearts were warm in the cause of God, they would sing the songs of Zion, and pray earnestly for one another. I felt great delight in attending their meeting, which I did as often as possible. I had not attended these meetings a great while before I became somewhat serious. I listened with great attention to the word of God, and though only eight years of age I was resolved to become better. I was encouraged by many of the people—they did every thing they could to cheer me. This had so good an effect upon me, that I felt determined to get about the work of repentance. I had very strange feelings for a child of my age. One day the preacher selected for the foundation of his sermon a text relating to the future state of mankind. He spoke much on the eternal happiness of the righteous, and the everlasting misery of the ungodly, and his observations sunk with awful weight upon my mind, and I was led to make many serious enquiries about the way of salvation. In these days of young desires and youthful aspirations, I found Mrs. Furman

8. Named after the infamous English prison at Newgate and Old Bailey Street in London, this Connecticut prison opened in the 1770s and closed in 1827. It is presently a historic site in East Granby, Connecticut.

9. "The Christians" were probably another group of dissenting Methodists.

ever ready to give me good advice. My mind was intent upon learning the lesson of righteousness, in order that I might learn to walk in the good way, and cease to do evil. My mind for one so young was greatly drawn out to seek the Lord. This spirit was manifested in my daily walk; and the friends of Christ noticed my afflictions; they knew that I was sincere because my spirits were depressed. When I was in church I could not at times avoid giving vent to my feelings, and often have I wept sorely before the Lord and his people. The people in the neighbourhood, of course, observed this change in my conduct—they knew I had been a rude child, and that efforts were made to bring me up in a proper manner, but the change in my deportment they did not ascribe to the influence of divine grace, inasmuch as they all considered me too young to be impressed with a sense of divine things. They were filled with unbelief. I need not describe the peculiar feelings of my soul.

I became very fond of attending meetings; so much so that Mr. Furman forbid me. He supposed that I only went for the purpose of seeing the boys and playing with them. This thing caused me a great deal of grief; I went for many days with my head and heart bowed down. No one had any idea of the mental agony I suffered, and perhaps the mind of no untutored child of my age was ever more seriously exercised. Sometimes I was tried and tempted—then I would be overcome by the fear of death. By day and by night I was in a continual ferment. To add to my fears about this time, death entered the family of Mr. Furman and removed his mother-in-law. I was much affected, as the old lady was the first corpse I had ever seen. I was much concerned for the family and mourned with them. She had always been so kind to me that I missed her quite as much as her children. The old lady had allowed me to call her mother.

Shortly after this occurrence I was taken ill. I then thought I should surely die. The distress of body and the anxiety of mind wore me down. Now I think that the disease with which I was afflicted was a very curious one. The physician could not account for it, and how should I be able to do it, and neither had those who were about me ever witnessed any disorder of the kind. Whenever I would try to lay down, it would seem as if something was choking me to death, and if I attempted to sit up, the wind would rise in my throat and nearly strangle me. I felt continually as if I was about being suffocated. I was consequently a great deal of trouble to the family, as some one had to be with me. One day Mr. Furman thought he would frighten the disease out of me. Accordingly he told me that all that ailed me was this—that the devil had taken complete possession of me, and that he was determined to flog him out. This threat had not the desired effect. One night, however, I got up, and went out, although I was afraid to be alone, and continued out by the door until after the family had retired to bed. After a while Mr. F. got up and gave me a dreadful whipping. He really thought, I believe that the devil was in me, and supposed that the birch was the best mode of ejecting him. But the flogging was as fruitless as the preceding threat in the accomplishment of his object, and he poor man found out his mistake, like many others who act without discretion.

One morning after this I went out in the yard to assist Mrs. Furman [to] milk the cows. We had not been out long before I felt very singular, and began to make a strange noise. I believed that I was going to die, and ran up to the house; she followed me immediately, expecting me to breathe my last. Every effort to breathe was accompanied by this strange noise, which was so loud as to be heard fifteen or twenty rods off. After a while, however, contrary to all expectation I began to revive, and from that very day my disorder began to abate, and I gradually regained my former health.

Soon after I recovered from my sickness, I went astray, associated again with my old school fellows, and on some occasions profaned the [S]abbath day. I did not do so without warning, as conscience would speak to me when I did wrong. Nothing very extraordinary occurred until I had reached the age of eleven years. At this time it was fashionable for boys to run away, and the devil put it into the head of the oldest boy on the farm to persuade me to follow the fashion. He told me that I could take care of myself, and get my own living. I thought it was a very pretty notion to be a man—to do business for myself and become rich. Like a fool I concluded to make the experiment, and accordingly began to pack up my clothes as deliberately as could be, in which my adviser assisted. I had been once or twice at New London, where I saw, as I thought, every thing wonderful: thither I determined to bend my course, as I expected, that on reaching the town I should be metamorphosed into a person of consequence; I had the world and every thing my little heart could desire in a string, when behold, my companion who had persuaded me to act thus, informed my master that I was going to run off. At first he would not believe the boy, but my clothing already packed up was ample evidence of my intention. On being questioned I acknowledged the fact. I did not wish to leave them—told Mr. Furman so; he believed me, but thought best that for a while I should have another master. He accordingly agreed to transfer my indentures to Judge Hillhouse[1] for the sum of twenty dollars. Of course after the bargain was made, my consent was to be obtained, but I was as unwilling to go now, as I had been anxious to run away before. After some persuasion, I agreed to try it for a fortnight, on condition that I should take my dog with me, and my request being granted, I was soon under the old man's roof, as he only lived about six miles off. Here every thing was done to make me contented, because they thought to promote their own interests by securing my services. They fed me with nicknacks, and soon after I went among them, I had a jack knife presented to me, which was the first one I had ever seen. Like other boys, I spent my time in whittling and playing with my dog, and was withal very happy. But I was home sick at heart, and as soon as my fortnight had expired, I went home without ceremony. Mr. Furman's family were surprized to see me, but that surprise was mutual joy, in which my faithful dog appeared to participate.

The joy I felt on returning home as I hoped, was turned to sorrow on being informed that I had been sold to the judge, and must instantly return. This I was compelled to do. And reader, all this sorrow was in consequence of being led away by a bad boy: if I had not listened to him I should not have lost my home. Such treatment I conceive to be the best means to accomplish the ruin of a child, as the reader will see in the sequel. I was sold to the judge at a time when age had rendered him totally unfit to manage an unruly lad. If he undertook to correct me, which he did at times, I did not

1. William Hillhouse (1728–1816) was chief judge of the county court. He had fought in the American Revolution and been a member of the Continental Congress.

regard it as I knew that I could run off from him if he was too severe, and besides I could do what I pleased in defiance of his authority. Now the old gentleman was a member of the Presbyterian church, and withal a very strict one. He never neglected family prayer, and he always insisted on my being present. I did not believe, or rather had no faith in his prayers, because it was the same thing from day to day, and I had heard it repeated so often, that I knew it as well as he. Although I was so young, I did not believe that Christians ought to learn their prayers, and knowing that he repeated the same thing from day to day, is, I think, the very reason why his petitions did me no good. I could fix no value on his prayers.

After a little while the conduct of my new guardians was changed towards me. Once secured, I was no longer the favourite. The few clothes I had were not taken care of, by which I mean, no pains were taken to keep them clean and whole, and the consequence was that in a little time they were all "tattered and torn," and I was not fit to be seen in decent company. I had not the opportunity of attending meeting as before. Yet as the divine and reclaiming impression had not been entirely defaced, I would frequently retire behind the barn, and attempt to pray in my weak manner. I now became quite anxious to attend evening meetings a few miles off: I asked the judge if I should go and take one of the horses, to which he consented. This promise greatly delighted me—but when it was time for me to go, all my hopes were dashed at once, as the judge had changed his mind. I was not to be foiled so easily; I watched the first opportunity and slipped off with one of the horses, reached the meeting, and returned in safety. Here I was to blame; if he acted wrong, it did not justify me in doing so; but being successful in one grand act of disobedience, I was encouraged to make another similar attempt, whenever my unsanctified dispositions prompted; for the very next time I wished to go to meeting, I thought I would take the horse again, and in the same manner too, without the knowledge of my master. As he was by some means apprized of my intention, he prevented my doing so, and had the horses locked up in the stable. He then commanded me to give him the bridle; I was obstinate for a time, then threw it at the old gentleman, and run off. I did not return until the next day, when I received a flogging for my bad conduct, which determined me to run away. Now the judge was partly to blame for all this. He had in the first place treated me with the utmost kindness until he had made sure of me. Then the whole course of his conduct changed, and I believed he fulfilled only one item of the transferred indentures, and that was work. Of this there was no lack. To be sure, I had enough to eat, such as it was, but he did not send me to school as he promised.

A few days found me on my way to New London, where I staid awhile. I then pushed on to Waterford, and as my father lived about twenty miles off, I concluded to go and see him. I got there safely, and told him I had come on a visit, and that I should stay one week. At the expiration of the week he bid me go home, and I obeyed him. On my return I was treated rather coolly, and this not suiting my disposition, I run off again, but returned in a few days. Now, as the judge found he could not control me, he got heartily tired of me, and wished to hand me over to some one else, so he obtained a place for me in New London. I knew nothing of it, and I was greatly mortified to think that I was sold in this way. If my consent had been solicited as a matter of form, I should not have felt so bad. But to be sold to, and treated unkindly, by those who had got our father's lands for nothing, was too much to bear. When all things were ready, the judge told me that he wanted me to go to New London with a neighbour, to purchase salt. I was delighted, and went with the man, expecting to return that night. When I reached the place I found my mistake. The name of the person to whom I was transferred this time, was Gen. William Williams,[2] and as my treatment at the Judge's was none of the best, I went home with him contentedly. Indeed I felt glad that I had changed masters, and more especially that I was to reside in the city. The finery and show caught my eye, and captivated my heart. I can truly say that my situation was better now than it had been previously to my residence in New London. In a little time I was furnished with good new clothes. I had enough to eat, both as it respects quality and quantity, and my work was light. The whole family treated me kindly, and the only difficulty of moment was that they all wished to be masters. But I would not obey all of them. There was a French boy in the family, who one day told Mr. Williams a wilful lie about me, which he believed, and gave me a horse-whipping, without asking me a single question about it. Now I do not suppose that he whipped me so much on account of what the boy told him as he did from the influence of the Judge's directions. He used the falsehood as a pretext for flogging me, as from what he said he was determined to make a good boy of me at once—as if stripes were calculated to effect that which love, kindness and instruction can only successfully accomplish. He told me that if I ever ran away from him he would follow me to the uttermost parts of the earth. I knew from this observation that the Judge had told him I was a runaway. However cruel this treatment appeared, for the accusation was false, yet it did me much good, as I was always ready to obey the general and his lady at all times. But I could not and would not obey any but my superiors. In short, I got on very smoothly for a season.

The general attended the Presbyterian church, and was exact in having all his family with him in the house of God. I of course formed one of the number. Though I did not profess religion, I observed and felt that their ways were not like the ways of the Christians.[3] It appeared inconsistent to me for a minister to read his sermon—to turn over leaf after leaf, and at the conclusion say Amen, seemed to me like an "empty sound and a tinkling cymbal."[4] I was not benefitted by his reading. It did not arouse me to a sense of my danger—and I am of the opinion that it had no better effect on the people of his charge. I liked to attend church, as I had been taught in my younger years to venerate the Sabbath day; and although young I could plainly perceive the difference between the preachers I had formerly heard and the minister at whose church I attended. I thought, as near as I can remember, that the Christians depended on the Holy Spirit's influence entirely, while this minister depended as much upon his learning. I would not be understood as saying any thing against knowledge; in its place it is

2. General William Williams (1731–1811) was a veteran of the Revolutionary War, a signer of the Declaration of Independence, a member of the Continental Congress, and a founder of Williams College.

3. Like Judge Hillhouse and many of the most prominent people of the time, General Williams is a Presbyterian. Apess finds his manner of prayer inferior to that of the evangelical "Christians."

4. From 1 Corinthians 13.1.

good, and highly necessary to a faithful preacher of righteousness. What I object to is, placing too much reliance in it, making a god of it, &c.

Every thing went on smoothly for two or three years. About this time the Methodists began to hold meetings in the neighbourhood, and consequently a storm of persecution gathered; the Pharisee[5] and the worldling united heartily in abusing them. The gall and wormwood of sectarian malice were emitted, and every evil report prejudicial to this pious people was freely circulated. And it was openly said that the character of a respectable man would receive a stain, and a deep one too, by attending one of their meetings. Indeed the stories circulated about them were bad enough to deter people of "Character!" from attending the Methodist ministry. But it had no effect on me. I thought I had no character to lose in the estimation of those who were accounted great. But what cared they for me. They had possession of the red man's inheritance, and had deprived me of liberty; with this they were satisfied, and could do as they pleased; therefore I thought I would do as I pleased, measurably. I therefore went to hear the noisy Methodist. When I reached the house I found a clever company. They did not appear to differ much from "respectable" people. They were clever, neatly and decently clothed, and I could not see that they differed from other people except in their behavior, which was more kind and gentlemanly. Their countenance was heavenly, their songs were like sweetest music—in their manners they were plain. Their language was not fashioned after the wisdom of men. When the minister preached he spoke as one having authority.[6] The exercises were accompanied by the power of God. His people shouted for joy—while sinners wept. This being the first time I had ever attended Methodist meeting, all things of course appeared new to me. I was very far from forming the opinion that most of the neighbourhood entertained about them. From this time I became more serious, and soon went to hear the Methodists again, and I was constrained to believe that they were the true people of God. One person asked me how I knew it? I replied that I was convinced in my own mind that they possessed something more than the power of the devil.

I now attended Methodist meeting constantly, and although I was a sinner before God, yet I felt no disposition to laugh or scoff. I make this observation because so many people went to these meetings to make fun. This was a common thing, and I often wondered how persons who professed to be considered great, i. e. "ladies and gentlemen," would so far disgrace themselves as to scoff in the house of God, and at his holy services. Such persons let themselves down below the heathen, in point of moral conduct—below the heathen, yes, and below the level of the brute creation, who answer the end for which they were made.

But notwithstanding the people were so bad, yet the Lord had respect unto the labours of his servants; his ear was open to their daily supplications, and in answer to prayer he was pleased to revive his work. The power of the

5. The Pharisees were a Jewish sect that emphasized strict interpretation of religious law. The term "Pharisee" has become a synonym for a hypocrite who values the letter over the spirit of the law.

6. Apess is expressing his preference for the more improvisational style of the Methodist revivalist preachers whose "authority" does not derive from any printed text but from divine inspiration. The older, more formal congregations tended to be "up in arms against the Methodists," as Apess later writes.

Holy Ghost moved forth among the people—the spirit's influence was felt at every meeting—the people of God were built up in the faith—their confidence in the Lord of hosts gathered strength, while many sinners were alarmed, and began to cry aloud for mercy. In a little time the work rolled onward like an overwhelming flood. I attended meeting as often as I could. Now the Methodists and all who attended their meetings were greatly persecuted. All denominations were up in arms against the Methodists, because the Lord was blessing their labours, and making them (a poor despised people) his instruments in the conversion of sinners. But all opposition had no other effect than of cementing the brethren more closely together; the work went on, as the Lord was with them of a truth, and signally owned and blessed their labours. At one of these meetings I was induced to laugh, I believe it must have been to smother my conviction, as it did not come from my heart. My heart was troubled on account of sin, and when conviction pressed upon me, I endeavoured not only to be cheerful, but to laugh; and thus drive away all appearance of being wrought upon. Shortly after this I was affected even unto tears. This the people of the world observed and immediately enquired if I was one of the Lamb's children. Brother Hill was then speaking from this passage of scripture—*Behold the Lamb of God, that laketh away the sins of the world.*[7] He spoke feelingly of his sufferings upon the cross—of the precious blood that flowed like a purifying river from his side—of his sustaining the accumulated weight of the sins of the whole world, and dying to satisfy the demands of that justice which could only be appeased by an infinite atonement. I felt convinced that Christ died for all mankind—that age, sect, colour, country, or situation, made no difference. I felt an assurance that I was included in the plan of redemption with all my brethren. No one can conceive with what joy I hailed this *new* doctrine as it was called—It removed every excuse, and I freely believed that all I had to do was to look in faith upon the Lamb of God that made himself a free-will offering for my unregenerate and wicked soul upon the cross. My spirits were depressed—my crimes were arrayed before me, and no tongue can tell the anguish of soul I felt.

After meeting I returned home with a heavy heart, determined to seek the salvation of my soul. This night I slept but little—at times I would be melted down to tenderness and tears, and then again my heart would seem as hard as adamant. I was greatly tempted. The evil one would try to persuade me that I was not in the pale of mercy. I fancied that evil spirits stood around my bed—my condition was deplorably awful—and I longed for the day to break as much as the tempest tost mariner who expects every moment to be washed from the wreck to which he fondly clings. So it was with me upon the wreck of the world—buffetted by temptations—assailed by the devil—sometimes in despair—then believing against hope. My heart seemed at times almost ready to break, while the tears of contrition coursed rapidly down my cheeks. But sin was the cause of this, and no wonder I groaned and wept. I had often sinned, and my accumulated transgressions had piled

7. "Behold the Lamb of God" (John 1.29), referring to Jesus. The next several pages describe Apess's personal experience of a type of conversion that had been recorded by others. Although he had probably not read conversion narratives at the time of his own conversion, he may have known some when he came to write his autobiography.

themselves as a rocky mountain on my heart, and how could I endure it? The weight thereof seemed to crush me down. In the night season I had frightful visions, and would often start from my sleep and gaze round the room, as I was ever in dread of seeing the evil one ready to carry me off. I continued in this frame of mind for more than seven weeks.

My distress finally became so acute that the family took notice of it. Some of them persecuted me because I was serious and fond of attending meeting. Now, persecution raged on every hand, within and without, and I had none to take me by the hand and say, "go with us and we will do thee good." But in the midst of difficulties so great to one only fifteen years of age, I ceased not to pray for the salvation of my soul. Very often my exercises were so great that sleep departed from me—I was fearful that I should wake up in hell. And one night when I was in bed, mourning like the dove for her absent mate.[8] I fell into a doze. I thought I saw the world of fire—it resembled a large solid bed of coals—red and glowing with heat. I shall never forget the impression it made upon my mind. No tongue can possibly describe the agony of my soul, for now I was greatly in fear of dropping into that awful place, the smoke of the torment of which ascendeth up for ever and ever. I cried earnestly for mercy. Then I was carried to another place, where perfect happiness appeared to pervade every part, and the inhabitants thereof. O how I longed to be among that happy company. I sighed to be free from misery and pain. I knew that nothing but the attenuated thread of life kept me from falling into the awful lake I beheld. I cannot think that it is in the power of human language to describe the feelings that rushed upon my mind, or thrilled through my veins. Every thing appeared to bear the signet of reality; when I awoke [I] heartily rejoiced to find it nothing but a dream.

I went on from day to day with my head and heart bowed down, seeking the Saviour of sinners, but without success. The heavens appeared to be brass; my prayers wanted the wings of faith to waft them to the skies; the disease of my heart increased; the heavenly physician had not stretched forth his hand and poured upon my soul the panacea of the gospel; the scales had not fallen from my eyes, and no ray of celestial light had dispelled the darkness that gathered around my soul. The cheering sound of sincere friendship fell not upon my ear. It seemed as if I were friendless, unpitied, and unknown, and at times I wished to become a dweller in the wilderness. No wonder then, that I was almost desponding. Surrounded by difficulties and apparent dangers, I was resolved to seek the salvation of my soul with all my heart—to trust entirely to the Lord, and if I failed, to perish pleading for mercy at the foot of the throne. I now hung all my hope on the Redeemer, and clung with indescribable tenacity to the cross on which he purchased salvation for the "vilest of the vile." The result was such as is always to be expected, when a lost and ruined sinner throws himself entirely on the Lord—*perfect freedom.* On the fifteenth day of March, in the year of our Lord, eighteen hundred and thirteen, I heard a voice in soft and soothing accents, saying unto me, *Arise, thy sins which were many are all forgiven thee, go in peace and sin no more!*[9]

8. The Mourning Dove's plaintive sound had been attributed by many poets to the absence of her mate.

9. Apess is echoing passages in the New Testament (e.g., Matthew 9.5, Mark 2.9, Luke 5.23) asking whether it is easier to say to the sinner, "Arise, thy sins are forgiven," or to say to the paralytic, "Arise, take up thy bed and walk."

There was nothing very singular, (save the fact that the Lord stooped to lift me up,) in my conversion. I had been sent into the garden to work, and while there I lifted up my heart to God, when all at once my burden and fears left me—my heart melted into tenderness—my soul was filled with love—love to God, and love to all mankind. Oh how my poor heart swelled with joy—and I could cry from my very soul, Glory to God in the highest!!! There was not only a change in my heart but in every thing around me. The scene was entirely altered. The works of God praised Him, and I saw him in every thing that he had made. My love now embraced the whole human family. The children of God I loved most affectionately. Oh how I longed to be with them, and when any of them passed by me, I could gaze at them until they were lost in the distance. I could have pressed them to my bosom, as they were more precious to me than gold, and I was always loth to part with them whenever we met together. The change too was visible in my very countenance.

I enjoyed great peace of mind, and that peace was like a river full, deep, and wide, and flowing continually, my mind was employed in contemplating the wonderful works of God, and in praising his holy name, dwelt so continually upon his mercy and goodness that I could praise him aloud even in my sleep. I continued in this happy frame of mind for some months. It was very pleasant to live in the enjoyment of pure and undefiled religion.

At last the devil became dissatisfied with my uninterrupted happiness, for my peace flowed as a river, and he began to tempt me. The fire of persecution was rekindled. Some members of the family endeavoured to make me think that I was too young to be religious—that I was under a delusion, and Mr. Williams thought I had better not attend Methodist meetings. This restriction was the more galling, as I had joined the class and was extremely fond of this means of grace. I generally attended once in each week, so when the time come round I went off to the meeting, without permission. When I returned, Mrs. Williams prepared to correct me for acting contrary to my orders; in the first place however, she asked me where I had been, I frankly told her that I had been to meeting to worship God. This reply completely disarmed her, and saved me a flogging for the time. But this was not the end of my persecution or my troubles.

The devil I believe was in the chamber maid—she was in truth a treacherous woman, her heart appeared to me to be filled with deceit and guile, and she persecuted me with as much bitterness as Paul did the disciples of old. She had a great dislike towards me, and would not hesitate to tell a lie in order to have me whipped. But my mind was stayed upon God, and I had much comfort in reading the holy Scriptures. One day after she had procured me a flogging, and no very mild one either, she pushed me down a long flight of stairs. In the fall I was greatly injured, especially my head: in consequence of this I was disabled and laid up for a long time. When I told Mr. Williams that the maid had pushed me down stairs, she denied it, but I succeeded in making them believe it. In all this trouble the Lord was with me of a truth. I was happy in the enjoyment of his love. The abuse heaped on me was in consequence of my being a Methodist.

Sometimes I would get permission to attend meetings in the evening, and once or twice on the Sabbath. And oh, how thankful I felt for these opportunities for hearing the word of God. But the waves of persecution, and affliction and sorrow, rolled on, and gathered strength in their progress, and for a season overwhelmed my dispirited soul. I was flogged several times very unjustly for what the maid said respecting me. My treatment in this respect was so bad that I could not brook it, and in an evil hour I listened to the suggestions of the devil who was not slow in prompting me to pursue a course directly at variance with the gospel. He put it into my head to abscond from my master, and I made arrangements with a boy of my acquaintance to accompany me. So one day Mr. Williams had gone to Stonington, I left his house, notwithstanding he had previously threatened if I did so, to follow me to the ends of the earth. While my companion was getting ready I hid my clothes in a barn, and went to buy some bread and cheese, and while at the store, notwithstanding I had about four dollars in my pocket, I so far forgot myself, as to buy a pair of shoes on my master's account. Then it was that I began to lose sight of religion and of God. We now set out it being a rainy night, we bought a bottle of rum, of which poisonous stuff I drank heartily. Now it was that the shadows of spiritual death, began to gather around my soul. It was half past nine o'clock at night when we started, and to keep up our courage we took another drink of the liquor. As soon as we left the city, that is, as we descended the hill, it became very dark, and my companion who was always fierce enough by daylight, began to hang back. I saw that his courage was failing, and endeavoured to cheer him up. Sometimes I would take a drink of rum to drown my sorrows—but in vain, it appears to me now as if my sorrows neutralised the effects of the liquor.

This night we travelled about seven miles, and being weary and wet with the rain, we crept into a barn by the way side, and for fear of being detected in the morning, if we should happen to sleep too long, we burrowed into the hay a considerable depth. We were aroused in the morning by the people feeding their cattle; we laid still and they did not discover us. After they had left the barn we crawled out, made our breakfast on rum, bread and cheese, and set off for Colchester about fourteen miles distant, which we reached that night. Here we ventured to put up at a tavern. The next morning we started for my father's about four miles off. I told him that we had come to stay only one week, and when that week had expired he wished me to redeem my promise and return home. So I had to comply, and when we had packed up our clothes, he said he would accompany us part of the way, and when we parted I thought he had some suspicions of my intention to take another direction, as he begged me to go straight home. He then sat down on the way side and looked after us as long as we were to be seen. At last we descended a hill, and as soon as we lost sight of him, we struck into the woods. I did not see my father again for eight years. At this time, I felt very much disturbed. I was just going to step out on the broad theatre of the world, as it were without father, mother, or friends.

After travelling some distance in the woods, we shaped our course towards Hartford. We were fearful of being taken up, and my companion coined a story which he thought would answer very well. It was this, to represent ourselves, whenever questioned, as having belonged to a privateer,[1] which was captured by the British, who kindly sent us on shore near New-London;

1. A privateer was a private warship authorized by the government during time of war to attack enemy ships, and, if successful to appropriate both ship and cargo for sale.

that our parents lived in the city of New-York, and that we were travelling thither to see them.

Now John was a great liar. He was brought up by dissipated parents, and accustomed in the way of the world to all kinds of company. He had a good memory, and having been w[h]ere he heard war songs and tales of blood and carnage, he treasured them up. He therefore agreed to be spokesman, and I assure my dear reader that I was perfectly willing, for abandoned as I was I could not lie without feeling my conscience smite me. This part of the business being arranged, it was agreed that I should sell part of my clothing, to defray our expenses. Our heads were full of schemes, and we journeyed on until night overtook us. We then went into a farmhouse to test our plan. The people soon began to ask us questions, and John as readily answered them. He gave them a great account of our having been captured by the enemy, and so straight, that they believed the whole of it. After supper we went to bed, and in the morning they gave us a good breakfast, and some bread and cheese, and we went on our way, satisfied with our exploits. John now studied to make his story appear as correct as possible. The people pitied us, and sometimes we had a few shillings put into our hands. We did not suffer for the want of food. At Hartford we staid some time, and we here agreed to work our passage down to New-York on board of a brig—but learning that the British fleet was on the coast, the captain declined going. We then set out to reach New-York by land. We thought it a good way to walk. We went by way of New-Haven, expecting to reach the city from that place by water. Again we were disappointed. We fell in company with some sailors who had been exchanged, and we listened to their story—it was an affecting one, and John concluded to incorporate a part of it with his own. So shortly afterwards he told some people that while we were prisoners, we had to eat bread mixed with pounded glass. The people were foolish enough to believe us. At Kingsbridge an old lady gave us several articles of clothing. Here we agreed with the captain of a vessel to work our way to New-York. When we got under weigh, John undertook to relate our sufferings to the crew. They appeared to believe it all, until he came to the incredible story of the "glass bread." This convinced the captain that all he said was false. He told us that he knew that we were runaways, and pressed us to tell him, but we declined. At length he told us that we were very near to Hell-gate, (Hurl-gate)—that when we reached it the devil would come on board in a stone canoe, with an iron paddle, and make a terrible noise, and that he intended to give us to him. I thought all he said was so. I therefore confessed that we were runaways—where, and with whom we had lived. He said he would take me back to New-London, as my master was rich and would pay him a good price. Here the devil prompted me to tell a lie, and I replied that the General had advertised me one cent reward. He then said that he would do nothing with me, further than to keep my clothes until we paid him. When the vessel reached the dock, John slipped off, and I was not slow to follow. In a few days we got money to redeem our clothing; we took board in Cherry-street, at two dollars per week; we soon obtained work, and received sixty-two and a half cents per day. While this continued, we had no difficulty in paying our board. My mind now became tolerably calm, but in the midst of this I was greatly alarmed; as I was informed that my master had offered fifteen dollars reward for me, and that the captain of one of the packets was looking for me. I dared not go back, and therefore determined to go to Philadelphia; to this John objected, and advised me to go to sea, but I could find no vessel. He entered on board a privateer, and I was thus left entirely alone in a strange city. Wandering about, I fell in company with a sergeant and a file of men who were enlisting soldiers for the United States army. They thought I would answer their purpose, but how to get me was the thing. Now they began to talk to me, then treated me to some spirits, and when that began to operate, they told me all about the war, and what a fine thing it was to be a soldier. I was pleased with the idea of being a soldier, took some more liquor, and some money, had a cockade fastened on my hat, and went off in fine spirits for my uniform. Now my enlistment was against the law,[2] but I did not know it; but I could not think why I should risk my life and limbs in fighting for the white man, who had cheated my forefathers out of their land. By this time I had acquired many bad practices. I was sent over to Governor's Island, opposite the city, and here I remained some time. Too much liquor was dealt out to the soldiers, who got drunk very often. Indeed the island was like a hell upon earth, in consequence of the wickedness of the soldiers. I have known sober men to enlist, who afterwards became confirmed drunkards, and appear like fools upon the earth. So it was among the soldiers, and what should a child do, who was entangled in their net. Now, although I made no profession of religion, yet I could not bear to hear sacred things spoken of lightly, or the sacred name of God blasphemed; and I often spoke to the soldiers about it, and in general they listened attentively to what I had to say. I did not tell them that I had ever made a profession of religion. In a little time I became almost as bad as any of them; could drink rum, play cards, and act as wickedly as any of them. I was at times tormented with the thoughts of death, but God had mercy on me, and spared my life, and for this I feel thankful to the present day. Some people are of opinion that if a person is once born of the Spirit of God he can never fall away entirely, and because I acted thus, they may pretend to say that I had not been converted to the faith. I believe firmly, that if ever Paul[3] was born again, I was; if not, from whence did I derive all the light and happiness I had heretofore experienced? To be sure it was not to be compared to Paul's—but the change I felt in my very soul.

I felt anxious to obtain forgiveness from every person I had injured in any manner whatever. Sometimes I thought I would write to my old friends and request forgiveness—then I thought I had done right. I could not bear to hear any order of Christians ridiculed, especially the Methodists—it grieved me to the heart. But to proceed.

Chapter III

After I had been some time on the island, I took much comfort in beating on an old drum; this was my business, as I was enlisted for a drummer. About this time I was greatly alarmed on account of the execution of a soldier, who

2. It was against the law because Apess was only fifteen years old and could not legally enlist before his seventeenth birthday. His enlistment papers were forged. He says that he "could not think why I should risk my life and limbs in fighting for the white man, who had cheated my forefathers of their land," but does not go on to explore the contradiction of his enlistment to fight the English in what came to be known as the War of 1812.

3. Paul of Tarsus, eventually St. Paul, traveling on the road to Damascus, was "born again" after a life-changing vision of the resurrected Jesus.

was shot on Governor's Island for mutiny. I cannot tell how I felt when I saw the soldiers parade, and the condemned clothed in white with bibles in their hands, come forward. The band then struck up the dead march, and the procession moved with a mournful and measured tread to the place of execution, where the poor creatures were compelled to kneel on their coffins, which were along side their newly dug graves. While in this position the chaplain went forward and conversed with them—after he had retired a soldier went up and drew their caps over their faces; thus blindfolded he led one of them some distance from the other. An officer then advanced, and raised his handkerchief as a signal to the platoon to prepare to fire—he then made another for them to aim at the wretch who had been left kneeling on his coffin, and at a third signal the platoon fired, and the immortal essence of the offender in an instant was in the spirit-land. To me this was an awful day—my heart seemed to leap into my throat. Death never appeared so awful. But what must have been the feelings of the unhappy man, who had so narrowly escaped the grave? He was completely overcome, and wept like a child, and it was found necessary to help him back to his quarters. This spectacle made me serious; but it wore off in a few days.

Shortly after this we were ordered to Staten Island, where we remained about two months.—Then we were ordered to join the army destined to conquer Canada.[4] As the soldiers were tired of the island, this news animated them very much. They thought it a great thing to march through the country and assist in taking the enemy's land. As soon as our things were ready we embarked on board a sloop for Albany, and then went on to Greenbush, where we were quartered. In the mean time I had been transferred to the ranks. This I did not like; to carry a musket was too fatiguing, and I had a positive objection to being placed on the guard, especially at night. As I had only enlisted for a drummer, I thought that this change by the officer was contrary to law, and as the bond was broken, liberty was granted me; therefore being heartily tired of a soldier's life, and having a desire to see my father once more, I went off very deliberately; I had no idea that they had a lawful claim on me, and was greatly surprised as well as alarmed, when arrested as a deserter from the army. Well, I was taken up and carried back to the camp, where the officers put me under guard. We shortly after marched for Canada, and during this dreary march the officers tormented me by telling me that it was their intention to make a fire in the woods, stick my skin full of pine splinters, and after having an Indian pow wow over me, burn me to death. Thus they tormented me day after day.

We halted for some time at Burlington: but resumed our march and went into winter quarters at Plattsburgh. All this time God was very good to me, as I had not a sick day. I had by this time become very bad. I had previously learned to drink rum, play cards and commit other acts of wickedness, but it was here that I first took the name of the Lord in vain, and oh, what a sting it left behind. We continued here until the ensuing fall, when we received orders to join the main army under Gen. Hampton.[5] Another change now

4. Apess's comment that "we were ordered to join the army destined to conquer Canada" may be ironically intended, since he knows well at the time of this writing that the army did not conquer Canada.

5. General Wade Hampton (c. 1752–1835) was a Southerner who had fought in the Revolutionary War and then retired to run several plantations in South Carolina, Mississippi, and Louisiana. He volunteered for duty in the War of 1812, and

took place,—we had several pieces of heavy artillery with us, and of course horses were necessary to drag them, and I was taken from the ranks and ordered to take charge of one team. This made my situation rather better. I now had the privilege of riding. The soldiers were badly off, as the officers were very cruel to them, and for every little offence they would have them flogged. One day the officer of our company got angry at me, and pricked my ear with the point of his sword.

We soon joined the main army, and pitched our tents with them. It was now very cold, and we had nothing but straw to lay on. There was also a scarcity of provisions, and we were not allowed to draw our full rations. Money would not procure food—and when any thing was to be obtained the officers had always the preference, and they, poor souls, always wanted the whole for themselves. The people generally, have no idea of the extreme sufferings of the soldiers on the frontiers during the last war; they were indescribable; the soldiers eat with the utmost greediness, raw corn and every thing eatable that fell in their way. In the midst of our afflictions, our valiant general ordered us to march forward to subdue the country in a trice. The pioneers had great difficulty in clearing the way—the enemy retreated burning every thing as they fled. They destroyed every thing, so that we could not find forage for the horses. We were now cutting our way through a wilderness, and were very often benumbed with the cold. Our sufferings now for the want of food were extreme—the officers too began to feel it, and one of them offered me two dollars for a little flour, but I did not take his money, and he did not get my flour; I would not have given it to *him* for fifty dollars. The soldiers united their flour and baked unleavened bread, of this we made a delicious repast.

After we had proceeded about thirty miles, we fell in with a body of Canadians and Indians—the woods fairly resounded with their yells. Our "brave and chivalrous" general ordered a picked troop to disperse them; we fired but one cannon and a retreat was sounded to the great mortification of the soldiers, who were ready and willing to fight. But as our general did not fancy the smell of gunpowder, he thought it best to close the campaign, by retreating with seven thousand men, before a "host" of seven hundred. Thus were many a poor fellow's hopes of conquest and glory blasted by the timidity of one man. This little brush with an enemy that we could have crushed in a single moment cost us several men in killed and wounded. The army now fell back on Plattsburgh, where we remained during the winter; we suffered greatly for the want of barracks, having to encamp in the open fields a good part of the time. My health, through the goodness of God, was preserved, notwithstanding many of the poor soldiers sickened and died. So fast did they go off, that it appeared to me as if the plague was raging among them.

When the spring opened, we were employed in building forts. We erected three in a very short time. We soon received orders to march, and joined the army under Gen. Wilkinson,[6] to reduce Montreal. We marched to Odletown

served under General James Wilkinson (see n. 6), who held him responsible for the disastrous attack on Montreal. Although the Department of War exonerated Hampton, he resigned his commission in 1814 and returned home. By the time of his death, he was the owner of more slaves than anyone else in the United States.

6. General James Wilkinson (1757–1825) had fought in the Revolutionary War and been promoted to the rank of general shortly before his twentieth birthday. Initially involved with Aaron Burr in treasonous activities, he ultimately

in great splendor, "Heads up and eyes right," with a noble commander at our head, and the splendid city of Montreal in our view. The city no doubt presented a scene of the wildest uproar and confusion; the people were greatly alarmed as we moved on with all the pomp and glory of an army flushed with many victories. But when we reached Odletown, John Bull[7] met us with a picked troop. They soon retreated, and some took refuge in an old fortified mill, which we pelted with a goodly number of cannon balls. It appeared as if we were determined to sweep every thing before us. It was really amusing to see our feminine general with his night-cap on his head, and a dishcloth tied round his precious body, crying out to his men "Come on, my brave boys, we will give John Bull a bloody nose." We did not succeed in taking the mill, and the British kept up an incessant cannonade from the fort. Some of the balls cut down the trees, so that we had frequently to spring out of their way when falling. I thought it was a hard time, and I had reason too, as I was in the front of the battle, assisting in working a twelve pounder and the British aimed directly at us. Their balls whistled around us, and hurried a good many of the soldiers into the eternal world, while others were most horribly mangled. Indeed they were so hot upon us, that we had not time to remove the dead as they fell. The horribly disfigured bodies of the dead—the piercing groans of the wounded and the dying—the cries of help and succor from those who could not help themselves—were most appalling. I can never forget it. We continued fighting until near sundown, when a retreat was sounded along our line, and instead of marching forward to Montreal, we wheeled about, and having once set our faces towards Plattsburgh, and turned our backs ingloriously on the enemy, we hurried off with all possible speed. We carried our dead and wounded with us. Oh, it was a dreadful sight to behold so many brave men sacrificed in this manner. In this way our campaign closed. During the whole of this time the Lord was merciful to me, as I was not suffered to be hurt. We once more reached Plattsburgh, and pitched our tents in the neighbourhood. While here, intelligence of the capture of Washington was received. Now, says the orderly sergeant, the British have burnt up all the papers at Washington,[8] and our enlistment for the war among them, we had better give in our names as having enlisted for five years.

We were again under marching orders, as the enemy it was thought contemplated an attack on Plattsburgh. Thither we moved without delay, and were posted in one of the forts. By the time we were ready for them, the enemy made his appearance on Lake Champlain, with his vessels of war. It was a fine thing to see their noble vessels moving like things of life upon this mimic sea, with their streamers floating in the wind. This armament was intended to co-operate with the army, which numbered fourteen thousand men, under the command of the captain general of Canada, and at that very time in view of our troops. They presented a very imposing aspect. Their red uniform[s], and the instruments of death which they bore in their

became one of Burr's principal accusers. All this time he was secretly a paid agent of Spain. Sometimes described as a man who never won a battle nor lost a court martial (he was court martialed at the order of James Madison but cleared of all charges), he was defeated in two battles in Canada during the War of 1812. Like Hampton, he was exonerated but resigned from the army.

7. The English, or any Englishman; here, the British army.

8. After the American defeat at the battle of Bladensburg, Washington, D.C., was captured and burned by the British on August 18, 1814.

hands, glittered in the sun beams of heaven, like so many sparkling diamonds. Very fortunately for us and for the country, a brave and noble commander had placed himself at the head of the army.[9] It was not an easy task to frighten him. For notwithstanding his men were inferior in point of number to those of the enemy, say as one to seven, yet relying on the bravery of his men, he determined to fight to the last extremity. The enemy in all the pomp and pride of war, had sat down before the town and its slender fortifications, and he commenced a cannonade, which we returned without much ceremony. Congreve rockets,[1] bomb shells, and cannon balls, poured upon us like a hail storm. There was scarcely any intermission, and for six days and nights we did not leave our guns, and during that time the work of death paused not, as every day some shot took effect. During the engagement, I had charge of a small magazine. All this time our fleet, under the command of the gallant M'Donough, was lying on the peaceful waters of Champlain.[2] But this little fleet was to be taken, or destroyed: it was necessary, in the accomplishment of their plans. Accordingly the British commander bore down on our vessels in gallant style. As soon as the enemy showed fight, our men flew to their guns. Then the work of death and carnage commenced. The adjacent shores resounded with the alternate shouts of the sons of liberty, and the groans of their parting spirits. A cloud of smoke mantled the heavens, shutting out the light of day—while the continual roar of artillery, added to the sublime horrors of the scene. At length the boasted valour of the haughty Britons failed them—they quailed before the incessant and well directed [f]ire of our brave and hardy tars, and after a hard fought battle, surrendered to that foe they had been sent to crush. On land the battle raged pretty fiercely. On our side the Green mountain boys behaved[3] with the greatest bravery. As soon as the British commander had seen the fleet fall into the hands of the Americans, his boasted courage forsook him, and he ordered his army of heroes, fourteen thousand strong, to retreat before a handful of militia.

This was indeed a proud day for our country. We had met a superior force on the Lake, and "they were ours."[4] On land we had compelled the enemy to seek safety in flight. Our army did not lose many men, but on the lake many a brave man fell—fell in the defence of his country's rights. The British moved off about sundown.

We remained in Plattsburgh until the peace.[5] As soon as it was known that the war had terminated, and the army disbanded, the soldiers were

9. The American forces were commanded by General Alexander Macomb (1782–1841). On September 11, 1814, he led a vastly outnumbered American force against the British at the Battle of Plattsburgh and by means of subterfuges negated the British advantage. The British were about to launch a major attack when they learned of their defeat in the Battle of Lake Champlain, which Apess describes below.

1. Congreve rockets were solid-fuel rockets invented by Sir William Congreve in 1805. They had been used to advantage in the British victory at the Battle of Bladensburg.

2. Captain Thomas Macdonough (1783–1825) commanded the four U.S. ships that sailed against a superior fleet led by Captain Downey of the British navy in the battle of Lake Champlain. Downey was killed early in the battle; Macdonough, though knocked down more than once, proved victorious.

3. Established before the American Revolution, the Green Mountain Boys became the militia of the Vermont Republic in 1777. They returned to action in the War of 1812, and Vermont's National Guard today is called by their name.

4. A reference to a message sent by U.S. Navy Commodore Oliver Hazard Perry after his victory over the British at the Battle of Lake Erie in 1814: "We have met the enemy, and they are ours."

5. The Treaty of Ghent, concluding the War of 1812, was signed at the end of December 1814. Because the news did not reach the United States until some months later, sporadic fighting continued into the new year.

clamorous for their discharge, but it was concluded to retain our company in the service—I, however, obtained my release.[6] Now, according to the act of enlistment, I was entitled to forty dollars bounty money, and one hundred and sixty acres of land. The government also owed me for fifteen months pay. I have not seen any thing of bounty money, land, or arrearages,[7] from that day to this. I am not, however, alone in this—hundreds were served in the same manner. But I could never think that the government acted right towards the "*Natives*," not merely in refusing to pay us, but in claiming our services in cases of perilous emergency, and still deny us the right of citizenship; and as long as our nation is debarred the privilege of voting for civil officers, I shall believe that the government has no claim on our services.[8]

1829

An Indian's Looking-Glass for the White Man[1]

Having a desire to place a few things before my fellow creatures who are traveling with me to the grave, and to that God who is the maker and preserver both of the white man and the Indian, whose abilities are the same and who are to be judged by one God, who will show no favor to outward appearances but will judge righteousness. Now I ask if degradation has not been heaped long enough upon the Indians? And if so, can there not be a compromise? Is it right to hold and promote prejudices? If not, why not put them all away? I mean here, among those who are civilized. It may be that many are ignorant of the situation of many of my brethren within the limits of New England. Let me for a few moments turn your attention to the reservations in the different states of New England, and, with but few exceptions, we shall find them as follows: the most mean, abject, miserable race of beings in the world—a complete place of prodigality and prostitution.

Let a gentleman and lady of integrity and respectability visit these places, and they would be surprised; as they wandered from one hut to the other they would view, with the females who are left alone, children half-starved and some almost as naked as they came into the world. And it is a fact that I have seen them as much so—while the females are left without protection, and are seduced by white men, and are finally left to be common prostitutes for them and to be destroyed by that burning, fiery curse, that has swept millions, both of red and white men, into the grave with sorrow and disgrace—rum. One reason why they are left so is because their most sensible and active men are absent at sea. Another reason is because they are made to believe

6. Apess's company was not disbanded at the end of the war, although as he says, he "obtained [his] release" in the fall of 1815—by deserting. That he did desert may explain why, as he says just below, he never saw "any thing of bounty money, land, or arrearages, from that day to this."

7. Unpaid, overdue debts.

8. American Indians were not granted American citizenship until 1924, although some had obtained it earlier by military service, or various acts of assimilation. While citizenship was sought by many Native people, others were not eager to be American citizens, preferring to emphasize their membership in tribal nations. Many Mohawks today, for example, claim either Mohawk citizenship only or dual citizenship.

1. The text is from *The Experiences of Five Christian Indians of the Pequot Tribe* (1833), reprinted in *On Our Own Ground: The Complete Writings of William Apess, a Pequot*, ed. Barry O'Connell (1992).

they are minors and have not the abilities given them from God to take care of themselves, without it is to see to a few little articles, such as baskets and brooms. Their land is in common stock, and they have nothing to make them enterprising.

Another reason is because those men who are Agents,[2] many of them are unfaithful and care not whether the Indians live or die; they are much imposed upon by their neighbors, who have no principle. They would think it no crime to go upon Indian lands and cut and carry off their most valuable timber, or anything else they chose; and I doubt not but they think it clear gain. Another reason is because they have no education to take care of themselves; if they had, I would risk them to take care of their own property.

Now I will ask if the Indians are not called the most ingenious people among us. And are they not said to be men of talents? And I would ask: Could there be a more efficient way to distress and murder them by inches than the way they have taken? And there is no people in the world but who may be destroyed in the same way. Now, if these people are what they are held up in our view to be, I would take the liberty to ask why they are not brought forward and pains taken to educate them, to give them all a common education, and those of the brightest and first-rate talents put forward and held up to office. Perhaps some unholy, unprincipled men would cry out, "The skin was not good enough"; but stop, friends—I am not talking about the skin but about principles. I would ask if there cannot be as good feelings and principles under a red skin as there can be under a white. And let me ask: Is it not on the account of a bad principle that we who are red children have had to suffer so much as we have? And let me ask: Did not this bad principle proceed from the whites or their forefathers? And I would ask: Is it worthwhile to nourish it any longer? If not, then let us have a change, although some men no doubt will spout their corrupt principles against it, that are in the halls of legislation and elsewhere. But I presume this kind of talk will seem surprising and horrible. I do not see why it should so long as they (the whites) say that they think as much of us as they do of themselves.

This I have heard repeatedly, from the most respectable gentlemen and ladies—and having heard so much precept, I should now wish to see the example. And I would ask who has a better right to look for these things than the naturalist[3] himself—the candid man would say none.

I know that many say that they are willing, perhaps the majority of the people, that we should enjoy our rights and privileges as they do. If so, I would ask, Why are not we protected in our persons and property throughout the Union? Is it not because there reigns in the breast of many who are leaders a most unrighteous, unbecoming, and impure black principle, and as corrupt and unholy as it can be—while these very same unfeeling, self-esteemed characters pretend to take the skin as a pretext to keep us from our unalienable and lawful rights? I would ask you if you would like to be disfranchised from all your rights, merely because your skin is white, and for no other crime. I'll venture to say, these very characters who hold the

2. Those appointed by the Commonwealth of Massachusetts to oversee Indian affairs in such towns as Mashpee.

3. I.e., the American Indian; a play on the view of Indians as children of nature or "sons of the forest".

skin to be such a barrier in the way would be the first to cry out, "Injustice! awful injustice!"

But, reader, I acknowledge that this is a confused world, and I am not seeking for office, but merely placing before you the black inconsistency that you place before me—which is ten times blacker than any skin that you will find in the universe. And now let me exhort you to do away that principle, as it appears ten times worse in the sight of God and candid men than skins of color—more disgraceful than all the skins that Jehovah ever made. If black or red skins or any other skin of color is disgraceful to God, it appears that he has disgraced himself a great deal—for he has made fifteen colored people to one white and placed them here upon this earth.

Now let me ask you, white man, if it is a disgrace for to eat, drink, and sleep with the image of God, or sit, or walk and talk with them. Or have you the folly to think that the white man, being one in fifteen or sixteen, are the only beloved images of God? Assemble all nations together in your imagination, and then let the whites be seated among them, and then let us look for the whites, and I doubt not it would be hard finding them; for to the rest of the nations, they are still but a handful. Now suppose these skins were put together, and each skin had its national crimes written upon it—which skin do you think would have the greatest? I will ask one question more. Can you charge the Indians with robbing a nation almost of their whole continent, and murdering their women and children, and then depriving the remainder of their lawful rights, that nature and God require them to have? And to cap the climax, rob another nation to till their grounds and welter out their days under the lash with hunger and fatigue under the scorching rays of a burning sun?[4] I should look at all the skins, and I know that when I cast my eye upon that white skin, and if I saw those crimes written upon it, I should enter my protest against it immediately and cleave to that which is more honorable. And I can tell you that I am satisfied with the manner of my creation, fully—whether others are or not.

But we will strive to penetrate more fully into the conduct of those who profess to have pure principles and who tell us to follow Jesus Christ and imitate him and have his Spirit. Let us see if they come anywhere near him and his ancient disciples. The first thing we are to look at are his precepts, of which we will mention a few. "Thou shalt love the Lord thy God with all thy heart, with all thy soul, with all thy mind, and with all thy strength. The second is like unto it. Thou shalt love thy neighbor as thyself. On these two precepts hang all the law and the prophets" (Matthew 22.37, 38, 39, 40). "By this shall all men know that they are my disciples, if ye have love one to another" (John 13.35). Our Lord left this special command with his followers, that they should love one another.

Again, John in his Epistles says, "He who loveth God loveth his brother also" (1 John 4.21). "Let us not love in word but in deed" (1 John 3.18). "Let your love be without dissimulation. See that ye love one another with a pure heart fervently" (1 Peter 1.22). "If any man say, I love God, and hateth his brother, he is a liar" (1 John 4.20). "Whosoever hateth his brother is a mur-

4. The reference is to the "nation" of Africa, many of whose people were brought to the United States as slaves.

derer, and no murderer hath eternal life abiding in him" (1 John 3.15). The first thing that takes our attention is the saying of Jesus, "Thou shalt love," etc. The first question I would ask my brethren in the ministry, as well as that of the membership: What is love, or its effects? Now, if they who teach are not essentially affected with pure love, the love of God, how can they teach as they ought? Again, the holy teachers of old said, "Now if any man have not the spirit of Christ, he is none of his" (Romans 8.9). Now, my brethren in the ministry, let me ask you a few sincere questions. Did you ever hear or read of Christ teaching his disciples that they ought to despise one because his skin was different from theirs? Jesus Christ being a Jew, and those of his Apostles certainly were not whites—and did not he who completed the plan of salvation complete it for the whites as well as for the Jews, and others? And were not the whites the most degraded people on the earth at that time? And none were more so, for they sacrificed their children to dumb idols![5] And did not St. Paul labor more abundantly for building up a Christian nation among you than any of the Apostles? And you know as well as I that you are not indebted to a principle beneath a white skin for your religious services but to a colored one.

What then is the matter now? Is not religion the same now under a colored skin as it ever was? If so, I would ask, why is not a man of color respected? You may say, as many say, we have white men enough. But was this the spirit of Christ and his Apostles? If it had been, there would not have been one white preacher in the world—for Jesus Christ never would have imparted his grace or word to them, for he could forever have withheld it from them. But we find that Jesus Christ and his Apostles never looked at the outward appearances. Jesus in particular looked at the hearts, and his Apostles through him, being discerners of the spirit, looked at their fruit without any regard to the skin, color, or nation; as St. Paul himself speaks, "Where there is neither Greek nor Jew, circumcision nor uncircumcision, Barbarian nor Scythian, bond nor free—but Christ is all, and in all" (Colossians 3.11). If you can find a spirit like Jesus Christ and his Apostles prevailing now in any of the white congregations, I should like to know it. I ask: Is it not the case that everybody that is not white is treated with contempt and counted as barbarians? And I ask if the word of God justifies the white man in so doing. When the prophets prophesied, of whom did they speak? When they spoke of heathens, was it not the whites and others who were counted Gentiles? And I ask if all nations with the exception of the Jews were not counted heathens. And according to the writings of some, it could not mean the Indians, for they are counted Jews.[6] And now I would ask: Why is all this distinction made among these Christian societies? I would ask: What is all this ado about missionary societies, if it be not to Christianize those who are not Christians? And what is it for? To degrade them worse, to bring them into society where they must welter out their days in disgrace merely because their skin is of a different complexion. What folly it is to try to make the state of human society worse than it is. How astonished some

5. The ancient Hebrews considered various Middle Eastern peoples idolators whose practices presumably included child sacrifice.

6. A reference to the (mistaken) notion that Native Americans were descended from the ten lost tribes of Israel.

may be at this—but let me ask: Is it not so? Let me refer you to the churches only. And, my brethren, is there any agreement? Do brethren and sisters love one another? Do they not rather hate one another? Outward forms and ceremonies, the lusts of the flesh, the lusts of the eye, and pride of life is of more value to many professors[7] than the love of God shed abroad in their hearts, or an attachment to his altar, to his ordinances, or to his children. But you may ask: Who are the children of God? Perhaps you may say, none but white. If so, the word of the Lord is not true.

I will refer you to St. Peter's precepts (Acts 10): "God is no respecter of persons," etc. Now if this is the case, my white brother, what better are you than God? And if no better, why do you, who profess his Gospel and to have his spirit, act so contrary to it? Let me ask why the men of a different skin are so despised. Why are not they educated and placed in your pulpits? I ask if his services well performed are not as good as if a white man performed them. I ask if a marriage or a funeral ceremony or the ordinance of the Lord's house would not be as acceptable in the sight of God as though he was white. And if so, why is it not to you? I ask again: Why is it not as acceptable to have men to exercise their office in one place as well as in another? Perhaps you will say that if we admit you to all of these privileges you will want more. I expect that I can guess what that is—Why, say you, there would be intermarriages. How that would be I am not able to say—and if it should be, it would be nothing strange or new to me; for I can assure you that I know a great many that have intermarried, both of the whites and the Indians—and many are their sons and daughters and people, too, of the first respectability. And I could point to some in the famous city of Boston and elsewhere. You may look now at the disgraceful act in the statute law passed by the legislature of Massachusetts, and behold the fifty-pound fine levied upon any clergyman or justice of the peace that dare to encourage the laws of God and nature by a legitimate union in holy wedlock between the Indians and whites. I would ask how this looks to your lawmakers. I would ask if this corresponds with your sayings—that you think as much of the Indians as you do of the whites. I do not wonder that you blush, many of you, while you read; for many have broken the ill-fated laws made by man to hedge up the laws of God and nature. I would ask if they who have made the law have not broken it—but there is no other state in New England that has this law but Massachusetts; and I think, as many of you do not, that you have done yourselves no credit.

But as I am not looking for a wife, having one of the finest cast, as you no doubt would understand while you read her experience and travail of soul in the way to heaven, you will see that it is not my object. And if I had none, I should not want anyone to take my right from me and choose a wife for me; for I think that I or any of my brethren have a right to choose a wife for themselves as well as the whites—and as the whites have taken the liberty to choose my brethren, the Indians, hundreds and thousands of them, as partners in life, I believe the Indians have as much right to choose their partners among the whites if they wish. I would ask you if you can see any-

7. I.e., those who profess the Christian faith.

thing inconsistent in your conduct and talk about the Indians. And if you do, I hope you will try to become more consistent. Now, if the Lord Jesus Christ, who is counted by all to be a Jew—and it is well known that the Jews are a colored people,[8] especially those living in the East, where Christ was born—and if he should appear among us, would he not be shut out of doors by many, very quickly? And by those too who profess religion?

By what you read, you may learn how deep your principles are. I should say they were skin-deep. I should not wonder if some of the most selfish and ignorant would spout a charge of their principles now and then at me. But I would ask: How are you to love your neighbors as yourself? Is it to cheat them? Is it to wrong them in anything? Now, to cheat them out of any of their rights is robbery. And I ask: Can you deny that you are not robbing the Indians daily, and many others? But at last you may think I am what is called a hard and uncharitable man. But not so. I believe there are many who would not hesitate to advocate our cause; and those too who are men of fame and respectability—as well as ladies of honor and virtue. There is a Webster, an Everett, and a Wirt,[9] and many others who are distinguished characters—besides a host of my fellow citizens, who advocate our cause daily. And how I congratulate such noble spirits—how they are to be prized and valued; for they are well calculated to promote the happiness of mankind. They well know that man was made for society, and not for hissing-stocks[1] and outcasts. And when such a principle as this lies within the hearts of men, how much it is like its God—and how it honors its Maker—and how it imitates the feelings of the Good Samaritan, that had his wounds bound up, who had been among thieves and robbers.

Do not get tired, ye noble-hearted—only think how many poor Indians want their wounds done up daily; the Lord will reward you, and pray you stop not till this tree of distinction shall be leveled to the earth, and the mantle of prejudice torn from every American heart—then shall peace pervade the Union.

1833

8. Referring to the belief that Moses and the biblical Hebrews, including Jesus, were people of color.

9. William Wirt (1772–1834), lawyer, politician, orator, and writer; he served as attorney general under President James Monroe and was nominated by the Whig Party for president. Daniel Webster (1782–1852), orator, legislator, statesman, and interpreter of the Constitution; he served as congressman from New Hampshire, senator from Massachusetts, and secretary of state under President William Henry Harrison. Edward Everett (1794–1865), the first Eliot Professor of Greek at Harvard and the editor of the prestigious *North American Review*; he served in Congress and as governor of Massachusetts.

1. Those who are laughed at or hissed at (i.e., laughingstocks).

JANE JOHNSTON SCHOOLCRAFT
1800–1842

Jane Johnston Schoolcraft, a mixed-blood, or *metis,* woman—her mother was Anishinabe or Chippewa/Ojibwe and her father was Irish—is the first known Native American literary writer. Although the Mohegan minister Samson Occom had written a short account of his life and published some sermons and hymns in the eighteenth century, and Schoolcraft's near contemporary the Pequot minister William Apess published accounts of his life, the lives of other Christian Indians, and a variety of historical and polemical texts, it is unlikely that either of them saw their writing as *literature.* Schoolcraft, however, wrote poems and short fiction. She published none of these in her lifetime, although her well-known husband, Henry Rowe Schoolcraft, did include some of her work—often heavily edited—in his own publications. It is only recently that an edition of Schoolcraft's writing has appeared, edited by Robert Dale Parker, to whose extensive research the editors are much indebted.

Jane Johnston's Ojibwe name was Bamewawagezhikaquay, "Woman of the Sound the Stars Make Rushing through the Sky." Her mother was Ozhagusodaywayquay, or Susan Johnston, and her father was John Johnston, an immigrant from Ireland. She was born at Sault Ste. Marie in what was then the extensive Michigan Territory (which included present-day Wisconsin and Minnesota). Her father was a fur trader who prospered not only from his own labor and acumen but from that of his wife and the kinship networks he could engage through her. The Johnston household was trilingual—Ojibwe, English, and French—and included a library that John Johnston had accumulated, containing the Greek and Roman classics, Shakespeare, historical and religious texts, and a range of contemporary authors. Much of Jane's education came from this library; except for a brief and unhappy period in Ireland and England when she was nine and ten, she had no formal schooling.

In 1822, Henry Rowe Schoolcraft arrived in the territory as the federally appointed agent in charge of Indian affairs. Henry was ambitious and a very eligible bachelor; Jane was a young woman of a prominent family and equally eligible. The two married in 1823. Henry was interested in Indians, but, like many whites in his time, he saw them as an inferior and vanishing race and certainly he did not see women as the equals of men. Nonetheless, there is much to suggest that—with some qualifications—the marriage was for the most part a happy one. Much of the writing Henry published on the Indians of the period benefited from Jane's help and the help of her mother's family. And Henry seems to have encouraged his wife's literary endeavors; indeed, if not for Henry, little of Jane's work would have survived.

Jane Schoolcraft's writing is of several kinds. From early in her life she composed poetry in English, frequently using iambic tetrameter lines, as well as the rhyme schemes and stanza forms conventional at the time. In 1827 her son William Henry Schoolcraft died at age two; she wrote, over a number of years, four poems commemorating his death. She thus joins a long line of women from Anne Bradstreet forward who grieved in verse over the loss of a young child. Schoolcraft is also the first known Indian writer to attempt literary composition in a Native language, as in "To the Pine Tree," which exists in an Ojibwe and an English version. "Lines Written at Castle Island" apparently had an Ojibwe original, which has not survived. Schoolcraft also wrote prose stories. It is not clear whether these were original compositions based on stories she had heard or somewhat nearer to literal translations of traditional material. Thus her work on the one hand fits well within the tradition of American antebellum women's poetry; on the other hand, it challenges our understanding of literary tradition by complicating our notions of such things as the distinction between translation and original composition as well as between poetry and prose.

The prose selections are from Robert Dale Parker, ed., *The Sound the Stars Make Rushing through the Sky: The Writings of Jane Johnston Schoolcraft* (2007) and the poetry selections are from a manuscript of Schoolcraft's poetry at the Abraham Lincoln Presidential Library in Springfield, Illinois.

Sweet Willy

A hundred moons and more have past,[1]
 Since erst upon this day,
They bore thee from my anguished sight,
 And from my home away
And pensively they carried thee
 And set the burial stone,
And left thy father and myself,
 Forsaken and alone.

A hundred moons and more have past
 And every year have we,
With pious steps gone out to sit
 Beneath thy graveyard tree
And often, with remembrance
 Of our darling little boy
Repeated—"they that sow in tears
 "Shall reap again in joy."[2]

Lo! children are a heritage
 A fruit and a reward,[3]
Bestowed in sovreign mercy
 By the fecit[4] of the Lord
But he, that giveth gifts to men
 May take away the same
And righteous is the holy act,
 And blessed be his name.

For still it is a mercy,
 And a mercy we can view,
For whom the Lord chastiseth
 He in love regardeth too.
And sweetly in remembrance
 Of our darling little boy
Bethink we still, that sorrow's tears
 Shall spring in beds of joy.

1. William Henry Schoolcraft died on March 13, 1827, at the age of two years and eight months. This line suggests that the poem was written sometime after the summer of 1835.

2. Psalm 126.5.

3. Psalm 127.3.

4. Made by or done (Latin). The sense is: by the act or deed of the Lord.

And aye, that Word is precious
  As the apple of the eye
That looketh up to mansions
  Which are builded in the sky
That palleth[5] with this scene of tears
  And vanities and strife,
And seeketh for that better home
  Where truly there is life.

I cling no more to life below,
  It hath no charm for me,
Yet strive to fill my duty here,
  While here below I be.
And often comes the memory
  Of my darling little boy,
For he was sown in bitter tears,
  And shall be reaped in joy.

To the Pine Tree[1]

on first seeing it
on returning from Europe

Shing wauk! Shing wauk! nin ge ik id,
Waish kee wau bum ug, shing wauk
Tuh quish in aun nau aub, ain dak nuk i yaun.
Shing wauk, shing wauk No sa
Shi e gwuh ke do dis au naun
Kau gega way zhau wus co zid.

Mes ah nah, shi egwuh tah gwish en aung
Sin dak mik ke aum baun
Kagait suh, ne meen wain dum
Me nah wau, wau bun dah maun
Gi yut wi au, wau bun dah maun een
Shing wauk, shing wauk no sa
Shi e gwuh ke do dis an naun.

Ka ween ga go, kau wau bun duh e yun
Tib ish co, izz henau gooz ze no an
Shing wauk wah zhau wush co zid
Ween Ait ah kwanaudj e we we
Kau ge gay wa zhau soush ko zid

5. Covers or shrouds; like a pall, the cloth that covers a coffin.

1. Schoolcraft had been taken to England and Ireland to be educated when she was nine. She was unhappy so far from home and at an unknown later date composed this poem. She addresses the pine tree in her Native language before offering an English version.

TRANSLATION

The pine! the pine! I eager cried,
The pine, my father! see it stand,
As first that cherished tree I spied,
Returning to my native land.
The pine! the pine! oh lovely scene!
The pine, that is forever green.

Ah beauteous tree! ah happy sight!
That greets me on my native strand
And hails me, with a friend's delight,
To my own dear bright mother land
Oh 'tis to me a heart-sweet scene,
The pine—the pine! that's ever green.

Not all the trees of England bright,
Not Erin's[2] lawns of green and light
Are half so sweet to memory's eye,
As this dear type of northern sky

Lines Written at Castle Island, Lake Superior[1]

1838

Here, in my native inland sea,
From pain and sickness would I flee
And from its shores and island bright,
Gather a store of sweet delight.
Lone islet of the saltless sea
How vast is all around—how free!
The waves come dashing clear and bright
The heavens are blue—the sky is bright
And all unites in sweetest strains
To tell, here nature only reigns.
Ah, nature, here forever sway
Far from the haunts of men away
For here there are no false displays,
No lures to lead in folly's maze
Or fashion's rounds to hurt or kill,
No laws to treat my people ill,
But all is glorious, free, and grand,
Fresh from the great Creator's hand.

2. Ireland's.

1. Schoolcraft did not know an Ojibwe name for this island and named it Castle Island. She apparently wrote the poem first in Ojibwe although no manuscript has been found.

Moowis, the Indian Coquette[1]

There was a village full of Indians, and a noted belle or *muh muh daw go qua* was living there. A noted beau or *muh muh daw go, nin nie* was there also. He and another young man went to court this young woman, and laid down beside her, when she scratched the face of the handsome beau. He went home and would not rise till the family prepared to depart, and he would not then arise. They then left him, as he felt ashamed to be seen even by his own relations. It was winter, and the young man, his rival, who was his cousin, tried all he could to persuade him to go with the family, for it was now winter, but to no purpose, till the whole village had decamped and had gone away. He then rose and gathered all the bits of clothing, and ornaments of beads and other things, that had been left. He then made a coat and leggins of the same, nicely trimmed with the beads, and the suit was fine and complete. After making a pair of moccasins, nicely trimmed, he also made a bow and arrows. He then collected the dirt of the village, and filled the garments he had made, so as to appear as a man, and put the bow and arrows in its hands, and it came to life. He then desired the dirt image to follow him to the camp of those who had left him, who thinking him dead by this time, were surprized to see him. One of the neighbors took in the dirt-man and entertained him. The belle saw them come and immediately fell in love with him. The family that took him in made a large fire to warm him, as it was winter. The image said to one of the children, "sit between me and the fire, it is too hot," and the child did so, but all smelt the dirt. Some said, "some one has trod on, and brought in dirt." The master of the family said to the child sitting in front of the guest, "get away from before our guest, you keep the heat from him." The boy answered saying, "he told me to sit between him and the fire." In the meantime, the belle wished the stranger would visit her. The image went to his master, and they went out to different lodges, the image going as directed to the belle[']s. Towards morning, the image said to the young woman (as he had succeeded) "I must now go away," but she said, "I will go with you." He said "it is too far." She answered, "it is not so far but that I can go with you." He first went to the lodge where he was entertained, and then to his master, and told him of all that had happened, and that he was going off with her. The young man thought it a pity she had treated him so, and how sadly she would be punished. They went off, she following behind. He left her a great way behind, but she continued to follow him. When the sun rose high, she found one of his mittens and picked it up, but to her astonishment, found it full of dirt. She, however took it up and wiped it, and going on further, she found the other mitten in the same condition. She thought, "fie!! why does he do so," thinking he dirtied in them. She kept finding different articles of his dress, on the way all day, in the same condition. He kept ahead of her till towards evening, when the snow was like

1. The text was printed in the *Literary Voyager* of 1827, by "Leelinau," one of Schoolcraft's pen names. The *Literary Voyager*, or *The Muzzeniegun* (Ojibwe for "book") was a handwritten journal that Henry Schoolcraft produced in the winter of 1826–27; it contained mainly his work but also the work of Jane and others. "Moowis": excrement, dirt. In other versions, the text has been sanitized; a sanitized version appears in Henry Wadsworth Longfellow's *Evangeline* (1847).

water, having melted by the heat of the day. No signs of her husband appearing, after having collected all the cloth[e]s that held him together, she began to cry, not knowing where to go, as their track was lost, on account of the snow's melting. She kept crying *Moowis* has led me astray, and she kept singing and crying Moowis nin ge won e win ig, ne won e win ig.[2]

The Little Spirit, or Boy-Man[1]

An Odjibwa Tale

There was once a little boy, remarkable for the smallness of his stature. He was living alone with his sister older than himself. They were orphans, and they lived in a beautiful spot on the Lake shore. Many large rocks were scattered around their habitation. The boy never grew larger as he advanced in years. One day in winter, he asked his sister to make him a ball to play with along shore on the clear ice. She made one for him but cautioned him not to go too far.—Off he went in high glee, throwing his ball before him and running after it at full speed and he went as fast as his ball. At last his ball flew to a great distance. He followed it as fast as he could. After he had run for some time, he saw four dark substances on the ice straight before him. When he came up to the spot he was surprised to see four large, tall men lying on the ice spearing fish. When he went up to them, the nearest looked up and in turn was surprised to see such a diminutive being, and turning to his brothers, he said, "Tia! look, see what a little fellow is here!" After they had all looked a moment, they resumed their position, covered their heads intent in searching for fish. The boy thought to himself, they imagine me too insignificant for common courtesy because they are tall and large. I shall teach them notwithstanding, that I am not to be treated so lightly. After they were covered up the boy saw they had each a large trout lying beside them. He slyly took the one nearest him and placing his fingers in the gills and tossing his ball before him ran off at full speed. When the man to whom the fish belonged looked up, he saw his trout sliding away as if of itself at a great rate, the boy being so small he was not distinguished from the fish. He addressed his brothers and said, "See how that tiny boy has stolen my fish; what a shame it is he should do so"—The boy reached home, and told his sister to go out and get the fish he had brought home. She exclaimed, "Where could you have got it? I hope you have not stolen it." "O! no," he replied, "I found it on the ice." "How," persisted the Sister, "could you have got it there?"—"No matter," said the boy, "go and cook it." He disdained to answer her again, but thought he would one day show her how to appreciate him. She went to the place he left it and there indeed she found a monstrous Trout. She did as she was bid and cooked it for that day's consumption.—Next morning he went off again as at first. When he came near the large men, who fished every day, he threw his ball with such force that it rolled into the ice-hole of the man of

2. You have led me astray, you are leading me astray (Ojibwe).

1. The text appears in the papers of Henry Schoolcraft in the Library of Congress in Jane's hand.

whom he had stolen the day before. As he happened to raise himself at the time, the boy said, "Nejee, pray hand me my ball." "No indeed" answered the man, "I shall not," and thrust the ball under the ice. The boy took hold of his arm and broke it in two in a moment and threw him to one side and picked up his ball which had bounded back from under the ice and tossed it as usual before him. Outstripping its speed, he got home and remained within till the next morning. The man whose arm he had broken hallooed out to his brothers and told them his case and deplored his fate. They hurried to their brother, and as loud as they could roar threatened vengeance on the morrow, knowing the boy's speed that they could not overtake him and he was near out of sight, yet he heard their threats and awaited their coming in perfect indifference. The four brothers the next morning prepared to take their revenge. Their old mother begged them not to go. "Better" said she, "one only should suffer, than that all should perish, for he must be a Monedo,[2] or he could not perform such feats," but her sons would not listen and taking their wounded brother along, started for the boy's lodge having learnt that he lived at the place of rocks. The boy's Sister thought she heard the noise of snow-shoes on the crusted snow at a distance. Advancing, she saw the large, tall men coming straight to their lodge, or rather cave for they lived in a large rock. She ran in with great fear and told her brother the fact. He said, "Why do you mind them? Give me something to eat." "How can you think of eating at such a time," she replied—"Do as I request you, and be quick." She then gave him his dish, which was a large *mis-qua-dace* shell and he commenced eating. Just then the men came to the door and were about lifting the curtain placed there when the boy-man turned his dish upside-down and immediately the door was closed with a stone. The men tried hard with their clubs to crack it; at length they succeeded in making a slight opening. When one of them peeped in with one eye, the boy-man shot his arrow into his eye and brain and he dropped down dead. The others not knowing what had happened to their brother did the same, and all fell in like manner. Their curiosity was so great to see what the boy was about so they all shared the same fate. After they were killed the boy-man told his sister to go out and see them; she opened the door but feared they were not dead and entered back again hastily and told her fears to her brother. He went out and hacked them in small pieces saying "Henceforth let no man be larger than you are now," so men became of the present size. When spring came on the boy-man said to his sister, "Make me a new set of arrows and bow." She obeyed, as he never did any thing himself of a nature that required manual labour. Though he provided for their sustenance, after she made them she again cautioned him not to shoot into the lake; but disregardless of all admonition, he on purpose shot his arrow into the Lake, and waded some distance till he got into deep water and paddled about for his arrow so as to attract the attention of his Sister. She came in haste to the shore calling him to return, but instead of minding her he called out, "Ma-mis-quan-ge-gun-a, be-nau-wa-con-zhe-shin," that is, "*You*, of the *red fins* come and swallow me." Immediately that monstrous fish came and swallowed him; and seeing his sister standing on the shore in despair he hallooed out to her, "Me-zush-ke-zin-ance." She wondered

2. Spirit, spirit power.

what he meant, but on reflection she thought it must be an old mockisin. She accordingly tied the old mockisin to a string and fastened it to a tree. The fish said to the Boy-man, under water, "What is that floating?" The Boy-man, said to the fish "Go, take hold of it, swallow it as fast as you can." The fish darted towards the old shoe and swallowed it. The Boy-man laughed in himself, but said nothing, till the fish was fairly caught. He then took hold of the line and began to pull himself and fish to shore. The Sister, who was watching, was surprised to see so large a fish, and hauling it ashore she took her knife and commenced cutting it open. When she heard her brother's voice inside of the fish, saying, "Make haste and release me from this nasty place," his sister was in such haste that she almost hit his head with her knife but succeeded in making an opening large enough for her Brother to get out. When he was fairly out, he told his sister to cut up the fish and dry it as it would last a long time for their sustenance, and said to her, never, never more to doubt his ability in any way. So ends the Story.

c. 1839

CAROLINE STANSBURY KIRKLAND
1801–1864

Caroline Kirkland's *A New Home—Who'll Follow? or, Glimpses of Western Life* (1839) is a pioneering work in American literary history, one of the earliest descriptions of life away from the settled East that refused to romanticize what was then thought of as "the West." Countering James Hall's *Legends of the West* (1833), Charles Fenno Hoffman's *A Winter in the West* (1835), and other popular works, Kirkland wrote what she called an "Emigrant's Guide" that was satirical, novelistic, and keenly interested in depicting the difficulties faced by women in the Michigan village she presents as something of a "mud-hole." As the critic Annette Kolodny has noted, *A New Home* had a key role in making "the west available for literary treatment by women," influencing such works as Margaret Fuller's *Summer on the Lakes* (1844) and later writings by women regionalist authors. However satirical her vision of life in the West, Kirkland saw great promise in the natural beauty and democratic potential of the new settlements, and thought women could play a particularly valuable role as western pioneers.

Kirkland was born in New York City on January 11, 1801, to a family that valued education and literature. Her maternal grandfather, the English-born Joseph Stansbury (1750–1809), became infamous during the American Revolution for his Loyalist verse satirizing the revolutionary cause; her mother, Eliza Alexander Stansbury, wrote poetry, fiction, and sketches. At the age of eight, Caroline Matilda Stansbury began her formal education at a school in Manhattan run by her father's sister, Lydia Mott; there she was educated in classical and modern languages. By the time she was a teenager, she was teaching classes in the school, and in 1822 she accepted a teaching position in Clinton, New York, at another school that was owned and managed by

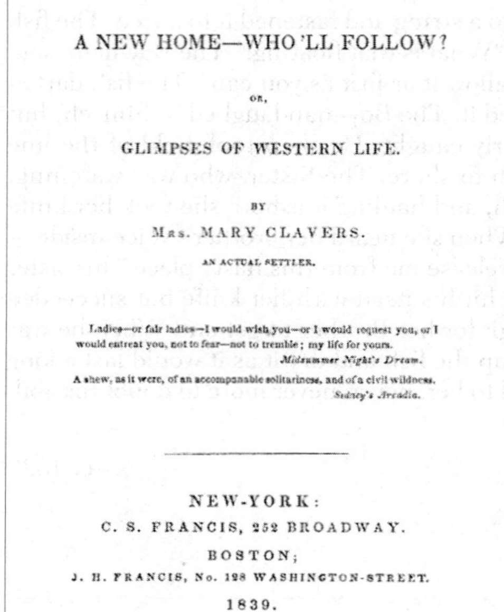

A NEW HOME—WHO'LL FOLLOW?

OR,

GLIMPSES OF WESTERN LIFE.

BY

MRS. MARY CLAVERS.

AN ACTUAL SETTLER.

Ladies—or fair ladies—I would wish you—or I would request you, or I would entreat you, not to fear—not to tremble; my life for yours.
Midsummer Night's Dream.

A shew, as it were, of an accompanable solitariness, and of a civil wildness.
Sidney's Arcadia.

NEW-YORK:
C. S. FRANCIS, 252 BROADWAY.
BOSTON;
J. H. FRANCIS, No. 128 WASHINGTON-STREET.
1839.

A New Home—Who'll Follow? Title page of the first edition.

the same aunt. There she met William Kirkland, a tutor at Hamilton College, whom she married in 1828. Together they founded a girl's school near Utica, New York, then moved to Detroit in 1835 to head the Detroit Female Seminary. In 1837 William bought eight hundred acres in Michigan Territory, much of it woodland and swamp, hoping that an upsurge of western emigration would push up land values and allow him to make a quick profit. Acquiring an additional five hundred acres from his father, he began developing a new village in the area, which he named Pinckney, while continuing to purchase land on speculation. Alternately bored and fascinated by life in Pinckney, Caroline Kirkland sent her eastern friends satirical letters about the community; and in 1839 she published the equally satirical *A New Home—Who'll Follow?* under the pseudonym of Mary Clavers. Blending realism and humor, Kirkland's book, which provided the comic perspective of a well educated woman struggling to run a household and keep her mind active in an isolated backwoods community, captured the attention of eastern readers and reviewers and angered some of her neighbors. She followed *A New Home* with a book that was more flatteringly descriptive of the Midwest, *Forest Life* (1843), a collection of sketches that Lydia Maria Child promptly serialized in the *National Anti-Slavery Standard*.

The Kirklands moved to New York City in 1843, in large part because William had been swindled out of his money by the land agent he had entrusted to develop his settlement. They both also missed the cosmopolitanism of the city. In New York, they taught and wrote for magazines. Some of Caroline Kirkland's magazine work went into *Western Clearings* (1845), which Evert A. Duyckinck chose as the first book by a woman in his Wiley & Putnam series, Library of American Books, along with books by Nathaniel Hawthorne, Edgar Allan Poe, Herman Melville, and others. In *Godey's Lady's Book* (August 1846), Poe acknowledged the impact Kirkland had made with her "picturesque description," "racy humor," and "animated individual portraiture" but insisted that her uniqueness lay in her realistic portrayal of the "veritable settlers of the forest, with all their peculiarities," so that eastern readers could become acquainted "with the *home* and home-life of the backwoodsman."

In 1846, just as Kirkland was establishing herself in New York literary circles, her husband died, leaving her to support their four children. She did so by taking on a variety of literary projects, including editing a magazine and publishing such works as *Holidays Abroad* (1849), *Personal Memoirs of George Washington* (1857), and *The School-Girl's Garland* (1864). Engaged with various social reforms, including abolitionism, she published an appeal for prison reform in 1853, *The Helping Hand. Comprising an Account of the Home for Discharged Female Convicts and an Appeal in Behalf of that Institution.* Kirkland's last philanthropic and patriotic efforts were devoted to improving conditions for injured soldiers during the Civil War; while working heroically in this cause she died suddenly of a stroke.

The text is that of the first edition, published in New York and Boston in 1839.

From A New Home—Who'll Follow? or, Glimpses of Western Life

Preface

I am glad to be told by those who live in the world, that it has lately become fashionable to read prefaces. I wished to say a few words, by way of introduction, to a work which may be deemed too slight to need a preface, but which will doubtless be acknowledged to require some recommendation.

I claim for these straggling and cloudy crayon-sketches of life and manners in the remoter parts of Michigan, the merit of general truth of outline. Beyond this I venture not to aspire. I felt somewhat tempted to set forth my little book as being entirely, what it is very nearly—a veritable history; an unimpeachable transcript of reality; a rough picture, in detached parts, but pentagraphed[1] from the life; a sort of "Emigrant's Guide:"—considering with myself that these my adventurous journeyings and tarryings beyond the confines of civilization, might fairly be held to confer the traveller's privilege. But conscience prevailed, and I must honestly confess, that there be glosses, and colourings, and lights, if not shadows, for which the author is alone accountable. Journals published entire and unaltered, should be Parthian[2] darts, sent abroad only when one's back is turned. To throw them in the teeth of one's every-day associates might diminish one's popularity rather inconveniently. I would desire the courteous reader to bear in mind, however, that whatever is quite unnatural, or absolutely incredible, in the few incidents which diversify the following pages, is to be received as literally true. It is only in the most commonplace parts (if there be comparisons) that I have any leasing-making[3] to answer for.

It will of course be observed that Miss Mitford's[4] charming sketches of village life must have suggested the form of my rude attempt. I dare not flatter myself that any one will be led to accuse me of further imitation of a deservedly popular writer. And with such brief salvo, I make my humble curtsey.

M. C.[5]

1. A pantograph is a mechanical instrument used to copy scale measurements onto a map.
2. Parthia was an ancient kingdom in western Asia known for its skilled warriors.
3. The stating of lies or libel.
4. Mary Russell Mitford (1787–1855), English writer who was best known for *Our Village* (1824–32), stories and sketches of country life collected in five small volumes.
5. On the title page, the author of *A New Home* is said to be "Mrs. Mary Clavers, An Actual Settler." Pen names were common at the time, though Kirkland may have used a pseudonym because she knew her book would anger her Michigan neighbors.

From *Chapter I*

Here are seen
No traces of man's pomp and pride; no silks
Rustle; nor jewels shine, nor envious eyes
Encounter * * * * *
Oh, there is not lost
One of earth's charms; upon her bosom yet
After the flight of untold centuries
The freshness of her far beginning lies.
BRYANT.[1]

* * *

When I made my first visit to these remote and lonely regions, the scattered woods through which we rode for many miles were gay in their first gosling-green suit of half-opened leaves, and the forest odours which exhaled with the dews of morning and evening, were beyond measure delicious to one "long in populous cities pent."[2] I desired much to be a little sentimental at the time, and feel tempted to indulge to some small extent even here—but I forbear; and shall adhere closely to matters more in keeping with my subject.

I think, to be precise, the time was the last, the very last of April, and I recollect well that even at that early season, by availing myself with sedulous application, of those times when I was fain to quit the vehicle through fear of the perilous mud-holes, or still more perilous half-bridged marshes, I picked upwards of twenty varieties of wild-flowers—some of them of rare and delicate beauty;—and sure I am, that if I had succeeded in inspiring my companion with one spark of my own floral enthusiasm, one hundred miles of travel would have occupied a week's time.

The wild flowers of Michigan deserve a poet of their own. Shelley, who sang so quaintly of "the pied wind-flowers and the tulip tall,"[3] would have found many a fanciful comparison and deep-drawn meaning for the thousand gems of the road-side. Charles Lamb[4] could have written charming volumes about the humblest among them. Bulwer would find means to associate the common three-leaved white lily so closely with the Past, the Present, and the Future—the Wind, the stars, and the tripod of Delphos, that all future botanists, and eke all future philosophers, might fail to unravel the "linked sweetness."[5] We must have a poet of our own.

Since I have casually alluded to a Michigan mud-hole, I may as well enter into a detailed memoir on the subject, for the benefit of future travellers, who, flying over the soil on rail-roads, may look slightingly back upon the achievements of their predecessors. In the "settlements," a mud-hole is considered as apt to occasion an unpleasant jolt—a breaking of the thread of one's reverie—or in extreme cases, a temporary stand-still or even an overturn of the rash or the unwary. Here, on approaching one of these characteristic features of the "West"—(How much does that expression mean to

1. From William Cullen Bryant's "A Forest Hymn" (1825).
2. From *Paradise Lost* (1667, 1674), 9.445, by John Milton (1608–1674).
3. From "The Sensitive Plant" (1820), by Percy Bysshe Shelley (1792–1822).
4. English essayist (1775–1834).
5. From Milton's "L'Allegro" (1631). Edward George Bulwer-Lytton (1803–1873), English historical novelist. Kirkland refers to symbols associated with the oracle at Delphi of Greek myth.

include? I never have been able to discover its limits)—the driver stops—alights—walks up to the dark gulf—and around it if he can get round it. He then seeks a long pole and sounds it, measures it across to ascertain how its width compares with the length of his wagon—tries whether its sides are perpendicular, as is usually the case if the road is much used. If he find it not more than three feet deep, he remounts cheerily, encourages his team, and in they go, with a plunge and a shock rather apt to damp the courage of the inexperienced. If the hole be narrow the hinder wheels will be quite lifted off the ground by the depression of their precedents, and so remain until by unwearied chirruping and some judicious touches of "the string" the horses are induced to struggle as for their lives; and if the fates are propitious they generally emerge on the opposite side, dragging the vehicle, or at least the fore wheels after them. When I first "penetrated the interior" (to use an indigenous phrase) all I knew of the wilds was from Hoffman's tour or Captain Hall's "graphic" delineations: I had some floating idea of "driving a barouche-and-four anywhere through the oak-openings"—and seeing "the murdered Banquos[6] of the forest" haunting the scenes of their departed strength and beauty. But I confess, these pictures, touched by the glowing pencil of fancy, gave me but incorrect notions of a real journey through Michigan.

Our vehicle was not perhaps very judiciously chosen;—at least we have since thought so. It was a light high-hung carriage—of the description commonly known as a buggy or shandrydan—names of which I would be glad to learn the etymology. I seriously advise any of my friends who are about flitting to Wisconsin or Oregon, to prefer a heavy lumber-wagon, even for the use of the ladies of the family; very little aid or consolation being derived from making a "genteel" appearance in such cases.

At the first encounter of such a mud-hole as I have attempted to describe, we stopped in utter despair. My companion indeed would fain have persuaded me that the many wheel tracks which passed through the formidable gulf were proof positive that it might be forded. I insisted with all a woman's obstinancy that I could not and would not make the attempt, and alighted accordingly, and tried to find a path on one side or the other. But in vain, even putting out of the question my paper-soled shoes—sensible things for the woods. The ditch on each side was filled with water and quite too wide to jump over; and we were actually contemplating a return, when a man in an immense bear-skin cap and a suit of deer's hide, sprang from behind a stump just within the edge of the forest. He "poled" himself over the ditch in a moment, and stood beside us, rifle in hand, as wild and rough a specimen of humanity as one would wish to encounter in a strange and lonely road, just at the shadowy dusk of the evening. I did *not* scream, though I own I was prodigiously frightened. But our stranger said immediately, in a gentle tone and with a French accent, "Me watch deer—you want to cross?" On receiving an answer in the affirmative, he ran in search of a rail which he threw over the terrific mud-hole—aided me to walk across by the help of his pole—showed my husband where to plunge—waited till he had gone safely through and

6. Banquo's ghost appears in Shakespeare's *Macbeth*. Charles Fenno Hoffman (1806–1884), author of *Winter in the West* (1835). James Hall (1793–1868), author of *Sketches of History, Life, and Manners in the West* (1834). Like Kirkland's, Hoffman's and Hall's books focus on what is now called the Midwest. "Oak-openings": clearings; described in Hoffman's *Winter in the West*.

"slow circles dimpled o'er the quaking mud"[7]—then took himself off by the way he came, declining any compensation with a most polite "rien, rien!"[8] This instance of true and genuine and generous politeness I record for the benefit of all bearskin caps, leathern jerkins and cowhide boots, which ladies from the eastward world may hereafter encounter in Michigan.

Our journey was marked by no incident more alarming than the one I have related, though one night passed in a wretched inn, deep in the "timbered land"—as all woods are called in Michigan—was not without its terrors, owing to the horrible drunkenness of the master of the house, whose wife and children were in constant fear of their lives, from his insane fury. I can never forget the countenance of that desolate woman, sitting trembling and with white, compressed lips in the midst of her children. The father raving all night, and coming through our sleeping apartment with the earliest ray of morning, in search of more of the poison already boiling in his veins. The poor wife could not forbear telling me her story—her change of lot—from a well-stored and comfortable home in Connecticut to this wretched den in the wilderness—herself and children worn almost to shadows with the ague, and her husband such as I have described him. I may mention here that not very long after I heard of this man in prison in Detroit, for stabbing a neighbour in a drunken brawl, and ere the year was out he died of delirium tremens, leaving his family destitute. So much for turning our fields of golden grain into "fire water"—a branch of business in which Michigan is fast improving.

Our ride being a deliberate one, I felt, after the third day, a little wearied, and began to complain of the sameness of the oak-openings and to wish we were fairly at our journey's end. We were crossing a broad expanse of what seemed at a little distance a smooth shaven lawn of the most brilliant green, but which proved on trial little better than a quaking bog—embracing within its ridgy circumference all possible varieties of

"Muirs, and mosses, slaps and styles"—

I had just indulged in something like a yawn, and wished that I could see our hotel. At the word, my companion's face assumed rather a comical expression, and I was preparing to inquire somewhat testily what there was so laughable—I was getting tired and cross, reader—when down came our good horse to the very chin in a bog-hole, green as Erin[9] on the top, but giving way on a touch, and seeming deep enough to have engulphed us entirely if its width had been proportionate. Down came the horse—and this was not all—down came the driver; and I could not do less than follow, though at a little distance—our good steed kicking and floundering—covering us with hieroglyphics, which would be readily decyphered by any Wolverine[1] we should meet, though perchance strange to the eyes of our friends at home. This mishap was soon amended. Tufts of long marsh grass served to assoilize[2] our habiliments a little, and a clear stream which rippled through the marsh aided in removing the eclipse from our faces. We journeyed on cheerily, watching the splendid changes in the west, but keeping a bright look-out for bog-holes.

* * *

7. From Pope's *Dunciad* (1728).
8. Nothing (French).
9. Ireland.
1. Longtime Michigan resident.
2. Cleanse.

Chapter XVI

Art thou so confident? within what space
Hop'st thou my cure?
All's well that ends well.[1]

Mr. Clavers[2] at length returned; and the progress of the village, though materially retarded by the obliquities of Mr. Mazard's course, was still not entirely at a stand. If our own operations were slow and doubtful, there were others whose building and improving went on at a rapid rate; and before the close of summer, several small tenements were enclosed and rendered in some sort habitable. A store and a public house were to be ready for business in a very short time.

I had the pleasure of receiving early in the month of September, a visit from a young city friend, a charming lively girl, who unaffectedly enjoyed the pleasures of the country, and whose taste for long walks and rides was insatiable. I curtained off with the unfailing cotton sheets a snow-white bower for her in the loft, and spread a piece of carpeting, a relic of former magnificence, over the loose boards that served for a floor. The foot square window was shaded by a pink curtain, and a bed-side chair and a candle-stand completed a sleeping apartment which she declared was perfectly delightful.

So smoothly flowed our days during that charming visit that I had begun to fear my fair guest would be obliged to return to ——— without a single adventure worth telling, when one morning as we sat sewing, Arthur ran in with a prodigious snake-story, to which, though we were at first disposed to pay no attention, we were at length obliged to listen.

"A most beautiful snake," he declared, "was coming up to the back door."

To the back door we ran; and there, to be sure, was a large rattle-snake, or massasauga; lazily winding its course towards the house, Alice standing still to admire it, too ignorant to fear.

My young friend snatched up a long switch, whose ordinary office was to warn the chickens from the dinner-table, and struck at the reptile which was not three feet from the door. It reared its head at once, made several attempts to strike, or spring, as it is called here, though it never really springs. Fanny continued to strike; and at length the snake turned for flight, not however without a battle of at least two minutes.

"Here's the axe, cousin Fanny," said Arthur, "don't let him run away!" and while poor I stood in silent terror, the brave girl followed, struck once ineffectually, and with another blow divided the snake, whose writhings turned to the sun as many hues as the windings of Broadway on a spring morning—and Fanny was a heroine.

It is my opinion that next to having a cougar spring at one, the absolute killing of a rattle-snake is peculiarly appropriate to constitute a Michigan heroine;—and the cream of my snake-story is, that it might be sworn to, chapter and verse, before the nearest justice. What cougar story can say as much?

1. Shakespeare, *All's Well that Ends Well* (1604), 2.1.159–60.

2. At this point in the narrative, the Clavers (Kirklands) have moved into a makeshift cabin. Mr. Mazard is the main designer and surveyor of the village. Mrs. Danforth is the proprietor of the local inn. Mrs. Jennings is working as the Clavers' domestic. The Jenkinses are neighbors. Arthur, Alice, and Bell are the children.

But the nobler part of the snake ran away with far more celerity than it had displayed while it "could a *tail* unfold," and we exalted the *coda* to a high station on the logs at the corner of the house—for fear none of the scornful sex would credit our prowess.

That snake absolutely haunted us for a day or two; we felt sure that there were more near the house, and our ten days of happiness seemed cut short like those of Seged,[3] and by a cause not very dissimilar. But the gloom consequent upon confining ourselves, children and all, to the house, in delicious weather, was too much for our prudence; and we soon began to venture out a little, warily inspecting every nook, and harassing the poor children with incessant cautions.

We had been watching the wheelings and flittings of a flock of prairie hens, which had alighted in Mr. Jenkins's corn-field, turning ever and anon a delighted glance westward at the masses of purple and crimson which make sunset so splendid in the region of the great lakes. I felt the dew, and warning all my companions, stepped into the house. I had reached the middle of the room, when I trod full upon something soft, which eluded my foot. I shrieked "a snake! a snake!" and fell senseless on the floor.

When I recovered myself I was on the bed, and well sprinkled with camphor, that never failing specific in the woods.

"Where is it?" said I, as soon as I could utter a word. There was a general smile. "Why, mamma," said Alice, who was exalted to a place on the bed, "dont you recollect that great toad that always sits behind the flour-barrel in the corner?"

I did not repent my fainting though it was not a snake, for if there is anything besides a snake that curdles the blood in my veins it is a toad. The harmless wretch was carried to a great distance from the house, but the next morning, there it sat again in the corner catching flies. I have been told by some persons here that they "liked to have toads in the room in fly time." Truly may it be said, "What's one man's meat———" Shade of Chesterfield,[4] forgive me!—but that any body *can* be willing to live with a toad! To my thinking nothing but a *toady* can be more odious.

The next morning I awoke with a severe head-ache, and racking pains in every bone. Dame Jennings said it was the *"agur."* I insisted that it could be nothing but the toad. The fair Fanny was obliged to leave us this day, or lose her escort home—a thing not to be risked in the wilderness. I thought I should get up to dinner, and in that hope bade her a gay farewell, with a charge to make the most of the snake story for the honour of the woods.

I did *not* get up to dinner, for the simple reason that I could not stand—and Mrs. Jennings consoled me by telling me every ten minutes, "Why, you've got th' agur! woman alive! Why, I know the fever-agur as well as I know beans! It a'n't nothin' else!"

3. In *The Rambler* (1750–52), the English writer Samuel Johnson (1709–1784) tells the fictional story of Seged, emperor of Ethiopia, who fails in his attempt to banish misery over a ten-day period.

4. Philip Dormer Stanhope, fourth earl of Chesterfield (1694–1771), was known for his sophistication and manners on account of his letters to his son (first published in 1774).

But no chills came. My pains and my fever became intense, and I knew but little about it after the first day, for there was an indistinctness about my perceptions, which almost, although not quite, amounted to delirium.

A physician was sent for, and we expected, of course, some village Galen,[5] who knew just enough to bleed and blister, for all mortal ills. No such thing! A man of first-rate education, who had walked European hospitals, and who had mother-wit in abundance, to enable him to profit by his advantages. It is surprising how many such people one meets in Michigan. Some, indeed, we have been led to suppose, from some traits in their American history, might have "left their country for their country's good:"—others appear to have forsaken the old world, either in consequence of some temporary disgust, or through romantic notions of the liberty to be enjoyed in this favoured land. I can at this moment call to mind, several among our ten-mile neighbours, who can boast University honours, either European or American, and who are reading men, even now. Yet one might pass any one of these gentlemen in the road without distinguishing between him and the Corydon[6] who curries his horses, so complete is their outward transformation.

Our medical friend, treated me very judiciously; and by his skill, the severe attack of rheumatic-fever, which my sunset and evening imprudences had been kindling in my veins, subsided after a week, into a daily ague; but Mrs. Jennings was not there to exult in this proof of her sagacity. She had been called away to visit a daughter, who had been taken ill at a distance from home, and I was left without a nurse.

My neighbours showed but little sympathy on the occasion. They had imbibed the idea that we held ourselves above them, and chose to take it for granted, that we did not need their aid. There were a good many cases of ague too, and, of course, people had their own troubles to attend to. The result was, that we were in a sad case enough. Oh! for one of those feminine men, who can make good gruel, and wash the children's faces! Mr. Clavers certainly did his best, and who can more? But the hot side of the bowl always *would* come to his fingers—and the sauce-pan *would* overset, let him balance it ever so nicely. And then—such hungry children! They wanted to eat all the time. After a day's efforts, he began to complain that stooping over the fire made him very dizzy. I was quite self-absorbed, or I should have noticed such a complaint from one who makes none without cause; but the matter went on, until, when I asked for my gruel, he had very nearly fallen on the coals, in the attempt to take it from the fire. He staggered to the bed, and was unable to sit up for many days after.

When matters reached this pitch—when we had, literally, no one to prepare food, or look after the children—little Bell added to the sick-list, too—our physician proved our good genius. He procured a nurse from a considerable distance; and it was through his means that good Mrs. Danforth heard of our sad condition, and sent us a maiden of all-work, who materially amended the aspect of our domestic affairs.

5. Greek physician and philosopher (130–200 C.E.) whose ideas permeated medical practices for centuries.

6. Conventional name for a shepherd in pastoral poetry.

Our agues were tremendous. I used to think I should certainly die in my ten or twelve hours' fever—and Mr. Clavers confidently asserted, several times, that the upper half of his head was taking leave of the lower. But the event proved that we were both mistaken; for our physician verified his own assertion, that an ague was as easily managed as a common cold, by curing us both in a short time after our illness had assumed the intermittent form. There is, however, one important distinction to be observed between a cold and the ague—the former does not recur after every trifling exertion, as the latter is sure to do. Again and again, after we seemed entirely cured, did the insidious enemy renew his attacks. A short ride, a walk, a drive of two or three miles, and we were prostrated for a week or two. Even a slight alarm, or any thing that occasioned an unpleasant surprise, would be followed by a chill and fever.

These things are, it must be conceded, very discouraging. One learns to feel as if the climate must be a wretched one, and it is not till after these first clouds have blown over, that we have resolution to look around us—to estimate the sunny skies of Michigan, and the ruddy countenances of its older inhabitants as they deserve.

The people are obstinately attached to some superstitious notions respecting agues. They hold that it is unlucky to break them. "You should let them run on," say they, "till they wear themselves out." This has probably arisen from some imprudent use of quinine, (or "Queen Ann,") and other powerful tonics, which are often taken before the system is properly prepared. There is also much prejudice against "Doctor's physic;"[7] while Lobelia, and other poisonous plants, which happen to grow wild in the woods are used with the most reckless rashness. The opinion that each region produces the medicines which its own diseases require, prevails extensively,—a notion which, though perhaps theoretically correct to a certain extent, is a most dangerous one for the ignorant to practise upon.

These agues are, as yet, the only diseases of the country. Consumption is almost unknown, as a Michigan evil. Indeed many, who have been induced to forsake the sea-board, by reason of too sensitive lungs, find themselves renovated after a year in the Peninsula. Our sickly season, from August till October, passed over without a single death within our knowledge.

To be sure, a neighbour told me, not long ago, that her old man had a complaint of "the lights," and that "to try to work any, gits his lights all up in a heap." But as this is a disease beyond the bounds of my medical knowledge, I can only "say the tale as 't was said to me," hoping, that none of my emigrating friends may find it contagious:—any disease which is brought on by *working*, being certainly much to be dreaded in this Western country!

7. I.e., a laxative.

Chapter XVII

The house's form within was rude and strong,
  Like an huge cave hewn out of rocky clift;
From whose rough vault the ragged breaches hung:—

* * *

And over them Arachne high did lift
  Her cunning web, and spread her subtle net,
Enwrapped in foul smoke, and clouds more black than jet.[1]
SPENCER.—*Faery Queene.*

It were good that men, in their innovations, would follow the example of time itself, which, indeed, innovateth greatly, but quietly, and by degrees scarce to be perceived. —BACON.[2]

It was on one of our superlatively doleful ague days, when a cold drizzling rain had sent mildew into our unfortunate bones; and I lay in bed, burning with fever, while my stronger half sat by the fire, taking his chill with his great-coat, hat, and boots on, that Mr. Rivers came to introduce his young daughter-in-law.[3] I shall never forget the utterly disconsolate air, which, in spite of the fair lady's politeness, would make itself visible in the pauses of our conversation. She *did* try not to cast a curious glance round the room. She fixed her eyes on the fire-place—but there were the clay-filled sticks, instead of a chimney-piece—the half-consumed wooden *crane*, which had, more than once, let our dinner fall—the Rocky-Mountain hearth, and the reflector, baking biscuits for tea—so she thought it hardly polite to appear to dwell too long there. She turned towards the window: there were the shelves, with our remaining crockery, a grotesque assortment! and, just beneath, the unnameable iron and tin affairs, that are reckoned among the indispensables, even of the half-civilized state. She tried the other side, but there was the ladder, the flour-barrel, and a host of other things—rather odd parlour furniture—and she cast her eyes on the floor, with its gaping cracks, wide enough to admit a massasauga[4] from below, and its inequalities, which might trip any but a sylph. The poor thing looked absolutely confounded, and I exerted all the energy my fever had left me, to try to say something a little encouraging.

"Come to-morrow morning, Mrs. Rivers," said I, "and you shall see the aspect of things quite changed; and I shall be able to tell you a great deal in favour of this wild life."

She smiled faintly, and tried not to look miserable, but I saw plainly that she was sadly depressed, and I could not feel surprised that she should be so. Mr. Rivers spoke very kindly to her, and filled up all the pauses in our forced talk with such cheering observations as he could muster.

He had found lodgings, he said, in a farm-house, not far from us, and his son's house would, ere long, be completed, when we should be quite near neighbours.

1. From Book II ("Temperance") of *The Faerie Queene* (1590), by the English poet Edmund Spenser (1522–1599).
2. From "Of Innovations," in *Essays or Counsels* (1625), by the English writer Francis Bacon (1561–1625).
3. The Rivers are neighbors, and Anna Rivers, whom Mary Clavers (Kirkland) takes under her wing, is newly arrived to the still-developing village.
4. Rattlesnake.

I saw tears swelling in the poor girl's eyes, as she took leave, and I longed to be well for her sake. In this newly-formed world, the earlier settler has a feeling of hostess-ship toward the new comer. I speak only of women—men look upon each one, newly arrived, merely as an additional business-automaton—a somebody more with whom to try the race of enterprize, i.e. money-making.

The next day Mrs. Rivers came again, and this time her husband was with her. Then I saw at a glance why it was that life in the wilderness looked so peculiarly gloomy to her. Her husband's face shewed but too plainly the marks of early excess;[5] and there was at intervals, in spite of an evident effort to play the agreeable, an appearance of absence, of indifference, which spoke volumes of domestic history. He made innumerable inquiries, touching the hunting and fishing facilities of the country around us, expressed himself enthusiastically fond of those sports, and said the country was a living death without them, regretting much that Mr. Clavers was not of the same mind.

Meanwhile I had begun to take quite an interest in his little wife. I found that she was as fond of novels and poetry, as her husband was of field-sports. Some of her flights of sentiment went quite beyond my sobered-down views. But I saw we should get on admirably, and so we have done ever since. I did not mistake that pleasant smile, and that soft sweet voice. They are even now as attractive as ever. And I had a neighbour.

Before the winter had quite set in, our little nest was finished, or as nearly finished as anything in Michigan; and Mr. and Mrs. Rivers took possession of their new dwelling, on the very same day that we smiled our adieux to the loggery.

Our new house was merely the beginning of a house, intended for the reception of a front-building, Yankee-fashion, whenever the owner should be able to enlarge his borders. But the contrast with our sometime dwelling, made even this humble cot seem absolutely sumptuous. The children could do nothing but admire the conveniences it afforded. Robinson Crusoe exulted not more warmly in his successive acquisitions than did Alice in "a kitchen, a real kitchen! and a pantry to put the dishes!" while Arthur found much to praise in the wee bed-room which was allotted as his sanctum in the "hic, hæc, hoc,"[6] hours. Mrs. Rivers, who was fresh from "the settlements," often curled her pretty lip at the deficiencies in her little mansion, but we had learned to prize any thing which was even a shade above the wigwam, and dreamed not of two parlours or a piazza.

Other families removed to Montacute[7] in the course of the winter. Our visiting list was considerably enlarged, and I used all my influence with Mrs. Rivers to persuade her that her true happiness lay in making friends of her neighbours. She was very shy, easily shocked by those sins against Chesterfield,[8] which one encounters here at every turn, did not conceal her

5. Throughout *A New Home*, Kirkland underscores the problem, particularly for women, of men's excessive drinking in the settlements.

6. Latin forms of "this." Having left their smaller older cabin, the "loggery," the Clavers' children Alice and Arthur have more room in their new house to study and play. "Robinson Crusoe": the shipwrecked hero of the English novelist Daniel Defoe's (c. 1661–1731) novel (1719).

7. The name Kirkland gives to the makeshift town, Pinckney, that William Kirkland is developing.

8. See p. 174, n. 4.

fatigue when a neighbour happened in after breakfast to make a three hours' call, forgot to ask those who came at one o'clock to take off their things and stay to tea, even though the knitting needles might peep out beneath the shawl. For these and similar omissions I lectured her continually but with little effect. It was with the greatest difficulty I could persuade her to enter any house but ours, although I took especial care to be impartial in my own visiting habits, determined at all sacrifice to live down the impression that I felt *above* my neighbours. In fact, however we may justify certain exclusive habits in populous places, they are strikingly and confessedly ridiculous in the wilderness. What can be more absurd than a feeling of proud distinction, where a stray spark of fire, a sudden illness, or a day's contre-temps, may throw you entirely upon the kindness of your humblest neighbour? If I treat Mrs. Timson with neglect to-day can I with any face borrow her broom to-morrow? And what would become of me, if in revenge for my declining her invitation to tea this afternoon, she should decline coming to do my washing on Monday?

It was as a practical corollary to these my lectures, that I persuaded Mrs. Rivers to accept an invitation that we received for the wedding of a young girl, the sister of our cooper, Mr. Whitefield. I attired myself in white, considered here as the extreme of festal elegance, to do honour to the occasion; and called for Mrs. Rivers in the ox-cart at two o'clock.

I found her in her ordinary neat home-dress; and it required some argument on my part to induce her to exchange it for a gay chally[9] with appropriate ornaments.

"It really seems ridiculous," she said, "to *dress* for such a place! and besides, my dear Mrs. Clavers, I am afraid we shall be suspected of a desire to outshine."

I assured her we were in more danger of that other and far more dangerous suspicion of undervaluing our rustic neighbours.

"I s'pose they did n't think it worth while to put on their best gowns for country-folks!"

I assumed the part of Mentor on this and many similar occasions; considering myself by this time quite an old resident, and of right entitled to speak for the natives.

Mrs. Rivers was a little disposed to laugh at the oxcart; but I soon convinced her that, with its cushion of straw overspread with a buffalo-robe, it was far preferable to a more ambitious carriage.

"No letting down of steps, no ruining one's dress against a muddy wheel! no gay horses tipping one into the gutter!"

She was obliged to acknowledge the superiority of our vehicle, and we congratulated ourselves upon reclining *à la* Lalla Rookh and Lady Mary Wortley Montague.[1] Certainly a cart is next to a palanquin.[2]

The pretty bride was in white cambric, worn over pink glazed muslin. The prodigiously stiff under-dress with its large cords (not more than three or

9. A woolen or silk dress.

1. English aristocrat and writer (1689–1762), known for her widely published letters from Turkey. "Lalla Rookh": the daughter of a Persian emperor and the heroine of a poem of that name (1817) by the Irish poet Thomas Moore (1779–1852).

2. Covered litter or couch typically carried on the shoulders of servants.

four years behind the fashion) gave additional slenderness to her taper waist, bound straitly with a sky-blue zone. The fair hair was decorated, not covered, with a cap, the universal adjunct of full dress in the country, placed far behind the ears, and displaying the largest puffs, set off by sundry gilt combs. The unfailing high-heeled prunelle shoe gave the finishing-touch, and the whole was scented, *à l'outrance*,[3] with essence of lemon.

After the ceremony, which occupied perhaps three minutes, fully twice as long as is required by our state laws, tea was served, absolutely handed on a salver, and by the master of the house, a respectable farmer. Mountains of cake followed. I think either pile might have measured a foot in height, and each piece would have furnished a meal for a hungry school-boy. Other things were equally abundant, and much pleasant talk followed the refreshments. I returned home highly delighted, and tried to persuade my companion to look on the rational side of the thing, which she scarcely seemed disposed to do, so *outre*[4] did the whole appear to her. I, who had begun to claim for myself the dignified character of a cosmopolite, a philosophical observer of men and things, consoled myself for this derogatory view of Montacute gentility, by thinking, "All city people are so cockneyish!"[5]

1839

3. Unsparingly (French).
4. Excessive, extreme (French).
5. Derogatory or comical term for working-class Londoners.

LYDIA MARIA CHILD
1802–1880

During a literary career that spanned fifty-five years, Lydia Maria Child published forty-seven books, including four novels and numerous uncollected short stories and essays. She wrote on behalf of women's rights and the rights of Native Americans and was among the most prominent antislavery writers of the nineteenth century. Her New York City newspaper column of the 1840s was read by thousands and helped to create new opportunities for women journalists in the United States. Hailed as "the first woman in the republic" by the abolitionist William Lloyd Garrison, Child inspired (and sometimes outraged) her readers while influencing such writers as Catharine Sedgwick, Margaret Fuller, Nathaniel Hawthorne, Fanny Fern, and William Wells Brown.

Child was born Lydia Francis on February 11, 1802, the youngest of the five surviving children of Susannah Rand and Convers Francis, a strict Calvinist and prosperous baker in the Boston suburb of Medford, Massachusetts. In 1814 her mother died of tuberculosis, and a year later she was sent to Norridgewock, Maine (at that time still a province of Massachusetts), to live with her married sister, Mary Francis Preston, and attend school. She returned to Massachusetts in 1821, moving in with her brother Convers Francis Jr., who had graduated from Harvard and was then an ordained Unitarian minister in Watertown, Massachusetts. At Convers's urging, in the summer of 1821 she was received into the Unitarian Church under a new name,

Lydia Maria Francis, thus formally breaking from her father's Calvinist heritage. Henceforth, she preferred to be known by her chosen name, Maria.

Child began her literary career in 1824 with the historical novel *Hobomok: A Tale of Early Times*, set in 1670s Salem, Massachusetts, during a time of war between the colonists and the Indians led by Metacom (also known as "King Philip"). The aspect of the novel that most caught her contemporaries' attention was its favorable representation of a marriage between the Wampanoag Indian Hobomok and the white heroine Mary Conant. The reviewer for the *North American Review* was appalled, proclaiming that the relationship was "not only unnatural, but revolting . . . to every feeling of delicacy in man or woman." Child took a safer route with her second historical novel, *The Rebels, or Boston before the Revolution* (1825). Despite the controversy surrounding *Hobomok*, the two works helped to secure Child's reputation as a leading novelist of the time.

In 1828 she married the lawyer and abolitionist David Child. His perpetual money problems strained the marriage and placed much of the responsibility for family finances on Maria Child. As editor of the *Juvenile Miscellany*, the nation's first successful children's magazine (founded by Maria Child in 1826), she had a small income, which she augmented through such popular domestic treatises as *The Frugal Housewife* (1829) and *The Mother's Book* (1831), the first handbook published in the United States on the stages of child-rearing. These popular works, while extolling women's important roles as homemakers and mothers, were also characterized by a concern for women's rights that culminated in her 1835 *History of the Condition of Women, in Various Nations and Ages*. Margaret Fuller, Elizabeth Cady Stanton, and many other feminists were inspired by this pathbreaking history. That same year Child published her third novel, *Philothea* (1835), set in classical Greece; it was greatly admired by Poe.

Child had written antislavery sketches and essays as early as 1824, but following her marriage to David Child and her introduction to Garrison in 1830, her politics became increasingly radical. She began publishing antislavery fiction in her *Juvenile Miscellany*; and in 1833 she published *An Appeal in Favor of That Class of Americans Called Africans*, the first full-scale analysis of slavery and race in the United States. In that book she adopted Garrison's abolitionist politics, calling for the immediate abolition of slavery in the South; she also attacked northern racism. At a time when radical abolitionism was distrusted in the North, Child bravely took risks and suffered the consequences. After publication of the *Appeal*, subscriptions to the *Juvenile Miscellany* fell so sharply that she had to give up editing the journal; moreover, the Boston Athenaeum withdrew her borrowing privileges. Nevertheless, Child remained true to her antislavery convictions, publishing *The Evils of Slavery, and the Cure for Slavery* in 1836, along with a number of antislavery essays and stories during the late 1830s and early 1840s, including "The Quadroons" (1842), which William Wells Brown liberally drew on for his 1853 antislavery novel *Clotel*.

Living apart from her husband for much of the 1840s (the couple had no children), Child moved to New York City in 1841 to edit the Garrisonian *National Anti-Slavery Standard*. Among features that she added to the paper was her column "Letters from New-York," which she initiated in the issue of August 19, 1841. In May 1843 she resigned from the editorship because of her weariness with factional debates within the newspaper; and in August 1843 she published at her own expense *Letters from New-York*, a collection of forty-eight of her columns. The first printing of fifteen hundred copies of *Letters* sold out by December, and over the next several years the book went through eleven printings, helping her win back the audience she had lost with *Appeal*. She wrote a similar column for the *Boston-Courier* and in 1845 published the equally popular *Letters from New York, Second Series*. In both volumes, Child provided revealing portraits of New York City as it was in the process of eclipsing Boston as the nation's leading urban center. Addressing such topics as poverty among women and children, popular entertainment, street life, the history of New

York City, temperance reform, technological change, and capital punishment, the "Letters" were held together by Child's belief in the redemptive power of religion, sympathy, and the values associated with domesticity. This middle-class perspective on the special status of feminine values was a powerful spur to all kinds of nineteenth-century reforms and remained an impetus to feminism throughout the nineteenth and twentieth centuries. The journalism of Margaret Fuller and Fanny Fern was informed by a similar sense that women could make a distinctive impact on the culture, and owed a considerable debt to Child's pioneering efforts to examine the full range of urban life.

By the mid-1840s Child had stopped working for antislavery societies, but her antislavery writing continued unabated, as did her writing on a variety of other topics. She published a collection of her short fiction, *Fact and Fiction* (1846); several children's books; a biography of the Quaker abolitionist Isaac T. Hopper (1853); a three-volume comparative history of religion, *The Progress of Religious Ideas* (1855); and a second volume of short stories, *Autumnal Leaves* (1856). As sectional tensions intensified during the 1850s, Child engaged the slavery conflict with a new vigor, publishing antislavery works in the *New York Tribune* and the antislavery periodical *Liberty Bell* and also the tracts *The Patriarchal Institution* (1860) and *The Duty of Disobedience to the Fugitive Slave Law* (1860). Her most widely read text, *Correspondence between Lydia Maria Child and Gov. Wise and Mrs. Mason*, was also published in 1860 and sold over three hundred thousand copies. In *Correspondence*, Child defended John Brown, who had raided a federal arsenal in Virginia in 1859 with the hope of inspiring a slave revolt. Later in 1860 Child helped Harriet Jacobs edit her slave narrative, *Incidents in the Life of a Slave Girl* (1861), and arranged for its publication.

The abolition of slavery was a personal triumph for Child. In an effort to help newly freed blacks rise in the culture, she published *The Freedman's Book* (1865), a reader with selections by white and black writers about the achievements of people of African descent. Even at this promising moment, however, Child remained concerned about the persistence of whites' antiblack racial prejudice. In 1867 she published her fourth and final novel, *The Romance of the Republic*, which, in the tradition of *Hobomok*, presented interracial marriage as a possible solution to the problem of racial conflict in the United States. One year later, in *An Appeal for the Indians*, she called for social justice for the nation's Native Americans. In 1870, Child and her husband attended a ritual closing meeting of the Massachusetts Antislavery Society; David Child died four years later. Lydia Maria Child's final publication in her lifetime was an appreciation of Garrison in the August 1879 issue of the *Atlantic Monthly*. She died of a heart attack in Wayland, Massachusetts, on October 20, 1880. Shortly after her death, her friends brought out a volume of her collected letters. The reviewer for the *New York Times* spoke for Child's many admirers: "Here was a most remarkable woman, one who lived a great life, but lived it so simply and with such limited consideration for herself that the more you study it the more it grows to be perhaps the truest life that an American woman has yet lived."

The Quadroons[1]

> "I promised thee a sister tale
> Of man's perfidious cruelty;
> Come then and hear what cruel wrong
> Befell the dark Ladie." —*Coleridge*.[2]

Not far from Augusta, Georgia, there is a pleasant place called Sand-Hills, appropriated almost exclusively to summer residences for the wealthy inhabitants of the neighboring city. Among the beautiful cottages that adorn it was one far retired from the public roads, and almost hidden among the trees. It was a perfect model of rural beauty. The piazzas that surrounded it were covered with Clematis and Passion flower. The Pride of China mixed its oriental-looking foliage with the majestic magnolia, and the air was redolent with the fragrance of flowers, peeping out from every nook, and nodding upon you in bye places, with a most unexpected welcome. The tasteful hand of Art had not learned to *imitate* the lavish beauty and harmonious disorder of Nature, but they lived together in loving unity, and spoke in according tones. The gateway rose in a Gothic arch, with graceful tracery in iron-work, surmounted by a Cross, around which fluttered and played the Mountain Fringe, that lightest and most fragile of vines.

The inhabitants of this cottage remained in it all the year round; and perhaps enjoyed most the season that left them without neighbors. To one of the parties, indeed, the fashionable summer residents, that came and went with the butterflies, were merely neighbors-in-law. The edicts of society had built up a wall of separation between her and them; for she was a quadroon;[3] the daughter of a wealthy merchant of New Orleans, highly cultivated in mind and manners, graceful as an antelope, and beautiful as the evening star. She had early attracted the attention of a handsome and wealthy young Georgian; and as their acquaintance increased, the purity and bright intelligence of her mind, inspired him with a far deeper sentiment than belongs merely to excited passion. It was in fact Love in its best sense—that most perfect landscape of our complex nature, where earth everywhere kisses the sky, but the heavens embrace all; and the lowliest dew-drop reflects the image of the highest star.

The tenderness of Rosalie's conscience required an outward form of marriage; though she well knew that a union with her proscribed race was unrecognised by law, and therefore the ceremony gave her no legal hold on Edward's constancy. But her high, poetic nature regarded the reality rather than the semblance of things; and when he playfully asked how she could keep him if he wished to run away, she replied, "Let the church that my mother loved sanction our union, and my own soul will be satisfied, without the protection of the state. If your affections fall from me, I would not, if I could, hold you by a legal fetter."

1. First printed in the antislavery compendium *The Liberty Bell* (1842), the source of the text printed here. Child later reprinted the story in her *Fact and Fiction: A Collection of Stories* (1846).
2. From "Introduction to the Tale of the Dark Ladie" (1799), by the English poet Samuel T. Coleridge (1772–1834).
3. Term used in the nineteenth century (less often in the twentieth century) for people thought to be one-fourth black; more generally, "quadroon," like "mulatto," was used for light-skinned people of mixed racial ancestry.

It was a marriage sanctioned by Heaven, though unrecognised on earth. The picturesque cottage at Sand-Hills was built for the young bride under her own directions; and there they passed ten as happy years as ever blessed the heart of mortals. It was Edward's fancy to name their eldest child Xarifa; in commemoration of a Spanish song,[4] which had first conveyed to his ears the sweet tones of her mother's voice. Her flexile form and nimble motions were in harmony with the breezy sound of the name; and its Moorish[5] origin was most appropriate to one so emphatically "a child of the sun." Her complexion, of a still lighter brown than Rosalie's, was rich and glowing as an autumnal leaf. The iris of her large, dark eye had the melting, mezzotinto[6] outline, which remains the last vestige of African ancestry, and gives that plaintive expression, so often observed, and so appropriate to that docile and injured race.

Xarifa learned no lessons of humility or shame, within her own happy home; for she grew up in the warm atmosphere of father's and mother's love, like a flower open to the sunshine, and sheltered from the winds. But in summer walks with her beautiful mother, her young cheek often mantled at the rude gaze of the young men, and her dark eye flashed fire, when some contemptuous epithet met her ear, as white ladies passed them by, in scornful pride and ill-concealed envy.

Happy as Rosalie was in Edward's love, and surrounded by an outward environment of beauty, so well adapted to her poetic spirit, she felt these incidents with inexpressible pain. For herself, she cared but little; for she had found a sheltered home in Edward's heart, which the world might ridicule, but had no power to profane. But when she looked at her beloved Xarifa, and reflected upon the unavoidable and dangerous position which the tyranny of society had awarded her, her soul was filled with anguish. The rare loveliness of the child increased daily, and was evidently ripening into most marvellous beauty. The father rejoiced in it with unmingled pride; but in the deep tenderness of the mother's eye there was an indwelling sadness, that spoke of anxious thoughts and fearful foreboding.

When Xarifa entered her ninth year, these uneasy feelings found utterance in earnest solicitations that Edward would remove to France, or England.[7] This request excited but little opposition, and was so attractive to his imagination, that he might have overcome all intervening obstacles, had not "a change come o'er the spirit of his dream."[8] He still loved Rosalie; but he was now twenty-eight years old, and, unconsciously to himself, ambition had for some time been slowly gaining an ascendency over his other feelings. The contagion of example had led him into the arena where so much American strength is wasted; he had thrown himself into political excitement, with all the honest fervor of youthful feeling. His motives had been unmixed with selfishness, nor could he ever define to himself when or how sincere patrio-

4. In the 15th-century Spanish ballad "The Bride of Andalla" (translated into English by John Gibson Lockhart), Xarifa is a "Moorish maiden." The name means "a learned woman" in Arabic.
5. In the style of the Moors—Muslims of northwest Africa known for their art and architecture—and associated with Morocco.
6. Literally, a half tint between whiteness and blackness (Italian).
7. Many American abolitionists believed that attitudes about race were more enlightened in Europe than in the United States. Slavery was abolished in the British Empire in 1834, and France ended slavery in its colonies in 1848.
8. From "The Dream" (1816), by the English poet Lord Byron (1788–1824).

tism took the form of personal ambition. But so it was, that at twenty-eight years old, he found himself an ambitious man, involved in movements which his frank nature would have once abhorred, and watching the doubtful game of mutual cunning with all the fierce excitement of a gambler.

Among those on whom his political success most depended was a very popular and wealthy man, who had an only daughter. His visits to the house were at first of a purely political nature; but the young lady was pleasing, and he fancied he discovered in her a sort of timid preference for himself. This excited his vanity, and awakened thoughts of the great worldly advantages connected with a union. Reminiscences of his first love kept these vague ideas in check for several months; but Rosalie's image at last became an unwelcome intruder; for with it was associated the idea of restraint. Moreover Charlotte, though inferior in beauty, was yet a pretty contrast to her rival. Her light hair fell in silken profusion, her blue eyes were gentle, though inexpressive, and her healthy cheeks were like opening rose-buds.

He had already become accustomed to the dangerous experiment of resisting his own inward convictions; and this new impulse to ambition, combined with the strong temptation of variety in love, met the ardent young man weakened in moral principle, and unfettered by laws of the land. The change wrought upon him was soon noticed by Rosalie.

> "In many ways does the full heart reveal
> The presence of the love it would conceal;
> But in far more the estranged heart lets know
> The absence of the love, which yet it fain would show."[9]

At length the news of his approaching marriage met her ear. Her head grew dizzy, and her heart fainted within her; but, with a strong effort at composure, she inquired all the particulars; and her pure mind at once took its resolution. Edward came that evening, and though she would have fain met him as usual, her heart was too full not to throw a deep sadness over her looks and tones. She had never complained of his decreasing tenderness, or of her own lonely hours; but he felt that the mute appeal of her heart-broken looks was more terrible than words. He kissed the hand she offered, and with a countenance almost as sad as her own, led her to a window in the recess shadowed by a luxuriant Passion Flower. It was the same seat where they had spent the first evening in this beautiful cottage, consecrated to their youthful loves. The same calm, clear moonlight looked in through the trellis. The vine then planted had now a luxuriant growth; and many a time had Edward fondly twined its sacred blossoms with the glossy ringlets of her raven hair. The rush of memory almost overpowered poor Rosalie; and Edward felt too much oppressed and ashamed to break the long, deep silence. At length, in words scarcely audible, Rosalie said, "Tell me, dear Edward, are you to be married next week?" He dropped her hand, as if a rifle-ball had struck him; and it was not until after long hesitation, that he began to make some reply about the necessity of circumstances. Mildly, but earnestly, the poor girl begged him to spare apologies. It was enough that he no longer loved her, and that they must bid farewell. Trusting to the yielding tenderness of her character, he ventured, in the most

9. From Coleridge's "Prose in Rhyme" (1828).

soothing accents, to suggest that as he still loved her better than all the world, she would ever be his real wife, and they might see each other frequently. He was not prepared for the storm of indignant emotion his words excited. Hers was a passion too absorbing to admit of partnership; and her spirit was too pure to form a selfish league with crime.

At length this painful interview came to an end. They stood together by the Gothic gate, where they had so often met and parted in the moonlight. Old remembrances melted their souls. "Farewell, dearest Edward," said Rosalie. "Give me a parting kiss." Her voice was choked for utterance, and the tears flowed freely, as she bent her lips toward him. He folded her convulsively in his arms, and imprinted a long, impassioned kiss on that mouth, which had never spoken to him but in love and blessing.

With effort like a death-pang, she at length raised her head from his heaving bosom, and turning from him with bitter sobs, she said, "It is our *last*. To meet thus is henceforth crime. God bless you. I would not have you so miserable as I am. Farewell. A *last* farewell." "The *last!*" exclaimed he, with a wild shriek. "Oh God, Rosalie, do not say that!" and covering his face with his hands, he wept like a child.

Recovering from his emotion, he found himself alone. The moon looked down upon him mild, but very sorrowful; as the Madonna seems to gaze on her worshipping children, bowed down with consciousness of sin. At that moment he would have given worlds to have disengaged himself from Charlotte; but he had gone so far, that blame, disgrace, and duels with angry relatives, would now attend any effort to obtain his freedom. Oh, how the moonlight oppressed him with its friendly sadness! It was like the plaintive eye of his forsaken one,—like the music of sorrow echoed from an unseen world.

Long and earnestly he gazed at that dwelling, where he had so long known earth's purest foretaste of heavenly bliss. Slowly he walked away; then turned again to look on that charmed spot, the nestling-place of his young affections. He caught a glimpse of Rosalie, weeping beside a magnolia, which commanded a long view of the path leading to the public road. He would have sprung toward her, but she darted from him, and entered the cottage. That graceful figure, weeping in the moonlight, haunted him for years. It stood before his closing eyes, and greeted him with the morning dawn.

Poor Charlotte! had she known all, what a dreary lot would hers have been; but fortunately, she could not miss the impassioned tenderness she had never experienced; and Edward was the more careful in his kindness, because he was deficient in love. Once or twice she heard him murmur, "dear Rosalie," in his sleep; but the playful charge she brought was playfully answered, and the incident gave her no real uneasiness. The summer after their marriage, she proposed a residence at Sand-Hills; little aware what a whirlwind of emotion she excited in her husband's heart. The reasons he gave for rejecting the proposition appeared satisfactory; but she could not quite understand why he was never willing that their afternoon drives should be in the direction of those pleasant rural residences, which she had heard him praise so much. One day, as their barouche[1] rolled along a wind-

1. A four-wheeled carriage with facing double seats and a seat for the driver.

ing road that skirted Sand-Hills, her attention was suddenly attracted by two figures among the trees by the way-side; and touching Edward's arm, she exclaimed, "Do look at that beautiful child!" He turned, and saw Rosalie and Xarifa. His lips quivered, and his face became deadly pale. His young wife looked at him intently, but said nothing. There were points of resemblance in the child, that seemed to account for his sudden emotion. Suspicion was awakened, and she soon learned that the mother of that lovely girl bore the name of Rosalie; with this information came recollections of the "dear Rosalie," murmured in uneasy slumbers. From gossiping tongues she soon learned more than she wished to know. She wept, but not as poor Rosalie had done, for she never had loved, and been beloved, like her; and her nature was more proud. Henceforth a change came over her feelings and her manners; and Edward had no further occasion to assume a tenderness in return for hers. Changed as he was by ambition, he felt the wintry chill of her polite propriety, and sometimes in agony of heart, compared it with the gushing love of her who was indeed his wife.

But these, and all his emotions, were a sealed book to Rosalie, of which she could only guess the contents. With remittances for her and her child's support, there sometimes came earnest pleadings that she would consent to see him again; but these she never answered, though her heart yearned to do so. She pitied his fair young bride, and would not be tempted to bring sorrow into her household by any fault of hers. Her earnest prayer was that she might never know of her existence. She had not looked on Edward since she watched him under the shadow of the magnolia, until his barouche passed her in her rambles some months after. She saw the deadly paleness of his countenance, and had he dared to look back, he would have seen her tottering with faintness. Xarifa brought water from a little rivulet, and sprinkled her face. When she revived, she clasped the beloved child to her heart with a vehemence that made her scream. Soothingly she kissed away her fears, and gazed into her beautiful eyes with a deep, deep sadness of expression, which Xarifa never forgot. Wild were the thoughts that pressed around her aching heart, and almost maddened her poor brain; thoughts which had almost driven her to suicide the night of that last farewell. For her child's sake she conquered the fierce temptation then; and for her sake, she struggled with it now. But the gloomy atmosphere of their once happy home overclouded the morning of Xarifa's life.

> "She from her mother learnt the trick of grief,
> And sighed among her playthings."[2]

Rosalie perceived this; and it gave her gentle heart unutterable pain. At last, the conflicts of her spirit proved too strong for the beautiful frame in which it dwelt. About a year after Edward's marriage, she was found dead in her bed, one bright autumnal morning. She had often expressed to her daughter a wish to be buried under a spreading oak, that shaded a rustic garden-chair, in which she and Edward had spent many happy evenings. And there she was buried; with a small white cross at her head, twined with the cypress vine. Edward came to the funeral, and wept long, very long, at

2. From *The Excursion* (1814), by the English poet William Wordsworth (1770–1850).

the grave. Hours after midnight, he sat in the recess-window, with Xarifa folded to his heart. The poor child sobbed herself to sleep on his bosom; and the convicted murderer had small reason to envy that wretched man, as he gazed on the lovely countenance, that so strongly reminded him of his early and his only love.

From that time, Xarifa was the central point of all his warmest affections. He employed an excellent old negress to take charge of the cottage, from which he promised his darling child that she should never be removed. He employed a music master, and dancing master, to attend upon her; and a week never passed without a visit from him, and a present of books, pictures, or flowers. To hear her play upon the harp, or repeat some favorite poem in her mother's earnest accents and melodious tones, or to see her flexile figure float in the garland-dance, seemed to be the highest enjoyment of his life. Yet was the pleasure mixed with bitter thoughts. What would be the destiny of this fascinating young creature, so radiant with life and beauty? She belonged to a proscribed race; and though the brown color on her soft cheek was scarcely deeper than the sunny side of a golden pear, yet was it sufficient to exclude her from virtuous society. He thought of Rosalie's wish to carry her to France; and he would have fulfilled it, had he been unmarried. As it was, he inwardly resolved to make some arrangement to effect it, in a few years, even if it involved separation from his darling child.

But alas for the calculations of man! From the time of Rosalie's death, Edward had sought relief for his wretched feelings in the free use of wine. Xarifa was scarcely fifteen, when her father was found dead by the road-side; having fallen from his horse, on his way to visit her. He left no will; but his wife with kindness of heart worthy of a happier domestic fate, expressed a decided reluctance to change any of the plans he had made for the beautiful child at Sand-Hills.

Xarifa mourned her indulgent father; but not as one utterly desolate. True she had lived "like a flower deep hid in rocky cleft;"[3] but the sunshine of love had already peeped in upon her. Her teacher on the harp was a handsome and agreeable young man of twenty, the only son of an English widow. Perhaps Edward had not been altogether unmindful of the result, when he first invited him to the flowery cottage. Certain it is, he had more than once thought what a pleasant thing it would be, if English freedom from prejudice should lead him to offer legal protection to his graceful and winning child. Being thus encouraged, rather than checked, in his admiration, George Elliot could not be otherwise than strongly attracted toward his beautiful pupil. The lonely and unprotected state in which her father's death left her, deepened this feeling into tenderness. And lucky was it for her enthusiastic and affectionate nature; for she could not live without an atmosphere of love. In her innocence, she knew nothing of the dangers in her path; and she trusted George with an undoubting simplicity, that rendered her sacred to his noble and generous soul. It seemed as if that flower-embosomed nest was consecrated by the Fates to Love. The French have well named it *La Belle Passion*; for without it life were "a year without spring, or a spring without roses."[4] Except the loveliness of infancy, what

3. From "A Poem on the Death of Charlotte Princess of Wales," by the English poet Rann Kennedy (1772–1851).

4. Francis I, king of France (1494–1547), is reputed to have said that "a court without ladies is a year without spring, or a spring without roses."

does earth offer so much like Heaven, as the happiness of two young, pure, and beautiful beings, living in each other's hearts?

Xarifa inherited her mother's poetic and impassioned temperament; and to her, above others, the first consciousness of these sweet emotions was like a golden sunrise on the sleeping flowers.

> "Thus stood she at the threshold of the scene
> Of busy life.
>
> * * *
>
> How fair it lay in solemn shade and sheen!
> And he beside her, like some angel, posted
> To lead her out of childhood's fairy land,
> On to life's glancing summit, hand in hand."[5]

Alas, the tempest was brooding over their young heads. Rosalie, though she knew it not, had been the daughter of a slave; whose wealthy master, though he remained attached to her to the end of her days, had carelessly omitted to have papers of manumission recorded. His heirs had lately failed, under circumstances, which greatly exasperated their creditors; and in an unlucky hour, they discovered their claim on Angelique's grand-child.

The gentle girl, happy as the birds in springtime, accustomed to the fondest indulgence, surrounded by all the refinements of life, timid as a young fawn, and with a soul full of romance, was ruthlessly seized by a sheriff, and placed on the public auction-stand in Savannah. There she stood, trembling, blushing, and weeping; compelled to listen to the grossest language, and shrinking from the rude hands that examined the graceful proportions of her beautiful frame. "Stop that," exclaimed a stern voice, "I bid two thousand dollars for her, without asking any of their d—d questions." The speaker was probably about forty years of age, with handsome features, but a fierce and proud expression. An older man, who stood behind him, bid two thousand five hundred. The first bid higher; then a third, a dashing young man, bid three thousand; and thus they went on, with the keen excitement of gamblers, until the first speaker obtained the prize, for the moderate sum of five thousand dollars.

And where was George, during this dreadful scene? He was absent on a visit to his mother, at Mobile. But, had he been at Sand-Hills, he could not have saved his beloved from the wealthy profligate, who was determined to obtain her at any price. A letter of agonized entreaty from her brought him home on the wings of the wind. But what could he do? How could he ever obtain a sight of her, locked up as she was in the princely mansion of her master? At last by bribing one of the slaves, he conveyed a letter to her, and received one in return. As yet, her purchaser treated her with respectful gentleness, and sought to win her favor, by flattery and presents; but she dreaded every moment, lest the scene should change, and trembled at the sound of every footfall. A plan was laid for escape. The slave agreed to drug his master's wine; a ladder of ropes was prepared, and a swift boat was in readiness. But the slave, to obtain a double reward, was treacherous. Xarifa had scarcely given an answering signal to the low, cautious whistle of her

5. From *The Death of Wallenstein* (1799), a play by the German author Friedrich Schiller (1759–1805).

lover, when the sharp sound of a rifle was followed by a deep groan, and a heavy fall on the pavement of the court-yard. With frenzied eagerness she swung herself down by the ladder of ropes, and, by the glancing light of lanthorns,[6] saw George, bleeding and lifeless at her feet. One wild shriek, that pierced the brains of those who heard it, and she fell senseless by his side.

For many days she had a confused consciousness of some great agony, but knew not where she was, or by whom she was surrounded. The slow recovery of her reason settled into the most intense melancholy, which moved the compassion even of her cruel purchaser. The beautiful eyes, always pleading in expression, were now so heart-piercing in their sadness, that he could not endure to look upon them. For some months, he sought to win her smiles by lavish presents, and delicate attentions. He bought glittering chains of gold, and costly bands of pearl. His victim scarcely glanced at them, and the slave laid them away, unheeded and forgotten. He purchased the furniture of the cottage at Sand-Hills, and one morning Xarifa found her harp at the bed-side, and the room filled with her own books, pictures, and flowers. She gazed upon them with a pang unutterable, and burst into an agony of tears; but she gave her master no thanks, and her gloom deepened.

At last his patience was exhausted. He grew weary of her obstinacy, as he was pleased to term it; and threats took the place of persuasion.

In a few months more, poor Xarifa was a raving maniac. That pure temple was desecrated; that loving heart was broken; and that beautiful head fractured against the wall in the frenzy of despair. Her master cursed the useless expense she had cost him; the slaves buried her; and no one wept at the grave of her who had been so carefully cherished, and so tenderly beloved.

Reader, do you complain that I have written fiction? Believe me, scenes like these are of no unfrequent occurrence at the South. The world does not afford such materials for tragic romance, as the history of the Quadroons.

1842

From Letters from New-York[1]

Letter XIV

[BURYING GROUND OF THE POOR]

February 17, 1842.

I was always eager for the spring-time, but never so much as now.

Patience yet a little longer! and I shall find delicate bells of the trailing arbutus,[2] fragrant as an infant's breath, hidden deep, under their coverlid of autumn leaves, like modest worth in this pretending world. My spirit is

6. Lanterns (archaic).

1. All selections are from the first edition, published in New York and Boston in 1843. The letters initially appeared in the New York weekly *National Anti-Slavery Standard*. Child made small revisions in all of the letters republished in *Letters from New-York*.

2. Flowering herb.

weary for rural rambles. It is sad walking in the city. The streets shut out the sky, even as commerce comes between the soul and heaven. The busy throng, passing and repassing, fetter freedom, while they offer no sympathy. The loneliness of the soul is deeper, and far more restless, than in the solitude of the mighty forest. Wherever are woods and fields I find a home; each tinted leaf and shining pebble is to me a friend; and wherever I spy a wild flower, I am ready to leap up, clap my hands, and exclaim, "Cockatoo! he know me very well!" as did the poor New Zealander, when he recognised a bird of his native clime, in the menageries of London.

But amid these magnificent masses of sparkling marble, hewn *in prison*, I am all alone. For eight weary months, I have met in the crowded streets but two faces I had ever seen before. Of some, I would I could say that I should never see them again; but they haunt me in my sleep, and come between me and the morning. Beseeching looks, begging the comfort and the hope I have no power to give. Hungry eyes, that look as if they had pleaded long for sympathy, and at last gone mute in still despair. Through what woful, what frightful masks, does the human soul look forth, leering, peeping, and defying, in this thoroughfare of nations. Yet in each and all lie the capacities of an archangel; as the majestic oak lies enfolded in the acorn that we tread carelessly under foot, and which decays, perchance, for want of soil to root in.

The other day, I went forth for exercise merely, without other hope of enjoyment than a farewell to the setting sun, on the now deserted Battery,[3] and a fresh kiss from the breezes of the sea, ere they passed through the polluted city, bearing healing on their wings. I had not gone far, when I met a little ragged urchin, about four years old, with a heap of newspapers, "more big as he could carry," under his little arm, and another clenched in his small, red fist.[4] The sweet voice of childhood was prematurely cracked into shrillness, by screaming street cries, at the top of his lungs; and he looked blue, cold, and disconsolate. May the angels guard him! How I wanted to warm him in my heart. I stood, looking after him, as he went shivering along. Imagination followed him to the miserable cellar where he probably slept on dirty straw; I saw him flogged, after his day of cheerless toil, because he had failed to bring home pence enough for his parents' grog;[5] I saw wicked ones come muttering and beckoning between his young soul and heaven; they tempted him to steal, to avoid the dreaded beating. I saw him, years after, bewildered and frightened, in the police-office, surrounded by hard faces. Their law-jargon conveyed no meaning to his ear, awakened no slumbering moral sense, taught him no clear distinction between right and wrong; but from their cold, harsh tones, and heartless merriment, he drew the inference that they were enemies; and, as such, he hated them. At that moment, one tone like a mother's voice might have wholly changed his earthly destiny; one kind word of friendly counsel might have saved him—as if an angel, standing in the genial sunlight, had thrown to him one end of a garland, and gently diminishing the distance between

3. The neighborhood by New York Harbor at the southern tip of Manhattan.
4. During this time, very young children, often from poor immigrant families, were employed to sell the increasingly popular penny newspapers.
5. Cheap alcoholic drink.

them, had drawn him safely out of the deep and tangled labyrinth, where false echoes and winding paths conspired to make him lose his way.

But watchmen and constables were around him, and they have small fellowship with angels. The strong impulses that might have become overwhelming love for his race, are perverted to the bitterest hatred. He tries the universal resort of weakness against force; if they are too strong for *him*, he will be too cunning for *them*. *Their* cunning is roused to detect *his* cunning: and thus the gallows game is played, with interludes of damnable merriment from police reports, whereat the heedless multitude laugh; while angels weep over the slow murder of a human soul.

When, oh when, will men learn that society makes and cherishes the very crimes it so fiercely punishes, and *in* punishing reproduces?

> "The key of knowledge first ye take away,
> And then, because ye've robbed him, ye enslave;
> Ye shut out from him the sweet light of day,
> And then, because he's in the dark, ye pave
> The road, that leads him to his wished-for grave,
> With stones of stumbling: then, if he but tread
> Darkling and slow, ye call him "fool" and "knave"—
> Doom him to toil, and yet deny him bread:
> Chains round his limbs ye throw, and curses on his head."[6]

God grant the little shivering carrier-boy a brighter destiny than I have foreseen for him.

A little further on, I encountered two young boys fighting furiously for some coppers,[7] that had been given them and had fallen on the pavement. They had matted black hair, large, lustrous eyes, and an olive complexion. They were evidently foreign children, from the sunny clime of Italy or Spain, and nature had made them subjects for an artist's dream. Near by on the cold stone steps, sat a ragged, emaciated woman, whom I conjectured, from the resemblance of her large, dark eyes, might be their mother; but she looked on their fight with languid indifference, as if seeing, she saw it not. I spoke to her, and she shook her head in a mournful way, that told me she did not understand my language. Poor, forlorn wanderer! would I could place thee and thy beautiful boys under shelter of sun-ripened vines, surrounded by the music of thy mother-land! Pence I will give thee, though political economy reprove the deed.[8] They can but appease the hunger of the body; they cannot soothe the hunger of thy heart; that I obey the kindly impulse may make the world none the better—perchance some iota the worse; yet I must needs follow it—I cannot otherwise.

I raised my eyes above the woman's weather-beaten head, and saw behind the window, of clear, plate glass, large vases of gold and silver, curiously wrought. They spoke significantly of the sad contrasts in this disordered world; and excited in my mind whole volumes, not of political, but of angelic economy. "Truly," said I, "if the Law of Love prevailed, vases of gold and silver might even more abound—but no homeless outcast would sit shivering

6. All verses in the letters reprinted here are probably by Child unless otherwise noted.
7. Pennies.
8. Child refers to the prevailing idea that giving charity to the poor encourages dependency and keeps them poor.

beneath their glittering mockery. All would be richer, and no man the poorer. When will the world learn its best wisdom? When will the mighty discord come into heavenly harmony?" I looked at the huge stone structures of commercial wealth, and they gave an answer that chilled my heart. Weary of city walks, I would have turned homeward; but nature, ever true and harmonious, beckoned to me from the Battery, and the glowing twilight gave me friendly welcome. It seemed as if the dancing Spring Hours had thrown their rosy mantles on old silvery winter in the lavishness of youthful love.

I opened my heart to the gladsome influence, and forgot that earth was not a mirror of the heavens. It was but for a moment; for there under the leafless trees, lay two ragged little boys, asleep in each other's arms. I remembered having read in the police reports, the day before, that two little children, thus found, had been taken up as vagabonds. They told, with simple pathos, how both their mothers had been dead for months; how they had formed an intimate friendship, had begged together, ate together, hungered together and together slept uncovered beneath the steel-cold stars.

The twilight seemed no longer warm; and brushing away a tear, I walked hastily homeward. As I turned into the street where God has provided me with a friendly shelter, something lay across my path. It was a woman, apparently dead; with garments all draggled in New-York gutters, blacker than waves of the infernal rivers. Those who gathered around, said she had fallen in intoxication, and was rendered senseless by the force of the blow. They carried her to the watch-house,[9] and the doctor promised she should be well attended. But, alas, for watch-house charities to a breaking heart! I could not bring myself to think otherwise than that hers *was* a breaking heart. Could she but give a full revelation of early emotions checked in their full and kindly flow, of affections repressed, of hopes blighted, and energies misemployed through ignorance, the heart would kindle and melt, as it does when genius stirs its deepest recesses.

It seemed as if the voice of human wo was destined to follow me through the whole of that unblest day. Late in the night I heard the sound of voices in the street, and raising the window, saw a poor, staggering woman in the hands of a watchman. My ear caught the words, "Thank you kindly, sir. I should *like* to go home." The sad and humble accents in which the simple phrase was uttered, the dreary image of the watch-house, which that poor wretch dreamed was her *home*, proved too much for my overloaded sympathies. I hid my face in the pillow, and wept; for "my heart was almost breaking with the misery of my kind."

I thought, then, that I would walk no more abroad, till the fields were green. But my mind and body grow alike impatient of being enclosed within walls; both ask for the free breeze, and the wide, blue dome that overarches and embraces *all*. Again I rambled forth, under the February sun, as mild and genial as the breath of June. Heart, mind, and frame grew glad and strong, as we wandered on, past the old Stuyvesant church,[1] which a few years agone

9. A place where those under temporary arrest or in need of assistance were kept.

1. Built in 1799 in the Bowery neighborhood of lower Manhattan on what had been the estate of Peter Stuyvesant (1592–1672), the Dutch colonial governor of New Amsterdam. Stuyvesant himself is entombed in the church's graveyard.

was surrounded by fields and Dutch farm-houses, but now stands in the midst of peopled streets;—and past the trim, new houses, with their green verandahs, in the airy suburbs. Following the railroad, which lay far beneath our feet, as we wound our way over the hills, we came to the burying-ground of the poor. Weeds and brambles grew along the sides, and the stubble of last year's grass waved over it, like dreary memories of the past; but the sun smiled on it, like God's love on the desolate soul. It was inexpressibly touching to see the frail memorials of affection, placed there by hearts crushed under the weight of poverty. In one place was a small rude cross of wood, with the initials J.S. cut with a penknife, and apparently filled with ink. In another a small hoop had been bent into the form of a heart, painted green, and nailed on a stick at the head of the grave. On one upright shingle was painted only "MUTTER;" the German word for MOTHER. On another was scrawled, as if with charcoal, *"So ruhe wohl, du unser liebes kind."* (Rest well, our beloved child.) One recorded life's brief history thus: "H.G. born in Bavaria; died in New-York." Another short epitaph, in French, told that the sleeper came from the banks of the Seine.

The predominance of foreign epitaphs affected me deeply. Who could now tell with what high hopes those departed ones had left the heart-homes of Germany, the sunny hills of Spain, the laughing skies of Italy, or the wild beauty of Switzerland? Would not the friends they had left in their childhood's home, weep scalding tears to find them in a pauper's grave, with their initials rudely carved on a fragile shingle? Some had not even these frail memorials. It seemed there was none to care whether they lived or died. A wide, deep trench was open; and there I could see piles of unpainted coffins heaped one upon the other, left uncovered with earth, till the yawning cavity was filled with its hundred tenants.

Returning homeward, we passed a Catholic burying-ground. It belonged to the upper classes, and was filled with marble monuments, covered with long inscriptions. But none of them touched my heart like that rude shingle, with the simple word "Mutter" inscribed thereon. The gate was open, and hundreds of Irish, in their best Sunday clothes, were stepping reverently among the graves, and kissing the very sods. Tenderness for the dead is one of the loveliest features of their nation and their church.

The evening was closing in, as we returned, thoughtful, but not gloomy. Bright lights shone through crimson, blue, and green, in the apothecaries' windows, and were reflected in prismatic beauty from the dirty pools in the street. It was like poetic thoughts in the minds of the poor and ignorant; like the memory of pure aspirations in the vicious; like a rainbow of promise, that God's spirit never leaves even the most degraded soul. I smiled, as my spirit gratefully accepted this love-token from the outward; and I thanked our heavenly Father for a world beyond this.

Letter XX

[BIRDS]

June 9, 1842.

There is nothing which makes me feel the imprisonment of a city, like the absence of birds. Blessings on the little warblers! Lovely types are they of all winged and graceful thoughts. Dr. Follen[2] used to say, "I feel dependent for a vigorous and hopeful spirit on now and then a kind word, the loud laugh of a child, or the silent greeting of a flower." Fully do I sympathize with this utterance of his gentle, and loving spirit; but more than the benediction of the flower, more perhaps than even the mirth of childhood, is the clear, joyous note of the bird, a refreshment to my soul.

"The birds! the birds of summer hours
  They bring a gush of glee,
To the child among the fragrant flowers,
  To the sailor on the sea.
We hear their thrilling voices
  In their swift and airy flight,
And the inmost heart rejoices
  With a calm and pure delight.
Amid the morning's fragrant dew,
  Amidst the mists of even,
They warble on, as if they drew
  Their music down from Heaven.
And when their holy anthems
  Come pealing through the air,
Our hearts leap forth to meet them,
  With a blessing and a prayer."

But alas! like the free voices of fresh youth, they come not on the city air. Thus should it be; where mammon imprisons all thoughts and feelings that would fly upward, their winged types should be in cages too. Walk down Mulberry street,[3] and you may see, in one small room, hundreds of little feathered songsters, each hopping about restlessly in his gilded and garlanded cage, like a dyspeptic merchant in his marble mansion. I always turn my head away when I pass; for the sight of the little captives goes through my heart like an arrow. The darling little creatures have such visible delight in freedom;

"In the joyous song they sing;
  In the liquid air they cleave;
In the sunshine; in the shower;
  In the nests they weave."

I seldom see a bird encaged, without being reminded of Petion,[4] a truly great man, the popular idol of Haiti, as Washington is of the United States.

2. The first professor of German literature at Harvard University, the German émigré Charles Follen (1796–1840) lost his job in 1835 after he espoused antislavery sentiments. He died in a steamboat accident in 1840.

3. In lower Manhattan near what was then the crime-ridden area of Five Points.

4. The revolutionary leader Alexandre Pétion (1770–1818) was the first president of the Republic of Haiti after the nation gained its independence from France.

While Petion administered the government of the island, some distinguished foreigner sent his little daughter a beautiful bird, in a very handsome cage. The child was delighted, and with great exultation exhibited the present to her father. "It is indeed very beautiful, my daughter," said he; "but it makes my heart ache to look at it. I hope you will never show it to me again."

With great astonishment, she inquired his reasons. He replied, "When this island was called St. Domingo, we were all slaves. It makes me think of it to look at that bird; for *he* is a slave."

The little girl's eyes filled with tears, and her lips quivered, as she exclaimed, "Why, father! he has such a large, handsome cage; and as much as ever he can eat and drink."

"And would *you* be a slave," said he, "if you could live in a great house, and be fed on frosted cake?"

After a moment's thought, the child began to say, half reluctantly, "Would he be happier, if I opened the door of his cage?" "He would be *free*!" was the emphatic reply. Without another word, she took the cage to the open window, and a moment after, she saw her prisoner playing with the humming-birds among the honey-suckles.

One of the most remarkable cases of instinctive knowledge in birds was often related by my grandfather, who witnessed the fact with his own eyes. He was attracted to the door, one summer day, by a troubled twittering, indicating distress and terror. A bird, who had built her nest in a tree near the door, was flying back and forth with the utmost speed, uttering wailing cries as she went. He was at first at a loss to account for her strange movements; but they were soon explained by the sight of a snake slowly winding up the tree.

Animal magnetism was then unheard of; and whosoever had dared to mention it, would doubtless have been hung on Witch's Hill,[5] without benefit of clergy. Nevertheless, marvellous and altogether unaccountable stories had been told of the snake's power to charm birds. The popular belief was that the serpent charmed the bird by *looking steadily at it; and that such a sympathy was thereby established, that if the snake were struck, the bird felt the blow, and writhed under it.*

These traditions excited my grandfather's curiosity to watch the progress of things; but, being a humane man, he resolved to kill the snake before he had a chance to despoil the nest. The distressed mother meanwhile continued her rapid movements and troubled cries; and he soon discovered that she went and came continually, with something in her bill, from one particular tree—a white ash. The snake wound his way up; but the instant his head came near the nest, his folds relaxed, and he fell to the ground rigid, and apparently lifeless. My grandfather made sure of his death by cutting off his head, and then mounted the tree to examine into the mystery. The snug little nest was filled with eggs, and covered with leaves of the white ash!

That little bird knew, if my readers do not, that contact with the white ash is deadly to a snake. This is no idle superstition, but a veritable fact in natural history. The Indians are aware of it, and twist garlands of white ash leaves about their ankles, as a protection against rattlesnakes. Slaves often

5. The name given to the site in Salem, Massachusetts, where those accused of witchcraft were executed during the trials of 1692. "Animal magnetism": mesmerism, a form of hypnotism.

take the same precaution when they travel through swamps and forests, guided by the north star; or to the cabin of some poor white man, who teaches them to read and write by the light of pine splinters, and receives his pay in "massa's" corn or tobacco.

I have never heard any explanation of the effect produced by the white ash; but I know that settlers in the wilderness like to have these trees round their log houses, being convinced that no snake will voluntarily come near them. When touched with the boughs, they are said to grow suddenly rigid, with strong convulsions; after a while they slowly recover, but seem sickly for some time.

The following well authenticated anecdote has something wonderfully human about it:

A parrot had been caught young, and trained by a Spanish lady, who sold it to an English sea-captain. For a time the bird seemed sad among the fogs of England, where birds and men all spoke to her in a foreign tongue. By degrees, however, she learned the language, forgot her Spanish phrases, and seemed to feel at home. Years passed on, and found Pretty Poll the pet of the captain's family. At last her brilliant feathers began to turn gray with age; she could take no food but soft pulp, and had not strength enough to mount her perch. But no one had the heart to kill the old favourite, she was entwined with so many pleasant household recollections. She had been some time in this feeble condition, when a Spanish gentleman called one day to see her master. It was the first time she had heard the language for many years. It probably brought back to memory the scenes of her youth in that beautiful region of vines and sunshine. She spread forth her wings with a wild scream of joy, rapidly ran over the Spanish phrases, which she had not uttered for years, and fell down dead.

There is something strangely like reason in this. It makes one want to know whence comes the bird's soul, and whither goes it.

There are different theories on the subject of instinct. Some consider it a special revelation to each creature; others believe it is founded on traditions handed down among animals, from generation to generation, and is therefore a matter of education. My own observation, two years ago, tends to confirm the latter theory. Two barn-swallows came into our wood-shed in the spring time. Their busy, earnest twitterings led me at once to suspect that they were looking out a building-spot; but as a carpenter's bench was under the window, and frequent hammering, sawing, and planing were going on, I had little hope they would choose a location under our roof. To my surprise, however, they soon began to build in the crotch of a beam, over the open door-way. I was delighted, and spent more time watching them, than "penny-wise" people would have approved. It was, in fact, a beautiful little drama of domestic love. The mother-bird was *so* busy, and *so* important; and her mate was *so* attentive! Never did any newly-married couple take more satisfaction with their first nicely-arranged drawer of baby-clothes, than these did in fashioning their little woven cradle.

The father-bird scarcely ever left the side of the nest. There he was, all day long, twittering in tones that were most obviously the outpourings of love. Sometimes he would bring in a straw, or a hair, to be inwoven in the precious little fabric. One day my attention was arrested by a very unusual twittering, and I saw him circling round with a large downy feather in his bill. He bent over the unfinished nest, and offered it to his mate with the most graceful and loving air imaginable; and when she put up her mouth to take it, he poured forth *such* a gush of gladsome sound! It seemed as if pride and affection had swelled his heart, till it was almost too big for his little bosom. The whole transaction was the prettiest piece of fond coquetry, on both sides, that it was ever my good luck to witness.

It was evident that the father-bird had formed correct opinions on "the woman question;"[6] for during the process of incubation he volunteered to perform his share of household duty. Three or four times a day would he, with coaxing twitterings, persuade his patient mate to fly abroad for food; and the moment she left the eggs, he would take the maternal station, and give a loud alarm whenever cat or dog came about the premises. He certainly performed the office with far less ease and grace than she did; it was something in the style of an old bachelor tending a babe; but nevertheless it showed that his heart was kind, and his principles correct, concerning division of labour. When the young ones came forth, he pursued the same equalizing policy, and brought at least half the food for his greedy little family.

But when they became old enough to fly, the veriest misanthrope would have laughed to watch their manœuvres! Such chirping and twittering! Such diving down from the nest, and flying up again! Such wheeling round in circles, talking to the young ones all the while! Such clinging to the sides of the shed with their sharp claws, to show the timid little fledgelings that there was no need of falling!

For three days all this was carried on with increasing activity. It was obviously an infant flying school. But all their talking and fussing was of no avail. The little downy things looked down, and then looked up, and alarmed at the infinity of space, sunk down into the nest again. At length the parents grew impatient, and summoned their neighbours. As I was picking up chips one day, I found my head encircled with a swarm of swallows. They flew up to the nest, and chatted away to the young ones; they clung to the walls, looking back to tell how the thing was done; they dived, and wheeled, and balanced, and floated, in a manner perfectly beautiful to behold.

The pupils were evidently much excited. They jumped up on the edge of the nest, and twittered, and shook their feathers, and waved their wings; and then hopped back again, saying, "It's pretty sport, but we can't do it."

Three times the neighbours came in and repeated their graceful lessons. The third time, two of the young birds gave a sudden plunge downward, and then fluttered and hopped, till they alighted on a small upright log. And oh, such praises as were warbled by the whole troop! The air was filled with their joy! Some were flying round, swift as a ray of light; others were perched on the hoe-handle, and the teeth of the rake; multitudes clung to the wall, after the fashion of their pretty kind; and two were swinging, in most graceful style, on a pendant hoop. Never while memory lasts, shall I forget that swallow party! I have frolicked with blessed Nature much and often; but this, above all her gambols, spoke into my inmost heart, like the glad voices of little children. That beautiful family continued to be our playmates, until the falling leaves gave token of approaching winter. For some time, the little

6. Women's rights; see "Letter XXXIV" on p. 199.

ones came home regularly to their nest at night. I was ever on the watch to welcome them, and count that none were missing. A sculptor might have taken a lesson in his art, from those little creatures perched so gracefully on the edge of their clay-built cradle, fast asleep, with heads hidden under their folded wings. Their familiarity was wonderful. If I hung my gown on a nail, I found a little swallow perched on the sleeve. If I took a nap in the afternoon, my waking eyes were greeted by a swallow on the bed-post; in the summer twilight, they flew about the sitting-room in search of flies, and sometimes lighted on chairs and tables. I almost thought they knew how much I loved them. But at last they flew away to more genial skies, with a whole troop of relations and neighbours. It was a deep pain to me, that I should never know them from other swallows, and that they would have no recollection of me. We had lived so friendly together, that I wanted to meet them in another world, if I could not in this; and I wept, as a child weeps at its first grief.

There was somewhat, too, in their beautiful life of loving freedom which was a reproach to me. Why was not *my* life as happy and as graceful as theirs? Because they were innocent, confiding, and unconscious, they fulfilled all the laws of their being without obstruction.

"Inward, inward to thy heart,
  Kindly Nature, take me;
Lovely, even as thou art,
  Full of loving, make me.
Thou knowest nought of dead-cold forms,
  Knowest nought of littleness;
Lifeful truth *thy* being warms,
  Majesty and earnestness."

The old Greeks observed a beautiful festival, called "The Welcome of the Swallows." When these social birds first returned in the spring-time, the children went about in procession, with music and garlands; receiving presents at every door, where they stopped to sing a welcome to the swallows, in that graceful old language, so melodious even in its ruins, that the listener feels as if the brilliant azure of Grecian skies, the breezy motion of their olive groves, and the gush of their silvery fountains, had all passed into a monument of liquid and harmonious sounds.

Letter XXXIV

[WOMEN'S RIGHTS]

January, 1843.[7]

You ask what are my opinions about "Women's Rights." I confess, a strong distaste to the subject, as it has been generally treated. On no other theme, probably, has there been uttered so much of false, mawkish sentiment, shallow philosophy, and sputtering, farthing-candle wit. If the style of its advocates has often been offensive to taste, and unacceptable to reason, assuredly that of its opponents have been still more so. College boys have

7. Though Child gives the date as January 1843, this letter draws on her columns of February 16, 1843, and February 23, 1843, in the *National Anti-Slavery Standard*.

amused themselves with writing dreams, in which they saw women in hotels, with their feet hoisted, and chairs tilted back, or growling and bickering at each other in legislative halls, or fighting at the polls, with eyes blackened by fisticuffs. But it never seems to have occurred to these facetious writers, that the proceedings which appear so ludicrous and improper in *women*, are also ridiculous and disgraceful in *men*. It were well that *men* should learn not to hoist their feet above their heads, and tilt their chairs backward, not to growl and snap in the halls of legislation, or give each other black eyes at the polls.

Maria Edgeworth[8] says, "We are disgusted when we see a woman's mind overwhelmed with a torrent of learning; that the tide of literature has passed over it should be betrayed only by its fertility." This is beautiful and true; but is it not likewise applicable to man? The truly great never seek to display themselves. If they carry their heads high above the crowd, it is only made manifest to others by accidental revelations of their extended vision. "Human duties and proprieties do not lie so very far apart," said Harriet Martineau;[9] "if they did, there would be two gospels, and two teachers, one for man, and another for woman."

It would seem, indeed, as if men were willing to give women the exclusive benefit of gospel-teaching. "*Women* should be gentle," say the advocates of subordination; but when Christ said, "Blessed are the meek,"[1] did he preach to women only? "*Girls* should be modest," is the language of common teaching, continually uttered in words and customs. Would it not be an improvement for men, also, to be scrupulously pure in manners, conversation, and life? Books addressed to young married people abound with advice to the *wife*, to control her temper, and never to utter wearisome complaints, or vexatious words, when the husband comes home fretful or unreasonable, from his out-of-doors conflicts with the world. Would not the advice be as excellent and appropriate, if the husband were advised to conquer *his* fretfulness, and forbear *his* complaints, in consideration of his wife's ill-health, fatiguing cares, and the thousand disheartening influences of domestic routine? In short, whatsoever can be named as loveliest, best, and most graceful in woman, would likewise be good and graceful in man. You will perhaps remind me of courage. If you use the word in its highest signification, I answer that woman, above others, has abundant need of it, in her pilgrimage; and the true woman wears it with a quiet grace. If you mean mere animal courage, *that* is not mentioned in the Sermon on the Mount, among those qualities which enable us to inherit the earth, or become the children of God. That the feminine ideal approaches much nearer to the gospel standard, than the prevalent idea of manhood, is shown by the universal tendency to represent the Saviour and his most beloved disciple with mild, meek expression, and feminine beauty. None speak of the bravery, the might, or the intellect of Jesus; but the devil is always imagined as a being of acute intellect, political

8. Child paraphrases from *Letters for Literary Ladies* (1795) by the Irish author Maria Edgeworth (1767–1849), who was also known for her novels and children's books.

9. English writer (1802–1876) who supported the abolitionist cause, defended Child's antislavery activities in an 1838 issue of the *Westminster Review*, and achieved notoriety in the United States for her travel narrative *Society in America* (1837), which was highly critical of American society. In *Society in America*, the likely source of Child's paraphrased quotation, she also addressed issues of women's rights.

1. Matthew 5.5, from Jesus' sermon on virtue, known as the Sermon on the Mount.

cunning, and the fiercest courage. These universal and instinctive tendencies of the human mind reveal much.

That the present position of women in society is the result of physical force, is obvious enough; whosoever doubts it, let her reflect why she is afraid to go out in the evening without the protection of a man. What constitutes the danger of aggression? Superior physical strength, uncontrolled by the moral sentiments. If physical strength were in complete subjection to moral influence, there would be no need of outward protection. That animal instinct and brute force now govern the world, is painfully apparent in the condition of women everywhere; from the Morduan Tartars,[2] whose ceremony of marriage consists in placing the bride on a mat, and consigning her to the bridegroom, with the words, "Here, wolf, take thy lamb,"—to the German remark, that "stiff ale, stinging tobacco, and a girl in her smart dress, are the best things." The same thing, softened by the refinements of civilization, peeps out in Stephen's remark, that "woman never looks so interesting, as when leaning on the arm of a soldier:" and in Hazlitt's complaint that "it is not easy to keep up a conversation with women in company. It is thought a piece of rudeness to differ from them; it is not quite fair to ask them a *reason* for what they say."[3]

This sort of politeness to women is what men call gallantry; an odious word to every sensible woman, because she sees that it is merely the flimsy veil which foppery throws over sensuality, to conceal its grossness. So far is it from indicating sincere esteem and affection for women, that the profligacy of a nation may, in general, be fairly measured by its gallantry. This taking away *rights*, and *condescending* to grant *privileges*, is an old trick of the physical force principle; and with the immense majority, who only look on the surface of things, this mask effectually disguises an ugliness, which would otherwise be abhorred. The most inveterate slaveholders are probably those who take most pride in dressing their household servants handsomely, and who would be most ashamed to have the name of being *unnecessarily* cruel. And profligates, who form the lowest and most sensual estimate of women, are the very ones to treat them with an excess of outward deference.

There are few books, which I can read through, without feeling insulted as a woman; but this insult is almost universally conveyed through that which was intended for praise. Just imagine, for a moment, what impression it would make on men, if women authors should write about *their* "rosy lips," and "melting eyes," and "voluptuous forms," as they write about *us*! That women in general do not feel this kind of flattery to be an insult, I readily admit; for, in the first place, they do not perceive the gross chattel-principle,[4] of which it is the utterance; moreover, they have, from long habit, become accustomed to consider themselves as household conveniences, or gilded toys. Hence, they consider it feminine and pretty to abjure all such use of their faculties, as would make them co-workers with man in the advancement of those great principles, on which the progress of society depends. "There is perhaps no

2. Turkic-speaking people of central Asia.
3. From the English essayist William Hazlitt (1778–1830), though, because of the paraphrasing, the actual source is obscure. Stephen's: Child may have been referring to the popular travel writer John Lloyd Stephens (1805–1852), author of *Incidents of Travel in Greece, Turkey, Russia, and Poland* (1838) and several other works.
4. To be regarded as property, like a slave.

animal," say Hannah More,[5] "so much indebted to subordination, for its good behaviour, as woman." Alas, for the animal age, in which such utterance could be tolerated by public sentiment!

Martha More,[6] sister of Hannah, describing a very impressive scene at the funeral of one of her Charity School teachers, says: "The spirit within seemed struggling to speak, and I was in a sort of agony; but I recollected that I had heard, somewhere, a woman must not speak in the *church*. Oh, had she been buried in the church *yard*, a messenger from Mr. Pitt[7] himself should not have restrained me; for I seemed to have received a message from a higher Master within."

This application of theological teaching carries its own commentary.

I have said enough to show that I consider prevalent opinions and customs highly unfavourable to the moral and intellectual development of women: and I need not say, that, in proportion to their true culture, women will be more useful and happy, and domestic life more perfected. True culture, in them, as in men, consists in the full and free development of individual character, regulated by their *own* perceptions of what is true, and their *own* love of what is good.

This individual responsibility is rarely acknowledged, even by the most refined, as necessary to the spiritual progress of women. I once heard a very beautiful lecture from R.W. Emerson, on Being and Seeming.[8] In the course of many remarks, as true as they were graceful, he urged women to *be*, rather than *seem*. He told them that all their laboured education of forms, strict observance of genteel etiquette, tasteful arrangement of the toilette, &c, all this *seeming* would not *gain hearts* like *being* truly what God made them; that earnest simplicity, the sincerity of nature, would kindle the eye, light up the countenance, and give an inexpressible charm to the plainest features.

The advice was excellent, but the motive, by which it was urged, brought a flush of indignation over my face. *Men* were exhorted to *be*, rather than to *seem*, that they might fulfil the sacred mission for which their souls were embodied; that they might, in God's freedom, grow up into the full stature of spiritual manhood; but *women* were urged to simplicity and truthfulness, that they might become more *pleasing*.

Are we not all immortal beings? Is not each one responsible for himself and herself? There is no measuring the mischief done by the prevailing tendency to teach women to be virtuous as a duty to *man*, rather than to *God*—for the sake of pleasing the creature, rather than the Creator. "*God* is thy law, *thou* mine," said Eve to Adam.[9] May Milton be forgiven for sending that thought "out into everlasting time" in such a jewelled setting. What weakness, vanity, frivolity, infirmity of moral purpose, sinful flexibility of

5. The English evangelical writer (1745–1833) who argued in favor of aspects of women's subordination. Her best-known work was *Strictures on the Modern System of Female Education* (1799), the probable source of Child's paraphrase.

6. More (1746–1819) worked with her better-known sister on educational projects, including schools for the poor ("Charity Schools"). The source for the quote is unclear.

7. English statesman William Pitt (1759–1806), celebrated for his oratory.

8. Emerson first delivered this lecture in Boston on January 10, 1838.

9. In Book 4 of Milton's *Paradise Lost* (1667, 1674), Eve declares to Adam before they fall asleep: "God is thy law, thou mine: to know no more is woman's happiest knowledge and her praise" (lines 637–38).

principle—in a word, what soul-stifling, has been the result of thus putting man in the place of God!

But while I see plainly that society is on a false foundation, and that prevailing views concerning women indicate the want of wisdom and purity, which they serve to perpetuate—still, I must acknowledge that much of the talk about Women's Rights offends both my reason and my taste. I am not of those who maintain there is no sex in souls; nor do I like the results deducible from that doctrine. Kinmont,[1] in his admirable book, called the Natural History of Man, speaking of the warlike courage of the ancient German women, and of their being respectfully consulted on important public affairs, says: "You ask me if I consider all this right, and deserving of approbation? or that women were here engaged in their appropriate tasks? I answer, yes; it is just *as* right that they should take this interest in the honour of their country, as the other sex. Of course, I do not think that women were *made* for war and battle; neither do I believe that *men* were. But since the fashion of the times had made it so, and settled it that war was a necessary element of greatness, and that no safety was to be procured without it, I argue that it shows a healthful state of feeling in other respects, that the feelings of both sexes were *equally* enlisted in the cause; that there was no *division* in the house, or the State; and that the serious pursuits and objects of the one were also the serious pursuits and objects of the other."[2]

The nearer society approaches to divine order, the less separation will there be in the characters, duties, and pursuits of men and women. Women will not become less gentle and graceful, but men will become more so. Women will not neglect the care and education of their children, but men will find themselves ennobled and refined by sharing those duties with them; and will receive, in return, co-operation and sympathy in the discharge of various other duties, now deemed inappropriate to women. The more women become rational companions, partners in business and in thought, as well as in affection and amusement, the more highly will men appreciate *home*—that blessed word, which opens to the human heart the most perfect glimpse of Heaven, and helps to carry it thither, as on an angel's wings.

"Domestic bliss,
That can, the world eluding, be itself
A world enjoyed; that wants no witnesses
But its own sharers, and approving heaven;
That, like a flower deep hid in rocky cleft,
Smiles, though 'tis looking only at the sky."

Alas, for these days of Astor houses, and Tremonts, and Albions![3] where families exchange comfort for costliness, fireside retirement for flirtation and flaunting, and the simple, healthful, cozy meal, for gravies and gout, dainties and dyspepsia. There is no characteristic of my countrymen which I regret so deeply, as their slight degree of adhesiveness to home. Closely intertwined with this instinct, is the religion of a nation. The Home and the Church bear a near relation to each other. The French have no such word

1. Alexander Kinmont (1799–1838), American ethnologist.
2. Kinmont's *Twelve Lectures on the National History of Man, and the Rise and Progress of Philosophy* (1839).
3. Allusion to the great urban hotels of the time.

as home in their language, and I believe they are the least reverential and religious of all the Christian nations. A Frenchman had been in the habit of visiting a lady constantly for several years, and being alarmed at a report that she was sought in marriage, he was asked why he did not marry her himself. "*Marry* her!" exclaimed he; "Good heavens! *where should I spend my evenings?*" The idea of domestic happiness was altogether a foreign idea to his soul, like a word that conveyed no meaning. Religious sentiment in France leads the same roving life as the domestic affections; breakfasting at one restaurateur's, and supping at another's. When some wag in Boston reported that Louis Philippe had sent over for Dr. Channing[4] to manufacture a religion for the French people, the witty significance of the joke was generally appreciated.

There is a deep spiritual reason why all that relates to the domestic affections should ever be found in close proximity with religious faith. The age of chivalry was likewise one of unquestioning veneration, which led to the crusade for the holy sepulchre. The French Revolution, which tore down churches, and voted that there was no God, likewise annulled marriage; and the doctrine that there is no sex in souls has usually been urged by those of infidel tendencies. Carlyle says: "But what feeling it was in the ancient, devout, deep soul, which of marriage made a *sacrament*, this, of all things in the world, is what Diderot will think of for æons without discovering; unless, perhaps, it were to increase the *vestry fees*."[5]

The conviction that woman's present position in society is a false one, and therefore re-acts disastrously on the happiness and improvement of man, is pressing, by slow degrees, on the common consciousness, through all the obstacles of bigotry, sensuality, and selfishness. As man approaches to the truest life, he will perceive more and more that there is no separation or discord in their mutual duties. They will be one; but it will be as affection and thought are one; the treble and bass of the same harmonious tune.

Letter XXXVI

[BARNUM'S AMERICAN MUSEUM]

March, 1843.[6]

I went, a few evenings ago, to the American Museum, to see fifteen Indians, fresh from the western forest.[7] Sacs, Fox, and Iowas;[8] really important people in their respective tribes. Nan-Nouce-Fush-E-To, which means the

4. American Unitarian minister and author, William Ellery Channing (1780–1842) emphasized religious tolerance. Louis Philippe (1773–1850) was king of France from 1840 to 1848, when he was deposed.

5. Payment for the use of a chapel or church seat. The Scottish-born author Thomas Carlyle (1795–1881) detested the philosophy of the French writer Denis Diderot (1713–1784) and other exemplars of the radical Enlightenment; see his 1833 essay "Diderot," the source of Child's paraphrase.

6. This letter draws on three columns Child published in the *National Anti-Slavery Standard*: January 5, 1843; March 2, 1843; March 23, 1843.

7. The American impresario P.T. Barnum (1810–1891) established the American Museum in lower Manhattan, at the intersection of Broadway and Ann, in 1841. He made it a popular destination by combining sideshows, exhibitions of scientific curiosities, and live performances. The Indians had come from Iowa to negotiate treaties with the U.S. government; Barnum had them "perform" in his lecture hall.

8. The Sac (or Sauk) and Fox tribes, from the Michigan and Wisconsin Great Lakes region, were removed to Iowa in 1833, where they joined the Iowas, the original inhabitants of the state that bears their name.

Buffalo King, is a famous Sac chief, sixty years old, covered with scars, and grim as a Hindoo god, or pictures of the devil on a Portuguese contribution box, to help sinners through purgatory. It is said that he has killed with his own hand one hundred Osages, three Mohawks, two Kas, two Sioux, and one Pawnee; and if we may judge by his organ of destructiveness, the story is true; a more enormous bump I never saw in that region of the skull.[9] He speaks nine Indian dialects, has visited almost every existing tribe of his race, and is altogether a remarkable personage. Mon-To-Gah, the White Bear, wears a medal from President Monroe,[1] for certain services rendered to the whites. Wa-Con-To-Kitch-Er, is an Iowa chief, of grave and thoughtful countenance, held in much veneration as the Prophet of his tribe. He sees visions, which he communicates to them for their spiritual instruction. Among the squaws is No-Nos-See, the She Wolf, a niece of the famous Black Hawk,[2] and very proud of the relationship; and Do-Hum-Me, the Productive Pumpkin, a very handsome woman, with a great deal of heart and happiness in her countenance.

> "Smiles settled on her sun-flecked cheeks,
> Like noon upon the mellow apricot."

She was married about a fortnight ago, at Philadelphia, to Cow-Hick-He, son of the principal chief of the Iowas, and as noble a specimen of manhood as I ever looked upon. Indeed I have never seen a group of human beings so athletic, well-proportioned, and majestic. They are a keen satire on our civilized customs, which produce such feeble forms and pallid faces. The unlimited pathway, the broad horizon, the free grandeur of the forest, has passed into their souls, and so stands revealed in their material forms.

We who have robbed the Indians of their lands, and worse still, of *themselves*, are very fond of proving their inferiority. We are told that the *facial angle*[3] in the

Caucasian race is	- - - -	85 degrees.
Asiatic	- - - -	78 "
American Indian	- - - -	73 "
Ethiopian	- - - -	70 "
Ourang Outang	- - - -	67 "

This simply proves that the Caucasian race, through a succession of ages, has been exposed to influences eminently calculated to develop the moral and intellectual faculties. That they started *first* in the race, might have been owing to a finer and more susceptible nervous organization, originating in climate, perhaps, but serving to bring the physical organization into more harmonious relation with the laws of spiritual reception. But by whatever agency it might have been produced, the nation, or race that perceived even one spiritual idea in advance of others, would necessarily go on improving

9. According to the then-popular "science" of phrenology, features of the skull, such as bumps on the head, could be read as determinants of character.
1. James Monroe (1758–1831), the fifth president of the United States (1817–25).
2. Sauk war chief (1767–1838) who fought to maintain Indian lands in Illinois and elsewhere against the encroachments of white settlers.
3. The concept that the ideal, or most beautiful, head produced the greatest vertical angle from the chin to the forehead was proposed by the Dutch naturalist Petrus Camper (1722–1789). Camper had a significant influence on the development of phrenology in the United States.

in geometric ratio, through the lapse of ages. For *our* Past, we have the oriental fervour, gorgeous imagery, and deep reverence of the Jews, flowing from that high fountain, the perception of the oneness and invisibility of God. From the Greeks we receive the very Spirit of Beauty, flowing into all forms of Philosophy and Art, encircled by a golden halo of Platonism, which

"Far over many a land and age hath shone,
And mingles with the light that beams from God's own throne."[4]

These have been transmitted to us in their own forms, and again reproduced through the classic strength and high cultivation of Rome, and the romantic minstrelsy and rich architecture of the middle ages. Thus we stand, a congress of ages, each with a glory on its brow, peculiar to itself, yet in part reflected from the glory that went before.

But what have the African savage, and the wandering Indian for *their* Past? To fight for food, and grovel in the senses, has been the employment of *their* ancestors. The Past reproduced in them, mostly belongs to the animal part of our mixed nature. They have indeed come in contact with the race on which had dawned higher ideas; but *how* have they come in contact? As *victims*, not as *pupils*. Rum, gunpowder, the horrors of slavery, the unblushing knavery of trade, these have been their teachers! And because these have failed to produce a high degree of moral and intellectual cultivation, we coolly declare that the negroes are made for slaves, that the Indians cannot be civilized; and that when either of the races come in contact with us, they must either consent to be our beasts of burden, or be driven to the wall, and perish.

That the races of mankind are different, spiritually as well as physically, there is, of course, no doubt; but it is as the difference between trees of the same forest, not as between trees and minerals. The facial angle and shape of the head, is various in races and nations; but these are the *effects* of spiritual influences, long operating on character, and in their turn becoming *causes*; thus intertwining, as Past and Future ever do.

But it is urged that Indians who have been put to schools and colleges, still remained attached to a roving life; away from all these advantages,

"His blanket tied with yellow strings, the Indian of the forest went."[5]

And what if he did? Do not white, young men who have been captured by savages in infancy, show an equally strong disinclination to take upon themselves the restraints of civilized life? Does anybody urge that this well-known fact proves the *white* race incapable of civilization?

You ask, perhaps, what becomes of my theory that races and individuals are the product of ages, if the influences of half a life produce the same effects on the Caucasian and the Indian? I answer, that white children brought up among Indians, though they strongly imbibe the habits of the race, are generally prone to be the geniuses and prophets of their tribe. The organization of nerve and brain has been changed by a more harmonious relation between the animal and the spiritual; and this comparative harmony has

4. From "The Ages" (1821), by William Cullen Bryant (1794–1878).

5. From "Indian Student" (1788), by Philip Freneau (1752–1832).

been produced by the influences of Judea, and Greece, and Rome, and the age of chivalry; though of all these things the young man never heard.

Similar influences brought to bear on the Indians or the Africans, as a race, would gradually change the structure of their skulls, and enlarge their perceptions of moral and intellectual truth. The *same* influences cannot be brought to bear upon them; for *their* Past is not *our* Past; and of course never can be. But let ours mingle with theirs, and you will find the result variety, without inferiority. They will be flutes on different notes, and so harmonize the better.

And how is this elevation of all races to be effected? By that which worketh *all* miracles, in the name of Jesus.—The LAW OF LOVE. We must not teach as superiors; we must *love as brothers*. Here is the great deficiency in all our efforts for the ignorant and the criminal. We stand apart from them, and expect them to feel grateful for our condescension in noticing them at all. We do not embrace them warmly with our sympathies, and put our souls into their soul's stead.

But even under this great disadvantage; accustomed to our smooth, deceitful talk, when we want their lands, and to the cool villany with which we break treaties when our purposes are gained; receiving gunpowder and rum from the very hands which retain from them all the better influences of civilized life; cheated by knavish agents, cajoled by government, and hunted with bloodhounds—still, under all *these* disadvantages, the Indians have shown that they can be civilized. Of this, the Choctaws and Cherokees are admirable proofs.[6] Both these tribes have a regularly-organized, systematic government, in the democratic form, and a printed constitution. The right of trial by jury, and other principles of a free government, are established on a permanent basis. They have good farms, cotton-gins, saw-mills, schools, and churches. Their dwellings are generally comfortable, and some of them are handsome. The last annual message of the chief of the Cherokees is a highly-interesting document, which would not compare disadvantageously with any of our governors' messages. It states that more than $2,500,000 are due to them from the United States; and recommends that this sum be obtained, and in part distributed among the people; but that the interest of the school fund be devoted to the maintenance of schools, and the diffusion of knowledge.

There was a time when *our* ancestors, the ancient Britons, went nearly without clothing, painted their bodies in fantastic fashion, offered up human victims to uncouth idols, and lived in hollow trees, or rude habitations, which we should now consider unfit for cattle. Making all due allowance for the different state of the world, it is much to be questioned whether they made more rapid advancement than the Cherokees and Choctaws.

It always fills me with sadness to see Indians surrounded by the false environment of civilized life; but I never felt so deep a sadness, as I did in looking upon these western warriors; for they were evidently the noblest of their dwindling race, unused to restraint, accustomed to sleep beneath the

6. Following the passage of the Indian Removal Act (1830), several tribes, including the Choctaws and Cherokees, were forced to move from the southern Appalachian area to what is now Oklahoma. The forced removal in a long winter march resulted in the deaths of an estimated three to four thousand Indians in what was called the Trail of Tears. Child had argued for the Indians' rights to remain in their homeland.

stars. And here they were, set up for a two-shilling show, with monkeys, flamingoes, dancers, and buffoons! If they understood our modes of society well enough to be aware of their degraded position, they would doubtless quit it, with burning indignation at the insult. But as it is, they allow women to examine their beads, and children to play with their wampum, with the most philosophic indifference. In their imperturbable countenances, I thought I could once or twice detect a slight expression of scorn at the eager curiosity of the crowd. The Albiness,[7] a short woman, with pink eyes, and hair like white floss, was the only object that visibly amused them. The young chiefs nodded to her often, and exchanged smiling remarks with each other, as they looked at her. Upon all the buffooneries and ledgerdermain tricks of the "Museum," they gazed as unmoved as John Knox[8] himself could have done. I would have given a good deal to know their thoughts, as mimic cities, and fairy grottoes, and mechanical dancing figures, rose and sunk before them. The mechanical figures were such perfect imitations of life, and went through so many wonderful evolutions, that they might well surprise even those accustomed to the marvels of mechanism. But Indians, who pay religious honours to venerable rocks, and moss-grown trees, who believe that brutes have souls, as well as men, and that all nature is filled with spirits, might well doubt whether there was not here some supernatural agency, either good or evil. I would suffer almost anything, if my soul could be transmigrated into the She Wolf, or the Productive Pumpkin, and their souls pass consciously into my frame, for a few days, that I might experience the fashion of their thoughts and feelings. Was there ever such a foolish wish! The soul *is* ME, and *is* Thee. I might as well put on their blankets, as their bodies, for purposes of spiritual insight. In that other world, shall we be enabled to know exactly how heaven, and earth, and hell, appear to other persons, nations, and tribes? I would it might be so; for I have an intense desire for such revelations. I do not care to travel to Rome, or St. Petersburg, because I can only look *at* people; and I want to look *into* them; and *through* them; to know how things appear to *their* spiritual eyes, and sound to *their* spiritual ears. This is a universal want; hence the intense interest taken in autobiography, by all classes of readers. Oh, if any one had but the courage to write the *whole* truth of himself, undisguised, as it appears before the eye of God and angels, the WORLD would read it, and it would soon be translated into all the dialects of the universe.

But these children of the forest, do not even give us glimpses of their inner life; for they consider that the body was given to *conceal* the emotions of the soul. The stars look down into their hearts, as into mine, the broad ocean, glittering in the moonbeams, speaks to them of the Infinite; and doubtless the wild flowers and the sea-shells, "talk to them a thought." But *what* thoughts, *what* revelations of the infinite? This would I give the world to know; but the world cannot buy an answer.

How foreign is my soul to that of the beautiful Do-Hum-Me! How helpless should I be in situations where she would be a heroine; and how little could she comprehend my eager thought, which seeks the creative three-in-one throughout the universe, and finds it in every blossom, and every

7. Barnum's coinage of the feminine form of *albino*, a person lacking in pigmentation.

8. Scottish Protestant reformer (1505–1572).

mineral. Between Wa-Con-To-Kitch-Er, and the German Herder,[9] what a distance! Yet are they both prophets; and though one looks through nature with the pitch-pine torch of the wilderness, and the other is lighted by a whole constellation of suns, yet have both learned, in their degree, that matter is only the time-garment of the spirit. The stammering utterance with which the Iowa seer reveals this, it were worth a kingdom to hear, if we could but borrow the souls of his tribe, while they listen to his visions.

It is a general trait with the Indian tribes to recognise the Great Spirit in every little child. They rarely refuse a child anything. When their revenge is most implacable, a little one is often sent to them, adorned with flowers and shells, and taught to lisp a prayer that the culprit may be forgiven; and such mediation is rarely without effect, even on the sternest warrior. This trait alone is sufficient to establish their relationship with Herder, Richter,[1] and other spirits of angel-stature. Nay, if we could look back a few centuries, we should find the ancestors of Shakspeare, and the fastidiously-refined Göethe, with painted cheeks, wolves' teeth for jewels, and boars' hides for garments. Perhaps the universe could not have passed before the vision of those star-like spirits, except through the forest life of such wild ancestry.

Some theorists say that the human brain, in its formation, "changes with a steady rise, through a likeness to one animal and then another, till it is perfected in that of man, the highest animal." It seems to be so with the nations, in their progressive rise out of barbarism. I was never before so much struck with the animalism of Indian character, as I was in the frightful war-dance of these chiefs. Their gestures were as furious as wild-cats, they howled like wolves, screamed like prairie dogs, and tramped like buffaloes. Their faces were painted fiery red, or with cross-bars of green and red, and they were decorated with all sorts of uncouth trappings of hair, and bones, and teeth. That which regulated their movements, in lieu of music, was a discordant clash; and altogether they looked and acted more like demons from the pit, than anything I ever imagined. It was the natural and appropriate language of War. The wolfish howl, and the wild-cat leap, represent it more truly than graceful evolutions, and the Marseilles hymn.[2] *That* music rises above mere brute vengeance; it breathes, in fervid ecstacy, the *soul's* aspiration after freedom—the struggle of will with fate. It is the Future setting sail from old landings, and merrily piping all hands on board. It is too noble a voice to belong to physical warfare; the shrill howl of old Nan-Nouce-Fush-E-To, is good enough for such brutish work; it clove the brain like a tomahawk; and was hot with hatred.

In truth, that war-dance was terrific both to eye and ear. I looked at the door, to see if escape were easy, in case they really worked themselves up to the scalping point. For the first time, I fully conceived the sacrifices and perils of Puritan settlers. Heaven have mercy on the mother who heard those dreadful yells when they really foreboded murder! or who suddenly met such a group of grotesque demons in the loneliness of the forest!

But instantly I felt that I was wronging them in my thought. Through paint and feathers, I saw gleams of right honest and friendly expression;

9. Johann Gottfried von Herder (1744–1803), influential German historian and philosopher.
1. Jean Paul Richter (1763–1825), German novelist.
2. French national song composed in 1792 during the French Revolution.

and I said, we are children of the same Father, seeking the same home. If the Puritans suffered from their savage hatred, it was because they met them with savage weapons, and a savage spirit. Then I thought of William Penn's treaty with the Indians;[3] "the only one ever formed without an oath, and the only one that was never broken." I thought of the deputation of Indians, who, some years ago, visited Philadelphia, and knelt with one spontaneous impulse around the monument of Penn.

Again I looked at the yelling savages in their grim array, stamping through the war-dance, with a furious energy that made the floor shake, as by an earthquake; and I said, These, too, would bow, like little children, before the persuasive power of Christian love! Alas, if we had but faith in this divine principle, what mountains of evil might be removed into the depths of the sea.

P.S. Alas, poor Do-Hum-Me is dead; so is No-See, Black Hawk's niece; and several of the chiefs are indisposed. Sleeping by hot anthracite fires, and then exposed to the keen encounters of the wintry wind; one hour, half stifled in the close atmosphere of theatres and crowded saloons, and the next, driving through snowy streets and the midnight air; this is a process which kills civilized people by inches, but savages at a few strokes.

Do-Hum-Me was but nineteen years old, in vigorous health, when I saw her a few days since, and obviously so happy in her newly wedded love, that it ran over at her expressive eyes, and mantled her handsome face like a veil of sunshine. Now she rests among the trees, in Greenwood Cemetery;[4] not the trees that whispered to her childhood. Her coffin was decorated according to Indian custom, and deposited with the ceremonies peculiar to her people. Alas, for the handsome one, how lonely she sleeps here! Far, far away from him, to whom her eye turned constantly, as the sunflower to the light!

Sick, and sad at heart, this noble band of warriors, with melancholy steps, left the pestilential city last week, for their own broad prairies in the West. Do-Hum-Me was the pride and idol of them all. The old Iowa chief, the head of the deputation, was her father; and notwithstanding the stoicism of Indian character, it is said that both he and the bereaved young husband were overwhelmed with an agony of grief. They obviously loved each other most strongly. May the Great Spirit grant them a happy meeting in their "fair hunting grounds" beyond the sky.

1843

3. In 1682 William Penn (1644–1718) and the Leni Lenape (Delaware) Indians negotiated a treaty that was, according to popular lore, never broken by either side; no signed copy of this treaty exists.

4. Famous cemetery in Brooklyn, New York.

RALPH WALDO EMERSON
1803–1882

Ralph Waldo Emerson is arguably the most influential American writer of the nineteenth century—the writer with whom numerous other significant writers of the time sought to come to terms. Without Emerson's inspirational essays on nonconformity, self-reliance, and anti-institutionalism, Henry David Thoreau's and Margaret Fuller's careers may have followed different paths; and without Emerson's call for an American bard whose poetry "speaks somewhat wildly" in addressing the nation's "ample geography," Whitman's great poetry might never have been written. Though Melville rejected Emerson's optimism, satirizing him in *The Confidence-Man* (1857) as a philosophical con man, he termed him a "deep diver" as well; Emerson's conception of nature as a sign of spirit permeates Melville's dynamic representations of the whale and the natural world in *Moby-Dick* (1851). Emerson's persisting influence on late-nineteenth- and twentieth-century American writers is evident in astonishing permutations, on figures as diverse as Emily Dickinson, Louisa May Alcott, William James, Theodore Dreiser, Robert Frost, John Dewey, and his namesake Ralph Waldo Ellison.

Emerson was born in Boston on May 25, 1803, the son of a Unitarian minister and the second of five surviving boys. He was eight years old when his father died. Determined to send as many sons as she could to Harvard—the traditional route for ministers-in-training—Emerson's mother kept a succession of boardinghouses. Around this time, Emerson's brilliant, eccentric aunt, Mary Moody Emerson (1774–1863), stepped in to become his principal educator and inspiration, guiding his reading and challenging his thinking over the next several decades. In the more conventional setting of Boston Public Latin School, where he was sent at age nine, and Harvard College, which he attended from 1817 to 1821, Emerson showed no particular promise. Graduating from Harvard thirtieth in a class of fifty-nine, Emerson served, as he put it, as "a hopeless Schoolmaster" in several Boston-area schools. Turning to the study of theology in 1825 at Harvard's Divinity School, he began preaching as a Unitarian in October 1826, and early in 1829 he was ordained by the Unitarians as a junior pastor at Boston's Second Church. In July of that year, he was promoted to pastor.

Boston Unitarianism, led in the 1820s by William Ellery Channing (1780–1842), accepted the Bible as the revelation of God's intentions but no longer held that human beings were innately depraved; some Unitarians, like Channing, came close to suggesting that Jesus was not a god but rather the highest expression of humanity. Emerson was deeply influenced by Channing, and his skepticism toward historical Christianity was strengthened by his exposure to the German "higher criticism," which regarded the Judeo-Christian Bible as a document produced in a specific historical time, rather than as the direct word of God, and interpreted biblical miracles as stories comparable to the myths of other cultures. Emerson was gradually developing a greater faith in individual moral sentiment and intuition than in revealed religion.

In 1831 Emerson faced a personal crisis: his wife, Ellen Tucker Emerson, whom he had married in 1829, died of tuberculosis on February 8, at the age of nineteen. Grief-stricken, Emerson wrote his aunt Mary: "My angel is gone to heaven this morning & I am alone in the world." Emerson also faced a spiritual crisis, perhaps precipitated by the death of Ellen, as his thinking developed into a full-fledged disillusionment with his position as pastor and with Unitarianism itself. Early in 1832 Emerson notified his church that he had become so skeptical of the validity of the Lord's Supper that he could no longer administer the sacrament, regarding it, as he remarked in his journal, as "worship in the dead forms of our forefathers." He resigned his pastorate on December 22, 1832, and on Christmas Day sailed for Europe, where he would remain until October 1833. During his European tour, he called on a number of well-known writers, in Italy meeting Walter Savage Landor, in England Samuel Coleridge and William Wordsworth, and in Scotland Thomas Carlyle, with whom he began a lifelong intellectual friendship.

Shortly after his return from Europe in late 1833, Emerson settled a legal dispute with the Tucker family and received the first installment of his wife's legacy. Soon he was assured of more than a thousand dollars annually, a considerable sum for that time. Without the need to produce a constant income, he began a new careeer as a lecturer, speaking around New England in the lyceums—public halls that brought a variety of speakers and performers to cities and smaller towns. In 1835, after a ten-month courtship, he married Lydia Jackson of Plymouth, and they moved to rural Concord, Massachusetts, where the Emerson family had property. There, Emerson completed his first book, *Nature*, which was published anonymously and at Emerson's own expense in 1836. This little book did not immediately establish Emerson as an important American writer, but, even with its philosophical complexities, it did confirm his future as a prose writer. As the reviewers understood, *Nature* was not a Christian book but one influenced by a range of idealistic philosophies, ancient and modern, Transcendentalism being merely the latest name for a way of thinking going back to Plato and more recently refashioned by a number of European romantics.

Although the favorable reception of *Nature* in England encouraged some American journalists to take Emerson seriously as an intellectual force, Emerson's immediate reward was having the book become the unofficial manifesto for a number of his like-minded friends, who, over the next eight years, would meet irregularly and informally in Emerson's study and elsewhere. Termed "Transcendentalists" by mocking outsiders, the group was composed mainly of ministers who rejected the view of the philosopher John Locke (1643–1704) that the mind was a merely passive receptor of sense impressions, endorsing Samuel Coleridge's and other romantics' alternative conception of the mind as actively intuitive and creative. Participants included the educators Bronson Alcott (1799–1888) and Elizabeth Palmer Peabody (1804–1894), the abolitionist and Unitarian minister Theodore Parker (1810–1860), the Unitarian minister (later an influential American Catholic) Orestes A. Brownson (1803–1876), Margaret Fuller, and Henry David Thoreau. The group began its own journal, *The Dial* (1840–44), edited for the most part by Emerson, Fuller, and Thoreau.

Nature reached a smaller audience than did many of Emerson's lectures, which were often written up in newspapers; his formal Harvard addresses to the Phi Beta Kappa Society in 1837 on the American scholar and to the Divinity School graduates in 1838 on the state of Christianity were both printed as pamphlets. Conservative ministers attacked "The Divinity School Adress" for its rejection of historical Christianity and its bold questioning of the claims made for Christ as a divine savior. But with the publication of *Essays* (1841), Emerson's lasting reputation began to take shape. Far more than *Nature*, this book was directed to a popular audience. The twelve essays in the volume had been tried out, in whole or in part, in his lectures, so that their final form was shaped by the responses of his many audiences.

Early in 1842 Emerson's first son, Waldo, died at the age of five, a loss from which Emerson never fully recovered. Writing in his journal the day after Waldo's death, he expressed his grief and confusion: "Sorrow makes us all children again[,] destroys all differences of intellect[.] The wisest know nothing[.]" For the philosopher of idealism who had argued that the world can be apprehended mainly through intuition, the death of a beloved son pushed him toward the skepticism expressed most powerfully in "Experience" (1844), an essay presenting individuals as perpetually skating on surfaces. At the conclusion of the essay, however, Emerson, in an anticipation of the American school of pragmatism that he would profoundly influence, insisted on the importance of continuing to act in the world, however elusive and tragic that world might be.

Emerson continued to work steadily on essays derived from his extensive journals and his lecturing. In 1844 he brought out a second series of essays, including his influential "The Poet," which grappled with aesthetic issues of form and meter and foretold—indeed provided the blueprints for—the style and subject matter of some of the great national poets to come. Meter does not make the argument, he wrote, in striking contrast to his contemporary Edgar Allan Poe, but the argument (or poetic idea or vision) makes its own meter; thus he inspired Whitman to break with poetic tradition by introducing the idea of "open form" poetry. Emerson lectured in Boston, across the Northeast, in the South, and even (after the completion of the transcontinental railroad in 1869) in California, giving more than fifteen hundred lectures over the course of his career. These as much as his essays helped develop his reputation.

As Emerson's reputation continued to grow, he gained modest recognition for his own poems, which he collected at the end of 1846. In 1847–48 he took a second trip to Europe, delivering approximately seventy lectures in England and Scotland. One eventual result of that tour was the publication in 1856 of *English Traits*, an inquiry into the supposed racial, historical, and cultural characteristics of Anglo-Saxonism. (Like many thinkers of the time, Emerson accepted the idea of racial differences and hierarchies.) Two other books emerged from his lectures: *Representative Men* (1850), which examined exemplary intellectual and cultural figures, such as Shakespeare and Napoleon; and *The Conduct of Life* (1860), which examined tensions between thought and delimiting worldly forces, even as Emerson reaffirmed the power of self-culture and the individual mind.

Precisely because he so valued individual self-culture, Emerson was skeptical of social reforms that required group participation. In the early 1840s he refused to participate in the reformist, socialistic community Brook Farm in West Roxbury, Massachusetts, which drew a number of the Transcendentalists associated with *The Dial*. Abolitionism did engage his attention, however, and in 1844 he delivered a passionate antislavery address, "Emancipation of the Negroes in the British West Indies," at the Concord Court House on August 1, 1844. Appalled by the Fugitive Slave Law of 1850, Emerson became more fervent in his views during the 1850s, offering scathing attacks on Northern supporters of what he termed "this filthy law." In his 1855 "Lecture on Slavery," presented before the Massachusetts Anti-Slavery Society at the Tremont Temple in Boston, Emerson declaimed against the "outrage of giving back a stolen and plundered man to his thieves." Valuing individual rights and believing in the individual mind (or soul) as divine, Emerson regarded slavery as abhorrent. He also argued in favor of women's rights. In 1855, the same year he attacked slavery at Boston's Tremont Temple, he spoke before a women's rights convention to support women's right to vote, to "hold their property as men do theirs," and to "enter a school as freely as a church." Although Emerson never achieved national prominence as a social reformer, his lectures and essays motivated many of his admirers to become political and social activists.

Emerson's contemporary reputation rested on his lectures and essays, but all along he had been producing another major body of writings, his journals, which he called his "savings bank." The journals were not published in full until the late twentieth century, under the title *Journals and Miscellaneous Notebooks*. A historical record of responses to people and events, the journals, as critics are increasingly recognizing, are among the best accounts of the intellectual and spiritual life of a nineteenth-century American writer. Following the Civil War, Emerson cut back on his writing, partly for health reasons (as he aged he began to display the symptoms of senility). But he had his vigorous moments. In 1871 he traveled to California, and in late 1872 and into 1873, following a fire that severely damaged his house, he traveled to Europe and Egypt with his daughter Ellen and met with Carlyle one last time. Upon his return to Concord, he lectured occasionally in Boston and Concord. He died on April 27, 1882, and was buried in Concord's Sleepy Hollow Cemetery.

In a journal entry of 1836, Emerson wrote: "There is creative reading as well as creative writing." As a creative writer, Emerson attempted to get his whole philosophy into every essay, and even into single sentences. At the same time, he was skeptical of the capacity of language to embody truths, so he presented his essays as epistemological quests of sorts that, in the twistings and turnings and circlings of his thought, made enormous demands on his readers. Emerson's language can be elliptical and sometimes maddeningly abstract, but there is no American writer who placed greater importance on the reader's active interpretive role in generating new meanings and new ways of seeing the world. Emerson's respect for the independent spirit of his readers, his prompting of readers to trust their ideas and take them in new and even different directions—the main point of "Self Reliance," perhaps his most famous essay—may in fact be the key to his broad literary and cultural influence.

Nature[1]

> "Nature is but an image or imitation of wisdom, the last thing of the soul; nature being a thing which doth only do, but not know."
>
> —PLOTINUS[2]

Introduction

Our age is retrospective. It builds the sepulchres of the fathers. It writes biographies, histories, and criticism. The foregoing generations beheld God and nature face to face; we, through their eyes. Why should not we also enjoy an original relation to the universe? Why should not we have a poetry and philosophy of insight and not of tradition, and a religion by revelation to us, and not the history of theirs? Embosomed for a season in nature, whose floods of life stream around and through us, and invite us by the powers they supply, to action proportioned to nature, why should we grope among the dry bones of the past,[3] or put the living generation into masquerade out of its faded wardrobe? The sun shines to-day also. There is more wool and flax in the fields. There are new lands, new men, new thoughts. Let us demand our own works and laws and worship.

1. *Nature* was published anonymously in 1836 by James Monroe and Company of Boston, paid for by Emerson himself (the company published a thousand copies for Emerson's approximately one-hundred-dollar payment). Emerson gave copies to friends, and the book was also advertised in local newspapers. The text used here is that of the first 1836 edition. A few obvious typographical errors have been corrected; and the changes that Emerson himself made in presentation copies to the opening of Chapter 4 have been adopted. Otherwise, the occasional oddities of punctuation, spelling, and subject–verb agreements that appeared in the 1836 text remain in this reprinting.

2. Emerson found the motto from the Roman philosopher Plotinus (205?–270?) in his copy of Ralph Cudworth's *The True Intellectual System of the Universe* (1820).

3. An echo of Ezekiel 37.1–14, especially 37.4, where God tells Ezekiel to "Prophesy upon these bones, and say unto them, O ye dry bones, hear the word of the Lord."

Undoubtedly we have no questions to ask which are unanswerable. We must trust the perfection of the creation so far, as to believe that whatever curiosity the order of things has awakened in our minds, the order of things can satisfy. Every man's condition is a solution in hieroglyphic to those inquiries he would put. He acts it as life, before he apprehends it as truth. In like manner, nature is already, in its forms and tendencies, describing its own design. Let us interrogate the great apparition, that shines so peacefully around us. Let us inquire, to what end is nature?

All science has one aim, namely, to find a theory of nature. We have theories of races and of functions, but scarcely yet a remote approximation to an idea of creation. We are now so far from the road to truth, that religious teachers dispute and hate each other, and speculative men are esteemed unsound and frivolous. But to a sound judgment, the most abstract truth is the most practical. Whenever a true theory appears, it will be its own evidence. Its test is, that it will explain all phenomena. Now many are thought not only unexplained but inexplicable; as language, sleep, dreams, beasts, sex.

Philosophically considered, the universe is composed of Nature and the Soul. Strictly speaking, therefore, all that is separate from us, all which Philosophy distinguishes as the NOT ME,[4] that is, both nature and art, all other men and my own body, must be ranked under this name, NATURE. In enumerating the values of nature and casting up their sum, I shall use the word in both senses;—in its common and in its philosophical import. In inquiries so general as our present one, the inaccuracy is not material; no confusion of thought will occur. *Nature*, in the common sense, refers to essences unchanged by man; space, the air, the river, the leaf. *Art* is applied to the mixture of his will with the same things, as in a house, a canal, a statue, a picture. But his operations taken together are so insignificant, a little chipping, baking, patching, and washing, that in an impression so grand as that of the world on the human mind, they do not vary the result.

Chapter I. Nature

To go into solitude, a man needs to retire as much from his chamber as from society. I am not solitary whilst I read and write, though nobody is with me. But if a man would be alone, let him look at the stars. The rays that come from those heavenly worlds, will separate between him and vulgar things. One might think the atmosphere was made transparent with this design, to give man, in the heavenly bodies, the perpetual presence of the sublime. Seen in the streets of cities, how great they are! If the stars should appear one night in a thousand years, how would men believe and adore; and preserve for many generations the remembrance of the city of God which had been shown! But every night come out these preachers of beauty, and light the universe with their admonishing smile.

The stars awaken a certain reverence, because though always present, they are always inaccessible; but all natural objects make a kindred impression, when the mind is open to their influence. Nature never wears a mean

4. Emerson draws on Thomas Carlyle's *Sartor Resartus* (1833–34) for his idea of "NOT ME," which Carlyle presents as similar to the German philosophical concept of "everything but the self."

Shortly after the publication of *Nature*, Emerson's friend, the artist and poet Christopher Cranch (1813–1893), depicted him as a **"transparent eye-ball"** in "Illustrations of the New Philosophy" (c. 1836).

appearance. Neither does the wisest man extort all her secret, and lose his curiosity by finding out all her perfection. Nature never became a toy to a wise spirit. The flowers, the animals, the mountains, reflected all the wisdom of his best hour, as much as they had delighted the simplicity of his childhood.

When we speak of nature in this manner, we have a distinct but most poetical sense in the mind. We mean the integrity of impression made by manifold natural objects. It is this which distinguishes the stick of timber of the wood-cutter, from the tree of the poet. The charming landscape which I saw this morning, is indubitably made up of some twenty or thirty farms. Miller owns this field, Locke that, and Manning the woodland beyond. But none of them owns the landscape. There is a property in the horizon which no man has but he whose eye can integrate all the parts, that is, the poet. This is the best part of these men's farms, yet to this their land-deeds give them no title.

To speak truly, few adult persons can see nature. Most persons do not see the sun. At least they have a very superficial seeing. The sun illuminates only the eye of the man, but shines into the eye and the heart of the child. The lover of nature is he whose inward and outward senses are still truly adjusted to each other; who has retained the spirit of infancy even into the era of manhood.[5] His intercourse with heaven and earth, becomes part of his daily food. In the presence of nature, a wild delight runs through the man, in spite of real sorrows. Nature says,—he is my creature, and maugre[6] all his impertinent griefs, he shall be glad with me. Not the sun or the summer alone, but every hour and season yields its tribute of delight; for every hour and change corresponds to and authorizes a different state of the mind, from breathless noon to grimmest midnight. Nature is a setting that fits equally well a comic or a mourning piece. In good health, the air is a cordial of incredible virtue. Crossing a bare common, in snow puddles, at twilight, under a clouded sky, without having in my thoughts any occurrence of special good fortune, I have enjoyed a perfect exhilaration. Almost I fear to think how glad I am. In the woods too, a man casts off his years, as the snake his slough, and at what period soever of life, is always a child. In the woods, is perpetual youth. Within these plantations of God, a decorum and sanctity reign, a perennial festival is dressed, and the guest sees not how he should tire of them in a thousand years. In the woods, we return to reason and faith. There I feel that nothing can befal me in life,—no disgrace, no calamity, (leaving me my eyes,) which nature cannot repair. Standing on the bare ground,—my head bathed by the blithe air, and uplifted into infinite space,—all mean egotism vanishes. I become a transparent eye-ball. I am nothing. I see all. The currents of the Universal Being circulate through me; I am part or particle of God. The name of the nearest friend sounds then foreign and accidental. To be brothers, to be acquaintances,—master or servant, is then a trifle and a disturbance. I am the lover of uncontained and immortal beauty. In the wilderness, I find something more dear and connate[7] than in streets or villages. In the tranquil landscape, and especially in the distant line of the horizon, man beholds somewhat as beautiful as his own nature.

The greatest delight which the fields and woods minister, is the suggestion of an occult relation between man and the vegetable. I am not alone and unacknowledged. They nod to me and I to them. The waving of the boughs in the storm, is new to me and old. It takes me by surprise, and yet is not unknown. Its effect is like that of a higher thought or a better emotion coming over me, when I deemed I was thinking justly or doing right.

Yet it is certain that the power to produce this delight, does not reside in nature, but in man, or in a harmony of both. It is necessary to use these pleasures with great temperance. For, nature is not always tricked in holiday attire, but the same scene which yesterday breathed perfume and glittered as for the frolic of the nymphs, is overspread with melancholy today. Nature always wears the colors of the spirit. To a man laboring under calamity, the heat of his own fire hath sadness in it. Then, there is a kind of contempt of the landscape felt by him who has just lost by death a dear friend. The sky is less grand as it shuts down over less worth in the population.

5. An echo of Samuel Taylor Coleridge's *Biographia Literaria* (1817), ch. 4, in which Coleridge defines the character and privilege of genius as the ability to carry the feelings of childhood into adulthood.

6. Despite (archaic).

7. Related.

Chapter II. Commodity

Whoever considers the final cause[8] of the world, will discern a multitude of uses that enter as parts into that result. They all admit of being thrown into one of the following classes; Commodity; Beauty; Language; and Discipline.

Under the general name of Commodity, I rank all those advantages which our senses owe to nature. This, of course, is a benefit which is temporary and mediate, not ultimate, like its service to the soul. Yet although low, it is perfect in its kind, and is the only use of nature which all men apprehend. The misery of man appears like childish petulance, when we explore the steady and prodigal provision that has been made for his support and delight on this green ball which floats him through the heavens. What angels invented these splendid ornaments, these rich conveniences, this ocean of air above, this ocean of water beneath, this firmament of earth between? this zodiac of lights, this tent of dropping clouds, this striped coat of climates, this fourfold year? Beasts, fire, water, stones, and corn serve him. The field is at once his floor, his work-yard, his play-ground, his garden, and his bed.

"More servants wait on man
Than he'll take notice of."———[9]

Nature, in its ministry to man, is not only the material, but is also the process and the result. All the parts incessantly work into each other's hands for the profit of man. The wind sows the seed; the sun evaporates the sea; the wind blows the vapor to the field; the ice, on the other side of the planet, condenses rain on this; the rain feeds the plant; the plant feeds the animal; and thus the endless circulations of the divine charity nourish man.

The useful arts are but reproductions or new combinations by the wit of man, of the same natural benefactors. He no longer waits for favoring gales, but by means of steam, he realizes the fable of Æolus's bag,[1] and carries the two and thirty winds in the boiler of his boat. To diminish friction, he paves the road with iron bars, and, mounting a coach with a ship-load of men, animals, and merchandise behind him, he darts through the country, from town to town, like an eagle or a swallow through the air. By the aggregate of these aids, how is the face of the world changed, from the era of Noah to that of Napoleon! The private poor man hath cities, ships, canals, bridges, built for him. He goes to the post-office, and the human race run on his errands; to the book-shop, and the human race read and write of all that happens, for him; to the court-house, and nations repair his wrongs. He sets his house upon the road, and the human race go forth every morning, and shovel out the snow, and cut a path for him.

But there is no need of specifying particulars in this class of uses. The catalogue is endless, and the examples so obvious, that I shall leave them to the reader's reflection, with the general remark, that this mercenary benefit is one which has respect to a farther good. A man is fed, not that he may be fed, but that he may work.

8. In the sense of "purpose."
9. From "Man" (1633), by the English poet George Herbert (1593–1633), quoted at length in chapter VIII, "Prospects."
1. In Homer's *Odyssey* 10, Aeolus, the god of winds, gives Odysseus a bag containing favorable winds, but they create a storm when his unwary sailors let them all out at once. "Realizes": brings into real existence.

Chapter III. Beauty

A nobler want of man is served by nature, namely, the love of Beauty.

The ancient Greeks called the world κόσμος[2] beauty. Such is the constitution of all things, or such the plastic[3] power of the human eye, that the primary forms, as the sky, the mountain, the tree, the animal, give us a delight *in and for themselves*; a pleasure arising from outline, color, motion, and grouping. This seems partly owing to the eye itself. The eye is the best of artists. By the mutual action of its structure and of the laws of light, perspective is produced, which integrates every mass of objects, of what character soever, into a well colored and shaded globe, so that where the particular objects are mean and unaffecting, the landscape which they compose, is round and symmetrical. And as the eye is the best composer, so light is the first of painters. There is no object so foul that intense light will not make beautiful. And the stimulus it affords to the sense, and a sort of infinitude which it hath, like space and time, make all matter gay. Even the corpse hath its own beauty. But beside this general grace diffused over nature, almost all the individual forms are agreeable to the eye, as is proved by our endless imitations[4] of some of them, as the acorn, the grape, the pine-cone, the wheat-ear, the egg, the wings and forms of most birds, the lion's claw, the serpent, the butterfly, sea-shells, flames, clouds, buds, leaves, and the forms of many trees, as the palm.

For better consideration, we may distribute the aspects of Beauty in a threefold manner.

1. First, the simple perception of natural forms is a delight. The influence of the forms and actions in nature, is so needful to man, that, in its lowest functions, it seems to lie on the confines of commodity and beauty. To the body and mind which have been cramped by noxious work or company, nature is medicinal and restores their tone. The tradesman, the attorney comes out of the din and craft[5] of the street, and sees the sky and the woods, and is a man again. In their eternal calm, he finds himself. The health of the eye seems to demand a horizon. We are never tired, so long as we can see far enough.

But in other hours, Nature satisfies the soul purely by its loveliness, and without any mixture of corporeal benefit. I have seen the spectacle of morning from the hill-top over against my house, from day-break to sun-rise, with emotions which an angel might share. The long slender bars of cloud float like fishes in the sea of crimson light. From the earth, as a shore, I look out into that silent sea. I seem to partake its rapid transformations: the active enchantment reaches my dust, and I dilate and conspire with[6] the morning wind. How does Nature deify us with a few and cheap elements! Give me health and a day, and I will make the pomp of emperors ridiculous. The dawn is my Assyria; the sun-set and moon-rise my Paphos, and unimaginable realms of faerie, broad noon shall be my England of the senses and the understanding; the night shall be my Germany of mystic philosophy and dreams.[7]

2. Cosmos, or order (Greek).
3. Creative.
4. As in architectural and furniture design and decoration.
5. Craftiness, materialism.
6. Breathe with.
7. Emerson is contrasting the rational empiricism of Scottish Common Sense philosophy with the mystical idealism of post-Kantian German philosophy. "Assyria": an ancient Near Eastern empire. "Paphos": an ancient city in Cyprus (site of worship of Aphrodite).

Not less excellent, except for our less susceptibility in the afternoon, was the charm, last evening, of a January sunset. The western clouds divided and subdivided themselves into pink flakes modulated with tints of unspeakable softness; and the air had so much life and sweetness, that it was a pain to come within doors. What was it that nature would say? Was there no meaning in the live repose of the valley behind the mill, and which Homer or Shakspeare could not re-form for me in words? The leafless trees become spires of flame in the sunset, with the blue east for their background, and the stars of the dead calices of flowers, and every withered stem and stubble rimed[8] with frost, contribute something to the mute music.

The inhabitants of cities suppose that the country landscape is pleasant only half the year. I please myself with observing the graces of the winter scenery, and believe that we are as much touched by it as by the genial influences of summer. To the attentive eye, each moment of the year has its own beauty, and in the same field, it beholds, every hour, a picture which was never seen before, and which shall never be seen again. The heavens change every moment, and reflect their glory or gloom on the plains beneath. The state of the crop in the surrounding farms alters the expression of the earth from week to week. The succession of native plants in the pastures and roadsides, which make the silent clock by which time tells the summer hours, will make even the divisions of the day sensible to a keen observer. The tribes of birds and insects, like the plants punctual to their time, follow each other, and the year has room for all. By water-courses, the variety is greater. In July, the blue pontederia or pickerel-weed blooms in large beds in the shallow parts of our pleasant river,[9] and swarms with yellow butterflies in continual motion. Art cannot rival this pomp of purple and gold. Indeed the river is a perpetual gala, and boasts each month a new ornament.

But this beauty of Nature which is seen and felt as beauty, is the least part. The shows of day, the dewy morning, the rainbow, mountains, orchards in blossom, stars, moonlight, shadows in still water, and the like, if too eagerly hunted, become shows merely, and mock us with their unreality. Go out of the house to see the moon, and 't is mere tinsel; it will not please as when its light shines upon your necessary journey. The beauty that shimmers in the yellow afternoons of October, who ever could clutch it? Go forth to find it, and it is gone: 't is only a mirage as you look from the windows of the diligence.

2. The presence of a higher, namely, of the spiritual element is essential to its perfection. The high and divine beauty which can be loved without effeminacy, is that which is found in combination with the human will, and never separate. Beauty is the mark God sets upon virtue. Every natural action is graceful. Every heroic act is also decent,[1] and causes the place and the bystanders to shine. We are taught by great actions that the universe is the property of every individual in it. Every rational creature has all nature for his dowry and estate. It is his, if he will. He may divest himself of it; he may creep into a corner, and abdicate his kingdom, as most men do, but he is entitled to the world by his constitution. In proportion to the energy of his thought and will, he takes up the world into himself. "All those things for

8. Coated. "Calices": i.e., calyxes; the outer whorls of leaves or sepals at the bases of flowers.

9. The Concord River.

1. Beautiful.

which men plough, build, or sail, obey virtue;" said an ancient historian.[2] "The winds and waves," said Gibbon,[3] "are always on the side of the ablest navigators." So are the sun and moon and all the stars of heaven. When a noble act is done,—perchance in a scene of great natural beauty; when Leonidas and his three hundred martyrs consume one day in dying, and the sun and moon come each and look at them once in the steep defile of Thermopylæ; when Arnold Winkelried,[4] in the high Alps, under the shadow of the avalanche, gathers in his side a sheaf of Austrian spears to break the line for his comrades; are not these heroes entitled to add the beauty of the scene to the beauty of the deed? When the bark of Columbus nears the shore of America;—before it, the beach lined with savages, fleeing out of all their huts of cane; the sea behind; and the purple mountains of the Indian Archipelago around, can we separate the man from the living picture? Does not the New World clothe his form with her palm-groves and savannahs as fit drapery? Ever does natural beauty steal in like air, and envelope great actions. When Sir Harry Vane[5] was dragged up the Tower-hill, sitting on a sled, to suffer death, as the champion of the English laws, one of the multitude cried out to him, "You never sate on so glorious a seat." Charles II., to intimidate the citizens of London, caused the patriot Lord Russel[6] to be drawn in an open coach, through the principal streets of the city, on his way to the scaffold. "But," to use the simple narrative of his biographer, "the multitude imagined they saw liberty and virtue sitting by his side." In private places, among sordid objects, an act of truth or heroism seems at once to draw to itself the sky as its temple, the sun as its candle. Nature stretcheth out her arms to embrace man, only let his thoughts be of equal greatness. Willingly does she follow his steps with the rose and the violet, and bend her lines of grandeur and grace to the decoration of her darling child. Only let his thoughts be of equal scope, and the frame will suit the picture. A virtuous man, is in unison with her works, and makes the central figure of the visible sphere. Homer, Pindar, Socrates, Phocion,[7] associate themselves fitly in our memory with the whole geography and climate of Greece. The visible heavens and earth sympathize with Jesus. And in common life, whosoever has seen a person of powerful character and happy genius, will have remarked how easily he took all things along with him,—the persons, the opinions, and the day, and nature became ancillary to a man.

3. There is still another aspect under which the beauty of the world may be viewed, namely, as it becomes an object of the intellect. Beside the relation of things to virtue, they have a relation to thought. The intellect searches out the absolute order of things as they stand in the mind of God, and without the colors of affection. The intellectual and the active powers seem to succeed each other in man, and the exclusive activity of the one,

2. Sallust (1st century B.C.E.), Roman historian, in "The Conspiracy of Cataline," ch. 2.

3. Edward Gibbon (1737–1794), English historian, from *The Decline and Fall of the Roman Empire*, ch. 68.

4. Arnold von Winkelried, a Swiss hero, was killed (1386) in a battle against the Austrians at Sempach. Leonidas, king of Sparta, was killed (c. 480 B.C.E.) defending the pass at Thermopylae against the Persian army led by Xerxes.

5. English Puritan leader (1613–1662) who was executed for treason by the Restoration government because he was suspected of conspiring against King Charles II (1630–1685).

6. William Lord Russel (1639–1683) was executed by English authorities for allegedly plotting to kill Charles II.

7. Athenian statesman and general of the 4th century B.C.E. Emerson knew of him from Plutarch's *Lives*. Pindar was a Greek lyric poet of the 5th and 6th centuries B.C.E. Socrates was a Greek philosopher of the 5th century B.C.E.

generates the exclusive activity of the other. There is something unfriendly in each to the other, but they are like the alternate periods of feeding and working in animals; each prepares and certainly will be followed by the other. Therefore does beauty, which, in relation to actions, as we have seen comes unsought, and comes because it is unsought, remain for the apprehension and pursuit of the intellect; and then again, in its turn, of the active power. Nothing divine dies. All good is eternally reproductive. The beauty of nature reforms itself in the mind, and not for barren contemplation, but for new creation.

All men are in some degree impressed by the face of the world. Some men even to delight. This love of beauty is Taste. Others have the same love in such excess, that, not content with admiring, they seek to embody it in new forms. The creation of beauty is Art.

The production of a work of art throws a light upon the mystery of humanity. A work of art is an abstract or epitome of the world. It is the result or expression of nature, in miniature. For although the works of nature are innumerable and all different, the result or the expression of them all is similar and single. Nature is a sea of forms radically alike and even unique. A leaf, a sun-beam, a landscape, the ocean, make an analogous impression on the mind. What is common to them all,—that perfectness and harmony, is beauty. Therefore the standard of beauty, is the entire circuit of natural forms,—the totality of nature; which the Italians expressed by defining beauty "il piu nell' uno."[8] Nothing is quite beautiful alone: nothing but is beautiful in the whole. A single object is only so far beautiful as it suggests this universal grace. The poet, the painter, the sculptor, the musician, the architect seek each to concentrate this radiance of the world on one point, and each in his several work to satisfy the love of beauty which stimulates him to produce. Thus is Art, a nature passed through the alembic[9] of man. Thus in art, does nature work through the will of a man filled with the beauty of her first works.

The world thus exists to the soul to satisfy the desire of beauty. Extend this element to the uttermost, and I call it an ultimate end. No reason can be asked or given why the soul seeks beauty. Beauty, in its largest and profoundest sense, is one expression for the universe. God is the all-fair. Truth, and goodness, and beauty, are but different faces of the same All. But beauty in nature is not ultimate. It is the herald of inward and eternal beauty, and is not alone a solid and satisfactory good. It must therefore stand as a part and not as yet the last or highest expression of the final cause of Nature.

Chapter IV. Language

A third use which Nature subserves to man is that of Language. Nature is the vehicle of thought, and in a simple, double, and threefold degree.

1. Words are signs of natural facts.
2. Particular natural facts are symbols of particular spiritual facts.
3. Nature is the symbol of spirit.

8. The many in one (Italian); a borrowing from Coleridge.

9. A distilling apparatus.

1. Words are signs of natural facts. The use of natural history is to give us aid in supernatural history. The use of the outer creation is to give us language for the beings and changes of the inward creation. Every word which is used to express a moral or intellectual fact, if traced to its root, is found to be borrowed from some material appearance. *Right* originally means *straight*; *wrong* means *twisted*. *Spirit* primarily means *wind*; *transgression*, the crossing of a *line*; *supercilious*, the *raising of the eye-brow*. We say the *heart* to express emotion, the *head* to denote thought; and *thought* and *emotion* are, in their turn, words borrowed from sensible things, and now appropriated to spiritual nature. Most of the process by which this transformation is made, is hidden from us in the remote time when language was framed; but the same tendency may be daily observed in children. Children and savages use only nouns or names of things, which they continually convert into verbs, and apply to analogous mental acts.

2. But this origin of all words that convey a spiritual import,—so conspicuous a fact in the history of language,—is our least debt to nature. It is not words only that are emblematic; it is things which are emblematic. Every natural fact is a symbol of some spiritual fact.[1] Every appearance in nature corresponds to some state of the mind, and that state of the mind can only be described by presenting that natural appearance as its picture. An enraged man is a lion, a cunning man is a fox, a firm man is a rock, a learned man is a torch. A lamb is innocence; a snake is subtle spite; flowers express to us the delicate affections. Light and darkness are our familiar expression for knowledge and ignorance; and heat for love. Visible distance behind and before us, is respectively our image of memory and hope.

Who looks upon a river in a meditative hour, and is not reminded of the flux of all things? Throw a stone into the stream, and the circles that propagate themselves are the beautiful type of all influence. Man is conscious of a universal soul within or behind his individual life, wherein, as in a firmament, the natures of Justice, Truth, Love, Freedom, arise and shine. This universal soul, he calls Reason: it is not mine or thine or his, but we are its; we are its property and men.[2] And the blue sky in which the private earth is buried, the sky with its eternal calm, and full of everlasting orbs, is the type of Reason. That which, intellectually considered, we call Reason, considered in relation to nature, we call Spirit. Spirit is the Creator. Spirit hath life in itself. And man in all ages and countries, embodies it in his language, as the FATHER.

It is easily seen that there is nothing lucky or capricious in these analogies, but that they are constant, and pervade nature. These are not the dreams of a few poets, here and there, but man is an analogist, and studies relations in all objects. He is placed in the centre of beings, and a ray of relation passes from every other being to him. And neither can man be understood without these objects, nor these objects without man. All the facts in natural history taken by themselves, have no value, but are barren like a single sex. But marry it to human history, and it is full of life. Whole Floras, all Linnæus'

1. This passage invokes the doctrine of correspondences between the spiritual and natural worlds developed by the Swedish theologian and mystic Emanuel Swedenborg (1688–1772).

2. By *reason*, Emerson means something like the intuitive powers of the mind; by *understanding*, he means logical and empirical reasoning. For Emerson, a suprarational reason is the higher faculty. Emerson probably derived these Kantian terms from Samuel Taylor Coleridge's *Biographia Literaria* (1817).

and Buffon's[3] volume, are but dry catalogues of facts; but the most trivial of these facts, the habit of a plant, the organs, or work, or noise of an insect, applied to the illustration of a fact in intellectual philosophy, or, in any way associated to human nature, affects us in the most lively and agreeable manner. The seed of a plant,—to what affecting analogies in the nature of man, is that little fruit made use of, in all discourse, up to the voice of Paul, who calls the human corpse a seed,—"It is sown a natural body; it is raised a spiritual body."[4] The motion of the earth round its axis, and round the sun, makes the day, and the year. These are certain amounts of brute light and heat. But is there no intent of an analogy between man's life and the seasons? And do the seasons gain no grandeur or pathos from that analogy? The instincts of the ant are very unimportant considered as the ant's; but the moment a ray of relation is seen to extend from it to man, and the little drudge is seen to be a monitor, a little body with a mighty heart, then all its habits, even that said to be recently observed, that it never sleeps, become sublime.

Because of this radical[5] correspondence between visible things and human thoughts, savages, who have only what is necessary, converse in figures. As we go back in history, language becomes more picturesque, until its infancy, when it is all poetry; or, all spiritual facts are represented by natural symbols. The same symbols are found to make the original elements of all languages. It has moreover been observed, that the idioms of all languages approach each other in passages of the greatest eloquence and power. And as this is the first language, so is it the last. This immediate dependence of language upon nature, this conversion of an outward phenomenon into a type of somewhat in human life, never loses its power to affect us. It is this which gives that piquancy to the conversation of a strong-natured farmer or back-woodsman, which all men relish.

Thus is nature an interpreter, by whose means man converses with his fellow men. A man's power to connect his thought with its proper symbol, and so utter it, depends on the simplicity of his character, that is, upon his love of truth and his desire to communicate it without loss. The corruption of man is followed by the corruption of language. When simplicity of character and the sovereignty of ideas is broken up by the prevalence of secondary desires, the desire of riches, the desire of pleasure, the desire of power, the desire of praise,—and duplicity and falsehood take place of simplicity and truth, the power over nature as an interpreter of the will, is in a degree lost; new imagery ceases to be created, and old words are perverted to stand for things which are not; a paper currency is employed when there is no bullion in the vaults. In due time, the fraud is manifest, and words lose all power to stimulate the understanding or the affections. Hundreds of writers may be found in every long-civilized nation, who for a short time believe, and make others believe, that they see and utter truths, who do not of themselves clothe one thought in its natural garment, but who feed unconsciously upon the language created by the primary writers of the country, those, namely, who hold primarily on nature.

3. French naturalist (1707–1788). Linnæus was Carl von Linné (1707–1778), Swedish botanist. Both were developing systems of classification for natural objects.

4. 1 Corinthians 15.44.

5. Fundamental (literally "from the root").

But wise men pierce this rotten diction and fasten words again to visible things; so that picturesque language is at once a commanding certificate that he who employs it, is a man in alliance with truth and God. The moment our discourse rises above the ground line of familiar facts, and is inflamed with passion or exalted by thought, it clothes itself in images. A man conversing in earnest, if he watch his intellectual processes, will find that always a material image, more or less luminous, arises in his mind, contemporaneous with every thought, which furnishes the vestment of the thought. Hence, good writing and brilliant discourse are perpetual allegories. This imagery is spontaneous. It is the blending of experience with the present action of the mind. It is proper creation. It is the working of the Original Cause through the instruments he has already made.

These facts may suggest the advantage which the country-life possesses for a powerful mind, over the artificial and curtailed life of cities. We know more from nature than we can at will communicate. Its light flows into the mind evermore, and we forget its presence. The poet, the orator, bred in the woods, whose scenes have been nourished by their fair and appeasing changes, year after year, without design and without heed,—shall not lose their lesson altogether, in the roar of cities or the broil of politics. Long hereafter, amidst agitation and terror in national councils,—in the hour of revolution,—these solemn images shall reappear in their morning lustre, as fit symbols and words of the thoughts which the passing events shall awaken. At the call of a noble sentiment, again the woods wave, the pines murmur, the river rolls and shines, and the cattle low upon the mountains, as he saw and heard them in his infancy. And with these forms, the spells of persuasion, the keys of power are put into his hands.

3. We are thus assisted by natural objects in the expression of particular meanings. But how great a language to convey such pepper-corn[6] informations! Did it need such noble races of creatures, this profusion of forms, this host of orbs in heaven, to furnish man with the dictionary and grammar of his municipal speech? Whilst we use this grand cipher to expedite the affairs of our pot and kettle, we feel that we have not yet put it to its use, neither are able. We are like travellers using the cinders of a volcano to roast their eggs. Whilst we see that it always stands ready to clothe what we would say, we cannot avoid the question, whether the characters are not significant of themselves. Have mountains, and waves, and skies, no significance but what we consciously give them, when we employ them as emblems of our thoughts? The world is emblematic. Parts of speech are metaphors because the whole of nature is a metaphor of the human mind. The laws of moral nature answer to those of matter as face to face in a glass. "The visible world and the relation of its parts, is the dial plate of the invisible."[7] The axioms of physics translate the laws of ethics.[8] Thus, "the whole is greater than its part;" "reaction is equal to action;" "the smallest weight may be made to lift the greatest, the difference of weight being compensated by time;" and many the like propositions, which have an ethical as well as physical sense. These

6. Ordinary, everyday.

7. Emerson copied the Swedenborg quotation from the *New Jerusalem Magazine* (July 1832).

8. Adapted from Mme. De Staël's "Germany" (1813): "Even a mathematical axiom is a moral rule."

propositions have a much more extensive and universal sense when applied to human life, than when confined to technical use.

In like manner, the memorable words of history, and the proverbs of nations, consist usually of a natural fact, selected as a picture or parable of a moral truth. Thus; A rolling stone gathers no moss; A bird in the hand is worth two in the bush; A cripple in the right way, will beat a racer in the wrong; Make hay whilst the sun shines; 'T is hard to carry a full cup even; Vinegar is the son of wine; The last ounce broke the camel's back; Long-lived trees make roots first;—and the like.[9] In their primary sense these are trivial facts, but we repeat them for the value of their analogical import. What is true of proverbs, is true of all fables, parables, and allegories.

This relation between the mind and matter is not fancied by some poet, but stands in the will of God, and so is free to be known by all men. It appears to men, or it does not appear. When in fortunate hours we ponder this miracle, the wise man doubts, if, at all other times, he is not blind and deaf;

——"Can these things be,
And overcome us like a summer's cloud,
Without our special wonder?"[1]

for the universe becomes transparent, and the light of higher laws than its own, shines through it. It is the standing problem which has exercised the wonder and the study of every fine genius since the world began; from the era of the Egyptians and the Brahmins, to that of Pythagoras, of Plato, of Bacon, of Leibnitz,[2] of Swedenborg. There sits the Sphinx at the road-side, and from age to age, as each prophet comes by, he tries his fortune at reading her riddle.[3] There seems to be a necessity in spirit to manifest itself in material forms; and day and night, river and storm, beast and bird, acid and alkali, preëxist in necessary Ideas in the mind of God, and are what they are by virtue of preceding affections, in the world of spirit. A Fact is the end or last issue of spirit. The visible creation is the terminus or the circumference of the invisible world. "Material objects," said a French philosopher, "are necessarily kinds of *scoriæ* of the substantial thoughts of the Creator, which must always preserve an exact relation to their first origin; in other words, visible nature must have a spiritual and moral side."[4]

This doctrine is abstruse, and though the images of "garment," "scoriæ," "mirror," &c., may stimulate the fancy, we must summon the aid of subtler and more vital expositors to make it plain. "Every scripture is to be inter-

9. Proverbs drawn from several writers, including Francis Bacon, *The Advancement of Learning* (1605), and Scottish theologian Robert Leighton (1611–1684), *Select Works* (1832).
1. Shakespeare's *Macbeth* 3.4.110–12.
2. Gottfried Wilhelm Leibnitz (1646–1716), German mathematician who championed philosophical idealism and symbolic logic. Pythagorus (c. 582–ca. 507 B.C.E.), Greek philosopher who believed in the transmigration of souls. Plato (c. 427–347 B.C.E.), Greek philosopher who was the founder of philosophical idealism. Sir Francis Bacon (1561–1626), English philosopher who developed inductive and empirical approaches to science.
3. In Greek mythology, a winged monster with a lion's body and head of a woman, who challenged those entering Thebes with a riddle; when they answered incorrectly, she killed them. But when Oedipus answered correctly, the Sphinx was so distraught that she killed herself, much to the delight of the Theban people, who named Oedipus their king.
4. From the French Swedenborgian Guillaume Oegger's "The True Messiah" (1829), which Emerson had seen in a manuscript translation, perhaps by Elizabeth Peabody. *Scoriæ*: i.e., scoria; slag or refuse left after metal has been smelted from ore.

preted by the same spirit which gave it forth,"—is the fundamental law of criticism.[5] A life in harmony with nature, the love of truth and of virtue, will purge the eyes to understand her text. By degrees we may come to know the primitive sense of the permanent objects of nature, so that the world shall be to us an open book, and every form significant of its hidden life and final cause.

A new interest surprises us, whilst, under the view now suggested, we contemplate the fearful extent and multitude of objects; since "every object rightly seen, unlocks a new faculty of the soul."[6] That which was unconscious truth, becomes, when interpreted and defined in an object, a part of the domain of knowledge,—a new amount to the magazine[7] of power.

Chapter V. Discipline

In view of this significance of nature, we arrive at once at a new fact, that nature is a discipline. This use of the world includes the preceding uses, as parts of itself.

Space, time, society, labor, climate, food, locomotion, the animals, the mechanical forces, give us sincerest lessons, day by day, whose meaning is unlimited. They educate both the Understanding and the Reason. Every property of matter is a school for the understanding,—its solidity or resistance, its inertia, its extension, its figure, its divisibility. The understanding adds, divides, combines, measures, and finds everlasting nutriment and room for its activity in this worthy scene. Meantime, Reason transfers all these lessons into its own world of thought, by perceiving the analogy that marries Matter and Mind.

1. Nature is a discipline of the understanding in intellectual truths. Our dealing with sensible objects is a constant exercise in the necessary lessons of difference, of likeness, of order, of being and seeming, of progressive arrangement; of ascent from particular to general; of combination to one end of manifold forces. Proportioned to the importance of the organ to be formed, is the extreme care with which its tuition is provided,—a care pretermitted[8] in no single case. What tedious training, day after day, year after year, never ending, to form the common sense; what continual reproduction of annoyances, inconveniences, dilemmas; what rejoicing over us of little men; what disputing of prices, what reckonings of interest,—and all to form the Hand of the mind;—to instruct us that "good thoughts are no better than good dreams, unless they be executed!"[9]

The same good office is performed by Property and its filial systems of debt and credit. Debt, grinding debt, whose iron face the widow, the orphan, and the sons of genius fear and hate;—debt, which consumes so much time, which so cripples and disheartens a great spirit with cares that seem so base, is a preceptor whose lessons cannot be foregone, and is needed most by those who suffer from it most. Moreover, property, which has been well compared to snow,—"if it fall level to-day, it will be blown into drifts tomorrow,"—is

5. From the English Quaker George Fox (1624–1691). Emerson's probable source for this quote is William Sewel's *History of the Rise, Increase, and Progress of the Christian People called Quakers* (1722).

6. From Coleridge's *Aids to Reflection* (1829).

7. Storehouse.

8. Neglected. "Tuition": guardianship.

9. Adapted from Bacon's "Of Great Place," in *Essays* (1625).

merely the surface action of internal machinery, like the index on the face of a clock. Whilst now it is the gymnastics of the understanding, it is hiving in the foresight of the spirit, experience in profounder laws.

The whole character and fortune of the individual is affected by the least inequalities in the culture of the understanding; for example, in the perception of differences. Therefore is Space, and therefore Time, that man may know that things are not huddled and lumped, but sundered and individual. A bell and a plough have each their use, and neither can do the office of the other. Water is good to drink, coal to burn, wool to wear; but wool cannot be drunk, nor water spun, nor coal eaten. The wise man shows his wisdom in separation, in gradation, and his scale of creatures and of merits, is as wide as nature. The foolish have no range in their scale, but suppose every man is as every other man. What is not good they call the worst, and what is not hateful, they call the best.

In like manner, what good heed, nature forms in us! She pardons no mistakes. Her yea is yea, and her nay, nay.

The first steps in Agriculture, Astronomy, Zoölogy, (those first steps which the farmer, the hunter, and the sailor take,) teach that nature's dice are always loaded; that in her heaps and rubbish are concealed sure and useful results.

How calmly and genially the mind apprehends one after another the laws of physics! What noble emotions dilate the mortal as he enters into the counsels of the creation, and feels by knowledge the privilege to BE! His insight refines him. The beauty of nature shines in his own breast. Man is greater that he can see this, and the universe less, because Time and Space relations vanish as laws are known.

Here again we are impressed and even daunted by the immense Universe to be explored. 'What we know, is a point to what we do not know.'[1] Open any recent journal of science, and weigh the problems suggested concerning Light, Heat, Electricity, Magnetism, Physiology, Geology, and judge whether the interest of natural science is likely to be soon exhausted.

Passing by many particulars of the discipline of nature we must not omit to specify two.

The exercise of the Will or the lesson of power is taught in every event. From the child's successive possession of his several senses up to the hour when he saith, "thy will be done!"[2] he is learning the secret, that he can reduce under his will, not only particular events, but great classes, nay the whole series of events, and so conform all facts to his character. Nature is thoroughly mediate. It is made to serve. It receives the dominion of man as meekly as the ass on which the Saviour rode.[3] It offers all its kingdoms to man as the raw material which he may mould into what is useful. Man is never weary of working it up. He forges the subtile and delicate air into wise and melodious words, and gives them wing as angels of persuasion and command. More and more, with every thought, does his kingdom stretch over things, until the world becomes, at last, only a realized will,—the double of the man.

1. A saying ascribed both to Sir Isaac Newton (1642–1727), English mathematician and philosopher, and to Bishop Joseph Butler (1692–1752), English moralist.
2. Matthew 6.10 and 26.42.
3. Matthew 21.5.

2. Sensible objects conform to the premonitions of Reason and reflect the conscience. All things are moral; and in their boundless changes have an unceasing reference to spiritual nature. Therefore is nature glorious with form, color, and motion, that every globe in the remotest heaven; every chemical change from the rudest crystal up to the laws of life; every change of vegetation from the first principle of growth in the eye of a leaf, to the tropical forest and antediluvian[4] coal-mine; every animal function from the sponge up to Hercules,[5] shall hint or thunder to man the laws of right and wrong, and echo the Ten Commandments. Therefore is nature always the ally of Religion: lends all her pomp and riches to the religious sentiment. Prophet and priest, David, Isaiah,[6] Jesus, have drawn deeply from this source.

This ethical character so penetrates the bone and marrow of nature, as to seem the end for which it was made. Whatever private purpose is answered by any member or part, this is its public and universal function, and is never omitted. Nothing in nature is exhausted in its first use. When a thing has served an end to the uttermost, it is wholly new for an ulterior service. In God, every end is converted into a new means. Thus the use of Commodity, regarded by itself, is mean and squalid. But it is to the mind an education in the great doctrine of Use, namely, that a thing is good only so far as it serves; that a conspiring of parts and efforts to the production of an end, is essential to any being. The first and gross manifestation of this truth, is our inevitable and hated training in values and wants, in corn and meat.

It has already been illustrated, in treating of the significance of material things, that every natural process is but a version of a moral sentence. The moral law lies at the centre of nature and radiates to the circumference. It is the pith and marrow of every substance, every relation, and every process. All things with which we deal, preach to us. What is a farm but a mute gospel? The chaff and the wheat, weeds and plants, blight, rain, insects, sun,—it is a sacred emblem from the first furrow of spring to the last stack which the snow of winter overtakes in the fields. But the sailor, the shepherd, the miner, the merchant, in their several resorts, have each an experience precisely parallel and leading to the same conclusions. Because all organizations are radically alike. Nor can it be doubted that this moral sentiment which thus scents the air, and grows in the grain, and impregnates the waters of the world, is caught by man and sinks into his soul. The moral influence of nature upon every individual is that amount of truth which it illustrates to him. Who can estimate this? Who can guess how much firmness the sea-beaten rock has taught the fisherman? how much tranquillity has been reflected to man from the azure sky, over whose unspotted deeps the winds forevermore drive flocks of stormy clouds, and leave no wrinkle or stain? how much industry and providence and affection we have caught from the pantomime of brutes? What a searching preacher of self-command is the varying phenomenon of Health!

Herein is especially apprehended the Unity of Nature,—the Unity in Variety,—which meets us everywhere. All the endless variety of things make

4. Before the Flood, which destroyed all living creatures not in Noah's ark (Genesis 6–9).

5. Roman name for the Greek mythological hero Heracles, renowned for feats of strength.

6. Old Testament prophet. David was the second king of Israel.

a unique, an identical impression. Xenophanes[7] complained in his old age, that, look where he would, all things hastened back to Unity. He was weary of seeing the same entity in the tedious variety of forms. The fable of Proteus has a cordial[8] truth. Every particular in nature, a leaf, a drop, a crystal, a moment of time is related to the whole, and partakes of the perfection of the whole. Each particle is a microcosm, and faithfully renders the likeness of the world.

Not only resemblances exist in things whose analogy is obvious, as when we detect the type of the human hand in the flipper of the fossil saurus, but also in objects wherein there is great superficial unlikeness. Thus architecture is called 'frozen music,' by De Stael and Goethe.[9] 'A Gothic church,' said Coleridge,[1] 'is a petrified religion.' Michael Angelo maintained, that, to an architect, a knowledge of anatomy is essential.[2] In Haydn's[3] oratorios, the notes present to the imagination not only motions, as, of the snake, the stag, and the elephant, but colors also; as the green grass. The granite is differenced in its laws only by the more or less of heat, from the river that wears it away. The river, as it flows, resembles the air that flows over it; the air resembles the light which traverses it with more subtile currents; the light resembles the heat which rides with it through Space. Each creature is only a modification of the other; the likeness in them is more than the difference, and their radical law is one and the same. Hence it is, that a rule of one art, or a law of one organization, holds true throughout nature. So intimate is this Unity, that, it is easily seen, it lies under the undermost garment of nature, and betrays its source in universal Spirit. For, it pervades Thought also. Every universal truth which we express in words, implies or supposes every other truth. *Omne verum vero consonat.*[4] It is like a great circle on a sphere, comprising all possible circles; which, however, may be drawn, and comprise it, in like manner. Every such truth is the absolute Ens[5] seen from one side. But it has innumerable sides.

The same central Unity is still more conspicuous in actions. Words are finite organs of the infinite mind. They cannot cover the dimensions of what is in truth. They break, chop, and impoverish it. An action is the perfection and publication of thought. A right action seems to fill the eye, and to be related to all nature. "The wise man, in doing one thing, does all; or, in the one thing he does rightly, he sees the likeness of all which is done rightly."[6]

Words and actions are not the attributes of mute and brute nature. They introduce us to that singular form which predominates over all other forms. This is the human. All other organizations appear to be degradations of the human form. When this organization appears among so many that surround it, the spirit prefers it to all others. It says, 'From such as this, have I drawn joy and knowledge. In such as this, have I found and beheld myself. I will speak to it. It can speak again. It can yield me thought already formed

7. Greek philosopher of 5th and 6th centuries B.C.E. who taught the unity of all existence.
8. Vital, heartwarming. Proteus was a sea god who could change his shape to evade any captor.
9. Johann Wolfgang von Goethe (1749–1832), in his *Conversations with Eckermann*. Mme. de Staël (1766–1817), in *Corinne*, book 4, chapter 3.
1. In his "Lecture on the General Character of the Gothic Mind in the Middle Ages" (1836).
2. From the sketch of Michelangelo (1475–1564) in *Lives of Eminent Persons* (1833).
3. Joseph Haydn (1732–1809), Austrian composer.
4. Every truth is consonant with every other truth (Latin).
5. Abstract being (Latin).
6. Paraphrase of Goethe's *Wilhelm Meister* (1795–96).

and alive.' In fact, the eye,—the mind,—is always accompanied by these forms, male and female; and these are incomparably the richest informations[7] of the power and order that lie at the heart of things. Unfortunately, every one of them bears the marks as of some injury; is marred and superficially defective. Nevertheless, far different from the deaf and dumb nature around them, these all rest like fountain-pipes on the unfathomed sea of thought and virtue whereto they alone, of all organizations, are the entrances.

It were a pleasant inquiry to follow into detail their ministry to our education, but where would it stop? We are associated in adolescent and adult life with some friends, who, like skies and waters, are coextensive with our idea; who, answering each to a certain affection of the soul, satisfy our desire on that side; whom we lack power to put at such focal distance from us, that we can mend or even analyze them. We cannot chuse but love them. When much intercourse with a friend has supplied us with a standard of excellence, and has increased our respect for the resources of God who thus sends a real person to outgo our ideal; when he has, moreover, become an object of thought, and, whilst his character retains all its unconscious effect, is converted in the mind into solid and sweet wisdom,—it is a sign to us that his office is closing, and he is commonly withdrawn from our sight in a short time.

Chapter VI. Idealism

Thus is the unspeakable but intelligible and practicable meaning of the world conveyed to man, the immortal pupil, in every object of sense. To this one end of Discipline, all parts of nature conspire.

A noble doubt perpetually suggests itself, whether this end be not the Final Cause of the Universe; and whether nature outwardly exists. It is a sufficient account of that Appearance we call the World, that God will teach a human mind, and so makes it the receiver of a certain number of congruent sensations, which we call sun and moon, man and woman, house and trade. In my utter impotence to test the authenticity of the report of my senses, to know whether the impressions they make on me correspond with outlying objects, what difference does it make, whether Orion[8] is up there in heaven, or some god paints the image in the firmament of the soul? The relations of parts and the end of the whole remaining the same, what is the difference, whether land and sea interact, and worlds revolve and intermingle without number or end,—deep yawning under deep,[9] and galaxy balancing galaxy, throughout absolute space, or, whether, without relations of time and space, the same appearances are inscribed in the constant faith of man. Whether nature enjoy a substantial existence without, or is only in the apocalypse[1] of the mind, it is alike useful and alike venerable to me. Be it what it may, it is ideal to me, so long as I cannot try the accuracy of my senses.

The frivolous make themselves merry with the Ideal theory,[2] as if its consequences were burlesque; as if it affected the stability of nature. It surely

7. Products of the inward, form-giving capacity.
8. Constellation named for the mythical Greek hunter.
9. From Psalm 42.7: "Deep calleth unto deep at the noise of thy waterspouts: all thy waves and thy billows are gone over me."
1. Revelation (Greek).
2. The idea that the mind cannot know anything except its own ideas and thus cannot know material things in themselves is associated with Bishop George Berkeley (1685–1753), whose writings were an important influence on Emerson.

does not. God never jests with us, and will not compromise the end of nature, by permitting any inconsequence in its procession. Any distrust of the permanence of laws, would paralyze the faculties of man. Their permanence is sacredly respected, and his faith therein is perfect. The wheels and springs of man are all set to the hypothesis of the permanence of nature. We are not built like a ship to be tossed, but like a house to stand. It is a natural consequence of this structure, that, so long as the active powers predominate over the reflective, we resist with indignation any hint that nature is more short-lived or mutable than spirit. The broker, the wheelwright, the carpenter, the tollman, are much displeased at the intimation.

But whilst we acquiesce entirely in the permanence of natural laws, the question of the absolute existence of nature, still remains open. It is the uniform effect of culture on the human mind, not to shake our faith in the stability of particular phenomena, as of heat, water, azote;[3] but to lead us to regard nature as a phenomenon, not a substance; to attribute necessary existence to spirit; to esteem nature as an accident and an effect.

To the senses and the unrenewed understanding, belongs a sort of instinctive belief in the absolute existence of nature. In their view, man and nature are indissolubly joined. Things are ultimates, and they never look beyond their sphere. The presence of Reason mars this faith. The first effort of thought tends to relax this despotism of the senses, which binds us to nature as if we were a part of it, and shows us nature aloof, and, as it were, afloat. Until this higher agency intervened, the animal eye sees, with wonderful accuracy, sharp outlines and colored surfaces. When the eye of Reason opens, to outline and surface are at once added, grace and expression. These proceed from imagination and affection, and abate somewhat of the angular distinctness of objects. If the Reason be stimulated to more earnest vision, outlines and surfaces become transparent, and are no longer seen; causes and spirits are seen through them. The best, the happiest moments of life, are these delicious awakenings of the higher powers, and the reverential withdrawing of nature before its God.

Let us proceed to indicate the effects of culture. 1. Our first institution[4] in the Ideal philosophy is a hint from nature herself.

Nature is made to conspire with spirit to emancipate us. Certain mechanical changes, a small alteration in our local position apprizes us of a dualism. We are strangely affected by seeing the shore from a moving ship, from a balloon, or through the tints of an unusual sky. The least change in our point of view, gives the whole world a pictorial air. A man who seldom rides, needs only to get into a coach and traverse his own town, to turn the street into a puppet-show. The men, the women,—talking, running, bartering, fighting,—the earnest mechanic, the lounger, the beggar, the boys, the dogs, are unrealized[5] at once, or, at least, wholly detached from all relation to the observer, and seen as apparent, not substantial beings. What new thoughts are suggested by seeing a face of country quite familiar, in the rapid movement of the railroad car! Nay, the most wonted objects, (make a very slight change in

3. Nitrogen.
4. Instruction. "Effects of culture": in the sense of the effects of awakening thought.
5. Made unsubstantial. "Mechanic": manual laborer.

the point of vision,) please us most. In a camera obscura,[6] the butcher's cart, and the figure of one of our own family amuse us. So a portrait of a well-known face gratifies us. Turn the eyes upside down, by looking at the landscape through your legs, and how agreeable is the picture, though you have seen it any time these twenty years!

In these cases, by mechanical means, is suggested the difference between the observer and the spectacle,—between man and nature. Hence arises a pleasure mixed with awe; I may say, a low degree of the sublime is felt from the fact, probably, that man is hereby apprized, that, whilst the world is a spectacle, something in himself is stable.

2. In a higher manner, the poet communicates the same pleasure. By a few strokes he delineates, as on air, the sun, the mountain, the camp, the city, the hero, the maiden, not different from what we know them, but only lifted from the ground and float before the eye. He unfixes the land and the sea, makes them revolve around the axis of his primary thought, and disposes them anew. Possessed himself by a heroic passion, he uses matter as symbols of it. The sensual man conforms thoughts to things; the poet conforms things to his thoughts.[7] The one esteems nature as rooted and fast; the other, as fluid, and impresses his being thereon. To him, the refractory world is ductile and flexible; he invests dusts and stones with humanity and makes them the words of the Reason. The imagination may be defined to be, the use which the Reason makes of the material world. Shakspeare possesses the power of subordinating nature for the purposes of expression, beyond all poets. His imperial muse tosses the creation like a bauble from hand to hand, to embody any capricious shade of thought that is uppermost in his mind. The remotest spaces of nature are visited, and the farthest sundered things are brought together, by a subtile spiritual connexion. We are made aware that magnitude of material things is merely relative, and all objects shrink and expand to serve the passion of the poet. Thus, in his sonnets, the lays of birds, the scents and dyes of flowers, he finds to be the *shadow* of his beloved; time, which keeps her from him, is his *chest*; the suspicion she has awakened, is her *ornament*;[8]

> The ornament of beauty is Suspect,
> A crow which flies in heaven's sweetest air.[9]

His passion is not the fruit of chance; it swells, as he speaks, to a city, or a state.

> No, it was builded far from accident;
> It suffers not in smiling pomp, nor falls
> Under the brow of thralling discontent;
> It fears not policy, that heretic,
> That works on leases of short numbered hours,
> But all alone stands hugely politic.[1]

6. Dark chamber or box with a lens or opening through which an image is projected in natural colors onto an opposite surface.
7. From Bacon's "The Advancement of Learning" (2.4.2), but more directly from William Hazlitt's adaptation.
8. Emerson summarizes Shakespeare's Sonnet 98 and refers to Sonnet 65 ("Shall Time's best jewel from Time's chest lie hid?").
9. Shakespeare's Sonnet 70.
1. Shakespeare's Sonnet 124.

In the strength of his constancy, the Pyramids[2] seem to him recent and transitory. And the freshness of youth and love dazzles him with its resemblance to morning.

> Take those lips away
> Which so sweetly were forsworn;
> And those eyes,—the break of day,
> Lights that do mislead the morn.[3]

The wild beauty of this hyperbole, I may say, in passing, it would not be easy to match in literature.

This transfiguration which all material objects undergo through the passion of the poet,—this power which he exerts, at any moment, to magnify the small, to micrify the great,—might be illustrated by a thousand examples from his Plays. I have before me the Tempest, and will cite only these few lines.

> PROSPERO. The strong based promontory
> Have I made shake, and by the spurs plucked up
> The pine and cedar.[4]

Prospero calls for music to sooth the frantic Alonzo, and his companions;

> A solemn air, and the best comforter
> To an unsettled fancy, cure thy brains
> Now useless, boiled within thy skull.

Again;

> The charm dissolves space
> And, as the morning steals upon the night,
> Melting the darkness, so their rising senses
> Begin to chase the ignorant fumes that mantle
> Their clearer reason.

> Their understanding
> Begins to swell: and the approaching tide
> Will shortly fill the reasonable shores
> That now lie foul and muddy.

The perception of real affinities between events, (that is to say, of *ideal* affinities, for those only are real,) enables the poet thus to make free with the most imposing forms and phenomena of the world, and to assert the predominance of the soul.

3. Whilst thus the poet delights us by animating[5] nature like a creator, with his own thoughts, he differs from the philosopher only herein, that the one proposes Beauty as his main end; the other Truth. But, the philosopher, not less than the poet, postpones the apparent order and relations of things to the empire of thought. "The problem of philosophy," according to Plato,

2. Shakespeare's Sonnet 123: "No, Time, thou shalt not boast that I do change: / Thy pyramids built up with newer might / To me are nothing novel, nothing strange: / They are but dressings of a former sight."

3. From Shakespeare's *Measure for Measure* 5.1.1–4.

4. Shakespeare's *The Tempest* 5.1.46–48; later quotations are from 5.1.58–60, 64–68, and 79–82.

5. Giving life to.

"is, for all that exists conditionally, to find a ground unconditioned and absolute."[6] It proceeds on the faith that a law determines all phenomena, which being known, the phenomena can be predicted. That law, when in the mind, is an idea. Its beauty is infinite. The true philosopher and the true poet are one, and a beauty, which is truth, and a truth, which is beauty, is the aim of both. Is not the charm of one of Plato's or Aristotle's definitions, strictly like that of the Antigone of Sophocles?[7] It is, in both cases, that a spiritual life has been imparted to nature; that the solid seeming block of matter has been pervaded and dissolved by a thought; that this feeble human being has penetrated the vast masses of nature with an informing soul, and recognised itself in their harmony, that is, seized their law. In physics, when this is attained, the memory disburthens itself of its cumbrous catalogues of particulars, and carries centuries of observation in a single formula.

Thus even in physics, the material is ever degraded before the spiritual. The astronomer, the geometer, rely on their irrefragable analysis, and disdain the results of observation. The sublime remark of Euler[8] on his law of arches, "This will be found contrary to all experience, yet it is true;" had already transferred nature into the mind, and left matter like an outcast corpse.

4. Intellectual science has been observed to beget invariably a doubt of the existence of matter. Turgot[9] said, "He that has never doubted the existence of matter, may be assured he has no aptitude for metaphysical inquiries." It fastens the attention upon immortal necessary uncreated natures, that is, upon Ideas; and in their beautiful and majestic presence, we feel that our outward being is a dream and a shade. Whilst we wait in this Olympus of gods, we think of nature as an appendix to the soul. We ascend into their region, and know that these are the thoughts of the Supreme Being. "These are they who were set up from everlasting, from the beginning, or ever the earth was. When he prepared the heavens, they were there; when he established the clouds above, when he strengthened the fountains of the deep. Then they were by him, as one brought up with him. Of them took he counsel."[1]

Their influence is proportionate. As objects of science, they are accessible to few men. Yet all men are capable of being raised by piety or by passion, into their region. And no man touches these divine natures, without becoming, in some degree, himself divine. Like a new soul, they renew the body. We become physically nimble and lightsome; we tread on air; life is no longer irksome, and we think it will never be so. No man fears age or misfortune or death, in their serene company, for he is transported out of the district of change. Whilst we behold unveiled the nature of Justice and Truth, we learn the difference between the absolute and the conditional or relative. We apprehend the absolute. As it were, for the first time, *we exist*. We become immortal, for we learn that time and space are relations of matter; that, with a perception of truth, or a virtuous will, they have no affinity.

6. Emerson draws this quotation from Coleridge's "The Friend" (1818).
7. Greek dramatist of the 5th century B.C.E.; in his tragedy *Antigone* the title character chooses death rather than violate her sacred duty to perform funeral rites for her slain brother.
8. Leonhard Euler (1707–1783), Swiss mathematician and physicist. Emerson took the quotation from Coleridge's *Aids to Reflection* (1829).
9. Anne Robert Jacques Turgot (1727–1781), French economist and author of a book on proofs of the existence of God.
1. Cf. Proverbs 8.23–30.

5. Finally, religion and ethics, which may be fitly called,—the practice of ideas, or the introduction of ideas into life,—have an analogous effect with all lower culture, in degrading nature and suggesting its dependence on spirit. Ethics and religion differ herein; that the one is the system of human duties commencing from man; the other, from God. Religion includes the personality of God; Ethics does not. They are one to our present design. They both put nature under foot. The first and last lesson of religion is, "The things that are seen, are temporal; the things that are unseen are eternal."[2] It puts an affront upon nature. It does that for the unschooled, which philosophy does for Berkeley and Viasa.[3] The uniform language that may be heard in the churches of the most ignorant sects, is,—'Contemn the unsubstantial shows of the world; they are vanities, dreams, shadows, unrealities; seek the realities of religion.' The devotee flouts nature. Some theosophists[4] have arrived at a certain hostility and indignation towards matter, as the Manichean and Plotinus. They distrusted in themselves any looking back to these flesh-pots of Egypt. Plotinus was ashamed of his body.[5] In short, they might all better say of matter, what Michael Angelo said of external beauty, "it is the frail and weary weed, in which God dresses the soul, which he has called into time."[6]

It appears that motion, poetry, physical and intellectual science, and religion, all tend to affect our convictions of the reality of the external world. But I own there is something ungrateful in expanding too curiously the particulars of the general proposition, that all culture tends to imbue us with idealism. I have no hostility to nature, but a child's love to it. I expand and live in the warm day like corn and melons. Let us speak her fair. I do not wish to fling stones at my beautiful mother, nor soil my gentle nest. I only wish to indicate the true position of nature in regard to man, wherein to establish man, all right education tends; as the ground which to attain is the object of human life, that is, of man's connexion with nature. Culture inverts the vulgar views of nature, and brings the mind to call that apparent, which it uses to call real, and that real, which it uses to call visionary. Children, it is true, believe in the external world. The belief that it appears only, is an afterthought, but with culture, this faith will as surely arise on the mind as did the first.

The advantage of the ideal theory over the popular faith, is this, that it presents the world in precisely that view which is most desirable to the mind. It is, in fact, the view which Reason, both speculative and practical, that is, philosophy and virtue, take. For, seen in the light of thought, the world always is phenomenal;[7] and virtue subordinates it to the mind. Idealism sees the world in God. It beholds the whole circle of persons and things, of actions and events, of country and religion, not as painfully accumulated, atom after atom, act after act, in an aged creeping Past, but as one vast picture, which God paints on the instant eternity, for the contemplation of the soul. Therefore the soul holds itself off from a too trivial and microscopic study of the

2. 2 Corinthians 4.18.
3. Reputed author of the Vedas, the ancient sacred literature of Hinduism. George Berkeley (1685–1753), Irish idealist philosopher.
4. In the broad sense of those who attempt to establish direct contact with divine principle through contemplation and revelation.
5. Plotinus was associated with Neoplatonism, a doctrine merging features from Greek philosophies with those of Judaism and Christianity.
6. Michelangelo's Sonnet 51 (c. 1530).
7. Only an appearance.

universal tablet. It respects the end too much, to immerse itself in the means. It sees something more important in Christianity, than the scandals of ecclesiastical history or the niceties of criticism; and, very incurious concerning persons or miracles, and not at all disturbed by chasms of historical evidence, it accepts from God the phenomenon, as it finds it, as the pure and awful form of religion in the world. It is not hot and passionate at the appearance of what it calls its own good or bad fortune, at the union or opposition of other persons. No man is its enemy. It accepts whatsoever befalls, as part of its lesson. It is a watcher more than a doer, and it is a doer, only that it may the better watch.

Chapter VII. Spirit

It is essential to a true theory of nature and of man, that it should contain somewhat progressive. Uses that are exhausted or that may be, and facts that end in the statement, cannot be all that is true of this brave lodging wherein man is harbored, and wherein all his faculties find appropriate and endless exercise. And all the uses of nature admit of being summed in one, which yields the activity of man an infinite scope. Through all its kingdoms, to the suburbs and outskirts of things, it is faithful to the cause whence it had its origin. It always speaks of Spirit. It suggests the absolute. It is a perpetual effect. It is a great shadow pointing always to the sun behind us.

The aspect of nature is devout. Like the figure of Jesus, she stands with bended head, and hands folded upon the breast. The happiest man is he who learns from nature the lesson of worship.

Of that ineffable essence which we call Spirit, he that thinks most, will say least. We can foresee God in the coarse and, as it were, distant phenomena of matter; but when we try to define and describe himself, both language and thought desert us, and we are as helpless as fools and savages. That essence refuses to be recorded in propositions, but when man has worshipped him intellectually, the noblest ministry of nature is to stand as the apparition[8] of God. It is the great organ through which the universal spirit speaks to the individual, and strives to lead back the individual to it.

When we consider Spirit, we see that the views already presented do not include the whole circumference of man. We must add some related thoughts.

Three problems are put by nature to the mind; What is matter? Whence is it? and Whereto? The first of these questions only, the ideal theory answers. Idealism saith: matter is a phenomenon, not a substance. Idealism acquaints us with the total disparity between the evidence of our own being, and the evidence of the world's being. The one is perfect, the other, incapable of any assurance; the mind is a part of the nature of things; the world is a divine dream, from which we may presently awake to the glories and certainties of day. Idealism is a hypothesis to account for nature by other principles than those of carpentry and chemistry. Yet, if it only deny the existence of matter, it does not satisfy the demands of the spirit. It leaves God out of me. It leaves me in the splendid labyrinth of my perceptions, to wander without end. Then the heart resists it, because it baulks the affections in denying substantive

8. Visible state.

being to men and women. Nature is so pervaded with human life, that there is something of humanity in all, and in every particular. But this theory makes nature foreign to me, and does not account for that consanguinity which we acknowledge to it.

Let it stand then, in the present state of our knowledge, merely as a useful introductory hypothesis, serving to apprize us of the eternal distinction between the soul and the world.

But when, following the invisible steps of thought, we come to inquire, Whence is matter? and Whereto? many truths arise to us out of the recesses of consciousness. We learn that the highest is present to the soul of man, that the dread universal essence, which is not wisdom, or love, or beauty, or power, but all in one, and each entirely, is that for which all things exist, and that by which they are; that spirit creates; that behind nature, throughout nature, spirit is present; that spirit is one and not compound; that spirit does not act upon us from without, that is, in space and time, but spiritually, or through ourselves. Therefore, that spirit, that is, the Supreme Being, does not build up nature around us, but puts it forth through us, as the life of the tree puts forth new branches and leaves through the pores of the old. As a plant upon the earth, so a man rests upon the bosom of God: he is nourished by unfailing fountains, and draws, at his need, inexhaustible power. Who can set bounds to the possibilities of man? Once inspire the infinite, by being admitted to behold the absolute natures of justice and truth, and we learn that man has access to the entire mind of the Creator, is himself the creator in the finite. This view, which admonishes me where the sources of wisdom and power lie, and points to virtue as to

"The golden key
Which opes the palace of eternity,"[9]

carries upon its face the highest certificate of truth, because it animates me to create my own world through the purification of my soul.

The world proceeds from the same spirit as the body of man. It is a remoter and inferior incarnation of God, a projection of God in the unconscious. But it differs from the body in one important respect. It is not, like that, now subjected to the human will. Its serene order is inviolable by us. It is therefore, to us, the present expositor of the divine mind. It is a fixed point whereby we may measure our departure. As we degenerate, the contrast between us and our house is more evident. We are as much strangers in nature, as we are aliens from God. We do not understand the notes of the birds. The fox and the deer run away from us; the bear and tiger rend us. We do not know the uses of more than a few plants, as corn and the apple, the potato and the vine. Is not the landscape, every glimpse of which hath a grandeur, a face of him? Yet this may show us what discord is between man and nature, for you cannot freely admire a noble landscape, if laborers are digging in the field hard by. The poet finds something ridiculous in his delight, until he is out of the sight of men.

9. From Milton's *Comus* 13–14.

Chapter VIII. Prospects

In inquiries respecting the laws of the world and the frame of things, the highest reason is always the truest. That which seems faintly possible—it is so refined, is often faint and dim because it is deepest seated in the mind among the eternal verities. Empirical science is apt to cloud the sight, and, by the very knowledge of functions and processes, to bereave the student of the manly contemplation of the whole. The savant[1] becomes unpoetic. But the best read naturalist who lends an entire and devout attention to truth, will see that there remains much to learn of his relation to the world, and that it is not to be learned by any addition or subtraction or other comparison of known quantities, but is arrived at by untaught sallies of the spirit, by a continual self-recovery, and by entire humility. He will perceive that there are far more excellent qualities in the student than preciseness and infallibility; that a guess is often more fruitful than an indisputable affirmation, and that a dream may let us deeper into the secret of nature than a hundred concerted experiments.

For, the problems to be solved are precisely those which the physiologist and the naturalist omit to state. It is not so pertinent to man to know all the individuals of the animal kingdom, as it is to know whence and whereto is this tyrannizing unity in his constitution, which evermore separates and classifies things, endeavouring to reduce the most diverse to one form. When I behold a rich landscape, it is less to my purpose to recite correctly the order and super-position of the strata, than to know why all thought of multitude is lost in a tranquil sense of unity. I cannot greatly honor minuteness in details, so long as there is no hint to explain the relation between things and thoughts; no ray upon the *metaphysics* of conchology, of botany, of the arts, to show the relation of the forms of flowers, shells, animals, architecture, to the mind, and build science upon ideas. In a cabinet[2] of natural history, we become sensible of a certain occult recognition and sympathy in regard to the most bizarre forms of beast, fish, and insect. The American who has been confined, in his own country, to the sight of buildings designed after foreign models, is surprised on entering York Minster or St. Peter's at Rome, by the feeling that these structures are imitations also,—faint copies of an invisible archetype. Nor has science sufficient humanity, so long as the naturalist overlooks that wonderful congruity which subsists between man and the world; of which he is lord, not because he is the most subtile inhabitant, but because he is its head and heart, and finds something of himself in every great and small thing, in every mountain stratum, in every new law of color, fact of astronomy, or atmospheric influence which observation or analysis lay open. A perception of this mystery inspires the muse of George Herbert, the beautiful psalmist of the seventeenth century. The following lines are part of his little poem on Man.[3]

> "Man is all symmetry,
> Full of proportions, one limb to another,
> And to all the world besides.

1. Learned person.
2. Display case, or room containing many display cases.
3. Stanzas 1–4 and 6 of "Man" (1633).

Each part may call the farthest, brother;
For head with foot hath private amity,
And both with moons and tides.

"Nothing hath got so far
But man hath caught and kept it as his prey;
His eyes dismount the highest star;
He is in little all the sphere.
Herbs gladly cure our flesh, because that they
Find their acquaintance there.

"For us, the winds do blow.
The earth doth rest, heaven move, and fountains flow;
Nothing we see, but means our good,
As our delight, or as our treasure;
The whole is either our cupboard of food,
Or cabinet of pleasure.

"The stars have us to bed;
Night draws the curtain; which the sun withdraws.
Music and light attend our head.
All things unto our flesh are kind,
In their descent and being; to our mind,
In their ascent and cause.

"More servants wait on man
Than he'll take notice of. In every path,
He treads down that which doth befriend him
When sickness makes him pale and wan.
Oh mighty love! Man is one world, and hath
Another to attend him."

The perception of this class of truths makes the eternal attraction which draws men to science, but the end is lost sight of in attention to the means. In view of this half-sight of science, we accept the sentence of Plato, that, "poetry comes nearer to vital truth than history."[4] Every surmise and vaticination[5] of the mind is entitled to a certain respect, and we learn to prefer imperfect theories, and sentences, which contain glimpses of truth, to digested systems which have no one valuable suggestion. A wise writer will feel that the ends of study and composition are best answered by announcing undiscovered regions of thought, and so communicating, through hope, new activity to the torpid spirit.

I shall therefore conclude this essay with some traditions of man and nature, which a certain poet[6] sang to me; and which, as they have always been in the world, and perhaps reappear to every bard, may be both history and prophecy.

4. In copying two quotations from the *Edinburgh Review* Emerson blurred the attributions; here he quotes not from Plato, but from section 9 of Aristotle's *Poetics*.
5. Foretelling, prophesying.
6. Perhaps a joking reference to Bronson Alcott (1799–1888), Emerson's neighbor and Trancendentalist friend, who authored his own "Orphic Sayings" (though these poetic passages are by Emerson).

'The foundations of man are not in matter, but in spirit. But the element of spirit is eternity. To it, therefore, the longest series of events, the oldest chronologies are young and recent. In the cycle of the universal man, from whom the known individuals proceed, centuries are points, and all history is but the epoch of one degradation.

'We distrust and deny inwardly our sympathy with nature. We own and disown our relation to it, by turns. We are, like Nebuchadnezzar, dethroned, bereft of reason, and eating grass like an ox.[7] But who can set limits to the remedial force of spirit?

'A man is a god in ruins. When men are innocent, life shall be longer, and shall pass into the immortal, as gently as we awake from dreams. Now, the world would be insane and rabid, if these disorganizations should last for hundreds of years. It is kept in check by death and infancy. Infancy is the perpetual Messiah, which comes into the arms of fallen men, and pleads with them to return to paradise.

'Man is the dwarf of himself. Once he was permeated and dissolved by spirit. He filled nature with his overflowing currents. Out from him sprang the sun and moon; from man, the sun; from woman, the moon. The laws of his mind, the periods of his actions externized themselves into day and night, into the year and the seasons. But, having made for himself this huge shell, his waters retired; he no longer fills the veins and veinlets; he is shrunk to a drop. He sees, that the structure still fits him, but fits him colossally. Say, rather, once it fitted him, now it corresponds to him from far and on high. He adores timidly his own work. Now is man the follower of the sun, and woman the follower of the moon. Yet sometimes he starts in his slumber, and wonders at himself and his house, and muses strangely at the resemblance betwixt him and it. He perceives that if his law is still paramount, if still he have elemental power, "if his word is sterling yet in nature," it is not conscious power, it is not inferior but superior to his will. It is Instinct.' Thus my Orphic poet sang.

At present, man applies to nature but half his force. He works on the world with his understanding alone. He lives in it, and masters it by a penny-wisdom; and he that works most in it, is but a half-man and whilst his arms are strong and his digestion good, his mind is imbruted and he is a selfish savage. His relation to nature, his power over it, is through the understanding; as by manure; the economic use of fire, wind, water, and the mariner's needle; steam, coal, chemical agriculture; the repairs of the human body by the dentist and the surgeon. This is such a resumption of power, as if a banished king should buy his territories inch by inch, instead of vaulting at once into his throne. Meantime, in the thick darkness, there are not wanting gleams of a better light,—occasional examples of the action of man upon nature with his entire force,—with reason as well as understanding. Such examples are; the traditions of miracles in the earliest antiquity of all nations; the history of Jesus Christ; the achievements of a principle, as in religious and political revolutions, and in the abolition of the Slave-trade; the miracles of enthusiasm,[8] as those reported of Swedenborg, Hohenlohe, and the

7. The Babylonian king Nebuchadnezzar (d. 562 B.C.E.) "was driven from men, and did eat grass as oxen" (Daniel 4.33).

8. State of supernatural ecstasy or possession.

Shakers;[9] many obscure and yet contested facts, now arranged under the name of Animal Magnetism;[1] prayer; eloquence, self-healing; and the wisdom of children. These are examples of Reason's momentary grasp of the sceptre, the exertions of a power which exists not in time or space, but an instantaneous in-streaming causing power. The difference between the actual and the ideal force of man is happily figured by the schoolmen,[2] in saying, that the knowledge of man is an evening knowledge, *vespertina cognitio*, but that of God is a morning knowledge, *matutina cognitio*.

The problem of restoring to the world original and eternal beauty, is solved by the redemption of the soul. The ruin or the blank, that we see when we look at nature, is in our own eye. The axis of vision is not coincident with the axis of things, and so they appear not transparent but opake. The reason why the world lacks unity, and lies broken and in heaps, is, because man is disunited with himself. He cannot be a naturalist, until he satisfies all the demands of the spirit. Love is as much its demand, as perception. Indeed, neither can be perfect without the other. In the uttermost meaning of the words, thought is devout, and devotion is thought. Deep calls unto deep.[3] But in actual life, the marriage is not celebrated. There are innocent men who worship God after the tradition of their fathers, but their sense of duty has not yet extended to the use of all their faculties. And there are patient naturalists, but they freeze their subject under the wintry light of the understanding. Is not prayer also a study of truth,—a sally of the soul into the unfound infinite? No man ever prayed heartily, without learning something. But when a faithful thinker, resolute to detach every object from personal relations, and see it in the light of thought, shall, at the same time, kindle science with the fire of the holiest affections, then will God go forth anew into the creation.

It will not need, when the mind is prepared for study, to search for objects. The invariable mark of wisdom is to see the miraculous in the common. What is a day? What is a year? What is summer? What is woman? What is a child? What is sleep? To our blindness, these things seem unaffecting. We make fables to hide the baldness of the fact and conform it, as we say, to the higher law of the mind. But when the fact is seen under the light of an idea, the gaudy fable fades and shrivels. We behold the real higher law. To the wise, therefore, a fact is true poetry, and the most beautiful of fables. These wonders are brought to our own door. You also are a man. Man and woman, and their social life, poverty, labor, sleep, fear, fortune, are known to you. Learn that none of these things is superficial, but that each phenomenon hath its roots in the faculties and affections of the mind. Whilst the abstract question occupies your intellect, nature brings it in the concrete to be solved by your hands. It were a wise inquiry for the closet,[4] to compare, point by point, especially at remarkable crises in life, our daily history, with the rise and progress of ideas in the mind.

9. A Protestant millenarian sect known for its commitments to sexual equality and celibacy, the Shakers were founded in England in 1747 and moved to America in 1774; like the Quakers, they preached the importance of attending to one's inner light. Leopold Franz Emmerich, prince of Hohenlohe (1794–1849), reputed miracle healer.

1. Hypnotism.
2. Medieval scholastic philosophers.
3. Psalm 42.7.
4. The scholar's private workroom.

So shall we come to look at the world with new eyes. It shall answer the endless inquiry of the intellect,—What is truth? and of the affections,—What is good? by yielding itself passive to the educated Will. Then shall come to pass what my poet said; 'Nature is not fixed but fluid. Spirit alters, moulds, makes it. The immobility or bruteness of nature, is the absence of spirit; to pure spirit, it is fluid, it is volatile, it is obedient. Every spirit builds itself a house; and beyond its house, a world; and beyond its world, a heaven. Know then, that the world exists for you. For you is the phenomenon perfect. What we are, that only can we see. All that Adam had, all that Cæsar could, you have and can do. Adam called his house, heaven and earth; Cæsar called his house, Rome; you perhaps call yours, a cobler's trade; a hundred acres of ploughed land; or a scholar's garret. Yet line for line and point for point, your dominion is as great as theirs, though without fine names. Build, therefore your own world. As fast as you can conform your life to the pure idea in your mind, that will unfold its great proportions. A correspondent revolution in things will attend the influx of the spirit. So fast will disagreeable appearances, swine, spiders, snakes, pests, mad-houses, prisons, enemies, vanish; they are temporary and shall be no more seen. The sordor and filths of nature, the sun shall dry up, and the wind exhale. As when the summer comes from the south, the snow-banks melt, and the face of the earth becomes green before it, so shall the advancing spirit create its ornaments along its path, and carry with it the beauty it visits, and the song which enchants it; it shall draw beautiful faces, and warm hearts, and wise discourse, and heroic acts, around its way, until evil is no more seen. The kingdom of man over nature, which cometh not with observation,[5]—a dominion such as now is beyond his dream of God,—he shall enter without more wonder than the blind man feels who is gradually restored to perfect sight.'

1836

The American Scholar[1]

Mr. President, and Gentlemen,

I greet you on the re-commencement of our literary year.[2] Our anniversary is one of hope, and, perhaps, not enough of labor. We do not meet for games of strength or skill, for the recitation of histories, tragedies and odes, like the ancient Greeks; for parliaments of love and poesy, like the Troubadours;[3] nor for the advancement of science, like our cotemporaries in the British and European capitals. Thus far, our holiday has been simply a friendly sign of the survival of the love of letters amongst a people too busy to give to letters any more. As such, it is precious as the sign of an indestructible instinct. Perhaps the time is already come, when it ought to be, and will be something else;

5. Luke 17.20.

1. The text printed here is that of the first publication (1837) as a pamphlet titled *An Oration, Delivered before the Phi Beta Kappa Society at Cambridge, August 31, 1837.* By changing the title to "The American Scholar" when he republished it in *Nature, Addresses, and Lectures* (1849), Emerson made clear that he was addressing a larger audience than this first group.

2. Also a reference to the academic year traditionally beginning in September.

3. Poets of southern France, especially Provence, in the 12th and 13th centuries.

when the sluggard intellect of this continent will look from under its iron lids and fill the postponed expectation of the world with something better than the exertions of mechanical skill. Our day of dependence, our long apprenticeship to the learning of other lands, draws to a close. The millions that around us are rushing into life, cannot always be fed on the sere remains of foreign harvests. Events, actions arise, that must be sung, that will sing themselves. Who can doubt that poetry will revive and lead in a new age, as the star in the constellation Harp which now flames in our zenith, astronomers announce, shall one day be the pole-star[4] for a thousand years.

In the light of this hope, I accept the topic which not only usage, but the nature of our association, seem to prescribe to this day,—the AMERICAN SCHOLAR. Year by year, we come up hither to read one more chapter of his biography. Let us inquire what new lights, new events and more days have thrown on his character, his duties and his hopes.

It is one of those fables, which out of an unknown antiquity, convey an unlooked for wisdom, that the gods, in the beginning, divided Man into men, that he might be more helpful to himself;[5] just as the hand was divided into fingers, the better to answer its end.

The old fable covers a doctrine ever new and sublime; that there is One Man,—present to all particular men only partially, or through one faculty; and that you must take the whole society to find the whole man. Man is not a farmer, or a professor, or an engineer, but he is all. Man is priest, and scholar, and statesman, and producer, and soldier. In the *divided* or social state, these functions are parcelled out to individuals, each of whom aims to do his stint of the joint work, whilst each other performs his. The fable implies that the individual to possess himself, must sometimes return from his own labor to embrace all the other laborers. But unfortunately, this original unit, this fountain of power, has been so distributed to multitudes, has been so minutely subdivided and peddled out, that it is spilled into drops, and cannot be gathered. The state of society is one in which the members have suffered amputation from the trunk, and strut about so many walking monsters,—a good finger, a neck, a stomach, an elbow, but never a man.

Man is thus metamorphosed into a thing, into many things. The planter, who is Man sent out into the field to gather food, is seldom cheered by any idea of the true dignity of his ministry. He sees his bushel and his cart, and nothing beyond, and sinks into the farmer, instead of Man on the farm. The tradesman scarcely ever gives an ideal worth to his work, but is ridden by the routine of his craft, and the soul is subject to dollars. The priest becomes a form; the attorney, a statute-book; the mechanic, a machine; the sailor, a rope of a ship.

In this distribution of functions, the scholar is the delegated intellect. In the right state, he is, *Man Thinking*. In the degenerate state, when the victim of society, he tends to become a mere thinker, or, still worse, the parrot of other men's thinking.

In this view of him, as Man Thinking, the whole theory of his office[6] is contained. Him nature solicits, with all her placid, all her monitory pictures.

4. The North Star. "Harp": Lyra, a northern constellation, which includes the bright star Vega.
5. Emerson knew one such fable from Plato's *Symposium*.
6. Function.

Him the past instructs. Him the future invites. Is not, indeed, every man a student, and do not all things exist for the student's behoof? And, finally, is not the true scholar the only true master? But, as the old oracle said, "All things have two handles. Beware of the wrong one."[7] In life, too often, the scholar errs with mankind and forfeits his privilege. Let us see him in his school, and consider him in reference to the main influences he receives.

I. The first in time and the first in importance of the influences upon the mind is that of nature. Every day, the sun; and, after sunset, night and her stars. Ever the winds blow; ever the grass grows. Every day, men and women, conversing, beholding and beholden. The scholar must needs stand wistful and admiring before this great spectacle. He must settle its value in his mind. What is nature to him? There is never a beginning, there is never an end to the inexplicable continuity of this web of God, but always circular power returning into itself. Therein it resembles his own spirit, whose beginning, whose ending he never can find—so entire, so boundless. Far, too, as her splendors shine, system on system shooting like rays, upward, downward, without centre, without circumference,—in the mass and in the particle nature hastens to render account of herself to the mind. Classification begins. To the young mind, every thing is individual, stands by itself. By and by, it finds how to join two things, and see in them one nature; then three, then three thousand; and so, tyrannized over by its own unifying instinct, it goes on tying things together, diminishing anomalies, discovering roots running under ground, whereby contrary and remote things cohere, and flower out from one stem. It presently learns, that, since the dawn of history, there has been a constant accumulation and classifying of facts. But what is classification but the perceiving that these objects are not chaotic, and are not foreign, but have a law which is also a law of the human mind? The astronomer discovers that geometry, a pure abstraction of the human mind, is the measure of planetary motion. The chemist finds proportions and intelligible method throughout matter: and science is nothing but the finding of analogy, identity in the most remote parts. The ambitious soul sits down before each refractory fact; one after another, reduces all strange constitutions, all new powers, to their class and their law, and goes on forever to animate the last fibre of organization, the outskirts of nature, by insight.

Thus to him, to this school-boy under the bending dome of day, is suggested, that he and it proceed from one root; one is leaf and one is flower; relation, sympathy, stirring in every vein. And what is that Root? Is not that the soul of his soul?—A thought too bold—a dream too wild. Yet when this spiritual light shall have revealed the law of more earthly natures,—when he has learned to worship the soul, and to see that the natural philosophy that now is, is only the first gropings of its gigantic hand, he shall look forward to an ever expanding knowledge as to a becoming creator. He shall see that nature is the opposite of the soul, answering to it part for part. One is seal, and one is print. Its beauty is the beauty of his own mind. Its laws are the laws of his own mind. Nature then becomes to him the measure of his attainments. So much of nature as he is ignorant of, so much of his own

7. From the Greek philosopher Epictetus (c. 50–c. 138 C.E.), who taught that the true good is within oneself.

mind does he not yet possess. And, in fine, the ancient precept, "Know thyself," and the modern precept, "Study nature," become at last one maxim.

II. The next great influence[8] into the spirit of the scholar, is, the mind of the Past,—in whatever form, whether of literature, of art, of institutions, that mind is inscribed. Books are the best type of the influence of the past, and perhaps we shall get at the truth—learn the amount of this influence more conveniently—by considering their value alone.

The theory of books is noble. The scholar of the first age received into him the world around; brooded thereon; gave it the new arrangement of his own mind, and uttered it again. It came into him—life; it went out from him—truth. It came to him—short-lived actions; it went out from him—immortal thoughts. It came to him—business; it went from him—poetry. It was—dead fact; now, it is quick[9] thought. It can stand, and it can go. It now endures, it now flies, it now inspires.[1] Precisely in proportion to the depth of mind from which it issued, so high does it soar, so long does it sing.

Or, I might say, it depends on how far the process had gone, of transmuting life into truth. In proportion to the completeness of the distillation, so will the purity and imperishableness of the product be. But none is quite perfect. As no air-pump can by any means make a perfect vacuum, so neither can any artist entirely exclude the conventional, the local, the perishable from his book, or write a book of pure thought that shall be as efficient, in all respects, to a remote posterity, as to cotemporaries, or rather to the second age. Each age, it is found, must write its own books; or rather, each generation for the next succeeding. The books of an older period will not fit this.

Yet hence arises a grave mischief. The sacredness which attaches to the act of creation,—the act of thought,—is instantly transferred to the record. The poet chanting, was felt to be a divine man. Henceforth the chant is divine also. The writer was a just and wise spirit. Henceforward it is settled, the book is perfect; as love of the hero corrupts into worship of his statue. Instantly, the book becomes noxious. The guide is a tyrant. We sought a brother, and lo, a governor. The sluggish and perverted mind of the multitude, always slow to open to the incursions of Reason, having once so opened, having once received this book, stands upon it, and makes an outcry, if it is disparaged. Colleges are built on it. Books are written on it by thinkers, not by Man Thinking; by men of talent, that is, who start wrong, who set out from accepted dogmas, not from their own sight of principles. Meek young men grow up in libraries, believing it their duty to accept the views which Cicero, which Locke, which Bacon have given, forgetful that Cicero, Locke and Bacon were only young men in libraries when they wrote these books.[2]

Hence, instead of Man Thinking, we have the bookworm. Hence, the book-learned class, who value books, as such; not as related to nature and the human constitution, but as making a sort of Third Estate[3] with the world and

8. Inflowing.
9. Living. "Business": busyness, activity.
1. Breathes in. "Go": walk.
2. As a young man Marcus Tullius Cicero (106–143 B.C.E.), Roman statesman, was renowned for his oratory. John Locke (1632–1704), English philosopher and political thinker, wrote *Essay Concerning Human Understanding* (1690) before he was forty. Sir Francis Bacon (1561–1626), English statesman and philosopher, is best known for his essays.
3. The term "Third Estate" is based on an obsolete social classification: first the clergy, second the nobility, third the common people.

the soul. Hence, the restorers of readings, the emendators, the bibliomaniacs of all degrees.

This is bad; this is worse than it seems. Books are the best of things, well used; abused, among the worst. What is the right use? What is the one end which all means go to effect? They are for nothing but to inspire. I had better never see a book than to be warped by its attraction clean out of my own orbit, and made a satellite instead of a system. The one thing in the world of value, is, the active soul,—the soul, free, sovereign, active. This every man is entitled to; this every man contains within him, although in almost all men, obstructed, and as yet unborn. The soul active sees absolute truth; and utters truth, or creates. In this action, it is genius; not the privilege of here and there a favorite, but the sound estate of every man. In its essence, it is progressive. The book, the college, the school of art, the institution of any kind, stop with some past utterance of genius. This is good, say they,—let us hold by this. They pin me down. They look backward and not forward. But genius always looks forward. The eyes of man are set in his forehead, not in his hindhead. Man hopes. Genius creates. To create,—to create,—is the proof of a divine presence. Whatever talents may be, if the man create not, the pure efflux[4] of the Deity is not his:—cinders and smoke, there may be, but not yet flame. There are creative manners, there are creative actions, and creative words; manners, actions, words, that is, indicative of no custom or authority, but springing spontaneous from the mind's own sense of good and fair.

On the other part, instead of being its own seer, let it receive always from another mind its truth, though it were in torrents of light, without periods of solitude, inquest and self-recovery, and a fatal disservice is done. Genius is always sufficiently the enemy of genius by over-influence. The literature of every nation bear me witness. The English dramatic poets have Shakspearized now for two hundred years.

Undoubtedly, there is a right way of reading,—so it be sternly subordinated. Man Thinking must not be subdued by his instruments. Books are for the scholar's idle times. When he can read God directly, the hour is too precious to be wasted in other men's transcripts of their readings. But when the intervals of darkness come, as come they must,—when the soul seeth not, when the sun is hid, and the stars withdraw their shining,—we repair to the lamps which were kindled by their ray to guide our steps to the East again, where the dawn is. We hear that we may speak. The Arabian proverb says, "A fig tree looking on a fig tree, becometh fruitful."

It is remarkable, the character of the pleasure we derive from the best books. They impress us ever with the conviction that one nature wrote and the same reads. We read the verses of one of the great English poets, of Chaucer, of Marvell, of Dryden,[5] with the most modern joy,—with a pleasure, I mean, which is in great part caused by the abstraction of all *time* from their verses. There is some awe mixed with the joy of our surprise, when this poet, who lived in some past world, two or three hundred years ago, says that which lies close to my own soul, that which I also had well nigh thought and said. But for the evidence thence afforded to the philosophical doctrine of the identity of all minds, we should suppose some

4. Flowing forth.
5. English poets: Geoffrey Chaucer (1340–1400), Andrew Marvell (1621–1678), and John Dryden (1631–1700).

pre-established harmony, some foresight of souls that were to be, and some preparation of stores for their future wants, like the fact observed in insects, who lay up food before death for the young grub they shall never see.

I would not be hurried by any love of system, by any exaggeration of instincts, to underrate the Book. We all know, that as the human body can be nourished on any food, though it were boiled grass and the broth of shoes, so the human mind can be fed by any knowledge. And great and heroic men have existed, who had almost no other information than by the printed page. I only would say, that it needs a strong head to bear that diet. One must be an inventor to read well. As the proverb says, "He that would bring home the wealth of the Indies, must carry out the wealth of the Indies." There is then creative reading, as well as creative writing. When the mind is braced by labor and invention, the page of whatever book we read becomes luminous with manifold allusion. Every sentence is doubly significant, and the sense of our author is as broad as the world. We then see, what is always true, that as the seer's hour of vision is short and rare among heavy days and months, so is its record, perchance, the least part of his volume. The discerning will read in his Plato or Shakspeare, only that least part,—only the authentic utterances of the oracle,—and all the rest he rejects, were it never so many times Plato's and Shakspeare's.

Of course, there is a portion of reading quite indispensable to a wise man. History and exact science he must learn by laborious reading. Colleges, in like manner, have their indispensable office,—to teach elements. But they can only highly serve us, when they aim not to drill, but to create; when they gather from far every ray of various genius to their hospitable halls, and, by the concentrated fires, set the hearts of their youth on flame. Thought and knowledge are natures in which apparatus and pretension avail nothing. Gowns, and pecuniary foundations, though of towns of gold, can never countervail the least sentence or syllable of wit.[6] Forget this, and our American colleges will recede in their public importance whilst they grow richer every year.

III. There goes in the world a notion that the scholar should be a recluse, a valetudinarian,[7]—as unfit for any handiwork or public labor, as a penknife for an axe. The so called "practical men" sneer at speculative men, as if, because they speculate or *see*, they could do nothing. I have heard it said that the clergy,—who are always more universally than any other class, the scholars of their day,—are addressed as women: that the rough, spontaneous conversation of men they do not hear, but only a mincing and diluted speech. They are often virtually disfranchised; and, indeed, there are advocates for their celibacy. As far as this is true of the studious classes, it is not just and wise. Action is with the scholar subordinate, but it is essential. Without it, he is not yet man. Without it, thought can never ripen into truth. Whilst the world hangs before the eye as a cloud of beauty, we can not even see its beauty. Inaction is cowardice, but there can be no scholar without the heroic mind. The preamble of thought, the transition through which it passes from the unconscious to the conscious, is action. Only so much do

6. Intelligence. "Gowns": academic robes.

7. Invalid.

I know, as I have lived. Instantly, we know whose words are loaded with life, and whose not.

The world,—this shadow of the soul, or *other me*, lies wide around. Its attractions are the keys which unlock my thoughts and make me acquainted with myself. I launch eagerly into this resounding tumult. I grasp the hands of those next me, and take my place in the ring to suffer and to work, taught by an instinct that so shall the dumb abyss be vocal with speech. I pierce its order; I dissipate its fear; I dispose of it within the circuit of my expanding life. So much only of life as I know by experience, so much of the wilderness have I vanquished and planted, or so far have I extended my being, my dominion. I do not see how any man can afford, for the sake of his nerves and his nap, to spare any action in which he can partake. It is pearls and rubies to his discourse. Drudgery, calamity, exasperation, want, are instructers in eloquence and wisdom. The true scholar grudges every opportunity of action past by, as a loss of power.

It is the raw material out of which the intellect moulds her splendid products. A strange process too, this, by which experience is converted into thought, as a mulberry leaf is converted into satin.[8] The manufacture goes forward at all hours.

The actions and events of our childhood and youth are now matters of calmest observation. They lie like fair pictures in the air. Not so with our recent actions,—with the business which we now have in hand. On this we are quite unable to speculate. Our affections as yet circulate through it. We no more feel or know it, than we feel the feet, or the hand, or the brain of our body. The new deed is yet a part of life,—remains for a time immersed in our unconscious life. In some contemplative hour, it detaches itself from the life like a ripe fruit, to become a thought of the mind. Instantly, it is raised, transfigured; the corruptible has put on incorruption.[9] Always now it is an object of beauty, however base its origin and neighborhood. Observe, too, the impossibility of antedating this act. In its grub state, it cannot fly, it cannot shine,—it is a dull grub. But suddenly, without observation, the selfsame thing unfurls beautiful wings, and is an angel of wisdom. So is there no fact, no event, in our private history, which shall not, sooner or later, lose its adhesive inert form, and astonish us by soaring from our body into the empyrean.[1] Cradle and infancy, school and playground, the fear of boys, and dogs, and ferules,[2] the love of little maids and berries, and many another fact that once filled the whole sky, are gone already; friend and relative, profession and party, town and country, nation and world, must also soar and sing.

Of course, he who has put forth his total strength in fit actions, has the richest return of wisdom. I will not shut myself out of this globe of action and transplant an oak into a flower pot, there to hunger and pine; nor trust the revenue of some single faculty, and exhaust one vein of thought, much like those Savoyards,[3] who, getting their livelihood by carving shepherds, shepherdesses, and smoking Dutchmen, for all Europe, went out one day to

8. A form of silk produced by silkworms, which feed on mulberry leaves.
9. "For this corruptible must put on incorruption, and this mortal must put on immortality" (I Corinthians 15.53).
1. The highest reaches of heaven.
2. Rods used for punishing children.
3. Savoy is in the western Alps, where France, Italy, and Switzerland converge.

the mountain to find stock, and discovered that they had whittled up the last of their pine trees. Authors we have in numbers, who have written out their vein, and who, moved by a commendable prudence, sail for Greece or Palestine, follow the trapper into the prairie, or ramble round Algiers to replenish their merchantable stock.[4]

If it were only for a vocabulary the scholar would be covetous of action. Life is our dictionary. Years are well spent in country labors; in town—in the insight into trades and manufactures; in frank intercourse with many men and women; in science; in art; to the one end of mastering in all their facts a language, by which to illustrate and embody our perceptions. I learn immediately from any speaker how much he has already lived, through the poverty or the splendor of his speech. Life lies behind us as the quarry from whence we get tiles and copestones for the masonry of to-day. This is the way to learn grammar. Colleges and books only copy the language which the field and the workyard made.

But the final value of action, like that of books, and better than books, is, that it is a resource. That great principle of Undulation in nature, that shows itself in the inspiring and expiring of the breath; in desire and satiety; in the ebb and flow of the sea, in day and night, in heat and cold, and as yet more deeply ingrained in every atom and every fluid, is known to us under the name of Polarity,—these "fits of easy transmission and reflection," as Newton[5] called them, are the law of nature because they are the law of spirit.

The mind now thinks; now acts; and each fit reproduces the other. When the artist has exhausted his materials, when the fancy no longer paints, when thoughts are no longer apprehended, and books are a weariness,—he has always the resource to *live*. Character is higher than intellect. Thinking is the function. Living is the functionary. The stream retreats to its source. A great soul will be strong to live, as well as strong to think. Does he lack organ or medium to impart his truths? He can still fall back on this elemental force of living them. This is a total act. Thinking is a partial act. Let the grandeur of justice shine in his affairs. Let the beauty of affection cheer his lowly roof. Those "far from fame" who dwell and act with him, will feel the force of his constitution in the doings and passages of the day better than it can be measured by any public and designed display. Time shall teach him that the scholar loses no hour which the man lives. Herein he unfolds the sacred germ of his instinct screened from influence. What is lost in seemliness is gained in strength. Not out of those on whom systems of education have exhausted their culture, comes the helpful giant to destroy the old or to build the new, but out of unhandselled[6] savage nature, out of terrible Druids and Berserkirs, come at last Alfred[7] and Shakspear.

I hear therefore with joy whatever is beginning to be said of the dignity and necessity of labor to every citizen. There is virtue yet in the hoe and the spade, for learned as well as for unlearned hands. And labor is every where

4. Likely references to Emerson's contemporaries: Nathaniel Parker Willis (1806–1867), editor and travel writer; Washington Irving, whose *A Tour on the Prairies* appeared in 1835; and James Fenimore Cooper, whose *The Prairie* was published in 1827.

5. From the *Optics* (1704) of Sir Isaac Newton (1642–1727), English scientist and mathematician.

6. A handsel is a gift to express good wishes at the outset of some enterprise; apparently Emerson uses "unhandselled" to mean something like unauspicious.

7. The enlightened 9th-century king of the West Saxons. "Terrible Druids and Berserkirs": uncivilized Celts and Anglo-Saxons.

welcome; always we are invited to work; only be this limitation observed, that a man shall not for the sake of wider activity sacrifice any opinion to the popular judgments and modes of action.

I have now spoken of the education of the scholar by nature, by books, and by action. It remains to say somewhat of his duties.

They are such as become Man Thinking. They may all be comprised in self-trust. The office of the scholar is to cheer, to raise, and to guide men by showing them facts amidst appearances. He plies the slow, unhonored, and unpaid task of observation. Flamsteed and Herschel, in their glazed[8] observatory, may catalogue the stars with the praise of all men, and the results being splendid and useful, honor is sure. But he, in his private observatory, cataloguing obscure and nebulous stars of the human mind, which as yet no man has thought of as such,—watching days and months, sometimes, for a few facts; correcting still his old records;—must relinquish display and immediate fame. In the long period of his preparation, he must betray often an ignorance and shiftlessness in popular arts, incurring the disdain of the able who shoulder him aside. Long he must stammer in his speech; often forego the living for the dead. Worse yet, he must accept—how often! poverty and solitude. For the ease and pleasure of treading the old road, accepting the fashions, the education, the religion of society, he takes the cross of making his own, and, of course, the self accusation, the faint heart, the frequent uncertainty and loss of time which are the nettles and tangling vines in the way of the self-relying and self-directed; and the state of virtual hostility in which he seems to stand to society, and especially to educated society. For all this loss and scorn, what offset? He is to find consolation in exercising the highest functions of human nature. He is one who raises himself from private considerations, and breathes and lives on public and illustrious thoughts. He is the world's eye. He is the world's heart. He is to resist the vulgar prosperity that retrogrades ever to barbarism, by preserving and communicating heroic sentiments, noble biographies, melodious verse, and the conclusions of history. Whatsoever oracles the human heart in all emergencies, in all solemn hours has uttered as its commentary on the world of actions,—these he shall receive and impart. And whatsoever new verdict Reason from her inviolable seat pronounces on the passing men and events of to-day,—this he shall hear and promulgate.

These being his functions, it becomes him to feel all confidence in himself, and to defer never to the popular cry. He and he only knows the world. The world of any moment is the merest appearance. Some great decorum, some fetish of a government, some ephemeral trade, or war, or man, is cried up by half mankind and cried down by the other half, as if all depended on this particular up or down. The odds are that the whole question is not worth the poorest thought which the scholar has lost in listening to the controversy. Let him not quit his belief that a popgun is a popgun, though the ancient and honorable of the earth affirm it to be the crack of doom. In silence, in steadiness, in severe abstraction, let him hold by himself; add observation to observation; patient of neglect, patient of reproach, and bide his own time,—happy enough if he can satisfy himself alone that this day he has

8. Glass-roofed. John Flamsteed (1646–1719), English astronomer, first royal astronomer at Greenwich Observatory. Sir William Herschel (1738–1822), German-born English astronomer.

seen something truly. Success treads on every right step. For the instinct is sure that prompts him to tell his brother what he thinks. He then learns that in going down into the secrets of his own mind, he has descended into the secrets of all minds. He learns that he who has mastered any law in his private thoughts, is master to that extent of all men whose language he speaks, and of all into whose language his own can be translated. The poet in utter solitude remembering his spontaneous thoughts and recording them, is found to have recorded that which men in "cities vast" find true for them also. The orator distrusts at first the fitness of his frank confessions,—his want of knowledge of the persons he addresses,—until he finds that he is the complement of his hearers;—that they drink his words because he fulfils for them their own nature; the deeper he dives into his privatest secretest presentiment,—to his wonder he finds, this is the most acceptable, most public, and universally true. The people delight in it; the better part of every man feels, This is my music: this is myself.

In self-trust, all the virtues are comprehended. Free should the scholar be,—free and brave. Free even to the definition of freedom, "without any hindrance that does not arise out of his own constitution." Brave; for fear is a thing which a scholar by his very function puts behind him. Fear always springs from ignorance. It is a shame to him if his tranquillity, amid dangerous times, arise from the presumption that like children and women, his is a protected class; or if he seek a temporary peace by the diversion of his thoughts from politics or vexed questions, hiding his head like an ostrich in the flowering bushes, peeping into microscopes, and turning rhymes, as a boy whistles to keep his courage up. So is the danger a danger still: so is the fear worse. Manlike let him turn and face it. Let him look into its eye and search its nature, inspect its origin—see the whelping of this lion,—which lies no great way back; he will then find in himself a perfect comprehension of its nature and extent; he will have made his hands meet on the other side, and can henceforth defy it, and pass on superior. The world is his who can see through its pretension. What deafness, what stone-blind custom, what overgrown error you behold, is there only by sufferance,—by your sufferance. See it to be a lie, and you have already dealt it its mortal blow.

Yes, we are the cowed,—we the trustless. It is a mischievous notion that we are come late into nature; that the world was finished a long time ago. As the world was plastic and fluid in the hands of God, so it is ever to so much of his attributes as we bring to it. To ignorance and sin, it is flint. They adapt themselves to it as they may; but in proportion as a man has anything in him divine, the firmament flows before him, and takes his signet[9] and form. Not he is great who can alter matter, but he who can alter my state of mind. They are the kings of the world who give the color of their present thought to all nature and all art, and persuade men by the cheerful serenity of their carrying the matter, that this thing which they do, is the apple which the ages have desired to pluck, now at last ripe, and inviting nations to the harvest. The great man makes the great thing. Wherever Macdonald sits, there is the head of the table.[1] Linnæus makes botany the most alluring of studies and wins it from the farmer and the herb-woman. Davy, chemistry: and

9. Seal.

1. An old proverb says, "Where Macgregor sits, there is the head of the table"; Emerson substitutes another typical name for a Scottish chief.

Cuvier,[2] fossils. The day is always his, who works in it with serenity and great aims. The unstable estimates of men crowd to him whose mind is filled with a truth, as the heaped waves of the Atlantic follow the moon.

For this self-trust, the reason is deeper than can be fathomed,—darker than can be enlightened. I might not carry with me the feeling of my audience in stating my own belief. But I have already shown the ground of my hope, in adverting to the doctrine that man is one. I believe man has been wronged: he has wronged himself. He has almost lost the light that can lead him back to his prerogatives. Men are become of no account. Men in history, men in the world of to-day are bugs, are spawn, and are called "the mass" and "the herd." In a century, in a millennium, one or two men; that is to say—one or two approximations to the right state of every man. All the rest behold in the hero or the poet their own green and crude being—ripened; yes, and are content to be less, so *that* may attain to its full stature. What a testimony—full of grandeur, full of pity, is borne to the demands of his own nature, by the poor clansman, the poor partisan, who rejoices in the glory of his chief. The poor and the low find some amends to their immense moral capacity, for their acquiescence in a political and social inferiority. They are content to be brushed like flies from the path of a great person, so that justice shall be done by him to that common nature which it is the dearest desire of all to see enlarged and glorified. They sun themselves in the great man's light, and feel it to be their own element. They cast the dignity of man from their downtrod selves upon the shoulders of a hero, and will perish to add one drop of blood to make that great heart beat, those giant sinews combat and conquer. He lives for us, and we live in him.

Men such as they are, very naturally seek money or power; and power because it is as good as money,—the "spoils," so called, "of office." And why not? for they aspire to the highest, and this, in their sleep-walking, they dream is highest. Wake them, and they shall quit the false good and leap to the true, and leave government to clerks and desks. This revolution is to be wrought by the gradual domestication of the idea of Culture. The main enterprise of the world for splendor, for extent, is the upbuilding of a man. Here are the materials strown along the ground. The private life of one man shall be a more illustrious monarchy,—more formidable to its enemy, more sweet and serene in its influence to its friend, than any kingdom in history. For a man, rightly viewed, comprehendeth the particular natures of all men. Each philosopher, each bard, each actor, has only done for me, as by a delegate, what one day I can do for myself. The books which once we valued more than the apple of the eye, we have quite exhausted. What is that but saying that we have come up with the point of view which the universal mind took through the eyes of that one scribe; we have been that man, and have passed on. First, one; then another; we drain all cisterns, and waxing greater by all these supplies, we crave a better and more abundant food. The man has never lived that can feed us ever. The human mind cannot be enshrined in a person who shall set a barrier on any one side to this unbounded, unboundable empire. It is one central fire which flaming now out of the lips

2. Georges Cuvier (1769–1832), French pioneer in comparative anatomy and paleontology. Carl von Linné ("Linnæus") (1707–1778), Swedish botanist. Sir Humphry Davy (1778–1829), English chemist.

of Etna, lightens the capes of Sicily; and now out of the throat of Vesuvius,[3] illuminates the towers and vineyards of Naples. It is one light which beams out of a thousand stars. It is one soul which animates all men.

But I have dwelt perhaps tediously upon this abstraction of the Scholar. I ought not to delay longer to add what I have to say, of nearer reference to the time and to this country.

Historically, there is thought to be a difference in the ideas which predominate over successive epochs, and there are data for marking the genius of the Classic, of the Romantic, and now of the Reflective or Philosophical age. With the views I have intimated of the oneness or the identity of the mind through all individuals, I do not much dwell on these differences. In fact, I believe each individual passes through all three. The boy is a Greek; the youth, romantic; the adult, reflective. I deny not, however, that a revolution in the leading idea may be distinctly enough traced.

Our age is bewailed as the age of Introversion. Must that needs be evil? We, it seems, are critical. We are embarrassed with second thoughts. We cannot enjoy any thing for hankering to know whereof the pleasure consists. We are lined with eyes. We see with our feet. The time is infected with Hamlet's unhappiness,—

"Sicklied o'er with the pale cast of thought."[4]

Is it so bad then? Sight is the last thing to be pitied. Would we be blind? Do we fear lest we should outsee nature and God, and drink truth dry? I look upon the discontent of the literary class as a mere announcement of the fact that they find themselves not in the state of mind of their fathers, and regret the coming state as untried; as a boy dreads the water before he has learned that he can swim. If there is any period one would desire to be born in,—is it not the age of Revolution; when the old and the new stand side by side, and admit of being compared; when the energies of all men are searched by fear and by hope; when the historic glories of the old, can be compensated by the rich possibilities of the new era? This time, like all times, is a very good one, if we but know what to do with it.

I read with joy some of the auspicious signs of the coming days as they glimmer already through poetry and art, through philosophy and science, through church and state.

One of these signs is the fact that the same movement which effected the elevation of what was called the lowest class in the state, assumed in literature a very marked and as benign an aspect. Instead of the sublime and beautiful, the near, the low, the common, was explored and poetised. That which had been negligently trodden under foot by those who were harnessing and provisioning themselves for long journeys into far countries, is suddenly found to be richer than all foreign parts. The literature of the poor, the feelings of the child, the philosophy of the street, the meaning of household life, are the topics of the time. It is a great stride. It is a sign—is it not? of new vigor, when the extremities are made active, when currents of warm life run into the hands and the feet. I ask not for the great, the remote, the romantic; what is doing in Italy or Arabia; what is Greek art, or

3. Active volcanoes in eastern Sicily and southern Italy.

4. Shakespeare's *Hamlet* 3.1.85.

Provençal Minstrelsy;[5] I embrace the common, I explore and sit at the feet of the familiar, the low. Give me insight into to-day, and you may have the antique and future worlds. What would we really know the meaning of? The meal in the firkin;[6] the milk in the pan; the ballad in the street; the news of the boat; the glance of the eye; the form and the gait of the body;—show me the ultimate reason of these matters;—show me the sublime presence of the highest spiritual cause lurking, as always it does lurk, in these suburbs and extremities of nature; let me see every trifle bristling with the polarity that ranges it instantly on an eternal law; and the shop, the plough, and the ledger, referred to the like cause by which light undulates and poets sing;—and the world lies no longer a dull miscellany and lumber room,[7] but has form and order; there is no trifle; there is no puzzle; but one design unites and animates the farthest pinnacle and the lowest trench.

This idea has inspired the genius of Goldsmith, Burns, Cowper, and in a newer time, of Goethe, Wordsworth, and Carlyle.[8] This idea they have differently followed and with various success. In contrast with their writing, the style of Pope, of Johnson, of Gibbon,[9] looks cold and pedantic. This writing is blood-warm. Man is surprised to find that things near are not less beautiful and wondrous than things remote. The near explains the far. The drop is a small ocean. A man is related to all nature. This perception of the worth of the vulgar, is fruitful in discoveries. Goethe, in this very thing the most modern of the moderns, has shown us, as none ever did, the genius of the ancients.

There is one man of genius who has done much for this philosophy of life, whose literary value has never yet been rightly estimated;—I mean Emanuel Swedenborg.[1] The most imaginative of men, yet writing with the precision of a mathematician, he endeavored to engraft a purely philosophical Ethics on the popular Christianity of his time. Such an attempt, of course, must have difficulty which no genius could surmount. But he saw and showed the connexion between nature and the affections of the soul. He pierced the emblematic or spiritual character of the visible, audible, tangible world. Especially did his shade-loving muse hover over and interpret the lower parts of nature; he showed the mysterious bond that allies moral evil to the foul material forms, and has given in epical parables a theory of insanity, of beasts, of unclean and fearful things.

Another sign of our times, also marked by an analogous political movement is, the new importance given to the single person. Every thing that tends to insulate the individual,—to surround him with barriers of natural respect, so that each man shall feel the world is his, and man shall treat with man as a sovereign state with a sovereign state;—tends to true union as well as greatness. "I learned," said the melancholy Pestalozzi,[2] "that no man in God's wide earth is either willing or able to help any other man."

5. Music of the medieval troubadours of Provence, in southeastern France.
6. Small wooden vessel.
7. Junk room.
8. Emerson contrasts the so-called pre-Romantics Oliver Goldsmith (1730–1794), Robert Burns (1759–1796), and William Cowper (1731–1800) with the Romantics Johann Wolfgang von Goethe (1749–1832), William Wordsworth (1770–1850), and Thomas Carlyle (1795–1881).
9. The 18th-century British writers Alexander Pope (1688–1744), Samuel Johnson (1709–1784), and Edward Gibbon (1737–1794).
1. Swedish scientist, theologian, and mystic (1688–1772). Emerson was inspired by Swedenborg's notion of the correspondence between the natural and spiritual worlds.
2. Johann Heinrich Pestalozzi (1746–1827), Swiss educator who was an early advocate of kindergarten education. His theories influenced several of Emerson's friends.

Help must come from the bosom alone. The scholar is that man who must take up into himself all the ability of the time, all the contributions of the past, all the hopes of the future. He must be an university of knowledges. If there be one lesson more than another which should pierce his ear, it is, The world is nothing, the man is all; in yourself is the law of all nature, and you know not yet how a globule of sap ascends; in yourself slumbers the whole of Reason; it is for you to know all, it is for you to dare all. Mr. President and Gentlemen, this confidence in the unsearched might of man, belongs by all motives, by all prophecy, by all preparation, to the American Scholar. We have listened too long to the courtly muses of Europe. The spirit of the American freeman is already suspected to be timid, imitative, tame. Public and private avarice make the air we breathe thick and fat. The scholar is decent, indolent, complaisant. See already the tragic consequence. The mind of this country taught to aim at low objects, eats upon itself. There is no work for any but the decorous and the complaisant. Young men of the fairest promise, who begin life upon our shores, inflated by the mountain winds, shined upon by all the stars of God, find the earth below not in unison with these,—but are hindered from action by the disgust which the principles on which business is managed inspire, and turn drudges, or die of disgust,—some of them suicides. What is the remedy? They did not yet see, and thousands of young men as hopeful now crowding to the barriers for the career, do not yet see, that if the single man plant himself indomitably on his instincts, and there abide, the huge world will come round to him. Patience—patience;—with the shades of all the good and great for company; and for solace, the perspective of your own infinite life; and for work, the study and the communication of principles, the making those instincts prevalent, the conversion of the world. Is it not the chief disgrace in the world, not to be an unit;—not to be reckoned one character;—not to yield that peculiar fruit which each man was created to bear, but to be reckoned in the gross, in the hundred, or the thousand, of the party, the section, to which we belong; and our opinion predicted geographically, as the north, or the south. Not so, brothers and friends,—please God, ours shall not be so. We will walk on our own feet; we will work with our own hands; we will speak our own minds. Then shall man be no longer a name for pity, for doubt, and for sensual indulgence. The dread of man and the love of man shall be a wall of defence and a wreath of love around all. A nation of men will for the first time exist, because each believes himself inspired by the Divine Soul which also inspires all men.

1837

The Divinity School Address[1]

In this refulgent summer it has been a luxury to draw the breath of life. The grass grows, the buds burst, the meadow is spotted with fire and gold in

1. "An Address Delivered before the Senior Class in Divinity College, Cambridge, Sunday Evening 15 July, 1838" was published as a pamphlet in Boston soon after it was given. That original text

the tint of flowers. The air is full of birds, and sweet with the breath of the pine, the balm-of-Gilead,[2] and the new hay. Night brings no gloom to the heart with its welcome shade. Through the transparent darkness pour the stars their almost spiritual rays. Man under them seems a young child, and his huge globe a toy. The cool night bathes the world as with a river, and prepares his eyes again for the crimson dawn. The mystery of nature was never displayed more happily. The corn and the wine have been freely dealt to all creatures, and the never-broken silence with which the old bounty goes forward, has not yielded yet one word of explanation. One is constrained to respect the perfection of this world, in which our senses converse. How wide; how rich; what invitation from every property it gives to every faculty of man! In its fruitful soils; in its navigable sea; in its mountains of metal and stone; in its forests of all woods; in its animals; in its chemical ingredients; in the powers and path of light, heat, attraction, and life, is it well worth the pith and heart of great men to subdue and enjoy it. The planters, the mechanics, the inventors, the astronomers, the builders of cities, and the captains, history delights to honor.

But the moment the mind opens, and reveals the laws which traverse the universe, and make things what they are, then shrinks the great world at once into a mere illustration and fable of this mind. What am I? and What is? asks the human spirit with a curiosity new-kindled, but never to be quenched. Behold these outrunning laws, which our imperfect apprehension can see tend this way and that, but not come full circle. Behold these infinite relations, so like, so unlike; many, yet one. I would study, I would know, I would admire forever. These works of thought have been the entertainments of the human spirit in all ages.

A more secret, sweet, and overpowering beauty appears to man when his heart and mind open to the sentiment of virtue. Then instantly he is instructed in what is above him. He learns that his being is without bound; that, to the good, to the perfect, he is born, low as he now lies in evil and weakness. That which he venerates is still his own, though he has not realized it yet. *He ought.* He knows the sense of that grand word, though his analysis fails entirely to render account of it. When in innocency, or when by intellectual perception, he attains to say,—'I love the Right; Truth is beautiful within and without, forevermore. Virtue, I am thine: save me: use me: thee will I serve, day and night, in great, in small, that I may be not virtuous, but virtue;'—then is the end of the creation answered, and God is well pleased.

The sentiment of virtue is a reverence and delight in the presence of certain divine laws. It perceives that this homely game of life we play, covers, under what seem foolish details, principles that astonish. The child amidst his baubles, is learning the action of light, motion, gravity, muscular force; and in the game of human life, love, fear, justice, appetite, man, and God, interact. These laws refuse to be adequately stated. They will not by us or

---

is followed here, though with the title used in *Nature, Addresses, and Lectures* (1849). Attacks on Emerson for questioning the unique divinity of Jesus Christ appeared in newspapers and pamphlets, and Emerson cautioned himself in his journal to remain "steady." He retracted nothing privately or publicly and was not invited back to Harvard for three decades.

2. An aromatic poplar tree, named for the curative resin associated with Gilead in Jeremiah 8.22: "Is there no balm in Gilead; is there no physician there?"

for us be written out on paper, or spoken by the tongue. They elude, evade our persevering thought, and yet we read them hourly in each other's faces, in each other's actions, in our own remorse. The moral traits which are all globed into every virtuous act and thought,—in speech, we must sever, and describe or suggest by painful enumeration of many particulars. Yet, as this sentiment is the essence of all religion, let me guide your eyes to the precise objects of the sentiment, by an enumeration of some of those classes of facts in which this element is conspicuous.

The intuition of the moral sentiment is an insight of the perfection of the laws of the soul. These laws execute themselves. They are out of time, out of space, and not subject to circumstance. Thus; in the soul of man there is a justice whose retributions are instant and entire. He who does a good deed, is instantly ennobled himself. He who does a mean deed, is by the action itself contracted. He who puts off impurity, thereby puts on purity. If a man is at heart just, then in so far is he God; the safety of God, the immortality of God, the majesty of God do enter into that man with justice. If a man dissemble, deceive, he deceives himself, and goes out of acquaintance with his own being. A man in the view of absolute goodness, adores, with total humility. Every step so downward, is a step upward. The man who renounces himself, comes to himself by so doing.

See how this rapid intrinsic energy worketh everywhere, righting wrongs, correcting appearances, and bringing up facts to a harmony with thoughts. Its operation in life, though slow to the senses, is, at last, as sure as in the soul. By it, a man is made the Providence to himself, dispensing good to his goodness, and evil to his sin. Character is always known. Thefts never enrich; alms never impoverish; murder will speak out of stone walls. The least admixture of a lie,—for example, the smallest mixture of vanity, the least attempt to make a good impression, a favorable appearance,—will instantly vitiate the effect. But speak the truth, and all nature and all spirits help you with unexpected furtherance. Speak the truth, and all things alive or brute are vouchers, and the very roots of the grass underground there, do seem to stir and move to bear you witness. See again the perfection of the Law as it applies itself to the affections, and becomes the law of society. As we are, so we associate. The good, by affinity, seek the good; the vile, by affinity, the vile. Thus of their own volition, souls proceed into heaven, into hell.

These facts have always suggested to man the sublime creed, that the world is not the product of manifold power, but of one will, of one mind; and that one mind is everywhere, in each ray of the star, in each wavelet of the pool, active; and whatever opposes that will, is everywhere baulked and baffled, because things are made so, and not otherwise. Good is positive. Evil is merely privative,[3] not absolute. It is like cold, which is the privation of heat. All evil is so much death or nonentity. Benevolence is absolute and real. So much benevolence as a man hath, so much life hath he. For all things proceed out of this same spirit, which is differently named love, justice, temperance, in its different applications, just as the ocean receives different names on the several shores which it washes. All things proceed out of the same spirit, and all things conspire with it. Whilst a man seeks good ends,

3. I.e., not an active power, but the absence of a power.

he is strong by the whole strength of nature. In so far as he roves from these ends, he bereaves himself of power, of auxiliaries; his being shrinks out of all remote channels, he becomes less and less, a mote, a point, until absolute badness is absolute death.

The perception of this law of laws always awakens in the mind a sentiment which we call the religious sentiment, and which makes our highest happiness. Wonderful is its power to charm and to command. It is a mountain air. It is the embalmer of the world. It is myrrh and storax, and chlorine and rosemary.[4] It makes the sky and the hills sublime, and the silent song of the stars is it. By it, is the universe made safe and habitable, not by science or power. Thought may work cold and intransitive in things, and find no end or unity. But the dawn of the sentiment of virtue on the heart, gives and is the assurance that Law is sovereign over all natures; and the worlds, time, space, eternity, do seem to break out into joy.

This sentiment is divine and deifying. It is the beatitude of man. It makes him illimitable. Through it, the soul first knows itself. It corrects the capital mistake of the infant man, who seeks to be great by following the great, and hopes to derive advantages *from another*,—by showing the fountain of all good to be in himself, and that he, equally with every man, is a door into the deeps of Reason. When he says, "I ought;" when love warms him; when he chooses, warned from on high, the good and great deed; then, deep melodies wander through his soul from Supreme Wisdom. Then he can worship, and be enlarged by his worship; for he can never go behind this sentiment. In the sublimest flights of the soul, rectitude is never surmounted, love is never outgrown.

This sentiment lies at the foundation of society, and successively creates all forms of worship. The principle of veneration never dies out. Man fallen into superstition, into sensuality, is never wholly without the visions of the moral sentiment. In like manner, all the expressions of this sentiment are sacred and permanent in proportion to their purity. The expressions of this sentiment affect us deeper, greatlier, than all other compositions. The sentences of the oldest time, which ejaculate this piety, are still fresh and fragrant. This thought dwelled always deepest in the minds of men in the devout and contemplative East; not alone in Palestine, where it reached its purest expression, but in Egypt, in Persia, in India, in China. Europe has always owed to oriental genius, its divine impulses. What these holy bards said, all sane men found agreeable and true. And the unique impression of Jesus upon mankind, whose name is not so much written as ploughed into the history of this world, is proof of the subtle virtue of this infusion.

Meantime, whilst the doors of the temple stand open, night and day, before every man, and the oracles of this truth cease never, it is guarded by one stern condition; this, namely; it is an intuition. It cannot be received at second hand. Truly speaking, it is not instruction, but provocation, that I can receive from another soul. What he announces, I must find true in me, or wholly reject; and on his word, or as his second, be he who he may, I can accept nothing. On the contrary, the absence of this primary faith is the presence of degradation. As is the flood so is the ebb. Let this faith depart,

4. An aromatic evergreen herb used in cookery and perfumery. "Myrrh": one of the gifts the wise men brought to Jesus, a perfume made from aromatic resins. "Storax": an aromatic resin. "Chlorine": in this sense, a greenish yellow gas used for purification.

and the very words it spake, and the things it made, become false and hurtful. Then falls the church, the state, art, letters, life. The doctrine of the divine nature being forgotten, a sickness infects and dwarfs the constitution. Once man was all; now he is an appendage, a nuisance. And because the indwelling Supreme Spirit cannot wholly be got rid of, the doctrine of it suffers this perversion, that the divine nature is attributed to one or two persons, and denied to all the rest, and denied with fury. The doctrine of inspiration is lost; the base doctrine of the majority of voices, usurps the place of the doctrine of the soul. Miracles, prophecy, poetry, the ideal life, the holy life, exist as ancient history merely; they are not in the belief, nor in the aspiration of society; but, when suggested, seem ridiculous. Life is comic or pitiful, as soon as the high ends of being fade out of sight, and man becomes near-sighted, and can only attend to what addresses the senses.

These general views, which, whilst they are general, none will contest, find abundant illustration in the history of religion, and especially in the history of the Christian church. In that, all of us have had our birth and nurture. The truth contained in that, you, my young friends, are now setting forth to teach. As the Cultus, or established worship of the civilized world, it has great historical interest for us. Of its blessed words, which have been the consolation of humanity, you need not that I should speak. I shall endeavor to discharge my duty to you, on this occasion, by pointing out two errors in its administration, which daily appear more gross from the point of view we have just now taken.

Jesus Christ belonged to the true race of prophets. He saw with open eye the mystery of the soul. Drawn by its severe harmony, ravished with its beauty, he lived in it, and had his being there. Alone in all history, he estimated the greatness of man. One man was true to what is in you and me. He saw that God incarnates himself in man, and evermore goes forth anew to take possession of his world. He said, in this jubilee of sublime emotion, 'I am divine. Through me, God acts; through me, speaks. Would you see God, see me; or, see thee, when thou also thinkest as I now think.' But what a distortion did his doctrine and memory suffer in the same, in the next, and the following ages! There is no doctrine of the Reason which will bear to be taught by the Understanding.[5] The understanding caught this high chant from the poet's lips, and said, in the next age, 'This was Jehovah come down out of heaven. I will kill you, if you say he was a man.' The idioms of his language, and the figures of his rhetoric, have usurped the place of his truth; and churches are not built on his principles, but on his tropes. Christianity became a Mythus,[6] as the poetic teaching of Greece and of Egypt, before. He spoke of miracles; for he felt that man's life was a miracle, and all that man doth, and he knew that this daily miracle shines, as the man is diviner. But the very word Miracle, as pronounced by Christian churches, gives a false impression; it is Monster. It is not one with the blowing clover and the falling rain.

5. Emerson reverses the common meaning of *reason*, using it in the sense of intuitive, suprarational knowledge, while by *understanding* he means knowledge arrived at through logical reasoning. Emerson probably derived these concepts from Samuel Taylor Coleridge's *Biographia Literaria* (1817).

6. Cult.

He felt respect for Moses and the prophets; but no unfit tenderness at postponing their initial revelations, to the hour and the man that now is; to the eternal revelation in the heart. Thus was he a true man. Having seen that the law in us is commanding, he would not suffer it to be commanded. Boldly, with hand, and heart, and life, he declared it was God. Thus was he a true man. Thus is he, as I think, the only soul in history who has appreciated the worth of a man.

1. In thus contemplating Jesus, we become very sensible of the first defect of historical Christianity. Historical Christianity has fallen into the error that corrupts all attempts to communicate religion. As it appears to us, and as it has appeared for ages, it is not the doctrine of the soul, but an exaggeration of the personal, the positive, the ritual. It has dwelt, it dwells, with noxious exaggeration about the *person* of Jesus. The soul knows no persons. It invites every man to expand to the full circle of the universe, and will have no preferences but those of spontaneous love. But by this eastern monarchy of a Christianity, which indolence and fear have built, the friend of man is made the injurer of man. The manner in which his name is surrounded with expressions, which were once sallies of admiration and love, but are now petrified into official titles, kills all generous sympathy and liking. All who hear me, feel, that the language that describes Christ to Europe and America, is not the style of friendship and enthusiasm to a good and noble heart, but is appropriated and formal,—paints a demigod, as the Orientals or the Greeks would describe Osiris or Apollo.[7] Accept the injurious impositions of our early catachetical instruction, and even honesty and self-denial were but splendid sins, if they did not wear the Christian name. One would rather be

'A pagan suckled in a creed outworn,'[8]

than to be defrauded of his manly right in coming into nature, and finding not names and places, not land and professions, but even virtue and truth foreclosed and monopolized. You shall not be a man even. You shall not own the world; you shall not dare, and live after the infinite Law that is in you, and in company with the infinite Beauty which heaven and earth reflect to you in all lovely forms; but you must subordinate your nature to Christ's nature; you must accept our interpretations; and take his portrait as the vulgar draw it.

That is always best which gives me to myself. The sublime is excited in me by the great stoical doctrine, Obey thyself. That which shows God in me, fortifies me. That which shows God out of me, makes me a wart and a wen.[9] There is no longer a necessary reason for my being. Already the long shadows of untimely oblivion creep over me, and I shall decease forever.

The divine bards are the friends of my virtue, of my intellect, of my strength. They admonish me, that the gleams which flash across my mind, are not mine, but God's; that they had the like, and were not disobedient to the heavenly vision.[1] So I love them. Noble provocations go out from them,

7. Gods associated with the sun and rebirth from two ancient religious traditions: Egyptian and Greek, respectively.

8. From Wordsworth's sonnet "The World Is Too Much with Us" (1807).

9. Cyst.

1. "I was not disobedient unto the heavenly vision" (Acts 26.19).

inviting me also to emancipate myself; to resist evil; to subdue the world; and to Be. And thus by his holy thoughts, Jesus serves us, and thus only. To aim to convert a man by miracles, is a profanation of the soul. A true conversion, a true Christ, is now, as always, to be made, by the reception of beautiful sentiments. It is true that a great and rich soul, like his, falling among the simple, does so preponderate, that, as his did, it names the world. The world seems to them to exist for him, and they have not yet drunk so deeply of his sense, as to see that only by coming again to themselves, or to God in themselves, can they grow forevermore. It is a low benefit to give me something; it is a high benefit to enable me to do somewhat of myself. The time is coming when all men will see, that the gift of God to the soul is not a vaunting, overpowering, excluding sanctity, but a sweet, natural goodness, a goodness like thine and mine, and that so invites thine and mine to be and to grow.

The injustice of the vulgar tone of preaching is not less flagrant to Jesus, than it is to the souls which it profanes. The preachers do not see that they make his gospel not glad, and shear him of the locks of beauty and the attributes of heaven. When I see a majestic Epaminondas,[2] or Washington; when I see among my contemporaries, a true orator, an upright judge, a dear friend; when I vibrate to the melody and fancy of a poem; I see beauty that is to be desired. And so lovely, and with yet more entire consent of my human being, sounds in my ear the severe music of the bards that have sung of the true God in all ages. Now do not degrade the life and dialogues of Christ out of the circle of this charm, by insulation and peculiarity. Let them lie as they befel, alive and warm, part of human life, and of the landscape, and of the cheerful day.

2. The second defect of the traditionary and limited way of using the mind of Christ is a consequence of the first; this, namely; that the Moral Nature, that Law of laws, whose revelations introduce greatness,—yea, God himself, into the open soul, is not explored as the fountain of the established teaching in society. Men have come to speak of the revelation as somewhat long ago given and done, as if God were dead. The injury to faith throttles the preacher; and the goodliest of institutions becomes an uncertain and inarticulate voice.

It is very certain that it is the effect of conversation with the beauty of the soul, to beget a desire and need to impart to others the same knowledge and love. If utterance is denied, the thought lies like a burden on the man. Always the seer is a sayer. Somehow his dream is told. Somehow he publishes it with solemn joy. Sometimes with pencil on canvas; sometimes with chisel on stone; sometimes in towers and aisles of granite, his soul's worship is builded; sometimes in anthems of indefinite music; but clearest and most permanent, in words.

The man enamored of this excellency, becomes its priest or poet. The office is coeval with the world. But observe the condition, the spiritual limitation of the office. The spirit only can teach. Not any profane man, not any sensual, not any liar, not any slave can teach, but only he can give, who has; he only can create, who is. The man on whom the soul descends, through whom the soul speaks, alone can teach. Courage, piety, love, wisdom, can

2. Theban general (418?–362 B.C.E.) whose military innovations helped end Sparta's dominance in Greece.

teach; and every man can open his door to these angels, and they shall bring him the gift of tongues. But the man who aims to speak as books enable, as synods use, as the fashion guides, and as interest commands, babbles. Let him hush.

To this holy office, you propose to devote yourselves. I wish you may feel your call in throbs of desire and hope. The office is the first in the world. It is of that reality, that it cannot suffer the deduction of any falsehood. And it is my duty to say to you, that the need was never greater of new revelation than now. From the views I have already expressed, you will infer the sad conviction, which I share, I believe, with numbers, of the universal decay and now almost death of faith in society. The soul is not preached. The Church seems to totter to its fall, almost all life extinct. On this occasion, any complaisance, would be criminal, which told you, whose hope and commission it is to preach the faith of Christ, that the faith of Christ is preached.

It is time that this ill-suppressed murmur of all thoughtful men against the famine of our churches; this moaning of the heart because it is bereaved of the consolation, the hope, the grandeur, that come alone out of the culture of the moral nature; should be heard through the sleep of indolence, and over the din of routine. This great and perpetual office of the preacher is not discharged. Preaching is the expression of the moral sentiment in application to the duties of life. In how many churches, by how many prophets, tell me, is man made sensible that he is an infinite Soul; that the earth and heavens are passing into his mind; that he is drinking forever the soul of God? Where now sounds the persuasion, that by its very melody imparadises my heart, and so affirms its own origin in heaven? Where shall I hear words such as in elder ages drew men to leave all and follow,—father and mother, house and land, wife and child?[3] Where shall I hear these august laws of moral being so pronounced, as to fill my ear, and I feel ennobled by the offer of my uttermost action and passion? The test of the true faith, certainly, should be its power to charm and command the soul, as the laws of nature control the activity of the hands,—so commanding that we find pleasure and honor in obeying. The faith should blend with the light of rising and of setting suns, with the flying cloud, the singing bird, and the breath of flowers. But now the priest's Sabbath has lost the splendor of nature; it is unlovely; we are glad when it is done; we can make, we do make, even sitting in our pews, a far better, holier, sweeter, for ourselves.

Whenever the pulpit is usurped by a formalist, then is the worshipper defrauded and disconsolate. We shrink as soon as the prayers begin, which do not uplift, but smite and offend us. We are fain to wrap our cloaks about us, and secure, as best we can, a solitude that hears not. I once heard a preacher who sorely tempted me to say, I would go to church no more. Men go, thought I, where they are wont to go, else had no soul entered the temple in the afternoon. A snowstorm was falling around us. The snowstorm was real; the preacher merely spectral; and the eye felt the sad contrast in looking at him, and then out of the window behind him, into the beautiful

3. See Matthew 19.28–29: "And Jesus said unto them, Verily I say unto you, That ye which have followed me, in the regeneration when the Son of man shall sit in the throne of his glory, ye also shall sit upon twelve thrones, judging the twelve tribes of Israel. And every one that hath forsaken houses, or brethren, or sisters, or father, or mother, or wife, or children, or lands, for my name's sake, shall receive an hundredfold, and shall inherit everlasting life."

meteor of the snow. He had lived in vain. He had no one word intimating that he had laughed or wept, was married or in love, had been commended, or cheated, or chagrined. If he had ever lived and acted, we were none the wiser for it. The capital secret of his profession, namely, to convert life into truth, he had not learned. Not one fact in all his experience, had he yet imported into his doctrine. This man had ploughed, and planted, and talked, and bought, and sold; he had read books; he had eaten and drunken; his head aches; his heart throbs; he smiles and suffers; yet was there not a surmise, a hint, in all the discourse, that he had ever lived at all. Not a line did he draw out of real history. The true preacher can always be known by this, that he deals out to the people his life,—life passed through the fire of thought. But of the bad preacher, it could not be told from his sermon, what age of the world he fell in; whether he had a father or a child; whether he was a freeholder or a pauper; whether he was a citizen or a countryman; or any other fact of his biography.

It seemed strange that the people should come to church. It seemed as if their houses were very unentertaining, that they should prefer this thoughtless clamor. It shows that there is a commanding attraction in the moral sentiment, that can lend a faint tint of light to dulness and ignorance, coming in its name and place. The good hearer is sure he has been touched sometimes; is sure there is somewhat to be reached, and some word that can reach it. When he listens to these vain words, he comforts himself by their relation to his remembrance of better hours, and so they clatter and echo unchallenged.

I am not ignorant that when we preach unworthily, it is not always quite in vain. There is a good ear, in some men, that draws supplies to virtue out of very indifferent nutriment. There is poetic truth concealed in all the common-places of prayer and of sermons, and though foolishly spoken, they may be wisely heard; for, each is some select expression that broke out in a moment of piety from some stricken or jubilant soul, and its excellency made it remembered. The prayers and even the dogmas of our church, are like the zodiac of Denderah,[4] and the astronomical monuments of the Hindoos, wholly insulated from anything now extant in the life and business of the people. They mark the height to which the waters once rose. But this docility is a check upon the mischief from the good and devout. In a large portion of the community, the religious service gives rise to quite other thoughts and emotions. We need not chide the negligent servant. We are struck with pity, rather, at the swift retribution of his sloth. Alas for the unhappy man that is called to stand in the pulpit, and *not* give bread of life. Everything that befals, accuses him. Would he ask contributions for the missions, foreign or domestic? Instantly his face is suffused with shame, to propose to his parish, that they should send money a hundred or a thousand miles, to furnish such poor fare as they have at home, and would do well to go the hundred or the thousand miles, to escape. Would he urge people to a godly way of living;—and can he ask a fellow creature to come to Sabbath meetings, when he and they all know what is the poor uttermost they can hope for therein? Will he invite them privately to the Lord's Supper? He dares

4. At Dandarah, a village in Upper Egypt, astronomical scenes are sculpted on the ceiling of a ruined ancient temple.

not. If no heart warm this rite, the hollow, dry, creaking formality is too plain, than that he can face a man of wit and energy, and put the invitation without terror. In the street, what has he to say to the bold village blasphemer? The village blasphemer sees fear in the face, form, and gait of the minister.

Let me not taint the sincerity of this plea by any oversight of the claims of good men. I know and honor the purity and strict conscience of numbers of the clergy. What life the public worship retains, it owes to the scattered company of pious men, who minister here and there in the churches, and who, sometimes accepting with too great tenderness the tenet of the elders, have not accepted from others, but from their own heart, the genuine impulses of virtue, and so still command our love and awe, to the sanctity of character. Moreover, the exceptions are not so much to be found in a few eminent preachers, as in the better hours, the truer inspirations of all,—nay, in the sincere moments of every man. But with whatever exception, it is still true, that tradition characterizes the preaching of this country; that it comes out of the memory, and not out of the soul; that it aims at what is usual, and not at what is necessary and eternal; that thus, historical Christianity destroys the power of preaching, by withdrawing it from the exploration of the moral nature of man, where the sublime is, where are the resources of astonishment and power. What a cruel injustice it is to that Law, the joy of the whole earth, which alone can make thought dear and rich; that Law whose fatal sureness the astronomical orbits poorly emulate, that it is travestied and depreciated, that it is behooted and behowled, and not a trait, not a word of it articulated. The pulpit in losing sight of this Law, loses all its inspiration, and gropes after it knows not what. And for want of this culture, the soul of the community is sick and faithless. It wants nothing so much as a stern, high, stoical, Christian discipline, to make it know itself and the divinity that speaks through it. Now man is ashamed of himself; he skulks and sneaks through the world, to be tolerated, to be pitied, and scarcely in a thousand years does any man dare to be wise and good, and so draw after him the tears and blessings of his kind.

Certainly there have been periods when, from the inactivity of the intellect on certain truths, a greater faith was possible in names and persons. The Puritans in England and America, found in the Christ of the Catholic Church, and in the dogmas inherited from Rome, scope for their austere piety, and their longings for civil freedom. But their creed is passing away, and none arises in its room. I think no man can go with his thoughts about him, into one of our churches, without feeling that what hold the public worship had on men, is gone or going. It has lost its grasp on the affection of the good, and the fear of the bad. In the country,—neighborhoods, half parishes are *signing off*,—to use the local term. It is already beginning to indicate character and religion to withdraw from the religious meetings. I have heard a devout person, who prized the Sabbath, say in bitterness of heart, "On Sundays, it seems wicked to go to church." And the motive, that holds the best there, is now only a hope and a waiting. What was once a mere circumstance, that the best and the worst men in the parish, the poor and the rich, the learned and the ignorant, young and old, should meet one day as fellows in one house, in sign of an equal right in the soul,—has come to be a paramount motive for going thither.

My friends, in these two errors, I think, I find the causes of that calamity of a decaying church and a wasting unbelief, which are casting malignant influences around us, and making the hearts of good men sad. And what greater calamity can fall upon a nation, than the loss of worship? Then all things go to decay. Genius leaves the temple, to haunt the senate, or the market. Literature becomes frivolous. Science is cold. The eye of youth is not lighted by the hope of other worlds, and age is without honor. Society lives to trifles, and when men die, we do not mention them.

And now, my brothers, you will ask, What in these desponding days can be done by us? The remedy is already declared in the ground of our complaint of the Church. We have contrasted the Church with the Soul. In the soul, then, let the redemption be sought. In one soul, in your soul, there are resources for the world. Wherever a man comes, there comes revolution. The old is for slaves. When a man comes, all books are legible, all things transparent, all religions are forms. He is religious. Man is the wonderworker. He is seen amid miracles. All men bless and curse. He saith yea and nay, only. The stationariness of religion; the assumption that the age of inspiration is past, that the Bible is closed; the fear of degrading the character of Jesus by representing him as a man; indicate with sufficient clearness the falsehood of our theology. It is the office of a true teacher to show us that God is, not was; that He speaketh, not spake. The true Christianity,—a faith like Christ's in the infinitude of man,—is lost. None believeth in the soul of man, but only in some man or person old and departed. Ah me! no man goeth alone. All men go in flocks to this saint or that poet, avoiding the God who seeth in secret. They cannot see in secret; they love to be blind in public. They think society wiser than their soul, and know not that one soul, and their soul, is wiser than the whole world. See how nations and races flit by on the sea of time, and leave no ripple to tell where they floated or sunk, and one good soul shall make the name of Moses, or of Zeno, or of Zoroaster,[5] reverend forever. None assayeth the stern ambition to be the Self of the nation, and of nature, but each would be an easy secondary to some Christian scheme, or sectarian connexion, or some eminent man. Once leave your own knowledge of God, your own sentiment, and take secondary knowledge, as St. Paul's, or George Fox's, or Swedenborg's,[6] and you get wide from God with every year this secondary form lasts, and if, as now, for centuries,—the chasm yawns to that breadth, that men can scarcely be convinced there is in them anything divine.

Let me admonish you, first of all, to go alone; to refuse the good models, even those most sacred in the imagination of men, and dare to love God without mediator or veil. Friends enough you shall find who will hold up to your emulation Wesleys and Oberlins,[7] Saints and Prophets. Thank God for these good men, but say, 'I also am a man.' Imitation cannot go above its

5. Persian prophet, philosopher, and religious reformer (6th century B.C.E.). Moses, Hebrew lawgiver who led the exodus from Egypt. Zeno (342?–270? B.C.E.), Greek philosopher and founder of Stoicism.

6. Emanuel Swedenborg (1688–1772), Swedish scientist and theologian. St. Paul, the apostle to the Gentiles, hero of the Book of Acts, and author of other books of the New Testament. George Fox (1624–1691), English founder of the Society of Friends (Quakers).

7. Jean Frédéric Oberlin (1740–1826), Alsatian Lutheran clergyman and philanthropist, innovator in children's education; the town and college in Ohio are named in his honor. John Wesley (1703–1791) and his brother Charles (1707–1788) founded the Methodist movement in the Church of England.

model. The imitator dooms himself to hopeless mediocrity. The inventor did it, because it was natural to him, and so in him it has a charm. In the imitator, something else is natural, and he bereaves himself of his own beauty, to come short of another man's.

Yourself a newborn bard of the Holy Ghost,—cast behind you all conformity, and acquaint men at first hand with Deity. Be to them a man. Look to it first and only, that you are such; that fashion, custom, authority, pleasure, and money are nothing to you,—are not bandages over your eyes, that you cannot see,—but live with the privilege of the immeasurable mind. Not too anxious to visit periodically all families and each family in your parish connexion,—when you meet one of these men or women, be to them a divine man; be to them thought and virtue; let their timid aspirations find in you a friend; let their trampled instincts be genially tempted out in your atmosphere; let their doubts know that you have doubted, and their wonder feel that you have wondered. By trusting your own soul, you shall gain a greater confidence in other men. For all our penny-wisdom, for all our soul-destroying slavery to habit, it is not to be doubted, that all men have sublime thoughts; that all men do value the few real hours of life; they love to be heard; they love to be caught up into the vision of principles. We mark with light in the memory the few interviews, we have had in the dreary years of routine and of sin, with souls that made our souls wiser; that spoke what we thought; that told us what we knew; that gave us leave to be what we inly were. Discharge to men the priestly office, and, present or absent, you shall be followed with their love as by an angel.

And, to this end, let us not aim at common degrees of merit. Can we not leave, to such as love it, the virtue that glitters for the commendation of society, and ourselves pierce the deep solitudes of absolute ability and worth? We easily come up to the standard of goodness in society. Society's praise can be cheaply secured, and almost all men are content with those easy merits; but the instant effect of conversing with God, will be, to put them away. There are sublime merits; persons who are not actors, not speakers, but influences; persons too great for fame, for display; who disdain eloquence; to whom all we call art and artist, seems too nearly allied to show and by-ends, to the exaggeration of the finite and selfish, and loss of the universal. The orators, the poets, the commanders encroach on us only as fair women do, by our allowance and homage. Slight them by preoccupation of mind, slight them, as you can well afford to do, by high and universal aims, and they instantly feel that you have right, and that it is in lower places that they must shine. They also feel your right; for they with you are open to the influx of the all-knowing Spirit, which annihilates before its broad noon the little shades and gradations of intelligence in the compositions we call wiser and wisest.

In such high communion, let us study the grand strokes of rectitude: a bold benevolence, an independence of friends, so that not the unjust wishes of those who love us, shall impair our freedom, but we shall resist for truth's sake the freest flow of kindness, and appeal to sympathies far in advance; and,—what is the highest form in which we know this beautiful element,—a certain solidity of merit, that has nothing to do with opinion, and which is so essentially and manifestly virtue, that it is taken for granted, that the right, the brave, the generous step will be taken by it, and nobody thinks of commending it. You would compliment a coxcomb[8] doing a good act, but you would not praise an angel. The silence that accepts merit as the most natural thing in the world, is the highest applause. Such souls, when they appear, are the Imperial Guard of Virtue, the perpetual reserve, the dictators of fortune. One needs not praise their courage,—they are the heart and soul of nature. O my friends, there are resources in us on which we have not drawn. There are men who rise refreshed on hearing a threat; men to whom a crisis which intimidates and paralyzes the majority—demanding not the faculties of prudence and thrift, but comprehension, immovableness, the readiness of sacrifice,—comes graceful and beloved as a bride. Napoleon said of Massena,[9] that he was not himself until the battle began to go against him; then, when the dead began to fall in ranks around him, awoke his powers of combination, and he put on terror and victory as a robe. So it is in rugged crises, in unweariable endurance, and in aims which put sympathy out of question, that the angel is shown. But these are heights that we can scarce remember and look up to, without contrition and shame. Let us thank God that such things exist.

And now let us do what we can to rekindle the smouldering, nigh quenched fire on the altar. The evils of that church that now is, are manifest. The question returns. What shall we do? I confess, all attempts to project and establish a Cultus with new rites and forms, seem to me vain. Faith makes us, and not we it, and faith makes its own forms. All attempts to contrive a system, are as cold as the new worship introduced by the French to the goddess of Reason—today, pasteboard and fillagree, and ending to-morrow in madness and murder.[1] Rather let the breath of new life be breathed by you through the forms already existing. For, if once you are alive, you shall find they shall become plastic[2] and new. The remedy to their deformity is, first, soul, and second, soul, and evermore, soul. A whole popedom[3] of forms, one pulsation of virtue can uplift and vivify. Two inestimable advantages Christianity has given us; first; the Sabbath, the jubilee of the whole world; whose light dawns welcome alike into the closet of the philosopher, into the garret of toil, and into prison cells, and everywhere suggests, even to the vile, a thought of the dignity of spiritual being. Let it stand forevermore, a temple, which new love, new faith, new sight shall restore to more than its first splendor to mankind. And secondly, the institution of preaching;—the speech of man to men,—essentially the most flexible of all organs, of all forms. What hinders that now, everywhere, in pulpits, in lecture-rooms, in houses, in fields, wherever the invitation of men or your own occasions lead you, you speak the very truth, as your life and conscience teach it, and cheer the waiting, fainting hearts of men with new hope and new revelation.

I look for the hour when that supreme Beauty, which ravished the souls of those Eastern men, and chiefly of those Hebrews, and through their lips spoke oracles to all time, shall speak in the West also. The Hebrew and Greek

8. Conceited fool.
9. André Masséna (1758–1817), marshal of the empire under Napoleon. The anecdote is taken from Barry Edward O'Meara's *Napoleon in Exile* (1823).
1. An allusion to the 1793–94 Reign of Terror, during which French revolutionary leaders ordered the guillotining or drowning of thousands of people.
2. Receptive to influences, capable of receiving new shapes.
3. I.e., rigid hierarchy.

Scriptures contain immortal sentences, that have been bread of life to millions. But they have no epical integrity; are fragmentary; are not shown in their order to the intellect. I look for the new Teacher, that shall follow so far those shining laws, that he shall see them come full circle; shall see their rounding complete grace; shall see the world to be the mirror of the soul; shall see the identity of the law of gravitation with purity of heart; and shall show that the Ought, that Duty, is one thing with Science, with Beauty, and with Joy.

1838, 1841

Self-Reliance[1]

Ne te quæsiveris extra.[2]

"Man is his own star, and the soul that can
Render an honest and a perfect man,
Command all light, all influence, all fate,
Nothing to him falls early or too late.
Our acts our angels are, or good or ill,
Our fatal shadows that walk by us still."
—Epilogue to Beaumont and Fletcher's
Honest Man's Fortune[3]

Cast the bantling[4] on the rocks,
Suckle him with the she-wolf's teat:
Wintered with the hawk and fox,
Power and speed be hands and feet.

I read the other day some verses written by an eminent painter[5] which were original and not conventional. Always the soul hears an admonition in such lines, let the subject be what it may. The sentiment they instil is of more value than any thought they may contain. To believe your own thought, to believe that what is true for you in your private heart, is true for all men,—that is genius. Speak your latent conviction and it shall be the universal sense; for always the inmost becomes the outmost,—and our first thought is rendered back to us by the trumpets of the Last Judgment. Familiar as the voice of the mind is to each, the highest merit we ascribe to Moses, Plato, and Milton, is that they set at naught books and traditions, and spoke not what men but what they thought. A man should learn to detect and watch that gleam of light which flashes across his mind from within, more than the lustre of the firmament of bards and sages. Yet he dismisses without notice his thought, because it is his. In every work of genius we recognize our own rejected thoughts: they come back to us with a certain alienated majesty. Great works of art have no more affecting lesson for us than this. They teach

1. First published in *Essays* (1841), the source of the present text.
2. The Roman poet Persius (34–62 C.E.), *Satire* 1.7: "Do not search outside yourself" (Latin), i.e., do not imitate.
3. Published in 1647, the play by the Jacobean dramatists Francis Beaumont (1584–1616) and John Fletcher (1579–1625) was written in 1613.
4. Baby. The stanza is Emerson's.
5. Probably the American painter Washington Alston (1779–1847), whose poetry Emerson praised in a journal entry of September 20, 1837.

us to abide by our spontaneous impression with good humored inflexibility then most when the whole cry of voices is on the other side. Else, to-morrow a stranger will say with masterly good sense precisely what we have thought and felt all the time, and we shall be forced to take with shame our own opinion from another.

There is a time in every man's education when he arrives at the conviction that envy is ignorance; that imitation is suicide; that he must take himself for better, for worse, as his portion; that though the wide universe is full of good, no kernel of nourishing corn can come to him but through his toil bestowed on that plot of ground which is given to him to till. The power which resides in him is new in nature, and none but he knows what that is which he can do, nor does he know until he has tried. Not for nothing one face, one character, one fact makes much impression on him, and another none. It is not without preëstablished harmony, this sculpture in the memory. The eye was placed where one ray should fall, that it might testify of that particular ray. Bravely let him speak the utmost syllable of his confession. We but half express ourselves, and are ashamed of that divine idea which each of us represents. It may be safely trusted as proportionate and of good issues, so it be faithfully imparted, but God will not have his work made manifest by cowards. It needs a divine man to exhibit any thing divine. A man is relieved and gay when he has put his heart into his work and done his best; but what he has said or done otherwise, shall give him no peace. It is a deliverance which does not deliver. In the attempt his genius deserts him; no muse befriends; no invention, no hope.

Trust thyself: every heart vibrates to that iron string. Accept the place the divine Providence has found for you; the society of your contemporaries, the connexion of events. Great men have always done so and confided themselves childlike to the genius of their age, betraying their perception that the Eternal was stirring at their heart, working through their hands, predominating in all their being. And we are now men, and must accept in the highest mind the same transcendent destiny; and not pinched in a corner, not cowards fleeing before a revolution, but redeemers and benefactors, pious aspirants to be noble clay plastic under the Almighty effort, let us advance and advance on Chaos and the Dark.

What pretty oracles nature yields us on this text in the face and behavior of children, babes and even brutes. That divided and rebel mind, that distrust of a sentiment because our arithmetic has computed the strength and means opposed to our purpose, these have not. Their mind being whole, their eye is as yet unconquered, and when we look in their faces, we are disconcerted. Infancy conforms to nobody: all conform to it, so that one babe commonly makes four or five out of the adults who prattle and play to it. So God has armed youth and puberty and manhood no less with its own piquancy and charm, and made it enviable and gracious and its claims not to be put by, if it will stand by itself. Do not think the youth has no force because he cannot speak to you and me. Hark! in the next room, who spoke so clear and emphatic? Good Heaven! it is he! it is that very lump of bashfulness and phlegm which for weeks has done nothing but eat when you were by, that now rolls out these words like bell-strokes. It seems he knows how to speak to his contemporaries. Bashful or bold, then, he will know how to make us seniors very unnecessary.

The nonchalance of boys who are sure of a dinner, and would disdain as much as a lord to do or say aught to conciliate one, is the healthy attitude of human nature. How is a boy the master of society; independent, irresponsible, looking out from his corner on such people and facts as pass by, he tries and sentences them on their merits, in the swift summary way of boys, as good, bad, interesting, silly, eloquent, troublesome. He cumbers himself never about consequences, about interests: he gives an independent, genuine verdict. You must court him: he does not court you. But the man is, as it were, clapped into jail by his consciousness. As soon as he has once acted or spoken with eclat, he is a committed person, watched by the sympathy or the hatred of hundreds whose affections must now enter into his account. There is no Lethe[6] for this. Ah, that he could pass again into his neutral, godlike independence! Who can thus lose all pledge, and having observed, observe again from the same unaffected, unbiased, unbribable, unaffrighted innocence, must always be formidable, must always engage the poet's and the man's regards. Of such an immortal youth the force would be felt. He would utter opinions on all passing affairs, which being seen to be not private but necessary, would sink like darts into the ear of men, and put them in fear.

These are the voices which we hear in solitude, but they grow faint and inaudible as we enter into the world. Society everywhere is in conspiracy against the manhood of every one of its members. Society is a joint-stock company[7] in which the members agree for the better securing of his bread to each shareholder, to surrender the liberty and culture of the eater. The virtue in most request is conformity. Self-reliance is its aversion. It loves not realities and creators, but names and customs.

Whoso would be a man must be a nonconformist. He who would gather immortal palms[8] must not be hindered by the name of goodness, but must explore if it be goodness. Nothing is at last sacred but the integrity of our own mind. Absolve you to yourself, and you shall have the suffrage of the world. I remember an answer which when quite young I was prompted to make to a valued adviser who was wont to importune me with the dear old doctrines of the church. On my saying, What have I to do with the sacredness of traditions, if I live wholly from within? my friend suggested—"But these impulses may be from below, not from above." I replied, 'They do not seem to me to be such; but if I am the devil's child, I will live then from the devil.' No law can be sacred to me but that of my nature. Good and bad are but names very readily transferable to that or this; the only right is what is after my constitution, the only wrong what is against it. A man is to carry himself in the presence of all opposition as if every thing were titular and ephemeral but he. I am ashamed to think how easily we capitulate to badges and names, to large societies and dead institutions. Every decent and well-spoken individual affects and sways me more than is right. I ought to go upright and vital, and speak the rude truth in all ways. If malice and vanity wear the coat of philanthropy, shall that pass? If an angry bigot assumes this bountiful cause of Abolition, and comes to me with his last news from Barbadoes,[9] why should

6. Oblivion-producing water from the river of the underworld in Greek mythology.
7. Business for which the capital is held by its joint owners in transferable shares.
8. Great honors.
9. Island in the eastern Caribbean where slavery was officially abolished in 1834. Despite his apparent skepticism here, Emerson became increasingly committed to abolitionism during the 1840s.

I not say to him, 'Go love thy infant; love thy wood-chopper: be good-natured and modest: have that grace; and never varnish your hard, uncharitable ambition with this incredible tenderness for black folk a thousand miles off. Thy love afar is spite at home.' Rough and graceless would be such greeting, but truth is handsomer than the affectation of love. Your goodness must have some edge to it—else it is none. The doctrine of hatred must be preached as the counteraction of the doctrine of love when that pules[1] and whines. I shun father and mother and wife and brother, when my genius calls me.[2] I would write on the lintels of the door-post, *Whim.*[3] I hope it is somewhat better than whim at last, but we cannot spend the day in explanation. Expect me not to show cause why I seek or why I exclude company. Then, again, do not tell me, as a good man did to-day, of my obligation to put all poor men in good situations. Are they *my* poor? I tell thee, thou foolish philanthropist, that I grudge the dollar, the dime, the cent I give to such men as do not belong to me and to whom I do not belong. There is a class of persons to whom by all spiritual affinity I am bought and sold; for them I will go to prison, if need be; but your miscellaneous popular charities; the education at college of fools; the building of meeting-houses to the vain end to which many now stand; alms to sots; and the thousandfold Relief Societies;—though I confess with shame I sometimes succumb and give the dollar, it is a wicked dollar which by-and-by I shall have the manhood to withhold.

Virtues are in the popular estimate rather the exception than the rule. There is the man *and* his virtues. Men do what is called a good action, as some piece of courage or charity, much as they would pay a fine in expiation of daily non-appearance on parade. Their works are done as an apology or extenuation of their living in the world,—as invalids and the insane pay a high board. Their virtues are penances. I do not wish to expiate, but to live. My life is not an apology, but a life. It is for itself and not for a spectacle. I much prefer that it should be of a lower strain, so it be genuine and equal, than that it should be glittering and unsteady. I wish it to be sound and sweet, and not to need diet and bleeding.[4] My life should be unique; it should be an alms, a battle, a conquest, a medicine. I ask primary evidence that you are a man, and refuse this appeal from the man to his actions. I know that for myself it makes no difference whether I do or forbear those actions which are reckoned excellent. I cannot consent to pay for a privilege where I have intrinsic right. Few and mean as my gifts may be, I actually am, and do not need for my own assurance or the assurance of my fellows any secondary testimony.

What I must do, is all that concerns me, not what the people think. This rule, equally arduous in actual and in intellectual life, may serve for the whole distinction between greatness and meanness. It is the harder, because you will always find those who think they know what is your duty better than you know it. It is easy in the world to live after the world's opinion; it is easy in solitude to live after our own; but the great man is he who in the midst of the crowd keeps with perfect sweetness the independence of solitude.

1. Whimpers.
2. For shunning family to obey a divine command, see Matthew 10.34–37.
3. See Exodus 12 for God's instructions to Moses on marking with blood the "two side posts" and the "upper door post" (or lintel) of houses so that God would spare those within when He came to "smite all the firstborn in the land of Egypt, both man and beast."
4. The old medical treatment of bloodletting.

The objection to conforming to usages that have become dead to you, is, that it scatters your force. It loses your time and blurs the impression of your character. If you maintain a dead church, contribute to a dead Bible-Society, vote with a great party either for the Government or against it, spread your table like base housekeepers,—under all these screens, I have difficulty to detect the precise man you are. And, of course, so much force is withdrawn from your proper life. But do your thing, and I shall know you. Do your work, and you shall reinforce yourself. A man must consider what a blindman's-bluff is this game of conformity. If I know your sect, I anticipate your argument. I hear a preacher announce for his text and topic the expediency of one of the institutions of his church. Do I not know beforehand that not possibly can he say a new and spontaneous word? Do I not know that with all this ostentation of examining the grounds of the institution, he will do no such thing? Do I not know that he is pledged to himself not to look but at one side; the permitted side, not as a man, but as a parish minister? He is a retained attorney, and these airs of the bench are the emptiest affectation. Well, most men have bound their eyes with one or another handkerchief, and attached themselves to some one of these communities of opinion. This conformity makes them not false in a few particulars, authors of a few lies, but false in all particulars. Their every truth is not quite true. Their two is not the real two, their four not the real four: so that every word they say chagrins us, and we know not where to begin to set them right. Meantime nature is not slow to equip us in the prison-uniform of the party to which we adhere. We come to wear one cut of face and figure, and acquire by degrees the gentlest asinine expression. There is a mortifying experience in particular which does not fail to wreak itself also in the general history; I mean, "the foolish face of praise,"[5] the forced smile which we put on in company where we do not feel at ease in answer to conversation which does not interest us. The muscles, not spontaneously moved, but moved by a low usurping wilfulness, grow tight about the outline of the face and make the most disagreeable sensation, a sensation of rebuke and warning which no brave young man will suffer twice.

For non-conformity the world whips you with its displeasure. And therefore a man must know how to estimate a sour face. The bystanders look askance on him in the public street or in the friend's parlor. If this aversation had its origin in contempt and resistance like his own, he might well go home with a sad countenance; but the sour faces of the multitude, like their sweet faces, have no deep cause,—disguise no god, but are put on and off as the wind blows, and a newspaper directs. Yet is the discontent of the multitude more formidable than that of the senate and the college. It is easy enough for a firm man who knows the world to brook the rage of the cultivated classes. Their rage is decorous and prudent, for they are timid as being very vulnerable themselves. But when to their feminine rage the indignation of the people is added, when the ignorant and the poor are aroused, when the unintelligent brute force that lies at the bottom of society is made to growl and mow,[6] it needs the habit of magnanimity and religion to treat it godlike as a trifle of no concernment.

5. Alexander Pope's "Epistle to Dr. Arbuthnot" (1735), line 212.

6. Grimace.

The other terror that scares us from self-trust is our consistency; a reverence for our past act or word, because the eyes of others have no other data for computing our orbit than our past acts, and we are loath to disappoint them.

But why should you keep your head over your shoulder? Why drag about this monstrous corpse of your memory, lest you contradict somewhat you have stated in this or that public place? Suppose you should contradict yourself; what then? It seems to be a rule of wisdom never to rely on your memory alone, scarcely even in acts of pure memory, but bring the past for judgment into the thousand-eyed present, and live ever in a new day. Trust your emotion. In your metaphysics you have denied personality to the Deity: yet when the devout motions of the soul come, yield to them heart and life, though they should clothe God with shape and color. Leave your theory as Joseph his coat in the hand of the harlot, and flee.[7]

A foolish consistency is the hobgoblin of little minds, adored by little statesmen and philosophers and divines. With consistency a great soul has simply nothing to do. He may as well concern himself with his shadow on the wall. Out upon your guarded lips! Sew them up with packthread, do. Else, if you would be a man, speak what you think to-day in words as hard as cannon balls, and to-morrow speak what to-morrow thinks in hard words again, though it contradict every thing you said to-day. Ah, then, exclaim the aged ladies, you shall be sure to be misunderstood. Misunderstood! It is a right fool's word. Is it so bad then to be misunderstood? Pythagoras was misunderstood, and Socrates, and Jesus, and Luther, and Copernicus, and Galileo, and Newton,[8] and every pure and wise spirit that ever took flesh. To be great is to be misunderstood.

I suppose no man can violate his nature. All the sallies of his will are rounded in by the law of his being as the inequalities of Andes and Himmaleh[9] are insignificant in the curve of the sphere. Nor does it matter how you gauge and try him. A character is like an acrostic or Alexandrian stanza;[1]—read it forward, backward, or across, it still spells the same thing. In this pleasing contrite wood-life which God allows me, let me record day by day my honest thought without prospect or retrospect, and, I cannot doubt, it will be found symmetrical, though I mean it not, and see it not. My book should smell of pines and resound with the hum of insects. The swallow over my window should interweave that thread or straw he carries in his bill into my web also. We pass for what we are. Character teaches above our wills. Men imagine that they communicate their virtue or vice only by overt actions and do not see that virtue or vice emit a breath every moment.

Fear never but you shall be consistent in whatever variety of actions, so they be each honest and natural in their hour. For of one will, the actions

7. When Potiphar's wife demanded that Joseph sleep with her, "he left his garment in her hand, and fled" (Genesis 39.12).
8. Sir Isaac Newton (1642–1727), English mathematician and scientist who developed the laws of gravity and motion. Pythagorus (c. 582–c. 507 B.C.E.), Greek philosopher and mathematician who elaborated a theory of numbers. Martin Luther (1483–1546), German leader of the Protestant Reformation. Nicholas Copernicus (1473–1543), Polish astronomer who argued that the planets revolve around a stationary sun. Galileo Galilei (1564–1662), Italian astronomer, mathematician, and physicist who supported the Copernican system and laid the foundations for modern science.
9. Mountain ranges in South America and Asia.
1. A palindrome, reading the same backward as forward.

will be harmonious, however unlike they seem. These varieties are lost sight of when seen at a little distance, at a little height of thought. One tendency unites them all. The voyage of the best ship is a zigzag line of a hundred tacks. This is only microscopic criticism. See the line from a sufficient distance, and it straightens itself to the average tendency. Your genuine action will explain itself and will explain your other genuine actions. Your conformity explains nothing. Act singly, and what you have already done singly, will justify you now. Greatness always appeals to the future. If I can be great enough now to do right and scorn eyes, I must have done so much right before, as to defend me now. Be it how it will, do right now. Always scorn appearances, and you always may. The force of character is cumulative. All the foregone days of virtue work their health into this. What makes the majesty of the heroes of the senate and the field, which so fills the imagination? The consciousness of a train of great days and victories behind. There they all stand and shed an united light on the advancing actor. He is attended as by a visible escort of angels to every man's eye. That is it which throws thunder into Chatham's voice, and dignity into Washington's port, and America into Adams's[2] eye. Honor is venerable to us because it is no ephemeris. It is always ancient virtue. We worship it to-day, because it is not of to-day. We love it and pay it homage, because it is not a trap for our love and homage, but is self-dependent, self-derived, and therefore of an old immaculate pedigree, even if shown in a young person.

I hope in these days we have heard the last of conformity and consistency. Let the words be gazetted[3] and ridiculous henceforward. Instead of the gong for dinner, let us hear a whistle from the Spartan fife.[4] Let us bow and apologize never more. A great man is coming to eat at my house. I do not wish to please him: I wish that he should wish to please me. I will stand here for humanity, and though I would make it kind, I would make it true. Let us affront and reprimand the smooth mediocrity and squalid contentment of the times, and hurl in the face of custom, and trade, and office, the fact which is the upshot of all history, that there is a great responsible Thinker and Actor moving wherever moves a man; that a true man belongs to no other time or place, but is the centre of things. Where he is, there is nature. He measures you, and all men, and all events. You are constrained to accept his standard. Ordinarily every body in society reminds us of somewhat else or of some other person. Character, reality, reminds you of nothing else. It takes place of the whole creation. The man must be so much that he must make all circumstances indifferent,—put all means into the shade. This all great men are and do. Every true man is a cause, a country, and an age; requires infinite spaces and numbers and time fully to accomplish his thought;—and posterity seem to follow his steps as a procession. A man Cæsar is born, and for ages after, we have a Roman Empire. Christ is born, and millions of minds so grow and cleave to his genius, that he is confounded with virtue and the possible of man. An institution is the lengthened shadow of one man; as, the

2. Probably John Quincy Adams (1767–1848), sixth president of the United States and, afterward, long-time member of the House of Representatives, known as "Old Man Eloquence." William Pitt, first Earl of Chatham (1708–1778), English statesman and great orator. George Washington (1732–1799), first president of the United States. "Port": carriage or physical bearing.

3. Printed in a newspaper or other public forum.

4. The Spartans were known for their military discipline and willingness to endure physical hardships.

Reformation, of Luther; Quakerism, of Fox; Methodism, of Wesley; Abolition, of Clarkson.[5] Scipio,[6] Milton called "the height of Rome;" and all history resolves itself very easily into the biography of a few stout and earnest persons.

Let a man then know his worth, and keep things under his feet. Let him not peep or steal, or skulk up and down with the air of a charity-boy, a bastard, or an interloper, in the world which exists for him. But the man in the street finding no worth in himself which corresponds to the force which built a tower or sculptured a marble god, feels poor when he looks on these. To him a palace, a statue, or a costly book have an alien and forbidding air, much like a gay equipage, and seem to say like that, 'Who are you, sir?' Yet they all are his, suitors for his notice, petitioners to his faculties that they will come out and take possession. The picture waits for my verdict: it is not to command me, but I am to settle its claims to praise. That popular fable of the sot who was picked up dead drunk in the street, carried to the duke's house, washed and dressed and laid in the duke's bed, and, on his waking, treated with all obsequious ceremony like the duke, and assured that he had been insane,[7]—owes its popularity to the fact, that it symbolizes so well the state of man, who is in the world a sort of sot, but now and then wakes up, exercises his reason, and finds himself a true prince.

Our reading is mendicant and sycophantic. In history, our imagination makes fools of us, plays us false. Kingdom and lordship, power and estate are a gaudier vocabulary than private John and Edward in a small house and common day's work: but the things of life are the same to both: the sum total of both is the same. Why all this deference to Alfred, and Scanderbeg, and Gustavus?[8] Suppose they were virtuous: did they wear out virtue? As great a stake depends on your private act to-day, as followed their public and renowned steps. When private men shall act with vast views, the lustre will be transferred from the actions of kings to those of gentlemen.

The world has indeed been instructed by its kings, who have so magnetized the eyes of nations. It has been taught by this colossal symbol the mutual reverence that is due from man to man. The joyful loyalty with which men have every where suffered the king, the noble, or the great proprietor to walk among them by a law of his own, make his own scale of men and things, and reverse theirs, pay for benefits not with money but with honor, and represent the Law in his person, was the hieroglyphic by which they obscurely signified their consciousness of their own right and comeliness, the right of every man.

The magnetism which all original action exerts is explained when we inquire the reason of self-trust. Who is the Trustee? What is the aboriginal Self on which a universal reliance may be grounded? What is the nature and power of that science-baffling star, without parallax,[9] without calculable elements, which shoots a ray of beauty even into trivial and impure actions, if

5. These founders are George Fox (1624–1691), John Wesley (1703–1791), and Thomas Clarkson (1760–1846).

6. Scipio Africanus (237–183 B.C.E.), the conqueror of Carthage.

7. See the "Induction" to Shakespeare's *The Taming of the Shrew.*

8. National heroes: Alfred (849–899), of England; Scanderbeg (1404?–1468), of Albania; and Gustavus (1594–1632), of Sweden.

9. An apparent change in the direction of an object caused by a change in the position from which it is observed. Emerson means without an observational position.

the least mark of independence appear? The inquiry leads us to that source, at once the essence of genius, the essence of virtue, and the essence of life, which we call Spontaneity or Instinct. We denote this primary wisdom as Intuition, whilst all later teachings are tuitions. In that deep force, the last fact behind which analysis cannot go, all things find their common origin. For the sense of being which in calm hours rises, we know not how, in the soul, is not diverse from things, from space, from light, from time, from man, but one with them, and proceedeth obviously from the same source whence their life and being also proceedeth. We first share the life by which things exist, and afterwards see them as appearances in nature, and forget that we have shared their cause. Here is the fountain of action and the fountain of thought. Here are the lungs of that inspiration which giveth man wisdom, of that inspiration of man which cannot be denied without impiety and atheism. We lie in the lap of immense intelligence, which makes us organs of its activity and receivers of its truth. When we discern justice, when we discern truth, we do nothing of ourselves, but allow a passage to its beams. If we ask whence this comes, if we seek to pry into the soul that causes,—all metaphysics, all philosophy is at fault. Its presence or its absence is all we can affirm. Every man discerns between the voluntary acts of his mind, and his involuntary perceptions. And to his involuntary perceptions, he knows a perfect respect is due. He may err in the expression of them, but he knows that these things are so, like day and night, not to be disputed. All my wilful actions and acquisitions are but roving;—the most trivial reverie, the faintest native emotion are domestic and divine. Thoughtless people contradict as readily the statement of perceptions as of opinions, or rather much more readily; for, they do not distinguish between perception and notion. They fancy that I choose to see this or that thing. But perception is not whimsical, but fatal. If I see a trait, my children will see it after me, and in course of time, all mankind,—although it may chance that no one has seen it before me. For my perception of it is as much a fact as the sun.

The relations of the soul to the divine spirit are so pure that it is profane to seek to interpose helps. It must be that when God speaketh, he should communicate not one thing, but all things; should fill the world with his voice; should scatter forth light, nature, time, souls from the centre of the present thought; and new date and new create the whole. Whenever a mind is simple, and receives a divine wisdom, then old things pass away,—means, teachers, texts, temples fall; it lives now and absorbs past and future into the present hour. All things are made sacred by relation to it,—one thing as much as another. All things are dissolved to their centre by their cause, and in the universal miracle petty and particular miracles disappear. This is and must be. If, therefore, a man claims to know and speak of God, and carries you backward to the phraseology of some old mouldered nation in another country, in another world, believe him not. Is the acorn better than the oak which is its fulness and completion? Is the parent better than the child into whom he has cast his ripened being? Whence then this worship of the past? The centuries are conspirators against the sanity and majesty of the soul. Time and space are but physiological colors which the eye maketh, but the soul is light; where it is, is day; where it was, is night; and history is an impertinence and an injury, if it be anything more than a cheerful apologue or parable of my being and becoming.

Man is timid and apologetic. He is no longer upright. He dares not say 'I think,' 'I am,' but quotes some saint or sage. He is ashamed before the blade of grass or the blowing rose. These roses under my window make no reference to former roses or to better ones; they are for what they are; they exist with God to-day. There is no time to them. There is simply the rose; it is perfect in every moment of its existence. Before a leaf-bud has burst, its whole life acts; in the full-blown flower, there is no more; in the leafless root, there is no less. Its nature is satisfied, and it satisfies nature, in all moments alike. There is no time to it. But man postpones or remembers; he does not live in the present, but with reverted eye laments the past, or, heedless of the riches that surround him, stands on tiptoe to foresee the future. He cannot be happy and strong until he too lives with nature in the present, above time.

This should be plain enough. Yet see what strong intellects dare not yet hear God himself, unless he speak the phraseology of I know not what David, or Jeremiah, or Paul.[1] We shall not always set so great a price on a few texts, on a few lines. We are like children who repeat by rote the sentences of grandames and tutors, and, as they grow older, of the men of talents and character they chance to see,—painfully recollecting the exact words they spoke; afterwards, when they come into the point of view which those had who uttered these sayings, they understand them, and are willing to let the words go; for, at any time, they can use words as good, when occasion comes. So was it with us, so will it be, if we proceed. If we live truly, we shall see truly. It is as easy for the strong man to be strong, as it is for the weak to be weak. When we have new perception, we shall gladly disburthen the memory of its hoarded treasures as old rubbish. When a man lives with God, his voice shall be as sweet as the murmur of the brook and the rustle of the corn.

And now at last the highest truth on this subject remains unsaid; probably, cannot be said; for all that we say is the far off remembering of the intuition. That thought, by what I can now nearest approach to say it, is this. When good is near you, when you have life in yourself,—it is not by any known or appointed way; you shall not discern the foot-prints of any other; you shall not see the face of man; you shall not hear any name;—the way, the thought, the good shall be wholly strange and new. It shall exclude all other being. You take the way from man not to man. All persons that ever existed are its fugitive ministers. There shall be no fear in it. Fear and hope are alike beneath it. It asks nothing. There is somewhat low even in hope. We are then in vision. There is nothing that can be called gratitude nor properly joy. The soul is raised over passion. It seeth identity and eternal causation. It is a perceiving that Truth and Right are. Hence it becomes a Tranquillity out of the knowing that all things go well. Vast spaces of nature; the Atlantic Ocean, the South Sea; vast intervals of time, years, centuries, are of no account. This which I think and feel, underlay that former state of life and circumstances, as it does underlie my present, and will always all circumstance, and what is called life, and what is called death.

Life only avails, not the having lived. Power ceases in the instant of repose; it resides in the moment of transition from a past to a new state; in the shooting of the gulf; in the darting to an aim. This one fact the world hates, that

1. Biblical authors of the Book of Psalms, the Book of Jeremiah, and various New Testament Epistles, respectively.

the soul *becomes*; for, that forever degrades the past; turns all riches to poverty; all reputation to a shame; confounds the saint with the rogue; shoves Jesus and Judas equally aside. Why then do we prate of self-reliance? Inasmuch as the soul is present, there will be power not confident but agent. To talk of reliance, is a poor external way of speaking. Speak rather of that which relies, because it works and is. Who has more soul than I, masters me, though he should not raise his finger. Round him I must revolve by the gravitation of spirits; who has less, I rule with like facility. We fancy it rhetoric when we speak of eminent virtue. We do not yet see that virtue is Height, and that a man or a company of men plastic and permeable to principles, by the law of nature must overpower and ride all cities, nations, kings, rich men, poets, who are not.

This is the ultimate fact which we so quickly reach on this as on every topic, the resolution of all into the ever blessed ONE. Virtue is the governor, the creator, the reality. All things real are so by so much of virtue as they contain. Hardship, husbandry, hunting, whaling, war, eloquence, personal weight, are somewhat, and engage my respect as examples of the soul's presence and impure action. I see the same law working in the nature for conservation and growth. The poise of a planet, the bended tree recovering itself from the strong wind, the vital resources of every vegetable and animal, are also demonstrations of the self-sufficing, and therefore self-relying soul. All history from its highest to its trivial passages is the various record of this power.

Thus all concentrates; let us not rove; let us sit at home with the cause. Let us stun and astonish the intruding rabble of men and books and institutions by a simple declaration of the divine fact. Bid them take the shoes from off their feet,[2] for God is here within. Let our simplicity judge them, and our docility to our own law demonstrate the poverty of nature and fortune beside our native riches.

But now we are a mob. Man does not stand in awe of man, nor is the soul admonished to stay at home, to put itself in communication with the internal ocean, but it goes abroad to beg a cup of water of the urns of men. We must go alone. Isolation must precede true society. I like the silent church before the service begins, better than any preaching. How far off, how cool, how chaste the persons look, begirt each one with a precinct or sanctuary. So let us always sit. Why should we assume the faults of our friend, or wife, or father, or child, because they sit around our hearth, or are said to have the same blood? All men have my blood, and I have all men's. Not for that will I adopt their petulance or folly, even to the extent of being ashamed of it. But your isolation must not be mechanical, but spiritual, that is, must be elevation. At times the whole world seems to be in conspiracy to importune you with emphatic trifles. Friend, client, child, sickness, fear, want, charity, all knock at once at thy closet door and say, 'Come out unto us.'—Do not spill thy soul; do not all descend; keep thy state; stay at home in thine own heaven; come not for a moment into their facts, into their hubbub of conflicting appearances, but let in the light of thy law on their confusion. The power men possess to annoy me, I give them by a weak curiosity. No man can come

2. In Exodus 3.5, God commands Moses "to put off thy shoes from off thy feet, for the place whereon thou standest is holy ground."

near me but through my act. "What we love that we have, but by desire we bereave ourselves of the love."[3]

If we cannot at once rise to the sanctities of obedience and faith, let us at least resist our temptations, let us enter into the state of war, and wake Thor and Woden,[4] courage and constancy in our Saxon breasts. This is to be done in our smooth times by speaking the truth. Check this lying hospitality and lying affection. Live no longer to the expectation of these deceived and deceiving people with whom we converse. Say to them, O father, O mother, O wife, O brother, O friend, I have lived with you after appearances hitherto. Henceforward I am the truth's. Be it known unto you that henceforward I obey no law less than the eternal law. I will have no covenants but proximities. I shall endeavor to nourish my parents, to support my family, to be the chaste husband of one wife,—but these relations I must fill after a new and unprecedented way. I appeal from your customs. I must be myself. I cannot break myself any longer for you, or you. If you can love me for what I am, we shall be the happier. If you cannot, I will still seek to deserve that you should. I must be myself. I will not hide my tastes or aversions. I will so trust that what is deep is holy, that I will do strongly before the sun and moon whatever inly rejoices me, and the heart appoints. If you are noble, I will love you; if you are not, I will not hurt you and myself by hypocritical attentions. If you are true, but not in the same truth with me, cleave to your companions; I will seek my own. I do this not selfishly, but humbly and truly. It is alike your interest and mine and all men's, however long we have dwelt in lies, to live in truth. Does this sound harsh to-day? You will soon love what is dictated by your nature as well as mine, and if we follow the truth, it will bring us out safe at last.—But so you may give these friends pain. Yes, but I cannot sell my liberty and my power, to save their sensibility. Besides, all persons have their moments of reason when they look out into the region of absolute truth; then will they justify me and do the same thing.

The populace think that your rejection of popular standards is a rejection of all standard, and mere antinomianism;[5] and the bold sensualist will use the name of philosophy to gild his crimes. But the law of consciousness abides. There are two confessionals, in one or the other of which we must be shriven. You may fulfil your round of duties by clearing yourself in the *direct*, or, in the *reflex* way. Consider whether you have satisfied your relations to father, mother, cousin, neighbor, town, cat, and dog; whether any of these can upbraid you. But I may also neglect this reflex standard, and absolve me to myself. I have my own stern claims and perfect circle. It denies the name of duty to many offices that are called duties. But if I can discharge its debts, it enables me to dispense with the popular code. If any one imagines that this law is lax, let him keep its commandment one day.

And truly it demands something godlike in him who has cast off the common motives of humanity, and has ventured to trust himself for a taskmaster. High be his heart, faithful his will, clear his sight, that he may in

3. In his notebook, Emerson attributed this quotation to the German poet and dramatist Friedrich Schiller (1759–1805).

4. Norse gods, here taken as ancestral gods of the Anglo-Saxon as well, associated respectively with courage and endurance.

5. Doctrine of salvation by faith alone.

good earnest be doctrine, society, law to himself, that a simple purpose may be to him as strong as iron necessity is to others.

If any man consider the present aspects of what is called by distinction *society*, he will see the need of these ethics. The sinew and heart of man seem to be drawn out, and we are become timorous desponding whimperers. We are afraid of truth, afraid of fortune, afraid of death, and afraid of each other. Our age yields no great and perfect persons. We want men and women who shall renovate life and our social state, but we see that most natures are insolvent; cannot satisfy their own wants, have an ambition out of all proportion to their practical force, and so do lean and beg day and night continually. Our housekeeping is mendicant, our arts, our occupations, our marriages, our religion we have not chosen, but society has chosen for us. We are parlor soldiers. The rugged battle of fate, where strength is born, we shun.

If our young men miscarry in their first enterprizes, they lose all heart. If the young merchant fails, men say he is *ruined*. If the finest genius studies at one of our colleges, and is not installed in an office within one year afterwards in the cities or suburbs of Boston or New York, it seems to his friends and to himself that he is right in being disheartened and in complaining the rest of his life. A sturdy lad from New Hampshire or Vermont, who in turn tries all the professions, who *teams it, farms it, peddles*, keeps a school, preaches, edits a newspaper, goes to Congress, buys a township, and so forth, in successive years, and always, like a cat, falls on his feet, is worth a hundred of these city dolls. He walks abreast with his days, and feels no shame in not 'studying a profession,' for he does not postpone his life, but lives already. He has not one chance, but a hundred chances. Let a stoic arise who shall reveal the resources of man, and tell men they are not leaning willows, but can and must detach themselves; that with the exercise of self-trust, new powers shall appear; that a man is the word made flesh, born to shed healing to the nations, that he should be ashamed of our compassion, and that the moment he acts from himself, tossing the laws, the books, idolatries, and customs out of the window,—we pity him no more but thank and revere him,—and that teacher shall restore the life of man to splendor, and make his name dear to all History.

It is easy to see that a greater self-reliance,—a new respect for the divinity in man,—must work a revolution in all the offices and relations of men; in their religion; in their education; in their pursuits; their modes of living; their association; in their property; in their speculative views.

1. In what prayers do men allow themselves! That which they call a holy office, is not so much as brave and manly. Prayer looks abroad and asks for some foreign addition to come through some foreign virtue, and loses itself in endless mazes of natural and supernatural, and mediatorial and miraculous. Prayer that craves a particular commodity—any thing less than all good, is vicious. Prayer is the contemplation of the facts of life from the highest point of view. It is the soliloquy of a beholding and jubilant soul. It is the spirit of God pronouncing his works good. But prayer as a means to effect a private end, is theft and meanness. It supposes dualism and not unity in nature and consciousness. As soon as the man is at one with God, he will not beg. He will then see prayer in all action. The prayer of the farmer kneeling in his field to weed it, the prayer of the rower kneeling with the stroke of his oar, are true prayers heard throughout nature, though for cheap ends. Caratach, in

Fletcher's Bonduca, when admonished to inquire the mind of the god Audate, replies,

> "His hidden meaning lies in our endeavors,
> Our valors are our best gods."[6]

Another sort of false prayers are our regrets. Discontent is the want of self-reliance; it is infirmity of will. Regret calamities, if you can thereby help the sufferer; if not, attend your own work, and already the evil begins to be repaired. Our sympathy is just as base. We come to them who weep foolishly, and sit down and cry for company, instead of imparting to them truth and health in rough electric shocks, putting them once more in communication with the soul. The secret of fortune is joy in our hands. Welcome evermore to gods and men is the self-helping man. For him all doors are flung wide. Him all tongues greet, all honors crown, all eyes follow with desire. Our love goes out to him and embraces him, because he did not need it. We solicitously and apologetically caress and celebrate him, because he held on his way and scorned our disapprobation. The gods love him because men hated him. "To the persevering mortal," said Zoroaster,[7] "the blessed Immortals are swift."

As men's prayers are a disease of the will, so are their creeds a disease of the intellect. They say with those foolish Israelites, 'Let not God speak to us, lest we die. Speak thou, speak any man with us, and we will obey.'[8] Everywhere I am bereaved of meeting God in my brother, because he has shut his own temple doors, and recites fables merely of his brother's, or his brother's brother's God. Every new mind is a new classification. If it prove a mind of uncommon activity and power, a Locke, a Lavoisier, a Hutton, a Bentham, a Spurzheim,[9] it imposes its classification on other men, and lo! a new system. In proportion always to the depth of the thought, and so to the number of the objects it touches and brings within reach of the pupil, is his complacency. But chiefly is this apparent in creeds and churches, which are also classifications of some powerful mind acting on the great elemental thought of Duty, and man's relation to the Highest. Such is Calvinism, Quakerism, Swedenborgianism.[1] The pupil takes the same delight in subordinating every thing to the new terminology that a girl does who has just learned botany, in seeing a new earth and new seasons thereby. It will happen for a time, that the pupil will feel a real debt to the teacher,—will find his intellectual power has grown by the study of his writings. This will continue until he has exhausted his master's mind. But in all unbalanced minds, the classification is idolized, passes for the end, and not for a speedily exhaustible means, so that the walls of the system blend to their eye in the remote horizon with the walls of the universe; the luminaries of heaven seem to them hung on the

6. Lines 1294–95; the play by the English playwright John Fletcher (1579–1625) was produced around 1614.
7. Religious prophet of ancient Persia.
8. See the fearful words of the Hebrews after God gave Moses the Ten Commandments, Exodus 20.19: "And they said unto Moses, Speak thou with us, and we will hear: but let not God speak with us, lest we die."
9. These innovators are John Locke (1632–1704), English philosopher; Antoine Lavoisier (1743–1797), French chemist; James Hutton (1726–1797), Scottish geologist; Jeremy Bentham (1748–1832), English philosopher; and Johann Kaspar Spurzheim (1776–1832), German physician whose work led to the pseudoscience of phrenology, assessing character by interpreting the bumps on the skull.
1. Three widely varying religious movements founded by or based on the teachings of, respectively, John Calvin (1509–1564), French theologian; George Fox (1624–1691), English clergyman; and Emanuel Swedenborg (1688–1772), Swedish scientist and theologian.

arch their master built. They cannot imagine how you aliens have any right to see,—how you can see; 'It must be somehow that you stole the light from us.' They do not yet perceive, that, light unsystematic, indomitable, will break into any cabin, even into theirs. Let them chirp awhile and call it their own. If they are honest and do well, presently their neat new pinfold[2] will be too strait and low, will crack, will lean, will rot and vanish, and the immortal light, all young and joyful, million-orbed, million-colored, will beam over the universe as on the first morning.

2. It is for want of self-culture that the idol of Travelling, the idol of Italy, of England, of Egypt, remains for all educated Americans. They who made England, Italy, or Greece venerable in the imagination, did so not by rambling round creation as a moth round a lamp, but by sticking fast where they were, like an axis of the earth. In manly hours, we feel that duty is our place, and that the merrymen of circumstance should follow as they may. The soul is no traveller: the wise man stays at home with the soul, and when his necessities, his duties, on any occasion call him from his house, or into foreign lands, he is at home still, and is not gadding abroad from himself, and shall make men sensible by the expression of his countenance, that he goes the missionary of wisdom and virtue, and visits cities and men like a sovereign, and not like an interloper or a valet.

I have no churlish objection to the circumnavigation of the globe, for the purposes of art, of study, and benevolence, so that the man is first domesticated, or does not go abroad with the hope of finding somewhat greater than he knows. He who travels to be amused, or to get somewhat which he does not carry, travels away from himself, and grows old even in youth among old things. In Thebes, in Palmyra,[3] his will and mind have become old and dilapidated as they. He carries ruins to ruins.

Travelling is a fool's paradise. We owe to our first journeys the discovery that place is nothing. At home I dream that at Naples, at Rome, I can be intoxicated with beauty, and lose my sadness. I pack my trunk, embrace my friends, embark on the sea, and at last wake up in Naples, and there beside me is the stern Fact, the sad self, unrelenting, identical, that I fled from. I seek the Vatican, and the palaces. I affect to be intoxicated with sights and suggestions, but I am not intoxicated. My giant goes with me wherever I go.

3. But the rage of travelling is itself only a symptom of a deeper unsoundness affecting the whole intellectual action. The intellect is vagabond, and the universal system of education fosters restlessness. Our minds travel when our bodies are forced to stay at home. We imitate; and what is imitation but the travelling of the mind? Our houses are built with foreign taste; our shelves are garnished with foreign ornaments; our opinions, our tastes, our whole minds lean, and follow the Past and the Distant, as the eyes of a maid follow her mistress. The soul created the arts wherever they have flourished. It was in his own mind that the artist sought his model. It was an application of his own thought to the thing to be done and the conditions to be observed. And why need we copy the Doric or the Gothic model?[4] Beauty, convenience, grandeur of thought, and quaint expression are as near to us as

2. Enclosure for animals.

3. Ruins of ancient cities in Egypt and Syria, respectively.

4. I.e., ancient Greek or medieval European architecture.

to any, and if the American artist will study with hope and love the precise thing to be done by him, considering the climate, the soil, the length of the day, the wants of the people, the habit and form of the government, he will create a house in which all these will find themselves fitted, and taste and sentiment will be satisfied also.

Insist on yourself; never imitate. Your own gift you can present every moment with the cumulative force of a whole life's cultivation; but of the adopted talent of another, you have only an extemporaneous, half possession. That which each can do best, none but his Maker can teach him. No man yet knows what it is, nor can, till that person has exhibited it. Where is the master who could have taught Shakspeare? Where is the master who could have instructed Franklin, or Washington, or Bacon, or Newton? Every great man is an unique. The Scipionism[5] of Scipio is precisely that part he could not borrow. If any body will tell me whom the great man imitates in the original crisis when he performs a great act, I will tell him who else than himself can teach him. Shakspeare will never be made by the study of Shakspeare. Do that which is assigned thee, and thou canst not hope too much or dare too much. There is at this moment, there is for me an utterance bare and grand as that of the colossal chisel of Phidias,[6] or trowel of the Egyptians, or the pen of Moses, or Dante, but different from all these. Now possibly will the soul all rich, all eloquent, with thousand-cloven tongue, deign to repeat itself; but if I can hear what these patriarchs say, surely I can reply to them in the same pitch of voice: for the ear and the tongue are two organs of one nature. Dwell up there in the simple and noble regions of thy life, obey thy heart, and thou shalt reproduce the Foreworld again.

4. As our Religion, our Education, our Art look abroad, so does our spirit of society. All men plume themselves on the improvement of society, and no man improves.

Society never advances. It recedes as fast on one side as it gains on the other. Its progress is only apparent, like the workers of a treadmill. It undergoes continual changes: it is barbarous, it is civilized, it is christianized, it is rich, it is scientific; but this change is not amelioration. For every thing that is given, something is taken. Society acquires new arts and loses old instincts. What a contrast between the well-clad, reading, writing, thinking American, with a watch, a pencil, and a bill of exchange in his pocket, and the naked New Zealander, whose property is a club, a spear, a mat, and an undivided twentieth of a shed to sleep under. But compare the health of the two men, and you shall see that his aboriginal strength the white man has lost. If the traveller tell us truly, strike the savage with a broad axe, and in a day or two the flesh shall unite and heal as if you struck the blow into soft pitch, and the same blow shall send the white to his grave.

The civilized man has built a coach, but has lost the use of his feet. He is supported on crutches, but loses so much support of muscle. He has got a fine Geneva watch, but he has lost the skill to tell the hour by the sun. A Greenwich nautical almanac he has, and so being sure of the information when he wants it, the man in the street does not know a star in the sky. The solstice he does not observe; the equinox he knows as little; and the whole bright calendar of the year is without a dial in his mind. His notebooks impair his mem-

5. I.e., the essence of the man.

6. Greek sculptor of the 5th century B.C.E.

ory; his libraries overload his wit; the insurance office increases the number of accidents; and it may be a question whether machinery does not encumber; whether we have not lost by refinement some energy, by a christianity entrenched in establishments and forms, some vigor of wild virtue. For every stoic was a stoic;[7] but in Christendom where is the Christian?

There is no more deviation in the moral standard than in the standard of height or bulk. No greater men are now than ever were. A singular equality may be observed between the great men of the first and of the last ages; nor can all the science, art, religion and philosophy of the nineteenth century avail to educate greater men than Plutarch's heroes,[8] three or four and twenty centuries ago. Not in time is the race progressive. Phocion, Socrates, Anaxagoras, Diogenes,[9] are great men, but they leave no class. He who is really of their class will not be called by their name, but be wholly his own man, and, in his turn the founder of a sect. The arts and inventions of each period are only its costume, and do not invigorate men. The harm of the improved machinery may compensate its good. Hudson and Behring[1] accomplished so much in their fishing-boats, as to astonish Parry and Franklin,[2] whose equipment exhausted the resources of science and art. Galileo, with an opera-glass, discovered a more splendid series of facts than any one since. Columbus found the New World in an undecked boat. It is curious to see the periodical disuse and perishing of means and machinery which were introduced with loud laudation, a few years or centuries before. The great genius returns to essential man. We reckoned the improvements of the art of war among the triumphs of science, and yet Napoleon conquered Europe by the Bivouac,[3] which consisted of falling back on naked valor, and disencumbering it of all aids. The Emperor held it impossible to make a perfect army, says Las Cases,[4] "without abolishing our arms, magazines, commissaries, and carriages, until in imitation of the Roman custom, the soldier should receive his supply of corn, grind it in his hand-mill, and bake his bread himself."

Society is a wave. The wave moves onward, but the water of which it is composed, does not. The same particle does not rise from the valley to the ridge. Its unity is only phenomenal. The persons who make up a nation today, next year die, and their experience with them.

And so the reliance on Property, including the reliance on governments which protect it, is the want of self-reliance. Men have looked away from themselves and at things so long, that they have come to esteem what they call the soul's progress, namely, the religious, learned, and civil institutions, as guards of property, and they deprecate assaults on these, because they feel them to be assaults on property. They measure their esteem of each other, by what each has, and not by what each is. But a cultivated man becomes

7. Emerson refers particularly to the Stoics, members of the Greek school of philosophy founded by Zeno about 308 B.C.E. It taught the ideal of a calm, self-controlled existence in which every occurrence is accepted as fated.

8. The lives of famous Greeks and Romans written by Plutarch (46?–120? C.E.), Greek biographer.

9. Four Greek philosophers: Phocion (402?–317 B.C.E.), Socrates (470?–399 B.C.E.), Anaxagoras (500?–428 B.C.E.), and Diogenes (412?–323 B.C.E.).

1. Vitus Jonassen Bering (1680–1741), Danish navigator who explored the northern Pacific Ocean. Henry Hudson (d. 1611), English navigator (sometimes in service of the Dutch).

2. Sir William Edward Perry (1790–1855) and Sir John Franklin (1786–1847), English explorers of the Arctic.

3. Temporary military camp.

4. Comte Emmanuel de Las Cases (1766–1842), author of a book recording his conversations with the exiled Napoleon at St. Helena.

ashamed of his property, ashamed of what he has, out of new respect for his being. Especially, he hates what he has, if he see that it is accidental,—came to him by inheritance, or gift, or crime; then he feels that it is not having; it does not belong to him, has no root in him, and merely lies there, because no revolution or no robber takes it away. But that which a man is, does always by necessity acquire, and what the man acquires is permanent and living property, which does not wait the beck of rulers, or mobs, or revolutions, or fire, or storm, or bankruptcies, but perpetually renews itself wherever the man is put. "Thy lot or portion of life," said the Caliph Ali,[5] "is seeking after thee; therefore be at rest from seeking after it." Our dependence on these foreign goods leads us to our slavish respect for numbers. The political parties meet in numerous conventions; the greater the concourse, and with each new uproar of announcement, The delegation from Essex![6] The Democrats from New Hampshire! The Whigs of Maine! the young patriot feels himself stronger than before by a new thousand of eyes and arms. In like manner the reformers summon conventions, and vote and resolve in multitude. But not so, O friends! will the God deign to enter and inhabit you, but by a method precisely the reverse. It is only as a man puts off from himself all external support, and stands alone, that I see him to be strong and to prevail. He is weaker by every recruit to his banner. Is not a man better than a town? Ask nothing of men, and in the endless mutation, thou only firm column must presently appear the upholder of all that surrounds thee. He who knows that power is in the soul, that he is weak only because he has looked for good out of him and elsewhere, and so perceiving, throws himself unhesitatingly on his thought, instantly rights himself, stands in the erect position, commands his limbs, works miracles; just as a man who stands on his feet is stronger than a man who stands on his head.

So use all that is called Fortune. Most men gamble with her, and gain all, and lose all, as her wheel rolls. But do thou leave as unlawful these winnings, and deal with Cause and Effect, the chancellors of God. In the Will work and acquire, and thou hast chained the wheel of Chance, and shalt always drag her after thee. A political victory, a rise of rents, the recovery of your sick, or the return of your absent friend, or some other quite external event, raises your spirits, and you think good days are preparing for you. Do not believe it. It can never be so. Nothing can bring you peace but yourself. Nothing can bring you peace but the triumph of principles.

1841

Circles[1]

The eye is the first circle; the horizon which it forms is the second; and throughout nature this primary figure is repeated without end. It is the highest emblem in the cipher of the world. St. Augustine[2] described the nature of

5. Fourth Muslim caliph of Mecca (602?–661).
6. County in Massachusetts.
1. First published in *Essays* (1841), the source of the present text.
2. Roman Catholic theologian (354–430 C.E.). The passage Emerson refers to here has not been located in St. Augustine's writings.

God as a circle whose centre was everywhere, and its circumference nowhere. We are all our lifetime reading the copious sense of this first of forms. One moral we have already deduced in considering the circular or compensatory character of every human action. Another analogy we shall now trace; that every action admits of being outdone. Our life is an apprenticeship to the truth, that around every circle another can be drawn; that there is no end in nature, but every end is a beginning; that there is always another dawn risen on mid-noon, and under every deep a lower deep opens.

This fact, as far as it symbolizes the moral fact of the Unattainable, the flying Perfect, around which the hands of man can never meet, at once the inspirer and the condemner of every success, may conveniently serve us to connect many illustrations of human power in every department.

There are no fixtures in nature. The universe is fluid and volatile. Permanence is but a word of degrees. Our globe seen by God, is a transparent law, not a mass of facts. The law dissolves the fact and holds it fluid. Our culture is the predominance of an idea which draws after it all this train of cities and institutions. Let us rise into another idea: they will disappear. The Greek sculpture is all melted away, as if it had been statues of ice: here and there a solitary figure or fragment remaining, as we see flecks and scraps of snow left in cold dells and mountain clefts, in June and July. For, the genius that created it, creates now somewhat else. The Greek letters last a little longer, but are already passing under the same sentence, and tumbling into the inevitable pit which the creation of new thought opens for all that is old. The new continents are built out of the ruins of an old planet: the new races fed out of the decomposition of the foregoing. New arts destroy the old. See the investment of capital in aqueducts, made useless by hydraulics; fortifications, by gunpowder; roads and canals, by railways; sails, by steam; steam by electricity.

You admire this tower of granite, weathering the hurts of so many ages. Yet a little waving hand built this huge wall, and that which builds, is better than that which is built. The hand that built, can topple it down much faster. Better than the hand, and nimbler, was the invisible thought which wrought through it, and thus ever behind the coarse effect, is a fine cause, which, being narrowly seen, is itself the effect of a finer cause. Every thing looks permanent until its secret is known. A rich estate appears to women and children, a firm and lasting fact; to a merchant, one easily created out of any materials, and easily lost. An orchard, good tillage, good grounds, seem a fixture, like a gold mine, or a river, to a citizen, but to a large farmer, not much more fixed than the state of the crop. Nature looks provokingly stable and secular,[3] but it has a cause like all the rest; and when once I comprehend that, will these fields stretch so immovably wide, these leaves hang so individually considerable? Permanence is a word of degrees. Every thing is medial.[4] Moons are no more bounds to spiritual power than bat-balls.

The key to every man is his thought. Sturdy and defying though he look, he has a helm which he obeys, which is, the idea after which all his facts are classified. He can only be reformed by showing him a new idea which commands his own. The life of man is a self-evolving circle, which, from a

3. In the sense of lasting or continuing through centuries.

4. Situated in or near the middle.

ring imperceptibly small, rushes on all sides outwards to new and larger circles, and that without end. The extent to which this generation of circles, wheel without wheel will go, depends on the force or truth of the individual soul. For, it is the inert effort of each thought having formed itself into a circular wave of circumstance, as, for instance, an empire, rules of an art, a local usage, a religious rite, to heap itself on that ridge, and to solidify, and hem in the life. But if the soul is quick and strong, it bursts over that boundary on all sides, and expands another orbit on the great deep, which also runs up into a high wave, with attempt again to stop and to bind. But the heart refuses to be imprisoned; in its first and narrowest pulses, it already tends outward with a vast force, and to immense and innumerable expansions.

Every ultimate fact is only the first of a new series. Every general law only a particular fact of some more general law presently to disclose itself. There is no outside, no enclosing wall, no circumference to us. The man finishes his story,—how good! How final! how it puts a new face on all things! He fills the sky. Lo, on the other side, rises also a man, and draws a circle around the circle we had just pronounced the outline of the sphere. Then already is our first speaker, not man, but only a first speaker. His only redress is forthwith to draw a circle outside of his antagonist. And so men do by themselves. The result of to-day which haunts the mind and cannot be escaped, will presently be abridged into a word, and the principle that seemed to explain nature, will itself be included as one example of a bolder generalization. In the thought of tomorrow there is a power to upheave all thy creed, all the creeds, all the literatures of the nations, and marshal thee to a heaven which no epic dream has yet depicted. Every man is not so much a workman in the world, as he is a suggestion of that he should be. Men walk as prophecies of the next age.

Step by step we scale this mysterious ladder: the steps are actions; the new prospect is power. Every several result is threatened and judged by that which follows. Every one seems to be contradicted by the new; it is only limited by the new. The new statement is always hated by the old, and, to those dwelling in the old, comes like an abyss of skepticism. But the eye soon gets wonted to it, for the eye and it are effects of one cause; then its innocency and benefit appear, and, presently, all its energy spent, it pales and dwindles before the revelation of the new hour.

Fear not the new generalization. Does the fact look crass and material, threatening to degrade thy theory of spirit? Resist it not; it goes to refine and raise thy theory of matter just as much.

There are no fixtures to men, if we appeal to consciousness. Every man supposes himself not to be fully understood; and if there is any truth in him, if he rests at last on the divine soul, I see not how it can be otherwise. The last chamber, the last closet, he must feel, was never opened; there is always a residuum unknown, unanalyzable. That is, every man believes that he has a greater possibility.

Our moods do not believe in each other. To-day, I am full of thoughts, and can write what I please. I see no reason why I should not have the same thought, the same power of expression to-morrow. What I write, whilst I write it, seems the most natural thing in the world: but, yesterday, I saw a dreary vacuity in this direction in which now I see so much; and a month hence, I doubt not, I shall wonder who he was that wrote so many continuous pages. Alas for this infirm faith, this will not strenuous, this vast ebb of a vast flow! I am God in nature; I am a weed by the wall.

The continual effort to raise himself above himself, to work a pitch above his last height, betrays itself in a man's relations. We thirst for approbation, yet cannot forgive the approver. The sweet of nature is love; yet if I have a friend, I am tormented by my imperfections. The love of me accuses the other party. If he were high enough to slight me, then could I love him, and rise by my affection to new heights. A man's growth is seen in the successive choirs of his friends. For every friend whom he loses for truth, he gains a better. I thought, as I walked in the woods and mused on my friends, why should I play with them this game of idolatry? I know and see too well, when not voluntarily blind, the speedy limits of persons called high and worthy. Rich, noble, and great they are by the liberality of our speech, but truth is sad. O blessed Spirit, whom I forsake for these, they are not thee! Every personal consideration that we allow, costs us heavenly state. We sell the thrones of angels for a short and turbulent pleasure.

How often must we learn this lesson? Men cease to interest us when we find their limitations. The only sin is limitation. As soon as you once come up with a man's limitations, it is all over with him. Has he talents? has he enterprises? has he knowledge? it boots not. Infinitely alluring and attractive was he to you yesterday, a great hope, a sea to swim in; now, you have found his shores, found it a pond, and you care not if you never see it again.

Each new step we take in thought reconciles twenty seemingly discordant facts, as expressions of one law. Aristotle and Plato are reckoned the respective heads of two schools. A wise man will see that Aristotle Platonizes.[5] By going one step farther back in thought, discordant opinions are reconciled, by being seen to be two extremes of one principle, and we can never go so far back as to preclude a still higher vision.

Beware when the great God lets loose a thinker on this planet. Then all things are at risk. It is as when a conflagration has broken out in a great city, and no man knows what is safe, or where it will end. There is not a piece of science, but its flank may be turned to-morrow; there is not any literary reputation, not the so-called eternal names of fame, that may not be revised and condemned. The very hopes of man, the thoughts of his heart, the religion of nations, the manners and morals of mankind, are all at the mercy of a new generalization. Generalization is always a new influx of the divinity into the mind. Hence the thrill that attends it.

Valor consists in the power of self-recovery, so that a man cannot have his flank turned, cannot be outgeneraled, but put him where you will, he stands. This can only be by his preferring truth to his past apprehension of truth; and his alert acceptance of it from whatever quarter; the intrepid conviction that his laws, his relations to society, his christianity, his world, may at any time be superseded and decease.

There are degrees in idealism. We learn first to play with it academically, as the magnet was once a toy. Then we see in the heyday of youth and poetry

5. The Greek philosopher Aristotle (384–322 B.C.E.) was actually a student of Plato (429–347 B.C.E.).

that it may be true, that it is true in gleams and fragments. Then, its countenance waxes stern and grand, and we see that it must be true. It now shows itself ethical and practical. We learn that God IS; that he is in me; and that all things are shadows of him. The idealism of Berkeley[6] is only a crude statement of the idealism of Jesus, and that, again, is a crude statement of the fact that all nature is the rapid efflux of goodness executing and organizing itself. Much more obviously is history and the state of the world at any one time, directly dependent on the intellectual classification then existing in the minds of men. The things which are dear to men at this hour, are so on account of the ideas which have emerged on their mental horizon, and which cause the present order of things as a tree bears its apples. A new degree of culture would instantly revolutionize the entire system of human pursuits.

Conversation is a game of circles. In conversation we pluck up the *termini*[7] which bound the common of silence on every side. The parties are not to be judged by the spirit they partake and even express under this Pentecost.[8] To-morrow they will have receded from this high-water mark. To-morrow you shall find them stooping under the old packsaddles. Yet let us enjoy the cloven flame[9] whilst it glows on our walls. When each new speaker strikes a new light, emancipates us from the oppression of the last speaker, to oppress us with the greatness and exclusiveness of his own thought, then yields us to another redeemer, we seem to recover our rights, to become men. O what truths profound and executable only in ages and orbs, are supposed in the announcement of every truth! In common hours, society sits cold and statuesque. We all stand waiting, empty,—knowing, possibly, that we can be full, surrounded by mighty symbols which are not symbols to us, but prose and trivial toys. Then cometh the god, and converts the statues into fiery men, and by a flash of his eye burns up the veil which shrouded all things, and the meaning of the very furniture, of cup and saucer, of chair and clock and tester,[1] is manifest. The facts which loomed so large in the fogs of yesterday,—property, climate, breeding, personal beauty, and the like, have strangely changed their proportions. All that we reckoned settled, shakes now and rattles; and literatures, cities, climates, religions, leave their foundations, and dance before our eyes. And yet here again see the swift circumscription. Good as is discourse, silence is better, and shames it. The length of the discourse indicates the distance of thought betwixt the speaker and the hearer. If they were at a perfect understanding in any part, no words would be necessary thereon. If at one in all parts, no words would be suffered.

Literature is a point outside of our hodiernal[2] circle, through which a new one may be described. The use of literature is to afford us a platform whence we may command a view of our present life, a purchase by which we may move it. We fill ourselves with ancient learning; install ourselves the best we can in Greek, in Punic,[3] in Roman houses, only that we may wiselier see French, English, and American houses and modes of living. In like man-

6. The Irish philosopher and bishop George Berkeley (1685–1753).
7. Ends (Latin).
8. The descent of the Holy Spirit, used in a spiritual sense not necessarily linked to Christianity.
9. See Acts 2.1–4.
1. Canopy over a bed.
2. Daily.
3. Relating to ancient Carthage.

ner, we see literature best from the midst of wild nature, or from the din of affairs, or from a high religion. The field cannot be well seen from within the field. The astronomer must have his diameter of the earth's orbit as a base to find the parallax of any star.

Therefore, we value the poet. All the argument, and all the wisdom, is not in the encyclopedia, or the treatise on metaphysics, or the Body of Divinity, but in the sonnet or the play. In my daily work I incline to repeat my old steps, and do not believe in remedial force, in the power of change and reform. But some Petrarch or Ariosto,[4] filled with the new wine of his imagination, writes me an ode, or a brisk romance, full of daring thought and action. He smites and arouses me with his shrill tones, breaks up my whole chain of habits, and I open my eye on my own possibilities. He claps wings to the sides of all the solid old lumber of the world, and I am capable once more of choosing a straight path in theory and practice.

We have the same need to command a view of the religion of the world. We can never see christianity from the catechism:—from the pastures, from a boat in the pond, from amidst the songs of wood-birds, we possibly may. Cleansed by the elemental light and wind, steeped in the sea of beautiful forms which the field offers us, we may chance to cast a right glance back upon biography. Christianity is rightly dear to the best of mankind; yet was there never a young philosopher whose breeding had fallen into the christian church, by whom that brave text of Paul's, was not specially prized, "Then shall also the Son be subject unto Him who put all things under him, that God may be all in all."[5] Let the claims and virtues of persons be never so great and welcome, the instinct of man presses eagerly onward to the impersonal and illimitable, and gladly arms itself against the dogmatism of bigots with this generous word, out of the book itself.

The natural world may be conceived of as a system of concentric circles, and we now and then detect in nature slight dislocations, which apprize us that this surface on which we now stand, is not fixed, but sliding. These manifold tenacious qualities, this chemistry and vegetation, these metals and animals, which seem to stand there for their own sake, are means and methods only, are words of God, and as fugitive as other words. Has the naturalist or chemist learned his craft, who has explored the gravity of atoms and the elective affinities, who has not yet discerned the deeper law whereof this is only a partial or approximate statement, namely, that like draws to like; and that the goods which belong to you, gravitate to you, and need not be pursued with pains and cost? Yet is that statement approximate also, and not final. Omnipresence is a higher fact. Not through subtle, subterranean channels, need friend and fact be drawn to their counterpart, but, rightly considered, these things proceed from the eternal generation of the soul. Cause and effect are two sides of one fact.

The same law of eternal procession ranges all that we call the virtues, and extinguishes each in the light of a better. The great man will not be prudent in the popular sense; all his prudence will be so much deduction from

4. The Italian poets Lodovico Ariosto (1475–1533) and Francesco Petrarca (1304–1374), known in English as Petrarch.
5. 1 Corinthians 15.28.

his grandeur. But it behoves each to see when he sacrifices prudence, to what god he devotes it; if to ease and pleasure, he had better be prudent still: if to a great trust, he can well spare his mule and panniers,[6] who has a winged chariot instead. Geoffrey draws on his boots to go through the woods, that his feet may be safer from the bite of snakes; Aaron never thinks of such a peril. In many years, neither is harmed by such an accident. Yet it seems to me that with every precaution you take against such an evil, you put yourself into the power of the evil. I suppose that the highest prudence is the lowest prudence. Is this too sudden a rushing from the centre to the verge of our orbit? Think how many times we shall fall back into pitiful calculations, before we take up our rest in the great sentiment, or make the verge of to-day the new centre. Besides, your bravest sentiment is familiar to the humblest men. The poor and the low have their way of expressing the last facts of philosophy as well as you. "Blessed be nothing," and "the worse things are, the better they are," are proverbs which express the transcendentalism of common life.

One man's justice is another's injustice; one man's beauty, another's ugliness; one man's wisdom, another's folly, as one beholds the same objects from a higher point of view. One man thinks justice consists in paying debts, and has no measure in his abhorrence of another who is very remiss in this duty, and makes the creditor wait tediously. But that second man has his own way of looking at things; asks himself, which debt must I pay first, the debt to the rich, or the debt to the poor? the debt of money, or the debt of thought to mankind, of genius to nature? For you, O broker, there is no other principle but arithmetic. For me, commerce is of trivial import; love, faith, truth of character, the aspiration of man, these are sacred: nor can I detach one duty, like you, from all other duties, and concentrate my forces mechanically on the payment of moneys. Let me live onward: you shall find that, though slower, the progress of my character will liquidate all these debts without injustice to higher claims. If a man should dedicate himself to the payment of notes, would not this be injustice? Owes he no debt but money? And are all claims on him to be postponed to a landlord's or a banker's?

There is no virtue which is final; all are initial. The virtues of society are vices of the saint. The terror of reform is the discovery that we must cast away our virtues, or what we have always esteemed such, into the same pit that has consumed our grosser vices.

> "Forgive his crimes, forgive his virtues too,
> Those smaller faults, half converts to the right."[7]

It is the highest power of divine moments that they abolish our contritions also. I accuse myself of sloth and unprofitableness, day by day; but when these waves of God flow into me, I no longer reckon lost time. I no longer poorly compute my possible achievement by what remains to me of the month or the year; for these moments confer a sort of omnipresence and omnipotence, which asks nothing of duration, but sees that the energy of the mind is commensurate with the work to be done, without time.

6. Large wicker baskets.
7. From *The Complaint: or, Night Thoughts* (1742–46), by the English poet Edward Young (1683–1765).

And thus, O circular philosopher, I hear some reader exclaim, you have arrived at a fine pyrrhonism,[8] at an equivalence and indifferency of all actions, and would fain teach us, that, *if we are true*, forsooth, our crimes may be lively stones out of which we shall construct the temple of the true God.

I am not careful to justify myself. I own I am gladdened by seeing the predominance of the saccharine principle throughout vegetable nature, and not less by beholding in morals that unrestrained inundation of the principle of good into every chink and hole that selfishness has left open, yea, into selfishness and sin itself; so that no evil is pure; nor hell itself without its extreme satisfactions. But lest I should mislead any when I have my own head, and obey my whims, let me remind the reader that I am only an experimenter. Do not set the least value on what I do, or the least discredit on what I do not, as if I pretended to settle anything as true or false. I unsettle all things. No facts are to me sacred; none are profane; I simply experiment, an endless seeker, with no Past at my back.

Yet this incessant movement and progression, which all things partake, could never become sensible to us, but by contrast to some principle of fixture or stability in the soul. Whilst the eternal generation of circles proceeds, the eternal generator abides. That central life is somewhat superior to creation, superior to knowledge and thought, and contains all its circles. Forever it labors to create a life and thought as large and excellent as itself; but in vain; for that which is made, instructs how to make a better.

Thus there is no sleep, no pause, no preservation, but all things renew, germinate, and spring. Why should we import rags and relics into the new hour? Nature abhors the old, and old age seems the only disease: all others run into this one. We call it by many names, fever, intemperance, insanity, stupidity, and crime: they are all forms of old age: they are rest, conservatism, appropriation, inertia, not newness, not the way onward. We grizzle every day. I see no need of it. Whilst we converse with what is above us, we do not grow old, but grow young. Infancy, youth, receptive, aspiring, with religious eye looking upward, counts itself nothing, and abandons itself to the instruction flowing from all sides. But the man and woman of seventy, assume to know all; throw up their hope; renounce aspiration; accept the actual for the necessary; and talk down to the young. Let them then become organs of the Holy Ghost; let them be lovers; let them behold truth; and their eyes are uplifted, their wrinkles smoothed, they are perfumed again with hope and power. This old age ought not to creep on a human mind. In nature, every moment is new; the past is always swallowed and forgotten; the coming only is sacred. Nothing is secure but life, transition, the energizing spirit. No love can be bound by oath or covenant to secure it against a higher love. No truth so sublime but it may be trivial tomorrow in the light of new thoughts. People wish to be settled: only as far as they are unsettled, is there any hope for them.

8. The Greek philosopher Pyrrho (c. 360–270 B.C.E.), founder of the school of Pyrrhonism, emphasized the importance of skepticism, or suspended judgment, insisting on the impossibility of attaining the highest truths.

Life is a series of surprises. We do not guess today the mood, the pleasure, the power of to-morrow, when we are building up our being. Of lower states,—of acts of routine and sense, we can tell somewhat, but the masterpieces of God, the total growths, and universal movements of the soul, he hideth; they are incalculable. I can know that truth is divine and helpful, but how it shall help me, I can have no guess, for, *so to be* is the sole inlet of *so to know.* The new position of the advancing man has all the powers of the old, yet has them all new. It carries in its bosom all the energies of the past, yet is itself an exhalation of the morning. I cast away in this new moment all my once hoarded knowledge, as vacant and vain. Now, for the first time, seem I to know any thing rightly. The simplest words,—we do not know what they mean, except when we love and aspire.

The difference between talents and character is adroitness to keep the old and trodden round, and power and courage to make a new road to new and better goals. Character makes an overpowering present, a cheerful, determined hour, which fortifies all the company, by making them see that much is possible and excellent, that was not thought of. Character dulls the impression of particular events. When we see the conqueror, we do not think much of any one battle or success. We see that we had exaggerated the difficulty. It was easy to him. The great man is not convulsible or tormentable. He is so much, that events pass over him without much impression. People say sometimes, 'See what I have overcome; see how cheerful I am; see how completely I have triumphed over these black events.' Not if they still remind me of the black event,—they have not yet conquered. Is it conquest to be a gay and decorated sepulchre, or a half-crazed widow hysterically laughing? True conquest is the causing the black event to fade and disappear as an early cloud of insignificant result in a history so large and advancing.

The one thing which we seek with insatiable desire, is to forget ourselves, to be surprised out of our propriety, to lose our sempiternal[9] memory, and to do something without knowing how or why; in short, to draw a new circle. Nothing great was ever achieved without enthusiasm. The way of life is wonderful. It is by abandonment. The great moments of history are the facilities of performance through the strength of ideas, as the works of genius and religion. "A man," said Oliver Cromwell, "never rises so high as when he knows not whither he is going."[1] Dreams and drunkenness, the use of opium and alcohol are the semblance and counterfeit of this oracular genius, and hence their dangerous attraction for men. For the like reason, they ask the aid of wild passions, as in gaming and war, to ape in some manner these flames and generosities of the heart.

1841

9. Enduring forever; eternal.

1. Attributed to Oliver Cromwell (1599–1658), military and political leader of the English Puritans, in Edward Hyde, Earl of Clarendon's *History of the Rebellion and Civil Wars in England* (1717).

The Poet[1]

A moody child and wildly wise
Pursued the game with joyful eyes,
Which chose, like meteors, their way,
And rived the dark with private ray:
They overleapt the horizon's edge,
Searched with Apollo's privilege;
Through man, and woman, and sea, and star,
Saw the dance of nature forward far;
Through worlds, and races, and terms, and times,
Saw musical order, and pairing rhymes.

Olympian bards who sung
Divine ideas below,
Which always find us young,
And always keep us so.

Those who are esteemed umpires of taste, are often persons who have acquired some knowledge of admired pictures or sculptures, and have an inclination for whatever is elegant; but if you inquire whether they are beautiful souls, and whether their own acts are like fair pictures, you learn that they are selfish and sensual. Their cultivation is local, as if you should rub a log of dry wood in one spot to produce fire, all the rest remaining cold. Their knowledge of the fine arts is some study of rules and particulars, or some limited judgment of color or form, which is exercised for amusement or for show. It is a proof of the shallowness of the doctrine of beauty, as it lies in the minds of our amateurs, that men seem to have lost the perception of the instant dependence of form upon soul. There is no doctrine of forms in our philosophy. We were put into our bodies, as fire is put into a pan, to be carried about; but there is no accurate adjustment between the spirit and the organ, much less is the latter the germination of the former. So in regard to other forms, the intellectual men do not believe in any essential dependence of the material world on thought and volition. Theologians think it a pretty air-castle to talk of the spiritual meaning of a ship or a cloud, of a city or a contract, but they prefer to come again to the solid ground of historical evidence; and even the poets are contented with a civil and conformed manner of living, and to write poems from the fancy, at a safe distance from their own experience. But the highest minds of the world have never ceased to explore the double meaning, or, shall I say, the quadruple, or the centuple, or much more manifold meaning, of every sensuous fact: Orpheus, Empedocles, Heraclitus, Plato, Plutarch, Dante, Swedenborg,[2] and the masters of sculpture, picture, and poetry. For we are not pans and barrows, nor even porters of the fire and torchbearers, but children of the fire, made of it, and only the same divinity transmuted, and at two or three removes, when we

1. First published in *Essays, Second Series* (1844), the source of the present text, "The Poet" contains the fullest elaboration of Emerson's aesthetic ideas and his most incisive comments on contemporary poetry and criticism. The first prefatory poem is from one of Emerson's uncompleted poems, and the second is from his "Ode to Beauty" (1843).

2. Emanuel Swedenborg (1688–1772), Swedish scientist and mystic. Orpheus, a legendary Greek poet. Empedocles (5th century B.C.E.), Heraclitus (6th century B.C.E.), and Plato (4th century B.C.E.) were Greek philosophers. Plutarch (1st century), Greek biographer. Dante (1265–1321), Italian poet.

know least about it. And this hidden truth, that the foundations whence all this river of Time, and its creatures, floweth, are intrinsically ideal and beautiful, draws us to the consideration of the nature and functions of the Poet, or the man of Beauty, to the means and materials he uses, and to the general aspect of the art in the present time.

The breadth of the problem is great, for the poet is representative. He stands among partial men for the complete man, and apprises us not of his wealth, but of the commonwealth. The young man reveres men of genius, because, to speak truly, they are more himself than he is. They receive of the soul as he also receives, but they more. Nature enhances her beauty, to the eye of loving men, from their belief that the poet is beholding her shows at the same time. He is isolated among his contemporaries, by truth and by his art, but with this consolation in his pursuits, that they will draw all men sooner or later. For all men live by truth, and stand in need of expression. In love, in art, in avarice, in politics, in labor, in games, we study to utter our painful secret. The man is only half himself, the other half is his expression.

Notwithstanding this necessity to be published, adequate expression is rare. I know not how it is that we need an interpreter; but the great majority of men seem to be minors, who have not yet come into possession of their own, or mutes, who cannot report the conversation they have had with nature. There is no man who does not anticipate a supersensual utility in the sun, and stars, earth, and water. These stand and wait to render him a peculiar service. But there is some obstruction, or some excess of phlegm in our constitution, which does not suffer them to yield the due effect. Too feeble fall the impressions of nature on us to make us artists. Every touch should thrill. Every man should be so much an artist, that he could report in conversation what had befallen him. Yet, in our experience, the rays or appulses[3] have sufficient force to arrive at the senses, but not enough to reach the quick, and compel the reproduction of themselves in speech. The poet is the person in whom these powers are in balance, the man without impediment, who sees and handles that which others dream of, traverses the whole scale of experience, and is representative of man, in virtue of being the largest power to receive and to impart.

For the Universe has three children, born at one time, which reappear, under different names, in every system of thought, whether they be called cause, operation, and effect; or, more poetically, Jove, Pluto, Neptune;[4] or, theologically, the Father, the Spirit, and the Son; but which we will call here, the Knower, the Doer, and the Sayer. These stand respectively for the love of truth, for the love of good, and for the love of beauty. These three are equal. Each is that which he is essentially, so that he cannot be surmounted or analyzed, and each of these three has the power of the others latent in him, and his own patent.

The poet is the sayer, the namer, and represents beauty. He is a sovereign, and stands on the centre. For the world is not painted or adorned, but is from the beginning beautiful; and God has not made some beautiful things, but Beauty is the creator of the universe. Therefore the poet is not any permissive potentate, but is emperor in his own right. Criticism is infested

3. Energies.
4. In Roman mythology, the supreme god, god of the underworld, and god of the sea, respectively.

with a cant of materialism, which assumes that manual skill and activity is the first merit of all men, and disparages such as say and do not, overlooking the fact that some men, namely, poets, are natural sayers, sent into the world to the end of expression, and confounds them with those whose province is action, but who quit it to imitate the sayers. But Homer's words are as costly and admirable to Homer, as Agamemnon's victories are to Agamemnon.[5] The poet does not wait for the hero or the sage, but, as they act and think primarily, so he writes primarily what will and must be spoken, reckoning the others, though primaries also, yet, in respect to him, secondaries and servants; as sitters or models in the studio of a painter, or as assistants who bring building materials to an architect.

For poetry was all written before time was, and whenever we are so finely organized that we can penetrate into that region where the air is music, we hear those primal warblings, and attempt to write them down, but we lose ever and anon a word, or a verse, and substitute something of our own, and thus miswrite the poem. The men of more delicate ear write down these cadences more faithfully, and these transcripts, though imperfect, become the songs of the nations. For nature is as truly beautiful as it is good, or as it is reasonable, and must as much appear, as it must be done, or be known. Words and deeds are quite indifferent modes of the divine energy. Words are also actions, and actions are a kind of words.

The sign and credentials of the poet are, that he announces that which no man foretold. He is the true and only doctor;[6] he knows and tells; he is the only teller of news, for he was present and privy to the appearance which he describes. He is a beholder of ideas, and an utterer of the necessary and causal. For we do not speak now of men of poetical talents, or of industry and skill in metre, but of the true poet. I took part in a conversation the other day, concerning a recent writer of lyrics, a man of subtle mind, whose head appeared to be a music-box of delicate tunes and rhythms, and whose skill, and command of language, we could not sufficiently praise. But when the question arose, whether he was not only a lyrist, but a poet, we were obliged to confess that he is plainly a contemporary, not an eternal man. He does not stand out of our low limitations, like a Chimborazo under the line,[7] running up from the torrid base through all the climates of the globe, with belts of the herbage of every latitude on its high and mottled sides; but this genius is the landscape-garden of a modern house, adorned with fountains and statues, with well-bred men and women standing and sitting in the walks and terraces. We hear, through all the varied music, the ground-tone of conventional life. Our poets are men of talents who sing, and not the children of music. The argument is secondary, the finish of the versus is primary.

For it is not metres, but a metre-making argument, that makes a poem,—a thought so passionate and alive, that, like the spirit of a plant or an animal, it has an architecture of its own, and adorns nature with a new thing. The thought and the form are equal in the order of time, but in the order of genesis the thought is prior to the form. The poet has a new thought: he has a whole new experience to unfold; he will tell us how it was with him, and all men will be the richer in his fortune. For, the experience of each new age

5. Emerson is comparing the author (Homer) with his character (Agamemnon, in *The Iliad*).

6. Teacher and healer.

7. Equator. Chimborazo is a mountain in Ecuador.

requires a new confession, and the world seems always waiting for its poet. I remember, when I was young, how much I was moved one morning by tidings that genius had appeared in a youth who sat near me at table. He had left his work, and gone rambling none knew whither, and had written hundreds of lines, but could not tell whether that which was in him was therein told: he could tell nothing but that all was changed,—man, beast, heaven, earth, and sea. How gladly we listened! how credulous! Society seemed to be compromised. We sat in the aurora of a sunrise which was to put out all the stars. Boston seemed to be at twice the distance it had the night before, or was much farther than that. Rome,—what was Rome! Plutarch and Shakspeare were in the yellow leaf, and Homer no more should be heard of. It is much to know that poetry has been written this very day, under this very roof, by your side. What! that wonderful spirit has not expired! these stony moments are still sparkling and animated! I had fancied that the oracles were all silent, and nature had spent her fires, and behold! all night, from every pore, these fine auroras have been streaming. Every one has some interest in the advent of the poet, and no one knows how much it may concern him. We know that the secret of the world is profound, but who or what shall be our interpreter, we know not. A mountain ramble, a new style of face, a new person, may put the key into our hands. Of course, the value of genius to us is in the veracity of its report. Talent may frolic and juggle; genius realizes and adds. Mankind, in good earnest, have availed so far in understanding themselves and their work, that the foremost watchman on the peak announces his news. It is the truest word ever spoken, and the phrase will be the fittest, most musical, and the unerring voice of the world for that time.

All that we call sacred history attests that the birth of a poet is the principal event in chronology. Man, never so often deceived, still watches for the arrival of a brother who can hold him steady to a truth, until he has made it his own. With what joy I begin to read a poem, which I confide in as an inspiration! And now my chains are to be broken; I shall mount above these clouds and opaque airs in which I live,—opaque, though they seem transparent,—and from the heaven of truth I shall see and comprehend my relations. That will reconcile me to life, and renovate nature, to see trifles animated by a tendency, and to know what I am doing. Life will no more be a noise; now I shall see men and women, and know the signs by which they may be discerned from fools and satans. This day shall be better than my birth-day: then I became an animal: now I am invited into the science of the real. Such is the hope, but the fruition is postponed. Oftener it falls, that this winged man, who will carry me into the heaven, whirls me into the clouds, then leaps and frisks about with me from cloud to cloud, still affirming that he is bound heavenward; and I, being myself a novice, am slow in perceiving that he does not know the way into the heavens, and is merely bent that I should admire his skill to rise, like a fowl or a flying fish, a little way from the ground or the water; but the all-piercing, all-feeding, and ocular[8] air of heaven, that man shall never inhabit. I tumble down again soon into my old nooks, and lead the life of exaggerations as before, and have lost my faith in the possibility of any guide who can lead me thither where I would be.

8. Visible.

But leaving these victims of vanity, let us, with new hope, observe how nature, by worthier impulses, has ensured the poet's fidelity to his office of announcement and affirming, namely, by the beauty of things, which becomes a new, and higher beauty, when expressed. Nature offers all her creatures to him as a picture-language. Being used as a type, a second wonderful value appears in the object, far better than its old value, as the carpenter's stretched cord, if you hold your ear close enough, is musical in the breeze. "Things more excellent than every image," says Jamblichus,[9] "are expressed through images." Things admit of being used as symbols, because nature is a symbol, in the whole, and in every part. Every line we can draw in the sand, has expression; and there is no body without its spirit or genius. All form is an effect of character; all condition, of the quality of the life; all harmony, of health; (and, for this reason, a perception of beauty should be sympathetic, or proper only to the good.) The beautiful rests on the foundations of the necessary. The soul makes the body, as the wise Spenser teaches:—

"So every spirit, as it is most pure,
And hath in it the more of heavenly light,
So it the fairer body doth procure
To habit in, and it more fairly dight,
With cheerful grace and amiable sight.
For, of the soul, the body form doth take,
For soul is form, and doth the body make."[1]

Here we find ourselves, suddenly, not in a critical speculation, but in a holy place, and should go very warily and reverently. We stand before the secret of the world, there where Being passes into Appearance, and Unity into Variety.

The Universe is the externisation of the soul. Wherever the life is, that bursts into appearance around it. Our science is sensual, and therefore superficial. The earth, and the heavenly bodies, physics, and chemistry, we sensually treat, as if they were self-existent; but these are the retinue of that Being we have. "The mighty heaven," said Proclus,[2] "exhibits, in its transfigurations, clear images of the splendor of intellectual perceptions; being moved in conjunction with the unapparent periods of intellectual natures." Therefore, science always goes abreast with the just elevation of the man, keeping step with religion and metaphysics; or, the state of science is an index of our self-knowledge. Since everything in nature answers to a moral power, if any phenomenon remains brute and dark, it is that the corresponding faculty in the observer is not yet active.

No wonder, then, if these waters be so deep, that we hover over them with a religious regard. The beauty of the fable proves the importance of the sense; to the poet, and to all others; or, if you please, every man is so far a poet as to be susceptible of these enchantments of nature: for all men have the thoughts whereof the universe is the celebration. I find that the fascination resides in the symbol. Who loves nature? Who does not? Is it only poets, and men of leisure and cultivation, who live with her? No; but also hunters, farmers, grooms, and butchers, though they express their affection in their

9. Neoplatonic philosopher of the 4th century C.E. (Neoplatonism is a mystical religious system combining features of Platonic and other Greek philosophies with features of Judaism and Christianity.)

1. "An Hymn in Honour of Beauty" (1596), by the English poet Edmund Spenser (1552–1599).

2. Greek Neoplatonic philosopher (411–485).

choice of life, and not in their choice of words. The writer wonders what the coachman or the hunter values in riding, in horses, and dogs. It is not superficial qualities. When you talk with him, he holds these at as slight a rate as you. His worship is sympathetic; he has no definitions, but he is commanded in nature, by the living power which he feels to be there present. No imitation, or playing of these things, would content him; he loves the earnest of the northwind, of rain, of stone, and wood, and iron. A beauty not explicable, is dearer than a beauty which we can see to the end of. It is nature the symbol, nature certifying the supernatural, body overflowed by life, which he worships, with coarse, but sincere rites.

The inwardness, and mystery, of this attachment, drives men of every class to the use of emblems. The schools of poets, and philosophers, are not more intoxicated with their symbols, than the populace with theirs. In our political parties, compute the power of badges and emblems. See the great ball which they roll from Baltimore to Bunker hill! In the political processions, Lowell goes in a loom, and Lynn in a shoe, and Salem in a ship.[3] Witness the ciderbarrel, the log-cabin, the hickory-stick, the palmetto,[4] and all the cognizances of party. See the power of national emblems. Some stars, lilies, leopards, a crescent, a lion, an eagle, or other figure, which came into credit God knows how, on an old rag of bunting, blowing in the wind, on a fort, at the ends of the earth, shall make the blood tingle under the rudest, or the most conventional exterior. The people fancy they hate poetry, and they are all poets and mystics!

Beyond this universality of the symbolic language, we are apprised of the divineness of this superior use of things, whereby the world is a temple, whose walls are covered with emblems, pictures, and commandments of the Deity, in this, that there is no fact in nature which does not carry the whole sense of nature; and the distinctions which we make in events, and in affairs, of low and high, honest and base, disappear when nature is used as a symbol. Thought makes every thing fit for use. The vocabulary of an omniscient man would embrace words and images excluded from polite conversation. What would be base, or even obscene, to the obscene, becomes illustrious, spoken in a new connexion of thought. The piety of the Hebrew prophets purges their grossness. The circumcision is an example of the power of poetry to raise the low and offensive. Small and mean things serve as well as great symbols. The meaner the type by which a law is expressed, the more pungent it is, and the more lasting in the memories of men: just as we choose the smallest box, or case, in which any needful utensil can be carried. Bare lists of words are found suggestive, to an imaginative and excited mind; as it is related of Lord Chatham, that he was accustomed to read in Bailey's Dictionary,[5] when he was preparing to speak in Parliament. The poorest experience is rich enough for all the purposes of expressing thought.

3. Towns are symbolized by major products. "The great ball": as a campaign stunt, William Henry Harrison's supporters during the 1840 presidential campaign rolled huge balls at rallies to cries of "Keep the ball a-rolling."

4. Allusions to the 1840 presidential election. Harrison's "Log Cabin and Hard Cider" campaign, which emphasized the candidate's humble roots while offering free alcohol to his supporters, helped him defeat Martin Van Buren. South Carolina, nicknamed the Palmetto State for its palm-like trees, claimed to be the birthplace of Andrew Jackson ("Old Hickory").

5. Nathan (or Nathaniel) Bailey (d. 1742) published *An Universal Etymological English Dictionary* (1721), which ran through many editions. Lord Chatham was William Pitt (1708–1778), English statesman famous for his oratory.

Why covet a knowledge of new facts? Day and night, house and garden, a few books, a few actions, serve us as well as would all trades and all spectacles. We are far from having exhausted the significance of the few symbols we use. We can come to use them yet with a terrible simplicity. It does not need that a poem should be long. Every word was once a poem. Every new relation is a new word. Also, we use defects and deformaties to a sacred purpose, so expressing our sense that the evils of the world are such only to the evil eye. In the old mythology, mythologists observe, defects are ascribed to divine natures, as lameness to Vulcan, blindness to Cupid, and the like, to signify exuberances.

For, as it is dislocation and detachment from the life of God, that makes things ugly, the poet, who re-attaches things to nature and the Whole,—re-attaching even artificial things, and violations of nature, to nature, by a deeper insight,—disposes very easily of the most disagreeable facts. Readers of poetry see the factory-village, and the railway, and fancy that the poetry of the landscape is broken up by these; for these works of art are not yet consecrated in their reading; but the poet sees them fall within the great Order not less than the bee-hive, or the spider's geometrical web. Nature adopts them very fast into her vital circles, and the gliding train of cars she loves like her own. Besides, in a centred mind, it signifies nothing how many mechanical inventions you exhibit. Though you add millions, and never so surprising, the fact of mechanics has not gained a grain's weight. The spiritual fact remains unalterable, by many or by few particulars; as no mountain is of any appreciable height to break the curve of the sphere. A shrewd country-boy goes to the city for the first time, and the complacent citizen is not satisfied with his little wonder. It is not that he does not see all the fine houses, and know that he never saw such before, but he disposes of them as easily as the poet finds place for the railway. The chief value of the new fact, is to enhance the great and constant fact of Life, which can dwarf any and every circumstance, and to which the belt of wampum, and the commerce of America, are alike.

The world being thus put under the mind for verb and noun, the poet is he who can articulate it. For, though life is great, and fascinates, and absorbs,—and though all men are intelligent of the symbols through which it is named,—yet they cannot originally use them. We are symbols, and inhabit symbols; workmen, work, and tools, words and things, birth and death, all are emblems; but we sympathize with the symbols, and, being infatuated with the economical uses of things, we do not know that they are thoughts. The poet, by an ulterior intellectual perception, gives them a power which makes their old use forgotten, and puts eyes, and a tongue, into every dumb and inanimate object. He perceives the independence of the thought on the symbol, the stability of the thought, the accidency and fugacity of the symbol. As the eyes of Lyncæus[6] were said to see through the earth, so the poet turns the world to glass, and shows us all things in their right series and procession. For, through that better perception, he stands one step nearer to things, and sees the flowing or metamorphosis; perceives that thought is multiform; that within the form of every creature is a force impelling it to ascend into a higher form; and, following with his eyes the life, uses the forms which

6. In Greek mythology, a keen-sighted crewman who sailed with Jason in search of the Golden Fleece.

express that life, and so his speech flows with the flowing of nature. All the facts of the animal economy, sex, nutriment, gestation, birth, growth, are symbols of the passage of the world into the soul of man, to suffer there a change, and re-appear a new and higher fact. He uses forms according to the life, and not according to the form. This is true science. The poet alone knows astronomy, chemistry, vegetation, and animation, for he does not stop at these facts, but employs them as signs. He knows why the plain, or meadow of space, was strown with these flowers we call suns, and moons, and stars; why the great deep is adorned with animals, with men, and gods; for, in every word he speaks he rides on them as the horses of thought.

By virtue of this science the poet is the Namer, or Language-maker, naming things sometimes after their appearance, sometimes after their essence, and giving to every one its own name and not another's, thereby rejoicing the intellect, which delights in detachment or boundary. The poets made all the words, and therefore language is the archives of history, and, if we must say it, a sort of tomb of the muses. For, though the origin of most of our words is forgotten, each word was at first a stroke of genius, and obtained currency, because for the moment it symbolized the world to the first speaker and to the hearer. The etymologist finds the deadest word to have been once a brilliant picture. Language is fossil poetry. As the limestone of the continent consists of infinite masses of the shells of animalcules, so language is made up of images, or tropes, which now, in their secondary use, have long ceased to remind us of their poetic origin. But the poet names the thing because he sees it, or comes one step nearer to it than any other. This expression, or naming, is not art, but a second nature, grown out of the first, as a leaf out of a tree. What we call nature, is a certain self-regulated motion, or change; and nature does all things by her own hands, and does not leave another to baptise her, but baptises herself; and this through the metamorphosis again. I remember that a certain poet[7] described it to me thus:

> Genius is the activity which repairs the decays of things, whether wholly or partly of a material and finite kind. Nature, through all her kingdoms, insures herself. Nobody cares for planting the poor fungus: so she shakes down from the gills of one agaric[8] countless spores, any one of which, being preserved, transmits new billions of spores to-morrow or next day. The new agaric of this hour has a chance which the old one had not. This atom of seed is thrown into a new place, not subject to the accidents which destroyed its parent two rods off. She makes a man; and having brought him to ripe age, she will no longer run the risk of losing this wonder at a blow, but she detaches from him a new self, that the kind may be safe from accidents to which the individual is exposed. So when the soul of the poet has come to ripeness of thought, she detaches and sends away from it its poems or songs,—a fearless, sleepless, deathless progeny, which is not exposed to the accidents of the weary kingdom of time: a fearless, vivacious offspring, clad with wings (such was the virtue of the soul out of which they came), which carry them fast and far, and infix them irrecoverably into the hearts of men. These wings are the beauty of the poet's soul. The songs, thus

7. A private joke: the poet is Emerson himself.

8. Fungus, such as a mushroom.

flying immortal from their mortal parent, are pursued by clamorous flights of censures, which swarm in far greater numbers, and threaten to devour them; but these last are not winged. At the end of a very short leap they fall plump down, and rot, having received from the souls out of which they came no beautiful wings. But the melodies of the poet ascend, and leap, and pierce into the deeps of infinite time.

So far the bard taught me, using his freer speech. But nature has a higher end, in the production of new individuals, than security, namely, *ascension*, or, the passage of the soul into higher forms. I knew, in my younger days, the sculptor who made the statue of the youth which stands in the public garden. He was, as I remember, unable to tell directly, what made him happy, or unhappy, but by wonderful indirections he could tell. He rose one day, according to his habit, before the dawn, and saw the morning break, grand as the eternity out of which it came, and, for many days after, he strove to express this tranquillity, and, lo! his chisel had fashioned out of marble the form of a beautiful youth, Phosphorus,[9] whose aspect is such, that, it is said, all persons who look on it become silent. The poet also resigns himself to his mood, and that thought which agitated him is expressed, but *alter idem*,[1] in a manner totally new. The expression is organic, or, the new type which things themselves take when liberated. As, in the sun, objects paint their images on the retina of the eye, so they, sharing the aspiration of the whole universe, tend to paint a far more delicate copy of their essence in his mind. Like the metamorphosis of things into higher organic forms, is their change into melodies. Over everything stands its dæmon, or soul, and, as the form of the thing is reflected by the eye, so the soul of the thing is reflected by a melody. The sea, the mountain-ridge, Niagara, and every flower-bed, pre-exist, or super-exist, in pre-cantations,[2] which sail like odors in the air, and when any man goes by with an ear sufficiently fine, he overhears them, and endeavors to write down the notes, without diluting or depraving them. And herein is the legitimation of criticism, in the mind's faith, that the poems are a corrupt version of some text in nature, with which they ought to be made to tally. A rhyme in one of our sonnets should not be less pleasing than the iterated nodes of a seashell, or the resembling difference of a group of flowers. The pairing of the birds is an idyl, not tedious as our idyls are; a tempest is a rough ode, without falsehood or rant: a summer, with its harvest sown, reaped, and stored, is an epic song, subordinating how many admirably executed parts. Why should not the symmetry and truth that modulate these, glide into our spirits, and we participate the invention of nature?

This insight, which expresses itself by what is called Imagination, is a very high sort of seeing, which does not come by study, but by the intellect being where and what it sees, by sharing the path, or circuit of things through forms, and so making them translucid to others. The path of things is silent. Will they suffer a speaker to go with them? A spy they will not suffer; a lover, a poet, is the transcendency of their own nature,—him they will suffer. The condition of true naming, on the poet's part, is his resigning himself to the divine *aura*[3] which breathes through forms, and accompanying that.

9. Greek god associated with the morning star.
1. The same yet different (Latin).
2. Prophetic incantations or spells.
3. I.e., all-pervading spirit.

It is a secret which every intellectual man quickly learns, that, beyond the energy of his possessed and conscious intellect, he is capable of a new energy (as of an intellect doubled on itself), by abandonment to the nature of things; that, beside his privacy of power as an individual man, there is a great public power, on which he can draw, by unlocking, at all risks, his human doors, and suffering the ethereal tides to roll and circulate through him: then he is caught up into the life of the Universe, his speech is thunder, his thought is law, and his words are universally intelligible as the plants and animals. The poet knows that he speaks adequately, then, only when he speaks somewhat wildly, or, "with the flower of the mind;" not with the intellect, used as an organ, but with the intellect released from all service, and suffered to take its direction from its celestial life; or, as the ancients were wont to express themselves, not with intellect alone, but with the intellect inebriated by nectar. As the traveller who has lost his way, throws his reins on his horse's neck, and trusts to the instinct of the animal to find his road, so must we do with the divine animal who carries us through this world. For if in any manner we can stimulate this instinct, new passages are opened for us into nature, the mind flows into and through things hardest and highest, and the metamorphosis is possible.

This is the reason why bards love wine, mead,[4] narcotics, coffee, tea, opium, the fumes of sandal-wood and tobacco, or whatever other species of animal exhilaration. All men avail themselves of such means as they can, to add this extraordinary power to their normal powers; and to this end they prize conversation, music, pictures, sculpture, dancing, theatres, travelling, war, mobs, fires, gaming, politics, or love, or science, or animal intoxication, which are several coarser or finer *quasi*-mechanical substitutes for the true nectar, which is the ravishment of the intellect by coming nearer to the fact. These are auxiliaries to the centrifugal tendency of a man, to his passage out into free space, and they help him to escape the custody of that body in which he is pent up, and of that jail-yard of individual relations in which he is enclosed. Hence a great number of such as were professionally expressors of Beauty, as painters, poets, musicians, and actors, have been more than others wont to lead a life of pleasure and indulgence; all but the few who received the true nectar; and, as it was a spurious mode of attaining freedom, as it was an emancipation not into the heavens, but into the freedom of baser places, they were punished for that advantage they won, by a dissipation and deterioration. But never can any advantage be taken of nature by a trick. The spirit of the world, the great calm presence of the creator, comes not forth to the sorceries of opium or of wine. The sublime vision comes to the pure and simple soul in a clean and chaste body. That is not an inspiration which we owe to narcotics, but some counterfeit excitement and fury. Milton says, that the lyric poet may drink wine and live generously, but the epic poet, he who shall sing of the gods, and their descent unto men, must drink water out of a wooden bowl.[5] For poetry is not 'Devil's wine,' but God's wine. It is with this as it is with toys. We fill the hands and nurseries of our children with all manner of dolls, drums, and horses, withdrawing their eyes from the plain

4. A beverage made from fermented honey, malt, yeast, and water.

5. In Milton's "Sixth Latin Elegy" (1629).

face and sufficing objects of nature, the sun, and moon, the animals, the water, and stones, which should be their toys. So the poet's habit of living should be set on a key so low and plain, that the common influences should delight him. His cheerfulness should be the gift of the sunlight; the air should suffice for his inspiration, and he should be tipsy with water. That spirit which suffices quiet hearts, which seems to come forth to such from every dry knoll of sere grass, from every pine-stump, and half-imbedded stone, on which the dull March sun shines, comes forth to the poor and hungry, and such as are of simple taste. If thou fill thy brain with Boston and New York, with fashion and covetousness, and wilt stimulate thy jaded senses with wine and French coffee, thou shalt find no radiance of wisdom in the lonely waste of the pinewoods.

If the imagination intoxicates the poet, it is not inactive in other men. The metamorphosis excites in the beholder an emotion of joy. The use of symbols has a certain power of emancipation and exhilaration for all men. We seem to be touched by a wand, which makes us dance and run about happily, like children. We are like persons who come out of a cave or cellar into the open air. This is the effect on us of tropes,[6] fables, oracles, and all poetic forms. Poets are thus liberating gods. Men have really got a new sense, and found within their world, another world, or nest of worlds; for, the metamorphosis once seen, we divine that it does not stop. I will not now consider how much this makes the charm of algebra and the mathematics, which also have their tropes, but it is felt in every definition; as, when Aristotle defines *space* to be an immovable vessel, in which things are contained;—or, when Plato defines a *line* to be a flowing point; or, *figure* to be a bound of solid; and many the like. What a joyful sense of freedom we have, when Vitruvius announces the old opinion of artists, that no architect can build any house well, who does not know something of anatomy. When Socrates, in Charmides, tells us that the soul is cured of its maladies by certain incantations, and that these incantations are beautiful reasons, from which temperance is generated in souls; when Plato calls the world an animal; and Timæus affirms that the plants also are animals; or affirms a man to be a heavenly tree, growing with his root, which is his head, upward; and, as George Chapman, following him, writes,—

> "So in our tree of man, whose nervie root
> Springs in his top;"

when Orpheus speaks of hoariness as "that white flower which marks extreme old age;" when Proclus calls the universe the statue of the intellect; when Chaucer, in his praise of 'Gentilesse,' compares good blood in mean condition to fire, which, though carried to the darkest house betwixt this and the mount of Caucasus, will yet hold its natural office, and burn as bright as if twenty thousand men did it behold; when John saw, in the apocalypse, the ruin of the world through evil, and the stars fall from heaven, as the figtree casteth her untimely fruit; when Æsop reports the whole catalogue of common daily relations through the masquerade of birds and beasts;—we take the cheerful hint of the immortality of our essence, and its versatile habit

6. Figures of speech.

and escapes, as when the gypsies say, "it is in vain to hang them, they cannot die."[7]

The poets are thus liberating gods. The ancient British bards had for the title of their order, "Those who are free throughout the world." They are free, and they make free. An imaginative book renders us much more service at first, by stimulating us through its tropes, than afterward, when we arrive at the precise sense of the author. I think nothing is of any value in books, excepting the transcendental and extraordinary. If a man is inflamed and carried away by his thought, to that degree that he forgets the authors and the public, and heeds only this one dream, which holds him like an insanity, let me read his paper, and you may have all the arguments and histories and criticism. All the value which attaches to Pythagoras, Paracelsus, Cornelius Agrippa, Cardan, Kepler, Swedenborg, Schelling, Oken,[8] or any other who introduces questionable facts into his cosmogony, as angels, devils, magic, astrology, palmistry, mesmerism,[9] and so on, is the certificate we have of departure from routine, and that here is a new witness. That also is the best success in conversation, the magic of liberty, which puts the world, like a ball, in our hands. How cheap even the liberty then seems; how mean to study, when an emotion communicates to the intellect the power to sap and upheave nature; how great the perspective! nations, times, systems, enter and disappear, like threads in tapestry of large figure and many colors; dream delivers us to dream, and, while the drunkenness lasts, we will sell our bed, our philosophy, our religion, in our opulence.

There is good reason why we should prize this liberation. The fate of the poor shepherd, who, blinded and lost in the snowstorm, perishes in a drift within a few feet of his cottage door, is an emblem of the state of man. On the brink of the waters of life and truth, we are miserably dying. The inaccessibleness of every thought but that we are in, is wonderful. What if you come near to it,—you are as remote, when you are nearest, as when you are farthest. Every thought is also a prison; every heaven is also a prison. Therefore we love the poet, the inventor, who in any form, whether in an ode, or in an action, or in looks and behavior, has yielded us a new thought. He unlocks our chains, and admits us to a new scene.

This emancipation is dear to all men, and the power to impart it, as it must come from greater depth and scope of thought, is a measure of intellect. Therefore all books of the imagination endure, all which ascend to that truth, that the writer sees nature beneath him, and uses it as his exponent.[1] Every verse or sentence, possessing this virtue, will take care of its own immortality. The religions of the world are the ejaculations[2] of a few imaginative men.

7. Vitruvius Pollio (50?–26 B.C.E.), Roman writer on architecture. *Charmides* and *Timaeus* are two of Plato's Dialogues. The Chapman quotation is from his dedication to his translation of Homer. Chaucer's praise of "gentilesse" is in "The Wife of Bath's Tale." John's vision is in Revelation 6.13. The Greek Aesop in the 6th century B.C.E. wrote beast fables that commented on human foibles. The saying attributed to gypsies comes from the English travel writer George Borrow's *The Zincali* (1841).

8. Lorenz Oken (1779–1851), German naturalist. Pythagoras (6th century B.C.E.), Greek mathematician and mystic philosopher. Paracelsus (1493–1541), German alchemist. Agrippa (1486–1535), German physician. Girolamo Cardano (1501–1576), Italian mathematician. Johannes Kepler (1571–1630), German astronomer. Swedenborg, see n. 2, p. 295. Friedrich Wilhelm Joseph von Schelling (1775–1854), German philosopher.

9. Hypnotism.

1. Means of expounding his beliefs.

2. Throwings forth.

But the quality of the imagination is to flow, and not to freeze. The poet did not stop at the color, or the form, but read their meaning; neither may he rest in this meaning, but he makes the same objects exponents of his new thought. Here is the difference betwixt the poet and the mystic, that the last nails a symbol to one sense, which was a true sense for a moment, but soon becomes old and false. For all symbols are fluxional; all language is vehicular and transitive, and is good, as ferries and horses are, for conveyance, not as farms and houses are, for homestead. Mysticism consists in the mistake of an accidental and individual symbol for an universal one. The morning-redness happens to be the favorite meteor to the eyes of Jacob Behmen,[3] and comes to stand to him for truth and faith; and he believes should stand for the same realities to every reader. But the first reader prefers as naturally the symbol of a mother and child, or a gardener and his bulb, or a jeweller polishing a gem. Either of these, or of a myriad more, are equally good to the person to whom they are significant. Only they must be held lightly, and be very willingly translated into the equivalent terms which others use. And the mystic must be steadily told,—All that you say is just as true without the tedious use of that symbol as with it. Let us have a little algebra, instead of this trite rhetoric,—universal signs, instead of these village symbols,—and we shall both be gainers. The history of hierarchies seems to show, that all religious error consisted in making the symbol too stark and solid, and, at last, nothing but an excess of the organ of language.

Swedenborg, of all men in the recent ages, stands eminently for the translator of nature into thought. I do not know the man in history to whom things stood so uniformly for words. Before him the metamorphosis continually plays. Everything on which his eye rests, obeys the impulses of moral nature. The figs become grapes whilst he eats them. When some of his angels affirmed a truth, the laurel twig which they held blossomed in their hands. The noise which, at a distance, appeared like gnashing and thumping, on coming nearer was found to be the voice of disputants. The men, in one of his visions, seen in heavenly light, appeared like dragons, and seemed in darkness: but, to each other, they appeared as men, and, when the light from heaven shone into their cabin, they complained of the darkness, and were compelled to shut the window that they might see.

There was this perception in him, which makes the poet or seer, an object of awe and terror, namely, that the same man, or society of men, may wear one aspect to themselves and their companions, and a different aspect to higher intelligences. Certain priests, whom he describes as conversing very learnedly together, appeared to the children, who were at some distance, like dead horses: and many the like misappearances. And instantly the mind inquires, whether these fishes under the bridge, yonder oxen in the pasture, those dogs in the yard, are immutably fishes, oxen, and dogs, or only so appear to me, and perchance to themselves appear upright men; and whether I appear as a man to all eyes. The Brahmins[4] and Pythagoras propounded the same question, and if any poet has witnessed the transformation, he doubtless found it in harmony with various experiences. We have all seen changes as considerable in wheat and caterpillars. He is the poet, and shall

3. German mystic (1575–1624).
4. The highest social caste in Hindu culture, from which all priests are drawn.

draw us with love and terror, who sees, through the flowing vest, the firm nature, and can declare it.

I look in vain for the poet whom I describe. We do not, with sufficient plainness, or sufficient profoundness, address ourselves to life, nor dare we chaunt our own times and social circumstance. If we filled the day with bravery, we should not shrink from celebrating it. Time and nature yield us many gifts, but not yet the timely man, the new religion, the reconciler, whom all things await. Dante's praise is, that he dared to write his autobiography in colossal cipher, or into universality. We have yet had no genius in America, with tyrannous eye, which knew the value of our incomparable materials, and saw, in the barbarism and materialism of the times, another carnival of the same gods whose picture he so much admires in Homer; then in the middle age; then in Calvinism. Banks and tariffs, the newspaper and caucus, methodism and unitarianism, are flat and dull to dull people, but rest on the same foundations of wonder as the town of Troy, and the temple of Delphos,[5] and are as swiftly passing away. Our logrolling, our stumps and their politics, our fisheries, our Negroes, and Indians, our boasts,[6] and our repudiations, the wrath of rogues, and the pusillanimity of honest men, the northern trade, the southern planting, the western clearing, Oregon, and Texas, are yet unsung. Yet America is a poem in our eyes; its ample geography dazzles the imagination, and it will not wait long for metres. If I have not found that excellent combination of gifts in my countrymen which I seek, neither could I aid myself to fix the idea of the poet by reading now and then in Chalmers's collection of five centuries of English poets.[7] These are wits, more than poets, though there have been poets among them. But when we adhere to the ideal of the poet, we have our difficulties even with Milton and Homer. Milton is too literary, and Homer too literal and historical.

But I am not wise enough for a national criticism, and must use the old largeness a little longer, to discharge my errand from the muse to the poet concerning his art.

Art is the path of the creator to his work. The paths, or methods, are ideal and eternal, though few men ever see them, not the artist himself for years, or for a lifetime, unless he comes into the conditions. The painter, the sculptor, the composer, the epic rhapsodist, the orator, all partake one desire, namely, to express themselves symmetrically and abundantly, not dwarfishly and fragmentarily. They found or put themselves in certain conditions, as, the painter and sculptor before some impressive human figures; the orator, into the assembly of the people; and the others, in such scenes as each has found exciting to his intellect; and each presently feels the new desire. He hears a voice, he sees a beckoning. Then he is apprised, with wonder, what herds of dæmons hem him in. He can no more rest; he says, with the old painter, "By God, it is in me, and must go forth of me." He pursues a beauty, half seen, which flies before him. The poet pours out verses in every solitude. Most of the things he says are conventional, no doubt; but by and by he says

5. The home of the Delphic oracle, or prophetess, in Greece. Troy is the site of the Trojan War in Asia Minor.

6. The common correction for the 1st edition's "boats." "Logrolling" seems to be used in the metaphorical sense of exchanging political favors. "Stumps" refers to the practice political orators had of addressing audiences from any makeshift platform, even a tree stump.

7. A popular collection of poetry compiled by Alexander Chalmers (1759–1834), Scottish journalist and biographer.

something which is original and beautiful. That charms him. He would say nothing else but such things. In our way of talking, we say, "That is yours, this is mine;" but the poet knows well that it is not his; that it is as strange and beautiful to him as to you; he would fain hear the like eloquence at length. Once having tasted this immortal ichor,[8] he cannot have enough of it, and, as an admirable creative power exists in these intellections, it is of the last importance that these things get spoken. What a little of all we know is said! What drops of all the sea of our science are bailed up! and by what accident it is that these are exposed, when so many secrets sleep in nature! Hence the necessity of speech and song; hence these throbs and heart-beatings in the orator, at the door of the assembly, to the end, namely, that thought may be ejaculated as Logos, or Word.

Doubt not, O Poet, but persist. Say, "It is in me, and shall out." Stand there, baulked and dumb, stuttering and stammering, hissed and hooted, stand and strive, until, at last, rage draw out of thee that *dream*-power which every night shows thee is thine own; a power transcending all limit and privacy, and by virtue of which a man is the conductor of the whole river of electricity. Nothing walks, or creeps, or grows, or exists, which must not in turn arise and walk before him as exponent of his meaning. Comes he to that power, his genius is no longer exhaustible. All the creatures, by pairs and by tribes, pour into his mind as into a Noah's ark, to come forth again to people a new world. This is like the stock of air for our respiration, or for the combustion of our fireplace, not a measure of gallons, but the entire atmosphere if wanted. And therefore the rich poets, as Homer, Chaucer, Shakspeare, and Raphael,[9] have obviously no limits to their works, except the limits of their lifetime, and resemble a mirror carried through the street, ready to render an image of every created thing.

O poet! a new nobility is conferred in groves and pastures, and not in castles, or by the sword-blade, any longer. The conditions are hard, but equal. Thou shalt leave the world, and know the muse only. Thou shalt not know any longer the times, customs, graces, politics, or opinions of men, but shalt take all from the muse. For the time of towns is tolled from the world by funereal chimes, but in nature the universal hours are counted by succeeding tribes of animals and plants, and by growth of joy on joy. God wills also that thou abdicate a manifold and duplex life, and that thou be content that others speak for thee. Others shall be thy gentlemen, and shall represent all courtesy and worldly life for thee; others shall do the great and resounding actions also. Thou shalt lie close hid with nature, and canst not be afforded to the Capitol or the Exchange.[1] The world is full of renunciations and apprenticeships, and this is thine: thou must pass for a fool and a churl for a long season. This is the screen and sheath in which Pan[2] has protected his well-beloved flower, and thou shalt be known only to thine own, and they shall console thee with tenderest love. And thou shalt not be able to rehearse the names of thy friends in thy verse, for an old shame before the holy ideal. And this is the reward: that the ideal shall be real to thee; and the

8. In Greek myth, blood of the gods, but Emerson may mean nectar, the drink of the gods.
9. Raphael Sanzio (1483–1520), renowned painter of the Italian Renaissance.
1. Stock exchange.
2. In Greek myth, the god of woods and fields, represented with goat's legs, horns, and ears.

impressions of the actual world shall fall like summer rain, copious, but not troublesome, to thy invulnerable essence. Thou shalt have the whole land for thy park and manor, the sea for thy bath and navigation, without tax and without envy; the woods and the rivers thou shalt own; and thou shalt possess that wherein others are only tenants and boarders. Thou true land-lord! sea-lord! air-lord! Wherever snow falls, or water flows, or birds fly, wherever day and night meet in twilight, wherever the blue heaven is hung by clouds, or sown with stars, wherever are forms with transparent boundaries, wherever are outlets into celestial space, wherever is danger, and awe, and love, there is Beauty, plenteous as rain, shed for thee, and though thou shouldest walk the world over, thou shalt not be able to find a condition inopportune or ignoble.

1844

Experience[1]

The lords of life, the lords of life,—
I saw them pass,
In their own guise,
Like and unlike,
Portly and grim,
Use and Surprise,
Surface and Dream,
Succession swift, and spectral Wrong,
Temperament without a tongue,
And the inventor of the game
Omnipresent without name;—
Some to see, some to be guessed,
They marched from east to west:
Little man, least of all,
Among the legs of his guardians tall,
Walked about with puzzled look:—
Him by the hand dear nature took;
Dearest nature, strong and kind,
Whispered, 'Darling, never mind!
Tomorrow they will wear another face,
The founder thou! these are thy race!"

Where do we find ourselves? In a series of which we do not know the extremes, and believe that it has none. We wake and find ourselves on a stair; there are stairs below us, which we seem to have ascended; there are stairs above us, many a one, which go upward and out of sight. But the Genius[2] which, according to the old belief, stands at the door by which we enter, and gives us the lethe[3] to drink, that we may tell no tales, mixed the cup too strongly, and we cannot shake off the lethargy now at noonday. Sleep lingers all our lifetime about our eyes; as night hovers all day in the boughs of the fir-tree. All things swim and glimmer. Our life is not so much threat-

1. First published in *Essays, Second Series* (1844), "Experience" emerged in 1843 and 1844 during Emerson's broodings following the death of his young son Waldo in January 1842. The epigraph is by Emerson.
2. Governing or guardian spirit.
3. Water from the river of forgetfulness in the underworld of Greek myth.

ened as our perception. Ghostlike we glide through nature, and should not know our place again. Did our birth fall in some fit of indigence and frugality in nature, that she was so sparing of her fire and so liberal of her earth, that it appears to us that we lack the affirmative principle, and though we have health and reason, yet we have no superfluity of spirit for new creation? We have enough to live and bring the year about, but not an ounce to impart or to invest. Ah that our Genius were a little more of a genius! We are like millers on the lower levels of a stream, when the factories above them have exhausted the water. We too fancy that the upper people must have raised their dams.

If any of us knew what we were doing, or where we are going, then when we think we best know! We do not know today whether we are busy or idle. In times when we thought ourselves indolent, we have afterwards discovered, that much was accomplished, and much was begun in us. All our days are so unprofitable while they pass, that 'tis wonderful where or when we ever got anything of this which we call wisdom, poetry, virtue. We never got it on any dated calendar day. Some heavenly days must have been intercalated somewhere, like those that Hermes won with dice of the Moon, that Osiris[4] might be born. It is said, all martyrdoms looked mean when they were suffered. Every ship is a romantic object, except that we sail in. Embark, and the romance quits our vessel, and hangs on every other sail in the horizon. Our life looks trivial, and we shun to record it. Men seem to have learned of the horizon the art of perpetual retreating and reference. 'Yonder uplands are rich pasturage, and my neighbor has fertile meadow, but my field,' says the querulous farmer, 'only holds the world together.' I quote another man's saying; unluckily, that other withdraws himself in the same way, and quotes me. 'Tis the trick of nature thus to degrade today; a good deal of buzz, and somewhere a result slipped magically in. Every roof is agreeable to the eye, until it is lifted; then we find tragedy and moaning women, and hard-eyed husbands, and deluges of lethe, and the men ask, 'What's the news?' as if the old were so bad. How many individuals can we count in society? how many actions? how many opinions? So much of our time is preparation, so much is routine, and so much retrospect, that the pith of each man's genius contracts itself to a very few hours. The history of literature—take the net result of Tiraboschi, Warton, or Schlegel,[5]—is a sum of very few ideas, and of very few original tales,—all the rest being variation of these. So in this great society wide lying around us, a critical analysis would find very few spontaneous actions. It is almost all custom and gross sense. There are even few opinions, and these seem organic in the speakers, and do not disturb the universal necessity.

What opium is instilled into all disaster! It shows formidable as we approach it, but there is at last no rough rasping friction, but the most slippery sliding surfaces. We fall soft on a thought. *Ate Dea*[6] is gentle,

4. Chief Egyptian god. The following story is told in Plutarch's *Morals*: the sun god forbade his wife, Rhea, to give birth on any day of the year, but Hermes won five new days from the moon, during which Osiris could be born. "Intercalated": inserted.

5. Either Friedrich von Schlegel (1772–1829) or his brother August Wilhelm von Schlegel (1767–1845), historians of European literature. Girolamo Tiraboschi (1731–1794), historian of Italian literature. Thomas Warton (1728–1790), historian of British literature.

6. The goddess of mischief or fatal recklessness.

"Over men's heads walking aloft,
With tender feet treading so soft."[7]

People grieve and bemoan themselves, but it is not half so bad with them as they say. There are moods in which we court suffering, in the hope that here, at least, we shall find reality, sharp peaks and edges of truth. But it turns out to be scene-painting and counterfeit. The only thing grief has taught me, is to know how shallow it is. That, like all the rest, plays about the surface, and never introduces me into the reality, for contact with which, we would even pay the costly price of sons and lovers. Was it Boscovich[8] who found out that bodies never come in contact? Well, souls never touch their objects. An innavigable sea washes with silent waves between us and the things we aim at and converse with. Grief too will make us idealists. In the death of my son, now more than two years ago, I seem to have lost a beautiful estate,—no more. I cannot get it nearer to me. If tomorrow I should be informed of the bankruptcy of my principal debtors, the loss of my property would be a great inconvenience to me, perhaps, for many years; but it would leave me as it found me,—neither better nor worse. So is it with this calamity: it does not touch me: some thing which I fancied was a part of me, which could not be torn away without tearing me, nor enlarged without enriching me, falls off from me, and leaves no scar. It was caducous.[9] I grieve that grief can teach me nothing, nor carry me one step into real nature. The Indian who was laid under a curse, that the wind should not blow on him, nor water flow to him, nor fire burn him, is a type of us all. The dearest events are summer-rain, and we the Para coats[1] that shed every drop. Nothing is left us now but death. We look to that with a grim satisfaction, saying, there at least is reality that will not dodge us.

I take this evanescence and lubricity of all objects, which lets them slip through our fingers then when we clutch hardest, to be the most unhandsome part of our condition. Nature does not like to be observed, and likes that we should be her fools and playmates. We may have the sphere for our cricket-ball, but not a berry for our philosophy. Direct strokes she never gave us power to make; all our blows glance, all our hits are accidents. Our relations to each other are oblique and casual.

Dream delivers us to dream, and there is no end to illusion. Life is a train of moods like a string of beads, and, as we pass through them, they prove to be many-colored lenses which paint the world their own hue, and each shows only what lies in its focus. From the mountain you see the mountain. We animate what we can, and we see only what we animate. Nature and books belong to the eyes that see them. It depends on the mood of the man, whether he shall see the sunset or the fine poem. There are always sunsets, and there is always genius; but only a few hours so serene that we can relish nature or criticism. The more or less depends on structure or temperament. Temperament is the iron wire on which the beads are strung. Of what use is fortune or talent to a cold and defective nature? Who cares what sensibility or discrimination a man has at some time shown, if he falls asleep in his chair? or

7. *The Iliad,* book 19.
8. Ruggiero Giuseppe Boscovich (1711–1787), Italian physicist who advanced a molecular theory of matter.
9. Not long lasting.
1. Rubber overcoats.

if he laugh and giggle? or if he apologize? or is affected with egotism? or thinks of his dollar? or cannot go by food? or has gotten a child in his boyhood? Of what use is genius, if the organ is too convex or too concave, and cannot find a focal distance within the actual horizon of human life? Of what use, if the brain is too cold or too hot, and the man does not care enough for results, to stimulate him to experiment, and hold him up in it? or if the web is too finely woven, too irritable by pleasure and pain, so that life stagnates from too much reception, without due outlet? Of what use to make heroic vows of amendment, if the same old law-breaker is to keep them? What cheer can the religious sentiment yield, when that is suspected to be secretly dependent on the seasons of the year, and the state of the blood? I knew a witty physician who found theology in the biliary duct, and used to affirm that if there was disease in the liver, the man became a Calvinist, and if that organ was sound, he became a Unitarian. Very mortifying is the reluctant experience that some unfriendly excess or imbecility neutralizes the promise of genius. We see young men who owe us a new world, so readily and lavishly they promise, but they never acquit the debt; they die young and dodge the account: or if they live, they lose themselves in the crowd.

Temperament also enters fully into the system of illusions, and shuts us in a prison of glass which we cannot see. There is an optical illusion about every person we meet. In truth, they are all creatures of given temperament, which will appear in a given character, whose boundaries they will never pass: but we look at them, they seem alive, and we presume there is impulse in them. In the moment it seems impulse; in the year, in the lifetime, it turns out to be a certain uniform tune which the revolving barrel of the music-box must play. Men resist the conclusion in the morning, but adopt it as the evening wears on, that temper prevails over everything of time, place, and condition, and is inconsumable in the flames of religion. Some modifications the moral sentiment avails to impose, but the individual texture holds its dominion, if not to bias the moral judgments, yet to fix the measure of activity and of enjoyment.

I thus express the law as it is read from the platform of ordinary life, but must not leave it without noticing the capital exception. For temperament is a power which no man willingly hears any one praise but himself. On the platform of physics, we cannot resist the contracting influences of so-called science. Temperament puts all divinity to rout. I know the mental proclivity of physicians. I hear the chuckle of the phrenologists.[2] Theoretic kidnappers and slave-drivers, they esteem each man the victim of another, who winds him round his finger by knowing the law of his being, and by such cheap signboards as the color of his beard, or the slope of his occiput, reads the inventory of his fortunes and character. The grossest ignorance does not disgust like this impudent knowingness. The physicians say, they are not materialists; but they are:—Spirit is matter reduced to an extreme thinness: O *so* thin!—But the definition of *spiritual* should be, *that which is its own evidence*. What notions do they attach to love! what to religion! One would not willingly pronounce these words in their hearing, and give them the occasion to profane them. I saw a gracious gentleman who adapts his

2. A method of deducing traits of character by analyzing the shape of the head.

conversation to the form of the head of the man he talks with! I had fancied that the value of life lay in its inscrutable possibilities; in the fact that I never know, in addressing myself to a new individual, what may befall me. I carry the keys of my castle in my hand, ready to throw them at the feet of my lord, whenever and in what disguise soever he shall appear. I know he is in the neighborhood hidden among vagabonds. Shall I preclude my future, by taking a high seat, and kindly adapting my conversation to the shape of heads? When I come to that, the doctors shall buy me for a cent.——'But, sir, medical history; the report to the Institute; the proven facts!'—I distrust the facts and the inferences. Temperament is the veto or limitation-power in the constitution, very justly applied to restrain an opposite excess in the constitution, but absurdly offered as a bar to original equity. When virtue is in presence, all subordinate powers sleep. On its own level, or in view of nature, temperament is final. I see not, if one be once caught in this trap of so-called sciences, any escape for the man from the links of the chain of physical necessity. Given such an embryo, such a history must follow. On this platform, one lives in a sty of sensualism, and would soon come to suicide. But it is impossible that the creative power should exclude itself. Into every intelligence there is a door which is never closed, through which the creator passes. The intellect, seeker of absolute truth, or the heart, lover of absolute good, intervenes for our succor, and at one whisper of these high powers, we awake from ineffectual struggles with this nightmare. We hurl it into its own hell, and cannot again contract ourselves to so base a state.

The secret of the illusoriness is in the necessity of a succession of moods or objects. Gladly we would anchor, but the anchorage is quicksand. This onward trick of nature is too strong for us: *Pero si muove.*[3] When, at night, I look at the moon and stars, I seem stationary, and they to hurry. Our love of the real draws us to permanence, but health of body consists in circulation, and sanity of mind in variety or facility of association. We need change of objects. Dedication to one thought is quickly odious. We house with the insane, and must humor them; then conversation dies out. Once I took such delight in Montaigne, that I thought I should not need any other book; before that, in Shakspeare; then in Plutarch; then in Plotinus; at one time in Bacon; afterwards in Goethe; even in Bettine;[4] but now I turn the pages of either of them languidly, whilst I still cherish their genius. So with pictures; each will bear an emphasis of attention once, which it cannot retain, though we fain would continue to be pleased in that manner. How strongly I have felt of pictures, that when you have seen one well, you must take your leave of it; you shall never see it again. I have had good lessons from pictures, which I have since seen without emotion or remark. A deduction must be made

3. It moves, all the same (Italian). According to legend, Galileo (1564–1642) muttered these words under his breath after publicly renouncing his theory that the earth moved around the sun, which he had been forced to do in 1633 to avoid condemnation as a heretic.

4. Elizabeth ("Bettine") von Arnim (1785–1859), whose letters to Goethe, which she never actually sent him, were published in 1835. Michel de Montaigne (1533–1592), French essayist. Plutarch (46?–120?), Greek biographer of famous Greeks and Romans. Plotinus (205?–270?), Egyptian-born Roman Neoplatonist philosopher. (Neoplatonism is a mystic religious system, combining features of Platonic and other Greek philosophies with features of Judaism and Christianity.) Sir Francis Bacon (1561–1626), English essayist, philosopher, and statesman. Johann Wolfgang von Goethe (1749–1832), German poet and dramatist.

from the opinion, which even the wise express of a new book or occurrence. Their opinion gives me tidings of their mood, and some vague guess at the new fact, but is nowise to be trusted as the lasting relation between that intellect and that thing. The child asks, 'Mamma, why don't I like the story as well as when you told it me yesterday?' Alas, child, it is even so with the oldest cherubim of knowledge. But will it answer thy question to say, Because thou wert born to a whole, and this story is a particular? The reason of the pain this discovery causes us (and we make it late in respect to works of art and intellect), is the plaint of tragedy which murmurs from it in regard to persons, to friendship and love.

That immobility and absence of elasticity which we find in the arts, we find with more pain in the artist. There is no power of expansion in men. Our friends early appear to us as representatives of certain ideas, which they never pass or exceed. They stand on the brink of the ocean of thought and power, but they never take the single step that would bring them there. A man is like a bit of Labrador spar,[5] which has no lustre as you turn it in your hand, until you come to a particular angle; then it shows deep and beautiful colors. There is no adaptation or universal applicability in men, but each has his special talent, and the mastery of successful men consists in adroitly keeping themselves where and when that turn shall be oftenest to be practised. We do what we must, and call it by the best names we can, and would fain have the praise of having intended the result which ensues. I cannot recall any form of man who is not superfluous sometimes. But is not this pitiful? Life is not worth the taking, to do tricks in.

Of course, it needs the whole society, to give the symmetry we seek. The parti-colored wheel must revolve very fast to appear white. Something is learned too by conversing with so much folly and defect. In fine, whoever loses, we are always of the gaining party. Divinity is behind our failures and follies also. The plays of children are nonsense, but very educative nonsense. So it is with the largest and solemnest things, with commerce, government, church, marriage, and so with the history of every man's bread, and the ways by which he is to come by it. Like a bird which alights nowhere, but hops perpetually from bough to bough, is the Power which abides in no man and in no woman, but for a moment speaks from this one, and for another moment from that one.

But what help from these fineries or pedantries? What help from thought? Life is not dialectics. We, I think, in these times, have had lessons enough of the futility of criticism. Our young people have thought and written much on labor and reform, and for all that they have written, neither the world nor themselves have got on a step. Intellectual tasting of life will not supersede muscular activity. If a man should consider the nicety of the passage of a piece of bread down his throat, he would starve. At Education-Farm,[6] the noblest theory of life sat on the noblest figures of young men and maidens, quite powerless and melancholy. It would not rake or pitch a ton of hay; it would not rub down a horse; and the men and maidens it left pale and hungry.

5. Labradorite, crystalline rock.

6. Brook Farm, the utopian community in West Roxbury, Massachusetts, founded by George Ripley (1802–1880) in 1841 and disbanded in 1847. Emerson declined an invitation to participate.

A political orator wittily compared our party promises to western roads, which opened stately enough, with planted trees on either side, to tempt the traveller, but soon became narrow and narrower, and ended in a squirrel-track, and ran up a tree. So does culture with us; it ends in head-ache. Unspeakably sad and barren does life look to those, who a few months ago were dazzled with the splendor of the promise of the times. "There is now no longer any right course of action, nor any self-devotion left among the Iranis."[7] Objections and criticism we have had our fill of. There are objections to every course of life and action, and the practical wisdom infers an indifferency, from the omnipresence of objection. The whole frame of things preaches indifferency. Do not craze yourself with thinking, but go about your business anywhere. Life is not intellectual or critical, but sturdy. Its chief good is for well-mixed people who can enjoy what they find, without question. Nature hates peeping and our mothers speak her very sense when they say, "Children, eat your victuals, and say no more of it." To fill the hour,—that is happiness; to fill the hour, and leave no crevice for a repentance or an approval. We live amid surfaces, and the true art of life is to skate well on them. Under the oldest mouldiest conventions, a man of native force prospers just as well as in the newest world, and that by skill of handling and treatment. He can take hold anywhere. Life itself is a mixture of power and form, and will not bear the least excess of either. To finish the moment, to find the journey's end in every step of the road, to live the greatest number of good hours, is wisdom. It is not the part of men, but of fanatics, or of mathematicians, if you will, to say, that, the shortness of life considered, it is not worth caring whether for so short a duration we were sprawling in want, or sitting high. Since our office is with moments, let us husband them. Five minutes of today are worth as much to me, as five minutes in the next millennium. Let us be poised, and wise, and our own, today. Let us treat the men and women well: treat them as if they were real: perhaps they are. Men live in their fancy, like drunkards whose hands are too soft and tremulous for successful labor. It is a tempest of fancies, and the only ballast I know, is a respect to the present hour. Without any shadow of doubt amidst this vertigo of shows and politics, I settle myself ever the firmer in the creed, that we should not postpone and refer and wish, but do broad justice where we are, by whomsoever we deal with, accepting our actual companions and circumstances, however humble or odious, as the mystic officials to whom the universe has delegated its whole pleasure for us. If these are mean and malignant, their contentment, which is the last victory of justice, is a more satisfying echo to the heart, than the voice of poets and the casual sympathy of admirable persons. I think that however a thoughtful man may suffer from the defects and absurdities of his company, he cannot without affectation deny to any set of men and women, a sensibility to extraordinary merit. The coarse and frivolous have an instinct of superiority, if they have not a sympathy, and honor it in their blind capricious way with sincere homage.

The fine young people despise life, but in me, and in such as with me are free from dyspepsia, and to whom a day is a sound and solid good, it is a great excess of politeness to look scornful and to cry for company. I am grown

7. From the Persian *Desatir*, ancient scriptures credited to Zoroaster (6th century B.C.E.), founder of the Parsee religion.

by sympathy a little eager and sentimental, but leave me alone, and I should relish every hour and what it brought me, the potluck of the day, as heartily as the oldest gossip in the bar-room. I am thankful for small mercies. I compared notes with one of my friends who expects everything of the universe, and is disappointed when anything is less than the best, and I found that I begin at the other extreme, expecting nothing, and am always full of thanks for moderate goods. I accept the clangor and jangle of contrary tendencies. I find my account in sots and bores also. They give a reality to the circumjacent picture, which such a vanishing meteorous appearance can ill spare. In the morning I awake, and find the old world, wife, babes, and mother, Concord and Boston, the dear old spiritual world, and even the dear old devil not far off. If we will take the good we find, asking no questions, we shall have heaping measures. The great gifts are not got by analysis. Everything good is on the highway. The middle region of our being is the temperate zone. We may climb into the thin and cold realm of pure geometry and lifeless science, or sink into that of sensation. Between these extremes is the equator of life, of thought, of spirit, of poetry,—a narrow belt. Moreover, in popular experience, everything good is on the highway. A collector peeps into all the picture-shops of Europe, for a landscape of Poussin, a crayon-sketch of Salvator; but the Transfiguration, the Last Judgment, the Communion of St. Jerome, and what are as transcendent as these, are on the walls of the Vatican, the Uffizii, or the Louvre, where every footman may see them;[8] to say nothing of nature's pictures in every street, of sunsets and sunrises every day, and the sculpture of the human body never absent. A collector recently bought at public auction, in London, for one hundred and fifty-seven guineas,[9] an autograph of Shakspeare: but for nothing a school-boy can read Hamlet, and can detect secrets of highest concernment yet unpublished therein. I think I will never read any but the commonest books,—the Bible, Homer, Dante, Shakspeare, and Milton. Then we are impatient of so public a life and planet, and run hither and thither for nooks and secrets. The imagination delights in the woodcraft of Indians, trappers, and bee-hunters. We fancy that we are strangers, and not so intimately domesticated in the planet as the wild man, and the wild beast and bird. But the exclusion reaches them also; reaches the climbing, flying, gliding, feathered and four-footed man. Fox and woodchuck, hawk and snipe, and bittern, when nearly seen, have no more root in the deep world than man, and are just such superficial tenants of the globe. Then the new molecular philosophy shows astronomical interspaces betwixt atom and atom, shows that the world is all outside: it has no inside.

The mid-world is best. Nature, as we know her, is no saint. The lights of the church, the ascetics, Gentoos and Grahamites,[1] she does not distinguish by any favor. She comes eating and drinking and sinning. Her darlings, the great, the strong, the beautiful, are not children of our law, do not come out

8. I.e., the collector hunts for minor paintings in out-of-the-way shops while the great paintings are in museums, where anyone may see them. Nicolas Poussin (1594–1665), French painter; Salvator Rosa (1615–1673), Italian painter of wild landscapes; the *Transfiguration* by Raphael, in Rome; the *Last Judgment* is Michelangelo's, in Florence; the *Communion of St. Jerome* is that by Domenichino, in Paris.

9. British coin no longer in use, worth a little more than a pound.

1. Sylvester Graham (1794–1851), vegetarian whose efforts at food reform are memorialized in the graham cracker. "Gentoos": Hindu sectarians.

of the Sunday School, nor weigh their food, nor punctually keep the commandments. If we will be strong with her strength, we must not harbor such disconsolate consciences, borrowed too from the consciences of other nations. We must set up the strong present tense against all the rumors of wrath, past or to come. So many things are unsettled which it is of the first importance to settle,—and, pending their settlement, we will do as we do. Whilst the debate goes forward on the equity of commerce, and will not be closed for a century or two, New and Old England may keep shop. Law of copyright and international copyright[2] is to be discussed, and, in the interim, we will sell our books for the most we can. Expediency of literature, reason of literature, lawfulness of writing down a thought, is questioned; much is to say on both sides, and, while the fight waxes hot, thou, dearest scholar, stick to thy foolish task, add a line every hour, and between whiles add a line. Right to hold land, right of property, is disputed, and the conventions convene, and before the vote is taken, dig away in your garden, and spend your earnings as a waif or godsend to all serene and beautiful purposes. Life itself is a bubble and a skepticism, and a sleep within a sleep. Grant it, and as much more as they will—but thou, God's darling! heed thy private dream: thou wilt not be missed in the scorning and skepticism: there are enough of them: stay there in thy closet, and toil, until the rest are agreed what to do about it. Thy sickness, they say, and thy puny habit, require that thou do this or avoid that, but know that thy life is a flitting state, a tent for a night, and do thou, sick or well, finish that stint. Thou art sick, but shalt not be worse, and the universe, which holds thee dear, shall be the better.

Human life is made up of the two elements, power and form, and the proportion must be invariably kept, if we would have it sweet and sound. Each of these elements in excess makes a mischief as hurtful as its defect. Everything runs to excess: every good quality is noxious, if unmixed, and, to carry the danger to the edge of ruin, nature causes each man's peculiarity to superabound. Here, among the farms, we adduce the scholars as examples of this treachery. They are nature's victims of expression. You who see the artist, the orator, the poet, too near, and find their life no more excellent than that of mechanics or farmers, and themselves victims of partiality, very hollow and haggard, and pronounce them failures,—not heroes, but quacks,—conclude very reasonably, that these arts are not for man, but are disease. Yet nature will not bear you out. Irresistible nature made men such, and makes legions more of such, every day. You love the boy reading in a book, gazing at a drawing, or a cast: yet what are these millions who read and behold, but incipient writers and sculptors? Add a little more of that quality which now reads and sees, and they will seize the pen and chisel. And if one remembers how innocently he began to be an artist, he perceives that nature joined with his enemy. A man is a golden impossibility. The line he must walk is a hair's breadth. The wise through excess of wisdom is made a fool.

How easily, if fate would suffer it, we might keep forever these beautiful limits, and adjust ourselves, once for all, to the perfect calculation of the kingdom of known cause and effect. In the street and in the newspapers, life

2. Not passed by the American Congress until 1891.

appears so plain a business, that manly resolution and adherence to the multiplication-table through all weathers, will insure success. But ah! presently comes a day, or is it only a half-hour, with its angel-whispering,—which discomfits the conclusions of nations and of years! Tomorrow again, everything looks real and angular, the habitual standards are reinstated, common sense is as rare as genius,—is the basis of genius, and experience is hands and feet to every enterprise;—and yet, he who should do his business on this understanding, would be quickly bankrupt. Power keeps quite another road than the turnpikes of choice and will, namely, the subterranean and invisible tunnels and channels of life. It is ridiculous that we are diplomatists, and doctors, and considerate people: there are no dupes like these. Life is a series of surprises, and would not be worth taking or keeping, if it were not. God delights to isolate us every day, and hide from us the past and the future. We would look about us, but with grand politeness he draws down before us an impenetrable screen of purest sky, and another behind us of purest sky. 'You will not remember,' he seems to say, 'and you will not expect.' All good conversation, manners, and action, come from a spontaneity which forgets usages, and makes the moment great. Nature hates calculators; her methods are saltatory and impulsive. Man lives by pulses; our organic movements are such; and the chemical and ethereal agents are undulatory and alternate; and the mind goes antagonizing on, and never prospers but by fits. We thrive by casualties. Our chief experiences have been casual. The most attractive class of people are those who are powerful obliquely, and not by the direct stroke: men of genius, but not yet accredited: one gets the cheer of their light, without paying too great a tax. Theirs is the beauty of the bird, or the morning light, and not of art. In the thought of genius there is always a surprise; and the moral sentiment is well called "the newness," for it is never other; as new to the oldest intelligence as to the young child.—"the kingdom that cometh without observation."[3] In like manner, for practical success, there must not be too much design. A man will not be observed in doing that which he can do best. There is a certain magic about his properest action, which stupefies your powers of observation, so that though it is done before you, you wist not of it. The art of life has a pudency, and will not be exposed. Every man is an impossibility, until he is born; every thing impossible, until we see a success. The ardors of piety agree at last with the coldest skepticism,—that nothing is of us or our works,—that all is of God. Nature will not spare us the smallest leaf of laurel. All writing comes by the grace of God, and all doing and having. I would gladly be moral, and keep due metes and bounds, which I dearly love, and allow the most to the will of man, but I have set my heart on honesty in this chapter, and I can see nothing at last, in success or failure, than more or less of vital force supplied from the Eternal. The results of life are uncalculated and uncalculable. The years teach much which the days never know. The persons who compose our company, converse, and come and go, and design and execute many things, and somewhat comes of it all, but an unlooked for result. The individual is always mistaken. He designed many things, and drew in other persons as coadjutors, quarrelled with some or all, blundered much, and something is done; all are a little advanced, but

3. Luke 17.20.

the individual is always mistaken. It turns out somewhat new, and very unlike what he promised himself.

The ancients, stuck with this irreducibleness of the elements of human life to calculation, exalted Chance into a divinity, but that is to stay too long at the spark,—which glitters truly at one point,—but the universe is warm with the latency of the same fire. The miracle of life which will not be expounded, but will remain a miracle, introduces a new element. In the growth of the embryo, Sir Everard Home,[4] I think, noticed that the evolution was not from one central point, but co-active from three or more points. Life has no memory. That which proceeds in succession might be remembered, but that which is co-existent, or ejaculated from a deeper cause, as yet far from being conscious, knows not its own tendency. So it is with us, now skeptical, or without unity, because immersed in forms and effects all seeming to be of equal yet hostile value, and now religious, whilst in the reception of spiritual law. Bear with these distractions, with this coetaneous[5] growth of the parts: they will one day be *members*, and obey one will. On that one will, on that secret cause, they nail our attention and hope. Life is hereby melted into an expectation or a religion. Underneath the inharmonious and trivial particulars, is a musical perfection, the Ideal journeying always with us, the heaven without rent or seam. Do but observe the mode of our illumination. When I converse with a profound mind, or if at any time being alone I have good thoughts, I do not at once arrive at satisfactions, as when, being thirsty, I drink water, or go to the fire, being cold: no! but I am at first apprised of my vicinity to a new and excellent region of life. By persisting to read or to think, this region gives further sign of itself, as it were in flashes of light, in sudden discoveries of its profound beauty and repose, as if the clouds that covered it parted at intervals, and showed the approaching traveller the inland mountains, with the tranquil eternal meadows spread at their base, whereon flocks graze, and shepherds pipe and dance. But every insight from this realm of thought is felt as initial, and promises a sequel. I do not make it; I arrive there, and behold what was there already. I make! O no! I clap my hands in infantine joy and amazement, before the first opening to me of this august magnificence, old with the love and homage of innumerable ages, young with the life of life, the sunbright Mecca[6] of the desert. And what a future it opens! I feel a new heart beating with the love of the new beauty. I am ready to die out of nature, and be born again into this new yet unapproachable America I have found in the West.

> "Since neither now nor yesterday began
> These thoughts, which have been ever, nor yet can
> A man be found who their first entrance knew."[7]

If I have described life as a flux of moods, I must now add, that there is that in us which changes not, and which ranks all sensations and states of mind. The consciousness in each man is a sliding scale, which identifies him now with the First Cause, and now with the flesh of his body; life above life, in

4. Scottish surgeon (1756–1832).
5. Simultaneous.
6. Located in Saudia Arabia, Mecca is the holiest city of Islam and the most important destination of Muslim pilgrims.
7. A free translation of the conclusion of one of the heroine's speeches in Sophocles' *Antigone* (c. 442 B.C.E.), lines 455–57.

infinite degrees. The sentiment from which it sprung determines the dignity of any deed, and the question ever is, not, what you have done or forborne, but, at whose command you have done or forborne it.

Fortune, Minerva,[8] Muse, Holy Ghost,—these are quaint names, too narrow to cover this unbounded substance. The baffled intellect must still kneel before this cause, which refuses to be named—ineffable cause, which every fine genius has essayed to represent by some emphatic symbol, as, Thales by water, Anaximenes by air, Anaxagoras by (*Noûs*) thought, Zoroaster[9] by fire, Jesus and the moderns by love: and the metaphor of each has become a national religion. The Chinese Mencius[1] has not been the least successful in his generalization. "I fully understand language," he said, "and nourish well my vast-flowing vigor."—"I beg to ask what you call vast-flowing vigor?"—said his companion. "The explanation," replied Mencius, "is difficult. This vigor is supremely great, and in the highest degree unbending. Nourish it correctly, and do it no injury, and it will fill up the vacancy between heaven and earth. This vigor accords with and assists justice and reason, and leaves no hunger."—In our more correct writing, we give to this generalization the name of Being, and thereby confess that we have arrived as far as we can go. Suffice it for the joy of the universe, that we have not arrived at a wall, but at interminable oceans. Our life seems not present, so much as prospective; not for the affairs on which it is wasted, but as a hint of this vast-flowing vigor. Most of life seems to be mere advertisement of faculty: information is given us not to sell ourselves cheap; that we are very great. So, in particulars, our greatness is always in a tendency or direction, not in an action. It is for us to believe in the rule, not in the exception. The noble are thus known from the ignoble. So in accepting the leading of the sentiments, it is not what we believe concerning the immortality of the soul, or the like, but *the universal impulse to believe*, that is the material circumstance, and is the principal fact in the history of the globe. Shall we describe this cause as that which works directly? The spirit is not helpless or needful of mediate organs. It has plentiful powers and direct effects. I am explained without explaining, I am felt without acting, and where I am not. Therefore all just persons are satisfied with their own praise. They refuse to explain themselves, and are content that new actions should do them that office. They believe that we communicate without speech, and above speech, and that no right action of ours is quite unaffecting to our friends, at whatever distance; for the influence of action is not to be measured by miles. Why should I fret myself, because a circumstance has occurred, which hinders my presence where I was expected? If I am not at the meeting, my presence where I am, should be as useful to the commonwealth of friendship and wisdom, as would be my presence in that place. I exert the same quality of power in all places. Thus journeys the mighty Ideal before us; it never was known to fall into the rear. No man ever came to an experience which was satiating, but his good is tidings of a better. Onward and onward! In liberated moments, we know that a new picture of life and duty is already possible; the

8. Roman goddess of wisdom.
9. The 6th-century Persian founder of the fire worship of the Parsees. Thales (7th century B.C.E.), Anaximenes (6th century B.C.E.), and Anaxagoras (5th century B.C.E), Greek philosophers.
1. Meng-tsu (3rd century B.C.E.), compiler of doctrines of Confucianism.

elements already exist in many minds around you, of a doctrine of life which shall transcend any written record we have. The new statement will comprise the skepticisms, as well as the faiths of society, and out of unbeliefs a creed shall be formed. For, skepticisms are not gratuitous or lawless, but are limitations of the affirmative statement, and the new philosophy must take them in, and make affirmations outside of them, just as much as it must include the oldest beliefs.

It is very unhappy, but too late to be helped, the discovery we have made, that we exist. That discovery is called the Fall of Man. Ever afterwards, we suspect our instruments. We have learned that we do not see directly, but mediately, and that we have no means of correcting these colored and distorting lenses which we are, or of computing the amount of their errors. Perhaps these subject-lenses have a creative power; perhaps there are no objects. Once we lived in what we saw; now, the rapaciousness of this new power, which threatens to absorb all things, engages us. Nature, art, persons, letters, religions,—objects, successively tumble in, and God is but one of its ideas. Nature and literature are subjective phenomena; every evil and every good thing is a shadow which we cast. The street is full of humiliations to the proud. As the fop contrived to dress his bailiffs in his livery, and make them wait on his guests at table, so the chagrins[2] which the bad heart gives off as bubbles, at once take form as ladies and gentlemen in the street, shopmen or barkeepers in hotels, and threaten or insult whatever is threatenable and insultable in us. 'Tis the same with our idolatries. People forget that it is the eye which makes the horizon, and the rounding mind's eye which makes this or that man a type or representative of humanity with the name of hero or saint. Jesus the "providential man," is a good man on whom many people are agreed that these optical laws shall take effect. By love on one part, and by forbearance to press objection on the other part, it is for a time settled, that we will look at him in the centre of the horizon, and ascribe to him the properties that will attach to any man so seen. But the longest love or aversion has a speedy term. The great and crescive[3] self, rooted in absolute nature, supplants all relative existence, and ruins the kingdom of mortal friendship and love. Marriage (in what is called the spiritual world) is impossible, because of the inequality between every subject and every object. The subject is the receiver of Godhead, and at every comparison must feel his being enhanced by that cryptic might. Though not in energy, yet by presence, this magazine[4] of substance cannot be otherwise than felt: nor can any force of intellect attribute to the object the proper deity which sleeps or wakes forever in every subject. Never can love make consciousness and ascription equal in force. There will be the same gulf between every me and thee, as between the original and the picture. The universe is the bride of the soul. All private sympathy is partial. Two human beings are like globes, which can touch only in a point, and, whilst they remain in contact, all other points of each of the spheres are inert; their turn must also come, and the longer a particular union lasts, the more energy of appetency[5] the parts not in union acquire.

2. Ill-humored feelings.
3. Increasing.
4. Stored supply.
5. Strong impulse toward union.

Life will be imaged, but cannot be divided nor doubled. Any invasion of its unity would be chaos. The soul is not twin-born, but the only begotten, and though revealing itself as child in time, child in appearance, is of a fatal and universal power, admitting no co-life. Every day, every act betrays the ill-concealed deity. We believe in ourselves, as we do not believe in others. We permit all things to ourselves, and that which we call sin in others, is experiment for us. It is an instance of our faith in ourselves, that men never speak of crime as lightly as they think: or, every man thinks a latitude safe for himself, which is nowise to be indulged to another. The act looks very differently on the inside, and on the outside; in its quality, and in its consequences. Murder in the murderer is no such ruinous thought as poets and romancers will have it; it does not unsettle him, or fright him from his ordinary notice of trifles: it is an act quite easy to be contemplated, but in its sequel, it turns out to be a horrible jangle and confounding of all relations. Especially the crimes that spring from love, seem right and fair from the actor's point of view, but, when acted, are found destructive of society. No man at last believes that he can be lost, nor that the crime in him is as black as in the felon. Because the intellect qualifies in our own case the moral judgments. For there is no crime to the intellect. That is antinomian or hypernomian,[6] and judges law as well as fact. "It is worse than a crime, it is a blunder," said Napoleon, speaking the language of the intellect. To it, the world is a problem in mathematics or the science of quantity, and it leaves out praise and blame, and all weak emotions. All stealing is comparative. If you come to absolutes, pray who does not steal? Saints are sad, because they behold sin, (even when they speculate,) from the point of view of the conscience, and not of the intellect; a confusion of thought. Sin seen from the thought, is a diminution or *less*: seen from the conscience or will, it is pravity or *bad*. The intellect names it shade, absence of light, and no essence. The conscience must feel it as essence, essential evil. This it is not: it has an objective existence, but no subjective.

Thus inevitably does the universe wear our color, and every object fall successively into the subject itself. The subject exists, the subject enlarges; all things sooner or later fall into place. As I am, so I see; use what language we will, we can never say anything but what we are; Hermes, Cadmus, Columbus, Newton, Buonaparte, are the mind's ministers.[7] Instead of feeling a poverty when we encounter a great man, let us treat the new comer like a travelling geologist, who passes through our estate, and shows us good slate, or limestone, or anthracite, in our brush pasture. The partial action of each strong mind in one direction, is a telescope for the objects on which it is pointed. But every other part of knowledge is to be pushed to the same extravagance, ere the soul attains her due sphericity. Do you see that kitten chasing so prettily her own tail? If you could look with her eyes, you might see her surrounded with hundreds of figures performing complex dramas, with tragic and comic issues, long conversations, many characters, many ups

6. Against or beyond the control of law.

7. I.e., great gods or men of legend and history are servants of the human mind because our subjectivity uses them to light up areas of our own being. Hermes is the Greek god of invention. Cadmus is the mythical inventor of the alphabet and creator of the Thebans by sowing dragon's teeth. Columbus sailed to America. Newton discovered the law of gravity. Napoleon Bonaparte, in Emerson's childhood, was the conquerer of much of Europe.

and downs of fate,—and meantime it is only puss and her tail. How long before our masquerade will end its noise of tamborines, laughter, and shouting, and we shall find it was a solitary performance?—A subject and an object,—it takes so much to make the galvanic circuit complete, but magnitude adds nothing. What imports it whether it is Kepler[8] and the sphere; Columbus and America; a reader and his book; or puss with her tail?

It is true that all the muses and love and religion hate these developments, and will find a way to punish the chemist, who publishes in the parlor the secrets of the laboratory. And we cannot say too little of our constitutional necessity of seeing things under private aspects, or saturated with our humors. And yet is the God the native of these bleak rocks. That need makes in morals the capital virtue of self-trust. We must hold hard to this poverty, however scandalous, and by more vigorous self-recoveries, after the sallies of action, possess our axis more firmly. The life of truth is cold, and so far mournful; but it is not the slave of tears, contritions, and perturbations. It does not attempt another's work, nor adopt another's facts. It is a main lesson of wisdom to know your own from another's. I have learned that I cannot dispose of other people's facts; but I possess such a key to my own, as persuades me against all their denials, that they also have a key to theirs. A sympathetic person is placed in the dilemma of a swimmer among drowning men, who all catch at him, and if he give so much as a leg or a finger, they will drown him. They wish to be saved from the mischiefs of their vices, but not from their vices. Charity would be wasted on this poor waiting on the symptoms. A wise and hardy physician will say, *Come out of that*, as the first condition of advice.

In this our talking America, we are ruined by our good nature and listening on all sides. This compliance takes away the power of being greatly useful. A man should not be able to look other than directly and forthright. A preoccupied attention is the only answer to the importunate frivolity of other people: an attention, and to an aim which makes their wants frivolous. This is a divine answer, and leaves no appeal, and no hard thoughts. In Flaxman's drawing of the Eumenides of Æschylus,[9] Orestes supplicates Apollo, whilst the Furies sleep on the threshold. The face of the god expresses a shade of regret and compassion, but calm with the conviction of the irreconcilableness of the two spheres. He is born into other politics, into the eternal and beautiful. The man at his feet asks for his interest in turmoils of the earth, into which his nature cannot enter. And the Eumenides there lying express pictorially this disparity. The god is surcharged with his divine destiny.

Illusion, Temperament, Succession, Surface, Surprise, Reality, Subjectiveness,—these are threads on the loom of time, these are the lords of life. I dare not assume to give their order, but I name them as I find them in my way. I know better than to claim any completeness for my picture. I am a fragment, and this is a fragment of me. I can very confidently announce

8. Johannes Kepler (1571–1630), German astronomer who developed the mathematical statements describing the revolutions of the planets around the sun.

9. John Flaxman (1755–1826), English illustrator. In the clearer modern usage, the title of Aeschylus's play *The Eumenides* (c. 458 B.C.E.) would be italicized. In the scene depicted by Flaxman, the Furies, or Eumenides, who have pursued Orestes since his murder of his adulterous mother, are temporarily lulled by the power of Apollo, who sanctioned the murder.

one or another law, which throws itself into relief and form, but I am too young yet by some ages to compile a code. I gossip for my hour concerning the eternal politics. I have seen many fair pictures not in vain. A wonderful time I have lived in. I am not the novice I was fourteen, nor yet seven years ago. Let who will ask, where is the fruit? I find a private fruit sufficient. This is a fruit,—that I should not ask for a rash effect from meditations, counsels, and the hiving of truths. I should feel it pitiful to demand a result on this town and county, an overt effect on the instant month and year. The effect is deep and secular[1] as the cause. It works on periods in which mortal lifetime is lost. All I know is reception; I am and I have: but I do not get, and when I have fancied I had gotten anything, I found I did not. I worship with wonder the great Fortune. My reception has been so large, that I am not annoyed by receiving this or that superabundantly. I say to the Genius, if he will pardon the proverb, *In for a mill, in for a million.* When I receive a new gift, I do not macerate[2] my body to make the account square, for, if I should die, I could not make the account square. The benefit overran the merit the first day, and has overran the merit ever since. The merit itself, so-called, I reckon part of the receiving.

Also, that hankering after an overt or practical effect seems to me an apostasy. In good earnest, I am willing to spare this most unnecessary deal of doing. Life wears to me a visionary face. Hardest, roughest action is visionary also. It is but a choice between soft and turbulent dreams. People disparage knowing and the intellectual life, and urge doing. I am very content with knowing, if only I could know. That is an august entertainment, and would suffice me a great while. To know a little, would be worth the expense of this world. I hear always the law of Adrastia,[3] "that every soul which had acquired any truth, should be safe from harm until another period."

I know that the world I converse with in the city and in the farms, is not the world I *think*. I observe that difference, and shall observe it. One day, I shall know the value and law of this discrepance. But I have not found that much was gained by manipular attempts to realize the world of thought. Many eager persons successively make an experiment in this way, and make themselves ridiculous. They acquire democratic manners, they foam at the mouth, they hate and deny. Worse, I observe, that, in the history of mankind, there is never a solitary example of success,—taking their own tests of success. I say this polemically, or in reply to the inquiry, why not realize your world? But far be from me the despair which prejudges the law by a paltry empiricism,—since there never was a right endeavor, but it succeeded. Patience and patience, we shall win at the last. We must be very suspicious of the deceptions of the element of time. It takes a good deal of time to eat or to sleep, or to earn a hundred dollars, and a very little time to entertain a hope and an insight which becomes the light of our life. We dress our garden, eat our dinners, discuss the household with our wives, and these things make no impression, are forgotten next week; but in the solitude to which every man is always returning, he has a sanity and revelations, which in his passage into new worlds he will carry with him. Never mind the ridicule, never mind the defeat: up again, old heart!—it seems to say,—there is victory yet for all

1. Lasting from century to century.
2. Waste away by fasting.
3. Another name for Nemesis or Destiny. The quotation is from the *Phaedrus* by Plato.

justice; and the true romance which the world exists to realize, will be the transformation of genius into practical power.

1844

John Brown[1]

Mr. Chairman: I have been struck with one fact, that the best orators who have added their praise to his fame—and I need not go out of this house to find the purest eloquence in the country—have one rival who comes off a little better, and that is JOHN BROWN. Every thing that is said of him leaves people a little dissatisfied; but as soon as they read his own speeches and letters they are heartily contented—such is the singleness of purpose which justifies him to the head and the heart of all. Taught by this experience, I mean, in the few remarks I have to make, to cling to his history, or let him speak for himself.

John Brown, the founder of liberty in Kansas, was born in Sorrington, Litchfield County, Conn., in 1800. When he was five years old his father emigrated to Ohio, and the boy was there set to keep sheep, and to look after cattle, and dress skins; he went bareheaded and barefooted, and clothed in buckskin. He said that he loved rough play, could never have rough play enough; could not see a seedy hat without wishing to pull it off. But for this it needed that the playmates should be equal; not one in fine clothes and the other in buckskin; not one his own master, hale and hearty, and the other watched and whipped. But it chanced that in Pennsylvania, where he was sent by his father to collect cattle, he fell in with a boy whom he heartily liked, and whom he looked upon as his superior. This boy was a slave; he saw him beaten with an iron shovel, and otherwise maltreated; he saw that this boy had nothing better to look forward to in life, whilst he himself was petted and made much of; for he was much considered in the family where he then stayed, from the circumstance that this boy of twelve years had conducted alone a drove of cattle a hundred miles. But the colored boy had no friend, and no future. This worked such indignation in him that he swore an oath of resistance to Slavery as long as he lived. And thus his enterprise to go into Virginia and run off five hundred or a thousand slaves, was not a piece of spite or revenge, a plot of two years or of twenty years, but the keeping of an oath made to heaven and earth forty-seven years before. Forty-seven years at least, though I incline to accept his own account of the matter, at Charlestown,[2] which makes the date a little older, when he said, "This was all settled millions of years before the world was made."

1. The text is taken from *Echoes of Harper's Ferry* (1860), edited by the Scottish American abolitionist James Redpath (1833–1891). On October 16, 1859, the militant abolitionist John Brown (1800–1859) led twenty-one men, including five African Americans, in an attack on an unguarded federal arsenal at Harpers Ferry in western Virginia in an effort to secure arms for a slave revolt he hoped to inspire. Within two days his group was defeated by American troops and he surrendered. Convicted of treason against the state of Virginia, he was hanged on December 2, 1859. Emerson delivered this speech at a fund-raising meeting for the Brown family held at Salem, Massachusetts, on January 6, 1860; there is no surviving manuscript.

2. Brown was tried and hanged in Charlestown, Virginia. Emerson probably derived much of his

He grew up a religious and manly person in severe poverty; a fair specimen of the best stock of New England; having that force of thought and that sense of right which are the warp and woof of greatness. Our farmers were Orthodox Calvinists,[3] mighty in the Scriptures; had learned that life was a preparation, a "probation," to use their word, for a higher world, and was to be spent in loving and serving mankind.

Thus was formed a romantic character absolutely without any vulgar trait; living to ideal ends, without any mixture of self-indulgence or compromise, such as lowers the value of benevolent and thoughtful men we know; abstemious, refusing luxuries, not sourly and reproachfully, but simply as unfit for his habit; quiet and gentle as a child in the house. And, as happens usually to men of romantic character, his fortunes were romantic. Walter Scott[4] would have delighted to draw his picture and trace his adventurous career. A shepherd and herdsman, he learned the manners of animals, and knew the secret signals by which animals communicate. He made his hard bed on the mountains with them; he learned to drive his flock through thickets all but impassable; he had all the skill of a shepherd by choice of breed, and by wise husbandry to obtain the best wool, and that for a course of years. And the anecdotes preserved show a far-seeing skill and conduct which, in spite of adverse accidents, should secure, one year with another, an honest reward, first to the farmer, and afterwards to the dealer. If he kept sheep, it was with a royal mind; and if he traded in wool, he was a merchant prince, not in the amount of wealth, but in the protection of the interests confided to him.

I am not a little surprised at the easy effrontery with which political gentlemen, in and out of Congress, take it upon them to say that there are not a thousand men in the North who sympathize with John Brown. It would be far safer and nearer the truth to say that all people, in proportion to their sensibility and self-respect, sympathize with him. For it is impossible to see courage, and disinterestedness, and the love that casts out fear, without sympathy.

All women are drawn to him by their predominance of sentiment. All gentlemen, of course, are on his side. I do not mean by "gentlemen," people of scented hair and perfumed handkerchiefs, but men of gentle blood and generosity, "fulfilled with all nobleness," who, like the Cid, give the outcast leper a share of their bed; like the dying Sidney,[5] pass the cup of cold water to the wounded soldier who needs it more. For what is the oath of gentle blood and knighthood? What but to protect the weak and lowly against the strong oppressor?

Nothing is more absurd than to complain of this sympathy, or to complain of a party of men united in opposition to Slavery. As well complain of gravity, or the ebb of the tide. Who makes the Abolitionist? The Slaveholder.

---

information about Brown from Redpath's articles published in the *Boston Atlas and Daily Bee*. Redpath published *The Public Life of Captain John Brown* in 1860.

3. Followers of the Protestant reformer John Calvin (1509–1564).

4. Scottish novelist and poet (1771–1832); his first novel, *Waverley* (1814), had an important influence on the development of the historical novel in the United States.

5. Mortally wounded in a battle against the Spanish fought in the Netherlands, the English poet Sir Philip Sidney (1554–1586) reportedly refused a cup of water so that it could go to a needier dying soldier. El Cid Campeador (1040–1099), heroic Spanish soldier celebrated in the 12th-century epic *Poema del Cid*.

The sentiment of mercy is the natural recoil which the laws of the universe provide to protect mankind from destruction by savage passions. And our blind statesmen go up and down, with committees of vigilance and safety, hunting for the origin of this new heresy. They will need a very vigilant committee indeed to find its birthplace, and a very strong force to root it out. For the arch-Abolitionist, older than Brown, and older than the Shenandoah Mountains, is Love, whose other name is Justice, which was before Alfred, before Lycurgus,[6] before Slavery, and will be after it.

1860

Thoreau[1]

Henry David Thoreau was the last male descendant of a French ancestor who came to this country from the Isle of Guernsey.[2] His character exhibited occasional traits drawn from this blood in singular combination with a very strong Saxon genius.[3]

He was born in Concord, Massachusetts, on the 12th of July, 1817. He was graduated at Harvard College in 1837, but without any literary distinction. An iconoclast in literature, he seldom thanked colleges for their service to him, holding them in small esteem, whilst yet his debt to them was important. After leaving the University, he joined his brother in teaching a private school, which he soon renounced. His father was a manufacturer of lead-pencils, and Henry applied himself for a time to this craft, believing he could make a better pencil than was then in use. After completing his experiments, he exhibited his work to chemists and artists in Boston, and having obtained their certificates to its excellence and to its equality with the best London manufacture, he returned home contented. His friends congratulated him that he had now opened his way to fortune. But he replied, that he should never make another pencil. "Why should I? I would not do again what I have done once." He resumed his endless walks and miscellaneous studies, making every day some new acquaintance with Nature, though as yet never speaking of zoölogy or botany, since, though very studious of natural facts, he was incurious of technical and textual science.

At this time, a strong, healthy youth, fresh from college, whilst all his companions were choosing their profession, or eager to begin some lucrative employment, it was inevitable that his thoughts should be exercised on the same question, and it required rare decision to refuse all the accustomed paths, and keep his solitary freedom at the cost of disappointing the natural expectations of his family and friends: all the more difficult that he had a perfect probity, was exact in securing his own independence, and in holding every man to the like duty. But Thoreau never faltered. He was a born protestant. He declined to give up his large ambition of knowledge and action

6. Legendary founder (c. 600 B.C.E.) of the laws and institutions of ancient Sparta. Alfred the Great (849–899), king of Wessex, was celebrated for his love of law and literature.

1. Emerson delivered an address at Thoreau's funeral on May 9, 1862, and shortened it to the version used here, published in the August 1862 *Atlantic Monthly*.

2. Island in the English Channel.

3. Emerson's racial assumptions are typical of the period.

for any narrow craft or profession, aiming at a much more comprehensive calling, the art of living well. If he slighted and defied the opinions of others, it was only that he was more intent to reconcile his practice with his own belief. Never idle or self-indulgent, he preferred, when he wanted money, earning it by some piece of manual labor agreeable to him, as building a boat or a fence, planting, grafting, surveying, or other short work, to any long engagements. With his hardy habits and few wants, his skill in wood-craft, and his powerful arithmetic, he was very competent to live in any part of the world. It would cost him less time to supply his wants than another. He was therefore secure of his leisure.

A natural skill for mensuration,[4] growing out of his mathematical knowledge, and his habit of ascertaining the measures and distance of objects which interested him, the size of trees, the depth and extent of ponds and rivers, the height of mountains, and the air-line distance of his favorite summits,—this, and his intimate knowledge of the territory about Concord, made him drift into the profession of land-surveyor. It had the advantage for him that it led him continually into new and secluded grounds, and helped his studies of Nature. His accuracy and skill in this work were readily appreciated, and he found all the employment he wanted.

He could easily solve the problems of the surveyor, but he was daily beset with graver questions, which he manfully confronted. He interrogated every custom, and wished to settle all his practice on an ideal foundation. He was a protestant *à l'outrance*,[5] and few lives contain so many renunciations. He was bred to no profession; he never married; he lived alone; he never went to church; he never voted; he refused to pay a tax to the State; he ate no flesh, he drank no wine, he never knew the use of tobacco; and, though a naturalist, he used neither trap nor gun. He chose, wisely, no doubt, for himself, to be the bachelor of thought and Nature. He had no talent for wealth, and knew how to be poor without the least hint of squalor or inelegance. Perhaps he fell into his way of living without forecasting it much, but approved it with later wisdom. "I am often reminded," he wrote in his journal, "that, if I had bestowed on me the wealth of Crœsus,[6] my aims must be still the same, and my means essentially the same." He had no temptations to fight against,—no appetites, no passions, no taste for elegant trifles. A fine house, dress, the manners and talk of highly cultivated people were all thrown away on him. He much preferred a good Indian, and considered these refinements as impediments to conversation, wishing to meet his companion on the simplest terms. He declined invitations to dinner-parties, because there each was in every one's way, and he could not meet the individuals to any purpose. "They make their pride," he said, "in making their dinner cost much; I make my pride in making my dinner cost little." When asked at table what dish he preferred, he answered, "The nearest." He did not like the taste of wine, and never had a vice in his life. He said,—"I have a faint recollection of pleasure derived from smoking dried lily-stems, before I was a man. I had commonly a supply of these. I have never smoked anything more noxious."

4. Measuring.
5. I.e., an extreme Protestant (French).
6. King of Lydia (6th century B.C.E.), in Asia Minor, fabled to have been the richest man in the world.

He chose to be rich by making his wants few, and supplying them himself. In his travels, he used the railroad only to get over so much country as was unimportant to the present purpose, walking hundreds of miles, avoiding taverns, buying a lodging in farmers' and fishermen's houses, as cheaper, and more agreeable to him, and because there he could better find the men and the information he wanted.

There was somewhat military in his nature not to be subdued, always manly and able, but rarely tender, as if he did not feel himself except in opposition. He wanted a fallacy to expose, a blunder to pillory, I may say required a little sense of victory, a roll of the drum, to call his powers into full exercise. It cost him nothing to say No; indeed, he found it much easier than to say Yes. It seemed as if his first instinct on hearing a proposition was to controvert it, so impatient was he of the limitations of our daily thought. This habit, of course, is a little chilling to the social affections; and though the companion would in the end acquit him of any malice or untruth, yet it mars conversation. Hence, no equal companion stood in affectionate relations with one so pure and guileless. "I love Henry," said one of his friends, "but I cannot like him; and as for taking his arm, I should as soon think of taking the arm of an elm-tree."

Yet, hermit and stoic as he was, he was really fond of sympathy, and threw himself heartily and childlike into the company of young people whom he loved, and whom he delighted to entertain, as he only could, with the varied and endless anecdotes of his experiences by field and river. And he was always ready to lead a huckleberry-party or a search for chestnuts or grapes. Talking, one day, of a public discourse, Henry remarked, that whatever succeeded with the audience was bad. I said, "Who would not like to write something which all can read, like 'Robinson Crusoe'? and who does not see with regret that his page is not solid with a right materialistic treatment, which delights everybody?" Henry objected, of course, and vaunted the better lectures which reached only a few persons. But, at supper, a young girl, understanding that he was to lecture at the Lyceum,[7] sharply asked him, "whether his lecture would be a nice, interesting story, such as she wished to hear, or whether it was one of those old philosophical things that she did not care about." Henry turned to her, and bethought himself, and, I saw, was trying to believe that he had matter that might fit her and her brother, who were to sit up and go to the lecture, if it was a good one for them.

He was a speaker and actor of the truth,—born such,—and was ever running into dramatic situations from this cause. In any circumstance, it interested all bystanders to know what part Henry would take, and what he would say; and he did not disappoint expectation, but used an original judgment on each emergency. In 1845 he built himself a small framed house on the shores of Walden Pond, and lived there two years alone, a life of labor and study. This action was quite native and fit for him. No one who knew him would tax him with affectation. He was more unlike his neighbors in his thought than in his action. As soon as he had exhausted the advantages of that solitude, he abandoned it. In 1847, not approving some uses to which the public expenditure was applied, he refused to pay his town tax, and was put in jail. A friend[8]

7. Public hall where lectures were given.
8. The identity of this person is unknown. The year was actually 1846.

paid the tax for him, and he was released. The like annoyance was threatened the next year. But, as his friends paid the tax, notwithstanding his protest, I believe he ceased to resist. No opposition or ridicule had any weight with him. He coldly and fully stated his opinion without affecting to believe that it was the opinion of the company. It was of no consequence, if every one present held the opposite opinion. On one occasion he went to the University Library to procure some books. The librarian refused to lend them. Mr. Thoreau repaired to the President, who stated to him the rules and usages, which permitted the loan of books to resident graduates, to clergymen who were alumni, and to some others resident within a circle of ten miles' radius from the College. Mr. Thoreau explained to the President that the railroad had destroyed the old scale of distances,—that the library was useless, yes, and President and College useless, on the terms of his rules,—that the one benefit he owed to the College was its library,—that, at this moment, not only his want of books was imperative, but he wanted a large number of books, and assured him that he, Thoreau, and not the librarian, was the proper custodian of these. In short, the President found the petitioner so formidable, and the rules getting to look so ridiculous, that he ended by giving him a privilege which in his hands proved unlimited thereafter.

No truer American existed than Thoreau. His preference of his country and condition was genuine, and his aversation from English and European manners and tastes almost reached contempt. He listened impatiently to news or *bon mots*[9] gleaned from London circles; and though he tried to be civil, these anecdotes fatigued him. The men were all imitating each other, and on a small mould. Why can they not live as far apart as possible, and each be a man by himself? What he sought was the most energetic nature; and he wished to go to Oregon, not to London. "In every part of Great Britain," he wrote in his diary, "are discovered traces of the Romans, their funereal urns, their camps, their roads, their dwellings. But New England, at least, is not based on any Roman ruins. We have not to lay the foundations of our houses on the ashes of a former civilization."

But, idealist as he was, standing for abolition of slavery, abolition of tariffs, almost for abolition of government, it is needless to say he found himself not only unrepresented in actual politics, but almost equally opposed to every class of reformers. Yet he paid the tribute of his uniform respect to the Anti-Slavery party. One man, whose personal acquaintance he had formed, he honored with exceptional regard. Before the first friendly word had been spoken for Captain John Brown,[1] he sent notices to most houses in Concord, that he would speak in a public hall on the condition and charter of John Brown, on Sunday evening, and invited all people to come. The Republican Committee, the Abolitionist Committee, sent him word that it was premature and not advisable. He replied,—"I did not send to you for advice, but to announce that I am to speak." The hall was filled at an early hour by people of all parties, and his earnest eulogy of the hero was heard by all respectfully, by many with a sympathy that surprised themselves.

9. Clever remarks (French).
1. The militant American abolitionist (1800–1859) who on October 16, 1859, led twenty-one men, including five African Americans, in an attempt to seize control of the federal arsenal at Harpers Ferry in western Virginia and inspire a massive slave uprising. Brown was convicted of treason against the state of Virginia and was hanged on December 2, 1859.

It was said of Plotinus[2] that he was ashamed of his body, and 't is very likely he had good reason for it,—that his body was a bad servant, and he had not skill in dealing with the material world, as happens often to men of abstract intellect. But Mr. Thoreau was equipped with a most adapted and serviceable body. He was of short stature, firmly built, of light complexion, with strong, serious blue eyes, and a grave aspect,—his face covered in the late years with a becoming beard. His senses were acute, his frame well-knit and hardy, his hands strong and skilful in the use of tools. And there was a wonderful fitness of body and mind. He could pace sixteen rods more accurately than another man could measure them with rod and chain. He could find his path in the woods at night, he said, better by his feet than his eyes. He could estimate the measure of a tree very well by his eye; he could estimate the weight of a calf or a pig, like a dealer. From a box containing a bushel or more of loose pencils, he could take up with his hands fast enough just a dozen pencils at every grasp. He was a good swimmer, runner, skater, boatman, and would probably outwalk most countrymen in a day's journey. And the relation of body to mind was still finer than we have indicated. He said he wanted every stride his legs made. The length of his walk uniformly made the length of his writing. If shut up in the house, he did not write at all.

He had a strong common sense, like that which Rose Flammock,[3] the weaver's daughter, in Scott's romance, commends in her father, as resembling a yardstick, which, whilst it measures dowlas and diaper, can equally well measure tapestry and cloth of gold. He had always a new resource. When I was planting forest-trees, and had procured half a peck of acorns, he said that only a small portion of them would be sound, and proceeded to examine them, and select the sound ones. But finding this took time, he said, "I think, if you put them all into water, the good ones will sink"; which experiment we tried with success. He could plan a garden, or a house, or a barn; would have been competent to lead a "Pacific Exploring Expedition"; could give judicious counsel in the gravest private or public affairs.

He lived for the day, not cumbered and mortified by his memory. If he brought you yesterday a new proposition, he would bring you to-day another not less revolutionary. A very industrious man, and setting, like all highly organized men, a high value on his time, he seemed the only man of leisure in town, always ready for any excursion that promised well, or for conversation prolonged into late hours. His trenchant sense was never stopped by his rules of daily prudence, but was always up to the new occasion. He liked and used the simplest food, yet, when someone urged a vegetable diet, Thoreau thought all diets a very small matter, saying that "the man who shoots the buffalo lives better than the man who boards at the Graham House."[4] He said,—"You can sleep near the railroad, and never be disturbed: Nature knows very well what sounds are worth attending to, and has made up her mind not to hear the railroad-whistle. But things respect the devout mind, and a mental ecstasy was never interrupted." He noted, what repeatedly

2. Egyptian-born Roman philosopher (205?–270), the leading exponent of Neoplatonism, a religious system combining elements of numerous doctrines of the time.

3. Character in Sir Walter Scott's *The Betrothed* (1825).

4. Boston boardinghouse run on Sylvester Graham's dietary system (one part of which remains in the national diet as the graham cracker).

befell him, that, after receiving from a distance a rare plant, he would presently find the same in his own haunts. And those pieces of luck which happen only to good players happened to him. One day, walking with a stranger, who inquired where Indian arrow-heads could be found, he replied, "Everywhere," and, stooping forward, picked one on the instant from the ground. At Mount Washington, in Tuckerman's Ravine, Thoreau had a bad fall, and sprained his foot. As he was in the act of getting up from his fall, he saw for the first time the leaves of the *Arnica mollis.*[5]

His robust common sense, armed with stout hands, keen perceptions, and strong will, cannot yet account for the superiority which shone in his simple and hidden life. I must add the cardinal fact, that there was an excellent wisdom in him, proper to a rare class of men, which showed him the material world as a means and symbol. This discovery, which sometimes yields to poets a certain casual and interrupted light, serving for the ornament of their writing, was in him an unsleeping insight; and whatever faults or obstructions of temperament might cloud it, he was not disobedient to the heavenly vision. In his youth, he said, one day, "The other world is all my art: my pencils will draw no other; my jack-knife will cut nothing else; I do not use it as a means." This was the muse and genius that ruled his opinions, conversation, studies, work, and course of life. This made him a searching judge of men. At first glance he measured his companion, and, though insensible to some fine traits of culture, could very well report his weight and calibre. And this made the impression of genius which his conversation sometimes gave.

He understood the matter in hand at a glance, and saw the limitations and poverty of those he talked with, so that nothing seemed concealed from such terrible eyes. I have repeatedly known young men of sensibility converted in a moment to the belief that this was the man they were in search of, the man of men, who could tell them all they should do. His own dealing with them was never affectionate, but superior, didactic,—scorning their petty ways,—very slowly conceding, or not conceding at all, the promise of his society at their houses, or even at his own. "Would he not walk with them?" "He did not know. There was nothing so important to him as his walk; he had no walks to throw away on company." Visits were offered him from respectful parties, but he declined them. Admiring friends offered to carry him at their own cost to the Yellow-Stone River,—to the West Indies,—to South America. But though nothing could be more grave or considered than his refusals, they remind one in quite new relations of that fop Brummel's[6] reply to the gentleman who offered him his carriage in a shower, "But where will *you* ride, then?"—and what accusing silences, and what searching and irresistible speeches, battering down all defences, his companions can remember!

Mr. Thoreau dedicated his genius with such entire love to the fields, hills, and waters of his native town, that he made them known and interesting to all reading Americans, and to people over the sea. The river on whose banks he was born and died he knew from its springs to its confluence with the Merrimack. He had made summer and winter observations on it for many years, and at every hour of the day and the night. The result of the

5. Thistle used medicinally.
6. George "Beau" Brummell (1778–1840), British dandy.

recent survey of the Water Commissioners appointed by the State of Massachusetts he had reached by his private experiments, several years earlier. Every fact which occurs in the bed, on the banks, or in the air over it; the fishes, and their spawning and nests, their manners, their food; the shadflies which fill the air on a certain evening once a year, and which are snapped at by the fishes so ravenously that many of these die of repletion; the conical heaps of small stones on the river-shallows, one of which heaps will sometimes overfill a cart,—these heaps the huge nests of small fishes; the birds which frequent the stream, heron, duck, sheldrake, loon, osprey; the snake, muskrat, otter, woodchuck, and fox, on the banks; the turtle, frog, hyla, and cricket, which make the banks vocal,—were all known to him, and, as it were, townsmen and fellow-creatures; so that he felt an absurdity or violence in any narrative of one of these by itself apart, and still more of its dimensions on an inch-rule, or in the exhibition of its skeleton, or the specimen of a squirrel or a bird in brandy. He liked to speak of the manners of the river, as itself a lawful creature, yet with exactness, and always to an observed fact. As he knew the river, so the ponds in this region.

One of the weapons he used, more important than microscope or alcohol-receiver to other investigators, was a whim which grew on him by indulgence, yet appeared in gravest statement, namely, of extolling his own town and neighborhood as the most favored centre for natural observation. He remarked that the Flora of Massachusetts embraced almost all the important plants of America,—most of the oaks, most of the willows, the best pines, the ash, the maple, the beech, the nuts. He returned Kane's[7] "Arctic Voyage" to a friend of whom he had borrowed it, with the remark, that "most of the phenomena noted might be observed in Concord." He seemed a little envious of the Pole, for the coincident sunrise and sunset, or five minutes' day after six months: a splendid fact, which Annursnuc[8] had never afforded him. He found red snow in one of his walks, and told me that he expected to find yet the *Victoria regia*[9] in Concord. He was the attorney of the indigenous plants, and owned to a preference of the weeds to the imported plants, as of the Indian to the civilized man,—and noticed, with pleasure, that the willow bean-poles of his neighbor had grown more than his beans. "See these weeds," he said, "which have been hoed at by a million farmers all spring and summer, and yet have prevailed, and just now come out triumphant over all lanes, pastures, fields, and gardens, such is their vigor. We have insulted them with low names, too,—as Pigweed, Wormwood, Chickweed, Shad-Blossom." He says, "They have brave names, too,—Ambrosia, Stellaria, Amelanchia, Amaranth, etc."

I think his fancy for referring everything to the meridian of Concord did not grow out of any ignorance or depreciation of other longitudes or latitudes, but was rather a playful expression of his conviction of the indifferency of all places, and that the best place for each is where he stands. He expressed it once in this wise:—"I think nothing is to be hoped from you, if this bit of mould under your feet is not sweeter to you to eat than any other in this world, or in any world."

7. Elisha Kent Kane (1820–1857), American naval officer and explorer of a route to the North Pole.

8. A hill in Concord.

9. South American water lily.

The other weapon with which he conquered all obstacles in science was patience. He knew how to sit immovable, a part of the rock he rested on, until the bird, the reptile, the fish, which had retired from him, should come back, and resume its habits, nay, moved by curiosity, should come to him and watch him.

It was a pleasure and a privilege to walk with him. He knew the country like a fox or a bird, and passed through it as freely by paths of his own. He knew every track in the snow or on the ground, and what creature had taken this path before him. One must submit abjectly to such a guide, and the reward was great. Under his arm he carried an old music-book to press plants; in his pocket, his diary and pencil, a spy-glass for birds, microscope, jack-knife, and twine. He wore straw hat, stout shoes, strong gray trousers, to brave shrub-oaks and smilax, and to climb a tree for a hawk's or a squirrel's nest. He waded into the pool for the water-plants, and his strong legs were no insignificant part of his armor. On the day I speak of he looked for the Menyanthes,[1] detected it across the wide pool, and, on examination of the florets, decided that it had been in flower five days. He drew out of his breast-pocket his diary, and read the names of all the plants that should bloom on this day, whereof he kept account as a banker when his notes fall due. The Cypripedium[2] not due till to-morrow. He thought, that, if waked up from a trance, in this swamp, he could tell by the plants what time of the year it was within two days. The redstart was flying about, and presently the fine grosbeaks, whose brilliant scarlet makes the rash gazer wipe his eye,[3] and whose fine clear note Thoreau compared to that of a tanager which has got rid of its hoarseness. Presently he heard a note which he called that of the night-warbler, a bird he had never identified, had been in search of twelve years, which always, when he saw it, was in the act of diving down into a tree or bush, and which it was vain to seek; the only bird that sings indifferently by night and by day. I told him he must beware of finding and booking it, lest life should have nothing more to show him. He said, "What you seek in vain for, half your life, one day you come full upon all the family at dinner. You seek it like a dream, and as soon as you find it you become its prey."

His interest in the flower or the bird lay very deep in his mind, was connected with Nature,—and the meaning of Nature was never attempted to be defined by him. He would not offer a memoir of his observations to the Natural History Society. "Why should I? To detach the description from its connections in my mind would make it no longer true or valuable to me: and they do not wish what belongs to it." His power of observation seemed to indicate additional senses. He saw as with microscope, heard as with ear-trumpet, and his memory was a photographic register of all he saw and heard. And yet none knew better than he that it is not the fact that imports, but the impression or effect of the fact on your mind. Every fact lay in glory in his mind, a type of the order and beauty of the whole.

His determination on Natural History was organic. He confessed that he sometimes felt like a hound or a panther, and, if born among Indians, would have been a fell hunter. But, restrained by his Massachusetts culture, he played out the game in this mild form of botany and ichthyology. His

1. Flowering bean that grows in boglike areas.
2. Lady's slipper.
3. An allusion to George Herbert's "Virtue" (1633).

intimacy with animals suggested what Thomas Fuller[4] records of Butler the apiologist, that "either he had told the bees things or the bees had told him." Snakes coiled round his leg; the fishes swam into his hand, and he took them out of the water; he pulled the woodchuck out of its hole by the tail, and took the foxes under his protection from the hunters. Our naturalist had perfect magnanimity; he had no secrets: he would carry you to the heron's haunt, or even to his most prized botanical swamp,—possibly knowing that you could never find it again, yet willing to take his risks.

No college ever offered him a diploma, or a professor's chair; no academy made him its corresponding secretary, its discoverer, or even its member. Perhaps these learned bodies feared the satire of his presence. Yet so much knowledge of Nature's secret and genius few others possessed, none in a more large and religious synthesis. For not a particle of respect had he to the opinions of any man or body of men, but homage solely to the truth itself; and as he discovered everywhere among doctors some leaning of courtesy, it discredited them. He grew to be revered and admired by his townsmen, who had at first known him only as an oddity. The farmers who employed him as a surveyor soon discovered his rare accuracy and skill, his knowledge of their lands, of trees, of birds, of Indian remains, and the like, which enabled him to tell every farmer more than he knew before of his own farm; so that he began to feel a little as if Mr. Thoreau had better rights in his land than he. They felt, too, the superiority of character which addressed all men with a native authority.

Indian relics abound in Concord,—arrow-heads, stone chisels, pestles, and fragments of pottery; and on the river-bank, large heaps of clam-shells and ashes mark spots which the savages frequented. These, and every circumstance touching the Indian, were important in his eyes. His visits to Maine were chiefly for love of the Indian. He had the satisfaction of seeing the manufacture of the bark-canoe, as well as of trying his hand in its management on the rapids. He was inquisitive about the making of the stone arrow-head, and in his last days charged a youth setting out for the Rocky Mountains to find an Indian who could tell him that: "It was well worth a visit to California to learn it." Occasionally, a small party of Penobscot Indians would visit Concord, and pitch their tents for a few weeks in summer on the river-bank. He failed not to make acquaintance with the best of them; though he well knew that asking questions of Indians is like catechizing beavers and rabbits. In his last visit to Maine he had great satisfaction from Joseph Polis, an intelligent Indian of Oldtown, who was his guide for some weeks.

He was equally interested in every natural fact. The depth of his perception found likeness of law throughout Nature, and I know not any genius who so swiftly inferred universal law from the single fact. He was no pedant of a department. His eye was open to beauty, and his ear to music. He found these, not in rare conditions, but wheresoever he went. He thought the best of music was in single strains; and he found poetic suggestion in the humming of the telegraph-wire.

4. Author (1608–1661) of *The History of the Worthies of England* (1662).

His poetry might be bad or good; he no doubt wanted a lyric facility and technical skill; but he had the source of poetry in his spiritual perception. He was a good reader and critic, and his judgment on poetry was to the ground of it. He could not be deceived as to the presence or absence of the poetic element in any composition, and his thirst for this made him negligent and perhaps scornful of superficial graces. He would pass by many delicate rhythms, but he would have detected every live stanza or line in a volume, and knew very well where to find an equal poetic charm in prose. He was so enamored of the spiritual beauty that he held all actual written poems in very light esteem in the comparison. He admired Æschylus and Pindar;[5] but, when some one was commending them, he said that "Æschylus and the Greeks, in describing Apollo and Orpheus, had given no song, or no good one. They ought not to have moved trees, but to have chanted to the gods such a hymn as would have sung all their old ideas out of their heads, and new ones in." His own verses are often rude and defective. The gold does not yet run pure, is drossy and crude. The thyme and marjoram are not yet honey. But if he want lyric fineness and technical merits, if he have not the poetic temperament, he never lacks the causal thought, showing that his genius was better than his talent. He knew the worth of the Imagination for the uplifting and consolation of human life, and liked to throw every thought into a symbol. The fact you tell is of no value, but only the impression. For this reason his presence was poetic, always piqued the curiosity to know more deeply the secrets of his mind. He had many reserves, an unwillingness to exhibit to profane eyes what was still sacred in his own, and knew well how to throw a poetic veil over his experience. All readers of "Walden" will remember his mythical record of his disappointments:—

"I long ago lost a hound, a bay horse, and a turtle-dove, and am still on their trail. Many are the travellers I have spoken concerning them, describing their tracks, and what calls they answered to. I have met one or two who had heard the hound, and the tramp of the horse, and even seen the dove disappear behind a cloud; and they seemed as anxious to recover them as if they had lost them themselves."[6]

His riddles were worth the reading, and I confide, that, if at any time I do not understand the expression, it is yet just. Such was the wealth of his truth that it was not worth his while to use words in vain. His poem entitled "Sympathy" reveals the tenderness under that triple steel of stoicism, and the intellectual subtilty it could animate. His classic poem on "Smoke" suggests Simonides,[7] but is better than any poem of Simonides. His biography is in his verses. His habitual thought makes all his poetry a hymn to the Cause of causes, the Spirit which vivifies and controls his own.

> "I hearing get, who had but ears,
> And sight, who had but eyes before;
> I moments live, who lived but years;
> And truth discern, who knew but learning's lore."

5. Greek lyric poet (c. 518–c. 438 B.C.E.) celebrated for his mastery of the ode. Aeschylus (525–456 B.C.E.), Greek tragedian.

6. See *Walden*, p. 981.

7. Greek lyric poet of the 6th century B.C.E.

And still more in these religious lines:—

> "Now chiefly is my natal hour,
> And only now my prime of life;
> I will not doubt the love untold,
> Which not my worth or want hath bought,
> Which wooed me young, and wooes me old,
> And to this evening hath me brought."[8]

Whilst he used in his writings a certain petulance of remark in reference to churches or churchmen, he was a person of a rare, tender, and absolute religion, a person incapable of any profanation, by act or by thought. Of course, the same isolation which belonged to his original thinking and living detached him from the social religious forms. This is neither to be censured nor regretted. Aristotle long ago explained it, when he said, "One who surpasses his fellow-citizens in virtue is no longer a part of the city. Their law is not for him, since he is a law to himself."[9]

Thoreau was sincerity itself, and might fortify the convictions of prophets in the ethical laws by his holy living. It was an affirmative experience which refused to be set aside. A truth-speaker he, capable of the most deep and strict conversation; a physician to the wounds of any soul; a friend, knowing not only the secret of friendship, but almost worshipped by those few persons who resorted to him as their confessor and prophet, and knew the deep value of his mind and great heart. He thought that without religion or devotion of some kind nothing great was ever accomplished: and he thought that the bigoted sectarian had better bear this in mind.

His virtues, of course, sometimes ran into extremes. It was easy to trace to the inexorable demand on all for exact truth that austerity which made this willing hermit more solitary even than he wished. Himself of a perfect probity, he required not less of others. He had a disgust at crime, and no worldly success would cover it. He detected paltering as readily in dignified and prosperous persons as in beggars, and with equal scorn. Such dangerous frankness was in his dealing that his admirers called him "that terrible Thoreau," as if he spoke when silent, and was still present when he had departed. I think the severity of his ideal interfered to deprive him of a healthy sufficiency of human society.

The habit of a realist to find things the reverse of their appearance inclined him to put every statement in a paradox. A certain habit of antagonism defaced his earlier writings,—a trick of rhetoric not quite outgrown in his later, of substituting for the obvious word and thought its diametrical opposite. He praised wild mountains and winter forests for their domestic air, in snow and ice he would find sultriness, and commended the wilderness for resembling Rome and Paris. "It was so dry, that you might call it wet."

The tendency to magnify the moment, to read all the laws of Nature in the one object or one combination under your eye, is of course comic to those who do not share the philosopher's perception of identity. To him there was no such thing as size. The pond was a small ocean; the Atlantic, a large Walden Pond. He referred every minute fact to cosmical laws. Though he

8. Both quotations are from Thoreau's "Inspiration" in *A Week on the Concord and Merrimack Rivers* (1849).

9. The source of this quotation remains obscure.

meant to be just, he seemed haunted by a certain chronic assumption that the science of the day pretended completeness, and he had just found out that the *savans*[1] had neglected to discriminate a particular botanical variety, had failed to describe the seeds or count the sepals. "That is to say," we replied, "the blockheads were not born in Concord; but who said they were? It was their unspeakable misfortune to be born in London, or Paris, or Rome; but, poor fellows, they did what they could, considering that they never saw Bateman's Pond, or Nine-Acre Corner, or Becky-Stow's Swamp. Besides, what were you sent into the world for, but to add this observation?"

Had his genius been only contemplative, he had been fitted to his life, but with his energy and practical ability he seemed born for great enterprise and for command; and I so much regret the loss of his rare powers of action, that I cannot help counting it a fault in him that he had no ambition. Wanting this, instead of engineering for all America, he was the captain of a huckleberry-party. Pounding beans is good to the end of pounding empires one of these days; but if, at the end of years, it is still only beans!

But these foibles, real or apparent, were fast vanishing in the incessant growth of a spirit so robust and wise, and which effaced its defeats with new triumphs. His study of Nature was a perpetual ornament to him, and inspired his friends with curiosity to see the world through his eyes, and to hear his adventures. They possessed every kind of interest.

He had many elegances of his own, whilst he scoffed at conventional elegance. Thus, he could not bear to hear the sound of his own steps, the grit of gravel; and therefore never willingly walked in the road, but in the grass, on mountains and in woods. His senses were acute, and he remarked that by night every dwelling-house gives out bad air, like a slaughterhouse. He liked the pure fragrance of melilot.[2] He honored certain plants with special regard, and, over all, the pond-lily,—then, the gentian, and the *Mikania scandens*,[3] and "life-everlasting," and a bass-tree which he visited every year when it bloomed, in the middle of July. He thought the scent a more oracular inquisition than the sight,—more oracular and trustworthy. The scent, of course, reveals what is concealed from the other senses. By it he detected earthiness. He delighted in echoes, and said they were almost the only kind of kindred voices that he heard. He loved Nature so well, was so happy in her solitude, that he became very jealous of cities, and the sad work which their refinements and artifices made with man and his dwelling. The axe was always destroying his forest. "Thank God," he said, "they cannot cut down the clouds!" "All kinds of figures are drawn on the blue ground with this fibrous white paint."

I subjoin a few sentences taken from his unpublished manuscripts, not only as records of his thought and feeling, but for their power of description and literary excellence.

"Some circumstantial evidence is very strong, as when you find a trout in the milk."

"The chub is a soft fish, and tastes like boiled brown paper salted."

1. Learned ones (French).
2. Sweet clover.
3. Climbing hempweed.

"The youth gets together his materials to build a bridge to the moon, or, perchance, a palace or temple on the earth, and at length the middle-aged man concludes to build a wood-shed with them."

"The locust z-ing."

"Devil's-needles zigzagging along the Nut-Meadow brook."

"Sugar is not so sweet to the palate as sound to the healthy ear."

"I put on some hemlock-boughs, and the rich salt crackling of their leaves was like mustard to the ear, the crackling of uncountable regiments. Dead trees love the fire."

"The bluebird carries the sky on his back."

"The tanager flies through the green foliage as if it would ignite the leaves."

"If I wish for a horse-hair for my compass-sight, I must go to the stable; but the hair-bird, with her sharp eyes, goes to the road."

"Immortal water, alive even to the superficies."

"Fire is the most tolerable third party."

"Nature made ferns for pure leaves, to show what she could do in that line."

"No tree has so fair a bole and so handsome an instep as the beech."

"How did these beautiful rainbow-tints get into the shell of the fresh-water clam, buried in the mud at the bottom of our dark river?"

"Hard are the times when the infant's shoes are second-foot."

"We are strictly confined to our men to whom we give liberty."

"Nothing is so much to be feared as fear. Atheism may comparatively be popular with God himself."

"Of what significance the things you can forget? A little thought is sexton[4] to all the world."

"How can we expect a harvest of thought who have not had a seed-time of character?"

"Only he can be trusted with gifts who can present a face of bronze to expectations."

"I ask to be melted. You can only ask of the metals that they be tender to the fire that melts them. To nought else can they be tender."

There is a flower known to botanists, one of the same genus with our summer plant called "Life-Everlasting," a *Gnaphalium* like that, which grows on the most inaccessible cliffs of the Tyrolese mountains, where the chamois dare hardly venture, and which the hunter, tempted by its beauty, and by his love, (for it is immensely valued by the Swiss maidens), climbs the cliffs to gather, and is sometimes found dead at the foot, with the flower in his hand. It is called by botanists the *Gnaphalium leontopodium*, but by the Swiss *Edelweisse*, which signifies *Noble Purity.* Thoreau seemed to me living in the hope to gather this plant, which belonged to him of right. The scale on which his studies proceeded was so large as to require longevity, and we were the less prepared for his sudden disappearance. The country knows not yet, or in the least part, how great a son it has lost. It seems an injury that he should leave in the midst his broken task, which none else can finish,—a kind of indignity to so noble a soul, that it should depart out of Nature before yet he has been really shown to his peers for what he is. But he, at least, is content. His soul was made for the noblest society; he had in a short life exhausted

4. Officer or employee responsible for overseeing the workings of a church, including bell ringing.

the capabilities of this world; wherever there is knowledge, wherever there is virtue, wherever there is beauty, he will find a home.

1862

Each and All[1]

Little thinks, in the field, you red-cloaked clown[2]
Of thee from the hill-top looking down;
The heifer that lows in the upland farm,
Far-heard, lows not thine ear to charm;
The sexton, tolling his bell at noon
Deems not that great Napoleon
Stops his horse, and lists with delight,
Whilst his files sweep round yon Alpine height;
Nor knowest thou what argument
Thy life to thy neighbor's creed has lent.
All are needed by each one;
Nothing is fair or good alone.
I thought the sparrow's note from heaven,
Singing at dawn on the alder bough;
I brought him home, in his nest at even;[3]
He sings the song, but it cheers not now,
For I did not bring home the river and sky;—
He sang to my ear,—they sang to my eye,
The delicate shells lay on the shore;
The bubbles of the latest wave
Fresh pearls to their enamel gave;
And the bellowing of the savage sea
Greeted their safe escape to me.
I wiped away the weeds and foam,
I fetched my sea-born treasures home;
But the poor, unsightly, noisome[4] things
Had left their beauty on the shore;
With the sun, and the sand, and the wild uproar.
The lover watched his graceful maid,
As 'mid the virgin train she strayed,
Nor knew her beauty's best attire
Was woven still by the snow-white choir.
At last she came to his hermitage,
Like the bird from the woodlands to the cage;—
The gay enchantment was undone,
A gentle wife, but fairy none.
Then I said, 'I covet truth;
Beauty is unripe childhood's cheat;
I leave it behind with the games of youth.'—

1. First published in *Western Messenger* (February 1839) as "Each in All." The text is from Emerson's *Poems* (1847).

2. Rustic.
3. Evening.
4. Having an offensive smell.

As I spoke, beneath my feet
The ground-pine curled its pretty wreath,
Running over the club-moss burrs;
I inhaled the violet's breath;
Around me stood the oaks and firs;
Pine-cones and acorns lay on the ground;
Over me soared the eternal sky,
Full of light and of deity;
Again I saw, again I heard,
The rolling river, the morning bird;—
Beauty through my senses stole;
I yielded myself to the perfect whole.

1839, 1847

The Snow-Storm[1]

Announced by all the trumpets of the sky,
Arrives the snow, and, driving o'er the fields,
Seems nowhere to alight: the whited air
Hides hills and woods, the river, and the heaven,
And veils the farm-house at the garden's end.
The sled and traveller stopped, the courier's feet
Delayed, all friends shut out, the housemates sit
Around the radiant fireplace, enclosed
In a tumultuous privacy of storm.
  Come see the north-wind's masonry.
Out of an unseen quarry evermore
Furnished with tile, the fierce artificer
Curves his white bastions with projected roof
Round every windward stake, or tree, or door.
Speeding, the myriad-handed, his wild work
So fanciful, so savage, naught cares he
For number or proportion. Mockingly,
On coop or kennel he hangs Parian[2] wreaths;
A swan-like form invests the hidden thorn;
Fills up the farmer's lane from wall to wall,
Maugre[3] the farmer's sighs; and, at the gate,
A tapering turret overtops the work.
And when his hours are numbered, and the world
Is all his own, retiring, as he were not,
Leaves, when the sun appears, astonished Art
To mimic in slow structures, stone by stone,
Built in an age, the mad wind's night-work,
The frolic architecture of the snow.

1841, 1847

1. First published in *The Dial* (January 1841); the text is from *Poems* (1847).
2. A white marble from the Aegean island of Paros.
3. Notwithstanding, in spite of (archaic).

Bacchus[1]

Bring me wine, but wine which never grew
In the belly of the grape,
Or grew on vine whose tap-roots, reaching through
Under the Andes to the Cape,[2]
Suffered no savor of the earth to scape.

Let its grapes the morn salute
From a nocturnal root,
Which feels the acrid juice
Of Styx and Erebus;[3]
And turns the woe of Night,
By its own craft, to a more rich delight.

We buy ashes for bread;
We buy diluted wine;
Give me of the true,—
Whose ample leaves and tendrils curled
Among the silver hills of heaven,
Draw everlasting dew;
Wine of wine,
Blood of the world,
Form of forms, and mould of statures,
That I intoxicated,
And by the draught assimilated,
May float at pleasure through all natures;
The bird-language rightly spell,
And that which roses say so well.

Wine that is shed
Like the torrents of the sun
Up the horizon walls,
Or like the Atlantic streams, which run
When the South Sea calls.

Water and bread,
Food which needs no transmuting,
Rainbow-flowering, wisdom-fruiting,
Wine which is already man,
Food which teach and reason can.

Wine which Music is,—
Music and wine are one,—
That I, drinking this,
Shall hear far Chaos talk with me;

1. The text is from *Poems* (1847). "Bacchus": Greek god of wine, also called Dionysus.
2. Cape Horn, at the southern tip of South America.
3. In Greek myth, Styx is the river across which the souls of the dead were ferried, and Erebus is a region of darkness below the earth.

Kings unborn shall walk with me;
And the poor grass shall plot and plan
What it will do when it is man.
Quickened so, will I unlock
Every crypt of every rock.

I thank the joyful juice
For all I know;—
Winds of remembering
Of the ancient being blow,
And seeming-solid walls of use
Open and flow.

Pour, Bacchus! the remembering wine;
Retrieve the loss of me and mine!
Vine for vine be antidote,
And the grape requite the lote!
Haste to cure the old despair,—
Reason in Nature's lotus[4] drenched,
The memory of ages quenched;
Give them again to shine;
Let wine repair what this undid;
And where the infection slid,
A dazzling memory revive;
Refresh the faded tints,
Recut the aged prints,
And write my old adventures with the pen
Which on the first day drew,
Upon the tablets blue
The dancing Pleiads[5] and eternal men.

1847

Merlin[1]

I

Thy trivial harp will never please
Or fill my craving ear;
Its chords should ring as blows the breeze,
Free, peremptory, clear.
No jingling serenader's art,
Nor tinkle of piano strings,
Can make the wild blood start
In its mystic springs.

4. Plant of Greek legend whose fruit, or wine made from the fruit, produced a dreamy forgetfulness in those who consumed it.
5. A constellation that, according to Greek myth, consists of the seven daughters of Atlas, the rebellious Titan who was condemned by Zeus to support the sky on his shoulders.
1. The text is from *Poems* (1847). "Merlin": prophet and magician who has a central role in the legends associated with the 6th-century King Arthur and his court.

The kingly bard
Must smite the chords rudely and hard,
As with hammer or with mace;

That they may render back
Artful thunder, which conveys
Secrets of the solar track,
Sparks of the supersolar blaze.
Merlin's blows are strokes of fate,
Chiming with the forest tone
When boughs buffet boughs in the wood;
Chiming with the gasp and moan
Of the ice-imprisoned flood;
With the pulse of manly hearts;
With the voice of orators;
With the din of city arts;
With the cannonade of wars;
With the marches of the brave;
And prayers of might from martyrs' cave.

Great is the art,
Great be the manners, of the bard.
He shall not his brain encumber
With the coil of rhythm and number;
But, leaving rule and pale forethought,
He shall aye[2] climb
For his rhyme.
'Pass in, pass in,' the angels say,
'In to the upper doors,
Nor count compartments of the floors,
But mount to paradise
By the stairway of surprise.'

Blameless master of the games,
King of sport that never shames,
He shall daily joy dispense
Hid in song's sweet influence.
Things more cheerly live and go,
What time the subtle mind
Sings aloud the tune whereto
Their pulses beat,
And march their feet,
And their members are combined.

By Sybarites[3] beguiled,
He shall no task decline:
Merlin's mighty line
Extremes of nature reconciled,—
Bereaved a tyrant of his will,

2. Always.
3. Those devoted to pleasure, like the inhabitants of the ancient Greek city Sybaris.

And made the lion mild.[4]
Songs can the tempest still,
Scattered on the stormy air,
Mould the year to fair increase,[5]
And bring in poetic peace.

He shall not seek to weave,
In weak, unhappy times,
Efficacious rhymes;
Wait his returning strength.
Bird, that from the nadir's floor
To the zenith's top can soar,
The soaring orbit of the muse exceeds that journey's
length.
Nor profane affect to hit
Or compass[6] that, by meddling wit,
Which only the propitious mind
Publishes when 't is inclined.
There are open hours
When the God's will sallies free,
And the dull idiot might see
The flowing fortunes of a thousand years;—
Sudden, at unawares,
Self-moved, fly-to the doors,
Nor sword of angels could reveal
What they conceal.

II

The rhyme of the poet
Modulates the king's affairs;
Balance-loving Nature
Made all things in pairs.
To every foot its antipode;[7]
Each color with its counter glowed;
To every tone beat answering tones,
Higher or graver;
Flavor gladly blends with flavor;
Leaf answers leaf upon the bough;[8]
And match the paired cotyledons.
Hands to hands, and feet to feet,
In one body grooms and brides;
Eldest rite, two married sides
In every mortal meet.
Light's far furnace shines,
Smelting balls and bars,
Forging double stars,

4. Allusion to Isaiah 11, which foresees the Messiah bringing about peace between the wolf and the lamb.
5. Productivity.
6. Achieve.
7. Opposing foot.
8. Pair of leaves developed by the embryo of a seed plant.

Glittering twins and trines.[9]
The animals are sick with love,
Lovesick with rhyme;
Each with all propitious time
Into chorus wove.

Like the dancers' ordered band,
Thoughts come also hand in hand;
In equal couples mated,
Or else alternated;
Adding by their mutual gage,
One to other, health and age.
Solitary fancies go
Short-lived wandering to and fro,
Most like to bachelors,
Or an ungiven maid,
Not ancestors,
With no posterity to make the lie afraid,
Or keep truth undecayed.
Perfect-paired as eagle's wings,
Justice is the rhyme of things;
Trade and counting use
The self-same tuneful muse;
And Nemesis,[1]
Who with even matches odd,
Who athwart space redresses
The partial wrong,
Fills the just period,
And finishes the song.
Subtle rhymes, with ruin rife,
Murmur in the house of life,
Sung by the Sisters[2] as they spin;
In perfect time and measure they
Build and unbuild our echoing clay,
As the two twilights[3] of the day
Fold us music-drunken in.

1847

Brahma[1]

If the red slayer think he slays,
  Or if the slain think he is slain,
They know not well the subtle ways
  I keep, and pass, and turn again.

9. Sets of three.
1. Greek goddess of retribution and justice.
2. Greek goddesses; the three Fates, who determine fate through their sewing.
3. Dawn and dusk.
1. The text is from the November 1857 *Atlantic Monthly*. "Brahma": the creator god of sacred Hindu texts.

Far or forgot to me is near;
  Shadow and sunlight are the same;
The vanished gods to me appear;
  And one to me are shame and fame.

They reckon ill who leave me out;
  When me they fly, I am the wings;
I am the doubter and the doubt,
  And I the hymn the Brahmin[2] sings.

The strong gods pine for my abode,
  And pine in vain the sacred Seven;[3]
But thou, meek lover of the good!
  Find me, and turn thy back on heaven.

1857

Letter to Walt Whitman[1]

Concord Masstts 21 July 1855

Dear Sir,

I am not blind to the worth of the wonderful gift of "Leaves of Grass." I find it the most extraordinary piece of wit & wisdom that America has yet contributed. I am very happy in reading it, as great power makes us happy. It meets the demand I am always making of what seemed the sterile & stingy Nature, as if too much handiwork or too much lymph in the temperament were making our western wits fat & mean. I give you joy of your free & brave thought. I have great joy in it. I find incomparable things said incomparably well, as they must be. I find the courage of *treatment*, which so delights us, & which large perception only can inspire.

I greet you at the beginning of a great career, which yet must have had a long foreground somewhere, for such a start. I rubbed my eyes a little to see if this sunbeam were no illusion; but the solid sense of the book is a sober certainty. It has the best merits, namely, of fortifying & encouraging.

I did not know until I, last night, saw the book advertised in a newspaper, that I could trust the name as real & available for a Post-Office. I wish to see my benefactor, & have felt much like striking my tasks, & visiting New York to pay you my respects.

R. W. Emerson.

2. Members of the highest Hindu caste; originally the priests responsible for officiating at religious rites.

3. Seers or saints of ancient Hindu poetry.

1. The text is from *The Letters of Ralph Waldo Emerson* (1939), ed. Eleanor M. Tilton. Emerson wrote this admiring letter to Whitman after reading the first edition of *Leaves of Grass* (1855), which Whitman had sent him. Whitman may not have received the letter in New York until sometime in September of 1855, and he subsequently distressed Emerson by using the letter without his permission to promote the book, publishing it in the New York *Tribune* of October 10, 1855, and as an appendix to the 1856 edition of *Leaves of Grass*.

Native Americans: Removal and Resistance

Just as the great majority of Native American peoples had fought on the side of the British during the Revolutionary War, so too did many Native peoples take the British side in the War of 1812. The reason, at base, was straightforward: Native Americans risked losing much more of their land and their autonomy at the hands of the colonials (1776), later the Americans (1812), than they did at the hands of the British. When the treaty of Ghent ending the war with Britain was signed in 1814, the United States could at last feel no longer threatened by any European nation; but the American threat to Native nations was substantially increased.

If President James Monroe invited Indian people to the White House in 1822, things were to be different under his successor, Andrew Jackson. Jackson, who had fought against the Seminoles and Creeks in Florida, was elected president in 1828. "Indian removal"—the relocation of the southeastern tribes to lands west of the Mississippi—was an important part of his agenda. The Cherokees of Georgia were a major target for removal. By the time of Jackson's election, the Cherokees had a written language, a constitution modeled after that of the United States, and the first newspaper, the Cherokee *Phoenix*, to publish both in an indigenous language and in English. Although the Cherokees, in "memorials" to Congress and in editorials and articles in their newspaper, spoke out strongly against Jackson's removal policy, Congress nonetheless passed the Indian Removal Act in 1830, granting the president the authority to enter into treaties with the eastern tribes for their removal west of the Mississippi River. Finally, in 1838—in spite of frantic protest by many, including Ralph Waldo Emerson—the Cherokees were indeed forcibly removed by federal troops under General Winfield Scott. They were sent on what would be called the Trail of Tears to "Indian Country," present-day Oklahoma, a march in winter during which some four thousand people died, out of a population of about thirteen thousand.

Between the passage of the Removal Act and the Trail of Tears came the removal under different auspices of Black Hawk's Sauk people, the consequence of the so-called Black Hawk War of 1832, the last Indian war fought (for the most part) east of the Mississippi. Black Hawk's account of some of these matters, documenting removal and resistance, is included here.

BLACK HAWK

A member of the Sauk nation, Black Hawk (1767?–1838) was born at Saukenuk on the Rock River in western Illinois. The town was destroyed by American militiamen during the Revolutionary War, and this act may well have initiated Black Hawk's lifelong distrust of and distaste for the Americans. In 1804, when the United States took control of the Louisiana Purchase from France, the Sauk chief Quashquame and some few others were persuaded to sign a treaty at St. Louis ceding

Sauk lands east of the Mississippi to the federal government. The signers of the treaty believed that they would be permitted to remain on their lands forever in spite of the sale. They did not understand that the document they had signed permitted them to remain only until the government sold or otherwise disposed of those lands. In 1816 Black Hawk and other Sauk chiefs signed another treaty, this one confirming the provisions of the 1804 treaty, but again, as Black Hawk insists, they had no clear idea of what was involved.

By the 1820s, settlers had begun to press into Sauk territory on the Rock River, and by 1829, submitting to the pressures put on them by the advancing Americans, many Sauk agreed to remove west of the Mississippi. The few who remained were forced west by U.S. troops under the command of General Edmund Gaines. Nonetheless, in 1832 Black Hawk led a party back to the Rock River, surely knowing that American opposition would ensue, yet determined to reestablish his people on their traditional homelands. His hopes in this endeavor were strengthened by a half-Sauk, half-Winnebago man named Wabokieshiek or White Cloud, known as the Winnebago Prophet, who had told Black Hawk that the return would be supported by Pottawatomi allies as well as by some English from Canada. This was not at all the case.

Governor John Reynolds of Illinois proclaimed Black Hawk's return "an invasion of the state" and called up five brigades of volunteers (the young Abraham Lincoln was among them) to join General Gaines, who had orders to force Black Hawk and his people back across the Mississippi. The federal and Illinois troops pursued Black Hawk and his people from the end of June until August 1832. They caught up with them as they were attempting a retreat to the western shore of the Mississippi. The Steamboat *Warrior*, chartered by the U.S. Army, fired on Black Hawk's party as they attempted to cross the river, continuing to fire even as Black Hawk himself waved a white flag of surrender. Finally, on August 2, at Bad Axe, a junction of the Mississippi and the Bad Axe River in what is today Wisconsin, the remaining Sauk were attacked in a battle that turned into a massacre, with some three hundred of Black Hawk's band—many of them women and children—killed, and hundreds taken prisoner. Eight American soldiers died.

Black Hawk was imprisoned and taken east, where he twice met President Jackson. Returned, finally, to his people, he participated in the production of the *Life of Ma-ka-tai-me-she-kia-kiak, or Black Hawk . . . with an account of the cause and general history of the late war . . . dictated by himself*, a narrative of his life published in Cincinnati in 1833. It is not clear whether Black Hawk himself initiated the project—if he did, it was probably at the urging of many who had spoken with him in the East—or whether the initiator was John Barton Patterson, a young and ambitious local newspaper editor. Also involved in the making of Black Hawk's autobiography was Antoine LeClaire, part Pottawatomi, part French, who served as Black Hawk's interpreter. Upon the autobiography's publication, there was a predictable questioning of its authenticity. Roger Nichols's work convincingly makes the case that Black Hawk did indeed narrate the greater part of what we have, even managing, despite the cumbersome division of labor, to produce what Neil Schmitz has called "a Sauk history advocating a Sauk politics."

The selection printed here, from the 1833 text, published in Donald Jackson's edition, *Black Hawk: An Autobiography* (1964), presents Black Hawk's strong sense of himself, his ties to his people, and his broad critique of the Americans.

From Life of Ma-ka-tai-me-she-kia-kiak, or Black Hawk

* * *

The great chief[1] at St. Louis having sent word for us to go down and confirm the treaty of peace, we did not hesitate, but started immediately, that we might smoke the *peace-pipe* with him. On our arrival, we met the great chiefs in council. They explained to us the words of our Great Father at Washington, accusing us of heinous crimes and divers misdemeanors, particularly in not coming down when first invited. We knew very well that our *Great Father had deceived us*, and thereby *forced* us to join the British, and could not believe that he had put this speech into the mouths of these chiefs to deliver to us. I was not a civil chief, and consequently made no reply: but our chiefs told the commissioners that "what they had said was a *lie*!—that our Great Father had sent no such speech, he knowing the situation in which we had been placed had been *caused by him*!" The white chiefs appeared very angry at this reply, and said they "would break off the treaty with us, and *go to war*, as they would not be insulted."

Our chiefs had no intention of insulting them, and told them so—"that they merely wished to explain to them that *they had told a lie*, without making them angry; in the same manner that the whites do, when they do not believe what is told them!" The council then proceeded, and the pipe of peace was smoked.

Here, for the first time, I touched the goose quill to the treaty—not knowing, however, that, by that act, I consented to give away my village. Had that been explained to me, I should have opposed it, and never would have signed their treaty, as my recent conduct will clearly prove.[2]

What do we know of the manner of the laws and customs of the white people? They might buy our bodies for dissection, and we would touch the goose quill to confirm it, without knowing what we are doing. This was the case with myself and people in touching the goose quill the first time.

* * *

I returned to my hunting ground, after an absence of one moon. * * * In a short time we came up to our village, and found that the whites had not left it—but that others had come, and that the greater part of our corn-fields had been enclosed. When we landed, the whites appeared displeased because we had come back. We repaired the lodges that had been left standing, and built others. Ke-o-kuck came to the village; but his object was to persuade others to follow him to the Ioway. He had accomplished nothing towards making arrangements for us to remain, or to exchange other lands for our village. There was no more friendship existing between us. I looked upon him as a coward, and no brave, to abandon his village to be occupied by strangers. What *right* had these people to our village, and our fields, which the Great Spirit had given us to live upon?

1. William Clark [Jackson's note].
2. This was the treaty of May 13, 1816, in which the Sauk of the Rock River unconditionally assented to and confirmed the treaty of 1804—as the Missouri Sauk and the Fox had done the year before. And once more there was misunderstanding, as shown by Black Hawk's account [Jackson's note].

My reason teaches me that *land cannot be sold*. The Great Spirit gave it to his children to live upon, and cultivate, as far as is necessary for their subsistence; and so long as they occupy and cultivate it, they have the right to the soil—but if they voluntarily leave it, then any other people have a right to settle upon it. Nothing can be sold, but such things as can be carried away.

In consequence of the improvements of the intruders on our fields, we found considerable difficulty to get ground to plant a little corn. Some of the whites permitted us to plant small patches in the fields they had fenced, keeping all the best ground for themselves. Our women had great difficulty in climbing their fences, (being unaccustomed to the kind,) and were ill-treated if they left a rail down.

One of my old friends thought he was safe. His corn-field was on a small island of Rock river. He planted his corn; it came up well—but the white man saw it!—he wanted the island, and took his team over, ploughed up the corn, and re-planted it for himself! The old man shed tears; not for himself, but the distress his family would be in if they raised no corn.

The white people brought whisky into our village, made our people drunk, and cheated them out of their horses, guns, and traps! This fraudulent system was carried to such an extent that I apprehended serious difficulties might take place, unless a stop was put to it. Consequently, I visited all the whites and begged them not to sell whisky to my people. One of them continued the practice openly. I took a party of my young men, went to his house, and took out his barrel and broke in the head and turned out the whisky. I did this for fear some of the whites might be killed by my people when drunk.

Our people were treated badly by the whites on many occasions. At one time, a white man beat one of our women cruelly, for pulling a few suckers of corn out of his field, to suck, when hungry! At another time, one of our young men was beat with clubs by two white men for opening a fence which crossed our road, to take his horse through. His shoulder blade was broken, and his body badly bruised, from which he soon after *died!*

Bad, and cruel, as our people were treated by the whites, not one of them was hurt or molested by any of my band. I hope this will prove that we are a peaceable people—having permitted ten men to take possession of our corn-fields; prevent us from planting corn; burn and destroy our lodges; ill-treat our women; and *beat to death* our men, without offering resistance to their barbarous cruelties. This is a lesson worthy for the white man to learn: to use forbearance when injured.

We acquainted our agent daily with our situation, and through him, the great chief at St. Louis—and hoped that something would be done for us. The whites were *complaining* at the same time that *we* were *intruding* upon *their rights!* THEY made themselves out the *injured* party, and *we* the *intruders!* and called loudly to the great war chief to protect *their* property!

How smooth must be the language of the whites, when they can make right look like wrong, and wrong like right.

During this summer, I happened at Rock Island, when a great chief arrived, (whom I had known as the great chief of Illinois, [governor Cole,] in company with another chief, who, I have been told, is a great writer, [judge Jas. Hall.] I called upon them and begged to explain to them the grievances under which me and my people were laboring, hoping that they could do something for us. The great chief, however, did not seem disposed to council with me. He said he was no longer the great chief of Illinois—that his children had selected another father in his stead, and that he now only ranked as they did. I was surprised at this talk, as I had always heard that he was a good, brave, and great chief. But the white people never appear to be satisfied. When they get a good father, they hold councils, (at the suggestion of some bad, ambitious man, who wants the place himself,) and conclude, among themselves, that this man, or some other equally ambitious, would make a better father than they have, and nine times out of ten they don't get as good a one again.

I insisted on explaining to these two chiefs the true situation of my people. They gave their assent: I rose and made a speech, in which I explained to them the treaty made by Quàsh-quà-me, and three of our braves, according to the manner the trader and others had explained it to me. I then told them that Quàsh-quà-me and his party *denied,* positively, having ever sold my village; and that, as I had never known them to *lie,* I was determined to keep it in possession.

I told them that the white people had already entered our village, *burnt our lodges, destroyed our fences, ploughed up our corn, and beat our people:* that they had brought *whisky* into our country, *made our people drunk,* and taken from them their *horses, guns,* and *traps;* and that I had borne all this injury, without suffering any of my braves to raise a hand against the whites.

My object in holding this council, was to get the opinion of these two chiefs, as to the best course for me to pursue. I had appealed in vain, time after time, to our agent, who regularly represented our situation to the great chief at St. Louis, whose duty it was to call upon our Great Father to have justice done to us; but instead of this, we are told *that the white people want our country, and we must leave it to them!*

I did not think it possible that our Great Father wished us to leave our village, where we had lived so long, and where the bones of so many of our people had been laid. The great chief said that, as he was no longer a chief, he could do nothing for us; and felt sorry that it was not in his power to aid us—nor did he know how to advise us. Neither of them could do any thing for us; but both evidently appeared very sorry. It would give me great pleasure, at all times, to take these two chiefs by the hand.

That fall I paid a visit to the agent, before we started to our hunting grounds, to hear if he had any good news for me. He had news! He said that the land on which our village stood was now ordered to be sold to individuals; and that, when sold, *our right* to remain, by treaty, would be at an end, and that if we returned next spring, we would be *forced* to remove!

1833

PETALESHARO

Petalesharo (1797?–1874)—the name means "generous chief" or "man chief"—was a Skidi (also called Loup) Pawnee, one of four bands of the Pawnee nation, which occupied lands in the old Missouri Territory. From October 1821 until March 1822, he was one of several Native people brought to Washington for an extended visit. During that time, the *National Daily Intelligencer* published an article called "Anecdote of a Pawnee Chief," which told of Petalesharo's successful efforts, in 1817 and 1820, to prevent young women captured from other tribes from being sacrificed in the Morning Star Ceremony. (The Skidi Pawnees were one of the very few tribes north of what is now the Mexican border to practice human sacrifice.) This account made him a most sought-after person. Petalesharo was one of the first Native people to be painted by Charles Bird King for the McKenney-Hall Indian Gallery (the paintings were reproduced in the gallery's *History of the Indian Tribes of North America* published in 1838–44); he was also painted by Samuel F.B. Morse, better known for his invention of Morse Code.

The speeches printed here were delivered on February 4, 1822, at a conference attended by President James Monroe. They were first published by James Buchanan, British consul for the state of New York, in his *Sketches of the North American Indians* (1824). The first, which is identified as having been delivered by "The Pawnee Chief," is the speech usually referred to as "Petalesharo's Speech." But it is followed in Buchanan by a speech assigned to a "Pawnee Loup Chief," a more likely designation for Petalesharo. Although the date and the occasion for both of these are certain, it is not clear who translated and transcribed the speeches—and, it should be stressed, we do not know whether "Petalesharo's speech" was in fact delivered by him or by an unnamed "Pawnee Chief." The speaker, whoever he may be, like Red Jacket (and others) before him, offers a "separatist" view of religion and culture, asserting that while the Great Father of the whites may be fine for them, "there is still *another* Great Father . . . *the Father of us all*," and it is to him that Native peoples continue to adhere. The second speech combines what is probably intended simply as good advice for the whites with a warrior's brief statement of his prowess.

The text is from Buchanan's *Sketches of the North American Indians* (1824).

Speech of the Pawnee Chief

My Great Father:—I have travelled a great distance to see you—I have seen you and my heart rejoices. I have heard your words—they have entered one ear and shall not escape the other, and I will carry them to my people as pure as they came from your mouth.

My Great Father:—I am going to speak the truth. The Great Spirit looks down upon us, and I call *Him* to witness all that may pass between us on this occasion. If I am here now and have seen your people, your houses, your vessels on the big lake, and a great many wonderful things far beyond my comprehension, which appear to have been made by the Great Spirit and placed in your hands, I am indebted to my Father here, who invited me from home, under whose wings I have been protected.[1] Yes, my Great Father, I have travelled with your chief; I have followed him, and trod in his tracks; but there is still *another* Great Father *to whom I am much indebted—it is the Father of us all.* Him who made us and placed us on this earth. I feel grateful to the Great Spirit for strengthening my heart for such an undertaking, and for preserving the life which he gave me. The Great Spirit made us all—he made my skin red, and yours white; he placed us on this earth, and intended that we should live differently from each other.

He made the whites to cultivate the earth, and feed on domestic animals; but he made us, red skins, to rove through the uncultivated woods and plains; to feed on wild animals; and to dress with their skins. He also intended that we should go to war—to take scalps—*steal horses from* and triumph over our enemies—cultivate peace at home, and promote the happiness of each other. I believe there are no people of any colour on this earth who do not believe in the Great Spirit—in rewards, and in punishments. We worship him, but we worship him not as you do. We differ from you in appearance and manners as well as in our customs; and we differ from you in our religion; we have no large houses as you have to worship the Great Spirit in; if we had them to-day, we should want others to-morrow, for we have not, like you, a fixed habitation—we have no settled home except our villages, where we remain but two moons in twelve. We, like animals, rove through the country, whilst you whites reside between us and heaven but still, my Great Father, we love the Great Spirit—we acknowledge his supreme power—our peace, our health, and our happiness depend upon him, and our lives belong to him—he made us and he can destroy us.

My Great Father:—Some of your good chiefs, as they are called (missionaries,) have proposed to send some of their good people among us to change our habits, to make us work and live like the white people. I will not tell a lie—I am going to tell the truth. You love your country—you love your people—you love the manner in which they live, and you think your people brave.—I am like you, my Great Father, I love my country—I love my people—I love the manner in which we live, and think myself and warriors brave. Spare me then, my Father; let me enjoy my country, and pursue the buffalo, and the beaver, and the other wild animals of our country, and I will trade their skins with your people. I have grown up, and lived thus long without work—I am in hopes you will suffer me to die without it. We have plenty of buffalo, beaver, deer and other wild animals—we have also an abundance of horses—we have every thing we want—we have plenty of land, if you will keep your people off of it. My father has a piece on which he lives (Council Bluffs) and we wish him to enjoy it—we have enough without it—but we wish him to live near us to give us good counsel—to keep our ears and eyes open that we may continue to pursue the right road—the road to happiness. He settles all differences between us and the whites, between the red skins themselves—he makes the whites do justice to the red skins, and he makes the red skins do justice to the whites. He saves the effusion of human blood, and restores peace and happiness on the land. You have already sent us a father; it is enough he knows us and we know him—we have confidence in

1. Pointing to Major O'Fallon [Buchanan's note].

him—we keep our eye constantly upon him, and since we have heard your words, we will listen more attentively to *his*.

It is too soon, my Great Father, to send those good men among us. *We are not starving yet*—we wish you to permit us to enjoy the chase until the game of our country is exhausted—until the wild animals become extinct. Let us exhaust our present resources before you make us toil and interrupt our happiness—let me continue to live as I have done, and after I have passed to the Good or Evil Spirit from off the wilderness of my present life, the subsistence of my children may become so precarious as to need and embrace the assistance of those good people.

There was a time when we did not know the whites—our wants were then fewer than they are now. They were always within our controul—we had then seen nothing which we could not get. Before our intercourse with the *whites* (who have caused such a destruction in our game,) we could lie down to sleep, and when we awoke we would find the buffalo feeding around our camp—but now we are killing them for their skins, and feeding the wolves with their flesh, to make our children cry over their bones.

Here, My Great Father, is a pipe which I present you, as I am accustomed to present pipes to all the red skins in peace with us. It is filled with such tobacco as we were accustomed to smoke before we knew the white people. It is pleasant, and the spontaneous growth of the most remote parts of our country. I know that the robes, leggins, mockasins, bear-claws, &c., are of little value to you, but we wish you to have them deposited and preserved in some conspicuous part of your lodge, so that when we are gone and the sod turned over our bones, if our children should visit this place, as we do now, they may see and recognize with pleasure the deposites of their fathers; and reflect on the times that are past.

Speech of the Pawnee Loup Chief

My Great Father:—Whenever I see a white man amongst us without a protector, I tremble for him. I am aware of the ungovernable disposition of some of our young men, and when I see an inexperienced white man, I am always afraid they will make me cry. I now begin to love your people, and, as I love my own people too, I am unwilling that any blood should be spilt between us. You are unacquainted with our fashions, and we are unacquainted with yours; and when any of your people come among us, I am always afraid that they will be struck on the head like dogs, as we should be here amongst you, but for our father in whose tracks we tread. When your people come among us, they should come as we come among you, with some one to protect them, whom we know and who knows us. Until this chief came amongst us, three winters since, we roved through the plains only thirsting for each other's blood—we were blind—we could not see the right road, and we hunted to destroy each other. We were always feeling for obstacles, and every thing we felt we thought one. Our warriors were always going to and coming from war. I myself have killed and scalped in every direction. I have often triumphed over my enemies.

ELIAS BOUDINOT

Elias Boudinot (1804?–1839) was born at Oothcaloga, a Cherokee "progressive" town, in northwestern Georgia. His birth name was Gallegina, and he was also called Buck Watie. His father, Oo'watie, or David Watie, sent him at the age of six to a nearby Moravian Mission School, where he continued until he was seventeen, at which time he set out north for another mission school, this one in Cornwall, Connecticut. It was on this trip that Buck Watie met the elderly Elias Boudinot, who had been a member of the Continental Congress and was at the time president of the American Bible Society. Consistent with an old Cherokee practice of changing names and with a newer Cherokee practice of adopting the names of prominent whites, Buck Watie became Elias Boudinot.

Although his family was staunchly progressive—his uncle was Major Ridge, whose picture says a good deal about him (see the color insert to this volume), and his younger brother, Stand Watie, joined white southerners to become the last Confederate general to surrender to the North in the Civil War (that both Buck and Stand took their father's surname indicates a movement away from traditional Cherokee matrilineal practice)—Boudinot opposed removal until some time in 1832. In what is probably his best-known work, "An Address to the Whites," delivered in Philadelphia in 1826, Boudinot makes the same case that the "Memorial" of the Cherokee Council would make to Congress opposing removal: he insists that not only are his people able to attain Christianity and "civilization" but that they are well on the way to those attainments. About two years after the passage of the Indian Removal Act in 1830 and, in particular, once Georgia had instituted a lottery to dispose of Cherokee lands to white citizens of the state, Boudinot concluded that further resistance to removal was hopeless.

In 1835, he, his uncle Major Ridge, and a small number of wealthy Cherokee planters met at New Echota, where, on December 29, they signed the Treaty of New Echota, agreeing to exchange Cherokee lands in the southeast for land in Indian Country, present-day Oklahoma. Boudinot and his family went west before the Trail of Tears and so were already established when the last of the Cherokee people to survive the forced march arrived in Indian Country in early spring 1839. In June of that year, several Cherokees came to Boudinot to ask for medicine. Two followed him as he led them to the mission dispensary and then attacked him with a knife and a tomahawk, leaving him to die. That same day, his relatives Major Ridge and John Ridge were also killed for their part in signing the treaty. The murderers very likely acted in accord with a traditional practice of vengeance, taking lives in recompense for the lives of those who had died on the trail, and also in accord with a law passed by the Cherokee Council in 1829 making it a capital crime to cede Cherokee lands.

The selection printed here is from the first issue of the *Cherokee Phoenix,* dated February 21, 1828, as it appears in *Cherokee Editor: The Writings of Elias Boudinot* (1996), edited by Theda Purdue. Boudinot edited the paper until 1832, when the Cherokee Council asked him to withdraw because of his support for removal. The *Phoenix* was the first American newspaper to print an Indian language (in the syllabary Sequoyah had invented in 1821); it also printed articles in English. Boudinot alerts his readers, white and Indian, to the fact that "the design of this paper . . . is [for] the benefit of the Cherokees."

From the Cherokee Phoenix

To the Public

FEBRUARY 21, 1828

We are happy in being able, at length, to issue the first number of our paper, although after a longer delay than we anticipated. This delay has been owing to unavoidable circumstances, which, we think, will be sufficient to acquit us, and though our readers and patrons may be wearied in the expectation of gratifying their eyes on this paper of no ordinary novelty, yet we hope their patience will not be so exhausted, but that they will give it a calm perusal and pass upon it a candid judgment. It is far from our expectation that it will meet with entire and universal approbation, particularly from those who consider learning and science necessary to the merits of newspapers. Such must not expect to be gratified here, for the merits, (if merits they can be called,) on which our paper is expected to exist, are not alike with those which keep alive the political and religious papers of the day. We lay no claim to extensive information; and we sincerely hope, this public disclosure will save us from the severe criticisms, to which our ignorance of many things, will frequently expose us, in the future of our editorial labors.— Let the public but consider our motives, and the design of this paper, which is, the benefit of the Cherokees, and we are sure, those who wish well to the Indian race, will keep out of view all failings and deficiencies of the Editor, and give a prompt support to the first paper ever published in an Indian country, and under the direction of some remnants of those, who by the most mysterious course of providence, have dwindled into oblivion. To prevent us from the like destiny, is certainly a laudable undertaking, which the Christian, the Patriot, and the Philanthropist will not be ashamed to aid. Many are now engaged, by various means and with various success, in attempting to rescue, not only us, but all our kindred tribes, from the impending danger which has been so fatal to our forefathers; and we are happy to be in a situation to tender them our public acknowledgments for their unwearied efforts. Our present undertaking is intended to be nothing more than a feeble auxiliary to these efforts. Those therefore, who are engaged for the good of the Indians of every tribe, and who pray that salvation, peace, and the comforts of civilized life may be extended to every Indian fire side on this continent, will consider us as co-workers together in their benevolent labors. To them we make our appeal for patronage, and pledge ourselves to encourage and assist them, in whatever appears to be for the benefit of the Aborigines.

In the commencement of our labours, it is due to our readers that we should acquaint them with the general principles, which we have prescribed to ourselves as rules in conducting this paper. These principles we shall accordingly state briefly. It may, however, be proper to observe that the establishment which has been lately purchased, principally with the charities of our white brethren, is the property of the Nation, and that the paper, which is now offered to the public, is patronized by, and under the direction of, the Cherokee Legislature, as will be seen in the Prospectus already before the public. As servants, we are bound to that body, from which, however, we have not received any instructions, but are left at liberty to form such regulations

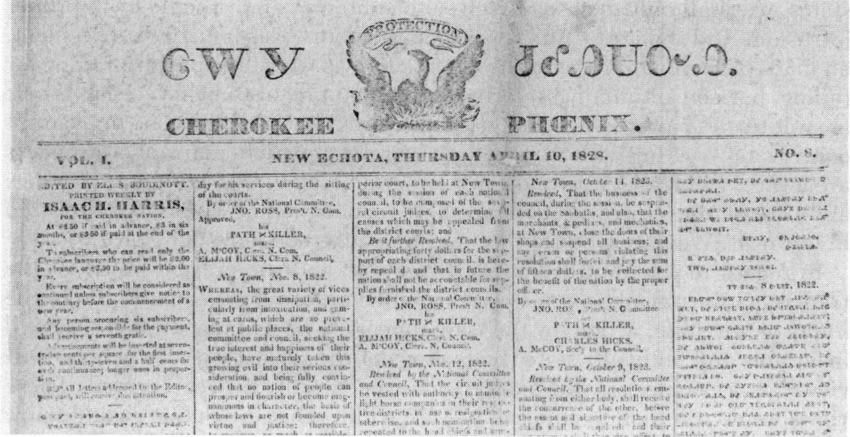

ᏣᎳᎩ PROTECTION ᏧᎴᎯᏌᏅᎯ.

CHEROKEE PHOENIX.

VOL. I. NEW ECHOTA, THURSDAY APRIL 10, 1828. NO. 8.

EDITED BY ELIAS BOUDINOTT.
PRINTED WEEKLY BY
ISAAC H. HARRIS,
FOR THE CHEROKEE NATION.

At $2 50 if paid in advance, $3 in six months, or $3 50 if paid at the end of the year.

To subscribers who can read only the Cherokee language the price will be $2,00 in advance, or $2,50 to be paid within the year.

Every subscription will be considered as continued unless subscribers give notice to the contrary before the commencement of a new year.

Any person procuring six subscribers, and becoming responsible for the payment, shall receive a seventh gratis.

Advertisements will be inserted at seventy-five cents per square for the first insertion, and thirty-seven and a half cents for each continuance; longer ones in proportion.

All letters addressed to the Editor, post paid, will receive due attention.

[illegible]

day for his services during the sitting of the courts.

By order of the National Committee,
JNO. ROSS, Pres't. N. Com.
Approved,
his
PATH ✕ KILLER,
mark.
A. M'COY, Clerk N. Com.
ELIJAH HICKS, Clerk N. Council,

New Town, Nov. 8, 1822.

WHEREAS, the great variety of vices emanating from dissipation, particularly from intoxication, and gaming at cards, which are so prevalent at public places, the national committee and council, seeking the true interest and happiness of their people, have maturely taken this growing evil into their serious consideration, and being fully convinced that no nation of people can prosper and flourish or become magnanimous in character, the basis of whose laws are not founded upon virtue and justice: therefore, [illegible]

perior court, to be held at New Town, during the session of each national council, to be composed of the several circuit judges, to determine all causes which may be appealed from the district courts; and

Be it further Resolved, That the law appropriating forty dollars for the support of each district council, is hereby repealed; and that in future the nation shall not be accountable for supplies furnished the district councils.

By order of the National Committee,
JNO. ROSS, Pres't N. Com.
his
PATH ✕ KILLER,
mark.
ELIJAH HICKS, Clerk N. Com.
A. M'COY, Clerk N. Council.

New Town, Nov. 12, 1822.

Resolved by the National Committee and Council, That the circuit judges be vested with authority to nominate light horse companies in their respective districts, in case of resignation or otherwise, and such nomination be [illegible] repeated to the head chiefs and [illegible]

New Town, October 14, 1823.

Resolved, That the business of the council, during the session, be suspended on the sabbaths, and also, that the merchants & pedlars, and mechanics, at New Town, close the doors of their shops and suspend all business; and any person or persons violating this resolution shall forfeit and pay the sum of fifteen dollars, to be collected for the benefit of the nation by the proper officer.

By order of the National Committee,
JNO. ROSS, Pres't N. Committee.
his
PATH ✕ KILLER,
mark.
CHARLES HICKS.
A. McCOY, Sec'y to the Council.

New Town, October 9, 1823.

Resolved by the National Committee and Council, That all resolutions emanating from either body, shall receive the concurrence of the other, before the assent and signature of the head chiefs shall be required: and their [illegible]

[illegible]

New Town, Nov. 8, 1822.

The masthead of the ***Cherokee Phoenix,*** the first newspaper in both a Native language and English, illustrates the complex cultural and political situation of the Cherokee Nation at the time. The two words on either side of the phoenix are in the Cherokee syllabary invented by Sequoyah (George Guess). They are pronounced roughly *Tsa-la-gi Tsi-le-hi-sa-ni*. The first word means "Cherokee"—as in the English below it—but the second word—unlike the English below it—does not mean "Phoenix" (there is no word in Cherokee for the Phoenix, but, rather, "I was down and I have risen" or "I will rise again" (the latter invokes both the Phoenix *and* Christ). In putting the word PROTECTION between the bird's wings, the Cherokees mean to remind the federal government of its responsibility to protect them from the threats of the state of Georgia.

for our conduct as will appear to us most conducive to the interests of the people, for whose benefit, this paper has been established.

As the Phoenix is a national newspaper, we shall feel ourselves bound to devote it to national purposes. "The laws and public documents of the Nation," and matters relating to the welfare and condition of the Cherokees as a people, will be faithfully published in English and Cherokee.

As the liberty of the press is so essential to the improvement of the mind, we shall consider our paper, a *free paper*, with, however, proper and usual restrictions. We shall reserve to ourselves the liberty of rejecting such communications as tend to evil, and such as are too intemperate and too personal. But the columns of this paper shall always be open to free and temperate discussions on matters of politics, religion, &c.

We shall avoid as much as possible, controversy on disputed doctrinal points in religion. Though we have our particular belief on this important subject, and perhaps are as strenuous upon it, as some of our brethren of a different faith, yet we conscientiously think, & in this thought we are supported by men of judgment that it would be injudicious, perhaps highly pernicious, to introduce to this people, the various minor differences of Christians. Our object is not sectarian, and if we had a wish to support, in our paper, the denomination with which we have the honor and privilege of being connected, yet we know our incompetency for the task.

We will not unnecessarily intermeddle with the politics and affairs of our neighbors. As we have no particular interest in the concerns of the surrounding states, we shall only expose ourselves to contempt and ridicule by improper intrusion. And though at times, we should do ourselves injustice, to be silent, on matters of great interest to the Cherokees, yet we will not return railing for railing, but consult mildness, for we have been taught to believe, that "A soft answer turneth away wrath; but grievous words stir up anger." The unpleasant controversy existing with the state of Georgia, of which, many of our readers are aware, will frequently make our situation trying, by having hard sayings and threatenings thrown out against us, a specimen of which will be found in our next. We pray God that we may be delivered from such spirit.

In regard to the controversy with Georgia, and the present policy of the General Government, in removing, and concentrating the Indians, out of the limits of any state, which, by the way, appears to be gaining strength, we will invariably and faithfully state the feelings of the majority of our people. Our views, as a people, on this subject, have been sadly misrepresented. These views we do not wish to conceal, but are willing that the public should know what we think of this policy, which, in our opinion, if carried into effect, will prove pernicious to us.

* * *

In fine, we shall pay a sacred regard to truth, and avoid, as much as possible, that partiality to which we shall be exposed. In relating facts of a local nature, whether political, moral, or religious, we shall take care that exaggeration shall not be our crime. We shall also feel ourselves bound to correct all mistatements, relating to the present condition of the Cherokees.

How far we shall be successful in advancing the improvement of our people, is not now for us to decide. We hope, however, our efforts will not be altogether in vain.—Now is the moment when mere speculation on the practicability of civilizing us is out of the question. Sufficient and repeated evidence has been given, that Indians can be reclaimed from a savage state, and that with proper advantages, they are as capable of improvement in mind as any other people; and let it be remembered, notwithstanding the assertions of those who talk to the contrary, that this improvement can be made, not only by the Cherokees, but by all the Indians, *in their present locations*. We are rendered bold in making this assertion, by considering the history of our people within the last fifteen years. There was a time within our remembrance, when darkness was sadly prevalent, and ignorance abounded amongst us—when strong and deep rooted prejudices were directed against many things relating to civilized life—and when it was thought a disgrace, for a Cherokee to appear in the costume of a white man. We mention these things not by way of boasting, but to shew our readers that it is not a visionary thing to attempt to civilize and christianize all the Indians, but highly practicable.

* * *

We would now commit our feeble efforts to the good will and indulgence of the public, praying that God will attend them with his blessings, and hoping for that happy period, when all the Indian tribes of America shall arise, Phoenix like, from their ashes, and when the terms, "Indian depredation," "warwhoop," "scalping knife" and the like, shall become obsolete, and for ever be "buried deep under ground."

THE CHEROKEE MEMORIALS

In 1828, Andrew Jackson, largely on his reputation as an Indian fighter, was elected president of the United States. In 1829, gold was discovered in Dahlonega on the western boundary of the Cherokee Nation in the state of Georgia. Georgia had for some time wished to rid itself of its Indian population, and the time seemed right to press the issue. Bills for the removal of the eastern Indians were introduced in both houses of Congress early in 1830; debate on the Removal Bill had begun in the House on February 24.

Anticipating these developments, the Cherokee Council had prepared a "memorial"—essentially a petition to Congress—as early as November 1829, which was received by the House in February of the following year, shortly before the official debate began. The memorial was probably authored for the most part by the clerk of the council, John Ridge, who had not yet broken with the "traditionalist" Cherokees, led by the principal chief John Ross, who were firmly opposed to removal. The memorial begins with what must be an intentional, although unstated reference to the Declaration of Independence. Whereas the Declaration made known to the world the "long rain of abuses and usurpations" for which the British king George III was responsible, the Cherokee memorial establishes the wrongs done by his namesake state, Georgia, petitioning the Congress of the United States—the same body that had adopted the Declaration—for redress of grievances. Although the American colonists had had to *declare* their independence, the Cherokees instead *affirm* theirs. As they demonstrate, they have always been treated by the American colonials and the United States as a sovereign nation.

Acknowledging that Georgia and the president have the power to force them to unfamiliar land west of the Mississippi, the Cherokee Council insists that the use of such power would lead to an unjust and unhappy fate for the Cherokee Nation. In the florid language of the period, the council offers its vision of Cherokee advancement "in civilized life . . . science and Christian knowledge," on the lands they have for long occupied.

This vision did not prevail. Basing his authority on the Treaty of New Echota—signed in 1835 by a minority of Cherokees—Jackson ordered the Cherokees to remove by the spring of 1838. Some moved west before that date. But the vast majority of the eastern Cherokee Nation refused to leave their homes. Thus it was that federal troops under the command of General Winfield Scott came to enforce the treaty. In the fall and winter of 1838–39, some thirteen thousand Cherokees were driven westward on what has come to be known as the Trail of Tears. Roughly one-third of them, about four thousand people, died en route. The survivors reached Indian Country, in what would eventually become Oklahoma, in the early spring of 1839.

Memorial of the Cherokee Council, November 5, 1829

To the Honorable Senate and House of Representatives of the United States of America in Congress assembled:

We, the representatives of the people of the Cherokee nation, in general council convened, compelled by a sense of duty we owe to ourselves and nation, and confiding in the justice of your honorable bodies, address and make known to you the grievances which disturb the quiet repose and harmony of our citizens, and the dangers by which we are surrounded. Extraordinary as this course may appear to you, the circumstances that have imposed upon us this duty we deem sufficient to justify the measure; and our safety as individuals, and as a nation, require that we should be heard by the immediate representatives of the people of the United States, whose humanity and magnanimity, by permission and will of Heaven, may yet preserve us from ruin and extinction.

The authorities of Georgia have recently and unexpectedly assumed a doctrine, horrid in its aspect, and fatal in its consequences to us, and utterly at variance with the laws of nations, of the United States, and the subsisting treaties between us, and the known history of said State, of this nation, and of the United States. She claims the exercise of sovereignty over this nation; and has threatened and decreed the extension of her jurisdictional limits over our people. The Executive of the United States, through the Secretary of War,[1] in a letter to our delegation of the 18th April last, has recognised this right to be abiding in, and possessed by, the State of Georgia; by the Declaration of Independence, and the treaty of peace concluded between the United States and Great Britain in 1783; and which it is urged vested in her all the rights of sovereignty pertaining to Great Britain, and which, in time previously, she claimed and exercised, within the limits of what constituted the "thirteen United States." It is a subject of vast importance to know whether the power of self-government abided in the Cherokee nation at the discovery of America, three hundred and thirty-seven years ago; and whether it was in any manner affected or destroyed by the charters of European potentates. It is evident from facts deducible from known history, that the Indians were found here by the white man, in the enjoyment of plenty and peace, and all the rights of soil and domain, inherited from their ancestors from time immemorial, well furnished with kings, chiefs, and warriors, the bulwarks of liberty, and the pride of their race. Great Britain established with them relationships of friendship and alliance, and at no time did she treat them as subjects, and as tenants at will, to her power. In war she fought them as a separate people, and they resisted her as a nation. In peace, she spoke the language of friendship, and they replied in the voice of independence, and frequently assisted her as allies, at their choice to fight her enemies in their own way and discipline, subject to the control of their own chiefs, and unaccountable to European officers and military law. Such was the connexion of this nation to Great Britain, to wit, that of friendship, and not allegiance, to the period of the declaration of Independence by the United States, and during the Revolutionary contest, down to the treaty of peace between the United States and Great Britain, forty-six years ago, when she abandoned all hopes of conquest, and at the same time abandoned her Cherokee allies to the difficulties in which they had been involved, either to continue the war, or procure peace on the best

1. I.e., John Eaton. President Andrew Jackson (the "Executive of the United States") believed that treating the Indians as sovereign nations was a mistake and that Indian occupancy of lands within the United States was simply owing to the generosity and goodwill of the federal government and the states in question.

terms they could, and close the scenes of carnage and blood, that had so long been witnessed and experienced by both parties. Peace was at last concluded at Hopewell, in '85, under the administration of Washington, by "the Commissioners, Plenipotentiaries of the United States in Congress assembled"; and the Cherokees were received "into the favor and protection of the United States of America." It remains to be proved, under a view of all these circumstances, and the knowledge we have of history, how our right to self-government was affected and destroyed by the Declaration of Independence, which never noticed the subject of Cherokee sovereignty; and the treaty of peace, in '83, between Great Britain and the United States, to which the Cherokees were not a party; but maintained hostilities on their part to the treaty of Hopewell, afterwards concluded. If, as it is stated by the Hon. Secretary of War, that the Cherokees were mere tenants at will,[2] and only permitted to enjoy possession of the soil to pursue game; and if the States of North Carolina and Georgia were sovereigns in truth and in right over us; why did President Washington send "Commissioners Plenipotentiaries" to treat with the subjects of those States? Why did they permit the chiefs and warriors to enter into treaty, when, if they were subjects, they had grossly rebelled and revolted from their allegiance? And why did not those sovereigns make their lives pay the forfeit of their guilt, agreeably to the laws of said States? The answer must be plain—they were not subjects, but a distinct nation, and in that light viewed by Washington, and by all the people of the Union, at that period. In the first and second articles of the Hopewell treaty, and the third article of the Holston treaty,[3] the United States and the Cherokee nation were bound to a mutual exchange of prisoners taken during the war; which incontrovertibly proves the possession of sovereignty by *both* contracting parties. It ought to be remembered too, in the conclusions of the treaties to which we have referred, and most of the treaties subsisting between the United States and this nation, that the phraseology, composition, etc. was always written by the Commissioners, on the part of the United States, for obvious reasons: as the Cherokees were unacquainted with letters. Again, in the Holston treaty, eleventh article, the following remarkable evidence is contained that our nation is not under the jurisdiction of any State: "If any citizen or inhabitant of the United States, or of either of the territorial districts of the United States, shall go into any town, settlement, or territory, belonging to the Cherokees, and shall there commit any crime upon, or trespass against, the person or

2. I.e., the will of the states and the federal government "to allow" the Cherokees to live on their own ancestral lands. These lands came into the possession of the United States as a result of the Declaration of Independence and victory in the Revolutionary War. The Treaty of Hopewell, signed November 28, 1785, was the first treaty between the Cherokees and the United States enacted after the Revolutionary War. It established the boundaries of Cherokee lands and was negotiated as an agreement between two sovereign nations. The Cherokees refer to the treaty to show that they were formerly recognized as an independent nation and should still be treated as such. This argument remains in force today.

3. Signed July 2, 1791, this treaty gave the federal government (not the states) exclusive right to regulate all citizens' trade with the Cherokees and redrew the boundaries, much encroached on by the settlers, of Cherokee lands. It also affirmed "Perpetual peace between the United States and the Cherokee Nation," and forbade non-Cherokee persons from hunting on or traversing Cherokee lands without a passport issued by the federal government. The Cherokees cite this as further evidence of their having been treated as a sovereign nation in the past.

property of any peaceable and friendly Indian or Indians, which, *if committed within the jurisdiction of any State, or within the jurisdiction of either of the said districts*, against a citizen or any white inhabitant thereof, would be punishable by the laws of such State or district, such offender or offenders shall be proceeded against in the same manner as if the offence had been committed *within the jurisdiction of the State or district* to which he or they may belong, against a citizen or white inhabitant thereof." The power of a State may put our national existence under its feet, and coerce us into her jurisdiction; but it would be contrary to legal right, and the plighted faith of the United States' Government. It is said by Georgia and the Honorable Secretary of War, that one sovereignty cannot exist within another, and, therefore, we must yield to the stronger power; but is not this doctrine favorable to our Government, which does not interfere with that of any other? Our sovereignty and right of enforcing legal enactments, extend no further than our territorial limits, and that of Georgia is, and has always terminated at, her limits. The constitution of the United States (article 6) contains these words: "All treaties made under the authority of the United States shall be the supreme law of the land, and the judges in every State shall be bound thereby, any thing in the laws or constitution of any State to the contrary notwithstanding." The sacredness of treaties, made under the authority of the United States, is paramount and supreme, stronger than the laws and constitution of any State. The jurisdiction, then, of our nation over its soil is settled by the laws, treaties, and constitution of the United States, and has been exercised from time out of memory.

Georgia has objected to the adoption, on our part, of a constitutional form of government, and which has in no wise violated the intercourse and connexion which bind us to the United States, its constitution, and the treaties thereupon founded, and in existence between us. As a distinct nation, notwithstanding any unpleasant feelings it might have created to a neighboring State, we had a right to improve our Government, suitable to the moral, civil, and intellectual advancement of our people; and had we anticipated any notice of it, it was the voice of encouragement by an approving world. We would, also, while on this subject, refer your attention to the memorial and protest submitted before your honorable bodies, during the last session of Congress, by our delegation then at Washington.

Permit us, also, to make known to you the aggrieved and unpleasant situation under which we are placed by the claim which Georgia has set up to a large portion of our territory, under the treaty of the Indian Springs concluded with the late General M'Intosh[4] and his party; and which was declared void, and of no effect, by a subsequent treaty between the Creek Nation and the United States, at Washington City. The President of the United States, through the Secretary of War, assured our delegation, that, so far as he understood the Cherokees had rights, protection should be afforded; and, respecting the intrusions on our lands, he had been advised,

4. General William McIntosh was a Creek Indian leader who signed the Treaty of Indian Springs on February 12, 1785. The treaty ceded Creek lands to the state of Georgia and agreed to the removal of the Creeks to west of the Mississippi. But the Creeks had earlier denied McIntosh's right to act on their behalf and did not honor the treaty. McIntosh was assassinated, and John Ridge and David Vann were engaged to negotiate a new treaty, the "subsequent treaty" referred to later in the sentence.

"and instructions had been forwarded to the agent of the Cherokees, directing him to cause their removal; and earnestly hoped, that, on this matter, all cause for future complaint would cease, and the order prove effectual." In consequence of the agent's neglecting to comply with the instructions, and a suspension of the order made by the Secretary afterwards, our border citizens are at this time placed under the most unfortunate circumstances, by the intrusions of citizens of the United States, and which are almost daily increasing, in consequence of the suspension of the once contemplated "effectual order." Many of our people are experiencing all the evils of personal insult, and, in some instances, expulsion from their homes, and loss of property, from the unrestrained intruders let loose upon us, and the encouragement they are allowed to enjoy, under the last order to the agent for this nation, which amounts to a suspension of the force of treaties, and the wholesome operation of the intercourse laws[5] of the United States. The reason alleged by the War Department for this suspension is, that it had been requested so to do, until the claim the State of Georgia has made to a portion of the Cherokee country be determined; and the intruders are to remain unmolested within the border limits of this nation. We beg leave to protest against this unprecedented procedure. If the State of Georgia has a claim to any portion of our lands, and is entitled by law and justice to them, let her seek through a legal channel to establish it; and we do hope that the United States will not suffer her to take possession of them forcibly, and investigate her claim afterwards.

Arguments to effect the emigration of our people, and to escape the troubles and disquietudes incident to a residence contiguous to the whites, have been urged upon us, and the arm of protection has been withheld, that we may experience still deeper and ampler proofs of the correctness of the doctrine; but we still adhere to what is right and agreeable to ourselves; and our attachment to the soil of our ancestors is too strong to be shaken. We have been invited to a retrospective view of the past history of Indians, who have melted away before the light of civilization, and the mountains of difficulties that have opposed our race in their advancement in civilized life. We have done so; and, while we deplore the fate of thousands of our complexion and kind, we rejoice that our nation stands and grows a lasting monument of God's mercy, and a durable contradiction to the misconceived opinion that the aborigines are incapable of civilization. The opposing mountains, that cast fearful shadows in the road of Cherokee improvement, have dispersed into vernal clouds; and our people stand adorned with the flowers of achievement flourishing around them, and are encouraged to secure the attainment of all that is useful in science and Christian knowledge.

Under the fostering care of the United States we have thus prospered; and shall we expect approbation, or shall we sink under the displeasure and rebukes of our enemies?

We now look with earnest expectation to your honorable bodies for redress, and that our national existence may not be extinguished before a prompt and effectual interposition is afforded in our behalf. The faith of your Government is solemnly pledged for our protection against all illegal

5. Laws regulating trade.

oppressions, so long as we remain firm to our treaties; and that we have, for a long series of years, proved to be true and loyal friends, the known history of past events abundantly proves. Your Chief Magistrate himself[6] has borne testimony of our devotedness in supporting the cause of the United States, during their late conflict with a foreign foe. It is with reluctant and painful feelings that circumstances have at length compelled us to seek from you the promised protection, for the preservation of our rights and privileges. This resort to us is a last one, and nothing short of the threatening evils and dangers that beset us could have forced it upon the nation but it is a right we surely have, and in which we cannot be mistaken—that of appealing for justice and humanity to the United States, under whose kind and fostering care we have been led to the present degree of civilization, and the enjoyment of its consequent blessings. Having said thus much, with patience we shall await the final issue of your wise deliberations.

6. John Marshall, chief justice of the Supreme Court.

RALPH WALDO EMERSON

Ralph Waldo Emerson (1803–1882) was perhaps the most important American thinker of the first half of the nineteenth century and a strong influence on Thoreau and Walt Whitman, among others. Although he knew some of the New England abolitionists, he did not himself become active in the cause until the 1850s. In regard to the American Indians, Emerson seems to have shared the general eastern distaste for President Andrew Jackson's removal policies, although it is only in his letter to Jackson's successor, Martin Van Buren, reprinted here, that he committed himself publicly to the Cherokees' cause.

Emerson seems to have learned of the imminent removal of the Cherokees only on April 19, 1838, writing in his journal, "I can do nothing. Why shriek? Why strike ineffectual blows?" Yet the following day he composed the first draft of his letter to Van Buren, noting in his journal, "The amount of [it], [to] be sure, is merely a Scream but sometimes a scream is better than a thesis." The following day he recorded his sense that this was "A deliverance that does not deliver the soul." Clearly, writing this letter was not an easy thing for him to do.

The letter does not seem ever to have been sent directly to Van Buren. Under the heading of "Communication," it was published, "with some reluctance" on the part of the proprietors of the *National Daily Intelligencer*, in the issue of May 14, 1838, next appearing on May 19 in the *Yeoman's Gazette* in Concord. The earliest version we have been able to find is from the *New Bedford Mercury* of May 25, 1838, the source of the text below.

Letter to Martin Van Buren

President of the United States

Concord, Mass. 23d April, 1838.

Sir—The seat you fill, places you in a relation of credit and dearness to every citizen. By right, and natural position, every citizen is your friend. Before any acts contrary to his own judgement or interest have repelled the affections of any man, each may look with trust and loving anticipations to your government. Each has the highest right to call your attention to such subjects as are of a public nature and properly belong to the chief magistrate; and the good magistrate will feel a joy in meeting such confidence. In this belief, and at the instance of a few of my friends and neighbors, I crave of your patience a short hearing for their sentiments and my own; and the circumstance that my name will be utterly unknown to you, will only give the fairer chance to your equitable construction of what I have to say.

Sir, my communication respects the sinister rumours that fill this part of the country concerning the Cherokee people. The interest always felt in the Aboriginal Population—an interest naturally growing as that decays—has been heightened in regard to this tribe. Even in our distant state, some good rumor of their worth and civility has arrived. We have learned with joy their improvement in social arts. We have read their newspapers. We have seen some of them in our schools and colleges. In common with the great body of the American people we have witnessed with sympathy the painful labors of these red men to redeem their own race from the doom of eternal inferiority, and to borrow and domesticate in the tribe, the arts and customs of the caucasian race. And notwithstanding the unaccountable apathy with which of late years the Indians have been sometimes abandoned to their enemies, it is not to be doubted that it is the good pleasure and the understanding of all humane persons in the republic—of the men and the matrons sitting in the thriving independent families all over the land, that they shall be duly cared for, that they shall taste justice and love from all to whom we have delegated the office of dealing with them.

The newspapers now inform us, that, in December 1835, a treaty contracting for the exchange of all the Cherokee territory, was pretended to be made by an agent on the part of the United States with some persons appearing on the part of the Cherokees; that the fact afterwards transpired that these deputies did by no means represent the will of the nation, and that out of eighteen thousand souls composing the nation, fifteen thousand six hundred and sixty eight have protested against the so called Treaty. It now appears that the Government of the United States choose to hold the Cherokees to this sham treaty, and are proceeding to execute the same. Almost the entire Cherokee nation stand up and say, "This is not our act. Behold us. Here are we. Do not mistake that handful of deserters for us," and the American President and his Cabinet, the Senate and the House of Representatives neither hear these men nor see them, and are contracting to put this nation into carts and boats and to drag them over mountains and rivers to a wilderness at a vast distance beyond the Mississippi.—And a paper purporting to be an army order, taxes a month from this day, as the hour for this doleful removal.

In the name of God, Sir, we ask you if this be so? Do the newspapers rightly inform us? Men and women with pale and perplexed faces meet one another in streets and churches here, and ask if this be so? We have inquired if this be a gross misrepresentation from the party opposed to the Government and anxious to blacken it with the people. We have looked in newspapers of different parties, and find a horrid confirmation of the tale. We are slow to believe it. We hoped the Indians were misinformed and their remonstrance was premature, and will turn out to be a needless act of terror. The piety, the principle that is left in these United States,—if only its coarsest form, a regard to the speech of men, forbid us to entertain it as a fact. Such a dereliction of all faith and virtue, such a denial of justice and such deafness to screams for mercy, were never heard of in times of peace, and in the dealing of a nation with its own allies and wards, since the earth was made. Sir, does this Government think that the people of the United States are become savage and mad? From their mind are the sentiments of love and of a good nature nature wiped clean out? The soul of man, the justice the mercy, that is the heart's heart in all men from Maine to Georgia, does abhor this business.

In speaking thus the sentiments of my neighbors and my own, perhaps I overstep the bounds of decorum. But would it not be a higher indecorum, coldly to argue a matter like this? We only state the fact that a crime is projected that confounds our understandings by its magnitude,—a crime that really deprives us as well as the Cherokees of a country, for how could we call the conspiracy that should crush these poor Indians, our Government, or the land that was cursed by their parting and dying imprecations, our country, any more? You, Sir, will bring down that renowned chair in which you sit into infamy, if your seal is set to this instrument of perfidy, and the name of this nation, hitherto the sweet omen of religion and liberty, will stink to the world.

You will not do us the injustice of connecting this remonstrance with any sectional or party feeling.—It is in our hearts the simplest commandment of brotherly love. We will not have this great and solemn claim upon national and human justice huddled aside under the flimsy plea of its being a party act. Sir, to us the questions upon which the government and the people have been agitated during the past year touching the prostration of the currency and of trade, seem but motes in comparison. The hard times, it is true, have brought this discussion home to every farmhouse and poor man's house in this town; but it is the chirping of grasshoppers beside the immortal question whether justice shall be done by the race of civilized, to the race of savage man; whether all the attributes of reason, of civility, of justice, and even of mercy, shall be put off by the American people, and so vast an outrage upon the Cherokee nation, and upon human nature, shall be consummated.

One circumstance lessens the reluctance with which I intrude at this time on your attention, my conviction that the government ought to be admonished of a new historical fact which the discussion of this question has disclosed, namely that there exists in a great part of the northern people, a gloomy diffidence in the *moral* character of the government. On the broaching of this question, a general expression of despondency,—of disbelief that any good will accrue from a remonstrance on an act of fraud and robbery—appeared in those men to whom we naturally turn for aid and counsel. Will the American Government steal? Will it lie? Will it kill?—we ask triumphantly. Our wise men shake their heads dubiously. Our counsellers and old statesmen here, say, that ten years ago, they would have staked their life on the affirmation that the proposed Indian measures could not be executed, that the unanimous country would put them down. And now the steps of this crime follow each other so fast,—at such fatally quick time,—that the millions of virtuous citizens, whose agents the Government are, have no place to interpose, and must shut their eyes until the last howl and wailing of these poor tormented villages and tribes shall afflict the ear of the world.

I will not hide from you as an indication of this alarming distrust that a letter addressed as mine is, and suggesting to the mind of the Executive the plain obligations of man, has a burlesque character in the apprehension of some of my friends. I, sir, will not beforehand treat you with contumely of this distrust. I will at least state to you this fact and show you how plain and humane people whose love would be honor, regard the policy of the Government, and what injurious inferences they draw as to the mind of the Governors. A man with your experience in affairs must have seen cause to appreciate the futility of opposition to the moral sentiment. However feeble the sufferer, and however great the oppressor, it is in the nature of things that the blow should recoil on the aggressor. For God is in the sentiment, and it cannot be withstood. The potentate and the people perish before it; but with it, and as its executors, they are omnipotent.

I write thus, Sir, to inform you of the state of mind these Indian tidings have awakened here, and to pray with one voice more that you whose hands are strong with the delegated power of fifteen millions of men will avert with that might the terrific injury which threatens the Cherokee tribe.

With great respect, Sir,
I am your fellow-citizen,
Ralph Waldo Emerson

NATHANIEL HAWTHORNE
1804–1864

In 1879, the author Henry James called Nathaniel Hawthorne "the most valuable example of American genius," expressing the widely held belief that he was the most significant fiction writer of the antebellum period. Readers continue to celebrate Hawthorne for his prose style, his perceptive renderings of New England history, his psychological acuity, and his vivid characterizations—especially of female characters. Still, for many, he remains tantalizingly elusive, a writer who—as he remarked in the "Custom-House" introduction to *The Scarlet Letter*—wished to keep "the inmost Me behind its veil." He was, to be sure, a deeply private man, but the elusiveness of his fiction stems from a deliberate aesthetic of ambiguity, a refusal to "stick a pin through a butterfly" (as he put it in the preface to *The House of the Seven Gables*) by imposing a single moral on a story. Withholding interpretation—or offering multiple and conflicting interpretations—Hawthorne not only makes readers do their own interpretive work but also shows how interpretation is often a form of self-expression.

Hawthorne was born on July 4, 1804, in Salem, Massachusetts. His prominent Puritan ancestors on the Hawthorne side of the family were among the first settlers of Massachusetts and included a judge in the Salem witchcraft trials of 1692. The men in his mother's family, the Mannings, were tradesmen and businessmen. When Hawthorne's sea-captain father died in Surinam of yellow fever in 1808, his mother, Elizabeth Manning Hawthorne, moved with her three children into the Manning family's commodious house in Salem. There, with his mother, sisters, grandparents, two aunts, and five uncles, Hawthorne discovered his love of reading, displaying particular interest as a boy in John Bunyan's Puritan allegory *The Pilgrim's Progress.* In 1813 he injured his foot in an accident, was fitted with a protective boot and crutches and, while remaining home from school during the long recuperation period, continued to read extensively. By his midteens he was reading the British novelists Henry Fielding, Tobias Smollet, William Godwin, and Sir Walter Scott, while forming an ambition, as he wrote his sister Elizabeth when he was sixteen, of "becoming an Author, and relying for support upon my pen." Hawthorne enjoyed long visits to the Manning properties at Sebago Lake, Maine, and at age seventeen enrolled at Bowdoin College in Brunswick, Maine. At Bowdoin he developed what would become lifelong friendships with Horatio Bridge, Franklin Pierce, and other members of the nascent Democratic Party. These friends would later help further his literary career by providing him with patronage jobs and funds. Henry Wadsworth Longfellow, another Bowdoin classmate, belonged to the more conservative Federalist Society. At the graduation ceremonies in 1825, Longfellow spoke of the possibility that "Our Native Writers" could achieve lasting fame; and twelve years later he would enthusiastically review Hawthorne's *Twice-Told Tales* in the prestigious *North American Review,* calling the collection of tales and sketches a "sweet, sweet book."

During the years between Hawthorne's graduation from Bowdoin in 1825 and the publication of *Twice-Told Tales* in 1837, Hawthorne seems to have lived quietly at home in Salem with his mother and sisters. He read extensively in colonial histories and documents, which would become important sources for such historical tales as "My Kinsman, Major Molineaux" (1832) and "Young Goodman Brown" (1835), while keeping a close eye on his contemporary world, which would supply him with material for such popular sketches as "Little Annie's Ramble" (1835) and "A Rill from the Town Pump" (1835). In 1828 Hawthorne published his first novel, *Fanshawe,* at his own expense. Set at a college resembling Bowdoin, the novel was reviewed so negatively that he attempted to suppress its distribution. Over the next several years Hawthorne tried unsuccessfully to find a publisher for collections of the tales he was writing. He may have destroyed one collection, "Seven Tales of My Native Land"; in 1829 he failed to find a publisher for a volume called "Provincial Tales," which included "The Gentle Boy" and perhaps "My Kinsman, Major Molineaux." A proposed third volume called "The Story Teller," in which the title character wandered about New England telling his stories in dramatic settings and circumstances, also foundered.

During the early 1830s, however, Hawthorne managed to publish many of these early tales and sketches in the literary annuals that were issued every fall as Christmas gifts. Still, he received only a few dollars for each tale and no recognition, since publication in the annuals was anonymous. In 1836 he edited the *American Magazine of Useful and Entertaining Knowledge,* a job he secured through the Boston publisher Samuel Goodrich, whose annual, *The Token,* regularly published his tales. That same year, with the help of his sister Elizabeth, he wrote a children's reference work for Goodrich, *Peter Parley's Universal History on the Basis of Geography.* Unbeknownst to

Hawthorne, his Bowdoin friend Horatio Bridge persuaded Goodrich to publish a collection of Hawthorne's tales by promising to repay any losses. This volume, *Twice-Told Tales*, appeared in March 1837 and was favorably reviewed in England as well as the United States. A notebook entry written sometime in 1836 was only a little premature: "In this dismal and sordid chamber FAME was won."

There is considerable uncertainty about Hawthorne's private affairs around the time of the publication of *Twice-Told Tales*. According to family lore, he may have challenged the future editor of the *Democratic Review*, John O'Sullivan, to a duel over Mary Silsbee of Salem. (During the 1840s O'Sullivan would publish over twenty of Hawthorne's stories in his journal.) Hawthorne may have also been enamored of Elizabeth Peabody, a Salemite who would become a major force in American educational reform as well as other progressive causes, and to whom he presented a copy of *Twice-Told Tales* in the fall of 1837. Sometime in late 1837 or 1838 Hawthorne met Elizabeth's youngest sister, Sophia Peabody, a painter whose migraine headaches often made her a virtual invalid; they were secretly engaged within a few months of the meeting. To save money for married life, Hawthorne accepted a patronage appointment as salt and coal measurer at the Boston Custom House during 1839 and 1840, and then invested some of his limited funds in the utopian community Brook Farm, located in West Roxbury, Massachusetts, where he spent seven months in 1841. During this period he published several children's books on colonial and revolutionary history—*Grandfather's Chair* (1841), *Famous Old People* (1841), *Liberty Tree* (1841), and *Biographical Stories for Children* (1842)—along with a revised and expanded edition of *Twice-Told Tales* (1842). He and Sophia Peabody were married in 1842; the couple rented a house in Concord named the "Old Manse" (owned by Emerson's family) and became friends with the notable writers and intellectuals of the area—Emerson, Thoreau, Margaret Fuller, and Ellery Channing, among others. The Hawthornes' first child, Una, was born in 1844. While a hoped-for novel failed to materialize, Hawthorne continued to publish sketches and tales. In 1845, he edited his friend Bridge's *Journal of an African Cruiser*, but little money came of this enterprise, and Hawthorne had to move his family back to Salem to live with his mother and sisters. The following year he published *Mosses from an Old Manse*, which added a number of his recent periodical publications to some earlier work.

The Hawthornes' second child, Julian, was born in 1846. Desperately in need of money, Hawthorne turned to his Democratic friends. The Democrats' local party leader, the historian George Bancroft, found work for Hawthorne as surveyor of the Salem Custom House, a position that Hawthorne assumed in April 1846. The work was not demanding, but the routine stifled Hawthorne's creative energies. Even though he wrote little in these years, Hawthorne resented being thrown out of office by the new Whig administration in June 1849 and was pleased that his ouster led to a furious controversy in the newspapers. He then spent a summer of "great diversity and severity of emotion" (as he wrote in a journal entry of 1855), climaxed by his mother's death on July 31. In September he was at work on *The Scarlet Letter*, which he planned as a long tale to make up half a volume called "Old Time Legends; together with Sketches, Experimental and Ideal." Besides the long introduction, "The Custom-House," which was Hawthorne's means of revenging himself on the Salem Whigs who had "decapitated" him, he planned to include several tales. On the lookout for New England novelistic talent, James Fields, the young associate of the publisher William D. Ticknor, persuaded Hawthorne to drop the stories. The novel was published by the Boston house of Ticknor, Reed, and Fields in 1850.

Although some reviewers denounced *The Scarlet Letter* as licentious or morbid for its treatment of adultery, the novel was nevertheless a literary success in the United States and Great Britain, and Hawthorne was celebrated for his brilliant prose style and uncanny ability to recreate the past. Hawthorne used the setting of Puritan Boston to address the politics of revolution, community, and government central to the emerging nation; he also used the setting to explore matters of sexuality, gender, and psychology in their historical complexity. In this dark novel of love and revenge, Hawthorne evokes emotional sympathy for the heroine, Hester Prynne, even as he appears to condemn her actions. Despite the appearance of condemnation, Hester, for many readers over the years, has emerged as more vibrantly alive and appealing than the male characters of the novel. Hester's status as heroine was apparent from the beginning; as the feminist-abolitionist Jane Swisshelm observed in her 1850 review of the novel, if Hawthorne wanted to teach a lesson about the putative sins of Hester, "he had better try again. For our part if we knew there was such another woman as Hester Prynne in Boston now, we should travel all the way there to pay our respects." Strong women characters—Hepzibah in *The House of the Seven Gables* (1851), Zenobia (modeled on Margaret Fuller) in *The Blithedale Romance* (1852), and Miriam in *The Marble Faun* (1860)—would remain central to Hawthorne's long fictions. Though some recent commentators have reviled Hawthorne for his 1855 complaint to his publisher Ticknor about the "d——d mob of scribbling women," the fact is that, as evidenced by such stories as "The Birthmark" and "Rappaccinni's Daughter" and all of the novels, few writers of the mid-nineteenth century were more insightful about the damage patriarchal culture can do to women.

Following the publication of *The Scarlet Letter*, the Hawthornes moved to Lenox, Massachusetts, in the Berkshire Mountains, in part to escape from the controversy surrounding the satirical "Custom-House" sketch, which had angered many in Salem. During a year and a half in Lenox, Hawthorne developed a complicated friendship with Herman Melville, who championed Hawthorne as a great American writer in his 1850 "Hawthorne and His Mosses" and dedicated *Moby-Dick* to him. Hawthorne, over time, pulled back from Melville, and their paths seldom crossed after 1852, when the Hawthornes moved to West Newton and then back to Concord. Hawthorne was especially productive during the early 1850s, publishing *The House of the Seven Gables*, a romance with a contemporary Salem setting, and *The Blithedale Romance*, which drew on Hawthorne's experiences at Brook Farm. Hawthorne also published *The Snow-Image and other Twice-Told Tales* (1852), two books of tales and myths for children (*A Wonder-Book* [1852] and *The Tanglewood Tales* [1853]), and *The Life of Franklin Pierce*, a presidential campaign biography for his Bowdoin friend. The victorious Pierce appointed Hawthorne American consul at Liverpool, a job that again pulled Hawthorne away from his writing but that helped him support a family augmented by the birth of a third child in 1850, his daughter Rose.

At Liverpool (1853–57) Hawthorne, an industrious consul, was particularly concerned to gain greater protections for American sailors from abusive officers. Hawthorne resigned the position early in 1857 after Pierce failed to gain the Democrats' nomination for a second term, and remained in Europe to travel with his family. A stay in Italy—starting in the miserably cold early months of 1858—turned into a nightmare when malaria nearly killed his daughter Una. Hawthorne kept a minutely detailed tourist's account of his travels in Italy, and he drew on these notebooks for the romance he began in Florence in 1858 and finished late in 1859 after his return to England. This novel, inspired by the statue of a faun attributed to the classical Greek sculptor Praxiteles, was published in London in February 1860 as *Transformation* and one month later in the United States under Hawthorne's preferred title, *The Marble Faun*. Acclaimed by reviewers, the novel proved to be especially popular with American travelers to Rome later in the nineteenth century, who enjoyed using it as a guidebook.

The Hawthornes returned to their Concord home, which Hawthorne had named The Wayside, in June 1860. Hawthorne's final years in the United States were an unhappy time for him. Una remained sickly, and Hawthorne's own health began to decline. Increasingly depressed, he began a romance about an American claimant to an ancestral English estate, then put it aside to begin a romance about the search for an elixir of life, and then put that one aside as well to start another. Meanwhile, the Jacksonian Democrat Hawthorne was baffled and disturbed by the coming of the Civil War, regarding the Northern declaration of war not as an idealistic campaign to bring about the end of slavery, which he viewed as an evil, but as a frenzied form of aggression. Following a visit to Washington, D.C., in which he met Abraham Lincoln, Hawthorne published "Chiefly about War-Matters" in the July 1862 issue of the *Atlantic*; the essay satirized Lincoln and conveyed Hawthorne's critique of a nation gone mad with war. Fields, the editor of the *Atlantic*, paid well for this and other of Hawthorne's contributions, but Hawthorne was increasingly unable to respond to Fields's demands. In 1863 Hawthorne published *Our Old Home*, a collection of his English sketches, which he loyally dedicated to Franklin Pierce, who, because of his Southern sympathies, was now anathema to many Northerners. Harriet Beecher Stowe expressed disbelief that Hawthorne would dedicate a book to "that arch-traitor Pierce"; and according to Annie Fields, the wife of Hawthorne's publisher, Emerson and many others who received complimentary copies of the book reported that they had cut out the dedication page. Suffering from health problems, a frail and somewhat isolated Hawthorne embarked on a trip to New Hampshire with his old friend Pierce early in May 1864, and died in his sleep, at a hotel, later that month. He was buried in the Sleepy Hollow Cemetery at Concord. Emerson, Longfellow, Fields, James Russell Lowell, and Oliver Wendell Holmes were among his pallbearers.

My Kinsman, Major Molineux[1]

After the kings of Great Britain had assumed the right of appointing the colonial governors,[2] the measures of the latter seldom met with the ready and general approbation, which had been paid to those of their predecessors, under the original charters. The people looked with most jealous scrutiny to the exercise of power, which did not emanate from themselves, and they usually rewarded the rulers with slender gratitude, for the compliances, by which, in softening their instructions from beyond the sea, they had incurred the reprehension of those who gave them. The annals of Massachusetts Bay will inform us, that of six governors, in the space of about forty years from the surrender of the old charter, under James II, two were imprisoned by a popular insurrection; a third, as Hutchinson[3] inclines to believe, was driven from the province by the whizzing of a musket ball; a fourth, in the opinion of the same historian, was hastened to his grave by continual bickerings with the house of representatives; and the remaining two, as well as their successors, till the Revolution, were favored with few and brief intervals of peaceful sway. The inferior members of the court party,[4] in times of high political excitement, led scarcely a more desirable life. These remarks may serve as preface to the following adventures, which chanced upon a summer night, not far from a hundred years ago. The reader, in order to avoid a long and dry detail of colonial affairs, is requested

1. The text is that of the first printing in *The Token* (1832).
2. In 1684 King Charles II (r. 1660–85) annulled the original Massachusetts Charter, which had allowed the colony to elect its own governor. King James II (r. 1685–88) appointed the colony's first royal governor in 1685.
3. Thomas Hutchinson (1711–1780), the last royal governor. The particular annals, or year-by-year histories, that Hawthorne has in mind are *The History of the Colony and Province of Massachusetts-Bay* (1764, 1767) by Hutchinson. James II (1633–1701) reigned briefly (1685–88) before being exiled to France in the Glorious Revolution.
4. The pro-Crown party.

to dispense with an account of the train of circumstances, that had caused much temporary inflammation of the popular mind.

It was near nine o'clock of a moonlight evening, when a boat crossed the ferry with a single passenger, who had obtained his conveyance, at that unusual hour, by the promise of an extra fare. While he stood on the landing-place, searching in either pocket for the means of fulfilling his agreement, the ferryman lifted a lantern, by the aid of which, and the newly risen moon, he took a very accurate survey of the stranger's figure. He was a youth of barely eighteen years, evidently country-bred, and now, as it should seem, upon his first visit to town. He was clad in a coarse grey coat, well worn, but in excellent repair; his under garments[5] were durably constructed of leather, and sat tight to a pair of serviceable and well-shaped limbs; his stockings of blue yarn, were the incontrovertible handiwork of a mother or a sister; and on his head was a three-cornered hat, which in its better days had perhaps sheltered the graver brow of the lad's father. Under his left arm was a heavy cudgel, formed of an oak sapling, and retaining a part of the hardened root; and his equipment was completed by a wallet,[6] not so abundantly stocked as to incommode the vigorous shoulders on which it hung. Brown, curly hair, well-shaped features, and bright, cheerful eyes, were nature's gifts, and worth all that art could have done for his adornment.

The youth, one of whose names was Robin, finally drew from his pocket the half of a little province-bill[7] of five shillings, which, in the depreciation of that sort of currency, did but satisfy the ferryman's demand, with the surplus of a sexangular piece of parchment valued at three pence. He then walked forward into the town, with as light a step, as if his day's journey had not already exceeded thirty miles, and with as eager an eye, as if he were entering London city, instead of the little metropolis of a New England colony. Before Robin had proceeded far, however, it occurred to him, that he knew not whither to direct his steps; so he paused, and looked up and down the narrow street, scrutinizing the small and mean wooden buildings, that were scattered on either side.

'This low hovel cannot be my kinsman's dwelling,' thought he, 'nor yonder old house, where the moonlight enters at the broken casement; and truly I see none hereabouts that might be worthy of him. It would have been wise to inquire my way of the ferryman, and doubtless he would have gone with me, and earned a shilling from the Major for his pains. But the next man I meet will do as well.'

He resumed his walk, and was glad to perceive that the street now became wider, and the houses more respectable in their appearance. He soon discerned a figure moving on moderately in advance, and hastened his steps to overtake it. As Robin drew nigh, he saw that the passenger was a man in years, with a full periwig of grey hair, a wide-skirted coat of dark cloth, and silk stockings rolled about his knees. He carried a long and polished cane, which he struck down perpendicularly before him, at every step; and at regular intervals he uttered two successive hems, of a peculiarly solemn and sepulchral intonation. Having made these observations, Robin laid hold of

5. Clothes worn on the lower part of the body.
6. Knapsack.
7. Local paper money.

the skirt of the old man's coat, just when the light from the open door and windows of a barber's shop, fell upon both their figures.

'Good evening to you, honored Sir,' said he, making a low bow, and still retaining his hold of the skirt. 'I pray you to tell me whereabouts is the dwelling of my kinsman, Major Molineux?'

The youth's question was uttered very loudly; and one of the barbers, whose razor was descending on a well-soaped chin, and another who was dressing a Ramillies wig,[8] left their occupations, and came to the door. The citizen, in the meantime, turned a long favored countenance upon Robin, and answered him in a tone of excessive anger and annoyance. His two sepulchral hems, however, broke into the very centre of his rebuke, with most singular effect, like a thought of the cold grave obtruding among wrathful passions.

'Let go my garment, fellow! I tell you. I know not the man you speak of. What! I have authority, I have—hem, hem—authority; and if this be the respect you show your betters, your feet shall be brought acquainted with the stocks,[9] by daylight, tomorrow morning!'

Robin released the old man's skirt, and hastened away, pursued by an ill-mannered roar of laughter from the barber's shop. He was at first considerably surprised by the result of his question, but, being a shrewd youth, soon thought himself able to account for the mystery.

'This is some country representative,' was his conclusion, 'who has never seen the inside of my kinsman's door, and lacks the breeding to answer a stranger civilly. The man is old, or verily—I might be tempted to turn back and smite him on the nose. Ah, Robin, Robin! even the barber's boys laugh at you, for choosing such a guide! You will be wiser in time, friend Robin.'

He now became entangled in a succession of crooked and narrow streets, which crossed each other, and meandered at no great distance from the water-side. The smell of tar was obvious to his nostrils, the masts of vessels pierced the moonlight above the tops of the buildings, and the numerous signs, which Robin paused to read, informed him that he was near the centre of business. But the streets were empty, the shops were closed, and lights were visible only in the second stories of a few dwelling-houses. At length, on the corner of a narrow lane, through which he was passing, he beheld the broad countenance of a British hero swinging before the door of an inn, whence proceeded the voices of many guests. The casement of one of the lower windows was thrown back, and a very thin curtain permitted Robin to distinguish a party at supper, round a well-furnished table. The fragrance of good cheer steamed forth into the outer air, and the youth could not fail to recollect, that the last remnant of his travelling stock of provision had yielded to his morning appetite, and that noon had found, and left him, dinnerless.

'Oh, that a parchment three-penny might give me a right to sit down at yonder table,' said Robin, with a sigh. 'But the Major will make me welcome to the best of his victuals; so I will even step boldly in, and inquire my way to his dwelling.'

8. Elaborately braided wig named for Ramillies, Belgium.

9. Wood-framed instrument of punishment with holes for confining the ankles and sometimes the wrists as well.

He entered the tavern, and was guided by the murmur of voices, and fumes of tobacco, to the public room. It was a long and low apartment, with oaken walls, grown dark in the continual smoke, and a floor, which was thickly sanded, but of no immaculate purity. A number of persons, the larger part of whom appeared to be mariners, or in some way connected with the sea, occupied the wooden benches, or leather-bottomed chairs, conversing on various matters, and occasionally lending their attention to some topic of general interest. Three or four little groups were draining as many bowls of punch, which the great West India trade[1] had long since made a familiar drink in the colony. Others, who had the aspect of men who lived by regular and laborious handicraft, preferred the insulated bliss of an unshared potation, and became more taciturn under its influence. Nearly all, in short, evinced a predilection for the Good Creature in some of its various shapes, for this is a vice, to which, as the Fast-day[2] sermons of a hundred years ago will testify, we have a long hereditary claim. The only guests to whom Robin's sympathies inclined him, were two or three sheepish countrymen, who were using the inn somewhat after the fashion of a Turkish Caravansary; they had gotten themselves into the darkest corner of the room, and, heedless of the Nicotian[3] atmosphere, were supping on the bread of their own ovens, and the bacon cured in their own chimney-smoke. But though Robin felt a sort of brotherhood with these strangers, his eyes were attracted from them, to a person who stood near the door, holding whispered conversation with a group of ill-dressed associates. His features were separately striking almost to grotesqueness, and the whole face left a deep impression in the memory. The forehead bulged out into a double prominence, with a vale between; the nose came boldly forth in an irregular curve, and its bridge was of more than a finger's breadth; the eyebrows were deep and shaggy, and the eyes glowed beneath them like fire in a cave.

While Robin deliberated of whom to inquire respecting his kinsman's dwelling, he was accosted by the innkeeper, a little man in a stained white apron, who had come to pay his professional welcome to the stranger. Being in the second generation from a French protestant, he seemed to have inherited the courtesy of his parent nation; but no variety of circumstance was ever known to change his voice from the one shrill note in which he now addressed Robin.

'From the country, I presume, Sir?' said he, with a profound bow. 'Beg to congratulate you on your arrival, and trust you intend a long stay with us. Fine town here, Sir, beautiful buildings, and much that may interest a stranger. May I hope for the honor of your commands in respect to supper?'

'The man sees a family likeness! the rogue has guessed that I am related to the Major!' thought Robin, who had hitherto experienced little superfluous civility.

All eyes were now turned on the country lad, standing at the door, in his worn three-cornered hat, grey coat, leather breeches, and blue yarn stockings, leaning on an oaken cudgel, and bearing a wallet on his back. Robin

1. West Indian molasses was shipped to New England and there made into rum.
2. Days set apart for public penitence. "Good Creature": rum. Hawthorne is alluding to 1 Timothy 4.4: "For every creature of God is good, and nothing to be refused, if it be received with thanksgiving."
3. Synonym for nicotine. "Caravansary": an inn built around a court for accommodating caravans.

replied to the courteous innkeeper, with such an assumption of consequence, as befitted the Major's relative.

'My honest friend,' he said, 'I shall make it a point to patronise your house on some occasion, when—' here he could not help lowering his voice—'I may have more than a parchment three-pence in my pocket. My present business,' continued he, speaking with lofty confidence, 'is merely to inquire the way to the dwelling of my kinsman, Major Molineux.'

There was a sudden and general movement in the room, which Robin interpreted as expressing the eagerness of each individual to become his guide. But the innkeeper turned his eyes to a written paper on the wall, which he read, or seemed to read, with occasional recurrences to the young man's figure.

'What have we here?' said he, breaking his speech into little dry fragments, "Left the house of the subscriber, bounden servant,[4] Hezekiah Mudge—had on when he went away, grey coat, leather breeches, master's third best hat. One pound currency reward to whoever shall lodge him in any jail in the province." 'Better trudge, boy, better trudge.'

Robin had begun to draw his hand towards the lighter end of the oak cudgel, but a strange hostility in every countenance, induced him to relinquish his purpose of breaking the courteous innkeeper's head. As he turned to leave the room, he encountered a sneering glance from the bold-featured personage whom he had before noticed; and no sooner was he beyond the door, than he heard a general laugh, in which the innkeeper's voice might be distinguished, like the dropping of small stones in a kettle.

'Now is it not strange,' thought Robin, with his usual shrewdness, 'is it not strange, that the confession of an empty pocket, should outweigh the name of my kinsman, Major Molineux? Oh, if I had one of these grinning rascals in the woods, where I and my oak sapling grew up together, I would teach him that my arm is heavy, though my purse be light!'

On turning the corner of the narrow lane, Robin found himself in a spacious street, with an unbroken line of lofty houses on each side, and a steepled building at the upper end, whence the ringing of a bell announced the hour of nine. The light of the moon, and the lamps from numerous shop windows, discovered people promenading on the pavement, and amongst them, Robin hoped to recognise his hitherto inscrutable relative. The result of his former inquiries made him unwilling to hazard another, in a scene of such publicity, and he determined to walk slowly and silently up the street, thrusting his face close to that of every elderly gentleman, in search of the Major's lineaments. In his progress, Robin encountered many gay and gallant figures. Embroidered garments, of showy colors, enormous periwigs, gold-laced hats, and silver hilted swords, glided past him and dazzled his optics. Travelled youths, imitators of the European fine gentlemen of the period, trod jauntily along, half-dancing to the fashionable tunes which they hummed, and making poor Robin ashamed of his quiet and natural gait. At length, after many pauses to examine the gorgeous display of goods in the shop windows, and after suffering some rebukes for the impertinence of his scrutiny into people's faces, the Major's kinsman found himself near the steepled

4. A person bound, or "indentured," by contract to servitude for seven years (or another set period), usually in repayment for transportation to the colonies.

building, still unsuccessful in his search. As yet, however, he had seen only one side of the thronged street; so Robin crossed, and continued the same sort of inquisition down the opposite pavement, with stronger hopes than the philosopher seeking an honest man,[5] but with no better fortune. He had arrived about midway towards the lower end, from which his course began, when he overheard the approach of some one, who struck down a cane on the flag-stones at every step, uttering, at regular intervals, two sepulchral hems.

'Mercy on us!' quoth Robin, recognising the sound.

Turning a corner, which chanced to be close at his right hand, he hastened to pursue his researches, in some other part of the town. His patience was now wearing low, and he seemed to feel more fatigue from his rambles since he crossed the ferry, than from his journey of several days on the other side. Hunger also pleaded loudly within him, and Robin began to balance the propriety of demanding, violently and with lifted cudgel, the necessary guidance from the first solitary passenger, whom he should meet. While a resolution to this effect was gaining strength, he entered a street of mean appearance, on either side of which, a row of ill-built houses was straggling towards the harbor. The moonlight fell upon no passenger along the whole extent, but in the third domicile which Robin passed, there was a half-opened door, and his keen glance detected a woman's garment within.

'My luck may be better here,' said he to himself.

Accordingly, he approached the door, and beheld it shut closer as he did so; yet an open space remained, sufficing for the fair occupant to observe the stranger, without a corresponding display on her part. All that Robin could discern was a strip of scarlet petticoat, and the occasional sparkle of an eye, as if the moonbeams were trembling on some bright thing.

'Pretty mistress,'—for I may call her so with a good conscience, thought the shrewd youth, since I know nothing to the contrary—'my sweet pretty mistress, will you be kind enough to tell me whereabouts I must seek the dwelling of my kinsman, Major Molineux?'

Robin's voice was plaintive and winning, and the female, seeing nothing to be shunned in the handsome country youth, thrust open the door, and came forth into the moonlight. She was a dainty little figure, with a white neck, round arms, and a slender waist, at the extremity of which her scarlet petticoat jutted out over a hoop, as if she were standing in a balloon. Moreover, her face was oval and pretty, her hair dark beneath the little cap, and her bright eyes possessed a sly freedom, which triumphed over those of Robin.

'Major Molineux dwells here,' said this fair woman.

Now her voice was the sweetest Robin had heard that night, the airy counterpart of a stream of melted silver; yet he could not help doubting whether that sweet voice spoke gospel truth. He looked up and down the mean street, and then surveyed the house before which they stood. It was a small, dark edifice of two stories, the second of which projected over the lower floor; and the front apartment had the aspect of a shop for petty commodities.

'Now truly I am in luck,' replied Robin, cunningly, 'and so indeed is my kinsman, the Major, in having so pretty a housekeeper. But I prithee trou-

5. Diogenes, the Greek philosopher (412?–323 B.C.E.), carried a lantern about in daytime in his search for an honest man.

ble him to step to the door; I will deliver him a message from his friends in the country, and then go back to my lodgings at the inn.'

'Nay, the Major has been a-bed this hour or more, said the lady of the scarlet petticoat; 'and it would be to little purpose to disturb him to night, seeing his evening draught was of the strongest. But he is a kind-hearted man, and it would be as much as my life's worth, to let a kinsman of his turn away from the door. You are the good old gentleman's very picture, and I could swear that was his rainy-weather hat. Also, he has garments very much resembling those leather—But come in, I pray, for I bid you hearty welcome in his name.'

So saying, the fair and hospitable dame took our hero by the hand; and though the touch was light, and the force was gentleness, and though Robin read in her eyes what he did not hear in her words, yet the slender waisted woman, in the scarlet petticoat, proved stronger than the athletic country youth. She had drawn his half-willing footsteps nearly to the threshold, when the opening of a door in the neighborhood, startled the Major's housekeeper, and, leaving the Major's kinsman, she vanished speedily into her own domicile. A heavy yawn preceded the appearance of a man, who, like the Moonshine of Pyramus and Thisbe, carried a lantern,[6] needlessly aiding his sister luminary in the heavens. As he walked sleepily up the street, he turned his broad, dull face on Robin, and displayed a long staff, spiked at the end.

'Home, vagabond, home!' said the watchman, in accents that seemed to fall asleep as soon as they were uttered. 'Home, or we'll set you in the stocks by peep of day!'

'This is the second hint of the kind,' thought Robin. 'I wish they would end my difficulties, by setting me there to-night.'

Nevertheless, the youth felt an instinctive antipathy towards the guardian of midnight order, which at first prevented him from asking his usual question. But just when the man was about to vanish behind the corner, Robin resolved not to lose the opportunity, and shouted lustily after him—

'I say, friend! will you guide me to the house of my kinsman, Major Molineux?'

The watchman made no reply, but turned the corner and was gone; yet Robin seemed to hear the sound of drowsy laughter stealing along the solitary street. At that moment, also, a pleasant titter saluted him from the open window above his head; he looked up, and caught the sparkle of a saucy eye; a round arm beckoned to him, and next he heard light footsteps descending the staircase within. But Robin, being of the household of a New England clergyman, was a good youth, as well as a shrewd one; so he resisted temptation, and fled away.

He now roamed desperately, and at random, through the town, almost ready to believe that a spell was on him, like that, by which a wizard of his country, had once kept three pursuers wandering, a whole winter night, within twenty paces of the cottage which they sought. The streets lay before him, strange and desolate, and the lights were extinguished in almost every house. Twice, however, little parties of men, among whom Robin distinguished individuals in outlandish attire, came hurrying along, but though

6. In the play-within-a-play in Shakespeare's *Midsummer Night's Dream* 5.1, the character Moonshine carries a lantern representing the moonlight that shines on the lovers Pyramus and Thisbe.

on both occasions they paused to address him, such intercourse did not at all enlighten his perplexity. They did but utter a few words in some language of which Robin knew nothing, and perceiving his inability to answer, bestowed a curse upon him in plain English, and hastened away. Finally, the lad determined to knock at the door of every mansion that might appear worthy to be occupied by his kinsman, trusting that perseverance would overcome the fatality which had hitherto thwarted him. Firm in this resolve, he was passing beneath the walls of a church, which formed the corner of two streets, when, as he turned into the shade of its steeple, he encountered a bulky stranger, muffled in a cloak. The man was proceeding with the speed of earnest business, but Robin planted himself full before him, holding the oak cudgel with both hands across his body, as a bar to further passage.

'Halt, honest man, and answer me a question,' said he, very resolutely, 'Tell me, this instant, whereabouts is the dwelling of my kinsman, Major Molineux?'

'Keep your tongue between your teeth, fool, and let me pass,' said a deep, gruff voice, which Robin partly remembered. 'Let me pass, I say, or I'll strike you to the earth!'

'No, no, neighbor!' cried Robin, flourishing his cudgel, and then thrusting its larger end close to the man's muffled face. 'No, no, I'm not the fool you take me for, nor do you pass, till I have an answer to my question. Whereabouts is the dwelling of my kinsman, Major Molineux?'

The stranger, instead of attempting to force his passage, stept back into the moonlight, unmuffled his own face and stared full into that of Robin.

'Watch here an hour, and Major Molineux will pass by,' said he.

Robin gazed with dismay and astonishment, on the unprecedented physiognomy of the speaker. The forehead with its double prominence, the broad-hooked nose, the shaggy eyebrows, and fiery eyes, were those which he had noticed at the inn, but the man's complexion had undergone a singular, or more properly, a two-fold change. One side of the face blazed of an intense red, while the other was black as midnight, the division line being in the broad bridge of the nose; and a mouth, which seemed to extend from ear to ear, was black or red, in contrast to the color of the cheek. The effect was as if two individual devils, a fiend of fire and a fiend of darkness, had united themselves to form this infernal visage. The stranger grinned in Robin's face, muffled his party-colored features, and was out of sight in a moment.

'Strange things we travellers see!' ejaculated Robin.

He seated himself, however, upon the steps of the church-door, resolving to wait the appointed time for his kinsman's appearance. A few moments were consumed in philosophical speculations, upon the species of the *genus homo*, who had just left him, but having settled this point shrewdly, rationally, and satisfactorily, he was compelled to look elsewhere for amusement. And first he threw his eyes along the street; it was of more respectable appearance than most of those into which he had wandered, and the moon, 'creating, like the imaginative power, a beautiful strangeness in familiar objects,' gave something of romance to a scene, that might not have possessed it in the light of day. The irregular, and often quaint architecture of the houses, some of whose roofs were broken into numerous little peaks; while others ascended, steep and narrow, into a single point; and others again were square; the pure milk-white of some of their complexions, the aged darkness of others, and the thousand sparklings, reflected from bright substances in the plastered walls of many; these matters engaged Robin's attention for awhile, and then began to grow wearisome. Next he endeavored to define the forms of distant objects, starting away with almost ghostly indistinctness, just as his eye appeared to grasp them; and finally he took a minute survey of an edifice, which stood on the opposite side of the street, directly in front of the church-door, where he was stationed. It was a large square mansion, distinguished from its neighbors by a balcony, which rested on tall pillars, and by an elaborate gothic window, communicating therewith.

'Perhaps this is the very house I have been seeking,' thought Robin.

Then he strove to speed away the time, by listening to a murmur, which swept continually along the street, yet was scarcely audible, except to an unaccustomed ear like his; it was a low, dull, dreamy sound, compounded of many noises, each of which was at too great a distance to be separately heard. Robin marvelled at this snore of a sleeping town, and marvelled more, whenever its continuity was broken, by now and then a distant shout, apparently loud where it originated. But altogether it was a sleep-inspiring sound, and to shake off its drowsy influence, Robin arose, and climbed a window-frame, that he might view the interior of the church. There the moonbeams came trembling in, and fell down upon the deserted pews, and extended along the quiet aisles. A fainter, yet more awful radiance, was hovering round the pulpit, and one solitary ray had dared to rest upon the opened page of the great bible. Had Nature, in that deep hour, become a worshipper in the house, which man had builded? Or was that heavenly light the visible sanctity of this place, visible because no earthly and impure feet were within the walls? The scene made Robin's heart shiver with a sensation of loneliness, stronger than he had ever felt in the remotest depths of his native woods; so he turned away, and sat down again before the door. There were graves around the church, and now an uneasy thought obtruded into Robin's breast. What if the object of his search, which had been so often and so strangely thwarted, were all the time mouldering in his shroud? What if his kinsman should glide through yonder gate, and nod and smile to him in passing dimly by?

'Oh, that any breathing thing were here with me!' said Robin.

Recalling his thoughts from this uncomfortable track, he sent them over forest, hill, and stream, and attempted to imagine how that evening of ambiguity and weariness, had been spent by his father's household. He pictured them assembled at the door, beneath the tree, the great old tree, which had been spared for its huge twisted trunk, and venerable shade, when a thousand leafy brethren fell. There, at the going down of the summer sun, it was his father's custom to perform domestic worship, that the neighbors might come and join with him like brothers of the family, and that the wayfaring man might pause to drink at that fountain, and keep his heart pure by freshening the memory of home. Robin distinguished the seat of every individual of the little audience; he saw the good man in the midst, holding the scriptures in the golden light that shone from the western clouds; he beheld him close the book, and all rise up to pray. He heard the old thanksgivings for daily mercies, the old supplications for their continuance, to which he had so often listened in weariness, but which were now among his dear remembrances. He perceived the slight inequality of his father's voice when he came to speak of the Absent One; he noted how his mother turned her face to the broad and knotted trunk, how his elder brother scorned, because the beard was rough upon his upper lip, to permit his features to be moved; how his younger sister drew down a low hanging branch before her eyes; and how the little one of all, whose sports had hitherto broken the decorum of the scene, understood the prayer for her playmate, and burst into clamorous grief. Then he saw them go in at the door; and when Robin would have entered also, the latch tinkled into its place, and he was excluded from his home.

'Am I here, or there?' cried Robin, starting; for all at once, when his thoughts had become visible and audible in a dream, the long, wide, solitary street shone out before him.

He aroused himself, and endeavored to fix his attention steadily upon the large edifice which he had surveyed before. But still his mind kept vibrating between fancy and reality; by turns, the pillars of the balcony lengthened into the tall, bare stems of pines, dwindled down to human figures, settled again in their true shape and size, and then commenced a new succession of changes. For a single moment, when he deemed himself awake, he could have sworn that a visage, one which he seemed to remember, yet could not absolutely name as his kinsman's, was looking towards him from the Gothic window. A deeper sleep wrestled with, and nearly overcame him, but fled at the sound of footsteps along the opposite pavement. Robin rubbed his eyes, discerned a man passing at the foot of the balcony, and addressed him in a loud, peevish, and lamentable cry.

'Halloo, friend! must I wait here all night for my kinsman, Major Molineux?'

The sleeping echoes awoke, and answered the voice; and the passenger, barely able to discern a figure sitting in the oblique shade of the steeple, traversed the street to obtain a nearer view. He was himself a gentleman in his prime, of open, intelligent, cheerful and altogether prepossessing countenance. Perceiving a country youth, apparently homeless and without friends, he accosted him in a tone of real kindness, which had become strange to Robin's ears.

'Well, my good lad, why are you sitting here?' inquired he. 'Can I be of service to you in any way?'

'I am afraid not, Sir,' replied Robin, despondingly; 'yet I shall take it kindly, if you'll answer me a single question. I've been searching half the night for one Major Molineux; now, Sir, is there really such a person in these parts, or am I dreaming?'

'Major Molineux! The name is not altogether strange to me,' said the gentleman smiling. 'Have you any objection to telling me the nature of your business with him?'

Then Robin briefly related that his father was a clergyman, settled on a small salary, at a long distance back in the country, and that he and Major Molineux were brothers' children. The Major, having inherited riches, and acquired civil and military rank, had visited his cousin in great pomp a year or two before; had manifested much interest in Robin and an elder brother, and, being childless himself, had thrown out hints respecting the future establishment of one of them in life. The elder brother was destined to succeed to the farm, which his father cultivated, in the interval of sacred duties; it was therefore determined that Robin should profit by his kinsman's generous intentions, especially as he had seemed to be rather the favorite, and was thought to possess other necessary endowments.

'For I have the name of being a shrewd youth,' observed Robin, in this part of his story.

'I doubt not you deserve it,' replied his new friend, good naturedly; 'but pray proceed.'

'Well, Sir, being nearly eighteen years old, and well grown, as you see,' continued Robin, raising himself to his full height, 'I thought it high time to begin the world. So my mother and sister put me in handsome trim, and my father gave me half the remnant of his last year's salary, and five days ago I started for this place, to pay the Major a visit. But would you believe it, Sir? I crossed the ferry a little after dusk, and have yet found nobody that would show me the way to his dwelling; only an hour or two since, I was told to wait here, and Major Molineux would pass by.'

'Can you describe the man who told you this?' inquired the gentleman.

'Oh, he was a very ill-favored fellow, Sir,' replied Robin, 'with two great bumps on his forehead, a hook nose, fiery eyes, and, what struck me as the strangest, his face was of two different colors. Do you happen to know such a man, Sir?'

'Not intimately,' answered the stranger, 'but I chanced to meet him a little time previous to your stopping me. I believe you may trust his word, and that the Major will very shortly pass through this street. In the mean time, as I have a singular curiosity to witness your meeting, I will sit down here upon the steps, and bear you company.'

He seated himself accordingly, and soon engaged his companion in animated discourse. It was but of brief continuance, however, for a noise of shouting, which had long been remotely audible, drew so much nearer, that Robin inquired its cause.

'What may be the meaning of this uproar?' asked he. 'Truly, if your town be always as noisy, I shall find little sleep, while I am an inhabitant.'

'Why, indeed, friend Robin, there do appear to be three or four riotous fellows abroad to-night,' replied the gentleman. 'You must not expect all the stillness of your native woods, here in our streets. But the watch will shortly be at the heels of these lads, and—'

'Aye, and set them in the stocks by peep of day,' interrupted Robin, recollecting his own encounter with the drowsy lantern-bearer. 'But, dear Sir, if I may trust my ears, an army of watchmen would never make head against such a multitude of rioters. There were at least a thousand voices went to make up that one shout.'

'May not one man have several voices, Robin, as well as two complexions?' said his friend.

'Perhaps a man may; but heaven forbid that a woman should!' responded the shrewd youth, thinking of the seductive tones of the Major's housekeeper.

The sounds of a trumpet in some neighboring street, now became so evident and continual, that Robin's curiosity was strongly excited. In addition to the shouts, he heard frequent bursts from many instruments of discord, and a wild and confused laughter filled up the intervals. Robin rose from the steps, and looked wistfully towards a point, whither several people seemed to be hastening.

'Surely some prodigious merrymaking is going on,' exclaimed he. 'I have laughed very little since I left home, Sir, and should be sorry to lose an opportunity. Shall we just step round the corner by that darkish house, and take our share of the fun?'

'Sit down again, sit down, good Robin,' replied the gentleman, laying his hand on the skirt of the grey coat. 'You forget that we must wait here for your kinsman; and there is reason to believe that he will pass by, in the course of a very few moments.'

The near approach of the uproar had now disturbed the neighborhood; windows flew open on all sides; and many heads, in the attire of the pillow, and confused by sleep suddenly broken, were protruded to the gaze of whoever had leisure to observe them. Eager voices hailed each other from house to house, all demanding the explanation, which not a soul could give. Half-dressed men hurried towards the unknown commotion, stumbling as they went over the stone steps, that thrust themselves into the narrow foot-walk. The shouts, the laughter, and the tuneless bray, the antipodes of music, came onward with increasing din, till scattered individuals, and then denser bodies, began to appear round a corner, at a distance of a hundred yards.

'Will you recognise your kinsman, Robin, if he passes in this crowd?' inquired the gentleman.

'Indeed, I can't warrant it, Sir; but I'll take my stand here, and keep a bright look out,' answered Robin, descending to the outer edge of the pavement.

A mighty stream of people now emptied into the street, and came rolling slowly towards the church. A single horseman wheeled the corner in the midst of them, and close behind him came a band of fearful wind-instruments, sending forth a fresher discord, now that no intervening buildings kept it from the ear. Then a redder light disturbed the moonbeams, and a dense multitude of torches shone along the street, concealing by their glare whatever object they illuminated. The single horseman, clad in a military dress, and bearing a drawn sword, rode onward as the leader, and, by his fierce and variegated countenance, appeared like war personified; the red of one cheek was an emblem of fire and sword; the blackness of the other betokened the mourning which attends them. In his train, were wild figures in the Indian dress, and many fantastic shapes without a model, giving the whole march a visionary air, as if a dream had broken forth from some feverish brain, and were sweeping visibly through the midnight streets. A mass of people, inactive, except as applauding spectators, hemmed the procession in, and several women ran along the sidewalks, piercing the confusion of heavier sounds, with their shrill voices of mirth or terror.[7]

'The double-faced fellow has his eye upon me,' muttered Robin, with an indefinite but uncomfortable idea, that he was himself to bear a part in the pageantry.

The leader turned himself in the saddle, and fixed his glance full upon the country youth, as the steed went slowly by. When Robin had freed his eyes from those fiery ones, the musicians were passing before him, and the torches were close at hand; but the unsteady brightness of the latter formed a veil which he could not penetrate. The rattling of wheels over the stones some-

7. Though set during the 1730s, the actions of the mob resemble those of the Boston Sons of Liberty during the Stamp Act crisis in 1765.

times found its way to his ear, and confused traces of a human form appeared at intervals, and then melted into the vivid light. A moment more, and the leader thundered a command to halt; the trumpets vomited a horrid breath, and held their peace; the shouts and laughter of the people died away, and there remained only an universal hum, nearly allied to silence. Right before Robin's eyes was an uncovered cart. There the torches blazed the brightest, there the moon shone out like day, and there, in tar-and-feathery dignity, sate his kinsman, Major Molineux!

He was an elderly man, of large and majestic person, and strong, square features, betokening a steady soul; but steady as it was, his enemies had found the means to shake it. His face was pale as death, and far more ghastly; the broad forehead was contracted in his agony, so that the eyebrows formed one dark grey line; his eyes were red and wild, and the foam hung white upon his quivering lip. His whole frame was agitated by a quick, and continual tremor, which his pride strove to quell, even in those circumstances of overwhelming humiliation. But perhaps the bitterest pang of all was when his eyes met those of Robin; for he evidently knew him on the instant, as the youth stood witnessing the foul disgrace of a head that had grown grey in honor. They stared at each other in silence, and Robin's knees shook, and his hair bristled, with a mixture of pity and terror. Soon, however, a bewildering excitement began to seize upon his mind; the preceding adventures of the night, the unexpected appearance of the crowd, the torches, the confused din, and the hush that followed, the spectre of his kinsman reviled by that great multitude, all this, and more than all, a perception of tremendous ridicule in the whole scene, affected him with a sort of mental inebriety. At that moment a voice of sluggish merriment saluted Robin's ears; he turned instinctively, and just behind the corner of the church stood the lantern-bearer, rubbing his eyes, and drowsily enjoying the lad's amazement. Then he heard a peal of laughter like the ringing of silvery bells; a woman twitched his arm, a saucy eye met his, and he saw the lady of the scarlet petticoat. A sharp, dry cachinnation appealed to his memory, and, standing on tiptoe in the crowd, with his white apron over his head, he beheld the courteous little innkeeper. And lastly, there sailed over the heads of the multitude a great, broad laugh, broken in the midst by two deep sepulchral hems; thus—

'Haw, haw, haw—hem, hem—haw, haw, haw, haw!'

The sound proceeded from the balcony of the opposite edifice, and thither Robin turned his eyes. In front of the Gothic window stood the old citizen, wrapped in a wide gown, his grey periwig exchanged for a nightcap, which was thrust back from his forehead, and his silk stockings hanging down about his legs. He supported himself on his polished cane in a fit of convulsive merriment, which manifested itself on his solemn old features, like a funny inscription on a tomb-stone. Then Robin seemed to hear the voices of the barbers; of the guests of the inn; and of all who had made sport of him that night. The contagion was spreading among the multitude, when, all at once, it seized upon Robin, and he sent forth a shout of laughter that echoed through the street; every man shook his sides, every man emptied his lungs, but Robin's shout was the loudest there. The cloud-spirits peeped from their silvery islands, as the congregated mirth went roaring up the sky! The Man in the Moon heard the far bellow; 'Oho,' quoth he, 'the old Earth is frolicsome to-night!'

When there was a momentary calm in that tempestuous sea of sound, the leader gave the sign, and the procession resumed its march. On they went, like fiends that throng in mockery round some dead potentate, mighty no more, but majestic still in his agony. On they went, in counterfeited pomp, in senseless uproar, in frenzied merriment, trampling all on an old man's heart. On swept the tumult, and left a silent street behind.

• • • • •

'Well, Robin, are you dreaming?' inquired the gentleman, laying his hand on the youth's shoulder.

Robin started, and withdrew his arm from the stone post, to which he had instinctively clung, while the living stream rolled by him. His cheek was somewhat pale, and his eye not quite so lively as in the earlier part of the evening.

'Will you be kind enough to show me the way to the Ferry?' said he, after a moment's pause.

'You have then adopted a new subject of inquiry?' observed his companion, with a smile.

'Why, yes, Sir,' replied Robin, rather dryly. 'Thanks to you, and to my other friends, I have at last met my kinsman, and he will scarce desire to see my face again. I begin to grow weary of a town life, Sir. Will you show me the way to the Ferry?'

'No, my good friend Robin, not to-night, at least,' said the gentleman. 'Some few days hence, if you continue to wish it, I will speed you on your journey. Or, if you prefer to remain with us, perhaps, as you are a shrewd youth, you may rise in the world, without the help of your kinsman, Major Molineux.'

1832

Young Goodman Brown[1]

Young goodman Brown came forth, at sunset, into the street of Salem village,[2] but put his head back, after crossing the threshold, to exchange a parting kiss with his young wife. And Faith, as the wife was aptly named, thrust her own pretty head into the street, letting the wind play with the pink ribbons of her cap, while she called to goodman Brown.

'Dearest heart,' whispered she, softly and rather sadly, when her lips were close to his ear, 'pr'y thee, put off your journey until sunrise, and sleep in your own bed to-night. A lone woman is troubled with such dreams and such thoughts, that she's afeard of herself, sometimes. Pray, tarry with me this night, dear husband, of all nights in the year!'

'My love and my Faith,' replied young goodman Brown, 'of all nights in the year, this one night must I tarry away from thee. My journey, as thou callest it, forth and back again, must needs be done 'twixt now and sunrise. What,

1. The text is that of the first publication in the *New-England Magazine* (April 1835). "Goodman": title used to address a man of humble birth.

2. In Massachusetts; the site of the witchcraft trials and executions of 1692.

my sweet, pretty wife, dost thou doubt me already, and we but three months married!'

'Then, God bless you!' said Faith, with the pink ribbons, 'and may you find all well, when you come back.'

'Amen!' cried goodman Brown. 'Say thy prayers, dear Faith, and go to bed at dusk, and no harm will come to thee.'

So they parted; and the young man pursued his way, until, being about to turn the corner by the meeting-house, he looked back, and saw the head of Faith still peeping after him, with a melancholy air, in spite of her pink ribbons.

'Poor little Faith!' thought he, for his heart smote him. 'What a wretch am I, to leave her on such an errand! She talks of dreams, too. Methought, as she spoke, there was trouble in her face, as if a dream had warned her what work is to be done to-night. But, no, no! 't would kill her to think it. Well; she's a blessed angel on earth; and after this one night, I'll cling to her skirts and follow her to Heaven.'

With this excellent resolve for the future, goodman Brown felt himself justified in making more haste on his present evil purpose. He had taken a dreary road, darkened by all the gloomiest trees of the forest, which barely stood aside to let the narrow path creep through, and closed immediately behind. It was all as lonely as could be; and there is this peculiarity in such a solitude, that the traveler knows not who may be concealed by the innumerable trunks and the thick boughs overhead; so that, with lonely footsteps, he may yet be passing through an unseen multitude.

'There may be a devilish Indian behind every tree,' said goodman Brown, to himself; and he glanced fearfully behind him, as he added, 'What if the devil himself should be at my very elbow!'

His head being turned back, he passed a crook of the road, and looking forward again, beheld the figure of a man, in grave and decent attire, seated at the foot of an old tree. He arose, at goodman Brown's approach, and walked onward, side by side with him.

'You are late, goodman Brown,' said he. 'The clock of the Old South was striking as I came through Boston; and that is full fifteen minutes agone.'[3]

'Faith kept me back awhile,' replied the young man, with a tremor in his voice, caused by the sudden appearance of his companion, though not wholly unexpected.

It was now deep dusk in the forest, and deepest in that part of it where these two were journeying. As nearly as could be discerned, the second traveler was about fifty years old, apparently in the same rank of life as goodman Brown, and bearing a considerable resemblance to him, though perhaps more in expression than features. Still, they might have been taken for father and son. And yet, though the elder person was as simply clad as the younger, and as simple in manner too, he had an indescribable air of one who knew the world, and would not have felt abashed at the governor's dinner-table, or in king William's[4] court, were it possible that his affairs should

3. Boston's Old South Church, built in 1669, was approximately sixteen miles from Salem. That the "figure" could make the journey from Old South to Salem in fifteen minutes signifies supernatural powers.

4. Beginning in 1689, King William III (1650–1702) ruled England with his wife, Queen Mary II, until her death in 1694.

call him thither. But the only thing about him, that could be fixed upon as remarkable, was his staff, which bore the likeness of a great black snake, so curiously wrought, that it might almost be seen to twist and wriggle itself, like a living serpent. This, of course, must have been an ocular deception, assisted by the uncertain light.

'Come, goodman Brown!' cried his fellow-traveler, 'this is a dull pace for the beginning of a journey. Take my staff, if you are so soon weary.'

'Friend,' said the other, exchanging his slow pace for a full stop, 'having kept covenant by meeting thee here, it is my purpose now to return whence I came. I have scruples, touching the matter thou wot'st[5] of.'

'Sayest thou so?' replied he of the serpent, smiling apart. 'Let us walk on, nevertheless, reasoning as we go, and if I convince thee not, thou shalt turn back. We are but a little way in the forest, yet.'

'Too far, too far!' exclaimed the goodman, unconsciously resuming his walk. 'My father never went into the woods on such an errand, nor his father before him. We have been a race of honest men and good Christians, since the days of the martyrs.[6] And shall I be the first of the name of Brown, that ever took this path, and kept'—

'Such company, thou wouldst say,' observed the elder person, interpreting his pause. 'Good, goodman Brown! I have been as well acquainted with your family as with ever a one among the Puritans; and that's no trifle to say. I helped your grandfather, the constable, when he lashed the Quaker woman so smartly through the streets of Salem.[7] And it was I that brought your father a pitch-pine knot, kindled at my own hearth, to set fire to an Indian village, in king Philip's[8] war. They were my good friends, both; and many a pleasant walk have we had along this path, and returned merrily after midnight. I would fain be friends with you, for their sake.'

'If it be as thou sayest,' replied goodman Brown, 'I marvel they never spoke of these matters. Or, verily, I marvel not, seeing that the least rumor of the sort would have driven them from New-England. We are a people of prayer, and good works, to boot, and abide no such wickedness.'

'Wickedness or not,' said the traveler with the twisted staff, 'I have a very general acquaintance here in New-England. The deacons of many a church have drunk the communion wine with me; the selectmen, of divers towns, make me their chairman; and a majority of the Great and General Court[9] are firm supporters of my interest. The governor and I, too—but these are state-secrets.'

'Can this be so!' cried goodman Brown, with a stare of amazement at his undisturbed companion. 'Howbeit, I have nothing to do with the governor and council; they have their own ways, and are no rule for a simple husbandman,[1] like me. But, were I to go on with thee, how should I meet the eye of

5. Wotest; to know (archaic).

6. I.e., during the reign of the Catholic Mary Tudor of England (r. 1553–58), called "Bloody Mary" for her persecution of Protestants. Common reading in New England was John Foxe's *Acts and Monuments* (1563), soon known as the *Book of Martyrs*; it concluded with detailed accounts of martyrdom under Mary.

7. Hawthorne's paternal great-great-grandfather, William Hathorne (1606–1681), had ordered the whipping of a Quaker woman in Salem. Hawthorne mentions this incident in "The Custom-House" preface to *The Scarlet Letter*.

8. Leader of the Wampanoag Indians, Metacomet (d. 1676), called Philip by the English, led a bloody and ultimately unsuccessful war (1675–76) against the New England colonists.

9. The legislature.

1. Usually, farmer; here, man of ordinary status.

that good old man, our minister, at Salem village? Oh, his voice would make me tremble, both Sabbath-day and lecture-day!'[2]

Thus far, the elder traveler had listened with due gravity, but now burst into a fit of irrepressible mirth, shaking himself so violently, that his snake-like staff actually seemed to wriggle in sympathy.

'Ha! ha! ha!' shouted he, again and again; then composing himself, 'Well, go on, goodman Brown, go on; but, pr'y thee, don't kill me with laughing!'

'Well, then, to end the matter at once,' said goodman Brown, considerably nettled, 'there is my wife, Faith. It would break her dear little heart; and I'd rather break my own!'

'Nay, if that be the case,' answered the other, 'e'en go thy ways, goodman Brown. I would not, for twenty old women like the one hobbling before us, that Faith should come to any harm.'

As he spoke, he pointed his staff at a female figure on the path, in whom goodman Brown recognized a very pious and exemplary dame, who had taught him his catechism, in youth, and was still his moral and spiritual adviser, jointly with the minister and deacon Gookin.[3]

'A marvel, truly, that goody Cloyse[4] should be so far in the wilderness, at night-fall!' said he. 'But, with your leave, friend, I shall take a cut through the woods, until we have left this Christian woman behind. Being a stranger to you, she might ask whom I was consorting with, and whither I was going.'

'Be it so,' said his fellow-traveler. 'Betake you to the woods, and let me keep the path.'

Accordingly, the young man turned aside, but took care to watch his companion, who advanced softly along the road, until he had come within a staff's length of the old dame. She, meanwhile, was making the best of her way, with singular speed for so aged a woman, and mumbling some indistinct words, a prayer, doubtless, as she went. The traveler put forth his staff, and touched her withered neck with what seemed the serpent's tail.

'The devil!' screamed the pious old lady.

'Then goody Cloyse knows her old friend?' observed the traveler, confronting her, and leaning on his writhing stick.

'Ah, forsooth, and is it your worship, indeed?' cried the good dame. 'Yea, truly is it, and in the very image of my old gossip, goodman Brown, the grandfather of the silly fellow that now is. But, would your worship believe it? my broomstick hath strangely disappeared, stolen, as I suspect, by that unhanged witch, goody Cory,[5] and that, too, when I was all anointed with the juice of smallage and cinque-foil and wolf's-bane'[6]—

'Mingled with fine wheat and the fat of a new-born babe,' said the shape of old goodman Brown.

'Ah, your worship knows the receipt,'[7] cried the old lady, cackling aloud. 'So, as I was saying, being all ready for the meeting, and no horse to ride on,

2. Midweek sermon day, Wednesday or Thursday.

3. Daniel Gookin (1612–1687), colonial magistrate who looked after Indian affairs. Throughout the story Hawthorne uses historical names associated with Salem and the witchcraft trial.

4. Sarah Cloyce was accused of witchcraft and imprisoned during the Salem witch trials; she was released when the trials were suspended. "Goody": i.e., goodwife; the polite title for a married woman of humble rank.

5. A woman named Martha Cory was hanged for witchcraft on September 22, 1692.

6. Plants associated with witchcraft. "Smallage": wild celery or parsley. "Cinque-foil": a five-lobed plant of the rose family (from the Latin for "five fingers"). "Wolf's-bane": hooded, poisonous plant known as monkshood (*bane* means "poison").

7. Recipe.

I made up my mind to foot it; for they tell me, there is a nice young man to be taken into communion to-night. But now your good worship will lend me your arm, and we shall be there in a twinkling.'

'That can hardly be,' answered her friend. 'I may not spare you my arm, goody Cloyse, but here is my staff, if you will.'

So saying, he threw it down at her feet, where, perhaps, it assumed life, being one of the rods which its owner had formerly lent to the Egyptian Magi.[8] Of this fact, however, goodman Brown could not take cognizance. He had cast up his eyes in astonishment, and looking down again, beheld neither goody Cloyse nor the serpentine staff, but his fellow-traveler alone, who waited for him as calmly as if nothing had happened.

'That old woman taught me my catechism!' said the young man; and there was a world of meaning in this simple comment.

They continued to walk onward, while the elder traveler exhorted his companion to make good speed and persevere in the path, discoursing so aptly, that his arguments seemed rather to spring up in the bosom of his auditor, than to be suggested by himself. As they went, he plucked a branch of maple, to serve for a walking-stick, and began to strip it of the twigs and little boughs, which were wet with evening dew. The moment his fingers touched them, they became strangely withered and dried up, as with a week's sunshine. Thus the pair proceeded, at a good free pace, until suddenly, in a gloomy hollow of the road, goodman Brown sat himself down on the stump of a tree, and refused to go any farther.

'Friend,' said he, stubbornly, 'my mind is made up. Not another step will I budge on this errand. What if a wretched old woman do choose to go to the devil, when I thought she was going to Heaven! Is that any reason why I should quit my dear Faith, and go after her?'

'You will think better of this, by-and-by,' said his acquaintance, composedly. 'Sit here and rest yourself awhile; and when you feel like moving again, there is my staff to help you along.'

Without more words, he threw his companion the maple stick, and was as speedily out of sight, as if he had vanished into the deepening gloom. The young man sat a few moments, by the roadside, applauding himself greatly, and thinking with how clear a conscience he should meet the minister, in his morning-walk, nor shrink from the eye of good old deacon Gookin. And what calm sleep would be his, that very night, which was to have been spent so wickedly, but purely and sweetly now, in the arms of Faith! Amidst these pleasant and praiseworthy meditations, goodman Brown heard the tramp of horses along the road, and deemed it advisable to conceal himself within the verge of the forest, conscious of the guilty purpose that had brought him thither, though now so happily turned from it.

On came the hoof-tramps and the voices of the riders, two grave old voices, conversing soberly as they drew near. These mingled sounds appeared to pass along the road, within a few yards of the young man's hiding-place; but owing, doubtless, to the depth of the gloom, at that particular spot, neither the travelers nor their steeds were visible. Though their figures brushed the small boughs by the way-side, it could not be seen that they intercepted, even

8. Exodus 7.11 describes the magicians of Egypt who duplicated Aaron's feat of casting down his rod before Pharaoh and making it turn into a serpent.

for a moment, the faint gleam from the strip of bright sky, athwart which they must have passed. Goodman Brown alternately crouched and stood on tiptoe, pulling aside the branches, and thrusting forth his head as far as he durst, without discerning so much as a shadow. It vexed him the more, because he could have sworn, were such a thing possible, that he recognized the voices of the minister and deacon Gookin, jogging along quietly, as they were wont to do, when bound to some ordination or ecclesiastical council. While yet within hearing, one of the riders stopped to pluck a switch.

'Of the two, reverend Sir,' said the voice like the deacon's, 'I had rather miss an ordination-dinner than to-night's meeting. They tell me that some of our community are to be here from Falmouth and beyond, and others from Connecticut and Rhode-Island; besides several of the Indian powows,[9] who, after their fashion, know almost as much deviltry as the best of us. Moreover, there is a goodly young woman to be taken into communion.'

'Mighty well, deacon Gookin!' replied the solemn old tones of the minister. 'Spur up, or we shall be late. Nothing can be done, you know, until I get on the ground.'

The hoofs clattered again, and the voices, talking so strangely in the empty air, passed on through the forest, where no church had ever been gathered, nor solitary Christian prayed. Whither, then, could these holy men be journeying, so deep into the heathen wilderness? Young goodman Brown caught hold of a tree, for support, being ready to sink down on the ground, faint and overburthened with the heavy sickness of his heart. He looked up to the sky, doubting whether there really was a Heaven above him. Yet, there was the blue arch, and the stars brightening in it.

'With Heaven above, and Faith below, I will yet stand firm against the devil!' cried goodman Brown.

While he still gazed upward, into the deep arch of the firmament, and had lifted his hands to pray, a cloud, though no wind was stirring, hurried across the zenith, and hid the brightening stars. The blue sky was still visible, except directly overhead, where this black mass of cloud was sweeping swiftly northward. Aloft in the air, as if from the depths of the cloud, came a confused and doubtful sound of voices. Once, the listener fancied that he could distinguish the accents of town's-people of his own, men and women, both pious and ungodly, many of whom he had met at the communion-table, and had seen others rioting at the tavern. The next moment, so indistinct were the sounds, he doubted whether he had heard aught but the murmur of the old forest, whispering without a wind. Then came a stronger swell of those familiar tones, heard daily in the sunshine, at Salem village, but never, until now, from a cloud of night. There was one voice, of a young woman, uttering lamentations, yet with an uncertain sorrow, and entreating for some favor, which, perhaps, it would grieve her to obtain. And all the unseen multitude, both saints and sinners, seemed to encourage her onward.

'Faith!' shouted goodman Brown, in a voice of agony and desperation; and the echoes of the forest mocked him, crying—'Faith! Faith!' as if bewildered wretches were seeking her, all through the wilderness.

9. Medicine men; usually spelled "pow-wow" and later used to refer to any conference or gathering. Falmouth is a town on Cape Cod, about seventy miles from Salem.

The cry of grief, rage, and terror, was yet piercing the night, when the unhappy husband held his breath for a response. There was a scream, drowned immediately in a louder murmur of voices, fading into far-off laughter, as the dark cloud swept away, leaving the clear and silent sky above goodman Brown. But something fluttered lightly down through the air, and caught on the branch of a tree. The young man seized it, and beheld a pink ribbon.

'My Faith is gone!' cried he, after one stupefied moment. 'There is no good on earth; and sin is but a name. Come, devil! for to thee is this world given.'

And maddened with despair, so that he laughed loud and long, did goodman Brown grasp his staff and set forth again, at such a rate, that he seemed to fly along the forest-path, rather than to walk or run. The road grew wilder and drearier, and more faintly traced, and vanished at length, leaving him in the heart of the dark wilderness, still rushing onward, with the instinct that guides mortal man to evil. The whole forest was peopled with frightful sounds; the creaking of the trees, the howling of wild beasts, and the yell of Indians; while, sometimes, the wind tolled like a distant church-bell, and sometimes gave a broad roar around the traveler, as if all Nature were laughing him to scorn. But he was himself the chief horror of the scene, and shrank not from its other horrors.

'Ha! ha! ha!' roared goodman Brown, when the wind laughed at him. 'Let us hear which will laugh loudest! Think not to frighten me with your deviltry! Come witch, come wizard, come Indian powow, come devil himself! and here comes goodman Brown. You may as well fear him as he fear you!'

In truth, all through the haunted forest, there could be nothing more frightful than the figure of goodman Brown. On he flew, among the black pines, brandishing his staff with frenzied gestures, now giving vent to an inspiration of horrid blasphemy, and now shouting forth such laughter, as set all the echoes of the forest laughing like demons around him. The fiend in his own shape is less hideous, than when he rages in the breast of man. Thus sped the demoniac on his course, until, quivering among the trees, he saw a red light before him, as when the felled trunks and branches of a clearing have been set on fire, and throw up their lurid blaze against the sky, at the hour of midnight. He paused, in a lull of the tempest that had driven him onward, and heard the swell of what seemed a hymn, rolling solemnly from a distance, with the weight of many voices. He knew the tune; it was a familiar one in the choir of the village meeting-house. The verse died heavily away, and was lengthened by a chorus, not of human voices, but of all the sounds of the benighted wilderness, pealing in awful harmony together. Goodman Brown cried out; and his cry was lost to his own ear, by its unison with the cry of the desert.

In the interval of silence, he stole forward, until the light glared full upon his eyes. At one extremity of an open space, hemmed in by the dark wall of the forest, arose a rock, bearing some rude, natural resemblance either to an altar or a pulpit, and surrounded by four blazing pines, their tops a flame, their stems untouched, like candles at an evening meeting. The mass of foliage, that had overgrown the summit of the rock, was all on fire, blazing high into the night, and fitfully illuminating the whole field. Each pendent twig and leafy festoon was in a blaze. As the red light arose and fell, a numerous congregation alternately shone forth, then disappeared in shadow, and again grew, as it were, out of the darkness, peopling the heart of the solitary woods at once.

'A grave and dark-clad company!' quoth goodman Brown.

In truth, they were such. Among them, quivering to-and-fro, between gloom and splendor, appeared faces that would be seen, next day, at the council-board of the province, and others which, Sabbath after Sabbath, looked devoutly heavenward, and benignantly over the crowded pews, from the holiest pulpits in the land. Some affirm, that the lady of the governor was there. At least, there were high dames well known to her, and wives of honored husbands, and widows, a great multitude, and ancient maidens, all of excellent repute, and fair young girls, who trembled, lest their mothers should espy them. Either the sudden gleams of light, flashing over the obscure field, bedazzled goodman Brown, or he recognized a score of the church-members of Salem village, famous for their especial sanctity. Good old deacon Gookin had arrived, and waited at the skirts of that venerable saint, his revered pastor. But, irreverently consorting with these grave, reputable, and pious people, these elders of the church, these chaste dames and dewy virgins, there were men of dissolute lives and women of spotted fame, wretches given over to all mean and filthy vice, and suspected even of horrid crimes. It was strange to see, that the good shrank not from the wicked, nor were the sinners abashed by the saints. Scattered, also, among their pale-faced enemies, were the Indian priests, or powows, who had often scared their native forest with more hideous incantations than any known to English witchcraft.

'But, where is Faith?' thought goodman Brown; and, as hope came into his heart, he trembled.

Another verse of the hymn arose, a slow and solemn strain, such as the pious love, but joined to words which expressed all that our nature can conceive of sin, and darkly hinted at far more. Unfathomable to mere mortals is the lore of fiends. Verse after verse was sung, and still the chorus of the desert swelled between, like the deepest tone of a mighty organ. And, with the final peal of that dreadful anthem, there came a sound, as if the roaring wind, the rushing streams, the howling beasts, and every other voice of the unconverted wilderness, were mingling and according with the voice of guilty man, in homage to the prince of all. The four blazing pines threw up a loftier flame, and obscurely discovered shapes and visages of horror on the smoke-wreaths, above the impious assembly. At the same moment, the fire on the rock shot redly forth, and formed a glowing arch above its base, where now appeared a figure. With reverence be it spoken, the apparition bore no slight similitude, both in garb and manner, to some grave divine of the New-England churches.

'Bring forth the converts!' cried a voice, that echoed through the field and rolled into the forest.

At the word, goodman Brown stept forth from the shadow of the trees, and approached the congregation, with whom he felt a loathful brotherhood, by the sympathy of all that was wicked in his heart. He could have well nigh sworn, that the shape of his own dead father[1] beckoned him to advance,

1. The Salem witch trials came to focus on the question of "specter evidence"—whether the devil could take on the "shape" of innocent people. If he could, then many supposed appearances of the accused might have been impersonations. An increasing suspicion of the value of spectral evidence was among the factors leading to the suspension of the trials.

looking downward from a smoke-wreath, while a woman, with dim features of despair, threw out her hand to warn him back. Was it his mother? But he had no power to retreat one step, nor to resist, even in thought, when the minister and good old deacon Gookin, seized his arms, and led him to the blazing rock. Thither came also the slender form of a veiled female, led between goody Cloyse, that pious teacher of the catechism, and Martha Carrier, who had received the devil's promise to be queen of hell.[2] A rampant hag was she! And there stood the proselytes, beneath the canopy of fire.

'Welcome, my children,' said the dark figure, 'to the communion of your race![3] Ye have found, thus young, your nature and your destiny. My children, look behind you!'

They turned; and flashing forth, as it were, in a sheet of flame, the fiend-worshippers were seen; the smile of welcome gleamed darkly on every visage.

'There,' resumed the sable form, 'are all whom ye have reverenced from youth. Ye deemed them holier than yourselves, and shrank from your own sin, contrasting it with their lives of righteousness, and prayerful aspirations heavenward. Yet, here are they all, in my worshipping assembly! This night it shall be granted you to know their secret deeds; how hoary-bearded elders of the church have whispered wanton words to the young maids of their households; how many a woman, eager for widow's weeds, has given her husband a drink at bed-time, and let him sleep his last sleep in her bosom; how beardless youths have made haste to inherit their fathers' wealth; and how fair damsels—blush not, sweet ones!—have dug little graves in the garden, and bidden me, the sole guest, to an infant's funeral. By the sympathy of your human hearts for sin, ye shall scent out all the places—whether in church, bed-chamber, street, field, or forest—where crime has been committed, and shall exult to behold the whole earth one stain of guilt, one mighty blood-spot. Far more than this! It shall be yours to penetrate, in every bosom, the deep mystery of sin, the fountain of all wicked arts, and which, inexhaustibly supplies more evil impulses than human power—than my power, at its utmost!—can make manifest in deeds. And now, my children, look upon each other.'

They did so; and, by the blaze of the hell-kindled torches, the wretched man beheld his Faith, and the wife her husband, trembling before that unhallowed altar.

'Lo! there ye stand, my children,' said the figure, in a deep and solemn tone, almost sad, with its despairing awfulness, as if his once angelic nature could yet mourn for our miserable race. 'Depending upon one another's hearts, ye had still hoped, that virtue were not all a dream. Now are ye undeceived! Evil is the nature of mankind. Evil must be your only happiness. Welcome, again, my children, to the communion of your race!'

'Welcome!' repeated the fiend-worshippers, in one cry of despair and triumph.

And there they stood, the only pair, as it seemed, who were yet hesitating on the verge of wickedness, in this dark world. A basin was hollowed, naturally, in the rock. Did it contain water, reddened by the lurid light? or was it

2. During her trial, the historical Martha Carrier told of how the devil promised that she could become the queen of hell; she was convicted and hanged for witchcraft on August 19, 1692.

3. The *New-England Magazine* erroneously printed "grave," corrected to "race" in *Mosses from an Old Manse* (1846).

blood? or, perchance, a liquid flame? Herein did the Shape of Evil dip his hand, and prepare to lay the mark of baptism upon their foreheads, that they might be partakers of the mystery of sin, more conscious of the secret guilt of others, both in deed and thought, than they could now be of their own. The husband cast one look at his pale wife, and Faith at him. What polluted wretches would the next glance shew them to each other, shuddering alike at what they disclosed and what they saw!

'Faith! Faith!' cried the husband. 'Look up to Heaven, and resist the Wicked One!'

Whether Faith obeyed, he knew not. Hardly had he spoken, when he found himself amid calm night and solitude, listening to a roar of the wind, which died heavily away through the forest. He staggered against the rock and felt it chill and damp, while a hanging twig, that had been all on fire, besprinkled his cheek with the coldest dew.

The next morning, young goodman Brown came slowly into the street of Salem village, staring around him like a bewildered man. The good old minister was taking a walk along the graveyard, to get an appetite for breakfast and meditate his sermon, and bestowed a blessing, as he passed, on goodman Brown. He shrank from the venerable saint, as if to avoid an anathema. Old deacon Gookin was at domestic worship, and the holy words of his prayer were heard through the open window. 'What God doth the wizard pray to?' quoth goodman Brown. Goody Cloyse, that excellent old Christian, stood in the early sunshine, at her own lattice, catechising a little girl, who had brought her a pint of morning's milk. Goodman Brown snatched away the child, as from the grasp of the fiend himself. Turning the corner by the meeting-house, he spied the head of Faith, with the pink ribbons, gazing anxiously forth, and bursting into such joy at sight of him, that she skipt along the street, and almost kissed her husband before the whole village. But, goodman Brown looked sternly and sadly into her face, and passed on without a greeting.

Had goodman Brown fallen asleep in the forest, and only dreamed a wild dream of a witch-meeting?

Be it so, if you will. But, alas! it was a dream of evil omen for young goodman Brown. A stern, a sad, a darkly meditative, a distrustful, if not a desperate man, did he become, from the night of that fearful dream. On the Sabbath-day, when the congregation were singing a holy psalm, he could not listen, because an anthem of sin rushed loudly upon his ear, and drowned all the blessed strain. When the minister spoke from the pulpit, with power and fervid eloquence, and, with his hand on the open bible, of the sacred truths of our religion, and of saint-like lives and triumphant deaths, and of future bliss or misery unutterable, then did goodman Brown turn pale, dreading, lest the roof should thunder down upon the gray blasphemer and his hearers. Often, awakening suddenly at midnight, he shrank from the bosom of Faith, and at morning or eventide, when the family knelt down at prayer, he scowled, and muttered to himself, and gazed sternly at his wife, and turned away. And when he had lived long, and was borne to his grave, a hoary corpse, followed by Faith, an aged woman, and children and grandchildren, a goodly procession, besides neighbors, not a few, they carved no hopeful verse upon his tomb-stone; for his dying hour was gloom.

1835

Wakefield[1]

In some old magazine or newspaper, I recollect a story, told as truth, of a man—let us call him Wakefield—who absented himself for a long time, from his wife. The fact, thus abstractedly stated, is not very uncommon, nor—without a proper distinction of circumstances—to be condemned either as naughty or nonsensical. Howbeit, this, though far from the most aggravated, is perhaps the strangest instance, on record, of marital delinquency; and, moreover, as remarkable a freak as may be found in the whole list of human oddities. The wedded couple lived in London. The man, under pretence of going a journey, took lodgings in the next street to his own house, and there, unheard of by his wife or friends, and without the shadow of a reason for such self-banishment, dwelt upwards of twenty years. During that period, he beheld his home every day, and frequently the forlorn Mrs. Wakefield. And after so great a gap in his matrimonial felicity—when his death was reckoned certain, his estate settled, his name dismissed from memory, and his wife, long, long ago, resigned to her autumnal widowhood—he entered the door one evening, quietly, as from a day's absence, and became a loving spouse until death.

This outline is all that I remember. But the incident, though of the purest originality, unexampled, and probably never to be repeated, is one, I think, which appeals to the general sympathies of mankind. We know, each for himself, that none of us would perpetrate such a folly, yet feel as if some other might. To my own contemplations, at least, it has often recurred, always exciting wonder, but with a sense that the story must be true, and a conception of its hero's character. Whenever any subject so forcibly affects the mind, time is well spent in thinking of it. If the reader choose, let him do his own meditation; or if he prefer to ramble with me through the twenty years of Wakefield's vagary, I bid him welcome; trusting that there will be a pervading spirit and a moral, even should we fail to find them, done up neatly, and condensed into the final sentence. Thought has always its efficacy, and every striking incident its moral.

What sort of a man was Wakefield? We are free to shape out our own idea, and call it by his name. He was now in the meridian of life; his matrimonial affections, never violent, were sobered into a calm, habitual sentiment; of all husbands, he was likely to be the most constant, because a certain sluggishness would keep his heart at rest, wherever it might be placed. He was intellectual, but not actively so; his mind occupied itself in long and lazy musings, that tended to no purpose, or had not vigor to attain it; his thoughts were seldom so energetic as to seize hold of words. Imagination, in the proper meaning of the term, made no part of Wakefield's gifts. With a cold, but not depraved nor wandering heart, and a mind never feverish with riotous thoughts, nor perplexed with originality, who could have anticipated, that our friend would entitle himself to a foremost place among the doers of eccentric deeds? Had his acquaintances been asked, who was the man in London, the surest to perform nothing to-day which should be remembered on the

1. The text is from *The New-England Magazine* (May 1835).

morrow, they would have thought of Wakefield. Only the wife of his bosom might have hesitated. She, without having analyzed his character, was partly aware of a quiet selfishness, that had rusted into his inactive mind—of a peculiar sort of vanity, the most uneasy attribute about him—of a disposition to craft, which had seldom produced more positive effects than the keeping of petty secrets, hardly worth revealing—and, lastly, of what she called a little strangeness, sometimes, in the good man. This latter quality is indefinable, and perhaps non-existent.

Let us now imagine Wakefield bidding adieu to his wife. It is the dusk of an October evening. His equipment is a drab great-coat, a hat covered with an oil-cloth, top-boots, an umbrella in one hand and a small portmanteau[2] in the other. He has informed Mrs. Wakefield that he is to take the night-coach into the country. She would fain inquire the length of his journey, its object, and the probable time of his return; but, indulgent to his harmless love of mystery, interrogates him only by a look. He tells her not to expect him positively by the return coach, nor to look alarmed should he tarry three or four days; but, at all events, to look for him at supper on Friday evening. Wakefield himself, be it considered, has no suspicion of what is before him. He holds out his hand; she gives her own, and meets his parting kiss, in the matter-of-course way of a ten years' matrimony; and forth goes the middle-aged Mr. Wakefield, almost resolved to perplex his good lady by a whole week's absence. After the door has closed behind him, she perceives it thrust partly open, and a vision of her husband's face, through the aperture, smiling on her, and gone in a moment. For the time, this little incident is dismissed without a thought. But, long afterwards, when she has been more years a widow than a wife, that smile recurs, and flickers across all her reminiscences of Wakefield's visage. In her many musings, she surrounds the original smile with a multitude of fantasies, which make it strange and awful; as, for instance, if she imagines him in a coffin, that parting look is frozen on his pale features; or, if she dreams of him in Heaven, still his blessed spirit wears a quiet and crafty smile. Yet, for its sake, when all others have given him up for dead, she sometimes doubts whether she is a widow.

But, our business is with the husband. We must hurry after him, along the street, ere he lose his individuality, and melt into the great mass of London life. It would be vain searching for him there. Let us follow close at his heels, therefore, until, after several superfluous turns and doublings, we find him comfortably established by the fireside of a small apartment, previously bespoken. He is in the next street to his own, and at his journey's end. He can scarcely trust his good fortune, in having got thither unperceived—recollecting that, at one time, he was delayed by the throng, in the very focus of a lighted lantern; and, again, there were foot-steps, that seemed to tread behind his own, distinct from the multitudinous tramp around him; and, anon, he heard a voice shouting afar, and fancied that it called his name. Doubtless, a dozen busy-bodies had been watching him, and told his wife the whole affair. Poor Wakefield! Little knowest thou thine own insignificance in this great world! No mortal eye but mine has traced thee. Go quietly to thy bed, foolish man; and, on the morrow, if thou wilt be wise, get

2. Traveling bag, suitcase.

thee home to good Mrs. Wakefield, and tell her the truth. Remove not thyself, even for a little week, from thy place in her chaste bosom. Were she, for a single moment, to deem thee dead, or lost, or lastingly divided from her, thou wouldst be woefully conscious of a change in thy true wife, forever after. It is perilous to make a chasm in human affections; not that they gape so long and wide—but so quickly close again!

Almost repenting of his frolic, or whatever it may be termed, Wakefield lies down betimes, and starting from his first nap, spreads forth his arms into the wide and solitary waste of the unaccustomed bed. 'No'—thinks he, gathering the bed-clothes about him—'I will not sleep alone another night.'

In the morning, he rises earlier than usual, and sets himself to consider what he really means to do. Such are his loose and rambling modes of thought, that he has taken this very singular step, with the consciousness of a purpose, indeed, but without being able to define it sufficiently for his own contemplation. The vagueness of the project, and the convulsive effort with which he plunges into the execution of it, are equally characteristic of a feeble-minded man. Wakefield sifts his ideas, however, as minutely as he may, and finds himself curious to know the progress of matters at home—how his exemplary wife will endure her widowhood, of a week; and, briefly, how the little sphere of creatures and circumstances, in which he was a central object, will be affected by his removal. A morbid vanity, therefore, lies nearest the bottom of the affair. But, how is he to attain his ends? Not, certainly, by keeping close in this comfortable lodging, where, though he slept and awoke in the next street to his home, he is as effectually abroad, as if the stage-coach had been whirling him away all night. Yet, should he reappear, the whole project is knocked in the head. His poor brains being hopelessly puzzled with this dilemma, he at length ventures out, partly resolving to cross the head of the street, and send one hasty glance towards his forsaken domicile. Habit—for he is a man of habits—takes him by the hand, and guides him, wholly unaware, to his own door, where, just at the critical moment, he is aroused by the scraping of his foot upon the step. Wakefield! whither are you going?

At that instant, his fate was turning on the pivot. Little dreaming of the doom to which his first backward step devotes him, he hurries away, breathless with agitation hitherto unfelt, and hardly dares turn his head, at the distant corner. Can it be, that nobody caught sight of him? Will not the whole household—the decent Mrs. Wakefield, the smart maid-servant, and the dirty little foot-boy—raise a hue-and-cry, through London streets, in pursuit of their fugitive lord and master? Wonderful escape! He gathers courage to pause and look homeward, but is perplexed with a sense of change about the familiar edifice, such as affects us all, when, after a separation of months or years, we again see some hill or lake, or work of art, with which we were friends, of old. In ordinary cases, this indescribable impression is caused by the comparison and contrast between our imperfect reminiscences and the reality. In Wakefield, the magic of a single night has wrought a similar transformation, because, in that brief period, a great moral change has been effected. But this is a secret from himself. Before leaving the spot, he catches a far and momentary glimpse of his wife, passing athwart the front window, with her face turned towards the head of the street. The crafty nincompoop takes to his heels, scared with the idea, that, among a thousand such atoms of mortality, her eye must have detected him. Right glad is his heart, though his brain be somewhat dizzy, when he finds himself by the coal-fire of his lodgings.

So much for the commencement of this long whim-wham. After the critical conception, and the stirring up of the man's sluggish temperament to put it in practice, the whole matter evolves itself in a natural train. We may suppose him, as the result of deep deliberation, buying a new wig, of reddish hair, and selecting sundry garments, in a fashion unlike his customary suit of brown, from a Jew's old-clothes bag. It is accomplished. Wakefield is another man. The new system being now established, a retrograde movement to the old would be almost as difficult as the step that placed him in his unparalleled position. Furthermore, he is rendered obstinate by a sulkiness, occasionally incident to his temper, and brought on, at present, by the inadequate sensation which he conceived to have been produced in the bosom of Mrs. Wakefield. He will not go back until she be frightened half to death. Well; twice or thrice has she passed before his sight, each time with a heavier step, a paler cheek, and more anxious brow; and, in the third week of his non-appearance, he detects a portent of evil entering the house, in the guise of an apothecary. Next day, the knocker is muffled. Towards night-fall, comes the chariot of a physician, and deposits its big-wigged and solemn burthen at Wakefield's door, whence, after a quarter of an hour's visit, he emerges, perchance the herald of a funeral. Dear woman! Will she die? By this time, Wakefield is excited to something like energy of feeling, but still lingers away from his wife's bedside, pleading with his conscience, that she must not be disturbed at such a juncture. If aught else restrains him, he does not know it. In the course of a few weeks, she gradually recovers; the crisis is over; her heart is sad, perhaps, but quiet; and, let him return soon or late, it will never be feverish for him again. Such ideas glimmer through the mist of Wakefield's mind, and render him indistinctly conscious, that an almost impassable gulf divides his hired apartment from his former home. 'It is but in the next street!' he sometimes says. Fool! it is in another world. Hitherto, he has put off his return from one particular day to another; henceforward, he leaves the precise time undetermined. Not to-morrow—probably next week—pretty soon. Poor man! The dead have nearly as much chance of re-visiting their earthly homes, as the self-banished Wakefield.

Would that I had a folio to write, instead of a brief article in the New-England! Then might I exemplify how an influence, beyond our control, lays its strong hand on every deed which we do, and weaves its consequences into an iron tissue of necessity. Wakefield is spell-bound. We must leave him, for ten years or so, to haunt around his house, without once crossing the threshold, and to be faithful to his wife, with all the affection of which his heart is capable, while he is slowly fading out of hers. Long since, it must be remarked, he has lost the perception of singularity in his conduct.

Now for a scene! Amid the throng of a London street, we distinguish a man, now waxing elderly, with few characteristics to attract careless observers, yet bearing, in his whole aspect, the hand-writing of no common fate, for such as have the skill to read it. He is meagre; his low and narrow forehead is deeply wrinkled; his eyes, small and lustreless, sometimes wander apprehensively about him, but oftener seem to look inward. He bends his head, and moves with an indescribable obliquity of gait, as if unwilling to display his full front to the world. Watch him, long enough to see what we have described, and you will allow, that circumstances—which often produce remarkable men from nature's ordinary handiwork—have produced one such here. Next, leaving him to sidle along the foot-walk, cast your eyes in the opposite direction, where a portly female, considerably in the wane of life, with a prayer-book in her hand, is proceeding to yonder church. She has the placid mien of settled widowhood. Her regrets have either died away, or have become so essential to her heart, that they would be poorly exchanged for joy. Just as the lean man and well conditioned woman are passing, a slight obstruction occurs, and brings these two figures directly in contact. Their hands touch; the pressure of the crowd forces her bosom against his shoulder; they stand, face to face, staring into each other's eyes. After a ten years' separation, thus Wakefield meets his wife!

The throng eddies away, and carries them asunder. The sober widow, resuming her former pace, proceeds to church, but pauses in the portal, and throws a perplexed glance along the street. She passes in, however, opening her prayer-book as she goes. And the man? With so wild a face, that busy and selfish London stands to gaze after him, he hurries to his lodgings, bolts the door, and throws himself upon the bed. The latent feelings of years break out; his feeble mind acquires a brief energy from their strength; all the miserable strangeness of his life is revealed to him at a glance; and he cries out, passionately—'Wakefield! Wakefield! You are mad!'

Perhaps he was so. The singularity of his situation must have so moulded him to itself, that, considered in regard to his fellow-creatures and the business of life, he could not be said to possess his right mind. He had contrived, or rather he had happened, to dissever himself from the world—to vanish—to give up his place and privileges with living men, without being admitted among the dead. The life of a hermit is nowise parallel to his. He was in the bustle of the city, as of old; but the crowd swept by, and saw him not; he was, we may figuratively say, always beside his wife, and at his hearth, yet must never feel the warmth of the one, nor the affection of the other. It was Wakefield's unprecedented fate, to retain his original share of human sympathies, and to be still involved in human interests, while he had lost his reciprocal influence on them. It would be a most curious speculation, to trace out the effect of such circumstances on his heart and intellect, separately, and in unison. Yet, changed as he was, he would seldom be conscious of it, but deem himself the same man as ever; glimpses of the truth, indeed, would come, but only for the moment; and still he would keep saying—'I shall soon go back!'—nor reflect, that he had been saying so for twenty years.

I conceive, also, that these twenty years would appear, in the retrospect, scarcely longer than the week to which Wakefield had at first limited his absence. He would look on the affair as no more than an interlude in the main business of his life. When, after a little while more, he should deem it time to re-enter his parlor, his wife would clap her hands for joy, on beholding the middle-aged Mr. Wakefield. Alas, what a mistake! Would Time but await the close of our favorite follies, we should be young men, all of us, and till Doom's Day.

One evening, in the twentieth year since he vanished, Wakefield is taking his customary walk towards the dwelling which he still calls his own. It is a gusty night of autumn, with frequent showers, that patter down upon the pavement, and are gone, before a man can put up his umbrella. Pausing near the house, Wakefield discerns, through the parlor-windows of the second floor, the red glow, and the glimmer and fitful flash, of a comfortable fire. On the ceiling, appears a grotesque shadow of good Mrs. Wakefield. The cap, the nose and chin, and the broad waist, form an admirable caricature, which dances, moreover, with the up-flickering and down-sinking blaze, almost too merrily for the shade of an elderly widow. At this instant, a shower chances to fall, and is driven, by the unmannerly gust, full into Wakefield's face and bosom. He is quite penetrated with its autumnal chill. Shall he stand, wet and shivering here, when his own hearth has a good fire to warm him, and his own wife will run to fetch the gray coat and small-clothes,[3] which, doubtless, she has kept carefully in the closet of their bed-chamber? No! Wakefield is no such fool. He ascends the steps—heavily!—for twenty years have stiffened his legs, since he came down—but he knows it not. Stay, Wakefield! Would you go to the sole home that is left you? Then step into your grave! The door opens. As he passes in, we have a parting glimpse of his visage, and recognize the crafty smile, which was the precursor of the little joke, that he has ever since been playing off at his wife's expense. How unmercifully has he quizzed[4] the poor woman! Well; a good night's rest to Wakefield!

This happy event—supposing it to be such—could only have occurred at an unpremeditated moment. We will not follow our friend across the threshold. He has left us much food for thought, a portion of which shall lend its wisdom to a moral, and be shaped into a figure. Amid the seeming confusion of our mysterious world, individuals are so nicely adjusted to a system, and systems to one another, and to a whole, that, by stepping aside for a moment, a man exposes himself to a fearful risk of losing his place forever. Like Wakefield, he may become, as it were, the Outcast of the Universe.

1835

The May-Pole of Merry Mount[1]

> There is an admirable foundation for a philosophic romance, in the curious history of the early settlement of Mount Wallaston, or Merry Mount. In the slight sketch here attempted, the facts, recorded on the grave pages of our New England annalists, have wrought themselves, almost spontaneously, into a sort of allegory. The masques, mummeries, and festive customs, described in the text, are in accordance with the manners of the age. Authority, on these points may be found in Strutt's Book of English Sports and Pastimes.[2]

Bright were the days at Merry Mount, when the May-Pole was the banner-staff of that gay colony! They who reared it, should their banner be triumphant, were to pour sun-shine over New England's rugged hills, and scatter

3. Knee-length pants.
4. Played a joke on.
1. The text is that of the first printing in *The Token* (1836). "May-pole": in English tradition, the tall pole placed in a village around which flower-bedecked people danced to celebrate May Day (the coming of spring). Puritans condemned the custom as pagan.
2. Joseph Strutt, *The Sports and Pastimes of the People of England* (1801). Hawthorne also knew

flower-seeds throughout the soil. Jollity and gloom were contending for an empire. Midsummer eve[3] had come, bringing deep verdure to the forest, and roses in her lap, of a more vivid hue than the tender buds of Spring. But May, or her mirthful spirit, dwelt all the year round at Merry Mount, sporting with the Summer months, and revelling with Autumn, and basking in the glow of Winter's fireside. Through a world of toil and care, she flitted with a dreamlike smile, and came hither to find a home among the lightsome hearts of Merry Mount.

Never had the May-Pole been so gaily decked as at sunset on mid-summer eve. This venerated emblem was a pine tree, which had preserved the slender grace of youth, while it equalled the loftiest height of the old wood monarchs. From its top streamed a silken banner, colored like the rainbow. Down nearly to the ground, the pole was dressed with birchen boughs, and others of the liveliest green, and some with silvery leaves, fastened by ribbons that fluttered in fantastic knots of twenty different colors, but no sad ones. Garden flowers, and blossoms of the wilderness, laughed gladly forth amid the verdure, so fresh and dewy, that they must have grown by magic on that happy pine tree. Where this green and flowery splendor terminated, the shaft of the May-Pole was stained with the seven brilliant hues of the banner at its top. On the lowest green bough hung an abundant wreath of roses, some that had been gathered in the sunniest spots of the forest, and others, of still richer blush, which the colonists had reared from English seed. Oh, people of the Golden Age, the chief of your husbandry, was to raise flowers!

But what was the wild throng that stood hand in hand about the May-Pole? It could not be, that the Fauns and Nymphs, when driven from their classic groves and homes of ancient fable, had sought refuge, as all the persecuted did, in the fresh woods of the West. These were Gothic monsters, though perhaps of Grecian ancestry. On the shoulders of a comely youth, uprose the head and branching antlers of a stag; a second, human in all other points, had the grim visage of a wolf; a third, still with the trunk and limbs of a mortal man, showed the beard and horns of a venerable he-goat. There was the likeness of a bear erect, brute in all but his hind legs, which were adorned with pink silk stockings. And here again, almost as wondrous, stood a real bear of the dark forest, lending each of his fore paws to the grasp of a human hand, and as ready for the dance as any in that circle. This inferior nature rose half-way, to meet his companions as they stooped. Other faces wore the similitude of man or woman, but distorted or extravagant, with red noses pendulous before their mouths, which seemed of awful depth, and stretched from ear to ear in an eternal fit of laughter. Here might be seen the Salvage Man,[4] well known in heraldry, hairy as a baboon, and girdled with green leaves. By his side, a nobler figure, but still a counterfeit, appeared an Indian

Nathaniel Morton's *New England Memorial* (1669), which drew on William Bradford's manuscript history *Of Plymouth Plantation.* Hawthorne's tale works loosely with the historical conflict between the colony of fur traders at Mount Wollaston, now Quincy, Massachusetts, and the religious leaders of Plymouth and Salem from 1625 to 1630. Thomas Morton (ca. 1579–1647), one of the traders, had dubbed Mount Wollaston "Merry Mount" and in 1627 encouraged the use of the maypole. In 1628 John Endicott (1589?–1665), the governor of the Massachusetts Colony, led an expedition that cut down the maypole shortly after Morton was deported to England for trafficking firearms to the Indians. Morton presents his side of the conflict in *New English Canaan* (1637).

3. June 20, the day before the longest day of the year.

4. Person clad in foliage to represent a savage, as in medieval and Renaissance pageantry.

hunter, with feathery crest and wampum belt. Many of this strange company wore fools-caps, and had little bells appended to their garments, tinkling with a silvery sound, responsive to the inaudible music of their gleesome spirits. Some youths and maidens were of soberer garb, yet well maintained their places in the irregular throng, by the expression of wild revelry upon their features. Such were the colonists of Merry Mount, as they stood in the broad smile of sunset, round their venerated May-Pole.

Had a wanderer, bewildered in the melancholy forest, heard their mirth, and stolen a half-affrighted glance, he might have fancied them the crew of Comus,[5] some already transformed to brutes, some midway between man and beast, and the others rioting in the flow of tipsey jollity that foreran the change. But a band of Puritans, who watched the scene, invisible themselves, compared the masques to those devils and ruined souls, with whom their superstition peopled the black wilderness.

Within the ring of monsters, appeared the two airiest forms, that had ever trodden on any more solid footing than a purple and golden cloud. One was a youth, in glistening apparel, with a scarf of the rainbow pattern crosswise on his breast. His right hand held a gilded staff, the ensign[6] of high dignity among the revellous, and his left grasped the slender fingers of a fair maiden, not less gaily decorated than himself. Bright roses glowed in contrast with the dark and glossy curls of each, and were scattered round their feet, or had sprung up spontaneously there. Behind this lightsome couple, so close to the May-Pole that its boughs shaded his jovial face, stood the figure of an English priest, canonically dressed, yet decked with flowers, in Heathen fashion, and wearing a chaplet of the native vine leaves. By the riot of his rolling eye, and the pagan decorations of his holy garb, he seemed the wildest monster there, and the very Comus of the crew.

'Votaries of the May-Pole,' cried the flower-decked priest, 'merrily, all day long, have the woods echoed to your mirth. But be this your merriest hour, my hearts! Lo, here stand the Lord and Lady of the May, whom I, a clerk[7] of Oxford, and high priest of Merry Mount, am presently to join in holy matrimony. Up with your nimble spirits, ye morrice-dancers, green-men, and glee-maidens,[8] bears and wolves, and horned gentlemen! Come; a chorus now, rich with the old mirth of Merry England, and the wilder glee of this fresh forest; and then a dance, to show the youthful pair what life is made of, and how airily they should go through it! All ye that love the May-Pole, lend your voices to the nuptial song of the Lord and Lady of the May!'

This wedlock was more serious than most affairs of Merry Mount, where jest and delusion, trick and fantasy, kept up a continual carnival. The Lord and Lady of the May, though their titles must be laid down at sunset, were really and truly to be partners for the dance of life, beginning the measure that same bright eve. The wreath of roses, that hung from the lowest green bough of the May-Pole, had been twined for them, and would be thrown over both their heads, in symbol of their flowery union. When the priest had spoken, therefore, a riotous uproar burst from the rout of monstrous figures.

5. The god of revelry, here associated with Milton's *Comus* (1634), whose magical potions turn unsuspecting travelers in the woods into monstrous figures who join his crew.
6. Sign, token.
7. In Anglican usage, lay minister who assists the parish clergyman.
8. Women singers. "Morrice-dancers": participants in an English folk dance, originally "Moorish dance." "Green-men": men bedecked in greenery.

'Begin you the stave,[9] reverend Sir,' cried they all; 'and never did the woods ring to such a merry peal, as we of the May-Pole shall send up!'

Immediately a prelude of pipe, cittern,[1] and viol, touched with practised minstrelsy, began to play from a neighboring thicket, in such a mirthful cadence, that the boughs of the May-Pole quivered to the sound. But the May Lord, he of the gilded staff, chancing to look into his Lady's eyes, was wonderstruck at the almost pensive glance that met his own.

'Edith, sweet Lady of the May,' whispered he, reproachfully, 'is your wreath of roses a garland to hang above our graves, that you look so sad? Oh, Edith, this is our golden time! Tarnish it not by any pensive shadow of the mind; for it may be, that nothing of futurity will be brighter than the mere remembrance of what is now passing.'

'That was the very thought that saddened me! How came it in your mind too?' said Edith, in a still lower tone than he; for it was high treason to be sad at Merry Mount. 'Therefore do I sigh amid this festive music. And besides, dear Edgar, I struggle as with a dream, and fancy that these shapes of our jovial friends are visionary, and their mirth unreal, and that we are no true Lord and Lady of the May. What is the mystery in my heart?'

Just then, as if a spell had loosened them, down came a little shower of withering rose leaves from the May-Pole. Alas, for the young lovers! No sooner had their hearts glowed with real passion, than they were sensible of something vague and unsubstantial in their former pleasures, and felt a dreary presentiment of inevitable change. From the moment that they truly loved, they had subjected themselves to earth's doom of care, and sorrow, and troubled joy, and had no more a home at Merry Mount. That was Edith's mystery. Now leave we the priest to marry them, and the masquers to sport round the May-Pole, till the last sunbeam be withdrawn from its summit, and the shadows of the forest mingle gloomily in the dance. Meanwhile, we may discover who these gay people were.

Two hundred years ago, and more, the old world and its inhabitants became mutually weary of each other. Men voyaged by thousands to the West; some to barter glass beads, and such like jewels, for the furs of the Indian hunter; some to conquer virgin empires; and one stern band to pray. But none of these motives had much weight with the colonists of Merry Mount. Their leaders were men who had sported so long with life, that when Thought and Wisdom came, even these unwelcome guests were led astray, by the crowd of vanities which they should have put to flight. Erring Thought and perverted Wisdom were made to put on masques, and play the fool. The men of whom we speak, after losing the heart's fresh gaiety, imagined a wild philosophy of pleasure, and came hither to act out their latest day-dream. They gathered followers from all that giddy tribe, whose whole life is like the festal days of soberer men. In their train were minstrels, not unknown in London streets; wandering players, whose theatres had been the halls of noblemen; mummeries, rope-dancers, and mountebanks,[2] who would long be missed at wakes, church-ales, and fairs; in a word, mirth-makers of every sort, such as abounded in that age, but now began to be discountenanced

9. Stanza or verse.
1. Guitar with pear-shaped body.
2. Showmen who "mount benches" to sell medicines or (as here) to tell stories or do tricks. "Mummeries": masked actors. "Rope-dancers": tightrope walkers.

by the rapid growth of Puritanism. Light had their footsteps been on land, and as lightly they came across the sea. Many had been maddened by their previous troubles into a gay despair; others were as madly gay in the flush of youth, like the May Lord and his Lady; but whatever might be the quality of their mirth, old and young were gay at Merry Mount. The young deemed themselves happy. The elder spirits, if they knew that mirth was but the counterfeit of happiness, yet followed the false shadow wilfully, because at least her garments glittered brightest. Sworn triflers of a life-time, they would not venture among the sober truths of life, not even to be truly blest.

All the hereditary pastimes of Old England were transplanted hither. The King of Christmas was duly crowned, and the Lord of Misrule[3] bore potent sway. On the eve of Saint John,[4] they felled whole acres of the forest to make bonfires, and danced by the blaze all night, crowned with garlands, and throwing flowers into the flame. At harvest time, though their crop was of the smallest, they made an image with the sheaves of Indian corn, and wreathed it with autumnal garlands, and bore it home triumphantly. But what chiefly characterized the colonists of Merry Mount, was their veneration for the May-Pole. It has made their true history a poet's tale. Spring decked the hallowed emblem with young blossoms and fresh green boughs; Summer brought roses of the deepest blush, and the perfected foliage of the forest; Autumn enriched it with that red and yellow gorgeousness, which converts each wildwood leaf into a painted flower; and Winter silvered it with sleet, and hung it round with icicles, till it flashed in the cold sunshine, itself a frozen sunbeam. Thus each alternate season did homage to the May-Pole, and paid it a tribute of its own richest splendor. Its votaries danced round it, once, at least, in every month; sometimes they called it their religion, or their altar; but always, it was the banner-staff of Merry Mount.

Unfortunately, there were men in the new world, of a sterner faith than these May-Pole worshippers. Not far from Merry Mount was a settlement of Puritans, most dismal wretches, who said their prayers before daylight, and then wrought in the forest or the cornfield, till evening made it prayer time again. Their weapons were always at hand, to shoot down the straggling savage. When they met in conclave, it was never to keep up the old English mirth, but to hear sermons three hours long, or to proclaim bounties on the heads of wolves and the scalps of Indians. Their festivals were fast-days, and their chief pastime the singing of psalms. Woe to the youth or maiden, who did but dream of a dance! The selectman nodded to the constable; and there sat the light-heeled reprobate in the stocks; or if he danced, it was round the whipping-post, which might be termed the Puritan May-Pole.

A party of these grim Puritans, toiling through the difficult woods, each with a horse-load of iron armor to burthen his footsteps, would sometimes draw near the sunny precincts of Merry Mount. There were the silken colonists, sporting round their May-Pole; perhaps teaching a bear to dance, or striving to communicate their mirth to the grave Indian; or masquerading in the skins of deer and wolves, which they had hunted for that especial purpose. Often, the whole colony were playing at blindman's bluff, magistrates and all with their eyes bandaged, except a single scape-goat, whom the

3. Person appointed to preside over the traditional Christmas revelry.

4. Midsummer eve.

blinded sinners pursued by the tinkling of the bells at his garments. Once, it is said, they were seen following a flower-decked corpse, with merriment and festive music, to his grave. But did the dead man laugh? In their quietest times, they sang ballads and told tales, for the edification of their pious visiters; or perplexed them with juggling tricks; or grinned at them through horse-collars; and when sport itself grew wearisome, they made game of their own stupidity, and began a yawning match. At the very least of these enormities, the men of iron shook their heads and frowned so darkly, that the revellers looked up, imagining that a momentary cloud had overcast the sunshine, which was to be perpetual there. On the other hand, the Puritans affirmed, that, when a psalm was pealing from their place of worship, the echo, which the forest sent them back, seemed often like the chorus of a jolly catch, closing with a roar of laughter. Who but the fiend, and his fond slaves, the crew of Merry Mount, had thus disturbed them! In due time, a feud arose, stern and bitter on one side, and as serious on the other as any thing could be, among such light spirits as had sworn allegiance to the May-Pole. The future complexion of New England was involved in this important quarrel. Should the grisly saints establish their jurisdiction over the gay sinners, then would their spirits darken all the clime, and make it a land of clouded visages, of hard toil, of sermon and psalm, forever. But should the banner-staff of Merry Mount be fortunate, sunshine would break upon the hills, and flowers would beautify the forest, and late posterity do homage to the May-Pole!

After these authentic passages from history, we return to the nuptials of the Lord and Lady of the May. Alas! we have delayed too long, and must darken our tale too suddenly. As we glanced again at the May-Pole, a solitary sun-beam is fading from the summit, and leaves only a faint golden tinge, blended with the hues of the rainbow banner. Even that dim light is now withdrawn, relinquishing the whole domain of Merry Mount to the evening gloom, which has rushed so instantaneously from the black surrounding woods. But some of these black shadows have rushed forth in human shape.

Yes: with the setting sun, the last day of mirth had passed from Merry Mount. The ring of gay masquers was disordered and broken; the stag lowered his antlers in dismay; the wolf grew weaker than a lamb; the bells of the morrice-dancers tinkled with tremulous affright. The Puritans had played a characteristic part in the May-Pole mummeries. Their darksome figures were intermixed with the wild shapes of their foes, and made the scene a picture of the moment, when waking thoughts start up amid the scattered fantasies of a dream. The leader of the hostile party stood in the centre of the circle, while the rout of monsters cowered around him, like evil spirits in the presence of a dread magician. No fantastic foolery could look him in the face. So stern was the energy of his aspect, that the whole man, visage, frame, and soul, seemed wrought of iron, gifted with life and thought, yet all of one substance with his head-piece and breast-plate. It was the Puritan of Puritans; it was Endicott himself!

'Stand off, priest of Baal!'[5] said he, with a grim frown, and laying no reverent hand upon the surplice. 'I know thee, Claxton![6] Thou art the man, who

5. The slaying of the prophets of the fertility god Baal is described in 1 Kings 18.

6. "Did Governor Endicott speak less positively, we should suspect a mistake here. The Reverend Mr. Claxton, though an eccentric, is not known to have been an immoral man. We rather doubt his

couldst not abide the rule even of thine own corrupted church,[7] and hast come hither to preach iniquity, and to give example of it in thy life. But now shall it be seen that the Lord hath sanctified this wilderness for his peculiar people. Woe unto them that would defile it! And first for this flower-decked abomination, the altar of thy worship!'

And with his keen sword, Endicott assaulted the hallowed May-Pole. Nor long did it resist his arm. It groaned with a dismal sound; it showered leaves and rose-buds upon the remorseless enthusiast; and finally, with all its green boughs, and ribbons, and flowers, symbolic of departed pleasures, down fell the banner-staff of Merry Mount. As it sank, tradition says, the evening sky grew darker, and the woods threw forth a more sombre shadow.

'There,' cried Endicott, looking triumphantly on his work, 'there lies the only May-Pole in New England! The thought is strong within me, that, by its fall, is shadowed forth the fate of light and idle mirth-makers, amongst us and our posterity. Amen, saith John Endicott!'

'Amen!' echoed his followers.

But the votaries of the May-Pole gave one groan for their idol. At the sound, the Puritan leader glanced at the crew of Comus, each a figure of broad mirth, yet, at this moment, strangely expressive of sorrow and dismay.

'Valiant captain,' quoth Peter Palfrey, the Ancient[8] of the band, 'what order shall be taken with the prisoners?'

'I thought not to repent me of cutting down a May-Pole,' replied Endicott, 'yet now I could find in my heart to plant it again, and give each of these bestial pagans one other dance round their idol. It would have served rarely for a whipping-post!'

'But there are pine trees enow,' suggested the lieutenant.

'True, good Ancient,' said the leader. 'Wherefore, bind the heathen crew, and bestow on them a small matter of stripes apiece, as earnest[9] of our future justice. Set some of the rogues in the stocks to rest themselves, so soon as Providence shall bring us to one of our own well-ordered settlements, where such accommodations may be found. Further penalties, such as branding and cropping of ears, shall be thought of hereafter.'

'How many stripes for the priest?' inquired Ancient Palfrey.

'None as yet,' answered Endicott, bending his iron frown upon the culprit. 'It must be for the Great and General Court[1] to determine, whether stripes and long imprisonment, and other grievous penalty, may atone for his transgressions. Let him look to himself! For such as violate our civil order, it may be permitted us to show mercy. But woe to the wretch that troubleth our religion!'

'And this dancing bear,' resumed the officer. 'Must he share the stripes of his fellows?'

'Shoot him through the head!' said the energetic Puritan. 'I suspect witchcraft in the beast.'

identity with the priest of Merry Mount" [Hawthorne's note]. An eccentric clergyman, William Blackstone was known for quarreling with both the Merry Mounters and the Puritans.

7. The Anglican Church.

8. Lieutenant or standard bearer. Palfrey (d. 1663), one of the first English settlers of Salem, which had broken away from the Plymouth Colony in 1629.

9. Pledge.

1. Massachusetts legislature.

'Here be a couple of shining ones,' continued Peter Palfrey, pointing his weapon at the Lord and Lady of the May. 'They seem to be of high station among these mis-doers. Methinks their dignity will not be fitted with less than a double share of stripes.'

Endicott rested on his sword, and closely surveyed the dress and aspect of the hapless pair. There they stood, pale, downcast, and apprehensive. Yet there was an air of mutual support, and of pure affection, seeking aid and giving it, that showed them to be man and wife, with the sanction of a priest upon their love. The youth, in the peril of the moment, had dropped his gilded staff, and thrown his arm about the Lady of the May, who leaned against his breast, too lightly to burthen him, but with weight enough to express that their destinies were linked together, for good or evil. They looked first at each other, and then into the grim captain's face. There they stood, in the first hour of wedlock, while the idle pleasures, of which their companions were the emblems, had given place to the sternest cares of life, personified by the dark Puritans. But never had their youthful beauty seemed so pure and high, as when its glow was chastened by adversity.

'Youth,' said Endicott, 'ye stand in an evil case, thou and thy maiden wife. Make ready presently; for I am minded that ye shall both have a token to remember your wedding-day!'

'Stern man,' exclaimed the May Lord, 'How can I move thee? Were the means at hand, I would resist to the death. Being powerless, I entreat! Do with me as thou wilt; but let Edith go untouched!'

'Not so,' replied the immitigable zealot. 'We are not wont to show an idle courtesy to that sex, which requireth the stricter discipline. What sayest thou, maid? Shall thy silken bridegroom suffer thy share of the penalty, besides his own?'

'Be it death,' said Edith, 'and lay it all on me!'

Truly, as Endicott had said, the poor lovers stood in a woeful case. Their foes were triumphant, their friends captive and abased, their home desolate, the benighted wilderness around them, and a rigorous destiny, in the shape of the Puritan leader, their only guide. Yet the deepening twilight could not altogether conceal, that the iron man was softened; he smiled, at the fair spectacle of early love; he almost sighed, for the inevitable blight of early hopes.

'The troubles of life have come hastily on this young couple,' observed Endicott. 'We will see how they comport themselves under their present trials, ere we burthen them with greater. If, among the spoil, there be any garments of a more decent fashion, let them be put upon this May Lord and his Lady, instead of their glistening vanities. Look to it, some of you.'

'And shall not the youth's hair be cut?' asked Peter Palfrey, looking with abhorrence at the love-lock and long glossy curls of the young man.

'Crop it forthwith, and that in the true pumpkin shell fashion,'[2] answered the captain. 'Then bring them along with us, but more gently than their fellows. There be qualities in the youth, which may make him valiant to fight, and sober to toil, and pious to pray; and in the maiden, that may fit her to become a mother in our Israel,[3] bringing up babes in better nurture

2. Roundhead style; relatively close-cropped in Puritan fashion.

3. Endicott makes the standard 17th-century Puritan identification of the New England settlers with the Jews, whom he regarded as another persecuted, God-chosen group.

than her own hath been. Nor think ye, young ones, that they are the happiest, even in our lifetime of a moment, who misspend it in dancing round a May-Pole!'

And Endicott, the severest Puritan of all who laid the rock-foundation of New England, lifted the wreath of roses from the ruin of the May-Pole, and threw it, with his own gauntleted hand, over the heads of the Lord and Lady of the May. It was a deed of prophecy. As the moral gloom of the world overpowers all systematic gaiety, even so was their home of wild mirth made desolate amid the sad forest. They returned to it no more. But, as their flowery garland was wreathed of the brightest roses that had grown there, so, in the tie that united them, were intertwined all the purest and best of their early joys. They went heavenward, supporting each other along the difficult path which it was their lot to tread, and never wasted one regretful thought on the vanities of Merry Mount.

1835

The Minister's Black Veil[1]

A Parable[2]

BY THE AUTHOR OF 'SIGHTS FROM A STEEPLE'

The sexton stood in the porch of Milford[3] meeting-house, pulling lustily at the bell-rope. The old people of the village came stooping along the street. Children, with bright faces, tript merrily beside their parents, or mimicked a graver gait, in the conscious dignity of their sunday clothes. Spruce bachelors looked sidelong at the pretty maidens, and fancied that the sabbath sunshine made them prettier than on week-days. When the throng had mostly streamed into the porch, the sexton began to toll the bell, keeping his eye on the Reverend Mr. Hooper's door. The first glimpse of the clergyman's figure was the signal for the bell to cease its summons.

'But what has good Parson Hooper got upon his face?' cried the sexton in astonishment.

All within hearing immediately turned about, and beheld the semblance of Mr. Hooper, pacing slowly his meditative way towards the meeting-house. With one accord they started, expressing more wonder than if some strange minister were coming to dust the cushions of Mr. Hooper's pulpit.

'Are you sure it is our parson?' inquired Goodman Gray of the sexton.

'Of a certainty it is good Mr. Hooper,' replied the sexton. 'He was to have exchanged pulpits with Parson Shute of Westbury; but Parson Shute sent to excuse himself yesterday, being to preach a funeral sermon.'

The cause of so much amazement may appear sufficiently slight. Mr. Hooper, a gentlemanly person of about thirty, though still a bachelor, was

1. The text is that of the first printing in *The Token* (1836).

2. Another clergyman in New-England, Mr. Joseph Moody, of York, Maine, who died about eighty years since, made himself remarkable by the same eccentricity that is here related of the Reverend Mr. Hooper. In his case, however, the symbol had a different import. In early life he had accidentally killed a beloved friend; and from that day till the hour of his own death, he hid his face from men [Hawthorne's note].

3. Town southwest of Boston.

dressed with due clerical neatness, as if a careful wife had starched his band,[4] and brushed the weekly dust from his Sunday's garb. There was but one thing remarkable in his appearance. Swathed about his forehead, and hanging down over his face, so low as to be shaken by his breath, Mr. Hooper had on a black veil. On a nearer view, it seemed to consist of two folds of crape,[5] which entirely concealed his features, except the mouth and chin, but probably did not intercept his sight, farther than to give a darkened aspect to all living and inanimate things. With this gloomy shade before him, good Mr. Hooper walked onward, at a slow and quiet pace, stooping somewhat and looking on the ground, as is customary with abstracted men, yet nodding kindly to those of his parishioners who still waited on the meeting-house steps. But so wonder-struck were they, that his greeting hardly met with a return.

'I can't really feel as if good Mr. Hooper's face was behind that piece of crape,' said the sexton.

'I don't like it,' muttered an old woman, as she hobbled into the meeting-house. 'He has changed himself into something awful, only by hiding his face.'

'Our parson has gone mad!' cried Goodman Gray, following him across the threshold.

A rumor of some unaccountable phenomenon had preceded Mr. Hooper into the meeting-house, and set all the congregation astir. Few could refrain from twisting their heads towards the door; many stood upright, and turned directly about; while several little boys clambered upon the seats, and came down again with a terrible racket. There was a general bustle, a rustling of the women's gowns and shuffling of the men's feet, greatly at variance with that hushed repose which should attend the entrance of the minister. But Mr. Hooper appeared not to notice the perturbation of his people. He entered with an almost noiseless step, bent his head mildly to the pews on each side, and bowed as he passed his oldest parishioner, a white-haired great-grandsire, who occupied an arm-chair in the centre of the aisle. It was strange to observe, how slowly this venerable man became conscious of something singular in the appearance of his pastor. He seemed not fully to partake of the prevailing wonder, till Mr. Hooper had ascended the stairs, and showed himself in the pulpit, face to face with his congregation, except for the black veil. That mysterious emblem was never once withdrawn. It shook with his measured breath as he gave out the psalm; it threw its obscurity between him and the holy page, as he read the Scriptures; and while he prayed, the veil lay heavily on his uplifted countenance. Did he seek to hide it from the dread Being whom he was addressing?

Such was the effect of this simple piece of crape, that more than one woman of delicate nerves was forced to leave the meeting-house. Yet perhaps the pale-faced congregation was almost as fearful a sight to the minister, as his black veil to them.

Mr. Hooper had the reputation of a good preacher, but not an energetic one: he strove to win his people heavenward, by mild persuasive influences, rather than to drive them thither, by the thunders of the Word. The sermon

4. Collar of a clerical gown.

5. Crepe; a light, semitransparent fabric.

which he now delivered, was marked by the same characteristics of style and manner, as the general series of his pulpit oratory. But there was something, either in the sentiment of the discourse itself, or in the imagination of the auditors, which made it greatly the most powerful effort that they had ever heard from their pastor's lips. It was tinged, rather more darkly than usual, with the gentle gloom of Mr. Hooper's temperament. The subject had reference to secret sin, and those sad mysteries which we hide from our nearest and dearest, and would fain conceal from our own consciousness, even forgetting that the Omniscient can detect them. A subtle power was breathed into his words. Each member of the congregation, the most innocent girl, and the man of hardened breast, felt as if the preacher had crept upon them, behind his awful veil, and discovered their hoarded iniquity of deed or thought. Many spread their clasped hands on their bosoms. There was nothing terrible in what Mr. Hooper said; at least, no violence; and yet, with every tremor of his melancholy voice, the hearers quaked. An unsought pathos came hand in hand with awe. So sensible were the audience of some unwonted attribute in their minister, that they longed for a breath of wind to blow aside the veil, almost believing that a stranger's visage would be discovered, though the form, gesture, and voice were those of Mr. Hooper.

At the close of the services, the people hurried out with indecorous confusion, eager to communicate their pent-up amazement, and conscious of lighter spirits, the moment they lost sight of the black veil. Some gathered in little circles, huddled closely together, with their mouths all whispering in the centre; some went homeward alone, wrapt in silent meditation; some talked loudly, and profaned the Sabbath-day with ostentatious laughter. A few shook their sagacious heads, intimating that they could penetrate the mystery; while one or two affirmed that there was no mystery at all, but only that Mr. Hooper's eyes were so weakened by the midnight lamp, as to require a shade. After a brief interval, forth came good Mr. Hooper also, in the rear of his flock. Turning his veiled face from one group to another, he paid due reverence to the hoary heads, saluted the middle-aged with kind dignity, as their friend and spiritual guide, greeted the young with mingled authority and love, and laid his hands on the little children's heads to bless them. Such was always his custom on the Sabbath-day. Strange and bewildered looks repaid him for his courtesy. None, as on former occasions, aspired to the honor of walking by their pastor's side. Old Squire Saunders, doubtless by an accidental lapse of memory, neglected to invite Mr. Hooper to his table, where the good clergyman had been wont to bless the food, almost every Sunday since his settlement. He returned, therefore, to the parsonage, and, at the moment of closing the door, was observed to look back upon the people, all of whom had their eyes fixed upon the minister. A sad smile gleamed faintly from beneath the black veil, and flickered about his mouth, glimmering as he disappeared.

'How strange,' said a lady, 'that a simple black veil, such as any woman might wear on her bonnet, should become such a terrible thing on Mr. Hooper's face!'

'Something must surely be amiss with Mr. Hooper's intellects,' observed her husband, the physician of the village. 'But the strangest part of the affair is the effect of this vagary, even on a sober-minded man like myself. The black veil, though it covers only our pastor's face, throws its influence over his whole person, and makes him ghost-like from head to foot. Do you not feel it so?'

'Truly do I,' replied the lady; 'and I would not be alone with him for the world. I wonder he is not afraid to be alone with himself!'

'Men sometimes are so,' said her husband.

The afternoon service was attended with similar circumstances. At its conclusion, the bell tolled for the funeral of a young lady. The relatives and friends were assembled in the house, and the more distant acquaintances stood about the door, speaking of the good qualities of the deceased, when their talk was interrupted by the appearance of Mr. Hooper, still covered with his black veil. It was now an appropriate emblem. The clergyman stepped into the room where the corpse was laid, and bent over the coffin, to take a last farewell of his deceased parishioner. As he stooped, the veil hung straight down from his forehead, so that, if her eye-lids had not been closed for ever, the dead maiden might have seen his face. Could Mr. Hooper be fearful of her glance, that he so hastily caught back the black veil? A person, who watched the interview between the dead and living, scrupled not to affirm, that, at the instant when the clergyman's features were disclosed, the corpse had slightly shuddered, rustling the shroud and muslin cap, though the countenance retained the composure of death. A superstitious old woman was the only witness of this prodigy. From the coffin, Mr. Hooper passed into the chambers of the mourners, and thence to the head of the staircase, to make the funeral prayer. It was a tender and heart-dissolving prayer, full of sorrow, yet so imbued with celestial hopes, that the music of a heavenly harp, swept by the fingers of the dead, seemed faintly to be heard among the saddest accents of the minister. The people trembled, though they but darkly understood him, when he prayed that they, and himself, and all of mortal race, might be ready, as he trusted this young maiden had been, for the dreadful hour that should snatch the veil from their faces. The bearers went heavily forth, and the mourners followed, saddening all the street, with the dead before them, and Mr. Hooper in his black veil behind.

'Why do you look back?' said one in the procession to his partner.

'I had a fancy,' replied she, 'that the minister and the maiden's spirit were walking hand in hand.'

'And so had I, at the same moment,' said the other.

That night, the handsomest couple in Milford village were to be joined in wedlock. Though reckoned a melancholy man, Mr. Hooper had a placid cheerfulness for such occasions, which often excited a sympathetic smile, where livelier merriment would have been thrown away. There was no quality of his disposition which made him more beloved than this. The company at the wedding awaited his arrival with impatience, trusting that the strange awe, which had gathered over him throughout the day, would now be dispelled. But such was not the result. When Mr. Hooper came, the first thing that their eyes rested on was the same horrible black veil, which had added deeper gloom to the funeral, and could portend nothing but evil to the wedding. Such was its immediate effect on the guests, that a cloud seemed to have rolled duskily from beneath the black crape, and dimmed the light of the candles. The bridal pair stood up before the minister. But the bride's cold fingers quivered in the tremulous hand of the bridegroom, and her death-like paleness caused a whisper, that the maiden who had been buried a few hours before, was come from her grave to be married. If ever another wedding were so dismal, it was that famous one, where they tolled the wedding-knell.[6] After performing the ceremony, Mr. Hooper raised a glass of wine to his lips, wishing happiness to the new-married couple, in a strain of mild pleasantry that ought to have brightened the features of the guests, like a cheerful gleam from the hearth. At that instant, catching a glimpse of his figure in the looking-glass, the black veil involved his own spirit in the horror with which it overwhelmed all others. His frame shuddered—his lips grew white—he spilt the untasted wine upon the carpet—and rushed forth into the darkness. For the Earth, too, had on her Black Veil.

The next day, the whole village of Milford talked of little else than Parson Hooper's black veil. That, and the mystery concealed behind it, supplied a topic for discussion between acquaintances meeting in the street, and good women gossiping at their open windows. It was the first item of news that the tavern-keeper told to his guests. The children babbled of it on their way to school. One imitative little imp covered his face with an old black handkerchief, thereby so affrighting his playmates, that the panic seized himself, and he well nigh lost his wits by his own waggery.

It was remarkable, that, of all the busy-bodies and impertinent people in the parish, not one ventured to put the plain question to Mr. Hooper, wherefore he did this thing. Hitherto, whenever there appeared the slightest call for such interference, he had never lacked advisers, nor shown himself averse to be guided by their judgment. If he erred at all, it was by so painful a degree of self-distrust, that even the mildest censure would lead him to consider an indifferent action as a crime. Yet, though so well acquainted with this amiable weakness, no individual among his parishioners chose to make the black veil a subject of friendly remonstrance. There was a feeling of dread, neither plainly confessed nor carefully concealed, which caused each to shift the responsibility upon another, till at length it was found expedient to send a deputation of the church, in order to deal with Mr. Hooper about the mystery, before it should grow into a scandal. Never did an embassy so ill discharge its duties. The minister received them with friendly courtesy, but became silent, after they were seated, leaving to his visitors the whole burthen[7] of introducing their important business. The topic, it might be supposed, was obvious enough. There was the black veil, swathed round Mr. Hooper's forehead, and concealing every feature above his placid mouth, on which, at times, they could perceive the glimmering of a melancholy smile. But that piece of crape, to their imagination, seemed to hang down before his heart, the symbol of a fearful secret between him and them. Were the veil but cast aside, they might speak freely of it, but not till then. Thus they sat a considerable time, speechless, confused, and shrinking uneasily from Mr. Hooper's eye, which they felt to be fixed upon them with an invisible glance. Finally, the deputies returned abashed to their constituents, pronouncing the matter too weighty to be handled, except by a council of the churches, if, indeed, it might not require a general synod.

But there was one person in the village, unappalled by the awe with which the black veil had impressed all beside herself. When the deputies returned

6. A reference to Hawthorne's "The Wedding Knell," which appeared in *The Token* for 1836 along with this story.

7. Burden.

without an explanation, or even venturing to demand one, she, with the calm energy of her character, determined to chase away the strange cloud that appeared to be settling round Mr. Hooper, every moment more darkly than before. As his plighted wife, it should be her privilege to know what the black veil concealed. At the minister's first visit, therefore, she entered upon the subject, with a direct simplicity, which made the task easier both for him and her. After he had seated himself, she fixed her eyes steadfastly upon the veil, but could discern nothing of the dreadful gloom that had so overawed the multitude: it was but a double fold of crape, hanging down from his forehead to his mouth, and slightly stirring with his breath.

'No,' said she aloud, and smiling, 'there is nothing terrible in this piece of crape, except that it hides a face which I am always glad to look upon. Come, good sir, let the sun shine from behind the cloud. First lay aside your black veil: then tell me why you put it on.'

Mr. Hooper's smile glimmered faintly.

'There is an hour to come,' said he, 'when all of us shall cast aside our veils. Take it not amiss, beloved friend, if I wear this piece of crape till then.'

'Your words are a mystery too,' returned the young lady. 'Take away the veil from them, at least.'

'Elizabeth, I will,' said he, 'so far as my vow may suffer me. Know, then, this veil is a type[8] and a symbol, and I am bound to wear it ever, both in light and darkness, in solitude and before the gaze of multitudes, and as with strangers, so with my familiar friends. No mortal eye will see it withdrawn. This dismal shade must separate me from the world: even you, Elizabeth, can never come behind it!'

'What grievous affliction hath befallen you,' she earnestly inquired, 'that you should thus darken your eyes for ever?'

'If it be a sign of mourning,' replied Mr. Hooper, 'I, perhaps, like most other mortals, have sorrows dark enough to be typified by a black veil.'

'But what if the world will not believe that it is the type of an innocent sorrow?' urged Elizabeth. 'Beloved and respected as you are, there may be whispers, that you hide your face under the consciousness of secret sin. For the sake of your holy office, do away this scandal!'

The color rose into her cheeks, as she intimated the nature of the rumors that were already abroad in the village. But Mr. Hooper's mildness did not forsake him. He even smiled again—that same sad smile, which always appeared like a faint glimmering of light, proceeding from the obscurity beneath the veil.

'If I hide my face for sorrow, there is cause enough,' he merely replied; 'and if I cover it for secret sin, what mortal might not do the same?'

And with this gentle, but unconquerable obstinacy, did he resist all her entreaties. At length Elizabeth sat silent. For a few moments she appeared lost in thought, considering, probably, what new methods might be tried, to withdraw her lover from so dark a fantasy, which, if it had no other meaning, was perhaps a symptom of mental disease. Though of a firmer character than his own, the tears rolled down her cheeks. But, in an instant, as it were, a new feeling took the place of sorrow: her eyes were fixed insensibly

8. Object that symbolically embodies or reveals a religious idea.

on the black veil, when, like a sudden twilight in the air, its terrors fell around her. She arose, and stood trembling before him.

'And do you feel it then at last?' said he mournfully.

She made no reply, but covered her eyes with her hand, and turned to leave the room. He rushed forward and caught her arm.

'Have patience with me, Elizabeth!' cried he passionately. 'Do not desert me, though this veil must be between us here on earth. Be mine, and hereafter there shall be no veil over my face, no darkness between our souls! It is but a mortal veil—it is not for eternity! Oh, you know not how lonely I am and how frightened to be alone behind my black veil. Do not leave me in this miserable obscurity for ever!'

'Lift the veil but once, and look me in the face,' said she.

'Never! It cannot be!' replied Mr. Hooper.

'Then, farewell!' said Elizabeth.

She withrew her arm from his grasp, and slowly departed, pausing at the door, to give one long, shuddering gaze, that seemed almost to penetrate the mystery of the black veil. But, even amid his grief, Mr. Hooper smiled to think that only a material emblem had separated him from happiness, though the horrors which it shadowed forth, must be drawn darkly between the fondest of lovers.

From that time no attempts were made to remove Mr. Hooper's black veil, or, by a direct appeal, to discover the secret which it was supposed to hide. By persons who claimed a superiority to popular prejudice, it was reckoned merely an eccentric whim, such as often mingles with the sober actions of men otherwise rational, and tinges them all with its own semblance of insanity. But with the multitude, good Mr. Hooper was irreparably a bugbear.[9] He could not walk the street with any peace of mind, so conscious was he that the gentle and timid would turn aside to avoid him, and that others would make it a point of hardihood to throw themselves in his way. The impertinence of the latter class compelled him to give up his customary walk, at sunset, to the burial ground; for when he leaned pensively over the gate, there would always be faces behind the grave-stones, peeping at his black veil. A fable went the rounds, that the stare of the dead people drove him thence. It grieved him, to the very depth of his kind heart, to observe how the children fled from his approach, breaking up their merriest sports, while his melancholy figure was yet afar off. Their instinctive dread caused him to feel, more strongly than aught else, that a preternatural horror was interwoven with the threads of the black crape. In truth, his own antipathy to the veil was known to be so great, that he never willingly passed before a mirror, nor stooped to drink at a still fountain, lest, in its peaceful bosom, he should be affrighted by himself. This was what gave plausibility to the whispers, that Mr. Hooper's conscience tortured him for some great crime, too horrible to be entirely concealed, or otherwise than so obscurely intimated. Thus, from beneath the black veil, there rolled a cloud into the sunshine, an ambiguity of sin or sorrow, which enveloped the poor minister, so that love or sympathy could never reach him. It was said, that ghost and fiend consorted with him there. With self-shudderings and outward terrors, he walked continually in

9. Object of dread.

its shadow, groping darkly within his own soul, or gazing through a medium that saddened the whole world. Even the lawless wind, it was believed, respected his dreadful secret, and never blew aside the veil. But still good Mr. Hooper sadly smiled, at the pale visages of the worldly throng as he passed by.

Among all its bad influences, the black veil had the one desirable effect, of making its wearer a very efficient clergyman. By the aid of his mysterious emblem—for there was no other apparent cause—he became a man of awful power, over souls that were in agony for sin. His converts always regarded him with a dread peculiar to themselves, affirming, though but figuratively, that, before he brought them to celestial light, they had been with him behind the black veil. Its gloom, indeed, enabled him to sympathize with all dark affections. Dying sinners cried aloud for Mr. Hooper, and would not yield their breath till he appeared; though ever, as he stooped to whisper consolation, they shuddered at the veiled face so near their own. Such were the terrors of the black veil, even when death had bared his visage! Strangers came long distances to attend service at his church, with the mere idle purpose of gazing at his figure, because it was forbidden them to behold his face. But many were made to quake ere they departed! Once, during Governor Belcher's administration, Mr. Hooper was appointed to preach the election sermon.[1] Covered with his black veil, he stood before the chief magistrate, the council, and the representatives, and wrought so deep an impression, that the legislative measures of that year, were characterized by all the gloom and piety of our earliest ancestral sway.

In this manner Mr. Hooper spent a long life, irreproachable in outward act, yet shrouded in dismal suspicions; kind and loving, though unloved, and dimly feared; a man apart from men, shunned in their health and joy, but ever summoned to their aid in mortal anguish. As years wore on, shedding their snows above his sable veil, he acquired a name throughout the New-England churches, and they called him Father Hooper. Nearly all his parishioners, who were of mature age when he was settled, had been borne away by many a funeral: he had one congregation in the church, and a more crowded one in the church-yard; and having wrought so late into the evening, and done his work so well, it was now good Father Hooper's turn to rest.

Several persons were visible by the shaded candlelight, in the death-chamber of the old clergyman. Natural connections he had none. But there was the decorously grave, though unmoved physician, seeking only to mitigate the last pangs of the patient whom he could not save. There were the deacons, and other eminently pious members of his church. There, also, was the Reverend Mr. Clark, of Westbury, a young and zealous divine, who had ridden in haste to pray by the bed-side of the expiring minister. There was the nurse, no hired handmaiden of death, but one whose calm affection had endured thus long, in secresy, in solitude, amid the chill of age, and would not perish, even at the dying hour. Who, but Elizabeth! And there lay the hoary head of good Father Hooper upon the death-pillow, with the black veil still swathed about his brow and reaching down over his face, so that each more difficult gasp of his faint breath caused it to stir. All through life

1. Sermon preached at the start of a governor's term. Jonathan Belcher (1682–1757) was governor of Massachusetts and New Hampshire (1730–41).

that piece of crape had hung between him and the world: it had separated him from cheerful brotherhood and woman's love, and kept him in that saddest of all prisons, his own heart; and still it lay upon his face, as if to deepen the gloom of his darksome chamber, and shade him from the sunshine of eternity.

For some time previous, his mind had been confused, wavering doubtfully between the past and the present, and hovering forward, as it were, at intervals, into the indistinctness of the world to come. There had been feverish turns, which tossed him from side to side, and wore away what little strength he had. But in his most convulsive struggles, and in the wildest vagaries of his intellect, when no other thought retained its sober influence, he still showed an awful solicitude lest the black veil should slip aside. Even if his bewildered soul could have forgotten, there was a faithful woman at his pillow, who, with averted eyes, would have covered that aged face, which she had last beheld in the comeliness of manhood. At length the death-stricken old man lay quietly in the torpor of mental and bodily exhaustion, with an imperceptible pulse, and breath that grew fainter and fainter, except when a long, deep, and irregular inspiration seemed to prelude the flight of his spirit.

The minister of Westbury approached the bedside.

'Venerable Father Hooper,' said he, 'the moment of your release is at hand. Are you ready for the lifting of the veil, that shuts in time from eternity?'

Father Hooper at first replied merely by a feeble motion of his head; then, apprehensive, perhaps, that his meaning might be doubtful, he exerted himself to speak.

'Yea,' said he, in faint accents, 'my soul hath a patient weariness until that veil be lifted.'

'And is it fitting,' resumed the Reverend Mr. Clark, 'that a man so given to prayer, of such a blameless example, holy in deed and thought, so far as mortal judgment may pronounce; is it fitting that a father in the church should leave a shadow on his memory, that may seem to blacken a life so pure? I pray you, my venerable brother, let not this thing be! Suffer us to be gladdened by your triumphant aspect, as you go to your reward. Before the veil of eternity be lifted, let me cast aside this black veil from your face!'

And thus speaking, the reverend Mr. Clark bent forward to reveal the mystery of so many years. But, exerting a sudden energy, that made all the beholders stand aghast, Father Hooper snatched both his hands from beneath the bed-clothes, and pressed them strongly on the black veil, resolute to struggle, if the minister of Westbury would contend with a dying man.

'Never!' cried the veiled clergyman. 'On earth, never!'

'Dark old man!' exclaimed the affrighted minister, 'with what horrible crime upon your soul are you now passing to the judgment?'

Father Hooper's breath heaved; it rattled in his throat; but, with a mighty effort, grasping forward with his hands, he caught hold of life, and held it back till he should speak. He even raised himself in bed; and there he sat, shivering with the arms of death around him, while the black veil hung down, awful, at that last moment, in the gathered terrors of a life-time. And yet the faint, sad smile, so often there, now seemed to glimmer from its obscurity, and linger on Father Hooper's lips.

'Why do you tremble at me alone?' cried he, turning his veiled face round the circle of pale spectators. 'Tremble also at each other! Have men avoided me, and women shown no pity, and children screamed and fled, only for my black veil? What, but the mystery which it obscurely typifies, has made this piece of crape so awful? When the friend shows his inmost heart to his friend; the lover to his best-beloved; when man does not vainly shrink from the eye of his Creator, loathsomely treasuring up the secret of his sin; then deem me a monster, for the symbol beneath which I have lived, and die! I look around me, and lo! on every visage a black veil!'

While his auditors shrank from one another, in mutual affright, Father Hooper fell back upon his pillow, a veiled corpse, with a faint smile lingering on the lips. Still veiled, they laid him in his coffin, and a veiled corpse they bore him to the grave. The grass of many years has sprung up and withered on that grave, the burial-stone is moss-grown, and good Mr. Hooper's face is dust; but awful is still the thought, that it mouldered beneath the black veil!

1836

The Birth-Mark[1]

In the latter part of the last century, there lived a man of science—an eminent proficient in every branch of natural philosophy—who, not long before our story opens, had made experience of a spiritual affinity, more attractive than any chemical one. He had left his laboratory to the care of an assistant, cleared his fine countenance from the furnace-smoke, washed the stain of acids from his fingers, and persuaded a beautiful woman to become his wife. In those days, when the comparatively recent discovery of electricity, and other kindred mysteries of nature, seemed to open paths into the region of miracle, it was not unusual for the love of science to rival the love of woman, in its depth and absorbing energy. The higher intellect, the imagination, the spirit, and even the heart, might all find their congenial aliment in pursuits which, as some of their ardent votaries[2] believed, would ascend from one step of powerful intelligence to another, until the philosopher should lay his hand on the secret of creative force, and perhaps make new worlds for himself. We know not whether Aylmer possessed this degree of faith in man's ultimate control over nature. He had devoted himself, however, too unreservedly to scientific studies, ever to be weaned from them by any second passion. His love for his young wife might prove the stronger of the two; but it could only be by intertwining itself with his love of science, and uniting the strength of the latter to its own.

Such a union accordingly took place, and was attended with truly remarkable consequences, and a deeply impressive moral. One day, very soon after their marriage, Aylmer sat gazing at his wife, with a trouble in his countenance that grew stronger, until he spoke.

"Georgiana," said he, "has it never occurred to you that the mark upon your cheek might be removed?"

1. First published in the *Pioneer* (March 1843), the source of the present text; the reprinting in *Mosses from an Old Manse* (1846) contains a few variants as well as two corrections (adopted and noted here).

2. Devoted admirers. "Aliment": nourishment.

"No, indeed," said she, smiling; but perceiving the seriousness of his manner, she blushed deeply. "To tell you the truth, it has been so often called a charm, that I was simple enough to imagine it might be so."

"Ah, upon another face, perhaps it might," replied her husband. "But never on yours! No, dearest Georgiana, you came so nearly perfect from the hand of Nature, that this slightest possible defect—which we hesitate whether to term a defect or a beauty—shocks me, as being the visible mark of earthly imperfection."

"Shocks you, my husband!" cried Georgiana, deeply hurt; at first reddening with momentary anger, but then bursting into tears. "Then why did you take me from my mother's side? You cannot love what shocks you!"

To explain this conversation, it must be mentioned, that, in the centre of Georgiana's left cheek, there was a singular mark, deeply interwoven, as it were, with the texture and substance of her face. In the usual state of her complexion,—a healthy, though delicate bloom,—the mark wore a tint of deeper crimson, which imperfectly defined its shape amid the surrounding rosiness. When she blushed, it gradually became more indistinct, and finally vanished amid the triumphant rush of blood, that bathed the whole cheek with its brilliant glow. But, if any shifting emotion caused her to turn pale, there was the mark again, a crimson stain upon the snow, in what Aylmer sometimes deemed an almost fearful distinctness. Its shape bore not a little similarity to the human hand, though of the smallest pigmy size. Georgiana's lovers were wont to say, that some fairy, at her birth-hour, had laid her tiny hand upon the infant's cheek, and left this impress there, in token of the magic endowments that were to give her such sway over all hearts. Many a desperate swain would have risked life for the privilege of pressing his lips to the mysterious hand. It must not be concealed, however, that the impression wrought by this fairy sign-manual varied exceedingly; according to the difference of temperament in the beholders. Some fastidious persons—but they were exclusively of her own sex—affirmed that the Bloody Hand, as they chose to call it, quite destroyed the effect of Georgiana's beauty, and rendered her countenance even hideous. But it would be as reasonable to say, that one of those small blue stains, which sometimes occur in the purest statuary marble, would convert the Eve of Powers[3] to a monster. Masculine observers, if the birth-mark did not heighten their admiration, contented themselves with wishing it away, that the world might possess one living specimen of ideal loveliness, without the semblance of a flaw. After his marriage—for he thought little or nothing of the matter before—Aylmer discovered that this was the case with himself.

Had she been less beautiful—if Envy's self could have found aught else to sneer at—he might have felt his affection heightened by the prettiness of this mimic hand, now vaguely portrayed, now lost, now stealing forth again, and glimmering to-and-fro with every pulse of emotion that throbbed within her heart. But, seeing her otherwise so perfect, he found this one defect grow more and more intolerable, with every moment of their united lives. It was the fatal flaw of humanity, which Nature, in one shape or another, stamps ineffaceably on all her productions, either to imply that they are temporary

3. *Eve before the Fall*, a sculpture by the American Hiram Powers (1805–1873).

and finite, or that their perfection must be wrought by toil and pain. The Crimson Hand expressed the ineludible gripe,[4] in which mortality clutches the highest and purest of earthly mould, degrading them into kindred with the lowest, and even with the very brutes, like whom their visible frames return to dust. In this manner, selecting it as the symbol of his wife's liability to sin, sorrow, decay, and death, Aylmer's sombre imagination was not long in rendering the birth-mark a frightful object, causing him more trouble and horror than ever Georgiana's beauty, whether of soul or sense, had given him delight.

At all the seasons which should have been their happiest, he invariably, and without intending it—nay, in spite of a purpose to the contrary—reverted to this one disastrous topic. Trifling as it at first appeared, it so connected itself with innumerable trains of thought, and modes of feeling, that it became the central point of all. With the morning twilight, Aylmer opened his eyes upon his wife's face, and recognised the symbol of imperfection; and when they sat together at the evening hearth, his eyes wandered stealthily to her cheek, and beheld, flickering with the blaze of the wood fire, the spectral Hand that wrote mortality, where he would fain have worshipped. Georgiana soon learned to shudder at his gaze. It needed but a glance, with the peculiar expression that his face often wore, to change the roses of her cheek into a deathlike paleness, amid which the Crimson Hand was brought strongly out, like a bas-relief[5] of ruby on the whitest marble.

Late, one night, when the lights were growing dim, so as hardly to betray the stain on the poor wife's cheek, she herself, for the first time, voluntarily took up the subject.

"Do you remember, my dear Aylmer," said she, with a feeble attempt at a smile—"have you any recollection of a dream, last night, about this odious Hand?"

"None!—none whatever!" replied Aylmer, starting; but then he added in a dry, cold tone, affected for the sake of concealing the real depth of his emotion:—"I might well dream of it; for, before I fell asleep, it had taken a pretty firm hold of my fancy."

"And you did dream of it," continued Georgiana, hastily; for she dreaded lest a gush of tears should interrupt what she had to say—"A terrible dream! I wonder that you can forget it. Is it possible to forget this one expression?—'It is in her heart now—we must have it out!'—Reflect, my husband; for by all means I would have you recall that dream."

The mind is in a sad state, when Sleep, the all-involving, cannot confine her spectres within the dim region of her sway, but suffers them to break forth, affrighting this actual life with secrets that perchance belong to a deeper one. Aylmer now remembered his dream. He had fancied himself, with his servant Aminidab, attempting an operation for the removal of the birth-mark. But the deeper went the knife, the deeper sank the Hand, until at length its tiny grasp appeared to have caught hold of Georgiana's heart; whence, however, her husband was inexorably resolved to cut or wrench it away.

4. Grip (variant spelling).

5. Low-relief; slightly raised.

When the dream had shaped itself perfectly in his memory, Aylmer sat in his wife's presence with a guilty feeling. Truth often finds its way to the mind close-muffled in robes of sleep, and then speaks with uncompromising directness of matters in regard to which we practise an unconscious self-deception, during our waking moments. Until now, he had not been aware of the tyrannizing influence acquired by one idea over his mind, and of the lengths which he might find in his heart to go, for the sake of giving himself peace.

"Aylmer," resumed Georgiana, solemnly, "I know not what may be the cost to both of us, to rid me of this fatal birth-mark. Perhaps its removal may cause cureless deformity. Or, it may be, the stain goes as deep as life itself. Again, do we know that there is a possibility, on any terms, of unclasping the firm gripe of this little Hand, which was laid upon me before I came into the world?"

"Dearest Georgiana, I have spent much thought upon the subject," hastily interrupted Aylmer—"I am convinced of the perfect practicability of its removal."

"If there be the remotest possibility of it," continued Georgiana, "let the attempt be made, at whatever risk. Danger is nothing to me; for life—while this hateful mark makes me the object of your horror and disgust—life is a burthen[6] which I would fling down with joy. Either remove this dreadful Hand, or take my wretched life! You have deep science! All the world bears witness of it. You have achieved great wonders! Cannot you remove this little, little mark, which I cover with the tips of two small fingers? Is this beyond your power, for the sake of your own peace, and to save your poor wife from madness?"

"Noblest—dearest—tenderest wife!" cried Aylmer, rapturously. "Doubt not my power. I have already given this matter the deepest thought—thought which might almost have enlightened me to create a being less perfect than yourself. Georgiana, you have led me deeper than ever into the heart of science. I feel myself fully competent to render this dear cheek as faultless as its fellow; and then, most beloved, what will be my triumph, when I shall have corrected what Nature left imperfect, in her fairest work! Even Pygmalion,[7] when his sculptured woman assumed life, felt not greater ecstasy than mine will be."

"It is resolved, then," said Georgiana, faintly smiling,—"And, Aylmer, spare me not, though you should find the birth-mark take refuge in my heart at last."

Her husband tenderly kissed her cheek—her right cheek—not that which bore the impress of the Crimson Hand.

The next day, Aylmer apprized his wife of a plan that he had formed, whereby he might have opportunity for the intense thought and constant watchfulness, which the proposed operation would require; while Georgiana, likewise, would enjoy the perfect repose essential to its success. They were to seclude themselves in the extensive apartments occupied by Aylmer as a laboratory, and where, during his toilsome youth, he had made discoveries in the elemental powers of nature, that had roused the admiration of all the

6. Burden.
7. In Greek myth, a king and sculptor who fell so deeply in love with his statue that Aphrodite granted his prayers and gave it life.

learned societies in Europe. Seated calmly in this laboratory, the pale philosopher had investigated the secrets of the highest cloud-region, and of the profoundest mines; he had satisfied himself of the causes that kindled and kept alive the fires of the volcano; and had explained the mystery of fountains, and how it is that they gush forth, some so bright and pure, and others with such rich medicinal[8] virtues, from the dark bosom of the earth. Here, too, at an earlier period, he had studied the wonders of the human frame, and attempted to fathom the very process by which Nature assimilates all her precious influences from earth and air, and from the spiritual world, to create and foster Man, her masterpiece. The latter pursuit, however, Aylmer had long laid aside, in unwilling recognition of the truth, against which all seekers sooner or later stumble, that our great creative Mother, while she amuses us with apparently working in the broadest sunshine, is yet severely careful to keep her own secrets, and, in spite of her pretended openness, shows us nothing but results. She permits us, indeed, to mar, but seldom to mend, and, like a jealous patentee, on no account to make. Now, however, Aylmer resumed these half-forgotten investigations; not, of course, with such hopes or wishes as first suggested them; but because they involved much physiological truth, and lay in the path of his proposed scheme for the treatment of Georgiana.

As he led her over the threshold of the laboratory, Georgiana was cold and tremulous. Aylmer looked cheerfully into her face, with intent to reassure her, but was so startled with the intense glow of the birth-mark upon the whiteness of her cheek, that he could not restrain a strong convulsive shudder. His wife fainted.

"Aminidab! Aminidab!" shouted Aylmer, stamping violently on the floor.

Forthwith, there issued from an inner apartment a man of low stature, but bulky frame, with shaggy hair hanging about his visage, which was grimed with the vapors of the furnace. This personage had been Aylmer's underworker during his whole scientific career, and was admirably fitted for that office by his great mechanical readiness, and the skill with which, while incapable of comprehending a single principle, he executed all the practical details of his master's experiments. With his vast strength, his shaggy hair, his smoky aspect, and the indescribable earthiness that incrusted him, he seemed to represent man's physical nature; while Aylmer's slender figure, and pale, intellectual face, were no less apt a type of the spiritual element.

"Throw open the door of the boudoir, Aminidab," said Aylmer, "and burn a pastille."[9]

"Yes, master," answered Aminidab, looking intently at the lifeless form of Georgiana; and then he muttered to himself;—"If she were my wife, I'd never part with that birth-mark."

When Georgiana recovered consciousness, she found herself breathing an atmosphere of penetrating fragrance, the gentle potency of which had recalled her from her deathlike faintness. The scene around her looked like enchantment. Aylmer had converted those smoky, dingy, sombre rooms, where he had spent his brightest years in recondite pursuits, into a series of

8. This 1846 reading replaces the 1843 *medical*.

9. A tablet burned to perfume the air.

beautiful apartments, not unfit to be the secluded abode of a lovely woman. The walls were hung with gorgeous curtains, which imparted the combination of grandeur and grace, that no other species of adornment can achieve; and as they fell from the ceiling to the floor, their rich and ponderous folds, concealing all angles and straight lines, appeared to shut in the scene from infinite space. For aught Georgiana knew, it might be a pavilion among the clouds. And Aylmer, excluding the sunshine, which would have interfered with his chemical processes, had supplied its place with perfumed lamps, emitting flames of various hue, but all uniting in a soft, empurpled radiance. He now knelt by his wife's side, watching her earnestly, but without alarm; for he was confident in his science, and felt that he could draw a magic circle round her, within which no evil might intrude.

"Where am I?—Ah, I remember!" said Georgiana, faintly; and she placed her hand over her cheek, to hide the terrible mark from her husband's eyes.

"Fear not, dearest!" exclaimed he, "Do not shrink from me! Believe me, Georgiana, I even rejoice in this single imperfection, since it will be such rapture to remove it."

"Oh, spare me!" sadly replied his wife—"Pray do not look at it again. I never can forget that convulsive shudder."

In order to soothe Georgiana, and, as it were, to release her mind from the burthen of actual things, Aylmer now put in practice some of the light and playful secrets, which science had taught him among its profounder lore. Airy figures, absolutely bodiless ideas, and forms of unsubstantial beauty, came and danced before her, imprinting their momentary footsteps on beams of light. Though she had some indistinct idea of the method of these optical phenomena, still the illusion was almost perfect enough to warrant the belief, that her husband possessed sway over the spiritual world. Then again, when she felt a wish to look forth from her seclusion, immediately, as if her thoughts were answered, the procession of external existence flitted across a screen. The scenery and the figures of actual life were perfectly represented, but with that bewitching, yet indescribable difference, which always makes a picture, an image, or a shadow, so much more attractive than the original. When wearied of this, Aylmer bade her cast her eyes upon a vessel, containing a quantity of earth. She did so, with little interest at first, but was soon startled, to perceive the germ of a plant, shooting upward from the soil. Then came the slender stalk—the leaves gradually unfolded themselves—and amid them was a perfect and lovely flower.

"It is magical!" cried Georgiana, "I dare not touch it."

"Nay, pluck it," answered Aylmer, "pluck it, and inhale its brief perfume while you may. The flower will wither in a few moments, and leave nothing save its brown seed-vessels—but thence may be perpetuated a race as ephemeral as itself."

But Georgiana had no sooner touched the flower than the whole plant suffered a blight, its leaves turning coal-black, as if by the agency of fire.

"There was too powerful a stimulus," said Aylmer thoughtfully.

To make up for this abortive experiment, he proposed to take her portrait by a scientific process of his own invention. It was to be effected by rays of light striking upon a polished plate of metal. Georgiana assented—but, on looking at the result, was affrighted to find the features of the portrait blurred and indefinable; while the minute figure of a hand appeared where the cheek should have been. Aylmer snatched the metallic plate, and threw it into a jar of corrosive acid.

Soon, however, he forgot these mortifying failures. In the intervals of study and chemical experiment, he came to her, flushed and exhausted, but seemed invigorated by her presence, and spoke in glowing language of the resources of his art. He gave a history of the long dynasty of the Alchemists, who spent so many ages in quest of the universal solvent, by which the Golden Principle might be elicited from all things vile and base.[1] Aylmer appeared to believe, that, by the plainest scientific logic, it was altogether within the limits of possibility to discover this long-sought medium; but, he added, a philosopher who should go deep enough to acquire the power, would attain too lofty a wisdom to stoop to the exercise of it. Not less singular were his opinions in regard to the Elixir Vitæ.[2] He more than intimated, that it was at his option to concoct a liquid that should prolong life for years—perhaps interminably—but that it would produce a discord in nature, which all the world, and chiefly the quaffer of the immortal nostrum, would find cause to curse.

"Aylmer, are you in earnest?" asked Georgiana, looking at him with amazement and fear; "it is terrible to possess such power, or even to dream of possessing it!"

"Oh, do not tremble, my love!" said her husband, "I would not wrong either you or myself, by working such inharmonious effects upon our lives. But I would have you consider how trifling, in comparison, is the skill requisite to remove this little Hand."

At the mention of the birth-mark, Georgiana, as usual, shrank, as if a red-hot iron had touched her cheek.

Again Aylmer applied himself to his labors. She could hear his voice in the distant furnace-room, giving directions to Aminidab, whose harsh, uncouth, misshapen tones were audible in response, more like the grunt or growl of a brute than human speech. After hours of absence, Aylmer re-appeared, and proposed that she should now examine his cabinet of chemical products, and natural treasures of the earth. Among the former he showed her a small vial, in which, he remarked, was contained a gentle, yet most powerful fragrance, capable of impregnating all the breezes that blow across a kingdom. They were of inestimable value, the contents of that little vial; and, as he said so, he threw some of the perfume into the air, and filled the room with piercing and invigorating delight.

"And what is this?" asked Georgiana, pointing to a small crystal globe, containing a gold-colored liquid. "It is so beautiful to the eye, that I could imagine it the Elixir of Life."

"In one sense it is," replied Aylmer, "or rather the Elixir of Immortality. It is the most precious poison that ever was concocted in this world. By its aid, I could apportion the lifetime of any mortal at whom you might point your finger. The strength of the dose would determine whether he were to linger out years, or drop dead in the midst of a breath. No king, on his guarded throne, could keep his life, if I, in my private station, should deem that the welfare of millions justified me in depriving him of it."

1. The goal of many alchemists was to turn base metal into gold.

2. Elixir of life (Latin); a potion with the power to prolong life indefinitely.

"Why do you keep such a terrific drug?" inquired Georgiana in horror.

"Do not mistrust me, dearest!" said her husband, smiling; "its virtuous potency is yet greater than its harmful one. But, see! here is a powerful cosmetic. With a few drops of this, in a vase of water, freckles may be washed away as easily as the hands are cleansed. A stronger infusion would take the blood out of the cheek, and leave the rosiest beauty a pale ghost."

"Is it with this lotion that you intend to bathe my cheek?' asked Georgiana anxiously.

"Oh, no!" hastily replied her husband—"this is merely superficial. Your case demands a remedy that shall go deeper."

In his interviews with Georgiana, Aylmer generally made minute inquiries as to her sensations, and whether the confinement of the rooms, and the temperature of the atmosphere, agreed with her. These questions had such a particular drift, that Georgiana began to conjecture that she was already subjected to certain physical influences, either breathed in with the fragrant air, or taken with her food. She fancied, likewise—but it might be altogether fancy—that there was a stirring up of her system,—a strange, indefinite sensation creeping through her veins, and tingling, half painfully, half pleasurably, at her heart. Still, whenever she dared to look into the mirror, there she beheld herself, pale as a white rose, and with the crimson birth-mark stamped upon her cheek. Not even Aylmer now hated it so much as she.

To dispel the tedium of the hours which her husband found it necessary to devote to the processes of combination and analysis, Georgiana turned over the volumes of his scientific library. In many dark old tomes, she met with chapters full of romance and poetry. They were the works of the philosophers of the middle ages, such as Albertus Magnus, Cornelius Agrippa, Paracelsus, and the famous friar who created the prophetic Brazen Head.[3] All these antique naturalists stood in advance of their centuries, yet were imbued with some of their[4] credulity, and therefore were believed, and perhaps imagined themselves, to have acquired from the investigation of nature a power above nature, and from physics a sway over the spiritual world. Hardly less curious and imaginative were the early volumes of the Transactions of the Royal Society,[5] in which the members, knowing little of the limits of natural possibility, were continually recording wonders, or proposing methods whereby wonders might be wrought.

But, to Georgiana, the most engrossing volume was a large folio from her husband's own hand, in which he had recorded every experiment of his scientific career, with its original aim, the methods adopted for its development, and its final success or failure, with the circumstances to which either event was attributable. The book, in truth, was both the history and emblem of his ardent, ambitious, imaginative, yet practical and laborious, life. He handled physical details, as if there were nothing beyond them; yet spiritualized them all, and redeemed himself from materialism, by his strong and eager aspiration towards the infinite. In his grasp, the veriest clod of earth

3. I.e., Roger Bacon (1214?–1294), English Franciscan monk interested in science and alchemy, who fashioned a head of bronze said to predict changes in climate and health. Magnus (1206?–1280), German theologian and alchemist. Agrippa (1486–1535), German theologian and writer. Philippus Aureolus Paracelsus (1493–1541), Swiss alchemist and physician.

4. This 1846 reading replaces the 1843 *its*.

5. The Royal Society of London, chartered in 1662 to advance scientific inquiry.

assumed a soul. Georgiana, as she read, reverenced Aylmer, and loved him more profoundly than ever, but with a less entire dependence on his judgment than heretofore. Much as he had accomplished, she could not but observe that his most splendid successes were almost invariably failures, if compared with the ideal at which he aimed. His brightest diamonds were the merest pebbles, and felt to be so by himself, in comparison with the inestimable gems which lay hidden beyond his reach. The volume, rich with achievements that had won renown for its author, was yet as melancholy a record as ever mortal hand had penned. It was the sad confession, and continual exemplification, of the short-comings of the composite man—the spirit burthened with clay and working in matter—and of the despair that assails the higher nature, at finding itself so miserably thwarted by the earthly part. Perhaps every man of genius, in whatever sphere, might recognise the image of his own experience in Aylmer's journal.

So deeply did these reflections affect Georgiana, that she laid her face upon the open volume, and burst into tears. In this situation she was found by her husband.

"It is dangerous to read in a sorcerer's books," said he, with a smile, though his countenance was uneasy and displeased. "Georgiana, there are pages in that volume, which I can scarcely glance over and keep my senses. Take heed lest it prove as detrimental to you!"

"It has made me worship you more than ever," said she.

"Ah! wait for this one success," rejoined he, "then worship me if you will. I shall deem myself hardly unworthy of it. But, come! I have sought you for the luxury of your voice. Sing to me, dearest!"

So she poured out the liquid music of her voice to quench the thirst of his spirit. He then took his leave, with a boyish exuberance of gaiety, assuring her that her seclusion would endure but a little longer, and that the result was already certain. Scarcely had he departed, when Georgiana felt irresistibly impelled to follow him. She had forgotten to inform Aylmer of a symptom, which, for two or three hours past, had begun to excite her attention. It was a sensation in the fatal birth-mark, not painful, but which induced a restlessness throughout her system. Hastening after her husband, she intruded, for the first time, into the laboratory.

The first thing that struck her eye was the furnace, that hot and feverish worker, with the intense glow of its fire, which, by the quantities of soot clustered above it, seemed to have been burning for ages. There was a distilling apparatus in full operation. Around the room were retorts,[6] tubes, cylinders, crucibles, and other apparatus of chemical research. An electrical machine stood ready for immediate use. The atmosphere felt oppressively close, and was tainted with gaseous odors, which had been tormented forth by the processes of science. The severe and homely simplicity of the apartment, with its naked walls and brick pavement, looked strange, accustomed as Georgiana had become to the fantastic elegance of her boudoir. But what chiefly, indeed almost solely, drew her attention, was the aspect of Aylmer himself.

He was pale as death, anxious, and absorbed, and hung over the furnace as if it depended upon his utmost watchfulness whether the liquid, which it

6. Glass vessels used for distillation.

was distilling, should be the draught of immortal happiness or misery. How different from the sanguine and joyous mien that he had assumed for Georgiana's encouragement!

"Carefully now, Aminidab! Carefully, thou human machine! Carefully, thou man of clay!" muttered Aylmer, more to himself than his assistant. "Now, if there be a thought too much or too little, it is all over!"

"Hoh! hoh!" mumbled Aminidab—"look, master, look!"

Aylmer raised his eyes hastily, and at first reddened, then grew paler than ever, on beholding Georgiana. He rushed towards her, and seized her arm with a gripe that left the print of his fingers upon it.

"Why do you come hither? Have you no trust in your husband?" cried he impetuously. "Would you throw the blight of that fatal birth-mark over my labors? It is not well done. Go, prying woman, go!"

"Nay, Aylmer," said Georgiana, with the firmness of which she possessed no stinted endowment, "it is not you that have a right to complain. You mistrust your wife! You have concealed the anxiety with which you watch the development of this experiment. Think not so unworthily of me, my husband! Tell me all the risk we run; and fear not that I shall shrink, for my share in it is far less than your own!"

"No, no, Georgiana!" said Aylmer impatiently, "it must not be."

"I submit," replied she, calmly. "And, Aylmer, I shall quaff whatever draught you bring me; but it will be on the same principle that would induce me to take a dose of poison, if offered by your hand."

"My noble wife," said Aylmer, deeply moved, "I knew not the height and depth of your nature, until now: Nothing shall be concealed. Know, then, that this Crimson Hand, superficial as it seems, has clutched its grasp, into your being, with a strength of which I had no previous conception. I have already administered agents powerful enough to do aught except to change your entire physical system. Only one thing remains to be tried. If that fail us, we are ruined!"

"Why did you hesitate to tell me this?" asked she.

"Because, Georgiana," said Aylmer, in a low voice, "there is danger!"

"Danger? There is but one danger—that this horrible stigma shall be left upon my cheek!" cried Georgiana. "Remove it! remove it!—whatever be the cost—or we shall both go mad!"

"Heaven knows, your words are too true," said Aylmer, sadly. "And now, dearest, return to your boudoir. In a little while, all will be tested."

He conducted her back, and took leave of her with a solemn tenderness, which spoke far more than his words how much was now at stake. After his departure, Georgiana became wrapt in musings. She considered the character of Aylmer, and did it completer justice than at any previous moment. Her heart exulted, while it trembled, at his honorable love, so pure and lofty that it would accept nothing less than perfection, nor miserably make itself contented with an earthlier nature than he had dreamed of. She felt how much more precious was such a sentiment, than that meaner kind which would have borne with the imperfection for her sake, and have been guilty of treason to holy love, by degrading its perfect idea to the level of the actual. And, with her whole spirit, she prayed, that, for a single moment, she might satisfy his highest and deepest conception. Longer than one moment, she well knew, it could not be; for his spirit was ever on the march—ever ascending—and each instant required something that was beyond the scope of the instant before.

The sound of her husband's footsteps aroused her. He bore a crystal goblet, containing a liquor colorless as water, but bright enough to be the draught of immortality. Aylmer was pale; but it seemed rather the consequence of a highly wrought state of mind, and tension of spirit, than of fear or doubt.

"The concoction of the draught has been perfect," said he, in answer to Georgiana's look. "Unless all my science have deceived me, it cannot fail."

"Save on your account, my dearest Aylmer," observed his wife, "I might wish to put off this birth-mark of mortality by relinquishing mortality itself, in preference to any other mode. Life is but a sad possession to those who have attained precisely the degree of moral advancement at which I stand. Were I weaker and blinder, it might be happiness. Were I stronger, it might be endured hopefully. But, being what I find myself, methinks I am of all mortals the most fit to die."

"You are fit for heaven without tasting death!" replied her husband. "But why do we speak of dying? The draught cannot fail. Behold its effect upon this plant!"

On the window-seat there stood a geranium, diseased with yellow blotches, which had overspread all its leaves. Aylmer poured a small quantity of the liquid upon the soil in which it grew. In a little time, when the roots of the plant had taken up the moisture, the unsightly blotches began to be extinguished in a living verdure.

"There needed no proof," said Georgiana, quietly. "Give me the goblet. I joyfully stake all upon your word."

"Drink, then, thou lofty creature!" exclaimed Aylmer, with fervid admiration. "There is no taint of imperfection on thy spirit. Thy sensible frame, too, shall soon be all perfect!"

She quaffed the liquid, and returned the goblet to his hand.

"It is grateful," said she with a placid smile. "Methinks it is like water from a heavenly fountain; for it contains I know not what of unobtrusive fragrance and deliciousness. It allays a feverish thirst, that had parched me for many days. Now, dearest, let me sleep. My earthly senses are closing over my spirit, like the leaves round the heart of a rose, at sunset."

She spoke the last words with a gentle reluctance, as if it required almost more energy than she could command to pronounce the faint and lingering syllables. Scarcely had they loitered through her lips, ere she was lost in slumber. Aylmer sat by her side, watching her aspect with the emotions proper to a man, the whole value of whose existence was involved in the process now to be tested. Mingled with this mood, however, was the philosophic investigation, characteristic of the man of science. Not the minutest symptom escaped him. A heightened flush of the cheek—a slight irregularity of breath—a quiver of the eye-lid—a hardly perceptible tremor through the frame—such were the details which, as the moments passed, he wrote down in his folio volume. Intense thought had set its stamp upon every previous page of that volume; but the thoughts of years were all concentrated upon the last.

While thus employed, he failed not to gaze often at the fatal Hand, and not without a shudder. Yet once, by a strange and unaccountable impulse, he pressed it with his lips. His spirit recoiled, however, in the very act, and Georgiana, out of the midst of her deep sleep, moved uneasily and murmured, as if in remonstrance. Again, Aylmer resumed his watch. Nor was it without avail. The Crimson Hand, which at first had been strongly visible upon the marble paleness of Georgiana's cheek, now grew more faintly outlined. She remained not less pale than ever; but the birth-mark, with every breath that came and went, lost somewhat of its former distinctness. Its presence had been awful; its departure was more awful still. Watch the stain of the rainbow fading out of the sky; and you will know how that mysterious symbol passed away.

"By Heaven, it is well nigh gone!" said Aylmer to himself, in almost irrepressible ecstasy. "I can scarcely trace it now. Success! Success! And now it is like the faintest rose-color. The slightest flush of blood across her cheek would overcome it. But she is so pale!"

He drew aside the window-curtain, and suffered the light of natural day to fall into the room, and rest upon her cheek. At the same time, he heard a gross, hoarse chuckle, which he had long known as his servant Aminidab's expression of delight.

"Ah, clod! Ah, earthly mass!" cried Aylmer, laughing in a sort of frenzy. "You have served me well! Matter and Spirit—Earth and Heaven—have both done their part in this! Laugh, thing of the senses! You have earned the right to laugh."

These exclamations broke Georgiana's sleep. She slowly unclosed her eyes, and gazed into the mirror, which her husband had arranged for that purpose. A faint smile flitted over her lips, when she recognised how barely perceptible was now that Crimson Hand, which had once blazed forth with such disastrous brilliancy as to scare away all their happiness. But then her eyes sought Aylmer's face, with a trouble and anxiety that he could by no means account for.

"My poor Aylmer!" murmured she.

"Poor? Nay, richest! Happiest! Most favored!" exclaimed he. "My peerless bride, it is successful! You are perfect!"

"My poor Aylmer!" she repeated, with a more than human tenderness. "You have aimed loftily!—you have done nobly! Do not repent, that, with so high and pure a feeling, you have rejected the best that earth could offer. Aylmer—dearest Aylmer—I am dying!"

Alas, it was too true! The fatal Hand had grappled with the mystery of life, and was the bond by which an angelic spirit kept itself in union with a mortal frame. As the last crimson tint of the birth-mark—that sole token of human imperfection—faded from her cheek, the parting breath of the now perfect woman passed into the atmosphere, and her soul, lingering a moment near her husband, took its heavenward flight. Then a hoarse, chuckling laugh was heard again! Thus ever does the gross Fatality of Earth exult in its invariable triumph over the immortal essence, which, in this dim sphere of half-development, demands the completeness of a higher state. Yet, had Aylmer reached a profounder wisdom, he need not thus have flung away the happiness, which would have woven his mortal life of the self-same texture with the celestial. The momentary circumstance was too strong for him; he failed to look beyond the shadowy scope of Time, and living once for all in Eternity, to find the perfect Future in the present.

1843, 1846

Rappaccini's Daughter[1]

Writings of Aubépine

We do not remember to have seen any translated specimens of the productions of M. de l'Aubépine;[2] a fact the less to be wondered at, as his very name is unknown to many of his own countrymen, as well as to the student of foreign literature. As a writer, he seems to occupy an unfortunate position between the Transcendentalists (who, under one name or another, have their share in all the current literature of the world), and the great body of pen-and-ink men who address the intellect and sympathies of the multitude. If not too refined, at all events too remote, too shadowy and unsubstantial in his modes of development, to suit the taste of the latter class, and yet too popular to satisfy the spiritual or metaphysical requisitions of the former, he must necessarily find himself without an audience; except here and there an individual, or possibly an isolated clique. His writings, to do them justice, are not altogether destitute of fancy and originality; they might have won him greater reputation but for an inveterate love of allegory, which is apt to invest his plots and characters with the aspect of scenery and people in the clouds, and to steal away the human warmth out of his conceptions. His fictions are sometimes historical, sometimes of the present day, and sometimes, so far as can be discovered, have little or no reference either to time or space. In any case, he generally contents himself with a very slight embroidery of outward manners,—the faintest possible counterfeit of real life,—and endeavors to create an interest by some less obvious peculiarity of the subject. Occasionally, a breath of nature, a rain-drop of pathos and tenderness, or a gleam of humor, will find its way into the midst of his fantastic imagery, and make us feel as if, after all, we were yet within the limits of our native earth. We will only add to this very cursory notice, that M. de l'Aubépine's productions, if the reader chance to take them in precisely the proper point of view, may amuse a leisure hour as well as those of a brighter man; if otherwise, they can hardly fail to look excessively like nonsense.

Our author is voluminous; he continues to write and publish with as much praiseworthy and indefatigable prolixity, as if his efforts were crowned with the brilliant success that so justly attends those of Eugene Sue.[3] His first appearance was by a collection of stories, in a long series of volumes, entitled "*Contes deux fois racontées.*"[4] The titles of some of his more recent works (we quote from memory) are as follows:—"*Le Voyage Céleste à Chemin de Fer,*" 3 tom. 1838. "*Le nouveau père Adam et la nouvelle mère Eve,*" 2 tom. 1839. "*Roderic; ou le Serpent à l'estomac,*" 2 tom. 1840. "*Le Culte du Feu,*" a folio volume of ponderous research into the religion and ritual of the old Persian Ghebers, published in 1841. "*La Soirée du Château en Espagne,*" 1 tom. 8vo. 1842; and "*L'Artiste du Beau; ou le Papillon Mécanique,*" 5 tom. 4to. 1843.[5]

1. The text is from the first publication in *The Democratic Review* (December 1844).
2. French for "Hawthorne." What follows is a tongue-in-cheek account of Hawthorne's own career.
3. French novelist (1804–1857), author of *The Wandering Jew* and other popular works.
4. *Twice-Told Tales* (French), Hawthorne's first volume (1837) after the anonymous *Fanshawe* (1828).
5. In these mock bibliographical citations, "tom." (French abbreviation for *tome*, "volume") and "8vo." (octavo) and "4vo." (quarto) are jokes: Hawthorne's tales took up only a few magazine pages

Our somewhat wearisome persual of this startling catalogue of volumes has left behind it a certain personal affection and sympathy, though by no means admiration, for M. de l'Aubépine; and we would fain do the little in our power towards introducing him favorably to the American public. The ensuing tale is a translation of his *"Béatrice; ou La Belle Empoisonneuse,"*[6] recently published in *"La Revue Anti-Aristocratique."* This journal, edited by the Comte de Bearhaven,[7] has, for some years past, led the defence of liberal principles and popular rights, with a faithfulness and ability worthy of all praise.

Rappaccini's Daughter

A young man, named Giovanni Guasconti, came, very long ago, from the more southern region of Italy, to pursue his studies at the University of Padua. Giovanni, who had but a scanty supply of gold ducats in his pocket, took lodgings in a high and gloomy chamber of an old edifice, which looked not unworthy to have been the palace of a Paduan noble, and which, in fact, exhibited over its entrance the armorial bearings of a family long since extinct. The young stranger, who was not unstudied in the great poem of his country, recollected that one of the ancestors of this family, and perhaps an occupant of this very mansion, had been pictured by Dante[8] as a partaker of the immortal agonies of his Inferno. These reminiscences and associations, together with the tendency to heart-break natural to a young man for the first time out of his native sphere, caused Giovanni to sigh heavily, as he looked around the desolate and ill-furnished apartment.

"Holy Virgin, signor," cried old dame Lisabetta, who, won by the youth's remarkable beauty of person, was kindly endeavoring to give the chamber a habitable air, "what a sigh was that to come out of a young man's heart! Do you find this old mansion gloomy? For the love of heaven, then, put your head out of the window, and you will see as bright sunshine as you have left in Naples."

Guasconti mechanically did as the old woman advised, but could not quite agree with her that the Lombard sunshine was as cheerful as that of southern Italy. Such as it was, however, it fell upon a garden beneath the window, and expended its fostering influences on a variety of plants, which seemed to have been cultivated with exceeding care.

"Does this garden belong to the house?" asked Giovanni.

"Heaven forbid, signor!—unless it were fruitful of better pot-herbs than any that grow there now," answered old Lisabetta. "No: that garden is cultivated by the own hands of Signor Giacomo Rappaccini, the famous Doctor, who, I warrant him, has been heard of as far as Naples. It is said he distils these plants into medicines that are as potent as a charm. Oftentimes you may see the signor Doctor at work, and perchance the signora his daughter, too, gathering the strange flowers that grow in the garden."

each. All but one of these French titles refer to stories by Hawthorne. In order, the titles are "The Celestial Railroad," "The New Adam and Eve," "Egotism; or, The Bosom-Serpent," "Fire-Worship," "Evening in a Castle in Spain" (imaginary), and "The Artist of the Beautiful."

6. *Beatrice; or the Poisonous Beauty.*

7. Hawthorne's friend John O'Sullivan (1813–1895), editor of *The Democratic Review* (here, "*La Revue Anti-Aristocratique*").

8. Dante Alighieri (1265–1321), author of the three-part epic poem the *Divine Comedy*, the first part of which is the *Inferno*. This famous poem follows the author in an imaginary journey from Hell to Purgatory to Paradise.

The old woman had now done what she could for the aspect of the chamber, and, commending the young man to the protection of the saints, took her departure.

Giovanni still found no better occupation than to look down into the garden beneath his window. From its appearance, he judged it to be one of those botanic gardens, which were of earlier date in Padua than elsewhere in Italy, or in the world. Or, not improbably, it might once have been the pleasure-place of an opulent family; for there was the ruin of a marble fountain in the centre, sculptured with rare art, but so woefully shattered that it was impossible to trace the original design from the chaos of remaining fragments. The water, however, continued to gush and sparkle into the sunbeams as cheerfully as ever. A little gurgling sound ascended to the young man's window, and made him feel as if the fountain were an immortal spirit, that sung its song unceasingly, and without heeding the vicissitudes around it; while one century embodied it in marble, and another scattered the garniture on the soil. All about the pool into which the water subsided, grew various plants, that seemed to require a plentiful supply of moisture for the nourishment of gigantic leaves, and, in some instances, flowers gorgeously magnificent. There was one shrub in particular, set in a marble vase in the midst of the pool, that bore a profusion of purple blossoms, each of which had the lustre and richness of a gem; and the whole together made a show so resplendent that it seemed enough to illuminate the garden, even had there been no sunshine. Every portion of the soil was peopled with plants and herbs, which, if less beautiful, still bore tokens of assiduous care; as if all had their individual virtues, known to the scientific mind that fostered them. Some were placed in urns, rich with old carving, and others in common garden-pots; some crept serpent-like along the ground, or climbed on high, using whatever means of ascent was offered them. One plant had wreathed itself round a statue of Vertumnus,[9] which was thus quite veiled and shrouded in a drapery of hanging foliage, so happily arranged that it might have served a sculptor for a study.

While Giovanni stood at the window, he heard a rustling behind a screen of leaves, and became aware that a person was at work in the garden. His figure soon emerged into view, and showed itself to be that of no common laborer, but a tall, emaciated, sallow, and sickly-looking man, dressed in a scholar's garb of black. He was beyond the middle term of life, with grey hair, a thin grey beard, and a face singularly marked with intellect and cultivation, but which could never, even in his more youthful days, have expressed much warmth of heart.

Nothing could exceed the intentness with which this scientific gardener examined every shrub which grew in his path; it seemed as if he was looking into their inmost nature, making observations in regard to their creative essence, and discovering why one leaf grew in this shape, and another in that, and wherefore such and such flowers differed among themselves in hue and perfume. Nevertheless, in spite of the deep intelligence on his part, there was no approach to intimacy between himself and these vegetable existences. On the contrary, he avoided their actual touch, or the direct inhaling of their

9. The Roman god of the seasons (and vegetation produced by the changing seasons).

odors, with a caution that impressed Giovanni most disagreeably; for the man's demeanor was that of one walking among malignant influences, such as savage beasts, or deadly snakes, or evil spirits, which, should he allow them one moment of license, would wreak upon him some terrible fatality. It was strangely frightful to the young man's imagination, to see this air of insecurity in a person cultivating a garden, that most simple and innocent of human toils, and which had been alike the joy and labor of the unfallen parents of the race. Was this garden, then, the Eden of the present world?—and this man, with such a perception of harm in what his own hands caused to grow, was he the Adam?

The distrustful gardener, while plucking away the dead leaves or pruning the too luxuriant growth of the shrubs, defended his hands with a pair of thick gloves. Nor were these his only armor. When, in his walk through the garden, he came to the magnificent plant that hung its purple gems beside the marble fountain, he placed a kind of mask over his mouth and nostrils, as if all this beauty did but conceal a deadlier malice. But finding his task still too dangerous, he drew back, removed the mask, and called loudly, but in the infirm voice of a person affected with inward disease:

"Beatrice![1]—Beatrice!"

"Here am I, my father! What would you?" cried a rich and youthful voice from the window of the opposite house; a voice as rich as a tropical sunset, and which made Giovanni, though he knew not why, think of deep hues of purple or crimson, and of perfumes heavily delectable.—"Are you in the garden?"

"Yes, Beatrice," answered the gardener, "and I need your help."

Soon there emerged from under a sculptured portal the figure of a young girl, arrayed with as much richness of taste as the most splendid of the flowers, beautiful as the day, and with a bloom so deep and vivid that one shade more would have been too much. She looked redundant with life, health, and energy; all of which attributes were bound down and compressed, as it were, and girdled tensely, in their luxuriance, by her virgin zone.[2] Yet Giovanni's fancy must have grown morbid, while he looked down into the garden; for the impression which the fair stranger made upon him was as if here were another flower, the human sister of those vegetable ones, as beautiful as they—more beautiful than the richest of them—but still to be touched only with a glove, nor to be approached without a mask. As Beatrice came down the garden-path, it was observable that she handled and inhaled the odor of several of the plants, which her father had most sedulously avoided.

"Here, Beatrice," said the latter,—"see how many needful offices require to be done to our chief treasure. Yet, shattered as I am, my life might pay the penalty of approaching it so closely as circumstances demand. Henceforth, I fear, this plant must be consigned to your sole charge."

"And gladly will I undertake it," cried again the rich tones of the young lady, as she bent towards the magnificent plant, and opened her arms as if to embrace it. "Yes, my sister, my splendor, it shall be Beatrice's task to nurse

1. Perhaps an allusion to Beatrice Portinari (1266–1290), the inspiration for the *Divine Comedy*'s idealized Beatrice, who leads Dante the pilgrim to Paradise.

2. Wide belt customarily worn by young unmarried women.

and serve thee; and thou shalt reward her with thy kisses and perfumed breath, which to her is as the breath of life!"

Then, with all the tenderness in her manner that was so strikingly expressed in her words, she busied herself with such attentions as the plant seemed to require; and Giovanni, at his lofty window, rubbed his eyes, and almost doubted whether it were a girl tending her favorite flower, or one sister performing the duties of affection to another. The scene soon terminated. Whether Doctor Rappaccini had finished his labors in the garden, or that his watchful eye had caught the stranger's face, he now took his daughter's arm and retired. Night was already closing in; oppressive exhalations seemed to proceed from the plants, and steal upward past the open window; and Giovanni, closing the lattice, went to his couch, and dreamed of a rich flower and beautiful girl. Flower and maiden were different and yet the same, and fraught with some strange peril in either shape.

But there is an influence in the light of morning that tends to rectify whatever errors of fancy, or even of judgment, we may have incurred during the sun's decline, or among the shadows of the night, or in the less wholesome glow of moonshine. Giovanni's first movement on starting from sleep, was to throw open the window, and gaze down into the garden which his dreams had made so fertile of mysteries. He was surprised, and a little ashamed, to find how real and matter-of-fact an affair it proved to be, in the first rays of the sun, which gilded the dew-drops that hung upon leaf and blossom, and, while giving a brighter beauty to each rare flower, brought everything within the limits of ordinary experience. The young man rejoiced, that, in the heart of the barren city, he had the privilege of overlooking this spot of lovely and luxuriant vegetation. It would serve, he said to himself, as a symbolic language, to keep him in communion with nature. Neither the sickly and thought-worn Doctor Giacomo Rappaccini, it is true, nor his brilliant daughter were now visible; so that Giovanni could not determine how much of the singularity which he attributed to both, was due to their own qualities, and how much to his wonder-working fancy. But he was inclined to take a most rational view of the whole matter.

In the course of the day, he paid his respects to Signor Pietro Baglioni, professor of medicine in the University, a physician of eminent repute, to whom Giovanni had brought a letter of introduction. The professor was an elderly personage, apparently of genial nature, and habits that might almost be called jovial; he kept the young man to dinner, and made himself very agreeable by the freedom and liveliness of his conversation, especially when warmed by a flask or two of Tuscan wine. Giovanni, conceiving that men of science, inhabitants of the same city, must needs be on familiar terms with one another, took an opportunity to mention the name of Dr. Rappaccini. But the professor did not respond with so much cordiality as he had anticipated.

"Ill would it become a teacher of the divine art of medicine," said Professor Pietro Baglioni, in answer to a question of Giovanni, "to withhold due and well-considered praise of a physician so eminently skilled as Rappaccini. But, on the other hand, I should answer it but scantily to my conscience, were I to permit a worthy youth like yourself, Signor Giovanni, the son of an ancient friend, to imbibe erroneous ideas respecting a man who might hereafter chance to hold your life and death in his hands. The truth is, our worshipful Doctor Rappaccini has as much science as any member of the faculty—with perhaps one single exception—in Padua, or all Italy. But there are certain grave objections to his professional character."

"And what are they?" asked the young man.

"Has my friend Giovanni any disease of body or heart, that he is so inquisitive about physicians?" said the Professor, with a smile. "But as for Rappaccini, it is said of him—and I, who know the man well, can answer for its truth—that he cares infinitely more for science than for mankind. His patients are interesting to him only as subjects for some new experiment. He would sacrifice human life, his own among the rest, or whatever else was dearest to him, for the sake of adding so much as a grain of mustard-seed to the great heap of his accumulated knowledge."

"Methinks he is an awful[3] man, indeed," remarked Guasconti, mentally recalling the cold and purely intellectual aspect of Rappaccini. "And yet, worshipful Professor, is it not a noble spirit? Are there many men capable of so spiritual a love of science?"

"God forbid," answered the Professor, somewhat testily—"at least, unless they take sounder views of the healing art than those adopted by Rappaccini. It is his theory, that all medicinal virtues are comprised within those substances which we term vegetable poisons. These he cultivates with his own hands, and is said even to have produced new varieties of poison, more horribly deleterious than Nature, without the assistance of this learned person, would ever have plagued the world with. That the signor Doctor does less mischief than might be expected, with such dangerous substances, is undeniable. Now and then, it must be owned, he has effected—or seemed to effect—a marvellous cure. But, to tell you my private mind, Signor Giovanni, he should receive little credit for such instances of success—they being probably the work of chance—but should be held strictly accountable for his failures, which may justly be considered his own work."

The youth might have taken Baglioni's opinions with many grains of allowance, had he known that there was a professional warfare of long continuance between him and Doctor Rappaccini, in which the latter was generally thought to have gained the advantage. If the reader be inclined to judge for himself, we refer him to certain black-letter tracts on both sides, preserved in the medical department of the University of Padua.

"I know not, most learned Professor," returned Giovanni, after musing on what had been said of Rappaccini's exclusive zeal for science—"I know not how dearly this physician may love his art; but surely there is one object more dear to him. He has a daughter."

"Aha!" cries the Professor with a laugh. "So now our friend Giovanni's secret is out. You have heard of this daughter, whom all the young men in Padua are wild about, though not half a dozen have ever had the good hap to see her face. I know little of the Signora Beatrice, save that Rappaccini is said to have instructed her deeply in his science, and that, young and beautiful as fame reports her, she is already qualified to fill a professor's chair. Perchance her father destines her for mine! Other absurd rumors there be, not worth talking about, or listening to. So now, Signor Giovanni, drink off your glass of Lacryma."[4]

3. As in "awe-striking."

4. An Italian wine.

Guasconti returned to his lodgings somewhat heated with the wine he had quaffed, and which caused his brain to swim with strange fantasies in reference to Doctor Rappaccini and the beautiful Beatrice. On his way, happening to pass by a florist's, he bought a fresh bouquet of flowers.

Ascending to his chamber, he seated himself near the window, but within the shadow thrown by the depth of the wall, so that he could look down into the garden with little risk of being discovered. All beneath his eye was a solitude. The strange plants were basking in the sunshine, and now and then nodding gently to one another, as if in acknowledgment of sympathy and kindred. In the midst, by the shattered fountain, grew the magnificent shrub, with its purple gems clustering all over it; they glowed in the air, and gleamed back again out of the depths of the pool, which thus seemed to overflow with colored radiance from the rich reflection that was steeped in it. At first, as we have said, the garden was a solitude. Soon, however,—as Giovanni had half-hoped, half-feared, would be the case,—a figure appeared beneath the antique sculptured portal, and came down between the rows of plants, inhaling their various perfumes, as if she were one of those beings of old classic fable, that lived upon sweet odors. On again beholding Beatrice, the young man was even startled to perceive how much her beauty exceeded his recollection of it; so brilliant, so vivid in its character, that she glowed amid the sunlight, and, as Giovanni whispered to himself, positively illuminated the more shadowy intervals of the garden path. Her face being now more revealed than on the former occasion, he was struck by its expression of simplicity and sweetness; qualities that had not entered into his idea of her character, and which made him ask anew, what manner of mortal she might be. Nor did he fail again to observe, or imagine, an analogy between the beautiful girl and the gorgeous shrub that hung its gem-like flowers over the fountain; a resemblance which Beatrice seemed to have indulged a fantastic humor in heightening, both by the arrangement of her dress and the selection of its hues.

Approaching the shrub, she threw open her arms, as with a passionate ardor, and drew its branches into an intimate embrace; so intimate, that her features were hidden in its leafy bosom, and her glistening ringlets all intermingled with the flowers.

"Give me thy breath, my sister," exclaimed Beatrice; "for I am faint with common air! And give me this flower of thine, which I separate with gentlest fingers from the stem, and place it close beside my heart."

With these words, the beautiful daughter of Rappaccini plucked one of the richest blossoms of the shrub, and was about to fasten it in her bosom. But now, unless Giovanni's draughts of wine had bewildered his senses, a singular incident occurred. A small orange-colored reptile of the lizard or chameleon species, chanced to be creeping along the path, just at the feet of Beatrice. It appeared to Giovanni—but, at the distance from which he gazed, he could scarcely have seen anything so minute—it appeared to him, however, that a drop or two of moisture from the broken stem of the flower descended upon the lizard's head. For an instant, the reptile contorted itself violently, and then lay motionless in the sunshine. Beatrice observed this remarkable phenomenon, and crossed herself, sadly, but without surprise; nor did she therefore hesitate to arrange the fatal flower in her bosom. There it blushed, and almost glimmered with the dazzling effect of a precious stone, adding to her dress and aspect the one appropriate charm, which nothing else in the world could have supplied. But Giovanni, out of the shadow of his window bent forward and shrank back, and murmured and trembled.

"Am I awake? Have I my senses?" said he to himself. "What is this being?—beautiful, shall I call her?—or inexpressibly terrible?"

Beatrice now strayed carelessly through the garden, approaching closer beneath Giovanni's window, so that he was compelled to thrust his head quite out of its concealment in order to gratify the intense and painful curiosity which she excited. At this moment, there came a beautiful insect over the garden wall; it had perhaps wandered through the city and found no flowers nor verdure among those antique haunts of men, until the heavy perfumes of Doctor Rappaccini's shrubs had lured it from afar. Without alighting on the flowers, this winged brightness seemed to be attracted by Beatrice, and lingered in the air and fluttered about her head. Now here it could not be but that Giovanni Guasconti's eyes deceived him. Be that as it might, he fancied that while Beatrice was gazing at the insect with childish delight, it grew faint and fell at her feet!—its bright wings shivered! it was dead!—from no cause that he could discern, unless it were the atmosphere of her breath. Again Beatrice crossed herself and sighed heavily, as she bent over the dead insect.

An impulsive movement of Giovanni drew her eyes to the window. There she beheld the beautiful head of the young man—rather a Grecian than an Italian head, with fair, regular features, and a glistening of gold among his ringlets—gazing down upon her like a being that hovered in mid-air. Scarcely knowing what he did, Giovanni threw down the bouquet which he had hitherto held in his hand.

"Signora," said he, "there are pure and healthful flowers. Wear them for the sake of Giovanni Guasconti!"

"Thanks, Signor," replied Beatrice, with her rich voice, that came forth as it were like a gush of music; and with a mirthful expression half childish and half woman-like. "I accept your gift, and would fain recompense it with this precious purple flower; but if I toss it into the air, it will not reach you. So Signor Guasconti must even content himself with my thanks."

She lifted the bouquet from the ground, and then as if inwardly ashamed at having stepped aside from her maidenly reserve to respond to a stranger's greeting, passed swiftly homeward through the garden. But, few as the moments were, it seemed to Giovanni when she was on the point of vanishing beneath the sculptured portal, that his beautiful bouquet was already beginning to wither in her grasp. It was an idle thought; there could be no possibility of distinguishing a faded flower from a fresh one at so great a distance.

For many days after the incident, the young man avoided the window that looked into Doctor Rappaccini's garden, as if something ugly and monstrous would have blasted his eye-sight, had he been betrayed into a glance. He felt conscious of having put himself, to a certain extent, within the influence of an unintelligible power, by the communication which he had opened with Beatrice. The wisest course would have been, if his heart were in any real danger, to quit his lodgings and Padua itself, at once; the next wiser, to have accustomed himself, as far as possible, to the familiar and day-light view of Beatrice; thus bringing her rigidly and systematically within the limits of ordinary experience. Least of all, while avoiding her sight, should Giovanni have remained so near this extraordinary being, that the proximity and possibility even of intercourse, should give a kind of substance and reality to the wild vagaries which his imagination ran riot continually in producing. Guasconti had not a deep heart—or at all events, its depths were not sounded now—but he had a quick fancy, and an ardent southern temperament, which rose every instant to a higher fever-pitch. Whether or no Beatrice possessed those terrible attributes—that fatal breath—the affinity with those so beautiful and deadly flowers—which were indicated by what Giovanni had witnessed, she had at least instilled a fierce and subtle poison into his sytem. It was not love, although her rich beauty was a madness to him; nor horror, even while he fancied her spirit to be imbued with the same baneful essence that seemed to pervade her physical frame; but a wild offspring of both love and horror that had each parent in it, and burned like one and shivered like the other. Giovanni knew not what to dread; still less did he know what to hope; *hope* and *dread* kept a continual warfare in his breast, alternately vanquishing one another and starting up afresh to renew the contest. Blessed are all simple emotions, be they dark or bright! It is the lurid intermixture of the two that produces the illuminating blaze of the infernal regions.

Sometimes he endeavored to assuage the fever of his spirit by a rapid walk through the streets of Padua, or beyond its gates; his footsteps kept time with the throbbings of his brain, so that the walk was apt to accelerate itself to a race. One day, he found himself arrested; his arm was seized by a portly personage who had turned back on recognizing the young man, and expended much breath in overtaking him.

"Signor Giovanni!—stay, my young friend!" cried he. "Have you forgotten me? That might well be the case, if I were as much altered as yourself."

It was Baglioni, whom Giovanni had avoided, ever since their first meeting, from a doubt that the professor's sagacity would look too deeply into his secrets. Endeavoring to recover himself, he stared forth wildly from his inner world into the outer one, and spoke like a man in a dream:

"Yes; I am Giovanni Guasconti. You are Professor Pietro Baglioni. Now let me pass!"

"Not yet—not yet, Signor Giovanni Guasconti," said the Professor, smiling, but at the same time scrutinizing the youth with an earnest glance.—"What; did I grow up side by side with your father, and shall his son pass me like a stranger, in these old streets of Padua? Stand still, Signor Giovanni; for we must have a word or two, before we part."

"Speedily, then, most worshipful Professor, speedily!" said Giovanni, with feverish impatience. "Does not your worship see that I am in haste?"

Now, while he was speaking, there came a man in black along the street, stooping and moving feebly, like a person in inferior health. His face was all overspread with a most sickly and sallow hue, but yet so pervaded with an expression of piercing and active intellect, that an observer might easily have overlooked the merely physical attributes, and have seen only this wonderful energy. As he passed, this person exchanged a cold and distant salutation with Baglioni, but fixed his eyes upon Giovanni with an intentness that seemed to bring out whatever was within him worthy of notice. Nevertheless, there was a peculiar quietness in the look, as if taking merely a speculative, not a human interest, in the young man.

"It is Doctor Rappaccini!" whispered the Professor, when the stranger had passed.—"Has he ever seen your face before?"

"Not that I know," answered Giovanni, starting at the name.

"He *has* seen you!—he must have seen you!" said Baglioni, hastily. "For some purpose or other, this man of science is making a study of you. I know that look of his! It is the same that coldly illuminates his face, as he bends over a bird, a mouse, or a butterfly, which, in pursuance of some experiment, he has killed by the perfume of a flower;—a look as deep as nature itself, but without nature's warmth of love. Signor Giovanni, I will stake my life upon it, you are the subject of one of Rappaccini's experiments!"

"Will you make a fool of me?" cried Giovanni, passionately. "*That,* Signor Professor, were an untoward experiment."

"Patience, patience!" replied the imperturbable Professor.—"I tell thee, my poor Giovanni, that Rappaccini has a scientific interest in thee. Thou hast fallen into fearful hands! And the Signora Beatrice? What part does she act in this mystery?"

But Guasconti, finding Baglioni's pertinacity intolerable, here broke away, and was gone before the Professor could again seize his arm. He looked after the young man intently, and shook his head.

"This must not be," said Baglioni to himself. "The youth is the son of my old friend, and should not come to any harm from which the arcana of medical science can preserve him. Besides, it is too insufferable an impertinence in Rappaccini, thus to snatch the bud out of my own hands, as I may say, and make use of him for his infernal experiments. This daughter of his! It shall be looked to. Perchance, most learned Rappaccini, I may foil you where you little dream of it!"

Meanwhile, Giovanni had pursued a circuitous route, and at length found himself at the door of his lodgings. As he crossed the threshold, he was met by old Lisabetta, who smirked and smiled, and was evidently desirous to attract his attention; vainly, however, as the ebullition of his feelings had momentarily subsided into a cold and dull vacuity. He turned his eyes full upon the withered face that was puckering itself into a smile, but seemed to behold it not. The old dame, therefore, laid her grasp upon his cloak.

"Signor!—Signor!" whispered she, still with a smile over the whole breadth of her visage, so that it looked not unlike a grotesque carving in wood, darkened by centuries—"Listen, Signor! There is a private entrance into the garden!"

"What do you say?" exclaimed Giovanni, turning quickly about, as if an inanimate thing should start into feverish life.—"A private entrance into Doctor Rappaccini's garden!"

"Hush! hush!—not so loud!" whispered Lisabetta, putting her hand over his mouth. "Yes; into the worshipful Doctor's garden, where you may see all his fine shrubbery. Many a young man in Padua would give gold to be admitted among those flowers."

Giovanni put a piece of gold into her hand.

"Show me the way," said he.

A surmise, probably excited by his conversation with Baglioni, crossed his mind, that this interposition of old Lisabetta might perchance be connected with the intrigue, whatever were its nature, in which the Professor seemed to suppose that Doctor Rappaccini was involving him. But such a suspicion, though it disturbed Giovanni, was inadequate to restrain him. The instant he was aware of the possibility of approaching Beatrice, it seemed an absolute necessity of his existence to do so. It mattered not whether she were angel or demon; he was irrevocably within her sphere, and must obey the law that whirled him onward, in ever lessening circles, towards a result which he did not attempt to foreshadow. And yet, strange to say, there came across him a sudden doubt, whether this intense interest on his part were not delusory—whether it were really of so deep and positive a nature as to justify him in now thrusting himself into an incalculable position—whether it were not merely the fantasy of a young man's brain, only slightly, or not at all, connected with his heart!

He paused—hesitated—turned half about—but again went on. His withered guide led him along several obscure passages, and finally undid a door, through which, as it was opened, there came the sight and sound of rustling leaves, with the broken sunshine glimmering among them. Giovanni stepped forth, and forcing himself through the entanglement of a shrub that wreathed its tendrils over the hidden entrance, he stood beneath his own window, in the open area of Doctor Rappaccini's garden.

How often is it the case, that, when impossibilities have come to pass, and dreams have condensed their misty substance into tangible realities, we find ourselves calm, and even coldly self-possessed, amid circumstances which it would have been a delirium of joy or agony to anticipate! Fate delights to thwart us thus. Passion will choose his own time to rush upon the scene, and lingers sluggishly behind, when an appropriate adjustment of events would seem to summon his appearance. So was it now with Giovanni. Day after day, his pulses had throbbed with feverish blood, at the improbable idea of an interview with Beatrice, and of standing with her, face to face, in this very garden, basking in the oriental sunshine of her beauty, and snatching from her full gaze the mystery which he deemed the riddle of his own existence. But now there was a singular and untimely equanimity within his breast. He threw a glance around the garden to discover if Beatrice or her father were present, and perceiving that he was alone, began a critical observation of the plants.

The aspect of one and all of them dissatisfied him; their gorgeousness seemed fierce, passionate, and even unnatural. There was hardly an individual shrub which a wanderer, straying by himself through a forest, would not have been startled to find growing wild, as if an unearthly face had glared at him out of the thicket. Several, also, would have shocked a delicate instinct by an appearance of artificialness, indicating that there had been such commixture, and, as it were, adultery of various vegetable species, that the production was no longer of God's making, but the monstrous offspring of man's depraved fancy, glowing with only an evil mockery of beauty. They were probably the result of experiment, which, in one or two cases, had succeeded in mingling plants individually lovely into a compound possessing the questionable and ominous character that distinguished the whole growth of the garden. In fine, Giovanni recognized but two or three plants in the collection, and those of a kind that he well knew to be poisonous. While busy with these contemplations, he heard the rustling of a silken garment, and turning, beheld Beatrice emerging from beneath the sculptured portal.

Giovanni had not considered with himself what should be his deportment; whether he should apologize for his intrusion into the garden, or assume that he was there with the privity, at least, if not the desire of Doctor Rappaccini or his daughter. But Beatrice's manner placed him at his ease, though leaving him still in doubt by what agency he had gained admittance. She came lightly along the path, and met him near the broken fountain. There was surprise in her face, but brightened by a simple and kind expression of pleasure.

"You are a connoisseur in flowers, Signor," said Beatrice with a smile, alluding to the bouquet which he had flung her from the window. "It is no marvel, therefore, if the sight of my father's rare collection has tempted you to take a nearer view. If he were here, he could tell you many strange and interesting facts as to the nature and habits of these shrubs, for he has spent a life-time in such studies, and this garden is his world."

"And yourself, lady"—observed Giovanni—"if fame says true—you, likewise, are deeply skilled in the virtues indicated by these rich blossoms, and these spicy perfumes. Would you deign to be my instructress, I should prove an apter scholar than under Signor Rappaccini himself."

"Are there such idle rumors?" asked Beatrice, with the music of a pleasant laugh. "Do people say that I am skilled in my father's science of plants? What a jest is there! No; though I have grown up among these flowers, I know no more of them than their hues and perfume; and sometimes, methinks I would fain rid myself of even that small knowledge. There are many flowers here, and those not the least brilliant, that shock and offend me, when they meet my eye. But, pray, Signor, do not believe these stories about my science. Believe nothing of me save what you see with your own eyes."

"And must I believe all that I have seen with my own eyes?" asked Giovanni pointedly, while the recollection of former scenes made him shrink. "No, Signora, you demand too little of me. Bid me believe nothing, save what comes from your own lips."

It would appear that Beatrice understood him. There came a deep flush to her cheek; but she looked full into Giovanni's eyes, and responded to his gaze of uneasy suspicion with a queen-like haughtiness.

"I do so bid you, Signor!" she replied. "Forget whatever you may have fancied in regard to me. If true to the outward senses, still it may be false in its essence. But the words of Beatrice Rappaccini's lips are true from the heart outward. Those you may believe!"

A fervor glowed in her whole aspect, and beamed upon Giovanni's consciousness like the light of truth itself. But while she spoke, there was a fragrance in the atmosphere around her, rich and delightful, though evanescent, yet which the young man, from an indefinable reluctance, scarcely dared to draw into his lungs. It might be the odor of the flowers. Could it be Beatrice's breath, which thus embalmed her words with a strange richness, as if by steeping them in her heart? A faintness passed like a shadow over Giovanni, and flitted away; he seemed to gaze through the beautiful girl's eyes into her transparent soul, and felt no more doubt or fear.

The tinge of passion that had colored Beatrice's manner vanished; she became gay, and appeared to derive a pure delight from her communion with the youth, not unlike what the maiden of a lonely island might have felt, conversing with a voyager from the civilized world. Evidently her experience of life had been confined within the limits of that garden. She talked now about matters as simple as the day-light or summer-clouds, and now asked questions in reference to the city, or Giovanni's distant home, his friends, his mother, and his sisters; questions indicating such seclusion, and such lack of familiarity with modes and forms, that Giovanni responded as if to an infant. Her spirit gushed out before him like a fresh rill, that was just catching its first glimpse of the sunlight, and wondering at the reflections of earth and sky which were flung into its bosom. There came thoughts, too, from a deep source, and fantasies of a gem-like brilliancy, as if diamonds and rubies sparkled upward among the bubbles of the fountain. Ever and anon, there gleamed across the young man's mind a sense of wonder, that he should be walking side by side with the being who had so wrought upon his imagination—whom he had idealized in such hues of terror—in whom he had positively witnessed such manifestations of dreadful attributes—that he should be conversing with Beatrice like a brother, and should find her so human and so maiden-like. But such reflections were only momentary; the effect of her character was too real, not to make itself familiar at once.

In this free intercourse, they had strayed through the garden, and now, after many turns among its avenues, were come to the shattered fountain, beside which grew the magnificent shrub with its treasury of glowing blossoms. A fragrance was diffused from it, which Giovanni recognized as identical with that which he had attributed to Beatrice's breath, but incomparably more powerful. As her eyes fell upon it, Giovanni beheld her press her hand to her bosom, as if her heart were throbbing suddenly and painfully.

"For the first time in my life," murmured she, addressing the shrub, "I had forgotten thee!"

"I remember, Signora," said Giovanni, "that you once promised to reward me with one of these living gems for the bouquet, which I had the happy boldness to fling to your feet. Permit me now to pluck it as a memorial of this interview."

He made a step towards the shrub, with extended hand. But Beatrice darted forward, uttering a shriek that went through his heart like a dagger. She caught his hand, and drew it back with the whole force of her slender figure. Giovanni felt her touch thrilling through his fibres.

"Touch it not!" exclaimed she, in a voice of agony. "Not for thy life! It is fatal!"

Then, hiding her face, she fled from him, and vanished beneath the sculptured portal. As Giovanni followed her with his eyes, he beheld the emaciated figure and pale intelligence of Doctor Rappaccini, who had been watching the scene, he knew not how long, within the shadow of the entrance.

No sooner was Guasconti alone in his chamber, than the image of Beatrice came back to his passionate musings, invested with all the witchery that had been gathering around it ever since his first glimpse of her, and now likewise imbued with a tender warmth of girlish womanhood. She was human: her nature was endowed with all gentle and feminine qualities; she was worthiest to be worshipped; she was capable, surely, on her part, of the height and heroism of love. Those tokens, which he had hitherto considered as proofs of a frightful peculiarity in her physical and moral system, were now either forgotten, or, by the subtle sophistry of passion, transmuted into a golden crown of enchantment, rendering Beatrice the more admirable, by so much as she was the more unique. Whatever had looked ugly, was now beautiful; or, if incapable of such a change, it stole away and hid itself among those shapeless half-ideas, which throng the dim region beyond the day-light of our perfect consciousness. Thus did Giovanni spend the night, nor fell asleep, until the dawn had begun to awake the slumbering flowers in Doctor Rappaccini's garden, whither his dreams doubtless led him. Up rose the sun in his due season, and flinging his beams upon the young man's eyelids, awoke him to a sense of pain. When thoroughly aroused, he became sensible of a burning and tingling agony in his hand—in his right hand—the very hand which Beatrice had grasped in her own, when he was on the point of plucking one of the gem-like flowers. On the back of that hand there was now a purple print, like that of four small fingers, and the likeness of a slender thumb upon his wrist.

Oh, how stubbornly does love—or even that cunning semblance of love which flourishes in the imagination, but strikes no depth of root into the heart—how stubbornly does it hold its faith, until the moment come, when it is doomed to vanish into thin mist! Giovanni wrapt a handkerchief about his hand, and wondered what evil thing had stung him, and soon forgot his pain in a reverie of Beatrice.

After the first interview, a second was in the inevitable course of what we call fate. A third; a fourth; and a meeting with Beatrice in the garden was no longer an incident in Giovanni's daily life, but the whole space in which he might be said to live; for the anticipation and memory of that ecstatic hour made up the remainder. Nor was it otherwise with the daughter of Rappaccini. She watched for the youth's appearance, and flew to his side with confidence as unreserved as if they had been playmates from early infancy—as if they were such playmates still. If, by any unwonted chance, he failed to come at the appointed moment, she stood beneath the window, and sent up the rich sweetness of her tones to float around him in his chamber, and echo and reverberate throughout his heart—"Giovanni! Giovanni! Why tarriest thou? Come down!"—And down he hastened into that Eden of poisonous flowers.

But, with all this intimate familiarity, there was still a reserve in Beatrice's demeanor, so rigidly and invariably sustained, that the idea of infringing it scarcely occurred to his imagination. By all appreciable signs, they loved; they had looked love, with eyes that conveyed the holy secret from the depths of one soul into the depths of the other, as if it were too sacred to be whispered by the way; they had even spoken love, in those gushes of passion when their spirits darted forth in articulated breath, like tongues of long-hidden flame; and yet there had been no seal of lips, no clasp of hands, nor any slightest caress, such as love claims and hallows. He had never touched one of the gleaming ringlets of her hair; her garment—so marked was the physical barrier between them—had never been waved against him by a breeze. On the few occasions when Giovanni had seemed tempted to overstep the limit, Beatrice grew so sad, so stern, and withal wore such a look of desolate separation, shuddering at itself, that not a spoken word was requisite to repel him. At such times, he was startled at the horrible suspicions that rose, monster-like, out of the caverns of his heart, and stared him in the face; his love grew thin and faint as the morning-mist; his doubts alone had substance. But when Beatrice's face brightened again, after the momentary shadow, she was transformed at once from the mysterious, questionable being, whom he had watched with so much awe and horror; she was now the beautiful and unsophisticated girl, whom he felt that his spirit knew with a certainty beyond all other knowledge.

A considerable time had now passed since Giovanni's last meeting with Baglioni. One morning, however, he was disagreeably surprised by a visit from the Professor, whom he had scarcely thought of for whole weeks, and would willingly have forgotten still longer. Given up, as he had long been, to a pervading excitement, he could tolerate no companions, except upon condition of their perfect sympathy with his present state of feeling. Such sympathy was not to be expected from Professor Baglioni.

The visitor chatted carelessly, for a few moments, about the gossip of the city and the University, and then took up another topic.

"I have been reading an old classic author lately," said he, "and met with a story[5] that strangely interested me. Possibly you may remember it. It is of an Indian prince, who sent a beautiful woman as a present to Alexander the Great.[6] She was as lovely as the dawn, and gorgeous as the sunset; but what especially distinguished her was a certain rich perfume in her breath—richer than a garden of Persian roses. Alexander, as was natural to a youthful conqueror, fell in love at first sight with this magnificent stranger. But a certain sage physician, happening to be present, discovered a terrible secret in regard to her."

"And what was that?" asked Giovanni, turning his eyes downward to avoid those of the Professor.

"That this lovely woman," continued Baglioni, with emphasis, "had been nourished with poisons from her birth upward, until her whole nature was so imbued with them, that she herself had become the deadliest poison in existence. Poison was her element of life. With that rich perfume of her breath, she blasted the very air. Her love would have been poison!—her embrace death! Is not this a marvellous tale?"

"A childish fable," answered Giovanni, nervously starting from his chair. "I marvel how your worship finds time to read such nonsense, among your graver studies."

"By the by," said the Professor, looking uneasily about him, "what singular fragrance is this in your apartment? Is it the perfume of your gloves? It is faint, but delicious, and yet, after all, by no means agreeable. Were I to breathe it long, methinks it would make me ill. It is like the breath of a flower—but I see no flowers in the chamber."

"Nor are there any," replied Giovanni, who had turned pale as the Professor spoke; "nor, I think, is there any fragrance, except in your worship's imagination. Odors, being a sort of element combined of the sensual and the spiritual, are apt to deceive us in this manner. The recollection of a perfume—the bare idea of it—may easily be mistaken for a present reality."

"Aye; but my sober imagination does not often play such tricks," said Baglioni; "and were I to fancy any kind of odor, it would be that of some vile apothecary drug, wherewith my fingers are likely enough to be imbued. Our

5. From Sir Thomas Browne's *Vulgar Errors* (1646), book VII.

6. Alexander the Great, king of Macedon (356–323 B.C.E.), conquered Egypt, Persia, and northern India.

worshipful friend Rappaccini, as I have heard, tinctures his medicaments with odors richer than those of Araby. Doubtless, likewise, the fair and learned Signora Beatrice would minister to her patients with draughts as sweet as a maiden's breath. But wo to him that sips them!"

Giovanni's face evinced many contending emotions. The tone in which the Professor alluded to the pure and lovely daughter of Rappaccini was a torture to his soul; and yet, the intimation of a view of her character, opposite to his own, gave instantaneous distinctness to a thousand dim suspicions, which now grinned at him like so many demons. But he strove hard to quell them, and to respond to Baglioni with a true lover's perfect faith.

"Signor Professor," said he, "you were my father's friend—perchance, too, it is your purpose to act a friendly part towards his son. I would fain feel nothing towards you, save respect and deference. But I pray you to observe, Signor, that there is one subject on which we must not speak. You know not the Signora Beatrice. You cannot, therefore, estimate the wrong—the blasphemy, I may even say—that is offered to her character by a light or injurious word."

"Giovanni!—my poor Giovanni!" answered the Professor, with a calm expression of pity, "I know this wretched girl far better than yourself. You shall hear the truth in respect to the poisoner Rappaccini, and his poisonous daughter. Yes; poisonous as she is beautiful! Listen; for even should you do violence to my grey hairs, it shall not silence me. That old fable of the Indian woman has become a truth, by the deep and deadly science of Rappaccini, and in the person of the lovely Beatrice!"

Giovanni groaned and hid his face.

"Her father," continued Baglioni, "was not restrained by natural affection from offering up his child, in this horrible manner, as the victim of his insane zeal for science. For—let us do him justice—he is as true a man of science as ever distilled his own heart in an alembic.[7] What, then, will be your fate? Beyond a doubt, you are selected as the material of some new experiment. Perhaps the result is to be death—perhaps a fate more awful still! Rappaccini, with what he calls the interest of science before his eyes, will hesitate at nothing."

"It is a dream!" muttered Giovanni to himself, "surely it is a dream!"

"But," resumed the professor, "be of good cheer, son of my friend! It is not yet too late for the rescue. Possibly, we may even succeed in bringing back this miserable child within the limits of ordinary nature, from which her father's madness has estranged her. Behold this little silver vase! It was wrought by the hands of the renowned Benvenuto Cellini,[8] and is well worthy to be a love-gift to the fairest dame in Italy. But its contents are invaluable. One little sip of this antidote would have rendered the most virulent poisons of the Borgias[9] innocuous. Doubt not that it will be as efficacious against those of Rappaccini. Bestow the vase, and the precious liquid within it, on your Beatrice, and hopefully await the result."

Baglioni laid a small, exquisitely wrought silver phial on the table, and withdrew, leaving what he had said to produce its effect upon the young man's mind.

7. Device that distills liquids.
8. Italian goldsmith and sculptor (1500–1571).
9. Influential Renaissance family notorious for cruelty and licentiousness

"We will thwart Rappaccini yet!" thought he, chuckling to himself, as he descended the stairs. "But, let us confess the truth of him, he is a wonderful man!—a wonderful man indeed! A vile empiric,[1] however, in his practice, and therefore not to be tolerated by those who respect the good old rules of the medical profession!"

Throughout Giovanni's whole acquaintance with Beatrice, he had occasionally, as we have said, been haunted by dark surmises as to her character. Yet, so thoroughly had she made herself felt by him as a simple, natural, most affectionate and guileless creature, that the image now held up by Professor Baglioni, looked as strange and incredible, as if it were not in accordance with his own original conception. True, there were ugly recollections connected with his first glimpses of the beautiful girl; he could not quite forget the bouquet that withered in her grasp, and the insect that perished amid the sunny air, by no ostensible agency, save the fragrance of her breath. These incidents, however, dissolving in the pure light of her character, had no longer the efficacy of facts, but were acknowledged as mistaken fantasies, by whatever testimony of the senses they might appear to be substantiated. There is something truer and more real, than what we can see with the eyes, and touch with the finger. On such better evidence, had Giovanni founded his confidence in Beatrice, though rather by the necessary force of her high attributes, than by any deep and generous faith, on his part. But, now, his spirit was incapable of sustaining itself at the height to which the early enthusiasm of passion had exalted it; he fell down, grovelling among earthly doubts, and defiled therewith the pure whiteness of Beatrice's image. Not that he gave her up; he did but distrust. He resolved to institute some decisive test that should satisfy him, once for all, whether there were those dreadful peculiarities in her physical nature, which could not be supposed to exist without some corresponding monstrosity of soul. His eyes, gazing down afar, might have deceived him as to the lizard, the insect, and the flowers. But if he could witness, at the distance of a few paces, the sudden blight of one fresh and healthful flower in Beatrice's hand, there would be room for no further question. With this idea, he hastened to the florist's, and purchased a bouquet that was still gemmed with the morning dew-drops.

It was now the customary hour of his daily interview with Beatrice. Before descending into the garden, Giovanni failed not to look at his figure in the mirror; a vanity to be expected in a beautiful young man, yet, as displaying itself at that troubled and feverish moment, the token of a certain shallowness of feeling and insincerity of character. He did gaze, however, and said to himself, that his features had never before possessed so rich a grace, nor his eyes such vivacity, nor his cheeks so warm a hue of superabundant life.

"At least," thought he, "her poison has not yet insinuated itself into my system. I am no flower to perish in her grasp!"

With that thought, he turned his eyes on the bouquet, which he had never once laid aside from his hand. A thrill of indefinable horror shot through his frame, on perceiving that those dewy flowers were already beginning to droop; they wore the aspect of things that had been fresh and lovely, yesterday. Giovanni grew white as marble, and stood motionless before the mirror,

1. A follower of the empirical method (relying on practice and observation rather than theory), and thus, in Baglioni's view, a charlatan who threatens the established order.

staring at his own reflection there, as at the likeness of something frightful. He remembered Baglioni's remark about the fragrance that seemed to pervade the chamber. It must have been the poison in his breath! Then he shuddered—shuddered at himself! Recovering from his stupor, he began to watch, with curious eye, a spider that was busily at work, hanging its web from the antique cornice of the apartment, crossing and re-crossing the artful system of interwoven lines, as vigorous and active a spider as ever dangled from an old ceiling. Giovanni bent towards the insect, and emitted a deep, long breath. The spider suddenly ceased its toil; the web vibrated with a tremor originating in the body of the small artizan. Again Giovanni sent forth a breath, deeper, longer, and imbued with a venomous feeling out of his heart; he knew not whether he were wicked or only desperate. The spider made a convulsive gripe with his limbs, and hung dead across the window.

"Accursed! Accursed!" muttered Giovanni, addressing himself. "Hast thou grown so poisonous, that this deadly insect perishes by the breath?"

At that moment, a rich, sweet voice came floating up from the garden:—

"Giovanni! Giovanni! It is past the hour! Why tarriest thou! Come down!"

"Yes," muttered Giovanni again. "She is the only being whom my breath may not slay! Would that it might!"

He rushed down, and in an instant, was standing before the bright and loving eyes of Beatrice. A moment ago, his wrath and despair had been so fierce that he could have desired nothing so much as to wither her by a glance. But, with her actual presence, there came influences which had too real an existence to be at once shaken off; recollections of the delicate and benign power of her feminine nature, which had so often enveloped him in a religious calm; recollections of many a holy and passionate outgush of her heart, when the pure fountain had been unsealed from its depths, and made visible in its transparency to his mental eye; recollections which, had Giovanni known how to estimate them, would have assured him that all this ugly mystery was but an earthly illusion, and that, whatever mist of evil might seem to have gathered over her, the real Beatrice was a heavenly angel. Incapable as he was of such high faith, still her presence had not utterly lost its magic. Giovanni's rage was quelled into an aspect of sullen insensibility. Beatrice, with a quick spiritual sense, immediately felt that there was a gulf of blackness between them, which neither he nor she could pass. They walked on together, sad and silent, and came thus to the marble fountain, and to its pool of water on the ground, in the midst of which grew the shrub that bore gem-like blossoms. Giovanni was affrighted at the eager enjoyment—the appetite, as it were—with which he found himself inhaling the fragrance of the flowers.

"Beatrice," asked he abruptly, "whence came this shrub?"

"My father created it," answered she, with simplicity.

"Created it! created it!" repeated Giovanni. "What mean you, Beatrice?"

"He is a man fearfully acquainted with the secrets of nature," replied Beatrice; "and, at the hour when I first drew breath, this plant sprang from the soil, the offspring of his science, of his intellect, while I was but his earthly child. Approach it not!" continued she, observing with terror that Giovanni was drawing nearer to the shrub. "It has qualities that you little dream of. But I, dearest Giovanni,—I grew up and blossomed with the plant, and was nourished with its breath. It was my sister, and I loved it with a human affection: for—alas! hast thou not suspected it? there was an awful doom."

Here Giovanni frowned so darkly upon her that Beatrice paused and trembled. But her faith in his tenderness re-assured her, and made her blush that she had doubted for an instant.

"There was an awful doom," she continued,—"the effect of my father's fatal love of science—which estranged me from all society of any kind. Until Heaven sent thee, dearest Giovanni, Oh! how lonely was thy poor Beatrice!"

"Was it a hard doom?" asked Giovanni, fixing his eyes upon her.

"Only of late have I known how hard it was," answered she tenderly. "Oh, yes; but my heart was torpid, and therefore quiet."

Giovanni's rage broke forth from his sullen gloom like a lightning-flash out of a dark cloud.

"Accursed one!" cried he, with venomous scorn and anger. "And finding thy solitude wearisome, thou hast severed me, likewise, from all the warmth of life, and enticed me into thy region of unspeakable horror!"

"Giovanni!" exclaimed Beatrice, turning her large bright eyes upon his face. The force of his words had not found its way into her mind; she was merely wonder-struck.

"Yes, poisonous thing!" repeated Giovanni, beside himself with passion. "Thou hast done it! Thou hast blasted me! Thou hast filled my veins with poison! Thou hast made me as hateful, as ugly, as loathsome and deadly a creature as thyself,—a world's wonder of hideous monstrosity! Now—if our breath be happily as fatal to ourselves as to all others—let us join our lips in one kiss of unutterable hatred, and so die!"

"What has befallen me?" murmured Beatrice, with a low moan out of her heart. "Holy Virgin pity me, a poor heart-broken child!"

"Thou! Dost thou pray?" cried Giovanni, still with the same fiendish scorn. "Thy very prayers, as they come from thy lips, taint the atmosphere with death. Yes, yes; let us pray! Let us to church, and dip our fingers in the holy water at the portal! They that come after us will perish as by a pestilence. Let us sign crosses in the air! It will be scattering curses abroad in the likeness of holy symbols!"

"Giovanni," said Beatrice calmly, for her grief was beyond passion, "why dost thou join thyself with me thus in those terrible words? I, it is true, am the horrible thing thou namest me. But thou!—what hast thou to do, save with one other shudder at my hideous misery, to go forth out of the garden and mingle with thy race, and forget that there ever crawled on earth such a monster as poor Beatrice?"

"Dost thou pretend ignorance?" asked Giovanni, scowling upon her. "Behold! This power have I gained from the pure daughter of Rappaccini!"

There was a swarm of summer-insects flitting through the air, in search of the food promised by the flower-odors of the fatal garden. They circled round Giovanni's head, and were evidently attracted towards him by the same influence which had drawn them, for an instant, within the sphere of several of the shrubs. He sent forth a breath among them, and smiled bitterly at Beatrice, as at least a score of the insects fell dead upon the ground.

"I see it! I see it!" shrieked Beatrice. "It is my father's fatal science! No, no, Giovanni; it was not I! Never, never! I dreamed only to love thee, and be with thee a little time, and so to let thee pass away, leaving but thine image in mine heart. For, Giovanni—believe it—though my body be nourished with poison, my spirit is God's creature, and craves love as its daily food. But my father!—he has united us in this fearful sympathy. Yes; spurn me!—tread upon me!—kill me! Oh, what is death, after such words as thine? But it was not I! Not for a world of bliss would I have done it!"

Giovanni's passion had exhausted itself in its outburst from his lips. There now came across a sense, mournful, and not without tenderness, of the intimate and peculiar relationship between Beatrice and himself. They stood, as it were, in an utter solitude, which would be made none the less solitary by the densest throng of human life. Ought not, then, the desert of humanity around them to press this insulated pair close together? If they should be cruel to one another, who was there to be kind to them? Besides, thought Giovanni, might there not still be a hope of his returning within the limits of ordinary nature, and leading Beatrice—the redeemed Beatrice—by the hand? Oh, weak, and selfish, and unworthy spirit, that could dream of an earthly union and earthly happiness as possible, after such deep love had been so bitterly wronged as was Beatrice's love by Giovanni's blighting words! No, no; there could be no such hope. She must pass heavily, with that broken heart, across the borders—she must bathe her hurts in some fount of Paradise, and forget her grief in the light of immortality—and *there* be well!

But Giovanni did not know it.

"Dear Beatrice," said he, approaching her, while she shrank away, as always at his approach, but now with a different impulse—"dearest Beatrice, our fate is not yet so desperate. Behold! There is a medicine, potent, as a wise physician has assured me, and almost divine in its efficacy. It is composed of ingredients the most opposite to those by which thy awful father has brought this calamity upon thee and me. It is distilled of blessed herbs. Shall we not quaff it together, and thus be purified from evil?"

"Give it me!" said Beatrice, extending her hand to receive the little silver phial which Giovanni took from his bosom. She added, with a peculiar emphasis; "I will drink—but do thou await the result."

She put Baglioni's antidote to her lips; and, at the same moment, the figure of Rappaccini emerged from the portal, and came slowly towards the marble fountain. As he drew near, the pale man of science seemed to gaze with a triumphant expression at the beautiful youth and maiden, as might an artist who should spend his life in achieving a picture or a group of statuary, and finally be satisfied with his success. He paused—his bent form grew erect with conscious power, he spread out his hand over them, in the attitude of a father imploring a blessing upon his children. But those were the same hands that had thrown poison into the stream of their lives! Giovanni trembled. Beatrice shuddered nervously, and pressed her hand upon her heart.

"My daughter," said Rappaccini, "thou art no longer lonely in the world! Pluck one of those precious gems from thy sister shrub, and bid thy bridegroom wear it in his bosom. It will not harm him now! My science, and the sympathy between thee and him, have so wrought within his system, that he now stands apart from common men, as thou dost, daughter of my pride and triumph, from ordinary women. Pass on, then, through the world, most dear to one another, and dreadful to all besides!"

"My father," said Beatrice, feebly—and still, as she spoke, she kept her hand upon her heart—"wherefore didst thou inflict this miserable doom upon thy child?"

"Miserable!" exclaimed Rappaccini. "What mean you, foolish girl? Dost thou deem it misery to be endowed with marvellous gifts, against which no power nor strength could avail an enemy? Misery, to be able to quell the mightiest with a breath? Misery, to be as terrible as thou art beautiful? Wouldst thou, then, have preferred the condition of a weak woman, exposed to all evil, and capable of none?"

"I would fain have been loved, not feared," murmured Beatrice, sinking down upon the ground.—"But now it matters not; I am going, father, where the evil, which thou hast striven to mingle with my being, will pass away like a dream—like the fragrance of these poisonous flowers, which will no longer taint my breath among the flowers of Eden. Farewell, Giovanni! Thy words of hatred are like lead within my heart—but they, too, will fall away as I ascend. Oh, was there not, from the first, more poison in thy nature than in mine?"

To Beatrice—so radically had her earthly part been wrought upon by Rappaccini's skill—as poison had been life, so the powerful antidote was death. And thus the poor victim of man's ingenuity and of thwarted nature, and of the fatality that attends all such efforts of perverted wisdom, perished there, at the feet of her father and Giovanni. Just at that moment, Professor Pietro Baglioni looked forth from the window, and called loudly, in a tone of triumph mixed with horror, to the thunder-stricken man of science:

"Rappaccini! Rappaccini! And is *this* the upshot of your experiment?"

1844

The Scarlet Letter[1]

The Custom-House

INTRODUCTORY TO "THE SCARLET LETTER"

It is a little remarkable, that—though disinclined to talk overmuch of myself and my affairs at the fireside, and to my personal friends—an autobiographical impulse should twice in my life[2] have taken possession of me, in addressing the public. The first time was three or four years since, when I favored the reader—inexcusably, and for no earthly reason, that either the indulgent reader or the intrusive author could imagine—with a description of my way of life in the deep quietude of an Old Manse. And now—because, beyond my deserts, I was happy enough to find a listener or two on the former occasion—I again seize the public by the button, and talk of my three years' experience in a Custom-House. The example of the famous "P.P., Clerk of this Parish,"[3] was never more faithfully followed. The truth seems to be,

1. The source of this text is the 1st edition (1850).
2. The "first time" was in "The Author Makes the Reader Acquainted with his Abode," the introduction to *Mosses from an Old Manse* (1846). Hawthorne and his wife, Sophia, lived in a house called the Old Manse in Concord, Massachusetts, from 1842 to 1845.
3. In 1728 Alexander Pope (1688–1744) published an anonymous mock autobiography spoofing Bishop Gilbert Burnet's pompous *History of My Own Time* (1724).

however, that, when he casts his leaves forth upon the wind, the author addresses, not the many who will fling aside his volume, or never take it up, but the few who will understand him, better than most of his schoolmates and lifemates. Some authors, indeed, do far more than this, and indulge themselves in such confidential depths of revelation as could fittingly be addressed, only and exclusively, to the one heart and mind of perfect sympathy; as if the printed book, thrown at large on the wide world, were certain to find out the divided segment of the writer's own nature, and complete his circle of existence by bringing him into communion with it. It is scarcely decorous, however, to speak all, even where we speak impersonally. But—as thoughts are frozen and utterance benumbed, unless the speaker stand in some true relation with his audience—it may be pardonable to imagine that a friend, a kind and apprehensive, though not the closest friend, is listening to our talk; and then, a native reserve being thawed by this genial consciousness, we may prate of the circumstances that lie around us, and even of ourself, but still keep the inmost Me behind its veil. To this extent and within these limits, an author, methinks, may be autobiographical, without violating either the reader's rights or his own.

It will be seen, likewise, that this Custom-House sketch has a certain propriety, of a kind always recognized in literature, as explaining how a large portion of the following pages came into my possession, and as offering proofs of the authenticity of a narrative therein contained. This, in fact,—a desire to put myself in my true position as editor, or very little more, of the most prolix among the tales that make up my volume,[4]—this, and no other, is my true reason for assuming a personal relation with the public. In accomplishing the main purpose, it has appeared allowable, by a few extra touches, to give a faint representation of a mode of life not heretofore described, together with some of the characters that move in it, among whom the author happened to make one.

In my native town of Salem, at the head of what, half a century ago, in the days of old King Derby,[5] was a bustling wharf,—but which is now burdened with decayed wooden warehouses, and exhibits few or no symptoms of commercial life; except, perhaps, a bark or brig, half-way down its melancholy length, discharging hides; or, nearer at hand, a Nova Scotia schooner, pitching out her cargo of firewood,—at the head, I say, of this dilapidated wharf, which the tide often overflows, and along which, at the base and in the rear of the row of buildings, the track of many languid years is seen in a border of unthrifty grass,—here, with a view from its front windows adown this not very enlivening prospect, and thence across the harbour, stands a spacious edifice of brick. From the loftiest point of its roof, during precisely three and a half hours of each forenoon, floats or droops, in breeze or calm, the banner of the republic; but with the thirteen stripes turned vertically, instead of horizontally, and thus indicating that a civil, and not a military post of Uncle Sam's government, is here established. Its front is ornamented with a portico of half a dozen wooden pillars, supporting a balcony, beneath which a flight of wide granite steps descends towards the street. Over the entrance

4. Hawthorne had planned to print several other stories together with *The Scarlet Letter* but was persuaded by his publisher to publish the novel separately.

5. Elias Hasket Derby (1739–1799), wealthy Salem shipowner.

hovers an enormous specimen of the American eagle, with outspread wings, a shield before her breast, and, if I recollect aright, a bunch of intermingled thunderbolts and barbed arrows in each claw. With the customary infirmity of temper that characterizes this unhappy fowl, she appears, by the fierceness of her beak and eye and the general truculency of her attitude, to threaten mischief to the inoffensive community; and especially to warn all citizens, careful of their safety, against intruding on the premises which she overshadows with her wings. Nevertheless, vixenly as she looks, many people are seeking, at this very moment, to shelter themselves under the wing of the federal eagle; imagining, I presume, that her bosom has all the softness and snugness of an eider-down pillow. But she has no great tenderness, even in her best of moods, and, sooner or later,—oftener soon than late,—is apt to fling off her nestlings with a scratch of her claw, a dab of her beak, or a rankling wound from her barbed arrows.

The pavement round about the above-described edifice—which we may as well name at once as the Custom-House of the port—has grass enough growing in its chinks to show that it has not, of late days, been worn by any multitudinous resort of business. In some months of the year, however, there often chances a forenoon when affairs move onward with a livelier tread. Such occasions might remind the elderly citizen of that period, before the last war with England,[6] when Salem was a port by itself; not scorned, as she is now, by her own merchants and ship-owners, who permit her wharves to crumble to ruin, while their ventures go to swell, needlessly and imperceptibly, the mighty flood of commerce at New York or Boston. On some such morning, when three or four vessels happen to have arrived at once,—usually from Africa or South America,—or to be on the verge of their departure thitherward, there is a sound of frequent feet, passing briskly up and down the granite steps. Here, before his own wife has greeted him, you may greet the sea-flushed ship-master, just in port, with his vessel's papers under his arm in a tarnished tin box. Here, too, comes his owner, cheerful or sombre, gracious or in the sulks, accordingly as his scheme of the now accomplished voyage has been realized in merchandise that will readily be turned to gold, or has buried him under a bulk of incommodities, such as nobody will care to rid him of. Here, likewise,—the germ of the wrinkle-browed, grizzly-bearded, careworn merchant,—we have the smart young clerk, who gets the taste of traffic as a wolf-cub does of blood, and already sends adventures in his master's ships, when he had better be sailing mimic boats upon a mill-pond. Another figure in the scene is the outward-bound sailor, in quest of a protection;[7] or the recently arrived one, pale and feeble, seeking a passport to the hospital. Nor must we forget the captains of the rusty little schooners that bring firewood from the British provinces; a rough-looking set of tarpaulins, without the alertness of the Yankee aspect, but contributing an item of no slight importance to our decaying trade.

Cluster all these individuals together, as they sometimes were, with other miscellaneous ones to diversify the group, and, for the time being, it made the Custom-House a stirring scene. More frequently, however, on ascending the steps, you would discern—in the entry, if it were summer time, or in their

6. The War of 1812.

7. A passport.

The Custom House. The U.S. Custom House in Salem, Massachusetts, built in 1819.

appropriate rooms, if wintry or inclement weather—a row of venerable figures, sitting in old-fashioned chairs, which were tipped on their hind legs back against the wall. Oftentimes they were asleep, but occasionally might be heard talking together, in voices between speech and a snore, and with that lack of energy that distinguishes the occupants of alms-houses, and all other human beings who depend for subsistence on charity, on monopolized labor, or any thing else but their own independent exertions. These old gentlemen—seated, like Matthew, at the receipt of custom, but not very liable to be summoned thence, like him, for apostolic errands—were Custom-House officers.[8]

Furthermore, on the left hand as you enter the front door, is a certain room or office, about fifteen feet square, and of a lofty height; with two of its arched windows commanding a view of the aforesaid dilapidated wharf, and the third looking across a narrow lane, and along a portion of Derby Street. All three give glimpses of the shops of grocers, block-makers, slop-sellers, and ship-chandlers; around the doors of which are generally to be seen, laughing and gossiping, clusters of old salts, and such other wharf-rats as haunt the Wapping[9] of a seaport. The room itself is cobwebbed, and dingy with old paint; its floor is strewn with gray sand, in a fashion that has elsewhere fallen into long disuse; and it is easy to conclude, from the general slovenliness of the place, that this is a sanctuary into which womankind,

8. "And as Jesus passed forth from thence, he saw a man, named Matthew, sitting at the receipt of custom: and he saith unto him, Follow me. And he arose, and followed him" (Matthew 9.9). The joke involves the common suspicion that customs officers are corrupt.

9. Rundown area of any seaport, from an area of the London wharves. "Block-makers": pulley makers. "Slop-sellers": clothiers. "Ship-chandlers": general outfitters for ship supplies.

with her tools of magic, the broom and mop, has very infrequent access. In the way of furniture, there is a stove with a voluminous funnel; an old pine desk, with a three-legged stool beside it; two or three wooden-bottom chairs, exceedingly decrepit and infirm; and,—not to forget the library,—on some shelves, a score or two of volumes of the Acts of Congress, and a bulky Digest of the Revenue Laws. A tin pipe ascends through the ceiling, and forms a medium of vocal communication with other parts of the edifice. And here, some six months ago,—pacing from corner to corner, or lounging on the long-legged stool, with his elbow on the desk, and his eyes wandering up and down the columns of the morning newspaper,—you might have recognized, honored reader, the same individual who welcomed you into his cheery little study, where the sunshine glimmered so pleasantly through the willow branches, on the western side of the Old Manse. But now, should you go thither to seek him, you would inquire in vain for the Loco-foco Surveyor.[1] The besom[2] of reform has swept him out of office; and a worthier successor wears his dignity and pockets his emoluments.

This old town of Salem—my native place, though I have dwelt much away from it, both in boyhood and maturer years—possesses, or did possess, a hold on my affections, the force of which I have never realized during my seasons of actual residence here. Indeed, so far as its physical aspect is concerned, with its flat, unvaried surface, covered chiefly with wooden houses, few or none of which pretend to architectural beauty,—its irregularity, which is neither picturesque nor quaint, but only tame,—its long and lazy street, lounging wearisomely through the whole extent of the peninsula, with Gallows Hill and New Guinea[3] at one end, and a view of the alms-house at the other,—such being the features of my native town, it would be quite as reasonable to form a sentimental attachment to a disarranged checkerboard. And yet, though invariably happiest elsewhere, there is within me a feeling for old Salem, which, in lack of a better phrase, I must be content to call affection. The sentiment is probably assignable to the deep and aged roots which my family has struck into the soil. It is now nearly two centuries and a quarter since the original Briton, the earliest emigrant of my name,[4] made his appearance in the wild and forest-bordered settlement, which has since become a city. And here his descendants have been born and died, and have mingled their earthy substance with the soil; until no small portion of it must necessarily be akin to the mortal frame wherewith, for a little while, I walk the streets. In part, therefore, the attachment which I speak of is the mere sensuous sympathy of dust for dust. Few of my countrymen can know what it is; nor, as frequent transplantation is perhaps better for the stock, need they consider it desirable to know.

But the sentiment has likewise its moral quality. The figure of that first ancestor, invested by family tradition with a dim and dusky grandeur, was

1. Supervisor. "Loco-foco": term of ridicule for any Democrat, although properly it applies to a reform faction of the New York Democrats who in 1835 carried on a meeting after lights were doused by producing the then-new lucifer matches ("locofocos") and burning them during the rest of the meeting.
2. Bundle of twigs bound to a handle and used as a broom.
3. Areas in the town of Salem. Gallows Hill was where those found guilty of witchcraft were executed in 1692.
4. William Hathorne (c. 1606–1681), Hawthorne's great-great grandfather, emigrated from England in 1630 and became a notable public figure in Salem. (Nathaniel Hawthorne added the *w* to his own name.)

present to my boyish imagination, as far back as I can remember. It still haunts me, and induces a sort of home-feeling with the past, which I scarcely claim in reference to the present phase of the town. I seem to have a stronger claim to a residence here on account of this grave, bearded, sable-cloaked, and steeple-crowned progenitor,—who came so early, with his Bible and his sword, and trode the unworn street with such a stately port, and made so large a figure, as a man of war and peace,—a stronger claim than for myself, whose name is seldom heard and my face hardly known. He was a soldier, legislator, judge; he was a ruler in the Church; he had all the Puritanic traits, both good and evil. He was likewise a bitter persecutor; as witness the Quakers, who have remembered him in their histories, and relate an incident of his hard severity towards a woman of their sect, which will last longer, it is to be feared, than any record of his better deeds, although these were many.[5] His son, too, inherited the persecuting spirit, and made himself so conspicuous in the martyrdom of the witches, that their blood may fairly be said to have left a stain upon him.[6] So deep a stain, indeed, that his old dry bones, in the Charter Street burial-ground, must still retain it, if they have not crumbled utterly to dust! I know not whether these ancestors of mine bethought themselves to repent, and ask pardon of Heaven for their cruelties; or whether they are now groaning under the heavy consequences of them, in another state of being. At all events, I, the present writer, as their representative, hereby take shame upon myself for their sakes, and pray that any curse incurred by them—as I have heard, and as the dreary and unprosperous condition of the race, for many a long year back, would argue to exist—may be now and henceforth removed.

Doubtless, however, either of these stern and black-browed Puritans would have thought it quite a sufficient retribution for his sins, that, after so long a lapse of years, the old trunk of the family tree, with so much venerable moss upon it, should have borne, as its topmost bough, an idler like myself. No aim, that I have ever cherished, would they recognize as laudable; no success of mine—if my life, beyond its domestic scope, had ever been brightened by success—would they deem otherwise than worthless, if not positively disgraceful. "What is he?" murmurs one gray shadow of my forefathers to the other. "A writer of story-books! What kind of a business in life,—what mode of glorifying God, or being serviceable to mankind in his day and generation,—may that be? Why, the degenerate fellow might as well have been a fiddler!" Such are the compliments bandied between my great-grandsires and myself, across the gulf of time! And yet, let them scorn me as they will, strong traits of their nature have intertwined themselves with mine.

Planted deep, in the town's earliest infancy and childhood, by these two earnest and energetic men, the race has ever since subsisted here; always, too, in respectability; never, so far as I have known, disgraced by a single unworthy member; but seldom or never, on the other hand, after the first two generations, performing any memorable deed, or so much as putting forward a claim to public notice. Gradually, they have sunk almost out of sight; as old houses, here and there about the streets, get covered half-way

5. William Hathorne ordered the whipping of the Quaker Ann Coleman. Hathorne figures as a villain in William Sewel's *History of the Christian People Called Quakers* (1722).
6. John Hathorne (1641–1717), a judge during the Salem witchcraft trials in 1692.

to the eaves by the accumulation of new soil. From father to son, for above a hundred years, they followed the sea; a gray-headed shipmaster, in each generation, retiring from the quarter-deck to the homestead, while a boy of fourteen took the hereditary place before the mast, confronting the salt spray and the gale, which had blustered against his sire and grandsire. The boy, also, in due time, passed from the forecastle to the cabin,[7] spent a tempestuous manhood, and returned from his world-wanderings, to grow old, and die, and mingle his dust with the natal earth. This long connection of a family with one spot, as its place of birth and burial, creates a kindred between the human being and the locality, quite independent of any charm in the scenery or moral circumstances that surround him. It is not love, but instinct. The new inhabitant—who came himself from a foreign land, or whose father or grandfather came—has little claim to be called a Salemite; he has no conception of the oyster-like tenacity with which an old settler, over whom his third century is creeping, clings to the spot where his successive generations have been imbedded. It is no matter that the place is joyless for him; that he is weary of the old wooden houses, the mud and dust, the dead level of site and sentiment, the chill east wind, and the chillest of social atmospheres;—all these, and whatever faults besides he may see or imagine, are nothing to the purpose. The spell survives, and just as powerfully as if the natal spot were an earthly paradise. So has it been in my case. I felt it almost as a destiny to make Salem my home; so that the mould of features and cast of character which had all along been familiar here—ever, as one representative of the race lay down in his grave, another assuming, as it were, his sentry-march along the Main Street—might still in my little day be seen and recognized in the old town. Nevertheless, this very sentiment is an evidence that the connection, which has become an unhealthy one, should at last be severed. Human nature will not flourish, any more than a potato, if it be planted and replanted, for too long a series of generations, in the same worn-out soil. My children have had other birthplaces, and, so far as their fortunes may be within my control, shall strike their roots into unaccustomed earth.

On emerging from the Old Manse, it was chiefly this strange, indolent, unjoyous attachment for my native town, that brought me to fill a place in Uncle Sam's brick edifice,[8] when I might as well, or better, have gone somewhere else. My doom was on me. It was not the first time, nor the second, that I had gone away,—as it seemed, permanently,—but yet returned, like the bad half-penny; or as if Salem were for me the inevitable centre of the universe. So, one fine morning, I ascended the flight of granite steps, with the President's commission in my pocket, and was introduced to the corps of gentlemen who were to aid me in my weighty responsibility, as chief executive officer of the Custom-House.

I doubt greatly—or rather, I do not doubt at all—whether any public functionary of the United States, either in the civil or military line, has ever had such a patriarchal body of veterans under his orders as myself. The whereabouts of the Oldest Inhabitant was at once settled, when I looked at them. For upwards of twenty years before this epoch, the independent posi-

7. I.e., from ordinary seaman to captain.

8. The custom house.

tion of the Collector had kept the Salem Custom-House out of the whirlpool of political vicissitude, which makes the tenure of office generally so fragile. A soldier,—New England's most distinguished soldier,[9]—he stood firmly on the pedestal of his gallant services; and, himself secure in the wise liberality of the successive administrations through which he had held office, he had been the safety of his subordinates in many an hour of danger and heart-quake. General Miller was radically conservative; a man over whose kindly nature habit had no slight influence; attaching himself strongly to familiar faces, and with difficulty moved to change, even when change might have brought unquestionable improvement. Thus, on taking charge of my department, I found few but aged men. They were ancient sea-captains, for the most part, who, after being tost on every sea, and standing up sturdily against life's tempestuous blast, had finally drifted into this quiet nook; where, with little to disturb them, except the periodical terrors of a Presidential election, they one and all acquired a new lease of existence. Though by no means less liable than their fellow-men to age and infirmity, they had evidently some talisman or other that kept death at bay. Two or three of their number, as I was assured, being gouty and rheumatic, or perhaps bed-ridden, never dreamed of making their appearance at the Custom-House, during a large part of the year; but, after a torpid winter, would creep out into the warm sunshine of May or June, go lazily about what they termed duty, and, at their own leisure and convenience, betake themselves to bed again. I must plead guilty to the charge of abbreviating the official breath of more than one of these venerable servants of the republic. They were allowed, on my representation, to rest from their arduous labors, and soon afterwards—as if their sole principle of life had been zeal for their country's service; as I verily believe it was—withdrew to a better world. It is a pious consolation to me, that, through my interference, a sufficient space was allowed them for repentance of the evil and corrupt practices, into which, as a matter of course, every Custom-House officer must be supposed to fall. Neither the front nor the back entrance of the Custom-House opens on the road to Paradise.

The greater part of my officers were Whigs.[1] It was well for their venerable brotherhood, that the new Surveyor was not a politician, and, though a faithful Democrat in principle, neither received nor held his office with any reference to political services.[2] Had it been otherwise,—had an active politician been put into this influential post, to assume the easy task of making head against a Whig Collector, whose infirmities withheld him from the personal administration of his office,—hardly a man of the old corps would have drawn the breath of official life, within a month after the exterminating angel had come up the Custom-House steps. According to the received code in such matters, it would have been nothing short of duty, in a politician, to bring every one of those white heads under the axe of the guillotine. It was plain enough to discern, that the old fellows dreaded some such

9. General James F. Miller (1776–1851), a hero of the War of 1812, served as collector, or chief officer, of the Salem custom house (1825–49).

1. The party that opposed the Democrats between the demise of the National Republicans in the early 1830s and the rise of the Republican Party in the 1850s.

2. Although Hawthorne was no less politically active than other appointees to this position, in "The Custom-House" he portrays himself as above politics.

discourtesy at my hands. It pained, and at the same time amused me, to behold the terrors that attended my advent; to see a furrowed cheek, weather-beaten by half a century of storm, turn ashy pale at the glance of so harmless an individual as myself; to detect, as one or another addressed me, the tremor of a voice, which, in long-past days, had been wont to bellow through a speaking-trumpet, hoarsely enough to frighten Boreas[3] himself to silence. They knew, these excellent old persons, that, by all established rule,—and, as regarded some of them, weighed by their own lack of efficiency for business,—they ought to have given place to younger men, more orthodox in politics, and altogether fitter than themselves to serve our common Uncle. I knew it too, but could never quite find in my heart to act upon the knowledge. Much and deservedly to my own discredit, therefore, and considerably to the detriment of my official conscience, they continued, during my incumbency, to creep about the wharves, and loiter up and down the Custom-House steps. They spent a good deal of time, also, asleep in their accustomed corners, with their chairs tilted back against the wall; awaking, however, once or twice in a forenoon, to bore one another with the several thousandth repetition of old sea-stories, and mouldy jokes, that had grown to be pass-words and countersigns among them.

The discovery was soon made, I imagine, that the new Surveyor had no great harm in him. So, with lightsome hearts, and the happy consciousness of being usefully employed,—in their own behalf, at least, if not for our beloved country,—these good old gentlemen went through the various formalities of office. Sagaciously, under their spectacles, did they peep into the holds of vessels! Mighty was their fuss about little matters, and marvellous, sometimes, the obtuseness that allowed greater ones to slip between their fingers! Whenever such a mischance occurred,—when a wagon-load of valuable merchandise had been smuggled ashore, at noonday, perhaps, and directly beneath their unsuspicious noses,—nothing could exceed the vigilance and alacrity with which they proceeded to lock, and double-lock, and secure with tape and sealing-wax, all the avenues of the delinquent vessel. Instead of a reprimand for their previous negligence, the case seemed rather to require an eulogium on their praiseworthy caution, after the mischief had happened; a grateful recognition of the promptitude of their zeal, the moment that there was no longer any remedy!

Unless people are more than commonly disagreeable, it is my foolish habit to contract a kindness for them. The better part of my companion's character, if it have a better part, is that which usually comes uppermost in my regard, and forms the type whereby I recognize the man. As most of these old Custom-House officers had good traits, and as my position in reference to them, being paternal and protective, was favorable to the growth of friendly sentiments, I soon grew to like them all. It was pleasant, in the summer forenoons,—when the fervent heat, that almost liquefied the rest of the human family, merely communicated a genial warmth to their half-torpid systems,—it was pleasant to hear them chatting in the back entry, a row of them all tipped against the wall, as usual; while the frozen witticisms of past generations were thawed out, and came bubbling with laughter from their

3. In Greek mythology, god of the north wind.

lips. Externally, the jollity of aged men has much in common with the mirth of children; the intellect, any more than a deep sense of humor, has little to do with the matter; it is, with both, a gleam that plays upon the surface, and imparts a sunny and cheery aspect alike to the green branch, and gray, mouldering trunk. In one case, however, it is real sunshine; in the other, it more resembles the phosphorescent glow of decaying wood.

It would be sad injustice, the reader must understand, to represent all my excellent old friends as in their dotage. In the first place, my coadjutors were not invariably old; there were men among them in their strength and prime, of marked ability and energy, and altogether superior to the sluggish and dependent mode of life on which their evil stars had cast them. Then, moreover, the white locks of age were sometimes found to be the thatch of an intellectual tenement in good repair. But, as respects the majority of my corps of veterans, there will be no wrong done, if I characterize them generally as a set of wearisome old souls, who had gathered nothing worth preservation from their varied experience of life. They seemed to have flung away all the golden grain of practical wisdom, which they had enjoyed so many opportunities of harvesting, and most carefully to have stored their memories with the husks. They spoke with far more interest and unction of their morning's breakfast, or yesterday's, to-day's, or to-morrow's dinner, than of the shipwreck of forty or fifty years ago, and all the world's wonders which they had witnessed with their youthful eyes.

The father of the Custom-House—the patriarch, not only of this little squad of officials, but, I am bold to say, of the respectable body of tide-waiters all over the United States—was a certain permanent Inspector.[4] He might truly be termed a legitimate son of the revenue system, dyed in the wool, or rather, born in the purple; since his sire, a Revolutionary colonel, and formerly collector of the port, had created an office for him, and appointed him to fill it, at a period of the early ages which few living men can now remember. This Inspector, when I first knew him, was a man of fourscore years, or thereabouts, and certainly one of the most wonderful specimens of wintergreen that you would be likely to discover in a lifetime's search. With his florid cheek, his compact figure, smartly arrayed in a bright-buttoned blue coat, his brisk and vigorous step, and his hale and hearty aspect, altogether, he seemed—not young, indeed—but a kind of new contrivance of Mother Nature in the shape of man, whom age and infirmity had no business to touch. His voice and laugh, which perpetually reëchoed through the Custom-House, had nothing of the tremulous quaver and cackle of an old man's utterance; they came strutting out of his lungs, like the crow of a cock, or the blast of a clarion. Looking at him merely as an animal,—and there was very little else to look at,—he was a most satisfactory object, from the thorough healthfulness and wholesomeness of his system, and his capacity, at that extreme age, to enjoy all, or nearly all, the delights which he had ever aimed at, or conceived of. The careless security of his life in the Custom-House, on a regular income, and with but slight and infrequent apprehensions of removal, had no doubt contributed to make time pass lightly over him. The original and more potent causes, however, lay in the rare perfection of his animal

4. William Lee (1771–1851), who was offended by Hawthorne's satirical sketch. "Tide-waiters": custom officers who board incoming ships at harbor.

nature, the moderate proportion of intellect, and the very trifling admixture of moral and spiritual ingredients; these latter qualities, indeed, being in barely enough measure to keep the old gentleman from walking on all-fours. He possessed no power of thought, no depth of feeling, no troublesome sensibilities; nothing, in short, but a few commonplace instincts, which, aided by the cheerful temper that grew inevitably out of his physical well-being, did duty very respectably, and to general acceptance, in lieu of a heart. He had been the husband of three wives, all long since dead; the father of twenty children, most of whom, at every age of childhood or maturity, had likewise returned to dust. Here, one would suppose, might have been sorrow enough to imbue the sunniest disposition, through and through, with a sable tinge. Not so with our old Inspector! One brief sigh sufficed to carry off the entire burden of these dismal reminiscences. The next moment, he was as ready for sport as any unbreeched infant; far readier than the Collector's junior clerk, who, at nineteen years, was much the elder and graver man of the two.

I used to watch and study this patriarchal personage with, I think, livelier curiosity than any other form of humanity there presented to my notice. He was, in truth, a rare phenomenon; so perfect in one point of view; so shallow, so delusive, so impalpable, such an absolute nonentity, in every other. My conclusion was that he had no soul, no heart, no mind; nothing, as I have already said, but instincts; and yet, withal, so cunningly had the few materials of his character been put together, that there was no painful perception of deficiency, but, on my part, an entire contentment with what I found in him. It might be difficult—and it was so—to conceive how he should exist hereafter, so earthy and sensuous did he seem; but surely his existence here, admitting that it was to terminate with his last breath, had been not unkindly given; with no higher moral responsibilities than the beasts of the field, but with a larger scope of enjoyment than theirs, and with all their blessed immunity from the dreariness and duskiness of age.

One point, in which he had vastly the advantage over his four-footed brethren, was his ability to recollect the good dinners which it had made no small portion of the happiness of his life to eat. His gourmandism was a highly agreeable trait; and to hear him talk of roast-meat was as appetizing as a pickle or an oyster. As he possessed no higher attribute, and neither sacrificed nor vitiated any spiritual endowment by devoting all his energies and ingenuities to subserve the delight and profit of his maw, it always pleased and satisfied me to hear him expatiate on fish, poultry, and butcher's meat, and the most eligible methods of preparing them for the table. His reminiscences of good cheer, however ancient the date of the actual banquet, seemed to bring the savor of pig or turkey under one's very nostrils. There were flavors on his palate, that had lingered there not less than sixty or seventy years, and were still apparently as fresh as that of the mutton-chop which he had just devoured for his breakfast. I have heard him smack his lips over dinners, every guest at which, except himself, had long been food for worms. It was marvellous to observe how the ghosts of bygone meals were continually rising up before him; not in anger or retribution, but as if grateful for his former appreciation, and seeking to reduplicate an endless series of enjoyment, at once shadowy and sensual. A tenderloin of beef, a hind-quarter of veal, a spare-rib of pork, a particular chicken, or a remarkably praiseworthy turkey, which had perhaps adorned his board in the days of the elder Adams,[5] would be remembered; while all the subsequent experience of our race, and all the events that brightened or darkened his individual career, had gone over him with as little permanent effect as the passing breeze. The chief tragic event of the old man's life, so far as I could judge, was his mishap with a certain goose, which lived and died some twenty or forty years ago; a goose of most promising figure, but which, at table, proved so inveterately tough that the carving-knife would make no impression on its carcass; and it could only be divided with an axe and handsaw.

But it is time to quit this sketch; on which, however, I should be glad to dwell at considerably more length, because, of all men whom I have ever known, this individual was fittest to be a Custom-House officer. Most persons, owing to causes which I may not have space to hint at, suffer moral detriment from this peculiar mode of life. The old Inspector was incapable of it, and, were he to continue in office to the end of time, would be just as good as he was then, and sit down to dinner with just as good an appetite.

There is one likeness, without which my gallery of Custom-House portraits would be strangely incomplete; but which my comparatively few opportunities for observation enable me to sketch only in the merest outline. It is that of the Collector, our gallant old General, who, after his brilliant military service, subsequently to which he had ruled over a wild Western territory,[6] had come hither, twenty years before, to spend the decline of his varied and honorable life. The brave soldier had already numbered, nearly or quite, his threescore years and ten, and was pursuing the remainder of his earthly march, burdened with infirmities which even the martial music of his own spirit-stirring recollections could do little towards lightening. The step was palsied now, that had been foremost in the charge. It was only with the assistance of a servant, and by leaning his hand heavily on the iron balustrade, that he could slowly and painfully ascend the Custom-House steps, and, with a toilsome progress across the floor, attain his customary chair beside the fireplace. There he used to sit, gazing with a somewhat dim serenity of aspect at the figures that came and went; amid the rustle of papers, the administering of oaths, the discussion of business, and the casual talk of the office; all which sounds and circumstances seemed but indistinctly to impress his senses, and hardly to make their way into his inner sphere of contemplation. His countenance, in this repose, was mild and kindly. If his notice was sought, an expression of courtesy and interest gleamed out upon his features; proving that there was light within him, and that it was only the outward medium of the intellectual lamp that obstructed the rays in their passage. The closer you penetrated to the substance of his mind, the sounder it appeared. When no longer called upon to speak, or listen, either of which operations cost him an evident effort, his face would briefly subside into its former not uncheerful quietude. It was not painful to behold this look; for, though dim, it had not the imbecility of decaying age. The framework of his nature, originally strong and massive, was not yet crumbled into ruin.

5. From 1797 to 1801, the term of John Adams, the second president, father of John Quincy Adams, the sixth president.

6. James Miller was governor of Arkansas Territory (1819–25).

To observe and define his character, however, under such disadvantages, was as difficult a task as to trace out and build up anew, in imagination, an old fortress, like Ticonderoga,[7] from a view of its gray and broken ruins. Here and there, perchance, the walls may remain almost complete; but elsewhere may be only a shapeless mound, cumbrous with its very strength, and overgrown, through long years of peace and neglect, with grass and alien weeds.

Nevertheless, looking at the old warrior with affection,—for, slight as was the communication between us, my feeling towards him, like that of all bipeds and quadrupeds who knew him, might not improperly be termed so,—I could discern the main points of his portrait. It was marked with the noble and heroic qualities which showed it to be not by a mere accident, but of good right, that he had won a distinguished name. His spirit could never, I conceive, have been characterized by an uneasy activity; it must, at any period of his life, have required an impulse to set him in motion; but, once stirred up, with obstacles to overcome, and an adequate object to be attained, it was not in the man to give out or fail. The heat that had formerly pervaded his nature, and which was not yet extinct, was never of the kind that flashes and flickers in a blaze, but, rather, a deep, red glow, as of iron in a furnace. Weight, solidity, firmness; this was the expression of his repose, even in such decay as had crept untimely over him, at the period of which I speak. But I could imagine, even then, that, under some excitement which should go deeply into his consciousness,—roused by a trumpet-peal, loud enough to awaken all of his energies that were not dead, but only slumbering,—he was yet capable of flinging off his infirmities like a sick man's gown, dropping the staff of age to seize a battle-sword, and starting up once more a warrior. And, in so intense a moment, his demeanour would have still been calm. Such an exhibition, however, was but to be pictured in fancy; not to be anticipated, nor desired. What I saw in him—as evidently as the indestructible ramparts of Old Ticonderoga, already cited as the most appropriate simile—were the features of stubborn and ponderous endurance, which might well have amounted to obstinacy in his earlier days; of integrity, that, like most of his other endowments, lay in a somewhat heavy mass, and was just as unmalleable and unmanageable as a ton of iron ore; and of benevolence, which, fiercely as he led the bayonets on at Chippewa or Fort Erie,[8] I take to be of quite as genuine a stamp as what actuates any or all the polemical philanthropists of the age. He had slain men with his own hand, for aught I know;—certainly, they had fallen, like blades of grass at the sweep of the scythe, before the charge to which his spirit imparted its triumphant energy;—but, be that as it might, there was never in his heart so much cruelty as would have brushed the down off a butterfly's wing. I have not known the man, to whose innate kindliness I would more confidently make an appeal.

Many characteristics—and those, too, which contribute not the least forcibly to impart resemblance in a sketch—must have vanished, or been obscured, before I met the General. All merely graceful attributes are usually the most evanescent; nor does Nature adorn the human ruin with blossoms of new beauty, that have their roots and proper nutriment only in the

7. Ethan Allen and Benedict Arnold (not yet a traitor) captured Fort Ticonderoga in upstate New York from the British in 1775.

8. Battles in upstate New York in 1814, which were crucial to the U.S. victory over the British in the War of 1812.

chinks and crevices of decay, as she sows wall-flowers over the ruined fortress of Ticonderoga. Still, even in respect of grace and beauty, there were points well worth noting. A ray of humor, now and then, would make its way through the veil of dim obstruction, and glimmer pleasantly upon our faces. A trait of native elegance, seldom seen in the masculine character after childhood or early youth, was shown in the General's fondness for the sight and fragrance of flowers. An old soldier might be supposed to prize only the bloody laurel on his brow; but here was one, who seemed to have a young girl's appreciation of the floral tribe.

There, beside the fireplace, the brave old General used to sit; while the Surveyor—though seldom, when it could be avoided, taking upon himself the difficult task of engaging him in conversation—was fond of standing at a distance, and watching his quiet and almost slumberous countenance. He seemed away from us, although we saw him but a few yards off; remote, though we passed close beside his chair; unattainable, though we might have stretched forth our hands and touched his own. It might be, that he lived a more real life within his thoughts, than amid the unappropriate environment of the Collector's office. The evolutions of the parade; the turmult of the battle; the flourish of old, heroic music, heard thirty years before;—such scenes and sounds, perhaps, were all alive before his intellectual sense. Meanwhile, the merchants and ship-masters, the spruce clerks, and uncouth sailors, entered and departed; the bustle of this commercial and Custom-House life kept up its little murmur round about him; and neither with the men nor their affairs did the General appear to sustain the most distant relation. He was as much out of place as an old sword—now rusty, but which had flashed once in the battle's front, and showed still a bright gleam along its blade—would have been, among the inkstands, paper-folders, and mahogany rulers, on the Deputy Collector's desk.

There was one thing that much aided me in renewing and re-creating the stalwart soldier of the Niagara frontier,—the man of true and simple energy. It was the recollection of those memorable words of his,—"I'll try, Sir!"[9]—spoken on the very verge of a desperate and heroic enterprise, and breathing the soul and spirit of New England hardihood, comprehending all perils, and encountering all. If, in our country, valor were rewarded by heraldic honor, this phrase—which it seems so easy to speak, but which only he, with such a task of danger and glory before him, has ever spoken—would be the best and fittest of all mottoes for the General's shield of arms.

It contributes greatly towards a man's moral and intellectual health, to be brought into habits of companionship with individuals unlike himself, who care little for his pursuits, and whose sphere and abilities he must go out of himself to appreciate. The accidents of my life have often afforded me this advantage, but never with more fulness and variety than during my continuance in office. There was one man,[1] especially, the observation of whose character gave me a new idea of talent. His gifts were emphatically those of a man of business; prompt, acute, clear-minded; with an eye that saw through

9. Miller's reported response to General Winfield Scott's order to storm a British battery of seven cannons at Lundy's Lane in Ontario, near Niagara Falls in 1814.

1. A reference to Hawthorne's friend Zachariah Burchmore (1809–1884), a custom-house clerk who also served as secretary of Salem's Democratic Party.

all perplexities, and a faculty of arrangement that made them vanish, as by the waving of an enchanter's wand. Bred up from boyhood in the Custom-House, it was his proper field of activity; and the many intricacies of business, so harassing to the interloper, presented themselves before him with the regularity of a perfectly comprehended system. In my contemplation, he stood as the ideal of his class. He was, indeed, the Custom-House in himself; or, at all events, the main-spring that kept its variously revolving wheels in motion; for, in an institution like this, where its officers are appointed to subserve their own profit and convenience, and seldom with a leading reference to their fitness for the duty to be performed, they must perforce seek elsewhere the dexterity which is not in them. Thus, by an inevitable necessity, as a magnet attracts steel-filings, so did our man of business draw to himself the difficulties which everybody met with. With an easy condescension, and kind forbearance towards our stupidity,—which, to his order of mind, must have seemed little short of crime,—would he forthwith, by the merest touch of his finger, make the incomprehensible as clear as daylight. The merchants valued him not less than we, his esoteric friends. His integrity was perfect; it was a law of nature with him, rather than a choice or a principle; nor can it be otherwise than the main condition of an intellect so remarkably clear and accurate as his, to be honest and regular in the administration of affairs. A stain on his conscience, as to any thing that came within the range of his vocation, would trouble such a man very much in the same way, though to a far greater degree, than an error in the balance of an account, or an ink-blot on the fair page of a book of record. Here, in a word,—and it is a rare instance in my life,—I had met with a person thoroughly adapted to the situation which he held.

Such were some of the people with whom I now found myself connected. I took it in good part at the hands of Providence, that I was thrown into a position so little akin to my past habits; and set myself seriously to gather from it whatever profit was to be had. After my fellowship of toil and impracticable schemes, with the dreamy brethren of Brook Farm; after living for three years within the subtile influence of an intellect like Emerson's; after those wild, free days on the Assabeth,[2] indulging fantastic speculations beside our fire of fallen boughs, with Ellery Channing; after talking with Thoreau about pine-trees and Indian relics, in his hermitage at Walden; after growing fastidious by sympathy with the classic refinement of Hillard's culture; after becoming imbued with poetic sentiment at Longfellow's hearth-stone;—it was time, at length, that I should exercise other faculties of my nature, and nourish myself with food for which I had hitherto had little appetite. Even the old Inspector was desirable, as a change of diet, to a man who had known Alcott.[3] I looked upon it as an evidence, in some measure, of a system naturally well balanced, and lacking no essential part of a thorough organization, that, with such associates to remember, I could mingle

2. A tributary that joins the Concord River near Concord, Massachusetts. "Brook Farm": the reformist agricultural community near Boston that Hawthorne participated in during 1841 and that provided the inspiration for *The Blithedale Romance* (1852).

3. The father of Louisa May Alcott, Bronson Alcott (1799–1888), was an innovative educator and sometimes-ridiculed reformer, whom Hawthorne knew in Concord. Emerson, Thoreau, and the writer Channing (1818–1901) also lived in Concord. In Boston Hawthorne could visit his friend the lawyer George Stillman Hillard (1808–1879), and at Cambridge he could visit his acquaintance Henry Wadsworth Longfellow.

at once with men of altogether different qualities, and never murmur at the change.

Literature, its exertions and objects, were now of little moment in my regard. I cared not, at this period, for books; they were apart from me. Nature,—except it were human nature,—the nature that is developed in earth and sky, was, in one sense, hidden from me; and all the imaginative delight, wherewith it had been spiritualized, passed away out of my mind. A gift, a faculty, if it had not departed, was suspended and inanimate within me. There would have been something sad, unutterably dreary, in all this, had I not been conscious that it lay at my own option to recall whatever was valuable in the past. It might be true, indeed, that this was a life which could not, with impunity, be lived too long; else, it might make me permanently other than I had been, without transforming me into any shape which it would be worth my while to take. But I never considered it as other than a transitory life. There was always a prophetic instinct, a low whisper in my ear, that, within no long period, and whenever a new change of custom should be essential to my good, a change would come.

Meanwhile, there I was, a Surveyor of the Revenue, and, so far as I have been able to understand, as good a Surveyor as need be. A man of thought, fancy, and sensibility, (had he ten times the Surveyor's proportion of those qualities,) may, at any time, be a man of affairs, if he will only choose to give himself the trouble. My fellow-officers, and the merchants and sea-captains with whom my official duties brought me into any manner of connection, viewed me in no other light, and probably knew me in no other character. None of them, I presume, had ever read a page of my inditing, or would have cared a fig the more for me, if they had read them all; nor would it have mended the matter, in the least, had those same unprofitable pages been written with a pen like that of Burns or of Chaucer,[4] each of whom was a Custom-House officer in his day, as well as I. It is a good lesson—though it may often be a hard one—for a man who has dreamed of literary fame, and of making for himself a rank among the world's dignitaries by such means, to step aside out of the narrow circle in which his claims are recognized, and to find how utterly devoid of significance, beyond that circle, is all that he achieves, and all he aims at. I know not that I especially needed the lesson, either in the way of warning or rebuke; but, at any rate, I learned it thoroughly; nor, it gives me pleasure to reflect, did the truth, as it came home to my perception, ever cost me a pang, or require to be thrown off in a sigh. In the way of literary talk, it is true, the Naval Officer—an excellent fellow, who came into office with me, and went out only a little later—would often engage me in a discussion about one or the other of his favorite topics, Napoleon or Shakspeare. The Collector's junior clerk too,—a young gentleman who, it was whispered, occasionally covered a sheet of Uncle Sam's letter-paper with what, (at the distance of a few yards,) looked very much like poetry,—used now and then to speak to me of books, as matters with which I might possibly be conversant. This was my all of lettered intercourse; and it was quite sufficient for my necessities.

4. Poets. Geoffrey Chaucer (1340?–1400) was controller of customs in London (1374–86). Robert Burns was collector of excise taxes (1789–91) in Dumfries, Scotland.

No longer seeking nor caring that my name should be blazoned abroad on title-pages, I smiled to think that it had now another kind of vogue. The Custom-House marker imprinted it, with a stencil and black paint, on pepper-bags, and baskets of anatto,[5] and cigar-boxes, and bales of all kinds of dutiable merchandise, in testimony that these commodities had paid the impost, and gone regularly through the office. Borne on such queer vehicle of fame, a knowledge of my existence, so far as a name conveys it, was carried where it had never been before, and, I hope, will never go again.

But the past was not dead. Once in a great while, the thoughts, that had seemed so vital and so active, yet had been put to rest so quietly, revived again. One of the most remarkable occasions, when the habit of bygone days awoke in me, was that which brings it within the law of literary propriety to offer the public the sketch which I am now writing.

In the second story of the Custom-House, there is a large room, in which the brick-work and naked rafters have never been covered with panelling and plaster. The edifice—originally projected on a scale adapted to the old commercial enterprise of the port, and with an idea of subsequent prosperity destined never to be realized—contains far more space than its occupants know what to do with. This airy hall, therefore, over the Collector's apartments, remains unfinished to this day, and, in spite of the aged cobwebs that festoon its dusky beams, appears still to await the labor of the carpenter and mason. At one end of the room, in a recess, were a number of barrels, piled one upon another, containing bundles of official documents. Large quantities of similar rubbish lay lumbering[6] the floor. It was sorrowful to think how many days, and weeks, and months, and years of toil, had been wasted on these musty papers, which were now only an encumbrance of earth, and were hidden away in this forgotten corner, never more to be glanced at by human eyes. But, then, what reams of other manuscripts—filled, not with the dulness of official formalities, but with the thought of inventive brains and the rich effusion of deep hearts—had gone equally to oblivion; and that, moreover, without serving a purpose in their day, as these heaped up papers had, and—saddest of all—without purchasing for their writers the comfortable livelihood which the clerks of the Custom-House had gained by these worthless scratchings of the pen! Yet not altogether worthless, perhaps, as materials of local history. Here, no doubt, statistics of the former commerce of Salem might be discovered, and memorials of her princely merchants,—old King Derby,—old Billy Gray,—old Simon Forrester,[7]—and many another magnate in his day; whose powdered head, however, was scarcely in the tomb, before his mountain-pile of wealth began to dwindle. The founders of the greater part of the families which now compose the aristocracy of Salem might here be traced, from the petty and obscure beginnings of their traffic, at periods generally much posterior to the Revolution, upward to what their children look upon as long-established rank.

5. Yellowish dye (usually spelled "annatto"). The trowel-shaped stencil was daubed with ink to imprint Hawthorne's name on goods passing through the port.
6. Cluttering.
7. Captain Simon Forrester (1776–1851), rich relative of the Hawthornes. William Gray (1750–1825) had become lieutenant governor of Massachusetts. Elias Haskett Derby (1739–1799) helped establish Salem as an important maritime trading center.

Prior to the Revolution, there is a dearth of records; the earlier documents and archives of the Custom-House having, probably, been carried off to Halifax, when all the King's officials accompanied the British army in its flight from Boston.[8] It has often been a matter of regret with me; for, going back, perhaps, to the days of the Protectorate,[9] those papers must have contained many references to forgotten or remembered men, and to antique customs, which would have affected me with the same pleasure as when I used to pick up Indian arrow-heads in the field near the Old Manse.

But, one idle and rainy day, it was my fortune to make a discovery of some little interest. Poking and burrowing into the heaped-up rubbish in the corner; unfolding one and another document, and reading the names of vessels that had long ago foundered at sea or rotted at the wharves, and those of merchants, never heard of now on 'Change,[1] nor very readily decipherable on their mossy tombstones; glancing at such matters with the saddened, weary, half-reluctant interest which we bestow on the corpse of dead activity,—and exerting my fancy, sluggish with little use, to raise up from these dry bones an image of the old town's brighter aspect, when India was a new region, and only Salem knew the way thither,—I chanced to lay my hand on a small package, carefully done up in a piece of ancient yellow parchment. This envelope had the air of an official record of some period long past, when clerks engrossed their stiff and formal chirography on more substantial materials than at present. There was something about it that quickened an instinctive curiosity, and made me undo the faded red tape, that tied up the package, with the sense that a treasure would here be brought to light. Unbending the rigid folds of the parchment cover, I found it to be a commission, under the hand and seal of Governor Shirley, in favor of one Jonathan Pue,[2] as Surveyor of his Majesty's Customs for the port of Salem, in the Province of Massachusetts Bay. I remembered to have read (probably in Felt's Annals) a notice of the decease of Mr. Surveyor Pue, about fourscore years ago; and likewise, in a newspaper of recent times, an account of the digging up of his remains in the little grave-yard of St. Peter's Church,[3] during the renewal of that edifice. Nothing, if I rightly call to mind, was left of my respected predecessor, save an imperfect skeleton, and some fragments of apparel, and a wig of majestic frizzle; which, unlike the head that it once adorned, was in very satisfactory preservation. But, on examining the papers which the parchment commission served to envelop, I found more traces of Mr. Pue's mental part, and the internal operations of his head, than the frizzled wig had contained of the venerable skull itself.

They were documents, in short, not official, but of a private nature, or, at least, written in his private capacity, and apparently with his own hand. I could account for their being included in the heap of Custom-House lumber only by the fact, that Mr. Pue's death had happened suddenly; and that these

8. General William Howe (1729–1814) had evacuated the British troops to Halifax, Nova Scotia, when Washington besieged Boston in 1776, but his transfer of the Salem records is undocumented.
9. The years 1653–60, when Oliver Cromwell (1599–1658) and then his son Richard (1626–1712) ruled as lord protector of England.
1. Exchange, equivalent of the modern stock exchange.
2. In Joseph B. Felt's *Annals of Salem* (1827), Hawthorne read that Jonathan Pue was appointed customs surveyor in 1752 and died in 1760. William Shirley (1694–1771), royal governor of Massachusetts (1741–49, 1753–56).
3. The first Anglican Church in Salem, which was begun in 1633.

papers, which he probably kept in his official desk, had never come to the knowledge of his heirs, or were supposed to relate to the business of the revenue. On the transfer of the archives to Halifax, this package, proving to be of no public concern, was left behind, and had remained ever since unopened.

The ancient Surveyor—being little molested, I suppose, at that early day, with business pertaining to his office—seems to have devoted some of his many leisure hours to researches as a local antiquarian, and other inquisitions of a similar nature. These supplied material for petty activity to a mind that would otherwise have been eaten up with rust. A portion of his facts, by the by, did me good service in the preparation of the article entitled "MAIN STREET," included in the present volume.[4] The remainder may perhaps be applied to purposes equally valuable, hereafter; or not impossibly may be worked up, so far as they go, into a regular history of Salem, should my veneration for the natal soil ever impel me to so pious a task. Meanwhile, they shall be at the command of any gentleman, inclined, and competent, to take the unprofitable labor off my hands. As a final disposition, I contemplate depositing them with the Essex Historical Society.[5]

But the object that most drew my attention, in the mysterious package, was a certain affair of fine red cloth, much worn and faded. There were traces about it of gold embroidery, which, however, was greatly frayed and defaced; so that none, or very little, of the glitter was left. It had been wrought, as was easy to perceive, with wonderful skill of needlework; and the stitch (as I am assured by ladies conversant with such mysteries) gives evidence of a now forgotten art, not to be recovered even by the process of picking out the threads. This rag of scarlet cloth,—for time, and wear, and a sacrilegious moth, had reduced it to little other than a rag,—on careful examination, assumed the shape of a letter. It was the capital letter A. By an accurate measurement, each limb proved to be precisely three inches and a quarter in length. It had been intended, there could be no doubt, as an ornamental article of dress; but how it was to be worn, or what rank, honor, and dignity, in by-past times, were signified by it, was a riddle which (so evanescent are the fashions of the world in these particulars) I saw little hope of solving. And yet it strangely interested me. My eyes fastened themselves upon the old scarlet letter, and would not be turned aside. Certainly, there was some deep meaning in it, most worthy of interpretation, and which, as it were, streamed forth from the mystic symbol, subtly communicating itself to my sensibilities, but evading the analysis of my mind.

While thus perplexed,—and cogitating, among other hypotheses, whether the letter might not have been one of those decorations which the white men used to contrive, in order to take the eyes of Indians,—I happened to place it on my breast. It seemed to me,—the reader may smile, but must not doubt my word,—it seemed to me, then, that I experienced a sensation not altogether physical, yet almost so, as of burning heat; and as if the letter were not of red cloth, but red-hot iron. I shuddered, and involuntarily let it fall upon the floor.

4. Another vestige of the earlier intention to publish several stories and sketches along with *The Scarlet Letter.*

5. A real institution, which does not contain Hawthorne's imaginary documents.

In the absorbing contemplation of the scarlet letter, I had hitherto neglected to examine a small roll of dingy paper, around which it had been twisted. This I now opened, and had the satisfaction to find, recorded by the old Surveyor's pen, a reasonably complete explanation of the whole affair. There were several foolscap sheets,[6] containing many particulars respecting the life and conversation of one Hester Prynne, who appeared to have been rather a noteworthy personage in the view of our ancestors. She had flourished during a period between the early days of Massachusetts and the close of the seventeenth century. Aged persons, alive in the time of Mr. Surveyor Pue, and from whose oral testimony he had made up his narrative, remembered her, in their youth, as a very old, but not decrepit woman, of a stately and solemn aspect. It had been her habit, from an almost immemorial date, to go about the country as a kind of voluntary nurse, and doing whatever miscellaneous good she might; taking upon herself, likewise, to give advice in all matters, especially those of the heart; by which means, as a person of such propensities inevitably must, she gained from many people the reverence due to an angel, but, I should imagine, was looked upon by others as an intruder and a nuisance. Prying farther into the manuscript, I found the record of other doings and sufferings of this singular woman, for most of which the reader is referred to the story entitled "The Scarlet Letter"; and it should be borne carefully in mind, that the main facts of that story are authorized and authenticated by the document of Mr. Surveyor Pue. The original papers, together with the scarlet letter itself,—a most curious relic,—are still in my possession, and shall be freely exhibited to whomsoever, induced by the great interest of the narrative, may desire a sight of them. I must not be understood as affirming, that, in the dressing up of the tale, and imagining the motives and modes of passion that influenced the characters who figure in it, I have invariably confined myself within the limits of the old Surveyor's half a dozen sheets of foolscap. On the contrary, I have allowed myself, as to such points, nearly or altogether as much license as if the facts had been entirely of my own invention. What I contend for is the authenticity of the outline.

This incident recalled my mind, in some degree, to its old track. There seemed to be here the groundwork of a tale. It impressed me as if the ancient Surveyor, in his garb of a hundred years gone by, and wearing his immortal wig,—which was buried with him, but did not perish in the grave,—had met me in the deserted chamber of the Custom-House. In his port[7] was the dignity of one who had borne his Majesty's commission, and who was therefore illuminated by a ray of the splendor that shone so dazzlingly about the throne. How unlike, alas! the hang-dog look of a republican official, who, as the servant of the people, feels himself less than the least, and below the lowest, of his masters. With his own ghostly hand, the obscurely seen, but majestic, figure had imparted to me the scarlet symbol, and the little roll of explanatory manuscript. With his own ghostly voice, he had exhorted me, on the sacred consideration of my filial duty and reverence towards him,—who might reasonably regard himself as my official ancestor,—to bring his

6. Sheets of paper 13 by 16 inches, unfolded; often folded to make four 13 by 8 pages.

7. Deportment; bearing.

mouldy and moth-eaten lucubrations[8] before the public. "Do this," said the ghost of Mr. Surveyor Pue, emphatically nodding the head that looked so imposing within its memorable wig, "do this, and the profit shall be all your own! You will shortly need it; for it is not in your days as it was in mine, when a man's office was a life-lease, and oftentimes an heirloom. But, I charge you, in this matter of old Mistress Prynne, give to your predecessor's memory the credit which will be rightfully its due!" And I said to the ghost of Mr. Surveyor Pue,—"I will!"

On Hester Prynne's story, therefore, I bestowed much thought. It was the subject of my meditations for many an hour, while pacing to and fro across my room, or traversing, with a hundredfold repetition, the long extent from the front-door of the Custom-House to the side-entrance, and back again. Great were the weariness and annoyance of the old Inspector and the Weighers and Gaugers, whose slumbers were disturbed by the unmercifully lengthened tramp of my passing and returning footsteps. Remembering their own former habits, they used to say that the Surveyor was walking the quarter-deck. They probably fancied that my sole object—and, indeed, the sole object for which a sane man could ever put himself into voluntary motion—was, to get an appetite for dinner. And to say the truth, an appetite, sharpened by the east-wind that generally blew along the passage, was the only valuable result of so much indefatigable exercise. So little adapted is the atmosphere of a Custom-House to the delicate harvest of fancy and sensibility, that, had I remained there through ten Presidencies yet to come, I doubt whether the tale of "The Scarlet Letter" would ever have been brought before the public eye. My imagination was a tarnished mirror. It would not reflect, or only with miserable dimness, the figures with which I did my best to people it. The characters of the narrative would not be warmed and rendered malleable, by any heat that I could kindle at my intellectual forge. They would take neither the glow of passion nor the tenderness of sentiment, but retained all the rigidity of dead corpses, and stared me in the face with a fixed and ghastly grin of contemptuous defiance. "What have you to do with us?" that expression seemed to say. "The little power you might once have possessed over the tribe of unrealities is gone! You have bartered it for a pittance of the public gold. Go, then, and earn your wages!" In short, the almost torpid creatures of my own fancy twitted me with imbecility, and not without fair occasion.

It was not merely during the three hours and a half which Uncle Sam claimed as his share of my daily life, that this wretched numbness held possession of me. It went with me on my sea-shore walks and rambles into the country, whenever—which was seldom and reluctantly—I bestirred myself to seek that invigorating charm of Nature, which used to give me such freshness and activity of thought, the moment that I stepped across the threshold of the Old Manse. The same torpor, as regarded the capacity for intellectual effort, accompanied me home, and weighed upon me in the chamber which I most absurdly termed my study. Nor did it quit me, when, late at night, I sat in the deserted parlour, lighted only by the glimmering coal-fire and the

8. Laborious or pedantic writing (from the Latin for working by candlelight, at night).

moon, striving to picture forth imaginary scenes, which, the next day, might flow out on the brightening page in many-hued description.

If the imaginative faculty refused to act at such an hour, it might well be deemed a hopeless case. Moonlight, in a familiar room, falling so white upon the carpet, and showing all its figures so distinctly,—making every object so minutely visible, yet so unlike a morning or noontide visibility,—is a medium the most suitable for a romance-writer to get acquainted with his illusive guests. There is the little domestic scenery of the well-known apartment; the chairs, with each its separate individuality; the centre-table, sustaining a work-basket, a volume or two, and an extinguished lamp; the sofa; the book-case; the picture on the wall;—all these details, so completely seen, are so spiritualized by the unusual light, that they seem to lose their actual substance, and become things of intellect. Nothing is too small or too trifling to undergo this change, and acquire dignity thereby. A child's shoe; the doll, seated in her little wicker carriage; the hobby-horse;—whatever, in a word, has been used or played with, during the day, is now invested with a quality of strangeness and remoteness, though still almost as vividly present as by daylight. Thus, therefore, the floor of our familiar room has become a neutral territory, somewhere between the real world and fairy-land, where the Actual and the Imaginary may meet, and each imbue itself with the nature of the other. Ghosts might enter here, without affrighting us. It would be too much in keeping with the scene to excite surprise, were we to look about us and discover a form, beloved, but gone hence, now sitting quietly in a streak of this magic moonshine, with an aspect that would make us doubt whether it had returned from afar, or had never once stirred from our fireside.

The somewhat dim coal-fire has an essential influence in producing the effect which I would describe. It throws its unobtrusive tinge throughout the room, with a faint ruddiness upon the walls and ceiling, and a reflected gleam from the polish of the furniture. This warmer light mingles itself with the cold spirituality of the moonbeams, and communicates, as it were, a heart and sensibilities of human tenderness to the forms which fancy summons up. It converts them from snow-images into men and women. Glancing at the looking-glass, we behold—deep within its haunted verge—the smouldering glow of the half-extinguished anthracite, the white moonbeams on the floor, and a repetition of all the gleam and shadow of the picture, with one remove farther from the actual, and nearer to the imaginative. Then, at such an hour, and with this scene before him, if a man, sitting all alone, cannot dream strange things, and make them look like truth, he need never try to write romances.

But, for myself, during the whole of my Custom-House experience, moonlight and sunshine, and the glow of fire-light, were just alike in my regard; and neither of them was of one whit more avail than the twinkle of a tallow-candle. An entire class of susceptibilities, and a gift connected with them,—of no great richness or value, but the best I had,—was gone from me.

It is my belief, however, that, had I attempted a different order of composition, my faculties would not have been found so pointless and inefficacious. I might, for instance, have contented myself with writing out the narratives of a veteran shipmaster, one of the Inspectors, whom I should be most ungrateful not to mention; since scarcely a day passed that he did not stir me to laughter and admiration by his marvellous gifts as a story-teller. Could I have preserved the picturesque force of his style, and the humorous coloring which nature taught him how to throw over his descriptions, the result, I honestly believe, would have been something new in literature. Or I might readily have found a more serious task. It was a folly, with the materiality of this daily life pressing so intrusively upon me, to attempt to fling myself back into another age; or to insist on creating the semblance of a world out of airy matter, when, at every moment, the impalpable beauty of my soap-bubble was broken by the rude contact of some actual circumstance. The wiser effort would have been, to diffuse thought and imagination through the opaque substance of to-day, and thus to make it a bright transparency; to spiritualize the burden that began to weigh so heavily; to seek, resolutely, the true and indestructible value that lay hidden in the petty and wearisome incidents, and ordinary characters, with which I was now conversant. The fault was mine. The page of life that was spread out before me seemed dull and commonplace, only because I had not fathomed its deeper import. A better book than I shall ever write was there; leaf after leaf presenting itself to me, just as it was written out by the reality of the flitting hour, and vanishing as fast as written, only because my brain wanted the insight and my hand the cunning to transcribe it. At some future day, it may be, I shall remember a few scattered fragments and broken paragraphs, and write them down, and find the letters turn to gold upon the page.

These perceptions have come too late. At the instant, I was only conscious that what would have been a pleasure once was now a hopeless toil. There was no occasion to make much moan about this state of affairs. I had ceased to be a writer of tolerably poor tales and essays, and had become a tolerably good Surveyor of the Customs. That was all. But, nevertheless, it is any thing but agreeable to be haunted by a suspicion that one's intellect is dwindling away; or exhaling, without your consciousness, like ether out of a phial; so that, at every glance, you find a smaller and less volatile residuum. Of the fact, there could be no doubt; and, examining myself and others, I was led to conclusions in reference to the effect of public office on the character, not very favorable to the mode of life in question. In some other form, perhaps, I may hereafter develop these effects. Suffice it here to say, that a Custom-House officer, of long continuance, can hardly be a very praiseworthy or respectable personage, for many reasons; one of them, the tenure by which he holds his situation, and another, the very nature of his business, which—though, I trust, an honest one—is of such a sort that he does not share in the united effort of mankind.

An effect—which I believe to be observable, more or less, in every individual who has occupied the position—is, that, while he leans on the mighty arm of the Republic, his own proper strength departs from him. He loses, in an extent proportioned to the weakness or force of his original nature, the capability of self-support. If he possess an unusual share of native energy, or the enervating magic of place do not operate too long upon him, his forfeited powers may be redeemable. The ejected officer—fortunate in the unkindly shove that sends him forth betimes, to struggle amid a struggling world—may return to himself, and become all that he has ever been. But this seldom happens. He usually keeps his ground just long enough for his own ruin, and is then thrust out, with sinews all unstrung, to totter along the difficult footpath of life as he best may. Conscious of his own infirmity,—that his tempered steel and elasticity are lost,—he for ever afterwards looks wistfully about him in quest of support external to himself. His pervading and continual hope—a hallucination, which, in the face of all discouragement, and making light of impossibilities, haunts him while he lives, and, I fancy, like the convulsive throes of the cholera, torments him for a brief space after death—is, that, finally, and in no long time, by some happy coincidence of circumstances, he shall be restored to office. This faith, more than any thing else, steals the pith and availability out of whatever enterprise he may dream of undertaking. Why should he toil and moil, and be at so much trouble to pick himself up out of the mud, when, in a little while hence, the strong arm of his Uncle will raise and support him? Why should he work for his living here, or go to dig gold in California,[9] when he is so soon to be made happy, at monthly intervals, with a little pile of glittering coin out of his Uncle's pocket? It is sadly curious to observe how slight a taste of office suffices to infect a poor fellow with this singular disease. Uncle Sam's gold—meaning no disrespect to the worthy old gentleman—has, in this respect, a quality of enchantment like that of the Devil's wages. Whoever touches it should look well to himself, or he may find the bargain to go hard against him, involving, if not his soul, yet many of its better attributes; its sturdy force, its courage and constancy, its truth, its self-reliance, and all that gives the emphasis to manly character.

Here was a fine prospect in the distance! Not that the Surveyor brought the lesson home to himself, or admitted that he could be so utterly undone, either by continuance in office, or ejectment. Yet my reflections were not the most comfortable. I began to grow melancholy and restless; continually prying into my mind, to discover which of its poor properties were gone, and what degree of detriment had already accrued to the remainder. I endeavoured to calculate how much longer I could stay in the Custom-House, and yet go forth a man. To confess the truth, it was my greatest apprehension,—as it would never be a measure of policy to turn out so quiet an individual as myself, and it being hardly in the nature of a public officer to resign,—it was my chief trouble, therefore, that I was likely to grow gray and decrepit in the Surveyorship, and become much such another animal as the old Inspector. Might it not, in the tedious lapse of official life that lay before me, finally be with me as it was with this venerable friend,—to make the dinner-hour the nucleus of the day, and to spend the rest of it, as an old dog spends it, asleep in the sunshine or the shade? A dreary look-forward this, for a man who felt it to be the best definition of happiness to live throughout the whole range of his faculties and sensibilities! But, all this while, I was giving myself very unnecessary alarm. Providence had meditated better things for me than I could possibly imagine for myself.

A remarkable event of the third year of my Surveyorship—to adopt the tone of "P.P."—was the election of General Taylor to the Presidency.[1] It is essential, in order to a complete estimate of the advantages of official life, to view the incumbent at the in-coming of a hostile administration. His position is then one of the most singularly irksome, and, in every contingency,

9. Gold was discovered in California in 1848, setting off the Gold Rush of 1849.

1. Zachary Taylor (1784–1850), Whig president whose election in 1848 brought about Hawthorne's dismissal; Taylor died July 9, 1850, a few months after *The Scarlet Letter* was published.

disagreeable, that a wretched mortal can possibly occupy; with seldom an alternative of good, on either hand, although what presents itself to him as the worst event may very probably be the best. But it is a strange experience, to a man of pride and sensibility, to know that his interests are within the control of individuals who neither love nor understand him, and by whom, since one or the other must needs happen, he would rather be injured than obliged. Strange, too, for one who has kept his calmness throughout the contest, to observe the bloodthirstiness that is developed in the hour of triumph, and to be conscious that he is himself among its objects! There are few uglier traits of human nature than this tendency—which I now witnessed in men no worse than their neighbours—to grow cruel, merely because they possessed the power of inflicting harm. If the guillotine, as applied to office-holders, were a literal fact, instead of one of the most apt of metaphors, it is my sincere belief, that the active members of the victorious party were sufficiently excited to have chopped off all our heads, and have thanked Heaven for the opportunity! It appears to me—who have been a calm and curious observer, as well in victory as defeat—that this fierce and bitter spirit of malice and revenge has never distinguished the many triumphs of my own party as it now did that of the Whigs. The Democrats take the offices, as a general rule, because they need them, and because the practice of many years has made it the law of political warfare, which, unless a different system be proclaimed, it were weakness and cowardice to murmur at. But the long habit of victory has made them generous. They know how to spare, when they see occasion; and when they strike, the axe may be sharp, indeed, but its edge is seldom poisoned with ill-will; nor is it their custom ignominiously to kick the head which they have just struck off.

In short, unpleasant as was my predicament, at best, I saw much reason to congratulate myself that I was on the losing side, rather than the triumphant one. If, heretofore, I had been none of the warmest of partisans, I began now, at this season of peril and adversity, to be pretty acutely sensible with which party my predilections lay; nor was it without something like regret and shame, that, according to a reasonable calculation of chances, I saw my own prospect of retaining office to be better than those of my Democratic brethren. But who can see an inch into futurity, beyond his nose? My own head was the first that fell!

The moment when a man's head drops off is seldom or never, I am inclined to think, precisely the most agreeable of his life. Nevertheless, like the greater part of our misfortunes, even so serious a contingency brings its remedy and consolation with it, if the sufferer will but make the best, rather than the worst, of the accident which has befallen him. In my particular case, the consolatory topics were close at hand, and, indeed, had suggested themselves to my meditations a considerable time before it was requisite to use them. In view of my previous weariness of office, and vague thoughts of resignation, my fortune somewhat resembled that of a person who should entertain an idea of committing suicide, and, altogether beyond his hopes, meet with the good hap to be murdered. In the Custom-House, as before in the Old Manse, I had spent three years; a term long enough to rest a weary brain; long enough to break off old intellectual habits, and make room for new ones; long enough, and too long, to have lived in an unnatural state, doing what was really of no advantage nor delight to any human being, and withholding myself from toil that would, at least, have stilled an unquiet impulse in me. Then, moreover, as regarded his unceremonious ejectment, the late Surveyor was not altogether ill-pleased to be recognized by the Whigs as an enemy; since his inactivity in political affairs,—his tendency to roam, at will, in that broad and quiet field where all mankind may meet, rather than confine himself to those narrow paths where brethren of the same household must diverge from one another,—had sometimes made it questionable with his brother Democrats whether he was a friend. Now, after he had won the crown of martyrdom, (though with no longer a head to wear it on,) the point might be looked upon as settled. Finally, little heroic as he was, it seemed more decorous to be overthrown in the downfall of the party with which he had been content to stand, than to remain a forlorn survivor, when so many worthier men were falling; and, at last, after subsisting for four years on the mercy of a hostile administration, to be compelled then to define his position anew, and claim the yet more humiliating mercy of a friendly one.

Meanwhile, the press had taken up my affair, and kept me, for a week or two, careering through the public prints, in my decapitated state, like Irving's Headless Horseman;[2] ghastly and grim, and longing to be buried, as a politically dead man ought. So much for my figurative self. The real human being, all this time, with his head safely on his shoulders, had brought himself to the comfortable conclusion, that every thing was for the best; and, making an investment in ink, paper, and steel-pens, had opened his long-disused writing-desk, and was again a literary man.

Now it was, that the lucubrations of my ancient predecessor, Mr. Surveyor Pue, came into play. Rusty through long idleness, some little space was requisite before my intellectual machinery could be brought to work upon the tale, with an effect in any degree satisfactory. Even yet, though my thoughts were ultimately much absorbed in the task, it wears, to my eye, a stern and sombre aspect; too much ungladdened by genial sunshine; too little relieved by the tender and familiar influences which soften almost every scene of nature and real life, and, undoubtedly, should soften every picture of them. This uncaptivating effect is perhaps due to the period of hardly accomplished revolution, and still seething turmoil, in which the story shaped itself. It is no indication, however, of a lack of cheerfulness in the writer's mind; for he was happier, while straying through the gloom of these sunless fantasies, than at any time since he had quitted the Old Manse. Some of the briefer articles, which contribute to make up the volume, have likewise been written since my involuntary withdrawal from the toils and honors of public life, and the remainder are gleaned from annuals and magazines, of such antique date that they have gone round the circle, and come back to novelty again.[3] Keeping up the metaphor of the political guillotine, the whole may be considered as the POSTHUMOUS PAPERS OF A DECAPITATED SURVEYOR; and the sketch which I am now bringing to a close, if too autobiographical for a modest person to publish in his lifetime, will readily be excused in a gentleman who writes from beyond

2. In Washington Irving's "The Legend of Sleepy Hollow." "Careering": running headlong.

3. At the time of writing this article, the author intended to publish, along with 'The Scarlet Letter,' several shorter tales and sketches. These it has been thought advisable to defer [Hawthorne's note].

the grave. Peace be with all the world! My blessing on my friends! My forgiveness to my enemies! For I am in the realm of quiet!

The life of the Custom-House lies like a dream behind me. The old Inspector,—who, by the by, I regret to say, was overthrown and killed by a horse, some time ago; else he would certainly have lived for ever,—he, and all those other venerable personages who sat with him at the receipt of custom, are but shadows in my view; white-headed and wrinkled images, which my fancy used to sport with, and has now flung aside for ever. The merchants,—Pingree, Phillips, Shepard, Upton, Kimball, Bertram, Hunt,—these, and many other names, which had such a classic familiarity for my ear six months ago,—these men of traffic, who seemed to occupy so important a position in the world,—how little time has it required to disconnect me from them all, not merely in act, but recollection! It is with an effort that I recall the figures and appellations of these few. Soon, likewise, my old native town will loom upon me through the haze of memory, a mist brooding over and around it; as if it were no portion of the real earth, but an overgrown village in cloud-land, with only imaginary inhabitants to people its wooden houses, and walk its homely lanes, and the unpicturesque prolixity of its main street. Henceforth, it ceases to be a reality of my life. I am a citizen of somewhere else. My good townspeople will not much regret me; for—though it has been as dear an object as any, in my literary efforts, to be of some importance in their eyes, and to win myself a pleasant memory in this abode and burial-place of so many of my forefathers—there has never been, for me, the genial atmosphere which a literary man requires, in order to ripen the best harvest of his mind. I shall do better amongst other faces; and these familiar ones, it need hardly be said, will do just as well without me.

It may be, however,—O, transporting and triumphant thought!—that the great-grandchildren of the present race may sometimes think kindly of the scribbler of bygone days, when the antiquary of days to come, among the sites memorable in the town's history, shall point out the locality of THE TOWN-PUMP![4]

The Scarlet Letter

I. The Prison-door

A throng of bearded men, in sad-colored garments and gray, steeple-crowned hats, intermixed with women, some wearing hoods, and others bareheaded, was assembled in front of a wooden edifice, the door of which was heavily timbered with oak, and studded with iron spikes.

The founders of a new colony, whatever Utopia of human virtue and happiness they might originally project, have invariably recognized it among their earliest practical necessities to allot a portion of the virgin soil as a cemetery, and another portion as the site of a prison. In accordance with this rule, it may safely be assumed that the forefathers of Boston had built the first prison-house, somewhere in the vicinity of Cornhill, almost as sea-

4. "A Rill from the Town-Pump" (1835), one of Hawthorne's best-known sketches at the time.

sonably as they marked out the first burial-ground, on Isaac Johnson's lot and round about his grave, which subsequently became the nucleus of all the congregated sepulchres in the old church-yard of King's Chapel.[1] Certain it is, that, some fifteen or twenty years[2] after the settlement of the town, the wooden jail was already marked with weather-stains and other indications of age, which gave a yet darker aspect to its beetle-browed and gloomy front. The rust on the ponderous iron-work of its oaken door looked more antique than any thing else in the new world. Like all that pertains to crime, it seemed never to have known a youthful era. Before this ugly edifice, and between it and the wheel-track of the street, was a grass-plot, much overgrown with burdock, pig-weed, apple-peru, and such unsightly vegetation, which evidently found something congenial in the soil that had so early borne the black flower of civilized society, a prison. But, on one side of the portal, and rooted almost at the threshold, was a wild rose-bush, covered, in this month of June, with its delicate gems, which might be imagined to offer their fragrance and fragile beauty to the prisoner as he went in, and to the condemned criminal as he came forth to his doom, in token that the deep heart of Nature could pity and be kind to him.

This rose-bush, by a strange chance, has been kept alive in history; but whether it had merely survived out of the stern old wilderness, so long after the fall of the gigantic pines and oaks that originally overshadowed it,—or whether, as there is fair authority for believing, it had sprung up under the footsteps of the sainted Ann Hutchinson,[3] as she entered the prison-door,—we shall not take upon us to determine. Finding it so directly on the threshold of our narrative, which is now about to issue from that inauspicious portal, we could hardly do otherwise than pluck one of its flowers and present it to the reader. It may serve, let us hope, to symbolize some sweet moral blossom, that may be found along the track, or relieve the darkening close of a tale of human frailty and sorrow.

II. The Market-place

The grass-plot before the jail, in Prison Lane, on a certain summer morning, not less than two centuries ago, was occupied by a pretty large number of the inhabitants of Boston; all with their eyes intently fastened on the iron-clamped oaken door. Amongst any other population, or at a later period in the history of New England, the grim rigidity that petrified the bearded physiognomies of these good people would have augured some awful business in hand. It could have betokened nothing short of the anticipated execution of some noted culprit, on whom the sentence of a legal tribunal had but confirmed the verdict of public sentiment. But, in that early severity of the Puritan character, an inference of this kind could not so indubitably be drawn. It might be that a sluggish bond-servant, or an undutiful child, whom his

1. The first Anglican Church in Boston, built in 1688. Isaac Johnson (1601–1630) died in the first year of the settlement of Boston; his land went to public uses.
2. "Some fifteen or twenty years" would mean roughly 1645–50, but Hawthorne's use of Governor Winthrop's death in ch. 12 suggests that the action of the novel (except the "Conclusion") covers 1642 to 1649.
3. Hutchinson (1591–1643) hosted prayer meetings for women and criticized Boston's Puritan ministers for allegedly emphasizing the importance of good works over faith. In 1638 she was banished to Rhode Island where she was later killed by American Indians.

parents had given over to the civil authority, was to be corrected at the whipping-post. It might be, that an Antinomian,[4] a Quaker, or other heterodox religionist, was to be scourged out of the town, or an idle and vagrant Indian, whom the white man's fire-water had made riotous about the streets, was to be driven with stripes into the shadow of the forest. It might be, too, that a witch, like old Mistress Hibbins,[5] the bitter-tempered widow of the magistrate, was to die upon the gallows. In either case, there was very much the same solemnity of demeanour on the part of the spectators; as befitted a people amongst whom religion and law were almost identical, and in whose character both were so thoroughly interfused, that the mildest and the severest acts of public discipline were alike made venerable and awful. Meagre, indeed, and cold, was the sympathy that a transgressor might look for, from such bystanders at the scaffold. On the other hand, a penalty which, in our days, would infer a degree of mocking infamy and ridicule, might then be invested with almost as stern a dignity as the punishment of death itself.

It was a circumstance to be noted, on the summer morning when our story begins its course, that the women, of whom there were several in the crowd, appeared to take a peculiar interest in whatever penal infliction might be expected to ensue. The age had not so much refinement, that any sense of impropriety restrained the wearers of petticoat and farthingale[6] from stepping forth into the public ways, and wedging their not unsubstantial persons, if occasion were, into the throng nearest to the scaffold at an execution. Morally, as well as materially, there was a coarser fibre in those wives and maidens of old English birth and breeding, than in their fair descendants, separated from them by a series of six or seven generations; for, throughout that chain of ancestry, every successive mother has transmitted to her child a fainter bloom, a more delicate and briefer beauty, and a slighter physical frame, if not a character of less force and solidity, than her own. The women, who were now standing about the prison-door, stood within less than half a century of the period when the man-like Elizabeth[7] had been the not altogether unsuitable representative of the sex. They were her countrywomen; and the beef and ale of their native land, with a moral diet not a whit more refined, entered largely into their composition. The bright morning sun, therefore, shone on broad shoulders and well-developed busts, and on round and ruddy cheeks, that had ripened in the far-off island, and had hardly yet grown paler or thinner in the atmosphere of New England. There was, moreover, a boldness and rotundity of speech among these matrons, as most of them seemed to be, that would startle us at the present day, whether in respect to its purport or its volume of tone.

"Goodwives," said a hard-featured dame of fifty, "I'll tell ye a piece of my mind. It would be greatly for the public behoof,[8] if we women, being of mature age and church-members in good repute, should have the handling of such malefactresses as this Hester Prynne. What think ye, gossips?[9] If the hussy stood up for judgment before us five, that are now here in a knot

4. One who believes that salvation comes through grace rather than good works.
5. A real Ann Hibbins was tried for witchcraft in 1655 and executed in 1656.
6. Hoop skirt.
7. Queen Elizabeth I reigned from 1558 to 1603.
8. Benefit.
9. Friends or companions (female); originally, kinspeople.

together, would she come off with such a sentence as the worshipful magistrates have awarded? Marry, I trow[1] not!"

"People say," said another, "that the Reverend Master Dimmesdale, her godly pastor, takes it very grievously to heart that such a scandal should have come upon his congregation."

"The magistrates are God-fearing gentlemen, but merciful overmuch,—that is a truth," added a third autumnal matron. "At the very least, they should have put the brand of a hot iron on Hester Prynne's forehead. Madam Hester would have winced at that, I warrant me. But she,—the naughty baggage,—little will she care what they put upon the bodice of her gown! Why, look you, she may cover it with a brooch, or such like heathenish adornment, and so walk the streets as brave as ever!"

"Ah, but," interposed, more softly, a young wife, holding a child by the hand, "let her cover the mark as she will, the pang of it will be always in her heart."

"What do we talk of marks and brands, whether on the bodice of her gown, or the flesh of her forehead?" cried another female, the ugliest as well as the most pitiless of these self-constituted judges. "This woman has brought shame upon us all, and ought to die. Is there not law for it? Truly there is, both in the Scripture[2] and the statute-book. Then let the magistrates, who have made it of no effect, thank themselves if their own wives and daughters go astray!"

"Mercy on us, goodwife," exclaimed a man in the crowd, "is there no virtue in woman, save what springs from a wholesome fear of the gallows? That is the hardest word yet! Hush, now, gossips; for the lock is turning in the prison-door, and here comes Mistress Prynne herself."

The door of the jail being flung open from within, there appeared, in the first place, like a black shadow emerging into the sunshine, the grim and grisly presence of the town-beadle,[3] with a sword by his side and his staff of office in his hand. The personage prefigured and represented in his aspect the whole dismal severity of the Puritanic code of law, which it was his business to administer in its final and closest application to the offender. Stretching forth the official staff in his left hand, he laid his right upon the shoulder of a young woman, whom he thus drew forward; until, on the threshold of the prison-door, she repelled him, by an action marked with natural dignity and force of character, and stepped into the open air, as if by her own free-will. She bore in her arms a child, a baby of some three months old, who winked and turned aside its little face from the too vivid light of day; because its existence, heretofore, had brought it acquainted only with the gray twilight of a dungeon, or other darksome apartment of the prison.

When the young woman—the mother of this child—stood fully revealed before the crowd, it seemed to be her first impulse to clasp the infant closely to her bosom; not so much by an impulse of motherly affection, as that she might thereby conceal a certain token, which was wrought or fastened into her dress. In a moment, however, wisely judging that one token of her shame

1. Think, suppose.
2. "And the man that committeth adultery with another man's wife, even he that committeth adultery with his neighbor's wife, the adulterer and the adulteress shall surely be put to death" (Leviticus 20.10).
3. A constable.

would but poorly serve to hide another, she took the baby on her arm, and, with a burning blush, and yet a haughty smile, and a glance that would not be abashed, looked around at her townspeople and neighbours. On the breast of her gown, in fine red cloth, surrounded with an elaborate embroidery and fantastic flourishes of gold thread, appeared the letter A. It was so artistically done, and with so much fertility and gorgeous luxuriance of fancy, that it had all the effect of a last and fitting decoration to the apparel which she wore; and which was of a splendor in accordance with the taste of the age, but greatly beyond what was allowed by the sumptuary regulations[4] of the colony.

The young woman was tall, with a figure of perfect elegance, on a large scale. She had dark and abundant hair, so glossy that it threw off the sunshine with a gleam, and a face which, besides being beautiful from regularity of feature and richness of complexion, had the impressiveness belonging to a marked brow and deep black eyes. She was lady-like, too, after the manner of the feminine gentility of those days; characterized by a certain state and dignity, rather than by the delicate, evanescent, and indescribable grace, which is now recognized as its indication. And never had Hester Prynne appeared more lady-like, in the antique interpretation of the term, than as she issued from the prison. Those who had before known her, and had expected to behold her dimmed and obscured by a disastrous cloud, were astonished, and even startled, to perceive how her beauty shone out, and made a halo of the misfortune and ignominy in which she was enveloped. It may be true, that, to a sensitive observer, there was something exquisitely painful in it. Her attire, which, indeed, she had wrought for the occasion, in prison, and had modelled much after her own fancy, seemed to express the attitude of her spirit, the desperate recklessness of her mood, by its wild and picturesque peculiarity. But the point which drew all eyes, and, as it were, transfigured the wearer,—so that both men and women, who had been familiarly acquainted with Hester Prynne, were now impressed as if they beheld her for the first time,—was that SCARLET LETTER, so fantastically embroidered and illuminated upon her bosom. It had the effect of a spell, taking her out of the ordinary relations with humanity, and inclosing her in a sphere by herself.

"She hath good skill at her needle, that's certain," remarked one of the female spectators; "but did ever a woman, before this brazen hussy, contrive such a way of showing it! Why, gossips, what is it but to laugh in the faces of our godly magistrates, and make a pride out of what they, worthy gentlemen, meant for a punishment?"

"It were well," muttered the most iron-visaged of the old dames, "if we stripped Madam Hester's rich gown off her dainty shoulders; and as for the red letter, which she hath stitched so curiously, I'll bestow a rag of mine own rheumatic flannel, to make a fitter one!"

"O, peace, neighbours, peace!" whispered their youngest companion. "Do not let her hear you! Not a stitch in that embroidered letter, but she has felt it in her heart."

The grim beadle now made a gesture with his staff.

4. Regulations governing elaborateness of apparel allowed to various social ranks.

"Make way, good people, make way, in the King's name," cried he. "Open a passage; and, I promise ye, Mistress Prynne shall be set where man, woman, and child may have a fair sight of her brave apparel, from this time till an hour past meridian. A blessing on the righteous Colony of the Massachusetts, where iniquity is dragged out into the sunshine! Come along, Madam Hester, and show your scarlet letter in the market-place!"

A lane was forthwith opened through the crowd of spectators. Preceded by the beadle, and attended by an irregular procession of stern-browed men and unkindly-visaged women, Hester Prynne set forth towards the place appointed for her punishment. A crowd of eager and curious schoolboys, understanding little of the matter in hand, except that it gave them a half-holiday, ran before her progress, turning their heads continually to stare into her face, and at the winking baby in her arms, and at the ignominious letter on her breast. It was no great distance, in those days, from the prison-door to the market-place. Measured by the prisoner's experience, however, it might be reckoned a journey of some length; for, haughty as her deameanour was, she perchance underwent an agony from every footstep of those that thronged to see her, as if her heart had been flung into the street for them all to spurn and trample upon. In our nature, however, there is a provision, alike marvellous and merciful, that the sufferer should never know the intensity of what he endures by its present torture, but chiefly by the pang that rankles after it. With almost a serene deportment, therefore, Hester Prynne passed through this portion of her ordeal, and came to a sort of scaffold, at the western extremity of the market-place. It stood nearly beneath the eaves of Boston's earliest church, and appeared to be a fixture there.

In fact, this scaffold constituted a portion of a penal machine, which now, for two or three generations past, has been merely historical and traditionary among us, but was held, in the old time, to be as effectual an agent in the promotion of good citizenship, as ever was the guillotine among the terrorists of France.[5] It was, in short, the platform of the pillory; and above it rose the framework of that instrument of discipline, so fashioned as to confine the human head in its tight grasp, and thus hold it up to the public gaze. The very ideal of ignominy was embodied and made manifest in this contrivance of wood and iron. There can be no outrage, methinks, against our common nature,—whatever be the delinquencies of the individual,—no outrage more flagrant than to forbid the culprit to hide his face for shame; as it was the essence of this punishment to do. In Hester Prynne's instance, however, as not unfrequently in other cases, her sentence bore, that she should stand a certain time upon the platform, but without undergoing that gripe[6] about the neck and confinement of the head, the proneness to which was the most devilish characteristic of this ugly engine. Knowing well her part, she ascended a flight of wooden steps, and was thus displayed to the surrounding multitude, at about the height of a man's shoulders above the street.

Had there been a Papist among the crowd of Puritans, he might have seen in this beautiful woman, so picturesque in her attire and mien, and with the infant at her bosom, an object to remind him of the image of Divine Maternity, which so many illustrious painters have vied with one another to

5. During the Reign of Terror (1793–94).

6. Grip (variant spelling).

represent; something which should remind him, indeed, but only by contrast, of that sacred image of sinless motherhood, whose infant was to redeem the world. Here, there was the taint of deepest sin in the most sacred quality of human life, working such effect, that the world was only the darker for this woman's beauty, and the more lost for the infant that she had borne.

The scene was not without a mixture of awe, such as must always invest the spectacle of guilt and shame in a fellow-creature, before society shall have grown corrupt enough to smile, instead of shuddering, at it. The witnesses of Hester Prynne's disgrace had not yet passed beyond their simplicity. They were stern enough to look upon her death, had that been the sentence, without a murmur at its severity, but had none of the heartlessness of another social state, which would find only a theme for jest in an exhibition like the present. Even had there been a disposition to turn the matter into ridicule, it must have been repressed and overpowered by the solemn presence of men no less dignified than the Governor, and several of his counsellors, a judge, a general, and the ministers of the town; all of whom sat or stood in a balcony of the meeting-house, looking down upon the platform. When such personages could constitute a part of the spectacle, without risking the majesty or reverence of rank and office, it was safely to be inferred that the infliction of a legal sentence would have an earnest and effectual meaning. Accordingly, the crowd was sombre and grave. The unhappy culprit sustained herself as best a woman might, under the heavy weight of a thousand unrelenting eyes, all fastened upon her, and concentred at her bosom. It was almost intolerable to be borne. Of an impulsive and passionate nature, she had fortified herself to encounter the stings and venomous stabs of public contumely, wreaking itself in every variety of insult; but there was a quality so much more terrible in the solemn mood of the popular mind, that she longed rather to behold all those rigid countenances contorted with scornful merriment, and herself the object. Had a roar of laughter burst from the multitude,—each man, each woman, each little shrill-voiced child, contributing their individual parts,—Hester Prynne might have repaid them all with a bitter and disdainful smile. But, under the leaden infliction which it was her doom to endure, she felt, at moments, as if she must needs shriek out with the full power of her lungs, and cast herself from the scaffold down upon the ground, or else go mad at once.

Yet there were intervals when the whole scene, in which she was the most conspicuous object, seemed to vanish from her eyes, or, at least, glimmered indistinctly before them, like a mass of imperfectly shaped and spectral images. Her mind, and especially her memory, was preternaturally active, and kept bringing up other scenes than this roughly hewn street of a little town, on the edge of the Western wilderness; other faces than were lowering upon her from beneath the brims of those steeple-crowned hats. Reminiscences, the most trifling and immaterial, passages of infancy and school-days, sports, childish quarrels, and the little domestic traits of her maiden years, came swarming back upon her, intermingled with recollections of whatever was gravest in her subsequent life; one picture precisely as vivid as another; as if all were of similar importance, or all alike a play. Possibly, it was an instinctive device of her spirit, to relieve itself, by the exhibition of these phantasmagoric forms, from the cruel weight and hardness of the reality.

Be that as it might, the scaffold of the pillory was a point of view that revealed to Hester Prynne the entire track along which she had been treading, since her happy infancy. Standing on that miserable eminence, she saw again her native village, in Old England, and her paternal home; a decayed house of gray stone, with a poverty-stricken aspect, but retaining a half-obliterated shield of arms over the portal, in token of antique gentility. She saw her father's face, with its bald brow, and reverend white beard, that flowed over the old-fashioned Elizabethan ruff;[7] her mother's, too, with the look of heedful and anxious love which it always wore in her remembrance, and which, even since her death, had so often laid the impediment of a gentle remonstrance in her daughter's pathway. She saw her own face, glowing with girlish beauty, and illuminating all the interior of the dusky mirror in which she had been wont to gaze at it. There she beheld another countenance, of a man well stricken in years, a pale, thin, scholar-like visage, with eyes dim and bleared by the lamp-light that had served them to pore over many ponderous books. Yet those same bleared optics had a strange, penetrating power, when it was their owner's purpose to read the human soul. This figure of the study and the cloister, as Hester Prynne's womanly fancy failed not to recall, was slightly deformed, with the left shoulder a trifle higher than the right. Next rose before her, in memory's picture-gallery, the intricate and narrow thoroughfares, the tall, gray houses, the huge cathedrals, and the public edifices, ancient in date and quaint in architecture, of a Continental city,[8] where a new life had awaited her, still in connection with the misshapen scholar; a new life, but feeding itself on time-worn materials, like a tuft of green moss on a crumbling wall. Lastly, in lieu of these shifting scenes, came back the rude market-place of the Puritan settlement, with all the townspeople assembled and levelling their stern regards at Hester Prynne,—yes, at herself,—who stood on the scaffold of the pillory, an infant on her arm, and the letter A, in scarlet, fantastically embroidered with gold thread, upon her bosom!

Could it be true? She clutched the child so fiercely to her breast, that it sent forth a cry; she turned her eyes downward at the scarlet letter, and even touched it with her finger, to assure herself that the infant and the shame were real. Yes!—these were her realities,—all else had vanished!

III. The Recognition

From this intense consciousness of being the object of severe and universal observation, the wearer of the scarlet letter was at length relieved by discerning, on the outskirts of the crowd, a figure which irresistibly took possession of her thoughts. An Indian, in his native garb, was standing there; but the red men were not so infrequent visitors of the English settlements, that one of them would have attracted any notice from Hester Prynne, at such a time; much less would he have excluded all other objects and ideas from her mind. By the Indian's side, and evidently sustaining a companionship

7. Elaborate, stiffly starched collar worn by the wealthier classes (men and women) in the 16th and 17th centuries.
8. Amsterdam (as noted in the next chapter), where many English Separatists and Puritans gathered before gaining permission to settle in the colonies.

with him, stood a white man, clad in a strange disarray of civilized and savage costume.

He was small in stature, with a furrowed visage, which, as yet, could hardly be termed aged. There was a remarkable intelligence in his features, as of a person who had so cultivated his mental part that it could not fail to mould the physical to itself, and become manifest by unmistakable tokens. Although, by a seemingly careless arrangement of his heterogeneous garb, he had endeavoured to conceal or abate the peculiarity, it was sufficiently evident to Hester Prynne, that one of this man's shoulders rose higher than the other. Again, at the first instant of perceiving that thin visage, and the slight deformity of the figure, she pressed her infant to her bosom, with so convulsive a force that the poor babe uttered another cry of pain. But the mother did not seem to hear it.

At his arrival in the market-place, and some time before she saw him, the stranger had bent his eyes on Hester Prynne. It was carelessly, at first, like a man chiefly accustomed to look inward, and to whom external matters are of little value and import, unless they bear relation to something within his mind. Very soon, however, his look became keen and penetrative. A writhing horror twisted itself across his features, like a snake gliding swiftly over them, and making one little pause, with all its wreathed intervolutions in open sight. His face darkened with some powerful emotion, which, nevertheless, he so instantaneously controlled by an effort of his will, that, save at a single moment, its expression might have passed for calmness. After a brief space, the convulsion grew almost imperceptible, and finally subsided into the depths of his nature. When he found the eyes of Hester Prynne fastened on his own, and saw that she appeared to recognize him, he slowly and calmly raised his finger, made a gesture with it in the air, and laid it on his lips.

Then, touching the shoulder of a townsman who stood next to him, he addressed him in a formal and courteous manner.

"I pray you, good Sir," said he, "who is this woman?—and wherefore is she here set up to public shame?"

"You must needs be a stranger in this region, friend," answered the townsman, looking curiously at the questioner and his savage companion; "else you would surely have heard of Mistress Hester Prynne, and her evil doings. She hath raised a great scandal, I promise you, in godly Master Dimmesdale's church."

"You say truly," replied the other. "I am a stranger, and have been a wanderer, sorely against my will. I have met with grievous mishaps by sea and land, and have been long held in bonds among the heathen-folk, to the southward; and am now brought hither by this Indian, to be redeemed out of my captivity. Will it please you, therefore, to tell me of Hester Prynne's,—have I her name rightly?—of this woman's offences, and what has brought her to yonder scaffold?"

"Truly, friend, and methinks it must gladden your heart, after your troubles and sojourn in the wilderness," said the townsman, "to find yourself, at length, in a land where iniquity is searched out, and punished in the sight of rulers and people; as here in our godly New England. Yonder woman, Sir, you must know, was the wife of a certain learned man, English by birth, but who had long dwelt in Amsterdam, whence, some good time agone, he was minded to cross over and cast in his lot with us of the Massachusetts. To this purpose, he sent his wife before him, remaining himself to look after some necessary affairs. Marry, good Sir, in some two years, or less, that the woman has been a dweller here in Boston, no tidings have come of this learned gentleman, Master Prynne; and his young wife, look you, being left to her own misguidance——"

"Ah!—aha!—I conceive you," said the stranger, with a bitter smile. "So learned a man as you speak of should have learned this too in his books. And who, by your favor, Sir, may be the father of yonder babe—it is some three or four months old, I should judge—which Mistress Prynne is holding in her arms?"

"Of a truth, friend, that matter remaineth a riddle; and the Daniel who shall expound it is yet a-wanting,"[9] answered the townsman. "Madam Hester absolutely refuseth to speak, and the magistrates have laid their heads together in vain. Peradventure the guilty one stands looking on at this sad spectacle, unknown of man, and forgetting that God sees him."

"The learned man," observed the stranger, with another smile, "should come himself to look into the mystery."

"It behooves him well, if he be still in life," responded the townsman. "Now, good Sir, our Massachusetts magistracy, bethinking themselves that this woman is youthful and fair, and doubtless was strongly tempted to her fall;—and that, moreover, as is most likely, her husband may be at the bottom of the sea;—they have not been bold to put in force the extremity of our righteous law against her. The penalty thereof is death. But, in their great mercy and tenderness of heart, they have doomed Mistress Prynne to stand only a space of three hours on the platform of the pillory, and then and thereafter, for the remainder of her natural life, to wear a mark of shame upon her bosom."

"A wise sentence!" remarked the stranger, gravely bowing his head. "Thus she will be a living sermon against sin, until the ignominious letter be engraved upon her tombstone. It irks me, nevertheless, that the partner of her iniquity should not, at least, stand on the scaffold by her side. But he will be known!—he will be known!—he will be known!"

He bowed courteously to the communicative townsman, and, whispering a few words to his Indian attendant, they both made their way through the crowd.

While this passed, Hester Prynne had been standing on her pedestal, still with a fixed gaze towards the stranger; so fixed a gaze, that, at moments of intense absorption, all other objects in the visible world seemed to vanish, leaving only him and her. Such an interview, perhaps, would have been more terrible than even to meet him as she now did, with the hot, midday sun burning down upon her face, and lighting up its shame; with the scarlet token of infamy on her breast; with the sin-born infant in her arms; with a whole people, drawn forth as to a festival, staring at the features that should have been seen only in the quiet gleam of the fireside, in the happy shadow of a home, or beneath a matronly veil, at church. Dreadful as it was, she was conscious of a shelter in the presence of these thousand witnesses. It was better to stand thus, with so many betwixt him and her, than to greet him, face

9. Allusion to Daniel's interpretation of the handwriting on the wall during the Babylonian king Belshazzar's great feast (Daniel 5.12).

to face, they two alone. She fled for refuge, as it were, to the public exposure, and dreaded the moment when its protection should be withdrawn from her. Involved in these thoughts, she scarcely heard a voice behind her, until it had repeated her name more than once, in a loud and solemn tone, audible to the whole multitude.

"Hearken unto me, Hester Prynne!" said the voice.

It has already been noticed, that directly over the platform on which Hester Prynne stood was a kind of balcony, or open gallery, appended to the meeting-house. It was the place whence proclamations were wont to be made, amidst an assemblage of the magistracy, with all the ceremonial that attended such public observances in those days. Here, to witness the scene which we are describing, sat Governor Bellingham himself with four sergeants about his chair, bearing halberds,[1] as a guard of honor. He wore a dark feather in his hat, a border of embroidery on his cloak, and a black velvet tunic beneath; a gentleman advanced in years, and with a hard experience written in his wrinkles. He was not ill fitted to be the head and representative of a community, which owed its origin and progress, and its present state of development, not to the impulses of youth, but to the stern and tempered energies of manhood, and the sombre sagacity of age; accomplishing so much, precisely because it imagined and hoped so little. The other eminent characters, by whom the chief ruler was surrounded, were distinguished by a dignity of mien, belonging to a period when the forms of authority were felt to possess the sacredness of divine institutions. They were, doubtless, good men, just, and sage. But, out of the whole human family, it would not have been easy to select the same number of wise and virtuous persons, who should be less capable of sitting in judgment on an erring woman's heart, and disentangling its mesh of good and evil, than the sages of rigid aspect towards whom Hester Prynne now turned her face. She seemed conscious, indeed, that whatever sympathy she might expect lay in the larger and warmer heart of the multitude; for, as she lifted her eyes towards the balcony, the unhappy woman grew pale and trembled.

The voice which had called her attention was that of the reverend and famous John Wilson,[2] the eldest clergyman of Boston, a great scholar, like most of his contemporaries in the profession, and withal a man of kind and genial spirit. This last attribute, however, had been less carefully developed than his intellectual gifts, and was, in truth, rather a matter of shame than self-congratulation with him. There he stood, with a border of grizzled locks beneath his skull-cap; while his gray eyes, accustomed to the shaded light of his study, were winking, like those of Hester's infant, in the unadulterated sunshine. He looked like the darkly engraved portraits which we see prefixed to old volumes of sermons; and had no more right than one of those portraits would have, to step forth, as he now did, and meddle with a question of human guilt, passion, and anguish.

1. Long-handled weapons with an ax on one side and a steel spike on the other. The historical Richard Bellingham (c. 1592–1672) came to Boston in 1634 and was governor in 1641, 1654, and 1665–72.

2. The historical John Wilson (1588–1667) was a Congregational minister who came to Boston with the first settlers, in 1630. Hutchinson had criticized the preaching of Wilson in particular; at Hutchinson's trial of 1638, it was Wilson who excommunicated her.

"Hester Prynne," said the clergyman, "I have striven with my young brother here, under whose preaching of the word you have been privileged to sit,"—here Mr. Wilson laid his hand on the shoulder of a pale young man beside him,—"I have sought, I say, to persuade this godly youth, that he should deal with you, here in the face of Heaven, and before these wise and upright rulers, and in hearing of all the people, as touching the vileness and blackness of your sin. Knowing your natural temper better than I, he could the better judge what arguments to use, whether of tenderness or terror, such as might prevail over your hardness and obstinacy; insomuch that you should no longer hide the name of him who tempted you to this grievous fall. But he opposes to me, (with a young man's oversoftness, albeit wise beyond his years,) that it were wronging the very nature of woman to force her to lay open her heart's secrets in such broad daylight, and in presence of so great a multitude. Truly, as I sought to convince him, the shame lay in the commission of the sin, and not in the showing of it forth. What say you to it, once again, brother Dimmesdale? Must it be thou or I that shall deal with this poor sinner's soul?"

There was a murmur among the dignified and reverend occupants of the balcony; and Governor Bellingham gave expression to its purport, speaking in an authoritative voice, although tempered with respect towards the youthful clergyman whom he addressed.

"Good Master Dimmesdale," said he, "the responsibility of this woman's soul lies greatly with you. It behooves you, therefore, to exhort her to repentance, and to confession, as a proof and consequence thereof."

The directness of this appeal drew the eyes of the whole crowd upon the Reverend Mr. Dimmesdale; a young clergyman, who had come from one of the great English universities, bringing all the learning of the age into our wild forest-land. His eloquence and religious fervor had already given the earnest of high eminence in his profession. He was a person of very striking aspect, with a white, lofty, and impending brow, large, brown, melancholy eyes, and a mouth which, unless when he forcibly compressed it, was apt to be tremulous, expressing both nervous sensibility and a vast power of self-restraint. Notwithstanding his high native gifts and scholar-like attainments, there was an air about this young minister,—an apprehensive, a startled, a half-frightened look,—as of a being who felt himself quite astray and at a loss in the pathway of human existence, and could only be at ease in some seclusion of his own. Therefore, so far as his duties would permit, he trode in the shadowy by-paths, and thus kept himself simple and childlike; coming forth, when occasion was, with a freshness, and fragrance, and dewy purity of thought, which, as many people said, affected them like the speech of an angel.

Such was the young man whom the Reverend Mr. Wilson and the Governor had introduced so openly to the public notice, bidding him speak, in the hearing of all men, to that mystery of a woman's soul, so sacred even in its pollution. The trying nature of his position drove the blood from his cheek, and made his lips tremulous.

"Speak to the woman, my brother," said Mr. Wilson. "It is of moment to her soul, and therefore, as the worshipful Governor says, momentous to thine own, in whose charge hers is. Exhort her to confess the truth!"

The Reverend Mr. Dimmesdale bent his head, in silent prayer, as it seemed, and then came forward.

"Hester Prynne," said he, leaning over the balcony, and looking down steadfastly into her eyes, "thou hearest what this good man says, and seest the accountability under which I labor. If thou feelest it to be for thy soul's peace, and that thy earthly punishment will thereby be made more effectual to salvation, I charge thee to speak out the name of thy fellow-sinner and fellow sufferer! Be not silent from any mistaken pity and tenderness for him; for, believe me, Hester, though he were to step down from a high place, and stand there beside thee, on thy pedestal of shame, yet better were it so, than to hide a guilty heart through life. What can thy silence do for him, except it tempt him—yea, compel him, as it were—to add hypocrisy to sin? Heaven hath granted thee an open ignominy, that thereby thou mayest work out an open triumph over the evil within thee, and the sorrow without. Take heed how thou deniest to him—who, perchance, hath not the courage to grasp it for himself—the bitter, but wholesome, cup that is now presented to thy lips!"

The young pastor's voice was tremulously sweet, rich, deep, and broken. The feeling that it so evidently manifested, rather than the direct purport of the words, caused it to vibrate within all hearts, and brought the listeners into one accord of sympathy. Even the poor baby, at Hester's bosom, was affected by the same influence; for it directed its hitherto vacant gaze towards Mr. Dimmesdale, and held up its little arms, with half pleased, half plaintive murmur. So powerful seemed the minister's appeal, that the people could not believe but that Hester Prynne would speak out the guilty name; or else that the guilty one himself, in whatever high or lowly place he stood, would be drawn forth by an inward and inevitable necessity, and compelled to ascend the scaffold.

Hester shook her head.

"Woman, transgress not beyond the limits of Heaven's mercy!" cried the Reverend Mr. Wilson, more harshly than before. "That little babe hath been gifted with a voice, to second and confirm the counsel which thou hast heard. Speak out the name! That, and thy repentance, may avail to take the scarlet letter off thy breast."

"Never!" replied Hester Prynne, looking, not at Mr. Wilson, but into the deep and troubled eyes of the younger clergyman. "It is too deeply branded. Ye cannot take it off. And would that I might endure his agony, as well as mine!"

"Speak, woman!" said another voice, coldly and sternly, proceeding from the crowd about the scaffold. "Speak; and give your child a father!"

"I will not speak!" answered Hester, turning pale as death, but responding to this voice, which she too surely recognized. "And my child must seek a heavenly Father; she shall never know an earthly one!"

"She will not speak!" murmured Mr. Dimmesdale, who, leaning over the balcony, with his hand upon his heart, had awaited the result of his appeal. He now drew back, with a long respiration. "Wondrous strength and generosity of a woman's heart! She will not speak!"

Discerning the impracticable state of the poor culprit's mind, the elder clergyman, who had carefully prepared himself for the occasion, addressed to the multitude a discourse on sin, in all its branches, but with continual reference to the ignominious letter. So forcibly did he dwell upon this symbol, for the hour or more during which his periods were rolling over the people's heads, that it assumed new terrors in their imagination, and seemed to derive its scarlet hue from the flames of the infernal pit. Hester Prynne, meanwhile, kept her place upon the pedestal of shame, with glazed eyes, and an air of weary indifference. She had borne, that morning, all that nature could endure; and as her temperament was not of the order that escapes from too intense suffering by a swoon, her spirit could only shelter itself beneath a stony crust of insensibility, while the faculties of animal life remained entire. In this state, the voice of the preacher thundered remorselessly, but unavailingly, upon her ears. The infant, during the latter portion of her ordeal, pierced the air with its wailings and screams; she strove to hush it, mechanically, but seemed scarcely to sympathize with its trouble. With the same hard demeanour, she was led back to prison, and vanished from the public gaze within its iron-clamped portal. It was whispered, by those who peered after her, that the scarlet letter threw a lurid gleam along the dark passage-way of the interior.

IV. The Interview

After her return to the prison, Hester Prynne was found to be in a state of nervous excitement that demanded constant watchfulness, lest she should perpetrate violence on herself, or do some half-frenzied mischief to the poor babe. As night approached, it proving impossible to quell her insubordination by rebuke or threats of punishment, Master Brackett, the jailer, thought fit to introduce a physician. He described him as a man of skill in all Christian modes of physical science, and likewise familiar with whatever the savage people could teach, in respect to medicinal herbs and roots that grew in the forest. To say the truth, there was much need of professional assistance, not merely for Hester herself, but still more urgently for the child; who, drawing its sustenance from the maternal bosom, seemed to have drank in with it all the turmoil, the anguish, and despair, which pervaded the mother's system. It now writhed in convulsions of pain, and was a forcible type,[3] in its little frame, of the moral agony which Hester Prynne had borne throughout the day.

Closely following the jailer into the dismal apartment, appeared that individual, of singular aspect, whose presence in the crowd had been of such deep interest to the wearer of the scarlet letter. He was lodged in the prison, not as suspected of any offence, but as the most convenient and suitable mode of disposing of him, until the magistrates should have conferred with the Indian sagamores[4] respecting his ransom. His name was announced as Roger Chillingworth. The jailer, after ushering him into the room, remained a moment, marvelling at the comparative quiet that followed his entrance; for Hester Prynne had immediately become as still as death, although the child continued to moan.

"Prithee, friend, leave me alone with my patient," said the practitioner. "Trust me, good jailer, you shall briefly have peace in your house; and, I promise you, Mistress Prynne shall hereafter be more amenable to just authority than you may have found her heretofore."

3. Symbol or emblem.

4. Chiefs.

"Nay, if your worship can accomplish that," answered Master Brackett, "I shall own you for a man of skill indeed! Verily, the woman hath been like a possessed one; and there lacks little, that I should take in hand to drive Satan out of her with stripes."

The stranger had entered the room with the characteristic quietude of the profession to which he announced himself as belonging. Nor did his demeanour change, when the withdrawal of the prison-keeper left him face to face with the woman, whose absorbed notice of him, in the crowd, had intimated so close a relation between himself and her. His first care was given to the child; whose cries, indeed, as she lay writhing on the trundle-bed, made it of peremptory necessity to postpone all other business to the task of soothing her. He examined the infant carefully, and then proceeded to unclasp a leathern case, which he took from beneath his dress. It appeared to contain certain medical preparations, one of which he mingled with a cup of water.

"My old studies in alchemy," observed he, "and my sojourn, for above a year past, among a people well versed in the kindly properties of simples,[5] have made a better physician of me than many that claim the medical degree. Here, woman! The child is yours,—she is none of mine,—neither will she recognize my voice or aspect as a father's. Administer this draught, therefore, with thine own hand."

Hester repelled the offered medicine, at the same time gazing with strongly marked apprehension into his face.

"Wouldst thou avenge thyself on the innocent babe?" whispered she.

"Foolish woman!" responded the physician, half coldly, half soothingly. "What should ail me to harm this misbegotten and miserable babe? The medicine is potent for good; and were it my child,—yea, mine own, as well as thine!—I could do no better for it."

As she still hesitated, being, in fact, in no reasonable state of mind, he took the infant in his arms, and himself administered the draught. It soon proved its efficacy, and redeemed the leech's[6] pledge. The moans of the little patient subsided; its convulsive tossings gradually ceased; and in a few moments, as is the custom of young children after relief from pain, it sank into a profound and dewy slumber. The physician, as he had a fair right to be termed, next bestowed his attention on the mother. With calm and intent scrutiny, he felt her pulse, looked into her eyes,—a gaze that made her heart shrink and shudder, because so familiar, and yet so strange and cold,—and, finally, satisfied with his investigation, proceeded to mingle another draught.

"I know not Lethe nor Nepenthe," remarked he; "but I have learned many new secrets in the wilderness, and here is one of them,—a recipe that an Indian taught me, in requital of some lessons of my own, that were as old as Paracelsus.[7] Drink it! It may be less soothing than a sinless conscience. That I cannot give thee. But it will calm the swell and heaving of thy passion, like oil thrown on the waves of a tempestuous sea."

5. Herbal medicines.
6. Doctor; from the use of leeches (usually freshwater worms) in drawing blood from patients at a time when bloodletting was commonly prescribed for many illnesses.
7. Swiss alchemist (1493–1541). In Greek mythology the water of Lethe, a river in the underworld, caused oblivion. "Nepenthe": an ancient drug (perhaps opium) that induced forgetfulness of pain.

He presented the cup to Hester, who received it with a slow, earnest look into his face; not precisely a look of fear, yet full of doubt and questioning, as to what his purposes might be. She looked also at her slumbering child.

"I have thought of death," said she,—"have wished for it,—would even have prayed for it, were it fit that such as I should pray for any thing. Yet, if death be in this cup, I bid thee think again, ere thou beholdest me quaff it. See! It is even now at my lips."

"Drink, then," replied he, still with the same cold composure. "Dost thou know me so little, Hester Prynne? Are my purposes wont to be so shallow? Even if I imagine a scheme of vengeance, what could I do better for my object than to let thee live,—than to give thee medicines against all harm and peril of life,—so that this burning shame may still blaze upon thy bosom?"—As he spoke, he laid his long forefinger on the scarlet letter, which forthwith seemed to scorch into Hester's breast, as if it had been red-hot. He noticed her involuntary gesture, and smiled.—"Live, therefore, and bear about thy doom with thee, in the eyes of men and women,—in the eyes of him whom thou didst call thy husband,—in the eyes of yonder child! And, that thou mayest live, take off this draught."

Without further expostulation or delay, Hester Prynne drained the cup, and, at the motion of the man of skill, seated herself on the bed where the child was sleeping; while he drew the only chair which the room afforded, and took his own seat beside her. She could not but tremble at these preparations; for she felt that—having now done all that humanity, or principle, or, if so it were, a refined cruelty, impelled him to do, for the relief of physical suffering—he was next to treat with her as the man whom she had most deeply and irreparably injured.

"Hester," said he, "I ask not wherefore, nor how, thou hast fallen into the pit, or say rather, thou hast ascended to the pedestal of infamy, on which I found thee. The reason is not far to seek. It was my folly, and thy weakness. I,—a man of thought,—the bookworm of great libraries,—a man already in decay, having given my best years to feed the hungry dream of knowledge,—what had I to do with youth and beauty like thine own! Misshapen from my birth-hour, how could I delude myself with the idea that intellectual gifts might veil physical deformity in a young girl's fantasy! Men call me wise. If sages were ever wise in their own behoof, I might have foreseen all this. I might have known that, as I came out of the vast and dismal forest, and entered this settlement of Christian men, the very first object to meet my eyes would be thyself, Hester Prynne, standing up, a statue of ignominy, before the people. Nay, from the moment when we came down the old church-steps together, a married pair, I might have beheld the bale-fire[8] of that scarlet letter blazing at the end of our path!"

"Thou knowest," said Hester,—for, depressed as she was, she could not endure this last quiet stab at the token of her shame,—"thou knowest that I was frank with thee. I felt no love, nor feigned any."

"True!" replied he. "It was my folly! I have said it. But, up to that epoch of my life, I had lived in vain. The world had been so cheerless! My heart was a habitation large enough for many guests, but lonely and chill, and without

8. Originally, funeral pyre; here, something like "hellish fire."

a household fire. I longed to kindle one! It seemed not so wild a dream,—old as I was, and sombre as I was, and misshapen as I was,—that the simple bliss, which is scattered far and wide, for all mankind to gather up, might yet be mine. And so, Hester, I drew thee into my heart, into its innermost chamber, and sought to warm thee by the warmth which thy presence made there!"

"I have greatly wronged thee," murmured Hester.

"We have wronged each other," answered he. "Mine was the first wrong, when I betrayed thy budding youth into a false and unnatural relation with my decay. Therefore, as a man who has not thought and philosophized in vain, I seek no vengeance, plot no evil against thee. Between thee and me, the scale hangs fairly balanced. But, Hester, the man lives who has wronged us both! Who is he?"

"Ask me not!" replied Hester Prynne, looking firmly into his face. "That thou shalt never know!"

"Never, sayest thou?" rejoined he, with a smile of dark and self-relying intelligence. "Never know him! Believe me, Hester, there are few things,—whether in the outward world, or, to a certain depth, in the invisible sphere of thought,—few things hidden from the man, who devotes himself earnestly and unreservedly to the solution of a mystery. Thou mayest cover up thy secret from the prying multitude. Thou mayest conceal it, too, from the ministers and magistrates, even as thou didst this day, when they sought to wrench the name out of thy heart, and give thee a partner on thy pedestal. But, as for me, I come to the inquest with other senses than they possess. I shall seek this man, as I have sought truth in books; as I have sought gold in alchemy. There is a sympathy that will make me conscious of him. I shall see him tremble. I shall feel myself shudder, suddenly and unawares. Sooner or later, he must needs be mine!"

The eyes of the wrinkled scholar glowed so intensely upon her, that Hester Prynne clasped her hands over her heart, dreading lest he should read the secret there at once.

"Thou wilt not reveal his name? Not the less he is mine," resumed he, with a look of confidence, as if destiny were at one with him. "He bears no letter of infamy wrought into his garment, as thou dost; but I shall read it on his heart. Yet fear not for him! Think not that I shall interfere with Heaven's own method of retribution, or, to my own loss, betray him to the gripe of human law. Neither do thou imagine that I shall contrive aught against his life, no, nor against his fame; if, as I judge, he be a man of fair repute. Let him live! Let him hide himself in outward honor, if he may! Not the less he shall be mine!"

"Thy acts are like mercy," said Hester, bewildered and appalled. "But thy words interpret thee as a terror!"

"One thing, thou that wast my wife, I would enjoin upon thee," continued the scholar. "Thou hast kept the secret of thy paramour. Keep, likewise, mine! There are none in this land that know me. Breathe not, to any human soul, that thou didst ever call me husband! Here, on this wild outskirt of the earth, I shall pitch my tent; for, elsewhere a wanderer, and isolated from human interests, I find here a woman, a man, a child, amongst whom and myself there exist the closest ligaments. No matter whether of love or hate; no matter whether of right or wrong! Thou and thine, Hester

Prynne, belong to me. My home is where thou art, and where he is. But betray me not!"

"Wherefore dost thou desire it?" inquired Hester, shrinking, she hardly knew why, from this secret bond. "Why not announce thyself openly, and cast me off at once?"

"It may be," he replied, "because I will not encounter the dishonor that besmirches the husband of a faithless woman. It may be for other reasons. Enough, it is my purpose to live and die unknown. Let, therefore, thy husband be to the world as one already dead, and of whom no tidings shall ever come. Recognize me not, by word, by sign, by look! Breathe not the secret, above all, to the man thou wottest[9] of. Shouldst thou fail me in this, beware! His fame, his position, his life, will be in my hands. Beware!"

"I will keep thy secret, as I have his," said Hester.

"Swear it!" rejoined he.

And she took the oath.

"And now, Mistress Prynne," said old Roger Chillingworth, as he was hereafter to be named, "I leave thee alone; alone with thy infant, and the scarlet letter! How is it, Hester? Doth thy sentence bind thee to wear the token in thy sleep? Art thou not afraid of nightmares and hideous dreams?"

"Why dost thou smile so at me?" inquired Hester, troubled at the expression of his eyes. "Art thou like the Black Man[1] that haunts the forest round about us? Hast thou enticed me into a bond that will prove the ruin of my soul?"

"Not thy soul," he answered, with another smile. "No, not thine!"

V. Hester at Her Needle

Hester Prynne's term of confinement was now at an end. Her prison-door was thrown open, and she came forth into the sunshine, which, falling on all alike, seemed, to her sick and morbid heart, as if meant for no other purpose than to reveal the scarlet letter on her breast. Perhaps there was a more real torture in her first unattended footsteps from the threshold of the prison, than even in the procession and spectacle that have been described, where she was made the common infamy, at which all mankind was summoned to point its finger. Then, she was supported by an unnatural tension of the nerves, and by all the combative energy of her character, which enabled her to convert the scene into a kind of lurid triumph. It was, moreover, a separate and insulated event, to occur but once in her lifetime, and to meet which, therefore, reckless of economy, she might call up the vital strength that would have sufficed for many quiet years. The very law that condemned her—a giant of stern features, but with vigor to support, as well as to annihilate, in his iron arm—had held her up, through the terrible ordeal of her ignominy. But now, with this unattended walk from her prison-door, began the daily custom, and she must either sustain and carry it forward by the ordinary resources of her nature, or sink beneath it. She could no longer borrow from the future, to help her through the present grief. To-morrow would bring its own trial with it; so would the next day, and so

9. Know.

1. Devil.

would the next; each its own trial, and yet the very same that was now so unutterably grievous to be borne. The days of the far-off future would toil onward, still with the same burden for her to take up, and bear along with her, but never to fling down; for the accumulating days, and added years, would pile up their misery upon the heap of shame. Throughout them all, giving up her individuality, she would become the general symbol at which the preacher and moralist might point, and in which they might vivify and embody their images of woman's frailty and sinful passion. Thus the young and pure would be taught to look at her, with the scarlet letter flaming on her breast,—at her, the child of honorable parents,—at her, the mother of a babe, that would hereafter be a woman,—at her, who had once been innocent,—as the figure, the body, the reality of sin. And over her grave, the infamy that she must carry thither would be her only monument.

It may seem marvellous, that, with the world before her,—kept by no restrictive clause of her condemnation within the limits of the Puritan settlement, so remote and so obscure,—free to return to her birthplace, or to any other European land, and there hide her character and identity under a new exterior, as completely as if emerging into another state of being,—and having also the passes of the dark, inscrutable forest open to her, where the wildness of her nature might assimilate itself with a people whose customs and life were alien from the law that had condemned her,—it may seem marvellous, that this woman should still call that place her home, where, and where only, she must needs be the type of shame. But there is a fatality, a feeling so irresistible and inevitable that it has the force of doom, which almost invariably compels human beings to linger around and haunt, ghost-like, the spot where some great and marked event has given the color to their lifetime; and still the more irresistibly, the darker the tinge that saddens it. Her sin, her ignominy, were the roots which she had struck into the soil. It was as if a new birth, with stronger assimilations than the first, had converted the forest-land, still so uncongenial to every other pilgrim and wanderer, into Hester Prynne's wild and dreary, but life-long home. All other scenes of earth—even that village of rural England, where happy infancy and stainless maidenhood seemed yet to be in her mother's keeping, like garments put off long ago—were foreign to her, in comparison. The chain that bound her here was of iron links, and galling to her inmost soul, but never could be broken.

It might be, too,—doubtless it was so, although she hid the secret from herself, and grew pale whenever it struggled out of her heart, like a serpent from its hole,—it might be that another feeling kept her within the scene and pathway that had been so fatal. There dwelt, there trode the feet of one with whom she deemed herself connected in a union, that, unrecognized on earth, would bring them together before the bar of final judgment, and make that their marriage-altar, for a joint futurity of endless retribution. Over and over again, the tempter of souls had thrust this idea upon Hester's contemplation, and laughed at the passionate and desperate joy with which she seized, and then strove to cast it from her. She barely looked the idea in the face, and hastened to bar it in its dungeon. What she compelled herself to believe,—what, finally, she reasoned upon, as her motive for continuing a resident of New England,—was half a truth, and half a self-delusion. Here, she said to herself, had been the scene of her guilt, and here should be the scene of her earthly punishment; and so, perchance, the torture of her daily shame would at length purge her soul, and work out another purity than that which she had lost; more saint-like, because the result of martyrdom.

Hester Prynne, therefore, did not flee. On the outskirts of the town, within the verge of the peninsula, but not in close vicinity to any other habitation, there was a small thatched cottage. It had been built by an earlier settler, and abandoned, because the soil about it was too sterile for cultivation, while its comparative remoteness put it out of the sphere of that social activity which already marked the habits of the emigrants. It stood on the shore, looking across a basin of the sea at the forest-covered hills, towards the west. A clump of scrubby trees, such as alone grew on the peninsula, did not so much conceal the cottage from view, as seem to denote that here was some object which would fain have been, or at least ought to be, concealed. In this little, lonesome dwelling, with some slender means that she possessed, and by the license of the magistrates, who still kept an inquisitorial watch over her, Hester established herself, with her infant child. A mystic shadow of suspicion immediately attached itself to the spot. Children, too young to comprehend wherefore this woman should be shut out from the sphere of human charities, would creep nigh enough to behold her plying her needle at the cottage-window, or standing in the door-way, or laboring in her little garden, or coming forth along the pathway that led townward; and, discerning the scarlet letter on her breast, would scamper off, with a strange, contagious fear.

Lonely as was Hester's situation, and without a friend on earth who dared to show himself, she, however, incurred no risk of want. She possessed an art that sufficed, even in a land that afforded comparatively little scope for its exercise, to supply food for her thriving infant and herself. It was the art—then, as now, almost the only one within a woman's grasp—of needlework. She bore on her breast, in the curiously embroidered letter, a specimen of her delicate and imaginative skill, of which the dames of a court might gladly have availed themselves, to add the richer and more spiritual adornment of human ingenuity to their fabrics of silk and gold. Here, indeed, in the sable simplicity that generally characterized the Puritanic modes of dress, there might be an infrequent call for the finer productions of her handiwork. Yet the taste of the age, demanding whatever was elaborate in compositions of this kind, did not fail to extend its influence over our stern progenitors, who had cast behind them so many fashions which it might seem harder to dispense with. Public ceremonies, such as ordinations, the installation of magistrates, and all that could give majesty to the forms in which a new government manifested itself to the people, were, as a matter of policy, marked by a stately and well-conducted ceremonial, and a sombre, but yet a studied magnificence. Deep ruffs, painfully wrought bands, and gorgeously embroidered gloves, were all deemed necessary to the official state of men assuming the reins of power; and were readily allowed to individuals dignified by rank or wealth, even while sumptuary laws forbade these and similar extravagances to the plebeian order. In the array of funerals, too,—whether for the apparel of the dead body, or to typify, by manifold emblematic devices of sable cloth and snowy lawn,[2] the sorrow of the

2. Fine, light cotton or linen fabric. "Sable cloth": black cloth, of any kind.

survivors,—there was a frequent and characteristic demand for such labor as Hester Prynne could supply. Baby-linen—for babies then wore robes of state—afforded still another possibility of toil and emolument.

By degrees, nor very slowly, her handiwork became what would now be termed the fashion. Whether from commiseration for a woman of so miserable a destiny; or from the morbid curiosity that gives a fictitious value even to common or worthless things; or by whatever other intangible circumstance was then, as now, sufficient to bestow, on some persons, what others might seek in vain; or because Hester really filled a gap which must otherwise have remained vacant; it is certain that she had ready and fairly requited employment for as many hours as she saw fit to occupy with her needle. Vanity, it may be, chose to mortify itself, by putting on, for ceremonials of pomp and state, the garments that had been wrought by her sinful hands. Her needle-work was seen on the ruff of the Governor; military men wore it on their scarfs, and the minister on his band; it decked the baby's little cap; it was shut up, to be mildewed and moulder away, in the coffins of the dead. But it is not recorded that, in a single instance, her skill was called in aid to embroider the white veil which was to cover the pure blushes of a bride. The exception indicated the ever relentless vigor with which society frowned upon her sin.

Hester sought not to acquire any thing beyond a subsistence, of the plainest and most ascetic description, for herself, and a simple abundance for her child. Her own dress was of the coarsest materials and the most sombre hue; with only that one ornament,—the scarlet letter,—which it was her doom to wear. The child's attire, on the other hand, was distinguished by a fanciful, or, we might rather say, a fantastic ingenuity, which served, indeed, to heighten the airy charm that early began to develop itself in the little girl, but which appeared to have also a deeper meaning. We may speak further of it hereafter. Except for that small expenditure in the decoration of her infant, Hester bestowed all her superfluous means in charity, on wretches less miserable than herself, and who not unfrequently insulted the hand that fed them. Much of the time, which she might readily have applied to the better efforts of her art, she employed in making coarse garments for the poor. It is probable that there was an idea of penance in this mode of occupation, and that she offered up a real sacrifice of enjoyment, in devoting so many hours to such rude handiwork. She had in her nature a rich, voluptuous, Oriental characteristic,—a taste for the gorgeously beautiful, which, save in the exquisite productions of her needle, found nothing else, in all the possibilities of her life, to exercise itself upon. Women derive a pleasure, incomprehensible to the other sex, from the delicate toil of the needle. To Hester Prynne it might have been a mode of expressing, and therefore soothing, the passion of her life. Like all other joys, she rejected it as sin. This morbid meddling of conscience with an immaterial matter betokened, it is to be feared, no genuine and stedfast penitence, but something doubtful, something that might be deeply wrong, beneath.

In this manner, Hester Prynne came to have a part to perform in the world. With her native energy of character, and rare capacity, it could not entirely cast her off, although it had set a mark upon her, more intolerable to a woman's heart than that which branded the brow of Cain.[3] In all her intercourse with society, however, there was nothing that made her feel as if she belonged to it. Every gesture, every word, and even the silence of those with whom she came in contact, implied, and often expressed, that she was banished, and as much alone as if she inhabited another sphere, or communicated with the common nature by other organs and senses than the rest of human kind. She stood apart from mortal interests, yet close beside them, like a ghost that revisits the familiar fireside, and can no longer make itself seen or felt; no more smile with the household joy, nor mourn with the kindred sorrow; or, should it succeed in manifesting its forbidden sympathy, awakening only terror and horrible repugnance. These emotions, in fact, and its bitterest scorn besides, seemed to be the sole portion that she retained in the universal heart. It was not an age of delicacy; and her position, although she understood it well, and was in little danger of forgetting it, was often brought before her vivid self-perception, like a new anguish, by the rudest touch upon the tenderest spot. The poor, as we have already said, whom she sought out to be the objects of her bounty, often reviled the hand that was stretched forth to succor them. Dames of elevated rank, likewise, whose doors she entered in the way of her occupation, were accustomed to distil drops of bitterness into her heart; sometimes through that alchemy of quiet malice, by which women can concoct a subtile poison from ordinary trifles; and sometimes, also, by a coarser expression, that fell upon the sufferer's defenceless breast like a rough blow upon an ulcerated wound. Hester had schooled herself long and well; she never responded to these attacks, save by a flush of crimson that rose irrepressibly over her pale cheek, and again subsided into the depths of her bosom. She was patient,—a martyr, indeed,—but she forbore to pray for her enemies; lest, in spite of her forgiving aspirations, the words of the blessing should stubbornly twist themselves into a curse.

Continually, and in a thousand other ways, did she feel the innumerable throbs of anguish that had been so cunningly contrived for her by the undying, the ever-active sentence of the Puritan tribunal. Clergymen paused in the street to address words of exhortation, that brought a crowd, with its mingled grin and frown, around the poor, sinful woman. If she entered a church, trusting to share the Sabbath smile of the Universal Father, it was often her mishap to find herself the text of the discourse. She grew to have a dread of children; for they had imbibed from their parents a vague idea of something horrible in this dreary woman, gliding silently through the town, with never any companion but one only child. Therefore, first allowing her to pass, they pursued her at a distance with shrill cries, and the utterance of a word that had no distinct purport to their own minds, but was none the less terrible to her, as proceeding from lips that babbled it unconsciously. It seemed to argue so wide a diffusion of her shame, that all nature knew of it; it could have caused her no deeper pang, had the leaves of the trees whispered the dark story among themselves,—had the summer breeze murmured

3. For murdering his brother Abel, Cain was sentenced to be a perpetual fugitive. When Cain protested that he would be murdered himself, "the Lord set a mark upon Cain, lest any finding him should kill him" (Genesis 4.15).

about it,—had the wintry blast shrieked it aloud! Another peculiar torture was felt in the gaze of a new eye. When strangers looked curiously at the scarlet letter,—and none ever failed to do so,—they branded it afresh into Hester's soul; so that, oftentimes, she could scarcely refrain, yet always did refrain, from covering the symbol with her hand. But then, again, an accustomed eye had likewise its own anguish to inflict. Its cool stare of familiarity was intolerable. From first to last, in short, Hester Prynne had always this dreadful agony in feeling a human eye upon the token; the spot never grew callous; it seemed, on the contrary, to grow more sensitive with daily torture.

But sometimes, once in many days, or perchance in many months, she felt an eye—a human eye—upon the ignominious brand, that seemed to give a momentary relief, as if half of her agony were shared. The next instant, back it all rushed again, with still a deeper throb of pain; for, in that brief interval, she had sinned anew. Had Hester sinned alone?

Her imagination was somewhat affected, and, had she been of a softer moral and intellectual fibre, would have been still more so, by the strange and solitary anguish of her life. Walking to and fro, with those lonely footsteps, in the little world with which she was outwardly connected, it now and then appeared to Hester,—if altogether fancy, it was nevertheless too potent to be resisted,—she felt or fancied, then, that the scarlet letter had endowed her with a new sense. She shuddered to believe, yet could not help believing, that it gave her a sympathetic knowledge of the hidden sin in other hearts. She was terror-stricken by the revelations that were thus made. What were they? Could they be other than the insidious whispers of the bad angel,[4] who would fain have persuaded the struggling woman, as yet only half his victim, that the outward guise of purity was but a lie, and that, if truth were everywhere to be shown, a scarlet letter would blaze forth on many a bosom besides Hester Prynne's? Or, must she receive those intimations—so obscure, yet so distinct—as truth? In all her miserable experience, there was nothing else so awful and so loathsome as this sense. It perplexed, as well as shocked her, by the irreverent inopportuneness of the occasions that brought it into vivid action. Sometimes, the red infamy upon her breast would give a sympathetic throb, as she passed near a venerable minister or magistrate, the model of piety and justice, to whom that age of antique reverence looked up, as to a mortal man in fellowship with angels. "What evil thing is at hand?" would Hester say to herself. Lifting her reluctant eyes, there would be nothing human within the scope of view, save the form of this earthly saint! Again, a mystic sisterhood would contumaciously[5] assert itself, as she met the sanctified frown of some matron, who, according to the rumor of all tongues, had kept cold snow within her bosom throughout life. That unsunned snow in the matron's bosom, and the burning shame on Hester Prynne's,—what had the two in common? Or, once more, the electric thrill would give her warning,—"Behold, Hester, here is a companion!"—and, looking up, she would detect the eyes of a young maiden glancing at the scarlet letter, shyly and aside, and quickly averted, with a faint, chill crimson in her cheeks; as if her purity were somewhat sullied by that momentary glance. O Fiend, whose talisman was that fatal

4. Satan.

5. Rebelliously.

symbol, wouldst thou leave nothing, whether in youth or age, for this poor sinner to revere?—Such loss of faith is ever one of the saddest results of sin. Be it accepted as a proof that all was not corrupt in this poor victim of her own frailty, and man's hard law, that Hester Prynne yet struggled to believe that no fellow-mortal was guilty like herself.

The vulgar, who, in those dreary old times, were always contributing a grotesque horror to what interested their imaginations, had a story about the scarlet letter which we might readily work up into a terrific legend. They averred, that the symbol was not mere scarlet cloth, tinged in an earthly dye-pot, but was red-hot with infernal fire, and could be seen glowing all alight, whenever Hester Prynne walked abroad in the night-time. And we must needs say, it seared Hester's bosom so deeply, that perhaps there was more truth in the rumor than our modern incredulity may be inclined to admit.

VI. Pearl

We have as yet hardly spoken of the infant; that little creature, whose innocent life had sprung, by the inscrutable decree of Providence, a lovely and immortal flower, out of the rank luxuriance of a guilty passion. How strange it seemed to the sad woman, as she watched the growth, and the beauty that became every day more brilliant, and the intelligence that threw its quivering sunshine over the tiny features of this child! Her Pearl!—For so had Hester called her; not as a name expressive of her aspect, which had nothing of the calm, white, unimpassioned lustre that would be indicated by the comparison. But she named the infant "Pearl," as being of great price,[6] purchased with all she had,—her mother's only treasure. How strange, indeed! Man had marked this woman's sin by a scarlet letter, which had such potent and disastrous efficacy that no human sympathy could reach her, save it were sinful like herself. God, as a direct consequence of the sin which man thus punished, had given her a lovely child, whose place was on that same dishonored bosom, to connect her parent for ever with the race and descent of mortals, and to be finally a blessed soul in heaven! Yet these thoughts affected Hester Prynne less with hope than apprehension. She knew that her deed had been evil; she could have no faith, therefore, that its result would be for good. Day after day, she looked fearfully into the child's expanding nature; ever dreading to detect some dark and wild peculiarity, that should correspond with the guiltiness to which she owed her being.

Certainly, there was no physical defect. By its perfect shape, its vigor, and its natural dexterity in the use of all its untried limbs, the infant was worthy to have been brought forth in Eden; worthy to have been left there, to be the plaything of the angels, after the world's first parents were driven out. The child had a native grace which does not invariably coexist with faultless beauty; its attire, however simple, always impressed the beholder as if it were the very garb that precisely became it best. But little Pearl was not clad in rustic weeds. Her mother, with a morbid purpose that may be better understood hereafter, had bought the richest tissues that could be

6. "Again, the kingdom of heaven is like unto a merchant man, seeking goodly pearls: Who, when he had found one pearl of great price, went and sold all that he had, and bought it" (Matthew 13.45–46).

procured, and allowed her imaginative faculty its full play in the arrangement and decoration of the dresses which the child wore, before the public eye. So magnificent was the small figure, when thus arrayed, and such was the splendor of Pearl's own proper beauty, shining through the gorgeous robes which might have extinguished a paler loveliness, that there was an absolute circle of radiance around her, on the darksome cottage-floor. And yet a russet gown, torn and soiled with the child's rude play, made a picture of her just as perfect. Pearl's aspect was imbued with a spell of infinite variety; in this one child there were many children, comprehending the full scope between the wild-flower prettiness of a peasant-baby, and the pomp, in little, of an infant princess. Throughout all, however, there was a trait of passion, a certain depth of hue, which she never lost; and if, in any of her changes, she had grown fainter or paler, she would have ceased to be herself;—it would have been no longer Pearl!

This outward mutability indicated, and did not more than fairly express, the various properties of her inner life. Her nature appeared to possess depth, too, as well as variety; but—or else Hester's fears deceived her—it lacked reference and adaptation to the world into which she was born. The child could not be made amenable to rules. In giving her existence, a great law had been broken; and the result was a being, whose elements were perhaps beautiful and brilliant, but all in disorder; or with an order peculiar to themselves, amidst which the point of variety and arrangement was difficult or impossible to be discovered. Hester could only account for the child's character—and even then, most vaguely and imperfectly—by recalling what she herself had been, during that momentous period while Pearl was imbibing her soul from the spiritual world, and her bodily frame from its material of earth. The mother's impassioned state had been the medium through which were transmitted to the unborn infant the rays of its moral life; and, however white and clear originally, they had taken the deep stains of crimson and gold, the fiery lustre, the black shadow, and the untempered light, of the intervening substance. Above all, the warfare of Hester's spirit, at that epoch, was perpetuated in Pearl. She could recognize her wild, desperate, defiant mood, the flightiness of her temper, and even some of the very cloud-shapes of gloom and despondency that had brooded in her heart. They were now illuminated by the morning radiance of a young child's disposition, but, later in the day of earthly existence, might be prolific of the storm and whirlwind.

The discipline of the family, in those days, was of a far more rigid kind than now. The frown, the harsh rebuke, the frequent application of the rod, enjoined by Scriptural authority,[7] were used, not merely in the way of punishment for actual offences, but as a wholesome regimen for the growth and promotion of all childish virtues. Hester Prynne, nevertheless, the lonely mother of this one child, ran little risk of erring on the side of undue severity. Mindful, however, of her own errors and misfortunes, she early sought to impose a tender, but strict, control over the infant immortality that was committed to her charge. But the task was beyond her skill. After testing both smiles and frowns, and proving that neither mode of treatment possessed any calculable influence, Hester was ultimately compelled to stand

7. "He that spareth his rod hateth his son: but he that loveth him chasteneth him betimes" (Proverbs 13.24).

aside, and permit the child to be swayed by her own impulses. Physical compulsion or restraint was effectual, of course, while it lasted. As to any other kind of discipline, whether addressed to her mind or heart, little Pearl might or might not be within its reach, in accordance with the caprice that ruled the moment. Her mother, while Pearl was yet an infant, grew acquainted with a certain peculiar look, that warned her when it would be labor thrown away to insist, persuade, or plead. It was a look so intelligent, yet inexplicable, so perverse, sometimes so malicious, but generally accompanied by a wild flow of spirits, that Hester could not help questioning, at such moments, whether Pearl was a human child. She seemed rather an airy sprite, which, after playing its fantastic sports for a little while upon the cottage-floor, would flit away with a mocking smile. Whenever that look appeared in her wild, bright, deeply black eyes, it invested her with a strange remoteness and intangibility; it was as if she were hovering in the air and might vanish, like a glimmering light that comes we know not whence, and goes we know not whither. Beholding it, Hester was constrained to rush towards the child,—to pursue the little elf in the flight which she invariably began,—to snatch her to her bosom, with a close pressure and earnest kisses,—not so much from overflowing love, as to assure herself that Pearl was flesh and blood, and not utterly delusive. But Pearl's laugh, when she was caught, though full of merriment and music, made her mother more doubtful than before.

Heart-smitten at this bewildering and baffling spell, that so often came between herself and her sole treasure, whom she had bought so dear, and who was all her world, Hester sometimes burst into passionate tears. Then, perhaps,—for there was no foreseeing how it might affect her,—Pearl would frown, and clench her little fist, and harden her small features into a stern, unsympathizing look of discontent. Not seldom, she would laugh anew, and louder than before, like a thing incapable and unintelligent of human sorrow. Or—but this more rarely happened—she would be convulsed with a rage of grief, and sob out her love for her mother, in broken words, and seem intent on proving that she had a heart, by breaking it. Yet Hester was hardly safe in confiding herself to that gusty tenderness; it passed, as suddenly as it came. Brooding over all these matters, the mother felt like one who has evoked a spirit, but, by some irregularity in the process of conjuration, has failed to win the master-word that should control this new and incomprehensible intelligence. Her only real comfort was when the child lay in the placidity of sleep. Then she was sure of her, and tasted hours of quiet, sad, delicious happiness; until—perhaps with that perverse expression glimmering from beneath her opening lids—little Pearl awoke!

How soon—with what strange rapidity, indeed!—did Pearl arrive at an age that was capable of social intercourse, beyond the mother's ever-ready smile and nonsense-words! And then what a happiness would it have been, could Hester Prynne have heard her clear, bird-like voice mingling with the uproar of other childish voices, and have distinguished and unravelled her own darling's tones, amid all the entangled outcry of a group of sportive children! But this could never be. Pearl was a born outcast of the infantile world. An imp of evil, emblem and product of sin, she had no right among christened infants. Nothing was more remarkable than the instinct, as it seemed, with which the child comprehended her loneliness; the destiny that had drawn an inviolable circle round about her; the whole peculiarity, in short, of her position in respect to other children. Never, since her release from prison, had Hester met the public gaze without her. In all her walks about the town, Pearl, too, was there; first as the babe in arms, and afterwards as the little girl, small companion of her mother, holding a forefinger with her whole grasp, and tripping along at the rate of three or four footsteps to one of Hester's. She saw the children of the settlement, on the grassy margin of the street, or at the domestic thresholds, disporting themselves in such grim fashion as the Puritanic nurture would permit; playing at going to church, perchance; or at scourging Quakers; or taking scalps in a sham-fight with the Indians; or scaring one another with freaks of imitative witchcraft. Pearl saw, and gazed intently, but never sought to make acquaintance. If spoken to, she would not speak again. If the children gathered about her, as they sometimes did, Pearl would grow positively terrible in her puny wrath, snatching up stones to fling at them, with shrill, incoherent exclamations that made her mother tremble, because they had so much the sound of a witch's anathemas in some unknown tongue.

The truth was, that the little Puritans, being of the most intolerant brood that ever lived, had got a vague idea of something outlandish, unearthly, or at variance with ordinary fashions, in the mother and child; and therefore scorned them in their hearts, and not unfrequently reviled them with their tongues. Pearl felt the sentiment, and requited it with the bitterest hatred that can be supposed to rankle in a childish bosom. These outbreaks of a fierce temper had a kind of value, and even comfort, for her mother; because there was at least an intelligible earnestness in the mood, instead of the fitful caprice that so often thwarted her in the child's manifestations. It appalled her, nevertheless, to discern here, again, a shadowy reflection of the evil that had existed in herself. All this enmity and passion had Pearl inherited, by inalienable right, out of Hester's heart. Mother and daughter stood together in the same circle of seclusion from human society; and in the nature of the child seemed to be perpetuated those unquiet elements that had distracted Hester Prynne before Pearl's birth, but had since begun to be soothed away by the softening influences of maternity.

At home, within and around her mother's cottage, Pearl wanted not a wide and various circle of acquaintance. The spell of life went forth from her ever creative spirit, and communicated itself to a thousand objects, as a torch kindles a flame wherever it may be applied. The unlikeliest materials, a stick, a bunch of rags, a flower, were the puppets of Pearl's witchcraft, and, without undergoing any outward change, became spiritually adapted to whatever drama occupied the stage of her inner world. Her one baby-voice served a multitude of imaginary personages, old and young, to talk withal. The pine-trees, aged, black, and solemn, and flinging groans and other melancholy utterances on the breeze, needed little transformation to figure as Puritan elders; the ugliest weeds of the garden were their children, whom Pearl smote down and uprooted, most unmercifully. It was wonderful, the vast variety of forms into which she threw her intellect, with no continuity, indeed, but darting up and dancing, always in a state of preternatural activity,—soon sinking down, as if exhausted by so rapid and feverish a tide of life,—and succeeded by other shapes of a similar wild energy. It was like nothing so much as the phantasmagoric play of the northern lights. In the mere exercise of the fancy, however, and the sportiveness of a growing mind, there might be little more than was observable in other children of bright faculties; except as Pearl, in the dearth of human playmates, was thrown more upon the visionary throng which she created. The singularity lay in the hostile feelings with which the child regarded all these offspring of her own heart and mind. She never created a friend, but seemed always to be sowing broadcast the dragon's teeth, whence sprung a harvest of armed enemies, against whom she rushed to battle.[8] It was inexpressibly sad—then what depth of sorrow to a mother, who felt in her own heart the cause!—to observe, in one so young, this constant recognition of an adverse world, and so fierce a training of the energies that were to make good her cause, in the contest that must ensue.

Gazing at Pearl, Hester Prynne often dropped her work upon her knees, and cried out, with an agony which she would fain have hidden, but which made utterance for itself, betwixt speech and a groan,—"O Father in Heaven,—if Thou art still my Father,—what is this being which I have brought into the world!" And Pearl, overhearing the ejaculation, or aware, through some more subtile channel, of those throbs of anguish, would turn her vivid and beautiful little face upon her mother, smile with sprite-like intelligence, and resume her play.

One peculiarity of the child's deportment remains yet to be told. The very first thing which she had noticed, in her life, was—what?—not the mother's smile, responding to it, as other babies do, by that faint, embryo smile of the little mouth, remembered so doubtfully afterwards, and with such fond discussion whether it were indeed a smile. By no means! But that first object of which Pearl seemed to become aware was—shall we say it?—the scarlet letter on Hester's bosom! One day, as her mother stooped over the cradle, the infant's eyes had been caught by the glimmering of the gold embroidery about the letter; and, putting up her little hand, she grasped at it, smiling, not doubtfully, but with a decided gleam that gave her face the look of a much older child. Then, gasping for breath, did Hester Prynne clutch the fatal token, instinctively endeavouring to tear it away; so infinite was the torture inflicted by the intelligent touch of Pearl's baby-hand. Again, as if her mother's agonized gesture were meant only to make sport for her, did little Pearl look into her eyes, and smile! From that epoch, except when the child was asleep, Hester had never felt a moment's safety; not a moment's calm enjoyment of her. Weeks, it is true, would sometimes elapse, during which Pearl's gaze might never once be fixed upon the scarlet letter; but then, again, it would come at unawares, like the stroke of sudden death, and always with that peculiar smile, and odd expression of the eyes.

Once, this freakish, elvish cast came into the child's eyes, while Hester was looking at her own image in them, as mothers are fond of doing; and, suddenly,—for women in solitude, and with troubled hearts, are pestered with unaccountable delusions,—she fancied that she beheld, not her own miniature portrait, but another face in the small black mirror of Pearl's eye. It was a face, fiend-like, full of smiling malice, yet bearing the semblance of features that she had known full well, though seldom with a smile, and never with malice, in them. It was as if an evil spirit possessed the child,

8. In Greek mythology, Cadmus killed a dragon and planted its teeth, from which sprang armed men who fought each other; the survivors helped him build the Cadmeia or citadel of Thebes.

and had just then peeped forth in mockery. Many a time afterwards had Hester been tortured, though less vividly, by the same illusion.

In the afternoon of a certain summer's day, after Pearl grew big enough to run about, she amused herself with gathering handfuls of wild-flowers, and flinging them, one by one, at her mother's bosom; dancing up and down, like a little elf, whenever she hit the scarlet letter. Hester's first motion had been to cover her bosom with her clasped hands. But, whether from pride or resignation, or a feeling that her penance might best be wrought out by this unutterable pain, she resisted the impulse, and sat erect, pale as death, looking sadly into little Pearl's wild eyes. Still came the battery of flowers, almost invariably hitting the mark, and covering the mother's breast with hurts for which she could find no balm in this world, nor knew how to seek it in another. At last, her shot being all expended, the child stood still and gazed at Hester, with that little, laughing image of a fiend peeping out—or, whether it peeped or no, her mother so imagined it—from the unsearchable abyss of her black eyes.

"Child, what art thou?" cried the mother.

"O, I am your little Pearl!" answered the child.

But, while she said it, Pearl laughed and began to dance up and down with the humorsome gesticulation of a little imp, whose next freak[9] might be to fly up the chimney.

"Art thou my child, in very truth?" asked Hester.

Nor did she put the question altogether idly, but, for the moment, with a portion of genuine earnestness; for, such was Pearl's wonderful intelligence, that her mother half doubted whether she were not acquainted with the secret spell of her existence, and might not now reveal herself.

"Yes; I am little Pearl!" repeated the child, continuing her antics.

"Thou art not my child! Thou art no Pearl of mine!" said the mother, half playfully; for it was often the case that a sportive impulse came over her, in the midst of her deepest suffering. "Tell me, then, what thou art, and who sent thee hither?"

"Tell me, mother!" said the child, seriously, coming up to Hester, and pressing herself close to her knees. "Do thou tell me!"

"Thy Heavenly Father sent thee!" answered Hester Prynne.

But she said it with a hesitation that did not escape the acuteness of the child. Whether moved only by her ordinary freakishness, or because an evil spirit prompted her, she put up her small forefinger, and touched the scarlet letter.

"He did not send me!" cried she, positively. "I have no Heavenly Father!"

"Hush, Pearl, hush! Thou must not talk so!" answered the mother, suppressing a groan. "He sent us all into this world. He sent even me, thy mother. Then, much more, thee! Or, if not, thou strange and elfish child, whence didst thou come?"

"Tell me! Tell me!" repeated Pearl, no longer seriously, but laughing, and capering about the floor. "It is thou that must tell me!"

But Hester could not resolve the query, being herself in a dismal labyrinth of doubt. She remembered—betwixt a smile and a shudder—the talk

9. Sudden, impulsive act or gesture.

of the neighbouring townspeople; who, seeking vainly elsewhere for the child's paternity, and observing some of her odd attributes, had given out that poor little Pearl was a demon offspring; such as, ever since old Catholic times[1] had occasionally been seen on earth, through the agency of their mothers' sin, and to promote some foul and wicked purpose. Luther,[2] according to the scandal of his monkish enemies, was a brat of that hellish breed; nor was Pearl the only child to whom this inauspicious origin was assigned, among the New England Puritans.

VII. The Governor's Hall

Hester Prynne went, one day, to the mansion of Governor Bellingham, with a pair of gloves, which she had fringed and embroidered to his order, and which were to be worn on some great occasion of state; for, though the chances of a popular election had caused this former ruler to descend a step or two from the highest rank, he still held an honorable and influential place among the colonial magistracy.

Another and far more important reason than the delivery of a pair of embroidered gloves impelled Hester, at this time, to seek an interview with a personage of so much power and activity in the affairs of the settlement. It had reached her ears, that there was a design on the part of some of the leading inhabitants, cherishing the more rigid order of principles in religion and government, to deprive her of her child. On the supposition that Pearl, as already hinted, was of demon origin, these good people not unreasonably argued that a Christian interest in the mother's soul required them to remove such a stumbling-block from her path. If the child, on the other hand, were really capable of moral and religious growth, and possessed the elements of ultimate salvation, then, surely, it would enjoy all the fairer prospect of these advantages by being transferred to wiser and better guardianship than Hester Prynne's. Among those who promoted the design, Governor Bellingham was said to be one of the most busy. It may appear singular, and, indeed, not a little ludicrous, that an affair of this kind, which, in later days, would have been referred to no higher jurisdiction than that of the selectmen of the town, should then have been a question publicly discussed, and on which statesmen of eminence took sides. At that epoch of pristine simplicity, however, matters of even slighter public interest, and of far less intrinsic weight than the welfare of Hester and her child, were strangely mixed up with the deliberations of legislators and acts of state. The period was hardly, if at all, earlier than that of our story, when a dispute concerning the right of property in a pig, not only caused a fierce and bitter contest in the legislative body of the colony, but resulted in an important modification of the framework itself of the legislature.[3]

Full of concern, therefore,—but so conscious of her own right, that it seemed scarcely an unequal match between the public, on the one side, and a lonely woman, backed by the sympathies of nature, on the other,—Hester

1. Before the 16th century, when Protestant churches broke away from the Roman Catholic Church.
2. Martin Luther (1483–1546), leader of the Protestant Reformation in Germany.
3. The so-called Sow Case (*Sherman v. Keayne*, 1643–44) led to the dividing of the Massachusetts General Court into two legislative bodies.

Prynne set forth from her solitary cottage. Little Pearl, of course, was her companion. She was now of an age to run lightly along by her mother's side, and, constantly in motion from morn till sunset, could have accomplished a much longer journey than that before her. Often, nevertheless, more from caprice than necessity, she demanded to be taken up in arms, but was soon as imperious to be set down again, and frisked onward before Hester on the grassy pathway, with many a harmless trip and tumble. We have spoken of Pearl's rich and luxuriant beauty; a beauty that shone with deep and vivid tints; a bright complexion, eyes possessing intensity both of depth and glow, and hair already of a deep, glossy brown, and which, in after years, would be nearly akin to black. There was fire in her and throughout her; she seemed the unpremeditated offshoot of a passionate moment. Her mother, in contriving the child's garb, had allowed the gorgeous tendencies of her imagination their full play; arraying her in a crimson velvet tunic, of a peculiar cut, abundantly embroidered with fantasies and flourishes of gold thread. So much strength of coloring, which must have given a wan and pallid aspect to cheeks of a fainter bloom, was admirably adapted to Pearl's beauty, and made her the very brightest little jet of flame that ever danced upon the earth.

But it was a remarkable attribute of this garb, and, indeed, of the child's whole appearance, that it irresistably and inevitably reminded the beholder of the token which Hester Prynne was doomed to wear upon her bosom. It was the scarlet letter in another form; the scarlet letter endowed with life! The mother herself—as if the red ignominy were so deeply scorched into her brain, that all her conceptions assumed its form—had carefully wrought out the similitude; lavishing many hours of morbid ingenuity, to create an analogy between the object of her affection, and the emblem of her guilt and torture. But, in truth, Pearl was the one, as well as the other; and only in consequence of that identity had Hester contrived so perfectly to represent the scarlet letter in her appearance.

As the two wayfarers came within the precincts of the town, the children of the Puritans looked up from their play,—or what passed for play with those sombre little urchins,—and spake gravely one to another:—

"Behold, verily, there is the woman of the scarlet letter; and, of a truth, moreover, there is the likeness of the scarlet letter running along by her side! Come, therefore, and let us fling mud at them!"

But Pearl, who was a dauntless child, after frowning, stamping her foot, and shaking her little hand with a variety of threatening gestures, suddenly made a rush at the knot of her enemies, and put them all to flight. She resembled, in her fierce pursuit of them, an infant pestilence,—the scarlet fever, or some such half-fledged angel of judgment,—whose mission was to punish the sins of the rising generation. She screamed and shouted, too, with a terrific volume of sound, which doubtless caused the hearts of the fugitives to quake within them. The victory accomplished, Pearl returned quietly to her mother, and looked up smiling into her face.

Without further adventure, they reached the dwelling of Governor Bellingham. This was a large wooden house, built in a fashion of which there are specimens still extant in the streets of our elder towns; now moss-grown, crumbling to decay, and melancholy at heart with the many sorrowful or joyful occurrences remembered or forgotten, that have happened, and passed away, within their dusky chambers. Then, however, there was the freshness of the passing year on its exterior, and the cheerfulness, gleaming forth from the sunny windows, of a human habitation into which death had never entered. It had indeed a very cheery aspect; the walls being overspread with a kind of stucco, in which fragments of broken glass were plentifully intermixed; so that, when the sunshine fell aslant-wise over the front of the edifice, it glittered and sparkled as if diamonds had been flung against it by the double handful. The brilliancy might have befitted Aladdin's palace, rather than the mansion of a grave old Puritan ruler. It was further decorated with strange and seemingly cabalistic figures and diagrams, suitable to the quaint taste of the age, which had been drawn in the stucco when newly laid on, and had now grown hard and durable, for the admiration of after times.

Pearl, looking at this bright wonder of a house, began to caper and dance, and imperatively required that the whole breadth of sunshine should be stripped off its front, and given her to play with.

"No, my little Pearl!" said her mother. "Thou must gather thine own sunshine. I have none to give thee!"

They approached the door; which was of an arched form, and flanked on each side by a narrow tower or projection of the edifice, in both of which were lattice-windows, with wooden shutters to close over them at need. Lifting the iron hammer that hung at the portal, Hester Prynne gave a summons, which was answered by one of the Governor's bond-servants; a free-born Englishman, but now a seven years' slave. During that term he was to be the property of his master, and as much a commodity of bargain and sale as an ox, or a joint-stool. The serf wore the blue coat, which was the customary garb of serving-men at that period, and long before, in the old hereditary halls of England.

"Is the worshipful Governor Bellingham within?" inquired Hester.

"Yea, forsooth," replied the bond-servant, staring with wide-open eyes at the scarlet letter, which, being a new-comer in the country, he had never before seen. "Yea, his honorable worship is within. But he hath a godly minister or two with him, and likewise a leech. Ye may not see his worship now."

"Nevertheless, I will enter," answered Hester Prynne; and the bond-servant, perhaps judging from the decision of her air and the glittering symbol in her bosom, that she was a great lady in the land, offered no opposition.

So the mother and little Pearl were admitted into the hall of entrance. With many variations, suggested by the nature of his building-materials, diversity of climate, and a different mode of social life, Governor Bellingham had planned his new habitation after the residences of gentlemen of fair estate in his native land. Here, then, was a wide and reasonably lofty hall, extending through the whole depth of the house, and forming a medium of general communication, more or less directly, with all the other apartments. At one extremity, this spacious room was lighted by the windows of the two towers, which formed a small recess on either side of the portal. At the other end, though partly muffled by a curtain, it was more powerfully illuminated by one of those embowed hall-windows which we read of in old books, and which was provided with a deep and cushioned seat. Here, on the cushion, lay a folio tome, probably of the Chronicles of England,[4] or

4. Raphael Holinshed's *Chronicles of England, Scotland, and Ireland* (1577).

other such substantial literature; even as, in our own days, we scatter gilded volumes on the centre-table, to be turned over by the casual guest. The furniture of the hall consisted of some ponderous chairs, the backs of which were elaborately carved with wreaths of oaken flowers; and likewise a table in the same taste; the whole being of the Elizabethan age, or perhaps earlier, and heirlooms, transferred hither from the Governor's paternal home. On the table—in token that the sentiment of old English hospitality had not been left behind—stood a large pewter tankard, at the bottom of which, had Hester or Pearl peeped into it, they might have seen the frothy remnant of a recent draught of ale.

On the wall hung a row of portraits, representing the forefathers of the Bellingham lineage, some with armour on their breasts, and others with stately ruffs and robes of peace. All were characterized by the sternness and severity which old portraits so invariably put on; as if they were the ghosts, rather than the pictures, of departed worthies, and were gazing with harsh and intolerant criticism at the pursuits and enjoyments of living men.

At about the centre of the oaken panels, that lined the hall, was suspended a suit of mail, not, like the pictures, an ancestral relic, but of the most modern date; for it had been manufactured by a skilful armourer in London, the same year in which Governor Bellingham came over to New England. There was a steel head-piece, a cuirass, a gorget, and greaves,[5] with a pair of gauntlets and a sword hanging beneath; all, and especially the helmet and breastplate, so highly burnished as to glow with white radiance, and scatter an illumination everywhere about upon the floor. This bright panoply was not meant for mere idle show, but had been worn by the Governor on many a solemn muster and training field, and had glittered, moreover, at the head of a regiment in the Pequod war.[6] For, though bred a lawyer, and accustomed to speak of Bacon, Coke, Noye, and Finch,[7] as his professional associates, the exigencies of this new country had transformed Governor Bellingham into a soldier, as well as a statesman and ruler.

Little Pearl—who was as greatly pleased with the gleaming armour as she had been with the glittering frontispiece of the house—spent some time looking into the polished mirror of the breastplate.

"Mother," cried she, "I see you here. Look! Look!"

Hester looked, by way of humoring the child; and she saw that, owing to the peculiar effect of this convex mirror, the scarlet letter was represented in exaggerated and gigantic proportions, so as to be greatly the most prominent feature of her appearance. In truth, she seemed absolutely hidden behind it. Pearl pointed upward, also, at a similar picture in the head-piece; smiling at her mother, with the elfish intelligence that was so familiar an expression on her small physiognomy. That look of naughty merriment was likewise reflected in the mirror, with so much breadth and intensity of effect, that it made Hester Prynne feel as if it could not be the image of her own child, but of an imp who was seeking to mould itself into Pearl's shape.

5. Parts of armor. "Cuirass": breastplate. "Gorget": collar. "Greaves": shin protectors.
6. There is no evidence that the historical Bellingham actually participated in the Puritans' War against the Pequots in 1637, which nearly annihilated the tribe.
7. Sir John Finch (1584–1660), speaker of the House of Commons and chief justice. Francis Bacon (1561–1626), lord chancellor of England. Sir Edward Coke (1552–1634), lord chief justice. William Noye (1577–1634), attorney general.

"Come along, Pearl!" said she, drawing her away. "Come and look into this fair garden. It may be, we shall see flowers there; more beautiful ones than we find in the woods."

Pearl, accordingly, ran to the bow-window, at the farther end of the hall, and looked along the vista of a garden-walk, carpeted with closely shaven grass, and bordered with some rude and immature attempt at shrubbery. But the proprietor appeared already to have relinquished, as hopeless, the effort to perpetuate on this side of the Atlantic, in a hard soil and amid the close struggle for subsistence, the native English taste for ornamental gardening. Cabbages grew in plain sight; and a pumpkin vine, rooted at some distance, had run across the intervening space, and deposited one of its gigantic products directly beneath the hall-window; as if to warn the Governor that this great lump of vegetable gold was as rich an ornament as New England earth would offer him. There were a few rose-bushes, however, and a number of apple-trees, probably the descendants of those planted by the Reverend Mr. Blackstone,[8] the first settler of the peninsula; that half mythological personage who rides through our early annals, seated on the back of a bull.

Pearl, seeing the rose-bushes, began to cry for a red rose, and would not be pacified.

"Hush, child, hush!" said her mother earnestly. "Do not cry, dear little Pearl! I hear voices in the garden. The Governor is coming, and gentlemen along with him!"

In fact, adown the vista of the garden-avenue, a number of persons were seen approaching towards the house. Pearl, in utter scorn of her mother's attempt to quiet her, gave an eldritch[9] scream, and then became silent; not from any notion of obedience, but because the quick and mobile curiosity of her disposition was excited by the appearance of these new personages.

VIII. The Elf-Child and the Minister

Governor Bellingham, in a loose gown and easy cap,—such as elderly gentlemen loved to indue themselves with, in their domestic privacy,—walked foremost, and appeared to be showing off his estate, and expatiating on his projected improvements. The wide circumference of an elaborate ruff, beneath his gray beard, in the antiquated fashion of King James's reign, caused his head to look not a little like that of John the Baptist in a charger.[1] The impression made by his aspect, so rigid and severe, and frost-bitten with more than autumnal age, was hardly in keeping with the appliances of worldly enjoyment wherewith he had evidently done his utmost to surround himself. But it is an error to suppose that our grave forefathers—though accustomed to speak and think of human existence as a state merely of trial and warfare, and though unfeignedly prepared to sacrifice goods and life at the behest of duty—made it a matter of conscience to reject such means of comfort, or even luxury, as lay fairly within their grasp. This creed was never

8. The Anglican minister William Blackstone (1595–1675), also known as William Blaxton, settled in Boston a few years before the arrival of the Puritans in the late 1620s. He moved to Rhode Island during the 1630s when he found that he could not coexist with Puritan leaders. He made a brief return to Boston in 1659, riding on a bull.

9. Weird, unearthly.

1. Platter. James I reigned in England from 1603 to 1625. For the beheading of John the Baptist, see Matthew 14.1–12.

taught, for instance, by the venerable pastor, John Wilson, whose beard, white as a snow-drift, was seen over Governor Bellingham's shoulder; while its wearer suggested that pears and peaches might yet be naturalized in the New England climate, and that purple grapes might possibly be compelled to flourish, against the sunny garden-wall. The old clergyman, nurtured at the rich bosom of the English Church, had a long established and legitimate taste for all good and comfortable things; and however stern he might show himself in the pulpit, or in his public reproof of such transgressions as that of Hester Prynne, still, the genial benevolence of his private life had won him warmer affection than was accorded to any of his professional contemporaries.

Behind the Governor and Mr. Wilson came two other guests; one, the Reverend Arthur Dimmesdale, whom the reader may remember, as having taken a brief and reluctant part in the scene of Hester Prynne's disgrace; and, in close companionship with him, old Roger Chillingworth, a person of great skill in physic,[2] who, for two or three years past, had been settled in the town. It was understood that this learned man was the physician as well as friend of the young minister, whose health had severely suffered, of late, by his too unreserved self-sacrifice to the labors and duties of the pastoral relation.

The Governor, in advance of his visitors, ascended one or two steps, and, throwing open the leaves of the great hall window, found himself close to little Pearl. The shadow of the curtain fell on Hester Prynne, and partially concealed her.

"What have we here?" said Governor Bellingham, looking with surprise at the scarlet little figure before him. "I profess, I have never seen the like, since my days of vanity, in old King James's time, when I was wont to esteem it a high favor to be admitted to a court mask! There used to be a swarm of these small apparitions, in holiday-time; and we called them children of the Lord of Misrule.[3] But how gat such a guest into my hall?"

"Ay, indeed!" cried good old Mr. Wilson. "What little bird of scarlet plumage may this be? Methinks I have seen just such figures, when the sun has been shining through a richly painted window, and tracing out the golden and crimson images across the floor. But that was in the old land. Prithee, young one, who art thou, and what has ailed thy mother to bedizen thee in this strange fashion? Art thou a Christian child,—ha? Dost know thy catechism? Or art thou one of those naughty elfs or fairies, whom we thought to have left behind us, with other relics of Papistry, in merry old England?"

"I am mother's child," answered the scarlet vision, "and my name is Pearl!"

"Pearl?—Ruby, rather!—or Coral!—or Red Rose, at the very least, judging from thy hue!" responded the old minister, putting forth his hand in a vain attempt to pat little Pearl on the cheek. "But where is this mother of thine? Ah! I see," he added; and, turning to Governor Bellingham, whispered,—"This is the selfsame child of whom we have held speech together; and behold here the unhappy woman, Hester Prynne, her mother!"

"Sayest thou so?" cried the Governor. "Nay, we might have judged that such a child's mother must needs be a scarlet woman, and a worthy type of

2. Medicine or healing.
3. Leader of Christmas revels in England as celebrated from medieval times to the early seventeenth century.

her of Babylon![4] But she comes at a good time; and we will look into this matter forthwith."

Governor Bellingham stepped through the window into the hall, followed by his three guests.

"Hester Prynne," said he, fixing his naturally stern regard on the wearer of the scarlet letter, "there hath been much question concerning thee, of late. The point hath been weightily discussed, whether we, that are of authority and influence, do well discharge our consciences by trusting an immortal soul, such as there is in yonder child, to the guidance of one who hath stumbled and fallen, amid the pitfalls of this world. Speak thou, the child's own mother! Were it not, thinkest thou, for thy little one's temporal and eternal welfare, that she be taken out of thy charge, and clad soberly, and disciplined strictly, and instructed in the truths of heaven and earth? What canst thou do for the child, in this kind?"

"I can teach my little Pearl what I have learned from this!" answered Hester Prynne, laying her finger on the red token.

"Woman, it is thy badge of shame!" replied the stern magistrate. "It is because of the stain which that letter indicates, what we would transfer thy child to other hands."

"Nevertheless," said the mother calmly, though growing more pale, "this badge hath taught me,—it daily teaches me,—it is teaching me at this moment,—lessons whereof my child may be the wiser and better, albeit they can profit nothing to myself."

"We will judge warily," said Bellingham, "and look well what we are about to do. Good Master Wilson, I pray you, examine this Pearl,—since that is her name,—and see whether she hath had such Christian nurture as befits a child of her age."

The old minister seated himself in an arm-chair, and made an effort to draw Pearl betwixt his knees. But the child, unaccustomed to the touch or familiarity of any but her mother, escaped through the open window and stood on the upper step, looking like a wild, tropical bird, of rich plumage, ready to take flight into the upper air. Mr. Wilson, not a little astonished at this outbreak,—for he was a grandfatherly sort of personage, and usually a vast favorite with children,—essayed, however, to proceed with the examination.

"Pearl," said he, with great solemnity, "thou must take heed to instruction, that so, in due season, thou mayest wear in thy bosom the pearl of great price.[5] Canst thou tell me, my child, who made thee?"

Now Pearl knew well enough who made her; for Hester Prynne, the daughter of a pious home, very soon after her talk with the child about her Heavenly Father, had begun to inform her of those truths which the human spirit, at whatever stage of immaturity, imbibes with such eager interest. Pearl, therefore, so large were the attainments of her three years' lifetime, could have borne a fair examination in the New England Primer, or the first column of the Westminster Catechism,[6] although unacquainted with the

4. Bellingham likens Hester to the Whore of Babylon of the Bible (Revelation 17.3–5).
5. See p. 499, n. 6.
6. Question-and-answer compendium of Calvinistic doctrine based on principles adopted at Westminster, England, 1645–47. "New England Primer": booklet for teaching the alphabet through woodcut illustrations and pious verses such as (for the letter *A*) "In Adam's fall we sinnèd all."

outward form of either of those celebrated works. But that perversity, which all children have more or less of, and of which little Pearl had a tenfold portion, now, at the most inopportune moment, took thorough possession of her, and closed her lips, or impelled her to speak words amiss. After putting her finger in her mouth, with many ungracious refusals to answer good Mr. Wilson's question, the child finally announced that she had not been made at all, but had been plucked by her mother off the bush of wild roses, that grew by the prison-door.

This fantasy was probably suggested by the near proximity of the Governor's red roses, as Pearl stood outside of the window; together with her recollection of the prison rose-bush, which she had passed in coming hither.

Old Roger Chillingworth, with a smile on his face, whispered something in the young clergyman's ear. Hester Prynne looked at the man of skill, and even then, with her fate hanging in the balance, was startled to perceive what a change had come over his features,—how much uglier they were,—how his dark complexion seemed to have grown duskier, and his figure more misshapen,—since the days when she had familiarly known him. She met his eyes for an instant, but was immediately constrained to give all her attention to the scene now going forward.

"This is awful!" cried the Governor, slowly recovering from the astonishment into which Pearl's response had thrown him. "Here is a child of three years old, and she cannot tell who made her! Without question, she is equally in the dark as to her soul, its present depravity, and future destiny! Methinks, gentlemen, we need inquire no further."

Hester caught hold of Pearl, and drew her forcibly into her arms, confronting the old Puritan magistrate with almost a fierce expression. Alone in the world, cast off by it, and with this sole treasure to keep her heart alive, she felt that she possessed indefeasible rights against the world, and was ready to defend them to the death.

"God gave me the child!" cried she. "He gave her, in requital of all things else, which ye had taken from me. She is my happiness!—she is my torture, none the less! Pearl keeps me here in life! Pearl punishes me too! See ye not, she is the scarlet letter, only capable of being loved, and so endowed with a million-fold the power of retribution for my sin! Ye shall not take her! I will die first!"

"My poor woman," said the not unkind old minister, "the child shall be well cared for!—far better than thou canst do it."

"God gave her into my keeping," repeated Hester Prynne, raising her voice almost to a shriek. "I will not give her up!"—And here, by a sudden impulse, she turned to the young clergyman, Mr. Dimmesdale, at whom, up to this moment, she had seemed hardly so much as once to direct her eyes.—"Speak thou for me!" cried she. "Thou wast my pastor, and hadst charge of my soul, and knowest me better than these men can. I will not lose the child! Speak for me! Thou knowest,—for thou hast sympathies which these men lack!—thou knowest what is in my heart, and what are a mother's rights, and how much the stronger they are, when that mother has but her child and the scarlet letter! Look thou to it! I will not lose the child! Look to it!"

At this wild and singular appeal, which indicated that Hester Prynne's situation had provoked her to little less than madness, the young minister at once came forward, pale, and holding his hand over his heart, as was his custom whenever his peculiarly nervous temperament was thrown into agitation. He looked now more careworn and emaciated than as we described him at the scene of Hester's public ignominy; and whether it were his failing health, or whatever the cause might be, his large dark eyes had a world of pain in their troubled and melancholy depth.

"There is truth in what she says," began the minister, with a voice sweet, tremulous, but powerful, insomuch that the hall reëchoed, and the hollow armour rang with it,—"truth in what Hester says, and in the feeling which inspires her! God gave her the child, and gave her, too, an instinctive knowledge of its nature and requirements,—both seemingly so peculiar,—which no other mortal being can possess. And, moreover, is there not a quality of awful sacredness in the relation between this mother and this child?"

"Ay!—how is that, good Master Dimmesdale?" interrupted the Governor. "Make that plain, I pray you!"

"It must be even so," resumed the minister. "For, if we deem it otherwise, do we not thereby say that the Heavenly Father, the Creator of all flesh, hath lightly recognized a deed of sin, and made of no account the distinction between unhallowed lust and holy love? This child of its father's guilt and its mother's shame hath come from the hand of God, to work in many ways upon her heart, who pleads so earnestly, and with such bitterness of spirit, the right to keep her. It was meant for a blessing; for the one blessing of her life! It was meant, doubtless, as the mother herself hath told us, for a retribution too; a torture, to be felt at many an unthought of moment; a pang, a sting, an ever-recurring agony, in the midst of a troubled joy! Hath she not expressed this thought in the garb of the poor child, so forcibly reminding us of that red symbol which sears her bosom?"

"Well said, again!" cried good Mr. Wilson. "I feared the woman had no better thought than to make a mountebank[7] of her child!"

"O, not so!—not so!" continued Mr. Dimmesdale. "She recognizes, believe me, the solemn miracle which God hath wrought, in the existence of that child. And may she feel, too,—what, methinks, is the very truth,—that this boon was meant, above all things else, to keep the mother's soul alive, and to preserve her from blacker depths of sin into which Satan might else have sought to plunge her! Therefore it is good for this poor, sinful woman that she hath an infant immortality, a being capable of eternal joy or sorrow, confided to her care,—to be trained up by her to righteousness,—to remind her, at every moment, of her fall,—but yet to teach her, as it were by the Creator's sacred pledge, that, if she bring the child to heaven, the child also will bring its parent thither! Herein is the sinful mother happier than the sinful father. For Hester Prynne's sake, then, and no less for the poor child's sake, let us leave them as Providence hath seen fit to place them!"

"You speak, my friend, with a strange earnestness," said old Roger Chillingworth, smiling at him.

"And there is weighty import in what my young brother hath spoken," added the Reverend Mr. Wilson. "What say you, worshipful Master Bellingham? Hath he not pleaded well for the poor woman?"

7. A fraud or charlatan.

"Indeed hath he," answered the magistrate, "and hath adduced such arguments, that we will even leave the matter as it now stands; so long, at least, as there shall be no further scandal in the woman. Care must be had, nevertheless, to put the child to due and stated examination in the catechism at thy hands or Master Dimmesdale's. Moreover, at a proper season, the tithing-men[8] must take heed that she go both to school and to meeting."

The young minister, on ceasing to speak, had withdrawn a few steps from the group, and stood with his face partially concealed in the heavy folds of the window-curtain; while the shadow of his figure, which the sunlight cast upon the floor, was tremulous with the vehemence of his appeal. Pearl, that wild and flighty little elf, stole softly towards him, and taking his hand in the grasp of both her own, laid her cheek against it; a caress so tender, and withal so unobtrusive, that her mother, who was looking on, asked herself,—"Is that my Pearl?" Yet she knew that there was love in the child's heart, although it mostly revealed itself in passion, and hardly twice in her lifetime had been softened by such gentleness as now. The minister,—for, save the long-sought regards of woman, nothing is sweeter than these marks of childish preference, accorded spontaneously by a spiritual instinct, and therefore seeming to imply in us something truly worthy to be loved,—the minister looked round, laid his hand on the child's head, hesitated an instant, and then kissed her brow. Little Pearl's unwonted mood of sentiment lasted no longer; she laughed, and went capering down the hall, so airily, that old Mr. Wilson raised a question whether even her tiptoes touched the floor.

"The little baggage hath witchcraft in her, I profess," said he to Mr. Dimmesdale. "She needs no old woman's broomstick to fly withal!"

"A strange child!" remarked old Roger Chillingworth. "It is easy to see the mother's part in her. Would it be beyond a philosopher's research, think ye, gentlemen, to analyze the child's nature, and, from its make and mould, to give a shrewd guess at the father?"

"Nay; it would be sinful, in such a question, to follow the clew of profane philosophy," said Mr. Wilson. "Better to fast and pray upon it; and still better, it may be, to leave the mystery as we find it, unless Providence reveal it of its own accord. Thereby, every good Christian man hath a title to show a father's kindness towards the poor, deserted babe."

The affair being so satisfactorily concluded, Hester Prynne, with Pearl, departed from the house. As they descended the steps, it is averred that the lattice of a chamber-window was thrown open, and forth into the sunny day was thrust the face of Mistress Hibbins, Governor Bellingham's bitter-tempered sister, and the same who, a few years later, was executed as a witch.

"Hist, hist!" said she, while her ill-omened physiognomy seemed to cast a shadow over the cheerful newness of the house. "Wilt thou go with us to-night? There will be a merry company in the forest; and I wellnigh promised the Black Man that comely Hester Prynne should make one."

"Make my excuse to him, so please you!" answered Hester, with a triumphant smile. "I must tarry at home, and keep watch over my little Pearl. Had they taken her from me, I would willingly have gone with thee into the forest,

8. Parish officers.

and signed my name in the Black Man's book too, and that with mine own blood!"

"We shall have thee there anon!" said the witch-lady, frowning, as she drew back her head.

But here—if we suppose this interview betwixt Mistress Hibbins and Hester Prynne to be authentic, and not a parable—was already an illustration of the young minister's argument against sundering the relation of a fallen mother to the offspring of her frailty. Even thus early had the child saved her from Satan's snare.

IX. The Leech

Under the appellation of Roger Chillingworth, the reader will remember, was hidden another name, which its former wearer had resolved should never more be spoken. It has been related, how, in the crowd that witnessed Hester Prynne's ignominious exposure, stood a man, elderly, travel-worn, who, just emerging from the perilous wilderness, beheld the woman, in whom he hoped to find embodied the warmth and cheerfulness of home, set up as a type of sin before the people. Her matronly fame was trodden under all men's feet. Infamy was babbling around her in the public market-place. For her kindred, should the tidings ever reach them, and for the companions of her unspotted life, there remained nothing but the contagion of her dishonor; which would not fail to be distributed in strict accordance and proportion with the intimacy and sacredness of their previous relationship. Then why—since the choice was with himself—should the individual, whose connection with the fallen woman had been the most intimate and sacred of them all, come forward to vindicate his claim to an inheritance so little desirable? He resolved not to be pilloried beside her on her pedestal of shame. Unknown to all but Hester Prynne, and possessing the lock and key of her silence, he chose to withdraw his name from the roll of mankind, and, as regarded his former ties and interests, to vanish out of life as completely as if he indeed lay at the bottom of the ocean, whither rumor had long ago consigned him. This purpose once effected, new interests would immediately spring up, and likewise a new purpose; dark, it is true, if not guilty, but of force enough to engage the full strength of his faculties.

In pursuance of this resolve, he took up his residence in the Puritan town, as Roger Chillingworth, without other introduction than the learning and intelligence of which he possessed more than a common measure. As his studies, at a previous period of his life, had made him extensively acquainted with the medical science of the day, it was as a physician that he presented himself, and as such was cordially received. Skilful men, of the medical and chirurgical[9] profession, were of rare occurrence in the colony. They seldom, it would appear, partook of the religious zeal that brought other emigrants across the Atlantic. In their researches into the human frame, it may be that the higher and more subtile faculties of such men were materialized, and that they lost the spiritual view of existence amid the intricacies of that wondrous mechanism, which seemed to involve art enough to comprise all of life

9. Surgical.

within itself. At all events, the health of the good town of Boston, so far as medicine had aught to do with it, had hitherto lain in the guardianship of an aged deacon and apothecary, whose piety and godly deportment were stronger testimonials in his favor, than any that he could have produced in the shape of a diploma. The only surgeon was one who combined the occasional exercise of that noble art with the daily and habitual flourish of a razor. To such a professional body Roger Chillingworth was a brilliant acquisition. He soon manifested his familiarity with the ponderous and imposing machinery of antique physic; in which every remedy contained a multitude of far-fetched and heterogeneous ingredients, as elaborately compounded as if the proposed result had been the Elixir of Life.[1] In his Indian captivity, moreover, he had gained much knowledge of the properties of native herbs and roots; nor did he conceal from his patients, that these simple medicines, Nature's boon to the untutored savage, had quite as large a share of his own confidence as the European pharmacopœia,[2] which so many learned doctors had spent centuries in elaborating.

This learned stranger was exemplary, as regarded at least the outward forms of a religious life, and, early after his arrival, had chosen for his spiritual guide the Reverend Mr. Dimmesdale. The young divine, whose scholar-like renown still lived in Oxford, was considered by his more fervent admirers as little less than a heaven-ordained apostle, destined, should he live and labor for the ordinary term of life, to do as great deeds for the now feeble New England Church, as the early Fathers had achieved for the infancy of the Christian faith. About this period, however, the health of Mr. Dimmesdale had evidently begun to fail. By those best acquainted with his habits, the paleness of the young minister's cheek was accounted for by his too earnest devotion to study, his scrupulous fulfilment of parochial duty, and, more than all, by the fasts and vigils of which he made a frequent practice, in order to keep the grossness of this earthly state from clogging and obscuring his spiritual lamp. Some declared, that, if Mr. Dimmesdale were really going to die, it was cause enough, that the world was not worthy to be any longer trodden by his feet. He himself, on the other hand, with characteristic humility, avowed his belief, that, if Providence should see fit to remove him, it would be because of his own unworthiness to perform its humblest mission here on earth. With all this difference of opinion as to the cause of his decline, there could be no question of the fact. His form grew emaciated; his voice, though still rich and sweet, had a certain melancholy prophecy of decay in it; he was often observed, on any slight alarm or other sudden accident, to put his hand over his heart, with first a flush and then a paleness, indicative of pain.

Such was the young clergyman's condition, and so imminent the prospect that his dawning light would be extinguished, all untimely, when Roger Chillingworth made his advent to the town. His first entry on the scene, few people could tell whence, dropping down, as it were, out of the sky, or starting from the nether earth, had an aspect of mystery, which was easily heightened to the miraculous. He was now known to be a man of skill; it was observed that he gathered herbs, and the blossoms of wild-flowers, and dug up roots and plucked off twigs from the forest-trees, like one acquainted

1. Substance thought capable of giving eternal life.

2. Collection of approved drugs.

with hidden virtues in what was valueless to common eyes. He was heard to speak of Sir Kenelm Digby,[3] and other famous men,—whose scientific attainments were esteemed hardly less than supernatural,—as having been his correspondents or associates. Why, with such rank in the learned world, had he come hither? What could he, whose sphere was in great cities, be seeking in the wilderness? In answer to this query, a rumor gained ground,—and, however absurd, was entertained by some very sensible people,—that Heaven had wrought an absolute miracle, by transporting an eminent Doctor of Physic, from a German university, bodily through the air, and setting him down at the door of Mr. Dimmesdale's study! Individuals of wiser faith, indeed, who knew that Heaven promotes its purposes without aiming at the stage-effect of what is called miraculous interposition, were inclined to see a providential hand in Roger Chillingworth's so opportune arrival.

This idea was countenanced by the strong interest which the physician ever manifested in the young clergyman; he attached himself to him as a parishioner, and sought to win a friendly regard and confidence from his naturally reserved sensibility. He expressed great alarm at his pastor's state of health, but was anxious to attempt the cure, and, if early undertaken, seemed not despondent of a favorable result. The elders, the deacons, the motherly dames, and the young and fair maidens, of Mr. Dimmesdale's flock, were alike importunate that he should make trial of the physician's frankly offered skill. Mr. Dimmesdale gently repelled their entreaties.

"I need no medicine," said he.

But how could the young minister say so, when, with every successive Sabbath, his cheek was paler and thinner, and his voice more tremulous than before,—when it had now become a constant habit, rather than a casual gesture, to press his hand over his heart? Was he weary of his labors? Did he wish to die? These questions were solemnly propounded to Mr. Dimmesdale by the elder ministers of Boston and the deacons of his church, who, to use their own phrase, "dealt with him" on the sin of rejecting the aid which Providence so manifestly held out. He listened in silence, and finally promised to confer with the physician.

"Were it God's will," said the Reverend Mr. Dimmesdale, when, in fulfilment of this pledge, he requested old Roger Chillingworth's professional advice, "I could be well content, that my labors, and my sorrows, and my sins, and my pains, should shortly end with me, and what is earthly of them be buried in my grave, and the spiritual go with me to my eternal state, rather than that you should put your skill to the proof in my behalf."

"Ah," replied Roger Chillingworth, with that quietness which, whether imposed or natural, marked all his deportment, "it is thus that a young clergyman is apt to speak. Youthful men, not having taken a deep root, give up their hold of life so easily! And saintly men, who walk with God on earth, would fain be away, to walk with him on the golden pavements of the New Jerusalem."

"Nay," rejoined the young minister, putting his hand to his heart, with a flush of pain flitting over his brow, "were I worthier to walk there, I could be better content to toil here."

3. English naval officer, diplomat, and scientist (1603–1665).

"Good men ever interpret themselves too meanly," said the physician.

In this manner, the mysterious old Roger Chillingworth became the medical adviser of the Reverend Mr. Dimmesdale. As not only the disease interested the physician, but he was strongly moved to look into the character and qualities of the patient, these two men, so different in age, came gradually to spend much time together. For the sake of the minister's health, and to enable the leech to gather plants with healing balm in them, they took long walks on the seashore, or in the forest; mingling various talk with the plash and murmur of the waves, and the solemn wind-anthem among the tree-tops. Often, likewise, one was the guest of the other, in his place of study and retirement. There was a fascination for the minister in the company of the man of science, in whom he recognized an intellectual cultivation of no moderate depth or scope; together with a range and freedom of ideas, that he would have vainly looked for among the members of his own profession. In truth, he was startled, if not shocked, to find this attribute in the physician. Mr. Dimmesdale was a true priest, a true religionist, with the reverential sentiment largely developed, and an order of mind that impelled itself powerfully along the track of a creed, and wore its passage continually deeper with the lapse of time. In no state of society would he have been what is called a man of liberal views; it would always be essential to his peace to feel the pressure of a faith about him, supporting, while it confined him within its iron framework. Not the less, however, though with a tremulous enjoyment, did he feel the occasional relief of looking at the universe through the medium of another kind of intellect than those with which he habitually held converse. It was as if a window were thrown open, admitting a freer atmosphere into the close and stifled study, where his life was wasting itself away, amid lamp-light, or obstructed daybeams, and the musty fragrance, be it sensual or moral, that exhales from books. But the air was too fresh and chill to be long breathed, with comfort. So the minister, and the physician with him, withdrew again within the limits of what their church defined as orthodox.

Thus Roger Chillingworth scrutinized his patient carefully, both as he saw him in his ordinary life, keeping an accustomed pathway in the range of thoughts familiar to him, and as he appeared when thrown amidst other moral scenery, the novelty of which might call out something new to the surface of his character. He deemed it essential, it would seem, to know the man, before attempting to do him good. Wherever there is a heart and an intellect, the diseases of the physical frame are tinged with the peculiarities of these. In Arthur Dimmesdale, thought and imagination were so active, and sensibility so intense, that the bodily infirmity would be likely to have its groundwork there. So Roger Chillingworth—the man of skill, the kind and friendly physician—strove to go deep into his patient's bosom, delving among his principles, prying into his recollections, and probing every thing with a cautious touch, like a treasure-seeker in a dark cavern. Few secrets can escape an investigator, who has opportunity and license to undertake such a quest, and skill to follow it up. A man burdened with a secret should especially avoid the intimacy of his physician. If the latter possess native sagacity, and a nameless something more,—let us call it intuition; if he show no intrusive egotism, nor disagreeably prominent characteristics of his own; if he have the power, which must be born with him, to bring his mind into such affinity with his patient's, that this last shall unawares have spoken what he imagines himself only to have thought; if such revelations be received without tumult, and acknowledged not so often by an uttered sympathy, as by silence, an inarticulate breath, and here and there a word, to indicate that all is understood; if, to these qualifications of a confidant be joined the advantages afforded by his recognized character as a physician;—then, at some inevitable moment, will the soul of the sufferer be dissolved, and flow forth in a dark, but transparent stream, bringing all its mysteries into the daylight.

Roger Chillingworth possessed all, or most, of the attributes above enumerated. Nevertheless, time went on; a kind of intimacy, as we have said, grew up between these two cultivated minds, which had as wide a field as the whole sphere of human thought and study, to meet upon; they discussed every topic of ethics and religion, of public affairs, and private character; they talked much, on both sides, of matters that seemed personal to themselves; and yet no secret, such as the physician fancied must exist there, ever stole out of the minister's consciousness into his companion's ear. The latter had his suspicions, indeed, that even the nature of Mr. Dimmesdale's bodily disease had never fairly been revealed to him. It was a strange reserve!

After a time, at a hint from Roger Chillingworth, the friends of Mr. Dimmesdale effected an arrangement by which the two were lodged in the same house; so that every ebb and flow of the minister's life-tide might pass under the eye of his anxious and attached physician. There was much joy throughout the town, when this greatly desirable object was attained. It was held to be the best possible measure for the young clergyman's welfare; unless, indeed, as often urged by such as felt authorized to do so, he had selected some one of the many blooming damsels, spiritually devoted to him, to become his devoted wife. This latter step, however, there was no present prospect that Arthur Dimmesdale would be prevailed upon to take; he rejected all suggestions of the kind, as if priestly celibacy were one of his articles of church-discipline. Doomed by his own choice, therefore, as Mr. Dimmesdale so evidently was, to eat his unsavory morsel always at another's board, and endure the life-long chill which must be his lot who seeks to warm himself only at another's fireside, it truly seemed that this sagacious, experienced, benevolent, old physician, with his concord of paternal and reverential love for the young pastor, was the very man, of all mankind, to be constantly within reach of his voice.

The new abode of the two friends was with a pious widow, of good social rank, who dwelt in a house covering pretty nearly the site on which the venerable structure of King's Chapel has since been built. It had the grave-yard, originally Isaac Johnson's home-field, on one side, and so was well adapted to call up serious reflections, suited to their respective employments, in both minister and man of physic. The motherly care of the good widow assigned to Mr. Dimmesdale a front apartment, with a sunny exposure, and heavy window-curtains to create a noontide shadow, when desirable. The walls were hung round with tapestry, said to be from the Gobelin looms,[4] and, at all events, representing the Scriptural story of David and Bathsheba, and Nathan the Prophet, in colors still unfaded, but which made the fair woman

4. Looms of the great Parisian tapestry-making family of the 15th century.

of the scene almost as grimly picturesque as the woe-denouncing seer. Here, the pale clergyman piled up his library, rich with parchment-bound folios of the Fathers,[5] and the lore of Rabbis, and monkish erudition, of which the Protestant divines, even while they vilified and decried that class of writers, were yet constrained often to avail themselves. On the other side of the house, old Roger Chillingworth arranged his study and laboratory; not such as a modern man of science would reckon even tolerably complete, but provided with a distilling apparatus, and the means of compounding drugs and chemicals, which the practised alchemist knew well how to turn to purpose. With such commodiousness of situation, these two learned persons sat themselves down, each in his own domain, yet familiarly passing from one apartment to the other, and bestowing a mutual and not incurious inspection into one another's business.

And the Reverend Arthur Dimmesdale's best discerning friends, as we have intimated, very reasonably imagined that the hand of Providence had done all this, for the purpose—besought in so many public, and domestic, and secret prayers—of restoring the young minister to health. But—it must now be said—another portion of the community had latterly begun to take its own view of the relation betwixt Mr. Dimmesdale and the mysterious old physician. When an uninstructed multitude attempts to see with its eyes, it is exceedingly apt to be deceived. When, however, it forms its judgment, as it usually does, on the intuitions of its great and warm heart, the conclusions thus attained are often so profound and so unerring, as to possess the character of truths supernaturally revealed. The people, in the case of which we speak, could justify its prejudice against Roger Chillingworth by no fact or argument worthy of serious refutation. There was an aged handicraftsman, it is true, who had been a citizen of London at the period of Sir Thomas Overbury's murder, now some thirty years agone; he testified to having seen the physician, under some other name, which the narrator of the story had now forgotten, in company with Doctor Forman, the famous old conjurer, who was implicated in the affair of Overbury.[6] Two or three individuals hinted, that the man of skill, during his Indian captivity, had enlarged his medical attainments by joining in the incantations of the savage priests; who were universally acknowledged to be powerful enchanters, often performing seemingly miraculous cures by their skill in the black art. A large number—and many of these were persons of such sober sense and practical observation, that their opinions would have been valuable, in other matters—affirmed that Roger Chillingworth's aspect had undergone a remarkable change while he had dwelt in town, and especially since his abode with Mr. Dim-

5. Christians in early centuries after Jesus' death who formulated doctrines and observances. Samuel 11–12 describes how the prophet Nathan denounced David, Israel's second king, for sending Bathsheba's husband to certain death in battle so that he could marry her.

6. Sir Thomas Overbury (1581–1613) was involved in a notorious scandal during the reign of James I. When he attempted to stop his employer, Viscount Rochester, from marrying the countess of Essex because of her reputed licentiousness, she manipulated events to make Overbury appear disrespectful of royalty. Eventually, James I ordered Overbury imprisoned in the Tower of London for rejecting an ambassadorial position, and he died there in 1613 from ingesting poison mixed with his food. A subsequent trial revealed that the countess had been behind the plot, ordering Ann Turner (a friend of Ann Hibbins and the wife of a physician) to administer the poison. Turner and three co-conspirators were hanged, but the countess was pardoned. Earlier Dr. Simon Forman (1552–1611), keeper of a historically valuable diary, had connived with the countess in seeking Overbury's death by witchcraft.

mesdale. At first, his expression had been calm, meditative, scholar-like. Now, there was something ugly and evil in his face, which they had not previously noticed, and which grew still the more obvious to sight, the oftener they looked upon him. According to the vulgar idea, the fire in his laboratory had been brought from the lower regions, and was fed with infernal fuel; and so, as might be expected, his visage was getting sooty with the smoke.

To sum up the matter, it grew to be a widely diffused opinion, that the Reverend Arthur Dimmesdale, like many other personages of especial sanctity, in all ages of the Christian world, was haunted either by Satan himself, or Satan's emissary, in the guise of old Roger Chillingworth. This diabolical agent had the Divine permission, for a season, to burrow into the clergyman's intimacy, and plot against his soul. No sensible man, it was confessed, could doubt on which side the victory would turn. The people looked, with an unshaken hope, to see the minister come forth out of the conflict, transfigured with the glory which he would unquestionably win. Meanwhile, nevertheless, it was sad to think of the perchance mortal agony through which he must struggle towards his triumph.

Alas, to judge from the gloom and terror in the depths of the poor minister's eyes, the battle was a sore one, and the victory any thing but secure!

X. *The Leech and his Patient*

Old Roger Chillingworth, throughout life, had been calm in temperament, kindly, though not of warm affections, but ever, and in all his relations with the world, a pure and upright man. He had begun an investigation, as he imagined, with the severe and equal integrity of a judge, desirous only of truth, even as if the question involved no more than the air-drawn lines and figures of a geometrical problem, instead of human passions, and wrongs inflicted on himself. But, as he proceeded, a terrible fascination, a kind of fierce, though still calm, necessity seized the old man within its gripe, and never set him free again, until he had done all its bidding. He now dug into the poor clergyman's heart, like a miner searching for gold; or, rather, like a sexton[7] delving into a grave, possibly in quest of a jewel that had been buried on the dead man's bosom, but likely to find nothing save mortality and corruption. Alas for his own soul, if these were what he sought!

Sometimes, a light glimmered out of the physician's eyes, burning blue and ominous, like the reflection of a furnace, or, let us say, like one of those gleams of ghastly fire that darted from Bunyan's awful doorway in the hillside,[8] and quivered on the pilgrim's face. The soil where this dark miner was working had perchance shown indications that encouraged him.

"This man," said he, at one such moment, to himself, "pure as they deem him,—all spiritual as he seems,—hath inherited a strong animal nature from his father or his mother. Let us dig a little farther in the direction of this vein!"

Then, after long search into the minister's dim interior, and turning over many precious materials, in the shape of high aspirations for the welfare of

7. Man in charge of maintaining a church, especially responsible for digging graves in the churchyard and supervising burials there.

8. In John Bunyan's *Pilgrim's Progress* (1678), the eighth stage of Christian's pilgrimage, the "by-way to hell" through which hypocrites enter.

his race, warm love of souls, pure sentiments, natural piety, strengthened by thought and study, and illuminated by revelation,—all of which invaluable gold was perhaps no better than rubbish to the seeker,—he would turn back, discouraged, and begin his quest towards another point. He groped along as stealthily, with as cautious a tread, and as wary an outlook, as a thief entering a chamber where a man lies only half asleep,—or, it may be, broad awake,—with purpose to steal the very treasure which this man guards as the apple of his eye. In spite of his premeditated carefulness, the floor would now and then creak; his garments would rustle; the shadow of his presence, in a forbidden proximity, would be thrown across his victim. In other words, Mr. Dimmesdale, whose sensibility of nerve often produced the effect of spiritual intuition, would become vaguely aware that something inimical to his peace had thrust itself into relation with him. But old Roger Chillingworth, too, had perceptions that were almost intuitive; and when the minister threw his startled eyes towards him, there the physician sat; his kind, watchful, sympathizing, but never intrusive friend.

Yet Mr. Dimmesdale would perhaps have seen this individual's character more perfectly, if a certain morbidness, to which sick hearts are liable, had not rendered him suspicious of all mankind. Trusting no man as his friend, he could not recognize his enemy when the latter actually appeared. He therefore still kept up a familiar intercourse with him, daily receiving the old physician in his study; or visiting the laboratory, and, for recreation's sake, watching the processes by which weeds were converted into drugs of potency.

One day, leaning his forehead on his hand, and his elbow on the sill of the open window, that looked towards the grave-yard, he talked with Roger Chillingworth, while the old man was examining a bundle of unsightly plants.

"Where," asked he, with a look askance at them,—for it was the clergyman's peculiarity that he seldom, now-a-days, looked straightforth at any object, whether human or inanimate,—"Where, my kind doctor, did you gather those herbs, with such a dark, flabby leaf?"

"Even in the grave-yard, here at hand" answered the physician, continuing his employment. "They are new to me. I found them growing on a grave, which bore no tombstone, nor other memorial of the dead man, save these ugly weeds that have taken upon themselves to keep him in remembrance. They grew out of his heart, and typify, it may be, some hideous secret that was buried with him, and which he had done better to confess during his lifetime."

"Perchance," said Mr. Dimmesdale, "he earnestly desired it, but could not."

"And wherefore?" rejoined the physician. "Wherefore not; since all the powers of nature call so earnestly for the confession of sin, that these black weeds have sprung up out of a buried heart, to make manifest an unspoken crime?"

"That, good Sir, is but a fantasy of yours," replied the minister. "There can be, if I forebode aright, no power, short of the Divine mercy, to disclose, whether by uttered words, or by type or emblem, the secrets that may be buried with a human heart. The heart, making itself guilty of such secrets, must perforce hold them, until the day when all hidden things shall be revealed. Nor have I so read or interpreted Holy Writ, as to understand that the disclosure of human thoughts and deeds, then to be made, is intended as a part of the retribution. That, surely, were a shallow view of it. No; these revelations, unless I greatly err, are meant merely to promote the intellectual satisfaction of all intelligent beings, who will stand waiting, on that day, to see the dark problem of this life made plain. A knowledge of men's hearts will be needful to the completest solution of that problem. And I conceive, moreover, that the hearts holding such miserable secrets as you speak of will yield them up, at that last day,[9] not with reluctance, but with a joy unutterable."

"Then why not reveal them here?" asked Roger Chillingworth, glancing quietly aside at the minister. "Why should not the guilty ones sooner avail themselves of this unutterable solace?"

"They mostly do," said the clergyman, griping hard at his breast, as if afflicted with an importunate throb of pain. "Many, many a poor soul hath given its confidence to me, not only on the deathbed, but while strong in life, and fair in reputation. And ever, after such an outpouring, O, what a relief have I witnessed in those sinful brethren! even as in one who at last draws free air, after long stifling with his own polluted breath. How can it be otherwise? Why should a wretched man, guilty, we will say, of murder, prefer to keep the dead corpse buried in his own heart, rather than fling it forth at once, and let the universe take care of it!"

"Yet some men bury their secrets thus," observed the calm physician.

"True; there are such men," answered Mr. Dimmesdale. "But, not to suggest more obvious reasons, it may be that they are kept silent by the very constitution of their nature. Or,—can we not suppose it?—guilty as they may be, retaining, nevertheless, a zeal for God's glory and man's welfare, they shrink from displaying themselves black and filthy in the view of men; because, thenceforward, no good can be achieved by them; no evil of the past be redeemed by better service. So, to their own unutterable torment, they go about among their fellow-creatures, looking pure as new-fallen snow; while their hearts are all speckled and spotted with iniquity of which they cannot rid themselves."

"These men deceive themselves," said Roger Chillingworth, with somewhat more emphasis than usual, and making a slight gesture with his forefinger. "They fear to take up the shame that rightfully belongs to them. Their love for man, their zeal for God's service,—these holy impulses may or may not coexist in their hearts with the evil inmates to which their guilt has unbarred the door, and which must needs propagate a hellish breed within them. But, if they seek to glorify God, let them not lift heavenward their unclean hands! If they would serve their fellow-men, let them do it by making manifest the power and reality of conscience, in constraining them to penitential self-abasement! Wouldst thou have me to believe, O wise and pious friend, that a false show can be better—can be more for God's glory, or man's welfare—than God's own truth? Trust me, such men deceive themselves!"

"It may be so," said the young clergyman indifferently, as waiving a discussion that he considered irrelevant or unseasonable. He had a ready faculty, indeed, of escaping from any topic that agitated his too sensitive and nervous temperament.—"But, now, I would ask of my well-skilled physician, whether, in good sooth, he deems me to have profited by his kindly care of this weak frame of mine?"

9. Judgment Day.

Before Roger Chillingworth could answer, they heard the clear, wild laughter of a young child's voice, proceeding from the adjacent burial-ground. Looking instinctively from the open window,—for it was summer-time,—the minister beheld Hester Prynne and little Pearl passing along the footpath that traversed the inclosure. Pearl looked as beautiful as the day, but was in one of those moods of perverse merriment which, whenever they occurred, seemed to remove her entirely out of the sphere of sympathy or human contact. She now skipped irreverently from one grave to another; until, coming to the broad flat, armourial tombstone of a departed worthy,—perhaps of Isaac Johnson himself,—she began to dance upon it. In reply to her mother's command and entreaty that she would behave more decorously, little Pearl paused to gather the prickly burrs from a tall burdock, which grew beside the tomb. Taking a handful of these, she arranged them along the lines of the scarlet letter that decorated the maternal bosom, to which the burrs, as their nature was, tenaciously adhered. Hester did not pluck them off.

Roger Chillingworth had by this time approached the window, and smiled grimly down.

"There is no law, nor reverence for authority, no regard for human ordinances or opinions, right or wrong, mixed up with that child's composition," remarked he, as much to himself as to his companion. "I saw her, the other day, bespatter the Governor himself with water, at the cattle-trough in Spring Lane. What, in Heaven's name, is she? Is the imp altogether evil? Hath she affections? Hath she any discoverable principle of being?"

"None,—save the freedom of a broken law," answered Mr. Dimmesdale, in a quiet way, as if he had been discussing the point within himself. "Whether capable of good, I know not."

The child probably overheard their voices; for, looking up to the window, with a bright, but naughty smile of mirth and intelligence, she threw one of the prickly burrs at the Reverend Mr. Dimmesdale. The sensitive clergyman shrunk, with nervous dread, from the light missile. Detecting his emotion, Pearl clapped her little hands in the most extravagant ecstasy. Hester Prynne, likewise, had involuntarily looked up; and all these four persons, old and young, regarded one another in silence, till the child laughed aloud, and shouted,—"Come away, mother! Come away, or yonder old Black Man will catch you! He hath got hold of the minister already. Come away, mother, or he will catch you! But he cannot catch little Pearl!"

So she drew her mother away, skipping, dancing, and frisking fantastically among the hillocks of the dead people, like a creature that had nothing in common with a bygone and buried generation, nor owned herself akin to it. It was as if she had been made afresh, out of new elements, and must perforce be permitted to live her own life, and be a law unto herself, without her eccentricities being reckoned to her for a crime.

"There goes a woman," resumed Roger Chillingworth, after a pause, "who, be her demerits what they may, hath none of that mystery of hidden sinfulness which you deem so grievous to be borne. Is Hester Prynne the less miserable, think you, for that scarlet letter on her breast?"

"I do verily believe it," answered the clergyman. "Nevertheless, I cannot answer for her. There was a look of pain in her face, which I would gladly have been spared the sight of. But still, methinks, it must needs be better for the sufferer to be free to show his pain, as this poor woman Hester is, than to cover it all up in his heart."

There was another pause; and the physician began anew to examine and arrange the plants which he had gathered.

"You inquired of me, a little time agone," said he, at length, "my judgment as touching your health."

"I did," answered the clergyman, "and would gladly learn it. Speak frankly, I pray you, be it for life or death."

"Freely, then, and plainly," said the physician, still busy with his plants, but keeping a wary eye on Mr. Dimmesdale, "the disorder is a strange one; not so much in itself, nor as outwardly manifested,—in so far, at least, as the symptoms have been laid open to my observation. Looking daily at you, my good Sir, and watching the tokens of your aspect, now for months gone by, I should deem you a man sore sick, it may be, yet not so sick but that an instructed and watchful physician might well hope to cure you. But—I know not what to say—the disease is what I seem to know, yet know it not."

"You speak in riddles, learned Sir," said the pale minister, glancing aside out of the window.

"Then, to speak more plainly," continued the physician, "and I crave pardon, Sir,—should it seem to require pardon,—for this needful plainness of my speech. Let me ask,—as your friend,—as one having charge, under Providence, of your life and physical well-being,—hath all the operation of this disorder been fairly laid open and recounted to me?"

"How can you question it?" asked the minister. "Surely, it were child's play to call in a physician, and then hide the sore!"

"You would tell me, then, that I know all?" said Roger Chillingworth, deliberately, and fixing an eye, bright with intense and concentrated intelligence, on the minister's face. "Be it so! But, again! He to whom only the outward and physical evil is laid open knoweth, oftentimes, but half the evil which he is called upon to cure. A bodily disease, which we look upon as whole and entire within itself, may, after all, be but a symptom of some ailment in the spiritual part. Your pardon, once again, good Sir, if my speech give the shadow of offence. You, Sir, of all men whom I have known, are he whose body is the closest conjoined, and imbued, and identified, so to speak, with the spirit whereof it is the instrument."

"Then I need ask no further," said the clergyman, somewhat hastily rising from his chair. "You deal not, I take it, in medicine for the soul!"

"Thus, a sickness," continued Roger Chillingworth, going on, in an unaltered tone, without heeding the interruption,—but standing up, and confronting the emaciated and white-cheeked minister with his low, dark, and misshapen figure,—"a sickness, a sore place, if we may so call it, in your spirit, hath immediately its appropriate manifestation in your bodily frame. Would you, therefore, that your physician heal the bodily evil? How may this be, unless you first lay open to him the wound or trouble in your soul?"

"No!—not to thee!—not to an earthly physician!" cried Mr. Dimmesdale, passionately, and turning his eyes, full and bright, and with a kind of fierceness, on old Roger Chillingworth. "Not to thee! But, if it be the soul's disease, then do I commit myself to the one Physician of the soul! He, if it stand with his good pleasure, can cure; or he can kill! Let him do with me as, in his justice and wisdom, he shall see good. But who art thou, that meddlest in this matter?—that dares thrust himself between the sufferer and his God?"

With a frantic gesture, he rushed out of the room.

"It is as well to have made this step," said Roger Chillingworth to himself, looking after the minister with a grave smile. "There is nothing lost. We shall be friends again anon. But see, now, how passion takes hold upon this man, and hurrieth him out of himself! As with one passion, so with another! He hath done a wild thing ere now, this pious Master Dimmesdale, in the hot passion of his heart!"

It proved not difficult to reëstablish the intimacy of the two companions, on the same footing and in the same degree as heretofore. The young clergyman, after a few hours of privacy, was sensible that the disorder of his nerves had hurried him into an unseemly outbreak of temper, which there had been nothing in the physician's words to excuse or palliate. He marvelled, indeed, at the violence with which he had thrust back the kind old man, when merely proffering the advice which it was his duty to bestow, and which the minister himself had expressly sought. With these remorseful feelings, he lost no time in making the amplest apologies, and besought his friend still to continue the care, which, if not successful in restoring him to health, had, in all probability, been the means of prolonging his feeble existence to that hour. Roger Chillingworth readily assented, and went on with his medical supervision of the minister; doing his best for him, in all good faith, but always quitting the patient's apartment, at the close of a professional interview, with a mysterious and puzzled smile upon his lips. This expression was invisible in Mr. Dimmesdale's presence, but grew strongly evident as the physician crossed the threshold.

"A rare case!" he muttered. "I must needs look deeper into it. A strange sympathy betwixt soul and body! Were it only for the art's sake, I must search this matter to the bottom!"

It came to pass, not long after the scene above recorded, that the Reverend Mr. Dimmesdale, at noon-day, and entirely unawares, fell into a deep, deep slumber, sitting in his chair, with a large black-letter[1] volume open before him on the table. It must have been a work of vast ability in the somniferous school of literature. The profound depth of the minister's repose was the more remarkable; inasmuch as he was one of those persons whose sleep, ordinarily, is as light, as fitful, and as easily scared away, as a small bird hopping on a twig. To such an unwonted remoteness, however, had his spirit now withdrawn into itself, that he stirred not in his chair, when old Roger Chillingworth, without any extraordinary precaution, came into the room. The physician advanced directly in front of his patient, laid his hand upon his bosom, and thrust aside the vestment, that, hitherto, had always covered it even from the professional eye.

Then, indeed, Mr. Dimmesdale shuddered, and slightly stirred.

After a brief pause, the physician turned away.

But with what a wild look of wonder, joy, and horror! With what a ghastly rapture, as it were, too mighty to be expressed only by the eye and features, and therefore bursting forth through the whole ugliness of his figure, and

1. An early typeface modeled on medieval script.

making itself even riotously manifest by the extravagant gestures with which he threw up his arms towards the ceiling, and stamped his foot upon the floor! Had a man seen old Roger Chillingworth, at that moment of his ecstacy, he would have had no need to ask how Satan comports himself, when a precious human soul is lost to heaven, and won into his kingdom.

But what distinguished the physician's ecstasy from Satan's was the trait of wonder in it!

XI. The Interior of a Heart

After the incident last described, the intercourse between the clergyman and the physician, though externally the same, was really of another character than it had previously been. The intellect of Roger Chillingworth had now a sufficiently plain path before it. It was not, indeed, precisely that which he had laid out for himself to tread. Calm, gentle, passionless, as he appeared, there was yet, we fear, a quiet depth of malice, hitherto latent, but active now, in this unfortunate old man, which led him to imagine a more intimate revenge than any mortal had ever wreaked upon an enemy. To make himself the one trusted friend, to whom should be confided all the fear, the remorse, the agony, the ineffectual repentance, the backward rush of sinful thoughts, expelled in vain! All that guilty sorrow, hidden from the world, whose great heart would have pitied and forgiven, to be revealed to him, the Pitiless, to him, the Unforgiving! All that dark treasure to be lavished on the very man, to whom nothing else could so adequately pay the debt of vengeance!

The clergyman's shy and sensitive reserve had balked this scheme. Roger Chillingworth, however, was inclined to be hardly, if at all, less satisfied with the aspect of affairs, which Providence—using the avenger and his victim for its own purposes, and, perchance, pardoning, where it seemed most to punish—had substituted for his black devices. A revelation, he could almost say, had been granted to him. It mattered little, for his object, whether celestial, or from what other region. By its aid, in all the subsequent relations betwixt him and Mr. Dimmesdale, not merely the external presence, but the very inmost soul of the latter seemed to be brought out before his eyes, so that he could see and comprehend its every movement. He became, thenceforth, not a spectator only, but a chief actor, in the poor minister's interior world. He could play upon him as he chose. Would he arouse him with a throb of agony? The victim was for ever on the rack; it needed only to know the spring that controlled the engine;—and the physician knew it well! Would he startle him with sudden fear? As at the waving of a magician's wand, uprose a grisly phantom,—uprose a thousand phantoms,—in many shapes, of death, or more awful shame, all flocking round about the clergyman, and pointing with their fingers at his breast!

All this was accomplished with a subtlety so perfect, that the minister, though he had constantly a dim perception of some evil influence watching over him, could never gain a knowledge of its actual nature. True, he looked doubtfully, fearfully,—even, at times, with horror and the bitterness of hatred,—at the deformed figure of the old physician. His gestures, his gait, his grizzled beard, his slightest and most indifferent acts, the very fashion of his garments, were odious in the clergyman's sight; a token, implicitly to be relied on, of a deeper antipathy in the breast of the latter than he was willing to acknowledge to himself. For, as it was impossible to assign a reason for such distrust and abhorrence, so Mr. Dimmesdale, conscious that the poison of one morbid spot was infecting his heart's entire substance, attributed all his presentiments to no other cause. He took himself to task for his bad sympathies in reference to Roger Chillingworth, disregarded the lesson that he should have drawn from them, and did his best to root them out. Unable to accomplish this, he nevertheless, as a matter of principle, continued his habits of social familiarity with the old man, and thus gave him constant opportunities for perfecting the purpose to which—poor, forlorn creature that he was, and more wretched than his victim—the avenger had devoted himself.

While thus suffering under bodily disease, and gnawed and tortured by some black trouble of the soul, and given over to the machinations of his deadliest enemy, the Reverend Mr. Dimmesdale had achieved a brilliant popularity in his sacred office. He won it, indeed, in great part, by his sorrows. His intellectual gifts, his moral perceptions, his power of experiencing and communicating emotion, were kept in a state of preternatural activity by the prick and anguish of his daily life. His fame, though still on its upward slope, already overshadowed the soberer reputations of his fellow-clergymen, eminent as several of them were. There were scholars among them, who had spent more years in acquiring abstruse lore, connected with the divine profession, than Mr. Dimmesdale had lived; and who might well, therefore, be more profoundly versed in such solid and valuable attainments than their youthful brother. There were men, too, of a sturdier texture of mind than his, and endowed with a far greater share of shrewd, hard, iron or granite understanding; which, duly mingled with a fair proportion of doctrinal ingredient, constitutes a highly respectable, efficacious, and unamiable variety of the clerical species. There were others, again, true saintly fathers, whose faculties had been elaborated by weary toil among their books, and by patient thought, and etherealized, moreover, by spiritual communications with the better world, into which their purity of life had almost introduced these holy personages, with their garments of mortality still clinging to them. All that they lacked was the gift that descended upon the chosen disciples, at Pentecost, in tongues of flame;[2] symbolizing, it would seem, not the power of speech in foreign and unknown languages, but that of addressing the whole human brotherhood in the heart's native language. These fathers, otherwise so apostolic, lacked Heaven's last and rarest attestation of their office, the Tongue of Flame. They would have vainly sought—had they ever dreamed of seeking—to express the highest truths through the humblest medium of familiar words and images. Their voices came down, afar and indistinctly, from the upper heights where they habitually dwelt.

Not improbably, it was to this latter class of men that Mr. Dimmesdale, by many of his traits of character, naturally belonged. To their high mountain-peaks of faith and sanctity he would have climbed, had not the tendency been thwarted by the burden, whatever it might be, of crime or anguish, beneath which it was his doom to totter. It kept him down, on a level with the lowest; him, the man of ethereal attributes, whose voice the angels might else have listened to and answered! But this very burden it was, that

2. See Acts 2.3 for the descent of the Holy Spirit to the disciples in the form of "cloven tongues like as of fire" on the day of the Pentecost, which enabled them to speak to all nations.

gave him sympathies so intimate with the sinful brotherhood of mankind; so that his heart vibrated in unison with theirs, and received their pain into itself, and sent its own throb of pain through a thousand other hearts, in gushes of sad, persuasive eloquence. Oftenest persuasive, but sometimes terrible! The people knew not the power that moved them thus. They deemed the young clergyman a miracle of holiness. They fancied him the mouth-piece of Heaven's messages of wisdom, and rebuke, and love. In their eyes, the very ground on which he trod was sanctified. The virgins of his church grew pale around him, victims of a passion so imbued with religious sentiment that they imagined it to be all religion, and brought it openly, in their white bosoms, as their most acceptable sacrifice before the altar. The aged members of his flock, beholding Mr. Dimmesdale's frame so feeble, while they were themselves so rugged in their infirmity, believed that he would go heavenward before them, and enjoined it upon their children, that their old bones should be buried close to their young pastor's holy grave. And, all this time, perchance, when poor Mr. Dimmesdale was thinking of his grave, he questioned with himself whether the grass would ever grow on it, because an accursed thing must there be buried!

It is inconceivable, the agony with which this public veneration tortured him! It was his genuine impulse to adore the truth, and to reckon all things shadow-like, and utterly devoid of weight or value, that had not its divine essence as the life within their life. Then, what was he?—a substance?—or the dimmest of all shadows? He longed to speak out, from his own pulpit, at the full height of his voice, and tell the people what he was. "I, whom you behold in these black garments of the priesthood,—I, who ascend the sacred desk, and turn my pale face heavenward, taking upon myself to hold communion, in your behalf, with the Most High Omniscience,—I, in whose daily life you discern the sanctity of Enoch,[3]—I, whose footsteps, as you suppose, leave a gleam along my earthly track, whereby the pilgrims that shall come after me may be guided to the regions of the blest,—I, who have laid the hand of baptism upon your children,—I, who have breathed the parting prayer over your dying friends, to whom the Amen sounded faintly from a world which they had quitted,—I, your pastor, whom you so reverence and trust, am utterly a pollution and a lie!"

More than once, Mr. Dimmesdale had gone into the pulpit, with a purpose never to come down its steps, until he should have spoken words like the above. More than once, he had cleared his throat, and drawn in the long, deep, and tremulous breath, which, when sent forth again, would come burdened with the black secret of his soul. More than once—nay, more than a hundred times—he had actually spoken! Spoken! But how? He had told his hearers that he was altogether vile, a viler companion of the vilest, the worst of sinners, an abomination, a thing of unimaginable iniquity; and that the only wonder was, that they did not see his wretched body shrivelled up before their eyes, by the burning wrath of the Almighty! Could there be plainer speech than this? Would not the people start up in their seats, by a simultaneous impulse, and tear him down out of the pulpit which he defiled? Not so, indeed! They heard it all, and did but reverence him the more. They little

3. In Genesis 5.21–24 Enoch is said to have "walked with God."

guessed what deadly purport lurked in those self-condemning words. "The godly youth!" said they among themselves. "The saint on earth! Alas, if he discern such sinfulness in his own white soul, what horrid spectacle would he behold in thine or mine!" The minister well knew—subtle, but remorseful hypocrite that he was!—the light in which his vague confession would be viewed. He had striven to put a cheat upon himself[4] by making the avowal of a guilty conscience, but had gained only one other sin, and a self-acknowledged shame, without the momentary relief of being self-deceived. He had spoken the very truth, and transformed it into the veriest falsehood. And yet, by the constitution of his nature, he loved the truth, and loathed the lie, as few men ever did. Therefore, above all things else, he loathed his miserable self!

His inward trouble drove him to practices, more in accordance with the old, corrupted faith of Rome, than with the better light of the church in which he had been born and bred. In Mr. Dimmesdale's secret closet, under lock and key, there was a bloody scourge.[5] Oftentimes, this Protestant and Puritan divine had plied it on his own shoulders; laughing bitterly at himself the while, and smiting so much the more pitilessly, because of that bitter laugh. It was his custom, too, as it has been that of many other pious Puritans, to fast,—not, however, like them, in order to purify the body and render it the fitter medium of celestial illumination,—but rigorously, and until his knees trembled beneath him, as an act of penance. He kept vigils, likewise, night after night, sometimes in utter darkness; sometimes with a glimmering lamp; and sometimes, viewing his own face in a looking-glass, by the most powerful light which he could throw upon it. He thus typified the constant introspection wherewith he tortured, but could not purify, himself. In these lengthened vigils, his brain often reeled, and visions seemed to flit before him; perhaps seen doubtfully, and by a faint light of their own, in the remote dimness of the chamber, or more vividly, and close beside him, within the looking-glass. Now it was a herd of diabolic shapes, that grinned and mocked at the pale minister, and beckoned him away with them; now a group of shining angels, who flew upward heavily, as sorrow-laden, but grew more ethereal as they rose. Now came the dead friends of his youth, and his white-bearded father, with a saint-like frown, and his mother, turning her face away as she passed by. Ghost of a mother, thinnest fantasy of a mother,—methinks she might yet have thrown a pitying glance towards her son! And now, through the chamber which these spectral thoughts had made so ghastly, glided Hester Prynne, leading along little Pearl, in her scarlet garb, and pointing her forefinger, first, at the scarlet letter on her bosom, and then at the clergyman's own breast.

None of these visions ever quite deluded him. At any moment, by an effort of his will, he could discern substances through their misty lack of substance, and convince himself that they were not solid in their nature, like yonder table of carved oak, or that big, square leathern-bound and brazen-clasped volume of divinity. But, for all that, they were, in one sense, the truest and most substantial things which the poor minister now dealt with. It is the unspeakable misery of a life so false as his, that it steals the pith and substance out of whatever realities there are around us, and which were meant

4. Label himself a cheat.

5. Whip.

by Heaven to be the spirit's joy and nutriment. To the untrue man, the whole universe is false,—it is impalpable,—it shrinks to nothing within his grasp. And he himself, in so far as he shows himself in a false light, becomes a shadow, or, indeed, ceases to exist. The only truth, that continued to give Mr. Dimmesdale a real existence on this earth, was the anguish in his inmost soul, and the undissembled expression of it in his aspect. Had he once found power to smile, and wear a face of gayety, there would have been no such man!

On one of those ugly nights, which we have faintly hinted at, but forborne to picture forth, the minister started from his chair. A new thought had struck him. There might be a moment's peace in it. Attiring himself with as much care as if it had been for public worship, and precisely in the same manner, he stole softly down the staircase, undid the door, and issued forth.

XII. The Minister's Vigil

Walking in the shadow of a dream, as it were, and perhaps actually under the influence of a species of somnambulism, Mr. Dimmesdale reached the spot, where, now so long since, Hester Prynne had lived through her first hour of public ignominy. The same platform or scaffold, black and weather-stained with the storm or sunshine of seven long years, and footworn, too, with the tread of many culprits who had since ascended it, remained standing beneath the balcony of the meeting-house. The minister went up the steps.

It was an obscure night of early May. An unvaried pall of cloud muffled the whole expanse of sky from zenith to horizon. If the same multitude which had stood as eyewitnesses while Hester Prynne sustained her punishment could now have been summoned forth, they would have discerned no face above the platform, nor hardly the outline of a human shape, in the dark gray of the midnight. But the town was all asleep. There was no peril of discovery. The minister might stand there, if it so pleased him, until morning should redden in the east, without other risk than that the dank and chill night-air would creep into his frame, and stiffen his joints with rheumatism, and clog his throat with catarrh and cough; thereby defrauding the expectant audience of to-morrow's prayer and sermon. No eye could see him, save that ever-wakeful one which had seen him in his closet, wielding the bloody scourge. Why, then, had he come hither? Was it but the mockery of penitence? A mockery, indeed, but in which his soul trifled with itself! A mockery at which angels blushed and wept, while fiends rejoiced, with jeering laughter! He had been driven hither by the impulse of that Remorse which dogged him everywhere, and whose own sister and closely linked companion was that Cowardice which invariably drew him back, with her tremulous gripe, just when the other impulse had hurried him to the verge of a disclosure. Poor, miserable man! what right had infirmity like his to burden itself with crime? Crime is for the iron-nerved, who have their choice either to endure it, or, if it press too hard, to exert their fierce and savage strength for a good purpose, and fling it off at once! This feeble and most sensitive of spirits could do neither, yet continually did one thing or another, which intertwined, in the same inextricable knot, the agony of heaven-defying guilt and vain repentance.

And thus, while standing on the scaffold, in this vain show of expiation, Mr. Dimmesdale was overcome with a great horror of mind, as if the universe were gazing at a scarlet token on his naked breast, right over his heart. On that spot, in very truth, there was, and there had long been, the gnawing and poisonous tooth of bodily pain. Without any effort of his will, or power to restrain himself, he shrieked aloud; an outcry that went pealing through the night, and was beaten back from one house to another, and reverberated from the hills in the background; as if a company of devils, detecting so much misery and terror in it, had made a plaything of the sound, and were bandying it to and fro.

"It is done!" muttered the minister, covering his face with his hands. "The whole town will awake, and hurry forth, and find me here!"

But it was not so. The shriek had perhaps sounded with a far greater power, to his own startled ears, than it actually possessed. The town did not awake; or, if it did, the drowsy slumberers mistook the cry either for something frightful in a dream, or for the noise of witches; whose voices, at that period, were often heard to pass over the settlements or lonely cottages, as they rode with Satan through the air. The clergyman, therefore, hearing no symptoms of disturbance, uncovered his eyes and looked about him. At one of the chamber-windows of Governor Bellingham's mansion, which stood at some distance, on the line of another street, he beheld the appearance of the old magistrate himself, with a lamp in his hand, a white night-cap on his head, and a long white gown enveloping his figure. He looked like a ghost, evoked unseasonably from the grave. The cry had evidently startled him. At another window of the same house, moreover, appeared old Mistress Hibbins, the Governor's sister, also with a lamp, which, even thus far off, revealed the expression of her sour and discontented face. She thrust forth her head from the lattice, and looked anxiously upward. Beyond the shadow of a doubt, this venerable witch-lady had heard Mr. Dimmesdale's outcry, and interpreted it, with its multitudinous echoes and reverberations, as the clamor of the fiends and night-hags, with whom she was well known to make excursions into the forest.

Detecting the gleam of Governor Bellingham's lamp, the old lady quickly extinguished her own, and vanished. Possibly, she went up among the clouds. The minister saw nothing further of her motions. The magistrate, after a wary observation of the darkness—into which, nevertheless, he could see but little farther than he might into a mill-stone—retired from the window.

The minister grew comparatively calm. His eyes, however, were soon greeted by a little, glimmering light, which, at first a long way off, was approaching up the street. It threw a gleam of recognition on here a post, and there a garden-fence, and here a latticed windowpane, and there a pump, with its full trough of water, and here, again, an arched door of oak, with an iron knocker, and a rough log for the door-step. The Reverend Mr. Dimmesdale noted all these minute particulars, even while firmly convinced that the doom of his existence was stealing onward, in the footsteps which he now heard; and that the gleam of the lantern would fall upon him, in a few moments more, and reveal his long-hidden secret. As the light drew nearer, he beheld, within its illuminated circle, his brother clergyman,—or, to speak more accurately, his professional father, as well as highly valued friend,—the Reverend Mr. Wilson; who, as Mr. Dimmesdale now conjectured, had been praying at the bedside of some dying man. And so he had. The good old minister came freshly from the death-chamber of Governor Winthrop, who had passed from earth to heaven within that very hour.[6] And now, surrounded, like the saint-like personages of olden times, with a radiant halo, that glorified him amid this gloomy night of sin,—as if the departed Governor had left him an inheritance of his glory, or as if he had caught upon himself the distant shine of the celestial city, while looking thitherward to see the triumphant pilgram pass within its gates,—now, in short, good Father Wilson was moving homeward, aiding his footsteps with a lighted lantern! The glimmer of this luminary suggested the above conceits to Mr. Dimmesdale, who smiled,—nay, almost laughed at them,—and then wondered if he were going mad.

As the Reverend Mr. Wilson passed beside the scaffold, closely muffling his Geneva cloak[7] about him with one arm, and holding the lantern before his breast with the other, the minister could hardly restrain himself from speaking.

"A good evening to you, venerable Father Wilson! Come up hither, I pray you, and pass a pleasant hour with me!"

Good heavens! Had Mr. Dimmesdale actually spoken? For one instant, he believed that these words had passed his lips. But they were uttered only within his imagination. The venerable Father Wilson continued to step slowly onward, looking carefully at the muddy pathway before his feet, and never once turning his head towards the guilty platform. When the light of the glimmering lantern had faded quite away, the minister discovered, by the faintness which came over him, that the last few moments had been a crisis of terrible anxiety; although his mind had made an involuntary effort to relieve itself by a kind of lurid playfulness.

Shortly afterwards, the like grisly sense of the humorous again stole in among the solemn phantoms of his thought. He felt his limbs growing stiff with the unaccustomed chilliness of the night, and doubted whether he should be able to descend the steps of the scaffold. Morning would break, and find him there. The neighbourhood would begin to rouse itself. The earliest riser, coming forth in the dim twilight, would perceive a vaguely defined figure aloft on the place of shame; and, half crazed betwixt alarm and curiosity, would go, knocking from door to door, summoning all the people to behold the ghost—as he needs must think it—of some defunct transgressor. A dusky tumult would flap its wings from one house to another. Then—the morning light still waxing stronger—old patriarchs would rise up in great haste, each in his flannel gown, and matronly dames, without pausing to put off their night-gear. The whole tribe of decorous personages, who had never heretofore been seen with a single hair of their heads awry, would start into public view, with the disorder of a nightmare in their aspects. Old Governor Bellingham would come grimly forth, with his King James's ruff fastened askew; and Mistress Hibbins, with some twigs of the forest clinging to her skirts, and looking sourer than ever, as having hardly got a wink of sleep after her night ride; and good Father Wilson, too, after spending half the night at

6. The historical John Winthrop died in March (not May) 1649.

7. Black ministerial cloak named for Geneva, Switzerland, where John Calvin spent his last years.

a death-bed, and liking ill to be disturbed, thus early, out of his dreams about the glorified saints. Hither, likewise, would come the elders and deacons of Mr. Dimmesdale's church, and the young virgins who so idolized their minister, and had made a shrine for him in their white bosoms; which, now, by the by, in their hurry and confusion, they would scantly have given themselves time to cover with their kerchiefs. All people, in a word, would come stumbling over their thresholds, and turning up their amazed and horror-stricken visages around the scaffold. Whom would they discern there, with the red eastern light upon his brow? Whom, but the Reverend Arthur Dimmesdale, half frozen to death, overwhelmed with shame, and standing where Hester Prynne had stood!

Carried away by the grotesque horror of this picture, the minister, unawares, and to his own infinite alarm, burst into a great peal of laughter. It was immediately responded to by a light, airy, childish laugh, in which, with a thrill of the heart,—but he knew not whether of exquisite pain, or pleasure as acute,—he recognized the tones of little Pearl.

"Pearl! Little Pearl!" cried he, after a moment's pause; then, suppressing his voice,—"Hester! Hester Prynne! Are you there?"

"Yes; it is Hester Prynne!" she replied, in a tone of surprise; and the minister heard her footsteps approaching from the sidewalk, along which she had been passing.—"It is I, and my little Pearl."

"Whence come you, Hester?" asked the minister. "What sent you hither?"

"I have been watching at a death-bed," answered Hester Prynne;—"at Governor Winthrop's death-bed, and have taken his measure for a robe, and am now going homeward to my dwelling."

"Come up hither, Hester, thou and little Pearl," said the Reverend Mr. Dimmesdale. "Ye have both been here before, but I was not with you. Come up hither once again, and we will stand all three together!"

She silently ascended the steps, and stood on the platform, holding little Pearl by the hand. The minister felt for the child's other hand, and took it. The moment that he did so, there came what seemed a tumultuous rush of new life, other life than his own, pouring like a torrent into his heart, and hurrying through all his veins, as if the mother and the child were communicating their vital warmth to his half-torpid system. The three formed an electric chain.

"Minister!" whispered little Pearl.

"What wouldst thou say, child?" asked Mr. Dimmesdale.

"Wilt thou stand here with mother and me, to-morrow noontide?" inquired Pearl.

"Nay; not so, my little Pearl!" answered the minister; for, with the new energy of the moment, all the dread of public exposure, that had so long been the anguish of his life, had returned upon him; and he was already trembling at the conjunction in which—with a strange joy, nevertheless—he now found himself. "Not so, my child. I shall, indeed, stand with thy mother and thee one other day, but not to-morrow!"

Pearl laughed, and attempted to pull away her hand. But the minister held it fast.

"A moment longer, my child!" said he.

"But wilt thou promise," asked Pearl, "to take my hand, and mother's hand, to-morrow noontide?"

"Not then, Pearl," said the minister, "but another time!"

"And what other time?" persisted the child.

"At the great judgment day!" whispered the minister,—and, strangely enough, the sense that he was a professional teacher of the truth impelled him to answer the child so. "Then, and there, before the judgment-seat, thy mother, and thou, and I, must stand together! But the daylight of this world shall not see our meeting!"

Pearl laughed again.

But, before Mr. Dimmesdale had done speaking, a light gleamed far and wide over all the muffled sky. It was doubtless caused by one of those meteors, which the night-watcher may so often observe burning out to waste, in the vacant regions of the atmosphere. So powerful was its radiance, that it thoroughly illuminated the dense medium of cloud betwixt the sky and earth. The great vault brightened, like the dome of an immense lamp. It showed the familiar scene of the street, with the distinctness of mid-day, but also with the awfulness that is always imparted to familiar objects by an unaccustomed light. The wooden houses, with their jutting stories and quaint gable-peaks; the door-steps and thresholds, with the early grass springing up about them; the garden-plots, black with freshly turned earth; the wheel-track, little worn, and, even in the market-place, margined with green on either side;—all were visible, but with a singularity of aspect that seemed to give another moral interpretation to the things of this world than they had ever borne before. And there stood the minister, with his hand over his heart; and Hester Prynne, with the embroidered letter glimmering on her bosom; and little Pearl, herself a symbol, and the connecting link between these two. They stood in the noon of that strange and solemn splendor, as if it were the light that is to reveal all secrets, and the daybreak that shall unite all who belong to one another.

There was witchcraft in little Pearl's eyes; and her face, as she glanced upward at the minister, wore that naughty smile which made its expression frequently so elvish. She withdrew her hand from Mr. Dimmesdale's, and pointed across the street. But he clasped both his hands over his breast, and cast his eyes towards the zenith.

Nothing was more common, in those days, than to interpret all meteoric appearances, and other natural phenomena, that occurred with less regularity than the rise and set of sun and moon, as so many revelations from a supernatural source. Thus, a blazing spear, a sword of flame, a bow, or a sheaf of arrows, seen in the midnight sky, prefigured Indian warfare. Pestilence was known to have been foreboded by a shower of crimson light. We doubt whether any marked event, for good or evil, ever befell New England, from its settlement down to Revolutionary times, of which the inhabitants had not been previously warned by some spectacle of this nature. Not seldom, it had been seen by multitudes. Oftener, however, its credibility rested on the faith of some lonely eyewitness, who beheld the wonder through the colored, magnifying, and distorting medium of his imagination, and shaped it more distinctly in his after-thought. It was, indeed, a majestic idea, that the destiny of nations should be revealed, in these awful hieroglyphics, on the cope[8] of heaven. A scroll so wide might not be deemed too expensive for

8. Canopy.

Providence to write a people's doom upon. The belief was a favorite one with our forefathers, as betokening that their infant commonwealth was under a celestial guardianship of peculiar intimacy and strictness. But what shall we say, when an individual discovers a revelation, addressed to himself alone, on the same vast sheet of record! In such a case, it could only be the symptom of a highly disordered mental state, when a man, rendered morbidly self-contemplative by long, intense, and secret pain, had extended his egotism over the whole expanse of nature, until the firmament itself should appear no more than a fitting page for his soul's history and fate.

We impute it, therefore, solely to the disease in his own eye and heart, that the minister, looking upward to the zenith, beheld there the appearance of an immense letter,—the letter A,—marked out in lines of dull red light. Not but the meteor may have shown itself at that point, burning duskily through a veil of cloud; but with no such shape as his guilty imagination gave it; or, at least, with so little definiteness, that another's guilt might have seen another symbol in it.

There was a singular circumstance that characterized Mr. Dimmesdale's psychological state, at this moment. All the time that he gazed upward to the zenith, he was, nevertheless, perfectly aware that little Pearl was pointing her finger towards old Roger Chillingworth, who stood at no great distance from the scaffold. The minister appeared to see him, with the same glance that discerned the miraculous letter. To his features, as to all other objects, the meteoric light imparted a new expression; or it might well be that the physician was not careful then, as at all other times, to hide the malevolence with which he looked upon his victim. Certainly, if the meteor kindled up the sky, and disclosed the earth, with an awfulness that admonished Hester Prynne and the clergyman of the day of judgment, then might Roger Chillingworth have passed with them for the arch-fiend, standing there, with a smile and scowl, to claim his own. So vivid was the expression, or so intense the minister's perception of it, that it seemed still to remain painted on the darkness, after the meteor had vanished, with an effect as if the street and all things else were at once annihilated.

"Who is that man, Hester?" gasped Mr. Dimmesdale, overcome with terror. "I shiver at him! Dost thou know the man? I hate him, Hester!"

She remembered her oath, and was silent.

"I tell thee, my soul shivers at him," muttered the minister again, "Who is he? Who is he? Canst thou do nothing for me? I have a nameless horror of the man."

"Minister," said little Pearl, "I can tell thee who he is!"

"Quickly, then, child!" said the minister, bending his ear close to her lips. "Quickly!—and as low as thou canst whisper."

Pearl mumbled something into his ear, that sounded, indeed, like human language, but was only such gibberish as children may be heard amusing themselves with, by the hour together. At all events, if it involved any secret information in regard to old Roger Chillingworth, it was in a tongue unknown to the erudite clergyman, and did but increase the bewilderment of his mind. The elvish child then laughed aloud.

"Dost thou mock me now?" said the minister.

"Thou wast not bold!—thou wast not true!" answered the child. "Thou wouldst not promise to take my hand, and mother's hand, to-morrow noontide!"

"Worthy Sir," said the physician, who had now advanced to the foot of the platform. "Pious Master Dimmesdale! can this be you? Well, well, indeed! We men of study, whose heads are in our books, have need to be straitly looked after! We dream in our waking moments, and walk in our sleep. Come, good Sir, and my dear friend, I pray you, let me lead you home!"

"How knewest thou that I was here?" asked the minister, fearfully.

"Verily, and in good faith," answered Roger Chillingworth, "I knew nothing of the matter. I had spent the better part of the night at the bedside of the worshipful Governor Winthrop, doing what my poor skill might to give him ease. He going home to a better world, I, likewise, was on my way homeward, when this strange light shone out. Come with me, I beseech you, Reverend Sir; else you will be poorly able to do Sabbath duty to-morrow. Aha! see now, how they trouble the brain,—these books!—these books! You should study less, good Sir, and take a little pastime; or these night-whimseys will grow upon you!"

"I will go home with you," said Mr. Dimmesdale.

With a chill despondency, like one awaking, all nerveless, from an ugly dream, he yielded himself to the physician, and was led away.

The next day, however, being the Sabbath, he preached a discourse which was held to be the richest and most powerful, and the most replete with heavenly influences, that had ever proceeded from his lips. Souls, it is said, more souls than one, were brought to the truth by the efficacy of that sermon, and vowed within themselves to cherish a holy gratitude towards Mr. Dimmesdale throughout the long hereafter. But, as he came down the pulpit-steps, the gray-bearded sexton met him, holding up a black glove, which the minister recognized as his own.

"It was found," said the sexton, "this morning, on the scaffold, where evildoers are set up to public shame. Satan dropped it there, I take it, intending a scurrilous jest against your reverence. But, indeed, he was blind and foolish, as he ever and always is. A pure hand needs no glove to cover it!"

"Thank you, my good friend," said the minister gravely, but startled at heart; for, so confused was his remembrance, that he had almost brought himself to look at the events of the past night as visionary. "Yes, it seems to be my glove indeed!"

"And, since Satan saw fit to steal it, your reverence must needs handle him without gloves, henceforward," remarked the old sexton, grimly smiling, "But did your reverence hear of the portent that was seen last night? A great red letter in the sky,—the letter A,—which we interpret to stand for Angel. For, as our good Governor Winthrop was made an angel this past night, it was doubtless held fit that there should be some notice thereof!"

"No," answered the minister, "I had not heard of it."

XIII. Another View of Hester

In her late singular interview with Mr. Dimmesdale, Hester Prynne was shocked at the condition to which she found the clergyman reduced. His nerve seemed absolutely destroyed. His moral force was abased into more than childish weakness. It grovelled helpless on the ground, even while his intellectual faculties retained their pristine strength, or had perhaps acquired a morbid energy, which disease only could have given them. With her knowledge of a train of circumstances hidden from all others, she could readily infer, that, besides the legitimate action of his own conscience, a terrible machinery had been brought to bear, and was still operating, on Mr. Dimmesdale's well-being and repose. Knowing what this poor, fallen man had once been, her whole soul was moved by the shuddering terror with which he had appealed to her,—the outcast woman,—for support against his instinctively discovered enemy. She decided, moreover, that he had a right to her utmost aid. Little accustomed, in her long seclusion from society, to measure her ideas of right and wrong by any standard external to herself, Hester saw—or seemed to see—that there lay a responsibility upon her, in reference to the clergyman, which she owed to no other, nor to the whole world besides. The links that united her to the rest of human kind—links of flowers, or silk, or gold, or whatever the material—had all been broken. Here was the iron link of mutual crime, which neither he nor she could break. Like all other ties, it brought along with it its obligations.

Hester Prynne did not now occupy precisely the same position in which we beheld her during the earlier periods of her ignominy. Years had come, and gone. Pearl was now seven years old. Her mother, with the scarlet letter on her breast, glittering in its fantastic embroidery, had long been a familiar object to the townspeople. As is apt to be the case when a person stands out in any prominence before the community, and, at the same time, interferes neither with public nor individual interests and convenience, a species of general regard had ultimately grown up in reference to Hester Prynne. It is to the credit of human nature, that, except where its selfishness is brought into play, it loves more readily than it hates. Hatred, by a gradual and quiet process, will even be transformed to love, unless the change be impeded by a continually new irritation of the original feeling of hostility. In this matter of Hester Prynne, there was neither irritation nor irksomeness. She never battled with the public, but submitted uncomplainingly to its worst usage; she made no claim upon it, in requital for what she suffered; she did not weigh upon its sympathies. Then, also, the blameless purity of her life, during all these years in which she had been set apart to infamy, was reckoned largely in her favor. With nothing now to lose, in the sight of mankind, and with no hope, and seemingly no wish, of gaining any thing, it could only be a genuine regard for virtue that had brought back the poor wanderer to its paths.

It was perceived, too, that, while Hester never put forward even the humblest title to share in the world's privileges,—farther than to breathe the common air, and earn daily bread for little Pearl and herself by the faithful labor of her hands,—she was quick to acknowledge her sisterhood with the race of man, whenever benefits were to be conferred. None so ready as she to give of her little substance to every demand of poverty; even though the bitter-hearted pauper threw back a gibe in requital of the food brought regularly to his door, or the garments wrought for him by the fingers that could have embroidered a monarch's robe. None so self-devoted as Hester, when pestilence stalked through the town. In all seasons of calamity, indeed, whether general or of individuals, the outcast of society at once found her place. She came, not as a guest, but as a rightful inmate, into the household that was darkened by trouble; as if its gloomy twilight were a medium in which she was entitled to hold intercourse with her fellow-creatures. There glimmered the embroidered letter, with comfort in its unearthly ray. Elsewhere the token of sin, it was the taper of the sick-chamber. It had even thrown its gleam, in the sufferer's hard extremity, across the verge of time. It had shown him where to set his foot, while the light of earth was fast becoming dim, and ere the light of futurity could reach him. In such emergencies, Hester's nature showed itself warm and rich; a well-spring of human tenderness, unfailing to every real demand, and inexhaustible by the largest. Her breast, with its badge of shame, was but the softer pillow for the head that needed one. She was self-ordained a Sister of Mercy; or, we may rather say, the world's heavy hand had so ordained her, when neither the world nor she looked forward to this result. The letter was the symbol of her calling. Such helpfulness was found in her,—so much power to do, and power to sympathize,—that many people refused to interpret the scarlet A by its original signification. They said that it meant Able; so strong was Hester Prynne, with a woman's strength.

It was only the darkened house that could contain her. When sunshine came again, she was not there. Her shadow had faded across the threshold. The helpful inmate had departed, without one backward glance to gather up the meed[9] of gratitude, if any were in the hearts of those whom she had served so zealously. Meeting them in the street, she never raised her head to receive their greeting. If they were resolute to accost her, she laid her finger on the scarlet letter, and passed on. This might be pride, but was so like humility, that it produced all the softening influence of the latter quality on the public mind. The public is despotic in its temper; it is capable of denying common justice, when too strenuously demanded as a right; but quite as frequently it awards more than justice, when the appeal is made, as despots love to have it made, entirely to its generosity. Interpreting Hester Prynne's deportment as an appeal of this nature, society was inclined to show its former victim a more benign countenance than she cared to be favored with, or, perchance, than she deserved.

The rulers, and the wise and learned men of the community, were longer in acknowledging the influence of Hester's good qualities than the people. The prejudices which they shared in common with the latter were fortified in themselves by an iron framework of reasoning, that made it a far tougher labor to expel them. Day by day, nevertheless, their sour and rigid wrinkles were relaxing into something which, in the due course of years, might grow to be an expression of almost benevolence. Thus it was with the men of rank, on whom their eminent position imposed the guardianship of the public morals. Individuals in private life, meanwhile, had quite forgiven Hester Prynne for her frailty; nay, more, they had begun to look upon the scarlet letter as the token, not of that one sin, for which she had borne so long and dreary a penance, but of her many good deeds since. "Do you see that woman with the embroidered badge?" they would say to strangers. "It is our Hester,—the town's own Hester,—who is so kind to the poor, so helpful to the sick, so comfortable to the afflicted!" Then, it is true, the propensity of human nature

9. Merited gift or reward.

to tell the very worst of itself, when embodied in the person of another, would constrain them to whisper the black scandal of bygone years. It was none the less a fact, however, that, in the eyes of the very men who spoke thus, the scarlet letter had the effect of the cross on a nun's bosom. It imparted to the wearer a kind of sacredness, which enabled her to walk securely amid all peril. Had she fallen among thieves, it would have kept her safe. It was reported, and believed by many, that an Indian had drawn his arrow against the badge, and that the missile struck it, but fell harmless to the ground.

The effect of the symbol—or rather, of the position in respect to society that was indicated by it—on the mind of Hester Prynne herself, was powerful and peculiar. All the light and graceful foliage of her character had been withered up by this red-hot brand, and had long ago fallen away, leaving a bare and harsh outline, which might have been repulsive, had she possessed friends or companions to be repelled by it. Even the attractiveness of her person had undergone a similar change. It might be partly owing to the studied austerity of her dress, and partly to the lack of demonstration in her manners. It was a sad transformation, too, that her rich and luxuriant hair had either been cut off, or was so completely hidden by a cap, that not a shining lock of it ever once gushed into the sunshine. It was due in part to all these causes, but still more to something else, that there seemed to be no longer any thing in Hester's face for Love to dwell upon; nothing in Hester's form, though majestic and statue-like, that Passion would ever dream of clasping in its embrace; nothing in Hester's bosom, to make it ever again the pillow of Affection. Some attribute had departed from her, the permanence of which had been essential to keep her a woman. Such is frequently the fate, and such the stern development, of the feminine character and person, when the woman has encountered, and lived through, an experience of peculiar severity. If she be all tenderness, she will die. If she survive, the tenderness will either be crushed out of her, or—and the outward semblance is the same—crushed so deeply into her heart that it can never show itself more. The latter is perhaps the truest theory. She who has once been woman, and ceased to be so, might at any moment become a woman again, if there were only the magic touch to effect the transfiguration. We shall see whether Hester Prynne were ever afterwards so touched, and so transfigured.

Much of the marble coldness of Hester's impression was to be attributed to the circumstance that her life had turned, in a great measure, from passion and feeling, to thought. Standing alone in the world,—alone, as to any dependence on society, and with little Pearl to be guided and protected,—alone, and hopeless of retrieving her position, even had she not scorned to consider it desirable,—she cast away the fragments of a broken chain. The world's law was no law for her mind. It was an age in which the human intellect, newly emancipated, had taken a more active and a wider range than for many centuries before. Men of the sword had overthrown nobles and kings.[1] Men bolder than these had overthrown and rearranged—not actually, but within the sphere of theory, which was their most real abode—the whole system of ancient prejudice, wherewith was linked much of ancient principle.

1. Hawthorne alludes to the English Civil War, whose dates (1642–49) parallel those of the novel. In January 1649, King Charles was beheaded by the Puritan revolutionaries led by Oliver Cromwell.

Hester Prynne imbibed this spirit. She assumed a freedom of speculation, then common enough on the other side of the Atlantic, but which our forefathers, had they known of it, would have held to be a deadlier crime than that stigmatized by the scarlet letter. In her lonesome cottage, by the seashore, thoughts visited her, such as dared to enter no other dwelling in New England; shadowy guests, that would have been as perilous as demons to their entertainer, could they have been seen so much as knocking at her door.

It is remarkable, that persons who speculate the most boldly often conform with the most perfect quietude to the external regulations of society. The thought suffices them, without investing itself in the flesh and blood of action. So it seemed to be with Hester. Yet, had little Pearl never come to her from the spiritual world, it might have been far otherwise. Then, she might have come down to us in history, hand in hand with Ann Hutchinson, as the foundress of a religious sect. She might, in one of her phases, have been a prophetess. She might, and not improbably would, have suffered death from the stern tribunals of the period, for attempting to undermine the foundations of the Puritan establishment. But, in the education of her child, the mother's enthusiasm of thought had something to wreak itself upon. Providence, in the person of this little girl, had assigned to Hester's charge the germ and blossom of womanhood, to be cherished and developed amid a host of difficulties. Every thing was against her. The world was hostile. The child's own nature had something wrong in it, which continually betokened that she had been born amiss,—the effluence of her mother's lawless passion,—and often impelled Hester to ask, in bitterness of heart, whether it were for ill or good that the poor little creature had been born at all.

Indeed, the same dark question often rose into her mind, with reference to the whole race of womanhood. Was existence worth accepting, even to the happiest among them? As concerned her own individual existence, she had long ago decided in the negative, and dismissed the point as settled. A tendency to speculation, though it may keep woman quiet, as it does man, yet makes her sad. She discerns, it may be, such a hopeless task before her. As a first step, the whole system of society is to be torn down, and built up anew. Then, the very nature of the opposite sex, or its long hereditary habit, which has become like nature, is to be essentially modified, before woman can be allowed to assume what seems a fair and suitable position. Finally, all other difficulties being obviated, woman cannot take advantage of these preliminary reforms, until she herself shall have undergone a still mightier change; in which, perhaps, the ethereal essence, wherein she has her truest life, will be found to have evaporated. A woman never overcomes these problems by any exercise of thought. They are not to be solved, or only in one way. If her heart chance to come uppermost, they vanish. Thus, Hester Prynne, whose heart had lost its regular and healthy throb, wandered without a clew in the dark labyrinth of mind; now turned aside by an insurmountable precipice; now starting back from a deep chasm. There was wild and ghastly scenery all around her, and a home and comfort nowhere. At times, a fearful doubt strove to possess her soul, whether it were not better to send Pearl at once to heaven, and go herself to such futurity as Eternal Justice should provide.

The scarlet letter had not done its office.

Now, however, her interview with the Reverend Mr. Dimmesdale, on the night of his vigil, had given her a new theme of reflection, and held up to her an object that appeared worthy of any exertion and sacrifice for its attainment. She had witnessed the intense misery beneath which the minister struggled, or, to speak more accurately, had ceased to struggle. She saw that he stood on the verge of lunacy, if he had not already stepped across it. It was impossible to doubt, that, whatever painful efficacy there might be in the secret sting of remorse, a deadlier venom had been infused into it by the hand that proffered relief. A secret enemy had been continually by his side, under the semblance of a friend and helper, and had availed himself of the opportunities thus afforded for tampering with the delicate springs of Mr. Dimmesdale's nature. Hester could not but ask herself, whether there had not originally been a defect of truth, courage, and loyalty, on her own part, in allowing the minister to be thrown into a position where so much evil was to be foreboded, and nothing auspicious to be hoped. Her only justification lay in the fact, that she had been able to discern no method of rescuing him from a blacker ruin than had overwhelmed herself, except by acquiescing in Roger Chillingworth's scheme of disguise. Under that impulse, she had made her choice, and had chosen, as it now appeared, the more wretched alternative of the two. She determined to redeem her error, so far as it might yet be possible. Strengthened by years of hard and solemn trial, she felt herself no longer so inadequate to cope with Roger Chillingworth as on that night, abased by sin, and half maddened by the ignominy that was still new, when they had talked together in the prison-chamber. She had climbed her way, since then, to a higher point. The old man, on the other hand, had brought himself nearer to her level, or perhaps below it, by the revenge which he had stooped for.

In fine, Hester Prynne resolved to meet her former husband, and do what might be in her power for the rescue of the victim on whom he had so evidently set his gripe. The occasion was not long to seek. One afternoon, walking with Pearl in a retired part of the peninsula, she beheld the old physician, with a basket on one arm, and a staff in the other hand, stooping along the ground, in quest of roots and herbs to concoct his medicines withal.

XIV. Hester and the Physician

Hester bade little Pearl run down to the margin of the water, and play with the shells and tangled seaweed, until she should have talked awhile with yonder gatherer of herbs. So the child flew away like a bird, and, making bare her small white feet, went pattering along the moist margin of the sea. Here and there, she came to a full stop, and peeped curiously into a pool, left by the retiring tide as a mirror for Pearl to see her face in. Forth peeped at her, out of the pool, with dark, glistening curls around her head, and an elf-smile in her eyes, the image of a little maid, whom Pearl, having no other playmate, invited to take her hand and run a race with her. But the visionary little maid, on her part, beckoned likewise, as if to say,—"This is a better place! Come thou into the pool!" And Pearl, stepping in, mid-leg deep, beheld her own white feet at the bottom; while, out of a still lower depth, came the gleam of a kind of fragmentary smile, floating to and fro in the agitated water.

Meanwhile, her mother had accosted the physician.

"I would speak a word with you," said she,—"a word that concerns us much."

"Aha! And is it Mistress Hester that has a word for old Roger Chillingworth?" answered he, raising himself from his stooping posture. "With all my heart! Why, Mistress, I hear good tidings of you on all hands! No longer ago than yester-eve, a magistrate, a wise and godly man, was discoursing of your affairs, Mistress Hester, and whispered me that there had been question concerning you in the council. It was debated whether or no, with safety to the common weal, yonder scarlet letter might be taken off your bosom. On my life, Hester, I made my entreaty to the worshipful magistrate that it might be done forthwith!"

"It lies not in the pleasure of the magistrates to take off this badge," calmly replied Hester. "Were I worthy to be quit of it, it would fall away of its own nature, or be transformed into something that should speak a different purport."

"Nay, then, wear it, if it suit you better," rejoined he. "A woman must needs follow her own fancy," touching the adornment of her person. "The letter is gayly embroidered, and shows right bravely on your bosom!"

All this while, Hester had been looking steadily at the old man, and was shocked, as well as wonder-smitten, to discern what a change had been wrought upon him within the past seven years. It was not so much that he had grown older; for though the traces of advancing life were visible, he bore his age well, and seemed to retain a wiry vigor and alertness. But the former aspect of an intellectual and studious man, calm and quiet, which was what she best remembered in him, had altogether vanished, and been succeeded by an eager, searching, almost fierce, yet carefully guarded look. It seemed to be his wish and purpose to mask this expression with a smile; but the latter played him false, and flickered over his visage so derisively, that the spectator could see his blackness all the better for it. Ever and anon, too, there came a glare of red light out of his eyes; as if the old man's soul were on fire, and kept on smouldering duskily within his breast, until, by some casual puff of passion, it was blown into a momentary flame. This he repressed as speedily as possible, and strove to look as if nothing of the kind had happened.

In a word, old Roger Chillingworth was a striking evidence of man's faculty of transforming himself into a devil, if he will only, for a reasonable space of time, undertake a devil's office. This unhappy person had effected such a transformation by devoting himself, for seven years, to the constant analysis of a heart full of torture, and deriving his enjoyment thence, and adding fuel to those fiery tortures which he analyzed and gloated over.

The scarlet letter burned on Hester Prynne's bosom. Here was another ruin, the responsibility of which came partly home to her.

"What see you in my face," asked the physician, "that you look at it so earnestly?"

"Something that would make me weep, if there were any tears bitter enough for it," answered she. "But let it pass! It is of yonder miserable man that I would speak."

"And what of him?" cried Roger Chillingworth eagerly, as if he loved the topic, and were glad of an opportunity to discuss it with the only person of whom he could make a confidant. "Not to hide the truth, Mistress Hester, my thoughts happen just now to be busy with the gentleman. So speak freely; and I will make answer."

"When we last spake together," said Hester, "now seven years ago, it was your pleasure to extort a promise of secrecy, as touching the former relation betwixt yourself and me. As the life and good fame of yonder man were in your hands, there seemed no choice to me, save to be silent, in accordance with your behest. Yet it was not without heavy misgivings that I thus bound myself; for, having cast off all duty towards other human beings, there remained a duty towards him; and something whispered me that I was betraying it, in pledging myself to keep your counsel. Since that day, no man is so near to him as you. You tread behind his every footstep. You are beside him, sleeping and waking. You search his thoughts. You burrow and rankle in his heart! Your clutch is on his life, and you cause him to die daily a living death; and still he knows you not. In permitting this, I have surely acted a false part by the only man to whom the power was left me to be true!"

"What choice had you?" asked Roger Chillingworth. "My finger, pointed at this man, would have hurled him from his pulpit into a dungeon,—thence, peradventure, to the gallows!"

"It had been better so!" said Hester Prynne.

"What evil have I done the man?" asked Roger Chillingworth again. "I tell thee, Hester Prynne, the richest fee that ever physician earned from monarch could not have brought such care as I have wasted on this miserable priest! But for my aid, his life would have burned away in torments, within the first two years after the perpetration of his crime and thine. For, Hester, his spirit lacked the strength that could have borne up, as thine has, beneath a burden like thy scarlet letter. O, I could reveal a goodly secret! But enough! What art can do, I have exhausted on him. That he now breathes, and creeps about on earth, is owing all to me!"

"Better he had died at once!" said Hester Prynne.

"Yea, woman, thou sayest truly!" cried old Roger Chillingworth, letting the lurid fire of his heart blaze out before her eyes. "Better had he died at once! Never did mortal suffer what this man has suffered. And all, all, in the sight of his worst enemy! He has been conscious of me. He has felt an influence dwelling always upon him like a curse. He knew, by some spiritual sense,—for the Creator never made another being so sensitive as this,—he knew that no friendly hand was pulling at his heart-strings, and that an eye was looking curiously into him, which sought only evil, and found it. But he knew not that the eye and hand were mine! With the superstition common to his brotherhood, he fancied himself given over to a fiend, to be tortured with frightful dreams, and desperate thoughts, the sting of remorse, and despair of pardon; as a foretaste of what awaits him beyond the grave. But it was the constant shadow of my presence!—the closest propinquity of the man whom he had most vilely wronged!—and who had grown to exist only by this perpetual poison of the direst revenge! Yea, indeed!—he did not err!—there was a fiend at his elbow! A mortal man, with once a human heart, has become a fiend for his especial torment!"

The unfortunate physician, while uttering these words, lifted his hands with a look of horror, as if he had beheld some frightful shape, which he could not recognize, usurping the place of his own image in a glass. It was one of those moments—which sometimes occur only at the interval of years—when a man's moral aspect is faithfully revealed to his mind's eye. Not improbably, he had never before viewed himself as he did now.

"Hast thou not tortured him enough?" said Hester, noticing the old man's look. "Has he not paid thee all?"

"No!—no!—He has but increased the debt!" answered the physician; and, as he proceeded, his manner lost its fiercer characteristics, and subsided into gloom. "Dost thou remember me, Hester, as I was nine years agone? Even then, I was in the autumn of my days, nor was it the early autumn. But all my life had been made up of earnest, studious, thoughtful, quiet years, bestowed faithfully for the increase of mine own knowledge, and faithfully, too, though this latter object was but casual to the other,—faithfully, for the advancement of human welfare. No life had been more peaceful and innocent than mine; few lives so rich with benefits conferred. Dost thou remember me? Was I not, though you might deem me cold, nevertheless a man thoughtful for others, craving little for himself,—kind, true, just, and of constant, if not warm affections? Was I not all this?"

"All this, and more," said Hester.

"And what am I now?" demanded he, looking into her face, and permitting the whole evil within him to be written on his features. "I have already told thee what I am! A fiend! Who made me so?"

"It was myself!" cried Hester, shuddering. "It was I, not less than he. Why hast thou not avenged thyself on me?"

"I have left thee to the scarlet letter," replied Roger Chillingworth. "If that have not avenged me, I can do no more!"

He laid his finger on it, with a smile.

"It has avenged thee!" answered Hester Prynne.

"I judged no less," said the physician. "And now, what wouldst thou with me touching this man?"

"I must reveal the secret," answered Hester, firmly. "He must discern thee in thy true character. What may be the result, I know not. But this long debt of confidence, due from me to him, whose bane and ruin I have been, shall at length be paid. So far as concerns the overthrow or preservation of his fair fame and his earthly state, and perchance his life, he is in thy hands. Nor do I,—whom the scarlet letter has disciplined to truth, though it be the truth of red-hot iron, entering into the soul,—nor do I perceive such advantage in his living any longer a life of ghastly emptiness, that I shall stoop to implore thy mercy. Do with him as thou wilt! There is no good for him,—no good for me,—no good for thee! There is no good for little Pearl! There is no path to guide us out of this dismal maze!"

"Woman, I could wellnigh pity thee!" said Roger Chillingworth, unable to restrain a thrill of admiration too; for there was a quality almost majestic in the despair which she expressed. "Thou hadst great elements. Peradventure, hadst thou met earlier with a better love than mine, this evil had not been. I pity thee, for the good that has been wasted in thy nature!"

"And I thee," answered Hester Prynne, "for the hatred that has transformed a wise and just man to a fiend! Wilt thou yet purge it out of thee, and be once more human? If not for his sake, then doubly for thine own! Forgive, and leave his further retribution to the Power that claims it! I said, but now, that there could be no good event for him, or thee, or me, who are here wandering together in this gloomy maze of evil, and stumbling, at every step, over the guilt wherewith we have strewn our path. It is not so! There might be good for thee, and thee alone, since thou hast been deeply wronged, and hast it at thy will to pardon. Wilt thou give up that only privilege? Wilt thou reject that priceless benefit?"

"Peace, Hester, peace!" replied the old man, with gloomy sternness. "It is not granted me to pardon. I have no such power as thou tellest me of. My old faith, long forgotten, comes back to me, and explains all that we do, and all we suffer. By thy first step awry, thou didst plant the germ of evil; but, since that moment, it has all been a dark necessity. Ye that have wronged me are not sinful, save in a kind of typical illusion; neither am I fiend-like, who have snatched a fiend's office from his hands. It is our fate. Let the black flower blossom as it may! Now go thy ways, and deal as thou wilt with yonder man."

He waved his hand, and betook himself again to his employment of gathering herbs.

XV. Hester and Pearl

So Roger Chillingworth—a deformed old figure, with a face that haunted men's memories longer than they liked—took leave of Hester Prynne, and went stooping away along the earth. He gathered here and there an herb, or grubbed up a root, and put it into the basket on his arm. His gray beard almost touched the ground, as he crept onward. Hester gazed after him a little while, looking with a half-fantastic curiosity to see whether the tender grass of early spring would not be blighted beneath him, and show the wavering track of his footsteps, sere and brown, across its cheerful verdure. She wondered what sort of herbs they were, which the old man was so sedulous to gather. Would not the earth, quickened to an evil purpose by the sympathy of his eye, greet him with poisonous shrubs, of species hitherto unknown, that would start up under his fingers? Or might it suffice him, that every wholesome growth should be converted into something deleterious and malignant at his touch? Did the sun, which shone so brightly everywhere else, really fall upon him? Or was there, as it rather seemed, a circle of ominous shadow moving along with his deformity, whichever way he turned himself? And whither was he now going? Would he not suddenly sink into the earth, leaving a barren and blasted spot, where in due course of time, would be seen deadly nightshade, dogwood, henbane,[2] and whatever else of vegetable wickedness the climate could produce, all flourishing with hideous luxuriance? Or would he spread bat's wings and flee away, looking so much the uglier, the higher he rose towards heaven?

"Be it sin or no," said Hester Prynne bitterly, as she still gazed after him, "I hate the man!"

She upbraided herself for the sentiment, but could not overcome or lessen it. Attempting to do so, she thought of those long-past days, in a distant land, when he used to emerge at eventide from the seclusion of his study, and sit down in the fire-light of their home, and in the light of her nuptial smile. He needed to bask himself in that smile, he said, in order that the chill of so many lonely hours among his books might be taken off the scholar's heart. Such scenes had once appeared not otherwise than happy, but now, as viewed through the dismal medium of her subsequent life, they classed themselves

2. Plants that are poisonous, produce poison, or are associated with witchcraft.

among her ugliest remembrances. She marvelled how such scenes could have been! She marvelled how she could ever have been wrought upon to marry him! She deemed it her crime most to be repented of, that she had ever endured, and reciprocated, the lukewarm grasp of his hand, and had suffered the smile of her lips and eyes to mingle and melt into his own. And it seemed a fouler offence committed by Roger Chillingworth, than any which had since been done him, that, in the time when her heart knew no better, he had persuaded her to fancy herself happy by his side.

"Yes, I hate him!" repeated Hester, more bitterly than before. "He betrayed me! He has done me worse wrong than I did him!"

Let men tremble to win the hand of woman, unless they win along with it the utmost passion of her heart! Else it may be their miserable fortune, as it was Roger Chillingworth's, when some mightier touch than their own may have awakened all her sensibilities, to be reproached even for the calm content, the marble image of happiness, which they will have imposed upon her as the warm reality. But Hester ought long ago to have done with this injustice. What did it betoken? Had seven long years, under the torture of the scarlet letter, inflicted so much of misery, and wrought out no repentance?

The emotions of that brief space, while she stood gazing after the crooked figure of old Roger Chillingworth, threw a dark light on Hester's state of mind, revealing much that she might not otherwise have acknowledged to herself.

He being gone, she summoned back her child.

"Pearl! Little Pearl! Where are you?"

Pearl, whose activity of spirit never flagged, had been at no loss for amusement while her mother talked with the old gatherer of herbs. At first, as already told, she had flirted fancifully with her own image in a pool of water, beckoning the phantom forth, and—as it declined to venture—seeking a passage for herself into its sphere of impalpable earth and unattainable sky. Soon finding, however, that either she or the image was unreal, she turned elsewhere for better pastime. She made little boats out of birch-bark, and freighted them with snail-shells, and sent out more ventures on the mighty deep than any merchant in New England; but the larger part of them foundered near the shore. She seized a live horseshoe by the tail, and made prize of several five-fingers,[3] and laid out a jelly-fish to melt in the warm sun. Then she took up the white foam, that streaked the line of the advancing tide, and threw it upon the breeze, scampering after it with winged footsteps, to catch the great snow-flakes ere they fell. Perceiving a flock of beach-birds, that fed and fluttered along the shore, the naughty child picked up her apron full of pebbles, and, creeping from rock to rock after these small sea-fowl, displayed remarkable dexterity in pelting them. One little gray bird, with a white breast, Pearl was almost sure, had been hit by a pebble, and fluttered away with a broken wing. But then the elf-child sighed, and gave up her sport; because it grieved her to have done harm to a little being that was as wild as the sea-breeze, or as wild as Pearl herself.

Her final employment was to gather sea-weed, of various kinds, and make herself a scarf, or mantle, and a head-dress, and thus assume the aspect of

3. Five-rayed starfish. "Horseshoe": horseshoe crab.

a little mermaid. She inherited her mother's gift for devising drapery and costume. As the last touch to her mermaid's garb, Pearl took some eel-grass, and imitated, as best she could, on her own bosom, the decoration with which she was so familiar on her mother's. A letter,—the letter A,—but freshly green, instead of scarlet! The child bent her chin upon her breast, and contemplated this device with strange interest; even as if the one only thing for which she had been sent into the world was to make out its hidden import.

"I wonder if mother will ask me what it means!" thought Pearl.

Just then, she heard her mother's voice, and, flitting along as lightly as one of the little sea-birds, appeared before Hester Prynne, dancing, laughing, and pointing her finger to the ornament upon her bosom.

"My little Pearl," said Hester, after a moment's silence, "the green letter, and on thy childish bosom, has no purport. But dost thou know, my child, what this letter means which thy mother is doomed to wear?"

"Yes, mother," said the child. "It is the great letter A. Thou hast taught it me in the horn-book."[4]

Hester looked steadily into her little face; but, though there was that singular expression which she had so often remarked in her black eyes, she could not satisfy herself whether Pearl really attached any meaning to the symbol. She felt a morbid desire to ascertain the point.

"Dost thou know, child, wherefore thy mother wears this letter?"

"Truly do I!" answered Pearl, looking brightly into her mother's face. "It is for the same reason that the minister keeps his hand over his heart!"

"And what reason is that?" asked Hester, half smiling at the absurd incongruity of the child's observation; but, on second thoughts, turning pale. "What has the letter to do with any heart, save mine?"

"Nay, mother, I have told all I know," said Pearl, more seriously than she was wont to speak. "Ask yonder old man whom thou hast been talking with! It may be he can tell. But in good earnest now, mother dear, what does this scarlet letter mean?—and why dost thou wear it on they bosom?—and why does the minister keep his hand over his heart?"

She took her mother's hand in both her own, and gazed into her eyes with an earnestness that was seldom seen in her wild and capricious character. The thought occurred to Hester, that the child might really be seeking to approach her with childlike confidence, and doing what she could, and as intelligently as she knew how, to establish a meeting-point of sympathy. It showed Pearl in an unwonted aspect. Heretofore, the mother, while loving her child with the intensity of a sole affection, had schooled herself to hope for little other return than the waywardness of an April breeze; which spends its time in airy sport, and has its gusts of inexplicable passion, and is petulant in its best of moods, and chills oftener than caresses you, when you take it to your bosom; in requital of which misdemeanours, it will sometimes, of its own vague purpose, kiss your cheek with a kind of doubtful tenderness, and play gently with your hair, and then begone about its other idle business, leaving a dreamy pleasure at your heart. And this, moreover, was a mother's estimate of the child's disposition. Any other observer might have seen few but unamiable traits, and have given them a far darker

4. A child's "first reader" or primer consisting of a single page, with the alphabet, religious materials, or the like protected by a transparent sheet made from an animal's horn.

coloring. But now the idea came strongly into Hester's mind, that Pearl, with her remarkable precocity and acuteness, might already have approached the age when she could be made a friend, and intrusted with as much of her mother's sorrows as could be imparted, without irreverence either to the parent or the child. In the little chaos of Pearl's character, there might be seen emerging—and could have been, from the very first—the stead-fast principles of an unflinching courage,—an uncontrollable will,—a sturdy pride, which might be disciplined into self-respect,—and a bitter scorn of many things, which, when examined, might be found to have the taint of falsehood in them. She possessed affections, too, though hitherto acrid and disagreeable, as are the richest flavors of unripe fruit. With all these sterling attributes, thought Hester, the evil which she inherited from her mother must be great indeed, if a noble woman do not grow out of this elfish child.

Pearl's inevitable tendency to hover about the enigma of the scarlet letter seemed an innate quality of her being. From the earliest epoch of her conscious life, she had entered upon this as her appointed mission. Hester had often fancied that Providence had a design of justice and retribution, in endowing the child with this marked propensity; but never, until now, had she bethought herself to ask, whether, linked with that design, there might not likewise be a purpose of mercy and beneficence. If little Pearl were entertained with faith and trust, as a spirit-messenger no less than an earthly child, might it not be her errand to soothe away the sorrow that lay cold in her mother's heart, and converted it into a tomb?—and to help her to overcome the passion, once so wild, and even yet neither dead nor asleep, but only imprisoned within the same tomb-like heart?

Such were some of the thoughts that now stirred in Hester's mind, with as much vivacity of impression as if they had actually been whispered into her ear. And there was little Pearl, all this while, holding her mother's hand in both her own, and turning her face upward, while she put these searching questions, once, and again, and still a third time.

"What does the letter mean, mother?—and why dost thou wear it?—and why does the minister keep his hand over his heart?"

"What shall I say?" thought Hester to herself.—"No! If this be the price of the child's sympathy, I cannot pay it!"

Then she spoke aloud.

"Silly Pearl," said she, "what questions are these? There are many things in this world that a child must not ask about. What know I of the minister's heart? And as for the scarlet letter, I wear it for the sake of its gold thread!"

In all the seven bygone years, Hester Prynne had never before been false to the symbol on her bosom. It may be that it was the talisman of a stern and severe, but yet a guardian spirit, who now forsook her; as recognizing that, in spite of his strict watch over her heart, some new evil had crept into it, or some old one had never been expelled. As for little Pearl, the earnestness soon passed out of her face.

But the child did not see fit to let the matter drop. Two or three times, as her mother and she went homeward, and as often at supper-time, and while Hester was putting her to bed, and once after she seemed to be fairly asleep, Pearl looked up, with mischief gleaming in her black eyes.

"Mother," said she, "what does the scarlet letter mean?"

And the next morning, the first indication the child gave of being awake was by popping up her head from the pillow, and making that other inquiry, which she had so unaccountably connected with her investigations about the scarlet letter:—

"Mother!—Mother!—Why does the minister keep his hand over his heart?"

"Hold thy tongue, naughty child!" answered her mother, with an asperity that she had never permitted to herself before. "Do not tease me; else I shall shut thee into the dark closet!"

XVI. A Forest Walk

Hester Prynne remained constant in her resolve to make known to Mr. Dimmesdale, at whatever risk of present pain or ulterior consequences, the true character of the man who had crept into his intimacy. For several days, however, she vainly sought an opportunity of addressing him in some of the meditative walks which she knew him to be in the habit of taking, along the shores of the peninsula, or on the wooded hills of the neighbouring country. There would have been no scandal, indeed, nor peril to the holy whiteness of the clergyman's good fame, had she visited him in his own study; where many a penitent, ere now, had confessed sins of perhaps as deep a die as the one betokened by the scarlet letter. But, partly that she dreaded the secret or undisguised interference of old Roger Chillingworth, and partly that her conscious heart imputed suspicion where none could have been felt, and partly that both the minister and she would need the whole wide world to breathe in, while they talked together,—for all these reasons, Hester never thought of meeting him in any narrower privacy than beneath the open sky.

At last, while attending in a sick-chamber, whither the Reverend Mr. Dimmesdale had been summoned to make a prayer, she learnt that he had gone, the day before, to visit the Apostle Eliot,[5] among his Indian converts. He would probably return, by a certain hour, in the afternoon of the morrow. Betimes, therefore, the next day, Hester took little Pearl,—who was necessarily the companion of all her mother's expeditions, however inconvenient her presence,—and set forth.

The road, after the two wayfarers had crossed from the peninsula to the mainland, was no other than a footpath. It straggled onward into the mystery of the primeval forest. This hemmed it in so narrowly, and stood so black and dense on either side, and disclosed such imperfect glimpses of the sky above, that, to Hester's mind, it imaged not amiss the moral wilderness in which she had so long been wandering. The day was chill and sombre. Overhead was a gray expanse of cloud, slightly stirred, however, by a breeze; so that a gleam of flickering sunshine might now and then be seen at its solitary play along the path. This flitting cheerfulness was always at the farther extremity of some long vista through the forest. The sportive sunlight—feebly sportive, at best, in the predominant pensiveness of the day and scene—withdrew itself as they came nigh, and left the spots where it had danced the drearier, because they had hoped to find them bright.

5. The historical John Eliot (1604–1690), self-appointed missionary to American Indians.

"Mother," said little Pearl, "the sunshine does not love you. It runs away and hides itself, because it is afraid of something on your bosom. Now, see! There it is, playing, a good way off. Stand you here, and let me run and catch it. I am but a child. It will not flee from me; for I wear nothing on my bosom yet!"

"Nor ever will, my child, I hope," said Hester.

"And why not, mother?" asked Pearl, stopping short, just at the beginning of her race. "Will not it come of its own accord, when I am a woman grown?"

"Run away, child," answered her mother, "and catch the sunshine! It will soon be gone."

Pearl set forth, at a great pace, and, as Hester smiled to perceive, did actually catch the sunshine, and stood laughing in the midst of it, all brightened by its splendor, and scintillating with the vivacity excited by rapid motion. The light lingered about the lonely child, as if glad of such a playmate, until her mother had drawn almost nigh enough to step into the magic circle too.

"It will go now!" said Pearl, shaking her head.

"See!" answered Hester, smiling. "Now I can stretch out my hand, and grasp some of it."

As she attempted to do so, the sunshine vanished; or, to judge from the bright expression that was dancing on Pearl's features, her mother could have fancied that the child had absorbed it into herself, and would give it forth again, with a gleam about her path, as they should plunge into some gloomier shade. There was no other attribute that so much impressed her with a sense of new and untransmitted vigor in Pearl's nature, as this never-failing vivacity of spirits; she had not the disease of sadness, which almost all children, in these latter days, inherit, with the scrofula,[6] from the troubles of their ancestors. Perhaps this too was a disease, and but the reflex of the wild energy with which Hester had fought against her sorrows, before Pearl's birth. It was certainly a doubtful charm, imparting a hard, metallic lustre to the child's character. She wanted—what some people want throughout life—a grief that should deeply touch her, and thus humanize and make her capable of sympathy. But there was time enough yet for little Pearl!

"Come, my child!" said Hester, looking about her, from the spot where Pearl had stood still in the sunshine. "We will sit down a little way within the wood, and rest ourselves."

"I am not aweary, mother," replied the little girl. "But you may sit down, if you will tell me a story meanwhile."

"A story, child!" said Hester. "And about what?"

"O, a story about the Black Man!" answered Pearl, taking hold of her mother's gown, and looking up, half earnestly, half mischievously, into her face. "How he haunts this forest, and carries a book with him,—a big, heavy book, with iron clasps; and how this ugly Black Man offers his book and an iron pen to every body that meets him here among the trees; and they are to write their names with their own blood. And then he sets his mark on their bosoms! Didst thou ever meet the Black Man, mother?"

"And who told you this story, Pearl?" asked her mother, recognizing a common superstition of the period.

6. Tubercular infection of the skin of the neck.

"It was the old dame in the chimney-corner, at the house where you watched last night," said the child. "But she fancied me asleep while she was talking of it. She said that a thousand and a thousand people had met him here, and had written in his book, and have his mark on them. And that ugly-tempered lady, old Mistress Hibbins, was one. And, mother, the old dame said that this scarlet letter was the Black Man's mark on thee, and that it glows like a red flame when thou meetest him at midnight, here in the dark wood. Is it true, mother? And dost thou go to meet him in the night-time?"

"Didst thou ever awake, and find thy mother gone?" asked Hester.

"Not that I remember," said the child. "If thou fearest to leave me in our cottage, thou mightest take me along with thee. I would very gladly go! But, mother, tell me now! Is there such a Black Man? And didst thou ever meet him? And is this his mark?"

"Wilt thou let me be at peace, if I once tell thee?" asked her mother.

"Yes, if thou tellest me all," answered Pearl.

"Once in my life I met the Black Man!" said her mother. "This scarlet letter is his mark!"

Thus conversing, they entered sufficiently deep into the wood to secure themselves from the observation of any casual passenger along the forest-track. Here they sat down on a luxuriant heap of moss; which, at some epoch of the preceding century, had been a gigantic pine, with its roots and trunk in the darksome shade, and its head aloft in the upper atmosphere. It was a little dell where they had seated themselves, with a leaf-strewn bank rising gently on either side, and a brook flowing through the midst, over a bed of fallen and drowned leaves. The trees impending over it had flung down great branches, from time to time, which choked up the current, and compelled it to form eddies and black depths at some points; while, in its swifter and livelier passages, there appeared a channel-way of pebbles, and brown, sparkling sand. Letting the eyes follow along the course of the stream, they could catch the reflected light from its water, at some short distance within the forest, but soon lost all traces of it amid the bewilderment of tree-trunks and underbrush, and here and there a huge rock, covered over with gray lichens. All these giant trees and boulders of granite seemed intent on making a mystery of the course of this small brook; fearing, perhaps, that, with its never-ceasing loquacity, it should whisper tales out of the heart of the old forest whence it flowed, or mirror its revelations on the smooth surface of a pool. Continually, indeed, as it stole onward, the streamlet kept up a babble, kind, quiet, soothing, but melancholy, like the voice of a young child that was spending its infancy without playfulness, and knew not how to be merry among sad acquaintance and events of sombre hue.

"O brook! O foolish and tiresome little brook!" cried Pearl, after listening awhile to its talk. "Why art thou so sad? Pluck up a spirit, and do not be all the time sighing and murmuring!"

But the brook, in the course of its little lifetime among the forest-trees, had gone through so solemn an experience that it could not help talking about it, and seemed to have nothing else to say. Pearl resembled the brook, inasmuch as the current of her life gushed from a well-spring as mysterious, and had flowed through scenes shadowed as heavily with gloom. But, unlike the little stream, she danced and sparkled, and prattled airily along her course.

"What does this sad little brook say, mother?" inquired she.

"If thou hadst a sorrow of thine own, the brook might tell thee of it," answered her mother, "even as it is telling me of mine! But now, Pearl, I hear a footstep along the path, and the noise of one putting aside the branches. I would have thee betake thyself to play, and leave me to speak with him that comes yonder."

"Is it the Black Man?" asked Pearl.

"Wilt thou go and play, child?" repeated her mother. "But do not stray far into the wood. And take heed that thou come at my first call."

"Yes, mother," answered Pearl. "But, if it be the Black Man, wilt thou not let me stay a moment, and look at him, with his big book under his arm?"

"Go, silly child!" said her mother, impatiently. "It is no Black Man! Thou canst see him now through the trees. It is the minister!"

"And so it is!" said the child. "And, mother, he has his hand over his heart! Is it because, when the minister wrote his name in the book, the Black Man set his mark in that place? But why does he not wear it outside his bosom, as thou dost, mother?"

"Go now, child, and thou shalt tease me as thou wilt another time," cried Hester Prynne. "But do not stray far. Keep where thou canst hear the babble of the brook."

The child went singing away, following up the current of the brook, and striving to mingle a more lightsome cadence with its melancholy voice. But the little stream would not be comforted, and still kept telling its unintelligible secret of some very mournful mystery that had happened—or making a prophetic lamentation about something that was yet to happen—within the verge of the dismal forest. So Pearl, who had enough of shadow in her own little life, chose to break off all acquaintance with this repining brook. She set herself, therefore, to gathering violets and wood-anemones, and some scarlet columbines that she found growing in the crevices of a high rock.

When her elf-child had departed, Hester Prynne made a step or two towards the track that led through the forest, but still remained under the deep shadow of the trees. She beheld the minister advancing along the path, entirely alone, and leaning on a staff which he had cut by the way-side. He looked haggard and feeble, and betrayed a nerveless despondency in his air, which had never so remarkably characterized him in his walks about the settlement, nor in any other situation where he deemed himself liable to notice. Here it was wofully visible, in this intense seclusion of the forest, which of itself would have been a heavy trial to the spirits. There was a listlessness in his gait; as if he saw no reason for taking one step farther, nor felt any desire to do so, but would have been glad, could he be glad of any thing, to fling himself down at the root of the nearest tree, and lie there passive for evermore. The leaves might bestrew him, and the soil gradually accumulate and form a little hillock over his frame, no matter whether there were life in it or no. Death was too definite an object to be wished for, or avoided.

To Hester's eye, the Reverend Mr. Dimmesdale exhibited no symptom of positive and vivacious suffering, except that, as little Pearl had remarked, he kept his hand over his heart.

XVII. The Pastor and His Parishioner

Slowly as the minister walked, he had almost gone by, before Hester Prynne could gather voice enough to attract his observation. At length, she succeeded.

"Arthur Dimmesdale!" she said, faintly at first; then louder, but hoarsely. "Arthur Dimmesdale!"

"Who speaks?" answered the minister.

Gathering himself quickly up, he stood more erect, like a man taken by surprise in a mood to which he was reluctant to have witnesses. Throwing his eyes anxiously in the direction of the voice, he indistinctly beheld a form under the trees, clad in garments so sombre, and so little relieved from the gray twilight into which the clouded sky and the heavy foliage had darkened the noontide, that he knew not whether it were a woman or a shadow. It may be, that his pathway through life was haunted thus, by a spectre that had stolen out from among his thoughts.

He made a step nigher, and discovered the scarlet letter.

"Hester! Hester Prynne!" said he. "Is it thou? Art thou in life?"

"Even so!" she answered. "In such life as has been mine these seven years past! And thou, Arthur Dimmesdale, dost thou yet live?"

It was no wonder that they thus questioned one another's actual and bodily existence, and even doubted of their own. So strangely did they meet, in the dim wood, that it was like the first encounter, in the world beyond the grave, of two spirits who had been intimately connected in their former life, but now stood coldly shuddering, in mutual dread; as not yet familiar with their state, nor wonted to the companionship of disembodied beings. Each a ghost, and awe-stricken at the other ghost! They were awe-stricken likewise at themselves; because the crisis flung back to them their consciousness, and revealed to each heart its history and experience, as life never does, except at such breathless epochs. The soul beheld its features in the mirror of the passing moment. It was with fear, and tremulously, and, as it were, by a slow, reluctant necessity, that Arthur Dimmesdale put forth his hand, chill as death, and touched the chill hand of Hester Prynne. The grasp, cold as it was, took away what was dreariest in the interview. They now felt themselves, at least, inhabitants of the same sphere.

Without a word more spoken,—neither he nor she assuming the guidance, but with an unexpressed consent,—they glided back into the shadow of the woods, whence Hester had emerged, and sat down on the heap of moss where she and Pearl had before been sitting. When they found voice to speak, it was, at first, only to utter remarks and inquiries such as any two acquaintance might have made, about the gloomy sky, the threatening storm, and, next, the health of each. Thus they went onward, not boldly, but step by step, into the themes that were brooding deepest in their hearts. So long estranged by fate and circumstances, they needed something slight and casual to run before, and throw open the doors of intercourse, so that their real thoughts might be led across the threshold.

After a while, the minister fixed his eyes on Hester Prynne's.

"Hester," said he, "hast thou found peace?"

She smiled drearily, looking down upon her bosom.

"Hast thou?" she asked.

"None!—nothing but despair!" he answered. "What else could I look for, being what I am, and leading such a life as mine? Were I an atheist,—a man devoid of conscience,—a wretch with coarse and brutal instincts,—I might have found peace, long ere now. Nay, I never should have lost it! But, as matters stand with my soul, whatever of good capacity there originally was in me, all of God's gifts that were the choicest have become the ministers of spiritual torment. Hester, I am most miserable!"

"The people reverence thee," said Hester. "And surely thou workest good among them! Doth this bring thee no comfort?"

"More misery, Hester!—only the more misery!" answered the clergyman, with a bitter smile. "As concerns the good which I may appear to do, I have no faith in it. It must needs be a delusion. What can a ruined soul, like mine, effect towards the redemption of other souls!—or a polluted soul, towards their purification? And as for the people's reverence, would that it were turned to scorn and hatred! Canst thou deem it, Hester, a consolation, that I must stand up in my pulpit, and meet so many eyes turned upward to my face, as if the light of heaven were beaming from it!—must see my flock hungry for the truth, and listening to my words as if a tongue of Pentecost were speaking!—and then look inward, and discern the black reality of what they idolize? I have laughed, in bitterness and agony of heart, at the contrast between what I seem and what I am! And Satan laughs at it!"

"You wrong yourself in this," said Hester, gently. "You have deeply and sorely repented. Your sin is left behind you, in the days long past. Your present life is not less holy, in very truth, than it seems in people's eyes. Is there no reality in the penitence thus sealed and witnessed by good works? And wherefore should it not bring you peace?"

"No, Hester, no!" replied the clergyman. "There is no substance in it! It is cold and dead, and can do nothing for me! Of penance I have had enough! Of penitence there has been none! Else, I should long ago have thrown off these garments of mock holiness, and have shown myself to mankind as they will see me at the judgment-seat. Happy are you, Hester, that wear the scarlet letter openly upon your bosom! Mine burns in secret! Thou little knowest what a relief it is, after the torment of a seven years' cheat, to look into an eye that recognizes me for what I am! Had I one friend,—or were it my worst enemy!—to whom, when sickened with the praises of all other men, I could daily betake myself, and be known as the vilest of all sinners, methinks my soul might keep itself alive thereby. Even thus much of truth would save me! But, now, it is all falsehood!—all emptiness!—all death!"

Hester Prynne looked into his face, but hesitated to speak. Yet, uttering his long-restrained emotions so vehemently as he did, his words here offered her the very point of circumstances in which to interpose what she came to say. She conquered her fears, and spoke.

"Such a friend as thou hast even now wished for," said she, "with whom to weep over thy sin, thou hast in me, the partner of it!"—Again she hesitated, but brought out the words with an effort.—"Thou hast long had such an enemy, and dwellest with him under the same roof!"

The minister started to his feet, gasping for breath, and clutching at his heart as if he would have torn it out of his bosom.

"Ha! What sayest thou?" cried he. "An enemy! And under mine own roof! What mean you?"

Hester Prynne was now fully sensible of the deep injury for which she was responsible to this unhappy man, in permitting him to lie for so many years, or, indeed, for a single moment, at the mercy of one, whose purposes could not be other than malevolent. The very contiguity of his enemy, beneath whatever mask the latter might conceal himself, was enough to disturb the magnetic sphere of a being so sensitive as Arthur Dimmesdale. There had been a period when Hester was less alive to this consideration; or, perhaps, in the misanthropy of her own trouble, she left the minister to bear what she might picture to herself as a more tolerable doom. But of late, since the night of his vigil, all her sympathies towards him had been both softened and invigorated. She now read his heart more accurately. She doubted not, that the continual presence of Roger Chillingworth,—the secret poison of his malignity, infecting all the air about him,—and his authorized interference, as a physician, with the minister's physical and spiritual infirmities,—that these bad opportunities had been turned to a cruel purpose. By means of them, the sufferer's conscience had been kept in an irritated state, the tendency of which was, not to cure by wholesome pain, but to disorganize and corrupt his spiritual being. Its result, on earth, could hardly fail to be insanity, and hereafter, that eternal alienation from the Good and True, of which madness is perhaps the earthly type.

Such was the ruin to which she had brought the man, once,—nay, why should we not speak it?—still so passionately loved! Hester felt that the sacrifice of the clergyman's good name, and death itself, as she had already told Roger Chillingworth, would have been infinitely preferable to the alternative which she had taken upon herself to choose. And now, rather than have had this grievous wrong to confess, she would gladly have lain down on the forest-leaves, and died there, at Arthur Dimmesdale's feet.

"O Arthur," cried she, "forgive me! In all things else, I have striven to be true! Truth was the one virtue which I might have held fast, and did hold fast through all extremity; save when thy good,—thy life,—thy fame,—were put in question! Then I consented to a deception. But a lie is never good, even though death threaten on the other side! Dost thou not see what I would say? That old man!—the physician!—he whom they call Roger Chillingworth!—he was my husband!"

The minister looked at her, for an instant, with all that violence of passion, which—intermixed, in more shapes than one, with his higher, purer, softer qualities—was, in fact, the portion of him which the Devil claimed, and through which he sought to win the rest. Never was there a blacker or a fiercer frown, than Hester now encountered. For the brief space that it lasted, it was a dark transfiguration. But his character had been so much enfeebled by suffering, that even its lower energies were incapable of more than a temporary struggle. He sank down on the ground, and buried his face in his hands.

"I might have known it!" murmured he. "I did know it! Was not the secret told me in the natural recoil of my heart, at the first sight of him, and as often as I have seen him since? Why did I not understand? O Hester Prynne, thou little, little knowest all the horror of this thing! And the shame!—the indelicacy!—the horrible ugliness of this exposure of a sick and guilty heart to the very eye that would gloat over it! Woman, woman, thou art accountable for this! I cannot forgive thee!"

"Thou shalt forgive me!" cried Hester, flinging herself on the fallen leaves beside him. "Let God punish! Thou shalt forgive!"

With sudden and desperate tenderness, she threw her arms around him, and pressed his head against her bosom; little caring though his cheek rested on the scarlet letter. He would have released himself, but strove in vain to do so. Hester would not set him free, lest he should look her sternly in the face. All the world had frowned on her,—for seven long years had it frowned upon this lonely woman,—and still she bore it all, nor ever once turned away her firm, sad eyes. Heaven, likewise, had frowned upon her, and she had not died. But the frown of this pale, weak, sinful, and sorrow-stricken man was what Hester could not bear, and live!

"Wilt thou yet forgive me?" she repeated, over and over again. "Wilt thou not frown? Wilt thou forgive?"

"I do forgive you, Hester," replied the minister, at length, with a deep utterance out of an abyss of sadness, but no anger. "I freely forgive you now. May God forgive us both! We are not, Hester, the worst sinners in the world. There is one worse than even the polluted priest! That old man's revenge has been blacker than my sin. He has violated, in cold blood, the sanctity of a human heart. Thou and I, Hester, never did so!"

"Never, never!" whispered she. "What we did had a consecration of its own. We felt it so! We said so to each other! Hast thou forgotten it?"

"Hush, Hester!" said Arthur Dimmesdale, rising from the ground. "No; I have not forgotten!"

They sat down again, side by side, and hand clasped in hand, on the mossy trunk of the fallen tree. Life had never brought them a gloomier hour; it was the point whither their pathway had so long been tending, and darkening ever, as it stole along;—and yet it inclosed a charm that made them linger upon it, and claim another, and another, and, after all, another moment. The forest was obscure around them, and creaked with a blast that was passing through it. The boughs were tossing heavily above their heads; while one solemn old tree groaned dolefully to another, as if telling the sad story of the pair that sat beneath, or constrained to forebode evil to come.

And yet they lingered. How dreary looked the forest-track that led backward to the settlement, where Hester Prynne must take up again the burden of her ignominy, and the minister the hollow mockery of his good name! So they lingered an instant longer. No golden light had ever been so precious as the gloom of this dark forest. Here, seen only by his eyes, the scarlet letter need not burn into the bosom of the fallen woman! Here, seen only by her eyes, Arthur Dimmesdale, false to God and man, might be, for one moment, true!

He started at a thought that suddenly occurred to him.

"Hester," cried he, "here is a new horror! Roger Chillingworth knows your purpose to reveal his true character. Will he continue, then, to keep our secret? What will now be the course of his revenge?"

"There is a strange secrecy in his nature," replied Hester, thoughtfully; "and it has grown upon him by the hidden practices of his revenge. I deem it not likely that he will betray the secret. He will doubtless seek other means of satiating his dark passion."

"And I!—how am I to live longer, breathing the same air with this deadly enemy?" exclaimed Arthur Dimmesdale, shrinking within himself, and pressing his hand nervously against his heart,—a gesture that had grown involuntary with him. "Think for me, Hester! Thou art strong. Resolve for me!"

"Thou must dwell no longer with this man," said Hester, slowly and firmly. "Thy heart must be no longer under his evil eye!"

"It were far worse than death!" replied the minister. "But how to avoid it? What choice remains to me? Shall I lie down again on these withered leaves, where I cast myself when thou didst tell me what he was? Must I sink down there, and die at once?"

"Alas, what a ruin has befallen thee!" said Hester, with the tears gushing into her eyes. "Wilt thou die for very weakness? There is no other cause!"

"The judgment of God is on me," answered the conscience-stricken priest. "It is too mighty for me to struggle with!"

"Heaven would show mercy," rejoined Hester, "hadst thou but the strength to take advantage of it."

"Be thou strong for me!" answered he. "Advise me what to do."

"Is the world then so narrow?" exclaimed Hester Prynne, fixing her deep eyes on the minister's, and instinctively exercising a magnetic power over a spirit so shattered and subdued, that it could hardly hold itself erect. "Doth the universe lie within the compass of yonder town, which only a little time ago was but a leaf-strewn desert, as lonely as this around us? Whither leads yonder forest-track? Backward to the settlement, thou sayest! Yes; but onward, too! Deeper it goes, and deeper, into the wilderness, less plainly to be seen at every step; until, some few miles hence, the yellow leaves will show no vestige of the white man's tread. There thou art free! So brief a journey would bring thee from a world where thou hast been most wretched, to one where thou mayest still be happy! Is there not shade enough in all this boundless forest to hide thy heart from the gaze of Roger Chillingworth?"

"Yes, Hester; but only under the fallen leaves!" replied the minister, with a sad smile.

"Then there is the broad pathway of the sea!" continued Hester. "It brought thee hither. If thou so choose, it will bear thee back again. In our native land, whether in some remote rural village or in vast London,—or, surely, in Germany, in France, in pleasant Italy,—thou wouldst be beyond his power and knowledge! And what hast thou to do with all these iron men, and their opinions? They have kept thy better part in bondage too long already!"

"It cannot be!" answered the minister, listening as if he were called upon to realize a dream. "I am powerless to go. Wretched and sinful as I am, I have had no other thought than to drag on my earthly existence in the sphere where Providence hath placed me. Lost as my own soul is, I would still do what I may for other human souls! I dare not quit my post, though an unfaithful sentinel, whose sure reward is death and dishonor, when his dreary watch shall come to an end!"

"Thou art crushed under this seven years' weight of misery," replied Hester, fervently resolved to buoy him up with her own energy. "But thou shalt leave it all behind thee! It shall not cumber thy steps, as thou treadest along the forest-path; neither shalt thou freight the ship with it, if thou prefer to cross the sea. Leave this wreck and ruin here where it hath happened! Meddle no more with it! Begin all anew! Hast thou exhausted possibility in the failure of this one trial? Not so! The future is yet full of trial and success.

There is happiness to be enjoyed! There is good to be done! Exchange this false life of thine for a true one. Be, if thy spirit summon thee to such a mission, the teacher and apostle of the red men. Or,—as is more thy nature,—be a scholar and a sage among the wisest and the most renowned of the cultivated world. Preach! Write! Act! Do any thing, save to lie down and die! Give up this name of Arthur Dimmesdale, and make thyself another, and a high one, such as thou canst wear without fear or shame. Why shouldst thou tarry so much as one other day in the torments that have so gnawed into thy life!—that have made thee feeble to will and to do!—that will leave thee powerless even to repent! Up, and away!"

"O Hester!" cried Arthur Dimmesdale, in whose eyes a fitful light, kindled by her enthusiasm, flashed up and died away, "thou tellest of running a race to a man whose knees are tottering beneath him! I must die here. There is not the strength or courage left me to venture into the wide, strange, difficult world, alone!"

It was the last expression of the despondency of a broken spirit. He lacked energy to grasp the better fortune that seemed within his reach.

He repeated the word.

"Alone, Hester!"

"Thou shalt not go alone!" answered she, in a deep whisper.

Then, all was spoken!

XVIII. A Flood of Sunshine

Arthur Dimmesdale gazed into Hester's face with a look in which hope and joy shone out, indeed, but with fear betwixt them, and a kind of horror at her boldness, who had spoken what he vaguely hinted at, but dared not speak.

But Hester Prynne, with a mind of native courage and activity, and for so long a period not merely estranged, but outlawed, from society, had habituated herself to such latitude of speculation as was altogether foreign to the clergyman. She had wandered, without rule or guidance, in a moral wilderness; as vast, as intricate and shadowy, as the untamed forest, amid the gloom of which they were now holding a colloquy that was to decide their fate. Her intellect and heart had their home, as it were, in desert places, where she roamed as freely as the wild Indian in his woods. For years past she had looked from this estranged point of view at human institutions, and whatever priests or legislators had established; criticizing all with hardly more reverence than the Indian would feel for the clerical band, the judicial robe, the pillory, the gallows, the fireside, or the church. The tendency of her fate and fortunes had been to set her free. The scarlet letter was her passport into regions where other women dared not tread. Shame, Despair, Solitude! These had been her teachers,—stern and wild ones,—and they had made her strong, but taught her much amiss.

The minister, on the other hand, had never gone through an experience calculated to lead him beyond the scope of generally received laws; although, in a single instance, he had so fearfully transgressed one of the most sacred of them. But this had been a sin of passion, not of principle, nor even purpose. Since that wretched epoch, he had watched, with morbid zeal and minuteness, not his acts,—for those it was easy to arrange,—but each breath of emotion, and his every thought. At the head of the social system, as the clergymen of that day stood, he was only the more trammelled by its regulations, its principles, and even its prejudices. As a priest, the framework of his order inevitably hemmed him in. As a man who had once sinned, but who kept his conscience all alive and painfully sensitive by the fretting of an unhealed wound, he might have been supposed safer within the line of virtue, than if he had never sinned at all.

Thus, we seem to see that, as regarded Hester Prynne, the whole seven years of outlaw and ignominy had been little other than a preparation for this very hour. But Arthur Dimmesdale! Were such a man once more to fall, what plea could be urged in extenuation of his crime? None; unless it avail him somewhat, that he was broken down by long and exquisite suffering; that his mind was darkened and confused by the very remorse which harrowed it; that, between fleeing as an avowed criminal, and remaining as a hypocrite, conscience might find it hard to strike the balance; that it was human to avoid the peril of death and infamy, and the inscrutable machinations of an enemy; that, finally, to this poor pilgrim, on his dreary and desert path, faint, sick, miserable, there appeared a glimpse of human affection and sympathy, a new life, and a true one, in exchange for the heavy doom which he was now expiating. And be the stern and sad truth spoken, that the breach which guilt has once made into the human soul is never, in this mortal state, repaired. It may be watched and guarded; so that the enemy shall not force his way again into the citadel, and might even, in his subsequent assaults, select some other avenue, in preference to that where he had formerly succeeded. But there is still the ruined wall, and, near it, the stealthy tread of the foe that would win over again his unforgotten triumph.

The struggle, if there were one, need not be described. Let it suffice, that the clergyman resolved to flee, and not alone.

"If, in all these past seven years," thought he, "I could recall one instant of peace or hope, I would yet endure, for the sake of that earnest of Heaven's mercy. But now,—since I am irrevocably doomed,—wherefore should I not snatch the solace allowed to the condemned culprit before his execution? Or, if this be the path to a better life, as Hester would persuade me, I surely give up no fairer prospect by pursuing it! Neither can I any longer live without her companionship; so powerful is she to sustain,—so tender to soothe! O Thou to whom I dare not lift mine eyes, wilt Thou yet pardon me!"

"Thou wilt go!" said Hester calmly, as he met her glance.

The decision once made, a glow of strange enjoyment threw its flickering brightness over the trouble of his breast. It was the exhilarating effect—upon a prisoner just escaped from the dungeon of his own heart—of breathing the wild, free atmosphere of an unredeemed, unchristianized, lawless region. His spirit rose, as it were, with a bound, and attained a nearer prospect of the sky, than throughout all the misery which had kept him grovelling on the earth. Of a deeply religious temperament, there was inevitably a tinge of the devotional in his mood.

"Do I feel joy again?" cried he, wondering at himself. "Methought the germ of it was dead in me! O Hester, thou art my better angel! I seem to have flung myself—sick, sin-stained, and sorrow-blackened—down upon these forest-leaves, and to have risen up all made anew, and with new powers to glorify Him that hath been merciful! This is already the better life! Why did we not find it sooner?"

"Let us not look back," answered Hester Prynne. "The past is gone! Wherefore should we linger upon it now? See! With this symbol, I undo it all, and make it as it had never been!"

So speaking, she undid the clasp that fastened the scarlet letter, and, taking it from her bosom, threw it to a distance among the withered leaves. The mystic token alighted on the hither verge of the stream. With a hand's breadth farther flight it would have fallen into the water, and have given the little brook another woe to carry onward, besides the unintelligible tale which it still kept murmuring about. But there lay the embroidered letter, glittering like a lost jewel, which some ill-fated wanderer might pick up, and thenceforth be haunted by strange phantoms of guilt, sinkings of the heart, and unaccountable misfortune.

The stigma gone, Hester heaved a long, deep sigh, in which the burden of shame and anguish departed from her spirit. O exquisite relief! She had not known the weight, until she felt the freedom! By another impulse, she took off the formal cap that confined her hair; and down it fell upon her shoulders, dark and rich, with at once a shadow and a light in its abundance, and imparting the charm of softness to her features. There played around her mouth, and beamed out of her eyes, a radiant and tender smile, that seemed gushing from the very heart of womanhood. A crimson flush was glowing on her cheek, that had been long so pale. Her sex, her youth, and the whole richness of her beauty, came back from what men call the irrevocable past, and clustered themselves, with her maiden hope, and a happiness before unknown, within the magic circle of this hour. And, as if the gloom of the earth and sky had been but the effluence of these two mortal hearts, it vanished with their sorrow. All at once, as with a sudden smile of heaven, forth burst the sunshine, pouring a very flood into the obscure forest, gladdening each green leaf, transmuting the yellow fallen ones to gold, and gleaming adown the gray trunks of the solemn trees. The objects that had made a shadow hitherto, embodied the brightness now. The course of the little brook might be traced by its merry gleam afar into the wood's heart of mystery, which had become a mystery of joy.

Such was the sympathy of Nature—that wild, heathen Nature of the forest, never subjugated by human law, nor illumined by higher truth—with the bliss of these two spirits! Love, whether newly born, or aroused from a deathlike slumber, must always create a sunshine, filling the heart so full of radiance, that it overflows upon the outward world. Had the forest still kept its gloom, it would have been bright in Hester's eyes, and bright in Arthur Dimmesdale's!

Hester looked at him with the thrill of another joy.

"Thou must know Pearl!" said she. "Our little Pearl! Thou hast seen her,—yes, I know it!—but thou wilt see her now with other eyes. She is a strange child! I hardly comprehend her! But thou wilt love her dearly, as I do, and wilt advise me how to deal with her."

"Dost thou think the child will be glad to know me?" asked the minister, somewhat uneasily. "I have long shrunk from children, because they often show a distrust,—a backwardness to be familiar with me. I have even been afraid of little Pearl!"

"Ah, that was sad!" answered the mother. "But she will love thee dearly, and thou her. She is not far off. I will call her! Pearl! Pearl!"

"I see the child," observed the minister. "Yonder she is, standing in a streak of sunshine, a good way off, on the other side of the brook. So thou thinkest the child will love me?"

Hester smiled, and again called to Pearl, who was visible, at some distance, as the minister had described her, like a bright-apparelled vision, in a sunbeam, which fell down upon her through an arch of boughs. The ray quivered to and fro, making her figure dim or distinct,—now like a real child, now like a child's spirit,—as the splendor went and came again. She heard her mother's voice, and approached slowly through the forest.

Pearl had not found the hour pass wearisomely, while her mother sat talking with the clergyman. The great black forest—stern as it showed itself to those who brought the guilt and troubles of the world into its bosom—became the playmate of the lonely infant, as well as it knew how. Sombre as it was, it put on the kindest of its moods to welcome her. It offered her the partridge-berries, the growth of the preceding autumn, but ripening only in the spring, and now red as drops of blood upon the withered leaves. These Pearl gathered, and was pleased with their wild flavor. The small denizens of the wilderness hardly took pains to move out of her path. A partridge, indeed, with a brood of ten behind her, ran forward threateningly, but soon repented of her fierceness, and clucked to her young ones not to be afraid. A pigeon, alone on a low branch, allowed Pearl to come beneath, and uttered a sound as much of greeting as alarm. A squirrel, from the lofty depths of his domestic tree, chattered either in anger or merriment,—for a squirrel is such a choleric and humorous little personage that it is hard to distinguish between his moods,—so he chattered at the child, and flung down a nut upon her head. It was a last year's nut, and already gnawed by his sharp tooth. A fox, startled from his sleep by her light foot-step on the leaves, looked inquisitively at Pearl, as doubting whether it were better to steal off, or renew his nap on the same spot. A wolf, it is said,—but here the tale has surely lapsed into the improbable,—came up, and smelt of Pearl's robe, and offered his savage head to be patted by her hand. The truth seems to be, however, that the mother-forest, and these wild things which it nourished, all recognized a kindred wildness in the human child.

And she was gentler here than in the grassy-margined streets of the settlement, or in her mother's cottage. The flowers appeared to know it; and one and another whispered, as she passed, "Adorn thyself with me, thou beautiful child, adorn thyself with me!"—and, to please them, Pearl gathered the violets, and anemones, and columbines, and some twigs of the freshest green, which the old trees held down before her eyes. With these she decorated her hair, and her young waist, and became a nymph-child, or an infant dryad,[7] or whatever else was in closest sympathy with the antique wood. In such guise had Pearl adorned herself, when she heard her mother's voice, and came slowly back.

Slowly; for she saw the clergyman!

7. Wood nymph.

XIX. The Child at the Brook-Side

"Thou wilt love her dearly," repeated Hester Prynne, as she and the minister sat watching little Pearl. "Dost thou not think her beautiful? And see with what natural skill she has made those simple flowers adorn her! Had she gathered pearls, and diamonds, and rubies, in the wood, they could not have become her better. She is a splendid child! But I know whose brow she has!"

"Dost thou know, Hester," said Arthur Dimmesdale, with an unquiet smile, "that this dear child, tripping about always at thy side, hath caused me many an alarm? Methought—O Hester, what a thought is that, and how terrible to dread it!—that my own features were partly repeated in her face, and so strikingly that the world might see them! But she is mostly thine!"

"No, no! Not mostly!" answered the mother with a tender smile. "A little longer, and thou needest not to be afraid to trace whose child she is. But how strangely beautiful she looks, with those wild flowers in her hair! It is as if one of the fairies, whom we left in our dear old England, had decked her out to meet us."

It was with a feeling which neither of them had ever before experienced, that they sat and watched Pearl's slow advance. In her was visible the tie that united them. She had been offered to the world, these seven years past, as the living hieroglyphic, in which was revealed the secret they so darkly sought to hide,—all written in this symbol,—all plainly manifest,—had there been a prophet or magician skilled to read the character of flame! And Pearl was the oneness of their being. Be the foregone evil what it might, how could they doubt that their earthly lives and future destinies were conjoined, when they beheld at once the material union, and the spiritual idea, in whom they met, and were to dwell immortally together? Thoughts like these—and perhaps other thoughts, which they did not acknowledge or define—threw an awe about the child, as she came onward.

"Let her see nothing strange—no passion nor eagerness—in thy way of accosting her," whispered Hester. "Our Pearl is a fitful and fantastic little elf, sometimes. Especially, she is seldom tolerant of emotion, when she does not fully comprehend the why and wherefore. But the child hath strong affections! She loves me, and will love thee!"

"Thou canst not think," said the minister, glancing aside at Hester Prynne, "how my heart dreads this interview, and yearns for it! But, in truth, as I already told thee, children are not readily won to be familiar with me. They will not climb my knee, nor prattle in my ear, nor answer to my smile; but stand apart, and eye me strangely. Even little babes, when I take them in my arms, weep bitterly. Yet Pearl, twice in her little lifetime, hath been kind to me! The first time,—thou knowest it well! The last was when thou ledst her with thee to the house of yonder stern old Governor."

"And thou didst plead so bravely in her behalf and mine!" answered the mother. "I remember it; and so shall little Pearl. Fear nothing! She may be strange and shy at first, but will soon learn to love thee!"

By this time Pearl had reached the margin of the brook, and stood on the farther side, gazing silently at Hester and the clergyman, who still sat together on the mossy tree-trunk, waiting to receive her. Just where she had paused the brook chanced to form a pool, so smooth and quiet that it reflected a perfect image of her little figure, with all the brilliant picturesqueness of her beauty, in its adornment of flowers and wreathed foliage, but more refined and spiritualized than the reality. This image, so nearly identical with the living Pearl, seemed to communicate somewhat of its own shadowy and intangible quality to the child herself. It was strange, the way in which Pearl stood, looking so steadfastly at them through the dim medium of the forest-gloom; herself, meanwhile, all glorified with a ray of sunshine, that was attracted thitherward as by a certain sympathy. In the brook beneath stood another child,—another and the same,—with likewise its ray of golden light. Hester felt herself, in some indistinct and tantalizing manner, estranged from Pearl; as if the child, in her lonely ramble through the forest, had strayed out of the sphere in which she and her mother dwelt together, and was now vainly seeking to return to it.

There was both truth and error in the impression; the child and mother were estranged, but through Hester's fault, not Pearl's. Since the latter rambled from her side, another inmate had been admitted within the circle of the mother's feelings, and so modified the aspect of them all, that Pearl, the returning wanderer, could not find her wonted place, and hardly knew where she was.

"I have a strange fancy," observed the sensitive minister, "that this brook is the boundary between two worlds, and that thou canst never meet thy Pearl again. Or is she an elfish spirit, who, as the legends of our childhood taught us, is forbidden to cross a running stream? Pray hasten her; for this delay has already imparted a tremor to my nerves."

"Come, dearest child!" said Hester encouragingly, and stretching out both her arms. "How slow thou art! When hast thou been so sluggish before now? Here is a friend of mine, who must be thy friend also. Thou wilt have twice as much love, henceforward, as thy mother alone could give thee! Leap across the brook and come to us. Thou canst leap like a young deer!"

Pearl, without responding in any manner to these honey-sweet expressions, remained on the other side of the brook. Now she fixed her bright, wild eyes on her mother, now on the minister, and now included them both in the same glance; as if to detect and explain to herself the relation which they bore to one another. For some unaccountable reason, as Arthur Dimmesdale felt the child's eyes upon himself, his hand—with that gesture so habitual as to have become involuntary—stole over his heart. At length, assuming a singular air of authority, Pearl stretched out her hand, with the small forefinger extended, and pointing evidently towards her mother's breast. And beneath, in the mirror of the brook, there was the flower-girdled and sunny image of little Pearl, pointing her small forefinger too.

"Thou strange child, why dost thou not come to me?" exclaimed Hester.

Pearl still pointed with her forefinger; and a frown gathered on her brow; the more impressive from the childish, the almost baby-like aspect of the features that conveyed it. As her mother still kept beckoning to her, and arraying her face in a holiday suit of unaccustomed smiles, the child stamped her foot with a yet more imperious look and gesture. In the brook, again, was the fantastic beauty of the image, with its reflected frown, its pointed finger, and imperious gesture, giving emphasis to the aspect of little Pearl.

"Hasten, Pearl; or I shall be angry with thee!" cried Hester Prynne, who, however inured to such behaviour on the elf-child's part at other seasons, was naturally anxious for a more seemly deportment now. "Leap across the brook, naughty child, and run hither! Else I must come to thee!"

But Pearl, not a whit startled at her mother's threats, any more than mollified by her entreaties, now suddenly burst into a fit of passion, gesticulating violently, and throwing her small figure into the most extravagant contortions. She accompanied this wild outbreak with piercing shrieks, which the woods reverberated on all sides; so that, alone as she was in her childish and unreasonable wrath, it seemed as if a hidden multitude were lending her their sympathy and encouragement. Seen in the brook, once more, was the shadowy wrath of Pearl's image, crowned and girdled with flowers, but stamping its foot, wildly gesticulating, and, in the midst of all, still pointing its small forefinger at Hester's bosom!

"I see what ails the child," whispered Hester to the clergyman, and turning pale in spite of a strong effort to conceal her trouble and annoyance. "Children will not abide any, the slightest, change in the accustomed aspect of things that are daily before their eyes. Pearl misses something which she has always seen me wear!"

"I pray you," answered the minister, "if thou hast any means of pacifying the child, do it forthwith! Save it were the cankered wrath of an old witch, like Mistress Hibbins," added he, attempting to smile. "I know nothing that I would not sooner encounter than this passion in a child. In Pearl's young beauty, as in the wrinkled witch, it has a preternatural effect. Pacify her, if thou lovest me!"

Hester turned again towards Pearl, with a crimson blush upon her cheek, a conscious glance aside at the clergyman, and then a heavy sigh; while, even before she had time to speak, the blush yielded to a deadly pallor.

"Pearl," said she, sadly, "look down at thy feet! There!—before thee!—on the hither side of the brook!"

The child turned her eyes to the point indicated; and there lay the scarlet letter, so close upon the margin of the stream, that the gold embroidery was reflected in it.

"Bring it hither!" said Hester.

"Come thou and take it up!" answered Pearl.

"Was ever such a child!" observed Hester aside to the minister. "O, I have much to tell thee about her. But, in very truth, she is right as regards this hateful token. I must bear its torture yet a little longer,—only a few days longer,—until we shall have left this region, and look back hither as to a land which we have dreamed of. The forest cannot hide it! The mid-ocean shall take it from my hand, and swallow it up for ever!"

With these words, she advanced to the margin of the brook, took up the scarlet letter, and fastened it again into her bosom. Hopefully, but a moment ago, as Hester had spoken of drowning it in the deep sea, there was a sense of inevitable doom upon her, as she thus received back this deadly symbol from the hand of fate. She had flung it into infinite space!—she had drawn an hour's free breath!—and here again was the scarlet misery, glittering on the old spot! So it ever is, whether thus typified or no, that an evil deed invests itself with the character of doom. Hester next gathered up the heavy tresses of her hair, and confined them beneath her cap. As if there were a withering spell in the sad letter, her beauty, the warmth and richness of her womanhood, departed, like fading sunshine; and a gray shadow seemed to fall across her.

When the dreary change was wrought, she extended her hand to Pearl.

"Dost thou know thy mother now, child!" asked she, reproachfully, but with a subdued tone. "Wilt thou come across the brook, and own thy mother, now that she has her shame upon her,—now that she is sad?"

"Yes; now I will!" answered the child, bounding across the brook, and clasping Hester in her arms. "Now thou art my mother indeed! And I am thy little Pearl!"

In a mood of tenderness that was not usual with her, she drew down her mother's head, and kissed her brow and both her cheeks. But then—by a kind of necessity that always impelled this child to alloy whatever comfort she might chance to give with a throb of anguish—Pearl put up her mouth, and kissed the scarlet letter too!

"That was not kind!" said Hester. "When thou hast shown me a little love, thou mockest me!"

"Why doth the minister sit yonder?" asked Pearl.

"He waits to welcome thee," replied her mother. "Come thou, and entreat his blessing! He loves thee, my little Pearl, and loves thy mother too. Wilt thou not love him? Come! he longs to greet thee!"

"Doth he love us?" said Pearl, looking up with acute intelligence into her mother's face. "Will he go back with us, hand in hand, we three together, into the town?"

"Not now, dear child," answered Hester. "But in days to come he will walk hand in hand with us. We will have a home and fireside of our own; and thou shalt sit upon his knee; and he will teach thee many things, and love thee dearly. Thou wilt love him; wilt thou not?"

"And will he always keep his hand over his heart?" inquired Pearl.

"Foolish child, what a question is that!" exclaimed her mother. "Come and ask his blessing!"

But, whether influenced by the jealousy that seems instinctive with every petted child towards a dangerous rival, or from whatever caprice of her freakish nature, Pearl would show no favour to the clergyman. It was only by an exertion of force that her mother brought her up to him, hanging back, and manifesting her reluctance by odd grimaces; of which, ever since her babyhood, she had possessed a singular variety, and could transform her mobile physiognomy into a series of different aspects, with a new mischief in them, each and all. The minister—painfully embarrassed, but hoping that a kiss might prove a talisman to admit him into the child's kindlier regards—bent forward, and impressed one on her brow. Hereupon, Pearl broke away from her mother, and running to the brook, stooped over it, and bathed her forehead, until the unwelcome kiss was quite washed off, and diffused through a long lapse of the gliding water. She then remained apart, silently watching Hester and the clergyman; while they talked together, and made such arrangements as were suggested by their new position, and the purposes soon to be fulfilled.

And now this fateful interview had come to a close. The dell was to be left a solitude among its dark, old trees, which, with their multitudinous tongues, would whisper long of what had passed there, and no mortal be the wiser. And the melancholy brook would add this other tale to the mystery with which its little heart was already overburdened, and whereof it still kept up a murmuring babble, with not a whit more cheerfulness of tone than for ages heretofore.

XX. The Minister in a Maze

As the minister departed, in advance of Hester Prynne and little Pearl, he threw a backward glance; half expecting that he should discover only some faintly traced features or outline of the mother and the child, slowly fading into the twilight of the woods. So great a vicissitude in his life could not at once be received as real. But there was Hester, clad in her gray robe, still standing beside the tree-trunk, which some blast had overthrown a long antiquity ago, and which time had ever since been covering with moss, so that these two fated ones, with earth's heaviest burden on them, might there sit down together, and find a single hour's rest and solace. And there was Pearl, too, lightly dancing from the margin of the brook,—now that the intrusive third person was gone,—and taking her old place by her mother's side. So the minister had not fallen asleep, and dreamed!

In order to free his mind from this indistinctness and duplicity of impression, which vexed it with a strange disquietude, he recalled and more thoroughly defined the plans which Hester and himself had sketched for their departure. It had been determined between them, that the Old World, with its crowds and cities, offered them a more eligible shelter and concealment than the wilds of New England, or all America, with its alternatives of an Indian wigwam, or the few settlements of Europeans, scattered thinly along the seaboard. Not to speak of the clergyman's health, so inadequate to sustain the hardships of a forest life, his native gifts, his culture, and his entire development would secure him a home only in the midst of civilization and refinement; the higher the state, the more delicately adapted to it the man. In furtherance of this choice, it so happened that a ship lay in the harbour; one of those questionable cruisers, frequent at that day, which, without being absolutely outlaws of the deep, yet roamed over its surface with a remarkable irresponsibility of character. This vessel had recently arrived from the Spanish Main, and, within three days' time, would sail for Bristol.[8] Hester Prynne—whose vocation, as a self-enlisted Sister of Charity, had brought her acquainted with the captain and crew—could take upon herself to secure the passage of two individuals and a child, with all the secrecy which circumstances rendered more than desirable.

The minister had inquired of Hester, with no little interest, the precise time at which the vessel might be expected to depart. It would probably be on the fourth day from the present. "That is most fortunate!" he had then said to himself. Now, why the Reverend Mr. Dimmesdale considered it so very fortunate, we hesitate to reveal. Nevertheless,—to hold nothing back from the reader,—it was because, on the third day from the present, he was to preach the Election Sermon;[9] and, as such an occasion formed an honorable epoch

8. In western England.
9. Sermon preached at the start of a governor's term of office.

in the life of a New England clergyman, he could not have chanced upon a more suitable mode and time of terminating his professional career. "At least, they shall say of me," thought this exemplary man, "that I leave no public duty unperformed, nor ill performed!" Sad, indeed, that an introspection so profound and acute as this poor minister's should be so miserably deceived! We have had, and may still have, worse things to tell of him; but none, we apprehend, so pitiably weak; no evidence, at once so slight and irrefragable,[1] of a subtle disease, that had long since begun to eat into the real substance of his character. No man, for any considerable period, can wear one face to himself, and another to the multitude, without finally getting bewildered as to which may be the true.

The excitement of Mr. Dimmesdale's feelings, as he returned from his interview with Hester, lent him unaccustomed physical energy, and hurried him townward at a rapid pace. The pathway among the woods seemed wilder, more uncouth with its rude natural obstacles, and less trodden by the foot of man, than he remembered it on his outward journey. But he leaped across the plashy places, thrust himself through the clinging underbrush, climbed the ascent, plunged into the hollow, and overcame, in short, all the difficulties of the track, with an unweariable activity that astonished him. He could not but recall how feebly, and with what frequent pauses for breath, he had toiled over the same ground only two days before. As he drew near the town, he took an impression of change from the series of familiar objects that presented themselves. It seemed not yesterday, not one, nor two, but many days, or even years ago, since he had quitted them. There, indeed, was each former trace of the street, as he remembered it, and all the peculiarities of the houses, with the due multitude of gable-peaks, and a weathercock at every point where his memory suggested one. Not the less, however, came this importunately obtrusive sense of change. The same was true as regarded the acquaintances whom he met, and all the well-known shapes of human life, about the little town. They looked neither older nor younger, now; the beards of the aged were no whiter, nor could the creeping babe of yesterday walk on his feet today; it was impossible to describe in what respect they differed from the individuals on whom he had so recently bestowed a parting glance; and yet the minister's deepest sense seemed to inform him of their mutability. A similar impression struck him most remarkably, as he passed under the walls of his own church. The edifice had so very strange, and yet so familiar, an aspect, that Mr. Dimmesdale's mind vibrated between two ideas; either that he had seen it only in a dream hitherto, or that he was merely dreaming about it now.

This phenomenon, in the various shapes which it assumed, indicated no external change, but so sudden and important a change in the spectator of the familiar scene, that the intervening space of a single day had operated on his consciousness like the lapse of years. The minister's own will, and Hester's will, and the fate that grew between them, had wrought this transformation. It was the same town as heretofore; but the same minister returned not from the forest. He might have said to the friends who greeted him,—"I am not the man for whom you take me! I left him yonder in the forest, with-

1. Irrefutable.

drawn into a secret dell, by a mossy tree-trunk, and near a melancholy brook! Go, seek your minister, and see if his emaciated figure, his thin cheek, his white, heavy, pain-wrinkled brow, be not flung down there like a cast-off garment!" His friends, no doubt, would still have insisted with him,—"Thou art thyself the man!"—but the error would have been their own, not his.

Before Mr. Dimmesdale reached home, his inner man gave him other evidences of a revolution in the sphere of thought and feeling. In truth, nothing short of a total change of dynasty and moral code, in that interior kingdom, was adequate to account for the impulses now communicated to the unfortunate and startled minister. At every step he was incited to do some strange, wild, wicked thing or other, with a sense that it would be at once involuntary and intentional; in spite of himself, yet growing out of a profounder self than that which opposed the impulse. For instance, he met one of his own deacons. The good old man addressed him with the paternal affection and patriarchal privilege, which his venerable age, his upright and holy character, and his station in the Church, entitled him to use; and, conjoined with this, the deep, almost worshipping respect, which the minister's professional and private claims alike demanded. Never was there a more beautiful example of how the majesty of age and wisdom may comport with the obeisance and respect enjoined upon it, as from a lower social rank and inferior order of endowment, towards a higher. Now, during a conversation of some two or three moments between the Reverend Mr. Dimmesdale and this excellent and hoary-bearded deacon, it was only by the most careful self-control that the former could refrain from uttering certain blasphemous suggestions that rose into his mind, respecting the communion-supper. He absolutely trembled and turned pale as ashes, lest his tongue should wag itself, in utterance of these horrible matters, and plead his own consent for so doing, without his having fairly given it. And, even with this terror in his heart, he could hardly avoid laughing to imagine how the sanctified old patriarchal deacon would have been petrified by his minister's impiety!

Again, another incident of the same nature. Hurrying along the street, the Reverend Mr. Dimmesdale encountered the eldest female member of his church; a most pious and exemplary old dame; poor, widowed, lonely, and with a heart as full of reminiscences about her dead husband and children, and her dead friends of long ago, as a burial-ground is full of storied gravestones. Yet all this, which would else have been such heavy sorrow, was made almost a solemn joy to her devout old soul by religious consolations and the truths of Scripture, wherewith she had fed herself continually for more than thirty years. And, since Mr. Dimmesdale had taken her in charge, the good grandam's chief earthly comfort—which, unless it had been likewise a heavenly comfort, could have been none at all—was to meet her pastor, whether casually, or of set purpose, and be refreshed with a word of warm, fragrant, heaven-breathing Gospel truth from his beloved lips into her dulled, but rapturously attentive ear. But, on this occasion, up to the moment of putting his lips to the old woman's ear, Mr. Dimmesdale, as the great enemy of souls would have it, could recall no text of Scripture, nor aught else, except a brief, pithy, and, as it then appeared to him, unanswerable argument against the immortality of the human soul. The instilment thereof into her mind would probably have caused this aged sister to drop down dead, at once, as by the effect of an intensely poisonous infusion. What he really did whisper, the minister could never afterwards recollect. There was, perhaps, a fortunate disorder in his utterance, which failed to impart any distinct idea to the good widow's comprehension, or which Providence interpreted after a method of its own. Assuredly, as the minister looked back, he beheld an expression of divine gratitude and ecstasy that seemed like the shine of the celestial city on her face, so wrinkled and ashy pale.

Again, a third instance. After parting from the old church-member, he met the youngest sister of them all. It was a maiden newly won—and won by the Reverend Mr. Dimmesdale's own sermon, on the Sabbath after his vigil—to barter the transitory pleasures of the world for the heavenly hope, that was to assume brighter substance as life grew dark around her, and which would gild the utter gloom with final glory. She was fair and pure as a lily that had bloomed in Paradise. The minister knew well that he was himself enshrined within the stainless sanctity of her heart, which hung its snowy curtains about his image, imparting to religion the warmth of love, and to love a religious purity. Satan, that afternoon, had surely led the poor young girl away from her mother's side, and thrown her into the pathway of this sorely tempted, or—shall we not rather say?—this lost and desperate man. As she drew nigh, the arch-fiend whispered him to condense into small compass and drop into her tender bosom a germ of evil that would be sure to blossom darkly soon, and bear black fruit betimes. Such was his sense of power over this virgin soul, trusting him as she did, that the minister felt potent to blight all the field of innocence with but one wicked look, and develop all its opposite with but a word. So—with a mightier struggle than he had yet sustained—he held his Geneva cloak before his face, and hurried onward, making no sign of recognition, and leaving the young sister to digest his rudeness as she might. She ransacked her conscience,—which was full of harmless little matters, like her pocket or her work-bag,—and took herself to task, poor thing, for a thousand imaginary faults; and went about her household duties with swollen eyelids the next morning.

Before the minister had time to celebrate his victory over this last temptation, he was conscious of another impulse, more ludicrous, and almost as horrible. It was,—we blush to tell it,—it was to stop short in the road, and teach some very wicked words to a knot of little Puritan children who were playing there, and had but just begun to talk. Denying himself this freak, as unworthy of his cloth, he met a drunken seaman, one of the ship's crew from the Spanish Main. And, here, since he had so valiantly forborne all other wickedness, poor Mr. Dimmesdale longed, at least, to shake hands with the tarry blackguard, and recreate himself with a few improper jests, such as dissolute sailors so abound with, and a volley of good, round, solid, satisfactory, and heaven-defying oaths! It was not so much a better principle, as partly his natural good taste, and still more his buckramed[2] habit of clerical decorum, that carried him safely through the latter crisis.

"What is it that haunts and tempts me thus?" cried the minister to himself, at length, pausing in the street, and striking his hand against his forehead. "Am I mad? or am I given over utterly to the fiend? Did I make a

2. Stiff, rigid.

contract with him in the forest, and sign it with my blood? And does he now summon me to its fulfilment, by suggesting the performance of every wickedness which his most foul imagination can conceive?"

At the moment when the Reverend Mr. Dimmesdale thus communed with himself, and struck his forehead with his hand, old Mistress Hibbins, the reputed witch-lady, is said to have been passing by. She made a very grand appearance; having on a high head-dress, a rich gown of velvet, and a ruff done up with the famous yellow starch, of which Ann Turner, her especial friend, had taught her the secret, before this last good lady had been hanged for Sir Thomas Overbury's murder.[3] Whether the witch had read the minister's thoughts, or no, she came to a full stop, looked shrewdly into his face, smiled craftily, and—though little given to converse with clergymen—began a conversation.

"So, reverend Sir, you have made a visit into the forest," observed the witch-lady, nodding her high head-dress at him. "The next time, I pray you to allow me only a fair warning, and I shall be proud to bear you company. Without taking overmuch upon myself, my good word will go far towards gaining any strange gentleman a fair reception from yonder potentate you wot of!"

"I profess, madam," answered the clergyman, with a grave obeisance, such as the lady's rank demanded, and his own good-breeding made imperative,—"I profess, on my conscience and character, that I am utterly bewildered as touching the purport of your words! I went not into the forest to seek a potentate; neither do I, at any future time, design a visit thither, with a view to gaining the favor of such personage. My one sufficient object was to greet that pious friend of mine, the Apostle Eliot, and rejoice with him over the many precious souls he hath won from heathendom!"

"Ha, ha, ha!" cackled the old witch-lady, still nodding her high head-dress at the minister. "Well, well, we must needs talk thus in the daytime! You carry it off like an old hand! But at midnight, and in the forest, we shall have other talk together!"

She passed on with her aged stateliness, but often turning back her head and smiling at him, like one willing to recognize a secret intimacy of connection.

"Have I then sold myself," thought the minister, "to the fiend whom, if men say true, this yellow-starched and velveted old hag has chosen for her prince and master!"

The wretched minister! He had made a bargain very like it! Tempted by a dream of happiness, he had yielded himself with deliberate choice, as he had never done before, to what he knew was deadly sin. And the infectious poison of that sin had been thus rapidly diffused throughout his moral system. It had stupefied all blessed impulses, and awakened into vivid life the whole brotherhood of bad ones. Scorn, bitterness, unprovoked malignity, gratuitous desire of ill, ridicule of whatever was good and holy, all awoke, to tempt, even while they frightened him. And his encounter with old Mistress Hibbins, if it were a real incident, did but show his sympathy and fellowship with wicked mortals and the world of perverted spirits.

3. See p. 520, n. 6.

He had by this time reached his dwelling, on the edge of the burial-ground, and, hastening up the stairs, took refuge in his study. The minister was glad to have reached this shelter, without first betraying himself to the world by any of those strange and wicked eccentricities to which he had been continually impelled while passing through the streets. He entered the accustomed room, and looked around him on its books, its windows, its fireplace, and the tapestried comfort of the walls, with the same perception of strangeness that had haunted him throughout his walk from the forest-dell into the town, and thitherward. Here he had studied and written; here, gone through fast and vigil, and come forth half alive; here, striven to pray; here, borne a hundred thousand agonies! There was the Bible, in its rich old Hebrew, with Moses and the Prophets speaking to him, and God's voice through all! There, on the table, with the inky pen beside it, was an unfinished sermon, with a sentence broken in the midst, where his thoughts had ceased to gush out upon the page two days before. He knew that it was himself, the thin and white-cheeked minister, who had done and suffered these things, and written thus far into the Election Sermon! But he seemed to stand apart, and eye this former self with scornful, pitying, but half-envious curiosity. That self was gone! Another man had returned out of the forest; a wiser one; with a knowledge of hidden mysteries which the simplicity of the former never could have reached. A bitter kind of knowledge that!

While occupied with these reflections, a knock came at the door of the study, and the minister said, "Come in!"—not wholly devoid of an idea that he might behold an evil spirit. And so he did! It was old Roger Chillingworth that entered. The minister stood, white and speechless, with one hand on the Hebrew Scriptures, and the other spread upon his breast.

"Welcome home, reverend Sir!" said the physician. "And how found you that godly man, the Apostle Eliot? But methinks, dear Sir, you look pale; as if the travel through the wilderness had been too sore for you. Will not my aid be requisite to put you in heart and strength to preach your Election Sermon?"

"Nay, I think not so," rejoined the Reverend Mr. Dimmesdale. "My journey, and the sight of the holy Apostle yonder, and the free air which I have breathed, have done me good, after so long confinement in my study. I think to need no more of your drugs, my kind physician, good though they be, and administered by a friendly hand."

All this time, Roger Chillingworth was looking at the minister with the grave and intent regard of a physician towards his patient. But, in spite of this outward show, the latter was almost convinced of the old man's knowledge, or, at least, his confident suspicion, with respect to his own interview with Hester Prynne. The physician knew, then, that, in the minister's regard, he was no longer a trusted friend, but his bitterest enemy. So much being known, it would appear natural that a part of it should be expressed. It is singular, however, how long a time often passes before words embody things; and with what security two persons, who choose to avoid a certain subject, may approach its very verge, and retire without disturbing it. Thus, the minister felt no apprehension that Roger Chillingworth would touch, in express words, upon the real position which they sustained towards one another. Yet did the physician, in his dark way, creep frightfully near the secret.

"Were it not better," said he, "that you use my poor skill to-night? Verily, dear Sir, we must take pains to make you strong and vigorous for this occasion of the Election discourse. The people look for great things from you; apprehending that another year may come about, and find their pastor gone."

"Yea, to another world," replied the minister, with pious resignation. "Heaven grant it be a better one; for, in good sooth, I hardly think to tarry with my flock through the flitting seasons of another year! But, touching your medicine, kind Sir, in my present frame of body I need it not."

"I joy to hear it," answered the physician. "It may be that my remedies, so long administered in vain, begin now to take due effect. Happy man were I, and well deserving of New England's gratitude, could I achieve this cure!"

"I thank you from my heart, most watchful friend," said the Reverend Mr. Dimmesdale, with a solemn smile. "I thank you, and can but requite your good deeds with my prayers."

"A good man's prayers are golden recompense!" rejoined old Roger Chillingworth, as he took his leave. "Yea, they are the current gold coin of the New Jerusalem, with the King's own mint-mark on them!"

Left alone, the minister summoned a servant of the house, and requested food, which, being set before him, he ate with ravenous appetite. Then, flinging the already written pages of the Election Sermon into the fire, he forthwith began another, which he wrote with such an impulsive flow of thought and emotion, that he fancied himself inspired; and only wondered that Heaven should see fit to transmit the grand and solemn music of its oracles through so foul an organ-pipe as he. However, leaving that mystery to solve itself, or go unsolved for ever, he drove his task onward, with earnest haste and ecstasy. Thus the night fled away, as if it were a winged steed, and he careering on it; morning came, and peeped blushing through the curtains; and at last sunrise threw a golden beam into the study, and laid it right across the minister's bedazzled eyes. There he was, with the pen still between his fingers, and a vast, immeasurable tract of written space behind him!

XXI. The New England Holiday

Betimes[4] in the morning of the day on which the new Governor was to receive his office at the hands of the people, Hester Prynne and little Pearl came into the market-place. It was already thronged with the craftsmen and other plebeian inhabitants of the town, in considerable numbers; among whom, likewise, were many rough figures, whose attire of deer-skins marked them as belonging to some of the forest settlements, which surrounded the little metropolis of the colony.

On this public holiday, as on all other occasions, for seven years past, Hester was clad in a garment of coarse gray cloth. Not more by its hue than by some indescribable peculiarity in its fashion, it had the effect of making her fade personally out of sight and outline; while, again, the scarlet letter brought her back from this twilight indistinctness, and revealed her under the moral aspect of its own illumination. Her face, so long familiar to the

4. Early.

townspeople, showed the marble quietude which they were accustomed to behold there. It was like a mask; or rather, like the frozen calmness of a dead woman's features; owing this dreary resemblance to the fact that Hester was actually dead, in respect to any claim of sympathy, and had departed out of the world with which she still seemed to mingle.

It might be, on this one day, that there was an expression unseen before, nor, indeed, vivid enough to be detected now; unless some preternaturally gifted observer should have first read the heart, and have afterwards sought a corresponding development in the countenance and mien. Such a spiritual seer might have conceived, that, after sustaining the gaze of the multitude through seven miserable years as a necessity, a penance, and something which it was a stern religion to endure, she now, for one last time more, encountered it freely and voluntarily, in order to convert what had so long been agony into a kind of triumph. "Look your last on the scarlet letter and its wearer!"—the people's victim and life-long bond-slave, as they fancied her, might say to them. "Yet a little while, and she will be beyond your reach! A few hours longer, and the deep, mysterious ocean will quench and hide for ever the symbol which ye have caused to burn upon her bosom!" Nor were it an inconsistency too improbable to be assigned to human nature, should we suppose a feeling of regret in Hester's mind, at the moment when she was about to win her freedom from the pain which had been thus deeply incorporated with her being. Might there not be an irresistible desire to quaff a last, long, breathless draught of the cup of wormwood and aloes, with which nearly all her years of womanhood had been perpetually flavored? The wine of life, henceforth to be presented to her lips, must be indeed rich, delicious, and exhilarating, in its chased[5] and golden beaker; or else leave an inevitable and weary languor, after the lees of bitterness wherewith she had been drugged, as with a cordial of intensest potency.

Pearl was decked out with airy gayety. It would have been impossible to guess that this bright and sunny apparition owed its existence to the shape of gloomy gray; or that a fancy, at once so gorgeous and so delicate as must have been requisite to contrive the child's apparel, was the same that had achieved a task perhaps more difficult, in imparting so distinct a peculiarity to Hester's simple robe. The dress, so proper was it to little Pearl, seemed an effluence, or inevitable development and outward manifestation of her character, no more to be separated from her than the many-hued brilliancy from a butterfly's wing, or the painted glory from the leaf of a bright flower. As with these, so with the child; her garb was all of one idea with her nature. On this eventful day, moreover, there was a certain singular inquietude and excitement in her mood, resembling nothing so much as the shimmer of a diamond, that sparkles and flashes with the varied throbbings of the breast on which it is displayed. Children have always a sympathy in the agitations of those connected with them; always, especially, a sense of any trouble or impending revolution, of whatever kind, in domestic circumstances; and therefore Pearl, who was the gem on her mother's unquiet bosom, betrayed, by the very dance of her spirits, the emotions which none could detect in the marble passiveness of Hester's brow.

5. Ornamented.

This effervescence made her flit with a bird-like movement, rather than walk by her mother's side. She broke continually into shouts of a wild, inarticulate, and sometimes piercing music. When they reached the market-place, she became still more restless, on perceiving the stir and bustle that enlivened the spot; for it was usually more like the broad and lonesome green before a village meeting-house, than the centre of a town's business.

"Why, what is this, mother?" cried she. "Wherefore have all the people left their work to-day? Is it a play-day for the whole world? See, there is the blacksmith! He has washed his sooty face, and put on his Sabbath-day clothes, and looks, as if he would gladly be merry, if any kind body would only teach him how! And there is Master Brackett, the old jailer, nodding and smiling at me. Why does he do so, mother?"

"He remembers thee a little babe, my child," answered Hester.

"He should not nod and smile at me, for all that,—the black, grim, ugly-eyed old man!" said Pearl. "He may nod at thee if he will; for thou are clad in gray, and wearest the scarlet letter. But, see, mother, how many faces of strange people, and Indians among them, and sailors! What have they all come to do here in the market-place?"

"They wait to see the procession pass," said Hester. "For the Governor and the magistrates are to go by, and the ministers, and all the great people and good people, with the music, and the soldiers marching before them."

"And will the minister be there?" asked Pearl. "And will he hold out both his hands to me, as when thou ledst me to him from the brook-side?"

"He will be there, child," answered her mother. "But he will not greet thee to-day; nor must thou greet him."

"What a strange, sad man is he!" said the child, as if speaking partly to herself. "In the dark night-time, he calls us to him, and holds thy hand and mine, as when we stood with him on the scaffold yonder! And in the deep forest, where only the old trees can hear, and the strip of sky see it, he talks with thee, sitting on a heap of moss! And he kisses my forehead, too, so that the little brook would hardly wash it off! But here in the sunny day, and among all the people, he knows us not; nor must we know him! A strange, sad man is he, with his hand always over his heart!"

"Be quiet, Pearl! Thou understandest not these things," said her mother. "Think not now of the minister, but look about thee, and see how cheery is every body's face to-day. The children have come from their schools, and the grown people from their workshops and their fields, on purpose to be happy. For, to-day, a new man is beginning to rule over them; and so—as has been the custom of mankind ever since a nation was first gathered—they make merry and rejoice; as if a good and golden year were at length to pass over the poor old world!"

It was as Hester said, in regard to the unwonted jollity that brightened the faces of the people. Into this festal season of the year—as it already was, and continued to be during the greater part of two centuries—the Puritans compressed whatever mirth and public joy they deemed allowable to human infirmity; thereby so far dispelling the customary cloud, that, for the space of a single holiday, they appeared scarcely more grave than most other communities at a period of general affliction.

But we perhaps exaggerate the gray or sable tinge, which undoubtedly characterized the mood and manners of the age. The persons now in the market-place of Boston had not been born to an inheritance of Puritanic gloom. They were native Englishmen, whose fathers had lived in the sunny richness of the Elizabethan epoch; a time when the life of England, viewed as one great mass, would appear to have been as stately, magnificent, and joyous, as the world has ever witnessed. Had they followed their hereditary taste, the New England settlers would have illustrated all events of public importance by bonfires, banquets, pageantries, and processions. Nor would it have been impracticable, in the observance of majestic ceremonies, to combine mirthful recreation with solemnity, and give, as it were, a grotesque and brilliant embroidery to the great robe of state, which a nation, at such festivals, puts on. There was some shadow of an attempt of this kind in the mode of celebrating the day on which the political year of the colony commenced. The dim reflection of a remembered splendor, a colorless and manifold diluted repetition of what they had beheld in proud old London,—we will not say at a royal coronation, but at a Lord Mayor's show,[6]—might be traced in the customs which our forefathers instituted, with reference to the annual installation of magistrates. The fathers and founders of the commonwealth—the statesman, the priest, and the soldier—deemed it a duty then to assume the outward state and majesty, which, in accordance with antique style, was looked upon as the proper garb of public or social eminence. All came forth, to move in procession before the people's eye, and thus impart a needed dignity to the simple framework of a government so newly constructed.

Then, too, the people were countenanced, if not encouraged, in relaxing the severe and close application to their various modes of rugged industry, which, at all other times, seemed of the same piece and material with their religion. Here, it is true, were none of the appliances which popular merriment would so readily have found in the England of Elizabeth's time, or that of James,[7]—no rude shows of a theatrical kind; no minstrel with his harp and legendary ballad, nor gleeman, with an ape dancing to his music; no juggler, with his tricks of mimic witchcraft; no Merry Andrew,[8] to stir up the multitude with jests, perhaps hundreds of years old, but still effective, by their appeals to the very broadest sources of mirthful sympathy. All such professors of the several branches of jocularity would have been sternly repressed, not only by the rigid discipline of law, but by the general sentiment which gives law its vitality. Not the less, however, the great, honest face of the people smiled, grimly, perhaps, but widely too. Nor were sports wanting, such as the colonists had witnessed, and shared in, long ago, at the country fairs and on the village-greens of England; and which it was thought well to keep alive on this new soil, for the sake of the courage and manliness that were essential in them. Wrestling-matches, in the differing fashions of Cornwall and Devonshire, were seen here and there about the market-place; in one corner, there was a friendly bout at quarterstaff; and—what attracted most interest of all—on the platform of the pillory, already so noted on our pages, two masters of defence were commencing an exhibition with the buckler[9] and broadsword. But, much to the disappointment of the

6. Procession and other ceremonies in honor of the inauguration of the lord mayor of London.
7. James I. Elizabeth I reigned from 1558 to 1603, James I from 1603 to 1625.
8. Jester or clown.
9. Small round shield, either carried or worn on the arm. "Quarterstaff": long wooden staff, used as a weapon.

crowd, this latter business was broken off by the interposition of the town beadle, who had no idea of permitting the majesty of the law to be violated by such an abuse of one of its consecrated places.

It may not be too much to affirm, on the whole, (the people being then in the first stages of joyless deportment, and the offspring of sires who had known how to be merry, in their day,) that they would compare favorably, in point of holiday keeping, with their descendants, even at so long an interval as ourselves. Their immediate posterity, the generation next to the early emigrants, wore the blackest shade of Puritanism, and so darkened the national visage with it, that all the subsequent years have not sufficed to clear it up. We have yet to learn again the forgotten art of gayety.

The picture of human life in the market-place, though its general tint was the sad gray, brown, or black of the English emigrants, was yet enlivened by some diversity of hue. A party of Indians—in their savage finery of curiously embroidered deer-skin robes, wampum-belts, red and yellow ochre, and feathers, and armed with the bow and arrow and stone-headed spear—stood apart, with countenances of inflexible gravity, beyond what even the Puritan aspect could attain. Nor, wild as were these painted barbarians, were they the wildest feature of the scene. This distinction could more justly be claimed by some mariners,—a part of the crew of the vessel from the Spanish Main,—who had come ashore to see the humors of Election Day. They were rough-looking desperadoes, with sun-blackened faces, and an immensity of beard; their wide, short trousers were confined about the waist by belts, often clasped with a rough plate of gold, and sustaining always a long knife, and, in some instances, a sword. From beneath their broad-brimmed hats of palm-leaf, gleamed eyes which, even in good nature and merriment, had a kind of animal ferocity. They transgressed, without fear or scruple, the rules of behaviour that were binding on all others; smoking tobacco under the beadle's very nose, although each whiff would have cost a townsman a shilling; and quaffing, at their pleasure, draughts of wine or aqua-vitæ[1] from pocket-flasks, which they freely tendered to the gaping crowd around them. It remarkably characterized the incomplete morality of the age, rigid as we call it, that a license was allowed the seafaring class, not merely for their freaks on shore, but for far more desperate deeds on their proper element. The sailor of that day would go near to be arraigned as a pirate in our own. There could be little doubt, for instance, that this very ship's crew, though no unfavorable specimens of the nautical brotherhood, had been guilty, as we should phrase it, of depredations on the Spanish commerce, such as would have perilled all their necks in a modern court of justice.

But the sea, in those old times, heaved, swelled, and foamed very much at its own will, or subject only to the tempestuous wind, with hardly any attempts at regulation by human law. The buccaneer on the wave might relinquish his calling, and become at once, if he chose, a man of probity and piety on land; nor, even in the full career of his reckless life, was he regarded as a personage with whom it was disreputable to traffic, or casually associate. Thus, the Puritan elders, in their black cloaks, starched bands, and steeple-crowned hats, smiled not unbenignantly at the clamor and rude deportment of these jolly seafaring men; and it excited neither surprise nor animadversion

1. Brandy.

when so reputable a citizen as old Roger Chillingworth, the physician, was seen to enter the market-place, in close and familiar talk with the commander of the questionable vessel.

The latter was by far the most showy and gallant figure, so far as apparel went, anywhere to be seen among the multitude. He wore a profusion of ribbons on his garment, and gold lace on his hat, which was also encircled by a gold chain, and surmounted with a feather. There was a sword at his side, and a sword-cut on his forehead, which, by the arrangement of his hair, he seemed anxious rather to display than hide. A landsman could hardly have worn this garb and shown this face, and worn and shown them both with such a galliard[2] air, without undergoing stern question before a magistrate, and probably incurring fine or imprisonment, or perhaps an exhibition in the stocks. As regarded the shipmaster, however, all was looked upon as pertaining to the character, as to a fish his glistening scales.

After parting from the physician, the commander of the Bristol ship strolled idly through the market-place; until, happening to approach the spot where Hester Prynne was standing, he appeared to recognize, and did not hesitate to address her. As was usually the case wherever Hester stood, a small, vacant area—a sort of magic circle—had formed itself about her, into which, though the people were elbowing one another at a little distance, none ventured, or felt disposed to intrude. It was a forcible type of the moral solitude in which the scarlet letter enveloped its fated wearer; partly by her own reserve, and partly by the instinctive, though no longer so unkindly, withdrawal of her fellow-creatures. Now, if never before, it answered a good purpose, by enabling Hester and the seaman to speak together without risk of being overheard; and so changed was Hester Prynne's repute before the public, that the matron in town most eminent for rigid morality could not have held such intercourse with less result of scandal than herself.

"So, mistress," said the mariner, "I must bid the steward make ready one more berth than you bargained for! No fear of scurvy or ship-fever, this voyage! What with the ship's surgeon and this other doctor, our only danger will be from drug or pill; more by token, as there is a lot of apothecary's stuff aboard, which I traded for with a Spanish vessel."

"What mean you?" inquired Hester, startled more than she permitted to appear. "Have you another passenger?"

"Why, know you not," cried the shipmaster, "that this physician here—Chillingworth, he calls himself—is minded to try my cabin-fare with you? Ay, ay, you must have known it; for he tells me he is of your party, and a close friend to the gentleman you spoke of,—he that is in peril from these sour old Puritan rulers!"

"They know each other well, indeed," replied Hester, with a mien of calmness, though in the utmost consternation. "They have long dwelt together."

Nothing further passed between the mariner and Hester Prynne. But, at that instant, she beheld old Roger Chillingworth himself, standing in the remotest corner of the market-place, and smiling on her; a smile which—across the wide and bustling square, and through all the talk and laughter, and various thoughts, moods, and interests of the crowd—conveyed secret and fearful meaning.

2. Lively.

XXII. *The Procession*

Before Hester Prynne could call together her thoughts, and consider what was practicable to be done in this new and startling aspect of affairs, the sound of military music was heard approaching along a contiguous street. It denoted the advance of the procession of magistrates and citizens, on its way towards the meeting-house; where, in compliance with a custom thus early established, and ever since observed, the Reverend Mr. Dimmesdale was to deliver an Election Sermon.

Soon the head of the procession showed itself, with a slow and stately march, turning a corner, and making its way across the market-place. First came the music. It comprised a variety of instruments, perhaps imperfectly adapted to one another, and played with no great skill, but yet attaining the great object for which the harmony of drum and clarion addresses itself to the multitude,—that of imparting a higher and more heroic air to the scene of life that passes before the eye. Little Pearl at first clapped her hands, but then lost, for an instant, the restless agitation that had kept her in a continual effervescence throughout the morning; she gazed silently, and seemed to be borne upward, like a floating sea-bird, on the long heaves and swells of sound. But she was brought back to her former mood by the shimmer of the sunshine on the weapons and bright armour of the military company, which followed after the music, and formed the honorary escort of the procession. This body of soldiery[3]—which still sustains a corporate existence, and marches down from past ages with an ancient and honorable fame—was composed of no mercenary materials. Its ranks were filled with gentlemen, who felt the stirrings of martial impulse, and sought to establish a kind of College of Arms, where, as in an association of Knights Templars,[4] they might learn the science, and, so far as peaceful exercise would teach them, the practices of war. The high estimation then placed upon the military character might be seen in the lofty port of each individual member of the company. Some of them, indeed, by their services in the Low Countries[5] and on other fields of European warfare, had fairly won their title to assume the name and pomp of soldiership. The entire array, moreover, clad in burnished steel, and with plumage nodding over their bright morions,[6] had a brilliancy of effect which no modern display can aspire to equal.

And yet the men of civil eminence, who came immediately behind the military escort, were better worth a thoughtful observer's eye. Even in outward demeanour they showed a stamp of majesty that made the warrior's haughty stride look vulgar, if not absurd. It was an age when what we call talent had far less consideration than now, but the massive materials which produce stability and dignity of character a great deal more. The people possessed, by hereditary right, the quality of reverence; which, in their descendants, if it survive at all, exists in smaller proportion, and with a vastly diminished force in the selection and estimate of public men. The change may be for good or ill, and is partly, perhaps, for both. In that old day, the

3. The Ancient and Honorable Artillery Company of Massachusetts.

4. A 12th-century order of crusaders. "College of Arms": the royal corporation instituted in 15th-century England to keep records of genealogies and coats of arms.

5. Belgium, the Netherlands, and Luxembourg.

6. Crested metal helmets with curved beaks at front and back.

English settler on these rude shores,—having left king, nobles, and all degrees of awful rank behind, while still the faculty and necessity of reverence were strong in him,—bestowed it on the white hair and venerable brow of age; on long-tried integrity; on solid wisdom and sad-colored experience; on endowments of that grave and weighty order, which gives the idea of permanence, and comes under the general definition of respectability. These primitive statesmen, therefore,—Bradstreet, Endicott, Dudley,[7] Bellingham, and their compeers,—who were elevated to power by the early choice of the people, seem to have been not often brilliant, but distinguished by a ponderous sobriety, rather than activity of intellect. They had fortitude and self-reliance, and, in time of difficulty or peril, stood up for the welfare of the state like a line of cliffs against a tempestuous tide. The traits of character here indicated were well represented in the square cast of countenance and large physical development of the new colonial magistrates. So far as a demeanour of natural authority was concerned, the mother country need not have been ashamed to see these foremost men of an actual democracy adopted into the House of Peers, or made the Privy Council[8] of the sovereign.

Next in order to the magistrates came the young and eminently distinguished divine, from whose lips the religious discourse of the anniversary was expected. His was the profession, at that era, in which intellectual ability displayed itself far more than in political life; for—leaving a higher motive out of the question—it offered inducements powerful enough, in the almost worshipping respect of the community, to win the most aspiring ambition into its service. Even political power—as in the case of Increase Mather[9]—was within the grasp of a successful priest.

It was the observation of those who beheld him now, that never, since Mr. Dimmesdale first set his foot on the New England shore, had he exhibited such energy as was seen in the gait and air with which he kept his pace in the procession. There was no feebleness of step, as at other times; his frame was not bent; nor did his hand rest ominously upon his heart. Yet, if the clergyman were rightly viewed, his strength seemed not of the body. It might be spiritual, and imparted to him by angelic ministrations. It might be the exhilaration of that potent cordial, which is distilled only in the furnace-glow of earnest and long-continued thought. Or, perchance, his sensitive temperament was invigorated by the loud and piercing music, that swelled heavenward, and uplifted him on its ascending wave. Nevertheless, so abstracted was his look, it might be questioned whether Mr. Dimmesdale even heard the music. There was his body, moving onward, and with an unaccustomed force. But where was his mind? Far and deep in its own region, busying itself, with preternatural activity, to marshal a procession of stately thoughts that were soon to issue thence; and so he saw nothing, heard nothing, knew nothing, of what was around him; but the spiritual element took up the feeble frame, and carried it along, unconscious of the burden, and converting it to spirit like itself. Men of uncommon intellect, who have

7. Early governors of New England colonies: Simon Bradstreet (1603–1697), John Endicott (1588–1665), Thomas Dudley (1576–1653).
8. The king's selected advisers. "House of Peers": the upper house in the British Parliament.
9. The Puritan Increase Mather (1639–1723) was president of Harvard College from 1685 to 1701. He had a prominent role in the witchcraft trials at Salem in 1692, urging moderation in the use of "specter evidence."

grown morbid, possess this occasional power of mighty effort, into which they throw the life of many days, and then are lifeless for as many more.

Hester Prynne, gazing steadfastly at the clergyman, felt a dreary influence come over her, but wherefore or whence she knew not; unless that he seemed so remote from her own sphere, and utterly beyond her reach. One glance of recognition, she had imagined, must needs pass between them. She thought of the dim forest, with its little dell of solitude, and love, and anguish, and the mossy tree-trunk, where, sitting hand in hand, they had mingled their sad and passionate talk with the melancholy murmur of the brook. How deeply had they known each other then! And was this the man? She hardly knew him now! He, moving proudly past, enveloped, as it were, in the rich music, with the procession of majestic and venerable fathers; he, so unattainable in his worldly position, and still more so in that far vista of his unsympathizing thoughts, through which she now beheld him! Her spirit sank with the idea that all must have been a delusion, and that, vividly as she had dreamed it, there could be no real bond betwixt the clergyman and herself. And thus much of woman was there in Hester, that she could scarcely forgive him,—least of all now, when the heavy footstep of their approaching Fate might be heard, nearer, nearer, nearer!—for being able so completely to withdraw himself from their mutual world; while she groped darkly, and stretched forth her cold hands, and found him not.

Pearl either saw and responded to her mother's feelings, or herself felt the remoteness and intangibility that had fallen around the minister. While the procession passed, the child was uneasy, fluttering up and down, like a bird on the point of taking flight. When the whole had gone by, she looked up into Hester's face.

"Mother," said she, "was that the same minister that kissed me by the brook?"

"Hold thy peace, dear little Pearl!" whispered her mother. "We must not always talk in the market-place of what happens to us in the forest."

"I could not be sure that it was he; so strange he looked," continued the child. "Else I would have run to him, and bid him kiss me now, before all the people; even as he did yonder among the dark old trees. What would the minister have said, mother? Would he have clapped his hand over his heart, and scowled on me, and bid me begone?"

"What should he say, Pearl," answered Hester, "save that it was no time to kiss, and that kisses are not to be given in the marketplace? Well for thee, foolish child, that thou didst not speak to him!"

Another shade of the same sentiment, in reference to Mr. Dimmesdale, was expressed by a person whose eccentricities—or insanity, as we should term it—led her to do what few of the townspeople would have ventured on; to begin a conversation with the wearer of the scarlet letter, in public. It was Mistress Hibbins, who, arrayed in great magnificence, with a triple ruff, a broidered stomacher, a gown of rich velvet, and a gold-headed cane, had come forth to see the procession. As this ancient lady had the renown (which subsequently cost her no less a price than her life) of being a principal actor in all the works of necromancy that were continually going forward, the crowd gave way before her, and seemed to fear the touch of her garment, as if it carried the plague among its gorgeous folds. Seen in conjunction with Hester Prynne,—kindly as so many now felt towards the latter,—the dread inspired by Mistress Hibbins was doubled, and caused a general movement from that part of the market-place in which the two women stood.

"Now, what mortal imagination could conceive it!" whispered the old lady confidentially to Hester. "Yonder divine man! That saint on earth, as the people uphold him to be, and as—I must needs say—he really looks! Who, now, that saw him pass in the procession, would think how little while it is since he went forth out of his study,—chewing a Hebrew text of Scripture in his mouth, I warrant,—to take an airing in the forest! Aha! we know what that means, Hester Prynne! But, truly, forsooth, I find it hard to believe him the same man. Many a church-member saw I, walking behind the music, that has danced in the same measure with me, when Somebody was fiddler, and, it might be, an Indian powwow or a Lapland[1] wizard changing hands with us! That is but a trifle, when a woman knows the world. But this minister! Couldst thou surely tell, Hester, whether he was the same man that encountered thee on the forest-path!"

"Madam, I know not of what you speak," answered Hester Prynne, feeling Mistress Hibbins to be of infirm mind; yet strangely startled and awe-stricken by the confidence with which she affirmed a personal connection between so many persons (herself among them) and the Evil One. "It is not for me to talk lightly of a learned and pious minister of the Word, like the Reverend Mr. Dimmesdale!"

"Fie, woman, fie!" cried the old lady, shaking her finger at Hester. "Dost thou think I have been to the forest so many times, and have yet no skill to judge who else has been there? Yea; though no leaf of the wild garlands, which they wore while they danced, be left in their hair! I know thee, Hester; for I behold the token. We may all see it in the sunshine; and it glows like a red flame in the dark. Thou wearest it openly; so there need be no question about that. But this minister! Let me tell thee in thine ear! When the Black Man sees one of his own servants, signed and sealed, so shy of owning to the bond as is the Reverend Mr. Dimmesdale, he hath a way of ordering matters so that the mark shall be disclosed in open daylight to the eyes of the world! What is it that the minister seeks to hide, with his hand always over his heart? Ha, Hester Prynne!"

"What is it, good Mistress Hibbins?" eagerly asked little Pearl. "Hast thou seen it?"

"No matter, darling!" responded Mistress Hibbins, making Pearl a profound reverence. "Thou thyself wilt see it, one time or another. They say, child, thou art of the lineage of the Prince of the Air![2] Wilt thou ride with me, some fine night, to see thy father? Then thou shalt know wherefore the minister keeps his hand over his heart!"

Laughing so shrilly that all the market-place could hear her, the weird old gentlewoman took her departure.

By this time the preliminary prayer had been offered in the meeting-house, and the accents of the Reverend Mr. Dimmesdale were heard commencing his discourse. An irresistible feeling kept Hester near the spot. As the sacred edifice was too much thronged to admit another auditor, she took up her position close beside the scaffold of the pillory. It was in sufficient proximity

1. Northern parts of Norway, Sweden, and Finland. "Indian powwow": medicine man.
2. Satan, described in Ephesians 2.2 as "the prince of the power of the air, the spirit that now worketh in the children of disobedience."

to bring the whole sermon to her ears, in the shape of an indistinct, but varied, murmur and flow of the minister's very peculiar voice.

This vocal organ was in itself a rich endowment; insomuch that a listener, comprehending nothing of the language in which the preacher spoke, might still have been swayed to and fro by the mere tone and cadence. Like all other music, it breathed passion and pathos, and emotions high or tender, in a tongue native to the human heart, wherever educated. Muffled as the sound was by its passage through the church-walls, Hester Prynne listened with such intentness, and sympathized so intimately, that the sermon had throughout a meaning for her, entirely apart from its indistinguishable words. These, perhaps, if more distinctly heard, might have been only a grosser medium, and have clogged the spiritual sense. Now she caught the low undertone, as of the wind sinking down to repose itself; then ascended with it, as it rose through progressive gradations of sweetness and power, until its volume seemed to envelop her with an atmosphere of awe and solemn grandeur. And yet, majestic as the voice sometimes became, there was for ever in it an essential character of plaintiveness. A loud or low expression of anguish,—the whisper, or the shriek, as it might be conceived, of suffering humanity, that touched a sensibility in every bosom! At times this deep strain of pathos was all that could be heard, and scarcely heard, sighing amid a desolate silence. But even when the minister's voice grew high and commanding,—when it gushed irrepressibly upward,—when it assumed its utmost breadth and power, so overfilling the church as to burst its way through the solid walls, and diffuse itself in the open air,—still, if the auditor listened intently, and for the purpose, he could detect the same cry of pain. What was it? The complaint of a human heart, sorrow-laden, perchance guilty, telling its secret, whether of guilt or sorrow, to the great heart of mankind; beseeching its sympathy or forgiveness,—at every moment,—in each accent,—and never in vain! It was this profound and continual undertone that gave the clergyman his most appropriate power.

During all this time Hester stood, statue-like, at the foot of the scaffold. If the minister's voice had not kept her there, there would nevertheless have been an inevitable magnetism in that spot, whence she dated the first hour of her life of ignominy. There was a sense within her,—too ill-defined to be made a thought, but weighing heavily on her mind,—that her whole orb of life, both before and after, was connected with this spot, as with the one point that gave it unity.

Little Pearl, meanwhile, had quitted her mother's side, and was playing at her own will about the market-place. She made the sombre crowd cheerful by her erratic and glistening ray; even as a bird of bright plumage illuminates a whole tree of dusky foliage by darting to and fro, half seen and half concealed, amid the twilight of the clustering leaves. She had an undulating, but, oftentimes, a sharp and irregular movement. It indicated the restless vivacity of her spirit, which to-day was doubly indefatigable in its tiptoe dance, because it was played upon and vibrated with her mother's disquietude. Whenever Pearl saw any thing to excite her ever active and wandering curiosity, she flew thitherward, and, as we might say, seized upon that man or thing as her own property, so far as she desired it; but without yielding the minutest degree of control over her motions in requital. The Puritans looked on, and, if they smiled, were none the less inclined to pronounce the child a demon offspring, from the indescribable charm of beauty and eccentricity that shone through her little figure, and sparkled with its activity. She ran and looked the wild Indian in the face; and he grew conscious of a nature wilder than his own. Thence, with native audacity, but still with a reserve as characteristic, she flew into the midst of a group of mariners, the swarthy-cheeked wild men of the ocean, as the Indians were of the land; and they gazed wonderingly and admiringly at Pearl, as if a flake of the sea-foam had taken the shape of a little maid, and were gifted with a soul of the sea-fire, that flashes beneath the prow in the night-time.

One of these seafaring men—the shipmaster, indeed, who had spoken to Hester Prynne—was so smitten with Pearl's aspect, that he attempted to lay hands upon her, with purpose to snatch a kiss. Finding it as impossible to touch her as to catch a humming-bird in the air, he took from his hat the gold chain that was twisted about it, and threw it to the child. Pearl immediately twined it around her neck and waist, with such happy skill, that, once seen there, it became a part of her, and it was difficult to imagine her without it.

"Thy mother is yonder woman with the scarlet letter," said the seaman. "Wilt thou carry her a message from me?"

"If the message pleases me I will," answered Pearl.

"Then tell her," rejoined he, "that I spake again with the black-a-visaged, hump-shouldered old doctor, and he engages to bring his friend, the gentleman she wots of, aboard with him. So let thy mother take no thought, save for herself and thee. Wilt thou tell her this, thou witch-baby?"

"Mistress Hibbins says my father is the Prince of the Air!" cried Pearl, with her naughty smile. "If thou callest me that ill name, I shall tell him of thee; and he will chase thy ship with a tempest!"

Pursuing a zigzag course across the market-place, the child returned to her mother, and communicated what the mariner had said. Hester's strong, calm, steadfastly enduring spirit almost sank, at last, on beholding this dark and grim countenance of an inevitable doom, which—at the moment when a passage seemed to open for the minister and herself out of their labyrinth of misery—showed itself, with an unrelenting smile, right in the midst of their path.

With her mind harrassed by the terrible perplexity in which the shipmaster's intelligence involved her, she was also subjected to another trial. There were many people present, from the country roundabout, who had often heard of the scarlet letter, and to whom it had been made terrific by a hundred false or exaggerated rumors, but who had never beheld it with their own bodily eyes. These, after exhausting other modes of amusement, now thronged about Hester Prynne with rude and boorish intrusiveness. Unscrupulous as it was, however, it could not bring them nearer than a circuit of several yards. At that distance they accordingly stood, fixed there by the centrifugal force of the repugnance which the mystic symbol inspired. The whole gang of sailors, likewise, observing the press of spectators, and learning the purport of the scarlet letter, came and thrust their sunburnt and desperado-looking faces into the ring. Even the Indians were affected by a sort of cold shadow of the white man's curiosity, and, gliding through the crowd, fastened their snake-like black eyes on Hester's bosom; conceiving, perhaps, that the wearer of this brilliantly embroidered badge must needs be a personage of high dignity among her people. Lastly, the inhabitants of the town (their own interest in this worn-out subject languidly reviving itself, by sympathy with what they saw others feel) lounged idly to the same quarter, and tormented Hester Prynne, perhaps more than all the rest, with their cool, well-acquainted gaze at her familiar shame. Hester saw and recognized the self-same faces of that group of matrons, who had awaited her forthcoming from the prison-door, seven years ago; all save one, the youngest and only compassionate among them, whose burial-robe she had since made. At the final hour, when she was so soon to fling aside the burning letter, it had strangely become the centre of more remark and excitement, and was thus made to sear her breast more painfully than at any time since the first day she put it on.

While Hester stood in that magic circle of ignominy, where the cunning cruelty of her sentence seemed to have fixed her for ever, the admirable preacher was looking down from the sacred pulpit upon an audience, whose very inmost spirits had yielded to his control. The sainted minister in the church! The woman of the scarlet letter in the market-place! What imagination would have been irreverent enough to surmise that the same scorching stigma was on them both?

XXIII. The Revelation of the Scarlet Letter

The eloquent voice, on which the souls of the listening audience had been borne aloft, as on the swelling waves of the sea, at length came to a pause. There was a momentary silence, profound as what should follow the utterance of oracles. Then ensued a murmur and half-hushed tumult; as if the auditors, released from the high spell that had transported them into the region of another's mind, were returning into themselves, with all their awe and wonder still heavy on them. In a moment more, the crowd began to gush forth from the doors of the church. Now that there was an end, they needed other breath, more fit to support the gross and earthly life into which they relapsed, than that atmosphere which the preacher had converted into words of flame, and had burdened with the rich fragrance of his thought.

In the open air their rapture broke into speech. The street and the market-place absolutely babbled, from side to side, with applauses of the minister. His hearers could not rest until they had told one another of what each knew better than he could tell or hear. According to their united testimony, never had man spoken in so wise, so high, and so holy a spirit, as he that spake this day; nor had inspiration ever breathed through mortal lips more evidently than it did through his. Its influence could be seen, as it were, descending upon him, and possessing him, and continually lifting him out of the written discourse that lay before him, and filling him with ideas that must have been as marvellous to himself as to his audience. His subject, it appeared, had been the relation between the Deity and the communities of mankind, with a special reference to the New England which they were here planting in the wilderness. And, as he drew towards the close, a spirit as of prophecy had come upon him, constraining him to its purpose as mightily as the old prophets of Israel were constrained; only with this difference, that, whereas the Jewish seers had denounced judgments and ruin on their country, it was his mission to foretell a high and glorious destiny for the newly gathered people of the Lord. But, throughout it all, and through the whole discourse, there had been a certain deep, sad undertone of pathos, which could not be interpreted otherwise than as the natural regret of one soon to pass away. Yes; their minister whom they so loved—and who so loved them all, that he could not depart heavenward without a sigh—had the foreboding of untimely death upon him, and would soon leave them in their tears! This idea of his transitory stay on earth gave the last emphasis to the effect which the preacher had produced; it was as if an angel, in his passage to the skies, had shaken his bright wings over the people for an instant,—at once a shadow and a splendor,—and had shed down a shower of golden truths upon them.

Thus, there had come to the Reverend Mr. Dimmesdale—as to most men, in their various spheres, though seldom recognized until they see it far behind them—an epoch of life more brilliant and full of triumph than any previous one, or than any which could hereafter be. He stood, at this moment, on the very proudest eminence of superiority, to which the gifts of intellect, rich lore, prevailing eloquence, and a reputation of whitest sanctity, could exalt a clergyman in New England's earliest days, when the professional character was of itself a lofty pedestal. Such was the position which the minister occupied, as he bowed his head forward on the cushions of the pulpit, at the close of his Election Sermon. Meanwhile, Hester Prynne was standing beside the scaffold of the pillory, with the scarlet letter still burning on her breast!

Now was heard again the clangor of the music, and the measured tramp of the military escort, issuing from the church-door. The procession was to be marshalled thence to the town-hall, where a solemn banquet would complete the ceremonies of the day.

Once more, therefore, the train of venerable and majestic fathers was seen moving through a broad pathway of the people, who drew back reverently, on either side, as the Governor and magistrates, the old and wise men, the holy ministers, and all that were eminent and renowned, advanced into the midst of them. When they were fairly in the market-place, their presence was greeted by a shout. This—though doubtless it might acquire additional force and volume from the childlike loyalty which the age awarded to its rulers—was felt to be an irrepressible outburst of the enthusiasm kindled in the auditors by that high strain of eloquence which was yet reverberating in their ears. Each felt the impulse in himself, and, in the same breath, caught it from his neighbour. Within the church, it had hardly been kept down; beneath the sky, it pealed upward to the zenith. There were human beings enough, and enough of highly wrought and symphonious feeling, to produce that more impressive sound than the organ-tones of the blast, or the thunder, or the roar of the sea; even that mighty swell of many voices, blended into one great voice by the universal impulse which makes likewise one vast heart out of the many. Never, from the soil of New England, had gone up such a shout! Never, on New England soil, had stood the man so honored by his mortal brethren as the preacher.

How fared it with him then? Were there not the brilliant particles of a halo in the air about his head? So etherealized by spirit as he was, and so apotheosized by worshipping admirers, did his footsteps in the procession really tread upon the dust of earth?

As the ranks of military men and civil fathers moved onward, all eyes were turned towards the point where the minister was seen to approach among them. The shout died into a murmur, as one portion of the crowd after another obtained a glimpse of him. How feeble and pale he looked amid all his triumph! The energy—or say, rather, the inspiration which had held him up, until he should have delivered the sacred message that brought its own strength along with it from heaven—was withdrawn, now that it had so faithfully performed its office. The glow, which they had just before beheld burning on his cheek, was extinguished, like a flame that sinks down hopelessly among the late-decaying embers. It seemed hardly the face of a man alive, with such a deathlike hue; it was hardly a man with life in him, that tottered on his path so nervelessly, yet tottered, and did not fall!

One of his clerical brethren,—it was the venerable John Wilson,—observing the state in which Mr. Dimmesdale was left by the retiring wave of intellect and sensibility, stepped forward hastily to offer his support. The minister tremulously, but decidedly, repelled the old man's arm. He still walked onward, if that movement could be so described, which rather resembled the wavering effort of an infant, with its mother's arms in view, outstretched to tempt him forward. And now, almost imperceptible as were the latter steps of his progress, he had come opposite the well-remembered and weather-darkened scaffold, where, long since, with all that dreary lapse of time between, Hester Prynne had encountered the world's ignominious stare. There stood Hester, holding little Pearl by the hand! And there was the scarlet letter on her breast! The minister here made a pause; although the music still played the stately and rejoicing march to which the procession moved. It summoned him onward,—onward to the festival!—but here he made a pause.

Bellingham, for the last few moments, had kept an anxious eye upon him. He now left his own place in the procession, and advanced to give assistance; judging from Mr. Dimmesdale's aspect that he must otherwise inevitably fall. But there was something in the latter's expression that warned back the magistrate, although a man not readily obeying the vague intimations that pass from one spirit to another. The crowd, meanwhile, looked on with awe and wonder. This earthly faintness was, in their view, only another phase of the minister's celestial strength; nor would it have seemed a miracle too high to be wrought for one so holy, had he ascended before their eyes, waxing dimmer and brighter, and fading at last into the light of heaven!

He turned towards the scaffold, and stretched forth his arms.

"Hester," said he, "come hither! Come, my little Pearl!"

It was a ghastly look with which he regarded them; but there was something at once tender and strangely triumphant in it. The child, with the birdlike motion which was one of her characteristics, flew to him, and clasped her arms about his knees. Hester Prynne—slowly, as if impelled by inevitable fate, and against her strongest will—likewise drew near, but paused before she reached him. At this instant old Roger Chillingworth thrust himself through the crowd,—or, perhaps, so dark, disturbed, and evil was his look, he rose up out of some nether region,—to snatch back his victim from what he sought to do! Be that as it might, the old man rushed forward and caught the minister by the arm.

"Madman, hold! What is your purpose?" whispered he. "Wave back that woman! Cast off this child! All shall be well! Do not blacken your fame, and perish in dishonor! I can yet save you! Would you bring infamy on your sacred profession?"

"Ha, tempter! Methinks thou art too late!" answered the minister, encountering his eye, fearfully, but firmly. "Thy power is not what it was! With God's help, I shall escape thee now!"

He again extended his hand to the woman of the scarlet letter.

"Hester Prynne," cried he, with a piercing earnestness, "in the name of Him, so terrible and so merciful, who gives me grace, at this last moment, to do what—for my own heavy sin and miserable agony—I withheld myself from doing seven years ago, come hither now, and twine thy strength about me! Thy strength, Hester; but let it be guided by the will which God hath granted me! This wretched and wronged old man is opposing it with all his might!—with all his own might and the fiend's! Come, Hester, come! Support me up yonder scaffold!"

The crowd was in a tumult. The men of rank and dignity, who stood more immediately around the clergyman, were so taken by surprise, and so perplexed as to the purport of what they saw,—unable to receive the explanation which most readily presented itself, or to imagine any other,—that they remained silent and inactive spectators of the judgment which Providence seemed about to work. They beheld the minister, leaning on Hester's shoulder and supported by her arm around him, approach the scaffold, and ascend its steps; while still the little hand of the sin-born child was clasped in his. Old Roger Chillingworth followed, as one intimately connected with the drama of guilt and sorrow in which they had all been actors, and well entitled, therefore, to be present at its closing scene.

"Hadst thou sought the whole earth over," said he, looking darkly at the clergyman, "there was no one place so secret,—no high place nor lowly place, where thou couldst have escaped me,—save on this very scaffold!"

"Thanks be to Him who hath led me hither!" answered the minister.

Yet he trembled, and turned to Hester with an expression of doubt and anxiety in his eyes, not the less evidently betrayed, that there was a feeble smile upon his lips.

"Is not this better," murmured he, "than what we dreamed of in the forest?"

"I know not! I know not!" she hurriedly replied. "Better? Yea; so we may both die, and little Pearl die with us!"

"For thee and Pearl, be it as God shall order," said the minister; "and God is merciful! Let me now do the will which he hath made plain before my sight. For, Hester, I am a dying man. So let me make haste to take my shame upon me."

Partly supported by Hester Prynne, and holding one hand of little Pearl's, the Reverend Mr. Dimmesdale turned to the dignified and venerable rulers; to the holy ministers, who were his brethren; to the people, whose great heart was thoroughly appalled, yet overflowing with tearful sympathy, as knowing that some deep life-matter—which, if full of sin, was full of anguish and repentance likewise—was now to be laid open to them. The sun, but little past its meridian, shone down upon the clergyman, and gave a distinctness to his figure, as he stood out from all the earth to put in his plea of guilty at the bar of Eternal Justice.

"People of New England!" cried he, with a voice that rose over them, high, solemn, and majestic,—yet had always a tremor through it, and sometimes a shriek, struggling up out of a fathomless depth of remorse and woe,—"ye, that have loved me!—ye, that have deemed me holy!—behold me here, the one sinner of the world! At last!—at last!—I stand upon the spot where, seven years since, I should have stood; here, with this woman, whose arm, more than the little strength wherewith I have crept hitherward, sustains me, at this dreadful moment, from grovelling down upon my face! Lo, the scarlet letter which Hester wears! Ye have all shuddered at it! Wherever her walk hath been,—wherever, so miserably burdened, she may have hoped to find repose,—it hath cast a lurid gleam of awe and horrible repugnance round about her. But there stood one in the midst of you, at whose brand of sin and infamy ye have not shuddered!"

It seemed, at this point, as if the minister must leave the remainder of his secret undisclosed. But he fought back the bodily weakness,—and, still more, the faintness of heart,—that was striving for the mastery with him. He threw off all assistance, and stepped passionately forward a pace before the woman and the child.

"It was on him!" he continued, with a kind of fierceness; so determined was he to speak out the whole. "God's eye beheld it! The angels were for ever pointing at it! The Devil knew it well, and fretted it continually with the touch of his burning finger! But he hid it cunningly from men, and walked among you with the mien of a spirit, mournful, because so pure in a sinful world!—and sad, because he missed his heavenly kindred! Now, at the death-hour, he stands up before you! He bids you look again at Hester's scarlet letter! He tells you, that, with all its mysterious horror, it is but the shadow of what he bears on his own breast, and that even this, his own red stigma, is no more than the type of what has seared his inmost heart! Stand any here that question God's judgment on a sinner? Behold! Behold a dreadful witness of it!"

With a convulsive motion he tore away the ministerial band from before his breast. It was revealed! But it were irreverent to describe that revelation. For an instant the gaze of the horror-stricken multitude was concentrated on the ghastly miracle; while the minister stood with a flush of triumph in his face, as one who, in the crisis of acutest pain, had won a victory. Then, down he sank upon the scaffold! Hester partly raised him, and supported his head against her bosom. Old Roger Chillingworth knelt down beside him, with a blank, dull countenance, out of which the life seemed to have departed.

"Thou hast escaped me!" he repeated more than once. "Thou hast escaped me!"

"May God forgive thee!" said the minister. "Thou, too, hast deeply sinned!"

He withdrew his dying eyes from the old man, and fixed them on the woman and the child.

"My little Pearl," said he feebly,—and there was a sweet and gentle smile over his face, as of a spirit sinking into deep repose; nay, now that the burden was removed, it seemed almost as if he would be sportive with the child,—"dear little Pearl, wilt thou kiss me now? Thou wouldst not yonder, in the forest! But now thou wilt?"

Pearl kissed his lips. A spell was broken. The great scene of grief, in which the wild infant bore a part, had developed all her sympathies; and as her tears fell upon her father's cheek, they were the pledge that she would grow up amid human joy and sorrow, nor for ever do battle with the world, but be a woman in it. Towards her mother, too, Pearl's errand as a messenger of anguish was all fulfilled.

"Hester," said the clergyman, "farewell!"

"Shall we not meet again?" whispered she, bending her face down close to his. "Shall we not spend our immortal life together? Surely, surely, we have ransomed one another, with all this woe! Thou lookest far into eternity, with those bright dying eyes! Then tell me what thou seest?"

"Hush, Hester, hush!" said he, with tremulous solemnity. "The law we broke!—the sin here so awfully revealed!—let these alone be in thy thoughts! I fear! I fear! It may be, that, when we forgot our God,—when we violated our reverence each for the other's soul,—it was thenceforth vain to hope that we could meet hereafter, in an everlasting and pure reunion. God knows; and He is merciful! He hath proved his mercy, most of all, in my afflictions. By giving me this burning torture to bear upon my breast! By sending yonder dark and terrible old man, to keep the torture always at red-heat! By bringing me hither, to die this death of triumphant ignominy before the people! Had either of these agonies been wanting, I had been lost for ever! Praised be his name! His will be done! Farewell!"

That final word came forth with the minister's expiring breath. The multitude, silent till then, broke out in a strange, deep voice of awe and wonder, which could not as yet find utterance, save in this murmur that rolled so heavily after the departed spirit.

XXIV. Conclusion

After many days, when time sufficed for the people to arrange their thoughts in reference to the foregoing scene, there was more than one account of what had been witnessed on the scaffold.

Most of the spectators testified to having seen, on the breast of the unhappy minister, a SCARLET LETTER—the very semblance of that worn by Hester Prynne—imprinted in the flesh. As regarded its origin, there were various explanations, all of which must necessarily have been conjectural. Some affirmed that the Reverend Mr. Dimmesdale, on the very day when Hester Prynne first wore her ignominious badge, had begun a course of penance,—which he afterwards, in so many futile methods, followed out,—by inflicting a hideous torture on himself. Others contended that the stigma had not been produced until a long time subsequent, when old Roger Chillingworth, being a potent necromancer, had caused it to appear, through the agency of magic and poisonous drugs. Others, again,—and those best able to appreciate the minister's peculiar sensibility, and the wonderful operation of his spirit upon the body,—whispered their belief, that the awful symbol was the effect of the ever active tooth of remorse, gnawing from the inmost heart outwardly, and at last manifesting Heaven's dreadful judgment by the visible presence of the letter. The reader may choose among these theories. We have thrown all the light we could acquire upon the portent, and would gladly, now that it has done its office, erase its deep print out of our own brain; where long meditation has fixed it in very undesirable distinctness.

It is singular, nevertheless, that certain persons, who were spectators of the whole scene, and professed never once to have removed their eyes from the Reverend Mr. Dimmesdale, denied that there was any mark whatever on his breast, more than on a new-born infant's. Neither, by their report, had his dying words acknowledged, nor even remotely implied, any, the slightest connection, on his part, with the guilt for which Hester Prynne had so long worn the scarlet letter. According to these highly respectable witnesses, the minister, conscious that he was dying,—conscious, also, that the reverence of the multitude placed him already among saints and angels,—had desired, by yielding up his breath in the arms of that fallen woman, to express to the world how utterly nugatory[3] is the choicest of man's own righteousness. After exhausting life in his efforts for mankind's spiritual good, he had made the manner of his death a parable, in order to impress on his admirers the mighty and mournful lesson, that, in the view of Infinite Purity, we are sinners all alike. It was to teach them, that the holiest among us has but attained so far above his fellows as to discern more clearly the Mercy which looks down, and repudiate more utterly the phantom of human merit, which would look aspiringly upward. Without disputing a truth so momentous, we must be allowed to consider this version of Mr. Dimmesdale's story as only an instance of that stubborn fidelity with which a man's friends—and especially a clergyman's—will sometimes uphold his character; when proofs, clear as the mid-day sunshine on the scarlet letter, establish him a false and sin-stained creature of the dust.

The authority which we have chiefly followed—a manuscript of old date, drawn up from the verbal testimony of individuals, some of whom had known Hester Prynne, while others had heard the tale from contemporary witnesses—fully confirms the view taken in the foregoing pages. Among many morals which press upon us from the poor minister's miserable experience, we put only this into a sentence:—"Be true! Be true! Be true! Show freely to the world, if not your worst, yet some trait whereby the worst may be inferred!"

Nothing was more remarkable than the change which took place, almost immediately after Mr. Dimmesdale's death, in the appearance and demeanour of the old man known as Roger Chillingworth. All his strength and energy—all his vital and intellectual force—seemed at once to desert him; insomuch that he positively withered up, shrivelled away, and almost vanished from mortal sight, like an uprooted weed that lies wilting in the sun. This unhappy man had made the very principle of his life to consist in the pursuit and systematic exercise of revenge; and when, by its completest triumph and consummation, that evil principle was left with no further material to support it,—when, in short, there was no more devil's work on earth for him to do, it only remained for the unhumanized mortal to betake himself whither his Master would find him tasks enough, and pay him his wages duly. But, to all these shadowy beings, so long our near acquaintances,—as well Roger Chillingworth as his companions,—we would fain be merciful. It is a curious subject of observation and inquiry, whether hatred and love be not the same thing at bottom. Each, in its utmost development, supposes a high degree of intimacy and heart-knowledge; each renders one individual dependent for the food of his affections and spiritual life upon another; each leaves the passionate lover, or the no less passionate hater, forlorn and desolate by the withdrawal of his object. Philosophically considered, therefore, the two passions seem essentially the same, except that one happens to be seen in a

3. Inconsequential.

celestial radiance, and the other in a dusky and lurid glow. In the spiritual world, the old physician and the minister—mutual victims as they have been—may, unawares, have found their earthly stock of hatred and antipathy transmuted into golden love.

Leaving this discussion apart, we have a matter of business to communicate to the reader. At old Roger Chillingworth's decease (which took place within the year), and by his last will and testament, of which Governor Bellingham and the Reverend Mr. Wilson were executors, he bequeathed a very considerable amount of property, both here and in England, to little Pearl, the daughter of Hester Prynne.

So Pearl—the elf-child,—the demon offspring, as some people, up to that epoch, persisted in considering her—became the richest heiress of her day, in the New World. Not improbably, this circumstance wrought a very material change in the public estimation; and, had the mother and child remained here, little Pearl, at a marriageable period of life, might have mingled her wild blood with the lineage of the devoutest Puritan among them all. But, in no long time after the physician's death, the wearer of the scarlet letter disappeared, and Pearl along with her. For many years, though a vague report would now and then find its way across the sea,—like a shapeless piece of driftwood tost ashore, with the initials of a name upon it,—yet no tidings of them unquestionably authentic were received. The story of the scarlet letter grew into a legend. Its spell, however, was still potent, and kept the scaffold awful where the poor minister had died, and likewise the cottage by the seashore, where Hester Prynne had dwelt. Near this latter spot, one afternoon, some children were at play, when they beheld a tall woman, in a gray robe, approach the cottage-door. In all those years it had never once been opened; but either she unlocked it, or the decaying wood and iron yielded to her hand, or she glided shadow-like through these impediments,—and, at all events, went in.

On the threshold she paused,—turned partly round,—for, perchance, the idea of entering, all alone, and all so changed, the home of so intense a former life, was more dreary and desolate than even she could bear. But her hesitation was only for an instant, though long enough to display a scarlet letter on her breast.

And Hester Prynne had returned, and taken up her long-forsaken shame. But where was little Pearl? If still alive, she must now have been in the flush and bloom of early womanhood. None knew—nor ever learned, with the fulness of perfect certainty—whether the elf-child had gone thus untimely to a maiden grave; or whether her wild, rich nature had been softened and subdued, and made capable of a woman's gentle happiness. But, through the remainder of Hester's life, there were indications that the recluse of the scarlet letter was the object of love and interest with some inhabitant of another land. Letters came, with armorial seals upon them, though of bearings unknown to English heraldry. In the cottage there were articles of comfort and luxury, such as Hester never cared to use, but which only wealth could have purchased, and affection have imagined for her. There were trifles, too, little ornaments, beautiful tokens of a continual remembrance, that must have been wrought by delicate fingers, at the impulse of a fond heart. And, once, Hester was seen embroidering a baby-garment, with such a lavish richness of golden fancy as would have raised a public tumult, had any infant, thus apparelled, been shown to our sobre-hued community.

In fine, the gossips of that day believed,—and Mr. Surveyor Pue, who made investigations a century later, believed,—and one of his recent successors in office, moreover, faithfully believes,—that Pearl was not only alive, but married, and happy, and mindful of her mother; and that she would most joyfully have entertained that sad and lonely mother at her fireside.

But there was a more real life for Hester Prynne, here, in New England, than in that unknown region where Pearl had found a home. Here had been her sin; here, her sorrow; and here was yet to be her penitence. She had returned, therefore, and resumed,—of her own free will, for not the sternest magistrate of that iron period would have imposed it,—resumed the symbol of which we have related so dark a tale. Never afterwards did it quit her bosom. But, in the lapse of the toilsome, thoughtful, and self-devoted years that made up Hester's life, the scarlet letter ceased to be a stigma which attracted the world's scorn and bitterness, and became a type of something to be sorrowed over, and looked upon with awe, yet with reverence too. And, as Hester Prynne had no selfish ends, nor lived in any measure for her own profit and enjoyment, people brought all their sorrows and perplexities, and besought her counsel, as one who had herself gone through a mighty trouble. Women, more especially,—in the continually recurring trials of wounded, wasted, wronged, misplaced, or erring and sinful passion,—or with the dreary burden of a heart unyielded, because unvalued and unsought,—came to Hester's cottage, demanding why they were so wretched, and what the remedy! Hester comforted and counselled them, as best she might. She assured them, too, of her firm belief, that, at some brighter period, when the world should have grown ripe for it, in Heaven's own time, a new truth would be revealed, in order to establish the whole relation between man and woman on a surer ground of mutual happiness. Earlier in life, Hester had vainly imagined that she herself might be the destined prophetess, but had long since recognized the impossibility that any mission of divine and mysterious truth should be confided to a woman stained with sin, bowed down with shame, or even burdened with a Life-long sorrow. The angel and apostle of the coming revelation must be a woman, indeed, but lofty, pure, and beautiful; and wise, moreover, not through dusky grief, but the ethereal medium of joy; and showing how sacred love should make us happy, by the truest test of a life successful to such an end!

So said Hester Prynne, and glanced her sad eyes downward at the scarlet letter. And, after many, many years, a new grave was delved, near an old and sunken one, in that burial-ground beside which King's Chapel has since been built. It was near that old and sunken grave, yet with a space between, as if the dust of the two sleepers had no right to mingle. Yet one tombstone served for both. All around, there were monuments carved with armorial bearings; and on this simple slab of slate—as the curious investigator may still discern, and perplex himself with the purport—there appeared the semblance of an engraved escutcheon.[4] It bore a device, a herald's wording of which might serve for a motto and brief description of our now concluded legend; so

4. A shield-shaped emblem.

sombre is it, and relieved only by one ever-glowing point of light gloomier than the shadow:—

"ON A FIELD, SABLE, THE LETTER A, GULES."[5]

THE END

1850

Preface to *The House of the Seven Gables*[1]

When a writer calls his work a Romance, it need hardly be observed that he wishes to claim a certain latitude, both as to its fashion and material, which he would not have felt himself entitled to assume, had he professed to be writing a Novel. The latter form of composition is presumed to aim at a very minute fidelity, not merely to the possible, but to the probable and ordinary course of man's experience. The former—while, as a work of art, it must rigidly subject itself to laws, and while it sins unpardonably so far as it may swerve aside from the truth of the human heart—has fairly a right to present that truth under circumstances, to a great extent, of the writer's own choosing or creation. If he think fit, also, he may so manage his atmospherical medium as to bring out or mellow the lights, and deepen and enrich the shadows, of the picture. He will be wise, no doubt, to make a very moderate use of the privileges here stated, and, especially, to mingle the Marvellous rather as a slight, delicate, and evanescent flavor, than as any portion of the actual substance of the dish offered to the public. He can hardly be said, however, to commit a literary crime, even if he disregard this caution.

In the present work, the author has proposed to himself—but with what success, fortunately, it is not for him to judge—to keep undeviatingly within his immunities. The point of view in which this tale comes under the Romantic definition lies in the attempt to connect a by-gone time with the very present that is flitting away from us. It is a legend, prolonging itself, from an epoch now gray in the distance, down into our own broad daylight, and bringing along with it some of its legendary mist, which the reader, according to his pleasure, may either disregard, or allow it to float almost imperceptibly about the characters and events, for the sake of a picturesque effect. The narrative, it may be, is woven of so humble a texture as to require this advantage, and, at the same time, to render it the more difficult of attainment.

Many writers lay very great stress upon some definite moral purpose, at which they profess to aim their works. Not to be deficient in this particular, the author has provided himself with a moral;—the truth, namely, that the wrong-doing of one generation lives into the successive ones, and, divesting itself of every temporary advantage, becomes a pure and uncontrollable mischief;—and he would feel it a singular gratification, if this romance might effectually convince mankind—or, indeed, any one man—of the folly of

5. On a black background, the letter *A*, in red.
1. The text is from *The House of the Seven Gables: A Romance* (1851).

tumbling down an avalanche of ill-gotten gold, or real estate, on the heads of an unfortunate posterity, thereby to maim and crush them, until the accumulated mass shall be scattered abroad in its original atoms. In good faith, however, he is not sufficiently imaginative to flatter himself with the slightest hope of this kind. When romances do really teach anything, or produce any effective operation, it is usually through a far more subtile process than the ostensible one. The author has considered it hardly worth his while, therefore, relentlessly to impale the story with its moral, as with an iron rod,—or, rather as by sticking a pin through a butterfly,—thus at once depriving it of life, and causing it to stiffen in an ungainly and unnatural attitude. A high truth, indeed, fairly, finely, and skilfully wrought out, brightening at every step, and crowning the final development of a work of fiction, may add an artistic glory, but is never any truer, and seldom any more evident, at the last page than at the first.

The reader may perhaps choose to assign an actual locality to the imaginary events of this narrative. If permitted by the historical connection,—which, though slight, was essential to his plan,—the author would very willingly have avoided anything of this nature. Not to speak of other objections, it exposes the romance to an inflexible and exceedingly dangerous species of criticism, by bringing his fancy-pictures almost into positive contact with the realities of the moment. It has been no part of his object, however, to describe local manners, nor in any way to meddle with the characteristics of a community for whom he cherishes a proper respect and a natural regard. He trusts not to be considered as unpardonably offending, by laying out a street that infringes upon nobody's private rights, and appropriating a lot of land which had no visible owner, and building a house, of materials long in use for constructing castles in the air. The personages of the tale—though they give themselves out to be of ancient stability and considerable prominence—are really of the author's own making, or, at all events, of his own mixing; their virtues can shed no lustre, nor their defects redound, in the remotest degree, to the discredit of the venerable town[2] of which they profess to be inhabitants. He would be glad, therefore, if—especially in the quarter to which he alludes—the book may be read strictly as a Romance, having a great deal more to do with the clouds overhead than with any portion of the actual soil of the County of Essex.

LENOX, *January 27, 1851.* 1851

2. Salem, Massachusetts.

HENRY WADSWORTH LONGFELLOW
1807–1882

Henry Wadsworth Longfellow was the most beloved American poet of the nineteenth century. His narrative poems *Evangeline* (1847), *The Song of Hiawatha* (1855), and *The Courtship of Miles Standish* (1858) went through numerous editions, and his collections of lyrics—*The Seaside and the Fireside* (1850), *Tales of a Wayside Inn* (1863), and many others—were also enormously popular. In Great Britain, Longfellow outsold England's poet laureate Alfred, Lord Tennyson; and shortly after Longfellow's death in 1882, he became the first American-born poet enshrined in Westminster Abbey's famed Poets' Corner. As literary modernism took hold in the twentieth century, Longfellow came to be seen as an unadventurous, timid poet; but such an assessment unfairly diminishes the achievement of a writer who saw value in working with (rather than against) established forms and traditions. Viewed in relation to his own culture and his own poetic aspirations, Longfellow exhibited a metrical complexity, a mastery of sound and atmosphere, a progressive social conscience, and a melancholy outlook for which his soothing words were especially appropriate, as though the poet were comforting himself as well as his audience.

Longfellow was born in Portland, Maine (then still a part of Massachusetts), on February 27, 1807, the second of eight children. Both of his parents encouraged his early interest in reading and writing, but when he was sent to Bowdoin College in 1821, the expectation was that the fourteen-year-old Longfellow would eventually become a lawyer like his father. Graduating at age eighteen in the class of 1825, which also included Nathaniel Hawthorne and the future president Franklin Pierce, Longfellow made the risky vocational decision to pursue his interest in literature. He was aided in this ambition by a college trustee who donated money to Bowdoin to hire Longfellow as a professor of modern languages, provided that Longfellow agreed to use his own funds to study languages in Europe. Supported by his father, Longfellow spent three years abroad, traveling in Germany, Italy, France, and Spain (where he met Washington Irving, the American writer he most admired). Returning to the United States in 1829 with a new fluency in four languages, the twenty-two-year-old Longfellow assumed the professorship at Bowdoin. In 1831 he married Mary Storer Potter; four years later he was appointed the Smith Professor of Modern Languages and Belles Lettres at Harvard University, with the understanding that he would need to improve his skills in Germanic languages. To that end, he traveled to Europe with his wife in 1835; while in Holland, Mary died of complications from a miscarriage. Just before returning to the United States in 1836, Longfellow toured Switzerland and Austria, meeting and falling in love with Fanny Appleton, the daughter of the wealthy Boston industrialist Nathan Appleton. After a seven-year courtship, they married in 1843. As a wedding gift, Longfellow's father-in-law bought the couple Craigie House in Cambridge, a mansion abutting Harvard Yard where Longfellow himself had been renting rooms.

Longfellow's first published poem appeared in Maine's *Portland Gazette* on November 17, 1820, when he was thirteen years old. He published poems and prose while in college, but in his initial years as a professor he focused on publishing scholarly articles in the *North American Review*, along with language textbooks and translations of European poetry. But he soon returned to his principal interest, which was writing his own poetry, publishing his first volume, *Voices of the Night*, in 1839. Other poetic volumes quickly followed, including *Ballads and Other Poems* (1841), *Poems on Slavery*

(1842), and *The Belfrey of Bruges and Other Poems* (1846). Longfellow's great commercial breakthrough came with the publication of his 1847 narrative poem *Evangeline*, which went through six printings in nine weeks. *Evangeline* weaves a tragic love story into a poetic narrative of the British dispossession of an Acadian French settlement in Nova Scotia during the French and Indian War (1756–63). At a time of increasing modernization, Longfellow tapped into the cultural nostalgia for times past that would also come to inform his popular Indian poetic narrative, *Hiawatha*. During these years Longfellow also published short and long prose pieces. Inspired by Irving's *Sketch-Book*, he brought out a collection of travel sketches, *Outre-Mer*, in 1835. In 1839 he published a two-volume prose romance, *Hyperion*; another prose romance, *Kavanagh*, appeared in 1849.

As a poet and a teacher, Longfellow took pride in his cosmopolitanism and transatlanticism. Rejecting the call by American literary nationalists for writing that drew mainly on native sources, Longfellow in his poetry worked with a wide range of sources—Homer and Virgil, for instance, for the hexameters of *Evangeline*, and Finnish mythologies and folk meter for *Hiawatha*. At Harvard, he taught European literatures of many periods and nationalities; he also published *The Poets and Poetry of Europe* (1845; rev. ed. 1871), a book of translations for the general reading public.

In 1854, Longfellow resigned from Harvard to devote himself completely to writing, editing, and translating. When he published *Hiawatha* one year after his resignation, the excellent sales (around thirty thousand copies in the first six months of publication) earned him his annual Harvard salary ($1,800) many times over. His 1858 *The Courtship of Miles Standish and Other Poems* sold twenty-five thousand copies in the United States over the first two months of publication, and ten thousand copies in London on its first day of publication. By the 1870s Longfellow's annual income from his writing was around $15,000, an enormous sum at that time and over $100,000 at today's value.

As with his first marriage, tragedy struck unexpectedly. In 1861 Fanny Longfellow burned to death when her dress caught fire while she was melting wax to preserve locks of her daughters' hair. Longfellow himself nearly died when he tried to smother the flames. In his grief Longfellow turned to translating the *Divine Comedy* of Dante, making the labor the occasion for regular meetings with friends such as James Russell Lowell and the young William Dean Howells; the volumes were published between 1865 and 1871. Longfellow made one last visit to Europe in 1868–69, during which Queen Victoria gave him a private audience and Oxford awarded him an honorary doctoral degree. On his return, he continued with his various writing and editing projects. His long religious poem *Christus: A Mystery*, the labor of many years, was published in 1872, and a number of other poetic volumes followed over the next decade, including a thirty-one-volume anthology, *Poems of Place* (1877–79). Longfellow died a month after his seventy-fifth birthday on March 24, 1882. At the time he was working on a long poem about Michelangelo; *Michael Angelo: A Fragment* was published posthumously in 1883. One year later his bust was unveiled in Poets' Corner.

A Psalm of Life[1]

'Life that shall send
A challenge to its end,
And when it comes, say, 'Welcome, friend.'[2]

What the Heart of the Young Man Said to the Psalmist

I

Tell me not, in mournful numbers,[3]
  Life is but an empty dream!
For the soul is dead that slumbers,
  And things are not what they seem.

II

Life is real—life is earnest—
  And the grave is not its goal:
Dust thou art, to dust returnest,
  Was not spoken of the soul.

III

Not enjoyment, and not sorrow,
  Is our destin'd end or way;
But to *act*, that each to-morrow
  Find us farther than to-day.

IV

Art is long, and time is fleeting,
  And our hearts, though stout and brave,
Still, like muffled drums, are beating
  Funeral marches to the grave.

V

In the world's broad field of battle,
  In the bivouac of Life,
Be not like dumb, driven cattle!
  Be a hero in the strife!

VI

Trust no Future, howe'er pleasant!
  Let the dead Past bury its dead!
Act—act in the glorious Present!
  Heart within, and God o'er head!

1. The text is that of the first publication, in the *Knickerbocker or New-York Monthly Magazine* (September 1838). The poem was collected in *Voices of the Night* (1839).

2. Adapted from "Wishes to His Supposed Mistress" by the English poet Richard Crashaw (c. 1613–1649).

3. Meters, rhythms.

VII

Lives of great men all remind us
We can make *our* lives sublime,
And, departing, leave behind us
Footsteps on the sands of time.

VIII

Footsteps, that, perhaps another,
Sailing o'er life's solemn main,
A forlorn and shipwreck'd brother,
Seeing, shall take heart again.

IX

Let us then be up and doing,
With a heart for any fate;
Still achieving, still pursuing,
Learn to labor and to wait.

1838, 1839

The Slave Singing at Midnight[1]

Loud he sang the psalm of David![2]
He, a Negro and enslaved,
Sang of Israel's victory,
Sang of Zion, bright and free.

In that hour, when night is calmest,
Sang he from the Hebrew Psalmist,
In a voice so sweet and clear
That I could not choose but hear,

Songs of triumph, and ascriptions,
Such as reached the swart Egyptians,
When upon the Red Sea coast
Perished Pharaoh and his host.[3]

And the voice of his devotion
Filled my soul with strange emotion;
For its tones by turns were glad,
Sweetly solemn, wildly sad.

1. From *Poems on Slavery* (1842).
2. Many of the psalms of the Old Testament have been attributed to David, the second of the Israelite kings, who reigned from c. 1000 B.C.E. to ca. 962 B.C.E.
3. The Israelites escaped from slavery when the Red Sea divided to let them pass and then closed to drown Pharaoh and his army (Exodus 15).

Paul and Silas, in their prison,
Sang of Christ, the Lord arisen,
And an earthquake's arm of might
Broke their dungeon-gates at night.[4]

But, alas! what holy angel
Brings the Slave this glad evangel?
And what earthquake's arm of might
Breaks his dungeon-gates at night?

1842

The Day Is Done[1]

The day is done, and the darkness
  Falls from the wings of Night,
As a feather is wafted downward
  From an eagle in his flight.

I see the lights of the village
  Gleam through the rain and the mist,
And a feeling of sadness comes o'er me,
  That my soul cannot resist:

A feeling of sadness and longing,
  That is not akin to pain,
And resembles sorrow only
  As the mist resembles the rain.

Come, read to me some poem,
  Some simple and heartfelt lay,
That shall soothe this restless feeling,
  And banish the thoughts of day.

Not from the grand old masters,
  Not from the bards sublime,
Whose distant footsteps echo
  Through the corridors of Time.

For, like strains of martial music,
  Their mighty thoughts suggest
Life's endless toil and endeavour;
  And to-night I long for rest.

Read from some humbler poet,
  Whose songs gushed from his heart,

4. See Acts 16.19–34 on the miraculous escape from prison of the Christian leaders Paul and Silas.

1. From *The Belfrey of Bruges and Other Poems* (1846).

As showers from the clouds of summer,
  Or tears from the eyelids start;

Who, through long days of labor,
  And nights devoid of ease,
Still heard in his soul the music
  Of wonderful melodies.

Such songs have power to quiet
  The restless pulse of care,
And come like the benediction
  That follows after prayer.

Then read from the treasured volume
  The poem of thy choice,
And lend to the rhyme of the poet
  The beauty of thy voice.

And the night shall be filled with music,
  And the cares, that infest the day,
Shall fold their tents, like the Arabs,
  And as silently steal away.

1846

From Evangeline, A Tale of Acadie[1]

[PROLOGUE]

This is the forest primeval. The murmuring pines and the hemlocks,
Bearded with moss, and in garments green, indistinct in the twilight,
Stand like Druids of eld,[2] with voices sad and prophetic,
Stand like harpers hoar,[3] with beards that rest on their bosoms.
Loud from its rocky caverns, the deep-voiced neighbouring ocean
Speaks, and in accents disconsolate answers the wail of the forest.

This is the forest primeval; but where are the hearts that beneath it
Leaped like the roe, when he hears in the woodland the voice of the
    huntsman?
Where is the thatch-roofed village, the home of Acadian farmers,—
Men whose lives glided on like rivers that water the woodlands,
Darkened by shadows of earth, but reflecting an image of heaven?
Waste are those pleasant farms, and the farmers forever departed!

1. From the first printing (1847). Written between 1845 and 1847, this book-length poem takes its inspiration from the 1755 expulsion of Acadians from the former French colony Acadie (present-day Nova Scotia, Canada) when they refused to offer their allegiance to the British Crown and renounce their Catholic faith. The process of loading the Acadians onto boats resulted in the separation of friends and families. Longfellow invented the tragic story of two Acadians, Evangeline and Gabriel, separated on their wedding; he used the prologue to set the mood of the overall poem, which went through six editions in its first nine weeks.

2. Old (archaic). "Druids": pre-Christian priests of ancient Ireland.

3. Ancient, venerable.

Scattered like dust and leaves, when the mighty blasts of October
Seize them, and whirl them aloft, and sprinkle them far o'er the ocean.
Naught but tradition remains of the beautiful village of Grand-Pré.[4]

Ye who believe in affection that hopes, and endures, and is patient,
Ye who believe in the beauty and strength of woman's devotion,[5]
List to the mournful tradition still sung by the pines of the forest;
List to a Tale of Love in Acadie, home of the happy.

1847

The Jewish Cemetery at Newport[1]

How strange it seems! These Hebrews in their graves.
Close by the street of this fair sea-port town;
Silent beside the never-silent waves,
At rest in all this moving up and down!

The trees are white with dust, that o'er their sleep
Wave their broad curtains in the south-wind's breath,
While underneath such leafy tents they keep
The long, mysterious Exodus of Death.

And these sepulchral stones, so old and brown,
That pave with level flags[2] their burial-place,
Are like the tablets of the Law, thrown down
And broken by Moses at the mountain's base.[3]

The very names recorded here are strange,
Of foreign accent, and of different climes;
Alvares and Rivera[4] interchange
With Abraham and Jacob of old times.

"Blessed be God! for he created Death!"
The mourners said: "and Death is rest and peace."
Then added, in the certainty of faith:
"And giveth Life, that never more shall cease."

Closed are the portals of their Synagogue,
No Psalms of David now the silence break,
No Rabbi reads the ancient Decalogue[5]
In the grand dialect the Prophets spake.

4. Historic Acadian farming site.
5. Evangeline devotes her life to searching for Gabriel, but does not find him until he is on his deathbed.
1. First published in *Putnam's Monthly* (July 1854), the source of the present text. The first Jewish settlers arrived in Newport, Rhode Island, in 1658, encouraged by the relatively tolerant religious attitudes of local leaders. During the colonial period, Newport had the second largest Jewish community in North America. The Touro Synagogue, the oldest still standing in the United States, dates from 1763. Longfellow visited Newport's Jewish Cemetery in July 1852.
2. Flagstones.
3. "Moses' anger waxed hot, and he cast the tables out of his hands, and brake them beneath the mount" (Exodus 32.19).
4. The Newport Jews were Sephardims, immigrants from Spain and Portugal, where they had acquired local names.
5. The Ten Commandments.

Gone are the living, but the dead remain,
 And not neglected, for a hand unseen,
Scattering its bounty, like a summer rain,
 Still keeps their graves and their remembrance green.

How came they here? What burst of Christian hate;
 What persecution, merciless, and blind,
Drove o'er the sea,—that desert, desolate—
 These Ishmaels and Hagars[6] of mankind?

They lived in narrow streets and lanes obscure,
 Ghetto or Judenstrass,[7] in mirk and mire;
Taught in the school of patience to endure
 The life of anguish and the death of fire.

All their lives long, with the unleavened bread
 And bitter herbs[8] of exile and its fears,
The wasting famine of the heart they fed,
 And slaked its thirst with marah[9] of their tears.

Anathema maranatha![1] was the cry
 That rang from town to town, from street to street;
At every gate the accursed Mordecai[2]
 Was mocked, and jeered, and spurned by Christian feet.

Pride and humiliation hand in hand
 Walked with them through the world, where'er they went;
Trampled and beaten were they as the sand,
 And yet unshaken as the continent.

For in the back-ground, figures vague and vast,
 Of patriarchs and of prophets rose sublime,
And all the great traditions of the Past
 They saw reflected in the coming time.

And thus for ever with reverted look,
 The mystic volume of the world they read,
Spelling it backward like a Hebrew book,[3]
 Till Life became a Legend of the Dead.

But ah! what once has been shall be no more!
 The groaning earth in travail and in pain

6. Outcasts. From Genesis 21, where Hagar, the concubine of Abraham, and their son, Ishmael, are driven from his household at the instigation of his wife, Sarah, after the birth of their son, Isaac.
7. Street of the Jews (German). "Ghetto": a section of a city to which Jews were restricted.
8. Foods eaten at Passover in remembrance of the exodus from slavery in Egypt.
9. Bitter water; see Exodus 15.22–25, which describes how the Hebrews, after crossing the Red Sea, came to Marah, where they found the water too bitter to drink until God showed Moses how to sweeten it with a tree.
1. "If any man love not the Lord Jesus Christ, let him be Anathema Maranatha" (1 Corinthians 16.22).
2. A Jewish leader abused by the Persians (Esther 2.5–6).
3. Hebrew is read from right to left.

Brings forth its races, but does not restore,
  and the dead nations never rise again.

1854

My Lost Youth[1]

Often I think of the beautiful town
  That is seated by the sea;
Often in thought go up and down
The pleasant streets of that dear old town,
  And my youth comes back to me.
    And a verse of a Lapland song
    Is haunting my memory still:
  "A boy's will is the wind's will,
And the thoughts of youth are long, long thoughts."[2]

I can see the shadowy lines of its trees,
  And catch, in sudden gleams,
The sheen of the far-surrounding seas,
And islands that were the Hesperides[3]
  Of all my boyish dreams.
    And the burden of that old song,
    It murmurs and whispers still:
  "A boy's will is the wind's will,
And the thoughts of youth are long, long thoughts."

I remember the black wharves and the slips,
  And the sea-tides tossing free;
And Spanish sailors with bearded lips,
And the beauty and mystery of the ships,
  And the magic of the sea.
    And the voice of that wayward song
    Is singing and saying still:
  "A boy's will is the wind's will,
And the thoughts of youth are long, long thoughts."

I remember the bulwarks by the shore,
  And the fort upon the hill;
The sun-rise gun, with its hollow roar,
The drum-beat repeated o'er and o'er,
  And the bugle wild and shrill.
    And the music of that old song
    Throbs in my memory still:

1. Longfellow wrote this poem about his hometown of Portland, Maine, in March 1855, at Cambridge. The text is that of the first printing in *Putnam's Monthly Magazine* (August 1855). It was reprinted in *The Courtship of Miles Standish and Other Poems* (1858).
2. Longfellow derived the refrain from lines in the English writer John Scheffer's *The History of Lapland* (1674): "A Youth's desire is the desire of the wind." Lapland is the area of northern Europe populated by the Finnic people of northern Norway, Sweden, Finland, and other nearby regions.
3. In Greek mythology, islands where the golden apples grew.

"A boy's will is the wind's will,
And the thoughts of youth are long, long thoughts."

I remember the sea-fight far away,
How it thundered o'er the tide![4]
And the dead captains, as they lay
In their graves, o'erlooking the tranquil bay,
Where they in battle died.
And the sound of that mournful song
Goes through me with a thrill:
"A boy's will is the wind's will,
And the thoughts of youth are long, long thoughts."

I can see the breezy dome of groves,
The shadows of Deering's Woods;[5]
And the friendships old and the early loves
Come back with a Sabbath sound, as of doves
In quiet neighborhoods.
And the verse of that sweet old song,
It flutters and murmurs still:
"A boy's will is the wind's will,
And the thoughts of youth are long, long thoughts."

I remember the gleams and glooms that dart
Across the schoolboy's brain;
The song and the silence in the heart,
That in part are prophecies, and in part
Are longings wild and vain.
And the voice of that fitful song
Sings on, and is never still:
"A boy's will is the wind's will,
And the thoughts of youth are long, long thoughts."

There are things of which I may not speak;
There are dreams that cannot die;
There are thoughts that make the strong heart weak,
And bring a pallor into the cheek,
And a mist before the eye.
And the words of that fatal song
Come over me like a chill:
"A boy's will is the wind's will,
And the thoughts of youth are long, long thoughts."

Strange to me now are the forms I meet
When I visit the dear old town;
But the native air is pure and sweet,
And the trees that o'ershadow each well-known street,
As they balance up and down,

4. The American *Enterprise* and the British *Boxer* fought near Portland in 1813. Both captains were killed and carried ashore for burial.

5. Wooded area in Portland now called Deering Oaks.

Are singing the beautiful song,
Are sighing and whispering still:
"A boy's will is the wind's will,
And the thoughts of youth are long, long thoughts."

And Deering's Woods are fresh and fair,
And with joy that is almost pain
My heart goes back to wander there,
And among the dreams of the days that were,
I find my lost youth again.
And the strange and beautiful song,
The groves are repeating it still:
"A boy's will is the wind's will,
And the thoughts of youth are long, long thoughts."

1855

Hawthorne[1]

MAY 23, 1864

How beautiful it was, that one bright day
In the long week of rain!
Though all its splendor could not chase away
The omnipresent pain.

The lovely town was white with apple-blooms,
And the great elms o'erhead
Dark shadows wove on their aerial looms,
Shot through with golden thread.

Across the meadows, by the gray old manse,[2]
The historic river flowed:
I was as one who wanders in a trance,
Unconscious of his road.

The faces of familiar friends seemed strange:
Their voices I could hear,
And yet the words they uttered seemed to change
Their meaning to my ear.

For the one face I looked for was not there,
The one low voice was mute;
Only an unseen presence filled the air,
And baffled my pursuit.

1. The poem first appeared in the August 1864 issue of the *Atlantic Monthly*, titled "Concord," and was reprinted as "Hawthorne" in Longfellow's *Flower-de-Luce* (1867), the source of the text here. Longfellow met Hawthorne at Bowdoin College (they were both in the class of 1825), and their friendship deepened during the 1850s and early 1860s. May 23, 1864, was the date of Hawthorne's funeral in Concord, Massachusetts, which Longfellow attended.

2. The Old Manse was the name Hawthorne gave to the house, a former parsonage, that he and his family lived in during his Concord years of 1842–45.

Now I look back, and meadow, manse, and stream
  Dimly my thought defines;
I only see—a dream within a dream—
  The hill-top hearsed with pines.

I only hear above his place of rest
  Their tender undertone,
The infinite longings of a troubled breast,
  The voice so like his own.

There in seclusion and remote from men
  The wizard hand lies cold,
Which at its topmost speed let fall the pen,
  And left the tale half told.[3]

Ah! who shall lift that wand of magic power,
  And the lost clew[4] regain?
The unfinished window in Aladdin's tower
  Unfinished must remain![5]

1864, 1867

The Cross of Snow[1]

In the long, sleepless watches of the night,
  A gentle face—the face of one long dead—
  Looks at me from the wall, where round its head
  The night-lamp casts a halo of pale light.
Here in this room she died; and soul more white
  Never through martyrdom of fire was led
  To its repose; nor can in books be read
  The legend of a life more benedight.[2]
There is a mountain in the distant West
  That, sun-defying, in its deep ravines
  Displays a cross of snow upon its side.[3]
Such is the cross I wear upon my breast
  These eighteen years, through all the changing scenes
  And seasons, changeless since the day she died.

1879, 1886

3. Reference to Hawthorne's *Twice-told Tales* (1837), which Longfellow had favorably reviewed in the July 1837 issue of the *North American Review*.
4. In Greek mythology, the ball of thread used by Theseus to find his way out of the labyrinth.
5. On the day of the funeral, the manuscript of one of Hawthorne's unfinished romances was placed on the coffin.
1. Longfellow wrote this poem on July 10, 1879, the eighteenth anniversary of the tragic death by fire of his second wife, Fanny; it was published posthumously by his brother Samuel in *Life of Henry Wadsworth Longfellow* (1886), from which the text is taken.
2. Blessed.
3. The Mountain of the Holy Cross, in the Rocky Mountains of Colorado, took its name from the snow-filled cross that appeared on its eastern face under certain weather conditions. In 1875, William Henry Jackson (1843–1942) took a photograph of the mountain, which Longfellow had probably seen.

JOHN GREENLEAF WHITTIER
1807–1892

John Greenleaf Whittier was born to a Quaker family on December 17, 1807, on a farm near Haverhill, Massachusetts. Although no longer persecuted in New England, Quakers were still a people apart, and Whittier grew up with a sense of being different from most of his neighbors. Labor on the debt-ridden farm overstrained his health in adolescence, and thereafter throughout his long life he suffered from intermittent physical collapses. At fourteen, having had only a meager education in a household suspicious of non-Quaker literature, he found in the Scottish poet Robert Burns (1759–1796) an initial source of inspiration. Like Burns, Whittier began writing poems that employed regional dialect, dealt with homely subjects, and displayed a democratic social conscience. His first poem was published in 1826 in a local newspaper run by another young man, William Lloyd Garrison (1805–1879), whose dedication to the antislavery movement was to affect Whittier's life profoundly. In 1827 Garrison helped persuade Whittier's father that the young poet deserved a formal education, and Whittier supported himself through two terms at Haverhill Academy. In 1836, six years after his father's death, Whittier and his mother and sisters moved from the farm to a house in nearby Amesbury, Massachusetts, which he owned until his death.

In his twenties Whittier became editor of various newspapers, some of regional importance. The turning point of his career came in 1833, when Garrison brought him into the abolitionist movement. In June 1833 Whittier published an antislavery pamphlet, *Justice and Expediency*, and later that year he helped found the American Anti-Slavery Society. In the tradition of such antislavery Quakers as Anthony Benezet (1713–1784) and John Woolman (1720–1793), Whittier believed that there was only one practicable and just scheme of emancipation: "Immediate abolition of slavery; an immediate acknowledgment of the great truth, that man cannot hold property in man; an immediate surrender of baneful prejudice to Christian love; an immediate practical obedience to the command of Jesus Christ: 'Whatsoever ye would that men should do unto you, do even so to them'" *Justice and Expediency*). In an effort to disseminate his views to the widest possible audience, Whittier published over a hundred antislavery poems and quickly emerged as the most popular poet of the abolitionist movement. His antislavery poetry was collected in 1837 in an unauthorized volume, *Poems Written during the Progress of the Abolition Question in the United States*, funded by abolitionists; one year later he oversaw the publication of *Poems* (1838), which included most of his antislavery poetry up to that time. That same year Whittier, in disguise, joined an antiabolitionist mob to save some of his papers as his office was being ransacked and burned.

From the 1830s through the 1850s, Whittier was a working editor and writer associated with abolitionist newspapers such as the Washington, D.C., weekly *National Era*, which serialized Harriet Beecher Stowe's *Uncle Tom's Cabin* from 1851 to 1852. During this time he published several additional volumes of poetry, including *Lays of My Home* (1843) and *The Chapel of Hermits and Other Poems* (1853), along with a serialized novel about New England's colonial past, *Leaves from Margaret Smith's Journal* (*National Era*, 1848–49). Like Nathaniel Hawthorne, Whittier had a keen interest in New England history. His first book, *Legends of New England* (1831), had explored New England's past in sketches and verse. In 1847 he published a sequel of sorts, the prose work *The Supernaturalism of New England*, which Hawthorne reviewed favorably in the New York monthly *Literary World*, terming it "no unworthy contribution from a poet to that species of literature which only a poet should meddle with." The New England writings of Hawthorne, Whittier, Catharine Sedgwick, and Stowe would have an important influence on the emergence of local-color regionalism later in the century.

Despite his wide-ranging interests in poetry, prose, and editing, Whittier well into the 1850s was generally regarded (contemptuously by some) as simply an abolitionist poet. His reputation underwent a change in the late 1850s, when abolitionism had become more accepted in the North, and when his poetry and humorous folk legends began to appear in the new (and very popular) *Atlantic Monthly*. With the outbreak of the Civil War, the nonviolent Quaker Whittier, whose progressive antislavery poems had contributed to northern militancy, became increasingly troubled by the carnage on the battlefield and sought refuge in a domestic poetry that recaptured an idealized, harmonic past. Grief-stricken at the death of his younger sister Elizabeth in 1865, he began work on *Snow-Bound*, which James T. Fields published as a book in 1866. In the aftermath of the Civil War, at a time of national mourning, readers responded enthusiastically to Whittier's nostalgic evocation of a historical moment when houses were not divided and all was mostly well with the world. Suddenly the poet on the margins emerged, along with Longfellow, as one of the nation's most-beloved poets. Whittier earned over $10,000 from the sales of *Snow-Bound*, an enormous sum for that time, and his subsequent volume, *The Tent on the Beach* (1867), was even more enthusiastically received, selling out its first printing of twenty thousand copies within the first three weeks of publication. During the final decades of his life, Whittier was regaled with honors, and even had a college in Iowa and a town in California named after him. On the occasion of his seventieth birthday, Stowe declared that Whittier's "life had been a consecration, his songs an inspiration, to all that is highest and best." In 1888 he helped edit a seven-volume edition of his collected works; his last volume, *At Sundown* (1890), was privately printed for friends. He died from a stroke in Hampton Falls, New Hampshire, on September 7, 1892.

The Hunters of Men[1]

Have ye heard of our hunting, o'er mountain and glen,
Through cane-brake[2] and forest—the hunting of men?
The lords of our land to this hunting have gone,
As the fox-hunter follows the sound of the horn:
Hark?—the cheer and the hallo!—the crack of the whip,
And the yell of the hound as he fastens his grip!
All blithe are our hunters, and noble their match—
Though *hundreds* are caught, there are *millions* to catch:
So speed to their hunting, o'er mountain and glen,
Through cane-brake and forest—the hunting of men!

Gay luck to our hunters!—how nobly they ride
In the glow of their zeal, and the strength of their pride!—

1. "Written on reading the report of the proceedings of the American Colonization Society, at its annual meeting in 1834" [Whittier's note]. Whittier first published the poem in 1835 and revised it in 1838 (adopting the question mark at the poem's end). The text is taken from *Poems* (1838). Founded in December 1816, the American Colonization Society sought to transport the free blacks to Africa. The focus of the poem, however, is on the practice of returning runaway slaves to their owners, which was mandated by the Fugitive Slave Law of 1793.

2. Rough or marshy land overgrown with bamboo-like grasses, such as sugarcane.

The Priest with his cassock flung back on the wind,
Just screening the politic Statesman behind—
The saint and the sinner, with cursing and prayer—
The drunk and the sober, ride merrily there.
And woman—kind woman—wife, widow and maid—
For *the good of the hunted,* is lending her aid:
Her foot's in the stirrup—her hand on the rein—
How blithely she rides to the hunting of men!

Oh! goodly and grand is our hunting to see,
In this "land of the brave and this home of the free."
Priest, warrior, and statesman, from Georgia to Maine,
All mounting the saddle—all grasping the rein—
Right merrily hunting the black man, whose sin
Is the curl of his hair and the hue of his skin!
Wo, now, to the hunted who turns him at bay!
Will our hunters be turn'd from their purpose and prey?
Will their hearts fail within them?—their nerves tremble, when
All roughly they ride to the hunting of men?

Ho!—ALMS for our hunters! all weary and faint
Wax the curse of the sinner and prayer of the saint.
The horn is wound faintly—the echoes are still
Over cane-brake and river, and forest and hill.
Haste—alms for our hunters! the hunted once more
Have turn'd from their flight with their backs to the shore:
What right have *they* here in the home of the white,
Shadow'd o'er by *our* banner of Freedom and Right?
Ho!—alms for the hunters! or never again
Will they ride in their pomp to the hunting of men!

ALMS—ALMS for our hunters! why *will* ye delay,
When their pride and their glory are melting away?
The parson has turn'd; for, on charge of his own,
Who goeth a warfare, or hunting, alone?
The politic statesman looks back with a sigh—
There is doubt in his heart—there is fear in his eye.
Oh! haste, lest that doubting and fear shall prevail,
And the head of his steed take the place of the tail.
Oh! haste, ere he leave us! for who will ride then,
For pleasure or gain, to the hunting of men?

1835, 1838

Ichabod![1]

So fallen! so lost! the light withdrawn
Which once he wore!
The glory from his gray hairs gone
Forevermore!

Revile him not—the Tempter hath
A snare for all;
And pitying tears, not scorn and wrath,
Befit his fall!

Oh! dumb be passion's stormy rage,
When he who might
Have lighted up and led his age,
Falls back in night.

Scorn! would the angels laugh, to mark
A bright soul driven,
Fiend-goaded, down the endless dark,
From hope and heaven!

Let not the land, once proud of him,
Insult him now,
Nor brand with deeper shame his dim,
Dishonored brow.

But let its humbled sons, instead,
From sea to lake,
A long lament, as for the dead,
In sadness make.

Of all we loved and honored, nought
Save power remains—
A fallen angel's pride of thought,
Still strong in chains.

All else is gone; from those great eyes
The soul has fled:
When faith is lost, when honor dies,
The man is dead!

Then, pay the reverence of old days
To his dead fame;
Walk backward, with averted gaze,
And hide the shame![2]

1850

1. "Ichabod!" is an attack on Daniel Webster, whose championing of the Fugitive Slave Bill (the part of the Compromise of 1850 making it a federal crime to assist runaway slaves) infuriated the abolitionists. The title is from 1 Samuel 4.21: "And she named the child Ichabod, saying, The glory is departed from Israel." The text is that of the first printing in *Songs of Labor, and Other Poems* (1850).

2. Alluding to Genesis 9.20–25, Whittier equates Webster's shame with that of Noah after his sons discovered him naked and drunk in his cave.

Snow-Bound: A Winter Idyl[1]

To the memory of the household it describes, this poem is dedicated by the author.

"As the Spirits of Darkness be stronger in the dark, so Good Spirits which be Angels of Light are augmented not only by the Divine light of the Sun, but also by our common Wood Fire: and as the celestial Fire drives away dark spirits, so also this our Fire of Wood doth the same."

—COR. AGRIPPA, *Occult Philosophy*, Book I. chap. v.[2]

"Announced by all the trumpets of the sky,
Arrives the snow; and, driving o'er the fields,
Seems nowhere to alight; the whited air
Hides hills and woods, the river and the heaven,
And veils the farm-house at the garden's end.
The sled and traveller stopped, the courier's feet
Delayed, all friends shut out, the housemates sit
Around the radiant fireplace, enclosed
In a tumultuous privacy of storm."

—EMERSON[3]

The sun that brief December day
Rose cheerless over hills of gray,
And, darkly circled, gave at noon
A sadder light than waning moon.

Slow tracing down the thickening sky
Its mute and ominous prophecy,
A portent seeming less than threat,
It sank from sight before it set.
A chill no coat, however stout,
Of homespun stuff could quite shut out,
A hard, dull bitterness of cold,
  That checked, mid-vein, the circling race
  Of life-blood in the sharpened face,
The coming of the snow-storm told.

The wind blew east: we heard the roar
Of Ocean on his wintry shore,
And felt the strong pulse throbbing there
Beat with low rhythm our inland air.

1. The text followed here is that of the 1st edition (1866). In a prefatory note to the 1891 edition, Whittier remarked that the "inmates of the family at the Whittier homestead who are referred to in the poem were my father, mother, my brother and two sisters, and my uncle and aunt, both unmarried. In addition, there was the district schoolmaster who boarded with us. The 'not unfeared, half-unwelcome guest' was Harriet Livermore, daughter of Judge Livermore, of New Hampshire, a young woman of fine natural ability, enthusiastic, eccentric." Harriet Livermore (1788–1868) became a well-known preacher, an unusual career for a woman at the time. A millenarian, she warned of a coming Apocalypse.

2. Heinrich Cornelius Agrippa (1486–1525) was a German physician and student of occult science. In his 1891 prefatory note, Whittier said that his family owned a 1651 edition of Agrippa's *Three Books of Occult Philosophy* (1532).

3. The opening of Emerson's "The Snow-Storm" (1841).

Meanwhile we did our nightly chores,—
Brought in the wood from out of doors,
Littered the stalls, and from the mows
Raked down the herd's-grass for the cows;
Heard the horse whinnying for his corn;
And, sharply clashing horn on horn,
Impatient down the stanchion rows
The cattle shake their walnut bows;[4]
While, peering from his early perch
Upon the scaffold's pole of birch,
The cock his crested helmet bent
And down his querulous challenge sent.

Unwarmed by any sunset light
The gray day darkened into night,
A night made hoary with the swarm
And whirl-dance of the blinding storm,
As zigzag wavering to and fro
Crossed and recrossed the wingéd snow:
And ere the early bed-time came
The white drift piled the window-frame,
And through the glass the clothes-line posts
Looked in like tall and sheeted ghosts.

So all night long the storm roared on:
The morning broke without a sun;
In tiny spherule traced with lines
Of Nature's geometric signs,
In starry flake, and pellicle,[5]
All day the hoary meteor fell;
And, when the second morning shone,
We looked upon a world unknown,
On nothing we could call our own.
Around the glistening wonder bent
The blue walls of the firmament,
No cloud above, no earth below,—
A universe of sky and snow!
The old familiar sights of ours
Took marvellous shapes; strange domes and towers
Rose up where sty or corn-crib stood,
Or garden wall, or belt of wood;
A smooth white mound the brush-pile showed,
A fenceless drift what once was road;
The bridle-post an old man sat
With loose-flung coat and high cocked hat;
The well-curb had a Chinese roof;
And even the long sweep,[6] high aloof,

4. Stanchions (here made of walnut and shaped like a bow) are adjustable braces set a few inches from stationary posts; they are pulled aside at the top to let a cow's head pass, then fixed against the neck so the cow cannot back out while being milked or fed.

5. A thin crust of crystals.

6. I.e., a well sweep; a pole attached to a pivot, with a bucket at one end for raising water.

In its slant splendor, seemed to tell
Of Pisa's leaning miracle.

A prompt, decisive man, no breath
Our father wasted: "Boys, a path!"
Well pleased, (for when did farmer boy
Count such a summons less than joy?)
Our buskins[7] on our feet we drew;
  With mittened hands, and caps drawn low,
  To guard our necks and ears from snow,
We cut the solid whiteness through.
And, where the drift was deepest, made
A tunnel walled and overlaid
With dazzling crystal: we had read
Of rare Aladdin's wondrous cave,
And to our own his name we gave,
With many a wish the luck were ours
To test his lamp's supernal powers.
We reached the barn with merry din,
And roused the prisoned brutes within.
The old horse thrust his long head out,
And grave with wonder gazed about;
The cock his lusty greeting said,
And forth his speckled harem led;
The oxen lashed their tails, and hooked,
And mild reproach of hunger looked;
The hornéd patriarch of the sheep,
Like Egypt's Amun[8] roused from sleep,
Shook his sage head with gesture mute,
And emphasized with stamp of foot.

All day the gusty north-wind bore
The loosening drift its breath before;
Low circling round its southern zone,
The sun through dazzling snow-mist shone.
No bell the hush of silence broke,
No neighboring chimney's social smoke
Curled over woods of snow-hung oak.
A solitude made more intense
By dreary voicéd elements,
The shrieking of the mindless wind,
The moaning tree-boughs swaying blind,
And on the glass the unmeaning beat
Of ghostly finger-tips of sleet.
Beyond the circle of our hearth
No welcome sound of toil or mirth
Unbound the spell, and testified
Of human life and thought outside.
We minded that the sharpest ear
The buried brooklet could not hear,

7. High-cut shoes, like a half boot.

8. Egyptian god with a ram's head.

The music of whose liquid lip
Had been to us companionship,
And, in our lonely life, had grown
To have an almost human tone.

As night drew on, and, from the crest
Of wooded knolls that ridged the west,
The sun, a snow-blown traveller, sank
From sight beneath the smothering bank,
We piled, with care, our nightly stack
Of wood against the chimney-back,—
The oaken log, green, huge, and thick,
And on its top the stout back-stick;
The knotty forestick laid apart,
And filled between with curious art
The ragged brush; then, hovering near,
We watched the first red blaze appear,
Heard the sharp crackle, caught the gleam
On whitewashed wall and sagging beam,
Until the old, rude-furnished room
Burst, flower-like, into rosy bloom;
While radiant with a mimic flame
Outside the sparkling drift became,
And through the bare-boughed lilac-tree
Our own warm hearth seemed blazing free.
The crane and pendent trammels[9] showed,
The Turks' heads[1] on the andirons glowed;
While childish fancy, prompt to tell
The meaning of the miracle,
Whispered the old rhyme: *"Under the tree,*
When fire outdoors burns merrily,
There the witches are making tea."
The moon above the eastern wood
Shone at its full; the hill-range stood
Transfigured in the silver flood,
Its blown snows flashing cold and keen,
Dead white, save where some sharp ravine
Took shadow, or the sombre green
Of hemlocks turned to pitchy black
Against the whiteness at their back.
For such a world and such a night
Most fitting that unwarming light,
Which only seemed where'er it fell
To make the coldness visible.

Shut in from all the world without,
We sat the clean-winged hearth about.
Content to let the north-wind roar
In baffled rage at pane and door,

9. Pot hooks hanging from the crane, or movable arm.

1. A favorite ornamentation, turbanlike knots in wrought iron.

While the red logs before us beat
The frost-line back with tropic heat;
And ever, when a louder blast
Shook beam and rafter as it passed,
The merrier up its roaring draught
The great throat of the chimney laughed.
The house-dog on his paws outspread
Laid to the fire his drowsy head,
The cat's dark silhouette on the wall
A couchant[2] tiger's seemed to fall;
And, for the winter fireside meet,
Between the andirons' straddling feet,
The mug of cider simmered slow,
The apples sputtered in a row,
And, close at hand, the basket stood
With nuts from brown October's wood.

What matter how the night behaved?
What matter how the north-wind raved?
Blow high, blow low, not all its snow
Could quench our hearth-fire's ruddy glow.
O Time and Change!—with hair as gray
As was my sire's that winter day,
How strange it seems, with so much gone
Of life and love, to still live on!
Ah, brother! only I and thou
Are left of all that circle now,—
The dear home faces whereupon
That fitful firelight paled and shone.
Henceforward, listen as we will,
The voices of that hearth are still;
Look where we may, the wide earth o'er,
Those lighted faces smile no more.
We tread the paths their feet have worn,
  We sit beneath their orchard-trees,
  We hear, like them, the hum of bees
And rustle of the bladed corn;
We turn the pages that they read,
  Their written words we linger o'er,
But in the sun they cast no shade,
No voice is heard, no sign is made,
  No step is on the conscious floor!
Yet Love will dream, and Faith will trust,
(Since He who knows our need is just,)
That somehow, somewhere, meet we must.
Alas for him who never sees
The stars shine through his cypress-trees!
Who, hopeless, lays his dead away,
Nor looks to see the breaking day
Across the mournful marbles[3] play!

2. Lying on stomach with head raised.

3. I.e., the gravestones.

Who hath not learned, in hours of faith,
  The truth to flesh and sense unknown,
That Life is ever lord of Death,
  And Love can never lose its own!

We sped the time with stories old,
Wrought puzzles out, and riddles told,
Or stammered from our school-book lore
"The Chief of Gambia's golden shore."[4]
How often since, when all the land
Was clay in Slavery's shaping hand,
As if a trumpet called, I've heard
Dame Mercy Warren's rousing word:
"Does not the voice of reason cry,
  Claim the first right which Nature gave,
From the red scourge of bondage fly,
  Nor deign to live a burdened slave!"
Our father rode again his ride
On Memphremagog's[5] wooded side;
Sat down again to moose and samp[6]
In trapper's hut and Indian camp;
Lived o'er the old idyllic ease
Beneath St. François'[7] hemlock-trees;
Again for him the moonlight shone
On Norman cap and bodiced zone;[8]
Again he heard the violin play
Which led the village dance away,
And mingled in its merry whirl
The grandam and the laughing girl.
Or, nearer home, our steps he led
Where Salisbury's[9] level marshes spread
  Mile-wide as flies the laden bee;
Where merry mowers, hale and strong,
Swept, scythe on scythe, their swaths along
  The low green prairies of the sea.
We shared the fishing off Boar's Head,
  And round the rocky Isles of Shoals[1]
  The hake-broil on the drift-wood coals;
The chowder on the sand-beach made,
Dipped by the hungry, steaming hot,
With spoons of clam-shell from the pot.
We heard the tales of witchcraft old,
And dream and sign and marvel told
To sleepy listeners as they lay
Stretched idly on the salted hay,

4. From "The African Chief," a widely reprinted antislavery poem by the Bostonian Sarah Wentworth Morton (1759–1846). In lines 220–23 Whittier quotes the poem but misidentifies the author as the Massachusetts historian Mercy Otis Warren (1728–1814).
5. A lake between Vermont and Quebec.
6. Cornmeal mush.
7. Village north of Lake Memphremagog.
8. Whittier's father is recalling the traditional clothes of women in French-Canadian settlements. (A "zone" is a belt or bodice.)
9. Nearby town in northeastern Massachusetts.
1. Off the New Hampshire coast.

Adrift along the winding shores,
When favoring breezes deigned to blow
The square sail of the gundalow[2]
And idle lay the useless oars.

Our mother, while she turned her wheel
Or run the new-knit stocking-heel,
Told how the Indian hordes came down
At midnight on Cochecho[3] town,
And how her own great-uncle bore
His cruel scalp-mark to fourscore.
Recalling, in her fitting phrase,
So rich and picturesque and free,
(The common unrhymed poetry
Of simple life and country ways,)
The story of her early days,—
She made for us the sunset shine
Aslant the tall columnar pine;
The river at her father's door
Its rippled moanings whispered o'er;
We heard the hawks at twilight play,
The boat-horn on Piscataqua,[4]
The loon's weird laughter far away.
So well she gleaned from earth and sky
That harvest of the ear and eye,
We almost felt the gusty air
That swept her native wood-paths bare,
Heard the far thresher's rhythmic flail,
The flapping of the fisher's sail,
Or saw, in sheltered cove and bay,
The ducks' black squadron anchored lay,
Or heard the wild geese calling loud
Beneath the gray November cloud.

Then, haply, with a look more grave,
And soberer tone, some tale she gave
From painful Sewell's[5] ancient tome,
Beloved in every Quaker home,
Of faith fire-winged by martyrdom,
Or Chalkley's Journal,[6] old and quaint,—
Gentlest of skippers, rare sea-saint!—
Who, when the dreary calms prevailed,
And water-butt and bread-cask failed,
And cruel, hungry eyes pursued
His portly presence mad for food,
With dark hints muttered under breath

2. Flat-bottomed boat.
3. Settlement near Dover, New Hampshire, on the Cochecho River.
4. I.e., foghorn on the Piscataqua River.
5. William Sewell or Sewel (1650–1725), author of a history of the Quakers. The history made painful reading because of the persecution and martyrdom many Quakers had suffered.
6. The *Journal* of the Quaker sea captain and preacher Thomas Chalkley (1675–1741) was published in 1747.

Of casting lots for life or death,
Offered, if Heaven withheld supplies,
To be himself the sacrifice.
Then, suddenly, as if to save
The good man from his living grave,
A ripple on the water grew,
A school of porpoise flashed in view.
"Take, eat," he said, "and be content;[7]
These fishes in my stead are sent
By Him who gave the tangled ram
To spare the child of Abraham."[8]
Our uncle, innocent of books,
But rich in lore of fields and brooks,
The ancient teachers never dumb
Of Nature's unhoused lyceum,[9]
In moons and tides and weather wise,
He read the clouds as prophecies,
And foul or fair could well divine,
By many an occult hint and sign,
Holding the cunning-warded[1] keys
To all the woodcraft mysteries;
Himself to Nature's heart so near
That all her voices in his ear
Of beast or bird had meanings clear,
Like Apollonius of old,
Who knew the tales the sparrows told,
Or Hermes,[2] who interpreted
What the sage cranes of Nilus[3] said;
A simple, guileless, childlike man,
Content to live where life began;
Strong only on his native grounds,
The little world of sights and sounds
Whose girdle was the parish bounds,
Whereof his fondly partial pride
The common features magnified,
As Surrey hills to mountains grew
In White of Selborne's[4] loving view,—
He told how teal and loon he shot,
And how the eagle's eggs he got,
The feats on pond and river done,
The prodigies of rod and gun;
Till, warming with the tales he told,
Forgotten was the outside cold,
The bitter wind unheeded blew,
From ripening corn the pigeons flew,

7. Matthew 26.26: "Take, eat: this is my body" (Jesus' words at Passover).
8. See Genesis 22.13.
9. Lecture hall.
1. Carefully guarded.
2. Hermes Trismegistus (3rd century C.E.), legendary author of Egyptian books of magic. Apollonius (1st century C.E.), Greek mystic.
3. Nile River.
4. Gilbert White (1720–1793), English naturalist who lived in the county of Surrey, in southern England, and wrote *The Natural History and Antiquities of Selborne* (1789).

The partridge drummed i' the wood, the mink
Went fishing down the river-brink.
In fields with bean or clover gay,
The woodchuck, like a hermit gray,
Peered from the doorway of his cell;
The muskrat plied the mason's trade,
And tier by tier his mud-walls laid;
And from the shagbark overhead
The grizzled squirrel dropped his shell.

Next, the dear aunt, whose smile of cheer
And voice in dreams I see and hear,—
The sweetest woman ever Fate
Perverse denied a household mate,
Who, lonely, homeless, not the less
Found peace in love's unselfishness,
And welcome wheresoe'er she went,
A calm and gracious element,
Whose presence seemed the sweet income
And womanly atmosphere of home,—
Called up her girlhood memories,
The huskings and the apple-bees,
The sleigh-rides and the summer sails,
Weaving through all the poor details
And homespun warp of circumstance
A golden woof-thread of romance.
For well she kept her genial mood
And simple faith of maidenhood;
Before her still a cloud-land lay,
The mirage loomed across her way;
The morning dew, that dries so soon
With others, glistened at her noon;
Through years of toil and soil and care
From glossy tress to thin gray hair,
All unprofaned she held apart
The virgin fancies of the heart.
Be shame to him of woman born
Who hath for such but thought of scorn.
There, too, our elder sister plied
Her evening task the stand beside;
A full, rich nature, free to trust,
Truthful and almost sternly just,
Impulsive, earnest, prompt to act,
And make her generous thought a fact,
Keeping with many a light disguise
The secret of self-sacrifice.
O heart sore-tried! thou hast the best
That Heaven itself could give thee,—rest,
Rest from all bitter thoughts and things!
  How many a poor one's blessing went
  With thee beneath the low green tent
Whose curtain never outward swings!

As one who held herself a part
Of all she saw, and let her heart
  Against the household bosom lean,
Upon the motley-braided mat
Our youngest and our dearest sat,
Lifting her large, sweet, asking eyes,
  Now bathed within the fadeless green
And holy peace of Paradise.
O, looking from some heavenly hill,
  Or from the shade of saintly palms,
  Or silver reach of river calms,
Do those large eyes behold me still?
With me one little year ago:—
The chill weight of the winter snow
  For months upon her grave has lain;
And now, when summer south-winds blow
  And brier and harebell bloom again,
I tread the pleasant paths we trod,
I see the violet-sprinkled sod
Whereon she leaned, too frail and weak
The hillside flowers she loved to seek,
Yet following me where'er I went
With dark eyes full of love's content.
The birds are glad; the brier-rose fills
The air with sweetness; all the hills
Stretch green to June's unclouded sky;
But still I wait with ear and eye
For something gone which should be nigh,
A loss in all familiar things,
In flower that blooms, and bird that sings.
And yet, dear heart! remembering thee,
  Am I not richer than of old?
Safe in thy immortality,
  What change can reach the wealth I hold?
  What chance can mar the pearl and gold
Thy love hath left in trust with me?
And while in life's late afternoon,
  Where cool and long the shadows grow,
I walk to meet the night that soon
  Shall shape and shadow overflow,
I cannot feel that thou art far,
Since near at need the angels are;
And when the sunset gates unbar,
  Shall I not see thee waiting stand,
And, white against the evening star,
  The welcome of thy beckoning hand?

Brisk wielder of the birch and rule,
The master of the district school
Held at the fire his favored place,
Its warm glow lit a laughing face
Fresh-hued and fair, where scarce appeared

The uncertain prophecy of beard.
He played the old and simple games
Our modern boyhood scarcely names,
Sang songs, and told us what befalls
In classic Dartmouth's college halls.
Born the wild Northern hills among,
From whence his yeoman father wrung
By patient toil subsistence scant,
Not competence and yet not want,
He early gained the power to pay
His cheerful, self-reliant way;
Could doff at ease his scholar's gown
To peddle wares from town to town;
Or through the long vacation's reach
In lonely lowland districts teach,
Where all the droll experience found
At stranger hearths in boarding round,
The moonlit skater's keen delight,
The sleigh-drive through the frosty night,
The rustic party, with its rough
Accompaniment of blind-man's-buff,
And whirling plate,[5] and forfeits paid,
His winter task a pastime made.
Happy the snow-locked homes wherein
He tuned his merry violin,
Or played the athlete in the barn,
Or held the good dame's winding yarn,
Or mirth-provoking versions told
Of classic legends rare and old,
Wherein the scenes of Greece and Rome
Had all the commonplace of home,
And little seemed at best the odds
'Twixt Yankee pedlers and old gods;
Where Pindus-born Araxes[6] took
The guise of any grist-mill brook,
And dread Olympus[7] at his will
Became a huckleberry hill.

A careless boy that night he seemed;
  But at his desk he had the look
And air of one who wisely schemed,
  And hostage from the future took
  In trainéd thought and lore of book.
Large-brained, clear-eyed,—of such as he
Shall Freedom's young apostles be,
Who, following in War's bloody trail,
Shall every lingering wrong assail;
All chains from limb and spirit strike,

5. Children's game of keeping a plate spinning on edge for as long as possible. "Blind-man's-buff": variant name for blind man's bluff, another children's game.

6. A Greek river, "born" in the Pindus Mountains.

7. Mountain that was the home of the Gods in Greek mythology.

Uplift the black and white alike;
Scatter before their swift advance
The darkness and the ignorance,
The pride, the lust, the squalid sloth,
Which nurtured Treason's monstrous growth,
Made murder pastime, and the hell
Of prison-torture possible;
The cruel lie of caste refute,
Old forms recast, and substitute
For Slavery's lash the freeman's will,
For blind routine, wise-handed skill;
A school-house plant on every hill,
Stretching in radiate nerve-lines thence
The quick wires of intelligence;[8]
Till North and South together brought
Shall own the same electric thought,
In peace a common flag salute,
And, side by side in labor's free
And unresentful rivalry,
Harvest the fields wherein they fought.

Another guest[9] that winter night
Flashed back from lustrous eyes the light.
Unmarked by time, and yet not young,
The honeyed music of her tongue
And words of meekness scarcely told
A nature passionate and bold,
Strong, self-concentred, spurning guide,
Its milder features dwarfed beside
Her unbent will's majestic pride.
She sat among us, at the best,
A not unfeared, half-welcome guest,
Rebuking with her cultured phrase
Our homeliness of words and ways.
A certain pard-like,[1] treacherous grace
   Swayed the lithe limbs and drooped the lash,
   Lent the white teeth their dazzling flash;
   And under low brows, black with night,
   Rayed out at times a dangerous light;
The sharp heat-lightnings of her face
Presaging ill to him whom Fate
Condemned to share her love or hate.
A woman tropical, intense
In thought and act, in soul and sense,
She blended in a like degree
The vixen and the devotee,
Revealing with each freak or feint
   The temper of Petruchio's Kate,[2]

8. Information, communication (the imagery is from the telegraph, then still a recent development).
9. The boarder Harriet Livermore.
1. Leopardlike.
2. The heroine of Shakespeare's *Taming of the Shrew*.

The raptures of Siena's saint.[3]
Her tapering hand and rounded wrist
Had facile power to form a fist;
The warm, dark languish of her eyes
Was never safe from wrath's surprise.
Brows saintly calm and lips devout
Knew every change of scowl and pout;
And the sweet voice had notes more high
And shrill for social battle-cry.

Since then what old cathedral town
Has missed her pilgrim staff and gown,
What convent-gate has held its lock
Against the challenge of her knock!
Through Smyrna's[4] plague-husked thoroughfares,
Up sea-set Malta's rocky stairs,
Gray olive slopes of hills that hem
Thy tombs and shrines, Jerusalem,
Or startling on her desert throne
The crazy Queen of Lebanon[5]
With claims fantastic as her own,
Her tireless feet have held their way;
And still, unrestful, bowed, and gray,
She watches under Eastern skies,
  With hope each day renewed and fresh,
  The Lord's quick coming in the flesh,
Whereof she dreams and prophesies!

Where'er her troubled path may be,
  The Lord's sweet pity with her go!
The outward wayward life we see,
  The hidden springs we may not know.
Nor is it given us to discern
  What threads the fatal sisters[6] spun,
  Through what ancestral years has run
The sorrow with the woman born,
What forged her cruel chain of moods,
What set her feet in solitudes,
  And held the love within her mute,
What mingled madness in the blood,
  A life-long discord and annoy,
  Water of tears with oil of joy,
And hid within the folded bud
  Perversities of flower and fruit.
It is not ours to separate
The tangled skein of will and fate,

3. St. Catharine (1347–1380) of Siena, in Tuscany, Italy.
4. Now Izmir in Turkey.
5. Lady Hester Stanhope (1776–1839), an Englishwoman who in 1810 settled in Lebanon, where she attempted to rule like a dictator over a small area. Whittier remarked in his 1891 preface to "Snow-Bound" that Harriet Livermore lived with Stanhope for a while before they quarreled over interpretations of Christ's Second Coming.
6. In Greek mythology the goddesses of destiny, the Fates.

To show what metes and bounds should stand
Upon the soul's debatable land,
And between choice and Providence
Divide the circle of events;
But He who knows our frame is just,[7]
  Merciful, and compassionate,
And full of sweet assurances
And hope for all the language is,
That He remembereth we are dust!

At last the great logs, crumbling low,
Sent out a dull and duller glow,
The bull's-eye watch[8] that hung in view,
Ticking its weary circuit through,
Pointed with mutely-warning sign
Its black hand to the hour of nine.
That sign the pleasant circle broke:
My uncle ceased his pipe to smoke,
Knocked from its bowl the refuse gray
And laid it tenderly away,
Then roused himself to safely cover
The dull red brands with ashes over.
And while, with care, our mother laid
The work aside, her steps she stayed
One moment, seeking to express
Her grateful sense of happiness
For food and shelter, warmth and health,
And love's contentment more than wealth,
With simple wishes (not the weak,
Vain prayers which no fulfilment seek,
But such as warm the generous heart,
O'er-prompt to do with Heaven its part)
That none might lack, that bitter night,
For bread and clothing, warmth and light.

Within our beds awhile we heard
The wind that round the gables roared,
With now and then a ruder shock,
Which made our very bedsteads rock.
We heard the loosened clapboards tost,
The board-nails snapping in the frost;
And on us, through the unplastered wall,
Felt the light sifted snow-flakes fall.
But sleep stole on, as sleep will do
When hearts are light and life is new;
Faint and more faint the murmurs grew,
Till in the summer-land of dreams
They softened to the sound of streams,

7. Psalm 103.14: "For he knoweth our frame; he remembereth that we are dust."

8. Watch with a thick glass face.

Low stir of leaves, and dip of oars,
And lapsing waves on quiet shores.

Next morn we wakened with the shout
Of merry voices high and clear;
And saw the teamsters[9] drawing near
To break the drifted highways out.
Down the long hillside treading slow
We saw the half-buried oxen go,
Shaking the snow from heads uptost,
Their straining nostrils white with frost.
Before our door the straggling train
Drew up, an added team to gain.
The elders threshed their hands a-cold,
  Passed, with the cider-mug, their jokes
  From lip to lip; the younger folks
Down the loose snow-banks, wrestling, rolled,
Then toiled again the cavalcade
  O'er windy hill, through clogged ravine,
  And woodland paths that wound between
Low drooping pine-boughs winter-weighed.
From every barn a team afoot,
At every house a new recruit,
Where, drawn by Nature's subtlest law,
Haply the watchful young men saw
Sweet doorway pictures of the curls
And curious eyes of merry girls,
Lifting their hands in mock defence
Against the snow-ball's compliments,
And reading in each missive tost
The charm with Eden never lost.
We heard once more the sleigh-bells' sound;
  And, following where the teamsters led,
The wise old Doctor went his round,
Just pausing at our door to say,
In the brief autocratic way
Of one who, prompt at Duty's call,
Was free to urge her claim on all,
  That some poor neighbor sick abed
At night our mother's aid would need.
For, one in generous thought and deed,
  What mattered in the sufferer's sight
  The Quaker matron's inward light,
The Doctor's mail[1] of Calvin's creed?
All hearts confess the saints elect
  Who, twain in faith, in love agree,
And melt not in an acid sect
  The Christian pearl of charity!

9. Those driving teams of oxen to plow snow.
1. Armor, with the suggestion that the French Protestant reformer John Calvin's (1509–1564) doctrines of predestination and Original Sin are less humane than the "whole armor of God" which Paul enjoins Christians to put on in Ephesians 6.11–17.

So days went on: a week had passed
Since the great world was heard from last.
The Almanac we studied o'er,
Read and reread our little store,
Of books and pamphlets, scarce a score;
One harmless novel, mostly hid
From younger eyes, a book forbid,
And poetry, (or good or bad,
A single book was all we had,)
Where Ellwood's meek, drab-skirted Muse,
  A stranger to the heathen Nine,[2]
  Sang, with a somewhat nasal whine,
The wars of David and the Jews.
At last the floundering carrier bore
The village paper to our door.
Lo! broadening outward as we read,
To warmer zones the horizon spread;
In panoramic length unrolled
We saw the marvels that it told.
Before us passed the painted Creeks,[3]
  And daft McGregor on his raids
  In dim Floridian everglades.[4]
And up Taygetos winding slow
Rode Ypsilanti's Mainote Greeks,
A Turk's head at each saddle-bow![5]
Welcome to us its week-old news,
Its corner for the rustic Muse,
  Its monthly gauge of snow and rain,
Its record, mingling in a breath
The wedding knell and dirge of death;
Jest, anecdote, and love-lorn tale,
The latest culprit sent to jail;
Its hue and cry of stolen and lost,
Its vendue[6] sales and goods at cost,
  And traffic calling loud for gain.
We felt the stir of hall and street,
The pulse of life that round us beat;
The chill embargo of the snow
Was melted in the genial glow;
Wide swung again our ice-locked door,
And all the world was ours once more!

2. Thomas Ellwood (1639–1714), English Quaker, wrote the *Davideis* (1712). Whittier has an essay on him in *Old Portraits and Modern Sketches* (1850). Here, Ellwood's source of inspiration wears "drab" Quaker clothes made of brownish yellow homespun, and knows nothing of the nine Greek goddesses who traditionally inspire artists and scientists.

3. Tribe of American Indians from Alabama who were subdued by Andrew Jackson in the Creek War (1813–14) and forced to resettle in present-day Oklahoma.

4. The Scottish adventurer Gregor McGregor (1786–1845) fought alongside Simón Bolívar (1783–1830) for the liberation of Venezuela from Spain, then in 1817 took possession of the Spanish-owned Amelia Island, off the Florida coast.

5. The Greek Revolutionary patriot Alexander Ypsilanti (1792–1828) defeated the Turks at Mount Taygetos in 1820; his saddle ornaments are heads of Turkish soldiers.

6. Auction.

Clasp, Angel of the backward look
  And folded wings of ashen gray
  And voice of echoes far away,
The brazen covers of thy book;
The weird palimpsest[7] old and vast,
Wherein thou hid'st the spectral past;
Where, closely mingling, pale and glow
The characters of joy and woe;
The monographs of outlived years,
Or smile-illumed or dim with tears,
  Green hills of life that slope to death,
And haunts of home, whose vistaed trees
Shade off to mournful cypresses
  With the white amaranths[8] underneath.
Even while I look, I can but heed
  The restless sands' incessant fall,
Importunate hours that hours succeed,
Each clamorous with its own sharp need,
  And duty keeping pace with all.
Shut down and clasp the heavy lids;
I hear again the voice that bids
The dreamer leave his dream midway
For larger hopes and graver fears:
Life greatens in these later years,
The century's aloe[9] flowers to-day!

Yet, haply, in some lull of life,
Some Truce of God which breaks its strife,
The worldling's eyes shall gather dew,
  Dreaming in throngful city ways
Of winter joys his boyhood knew;
And dear and early friends—the few
Who yet remain—shall pause to view
  These Flemish pictures[1] of old days;
Sit with me by the homestead hearth,
And stretch the hands of memory forth
  To warm them at the wood-fire's blaze!
And thanks untraced to lips unknown
Shall greet me like the odors blown
From unseen meadows newly mown,
Or lilies floating in some pond,
Wood-fringed, the wayside gaze beyond;
The traveller owns the grateful sense
Of sweetness near, he knows not whence,
And, pausing, takes with forehead bare
The benediction of the air.

1866

7. Parchment with earlier writing still visible beneath later writing.
8. Flowers associated with immortality.
9. The century plant, fabled to bloom only once every hundred years.
1. Dutch (Flemish) painters from the 17th century were known for their realistic domestic scenes.

EDGAR ALLAN POE
1809–1849

The facts of Poe's life, the most melodramatic of any of the major American writers of his generation, have been hard to determine; lurid legends about him circulated even before he died, some spread by Poe himself. Two days after Poe's death his supposed friend Rufus Griswold, a prominent anthologizer of American literature to whom Poe had entrusted his literary papers, began a campaign of character assassination, writing a vicious obituary and rewriting Poe's correspondence so as to alienate the public as well as his friends. Griswold's false claims and forgeries, unexposed for many years, significantly shaped Poe's reputation for decades.

Yet biographers now possess much reliable information about Poe's life. His mother, Elizabeth Arnold, was a prominent actress, touring the eastern seaboard in a profession that was then considered disreputable. In 1806, as a teenage widow, she married David Poe Jr., another actor. Edgar, the couple's second of three children, was born in Boston on January 19, 1809; a year later, David Poe deserted the family. In December 1811, Elizabeth Poe died at twenty-four while performing in Richmond, Virginia; the evidence suggests that her husband died soon afterward at the age of twenty-seven.

The disruptions of Poe's first two years were followed by years of security after John Allan, a young Richmond tobacco merchant, and his wife, Frances, took him in; his siblings (William Henry, born 1807, and Rosalie, born 1810) were sent to different foster parents. The Allans, who were childless, renamed the boy Edgar Allan and raised him as their son, but they never adopted him legally. Poe accompanied the family to England in 1815, where he attended good schools until the collapse of the London tobacco market forced the Allans back to Richmond in 1820. In 1824 Allan's firm failed and hostilities developed between Poe and his foster father. Allan lost interest in supporting Poe financially; even after inheriting all the property of a wealthy bachelor uncle, including several slave plantations, he provided only minimal funds to Poe for studying at the University of Virginia in 1826. Poe was a good student and wrote poetry on the side, but he ran into debt and began to drink. He gambled to pay his debts, instead losing as much as $2,000 (around $30,000 in current value). Allan refused to honor the debt, and Poe had to leave the

Edgar Allan Poe. Daguerreotype, 1848.

university before his first year was completed. In March 1827, after another quarrel between the two, Allan ordered Poe out of the house.

The eighteen-year-old outcast Poe went first to Baltimore, reuniting briefly with his brother, Henry, who would die of alcoholism and consumption in 1831; then he moved north to his birthplace, where he paid for the printing of *Tamerlane and Other Poems*, "By a Bostonian," in 1827. Even before its publication, "Edgar A. Perry" (he had changed his name to avoid creditors) had joined the army. Released from the army with the rank of sergeant major, Poe now sought Allan's influence to help him get into the military academy at West Point. While waiting for the appointment, Poe condensed *Tamerlane*, revised other poems, and added new ones to make up a second volume, *Al Aaraaf, Tamerlane, and Minor Poems*, published in Baltimore in December 1829. In a short but favorable review, the influential New England critic John Neal declared that Poe could become "*foremost* in the rank of *real* poets."

Admitted to West Point in June 1830, Poe quickly became known for his conviviality and skills in mathematics and French. Despite renewed conflict with Allan, he believed himself the heir to Allan's great fortune. But his expectations were dashed when Allan, less than two years after the death of Frances Allan, married the thirty-year-old Louisa Patterson in October 1830 and had a son in 1831 (in fact when Allan died in 1834, Poe was not mentioned in the will). The disillusioned Poe began to miss classes and roll calls and, as he anticipated, was expelled from school. Supportive friends among the cadets collected funds to publish his *Poems*, which appeared in May 1831. In this third book of his poetry Poe revised some earlier poems and for the first time included versions of both "To Helen" and "Israfel."

Poe's mature career—from his twenty-first year to his death in his fortieth year—was spent in four literary centers: Baltimore, Richmond, Philadelphia, and New York. The Baltimore years—mid-1831 to late 1835—were marked by hard work and comparative sobriety. Poe lived in poverty among his once-prosperous relatives, including his aunt Maria Poe Clemm and her daughter, Virginia. Poe's first story, "Metzengerstein," was published anonymously in the *Philadelphia Saturday Courier*, in January 1832; other stories appeared in the same paper throughout the year. Over the next two years, Poe placed stories and poems in the *Baltimore Saturday Visiter*. In January 1834 he made a significant breakthrough, publishing his tale "The Visionary" in *Godey's Lady's Book*, a popular Philadelphia monthly edited by Sarah J. Hale, for many years the nation's most prominent woman of letters. The writer and editor John P. Kennedy, who had read Poe's submissions to the *Saturday Visiter*, introduced the increasingly well-known Poe to Thomas W. White, publisher of the new Richmond-based *Southern Literary Messenger*. In August 1835, Poe became White's editorial assistant, moving back to Richmond where, for the next seventeen months, he played a significant role in the operations of the journal. Not only his stories and poems but also his often slashing reviews appeared in the *Messenger*, gaining him a reputation as the "Tomahawk Man," as White called him. Relations between Poe and White deteriorated when Poe resumed drinking. Returning to Baltimore briefly, Poe secretly married Virginia Clemm, and later publicly wed the thirteen-year-old Virginia in a May 1836 ceremony in Richmond. Thereafter, wherever he went, he lived with Virginia and her mother, whose loyalty to him was probably the only stable element in his tempestuous life.

Hoping to make the *Southern Literary Messenger* a nationally esteemed publication, Poe had to negotiate between the proslavery views of white Virginians and the growing opposition to such views in the free North. As a result, though the journal did occasionally print proslavery pieces (including an anonymous defense of slavery in a review of April 1836 that was long attributed to Poe but was almost certainly not written by him), it usually adopted a middle-of-the-road position linking slavery to states' rights rather than God's will. In Poe's writings overall, slavery and race remain highly problematical. Like many white writers of the time, Poe sometimes resorted to racial stereotypes, and he sometimes conveyed his fears of the possibilities of black violence. For the most part, however, the perverse killers of his tales are white men. Critics continue to debate Poe's views on slavery and race. Although he spent years in the South and even held hopes for inheriting the property of a slaveholder, the fact is that his relative silence on the political debate on slavery makes him notably different from most southern intellectuals of the time—William Gilmore Simms, Nathaniel Beverly Tucker, and many others—who went on record with their proslavery views.

White fired Poe early in 1837, citing Poe's drinking, his demands for a higher salary, and his regular clashes with White about the day-to-day operations of the journal. Poe then moved, with his aunt (now his mother-in-law as well) and his wife, to New York City, where Mrs. Clemm ran a boarding house to support them all. In Richmond he had written a short novel, *The Narrative of Arthur Gordon Pym*, of which White had run two installments in the *Messenger* early in 1837. *Harper's* published it in July 1838, but it earned him little money. In 1838 Poe moved to Philadelphia, where, despite extreme poverty, he continued writing. "Ligeia" appeared in the *Baltimore American Museum* in September 1838, where other stories and poems followed. In May 1839 he got his first steady job in more than two years, as co-editor of *Burton's Gentleman's Magazine*. There, in a job that paid him a small salary, he published book reviews and stories, including "The Fall of the House of Usher" and "William Wilson." Late in 1839, the Philadelphia firm of Lea and Blanchard published *Tales of the Grotesque and Arabesque*, a collection of the twenty-five stories Poe had written to that date. The mostly good reviews did not lead to good sales; the country was in the midst of a depression.

By the late 1830s, Poe was at the height of his powers as a writer of tales, though his personal and professional life continued to be unstable. William Burton fired him for drinking in May 1840 but recommended him to George Graham, who had bought out *Burton's* and created a new magazine called *Graham's*. Throughout 1841, Poe was with *Graham's* as a co-editor, courting subscribers by writing articles on cryptography—the art and science of code breaking. He also published "The Murders in the Rue Morgue," the first of what he termed his "tales of ratiocination" featuring detective August Dupin, a tale that many critics regard as the earliest example of detective fiction. In January 1842, Virginia Poe, not yet twenty, began hemorrhaging from her lungs while singing; she lived as a tubercular invalid only five more years. Poe continued reviewing for *Graham's*, but he resigned from the magazine in May 1842 after a dispute with Graham. His hope of his own journal—to be called *The Stylus*—was never realized.

In April 1844, Poe again moved his family to New York City, working as an editor on the *New York Evening Mirror*. Poe's most successful year was 1845. The February issue of *Graham's* contained an essay by James Russell Lowell declaring Poe a man of "*genius*"; and Poe's most popular work, "The Raven," appeared in the February *American Review* after advance publication in the *New York Evening Mirror*. One new literary acquaintance, the influential editor Evert A. Duyckinck, selected a dozen of Poe's stories for a collection brought out by Wiley & Putnam in June and arranged for the same firm to publish *The Raven and Other Poems* in November. Poe lectured on the poets of America and became a principal reviewer for a new weekly, the *Broadway Journal*, which also reprinted most of Poe's stories and poems. Still hoping to have his own magazine, in which he could be free of editorial interference, he purchased the *Broadway Journal* only to see it fail in January 1846.

While the tempo of Poe's life speeded up, with ever more literary feuds and drinking bouts, he maintained an undiminished commitment to his writing. During 1847, the year that Virginia died from tuberculosis, Poe was seriously ill himself. In 1848 he published *Eureka*, a philosophical prose work that presented God as the force behind all matter, and all matter as seeking a return to oneness. He also published "Ulalume," a poem inspired by his grief at the loss of Virginia. In 1848 he fell in love with the poet Sarah Helen Whitman, who refused his initial proposal, then agreed to a December

1848 marriage, and finally broke off the relationship. In his final year, during a two-month stay in Richmond, Poe joined a temperance society and got engaged to Elmira Royster Shelton, a widow whom he had known in his childhood. On a subsequent trip to Baltimore, Poe was found senseless near a polling place on Election Day (October 3). Taken to a hospital, he died on October 7, 1849, "of congestion of the brain." His poem "Annabel Lee" was published posthumously later that year.

Much of Poe's collected writings consists of his criticism, representing his abiding ambition to become a powerful critic and influence the course of American literary history. Just as he had modeled his poems and first tales on British examples (or British imitations of the German), he took his critical concepts from treatises on aesthetics by late-eighteenth-century Scottish Common Sense philosophers, who emphasized the aesthetic importance of moral sympathy. Later, he modified his approach with borrowings from A.W. Schlegel, Coleridge, and other Romantics, who emphasized the importance of intuitively conceived notions of the beautiful. But despite modulations in his theories, Poe's critical principles were consistent: he thought poetry should appeal only to the sense of beauty; informational poetry, poetry of ideas, or any sort of didactic poetry was, in his view, illegitimate. Holding that true poetic emotion was a vague sensory state inspired by the work of art itself, he set himself against realistic details in poetry, although the prose tale, with truth as one object, could profit from the discreet use of specifics. He believed that poems and tales should be short enough to be read in one sitting; otherwise the unity of effect would be dissipated. In his most famous artistic treatise, "The Philosophy of Composition," Poe makes clear that, unlike Emerson, he remains skeptical of the possibilities of transcendental vision untethered by the material realities of body and aesthetic form. In crucial ways, then, Poe split with Emerson and other transcendentalists in arguing that the vision that comes to the artist and reader is inextricably linked to the formal qualities of the work of art itself.

Poe's reputation today rests not on his criticism, however, but on his poetry—"The Raven," "Ulalume," and "To Helen" made him internationally famous even in his lifetime—and his tales. He has had immense influence on poets and prose writers both in the United States and abroad; among those who have followed his lead are such modernists as T.S. Eliot and William Faulkner. The tales have proven hard to classify—are they burlesque exaggerations of popular forms of fiction, or serious attempts to contribute to or alter those forms, or both of these at the same time? Poe's own comments deliberately obscured his intentions. Responding to a query from his literary admirer John P. Kennedy in 1836, who labeled his work as "seriotragicomic," he said that most of his tales "were *intended* for half banter, half satire—although I might not have fully acknowledged this to be their aim even to myself." At the core of this and other of Poe's comments on his fiction is the pragmatism of a professional writer who recognized the advent of a mass market and wanted to succeed in it. He worked hard at structuring his tales of aristocratic madmen, self-tormented murderers, neurasthenic necrophiliacs, and other deviant types so as to produce, as he wrote in "The Philosophy of Composition," the greatest possible *effect* on his readers. Poe, more than most, understood his audience—its distractedness, its fascination with the new and short-lived, its anomie and confusion—and sought ways to gain its attention for stories that, aside from their shock value, regularly addressed compelling philosophical, cultural, and pyschological issues: the place of irrationality, violence, and repression in human consciousness and social institutions; the alienation and dislocations attending democratic mass culture and the modernizing forces of the time; the tug and pull of the material and corporeal; the absolutely terrifying dimensions of one's own mind. Seriously as he took the writing of his tales, Poe always put his highest stock in poetry, which he called a "passion" and not merely a "purpose." As he remarked in "The Philosophy of Composition," poetry, even more than fiction, provides the possibility of taking the reader out of body, in effect out of time, through "that intense and pure elevation of *soul*" which can come with "the contemplation of the beautiful." In a life that was often a tangled mess, the pursuit of the beautiful in works of art motivated Poe's writing to the very end.

Sonnet—To Science[1]

SCIENCE! meet[2] daughter of old Time thou art
Who alterest all things with thy peering eyes!
Why prey'st thou thus upon the poet's heart,
Vulture! whose wings are dull realities!
How should he love thee—or how deem thee wise
Who woulds't not leave him, in his wandering,
To seek for treasure in the jewell'd skies
Albeit, he soar with an undaunted wing?
Hast thou not dragg'd Diana[3] from her car,
And driv'n the Hamadryad[4] from the wood
To seek a shelter in some happier star?
The gentle Naiad[5] from her fountain-flood?
The elfin from the green grass? and from me
The summer dream beneath the shrubbery?

1829, 1845

To Helen[1]

Helen, thy beauty is to me
Like those Nicéan barks[2] of yore,
That gently, o'er a perfumed sea,
The weary, way-worn wanderer bore
To his own native shore.

On desperate seas long wont to roam,
Thy hyacinth[3] hair, thy classic face,
Thy Naiad[4] airs have brought me home
To the glory that was Greece,
And the grandeur that was Rome.

Lo! in yon brilliant window-niche
How statue-like I see thee stand,
The agate lamp within thy hand!

1. The text is from *The Raven and Other Poems* (1845). The sonnet was initially printed as an untitled prefatory poem to Poe's 1829 volume *Al Aaraaf*: Poe added the title to an 1843 reprinting.
2. True, fitting.
3. Roman goddess of the moon (imaged as a chariot or car that she drives through the sky).
4. Wood nymph in Greek and Roman mythology, often thought of as living within a tree and perishing with it.
5. Nymph living in brooks or fountains.

1. The text is that of 1845, with two errors of indentation corrected. The poem was first published in 1831, where, among other differences, lines 9 and 10 read: "To the beauty of fair Greece, / And the grandeur of old Rome." The title invokes Helen of Troy, according to Greek myth the beautiful daughter of Zeus and the cause of the Trojan War.
2. Victorious ships (from the Greek *nike*).
3. Luxurious, curling.
4. Nymphlike, fairylike.

Ah, Psyche,[5] from the regions which
Are Holy-Land!

1831, 1845

Israfel[1]

In Heaven a spirit doth dwell
"Whose heart-strings are a lute;"
None sing so wildly well
As the angel Israfel,
And the giddy stars (so legends tell)
Ceasing their hymns, attend the spell
Of his voice, all mute.

Tottering above
In her highest noon,
The enamoured moon
Blushes with love,
While, to listen, the red levin[2]
(With the rapid Pleiads,[3] even,
Which were seven,)
Pauses in Heaven.

And they say (the starry choir
And the other listening things)
That Israfeli's fire
Is owing to that lyre
By which he sits and sings—
The trembling living wire
Of those unusual strings.

But the skies that angel trod,
Where deep thoughts are a duty—
Where Love's a grown-up God—
Where the Houri[4] glances are
Imbued with all the beauty
Which we worship in a star.

Therefore, thou art not wrong,
Israfeli, who despises
An unimpassioned song;
To thee the laurels belong,
Best bard, because the wisest!
Merrily live, and long!

5. Goddess of the soul.

1. "And the angel Israfel, whose heartstrings are a lute, and who has the sweetest voice of all God's creatures.—KORAN" [Poe's note]. A version of this poem appeared in the 1831 volume; the present text is from 1845.

2. Lightning.

3. In Greek mythology the seven daughters of Atlas became stars, making up a group called the Pleiades in the constellation Taurus.

4. Beautiful maiden waiting in paradise for the devout Muslim.

The ecstasies above
  With thy burning measures suit—
Thy grief, thy joy, thy hate, thy love,
  With the fervour of thy lute—
  Well may the stars be mute!

Yes, Heaven is thine; but this
  Is a world of sweets and sours;
  Our flowers are merely—flowers,
And the shadow of thy perfect bliss
  Is the sunshine of ours.

If I could dwell
Where Israfel
  Hath dwelt, and he where I,
He might not sing so wildly well
  A mortal melody,
While a bolder note than this might swell
  From my lyre within the sky.

1831, 1845

The City in the Sea[1]

Lo! Death has reared himself a throne
In a strange city lying alone
Far down within the dim West,
Where the good and the bad and the worst and the best
Have gone to their eternal rest.
There shrines and palaces and towers
(Time-eaten towers that tremble not!)
Resemble nothing that is ours.
Around, by lifting winds forgot,
Resignedly beneath the sky
The melancholy waters lie.

No rays from the holy heaven come down
On the long night-time of that town;
But light from out the lurid sea
Streams up the turrets silently—
Gleams up the pinnacles far and free—
Up domes—up spires—up kingly halls—
Up fanes—up Babylon-like walls[2]—
Up shadowy long-forgotten bowers
Of sculptured ivy and stone flowers—
Up many and many a marvellous shrine

1. The text is that of 1845; it was first published in 1831 as "The Doomed City."
2. According to the Old Testament, these walls were doomed to destruction along with the city of Babylon. "Fanes": temples.

Whose wreathéd friezes intertwine
The viol, the violet, and the vine.
Resignedly beneath the sky
The melancholy waters lie.
So blend the turrets and shadows there
That all seem pendulous in air,
While from a proud tower in the town
Death looks gigantically down.

There open fanes and gaping graves
Yawn level with the luminous waves;
But not the riches there that lie
In each idol's diamond eye—
Not the gaily-jewelled dead
Tempt the waters from their bed;
For no ripples curl, alas!
Along that wilderness of glass—
No swellings tell that winds may be
Upon some far-off happier sea—
No heavings hint that winds have been
On seas less hideously serene.

But lo, a stir is in the air!
The wave—there is a movement there!
As if the towers had thrust aside,
In slightly sinking, the dull tide—
As if their tops had feebly given
A void within the filmy Heaven.
The waves have now a redder glow—
The hours are breathing faint and low—
And when, amid no earthly moans,
Down, down that town shall settle hence,
Hell, rising from a thousand thrones,
Shall do it reverence.

1831, 1845

Alone[1]

From childhood's hour I have not been
As others were—I have not seen
As others saw—I could not bring
My passions from a common spring—
From the same source I have not taken
My sorrow—I could not awaken
My heart to joy at the same tone—
And all I lov'd—*I* lov'd alone—

1. Probably written in the early 1830s, "Alone" was first printed in *Scribner's Monthly Magazine* 12 (September 1875).

Then—in my childhood—in the dawn
Of a most stormy life—was drawn
From ev'ry depth of good and ill
The mystery which binds me still—
From the torrent, or the fountain—
From the red cliff of the mountain—
From the sun that round me roll'd
In its autumn tint of gold—
From the lightning in the sky
As it pass'd me flying by—
From the thunder, and the storm—
And the cloud that took the form
(When the rest of Heaven was blue)
Of a demon in my view—

1875

The Raven[1]

By —— Quarles

[*The following lines from a correspondent—besides the deep quaint strain of the sentiment, and the curious introduction of some ludicrous touches amidst the serious and impressive, as was doubtless intended by the author—appear to us one of the most felicitous specimens of unique rhyming which has for some time met our eye. The resources of English rhythm for varieties of melody, measure, and sound, producing corresponding diversities of effect, have been thoroughly studied, much more perceived, by very few poets in the language. While the classic tongues, especially the Greek, possess, by power of accent, several advantages for versification over our own, chiefly through greater abundance of spondaic feet,[2] we have other and very great advantages of sound by the modern usage of rhyme. Alliteration is nearly the only effect of that kind which the ancients had in common with us. It will be seen that much of the melody of "The Raven" arises from alliteration, and the studious use of similar sounds in unusual places. In regard to its measure, it may be noted that if all the verses were like the second, they might properly be placed merely in short lines, producing a not uncommon form; but the presence in all the others of one line—mostly the second in the verse—which flows continuously, with only an aspirate pause in the middle, like that before the short line in the Sapphic Adonic,[3] while the fifth has at the middle pause no similarity of sound with any part besides, gives the versification an entirely different effect. We could wish the capacities of our noble language, in prosody, were better understood.*—ED. AM. REV.]

Once upon a midnight dreary, while I pondered, weak and weary,
Over many a quaint and curious volume of forgotten lore,

1. This printing of Poe's most famous poem is taken from the *American Review: A Whig Journal of Politics, Literature, Art and Science* 1 (February 1845), where it was first set in type from Poe's manuscript; the New York *Evening Mirror* printed the poem on January 29, 1845, probably from the proof sheets of the *American Review*. The prefatory paragraph, signed as if it were by the editor of the *American Review*, is retained here because Poe most likely wrote some or all of it himself. Many minor variations appear in later texts.

2. A spondee is a metrical foot consisting of two stressed syllables.

3. A Greek lyric form. An adonic is a dactyl (a foot with one long syllable and two short ones) followed by a spondee.

While I nodded, nearly napping, suddenly there came a tapping,
As of some one gently rapping, rapping at my chamber door.
"'Tis some visiter," I muttered, "tapping at my chamber door—
Only this, and nothing more."

Ah, distinctly I remember it was in the bleak December,
And each separate dying ember wrought its ghost upon the floor.
Eagerly I wished the morrow;—vainly I had tried to borrow
From my books surcease of sorrow—sorrow for the lost Lenore—
For the rare and radiant maiden whom the angels name Lenore—
Nameless here for evermore.

And the silken sad uncertain rustling of each purple curtain
Thrilled me—filled me with fantastic terrors never felt before;
So that now, to still the beating of my heart, I stood repeating
"'Tis some visiter entreating entrance at my chamber door—
Some late visiter entreating entrance at my chamber door;—
This it is, and nothing more."

Presently my soul grew stronger; hesitating then no longer,
"Sir," said I, "or Madam, truly your forgiveness I implore;
But the fact is I was napping, and so gently you came rapping,
And so faintly you came tapping, tapping at my chamber door,
That I scarce was sure I heard you"—here I opened wide the door;—
Darkness there, and nothing more.

Deep into that darkness peering, long I stood there wondering, fearing,
Doubting, dreaming dreams no mortal ever dared to dream before;
But the silence was unbroken, and the darkness gave no token,
And the only word there spoken was the whispered word, "Lenore!"
This *I* whispered, and an echo murmured back the word, "Lenore!"
Merely this, and nothing more.

Then into the chamber turning, all my soul within me burning,
Soon I heard again a tapping somewhat louder than before.
"Surely," said I, "surely that is something at my window lattice;
Let me see, then, what thereat is, and this mystery explore—
Let my heart be still a moment and this mystery explore;—
'Tis the wind, and nothing more!"

Open here I flung the shutter, when, with many a flirt and flutter,
In there stepped a stately raven of the saintly days of yore;
Not the least obeisance made he; not an instant stopped or stayed he;
But, with mien of lord or lady, perched above my chamber door—
Perched upon a bust of Pallas[4] just above my chamber door—
Perched, and sat, and nothing more.

Then this ebony bird beguiling my sad fancy into smiling,
By the grave and stern decorum of the countenance it wore,
"Though thy crest be shorn and shaven, thou," I said, "art sure no craven,

4. Athena, the Greek goddess of wisdom and the arts.

Ghastly grim and ancient raven wandering from the Nightly shore—
Tell me what thy lordly name is on the Night's Plutonian[5] shore!"
Quoth the raven, "Nevermore."

Much I marvelled this ungainly fowl to hear discourse so plainly,
Though its answer little meaning—little relevancy bore;
For we cannot help agreeing that no sublunary[6] being
Ever yet was blessed with seeing bird above his chamber door—
Bird or beast upon the sculptured bust above his chamber door,
With such name as "Nevermore."

But the raven, sitting lonely on the placid bust, spoke only
That one word, as if his soul in that one word he did outpour.
Nothing farther then he uttered—not a feather then he fluttered—
Till I scarcely more than muttered, "Other friends have flown before—
On the morrow *he* will leave me, as my hopes have flown before."
Quoth the raven, "Nevermore."

Wondering at the stillness broken by reply so aptly spoken,
"Doubtless," said I, "what it utters is its only stock and store,
Caught from some unhappy master whom unmerciful Disaster
Followed fast and followed faster—so, when Hope he would adjure,
Stern Despair returned, instead of the sweet Hope he dared adjure—
That sad answer, "Nevermore!"[7]

But the raven still beguiling all my sad soul into smiling,
Straight I wheeled a cushioned seat in front of bird, and bust, and door;
Then upon the velvet sinking, I betook myself to linking
Fancy unto fancy, thinking what this ominous bird of yore—
What this grim, ungainly, ghastly, gaunt, and ominous bird of yore
Meant in croaking "Nevermore."

This I sat engaged in guessing, but no syllable expressing
To the fowl whose fiery eyes now burned into my bosom's core;
This and more I sat divining, with my head at ease reclining
On the cushion's velvet lining that the lamplight gloated o'er,
But whose velvet violet lining with the lamplight gloating o'er,
She shall press, ah, nevermore!

Then, methought, the air grew denser, perfumed from an unseen censer
Swung by angels whose faint foot-falls tinkled on the tufted floor.
"Wretch," I cried, "thy God hath lent thee—by these angels he hath sent thee
Respite—respite and Nepenthe[8] from thy memories of Lenore!
Let me quaff this kind Nepenthe and forget this lost Lenore!"
Quoth the raven, "Nevermore."

"Prophet!" said I, "thing of evil!—prophet still, if bird or devil!—
Whether Tempter sent, or whether tempest tossed thee here ashore,

5. Black, as in the underworld ruled by Pluto in Greek mythology.
6. Earthly, beneath the moon.
7. This stanza concluded in the 1845 volume with these lines: "Followed faster till his songs one burden bore— / Till the dirges of his Hope that melancholy burden bore / Of 'Never—nevermore.'"
8. Drug that induces oblivion.

Desolate, yet all undaunted, on this desert land enchanted—
On this home by Horror haunted—tell me truly, I implore—
Is there—*is* there balm in Gilead?[9]—tell me—tell me, I implore!"
Quoth the raven, "Nevermore."

"Prophet!" said I, "thing of evil!—prophet still, if bird or devil!
By that Heaven that bends above us—by that God we both adore—
Tell this soul with sorrow laden if, within the distant Aidenn,[1]
It shall clasp a sainted maiden whom the angels name Lenore—
Clasp a rare and radiant maiden whom the angels name Lenore."
Quoth the raven, "Nevermore."

"Be that word our sign of parting, bird or fiend!" I shrieked, upstarting—
"Get thee back into the tempest and the Night's Plutonian shore!
Leave no black plume as a token of that lie thy soul hath spoken!
Leave my loneliness unbroken—quit the bust above my door!
Take thy beak from out my heart, and take thy form from off my door!"
Quoth the raven, "Nevermore."

And the raven, never flitting, still is sitting, still is sitting
On the pallid bust of Pallas just above my chamber door;
And his eyes have all the seeming of a demon that is dreaming,
And the lamp-light o'er him streaming throws his shadow on the floor;
And my soul from out that shadow that lies floating on the floor
Shall be lifted—nevermore!

1845

To ———. Ulalume: A Ballad[1]

The skies they were ashen and sober;
The leaves they were crispéd and sere—
The leaves they were withering and sere;
It was night in the lonesome October
Of my most immemorial year;
It was hard by the dim lake of Auber,[2]
In the misty mid region of Weir—
It was down by the dank tarn[3] of Auber,
In the ghoul-haunted woodland of Weir.

Here once, through an alley Titanic,[4]
Of cypress, I roamed with my Soul—

9. An echo of the ironic words in Jeremiah 8.22: "Is there no balm in Gilead; is there no physician there?" Gilead is a mountainous area east of the Jordan River between the Sea of Galilee and the Dead Sea; evergreens growing there were a source of medicinal resins.

1. One of Poe's vaguely evocative place names, designed to suggest Eden.

1. This is the longer version of the poem; Poe sometimes dropped the tenth stanza. The source is the first printing in the *American Review* 6 (December 1847).

2. This, like many names in the poem (e.g., Weir, line 7), was probably chosen for its sound and associative values.

3. A small mountain lake.

4. The alley—the pathway—is titanic because the cypress trees on either side are enormous, on a scale to match that of the pre-Olympian Greek gods.

Of cypress, with Psyche, my Soul.
These were days when my heart was volcanic
As the scoriac rivers[5] that roll—
As the lavas that restlessly roll
Their sulphurous currents down Yaanek
In the ultimate climes of the pole—
That groan as they roll down Mount Yaanek
In the realms of the boreal pole.[6]

Our talk had been serious and sober,
But our thoughts they were palsied and sere—
Our memories were treacherous and sere—
For we knew not the month was October,
And we marked not the night of the year—
(Ah, night of all nights[7] in the year!)
We noted not the dim lake of Auber—
(Though once we had journeyed down here)—
We remembered not the dank tarn of Auber,
Nor the ghoul-haunted woodland of Weir.

And now, as the night was senescent[8]
And star-dials pointed to morn—
As the star-dials hinted of morn—
At the end of our path a liquescent
And nebulous lustre was born,
Out of which a miraculous crescent
Arose with a duplicate horn—
Astarte's[9] bediamonded crescent
Distinct with its duplicate horn.

And I said—"She is warmer than Dian:[1]
She rolls through an ether of sighs—
She revels in a region of sighs:
She has seen that the tears are not dry on
These cheeks, where the worm never dies,
And has come past the stars of the Lion[2]
To point us the path to the skies—
To the Lethean[3] peace of the skies—
Come up, in despite of the Lion,
To shine on us with her bright eyes—
Come up through the lair of the Lion
With Love in her luminous eyes."

But Psyche, uplifting her finger,
Said—"Sadly this star I mistrust—
Her pallor I strangely mistrust:—

5. Rivers of lava.
6. North pole.
7. All Hallow's Eve, or Halloween.
8. Becoming old.
9. Phoenician fertility and lunar goddess, often depicted with crescent horns.
1. The chaste Roman goddess of the moon.
2. The constellation Leo.
3. Absolute peace, as if bathed in the oblivion-giving waters of Lethe, one of the five rivers of Hades in Greek mythology

Oh, hasten!—oh, let us not linger!
Oh, fly!—let us fly!—for we must."
In terror she spoke, letting sink her
Wings till they trailed in the dust—
In agony sobbed, letting sink her
Plumes till they trailed in the dust—
Till they sorrowfully trailed in the dust.

I replied—"This is nothing but dreaming:
Let us on by this tremulous light!
Let us bathe in this crystalline light!
Its Sybillic[4] splendor is beaming
With Hope and in Beauty to-night:—
See!—it flickers up the sky through the night!
Ah, we safely may trust to its gleaming,
And be sure it will lead us aright—
We safely may trust to a gleaming
That cannot but guide us aright,
Since it flickers up to Heaven through the night."

Thus I pacified Psyche and kissed her,
And tempted her out of her gloom—
And conquered her scruples and gloom:
And we passed to the end of the vista,
And were stopped by the door of a tomb—
By the door of a legended tomb;
And I said—"What is written, sweet sister,
On the door of this legended tomb?"
She replied—"Ulalume—Ulalume—
'Tis the vault of thy lost Ulalume!"

Then my heart it grew ashen and sober
As the leaves that were crispéd and sere—
As the leaves that were withering and sere,
And I cried—"It was surely October
On *this* very night of last year
That I journeyed—I journeyed down here—
That I brought a dread burden down here—
On this night of all nights in the year,
Oh, what demon has tempted me here?
Well I know, now, this dim lake of Auber—
This misty mid region of Weir—
Well I know, now, this dank tarn of Auber,
In the ghoul-haunted woodland of Weir."

Said *we,* then—the two, then—"Ah, can it
Have been that the woodlandish ghouls—
The pitiful, the merciful ghouls—
To bar up our way and to ban it
From the secret that lies in these wolds[5]—

4. Mysteriously prophetic—now spelled "sibyllic."

5. Open, hilly areas.

From the thing that lies hidden in these wolds—
Had drawn up the spectre of a planet
From the limbo of lunary souls—
This sinfully scintillant[6] planet
From the Hell of the planetary souls?"

1847

Annabel Lee[1]

It was many and many a year ago,
In a kingdom by the sea
That a maiden there lived whom you may know
By the name of ANNABEL LEE;
And this maiden she lived with no other thought
Than to love and be loved by me.

I was a child and *she* was a child,
In this kingdom by the sea;
But we loved with a love that was more than love—
I and my ANNABEL LEE—
With a love that the wingèd seraphs of heaven
Coveted her and me.

And this was the reason that, long ago,
In this kingdom by the sea,
A wind blew out of a cloud, chilling
My beautiful ANNABEL LEE;
So that her highborn kinsmen came
And bore her away from me,
To shut her up in a sepulchre
In this kingdom by the sea.

The angels, not half so happy in heaven,
Went envying her and me—
Yes!—that was the reason (as all men know,
In this kingdom by the sea)
That the wind came out of the cloud by night,
Chilling and killing my ANNABEL LEE.

But our love it was stronger by far than the love
Of those who were older than we—
Of many far wiser than we—
And neither the angels in heaven above,
Nor the demons down under the sea,
Can ever dissever my soul from the soul
Of the beautiful ANNABEL LEE:

6. Sparkling, shining.
1. The text is that of the first printing, in an article by Rufus Griswold in the *New York Tribune* (October 9, 1849), signed "Ludwig," which was printed two days after Poe's death.

For the moon never beams, without bringing me dreams
Of the beautiful ANNABEL LEE;
And the stars never rise, but I feel the bright eyes
Of the beautiful ANNABEL LEE:
And so, all the night tide, I lie down by the side
Of my darling—my darling—my life and my bride,
In her sepulchre there by the sea—
In her tomb by the sounding sea.

1849

Ligeia[1]

And the will therein lieth, which dieth not. Who knoweth the mysteries of the will, with its vigour? For God is but a great will pervading all things by nature of its intentness. Man doth not yield himself to the angels, nor unto death utterly, save only through the weakness of his feeble will.

—Joseph Glanvill[2]

I cannot, for my soul, remember how, when, or even precisely where I first became acquainted with the lady Ligeia. Long years have since elapsed, and my memory is feeble through much suffering: or, perhaps, I cannot *now* bring these points to mind, because, in truth, the character of my beloved, her rare learning, her singular yet placid cast of beauty, and the thrilling and enthralling eloquence of her low, musical language, made their way into my heart by paces, so steadily and stealthily progressive, that they have been unnoticed and unknown. Yet I know that I met her most frequently in some large, old, decaying city near the Rhine. Of her family—I have surely heard her speak—that they are of a remotely ancient date cannot be doubted. Ligeia! Buried in studies of a nature, more than all else, adapted to deaden impressions of the outward world, it is by that sweet word alone—by Ligeia, that I bring before mine eyes in fancy the image of her who is no more. And now, while I write, a recollection flashes upon me that I have *never known* the paternal name of her who was my friend and my betrothed, and who became the partner of my studies, and eventually the wife of my bosom. Was it a playful charge on the part of my Ligeia? or was it a test of my strength of affection that I should institute no inquiries upon this point? or was it rather a caprice of my own—a wildly romantic offering on the shrine of the most passionate devotion? I but indistinctly recall the fact itself—what wonder that I have utterly forgotten the circumstances which originated or attended it? And indeed, if ever that spirit which is entitled *Romance*—if ever she, the wan, and the misty-winged *Ashtophet*[3] of idolatrous Egypt, presided, as they tell, over marriages ill-omened, then most surely she presided over mine.

1. "Ligeia" was first published in the *American Museum* 1 (September 1838), the source of the present text. Poe later revised the tale slightly and added to it the poem "The Conqueror Worm."
2. Like many of Poe's epigraphs (often added after first publication), this one is fabricated. Joseph Glanvill (1636–1680) was one of the Cambridge Platonists, 17th-century English religious philosophers who tried to reconcile Christianity and Renaissance science.
3. Variant of Ashtoreth, Phoenician goddess of fertility.

There is one dear topic, however, on which my memory faileth me not. It is the person of Ligeia. In stature she was tall, somewhat slender, and in her latter days even emaciated. I would in vain attempt to pourtray the majesty, the quiet ease of her demeanour, or the incomprehensible lightness and elasticity of her footfall. She came and departed like a shadow. I was never made aware of her entrance into my closed study save by the dear music of her low sweet voice, as she placed her delicate hand upon my shoulder. In beauty of face no maiden ever equalled her. It was the radiance of an opium dream—an airy and spirit-lifting vision more wildly divine than the phantasies which hovered about the slumbering souls of the daughters of Delos.[4] Yet her features were not of that regular mould which we have been falsely taught to worship in the classical labors of the Heathen. "There is no exquisite[5] beauty," saith Verülam, Lord Bacon, speaking truly of all the forms and *genera* of beauty, "without some *strangeness* in the proportions." Yet, although I saw that the features of Ligeia were not of classic regularity, although I perceived that her loveliness was indeed "exquisite," and felt that there was much of "strangeness" pervading it, yet I have tried in vain to detect the irregularity, and to trace home my own perception of "the strange." I examined the contour of the lofty and pale forehead—it was faultless—how cold indeed that word when applied to a majesty so divine! The skin rivaling the purest ivory, the commanding breadth and repose, the gentle prominence of the regions above the temples, and then the raven-black, the glossy, the luxuriant and naturally-curling tresses, setting forth the full force of the Homeric epithet, "hyacinthine;"[6] I looked at the delicate outlines of the nose—and nowhere but in the graceful medallions of the Hebrews had I beheld a similar perfection. There was the same luxurious smoothness of surface, the same scarcely perceptible tendency to the aquiline, the same harmoniously curved nostril speaking the free spirit. I regarded the sweet mouth. Here was indeed the triumph of all things heavenly—the magnificent turn of the short upper lip—the soft, voluptuous repose of the under—the dimples which sported, and the colour which spoke—the teeth glancing back, with a brilliancy almost startling, every ray of the holy light which fell upon them in her serene, and placid, yet most exultingly radiant of all smiles. I scrutinized the formation of the chin—and here, too, I found the gentleness of breadth, the softness and the majesty, the fulness and the spirituality, of the Greek, the contour which the God Apollo revealed but in a dream to Cleomenes, the son of the Athenian.[7] And then I peered into the large eyes of Ligeia.

For eyes we have no models in the remotely antique. It might have been, too, that in these eyes of my beloved lay the secret to which Lord Verülam alludes. They were, I must believe, far larger than the ordinary eyes of our race. They were even far fuller than the fullest of the Gazelle eyes of the tribe of the valley of Nourjahad.[8] Yet it was only at intervals—in moments of intense excitement—that this peculiarity became more than slightly

4. Probably the maidens attending Artemis, goddess of wild nature and the hunt; she was born on Delos, a Greek island in the Aegean Sea.
5. In his essay "Of Beauty" Francis Bacon, Baron Verulam (1561–1626), wrote "excellent," not "exquisite."
6. In the *Odyssey*, Homer compares Odysseus's curly hair to the flowering hyacinth plant.
7. Classical Greek sculptor whose name is affixed to the Venus de' Medici. The god Apollo was the patron of artists.
8. From the Asian romance *The History of Nourjahad* (1767), by the English writer Frances Sheridan (1724–1766).

noticeable in Ligeia. And at such moments was her beauty—in my heated fancy thus it appeared perhaps—the beauty of beings either above or apart from the earth—the beauty of the fabulous Houri[9] of the Turk. The colour of the orbs was the most brilliant of black, and far over them hung jetty lashes of great length. The brows, slightly irregular in outline, had the same hue. The "strangeness," however, which I have found in the eyes of my Ligeia was of a nature distinct from the formation, or the colour, or the brilliancy of the feature, and must, after all, be referred to the *expression*. Ah, word of no meaning! behind whose vast latitude of mere sound we intrench our ignorance of so much of the spiritual. The expression of the eyes of Ligeia! How, for long hours have I pondered upon it! How have I, through the whole of a mid-summer night, struggled to fathom it! What was it—that something more profound than the well of Democritus[1]—which lay far within the pupils of my beloved? What *was* it? I was possessed with a passion to discover. Those eyes! those large, those shining, those divine orbs! they became to me twin stars of Leda,[2] and I to them devoutest of astrologers. Not for a moment was the unfathomable meaning of their glance, by day or by night, absent from my soul.

There is no point, among the many incomprehensible anomalies of the science of mind, more thrillingly exciting than the fact—never, I believe noticed in the schools—that in our endeavours to recall to memory something long forgotten we often find ourselves *upon the very verge* of remembrance without being able, in the end, to remember. And thus, how frequently, in my intense scrutiny of Ligeia's eyes, have I felt approaching the full knowledge of the secret of their expression—felt it approaching—yet not quite be mine—and so at length utterly depart. And (strange, oh strangest mystery of all!) I found, in the commonest objects of the universe, a circle of analogies to that expression. I mean to say that, subsequently to the period when Ligeia's beauty passed into my spirit, there dwelling as in a shrine, I derived from many existences in the material world, a sentiment, such as I felt always aroused within me by her large and luminous orbs. Yet not the more could I define that sentiment, or analyze, or even steadily view it. I recognized it, let me repeat, sometimes in the commonest objects of the universe. It has flashed upon me in the survey of a rapidly-growing vine—in the contemplation of a moth, a butterfly, a chrysalis, a stream of running water. I have felt it in the ocean, in the falling of a meteor. I have felt it in the glances of unusually aged people. And there are one or two stars in heaven—(one especially, a star of the sixth magnitude, double and changeable, to be found near the large star in Lyra)[3] in a telescopic scrutiny of which I have been made aware of the feeling. I have been filled with it by certain sounds from stringed instruments, and not unfrequently by passages from books. Among innumerable other instances, I well remember something in a volume of Joseph Glanvill, which, perhaps merely from its quaintness—who shall say? never failed to inspire me with the sentiment.—"And the will therein lieth,

9. Beautiful maiden waiting in paradise for the devout Muslim.
1. Greek philosopher (5th century B.C.E.); one of his proverbs is "Truth lies at the bottom of a well."
2. Queen of Sparta whom Zeus, in the form of a swan, raped, thereby begetting Helen of Troy and (according to some versions) the twin sons Castor and Pollux, whom Zeus transformed into the constellation Gemini.
3. The lesser star is epsilon Lyrae, the large one Vega or alpha Lyrae.

which dieth not. Who knoweth the mysteries of the will, with its vigor? For God is but a great will pervading all things by nature of its intentness. Man doth not yield him to the angels, nor unto death utterly, but only through the weakness of his feeble will."

Length of years, and subsequent reflection, have enabled me to trace, indeed, some remote connexion between this passage in the old English moralist and a portion of the character of Ligeia. An *intensity* in thought, action, or speech was possibly, in her, a result, or at least an index, of that gigantic volition which, during our long intercourse, failed to give other and more immediate evidence of its existence. Of all women whom I have ever known, she, the outwardly calm, the ever placid Ligeia, was the most violently a prey to the tumultuous vultures of stern passion. And of such passion I could form no estimate, save by the miraculous expansion of those eyes which at once so delighted and appalled me, by the almost magical melody, modulation, distinctness and placidity of her very low voice, and by the fierce energy, (rendered doubly effective by contrast with her manner of utterance) of the words which she uttered.

I have spoken of the learning of Ligeia: it was immense—such as I have never known in woman. In all the classical tongues was she deeply proficient, and as far as my own acquaintance extended in regard to the modern dialects of Europe, I have never known her at fault. Indeed upon any theme of the most admired, because simply the most abstruse, of the boasted erudition of the academy, have I *ever* found Ligeia at fault? How singularly, how thrillingly, this one point in the nature of my wife has forced itself, at this late period, only, upon my attention! I said her knowledge was such as I had never known in woman. Where breathes the man who, like her, has traversed, and successfully, *all* the wide areas of moral, natural, and mathematical science? I saw not then what I now clearly perceive, that the acquisitions of Ligeia were gigantic, were astounding—yet I was sufficiently aware of her infinite supremacy to resign myself, with a childlike confidence, to her guidance through the chaotic world of metaphysical investigation at which I was most busily occupied during the earlier years of our marriage. With how vast a triumph—with how vivid a delight—with how much of all that is ethereal in hope—did I *feel*, as she bent over me, in studies but little sought for—but less known that delicious vista by slow but very perceptible degrees expanding before me, down whose long, gorgeous, and all untrodden path I might at length pass onward to the goal of a wisdom too divinely precious not to be forbidden!

How poignant, then, must have been the grief with which, after some years, I beheld my well-grounded expectations take wings to themselves and flee away! Without Ligeia I was but as a child groping benighted. Her presence, her readings alone, rendered vividly luminous the many mysteries of the transcendentalism in which we were immersed. Letters, lambent and golden, grew duller than Saturnian[4] lead wanting the radiant lustre of her eyes. And now those eyes shone less and less frequently upon the pages over which I poured. Ligeia grew ill. The wild eye blazed with a too—too glorious effulgence; the pale fingers became of the transparent waxen hue of the

4. Sluggish; in alchemy *saturnus* is the name for lead.

grave—and the blue veins upon the lofty forehead swelled and sunk impetuously with the tides of the most gentle emotion. I saw that she must die—and I struggled desperately in spirit with the grim Azrael.[5] And the struggles of the passionate Ligeia were, to my astonishment, even more energetic than my own. There had been much in her stern nature to impress me with the belief that, to her, death would have come without its terrors—but not so. Words are impotent to convey any just idea of the fierceness of resistance with which Ligeia wrestled with the dark shadow. I groaned in anguish at the pitiable spectacle. I would have soothed—I would have reasoned; but in the intensity of her wild desire for life—for life—*but* for life, solace and reason were alike the uttermost of folly. Yet not for an instant, amid the most convulsive writhings of her fierce spirit, was shaken the external placidity of her demeanor. Her voice grew more gentle—grew more low—yet I would not wish to dwell upon the wild meaning of the quietly-uttered words. My brain reeled as I hearkened, entranced, to a melody more than mortal—to assumptions and aspirations which mortality had never before known.

That Ligeia loved me, I should not have doubted; and I might have been easily aware that, in a bosom such as hers, love would have reigned no ordinary passion. But in death only, was I fully impressed with the intensity of her affection. For long hours, detaining my hand, would she pour out before me the overflowings of a heart whose more than passionate devotion amounted to idolatry. How had I deserved to be so blessed by such confessions.—How had I deserved to be so cursed with the removal of my beloved in the hour of her making them? But upon this subject I cannot bear to dilate. Let me say only, that in Ligeia's more than womanly abandonment to a love, alas, all unmerited, all unworthily bestowed; I at length recognised the principle of her longing, with so wildly earnest a desire for the life which was now fleeing so rapidly away. It is this wild longing—it is this eager intensity of desire for life—*but* for life—that I have no power to pourtray—no utterance capable to express. Methinks I again behold the terrific struggles of her lofty, her nearly idealized nature, with the might and the terror, and the majesty of the great Shadow. But she perished. The giant *will* succumbed to a power more stern. And I thought, as I gazed upon the corpse, of the wild passage in Joseph Glanvill. "The will therein lieth, which dieth not. Who knoweth the mysteries of the will, with its vigor? For God is but a great will pervading all things by nature of its intentness. Man doth not yield him to the angels, *nor unto death utterly*, save only through the weakness of his feeble will."

She died—and I, crushed into the very dust with sorrow, could no longer endure the lonely desolation of my dwelling in the dim and decaying city by the Rhine. I had no lack of what the world terms wealth—Ligeia had brought me far more, very far more, than falls ordinarily to the lot of mortals. After a few months, therefore, of weary and aimless wandering, I purchased, and put in some repair, an abbey, which I shall not name, in one of the wildest and least frequented portions of fair England. The gloomy and dreary grandeur of the building, the almost savage aspect of the domain, the many melancholy and time-honored memories connected with both, had much in uni-

5. The Angel of Death (in Judaism and Islam).

son with the feelings of utter abandonment which had driven me into that remote and unsocial region of the country. Yet, although the external abbey, with its verdant decay hanging about it suffered but little alteration, I gave way with a child-like perversity, and perchance with a faint hope of alleviating my sorrows, to a display of more than regal magnificence within. For such follies even in childhood I had imbibed a taste, and now they came back to me as if in the dotage of grief. Alas, I now feel how much even of incipient madness might have been discovered in the gorgeous and fantastic draperies, in the solemn carvings of Egypt, in the wild cornices and furniture of Arabesque,[6] in the bedlam patterns of the carpets of tufted gold! I had become a bounden slave in the trammels of opium, and my labors and my orders had taken a colouring from my dreams. But these absurdities I must not pause to detail. Let me speak only of that one chamber, ever accursed, whither, in a moment of mental alienation, I led from the altar as my bride—as the successor of the unforgotten Ligeia—the fair-haired and blue-eyed lady Rowena Trevanion, of Tremaine.

There is not any individual portion of the architecture and decoration of that bridal chamber which is not now visibly before me. Where were the souls of the haughty family of the bride, when, through thirst of gold, they permitted to pass the threshold of an apartment *so* bedecked, a maiden and a daughter so beloved? I have said that I minutely remember the details of the chamber—yet I am sadly forgetful on topics of deep moment—and here there was no system, no keeping, in the fantastic display, to take hold upon the memory. The room lay in a high turret of the castellated abbey, was pentagonal in shape, and of capacious size. Occupying the whole southern face of the pentagon was the sole window—an immense sheet of unbroken glass from Venice—a single pane, and tinted of a leaden hue, so that the rays of either the sun or moon, passing through it, fell with a ghastly lustre upon the objects within. Over the upper portion of this huge window extended the open trellice-work of an aged vine which clambered up the massy walls of the turret. The ceiling, of gloomy-looking oak, was excessively lofty, vaulted, and elaborately fretted with the wildest and most grotesque specimens of a semi-Gothic, semi-druidical[7] device. From out the most central recess of this melancholy vaulting, depended, by a single chain of gold, with long links, a huge censer of the same metal, Arabesque in pattern, and with many perforations so contrived that there writhed in and out of them, as if endued with a serpent vitality, a continual succession of parti-coloured fires. Some few ottomans and golden candelabras of Eastern figure were in various stations about—and there was the couch, too, the bridal couch, of an Indian model, and low, and sculptured of solid ebony, with a canopy above. In each of the angles of the chamber, stood on end a gigantic sarcophagus of black granite, from the tombs of the kings over against Luxor,[8] with their aged lids full of immemorial sculpture. But in the draping of the apartment lay, alas! the chief phantasy of all. The lofty walls—gigantic in height—even unproportionally so, were hung from summit to foot, in vast folds with a heavy and massy looking tapestry—tapestry of a material which was found alike as a

6. Ornamental style employing intricate patterns of lines and figures.
7. Druids are the legendary priests, or wizards, of ancient Britain and Ireland. "Fretted": ornamented with intersecting patterns.
8. In Egypt, near Thebes; site of famous ruins.

carpet on the floor, as a covering for the ottomans, and the ebony bed, as a canopy for the bed, and as the gorgeous volutes[9] of the curtains which partially shaded the window. This material was the richest cloth of gold. It was spotted all over, at irregular intervals, with Arabesque figures, of about a foot in diameter, and wrought upon the cloth in patterns of the most jetty black. But these figures partook of the true character of the Arabesque only when regarded from a single point of view. By a contrivance now common, and indeed traceable to a very remote period of antiquity, they were made changeable in aspect. To one entering the room they bore the appearance of ideal monstrosities; but, upon a farther advance, this appearance suddenly departed; and, step by step, as the visitor moved his station in the chamber, he saw himself surrounded by an endless succession of the ghastly forms which belong to the superstition of the Northman, or arise in the guilty slumbers of the monk. The phantasmagoric effect was vastly heightened by the artificial introduction of a strong continual current of wind behind the draperies—giving a hideous and uneasy vitality to the whole.

In halls such as these—in a bridal chamber such as this, I passed, with the lady of Tremaine, the unhallowed hours of the first month of our marriage—passed them with but little disquietude. That my wife dreaded the fierce moodiness of my temper—that she shunned me, and loved me but little, I could not help perceiving—but it gave me rather pleasure than otherwise. I loathed her with a hatred belonging more to demon than to man. My memory flew back, (oh, with what intensity of regret!) to Ligeia, the beloved, the beautiful, the entombed. I revelled in recollections of her purity, of her wisdom, of her lofty, her ethereal nature, of her passionate, her idolatrous love. Now, then, did my spirit fully and freely burn with more than all the fires of her own. In the excitement of my opium dreams (for I was habitually fettered in the iron shackles of the drug)[1] I would call aloud upon her name, during the silence of the night, or among the sheltered recesses of the glens by day, as if, by the wild eagerness, the solemn passion, the consuming intensity of my longing for the departed Ligeia, I could restore the departed Ligeia to the pathways she had abandoned upon earth.

About the commencement of the second month of the marriage, the lady Rowena was attacked with sudden illness from which her recovery was slow. The fever which consumed her, rendered her nights uneasy, and, in her perturbed state of half-slumber, she spoke of sounds, and of motions, in and about the chamber of the turret which had no origin save in the distemper of her fancy, or, perhaps, in the phantasmagoric influences of the chamber itself. She became at length convalescent—finally well. Yet but a brief period elapsed, ere a second more violent disorder again threw her upon a bed of suffering—and from this attack her frame, at all times feeble, never altogether recovered. Her illnesses were, after this period, of alarming character, and of more alarming recurrence, defying alike the knowledge and the great exertions of her medical men. With the increase of the chronic disease which had thus, apparently, taken too sure hold upon her constitution to be eradicated by human means, I could not fail to observe a similar increase in the nervous irritability of her temperament, and in her excitability

9. Scroll-like ornaments.
1. The *American Museum* has no punctuation after "dreams" or "drug" in this sentence; parentheses are added to the present text.

by trivial causes of fear. Indeed reason seemed fast tottering from her throne. She spoke again, and now more frequently and pertinaciously, of the sounds, of the slight sounds, and of the unusual motions among the tapestries, to which she had formerly alluded. It was one night near the closing in of September, when she pressed this distressing subject with more than usual emphasis upon my attention. She had just awakened from a perturbed slumber, and I had been watching, with feelings half of anxiety, half of a vague terror, the workings of her emaciated countenance. I sat by the side of her ebony bed, upon one of the ottomans of India. She partly arose, and spoke, in an earnest low whisper, of sounds which she *then* heard, but which I could not hear, of motions which she *then* saw, but which I could not perceive. The wind was rushing hurriedly behind the tapestries, and I wished to show her (what, let me confess it, I could not *all* believe) that those faint, almost articulate, breathings, and the very gentle variations of the figures upon the wall, were but the natural effects of that customary rushing of the wind. But a deadly pallor overspreading her face, had proved to me that my exertions to re-assure her would be fruitless. She appeared to be fainting, and no attendants were within call. I remembered where was deposited a decanter of some light wine which had been ordered by her physicians, and hastened across the chamber to procure it. But, as I stepped beneath the light of the censer, two circumstances of a startling nature attracted my attention. I had felt that some palpable object had passed lightly by my person; and I saw that there lay a faint, indefinite shadow upon the golden carpet in the very middle of the rich lustre, thrown from the censer. But I was wild with the excitement of an immoderate dose of opium, and heeded these things but little, nor spoke of them to Rowena. Finding the wine, I re-crossed the chamber, and poured out a goblet-ful, which I held to the lips of the fainting lady. But she had now partially recovered, and took, herself, the vessel, while I sank upon the ottoman near me, with my eyes rivetted upon her person. It was then that I became distinctly aware of a gentle foot-fall upon the carpet, and near the couch; and, in a second thereafter, as Rowena was in the act of raising the wine to her lips, I saw, or may have dreamed that I saw, fall within the goblet, as if from some invisible spring in the atmosphere of the room, three or four large drops of a brilliant and ruby colored fluid. If this I saw—not so Rowena. She swallowed the wine unhesitatingly, and I forbore to speak to her of a circumstance which must, after all, I considered, have been but the suggestion of a vivid imagination, rendered morbidly active by the terror of the lady, by the opium, and by the hour.

Yet I cannot conceal it from myself, after this period, a rapid change for the worse took place in the disorder of my wife, so that, on the third subsequent night, the hands of her menials prepared her for the tomb, and on the fourth, I sat alone, with her shrouded body, in that fantastical chamber which had received her as my bride. Wild visions, opium engendered, flitted, shadow-like, before me. I gazed with unquiet eye upon the sarcophagi in the angles of the room, upon the varying figures of the drapery, and upon the writhing of the parti-colored fires in the censer overhead. My eyes then fell, as I called to mind the circumstances of a former night, to the spot beneath the glare of the censer where I had beheld the faint traces of the shadow. It was there, however, no longer, and, breathing with greater freedom, I turned my glances to the pallid and rigid figure upon the bed. Then rushed upon me a thousand memories of Ligeia—and then came back upon my heart, with the turbulent violence of a flood, the whole of that unutterable woe with which I had regarded *her* thus enshrouded. The night waned; and still, with a bosom full of bitter thoughts of the one only and supremely beloved, I remained with mine eyes rivetted upon the body of Rowena.

It might have been midnight, or perhaps earlier, or later, for I had taken no note of time, when a sob, low, gentle, but very distinct, startled me from my revery. I *felt* that it came from the bed of ebony—the bed of death. I listened in an agony of superstitious terror—but there was no repetition of the sound; I strained my vision to detect any motion in the corpse, but there was not the slightest perceptible. Yet I could not have been deceived. I had heard the noise, however faint, and my whole soul was awakened within me, as I resolutely and perseveringly kept my attention rivetted upon the body. Many minutes elapsed before any circumstance occurred tending to throw light upon the mystery. At length it became evident that a slight, a very faint, and barely noticeable tinge of colour had flushed up within the cheeks, and along the sunken small veins of the eyelids. Through a species of unutterable horror and awe, for which the language of mortality has no sufficiently energetic expression, I felt my brain reel, my heart cease to beat, my limbs grow rigid where I sat. Yet a sense of duty finally operated to restore my self-possession. I could no longer doubt that we had been precipitate in our preparations for interment—that Rowena still lived. It was necessary that some immediate exertion be made; yet the turret was altogether apart from the portion of the Abbey tenanted by the servants—there were none within call, and I had no means of summoning them to my aid without leaving the room for many minutes—and this I could not venture to do. I therefore struggled alone in my endeavors to call back the spirit still hovering. In a short period it became evident however, that a relapse had taken place; the color utterly disappeared from both eyelid and cheek, leaving a wanness even more than that of marble; the lips became doubly shrivelled and pinched up in the ghastly expression of death; a coldness surpassing that of ice, overspread rapidly the surface of the body, and all the usual rigorous stiffness immediately supervened. I fell back with a shudder upon the ottoman from which I had been so startlingly aroused, and again gave myself up to passionate waking visions of Ligeia.

An hour thus elapsed when, (could it be possible?) I was a second time aware of some vague sound issuing from the region of the bed. I listened—in extremity of horror. The sound came again—it was a sigh. Rushing to the corpse, I saw—distinctly saw—a tremor upon the lips. In a minute after they slightly relaxed, disclosing a bright line of the pearly teeth. Amazement now struggled in my bosom with the profound awe which had hitherto reigned therein alone. I felt that my vision grew dim, that my brain wandered, and it was only by a convulsive effort that I at length succeeded in nerving myself to the task which duty thus, once more, had pointed out. There was now a partial glow upon the forehead, upon the cheek and throat—a perceptible warmth pervaded the whole frame—there was even a slight pulsation at the heart. The lady lived; and with redoubled ardour I betook myself to the task of restoration. I chafed, and bathed the temples, and the hands, and used every exertion which experience, and no little medical reading, could suggest. But in vain. Suddenly, the colour fled, the pulsation ceased, the lips resumed the expression of the dead, and, in an instant afterwards, the whole body took upon itself the icy chillness, the livid hue, the intense rigidity, the sunken outline, and each and all of the loathsome peculiarities of that which has been, for many days, a tenant of the tomb.

And again I sunk into visions of Ligeia—and again (what marvel that I shudder while I write?) *again* there reached my ears a low sob from the region of the ebony bed. But why shall I minutely detail the unspeakable horrors of that night? Why shall I pause to relate how, time after time, until near the period of the grey dawn, this hideous drama of revivification was repeated, and how each terrific relapse was only into a sterner and apparently more irredeemable death? Let me hurry to a conclusion.

The greater part of the fearful night had worn away, and the corpse of Rowena once again stirred—and now more vigorously than hitherto, although arousing from a dissolution more appalling in its utter hopelessness than any. I had long ceased to struggle or to move, and remained sitting rigidly upon the ottoman, a helpless prey to a whirl of violent emotions, of which extreme awe was perhaps the least terrible, the least consuming. The corpse, I repeat, stirred, and now more vigorously than before. The hues of life flushed up with unwonted energy into the countenance—the limbs relaxed—and, save that the eyelids were yet pressed heavily together, and that the bandages and draperies of the grave still imparted their charnel character to the figure, I might have dreamed that Rowena had indeed shaken off, utterly, the fetters of Death. But if this idea was not, even then, altogether adopted, I could, at least, doubt no longer, when, arising from the bed, tottering, with feeble steps, with closed eyes, and with the air of one bewildered in a dream, the lady of Tremaine stood bodily and palpably before me.

I trembled not—I stirred not—for a crowd of unutterable fancies connected with the air, the demeanour of the figure, rushing hurriedly through my brain, sent the purple blood ebbing in torrents from the temples to the heart. I stirred not—but gazed upon her who was before me. There was a mad disorder in my thoughts—a tumult unappeasable. Could it, indeed, be the *living* Rowena who confronted me? Why, *why* should I doubt it? The bandage lay heavily about the mouth—but then it was the mouth of the breathing lady of Tremaine. And the cheeks—there were the roses as in her noon of health—yes, these were indeed the fair cheeks of the living lady of Tremaine. And the chin, with its dimples, as in health, was it not hers?—but—but *had she then grown taller since her malady?* What inexpressible madness seized me with that thought? One bound, and I had reached her feet! Shrinking from my touch, she let fall from her head, unloosened, the ghastly cerements[2] which had confined it, and there streamed forth, into the rushing atmosphere of the chamber, huge masses of long and dishevelled hair. *It was blacker than the raven wings of the midnight!* And now the eyes opened of the figure which stood before me. "Here then at least," I shrieked aloud, "can I never—can I never be mistaken—these are the full, and the black, and the wild eyes of the lady—of the lady Ligeia!"

1838

2. Shrouds.

The Fall of the House of Usher[1]

During the whole of a dull, dark, and soundless day in the autumn of the year, when the clouds hung oppressively low in the heavens, I had been passing alone, on horseback, through a singularly dreary tract of country; and at length found myself, as the shades of the evening drew on, within view of the melancholy House of Usher. I know not how it was—but, with the first glimpse of the building, a sense of insufferable gloom pervaded my spirit. I say insufferable; for the feeling was unrelieved by any of that half-pleasurable, because poetic, sentiment, with which the mind usually receives even the sternest natural images of the desolate or terrible. I looked upon the scene before me—upon the mere house, and the simple landscape features of the domain—upon the bleak walls—upon the vacant eye-like windows—upon a few rank sedges—and upon a few white trunks of decayed trees—with an utter depression of soul which I can compare to no earthly sensation more properly than to the after-dream of the reveller upon opium—the bitter lapse into common life—the hideous dropping off of the veil. There was an iciness, a sinking, a sickening of the heart—an unredeemed dreariness of thought which no goading of the imagination could torture into aught of the sublime. What was it—I paused to think—what was it that so unnerved me in the contemplation of the House of Usher? It was a mystery all insoluble; nor could I grapple with the shadowy fancies that crowded upon me as I pondered. I was forced to fall back upon the unsatisfactory conclusion, that while, beyond doubt, there *are* combinations of very simple natural objects which have the power of thus affecting us, still the reason, and the analysis, of this power, lie among considerations beyond our depth. It was possible, I reflected, that a mere different arrangement of the particulars of the scene, of the details of this picture, would be sufficient to modify, or perhaps to annihilate its capacity for sorrowful impression; and, acting upon this idea, I reined my horse to the precipitous brink of a black and lurid tarn[2] that lay in unruffled lustre by the dwelling, and gazed down—but with a shudder even more thrilling than before—upon the re-modelled and inverted images of the gray sedge, and the ghastly tree-stems, and the vacant and eye-like windows.

Nevertheless, in this mansion of gloom I now proposed to myself a sojourn of some weeks. Its proprietor, Roderick Usher, had been one of my boon companions in boyhood; but many years had elapsed since our last meeting. A letter, however, had lately reached me in a distant part of the country—a letter from him—which, in its wildly importunate nature, had admitted of no other than a personal reply. The MS. gave evidence of nervous agitation. The writer spoke of acute bodily illness—of a pitiable mental idiosyncrasy which oppressed him—and of an earnest desire to see me, as his best, and indeed, his only personal friend, with a view of attempting, by the cheerfulness of my society, some alleviation of his malady. It was the manner in which all this, and much more, was said—it was the apparent *heart* that went with his request—which allowed me no room for hesitation—and I accordingly obeyed, what I still considered a very singular summons, forthwith.

1. The text is that of the first publication in *Burton's Gentleman's Magazine, and American Monthly Review* 5 (September 1839).
2. A small lake, usually in the mountains.

Although, as boys, we had been even intimate associates, yet I really knew little of my friend. His reserve had been always excessive and habitual. I was aware, however, that his very ancient family had been noted, time out of mind, for a peculiar sensibility of temperament, displaying itself, through long ages, in many works of exalted art, and manifested, of late, in repeated deeds of munificent yet unobtrusive charity, as well as in a passionate devotion to the intricacies, perhaps even more than to the orthodox and easily recognizable beauties, of musical science. I had learned, too, the very remarkable fact, that the stem of the Usher race, all time-honored as it was, had put forth, at no period, any enduring branch; in other words, that the entire family lay in the direct line of descent, and had always, with very trifling and very temporary variation, so lain. It was this deficiency, I considered, while running over in thought the perfect keeping of the character of the premises with the accredited character of the people, and while speculating upon the possible influence which the one, in the long lapse of centuries, might have exercised upon the other—it was this deficiency, perhaps, of collateral issue, and the consequent undeviating transmission, from sire to son, of the patrimony with the name, which had, at length, so identified the two as to merge the original title of the estate in the quaint and equivocal appellation of the "House of Usher"—an appellation which seemed to include, in the minds of the peasantry who used it, both the family and the family mansion.

I have said that the sole effect of my somewhat childish experiment, of looking down within the tarn, had been to deepen the first singular impression. There can be no doubt that the consciousness of the rapid increase of my superstition—for why should I not so term it?—served mainly to accelerate the increase itself. Such, I have long known, is the paradoxical law of all sentiments having terror as a basis. And it might have been for this reason only, that, when I again uplifted my eyes to the house itself, from its image in the pool, there grew in my mind a strange fancy—a fancy so ridiculous, indeed, that I but mention it to show the vivid force of the sensations which oppressed me. I had so worked upon my imagination as really to believe that around about the whole mansion and domain there hung an atmosphere peculiar to themselves and their immediate vicinity—an atmosphere which had no affinity with the air of heaven, but which had reeked up from the decayed trees, and the gray walls, and the silent tarn, in the form of an inelastic vapor or gas—dull, sluggish, faintly discernible, and leaden-hued. Shaking off from my spirit what *must* have been a dream, I scanned more narrowly the real aspect of the building. Its principal feature seemed to be that of an excessive antiquity. The discoloration of ages had been great. Minute fungi overspread the whole exterior, hanging in a fine tangled web-work from the eaves. Yet all this was apart from any extraordinary dilapidation. No portion of the masonry had fallen; and there appeared to be a wild inconsistency between its still perfect adaptation of parts, and the utterly porous, and evidently decayed condition of the individual stones. In this there was much that reminded me of the specious totality of old wood-work which has rotted for long years in some neglected vault, with no disturbance from the breath of the external air. Beyond this indication of extensive decay, however, the fabric gave little token of instability. Perhaps the eye of a scrutinizing observer might have discovered a barely perceptible fissure, which, extending from the roof of the building in front, made its way down the wall in a zigzag direction, until it became lost in the sullen waters of the tarn.

Noticing these things, I rode over a short causeway to the house. A servant in waiting took my horse, and I entered the Gothic archway of the hall. A valet, of stealthy step, thence conducted me, in silence, through many dark and intricate passages in my progress to the studio of his master. Much that I encountered on the way contributed, I know not how, to heighten the vague sentiments of which I have already spoken. While the objects around me—while the carvings of the ceilings, the sombre tapestries of the walls, the ebon blackness of the floors, and the phantasmagoric armorial trophies which rattled as I strode, were but matters to which, or to such as which, I had been accustomed from my infancy—while I hesitated not to acknowledge how familiar was all this—I still wondered to find how unfamiliar were the fancies which ordinary images were stirring up. On one of the staircases, I met the physician of the family. His countenance, I thought, wore a mingled expression of low cunning and perplexity. He accosted me with trepidation and passed on. The valet now threw open a door and ushered me into the presence of his master.

The room in which I found myself was very large and excessively lofty. The windows were long, narrow, and pointed, and at so vast a distance from the black oaken floor as to be altogether inaccessible from within. Feeble gleams of encrimsoned light made their way through the trelliced panes, and served to render sufficiently distinct the more prominent objects around; the eye, however, struggled in vain to reach the remoter angles of the chamber, or the recesses of the vaulted and fretted ceiling. Dark draperies hung upon the walls. The general furniture was profuse, comfortless, antique, and tattered. Many books and musical instruments lay scattered about, but failed to give any vitality to the scene. I felt that I breathed an atmosphere of sorrow. An air of stern, deep, and irredeemable gloom hung over and pervaded all.

Upon my entrance, Usher arose from a sofa upon which he had been lying at full length, and greeted me with a vivacious warmth which had much in it, I at first thought of an overdone cordiality—of the constrained effort of the ennuyé[3] man of the world. A glance, however, at his countenance convinced me of his perfect sincerity. We sat down; and for some moments, while he spoke not, I gazed upon him with a feeling half of pity, half of awe. Surely, man had never before so terribly altered, in so brief a period, as had Roderick Usher! It was with difficulty that I could bring myself to admit the identity of the wan being before me with the companion of my early boyhood. Yet the character of his face had been at all times remarkable. A cadaverousness of complexion; an eye large, liquid, and luminous beyond comparison; lips somewhat thin and very pallid, but of a surpassingly beautiful curve; a nose of a delicate Hebrew model, but with a breadth of nostril unusual in similar formations; a finely moulded chin, speaking, in its want of prominence, of a want of moral energy; hair of a more than web-like softness and tenuity; these features, with an inordinate expansion above the regions of the temple, made up altogether a countenance not easily to be forgotten. And now in the mere exaggeration of the prevailing character of these features,

3. Bored (French).

and of the expression they were wont to convey, lay so much of change that I doubted to whom I spoke. The now ghastly pallor of the skin, and the now miraculous lustre of the eye, above all things startled and even awed me. The silken hair, too, had been suffered to grow all unheeded, and as, in its wild gossamer texture, it floated rather than fell about the face, I could not, even with effort, connect its arabesque expression with any idea of simple humanity.

In the manner of my friend I was at once struck with an incoherence—an inconsistency; and I soon found this to arise from a series of feeble and futile struggles to overcome an habitual trepidancy, an excessive nervous agitation. For something of this nature I had indeed been prepared, no less by his letter, than by reminiscences of certain boyish traits, and by conclusions deduced from his peculiar physical conformation and temperament. His action was alternately vivacious and sullen. His voice varied rapidly from a tremulous indecision (when the animal spirits seemed utterly in abeyance) to that species of energetic concision—that abrupt, weighty, unhurried, and hollow-sounding enunciation—that leaden, self-balanced and perfectly modulated guttural utterance, which may be observed in the moments of the intensest excitement of the lost drunkard, or the irreclaimable eater of opium.

It was thus that he spoke of the object of my visit, of his earnest desire to see me, and of the solace he expected me to afford him. He entered, at some length, into what he conceived to be the nature of his malady. It was, he said, a constitutional and a family evil, and one for which he despaired to find a remedy—a mere nervous affection, he immediately added, which would undoubtedly soon pass off. It displayed itself in a host of unnatural sensations. Some of these, as he detailed them, interested and bewildered me—although, perhaps, the terms, and the general manner of the narration had their weight. He suffered much from a morbid acuteness of the senses; the most insipid food was alone endurable; he could wear only garments of certain texture; the odors of all flowers were oppressive; his eyes were tortured by even a faint light; and there were but peculiar sounds, and these from stringed instruments, which did not inspire him with horror.

To an anomalous species of terror I found him a bounden slave. "I shall perish," said he, "I *must* perish in this deplorable folly. Thus, thus, and not otherwise, shall I be lost. I dread the events of the future, not in themselves, but in their results. I shudder at the thought of any, even the most trivial, incident, which may operate upon this intolerable agitation of soul. I have, indeed, no abhorrence of danger, except in its absolute effect—in terror. In this unnerved—in this pitiable condition—I feel that I must inevitably abandon life and reason together in my struggles with some fatal demon of fear."

I learned, moreover, at intervals, and through broken and equivocal hints, another singular feature of his mental condition. He was enchained by certain superstitious impressions in regard to the dwelling which he tenanted, and from which, for many years, he had never ventured forth—in regard to an influence whose supposititious force was conveyed in terms too shadowy here to be restated—an influence which some peculiarities in the mere form and substance of his family mansion, had, by dint of long sufferance, he said, obtained over his spirit—an effect which the *physique* of the gray walls and turrets, and of the dim tarn into which they all looked down, had, at length, brought about upon the *morale* of his existence.

He admitted, however, although with hesitation, that much of the peculiar gloom which thus afflicted him could be traced to a more natural and far more palpable origin—to the severe and long-continued illness—indeed to the evidently approaching dissolution—of a tenderly beloved sister; his sole companion for long years—his last and only relative on earth. "Her decease," he said, with a bitterness which I can never forget, "would leave him (him the hopeless and the frail) the last of the ancient race of the Ushers." As he spoke, the lady Madeline (for so was she called) passed slowly through a remote portion of the apartment, and, without having noticed my presence, disappeared. I regarded her with an utter astonishment not unmingled with dread. Her figure, her air, her features—all, in their very minutest development were those—were identically (I can use no other sufficient term) were identically those of the Roderick Usher who sat beside me. A feeling of stupor oppressed me, as my eyes followed her retreating steps. As a door, at length, closed upon her exit, my glance sought instinctively and eagerly the countenance of the brother—but he had buried his face in his hands, and I could only perceive that a far more than ordinary wanness had overspread the emaciated fingers through which trickled many passionate tears.

The disease of the lady Madeline had long baffled the skill of her physicians. A settled apathy, a gradual wasting away of the person, and frequent although transient affections of a partially cataleptical[4] character, were the unusual diagnosis. Hitherto she had steadily borne up against the pressure of her malady, and had not betaken herself finally to bed; but, on the closing in of the evening of my arrival at the house, she succumbed, as her brother told me at night with inexpressible agitation, to the prostrating power of the destroyer—and I learned that the glimpse I had obtained of her person would thus probably be the last I should obtain—that the lady, at least while living, would be seen by me no more.

For several days ensuing, her name was unmentioned by either Usher or myself; and, during this period, I was busied in earnest endeavors to alleviate the melancholy of my friend. We painted and read together—or I listened, as if in a dream, to the wild improvisations of his speaking guitar. And thus, as a closer and still closer intimacy admitted me more unreservedly into the recesses of his spirit, the more bitterly did I perceive the futility of all attempt at cheering a mind from which darkness, as if an inherent positive quality, poured forth upon all objects of the moral and physical universe, in one unceasing radiation of gloom.

I shall ever bear about me, as Moslemin their shrouds at Mecca, a memory of the many solemn hours I thus spent alone with the master of the House of Usher. Yet I should fail in any attempt to convey an idea of the exact character of the studies, or of the occupations, in which he involved me, or led me the way. An excited and highly distempered ideality threw a sulphurous lustre over all. His long improvised dirges will ring for ever in my ears. Among other things, I bear painfully in mind a certain singular perversion and amplification of the wild air of the last waltz of Von Weber.[5] From the

4. A condition characterized by a loss of sensation and muscular paralysis.

5. Carl Maria von Weber (1786–1826), influential German composer of the Romantic school. "The Last Waltz of Von Weber" was composed by Carl Gottlieb Reissiger (1798–1859).

paintings over which his elaborate fancy brooded, and which grew, touch by touch, into vaguenesses at which I shuddered the more thrillingly, because I shuddered knowing not why, from these paintings (vivid as their images now are before me) I would in vain endeavor to educe more than a small portion which should lie within the compass of merely written words. By the utter simplicity, by the nakedness, of his designs, he arrested and overawed attention. If ever mortal painted an idea, that mortal was Roderick Usher. For me at least—in the circumstances then surrounding me—there arose out of the pure abstractions which the hypochondriac contrived to throw upon his canvas, an intensity of intolerable awe, no shadow of which felt I ever yet in the contemplation of the certainly glowing yet too concrete reveries of Fuseli.[6]

One of the phantasmagoric conceptions of my friend, partaking not so rigidly of the spirit of abstraction, may be shadowed forth, although feebly, in words. A small picture presented the interior of an immensely long and rectangular vault or tunnel, with low walls, smooth, white, and without interruption or device. Certain accessory points of the design served well to convey the idea that this excavation lay at an exceeding depth below the surface of the earth. No outlet was observed in any portion of its vast extent, and no torch, or other artificial source of light was discernible—yet a flood of intense rays rolled throughout, and bathed the whole in a ghastly and inappropriate splendor.

I have just spoken of that morbid condition of the auditory nerve which rendered all music intolerable to the sufferer, with the exception of certain effects of stringed instruments. It was, perhaps, the narrow limits to which he thus confined himself upon the guitar, which gave birth, in great measure, to the fantastic character of his performances. But the fervid *facility* of his impromptus could not be so accounted for. They must have been, and were, in the notes, as well as in the words of his wild fantasias, (for he not unfrequently accompanied himself with rhymed verbal improvisations,) the result of that intense mental collectedness and concentration to which I have previously alluded as observable only in particular moments of the highest artificial excitement. The words of one of these rhapsodies I have easily borne away in memory. I was, perhaps, the more forcibly impressed with it, as he gave it, because, in the under or mystic current of its meaning, I fancied that I perceived, and for the first time, a full consciousness on the part of Usher, of the tottering of his lofty reason upon her throne. The verses, which were entitled "The Haunted Palace," ran very nearly, if not accurately, thus:[7]

I

In the greenest of our valleys,
   By good angels tenanted,
Once a fair and stately palace—
   Snow-white palace—reared its head.
In the monarch Thought's dominion—

6. Henry Fuseli (1741–1825), Swiss painter noted for his interest in the supernatural.

7. In the original printing this note appeared at the end of the story: "The ballad of 'The Haunted Palace,' introduced in this tale, was published separately, some months ago, in the Baltimore 'Museum.'"

It stood there!
Never seraph spread a pinion
Over fabric half so fair.

II

Banners yellow, glorious, golden,
On its roof did float and flow;
(This—all this—was in the olden
Time long ago)
And every gentle air that dallied,
In that sweet day,
Along the ramparts plumed and pallid,
A winged odor went away.

III

Wanderers in that happy valley
Through two luminous windows saw
Spirits moving musically
To a lute's well-tunéd law,
Round about a throne, where sitting
(Porphyrogene!)[8]
In state his glory well befitting,
The sovereign of the realm was seen.

IV

And all with pearl and ruby glowing
Was the fair palace door,
Through which came flowing, flowing, flowing,
And sparkling evermore,
A troop of Echoes whose sole duty
Was but to sing,
In voices of surpassing beauty,
The wit and wisdom of their king.

V

But evil things, in robes of sorrow,
Assailed the monarch's high estate;
(Ah, let us mourn, for never morrow
Shall dawn upon him, desolate!)
And, round about his home, the glory
That blushed and bloomed
Is but a dim-remembered story
Of the old time entombed.

VI

And travellers now within that valley,
Through the red-litten windows, see

8. Born to the purple, of royal birth.

Vast forms that move fantastically
  To a discordant melody;
While, like a rapid ghastly river,
  Through the pale door,
A hideous throng rush out forever,
  And laugh—but smile no more.

I well remember that suggestions arising from this ballad led us into a train of thought wherein there became manifest an opinion of Usher's which I mention not so much on account of its novelty, (for other men have thought thus,) as on account of the pertinacity with which he maintained it. This opinion, in its general form, was that of the sentience of all vegetable things. But, in his disordered fancy, the idea had assumed a more daring character, and trespassed, under certain conditions, upon the kingdom of inorganization. I lack words to express the full extent, or the earnest *abandon* of his persuasion. The belief, however, was connected (as I have previously hinted) with the gray stones of the home of his forefathers. The condition of the sentience had been here, he imagined, fulfilled in the method of collocation of these stones—in the order of their arrangement, as well as in that of the many fungi which overspread them, and of the decayed trees which stood around—above all, in the long undisturbed endurance of this arrangement, and in its reduplication in the still waters of the tarn. Its evidence—the evidence of the sentience—was to be seen, he said, (and I here started as he spoke,) in *the gradual yet certain condensation of an atmosphere of their own about the waters and the walls*. The result was discoverable, he added, in that silent, yet importunate and terrible influence which for centuries had moulded the destinies of his family, and which made *him* what I now saw him—what he was. Such opinions need no comment, and I will make none.

Our books—the books which, for years, had formed no small portion of the mental existence of the invalid—were, as might be supposed, in strict keeping with this character of phantasm. We pored together over such works as the Ververt et Chartreuse of Gresset; the Belphegor of Machiavelli; the Selenography of Brewster; the Heaven and Hell of Swedenborg; the Subterranean Voyage of Nicholas Klimm de Holberg; the Chiromancy of Robert Flud, of Jean D'Indaginé, and of De la Chambre; the Journey into the Blue Distance of Tieck; and the City of the Sun of Campanella.[9] One favorite volume was a small octavo edition of the Directorium Inquisitorium, by the Dominican Eymeric de Gironne; and there were passages in Pomponius Mela, about the old African Satyrs and Œgipans, over which Usher would sit dreaming for hours. His chief delight, however, was found in the earnest and repeated perusal of an exceedingly rare and curious book in quarto

9. *The City of the Sun* by the Italian Tommaso Campanella (1568–1639) is a famous utopian work. Jean Baptiste Gresset (1709–1777) wrote the anticlerical *Vairvert* and *Ma Chartreuse*. In *Belphegor*, by Niccolò Machiavelli (1469–1527), a demon comes to earth to prove that women damn men to hell. Sir David Brewster (1781–1868), Scottish physicist who studied optics and light. Emanuel Swedenborg (1688–1772), Swedish scientist and mystic. Ludwig Holberg (1684–1754), Danish dramatist and historian, described a voyage to the land of death and back. The English physician Robert Flud (1574–1637) and two Frenchmen, Jean D'Indaginé (fl. early 16th century) and Maria Cireau de la Chambre (1594–1669), all wrote on chiromancy (palm reading). The German Ludwig Tieck (1773–1853) wrote *Das Alte Buch; oder Reise ins Blaue hinein*, which narrates a journey to another world.

Gothic—the manual of a forgotten church—the *Vigilae Mortuorum secundum Chorum Ecclesiae Maguntinae*.[1]

I could not help thinking of the wild ritual of this work, and of its probable influence upon the hypochondriac, when, one evening, having informed me abruptly that the lady Madeline was no more, he stated his intention of preserving her corpse for a fortnight, previously to its final interment, in one of the numerous vaults within the main walls of the building. The worldly reason, however, assigned for this singular proceeding, was one which I did not feel at liberty to dispute. The brother had been led to his resolution (so he told me) by considerations of the unusual character of the malady of the deceased, of certain obtrusive and eager inquiries on the part of her medical men, and of the remote and exposed situation of the burial ground of the family. I will not deny that when I called to mind the sinister countenance of the person whom I met upon the staircase, on the day of my arrival at the house, I had no desire to oppose what I regarded as at best but a harmless, and not by any means an unnatural precaution.[2]

At the request of Usher, I personally aided him in the arrangements for the temporary entombment. The body having been encoffined, we two alone bore it to its rest. The vault in which we placed it (and which had been so long unopened that our torches, half smothered in its oppressive atmosphere, gave us little opportunity for investigation) was small, damp, and utterly without means of admission for light; lying, at great depth, immediately beneath that portion of the building in which was my own sleeping apartment. It had been used, apparently, in remote feudal times, for the worst purposes of a donjon[3] keep, and, in later days, as a place of deposit for powder, or other highly combustible substance, as a portion of its floor, and the whole interior of a long archway through which we reached it, were carefully sheathed with copper. The door, of massive iron, had been, also, similarly protected. Its immense weight caused an unusually sharp grating sound, as it moved upon its hinges.

Having deposited our mournful burden upon tressels[4] within this region of horror, we partially turned aside the yet unscrewed lid of the coffin, and looked upon the face of the tenant. The exact similitude between the brother and sister even here again startled and confounded me. Usher, divining, perhaps, my thoughts, murmured out some few words from which I learned that the deceased and himself had been twins, and that sympathies of a scarcely intelligible nature had always existed between them. Our glances, however, rested not long upon the dead—for we could not regard her unawed. The disease which had thus entombed the lady in the maturity of youth, had left, as usual in all maladies of a strictly cataleptical character, the mockery of a faint blush upon the bosom and the face, and that suspiciously lingering smile upon the lip which is so terrible in death. We replaced and screwed down the lid, and, having secured the door of iron, made our

1. A book called *The Vigils of the Dead, According to the Church-Choir of Mayence* was printed in Switzerland around 1500. Nicholas Eymeric de Gerone, who was inquisitor-general for Castile in 1356, recorded procedures for torturing heretics. Pomponius Mela (1st century) was a Roman whose widely used book on geography (printed in Italy in 1471) described strange beasts ("œgipans" are African goat-men).
2. The shortage of corpses for dissection had led to the new profession of "resurrection men," who dug up fresh corpses and sold them to medical students and surgeons.
3. Dungeon.
4. Trestles; braced supports.

way, with toil, into the scarcely less gloomy apartments of the upper portion of the house.

And now, some days of bitter grief having elapsed, an observable change came over the features of the mental disorder of my friend. His ordinary manner had vanished. His ordinary occupations were neglected or forgotten. He roamed from chamber to chamber with hurried, unequal, and objectless step. The pallor of his countenance had assumed, if possible, a more ghastly hue—but the luminousness of his eye had utterly gone out. The once occasional huskiness of his tone was heard no more; and a tremulous quaver, as if of extreme terror, habitually characterized his utterance.—There were times, indeed, when I thought his unceasingly agitated mind was laboring with an oppressive secret, to divulge which he struggled for the necessary courage. At times, again, I was obliged to resolve all into the mere inexplicable vagaries of madness, as I beheld him gazing upon vacancy for long hours, in an attitude of the profoundest attention, as if listening to some imaginary sound. It was no wonder that his condition terrified—that it infected me. I felt creeping upon me, by slow yet certain degrees, the wild influences of his own fantastic yet impressive superstitions.

It was, most especially, upon retiring to bed late in the night of the seventh or eighth day after the entombment of the lady Madeline, that I experienced the full power of such feelings. Sleep came not near my couch—while the hours waned and waned away. I struggled to reason off the nervousness which had dominion over me. I endeavored to believe that much, if not all of what I felt, was due to the phantasmagoric influence of the gloomy furniture of the room—of the dark and tattered draperies, which, tortured into motion by the breath of a rising tempest, swayed fitfully to and fro upon the walls, and rustled uneasily about the decorations of the bed. But my efforts were fruitless. An irrepressible tremor gradually pervaded my frame; and, at length, there sat upon my very heart an incubus[5] of utterly causeless alarm. Shaking this off with a gasp and a struggle, I uplifted myself upon the pillows, and, peering earnestly within the intense darkness of the chamber, harkened—I know not why, except that an instinctive spirit prompted me—to certain low and indefinite sounds which came, through the pauses of the storm, at long intervals, I knew not whence. Overpowered by an intense sentiment of horror, unaccountable yet unendurable, I threw on my clothes with haste, for I felt that I should sleep no more during the night, and endeavored to arouse myself from the pitiable condition into which I had fallen, by pacing rapidly to and fro through the apartment.

I had taken but few turns in this manner, when a light step on an adjoining staircase arrested my attention. I presently recognized it as that of Usher. In an instant afterwards he rapped, with a gentle touch, at my door, and entered, bearing a lamp. His countenance was, as usual, cadaverously wan—but there was a species of mad hilarity in his eyes—an evidently restrained hysteria in his whole demeanor. His air appalled me—but any thing was preferable to the solitude which I had so long endured, and I even welcomed his presence as a relief.

5. An evil spirit supposed to lie upon people in their sleep.

"And you have not seen it?" he said abruptly, after having stared about him for some moments in silence—"you have not then seen it?—but, stay! you shall." Thus speaking, and having carefully shaded his lamp, he hurried to one of the gigantic casements, and threw it freely open to the storm.

The impetuous fury of the entering gust nearly lifted us from our feet. It was, indeed, a tempestuous yet sternly beautiful night, and one wildly singular in its terror and its beauty. A whirlwind had apparently collected its force in our vicinity; for there were frequent and violent alterations in the direction of the wind; and the exceeding density of the clouds (which hung so low as to press upon the turrets of the house) did not prevent our perceiving the life-like velocity with which they flew careering from all points against each other, without passing away into the distance. I say that even their exceeding density did not prevent our perceiving this—yet we had no glimpse of the moon or stars—nor was there any flashing forth of the lightning. But the under surfaces of the huge masses of agitated vapor, as well as all terrestrial objects immediately around us, were glowing in the unnatural light of a faintly luminous and distinctly visible gaseous exhalation which hung about and enshrouded the mansion.

"You must not—you shall not behold this!" said I, shudderingly, to Usher, as I led him, with a gentle violence, from the window to a seat. "These appearances, which bewilder you, are merely electrical phenomena not uncommon—or it may be that they have their ghastly origin in the rank miasma of the tarn. Let us close this casement—the air is chilling and dangerous to your frame. Here is one of your favorite romances. I will read, and you shall listen—and so we will pass away this terrible night together."

The antique volume which I had taken up was the "Mad Trist" of Sir Launcelot Canning[6]—but I had called it a favorite of Usher's more in sad jest than in earnest; for, in truth, there is little in its uncouth and unimaginative prolixity which could have had interest for the lofty and spiritual ideality of my friend. It was, however, the only book immediately at hand; and I indulged a vague hope that the excitement which now agitated the hypochondriac might find relief (for the history of mental disorder is full of similar anomalies) even in the extremeness of the folly which I should read. Could I have judged, indeed, by the wild, overstrained air of vivacity with which he harkened, or apparently harkened, to the words of the tale, I might have well congratulated myself upon the success of my design.

I had arrived at that well-known portion of the story where Ethelred, the hero of the Trist, having sought in vain for peaceable admission into the dwelling of the hermit, proceeds to make good an entrance by force. Here, it will be remembered, the words of the narrative run thus—

"And Ethelred, who was by nature of a doughty heart, and who was now mighty withal, on account of the powerfulness of the wine which he had drunken, waited no longer to hold parley with the hermit, who, in sooth, was of an obstinate and maliceful turn, but, feeling the rain upon his shoulders, and fearing the rising of the tempest, uplifted his mace outright, and, with blows, made quickly room in the plankings of the door for his gauntleted hand, and now pulling therewith sturdily, he so cracked, and ripped,

6. Not a real book. "Trist" here means meeting, or prearranged or fated encounter.

and tore all asunder, that the noise of the dry and hollow-sounding wood alarummed and reverberated throughout the forest."

At the termination of this sentence I started, and, for a moment, paused; for it appeared to me (although I at once concluded that my excited fancy had deceived me)—it appeared to me that, from some very remote portion of the mansion or of its vicinity, there came, indistinctly, to my ears, what might have been, in its exact similarity of character, the echo (but a stifled and dull one certainly) of the very cracking and ripping sound which Sir Launcelot had so particularly described. It was, beyond doubt, the coincidence alone which had arrested my attention; for, amid the rattling of the sashes of the casements, and the ordinary commingled noises of the still increasing storm, the sound, in itself, had nothing, surely, which should have interested or disturbed me. I continued the story.

"But the good champion Ethelred, now entering within the door, was sore enraged and amazed to perceive no signal of the maliceful hermit; but, in the stead thereof, a dragon of scaly and prodigious demeanor, and of a fiery tongue, which sate in guard before a palace of gold, with a floor of silver; and upon the wall there hung a shield of shining brass with this legend enwritten—

> Who entereth herein, a conqueror hath bin,
> Who slayeth the dragon, the shield he shall win.

And Ethelred uplifted his mace, and struck upon the head of the dragon, which fell before him, and gave up his pesty breath, with a shriek so horrid and harsh, and withal so piercing, that Ethelred had fain to close his ears with his hands against the dreadful noise of it, the like whereof was never before heard."

Here again I paused abruptly, and now with a feeling of wild amazement—for there could be no doubt whatever that, in this instance, I did actually hear (although from what direction it proceeded I found it impossible to say) a low and apparently distant, but harsh, protracted, and most unusual screaming or grating sound—the exact counterpart of what my fancy had already conjured up as the sound of the dragon's unnatural shriek as described by the romancer.

Oppressed, as I certainly was, upon the occurrence of this second and most extraordinary coincidence, by a thousand conflicting sensations, in which wonder and extreme terror were predominant, I still retained sufficient presence of mind to avoid exciting, by any observation, the sensitive nervousness of my companion. I was by no means certain that he had noticed the sounds in question; although, assuredly, a strange alteration had, during the last few minutes, taken place in his demeanor. From a position fronting my own, he had gradually brought round his chair, so as to sit with his face to the door of the chamber, and thus I could but partially perceive his features, although I saw that his lips trembled as if he were murmuring inaudibly. His head had dropped upon his breast—yet I knew that he was not asleep, from the wide and rigid opening of the eye, as I caught a glance of it in profile. The motion of his body, too, was at variance with his idea—for he rocked from side to side with a gentle yet constant and uniform sway. Having rapidly taken notice of all this, I resumed the narrative of Sir Launcelot, which thus proceeded:—

"And now, the champion, having escaped from the terrible fury of the dragon, bethinking himself of the brazen shield, and of the breaking up of the enchantment which was upon it, removed the carcass from out of the way before him, and approached valorously over the silver pavement of the castle to where the shield was upon the wall; which in sooth tarried not for his full coming, but fell down at his feet upon the silver floor, with a mighty great and terrible ringing sound."

No sooner had these syllables passed my lips, than—as if a shield of brass had indeed, at the moment, fallen heavily upon a floor of silver—I became aware of a distinct, hollow, metallic, and clangorous, yet apparently muffled reverberation. Completely unnerved, I started convulsively to my feet, but the measured rocking movement of Usher was undisturbed. I rushed to the chair in which he sat. His eyes were bent fixedly before him, and throughout his whole countenance there reigned a more than stony rigidity. But, as I laid my hand upon his shoulder, there came a strong shudder over his frame; a sickly smile quivered about his lips; and I saw that he spoke in a low, hurried, and gibbering murmur, as if unconscious of my presence. Bending closely over his person, I at length drank in the hideous import of his words.

"Not hear it?—yes, I hear it, and *have* heard it. Long—long—long—many minutes, many hours, many days, have I heard it—yet I dared not—oh, pity me, miserable wretch that I am!—I dared not—I *dared* not speak! *We have put her living in the tomb!* Said I not that my senses were acute?—I *now* tell you that I heard her first feeble movements in the hollow coffin. I heard them—many, many days ago—yet I dared not—*I dared not speak!* And now—to-night—Ethelred—ha! ha!—the breaking of the hermit's door, and the death-cry of the dragon, and the clangor of the shield—say, rather, the rending of the coffin, and the grating of the iron hinges, and her struggles within the coppered archway of the vault! Oh whither shall I fly? Will she not be here anon? Is she not hurrying to upbraid me for my haste? Have I not heard her footsteps on the stair? Do I not distinguish that heavy and horrible beating of her heart? Madman!"—here he sprung violently to his feet, and shrieked out his syllables, as if in the effort he were giving up his soul—"Madman! *I tell you that she now stands without the door!*"

As if in the superhuman energy of his utterance there had been found the potency of a spell—the huge antique pannels to which the speaker pointed, threw slowly back, upon the instant, their ponderous and ebony jaws. It was the work of the rushing gust—but then without those doors there *did* stand the lofty and enshrouded figure of the lady Madeline of Usher. There was blood upon her white robes, and the evidence of some bitter struggle upon every portion of her emaciated frame. For a moment she remained trembling and reeling to and fro upon the threshold—then, with a low moaning cry, fell heavily inward upon the person of her brother, and in her horrible and now final death-agonies, bore him to the floor a corpse, and a victim to the terrors he had dreaded.

From that chamber, and from that mansion, I fled aghast. The storm was still abroad in all its wrath as I found myself crossing the old causeway. Suddenly there shot along the path a wild light, and I turned to see whence a gleam so unusual could have issued—for the vast house and its shadows were alone behind me. The radiance was that of the full, setting, and blood-red moon, which now shone vividly through that once barely-discernible fissure, of which I have before spoken, as extending from the roof of the building, in a zig-zag direction, to the base. While I gazed, this fissure rapidly widened—there came a fierce breath of the whirlwind—the entire orb of the satellite burst at once upon my sight—my brain reeled as I saw the mighty walls rushing asunder—there was a long tumultuous shouting sound like the voice of a thousand waters—and the deep and dank tarn at my feet closed sullenly and silently over the fragments of the *"House of Usher."*

1839

William Wilson. A Tale[1]

What say of it? what say of conscience *grim,*
That spectre in my path?
—*Chamberlaine's Pharronida*[2]

Let me call myself, for the present, William Wilson. The fair page now lying before me need not be sullied with my real appellation. This has been already too much an object for the scorn, for the horror, for the detestation of my race. To the uttermost regions of the globe have not the indignant winds bruited its unparalleled infamy? oh, outcast of all outcasts most abandoned! To the earth art thou not for ever dead? to its honours, to its flowers, to its golden aspirations? and a cloud, dense, dismal, and limitless, does it not hang eternally between thy hopes and heaven?

I would not, if I could, here or to-day, embody a record of my later years of unspeakable misery, and unpardonable crime. This epoch—these later years—took unto themselves a sudden elevation in turpitude, whose origin alone it is my present purpose to assign. Men usually grow base by degrees. From me, in an instant, all virtue dropped bodily as a mantle. I shrouded my nakedness in triple guilt. From comparatively trivial wickedness I passed, with the stride of a giant, into more than the enormities of an Elah-Gabalus.[3] What chance, what one event brought this evil thing to pass, bear with me while I relate. Death approaches; and the shadow which foreruns him has thrown a softening influence over my spirit. I long, in passing through the dim valley, for the sympathy—I had nearly said for the pity—of my fellow-men. I would fain have them believe that I have been, in some measure, the slave of circumstances beyond human control. I would wish them to seek out for me, in the details I am about to give, some little oasis of *fatality* amid a wilderness of error. I would have them allow—what they cannot refrain from allowing—that, although temptation may have erewhile existed as great, man was never *thus*, at least, tempted before—certainly, never *thus* fell. And therefore has he never thus suffered. Have I not indeed been living in a dream? And am I not now dying a victim to the horror and the mystery of the wildest of all sub-lunary visions?

1. This tale is reprinted from its first appearance in the Philadelphia annual *The Gift*, dated 1840 but published in September 1839. Poe drew on memories of the school he attended at Stoke-Newington (Bransby was the name of his principal there).

2. The epigraph is not in this 1659 poem by the English poet William Chamberlayne (1619–1689); something like the epigraph does appear in his *Love's Victory* (1658).

3. Elagabalus (b. 204), boy emperor of Rome (r. 218–22), murdered by the imperial guards.

I am come of a race whose imaginative and easily excitable temperament has at all times rendered them remarkable; and, in my earliest infancy, I gave evidence of having fully inherited the family character. As I advanced in years it was more strongly developed; becoming, for many reasons, a cause of serious disquietude to my friends, and of positive injury to myself. I grew self-willed, addicted to the wildest caprices, and a prey to the most ungovernable passions. Weak-minded, and beset with constitutional infirmities akin to my own, my parents could do but little to check the evil propensities which distinguished me. Some feeble and ill-directed efforts resulted in complete failure on their part, and of course, in total triumph on mine. Thenceforward my voice was a household law; and at an age when few children have abandoned their leading-strings, I was left to the guidance of my own will, and became, in all but name, the master of my own actions.

My earliest recollections of a school-life are connected with a large, rambling, cottage-built, and somewhat decayed building in a misty-looking village of England, where were a vast number of gigantic and gnarled trees, and where all the houses were excessively ancient and inordinately tall. In truth, it was a dream-like and spirit-soothing place, that venerable old town. At this moment, in fancy, I feel the refreshing chilliness of its deeply-shadowed avenues, inhale the fragrance of its thousand shrubberies, and thrill anew with undefinable delight, at the deep, hollow note of the church-bell, breaking each hour, with sullen and sudden roar, upon the stillness of the dusky atmosphere in which the old, fretted, Gothic steeple lay imbedded and asleep.

It gives me, perhaps, as much of pleasure as I can now in any manner experience, to dwell upon minute recollections of the school and its concerns. Steeped in misery as I am—misery, alas! only too real—I shall be pardoned for seeking relief, however slight and temporary, in the weakness of a few rambling details. These, moreover, utterly trivial, and even ridiculous in themselves, assume, to my fancy, adventitious importance as connected with a period and a locality, when and where I recognise the first ambiguous monitions of the destiny which afterwards so fully overshadowed me. Let me then remember.

The house, I have said, was old, irregular, and cottage-built. The grounds were extensive, and an enormously high and solid brick wall, topped with a bed of mortar and broken glass, encompassed the whole. This prison-like rampart formed the limit of our domain; beyond it we saw but thrice a week—once every Saturday afternoon, when, attended by two ushers,[4] we were permitted to take brief walks in a body through some of the neighbouring fields—and twice during Sunday, when we were paraded in the same formal manner to the morning and evening service in the one church of the village. Of this church the principal of our school was pastor. With how deep a spirit of wonder and perplexity was I wont to regard him from our remote pew in the gallery, as, with step solemn and slow he ascended the pulpit! This reverend man, with countenance so demurely benign, with robes so glossy and so clerically flowing, with wig so minutely powdered, so rigid and so vast—could this be he who of late, with sour visage, and in

4. Assistant schoolmasters.

snuffy habiliments, administered, ferule in hand, the Draconian[5] laws of the academy? Oh, gigantic paradox too utterly monstrous for solution!

At an angle of the ponderous wall frowned a more ponderous gate. It was riveted and studded with iron bolts, and surmounted with jagged iron spikes. What impressions of deep awe it inspired! It was never opened save for the three periodical egressions and ingressions already mentioned; then, in every creak of its mighty hinges we found a plenitude of mystery, a world of matter for solemn remark, or for far more solemn meditation.

The extensive enclosure was irregular in form, having many capacious recesses. Of these, three or four of the largest constituted the play-ground. It was level, and covered with fine hard gravel. I well remember it had no trees, nor benches, nor any thing similar within it. Of course it was in the rear of the house. In front lay a small parterre,[6] planted with box and other shrubs; but through this sacred division we passed only upon rare occasions indeed, such as a first advent or final departure from school, or perhaps, when a parent or friend having called for us, we joyfully took our way home for the Christmas or Mid-summer holydays.

But the house—how quaint an old building was this!—to me how veritably a palace of enchantment! There was really no end to its windings, to its incomprehensible sub-divisions. It was impossible, at any given time, to say with certainty upon which of its two stories one happened to be. From each room to every other there were sure to be found three or four steps either in ascent or descent. Then the lateral branches were innumerable—inconceivable, and so returning in upon themselves, that our most exact ideas in regard to the whole mansion were not very far different from those with which we pondered upon infinity. During the five years of my residence here I was never able to ascertain with precision, in what remote locality lay the little sleeping apartment assigned to myself and some eighteen or twenty other scholars.

The school-room was the largest in the house—I could not help thinking, in the world. It was very long, narrow, and dismally low, with pointed Gothic windows and a ceiling of oak. In a remote and terror-inspiring angle was a square enclosure of eight or ten feet, comprising the sanctum, "during hours," of our principal, the Reverend Dr. Bransby. It was a solid structure, with massy door, sooner than open which in the absence of "the Dominie," we would all have willingly perished by the *peine forte et dure*.[7] In other angles were two other similar boxes, far less reverenced, indeed, but still greatly matters of awe. One of these was the pulpit of "the classical" usher, one of the "English and mathematical." Interspersed about the room, crossing and recrossing in endless irregularity, were innumerable benches and desks, black, ancient, and time-worn, piled desperately with much-bethumbed books, and so beseamed with initial letters, names at full length, meaningless gashes, grotesque figures, and other multiplied efforts of the knife, as to have utterly lost what little of original form might have been their portion in

5. Merciless and severe; derived from Draco, Athenian lawgiver, whose stringent code of laws (621? B.C.E.) set death as the penalty for numerous crimes.
6. Ornamental garden.
7. Hard and forceful punishment (French); refers to the practice of crushing people to death under large flat rocks. "Dominie": minister or schoolteacher (Bransby was both).

days long departed. A huge bucket with water stood at one extremity of the room, and a clock of stupendous dimensions at the other.

Encompassed by the massy walls of this venerable academy I passed, yet not in tedium or disgust, the years of the third lustrum[8] of my life. The teeming brain of childhood requires no external world of incident to occupy or amuse it, and the apparently dismal monotony of a school, was replete with more intense excitement than my riper youth has derived from luxury, or my full manhood from crime. Yet I must believe that my first mental developement had in it much of the uncommon, even much of the *outré*.[9] Upon mankind at large the events of very early existence rarely leave in mature age any definite impression. All is gray shadow—a weak and irregular remembrance—an indistinct regathering of feeble pleasures and phantasmagoric pains. With me this is not so. In childhood I must have felt with the energy of a man what I now find stamped upon memory in lines as vivid, as deep, and as durable as the exergues of the Carthaginian medals.[1]

Yet in fact—in the fact of the world's view—how little was there to remember! The morning's awakening, the nightly summons to bed; the connings,[2] the recitations; the periodical half-holidays and perambulations; the play-ground, with its broils, its pastimes, its intrigues—these, by a mental sorcery long forgotten, were made to involve a wilderness of sensation, a world of rich incident, an universe of varied emotion, of excitement the most passionate and spirit-stirring. *"Oh, le bon temps, que ce siecle de fer!"*[3]

In truth, the ardency, the enthusiasm, and the imperiousness of my disposition soon rendered me a marked character among my schoolmates, and by slow but natural gradations, gave me an ascendency over all not greatly older than myself—over all with one single exception. This exception was found in the person of a scholar, who although no relation, bore the same Christian and surname as myself—a circumstance, in truth, little remarkable, for, notwithstanding a noble descent, mine was one of those every-day appellations which seem, by prescriptive right, to have been, time out of mind, the common property of the mob. In this narrative I have therefore designated myself as William Wilson—a fictitious title not very dissimilar to the real. My namesake alone, of those who in school phraseology constituted "our set," presumed to compete with me in the studies of the class, in the sports and broils of the play-ground—to refuse implicit belief in my assertions, and submission to my will—indeed to interfere with my arbitrary dictation in any respect whatsoever. If there be on earth a supreme and unqualified despotism, it is the despotism of a master mind in boyhood over the less energetic spirits of his companions.

Wilson's rebellion was to me a source of the greatest embarrassment—the more so as, in spite of the bravado with which in public I made a point of treating him and his pretensions, I secretly felt that I feared him, and could not help thinking the equality which he maintained so easily with myself a proof of his true superiority, since not to be overcome cost me a

8. Five-year period.
9. Extreme, exaggerated (French).
1. Medals of Carthage (the ancient sea power on the Mediterranean near modern Tunis, defeated by Rome in the 2nd century B.C.E.). "Exergues": the spaces beneath the central design on the reverse of coins.
2. Memorizings.
3. From Voltaire's *Le Mondain* (1736): "Oh, this age of iron is a good time" (French). Iron implies dull utilitarianism.

perpetual struggle. Yet this superiority—even this equality—was in truth acknowledged by no one but myself; our companions, by some unaccountable blindness, seemed not even to suspect it. Indeed, his competition, his resistance, and especially his impertinent and dogged interference with my purposes, were not more pointed than private. He appeared to be utterly destitute alike of the ambition which urged, and of the passionate energy of mind which enabled me to excel. In his rivalry he might have been supposed actuated solely by a whimsical desire to thwart, astonish, or mortify myself; although there were times when I could not help observing, with a feeling made up of wonder, abasement, and pique, that he mingled with his injuries, his insults, or his contradictions, a certain most inappropriate, and assuredly most unwelcome *affectionateness* of manner. I could only conceive this singular behaviour to arise from a consummate self-conceit assuming the vulgar airs of patronage and protection.

Perhaps it was this latter trait in Wilson's conduct, conjoined with our identity of name, and the mere accident of our having entered the school upon the same day, which set afloat the notion that we were brothers, among the senior classes in the academy. These do not usually inquire with much strictness into the affairs of their juniors. I have before said, or should have said, that Wilson was not, in the most remote degree, connected with my family. But assuredly if we *had* been brothers we must have been twins, for, since leaving Dr. Bransby's, I casually learned that my namesake—a somewhat remarkable coincidence—was born on the nineteenth of January, 1811—and this is precisely the day of my own nativity.[4]

It may seem strange that in spite of the continual anxiety occasioned me by the rivalry of Wilson, and his intolerable spirit of contradiction, I could not bring myself to hate him altogether. We had, to be sure, nearly every day a quarrel, in which, yielding me publicly the palm of victory, he, in some manner, contrived to make me feel that it was he who had deserved it; yet a sense of pride upon my part, and a veritable dignity upon his own, kept us always upon what are called "speaking terms," while there were many points of strong congeniality in our tempers, operating to awake in me a sentiment which our position alone, perhaps, prevented from ripening into friendship. It is difficult, indeed, to define, or even to describe, my real feelings towards him. They were formed of a heterogeneous mixture—some petulant animosity, which was not yet hatred, some esteem, more respect, much fear, with a world of uneasy curiosity. To the moralist fully acquainted with the minute springs of human action, it will be unnecessary to say, in addition, that Wilson and myself were the most inseparable of companions.

It was no doubt the anomalous state of affairs existing between us which turned all my attacks upon him, and they were many, either open or covert, into the channel of banter or practical joke (giving pain while assuming the aspect of mere fun) rather than into that of a more serious and determined hostility. But my endeavours on this head were by no means uniformly successful, even when my plans were the most wittily concocted; for my namesake had much about him, in character, of that unassuming and quiet austerity which, while enjoying the poignancy of its own jokes, has no heel

4. Poe was born on January 19, 1809.

of Achilles[5] in itself, and absolutely refuses to be laughed at. I could find, indeed, but one vulnerable point, and that, lying in a personal peculiarity arising, perhaps, from constitutional disease, would have been spared by any antagonist less at his wit's end than myself—my rival had a weakness in the faucial or guttural organs which precluded him from raising his voice at any time *above a very low whisper.* Of this defect I did not fail to take what poor advantage lay in my power.

Wilson's retaliations in kind were many, and there was one form of his practical wit that disturbed me beyond measure. How his sagacity first discovered at all that so petty a thing would vex me is a question I never could solve—but, having discovered, he habitually practised the annoyance. I had always felt aversion to my uncourtly patronymic, and its very common, if not plebeian, praenomen. The words were venom in my ears; and when, upon the day of my arrival, a second William Wilson came also to the academy, I felt angry with him for bearing the name, and doubly disgusted with the name because a stranger bore it who would be the cause of its twofold repetition, who would be constantly in my presence, and whose concerns, in the ordinary routine of the school business, must, inevitably, on account of the detestable coincidence, be often confounded with my own.

The feeling of vexation thus engendered, grew stronger with every circumstance tending to show resemblance, moral or physical, between my rival and myself. I had not then discovered the remarkable fact that we were of the same age; but I saw that we were of the same height, and I perceived that we were not altogether unlike in general contour of person and outline of feature. I was galled, too, by the rumour touching a relationship which had grown current in the upper forms. In a word, nothing could more seriously disturb me, (although I scrupulously concealed such disturbance,) than any allusion to a similarity of mind, person, or condition existing between us. But, in truth, I had no reason to believe that (with the exception of the matter of relationship, and in the case of Wilson himself,) this similarity had ever been made a subject of comment, or even observed at all by our schoolfellows. That *he* observed it in all its bearings, and as fixedly as I, was apparent, but that he could discover in such circumstances so fruitful a field of annoyance for myself can only be attributed, as I said before, to his more than ordinary penetration.

His cue, which was to perfect an imitation of myself, lay both in words and in actions; and most admirably did he play his part. My dress it was an easy matter to copy; my gait and general manner were, without difficulty, appropriated; in spite of his constitutional defect, even my voice did not escape him. My louder tones were, of course, unattempted, but then the key, it was identical; *and his singular whisper, it grew the very echo of my own.*

How greatly this most exquisite portraiture harassed me, (for it could not justly be termed a caricature,) I will not now venture to describe. I had but one consolation—in the fact that the imitation, apparently, was noticed by myself alone, and that I had to endure only the knowing and strangely sarcastic smiles of my namesake himself. Satisfied with having produced in

5. I.e., no vulnerable spot. The mother of Achilles, the hero of Homer's *Iliad*, tried to make her son immortal by dipping him into the river Styx. But no water touched the heel she held him by, and that is where he received his death wound.

my bosom the intended effect, he seemed to chuckle in secret over the sting he had inflicted, and was characteristically disregardful of the public applause which the success of his witty endeavours might have so easily elicited. That the school, indeed, did not feel his design, perceive its accomplishment, and participate in his sneer, was, for many anxious months, a riddle I could not resolve. Perhaps the *gradation* of his copy rendered it not so readily perceptible, or, more possibly, I owed my security to the masterly air of the copyist, who, disdaining the letter, which in a painting is all the obtuse can see, gave but the full spirit of his original for my individual contemplation and chagrin.

I have already more than once spoken of the disgusting air of patronage which he assumed towards me, and of his frequent officious interference with my will. This interference often took the ungracious character of advice; advice not openly given, but hinted or insinuated. I received it with a repugnance which gained strength as I grew in years. Yet, at this distant day, let me do him the simple justice to acknowledge that I can recall no occasion when the suggestions of my rival were on the side of those errors or follies so usual to his immature age, and seeming inexperience; that his moral sense, at least, if not his general talents and worldly wisdom, was far keener than my own; and that I might, to-day, have been a better, and thus a happier man, had I more seldom rejected the counsels embodied in those meaning whispers which I then but too cordially hated, and too bitterly derided.

As it was, I at length grew restive in the extreme, under his distasteful supervision, and daily resented more and more openly what I considered his intolerable arrogance. I have said that, in the first years of our connexion as schoolmates, my feelings in regard to him might have been easily ripened into friendship; but, in the latter months of my residence at the academy, although the intrusion of his ordinary manner had, beyond doubt, in some measure, abated, my sentiments, in nearly similar proportion, partook very much of positive hatred. Upon one occasion he saw this, I think, and afterwards avoided, or made a show of avoiding me.

It was about the same period, if I remember aright, that, in an altercation of violence with him, in which he was more than usually thrown off his guard, and spoke and acted with an openness of demeanour rather foreign to his nature, I discovered, or fancied I discovered, in his accent, his air, and general appearance, a something which first startled, and then deeply interested me, by bringing to mind dim visions of my earliest infancy; wild, confused, and thronging memories of a time when memory herself was yet unborn. I cannot better describe the sensation which oppressed me than by saying that I could with difficulty shake off the belief that myself and the being who stood before me had been acquainted at some epoch very long ago; some point of the past even infinitely remote. The delusion, however, faded rapidly as it came; and I mention it at all but to define the day of the last conversation I there held with my singular namesake.

The huge old house, with its countless subdivisions, had several enormously large chambers communicating with each other, where slept the greater number of the students. There were, however, as must necessarily happen in a building so awkwardly planned, many little nooks or recesses, the odds and ends of the structure; and these the economic ingenuity of Dr. Bransby had also fitted up as dormitories—although, being the merest closets, they were capable of accommodating only a single individual. One of these small apartments was occupied by Wilson.

It was upon a gloomy and tempestuous night of an early autumn, about the close of my fifth year at the school, and immediately after the altercation just mentioned, that, finding every one wrapped in sleep, I arose from bed, and, lamp in hand, stole through a wilderness of narrow passages from my own bed-room to that of my rival. I had been long plotting one of those ill-natured pieces of practical wit at his expense in which I had hitherto been so uniformly unsuccessful. It was my intention, now, to put my scheme in operation, and I resolved to make him feel the whole extent of the malice with which I was imbued. Having reached his closet, I noiselessly entered, leaving the lamp with a shade over it, on the outside. I advanced a step, and listened to the sound of his tranquil breathing. Assured of his being asleep, I returned, took the light, and with it again approached the bed. Close curtains were around it, which, in the prosecution of my plan, I slowly and quietly withdrew, when the bright rays fell vividly upon the sleeper, and my eyes, at the same moment upon his countenance. I looked, and a numbness, an iciness of feeling instantly pervaded my frame. My breast heaved, my knees tottered, my whole spirit became possessed with an objectless yet intolerable horror. Gasping for breath, I lowered the lamp in still nearer proximity to the face. Were these—*these* the lineaments of William Wilson? I saw, indeed, that they were his, but I shook as with a fit of the ague in fancying they were not. What *was* there about them to confound me in this manner? I gazed—while my brain reeled with a multitude of incoherent thoughts. Not thus he appeared—assuredly not *thus*—in the vivacity of his waking hours. The same name; the same contour of person; the same day of arrival at the academy! And then his dogged and meaningless imitation of my gait, my voice, my habits, and my manner! Was it, in truth, within the bounds of human possibility that *what I now witnessed* was the result of the habitual practice of this sarcastic imitation? Awe-stricken, and with a creeping shudder, I extinguished the lamp, passed silently from the chamber, and left, at once, the halls of that old academy, never to enter them again.

After a lapse of some months, spent at home in mere idleness, I found myself a student at Eton. The brief interval had been sufficient to enfeeble my remembrance of the events at Dr. Bransby's, or at least, to effect a material change in the nature of the feelings with which I remembered them. The truth—the tragedy—of the drama was no more. I could now find room to doubt the evidence of my senses; and seldom called up the subject at all but with wonder at the extent of human credulity, and a smile at the vivid force of the imagination which I hereditarily possessed. Neither was this species of scepticism likely to be diminished by the character of the life I led at Eton. The vortex of thoughtless folly into which I there so immediately and so recklessly plunged, washed away all but the froth of my past hours—engulfed, at once, every solid or serious impression, and left to memory only the veriest levities of a former existence.

I do not wish, however, to trace the course of my miserable profligacy here—a profligacy which set at defiance the laws, while it eluded the vigilance of the institution. Three years of folly, passed without profit, had but given me rooted habits of vice, and added, in a somewhat unusual degree, to my bodily stature, when, after a week of soulless dissipation, I invited a small party of the most dissolute students to a secret carousal in my chamber. We met at a late hour of the night, for our debaucheries were to be faithfully protracted until morning. The wine flowed freely, and there were not wanting other, perhaps more dangerous, seductions; so that the gray dawn had already faintly appeared in the east, while our delirious extravagance was at its height. Madly flushed with cards and intoxication, I was in the act of insisting upon a toast of more than intolerable profanity, when my attention was suddenly diverted by the violent, although partial unclosing of the door of the apartment, and by the eager voice from without of a servant. He said that some person, apparently in great haste, demanded to speak with me in the hall.

Wildly excited with the potent *Vin de Barac*, the unexpected interruption rather delighted than surprised me. I staggered forward at once, and a few steps brought me to the vestibule of the building. In this low and small room there hung no lamp; and now no light at all was admitted, save that of the exceedingly feeble dawn which made its way through a semicircular window. As I put my foot over the threshold I became aware of the figure of a youth about my own height, and (what then peculiarly struck my mad fancy) habited in a white cassimere morning frock, cut in the novel fashion of the one I myself wore at the moment. This the faint light enabled me to perceive—but the features of his face I could not distinguish. Immediately upon my entering he strode hurriedly up to me, and, seizing me by the arm with a gesture of petulant impatience, whispered the words "William Wilson!" in my ear. I grew perfectly sober in an instant.

There was that in the manner of the stranger, and in the tremulous shake of his uplifted finger, as he held it between my eyes and the light, which filled me with unqualified amazement—but it was not this which had so violently moved me. It was the pregnancy of solemn admonition in the singular, low, hissing utterance; and, above all, it was the character, the tone, *the key*, of those few, simple, and familiar, yet whispered, syllables, which came with a thousand thronging memories of by-gone days, and struck upon my soul with the shock of a galvanic battery. Ere I could recover the use of my senses he was gone.

Although this event failed not of a vivid effect upon my disordered imagination, yet was it evanescent as vivid. For some weeks, indeed, I busied myself in earnest inquiry, or was wrapped in a cloud of morbid speculation. I did not pretend to disguise from my perception the identity of the singular individual who thus perseveringly interfered with my affairs, and harassed me with his insinuated counsel. But who and what was this Wilson?—and whence came he?—and what were his purposes? Upon neither of these points could I be satisfied—merely ascertaining, in regard to him, that a sudden accident in his family had caused his removal from Dr. Bransby's Academy on the afternoon of the day in which I myself had eloped. But in a brief period I ceased to think upon the subject; my attention being all absorbed in a contemplated departure for Oxford. Thither I soon went; the uncalculating vanity of my parents furnished me with an outfit, and annual establishment, which would enable me to indulge at will in the luxury already so dear to my heart—to vie in profuseness of expenditure with the haughtiest heirs of the wealthiest earldoms in Great Britain.

Excited by such appliances to vice, my constitutional temperament broke forth with redoubled ardour, and I spurned even the common restraints of decency in the mad infatuation of my revels. But it were absurd to pause in the detail of my extravagance. Let it suffice, that among spendthrifts I out-heroded Herod,[6] and that, giving name to a multitude of novel follies, I added no brief appendix to the long catalogue of vices then usual in the most dissolute university of Europe.

It could hardly be credited, however, that I had, even here, so utterly fallen from the gentlemanly estate as to seek acquaintance with the vilest arts of the gambler by profession, and, having become an adept in his despicable science, to practise it habitually as a means of increasing my already enormous income at the expense of the weak-minded among my fellow-collegians. Such, nevertheless, was the fact. And the very enormity of this offence against all manly and honourable sentiment proved, beyond doubt, the main, if not the sole reason of the impunity with which it was committed. Who, indeed, among my most abandoned associates, would not rather have disputed the clearest evidence of his senses, than have suspected of such courses the gay, the frank, the generous William Wilson—the noblest and most liberal commoner at Oxford—him whose follies (said his parasites) were but the follies of youth and unbridled fancy—whose errors but inimitable whim—whose darkest vice but a careless and dashing extravagance.

I had been now two years successfully busied in this way, when there came to the university a young *parvenu* nobleman, Glendinning—rich, said report, as Herodes Atticus[7]—his riches, too, as easily acquired. I soon found him of weak intellect, and, of course, marked him as a fitting subject for my skill. I frequently engaged him in play, and contrived, with a gambler's usual art, to let him win considerable sums, the more effectually to entangle him in my snares. At length, my schemes being ripe, I met him (with the full intention that this meeting should be final and decisive) at the chambers of a fellow-commoner, (Mr. Preston,) equally intimate with both, but who, to do him justice, entertained not even a remote suspicion of my design. To give to this a better colouring, I had contrived to have assembled a party of some eight or ten, and was solicitously careful that the introduction of cards should appear accidental, and originate in the proposal of my contemplated dupe himself. To be brief upon a vile topic, none of the low finesse was omitted, so customary upon similar occasions that it is a just matter for wonder how any are still found so besotted as to fall its victim.

We had protracted our sitting far into the night, and I had at length effected the manœuvre of getting Glendinning as my sole antagonist. The game, too, was my favourite écarté.[8] The rest of the company, interested in the extent of our play, had abandoned their own cards, and were standing around us as spectators. The *parvenu*, who had been induced by my artifices in the early part of the evening to drink deeply, now shuffled, dealt, or played with a wild nervousness of manner for which his intoxication, I thought, might partially, but could not altogether, account. In a very short period he had become my debtor to a large amount of money, when, having taken a long draught of port, he did precisely what I had been cooly anticipating,

6. To outdo Herod in wickedness. In medieval mystery plays a favorite luridly acted villain was Herod (75–4 B.C.E.), the cruel king of Judea who ordered the massacre of the young male children of Bethlehem (Matthew 2).

7. Athenian rhetorician (2nd century), proverbial for his extreme wealth. "Parvenu": upstart, newly rich (French).

8. Card game for two people.

proposed to double our already extravagant stakes. With a well feigned show of reluctance, and not until after my repeated refusal had seduced him into some angry words which gave a colour of *pique* to my compliance, did I finally comply. The result, of course, did but prove how entirely the prey was in my toils—in less than a single hour he had quadrupled his debt. For some time his countenance had been losing the florid tinge lent it by the wine—but now, to my astonishment, I perceived that it had grown to a pallor truly fearful. I say to my astonishment. Glendinning had been represented to my eager inquiries as immeasurably wealthy; and the sums which he had as yet lost, although in themselves vast, could not, I supposed, very seriously annoy, much less so violently affect him. That he was overcome by the wine just swallowed, was the idea which most readily presented itself; and, rather with a view to the preservation of my own character in the eyes of my associates, than from any less interested motive, I was about to insist, peremptorily, upon a discontinuance of the play, when some expressions at my elbow from among the company, and an ejaculation evincing utter despair on the part of Glendinning, gave me to understand that I had effected his total ruin under circumstances which, rendering him an object for the pity of all, should have protected him from the ill offices of a fiend.

What now might have been my conduct it is difficult to say. The pitiable condition of my dupe had thrown an air of embarrassed gloom over all, and, for some moments, a profound and unbroken silence was maintained, during which I could not help feeling my cheeks tingle with the many burning glances of scorn or reproach cast upon me by the less abandoned of the party. I will even own that an intolerable weight of anxiety was for a brief instant lifted from my bosom by the sudden and extraordinary interruption which ensued. The wide, heavy folding doors of the apartment were all at once thrown open, to their full extent, with a vigorous and rushing impetuosity that extinguished, as if by magic, every candle in the room. Their light, in dying, enabled us just to perceive that a stranger had entered of about my own height, and closely muffled in a cloak. The darkness, however, was now total; and we could only feel that he was standing in our midst. Before any one of us could recover from the extreme astonishment into which this rudeness had thrown all, we heard the voice of the intruder.

"Gentlemen"—he said, in a low, distinct, and never-to-be-forgotten *whisper* which thrilled to the very marrow of my bones—"Gentlemen, I make no apology for this behaviour, because in thus behaving I am but fulfilling a duty. You are, beyond doubt, uninformed of the true character of the person who has to-night won at écarté a large sum of money from Lord Glendinning. I will therefore put you upon an expeditious and decisive plan of obtaining this very necessary information. Please to examine, at your leisure, the inner linings of the cuff of his left sleeve, and the several little packages which may be found in the somewhat capacious pockets of his embroidered morning wrapper."

While he spoke, so profound was the stillness that one might have heard a pin dropping upon the floor. In ceasing, he at once departed, and as abruptly as he had entered. Can I—shall I describe my sensations?—must I say that I felt all the horrors of the damned? Most assuredly I had but little time given for reflection. Many hands roughly seized me upon the spot, and lights were immediately reprocured. A search ensued. In the lining of my sleeve were found all of the court-cards essential in écarté, and, in the pockets of my wrapper, a number of packs, fac-similes of those used at our sittings, with the single exception that mine were of the species called, technically, *arrondé*; the honours[9] being slightly convex at the ends, the lower cards slightly convex at the sides. In this disposition, the dupe who cuts, as customary, at the breadth of the pack, will invariably find that he cuts his antagonist an honour; while the gambler, cutting at the length, will, as certainly, cut nothing for his victim which may count in the records of the game.

Any outrageous burst of indignation upon this shameful discovery would have affected me less than the silent contempt, or the sarcastic composure with which it was received.

"Mr. Wilson," said our host, stooping to remove from beneath his feet an exceedingly luxurious cloak of rare furs, "Mr. Wilson, this is your property." (The weather was cold; and, upon quitting my own room, I had thrown a cloak over my dressing wrapper, putting it off upon reaching the scene of play.) "I presume it is supererogatory to seek here (eyeing the folds of the garment with a bitter smile,) for any farther evidence of your skill. Indeed we have had enough. You will see the necessity, I hope, of quitting Oxford—at all events, of quitting, instantly, my chambers."

Abased, humbled to the dust as I then was, it is probable that I should have resented this galling language by immediate personal violence, had not my whole attention been immediately arrested, by a fact of the most startling character. The cloak which I had worn was of a rare description of fur; how rare, how extravagantly costly, I shall not venture to say. Its fashion, too, was of my own fantastic invention; for I was fastidious, to a degree of absurd coxcombry, in matters of this frivolous nature. When, therefore, Mr. Preston reached me that which he had picked up upon the floor, and near the folding doors of the apartment, it was with an astonishment nearly bordering upon terror, that I perceived my own already hanging on my arm, (where I had no doubt unwittingly placed it,) and that the one presented me was but its exact counterpart in every, in even the minutest possible particular. The singular being who had so disastrously exposed me, had been muffled, I remembered, in a cloak; and none had been worn at all by any of the members of our party with the exception of myself. Retaining some presence of mind, I took the one offered me by Preston, placed it, unnoticed, over my own, left the apartment with a resolute scowl of defiance, and, next morning ere dawn of day, commenced a hurried journey from Oxford to the continent, in a perfect agony of horror and of shame.

I fled in vain. My evil destiny pursued me as if in exultation, and proved, indeed, that the exercise of its mysterious dominion had as yet only begun. Scarcely had I set foot in Paris ere I had fresh evidence of the detestable interest taken by this Wilson in my concerns. Years flew, while I experienced no relief. Villain!—at Rome, with how untimely, yet with how spectral an officiousness, stepped he in between me and my ambition! At Vienna, too, at Berlin, and at Moscow! Where, in truth, had I *not* bitter cause to curse him within my heart? From his inscrutable tyranny did I at length flee, panic-stricken, as from a pestilence; and to the very ends of the earth *I fled in vain.*

9. Face cards. *"Arrondé"*: rounded (French).

And again, and again, in secret communion with my own spirit, would I demand the questions "Who is he?—whence came he?—and what are his objects?" But no answer was there found. And now I scrutinized, with a minute scrutiny, the forms, and the methods, and the leading traits of his impertinent supervision. But even here there was very little upon which to base a conjecture. It was noticeable, indeed, that, in no one of the multiplied instances in which he had of late crossed my path, had he so crossed it except to frustrate those schemes, or to disturb those actions, which, fully carried out, might have resulted in bitter mischief. Poor justification this, in truth, for an authority so imperiously assumed! Poor indemnity for natural rights of self-agency so pertinaciously, so insultingly denied!

I had also been forced to notice that my tormentor, for a very long period of time, (while scrupulously and with miraculous dexterity maintaining his whim of an identity of apparel with myself,) had so contrived it, in the execution of his varied interference with my will, that I saw not, at any moment, the features of his face. Be Wilson what he might, *this*, at least, was but the veriest of affection, or of folly. Could he, for an instant, have supposed that, in my admonisher at Eton, in the destroyer of my honour at Oxford, in him who thwarted my ambition at Rome, my revenge in Paris, my passionate love at Naples, or what he falsely termed my avarice in Egypt, that in this, my arch-enemy and evil genius, I could fail to recognize the William Wilson of my schoolboy days, the namesake, the companion, the rival, the hated and dreaded rival at Dr. Bransby's? Impossible!—But let me hasten to the last eventful scene of the drama.

Thus far I had succumbed supinely to this imperious domination. The sentiments of deep awe with which I habitually regarded the elevated character, the majestic wisdom, the apparent omnipresence and omnipotence of Wilson, added to a feeling of even terror, with which certain other traits in his nature and assumptions inspired me, had operated, hitherto, to impress me with an idea of my own utter weakness and helplessness, and to suggest an implicit, although bitterly reluctant submission to his arbitrary will. But, of late days, I had given myself up entirely to wine; and its maddening influency upon my hereditary temper rendered me more and more impatient of control. I began to murmur, to hesitate, to resist. And was it only fancy which induced me to believe that, with the increase of my own firmness, that of my tormentor underwent a proportional diminution? Be this as it may, I now began to feel the inspirations of a burning hope, and at length nurtured in my secret thoughts a stern and desperate resolution that I would submit no longer to be enslaved.

It was at Rome, during the carnival of 18—, that I attended a masquerade in the palazzo of the Neapolitan Duke Di Broglio. I had indulged more freely than usual in the excesses of the wine-table; and now the suffocating atmosphere of the crowded rooms irritated me beyond endurance. The difficulty, too, of forcing my way through the mazes of the company contributed not a little to the ruffling of my temper; for I was anxiously seeking, let me not say with what unworthy motive, the young, the gay, the beautiful wife of the aged and doting Di Broglio. With a too unscrupulous confidence she had previously communicated to me the secret of the costume in which she would be habited, and now, having caught a glimpse of her person, I was hurrying to make my way into her presence. At this moment I felt a light hand laid upon my shoulder, and that ever-remembered, low, damnable whisper within my ear.

In a perfect whirlwind of wrath, I turned at once upon him who had thus interrupted me, and seized him violently by the collar. He was attired, as I expected, like myself; wearing a large Spanish cloak, and a mask of black silk which entirely covered his features.

"Scoundrel!" I said, in a voice husky with rage, while every syllable I uttered seemed as new fuel to my fury, "scoundrel! impostor! accursed villain! you shall not—you *shall not* dog me unto death! Follow me, or I stab you where I stand," and I broke my way from the room into a small antechamber adjoining, dragging him unresistingly with me as I went.

Upon entering, I thrust him furiously from me. He staggered against the wall, while I closed the door with an oath, and commanded him to draw. He hesitated but for an instant, then, with a slight sigh, drew in silence, and put himself upon his defence.

The contest was brief indeed. I was frantic with every species of wild excitement, and felt within my single arm the energy and the power of a multitude. In a few seconds I forced him by sheer strength against the wainscoting, and thus, getting him at mercy, plunged my sword, with brute ferocity, repeatedly through and through his bosom.

At this instant some person tried the latch of the door. I hastened to prevent an intrusion, and then immediately returned to my dying antagonist. But what human language can adequately portray *that* astonishment, *that* horror which possessed me at the spectacle then presented to view. The brief moment in which I averted my eyes had been sufficient to produce, apparently, a material change in the arrangements at the upper or farther end of the room. A large mirror, it appeared to me, now stood where none had been perceptible before; and, as I stepped up to it in extremity of terror, mine own image, but with features all pale and dabbled in blood, advanced, with a feeble and tottering gait, to meet me.

Thus it appeared, I say, but was not. It was my antagonist—it was Wilson, who then stood before me in the agonies of his dissolution. Not a line in all the marked and singular lineaments of that face which was not, even identically, mine own! His mask and cloak lay, where he had thrown them, upon the floor.

It was Wilson, but he spoke no longer in a whisper, and I could have fancied that I myself was speaking while he said—

"You have conquered, and I yield. Yet, henceforward art thou also dead—dead to the world and its hopes. In me didst thou exist—and, in my death, see by this image, which is thine, how utterly thou hast murdered thyself."

1839

The Man of the Crowd[1]

Ce grand malheur, de ne pouvoir être seul.
—La Bruyère[2]

It was well said of a certain German book that *"er lasst sich nicht lesen"*—it does not permit itself to be read. There are some secrets which do not permit themselves to be told. Men die nightly in their beds, wringing the hands of ghostly confessors, and looking them piteously in the eyes—die with despair of heart and convulsion of throat, on account of the hideousness of mysteries which will not *suffer themselves* to be revealed. Now and then, alas, the conscience of man takes up a burthen so heavy in horror that it can be thrown down only into the grave. And thus the essence of all crime is undivulged.

Not long ago, about the closing in of an evening in autumn, I sat at the large bow window of the D——Coffee-House in London. For some months I had been ill in health, but was now convalescent, and, with returning strength, found myself in one of those happy moods which are so precisely the converse of *ennui*[3]—moods of the keenest appetency, when the film from the mental vision departs—the αχλμ. ο. πζιυ επιπεν[4]—and the intellect, electrified, surpasses as greatly its every-day condition, as does the vivid, yet candid reason of Combe, the mad and flimsy rhetoric of Gorgias.[5] Merely to breathe was enjoyment; and I derived positive pleasure even from many of the legitimate sources of pain. I felt a calm but inquisitive interest in every thing. With a cigar in my mouth and a newspaper in my lap, I had been amusing myself for the greater part of the afternoon, now in poring over advertisements, now in observing the promiscuous company in the room, and now in peering through the smoky panes into the street.

This latter is one of the principal thoroughfares of the city, and had been very much crowded during the whole day. But, as the darkness came on, the throng momently increased; and by the time the lamps were well litten two dense and continuous tides of population were rushing past the door. At this particular period of the evening I had never before been in a similar situation, and the tumultuous sea of human heads filled me, therefore, with a delicious novelty of emotion. I gave up at length all care of things within the hotel, and became absorbed in contemplation of the scene without. At first my observations took an abstract and generalizing turn. I looked at the passengers in masses, and thought of them in their aggregate relations. Soon, however, I descended to details, and regarded with minute interest the innumerable varieties of figure, dress, air, gait, visage, and expression of countenance.

By far the greater number of those who went by had a satisfied business-like demeanor, and seemed to be thinking only of making their way through

1. First published in *Graham's Magazine* 7 (December 1840), the source of the present text.
2. This great misfortune, of not being able to be alone (French). Adapted from *Characters*, by Jean de La Bruyère (1645–1696).
3. Boredom (French).
4. The mist that was upon it before (Greek), from Homer's *Iliad*, book 5.
5. Greek skeptic (4th century B.C.E.), known for an excessive rhetoric that preened itself at the expense of reason. William Combe (1741–1823), English writer of a series of books about the adventures of a clergyman-teacher, "Dr. Syntax."

the press. Their brows were knit, and their eyes rolled quickly, when pushed against by fellow-wayfarers they envinced no symptom of impatience, but adjusted their clothes and hurried on. Others, still a numerous class, were restless in their movements, had flushed faces, and talked and gesticulated to themselves, as if feeling in solitude on account of the very denseness of the company around. When impeded in their progress these people suddenly ceased muttering, but redoubled their gesticulations, and awaited, with an absent and overdone smile upon the lips, the course of the persons impeding them. If jostled, they bowed profusely to the jostlers, and appeared overwhelmed with confusion.—There was nothing very distinctive about these two large classes beyond what I have noted. Their habiliments belonged to that order which is pointedly termed the decent. They were undoubtedly noblemen, merchants, attorneys, tradesmen, stockjobbers—the Eupatrids[6] and the common-places of society—men of leisure and men actively engaged in affairs of their own—conducting business upon their own responsibility. They did not greatly excite my attention.

The tribe of clerks was an obvious one, and here I discerned two remarkable divisions. There were the junior clerks of flash houses—young gentlemen with tight coats, bright boots, well-oiled hair, and supercilious lips. Setting aside a certain dapperness of carriage which may be termed deskism for want of a better word, the manner of these persons seemed to me an exact facsimile of what had been the perfection of *bon ton*[7] about twelve or eighteen months before. They wore the cast-off graces of the gentry—and this, I believe, involves the best definition of the class.

The division of the upper clerks of staunch firms, or of the "steady old fellows," it was not possible to mistake. These were known by their coats and pantaloons of black or brown, made to sit comfortably, with white cravats and waistcoats, broad solid-looking shoes, and thick hose, or gaiters.—They had all slightly bald heads, from which the right ears, long used to pen-holding, had an odd habit of standing off on end. I observed that they always removed or settled their hats with both hands, and wore watches, with short, gold chains of a substantial and ancient pattern. Theirs was the affectation of respectability—if indeed there be an affectation so honorable.

There were many individuals of dashing appearance, whom I easily set down as belonging to the race of swell pick-pockets, with which all great cities are infested. I watched these gentry with much inquisitiveness, and found it difficult to imagine how they should ever be mistaken for gentlemen by gentlemen themselves. Their voluminousness of wristband, with an air of excessive frankness, should betray them at once.

The gamblers, of whom I described not a few, were still more easily recognisable. They wore every variety of dress, from that of the desperate thimble-rig[8] bully, with velvet waistcoat, fancy neckerchief, gilt chains, and fillagreed buttons, to that of the scrupulously inornate clergyman, than which nothing could be less liable to suspicion. Still all were distinguished by a certain sodden swarthiness of complexion, a filmy dimness of eye, and pallor and compression of lip. There were two other traits, moreover, by which I could always detect them—a guarded lowness of tone in conversation, and a more

6. Aristocrats.
7. Fashion (French).
8. Shell game, a gambling scheme of con artists who use sleight of hand to deceive.

than ordinary extension of the thumb in a direction at right angles with the fingers.—Very often in company with these sharpers I observed an order of men somewhat different in habits, but still birds of kindred feather. They may be defined as the gentlemen who live by their wits. They seem to prey upon the public in two battallions—that of the dandies and that of the military men. Of the first grade the leading features are long locks and smiles; of the second frogged coats and frowns.

Descending in the scale of what is termed gentility, I found darker and deeper themes for speculation. I saw Jew pedlars, with hawk eyes flashing from countenances whose every other feature wore only an expression of abject humility; sturdy professional street beggars scowling upon mendicants of a better stamp, whom despair alone had driven forth into the night for charity; feeble and ghastly invalids, upon whom death had placed a sure hand, and who sidled and tottered through the mob looking every one beseechingly in the face, as if in search of some chance consolation, some lost hope; modest young girls returning from long and late labor to a cheerless home, and shrinking more tearfully than indignantly from the glances of ruffians, whose direct contact even could not be avoided; women of the town of all kinds and of all ages—the unequivocal beauty in the prime of her womanhood, putting one in mind of the statue of Lucian, with the surface of Parian marble, and the interior filled with filth[9]—the loathsome and utterly lost leper in rags—the wrinkled, bejewelled and paint-begrimed beldame, making a last effort at youth—the mere child of immature form, yet, from long association, an adept in the dreadful coquetries of her trade, and burning with a rabid ambition to be ranked the equal of her elders in vice; drunkards innumerable and indescribable—some in shreds and patches, reeling, inarticulate, with bruised visage and lack-lustre eyes—some in whole although filthy garments, with a slightly unsteady swagger, thick sensual lips, and hearty-looking rubicund faces—others clothed in materials which had once been good, and which even now were scrupulously well-brushed—men who walked with a more than naturally firm and springy step, but whose countenances were fearfully pale, whose eyes hideously wild and red, and who clutched with quivering fingers, as they strode through the crowd, at every object which came within their reach; beside these, pie-men, porters, coal-heavers, sweeps; organ-grinders, monkey-exhibiters and ballad mongers, those who vended with those who sang; ragged artizans and exhausted laborers of every description, and still all full of a noisy and inordinate vivacity which jarred discordantly upon the ear, and gave an aching sensation to the eye.

As the night deepened, so deepened to me the interest of the scene; for not only did the general character of the crowd materially alter (its gentler features retiring in the gradual withdrawal of the more orderly portion of the people, and its harsher ones coming out into bolder relief as the late hour brought forth every species of infamy from its den,) but the rays of the gas-lamps, feeble at first in their struggle with the dying day, had now at length gained ascendency, and threw over every thing a fitful and garish lustre. All was dark yet splendid—as that ebony to which has been likened the style of

9. Paraphrased from "The Cock," by the Greek satirist Lucian (125?–200?). Parian marble (from the island of Paros, in the Cyclades) was used in classical statuary.

Tertullian.[1] The wild effects of the light enchained me to an examination of individual faces; and although the rapidity with which the world of life flitted before the window prevented me from casting more than a glance upon each visage, still it seemed that, in my then peculiar mental state, I could frequently read, even in that brief interval of a glance, the history of long years. With my brow to the glass, I was thus occupied in scrutinising the mob, when suddenly there came into view a countenance (that of a decrepid old man, some sixty-five or seventy years of age,) a countenance which at once arrested and absorbed my whole attention, on account of the absolute idiosyncrasy of its expression. Any thing even remotely resembling that expression I had never seen before. I well remember that my first thought, upon beholding it, was that Retzch,[2] had he viewed it, would have greatly preferred it to his own pictural incarnations of the fiend. As I endeavored, during the brief minute of my original survey, to form some analysis of the meaning conveyed, there arose confusedly and paradoxically within my mind the ideas of vast mental power, of caution, of penuriousness, of avarice, of coolness, of malice, of blood-thirstiness, of triumph, of merriment, of excessive terror, of intense, of supreme despair. I felt singularly aroused, startled, fascinated. "How wild a history," I said to myself, "is written within that bosom!" Then came a craving desire to keep the man in view—to know more of him. Hurriedly putting on an overcoat, and seizing my hat and cane, I made my way into the street, and pushed through the crowd in the direction which I had seen him take; for he had already disappeared. With some little difficulty I at length came within sight of him, approached, and followed him closely, yet cautiously, so as not to attract his attention.

I had now a good opportunity of examining his person. He was short in stature, very thin, and apparently very feeble. His clothes, generally, were filthy and ragged; but as he came, now and then, within the strong glare of a lamp, I perceived that his linen, although dirty, was of beautiful texture; and my vision deceived me, or, through a rent in a closely-buttoned, and evidently second-handed roquelaire[3] which enveloped him, I caught a glimpse either of a diamond, or of a dagger. These observations heightened my curiosity, and I resolved to follow the stranger whithersoever he should go.

It was now fully night-fall, and a thick humid fog hung over the city, threatening to end in a settled and heavy rain. This change of weather had an odd effect upon the crowd, the whole of which was at once put into new commotion, and overshadowed by a world of umbrellas. The waver, the jostle, and the hum increased in a tenfold degree. For my own part I did not much regard the rain—the lurking of an old fever in my system rending the moisture somewhat too dangerously pleasant. Tying a handkerchief about my mouth I kept on. For half an hour the old man held his way with difficulty along the great thoroughfare; and I here walked close at his elbow through fear of losing sight of him. Never once turning his head to look back, he did not observe me. By and bye he passed into a cross street, which, although densely filled with people, was not quite so much thronged as the main one he had quitted. Here a change in his demeanor became evident. He walked more slowly and with less object than before—more hesitatingly.

1. Quintus Septimius Florens Tertullianus (160?–230?), an influential early Christian writer.

2. Moritz Retzsch (1779–1857), German artist.

3. Cloak.

He crossed and re-crossed the street way repeatedly without apparent aim; and the press was still so thick that at every such movement I was obliged to follow him closely. The street was a narrow and long one, and his course lay within it for nearly an hour, during which the passengers had gradually diminished to about that number which is ordinarily seen at noon in Broadway near the Park—so vast a difference is there between a London populace and that of the most frequented American city. A second turn brought us into a square, brilliantly litten, and overflowing with life. The old manner of the stranger re-appeared. His chin fell upon his breast, while his eyes rolled wildly from under his knit brows in every direction upon those who hemmed him in. He urged his way steadily and perseveringly. I was surprised, however, to find, upon his having made the circuit of the square, that he turned and retraced his steps.—Still more was I astonished to see him repeat the same walk several times—once nearly detecting me as he came round with a sudden movement.

In this exercise he spent about an hour, at the end of which we met with far less interruption from passengers than at first. The rain fell fast; the air grew cool; and the people were retiring to their homes. With a gesture of what seemed to be petulant impatience, the wanderer passed into a bye-street comparatively deserted. Down this, some quarter of a mile long, he rushed with an activity I could not have dreamed of seeing in one so aged, and which put me to much trouble in pursuit. A few minutes brought us to a large and busy bazaar, with the localities of which the stranger appeared well acquainted, and where his original demeanor again became apparent, as he forced his way to and fro, without aim, among the host of buyers and sellers.

During the hour and a half, or thereabouts, which we passed in this place, it required much caution on my part to keep him within reach without attracting his observation. Luckily I wore a pair of gum[4] over-shoes and could move about in perfect silence. At no moment did he see that I watched him. He entered shop after shop, priced nothing, spoke no word, and looked at all objects with a wild and vacant stare. I was now utterly amazed at his behavior, and firmly resolved that we should not part until I had satisfied myself in some measure respecting him.

A loud-toned clock struck eleven, and the company were fast deserting the bazaar. A shopkeeper, in putting up a shutter, jostled the old man, and at the instant I saw a strong shudder come over his frame. He hurried into the street, looked anxiously around him for an instant, and then ran with incredible swiftness through many crooked and people-less lanes, until we emerged once more upon the great thoroughfare whence we had started—the street of the D——Hotel. It no longer wore, however, the same aspect. It was still brilliant with gas; but the rain fell fiercely, and there were few persons to be seen. The stranger grew deadly pale. He walked moodily some paces up the once populous avenue, then, with a heavy sigh, turned in the direction of the river, and, plunging through a great variety of devious ways, came out at length in view of one of the principal theatres. It was about being closed, and the audience were thronging from the doors. I saw the old man gasp as if for breath while he threw himself amid the crowd; but I

4. Rubber.

thought that the intense agony of his countenance had, in some measure, abated. His head again fell upon his breast; he appeared as I had seen him at first. I observed that he now took the course in which had gone the greater number of the audience—but, upon the whole, I was at a loss to comprehend the waywardness of his actions.

As he proceeded, the company grew more scattered, and his old uneasiness and vacillation were resumed. For some time he followed closely a party of some ten or twelve roisterers; but from this number one by one dropped off, until three only remained together in a narrow and gloomy lane little frequented. The stranger paused, and, for a moment, seemed lost in thought; then, with every mark of agitation, pursued rapidly a route which brought us to the verge of the city, amid regions very different from those we had hitherto traversed. It was the most noisome[5] quarter of London, where every thing wore the worst impress of the most deplorable poverty, and of the most desperate crime. By the dim light of an accidental lamp, tall, antique, worm-eaten, wooden tenements were seen tottering to their fall in directions so many and capricious that scarce the semblance of a passage was discernible between them. The paving-stones lay at random, displaced from their beds by the rankly-growing grass. Horrible filth festered in the dammed-up gutters. The whole atmosphere teemed with desolation. Yet, as we proceeded, the sounds of human life revived by sure degrees, and at length large bands of the most abandoned of a London populace were seen reeling to and fro. The spirits of the old man again flickered up, as a lamp which is near its death-hour.—Once more he strode onward with elastic tread. Suddenly a corner was turned, a blaze of light burst upon our sight, and we stood before one of the huge suburban temples of Intemperance—one of the palaces of the fiend, Gin.

It was now nearly day-break; but a number of wretched inebriates still pressed in and out of the flaunting entrance. With a half shriek of joy the old man forced a passage within, resumed at once his original bearing, and stalked backward and forward, without apparent object, among the throng. He had not been thus long occupied, however, before a rush to the doors gave token that the host was closing them for the night. It was something even more intense than despair that I then observed upon the countenance of the singular being whom I had watched so pertinaciously. Yet he did not hesitate in his career, but with a mad energy retraced his steps at once, to the heart of the mighty London. Long and swiftly he fled, while I followed him in the wildest amazement, resolute not to abandon a scrutiny in which I now felt an interest all-absorbing. The sun arose while we proceeded, and, when we had once again reached that most thronged mart of the populous town, the street of the D——Hotel, it presented an appearance of human bustle and activity scarcely inferior to what I had seen on the evening before. And here, long, amid the momently increasing confusion, did I persist in my pursuit of the stranger. But, as usual, he walked to and fro, and during the day did not pass from out the turmoil of that street. And, as the shades of the second evening come on, I grew wearied unto death, and, stopping fully in front of the wanderer, gazed at him steadfastly in the face. He noticed me not, but resumed

5. Disgusting, with an offensive odor.

his solemn walk, while I, ceasing to follow, remained absorbed in contemplation. "This old man," I said at length, "is the type and the genius of deep crime. He refuses to be alone. *He is the man of the crowd.* It will be in vain to follow; for I shall learn no more of him, nor of his deeds. The worst heart of the world is a grosser book than the 'Hortulus Animæ,' and perhaps it is but one of the great mercies of God that *'er lasst sich nicht lesen.'*"[6]

1840

The Masque of the Red Death[1]

The "Red Death" had long devastated the country. No pestilence had been ever so fatal, or so hideous. Blood was its Avatar[2] and its seal—the redness and the horror of blood. There were sharp pains, and sudden dizziness, and then profuse bleedings at the pores, with dissolution. The scarlet stains upon the body and especially upon the face of the victim, were the pest-ban which shut him out from the aid and from the sympathy of his fellow-men. And the whole seizure, progress and termination of the disease were the incidents of half an hour.

But the Prince Prospero was happy and dauntless, and sagacious. When his dominions were half depopulated, he summoned to his presence a thousand, hale and light-hearted friends from among the knights and dames of his court, and with these retired to the deep seclusion of one of his castellated[3] abbeys. This was an extensive and magnificent structure, the creation of the prince's own eccentric yet august taste. A strong and lofty wall girdled it in. This wall had gates of iron. The courtiers, having entered, brought furnaces and massy hammers and welded the bolts. They resolved to leave means neither of ingress or egress to the sudden impulses of despair from without or of frenzy from within. The abbey was amply provisioned. With such precautions the courtiers might bid defiance to contagion. The external world could take care of itself. In the meantime it was folly to grieve, or to think. The prince had provided all the appliances of pleasure. There were buffoons, there were improvisatori,[4] there were ballet dancers, there were musicians, there were cards, there was Beauty, there was wine. All these and security were within. Without was the "Red Death."

It was towards the close of the fifth or sixth month of his seclusion, and while the pestilence raged most furiously abroad, that the Prince Prospero entertained his thousand friends at a masked ball of the most unusual magnificence. It was a voluptuous scene that masquerade.

But first let me tell of the rooms in which it was held. There were seven—an imperial suite. In many palaces, however, such suites form a long and straight vista, while the folding doors slide back nearly to the walls on either hand, so that the view of the whole extent is scarcely impeded. Here the case was very

6. "It does not permit itself to be read" (German); see the opening lines of the story. "Hortulus Animæ": a book by John Grunninger printed in Germany around 1500.

1. First published in *Graham's Magazine* (May 1842), the source of the present text.

2. In Hindu myth, an earthly embodiment of a god.

3. With turrets and battlements, like a castle.

4. Improvisers (Italian); those who invent, compose, or recite without preparation. "Buffoons": clowns.

different; as might have been expected from the duke's love of the *bizarre*. The apartments were so irregularly disposed that the vision embraced but little more than one at a time. There was a sharp turn at every twenty or thirty yards, and at each turn a novel effect. To the right and left, in the middle of each wall, a tall and narrow Gothic window looked out upon a closed corridor which pursued the windings of the suite. These windows were of stained glass whose color varied in accordance with the prevailing hue of the decorations of the chamber into which it opened. That at the eastern extremity was hung, for example, in blue—and vividly blue were its windows. The second chamber was purple in its ornaments and tapestries, and here the panes were purple. The third was green throughout, and so were the casements. The fourth was furnished and litten[5] with orange—the fifth with white—the sixth with violet. The seventh apartment was closely shrouded in black velvet tapestries that hung all over the ceiling and down the walls, falling in heavy folds upon a carpet of the same material and hue. But, in this chamber only, the color of the windows failed to correspond with the decorations. The panes here were scarlet—a deep blood color. Now in no one of the seven apartments was there any lamp or candelabrum, amid the profusion of golden ornaments that lay scattered to and fro or depended from the roof. There was no light of any kind emanating from lamp or candle within the suite of chambers. But in the corridors that followed the suite, there stood, opposite to each window, a heavy tripod, bearing a brasier of fire that projected its rays through the tinted glass and so glaringly illumined the room. And thus were produced a multitude of gaudy and fantastic appearances. But in the western or black chamber the effect of the fire-light that streamed upon the dark hangings through the blood-tinted panes, was ghastly in the extreme, and produced so wild a look upon the countenances of those who entered, that there were few of the company bold enough to set foot within its precincts at all.

It was in this apartment, also, that there stood against the western wall, a gigantic clock of ebony. Its pendulum swung to and fro with a dull, heavy, monotonous clang; and when its minute-hand made the circuit of the face, and the hour was to be stricken, there came forth from the brazen[6] lungs of the clock a sound which was clear and loud and deep and exceedingly musical, but of so peculiar a note and emphasis that, at each lapse of an hour, the musicians in the orchestra were constrained to pause, momently, in their performance, to hearken to the sound; and thus the waltzers perforce ceased their evolutions; and there was a brief disconcert of the whole gay company; and, while the chimes of the clock yet rang, it was observed that the giddiest grew pale, and that the more aged and sedate passed their hands over their brows as if in confused reverie or meditation. But when the echoes had fully ceased, a light laughter at once pervaded the assembly; the musicians looked at each other and smiled as if at their own nervousness and folly, and made whispering vows, each to the other, that the next chiming of the clock should produce in them no similar emotion; and then, after the lapse of sixty minutes, (which embrace three thousand and six hundred seconds of the Time

5. Lighted.

6. Brass.

that flies,) there came yet another chiming of the clock, and then there were the same disconcert and tremulousness and meditation as before.

But, in spite of these things, it was a gay and magnificent revel. The tastes of the duke were peculiar. He had a fine eye for colors and effects. He disregarded the *decora*[7] of mere fashion. His plans were bold and fiery, and his conceptions glowed with barbaric lustre. There are some who would have thought him mad. His followers felt that he was not. It was necessary to hear and see and touch him to be *sure* that he was not.

He had directed, in great part, the moveable embellishments of the seven chambers, upon occasion of this great *fête*, and it was his own guiding taste which had given character to the costumes of the masqueraders. Be sure they were grotesque. There were much glare and glitter and piquancy and phantasm—much of what has been since seen in "Hernani."[8] There were arabesque figures with unsuited limbs and appointments. There were delirious fancies such as the madman fashions. There was much of the beautiful, much of the wanton, much of the *bizarre*, something of the terrible, and not a little of that which might have excited disgust. To and fro in the seven chambers there stalked, in fact, a multitude of dreams. And these, the dreams—writhed in and about, taking hue from the rooms, and causing the wild music of the orchestra to seem as the echo of their steps. And, anon, there strikes the ebony clock which stands in the hall of the velvet. And then, momently, all is still, and all is silent save the voice of the clock. The dreams are stiff frozen as they stand. But the echoes of the chime die away—they have endured but an instant—and a light, half-subdued laughter floats after them as they depart. And now again the music swells, and the dreams live, and writhe to and fro more merrily than ever, taking hue from the many-tinted windows through which stream the rays from the tripods. But to the chamber which lies most westwardly of the seven there are now none of the maskers who venture; for the night is waning away; and there flows a ruddier light through the blood-colored panes; and the blackness of the sable drapery appals; and to him whose foot falls upon the sable carpet, there comes from the near clock of ebony a muffled peal more solemnly emphatic than any which reaches *their* ears who indulge in the more remote gaieties of the other apartments.

But these other apartments were densely crowded, and in them beat feverishly the heart of life. And the revel went whirlingly on, until at length was sounded the twelfth hour upon the clock. And then the music ceased, as I have told; and the evolutions of the waltzers were quieted; and there was an uneasy cessation of all things as before. But now there were twelve strokes to be sounded by the bell of the clock; and thus it happened, perhaps, that more of thought crept, with more of time, into the meditations of the thoughtful among those who revelled. And thus, again, it happened, perhaps, that before the last echoes of the last chime had utterly sunk into silence, there were many individuals in the crowd who had found leisure to become aware of the presence of a masked figure which had arrested the attention of no single individual before. And the rumor of this new presence having

7. Proprieties (Latin).

8. Play that established Victor Hugo (1802–1885), later famous as a novelist, as the leading French Romantic playwright. Set in 16th-century Spain, *Hernani* opens with the entrance of a masked man.

spread itself whisperingly around, there arose at length from the whole company a buzz, or murmur, expressive at first of disapprobation and surprise—then, finally, of terror, of horror, and of disgust.

In an assembly of phantasms such as I have painted, it may well be supposed that no ordinary appearance could have excited such sensation. In truth the masquerade license of the night was nearly unlimited; but the figure in question had out-Heroded Herod,[9] and gone beyond the bounds of even the prince's indefinite decorum. There are chords in the hearts of the most reckless which cannot be touched without emotion. Even with the utterly lost, to whom life and death are equally jests, there *are* matters of which no jest can be properly made. The whole company, indeed, seemed now deeply to feel that in the costume and bearing of the stranger neither wit nor propriety existed. The figure was tall and gaunt, and shrouded from head to foot in the habiliments[1] of the grave. The mask which concealed the visage was made so nearly to resemble the countenance of a stiffened corpse that the closest scrutiny must have had difficulty in detecting the cheat. And yet all this might have been endured, if not approved, by the mad revellers around. But the mummer[2] had gone so far as to assume the type of the Red Death. His vesture was dabbled in *blood*—and his broad brow, with all the features of the face, was besprinkled with the scarlet horror.

When the eyes of the Prince Prospero fell upon this spectral image (which with a slow and solemn movement, as if more fully to sustain its *rôle,* stalked to and fro among the waltzers) he was seen to be convulsed, in the first moment, with a strong shudder either of terror or distaste; but, in the next, his brow reddened with rage.

"Who dares?" he demanded hoarsely of the group that stood around him, "who dares thus to make mockery of our woes? Uncase the varlet[3] that we may know whom we have to hang to-morrow at sunrise from the battlements. Will no one stir at my bidding?—stop him and strip him, I say, of those reddened vestures of sacrilege!"

It was in the eastern or blue chamber in which stood the Prince Prospero as he uttered these words. They rang throughout the seven rooms loudly and clearly—for the prince was a bold and robust man, and the music had become hushed at the waving of his hand.

It was in the blue room where stood the prince, with a group of pale courtiers by his side. At first, as he spoke, there was a slight rushing movement of this group in the direction of the intruder, who at the moment was also near at hand, and now, with deliberate and stately step, made closer approach to the speaker. But from a certain nameless awe with which the mad assumptions of the mummer had inspired the whole party, there were found none who put forth hand to seize him; so that, unimpeded, he passed within a yard of the prince's person; and, while the vast assembly, as if with one impulse, shrank from the centres of the rooms to the walls, he made his way uninterruptedly, but with the same solemn and measured step which had distinguished him from the first, through the blue chamber to the purple—through the purple to the green—through the green to the orange,—through this again to the white—and even thence to the violet, ere a decided movement

9. See p. 676, n. 6.
1. Clothing.
2. One who performs in a mask and does not speak.
3. Worthless fellow. "Uncase": unmask.

had been made to arrest him. It was then, however, that the Prince Prospero, maddening with rage and the shame of his own momentary cowardice, rushed hurriedly through the six chambers—while none followed him on account of a deadly terror that had seized upon all. He bore aloft a drawn dagger, and had approached, in rapid impetuosity, to within three or four feet of the retreating figure, when the latter, having attained the extremity of the velvet apartment, turned suddenly round and confronted his pursuer. There was a sharp cry—and the dagger dropped gleaming upon the sable carpet, upon which instantly afterwards, fell prostrate in death the Prince Prospero. Then, summoning the wild courage of despair, a throng of the revellers at once threw themselves into the black apartment, and, seizing the mummer, whose tall figure stood erect and motionless within the shadow of the ebony clock, gasped in unutterable horror at finding the grave-cerements[4] and corpse-like mask which they handled with so violent a rudeness, untenanted by any tangible form.

And now was acknowledged the presence of the Red Death. He had come like a thief in the night. And one by one dropped the revellers in the blood-bedewed halls of their revel, and died each in the despairing posture of his fall. And the life of the ebony clock went out with that of the last of the gay. And the flames of the tripods expired. And Darkness and Decay and the Red Death held illimitable dominion over all.

1842

The Tell-Tale Heart[1]

Art is long and Time is fleeting,
   And our hearts, though stout and brave,
Still, like muffled drums, are beating
   Funeral marches to the grave.
                    —*Longfellow*[2]

True!—nervous—very, very dreadfully nervous I had been, and am; but why *will* you say that I am mad? The disease had sharpened my senses—not destroyed—not dulled them. Above all was the sense of hearing acute. I heard all things in the heaven and in the earth. I heard many things in hell. How, then, am I mad? Harken! and observe how healthily—how calmly I can tell you the whole story.

It is impossible to say how first the idea entered my brain; but, once conceived, it haunted me day and night. Object there was none. Passion there was none. I loved the old man. He had never wronged me. He had never given me insult. For his gold I had no desire. I think it was his eye!—yes, it was this! He had the eye of a vulture—a pale blue eye, with a film over it. Whenever it fell upon me, my blood ran cold; and so, by degrees—very gradually—I made up my mind to take the life of the old man, and thus rid myself of the eye forever.

4. Cloths used for wrapping the dead; shrouds.

1. First published in *The Pioneer* (January 1843), the source of the present text.

2. Henry Wadsworth Longfellow's "A Psalm of Life" (1838), lines 13–16.

Now this is the point. You fancy me mad. Madmen know nothing. But you should have seen *me*. You should have seen how wisely I proceeded—with what caution—with what foresight—with what dissimulation I went to work! I was never kinder to the old man than during the whole week before I killed him. And every night, about midnight, I turned the latch of his door and opened it—oh so gently! And then, when I had made an opening sufficient for my head, I first put in a dark lantern,[3] all closed, closed, so that no light shone out, and then I thrust in my head. Oh, you would have laughed to see how cunningly I thrust it in! I moved it slowly—very, very slowly, so that I might not disturb the old man's sleep. It took me an hour to place my whole head within the opening so far that I could see the old man as he lay upon his bed. Ha!—would a madman have been so wise as this? And then, when my head was well in the room, I undid the lantern cautiously—oh, so cautiously (for the hinges creaked)—I undid it just so much that a single thin ray fell upon the vulture eye. And this I did for seven long nights—every night just at midnight—but I found the eye always closed; and so it was impossible to do the work; for it was not the old man who vexed me, but his Evil Eye. And every morning, when the day broke, I went boldly into his chamber, and spoke courageously to him, calling him by name in a hearty tone, and inquiring how he had passed the night. So you see he would have been a very profound old man, indeed, to suspect that every night, just at twelve, I looked in upon him while he slept.

Upon the eighth night I was more than usually cautious in opening the door. A watch's minute-hand moves more quickly than did mine. Never, before that night, had I *felt* the extent of my own powers—of my sagacity. I could scarcely contain my feelings of triumph. To think that there I was, opening the door, little by little, and the old man not even to dream of my secret deeds or thoughts. I fairly chuckled at the idea. And perhaps the old man heard me; for he moved in the bed suddenly, as if startled. Now you may think that I drew back—but no. His room was as black as pitch with the thick darkness, (for the shutters were close fastened, through fear of robbers,) and so I knew that he could not see the opening of the door, and I kept on pushing it steadily, steadily.

I had got my head in, and was about to open the lantern, when my thumb slipped upon the tin fastening, and the old man sprang up in the bed, crying out—"Who's there?"

I kept quite still and said nothing. For another hour I did not move a muscle, and in the meantime I did not hear the old man lie down. He was still sitting up in the bed, listening;—just as I have done, night after night, hearkening to the death-watches[4] in the wall.

Presently I heard a slight groan, and I knew that it was the groan of mortal terror. It was not a groan of pain, or of grief—oh, no!—it was the low, stifled sound that arises from the bottom of the soul when overcharged with *awe*. I knew the sound well. Many a night, just at midnight, when all the world slept, it has welled up from my own bosom, deepening, with its dreadful echo, the terrors that distracted me. I say I knew it well. I knew

3. Lantern with a single opening and sliding panel that can cut off the light.

4. Beetles that make a hollow clicking sound by striking their heads against the wood into which they burrow.

what the old man felt, and pitied him, although I chuckled at heart. I knew that he had been lying awake ever since the first slight noise, when he had turned in the bed. His fears had been, ever since, growing upon him. He had been trying to fancy them causeless, but could not. He had been saying to himself—"It is nothing but the wind in the chimney—it is only a mouse crossing the floor," or "it is merely a cricket which has made a single chirp." Yes, he had been trying to comfort himself with these suppositions; but he had found all in vain. *All in vain*; because death, in approaching the old man, had stalked with his black shadow before him, and the shadow had now reached and enveloped the victim. And it was the mournful influence of the unperceived shadow that caused him to feel—although he neither saw nor heard me—to *feel* the presence of my head within the room.

When I had waited a long time, very patiently, without hearing the old man lie down, I resolved to open a little—a very, very little crevice in the lantern. So I opened it—you cannot imagine how stealthily, stealthily—until, at length, a single dim ray, like the thread of the spider, shot from out the crevice and fell full upon the vulture eye.

It was open—wide, wide open—and I grew furious as I gazed upon it. I saw it with perfect distinctness—all a dull blue, with a hideous veil over it that chilled the very marrow in my bones; but I could see nothing else of the old man's face or person; for I had directed the ray, as if by instinct, precisely upon the damned spot.

And now—have I not told you that what you mistake for madness is but over acuteness of the senses?—now, I say, there came to my ears *a low, dull, quick sound—much such a sound as a watch makes when enveloped in cotton*. I knew *that* sound well, too. It was the beating of the old man's heart. It increased my fury, as the beating of a drum stimulates the soldier into courage.

But even yet I refrained and kept still. I scarcely breathed. I held the lantern motionless. I tried how steadily I could maintain the ray upon the eye. Meantime the hellish tattoo[5] of the heart increased. It grew quicker, and louder and louder every instant. The old man's terror *must* have been extreme! It grew louder, I say, louder every moment:—do you mark me well? I have told you that I am nervous:—so I am. And now, at the dead hour of night, and amid the dreadful silence of that old house, so strange a noise as this excited me to uncontrollable wrath. Yet, for some minutes longer, I refrained and kept still. But the beating grew louder, *louder*! I thought the heart must burst! And now a new anxiety seized me—the sound would be heard by a neighbor! The old man's hour had come! With a loud yell, I threw open the lantern and leaped into the room. He shrieked once—once only. In an instant I dragged him to the floor, and pulled the heavy bed over him. I then sat upon the bed and smiled gaily, to find the deed so far done. But, for many minutes, the heart beat on, with a muffled sound. This, however, did not vex me; it would not be heard through the walls. At length it ceased. The old man was dead. I removed the bed and examined the corpse. Yes, he was stone, stone dead. I placed my hand upon the heart

5. Drumbeat.

and held it there many minutes. There was no pulsation. The old man was stone dead. His eye would trouble *me* no more.

If, still, you think me mad, you will think so no longer when I describe the wise precautions I took for the concealment of the body. The night waned, and I worked hastily, but in silence. First of all I dismembered the corpse. I cut off the head and the arms and the legs. I then took up three planks from the flooring of the chamber, and deposited all between the scantlings.[6] I then replaced the boards so cleverly, so cunningly, that no human eye—not even *his*—could have detected anything wrong. There was nothing to wash out—no stain of any kind—no blood-spot whatever. I had been too wary for that. A tub had caught all—ha! ha!

When I had made an end of these labors, it was four o'clock—still dark as midnight. As the bell sounded the hour, there came a knocking at the street door. I went down to open it with a light heart,—for what had I *now* to fear? There entered three men, who introduced themselves, with perfect suavity, as officers of the police. A shriek had been heard by a neighbor during the night; suspicion of foul play had been aroused; information had been lodged at the police-office, and they (the officers) had been deputed to search the premises.

I smiled,—for *what* had I to fear? I bade the gentlemen welcome. The shriek, I said, was my own in a dream. The old man, I mentioned, was absent in the country. I took my visiters all over the house. I bade them search—search *well*. I led them, at length, to *his* chamber. I showed them his treasures, secure, undisturbed. In the enthusiasm of my confidence, I brought chairs into the room, and desired them *here* to rest from their fatigues; while I myself, in the wild audacity of my perfect triumph, placed my own seat upon the very spot beneath which reposed the corpse of the victim.

The officers were satisfied. My *manner* had convinced them. I was singularly at ease. They sat, and, while I answered cheerily, they chatted of familiar things. But, ere long, I felt myself getting pale and wished them gone. My head ached, and I fancied a ringing in my ears: but still they sat and still chatted. The ringing became more distinct: I talked more freely, to get rid of the feeling; but it continued and gained definitiveness—until, at length, I found that the noise was *not* within my ears.

No doubt I now grew *very* pale;—but I talked more fluently, and with a heightened voice. Yet the sound increased—and what could I do? It was *a low, dull, quick sound—much such a sound as a watch makes when enveloped in cotton*. I gasped for breath—and yet the officers heard it not. I talked more quickly—more vehemently;—but the noise steadily increased. I arose, and argued about trifles, in a high key and with violent gesticulations;—but the noise steadily increased. Why *would* they not be gone? I paced the floor to and fro, with heavy strides, as if excited to fury by the observations of the men;—but the noise steadily increased. Oh God! what *could* I do? I foamed—I raved—I swore! I swung the chair upon which I had sat, and grated it upon the boards;—but the noise arose over all and continually increased. It grew louder—louder—*louder!* And still the men chatted pleasantly, and smiled. Was it possible they heard not? Almighty God! no, no! They heard!—they

6. Small planks.

suspected!—they *knew!*—they were making a mockery of my horror!—this I thought, and this I think. But anything better than this agony! Anything was more tolerable than this derision! I could bear those hypocritical smiles no longer! I felt that I must scream or die!—and now—again!—hark! louder! louder! louder! *louder!*—

"Villains!" I shrieked, "dissemble no more! I admit the deed!—tear up the planks!—here, here!—it is the beating of his hideous heart!"

1843

The Black Cat[1]

For the most wild, yet most homely narrative which I am about to pen, I neither expect nor solicit belief. Mad indeed would I be to expect it, in a case where my very senses reject their own evidence. Yet, mad am I not—and very surely do I not dream. But to-morrow I die, and to-day I would unburthen my soul. My immediate purpose is to place before the world, plainly, succinctly, and without comment, a series of mere household events. In their consequences, these events have terrified—have tortured—have destroyed me. Yet I will not attempt to expound them. To me, they have presented little but Horror—to many they will seem less terrible than *barroques*.[2] Hereafter, perhaps, some intellect may be found which will reduce my phantasm to the commonplace—some intellect more calm, more logical, and far less excitable than my own, which will perceive, in the circumstances I detail with awe, nothing more than an ordinary succession of very natural causes and effects.

From my infancy I was noted for the docility and humanity of my disposition. My tenderness of heart was even so conspicuous as to make me the jest of my companions. I was especially fond of animals, and was indulged by my parents with a great variety of pets. With these I spent most of my time, and never was so happy as when feeding and caressing them. This peculiarity of character grew with my growth, and, in my manhood, I derived from it one of my principal sources of pleasure. To those who have cherished an affection for a faithful and sagacious dog, I need hardly be at the trouble of explaining the nature or the intensity of the gratification thus derivable. There is something in the unselfish and self-sacrificing love of a brute, which goes directly to the heart of him who has had frequent occasion to test the paltry friendship and gossamer fidelity of mere *Man*.

I married early, and was happy to find in my wife a disposition not uncongenial with my own. Observing my partiality for domestic pets, she lost no opportunity of procuring those of the most agreeable kind. We had birds, gold-fish, a fine dog, rabbits, a small monkey, and *a cat*.

This latter was a remarkably large and beautiful animal, entirely black, and sagacious to an astonishing degree. In speaking of his intelligence, my wife, who at heart was not a little tinctured with superstition, made frequent

1. First published in the August 1843 *United States Saturday Post*, a Philadelphia weekly, and reprinted here from *Tales* (1845).

2. Odd (French).

allusion to the ancient popular notion, which regarded all black cats as witches in disguise. Not that she was ever *serious* upon this point—and I mention the matter at all for no better reason than that it happens, just now, to be remembered.

Pluto[3]—this was the cat's name—was my favorite pet and playmate. I alone fed him, and he attended me wherever I went about the house. It was even with difficulty that I could prevent him from following me through the streets.

Our friendship lasted, in this manner, for several years, during which my general temperament and character—through the instrumentality of the Fiend Intemperance—had (I blush to confess it) experienced a radical alteration for the worse. I grew, day by day, more moody, more irritable, more regardless of the feelings of others. I suffered myself to use intemperate language to my wife. At length, I even offered her personal violence. My pets, of course, were made to feel the change in my disposition. I not only neglected, but ill-used them. For Pluto, however, I still retained sufficient regard to restrain me from maltreating him, as I made no scruple of maltreating the rabbits, the monkey, or even the dog, when by accident, or through affection, they came in my way. But my disease grew upon me—for what disease is like Alcohol!—and at length even Pluto, who was now becoming old, and consequently somewhat peevish—even Pluto began to experience the effects of my ill temper.

One night, returning home, much intoxicated, from one of my haunts about town, I fancied that the cat avoided my presence. I seized him; when, in his fright at my violence, he inflicted a slight wound upon my hand with his teeth. The fury of a demon instantly possessed me. I knew myself no longer. My original soul seemed, at once, to take its flight from my body; and a more than fiendish malevolence, gin-nurtured, thrilled every fibre of my frame. I took from my waistcoat-pocket a pen-knife, opened it, grasped the poor beast by the throat, and deliberately cut one of its eyes from the socket! I blush, I burn, I shudder, while I pen the damnable atrocity.

When reason returned with the morning—when I had slept off the fumes of the night's debauch—I experienced a sentiment half of horror, half of remorse, for the crime of which I had been guilty; but it was, at best, a feeble and equivocal feeling, and the soul remained untouched. I again plunged into excess, and soon drowned in wine all memory of the deed.

In the meantime the cat slowly recovered. The socket of the lost eye presented, it is true, a frightful appearance, but he no longer appeared to suffer any pain. He went about the house as usual, but, as might be expected, fled in extreme terror at my approach. I had so much of my old heart left, as to be at first grieved by this evident dislike on the part of a creature which had once so loved me. But this feeling soon gave place to irritation. And then came, as if to my final and irrevocable overthrow, the spirit of PERVERSENESS. Of this spirit philosophy takes no account. Yet I am not more sure that my soul lives, than I am that perverseness is one of the primitive impulses of the human heart—one of the indivisible primary faculties, or sentiments, which give direction to the character of Man. Who has not, a hundred

3. In Roman mythology, god of the dead and ruler of the underworld.

times, found himself committing a vile or a silly action, for no other reason than because he knows he should *not*? Have we not a perpetual inclination, in the teeth of our best judgment, to violate that which is *Law*, merely because we understand it to be such? This spirit of perverseness, I say, came to my final overthrow. It was this unfathomable longing of the soul *to vex itself*—to offer violence to its own nature—to do wrong for the wrong's sake only—that urged me to continue and finally to consummate the injury I had inflicted upon the unoffending brute. One morning, in cool blood, I slipped a noose about its neck and hung it to the limb of a tree;—hung it with the tears streaming from my eyes, and with the bitterest remorse at my heart;—hung it *because* I knew that it had loved me, and *because* I felt it had given me no reason of offence;—hung it *because* I knew that in so doing I was committing a sin—a deadly sin that would so jeopardize my immortal soul as to place it—if such a thing were possible—even beyond the reach of the infinite mercy of the Most Merciful and Most Terrible God.

On the night of the day on which this cruel deed was done, I was aroused from sleep by the cry of fire. The curtains of my bed were in flames. The whole house was blazing. It was with great difficulty that my wife, a servant, and myself, made our escape from the conflagration. The destruction was complete. My entire worldly wealth was swallowed up, and I resigned myself thenceforward to despair.

I am above the weakness of seeking to establish a sequence of cause and effect, between the disaster and the atrocity. But I am detailing a chain of facts—and wish not to leave even a possible link imperfect. On the day succeeding the fire, I visited the ruins. The walls, with one exception, had fallen in. This exception was found in a compartment wall, not very thick, which stood about the middle of the house, and against which had rested the head of my bed. The plastering had here, in great measure, resisted the action of the fire—a fact which I attributed to its having been recently spread. About this wall a dense crowd were collected, and many persons seemed to be examining a particular portion of it with very minute and eager attention. The words "strange!" "singular!" and other similar expressions, excited my curiosity. I approached and saw, as if graven in *bas relief*[4] upon the white surface, the figure of a gigantic *cat*. The impression was given with an accuracy truly marvellous. There was a rope about the animal's neck.

When I first beheld this apparition—for I could scarcely regard it as less—my wonder and my terror were extreme. But at length reflection came to my aid. The cat, I remembered, had been hung in a garden adjacent to the house. Upon the alarm of fire, this garden had been immediately filled by the crowd—by some one of whom the animal must have been cut from the tree and thrown, through an open window, into my chamber. This had probably been done with the view of arousing me from sleep. The falling of other walls had compressed the victim of my cruelty into the substance of the freshly-spread plaster; the lime of which, with the flames, and the *ammonia* from the carcass, had then accomplished the portraiture as I saw it.

Although I thus readily accounted to my reason, if not altogether to my conscience, for the startling fact just detailed, it did not the less fail to

4. Low relief (French); the slight projection from a flat sculptural background.

make a deep impression upon my fancy. For months I could not rid myself of the phantasm of the cat; and, during this period, there came back into my spirit a half-sentiment that seemed, but was not, remorse. I went so far as to regret the loss of the animal, and to look about me, among the vile haunts which I now habitually frequented, for another pet of the same species, and of somewhat similar appearance, with which to supply its place.

One night as I sat, half stupified, in a den of more than infamy, my attention was suddenly drawn to some black object, reposing upon the head of one of the immense hogsheads[5] of Gin, or of Rum, which constituted the chief furniture of the apartment. I had been looking steadily at the top of this hogshead for some minutes, and what now caused me surprise was the fact that I had not sooner perceived the object thereupon. I approached it, and touched it with my hand. It was a black cat—a very large one—fully as large as Pluto, and closely resembling him in every respect but one. Pluto had not a white hair upon any portion of his body; but this cat had a large, although indefinite splotch of white, covering nearly the whole region of the breast.

Upon my touching him, he immediately arose, purred loudly, rubbed against my hand, and appeared delighted with my notice. This, then, was the very creature of which I was in search. I at once offered to purchase it of the landlord; but this person made no claim to it—knew nothing of it—had never seen it before.

I continued my caresses, and, when I prepared to go home, the animal evinced a disposition to accompany me. I permitted it to do so; occasionally stooping and patting it as I proceeded. When it reached the house it domesticated itself at once, and became immediately a great favorite with my wife.

For my own part, I soon found a dislike to it arising within me. This was just the reverse of what I had anticipated; but—I know not how or why it was—its evident fondness for myself rather disgusted and annoyed. By slow degrees, these feelings of disgust and annoyance rose into the bitterness of hatred. I avoided the creature; a certain sense of shame, and the remembrance of my former deed of cruelty, preventing me from physically abusing it. I did not, for some weeks, strike, or otherwise violently ill use it; but gradually—very gradually—I came to look upon it with unutterable loathing, and to flee silently from its odious presence, as from the breath of a pestilence.

What added, no doubt, to my hatred of the beast, was the discovery, on the morning after I brought it home, that, like Pluto, it also had been deprived of one of its eyes. This circumstance, however, only endeared it to my wife, who, as I have already said, possessed, in a high degree, that humanity of feeling which had once been my distinguishing trait, and the source of many of my simplest and purest pleasures.

With my aversion to this cat, however, its partiality for myself seemed to increase. It followed my footsteps with a pertinacity which it would be difficult to make the reader comprehend. Whenever I sat, it would crouch beneath my chair, or spring upon my knees, covering me with its loathsome caresses. If I arose to walk it would get between my feet and thus nearly throw me down, or, fastening its long and sharp claws in my dress, clamber, in this manner, to my breast. At such times, although I longed to destroy it

5. Large casks.

with a blow, I was yet withheld from so doing, partly by a memory of my former crime, but chiefly—let me confess it at once—by absolute *dread* of the beast.

This dread was not exactly a dread of physical evil—and yet I should be at a loss how otherwise to define it. I am almost ashamed to own—yes, even in this felon's cell, I am almost ashamed to own—that the terror and horror with which the animal inspired me, had been heightened by one of the merest chimæras[6] it would be possible to conceive. My wife had called my attention, more than once, to the character of the mark of white hair, of which I have spoken, and which constituted the sole visible difference between the strange beast and the one I had destroyed. The reader will remember that this mark, although large, had been originally very indefinite; but, by slow degrees—degrees nearly imperceptible, and which for a long time my Reason struggled to reject as fanciful—it had, at length, assumed a rigorous distinctness of outline. It was now the representation of an object that I shudder to name—and for this, above all, I loathed, and dreaded, and would have rid myself of the monster *had I dared*—it was now, I say, the image of a hideous—of a ghastly thing—of the GALLOWS!—oh, mournful and terrible engine of Horror and of Crime—of Agony and of Death!

And now was I indeed wretched beyond the wretchedness of mere Humanity. And *a brute beast*—whose fellow I had contemptuously destroyed—*a brute beast* to work out for *me*—for me a man, fashioned in the image of the High God—so much of insufferable wo! Alas! neither by day nor by night knew I the blessing of Rest any more! During the former the creature left me no moment alone; and, in the latter, I started, hourly, from dreams of unutterable fear, to find the hot breath of *the thing* upon my face, and its vast weight—an incarnate Night-Mare that I had no power to shake off—incumbent eternally upon my *heart*!

Beneath the pressure of torments such as these, the feeble remnant of the good within me succumbed. Evil thoughts became my sole intimates—the darkest and most evil of thoughts. The moodiness of my usual temper increased to hatred of all things and of all mankind; while, from the sudden, frequent, and ungovernable outbursts of a fury to which I now blindly abandoned myself, my uncomplaining wife, alas! was the most usual and the most patient of sufferers.

One day she accompanied me, upon some household errand, into the cellar of the old building which our poverty compelled us to inhabit. The cat followed me down the steep stairs, and, nearly throwing me headlong, exasperated me to madness. Uplifting an axe, and forgetting, in my wrath, the childish dread which had hitherto stayed my hand, I aimed a blow at the animal which, of course, would have proved instantly fatal had it descended as I wished. But this blow was arrested by the hand of my wife. Goaded, by the interference, into a rage more than demoniacal, I withdrew my arm from her grasp and buried the axe in her brain. She fell dead upon the spot, without a groan.

This hideous murder accomplished, I set myself forthwith, and with entire deliberation, to the task of concealing the body. I knew that I could not

6. Illusions.

remove it from the house, either by day or by night, without the risk of being observed by the neighbors. Many projects entered my mind. At one period I thought of cutting the corpse into minute fragments, and destroying them by fire. At another, I resolved to dig a grave for it in the floor of the cellar. Again, I deliberated about casting it in the well in the yard—about packing it in a box, as if merchandize, with the usual arrangements, and so getting a porter to take it from the house. Finally I hit upon what I considered a far better expedient than either of these. I determined to wall it up in the cellar—as the monks of the middle ages are recorded to have walled up their victims.

For a purpose such as this the cellar was well adapted. Its walls were loosely constructed, and had lately been plastered throughout with a rough plaster, which the dampness of the atmosphere had prevented from hardening. Moreover, in one of the walls was a projection, caused by a false chimney, or fireplace, that had been filled up, and made to resemble the rest of the cellar. I made no doubt that I could readily displace the bricks at this point, insert the corpse, and wall the whole up as before, so that no eye could detect any thing suspicious.

And in this calculation I was not deceived. By means of a crow-bar I easily dislodged the bricks, and, having carefully deposited the body against the inner wall, I propped it in that position, while, with little trouble, I re-laid the whole structure as it originally stood. Having procured mortar, sand, and hair, with every possible precaution, I prepared a plaster which could not be distinguished from the old, and with this I very carefully went over the new brick-work. When I had finished, I felt satisfied that all was right. The wall did not present the slightest appearance of having been disturbed. The rubbish on the floor was picked up with the minutest care. I looked around triumphantly, and said to myself—"Here at least, then, my labor has not been in vain."

My next step was to look for the beast which had been the cause of so much wretchedness; for I had, at length, firmly resolved to put it to death. Had I been able to meet with it, at the moment, there could have been no doubt of its fate; but it appeared that the crafty animal had been alarmed at the violence of my previous anger, and forebore to present itself in my present mood. It is impossible to describe, or to imagine, the deep, the blissful sense of relief which the absence of the detested creature occasioned in my bosom. It did not make its appearance during the night—and thus for one night at least, since its introduction into the house, I soundly and tranquilly slept; aye, *slept* even with the burden of murder upon my soul!

The second and the third day passed, and still my tormentor came not. Once again I breathed as a freeman. The monster, in terror, had fled the premises forever! I should behold it no more! My happiness was supreme! The guilt of my dark deed disturbed me but little. Some few inquiries had been made, but these had been readily answered. Even a search had been instituted—but of course nothing was to be discovered. I looked upon my future felicity as secured.

Upon the fourth day of the assassination, a party of the police came, very unexpectedly, into the house, and proceeded again to make rigorous investigation of the premises. Secure, however, in the inscrutability of my place of concealment, I felt no embarrassment whatever. The officers bade me accompany them in their search. They left no nook or corner unexplored.

At length, for the third or fourth time, they descended into the cellar. I quivered not in a muscle. My heart beat calmly as that of one who slumbers in innocence. I walked the cellar from end to end. I folded my arms upon my bosom, and roamed easily to and fro. The police were thoroughly satisfied and prepared to depart. The glee at my heart was too strong to be restrained. I burned to say if but one word, by way of triumph, and to render doubly sure their assurance of my guiltlessness.

"Gentlemen," I said at last, as the party ascended the steps, "I delight to have allayed your suspicions. I wish you all health, and a little more courtesy. By the bye, gentlemen, this—this is a very well constructed house." [In the rabid desire to say something easily, I scarcely knew what I uttered at all.]—"I may say an *excellently* well constructed house. These walls—are you going, gentlemen?—these walls are solidly put together;" and here, through the mere phrenzy of bravado, I rapped heavily, with a cane which I held in my hand, upon that very portion of the brick-work behind which stood the corpse of the wife of my bosom.

But may God shield and deliver me from the fangs of the Arch-Fiend! No sooner had the reverberation of my blows sunk into silence, than I was answered by a voice from within the tomb!—by a cry, at first muffled and broken, like the sobbing of a child, and then quickly swelling into one long, loud, and continuous scream, utterly anomalous and inhuman—a howl—a wailing shriek, half of horror and half of triumph, such as might have arisen only out of hell, conjointly from the throats of the damned in their agony and of the demons that exult in the damnation.

Of my own thoughts it is folly to speak. Swooning, I staggered to the opposite wall. For one instant the party upon the stairs remained motionless, through extremity of terror and of awe. In the next, a dozen stout arms were toiling at the wall. It fell bodily. The corpse, already greatly decayed and clotted with gore, stood erect before the eyes of the spectators. Upon its head, with red extended mouth and solitary eye of fire, sat the hideous beast whose craft had seduced me into murder, and whose informing voice had consigned me to the hangman. I had walled the monster up within the tomb!

1843, 1845

The Purloined Letter[1]

At Paris, just after dark one gusty evening in the autumn of 18—, I was enjoying the twofold luxury of meditation and a meerschaum,[2] in company with my friend C. Auguste Dupin, in his little back library, or book-closet, *au troisième,*[3] *No. 33, Rue Dunôt, Faubourg St. Germain.* For one hour at least we had maintained a profound silence; while each, to any casual observer, might have seemed intently and exclusively occupied with the

1. The text is that of the first publication in *The Gift*, a Philadelphia annual dated 1845 but for sale late in 1844. Historians of detective fiction usually cite Poe's three stories about C. Auguste Dupin as the first of the genre. This is the third Dupin story, the others being "The Murders in the Rue Morgue" (1841) and "The Mystery of Marie Rôget" (1842).

2. Tobacco pipe.

3. Actually the fourth floor (because the French do not count the first, the *rez-de-chaussée*).

curling eddies of smoke that oppressed the atmosphere of the chamber. For myself, however, I was mentally discussing certain topics which had formed matter for conversation between us at an earlier period of the evening; I mean the affair of the Rue Morgue, and the mystery attending the murder of Marie Roget.[4] I looked upon it, therefore, as something of coincidence, when the door of our apartment was thrown open and admitted our old acquaintance, Monsieur G——, the Prefect of the Parisian police.

We gave him a hearty welcome; for there was nearly half as much of the entertaining as of the contemptible about the man, and we had not seen him for several years. We had been sitting in the dark, and Dupin now arose for the purpose of lighting a lamp, but sat down again, without doing so, upon G.'s saying that he had called to consult us, or rather to ask the opinion of my friend, about some official business which had occasioned a great deal of trouble.

"If it is any point requiring reflection," observed Dupin, as he forebore to enkindle the wick, "we shall examine it to better purpose in the dark."

"That is another of your odd notions," said the Prefect, who had a fashion of calling every thing "odd" that was beyond his comprehension, and thus lived amid an absolute legion of "oddities."

"Very true," said Dupin, as he supplied his visiter with a pipe, and rolled towards him a very comfortable chair.

"And what is the difficulty now?" I asked. "Nothing more in the assassination way, I hope?"

"Oh no; nothing of that nature. The fact is, the business is *very* simple indeed, and I make no doubt that we can manage it sufficiently well ourselves; but then I thought Dupin would like to hear the details of it, because it is so excessively *odd*."

"Simple and odd," said Dupin.

"Why, yes; and not exactly that, either. The fact is, we have all been a good deal puzzled because the affair *is* so simple, and yet baffles us altogether."

"Perhaps it is the very simplicity of the thing which puts you at fault," said my friend.

"What nonsense you *do* talk!" replied the Prefect, laughing heartily.

"Perhaps the mystery is a little *too* plain," said Dupin.

"Oh, good heavens! who ever heard of such an idea?"

"A little *too* self-evident."

"Ha! ha! ha!—ha! ha! ha!—ho! ho! ho!" roared out our visiter, profoundly amused, "oh, Dupin, you will be the death of me yet!"

"And what, after all, *is* the matter on hand?" I asked.

"Why, I will tell you," replied the Prefect, as he gave a long, steady, and contemplative puff, and settled himself in his chair. "I will tell you in a few words; but, before I begin, let me caution you that this is an affair demanding the greatest secrecy, and that I should most probably lose the position I now hold, were it known that I confided it to any one."

"Proceed," said I.

"Or not," said Dupin.

4. The earlier cases solved by Dupin.

"Well, then; I have received personal information, from a very high quarter, that a certain document of the last importance, has been purloined from the royal apartments. The individual who purloined it is known; this beyond a doubt; he was seen to take it. It is known, also, that it still remains in his possession."

"How is this known?" asked Dupin.

"It is clearly inferred," replied the Prefect, "from the nature of the document, and from the non-appearance of certain results which would at once arise from its passing *out* of the robber's possession;—that is to say, from his employing it as he must design in the end to employ it."

"Be a little more explicit," I said.

"Well, I may venture so far as to say that the paper gives its holder a certain power in a certain quarter where such power is immensely valuable." The Prefect was fond of the cant of diplomacy.

"Still I do not quite understand," said Dupin.

"No? Well; the disclosure of the document to a third person, who shall be nameless, would bring in question the honour of a personage of most exalted station; and this fact gives the holder of the document an ascendancy over the illustrious personage whose honour and peace are so jeopardized."

"But this ascendancy," I interposed, "would depend upon the robber's knowledge of the loser's knowledge of the robber. Who would dare—"

"The thief," said G, "is the—Minister D——, who dares all things, those unbecoming as well as those becoming a man. The method of the theft was not less ingenious than bold. The document in question—a letter, to be frank—had been received by the personage robbed while alone in the royal *boudoir.* During its perusal she was suddenly interrupted by the entrance of the other exalted personage from whom especially it was her wish to conceal it. After a hurried and vain endeavour to thrust it in a drawer, she was forced to place it, open as it was, upon a table. The address, however, was uppermost, and the contents thus unexposed, the letter escaped notice. At this juncture enters the Minister D——. His lynx eye immediately perceives the paper, recognises the handwriting of the address, observes the confusion of the personage addressed, and fathoms her secret. After some business transactions, hurried through in his ordinary manner, he produces a letter somewhat similar to the one in question, opens it, pretends to read it, and then places it in close juxtaposition to the other. Again he converses, for some fifteen minutes, upon the public affairs. At length, in taking leave, he takes also from the table the letter to which he had no claim. Its rightful owner saw, but, of course, dared not call attention to the act, in the presence of the third personage who stood at her elbow. The minister decamped; leaving his own letter—one of no importance—upon the table."

"Here, then," said Dupin to me, "you have precisely what you demand to make the ascendancy complete—the robber's knowledge of the loser's knowledge of the robber."

"Yes," replied the Prefect; "and the power thus attained has, for some months past, been wielded, for political purposes, to a very dangerous extent. The personage robbed is more thoroughly convinced, every day, of the necessity of reclaiming her letter. But this, of course, cannot be done openly. In fine, driven to despair, she has committed the matter to me."

"Than whom," said Dupin, amid a perfect whirlwind of smoke, "no more sagacious agent could, I suppose, be desired, or even imagined."

"You flatter me," replied the Prefect; "but it is possible that some such opinion may have been entertained."

"It is clear," said I, "as you observe, that the letter is still in possession of the minister; since it is this possession, and not any employment, of the letter, which bestows the power. With the employment the power departs."

"True," said G——; "and upon this conviction I proceeded. My first care was to make thorough search of the minister's hotel; and here my chief embarrassment lay in the necessity of searching without his knowledge. Beyond all things, I have been warned of the danger which would result from giving him reason to suspect our design."

"But," said I, "you are quite *au fait*[5] in these investigations. The Parisian police have done this thing often before."

"O yes; and for this reason I did not despair. The habits of the minister gave me, too, a great advantage. He is frequently absent from home all night. His servants are by no means numerous. They sleep at a distance from their master's apartments, and, being chiefly Neapolitans, are readily made drunk. I have keys, as you know, with which I can open any chamber or cabinet in Paris. For three months a night has not passed, during the greater part of which I have not been engaged, personally, in ransacking the D——Hotel. My honour is interested, and, to mention a great secret, the reward is enormous. So I did not abandon the search until I had become fully satisfied that the thief is a more astute man than myself. I fancy that I have investigated every nook and corner of the premises in which it is possible that the paper can be concealed."

"But is it not possible," I suggested, "that although the letter may be in possession of the minister, as it unquestionably is, he may have concealed it elsewhere than upon his own premises?"

"This is barely possible," said Dupin. "The present peculiar condition of affairs at court, and especially of those intrigues in which D——is known to be involved, would render the instant availability of the document—its susceptibility of being produced at a moment's notice—a point of nearly equal importance with its possession."

"Its susceptibility of being produced?" said I.

"That is to say, of being *destroyed*," said Dupin.

"True," I observed; "the paper is clearly then upon the premises. As for its being upon the person of the minister, we may consider that as out of the question."

"Entirely," said the Prefect. "He has been twice waylaid, as if by footpads, and his person rigorously searched under my own inspection."

"You might have spared yourself this trouble," said Dupin. "D——, I presume, is not altogether a fool, and, if not, must have anticipated these waylayings, as a matter of course."

"Not *altogether* a fool," said G——, "but then he's a poet, which I take to be only one remove from a fool."

5. Informed about (French).

"True;" said Dupin, after a long and thoughtful whiff from his meerschaum, "although I have been guilty of certain doggerel myself."

"Suppose you detail," said I, "the particulars of your search."

"Why the fact is, we took our time, and we searched *every where.* I have had long experience in these affairs. I took the entire building, room by room; devoting the nights of a whole week to each. We examined, first, the furniture of each apartment. We opened every possible drawer; and I presume you know that, to a properly trained police agent, such a thing as a *secret* drawer is impossible. Any man is a dolt who permits a 'secret' drawer to escape him in a search of this kind. The thing is *so* plain. There is a certain amount of bulk—of space—to be accounted for in every cabinet. Then we have accurate rules. The fiftieth part of a line could not escape us. After the cabinets we took the chairs. The cushions we probed with the fine long needles you have seen me employ. From the tables we removed the tops."

"Why so?"

"Sometimes the top of a table, or other similarly arranged piece of furniture, is removed by the person wishing to conceal an article; then the leg is excavated, the article deposited within the cavity, and the top replaced. The bottoms and tops of bed-posts are employed in the same way."

"But could not the cavity be detected by sounding?" I asked.

"By no means, if, when the article is deposited, a sufficient wadding of cotton be placed around it. Besides, in our case, we were obliged to proceed without noise."

"But you could not have removed—you could not have taken to pieces *all* articles of furniture in which it would have been possible to make a deposit in the manner you mention. A letter may be compressed into a thin spiral roll, not differing much in shape or bulk from a large knitting-needle, and in this form it might be inserted into the rung of a chair, for example. You did not take to pieces all the chairs?"

"Certainly not; but we did better—we examined the rungs of every chair in the hotel, and, indeed, the jointings of every description of furniture, by the aid of a most powerful microscope.[6] Had there been any traces of recent disturbance we should not have failed to detect it *instanter.*[7] A single grain of gimlet-dust, or sawdust, for example, would have been as obvious as an apple. Any disorder in the glueing—any unusual gaping in the joints—would have sufficed to insure detection."

"Of course you looked to the mirrors, between the boards and the plates, and you probed the beds and the bed-clothes, as well as the curtains and carpets."

"That of course; and when we had absolutely completed every particle of the furniture in this way, then we examined the house itself. We divided its entire surface into compartments, which we numbered, so that none might be missed; then we scrutinized each individual square inch throughout the premises, including the two houses immediately adjoining, with the microscope, as before."

"The two houses adjoining!" I exclaimed; "you must have had a great deal of trouble."

6. A powerful magnifying glass.

7. Instantly (Latin).

"We had; but the reward offered is prodigious."

"You include the *grounds* about the houses?"

"All the grounds are paved with brick. They gave us comparatively little trouble. We examined the moss between the bricks, and found it undisturbed."

"And the roofs?"

"We surveyed every inch of the external surface, and probed carefully beneath every tile."

"You looked among D——'s papers, of course, and into the books of the library?"

"Certainly; we opened every package and parcel; we not only opened every book, but we turned over every leaf in each volume, not contenting ourselves with a mere shake, according to the fashion of some of our police officers. We also measured the thickness of every book-*cover*, with the most accurate admeasurement, and applied to them the most jealous scrutiny of the microscope. Had any of the bindings been recently meddled with, it would have been utterly impossible that the fact should have escaped observation. Some five or six volumes, just from the hands of the binder, we carefully probed, longitudinally, with the needles."

"You explored the floors beneath the carpets?"

"Beyond doubt. We removed every carpet, and examined the boards with the microscope."

"And the paper on the walls?"

"Yes."

"You looked into the cellars?"

"We did; and, as time and labour were no objects, we dug up every one of them to the depth of four feet."

"Then," I said, "you have been making a miscalculation, and the letter is *not* upon the premises, as you suppose."

"I fear you are right there," said the Prefect. "And now, Dupin, what would you advise me to do?"

"To make a thorough re-search of the premises."

"That is absolutely needless," replied G——. "I am not more sure that I breathe than I am that the letter is not at the Hotel."

"I have no better advice to give you," said Dupin. "You have, of course, an accurate description of the letter?"

"Oh yes!"—And here the Prefect, producing a memorandum-book, proceeded to read aloud a minute account of the internal, and especially of the external, appearance of the missing document. Soon after finishing the perusal of this description, he took his departure, more entirely depressed in spirits than I had ever known the good gentleman before.

In about a month afterwards he paid us another visit, and found us occupied very nearly as before. He took a pipe and a chair, and entered into some ordinary conversation. At length I said,—

"Well, but G——, what of the purloined letter? I presume you have at last made up your mind that there is no such thing as overreaching the Minister?"

"Confound him, say I—yes; I made the re-examination, however, as Dupin suggested—but it was all labour lost, as I knew it would be."

"How much was the reward offered, did you say?" asked Dupin.

"Why, a very great deal—a *very* liberal reward—I don't like to say how much, precisely; but one thing I *will* say, that I wouldn't mind giving my individual check for fifty thousand francs to any one who could obtain me that letter. The fact is, it is becoming of more and more importance every day; and the reward has been lately doubled. If it were trebled, however, I could do no more than I have done."

"Why, yes," said Dupin, drawlingly, between the whiffs of his meerschaum, "I really—think, G——, you have not exerted yourself—to the utmost in this matter. You might—do a little more, I think, eh?"

"How?—in what way?"

"Why—puff, puff—you might—puff, puff—employ counsel in the matter, eh?—puff, puff, puff. Do you remember the story they tell of Abernethy?"[8]

"No; hang Abernethy!"

"To be sure! hang him and welcome. But, once upon a time, a certain rich miser conceived the design of spunging upon this Abernethy for a medical opinion. Getting up, for this purpose, an ordinary conversation in a private company, he insinuated his case to the physician, as that of an imaginary individual.

"'We will suppose,' said the miser, 'that his symptoms are such and such; now, doctor, what would *you* have directed him to take?'

"'Take!' said Abernethy, 'why, take *advice*, to be sure.'"

"But," said the Prefect, a little discomposed, "*I* am *perfectly* willing to take advice, and to pay for it. I would *really* give fifty thousand francs, every *centime* of it, to any one who would aid me in the matter!"

"In that case," replied Dupin, opening a drawer, and producing a checkbook, "you may as well fill me up a check for the amount mentioned. When you have signed it, I will hand you the letter."

I was astounded. The Prefect appeared absolutely thunder-stricken. For some minutes he remained speechless and motionless, looking incredulously at my friend with open mouth, and eyes that seemed starting from their sockets; then, apparently recovering himself in some measure, he seized a pen, and after several pauses and vacant stares, finally filled up and signed a check for fifty thousand francs, and handed it across the table to Dupin. The latter examined it carefully and deposited it in his pocket-book; then, unlocking an *escritoire*,[9] took thence a letter and gave it to the Prefect. This functionary grasped it in a perfect agony of joy; opened it with a trembling hand, cast a rapid glance at its contents, and then, scrambling and struggling to the door, rushed at length unceremoniously from the room and from the house, without having uttered a solitary syllable since Dupin had requested him to fill up the check.

When he had gone, my friend entered into some explanations.

"The Parisian police," he said, "are exceedingly able in their way. They are persevering, ingenious, cunning, and thoroughly versed in the knowledge which their duties seem chiefly to demand. Thus when G—— detailed to us his mode of searching the premises at the Hotel D——, I felt the entire confidence in his having made a satisfactory investigation—so far as his labours extended."

8. Probably the English surgeon John Abernethy (1764–1831).

9. Writing desk (French).

"So far as his labours extended?" said I.

"Yes," said Dupin. "The measures adopted were not only the best of their kind, but carried out to absolute perfection. Had the letter been deposited within the range of their search, these fellows would, beyond a question, have found it."

I merely laughed—but he seemed quite serious in all that he said.

"The measures, then," he continued, "were good in their kind, and well executed; their defect lay in their being inapplicable to the case, and to the man. A certain set of highly ingenious resources are, with the Prefect, a sort of Procrustean bed,[1] to which he forcibly adapts his designs. But he perpetually errs by being too deep or too shallow, for the matter in hand; and many a schoolboy is a better reasoner than he. I knew one about eight years of age, whose success at guessing in the game of 'even and odd' attracted universal admiration. This game is simple, and is played with marbles. One player holds in his hand a number of these toys; and demands of another whether that number is even or odd. If the guess is right, the guesser wins one; if wrong, he loses one. The boy to whom I allude won all the marbles of the school. Of course he had some principle of guessing; and this lay in mere observation and admeasurement of the astuteness of his opponents. For example, an arrant simpleton is his opponent, and, holding up his closed hand, asks, 'are they even or odd?' Our schoolboy replies 'odd,' and loses; but upon the second trial he wins, for he then says to himself, 'the simpleton had them even upon the first trial, and his amount of cunning is just sufficient to make him have them odd upon the second; I will therefore guess odd;'—he guesses odd, and wins. Now, with a simpleton a degree above the first, he would have reasoned thus: 'this fellow finds that in the first instance I guessed odd, and, in the second, he will propose to himself, upon the first impulse, a simple variation from even to odd, as did the first simpleton; but then a second thought will suggest that this is too simple a variation, and finally he will decide upon putting it even as before. I will therefore guess even;'—he guesses even, and wins. Now this mode of reasoning in the schoolboy, whom his fellows termed 'lucky,'—what, in its last analysis, is it?"

"It is merely," I said, "an identification of the reasoner's intellect with that of his opponent."

"It is," said Dupin; "and, upon inquiring of the boy by what means he effected the *thorough* identification in which his success consisted, I received answer as follows: 'When I wish to find out how wise, or how stupid, or how good, or how wicked is any one, or what are his thoughts at the moment, I fashion the expression of my face, as accurately as possible, in accordance with the expression of his, and then wait to see what thoughts or sentiments arise in my mind or heart, as if to match or correspond with the expression.' This response of the schoolboy lies at the bottom of all the spurious profundity which has been attributed to Rochefoucault, to La Bougive, to Machiavelli, and to Campanella."[2]

1. Procrustes, legendary Greek bandit, made his victims fit the bed he bound them to, either by stretching them to the required length or by hacking off any surplus length in the feet and legs.

2. Philosophers of the 15th to 16th centuries who depicted human behavior as ultimately motivated by selfishness. Duc de la Rochefoucauld (1613–1680) and Jean de la Bruyère (1645–1696), French moralists. Niccolò Macchiavelli (1469–1527) and Tommaso Campanella (1568–

"And the identification," I said, "of the reasoner's intellect with that of his opponent, depends, if I understand you aright, upon the accuracy with which the opponent's intellect is admeasured."

"For its practical value it depends upon this," replied Dupin; "and the Prefect and his cohort fail so frequently, first, by default of this identification, and, secondly, by ill-admeasurement, or rather through non-admeasurement, of the intellect with which they are engaged. They consider only their *own* ideas of ingenuity; and, in searching for any thing hidden, advert only to the modes in which *they* would have hidden it. They are right in this much—that their own ingenuity is a faithful representative of that of *the mass;* but when the cunning of the individual felon is diverse in character from their own, the felon foils them, of course. This always happens when it is above their own, and very usually when it is below. They have no variation of principle in their investigations; at best, when urged by some unusual emergency—by some extraordinary reward—they extend or exaggerate their old modes of *practice,* without touching their principles. What, for example, in this case of D——, has been done to vary the principle of action? What is all this boring, and probing, and sounding, and scrutinizing with the microscope, and dividing the surface of the building into registered square inches—what is it all but an exaggeration *of the application* of the one principle or set of principles of search, which are based upon the one set of notions regarding human ingenuity, to which the Prefect, in the long routine of his duty, has been accustomed? Do you not see he has taken it for granted that *all* men proceed to conceal a letter,—not exactly in a gimlet-hole bored in a chair-leg—but, at least, in *some* out-of-the-way hole or corner suggested by the same tenor of thought which would urge a man to secrete a letter in a gimlet-hole bored in a chair-leg? And do you not see also, that such *recherchés*[3] nooks for concealment are adapted only for ordinary occasions, and would be adopted only by ordinary intellects; for, in all cases of concealment, a disposal of the article concealed—a disposal of it in this *recherché* manner,—is, in the very first instance, presumed and presumable; and thus its discovery depends, not at all upon the acumen, but altogether upon the mere care, patience, and determination of the seekers; and where the case is of importance—or, what amounts to the same thing in the policial eyes, when the reward is of magnitude, the qualities in question have *never* been known to fail. You will now understand what I meant in suggesting that, had the purloined letter been hidden any where within the limits of the Prefect's examination—in other words, had the principle of its concealment been comprehended within the principles of the Prefect—its discovery would have been a matter altogether beyond question. This functionary, however, has been thoroughly mystified; and the remote source of his defeat lies in the supposition that the Minister is a fool, because he has acquired renown as a poet. All fools are poets; this the Prefect *feels*; and he is merely guilty of a *non distributio medii*[4] in thence inferring that all poets are fools."

1639), Italian philosophers. Poe used a variant spelling for Rouchefoucauld, and his printer probably misread "La Bruyère" as "La Bougive."

3. Out of the ordinary, esoteric (French).

4. A logical fallacy.

"But is this really the poet?" I asked. "There are two brothers, I know; and both have attained reputation in letters. The Minister I believe has written learnedly on the Differential Calculus. He is a mathematician, and no poet."

"You are mistaken; I know him well; he is both. As poet *and* mathematician, he would reason well; as poet, profoundly; as mere mathematician, he could not have reasoned at all, and thus would have been at the mercy of the Prefect."

"You surprise me," I said, "by these opinions, which have been contradicted by the voice of the world. You do not mean to set at naught the well-digested idea of centuries. The mathematical reason has been long regarded as *the* reason *par excellence*."

"'Il y a à parièr,' replied Dupin, quoting from Chamfort, 'que toute idée publique, toute convention reçue, est une sottise, car elle a convenue au plus grand nombre.'[5] The mathematicians, I grant you, have done their best to promulgate the popular error to which you allude, and which is none the less an error for its promulgation as truth. With an art worthy a better cause, for example, they have insinuated the term 'analysis' into application to algebra. The French are the originators of this particular deception; but if a term is of any importance—if words derive any value from applicability—then 'analysis' conveys 'algebra' about as much as, in Latin, '*ambitus*' implies 'ambition,' '*religio*' 'religion,' or '*homines honesti*,' a set of *honourable* men."

"You have a quarrel on hand, I see," said I, "with some of the algebraists of Paris; but proceed."

"I dispute the availability, and thus the value, of that reason which is cultivated in any especial form other than the abstractly logical. I dispute, in particular, the reason educed by mathematical study. The mathematics are the science of form and quantity; mathematical reasoning is merely logic applied to observation upon form and quantity. The great error lies in supposing that even the truths of what is called *pure* algebra, are abstract or general truths. And this error is so egregious that I am confounded at the universality with which it has been received. Mathematical axioms are *not* axioms of general truth. What is true of *relation*—of form and quantity—is often grossly false in regard to morals, for example. In this latter science it is very usually *un*true that the aggregated parts are equal to the whole. In chemistry also the axiom fails. In the consideration of motive it fails; for two motives, each of a given value, have not, necessarily, a value when united, equal to the sum of their values apart. There are numerous other mathematical truths which are only truths within the limits of *relation*. But the mathematician argues, from his *finite truths*, through habit, as if they were of absolutely general applicability—as the world indeed imagines them to be. Bryant,[6] in his very learned 'Mythology,' mentions an analogous source of error, when he says that 'although the Pagan fables are not believed, yet we forget ourselves continually, and make inferences from them as existing realities.' With the algebraist, however, who are Pagans themselves, the 'Pagan fables' *are* believed, and the inferences are made, not so much through lapse of memory, as through an unaccountable addling of the brains. In short, I never yet encountered the

5. The odds are that every common notion, every accepted convention, is nonsense, because it has suited itself to the majority (French). Sébastian Roch Nicolas Chamfort (1741–1794), author of *Maximes et Pensées*.

6. Jacob Bryant (1715–1804), English scholar who wrote *A New System, or an Analysis of Antient Mythology* (1774–76).

mere mathematician who could be trusted out of equal roots, or one who did not clandestinely hold it as a point of his faith x^2+px was absolutely and unconditionally equal to q. Say to one of these gentlemen, by way of experiment, if you please, that you believe occasions may occur where x^2+px is *not* altogether equal to q, and, having made him understand what you mean, get out of his reach as speedily as convenient, for, beyond doubt, he will endeavour to knock you down.

"I mean to say," continued Dupin, while I merely laughed at his last observations, "that if the Minister had been no more than a mathematician, the Prefect would have been under no necessity of giving me this check. Had he been no more than a poet, I think it probable that he would have foiled us all. I knew him, however, as both mathematician and poet, and my measures were adapted to his capacity, with reference to the circumstances by which he was surrounded. I knew him as a courtier, too, and as a bold *intriguant.* Such a man, I considered, could not fail to be aware of the ordinary policial modes of action. He could not have failed to anticipate—and events have proved that he did not fail to anticipate—the waylayings to which he was subjected. He must have foreseen, I reflected, the secret investigations of his premises. His frequent absences from home at night, which were hailed by the Prefect as certain aids to his success, I regarded only as *ruses*, to afford opportunity for thorough search to the police, and thus the sooner to impress them with the conviction to which G——, in fact, did finally arrive—the conviction that the letter was not upon the premises. I felt, also, that the whole train of thought, which I was at some pains in detailing to you just now, concerning the invariable principle of policial action in searches for articles concealed—I felt that this whole train of thought would necessarily pass through the mind of the Minister. It would imperatively lead him to despise all the ordinary *nooks* of concealment. *He* could not, I reflected, be so weak as not to see that the most intricate and remote recess of his hotel would be as open as his commonest closets to the eyes, to the probes, to the gimlets, and to the microscopes of the Prefect. I saw, in fine, that he would be driven, as a matter of course, to *simplicity*, if not deliberately induced to it as a matter of choice. You will remember, perhaps how desperately the Prefect laughed when I suggested, upon our first interview, that it was just possible this mystery troubled him so much on account of its being so *very* self-evident."

"Yes," said I, "I remember his merriment well. I really thought he would have fallen into convulsions."

"The material world," continued Dupin, "abounds with very strict analogies to the immaterial; and thus some colour of truth has been given to the rhetorical dogma, that metaphor, or simile, may be made to strengthen an argument, as well as to embellish a description. The principle of the *vis inertiæ*,[7] for example, with the amount of *momentum* proportionate with it and consequent upon it, seems to be identical in physics and metaphysics. It is not more true in the former, that a large body is with more difficulty set in motion than a smaller one, and that its subsequent *impetus* is commensurate with this difficulty, than it is, in the latter, that intellects of the vaster capacity, while more forcible, more constant, and more eventful in their

7. The power of inertia (Latin).

movements than those of inferior grade, are yet the less readily moved, and more embarrassed and full of hesitation in the first few steps of their progress. Again: have you ever noticed which of the street signs, over the shop-doors, are the most attractive of attention?"

"I have never given the matter a thought," I said.

"There is a game of puzzles," he resumed, "which is played upon a map. One party playing requires another to find a given word—the name of town, river, state, or empire—any word, in short, upon the motley and perplexed surface of the chart. A novice in the game generally seeks to embarrass his opponents by giving them the most minutely lettered names; but the adept selects such words as stretch, in large characters, from one end of the chart to the other. These, like the over-largely lettered signs and placards of the street, escape observation by dint of being excessively obvious; and here the physical oversight is precisely analogous with the moral inapprehension by which the intellect suffers to pass unnoticed those considerations which are too obtrusively and too palpably self-evident. But this is a point, it appears, somewhat above or beneath the understanding of the Prefect. He never once thought it probable, or possible, that the Minister had deposited the letter immediately beneath the nose of the whole world, by way of best preventing any portion of that world from perceiving it.

"But the more I reflected upon the daring, dashing, and discriminating ingenuity of D——; upon the fact that the document must always have been *at hand*, if he intended to use it to good purpose; and upon the decisive evidence, obtained by the Prefect, that it was not hidden within the limits of that dignitary's ordinary search—the more satisfied I became that, to conceal this letter, the Minister had resorted to the comprehensive and sagacious expedient of not attempting to conceal it at all.

"Full of these ideas, I prepared myself with a pair of green spectacles, and called one fine morning, quite by accident, at the ministerial hotel. I found D—— at home, yawning, lounging, and dawdling as usual, and pretending to be in the last extremity of *ennui*.[8] He is, perhaps, the most really energetic human being now alive—but that is only when nobody sees him.

"To be even with him, I complained of my weak eyes, and lamented the necessity of the spectacles, under cover of which I cautiously and thoroughly surveyed the whole apartment, while seemingly intent only upon the conversation of my host.

"I paid especial attention to a large writing-table near which he sat, and upon which lay confusedly, some miscellanous letters and other papers, with one or two musical instruments and a few books. Here, however, after a long and very deliberate scrutiny, I saw nothing to excite particular suspicion.

"At length my eyes, in going the circuit of the room, fell upon a trumpery fillagree card-rack of pasteboard, that hung dangling by a dirty blue riband, from a little brass knob just beneath the middle of the mantel-piece. In this rack, which had three or four compartments, were five or six visiting-cards, and a solitary letter. This last was much soiled and crumpled. It was torn nearly in two, across the middle—as if a design, in the first instance, to tear it entirely up as worthless, had been altered, or stayed, in the second. It had

8. Boredom (French).

a large black seal, bearing the D—— cipher *very* conspicuously, and was addressed, in a diminutive female hand, to D——, the minister himself. It was thrust carelessly, and even, as it seemed, contemptuously, into one of the uppermost divisions of the rack.

"No sooner had I glanced at this letter, than I concluded it to be that of which I was in search. To be sure, it was, to all appearance, radically different from the one of which the Prefect had read us so minute a description. Here the seal was large and black, with the D—— cipher; there, it was small and red, with the ducal arms of the S—— family. Here, the address, to the minister, was diminutive and feminine; there, the superscription, to a certain royal personage, was markedly bold and decided; the size alone formed a point of correspondence. But, then, the *radicalness* of these differences, which was excessive; the dirt, the soiled and torn condition of the paper, so inconsistent with the *true* methodical habits of D——, and so suggestive of a design to delude the beholder into an idea of the worthlessness of the document; these things, together with the hyper-obtrusive situation of this document, full in the view of every visiter, and thus exactly in accordance with the conclusions to which I had previously arrived; these things, I say, were strongly corroborative of suspicion, in one who came with the intention to suspect.

"I protracted my visit as long as possible, and, while I maintained a most animated discussion with the minister, upon a topic which I knew well had never failed to interest and excite him, I kept my attention really riveted upon the letter. In this examination, I committed to memory its external appearance and arrangement in the rack; and also fell, at length, upon a discovery which set at rest whatever trivial doubt I might have entertained. In scrutinizing the edges of the paper, I observed them to be more *chafed* than seemed necessary. They presented the *broken* appearance which is manifested when a stiff paper, having been once folded and pressed with a folder, is refolded in a reversed direction, in the same creases or edges which had formed the original fold. This discovery was sufficient. It was clear to me that the letter had been turned, as a glove, inside out, re-directed, and re-sealed. I bade the minister good morning and took my departure at once, leaving a gold snuff-box upon the table.

"The next morning I called for the snuff-box, when we resumed, quite eagerly, the conversation of the preceding day. While thus engaged, however, a loud report, as if of a pistol, was heard immediately beneath the windows of the hotel, and was succeeded by a series of fearful screams, and the shoutings of a terrified mob. D—— rushed to a casement, threw it open, and looked out. In the meantime, I stepped to the card-rack, took the letter, put it in my pocket, and replaced it by a *fac-simile*, which I had carefully prepared at my lodgings—imitating the D—— cipher very readily, by means of a seal formed of bread.

"The disturbance in the street had been occasioned by the frantic behaviour of a man with a musket. He had fired it among a crowd of women and children. It proved, however, to have been without ball, and the fellow was suffered to go his way as a lunatic or a drunkard. When he had gone, D——came from the window, whither I had followed him immediately upon securing the object in view. Soon afterwards I bade him farewell. The pretended lunatic was a man in my own pay."

"But what purpose had you," I asked, "in replacing the letter by a *fac-simile*? Would it not have been better, at the first visit, to have seized it openly, and departed?"

"D——," replied Dupin, "is a desperate man, and a man of nerve. His hotel, too, is not without attendants devoted to his interests. Had I made the wild attempt you suggest, I should never have left the ministerial presence alive. The good people of Paris would have heard of me no more. But I had an object apart from these considerations. You know my political prepossessions. In this matter, I act as a partisan of the lady concerned. For eighteen months the minister has had her in his power. She has now him in hers—since, being unaware that the letter is not in his possession, he will proceed with his exactions as if it was. Thus will he inevitably commit himself, at once, to his political destruction. His downfall, too, will not be more precipitate than awkward. It is all very well to talk about the *facilis descensus Averni*;[9] but in all kinds of climbing, as Catalini[1] said of singing, it is far more easy to get up than to come down. In the present instance I have no sympathy—at least no pity for him who descends. He is that *monstrum horrendum*,[2] an unprincipled man of genius. I confess, however, that I should like very well to know the precise character of his thoughts, when, being defied by her whom the Prefect terms 'a certain personage,' he is reduced to opening the letter which I left for him in the card-rack."

"How? did you put any thing particular in it?"

"Why—it did not seem altogether right to leave the interior blank—that would have been insulting. To be sure, D——, at Vienna once, did me an evil turn, which I told him, quite good-humouredly, that I should remember. So, as I knew he would feel some curiosity in regard to the identity of the person who had outwitted him, I thought it a pity not to give him a clue. He is well acquainted with my MS., and I just copied into the middle of the blank sheet the words—

"'—Un dessein si funeste,
S'il n'est digne d'Atrée, est digne de Thyeste.'

They are to be found in Crébillon's 'Atrée.'"[3]

1844

The Cask of Amontillado[1]

The thousand injuries of Fortunato I had borne as I best could, but when he ventured upon insult I vowed revenge. You, who so well know the nature of my soul, will not suppose, however, that I gave utterance to a threat. *At*

9. From Virgil's *Aeneid*, book 6: "The descent to Avernus [Hell] is easy."
1. Angelica Catalani (1780–1849), Italian singer.
2. "Dreadful monstrosity" (Virgil's epithet for Polyphemus, the one-eyed man-eating giant, in book 3 of the *Aeneid*).
3. Prosper Jolyot de Crébillon (1674–1762) wrote *Atrée et Thyeste* (1707), in which the Greek mythological figure Thyestes seduces the wife of his brother Atreus, the king of Mycenae; in revenge Atreus murders the three sons of Thyestes and cooks them up to serve to their father at a feast. The quotation reads: "So baneful a scheme, / if not worthy of Atreus, is worthy of Thyestes" (French).
1. The text is that of the first publication, in *Godey's Magazine and Lady's Book* 33 (November 1846).

length I would be avenged; this was a point definitively settled—but the very definitiveness with which it was resolved precluded the idea of risk. I must not only punish but punish with impunity. A wrong is unredressed when retribution overtakes its redresser. It is equally unredressed when the avenger fails to make himself felt as such to him who has done the wrong.

It must be understood that neither by word nor deed had I given Fortunato cause to doubt my good will. I continued, as was my wont, to smile in his face, and he did not perceive that my smile *now* was at the thought of his immolation.

He had a weak point—this Fortunato—although in other regards he was a man to be respected and even feared. He prided himself upon his connoisseurship in wine. Few Italians have the true virtuoso spirit. For the most part their enthusiasm is adopted to suit the time and opportunity, to practice imposture upon the British and Austrian *millionaires.* In painting and gemmary, Fortunato, like his countrymen, was a quack, but in the matter of old wines he was sincere. In this respect I did not differ from him materially;—I was skilful in the Italian vintages myself, and bought largely whenever I could.

It was about dusk, one evening during the supreme madness of the carnival season, that I encountered my friend. He accosted me with excessive warmth, for he had been drinking much. The man wore motley.[2] He had on a tight-fitting parti-striped dress, and his head was surmounted by the conical cap and bells. I was so pleased to see him that I thought I should never have done wringing his hand.

I said to him—"My dear Fortunato, you are luckily met. How remarkably well you are looking to-day. But I have received a pipe of what passes for Amontillado,[3] and I have my doubts."

"How?" said he. "Amontillado? A pipe? Impossible! And in the middle of the carnival!"

"I have my doubts," I replied; "and I was silly enough to pay the full Amontillado price without consulting you in the matter. You were not to be found, and I was fearful of losing a bargain."

"Amontillado!"

"I have my doubts."

"Amontillado!"

"And I must satisfy them."

"Amontillado!"

"As you are engaged, I am on my way to Luchresi. If any one has a critical turn it is he. He will tell me——"

"Luchresi cannot tell Amontillado from Sherry."

"And yet some fools will have it that his taste is a match for your own."

"Come, let us go."

"Whither?"

"To your vaults."

"My friend, no; I will not impose upon your good nature. I perceive you have an engagement. Luchresi——"

"I have no engagement;—come."

2. A multicolored costume worn by clowns and jesters.

3. A light Spanish sherry. 'Pipe": a large barrel.

"My friend, no. It is not the engagement, but the severe cold with which I perceive you are afflicted. The vaults are insufferably damp. They are encrusted with nitre."[4]

"Let us go, nevertheless. The cold is merely nothing. Amontillado! You have been imposed upon. And as for Luchresi, he cannot distinguish Sherry from Amontillado."

Thus speaking, Fortunato possessed himself of my arm; and putting on a mask of black silk and drawing a *roquelaire*[5] closely about my person, I suffered him to hurry me to my palazzo.

There were no attendants at home; they had absconded to make merry in honour of the time. I had told them that I should not return until the morning, and had given them explicit orders not to stir from the house. These orders were sufficient, I well knew, to insure their immediate disappearance, one and all, as soon as my back was turned.

I took from their sconces two flambeaux,[6] and giving one to Fortunato, bowed him through several suites of rooms to the archway that led into the vaults. I passed down a long and winding staircase, requesting him to be cautious as he followed. We came at length to the foot of the descent, and stood together upon the damp ground of the catacombs of the Montresors.

The gait of my friend was unsteady, and the bells upon his cap jingled as he strode.

"The pipe," said he.

"It is farther on," said I; "but observe the white web-work which gleams from these cavern walls."

He turned towards me, and looked into my eyes with two filmy orbs that distilled the rheum of intoxication.

"Nitre?" he asked, at length.

"Nitre," I replied. "How long have you had that cough?"

"Ugh! ugh! ugh!—ugh! ugh! ugh!—ugh! ugh !ugh!—ugh! ugh! ugh!—ugh! ugh! ugh!"

My poor friend found it impossible to reply for many minutes.

"It is nothing," he said, at last.

"Come," I said, with decision, "we will go back; your health is precious. You are rich, respected, admired, beloved; you are happy, as once I was. You are a man to be missed. For me it is no matter. We will go back; you will be ill, and I cannot be responsible. Besides, there is Luchresi——"

"Enough," he said; "the cough is a mere nothing; it will not kill me. I shall not die of a cough."

"True—true," I replied; "and, indeed, I had no intention of alarming you unneccessarily—but you should use all proper caution. A draught of this Medoc[7] will defend us from the damps."

Here I knocked off the neck of a bottle which I drew from a long row of its fellows that lay upon the mould.

"Drink," I said, presenting him the wine.

He raised it to his lips with a leer. He paused and nodded to me familiarly, while his bells jingled.

"I drink," he said, "to the buried that repose around us."

4. Niter; potassium nitrate.
5. A knee-length cloak.
6. Flaming torches. "Sconces": holders.
7. Red wine from the Bordeaux region of France.

"And I to your long life."

He again took my arm, and we proceeded.

"These vaults," he said, "are extensive."

"The Montresors," I replied, "were a great and numerous family."

"I forget your arms."

"A huge human foot d'or, in a field azure; the foot crushes a serpent rampant whose fangs are imbedded in the heel."[8]

"And the motto?"

"Nemo me impune lacessit."[9]

"Good!" he said.

The wine sparkled in his eyes and the bells jingled. My own fancy grew warm with the Medoc. We had passed through long walls of piled skeletons, with casks and puncheons[1] intermingling, into the inmost recesses of the catacombs. I paused again, and this time I made bold to seize Fortunato by an arm above the elbow.

"The nitre!" I said; "see, it increases. It hangs like moss upon the vaults. We are below the river's bed. The drops of moisture trickle among the bones. Come, we will go back ere it is too late. Your cough——"

"It is nothing," he said; "let us go on. But first, another draught of the Medoc."

I broke and reached him a flaçon of De Grâve.[2] He emptied it at a breath. His eyes flashed with a fierce light. He laughed and threw the bottle upwards with a gesticulation I did not understand.

I looked at him in surprise. He repeated the movement—a grotesque one.

"You do not comprehend?" he said.

"Not I," I replied.

"Then you are not of the brotherhood."

"How?"

"You are not of the masons."[3]

"Yes, yes," I said; "yes, yes."

"You? Impossible! A mason?"

"A mason," I replied.

"A sign," he said, "a sign."

"It is this," I answered, producing from beneath the folds of my *roquelaire* a trowel.

"You jest," he exclaimed, recoiling a few paces. "But let us proceed to the Amontillado."

"Be it so," I said, replacing the tool beneath the cloak and again offering him my arm. He leaned upon it heavily. We continued our rout in search of the Amontillado. We passed through a range of low arches, descended, passed on, and descending again, arrived at a deep crypt, in which the foulness of the air caused our flambeaux rather to glow than flame.

8. On the coat of arms the golden foot is in a blue background; the foot crushes a serpent whose head is reared up and biting.
9. No one insults me with impunity (Latin).
1. Large casks.
2. A Bordeaux wine.
3. International and secretive fraternal organization thought to have originated among stonemasons and cathedral builders in the middle ages, whose members identified themselves to each other through hand signs.

At the most remote end of the crypt there appeared another less spacious. Its walls had been lined with human remains, piled to the vault overhead, in the fashion of the great catacombs of Paris. Three sides of this interior crypt were still ornamented in this manner. From the fourth side the bones had been thrown down, and lay promiscuously upon the earth, forming at one point a mound of some size. Within the wall thus exposed by the displacing of the bones, we perceived a still interior crypt or recess, in depth about four feet, in width three, in height six or seven. It seemed to have been constructed for no especial use within itself, but formed merely the interval between two of the colossal supports of the roof of the catacombs, and was backed by one of their circumscribing walls of solid granite.

It was in vain that Fortunato, uplifting his dull torch, endeavoured to pry into the depth of the recess. Its termination the feeble light did not enable us to see.

"Proceed," I said; "herein is the Amontillado. As for Luchresi——"

"He is an ignoramus," interrupted my friend, as he stepped unsteadily forward, while I followed immediately at his heels. In an instant he had reached the extremity of the niche, and finding his progress arrested by the rock, stood stupidly bewildered. A moment more and I had fettered him to the granite. In its surface were two iron staples, distant from each other about two feet, horizontally. From one of these depended a short chain, from the other a padlock. Throwing the links about his waist, it was but the work of a few seconds to secure it. He was too much astounded to resist. Withdrawing the key I stepped back from the recess.

"Pass your hand," I said, "over the wall; you cannot help feeling the nitre. Indeed, it is *very* damp. Once more let me *implore* you to return. No? Then I must positively leave you. But I will first render you all the little attentions in my power."

"The Amontillado!" ejaculated my friend, not yet recovered from his astonishment.

"True," I replied; "the Amontillado."

As I said these words I busied myself among the pile of bones of which I have before spoken. Throwing them aside, I soon uncovered a quantity of building stone and mortar. With these materials and with the aid of my trowel, I began vigorously to wall up the entrance of the niche.

I had scarcely laid the first tier of the masonry when I discovered that the intoxication of Fortunato had in great measure worn off. The earliest indication I had of this was a low moaning cry from the depth of the recess. It was *not* the cry of a drunken man. There was then a long and obstinate silence. I laid the second tier, and the third, and the fourth; and then I heard the furious vibration of the chain. The noise lasted for several minutes, during which, that I might hearken to it with the more satisfaction, I ceased my labours and sat down upon the bones. When at last the clanking subsided, I resumed the trowel, and finished without interruption the fifth, the sixth, and the seventh tier. The wall was now nearly upon a level with my breast. I again paused, and holding the flambeaux over the mason-work, threw a few feeble rays upon the figure within.

A succession of loud and shrill screams, bursting suddenly from the throat of the chained form, seemed to thrust me violently back. For a brief moment I hesitated, I trembled. Unsheathing my rapier, I began to grope with it about the recess; but the thought of an instant reassured me. I placed my hand upon the solid fabric of the catacombs and felt satisfied. I reapproached the wall. I replied to the yells of him who clamoured. I re-echoed, I aided, I surpassed them in volume and in strength. I did this, and the clamourer grew still.

It was now midnight, and my task was drawing to a close. I had completed the eighth, the ninth and the tenth tier. I had finished a portion of the last and the eleventh; there remained but a single stone to be fitted and plastered in. I struggled with its weight; I placed it partially in its destined position. But now there came from out the niche a low laugh that erected the hairs upon my head. It was succeeded by a sad voice, which I had difficulty in recognizing as that of the noble Fortunato. The voice said—

"Ha! ha! ha!—he! he! he!—a very good joke, indeed—an excellent jest. We will have many a rich laugh about it at the palazzo—he! he! he!—over our wine—he! he! he!"

"The Amontillado!" I said.

"He! he! he!—he! he! he!—yes, the Amontillado. But is it not getting late? Will not they be awaiting us at the palazzo—the Lady Fortunato and the rest? Let us be gone."

"Yes," I said, "let us be gone."

"For the love of God, Montresor!"

"Yes," I said, "for the love of God!"

But to these words I hearkened in vain for a reply. I grew impatient. I called aloud—

"Fortunato!"

No answer. I called again—

"Fortunato!"

No answer still. I thrust a torch through the remaining aperture and let it fall within. There came forth in return only a jingling of the bells. My heart grew sick; it was the dampness of the catacombs that made it so. I hastened to make an end of my labour. I forced the last stone into its position; I plastered it up. Against the new masonry I re-erected the old rampart of bones. For the half of a century no mortal has disturbed them. *In pace requiescat!*[4]

1846

The Philosophy of Composition[1]

Charles Dickens, in a note[2] now lying before me, alluding to an examination I once made of the mechanism of "Barnaby Rudge," says—"By the way, are you aware that Godwin wrote his 'Caleb Williams' backwards? He first involved his hero in a web of difficulties, forming the second volume, and

4. May he rest in peace! (Latin).

1. Poe wrote this as a lecture in hopes of capitalizing on the success of "The Raven." Poe, an advocate of rational composition rather than romantic effusions, here presents an account of how he wrote "The Raven" that may or may not be factual. In a letter of August 9, 1846, Poe called the essay his "best specimen of analysis." The text here is that of the first printing, in *Graham's Magazine* (April 1846).

2. Letter dated March 6, 1842.

then, for the first, cast about him for some mode of accounting for what had been done."[3]

I cannot think this the *precise* mode of procedure on the part of Godwin—and indeed what he himself acknowledges, is not altogether in accordance with Mr. Dickens' idea—but the author of "Caleb Williams" was too good an artist not to perceive the advantage derivable from at least a somewhat similar process. Nothing is more clear than that every plot, worth the name, must be elaborated to its *dénouement*[4] before any thing be attempted with the pen. It is only with the *dénouement* constantly in view that we can give a plot its indispensable air of consequence, or causation, by making the incidents, and especially the tone at all points, tend to the development of the intention.

There is a radical error, I think, in the usual mode of constructing a story. Either history affords a thesis—or one is suggested by an incident of the day—or, at best, the author sets himself to work in the combination of striking events to form merely the basis of his narrative—designing, generally, to fill in with description, dialogue, or autorial comment, whatever crevices of fact, or action, may, from page to page, render themselves apparent.

I prefer commencing with the consideration of an *effect*. Keeping originality *always* in view—for he is false to himself who ventures to dispense with so obvious and so easily attainable a source of interest—I say to myself, in the first place, "Of the innumerable effects, or impressions, of which the heart, the intellect, or (more generally) the soul is susceptible, what one shall I, on the present occasion, select?" Having chosen a novel, first, and secondly a vivid effect, I consider whether it can best be wrought by incident or tone—whether by ordinary incidents and peculiar tone, or the converse, or by peculiarity both of incident and tone—afterward looking about me (or rather within) for such combinations of event, or tone, as shall best aid me in the construction of the effect.

I have often thought how interesting a magazine paper might be written by any author who would—that is to say, who could—detail, step by step, the processes by which any one of his compositions attained its ultimate point of completion. Why such a paper has never been given to the world, I am much at a loss to say—but, perhaps, the autorial vanity has had more to do with the omission than any one other cause. Most writers—poets in especial—prefer having it understood that they compose by a species of fine frenzy[5]—an ecstatic intuition—and would positively shudder at letting the public take a peep behind the scenes, at the elaborate and vacillating crudities of thought—at the true purposes seized only at the last moment—at the innumerable glimpses of idea that arrived not at the maturity of full view—at the fully matured fancies discarded in despair as unmanageable—at the cautious selections and rejections—at the painful erasures and interpolations—in a word, at the wheels and pinions—the tackle for scene-shifting—

3. William Godwin makes this claim in his 1832 preface to *Caleb Williams* (first published in 1794). As *Barnaby Rudge* was being serialized in 1842, Poe published an analysis of the novel that identified the murderer and correctly predicted the ending.
4. The final revelation showing the outcome, or untying, of the plot. From *dénouer* (French), "to untie."
5. The character Theseus's description of the poet in Shakespeare's *Midsummer Night's Dream* 5.1.12: "The poet's eye, in a fine frenzy rolling, / Doth glance from heaven to earth, from earth to heaven / And as imagination bodies forth / The forms of things unknown, the poet's pen / Turns them to shapes, and gives to airy nothing / A local habitation and a name."

the step-ladders and demon-traps—the cock's feathers, the red paint and the black patches, which, in ninety-nine cases out of the hundred, constitute the properties of the literary *histrio*.[6]

I am aware, on the other hand, that the case is by no means common, in which an author is at all in condition to retrace the steps by which his conclusions have been attained. In general, suggestions, having arisen pell-mell, are pursued and forgotten in a similar manner.

For my own part, I have neither sympathy with the repugnance alluded to, nor, at any time, the least difficulty in recalling to mind the progressive steps of any of my compositions; and, since the interest of an analysis, or reconstruction, such as I have considered a *desideratum*,[7] is quite independent of any real or fancied interest in the thing analyzed, it will not be regarded as a breach of decorum on my part to show the *modus operandi*[8] by which some one of my own works was put together. I select "The Raven," as the most generally known. It is my design to render it manifest that no one point in its composition is referrible either to accident or intuition—that the work proceeded, step by step, to its completion with the precision and rigid consequence of a mathematical problem.

Let us dismiss, as irrelevant to the poem *per se*, the circumstance—or say the necessity—which, in the first place, gave rise to the intention of composing *a* poem that should suit at once the popular and the critical taste.

We commence, then, with this intention.

The initial consideration was that of extent. If any literary work is too long to be read at one sitting, we must be content to dispense with the immensely important effect derivable from unity of impression—for, if two sittings be required, the affairs of the world interfere, and every thing like totality is at once destroyed. But since, *ceteris paribus*,[9] no poet can afford to dispense with *any thing* that may advance his design, it but remains to be seen whether there is, in extent, any advantage to counterbalance the loss of unity which attends it. Here I say no, at once. What we term a long poem is, in fact, merely a succession of brief ones—that is to say, of brief poetical effects. It is needless to demonstrate that a poem is such, only inasmuch as it intensely excites, by elevating, the soul; and all intense excitements are, through a psychal necessity, brief. For this reason, at least one half of the "Paradise Lost"[1] is essentially prose—a succession of poetical excitements interspersed, *inevitably*, with corresponding depressions—the whole being deprived, through the extremeness of its length, of the vastly important artistic element, totality, or unity, of effect.

It appears evident, then, that there is a distinct limit, as regards length, to all works of literary art—the limit of a single sitting—and that, although in certain classes of prose composition, such as "Robinson Crusoe,"[2] (demanding no unity,) this limit may be advantageously overpassed, it can never properly be overpassed in a poem. Within this limit, the extent of a poem may be made to bear mathematical relation to its merit—in other words, to the excitement or elevation—again in other words, to the degree

6. Artist (Latin).
7. Something to be desired (Latin).
8. Method of procedure (Latin).
9. Other things being equal (Latin).
1. For Poe, John Milton's blank verse epic (1667) of some 10,500 lines is much too long to be poetry all the way through.
2. Daniel Defoe's novel of shipwreck in the Caribbean (1719).

of the true poetical effect which it is capable of inducing; for it is clear that the brevity must be in direct ratio of the intensity of the intended effect:—this, with one proviso—that a certain degree of duration is absolutely requisite for the production of any effect at all.

Holding in view these considerations, as well as that degree of excitement which I deemed not above the popular, while not below the critical, taste, I reached at once what I conceived the proper *length* for my intended poem—a length of about one hundred lines. It is, in fact, a hundred and eight.

My next thought concerned the choice of an impression, or effect, to be conveyed: and here I may as well observe that, throughout the construction, I kept steadily in view the design of rendering the work *universally* appreciable. I should be carried too far out of my immediate topic were I to demonstrate a point upon which I have repeatedly insisted, and which, with the poetical, stands not in the slightest need of demonstration—the point, I mean, that Beauty is the sole legitimate province of the poem. A few words, however, in elucidation of my real meaning, which some of my friends have evinced a disposition to misrepresent. That pleasure which is at once the most intense, the most elevating, and the most pure, is, I believe, found in the contemplation of the beautiful. When, indeed, men speak of Beauty, they mean, precisely, not a quality, as is supposed, but an effect—they refer, in short, just to that intense and pure elevation of *soul—not* of intellect, or of heart—upon which I have commented, and which is experienced in consequence of contemplating "the beautiful." Now I designate Beauty as the province of the poem, merely because it is an obvious rule of Art that effects should be made to spring from direct causes—that objects should be attained through means best adapted for their attainment—no one as yet having been weak enough to deny that the peculiar elevation alluded to, is *most readily* attained in the poem. Now the object, Truth, or the satisfaction of the intellect, and the object, Passion, or the excitement of the heart, are, although attainable, to a certain extent, in poetry, far more readily attainable in prose. Truth, in fact, demands a precision, and Passion, a *homeliness* (the truly passionate will comprehend me) which are absolutely antagonistic to that Beauty which, I maintain, is the excitement, or pleasurable elevation, of the soul. It by no means follows from any thing here said, that passion, or even truth, may not be introduced, and even profitably introduced, into a poem—for they may serve in elucidation, or aid the general effect, as do discords in music, by contrast—but the true artist will always contrive, first, to tone them into proper subservience to the predominant aim, and, secondly, to enveil them, as far as possible, in that Beauty which is the atmosphere and the essence of the poem.

Regarding, then, Beauty as my province, my next question referred to the *tone* of its highest manifestation—and all experience has shown that this tone is one of *sadness*. Beauty of whatever kind, in its supreme development, invariably excites the sensitive soul to tears. Melancholy is thus the most legitimate of all the poetical tones.

The length, the province, and the tone, being thus determined, I betook myself to ordinary induction, with the view of obtaining some artistic piquancy which might serve me as a key-note in the construction of the poem—some pivot upon which the whole structure might turn. In carefully thinking over all the usual artistic effects—or more properly *points*, in the theatrical sense—I did not fail to perceive immediately that no one had been so universally employed as that of the *refrain.* The universality of its employment sufficed to assure me of its intrinsic value, and spared me the necessity of submitting it to analysis. I considered it, however, with regard to its susceptibility of improvement, and soon saw it to be in a primitive condition. As commonly used, the *refrain*, or burden, not only is limited to lyric verse, but depends for its impression upon the force of monotone—both in sound and thought. The pleasure is deduced solely from the sense of identity—of repetition. I resolved to diversify, and so vastly heighten, the effect, by adhering, in general, to the monotone of sound, while I continually varied that of thought: that is to say, I determined to produce continuously novel effects, by the variation *of the application* of the *refrain*—the *refrain* itself remaining, for the most part, unvaried.

These points being settled, I next bethought me of the *nature* of my *refrain.* Since its application was to be repeatedly varied, it was clear that the *refrain* itself must be brief, for there would have been an insurmountable difficulty in frequent variations of application in any sentence of length. In proportion to the brevity of the sentence, would, of course, be the facility of the variation. This led me at once to a single word as the best *refrain.*

The question now arose as to the *character* of the word. Having made up my mind to a *refrain*, the division of the poem into stanzas was, of course, a corollary: the *refrain* forming the close to each stanza. That such a close, to have force, must be sonorous and susceptible of protracted emphasis, admitted no doubt: and these considerations inevitably led me to the long *o* as the most sonorous vowel, in connection with *r* as the most producible consonant.

The sound of the *refrain* being thus determined, it became necessary to select a word embodying this sound, and at the same time in the fullest possible keeping with that melancholy which I had predetermined as the tone of the poem. In such a search it would have been absolutely impossible to overlook the word "Nevermore." In fact, it was the very first which presented itself.

The next *desideratum* was a pretext for the continuous use of the one word "nevermore." In observing the difficulty which I at once found in inventing a sufficiently plausible reason for its continuous repetition, I did not fail to perceive that this difficulty arose solely from the pre-assumption that the word was to be so continuously or monotonously spoken by *a human* being—I did not fail to perceive, in short, that the difficulty lay in the reconciliation of this monotony with the exercise of reason on the part of the creature repeating the word. Here, then, immediately arose the idea of a *non*-reasoning creature capable of speech; and, very naturally, a parrot, in the first instance, suggested itself, but was superseded forthwith by a Raven, as equally capable of speech, and infinitely more in keeping with the intended *tone.*

I had now gone so far as the conception of a Raven—the bird of ill omen—monotonously repeating the one word, "Nevermore," at the conclusion of each stanza, in a poem of melancholy tone, and in length about one hundred lines. Now, never losing sight of the object *supremeness*, or perfection, at all points, I asked myself—"Of all melancholy topics, what, according to the *universal* understanding of mankind, is the *most* melancholy?" Death—was the obvious reply. "And when," I said, "is this most melancholy of topics most poetical?" From what I have already explained at some length, the answer, here also, is obvious—"When it most closely allies itself to *Beauty*: the death, then, of a beautiful woman is, unquestionably, the most poetical topic in the world—and equally is it beyond doubt that the lips best suited for such topic are those of a bereaved lover."

I had now to combine the two ideas, of a lover lamenting his deceased mistress and a Raven continuously repeating the word "Nevermore"—I had to combine these, bearing in mind my design of varying, at every turn, the *application* of the word repeated; but the only intelligible model of such combination is that of imagining the Raven employing the word in answer to the queries of the lover. And here it was that I saw at once the opportunity afforded for the effect on which I had been depending—that is to say, the effect of the *variation of application*. I saw that I could make the first query propounded by the lover—the first query to which the Raven should reply "Nevermore"—that I could make this first query a commonplace one—the second less so—the third still less, and so on—until at length the lover, startled from his original *nonchalance* by the melancholy character of the word itself—by its frequent repetition—and by a consideration of the ominous reputation of the fowl that uttered it—is at length excited to superstition, and wildly propounds queries of a far different character—queries whose solution he has passionately at heart—propounds them half in superstition and half in that species of despair which delights in self-torture—propounds them not altogether because he believes in the prophetic or demoniac character of the bird (which, reason assures him, is merely repeating a lesson learned by rote) but because he experiences a phrenzied pleasure in so modeling his questions as to receive from the *expected* "Nevermore" the most delicious because the most intolerable of sorrow. Perceiving the opportunity thus afforded me—or, more strictly, thus forced upon me in the progress of the construction—I first established in mind the climax, or concluding query—that to which "Nevermore" should be in the last place an answer—that in reply to which this word "Nevermore" should involve the utmost conceivable amount of sorrow and despair.

Here then the poem may be said to have its beginning—at the end, where all works of art should begin—for it was here, at this point of my preconsiderations, that I first put pen to paper in the composition of the stanza:

"Prophet," said I, "thing of evil! prophet still if bird or devil!
By that heaven that bends above us—by that God we both adore,
Tell this soul with sorrow laden, if within the distant Aidenn,
It shall clasp a sainted maiden whom the angels name Lenore—
Clasp a rare and radiant maiden whom the angels name Lenore."
Quoth the raven "Nevermore."

I composed this stanza, at this point, first that, by establishing the climax, I might the better vary and graduate, as regards seriousness and importance, the preceding queries of the lover—and, secondly, that I might definitely settle the rhythm, the metre, and the length and general arrangement of the stanza—as well as graduate the stanzas which were to precede, so that none of them might surpass this in rhythmical effect. Had I been able, in the subsequent composition, to construct more vigorous stanzas, I should, without scruple, have purposely enfeebled them, so as not to interfere with the climacteric effect.

And here I may as well say a few words of the versification. My first object (as usual) was originality. The extent to which this has been neglected, in versification, is one of the most unaccountable things in the world. Admitting that there is little possibility of variety in mere *rhythm*, it is still clear that the possible varieties of metre and stanza are absolutely infinite—and yet, *for centuries, no man, in verse, has ever done, or ever seemed to think of doing, an original thing.* The fact is, originality (unless in minds of very unusual force) is by no means a matter, as some suppose, of impulse or intuition. In general, to be found, it must be elaborately sought, and although a positive merit of the highest class, demands in its attainment less of invention than negation.

Of course, I pretend to no originality in either the rhythm or metre of the "Raven." The former is trochaic—the latter is octameter acatalectic, alternating with heptameter catalectic repeated in the *refrain* of the fifth verse, and terminating with tetrameter catalectic. Less pedantically—the feet employed throughout (trochees) consist of a long syllable followed by a short: the first line of the stanza consists of eight of these feet—the second of seven and a half (in effect two-thirds)—the third of eight—the fourth of seven and a half—the fifth the same—the sixth three and a half. Now, each of these lines, taken individually, has been employed before, and what originality the "Raven" has, is in their *combination into stanza*; nothing even remotely approaching this combination has ever been attempted. The effect of this originality of combination is aided by other unusual, and some altogether novel effects, arising from an extension of the application of the principles of rhyme and alliteration.

The next point to be considered was the mode of bringing together the lover and the Raven—and the first branch of this consideration was the *locale*. For this the most natural suggestion might seem to be a forest, or the fields—but it has always appeared to me that a close *circumscription of space* is absolutely necessary to the effect of insulated incident:—it has the force of a frame to a picture. It has an indisputable moral power in keeping concentrated the attention, and, of course, must not be confounded with mere unity of place.

I determined, then, to place the lover in his chamber—in a chamber rendered sacred to him by memories of her who had frequented it. The room is represented as richly furnished—this in mere pursuance of the ideas I have already explained on the subject of Beauty, as the sole true poetical thesis.

The *locale* being thus determined, I had now to introduce the bird—and the thought of introducing him through the window, was inevitable. The idea of making the lover suppose, in the first instance, that the flapping of the wings of the bird against the shutter, is a "tapping" at the door, originated in a wish to increase, by prolonging, the reader's curiosity, and in a desire to admit the incidental effect arising from the lover's throwing open the door, finding all dark, and thence adopting the half-fancy that it was the spirit of his mistress that knocked.

I made the night tempestuous, first, to account for the Raven's seeking admission, and secondly, for the effect of contrast with the (physical) serenity within the chamber.

I made the bird alight on the bust of Pallas,[3] also for the effect of contrast between the marble and the plumage—it being understood that the bust

3. Pallas Athena, the Greek goddess of wisdom and the arts.

was absolutely *suggested* by the bird—the bust of *Pallas* being chosen, first, as most in keeping with the scholarship of the lover, and, secondly, for the sonorousness of the word, Pallas, itself.

About the middle of the poem, also, I have availed myself of the force of contrast, with a view of deepening the ultimate impression. For example, an air of the fantastic—approaching as nearly to the ludicrous as was admissible—is given to the Raven's entrance. He comes in "with many a flirt and flutter."

Not the *least obeisance made he*—not a moment stopped or stayed he,
But with mien of lord or lady, perched above my chamber door.

In the two stanzas which follow, the design is more obviously carried out:—

Then this ebony bird beguiling my sad fancy into smiling
By the *grave and stern decorum of the countenance it wore,*
"Though thy *crest be shorn and shaven* thou," I said, "art sure no craven,
Ghastly grim and ancient Raven wandering from the nightly shore—
Tell me what thy lordly name is on the Night's Plutonian shore!"
Quoth the Raven "Nevermore."

Much I marvelled *this ungainly fowl* to hear discourse so plainly,
Though its answer little meaning—little relevancy bore;
For we cannot help agreeing that no living human being
Ever yet was blessed with seeing bird above his chamber door—
Bird or beast upon the sculptured bust above his chamber door,
With such name as "Nevermore."

The effect of the *dénouement* being thus provided for, I immediately drop the fantastic for a tone of the most profound seriousness:—this tone commencing in the stanza directly following the one last quoted, with the line,

But the Raven, sitting lonely on that placid bust, spoke only, etc.

From this epoch the lover no longer jests—no longer sees any thing even of the fantastic in the Raven's demeanor. He speaks of him as a "grim, ungainly, ghastly, gaunt, and ominous bird of yore," and feels the "fiery eyes" burning into his "bosom's core." This revolution of thought, or fancy, on the lover's part, is intended to induce a similar one on the part of the reader—to bring the mind into a proper frame for the *dénouement*—which is now brought about as rapidly and as *directly* as possible.

With the *dénouement* proper—with the Raven's reply, "Nevermore," to the lover's final demand if he shall meet his mistress in another world—the poem, in its obvious phase, that of a simple narrative, may be said to have its completion. So far, every thing is within the limits of the accountable—of the real. A raven, having learned by rote the single word "Nevermore," and having escaped from the custody of its owner, is driven, at midnight, through the violence of a storm, to seek admission at a window from which a light still gleams—the chamber-window of a student, occupied half in poring over a volume, half in dreaming of a beloved mistress deceased. The casement being thrown open at the fluttering of the bird's wings, the bird itself perches on the most convenient seat out of the immediate reach of the student, who, amused by the incident and the oddity of the visiter's demeanor, demands of it, in jest and without looking for a reply, its name. The raven addressed, answers with its customary word, "Nevermore"—a word which finds immediate echo in the melancholy heart of the student, who, giving utterance aloud to certain thoughts suggested by the occasion, is again startled by the fowl's repetition of "Nevermore." The student now guesses the state of the case, but is impelled, as I have before explained, by the human thirst for self-torture, and in part by superstition, to propound such queries to the bird as will bring him, the lover, the most of the luxury of sorrow, through the anticipated answer "Nevermore." With the indulgence, to the utmost extreme, of this self-torture, the narration, in what I have termed its first or obvious phase, has a natural termination, and so far there has been no overstepping of the limits of the real.

But in subjects so handled, however skilfully, or with however vivid an array of incident, there is always a certain hardness or nakedness, which repels the artistical eye. Two things are invariably required—first, some amount of complexity, or more properly, adaptation; and, secondly, some amount of suggestiveness—some under current, however indefinite of meaning. It is this latter, in especial, which imparts to a work of art so much of that *richness* (to borrow from colloquy a forcible term) which we are too fond of confounding with *the ideal*. It is the *excess* of the suggested meaning—it is the rendering this the upper instead of the under current of the theme—which turns into prose (and that of the very flattest kind) the so called poetry of the so called transcendentalists.

Holding these opinions, I added the two concluding stanzas of the poem—their suggestiveness being thus made to pervade all the narrative which has preceded them. The under-current of meaning is rendered first apparent in the lines—

"Take thy beak from out *my heart,* and take thy form from off my door!"
Quoth the Raven "Nevermore!"

It will be observed that the words, "from out my heart," involve the first metaphorical expression in the poem. They, with the answer, "Nevermore," dispose the mind to seek a moral in all that has been previously narrated. The reader begins now to regard the Raven as emblematical—but it is not until the very last line of the very last stanza, that the intention of making him emblematical of *Mournful and Never-ending Remembrance* is permitted distinctly to be seen:

And the Raven, never flitting, still is sitting, still is sitting,
On the pallid bust of Pallas just above my chamber door;
And his eyes have all the seeming of a demon's that is dreaming,
And the lamplight o'er him streaming throws his shadow on the floor;
And my soul *from out that shadow* that lies floating on the floor
Shall be lifted—nevermore.

1846

From The Poetic Principle[1]

In speaking of the Poetic Principle, I have no design to be either thorough or profound. While discussing, very much at random, the essentiality of what we call Poetry, my principal purpose will be to cite for consideration, some few of those minor English or American poems which best suit my own taste, or which, upon my own fancy, have left the most definite impression. By "minor poems" I mean, of course, poems of little length. And here, in the beginning, permit me to say a few words in regard to a somewhat peculiar principle, which, whether rightfully or wrongfully, has always had its influence in my own critical estimate of the poem. I hold that a long poem does not exist. I maintain that the phrase, "a long poem," is simply a flat contradiction in terms.

I need scarcely observe that a poem deserves its title only inasmuch as it excites, by elevating the soul. The value of the poem is in the ratio of this elevating excitement. But all excitements are, through a psychal necessity, transient. That degree of excitement which would entitle a poem to be so called at all, cannot be sustained throughout a composition of any great length. After the lapse of half an hour, at the very utmost, it flags—fails—a revulsion ensues—and then the poem is, in effect, and in fact, no longer such.

There are, no doubt, many who have found difficulty in reconciling the critical dictum that the "Paradise Lost" is to be devoutly admired throughout, with the absolute impossibility of maintaining for it, during perusal, the amount of enthusiasm which that critical dictum would demand. This great work, in fact, is to be regarded as poetical, only when, losing sight of that vital requisite in all works of Art, Unity, we view it merely as a series of minor poems. If, to preserve its Unity—its totality of effect or impression—we read it (as would be necessary) at a single sitting, the result is but a constant alternation of excitement and depression. After a passage of what we feel to be true poetry, there follows, inevitably, a passage of platitude which no critical pre-judgment can force us to admire; but if, upon completing the work, we read it again, omitting the first book—that is to say, commencing with the second—we shall be surprised at now finding that admirable which we before condemned—that damnable which we had previously so much admired. It follows from all this that the ultimate, aggregate, or absolute effect of even the best epic under the sun, is a nullity:—and this is precisely the fact.

In regard to the Iliad, we have, if not positive proof, at least very good reason for believing it intended as a series of lyrics; but, granting the epic intention, I can say only that the work is based in an imperfect sense of art. The modern epic is, of the supposititious ancient model, but an inconsiderate and blindfold imitation. But the day of these artistic anomalies is over. If, at any time, any very long poem *were* popular in reality, which I doubt, it is at least clear that no very long poem will ever be popular again.

That the extent of a poetical work is, *coeteris paribus*,[2] the measure of its merit, seems undoubtedly, when we thus state it, a proposition sufficiently

1. Poe delivered this as a lecture several times in the last two years of his life. The text is from *Sartain's Magazine* 7 (October 1850).

2. Other things being equal (Latin).

absurd—yet we are indebted for it to the Quarterly Reviews.[3] Surely there can be nothing in mere size, abstractly considered—there can be nothing in mere *bulk*, so far as a volume is concerned, which has so continuously elicited admiration from these saturnine pamphlets! A mountain, to be sure, by the mere sentiment of physical magnitude which it conveys, *does* impress us with a sense of the sublime—but no man is impressed after *this* fashion by the material grandeur of even "The Columbiad."[4] Even the Quarterlies have not instructed us to be so impressed by it. *As yet*, they have not *insisted* on our estimating Lamartine by the cubic foot, or Pollock by the pound[5]—but what else are we to infer from their continual prating about "sustained effort"? If, by "sustained effort," any little gentleman has accomplished an epic, let us frankly commend him for the effort—if this indeed be a thing commendable—but let us forbear praising the epic on the effort's account. It is to be hoped that common sense, in the time to come, will prefer deciding upon a work of art, rather by the impression it makes, by the effect it produces, than by the time it took to impress the effect, or by the amount of "sustained effort" which had been found necessary in effecting the impression. The fact is, that perseverance is one thing, and genius quite another; nor can all the Quarterlies in Christendom confound them. By and by, this proposition, with many which I have been just urging, will be received as self-evident. In the mean time, by being generally condemned as falsities, they will not be essentially damaged as truths.

On the other hand, it is clear that a poem may be improperly brief. Undue brevity degenerates into mere epigrammatism. A *very* short poem, while now and then producing a brilliant or vivid, never produces a profound or enduring effect. There must be the steady pressing down of the stamp upon the wax. De Béranger[6] has wrought innumerable things, pungent and spirit-stirring; but, in general, they have been too imponderous to stamp themselves deeply into the public attention; and thus, as so many feathers of fancy, have been blown aloft only to be whistled down the wind.

* * *

1850

3. The English and Scottish quarterlies, led by the *Edinburgh Review* (founded 1802) and the *Quarterly Review* (founded in 1809, also in Edinburgh).
4. An epic nationalistic poem about Columbus, published in 1807 by the American diplomat and writer Joel Barlow (1754–1812).
5. Alphonse de Lamartine (1790–1869), French poet; Robert Pollock (1798–1827), Scottish poet, author of the long *The Course of Time* (1827).
6. Pierre-Jean de Béranger (1780–1857), French lyric poet, author of a popular series of *Chansons*.

ABRAHAM LINCOLN
1809–1865

Abraham Lincoln, the sixteenth president of the United States (1861–65), presided over the bloodiest war in U.S. history—one that preserved the Union and ended slavery. He was also one of the era's great prose stylists. Drawing on his boyhood in Kentucky and Indiana and his young manhood in rural Illinois, he used American traditions of ordinary speech and backwoods humor to great political effect and, in so doing, placed these regional traits at the center of American discourse. At the same time, he was passionately committed to the egalitarian principles of the Declaration of Independence and the spiritual ideals of the Bible, and he would regularly invoke both the Declaration and the Bible when contesting slavery and thinking about the future of the United States. His vision of a national house divided by slavery was of a piece with Harriet Beecher Stowe's domestic and millennial vision, though in his late Civil War speeches, Lincoln was far more magnanimous toward the South than most antislavery writers. With his assassination in 1865, Lincoln, who had been reviled by many in the North and South, came to be regarded almost mystically as a Christ-like figure whose death held out the promise that the great bloodletting of the war would give birth to a redeemed nation.

Lincoln was born on February 12, 1809, in a cabin in Hardin County, Kentucky. His father, Thomas Lincoln, and his mother, Mary Hanks, were barely literate; Lincoln himself attended school only sporadically—probably for no more than a year altogether. Although his access to books was limited, his memory was remarkable; years later he was able to draw on his childhood reading of the King James Bible, Aesop's *Fables*, John Bunyan's *Pilgrim's Progress*, Daniel Defoe's *Robinson Crusoe*, and Mason Locke Weems's *Life of George Washington*. Lincoln never lost his love of reading, adding John Stuart Mill, Lord Byron, Robert Burns, and especially Shakespeare to his list of favorites.

Lincoln spent his impoverished youth in Kentucky and southern Indiana, where his father farmed for a living. His mother died when he was nine, but his stepmother, who soon joined the family with children of her own, seems to have singled him out for special affection; Lincoln later spoke of her as his "angel mother." In 1830 the family moved to Illinois. After trying various jobs, Lincoln decided in the early 1830s to prepare for a career in law. In 1834 he was elected to the first of four terms as an Illinois state legislator. He passed the state bar examination in 1836 and moved the next year to the new state capital in Springfield, where he prospered as a lawyer. In 1842 he married Mary Todd, from a wealthy Kentucky family then residing in Springfield. The couple had four sons, only one of whom survived to adulthood.

The political and historical developments of the 1840s and 1850s that would result in Lincoln's election were complicated, but the central issue was whether slavery would be permitted in the new territories, which eventually would become states. Lincoln was elected to the U.S. Congress in 1846; always concerned with mediating rather than inflaming disputes, he voted against abolitionist measures, which he believed might eventually threaten the Union. At the same time, recalling his own remarkable rise from poverty, he insisted that new territories be kept free as "places for poor people to go and better their condition." He also joined an unsuccessful vote to censure President Polk for engaging in the war against Mexico

(1846–48), a war he and many of his legislative colleagues believed to be both unjustified and unconstitutional. He did not run for reelection and it appeared that his political career had come to an end.

By 1854 the two major political parties of the time—the Whigs (to which Lincoln belonged) and the Democrats—had compromised on the extension of slavery into new territories and states. Strong antislavery elements in both parties, however, established independent organizations; and when, in 1854, the Republican Party was organized, Lincoln soon joined it. His new party lost the presidential election of 1856 to the Democrats, but in 1858 Lincoln reentered political life as the Republican candidate in the Illinois senatorial election. He opposed the Democrat Stephen A. Douglas, who had earlier sponsored the Kansas-Nebraska Bill, which left it to new territories to establish their status as slave or free when they achieved statehood. Lincoln may have won the famous series of debates with Douglas, but he lost the election. More important for the future, though, he had gained national recognition for his principled opposition to the extension of slavery and found a theme commensurate with his rapidly intensifying powers of thought and expression. As the "House Divided" speech suggests, Lincoln now added to the often biting satirical humor, and to the logic and natural grace of his earlier utterances, a resonance and moral purpose that mark his emergence as a national political leader and as a master of language.

This reputation was enhanced by the Cooper Union Address in 1860, his first in the East, in which Lincoln disputed the idea that slavery was endorsed by the Founding Fathers; and at the Republican presidential convention he won nomination on the third ballot. Lincoln was elected president of the United States in November 1860; but before he took office on March 4, 1861, seven Southern states had seceded from the Union to form the Confederacy. Little more than a month after his inauguration, the Civil War had begun. True to his long-standing commitment, he devoted himself to the preservation of the Union. To do this he had to develop an overall war strategy, devise a workable command system, and find the right personnel to execute his plans. All of this he was to accomplish by trial and error in the early months of the war. As months turned to years, he had to garner popular support for his purposes by using his extraordinary political and oratorical skills in times of high passion and internal division; in two of his most famous speeches, the Gettysburg Address and the Second Inaugural, he offered an almost biblical vision of a divided, suffering nation that would one day reunite to bring forth "a new birth of freedom."

Lincoln committed himself by degrees to the elimination of slavery throughout the country. Initially, he wished only to contain it; next, he proceeded cautiously with the 1863 Emancipation Proclamation, which freed only the slaves of the seceded Southern states; finally, he took the leading role in the passage of the Thirteenth Amendment, which outlawed slavery everywhere and forever in the United States. Elected to a second term in 1864, he had served scarcely a month of his new term when he was assassinated, while attending a play, by the actor John Wilkes Booth. He died on April 15, 1865. In subsequent weeks, mournful crowds gathered at the various stops on Lincoln's funeral train to pay homage to their fallen leader. Whitman spoke for the multitudes when he eulogized him in "When Lilacs Last in the Dooryard Bloom'd" (1865) as "the sweetest, wisest soul of all my days and lands."

A House Divided: Speech Delivered at Springfield, Illinois, at the Close of the Republican State Convention, June 16, 1858[1]

If we could first know *where* we are, and *whither* we are tending, we could better judge *what* to do, and *how* to do it.

We are now far into the *fifth* year, since a policy was initiated, with the *avowed* object, and *confident* promise, of putting an end to slavery agitation.[2]

Under the operation of that policy, that agitation has not only, *not ceased*, but has *constantly augmented*.

In my opinion, it *will* not cease, until a *crisis* shall have been reached, and passed—

"A house divided against itself cannot stand."[3]

I believe this government cannot endure, permanently half *slave* and half *free*.

I do not expect the Union to be *dissolved*—I do not expect the house to *fall*—but I *do* expect it will cease to be divided.

It will become *all* one thing, or *all* the other.

Either the *opponents* of slavery, will arrest the further spread of it, and place it where the public mind shall rest in the belief that it is in course of ultimate extinction; or its *advocates* will push it forward, till it shall become alike lawful in *all* the States, *old* as well as *new—North* as well as *South*.

Have we no *tendency* to the latter condition?

Let any one who doubts, carefully contemplate that now almost complete legal combination—piece of *machinery* so to speak—compounded of the Nebraska doctrine, and the Dred Scott decision.[4] Let him consider not only *what work* the machinery is adapted to do, and *how well* adapted; but also, let him study the history of its construction, and trace, if he can, or rather *fail*, if he can, to trace the evidences of design, and concert of action, among its chief bosses, from the beginning.

The new year of 1854 found slavery excluded from more than half the States by State Constitutions, and from most of the national territory by congressional prohibition.

Four days later, commenced the struggle, which ended in repealing that congressional prohibition.

This opened all the national territory to slavery; and was the first point gained.

But, so far, *Congress* only, had acted; and an *indorsement* by the people, *real* or *apparent*, was indispensible, to *save* the point already gained, and give chance for more.

1. First printed in the *Illinois Journal* on June 18, 1858. Lincoln delivered this speech after being nominated as the Republicans' candidate for U.S. senator.

2. Lincoln refers to the Compromise of 1850, which had balanced the number of slave and free states and instituted a new Fugitive Slave Law.

3. Mark 3.25: "If a house be divided against itself, that house cannot stand."

4. The Kansas-Nebraska Bill of 1854 overrode earlier legislation by allowing white male residents of newly established territories to vote on whether to permit slavery therein. As a result, antislavery New Englanders and proslavery Missourians both entered Kansas to settle there, engaging in hostilities that anticipated the Civil War. The Supreme Court's Dred Scott ruling of March 1857 effectively negated any possible antislavery consequences of the Kansas-Nebraska Bill by asserting that blacks could not become U.S. citizens and thus had no legal rights.

This necessity had not been overlooked; but had been provided for, as well as might be, in the notable argument of "squatter sovereignty," otherwise called *"sacred right of self government,"* which latter phrase, though expressive of the only rightful basis of any government, was so perverted in this attempted use of it as to amount to just this: That if any *one* man, choose to enslave *another*, no *third* man shall be allowed to object.

That argument was incorporated into the Nebraska bill itself, in the language which follows: *"It being the true intent and meaning of this act not to legislate slavery into any Territory or State, nor to exclude it therefrom; but to leave the people thereof perfectly free to form and regulate their domestic institutions in their own way, subject only to the Constitution of the United States."*

Then opened the roar of loose declamation in favor of 'Squatter Sovereignty," and "Sacred right of self government."

"But," said opposition members, "let us be more *specific*—let us *amend* the bill so as to expressly declare that the people of the Territory *may* exclude slavery." "Not we," said the friends of the measure; and down they voted the amendment.

While the Nebraska bill was passing through congress, a *law case*, involving the question of a negro's freedom, by reason of his owner having voluntarily taken him first into a free State and then a territory covered by the congressional prohibition, and held him as a slave for a long time in each, was passing through the U.S. Circuit Court for the District of Missouri; and both Nebraska bill and law suit were brought to a decision in the same month of May, 1854. The negro's name was "Dred Scott," which name now designates the decision finally made in the case.

Before the *then* next Presidential election, the law case came *to*, and was argued *in* the Supreme Court of the United States; but the *decision* of it was deferred until *after* the election. Still, *before* the election, Senator Trumbull, on the floor of the Senate, requests the leading advocate[5] of the Nebraska bill to state *his opinion* whether the people of a territory can constitutionally exclude slavery from their limits; and the latter answers, "That is a question for the Supreme Court."

The election came. Mr. Buchanan[6] was elected, and the *indorsement*, such as it was, secured. That was the *second* point gained. This indorsement, however, fell short of a clear popular majority by nearly four hundred thousand votes, and so, perhaps, was not over-whelmingly reliable and satisfactory.

The *outgoing* President,[7] in his last annual message, as impressively as possible *echoed back* upon the people the *weight* and *authority* of the indorsement.

The Supreme Court met again; *did not* announce their decision, but ordered a re-argument.

The Presidential inauguration came, and still no decision of the court; but the *incoming* President, in his inaugural address, fervently exhorted the people to abide by the forthcoming decision, *whatever it might be*.

Then, in a few days, came the decision.

5. Stephen A. Douglas (1813–1861), Lincoln's Democratic Party opponent for the Senate. Lyman Trumbull (1813–1896), Illinois senator (1855–73).

6. James Buchanan (1791–1868), fifteenth president of the United States (1857–61).

7. Franklin Pierce (1804–1869), fourteenth president of the United States (1853–57).

The reputed author of the Nebraska bill finds an early occasion to make a speech at this capitol indorsing the Dred Scott Decision, and vehemently denouncing all opposition to it.

The new President, too, seizes the early occasion of the Silliman letter[8] to indorse and strongly *construe* that decision, and to express his *astonishment* that any different view had ever been entertained.

At length a squabble springs up between the President and the author of the Nebraska bill, on the *mere* question of *fact*, whether the Lecompton constitution[9] was or was not, in any just sense, made by the people of Kansas; and in that quarrel the latter declares that all he wants is a fair vote for the people, and that he *cares* not whether slavery be voted *down* or voted *up*. I do not understand his declaration that he cares not whether slavery be voted down or voted up, to be intended by him other than as an *apt definition* of the *policy* he would impress upon the public mind—the *principle* for which he declares he has suffered much, and is ready to suffer to the end.

And well may he cling to that principle. If he has any parental feeling, well may he cling to it. That principle, is the only shred left of his original Nebraska doctrine. Under the Dred Scott decision, "squatter sovereignty" squatted out of existence, tumbled down like temporary scaffolding—like the mold at the foundry served through one blast and fell back into loose sand—helped to carry an election, and then was kicked to the winds. His late *joint* struggle with the Republicans, against the Lecompton Constitution, involves nothing of the original Nebraska doctrine. That struggle was made on a point, the right of a people to make their own constitution, upon which he and the Republicans have never differed.

The several points of the Dred Scott decision, in connection with Senator Douglas' "care not" policy, constitute the piece of machinery, in its *present* state of advancement.

The *working* points of that machinery are:

First, that no negro slave, imported as such from Africa, and no descendant of such slave can ever be a *citizen* of any State, in the sense of that term as used in the Constitution of the United States.

This point is made in order to deprive the negro, in every possible event, of the benefit of that provision of the United States Constitution, which declares that—

"the citizens of each State shall be entitled to all privileges and immunities of citizens in the several States."

Secondly, that "subject to the Constitution of the United States," neither *Congress* nor a *Territorial Legislature* can exclude slavery from any United States Territory.

The point is made in order that individual men may *fill up* the territories with slaves, without danger of losing them as property, and thus enhance the chances of *permanency* to the institution through all the future.

8. Written by Buchanan to Benjamin Silliman (1816–1885), the representative of forty prominent Connecticut educators and preachers who had protested Buchanan's support for the newly elected, largely proslavery delegates to the Kansas State constitutional convention and the laws they passed.

9. At an 1857 convention held in Lecompton, Kansas, proslavery delegates developed a constitution for Kansas that would have admitted it to the Union as a slave state. It was rejected by both the House of Representatives and the voters of Kansas.

Thirdly, that whether the holding a negro in actual slavery in a free State, makes him free, as against the holder, the United States courts will not decide, but will leave to be decided by the courts of any slave State the negro may be forced into by the master.

This point is made, not to be pressed *immediately*; but, if acquiesced in for a while, and apparently *indorsed* by the people at an election, *then* to sustain the logical conclusion that what Dred Scott's master might lawfully do with Dred Scott, in the free State of Illinois, every other master may lawfully do with any other *one* or one *thousand* slaves, in Illinois, or in any other free State.

Auxiliary to all this, and working hand in hand with it, the Nebraska doctrine, or what is left of it, is to *educate* and *mould* public opinion, at least *Northern* public opinion, to not *care* whether slavery is voted *down* or voted *up*.

This shows exactly where we now *are*; and *partially* also, whither we are tending.

It will throw additional light on the latter, to go back, and run the mind over the string of historical facts already stated. Several things will *now* appear less *dark* and *mysterious* than they did *when* they were transpiring. The people were to be left "perfectly free" "subject only to the Constitution." What the *Constitution* had to do with it, outsiders could not *then* see. Plainly enough *now,* it was an exactly fitted *nitch* for the Dred Scott decision to afterward come in, and declare that *perfect freedom* of the people, to be just no freedom at all.

Why was the amendment, expressly declaring the right of the people to exclude slavery, voted down? Plainly enough *now,* the adoption of it, would have spoiled the nitch for the Dred Scott decision.

Why was the court decision held up? Why, even a Senator's individual opinion withheld, till *after* the Presidential election? Plainly enough *now,* the speaking out *then* would have damaged the *"perfectly free"* argument upon which the election was to be carried.

Why the *outgoing* President's felicitation on the indorsement? Why the delay of a reargument? Why the incoming President's *advance* exhortation in favor of the decision?

These things *look* like the cautious *patting* and *petting* of a spirited horse, preparatory to mounting him, when it is dreaded that he may give the rider a fall.

And why the hasty after indorsements of the decision by the President and others?

We cannot absolutely *know* that all these exact adaptations are the result of preconcert. But when we see a lot of framed timbers, different portions of which we know have been gotten out at different times and places and by different workmen—Stephen, Franklin, Roger, and James, for instance—and we see these timbers joined together, and see they exactly make the frame of a house or a mill, all the tenons and mortises[1] exactly fitting, and all the lengths and proportions of the different pieces exactly adapted to

1. Grooves or slots in boards that hold projecting pieces ("tenons") from other boards, forming joints. Lincoln refers to Stephen Douglas, Democratic senator from Illinois; former president Franklin Pierce; Roger Brooke Taney (1777–1864), Chief Justice of the Supreme Court who had recently delivered the Dred Scott decision; and the current president, James Buchanan.

their respective places, and not a piece too many or too few—not omitting even scaffolding—or, if a single piece be lacking, we see the place in the frame exactly fitted and prepared to yet bring such piece in—in *such* a case, we find it impossible not to *believe* that Stephen and Franklin and Roger and James all understood one another from the beginning, and all worked upon a common *plan* or *draft* drawn up before the first lick was struck.

It should not be overlooked that, by the Nebraska bill, the people of a *State* as well as *Territory*, were to be left *"perfectly free" "subject only to the Constitution."*

Why mention a *State*? They were legislating for *territories*, and not *for* or *about* States. Certainly the people of a *State are* and *ought to be* subject to the Constitution of the United States; but why is mention of this *lugged* into this merely *territorial* law? Why are the people of a *territory* and the people of a *state* therein *lumped* together, and their relation to the Constitution therein treated as being *precisely* the same?

While the opinion of the Court, by Chief Justice Taney, in the Dred Scott case, and the separate opinions of all the concurring Judges, expressly declare that the Constitution of the United States neither permits Congress nor a territorial legislature to exclude slavery from any United States territory, they all *omit* to declare whether or not the same Constitution permits a state, or the people of a State, to exclude it.

Possibly, this is a mere *omission*; but who can be *quite* sure, if McLean or Curtis had sought to get into the opinion a declaration of unlimited power in the people of a state to exclude slavery from their limits, just as Chase and Mace[2] sought to get such declaration, in behalf of the people of a territory, into the Nebraska bill—I ask, who can be quite *sure* that it would not have been voted down, in the one case, as it had been in the other?

The nearest approach to the point of declaring the power of a State over slavery, is made by Judge Nelson.[3] He approaches it more than once, using the precise idea, and *almost* the language too, of the Nebraska act. On one occasion his exact language is, "except in cases where the power is restrained by the Constitution of the United States, the law of the State is supreme over the subject of slavery within its jurisdiction."

In what *cases* the power of the *states* is so restrained by the U.S. Constitution is left an *open* question, precisely as the same question, as to the restraint on the power of the *territories* was left open in the Nebraska act. Put *that* and *that* together, and we have another nice little nitch, which we may, ere long, see filled with another Supreme Court decision, declaring that the Constitution of the United States does not permit a state to exclude slavery from its limits.

And this may especially be expected if the doctrine of "care not whether slavery be voted *down* or voted *up*," shall gain upon the public mind sufficiently to give promise that such a decision can be maintained when made.

Such a decision is all that slavery now lacks of being alike lawful in all the States.

2. Daniel Mace (1811–1867), representative from Indiana. John McLean (1785–1861), American congressman, postmaster, and jurist; Benjamin Robbins Curtis (1809–1874), American jurist; Salmon Portland Chase (1808–1873), governor of Ohio, senator, secretary of the treasury, and chief justice of the Supreme Court.

3. Rensselaer Russell Nelson (1826–1904) was appointed an associate of the territorial supreme court of Minnesota in 1857 by Buchanan.

Welcome or unwelcome, such decision *is* probably coming, and will soon be upon us, unless the power of the present political dynasty shall be met and overthrown. We shall *lie down* pleasantly dreaming that the people of *Missouri* are on the verge of making their State *free*; and we shall *awake* to the *reality*, instead, that the *Supreme* Court has made *Illinois* a *slave* State.

To meet and overthrow the power of that dynasty, is the work now before all those who would prevent that consummation.

That is *what* we have to do.

But *how* can we best do it?

There are those who denounce us *openly* to their *own* friends, and yet whisper *us softly*, that *Senator Douglas* is the *aptest* instrument there is, with which to effect that object. *They* do *not* tell us, nor has *he* told us, that he *wishes* any such object to be effected. They wish us to *infer* all, from the facts, that he now has a little quarrel with the present head of the dynasty; and that he has regularly voted with us, on a single point, upon which, he and we, have never differed.

They remind us that *he* is a *great* man, and that the largest of *us* are very small ones. Let this be granted. But "a *living dog* is better than a *dead lion*."[4] Judge Douglas, if not a *dead* lion *for this work*, is at least a *caged* and *toothless* one. How can he oppose the advances of slavery? He don't *care* anything about it. His avowed *mission is impressing* the "public heart" to *care* nothing about it.

A leading Douglas Democratic newspaper thinks Douglas' superior talent will be needed to resist the revival of the African slave trade.[5]

Does Douglas believe an effort to revive that trade is approaching? He has not said so. Does he *really* think so? But if it is, how can he resist it? For years he has labored to prove it a *sacred right* of white men to take negro slaves into the new territories. Can he possibly show that it is *less* a sacred right to *buy* them where they can be bought cheapest? And, unquestionably they can be bought *cheaper* in *Africa* than in *Virginia*.

He has done all in his power to reduce the whole question of slavery to one of a mere *right of property*; and as such, how can *he* oppose the foreign slave trade—how can he refuse that trade in that "property" shall be "perfectly free"—unless he does it as a *protection* to the home production? And as the home *producers* will probably not *ask* the protection, he will be wholly without a ground of opposition.

Senator Douglas holds, we know, that a man may rightfully be *wiser today* than he was *yesterday*—that he may rightfully *change* when he finds himself wrong.

But, can we for that reason, run ahead, and *infer* that he *will* make any particular change, of which he, himself, has given no intimation? Can we *safely* base *our* action upon any such *vague* inference?

Now, as ever, I wish to not misrepresent Judge Douglas' *position*, question his *motives*, or do aught that can be personally offensive to him.

Whenever, *if ever*, he and we can come together on *principle* so that *our great cause* may have assistance from *his great ability*, I hope to have interposed no adventitious obstacle.

4. Ecclesiastes 9.4.
5. U.S. participation in the international African slave trade was banned by Congress in 1808; slave trade within the United States remained legal.

But clearly, he is not *now* with us—he does not *pretend* to be—he does not *promise* to *ever* be.

Our cause, then, must be intrusted to, and conducted by its own undoubted friends—those whose hands are free, whose hearts are in the work—who *do care* for the result.

Two years ago the Republicans of the nation mustered over thirteen hundred thousand strong.

We did this under the single impulse of resistance to a common danger, with every external circumstance against us.

Of *strange, discordant*, and even, *hostile* elements, we gathered from the four winds, and *formed* and fought the battle through, under the constant hot fire of a disciplined, proud, and pampered enemy.

Did we brave all *then* to *falter* now?—now—when that same enemy is *wavering*, dissevered, and belligerent?

1858

Address Delivered at the Dedication of the Cemetery at Gettysburg, November 19, 1863[1]

Four score and seven years ago our fathers brought forth on this continent, a new nation, conceived in Liberty, and dedicated to the proposition that all men are created equal.

Now we are engaged in a great civil war, testing whether that nation, or any nation so conceived and so dedicated, can long endure. We are met on a great battle-field of that war. We have come to dedicate a portion of that field, as a final resting place for those who here gave their lives that that nation might live. It is altogether fitting and proper that we should do this.

But, in a larger sense, we can not dedicate—we can not consecrate—we can not hallow—this ground. The brave men, living and dead, who struggled here, have consecrated it, far above our poor power to add or detract. The world will little note, nor long remember what we say here, but it can never forget what they did here. It is for us the living, rather, to be dedicated here to the unfinished work which they who fought here have thus far so nobly advanced. It is rather for us to be here dedicated to the great task remaining before us—that from these honored dead we take increased devotion to that cause for which they gave the last full measure of devotion—that we here highly resolve that these dead shall not have died in vain—that this nation, under God, shall have a new birth of freedom—and that government of the people, by the people, for the people, shall not perish from the earth.

ABRAHAM LINCOLN

1863

1. The source of the text printed here is the facsimile reproduced in W.F. Barton's *Lincoln at Gettysburg* (1930). Lincoln delivered the address approximately four months after the three-day battle between Robert E. Lee, with seventy thousand Southern troops, and George Gordon Meade, with more than ninety thousand Northern troops. The North was victorious in a battle that left over six thousand dead and thousands injured. Lincoln spoke at Cemetery Hill, which held the Union dead.

Second Inaugural Address, March 4, 1865[1]

At this second appearing to take the oath of the presidential office, there is less occasion for an extended address than there was at the first. Then a statement, somewhat in detail, of a course to be pursued, seemed fitting and proper. Now, at the expiration of four years, during which public declarations have been constantly called forth on every point and phase of the great contest which still absorbs the attention, and engrosses the energies of the nation, little that is new could be presented. The progress of our arms, upon which all else chiefly depends, is as well known to the public as to myself; and it is, I trust, reasonably satisfactory and encouraging to all. With high hope for the future, no prediction in regard to it is ventured.

On the occasion corresponding to this four years ago, all thoughts were anxiously directed to an impending civil war. All dreaded it—all sought to avert it. While the inaugural address was being delivered from this place, devoted altogether to *saving* the Union without war, insurgent agents were in the city seeking to *destroy* it without war—seeking to dissol[v]e the Union, and divide effects, by negotiation. Both parties deprecated war; but one of them would *make* war rather than let the nation survive; and the other would *accept* war rather than let it perish. And the war came.

One eighth of the whole population were colored slaves, not distributed generally over the Union, but localized in the Southern part of it. These slaves constituted a peculiar and powerful interest. All knew that this interest was, somehow, the cause of the war. To strengthen, perpetuate, and extend this interest was the object for which the insurgents would rend the Union, even by war; while the government claimed no right to do more than to restrict the territorial enlargement of it. Neither party expected for the war, the magnitude, or the duration, which it has already attained. Neither anticipated that the *cause* of the conflict might cease with, or even before, the conflict itself should cease. Each looked for an easier triumph, and a result less fundamental and astounding. Both read the same Bible, and pray to the same God; and each invokes His aid against the other. It may seem strange that any men should dare to ask a just God's assistance in wringing their bread from the sweat of other men's faces; but let us judge not that we be not judged. The prayers of both could not be answered; that of neither has been answered fully. The Almighty has his own purposes. "Woe unto the world because of offences! for it must needs be that offences come; but woe to that man by whom the offence cometh!"[2] If we shall suppose that American Slavery is one of those offences which, in the providence of God, must needs come, but which, having continued through His appointed time, He now wills to remove, and that He gives to both North and South, this terrible war, as the woe due to those by whom the offence came, shall we discern therein any departure from those divine attributes which the believers in a Living God always ascribe to Him? Fondly do we hope—fervently do

1. The text is based on photostats of the original manuscript, owned by the Abraham Lincoln Association. A little more than a month after Lincoln delivered this address, the Civil War came to an end at Appomattox, Virginia, on April 9, when Robert E. Lee formally surrendered to Ulysses S. Grant. Shortly after that, on April 14, Lincoln was fatally shot while attending a play at Ford's Theater in Washington, D.C.

2. Matthew 18.7.

we pray—that this mighty scourge of war may speedily pass away. Yet, if God wills that it continue, until all the wealth piled by the bond-man's two hundred and fifty years of unrequited toil shall be sunk, and until every drop of blood drawn with the lash, shall be paid by another drawn with the sword, as was said three thousand years ago, so still it must be said "the judgments of the Lord, are true and righteous altogether."[3]

With malice toward none; with charity for all; with firmness in the right, as God gives us to see the right, let us strive on to finish the work we are in; to bind up the nation's wounds; to care for him who shall have borne the battle, and for his widow, and his orphan—to do all which may achieve and cherish a just and lasting peace, among ourselves, and with all nations.

1865

3. Psalm 19.9.

MARGARET FULLER
1810–1850

In their six-volume *History of Woman Suffrage* (1881), the U.S. feminists Elizabeth Cady Stanton, Susan B. Anthony, and Matilda Joslyn Gage declared that Margaret Fuller "possessed more influence upon the thought of American women than any woman previous to her time." By the time of her relatively early death in a shipwreck at the age of forty, she had published approximately three hundred essays and reviews—emerging as one of the best literary critics of her day—as well as a major travel narrative, an important book on women's rights that predated the first women's suffrage convention by several years, and a collection of her writings. She had also edited the *Dial* (the semi-official journal of the Transcendentalists) and become one of the first female columnists and the first female overseas journalist for a U.S. daily newspaper, Horace Greeley's *New York Tribune*. She not only argued for the intellectual equality of women to men but, in her writings and personal life, presented herself as an example of women's abilities. At a time when no institutions of higher learning were open to women, her richly allusive writings displayed a knowledge of literary traditions, history, religion, and political and legal thought that one would associate with a university-educated scholar or teacher; and at a time when women were expected to remain within the domestic sphere—and never under any circumstances to compete with men—her activist public presence and confident persona troubled and fascinated her male friends. Influenced by Emerson's philosophy of self-culture and self-reliance, which she extended to women, Fuller continually challenged herself to move in new directions.

Sarah Margaret Fuller was born at Cambridgeport (now part of Cambridge), Massachusetts, on May 23, 1810, the first of the nine children of Margarett Crane and Timothy Fuller. Her father, a lawyer and four-term congressman, supervised her education, teaching her Latin, Greek, French, and Italian in a rigorous regime involving long hours of study and drill. In an autobiographical account written when she was thirty years old, Fuller complained of the nightmares and headaches that accompanied what she termed her "unnatural" childhood; but a few years later, in "The Great Lawsuit" (1843), she praised the father of "Miranda" (Fuller's fictionalized self-portrait in the essay) for regarding her "as a living mind" and thus freeing her from the culture's strictures against developing female intellect. By the time she was ten, she had read extensively in Virgil, Cicero, Tacitus, Shakespeare, and numerous other classic writers. In 1824, her parents sent her to Miss Susan Prescott's Young Ladies' Seminary in Groton, Massachusetts, a sort of finishing school, which she left after a year, returning to live with her family in Cambridge. During the late 1820s she began to read such influential European romantics as the French novelist and political theorist Germaine de Staël and the German novelist, dramatist, and poet Johann Wolfgang von Goethe. Timothy Fuller moved the family to a farm in Groton in 1833, thus removing Margaret from the Cambridge environment she had come to find so stimulating. She continued with her self-education, however, translating Goethe's drama *Torquato Tasso* and publishing her first essay, "In Defense of Brutus," in an 1834 issue of the *Boston Daily Advertiser & Patriot*.

Fuller wanted to become a full-time writer and translator—activities then opening up to women—but those plans had to be abandoned when her father died of cholera in October 1835. Her mother was sickly, and the bulk of the responsibility for financially supporting the family fell to Fuller. Setting aside her own ambitions, she turned to teaching, first at Bronson Alcott's progressive co-educational Temple School in Boston, and then at the prestigious Greene Street School in Providence, Rhode Island. In her little spare time, she continued her writing and translating, placing several reviews and essays in the *Western Messenger*, and publishing a translation of *Eckermann's Conversations with Goethe* in 1839. Realizing that she would not be able to devote herself to her literary interests while holding a full-time teaching job, she resigned from Greene Street School in 1839—by this time, her siblings were old enough to work—and moved back to Cambridge. To support herself, she established her "Conversations"—paid seminars for elite women of the Boston and Cambridge area in which dialogue, rather than rote learning or lecture, was the dominant pedagogy. These meetings anticipated the women's book-club movement of later in the century and were fondly remembered for years afterward by their participants. Over the next six years the group addressed such topics as Greek mythology, the fine arts, ethics, education, demonology, philosophical idealism, and the intellectual potential of women.

A friend of Emerson's since she first sought him out in 1836, Fuller edited the *Dial* from its founding in 1840 to 1842, while continuing to translate works by and about Goethe. In 1842 she resigned her editorship but kept on with her "Conversations" and writing. She did her first significant traveling in 1843, spending four months with friends touring the Great Lakes, Illinois, and the Wisconsin Territory. Upon her return, she researched the history of the old Northwest territories, wrote over thirty poems, and in 1844 brought out her first full-length book, *Summer on the Lakes, in 1843*, a volume of historical meditations, poetry, and travel narrative, which Edgar Allan Poe hailed as "remarkable." The New York editor Horace Greeley was so impressed with

Margaret Fuller, from a daguerreotype made in July 1846. This is the only known photograph of Fuller.

the book that he offered Fuller the position of full-time literary editor of the *New York Tribune*.

Fuller moved to New York City in late 1844, and during the next two years published over two hundred essays in the *Tribune*, including influential reviews of Poe, Hawthorne, Melville, and Frederick Douglass. (She republished a number of these reviews in her 1846 *Papers on Literature and Art*.) She also wrote columns on public questions—what we would now call investigative reporting—addressing such matters as the condition of the blind, of the insane, and of the female prisoners she had visited in New York's Sing Sing prison in late 1844. In 1845 Greeley published her *Woman in the Nineteenth Century*, which expanded her 1843 *Dial* essay "The Great Lawsuit: Man *versus* Men. Woman *versus* Women" into a full-length book. Taken together, the essay and book meditate powerfully on the ways that cultural constructions of gender limited both female and male potential. Providing examples of strong heroines and goddesses from history, literature, and mythology, she sought to inspire women readers to imagine greater possibilities for themselves. She also linked the situation of white domestic women to the situation of the slave, thus developing an overlapping critique of slavery and patriarchy. Lydia Maria Child declared in an 1845 review of *Woman in the Nineteenth Century* that Fuller raised important questions about whether under current conditions love is "a mockery, and marriage a sham." By the late nineteenth century both the book and "The Great Lawsuit" had emerged as landmarks in the history of feminist thought in the United States.

In August 1846, Fuller sailed for Europe, having arranged with Greeley to send back regular dispatches at the rate of ten dollars per column. Arriving first in England, she met the writer and philosopher Thomas Carlyle, whom she had long admired but who disappointed her by his reactionary political views and his cold response to the Italian revolutionary Giuseppe Mazzini, then a political refugee in England. In Paris she met the French woman novelist George Sand, whom she found more satisfactory than Carlyle, and another political revolutionary, the exiled Polish poet Adam Mickiewicz. She next went to Italy, at the time not a unified country but a collection of states—some independent, some controlled by the pope, and some controlled by Austria. Soon after settling in Rome she became romantically involved with Giovanni Angelo Ossoli, a nobleman eleven years her junior who supported the revolutionary cause of Italian unification (Risorgimento) led by Giuseppe Garibaldi and Mazzini. Her dispatches to the *Tribune* recorded her increasing preoccupation with the developing Italian revolution, which she linked to American ideals of republicanism that harked back to the original Roman republic, long her political ideal.

In December of 1847 Fuller became pregnant, but as a Protestant her marriage to the Catholic Ossoli seemed out of the question because of the opposition of his family and the difficulties of getting permission in Italy for an interfaith marriage. Through a dismal rainy season, she covered political events for the *Tribune* and became intimate with the Princess Belgioioso, a leader of the anti-Austrian faction who drew her still more deeply into Italian politics. When cities of northern Italy revolted against the Austrians in March 1848, Fuller described to her New York readers the joyous response of the Roman citizens. Emerson wrote from England urging her to return home before war broke out, but she was not ready to tell her Massachusetts connections about her pregnancy, and chose instead to wait for the child's birth in the countryside near Rome. Ossoli, who had become a member of the civic guard, was with her when their son, Angelo, was born on September 5. Leaving the baby with a wet nurse—a common practice for the era—Fuller returned to Rome late in November in time to cover the flight of the pope and, early in 1849, the arrival of the Italian nationalist Garibaldi, the proclamation of the Roman Republic, and Mazzini's arrival in Rome as well. The republic lasted less than a year: French troops entered Rome on June 30, 1849, and quickly restored the pope to power. During the bloody siege, Fuller served as the director of the Hospital of the Fate Bene Fratelli, doing heroic work for the wounded revolutionaries.

After the defeat of the republican forces, Fuller moved to Florence with Angelo and Ossoli and began to work on a history of the short-lived Roman Republic. She may have married Ossoli, as his sister later claimed and as she herself stated in some of her letters home. But there was doubt about this among her friends, who may have been just as alarmed by her marriage to a Catholic as by her having a sexual liaison as an unmarried woman. Convinced that she and Ossoli would have better economic prospects in the United States, Fuller arranged passage home, and on May 17, 1850, the three sailed for the United States. On July 19, two months and two days later—sailing ships took many weeks to cross the Atlantic—the ship was wrecked within sight of land off Fire Island, New York, and all three perished. Angelo's body washed ashore. A trunk containing some of Fuller's papers was later recovered, but not her history of Rome. Thoreau traveled to the site and sought vainly for her body; at home, Emerson wrote mournfully in his journal, "I have lost in her my audience." Hawthorne, who had been friends with Fuller during the 1840s, may have had her in mind when creating Hester in *The Scarlet Letter* (1850). Wishing to memorialize her career and yet confused about how to present this unconventional woman to a general audience, Fuller's male friends, who brought out *Memoirs of Margaret Fuller Ossoli* in 1852, emphasized her eccentricities, egotism, and aloofness. But if her refusal to stay within feminine bounds disturbed her male contemporaries, that very nonconformity—an instance of Emerson's own teachings, after all—had been crucial to her achievements as an intellectual and writer.

The Great Lawsuit: Man *versus* Men. Woman *versus* Women[1]

This great suit has now been carried on through many ages, with various results. The decisions have been numerous, but always followed by appeals to still higher courts. How can it be otherwise, when the law itself is the subject of frequent elucidation, constant revision? Man has, now and then, enjoyed a clear, triumphant hour, when some irresistible conviction warmed and purified the atmosphere of his planet. But, presently, he sought repose after his labors, when the crowd of pigmy adversaries bound him in his sleep. Long years of inglorious imprisonment followed, while his enemies reveled in his spoils, and no counsel could be found to plead his cause, in the absence of that all-promising glance, which had, at times, kindled the poetic soul to revelation of his claims, of his rights.

Yet a foundation for the largest claim is now established. It is known that his inheritance consists in no partial sway, no exclusive possession, such as his adversaries desire. For they, not content that the universe is rich, would, each one for himself, appropriate treasure; but in vain! The many-colored garment, which clothed with honor an elected son, when rent asunder for the many, is a worthless spoil. A band of robbers cannot live princely in the prince's castle; nor would he, like them, be content with less than all, though he would not, like them, seek it as fuel for riotous enjoyment, but as his principality, to administer and guard for the use of all living things therein.

1. Reprinted from the *Boston Dial* (July 1843). In 1845 Fuller published a revised, expanded version of this work under the title *Woman in the Nineteenth Century*.

He cannot be satisfied with any one gift of the earth, any one department of knowledge, or telescopic peep at the heavens. He feels himself called to understand and aid nature, that she may, through his intelligence, be raised and interpreted; to be a student of, and servant to, the universe-spirit; and only king of his planet, that, as an angelic minister, he may bring it into conscious harmony with the law of that spirit.

Such is the inheritance of the orphan prince, and the illegitimate children of his family will not always be able to keep it from him, for, from the fields which they sow with dragon's teeth, and water with blood, rise monsters, which he alone has power to drive away.

But it is not the purpose now to sing the prophecy of his jubilee. We have said that, in clear triumphant moments, this has many, many times been made manifest, and those moments, though past in time, have been translated into eternity by thought. The bright signs they left hang in the heavens, as single stars or constellations, and, already, a thickly-sown radiance consoles the wanderer in the darkest night. Heroes have filled the zodiac of beneficent labors, and then given up their mortal part[2] to the fire without a murmur. Sages and lawgivers have bent their whole nature to the search for truth, and thought themselves happy if they could buy, with the sacrifice of all temporal ease and pleasure, one seed for the future Eden. Poets and priests have strung the lyre with heart-strings, poured out their best blood upon the altar which, reared anew from age to age, shall at last sustain the flame which rises to highest heaven. What shall we say of those who, if not so directly, or so consciously, in connection with the central truth, yet, led and fashioned by a divine instinct, serve no less to develop and interpret the open secret of love passing into life, the divine energy creating for the purpose of happiness;—of the artist, whose hand, drawn by a preëxistent harmony to a certain medium, moulds it to expressions of life more highly and completely organized than are seen elsewhere, and, by carrying out the intention of nature, reveals her meaning to those who are not yet sufficiently matured to divine it; of the philosopher, who listens steadily for causes, and, from those obvious, infers those yet unknown; of the historian, who, in faith that all events must have their reason and their aim, records them, and lays up archives from which the youth of prophets may be fed. The man of science dissects the statement, verifies the facts, and demonstrates connection even where he cannot its purpose.

Lives, too, which bear none of these names, have yielded tones of no less significance. The candlestick, set in a low place, has given light as faithfully, where it was needed, as that upon the hill.[3] In close alleys, in dismal

2. Ovid, *Apotheosis of Hercules*, translated into clumsy English by Mr. Gay, as follows:
Jove said,
Be all your fears forborne, / Th' Œtean fires do thou, great hero, scorn; / Who vanquished all things, shall subdue the flame; / The part alone of gross *maternal* frame, /Fire shall devour, while that from me he drew / Shall live immortal, and its force renew; / That, when he's dead, I'll raise to realms above, / May all the powers the righteous act approve. / If any God dissent, and judge too great / The sacred honors of the heavenly seat, / Even he shall own his deeds deserve the sky, / Even he, reluctant, shall at length comply. / Th' assembled powers assent [Fuller's note; she also supplied the original Latin, which is not included here]. The translation by the English poet John Gay (1685–1732) comes from book 9 of *Metamorphoses*, by the Roman poet Ovid (43 B.C.E.–C. 17 C.E.).

3. From Jesus' Sermon on the Mount (Matthew 5.15–16): "Neither do men light a candle, and put it under a bushel, but on a candlestick; and it giveth light unto all that are in the house. Let your light so shine before men, that they may see your good works, and glorify your Father which is in heaven."

nooks, the Word has been read as distinctly, as when shown by angels to holy men in the dark prison. Those who till a spot of earth, scarcely larger than is wanted for a grave, have deserved that the sun should shine upon its sod till violets answer.

So great has been, from time to time, the promise, that, in all ages, men have said the Gods themselves came down to dwell with them; that the All-Creating wandered on the earth to taste in a limited nature the sweetness of virtue, that the All-Sustaining incarnated himself, to guard, in space and time, the destinies of his world; that heavenly genius dwelt among the shepherds, to sing to them and teach them how to sing. Indeed,

> "Der stets den Hirten gnädig sich bewies."
> "He has constantly shown himself favorable to shepherds."

And these dwellers in green pastures and natural students of the stars, were selected to hail, first of all, the holy child, whose life and death presented the type of excellence, which has sustained the heart of so large a portion of mankind in these later generations.

Such marks have been left by the footsteps of man, whenever he has made his way through the wilderness of men. And whenever the pygmies stepped in one of these, they felt dilate within the breast somewhat that promised larger stature and purer blood. They were tempted to forsake their evil ways, to forsake the side of selfish personal existence, of decrepit skepticism, and covetousness of corruptible possessions. Conviction flowed in upon them. They, too, raised the cry; God is living, all is his, and all created beings are brothers, for they are his children. These were the triumphant moments; but as we have said, man slept and selfishness awoke.

Thus he is still kept out of his inheritance, still a pleader, still a pilgrim. But his reinstatement is sure. And now, no mere glimmering consciousness, but a certainty, is felt and spoken, that the highest ideal man can form of his own capabilities is that which he is destined to attain. Knock, and it shall be opened; seek, and ye shall find. It is demonstrated, it is a maxim. He no longer paints his proper nature in some peculiar form and says, "Prometheus[4] had it," but "Man must have it." However disputed by many, however ignorantly used, or falsified, by those who do receive it, the fact of an universal, unceasing revelation, has been too clearly stated in words, to be lost sight of in thought, and sermons preached form the text, "Be ye perfect,"[5] are the only sermons of a pervasive and deep-searching influence.

But among those who meditate upon this text, there is great difference of view, as to the way in which perfection shall be sought.

Through the intellect, say some; Gather from every growth of life its seed of thought; look behind every symbol for its law. If thou canst *see* clearly, the rest will follow.

Through the life, say others; Do the best thou knowest to-day. Shrink not from incessant error, in this gradual, fragmentary state. Follow thy light for as much as it will show thee, be faithful as far as thou canst, in hope that faith presently will lead to sight. Help others, without blame that they need thy help. Love much, and be forgiven.

4. In Greek mythology, the Titan who gave humans the gift of fire out of pity for their misery.

5. "Be ye therefore perfect, even as your Father which is in heaven is perfect" (Matthew 5.48).

It needs not intellect, needs not experience, says a third. If you took the true way, these would be evolved in purity. You would not learn through them, but express through them a higher knowledge. In quietness, yield thy soul to the casual soul. Do not disturb its teachings by methods of thine own. Be still, seek not, but wait in obedience. Thy commission will be given.

Could we, indeed, say what we want, could we give a description of the child that is lost, he would be found. As soon as the soul can say clearly, that a certain demonstration is wanted, it is at hand. When the Jewish prophet described the Lamb, as the expression of what was required by the coming era, the time drew nigh.[6] But we say not, see not, as yet, clearly, what we would. Those who call for a more triumphant expression of love, a love that cannot be crucified, show not a perfect sense of what has already been expressed. Love has already been expressed, that made all things new, that gave the worm its ministry as well as the eagle; a love, to which it was alike to descend into the depths of hell, or to sit at the right hand of the Father.[7]

Yet, no doubt, a new manifestation is at hand, a new hour in the day of man. We cannot expect to see him a completed being, when the mass of men lie so entangled in the sod, or use the freedom of their limbs only with wolfish energy. The tree cannot come to flower till its root be freed from the cankering worm, and its whole growth open to air and light. Yet something new shall presently be shown of the life of man, for hearts crave it now, if minds do not know how to ask it.

Among the strains of prophecy, the following, by an earnest mind of a foreign land, written some thirty years ago, is not yet outgrown; and it has the merit of being a positive appeal from the heart, instead of a critical declaration what man shall *not* do.

> "The ministry of man implies, that he must be filled from the divine fountains which are being engendered through all eternity, so that, at the mere name of his Master, he may be able to cast all his enemies into the abyss; that he may deliver all parts of nature from the barriers that imprison them; that he may purge the terrestrial atmosphere from the poisons that infect it; that he may preserve the bodies of men from the corrupt influences that surround, and the maladies that afflict them; still more, that he may keep their souls pure from the malignant insinuations which pollute, and the gloomy images that obscure them; that we may restore its serenity to the Word, which false words of men fill with mourning and sadness; that he may satisfy the desires of the angels, who wait from him the development of the marvels of nature; that, in fine, his world may be filled with God, as eternity is."[8]

Another attempt we will give, by an obscure observer of our own day and country, to draw some lines of the desired image. It was suggested by seeing the design of Crawford's Orpheus,[9] and connecting with the circumstance of the

6. See Isaiah 7–11.
7. According to Mark 16.19, after the crucified and risen Jesus had preached to the disciples, "he was received up into heaven, and sat on the right hand of God."
8. St. Martin [Fuller's note]. Louis Claude de Saint-Martin (1743–1803), French philosopher, from *The Ministry of Man and Spirit* (1802).
9. In Greek mythology, a musician so powerful that with his lyre he cast a spell on Hades and almost succeeded in drawing his dead wife, Eurydice, back to the upper world. In 1839 Fuller saw the statue of Orpheus by Thomas Crawford (1814–1857) at the Allston Gallery in Boston and wrote a poem about it, which she incorporates into this essay just below.

American, in his garret at Rome, making choice of this subject, that of Americans here at home, showing such ambition to represent the character, by calling their prose and verse, Orphic sayings, Orphics. Orpheus was a lawgiver by theocratic commission. He understood nature, and made all her forms move to his music. He told her secrets in the form of hymns, nature as seen in the mind of God. Then it is the prediction, that to learn and to do, all men must be lovers, and Orpheus was, in a high sense, a lover. His soul went forth towards all beings, yet could remain sternly faithful to a chosen type of excellence. Seeking what he loved, he feared not death nor hell, neither could any presence daunt his faith in the power of the celestial harmony that filled his soul.

It seemed significant of the state of things in this country, that the sculptor should have chosen the attitude of shading his eyes. When we have the statue here, it will give lessons in reverence.

  Each Orpheus must to the depths descend,
For only thus the poet can be wise
  Must make the sad Persephone[1] his friend,
And buried love to second life arise;
  Again his love must lose through too much love,
Must lose his life by living life too true,
  For what he sought below is passed above,
Already done is all that he would do;
  Must tune all being with his single lyre,
Must melt all rocks free from their primal pain,
  Must search all nature with his one soul's fire,
Must bind anew all forms in heavenly chain.
  If he already sees what he must do,
Well may he shade his eyes from the far-shining view.

Meanwhile, not a few believe, and men themselves have expressed the opinion, that the time is come when Euridice is to call for an Orpheus, rather than Orpheus for Euridice; that the idea of man, however imperfectly brought out, has been far more so than that of woman, and that an improvement in the daughters will best aid the reformation of the sons of this age.

It is worthy of remark, that, as the principle of liberty is better understood and more nobly interpreted, a broader protest is made in behalf of woman. As men become aware that all men have not had their fair chance, they are inclined to say that no women have had a fair chance. The French revolution, that strangely disguised angel, bore witness in favor of woman, but interpreted her claims no less ignorantly than those of man. Its idea of happiness did not rise beyond outward enjoyment, unobstructed by the tyranny of others. The title it gave was Citoyen, Citoyenne,[2] and it is not unimportant to woman that even this species of equality was awarded her. Before, she could be condemned to perish on the scaffold for treason, but not as a citizen, but a subject. The right, with which this title then invested a human being, was that of bloodshed and license. The Goddess of Liberty was impure. Yet truth was prophesied in the ravings of that hideous fever induced by long ignorance

1. In Greek mythology, the wife of Pluto and the queen of the underworld.
2. Male citizen, female citizen (French). Men and women were equal under the law—one of the most promising early achievements of the French Revolution.

and abuse. Europe is conning a valued lesson from the blood-stained page. The same tendencies, farther unfolded, will bear good fruit in this country.

Yet, in this country, as by the Jews, when Moses was leading them to the promised land,[3] everything has been done that inherited depravity could, to hinder the promise of heaven from its fulfilment. The cross, here as elsewhere, has been planted only to be blasphemed by cruelty and fraud. The name of the Prince of Peace has been profaned by all kinds of injustice towards the Gentile whom he said he came to save. But I need not speak of what has been done towards the red man, the black man. These deeds are the scoff of the world; and they have been accompanied by such pious words, that the gentlest would not dare to intercede with, "Father forgive them, for they know not what they do."[4]

Here, as elsewhere, the gain of creation consists always in the growth of individual minds, which live and aspire, as flowers bloom and birds sing, in the midst of morasses; and in the continual development of that thought, the thought of human destiny, which is given to eternity to fulfil, and which ages of failure only seemingly impede. Only seemingly, and whatever seems to the contrary, this country is as surely destined to elucidate a great moral law, as Europe was to promote the mental culture of man.

Though the national independence be blurred by the servility of individuals; though freedom and equality have been proclaimed only to leave room for a monstrous display of slave dealing and slave keeping; though the free American so often feels himself free, like the Roman, only to pamper his appetites and his indolence through the misery of his fellow beings, still it is not in vain, that the verbal statement has been made, "All men are born free and equal."[5] There it stands, a golden certainty, wherewith to encourage the good, to shame the bad. The new world may be called clearly to perceive that it incurs the utmost penalty, if it reject the sorrowful brother. And if men are deaf, the angels hear. But men cannot be deaf. It is inevitable that an external freedom, such as has been achieved for the nation, should be so also for every member of it. That, which has once been clearly conceived in the intelligence, must be acted out. It has become a law, irrevocable as that of the Medes[6] in their ancient dominion. Men will privately sin against it, but the law so clearly expressed by a leading mind of the age,

"Tutti fatti a sembianza d' un Solo;
Figli tutti d' un solo riscatto,
In qual ora, in qual parte del suolo
Trascorriamo quest' aura vital,
Siam fratelli, siam stretti ad un patto:
Maladetto colui che lo infrange,
Che s' innalza sul fiacco che piange,
Che contrista uno spirto immortal."[7]

"All made in the likeness of the One,
All children of one ransom,

3. Fuller alludes to moments when the Jews strayed from Moses' teachings, such as when they worshiped the Golden Calf (Exodus 32).
4. Jesus' words in Luke 23.34, in reference to the Roman soldiers who had just nailed him to the cross.
5. As in the Declaration of Independence, second paragraph, "all men are created equal."
6. Media is now part of Iran.
7. Manzoni [Fuller's note]. Alessandro Manzoni (1785–1873), Italian poet and novelist.

In whatever hour, in whatever part of the soil
We draw this vital air,
We are brothers, we must be bound by one compact,
Accursed he who infringes it,
Who raises himself upon the weak who weep,
Who saddens an immortal spirit."

cannot fail of universal recognition.

We sicken no less at the pomp than at the strife of words. We feel that never were lungs so puffed with the wind of declamation, on moral and religious subjects, as now. We are tempted to implore these "word-heroes," these word-Catos, word-Christs,[8] to beware of cant above all things; to remember that hypocrisy is the most hopeless as well as the meanest of crimes, and that those must surely be polluted by it, who do not keep a little of all this morality and religion for private use.[9] We feel that the mind may "grow black and rancid in the smoke" even of altars. We start up from the harangue to go into our closet and shut the door. But, when it has been shut long enough, we remember that where there is so much smoke, there must be some fire; with so much talk about virtue and freedom must be mingled some desire for them; that it cannot be in vain that such have become the common topics of conversation among men; that the very newspapers should proclaim themselves Pilgrims, Puritans, Heralds of Holiness.[1] The king that maintains so costly a retinue cannot be a mere Count of Carabbas[2] fiction. We have waited here long in the dust; we are tired and hungry, but the triumphal procession must appear at last.

Of all its banners, none has been more steadily upheld, and under none has more valor and willingness for real sacrifices been shown, than that of the champions of the enslaved African. And this band it is, which, partly in consequence of a natural following out of principles, partly because many women have been prominent in that cause, makes, just now, the warmest appeal in behalf of woman.

Though there has been a growing liberality on this point, yet society at large is not so prepared for the demands of this party, but that they are, and will be for some time, coldly regarded as the Jacobins[3] of their day.

"Is it not enough," cries the sorrowful trader, "that you have done all you could to break up the national Union, and thus destroy the prosperity of our country, but now you must be trying to break up family union, to take my wife away from the cradle, and the kitchen hearth, to vote at polls, and preach from a pulpit? Of course, if she does such things, she cannot attend to those of her own sphere. She is happy enough as she is. She has more leisure than I have, every means of improvement, every indulgence."

"Have you asked her whether she was satisfied with these indulgences?"

8. Would-be reformers, whether of political and social morality like Marcus Porcius Cato (234–149 B.C.E.), Roman statesman, or of religion, in fancied imitation of Jesus.

9. Dr. Johnson's one piece of advice should be written on every door; "Clear your mind of cant." But Byron, to whom it was so acceptable, in clearing away the noxious vine, shook down the building too. Stirling's emendation is noteworthy, "Realize your cant, not cast it off" [Fuller's note]. The English man of letters Samuel Johnson (1707–1784), as quoted in James Boswell's *The Life of Samuel Johnson* (1791). John Sterling (1806–1844), English poet and dramatist.

1. Then-common names for newspapers in Massachusetts and elsewhere.

2. Type name for a pretentious nobleman (or fake nobleman, as in the nursery tale *Puss in Boots*).

3. Radical extremists, from the political group founded in Paris at the outset of the French Revolution in 1789 near the church of Saint-Jacques.

"No, but I know she is. She is too amiable to wish what would make me unhappy, and too judicious to wish to step beyond the sphere of her sex. I will never consent to have our peace disturbed by any such discussions."

"'Consent'—you? it is not consent from you that is in question, it is assent from your wife."

"Am I not the head of my house?"

"You are not the head of your wife. God has given her a mind of her own."

"I am the head and she the heart."

"God grant you play true to one another then. If the head represses no natural pulse of the heart, there can be no question as to your giving your consent. Both will be of one accord, and there needs but to present any question to get a full and true answer. There is no need of precaution, of indulgence, or consent. But our doubt is whether the heart consents with the head, or only acquiesces in its decree; and it is to ascertain the truth on this point, that we propose some liberating measures."

Thus vaguely are these questions proposed and discussed at present. But their being proposed at all implies much thought, and suggests more. Many women are considering within themselves what they need that they have not, and what they can have, if they find they need it. Many men are considering whether women are capable of being and having more than they are and have, and whether, if they are, it will be best to consent to improvement in their condition.

The numerous party, whose opinions are already labelled and adjusted too much to their mind to admit of any new light, strive, by lectures on some model-women of bridal-like beauty and gentleness, by writing or lending little treatises, to mark out with due precision the limits of woman's sphere, and woman's mission, and to prevent other than the rightful shepherd from climbing the wall, or the flock from using any chance gap to run astray.

Without enrolling ourselves at once on either side, let us look upon the subject from that point of view which to-day offers. No better, it is to be feared, than a high house-top. A high hill-top, or at least a cathedral spire, would be desirable.

It is not surprising that it should be the Anti-Slavery party that pleads for woman, when we consider merely that she does not hold property on equal terms with men; so that, if a husband dies without a will, the wife, instead of stepping at once into his place as head of the family, inherits only a part of his fortune, as if she were a child, or ward only, not an equal partner.

We will not speak of the innumerable instances, in which profligate or idle men live upon the earnings of industrious wives; or if the wives leave them and take with them the children, to perform the double duty of mother and father, follow from place to place, and threaten to rob them of the children, if deprived of the rights of a husband, as they call them, planting themselves in their poor lodgings, frightening them into paying tribute by taking from them the children, running into debt at the expense of these otherwise so overtasked helots.[4] Though such instances abound, the public opinion of his own sex is against the man, and when cases of extreme tyranny are made known, there is private action in the wife's favor. But if

4. Slaves. Fuller fairly describes the legal situation in her time.

woman be, indeed, the weaker party, she ought to have legal protection, which would make such oppression impossible.

And knowing that there exists, in the world of men, a tone of feeling towards women as towards slaves, such as is expressed in the common phrase, "Tell that to women and children;" that the infinite soul can only work through them in already ascertained limits; that the prerogative of reason, man's highest portion, is allotted to them in a much lower degree; that it is better for them to be engaged in active labor, which is to be furnished and directed by those better able to think, &c. &c.; we need not go further, for who can review the experience of last week, without recalling words which imply, whether in jest or earnest, these views, and views like these? Knowing this, can we wonder that many reformers think that measures are not likely to be taken in behalf of women, unless their wishes could be publicly represented by women?

That can never be necessary, cry the other side. All men are privately influenced by women; each has his wife, sister, or female friends, and is too much biased by these relations to fail of representing their interests. And if this is not enough, let them propose and enforce their wishes with the pen. The beauty of home would be destroyed, the delicacy of the sex be violated, the dignity of halls of legislation destroyed, by an attempt to introduce them there. Such duties are inconsistent with those of a mother; and then we have ludicrous pictures of ladies in hysterics at the polls, and senate chambers filled with cradles.

But if, in reply, we admit as truth that woman seems destined by nature rather to the inner circle, we must add that the arrangements of civilized life have not been as yet such as to secure it to her. Her circle, if the duller, is not the quieter. If kept from excitement, she is not from drudgery. Not only the Indian carries the burdens of the camp, but the favorites of Louis the Fourteenth accompany him in his journeys, and the washerwoman stands at her tub and carries home her work at all seasons, and in all states of health.[5]

As to the use of the pen, there was quite as much opposition to woman's possessing herself of that help to free-agency as there is now to her seizing on the rostrum or the desk; and she is likely to draw, from a permission to plead her cause that way, opposite inferences to what might be wished by those who now grant it.

As to the possibility of her filling, with grace and dignity, any such position, we should think those who had seen the great actresses, and heard the Quaker preachers of modern times, would not doubt, that woman can express publicly the fulness of thought and emotion, without losing any of the peculiar beauty of her sex.

As to her home, she is not likely to leave it more than she now does for balls, theatres, meetings for promoting missions, revival meetings, and others to which she flies, in hope of an animation for her existence, commensurate with what she sees enjoyed by men. Governors of Ladies' Fairs are no less engrossed by such a charge, than the Governor of the State by his; presidents of Washingtonian societies,[6] no less away from home than presidents of conventions. If men look straitly to it, they will find that, unless

5. In Fuller's view, courtesans and washerwomen are equally enslaved, however different their conditions.

6. General name for patriotic and temperance organizations of the time.

their own lives are domestic, those of the women will not be. The female Greek, of our day, is as much in the street as the male, to cry, What news? We doubt not it was the same in Athens of old. The women, shut out from the market-place, made up for it at the religious festivals. For human beings are not so constituted, that they can live without expansion; and if they do not get it one way, must another, or perish.

And, as to men's representing women fairly, at present, while we hear from men who owe to their wives not only all that is comfortable and graceful, but all that is wise in the arrangement of their lives, the frequent remark, "You cannot reason with a woman," when from those of delicacy, nobleness, and poetic culture, the contemptuous phrase, "Women and children," and that in no light sally of the hour, but in works intended to give a permanent statement of the best experiences, when not one man in the million, shall I say, no, not in the hundred million, can rise above the view that woman was made *for man*, when such traits as these are daily forced upon the attention, can we feel that man will always do justice to the interests of woman? Can we think that he takes a sufficiently discerning and religious view of her office and destiny, ever to do her justice, except when prompted by sentiment; accidentally or transiently, that is, for his sentiment will vary according to the relations in which he is placed. The lover, the poet, the artist, are likely to view her nobly. The father and the philosopher have some chance of liberality; the man of the world, the legislator for expediency, none.

Under these circumstances, without attaching importance in themselves to the changes demanded by the champions of woman, we hail them as signs of the times. We would have every arbitrary barrier thrown down. We would have every path laid open to woman as freely as to man. Were this done, and a slight temporary fermentation allowed to subside, we believe that the Divine would ascend into nature to a height unknown in the history of past ages, and nature, thus instructed, would regulate the spheres not only so as to avoid collision, but to bring forth ravishing harmony.

Yet then, and only then, will human beings be ripe for this, when inward and outward freedom for woman, as much as for man, shall be acknowledged as a right, not yielded as a concession. As the friend of the negro assumes that one man cannot, by right, hold another in bondage, should the friend of woman assume that man cannot, by right, lay even well-meant restrictions on woman. If the negro be a soul, if the woman be a soul, apparelled in flesh, to one master only are they accountable. There is but one law for all souls, and, if there is to be an interpreter of it, he comes not as man, or son of man, but as Son of God.

Were thought and feeling once so far elevated that man should esteem himself the brother and friend, but nowise the lord and tutor of woman, were he really bound with her in equal worship, arrangements as to function and employment would be of no consequence. What woman needs is not as a woman to act or rule, but as a nature to grow, as an intellect to discern, as a soul to live freely, and unimpeded to unfold such powers as were given her when we left our common home. If fewer talents were given her, yet, if allowed the free and full employment of these, so that she may render back to the giver his own with usury, she will not complain, nay, I dare to say she will bless and rejoice in her earthly birth-place, her earthly lot.

Let us consider what obstructions impede this good era, and what signs give reason to hope that it draws near.

I was talking on this subject with Miranda,[7] a woman, who, if any in the world, might speak without heat or bitterness of the position of her sex. Her father was a man who cherished no sentimental reverence for woman, but a firm belief in the equality of the sexes. She was his eldest child, and came to him at an age when he needed a companion. From the time she could speak and go[8] alone, he addressed her not as a plaything, but as a living mind. Among the few verses he ever wrote were a copy addressed to this child, when the first locks were cut from her head, and the reverence expressed on this occasion for that cherished head he never belied. It was to him the temple of immortal intellect. He respected his child, however, too much to be an indulgent parent. He called on her for clear judgment, for courage, for honor and fidelity, in short for such virtues as he knew. In so far as he possessed the keys to the wonders of this universe, he allowed free use of them to her, and by the incentive of a high expectation he forbade, as far as possible, that she should let the privilege lie idle.

Thus this child was eagerly led to feel herself a child of the spirit. She took her place easily, not only in the world of organized being, but in the world of mind. A dignified sense of self-dependence was given as all her portion, and she found it a sure anchor. Herself securely anchored, her relations with others were established with equal security. She was fortunate, in a total absence of those charms which might have drawn to her bewildering flatteries, and of a strong electric nature, which repelled those who did not belong to her, and attracted those who did. With men and women her relations were noble; affectionate without passion, intellectual without coldness. The world was free to her, and she lived freely in it. Outward adversity came, and inward conflict, but that faith and self-respect had early been awakened, which must always lead at last to an outward serenity, and an inward peace.

Of Miranda I had always thought as an example, that the restraints upon the sex were insuperable only to those who think them so, or who noisily strive to break them. She had taken a course of her own, and no man stood in her way. Many of her acts had been unusual, but excited no uproar. Few helped, but none checked her; and the many men, who knew her mind and her life, showed to her confidence as to a brother, gentleness as to a sister. And not only refined, but very coarse men approved one in whom they saw resolution and clearness of design. Her mind was often the leading one, always effective.

When I talked with her upon these matters, and had said very much what I have written, she smilingly replied, And yet we must admit that I have been fortunate, and this should not be. My good father's early trust gave the first bias, and the rest followed of course. It is true that I have had less outward aid, in after years, than most women, but that is of little consequence. Religion was early awakened in my soul, a sense that what the soul is capable to ask it must attain, and that, though I might be aided by others, I must depend on myself as the only constant friend. This self-dependence, which was honored in me, is deprecated as a fault in most women. They are taught to learn their rule from without, not to unfold it from within.

7. Fuller's own experiences are reflected in those of "Miranda."

8. Walk.

This is the fault of man, who is still vain, and wishes to be more important to woman than by right he should be.

Men have not shown this disposition towards you, I said.

No, because the position I early was enabled to take, was one of self-reliance. And were all women as sure of their wants as I was, the result would be the same. The difficulty is to get them to the point where they shall naturally develop self-respect, the question how it is to be done.

Once I thought that men would help on this state of things more than I do now. I saw so many of them wretched in the connections they had formed in weakness and vanity. They seemed so glad to esteem women whenever they could!

But early I perceived that men never, in any extreme of despair, wished to be women. Where they admired any woman they were inclined to speak of her as above her sex. Silently I observed this, and feared it argued a rooted skepticism, which for ages had been fastening on the heart, and which only an age of miracles could eradicate.

Ever I have been treated with great sincerity; and I look upon it as a most signal instance of this, that an intimate friend of the other sex said in a fervent moment, that I deserved in some star to be a man. Another used as highest praise, in speaking of a character in literature, the words "a manly woman."

It is well known that of every strong woman they say she has a masculine mind.[9]

This by no means argues a willing want of generosity towards woman. Man is as generous towards her, as he knows how to be.

Wherever she has herself arisen in national or private history, and nobly shone forth in any ideal of excellence, men have received her, not only willingly, but with triumph. Their encomiums indeed are always in some sense mortifying, they show too much surprise.

In every-day life the feelings of the many are stained with vanity. Each wishes to be lord in a little world, to be superior at least over one; and he does not feel strong enough to retain a life-long ascendant over a strong nature. Only a Brutus would rejoice in a Portia. Only Theseus could conquer before he wed the Amazonian Queen. Hercules wished rather to rest from his labors with Dejanira, and received the poisoned robe, as a fit guerdon.[1] The tale should be interpreted to all those who seek repose with the weak.

But not only is man vain and fond of power, but the same want of development, which thus affects him morally in the intellect, prevents his discerning the destiny of woman. The boy wants no woman, but only a girl to play ball with him, and mark his pocket handkerchief.

Thus in Schiller's Dignity of Woman,[2] beautiful as the poem is, there is no "grave and perfect man," but only a great boy to be softened and restrained by the influence of girls. Poets, the elder brothers of their race, have usually seen further; but what can you expect of every-day men, if Schiller was not

9. The 1843 text gives no indication where Fuller means Miranda's voice to stop, but the 1845 edition makes this sentence Miranda's last.

1. Reward. Shakespeare portrays the love between the republican-spirited Brutus and Portia in *Julius Caesar.* In Greek myth, Theseus was celebrated for his military heroics, and the justly jealous Dejanira innocently tried to win back Hercules' love by sending him a shirt imbued with an ointment given her by Nessus; proffered as a love potion, it was in fact a virulent poison that consumed Hercules' flesh.

2. This poem by Friedrich von Schiller (1759–1805) celebrates women's ability to constrain or control the passionate striving of men.

more prophetic as to what women must be? Even with Richter[3] one foremost thought about a wife was that she would "cook him something good."

The sexes should not only correspond to and appreciate one another, but prophesy to one another. In individual instances this happens. Two persons love in one another the future good which they aid one another to unfold. This is very imperfectly done as yet in the general life. Man has gone but little way, now he is waiting to see whether woman can keep step with him, but instead of calling out like a good brother; You can do it if you only think so, or impersonally; Any one can do what he tries to do, he often discourages with schoolboy brag; Girls cant do that, girls cant play ball. But let any one defy their taunts, break through, and be brave and secure, they rend the air with shouts.

No! man is not willingly ungenerous. He wants faith and love, because he is not yet himself an elevated being. He cries with sneering skepticism; Give us a sign. But if the sign appears, his eyes glisten, and he offers not merely approval, but homage.

The severe nation[4] which taught that the happiness of the race was forfeited through the fault of a woman, and showed its thought of what sort of regard man owed her, by making him accuse her on the first question to his God, who gave her to the patriarch as a handmaid, and, by the Mosaical law, bound her to allegiance like a serf, even they greeted, with solemn rapture, all great and holy women as heroines, prophetesses, nay judges in Israel; and, if they made Eve listen to the serpent, gave Mary to the Holy Spirit. In other nations it has been the same down to our day. To the woman, who could conquer, a triumph was awarded. And not only those whose strength was recommended to the heart by association with goodness and beauty, but those who were bad, if they were steadfast and strong, had their claims allowed. In any age a Semiramis, an Elizabeth of England, a Catharine of Russia[5] makes her place good, whether in a large or small circle.

How has a little wit, a little genius, always been celebrated in a woman! What an intellectual triumph was that of the lonely Aspasia,[6] and how heartily acknowledged! She, indeed, met a Pericles. But what annalist, the rudest of men, the most plebian of husbands, will spare from his page one of the few anecdotes of Roman women?—Sappho, Eloisa![7] The names are of thread-bare celebrity. The man habitually most narrow towards women will be flushed, as by the worst assault on Christianity, if you say it has made no improvement in her condition. Indeed, those most opposed to new acts in her favor are jealous of the reputation of those which have been done.

We will not speak of the enthusiasm excited by actresses, improvisatrici,[8] female singers, for here mingles the charm of beauty and grace, but female authors, even learned women, if not insufferably ugly and slovenly, from the Italian professor's daughter, who taught behind the curtain, down to

3. Jean Paul Richter (1763–1825), German novelist and tale writer, often portrayed women sympathetically, but his *Levana; or, The Doctrine of Education* (1807) is in part a compendium of sexist notions.
4. The Jews of the Old Testament.
5. Three powerful women: Semiramis was the legendary founder of Babylon; Elizabeth I (1558–1603), queen of England; Catharine (1762–1796), empress of Russia.
6. Greek (470?–410 B.C.E.), leader of a literary and philosophical salon; she became the mistress of Pericles (495–429 B.C.E.), the Athenian statesman and general.
7. French abbess (1101–1164), remembered for her romance with (and letters to) Abelard (1079–1142), French philosopher and theologian. Sappho (7th century B.C.E.), Greek lyric poet.
8. Female improvisers of dance or song.

Mrs. Carter and Madame Dacier,[9] are sure of an admiring audience, if they can once get a platform on which to stand.

But how to get this platform, or how to make it of reasonably easy access is the difficulty. Plants of great vigor will almost always struggle into blossom, despite impediments. But there should be encouragement, and a free, genial atmosphere for those of more timid sort, fair play for each in its own kind. Some are like the little, delicate flowers, which love to hide in the dripping mosses by the sides of mountain torrents, or in the shade of tall trees. But others require an open field, a rich and loosened soil, or they never show their proper hues.

It may be said man does not have his fair play either; his energies are repressed and distorted by the interposition of artificial obstacles. Aye, but he himself has put them there; they have grown out of his own imperfections. If there *is* a misfortune in woman's lot, it is in obstacles being interposed by men, which do *not* mark her state, and if they express her past ignorance, do not her present needs. As every man is of woman born, she has slow but sure means of redress, yet the sooner a general justness of thought makes smooth the path, the better.

Man is of woman born, and her face bends over him in infancy with an expression he can never quite forget. Eminent men have delighted to pay tribute to this image, and it is a hacknied observation, that most men of genius boast some remarkable development in the mother. The rudest tar brushes off a tear with his coat-sleeve at the hallowed name. The other day I met a decrepit old man of seventy, on a journey, who challenged the stage-company to guess where he was going. They guessed aright, "To see your mother." "Yes," said he, "she is ninety-two, but has good eye-sight still, they say. I've not seen her these forty years, and I thought I could not die in peace without." I should have liked his picture painted as a companion piece to that of a boisterous little boy, whom I saw attempt to declaim at a school exhibition.

> "O that those lips had language! Life has passed
> With me but roughly since I heard thee last."[1]

He got but very little way before sudden tears shamed him from the stage.

Some gleams of the same expression which shone down upon his infancy, angelically pure and benign, visit man again with hopes of pure love, of a holy marriage. Or if not before, in the eyes of the mother of his child they again are seen, and dim fancies pass before his mind, that woman may not have been born for him alone, but have come from heaven, a commissioned soul, a messenger of truth and love.

In gleams, in dim fancies, this thought visits the mind of common men. It is soon obscured by the mists of sensuality, the dust of routine, and he thinks it was only some meteor or ignis fatuus[2] that shone. But, as a Rosicrucian lamp, it burns unwearied,[3] though condemned to the solitude of

9. Anne LeFèvre Dacier (1654–1720), French scholar and translator of the classics. The Italian professor's daughter, if a historical person, is unidentified. Elizabeth Carter (1717–1806), English poet and translator.
1. From "On the Receipt of My Mother's Picture," by the English poet William Cowper (1731–1800).
2. False fire (Latin); term used to describe the fiery light seen over marshlands after sunset, attributable to decomposing matter. The term has come to refer to deceptive hopes or perceptions.
3. The ever-burning lamp is one of the rumored practices of the Rosicrucians, esoteric religious order supposedly founded in the 15th century and especially active in the 17th and 18th centuries.

tombs. And, to its permanent life, as to every truth, each age has, in some form, borne witness. For the truths, which visit the minds of careless men only in fitful gleams, shine with radiant clearness into those of the poet, the priest, and the artist.

Whatever may have been the domestic manners of the ancient nations, the idea of women was nobly manifested in their mythologies and poems, where she appeared as Sita in the Ramayana, a form of tender purity, in the Egyptian Isis,[4] of divine wisdom never yet surpassed. In Egypt, too, the Sphynx, walking the earth with lion tread, looked out upon its marvels in the calm, inscrutable beauty of a virgin's face, and the Greek could only add wings to the great emblem. In Greece, Ceres and Proserpine,[5] significantly termed "the great goddesses," were seen seated, side by side. They needed not to rise for any worshipper or any change; they were prepared for all things, as those initiated to their mysteries knew. More obvious is the meaning of those three forms, the Diana, Minerva, and Vesta.[6] Unlike in the expression of their beauty, but alike in this,—that each was self-sufficing. Other forms were only accessories and illustrations, none the complement to one like these. Another might indeed be the companion, and the Apollo and Diana set off one another's beauty. Of the Vesta, it is to be observed, that not only deep-eyed deep-discerning Greece, but ruder Rome, who represents the only form of good man (the always busy warrior) that could be indifferent to woman, confided the permanence of its glory to a tutelary goddess, and her wisest legislator spoke of Meditation as a nymph.

In Sparta, thought, in this respect as all others, was expressed in the characters of real life, and the women of Sparta were as much Spartans as the men. The Citoyen, Citoyenne, of France, was here actualized. Was not the calm equality they enjoyed well worth the honors of chivalry? They intelligently shared the ideal life of their nation.

Generally, we are told of these nations, that women occupied there a very subordinate position in actual life. It is difficult to believe this, when we see such range and dignity of thought on the subject in the mythologies, and find the poets producing such ideals as Cassandra, Iphigenia, Antigone, Macaria,[7] (though it is not unlike our own day, that men should revere those heroines of their great princely houses at theatres from which their women were excluded,) where Sibylline priestesses told the oracle of the highest god, and he could not be content to reign with a court of less than nine Muses.[8] Even Victory wore a female form.[9]

4. In Egyptian mythology, the goddess of fertility. "The Ramayana": In the *Life of Rama*, one of the two great national epic poems of India, written in Sanskrit c. 300 B.C.E., the god Rama wins Sita, the daughter of King Janaka, and rescues her after she is kidnapped.

5. The goddess of agriculture and her daughter, the goddess of the underworld, respectively.

6. Roman goddesses of the hunt, wisdom and the arts, and the home.

7. The "ideal" women are all from Greek mythology. Cassandra was the prophetess of Troy, whose fate it was to be disbelieved. Iphigenia was the daughter of Agamemnon, destined by her father for sacrifice but rescued by the goddess Artemis. Antigone was a Theban princess executed because she buried her brother's corpse against the orders of her uncle. Macaria was the daughter of Hercules, who sacrificed herself to save Athens. Fuller knew not only the original Greek epics and dramas in translation but also such German reworkings of Greek myth as Goethe's play *Iphigenia* (1786).

8. In Greek mythology, the nine sisters, daughters of Mnemosyne and Zeus, each of whom presided over a different art or science. "Sibylline priestesses": the votaries of Apollo who conveyed the god's messages to the oracle at Delphos.

9. In statuary, as in the second-century B.C.E. Greek marble sculpture *The Winged Victory of Samothrace*.

But whatever were the facts of daily life, I cannot complain of the age and nation, which represents its thought by such a symbol as I see before me at this moment. It is a zodiac of the busts of gods and goddesses, arranged in pairs. The circle breathes the music of a heavenly order. Male and female heads are distinct in expression, but equal in beauty, strength, and calmness. Each male head is that of a brother and a king, each female of a sister and a queen. Could the thought, thus expressed, be lived out, there would be nothing more to be desired. There would be unison in variety, congeniality in difference.

Coming nearer our own time, we find religion and poetry no less true in their revelations. The rude man, but just disengaged from the sod, the Adam, accuses woman to his God, and records her disgrace to their posterity. He is not ashamed to write that he could be drawn from heaven by one beneath him. But in the same nation, educated by time, instructed by successive prophets, we find woman in as high a position as she has ever occupied. And no figure, that has ever arisen to greet our eyes, has been received with more fervent reverence than that of the Madonna. Heine calls her the Dame du Comptoir[1] of the Catholic Church, and this jeer well expresses a serious truth.

And not only this holy and significant image was worshipped by the pilgrim, and the favorite subject of the artist, but it exercised an immediate influence on the destiny of the sex. The empresses, who embraced the cross, converted sons and husbands.[2] Whole calendars of female saints, heroic dames of chivalry, binding the emblem of faith on the heart of the best beloved, and wasting the bloom of youth in separation and loneliness, for the sake of duties they thought it religion to assume, with innumerable forms of poesy, trace their lineage to this one. Nor, however imperfect may be the action, in our day, of the faith thus expressed, and though we can scarcely think it nearer this ideal than that of India or Greece was near their ideal, is it in vain that the truth has been recognized, that woman is not only a part of man, bone of his bone and flesh of his flesh, born that men might not be lonely, but in themselves possessors of and possessed by immortal souls. This truth undoubtedly received a greater outward stability from the belief of the church, that the earthly parent of the Saviour of souls was a woman.

The Assumption of the Virgin, as painted by sublime artists, Petrarch's[3] Hymn to the Madonna, cannot have spoken to the world wholly without result, yet oftentimes those who had ears heard not.

Thus, the Idea of woman has not failed to be often and forcibly represented. So many instances throng on the mind, that we must stop here, lest the catalogue be swelled beyond the reader's patience.

Neither can she complain that she has not had her share of power. This, in all ranks of society, except the lowest, has been hers to the extent that vanity could crave, far beyond what wisdom would accept. In the very lowest, where man, pressed by poverty, sees in women only the partner of toils and cares, and cannot hope, scarcely has an idea of a comfortable home, he maltreats her, often, and is less influenced by her. In all ranks, those who are amiable

1. "Lady Chancellor of the Exchequer" or "Lady of the Counting-House" (French). Heinrich Heine (1797–1856), German lyric poet and satirist.
2. An allusion to Helena (c. 248–328), mother of the emperor Constantine the Great of Rome and reputed discoverer of Jesus' cross.
3. Francesco Petrarca (1304–1374), Italian lyric poet. "Assumption": the act of being taken up bodily into heaven. Catholic doctrine ascribes this fate to Mary, the mother of Jesus.

and uncomplaining, suffer much. They suffer long, and are kind; verily they have their reward.[4] But wherever man is sufficiently raised above extreme poverty, or brutal stupidity, to care for the comforts of the fireside, or the bloom and ornament of life, woman has always power enough, if she choose to exert it, and is usually disposed to do so in proportion to her ignorance and childish vanity. Unacquainted with the importance of life and its purposes, trained to a selfish coquetry and love of petty power, she does not look beyond the pleasure of making herself felt at the moment, and governments are shaken and commerce broken up to gratify the pique of a female favorite. The English shopkeeper's wife does not vote, but it is for her interest that the politician canvasses by the coarsest flattery. France suffers no woman on her throne, but her proud nobles kiss the dust at the feet of Pompadour and Dubarry, for such flare in the lighted foreground where a Roland would modestly aid in the closet.[5] Spain shuts up her women in the care of duennas, and allows them no book but the Breviary;[6] but the ruin follows only the more surely from the worthless favorite of a worthless queen.

It is not the transient breath of poetic incense, that women want; each can receive that from a lover. It is not life-long sway; it needs but to become a coquette, a shrew, or a good cook to be sure of that. It is not money, nor notoriety, nor the badges of authority, that men have appropriated to themselves. If demands made in their behalf lay stress on any of these particulars, those who make them have not searched deeply into the need. It is for that which at once includes all these and precludes them; which would not be forbidden power, lest there be temptation to steal and misuse it; which would not have the mind perverted by flattery from a worthiness of esteem. It is for that which is the birthright of every being capable to receive it,—the freedom, the religious, the intelligent freedom of the universe, to use its means, to learn its secret as far as nature has enabled them, with God alone for their guide and their judge.

Ye cannot believe it, men; but the only reason why women ever assume what is more appropriate to you, is because you prevent them from finding out what is fit for themselves. Were they free, were they wise fully to develop the strength and beauty of women, they would never wish to be men, or manlike. The well-instructed moon flies not from her orbit to seize on the glories of her partner. No; for she knows that one law rules, one heaven contains, one universe replies to them alike. It is with women as with the slave.

> "Vor dem Sklaven, wenn er die Kette bricht,
> Vor dem freien Menschen erzittert nicht."[7]
>
> Tremble not before the free man, but before the slave
> who has chains to break.

In slavery, acknowledged slavery, women are on a par with men. Each is a work-tool, an article of property,—no more! In perfect freedom, such as is

4. A distillation of parts of the Sermon on the Mount, especially Matthew 5.3–12.

5. Small private room. Jeanne Antoinette Poisson, Marquise de Pompadour (1721–1764), mistress of Louis XV of France. Marie Jeanne Bécu, Comtesse du Barry (1743–1793), last mistress of Louis XV, executed during the revolution. Marie Jeanne Roland (1754–1793), Jacobin wife of Jean Marie Roland (1734–1793), who killed himself after learning she had been guillotined.

6. Book containing hymns, offices, and prayers for the canonical hours (hours at which prayers are to be recited). "Duennas": elderly governesses and chaperones to the daughters of Spanish or Portuguese families.

7. From "Words of Faith" (1798) by Friedrich von Schiller.

painted in Olympus, in Swedenborg's angelic state,[8] in the heaven where there is no marrying nor giving in marriage,[9] each is a purified intelligence, an enfranchised soul,—no less!

> Jene himmlische Gestalten
> Sie fragen nicht nach Mann und Weib,
> Und keine Kleider, keine Falten
> Umgeben den verklärten Leib.[1]

The child who sang this was a prophetic form, expressive of the longing for a state of perfect freedom, pure love. She could not remain here, but was transplanted to another air. And it may be that the air of this earth will never be so tempered, that such can bear it long. But, while they stay, they must bear testimony to the truth they are constituted to demand.

That an era approaches which shall approximate nearer to such a temper than any has yet done, there are many tokens, indeed so many that only a few of the most prominent can here be enumerated.

The reigns of Elizabeth of England and Isabella of Castile foreboded this era.[2] They expressed the beginning of the new state, while they forwarded its progress. These were strong characters, and in harmony with the wants of their time. One showed that this strength did not unfit a woman for the duties of a wife and mother; the other, that it could enable her to live and die alone. Elizabeth is certainly no pleasing example. In rising above the weakness, she did not lay aside the weaknesses ascribed to her sex; but her strength must be respected now, as it was in her own time.

We may accept it as an omen for ourselves, that it was Isabella who furnished Columbus with the means of coming hither. This land must pay back its debt to woman, without whose aid it would not have been brought into alliance with the civilized world.

The influence of Elizabeth on literature was real, though, by sympathy with its finer productions, she was no more entitled to give name to an era than Queen Anne.[3] It was simply that the fact of having a female sovereign on the throne affected the course of a writer's thoughts. In this sense, the presence of a woman on the throne always makes its mark. Life is lived before the eyes of all men, and their imaginations are stimulated as to the possibilities of woman. "We will die for our King, Maria Theresa,"[4] cry the wild warriors, clashing their swords, and the sounds vibrate through the poems of that generation. The range of female character in Spenser alone might content us for one period. Britomart and Belphoebe have as much room in the canvass as Florimel; and where this is the case, the haughtiest Amazon will not murmur that Una[5] should be felt to be the highest type.

8. In the *Heaven and Hell* by Emanuel Swedenborg (1688–1772), Swedish statesman and mystic.
9. Jesus' words to the Sadducees: "For in the resurrection they neither marry, nor are given in marriage, but are as the angels of God in heaven" (Matthew 22.30).
1. In Goethe's *Wilhelm Meister* (1796), Mignon's song just before her death: "Yonder heavenly forms / They ask not whether one be man or woman, / And no garments, no folds / Enclose the transfigured body."
2. 1558–1603 and 1474–1504, respectively.
3. Queen of England (1702–14).
4. Maria Theresa (1717–1780), queen of Hungary and Bohemia, wife of the emperor Francis I.
5. From Spenser's *Faerie Queene* (1590). Britomart is the lady knight representing Chastity. Belphoebe is the huntress who flatteringly resembles Queen Elizabeth. Florimel is a witch. Una is the personification of Truth.

Unlike as was the English Queen to a fairy queen, we may yet conceive that it was the image of *a* queen before the poet's mind, that called up this splendid court of women.

Shakespeare's range is also great, but he has left out the heroic characters, such as the Macaria of Greece,[6] the Britomart of Spenser. Ford and Massinger[7] have, in this respect, shown a higher flight of feeling than he. It was the holy and heroic woman they most loved, and if they could not paint an Imogen, a Desdemona, a Rosalind,[8] yet in those of a stronger mould, they showed a higher ideal, though with so much less poetic power to represent it, than we see in Portia or Isabella.[9] The simple truth of Cordelia,[1] indeed, is of this sort. The beauty of Cordelia is neither male nor female: it is the beauty of virtue.

The ideal of love and marriage rose high in the mind of all the Christian nations who were capable of grave and deep feeling. We may take as examples of its English aspect, the lines,

> "I could not love thee, dear, so much,
> Loved I not honor more."[2]

The address of the Commonwealth's man to his wife as she looked out from the Tower window to see him for the last time on his way to execution. "He stood up in the cart, waved his hat, and cried, "To Heaven, my love, to Heaven! and leave you in the storm!'"

Such was the love of faith and honor, a love which stopped, like Colonel Hutchinson's, "on this side idolatry,"[3] because it was religious. The meeting of two such souls Donne describes as giving birth to an "abler soul."[4]

Lord Herbert wrote to his love,

> "Were not our souls immortal made,
> Our equal loves can make them such."[5]

In Spain the same thought is arrayed in a sublimity, which belongs to the somber and passionate genius of the nation. Calderon's Justina resists all the temptation of the Demon, and raises her lover with her above the sweet lures of mere temporal happiness.[6] Their marriage is vowed at the stake, their souls are liberated together by the martyr flame into "a purer state of sensation and existence."

In Italy, the great poets wove into their lives an ideal love which answered to the highest wants. It included those of the intellect and the affections, for it was a love of spirit for spirit. It was not ascetic and superhuman, but

6. The self-sacrificing daughter of Hercules.
7. John Ford (1586–1640) and Philip Massinger (1583–1640), English playwrights.
8. The gay, self-reliant heroine of *As You Like It*. Imogen is the gallant heroine of *Cymbeline*, a much-abused but forgiving wife. Desdemona is the innocent, loyal wife in *Othello*.
9. The chaste heroine of *Measure for Measure*, an acute reasoner and forceful speaker, like the Portia of *Merchant of Venice*. Portia is either the ideal Roman wife in *Julius Caesar* or the resourceful heiress in *Merchant of Venice*.
1. The honest, loving daughter in *King Lear*.
2. From "To Lucasta, Going to the Wars," by the English poet Richard Lovelace (1618–1657).
3. In his posthumously published *Timber*, Ben Jonson (1572–1637) says of Shakespeare: "I loved the man, and do honor his memory (on this side idolatry) as much as any." Colonel John Hutchinson (1615–1664), a pro-Commonwealth man during the English Civil War, whose widow, Lucy, wrote in his *Memoirs* of their mutual devotion.
4. In John Donne's "The Ecstasy," line 43.
5. Edward, Lord Herbert of Cherbury (1583–1648), "An Ode upon a Question Moved Whether Love Should Continue for Ever."
6. In *El Mágico Prodigioso* (*The Mighty Magician*) by Pedro Calderón de la Barca (1600–1681), Justina, daughter of an aged Christian in Antioch during Rome's persecution of the new sect, saves herself from Lucifer by a powerful appeal to Jesus.

interpreting all things, gave their proper beauty to details of the common life, the common day; the poet spoke of his love not as a flower to place in his bosom, or hold carelessly in his hand, but as a light towards which he must find wings to fly, or "a stair to heaven." He delighted to speak of her not only as the bride of his heart, but the mother of his soul, for he saw that, in cases where the right direction has been taken, the greater delicacy of her frame, and stillness of her life, left her more open to spiritual influx than man is. So he did not look upon her as betwixt him and earth, to serve his temporal needs, but rather betwixt him and heaven, to purify his affections and lead him to wisdom through her pure love. He sought in her not so much the Eve as the Madonna.

In these minds the thought, which glitters in all the legends of chivalry, shines in broad intellectual effulgence, not to be misinterpreted. And their thought is reverenced by the world, though it lies so far from them as yet, so far, that it seems as though a gulf of Death lay between.

Even with such men the practice was often widely different from the mental faith. I say mental, for if the heart were thoroughly alive with it, the practice could not be dissonant. Lord Herbert's was a marriage of convention, made for him at fifteen;[7] he was not discontented with it, but looked only to the advantages it brought of perpetuating his family on the basis of a great fortune. He paid, in act, what he considered a dutiful attention to the bond; his thoughts travelled elsewhere, and, while forming a high ideal of the companionship of minds in marriage, he seems never to have doubted that its realization must be postponed to some other stage of being. Dante, almost immediately after the death of Beatrice,[8] married a lady chosen for him by his friends.

Centuries have passed since, but civilized Europe is still in a transition state about marriage, not only in practice, but in thought. A great majority of societies and individuals are still doubtful whether earthly marriage is to be a union of souls, or merely a contract of convenience and utility. Were woman established in the rights of an immortal being, this could not be. She would not in some countries be given away by her father, with scarcely more respect for her own feelings than is shown by the Indian chief, who sells his daughter for a horse, and beats her if she runs away from her new home. Nor, in societies where her choice is left free, would she be perverted, by the current of opinion that seizes her, into the belief that she must marry, if it be only to find a protector, and a home of her own.

Neither would man, if he thought that the connection was of permanent importance, enter upon it so lightly. He would not deem it a trifle, that he was to enter into the closest relations with another soul, which, if not eternal in themselves, must eternally affect his growth.

Neither, did he believe woman capable of friendship, would he, by rash haste, lose the chance of finding a friend in the person who might, probably, live half a century by his side. Did love to his mind partake of infinity, he would not miss his chance of its revelations, that he might the sooner rest from his weariness by a bright fireside, and have a sweet and graceful atten-

7. He was married in 1599, when he was around sixteen.
8. Beatrice Portinari (1266–1290), a Florentine whom the poet Dante Alighieri (1265–1321) loved at first sight in childhood and used as the inspiration for *New Life* and later portrayed as his guide through Paradise in the *Divine Comedy*.

dant, "devoted to him alone." Were he a step higher, he would not carelessly enter into a relation, where he might not be able to do the duty of a friend, as well as a protector from external ill, to the other party, and have a being in his power pining for sympathy, intelligence, and aid, that he could not give.

Where the thought of equality has become pervasive, it shows itself in four kinds.

The household partnership. In our country the woman looks for a "smart but kind" husband, the man for a "capable, sweet tempered" wife.

The man furnishes the house, the woman regulates it. Their relation is one of mutual esteem, mutual dependence. Their talk is of business, their affection shows itself by practical kindness. They know that life goes more smoothly and cheerfully to each for the other's aid; they are grateful and content. The wife praises her husband as a "good provider," the husband in return compliments her as a "capital housekeeper." This relation is good as far as it goes.

Next comes a closer tie which takes the two forms, either of intellectual companionship, or mutual idolatry. The last, we suppose, is to no one a pleasing subject of contemplation. The parties weaken and narrow one another; they lock the gate against all the glories of the universe that they may live in a cell together. To themselves they seem the only wise, to all others steeped in infatuation, the gods smile as they look forward to the crisis of cure, to men the woman seems an unlovely syren, to women the man an effeminate boy.

The other form, of intellectual companionship, has become more and more frequent. Men engaged in public life, literary men, and artists have often found in their wives companions and confidants in thought no less than in feeling. And, as in the course of things the intellectual development of woman has spread wider and risen higher, they have, not unfrequently, shared the same employment. As in the case of Roland and his wife, who were friends in the household and the nation's councils, read together, regulated home affairs, or prepared public documents together indifferently.

It is very pleasant, in letters begun by Roland and finished by his wife, to see the harmony of mind and the difference of nature, one thought, but various ways of treating it.

This is one of the best instances of a marriage of friendship. It was only friendship, whose basis was esteem; probably neither party knew love, except by name.

Roland was a good man, worthy to esteem and be esteemed, his wife as deserving of admiration as able to do without it. Madame Roland is the fairest specimen we have yet of her class, as clear to discern her aim, as valiant to pursue it, as Spenser's Britomart,[9] austerely set apart from all that did not belong to her, whether as woman or as mind. She is an antetype of a class to which the coming time will afford a field, the Spartan[1] matron, brought by the culture of a book-furnishing age to intellectual consciousness and expansion.

Self-sufficing strength and clear-sightedness were in her combined with a power of deep and calm affection. The page of her life is one of unsullied dignity.

9. In Spenser's *The Fairie Queene*, the female knight Britomart represents chastity.

1. Resembling the ancient Greeks known for their austerity and military valor.

Her appeal to posterity is one against the injustice of those who committed such crimes in the name of liberty. She makes it in behalf of herself and her husband. I would put beside it on the shelf a little volume, containing a similar appeal from the verdict of contemporaries to that of mankind, that of Godwin in behalf of his wife, the celebrated, the by most men detested Mary Wolstonecraft.[2] In his view it was an appeal from the injustice of those who did such wrong in the name of virtue.

Were this little book interesting for no other cause, it would be so for the generous affection evinced under the peculiar circumstances. This man had courage to love and honor this woman in the face of the world's verdict, and of all that was repulsive in her own past history. He believed he saw of what soul she was, and that the thoughts she had struggled to act out were noble. He loved her and he defended her for the meaning and intensity of her inner life. It was a good fact.

Mary Wolstonecraft, like Madame Dudevant[3] (commonly known as George Sand) in our day, was a woman whose existence better proved the need of some new interpretation of woman's rights, than anything she wrote. Such women as these, rich in genius, of most tender sympathies, and capable of high virtue and a chastened harmony, ought not to find themselves by birth in a place so narrow, that in breaking bonds they become outlaws. Were there as much room in the world for such, as in Spenser's poem for Britomart, they would not run their heads so wildly against its laws. They find their way at last to purer air, but the world will not take off the brand it has set upon them. The champion of the rights of woman found in Godwin one who pleads her own cause like a brother. George Sand smokes, wears male attire, wishes to be addressed as Mon frère;[4] perhaps, if she found those who were as brothers indeed, she would not care whether she were brother or sister.

We rejoice to see that she, who expresses such a painful contempt for men in most of her works, as shows she must have known great wrong from them, in La Roche Mauprat[5] depicting one raised, by the workings of love, from the depths of savage sensualism to a moral and intellectual life. It was love for a pure object, for a steadfast woman, one of those who, the Italian said, could make the stair to heaven.

Women like Sand will speak now, and cannot be silenced; their characters and their eloquence alike foretell an era when such as they shall easier learn to lead true lives. But though such forebode, not such shall be the parents of it. Those who would reform the world must show that they do not speak in the heat of wild impulse; their lives must be unstained by passionate error; they must be severe lawgivers to themselves. As to their transgressions and opinions, it may be observed, that the resolve of Eloisa to be only the mistress of Abelard, was that of one who saw the contract of marriage a seal of degradation.[6] Wherever abuses of this sort are seen, the timid will suffer, the bold protest. But society is in the right to outlaw them till she

2. *Memoirs of the Author of "A Vindication of the Rights of Woman"* (1798) by the English author William Godwin (1756–1836). Mary Wollstonecraft (1759–1797) married Godwin shortly before her death in childbirth.
3. Amandine Aurore Lucile Dudevant (1804–1876), French Romantic novelist who adopted a male pen name, wore male clothing, and had a succession of male lovers.
4. Old friend and colleague (French); literally, "my brother."
5. An 1837 drama by George Sand.
6. In her famous letters written in the 12th century, Eloisa steadfastly refused to marry Abelard, because marriage would force him to give up his teaching of theology within the Church.

has revised her law, and she must be taught to do so, by one who speaks with authority, not in anger and haste.

If Godwin's choice of the calumniated authoress of the "Rights of Woman," for his honored wife, be a sign of a new era, no less so is an article of great learning and eloquence, published several years since in an English review, where the writer, in doing full justice to Eloisa, shows his bitter regret that she lives not now to love him, who might have known better how to prize her love than did the egotistical Abelard.

These marriages, these characters, with all their imperfections, express an onward tendency. They speak of aspiration of soul, of energy of mind, seeking clearness and freedom. Of a like promise are the tracts now publishing by Goodwyn Barmby[7] (the European Pariah as he calls himself) and his wife Catharine. Whatever we may think of their measures, we see them in wedlock, the two minds are wed by the only contract that can permanently avail, of a common faith, and a common purpose.

We might mention instances, nearer home, of minds, partners in work and in life, sharing together, on equal terms, public and private interests, and which have not on any side that aspect of offence which characterizes the attitude of the last named; persons who steer straight onward, and in our freer life have not been obliged to run their heads against any wall. But the principles which guide them might, under petrified or oppressive institutions, have made them warlike, paradoxical, or, in some sense, Pariahs. The phenomenon is different, the last the same, in all these cases. Men and women have been obliged to build their house from the very foundation. If they found stone ready in the quarry, they took it peaceably, otherwise they alarmed the country by pulling down old towers to get materials.

These are all instances of marriage as intellectual companionship. The parties meet mind to mind, and a mutual trust is excited which can buckler them against a million. They work together for a common purpose, and, in all these instances, with the same implement, the pen.

A pleasing expression in this kind is afforded by the union in the names of the Howitts.[8] William and Mary Howitt we heard named together for years, supposing them to be brother and sister; the equality of labors and reputation, even so, was auspicious, more so, now we find them man and wife. In his late work on Germany, Howitt mentions his wife with pride, as one among the constellation of distinguished English women, and in a graceful, simple manner.

In naming these instances we do not mean to imply that community of employment is an essential to union of this sort, more than to the union of friendship. Harmony exists no less in difference than in likeness, if only the same key-note govern both parts. Woman the poem, man the poet; woman the heart, man the head; such divisions are only important when they are never to be transcended. If nature is never bound down, nor the voice of inspiration stifled, that is enough. We are pleased that women should write and speak, if they feel the need of it, from having something to tell; but silence for a hundred years would be as well, if that silence be from divine command, and not from man's tradition.

7. English publisher (1820–1881) of socialist tracts who founded the London Communist Propaganda Society in 1841.

8. William Howitt (1792–1879) and Mary Howitt (1799–1888), prolific British authors and translators.

While Goetz von Berlichingen[9] rides to battle, his wife is busy in the kitchen; but difference of occupation does not prevent that community of life, that perfect esteem, with which he says,

"Whom God loves, to him gives he such a wife!"

Manzoni thus dedicates his Adelchi.[1]

> "To his beloved and venerated wife, Enrichetta Luigia Blondel, who, with conjugal affections and maternal wisdom, has preserved a virgin mind, the author dedicates this Adelchi, grieving that he could not, by a more splendid and more durable monument, honor the dear name and the memory of so many virtues."

The relation could not be fairer, nor more equal, if she too had written poems. Yet the position of the parties might have been the reverse as well; the woman might have sung the deeds, given voice to the life of the man, and beauty would have been the result, as we see in pictures of Arcadia[2] the nymph singing to the shepherds, or the shepherd with his pipe allures the nymphs, either makes a good picture. The sounding lyre requires not muscular strength, but energy of soul to animate the hand which can control it. Nature seems to delight in varying her arrangements, as if to show that she will be fettered by no rule, and we must admit the same varieties that she admits.

I have not spoken of the higher grade of marriage union, the religious, which may be expressed as pilgrimage towards a common shrine. This includes the others; home sympathies, and household wisdom, for these pilgrims must know how to assist one another to carry their burdens along the dusty way; intellectual communion, for how sad it would be on such a journey to have a companion to whom you could not communicate thoughts and aspirations, as they sprang to life, who would have no feeling for the more and more glorious prospects that open as we advance, who would never see the flowers that may be gathered by the most industrious traveler. It must include all these. Such a fellow pilgrim Count Zinzendorf[3] seems to have found in his countess of whom he thus writes:

> "Twenty-five years' experience has shown me that just the help-mate whom I have is the only one that could suit my vocation, Who else could have so carried through my family affairs? Who lived so spotlessly before the world? Who so wisely aided me in my rejection of a dry morality? Who so clearly set aside the Pharisaism[4] which, as years passed, threatened to creep in among us? Who so deeply discerned as to the spirits of delusion which sought to bewilder us? Who would have governed my whole economy so wisely, richly, and hospitably when circumstances commanded? Who have taken indifferently the part of servant or mis-

9. German knight (1481–1562), a sort of Robin Hood, familiar to Fuller from Goethe's play *Göetz von Berlichingen* (1773).
1. A tragedy (1822) by Alessandro Manzoni (1785–1873), Italian writer.
2. Pastoral district of the Peloponnesus in Greece, symbolic of rustic simplicity and contentment.
3. Nikolas Ludwig, Count von Zinzendorf (1700–1760), German leader of the Moravian Church, or the Bohemian Brethren, a Catholic heretical group founded in Bohemia around 1722, influential both in Europe and in the Moravian settlements in the American colonies, which he visited.
4. Self-righteous hypocrisy, from the Jewish sect whom Jesus condemned as whitened sepulchres (Matthew 23.27), "which indeed appear beautiful outward, but are within full of dead men's bones, and of all uncleanness."

tress, without on the one side affecting an especial spirituality, on the other being sullied by any worldly pride? Who, in a community where all ranks are eager to be on a level, would, from wise and real causes, have known how to maintain inward and outward distinctions? Who, without a murmur, have seen her husband encounter such dangers by land and sea? Who undertaken with him and sustained such astonishing pilgrimages? Who amid such difficulties always held up her head, and supported me? Who found so many hundred thousands and acquitted them on her own credit? And, finally, who, of all human beings, would so well understand and interpret to others my inner and outer being as this one, of such nobleness in her way of thinking, such great intellectual capacity, and free from the theological perplexities that enveloped me?"

An observer[5] adds this testimony.

"We may in many marriages regard it as the best arrangement, if the man has so much advantage over his wife that she can, without much thought of her own, be, by him, led and directed, as by a father. But it was not so with the Count and his consort. She was not made to be a copy; she was an original; and, while she loved and honored him, she thought for herself on all subjects with so much intelligence, that he could and did look on her as a sister and friend also."

Such a woman is the sister and friend of all beings, as the worthy man is their brother and helper.

Another sign of the time is furnished by the triumphs of female authorship. These have been great and constantly increasing. They have taken possession of so many provinces for which men had pronounced them unfit, that though these still declare there are some inaccessible to them, it is difficult to say just *where* they must stop.

The shining names of famous women have cast light upon the path of the sex, and many obstructions have been removed. When a Montague[6] could learn better than her brother, and use her lore to such purpose afterwards as an observer, it seemed amiss to hinder women from preparing themselves to see, or from seeing all they could when prepared. Since Somerville[7] has achieved so much, will any young girl be prevented from attaining a knowledge of the physical sciences, if she wishes it? De Staël's[8] name was not so clear of offence; she could not forget the woman in the thought; while she was instructing you as a mind, she wished to be admired as a woman. Sentimental tears often dimmed the eagle glance. Her intellect, too, with all its splendor, trained in a drawing room, fed on flattery, was tainted and flawed; yet its beams made the obscurest school house in New England warmer and lighter to the little rugged[9] girls, who are gathered together on its wooden bench. They may never through life hear her name, but she is not the less their benefactress.

5. Spangenberg [Fuller's note]. August Gotlieb Spangenberg (1704–1792), successor to Count von Zinzendorf. See p. 766, n. 3.

6. Lady Mary Wortley Montagu (1689–1762), famous as a letter writer.

7. Mary Somerville (1789–1872), British scientific writer.

8. Madame de Staël (1766–1817), French author and critic, famous for her literary-political salons.

9. Tough, uncouth.

This influence has been such that the aim certainly is, how, in arranging school instruction for girls, to give them as fair a field as boys. These arrangements are made as yet with little judgment or intelligence, just as the tutors of Jane Grey,[1] and the other famous women of her time, taught them Latin and Greek, because they knew nothing else themselves, so now the improvement in the education of girls is made by giving them gentlemen as teachers, who only teach what has been taught themselves at college, while methods and topics need revision for those new cases, which could better be made by those who had experienced the same wants. Women are often at the head of these institutions, but they have as yet seldom been thinking women, capable to organize a new whole for the wants of the time, and choose persons to officiate in the departments. And when some portion of education is got of a good sort from the school, the tone of society, the much larger proportion received from the world, contradicts its purport. Yet books have not been furnished, and a little elementary instruction been given in vain. Women are better aware how large and rich the universe is, not so easily blinded by the narrowness and partial view of a home circle.

Whether much or little has or will be done, whether women will add to the talent of narration, the power of systematizing, whether they will carve marble as well as draw, is not important. But that it should be acknowledged that they have intellect which needs developing, that they should be considered complete, if beings of affection and habit alone, is important.

Yet even this acknowledgment, rather obtained by woman than proffered by man, has been sullied by the usual selfishness. So much is said of women being better educated that they may be better companions and mothers *of men*! They should be fit for such companionship, and we have mentioned with satisfaction instances where it has been established. Earth knows no fairer, holier relation than that of a mother. But a being of infinite scope must not be treated with an exclusive view to any one relation. Give the soul free course, let the organization be freely developed, and the being will be fit for any and every relation to which it may be called. The intellect, no more than the sense of hearing, is to be cultivated, that she may be a more valuable companion to man, but because the Power who gave a power by its mere existence signifies that it must be brought out towards perfection.

In this regard, of self-dependence and a greater simplicity and fulness of being, we must hail as a preliminary the increase of the class contemptuously designated as old maids.

We cannot wonder at the aversion with which old bachelors and old maids have been regarded. Marriage is the natural means of forming a sphere, of taking root on the earth: it requires more strength to do this without such an opening, very many have failed to this, and their imperfections have been in every one's way. They have been more partial, more harsh, more officious and impertinent than others. Those, who have a complete experience of the human instincts, have a distrust as to whether they can be thoroughly human and humane, such as is hinted at in the saying,

1. Lady Jane Grey (1537–1554), married by her family to Guildford Dudley and proclaimed queen of England in 1553 on the death of Edward VI, was captured and executed when Mary Tudor established her own succession.

"Old maids' and bachelors' children are well cared for," which derides at once their ignorance and their presumption.

Yet the business of society has become so complex, that it could now scarcely be carried on without the presence of these despised auxiliaries, and detachments from the army of aunts and uncles are wanted to stop gaps in every hedge. They rove about, mental and moral Ishmaelites,[2] pitching their tents amid the fixed and ornamented habitations of men.

They thus gain a wider, if not so deep, experience. They are not so intimate with others, but thrown more upon themselves, and if they do not there find peace and incessant life, there is none to flatter them that they are not very poor and very mean.

A position, which so constantly admonishes, may be of inestimable benefit. The person may gain, undistracted by other relationships, a closer communion with the One. Such a use is made of it by Saints and sibyls. Or she may be one of the lay sisters of charity, or more humbly only the useful drudge of all men, or the intellectual interpreter of the varied life she sees.

Or she may combine all these. Not "needing to care that she may please a husband," a frail and limited being, all her thoughts may turn to the centre, and by steadfast contemplation enter into the secret of truth and love, use it for the use of men, instead of a chosen few, and interpret through it all the forms of life.

Saints and geniuses have often chosen a lonely position, in the faith that, if undisturbed by the pressure of near ties they could give themselves up to the inspiring spirit, it would enable them to understand and reproduce life better than actual experience could.

How many old maids take this high stand, we cannot say; it is an unhappy fact that too many of those who come before the eyes are gossips rather, and not always good-natured gossips. But, if these abuse, and none make the best of their vocation, yet, it has not failed to produce some good fruit. It has been seen by others, if not by themselves, that beings likely to be left alone need to be fortified and furnished within themselves, and education and thought have tended more and more to regard beings as related to absolute Being, as well as to other men. It has been seen that as the loss of no bond ought to destroy a human being, so ought the missing of none to hinder him from growing. And thus a circumstance of the time has helped to put woman on the true platform. Perhaps the next generation will look deeper into this matter, and find that contempt is put on old maids, or old women at all, merely because they do not use the elixir which will keep the soul always young. No one thinks of Michael Angelo's Persican Sibyl, or St. Theresa, or Tasso's Leonora, or the Greek Electra[3] as an old maid, though all had reached the period in life's course appointed to take that degree.

Even among the North American Indians, a race of men as completely engaged in mere instinctive life as almost any in the world, and where each

2. Outcasts, like the descendants of Ishmael, the eldest son of Abraham by Hagar, the handmaid of his wife, Sarah (Genesis 15–25).

3. In Greek mythology, Electra was the daughter of Agamemnon and Clytemnestra, who, with her brother Orestes, avenged the murder of her father by killing her mother and her mother's lover, Aegisthus. Michelangelo's Persican Sibyl (ancient prophetess), one of the five he painted in the Sistine Chapel; St. Teresa of Ávila (1515–1582), Spanish Carmelite nun; Princess Leonora d'Este, protector of the Italian poet Torquato Tasso (1544–1595), who was rumored to be in love with her.

chief, keeping many wives as useful servants, of course looks with no kind eye on celibacy in woman, it was excused in the following instance mentioned by Mrs. Jameson.[4] A woman dreamt in youth that she was betrothed to the sun. She built her a wigwam apart, filled it with emblems of her alliance and means of an independent life. There she passed her days, sustained by her own exertions, and true to her supposed engagement.

In any tribe, we believe, a woman, who lived as if she was betrothed to the sun, would be tolerated, and the rays which made her youth blossom sweetly would crown her with a halo in age.

There is on this subject a nobler view than heretofore, if not the noblest, and we greet improvement here, as much as on the subject of marriage. Both are fertile themes, but time permits not here to explore them.

If larger intellectual resources begin to be deemed necessary to woman, still more is a spiritual dignity in her, or even the mere assumption of it listened to with respect. Joanna Southcote, and Mother Anne Lee are sure of a band of disciples; Ecstatica, Dolorosa,[5] of enraptured believers who will visit them in their lowly huts, and wait for hours to revere them in their trances. The foreign noble traverses land and sea to hear a few words from the lips of the lowly peasant girl, whom he believes specially visited by the Most High. Very beautiful in this way was the influence of the invalid of St. Petersburg, as described by De Maistre.[6]

To this region, however misunderstood, and ill-developed, belong the phenomena of Magnetism, or Mesmerism,[7] as it is now often called, where the trance of the Ecstatica purports to be produced by the agency of one human being on another, instead of, as in her case, direct from the spirit.

The worldling has his sneer here as about the services of religion. "The churches can always be filled with women." "Show me a man in one of your magnetic states, and I will believe."

Women are indeed the easy victims of priestcraft, or self-delusion, but this might not be, if the intellect was developed in proportion to the other powers. They would then have a regulator and be in better equipoise, yet must retain the same nervous susceptibility, while their physical structure is such as it is.

It is with just that hope, that we welcome everything that tends to strengthen the fibre and develop the nature on more sides. When the intellect and affections are in harmony, when intellectual consciousness is calm and deep, inspiration will not be confounded with fancy.

The electrical, the magnetic element in woman has not been fairly developed at any period. Everything might be expected from it; she has far more of it than man. This is commonly expressed by saying, that her intuitions are more rapid and more correct.

4. Anna Brownell Jameson (1794–1860), Irish-born English writer whose *Winter Studies and Summer Rambles* was based on her months in Canada.

5. Ecstatica and Dolorosa are here used as type names for religious enthusiasts and sufferers. Southcote (1750–1814), an English religious enthusiast who in the 1790s announced herself as the woman spoken of in Revelation 12 and began "sealing" the 144,000 elect—for a price per head. Ann Lee (1736–1784), an English religious visionary who founded the Shaker movement.

6. The story of this invalid is unlocated. Joseph de Maistre (1754–1821), French émigré and author of the philosophical dialogue *Soirées de St. Petersbourg*, who for many years was the Sardinian minister to Russia and philosophical spokesman against the French Revolution. An intensely pious Catholic, he was drawn to mysticism.

7. Hypnotism.

But I cannot enlarge upon this here, except to say that on this side is highest promise. Should I speak of it fully, my title should be Cassandra, my topic the Seeress of Prevorst, the first, or the best observed subject of magnetism in our times, and who, like her ancestresses at Delphos, was roused to ecstasy or phrenzy by the touch of the laurel.[8]

In such cases worldlings sneer, but reverent men learn wondrous news, either from the person observed, or by the thoughts caused in themselves by the observation. Fenelon learns from Guyon,[9] Kerner from his Seeress what we fain would know. But to appreciate such disclosures one must be a child, and here the phrase, "women and children," may perhaps be interpreted aright, that only little children shall enter into the kingdom of heaven.[1]

All these motions of the time, tides that betoken a waxing moon, overflow upon our own land. The world at large is readier to let woman learn and manifest the capacities of her nature than it ever was before, and here is a less encumbered field, and freer air than anywhere else. And it ought to be so; we ought to pay for Isabella's jewels.[2]

The names of nations are feminine. Religion, Virtue, and Victory are feminine. To those who have a superstition as to outward signs, it is not without significance that the name of the Queen of our mother-land should at this crisis be Victoria. Victoria the First. Perhaps to us it may be given to disclose the era there outwardly presaged.

Women here are much better situated than men. Good books are allowed with more time to read them. They are not so early forced into the bustle of life, nor so weighed down by demands for outward success. The perpetual changes, incident to our society, make the blood circulate freely through the body politic, and, if not favorable at present to the grace and bloom of life, they are so to activity, resource, and would be to reflection but for a low materialist tendency, from which the women are generally exempt.

They have time to think, and no traditions chain them, and few conventionalities compared with what must be met in other nations. There is no reason why the fact of a constant revelation should be hid from them, and when the mind once is awakened by that, it will not be restrained by the past, but fly to seek the seeds of heavenly future.

Their employments are more favorable to the inward life than those of the men.

Woman is not addressed religiously here, more than elsewhere. She is told to be worthy to be the mother of a Washington, or the companion of some good man. But in many, many instances, she has already learnt that all bribes have the same flaw; that truth and good are to be sought for themselves alone. And already an ideal sweetness floats over many forms, shines in many eyes.

Already deep questions are put by young girls on the great theme, What shall I do to inherit eternal life?[3]

8. The ancient oracles of Delphi, on the slopes of Mount Parnassus in Greece, were devotees of Apollo, who foretold the future to mortal suppliants; the prophetesses chewed laurel leaves in their rites. Fuller took seriously the spiritualistic claims in the German poet Justinus Kerner's (1786–1862) *Seherin von Prevorst* (1829), a book she discusses at length in *Summer on the Lakes*.

9. François Fénelon (1651–1715), French archbishop, learned about the mystical Christian philosophy of Quietism from Jeanne Guyon (1648–1717).

1. Mark 10.14–15.

2. I.e., Americans ought to repay Europe for discovering the Western Hemisphere.

3. An allusion to the rich young man's question to Jesus in Matthew 19.16: "Good Master, what good thing shall I do, that I may have eternal life?"

Men are very courteous to them. They praise them often, check them seldom. There is some chivalry in the feelings towards "the ladies," which gives them the best seats in the stage-coach, frequent admission not only to lectures of all sorts, but to courts of justice, halls of legislature, reform conventions. The newspaper editor "would be better pleased that the Lady's Book[4] were filled up exclusively by ladies. It would, then, indeed, be a true gem, worthy to be presented by young men to the mistresses of their affections." Can gallantry go farther?

In this country is venerated, wherever seen, the character which Goethe spoke of as an Ideal. "The excellent woman is she, who, if the husband dies, can be a father to the children." And this, if rightly read, tells a great deal.

Women who speak in public, if they have a moral power, such as has been felt from Angelina Grimke and Abby Kelly,[5] that is, if they speak for conscience' sake, to serve a cause which they hold sacred, invariably subdue the prejudices of their hearers, and excite an interest proportionate to the aversion with which it had been the purpose to regard them.

A passage in a private letter so happily illustrates this, that I take the liberty to make use of it, though there is not opportunity to ask leave either of the writer or owner of the letter. I think they will pardon me when they see it in print; it is so good, that as many as possible should have the benefit of it.

> Abby Kelly in the Town-House of ——
>
> "The scene was not unheroic,—to see that woman, true to humanity and her own nature, a centre of rude eyes and tongues, even gentlemen feeling licensed to make part of a species of mob around a female out of her sphere. As she took her seat in the desk amid the great noise, and in the throng full, like a wave, of something to ensue, I saw her humanity in a gentleness and unpretension, tenderly open to the sphere around her, and, had she not been supported by the power of the will of genuineness and principle, she would have failed. It led her to prayer, which, in woman especially, is childlike; sensibility and will going to the side of God and looking up to him; and humanity was poured out in aspiration.
>
> "She acted like a gentle hero, with her mild decision and womanly calmness. All heroism is mild and quiet and gentle, for it is life and possession, and combativeness and firmness show a want of actualness. She is as earnest, fresh, and simple as when she first entered the crusade. I think she did much good, more than the men in her place could do, for woman feels more as being and reproducing; this brings the subject more into home relations. Men speak through and mostly from intellect, and this addresses itself in others, which creates and is combative."

Not easily shall we find elsewhere, or before this time, any written observations on the same subject, so delicate and profound.

The late Dr. Channing,[6] whose enlarged and tender and religious nature shared every onward impulse of his time, though his thoughts followed his wishes with a deliberative caution, which belonged to his habits and tem-

4. *Godey's Lady's Book*, popular Philadelphia magazine.

5. Massachusetts-born Quaker (1811–1887); after 1837 she became a lecturer on abolition. Grimké (1805–1879), antislavery advocate from South Carolina, author of *Appeal to the Christian Women of the South* (1836).

6. William Ellery Channing (1780–1842), clergyman and social reformer, one of the founders of Unitarianism.

perament, was greatly interested in these expectations for women. His own treatment of them was absolutely and thoroughly religious. He regarded them as souls, each of which had a destiny of its own, incalculable to other minds, and whose leading it must follow, guided by the light of a private conscience. He had sentiment, delicacy, kindness, taste, but they were all pervaded and ruled by this one thought, that all beings had souls, and must vindicate their own inheritance. Thus all beings were treated by him with an equal, and sweet, though solemn courtesy. The young and unknown, the woman and the child, all felt themselves regarded with an infinite expectation, from which there was no reaction to vulgar prejudice He demanded of all he met, to use his favorite phrase, "great truths."

His memory, every way dear and reverend, is by many especially cherished for this intercourse of unbroken respect.

At one time when the progress of Harriet Martineau through this country, Angelina Grimke's appearance in public, and the visit of Mrs. Jameson[7] had turned his thoughts to this subject, he expressed high hopes as to what the coming era would bring to woman. He had been much pleased with the dignified courage of Mrs. Jameson in taking up the defence of her sex, in a way from which women usually shrink, because, if they express themselves on such subjects with sufficient force and clearness to do any good, they are exposed to assaults whose vulgarity makes them painful. In intercourse with such a woman, he had shared her indignation at the base injustice, in many respects, and in many regions done to the sex; and been led to think of it far more than ever before. He seemed to think that he might some time write upon the subject. That his aid is withdrawn from the cause is a subject of great regret, for on this question, as on others, he would have known how to sum up the evidence and take, in the noblest spirit, middle ground. He always furnished a platform on which opposing parties could stand, and look at one another under the influence of his mildness and enlightened candor.

Two younger thinkers, men both, have uttered noble prophecies, auspicious for woman. Kinmont, all whose thoughts tended towards the establishment of the reign of love and peace, thought that the inevitable means of this would be an increased predominance given to the idea of woman. Had he lived longer to see the growth of the peace party, the reforms in life and medical practice which seek to substitute water for wine and drugs, pulse[8] for animal food, he would have been confirmed in his view of the way in which the desired changes are to be effected.

In this connection I must mention Shelley,[9] who, like all men of genius, shared the feminine development, and, unlike many, knew it. His life was one of the first pulse-beats in the present reform-growth. He, too, abhorred blood and heat, and, by his system and his song, tended to reinstate a plant-like gentleness in the development of energy. In harmony with this his ideas of marriage were lofty, and of course no less so of woman, her nature, and destiny.

7. Jameson passed through the Northeast in 1836, on her way to Canada. Fuller met Martineau (1802–1876), British author of *Illustrations of Political Economy*, in 1835 during Martineau's tour of the United States. The Grimké appearance was during the late 1830s.

8. Peas.

9. Percy Bysshe Shelley (1792–1822), English poet.

For woman, if by a sympathy as to outward condition, she is led to aid the enfranchisement of the slave, must no less so, by inward tendency, to favor measures which promise to bring the world more thoroughly and deeply into harmony with her nature. When the lamb takes place of the lion as the emblem of nations, both women and men will be as children of one spirit, perpetual learners of the word and doers thereof, not hearers only.

A writer in a late number of the New York Pathfinder, in two articles headed "Femality," has uttered a still more pregnant word than any we have named. He views woman truly from the soul, and not from society, and the depth and leading of his thoughts is proportionably remarkable. He views the feminine nature as a harmonizer of the vehement elements, and this has often been hinted elsewhere; but what he expresses most forcibly is the lyrical, the inspiring and inspired apprehensiveness of her being.

Had I room to dwell upon this topic, I could not say anything so precise, so near the heart of the matter, as may be found in that article; but, as it is, I can only indicate, not declare, my view.

There are two aspects of woman's nature, expressed by the ancients as Muse and Minerva.[1] It is the former to which the writer in the Pathfinder looks. It is the latter which Wordsworth has in mind, when he says,

"With a placid brow,
Which woman ne'er should forfeit, keep thy vow."[2]

The especial genius of woman I believe to be electrical in movement, intuitive in function, spiritual in tendency. She is great not so easily in classification, or re-creation, as in an instinctive seizure of causes, and a simple breathing out of what she receives that has the singleness of life, rather than the selecting or energizing of art.

More native to her is it to be the living model of the artist, than to set apart from herself any one form in objective reality; more native to inspire and receive the poem than to create it. In so far as soul is in her completely developed, all soul is the same; but as far as it is modified in her as woman, it flows, it breathes, it sings, rather than deposits soil, or finishes work, and that which is especially feminine flushes in blossom the face of earth, and pervades like air and water all this seeming solid globe, daily renewing and purifying its life. Such may be the especially feminine element, spoken of as Femality. But it is no more the order of nature that it should be incarnated pure in any form, than that the masculine energy should exist unmingled with it in any form.

Male and female represent the two sides of the great radical dualism. But, in fact, they are perpetually passing into one another. Fluid hardens to solid, solid rushes to fluid. There is no wholly masculine man, no purely feminine woman.

History jeers at the attempts of physiologists to bind great original laws by the forms which flow from them. They make a rule; they say from observation what can and cannot be. In vain! Nature provides exceptions to every rule. She sends women to battle, and sets Hercules spinning;[3] she enables

1. The poetical or artistic aspect, embodied in the Muses, goddesses of song and poetry and the arts and sciences, and the intellectually serene aspect, embodied in Minerva, goddess of wisdom.

2. Slightly misquoted from "Liberty: Sequel to the Preceding" (1835).

3. I.e., sets the strongest men to domestic tasks.

women to bear immense burdens, cold, and frost; she enables the man, who feels maternal love, to nourish his infant like a mother. Of late she plays still gayer pranks. Not only she deprives organizations, but organs, of a necessary end. She enables people to read with the top of the head, and see with the pit of the stomach. Presently she will make a female Newton, and a male Syren.[4]

Man partakes of the feminine in the Apollo, woman of the Masculine as Minerva.

Let us be wise and not impede the soul. Let her work as she will. Let us have one creative energy, one incessant revelation. Let it take what form it will, and let us not bind it by the past to man or woman, black or white. Jove sprang from Rhea, Pallas from Jove.[5] So let it be.

If it has been the tendency of the past remarks to call woman rather to the Minerva side,—if I, unlike the more generous writer, have spoken from society no less than the soul,—let it be pardoned. It is love that has caused this, love for many incarcerated souls, that might be freed could the idea of religious self-dependence be established in them, could the weakening habit of dependence on others be broken up.

Every relation, every gradation of nature, is incalculably precious, but only to the soul which is poised upon itself, and to whom no loss, no change, can bring dull discord, for it is in harmony with the central soul.

If any individual live too much in relations, so that he becomes a stranger to the resources of his own nature, he falls after a while into a distraction, or imbecility, from which he can only be cured by a time of isolation, which gives the renovating fountains time to rise up. With a society it is the same. Many minds, deprived of the traditionary or instinctive means of passing a cheerful existence, must find help in self-impulse or perish. It is therefore that while any elevation, in the view of union, is to be hailed with joy, we shall not decline celibacy as the great fact of the time. It is one from which no vow, no arrangement, can at present save a thinking mind. For now the rowers are pausing on their oars, they wait a change before they can pull together. All tends to illustrate the thought of a wise contemporary. Union is only possible to those who are units. To be fit for relations in time, souls, whether of man or woman, must be able to do without them in the spirit.

It is therefore that I would have woman lay aside all thought, such as she habitually cherishes, of being taught and led by men. I would have her, like the Indian girl, dedicate herself to the Sun, the Sun of Truth, and go no where if his beams did not make clear the path. I would have her free from compromise, from complaisance, from helplessness, because I would have her good enough and strong enough to love one and all beings, from the fulness, not the poverty of being.

Men, as at present instructed, will not help this work, because they also are under the slavery of habit. I have seen with delight their poetic impulses. A sister is the fairest ideal, and how nobly Wordsworth, and even Byron, have written of a sister.[6]

4. In this inversion of sexual stereotypes, a male would be as alluring as the Syrens (or Sirens), Greek sea nymphs who lured mariners into shipwreck on the rocks surrounding their island. Isaac Newton (1642–1727), English mathematician.

5. In Greek mythology, Rhea, the sister and wife of Cronus, and mother of Zeus (known to the Romans as Jove). Pallas Athena sprang from Jove's skull, fully grown and fully armed.

6. Fuller alludes to the various tributes by William Wordsworth to his sister Dorothy and Lord Byron to his half-sister Augusta Leigh.

There is no sweeter sight than to see a father with his little daughter. Very vulgar men become refined to the eye when leading a little girl by the hand. At that moment the right relation between the sexes seems established, and you feel as if the man would aid in the noblest purpose, if you ask him in behalf of his little daughter. Once two fine figures stood before me, thus. The father of very intellectual aspect, his falcon eye softened by affection as he looked down on his fair child, she the image of himself, only more graceful and brilliant in expression. I was reminded of Southey's Kehama,[7] when lo, the dream was rudely broken. They were talking of education, and he said.

"I shall not have Maria brought too forward. If she knows too much, she will never find a husband; superior women hardly ever can."

"Surely," said his wife, with a blush, "you wish Maria to be as good and wise as she can, whether it will help her to marriage or not."

"No," he persisted, "I want her to have a sphere and a home, and some one to protect her when I am gone."

It was a trifling incident, but made a deep impression. I felt that the holiest relations fail to instruct the unprepared and perverted mind. If this man, indeed, would have looked at it on the other side, he was the last that would have been willing to have been taken himself for the home and protection he could give, but would have been much more likely to repeat the tale of Alcibiades[8] with his phials.

But men do *not* look at both sides, and women must leave off asking them and being influenced by them, but retire within themselves, and explore the groundwork of being till they find their peculiar secret. Then when they come forth again, renovated and baptized, they will know how to turn all dross to gold, and will be rich and free though they live in a hut, tranquil, if in a crowd. Then their sweet singing shall not be from passionate impulse, but the lyrical overflow of a divine rapture, and a new music shall be elucidated from this many-chorded world.

Grant her then for a while the armor and the javelin.[9] Let her put from her the press of other minds and meditate in virgin loneliness. The same idea shall reappear in due time as Muse, or Ceres,[1] the all-kindly, patient Earth-Spirit.

I tire every one with my Goethean illustrations. But it cannot be helped.

Goethe, the great mind which gave itself absolutely to the leadings of truth, and let rise through him the waves which are still advancing through the century, was its intellectual prophet. Those who know him, see, daily, his thought fulfilled more and more, and they must speak of it, till his name weary and even nauseate, as all great names have in their time. And I cannot spare the reader, if such there be, his wonderful sight as to the prospects and wants of women.

As his Wilhelm grows in life and advances in wisdom, he becomes acquainted with women of more and more character, rising from Mariana to Macaria.[2]

7. *The Curse of Kehama* (1810), by the English writer Robert Southey (1774–1843).
8. Athenian general (c. 450–404 B.C.E.), who was convicted for drunkenly imitating sacred rituals.
9. The weapons of Athena, Greek goddess of wisdom.
1. The Roman goddess of agriculture.
2. Feminine characters in Johann Wolfgang von Goethe's *Wilhelm Meister's Apprenticeship* (1796); other female characters from the same book are named just below.

Macaria, bound with the heavenly bodies in fixed revolutions, the centre of all relations, herself unrelated, expresses the Minerva side.

Mignon, the electrical, inspired lyrical nature.

All these women, though we see them in relations, we can think of as unrelated. They all are very individual, yet seem nowhere restrained. They satisfy for the present, yet arouse an infinite expectation.

The economist Theresa, the benevolent Natalia, the fair Saint, have chosen a path, but their thoughts are not narrowed to it. The functions of life to them are not ends, but suggestions.

Thus to them all things are important, because none is necessary. Their different characters have fair play, and each is beautiful in its minute indications, for nothing is enforced or conventional, but everything, however slight, grows from the essential life of the being.

Mignon and Theresa wear male attire when they like, and it is graceful for them to do so, while Macaria is confined to her arm chair behind the green curtain, and the Fair Saint could not bear a speck of dust on her robe.

All things are in their places in this little world because all is natural and free, just as "there is room for everything out of doors." Yet all is rounded in by natural harmony which will always arise where Truth and Love are sought in the light of freedom.

Goethe's book bodes an era of freedom like its own, of "extraordinary generous seeking," and new revelations. New individualities shall be developed in the actual world, which shall advance upon it as gently as the figures come out upon his canvass.

A profound thinker has said "no married woman can represent the female world, for she belongs to her husband. The idea of woman must be represented by a virgin."

But that is the very fault of marriage, and of the present relation between the sexes, that the woman does belong to the man, instead of forming a whole with him. Were it otherwise there would be no such limitation to the thought.

Woman, self-centred, would never be absorbed by any relation; it would be only an experience to her as to man. It is a vulgar error that love, *a* love to woman is her whole existence; she also is born for Truth and Love in their universal energy. Would she but assume her inheritance, Mary would not be the only Virgin Mother. Not Manzoni[3] alone would celebrate in his wife the virgin mind with the maternal wisdom and conjugal affections. The soul is ever young, ever virgin.

And will not she soon appear? The woman who shall vindicate their birthright for all women; who shall teach them what to claim, and how to use what they obtain? Shall not her name be for her era Victoria, for her country and her life Virginia?[4] Yet predictions are rash; she herself must teach us to give her the fitting name.

1843

3. Another allusion to the preface to Manzoni's *Adelchi*.

4. I.e., shall not her character include power (such as made Victoria so fit a name for a queen) and purity?

Review of *Narrative of the Life of Frederick Douglass, An American Slave*[1]

Frederick Douglass has been for some time a prominent member of the Abolition party. He is said to be an excellent speaker—can speak from a thorough personal experience—and has upon the audience, beside, the influence of a strong character and uncommon talents. In the book before us he has put into the story of his life the thoughts, the feelings and the adventures that have been so affecting through the living voice; nor are they less so from the printed page. He has had the courage to name the persons, times and places, thus exposing himself to obvious danger, and setting the seal on his deep convictions as to the religious need of speaking the whole truth. Considered merely as a narrative, we have never read one more simple, true, coherent, and warm with genuine feeling. It is an excellent piece of writing, and on that score to be prized as a specimen of the powers of the Black Race, which Prejudice persists in disputing. We prize highly all evidence of this kind, and it is becoming more abundant. The Cross of the Legion of Honor has just been conferred in France on Dumas and Souliè,[2] both celebrated in the paths of light literature. Dumas, whose father was a General in the French Army, is a Mulatto; Souliè, a Quadroon. He went from New-Orleans, where, though to the eye a white man, yet, as known to have African blood in his veins, he could never have enjoyed the privileges due to a human being. Leaving the Land of Freedom, he found himself free to develope the powers that God has given.

Two wise and candid thinkers,—the Scotchman, Kinmont, prematurely lost to this country, of which he was so faithful and generous a student, and the late Dr. Channing,[3]—both thought that the African Race had in them a peculiar element, which, if it could be assimilated with those imported among us from Europe, would give to genius a development, and to the energies of character a balance and harmony beyond what has been seen heretofore in the history of the world. Such an element is indicated in their lowest estate by a talent for melody, a ready skill at imitation and adaptation, an almost indestructible elasticity of nature. It is to be remarked in the writings both of Souliè and Dumas, full of faults but glowing with plastic life and fertile in invention. The same torrid energy and saccharine fullness may be felt in the writings of this Douglass, though his life being one of action or resistance, was less favorable to *such* powers than one of a more joyous flow might have been.

The book is prefaced by two communications,—one from Garrison, and one from Wendell Phillips.[4] That from the former is in his usual over

1. The text is from the *New York Daily Tribune*, June 10, 1845.
2. The novelist and playwright Frédéric Souliè (1800–1847) was best known for his romance *The Memoirs of the Devil* (1837–38). Alexandre Dumas (1802–1870) was acclaimed for such historical novels as *The Three Musketeers* (1844) and *The Count of Monte Cristo* (1845–46).
3. Both the Boston Unitarian minister William Ellery Channing (1780–1842) and the Scottish-born philosopher Alexander Kinmont (1799–1838) argued that blacks had distinctive characteristics—such as loyalty to friends and family, and attachment to local places—helping to make them natural Christians. See Channing's "Slavery" (1836) and Kinmont's *Twelve Lectures on the Natural History of Man* (1837).
4. Prominent Boston abolitionist (1811–1884). William Lloyd Garrison (1805–1879), the most influential white abolitionist leader of the 1830s and 1840s, published Douglass's *Narrative*.

emphatic style. His motives and his course have been noble and generous. We look upon him with high respect, but he has indulged in violent invective and denunciation till he has spoiled the temper of his mind. Like a man who has been in the habit of screaming himself hoarse to make the deaf hear, he can no longer pitch his voice on a key agreeable to common ears. Mr. Phillips's remarks are equally decided, without this exaggeration in the tone. Douglass himself seems very just and temperate. We feel that his view, even of those who have injured him most, may be relied upon. He knows how to allow for motives and influences. Upon the subject of Religion, he speaks with great force, and not more than our own sympathies can respond to. The inconsistencies of Slaveholding professors of religion cry to Heaven. We are not disposed to detest, or refuse communion with them. Their blindness is but one form of that prevalent fallacy which substitutes a creed for a faith, a ritual for a life. We have seen too much of this system of atonement not to know that those who adopt it often began with good intentions, and are, at any rate, in their mistakes worthy of the deepest pity. But that is no reason why the truth should not be uttered, trumpet-tongued, about the thing. "Bring no more vain oblations";[5] sermons must daily be preached anew on that text. Kings, five hundred years ago, built Churches with the spoils of War; Clergymen to-day command Slaves to obey a Gospel which they will not allow them to read, and call themselves Christians amid the curses of their fellow men.—The world ought to get on a little faster than that, if there be really any principle of improvement in it. The Kingdom of Heaven may not at the beginning have dropped seed larger than a mustard-seed, but even from that we had a right to expect a fuller growth than can be believed to exist, when we read such a book as this of Douglass. Unspeakable affecting is the fact that he never saw his mother at all by day-light.

> "I do not recollect of ever seeing my mother by the light of day. She was with me in the night. She would lie down with me, and get me to sleep, but long before I waked she was gone."

The following extract[6] presents a suitable answer to the hacknied argument drawn by the defender of Slavery from the songs of the Slave, and is also a good specimen of the powers of observation and manly heart of the writer. We wish that every one may read his book and see what a mind might have been stifled in bondage,—what a man may be subjected to the insults of spendthrift dandies, or the blows of mercenary brutes, in whom there is no whiteness except of the skin, no humanity except in the outward form, and of whom the Avenger will not fail yet to demand—"Where is thy brother?"

1845

5. Isaiah 1.13.
6. Fuller reprinted much of chapter 2 of the *Narrative* immediately following her review.

Fourth of July[1]

The bells ring; the cannon rouse the echoes along the river shore: the boys sally forth with shouts and little flags and crackers enough to frighten all the people they meet from sunrise to sunset. The orator is conning for the last time the speech in which he has vainly attempted to season with some new spice the yearly panegyric upon our country; its happiness and glory; the audience is putting on its best bib and tucker,[2] and its blandest expression to listen.

And yet, no heart, we think, can beat to-day with one pulse of genuine, noble joy. Those who have obtained their selfish objects will not take especial pleasure in thinking of them to-day, while to unbiased minds must come sad thoughts of National Honor soiled in the eyes of other nations, of a great inheritance, risked, if not forfeited.

Much has been achieved in this country since the first Declaration of Independence. America is rich and strong; she has shown great talent and energy; vast prospects of aggrandizement open before her. But the noble sentiment which she expressed in her early youth is tarnished; she has shown that righteousness is not her chief desire, and her name is no longer a watchword for the highest hopes to the rest of the world. She knows this, but takes it very easily; she feels that she is growing richer and more powerful, and that seems to suffice her.

These facts are deeply saddening to those who can pronounce the words 'My Country' with pride and peace only so far as steadfast virtues, generous impulses find their home in that country. They cannot be satisfied with superficial benefits, with luxuries and the means of obtaining knowledge which are multiplied for them. They could rejoice in full hands and a busy brain, if the soul were expanding and the heart pure, but, the higher conditions being violated, what is done cannot be done for good.

Such thoughts shadow patriot minds as the cannon-peal burst upon the ear. This year, which declares that the people at large consent to cherish and extend Slavery as one of our "domestic institutions," takes from the patriot his home. This year, which attests their insatiate love of wealth and power, quenches the flame upon the altar.

Yet there remains the good part which cannot be taken away. If nations go astray, the narrow path may always be found and followed by the individual man. It is hard, hard indeed, when politics and trade are mixed up with evils so mighty that he scarcely dares touch them for fear of being defiled. He finds his activity checked in great natural outlets by the scruples of conscience. He cannot enjoy the free use of his limbs, glowing upon a favorable tide; but struggling, panting, must fix his eyes upon his aim and fight against the current to reach it. It is not easy, it is very hard just now to realize the blessings of Independence.

For what is Independence if it do not lead to Freedom?—Freedom from fraud and meanness, from selfishness, from public opinion so far as it does not consent with the still small voice of one's better self?

1. The text is from the *New York Daily Tribune*, July 4, 1845.

2. Best clothing (colloquial).

Yet there is still a great and worthy part to play. This country presents great temptations to ill, but also great inducements to good. Her health and strength are so remarkable; her youth so full of life that disease cannot yet have taken deep hold of her. It has bewildered her brain, made her steps totter, fevered, but not yet tainted, her blood. Things are still in that state when ten just men may save the city. A few men are wanted, able to think and act upon principles of an eternal value. The safety of the country must lie in a few such men—men who have achieved the genuine independence, independence of wrong, of violence, of falsehood.

We want individuals to whom all eyes may turn as an example of the practicability of virtue. We want shining examples. We want deeply rooted characters, who cannot be moved by flattery, by fear, even by hope, for they work in faith. The opportunity for such men is great, they will not be burnt at the stake in their prime for bearing witness to the truth, yet they will be tested most severely in their adherence to it. There is nothing to hinder them from learning what is true and best, no physical tortures will be inflicted on them for expressing it. Let men feel that in private lives, more than in public measures must the salvation of the country lie. If that country has so widely veered from the course she prescribed to herself and that the hope of the world prescribed to her, it must be because she had not men ripened and confirmed for better things. They leaned too carelessly on one another; they had not deepened and purified the private lives from which the public must spring, as the verdure of the plain from the fountains of the hills.

What a vast influence is given by sincerity alone? The bier of General Jackson[3] has just passed, upbearing a golden urn. The men who placed it there lament his departure and esteem the measures which had led this country to her present position wise and good. The other side esteem them unwise, unjust, and disastrous in their consequences. But both respect him thus far that his conduct was boldly sincere. The sage of Quincy![4] Men differ in their estimate of his abilities. None, probably, esteem his mind as one of the first magnitude. But both sides, all men, are influenced by the bold integrity of his character. Mr. Calhoun[5] speaks straight out what he thinks. So far as this straightforwardness goes, he confers the benefits of virtue. If a character be uncorrupted, whatever bias it takes, it thus far is good and does good. It may help others to a higher, wiser, larger independence than its own.

We know not where to look for an example of all or many of the virtues we would seek from the man who is to begin the new dynasty that is needed of Fathers of the Country. The Country needs to be born again; she is polluted with the lust of power, the lust of gain. She needs Fathers good enough to be God-fathers—men who will stand sponsors at the baptism with *all* they possess, with all the goodness they can cherish, and all the wisdom they can win, to lead this child the way she should go, and never one step in another. Are there not in schools and colleges the boys who will become such men? Are there not those on the threshold of manhood who have not

3. Andrew Jackson (1767–1845), seventh president of the United States (1829–37), had died on June 8, approximately a month before Fuller wrote this column.

4. John Quincy Adams (1767–1848), sixth president of the United States (1825–29). During the 1830s and 1840s, he served as a congressman and actively fought against the extension of slavery.

5. John C. Calhoun (1782–1850), South Carolina congressman who espoused states' rights and defended slavery.

yet chosen the broad way into which the multitude rushes, led by the banner on which, strange to say, the royal Eagle is blazoned, together with the word Expediency? Let him decline that road, and take the narrow, thorny path where Integrity leads, though with no prouder emblem than the dove. He may there find the needed remedy which, like the white root, the *Moly*, detected by the patient and resolved Odysseus,[6] shall have power to restore the herd of men, disguised by the enchantress to whom they had willingly yielded in the forms of brutes, to the stature and beauty of men.

1845

From Things and Thoughts in Europe[1]

Letter XVIII

This letter will reach the United States about the 1st of January; and it may not be impertinent to offer a few New-Year's reflections. Every new year, indeed, confirms the old thoughts, but also presents them under some new aspects.

The American in Europe, if a thinking mind, can only become more American. In some respects it is a great pleasure to be here. Although we have an independent political existence, our position toward Europe, as to Literature and the Arts, is still that of a colony, and one feels the same joy here that is experienced by the colonist in returning to the parent home. What was but picture to us becomes reality; remote allusions and derivations trouble no more: we see the pattern of the stuff, and understand the whole tapestry. There is a gradual clearing up on many points, and many baseless notions and crude fancies are dropped. Even the post-haste passage of the business American through the great cities, escorted by cheating couriers, and ignorant *valets de place*,[2] unable to hold intercourse with the natives of the country, and passing all his leisure hours with his countrymen, who know no more than himself, clears his mind of some mistakes—lifts some mists from his horizon.

There are three species: first, the servile American—a being utterly shallow, thoughtless, worthless. He comes abroad to spend his money and indulge his tastes. His object in Europe is to have fashionable clothes, good foreign cookery, to know some titled persons, and furnish himself with coffee-house gossip, which he wins importance at home by retailing among those less traveled, and as uninformed as himself.

I look with unspeakable contempt on this class—a class which has all the thoughtlessness and partiality of the exclusive classes in Europe, without any of their refinement, or the chivalric feeling which still sparkles among them here and there. However, though these willing serfs in a free age do

6. In Homer's *Odyssey*, Odysseus (Ulysses) is able to resist Circe's efforts to turn him into a swine by eating the magical herb moly.

1. The text is from the *New York Daily Tribune*, January 1, 1848. Between August 23, 1846 and January 6, 1850, Fuller published thirty-seven dispatches in the *Daily Tribune* under the title of "Things and Thoughts in Europe." She arrived in Rome in March 1847 and quickly became an enthusiastic supporter of the Italian revolutionaries calling for national unification and independence. This letter was written in Rome in November or December 1847.

2. Local servants (French).

some little hurt, and cause some annoyance at present, it cannot last: our country is fated to a grand, independent existence, and, as its laws develop, these parasites of a bygone period must whither and drop away.

Then there is the conceited American, instinctively bristling and proud of—he knows not what.—He does not see, not he, that the history of Humanity for many centuries is likely to have produced results it requires some training, some devotion, to appreciate and profit by. With his great clumsy hands, only fitted to work on a steam-engine, he seizes the old Cremona violin,[3] makes it shriek with anguish in his grasp, and then declares he thought it was all humbug before he came, and now he knows it; that there is not really any music in these old things; that the frogs in one of our swamps makes much finer, for *they* are young and alive. To him the etiquettes of courts and camps, the ritual of the Church, seem simply silly—and no wonder, profoundly ignorant as he is of their origin and meaning. Just so the legends which are the subjects of pictures, the profound myths which are represented in the antique marbles, amaze and revolt him; as, indeed, such things need to be judged of by another standard from that of the Connecticut Blue-Laws.[4] He criticises severely pictures, feeling quite sure that his natural senses are better means of judgment than the rules of connoisseurs—not feeling that to see such objects mental vision as well as fleshly eyes are needed, and that something is aimed at in Art beyond the imitation of the commonest forms of Nature.

This is Jonathan[5] in the sprawling state, the booby truant, not yet aspiring enough to be a good school-boy. Yet in his folly there is meaning; add thought and culture to his independence, and he will be a man of might: he is not a creature without hope, like the thick-skinned dandy of the class first specified.

The Artistes form a class by themselves. Yet among them, though seeking special aims by special means, may also be found the lineaments of these two classes, as well as of the third, of which I am now to speak.

3d. The thinking American—a man who, recognizing the immense advantage of being born to a new world and on a virgin soil, yet does not wish one seed from the Past to be lost. He is anxious to gather and carry back with him all that will bear a new climate and new culture. Some will dwindle; others will attain a bloom and stature unknown before. He wishes to gather them clean, free from noxious insects. He wishes to give them a fair trial in his new world. And that he may know the conditions under which he may best place them in that new world, he does not neglect to study their history in this.

The history of our planet in some moments seems so painfully mean and little, such trifling bafflings and failures to compensate some brilliant successes—such a crashing of the mass of men beneath the feet of a few, and these, too, often the least worthy—such a small drop of honey to each cup of gall, and, in many cases, so mingled, that it is never one moment in life purely tasted,—above all, so little achieved for Humanity as a whole, such tides of war and pestilence intervening to blot out the traces of each

3. Famous violin made in Cremona, Italy, by Antonio Amati (1555–1640).

4. Such laws demanded the closing of businesses on Sundays and were aimed at curbing the sale of alcohol.

5. Typical, ordinary American.

triumph, that no wonder if the strongest soul sometimes pauses aghast! No wonder if the many indolently console themselves with gross joys and frivolous prizes. Yes! those men *are* worthy of admiration who can carry this cross faithfully through fifty years; it is a great while for all the agonies that beset a lover of good, a lover of men; it makes a soul worthy of a speedier ascent, a more productive ministry in the next sphere. Blessed are they who ever keep that portion of pure, generous love with which they began life! How blessed those who have deepened the fountains, and have enough to spare for the thirst of others! Some such there are; and, feeling that, with all the excuses for failure, still only the sight of those who triumph gives a meaning to life or makes its pangs endurable, we must arise and follow.

Eighteen hundred years of this Christian culture in these European Kingdoms, a great theme never lost sight of, a mighty idea, an adorable history to which the hearts of men invariably cling, yet are genuine results rare as grains of gold in the river's sandy bed! Where is the genuine Democracy to which the rights of all men are holy? where the child-like wisdom learning all through life more and more of the will of God? where the aversion to falsehood in all its myriad disguises of cant, vanity, covetousness, so clear to be read in all the history of Jesus of Nazareth? Modern Europe is the sequel to that history, and see this hollow England, with its monstrous wealth and cruel poverty, its conventional life and low, practical aims; see this poor France, so full of talent, so adroit, yet so shallow and glossy still, which could not escape from a false position with all its baptism of blood; see that lost Poland and this Italy bound down by treacherous hands in all the force of genius; see Russia with its brutal Czar and innumerable slaves; see Austria and its royalty that represents nothing, and its people who, as people, are and have nothing! If we consider the amount of truth that has really been spoken out in the world, and the love that has beat in private hearts—how Genius has decked each springtime with such splendid flowers, conveying each one enough of instruction in its life of harmonious energy, and how continually, unquenchably the spark of faith has striven to burst into flame and light up the Universe—the public failure seems amazing, even monstrous.

Still Europe toils and struggles with her idea, and, at this moment, all things bode and declare a new outbreak of the fire, to destroy the old palaces of crime! May it fertilize also many vineyards!—Here at this moment a successor of St. Peter, after the lapse of two thousand years, is called "Utopian" by a part of this Europe, because he strives to get some food to the mouths of the *leaner* of his flock. A wonderful state of things, and which leaves as the best argument against despair that men do not, *cannot* despair amid such dark experiences—and thou, my country! will thou not be more true? does no greater success await thee? All things have so conspired to teach, to aid! A new world, a new chance, with oceans to wall in the new thought against interference from the old!—Treasures of all kinds, gold, silver, corn, marble, to provide for every physical need! A noble, constant, starlike soul, an Italian,[6] led the way to its shores, and, in the first days, the strong, the pure, those too brave, too sincere for the life of the Old World hastened to

6. Christopher Columbus (1451–1506), born in Genoa.

people them. A generous struggle then shook off what was foreign and gave the nation a glorious start for a worthy goal. Men rocked the cradle of its hopes, great, firm, disinterested men who saw, who wrote, as the basis of all that was to be done, a statement of the rights, the inborn rights of men, which, if fully interpreted and acted upon, leaves nothing to be desired.

Yet, oh Eagle, whose early flight showed this clear sight of the Sun, how often dost thou near the ground, how show the vulture in these later days! Thou wert to be the advance-guard of Humanity, the herald of all Progress; how often hast thou betrayed this high commission! Fain would the tongue in clear triumphant accents draw example from thy story, to encourage the hearts of those who almost faint and die beneath the old oppressions. But we must stammer and blush when we speak of many things. I take pride here that I may really say the Liberty of the Press works well, and that the checks and balances naturally evolve from it which suffice to its government. I may say the minds of our people are alert, and that Talent has a free chance to rise. It is much. But dare I say that political ambition is not as darkly sullied as in other countries? Dare I say that men of most influence in political life are those who represent most virtue or even intellectual power? Is it easy to find names in that career of which I can speak with enthusiasm? Must I not confess in my country to a boundless lust of gain? Must I not confess to the weakest vanity, which bristles and blusters at each foolish taunt of the foreign press; and must I not admit that the men who make these undignified rejoinders seek and find popularity so? Must I not confess that there is as yet no antidote cordially adopted that will defend even that great, rich country against the evils that have grown out of the commercial system in the old world? Can I say our social laws are generally better, or show a nobler insight to the wants of man and woman? I do, indeed, say what I believe, that voluntary association for improvement in these particulars will be the grand means for my nation to grow and give a nobler harmony to the coming age. But it is only of a small minority that I can say they as yet seriously take to heart these things; that they earnestly meditate on what is wanted for the country,—for mankind,—for our cause is, indeed, the cause of all mankind at present. Could we succeed, really succeed, combine a deep religious love with practical development, the achievements of Genius with the happiness of the multitude, we might believe Man had now reached a commanding point in his ascent, and would stumble and faint no more. Then there is this horrible cancer of Slavery, and this wicked War,[7] that has grown out of it. How dare I speak of these things here? I listen to the same arguments against the emancipation of Italy, that are used against the emancipation of our blacks; the same arguments in favor of the spollation[8] of Poland as for the conquest of Mexico. I find the cause of tyranny and wrong everywhere the same—and lo! my Country the darkest offender, because with the least excuse, foresworn to the high calling with which she was called,—no champion of the rights of men, but a robber and a jailor; the scourge hid behind her banner; her eyes fixed, not on the stars, but on the possession of other men.

7. The war with Mexico (1846–48), which many Northerners believed was intended to expand slavery into the southwestern territories.
8. Spoliation.

How it pleases me here to think of the Abolitionists! I could never endure to be with them at home, they were so tedious, often so narrow, always so rabid and exaggerated in their tone.

But, after all, they had a high motive, something eternal in their desire and life; and, if it was not the only thing worth thinking of it was really something worth living and dying for to free a great nation from such a terrible blot, such a threatening plague. God strengthen them and make them wise to achieve their purpose!

I please myself, too, with remembering some ardent souls among the American youth who, I trust, will yet expand and help to give soul to the huge, over fed, too hastily grown-up body. May they be constant. "Were Man but constant he were perfect!"[9] it has been said; and it is true that he who could be constant to those moments in which he has been truly human—not brutal, not mechanical—is on the sure path to his perfection and to effectual service of the Universe.

It is to the youth that Hope addresses itself, to those who yet burn with aspiration, who are not hardened in their sins. But I dare not expect too much of them. I am not very old, yet of those who, in life's morning, I saw touched by the light of a high hope, many have seceded. Some have become voluptuaries; some mere family men, who think it is quite life enough to win bread for half a dozen people and treat them decently; others are lost through indolence and vacillation. Yet some remain constant. "I have witnessed many a shipwreck, yet still beat noble hearts."

I have found many among the youth of England, of France—of Italy also—full of high desire, but will they have courage and purity to fight the battle through in the sacred, the immortal band? Of some of them I believe it and await the proof. If a few succeed amid the trial, we have not lived and loved in vain.

To these, the heart of my country, a Happy New Year! I do not know what I have written. I have merely yielded to my feelings in thinking of America; but something of true love must be in these lines—receive them kindly, my friends; it is, by itself, some merit for printed words to be sincere.

1848

9. Shakespeare's *The Two Gentlemen of Verona* 5.4.111–12.

Slavery, Race, and the Making of American Literature

In 1820 the English critic Sidney Smith became exasperated by the boasting of American literary nationalists, and in the pages of the *Edinburgh Review* he famously asked: "In the four quarters of the globe, who reads an American book? or goes to an American play? or looks at an American picture or statue?" His questions about Americans' self-proclaimed literary, cultural, and national superiority culminated with the most withering question of all: "Finally, under which of the old tyrannical governments of Europe is every sixth man a Slave, whom his fellow-creatures may buy and sell and torture?" For Smith, the making of American literature and culture could not be separated from the making of the nation itself. The paradoxical fact that a nation founded on the principles of equality would develop into a slaveholding republic was not lost on writers of the early national and antebellum period. The vast majority of the writers in this volume of *The Norton Anthology of American Literature* confronted issues of slavery and race at some point during their careers. Whether central to their writings, as was the case with Douglass, early Harriet Beecher Stowe, William Wells Brown, and others, or of peripheral interest, as was true, say, for Sedgwick and Fern, slavery could not be ignored. Tensions between the realities of slavery and the ideals of freedom inform much writing of the period.

The selections on slavery and race offered here take off from Thomas Jefferson, author of the first draft of the Declaration of Independence, who coined many of its most memorable phrases. Jefferson's *Notes on the State of Virginia* celebrated the democratic ideals of the Declaration while making clear that he regarded those ideals as best realized by whites. In the classificatory and hierarchical mode of the Enlightenment period, he presents black people as inferior to white people. Though he leaves the question of race open to further empirical analysis, his observations nevertheless helped give rise to the racial ethnological "science" of the nineteenth century, which invariably presented whites as superior to blacks. African American writers regularly sought to counter such claims, and in his *Appeal*, David Walker directly responds, or talks back, to Jefferson. Much African American writing of the period, and indeed much antislavery writing of the period, as we can see from the selection by William Lloyd Garrison, sought to abolish slavery and challenge the hierarchical claims of the racial ethnologists by invoking (or reclaiming) the principles of the Declaration. These principles were also insisted on by writers such as Emerson, Melville, Thoreau, and Whitman as they prodded readers to comprehend their own "enslavement" to cultural conventions. As Ishmael remarks at the opening of *Moby-Dick*: "Who aint a slave?" For many women writers of the period, from Lydia Maria Child to Harriet Beecher Stowe, slavery also raised questions about patriarchy and women's rights. As the selections from Angelina Grimké and Sojourner Truth suggest, women reformers saw themselves as especially qualified to contest slavery, which they regarded both as a specific institution in the slave South and as one of many manifestations of patriarchal power.

The best-selling literary work of the antebellum period was Harriet Beecher Stowe's antislavery novel *Uncle Tom's Cabin*; published in 1852, it sold around one million copies by the end of the decade. Inspired by feminist-abolitionists like Angelina Grimké, Stowe emphasized the importance of women to antislavery reform. In the manner of David Walker, Frederick Douglass, and numerous other African American writers, she lamented the unfinished work of the American Revolution by having the rebellious slave George Harris invoke the ideals of the Declaration. Like many Americans of the time, Stowe, even in a novel attacking slavery, seemed to accept notions of racial difference, presenting whites as unduly aggressive and blacks as domestic and religious to an extreme. The novel polarized the nation, spawning numerous other antislavery works in the North, along with a number of proslavery, anti–*Uncle Tom's Cabin* writings in the South. The debates on slavery exerted an especially strong influence on the literature of the 1840s and 1850s. Melville wrote a novella, "Benito Cereno," about a slave rebellion; Whitman in "Song of Myself" imagined himself offering succor to a fugitive slave; and Thoreau in "Slavery in Massachusetts" conceived of a Massachusetts that supported the Fugitive Slave Law of 1850 as a version of hell. Race, too, infused writings of the period, even texts that may not seem to be overtly about race. If whiteness was the culture's default and "superior" category of human existence, then, for many white writers blackness posed the threat (and sometimes appeal) of a dangerous otherness. Thus Poe's "The Black Cat" or Hawthorne's presentation of the "black" Chillingworth and Mistress Hibbens in *The Scarlet Letter* may well be inflected by anxieties about race.

In 1857, the Supreme Court ruled in the case of *Dred Scott v. Sanford* that blacks could never become U.S. citizens and were inferior to whites. That ruling, which robbed Jefferson's Declaration of Independence of its ambiguities and potential, made clear that the debates on slavery and race were debates about the nation. In the final selection here, the black nationalist Martin R. Delany, as if anticipating the Dred Scott decision, argues in his 1854 "Political Destiny" that disenfranchised African Americans should consider leaving the United States. Similarly, in William Wells Brown's *Clotel*, the surviving black characters choose to live in Europe; in Frederick Douglass's "The Heroic Slave," the black rebel Madison Washington ends up in Nassau. And though Harriet Jacobs manages to escape from slavery to New York City, she presents herself at the end of *Incidents in the Life of a Slave Girl* as continuing to live in a "free" state that is not as hospitable to black people as England. Most African American leaders committed themselves to the Civil War effort, but the problems raised by slavery and racism in the antebellum period would continue to engage writers of the Reconstruction era and beyond.

THOMAS JEFFERSON

The Declaration of Independence, drafted in 1776 by the Virginian Thomas Jefferson (1743–1826), declared that "all men are created equal." Those resonant words helped inspire the American Revolution and the subsequent development of the nation's democratic institutions. Several years after drafting the Declaration, Jefferson explored the possibility of ending slavery in Virginia, and at various times in his life he wrote about slavery as an evil, remarking in his 1787 *Notes on the State of Virginia*, for example, that the "whole commerce between master and slave is a perpetual exercise of the most boisterous passions, the most unremitting despotism on the one part, and degrading submission on the other." Yet Jefferson, the nation's third president (1801–9), was a slaveowner who, recent DNA evidence suggests, had at least one child with his slave Sally Hemings; at his death, he manumitted only slaves in the Hemings family. Some therefore view him as a hypocrite who celebrated human liberty while defending Southerners' rights to enslave black people; others regard him as a visionary Founding Father who, despite being influenced by the racist ideologies current in his day, gave the nation's democratic ideals their most powerful written expression. At the time that he wrote *Notes on the State of Virginia*, a book intended primarily for European readers, Jefferson disapproved of slavery, but his antislavery views were grounded in beliefs in whites' superiority to blacks. In later life, as he became economically dependent on his slaves, he became more of a defender of the South's rights to own slaves, though he hoped for a national future in which slavery would come to an end and blacks would be colonized to other countries. As the subsequent selection from David Walker makes clear, the free blacks of the antebellum period were particularly troubled by Jefferson's writings, even as they sought to reinvigorate the principles of his Declaration. The selection from *Notes* is taken from *The Works of Thomas Jefferson* (1904), ed. Paul Leicester Ford.

From Notes on the State of Virginia

* * *

It will probably be asked, Why not retain and incorporate the blacks into the state, and thus save the expence of supplying by importation of white settlers, the vacancies they will leave?[1] Deep rooted prejudices entertained by the whites; ten thousand recollections, by the blacks, of the injuries they have sustained; new provocations; the real distinctions which nature has made; and many other circumstances will divide us into parties, and produce convulsions, which will probably never end but in the extermination of the one or the other race.—To these objections, which are political, may be added others, which are physical and moral. The first difference which strikes us is that of colour. Whether the black of the negro resides in the reticular membrane between the skin and scarfskin,[2] or in the scarfskin itself; whether it proceeds from the colour of the blood, the colour of the bile, or from that of some other secretion, the difference is fixed in nature, and is as real as if its seat and cause were better known to us. And is this difference of no importance? Is it not the foundation of a greater or less share of beauty in the two races? Are not the fine mixtures of red and white, the expressions of every passion by greater or less suffusions of colour in the one, preferable to that eternal monotony, which reigns in the countenances, that immovable veil of black which covers all the emotions of the other race? Add to these, flowing hair, a more elegant symmetry of form, their own judgment in favour of the whites, declared by their preference of them as uniformly as in the preference of the Oran ootan[3] for the black woman over those of his own species. The circumstance of superior beauty, is thought worthy attention in the propagation of our horses, dogs, and other domestic animals; why not in that of man? Besides those of colour, figure and hair, there are other physical distinctions proving a difference of race. They have less hair on the face and body. They secrete less by the kidnies, and more by the glands of the skin, which gives them a very strong and disagreeable odour.

1. In the text, Jefferson had just proposed the possibility of emancipating some of the slaves and shipping them "to other parts of the world."

2. The outermost layer of skin.

3. Orangutan.

This greater degree of transpiration, renders them more tolerant of heat, and less so of cold than the whites. Perhaps too a difference of structure in the pulmonary apparatus, which a late ingenious experimentalist[4] has discovered to be the principal regulator of animal heat, may have disabled them from extricating, in the act of inspiration, so much of that fluid from the outer air, or obliged them in expiration, to part with more of it. They seem to require less sleep. A black after hard labour through the day, will be induced by the slightest amusements to sit up till midnight or later, though knowing he must be out with the first dawn of the morning. They are at least as brave, and more adventuresome. But this may perhaps proceed from a want of forethought, which prevents their seeing a danger till it be present. When present, they do not go through it with more coolness or steadiness than the whites. They are more ardent after their female; but love seems with them to be an eager desire, than a tender delicate mixture of sentiment and sensation. Their griefs are transient. Those numberless afflictions, which render it doubtful whether heaven has given life to us in mercy or in wrath, are less felt, and sooner forgotten with them. In general, their existence appears to participate more of sensation than reflection. To this must be ascribed their disposition to sleep when abstracted from their diversions, and unemployed in labour. An animal whose body is at rest, and who does not reflect, must be disposed to sleep of course. Comparing them by their faculties of memory, reason, and imagination, it appears to me that in memory they are equal to the whites; in reason much inferior, as I think one could scarcely be found capable of tracing and comprehending the investigations of Euclid:[5] and that in imagination they are dull, tasteless, and anomalous. It would be unfair to follow them to Africa for this investigation. We will consider them here, on the same stage with the whites, and where the facts are not apochryphal on which a judgment is to be formed. It will be right to make great allowances for the difference of condition, of education, of conversation, of the sphere in which they move. Many millions of them have been brought to, and born in America. Most of them, indeed, have been confined to tillage, to their own homes, and their own society: yet many have been so situated, that they might have availed themselves of the conversation of their masters; many have been brought up to the handicraft arts, and from that circumstance have always been associated with the whites. Some have been liberally educated, and all have lived in countries where the arts and sciences are cultivated to a considerable degree, and have had before their eyes samples of the best works from abroad. The Indians, with no advantages of this kind, will often carve figures on their pipes not destitute of design and merit. They will crayon out an animal, a plant, or a country, so as to prove the existence of a germ in their minds which only wants cultivation. They astonish you with strokes of the most sublime oratory; such as prove their reason and sentiment strong, their imagination glowing and elevated. But never yet could I find that a black had uttered a thought above the level of plain narration; never seen even an elementary trait of painting or sculpture. In music they are more generally gifted than the whites, with accurate

4. Adair Crawford (1748–1795), an English chemist best known for his *Experiments and Observations on Animal Heat* (1779).

5. Greek mathematician c. 300 B.C.E.

ears for tune and time, and they have been found capable of imagining a small catch.[6] Whether they will be equal to the composition of a more extensive run of melody, or of complicated harmony, is yet to be proved. Misery is often the parent of the most affecting touches in poetry.—Among the blacks is misery enough, God knows, but no poetry. Love is the peculiar œstrum[7] of the poet. Their love is ardent, but it kindles the senses only, not the imagination. Religion, indeed, has produced a Phyllis Whately;[8] but it could not produce a poet. The compositions published under her name are below the dignity of criticism.

* * *

To justify a general conclusion, requires many observations, even where the subject may be submitted to the Anatomical knife, to Optical glasses, to analysis by fire or by solvents. How much more then where it is a faculty, not a substance, we are examining; where it eludes the research of all the senses; where the conditions of its existence are various and variously combined; where the effects of those which are present or absent bid defiance to calculation; let me add too, as a circumstance of great tenderness, where our conclusion would degrade a whole race of men from the rank in the scale of beings which their Creator may perhaps have given them. To our reproach it must be said, that though for a century and a half we have had under our eyes the races of black and of red men, they have never yet been viewed by us as subjects of natural history. I advance it, therefore, as a suspicion only, that the blacks, whether originally a distinct race, or made distinct by time and circumstances, are inferior to the whites in the endowments both of body and mind. * * *

1785

6. The instrument proper to them is the Banjar, which they brought hither from Africa, and which is the original of the guitar, its chords being precisely the four lower chords of the guitar [Jefferson's note].

7. Passionate impulse.

8. Jefferson refers to the African American poet Phillis Wheatley (1753–1784), whose *Poems* (1773) was popular in England, going through at least four printings.

DAVID WALKER

Central to the development of African American writing of the antebellum period was a willingness to critique national ideologies and practices. Frederick Douglass's "What to the Slave Is the Fourth of July?" (1852), for example, pointed to the failure of the nation to live up to the ideals of the Declaration of Independence. Two decades before Douglass's most famous speech, David Walker (c. 1790–1830), a free black in Boston, maintained that the nation failed to live up to those ideals because the author of the Declaration was a racist. In *David Walker's Appeal, in Four Articles, Together with a Preamble, to the Colored Citizens of the World, But in Particular, and Very Expressly to those of the United States of America* (1829), Walker argued for African Americans' rights to freedom and dignity in the United

States; in developing his argument, he challenged assumptions about black inferiority, particularly as set forth in Jefferson's *Notes on the State of Virginia*. Though Jefferson had died three years before the publication of the *Appeal*, Walker structured much of his text as a debate with Jefferson, and he hoped to use his text to create black community in the North and the South. To that end, he attempted to smuggle the book into the South with the help of black sailors. The book became notorious for its militant assertion that blacks, when faced with possible enslavement, should "kill or be killed." While the volume appalled and terrified whites, it inspired black abolitionists such as Henry Highland Garnet (1815–1882), who in his 1843 "Address to the Slaves" exhorted the slaves to violently resist the masters. But the volume's main intention was not to push blacks into a race war (unless whites offered no other choice) but to argue for blacks' rights to U.S. citizenship. In 1848 the *Appeal* was republished as part of a volume titled *Walker's Appeal, With a Brief Sketch of His Life. By Henry Highland Garnet. And also Garnet's Address to the Slaves of the United States of America*, from which the selection below is taken.

From David Walker's Appeal in Four Articles

My beloved brethren: The Indians of North and of South America—the Greeks—the Irish subjected under the king of Great Britain—the Jews that ancient people of the Lord—the inhabitants of the islands of the sea—in fine, all the inhabitants of the earth, (except however, the sons of Africa) are called *men*, and of course are, and ought to be free. But *we*, (coloured people) and our children are *brutes*!! and of course are and ought to be SLAVES to the American people and their children forever! to dig their mines and work their farms; and thus go on enriching them, from one generation to another with our blood and our tears!!

I promised in a preceding page to demonstrate to the satisfaction of the most incredulous, that we, (coloured people of these United States of America) are the *most wretched*, *degraded* and abject set of beings that ever *lived* since the world began, and that the white Americans having reduced us to the wretched state of *slavery*, treat us in that condition *more cruel* (they being an enlightened and christian people) than any heathen nation did any people whom it had reduced to our condition. These affirmations are so well confirmed in the minds of all unprejudiced men who have taken the trouble to read histories, that they need no elucidation from me.

* * *

I have been for years troubling the pages of historians to find out what our fathers have done to the *white Christians of America*, to merit such condign punishment as they have inflicted on them, and do continue to inflict on us their children. But I must aver, that my researches have hitherto been to no effect. I have therefore come to the immovable conclusion, that they (Americans) have, and do continue to punish us for nothing else, but for enriching them and their country. For I cannot conceive of any thing else. Nor will I ever believe otherwise until the Lord shall convince me.

The world knows, that slavery as it existed among the Romans, (which was the primary cause of their destruction) was, comparatively speaking, no more than a *cypher*, when compared with ours under the Americans.

Indeed, I should not have noticed the Roman slaves, had not the very learned and penetrating Mr. Jefferson said, "When a master was murdered, all his slaves in the same house or within hearing, were condemned to death."[1]—Here let me ask Mr. Jefferson, (but he is gone to answer at the bar of God, for the deeds done in his body while living,) I therefore ask the whole American people, had I not rather die, or be put to death than to be a slave to any tyrant, who takes not only my own, but my wife and children's lives by the inches? Yea, would I meet death with avidity far! far!! in preference to such *servile submission* to the murderous hands of tyrants. Mr. Jefferson's very severe remarks on us have been so extensively argued upon by men whose attainments in literature, I shall never be able to reach, that I would not have meddled with it, were it not to solicit each of my brethren, who has the spirit of a man, to buy a copy of Mr. Jefferson's "Notes on Virginia," and put it in the hand of his son. For let no one of us suppose that the refutations which have been written by our white friends are enough—they are *whites*—we are *blacks*. We, and the world wish to see the charges of Mr. Jefferson refuted by the blacks *themselves*, according to their chance: for we must remember that what the whites have written respecting this subject, is other men's labors and did not emanate from the blacks. I know well, that there are some talents and learning among the coloured people of this country, which we have not a chance to develope, in consequence of oppression; but our oppression ought not to hinder us from acquiring all we can.—For we will have a chance to develope them by and by. God will not suffer us, always to be oppressed. Our sufferings will come to an *end*, in spite of all the Americans this side of *eternity*. Then we will want all the learning and talents among ourselves, and perhaps more, to govern ourselves.—"Every dog must have its day,"[2] the American's is coming to an end.

But let us review Mr. Jefferson's remarks respecting us some further. Comparing our miserable fathers, with the learned philosophers of Greece, he says: "Yet notwithstanding these and other discouraging circumstances among the Romans, their slaves were often their rarest artists. They excelled too in science, insomuch as to be usually employed as tutors to their master's children; Epictetus, Terence and Phædrus, were slaves,—but they were of the race of whites. It is not their *condition* then, but *nature*, which has produced the distinction."[3] See this, my brethren!! Do you believe that this assertion is swallowed by millions of the whites? Do you know that Mr. Jefferson was one of as great characters as ever lived among the whites? See his writings for the world, and public labors for the United States of America. Do you believe that the assertions of such a man, will pass away into oblivion unobserved by this people and the world? If you do you are much mistaken—See how the American people treat us—have we souls in our bodies? are we men who have any spirits at all? I know that there are many *swell-bellied* fellows among us whose greatest object is to fill their stomachs. Such I do not mean—I am after those who know and feel, that we are MEN as well as other people; to them, I say, that unless we try to refute Mr. Jefferson's arguments respecting us, we will only establish them.

1. See his notes on Virginia [Walker's note].
2. Attributed to John Heywood (1497?–1580?), English writer of proverbs and epigrams.
3. See his notes on Virginia [Walker's note].

But the slaves among the Romans. Every body who has read history, knows, that as soon as a slave among the Romans obtained his freedom, he could rise to the greatest eminence in the State, and there was no law instituted to hinder a slave from buying his freedom. Have not the Americans instituted laws to hinder us from obtaining our freedom. Do any deny this charge? Read the laws of Virginia, North Carolina, &c. Further: have not the Americans instituted laws to prohibit a man of colour from obtaining and holding any office whatever, under the government of the United States of America? Now, Mr. Jefferson tells us that our condition is not so hard, as the slaves were under the Romans!!!!

It is time for me to bring this article to a close. But before I close it, I must observe to my brethren that at the close of the first Revolution in this country with Great Britain, there were but thirteen States in the Union, now there are twenty-four, most of which are slave-holding States, and the whites are dragging us around in chains and hand-cuffs to their new States and Territories to work their mines and farms, to enrich them and their children, and millions of them believing firmly that we being a little darker than they, were made by our creator to be an inheritance to them and their children forever—the same as a parcel of *brutes!!*

Are we MEN!!—I ask you, O my brethren! are we MEN? Did our creator make us to be slaves to dust and ashes like ourselves? Are they not dying worms as well as we? Have they not to make their appearance before the tribunal of heaven, to answer for the deeds done in the body, as well as we? Have we any other master but Jesus Christ alone? Is he not their master as well as ours?—What right then, have we to obey and call any other master, but Himself? How we could be so *submissive* to a gang of men, whom we cannot tell whether they are as *good* as ourselves or not, I never could conceive. However, this is shut up with the Lord and we cannot precisely tell—but I declare, we judge men by their works.

The whites have always been an unjust, jealous unmerciful, avaricious and blood thirsty set of beings, always seeking after power and authority.—We view them all over the confederacy of Greece, where they were first known to be any thing, (in consequence of education) we see them there, cutting each other's throats—trying to subject each other to wretchedness and misery, to effect which they used all kinds of deceitful, unfair and unmerciful means. We view them next in Rome, where the spirit of tyranny and deceit rated still higher.—We view them in Gaul, Spain and in Britain—in fine, we view them all over Europe, together with what were scattered about in Asia and Africa, as heathens, and we see them acting more like devils than accountable men. But some may ask, did not the blacks of Africa, and the mulattoes of Asia, go on in the same way as did the whites of Europe. I answer no—they never were half so avaricious, deceitful and unmerciful as the whites, according to their knowledge.

But we will leave the whites or Europeans as heathens and take a view of them as christians, in which capacity we see them as cruel, if not more so than ever. In fact, take them as a body, they are ten times more cruel, avaricious and unmerciful than ever they were; for while they were heathens they were bad enough it is true, but it is positively a fact that they were not quite so audacious as to go and take vessel loads of men, women and children, and in cold blood and through devilishness, throw them into the sea, and murder them in all kind of ways. While they were heathens, they were too ignorant for such barbarity. But being christians, enlightened and sensible, they are completely prepared for such hellish cruelties. Now suppose God were to give them more sense, what would they do. If it were possible would they not *dethrone* Jehovah and seat themselves upon his throne? I therefore, in the name and fear of the Lord God of heaven and of earth, divested of prejudice either on the side of my colour or that of the whites, advance my suspicion, whether they are *as good by nature* as we are or not. Their actions, since they were known as a people, have been the reverse, I do indeed suspect them, but this, as I before observed, is shut up with the Lord, we cannot exactly tell, it will be proved in succeeding generations.

* * *

1829

WILLIAM LLOYD GARRISON

Born in Newburyport, Massachusetts, the white abolitionist William Lloyd Garrison (1805–1879) worked on the antislavery newspaper *The Genius of Universal Emancipation* during the late 1820s. In 1831 he established his own antislavery newspaper, the *Liberator*, which—published in Boston from January 1831 to December 1865—became the most influential antislavery newspaper of the time. The only near competitors were Frederick Douglass's the *North Star* and *Frederick Douglass' Paper*. In his newspaper editorials and other writings, Garrison advocated moral persuasion over violence, condemned the Constitution as a proslavery document, rejected union with slaveholders, and—most important—called for the immediate (not gradual) emancipation of the slaves. In 1833 he organized the American Anti-Slavery Society, which remained one of the most effective antislavery organizations of the period. Under its auspices, he published Douglass's *Narrative* in 1845; but Douglass broke with him around 1850 when he became convinced that Garrison's view of the Constitution as a proslavery document was incorrect. Garrison's antislavery activities, particularly the publication of his newspaper, infuriated Southerners and contributed to the increasingly heated sectional tensions of the antebellum period. That Nat Turner's bloody slave rebellion in Southampton, Virginia, occurred just months after Garrison began publishing the *Liberator* was not lost on his Southern critics, who called for the suppression of the newspaper and other antislavery publications. In the editorial "To the Public," which appeared in the January 1, 1831, inaugural issue of the *Liberator*, the source of the selection printed here, Garrison invokes the Declaration of Independence of the Southerner Jefferson to argue for the need to fulfill the mandate of the American Revolution by bringing equality to all.

To the Public

In the month of August, I issued proposals for publishing "THE LIBERATOR" in Washington city; but the enterprise, though hailed in different sections of the country, was palsied by public indifference. Since that time, the removal of the Genius of Universal Emancipation[1] to the Seat of Government has rendered less imperious the establishment of a similar periodical in that quarter.

During my recent tour for the purpose of exciting the minds of the people by a series of discourses on the subject of slavery, every place that I visited gave fresh evidence of the fact, that a greater revolution in public sentiment was to be effected in the free states—*and particularly in New-England*—than at the south. I found contempt more bitter, opposition more active, detraction more relentless, prejudice more stubborn, and apathy more frozen, than among slave owners themselves. Of course, there were individual exceptions to the contrary. This state of things afflicted, but did not dishearten me. I determined, at every hazard, to lift up the standard of emancipation in the eyes of the nation, *within sight of Bunker Hill*[2] *and in the birth place of liberty*. That standard is now unfurled; and long may it float unhurt by the spoliations of time or the missiles of a desperate foe—yea, till every chain be broken, and every bondman set free! Let southern oppressors tremble—let their secret abettors tremble—let their northern apologists tremble—let all the enemies of the persecuted blacks tremble.

I deem the publication of my original Prospectus unnecessary, as it has obtained a wide circulation. The principles therein inculcated will be steadily pursued in this paper, excepting that I shall not array myself as the political partisan of any man. In defending the great cause of human rights, I wish to derive the assistance of all religions and of all parties.

Assenting to the "self-evident truth" maintained in the American Declaration of Independence, "that all men are created equal, and endowed by their Creator with certain inalienable rights—among which are life, liberty and the pursuit of happiness," I shall strenuously contend for the immediate enfranchisement of our slave population. In Park-street Church, on the Fourth of July, 1829, in an address on slavery, I unreflectingly assented to the popular but pernicious doctrine of *gradual* abolition. I seize this opportunity to make a full and unequivocal recantation, and thus publicly to ask pardon of my God, of my country, and of my brethren the poor slaves, for having uttered a sentiment so full of timidity, injustice and absurdity. A similar recantation, from my pen, was published in the Genius of Universal Emancipation at Baltimore, in September, 1829. My conscience is now satisfied.

I am aware, that many object to the severity of my language; but is there not cause for severity? I *will be* as harsh as truth, and as uncompromising as justice. On this subject, I do not wish to think, or speak, or write, with moderation. No! no! Tell a man whose house is on fire, to give a moderate alarm; tell him to moderately rescue his wife from the hands of the ravisher;

1. An antislavery newspaper edited by Benjamin Lundy (1789–1839). Garrison served as an editor from 1829 to 1830.

2. The site of a famous Revolutionary War battle in Boston on June 17, 1775.

The Liberator. Detail from the masthead of Garrison's antislavery paper, May 28, 1831.

tell the mother to gradually extricate her babe from the fire into which it has fallen;—but urge me not to use moderation in a cause like the present. I am in earnest—I will not equivocate—I will not excuse—I will not retreat a single inch—AND I WILL BE HEARD. The apathy of the people is enough to make every statue leap from its pedestal, and to hasten the resurrection of the dead.

It is pretended, that I am retarding the cause of emancipation by the coarseness of my invective, and the precipitancy of my measures. *The charge is not true.* On this question my influence,—humble as it is,—is felt at this moment to a considerable extent, and shall be felt in coming years—not perniciously, but beneficially—not as a curse, but as a blessing; and posterity will bear testimony that I was right. I desire to thank God, that he enables me to disregard "the fear of man which bringeth a snare,"[3] and to speak his truth in its simplicity and power. And here I close with this fresh dedication:

Oppression! I have seen thee, face to face,
And met thy cruel eye and cloudy brow;
But thy soul-withering glance I fear not now—
For dread to prouder feelings doth give place
Of deep abhorrence! Scorning the disgrace
Of slavish knees that at thy footstool bow
I also kneel—but with far other vow
Do hail thee and thy hord of hirelings base:—
I swear, while life-blood warms my throbbing veins,
Still to oppose and thwart, with heart and hand,
Thy brutalising sway—till Afric's chains
Are burst, and Freedom rules the rescued land,—
Trampling Oppression and his iron rod:
Such is the vow I take—SO HELP ME GOD![4]

1831

3. Proverbs 29.25.

4. The poem is by Garrison.

ANGELINA E. GRIMKÉ

Born and raised in a slaveholding family in Charleston, South Carolina, Angelina E. Grimké (1805–1879) moved to Philadelphia in the 1820s and, by the 1830s, was a fervent supporter of Garrisonian abolitionism. At a time when women in her social class were expected to remain at home and embrace the private realm of domesticity, she was regarded as a particularly shocking cultural figure for her boldness in lecturing on abolitionism before mixed audiences of men and women. She found that her work in antislavery led her to champion women's rights as well. As she remarked in 1838: "The investigation of the rights of the slave has led me to a better understanding of my own." Other women writers of the period, such as Lydia Maria Child and Margaret Fuller, also saw connections between the causes of antislavery and women's rights. In *Appeal to the Christian Women of the South* (1836), the source of the selection printed here, Grimké, somewhat in the manner of Harriet Beecher Stowe in *Uncle Tom's Cabin*, urges Southern women to use their influence within the home to help bring about the end of slavery. Challenging key tenets of the proslavery argument, including the notion that emancipation would lead to a racial war of extermination (an argument that Jefferson made in *Notes in the State of Virginia*), Grimké in effect calls on Southern women to rebel against their own "enslavement" to patriarchy.

From Appeal to the Christian Women of the South

* * *

I have thus, I think, clearly proved to you seven propositions, viz.: First, that slavery is contrary to the declaration of our independence. Second, that it is contrary to the first charter of human rights given to Adam, and renewed to Noah. Third, that the fact of slavery having been the subject of prophecy, furnishes *no* excuse whatever to slavedealers. Fourth, that no such system existed under the patriarchal dispensation. Fifth, that *slavery never* existed under the Jewish dispensation; but so far otherwise, that every servant was placed under the *protection of law*, and care taken not only to prevent all *involuntary* servitude, but all *voluntary perpetual* bondage. Sixth, that slavery in America reduces a *man* to a *thing*, a "chattel personal," *robs him* of *all* his rights as a *human being*, fetters both his mind and body, and protects the *master* in the most unnatural and unreasonable power, whilst it *throws him out* of the protection of law. Seventh, that slavery is contrary to the example and precepts of our holy and merciful Redeemer, and of his apostles.

But perhaps you will be ready to query, why appeal to *women* on this subject? *We* do not make the laws which perpetuate slavery. *No* legislative power is vested in *us*; *we* can do nothing to overthrow the system, even if we wished to do so. To this I reply, I know you do not make the laws, but I also know that *you are the wives and mothers, the sisters and daughters of those who do*; and if you really suppose *you* can do nothing to overthrow slavery, you are greatly mistaken. You can do much in every way: four things I will name.

1st. You can read on this subject. 2d. You can pray over this subject. 3d. You can speak on this subject. 4th You can *act* on this subject. I have not placed reading before praying, because I regard it more important, but because, in order to pray aright, we must understand what we are praying for; it is only then we can "pray with the understanding and the spirit also."

1. Read then on the subject of slavery. Search the Scriptures daily, whether the things I have told you are true. Other books and papers might be a great help to you in this investigation, but they are not necessary, and it is hardly probable that your Committees of Vigilance[1] will allow you to have any other. The *Bible* then is the book I want you to read in the spirit of inquiry, and the spirit of prayer. Even the enemies of Abolitionists, acknowledge that their doctrines are drawn from it. In the great mob in Boston,[2] last autumn, when the books and papers of the Anti-Slavery Society, were thrown out of the windows of their office, one individual laid hold of the Bible and was about tossing it out to the ground, when another reminded him that it was the Bible he had in his hand. *"O! 'tis all one,"* he replied, and out went the sacred volume, along with the rest. We thank him for the acknowledgment. Yes, *"it is all one,"* for our books and papers are mostly commentaries on the Bible, and the Declaration. Read the *Bible* then, it contains the words of Jesus, and they are spirit and life. Judge for yourselves whether *he sanctioned* such a system of oppression and crime.

2. Pray over this subject. When you have entered into your closets, and shut to the doors, then pray to your father, who seeth in secret, that he would open your eyes to see whether slavery is *sinful*, and if it is, that he would enable you to bear a faithful, open and unshrinking testimony against it, and to do whatsoever your hands find to do, leaving the consequences entirely to him, who still says to us whenever we try to reason away duty from the fear of consequences, *"What is that to thee, follow thou me."*[3] Pray also for that poor slave, that he may be kept patient and submissive under his hard lot, until God is pleased to open the door of freedom to him without violence or bloodshed. Pray too for the master that his heart may be softened, and he made willing to acknowledge, as Joseph's brethren did, "Verily we are guilty concerning our brother," before he will be compelled to add in consequence of Divine judgment, "therefore is all this evil come upon us."[4] Pray also for all your brethren and sisters who are laboring in the righteous cause of Emancipation in the Northern States, England and the world. There is great encouragement for prayer in these words of our Lord. "Whatsoever ye shall ask the Father *in my name*, he *will give* it to you"[5]—Pray then without ceasing, in the closet and the social circle.

3. Speak on this subject. It is through the tongue, the pen, and the press, that truth is principally propagated. Speak then to your relatives, your friends, your acquaintances on the subject of slavery; be not afraid if you are conscientiously convinced it is *sinful*, to say so openly, but calmly, and to let your sentiments be known. If you are served by the slaves of others, try to ameliorate their condition as much as possible; never aggravate their faults,

1. Groups of Southern whites who attempted to suppress abolitionist writings.
2. In October 1835, a mob attacked William Lloyd Garrison and the English abolitionist George Thompson (1804–1878).
3. John 21.22.
4. Cf. Genesis 42.21.
5. John 16.23.

"Am I not a Woman . . . ?" In the early nineteenth century, British antislavery advocates popularized the image of the kneeling slave, with the caption "Am I not a Man and a Brother?" This image from George Bourne's *Slavery Illustrated in Its Effects upon Women* (1837) suggests the increasing interconnections between antislavery and the campaign for women's rights.

and thus add fuel to the fire of anger already kindled, in a master and mistress's bosom; remember their extreme ignorance, and consider them as your Heavenly Father does the *less* culpable on this account, even when they do wrong things. Discountenance *all* cruelty to them, all starvation, all corporal chastisement; these may brutalize and *break* their spirits, but will never bend them to willing, cheerful obedience. If possible, see that they are comfortably and *seasonably* fed, whether in the house or the field; it is unreasonable and cruel to expect slaves to wait for their breakfast until eleven o'clock, when they rise at five or six. Do all you can, to induce their owners to clothe them well, and to allow them many little indulgences which would contribute to their comfort. Above all, try to persuade your husband, father, brothers and sons, that *slavery is a crime against God and man*, and that it is a great sin to keep *human beings* in such abject ignorance; to deny them the privilege of learning to read and write. The Catholics are universally condemned, for denying the Bible to the common people, but, *slaveholders must not* blame them, for *they* are doing the *very same thing*, and for the very same reason, neither of these systems can bear the light which bursts from the pages of that Holy Book. And lastly, endeavour to inculcate submission on the part of the slaves, but whilst doing this be faithful in pleading the cause of the oppressed.

"Will *you* behold unheeding,
  Life's holiest feelings crushed,
Where *woman's* heart is bleeding,
  Shall *woman's* voice be hushed?"[6]

4. Act on this subject. Some of you *own* slaves yourselves. If you believe slavery is *sinful*, set them at liberty, "undo the heavy burdens and let the oppressed go free."[7] If they wish to remain with you, pay them wages, if not let them leave you. Should they remain teach them, and have them taught the common branches of an English education; they have minds and those

6. From "Think of Our Country's Glory," by Elizabeth Margaret Chandler (1807–1834), in *Poetical Works* (1836).
7. Isaiah 58.6.

minds, *ought to be improved*. So precious a talent as intellect, never was given to be wrapt in a napkin and buried in the earth. It is the *duty* of all, as far as they can, to improve their own mental faculties, because we are commanded to love God with *all our minds*, as well as with all our hearts, and we commit a great sin, if we *forbid or prevent* that cultivation of the mind in others, which would enable them to perform this duty. * * *

1836

SOJOURNER TRUTH

Born a slave in Ulster County in Upstate New York, Sojourner Truth (1797–1883) emerged as one of the nation's most flamboyant advocates of the rights of African Americans and women. At least five of her children were sold into slavery before New York State abolished slavery in 1827, and though she never learned to read or write, she successfully sued for the return of one of her sons in 1829. In 1843 she had a visionary experience that left her convinced God wanted her to speak the truth about the evils of Americans' sins against blacks and women. Like Angelina Grimké, she regularly spoke before mixed audiences of men and women, presenting the causes of antislavery and women's rights as inextricably intertwined. With the publication of the *Narrative of Sojourner Truth* in 1850, a life history that she dictated to Oliver Gilbert, she gained even greater renown. Harriet Beecher Stowe regarded Truth an inspiring example of the black Christian woman as antipatriarchal reformer, and she was not alone in being influenced by newspaper reports of Truth's dramatic speeches. In the summer of 1851, Truth addressed a women's rights convention in Akron, Ohio. The account that follows is from the June 21, 1851, issue of the *Anti-Slavery Bugle*.

Speech to the Women's Rights Convention in Akron, Ohio, 1851

One of the most unique and interesting speeches of the Convention was made by Sojourner Truth, an emancipated slave. It is impossible to transfer it to paper, or convey any adequate idea of the effect it produced upon the audience. Those only can appreciate it who saw her powerful form, her whole-souled, earnest gestures, and listened to her strong and truthful tones. She came forward to the platform and addressing the President said with great simplicity:

May I say a few words? Receiving an affirmative answer, she proceeded: I want to say a few words about this matter. I am a woman's rights. I have as much muscle as any man, and can do as much work as any man. I have plowed and reaped and husked and chopped and mowed, and can any man do more than that? I have heard much about the sexes being equal; I can carry as much as any man, and can cut as much too, if I can get it. I am as strong as any man that is now. As for intellect, all I can say is, if woman have a pint and man a quart—why cant she have her little pint full? You need not be afraid to give us our rights for fear we will take too much,—for we cant take more than our pint'll hold. The poor men seem to be all in confusion, and dont know what to do. Why children, if you have woman's rights give it to her and you will feel better. You will have your own rights, and they wont be so much trouble. I cant read, but I can hear. I have heard the bible and have learned that Eve caused man to sin. Well if woman upset the world, do give her a chance to set it rightside up again. The Lady has spoken about Jesus, how he never spurned woman from him, and she was right. When Lazarus[1] died, Mary and Martha came to him with faith and love and besought him to raise their brother. And Jesus wept—and Lazarus came forth. And how came Jesus into the world? Through God who created him and woman who bore him. Man, where is your part? But the women are coming up blessed be God and a few of the men are coming up with them. But man is in a tight place, the poor slave is on him, woman is coming on him, and he is surely between a hawk and a buzzard.

1851

1. Restored to life by Jesus (John 11.1–44).

MARTIN R. DELANY

During the antebellum period, a number of African American leaders argued that the United States would forever remain a nation of slavery and white supremacy and that beneath the contradictions in Jefferson's vision lay the reality that he and others among the nation's founders never intended for blacks to become citizens of the new republic. Angered and disillusioned by the Compromise of 1850, with its infamous Fugitive Slave Law requiring all citizens to assist in returning escaped slaves to their "owners," the black Pittsburgh leader Martin R. Delany (1812–1885) broke with his friend Frederick Douglass, with whom he had co-edited the antislavery newspaper the *North Star*, and began to call for African American emigration. In 1854 he convened a National Emigration Convention of Colored Men in Cleveland; his address at the convention, "Political Destiny," counseled African Americans to emigrate to Central or South America or to the Caribbean. His emigrationist vision inspired a number of African Americans, including William Wells Brown, who, in the wake of the Supreme Court's 1857 Dred Scott decision declaring that blacks could never become citizens of the United States, advocated African American emigration to Haiti. With the outbreak of the Civil War, however, most black emigrationists, including Delany and Brown, committed themselves to the Union cause, which they regarded as the cause of antislavery. Delany himself became the first black major in the Union Army. For the remainder of his life, however, he remained tempted by the prospect of black emigration to Africa. The text of his 1854 emigrationist speech is taken from *Proceedings of the National Emigration Convention of Colored People* (1854).

From Political Destiny of the Colored Race on the American Continent

Let it then be understood, as a great principle of political economy, that no people can be free who themselves do not constitute an essential part of the *ruling element* of the country in which they live. Whether this element be founded upon a true or false, a just or an unjust basis; this position in community is necessary to personal safety. The liberty of no man is secure, who controls not his own political destiny. What is true of an individual, is true of a family; and that which is true of a family, is also true concerning a whole people. To suppose otherwise, is that delusion which at once induces its victim, through a period of long suffering, patiently to submit to every species of wrong; trusting against probability, and hoping against all reasonable grounds of expectation, for the granting of privileges and enjoyment of rights, which never will be attained. This delusion reveals the true secret of the power which holds in peaceable subjection, all the oppressed in every part of the world.

A people, to be free, must necessarily be *their own rulers*: that is, *each individual* must, in himself, embody the *essential ingredient*—so to speak—of the *sovereign principle* which composes the *true basis* of his liberty. This principle, when not exercised by himself, may, at his pleasure, be delegated to another—his true representative.

Said a great French writer: "A free agent, in a free government, should be his own governor;"[1] that is, he must possess within himself the *acknowledged right to govern*: this constitutes him a *governor*, though he may delegate to another the power to govern himself.

No one, then, can delegate to another a power he never possessed; that is, he cannot *give an agency* in that which he never had a right. Consequently, the colored man in the United States, being deprived of the right of inherent sovereignty, cannot *confer* a suffrage, because he possesses none to confer. Therefore, where there is no suffrage, there can neither be *freedom* nor *safety* for the disfranchised. And it is a futile hope to suppose that the agent of another's concerns will take a proper interest in the affairs of those to whom he is under no obligations. Having no favors to ask or expect, he therefore has none to lose.

In other periods and parts of the world—as in Europe and Asia—the people being of one common, direct origin of race, though established on the presumption of difference by birth, or what was termed *blood*, yet the distinction between the superior classes and common people, could only be marked by the difference, in the dress and education of the two classes. To effect this, the interposition of government was necessary; consequently, the costume and education of the people became a subject of legal restriction, guarding carefully against the privileges of the common people.

In Rome, the Patrician and Plebeian were orders in the ranks of her people—all of whom were termed citizens (*cives*)—recognized by the laws of the country; their dress and education being determined by law, the better to

1. The most likely source is *Principles of Politics* (1815), by Benjamin Constant (1767–1830), French-Swiss political theorist.

fix the distinction. In different parts of Europe, at the present day, if not the same, the distinction among the people is similar, only on a modified—and in some kingdoms—probably more tolerant or deceptive policy.

In the United States, our degradation being once—as it has in a hundred instances been done—legally determined, our color is sufficient, independently of costume, education, or other distinguishing marks, to keep up that distinction.

In Europe, when an inferior is elevated to the rank of equality with the superior class, the law first comes to his aid, which, in its decrees, entirely destroys his identity as an inferior, leaving no trace of his former condition visible.

In the United States, among the whites, their color is made, by law and custom, the mark of distinction and superiority; while the color of the blacks is a badge of degradation, acknowledged by statute, organic law, and the common consent of the people.

With this view of the case—which we hold to be correct—to elevate to equality the degraded subject of law and custom, it can only be done, as in Europe, by an entire destruction of the identity of the former condition of the applicant. Even were this desirable—which we by no means admit—with the deep seated prejudices engendered by oppression, with which we have to contend, ages incalculable might reasonably be expected to roll around, before this could honorably be accomplished; otherwise, we should encourage and at once commence an indiscriminate concubinage and immoral commerce, of our mothers, sisters, wives and daughters, revolting to think of, and a physical curse to humanity.

If this state of things be to succeed, then, as in Egypt, under the dread of the inscrutable approach of the destroying angel, to appease the hatred of our oppressors, as a license to the passions of every white, let the lintel of each door of every black man, be stained with the blood of virgin purity and unsullied matron fidelity. Let it be written along the cornice in capitals, "The *will* of the white man is the rule of my household."[2] Remove the protection to our chambers and nurseries, that the places once sacred may henceforth become the unrestrained resort of the vagrant and rabble, always provided that the licensed commissioner of lust shall wear the indisputable impress of a *white* skin.

But we have fully discovered and comprehended the great political disease with which we are affected, the cause of its origin and continuance; and what is now left for us to do is to discover and apply a sovereign remedy—a healing balm to a sorely diseased body—a wrecked but not entirely shattered system. We propose for this disease a remedy. That remedy is Emigration. This Emigration should be well advised, and like remedies applied to remove the disease from the physical system of man, skillfully and carefully applied, within the proper time, directed to operate on that part of the system, whose greatest tendency shall be, to benefit the whole.

1854

2. Exodus 12.21–23 describes Moses instructing the Israelites to put the blood of the lamb just above their doorposts so God would know not to smite them.

HARRIET BEECHER STOWE
1811–1896

The author of the best-selling novel of the pre–Civil War period, Harriet Beecher Stowe was born in Litchfield, Connecticut, the seventh child and fourth daughter of Lyman Beecher, an eminent evangelical Calvinist minister, and Roxana Foote Beecher. After bearing two more children, Roxana died when Harriet was four; typically for this era, Lyman remarried quickly. Harriet Beecher found her stepmother aloof and overly formal, and continued to grieve for her mother. The family eventually numbered thirteen children, among whom Harriet was especially close to her brothers Henry Ward (1813–1887) and Charles (1815–1900), her sister Catharine (1800–1878), and her half-sister Isabella (1822–1907). Profoundly influenced by Lyman Beecher's ambitions to shape the nation along the lines of his Protestant evangelical vision, many of the children grew up to take on leadership roles in the culture. The men became ministers; the women became writers, teachers, and reformers. Catharine was a pioneer in women's education and teacher training; Isabella turned to suffragism and women's rights; Harriet wrote the most effective antislavery novel in the nation's history.

Between 1819 and 1824, Harriet Beecher studied at Sarah Pierce's Litchfield Female Academy, one of the earliest schools in the nation to offer serious academic training to women. Pierce (1806–1863) believed that properly trained women were ultimately destined (as she phrased it in a commencement address) to "instruct and enlighten the world." In 1823, Catharine Beecher, who had also attended Pierce's school, joined with another sister, Mary, to found a girls' academy in Hartford, Connecticut. Harriet Beecher began to study there in 1824 and became a teacher at the academy in 1827.

In 1832 the Beecher family moved to Cincinnati, where Lyman Beecher assumed the presidency of the new Lane Theological Seminary, convinced of the importance of doing Protestant evangelical work in the western states. Working with her father and her sister Harriet, Catharine Beecher founded the Western Female Institute in order to train "Protestant young women" to teach the children of farmers and workers in the burgeoning schools of the Midwest. Although the Beechers regretted leaving their beloved New England, they became part of an active home-based cultural life (scholars call this a "parlor culture") in Cincinnati, at that time the largest city in the West. Harriet Beecher began to write short stories in 1834. That same year she became acutely aware of the controversy over slavery when a number of Lane students, including the soon to be prominent abolitionist Theodore Dwight Weld, rebelled against Lyman Beecher's lukewarm antislavery position—he supported shipping free American blacks to a colony in Africa—and withdrew from the seminary.

In 1836, a year that saw major antiabolitionist riots in Cincinnati, Harriet Beecher married Calvin Stowe, a professor of biblical literature at Lane who was one of the best Hebrew scholars of his day. Because his salary was small and the Stowes began to rear a large family very quickly—twin girls (Eliza and Harriet) were born in 1836, a son (Henry) in 1838—Harriet Beecher Stowe continued to write for money even though she found childbirth extremely debilitating. Her first book—a collection of stories titled *The Mayflower*—appeared in 1843. Her first antislavery sketch, "Immediate Emancipation," appeared in 1845. The death of her baby boy Samuel, who succumbed to cholera in 1849 before he was a year old, was a great blow and infused her writing with sympathy for people who were helpless in the face of great personal loss. Although she had little firsthand knowledge of slavery, she had become increasingly interested in the abolitionist cause; now her deep sorrow forged an emotional link with the oppressed that was to push *Uncle Tom's Cabin* far beyond the standard abolitionist tract.

In 1849 Calvin Stowe accepted a position at Bowdoin College, in Maine, and the Stowes moved to New England in 1850. (In 1851, when the family moved again, he went to Andover Theological Seminary in Massachusetts.) Passage of the Fugitive Slave Act in 1850—which made it a federal crime to assist an escaping slave—had outraged Harriet Beecher Stowe and many other Northerners, who regarded the new law as having further implicated the North in the practice of slavery. For, if it was now a crime to help escaping slaves anywhere in the nation, one could no longer see slavery as simply a Southern institution. Fired by this development, she began writing *Uncle Tom's Cabin*, which was serialized during 1851–52 in the Washington, D.C., weekly antislavery journal, the *National Era*. In this setting, the novel was well received, but its audience was limited to adherents of the abolitionist cause.

The novel had an entirely different effect when it appeared in book form in 1852. It sold around three thousand copies the day of publication and more than three hundred thousand copies by the end of the year. (Comparable figures for today's population would have to be more than ten times larger.) As a reviewer in the *Literary World* put it: "No literary work of any character or merit, whether of poetry or prose, or imagination or observation, fancy or fact, truth or fiction, that has ever been written since there have been writers or readers, has ever commanded so great a popular success." Between 1852 and 1860 it was reprinted in twenty-two languages. The novel helped push abolitionism from the margins to the mainstream, and thus moved the nation closer to Civil War—an outcome that, in fact, Stowe had hoped to avert by her depictions of slave suffering. Her aim had been to inspire voluntary emancipation by demonstrating the evil and unchristian nature of slavery.

Uncle Tom's Cabin made Stowe a national and international celebrity. When she traveled to Europe in 1853 she was entertained and feted wherever she went. As a means of authenticating aspects of *Uncle Tom's Cabin*, she had published the book-length *Key to Uncle Tom's Cabin* before setting sail. Over the next several years she met with a number of black abolitionists, including Frederick Douglass, and came to regret that the ending of *Uncle Tom's Cabin*, where a number of the novel's prominent black characters choose to emigrate to Africa, seemed to support colonization (the policy of relocating free blacks to Africa). In her next antislavery novel, *Dred; A Tale of the Great Dismal Swamp* (1856), she depicted slave rebels who, following the death of their leader, made their way to New York and Canada. Though not as popular as *Uncle Tom's Cabin*, the novel nonetheless sold several hundred thousand copies and was praised by the British novelist George Eliot as "rare in both its intensity and range of power."

As the Civil War approached, Stowe continued to write on behalf of abolitionism in the *New York Independent* while turning to novels focused on New England culture and history. She made a pioneering contribution to regional writing in such books as *The Minister's Wooing* (1859), *The Pearl of Orr's Island* (1862), *Oldtown Folks* (1869), and *Poganuc People* (1878). Much of the power of these novels derives from Stowe's profoundly ambivalent tributes to the old New England character and its ways of life in the prerailroad days. She deplored New England's doctrinal severity, yet admired the region's homogeneous community life, which she strove to depict in meticulous, nostalgic detail. These novels developed the figure of an innocent young woman whose religious intuitions resist the bookish theologies of male religious authorities. A historical novel, *Agnes of Sorrento* (1862), which drew on her travels in Italy, featured the same kind of heroine in a fifteenth-century setting.

In 1863 Calvin Stowe retired, and the Stowes moved to Hartford, Connecticut. In this same year she became an Episcopalian, abandoning the rigors of Calvinism with which she had struggled for so long. Her life contained many sorrows; only three of her seven children—the twins and the youngest child, Charles, born in 1850—outlived her. Calvin Stowe died in 1886; in her last decade, Harriet Beecher Stowe suffered greatly from physical illness and mental exhaustion.

When the modernist movement championed a critical ethos of understatement and antisentimentality, denying that politics had any place in serious literature, *Uncle Tom's Cabin* became a target of critical abuse. Overtly emotional, fearlessly political, and appealing to the widest possible audience, it represented literary values that modernism abhorred. More recently the novel's racial politics have come under fire, as some have objected to the extent to which it draws on stereotypes. But if it had not been so much a part of its own time, *Uncle Tom's Cabin* could never have achieved its effects, and reconsideration of the novel has helped revive appreciation for literature that is politically engaged and popularly effective. Understanding the importance of this novel in American culture also reminds readers of how central women were to literary life before the Civil War, and how openly they engaged with topics that, supposedly, were outside their sphere.

The text is that of the first American edition of *Uncle Tom's Cabin* (1852).

From Uncle Tom's Cabin; or, Life among the Lowly[1]

Volume I

CHAPTER I. IN WHICH THE READER IS INTRODUCED TO A MAN OF HUMANITY

Late in the afternoon of a chilly day in February, two gentlemen were sitting alone over their wine, in a well-furnished dining parlor, in the town of P——, in Kentucky. There were no servants present, and the gentlemen, with chairs closely approaching, seemed to be discussing some subject with great earnestness.

For convenience sake, we have said, hitherto, two *gentlemen*. One of the parties, however, when critically examined, did not seem, strictly speaking, to come under the species. He was a short, thick-set man, with coarse, commonplace features, and that swaggering air of pretension which marks a low man who is trying to elbow his way upward in the world. He was much overdressed, in a gaudy vest of many colors, a blue neckerchief, bedropped gayly with yellow spots, and arranged with a flaunting tie, quite in keeping with the general air of the man. His hands, large and coarse, were plentifully bedecked with rings; and he wore a heavy gold watch-chain, with a bundle of seals of portentous size, and a great variety of colors, attached to it,—which, in the ardor of conversation, he was in the habit of flourishing and jingling with evident satisfaction. His conversation was in free and easy defiance of Murray's Grammar,[2] and was garnished at convenient intervals with various profane expressions, which not even the desire to be graphic in our account shall induce us to transcribe.

1. The novel follows the fortunes of two slaves from the Shelby plantation in Kentucky. The first plot concerns Tom, about thirty-five years old and a devout Christian; the second concerns Eliza, a young mother. "Uncle" does not mean an old person, but an honored person.

2. *English Grammar* (1795), by Lindley Murray (1745–1826), Pennsylvanian author of popular textbooks.

His companion, Mr. Shelby, had the appearance of a gentleman; and the arrangements of the house, and the general air of the housekeeping, indicated easy, and even opulent circumstances. As we before stated, the two were in the midst of an earnest conversation.

"That is the way I should arrange the matter," said Mr. Shelby.

"I can't make trade that way—I positively can't, Mr. Shelby," said the other, holding up a glass of wine between his eye and the light.

"Why, the fact is, Haley, Tom is an uncommon fellow; he is certainly worth that sum anywhere,—steady, honest, capable, manages my whole farm like a clock."

"You mean honest, as niggers go," said Haley, helping himself to a glass of brandy.

"No; I mean, really, Tom is a good, steady, sensible, pious fellow. He got religion at a camp-meeting,[3] four years ago; and I believe he really *did* get it. I've trusted him, since then, with everything I have,—money, house, horses,—and let him come and go round the country; and I always found him true and square in everything."

"Some folks don't believe there is pious niggers, Shelby," said Haley, with a candid flourish of his hand, "but *I do*. I had a fellow, now, in this yer last lot I took to Orleans[4]—'t was as good as a meetin, now, really, to hear that critter pray; and he was quite gentle and quiet like. He fetched me a good sum, too, for I bought him cheap of a man that was 'bliged to sell out; so I realized six hundred on him. Yes, I consider religion a valeyable thing in a nigger, when it's the genuine article, and no mistake."

"Well, Tom's got the real article, if ever a fellow had," rejoined the other. "Why, last fall, I let him go to Cincinnati alone, to do business for me, and bring home five hundred dollars. 'Tom,' says I to him, 'I trust you, because I think you're a Christian—I know you wouldn't cheat.' Tom comes back, sure enough; I knew he would. Some low fellows, they say, said to him—'Tom, why don't you make tracks for Canada?' 'Ah, master trusted me, and I couldn't,'—they told me about it. I am sorry to part with Tom, I must say. You ought to let him cover the whole balance of the debt; and you would, Haley, if you had any conscience."

"Well, I've got just as much conscience as any man in business can afford to keep,—just a little, you know, to swear by, as 't were," said the trader, jocularly; "and, then, I'm ready to do anything in reason to 'blige friends; but this yer, you see, is a leetle too hard on a fellow—a leetle too hard." The trader sighed contemplatively, and poured out some more brandy.

"Well, then, Haley, how will you trade?" said Mr. Shelby, after an uneasy interval of silence.

"Well, haven't you a boy or gal that you could throw in with Tom?"

"Hum!—none that I could well spare; to tell the truth, it's only hard necessity makes me willing to sell at all. I don't like parting with any of my hands, that's a fact."

Here the door opened, and a small quadroon[5] boy, between four and five years of age, entered the room. There was something in his appearance

3. Evangelical religious gathering, usually held outdoors and lasting several days.
4. New Orleans.
5. Technically, a person with one-quarter black ancestry; generally used in 19th-century culture for a light-skinned black.

remarkably beautiful and engaging. His black hair, fine as floss silk, hung in glossy curls about his round, dimpled face, while a pair of large dark eyes, full of fire and softness, looked out from beneath the rich, long lashes, as he peered curiously into the apartment. A gay robe of scarlet and yellow plaid, carefully made and neatly fitted, set off to advantage the dark and rich style of his beauty; and a certain comic air of assurance, blended with bashfulness, showed that he had been not unused to being petted and noticed by his master.

"Hulloa, Jim Crow!"[6] said Mr. Shelby, whistling, and snapping a bunch of raisins towards him, "pick that up, now!"

The child scampered, with all his little strength, after the prize, while his master laughed.

"Come here, Jim Crow," said he. The child came up, and the master patted the curly head, and chucked him under the chin.

"Now, Jim, show this gentleman how you can dance and sing." The boy commenced one of those wild, grotesque songs common among the negroes, in a rich, clear voice, accompanying his singing with many comic evolutions of the hands, feet, and whole body, all in perfect time to the music.

"Bravo!" said Haley, throwing him a quarter of an orange.

"Now, Jim, walk like old Uncle Cudjoe, when he has the rheumatism," said his master.

Instantly the flexible limbs of the child assumed the appearance of deformity and distortion, as, with his back humped up, and his master's stick in his hand, he hobbled about the room, his childish face drawn into a doleful pucker, and spitting from right to left, in imitation of an old man.

Both gentlemen laughed uproariously.

"Now, Jim," said his master, "show us how old Elder Robbins leads the psalm." The boy drew his chubby face down to a formidable length, and commenced toning a psalm tune through his nose, with imperturbable gravity.

"Hurrah! bravo! what a young 'un!" said Haley; "that chap's a case, I'll promise. Tell you what," said he, suddenly clapping his hand on Mr. Shelby's shoulder, "fling in that chap, and I'll settle the business—I will. Come, now, if that ain't doing the thing up about the rightest!"

At this moment, the door was pushed gently open, and a young quadroon woman, apparently about twenty-five, entered the room.

There needed only a glance from the child to her, to identify her as its mother. There was the same rich, full, dark eye, with its long lashes; the same ripples of silky black hair. The brown of her complexion gave way on the cheek to a perceptible flush, which deepened as she saw the gaze of the strange man fixed upon her in bold and undisguised admiration. Her dress was of the neatest possible fit, and set off to advantage her finely moulded shape;—a delicately formed hand and a trim foot and ankle were items of appearance that did not escape the quick eye of the trader, well used to run up at a glance the points of a fine female article.

"Well, Eliza?" said her master, as she stopped and looked hesitatingly at him.

6. The stereotypical image of a happily dancing black man or boy, derived from the blackface impersonations popularized in the minstrel shows of the 1840s and 1850s.

"I was looking for Harry, please, sir;" and the boy bounded toward her, showing his spoils, which he had gathered in the skirt of his robe.

"Well, take him away, then," said Mr. Shelby; and hastily she withdrew, carrying the child on her arm.

"By Jupiter," said the trader, turning to him in admiration, "there's an article, now! You might make your fortune on that ar gal in Orleans, any day. I've seen over a thousand, in my day, paid down for gals not a bit handsomer."

"I don't want to make my fortune on her," said Mr. Shelby, dryly; and, seeking to turn the conversation, he uncorked a bottle of fresh wine, and asked his companion's opinion of it.

"Capital, sir,—first chop!" said the trader; then turning, and slapping his hand familiarly on Shelby's shoulder, he added—

"Come, how will you trade about the gal?—what shall I say for her—what'll you take?"

"Mr. Haley, she is not to be sold," said Shelby. "My wife would not part with her for her weight in gold."

"Ay, ay! women always say such things, cause they ha'nt no sort of calculation. Just show 'em how many watches, feathers, and trinkets, one's weight in gold would buy, and that alters the case, *I* reckon."

"I tell you, Haley, this must not be spoken of; I say no, and I mean no," said Shelby, decidedly.

"Well, you'll let me have the boy, though," said the trader; "you must own I've come down pretty handsomely for him."

"What on earth can you want with the child?" said Shelby.

"Why, I've got a friend that's going into this yer branch of the business—wants to buy up handsome boys to raise for the market. Fancy articles entirely—sell for waiters, and so on, to rich 'uns, that can pay for handsome 'uns. It sets off one of yer great places—a real handsome boy to open door, wait, and tend. They fetch a good sum; and this little devil is such a comical, musical concern, he's just the article."

"I would rather not sell him," said Mr. Shelby, thoughtfully; "the fact is, sir, I'm a humane man, and I hate to take the boy from his mother, sir."

"O, you do?—La! yes—something of that ar natur. I understand, perfectly. It is mighty onpleasant getting on with women, sometimes. I al'ays hates these yer screachin', screamin' times. They are *mighty* onpleasant; but, as I manages business, I generally avoids 'em, sir. Now, what if you get the girl off for a day, or a week, or so; then the thing's done quietly,—all over before she comes home. Your wife might get her some ear-rings, or a new gown, or some such truck, to make up with her."

"I'm afraid not."

"Lor bless ye, yes! These critters an't like white folks, you know; they gets over things, only manage right. Now, they say," said Haley, assuming a candid and confidential air, "that this kind o' trade is hardening to the feelings; but I never found it so. Fact is, I never could do things up the way some fellers manage the business. I've seen 'em as would pull a woman's child out of her arms, and set him up to sell, and she screechin' like mad all the time;—very bad policy—damages the article—makes 'em quite unfit for service sometimes. I knew a real handsome gal once, in Orleans, as was entirely ruined by this sort o' handling. The fellow that was trading for her didn't want her baby; and she was one of your real high sort, when her blood was up. I tell you, she squeezed up her child in her arms, and talked, and went on real awful. It kinder makes my blood run cold to think on't; and when they carried off the child, and locked her up, she jest went ravin' mad, and died in a week. Clear waste, sir, of a thousand dollars, just for want of management,—there's where 't is. It's always best to do the humane thing, sir; that's been *my* experience." And the trader leaned back in his chair, and folded his arm, with an air of virtuous decision, apparently considering himself a second Wilberforce.[7]

The subject appeared to interest the gentleman deeply; for while Mr. Shelby was thoughtfully peeling an orange, Haley broke out afresh, with becoming diffidence, but as if actually driven by the force of truth to say a few words more.

"It don't look well, now, for a feller to be praisin' himself; but I say it jest because it's the truth. I believe I'm reckoned to bring in about the finest droves of niggers that is brought in,—at least, I've been told so; if I have once, I reckon I have a hundred times,—all in good case,—fat and likely, and I lose as few as any man in the business. And I lays it all to my management, sir; and humanity, sir, I may say, is the great pillar of *my* management."

Mr. Shelby did not know what to say, and so he said, "Indeed!"

"Now, I've been laughed at for my notions, sir, and I've been talked to. They an't pop'lar, and they an't common; but I stuck to 'em, sir; I've stuck to 'em, and realized well on 'em; yes, sir, they have paid their passage, I may say," and the trader laughed at his joke.

There was something so piquant and original in these elucidations of humanity, that Mr. Shelby could not help laughing in company. Perhaps you laugh too, dear reader; but you know humanity comes out in a variety of strange forms now-a-days, and there is no end to the odd things that humane people will say and do.

Mr. Shelby's laugh encouraged the trader to proceed.

"It's strange now, but I never could beat this into people's heads. Now, there was Tom Loker, my old partner, down in Natchez;[8] he was a clever fellow, Tom was, only the very devil with niggers,—on principle 't was, you see, for a better hearted feller never broke bread; 't was his *system*, sir. I used to talk to Tom. 'Why, Tom,' I used to say, 'when your gals takes on and cry, what's the use o' crackin on 'em over the head, and knockin' on 'em round? It's ridiculous,' says I, 'and don't do no sort o' good. Why, I don't see no harm in their cryin',' says I; 'it's natur,' says I, 'and if natur can't blow off one way, it will another. Besides, Tom,' says I, 'it jest spiles your gals; they get sickly, and down in the mouth; and sometimes they gets ugly,—particular yallow[9] gals do,—and it's the devil and all gettin' on 'em broke in. Now,' says I, 'why can't you kinder coax 'em up, and speak 'em fair? Depend on it, Tom, a little humanity, thrown in along, goes a heap further than all your jawin' and

7. William Wilberforce (1759–1833), British statesman widely credited as the architect of the 1833 emancipation bill abolishing slavery throughout the British Empire.

8. City in southwest Mississippi.

9. Derogatory reference to a mulatto (person of mixed racial ancestry).

crackin'; and it pays better,' says I, 'depend on 't.' But Tom couldn't get the hang on 't; and he spiled so many for me, that I had to break off with him, though he was a good-hearted fellow, and as fair a business hand as is goin'."

"And do you find your ways of managing do the business better than Tom's?" said Mr. Shelby.

"Why, yes, sir, I may say so. You see, when I any ways can, I takes a leetle care about the onpleasant parts like selling young uns and that,—get the gals out of the way—out of sight, out of mind, you know,—and when it's clean done, and can't be helped, they naturally gets used to it. 'Tan't, you know, as if it was white folks, that's brought up in the way of 'spectin' to keep their children and wives, and all that. Niggers, you know, that's fetched up properly, ha'n't no kind of 'spectations of no kind; so all these things comes easier."

"I'm afraid mine are not properly brought up, then," said Mr. Shelby.

"S'pose not; you Kentucky folks spile your niggers. You mean well by 'em, but 'tan't no real kindness, arter all. Now, a nigger, you see, what's got to be hacked and tumbled round the world, and sold to Tom, and Dick, and the Lord knows who, 'tan't no kindness to be givin' on him notions and expectations, and bringin' on him up too well, for the rough and tumble comes all the harder on him arter. Now, I venture to say, your niggers would be quite chop-fallen in a place where some of your plantation niggers would be singing and whooping like all possessed. Every man, you know, Mr. Shelby, naturally thinks well of his own ways; and I think I treat niggers just about as well as it's ever worth while to treat 'em."

"It's a happy thing to be satisfied," said Mr. Shelby, with a slight shrug, and some perceptible feelings of a disagreeable nature.

"Well," said Haley, after they had both silently picked their nuts[1] for a season, "what do you say?"

"I'll think the matter over, and talk with my wife," said Mr. Shelby. "Meantime, Haley, if you want the matter carried on in the quiet way you speak of, you'd best not let your business in this neighborhood be known. It will get out among my boys, and it will not be a particularly quiet business getting away any of my fellows, if they know it, I'll promise you."

"O! certainly, by all means, mum! of course. But I'll tell you, I'm in a devil of a hurry, and shall want to know, as soon as possible, what I may depend on," said he, rising and putting on his overcoat.

"Well, call up this evening, between six and seven, and you shall have my answer," said Mr. Shelby, and the trader bowed himself out of the apartment.

"I'd like to have been able to kick the fellow down the steps," said he to himself, as he saw the door fairly closed, "with his impudent assurance; but he knows how much he has me at advantage. If anybody had ever said to me that I should sell Tom down south to one of those rascally traders, I should have said, 'Is thy servant a dog, that he should do this thing?'[2] And now it must come, for aught I see. And Eliza's child, too! I know that I shall have

1. Pondered.

2. Cf. 2 Kings 8.13.

some fuss with wife about that; and, for that matter, about Tom, too. So much for being in debt,—heigho! The fellow sees his advantage, and means to push it."

Perhaps the mildest form of the system of slavery is to be seen in the State of Kentucky. The general prevalence of agricultural pursuits of a quiet and gradual nature, not requiring those periodic seasons of hurry and pressure that are called for in the business of more southern districts, makes the task of the negro a more healthful and reasonable one; while the master, content with a more gradual style of acquisition, has not those temptations to hardheartedness which always overcome frail human nature when the prospect of sudden and rapid gain is weighed in the balance, with no heavier counterpoise than the interests of the helpless and unprotected.

Whoever visits some estates there, and witnesses the goodhumored indulgence of some masters and mistresses, and the affectionate loyalty of some slaves, might be tempted to dream the oft-fabled poetic legend of a patriarchal institution, and all that; but over and above the scene there broods a portentous shadow—the shadow of *law*. So long as the law considers all these human beings, with beating hearts and living affections, only as so many *things* belonging to a master,—so long as the failure, or misfortune, or imprudence, or death of the kindest owner, may cause them any day to exchange a life of kind protection and indulgence for one of hopeless misery and toil,—so long it is impossible to make anything beautiful or desirable in the best regulated administration of slavery.

Mr. Shelby was a fair average kind of man, good-natured and kindly, and disposed to easy indulgence of those around him, and there had never been a lack of anything which might contribute to the physical comfort of the negroes on his estate. He had, however, speculated largely and quite loosely; had involved himself deeply, and his notes[3] to a large amount had come into the hands of Haley; and this small piece of information is the key to the preceding conversation.

Now, it had so happened that, in approaching the door, Eliza had caught enough of the conversation to know that a trader was making offers to her master for somebody.

She would gladly have stopped at the door to listen, as she came out; but her mistress just then calling, she was obliged to hasten away.

Still she thought she heard the trader make an offer for her boy;—could she be mistaken? Her heart swelled and throbbed, and she involuntarily strained him so tight that the little fellow looked up into her face in astonishment.

"Eliza, girl, what ails you to-day?" said her mistress, when Eliza had upset the wash-pitcher, knocked down the work-stand, and finally was abstractedly offering her mistress a long night-gown in place of the silk dress she had ordered her to bring from the wardrobe.

Eliza started. "O, missis!" she said, raising her eyes; then, bursting into tears, she sat down in a chair, and began sobbing.

"Why, Eliza, child! what ails you?" said her mistress.

3. IOUs, formally promising to repay a loan.

"O! missis, missis," said Eliza, "there's been a trader talking with master in the parlor! I heard him."

"Well, silly child, suppose there has."

"O, missis, *do* you suppose mas'r would sell my Harry?" And the poor creature threw herself into a chair, and sobbed convulsively.

"Sell him! No, you foolish girl! You know your master never deals with those southern traders, and never means to sell any of his servants, as long as they behave well. Why, you silly child, who do you think would want to buy your Harry? Do you think all the world are set on him as you are, you goosie? Come, cheer up, and hook my dress. There now, put my back hair up in that pretty braid you learnt the other day, and don't go listening at doors any more."

"Well, but, missis, *you* never would give your consent—to—to—"

"Nonsense, child! to be sure, I shouldn't. What do you talk so for? I would as soon have one of my own children sold. But really, Eliza, you are getting altogether too proud of that little fellow. A man can't put his nose into the door, but you think he must be coming to buy him."

Reassured by her mistress' confident tone, Eliza proceeded nimbly and adroitly with her toilet, laughing at her own fears, as she proceeded.

Mrs. Shelby was a woman of a high class, both intellectually and morally. To that natural magnanimity and generosity of mind which one often marks as characteristic of the women of Kentucky, she added high moral and religious sensibility and principle, carried out with great energy and ability into practical results. Her husband, who made no professions to any particular religious character, nevertheless reverenced and respected the consistency of hers, and stood, perhaps, a little in awe of her opinion. Certain it was that he gave her unlimited scope in all her benevolent efforts for the comfort, instruction, and improvement of her servants, though he never took any decided part in them himself. In fact, if not exactly a believer in the doctrine of the efficiency of the extra good works of saints, he really seemed somehow or other to fancy that his wife had piety and benevolence enough for two—to indulge a shadowy expectation of getting into heaven through her superabundance of qualities to which he made no particular pretension.

The heaviest load on his mind, after his conversation with the trader, lay in the foreseen necessity of breaking to his wife the arrangement contemplated,—meeting the importunities and opposition which he knew he should have reason to encounter.

Mrs. Shelby, being entirely ignorant of her husband's embarrassments, and knowing only the general kindliness of his temper, had been quite sincere in the entire incredulity with which she had met Eliza's suspicions. In fact, she dismissed the matter from her mind, without a second thought; and being occupied in preparations for an evening visit, it passed out of her thoughts entirely.

* * *

CHAPTER III.[4] THE HUSBAND AND FATHER

Mrs. Shelby had gone on her visit, and Eliza stood in the verandah, rather dejectedly looking after the retreating carriage, when a hand was laid on her shoulder. She turned, and a bright smile lighted up her fine eyes.

"George, is it you? How you frightened me! Well; I am so glad you's come! Missis is gone to spend the afternoon; so come into my little room, and we'll have the time all to ourselves."

Saying this, she drew him into a neat little apartment opening on the verandah, where she generally sat at her sewing, within call of her mistress.

"How glad I am!—why don't you smile?—and look at Harry—how he grows." The boy stood shyly regarding his father through his curls, holding close to the skirts of his mother's dress. "Isn't he beautiful?" said Eliza, lifting his long curls and kissing him.

"I wish he'd never been born!" said George, bitterly. "I wish I'd never been born myself!"

Surprised and frightened, Eliza sat down, leaned her head on her husband's shoulder, and burst into tears.

"There now, Eliza, it's too bad for me to make you feel so, poor girl!" said he, fondly; "it's too bad. O, how I wish you never had seen me—you might have been happy!"

"George! George! how can you talk so? What dreadful thing has happened, or is going to happen? I'm sure we've been very happy, till lately."

"So we have, dear," said George. Then drawing his child on his knee, he gazed intently on his glorious dark eyes, and passed his hands through his long curls.

"Just like you, Eliza; and you are the handsomest woman I ever saw, and the best one I ever wish to see; but, oh, I wish I'd never seen you, nor you me!"

"O, George, how can you!"

"Yes, Eliza, it's all misery, misery, misery! My life is bitter as wormwood;[5] the very life is burning out of me. I'm a poor, miserable, forlorn drudge; I shall only drag you down with me, that's all. What's the use of our trying to do anything, trying to know anything, trying to be anything? What's the use of living? I wish I was dead!"

"O, now, dear George, that is really wicked! I know how you feel about losing your place in the factory, and you have a hard master; but pray be patient, and perhaps something—"

"Patient!" said he, interrupting her; "haven't I been patient? Did I say a word when he came and took me away, for no earthly reason, from the place where everybody was kind to me? I'd paid him truly every cent of my earnings,—and they all say I worked well."

"Well, it *is* dreadful," said Eliza; "but, after all, he is your master, you know."

"My master! and who made him my master? That's what I think of—what right has he to me? I'm a man as much as he is. I'm a better man than he is. I know more about business than he does; I am a better manager than he is;

4. In this chapter, Eliza, still anxious that Shelby might sell her son to the slave trader Haley, meets her husband, George Harris, who lives on another plantation. (At the time, the South did not legally recognize slave marriages.)

5. Plant producing bitter dark green oil; allusion to Proverbs 5.3–4.

I can read better than he can; I can write a better hand,—and I've learned it all myself, and no thanks to him,—I've learned it in spite of him; and now what right has he to make a dray-horse[6] of me?—to take me from things I can do, and do better than he can, and put me to work that any horse can do? He tries to do it; he says he'll bring me down and humble me, and he puts me to just the hardest, meanest and dirtiest work, on purpose!"

"O, George! George! you frighten me! Why, I never heard you talk so; I'm afraid you'll do something dreadful. I don't wonder at your feelings, at all; but oh, do be careful—do, do—for my sake—for Harry's!"

"I have been careful, and I have been patient, but it's growing worse and worse; flesh and blood can't bear it any longer;—every chance he can get to insult and torment me, he takes. I thought I could do my work well, and keep on quiet, and have some time to read and learn out of work hours; but the more he sees I can do, the more he loads on. He says that though I don't say anything, he sees I've got the devil in me, and he means to bring it out; and one of these days it will come out in a way that he won't like, or I'm mistaken!"

"O dear! what shall we do?" said Eliza, mournfully.

"It was only yesterday," said George, "as I was busy loading stones into a cart, that young Mas'r Tom stood there, slashing his whip so near the horse that the creature was frightened. I asked him to stop, as pleasant as I could,—he just kept right on. I begged him again, and then he turned on me, and began striking me. I held his hand, and then he screamed and kicked and ran to his father, and told him that I was fighting him. He came in a rage, and said he'd teach me who was my master; and he tied me to a tree, and cut switches for young master, and told him that he might whip me till he was tired;—and he did do it! If I don't make him remember it, some time!" and the brow of the young man grew dark, and his eyes burned with an expression that made his young wife tremble. "Who made this man my master? That's what I want to know!" he said.

"Well," said Eliza, mournfully, "I always thought that I must obey my master and mistress, or I couldn't be a Christian."

"There is some sense in it, in your case; they have brought you up like a child, fed you, clothed you, indulged you, and taught you, so that you have a good education; that is some reason why they should claim you. But I have been kicked and cuffed and sworn at, and at the best only let alone; and what do I owe? I've paid for all my keeping a hundred times over. I *won't* bear it. No, I *won't*!" he said, clenching his hand with a fierce frown.

Eliza trembled, and was silent. She had never seen her husband in this mood before; and her gentle system of ethics seemed to bend like a reed in the surges of such passions.

"You know poor little Carlo, that you gave me," added George; "the creature has been about all the comfort that I've had. He has slept with me nights, and followed me around days, and kind o' looked at me as if he understood how I felt. Well, the other day I was just feeding him with a few old scraps I picked up by the kitchen door, and Mas'r came along, and said I was feeding him up at his expense, and that he couldn't afford to have every nigger keeping his dog, and ordered me to tie a stone to his neck and throw him in the pond."

6. Work horse. "Dray": cart used to carry loads.

"O, George, you didn't do it!"

"Do it? not I!—but he did. Mas'r and Tom pelted the poor drowning creature with stones. Poor thing! he looked at me so mournful, as if he wondered why I didn't save him. I had to take a flogging because I wouldn't do it myself. I don't care. Mas'r will find out that I'm one that whipping won't tame. My day will come yet, if he don't look out."

"What are you going to do? O, George, don't do anything wicked; if you only trust in God, and try to do right, he'll deliver you."

"I an't a Christian like you, Eliza; my heart's full of bitterness; I can't trust in God. Why does he let things be so?"

"O, George, we must have faith. Mistress says that when all things go wrong to us, we must believe that God is doing the very best."

"That's easy to say for people that are sitting on their sofas and riding in their carriages; but let 'em be where I am, I guess it would come some harder. I wish I could be good; but my heart burns, and can't be reconciled, anyhow. You couldn't, in my place,—you can't now, if I tell you all I've got to say. You don't know the whole yet."

"What can be coming now?"

"Well, lately Mas'r has been saying that he was a fool to let me marry off the place; that he hates Mr. Shelby and all his tribe, because they are proud, and hold their heads up above him, and that I've got proud notions from you; and he says he won't let me come here any more, and that I shall take a wife and settle down on his place. At first he only scolded and grumbled these things; but yesterday he told me that I should take Mina for a wife, and settle down in a cabin with her, or he would sell me down river."

"Why—but you were married to *me*, by the minister, as much as if you'd been a white man!" said Eliza, simply.

"Don't you know a slave can't be married? There is no law in this country for that; I can't hold you for my wife, if he chooses to part us. That's why I wish I'd never seen you,—why I wish I'd never been born; it would have been better for us both,—it would have been better for this poor child if he had never been born. All this may happen to him yet!"

"O, but master is so kind!"

"Yes, but who knows?—he may die—and then he may be sold to nobody knows who. What pleasure is it that he is handsome, and smart, and bright? I tell you, Eliza, that a sword will pierce through your soul for every good and pleasant thing your child is or has; it will make him worth too much for you to keep!"

The words smote heavily on Eliza's heart; the vision of the trader came before her eyes, and, as if some one had struck her a deadly blow, she turned pale and gasped for breath. She looked nervously out on the verandah, where the boy, tired of the grave conversation, had retired, and where he was riding triumphantly up and down on Mr. Shelby's walking-stick. She would have spoken to tell her husband her fears, but checked herself.

"No, no,—he has enough to bear, poor fellow!" she thought. "No, I won't tell him; besides, it an't true; Missis never deceives us."

"So, Eliza, my girl," said the husband, mournfully, "bear up, now; and good-by, for I'm going."

"Going, George! Going where?"

"To Canada," said he, straightening himself up; "and when I'm there, I'll buy you; that's all the hope that's left us. You have a kind master, that won't refuse to sell you. I'll buy you and the boy;—God helping me, I will!"

"O, dreadful! if you should be taken?"

"I won't be taken, Eliza; I'll *die* first! I'll be free, or I'll die!"

"You won't kill yourself!"

"No need of that. They will kill me, fast enough; they never will get me down the river alive!"

"O, George, for my sake, do be careful! Don't do anything wicked; don't lay hands on yourself, or anybody else! You are tempted too much—too much; but don't—go you must—but go carefully, prudently; pray God to help you."

"Well, then, Eliza, hear my plan. Mas'r took it into his head to send me right by here, with a note to Mr. Symmes, that lives a mile past. I believe he expected I should come here to tell you what I have. It would please him, if he thought it would aggravate 'Shelby's folks,' as he calls 'em. I'm going home quite resigned, you understand, as if all was over. I've got some preparations made,—and there are those that will help me; and, in the course of a week or so, I shall be among the missing, some day. Pray for me, Eliza; perhaps the good Lord will hear *you*."

"O, pray yourself, George, and go trusting in him; then you won't do anything wicked."

"Well, now, *good-by*," said George, holding Eliza's hands, and gazing into her eyes, without moving. They stood silent; then there were last words, and sobs, and bitter weeping,—such parting as those may make whose hope to meet again is as the spider's web,—and the husband and wife were parted.

* * *

CHAPTER VII. THE MOTHER'S STRUGGLE[7]

It is impossible to conceive of a human creature more wholly desolate and forlorn than Eliza, when she turned her footsteps from Uncle Tom's cabin.

Her husband's suffering and dangers, and the danger of her child, all blended in her mind, with a confused and stunning sense of the risk she was running, in leaving the only home she had ever known, and cutting loose from the protection of a friend whom she loved and revered. Then there was the parting from every familiar object,—the place where she had grown up, the trees under which she had played, the groves where she had walked many an evening in happier days, by the side of her young husband,—everything, as it lay in the clear, frosty starlight, seemed to speak reproachfully to her, and ask her whither could she go from a home like that?

But stronger than all was maternal love, wrought into a paroxysm of frenzy by the near approach of a fearful danger. Her boy was old enough to have walked by her side, and, in an indifferent case, she would only have led him by the hand; but now the bare thought of putting him out of her arms made her shudder, and she strained him to her bosom with a convulsive grasp, as she went rapidly forward.

7. At this point in the novel, Eliza has decided to run away with her son, Harry, rather than let him be sold to Haley. She has alerted Tom to his impending sale; he chooses to remain and allow himself to be sold to protect the other slave families on the plantation. As he knows, others would be sold in his place if he escaped.

The frosty ground creaked beneath her feet, and she trembled at the sound; every quaking leaf and fluttering shadow sent the blood backward to her heart, and quickened her footsteps. She wondered within herself at the strength that seemed to be come upon her; for she felt the weight of her boy as if it had been a feather, and every flutter of fear seemed to increase the supernatural power that bore her on, while from her pale lips burst forth, in frequent ejaculations, the prayer to a Friend above—"Lord, help! Lord, save me!"

If it were *your* Harry, mother, or your Willie, that were going to be torn from you by a brutal trader, to-morrow morning,—if you had seen the man, and heard that the papers were signed and delivered, and you had only from twelve o'clock till morning to make good your escape,—how fast could *you* walk? How many miles could you make in those few brief hours, with the darling at your bosom,—the little sleepy head on your shoulder,—the small, soft arms trustingly holding on to your neck?

For the child slept. At first, the novelty and alarm kept him waking; but his mother so hurriedly repressed every breath or sound, and so assured him that if he were only still she would certainly save him, that he clung quietly round her neck, only asking, as he found himself sinking to sleep,

"Mother, I don't need to keep awake, do I?"

"No, my darling; sleep, if you want to."

"But, mother, if I do get asleep, you won't let him get me?"

"No! so may God help me!" said his mother, with a paler cheek, and a brighter light in her large dark eyes.

"You're *sure*, an't you, mother?"

"Yes, *sure*!" said the mother, in a voice that startled herself; for it seemed to her to come from a spirit within, that was no part of her; and the boy dropped his little weary head on her shoulder, and was soon asleep. How the touch of those warm arms, the gentle breathings that came in her neck, seemed to add fire and spirit to her movements! It seemed to her as if strength poured into her in electric streams, from every gentle touch and movement of the sleeping, confiding child. Sublime is the dominion of the mind over the body, that, for a time, can make flesh and nerve impregnable, and string the sinews like steel, so that the weak become so mighty.

The boundaries of the farm, the grove, the wood-lot, passed by her dizzily, as she walked on; and still she went, leaving one familiar object after another, slacking not, pausing not, till reddening daylight found her many a long mile from all traces of any familiar objects upon the open highway.

She had often been, with her mistress, to visit some connections, in the little village of T——, not far from the Ohio river, and knew the road well. To go thither, to escape across the Ohio river, were the first hurried outlines of her plan of escape; beyond that, she could only hope in God.

When horses and vehicles began to move along the highway, with that alert perception peculiar to a state of excitement, and which seems to be a sort of inspiration, she became aware that her headlong pace and distracted air might bring on her remark and suspicion. She therefore put the boy on the ground, and, adjusting her dress and bonnet, she walked on at as rapid a pace as she thought consistent with the preservation of appearances. In her little bundle she had provided a store of cakes and apples, which she used as expedients for quickening the speed of the child, rolling the apple some yards before them, when the boy would run with all his might after it; and this ruse, often repeated, carried them over many a half-mile.

After a while, they came to a thick patch of woodland, through which murmured a clear brook. As the child complained of hunger and thirst, she climbed over the fence with him; and, sitting down behind a large rock which concealed them from the road, she gave him a breakfast out of her little package. The boy wondered and grieved that she could not eat; and when, putting his arms round her neck, he tried to wedge some of his cake into her mouth, it seemed to her that the rising in her throat would choke her.

"No, no, Harry darling! mother can't eat till you are safe! We must go on—on—till we come to the river!" And she hurried again into the road, and again constrained herself to walk regularly and composedly forward.

She was many miles past any neighborhood where she was personally known. If she should chance to meet any who knew her, she reflected that the well-known kindness of the family would be of itself a blind to suspicion, as making it an unlikely supposition that she could be a fugitive. As she was also so white as not to be known as of colored lineage, without a critical survey, and her child was white also, it was much easier for her to pass on unsuspected.

On this presumption, she stopped at noon at a neat farmhouse, to rest herself, and buy some dinner for her child and self; for, as the danger decreased with the distance, the supernatural tension of the nervous system lessened, and she found herself both weary and hungry.

The good woman, kindly and gossipping, seemed rather pleased than otherwise with having somebody come in to talk with; and accepted, without examination, Eliza's statement, that she "was going on a little piece, to spend a week with her friends,"—all which she hoped in her heart might prove strictly true.

An hour before sunset, she entered the village of T——, by the Ohio river, weary and foot-sore, but still strong in heart. Her first glance was at the river, which lay, like Jordan, between her and the Canaan[8] of liberty on the other side.

It was now early spring, and the river was swollen and turbulent; great cakes of floating ice were swinging heavily to and fro in the turbid waters. Owing to the peculiar form of the shore on the Kentucky side, the land bending far out into the water, the ice had been lodged and detained in great quantities, and the narrow channel which swept round the bend was full of ice, piled one cake over another, thus forming a temporary barrier to the descending ice, which lodged, and formed a great, undulating raft, filling up the whole river, and extending almost to the Kentucky shore.

Eliza stood, for a moment, contemplating this unfavorable aspect of things, which she saw at once must prevent the usual ferry-boat from running, and then turned into a small public house on the bank, to make a few inquiries.

The hostess, who was busy in various fizzing and stewing operations over the fire, preparatory to the evening meal, stopped, with a fork in her hand, as Eliza's sweet and plaintive voice arrested her.

"What is it?" she said.

8. In the Bible, the promised land for the Israelites, who wandered in the desert for forty years. The Jordan is the river they had to cross to get there.

"Isn't there any ferry or boat, that takes people over to B——, now?" she said.

"No, indeed!" said the woman; "the boats has stopped running."

Eliza's look of dismay and disappointment struck the woman, and she said, inquiringly,

"May be you're wanting to get over?—anybody sick? Ye seem mighty anxious?"

"I've got a child that's very dangerous,"[9] said Eliza. "I never heard of it till last night, and I've walked quite a piece to-day, in hopes to get to the ferry."

"Well, now, that's onlucky," said the woman, whose motherly sympathies were much aroused; "I'm re'lly consarned for ye. Solomon!" she called, from the window, towards a small back building. A man, in leather apron and very dirty hands, appeared at the door.

"I say, Sol," said the woman, "is that ar man going to tote them bar'ls over to-night?"

"He said he should try, if't was any way prudent," said the man.

"There's a man a piece down here, that's going over with some truck[1] this evening, if he durs'to; he'll be in here to supper to-night, so you'd better set down and wait. That's a sweet little fellow," added the woman, offering him a cake.

But the child, wholly exhausted, cried with weariness.

"Poor fellow! he isn't used to walking, and I've hurried him on so," said Eliza.

"Well, take him into this room," said the woman, opening into a small bedroom, where stood a comfortable bed. Eliza laid the weary boy upon it, and held his hands in hers till he was fast asleep. For her there was no rest. As a fire in her bones, the thought of the pursuer urged her on; and she gazed with longing eyes on the sullen, surging waters that lay between her and liberty.

Here we must take our leave of her for the present, to follow the course of her pursuers.

Though Mrs. Shelby had promised that the dinner should be hurried on table, yet it was soon seen, as the thing has often been seen before, that it required more than one to make a bargain. So, although the order was fairly given out in Haley's hearing, and carried to Aunt Chloe[2] by at least half a dozen juvenile messengers, that dignitary only gave certain very gruff snorts, and tosses of her head, and went on with every operation in an unusually leisurely and circumstantial manner.

For some singular reason, an impression seemed to reign among the servants generally that Missis would not be particularly disobliged by delay; and it was wonderful what a number of counter accidents occurred constantly, to retard the course of things. One luckless wight contrived to upset the gravy; and then gravy had to be got up *de novo*,[3] with due care and formality, Aunt Chloe watching and stirring with dogged precision, answering shortly, to all suggestions of haste, that she "warn't a going to have raw gravy on the table, to help nobody's catchings." One tumbled down with the water,

9. I.e., dangerously ill.

1. Goods.

2. Tom's wife, the Shelbys' cook. The entire household works together to delay Haley's departure in pursuit of Eliza.

3. From the beginning (Latin). "Wight": serving person, slave.

and had to go to the spring for more; and another precipitated the butter into the path of events; and there was from time to time giggling news brought into the kitchen that "Mas'r Haley was mighty oneasy, and that he couldn't sit in his cheer no ways, but was a walkin' and stalkin' to the winders and through the porch."

"Sarves him right!" said Aunt Chloe, indignantly. "He'll get wus nor oneasy, one of these days, if he don't mend his ways. *His* master'll be sending for him, and then see how he'll look!"

"He'll go to torment, and no mistake," said little Jake.

"He desarves it!" said Aunt Chloe, grimly; "he's broke a many, many, many hearts,—I tell ye all!" she said, stopping, with a fork uplifted in her hands; "it's like what Mas'r George reads in Ravelations,[4]—souls a callin' under the altar! and a callin' on the Lord for vengeance on sich!—and by and by the Lord he'll hear 'em—so he will!"

Aunt Chloe, who was much revered in the kitchen, was listened to with open mouth; and, the dinner being now fairly sent in, the whole kitchen was at leisure to gossip with her, and to listen to her remarks.

"Sich 'll be burnt up forever, and no mistake; won't ther?" said Andy.

"I'd be glad to see it, I'll be boun'," said little Jake.

"Chil'en!" said a voice, that made them all start. It was Uncle Tom, who had come in, and stood listening to the conversation at the door.

"Chil'en!" he said, "I'm afeard you don't know what ye're sayin'. Forever is a *dre'ful* word, chil'en; it's awful to think on 't. You oughtenter wish that ar to any human crittur."

"We wouldn't to anybody but the soul-drivers,"[5] said Andy; "nobody can help wishing it to them, they's so awful wicked."

"Don't natur herself kinder cry out on em?" said Aunt Chloe. "Don't dey tear der suckin' baby right off his mother's breast, and sell him, and der little children as is crying and holding on by her clothes,—don't dey pull 'em off and sells em? Don't dey tear wife and husband apart?" said Aunt Chloe, beginning to cry, "when it's jest takin' the very life on 'em?—and all the while does they feel one bit,—don't dey drink and smoke, and take it oncommon easy? Lor, if the devil don't get them, what's he good for?" And Aunt Chloe covered her face with her checked apron, and began to sob in good earnest.

"Pray for them that 'spitefully use you, the good book says," says Tom.[6]

"Pray for 'em!" said Aunt Chloe; "Lor, it's too tough! I can't pray for 'em."

"It's natur, Chloe, and natur's strong," said Tom, "but the Lord's grace is stronger; besides, you oughter think what an awful state a poor crittur's soul's in that'll do them ar things,—you oughter thank God that you an't *like* him, Chloe. I'm sure I'd rather be sold, ten thousand times over, than to have all that ar poor crittur's got to answer for."

"So'd I, a heap," said Jake. "Lor, *shouldn't* we cotch it, Andy?"

Andy shrugged his shoulders, and gave an acquiescent whistle.

"I'm glad Mas'r didn't go off this morning, as he looked to," said Tom; "that ar hurt me more than sellin', it did. Mebbe it might have been natural

4. The Book of Revelation, which contains symbolic prophecies of the end of the world. George is the Shelbys' son, who in Chapter IV reads the Bible to the slaves.

5. Slave owners or traders.

6. From Matthew 5.44: "Love your enemies, bless them that curse you, do good to them that hate you, and pray for them which despitefully use you, and persecute you."

for him, but 't would have come desp't hard on me, as has known him from a baby; but I've seen Mas'r, and I begin ter feel sort o' reconciled to the Lord's will now. Mas'r couldn't help hisself; he did right, but I'm feared things will be kinder goin' to rack, when I'm gone. Mas'r can't be spected to be a pryin' round everywhar, as I've done, a keepin' up all the ends. The boys all means well, but they's powerful car'less. That ar troubles me."

The bell here rang, and Tom was summoned to the parlor.

"Tom," said his master, kindly, "I want you to notice that I give this gentleman bonds to forfeit a thousand dollars if you are not on the spot when he wants you; he's going to-day to look after his other business, and you can have the day to yourself. Go anywhere you like, boy."

"Thank you, Mas'r," said Tom.

"And mind yerself," said the trader, "and don't come it over your master with any o' yer nigger tricks; for I'll take every cent out of him, if you an't thar. If he'd hear to me, he wouldn't trust any on ye—slippery as eels!"

"Mas'r," said Tom,—and he stood very straight,—"I was jist eight years old when ole Missis put you into my arms, and you wasn't a year old. 'Thar,' says she, 'Tom, that's to be *your* young Mas'r; take good care on him,' says she. And now I jist ask you, Mas'r, have I ever broke word to you, or gone contrary to you, 'specially since I was a Christian?"

Mr. Shelby was fairly overcome, and the tears rose to his eyes.

"My good boy," said he, "the Lord knows you say but the truth; and if I was able to help it, all the world shouldn't buy you."

"And sure as I am a Christian woman," said Mrs. Shelby, "you shall be redeemed as soon as I can any way bring together means. Sir," she said to Haley, "take good account of who you sell him to, and let me know."

"Lor, yes, for that matter," said the trader, "I may bring him up in a year, not much the wuss for wear, and trade him back."

"I'll trade with you then, and make it for your advantage," said Mrs. Shelby.

"Of course," said the trader, "all's equal with me; li'ves trade 'em up as down, so I does a good business. All I want is a livin', you know, ma'am; that's all any on us wants, I s'pose."

Mr. and Mrs. Shelby both felt annoyed and degraded by the familiar impudence of the trader, and yet both saw the absolute necessity of putting a constraint on their feelings. The more hopelessly sordid and insensible he appeared, the greater became Mrs. Shelby's dread of his succeeding in recapturing Eliza and her child, and of course the greater her motive for detaining him by every female artifice. She therefore graciously smiled, assented, chatted familiarly, and did all she could to make time pass imperceptibly.

At two o'clock Sam and Andy brought the horses up to the posts, apparently greatly refreshed and invigorated by the scamper of the morning.

Sam was there new oiled from dinner, with an abundance of zealous and ready officiousness. As Haley approached, he was boasting, in flourishing style, to Andy, of the evident and eminent success of the operation, now that he had "farly come to it."

"Your master, I s'pose, don't keep no dogs," said Haley, thoughtfully, as he prepared to mount.

"Heaps on 'em," said Sam, triumphantly; "thar's Bruno—he's a roarer! and, besides that, 'bout every nigger of us keeps a pup of some natur or uther."

"Poh!" said Haley,—and he said something else, too, with regard to the said dogs, at which Sam muttered,

"I don't see no use cussin' on 'em, no way."

"But your master don't keep no dogs (I pretty much know he don't) for trackin' out niggers."

Sam knew exactly what he meant, but he kept on a look of earnest and desperate simplicity.

"Our dogs all smells round considable sharp. I spect they's the kind, though they han't never had no practice. They's *far*[7] dogs, though, at most anything, if you'd get 'em started. Here, Bruno," he called, whistling to the lumbering Newfoundland, who came pitching tumultuously toward them.

"You go hang!" said Haley, getting up. "Come, tumble up now."

Sam tumbled up accordingly, dexterously contriving to tickle Andy as he did so, which occasioned Andy to split out into a laugh, greatly to Haley's indignation, who made a cut at him with his riding-whip.

"I's 'stonished at yer, Andy," said Sam, with awful gravity. "This yer's a seris bisness, Andy. Yer mustn't be a makin' game. This yer an't no way to help Mas'r."

"I shall take the straight road to the river," said Haley, decidedly, after they had come to the boundaries of the estate. "I know the way of all of 'em,—they makes tracks for the underground."[8]

"Sartin," said Sam, "dat's de idee. Mas'r Haley hits de thing right in de middle. Now, der's two roads to de river,—de dirt road and der pike,—which Mas'r mean to take?"

Andy looked up innocently at Sam, surprised at hearing this new geographical fact, but instantly confirmed what he said, by a vehement reiteration.

"Cause," said Sam, "I'd rather be 'clined to 'magine that Lizy'd take de dirt road, bein' it 's the least travelled."

Haley, notwithstanding that he was a very old bird, and naturally inclined to be suspicious of chaff, was rather brought up by this view of the case.

"If yer warn't both on yer such cussed liars, now!" he said, contemplatively, as he pondered a moment.

The pensive, reflective tone in which this was spoken appeared to amuse Andy prodigiously, and he drew a little behind, and shook so as apparently to run a great risk of falling off his horse, while Sam's face was immovably composed into the most doleful gravity.

"Course," said Sam, "Mas'r can do as he 'd ruther; go de straight road, if Mas'r thinks best,—it's all one to us. Now, when I study 'pon it, I think de straight road do best, *deridedly*."

"She would naturally go a lonesome way," said Haley, thinking aloud, and not minding Sam's remark.

"Dar an't no sayin'," said Sam; "gals is pecular; they never does nothin' ye thinks they will; mose gen'lly the contrar. Gals is nat'lly made contrary; and so, if you thinks they've gone one road, it is sartin you'd better go t' other, and then you'll be sure to find 'em. Now, my private 'pinion is, Lizy took der dirt road; so I think we'd better take de straight one."

7. Fair.
8. The Underground Railroad; the informal, secretive network of individuals whose homes were used by slaves escaping from the South to Canada.

This profound generic view of the female sex did not seem to dispose Haley particularly to the straight road; and he announced decidedly that he should go the other, and asked Sam when they should come to it.

"A little piece ahead," said Sam, giving a wink to Andy with the eye which was on Andy's side of the head; and he added, gravely, "but I've studded on de matter, and I'm quite clar we ought not to go dat ar way. I nebber been over it no way. It's despit lonesome, and we might lose our way,—whar we'd come to, de Lord only knows."

"Nevertheless," said Haley, "I shall go that way."

"Now I think on 't, I think I hearn 'em tell that dat ar road was all fenced up and down by der creek, and thar, an't it, Andy?"

Andy wasn't certain; he'd only "hearn tell" about that road, but never been over it. In short, he was strictly noncommittal.

Haley, accustomed to strike the balance of probabilities between lies of greater or lesser magnitude, thought that it lay in favor of the dirt road aforesaid. The mention of the thing he thought he perceived was involuntary on Sam's part at first, and his confused attempts to dissuade him he set down to a desperate lying on second thoughts, as being unwilling to implicate Eliza.

When, therefore, Sam indicated the road, Haley plunged briskly into it, followed by Sam and Andy.

Now, the road, in fact, was an old one, that had formerly been a thoroughfare to the river, but abandoned for many years after the laying of the new pike. It was open for about an hour's ride, and after that it was cut across by various farms and fences. Sam knew this fact perfectly well,—indeed, the road had been so long closed up, that Andy had never heard of it. He therefore rode along with an air of dutiful submission, only groaning and vociferating occasionally that 't was "desp't rough, and bad for Jerry's foot."

"Now, I jest give yer warning," said Haley, "I know yer; yer won't get me to turn off this yer road, with all yer fussin'—so you shet up!"

"Mas'r will go his own way!" said Sam, with rueful submission, at the same time winking most portentously to Andy, whose delight was now very near the explosive point.

Sam was in wonderful spirits,—professed to keep a very brisk look-out,—at one time exclaiming that he saw "a gal's bonnet" on the top of some distant eminence, or calling to Andy "if that thar wasn't 'Lizy' down in the hollow;" always making these exclamations in some rough or craggy part of the road, where the sudden quickening of speed was a special inconvenience to all parties concerned, and thus keeping Haley in a state of constant commotion.

After riding about an hour in this way, the whole party made a precipitate and tumultuous descent into a barn-yard belonging to a large farming establishment. Not a soul was in sight, all the hands being employed in the fields; but, as the barn stood conspicuously and plainly square across the road, it was evident that their journey in that direction had reached a decided finale.

"Wan't dat ar what I telled Mas'r?" said Sam, with an air of injured innocence. "How does strange gentleman spect to know more about a country dan de natives born and raised?"

"You rascal!" said Haley, "you knew all about this."

"Didn't I tell yer I *know'd*, and yer wouldn't believe me? I telled Mas'r 't was all shet up, and fenced up, and I didn't spect we could get through,—Andy heard me."

It was all too true to be disputed, and the unlucky man had to pocket his wrath with the best grace he was able, and all three faced to the right about, and took up their line of march for the highway.

In consequence of all the various delays, it was about three-quarters of an hour after Eliza had laid her child to sleep in the village tavern that the party came riding into the same place. Eliza was standing by the window, looking out in another direction, when Sam's quick eye caught a glimpse of her. Haley and Andy were two yards behind. At this crisis, Sam contrived to have his hat blown off, and uttered a loud and characteristic ejaculation, which startled her at once; she drew suddenly back; the whole train swept by the window, round to the front door.

A thousand lives seemed to be concentrated in that one moment to Eliza. Her room opened by a side door to the river. She caught her child, and sprang down the steps towards it. The trader caught a full glimpse of her, just as she was disappearing down the bank; and throwing himself from his horse, and calling loudly on Sam and Andy, he was after her like a hound after a deer. In that dizzy moment her feet to her scarce seemed to touch the ground, and a moment brought her to the water's edge. Right on behind they came; and, nerved with strength such as God gives only to the desperate, with one wild cry and flying leap, she vaulted sheer over the turbid current by the shore, on to the raft of ice beyond. It was a desperate leap—impossible to anything but madness and despair; and Haley, Sam, and Andy, instinctively cried out, and lifted up their hands, as she did it.

The huge green fragment of ice on which she alighted pitched and creaked as her weight came on it, but she staid there not a moment. With wild cries and desperate energy she leaped to another and still another cake;—stumbling—leaping—slipping—springing upwards again! Her shoes are gone—her stockings cut from her feet—while blood marked every step; but she saw nothing, felt nothing, till dimly, as in a dream, she saw the Ohio side, and a man helping her up the bank.

"Yer a brave gal, now, whoever ye ar!" said the man, with an oath.

Eliza recognized the voice and face of a man who owned a farm not far from her old home.

"O, Mr. Symmes!—save me—do save me—do hide me!" said Eliza.

"Why, what's this?" said the man. "Why, if 'tan't Shelby's gal!"

"My child!—this boy!—he'd sold him! There is his Mas'r," said she, pointing to the Kentucky shore. "O, Mr. Symmes, you've got a little boy!"

"So I have," said the man, as he roughly, but kindly, drew her up the steep bank. "Besides, you're a right brave gal. I like grit, wherever I see it."

When they had gained the top of the bank, the man paused.

"I'd be glad to do something for ye," said he; "but then there's nowhar I could take ye. The best I can do is to tell ye to go *thar*," said he, pointing to a large white house which stood by itself, off the main street of the village. "Go thar; they're kind folks. Thar's no kind o' danger but they'll help you,—they're up to all that sort o' thing."

"The Lord bless you!" said Eliza, earnestly.

"No 'casion, no 'casion in the world," said the man. "What I've done's of no 'count."

"And, oh, surely, sir, you won't tell any one!"

"Go to thunder, gal! What do you take a feller for? In course not," said the man. "Come, now, go along like a likely, sensible gal, as you are. You've arnt your liberty, and you shall have it, for all me."

The woman folded her child to her bosom, and walked firmly and swiftly away. The man stood and looked after her.

"Shelby, now, mebbe won't think this yer the most neighborly thing in the world; but what's a feller to do? If he catches one of my gals in the same fix, he's welcome to pay back. Somehow I never could see no kind o' critter a strivin' and pantin', and trying to clar theirselves, with the dogs arter 'em, and go agin 'em. Besides, I don't see no kind of 'casion for me to be hunter and catcher for other folks, neither."

So spoke this poor, heathenish Kentuckian, who had not been instructed in his constitutional relations,[9] and consequently was betrayed into acting in a sort of Christianized manner, which, if he had been better situated and more enlightened, he would not have been left to do.

Haley had stood a perfectly amazed spectator of the scene, till Eliza had disappeared up the bank, when he turned a blank, inquiring look on Sam and Andy.

"That ar was a tolable fair stroke of business," said Sam.

"The gal's got seven devils in her, I believe!" said Haley. "How like a wildcat she jumped!"

"Wal, now," said Sam, scratching his head, "I hope Mas'r'll 'scuse us tryin' dat ar road. Don't think I feel spry enough for dat ar, no way!" and Sam gave a hoarse chuckle.

"*You* laugh!" said the trader, with a growl.

"Lord bless you, Mas'r, I couldn't help it, now," said Sam, giving way to the long pent-up delight of his soul. "She looked so curi's, a leapin' and springin'—ice a crackin'—and only to hear her,—plump! ker chunk! ker splash! Spring! Lord! how she goes it!" and Sam and Andy laughed till the tears rolled down their cheeks.

"I'll make ye laugh t'other side yer mouths!" said the trader, laying about their heads with his riding-whip.

Both ducked, and ran shouting up the bank, and were on their horses before he was up.

"Good-evening, Mas'r!" said Sam, with much gravity. "I berry much spect Missis be anxious 'bout Jerry. Mas'r Haley won't want us no longer. Missis wouldn't hear of our ridin' the critters over Lizy's bridge to-night;" and, with a facetious poke into Andy's ribs, he started off, followed by the latter, at full speed,—their shouts of laughter coming faintly on the wind.

* * *

9. Allusion to the Fugitive Slave Law, recently passed by Congress as part of the Compromise of 1850, which made it a federal crime to aid fugitive slaves.

CHAPTER IX. IN WHICH IT APPEARS THAT A SENATOR IS BUT A MAN

The light of the cheerful fire shone on the rug and carpet of a cosey parlor, and glittered on the sides of the tea-cups and well-brightened tea-pot, as Senator Bird[1] was drawing off his boots, preparatory to inserting his feet in a pair of new handsome slippers, which his wife had been working for him while away on his senatorial tour. Mrs. Bird, looking the very picture of delight, was superintending the arrangements of the table, ever and anon mingling admonitory remarks to a number of frolicsome juveniles, who were effervescing in all those modes of untold gambol and mischief that have astonished mothers ever since the flood.

"Tom, let the door-knob alone,—there's a man! Mary! Mary! don't pull the cat's tail,—poor pussy! Jim, you mustn't climb on that table,—no, no!—You don't know, my dear, what a surprise it is to us all, to see you here to-night," said she, at last, when she found a space to say something to her husband.

"Yes, yes, I thought I'd just make a run down, spend the night, and have a little comfort at home. I'm tired to death, and my head aches!"

Mrs. Bird cast a glance at a camphor-bottle,[2] which stood in the half-open closet, and appeared to meditate an approach to it, but her husband interposed.

"No, no, Mary, no doctoring! a cup of your good hot tea, and some of our good home living, is what I want. It's a tiresome business, this legislating!"

And the senator smiled, as if he rather liked the idea of considering himself a sacrifice to his country.

"Well," said his wife, after the business of the tea-table was getting rather slack, "and what have they been doing in the Senate?"

Now, it was a very unusual thing for gentle little Mrs. Bird ever to trouble her head with what was going on in the house of the state, very wisely considering that she had enough to do to mind her own. Mr. Bird, therefore, opened his eyes in surprise, and said,

"Not very much of importance."

"Well; but is it true that they have been passing a law forbidding people to give meat and drink to those poor colored folks that come along?[3] I heard they were talking of some such law, but I didn't think any Christian legislature would pass it!"

"Why, Mary, you are getting to be a politician, all at once."

"No, nonsense! I wouldn't give a fip for all your politics, generally, but I think this is something downright cruel and unchristian. I hope, my dear, no such law has been passed."

"There has been a law passed forbidding people to help off the slaves that come over from Kentucky, my dear; so much of that thing has been done by these reckless Abolitionists, that our brethren in Kentucky are very strongly excited, and it seems necessary, and no more than Christian and kind, that something should be done by our state to quiet the excitement."

1. An Ohio state senator, returning from a session in Columbus, the state capital.
2. During the 19th century, camphor, a compound from a tree of the same name, was used for pain relief.
3. Such a state law would have added force to the federal Fugitive Slave Law.

"And what is the law? It don't forbid us to shelter these poor creatures a night, does it, and to give 'em something comfortable to eat, and a few old clothes, and send them quietly about their business?"

"Why, yes, my dear; that would be aiding and abetting, you know."

Mrs. Bird was a timid, blushing little woman, of about four feet in height, and with mild blue eyes, and a peach-blow[4] complexion, and the gentlest, sweetest voice in the world;—as for courage, a moderate-sized cock-turkey had been known to put her to rout at the very first gobble, and a stout house-dog, of moderate capacity, would bring her into subjection merely by a show of his teeth. Her husband and children were her entire world, and in these she ruled more by entreaty and persuasion than by command or argument. There was only one thing that was capable of arousing her, and that provocation came in on the side of her unusually gentle and sympathetic nature;—anything in the shape of cruelty would throw her into a passion, which was the more alarming and inexplicable in proportion to the general softness of her nature. Generally the most indulgent and easy to be entreated of all mothers, still her boys had a very reverent remembrance of a most vehement chastisement she once bestowed on them, because she found them leagued with several graceless boys of the neighborhood, stoning a defenceless kitten.

"I'll tell you what," Master Bill used to say, "I was scared that time. Mother came at me so that I thought she was crazy, and I was whipped and tumbled off to bed, without any supper, before I could get over wondering what had come about; and, after that, I heard mother crying outside the door, which made me feel worse than all the rest. I'll tell you what," he'd say, "we boys never stoned another kitten!"

On the present occasion, Mrs. Bird rose quickly, with very red cheeks, which quite improved her general appearance, and walked up to her husband, with quite a resolute air, and said, in a determined tone,

"Now, John, I want to know if you think such a law as that is right and Christian?"

"You won't shoot me, now, Mary, if I say I do!"

"I never could have thought it of you, John; you didn't vote for it?"

"Even so, my fair politician."

"You ought to be ashamed, John! Poor, homeless, houseless creatures! It's a shameful, wicked, abominable law, and I'll break it, for one, the first time I get a chance; and I hope I *shall* have a chance, I do! Things have got to a pretty pass, if a woman can't give a warm supper and a bed to poor, starving creatures, just because they are slaves, and have been abused and oppressed all their lives, poor things!"

"But, Mary, just listen to me. Your feelings are all quite right, dear, and interesting, and I love you for them; but, then, dear, we mustn't suffer our feelings to run away with our judgment; you must consider it's not a matter of private feeling,—there are great public interests involved,—there is such a state of public agitation rising, that we must put aside our private feelings."

"Now, John, I don't know anything about politics, but I can read my Bible; and there I see that I must feed the hungry, clothe the naked, and comfort the desolate; and that Bible I mean to follow."

4. Peach blossom.

"But in cases where your doing so would involve a great public evil—"

"Obeying God never brings on public evils. I know it can't. It's always safest, all round, to *do as He* bids us."

"Now, listen to me, Mary, and I can state to you a very clear argument, to show—"

"O, nonsense, John! you can talk all night, but you wouldn't do it. I put it to you, John,—would *you* now turn away a poor, shivering, hungry creature from your door, because he was a runaway? *Would* you, now?"

Now, if the truth must be told, our senator had the misfortune to be a man who had a particularly humane and accessible nature, and turning away anybody that was in trouble never had been his forte; and what was worse for him in this particular pinch of the argument was, that his wife knew it, and, of course, was making an assault on rather an indefensible point. So he had recourse to the usual means of gaining time for such cases made and provided; he said "ahem," and coughed several times, took out his pocket-handkerchief, and began to wipe his glasses. Mrs. Bird, seeing the defenceless condition of the enemy's territory, had no more conscience than to push her advantage.

"I should like to see you doing that, John—I really should! Turning a woman out of doors in a snow-storm, for instance; or, may be you'd take her up and put her in jail, wouldn't you? You would make a great hand at that!"

"Of course, it would be a very painful duty," began Mr. Bird, in a moderate tone.

"Duty, John! don't use that word! You know it isn't a duty—it can't be a duty! If folks want to keep their slaves from running away, let 'em treat 'em well,—that's my doctrine. If I had slaves (as I hope I never shall have), I'd risk their wanting to run away from me, or you either, John. I tell you folks don't run away when they are happy; and when they do run, poor creatures! they suffer enough with cold and hunger and fear, without everybody's turning against them; and, law or no law, I never will, so help me God!"

"Mary! Mary! My dear, let me reason with you."

"I hate reasoning, John,—especially reasoning on such subjects. There's a way you political folks have of coming round and round a plain right thing; and you don't believe in it yourselves, when it comes to practice. I know *you* well enough, John. You don't believe it's right any more than I do; and you wouldn't do it any sooner than I."

At this critical juncture, old Cudjoe, the black man-of-all-work, put his head in at the door, and wished "Missis would come into the kitchen;" and our senator, tolerably relieved, looked after his little wife with a whimsical mixture of amusement and vexation, and, seating himself in the arm-chair, began to read the papers.

After a moment, his wife's voice was heard at the door, in a quick, earnest tone,—"John! John! I do wish you'd come here, a moment."

He laid down his paper, and went into the kitchen, and started, quite amazed at the sight that presented itself:—A young and slender woman, with garments torn and frozen, with one shoe gone, and the stocking torn away from the cut and bleeding foot, was laid back in a deadly swoon upon two chairs. There was the impress of the despised race on her face, yet none could help feeling its mournful and pathetic beauty, while its stony sharpness, its cold, fixed, deathly aspect, struck a solemn chill over him. He drew his breath short, and stood in silence. His wife, and their only colored domestic, old Aunt Dinah, were busily engaged in restorative measures; while old Cudjoe had got the boy on his knee, and was busy pulling off his shoes and stockings, and chafing his little cold feet.

"Sure, now, if she an't a sight to behold!" said old Dinah, compassionately; " 'pears like 'twas the heat that made her faint. She was tol'able peart when she cum in, and asked if she couldn't warm herself here a spell; and I was just a askin' her where she cum from, and she fainted right down. Never done much hard work, guess, by the looks of her hands."

"Poor creature!" said Mrs. Bird, compassionately, as the woman slowly unclosed her large, dark eyes, and looked vacantly at her. Suddenly an expression of agony crossed her face, and she sprang up, saying, "O, my Harry! Have they got him?"

The boy, at this, jumped from Cudjoe's knee, and, running to her side, put up his arms. "O, he's here! he's here!" she exclaimed.

"O, ma'am!" said she, wildly, to Mrs. Bird, "do protect us! don't let them get him!"

"Nobody shall hurt you here, poor woman," said Mrs. Bird, encouragingly. "You are safe; don't be afraid."

"God bless you!" said the woman, covering her face and sobbing; while the little boy, seeing her crying, tried to get into her lap.

With many gentle and womanly offices, which none knew better how to render than Mrs. Bird, the poor woman was, in time, rendered more calm. A temporary bed was provided for her on the settle,[5] near the fire; and, after a short time, she fell into a heavy slumber, with the child, who seemed no less weary, soundly sleeping on her arm; for the mother resisted, with nervous anxiety, the kindest attempts to take him from her; and, even in sleep, her arm encircled him with an unrelaxing clasp, as if she could not even then be beguiled of her vigilant hold.

Mr. and Mrs. Bird had gone back to the parlor, where, strange as it may appear, no reference was made, on either side, to the preceding conversation; but Mrs. Bird busied herself with her knitting-work, and Mr. Bird pretended to be reading the paper.

"I wonder who and what she is!" said Mr. Bird, at last, as he laid it down.

"When she wakes up and feels a little rested, we will see," said Mrs. Bird.

"I say, wife!" said Mr. Bird, after musing in silence over his newspaper.

"Well, dear!"

"She couldn't wear one of your gowns, could she, by any letting down, or such matter? She seems to be rather larger than you are."

A quite perceptible smile glimmered on Mrs. Bird's face, as she answered, "We'll see."

Another pause, and Mr. Bird again broke out,

"I say, wife!"

"Well! What now?"

"Why, there's that old bombazin[6] cloak, that you keep on purpose to put over me when I take my afternoon's nap; you might as well give her that,— she needs clothes."

5. A small sofa.

6. Fabric woven of silk and wool.

At this instant, Dinah looked in to say that the woman was awake, and wanted to see Missis.

Mr. and Mrs. Bird went into the kitchen, followed by the two eldest boys, the smaller fry having, by this time, been safely disposed of in bed.

The woman was now sitting up on the settle, by the fire. She was looking steadily into the blaze, with a calm, heartbroken expression, very different from her former agitated wildness.

"Did you want me?" said Mrs. Bird, in gentle tones. "I hope you feel better now, poor woman!"

A long-drawn, shivering sigh was the only answer; but she lifted her dark eyes, and fixed them on her with such a forlorn and imploring expression, that the tears came into the little woman's eyes.

"You needn't be afraid of anything; we are friends here, poor woman! Tell me where you came from, and what you want," said she.

"I came from Kentucky," said the woman.

"When?" said Mr. Bird, taking up the interrogatory.

"To-night."

"How did you come?"

"I crossed on the ice."

"Crossed on the ice!" said every one present.

"Yes," said the woman, slowly, "I did. God helping me, I crossed on the ice; for they were behind me—right behind—and there was no other way!"

"Law, Missis," said Cudjoe, "the ice is all in broken-up blocks, a swinging and a tetering up and down in the water!"

"I know it was—I know it!" said she, wildly; "but I did it! I wouldn't have thought I could,—I didn't think I should get over, but I didn't care! I could but die, if I didn't. The Lord helped me; nobody knows how much the Lord can help 'em, till they try," said the woman, with a flashing eye.

"Were you a slave?" said Mr. Bird.

"Yes, sir; I belonged to a man in Kentucky."

"Was he unkind to you?"

"No, sir; he was a good master."

"And was your mistress unkind to you?"

"No, sir—no! my mistress was always good to me."

"What could induce you to leave a good home, then, and run away, and go through such dangers?"

The woman looked up at Mrs. Bird, with a keen, scrutinizing glance, and it did not escape her that she was dressed in deep mourning.

"Ma'am," she said, suddenly, "have you ever lost a child?"

The question was unexpected, and it was a thrust on a new wound; for it was only a month since a darling child of the family had been laid in the grave.

Mr. Bird turned around and walked to the window, and Mrs. Bird burst into tears; but, recovering her voice, she said,

"Why do you ask that? I have lost a little one."

"Then you will feel for me. I have lost two, one after another,—left 'em buried there when I came away; and I had only this one left. I never slept a night without him; he was all I had. He was my comfort and pride, day and night; and, ma'am, they were going to take him away from me,—to *sell* him,—sell him down south, ma'am, to go all alone,—a baby that had never been away from his mother in his life! I couldn't stand it, ma'am. I knew I never should be good for anything, if they did; and when I knew the papers were signed, and he was sold, I took him and came off in the night; and they chased me,—the man that bought him, and some of Mas'r's folks,—and they were coming down right behind me, and I heard 'em. I jumped right on to the ice; and how I got across, I don't know,—but, first I knew, a man was helping me up the bank."

The woman did not sob nor weep. She had gone to a place where tears are dry; but every one around her was, in some way characteristic of themselves, showing signs of hearty sympathy.

The two little boys, after a desperate rummaging in their pockets, in search of those pocket-handkerchiefs which mothers know are never to be found there, had thrown themselves disconsolately into the skirts of their mother's gown, where they were sobbing, and wiping their eyes and noses, to their hearts' content;—Mrs. Bird had her face fairly hidden in her pocket-handkerchief; and old Dinah, with tears streaming down her black, honest face, was ejaculating, "Lord have mercy on us!" with all the fervor of a camp-meeting;—while old Cudjoe, rubbing his eyes very hard with his cuffs, and making a most uncommon variety of wry faces, occasionally responded in the same key, with great fervor. Our senator was a statesman, and of course could not be expected to cry, like other mortals; and so he turned his back to the company, and looked out of the window, and seemed particularly busy in clearing his throat and wiping his spectacle-glasses, occasionally blowing his nose in a manner that was calculated to excite suspicion, had any one been in a state to observe critically.

"How came you to tell me you had a kind master?" he suddenly exclaimed, gulping down very resolutely some kind of rising in his throat, and turning suddenly round upon the woman.

"Because he *was* a kind master; I'll say that of him, any way;—and my mistress was kind; but they couldn't help themselves. They were owing money; and there was some way, I can't tell how, that a man had a hold on them, and they were obliged to give him his will. I listened, and heard him telling mistress that, and she begging and pleading for me,—and he told her he couldn't help himself, and that the papers were all drawn;—and then it was I took him and left my home, and came away. I knew 'twas no use of my trying to live, if they did it; for 't 'pears like this child is all I have."

"Have you no husband?"

"Yes, but he belongs to another man. His master is real hard to him, and won't let him come to see me, hardly ever; and he's grown harder and harder upon us, and he threatens to sell him down south;—it's like I'll never see *him* again!"

The quiet tone in which the woman pronounced these words might have led a superficial observer to think that she was entirely apathetic; but there was a calm, settled depth of anguish in her large, dark eye, that spoke of something far otherwise.

"And where do you mean to go, my poor woman?" said Mrs. Bird.

"To Canada, if I only knew where that was. Is it very far off, is Canada?" said she, looking up, with a simple, confiding air, to Mrs. Bird's face.

"Poor thing!" said Mrs. Bird, involuntarily.

"Is't a very great way off, think?" said the woman, earnestly.

"Much further than you think, poor child!" said Mrs. Bird; "but we will try to think what can be done for you. Here, Dinah, make her up a bed in your own room, close by the kitchen, and I'll think what to do for her in the morning. Meanwhile, never fear, poor woman; put your trust in God; he will protect you."

Mrs. Bird and her husband reentered the parlor. She sat down in her little rocking-chair before the fire, swaying thoughtfully to and fro. Mr. Bird strode up and down the room, grumbling to himself, "Pish! pshaw! confounded awkward business!" At length, striding up to his wife, he said,

"I say, wife, she'll have to get away from here, this very night. That fellow will be down on the scent bright and early to-morrow morning; if 'twas only the woman, she could lie quiet till it was over; but that little chap can't be kept still by a troop of horse and foot, I'll warrant me; he'll bring it all out, popping his head out of some window or door. A pretty kettle of fish it would be for me, too, to be caught with them both here, just now! No; they'll have to be got off to-night."

"To-night! How is it possible?—where to?"

"Well, I know pretty well where to," said the senator, beginning to put on his boots, with a reflective air; and, stopping when his leg was half in, he embraced his knee with both hands, and seemed to go off in deep meditation.

"It's a confounded awkward, ugly business," said he, at last, beginning to tug at his boot-straps again, "and that's a fact!" After one boot was fairly on, the senator sat with the other in his hand, profoundly studying the figure of the carpet. "It will have to be done, though, for aught I see,—hang it all!" and he drew the other boot anxiously on, and looked out of the window.

Now, little Mrs. Bird was a discreet woman,—a woman who never in her life said, "I told you so!" and, on the present occasion, though pretty well aware of the shape her husband's meditations were taking, she very prudently forbore to meddle with them, only sat very quietly in her chair, and looked quite ready to hear her liege lord's intentions, when he should think proper to utter them.

"You see," he said, "there's my old client, Van Trompe, has come over from Kentucky, and set all his slaves free; and he has bought a place seven miles up the creek, here, back in the woods, where nobody goes, unless they go on purpose; and it's a place that isn't found in a hurry. There she'd be safe enough; but the plague of the thing is, nobody could drive a carriage there to-night, but *me*."

"Why not? Cudjoe is an excellent driver."

"Ay, ay, but here it is. The creek has to be crossed twice; and the second crossing is quite dangerous, unless one knows it as I do. I have crossed it a hundred times on horseback, and know exactly the turns to take. And so, you see, there's no help for it. Cudjoe must put in the horses, as quietly as may be, about twelve o'clock, and I'll take her over; and then, to give color to the matter, he must carry me on to the next tavern, to take the stage[7] for Columbus, that comes by about three or four, and so it will look as if I had had the carriage only for that. I shall get into business bright and early in the morn-

7. Stagecoach.

ing. But I'm thinking I shall feel rather cheap there, after all that's been said and done; but, hang it, I can't help it!"

"Your heart is better than your head, in this case, John," said the wife, laying her little white hand on his. "Could I ever have loved you, had I not known you better than you know yourself?" And the little woman looked so handsome, with the tears sparkling in her eyes, that the senator thought he must be a decidedly clever fellow, to get such a pretty creature into such a passionate admiration of him; and so, what could he do but walk off soberly, to see about the carriage. At the door, however, he stopped a moment, and then coming back, he said, with some hesitation,

"Mary, I don't know how you'd feel about it, but there's that drawer full of things—of—of—poor little Henry's." So saying, he turned quickly on his heel, and shut the door after him.

His wife opened the little bed-room door adjoining her room, and, taking the candle, set it down on the top of a bureau there; then from a small recess she took a key, and put it thoughtfully in the lock of a drawer, and made a sudden pause, while two boys, who, boy like, had followed close on her heels, stood looking, with silent, significant glances, at their mother. And oh! mother that reads this, has there never been in your house a drawer, or a closet, the opening of which has been to you like the opening again of a little grave? Ah! happy mother that you are, if it has not been so.

Mrs. Bird slowly opened the drawer. There were little coats of many a form and pattern, piles of aprons, and rows of small stockings; and even a pair of little shoes, worn and rubbed at the toes, were peeping from the folds of a paper. There was a toy horse and wagon, a top, a ball,—memorials gathered with many a tear and many a heart-break! She sat down by the drawer, and, leaning her head on her hands over it, wept till the tears fell through her fingers into the drawer; then suddenly raising her head, she began, with nervous haste, selecting the plainest and most substantial articles, and gathering them into a bundle.

"Mamma," said one of the boys, gently touching her arm, "are you going to give away *those* things?"

"My dear boys," she said, softly and earnestly, "if our dear, loving little Henry looks down from heaven, he would be glad to have us do this. I could not find it in my heart to give them away to any common person—to anybody that was happy; but I give them to a mother more heart-broken and sorrowful than I am; and I hope God will send his blessings with them!"

There are in this world blessed souls, whose sorrows all spring up into joys for others; whose earthly hopes, laid in the grave with many tears, are the seed from which spring healing flowers and balm for the desolate and the distressed. Among such was the delicate woman who sits there by the lamp, dropping slow tears, while she prepares the memorials of her own lost one for the outcast wanderer.

After a while, Mrs. Bird opened a wardrobe, and, taking from thence a plain, serviceable dress or two, she sat down busily to her work-table, and, with needle, scissors, and thimble, at hand, quietly commenced the "letting down" process which her husband had recommended, and continued busily at it till the old clock in the corner struck twelve, and she heard the low rattling of wheels at the door.

"Mary," said her husband, coming in, with his overcoat in his hand, "you must wake her up now; we must be off."

Mrs. Bird hastily deposited the various articles she had collected in a small plain trunk, and locking it, desired her husband to see it in the carriage, and then proceeded to call the woman. Soon, arrayed in a cloak, bonnet, and shawl, that had belonged to her benefactress, she appeared at the door with her child in her arms. Mr. Bird hurried her into the carriage, and Mrs. Bird pressed on after her to the carriage steps. Eliza leaned out of the carriage, and put out her hand,—a hand as soft and beautiful as was given in return. She fixed her large, dark eyes, full of earnest meaning, on Mrs. Bird's face, and seemed going to speak. Her lips moved,—she tried once or twice, but there was no sound,—and pointing upward, with a look never to be forgotten, she fell back in the seat, and covered her face. The door was shut, and the carriage drove on.

What a situation, now, for a patriotic senator, that had been all the week before spurring up the legislature of his native state to pass more stringent resolutions against escaping fugitives, their harborers and abettors!

Our good senator in his native state had not been exceeded by any of his brethren at Washington, in the sort of eloquence which has won for them immortal renown! How sublimely he had sat with his hands in his pockets, and scouted[8] all sentimental weakness of those who would put the welfare of a few miserable fugitives before great state interests!

He was as bold as a lion about it, and "mightily convinced" not only himself, but everybody that heard him;—but then his idea of a fugitive was only an idea of the letters that spell the word,—or, at the most, the image of a little newspaper picture of a man with a stick and bundle, with "Ran away from the subscriber" under it. The magic of the real presence of distress,—the imploring human eye, the frail, trembling human hand, the despairing appeal of helpless agony,—these he had never tried. He had never thought that a fugitive might be a hapless mother, a defenceless child,—like that one which was now wearing his lost boy's little well-known cap; and so, as our poor senator was not stone or steel,—as he was a man, and a downright noblehearted one, too,—he was, as everybody must see, in a sad case for his patriotism. And you need not exult over him, good brother of the Southern States; for we have some inklings that many of you, under similar circumstances, would not do much better. We have reason to know, in Kentucky, as in Mississippi, are noble and generous hearts, to whom never was tale of suffering told in vain. Ah, good brother! is it fair for you to expect of us services which your own brave, honorable heart would not allow you to render, were you in our place?

Be that as it may, if our good senator was a political sinner, he was in a fair way to expiate it by his night's penance. There had been a long continuous period of rainy weather, and the soft, rich earth of Ohio, as every one knows, is admirably suited to the manufacture of mud,—and the road was an Ohio railroad of the good old times.

"And pray, what sort of a road may that be?" says some eastern traveller, who has been accustomed to connect no ideas with a railroad, but those of smoothness or speed.

8. Mocked.

Know, then, innocent eastern friend, that in benighted regions of the west, where the mud is of unfathomable and sublime depth, roads are made of round rough logs, arranged transversely side by side, and coated over in their pristine freshness with earth, turf, and whatsoever may come to hand, and then the rejoicing native calleth it a road, and straightway essayeth to ride thereupon. In process of time, the rains wash off all the turf and grass aforesaid, move the logs hither and thither, in picturesque positions, up, down and crosswise, with divers chasms and ruts of black mud intervening.

Over such a road as this our senator went stumbling along, making moral reflections as continuously as under the circumstances could be expected,—the carriage proceeding along much as follows,—bump! bump! bump! slush! down in the mud!—the senator, woman and child, reversing their positions so suddenly as to come, without any very accurate adjustment, against the windows of the down-hill side. Carriage sticks fast, while Cudjoe on the outside is heard making a great muster among the horses. After various ineffectual pullings and twitchings, just as the senator is losing all patience, the carriage suddenly rights itself with a bounce,—two front wheels go down into another abyss, and senator, woman, and child, all tumble promiscuously on to the front seat,—senator's hat is jammed over his eyes and nose quite unceremoniously, and he considers himself fairly extinguished;—child cries, and Cudjoe on the outside delivers animated addresses to the horses, who are kicking, and floundering, and straining, under repeated cracks of the whip. Carriage springs up, with another bounce,—down go the hind wheels,—senator, woman, and child, fly over on to the back seat, his elbows encountering her bonnet, and both her feet being jammed into his hat, which flies off in the concussion. After a few moments the "slough" is passed, and the horses stop, panting;—the senator finds his hat, the woman straightens her bonnet and hushes her child, and they brace themselves firmly for what is yet to come.

For a while only the continuous bump! bump! intermingled, just by way of variety, with divers side plunges and compound shakes; and they begin to flatter themselves that they are not so badly off, after all. At last, with a square plunge, which puts all on to their feet and then down into their seats with incredible quickness, the carriage stops,—and, after much outside commotion, Cudjoe appears at the door.

"Please, sir, it's powerful bad spot, this yer. I don't know how we's to get clar out. I'm a thinkin' we'll have to be a gettin' rails."[9]

The senator despairingly steps out, picking gingerly for some firm foothold; down goes one foot an immeasurable depth,—he tries to pull it up, loses his balance, and tumbles over into the mud, and is fished out, in a very despairing condition, by Cudjoe.

But we forbear, out of sympathy to our readers' bones. Western travellers, who have beguiled the midnight hour in the interesting process of pulling down rail fences, to pry their carriages out of mud holes, will have a respectful and mournful sympathy with our unfortunate hero. We beg them to drop a silent tear, and pass on.

9. A reference to the practice of removing boards from rail fences to make tracks to enable a carriage or cart to get out of the mud.

It was full late in the night when the carriage emerged, dripping and bespattered, out of the creek, and stood at the door of a large farm-house.

It took no inconsiderable perseverance to arouse the inmates; but at last the respectable proprietor appeared, and undid the door. He was a great, tall, bristling Orson of a fellow,[1] full six feet and some inches in his stockings, and arrayed in a red flannel hunting-shirt. A very heavy *mat* of sandy hair, in a decidedly tousled condition, and a beard of some days' growth, gave the worthy man an appearance, to say the least, not particularly prepossessing. He stood for a few minutes holding the candle aloft, and blinking on our travellers with a dismal and mystified expression that was truly ludicrous. It cost some effort of our senator to induce him to comprehend the case fully; and while he is doing his best at that, we shall give him a little introduction to our readers.

Honest old John Van Trompe was once quite a considerable land-holder and slave-owner in the State of Kentucky. Having "nothing of the bear about him but the skin,"[2] and being gifted by nature with a great, honest, just heart, quite equal to his gigantic frame, he had been for some years witnessing with repressed uneasiness the workings of a system equally bad for oppressor and oppressed. At last, one day, John's great heart had swelled altogether too big to wear his bonds any longer; so he just took his pocket-book out of his desk, and went over into Ohio, and bought a quarter of a township of good, rich land, made out free papers for all his people,—men, women, and children,—packed them up in wagons, and sent them off to settle down; and then honest John turned his face up the creek, and sat quietly down on a snug, retired farm, to enjoy his conscience and his reflections.

"Are you the man that will shelter a poor woman and child from slave-catchers?" said the senator, explicitly.

"I rather think I am," said honest John, with some considerable emphasis.

"I thought so," said the senator.

"If there's anybody comes," said the good man, stretching his tall, muscular form upward, "why here I'm ready for him: and I've got seven sons, each six foot high, and they'll be ready for 'em. Give our respects to 'em," said John; "tell 'em it's no matter how soon they call,—make no kinder difference to us," said John, running his fingers through the shock of hair that thatched his head, and bursting out into a great laugh.

Weary, jaded, and spiritless, Eliza dragged herself up to the door, with her child lying in a heavy sleep on her arm. The rough man held the candle to her face, and uttering a kind of compassionate grunt, opened the door of a small bedroom adjoining to the large kitchen where they were standing, and motioned her to go in. He took down a candle, and lighting it, set it upon the table, and then addressed himself to Eliza.

"Now, I say, gal, you needn't be a bit afeard, let who will come here. I'm up to all that sort o' thing," said he, pointing to two or three goodly rifles over the mantel-piece; "and most people that know me know that 't wouldn't be healthy to try to get anybody out o' my house when I'm agin it. So *now* you jist

1. A strong, wild man; from the story of "Orson and Valentine," an early French romance that appeared in English around 1550. Orson is the lost son of a king; abandoned in the woods, he was raised by a bear.

2. As recorded in James Boswell's *Life of Samuel Johnson* (1791), the Anglo-Irish author Oliver Goldsmith (1730–1794) proclaimed that the great English author and critic Johnson (1709–1784) "had nothing of the bear but his skin."

go to sleep now, as quiet as if yer mother was a rockin' ye," said he, as he shut the door.

"Why, this is an uncommon handsome un," he said to the senator. "Ah, well; handsome uns has the greatest cause to run, sometimes, if they has any kind o' feelin, such as decent women should. I know all about that."

The senator, in a few words, briefly explained Eliza's history.

"O! ou! aw! now, I want to know?" said the good man, pitifully; "sho! now sho! That's natur now, poor crittur! hunted down now like a deer,—hunted down, jest for havin' natural feelin's, and doin' what no kind o' mother could help a doin'! I tell ye what, these yer things make me come the nighest to swearin', now, o' most anything," said honest John, as he wiped his eyes with the back of a great, freckled, yellow hand. "I tell yer what, stranger, it was years and years before I'd jine the church, 'cause the ministers round in our parts used to preach that the Bible went in for these ere cuttings up,—and I couldn't be up to 'em with their Greek and Hebrew, and so I took up agin 'em, Bible and all. I never jined the church till I found a minister that was up to 'em all in Greek and all that, and he said right the contrary; and then I took right hold, and jined the church,—I did now, fact," said John, who had been all this time uncorking some very frisky bottled cider, which at this juncture he presented.

"Ye'd better jest put up here, now, till daylight," said he, heartily, "and I'll call up the old woman, and have a bed got ready for you in no time."

"Thank you, my good friend," said the senator, "I must be along, to take the night stage for Columbus."

"Ah! well, then, if you must, I'll go a piece with you, and show you a cross road that will take you there better than the road you came on. That road's mighty bad."

John equipped himself, and, with a lantern in hand, was soon seen guiding the senator's carriage towards a road that ran down in a hollow, back of his dwelling. When they parted, the senator put into his hand a ten-dollar bill.

"It's for her," he said, briefly.

"Ay, ay," said John, with equal conciseness.

They shook hands, and parted.

* * *

CHAPTER XII. SELECT INCIDENT OF LAWFUL TRADE

> "In Ramah there was a voice heard,—weeping, and lamentation, and great mourning; Rachel weeping for her children, and would not be comforted."[3]

Mr. Haley and Tom jogged onward in their wagon, each, for a time, absorbed in his own reflections. Now, the reflections of two men sitting side by side are a curious thing,—seated on the same seat, having the same eyes, ears, hands and organs of all sorts, and having pass before their eyes the same objects,—it is wonderful what a variety we shall find in these same reflections!

As, for example, Mr. Haley: he thought first of Tom's length, and breadth, and height, and what he would sell for, if he was kept fat and in good case

3. Paraphrase of Jeremiah 31.15.

till he got him into market. He thought of how he should make out his gang; he thought of the respective market value of certain supposititious men and women and children who were to compose it, and other kindred topics of the business; then he thought of himself, and how humane he was, that whereas other men chained their "niggers" hand and foot both, he only put fetters on the feet, and left Tom the use of his hands, as long as he behaved well; and he sighed to think how ungrateful human nature was, so that there was even room to doubt whether Tom appreciated his mercies. He had been taken in so by "niggers" whom he had favored; but still he was astonished to consider how good-natured he yet remained!

As to Tom, he was thinking over some words of an unfashionable old book, which kept running through his head again and again, as follows: "We have here no continuing city, but we seek one to come; wherefore God himself is not ashamed to be called our God; for he hath prepared for us a city."[4] These words of an ancient volume, got up principally by "ignorant and unlearned men," have, through all time, kept up, somehow, a strange sort of power over the minds of poor, simple fellows, like Tom. They stir up the soul from its depths, and rouse, as with trumpet call, courage, energy, and enthusiasm, where before was only the blackness of despair.

Mr. Haley pulled out of his pocket sundry newspapers, and began looking over their advertisements, with absorbed interest. He was not a remarkably fluent reader, and was in the habit of reading in a sort of recitative half-aloud, by way of calling in his ears to verify the deductions of his eyes. In this tone he slowly recited the following paragraph:

> "EXECUTOR'S SALE,—NEGROES!—Agreeably to order of court, will be sold, on Tuesday, February 20, before the Court-house door, in the town of Washington, Kentucky, the following negroes: Hagar, aged 60; John, aged 30; Ben, aged 21; Saul, aged 25; Albert, aged 14. Sold for the benefit of the creditors and heirs of the estate of Jesse Blutchford, Esq.
>
> SAMUEL MORRIS,
> THOMAS FLINT,
> *Executors.*"

"This yer I must look at," said he to Tom, for want of somebody else to talk to.

"Ye see, I'm going to get up a prime gang to take down with ye, Tom; it'll make it sociable and pleasant like,—good company will, ye know. We must drive right to Washington[5] first and foremost, and then I'll clap you into jail, while I does the business."

Tom received this agreeable intelligence quite meekly; simply wondering, in his own heart, how many of these doomed men had wives and children, and whether they would feel as he did about leaving them. It is to be confessed, too, that the naïve, off-hand information that he was to be thrown into jail by no means produced an agreeable impression on a poor fellow who had always prided himself on a strictly honest and upright course of life. Yes, Tom, we must confess it, was rather proud of his honesty, poor fellow,—not having very much else to be proud of;—if he had belonged to some of the higher walks of society, he, perhaps, would never have been reduced to such

4. Amalgam of Hebrews 11.16 and Hebrews 13.14.
5. Washington, Kentucky; upriver from New Orleans.

straits. However, the day wore on, and the evening saw Haley and Tom comfortably accommodated in Washington,—the one in a tavern, and the other in a jail.

About eleven o'clock the next day, a mixed throng was gathered around the court-house steps,—smoking, chewing, spitting, swearing, and conversing, according to their respective tastes and turns,—waiting for the auction to commence. The men and women to be sold sat in a group apart, talking in a low tone to each other. The woman who had been advertised by the name of Hagar was a regular African in feature and figure. She might have been sixty, but was older than that by hard work and disease, was partially blind, and somewhat crippled with rheumatism. By her side stood her only remaining son, Albert, a bright-looking little fellow of fourteen years. The boy was the only survivor of a large family, who had been successively sold away from her to a southern market. The mother held on to him with both her shaking hands, and eyed with intense trepidation every one who walked up to examine him.

"Don't be feard, Aunt Hagar," said the oldest of the men, "I spoke to Mas'r Thomas 'bout it, and he thought he might manage to sell you in a lot both together."

"Dey needn't call me worn out yet," said she, lifting her shaking hands. "I can cook yet, and scrub, and scour,—I'm wuth a buying, if I do come cheap;—tell em dat ar,—you *tell* em," she added, earnestly.

Haley here forced his way into the group, walked up to the old man, pulled his mouth open and looked in, felt of his teeth, made him stand and straighten himself, bend his back, and perform various evolutions to show his muscles; and then passed on to the next, and put him through the same trial. Walking up last to the boy, he felt of his arms, straightened his hands, and looked at his fingers, and made him jump, to show his agility.

"He an't gwine to be sold widout me!" said the old woman, with passionate eagerness; "he and I goes in a lot together; I's rail strong yet, Mas'r, and can do heaps o' work,—heaps on it, Mas'r."

"On plantation?" said Haley, with a contemptuous glance. "Likely story!" and, as if satisfied with his examination, he walked out and looked, and stood with his hands in his pocket, his cigar in his mouth, and his hat cocked on one side, ready for action.

"What think of 'em?" said a man who had been following Haley's examination, as if to make up his own mind from it.

"Wal," said Haley, spitting, "I shall put in, I think, for the youngerly ones and the boy."

"They want to sell the boy and the old woman together," said the man.

"Find it a tight pull;—why, she's an old rack o' bones,—not worth her salt."

"You wouldn't, then?" said the man.

"Anybody'd be a fool 't would. She's half blind, crooked with rheumatis, and foolish to boot."

"Some buys up these yer old critturs, and ses there's a sight more wear in 'em than a body'd think," said the man, reflectively.

"No go, 't all," said Haley; "wouldn't take her for a present,—fact,—I've *seen*, now."

"Wal, 'tis kinder pity, now, not to buy her with her son,—her heart seems so sot on him,—s'pose they fling her in cheap."

"Them that's got money to spend that ar way, it's all well enough. I shall bid off on that ar boy for a plantation-hand;—wouldn't be bothered with her, no way,—not if they'd give her to me," said Haley.

"She'll take on desp't," said the man.

"Nat'lly, she will," said the trader, coolly.

The conversation was here interrupted by a busy hum in the audience; and the auctioneer, a short, bustling, important fellow, elbowed his way into the crowd. The old woman drew in her breath, and caught instinctively at her son.

"Keep close to yer mammy, Albert,—close,—dey'll put us up togedder," she said.

"O, mammy, I'm feared they won't," said the boy.

"Dey must, child; I can't live, no ways, if they don't," said the old creature, vehemently.

The stentorian tones of the auctioneer, calling out to clear the way, now announced that the sale was about to commence. A place was cleared, and the bidding began. The different men on the list were soon knocked off at prices which showed a pretty brisk demand in the market; two of them fell to Haley.

"Come, now, young un," said the auctioneer, giving the boy a touch with his hammer, "be up and show your springs, now."

"Put us two up togedder, togedder,—do please, Mas'r," said the old woman, holding fast to her boy.

"Be off," said the man, gruffy, pushing her hands away; "you come last. Now, darkey, spring;" and, with the word, he pushed the boy toward the block, while a deep, heavy groan rose behind him. The boy paused, and looked back; but there was no time to stay, and, dashing the tears from his large, bright eyes, he was up in a moment.

His fine figure, alert limbs, and bright face, raised an instant competition, and half a dozen bids simultaneously met the ear of the auctioneer. Anxious, half-frightened, he looked from side to side, as he heard the clatter of contending bids,—now here, now there,—till the hammer fell. Haley had got him. He was pushed from the block toward his new master, but stopped one moment, and looked back, when his poor old mother, trembling in every limb, held out her shaking hands toward him.

"Buy me too, Mas'r, for de dear Lord's sake!—buy me,—I shall die if you don't!"

"You'll die if I do, that's the kink of it," said Haley,—"no!" And he turned on his heel.

The bidding for the poor old creature was summary. The man who had addressed Haley, and who seemed not destitute of compassion, bought her for a trifle, and the spectators began to disperse.

The poor victims of the sale, who had been brought up in one place together for years, gathered round the despairing old mother, whose agony was pitiful to see.

"Couldn't dey leave me one? Mas'r allers said I should have one,—he did," she repeated over and over, in heartbroken tones.

"Trust in the Lord, Aunt Hagar," said the oldest of the men, sorrowfully.

"What good will it do?" said she, sobbing passionately.

"Mother, mother,—don't! don't!" said the boy. "They say you's got a good master."

"I don't care,—I don't care. O, Albert! oh, my boy! you's my last baby. Lord, how ken I?"

"Come, take her off, can't some of ye?" said Haley, dryly; "don't do no good for her to go on that ar way."

The old men of the company, partly by persuasion and partly by force, loosed the poor creature's last despairing hold, and, as they led her off to her new master's wagon, strove to comfort her.

"Now!" said Haley, pushing his three purchases together, and producing a bundle of handcuffs, which he proceeded to put on their wrists; and fastening each handcuff to a long chain, he drove them before him to the jail.

A few days saw Haley, with his possessions, safely deposited on one of the Ohio boats. It was the commencement of his gang, to be augmented, as the boat moved on, by various other merchandise of the same kind, which he, or his agent, had stored for him in various points along shore.

The La Belle Rivière,[6] as brave and beautiful a boat as ever walked the waters of her namesake river, was floating gayly down the stream, under a brilliant sky, the stripes and stars of free America waving and fluttering over head; the guards crowded with well-dressed ladies and gentlemen walking and enjoying the delightful day. All was full of life, buoyant and rejoicing;—all but Haley's gang, who were stored, with other freight, on the lower deck, and who, somehow, did not seem to appreciate their various privileges, as they sat in a knot, talking to each other in low tones.

"Boys," said Haley, coming up, briskly, "I hope you keep up good heart, and are cheerful. Now, no sulks, ye see; keep stiff upper lip, boys; do well by me, and I'll do well by you."

The boys addressed responded the invariable "Yes, Mas'r," for ages the watchword of poor Africa; but it's to be owned they did not look particularly cheerful; they had their various little prejudices in favor of wives, mothers, sisters, and children, seen for the last time,—and though "they that wasted them required of them mirth,"[7] it was not instantly forthcoming.

"I've got a wife," spoke out the article enumerated as "John, aged thirty," and he laid his chained hand on Tom's knee,—"and she don't know a word about this, poor girl!"

"Where does she live?" said Tom.

"In a tavern a piece down here," said John; "I wish, now, I *could* see her once more in this world," he added.

Poor John! It *was* rather natural; and the tears that fell, as he spoke, came as naturally as if he had been a white man. Tom drew a long breath from a sore heart, and tried, in his poor way, to comfort him.

And over head, in the cabin, sat fathers and mothers, husbands and wives; and merry, dancing children moved round among them, like so many little butterflies, and everything was going on quite easy and comfortable.

"O, mamma," said a boy, who had just come up from below, "there's a negro trader on board, and he's brought four or five slaves down there."

"Poor creatures!" said the mother, in a tone between grief and indignation.

"What's that?" said another lady.

"Some poor slaves below," said the mother.

6. The Beautiful River (French).

7. Paraphrase of Psalm 137.3.

"And they've got chains on," said the boy.

"What a shame to our country that such sights are to be seen!" said another lady.

"O, there's a great deal to be said on both sides of the subject," said a genteel woman, who sat at her state-room door sewing, while her little girl and boy were playing round her. "I've been south, and I must say I think the negroes are better off than they would be to be free."

"In some respects, some of them are well off, I grant," said the lady to whose remark she had answered. "The most dreadful part of slavery, to my mind, is its outrages on the feelings and affections,—the separating of families, for example."

"That *is* a bad thing, certainly," said the other lady, holding up a baby's dress she had just completed, and looking intently on its trimmings; "but then, I fancy, it don't occur often."

"O, it does," said the first lady, eagerly; "I've lived many years in Kentucky and Virginia both, and I've seen enough to make any one's heart sick. Suppose, ma'am, your two children, there, should be taken from you, and sold?"

"We can't reason from our feelings to those of this class of persons," said the other lady, sorting out some worsteds on her lap.

"Indeed, ma'am, you can know nothing of them, if you say so," answered the first lady, warmly. "I was born and brought up among them. I know they *do* feel, just as keenly,—even more so, perhaps,—as we do."

The lady said "Indeed!" yawned, and looked out the cabin window, and finally repeated, for a finale, the remark with which she had begun,—"After all, I think they are better off than they would be to be free."

"It's undoubtedly the intention of Providence that the African race should be servants,—kept in a low condition," said a grave-looking gentleman in black, a clergyman, seated by the cabin door. "'Cursed be Canaan; a servant of servants shall he be,' the scripture says."[8]

"I say, stranger, is that ar what that text means?" said a tall man, standing by.

"Undoubtedly. It pleased Providence, for some inscrutable reason, to doom the race to bondage, ages ago; and we must not set up our opinion against that."

"Well, then, we'll all go ahead and buy up niggers," said the man, "if that's the way of Providence,—won't we, Squire?" said he, turning to Haley, who had been standing, with his hands in his pockets, by the stove, and intently listening to the conversation.

"Yes," continued the tall man, "we must all be resigned to the decrees of Providence. Niggers must be sold, and trucked round, and kept under; it's what they's made for. 'Pears like this yer view's quite refreshing, an't it, stranger?" said he to Haley.

"I never thought on 't," said Haley. "I couldn't have said as much, myself; I ha'nt no larning. I took up the trade just to make a living; if 't an't right, I calculated to 'pent on 't in time, *ye* know."

"And now you'll save yerself the trouble, won't ye?" said the tall man. "See what 't is, now, to know scripture. If ye'd only studied yer Bible, like this yer

8. Genesis 9.25, from the story of Noah and his son Ham; a passage cited by proslavery writers to justify slavery on the assumption that Africans were Ham's descendants.

good man, ye might have know'd it before, and saved ye a heap o' trouble. Ye could jist have said, 'Cussed be'—what's his name?—'and 't would all have come right.'" And the stranger, who was no other than the honest drover whom we introduced to our readers in the Kentucky tavern,[9] sat down, and began smoking, with a curious smile on his long, dry face.

A tall, slender young man, with a face expressive of great feeling and intelligence, here broke in, and repeated the words, "'All things whatsoever ye would that men should do unto you, do ye even so unto them.'[1] I suppose," he added, "*that* is scripture, as much as 'Cursed be Canaan.'"

"Wal, it seems quite *as* plain a text, stranger," said John the drover, "to poor fellows like us, now;" and John smoked on like a volcano.

The young man paused, looked as if he was going to say more, when suddenly the boat stopped, and the company made the usual steamboat rush, to see where they were landing.

"Both them ar chaps parsons?" said John to one of the men, as they were going out.

The man nodded.

As the boat stopped, a black woman came running wildly up the plank, darted into the crowd, flew up to where the slave gang sat, and threw her arms round that unfortunate piece of merchandise before enumerated—"John, aged thirty," and with sobs and tears bemoaned him as her husband.

But what needs tell the story, told too oft,—every day told,—of heart-strings rent and broken,—the weak broken and torn for the profit and convenience of the strong! It needs not to be told;—every day is telling it,—telling it, too, in the ear of One who is not deaf, though he be long silent.

The young man who had spoken for the cause of humanity and God before stood with folded arms, looking on this scene. He turned, and Haley was standing at his side. "My friend," he said, speaking with thick utterance, "how can you, how dare you, carry on a trade like this? Look at those poor creatures! Here I am, rejoicing in my heart that I am going home to my wife and child; and the same bell which is a signal to carry me onward towards them will part this poor man and his wife forever. Depend upon it, God will bring you into judgment for this."

The trader turned away in silence.

"I say, now," said the drover, touching his elbow, "there's differences in parsons, an't there? 'Cussed be Canaan' don't seem to go down with this 'un, does it?"

Haley gave an uneasy growl.

"And that ar an't the worse on 't," said John; "mabbe it won't go down with the Lord, neither, when ye come to settle with Him, one o' these days, as all on us must, I reckon."

Haley walked reflectively to the other end of the boat.

"If I make pretty handsomely on one or two next gangs," he thought, "I reckon I'll stop off this yer; it's really getting dangerous." And he took out his pocket-book, and began adding over his accounts,—a process which many gentlemen besides Mr. Haley have found a specific[2] for an uneasy conscience.

9. Mr. Symmes was introduced at the end of Chapter III. "Drover": cattle driver, farmer.

1. From the Sermon on the Mount (Matthew 7.12).

2. Healing tonic.

The boat swept proudly away from the shore, and all went on merrily, as before. Men talked, and loafed, and read, and smoked. Women sewed, and children played, and the boat passed on her way.

One day, when she lay to for a while at a small town in Kentucky, Haley went up into the place on a little matter of business.

Tom, whose fetters did not prevent his taking a moderate circuit, had drawn near the side of the boat, and stood listlessly gazing over the railings. After a time, he saw the trader returning, with an alert step, in company with a colored woman, bearing in her arms a young child. She was dressed quite respectably, and a colored man followed her, bringing along a small trunk. The woman came cheerfully onward, talking, as she came, with the man who bore her trunk, and so passed up the plank into the boat. The bell rung, the steamer whizzed, the engine groaned and coughed, and away swept the boat down the river.

The woman walked forward among the boxes and bales of the lower deck, and, sitting down, busied herself with chirruping to her baby.

Haley made a turn or two about the boat, and then, coming up, seated himself near her, and began saying something to her in an indifferent undertone.

Tom soon noticed a heavy cloud passing over the woman's brow; and that she answered rapidly, and with great vehemence.

"I don't believe it,—I won't believe it!" he heard her say. "You're jist a foolin with me."

"If you won't believe it, look here!" said the man, drawing out a paper; "this yer's the bill of sale, and there's your master's name to it; and I paid down good solid cash for it, too, I can tell you,—so, now!"

"I don't believe Mas'r would cheat me so; it can't be true!" said the woman, with increasing agitation.

"You can ask any of these men here, that can read writing. Here!" he said, to a man that was passing by, "jist read this yer, won't you! This yer gal won't believe me, when I tell her what 't is."

"Why, it's a bill of sale, signed by John Fosdick," said the man, "making over to you the girl Lucy and her child. It's all straight enough, for aught I see."

The woman's passionate exclamations collected a crowd around her, and the trader briefly explained to them the cause of the agitation.

"He told me that I was going down to Louisville, to hire out as cook to the same tavern where my husband works,—that's what Mas'r told me, his own self; and I can't believe he'd lie to me," said the woman.

"But he has sold you, my poor woman, there's no doubt about it," said a good-natured looking man, who had been examining the papers; "he has done it, and no mistake."

"Then it's no account talking," said the woman, suddenly growing quite calm; and, clasping her child tighter in her arms, she sat down on her box, turned her back round, and gazed listlessly into the river.

"Going to take it easy, after all!" said the trader. "Gal's got grit, I see."

The woman looked calm, as the boat went on; and a beautiful soft summer breeze passed like a compassionate spirit over her head,—the gentle breeze, that never inquires whether the brow is dusky or fair that it fans. And she saw sunshine sparkling on the water, in golden ripples, and heard gay voices, full of ease and pleasure, talking around her everywhere; but her heart lay as if a great stone had fallen on it. Her baby raised himself up against her, and stroked her cheeks with his little hands; and, springing up and down, crowing and chatting, seemed determined to arouse her. She strained him suddenly and tightly in her arms, and slowly one tear after another fell on his wondering, unconscious face; and gradually she seemed, and little by little, to grow calmer, and busied herself with tending and nursing him.

The child, a boy of ten months, was uncommonly large and strong of his age, and very vigorous in his limbs. Never, for a moment, still, he kept his mother constantly busy in holding him, and guarding his springing activity.

"That's a fine chap!" said a man, suddenly stopping opposite to him, with his hands in his pockets. "How old is he?"

"Ten months and a half," said the mother.

The man whistled to the boy, and offered him part of a stick of candy, which he eagerly grabbed at, and very soon had it in a baby's general depository, to wit, his mouth.

"Rum fellow!" said the man. "Knows what's what!" and he whistled, and walked on. When he had got to the other side of the boat, he came across Haley, who was smoking on top of a pile of boxes.

The stranger produced a match, and lighted a cigar, saying, as he did so,

"Decentish kind o' wench you've got round there, stranger."

"Why, I reckon she *is* tol'able fair," said Haley, blowing the smoke out of his mouth.

"Taking her down south?" said the man.

Haley nodded, and smoked on.

"Plantation hand?" said the man.

"Wal," said Haley, "I'm fillin' out an order for a plantation, and I think I shall put her in. They telled me she was a good cook; and they can use her for that, or set her at the cotton-picking. She's got the right fingers for that; I looked at 'em. Sell well, either way;" and Haley resumed his cigar.

"They won't want the young 'un on a plantation," said the man.

"I shall sell him, first chance I find," said Haley, lighting another cigar.

"S'pose you'd be selling him tol'able cheap," said the stranger, mounting the pile of boxes, and sitting down comfortably.

"Don't know 'bout that," said Haley; "he's a pretty smart young 'un,—straight, fat, strong; flesh as hard as a brick!"

"Very true, but then there's all the bother and expense of raisin'."

"Nonsense!" said Haley; "they is raised as easy as any kind of critter there is going; they an't a bit more trouble than pups. This yer chap will be running all round, in a month."

"I've got a good place for raisin', and I thought of takin' in a little more stock," said the man. "One cook lost a young 'un last week,—got drownded in a wash-tub, while she was a hangin' out clothes,—and I reckon it would be well enough to set her to raisin' this yer."

Haley and the stranger smoked a while in silence, neither seeming willing to broach the test question of the interview. At last the man resumed:

"You wouldn't think of wantin' more than ten dollars for that ar chap, seeing you *must* get him off yer hand, any how?"

Haley shook his head, and spit impressively.

"That won't do, no ways," he said, and began his smoking again.

"Well, stranger, what will you take?"

"Well, now," said Haley, "I *could* raise that ar chap myself, or get him raised; he's oncommon likely and healthy, and he'd fetch a hundred dollars, six months hence; and, in a year or two, he'd bring two hundred, if I had him in the right spot;—so I shan't take a cent less nor fifty for him now."

"O, stranger! that's rediculous, altogether," said the man.

"Fact!" said Haley, with a decisive nod of his head.

"I'll give thirty for him," said the stranger, "but not a cent more."

"Now, I'll tell ye what I will do," said Haley, spitting again, with renewed decision. "I'll split the difference, and say forty-five; and that's the most I will do."

"Well, agreed!" said the man, after an interval.

"Done!" said Haley. "Where do you land?"

"At Louisville," said the man.

"Louisville," said Haley. "Very fair, we get there about dusk. Chap will be asleep,—all fair,—get him off quietly, and no screaming,—happens beautiful,—I like to do everything quietly,—I hates all kind of agitation and fluster." And so, after a transfer of certain bills had passed from the man's pocket-book to the trader's, he resumed his cigar.

It was a bright, tranquil evening when the boat stopped at the wharf at Louisville. The woman had been sitting with her baby in her arms, now wrapped in a heavy sleep. When she heard the name of the place called out, she hastily laid the child down in a little cradle formed by the hollow among the boxes, first carefully spreading under it her cloak; and then she sprung to the side of the boat, in hopes that, among the various hotel-waiters who thronged the wharf, she might see her husband. In this hope, she pressed forward to the front rails, and, stretching far over them, strained her eyes intently on the moving heads on the shore, and the crowd pressed in between her and the child.

"Now's your time," said Haley, taking the sleeping child up, and handing him to the stranger. "Don't wake him up, and set him to crying, now; it would make a devil of a fuss with the gal." The man took the bundle carefully, and was soon lost in the crowd that went up the wharf.

When the boat, creaking, and groaning, and puffing, had loosed from the wharf, and was beginning slowly to strain herself along, the woman returned to her old seat. The trader was sitting there,—the child was gone!

"Why, why,—where?" she began, in bewildered surprise.

"Lucy," said the trader, "your child's gone; you may as well know it first as last. You see, I know'd you couldn't take him down south; and I got a chance to sell him to a first-rate family, that'll raise him better than you can."

The trader had arrived at that stage of Christian and political perfection which has been recommended by some preachers and politicians of the north, lately, in which he had completely overcome every humane weakness and prejudice. His heart was exactly where yours, sir, and mine could be brought, with proper effort and cultivation. The wild look of anguish and utter despair that the woman cast on him might have disturbed one less practised; but he was used to it. He had seen that same look hundreds of times. You can get used to such things, too, my friend; and it is the great object of recent efforts to make our whole northern community used to them, for the glory of the Union. So the trader only regarded the mortal anguish which he saw working in those dark features, those clenched hands, and suffocating breathings, as necessary incidents of the trade, and merely calculated whether she was going to scream, and get up a commotion on the boat; for, like other supporters of our peculiar institution, he decidedly disliked agitation.

But the woman did not scream. The shot had passed too straight and direct through the heart, for cry or tear.

Dizzily she sat down. Her slack hands fell lifeless by her side. Her eyes looked straight forward, but she saw nothing. All the noise and hum of the boat, the groaning of the machinery, mingled dreamily to her bewildered ear; and the poor, dumb-stricken heart had neither cry nor tear to show for its utter misery. She was quite calm.

The trader, who, considering his advantages, was almost as humane as some of our politicians, seemed to feel called on to administer such consolation as the case admitted of.

"I know this yer comes kinder hard, at first, Lucy," said he; "but such a smart, sensible gal as you are, won't give way to it. You see it's *necessary*, and can't be helped!"

"O! don't, Mas'r, don't!" said the woman, with a voice like one that is smothering.

"You're a smart wench, Lucy," he persisted; "I mean to do well by ye, and get ye a nice place down river; and you'll soon get another husband,—such a likely gal as you—"

"O! Mas'r, if you *only* won't talk to me now," said the woman, in a voice of such quick and living anguish that the trader felt that there was something at present in the case beyond his style of operation. He got up, and the woman turned away, and buried her head in her cloak.

The trader walked up and down for a time, and occasionally stopped and looked at her.

"Takes it hard, rather," he soliloquized, "but quiet, tho';—let her sweat a while; she'll come right, by and by!"

Tom had watched the whole transaction from first to last, and had a perfect understanding of its results. To him, it looked like something unutterably horrible and cruel, because, poor, ignorant black soul! he had not learned to generalize, and to take enlarged views. If he had only been instructed by certain ministers of Christianity, he might have thought better of it, and seen in it an every-day incident of a lawful trade; a trade which is the vital support of an institution which some American divines tell us has no evils but such as are inseparable from any other relations in social and domestic life. But Tom, as we see, being a poor, ignorant fellow, whose reading had been confined entirely to the New Testament, could not comfort and solace himself with views like these. His very soul bled within him for what seemed to him the *wrongs* of the poor suffering thing that lay like a crushed reed on the boxes; the feeling, living, bleeding, yet immortal *thing*, which American state law coolly classes with the bundles, and bales, and boxes, among which she is lying.

Tom drew near, and tried to say something; but she only groaned. Honestly, and with tears running down his own cheeks, he spoke of a heart of love in the skies, of a pitying Jesus, and an eternal home; but the ear was deaf with anguish, and the palsied heart could not feel.

Night came on,—night calm, unmoved, and glorious, shining down with her innumerable and solemn angel eyes, twinkling, beautiful, but silent. There was no speech nor language, no pitying voice nor helping hand, from that distant sky. One after another, the voices of business or pleasure died away; all on the boat were sleeping, and the ripples at the prow were plainly heard. Tom stretched himself out on a box, and there, as he lay, he heard, ever and anon, a smothered sob or cry from the prostate creature,—"O! what shall I do? O Lord! O good Lord, do help me!" and so, ever and anon, until the murmur died away in silence.

At midnight, Tom waked, with a sudden start. Something black passed quickly by him to the side of the boat, and he heard a splash in the water. No one else saw or heard anything. He raised his head,—the woman's place was vacant! He got up, and sought about him in vain. The poor bleeding heart was still, at last, and the river rippled and dimpled just as brightly as if it had not closed above it.

Patience! patience! ye whose hearts swell indignant at wrongs like these. Not one throb of anguish, not one tear of the oppressed, is forgotten by the Man of Sorrows, the Lord of Glory. In his patient, generous bosom he bears the anguish of a world. Bear thou, like him, in patience, and labor in love; for sure as he is God, "the year of his redeemed *shall* come."[3]

The trader waked up bright and early, and came out to see to his live stock. It was now his turn to look about in perplexity.

"Where alive is that gal?" he said to Tom.

Tom, who had learned the wisdom of keeping counsel, did not feel called on to state his observations and suspicions, but said he did not know.

"She surely couldn't have got off in the night at any of the landings, for I was awake, and on the look-out, whenever the boat stopped. I never trust these yer things to other folks."

This speech was addressed to Tom quite confidentially, as if it was something that would be specially interesting to him. Tom made no answer.

The trader searched the boat from stem to stern, among boxes, bales and barrels, around the machinery, by the chimneys, in vain.

"Now, I say, Tom, be fair about this yer," he said, when, after a fruitless search, he came where Tom was standing. "You know something about it, now. Don't tell me,—I know you do. I saw the gal stretched out here about ten o'clock, and ag'in at twelve, and ag'in between one and two; and then at four she was gone, and you was sleeping right there all the time. Now, you know something,—you can't help it."

"Well, Mas'r," said Tom, "towards morning something brushed by me, and I kinder half woke; and then I hearn a great splash, and then I clare woke up, and the gal was gone. That's all I know on 't."

The trader was not shocked nor amazed; because, as we said before, he was used to a great many things that you are not used to. Even the awful presence of Death struck no solemn chill upon him. He had seen Death many times,—met him in the way of trade, and got acquainted with him,—and he only thought of him as a hard customer, that embarrassed his property operations very unfairly; and so he only swore that the gal was a baggage,

3. Paraphrase of Isaiah 63.4.

and that he was devilish unlucky, and that, if things went on in this way, he should not make a cent on the trip. In short, he seemed to consider himself an ill-used man, decidedly; but there was no help for it, as the woman had escaped into a state which *never will* give up a fugitive,—not even at the demand of the whole glorious Union. The trader, therefore, sat discontentedly down, with his little account-book, and put down the missing body and soul under the head of *losses*!

"He's a shocking creature, isn't he,—this trader? so unfeeling! It's dreadful, really!"

"O, but nobody thinks anything of these traders! They are universally despised,—never received into any decent society."

But who, sir, makes the trader? Who is most to blame? The enlightened, cultivated, intelligent man, who supports the system of which the trader is the inevitable result, or the poor trader himself? You make the public sentiment that calls for his trade, that debauches and depraves him, till he feels no shame in it; and in what are you better than he?

Are you educated and he ignorant, you high and he low, you refined and he coarse, you talented and he simple?

In the day of a future Judgment, these very considerations may make it more tolerable for him than for you.

In concluding these little incidents of lawful trade, we must beg the world not to think that American legislators are entirely destitute of humanity, as might, perhaps, be unfairly inferred from the great efforts made in our national body to protect and perpetuate this species of traffic.

Who does not know how our great men are outdoing themselves, in declaiming against the *foreign* slave-trade. There are a perfect host of Clarksons[4] and Wilberforces risen up among us on that subject, most edifying to hear and behold. Trading negroes from Africa, dear reader, is so horrid! It is not to be thought of! But trading them from Kentucky,— that's quite another thing!

CHAPTER XIII. THE QUAKER SETTLEMENT[5]

A quiet scene now rises before us. A large, roomy, neatly-painted kitchen, its yellow floor glossy and smooth, and without a particle of dust; a neat, well-blacked cooking-stove; rows of shining tin, suggestive of unmentionable good things to the appetite; glossy green wood chairs, old and firm; a small flag-bottomed rocking-chair, with a patch-work cushion in it, neatly contrived out of small pieces of different colored woollen goods, and a larger sized one, motherly and old, whose wide arms breathed hospitable invitation, seconded by the solicitation of its feather cushions,—a real comfortable, persuasive old chair, and worth, in the way of honest, homely enjoyment, a dozen of your plush or brochetelle[6] drawing-room gentry; and in the chair, gently swaying back and forward, her eyes bent on some fine sewing, sat our old

4. The English abolitionist Thomas Clarkson (1760–1846), who with his countryman William Wilberforce was an architect of the 1807 act of Parliament abolishing the slave trade. A similar act was passed by the U.S. Congress the same year; it prohibited importation of slaves from abroad, which allowed the trade to flourish within the United States.

5. Located in Indiana. The Quakers, or Society of Friends, are a religious group known during the antebellum period for their pacifism and antislavery politics. Stowe emphasizes the matriarchal and familial nature of the settlement.

6. Brocatelle; a patterned fabric.

friend Eliza. Yes, there she is, paler and thinner than in her Kentucky home, with a world of quiet sorrow lying under the shadow of her long eyelashes, and marking the outline of her gentle mouth! It was plain to see how old and firm the girlish heart was grown under the discipline of heavy sorrow; and when, anon, her large dark eye was raised to follow the gambols of her little Harry, who was sporting, like some tropical butterfly, hither and thither over the floor, she showed a depth of firmness and steady resolve that was never there in her earlier and happier days.

By her side sat a woman with a bright tin pan in her lap, into which she was carefully sorting some dried peaches. She might be fifty-five or sixty; but hers was one of those faces that time seems to touch only to brighten and adorn. The snowy lisse crape[7] cap, made after the strait Quaker pattern,—the plain white muslin handkerchief, lying in placid folds across her bosom,—the drab shawl and dress,—showed at once the community to which she belonged. Her face was round and rosy, with a healthful downy softness, suggestive of a ripe peach. Her hair, partially silvered by age, was parted smoothly back from a high placid forehead on which time had written no inscription, except peace on earth, good will to men, and beneath shone a large pair of clear, honest, loving brown eyes; you only needed to look straight into them, to feel that you saw to the bottom of a heart as good and true as ever throbbed in woman's bosom. So much has been said and sung of beautiful young girls, why don't somebody wake up to the beauty of old women? If any want to get up an inspiration under this head, we refer them to our good friend Rachel Halliday, just as she sits there in her little rocking-chair. It had a turn for quacking and squeaking,—that chair had,—either from having taken cold in early life, or from some asthmatic affection, or perhaps from nervous derangement; but, as she gently swung backward and forward, the chair kept up a kind of subdued "creechy crawchy," that would have been intolerable in any other chair. But old Simeon Halliday often declared it was as good as any music to him, and the children all avowed that they wouldn't miss of hearing mother's chair for anything in the world. For why? for twenty years or more, nothing but loving words and gentle moralities, and motherly loving kindness, had come from that chair;—head-aches and heart-aches innumerable had been cured there,—difficulties spiritual and temporal solved there,—all by one good, loving woman, God bless her!

"And so thee still thinks of going to Canada, Eliza?" she said, as she was quietly looking over her peaches.

"Yes, ma'am," said Eliza, firmly. "I must go onward. I dare not stop."

"And what'll thee do, when thee gets there? Thee must think about that, my daughter."

"My daughter" came naturally from the lips of Rachel Halliday; for hers was just the face and form that made "mother" seem the most natural word in the world.

Eliza's hands trembled, and some tears fell on her fine work; but she answered, firmly,

"I shall do—anything I can find. I hope I can find something."

"Thee knows thee can stay here, as long as thee pleases," said Rachel.

7. Light decorative fabric.

"O, thank you," said Eliza, "but"—she pointed to Harry—"I can't sleep nights; I can't rest. Last night I dreamed I saw that man coming into the yard," she said, shuddering.

"Poor child!" said Rachel, wiping her eyes; "but thee mustn't feel so. The Lord hath ordered it so that never hath a fugitive been stolen from our village. I trust thine will not be the first."

The door here opened, and a little short, round, pincushiony woman stood at the door, with a cheery, blooming face, like a ripe apple. She was dressed, like Rachel, in sober gray, with the muslin folded neatly across her round, plump little chest.

"Ruth Stedman," said Rachel, coming joyfully forward; "how is thee, Ruth?" she said, heartily taking both her hands.

"Nicely," said Ruth, taking off her little drab bonnet, and dusting it with her handkerchief, displaying, as she did so, a round little head, on which the Quaker cap sat with a sort of jaunty air, despite all the stroking and patting of the small fat hands, which were busily applied to arranging it. Certain stray locks of decidedly curly hair, too, had escaped here and there, and had to be coaxed and cajoled into their place again; and then the new comer, who might have been five-and-twenty, turned from the small looking-glass, before which she had been making these arrangements, and looked well pleased,—as most people who looked at her might have been,—for she was decidedly a wholesome, whole-hearted, chirruping little woman, as ever gladdened man's heart withal.

"Ruth, this friend is Eliza Harris; and this is the little boy I told thee of."

"I am glad to see thee, Eliza,—very," said Ruth, shaking hands, as if Eliza were an old friend she had long been expecting; "and this is thy dear boy,—I brought a cake for him," she said, holding out a little heart to the boy, who came up, gazing through his curls, and accepted it shyly.

"Where's thy baby, Ruth?" said Rachel.

"O, he's coming; but thy Mary caught him as I came in, and ran off with him to the barn, to show him to the children."

At this moment, the door opened, and Mary, an honest, rosy-looking girl, with large brown eyes, like her mother's, came in with the baby.

"Ah! ha!" said Rachel, coming up, and taking the great, white, fat fellow in her arms; "how good he looks, and how he does grow!"

"To be sure, he does," said little bustling Ruth as she took the child, and began taking off a little blue silk hood, and various layers and wrappers of outer garments; and having given a twitch here, and a pull there, and variously adjusted and arranged him, and kissed him heartily, she set him on the floor to collect his thoughts. Baby seemed quite used to this mode of proceeding, for he put his thumb in his mouth (as if it were quite a thing of course), and seemed soon absorbed in his own reflections, while the mother seated herself, and taking out a long stocking of mixed blue and white yarn, began to knit with briskness.

"Mary, thee'd better fill the kettle, hadn't thee?" gently suggested the mother.

Mary took the kettle to the well, and soon reappearing, placed it over the stove, where it was soon purring and steaming, a sort of censer of hospitality and good cheer. The peaches, moreover, in obedience to a few gentle whispers from Rachel, were soon deposited, by the same hand, in a stew-pan over the fire.

Rachel now took down a snowy moulding-board, and, tying on an apron, proceeded quietly to making up some biscuits, first saying to Mary,—"Mary, hadn't thee better tell John to get a chicken ready?" and Mary disappeared accordingly.

"And how is Abigail Peters?" said Rachel, as she went on with her biscuits.

"O, she's better," said Ruth; "I was in, this morning; made the bed, tidied up the house. Leah Hills went in, this afternoon, and baked bread and pies enough to last some days and I engaged to go back to get her up, this evening."

"I will go in to-morrow, and do any cleaning there may be, and look over the mending," said Rachel.

"Ah! that is well," said Ruth. "I've heard," she added, "that Hannah Stanwood is sick. John was up there, last night,—I must go there tomorrow."

"John can come in here to his meals, if thee needs to stay all day," suggested Rachel.

"Thank thee, Rachel; will see, to-morrow; but, here comes Simeon."

Simeon Halliday, a tall, straight, muscular man, in drab coat and pantaloons, and broad-brimmed hat, now entered.

"How is thee, Ruth?" he said, warmly, as he spread his broad open hand for her little fat palm; "and how is John?"

"O! John is well, and all the rest of our folks," said Ruth, cheerily.

"Any news, father?" said Rachel, as she was putting her biscuits into the oven.

"Peter Stebbins told me that they should be along to-night, with *friends*," said Simeon, significantly, as he was washing his hands at a neat sink, in a little back porch.

"Indeed!" said Rachel, looking thoughtfully, and glancing at Eliza.

"Did thee say thy name was Harris?" said Simeon to Eliza, as he reentered.

Rachel glanced quickly at her husband, as Eliza tremulously answered "yes;" her fears, ever uppermost, suggesting that possibly there might be advertisements out for her.

"Mother!" said Simeon, standing in the porch, and calling Rachel out.

"What does thee want, father?" said Rachel, rubbing her floury hands, as she went into the porch.

"This child's husband is in the settlement, and will be here to-night," said Simeon.

"Now, thee doesn't say that, father?" said Rachel, all her face radiant with joy.

"It's really true. Peter was down yesterday, with the wagon, to the other stand, and there he found an old woman and two men; and one said his name was George Harris; and, from what he told of his history, I am certain who he is. He is a bright, likely fellow, too."

"Shall we tell her now?" said Simeon.

"Let's tell Ruth," said Rachel. "Here, Ruth,—come here."

Ruth laid down her knitting-work, and was in the back porch in a moment.

"Ruth, what does thee think?" said Rachel. "Father says Eliza's husband is in the last company, and will be here to-night."

A burst of joy from the little Quakeress interrupted the speech. She gave such a bound from the floor, as she clapped her little hands, that two stray curls fell from under her Quaker cap, and lay brightly on her white neckerchief.

"Hush thee, dear!" said Rachel, gently; "hush, Ruth! Tell us, shall we tell her now?"

"Now! to be sure,—this very minute. Why, now, suppose 'twas my John, how should I feel? Do tell her, right off."

"Thee uses thyself only to learn how to love thy neighbor, Ruth," said Simeon, looking, with a beaming face, on Ruth.

"To be sure. Isn't it what we are made for? If I didn't love John and the baby, I should not know how to feel for her. Come, now, do tell her,—do!" and she laid her hands persuasively on Rachel's arm. "Take her into thy bed-room, there, and let me fry the chicken while thee does it."

Rachel came out into the kitchen, where Eliza was sewing, and opening the door of a small bed-room, said, gently, "Come in here with me, my daughter; I have news to tell thee."

The blood flushed in Eliza's pale face; she rose, trembling with nervous anxiety, and looked towards her boy.

"No, no," said little Ruth, darting up, and seizing her hands. "Never thee fear; it's good news, Eliza,—go in, go in!" And she gently pushed her to the door, which closed after her; and then, turning round, she caught little Harry in her arms, and began kissing him.

"Thee'll see thy father, little one. Does thee know it? Thy father is coming," she said, over and over again, as the boy looked wonderingly at her.

Meanwhile, within the door, another scene was going on. Rachel Halliday drew Eliza toward her, and said, "The Lord hath had mercy on thee, daughter; thy husband hath escaped from the house of bondage."

The blood flushed to Eliza's cheek in a sudden glow, and went back to her heart with as sudden a rush. She sat down, pale and faint.

"Have courage, child," said Rachel, laying her hand on her head. "He is among friends, who will bring him here to-night."

"To-night!" Eliza repeated, "to-night!" The words lost all meaning to her; her head was dreamy and confused; all was mist for a moment.

When she awoke, she found herself snugly tucked up on the bed, with a blanket over her, and little Ruth rubbing her hands with camphor. She opened her eyes in a state of dreamy, delicious languor, such as one has who has long been bearing a heavy load, and now feels it gone, and would rest. The tension of the nerves, which had never ceased a moment since the first hour of her flight, had given way, and a strange feeling of security and rest came over her; and, as she lay, with her large, dark eyes open, she followed, as in a quiet dream, the motions of those about her. She saw the door open into the other room; saw the supper table, with its snowy cloth; heard the dreamy murmur of the singing tea-kettle, saw Ruth tripping backward and forward, with plates of cake and saucers of preserves, and ever and anon stopping to put a cake into Harry's hand, or pat his head, or twine his long curls round her snowy fingers. She saw the ample, motherly form of Rachel, as she ever and anon came to the bed-side, and smoothed and arranged something about the bed-clothes, and gave a tuck here and there, by way of expressing her good-will; and was conscious of a kind of sunshine beaming down upon her from her large, clear, brown eyes. She saw Ruth's husband come in,—saw her fly up to him, and commence whispering very earnestly, ever and anon, with impressive gesture, pointing her little finger toward the room. She saw her, with the baby in her arms, sitting down to tea; she saw them all at table, and little Harry in a high chair, under the shadow of Rachel's ample wing; there were low murmurs of talk, gentle tinkling of tea-spoons, and musical clatter of cups and saucers, and all mingled in a delightful dream of rest; and Eliza slept, as she had not slept before, since the fearful midnight hour when she had taken her child and fled through the frosty star-light.

She dreamed of a beautiful country,—a land, it seemed to her, of rest,—green shores, pleasant islands, and beautifully glittering water; and there, in a house which kind voices told her was a home, she saw her boy playing, a free and happy child. She heard her husband's footsteps; she felt him coming nearer; his arms were around her, his tears falling on her face, and she awoke! It was no dream. The daylight had long faded; her child lay calmly sleeping by her side; a candle was burning dimly on the stand, and her husband was sobbing by her pillow.

The next morning was a cheerful one at the Quaker house. "Mother" was up betimes, and surrounded by busy girls and boys, whom we had scarce time to introduce to our readers yesterday, and who all moved obediently to Rachel's gentle "Thee had better," or more gentle "Hadn't thee better?" in the work of getting breakfast; for a breakfast in the luxurious valleys of Indiana is a thing complicated and multiform, and, like picking up the rose-leaves and trimming the bushes in Paradise, asking other hands than those of the original mother. While, therefore, John ran to the spring for fresh water, and Simeon the second sifted meal for corn-cakes, and Mary ground coffee, Rachel moved gently and quietly about, making biscuits, cutting up chicken, and diffusing a sort of sunny radiance over the whole proceeding generally. If there was any danger of friction or collision from the ill-regulated zeal of so many young operators, her gentle "Come! come!" or "I wouldn't, now," was quite sufficient to allay the difficulty. Bards have written of the cestus of Venus,[8] that turned the heads of all the world in successive generations. We had rather, for our part, have the cestus of Rachel Halliday, that kept heads from being turned, and made everything go on harmoniously. We think it is more suited to our modern days, decidedly.

While all other preparations were going on, Simeon the elder stood in his shirt-sleeves before a little looking-glass in the corner, engaged in the anti-patriarchal operation of shaving. Everything went on so sociably, so quietly, so harmoniously, in the great kitchen,—it seemed so pleasant to every one to do just what they were doing, there was such an atmosphere of mutual confidence and good fellowship everywhere,—even the knives and forks had a social clatter as they went on to the table; and the chicken and ham had a cheerful and joyous fizzle in the pan, as if they rather enjoyed being cooked than otherwise;—and when George and Eliza and little Harry came out, they met such a hearty, rejoicing welcome, no wonder it seemed to them like a dream.

8. Roman goddess of love and beauty. "Cestus": woman's belt or girdle, worn by Venus to arouse desire.

At last, they were all seated at breakfast, while Mary stood at the stove, baking griddle-cakes, which, as they gained the true exact golden-brown tint of perfection, were transferred quite handily to the table.

Rachel never looked so truly and benignly happy as at the head of her table. There was so much motherliness and full-heartedness even in the way she passed a plate of cakes or poured a cup of coffee, that it seemed to put a spirit into the food and drink she offered.

It was the first time that ever George had sat down on equal terms at any white man's table; and he sat down, at first, with some constraint and awkwardness; but they all exhaled and went off like fog, in the genial morning rays of this simple, overflowing kindness.

This, indeed, was a home,—*home*,—a word that George had never yet known a meaning for; and a belief in God, and trust in his providence, began to encircle his heart, as, with a golden cloud of protection and confidence, dark, misanthropic, pining, atheistic doubts, and fierce despair, melted away before the light of a living Gospel, breathed in living faces, preached by a thousand unconscious acts of love and good will, which, like the cup of cold water given in the name of a disciple, shall never lose their reward.

"Father, what if thee should get found out again?" said Simeon second, as he buttered his cake.

"I should pay my fine," said Simeon, quietly.

"But what if they put thee in prison?"

"Couldn't thee and mother manage the farm?" said Simeon, smiling.

"Mother can do almost everything," said the boy. "But isn't it a shame to make such laws?"

"Thee mustn't speak evil of thy rulers, Simeon," said his father, gravely. "The Lord only gives us our worldly goods that we may do justice and mercy; if our rulers require a price of us for it, we must deliver it up."

"Well, I hate those old slaveholders!" said the boy, who felt as unchristian as became any modern reformer.

"I am surprised at thee, son," said Simeon; "thy mother never taught thee so. I would do even the same for the slaveholder as for the slave, if the Lord brought him to my door in affliction."

Simeon second blushed scarlet; but his mother only smiled, and said, "Simeon is my good boy; he will grow older, by and by, and then he will be like his father."

"I hope, my good sir, that you are not exposed to any difficulty on our account," said George, anxiously.

"Fear nothing, George, for therefore are we sent into the world. If we would not meet trouble for a good cause, we were not worthy of our name."

"But, for *me*," said George, "I could not bear it."

"Fear not, then, friend George; it is not for thee, but for God and man, we do it," said Simeon. "And now thou must lie by quietly this day, and to-night, at ten o'clock, Phineas Fletcher will carry thee onward to the next stand,—thee and the rest of thy company. The pursuers are hard after thee; we must not delay."

"If that is the case, why wait till evening?" said George.

"Thou art safe here by daylight, for every one in the settlement is a Friend, and all are watching. It has been found safer to travel by night."

CHAPTER XIV. EVANGELINE

"A young star! which shone
O'er life—too sweet an image for such glass!
A lovely being, scarcely formed or moulded;
A rose with all its sweetest leaves yet folded."[9]

The Mississippi! How, as by an enchanted wand, have its scenes been changed, since Chateaubriand[1] wrote his prose-poetic description of it, as a river of mighty, unbroken solitudes, rolling amid undreamed wonders of vegetable and animal existence.

But, as in an hour, this river of dreams and wild romance has emerged to a reality scarcely less visionary and splendid. What other river of the world bears on its bosom to the ocean the wealth and enterprise of such another country?—a country whose products embrace all between the tropics and the poles! Those turbid waters, hurrying, foaming, tearing along, an apt resemblance of that headlong tide of business which is poured along its wave by a race more vehement and energetic than any the old world ever saw. Ah! would that they did not also bear along a more fearful freight,—the tears of the oppressed, the sighs of the helpless, the bitter prayers of poor, ignorant hearts to an unknown God—unknown, unseen and silent, but who will yet "come out of his place to save all the poor of the earth!"[2]

The slanting light of the setting sun quivers on the sea-like expanse of the river; the shivery canes, and the tall, dark cypress, hung with wreaths of dark, funereal moss, glow in the golden ray, as the heavily-laden steamboat marches onward.

Piled with cotton-bales, from many a plantation, up over deck and sides, till she seems in the distance a square, massive block of gray, she moves heavily onward to the nearing mart. We must look some time among its crowded decks before we shall find again our humble friend Tom. High on the upper deck, in a little nook among the everywhere predominant cotton-bales, at last we may find him.

Partly from confidence inspired by Mr. Shelby's representations, and partly from the remarkably inoffensive and quiet character of the man, Tom had insensibly won his way far into the confidence even of such a man as Haley.

At first he had watched him narrowly through the day, and never allowed him to sleep at night unfettered; but the uncomplaining patience and apparent contentment of Tom's manner led him gradually to discontinue these restraints, and for some time Tom had enjoyed a sort of parole of honor, being permitted to come and go freely where he pleased on the boat.

Ever quiet and obliging, and more than ready to lend a hand in every emergency which occurred among the workmen below, he had won the good opinion of all the hands, and spent many hours in helping them with as hearty a good will as ever he worked on a Kentucky farm.

When there seemed to be nothing for him to do, he would climb to a nook among the cotton-bales of the upper deck, and busy himself in studying over his Bible,—and it is there we see him now.

9. From *Don Juan* 14.43 (1818–24), by the English poet George Gordon, Lord Byron (1788–1824).
1. François-René, Vicomte de Chateaubriand (1768–1848), French writer who journeyed in the United States in 1791 and incorporated descriptions from his travels into his writings.
2. Psalm 76.9.

For a hundred or more miles above New Orleans, the river is higher than the surrounding country, and rolls its tremendous volume between massive levees twenty feet in height. The traveller from the deck of the steamer, as from some floating castle top, overlooks the whole country for miles and miles around. Tom, therefore, had spread out full before him, in plantation after plantation, a map of the life to which he was approaching.

He saw the distant slaves at their toil; he saw afar their villages of huts gleaming out in long rows on many a plantation, distant from the stately mansions and pleasure-grounds of the master;—and as the moving picture passed on, his poor, foolish heart would be turning backward to the Kentucky farm, with its old shadowy beeches,—to the master's house, with its wide, cool halls, and, near by, the little cabin, overgrown with the multiflora and bignonia. There he seemed to see familiar faces of comrades, who had grown up with him from infancy; he saw his busy wife, bustling in her preparations for his evening meals; he heard the merry laugh of his boys at their play, and the chirrup of the baby at his knee; and then, with a start, all faded, and he saw again the cane-brakes[3] and cypresses and gliding plantations, and heard again the creaking and groaning of the machinery, all telling him too plainly that all that phase of life had gone by forever.

In such a case, you write to your wife, and send messages to your children; but Tom could not write,—the mail for him had no existence, and the gulf of separation was unbridged by even a friendly word or signal.

Is it strange, then, that some tears fall on the pages of his Bible, as he lays it on the cotton-bale, and, with patient finger, threading his slow way from word to word, traces out its promises? Having learned late in life, Tom was but a slow reader, and passed on laboriously from verse to verse. Fortunate for him was it that the book he was intent on was one which slow reading cannot injure,—nay, one whose words, like ingots of gold, seem often to need to be weighed separately, that the mind may take in their priceless value. Let us follow him a moment, as, pointing to each word, and pronouncing each half aloud, he reads,

"Let—not—your—heart—be—troubled. In—my—Father's—house—are—many—mansions. I—go—to—prepare—a—place—for—you."[4]

Cicero, when he buried his darling and only daughter, had a heart as full of honest grief as poor Tom's,—perhaps no fuller, for both were only men;—but Cicero could pause over no such sublime words of hope, and look to no such future reunion; and if he *had* seen them, ten to one he would not have believed,—he must fill his head first with a thousand questions of authenticity of manuscript, and correctness of translation.[5] But, to poor Tom, there it lay, just what he needed, so evidently true and divine that the possibility of a question never entered his simple head. It must be true; for, if not true, how could he live?

As for Tom's Bible, though it had no annotations and helps in margin from learned commentators, still it had been embellished with certain waymarks and guide-boards of Tom's own invention, and which helped him more

3. Thickets of sugarcane.
4. From John 14.1–2.
5. Marcus Tullius Cicero (106–43 B.C.E.), Roman statesman, orator, and philosopher, was devastated by the death of his daughter, Tullia. Stowe's point is that Cicero, despite his accomplishments, was a pagan who lacked the consolation of the Bible.

than the most learned expositions could have done. It had been his custom to get the Bible read to him by his master's children, in particular by young Master George; and, as they read, he would designate, by bold, strong marks and dashes, with pen and ink, the passages which more particularly gratified his ear or affected his heart. His Bible was thus marked through, from one end to the other, with a variety of styles and designations; so he could in a moment seize upon his favorite passages, without the labor of spelling out what lay between them;—and while it lay there before him, every passage breathing of some old home scene, and recalling some past enjoyment, his Bible seemed to him all of this life that remained, as well as the promise of a future one.

Among the passengers on the boat was a young gentleman of fortune and family, resident in New Orleans, who bore the name of St. Clare. He had with him a daughter between five and six years of age, together with a lady who seemed to claim relationship to both, and to have the little one especially under her charge.

Tom had often caught glimpses of this little girl,—for she was one of those busy, tripping creatures, that can be no more contained in one place than a sunbeam or a summer breeze,—nor was she one that, once seen, could be easily forgotten.

Her form was the perfection of childish beauty, without its usual chubbiness and squareness of outline. There was about it an undulating and aerial grace, such as one might dream of for some mythic and allegorical being. Her face was remarkable less for its perfect beauty of feature than for a singular and dreamy earnestness of expression, which made the ideal start when they looked at her, and by which the dullest and most literal were impressed, without exactly knowing why. The shape of her head and the turn of her neck and bust was peculiarly noble, and the long golden-brown hair that floated like a cloud around it, the deep spiritual gravity of her violet blue eyes, shaded by heavy fringes of golden brown,—all marked her out from other children, and made every one turn and look after her, as she glided hither and thither on the boat. Nevertheless, the little one was not what you would have called either a grave child or a sad one. On the contrary, an airy and innocent playfulness seemed to flicker like the shadow of summer leaves over her childish face, and around her buoyant figure. She was always in motion, always with a half smile on her rosy mouth, flying hither and thither, with an undulating and cloud-like tread, singing to herself as she moved as in a happy dream. Her father and female guardian were incessantly busy in pursuit of her,—but, when caught, she melted from them again like a summer cloud; and as no word of chiding or reproof ever fell on her ear for whatever she chose to do, she pursued her own way all over the boat. Always dressed in white, she seemed to move like a shadow through all sorts of places, without contracting spot or stain; and there was not a corner or nook, above or below, where those fairy footsteps had not glided, and that visionary golden head, with its deep blue eyes, fleeted along.

The fireman,[6] as he looked up from his sweaty toil, sometimes found those eyes looking wonderingly into the raging depths of the furnace, and fearfully

6. The person who operated the steamboat boilers, which were fueled by wood.

and pityingly at him, as if she thought him in some dreadful danger. Anon the steersman at the wheel paused and smiled, as the picture-like head gleamed through the window of the round house, and in a moment was gone again. A thousand times a day rough voices blessed her, and smiles of unwonted softness stole over hard faces, as she passed; and when she tripped fearlessly over dangerous places, rough, sooty hands were stretched involuntarily out to save her, and smooth her path.

Tom, who had the soft, impressible nature of his kindly race, ever yearning toward the simple and childlike, watched the little creature with daily increasing interest. To him she seemed something almost divine; and whenever her golden head and deep blue eyes peered out upon him from behind some dusky cotton-bale, or looked down upon him over some ridge of packages, he half believed that he saw one of the angels stepped out of his New Testament.[7]

Often and often she walked mournfully round the place where Haley's gang of men and women sat in their chains. She would glide in among them, and look at them with an air of perplexed and sorrowful earnestness; and sometimes she would lift their chains with her slender hands, and then sigh wofully, as she glided away. Several times she appeared suddenly among them, with her hands full of candy, nuts, and oranges, which she would distribute joyfully to them, and then be gone again.

Tom watched the little lady a great deal, before he ventured on any overtures towards acquaintanceship. He knew an abundance of simple acts to propitiate and invite the approaches of the little people, and he resolved to play his part right skilfully. He could cut cunning little baskets out of cherry-stones, could make grotesque faces on hickory-nuts, or odd-jumping figures out of elder-pith, and he was a very Pan[8] in the manufacture of whistles of all sizes and sorts. His pockets were full of miscellaneous articles of attraction, which he had hoarded in days of old for his master's children, and which he now produced, with commendable prudence and economy, one by one, as overtures for acquaintance and friendship.

The little one was shy, for all her busy interest in everything going on, and it was not easy to tame her. For a while, she would perch like a canary-bird on some box or package near Tom, while busy in the little arts afore-named, and take from him, with a kind of grave bashfulness, the little articles he offered. But at last they got on quite confidential terms.

"What's little missy's name?" said Tom, at last, when he thought matters were ripe to push such an inquiry.

"Evangeline St. Clare," said the little one, "though papa and everybody else call me Eva. Now, what's your name?"

"My name's Tom; the little chil'en used to call me Uncle Tom, way back thar in Kentuck."

"Then I mean to call you Uncle Tom, because, you see, I like you," said Eva. "So, Uncle Tom, where are you going?"

"I don't know, Miss Eva."

7. Later in the novel, Tom and Eva read the Bible together. For a famous painting of the two, based on an illustration in the first edition, see Robert Scott Duncanson's *Uncle Tom and Little Eva* (1853), in the color insert to this volume.

8. In Greek mythology, the goat-legged, flute-playing god of fields, forest, and revelry.

"Don't know?" said Eva.

"No. I am going to be sold to somebody. I don't know who."

"My papa can buy you," said Eva, quickly; "and if he buys you, you will have good times. I mean to ask him to, this very day."

"Thank you, my little lady," said Tom.

The boat here stopped at a small landing to take in wood, and Eva, hearing her father's voice, bounded nimbly away. Tom rose up, and went forward to offer his service in wooding, and soon was busy among the hands.

Eva and her father were standing together by the railings to see the boat start from the landing-place, the wheel had made two or three revolutions in the water, when, by some sudden movement, the little one suddenly lost her balance, and fell sheer over the side of the boat into the water. Her father, scarce knowing what he did, was plunging in after her, but was held back by some behind him, who saw that more efficient aid had followed his child.

Tom was standing just under her on the lower deck, as she fell. He saw her strike the water, and sink, and was after her in a moment. A broad-chested, strong-armed fellow, it was nothing for him to keep afloat in the water, till, in a moment or two, the child rose to the surface, and he caught her in his arms, and, swimming with her to the boat-side, handed her up, all dripping, to the grasp of hundreds of hands, which, as if they had all belonged to one man, were stretched eagerly out to receive her. A few moments more, and her father bore her, dripping and senseless, to the ladies' cabin, where, as is usual in cases of the kind, there ensued a very well-meaning and kind-hearted strife among the female occupants generally, as to who should do the most things to make a disturbance, and to hinder her recovery in every way possible.

It was a sultry, close day, the next day, as the steamer drew near to New Orleans. A general bustle of expectation and preparation was spread through the boat; in the cabin, one and another were gathering their things together, and arranging them, preparatory to going ashore. The steward and chambermaid, and all, were busily engaged in cleaning, furbishing, and arranging the splendid boat, preparatory to a grand entree.

On the lower deck sat our friend Tom, with his arms folded, and anxiously, from time to time, turning his eyes towards a group on the other side of the boat.

There stood the fair Evangeline, a little paler than the day before, but otherwise exhibiting no traces of the accident which had befallen her. A graceful, elegantly-formed young man stood by her, carelessly leaning one elbow on a bale of cotton, while a large pocket-book lay open before him. It was quite evident, at a glance, that the gentleman was Eva's father. There was the same noble cast of head, the same large blue eyes, the same golden-brown hair; yet the expression was wholly different. In the large, clear blue eyes, though in form and color exactly similar, there was wanting that misty, dreamy depth of expression; all was clear, bold, and bright, but with a light wholly of this world: the beautifully cut mouth had a proud and somewhat sarcastic expression, while an air of free-and-easy superiority sat not ungracefully in every turn and movement of his fine form. He was listening, with a good-humored, negligent air, half comic, half contemptuous, to Haley, who was very volubly expatiating on the quality of the article for which they were bargaining.

"All the moral and Christian virtues bound in black morocco,[9] complete!" he said, when Haley had finished. "Well, now, my good fellow, what's the damage, as they say in Kentucky; in short, what's to be paid out for this business? How much are you going to cheat me, now? Out with it!"

"Wal," said Haley, "if I should say thirteen hundred dollars for that ar fellow, I shouldn't but just save myself; I shouldn't, now, re'ly."

"Poor fellow!" said the young man, fixing his keen, mocking blue eye on him; "but I suppose you'd let me have him for that, out of a particular regard for me."

"Well, the young lady here seems to be sot on him, and nat'lly enough."

"O! certainly, there's a call on your benevolence, my friend. Now, as a matter of Christian charity, how cheap could you afford to let him go, to oblige a young lady that's particular sot on him?"

"Wal, now, just think on 't," said the trader; "just look at them limbs,—broad-chested, strong as a horse. Look at his head; them high forrads allays shows calculatin niggers, that'll do any kind o' thing. I've marked that ar. Now, a nigger of that ar heft and build is worth considerable, just, as you may say, for his body, supposin he's stupid; but come to put in his calculatin faculties, and them which I can show he has oncommon, why, of course, it makes him come higher. Why, that ar fellow managed his master's whole farm. He has a strornary talent for business."

"Bad, bad, very bad; knows altogether too much!" said the young man, with the same mocking smile playing about his mouth. "Never will do, in the world. Your smart fellows are always running off, stealing horses, and raising the devil generally. I think you'll have to take off a couple of hundred for his smartness."

"Wal, there might be something in that ar, if it warnt for his character; but I can show recommends from his master and others, to prove he is one of your real pious,—the most humble, prayin, pious crittur ye ever did see. Why, he's been called a preacher in them parts he came from."

"And I might use him for a family chaplain, possibly," added the young man, dryly. "That's quite an idea. Religion is a remarkably scarce article at our house."

"You're joking, now."

"How do you know I am? Didn't you just warrant him for a preacher? Has he been examined by any synod or council? Come, hand over your papers."

If the trader had not been sure, by a certain good-humored twinkle in the large blue eye, that all this banter was sure, in the long run, to turn out a cash concern, he might have been somewhat out of patience; as it was, he laid down a greasy pocket-book on the cotton-bales, and began anxiously studying over certain papers in it, the young man standing by, the while, looking down on him with an air of careless, easy drollery.

"Papa, do buy him! it's no matter what you pay," whispered Eva, softly, getting up on a package, and putting her arm around her father's neck. "You have money enough, I know. I want him."

9. A high-quality leather made from goatskin.

"What for, pussy? Are you going to use him for a rattle-box, or a rocking-horse, or what?"

"I want to make him happy."

"An original reason, certainly."

Here the trader handed up a certificate, signed by Mr. Shelby, which the young man took with the tips of his long fingers, and glanced over carelessly.

"A gentlemanly hand," he said, "and well spelt, too. Well, now, but I'm not sure, after all, about this religion," said he, the old wicked expression returning to his eye; "the country is almost ruined with pious white people: such pious politicians as we have just before elections,—such pious goings on in all departments of church and state, that a fellow does not know who'll cheat him next. I don't know, either, about religion's being up in the market, just now. I have not looked in the papers lately, to see how it sells. How many hundred dollars, now, do you put on for this religion?"

"You like to be a jokin, now," said the trader; "but, then, there's *sense* under all that ar. I know there's differences in religion. Some kinds is mis'rable: there's your meetin pious; there's your singin, roarin pious; them ar an't no account, in black or white;—but these rayly is; and I've seen it in niggers as often as any, your rail softly, quiet, stiddy, honest, pious, that the hull world couldn't tempt 'em to do nothing that they thinks is wrong; and ye see in this letter what Tom's old master says about him."

"Now," said the young man, stooping gravely over his book of bills, "if you can assure me that I really can buy *this* kind of pious, and that it will be set down to my account in the book up above, as something belonging to me, I wouldn't care if I did go a little extra for it. How d' ye say?"

"Wal, raily, I can't do that," said the trader. "I'm a thinkin that every man'll have to hang on his own hook, in them ar quarters."

"Rather hard on a fellow that pays extra on religion, and can't trade with it in the state where he wants it most, an't it, now?" said the young man, who had been making out a roll of bills while he was speaking. "There, count your money, old boy!" he added, as he handed the roll to the trader.

"All right," said Haley, his face beaming with delight; and pulling out an old inkhorn, he proceeded to fill out a bill of sale, which, in a few moments, he handed to the young man.

"I wonder, now, if I was divided up and inventoried," said the latter, as he ran over the paper, "how much I might bring. Say so much for the shape of my head, so much for a high forehead, so much for arms, and hands, and legs, and then so much for education, learning, talent, honesty, religion! Bless me! there would be small charge on that last, I'm thinking. But come, Eva," he said; and taking the hand of his daughter, he stepped across the boat, and carelessly putting the tip of his finger under Tom's chin, said good-humoredly, "Look up, Tom, and see how you like your new master."

Tom looked up. It was not in nature to look into that gay, young, handsome face, without a feeling of pleasure; and Tom felt the tears start in his eyes as he said, heartily, "God bless you, Mas'r!"

"Well, I hope he will. What's your name? Tom? Quite as likely to do it for your asking as mine, from all accounts. Can you drive horses, Tom?"

"I've been allays used to horses," said Tom. "Mas'r Shelby raised heaps on 'em."

"Well, I think I shall put you in coachy, on condition that you won't be drunk more than once a week, unless in cases of emergency, Tom."

Tom looked surprised, and rather hurt, and said, "I never drink, Mas'r."

"I've heard that story before, Tom; but then we'll see. It will be a special accommodation to all concerned, if you don't. Never mind, my boy," he added, good-humoredly, seeing Tom still looked grave; "I don't doubt you mean to do well."

"I sartin do, Mas'r," said Tom.

"And you shall have good times," said Eva. "Papa is very good to everybody, only he always will laugh at them."

"Papa is much obliged to you for his recommendation," said St. Clare, laughing, as he turned on his heel and walked away.

* * *

Volume II

CHAPTER XX. TOPSY

One morning, while Miss Ophelia[1] was busy in some of her domestic cares, St. Clare's voice was heard, calling her at the foot of the stairs.

"Come down here, Cousin; I've something to show you."

"What is it?" said Miss Ophelia, coming down, with her sewing in her hand.

"I've made a purchase for your department,—see here," said St. Clare; and, with the word, he pulled along a little negro girl, about eight or nine years of age.

She was one of the blackest of her race; and her round, shining eyes, glittering as glass beads, moved with quick and restless glances over everything in the room. Her mouth, half open with astonishment at the wonders of the new Mas'r's parlor, displayed a white and brilliant set of teeth. Her woolly hair was braided in sundry little tails, which stuck out in every direction. The expression of her face was an odd mixture of shrewdness and cunning, over which was oddly drawn, like a kind of veil, an expression of the most doleful gravity and solemnity. She was dressed in a single filthy, ragged garment, made of bagging; and stood with her hands demurely folded before her. Altogether, there was something odd and goblin-like about her appearance,—something, as Miss Ophelia afterwards said, "so heathenish," as to inspire that good lady with utter dismay; and, turning to St. Clare, she said,

"Augustine, what in the world have you brought that thing here for?"

"For you to educate, to be sure, and train in the way she should go.[2] I thought she was rather a funny specimen in the Jim Crow line.[3] Here, Topsy," he added, giving a whistle, as a man would to call the attention of a dog, "give us a song, now, and show us some of your dancing."

The black, glassy eyes glittered with a kind of wicked drollery, and the thing struck up, in a clear shrill voice, an odd negro melody, to which she

1. Ophelia is Augustine St. Clare's cousin from New England, who has joined the household in New Orleans to help with domestic affairs because Marie St. Clare, Augustine's wife and Evangeline's mother, claims to be an invalid.

2. Allusion to Proverbs 22.6: "Train up a child in the way he should go: and when he is old, he will not depart from it."

3. See p. 809, n. 6.

kept time with her hands and feet, spinning round, clapping her hands, knocking her knees together, in a wild, fantastic sort of time, and producing in her throat all those odd guttural sounds which distinguish the native music of her race; and finally, turning a summerset[4] or two, and giving a prolonged closing note, as odd and unearthly as that of a steam-whistle, she came suddenly down on the carpet, and stood with her hands folded, and a most sanctimonious expression of meekness and solemnity over her face, only broken by the cunning glances which she shot askance from the corners of her eyes.

Miss Ophelia stood silent, perfectly paralyzed with amazement.

St. Clare, like a mischievous fellow as he was, appeared to enjoy her astonishment; and, addressing the child again, said,

"Topsy, this is your new mistress. I'm going to give you up to her; see now that you behave yourself."

"Yes, Mas'r," said Topsy, with sanctimonious gravity, her wicked eyes twinkling as she spoke.

"You're going to be good, Topsy, you understand," said St. Clare.

"O yes, Mas'r," said Topsy, with another twinkle, her hands still devoutly folded.

"Now, Augustine, what upon earth is this for?" said Miss Ophelia. "Your house is so full of these little plagues, now, that a body can't set down their foot without treading on 'em. I get up in the morning, and find one asleep behind the door, and see one black head poking out from under the table, one lying on the door-mat,—and they are mopping and mowing and grinning between all the railings, and tumbling over the kitchen floor! What on earth did you want to bring this one for?"

"For you to educate—didn't I tell you? You're always preaching about educating. I thought I would make you a present of a fresh-caught specimen, and let you try your hand on her, and bring her up in the way she should go."

"*I* don't want her, I am sure;—I have more to do with 'em now than I want to."

"That's you Christians, all over!—you'll get up a society, and get some poor missionary to spend all his days among just such heathen. But let me see one of you that would take one into your house with you, and take the labor of their conversion on yourselves! No; when it comes to that, they are dirty and disagreeable, and it's too much care, and so on."

"Augustine, you know I didn't think of it in that light," said Miss Ophelia, evidently softening. "Well, it might be a real missionary work," said she, looking rather more favorably on the child.

St. Clare had touched the right string. Miss Ophelia's conscientiousness was ever on the alert. "But," she added, "I really didn't see the need of buying this one;—there are enough now, in your house, to take all my time and skill."

"Well, then, Cousin," said St. Clare, drawing her aside; "I ought to beg your pardon for my good-for-nothing speeches. You are so good, after all, that there's no sense in them. Why, the fact is, this concern belonged to a couple of drunken creatures that keep a low restaurant that I have to pass by every

4. Somersault.

1820–1865

The Return of Rip Van Winkle, John Quidor, 1829

A friend of Washington Irving, Quidor (1801–1881) depicted a key scene near the end of "Rip Van Winkle" (1819), capturing the fantastic quality of Rip's return to his village in New York's Catskill Mountains after sleeping through the American Revolution. In the background, the American flag and the image of George Washington on the tavern's sign suggest the post-Revolutionary moment. Rip appears both confused and in control amidst the curious crowd.

War News from Mexico, Richard Caton Woodville, 1848

Working at the time in Germany, Woodville (1822–1855) sent this painting to be exhibited in New York City. In a small town where a post office shares space with an "American Hotel," eight white men gather to read the news about the war with Mexico (1846–48). The excitement of the principal reader is offset by the excluded white woman in the shadows and by the seated black workingman and poorly dressed black girl, perhaps his daughter, who seem to convey a muted knowingness about the consequences of a war that promised to extend the realm of slavery.

Uncle Tom and Little Eva, Robert Scott Duncanson, 1853

Commissioned by a Detroit abolitionist to depict a scene from Harriet Beecher Stowe's best-selling *Uncle Tom's Cabin* (1852), the free-born African American landscapist Duncanson (1821–1872) wanted to show that interracial human kindness and spirituality, not violence, would help to end slavery. In this scene, based on a black-and-white engraving in the novel's first edition, Little Eva teaches Uncle Tom to read the family Bible in a lush tropical setting near Louisiana's Lake Pontchartrain. Eva points toward the heavens, declaring, "I'm going there . . . before long." The glimmering sky suggests her impending salvation.

Shake Hands?, Lily Martin Spencer, 1854

The first female genre painter in the nineteenth-century United States, Spencer (1822–1902) achieved great popular success with this painting. In a kitchen replete with chicken, cabbage, and apples, a self-possessed and thoroughly happy woman extends a dough-covered hand. Typically a male gesture of equality, the proffered handshake boldly suggests the woman's sense that she is equal to anyone who might be viewing her. That the painting could be interpreted both as a celebration of women's domesticity and as a radical statement about women's equality no doubt contributed to its popularity. It toured several cities and in 1857 was lithographed for wide distribution.

The Lackawanna Valley, George Innes, 1855

In the early 1850s Innes (1825–1894) was commissioned by the Delaware, Lackawanna and Western Railroad to celebrate its development in the Northeast. In this scene just past a roundhouse in Scranton, Pennsylvania, the train, with its smoke and forward energy, seems at first glance to be intruding onto a bucolic landscape. Overall, though, Innes, perhaps because he was under commission, sought to depict nature and machine as organically integrated. The golden glow of the painting, along with the reclining youthful figure who is unthreatened by the approaching train, conveys a hopeful sense that this is the dawn of a glorious new era in U.S. civilization.

The Oregon Trail, Albert Bierstadt, 1869

In the year that marked the completion of the first continental railroad, Bierstadt (1830–1902) presented a striking allegory of westward expansion. Drawing on his own encounter with German emigrants on their way to Oregon, Bierstadt uses the cliffs, trees, and glowing orange-red sky to suggest the spiritual imperative of the move west. The cattle, oxen, and other livestock, along with the covered wagon, create a nostalgic mood. The teepees in the distance are reminders of the Native American presence, but the overall intent of the image is to suggest the centrality of the whites' pioneer experiences to the national character.

day, and I was tired of hearing her screaming, and them beating and swearing at her. She looked bright and funny, too, as if something might be made of her;—so I bought her, and I'll give her to you. Try, now, and give her a good orthodox New England bringing up, and see what it'll make of her. You know I haven't any gift that way; but I'd like you to try."

"Well, I'll do what I can," said Miss Ophelia; and she approached her new subject very much as a person might be supposed to approach a black spider, supposing them to have benevolent designs toward it.

"She's dreadfully dirty, and half naked," she said.

"Well, take her down stairs, and make some of them clean and clothe her up."

Miss Ophelia carried her to the kitchen regions.

"Don't see what Mas'r St. Clare wants of 'nother nigger!" said Dinah,[5] surveying the new arrival with no friendly air. "Won't have her round under *my* feet, *I* know!"

"Pah!" said Rosa and Jane,[6] with supreme disgust; "let her keep out of our way! What in the world Mas'r wanted another of these low niggers for, I can't see!"

"You go long! No more nigger dan you be, Miss Rosa," said Dinah, who felt this last remark a reflection on herself. "You seem to tink yourself white folks. You an't nerry one, black *nor* white. I'd like to be one or turrer."

Miss Ophelia saw that there was nobody in the camp that would undertake to oversee the cleansing and dressing of the new arrival; and so she was forced to do it herself, with some very ungracious and reluctant assistance from Jane.

It is not for ears polite to hear the particulars of the first toilet of a neglected, abused child. In fact, in this world, multitudes must live and die in a state that it would be too great a shock to the nerves of their fellow-mortals even to hear described. Miss Ophelia had a good, strong, practical deal of resolution; and she went through all the disgusting details with heroic thoroughness, though, it must be confessed, with no very gracious air,—for endurance was the utmost to which her principles could bring her. When she saw, on the back and shoulders of the child, great welts and calloused spots, ineffaceable marks of the system under which she had grown up thus far, her heart became pitiful within her.

"See there!" said Jane, pointing to the marks, "don't that show she's a limb?[7] We'll have fine works with her, I reckon. I hate these nigger young uns! so disgusting! I wonder that Mas'r would buy her!"

The "young un" alluded to heard all these comments with the subdued and doleful air which seemed habitual to her, only scanning, with a keen and furtive glance of her flickering eyes, the ornaments which Jane wore in her ears. When arrayed at last in a suit of decent and whole clothing, her hair cropped short to her head, Miss Ophelia, with some satisfaction, said she looked more Christian-like than she did, and in her own mind began to mature some plans for her instruction.

Sitting down before her, she began to question her.

"How old are you, Topsy?"

5. The St. Clares' cook and slave.
6. Rosa and Jane are house slaves who feel superior to the other slaves.
7. Mischievous child (slang).

"Dun no, Missis," said the image, with a grin that showed all her teeth.

"Don't know how old you are? Didn't anybody ever tell you? Who was your mother?"

"Never had none!" said the child, with another grin.

"Never had any mother? What do you mean? Where were you born?"

"Never was born!" persisted Topsy, with another grin, that looked so goblin-like, that, if Miss Ophelia had been at all nervous, she might have fancied that she had got hold of some sooty gnome from the land of Diablerie;[8] but Miss Ophelia was not nervous, but plain and business-like, and she said, with some sternness,

"You mustn't answer me in that way, child; I'm not playing with you. Tell me where you were born, and who your father and mother were."

"Never was born," reiterated the creature, more emphatically; "never had no father nor mother, nor nothin'. I was raised by a speculator, with lots of others. Old Aunt Sue used to take car on us."

The child was evidently sincere; and Jane, breaking into a short laugh, said,

"Laws, Missis, there's heaps of 'em. Speculators buys 'em up cheap, when they's little, and gets 'em raised for market."

"How long have you lived with your master and mistress?"

"Dun no, Missis."

"Is it a year, or more, or less?"

"Dun no, Missis."

"Laws, Missis, those low negroes,—they can't tell; they don't know anything about time," said Jane; "they don't know what a year is; they don't know their own ages."

"Have you ever heard anything about God, Topsy?"

The child looked bewildered, but grinned as usual.

"Do you know who made you?"

"Nobody, as I knows on," said the child, with a short laugh.

The idea appeared to amuse her considerably; for her eyes twinkled, and she added,

"I spect I grow'd. Don't think nobody never made me."

"Do you know how to sew?" said Miss Ophelia, who thought she would turn her inquiries to something more tangible.

"No, Missis."

"What can you do?—what did you do for your master and mistress?"

"Fetch water, and wash dishes, and rub knives, and wait on folks."

"Were they good to you?"

"Spect they was," said the child, scanning Miss Ophelia cunningly.

Miss Ophelia rose from this encouraging colloquy; St. Clare was leaning over the back of her chair.

"You find virgin soil there, Cousin; put in your own ideas,—you won't find many to pull up."

Miss Ophelia's ideas of education, like all her other ideas, were very set and definite; and of the kind that prevailed in New England a century ago, and which are still preserved in some very retired and unsophisticated parts,

8. Deviltry (Creole French).

where there are no railroads. As nearly as could be expressed, they could be comprised in very few words: to teach them to mind when they were spoken to; to teach them the catechism,[9] sewing, and reading; and to whip them if they told lies. And though, of course, in the flood of light that is now poured on education, these are left far away in the rear, yet it is an undisputed fact that our grandmothers raised some tolerably fair men and women under this regime, as many of us can remember and testify. At all events, Miss Ophelia knew of nothing else to do; and, therefore, applied her mind to her heathen with the best diligence she could command.

The child was announced and considered in the family as Miss Ophelia's girl; and, as she was looked upon with no gracious eye in the kitchen, Miss Ophelia resolved to confine her sphere of operation and instruction chiefly to her own chamber. With a self-sacrifice which some of our readers will appreciate, she resolved, instead of comfortably making her own bed, sweeping and dusting her own chamber,—which she had hitherto done, in utter scorn of all offers of help from the chambermaid of the establishment,—to condemn herself to the martyrdom of instructing Topsy to perform these operations,—ah, woe the day! Did any of our readers ever do the same, they will appreciate the amount of her self-sacrifice.

Miss Ophelia began with Topsy by taking her into her chamber, the first morning, and solemnly commencing a course of instruction in the art and mystery of bed-making.

Behold, then, Topsy, washed and shorn of all the little braided tails wherein her heart had delighted, arrayed in a clean gown, with well-starched apron, standing reverently before Miss Ophelia, with an expression of solemnity well befitting a funeral.

"Now, Topsy, I'm going to show you just how my bed is to be made. I am very particular about my bed. You must learn exactly how to do it."

"Yes, ma'am," says Topsy, with a deep sigh, and a face of woful earnestness.

"Now, Topsy, look here;—this is the hem of the sheet,—this is the right side of the sheet, and this is the wrong;—will you remember?"

"Yes, ma'am," says Topsy, with another sigh.

"Well, now, the under sheet you must bring over the bolster,—so,—and tuck it clear down under the mattress nice and smooth,—so,—do you see?"

"Yes, ma'am," said Topsy, with profound attention.

"But the upper sheet," said Miss Ophelia, "must be brought down in this way, and tucked under firm and smooth at the foot,—so,—the narrow hem at the foot."

"Yes, ma'am," said Topsy, as before;—but we will add, what Miss Ophelia did not see, that, during the time when the good lady's back was turned, in the zeal of her manipulations, the young disciple had contrived to snatch a pair of gloves and a ribbon, which she had adroitly slipped into her sleeves, and stood with her hands dutifully folded, as before.

"Now, Topsy, let's see *you* do this," said Miss Ophelia, pulling off the clothes, and seating herself.

Topsy, with great gravity and adroitness, went through the exercise completely to Miss Ophelia's satisfaction; smoothing the sheets, patting out every

9. Question-and-answer formulation of religious doctrine used for instructional purposes.

wrinkle, and exhibiting, through the whole process, a gravity and seriousness with which her instructress was greatly edified. By an unlucky slip, however, a fluttering fragment of the ribbon hung out of one of her sleeves, just as she was finishing, and caught Miss Ophelia's attention. Instantly she pounced upon it. "What's this? You naughty, wicked child,—you've been stealing this!"

The ribbon was pulled out of Topsy's own sleeve, yet was she not in the least disconcerted; she only looked at it with an air of the most surprised and unconscious innocence.

"Laws! why, that ar's Miss Feely's[1] ribbon, an't it? How could it a got caught in my sleeve?"

"Topsy, you naughty girl, don't you tell me a lie,—you stole that ribbon!"

"Missis, I declar for 't, I didn't;—never seed it till dis yer blessed minnit."

"Topsy," said Miss Ophelia, "don't you know it's wicked to tell lies?"

"I never tells no lies, Miss Feely," said Topsy, with virtuous gravity; "it's jist the truth I've been a tellin now, and an't nothin else."

"Topsy, I shall have to whip you, if you tell lies so."

"Laws, Missis, if you's to whip all day, couldn't say no other way," said Topsy, beginning to blubber. "I never seed dat ar,—it must a got caught in my sleeve. Miss Feely must have left it on the bed, and it got caught in the clothes, and so got in my sleeve."

Miss Ophelia was so indignant at the barefaced lie, that she caught the child and shook her.

"Don't you tell me that again!"

The shake brought the gloves on to the floor, from the other sleeve.

"There, you!" said Miss Ophelia, "will you tell me now, you didn't steal the ribbon?"

Topsy now confessed to the gloves, but still persisted in denying the ribbon.

"Now, Topsy," said Miss Ophelia, "if you'll confess all about it, I won't whip you this time." Thus adjured, Topsy confessed to the ribbon and gloves, with woful protestations of penitence.

"Well, now, tell me. I know you must have taken other things since you have been in the house, for I let you run about all day yesterday. Now, tell me if you took anything, and I shan't whip you."

"Laws, Missis! I took Miss Eva's red thing she wars on her neck."

"You did, you naughty child!—Well, what else?"

"I took Rosa's yer-rings,—them red ones."

"Go bring them to me this minute, both of 'em."

"Laws, Missis! I can't,—they's burnt up!"

"Burnt up!—what a story! Go get 'em, or I'll whip you."

Topsy, with loud protestations, and tears, and groans, declared that she *could* not. "They's burnt up,—they was."

"What did you burn 'em up for?" said Miss Ophelia.

"Cause I's wicked,—I is. I's mighty wicked, any how. I can't help it."

Just at this moment, Eva came innocently into the room, with the identical coral necklace on her neck.

"Why, Eva, where did you get your necklace?" said Miss Ophelia.

"Get it? Why, I've had it on all day," said Eva.

1. Child's version of "Miss Ophelia."

"Did you have it on yesterday?"

"Yes; and what is funny, Aunty, I had it on all night. I forgot to take it off when I went to bed."

Miss Ophelia looked perfectly bewildered; the more so, as Rosa, at that instant, came into the room, with a basket of newly-ironed linen poised on her head, and the coral ear-drops shaking in her ears!

"I'm sure I can't tell anything what to do with such a child!" she said, in despair. "What in the world did you tell me you took those things for, Topsy?"

"Why, Missis said I must 'fess; and I couldn't think of nothin' else to 'fess," said Topsy, rubbing her eyes.

"But, of course, I didn't want you to confess things you didn't do," said Miss Ophelia; "that's telling a lie, just as much as the other."

"Laws, now, is it?" said Topsy, with an air of innocent wonder.

"La, there an't any such thing as truth in that limb," said Rosa, looking indignantly at Topsy. "If I was Mas'r St. Clare, I'd whip her till the blood run. I would,—I'd let her catch it!"

"No, no, Rosa," said Eva, with an air of command, which the child could assume at times; "you mustn't talk so, Rosa. I can't bear to hear it."

"La sakes! Miss Eva, you's so good, you don't know nothing how to get along with niggers. There's no way but to cut 'em well up, I tell ye."

"Rosa!" said Eva, "hush! Don't you say another word of that sort!" and the eye of the child flashed, and her cheek deepened its color.

Rosa was cowed in a moment.

"Miss Eva has got the St. Clare blood in her, that's plain. She can speak, for all the world, just like her papa," she said, as she passed out of the room.

Eva stood looking at Topsy.

There stood the two children, representatives of the two extremes of society. The fair, high-bred child, with her golden head, her deep eyes, her spiritual, noble brow, and prince-like movements; and her black, keen, subtle, cringing, yet acute neighbor. They stood the representatives of their races. The Saxon, born of ages of cultivation, command, education, physical and moral eminence; the Afric, born of ages of oppression, submission, ignorance, toil, and vice!

Something, perhaps, of such thoughts struggled through Eva's mind. But a child's thoughts are rather dim, undefined instincts; and in Eva's noble nature many such were yearning and working, for which she had no power of utterance. When Miss Ophelia expatiated on Topsy's naughty, wicked conduct, the child looked perplexed and sorrowful, but said, sweetly,

"Poor Topsy, why need you steal? You're going to be taken good care of, now. I'm sure I'd rather give you anything of mine, than have you steal it."

It was the first word of kindness the child had ever heard in her life; and the sweet tone and manner struck strangely on the wild, rude heart, and a sparkle of something like a tear shone in the keen, round, glittering eye; but it was followed by the short laugh and habitual grin. No! the ear that has never heard anything but abuse is strangely incredulous of anything so heavenly as kindness; and Topsy only thought Eva's speech something funny and inexplicable,—she did not believe it.

But what was to be done with Topsy? Miss Ophelia found the case a puzzler; her rules for bringing up didn't seem to apply. She thought she would take time to think of it; and, by the way of gaining time, and in hopes of some indefinite moral virtues supposed to be inherent in dark closets, Miss Ophelia shut Topsy up in one till she had arranged her ideas further on the subject.

"I don't see," said Miss Ophelia to St. Clare, "how I'm going to manage that child, without whipping her."

"Well, whip her, then, to your heart's content; I'll give you full power to do what you like."

"Children always have to be whipped," said Miss Ophelia; "I never heard of bringing them up without."

"O, well, certainly," said St. Clare: "do as you think best. Only I'll make one suggestion: I've seen this child whipped with a poker, knocked down with the shovel or tongs, whichever came handiest, &c.; and, seeing that she is used to that style of operation, I think your whippings will have to be pretty energetic, to make much impression."

"What is to be done with her, then?" said Miss Ophelia.

"You have started a serious question," said St. Clare; "I wish you'd answer it. What is to be done with a human being that can be governed only by the lash,—*that* fails,—it's a very common state of things down here!"

"I'm sure I don't know; I never saw such a child as this."

"Such children are very common among us, and such men and women, too. How are they to be governed?" said St. Clare.

"I'm sure it's more than I can say," said Miss Ophelia.

"Or I either," said St. Clare. "The horrid cruelties and outrages that once and a while find their way into the papers,—such cases as Prue's,[2] for example,—what do they come from? In many cases, it is a gradual hardening process on both sides,—the owner growing more and more cruel, as the servant more and more callous. Whipping and abuse are like laudanum;[3] you have to double the dose as the sensibilities decline. I saw this very early when I became an owner; and I resolved never to begin, because I did not know when I should stop,—and I resolved, at least, to protect my own moral nature. The consequence is, that my servants act like spoiled children; but I think that better than for us both to be brutalized together. You have talked a great deal about our responsibilities in educating, Cousin. I really wanted you to *try* with one child, who is a specimen of thousands among us."

"It is your system makes such children," said Miss Ophelia.

"I know it; but they are *made*,—they exist,—and what *is* to be done with them?"

"Well, I can't say I thank you for the experiment. But, then, as it appears to be a duty, I shall persevere and try, and do the best I can," said Miss Ophelia; and Miss Ophelia, after this, did labor, with a commendable degree of zeal and energy, on her new subject. She instituted regular hours and employments for her, and undertook to teach her to read and to sew.

In the former art, the child was quick enough. She learned her letters as if by magic, and was very soon able to read plain reading; but the sewing was a more difficult matter. The creature was as lithe as a cat, and as active as a monkey, and the confinement of sewing was her abomination; so she broke her needles, threw them slyly out of windows, or down in chinks of the

2. A slave on another plantation who had been whipped to death.

3. Tincture of opium, commonly used as a painkiller in the 19th century.

walls; she tangled, broke, and dirtied her thread, or, with a sly movement, would throw a spool away altogether. Her motions were almost as quick as those of a practised conjurer, and her command of her face quite as great; and though Miss Ophelia could not help feeling that so many accidents could not possibly happen in succession, yet she could not, without a watchfulness which would leave her no time for anything else, detect her.

Topsy was soon a noted character in the establishment. Her talent for every species of drollery, grimace, and mimicry,—for dancing, tumbling, climbing, singing, whistling, imitating every sound that hit her fancy,—seemed inexhaustible. In her play-hours, she invariably had every child in the establishment at her heels, open-mouthed with admiration and wonder,—not excepting Miss Eva, who appeared to be fascinated by her wild diablerie, as a dove is sometimes charmed by a glittering serpent. Miss Ophelia was uneasy that Eva should fancy Topsy's society so much, and implored St. Clare to forbid it.

"Poh! let the child alone," said St. Clare. "Topsy will do her good."

"But so depraved a child,—are you not afraid she will teach her some mischief?"

"She can't teach her mischief; she might teach it to some children, but evil rolls off Eva's mind like dew off a cabbage-leaf,—not a drop sinks in."

"Don't be too sure," said Miss Ophelia. "I know I'd never let a child of mine play with Topsy."

"Well, your children needn't," said St. Clare, "but mine may; if Eva could have been spoiled, it would have been done years ago."

Topsy was at first despised and contemned by the upper servants. They soon found reason to alter their opinion. It was very soon discovered that whoever cast an indignity on Topsy was sure to meet with some inconvenient accident shortly after;—either a pair of ear-rings or some cherished trinket would be missing, or an article of dress would be suddenly found utterly ruined, or the person would stumble accidentally into a pail of hot water, or a libation of dirty slop would unaccountably deluge them from above when in full gala dress;—and on all these occasions, when investigation was made, there was nobody found to stand sponsor for the indignity. Topsy was cited, and had up before all the domestic judicatories, time and again; but always sustained her examinations with most edifying innocence and gravity of appearance. Nobody in the world ever doubted who did the things; but not a scrap of any direct evidence could be found to establish the suppositions, and Miss Ophelia was too just to feel at liberty to proceed to any lengths without it.

The mischiefs done were always so nicely timed, also, as further to shelter the aggressor. Thus, the times for revenge on Rosa and Jane, the two chambermaids, were always chosen in those seasons when (as not unfrequently happened) they were in disgrace with their mistress, when any complaint from them would of course meet with no sympathy. In short, Topsy soon made the household understand the propriety of letting her alone; and she was let alone accordingly.

Topsy was smart and energetic in all manual operations, learning everything that was taught her with surprising quickness. With a few lessons, she had learned to do the proprieties of Miss Ophelia's chamber in a way with which even that particular lady could find no fault. Mortal hands could not lay spread smoother, adjust pillows more accurately, sweep and dust and arrange more perfectly, than Topsy, when she chose,—but she didn't very often choose. If Miss Ophelia, after three or four days of careful and patient supervision, was so sanguine as to suppose that Topsy had at last fallen into her way, could do without overlooking, and so go off and busy herself about something else, Topsy would hold a perfect carnival of confusion, for some one or two hours. Instead of making the bed, she would amuse herself with pulling off the pillow-cases, butting her woolly head among the pillows, till it would sometimes be grotesquely ornamented with feathers sticking out in various directions; she would climb the posts, and hang head downward from the tops; flourish the sheets and spreads all over the apartment; dress the bolster up in Miss Ophelia's night-clothes, and enact various scenic performances with that,—singing and whistling, and making grimaces at herself in the looking-glass; in short, as Miss Ophelia phrased it, "raising Cain" generally.

On one occasion, Miss Ophelia found Topsy with her very best scarlet India Canton crape shawl wound round her head for a turban, going on with her rehearsals before the glass in great style,—Miss Ophelia having, with carelessness most unheard-of in her, left the key for once in her drawer.

"Topsy!" she would say, when at the end of all patience, "what does make you act so?"

"Dunno, Missis,—I spects cause I's so wicked!"

"I don't know anything what I shall do with you, Topsy."

"Law, Missis, you must whip me; my old Missis allers whipped me. I an't used to workin' unless I gets whipped."

"Why, Topsy, I don't want to whip you. You can do well, if you've a mind to; what is the reason you won't?"

"Laws, Missis, I's used to whippin'; I spects it's good for me."

Miss Ophelia tried the recipe, and Topsy invariably made a terrible commotion, screaming, groaning and imploring, though half an hour afterwards, when roosted on some projection of the balcony, and surrounded by a flock of admiring "young uns," she would express the utmost contempt of the whole affair.

"Law, Miss Feely whip!—wouldn't kill a skeeter, her whippins. Oughter see how old Mas'r made the flesh fly; old Mas'r know'd how!"

Topsy always made great capital of her own sins and enormities, evidently considering them as something peculiarly distinguishing.

"Law, you niggers," she would say to some of her auditors, "does you know you's all sinners? Well, you is—everybody is. White folks is sinners too,—Miss Feely says so; but I spects niggers is the biggest ones; but lor! ye an't any on ye up to me. I's so awful wicked there can't nobody do nothin' with me. I used to keep old Missis a swarin' at me half de time. I spects I's the wickedest critter in the world;" and Topsy would cut a summerset, and come up brisk and shining on to a higher perch, and evidently plume herself on the distinction.

Miss Ophelia busied herself very earnestly on Sundays, teaching Topsy the catechism. Topsy had an uncommon verbal memory, and committed with a fluency that greatly encouraged her instructress.

"What good do you expect it is going to do her?" said St. Clare.

"Why, it always has done children good. It's what children always have to learn, you know," said Miss Ophelia.

"Understand it or not," said St. Clare.

"O, children never understand it at the time; but, after they are grown up, it'll come to them."

"Mine hasn't come to me yet," said St. Clare, "though I'll bear testimony that you put it into me pretty thoroughly when I was a boy."

"Ah, you were always good at learning, Augustine. I used to have great hopes of you," said Miss Ophelia.

"Well, haven't you now?" said St. Clare.

"I wish you were as good as you were when you were a boy, Augustine."

"So do I, that's a fact, Cousin," said St. Clare. "Well, go ahead and catechize Topsy; may be you'll make out something yet."

Topsy, who had stood like a black statue during this discussion, with hands decently folded, now, at a signal from Miss Ophelia, went on:

"Our first parents, being left to the freedom of their own will, fell from the state wherein they were created."

Topsy's eyes twinkled, and she looked inquiringly.

"What is it, Topsy?" said Miss Ophelia.

"Please, Missis, was dat ar state Kintuck?"

"What state, Topsy?"

"Dat state dey fell out of. I used to hear Mas'r tell how we came down from Kintuck."

St. Clare laughed.

"You'll have to give her a meaning, or she'll make one," said he. "There seems to be a theory of emigration suggested there."

"O! Augustine, be still," said Miss Ophelia; "how can I do anything, if you will be laughing?"

"Well, I won't disturb the exercises again, on my honor;" and St. Clare took his paper into the parlor, and sat down, till Topsy had finished her recitations. They were all very well, only that now and then she would oddly transpose some important words, and persist in the mistake, in spite of every effort to the contrary; and St. Clare, after all his promises of goodness, took a wicked pleasure in these mistakes, calling Topsy to him whenever he had a mind to amuse himself, and getting her to repeat the offending passages, in spite of Miss Ophelia's remonstrances.

"How do you think I can do anything with the child, if you will go on so, Augustine?" she would say.

"Well, it is too bad,—I won't again; but I do like to hear the droll little image stumble over those big words!"

"But you confirm her in the wrong way."

"What's the odds? One word is as good as another to her."

"You wanted me to bring her up right; and you ought to remember she is a reasonable creature, and be careful of your influence over her."

"O, dismal! so I ought; but, as Topsy herself says, 'I's so wicked!'"

In very much this way Topsy's training proceeded, for a year or two,—Miss Ophelia worrying herself, from day to day, with her, as a kind of chronic plague, to whose inflictions she became, in time, as accustomed, as persons sometimes do to the neuralgia or sick head-ache.

St. Clare took the same kind of amusement in the child that a man might in the tricks of a parrot or a pointer. Topsy, whenever her sins brought her into disgrace in other quarters, always took refuge behind his chair; and St. Clare, in one way or other, would make peace for her. From him she got many a stray picayune,[4] which she laid out in nuts and candies, and distributed, with careless generosity, to all the children in the family; for Topsy, to do her justice, was good-natured and liberal, and only spiteful in self-defence. She is fairly introduced into our *corps de ballet*,[5] and will figure, from time to time, in her turn, with other performers.

* * *

FROM CHAPTER XXVI. DEATH[6]

Weep not for those whom the veil of the tomb,
In life's early morning, hath bid from our eyes.[7]

* * *

"Mamma," said Eva, "I want to have some of my hair cut off,—a good deal of it."

"What for?" said Marie.

"Mamma, I want to give some away to my friends, while I am able to give it to them myself. Won't you ask aunty to come and cut it for me?"

Marie raised her voice, and called Miss Ophelia, from the other room.

The child half rose from her pillow as she came in, and, shaking down her long golden-brown curls, said, rather playfully, "Come, aunty, shear the sheep!"

"What's that?" said St. Clare, who just then entered with some fruit he had been out to get for her.

"Papa, I just want aunty to cut off some of my hair;—there's too much of it, and it makes my head hot. Besides, I want to give some of it away."

Miss Ophelia came, with her scissors.

"Take care,—don't spoil the looks of it!" said her father; "cut underneath, where it won't show. Eva's curls are my pride."

"O, papa!" said Eva, sadly.

"Yes, and I want them kept handsome against the time I take you up to your uncle's plantation, to see Cousin Henrique," said St. Clare, in a gay tone.

"I shall never go there, papa;—I am going to a better country. O, do believe me! Don't you see, papa, that I get weaker, every day?"

"Why do you insist that I shall believe such a cruel thing, Eva?" said her father.

"Only because it is *true*, papa: and, if you will believe it now, perhaps you will get to feel about it as I do."

St. Clare closed his lips, and stood gloomily eying the long, beautiful curls, which, as they were separated from the child's head, were laid, one by one, in

4. Small coin, such as a penny, nickle, or the Spanish picayune, which was used as currency in parts of the South until 1857.

5. The subordinate dancers in a ballet company (French, literal trans.); here the novel's cast of supporting characters.

6. Two years have passed. To escape the hot New Orleans summer, St. Clare has brought his family and slaves to his villa at Lake Pontchartrain in southeastern Louisiana. Eva, who has been showing signs of serious illness, has declared to Tom that she would be happy to die if her death would bring an end to the sufferings of the slaves.

7. From "Weep Not for Those" (1816), by the Irish poet Thomas Moore (1779–1852).

her lap. She raised them up, looked earnestly at them, twined them around her thin fingers, and looked, from time to time, anxiously at her father.

"It's just what I've been foreboding!" said Marie; "it's just what has been preying on my health, from day to day, bringing me downward to the grave, though nobody regards it. I have seen this, long. St. Clare, you will see, after a while, that I was right."

"Which will afford you great consolation, no doubt!" said St. Clare, in a dry, bitter tone.

Marie lay back on a lounge, and covered her face with her cambric handkerchief.

Eva's clear blue eye looked earnestly from one to the other. It was the calm, comprehending gaze of a soul half loosed from its earthly bonds; it was evident she saw, felt, and appreciated, the difference between the two.

She beckoned with her hand to her father. He came, and sat down by her.

"Papa, my strength fades away every day, and I know I must go. There are some things I want to say and do,—that I ought to do; and you are so unwilling to have me speak a word on this subject. But it must come; there's no putting it off. Do be willing I should speak now!"

"My child, I *am* willing!" said St. Clare, covering his eyes with one hand, and holding up Eva's hand with the other.

"Then, I want to see all our people together. I have some things I *must* say to them," said Eva.

"*Well*," said St. Clare, in a tone of dry endurance.

Miss Ophelia despatched a messenger, and soon the whole of the servants were convened in the room.

Eva lay back on her pillows; her hair hanging loosely about her face, her crimson cheeks contrasting painfully with the intense whiteness of her complexion and the thin contour of her limbs and features, and her large, soul-like eyes fixed earnestly on every one.

The servants were struck with a sudden emotion. The spiritual face, the long locks of hair cut off and lying by her, her father's averted face, and Marie's sobs, struck at once upon the feelings of a sensitive and impressible race; and, as they came in, they looked one on another, sighed, and shook their heads. There was a deep silence, like that of a funeral.

Eva raised herself, and looked long and earnestly round at every one. All looked sad and apprehensive. Many of the women hid their faces in their aprons.

"I sent for you all, my dear friends," said Eva, "because I love you. I love you all; and I have something to say to you, which I want you always to remember. . . . I am going to leave you. In a few more weeks, you will see me no more—"

Here the child was interrupted by bursts of groans, sobs, and lamentations, which broke from all present, and in which her slender voice was lost entirely. She waited a moment, and then, speaking in a tone that checked the sobs of all, she said,

"If you love me, you must not interrupt me so. Listen to what I say. I want to speak to you about your souls. . . . Many of you, I am afraid, are very careless. You are thinking only about this world. I want you to remember that there is a beautiful world, where Jesus is. I am going there, and you can go there. It is for you, as much as me. But, if you want to go there, you must not live idle, careless, thoughtless lives. You must be Christians. You must remember that each one of you can become angels, and be angels forever. . . . If you want to be Christians, Jesus will help you. You must pray to him; you must read—"

The child checked herself, looked piteously at them, and said, sorrowfully,

"O, dear! you *can't* read,—poor souls!" and she hid her face in the pillow and sobbed, while many a smothered sob from those she was addressing, who were kneeling on the floor, aroused her.

"Never mind," she said, raising her face and smiling brightly through her tears, "I have prayed for you; and I know Jesus will help you, even if you can't read. Try all to do the best you can; pray every day; ask Him to help you, and get the Bible read to you whenever you can; and I think I shall see you all in heaven."

"Amen," was the murmured response from the lips of Tom and Mammy, and some of the elder ones, who belonged to the Methodist church. The younger and more thoughtless ones, for the time completely overcome, were sobbing, with their heads bowed upon their knees.

"I know," said Eva, "you all love me."

"Yes; oh, yes! indeed we do! Lord bless her!" was the involuntary answer of all.

"Yes, I know you do! There isn't one of you that hasn't always been very kind to me; and I want to give you something that, when you look at, you shall always remember me. I'm going to give all of you a curl of my hair; and, when you look at it, think that I loved you and am gone to heaven, and that I want to see you all there."

It is impossible to describe the scene, as, with tears and sobs, they gathered round the little creature, and took from her hands what seemed to them a last mark of her love. They fell on their knees; they sobbed, and prayed, and kissed the hem of her garment; and the elder ones poured forth words of endearment, mingled in prayers and blessings, after the manner of their susceptible race.

As each one took their gift, Miss Ophelia, who was apprehensive for the effect of all this excitement on her little patient, signed to each one to pass out of the apartment.

At last, all were gone but Tom and Mammy.

"Here, Uncle Tom," said Eva, "is a beautiful one for you. O, I am so happy, Uncle Tom, to think I shall see you in heaven,—for I'm sure I shall; and Mammy,—dear, good, kind Mammy!" she said, fondly throwing her arms round her old nurse,—"I know you'll be there, too."

"O, Miss Eva, don't see how I can live without ye, no how!" said the faithful creature. "'Pears like it's just taking everything off the place to oncet!"[8] and Mammy gave way to a passion of grief.

Miss Ophelia pushed her and Tom gently from the apartment, and thought they were all gone; but, as she turned, Topsy was standing there.

"Where did you start up from?" she said, suddenly.

"I was here," said Topsy, wiping the tears from her eyes. "O, Miss Eva, I've been a bad girl; but won't you give *me* one, too?"

8. At once (colloquial).

"Yes, poor Topsy! to be sure, I will. There—every time you look at that, think that I love you, and wanted you to be a good girl!"

"O, Miss Eva, I *is* tryin!" said Topsy, earnestly; "but, Lor, it's so hard to be good! 'Pears like I an't used to it, no ways!"

"Jesus knows it, Topsy; he is sorry for you; he will help you."

Topsy, with her eyes hid in her apron, was silently passed from the apartment by Miss Ophelia; but, as she went, she hid the precious curl in her bosom.

* * *

Eva had been unusually bright and cheerful, that afternoon, and had sat raised in her bed, and looked over all her little trinkets and precious things, and designated the friends to whom she would have them given; and her manner was more animated, and her voice more natural, than they had known it for weeks. Her father had been in, in the evening, and had said that Eva appeared more like her former self than ever she had done since her sickness; and when he kissed her for the night, he said to Miss Ophelia,—"Cousin, we may keep her with us, after all; she is certainly better;" and he had retired with a lighter heart in his bosom than he had had there for weeks.

But at midnight,—strange, mystic hour!—when the veil between the frail present and the eternal future grows thin,—then came the messenger!

There was a sound in that chamber, first of one who stepped quickly. It was Miss Ophelia, who had resolved to sit up all night with her little charge, and who, at the turn of the night, had discerned what experienced nurses significantly call "a change." The outer door was quickly opened, and Tom, who was watching outside, was on the alert, in a moment.

"Go for the doctor, Tom! lose not a moment," said Miss Ophelia; and, stepping across the room, she rapped at St. Clare's door.

"Cousin," she said, "I wish you would come."

Those words fell on his heart like clods upon a coffin. Why did they? He was up and in the room in an instant, and bending over Eva, who still slept.

What was it he saw that made his heart stand still? Why was no word spoken between the two? Thou canst say, who hast seen that same expression on the face dearest to thee;—that look indescribable, hopeless, unmistakable, that says to thee that thy beloved is no longer thine.

On the face of the child, however, there was no ghastly imprint,—only a high and almost sublime expression,—the overshadowing presence of spiritual natures, the dawning of immortal life in that childish soul.

They stood there so still, gazing upon her, that even the ticking of the watch seemed too loud. In a few moments, Tom returned, with the doctor. He entered, gave one look, and stood silent as the rest.

"When did this change take place?" said he, in a low whisper, to Miss Ophelia.

"About the turn of the night," was the reply.

Marie, roused by the entrance of the doctor, appeared, hurriedly, from the next room.

"Augustine! Cousin!—O!—what!" she hurriedly began.

"Hush!" said St. Clare, hoarsely; "*she is dying*!"

Mammy heard the words, and flew to awaken the servants. The house was soon roused,—lights were seen, footsteps heard, anxious faces thronged the verandah, and looked tearfully through the glass doors; but St. Clare heard and said nothing,—he saw only *that look* on the face of the little sleeper.

"O, if she would only wake, and speak once more!" he said; and, stooping over her, he spoke in her ear,—"Eva, darling!"

The large blue eyes unclosed,—a smile passed over her face;—she tried to raise her head, and to speak.

"Do you know me, Eva?"

"Dear papa," said the child, with a last effort, throwing her arms about his neck. In a moment they dropped again; and, as St. Clare raised his head, he saw a spasm of mortal agony pass over the face,—she struggled for breath, and threw up her little hands.

"O, God, this is dreadful!" he said, turning away in agony, and wringing Tom's hand, scarce conscious what he was doing. "O, Tom, my boy, it is killing me!"

Tom had his master's hands between his own; and, with tears streaming down his dark cheeks, looked up for help where he had always been used to look.

"Pray that this may be cut short!" said St. Clare,—"this wrings my heart."

"O, bless the Lord! it's over,—it's over, dear Master!" said Tom; "look at her."

The child lay panting on her pillows, as one exhausted,—the large clear eyes rolled up and fixed. Ah, what said those eyes, that spoke so much of heaven? Earth was past, and earthly pain; but so solemn, so mysterious, was the triumphant brightness of that face, that it checked even the sobs of sorrow. They pressed around her, in breathless stillness.

"Eva," said St. Clare, gently.

She did not hear.

"O, Eva, tell us what you see! What is it?" said her father.

A bright, a glorious smile passed over her face, and she said, brokenly,—"O! love,—joy,—peace!" gave one sigh, and passed from death unto life!

"Farewell, beloved child! the bright, eternal doors have closed after thee; we shall see thy sweet face no more. O, woe for them who watched thy entrance into heaven, when they shall wake and find only the cold gray sky of daily life, and thou gone forever!"

* * *

CHAPTER XXX. THE SLAVE WAREHOUSE[9]

A slave warehouse! Perhaps some of my readers conjure up horrible visions of such a place. They fancy some foul, obscure den, some horrible *Tartarus "informis, ingens, cui lumen ademptum."*[1] But no, innocent friend; in these days men have learned the art of sinning expertly and genteelly, so as not to shock the eyes and senses of respectable society. Human property is high in the market; and is, therefore, well fed, well cleaned, tended, and looked after, that it may come to sale sleek, and strong, and shining. A slave-warehouse

9. At this point in the novel Tom has lost his protectors. Eva has died of tuberculosis, St. Clare has been killed while trying to break up a fight, and Ophelia is returning to New England with Topsy after having vainly urged Marie St. Clare to honor her late husband's wish to free their slaves. The group sent to the warehouse includes Tom and St. Clare's valet, Adolph.

1. "Frightful, formless, immense, with light removed" (Latin); from *The Aeneid* (3.658), the Latin epic by Virgil (70–19 B.C.E.). "Tartarus": in Greek mythology, a kind of hell.

in New Orleans is a house externally not much unlike many others, kept with neatness; and where every day you may see arranged, under a sort of shed along the outside, rows of men and women, who stand there as a sign of the property sold within.

Then you shall be courteously entreated to call and examine, and shall find an abundance of husbands, wives, brothers, sisters, fathers, mothers, and young children, to be "sold separately, or in lots to suit the convenience of the purchaser;" and that soul immortal, once bought with blood and anguish by the Son of God, when the earth shook, and the rocks rent, and the graves were opened, can be sold, leased, mortgaged, exchanged for groceries or dry goods, to suit the phases of trade, or the fancy of the purchaser.

It was a day or two after the conversation between Marie and Miss Ophelia, that Tom, Adolph, and about half a dozen others of the St. Clare estate, were turned over to the loving kindness of Mr. Skeggs, the keeper of a depot on —— street, to await the auction, next day.

Tom had with him quite a sizable trunk full of clothing, as had most others of them. They were ushered, for the night, into a long room, where many other men, of all ages, sizes and shades of complexion, were assembled, and from which roars of laughter and unthinking merriment were proceeding.

"Ah, ha! that's right. Go it, boys,—go it!" said Mr. Skeggs, the keeper. "My people are always so merry! Sambo, I see!" he said, speaking approvingly to a burly negro who was performing tricks of low buffoonery, which occasioned the shouts which Tom had heard.

As might be imagined, Tom was in no humor to join these proceedings; and, therefore, setting his trunk as far as possible from the noisy group, he sat down on it, and leaned his face against the wall.

The dealers in the human article make scrupulous and systematic efforts to promote noisy mirth among them, as a means of drowning reflection, and rendering them insensible to their condition. The whole object of the training to which the negro is put, from the time he is sold in the northern market till he arrives south, is systematically directed towards making him callous, unthinking, and brutal. The slave-dealer collects his gang in Virginia or Kentucky, and drives them to some convenient, healthy place,—often a watering place,—to be fattened. Here they are fed full daily; and, because some incline to pine, a fiddle is kept commonly going among them, and they are made to dance daily; and he who refuses to be merry—in whose soul thoughts of wife, or child, or home, are too strong for him to be gay—is marked as sullen and dangerous, and subjected to all the evils which the ill will of an utterly irresponsible and hardened man can inflict upon him. Briskness, alertness, and cheerfulness of appearance, especially before observers, are constantly enforced upon them, both by the hope of thereby getting a good master, and the fear of all that the driver may bring upon them, if they prove unsalable.

"What dat ar nigger doin here?" said Sambo, coming up to Tom, after Mr. Skeggs had left the room. Sambo was a full black, of great size, very lively, voluble, and full of trick and grimace.

"What you doin here?" said Sambo, coming up to Tom, and poking him facetiously in the side. "Meditatin', eh?"

"I am to be sold at the auction, to-morrow!" said Tom, quietly.

"Sold at auction,—haw! haw! boys, an't this yer fun? I wish't I was gwine that ar way!—tell ye, wouldn't I make em laugh? But how is it,—dis yer whole lot gwine to-morrow?" said Sambo, laying his hand freely on Adolph's shoulder.

"Please to let me alone!" said Adolph, fiercely, straightening himself up, with extreme disgust.

"Law, now, boys! dis yer's one o' yer white niggers,—kind o' cream color, ye know, scented!" said he, coming up to Adolph and snuffing. "O, Lor! he'd do for a tobaccer-shop; they could keep him to scent snuff! Lor, he'd keep a whole shope agwine,—he would!"

"I say, keep off, can't you?" said Adolph, enraged.

"Lor, now, how touchy we is,—we white niggers! Look at us, now!" and Sambo gave a ludicrous imitation of Adolph's manner; "here's de airs and graces. We's been in a good family, I specs."

"Yes," said Adolph; "I had a master that could have bought you all for old truck!"

"Laws, now, only think," said Sambo, "the gentlemens that we is!"

"I belonged to the St. Clare family," said Adolph, proudly.

"Lor, you did! Be hanged if they ar'n't lucky to get shet of ye. Spects they's gwine to trade ye off with a lot o' cracked tea-pots and sich like!" said Sambo, with a provoking grin.

Adolph, enraged at this taunt, flew furiously at his adversary, swearing and striking on every side of him. The rest laughed and shouted, and the uproar brought the keeper to the door.

"What now, boys? Order,—order!" he said, coming in and flourishing a large whip.

All fled in different directions, except Sambo, who, presuming on the favor which the keeper had to him as a licensed wag, stood his ground, ducking his head with a facetious grin, whenever the master made a dive at him.

"Lor, Mas'r, 'tan't us,—we's reglar stiddy,—it's these yer new hands; they's real aggravatin',—kinder pickin' at us, all time!"

The keeper, at this, turned upon Tom and Adolph, and distributing a few kicks and cuffs without much inquiry, and leaving general orders for all to be good boys and go to sleep, left the apartment.

While this scene was going on in the men's sleeping-room, the reader may be curious to take a peep at the corresponding apartment allotted to the women. Stretched out in various attitudes over the floor, he may see numberless sleeping forms of every shade of complexion, from the purest ebony to white, and of all years, from childhood to old age, lying now asleep. Here is a fine bright girl, of ten years, whose mother was sold out yesterday, and who to-night cried herself to sleep when nobody was looking at her. Here, a worn old negress, whose thin arms and callous fingers tell of hard toil, waiting to be sold to-morrow, as a cast-off article, for what can be got for her; and some forty or fifty others, with heads variously enveloped in blankets or articles of clothing, lie stretched around them. But, in a corner, sitting apart from the rest, are two females of a more interesting appearance than common. One of these is a respectably-dressed mulatto woman between forty and fifty, with soft eyes and a gentle and pleasing physiognomy. She has on her head a high-raised turban, made of a gay red Madras handkerchief, of the first quality, and her dress is neatly fitted, and of good material, showing that she has been provided for with a careful hand. By her side, and nestling closely to her, is a young girl of fifteen,—her daughter. She is a quadroon, as may be seen from her fairer complexion, though her likeness to her mother is quite discernible. She has the same soft, dark eye, with longer lashes, and her curling hair is of a luxuriant brown. She also is dressed with great neatness, and her white, delicate hands betray very little acquaintance with servile toil. These two are to be sold to-morrow, in the same lot with the St. Clare servants; and the gentleman to whom they belong, and to whom the money for their sale is to be transmitted, is a member of a Christian church in New York, who will receive the money, and go thereafter to the sacrament of his Lord and theirs, and think no more of it.

These two, whom we shall call Susan and Emmeline, had been the personal attendants of an amiable and pious lady of New Orleans, by whom they had been carefully and piously instructed and trained. They had been taught to read and write, diligently instructed in the truths of religion, and their lot had been as happy an one as in their condition it was possible to be. But the only son of their protectress had the management of her property; and, by carelessness and extravagance involved it to a large amount, and at last failed. One of the largest creditors was the respectable firm of B. & Co., in New York. B. & Co. wrote to their lawyer in New Orleans, who attached the real estate (these two articles and a lot of plantation hands formed the most valuable part of it), and wrote word to that effect to New York. Brother B., being, as we have said, a Christian man, and a resident in a free State, felt some uneasiness on the subject. He didn't like trading in slaves and souls of men,—of course, he didn't; but, then, there were thirty thousand dollars in the case, and that was rather too much money to be lost for a principle; and so, after much considering, and asking advice from those that he knew would advise to suit him, Brother B. wrote to his lawyer to dispose of the business in the way that seemed to him the most suitable, and remit the proceeds.

The day after the letter arrived in New Orleans, Susan and Emmeline were attached, and sent to the depot to await a general auction on the following morning; and as they glimmer faintly upon us in the moonlight which steals through the grated window, we may listen to their conversation. Both are weeping, but each quietly, that the other may not hear.

"Mother, just lay your head on my lap, and see if you can't sleep a little," says the girl, trying to appear calm.

"I haven't any heart to sleep, Em; I can't; it's the last night we may be together!"

"O, mother, don't say so! perhaps we shall get sold together,—who knows?"

"If't was anybody's else case, I should say so, too, Em," said the woman; "but I'm so feard of losin' you that I don't see anything but the danger."

"Why, mother, the man said we were both likely, and would sell well."

Susan remembered the man's looks and words. With a deadly sickness at her heart, she remembered how he had looked at Emmeline's hands, and lifted up her curly hair, and pronounced her a first-rate article. Susan had been trained as a Christian, brought up in the daily reading of the Bible, and had the same horror of her child's being sold to a life of shame that any other Christian mother might have; but she had no hope,—no protection.

"Mother, I think we might do first rate, if you could get a place as cook, and I as chamber-maid or seamstress, in some family. I dare say we shall. Let's both look as bright and lively as we can, and tell all we can do, and perhaps we shall," said Emmeline.

"I want you to brush your hair all back straight, to-morrow," said Susan.

"What for, mother? I don't look near so well, that way."

"Yes, but you'll sell better so."

"I don't see why!" said the child.

"Respectable families would be more apt to buy you, if they saw you looked plain and decent, as if you wasn't trying to look handsome. I know their ways better 'n you do," said Susan.

"Well, mother, then I will."

"And, Emmeline, if we shouldn't ever see each other again, after to-morrow,—if I'm sold way up on a plantation somewhere, and you somewhere else,—always remember how you've been brought up, and all Missis has told you; take your Bible with you, and your hymn-book; and if you're faithful to the Lord, he'll be faithful to you."

So speaks the poor soul, in sore discouragement; for she knows that to-morrow any man, however vile and brutal, however godless and merciless, if he only has money to pay for her, may become owner of her daughter, body and soul; and then, how is the child to be faithful? She thinks of all this, as she holds her daughter in her arms, and wishes that she were not handsome and attractive. It seems almost an aggravation to her to remember how purely and piously, how much above the ordinary lot, she has been brought up. But she has no resort but to *pray*; and many such prayers to God have gone up from those same trim, neatly-arranged, respectable slave-prisons,—prayers which God has not forgotten, as a coming day shall show; for it is written, "Whoso causeth one of these little ones to offend, it were better for him that a mill-stone were hanged about his neck, and that he were drowned in the depths of the sea."[2]

The soft, earnest, quiet moonbeam looks in fixedly marking the bars of the grated windows on the prostrate, sleeping forms. The mother and daughter are singing together a wild and melancholy dirge, common as a funeral hymn among the slaves:

"O, where is weeping Mary?
O, where is weeping Mary?
'Rived in the goodly land.
She is dead and gone to Heaven;
She is dead and gone to Heaven;
'Rived in the goodly land."[3]

These words, sung by voices of a peculiar and melancholy sweetness, in an air which seemed like the sighing of earthly despair after heavenly hope, floated through the dark prison rooms with a pathetic cadence, as verse after verse was breathed out:

"O, where are Paul and Silas?
O, where are Paul and Silas?
Gone to the goodly land.
They are dead and gone to Heaven;
They are dead and gone to Heaven;
'Rived in the goodly land."

2. Matthew 18.6.
3. This and the next stanza are derived from the popular camp-meeting song "Hebrew Children."

Sing on, poor souls! The night is short, and the morning will part you forever!

But now it is morning, and everybody is astir; and the worthy Mr. Skeggs is busy and bright, for a lot of goods is to be fitted out for auction. There is a brisk look-out on the toilet; injunctions passed around to every one to put on their best face and be spry; and now all are arranged in a circle for a last review, before they are marched up to the Bourse.[4]

Mr. Skeggs, with his palmetto on and his cigar in his mouth, walks around to put farewell touches on his wares.

"How's this?" he said, stepping in front of Susan and Emmeline. "Where's your curls, gal?"

The girl looked timidly at her mother, who, with the smooth adroitness common among her class, answers,

"I was telling her, last night, to put up her hair smooth and neat, and not havin' it flying about in curls; looks more respectable so."

"Bother!" said the man, peremptorily, turning to the girl; "you go right along, and curl yourself real smart!" He added, giving a crack to a rattan he held in his hand, "And be back in quick time, too!"

"You go and help her," he added, to the mother. "Them curls may make a hundred dollars difference in the sale of her."

Beneath a splendid dome were men of all nations, moving to and fro, over the marble pave. On every side of the circular area were little tribunes, or stations, for the use of speakers and auctioneers. Two of these, on opposite sides of the area, were now occupied by brilliant and talented gentlemen, enthusiastically forcing up, in English and French commingled,[5] the bids of connoisseurs in their various wares. A third one, on the other side, still unoccupied, was surrounded by a group, waiting the moment of sale to begin. And here we may recognize the St. Clare servants,—Tom, Adolph, and others; and there, too, Susan and Emmeline, awaiting their turn with anxious and dejected faces. Various spectators, intending to purchase, or not intending, as the case might be, gathered around the group, handling, examining, and commenting on their various points and faces with the same freedom that a set of jockeys discuss the merits of a horse.

"Hulloa, Alf! what brings you here?" said a young exquisite, slapping the shoulder of a sprucely-dressed young man, who was examining Adolph through an eye-glass.

"Well, I was wanting a valet, and I heard that St. Clare's lot was going. I thought I'd just look at his—"

"Catch me ever buying any of St. Clare's people! Spoilt niggers, every one. Impudent as the devil!" said the other.

"Never fear that!" said the first. "If I get 'em, I'll soon have their airs out of them; they'll soon find that they've another kind of master to deal with than Monsieur St. Clare. 'Pon my word, I'll buy that fellow. I like the shape of him."

"You'll find it'll take all you've got to keep him. He's deucedly extravagant!"

4. Market or stock exchange (French).
5. Both French and English are spoken in New Orleans.

"Yes, but my lord will find that he *can't* be extravagant with *me*. Just let him be sent to the calaboose[6] a few times, and thoroughly dressed down! I'll tell you if it don't bring him to a sense of his ways! O, I'll reform him, up hill and down,—you'll see. I buy him, that's flat!"

Tom had been standing wistfully examining the multitude of faces thronging around him, for one whom he would wish to call master. And if you should ever be under the necessity, sir, of selecting, out of two hundred men, one who was to become your absolute owner and disposer, you would, perhaps, realize, just as Tom did, how few there were that you would feel at all comfortable in being made over to. Tom saw abundance of men,—great, burly, gruff men; little, chirping, dried men; long-favored, lank, hard men; and every variety of stubbed-looking, commonplace men, who pick up their fellow-men as one picks up chips, putting them into the fire or a basket with equal unconcern, according to their convenience; but he saw no St. Clare.

A little before the sale commenced, a short, broad, muscular man, in a checked shirt considerably open at the bosom, and pantaloons much the worse for dirt and wear, elbowed his way through the crowd, like one who is going actively into a business; and, coming up to the group, began to examine them systematically. From the moment that Tom saw him approaching, he felt an immediate and revolting horror at him, that increased as he came near. He was evidently, though short, of gigantic strength. His round, bullet head, large, light-gray eyes, with their shaggy, sandy eye-brows, and stiff, wiry, sun-burned hair, were rather unprepossessing items, it is to be confessed; his large, coarse mouth was distended with tobacco, the juice of which, from time to time, he ejected from him with great decision and explosive force; his hands were immensely large, hairy, sunburned, freckled, and very dirty, and garnished with long nails, in a very foul condition. This man proceeded to a very free personal examination of the lot. He seized Tom by the jaw, and pulled open his mouth to inspect his teeth; made him strip up his sleeve, to show his muscle; turned him round, made him jump and spring, to show his paces.

"Where was you raised?" he added, briefly, to these investigations.

"In Kintuck, Mas'r," said Tom, looking about, as if for deliverance.

"What have you done?"

"Had care of Mas'r's farm," said Tom.

"Likely story!" said the other, shortly, as he passed on. He paused a moment before Dolph; then spitting a discharge of tobacco-juice on his well-blacked boots, and giving a contemptuous umph, he walked on. Again he stopped before Susan and Emmeline. He put out his heavy, dirty hand, and drew the girl towards him; passed it over her neck and bust, felt her arms, looked at her teeth, and then pushed her back against her mother, whose patient face showed the suffering she had been going through at every motion of the hideous stranger.

The girl was frightened, and began to cry.

"Stop that, you minx!" said the salesman; "no whimpering here,—the sale is going to begin." And accordingly the sale begun.

6. Jail (from the Spanish *calabozo*, "dungeon").

Adolph was knocked off, at a good sum, to the young gentleman who had previously stated his intention of buying him; and the other servants of the St. Clare lot went to various bidders.

"Now, up with you, boy! d'ye hear?" said the auctioneer to Tom.

Tom stepped upon the block, gave a few anxious looks round; all seemed mingled in a common, indistinct noise,—the clatter of the salesman crying off his qualifications in French and English, the quick fire of French and English bids; and almost in a moment came the final thump of the hammer, and the clear ring on the last syllable of the word "*dollars*," as the auctioneer announced his price, and Tom was made over.—He had a master!

He was pushed from the block;—the short, bullet-headed man seizing him roughly by the shoulder, pushed him to one side, saying, in a harsh voice, "Stand there, *you*!"

Tom hardly realized anything; but still the bidding went on,—rattling, clattering, now French, now English. Down goes the hammer again,—Susan is sold! She goes down from the block, stops, looks wistfully back,—her daughter stretches her hands towards her. She looks with agony in the face of the man who has bought her,—a respectable middle-aged man, of benevolent countenance.

"O, Mas'r, please do buy my daughter!"

"I'd like to, but I'm afraid I can't afford it!" said the gentleman, looking, with painful interest, as the young girl mounted the block, and looked around her with a frightened and timid glance.

The blood flushes painfully in her otherwise colorless cheek, her eye has a feverish fire, and her mother groans to see that she looks more beautiful than she ever saw her before. The auctioneer sees his advantage, and expatiates volubly in mingled French and English, and bids rise in rapid succession.

"I'll do anything in reason," said the benevolent-looking gentleman, pressing in and joining with the bids. In a few moments they have run beyond his purse. He is silent; the auctioneer grows warmer; but bids gradually drop off. It lies now between an aristocratic old citizen and our bullet-headed acquaintance. The citizen bids for a few turns, contemptuously measuring his opponent; but the bullet-head has the advantage over him, both in obstinacy and concealed length of purse, and the controversy lasts but a moment; the hammer falls,—he has got the girl, body and soul, unless God help her!

Her master is Mr. Legree, who owns a cotton plantation on the Red river.[7] She is pushed along into the same lot with Tom and two other men, and goes off, weeping as she goes.

The benevolent gentleman is sorry; but, then, the thing happens every day! One sees girls and mothers crying, at these sales, *always*! it can't be helped, &c.; and he walks off, with his acquisition, in another direction.

Two days after, the lawyer of the Christian firm of B. & Co., New York, sent on their money to them. On the reverse of that draft, so obtained, let them write these words of the great Paymaster, to whom they shall make up their account in a future day: "*When he maketh inquisition for blood, he forgetteth not the cry of the humble!*"[8]

7. Tributary of the Mississippi River, flowing through Arkansas and Louisiana.

8. Psalm 9.12.

CHAPTER XXXI. THE MIDDLE PASSAGE[9]

> "Thou art of purer eyes than to behold evil, and canst not look upon iniquity: wherefore lookest thou upon them that deal treacherously, and holdest thy tongue when the wicked devoureth the man that is more righteous than he?"
>
> —HAB. 1:13.

On the lower part of a small, mean boat, on the Red river, Tom sat,—chains on his wrists, chains on his feet, and a weight heavier than chains lay on his heart. All had faded from his sky,—moon and star; all had passed by him, as the trees and banks were now passing, to return no more. Kentucky home, with wife and children, and indulgent owners; St. Clare home, with all its refinements and splendors; the golden head of Eva, with its saint-like eyes; the proud, gay, handsome, seemingly careless, yet ever-kind St. Clare; hours of ease and indulgent leisure,—all gone! and in place thereof, *what* remains?

It is one of the bitterest apportionments of a lot of slavery, that the negro, sympathetic and assimilative, after acquiring, in a refined family, the tastes and feelings which form the atmosphere of such a place, is not the less liable to become the bond-slave of the coarsest and most brutal,—just as a chair or table, which once decorated the superb saloon, comes, at last, battered and defaced, to the bar-room of some filthy tavern, or some low haunt of vulgar debauchery. The great difference is, that the table and chair cannot feel, and the *man* can; for even a legal enactment that he shall be "taken, reputed, adjudged in law, to be a chattel personal,"[1] cannot blot out his soul, with its own private little world of memories, hopes, loves, fears, and desires.

Mr. Simon Legree, Tom's master, had purchased slaves at one place and another, in New Orleans, to the number of eight, and driven them, handcuffed, in couples of two and two, down to the good steamer Pirate, which lay at the levee, ready for a trip up the Red river.

Having got them fairly on board, and the boat being off, he came round, with that air of efficiency which ever characterized him, to take a review of them. Stopping opposite to Tom, who had been attired for sale in his best broadcloth suit, with well-starched linen and shining boots, he briefly expressed himself as follows:

"Stand up."

Tom stood up.

"Take off that stock!" and, as Tom, encumbered by his fetters, proceeded to do it, he assisted him, by pulling it, with no gentle hand, from his neck, and putting it in his pocket.

Legree now turned to Tom's trunk, which, previous to this, he had been ransacking, and, taking from it a pair of old pantaloons and a dilapidated coat, which Tom had been wont to put on about his stable-work, he said, liberating Tom's hands from the handcuffs, and pointing to a recess in among the boxes,

"You go there, and put these on."

9. The term used in the slave trade for the Atlantic voyage from Africa to the Americas; here Tom's river journey from New Orleans to the back country of Louisiana, where Legree's plantation is located.

1. Typical language from the slave codes of the Southern states.

Tom obeyed, and in a few moments returned.

"Take off your boots," said Mr. Legree.

Tom did so.

"There," said the former, throwing him a pair of coarse, stout shoes, such as were common among the slaves, "put these on."

In Tom's hurried exchange, he had not forgotten to transfer his cherished Bible to his pocket. It was well he did so; for Mr. Legree, having refitted Tom's handcuffs, proceeded deliberately to investigate the contents of his pockets. He drew out a silk handkerchief, and put it into his own pocket. Several little trifles, which Tom had treasured, chiefly because they had amused Eva, he looked upon with a contemptuous grunt, and tossed them over his shoulder into the river.

Tom's Methodist hymn-book, which, in his hurry, he had forgotten, he now held up and turned over.

"Humph! pious, to be sure. So, what's yer name,—you belong to the church, eh?"

"Yes, Mas'r," said Tom, firmly.

"Well, I'll soon have *that* out of you. I have none o' yer bawling, praying, singing niggers on my place; so remember. Now, mind yourself," he said, with a stamp and a fierce glance of his gray eye, directed at Tom, "*I'm* your church now! You understand,—you've got to be as *I* say."

Something within the silent black man answered *No!* and, as if repeated by an invisible voice, came the words of an old prophetic scroll, as Eva had often read them to him,—"Fear not! for I have redeemed thee. I have called thee by my name. Thou art MINE!"[2]

But Simon Legree heard no voice. That voice is one he never shall hear. He only glared for a moment on the downcast face of Tom, and walked off. He took Tom's trunk, which contained a very neat and abundant wardrobe, to the forecastle, where it was soon surrounded by various hands of the boat. With much laughing, at the expense of niggers who tried to be gentlemen, the articles very readily were sold to one and another, and the empty trunk finally put up at auction. It was a good joke, they all thought, especially to see how Tom looked after his things, as they were going this way and that; and then the auction of the trunk, that was funnier than all, and occasioned abundant witticisms.

This little affair being over, Simon sauntered up again to his property.

"Now, Tom, I've relieved you of any extra baggage, you see. Take mighty good care of them clothes. It'll be long enough 'fore you get more. I go in for making niggers careful; one suit has to do for one year, on my place."

Simon next walked up to the place where Emmeline was sitting, chained to another woman.

"Well, my dear," he said, chucking her under the chin, "keep up your spirits."

The involuntary look of horror, fright, and aversion, with which the girl regarded him, did not escape his eye. He frowned fiercely.

"None o' your shines, gal! you's got to keep a pleasant face, when I speak to ye,—d'ye hear? And you, you old yellow poco moonshine!" he said, giving

2. Isaiah 43.1.

a shove to the mulatto woman to whom Emmeline was chained, "don't you carry that sort of face! You's got to look chipper, I tell ye!"

"I say, all on ye," he said retreating a pace or two back, "look at me,—look at me,—look me right in the eye,—*straight*, now!" said he, stamping his foot at every pause.

As by a fascination, every eye was now directed to the glaring greenish-gray eye of Simon.

"Now," said he, doubling his great, heavy fist into something resembling a blacksmith's hammer, "d'ye see this fist? Heft it!" he said, bringing it down on Tom's hand. "Look at these yer bones! Well, I tell ye this yer fist has got as hard as iron *knocking down niggers*. I never see the nigger, yet, I couldn't bring down with one crack," said he, bringing his fist down so near to the face of Tom that he winked and drew back. "I don't keep none o' yer cussed overseers; I does my own overseeing; and I tell you things *is* seen to. You's every one on ye got to toe the mark, I tell ye; quick,—straight,—the moment I speak. That's the way to keep in with me. Ye won't find no soft spot in me, nowhere. So, now, mind yerselves; for I don't show no mercy!"

The women involuntarily drew in their breath, and the whole gang sat with downcast, dejected faces. Meanwhile, Simon turned on his heel, and marched up to the bar of the boat for a dram.[3]

"That's the way I begin with my niggers," he said, to a gentlemanly man, who had stood by him during his speech. "It's my system to begin strong,—just let 'em know what to expect."

"Indeed!" said the stranger, looking upon him with the curiosity of a naturalist studying some out-of-the-way specimen.

"Yes, indeed. I'm none o' yer gentlemen planters, with lily fingers, to slop round and be cheated by some old cuss of an overseer! Just feel of my knuckles, now; look at my fist. Tell ye, sir, the flesh on 't has come jest like a stone, practising on niggers,—feel on it."

The stranger applied his fingers to the implement in question, and simply said,

"'T is hard enough; and, I suppose," he added, "practice has made your heart just like it."

"Why, yes, I may say so," said Simon, with a hearty laugh. "I reckon there's as little soft in me as in any one going. Tell you, nobody comes it over me! Niggers never gets round me, neither with squalling nor soft soap,—that's a fact."

"You have a fine lot there."

"Real," said Simon. "There's that Tom, they telled me he was suthin' uncommon. I paid a little high for him, tendin' him for a driver and a managing chap; only get the notions out that he's larnt by bein' treated as niggers never ought to be, he'll do prime! The yellow woman I got took in. I rayther think she's sickly, but I shall put her through for what she's worth; she may last a year or two. I don't go for savin' niggers. Use up, and buy more, 's my way;—makes you less trouble, and I'm quite sure it comes cheaper in the end;" and Simon sipped his glass.

"And how long do they generally last?" said the stranger.

3. Small drink (typically alcoholic).

"Well, donno; 'cordin' as their constitution is. Stout fellers last six or seven years; trashy ones gets worked up in two or three. I used to, when I fust begun, have considerable trouble fussin' with 'em and trying to make 'em hold out,—doctorin' on 'em up when they's sick, and givin' on 'em clothes and blankets, and what not, tryin' to keep 'em all sort o' decent and comfortable. Law, 't wasn't no sort o' use; I lost money on 'em, and 't was heaps o' trouble. Now, you see, I just put 'em straight through, sick or well. When one nigger's dead, I buy another; and I find it comes cheaper and easier, every way."

The stranger turned away, and seated himself beside a gentleman, who had been listening to the conversation with repressed uneasiness.

"You must not take that fellow to be any specimen of Southern planters," said he.

"I should hope not," said the young gentleman, with emphasis.

"He is a mean, low, brutal fellow!" said the other.

"And yet your laws allow him to hold any number of human beings subject to his absolute will, without even a shadow of protection; and, low as he is, you cannot say that there are not many such."

"Well," said the other, "there are also many considerate and humane men among planters."

"Granted," said the young man; "but, in my opinion, it is you considerate, humane men, that are responsible for all the brutality and outrage wrought by these wretches; because, if it were not for your sanction and influence, the whole system could not keep foot-hold for an hour. If there were no planters except such as that one," said he, pointing with his finger to Legree, who stood with his back to them, "the whole thing would go down like a millstone. It is your respectability and humanity that licenses and protects his brutality."

"You certainly have a high opinion of my good nature," said the planter, smiling; "but I advise you not to talk quite so loud, as there are people on board the boat who might not be quite so tolerant to opinion as I am. You had better wait till I get up to my plantation, and there you may abuse us all, quite at your leisure."

The young gentleman colored and smiled, and the two were soon busy in a game of backgammon. Meanwhile, another conversation was going on in the lower part of the boat, between Emmeline and the mulatto woman with whom she was confined. As was natural, they were exchanging with each other some particulars of their history.

"Who did you belong to?" said Emmeline.

"Well, my Mas'r was Mr. Ellis,—lived on Levee-street. P'raps you've seen the house."

"Was he good to you?" said Emmeline.

"Mostly, till he tuk sick. He's lain sick, off and on, more than six months, and been orful oneasy. 'Pears like he warnt willin' to have nobody rest, day nor night; and got so curous, there couldn't nobody suit him. 'Pears like he just grew crosser, every day; kep me up nights till I got farly beat out, and couldn't keep awake no longer; and cause I got to sleep, one night, Lors, he talk so orful to me, and he tell me he'd sell me to just the hardest master he could find; and he'd promised me my freedom, too, when he died."

"Had you any friends?" said Emmeline.

"Yes, my husband,—he's a blacksmith. Mas'r gen'ly hired him out. They took me off so quick, I didn't even have time to see him; and I's got four children. O, dear me!" said the woman, covering her face with her hands.

It is a natural impulse, in every one, when they hear a tale of distress, to think of something to say by way of consolation. Emmeline wanted to say something, but she could not think of anything to say. What was there to be said? As by a common consent, they both avoided, with fear and dread, all mention of the horrible man who was now their master.

True, there is religious trust for even the darkest hour. The mulatto woman was a member of the Methodist church, and had an unenlightened but very sincere spirit of piety. Emmeline had been educated much more intelligently,—taught to read and write, and diligently instructed in the Bible, by the care of a faithful and pious mistress; yet, would it not try the faith of the firmest Christian, to find themselves abandoned, apparently, of God, in the grasp of ruthless violence? How much more must it shake the faith of Christ's poor little ones, weak in knowledge and tender in years!

The boat moved on,—freighted with its weight of sorrow—up the red, muddy, turbid current, through the abrupt, tortuous windings of the Red river; and sad eyes gazed wearily on the steep red-clay banks, as they glided by in dreary sameness. At last the boat stopped at a small town, and Legree, with his party, disembarked.

* * *

CHAPTER XXXIV. THE QUADROON'S STORY

> "And behold the tears of such as are oppressed; and on the side of their oppressors there was power. Wherefore I praised the dead that are already dead more than the living that are yet alive."
>
> —ECCL. 4:1.

It was late at night, and Tom lay groaning and bleeding alone,[4] in an old forsaken room of the gin-house, among pieces of broken machinery, piles of damaged cotton, and other rubbish which had there accumulated.

The night was damp and close, and the thick air swarmed with myriads of mosquitos, which increased the restless torture of his wounds; whilst a burning thirst—a torture beyond all others—filled up the uttermost measure of physical anguish.

"O, good Lord! *Do* look down,—give me the victory!—give me the victory over all!" prayed poor Tom, in his anguish.

A footstep entered the room, behind him, and the light of a lantern flashed on his eyes.

"Who's there? O, for the Lord's massy, please give me some water!"

The woman Cassy[5]—for it was she—set down her lantern, and, pouring water from a bottle, raised his head, and gave him drink. Another and another cup were drained, with feverish eagerness.

"Drink all ye want," she said; "I knew how it would be. It isn't the first time I've been out in the night, carrying water to such as you."

"Thank you, Missis," said Tom, when he had done drinking.

4. Tom has been beaten for refusing Legree's command to flog a slave woman.

5. Legree's mixed-race former housekeeper and concubine, whom he had abused sexually.

"Don't call me Missis! I'm a miserable slave, like yourself,—a lower one than you can ever be!" said she, bitterly; "but now," said she, going to the door, and dragging in a small pallaise,[6] over which she had spread linen cloths wet with cold water, "try, my poor fellow, to roll yourself on to this."

Stiff with wounds and bruises, Tom was a long time in accomplishing this movement; but, when done, he felt a sensible relief from the cooling application to his wounds.

The woman, whom long practice with the victims of brutality had made familiar with many healing arts, went on to make many applications to Tom's wounds, by means of which he was soon somewhat relieved.

"Now," said the woman, when she had raised his head on a roll of damaged cotton, which served for a pillow, "there's the best I can do for you."

Tom thanked her; and the woman, sitting down on the floor, drew up her knees, and embracing them with her arms, looked fixedly before her, with a bitter and painful expression of countenance. Her bonnet fell back, and long wavy streams of black hair fell around her singular and melancholy face.

"It's no use, my poor fellow!" she broke out, at last, "it's of no use, this you've been trying to do. You were a brave fellow,—you had the right on your side; but it's all in vain, and out of the question, for you to struggle. You are in the devil's hands;—he is the strongest, and you must give up!"

Give up! and, had not human weakness and physical agony whispered that, before? Tom started; for the bitter woman, with her wild eyes and melancholy voice, seemed to him an embodiment of the temptation with which he had been wrestling.

"O Lord! O Lord!" he groaned, "how can I give up?"

"There's no use calling on the Lord,—he never hears," said the woman, steadily; "there isn't any God, I believe; or, if there is, he's taken sides against us. All goes against us, heaven and earth. Everything is pushing us into hell. Why shouldn't we go?"

Tom closed his eyes, and shuddered at the dark, atheistic words.

"You see," said the woman, "*you* don't know anything about it;—I do. I've been on this place five years, body and soul, under this man's foot; and I hate him as I do the devil! Here you are, on a lone plantation, ten miles from any other, in the swamps; not a white person here, who could testify, if you were burned alive,—if you were scalded, cut into inch-pieces, set up for the dogs to tear, or hung up and whipped to death. There's no law here, of God or man, that can do you, or any one of us, the least good; and, this man! there's no earthly thing that he's too good to do. I could make any one's hair rise, and their teeth chatter, if I should only tell what I've seen and been knowing to, here,—and it's no use resisting! Did I *want* to live with him? Wasn't I a woman delicately bred; and he—God in heaven! what was he, and is he? And yet, I've lived with him, these five years, and cursed every moment of my life,—night and day! And now, he's got a new one,[7]—a young thing, only fifteen, and she brought up, she says, piously. Her good mistress taught her to read the Bible; and she's brought her Bible here—to hell with her!"—and the woman laughed a wild and doleful laugh, that rung, with a strange, supernatural sound, through the old ruined shed.

6. Thin mattress (Creole French).

7. Emmeline.

Tom folded his hands; all was darkness and horror.

"O Jesus! Lord Jesus! have you quite forgot us poor critturs?" burst forth, at last;—"help, Lord, I perish!"

The woman sternly continued:

"And what are these miserable low dogs you work with, that you should suffer on their account? Every one of them would turn against you, the first time they got a chance. They are all of 'em as low and cruel to each other as they can be; there's no use in your suffering to keep from hurting them."

"Poor critturs!" said Tom,—"what made 'em cruel?—and, if I give out, I shall get used to't, and grow, little by little, just like 'em! No, no, Missis! I've lost everything,—wife, and children, and home, and a kind Mas'r,—and he would have set me free, if he'd only lived a week longer; I've lost everything in *this* world, and it's clean gone, forever,—and now I *can't* lose Heaven, too; no, I can't get to be wicked, besides all!"

"But it can't be that the Lord will lay sin to our account," said the woman; "he won't charge it to us, when we're forced to it; he'll charge it to them that drove us to it."

"Yes," said Tom; "but that won't keep us from growing wicked. If I get to be as hard-hearted as that ar' Sambo, and as wicked, it won't make much odds to me how I come so; it's the *bein' so*,—that ar's what I'm a dreadin'."

The woman fixed a wild and startled look on Tom, as if a new thought had struck her; and then, heavily groaning, said,

"O God a' mercy! you speak the truth! O—O—O!"—and, with groans, she fell on the floor, like one crushed and writhing under the extremity of mental anguish.

There was a silence, a while, in which the breathing of both parties could be heard, when Tom faintly said, "O, please, Missis!"

The woman suddenly rose up, with her face composed to its usual stern, melancholy expression.

"Please, Missis, I saw 'em throw my coat in that ar' corner, and in my coat-pocket is my Bible;—if Missis would please get it for me."

Cassy went and got it. Tom opened, at once, to a heavily marked passage, much worn, of the last scenes in the life of Him by whose stripes we are healed.

"If Missis would only be so good as read that ar',—it's better than water."

Cassy took the book, with a dry, proud air, and looked over the passage. She then read aloud, in a soft voice, and with a beauty of intonation that was peculiar, that touching account of anguish and of glory. Often, as she read, her voice faltered, and sometimes failed her altogether, when she would stop, with an air of frigid composure, till she had mastered herself. When she came to the touching words, "Father forgive them, for they know not what they do,"[8] she threw down the book, and, burying her face in the heavy masses of her hair, she sobbed aloud, with a convulsive violence.

Tom was weeping, also, and occasionally uttering a smothered ejaculation.

"If we only could keep up to that ar'!" said Tom;—"it seemed to come so natural to him, and we have to fight so hard for 't! O Lord, help us! O blessed Lord Jesus, do help us!"

8. Christ's words on the Cross (Luke 23.34).

"Missis," said Tom, after a while, "I can see that, some how, you're quite 'bove me in everything; but there's one thing Missis might learn even from poor Tom. Ye said the Lord took sides against us, because he lets us be 'bused and knocked round; but ye see what come on his own Son,—the blessed Lord of Glory,—wan't he allays poor? and have we, any on us, yet come so low as he come? The Lord han't forgot us,—I'm sartin' o' that ar'. If we suffer with him, we shall also reign, Scripture says; but, if we deny Him, he also will deny us. Didn't they all suffer?—the Lord and all his? It tells how they was stoned and sawn asunder, and wandered about in sheep-skins and goat-skins, and was destitute, afflicted, tormented. Sufferin' an't no reason to make us think the Lord's turned agin us; but jest the contrary, if only we hold on to him, and doesn't give up to sin."

"But why does he put us where we can't help but sin?" said the woman.

"I think we *can* help it," said Tom.

"You'll see," said Cassy; "what'll you do? To-morrow they'll be at you again. I know 'em; I've seen all their doings; I can't bear to think of all they'll bring you to;—and they'll make you give out, at last!"

"Lord Jesus!" said Tom, "you *will* take care of my soul? O Lord, do!—don't let me give out!"

"O dear!" said Cassy; "I've heard all this crying and praying before; and yet, they've been broken down, and brought under. There's Emmeline, she's trying to hold on, and you're trying,—but what use? You must give up, or be killed by inches."

"Well, then, I *will* die!" said Tom. "Spin it out as long as they can, they can't help my dying, some time!—and, after that, they can't do no more. I'm clar, I'm set! I *know* the Lord'll help me, and bring me through."

The woman did not answer; she sat with her black eyes intently fixed on the floor.

"May be it's the way," she murmured to herself; "but those that *have* given up, there's no hope for them!—none! We live in filth, and grow loathsome, till we loathe ourselves! And we long to die, and we don't dare to kill ourselves!—No hope! no hope! no hope!—this girl now,—just as old as I was!

"You see me now," she said, speaking to Tom very rapidly; "see what I am! Well, I was brought up in luxury; the first I remember is, playing about, when I was a child, in splendid parlors;—when I was kept dressed up like a doll, and company and visiters used to praise me. There was a garden opening from the saloon windows; and there I used to play hide-and-go-seek, under the orange-trees, with my brothers and sisters. I went to a convent, and there I learned music, French and embroidery, and what not; and when I was fourteen, I came out to my father's funeral. He died very suddenly, and when the property came to be settled, they found that there was scarcely enough to cover the debts; and when the creditors took an inventory of the property, I was set down in it. My mother was a slave woman, and my father had always meant to set me free; but he had not done it, and so I was set down in the list. I'd always known who I was, but never thought much about it. Nobody ever expects that a strong, healthy man is a going to die. My father was a well man only four hours before he died;—it was one of the first cholera cases in New Orleans. The day after the funeral, my father's wife took her children, and went up to her father's plantation. I thought they treated me strangely, but didn't know. There was a young lawyer whom they left to settle the business; and he came every day, and was about the house, and spoke very politely to me. He brought with him, one day, a young man, whom I thought the handsomest I had ever seen. I shall never forget that evening. I walked with him in the garden. I was lonesome and full of sorrow, and he was so kind and gentle to me; and he told me that he had seen me before I went to the convent, and that he had loved me a great while, and that he would be my friend and protector;—in short, though he didn't tell me, he had paid two thousand dollars for me, and I was his property,—I became his willingly, for I loved him. Loved!" said the woman, stopping. "O, how I *did* love that man! How I love him now,—and always shall, while I breathe! He was so beautiful, so high, so noble! He put me into a beautiful house, with servants, horses, and carriages, and furniture, and dresses. Everything that money could buy, he gave me; but I didn't set any value on all that,—I only cared for him. I loved him better than my God and my own soul; and, if I tried, I couldn't do any other way from what he wanted me to.

"I wanted only one thing—I did want him to *marry* me. I thought, if he loved me as he said he did, and if I was what he seemed to think I was, he would be willing to marry me and set me free. But he convinced me that it would be impossible; and he told me that, if we were only faithful to each other, it was marriage before God. If that is true, wasn't I that man's wife? Wasn't I faithful? For seven years, didn't I study every look and motion, and only live and breathe to please him? He had the yellow fever, and for twenty days and nights I watched with him. I alone,—and gave him all his medicine, and did everything for him; and then he called me his good angel, and said I'd saved his life. We had two beautiful children. The first was a boy, and we called him Henry. He was the image of his father,—he had such beautiful eyes, such a forehead, and his hair hung all in curls around it; and he had all his father's spirit, and his talent, too. Little Elise, he said, looked like me. He used to tell me that I was the most beautiful woman in Louisiana, he was so proud of me and the children. He used to love to have me dress them up, and take them and me about in an open carriage, and hear the remarks that people would make on us; and he used to fill my ears constantly with the fine things that were said in praise of me and the children. O, those were happy days! I thought I was as happy as any one could be; but then there came evil times. He had a cousin come to New Orleans, who was his particular friend,—he thought all the world of him;—but, from the first time I saw him, I couldn't tell why, I dreaded him; for I felt sure he was going to bring misery on us. He got Henry to going out with him, and often he would not come home nights till two or three o'clock. I did not dare say a word; for Henry was so high-spirited, I was afraid to. He got him to the gaming-houses; and he was one of the sort that, when he once got a going there, there was no holding back. And then he introduced him to another lady, and I saw soon that his heart was gone from me. He never told me, but I saw it,—I knew it, day after day,—I felt my heart breaking, but I could not say a word! At this, the wretch offered to buy me and the children of Henry, to clear off his gambling debts, which stood in the way of his marrying as he wished;—and *he sold us*. He told me, one day, that he had business in the country, and should be gone two or three weeks. He spoke kinder than usual, and said he should come back; but it didn't deceive me. I knew that the time had come; I was just like one turned into stone; I couldn't speak, nor shed a tear. He kissed me and kissed the children, a good many times, and went out. I saw him get on his horse, and I watched him till he was quite out of sight; and then I fell down, and fainted.

"Then *he* came, the cursed wretch! he came to take possession. He told me that he had bought me and my children; and showed me the papers. I cursed him before God, and told him I'd die sooner than live with him.

"'Just as you please,' said he; 'but, if you don't behave reasonably, I'll sell both the children, where you shall never see them again.' He told me that he always had meant to have me, from the first time he saw me; and that he had drawn Henry on, and got him in debt, on purpose to make him willing to sell me. That he got him in love with another woman; and that I might know, after all that, that he should not give up for a few airs and tears, and things of that sort.

"I gave up, for my hands were tied. He had my children;—whenever I resisted his will anywhere, he would talk about selling them, and he made me as submissive as he desired. O, what a life it was! to live with my heart breaking, every day,—to keep on, on, on, loving, when it was only misery; and to be bound, body and soul, to one I hated. I used to love to read to Henry, to play to him, to waltz with him, and sing to him; but everything I did for this one was a perfect drag,—yet I was afraid to refuse anything. He was very imperious, and harsh to the children. Elise was a timid little thing; but Henry was bold and high-spirited, like his father, and he had never been brought under, in the least, by any one. He was always finding fault, and quarrelling with him; and I used to live in daily fear and dread. I tried to make the child respectful;—I tried to keep them apart, for I held on to those children like death; but it did no good. *He sold both those children.* He took me to ride, one day, and when I came home, they were nowhere to be found! He told me he had sold them; he showed me the money, the price of their blood. Then it seemed as if all good forsook me. I raved and cursed,—cursed God and man; and, for a while, I believe, he really was afraid of me. But he didn't give up so. He told me that my children were sold, but whether I ever saw their faces again, depended on him; and that, if I wasn't quiet, they should smart for it. Well, you can do anything with a woman, when you've got her children. He made me submit; he made me be peaceable; he flattered me with hopes that, perhaps, he would buy them back; and so things went on, a week or two. One day, I was out walking, and passed by the calaboose; I saw a crowd about the gate, and heard a child's voice,—and suddenly my Henry broke away from two or three men who were holding him, and ran, screaming, and caught my dress. They came up to him, swearing dreadfully; and one man, whose face I shall never forget, told him that he wouldn't get away so; that he was going with him into the calaboose, and he'd get a lesson there he'd never forget. I tried to beg and plead,—they only laughed; the poor boy screamed and looked into my face, and held on to me, until, in tearing him off, they tore the skirt of my dress half away; and they carried him in, screaming 'Mother! mother! mother!' There was one man stood there seemed to pity me. I offered him all the money I had, if he'd only interfere. He shook his head, and said that the man said the boy had been impudent and disobedient, ever since he bought him; that he was going to break him in, once for all. I turned and ran; and every step of the way, I thought that I heard him scream. I got into the house; ran, all out of breath, to the parlor, where I found Butler. I told him, and begged him to go and interfere. He only laughed, and told me the boy had got his deserts. He'd got to be broken in,—the sooner the better; 'what did I expect?' he asked.

"It seemed to me something in my head snapped, at that moment. I felt dizzy and furious. I remember seeing a great sharp bowie-knife on the table; I remember something about catching it, and flying upon him; and then all grew dark, and I didn't know any more—not for days and days.

"When I came to myself, I was in a nice room,—but not mine. An old black woman tended me; and a doctor came to see me, and there was a great deal of care taken of me. After a while, I found that he had gone away, and left me at this house to be sold; and that's why they took such pains with me.

"I didn't mean to get well, and hoped I shouldn't; but, in spite of me, the fever went off, and I grew healthy, and finally got up. Then, they made me dress up, every day; and gentlemen used to come in and stand and smoke their cigars, and look at me, and ask questions, and debate my price. I was so gloomy and silent, that none of them wanted me. They threatened to whip me, if I wasn't gayer, and didn't take some pains to make myself agreeable. At length, one day, came a gentleman named Stuart. He seemed to have some feeling for me; he saw that something dreadful was on my heart, and he came to see me alone, a great many times, and finally persuaded me to tell him. He bought me, at last, and promised to do all he could to find and buy back my children. He went to the hotel where my Henry was; they told him he had been sold to a planter up on Pearl river;[9] that was the last that I ever heard. Then he found where my daughter was; an old woman was keeping her. He offered an immense sum for her, but they would not sell her. Butler found out that it was for me he wanted her; and he sent me word that I should never have her. Captain Stuart was very kind to me; he had a splendid plantation, and took me to it. In the course of a year, I had a son born. O, that child!—how I loved it! How just like my poor Henry the little thing looked! But I had made up my mind,—yes, I had. I would never again let a child live to grow up! I took the little fellow in my arms, when he was two weeks old, and kissed him, and cried over him; and then I gave him laudanum, and held him close to my bosom, while he slept to death. How I mourned and cried over it! and who ever dreamed that it was anything but a mistake, that had made me give it the laudanum? but it's one of the few things that I'm glad of, now. I am not sorry, to this day; he, at least, is out of pain. What better than death could I give him, poor child! After a while, the cholera came, and Captain Stuart died; everybody died that wanted to live,—and I,—I, though I went down to death's door,—*I lived*! Then I was sold, and passed from hand to hand, till I grew faded and wrinkled, and I had a fever; and then this wretch bought me, and brought me here,—and here I am!"

The woman stopped. She had hurried on through her story, with a wild, passionate utterance; sometimes seeming to address it to Tom, and sometimes speaking as in a soliloquy. So vehement and overpowering was the force with which she spoke, that, for a season, Tom was beguiled even from the pain of his wounds, and, raising himself on one elbow, watched her as

9. River in central Mississippi.

she paced restlessly up and down, her long black hair swaying heavily about her, as she moved.

"You tell me," she said, after a pause, "that there is a God,—a God that looks down and sees all these things. May be it's so. The sisters in the convent used to tell me of a day of judgment, when everything is coming to light;—won't there be vengeance, then!

"They think it's nothing, what we suffer,—nothing, what our children suffer! It's all a small matter; yet I've walked the streets when it seemed as if I had misery enough in my one heart to sink the city. I've wished the houses would fall on me, or the stones sink under me. Yes! and, in the judgment day, I will stand up before God, a witness against those that have ruined me and my children, body and soul!

"When I was a girl, I thought I was religious; I used to love God and prayer. Now, I'm a lost soul, pursued by devils that torment me day and night; they keep pushing me on and on—and I'll do it, too, some of these days!" she said, clenching her hand, while an insane light glanced in her heavy black eyes. "I'll send him where he belongs,—a short way, too,—one of these nights, if they burn me alive for it!" A wild, long laugh, rang through the deserted room, and ended in a hysteric sob; she threw herself on the floor, in convulsive sobbings and struggles.

In a few moments the frenzy fit seemed to pass off; she rose slowly, and seemed to collect herself.

"Can I do anything more for you, my poor fellow?" she said, approaching where Tom lay; "shall I give you some more water?"

There was a graceful and compassionate sweetness in her voice and manner, as she said this, that formed a strange contrast with the former wildness.

Tom drank the water, and looked earnestly and pitifully into her face.

"O, Missis, I wish you'd go to him that can give you living waters!"

"Go to him! Where is he? Who is he?" said Cassy.

"Him that you read of to me,—the Lord."

"I used to see the picture of him, over the altar, when I was a girl," said Cassy, her dark eyes fixing themselves in an expression of mournful reverie; "but, *he isn't here!* there's nothing here, but sin and long, long, long despair! O!" She laid her hand on her breast and drew in her breath, as if to lift a heavy weight.

Tom looked as if he would speak again; but she cut him short, with a decided gesture.

"Don't talk, my poor fellow. Try to sleep, if you can." And, placing water in his reach, and making whatever little arrangements for his comfort she could, Cassy left the shed.

* * *

CHAPTER XL. THE MARTYR

"Deem not the just by Heaven forgot!
  Though life its common gifts deny,—
Though, with a crushed and bleeding heart,
  And spurned of man, he goes to die!
For God hath marked each sorrowing day,
  And numbered every bitter tear;
And heaven's long years of bliss shall pay
  For all his children suffer here."

BRYANT.[1]

The longest way must have its close,—the gloomiest night will wear on to a morning. An eternal, inexorable lapse of moments is ever hurrying the day of the evil to an eternal night, and the night of the just to an eternal day. We have walked with our humble friend thus far in the valley of slavery; first through flowery fields of ease and indulgence, then through heart-breaking separations from all that man holds dear. Again, we have waited with him in a sunny island, where generous hands concealed his chains with flowers; and, lastly, we have followed him when the last ray of earthly hope went out in night, and seen how, in the blackness of earthly darkness, the firmament of the unseen has blazed with stars of new and significant lustre.

The morning-star now stands over the tops of the mountains, and gales and breezes, not of earth, show that the gates of day are unclosing.

The escape of Cassy and Emmeline[2] irritated the before surly temper of Legree to the last degree; and his fury, as was to be expected, fell upon the defenceless head of Tom. When he hurriedly announced the tidings among his hands, there was a sudden light in Tom's eye, a sudden upraising of his hands, that did not escape him. He saw that he did not join the muster of the pursuers. He thought of forcing him to do it; but, having had, of old, experience of his inflexibility when commanded to take part in any deed of inhumanity, he would not, in his hurry, stop to enter into any conflict with him.

Tom, therefore, remained behind, with a few who had learned of him to pray, and offered up prayers for the escape of the fugitives.

When Legree returned, baffled and disappointed, all the long-working hatred of his soul towards his slave began to gather in a deadly and desperate form. Had not this man braved him,—steadily, powerfully, resistlessly,—ever since he bought him? Was there not a spirit in him which, silent as it was, burned on him like the fires of perdition?

"I *hate* him!" said Legree, that night, as he sat up in his bed; "I *hate* him! And isn't he MINE? Can't I do what I like with him? Who's to hinder, I wonder?" And Legree clenched his fist, and shook it, as if he had something in his hands that he could rend in pieces.

But, then, Tom was a faithful, valuable servant; and, although Legree hated him the more for that, yet the consideration was still somewhat of a restraint to him.

The next morning, he determined to say nothing, as yet; to assemble a party, from some neighboring plantations, with dogs and guns; to sur-

1. Adapted from "Blessed Are They That Mourn" (1832) by William Cullen Bryant (1794–1878).

2. Cassy and Emmeline hide in a garret that the superstitious Legree is afraid to enter (because he had murdered and perhaps sexually violated a slave woman there) and eventually escape during a night when he is drunk and worrying about his imminent death.

round the swamp, and go about the hunt systematically. If it succeeded, well and good; if not, he would summon Tom before him, and—his teeth clenched and his blood boiled—*then* he would break that fellow down, or—there was a dire inward whisper, to which his soul assented.

Ye say that the *interest* of the master is a sufficient safe-guard for the slave. In the fury of man's mad will, he will wittingly, and with open eye, sell his own soul to the devil to gain his ends; and will he be more careful of his neighbor's body?

"Well," said Cassy, the next day, from the garret, as she reconnoitered through the knot-hole, "the hunt's going to begin again, to-day!"

Three or four mounted horsemen were curvetting[3] about, on the space front of the house; and one or two leashes of strange dogs were struggling with the negroes who held them, baying and barking at each other.

The men are, two of them, overseers of plantations in the vicinity; and others were some of Legree's associates at the tavern-bar of a neighboring city, who had come for the interest of the sport. A more hard-favored set, perhaps, could not be imagined. Legree was serving brandy, profusely, round among them, as also among the negroes, who had been detailed from the various plantations for this service; for it was an object to make every service of this kind, among the negroes, as much of a holiday as possible.

Cassy placed her ear at the knot-hole; and, as the morning air blew directly towards the house, she could overhear a good deal of the conversation. A grave sneer overcast the dark, severe gravity of her face, as she listened, and heard them divide out the ground, discuss the rival merits of the dogs, give orders about firing, and the treatment of each, in case of capture.

Cassy drew back; and, clasping her hands, looked upward, and said, "O, great Almighty God! we are *all* sinners; but what have *we* done, more than all the rest of the world, that we should be treated so?"

There was a terrible earnestness in her face and voice, as she spoke.

"If it wasn't for *you*, child," she said, looking at Emmeline, "I'd *go* out to them; and I'd thank any one of them that *would* shoot me down; for what use will freedom be to me? Can it give me back my children, or make me what I used to be?"

Emmeline, in her child-like simplicity, was half afraid of the dark moods of Cassy. She looked perplexed, but made no answer. She only took her hand, with a gentle, caressing movement.

"Don't!" said Cassy, trying to draw it away; "you'll get me to loving you; and I never mean to love anything, again!"

"Poor Cassy!" said Emmeline, "don't feel so! If the Lord gives us liberty, perhaps he'll give you back your daughter; at any rate, I'll be like a daughter to you. I know I'll never see my poor old mother again! I shall love you, Cassy, whether you love me or not!"

The gentle, child-like spirit conquered. Cassy sat down by her, put her arm round her neck, stroked her soft, brown hair; and Emmeline then wondered at the beauty of her magnificent eyes, now soft with tears.

"O, Em!" said Cassy, "I've hungered for my children, and thirsted for them, and my eyes fail with longing for them! Here! here!" she said, striking her

3. Frolicking.

breast, "it's all desolate, all empty! If God would give me back my children, then I could pray."

"You must trust him, Cassy," said Emmeline; "he is our Father!"

"His wrath is upon us," said Cassy; "he has turned away in anger."

"No, Cassy! He will be good to us! Let us hope in Him," said Emmeline,—"I always have had hope."

The hunt was long, animated, and thorough, but unsuccessful; and, with grave, ironic exultation, Cassy looked down on Legree, as, weary and dispirited, he alighted from his horse.

"Now, Quimbo," said Legree, as he stretched himself down in the sitting-room, "you jest go and walk that Tom up here, right away! The old cuss is at the bottom of this yer whole matter; and I'll have it out of his old black hide, or I'll know the reason why!"

Sambo and Quimbo,[4] both, though hating each other, were joined in one mind by a no less cordial hatred of Tom. Legree had told them, at first, that he had bought him for a general overseer, in his absence; and this had begun an ill will, on their part, which had increased, in their debased and servile natures, as they saw him becoming obnoxious to their master's displeasure. Quimbo, therefore, departed, with a will, to execute his orders.

Tom heard the message with a forewarning heart; for he knew all the plan of the fugitives' escape, and the place of their present concealment;—he knew the deadly character of the man he had to deal with, and his despotic power. But he felt strong in God to meet death, rather than betray the helpless.

He sat his basket down by the row, and, looking up, said, "Into thy hands I commend my spirit! Thou has redeemed me, oh Lord God of truth!"[5] and then quietly yielded himself to the rough, brutal grasp with which Quimbo seized him.

"Ay, ay!" said the giant, as he dragged him along; "ye'll cotch it, now! I'll boun' Mas'r's back's up *high*! No sneaking out, now! Tell ye, ye'll get it, and no mistake! See how ye'll look, now, helpin' Mas'r's niggers to run away! See what ye'll get!"

The savage words none of them reached that ear!—a higher voice there was saying, "Fear not them that kill the body, and, after that, have no more that they can do."[6] Nerve and bone of that poor man's body vibrated to those words, as if touched by the finger of God; and he felt the strength of a thousand souls in one. As he passed along, the trees and bushes, the huts of his servitude, the whole scene of his degradation, seemed to whirl by him as the landscape by the rushing car. His soul throbbed,—his home was in sight,—and the hour of release seemed at hand.

"Well, Tom !" said Legree, walking up, and seizing him grimly by the collar of his coat, and speaking through his teeth, in a paroxysm of determined rage, "do you know I've made up my mind to KILL you?"

"It's very likely, Mas'r," said Tom, calmly.

"I *have*," said Legree, with grim, terrible calmness, "*done—just—that—thing*, Tom, unless you'll tell me what you know about these yer gals!"

4. Slaves whom Legree had trained to be overseers.

5. Similar to Christ's last words on the Cross: "Father, into thy hands I commend my spirit" (Luke 23.46).

6. Christ's words to the Apostles (Matthew 10.28).

Tom stood silent.

"D' ye hear?" said Legree, stamping, with a roar like that of an incensed lion. "Speak!"

"I han't got nothing to tell, Mas'r," said Tom, with a slow, firm, deliberate utterance.

"Do you dare to tell me, ye old black Christian, ye don't *know?"* said Legree.

Tom was silent.

"Speak!" thundered Legree, striking him furiously. "Do you know anything?"

"I know, Mas'r; but I can't tell anything. *I can die!"*

Legree drew in a long breath; and, suppressing his rage, took Tom by the arm, and, approaching his face almost to his, said, in a terrible voice, "Hark'e, Tom!—ye think, 'cause I've let you off before, I don't mean what I say; but, this time, I've *made up my mind*, and counted the cost. You've always stood it out agin' me: now, I'll *conquer ye, or kill ye!*—one or t'other. I'll count every drop of blood there is in you, and take 'em, one by one, till ye give up!"

Tom looked up to his master, and answered, "Mas'r, if you was sick, or in trouble, or dying, and I could save ye, I'd *give* ye my heart's blood; and, if taking every drop of blood in this poor old body would save your precious soul, I'd give 'em freely, as the Lord gave his for me. O, Mas'r! don't bring this great sin on your soul! It will hurt you more than 't will me! Do the worst you can, my troubles'll be over soon; but, if ye don't repent, yours won't *never* end!"

Like a strange snatch of heavenly music, heard in the lull of a tempest, this burst of feeling made a moment's blank pause. Legree stood aghast, and looked at Tom; and there was such a silence, that the tick of the old clock could be heard, measuring, with silent touch, the last moments of mercy and probation to that hardened heart.

It was but a moment. There was one hesitating pause,—one irresolute, relenting thrill,—and the spirit of evil came back, with seven-fold vehemence; and Legree, foaming with rage, smote his victim to the ground.

Scenes of blood and cruelty are shocking to our ear and heart. What man has nerve to do, man has not nerve to hear. What brother-man and brother-Christian must suffer, cannot be told us, even in our secret chamber, it so harrows up the soul! And yet, oh my country! these things are done under the shadow of thy laws! O, Christ! thy church sees them, almost in silence!

But, of old, there was One whose suffering changed an instrument of torture, degradation and shame, into a symbol of glory, honor, and immortal life; and, where His spirit is, neither degrading stripes, nor blood, nor insults, can make the Christian's last struggle less than glorious.

Was he alone, that long night, whose brave, loving spirit was bearing up, in that old shed, against buffeting and brutal stripes?

Nay! There stood by him ONE,—seen by him alone,—"like unto the Son of God."[7]

The tempter stood by him, too,—blinded by furious, despotic will,—every moment pressing him to shun that agony by the betrayal of the innocent. But

7. Hebrews 7.3.

the brave, true heart was firm on the Eternal Rock.[8] Like his Master, he knew that, if he saved others, himself he could not save; nor could utmost extremity wring from him words, save of prayer and holy trust.

"He's most gone, Mas'r," said Sambo, touched, in spite of himself, by the patience of his victim.

"Pay away, till he gives up! Give it to him!—give it to him!" shouted Legree. "I'll take every drop of blood he has, unless he confesses!"

Tom opened his eyes, and looked upon his master. "Ye poor miserable critter!" he said, "there an't no more ye can do! I forgive ye, with all my soul!" and he fainted entirely away.

"I b'lieve, my soul, he's done for, finally," said Legree, stepping forward, to look at him. "Yes, he is! Well, his mouth's shut up, at last,—that's one comfort!"

Yes, Legree; but who shall shut up that voice in thy soul? that soul, past repentance, past prayer, past hope, in whom the fire that never shall be quenched is already burning!

Yet Tom was not quite gone. His wondrous words and pious prayers had struck upon the hearts of the imbruted blacks, who had been the instruments of cruelty upon him; and, the instant Legree withdrew, they took him down, and, in their ignorance, sought to call him back to life,—as if *that* were any favor to him.

"Sartin, we's been doin' a drefful wicked thing!" said Sambo; "hopes Mas'r'll have to 'count for it, and not we."

They washed his wounds,—they provided a rude bed, of some refuse cotton, for him to lie down on; and one of them, stealing up to the house, begged a drink of brandy of Legree, pretending that he was tired, and wanted it for himself. He brought it back, and poured it down Tom's throat.

"O, Tom!" said Quimbo, "we's been awful wicked to ye!"

"I forgive ye, with all my heart!" said Tom, faintly.

"O, Tom! do tell us who is *Jesus*, anyhow?" said Sambo;—"Jesus, that's been a standin' by you so, all this night!—Who is he?"

The word roused the failing, fainting spirit. He poured forth a few energetic sentences of that wondrous One,—his life, his death, his everlasting presence, and power to save.

They wept,—both the two savage men.

"Why didn't I never hear this before?" said Sambo; "but I do believe!—can't help it! Lord Jesus, have mercy on us!"

"Poor critters!" said Tom, "I'd be willing to bar' all I have, if it'll only bring ye to Christ! O, Lord! give me these two more souls, I pray!"

That prayer was answered![9]

* * *

1852

8. Matthew 16.18.

9. In the subsequent chapter, George Shelby Jr. arrives at Legree's plantation just in time to witness Tom's death; he is inspired by Tom's Christlike goodness to emancipate all the slaves on the Kentucky plantation. At the end of the novel, Cassy, while taking a ship to Canada, meets George Harris and learns that Eliza is her long-lost daughter. George and his family eventually emigrate to Africa. In New England, Topsy embraces Christianity and decides to become a missionary to Africa.

FANNY FERN (SARAH WILLIS PARTON)
1811–1872

Sarah Payson Willis was born in Portland, Maine, on July 9, 1811, the fifth of nine children of Nathaniel Willis and Hannah Parker Willis. Two sons rose to prominence—Richard Storrs Willis as a music critic and Nathaniel Parker Willis as a poet, travel writer, journalist, and influential editor who had no sympathy for his sister's career efforts and, according to Sarah Willis's accounts, tried to thwart them whenever he could. Nevertheless, under the pseudonym "Fanny Fern," she became a newspaper columnist and novelist and for years was among the nation's best-paid and most famous authors. A master of the ironic vignette, Fern used a light touch to explore such difficult issues as gender inequalities in marriage, divorce law, prison reform, woman's suffrage, and the struggles of the working poor. In her most popular novel, *Ruth Hall: A Domestic Tale of the Present Time* (1855), she addressed a number of these social concerns; but, more important for the book's success, she also offered a thinly veiled autobiographical account of her rise to prominence as a writer despite severe personal hardships and the opposition (or indifference) of her family. The novel, like many other popular works by women in the decade, tapped into American traditions by applying Franklinesque and Emersonian notions of industry and self-reliance to women's lives; the specific autobiographical content illuminated the challenges faced by aspiring women writers who were also wives and mothers.

Sarah Willis learned something of the literary marketplace from her father, who in 1816 founded the *Boston Recorder*, an early religious newspaper, and in 1827 founded the *Youth's Companion*, a popular periodical for children, which he edited until 1862. Both publications were shaped by Nathaniel Willis's orthodox Calvinist beliefs, which his free-thinking daughter came to reject. Educated at the Adams Female Academy in Derry, New Hampshire, and from 1828 to 1831 at Catharine Beecher's Hartford Female Seminary, Sarah Willis excelled as a student and was renowned among her peers and teachers for her skills in composition. In 1837 she married Charles Harrington Eldredge, a cashier in a Boston bank. They had three daughters in a domestic life marked by debt and tragedy; the eldest, Mary, died in 1845 at age seven, and Charles himself died of typhoid fever in 1846 at the age of thirty-five. Neither her own father, recently remarried, nor her in-laws were willing or able to support her in a household of her own, nor did she move in with either set, as might have been expected of a new widow. Whatever the reason for this divergence from the norm, Sarah Eldredge attempted for a while to support herself and her daughters as a seamstress. In 1849, perhaps out of economic necessity, she married her father's friend Samuel P. Farrington, a Boston widower with two daughters. To judge from surviving documents and from the portrayal of the character John Stahle in her novel *Rose Clark* (1856), she quickly found Farrington jealous, tyrannical, and repulsive. She left him after two years, a revolutionary act for which she was ostracized by her own family. Farrington spread rumors about her misbehavior, refused to offer financial support, and in 1853 obtained a legal divorce in Chicago on the grounds of abandonment.

In 1851, Sarah Payson Willis Eldredge Farrington, having put her older daughter in the care of the Eldredges, began efforts to support herself by writing. She published her first sketch, "The Model Husband," in the June 28, 1851, issue of the *Boston Olive Branch*, earning fifty cents for it. When she submitted several unpublished sketches to her brother Nathaniel Willis, editor of New York City's fashionable *Home*

Journal, he rejected them, and according to her account, also discouraged other editors from accepting her work because of its supposed vulgarity and indecency. Continuing her low-paying writing for the *Olive Branch*, she developed as a writer, finding her tone (colloquial, flippant, ironic) and adopting a new name; as Fanny Fern in the *Olive Branch* and in the *New York Musical World and Times*, she became the talk of the literary world and a genuine celebrity who was able to negotiate ever more favorable contracts. In 1853 she collected her columns in *Fern Leaves from Fanny's Port-Folio*, which sold approximately a hundred thousand copies, an astonishing number for that time. Later that year, she moved to New York City and published the equally successful children's text *Little Ferns for Fanny's Little Friends* (1853) and then a sequel to her first volume, *Fern Leaves from Fanny's Port-Folio. Second Series* (1854).

Fern published her first novel, *Ruth Hall*, in 1855, with a prepublication release in December 1854. It became a sensation, mainly because of its hostile depictions of the heroine's family, whose names were known to many readers (its portrait of her editor brother, Nathaniel Willis, was satiric in the extreme). In addition *Ruth Hall* depicted a new sort of enterprising heroine, struggling for opportunities in a society whose laws gave husbands control of their wives' property. The feminist reformer Elizabeth Cady Stanton, for instance, praised Fern in print for showing that a woman can "work out her own destiny unaided and alone." Though some reviewers criticized Fern for embarrassing her family—the reviewer for the *New York Times* spoke for many in wondering how "a delicate, suffering woman can hunt down even her persecutors so remorselessly"—the negative publicity did not hurt sales; indeed, by calling attention to the novel's autobiographical elements, such publicity made readers all the more eager to purchase the book.

On the strength of her fame, in 1855 Robert Bonner, editor of the weekly *New York Ledger*, made Fern an unprecedented offer, inviting her to write a weekly column at $100 per column (a figure comparable to $2,000 in today's value). Her popularity was such that Bonner prospered under these terms, seeing the circulation of the *Ledger*—approximately a hundred thousand at the time Fern signed on—reach four hundred thousand by 1860, a large number for a journal even today. Like other forms of newsprint, each bought copy of the *Ledger* had several readers. In short, Fern had an enormous readership.

In 1856, at the height of her success, she married the journalist and biographer James Parton (1822–1891), soon to become famous for his 1860 multivolume biography of Andrew Jackson. (That Parton was more than a decade her junior was rightly perceived as a bold statement of Fern's politics of sexuality; in a similarly bold move, she insisted that Parton sign a prenuptial agreement disclaiming any rights to her income from writing.) Fern's second novel, *Rose Clark*, based in part on her disastrous second marriage, was published the year of her marriage to Parton but failed to have the impact of *Ruth Hall*. For the rest of her writing career, Fern, living with her husband and daughters in Manhattan, devoted herself mainly to her column for the *Ledger*, which gave her a prominent outlet for her shrewd feminist commentary on the social issues of her day. Collections of these columns—*Fresh Leaves* (1857), *Folly as It Flies* (1868), *Ginger Snaps* (1870), and *Caper-Sauce* (1872)—were popular with her contemporaries. She also published several books for children. She died of cancer in 1872. In 1873 James Parton published an edited collection of tributes, *Fanny Fern: A Memorial Volume*, which celebrated Fern's independence, artistry, and important role in expanding opportunities for women in American journalism.

Aunt Hetty on Matrimony[1]

"Now girls," said Aunt Hetty, "put down your embroidery and worsted work; do something sensible, and stop building air-castles, and talking of lovers and honey-moons. It makes me sick; it is perfectly antimonial.[2] Love is a farce; matrimony is a humbug; husbands are domestic Napoleons, Neroes, Alexanders[3]—sighing for other hearts to conquer, after they are sure of yours. The honey-moon is as short-lived as a lucifer-match;[4] after that you may wear your wedding-dress at breakfast, and your night-cap to meeting, and your husband wouldn't know it. You may pick up your own pocket-handkerchief, help yourself to a chair, and split your gown across the back reaching over the table to get a piece of butter, while he is laying in his breakfast as if it was the last meal he should eat in this world. When he gets through he will aid your digestion,—while you are sipping your first cup of coffee,—by inquiring what you'll have for dinner; whether the cold lamb was all ate yesterday; if the charcoal is all out, and what you gave for the last green tea you bought. Then he gets up from the table, lights his cigar with the last evening's paper, that you have not had a chance to read; gives two or three whiffs of smoke,—which are sure to give you a headache for the afternoon,—and, just as his coattail is vanishing through the door, apologizes for not doing 'that errand' for you yesterday,—thinks it doubtful if he can to-day,—'so pressed with business.' Hear of him at eleven o'clock, taking an ice-cream with some ladies at a confectioner's, while you are at home new-lining his coat-sleeves. Children by the ears all day; can't get out to take the air; feel as crazy as a fly in a drum. Husband comes home at night; nods a 'How d'ye do, Fan?' boxes Charley's ears; stands little Fanny in the corner; sits down in the easiest chair in the warmest nook; puts his feet up over the grate, shutting out all the fire, while the baby's little pug nose grows blue with the cold; reads the newspaper all to himself; solaces his inner man with a cup of tea, and, just as you are laboring under the hallucination that he will ask you to take a mouthful of fresh air with him, he puts on his dressing-gown and slippers, and begins to reckon up the family expenses; after which he lies down on the sofa, and you keep time with your needle, while he sleeps till nine o'clock. Next morning, ask him to leave you a 'little money,' he looks at you as if to be sure that you are in your right mind, draws a sigh long enough and strong enough to inflate a pair of bellows, and asks you 'what you want with it, and if a half-a-dollar won't do?' Gracious king! as if those little shoes, and stockings, and petticoats could be had for half-a-dollar! O, girls! set your affections on cats, poodles, parrots or lap-dogs; but let matrimony alone. It's the hardest way on earth of getting a living. You never know when your work is done. Think of carrying eight or nine children through the measles, chicken-pox, rash, mumps, and scarlet fever,—some of them twice over. It makes my head ache

1. From *Fern Leaves from Fanny's Port-Folio* (1853); the column first appeared in the December 6, 1851, issue of the *Olive Branch*.
2. During the 19th century, antimony was a drug commonly prescribed to treat fever and pneumonia.
3. Historical icons of male power: Napoleon (1769–1821), French general, attempted to conquer Europe; Nero (37–68), emperor of Rome; Alexander the Great (356–323 B.C.E.), king of Macedonia and the conqueror of the Greek city-states.
4. One of the first friction matches, developed in London during the 1820s.

to think of it. O, you may scrimp and save, and twist and turn, and dig and delve, and economize and die; and your husband will marry again, and take what you have saved to dress his second wife with; and she'll take your portrait for a fire-board!

"But, what's the use of talking? I'll warrant every one of you'll try it the first chance you get; for, somehow, there's a sort of bewitchment about it. I wish one half the world were not fools, and the other half idiots."

1851, 1853

Hungry Husbands[1]

"The hand that can make a pie is a continual feast to the husband that marries its owner."[2]

Well, it is a humiliating reflection, that the straightest road to a man's heart is through his palate. He is never so amiable as when he has discussed a roast turkey. Then's your time, "Esther," for "half his kingdom,"[3] in the shape of a new bonnet, cap, shawl, or dress. He's too complacent to dispute the matter. Strike while the iron is hot; petition for a trip to Niagara, Saratoga, the Mammoth Cave, the White Mountains,[4] or to London, Rome, or Paris. Should he demur about it, the next day cook him another turkey, and pack your trunk while he is eating it.

There's nothing on earth so savage—except a bear robbed of her cubs—as a hungry husband. It is as much as your life is worth to sneeze, till dinner is on the table, and his knife and fork are in vigorous play. Tommy will get his ears boxed, the ottoman will be kicked into the corner, your work-box be turned bottom upwards, and the poker and tongs will beat a tattoo on that grate that will be a caution to dilatory cooks.

After the first six mouthfuls you may venture to say your soul is your own; his eyes will lose their ferocity, his brow its furrows, and he will very likely recollect to help you to a cold potato! Never mind—*eat it*. You might have to swallow a worse pill—for instance, should he offer to kiss you!

Well, learn a lesson from it—keep him well fed and languid—live yourself on a low diet, and cultivate your thinking powers; and you'll be as spry as a cricket, and hop over all the objections and remonstances that his dead-and-alive energies can muster. Yes, feed him well, and he will stay contentedly in his cage, like a gorged anaconda. If he were my husband, wouldn't I make him heaps of *pison*[5] things! Bless me! I've made a mistake in the spelling; it should have been *pies and things*!

1853, 1854

1. From *Fern Leaves from Fanny's Port-Folio. Second Series* (1854); the column was first published in *True Flag*, April 23, 1853.
2. From a newspaper column or domestic advice manual by someone other than Fern. Fern began many of her columns with passages from the conventional writings of the day.
3. In the Bible, when the Persian king Ahasuerus offered the Jewish woman Esther half his kingdom while complimenting her in front of his court, she responded by offering to prepare him a banquet (Esther 5.1–5).
4. Popular vacation spots in New York, Kentucky, and New Hampshire, respectively.
5. I.e., poison; phonetic spelling, as the word might be pronounced in a local dialect.

"Leaves of Grass"[1]

Well baptized: fresh, hardy, and grown for the masses. Not more welcome is their natural type to the winter-bound, bed-ridden, and spring-emancipated invalid. "Leaves of Grass" thou art unspeakably delicious, after the forced, stiff, Parnassian[2] exotics for which our admiration has been vainly challenged.

Walt Whitman, the effeminate world needed thee. The timidest soul whose wings ever drooped with discouragement, could not choose but rise on thy strong pinions.

"Undrape—you are not guilty to me, nor stale nor discarded;
I see through the broadcloth and gingham whether or no."

* * *

"O despairer, here is my neck,
You shall *not* go down! Hang your whole weight upon me."

Walt Whitman, the world needed a "Native American" of thorough, out and out breed—enamored of *women* not *ladies, men* not *gentlemen*, something beside a mere Catholic-hating Know-Nothing;[3] it needed a man who dared speak out his strong, honest thoughts, in the face of pusillanimous, toadeying, republican aristocracy; dictionary-men, hypocrites, cliques and creeds; it needed a large-hearted, untainted, self-reliant, fearless son of the Stars and Stripes, who disdains to sell his birthright for a mess of pottage;[4] who does

"Not call one greater or one smaller,
That which fills its period and place being equal to any;"

who will

"Accept nothing which all cannot have their counterpart of
on the same terms."

Fresh "Leaves of Grass!" not submitted by the self-reliant author to the fingering of any publisher's critic, to be arranged, re-arranged and disarranged to his circumscribed liking, till they hung limp, tame, spiritless, and scentless. No. It were a spectacle worth seeing, this glorious Native American, who, when the daily labor of chisel and plane was over, himself, with toil-hardened fingers, handled the types to print the pages which wise and good men have since delighted to endorse and to honor. Small critics,

1. From the May 10, 1856, issue of the *New York Ledger*. Fern met Whitman a few months before she published this review, and, for a short time, they developed a literary friendship. Fern's husband, James Parton, had introduced the writers, and the friendship came to an end in 1857 when Whitman failed to repay money he had borrowed from Parton. In her review, Fern responds to the second edition of *Leaves of Grass*, published in 1856. All quotations are from poems in that volume.
2. In Greek mythology, Mount Parnassus was the home of the Muses.
3. The anti-Catholic Know-Nothing Party formed during the late 1840s and early 1850s in response to fears shared by some native-born Protestants about increasing Catholic immigration. At first it was a secretive party, with members urged to say, "I know nothing," if asked about the party's activities. Under the name of the American Party, the Know-Nothings did well in elections of the early 1850s, but the party fell apart in 1856 as a result of sectional divisions over its proslavery platform.
4. In Genesis 25, Esau, the son of Isaac and Rebekah, sells his birthright (or inheritance) to his brother, Jacob, for a mess of pottage (meal of lentils).

whose contracted vision could see no beauty, strength, or grace, in these "Leaves," have long ago repented that they so hastily wrote themselves down shallow by such a premature confession. Where an Emerson and a Howitt[5] have commended, my woman's voice of praise may not avail; but happiness was born a twin, and so I would fain share with others the unmingled delight which these "Leaves" have given me.

I say unmingled; I am not unaware that the charge of coarseness and sensuality has been affixed to them. My moral constitution may be hopelessly tainted or—too sound to be tainted, as the critic wills—but I confess that I extract no poison from these "Leaves"—to me they have brought only healing. Let him who can do so, shroud the eyes of the nursing babe lest it should see its mother's breast. Let him look carefully between the gilded covers of books, backed by high-sounding names, and endorsed by parson and priest, lying unrebuked upon his own family table; where the asp of sensuality lies coiled amid rhetorical flowers. Let him examine well the paper dropped weekly at his door, in which virtue and religion are rendered disgusting, save when they walk in satin slippers, or, clothed in purple and fine linen, kneel on a damask "*prie-dieu.*"[6]

Sensual!—No—the moral assassin looks you not boldly in the eye by broad daylight; but Borgia-like[7] takes you treacherously by the hand, while from the glittering ring on his finger he distils through your veins the subtle and deadly poison.

Sensual? The artist who would inflame, paints you not nude Nature, but stealing Virtue's veil, with artful artlessness now conceals, now exposes, the ripe and swelling proportions.

Sensual? Let him who would affix this stigma upon "Leaves of Grass," write upon his heart, in letters of fire, these noble words of its author.

> "In woman I see the bearer of the great fruit, which is immortality
> * * * * the good thereof is not tasted by *roues*, and never can be.
>
> * * *
>
> Who degrades or defiles the living human body is cursed,
> Who degrades or defiles the body of the dead is not more cursed."

Were I an artist, I would like no more suggestive subjects for my easel than Walt Whitman's pen has furnished.

> "The little one sleeps in its cradle,
> I lift the gauze and look a long time, and silently brush away flies
> with my hand.
> The farmer stops by the bars of a Sunday and looks at the oats and rye.
>
> * * *

5. The English critic William Howitt (1792–1879) favorably reviewed *Leaves of Grass* in the *London Weekly Dispatch*, and the review was reprinted in the April 19, 1856 issue of *Life Illustrated*, published in New York City. Emerson praised the first edition of *Leaves* in a letter to Whitman of July 21, 1855 (see p. 348), and Whitman included that letter in the second edition of *Leaves*.

6. Literally, "Pray to God" (French); low bench for kneeling.

7. Reference to prominent Italian Renaissance family legendary for corruption and treachery.

Earth of the slumbering and liquid trees!
Earth of the departed Sunset,
Earth of the mountains misty-topt!
Earth of the vitreous pour of the full moon just tinged with blue!
Earth of shine and dark mottling the tide of the river!
Earth of the limpid grey of clouds brighter and clearer for my sake!
Far swooping elbowed earth! Rich apple-blossomed earth!
Smile, for your lover comes!"

I quote at random, the following passages which appeal to me:

"A morning glory at my window, satisfies me more than the metaphysics of books.

* * *

Logic and sermons never convince.
The damp of the night drives deeper into my soul."

Speaking of animals, he says:

"I stand and look at them sometimes half the day long,
They do not make me sick, discussing their duty to God.

* * *

—Whoever walks a furlong without sympathy, walks to his own funeral dressed in his shroud.

* * *

I hate him that oppresses me,
I will either destroy him, or he shall release me.

* * *

I find letters from God dropped in the street, and every one is signed by God's name,
And I leave them where they are, for I know that others will punctually come forever and ever.

* * *

—Under Niagara, *the cataract falling like a veil over my countenance*."

Of the grass he says:

"It seems to me *the beautiful uncut hair of graves*."

I close the extracts from these "Leaves," which it were easy to multiply, for one is more puzzled what to leave unculled, than what to gather, with the following sentiments; for which, and for all the good things included between the covers of his book, Mr. Whitman will please accept the cordial grasp of a woman's hand:

"The wife—and she is not one jot less than the husband,
The daughter—and she is just as good as the son,
The mother—and she is every bit as much as the father."

1856

Male Criticism on Ladies' Books[1]

> Courtship and marriage, servants and children, these are the great objects of a woman's thoughts, and they necessarily form the staple topics of their writings and their conversation. We have no right to expect anything else in a woman's book.
>
> —N.Y. TIMES

Is it in feminine novels *only* that courtship, marriage, servants, and children are the staple? Is not this true of all novels?—of Dickens, of Thackeray, of Bulwer[2] and a host of others? Is it peculiar to feminine pens, most astute and liberal of critics? Would a novel be a novel if it did not treat of courtship and marriage? and if it could be so recognized, would it find readers? When I see such a narrow, snarling criticism as the above, I always say to myself, the writer is some unhappy man, who has come up without the refining influence of mother, or sister, or reputable female friends; who has divided his migratory life between boarding-houses, restaurants, and the outskirts of editorial sanctums; and who knows as much about reviewing a woman's book, as I do about navigating a ship, or engineering an omnibus from the South Ferry, through Broadway, to Union Park.[3] I think I see him writing that paragraph in a fit of spleen—of *male* spleen—in his small boarding-house upper chamber, by the cheerful light of a solitary candle, flickering alternately on cobwebbed walls, dusty wash-stand, begrimed bowl and pitcher, refuse cigar stumps, boot-jacks, old hats, buttonless coats, muddy trousers, and all the wretched accompaniments of solitary, selfish male existence, not to speak of his own puckered, unkissable face; perhaps, in addition, his boots hurt, his cravat-bow[4] persists in slipping under his ear for want of a pin, and a wife to pin it, (poor wretch!) or he has been refused by some pretty girl, as he deserved to be, (narrow-minded old vinegar-cruet!) or snubbed by some lady authoress; or, more trying than all to the male constitution, has had a weak cup of coffee for that morning's breakfast.

But seriously—we have had quite enough of this shallow criticism (?) on lady-books. Whether the book which called forth the remark above quoted, was a good book or a bad one, I know not: I should be inclined to think the *former* from the dispraise of such a pen. Whether ladies can write novels or not, is a question I do not intend to discuss; but that some of them have no difficulty in finding either publishers or readers, is a matter of history; and that gentlemen often write over feminine signatures would seem also to argue that feminine literature is, after all, in good odor with the reading public. Granting that lady-novels are not all that they should be—is such shallow, unfair, wholesale, sneering criticism (?) the way to reform them? Would it not be better and more manly to point out a better way kindly, justly, *and, above all, respectfully*? or—what would be a much harder task for such critics—write a better book!

1857

1. First printed in the *New York Ledger* on May 23, 1857, the source of the present text.
2. English novelists: Charles Dickens (1812–1870), William Makepeace Thackeray (1811–1863), and Edward George Earle Bulwer-Lytton (1803–1873).
3. A line of omnibuses (horse-drawn public vehicles) that started at the South Ferry terminal at the Battery, the southern tip of Manhattan, and ran north on Broadway to Union Park at Fourteenth Street, then considered uptown.
4. A form of bowtie.

"Fresh Leaves, by Fanny Fern"[1]

This little volume has just been laid upon our table. The publishers have done all they could for it, with regard to outward adorning. No doubt it will be welcomed by those who admire this lady's style of writing: we confess ourselves not to be of that number. We have never seen Fanny Fern, nor do we desire to do so. We imagine her, from her writings, to be a muscular, black-browed, grenadier-looking female, who would be more at home in a boxing gallery than in a parlor,—a vociferous, demonstrative, strong-minded horror,—a woman only by virtue of her dress. Bah! the very thought sickens us. We have read, or, rather, tried to read, her halloo-there effusions.[2] When we take up a woman's book we expect to find gentleness, timidity, and that lovely reliance on the patronage of our sex which constitutes a woman's greatest charm. We do not wish to be startled by bold expressions, or disgusted with exhibitions of masculine weaknesses. We do not desire to see a woman wielding the scimetar blade of sarcasm. If she be, unfortunately, endowed with a gift so dangerous, let her—as she values the approbation of our sex—fold it in a napkin. Fanny's strong-minded nose would probably turn up at this inducement. Thank heaven! there are still women who *are* women—who know the place Heaven assigned them, and keep it—who do not waste floods of ink and paper, brow-beating men and stirring up silly women;—who do not teach children that a game of romps is of as much importance as Blair's Philosophy;[3]—who have not the presumption to advise clergymen as to their duties, or lecture doctors, and savans;—who live for something else than to astonish a gaping, idiotic crowd. Thank heaven! there are women writers who do not disturb our complacence or serenity; whose books lull one to sleep like a strain of gentle music; who excite no antagonism, or angry feeling. Woman never was intended for an irritant: she should be oil upon the troubled waters of manhood—soft and amalgamating, a necessary but unobtrusive ingredient;—never challenging attention—never throwing the gauntlet of defiance to a beard, but softly purring beside it lest it bristle and scratch.

The very fact that Fanny Fern has, in the language of her admirers, "elbowed her way through unheard of difficulties," shows that she is an antagonistic, pugilistic female. One must needs, forsooth, get out of her way, or be pushed one side, or trampled down. How much more womanly to have allowed herself to be doubled up by adversity, and quietly laid away on the shelf of fate, than to have rolled up her sleeves, and gone to fisticuffs with it. Such a woman may conquer, it is true, but her victory will cost her dear; it will neither be forgotten nor forgiven—let her put that in her apron pocket.

As to Fanny Fern's grammar, rhetoric, and punctuation, they are beneath criticism. It is all very well for her to say, those who wish commas, semicolons and periods, must look for them in the printer's case, or that she who finds ideas must not be expected to find rhetoric or grammar; for our part, we should be gratified if we had even found any ideas!

1. First printed in the *New York Ledger* on October 10, 1857, the source of the text. In this piece Fern parodies the tone and content of reviews she may have anticipated.

2. Bold attention-getting articles.

3. *Moral Philosophy, etc.; On the Duties of the Young* (1798), by the Scottish writer Hugh Blair (1718–1800).

We regret to be obliged to speak thus of a lady's book: it gives us pleasure, when we can do so conscientiously, to pat lady writers on the head; but we owe a duty to the public which will not permit us to recommend to their favorable notice an aspirant who has been unwomanly enough so boldly to contest every inch of ground in order to reach them—an aspirant at once so high-stepping and so ignorant, so plausible, yet so pernicious. We have a conservative horror of this pop-gun, torpedo female; we predict for Fanny Fern's "Leaves" only a fleeting autumnal flutter.

1857

A Law More Nice Than Just[1]

Here I have been sitting twiddling the morning paper between my fingers this half hour, reflecting upon the following paragraph in it: "Emma Wilson was arrested yesterday for wearing man's apparel." Now, why this should be an actionable offense is past my finding out, or where's the harm in it, I am as much at a loss to see. Think of the old maids (and weep) who have to stay at home evening after evening, when, if they provided themselves with a coat, pants and hat, they might go abroad, instead of sitting there with their noses flattened against the window-pane, looking vainly for "the Coming Man."[2] Think of the married women who stay at home after their day's toil is done, waiting wearily for their thoughtless, truant husbands, when they might be taking the much needed independent walk in trowsers, which custom forbids to petticoats. And this, I fancy, may be the secret of this famous law—who knows? It *wouldn't* be pleasant for some of them to be surprised by a touch on the shoulder from some dapper young fellow, whose familiar treble voice belied his corduroys. That's it, now. What a fool I was not to think of it—not to remember that men who make the laws, make them to meet all these little emergencies.

Everybody knows what an everlasting drizzle of rain we have had lately, but nobody but a woman, and a woman who lives on fresh air and out-door exercise, knows the thraldom of taking her daily walk through a three weeks' rain, with skirts to hold up, and umbrella to hold down, and puddles to skip over, and gutters to walk round, and all the time in a fright lest, in an unguarded moment, her calves should become visible to some one of those rainy-day philanthropists who are interested in the public study of female anatomy.

One evening, after a long rainy day of scribbling, when my nerves were in double-twisted knots, and I felt as if myriads of little ants were leisurely traveling over me, and all for want of the walk which is my daily salvation, I stood at the window, looking at the slanting, persistent rain, and took my resolve. *"I'll do it,"* said I, audibly, planting my slipper upon the carpet. "Do what?" asked Mr. Fern, looking up from a big book. "Put on a suit of your clothes and take a tramp with you," was the answer. "You dare not," was the rejoinder;

1. First printed in the *New York Ledger* on July 10, 1858, the source of the text. "Nice": fastidious.

2. A suitor with good prospects for financial or professional advancement.

"you are a little coward, only saucy on paper." It was the work of a moment, with such a challenge, to fly up stairs and overhaul my philosopher's wardrobe. Of course we had fun. Tailors must be a stingy set, I remarked, to be so sparing of their cloth, as I struggled into a pair of their handiwork, undeterred by the vociferous laughter of the wretch who had solemnly vowed to "cherish me" through all my tribulations. "Upon my word, everything seems to be narrow where it ought to be broad, and the waist of this coat might be made for a hogshead;[3] and, ugh! this shirt-collar is cutting my ears off, and you have not a decent cravat in the whole lot, and your vests are frights, and what am I to do with my hair?" Still no reply from Mr. Fern, who lay on the floor, faintly ejaculating, between his fits of laughter, "Oh, my! by Jove!—oh! by Jupiter!"

Was that to hinder me? Of course not. Strings and pins, woman's never-failing resort, soon brought broadcloth and kerseymere[4] to terms. I parted my hair on one side, rolled it under, and then secured it with hair-pins; chose the best fitting coat, and cap-ping the climax with one of those soft, cosy hats, looked in the glass, where I beheld the very fac-simile of a certain musical gentleman, whose photograph hangs this minute in Brady's[5] entry.

Well, Mr. Fern seized his hat, and out we went together. "Fanny," said he, "you must not take my arm; you are a fellow." "True," said I, "I forgot; and you must not help me over the puddles, as you did just now, and do, for mercy's sake, stop laughing. There, there goes your hat—I mean *my* hat; confound the wind! and down comes my hair; lucky 'tis dark, isn't it? But oh, the delicious freedom of that walk, after we were well started! No skirts to hold up, or to draggle their wet folds against my ankles; no stifling vail flapping in my face, and blinding my eyes; no umbrella to turn inside out, but instead, the cool rain driving slap into my face, and the resurrectionized blood coursing through my veins, and tingling in my cheeks. To be sure, Mr. Fern occasionally loitered behind, and leaned up against the side of a house to enjoy a little private "guffaw," and I could now and then hear a gasping "Oh, Fanny!" "oh, my!" but none of these things moved me, and if I don't have a nicely-fitting suit of my own to wear rainy evenings, it is because—well, there *are* difficulties in the way. Who's the best tailor?

Now, if any male or female Miss Nancy[6] who reads this feels shocked, let 'em! Any woman who likes, may stay at home during a three weeks' rain, till her skin looks like parchment, and her eyes like those of a dead fish, or she may go out and get a consumption dragging round wet petticoats; I won't—I positively declare I won't. I shall begin *evenings* when *that* suit is made, and take private walking lessons with Mr. Fern, and they who choose may crook their backs at home for fashion, and then send for the doctor to straighten them; I prefer to patronize my shoe-maker and tailor. I've as good a right to preserve the healthy body God gave me, as if I were not a woman.

1858

3. Large cask.
4. Woolen cloth used in men's apparel.
5. Mathew B. Brady (1823–1896), pioneering photographer, had a studio in lower Manhattan at Broadway and Fulton. The "musical gentleman" may have been the great Italian baritone Giorgio Ronconi (1810–1890); several weeks before Fern published this article, New Yorkers lamented his departure for Europe.
6. A prude.

From Ruth Hall[1]

Chapter LIV

"What is it on the gate? Spell it, mother," said Katy, looking wistfully through the iron fence at the terraced banks, smoothly-rolled gravel walks, plats of flowers, and grape-trellised arbors; "what is it on the gate, mother?"

"'Insane Hospital,' dear; a place for crazy people."

"Want to walk round, ma'am?" asked the gate-keeper, as Katy poked her little head in; "can, if you like." Little Katy's eyes pleaded eloquently; flowers were to her another name for happiness, and Ruth passed in.

"I should like to live here, mamma," said Katy.

Ruth shuddered, and pointed to a pale face pressed close against the grated window. Fair rose the building in its architectural proportions; the well-kept lawn was beautiful to the eye; but, alas! there was helpless age, whose only disease was too long a lease of life for greedy heirs. There, too, was the fragile wife, to whom *love* was breath—being!—forgotten by the world and him in whose service her bloom had withered, insane—only in that her love had outlived his patience.

"Poor creatures!" exclaimed Ruth, as they peered out from one window after another. "Have you had many deaths here?" asked she of the gate-keeper.

"Some, ma'am. There is one corpse in the house now; a married lady, Mrs. Leon."[2]

"Good heavens!" exclaimed Ruth, "my friend Mary."

"Died yesterday, ma'am; her husband left her here for her health, while he went to Europe."

"Can I see the Superintendent," asked Ruth; "I must speak to him."

Ruth followed the gate-keeper up the ample steps into a wide hall, and from thence into a small parlor; after waiting what seemed to her an age of time, Mr. Tibbetts, the Superintendent, entered. He was a tall, handsome man, between forty and fifty, with a very imposing air and address.

"I am pained to learn," said Ruth, "that a friend of mine, Mrs. Leon, lies dead here; can I see the body?"

"Are you a relative of that lady?" asked Mr. Tibbetts, with a keen glance at Ruth.

"No," replied Ruth, "but she was very dear to me. The last time I saw her, not many months since, she was in tolerable health. Has she been long with you, Sir?"

"About two months," replied Mr. Tibbetts; "she was hopelessly crazy, refused food entirely, so that we were obliged to force it. Her husband, who is an intimate friend of mine, left her under my care, and went to the Continent. A very fine man, Mr. Leon."

1. From the first printing of *Ruth Hall: A Domestic Tale of the Present Time* (1855). The novel tells the story of the rise of a woman author somewhat resembling Fanny Fern herself. At this point in the novel, Ruth's first husband has died; and after being rejected by both her family and her husband's family, she is struggling to survive as a working-class woman while caring for her daughters, Katy and Nettie.

2. Earlier in the novel, before the death of her husband, Ruth had briefly befriended Mrs. Leon at a fashionable beach hotel where both of the women were taking rest cures. Mrs. Leon suffered from severe nervous headaches and "shuddered" at the mention of her husband's name.

Ruth did not feel inclined to respond to this remark, but repeated her request to see Mary.

"It is against the rules of our establishment to permit this to any but relatives," said Mr. Tibbetts.

"I should esteem it a great favor if you would break through your rules in my case," replied Ruth; "it will be a great consolation to me to have seen her once more;" and her voice faltered.

The appeal was made so gently, yet so firmly, that Mr. Tibbetts reluctantly yielded.

The matron of the establishment, Mrs. Bunce, (whose advent was heralded by the clinking of a huge bunch of keys at her waist,) soon after came in. Mrs. Bunce was gaunt, sallow and bony, with restless, yellowish, glaring black eyes, very much resembling those of a cat in the dark; her motions were quick, brisk, and angular; her voice loud, harsh, and wiry. Ruth felt an instantaneous aversion to her; which was not lessened by Mrs. Bunce asking, as they passed through the parlor-door:

"Fond of looking at corpses, ma'am? I've seen a great many in my day; I've laid out more'n twenty people, first and last, with my own hands. Relation of Mrs. Leon's, perhaps?" said she, curiously peering under Ruth's bonnet. "Ah, only a friend?"

"This way, if you please, ma'am;" and on they went, through one corridor, then another, the massive doors swinging heavily to on their hinges, and fastening behind them as they closed.

"Hark!" said Ruth, with a quick, terrified look, "what's that?"

"Oh, nothing," replied the matron, "only a crazy woman in that room yonder, screaming for her child. Her husband ran away from her and carried off her child with him, to spite her, and now she fancies every footstep she hears is his. Visitors always thinks she screams awful. She can't harm you, ma'am," said the matron, mistaking the cause of Ruth's shudder, "for she is chained. She went to law about the child, and the law, you see, as it generally is, was on the man's side; and it just upset her. She's a sight of trouble to manage. If she was to catch sight of your little girl out there in the garden, she'd spring at her through them bars like a panther; but we don't have to whip her *very* often."

"Down here," said the matron, taking the shuddering Ruth by the hand, and descending a flight of stone steps, into a dark passage-way. "Tired aren't you?"

"Wait a bit, please," said Ruth, leaning against the stone wall, for her limbs were trembling so violently that she could scarcely bear her weight.

"*Now,*" said she, (after a pause,) with a firmer voice and step.

"This way," said Mrs. Bunce, advancing towards a rough deal box which stood on a table in a niche of the cellar, and setting a small lamp upon it; "she didn't look no better than that, ma'am, for a long while before she died."

Ruth gave one hurried glance at the corpse, and buried her face in her hands. Well might she fail to recognize in that emaciated form, those sunken eyes and hollow cheeks, the beautiful Mary Leon. Well might she shudder, as the gibbering screams of the maniacs over head echoed through the stillness of that cold, gloomy vault.

"Were you with her at the last?" asked Ruth of the matron, wiping away her tears.

"No," replied she; "the afternoon she died she said, 'I want to be alone,' and, not thinking her near her end, I took my work and sat just outside the door. I looked in once, about half an hour after, but she lay quietly asleep, with her cheek in her hand,—so. By-and-by I thought I would speak to her, so I went in, and saw her lying just as she did when I looked at her before. I spoke to her, but she did not answer me; she was dead, ma'am."

O, how mournfully sounded in Ruth's ears those plaintive words, "I want to be alone." Poor Mary! aye, better even in death 'alone,' than gazed at by careless, hireling eyes, since he who should have closed those drooping lids, had wearied of their faded light.

"Did she speak of no one?" asked Ruth; "mention no one?"

"No—yes; I recollect now that she said something about calling Ruth; I didn't pay any attention, for they don't know what they are saying, you know. She scribbled something, too, on a bit of paper; I found it under her pillow, when I laid her out. I shouldn't wonder if it was in my pocket now; I haven't thought of it since. Ah! here it is," said Mrs. Bunce, as she handed the slip of paper to Ruth.

It ran thus:—"I am not crazy, Ruth, no, no—but I shall be; the air of this place stifles me; I grow weaker—weaker. I cannot die here; for the love of heaven, dear Ruth, come and take me away."

"Only three mourners,—a woman and two little girls," exclaimed a bystander, as Ruth followed Mary Leon to her long home.

* * *

Chapter LVI

It was a sultry morning in July. Ruth had risen early, for her cough seemed more troublesome in a reclining posture. "I wonder what that noise can be?" said she to herself; whir—whir—whir, it went, all day long in the attic overhead.[3] She knew that Mrs. Waters had one other lodger beside herself, an elderly gentleman by the name of Bond,[4] who cooked his own food, and whom she often met on the stairs, coming up with a pitcher of water, or a few eggs in a paper bag, or a pie that he had bought of Mr. Flake, at the little black grocery-shop at the corner. On these occasions he always stepped aside, and with a deferential bow waited for Ruth to pass. He was a thin, spare man, slightly bent; his hair and whiskers curiously striped like a zebra, one lock being jet black, while the neighboring one was as distinct a white. His dress was plain, but very neat and tidy. He never seemed to have any business outdoors, as he staid in his room all day, never leaving it at all till dark, when he paced up and down, with his hands behind him, before the house. "Whir—whir—whir." It was early sunrise; but Ruth had heard that odd noise for two hours at least. What *could* it mean? Just then a carrier passed on the other side of the street with the morning papers, and slipped one under the crack of the house door opposite.

3. The whirring sound may be a printing press, but that is never made clear. Ruth had recently moved to Mrs. Waters's boarding-house in lower Manhattan.

4. Mr. Bond remains a mystery in the novel.

A thought! why could not Ruth write for the papers? How very odd it had never occurred to her before? Yes, write for the papers—why not? She remembered that while at boarding-school, an editor of a paper in the same town used often to come in and take down her compositions in short-hand as she read them aloud, and transfer them to the columns of his paper. She certainly *ought* to write better now than she did when an inexperienced girl. She would begin that very night; but where to make a beginning? who would publish her articles? how much would they pay her? to whom should she apply first? There was her brother Hyacinth,[5] now the prosperous editor of the Irving Magazine; oh, if he would only employ her? Ruth was quite sure she could write as well as some of his correspondents, whom he had praised with no niggardly pen. She would prepare samples to send immediately, announcing her intention, and offering them for his acceptance. This means of support would be so congenial, so absorbing. At the needle one's mind could still be brooding over sorrowful thoughts.

Ruth counted the days and hours impatiently, as she waited for an answer. Hyacinth surely would not refuse *her* when in almost every number of his magazine he was announcing some new contributor; or, if *he* could not employ her *himself*, he surely would be brotherly enough to point out to her some one of the many avenues so accessible to a man of extensive newspaperial and literary acquaintance. She would so gladly support herself, so cheerfully toil day and night, if need be, could she only win an independence; and Ruth recalled with a sigh Katy's last visit to her father, and then she rose and walked the floor in her impatience; and then, her restless spirit urging her on to her fate, she went again to the post office to see if there were no letter. How long the clerk made her wait! Yes, there *was* a letter for her, and in her brother's hand-writing too. Oh, how long since she had seen it!

Ruth heeded neither the jostling of office-boys, porters, or draymen, as she held out her eager hand for the letter. Thrusting it hastily in her pocket, she hurried in breathless haste back to her lodgings. The contents were as follows:

> "I have looked over the pieces you sent me, Ruth. It is very evident that writing never can be *your* forte; you have no talent that way. You may possibly be employed by some inferior newspapers, but be assured your articles never will be heard of out of your own little provincial city. For myself I have plenty of contributors, nor do I know of any of my literary acquaintances who would employ you. I would advise you, therefore, to seek some *unobtrusive* employment. Your brother,
>
> "HYACINTH ELLET."

A bitter smile struggled with the hot tear that fell upon Ruth's cheek. "I have tried the unobtrusive employment," said Ruth; "the wages are six cents a day, Hyacinth;" and again the bitter smile disfigured her gentle lip.

"No talent!"

"At another tribunal than his will I appeal."

"Never be heard of out of my own little provincial city!" The cold, contemptuous tone stung her.

5. Fern's satirical portrayal of her brother, Nathaniel Parker Willis (1806–1867), who was then editor of New York's *Home Journal*.

"But they shall be heard of;" and Ruth leaped to her feet. "Sooner than he dreams of, too. I *can* do it, I *feel* it, I *will* do it," and she closed her lips firmly; "but there will be a desperate struggle first," and she clasped her hands over her heart as if it had already commenced; "there will be scant meals, and sleepless nights, and weary days, and a throbbing brow, and an aching heart; there will be the chilling tone, the rude repulse; there will be ten backward steps to one forward. *Pride* must sleep! but—" and Ruth glanced at her children—"it shall be *done*. They shall be proud of their mother. *Hyacinth shall yet be proud to claim his sister.*"

"What is it, mamma?" asked Katy, looking wonderingly at the strange expression of her mother's face.

"What is it, my darling?" and Ruth caught up the child with convulsive energy; "what is it? only that when you are a woman you shall remember this day, my little pet;" and as she kissed Katy's upturned brow a bright spot burned on her cheek, and her eye glowed like a star.

1855

HARRIET JACOBS
c. 1813–1897

The first African American woman known to have authored a slave narrative in the United States, Harriet Jacobs was born into slavery in Edenton, North Carolina. Her father was a skilled carpenter who was permitted to hire himself out, and her parents were allowed to live together even though they had different masters; therefore, as a child Jacobs was unaware that she was a slave. Her mother's death and a change of owners for both Jacobs and her father brought her into the family of Dr. and Mrs. James Norcom in 1825. There, as she grew to adulthood, she was sexually threatened by the doctor and abused by his jealous wife. As a defense against this treatment, Jacobs became involved with an unmarried white attorney, Samuel Tredwell Sawyer, with whom she had two children: Joseph, born in 1829, and Louisa Matilda, born in 1833. When Norcom sent her to a country plantation in 1835, she escaped back to Edenton, hiding for perhaps seven years in an attic crawl space in the home of her maternal grandmother, who had been emancipated some years earlier. While Jacobs was in hiding, Sawyer purchased, but did not emancipate, their two children. Jacobs finally escaped to the North in 1842, and later both her children came north as well. Life in the North remained insecure and perilous, however, because slave catchers were constantly hunting down escaped slaves to return them to the South, which they could do more aggressively after 1850 with the Fugitive Slave Law on their side.

For much of the next two decades Jacobs worked in the family of Nathaniel Parker Willis (1806–1867), one of the era's most popular writers and editors (and the brother of the popular writer Fanny Fern). She took care of his children and became particularly close to his second wife, Cornelia Grinnell Willis, a staunch abolitionist. In 1852 Cornelia Willis arranged to purchase Jacobs from Norcom's daughter, Jacobs's legal owner; then she emancipated Jacobs, who continued to work for Willis after he became a widower.

Jacobs spent most of 1849 in Rochester, New York, working for the Anti-Slavery Office run by her younger brother, who had also escaped slavery. She read through a large body of antislavery writings and also came to know a number of abolitionists, including many white women, among them the Quaker Amy Post, who became a mentor to her and in whose house she lived for nine months while her brother was away on lecture tours. Jacobs wanted to contribute her life story to the abolitionist cause in a way that would capture the attention of Northern white women in particular, to show them how slavery debased and demoralized women, at once subjecting them to white male lust and also depriving them of the right to make homes for their families. Yet this topic was difficult to discuss in an era when extreme sexual prudery was the norm, when standards of female sexual "purity" could result in blaming the unmarried slave mother rather than the man whose victim she was. In *Incidents in the Life of a Slave Girl* Jacobs tried to do more than create sympathy for her plight; she sought to win the respect and admiration of her readers for the courage with which she forestalled abuse and for the independence with which she chose a lover rather than having one forced on her. Her description of hiding in the attic, her emphasis on family life and maternal values, and her account of the difficulties of fugitive slaves in the North differentiate the book from the numerous slave narratives produced in the twenty years before the Civil War.

Encouraged by the success of Harriet Beecher Stowe's *Uncle Tom's Cabin* (1852)—one of whose heroines is the slave concubine Cassy—Jacobs began work on her narrative around 1853 and finished it by 1858. She was not successful in finding a publisher for it, however, until Lydia Maria Child (1802–1880), the well-known woman of letters and abolitionist, agreed to write a preface for it. Child became interested in the project, putting much editorial work into the manuscript; and when the contracted publishers went bankrupt, she arranged for its publication. The book came out under the pseudonym Linda Brent in 1861; it was sold by antislavery societies in the Northeast, was published in England in 1862, and received several favorable reviews. The outbreak of the Civil War made its message less pressing, however; and it sank from notice until the 1980s, when renewed interest in writings by African-American women and superb biographical scholarship by Jean Fagin Yellin, establishing that this was an autobiographical narrative and not a novel, brought belated acclaim to the work.

During and after the war Jacobs worked with the Quakers in their efforts to help freed slaves with direct aid and by organizing schools, orphanages, and nursing homes. She ran a boardinghouse in Cambridge, Massachusetts, and later moved to Washington, D.C., with her daughter. She is buried in Mount Auburn Cemetery in Cambridge.

From Incidents in the Life of a Slave Girl[1]

I. Childhood

I was born a slave; but I never knew it till six years of happy childhood had passed away. My father was a carpenter, and considered so intelligent and skilful in his trade, that, when buildings out of the common line were to be erected, he was sent for from long distances, to be head workman. On condition of paying his mistress two hundred dollars a year, and supporting

1. The text is that of the 1861 edition, edited by Jean Fagin Yellin (1987).

himself, he was allowed to work at his trade, and manage his own affairs. His strongest wish was to purchase his children; but, though he several times offered his hard earnings for that purpose, he never succeeded. In complexion my parents were a light shade of brownish yellow, and were termed mulattoes. They lived together in a comfortable home; and, though we were all slaves, I was so fondly shielded that I never dreamed I was a piece of merchandise, trusted to them for safe keeping, and liable to be demanded of them at any moment. I had one brother, William, who was two years younger than myself—a bright, affectionate child. I had also a great treasure in my maternal grandmother, who was a remarkable woman in many respects. She was the daughter of a planter in South Carolina, who, at his death, left her mother and his three children free, with money to go to St. Augustine,[2] where they had relatives. It was during the Revolutionary War; and they were captured on their passage, carried back, and sold to different purchasers. Such was the story my grandmother used to tell me; but I do not remember all the particulars. She was a little girl when she was captured and sold to the keeper of a large hotel.[3] I have often heard her tell how hard she fared during childhood. But as she grew older she evinced so much intelligence, and was so faithful, that her master and mistress could not help seeing it was for their interest to take care of such a valuable piece of property. She became an indispensable personage in the household, officiating in all capacities, from cook and wet nurse to seamstress. She was much praised for her cooking; and her nice crackers became so famous in the neighborhood that many people were desirous of obtaining them. In consequence of numerous requests of this kind, she asked permission of her mistress to bake crackers at night, after all the household work was done; and she obtained leave to do it, provided she would clothe herself and her children from the profits. Upon these terms, after working hard all day for her mistress, she began her midnight bakings, assisted by her two oldest children. The business proved profitable; and each year she laid by a little, which was saved for a fund to purchase her children. Her master died, and the property was divided among his heirs. The widow had her dower[4] in the hotel, which she continued to keep open. My grandmother remained in her service as a slave; but her children were divided among her master's children. As she had five, Benjamin, the youngest one, was sold, in order that each heir might have an equal portion of dollars and cents. There was so little difference in our ages that he seemed more like my brother than my uncle. He was a bright, handsome lad, nearly white; for he inherited the complexion my grandmother had derived from Anglo-Saxon ancestors. Though only ten years old, seven hundred and twenty dollars were paid for him. His sale was a terrible blow to my grandmother; but she was naturally hopeful, and she went to work with renewed energy, trusting in time to be able to purchase some of her children. She had laid up three hundred dollars, which her mistress one day begged as a loan, promising to pay her soon.

2. During the Revolutionary War, a British port town in what is now Florida.
3. *John Horniblow, who ran the* King's Arms hotel in Edenton, North Carolina. Jacobs's grandmother's legal name was Margaret (Molly) Horniblow (c. 1771–1853); as was typical for the era, Molly received the surname of her owner. *Incidents* never mentions a grandfather, and no information has been recovered relating to the paternal parentage of Molly's children.
4. Inheritance from her husband's estate.

The reader probably knows that no promise or writing given to a slave is legally binding; for, according to Southern laws, a slave, *being* property, can *hold* no property. When my grandmother lent her hard earnings to her mistress, she trusted solely to her honor. The honor of a slaveholder to a slave!

To this good grandmother I was indebted for many comforts. My brother Willie and I often received portions of the crackers, cakes, and preserves, she made to sell; and after we ceased to be children we were indebted to her for many more important services.

Such were the unusually fortunate circumstances of my early childhood. When I was six years old, my mother died, and then, for the first time, I learned, by the talk around me, that I was a slave. My mother's mistress was the daughter of my grandmother's mistress. She was the foster sister of my mother; they were both nourished at my grandmother's breast. In fact, my mother had been weaned at three months old, that the babe of the mistress might obtain sufficient food. They played together as children; and, when they became women, my mother was a most faithful servant to her whiter foster sister. On her death-bed her mistress promised that her children should never suffer for any thing; and during her lifetime she kept her word. They all spoke kindly of my dead mother, who had been a slave merely in name, but in nature was noble and womanly. I grieved for her, and my young mind was troubled with the thought who would now take care of me and my little brother. I was told that my home was now to be with her mistress; and I found it a happy one. No toilsome or disagreeable duties were imposed upon me. My mistress was so kind to me that I was always glad to do her bidding, and proud to labor for her as much as my young years would permit. I would sit by her side for hours, sewing diligently, with a heart as free from care as that of any free-born white child. When she thought I was tired, she would send me out to run and jump; and away I bounded, to gather berries or flowers to decorate her room. Those were happy days—too happy to last. The slave child had no thought for the morrow; but there came that blight, which too surely waits on every human being born to be a chattel.

When I was nearly twelve years old, my kind mistress sickened and died. As I saw the cheek grow paler, and the eye more glassy, how earnestly I prayed in my heart that she might live! I loved her; for she had been almost like a mother to me. My prayers were not answered. She died, and they buried her in the little churchyard, where, day after day, my tears fell upon her grave.

I was sent to spend a week with my grandmother. I was now old enough to begin to think of the future; and again and again I asked myself what they would do with me. I felt sure I should never find another mistress so kind as the one who was gone. She had promised my dying mother that her children should never suffer for any thing; and when I remembered that, and recalled her many proofs of attachment to me, I could not help having some hopes that she had left me free. My friends were almost certain it would be so. They thought she would be sure to do it, on account of my mother's love and faithful service. But, alas! we all know that the memory of a faithful slave does not avail much to save her children from the auction block.

After a brief period of suspense, the will of my mistress was read, and we learned that she had bequeathed me to her sister's daughter, a child of five years old. So vanished our hopes. My mistress had taught me the precepts of God's Word: "Thou shalt love thy neighbor as thyself."[5] "Whatsoever ye would that men should do unto you, do ye even so unto them."[6] But I was her slave, and I suppose she did not recognize me as her neighbor. I would give much to blot out from my memory that one great wrong. As a child, I loved my mistress; and, looking back on the happy days I spent with her, I try to think with less bitterness of this act of injustice. While I was with her, she taught me to read and spell; and for this privilege, which so rarely falls to the lot of a slave, I bless her memory.

She possessed but few slaves; and at her death those were all distributed among her relatives. Five of them were my grandmother's children, and had shared the same milk that nourished her mother's children. Notwithstanding my grandmother's long and faithful service to her owners, not one of her children escaped the auction block. These God-breathing machines are no more, in the sight of their masters, than the cotton they plant, or the horses they tend.

* * *

VII. The Lover

Why does the slave ever love? Why allow the tendrils of the heart to twine around objects which may at any moment be wrenched away by the hand of violence? When separations come by the hand of death, the pious soul can bow in resignation, and say, "Not my will, but thine be done, O Lord!"[7] But when the ruthless hand of man strikes the blow, regardless of the misery he causes, it is hard to be submissive. I did not reason thus when I was a young girl. Youth will be youth. I loved, and I indulged the hope that the dark clouds around me would turn out a bright lining. I forgot that in the land of my birth the shadows are too dense for light to penetrate. A land

> "Where laughter is not mirth; nor thought the mind;
> Nor words a language; no e'en men mankind.
> Where cries reply to curses, shrieks to blows,
> And each is tortured in his separate hell."[8]

There was in the neighborhood a young colored carpenter; a free born man. We had been well acquainted in childhood, and frequently met together afterwards. We became mutually attached, and he proposed to marry me. I loved him with all the ardor of a young girl's first love. But when I reflected that I was a slave, and that the laws gave no sanction to the marriage of such, my heart sank within me. My lover wanted to buy me; but I knew that Dr. Flint was too wilful and arbitrary a man to consent to that arrangement. From him, I was sure of experiencing all sorts of opposition, and I had nothing to hope from my mistress.[9] She would have been delighted to have got rid of me, but not in that way. It would have relieved her mind of a burden if she could have seen me sold to some distant state, but if I was married near home I should be just as much in her husband's power as I

5. Mark 12.31.
6. Matthew 7.12.
7. Matthew 26.39.
8. From *The Lament of Tasso* 4.7–10 (1817), by the English poet George Gordon, Lord Byron (1788–1824).
9. Dr. Flint is the father of Brent's owner, Emily Flint, who is a child at this time, giving Flint and his wife (whom Brent refers to as her mistress) legal power.

had previously been,—for the husband of a slave has no power to protect her.[1] Moreover, my mistress, like many others, seemed to think that slaves had no right to any family ties of their own; that they were created merely to wait upon the family of the mistress. I once heard her abuse a young slave girl, who told her that a colored man wanted to make her his wife. "I will have you peeled and pickled, my lady," said she, "if I ever hear you mention that subject again. Do you suppose that I will have you tending *my* children with the children of that nigger?" The girl to whom she said this had a mulatto child, of course not acknowledged by its father. The poor black man who loved her would have been proud to acknowledge his helpless offspring.

Many and anxious were the thoughts I revolved in my mind. I was at a loss what to do. Above all things, I was desirous to spare my lover the insults that had cut so deeply into my own soul. I talked with my grandmother about it, and partly told her my fears. I did not dare to tell her the worst. She had long suspected all was not right, and if I confirmed her suspicions I knew a storm would rise that would prove the overthrow of all my hopes.

This love-dream had been my support through many trials; and I could not bear to run the risk of having it suddenly dissipated. There was a lady in the neighborhood, a particular friend of Dr. Flint's, who often visited the house. I had a great respect for her, and she had always manifested a friendly interest in me. Grandmother thought she would have great influence with the doctor. I went to this lady, and told her my story. I told her I was aware that my lover's being a free-born man would prove a great objection; but he wanted to buy me; and if Dr. Flint would consent to that arrangement, I felt sure he would be willing to pay any reasonable price. She knew that Mrs. Flint disliked me; therefore, I ventured to suggest that perhaps my mistress would approve of my being sold, as that would rid her of me. The lady listened with kindly sympathy, and promised to do her utmost to promote my wishes. She had an interview with the doctor, and I believe she pleaded my cause earnestly; but it was all to no purpose.

How I dreaded my master now! Every minute I expected to be summoned to his presence; but the day passed, and I heard nothing from him. The next morning, a message was brought to me: "Master wants you in his study." I found the door ajar, and I stood a moment gazing at the hateful man who claimed a right to rule me, body and soul. I entered, and tried to appear calm. I did not want him to know how my heart was bleeding. He looked fixedly at me, with an expression which seemed to say, "I have half a mind to kill you on the spot." At last he broke the silence, and that was a relief to both of us.

"So you want to be married, do you?" said he, "and to a free nigger."

"Yes, sir."

"Well, I'll soon convince you whether I am your master, or the nigger fellow you honor so highly. If you *must* have a husband, you may take up with one of my slaves."

What a situation I should be in, as the wife of one of *his* slaves, even if my heart had been interested!

I replied, "Don't you suppose, sir, that a slave can have some preference about marrying? Do you suppose that all men are alike to her?"

1. Flint has been attempting to coerce Brent into sexual relations.

"Do you love this nigger?" said he, abruptly.

"Yes, sir."

"How dare you tell me so!" he exclaimed, in great wrath. After a slight pause, he added, "I supposed you thought more of yourself; that you felt above the insults of such puppies."

I replied, "If he is a puppy I am a puppy, for we are both of the negro race. It is right and honorable for us to love each other. The man you call a puppy never insulted me, sir; and he would not love me if he did not believe me to be a virtuous woman."

He sprang upon me like a tiger, and gave me a stunning blow. It was the first time he had ever struck me; and fear did not enable me to control my anger. When I had recovered a little from the effects, I exclaimed, "You have struck me for answering you honestly. How I despise you!"

There was silence for some minutes. Perhaps he was deciding what should be my punishment; or, perhaps, he wanted to give me time to reflect on what I had said, and to whom I had said it. Finally, he asked, "Do you know what you have said?"

"Yes, sir; but your treatment drove me to it."

"Do you know that I have a right to do as I like with you,—that I can kill you, if I please?"

"You have tried to kill me, and I wish you had; but you have no right to do as you like with me."

"Silence!" he exclaimed, in a thundering voice. "By heavens, girl, you forget yourself too far! Are you mad? If you are, I will soon bring you to your senses. Do you think any other master would bear what I have borne from you this morning? Many masters would have killed you on the spot. How would you like to be sent to jail for your insolence?"

"I know I have been disrespectful, sir," I replied; "but you drove me to it; I couldn't help it. As for the jail, there would be more peace for me there than there is here."

"You deserve to go there," he said, "and to be under such treatment, that you would forget the meaning of the word *peace*. It would do you good. It would take some of your high notions out of you. But I am not ready to send you there yet, notwithstanding your ingratitude for all my kindness and forbearance. You have been the plague of my life. I have wanted to make you happy, and I have been repaid with the basest ingratitude; but though you have proved yourself incapable of appreciating my kindness, I will be lenient towards you, Linda. I will give you one more chance to redeem your character. If you behave yourself and do as I require, I will forgive you and treat you as I always have done; but if you disobey me, I will punish you as I would the meanest slave on my plantation. Never let me hear that fellow's name mentioned again. If I ever know of your speaking to him, I will cowhide you both; and if I catch him lurking about my premises, I will shoot him as soon as I would a dog. Do you hear what I say? I'll teach you a lesson about marriage and free niggers! Now go, and let this be the last time I have occasion to speak to you on this subject."

Reader, did you ever hate? I hope not. I never did but once; and I trust I never shall again. Somebody has called it "the atmosphere of hell;" and I believe it is so.

For a fortnight the doctor did not speak to me. He thought to mortify me; to make me feel that I had disgraced myself by receiving the honorable addresses of a respectable colored man, in preference to the base proposals of a white man. But though his lips disdained to address me, his eyes were very loquacious. No animal ever watched its prey more narrowly than he watched me. He knew that I could write, though he had failed to make me read his letters; and he was now troubled lest I should exchange letters with another man. After a while he became weary of silence; and I was sorry for it. One morning, as he passed through the hall, to leave the house, he contrived to thrust a note into my hand. I thought I had better read it, and spare myself the vexation of having him read it to me. It expressed regret for the blow he had given me, and reminded me that I myself was wholly to blame for it. He hoped I had become convinced of the injury I was doing myself by incurring his displeasure. He wrote that he had made up his mind to go to Louisiana; that he should take several slaves with him, and intended I should be one of the number. My mistress would remain where she was; therefore I should have nothing to fear from that quarter. If I merited kindness from him, he assured me that it would be lavishly bestowed. He begged me to think over the matter, and answer the following day.

The next morning I was called to carry a pair of scissors to his room. I laid them on the table, with the letter beside them. He thought it was my answer, and did not call me back. I went as usual to attend my young mistress to and from school. He met me in the street, and ordered me to stop at his office on my way back. When I entered, he showed me his letter, and asked me why I had not answered it. I replied, "I am your daughter's property, and it is in your power to send me, or take me, wherever you please." He said he was very glad to find me so willing to go, and that we should start early in the autumn. He had a large practice in the town, and I rather thought he had made up the story merely to frighten me. However that might be, I was determined that I would never go to Louisiana with him.

Summer passed away, and early in the autumn, Dr. Flint's eldest son was sent to Louisiana to examine the country, with a view to emigrating. That news did not disturb me. I knew very well that I should not be sent with *him*. That I had not been taken to the plantation before this time, was owing to the fact that his son was there. He was jealous of his son; and jealousy of the overseer had kept him from punishing me by sending me into the fields to work. Is it strange that I was not proud of these protectors? As for the overseer, he was a man for whom I had less respect than I had for a bloodhound.

Young Mr. Flint did not bring back a favorable report of Louisiana, and I heard no more of that scheme. Soon after this, my lover met me at the corner of the street, and I stopped to speak to him. Looking up, I saw my master watching us from his window. I hurried home, trembling with fear. I was sent for, immediately, to go to his room. He met me with a blow. "When is mistress to be married?" said he, in a sneering tone. A shower of oaths and imprecations followed. How thankful I was that my lover was a free man! that my tyrant had no power to flog him for speaking to me in the street!

Again and again I revolved in my mind how all this would end. There was no hope that the doctor would consent to sell me on any terms. He had an iron will, and was determined to keep me, and to conquer me. My lover was an intelligent and religious man. Even if he could have obtained permission to marry me while I was a slave, the marriage would give him no power to protect me from my master. It would have made him miserable to witness the insults I should have been subjected to. And then, if we had children, I knew they must "follow the condition of the mother."[2] What a terrible blight that would be on the heart of a free, intelligent father! For *his* sake, I felt that I ought not to link his fate with my own unhappy destiny. He was going to Savannah to see about a little property left him by an uncle; and hard as it was to bring my feelings to it, I earnestly entreated him not to come back. I advised him to go to the Free States, where his tongue would not be tied, and where his intelligence would be of more avail to him. He left me, still hoping the day would come when I could be bought. With me the lamp of hope had gone out. The dream of my girlhood was over. I felt lonely and desolate.

Still I was not stripped of all. I still had my good grandmother, and my affectionate brother. When he put his arms round my neck, and looked into my eyes, as if to read there the troubles I dared not tell, I felt that I still had something to love. But even that pleasant emotion was chilled by the reflection that he might be torn from me at any moment, by some sudden freak of my master. If he had known how we love each other, I think he would have exulted in separating us. We often planned together how we could get to the north. But, as William remarked, such things are easier said than done. My movements were very closely watched, and we had no means of getting any money to defray our expenses. As for grandmother, she was strongly opposed to her children's undertaking any such project. She had not forgotten poor Benjamin's sufferings[3] and she was afraid that if another child tried to escape, he would have a similar or a worse fate. To me, nothing seemed more dreadful than my present life. I said to myself, "William *must* be free. He shall go to the north, and I will follow him." Many a slave sister has formed the same plans.

* * *

X. A Perilous Passage in the Slave Girl's Life

After my lover went away, Dr. Flint contrived a new plan. He seemed to have an idea that my fear of my mistress was his greatest obstacle. In the blandest tones, he told me that he was going to build a small house for me, in a secluded place, four miles away from the town. I shuddered; but I was constrained to listen, while he talked of his intention to give me a home of my own, and to make a lady of me. Hitherto, I had escaped my dreaded fate, by being in the midst of people. My grandmother had already had high words with my master about me. She had told him pretty plainly what she thought of his character, and there was considerable gossip in the neighborhood about our affairs, to which the open-mouthed jealousy of Mrs. Flint contributed not a little. When my master said he was going to build a house for me, and that he could do it with little trouble and expense, I was in hopes something would happen to frustrate his scheme; but I soon heard that the house was actually begun. I vowed before my Maker that I would never enter

2. In Southern law, the mother's legal status as slave or free determined the legal status of the child.

3. One of Brent's uncles, caught attempting to escape, was jailed for six months, then sold to a trader. He eventually escaped to New York City but never saw his mother again.

it. I had rather toil on the plantation from dawn till dark; I had rather live and die in jail, than drag on, from day to day, through such a living death. I was determined that the master, whom I so hated and loathed, who had blighted the prospects of my youth, and made my life a desert, should not, after my long struggle with him, succeed at last in trampling his victim under his feet. I would do any thing, every thing, for the sake of defeating him. What *could* I do? I thought and thought, till I became desperate, and made a plunge into the abyss.

And now, reader, I come to a period in my unhappy life, which I would gladly forget if I could. The remembrance fills me with sorrow and shame. It pains me to tell you of it; but I have promised to tell you the truth, and I will do it honestly, let it cost me what it may. I will not try to screen myself behind the plea of compulsion from a master; for it was not so. Neither can I plead ignorance or thoughtlessness. For years, my master had done his utmost to pollute my mind with foul images, and to destroy the pure principles inculcated by my grandmother, and the good mistress of my childhood. The influences of slavery had had the same effect on me that they had on other young girls; they had made me prematurely knowing, concerning the evil ways of the world. I knew what I did, and I did it with deliberate calculation.

But, O, ye happy women, whose purity has been sheltered from childhood, who have been free to choose the objects of your affection, whose homes are protected by law, do not judge the poor desolate slave girl too severely! If slavery had been abolished, I, also, could have married the man of my choice; I could have had a home shielded by the laws; and I should have been spared the painful task of confessing what I am now about to relate; but all my prospects had been blighted by slavery. I wanted to keep myself pure; and, under the most adverse circumstances, I tried hard to preserve my self-respect; but I was struggling alone in the powerful grasp of the demon Slavery; and the monster proved too strong for me. I felt as if I was forsaken by God and man; as if all my efforts must be frustrated; and I became reckless in my despair.

I have told you that Dr. Flint's persecutions and his wife's jealousy had given rise to some gossip in the neighborhood. Among others, it chanced that a white unmarried gentleman had obtained some knowledge of the circumstances in which I was placed. He knew my grandmother, and often spoke to me in the street. He became interested for me, and asked questions about my master, which I answered in part. He expressed a great deal of sympathy, and a wish to aid me. He constantly sought opportunities to see me, and wrote to me frequently. I was a poor slave girl, only fifteen years old.

So much attention from a superior person was, of course, flattering; for human nature is the same in all. I also felt grateful for his sympathy, and encouraged by his kind words. It seemed to me a great thing to have such a friend. By degrees, a more tender feeling crept into my heart. He was an educated and eloquent gentleman; too eloquent, alas, for the poor slave girl who trusted in him. Of course I saw whither all this was tending. I knew the impassable gulf between us; but to be an object of interest to a man who is not married, and who is not her master, is agreeable to the pride and feelings of a slave, if her miserable situation has left her any pride or sentiment. It seems less degrading to give one's self, than to submit to compulsion. There is something akin to freedom in having a lover who has no control over you, except that which he gains by kindness and attachment. A master may treat you as rudely as he pleases, and you dare not speak; moreover, the wrong does not seem so great with an unmarried man, as with one who has a wife to be made unhappy. There may be sophistry in all this; but the condition of a slave confuses all principles of morality, and, in fact, renders the practice of them impossible.

When I found that my master had actually begun to build the lonely cottage, other feelings mixed with those I have described. Revenge, and calculations of interest, were added to flattered vanity and sincere gratitude for kindness. I knew nothing would enrage Dr. Flint so much as to know that I favored another; and it was something to triumph over my tyrant even in that small way. I thought he would revenge himself by selling me, and I was sure my friend, Mr. Sands, would buy me.[4] He was a man of more generosity and feeling than my master, and I thought my freedom could be easily obtained from him. The crisis of my fate now came so near that I was desperate. I shuddered to think of being the mother of children that should be owned by my old tyrant. I knew that as soon as a new fancy took him, his victims were sold far off to get rid of them; especially if they had children. I had seen several women sold, with his babies at the breast. He never allowed his offspring by slaves to remain long in sight of himself and his wife. Of a man who was not my master I could ask to have my children well supported; and in this case, I felt confident I should obtain the boon. I also felt quite sure that they would be made free. With all these thoughts revolving in my mind, and seeing no other way of escaping the doom I so much dreaded, I made a headlong plunge. Pity me, and pardon me, O virtuous reader! You never knew what it is to be a slave; to be entirely unprotected by law or custom; to have the laws reduce you to the condition of a chattel, entirely subject to the will of another. You never exhausted your ingenuity in avoiding the snares, and eluding the power of a hated tyrant; you never shuddered at the sound of his footsteps, and trembled within hearing of his voice. I know I did wrong. No one can feel it more sensibly than I do. The painful and humiliating memory will haunt me to my dying day. Still, in looking back, calmly, on the events of my life, I feel that the slave woman ought not to be judged by the same standard as others.

The months passed on. I had many unhappy hours. I secretly mourned over the sorrow I was bringing on my grandmother, who had so tried to shield me from harm. I knew that I was the greatest comfort of her old age, and that it was a source of pride to her that I had not degraded myself, like most of the slaves. I wanted to confess to her that I was no longer worthy of her love; but I could not utter the dreaded words.

As for Dr. Flint, I had a feeling of satisfaction and triumph in the thought of telling *him*. From time to time he told me of his intended arrangements, and I was silent. At last, he came and told me the cottage was completed, and ordered me to go to it. I told him I would never enter it. He said, "I have heard enough of such talk as that. You shall go, if you are carried by force; and you shall remain there."

I replied, "I will never go there. In a few months I shall be a mother."

He stood and looked at me in dumb amazement, and left the house without a word. I thought I should be happy in my triumph over him. But now that

4. Brent misjudged Flint, who becomes even more possessive when he learns of her relationship with Sands.

the truth was out, and my relatives would hear of it, I felt wretched. Humble as were their circumstances, they had pride in my good character. Now, how could I look them in the face? My self-respect was gone! I had resolved that I would be virtuous, though I was a slave. I had said, "Let the storm beat! I will brave it till I die." And now, how humiliated I felt!

I went to my grandmother. My lips moved to make confession, but the words stuck in my throat. I sat down in the shade of a tree at her door and began to sew. I think she saw something unusual was the matter with me. The mother of slaves is very watchful. She knows there is no security for her children. After they have entered their teens she lives in daily expectation of trouble. This leads to many questions. If the girl is of a sensitive nature, timidity keeps her from answering truthfully, and this well-meant course has a tendency to drive her from maternal counsels. Presently, in came my mistress, like a mad woman, and accused me concerning her husband. My grandmother, whose suspicions had been previously awakened, believed what she said. She exclaimed, "O Linda! has it come to this? I had rather see you dead than to see you as you now are. You are a disgrace to your dead mother." She tore from my fingers my mother's wedding ring and her silver thimble. "Go away!" she exclaimed, "and never come to my house, again." Her reproaches fell so hot and heavy, that they left me no chance to answer. Bitter tears, such as the eyes never shed but once, were my only answer. I rose from my seat, but fell back again, sobbing. She did not speak to me; but the tears were running down her furrowed cheeks, and they scorched me like fire. She had always been so kind to me! *So* kind! How I longed to throw myself at her feet, and tell her all the truth! But she had ordered me to go, and never to come there again. After a few minutes, I mustered strength, and started to obey her. With what feelings did I now close that little gate, which I used to open with such an eager hand in my childhood! It closed upon me with a sound I never heard before.

Where could I go? I was afraid to return to my master's. I walked on recklessly, not caring where I went, or what would become of me. When I had gone four or five miles, fatigue compelled me to stop. I sat down on the stump of an old tree. The stars were shining through the boughs above me. How they mocked me, with their bright, calm light! The hours passed by, and as I sat there alone a chilliness and deadly sickness came over me. I sank on the ground. My mind was full of horrid thoughts. I prayed to die; but the prayer was not answered. At last, with great effort I roused myself, and walked some distance further, to the house of a woman who had been a friend of my mother. When I told her why I was there, she spoke soothingly to me; but I could not be comforted. I thought I could bear my shame if I could only be reconciled to my grandmother. I longed to open my heart to her. I thought if she could know the real state of the case, and all I had been bearing for years, she would perhaps judge me less harshly. My friend advised me to send for her. I did so; but days of agonizing suspense passed before she came. Had she utterly forsaken me? No. She came at last. I knelt before her, and told her the things that had poisoned my life; how long I had been persecuted; that I saw no way of escape; and in an hour of extremity I had become desperate. She listened in silence. I told her I would bear any thing and do any thing, if in time I had hopes of obtaining her forgiveness. I begged of her to pity me, for my dead mother's sake. And she did pity me.

She did not say, "I forgive you;" but she looked at me lovingly, with her eyes full of tears. She laid her old hand gently on my head, and murmured, "Poor child! Poor child!"

* * *

XIV. Another Link to Life

I had not returned to my master's house since the birth of my child. The old man raved to have me thus removed from his immediate power; but his wife vowed, by all that was good and great, she would kill me if I came back; and he did not doubt her word. Sometimes he would stay away for a season. Then he would come and renew the old threadbare discourse about his forbearance and my ingratitude. He labored, most unnecessarily, to convince me that I had lowered myself. The venomous old reprobate had no need of descanting on that theme. I felt humiliated enough. My unconscious babe was the ever-present witness of my shame. I listened with silent contempt when he talked about my having forfeited *his* good opinion; but I shed bitter tears that I was no longer worthy of being respected by the good and pure. Alas! slavery still held me in its poisonous grasp. There was no chance for me to be respectable. There was no prospect of being able to lead a better life.

Sometimes, when my master found that I still refused to accept what he called his kind offers, he would threaten to sell my child. "Perhaps that will humble you," said he.

Humble *me*! Was I not already in the dust?[5] But his threat lacerated my heart. I knew the law gave him power to fulfill it; for slaveholders have been cunning enough to enact that "the child shall follow the condition of the *mother*," not of the *father*; thus taking care that licentiousness shall not interfere with avarice. This reflection made me clasp my innocent babe all the more firmly to my heart. Horrid visions passed through my mind when I thought of his liability to fall into the slave trader's hands. I wept over him, and said, "O my child! perhaps they will leave you in some cold cabin to die, and then throw you into a hole, as if you were a dog."

When Dr. Flint learned that I was again to be a mother, he was exasperated beyond measure. He rushed from the house, and returned with a pair of shears. I had a fine head of hair; and he often railed about my pride of arranging it nicely. He cut every hair close to my head, storming and swearing all the time. I replied to some of his abuse, and he struck me. Some months before, he had pitched me down stairs in a fit of passion; and the injury I received was so serious that I was unable to turn myself in bed for many days. He then said, "Linda, I swear by God I will never raise my hand against you again;" but I knew that he would forget his promise.

After he discovered my situation, he was like a restless spirit from the pit. He came every day; and I was subjected to such insults as no pen can describe. I would not describe them if I could; they were too low, too revolting. I tried to keep them from my grandmother's knowledge as much as I could. I knew she had enough to sadden her life, without having my troubles to bear. When she saw the doctor treat me with violence, and heard him utter oaths terrible enough to palsy a man's tongue, she could not always hold her

5. Job 42.6.

peace. It was natural and motherlike that she should try to defend me; but it only made matters worse.

When they told me my new-born babe was a girl, my heart was heavier than it had ever been before. Slavery is terrible for men; but it is far more terrible for women. Superadded to the burden common to all, *they* have wrongs, and sufferings, and mortifications peculiarly their own.

Dr. Flint had sworn that he would make me suffer, to my last day, for this new crime against *him*, as he called it; and as long as he had me in his power he kept his word. On the fourth day after the birth of my babe, he entered my room suddenly, and commanded me to rise and bring my baby to him. The nurse who took care of me had gone out of the room to prepare some nourishment, and I was alone. There was no alternative. I rose, took up my babe, and crossed the room to where he sat. "Now stand there," said he, "till I tell you to go back!" My child bore a strong resemblance to her father, and to the deceased Mrs. Sands, her grandmother. He noticed this; and while I stood before him, trembling with weakness, he heaped upon me and my little one every vile epithet he could think of. Even the grandmother in her grave did not escape his curses. In the midst of his vituperations I fainted at his feet. This recalled him to his senses. He took the baby from my arms, laid it on the bed, dashed cold water in my face, took me up, and shook me violently, to restore my consciousness before any one entered the room. Just then my grandmother came in, and he hurried out of the house. I suffered in consequence of this treatment; but I begged my friends to let me die, rather than send for the doctor. There was nothing I dreaded so much as his presence. My life was spared; and I was glad for the sake of my little ones. Had it not been for these ties to life, I should have been glad to be released by death, though I had lived only nineteen years.

Always it gave me a pang that my children had no lawful claim to a name. Their father offered his; but, if I had wished to accept the offer, I dared not while my master lived. Moreover, I knew it would not be accepted at their baptism. A Christian name they were at least entitled to; and we resolved to call my boy for our dear good Benjamin, who had gone far away from us.

My grandmother belonged to the church, and she was very desirous of having the children christened. I knew Dr. Flint would forbid it, and I did not venture to attempt it. But chance favored me. He was called to visit a patient out of town, and was obliged to be absent during Sunday. "Now is the time," said my grandmother; "we will take the children to church, and have them christened."

When I entered the church, recollections of my mother came over me, and I felt subdued in spirit. There she had presented me for baptism, without any reason to feel ashamed. She had been married, and had such legal rights as slavery allows a slave. The vows had at least been sacred to *her*, and she had never violated them. I was glad she was not alive, to know under what different circumstances her grandchildren were presented for baptism. Why had my lot been so different from my mother's? *Her* master had died when she was a child; and she remained with her mistress till she married. She was never in the power of any master; and thus she escaped one class of the evils that generally fall upon slaves.

When my baby was about to be christened, the former mistress of my father stepped up to me, and proposed to give it her Christian name. To this

I added the surname of my father, who had himself no legal right to it; for my grandfather on the paternal side was a white gentleman. What tangled skeins are the genealogies of slavery![6] I loved my father; but it mortified me to be obliged to bestow his name on my children.

When we left the church, my father's old mistress invited me to go home with her. She clasped a gold chain around my baby's neck. I thanked her for this kindness; but I did not like the emblem. I wanted no chain to be fastened on my daughter, not even if its links were of gold. How earnestly I prayed that she might never feel the weight of slavery's chain, whose iron entereth into the soul.

* * *

XXI. The Loophole of Retreat[7]

A small shed had been added to my grandmother's house years ago. Some boards were laid across the joists at the top, and between these boards and the roof was a very small garret, never occupied by any thing but rats and mice. It was a pent roof, covered with nothing but shingles, according to the southern custom for such buildings. The garret was only nine feet long and seven wide. The highest part was three feet high, and sloped down abruptly to the loose board floor. There was no admission for either light or air. My uncle Phillip, who was a carpenter, had very skilfully made a concealed trap-door, which communicated with the storeroom. He had been doing this while I was waiting in the swamp. The storeroom opened upon a piazza. To this hole I was conveyed as soon as I entered the house. The air was stifling; the darkness total. A bed had been spread on the floor. I could sleep quite comfortably on one side; but the slope was so sudden that I could not turn on the other without hitting the roof. The rats and mice ran over my bed; but I was weary, and I slept such sleep as the wretched may, when a tempest has passed over them. Morning came. I knew it only by the noises I heard; for in my small den day and night were all the same. I suffered for air even more than for light. But I was not comfortless. I heard the voices of my children. There was joy and there was sadness in the sound. It made my tears flow. How I longed to speak to them! I was eager to look on their faces; but there was no hole, no crack, through which I could peep. This continued darkness was oppressive. It seemed horrible to sit or lie in a cramped position day after day, without one gleam of light. Yet I would have chosen this, rather than my lot as a slave, though white people considered it an easy one; and it was so compared with the fate of others. I was never cruelly over-worked; I was never lacerated with the whip from head to foot; I was never so beaten and bruised that I could not turn from one side to the other; I never had my heel-strings cut to prevent my running away; I was never chained to a log and forced to drag it about, while I toiled in the fields from morning till night; I was never branded with hot iron, or torn by bloodhounds. On the contrary, I had always been kindly treated, and tenderly cared for, until I came into the hands of Dr. Flint.

6. Jacobs stresses her mixed-race parentage not to claim that she is really white but to show the arbitrariness and absurdity of racial distinctions.

7. From *The Task* 4.88–90, a popular long poem (1785) by the English poet William Cowper (1731–1800). By this point in the narrative Brent has escaped from the Flint household and is hiding in a crawl space beneath the roof of her grandmother's house. The account states that she remains there for seven years.

I had never wished for freedom till then. But though my life in slavery was comparatively devoid of hardships, God pity the woman who is compelled to lead such a life!

My food was passed up to me through the trap-door my uncle had contrived; and my grandmother, my uncle Phillip, and aunt Nancy would seize such opportunities as they could, to mount up there and chat with me at the opening. But of course this was not safe in the daytime. It must all be done in darkness. It was impossible for me to move in an erect position, but I crawled about my den for exercise. One day I hit my head against something, and found it was a gimlet.[8] My uncle had left it sticking there when he made the trap-door. I was as rejoiced as Robinson Crusoe[9] could have been at finding such a treasure. It put a lucky thought into my head. I said to myself, "Now I will have some light. Now I will see my children." I did not dare to begin my work during the daytime, for fear of attracting attention. But I groped round; and having found the side next the street, where I could frequently see my children, I struck the gimlet in and waited for evening. I bored three rows of holes, one above another; then I bored out the interstices between. I thus succeeded in making one hole about an inch long and an inch broad. I sat by it till late into the night, to enjoy the little whiff of air that floated in. In the morning I watched for my children. The first person I saw in the street was Dr. Flint. I had a shuddering, superstitious feeling that it was a bad omen. Several familiar faces passed by. At last I heard the merry laugh of children, and presently two sweet little faces were looking up at me, as though they knew I was there, and were conscious of the joy they imparted. How I longed to *tell* them I was there!

My condition was now a little improved. But for weeks I was tormented by hundreds of little red insects, fine as a needle's point, that pierced through my skin, and produced an intolerable burning. The good grandmother gave me herb teas and cooling medicines, and finally I got rid of them. The heat of my den was intense, for nothing but thin shingles protected me from the scorching summer's sun. But I had my consolations. Through my peeping-hole I could watch the children, and when they were near enough, I could hear their talk. Aunt Nancy brought me all the news she could hear at Dr. Flint's. From her I learned that the doctor had written to New York to a colored woman, who had been born and raised in our neighborhood, and had breathed his contaminating atmosphere. He offered her a reward if she could find out any thing about me. I know not what was the nature of her reply; but he soon after started for New York in haste, saying to his family that he had business of importance to transact. I peeped at him as he passed on his way to the steamboat. It was a satisfaction to have miles of land and water between us, even for a little while; and it was a still greater satisfaction to know that he believed me to be in the Free States. My little den seemed less dreary than it had done. He returned, as he did from his former journey to New York, without obtaining any satisfactory information. When he passed our house next morning, Benny was standing at the gate. He had heard them say that he had gone to find me, and he called out, "Dr. Flint, did you bring my mother home? I want to see her." The doctor stamped his foot at him in a

8. Small tool for boring holes.
9. Hero of a novel of the same name (1719) by the English writer Daniel Defoe (1660–1731) about a man shipwrecked on a desert island.

rage, and exclaimed, "Get out of the way, you little damned rascal! If you don't, I'll cut off your head."

Benny ran terrified into the house, saying, "You can't put me in jail again. I don't belong to you now." It was well that the wind carried the words away from the doctor's ear. I told my grandmother of it, when we had our next conference at the trap-door; and begged of her not to allow the children to be impertinent to the irascible old man.

Autumn came, with a pleasant abatement of heat. My eyes had become accustomed to the dim light, and by holding my book or work in a certain position near the aperture I contrived to read and sew. That was a great relief to the tedious monotony of my life. But when winter came, the cold penetrated through the thin shingle roof, and I was dreadfully chilled. The winters there are not so long, or so severe, as in northern latitudes; but the houses are not built to shelter from cold, and my little den was peculiarly comfortless. The kind grandmother brought me bed-clothes and warm drinks. Often I was obliged to lie in bed all day to keep comfortable; but with all my precautions, my shoulders and feet were frostbitten. O, those long, gloomy days, with no object for my eye to rest upon, and no thoughts to occupy my mind, except the dreary past and the uncertain future! I was thankful when there came a day sufficiently mild for me to wrap myself up and sit at the loophole to watch the passers by. Southerners have the habit of stopping and talking in the streets, and I heard many conversations not intended to meet my ears. I heard slave-hunters planning how to catch some poor fugitive. Several times I heard allusions to Dr. Flint, myself, and the history of my children, who, perhaps, were playing near the gate. One would say, "I wouldn't move my little finger to catch her, as old Flint's property." Another would say, "I'll catch *any* nigger for the reward. A man ought to have what belongs to him, if he *is* a damned brute." The opinion was often expressed that I was in the Free States. Very rarely did any one suggest that I might be in the vicinity. Had the least suspicion rested on my grandmother's house, it would have been burned to the ground. But it was the last place they thought of. Yet there was no place, where slavery existed, that could have afforded me so good a place of concealment.

Dr. Flint and his family repeatedly tried to coax and bribe my children to tell something they had heard said about me. One day the doctor took them into a shop, and offered them some bright little silver pieces and gay handkerchiefs if they would tell where their mother was. Ellen shrank away from him, and would not speak; but Benny spoke up, and said, "Dr. Flint, I don't know where my mother is. I guess she's in New York; and when you go there again, I wish you'd ask her to come home, for I want to see her; but if you put her in jail, or tell her you'll cut her head off, I'll tell her to go right back."

* * *

XLI. Free at Last[1]

Mrs. Bruce, and every member of her family, were exceedingly kind to me. I was thankful for the blessings of my lot, yet I could not always wear a cheerful

1. This is the final chapter of *Incidents*. Having escaped from the South on a ship headed to Philadelphia, Brent finds employment with the Bruce family of New York City, but she remains in constant fear of being returned to the South under the provisions of the Fugitive Slave Act of 1793.

countenance. I was doing harm to no one; on the contrary, I was doing all the good I could in my small way; yet I could never go out to breathe God's free air without trepidation at my heart. This seemed hard; and I could not think it was a right state of things in any civilized country.

From time to time I received news from my good old grandmother. She could not write; but she employed others to write for her. The following is an extract from one of her last letters:—

> "Dear Daughter: I cannot hope to see you again on earth; but I pray to God to unite us above, where pain will no more rack this feeble body of mine; where sorrow and parting from my children will be no more.[2] God has promised these things if we are faithful unto the end. My age and feeble health deprive me of going to church now; but God is with me here at home. Thank your brother for his kindness. Give much love to him, and tell him to remember the Creator in the days of his youth,[3] and strive to meet me in the Father's kingdom. Love to Ellen and Benjamin. Don't neglect him. Tell him for me, to be a good boy. Strive, my child, to train them for God's children. May he protect and provide for you, is the prayer of your loving old mother."

These letters both cheered and saddened me. I was always glad to have tidings from the kind, faithful old friend of my unhappy youth; but her messages of love made my heart yearn to see her before she died, and I mourned over the fact that it was impossible. Some months after I returned from my flight to New England, I received a letter from her, in which she wrote, "Dr. Flint is dead. He has left a distressed family. Poor old man! I hope he made his peace with God."

I remembered how he had defrauded my grandmother of the hard earnings she had loaned; how he had tried to cheat her out of the freedom her mistress had promised her, and how he had persecuted her children; and I thought to myself that she was a better Christian than I was, if she could entirely forgive him. I cannot say, with truth, that the news of my old master's death softened my feelings towards him. There are wrongs which even the grave does not bury. The man was odious to me while he lived, and his memory is odious now.

His departure from this world did not diminish my danger. He had threatened my grandmother that his heirs should hold me in slavery after he was gone; that I never should be free so long as a child of his survived. As for Mrs. Flint, I had seen her in deeper afflictions than I supposed the loss of her husband would be, for she had buried several children; yet I never saw any signs of softening in her heart. The doctor had died in embarrassed circumstances, and had little to will to his heirs, except such property as he was unable to grasp. I was well aware what I had to expect from the family of Flints; and my fears were confirmed by a letter from the south, warning me to be on my guard, because Mrs. Flint openly declared that her daughter could not afford to lose so valuable a slave as I was.

I kept close watch of the newspapers for arrivals; but one Saturday night, being much occupied, I forgot to examine the Evening Express as usual.

2. Paraphrase of Revelation 21.4.

3. Ecclesiastes 12.1.

I went down into the parlor for it, early in the morning, and found the boy about to kindle a fire with it. I took it from him and examined the list of arrivals. Reader, if you have never been a slave, you cannot imagine the acute sensation of suffering at my heart, when I read the names of Mr. and Mrs. Dodge,[4] at a hotel in Courtland Street. It was a third-rate hotel, and that circumstance convinced me of the truth of what I had heard, that they were short of funds and had need of my value, as *they* valued me; and that was by dollars and cents. I hastened with the paper to Mrs. Bruce. Her heart and hand were always open to every one in distress, and she always warmly sympathized with mine. It was impossible to tell how near the enemy was. He might have passed and repassed the house while we were sleeping. He might at that moment be waiting to pounce upon me if I ventured out of doors. I had never seen the husband of my young mistress, and therefore I could not distinguish him from any other stranger. A carriage was hastily ordered; and, closely veiled, I followed Mrs. Bruce, taking the baby again with me into exile. After various turnings and crossings, and returnings, the carriage stopped at the house of one of Mrs. Bruce's friends, where I was kindly received. Mrs. Bruce returned immediately, to instruct the domestics what to say if any one came to inquire for me.

It was lucky for me that the evening paper was not burned up before I had a chance to examine the list of arrivals. It was not long after Mrs. Bruce's return to her house, before several people came to inquire for me. One inquired for me, another asked for my daughter Ellen, and another said he had a letter from my grandmother, which he was requested to deliver in person.

They were told, "She *has* lived here, but she has left."

"How long ago?"

"I don't know, sir."

"Do you know where she went?"

"I do not, sir." And the door was closed.

This Mr. Dodge, who claimed me as his property, was originally a Yankee pedler in the south; then he became a merchant, and finally a slaveholder. He managed to get introduced into what was called the first society, and married Miss Emily Flint. A quarrel arose between him and her brother, and the brother cowhided him. This led to a family feud, and he proposed to remove to Virginia. Dr. Flint left him no property, and his own means had become circumscribed, while a wife and children depended upon him for support. Under these circumstances, it was very natural that he should make an effort to put me into his pocket.

I had a colored friend, a man from my native place, in whom I had the most implicit confidence. I sent for him, and told him that Mr. and Mrs. Dodge had arrived in New York. I proposed that he should call upon them to make inquiries about his friends at the south, with whom Dr. Flint's family were well acquainted. He thought there was no impropriety in his doing so, and he consented. He went to the hotel, and knocked at the door of Mr. Dodge's room, which was opened by the gentleman himself, who gruffly inquired, "What brought you here? How came you to know I was in the city?"

4. Dodge is the married name of Emily Flint, Brent's legal owner.

"Your arrival was published in the evening papers, sir; and I called to ask Mrs. Dodge about my friends at home. I didn't suppose it would give any offence."

"Where's that negro girl, that belongs to my wife?"

"What girl, sir?"

"You know well enough. I mean Linda, that ran away from Dr. Flint's plantation, some years ago. I dare say you've seen her, and know where she is."

"Yes, sir, I've seen her, and know where she is. She is out of your reach, sir."

"Tell me where she is, or bring her to me, and I will give her a chance to buy her freedom."

"I don't think it would be of any use, sir. I have heard her say she would go to the ends of the earth, rather than pay any man or woman for her freedom, because she thinks she has a right to it. Besides, she couldn't do it, if she would, for she has spent her earnings to educate her children."

This made Mr. Dodge very angry, and some high words passed between them. My friend was afraid to come where I was; but in the course of the day I received a note from him. I supposed they had not come from the south, in the winter, for a pleasure excursion; and now the nature of their business was very plain.

Mrs. Bruce came to me and entreated me to leave the city the next morning. She said her house was watched, and it was possible that some clew to me might be obtained. I refused to take her advice. She pleaded with an earnest tenderness, that ought to have moved me; but I was in a bitter, disheartened mood. I was weary of flying from pillar to post. I had been chased during half my life, and it seemed as if the chase was never to end. There I sat, in that great city, guiltless of crime, yet not daring to worship God in any of the churches. I heard the bells ringing for afternoon service, and, with contemptuous sarcasm, I said, "Will the preachers take for their text, 'Proclaim liberty to the captive, and the opening of prison doors to them that are bound'?[5] or will they preach from the text, 'Do unto others as ye would they should do unto you'?"[6] Oppressed Poles and Hungarians could find a safe refuge in that city; John Mitchell[7] was free to proclaim in the City Hall his desire for "a plantation well stocked with slaves;" but there I sat, an oppressed American, not daring to show my face. God forgive the black and bitter thoughts I indulged on that Sabbath day! The Scripture says, "Oppression makes even a wise man mad;"[8] and I was not wise.

I had been told that Mr. Dodge said his wife had never signed away her right to my children, and if he could not get me, he would take them. This it was, more than any thing else, that roused such a tempest in my soul. Benjamin was with his uncle William in California, but my innocent young daughter had come to spend a vacation with me. I thought of what I had suffered in slavery at her age, and my heart was like a tiger's when a hunter tries to seize her young.

5. Isaiah 61.1.

6. Matthew 7.12.

7. Irish American (1815–1875) who founded the proslavery New York newspaper *The Citizen* and who argued that free blacks would take the jobs of Irish workers. "Poles and Hungarians": following the failed European revolutions of 1848, many political refugees settled in New York City and New England.

8. Ecclesiastes 7.7.

Dear Mrs. Bruce! I seem to see the expression of her face, as she turned away discouraged by my obstinate mood. Finding her expostulations unavailing, she sent Ellen to entreat me. When ten o'clock in the evening arrived and Ellen had not returned, this watchful and unwearied friend became anxious. She came to us in a carriage, bringing a well-filled trunk for my journey—trusting that by this time I would listen to reason. I yielded to her, as I ought to have done before.

The next day, baby and I set out in a heavy snow storm, bound for New England again. I received letters from the City of Iniquity,[9] addressed to me under an assumed name. In a few days one came from Mrs. Bruce, informing me that my new master was still searching for me, and that she intended to put an end to this persecution by buying my freedom. I felt grateful for the kindness that prompted this offer, but the idea was not so pleasant to me as might have been expected. The more my mind had become enlightened, the more difficult it was for me to consider myself an article of property; and to pay money to those who had so grievously oppressed me seemed like taking from my sufferings the glory of triumph. I wrote to Mrs. Bruce, thanking her, but saying that being sold from one owner to another seemed too much like slavery; that such a great obligation could not be easily cancelled; and that I preferred to go to my brother in California.

Without my knowledge, Mrs. Bruce employed a gentleman in New York to enter into negotiations with Mr. Dodge. He proposed to pay three hundred dollars down, if Mr. Dodge would sell me, and enter into obligations to relinquish all claim to me or my children forever after. He who called himself my master said he scorned so small an offer for such a valuable servant. The gentleman replied, "You can do as you choose, sir. If you reject this offer you will never get any thing; for the woman has friends who will convey her and her children out of the country."

Mr. Dodge concluded that "half a loaf was better than no bread," and he agreed to the proffered terms. By the next mail I received this brief letter from Mrs. Bruce: "I am rejoiced to tell you that the money for your freedom has been paid to Mr. Dodge. Come home to-morrow. I long to see you and my sweet babe."

My brain reeled as I read these lines. A gentleman near me said, "It's true; I have seen the bill of sale." "The bill of sale!" Those words struck me like a blow. So I was *sold* at last! A human being *sold* in the free city of New York! The bill of sale is on record, and future generations will learn from it that women were articles of traffic in New York, late in the nineteenth century of the Christian religion. It may hereafter prove a useful document to antiquaries, who are seeking to measure the progress of civilization in the United States. I well know the value of that bit of paper; but much as I love freedom, I do not like to look upon it. I am deeply grateful to the generous friend who procured it, but I despise the miscreant who demanded payment for what never rightfully belonged to him or his.

I had objected to having my freedom bought, yet I must confess that when it was done I felt as if a heavy load had been lifted from my weary

9. New York City, because it was the center of activity for hunters of fugitive slaves.

shoulders. When I rode home in the cars I was no longer afraid to unveil my face and look at people as they passed. I should have been glad to have met Daniel Dodge himself; to have had him seen me and known me, that he might have mourned over the untoward circumstances which compelled him to sell me for three hundred dollars.

When I reached home, the arms of my benefactress were thrown round me, and our tears mingled. As soon as she could speak, she said, "O Linda, I'm *so* glad it's all over! You wrote to me as if you thought you were going to be transferred from one owner to another. But I did not buy you for your services. I should have done just the same, if you had been going to sail for California tomorrow. I should, at least, have the satisfaction of knowing that you left me a free woman."

My heart was exceedingly full. I remembered how my poor father had tried to buy me, when I was a small child, and how he had been disappointed. I hoped his spirit was rejoicing over me now. I remembered how my good old grandmother had laid up her earnings to purchase me in later years, and how often her plans had been frustrated. How that faithful, loving old heart would leap for joy, if she could look on me and my children now that we were free! My relatives had been foiled in all their efforts, but God had raised me up a friend among strangers, who had bestowed on me the precious, long-desired boon. Friend! It is a common word, often lightly used. Like other good and beautiful things, it may be tarnished by careless handling; but when I speak of Mrs. Bruce as my friend, the word is sacred.

My grandmother lived to rejoice in my freedom; but not long after, a letter came with a black seal. She had gone "where the wicked cease from troubling, and the weary are at rest."[1]

Time passed on, and a paper came to me from the south, containing an obituary notice of my uncle Phillip. It was the only case I ever knew of such an honor conferred upon a colored person. It was written by one of his friends, and contained these words: "Now that death has laid him low, they call him a good man and a useful citizen; but what are eulogies to the black man, when the world has faded from his vision? It does not require man's praise to obtain rest in God's kingdom." So they called a colored man a *citizen!* Strange words to be uttered in that region![2]

Reader, my story ends with freedom; not in the usual way, with marriage.[3] I and my children are now free! We are as free from the power of slaveholders as are the white people of the north; and though that, according to my ideas, is not saying a great deal, it is a vast improvement in *my* condition. The dream of my life is not yet realized. I do not sit with my children in a home of my own. I still long for a hearthstone of my own, however humble. I wish it for my children's sake far more than for my own. But God so orders circumstances as to keep me with my friend Mrs. Bruce. Love, duty, gratitude, also bind me to her side. It is a privilege to serve her who pities my oppressed

1. Job 3.17.
2. Free blacks in North Carolina did not have the legal status of citizens.
3. Allusion to the way popular novels of the period typically ended with a happy marriage.

people, and who has bestowed the inestimable boon of freedom on me and my children.

It has been painful to me, in many ways, to recall the dreary years I passed in bondage. I would gladly forget them if I could. Yet the retrospection is not altogether without solace; for with those gloomy recollections come tender memories of my good old grandmother, like light, fleecy clouds floating over a dark and troubled sea.

1861

WILLIAM WELLS BROWN

1814–1884

One of the most renowned antislavery lecturers and reformers of the time, and the author of the first novel published by an African American, William Wells Brown was born into slavery on a plantation near Lexington, Kentucky, in 1814. His mother, Elizabeth, was a slave; his father was a white man, probably a relative of Dr. John Young, the owner of Elizabeth and her son. As a boy he spent several years in the Missouri territory with Young, and by 1827 he was living in St. Louis when Young purchased a farm there. After working a variety of jobs, ranging from house servant to assistant to the slave trader James Walker, Brown, accompanied by his mother, attempted to escape from slavery in 1833. Captured in Illinois, he was returned to Young and eventually sold to Enoch Price, a St. Louis merchant and steamboat owner. His mother, whom he would never see again, was sold and taken to New Orleans. Early in 1834, Brown made a second escape attempt, this time successful, traveling at night from Cincinnati to Cleveland and receiving invaluable assistance in Ohio from the Quakers Wells Brown and his wife. To celebrate his escape from slavery, William, who had been renamed "Sandford" when Young adopted a nephew named "William," reassumed his birth name and added to it the name of his Quaker benefactor. By the spring of 1834 Brown had a job on the Lake Erie steamer *Detroit*, and by the end of the summer he was married to the free black Elizabeth Schooner, with whom he would have two daughters. Over the next nine years he worked as a steamboatsman on Lake Erie, while surreptitiously helping fugitive slaves to escape to Canada.

Brown moved to Buffalo in 1836 and there initiated his career as a reformer, organizing and later serving as president of a black temperance society while continuing his work as a steamboatsman. He met Frederick Douglass at an antislavery convention in Buffalo in 1843, and that same year he began lecturing for the Western New York Anti-Slavery Society. In 1847 he moved to Boston to work as a paid lecturer for William Lloyd Garrison's Massachusetts Anti-Slavery Society. During the summer of 1847 Garrison published Brown's *Narrative of William W. Brown, A Fugitive Slave*, which rivaled Douglass's 1845 *Narrative* in popularity and consequently made him, as had been true for Douglass, a target for those who sought the cash bounty promised for returning fugitive slaves to their owners. Estranged from his wife, who would die in 1851, Brown traveled to Paris with his daughters to attend the 1849 International Peace Congress, subsequently toured Great Britain as an antislavery lecturer, and decided to stay in England when he learned that the Fugitive Slave Law had been approved by the U.S. Congress in 1850. After the British reformer Ellen Richardson (the same woman who had helped purchase Douglass's freedom in 1846) bought his manumission papers for $300, Brown was able to return to the United States in 1854.

Both before and after his manumission, Brown published widely, working in a number of genres. In addition to his 1847 *Narrative*, he published *A Lecture Delivered before the Female Anti-Slavery Society of Salem* (1847); *The Anti-Slavery Harp: A Collection of Songs for Anti-Slavery Meetings* (1848); a catalog description of antislavery drawings on canvas titled *A Description of William Wells Brown's Original Panoramic Views* (1850); a travel book, *Three Years in Europe* (1852); and the novel *Clotel; or, The President's Daughter* (1853). Brown would go on to publish three significantly revised versions of *Clotel—Miralda; or, The Beautiful Quadroon* (1860–61), *Clotelle: A Tale of the Southern States* (1864), and *Clotelle; or, The Colored Heroine* (1867)—three major histories of blacks in the United States, the play *The Escape; or A Leap for Freedom* (1857), several memoirs, and one of his most famous speeches, *St. Domingo: Its Revolution and Its Patriots* (1855). In a review of Brown's first history, *The Black Man, His Antecedents, His Genius, and His Achievements* (1863), Frederick Douglass hailed the book as a "valuable contribution to the colored literature of the country" and admiringly wondered "whence had this man this knowledge? He seems to have read and remembered nearly every thing which has been written or said respecting the ability of the negro." That extensive knowledge, which informed *Clotel* and other earlier works, would also come to inform his later histories, *The Negro in the American Rebellion* (1867) and *The Rising Son; or, The Antecedents and Advancement of the Colored Race* (1874). Brown's last published book, *My Southern Home* (1880), revisited the terrain of his earlier autobiographies, offering the hope for black and white reconciliation despite the failure of Reconstruction.

In his best known book, the novel *Clotel*, Brown engaged the ideological contradictions of a nation that celebrated itself as a bastion of republican freedom even as it continued to uphold the institution of slavery. Locating those contradictions in the founding father Thomas Jefferson, Brown conceived of Jefferson as both the father of the nation's egalitarian ideals, through his authorship of the Declaration of Independence, and the father of slaves, specifically the fictional Clotel and her sister, Althesa. For his depiction of Jefferson's fictional slave daughters, Brown took seriously the rumor that Jefferson, who owned a slave plantation in Virginia with approximately two hundred slaves, had had sexual relations and children with his slave Sally Hemings (DNA testing in 1998 and historical research suggest that the rumor had its source in fact). In addition to working with this rumor, Brown remarked in the closing chapter of *Clotel* that he created the novel by drawing on his personal experiences and wide reading, which he then "combined" into the narrative that "made up my story." Among the sources that he appropriated for *Clotel* were proslavery prayer books, Lydia Maria Child's 1842 short story "The Quadroons" (which can be found on pp. 183–90), a speech by Andrew Jackson, and numerous other discourses and texts that he artfully arranged and recontextualizd to suggest the limits of their truth-telling capacities and thus the limits (and blindnesses) of the dominant culture itself. As can be seen in the autobiographical selection printed here, Brown was something of a trickster. But he was also a shrewd cultural critic. In his various works, he presented himself as living proof of an African American's ability to become a learned man of letters capable of refuting a culture that denied blacks a basic recognition of their humanity.

From The Narrative of the Life and Escape of William Wells Brown[1]

[ESCAPE; SELF-EDUCATION]

* * *

It was winter-time; the day on which he started was the 1st of January, and, as it might be expected, it was intensely cold; he had no overcoat, no food, no friend, save the North Star, and the God which made it. How ardently must the love of freedom burn in the poor slave's bosom, when he will pass through so many difficulties, and even look death in the face, in winning his birth-right, freedom. But what crushed the poor slave's heart in his flight most was, not the want of food or clothing, but the thought that every white man was his deadly enemy. Even in the free states the prejudice against color is so strong, that there appears to exist a deadly antagonism between the white and coloured races.

William in his flight carried a tinder-box with him, and when he got very cold he would gather together dry leaves and stubble and make a fire, or certainly he would have perished. He was determined to enter into no house, fearing that he might meet a betrayer.

It must have been a picture which would have inspired an artist, to see the fugitive roasting the ears of corn that he found or took from barns during the night, at solitary fires in the deep solitudes of woods.

The suffering of the fugitive was greatly increased by the cold, from the fact of his having just come from the warm climate of New Orleans. Slaves seldom have more than one name, and William was not an exception to this, and the fugitive began to think of an additional name. A heavy rain of three days, in which it froze as fast as it fell, and by which the poor fugitive was completely drenched, and still more chilled, added to the depression of his spirits already created by his weary journey. Nothing but the fire of hope burning within his breast could have sustained him under such overwhelming trials,

> "Behind he left the whip and chains,
> Before him were sweet Freedom's plains."[2]

Through cold and hunger, William was now ill, and he could go no further. The poor fugitive resolved to seek protection, and accordingly hid himself in the woods near the road, until some one should pass. Soon a traveller came along, but the slave dared not speak. A few moments more and a second passed, the fugitive attempted to speak, but fear deprived him of voice. A third made his appearance. He wore a broad-brimmed hat and a long coat, and was evidently walking only for exercise. William scanned him well, and though not much skilled in physiognomy, he concluded he was the man.

1. From the first printing in the 1853 *Clotel*; Brown's third-person autobiographical narrative served as one of the prefaces to his novel. For this version of his autobiography, he drew on his 1847 *Narrative of William W. Brown, A Fugitive Slave*, while adding new material, such as an account, somewhat similar to Frederick Douglass's in his 1845 *Narrative*, of how he learned to read and write. This selection begins with Brown's efforts to escape from slavery in 1834. His master, Enoch Price, had docked his steamboat in Cincinnati, Ohio, and Brown, under cover of night, seeks to make his way to Cleveland.

2. From "The Flying Slave" (author unknown) in *The Anti-Slavery Harp* (1848), ed. William Wells Brown.

William approached him, and asked him if he knew any one who would help him, as he was sick? The gentleman asked whether he was not a slave. The poor slave hesitated; but, on being told that he had nothing to fear, he answered, "Yes." The gentleman told him he was in a pro-slaving neighbourhood, but, if he would wait a little, he would go and get a covered waggon, and convey him to his house. After he had gone, the fugitive meditated whether he should stay or not, being apprehensive that the broad-brimmed gentleman had gone for some one to assist him: he however concluded to remain.

After waiting about an hour—an hour big with fate to him—he saw the covered waggon making its appearance, and no one on it but the person he before accosted. Trembling with hope and fear, he entered the waggon, and was carried to the person's house. When he got there, he still halted between two opinions, whether he should enter or take to his heels; but he soon decided after seeing the glowing face of the wife. He saw something in her that bid him welcome, something that told him he would not be betrayed.

He soon found that he was under the shed of a Quaker, and a Quaker of the George Fox[3] stamp. He had heard of Quakers and their kindness; but was not prepared to meet with such hospitality as now greeted him. He saw nothing but kind looks, and heard nothing but tender words. He began to feel the pulsations of a new existence. White men always scorned him, but now a white benevolent woman felt glad to wait on him; it was a revolution in his experience. The table was loaded with good things, but he could not eat. If he were allowed the privilege of sitting in the kitchen, he thought he could do justice to the viands. The surprise being over his appetite soon returned.

"I have frequently been asked," says William, "how I felt upon finding myself regarded as a man by a white family; especially having just run away from one. I cannot say that I have ever answered the question yet. The fact that I was, in all probability, a freeman, sounded in my ears like a charm. I am satisfied that none but a slave could place such an appreciation upon liberty as I did at that time. I wanted to see my mother and sister, that I might tell them that 'I was free!' I wanted to see my fellow-slaves in St. Louis, and let them know that the chains were no longer upon my limbs. I wanted to see Captain Price, and let him learn from my own lips that I was no more a chattel, but a MAN. I was anxious, too, thus to inform Mrs. Price that she must get another coachman, and I wanted to see Eliza[4] more than I did Mr. Price or Mrs. Price. The fact that I was a freeman—could walk, talk, eat, and sleep as a man, and no one to stand over me with the blood-clotted cow-hide—all this made me feel that I was not myself."

The kind Quaker, who so hospitably entertained William, was called Wells Brown. He remained with him about a fortnight, during which time he was well fed and clothed. Before leaving, the Quaker asked him what was his name besides William? The fugitive told him he had no other. "Well," said he,

3. Fox (1624–1691), founder of the Quakers, or Society of Friends, a religious group known for its commitment to nonviolence and abolitionism.

4. According to Brown's 1847 *Narrative*, a maid belonging to the Enoch Price family. Mrs. Price hoped to secure Brown's loyalty by marrying him to Eliza.

"thee must have another name. Since thee has got out of slavery, thee has become a man, and men always have two names."

William told him that as he was the first man to extend the hand of friendship to him, he would give him the privilege of naming him.

"If I name thee," said he, "I shall call thee Wells Brown, like myself."

"But," said he, "I am not willing to lose my name of William. It was taken from me once against my will,[5] and I am not willing to part with it on any terms."

"Then," said the benevolent man, "I will call thee William Wells Brown."

"So be it," said William Wells Brown, and he has been known by this name ever since.

After giving the newly-christened freeman "a name," the Quaker gave him something to aid him to get "a local habitation."[6] So, after giving him some money, Brown again started for Canada. In four days he reached a public-house, and went in to warm himself. He soon found that he was not out of the reach of his enemies. While warming himself, he heard some men in an adjoining bar-room talking about some runaway slaves. He thought it was time to be off, and, suiting the action to the thought, he was soon in the woods out of sight. When night came, he returned to the road and walked on; and so, for two days and two nights, till he was faint and ready to perish of hunger.

In this condition he arrived in the town of Cleveland, Ohio, on the banks of Lake Erie, where he determined to remain until the spring of the year, and then to try and reach Canada. Here he was compelled to work merely for his food. "Having lived in that way," said he in a speech at a public meeting in Exeter Hall,[7] "for some weeks, I obtained a job, for which I received a shilling. This was not only the only shilling I had, but it was the first I had received after obtaining my freedom, and that shilling made me feel, indeed, as if I had a considerable stock in hand. What to do with my shilling I did not know. I would not put it into the bankers' hands, because, if they would have received it, I would not trust them. I would not lend it out, because I was afraid I should not get it back again. I carried the shilling in my pocket for some time, and finally resolved to lay it out; and after considerable thinking upon the subject, I laid out *6d.*[8] for a spelling-book, and the other *6d.* for sugar candy or barley sugar. Well, now, you will all say that the one *6d.* for the spelling-book was well laid out; and I am of opinion that the other was well laid out too; for the family in which I worked for my bread had two little boys, who attended the school every day, and I wanted to convert them into teachers; so I thought that nothing would act like a charm so much as a little barley sugar. The first day I got my book and stock in trade, I put the book into my bosom, and went to saw wood in the wood-house on a very cold day. One of the boys, a little after four o'clock, passed through the wood-house with a bag of books. I called to him, and I said to him, 'Johnny, do you see

5. The name "William" had been taken from Brown during his boyhood when his owner at the time, Dr John Young, adopted a nephew named William Moore.

6. Theseus declares in Shakespeare's *A Midsummer Night's Dream* (1600): "the poet's pen / . . . gives to airy nothing / A local habitation and a name" (5.1.15–17).

7. Opened in 1831 in London with a seating capacity of three thousand, the hall was regularly used for antislavery rallies.

8. I.e., six pence. There were twelve pence (d) to the shilling, which was approximately equivalent to the U.S. dime.

this?' taking a stick of barley sugar from my pocket and showing it to him. Says he, 'Yes; give me a taste of it.' Said I, 'I have got a spelling-book too,' and I showed that to him. 'Now,' said I, 'if you come to me in my room, and teach me my A, B, C, I will give you a whole stick.' 'Very well,' said he, 'I will; but let me taste it.' 'No; I can't.' 'Let me have it now.' Well, I thought I had better give him a little taste, until the right time came; and I marked the barley sugar about a quarter of an inch down, and told him to bite that far and no farther. He made a grab, and bit half the stick, and ran off laughing. I put the other piece in my pocket, and after a little while the other boy, little David, came through the wood-house with his books. I said nothing about the barley sugar, or my wish to get education. I knew the other lad would communicate the news to him. In a little while he returned, and said, 'Bill, John says you have got some barley sugar.' 'Well,' I said, 'what of that?' 'He said you gave him some; give me a little taste.' 'Well, if you come to-night and help me to learn my letters, I will give you a whole stick.' 'Yes; but let me taste it.' 'Ah! but you want to bite it.' 'No, I don't, but just let me taste it.' Well, I thought I had better show it to him. 'Now,' said he, 'let me touch my tongue against it.' I thought then that I had better give him a taste, but I would not trust him so far as I trusted John; so I called him to me, and got his head under my arm, and took him by the chin, and told him to hold out his tongue; and as he did so, I drew the barley sugar over very lightly. He said, 'That's very nice; just draw it over again. I could stand here and let you draw it across my tongue all day.' The night came on; the two boys came out of their room up into the attic where I was lodging, and there they commenced teaching me the letters of the alphabet. We all laid down upon the floor, covered with the same blanket; and first one would teach me a letter, and then the other, and I would pass the barley sugar from one side to the other. I kept those two boys on my sixpenny worth of barley sugar for about three weeks. Of course I did not let them know how much I had. I first dealt it out to them a quarter of a stick at a time. I worked along in that way, and before I left that place where I was working for my bread, I got so that I could spell. I had a book that had the word *baker* in it, and the boys used to think that when they got so far as that, they were getting on pretty well. I had often passed by the school-house, and stood and listened at the window to hear them spell, and I knew that when they could spell *baker* they thought something of themselves; and I was glad when I got that far. Before I left that place I could read. Finally, from that I went on until I could write. How do you suppose I first commenced writing? for you will understand that up to the present time I never spent a day in school in my life, for I had no money to pay for schooling, so that I had to get my learning first from one and then from another. I carried a piece of chalk in my pocket, and whenever I met a boy I would stop him and take out my chalk and get at a board fence and then commence. First I made some flourishes with no meaning, and called a boy up, and said, 'Do you see that? Can you beat that writing?' Said he, 'That's not writing.' Well, I wanted to get so as to write my own name. I had got out of slavery with only one name. While escaping, I received the hospitality of a very good man, who had spared part of his name to me, and finally my name got pretty long, and I wanted to be able to write it. 'Now, what do you call that?' said the boy, looking at my flourishes. I said, 'Is not that *William Wells Brown*?' 'Give me the chalk,' says he, and he wrote out in large letters '*William Wells Brown*,' and I marked up the fence for nearly a quarter of a mile, trying to copy, till I got so that I could write my name. Then I went on with my chalking, and, in fact, all board fences within half a mile of where I lived were marked over with some kind of figures I had made, in trying to learn how to write. I next obtained an arithmetic, and then a grammar, and I stand here to-night, without having had a day's schooling in my life." Such were some of the efforts made by a fugitive slave to obtain for himself an education.

* * *

1853

From Clotel; or, The President's Daughter[1]

Chapter I. The Negro Sale

"Why stands she near the auction stand,
That girl so young and fair?
What brings her to this dismal place,
Why stands she weeping there?"[2]

With the growing population of slaves in the Southern States of America, there is a fearful increase of half whites, most of whose fathers are slave-owners, and their mothers slaves. Society does not frown upon the man who sits with his mulatto child upon his knee, whilst its mother stands a slave behind his chair. The late Henry Clay,[3] some years since, predicted that the abolition of negro slavery would be brought about by the amalgamation of the races. John Randolph, a distinguished slaveholder of Virginia, and a prominent statesman, said in a speech in the legislature of his native state, that "the blood of the first American statesmen coursed through the veins of the slave of the South."[4] In all the cities and towns of the slave states, the real negro, or clear black, does not amount to more than one in every four of the slave population. This fact is, of itself, the best evidence of the degraded and immoral condition of the relation of master and slave in the United States of America.

In all the slave states, the law says:—"Slaves shall be deemed, sold, taken, reputed, and adjudged in law to be chattels[5] personal in the hands of their owners and possessors, and their executors, administrators and assigns, to all intents, constructions, and purposes whatsoever. A slave is one who is in the power of a master to whom he belongs. The master may sell him, dispose of

1. The text is that of the first edition (1853), published in London by Partridge & Oakey.
2. The opening stanza of "The Slave-Auction—A Fact" (author unknown), from *The Anti-Slavery Harp* (1848), ed. William Wells Brown.
3. The Kentucky congressman and perennial presidential candidate (1777–1852), who championed the American Colonization Society's efforts to ship free blacks to Africa. Committed to the preservation of the Union, Clay was one of the principal architects of the Compromise of 1850, which, among other things, mandated that all U.S. citizens assist in returning fugitive slaves to their masters. But the compromise only exacerbated sectional conflict.
4. An obscure and possibly apocryphal quotation from a speech by the Virginia political leader John Randolph (1773–1833), a fiery advocate of states' rights and the owner of one of Virginia's largest slave plantations. Nevertheless, Randolph went on record as opposing slavery, and in his will he freed his slaves.
5. Moveable property; possessions.

his person, his industry, and his labour. He can do nothing, possess nothing, nor acquire anything, but what must belong to his master. The slave is entirely subject to the will of his master, who may correct and chastise him, though not with unusual rigour, or so as to maim and mutilate him, or expose him to the danger of loss of life, or to cause his death. The slave, to remain a slave, must be sensible that there is no appeal from his master."[6] Where the slave is placed by law entirely under the control of the man who claims him, body and soul, as property, what else could be expected than the most depraved social condition? The marriage relation, the oldest and most sacred institution given to man by his Creator, is unknown and unrecognised in the slave laws of the United States. Would that we could say, that the moral and religious teaching in the slave states were better than the laws; but, alas! we cannot. A few years since, some slaveholders became a little uneasy in their minds about the rightfulness of permitting slaves to take to themselves husbands and wives, while they still had others living, and applied to their religious teachers for advice; and the following will show how this grave and important subject was treated:—

> "Is a servant, whose husband or wife has been sold by his or her master into a distant country, to be permitted to marry again?"

The query was referred to a committee, who made the following report; which, after discussion, was adopted:—

> "That, in view of the circumstances in which servants in this country are placed, the committee are unanimous in the opinion, that it is better to permit servants thus circumstanced to take another husband or wife."

Such was the answer from a committee of the "Shiloh Baptist Association;" and instead of receiving light, those who asked the question were plunged into deeper darkness!

A similar question was put to the "Savannah River Association,"[7] and the answer, as the following will show, did not materially differ from the one we have already given:—

> "Whether, in a case of involuntary separation, of such a character as to preclude all prospect of future intercourse, the parties ought to be allowed to marry again."

Answer—

> "That such separation among persons situated as our slaves are, is civilly a separation by death; and they believe that, in the sight of God, it would be so viewed. To forbid second marriages in such cases would be to expose the parties, not only to stronger hardships and strong temptation, but to church-censure for acting in obedience to their masters, who cannot be expected to acquiesce in a regulation at variance

6. The various slave statutes Brown quotes and paraphrases echo the famous ruling by Judge Thomas Ruffin (1787–1870), in the 1829 North Carolina case of *State v. Mann*, that "The power of the master must be absolute to render the submission of the slave perfect."

7. Like the Shiloh Baptist Association (previous paragraph), a Christian organization based in the South.

with justice to the slaves, and to the spirit of that command which regulates marriage among Christians. The slaves are not free agents; and a dissolution by death is not more entirely without their consent, and beyond their control, than by such separation."

Although marriage, as the above indicates, is a matter which the slave-holders do not think is of any importance, or of any binding force with their slaves, yet it would be doing that degraded class an injustice, not to acknowledge that many of them do regard it as a sacred obligation, and show a willingness to obey the commands of God on this subject. Marriage is, indeed, the first and most important institution of human existence—the foundation of all civilisation and culture—the root of church and state. It is the most intimate covenant of heart formed among mankind; and for many persons the only relation in which they feel the true sentiments of humanity. It gives scope for every human virtue, since each of these is developed from the love and confidence which here predominate. It unites all which ennobles and beautifies life,—sympathy, kindness of will and deed, gratitude, devotion, and every delicate, intimate feeling. As the only asylum for true education, it is the first and last sanctuary of human culture. As husband and wife through each other become conscious of complete humanity, and every human feeling, and every human virtue; so children, at their first awakening in the fond covenant of love between parents, both of whom are tenderly concerned for the same object, find an image of complete humanity leagued in free love. The spirit of love which prevails between them acts with creative power upon the young mind, and awakens every germ of goodness within it. This invisible and incalculable influence of parental life acts more upon the child than all the efforts of education, whether by means of instruction, precept, or exhortation. If this be a true picture of the vast influence for good of the institution of marriage, what must be the moral degradation of that people to whom marriage is denied? Not content with depriving them of all the higher and holier enjoyments of this relation, by degrading and darkening their souls, the slaveholder denies to his victim even that slight alleviation of his misery, which would result from the marriage relation being protected by law and public opinion. Such is the influence of slavery in the United States, that the ministers of religion, even in the so-called free states, are the mere echoes, instead of the correctors, of public sentiment.

We have thought it advisable to show that the present system of chattel slavery in America undermines the entire social condition of man, so as to prepare the reader for the following narrative of slave life, in that otherwise happy and prosperous country.

In all the large towns in the Southern States, there is a class of slaves who are permitted to hire their time of their owners, and for which they pay a high price. These are mulatto women, or quadroons,[8] as they are familiarly known, and are distinguished for their fascinating beauty. The handsomest usually pays the highest price for her time. Many of these women are the favourites of persons who furnish them with the means of paying their owners, and not

8. A term used in the 19th century to refer to a person with one quarter black ancestry or, more generally, a light-skinned black of mixed racial ancestry.

a few are dressed in the most extravagant manner. Reader, when you take into consideration the fact, that amongst the slave population no safeguard is thrown around virtue, and no inducement held out to slave women to be chaste, you will not be surprised when we tell you that immorality and vice pervade the cities of the Southern States in a manner unknown in the cities and towns of the Northern States. Indeed most of the slave women have no higher aspiration than that of becoming the finely-dressed mistress of some white man. And at negro balls and parties, this class of women usually cut the greatest figure.

At the close of the year —— the following advertisement appeared in a newspaper published in Richmond, the capital of the state of Virginia:— "Notice: Thirty-eight negroes will be offered for sale on Monday, November 10th, at twelve o'clock, being the entire stock of the late John Graves, Esq. The negroes are in good condition, some of them very prime; among them are several mechanics, able-bodied field hands, plough-boys, and women with children at the breast, and some of them very prolific in their generating qualities, affording a rare opportunity to any one who wishes to raise a strong and healthy lot of servants for their own use. Also several mulatto girls of rare personal qualities: two of them very superior. Any gentleman or lady wishing to purchase, can take any of the above slaves on trial for a week, for which no charge will be made."[9] Amongst the above slaves to be sold were Currer and her two daughters, Clotel and Althesa; the latter were the girls spoken of in the advertisement as "very superior." Currer was a bright mulatto, and of prepossessing appearance, though then nearly forty years of age. She had hired her time for more than twenty years, during which time she had lived in Richmond. In her younger days Currer had been the housekeeper of a young slaveholder; but of later years had been a laundress or washerwoman, and was considered to be a woman of great taste in getting up linen. The gentleman for whom she had kept house was Thomas Jefferson, by whom she had two daughters.[1] Jefferson being called to Washington to fill a government appointment, Currer was left behind, and thus she took herself to the business of washing, by which means she paid her master, Mr. Graves, and supported herself and two children. At the time of the decease of her master, Currer's daughters, Clotel and Althesa, were aged respectively sixteen and fourteen years, and both, like most of their own sex in America, were well grown. Currer early resolved to bring her daughters up as ladies, as she termed it, and therefore imposed little or no work upon them. As her daughters grew older, Currer had to pay a stipulated price for them; yet her notoriety as a laundress of the first class enabled her to put an extra price upon her charges, and thus she and her daughters lived in comparative luxury. To bring up Clotel and Althesa to attract attention, and especially at balls and parties, was the great aim of Currer. Although the term "negro ball" is applied to most of these gatherings, yet a majority of the attendants are often

9. Brown draws on an actual 1838 advertisement quoted in the abolitionist Theodore Weld's *Slavery as It Is* (1839).

1. Rumors that Thomas Jefferson (1743–1826), third president of the United States, had fathered children by his slave Sally Hemings (1773–1835) were first circulated in 1802 by James Callender, an alcoholic journalist angered by Jefferson's refusal to appoint him postmaster of Richmond, Virginia. By the 1830s these rumors had become an important part of abolitionist discourse.

whites. Nearly all the negro parties in the cities and towns of the Southern States are made up of quadroon and mulatto girls, and white men. These are democratic gatherings, where gentlemen, shopkeepers, and their clerks, all appear upon terms of perfect equality. And there is a degree of gentility and decorum in these companies that is not surpassed by similar gatherings of white people in the Slave States. It was at one of these parties that Horatio Green, the son of a wealthy gentleman of Richmond, was first introduced to Clotel. The young man had just returned from college, and was in his twenty-second year. Clotel was sixteen, and was admitted by all to be the most beautiful girl, coloured or white, in the city. So attentive was the young man to the quadroon during the evening that it was noticed by all, and became a matter of general conversation; while Currer appeared delighted beyond measure at her daughter's conquest. From that evening, young Green became the favourite visitor at Currer's house. He soon promised to purchase Clotel, as speedily as it could be effected, and make her mistress of her own dwelling; and Currer looked forward with pride to the time when she should see her daughter emancipated and free. It was a beautiful moonlight night in August, when all who reside in tropical climes are eagerly gasping for a breath of fresh air, that Horatio Green was seated in the small garden behind Currer's cottage, with the object of his affections by his side. And it was here that Horatio drew from his pocket the newspaper, wet from the press, and read the advertisement for the sale of the slaves to which we have alluded; Currer and her two daughters being of the number. At the close of the evening's visit, and as the young man was leaving, he said to the girl, "You shall soon be free and your own mistress."

As might have been expected, the day of sale brought an unusual large number together to compete for the property to be sold. Farmers who make a business of raising slaves for the market were there; slave-traders and speculators were also numerously represented; and in the midst of this throng was one who felt a deeper interest in the result of the sale than any other of the bystanders; this was young Green. True to his promise, he was there with a blank bank check in his pocket, awaiting with impatience to enter the list as a bidder for the beautiful slave. The less valuable slaves were first placed upon the auction block, one after another, and sold to the highest bidder. Husbands and wives were separated with a degree of indifference that is unknown in any other relation of life, except that of slavery. Brothers and sisters were torn from each other; and mothers saw their children leave them for the last time on this earth.

It was late in the day, when the greatest number of persons were thought to be present, that Currer and her daughters were brought forward to the place of sale. Currer was first ordered to ascend the auction stand, which she did with a trembling step. The slave mother was sold to a trader. Althesa, the youngest, and who was scarcely less beautiful than her sister, was sold to the same trader for one thousand dollars. Clotel was the last, and, as was expected, commanded a higher price than any that had been offered for sale that day. The appearance of Clotel on the auction block created a deep sensation amongst the crowd. There she stood, with a complexion as white as most of those who were waiting with a wish to become her purchasers; her features as finely defined as any of her sex of pure Anglo-Saxon; her long black wavy hair done up in the neatest manner; her form tall and graceful, and her whole appearance indicating one superior to her position.[2] The auctioneer commenced by saying, that "Miss Clotel had been reserved for the last, because she was the most valuable. How much gentlemen? Real Albino, fit for a fancy girl for any one. She enjoys good health, and has a sweet temper. How much do you say?" "Five hundred dollars." "Only five hundred for such a girl as this? Gentlemen, she is worth a deal more than that sum; you certainly don't know the value of the article you are bidding upon. Here, gentlemen, I hold in my hand a paper certifying that she has a good moral character." "Seven hundred." "Ah, gentlemen, that is something like. This paper also states that she is very intelligent." "Eight hundred." "She is a devoted Christian, and perfectly trustworthy." "Nine hundred." "Nine fifty." "Ten." "Eleven." "Twelve hundred." Here the sale came to a dead stand. The auctioneer stopped, looked around, and began in a rough manner to relate some anecdotes relative to the sale of slaves, which, he said, had come under his own observation. At this juncture the scene was indeed strange. Laughing, joking, swearing, smoking, spitting, and talking kept up a continual hum and noise amongst the crowd; while the slave-girl stood with tears in her eyes, at one time looking towards her mother and sister, and at another towards the young man whom she hoped would become her purchaser. "The chastity of this girl is pure; she has never been from under her mother's care; she is a virtuous creature." "Thirteen." "Fourteen." "Fifteen." "Fifteen hundred dollars," cried the auctioneer, and the maiden was struck for that sum. This was a Southern auction, at which the bones, muscles, sinews, blood, and nerves of a young lady of sixteen were sold for five hundred dollars; her moral character for two hundred; her improved intellect for one hundred; her Christianity for three hundred; and her chastity and virtue for four hundred dollars more. And this, too, in a city thronged with churches, whose tall spires look like so many signals pointing to heaven, and whose ministers preach that slavery is a God-ordained institution!

What words can tell the inhumanity, the atrocity, and the immorality of that doctrine which, from exalted office, commends such a crime to the favour of enlightened and Christian people? What indignation from all the world is not due to the government and people who put forth all their strength and power to keep in existence such an institution? Nature abhors it; the age repels it; and Christianity needs all her meekness to forgive it.

Clotel was sold for fifteen hundred dollars, but her purchaser was Horatio Green. Thus closed a negro sale, at which two daughters of Thomas Jefferson, the writer of the Declaration of American Independence, and one of the presidents of the great republic, were disposed of to the highest bidder!

"O God! my every heart-string cries,
 Dost thou these scenes behold
In this our boasted Christian land,
 And must the truth be told?

"Blush, Christian, blush! for e'en the dark,
 Untutored heathen see

2. By describing such a "white" person on the slave auction block, Brown invites white readers to identify with someone of a supposedly inferior race and at the same time suggests the tenuousness of racial difference.

Thy inconsistency; and, lo!
They scorn thy God, and thee!"[3]

* * *

[After purchasing Clotel, Horatio installs her in a cottage outside of Richmond, Virginia. They have a daughter, Mary, but Horatio's political ambitions lead him to ignore Clotel's plea that they emigrate to Europe; instead, he marries Gertrude, the white daughter of a wealthy man. Clotel is sold south, but she escapes and returns to Richmond in quest of her daughter.]

Chapter XXIV

THE ARREST

"The fearful storm—it threatens lowering,
Which God in mercy long delays;
Slaves yet may see their masters cowering,
While whole plantations smoke and blaze!"
Carter.[4]

It was late in the evening when the coach arrived at Richmond, and Clotel once more alighted in her native city. She had intended to seek lodgings somewhere in the outskirts of the town, but the lateness of the hour compelled her to stop at one of the principal hotels for the night. She had scarcely entered the inn, when she recognised among the numerous black servants one to whom she was well known; and her only hope was, that her disguise would keep her from being discovered. The imperturbable calm and entire forgetfulness of self which induced Clotel to visit a place from which she could scarcely hope to escape, to attempt the rescue of a beloved child, demonstrate that over-willingness of woman to carry out the promptings of the finer feelings of her heart. True to woman's nature, she had risked her own liberty for another.

She remained in the hotel during the night, and the next morning, under the plea of illness, she took her breakfast alone. That day the fugitive slave paid a visit to the suburbs of the town, and once more beheld the cottage in which she had spent so many happy hours. It was winter, and the clematis and passion flower were not there; but there were the same walks she had so often pressed with her feet, and the same trees which had so often shaded her as she passed through the garden at the back of the house. Old remembrances rushed upon her memory, and caused her to shed tears freely. Clotel was now in her native town, and near her daughter; but how could she communicate with her? How could she see her? To have made herself known, would have been a suicidal act; betrayal would have followed, and she arrested. Three days had passed away, and Clotel still remained in the hotel at which she had first put up; and yet she had got no tidings of her child. Unfortunately for Clotel, a disturbance had just broken out amongst the slave population in the state of Virginia, and all strangers were eyed with suspicion.

3. From "The Slave-Auction—A Fact." See p. 948, n. 2.

4. From Mrs. J. G. Carter's "Ye Sons of Freedom," in *The Anti-Slavery Harp*.

The evils consequent on slavery are not lessened by the incoming of one or two rays of light. If the slave only becomes aware of his condition, and conscious of the injustice under which he suffers, if he obtains but a faint idea of these things, he will seize the first opportunity to possess himself of what he conceives to belong to him. The infusion of Anglo-Saxon with African blood has created an insurrectionary feeling among the slaves of America hitherto unknown. Aware of their blood connection with their owners, these mulattoes labour under the sense of their personal and social injuries; and tolerate, if they do not encourage in themselves, low and vindictive passions. On the other hand, the slave owners are aware of their critical position, and are ever watchful, always fearing an outbreak among the slaves.[5]

True, the Free States are equally bound with the Slave States to suppress any insurrectionary movement that may take place among the slaves. The Northern freemen are bound by their constitutional obligations to aid the slaveholder in keeping his slaves in their chains. Yet there are, at the time we write, four millions of bond slaves in the United States. The insurrection to which we now refer was headed by a full-blooded negro, who had been born and brought up a slave. He had heard the twang of the driver's whip, and saw the warm blood streaming from the negro's body; he had witnessed the separation of parents and children, and was made aware, by too many proofs, that the slave could expect no justice at the hand of the slave owner. He went by the name of "Nat Turner."[6] He was a preacher amongst the negroes, and distinguished for his eloquence, respected by the whites, and loved and venerated by the negroes. On the discovery of the plan for the outbreak, Turner fled to the swamps, followed by those who had joined in the insurrection. Here the revolted negroes numbered some hundreds, and for a time bade defiance to their oppressors. The Dismal Swamps cover many thousands of acres of wild land, and a dense forest, with wild animals and insects, such as are unknown in any other part of Virginia. Here runaway negroes usually seek a hiding-place, and some have been known to reside here for years. The revolters were joined by one of these. He was a large, tall, full-blooded negro, with a stern and savage countenance; the marks on his face showed that he was from one of the barbarous tribes in Africa, and claimed that country as his native land; his only covering was a girdle around his loins, made of skins of wild beasts which he had killed; his only token of authority among those that he led, was a pair of epaulettes made from the tail of a fox, and tied to his shoulder by a cord. Brought from the coast of Africa when only fifteen years of age to the island of Cuba, he was smuggled from thence into Virginia. He had been two years in the swamps, and considered it his future home. He had met a negro woman who was also a runaway; and, after the fashion of his native land, had gone through the process of oiling[7] her as the marriage ceremony. They had built a cave on a rising mound in the swamp; this was their home. His name was Picquilo. His only weapon was a sword, made from the blade of a scythe, which he had stolen

5. For this paragraph, Brown borrowed from John Beard's *The Life of Toussaint L'Ouverture* (1853).

6. In August 1831, the slave Nat Turner (1800–1831) led a slave rebellion in Southampton County, Virginia, which resulted in the death of fifty-five whites. In retaliation, whites killed over twice that number of blacks. Southern whites blamed abolitionist meddling for the rebellion and subsequently strengthened the slave codes. Many Northern blacks regarded Turner as a hero.

7. African purification ritual typically involving spreading olive or palm oil over the bride's body.

from a neighbouring plantation. His dress, his character, his manners, his mode of fighting, were all in keeping with the early training he had received in the land of his birth. He moved about with the activity of a cat, and neither the thickness of the trees, nor the depth of the water could stop him. He was a bold, turbulent spirit; and from revenge imbrued his hands in the blood of all the whites he could meet. Hunger, thirst, fatigue, and loss of sleep he seemed made to endure as if by peculiarity of constitution. His air was fierce, his step oblique, his look sanguinary. Such was the character of one of the leaders in the Southampton insurrection.[8] All negroes were arrested who were found beyond their master's threshold, and all strange whites watched with a great degree of alacrity.

Such was the position in which Clotel found affairs when she returned to Virginia in search of her Mary. Had not the slave-owners been watchful of strangers, owing to the outbreak, the fugitive could not have escaped the vigilance of the police; for advertisements, announcing her escape and offering a large reward for her arrest, had been received in the city previous to her arrival, and the officers were therefore on the look-out for the runaway slave. It was on the third day, as the quadroon was seated in her room at the inn, still in the disguise of a gentleman, that two of the city officers entered the room, and informed her that they were authorised to examine all strangers, to assure the authorities that they were not in league with the revolted negroes. With trembling heart the fugitive handed the key of her trunk to the officers. To their surprise, they found nothing but woman's apparel in the box, which raised their curiosity, and caused a further investigation that resulted in the arrest of Clotel as a fugitive slave. She was immediately conveyed to prison, there to await the orders of her master. For many days, uncheered by the voice of kindness, alone, hopeless, desolate, she waited for the time to arrive when the chains were to be placed on her limbs, and she returned to her inhuman and unfeeling owner.

The arrest of the fugitive was announced in all the newspapers, but created little or no sensation. The inhabitants were too much engaged in putting down the revolt among the slaves; and although all the odds were against the insurgents, the whites found it no easy matter, with all their caution. Every day brought news of fresh outbreaks. Without scruple and without pity, the whites massacred all blacks found beyond their owners' plantations: the negroes, in return, set fire to houses, and put those to death who attempted to escape from the flames. Thus carnage was added to carnage, and the blood of the whites flowed to avenge the blood of the blacks. These were the ravages of slavery. No graves were dug for the negroes; their dead bodies became food for dogs and vultures, and their bones, partly calcined by the sun, remained scattered about, as if to mark the mournful fury of servitude and lust of power. When the slaves were subdued, except a few in the swamps, bloodhounds were put in this dismal place to hunt out the remaining revolters. Among the captured negroes was one of whom we shall hereafter make mention.[9]

8. For his description of the fictional Picquilo, Brown borrowed from John R. Beard's portrayal of the Haitian revolutionary Lamour de Rance in *The Life of Toussaint L'Ouverture* (1853).

9. Reference to George, a slave of Clotel's former owner, Horatio Green.

Chapter XXV. Death Is Freedom

"I asked but freedom, and ye gave
Chains, and the freedom of the grave."
—*Snelling*.[1]

There are, in the district of Columbia, several slave prisons, or "negro pens," as they are termed. These prisons are mostly occupied by persons to keep their slaves in, when collecting their gangs together for the New Orleans market. Some of them belong to the government, and one, in particular, is noted for having been the place where a number of free coloured persons have been incarcerated from time to time. In this district is situated the capitol of the United States. Any free coloured persons visiting Washington, if not provided with papers asserting and proving their right to be free, may be arrested and placed in one of these dens. If they succeed in showing that they are free, they are set at liberty, provided they are able to pay the expenses of their arrest and imprisonment; if they cannot pay these expenses, they are sold out. Through this unjust and oppressive law, many persons born in the Free States have been consigned to a life of slavery on the cotton, sugar, or rice plantations of the Southern States. By order of her master, Clotel was removed from Richmond and placed in one of these prisons, to await the sailing of a vessel for New Orleans. The prison in which she was put stands midway between the capitol at Washington and the president's house. Here the fugitive saw nothing but slaves brought in and taken out, to be placed in ships and sent away to the same part of the country to which she herself would soon be compelled to go. She had seen or heard nothing of her daughter while in Richmond, and all hope of seeing her now had fled. If she was carried back to New Orleans, she could expect no mercy from her master.

At the dusk of the evening previous to the day when she was to be sent off, as the old prison was being closed for the night, she suddenly darted past her keeper, and ran for her life. It is not a great distance from the prison to the Long Bridge, which passes from the lower part of the city across the Potomac, to the extensive forests and woodlands of the celebrated Arlington Place, occupied by that distinguished relative and descendant of the immortal Washington, Mr. George W. Custis.[2] Thither the poor fugitive directed her flight. So unexpected was her escape, that she had quite a number of rods the start before the keeper had secured the other prisoners, and rallied his assistants in pursuit. It was at an hour when, and in a part of the city where, horses could not be readily obtained for the chase; no bloodhounds were at hand to run down the flying woman; and for once it seemed as though there was to be a fair trial of speed and endurance between the slave and the slave-catchers. The keeper and his forces raised the hue and cry on her pathway close behind; but so rapid was the flight along the wide avenue, that the astonished citizens, as they poured forth from their dwellings to learn the cause of alarm, were only able to comprehend the nature of the case in time to fall in with the motley mass in pursuit, (as many a one did

1. From a poem by William J. Snelling (1804–1848), whose work regularly appeared in the antislavery newspaper the *Liberator*.
2. Custis (1781–1857), grandson of Martha Washington and an heir to Washington's Mount Vernon estate. "Long Bridge": built in 1835, the bridge crossed the Potomac River, linking Washington, D.C., to Virginia; it remained in use until 1903.

that night,) to raise an anxious prayer to heaven, as they refused to join in the pursuit, that the panting fugitive might escape, and the merciless soul dealer for once be disappointed of his prey. And now with the speed of an arrow—having passed the avenue—with the distance between her and her pursuers constantly increasing, this poor hunted female gained the *"Long Bridge,"* as it is called, where interruption seemed improbable, and already did her heart begin to beat high with the hope of success. She had only to pass three-fourths of a mile across the bridge, and she could bury herself in a vast forest, just at the time when the curtain of night would close around her, and protect her from the pursuit of her enemies.

But God by his Providence had otherwise determined. He had determined that an appalling tragedy should be enacted that night, within plain sight of the President's house and the capital of the Union, which should be an evidence wherever it should be known, of the unconquerable love of liberty the heart may inherit; as well as a fresh admonition to the slave dealer, of the cruelty and enormity of his crimes. Just as the pursuers crossed the high draw for the passage of sloops, soon after entering upon the bridge, they beheld three men slowly approaching from the Virginia side. They immediately called to them to arrest the fugitive, whom they proclaimed a runaway slave. True to their Virginian instincts as she came near, they formed in line across the narrow bridge, and prepared to seize her. Seeing escape impossible in that quarter, she stopped suddenly, and turned upon her pursuers. On came the profane and ribald crew, faster than ever, already exulting in her capture, and threatening punishment for her flight. For a moment she looked wildly and anxiously around to see if there was no hope of escape. On either hand, far down below, rolled the deep foamy waters of the Potomac, and before and behind the rapidly approaching step and noisy voices of pursuers,

THE DEATH OF CLOTEL. *Page* 218.

"The Death of Clotel." Illustration and caption from Brown's *Clotel* (London, 1853).

showing how vain would be any further effort for freedom. Her resolution was taken. She clasped her *hands* convulsively, and raised *them*, as she at the same time raised her *eyes* towards heaven, and begged for that mercy and compassion *there*, which had been denied her on earth; and then, with a single bound, she vaulted over the railings of the bridge, and sunk for ever beneath the waves of the river!

Thus died Clotel, the daughter of Thomas Jefferson, a president of the United States; a man distinguished as the author of the Declaration of American Independence, and one of the first statesmen of that country.

Had Clotel escaped from oppression in any other land, in the disguise in which she fled from the Mississippi to Richmond, and reached the United States, no honour within the gift of the American people would have been too good to have been heaped upon the heroic woman. But she was a slave, and therefore out of the pale of their sympathy. They have tears to shed over Greece and Poland; they have an abundance of sympathy for "poor Ireland;" they can furnish a ship of war to convey the Hungarian refugees from a Turkish prison to the "land of the free and home of the brave."[3] They boast that America is the "cradle of liberty;" if it is, I fear they have rocked the child to death. The body of Clotel was picked up from the bank of the river, where it had been washed by the strong current, a hole dug in the sand, and there deposited, without either inquest being held over it, or religious service being performed. Such was the life and such the death of a woman whose virtues and goodness of heart would have done honour to one in a higher station of life, and who, if she had been born in any other land but that of slavery, would have been honoured and loved. A few days after the death of Clotel, the following poem appeared in one of the newspapers:

"Now, rest for the wretched! the long day is past,
And night on yon prison descendeth at last.
Now lock up and bolt! Ha, jailor, look there!
Who flies like a wild bird escaped from the snare?
    A woman, a slave—up, out in pursuit,
        While linger some gleams of day!
    Let thy call ring out!—now a rabble rout
        Is at thy heels—speed away!

"A bold race for freedom!—On, fugitive, on!
Heaven help but the right, and thy freedom is won.
How eager she drinks the free air of the plains;
Every limb, every nerve, every fibre she strains;
    From Columbia's glorious capitol,
        Columbia's daughter flees
    To the sanctuary God has given—
        The sheltering forest trees.

"Now she treads the Long Bridge—joy lighteth her eye—
Beyond her the dense wood and darkening sky—

3. Brown here joins with many abolitionists in decrying Americans' tendencies to support European revolutionary movements while ignoring the plight of U.S. slaves. Brown was particularly disturbed by the hero's welcome accorded the Hungarian revolutionary Louis Kossuth (1802–1894) during his 1851–52 tour of the United States because Kossuth insisted on remaining neutral on abolitionism.

Wild hopes thrill her heart as she neareth the shore:
O, despair! there are *men* fast advancing before!
Shame, shame on their manhood! they hear, they heed
The cry, her flight to stay,
And like demon forms with their outstretched arms,
They wait to seize their prey!

"She pauses, she turns! Ah, will she flee back?
Like wolves, her pursuers howl loud on their track;
She lifteth to Heaven one look of despair—
Her anguish breaks forth in one hurried prayer—
Hark! her jailor's yell! like a bloodhound's bay
On the low night wind it sweeps!
Now, death or the chain! to the stream she turns,
And she leaps! O God, she leaps!

"The dark and the cold, yet merciful wave,
Receives to its bosom the form of the slave:
She rises—earth's scenes on her dim vision gleam,
Yet she struggleth not with the strong rushing stream:
And low are the death-cries her woman's heart gives,
As she floats adown the river,
Faint and more faint grows the drowning voice,
And her cries have ceased for ever!

"Now back, jailor, back to thy dungeons, again,
To swing the red lash and rivet the chain!
The form thou would'st fetter—returned to its God;
The universe holdeth no realm of night
More drear than her slavery—
More merciless fiends than here stayed her flight—
Joy! the hunted slave is free!

"That bond-woman's corse,[4]—let Potomac's proud wave
Go bear it along *by our Washington's grave*,
And heave it high up on that hallowed strand,
To tell of the freedom he won for our land.
A weak woman's corse by freemen chased down;
Hurrah for our country! hurrah!
To freedom she leaped, through drowning and death—
Hurrah for our country! hurrah!"[5]

* * *

1853

4. Corpse.

5. "The Leap from Long Bridge," by Sarah Jane Clarke (1823–1904)—who published under the name "Grace Greenwood"—included in her *Poems* (1851). Brown changed some of the wording and added the final stanza. By the end of the novel, Clotel's daughter, Mary, has escaped to Europe, where she is eventually reunited with her lover, the former slave George Green.

HENRY DAVID THOREAU
1817–1862

Henry David Thoreau aspired to write great literature by adventuring at home, traveling, as he put it, a good deal in Concord, Massachusetts. "As travelers go around the world and report natural objects and phenomena, so let another stay at home and report the phenomena of his own life," he remarked in a journal entry of August 1851. Known by some of his Concord neighbors as the Harvard graduate who never lived up to his potential, Thoreau presented himself in *Walden* as an exemplary figure who—by virtue of his philosophical questionings, economic good sense, nonconformity, and appreciative observation of the natural world—could serve as a model for others. Thoreau infuriated and inspired his Massachusetts neighbors and audiences while he lived; since his death, his writings have continued to provoke generations of readers to contemplate their obligations to society, nature, and themselves.

The third of four children of Cynthia (Dunbar) and John Thoreau, a storekeeper who opened a pencil-making business in the early 1820s, Thoreau was born in Concord on July 12, 1817. His sister Helen, five years his senior, was an important teacher in his childhood years; his brother, John, two years his senior, was his closest friend until John's untimely death in 1842; and his sister Sophia, two years his junior, cared for him at the end of his life. By the age of ten, Thoreau, who reveled in reading, had memorized passages from Shakespeare, John Bunyan, Samuel Johnson, and other writers. In 1828, he and his brother were enrolled in the private Concord Academy, and because Henry was regarded as the more academically promising of the two, the family, which was struggling economically (his mother ran their home as a boardinghouse to produce additional income), decided that he would be the one son to attend Harvard. Thoreau began his studies there in 1833, excelling in languages but otherwise failing to distinguish himself. After his 1837 graduation he returned to Concord, where he taught briefly at a local elementary school before resigning in protest when he was instructed to flog some of his students. In 1838 he took a teaching and administrative position at the Concord Academy, where a year later John joined him as a teacher and co-director of the school. The brothers had to close the Concord Academy in 1841 because of John's poor health. Paralyzed by tetanus from a razor cut, John died in Thoreau's arms on January 1, 1842. The grief at the loss of his beloved brother would inspire his elegiac *A Week on the Concord and Merrimack Rivers* (1849), which memorialized a two-week boating trip that the brothers took in 1839.

Thoreau met his fellow Concordian, Ralph Waldo Emerson, in 1836. Emerson, fourteen years his senior, became the most important influence and friendship in his life. Thoreau attended the informal meetings of the New England Transcendentalists that convened irregularly in Emerson's study and there met such people as Margaret Fuller and the education reformers Elizabeth Peabody and Bronson Alcott (father of Louisa May). With Emerson's encouragement, Thoreau also began to keep a journal, which served him as a sourcebook for some of his published writings and lectures, eventually growing to nearly two million words. Like Emerson's own journal, Thoreau's has emerged as one of his greatest literary achievements. In 1840, Thoreau commenced his efforts to make a name for himself as a published writer. He placed a poem and an essay in the inaugural issue of the *Dial*, the journal founded by the Concord Transcendentalist circle and edited by Margaret Fuller (and at times by Thoreau himself); he would publish over thirty essays, poems, and translations in the journal before it ceased operations in 1844. He never stopped reading, although contemporary writers meant little to him except for Emerson and Thomas Carlyle, whom he regarded as one of the great prophets of the era. He steeped himself in the classics—Greek, Latin, and English—and read the sacred writings of the Hindus in translation; they are an enormous influence on the cosmic vision of *Walden*.

Much of Thoreau's reading and writing during this time took place in Emerson's house, for beginning in 1841 Thoreau lived there on and off as a handyman and general help to Emerson's wife, Lydia, when Emerson himself was off on lecture tours. Thoreau moved to Staten Island in May 1843 to work as a tutor for the sons of Emerson's brother William, but unhappy with that work, he returned to Concord six months later, moving back to his family home, all the while keeping up his association with Emerson. In the spring he typically earned money as a surveyor, helping reestablish the boundaries of farms whose fences and walls had been washed away by melting snows. He also helped his father make pencils. Early in 1844 he delivered his first series of lectures, "The Conservative and the Reformer," in Boston's Armory Hall. To his great embarrassment, during a camping trip in April of that year, he accidentally set fire to the Concord woods near Walden Pond, burning approximately three hundred acres. Shortly after the fire, Thoreau decided to begin what he termed his "experiment" at Walden, building a cabin on land that Emerson owned near the pond and taking up residence there on July 4, 1845—a symbolic moment of personal liberation aligned with the celebration of national freedom. One of Thoreau's major goals in moving to the pond was to write a book about his 1839 boating journey with his brother (which he completed before he left after two years, two months, and two days). Only a couple of miles from town, his cabin became the destination of many local visitors, and he often went back to Concord for meals and conversation. During his time at Walden, Thoreau also spent one night of 1846 in the local jail when, in protest against what he regarded as the proslavery agenda of the war against Mexico, he refused to pay his poll tax. That experience would inspire "Resistance to Civil Government" (1849), which in due time would become a world-famous essay on the relationship of the individual to the state. He never disguised the fact that he was in jail for only one night but made that experience symbolic, just as he did with his sojourn at Walden Pond.

In 1849 Thoreau published the book he had drafted at Walden as *A Week on the Concord and Merrimack Rivers*, a work that mixes naturalist meditations, personal reflections, poetry, and scripture. Barely noticed by reviewers and readers, it sold fewer than three hundred of the thousand copies printed. Thoreau had subsidized the publication through his royalties, and in 1853, when he received the unsold books, he wrote in his journal: "I have now a library of nearly nine hundred volumes, over seven hundred of which I wrote myself." Despite the critical and financial setback of *A Week*, Thoreau worked intensively on *Walden* between 1847 and its publication in 1854. The prestigious Boston firm of Ticknor and Fields published the book in a small print run of two thousand copies, and by 1859 most of these copies had been sold. Encouraged by the relatively good reviews and sales, Thoreau over the next few years attempted to work up books from his Cape Cod travels of 1849 and 1850 and his Maine travels of 1857, bringing out sections of the Cape Cod manuscript in the 1855 *Putnam's Monthly Magazine*. None of the other books that Thoreau published or projected has achieved the influence and reputation of *Walden*, where Thoreau's whole literary character emerges—his love of nature, his rhetorical inventiveness, his humor, his philosophical adventurousness, his everyday nonconformity. In it he becomes, in the highest sense, a fully employed public servant, offering readers the fruits of his experience, thought, and artistic dedication.

His writing and lectures brought Thoreau a small but widening circle of admirers. His earlier journals had combined naturalistic observations with moral commentary; in the 1850s they increasingly recorded his observations of nature without comment and in great detail as he sought to understand the daily and seasonal rhythms of nature. Inspired by his reading during the early 1850s of the German naturalist Alexander von Humboldt (1769–1859) and the English naturalist Charles Darwin (1809–1882), he made himself into what critic Laura Dassow Walls has called "a scientific seer, walking, recording, measuring, and weaving the details of nature into meaning." Professors at Harvard, such as the geologist Louis Agassiz, found his scientific vision of interest. At the same time, Thoreau emerged as one of the most outspoken abolitionists in the Concord area. In 1854, the year of *Walden*'s publication, he delivered his best known antislavery speech, "Slavery in Massachusetts," at a rally in Framingham, Massachusetts, protesting the arrest of the fugitive slave Anthony Burns. Thoreau achieved his greatest prominence as an antislavery speaker with his defense of John Brown immediately after Brown's arrest at Harpers Ferry in October 1859. Before large audiences in Concord, Boston, and Worcester, Thoreau honored Brown's revolutionary antislavery aims. He thus welcomed the Civil War, with its promise of ridding the nation of slavery, even as he faced the difficulties of declining health brought on by tuberculosis, the great nineteenth-century killer of young adults. (His sister Helen had died of the disease in 1849.) In May 1861 Thoreau traveled to Minnesota with the hope of recovering his health, and there he collected botanical specimens and observed the Sioux Indians of the region. His health continuing to deteriorate, he returned to Concord and worked with his sister Sophia to prepare what he recognized would be posthumously published writings. He was forty-four when he died at Concord on May 6, 1862. The little fame he had achieved was as a social experimenter who applied Emerson's theoretical transcendentalism to daily life, and as John Brown's champion.

Recognition of Thoreau as an important writer was slow in coming, though the publication of *Walden* did occasion comment in some of the most widely read newspapers and magazines of the time. In the January 1856 issue of the highly respected *Westminster Review*, for instance, the English novelist George Eliot celebrated Thoreau as a writer of "great beauty," and urged her readers to take note of that "theoretic independence of formulæ, which is peculiar to some of the finer American minds." No essay in Thoreau's canon more powerfully exemplifies his independence than "Resistance to Civil Government," but outside of Thoreau's immediate circle at Concord, what little attention it received when initially published was negative. Thoreau's radical insistence that "under a government that imprisons any man unjustly, the true place for a just man is prison" alarmed local conservatives. The *Boston Post*, for instance, called the essay "crazy," and the reviewer for the *Boston Courier* urged him to "take a trip to France, and preach his doctrine of '*Resistance to Civil Government*' to the red republicans." Thoreau's most widely read works published during his lifetime were "Slavery in Massachusetts" (printed in William Lloyd Garrison's abolitionist newspaper the *Liberator* and reprinted in the *New York Tribune*) and "A Plea for Captain John Brown" (printed in *Echoes of Harpers Ferry* in 1860).

Between June 1862, the month after Thoreau's death, and November 1863, the Boston-based *Atlantic Monthly* published the essays "Walking," "Autumn Tints," "Wild Apples," "Life without Principle," and "Night and Moonlight." In 1862 Ticknor and Fields reissued *A Week* and *Walden* (which never again went out of print) and attempted to capitalize on the growing interest in Thoreau by publishing five new books: *Excursions* (1863), *The Maine Woods* (1864), *Cape Cod* (1864), *Letters to Various Persons* (1865), and *A Yankee in Canada, with Anti-Slavery and Reform Papers* (1866). An expanded version of Emerson's eulogy for Thoreau, published in the *Atlantic Monthly* for August 1863, confirmed Thoreau's growing reputation. By the early twentieth century, Thoreau was becoming widely recognized as a social philosopher, naturalist, and writer with few peers. In 1906 his journals were published for the first time in chronological order, in fourteen volumes as part of a twenty-volume set of his complete works. That same year, Mahatma Ghandi, in his African exile, read "Resistance to Civil Government" and later acknowledged its important influence on his thinking about how best to achieve Indian independence. Later in the century, Martin Luther King Jr. would similarly attest to the crucial influence of Thoreau on his adoption of nonviolent civil disobedience as a key to the civil rights movement.

By the middle of the twentieth century, Thoreau's literary reputation equaled or surpassed Emerson's, with *Walden* regarded as one of the masterpieces of American literature. It is a work that powerfully affected environmentalists like John Muir and Aldo Leopold, who greatly admired Thoreau for his concerns about the natural habitat; contemporary writers like Edward Abbey and Annie Dillard also cite him frequently. As crucial as environmental concerns, and even antislavery, were to Thoreau, however, he always insisted that all principled action had to be undertaken by the individual rather than through groups. It is important to recall that Thoreau described *Walden* as an "experiment"—an account of one possible way of viewing, representing, and acting in the world. In *Walden*'s punning wordplay, richly allusive sentences, and (with its numerous references to a panoply of Eastern and Western texts) truly global textual vision, Thoreau more than anything else attempted to push his readers to think—to "wake . . . up," as he put it in the book's epigraph. Life is short and life is miraculous, Thoreau insists, and it is incumbent on each individual to figure out how best to respond to the circumstances of the moment. Though there are considerable differences between Thoreau and Emerson, the most provocative literary expression of Emerson's call for self-reliance may well be Thoreau's bragging, visionary, down-to-earth *Walden*.

Resistance to Civil Government[1]

I heartily accept the motto,—"That government is best which governs least;"[2] and I should like to see it acted up to more rapidly and systematically. Carried out, it finally amounts to this, which also I believe,—"That government is best which governs not at all;" and when men are prepared for it, that will be the kind of government which they will have. Government is at best but an expedient; but most governments are usually, and all governments are sometimes, inexpedient. The objections which have been brought against a standing army, and they are many and weighty, and deserve to prevail, may also at last be brought against a standing government. The standing army is only an arm of the standing government. The government itself, which is only the mode which the people have chosen to execute their will, is equally liable to be abused and perverted before the people can act through it. Witness the present Mexican war, the work of comparatively a few individuals

1. "Resistance to Civil Government" is reprinted here from its first appearance, in *Aesthetic Papers* (1849), edited by the educational reformer Elizabeth Peabody (1804–1894). Thoreau had delivered a version of the essay as a lecture in January and again in February 1848 at the Concord Lyceum, under the title "The Rights and Duties of the Individual in Relation to Government." After his death it was reprinted in *A Yankee in Canada, with Anti-Slavery and Reform Papers* (1866) as "Civil Disobedience." That title, although commonly used, may not be authorial; the title of the first printing, as Thoreau indicates, was a play on "The Duty of Submission to Civil Government Explained," the title of one of the chapters in *Principles of Moral and Political Philosophy* (1785), a book by English theologian and moralist William Paley (1743–1805), that was one of Thoreau's Harvard textbooks.

2. These words appeared on the masthead of the *Democratic Review*, the New York magazine that published two early Thoreau pieces in 1843.

using the standing government as their tool; for, in the outset, the people would not have consented to this measure.[3]

This American government,—what is it but a tradition, though a recent one, endeavoring to transmit itself unimpaired to posterity, but each instant losing some of its integrity? It has not the vitality and force of a single living man; for a single man can bend it to his will. It is a sort of wooden gun to the people themselves; and, if ever they should use it in earnest as a real one against each other, it will surely split. But it is not the less necessary for this; for the people must have some complicated machinery or other, and hear its din, to satisfy that idea of government which they have. Governments show thus how successfully men can be imposed on, even impose on themselves, for their own advantage. It is excellent, we must all allow; yet this government never of itself furthered any enterprise, but by the alacrity with which it got out of its way. *It* does not keep the country free. *It* does not settle the West. *It* does not educate. The character inherent in the American people has done all that has been accomplished; and it would have done somewhat more, if the government had not sometimes got in its way. For government is an expedient by which men would fain succeed in letting one another alone; and, as has been said, when it is most expedient, the governed are most let alone by it. Trade and commerce, if they were not made of India rubber, would never manage to bounce over the obstacles which legislators are continually putting in their way; and, if one were to judge these men wholly by the effects of their actions, and not partly by their intentions, they would deserve to be classed and punished with those mischievous persons who put obstructions on the railroads.

But, to speak practically and as a citizen, unlike those who call themselves no-government men, I ask for, not at once no government, but *at once* a better government. Let every man make known what kind of government would command his respect, and that will be one step toward obtaining it.

After all, the practical reason why, when the power is once in the hands of the people, a majority are permitted, and for a long period continue, to rule, is not because they are most likely to be in the right, nor because this seems fairest to the minority, but because they are physically the strongest. But a government in which the majority rule in all cases cannot be based on justice, even as far as men understand it. Can there not be a government in which majorities do not virtually decide right and wrong, but conscience?—in which majorities decide only those questions to which the rule of expediency is applicable? Must the citizen ever for a moment, or in the least degree, resign his conscience to the legislator? Why has every man a conscience, then? I think that we should be men first, and subjects afterward. It is not desirable to cultivate a respect for the law, so much as for the right. The only obligation which I have a right to assume, is to do at any time what I think right. It is truly enough said,[4] that a corporation has no conscience; but a corporation of conscientious men is a corporation *with* a conscience. Law never made men a whit more just; and, by means of their respect for it, even the

3. The Mexican War (1846–48) was criticized by Whigs and some Democrats as an "executive's war" because President Polk commenced hostilities without a congressional declaration of war. Many New Englanders, including Thoreau, regarded the war as part of the South's effort to extend the territorial domain of slavery.

4. By the English jurist Sir Edward Coke (1552–1634), in a famous legal decision of 1612.

well-disposed are daily made the agents of injustice. A common and natural result of an undue respect for law is, that you may see a file of soldiers, colonel, captain, corporal, privates, powder-monkeys and all, marching in admirable order over hill and dale to the wars, against their wills, aye, against their common sense and consciences, which makes it very steep marching indeed, and produces a palpitation of the heart. They have no doubt that it is a damnable business in which they are concerned; they are all peaceably inclined. Now, what are they? Men at all? or small moveable forts and magazines, at the service of some unscrupulous man in power? Visit the Navy Yard, and behold a marine, such a man as an American government can make, or such as it can make a man with its black arts, a mere shadow and reminiscence of humanity, a man laid out alive and standing, and already, as one may say, buried under arms with funeral accompaniments, though it may be

"Not a drum was heard, nor a funeral note,
As his corse to the ramparts we hurried;
Not a soldier discharged his farewell shot
O'er the grave where our hero we buried."[5]

The mass of men serve the State thus, not as men mainly, but as machines, with their bodies. They are the standing army, and the militia, jailers, constables, *posse comitatus*,[6] &c. In most cases there is no free exercise whatever of the judgment or of the moral sense; but they put themselves on a level with wood and earth and stones; and wooden men can perhaps be manufactured that will serve the purpose as well. Such command no more respect than men of straw, or a lump of dirt. They have the same sort of worth only as horses and dogs. Yet such as these even are commonly esteemed good citizens. Others, as most legislators, politicians, lawyers, ministers, and office-holders, serve the State chiefly with their heads; and, as they rarely make any moral distinctions, they are as likely to serve the devil, without intending it, as God. A very few, as heroes, patriots, martyrs, reformers in the great sense, and *men*, serve the State with their consciences also, and so necessarily resist it for the most part; and they are commonly treated by it as enemies. A wise man will only be useful as a man, and will not submit to be "clay," and "stop a hole to keep the wind away,"[7] but leave that office to his dust at least:—

"I am too high-born to be propertied,
To be a secondary at control,
Or useful serving-man and instrument
To any sovereign state throughout the world."[8]

He who gives himself entirely to his fellow-men appears to them useless and selfish; but he who gives himself partially to them is pronounced a benefactor and philanthropist.

How does it become a man to behave toward this American government to-day? I answer that he cannot without disgrace be associated with it. I

5. From the Irish poet Charles Wolfe's "Burial of Sir John Moore at Corunna" (1817), a song Thoreau liked to sing. "Corse": corpse.

6. Sheriff's posse (Latin).

7. Shakespeare's *Hamlet* 5.1.236–37.

8. Shakespeare's *King John* 5.1.79–82.

cannot for an instant recognize that political organization as *my* government which is the *slave's* government also.

All men recognize the right of revolution; that is, the right to refuse allegiance to and to resist the government, when its tyranny or its inefficiency are great and unendurable. But almost all say that such is not the case now. But such was the case, they think, in the Revolution of '75. If one were to tell me that this was a bad government because it taxed certain foreign commodities brought to its ports, it is most probable that I should not make an ado about it, for I can do without them: all machines have their friction; and possibly this does enough good to counterbalance the evil. At any rate, it is a great evil to make a stir about it. But when the friction comes to have its machine, and oppression and robbery are organized, I say, let us not have such a machine any longer. In other words, when a sixth of the population of a nation which has undertaken to be the refuge of liberty are slaves, and a whole country is unjustly overrun and conquered by a foreign army, and subjected to military law, I think that it is not too soon for honest men to rebel and revolutionize. What makes this duty the more urgent is the fact, that the country so overrun is not our own, but ours is the invading army.

Paley, a common authority with many on moral questions, in his chapter on the "Duty of Submission to Civil Government," resolves all civil obligation into expediency; and he proceeds to say, "that so long as the interest of the whole society requires it, that is, so long as the established government cannot be resisted or changed without public inconveniency, it is the will of God that the established government be obeyed, and no longer."—"This principle being admitted, the justice of every particular case of resistance is reduced to a computation of the quantity of the danger and grievance on the one side, and of the probability and expense of redressing it on the other." Of this, he says, every man shall judge for himself. But Paley appears never to have contemplated those cases to which the rule of expediency does not apply, in which a people, as well as an individual, must do justice, cost what it may. If I have unjustly wrested a plank from a drowning man, I must restore it to him though I drown myself.[9] This, according to Paley, would be inconvenient. But he that would save his life, in such a case, shall lose it.[1] This people must cease to hold slaves, and to make war on Mexico, though it cost them their existence as a people.

In their practice, nations agree with Paley; but does any one think that Massachusetts does exactly what is right at the present crisis?

> "A drab of state, a cloth-o'-silver slut,
> To have her train borne up, and her soul trail in the dirt."[2]

Practically speaking, the opponents to a reform in Massachusetts are not a hundred thousand politicians at the South, but a hundred thousand merchants and farmers here,[3] who are more interested in commerce and agriculture than they are in humanity, and are not prepared to do justice to the slave and to Mexico, *cost what it may.* I quarrel not with far-off foes, but

9. A problem in situational ethics cited by Cicero (106–43 B.C.E.) in *De Officiis* 3, which Thoreau had studied.
1. Matthew 10.39; Luke 9.24.
2. Cyril Tourneur (1575?–1626), *The Revenger's Tragedy* 3.4.
3. Thoreau refers to the economic alliance of Southern cotton growers with Northern shippers, farmers, and manufacturers.

with those who, near at home, co-operate with, and do the bidding of those far away, and without whom the latter would be harmless. We are accustomed to say, that the mass of men are unprepared; but improvement is slow, because the few are not materially wiser or better than the many. It is not so important that many should be as good as you, as that there be some absolute goodness somewhere; for that will leaven the whole lump.[4] There are thousands who are *in opinion* opposed to slavery and to the war, who yet in effect do nothing to put an end to them; who, esteeming themselves children of Washington and Franklin, sit down with their hands in their pockets, and say that they know not what to do, and do nothing; who even postpone the question of freedom to the question of free-trade, and quietly read the prices-current along with the latest advices[5] from Mexico, after dinner, and, it may be, fall asleep over them both. What is the price-current of an honest man and patriot to-day? They hesitate, and they regret, and sometimes they petition; but they do nothing in earnest and with effect. They will wait, well disposed, for others to remedy the evil, that they may no longer have it to regret. At most, they give only a cheap vote, and a feeble countenance and God-speed, to the right, as it goes by them. There are nine hundred and ninety-nine patrons of virtue to one virtuous man; but it is easier to deal with the real possessor of a thing than with the temporary guardian of it.

All voting is a sort of gaming, like chequers or backgammon, with a slight moral tinge to it, a playing with right and wrong, with moral questions; and betting naturally accompanies it. The character of the voters is not staked. I cast my vote, perchance, as I think right; but I am not vitally concerned that that right should prevail. I am willing to leave it to the majority. Its obligation, therefore, never exceeds that of expediency. Even voting *for the right* is *doing* nothing for it. It is only expressing to men feebly your desire that it should prevail. A wise man will not leave the right to the mercy of chance, nor wish it to prevail through the power of the majority. There is but little virtue in the action of masses of men. When the majority shall at length vote for the abolition of slavery, it will be because they are indifferent to slavery, or because there is but little slavery left to be abolished by their vote. *They* will then be the only slaves. Only *his* vote can hasten the abolition of slavery who asserts his own freedom by his vote.

I hear of a convention to be held at Baltimore,[6] or elsewhere, for the selection of a candidate for the Presidency, made up chiefly of editors, and men who are politicians by profession; but I think, what is it to any independent, intelligent, and respectable man what decision they may come to, shall we not have the advantage of his wisdom and honesty, nevertheless? Can we not count upon some independent votes? Are there not many individuals in the country who do not attend conventions? But no: I find that the respectable man, so called, has immediately drifted from his position, and despairs of his country, when his country has more reason to despair of him. He forthwith adopts one of the candidates thus selected as the only *available* one, thus proving that he is himself *available* for any purposes of the demagogue. His

4. 1 Corinthians 5.6: "Know ye not that a little leaven leaveneth the whole lump?"

5. New dispatches. "Children of Washington and Franklin": i.e., patriotic Americans, children of rebels and revolutionaries.

6. The Democratic convention was held in Baltimore in May 1848.

vote is of no more worth than that of any unprincipled foreigner or hireling native, who may have been bought. Oh for a man who is a *man,* and, as my neighbor says, has a bone in his back which you cannot pass your hand through! Our statistics are at fault: the population has been returned too large. How many *men* are there to a square thousand miles in this country? Hardly one. Does not America offer any inducement for men to settle here? The American has dwindled into an Odd Fellow,—one who may be known by the development of his organ of gregariousness, and a manifest lack of intellect and cheerful self-reliance; whose first and chief concern, on coming into the world, is to see that the alms-houses are in good repair; and, before yet he has lawfully donned the virile garb,[7] to collect a fund for the support of the widows and orphans that may be; who, in short, ventures to live only by the aid of the mutual insurance company, which has promised to bury him decently.

It is not a man's duty, as a matter of course, to devote himself to the eradication of any, even the most enormous wrong; he may still properly have other concerns to engage him; but it is his duty, at least, to wash his hands of it, and, if he gives it no thought longer, not to give it practically his support. If I devote myself to other pursuits and contemplations, I must first see, at least, that I do not pursue them sitting upon another man's shoulders. I must get off him first, that he may pursue his contemplations too. See what gross inconsistency is tolerated. I have heard some of my townsmen say, "I should like to have them order me out to help put down an insurrection of the slaves, or to march to Mexico,—see if I would go;" and yet these very men have each, directly by their allegiance, and so indirectly, at least, by their money, furnished a substitute. The soldier is applauded who refuses to serve in an unjust war by those who do not refuse to sustain the unjust government which makes the war; is applauded by those whose own act and authority he disregards and sets at nought; as if the State were penitent to that degree that it hired one to scourge it while it sinned, but not to that degree that it left off sinning for a moment. Thus, under the name of order and civil government, we are all made at last to pay homage to and support our own meanness. After the first blush of sin, comes its indifference; and from immoral it becomes, as it were, *un*moral, and not quite unnecessary to that life which we have made.

The broadest and most prevalent error requires the most disinterested virtue to sustain it. The slight reproach to which the virtue of patriotism is commonly liable, the noble are most likely to incur. Those who, while they disapprove of the character and measures of a government, yield to it their allegiance and support, are undoubtedly its most conscientious supporters, and so frequently the most serious obstacles to reform. Some are petitioning the State to dissolve the Union, to disregard the requisitions of the President. Why do they not dissolve it themselves,—the union between themselves and the State,—and refuse to pay their quota into its treasury? Do not they stand in the same relation to the State, that the State does to the Union? And have

7. Adult clothes allowed for a Roman boy on reaching the age of fourteen. The Independent Order of Odd Fellows, a benevolent fraternal organization, was chosen by Thoreau for the satirical value of its name; in his view the archetypal American is not the individualist, the genuine odd fellow, but the conformist.

not the same reasons prevented the State from resisting the Union, which have prevented them from resisting the State?

How can a man be satisfied to entertain an opinion merely, and enjoy *it*? Is there any enjoyment in it, if his opinion is that he is aggrieved? If you are cheated out of a single dollar by your neighbor, you do not rest satisfied with knowing that you are cheated, or with saying that you are cheated, or even with petitioning him to pay you your due; but you take effectual steps at once to obtain the full amount, and see that you are never cheated again. Action from principle,—the perception and the performance of right,—changes things and relations; it is essentially revolutionary, and does not consist wholly with any thing which was. It not only divides states and churches, it divides families; aye, it divides the *individual*, separating the diabolical in him from the divine.

Unjust laws exist: shall we be content to obey them, or shall we endeavor to amend them, and obey them until we have succeeded, or shall we transgress them at once? Men generally, under such a government as this, think that they ought to wait until they have persuaded the majority to alter them. They think that, if they should resist, the remedy would be worse than the evil. But it is the fault of the government itself that the remedy *is* worse than the evil. *It* makes it worse. Why is it not more apt to anticipate and provide for reform? Why does it not cherish its wise minority? Why does it cry and resist before it is hurt? Why does it not encourage its citizens to be on the alert to point out its faults, and *do* better than it would have them? Why does it always crucify Christ, and excommunicate Copernicus and Luther,[8] and pronounce Washington and Franklin rebels?

One would think, that a deliberate and practical denial of its authority was the only offence never contemplated by government; else, why has it not assigned its definite, its suitable and proportionate penalty? If a man who has no property refuses but once to earn nine shillings[9] for the State, he is put in prison for a period unlimited by any law that I know, and determined only by the discretion of those who placed him there; but if he should steal ninety times nine shillings from the State, he is soon permitted to go at large again.

If the injustice is part of the necessary friction of the machine of government, let it go, let it go: perchance it will wear smooth,—certainly the machine will wear out. If the injustice has a spring, or a pulley, or a rope, or a crank, exclusively for itself, then perhaps you may consider whether the remedy will not be worse than the evil; but if it is of such a nature that it requires you to be the agent of injustice to another, then, I say, break the law. Let your life be a counter friction to stop the machine. What I have to do is to see, at any rate, that I do not lend myself to the wrong which I condemn.

As for adopting the ways which the State has provided for remedying the evil, I know not of such ways. They take too much time, and a man's life will be gone. I have other affairs to attend to. I came into this world, not chiefly

8. Thoreau cites as announcers of new truths Copernicus (1473–1543), the Polish astronomer who died too soon after the publication of his new system of astronomy to be excommunicated from the Catholic Church for writing it, and Martin Luther (1483–1546), the German leader of the Protestant Reformation who was excommunicated.

9. Because of sporadic coin shortages, the British shilling was still in use in parts of the United States during the 1840s; it was valued at approximately 20 U.S. cents. The amount of the tax, assessed on adult male citizens, was $1.50, approximately $30 in today's currency.

to make this a good place to live in, but to live in it, be it good or bad. A man has not every thing to do, but something; and because he cannot do *every thing*, it is not necessary that he should do *something* wrong. It is not my business to be petitioning the governor or the legislature any more than it is theirs to petition me; and, if they should not hear my petition, what should I do then? But in this case the State has provided no way: its very Constitution is the evil. This may seem to be harsh and stubborn and unconciliatory; but it is to treat with the utmost kindness and consideration the only spirit that can appreciate or deserves it. So is all change for the better, like birth and death which convulse the body.

I do not hesitate to say, that those who call themselves abolitionists should at once effectually withdraw their support, both in person and property, from the government of Massachusetts, and not wait till they constitute a majority of one, before they suffer the right to prevail through them. I think that it is enough if they have God on their side, without waiting for that other one. Moreover, any man more right than his neighbors, constitutes a majority of one already.[1]

I meet this American government, or its representative the State government, directly, and face to face, once a year, no more, in the person of its tax-gatherer; this is the only mode in which a man situated as I am necessarily meets it; and it then says distinctly, Recognize me; and the simplest, the most effectual, and, in the present posture of affairs, the indispensablest mode of treating with it on this head, of expressing your little satisfaction with and love for it, is to deny it then. My civil neighbor, the tax-gatherer,[2] is the very man I have to deal with,—for it is, after all, with men and not with parchment that I quarrel,—and he has voluntarily chosen to be an agent of the government. How shall he ever know well what he is and does as an officer of the government, or as a man, until he is obliged to consider whether he shall treat me, his neighbor, for whom he has respect, as a neighbor and well-disposed man, or as a maniac and disturber of the peace, and see if he can get over this obstruction to his neighborliness without a ruder and more impetuous thought or speech corresponding with his action? I know this well, that if one thousand, if one hundred, if ten men whom I could name,—if ten *honest* men only,—aye, if *one* HONEST man, in this State of Massachusetts, *ceasing to hold slaves*, were actually to withdraw from this copartnership, and be locked up in the county jail therefor, it would be the abolition of slavery in America. For it matters not how small the beginning may seem to be: what is once well done is done for ever. But we love better to talk about it: that we say is our mission. Reform keeps many scores of newspapers in its service, but not one man. If my esteemed neighbor, the State's ambassador,[3] who will devote his days to the settlement of the question of human rights in the Council Chamber, instead of being threatened with the prisons of Carolina, were to sit down the prisoner of Massachusetts, that State which is so anxious to foist the sin of slavery upon her sister,—though at present she can discover only an act of inhospitality to be the ground of

1. John Knox (1505?–1572), the Scottish religious reformer, said that "a man with God is always in the majority."
2. Sam Staples, who sometimes assisted Thoreau in his surveying.
3. Samuel Hoar (1778–1856), local political figure who as agent of the state of Massachusetts had been expelled from Charleston, South Carolina, in 1844 while interceding on behalf of imprisoned black seamen from Massachusetts.

a quarrel with her,—the Legislature would not wholly waive the subject the following winter.

Under a government which imprisons any unjustly, the true place for a just man is also a prison. The proper place to-day, the only place which Massachusetts has provided for her freer and less desponding spirits, is in her prisons, to be put out and locked out of the State by her own act, as they have already put themselves out by their principles. It is there that the fugitive slave, and the Mexican prisoner on parole, and the Indian come to plead the wrongs of his race, should find them; on that separate, but more free and honorable ground, where the State places those who are not *with* her but *against* her,—the only house in a slave-state in which a free man can abide with honor. If any think that their influence would be lost there, and their voices no longer afflict the ear of the State, that they would not be as an enemy within its walls, they do not know by how much truth is stronger than error, nor how much more eloquently and effectively he can combat injustice who has experienced a little in his own person. Cast your whole vote, not a strip of paper merely, but your whole influence. A minority is powerless while it conforms to the majority; it is not even a minority then; but it is irresistible when it clogs by its whole weight. If the alternative is to keep all just men in prison, or give up war and slavery, the State will not hesitate which to choose. If a thousand men were not to pay their tax-bills this year, that would not be a violent and bloody measure, as it would be to pay them, and enable the State to commit violence and shed innocent blood. This is, in fact, the definition of a peaceable revolution, if any such is possible. If the tax-gatherer, or any other public officer, asks me, as one has done, "But what shall I do?" my answer is, "If you really wish to do any thing, resign your office." When the subject has refused allegiance, and the officer has resigned his office, then the revolution is accomplished. But even suppose blood should flow. Is there not a sort of blood shed when the conscience is wounded? Through this wound a man's real manhood and immortality flow out, and he bleeds to an everlasting death. I see this blood flowing now.

I have contemplated the imprisonment of the offender, rather than the seizure of his goods,—though both will serve the same purpose,—because they who assert the purest right, and consequently are most dangerous to a corrupt State, commonly have not spent much time in accumulating property. To such the State renders comparatively small service, and a slight tax is wont to appear exorbitant, particularly if they are obliged to earn it by special labor with their hands. If there were one who lived wholly without the use of money, the State itself would hesitate to demand it of him. But the rich man—not to make any invidious comparison—is always sold to the institution which makes him rich. Absolutely speaking, the more money, the less virtue; for money comes between a man and his objects, and obtains them for him; and it was certainly no great virtue to obtain it. It puts to rest many questions which he would otherwise be taxed to answer; while the only new question which it puts is the hard but superfluous one, how to spend it. Thus his moral ground is taken from under his feet. The opportunities of living are diminished in proportion as what are called the "means" are increased. The best thing a man can do for his culture when he is rich is to endeavour to carry out those schemes which he entertained when he was poor. Christ answered the Herodians according to their condition. "Show me the tribute-money," said he;—and one took a penny out of his pocket;—If you use money which has the image of Cæsar on it, and which he has made current and valuable, that is, *if you are men of the State*, and gladly enjoy the advantages of Cæsar's government, then pay him back some of his own when he demands it: "Render therefore to Cæsar that which is Cæsar's, and to God those things which are God's,"[4]—leaving them no wiser than before as to which was which; for they did not wish to know.

When I converse with the freest of my neighbors, I perceive that, whatever they may say about the magnitude and seriousness of the question, and their regard for the public tranquillity, the long and the short of the matter is, that they cannot spare the protection of the existing government, and they dread the consequences of disobedience to it to their property and families. For my own part, I should not like to think that I ever rely on the protection of the State. But, if I deny the authority of the State when it presents its tax-bill, it will soon take and waste all my property, and so harass me and my children without end. This is hard. This makes it impossible for a man to live honestly and at the same time comfortably in outward respects. It will not be worth the while to accumulate property; that would be sure to go again. You must hire or squat somewhere, and raise but a small crop, and eat that soon. You must live within yourself, and depend upon yourself, always tucked up and ready for a start, and not have many affairs. A man may grow rich in Turkey even, if he will be in all respects a good subject of the Turkish government. Confucious said,—"If a State is governed by the principles of reason, poverty and misery are subjects of shame; if a State is not governed by the principles of reason, riches and honors are the subjects of shame."[5] No: until I want the protection of Massachusetts to be extended to me in some distant southern port, where my liberty is endangered, or until I am bent solely on building up an estate at home at peaceful enterprise, I can afford to refuse allegiance to Massachusetts, and her right to my property and life. It costs me less in every sense to incur the penalty of disobedience to the State, than it would to obey. I should feel as if I were worth less in that case.

Some years ago, the State met me in behalf of the church, and commanded me to pay a certain sum toward the support of a clergyman whose preaching my father attended, but never I myself. "Pay it," it said, "or be locked up in the jail." I declined to pay. But, unfortunately, another man saw fit to pay it. I did not see why the schoolmaster should be taxed to support the priest, and not the priest the schoolmaster; for I was not the State's schoolmaster, but I supported myself by voluntary subscription. I did not see why the lyceum should not present its tax-bill, and have the State to back its demand, as well as the church. However, at the request of the selectmen, I condescended to make some such statement as this in writing:—"Know all men by these presents, that I, Henry Thoreau, do not wish to be regarded as a member of any incorporated society which I have not joined." This I gave to the town-clerk; and he has it. The State, having thus learned that I did not wish to be regarded as a member of that church, has never made a like demand on me since; though it said that it must adhere to its original presumption that time. If I had known

4. Matthew 22.16–21. In their attempt to entrap Jesus, the Pharisees (a Jewish sect that held to Mosaic law) were using secular government functionaries of Herod, the king of Judea.

5. Confucius's *Analects* 8.13.

how to name them, I should then have signed off in detail from all the societies which I never signed on to; but I did not know where to find a complete list.

I have paid no poll-tax for six years.[6] I was put into a jail[7] once on this account, for one night; and, as I stood considering the walls of solid stone, two or three feet thick, the door of wood and iron, a foot thick, and the iron grating which strained the light, I could not help being struck with the foolishness of that institution which treated me as if I were mere flesh and blood and bones, to be locked up. I wondered that it should have concluded at length that this was the best use it could put me to, and had never thought to avail itself of my services in some way. I saw that, if there was a wall of stone between me and my townsmen, there was a still more difficult one to climb or break through, before they could get to be as free as I was. I did not for a moment feel confined, and the walls seemed a great waste of stone and mortar. I felt as if I alone of all my townsmen had paid my tax. They plainly did not know how to treat me, but behaved like persons who are underbred. In every threat and in every compliment there was a blunder; for they thought that my chief desire was to stand the other side of that stone wall. I could not but smile to see how industriously they locked the door on my meditations, which followed them out again without let or hinderance, and *they* were really all that was dangerous. As they could not reach me, they had resolved to punish my body; just as boys, if they cannot come at some person against whom they have a spite, will abuse his dog. I saw that the State was half-witted, that it was timid as a lone woman with her silver spoons, and that it did not know its friends from its foes, and I lost all my remaining respect for it, and pitied it.

Thus the State never intentionally confronts a man's sense, intellectual or moral, but only his body, his senses. It is not armed with superior wit or honesty, but with superior physical strength. I was not born to be forced. I will breathe after my own fashion. Let us see who is the strongest. What force has a multitude? They only can force me who obey a higher law than I. They force me to become like themselves. I do not hear of *men* being *forced* to live this way or that by masses of men. What sort of life were that to live? When I meet a government which says to me, "Your money or your life," why should I be in haste to give it my money? It may be in a great strait, and not know what to do: I cannot help that. It must help itself; do as I do. It is not worth the while to snivel about it. I am not responsible for the successful working of the machinery of society. I am not the son of the engineer. I perceive that, when an acorn and a chestnut fall side by side, the one does not remain inert to make way for the other, but both obey their own laws, and spring and grow and flourish as best they can, till one, perchance, overshadows and destroys the other. If a plant cannot live according to its nature, it dies; and so a man.

The night in prison was novel and interesting enough. The prisoners in their shirt-sleeves were enjoying a chat and the evening air in the door-way, when I entered. But the jailer said, "Come, boys, it is time to lock up;" and so they dispersed, and I heard the sound of their steps

6. I.e., since 1840.
7. The Middlesex County jail in Concord, a large three-story building.

returning into the hollow apartments. My room-mate was introduced to me by the jailer, as "a first-rate fellow and a clever man." When the door was locked, he showed me where to hang my hat, and how he managed matters there. The rooms were whitewashed once a month; and this one, at least, was the whitest, most simply furnished, and probably the neatest apartment in the town. He naturally wanted to know where I came from, and what brought me there; and, when I had told him, I asked him in my turn how he came there, presuming him to be an honest man, of course; and, as the world goes, I believe he was. "Why," said he, "they accuse me of burning a barn; but I never did it." As near as I could discover, he had probably gone to bed in a barn when drunk, and smoked his pipe there; and so a barn was burnt. He had the reputation of being a clever man, had been there some three months waiting for his trial to come on, and would have to wait as much longer; but he was quite domesticated and contented since he got his board for nothing, and thought that he was well treated.

He occupied one window, and I the other; and I saw, that, if one stayed there long, his principal business would be to look out the window. I had soon read all the tracts that were left there, and examined where former prisoners had broken out, and where a grate had been sawed off, and heard the history of the various occupants of that room; for I found that even here there was a history and a gossip which never circulated beyond the walls of the jail. Probably this is the only house in the town where verses are composed, which are afterward printed in a circular form, but not published. I was shown quite a long list of verses which were composed by some young men who had been detected in an attempt to escape, who avenged themselves by singing them.

I pumped my fellow-prisoner as dry as I could, for fear I should never see him again; but at length he showed me which was my bed, and left me to blow out the lamp.

It was like travelling into a far country, such as I had never expected to behold, to lie there for one night. It seemed to me that I never had heard the town-clock strike before, nor the evening sounds of the village; for we slept with the windows open, which were inside the grating. It was to see my native village in the light of the middle ages, and our Concord was turned into a Rhine stream, and visions of knights and castles passed before me. They were the voices of old burghers that I heard in the streets. I was an involuntary spectator and auditor of whatever was done and said in the kitchen of the adjacent village-inn,—a wholly new and rare experience to me. It was a closer view of my native town. I was fairly inside of it. I never had seen its institutions before. This is one of its peculiar institutions; for it is a shire town.[8] I began to comprehend what its inhabitants were about.

In the morning, our breakfasts were put through the hole in the door, in small oblong-square tin pans, made to fit, and holding a pint of chocolate, with brown bread, and an iron spoon. When they called for the vessels again, I was green enough to return what bread I had left; but my

8. Comparable to county seat.

comrade seized it, and said that I should lay that up for lunch or dinner. Soon after, he was let out to work at haying in a neighboring field, whither he went every day, and would not be back till noon; so he bade me good-day, saying that he doubted if he should see me again.

When I came out of prison,—for some one interfered, and paid the tax,[9]—I did not perceive that great changes had taken place on the common, such as he observed who went in a youth, and emerged a tottering and gray-headed man; and yet a change had to my eyes come over the scene,—the town, and State, and country,—greater than any that mere time could effect. I saw yet more distinctly the State in which I lived. I saw to what extent the people among whom I lived could be trusted as good neighbors and friends; that their friendship was for summer weather only; that they did not greatly purpose to do right; that they were a distinct race from me by their prejudices and superstitions, as the Chinamen and Malays are; that, in their sacrifices to humanity, they ran no risks, not even to their property; that, after all, they were not so noble but they treated the thief as he had treated them, and hoped, by a certain outward observance and a few prayers, and by walking in a particular straight though useless path from time to time, to save their souls. This may be to judge my neighbors harshly; for I believe that most of them are not aware that they have such an institution as the jail in their village.

It was formerly the custom in our village, when a poor debtor came out of jail, for his acquaintances to salute him, looking through their fingers, which were crossed to represent the grating of a jail window, "How do ye do?" My neighbors did not thus salute me, but first looked at me, and then at one another, as if I had returned from a long journey. I was put into jail as I was going to the shoemaker's to get a shoe which was mended. When I was let out the next morning, I proceeded to finish my errand, and, having put on my mended shoe, joined a huckleberry party, who were impatient to put themselves under my conduct; and in half an hour,—for the horse was soon tackled,[1]—was in the midst of a huckleberry field, on one of our highest hills, two miles off; and then the State was nowhere to be seen.

This is the whole history of "My Prisons."[2]

I have never declined paying the highway tax, because I am as desirous of being a good neighbor as I am of being a bad subject; and, as for supporting schools, I am doing my part to educate my fellow-countrymen now. It is for no particular item in the tax-bill that I refuse to pay it. I simply wish to refuse allegiance to the State, to withdraw and stand aloof from it effectually. I do not care to trace the course of my dollar, if I could, till it buys a man, or a musket to shoot one with,—the dollar is innocent,—but I am concerned to trace the effects of my allegiance. In fact, I quietly declare war with the State, after my fashion, though I will still make what use and get what advantage of her I can, as is usual in such cases.

If others pay the tax which is demanded of me, from a sympathy with the State, they do but what they have already done in their own case, or rather

9. The identity of this person is unknown.
1. Harnessed.
2. An allusion to the title of a book (1832) by the Italian poet Silvio Pellico (1789–1854) describing his years of hard labor in Austrian prisons.

they abet injustice to a greater extent than the State requires. If they pay the tax from a mistaken interest in the individual taxed, to save his property or prevent his going to jail, it is because they have not considered wisely how far they let their private feelings interfere with the public good.

This, then, is my position at present. But one cannot be too much on his guard in such a case, lest his action be biassed by obstinacy, or an undue regard for the opinions of men. Let him see that he does only what belongs to himself and to the hour.

I think sometimes, Why, this people mean well; they are only ignorant; they would do better if they knew how; why give your neighbors this pain to treat you as they are not inclined to? But I think, again, this is no reason why I should do as they do, or permit others to suffer much greater pain of a different kind. Again, I sometimes say to myself, When many millions of men, without heat, without ill-will, without personal feeling of any kind, demand of you a few shillings only, without the possibility, such is their constitution, of retracting or altering their present demand, and without the possibility, on your side, of appeal to any other millions, why expose yourself to this overwhelming brute force? You do not resist cold and hunger, the winds and the waves, thus obstinately; you quietly submit to a thousand similar necessities. You do not put your head into the fire. But just in proportion as I regard this as not wholly a brute force, but partly a human force, and consider that I have relations to those millions as to so many millions of men, and not of mere brute or inanimate things, I see that appeal is possible, first and instantaneously, from them to the Maker of them, and, secondly, from them to themselves. But, if I put my head deliberately into the fire, there is no appeal to fire or to the Maker of fire, and I have only myself to blame. If I could convince myself that I have any right to be satisfied with men as they are, and to treat them accordingly, and not according, in some respects, to my requisitions and expectations of what they and I ought to be, then, like a good Mussulman[3] and fatalist, I should endeavor to be satisfied with things as they are, and say it is the will of God. And, above all, there is this difference between resisting this and a purely brute or natural force, that I can resist this with some effect; but I cannot expect, like Orpheus,[4] to change the nature of the rocks and trees and beasts.

I do not wish to quarrel with any man or nation. I do not wish to split hairs, to make fine distinctions, or set myself up as better than my neighbors. I seek rather, I may say, even an excuse for conforming to the laws of the land. I am but too ready to conform to them. Indeed I have reason to suspect myself on this head; and each year, as the tax-gatherer comes round, I find myself disposed to review the acts and position of the general and state governments, and the spirit of the people, to discover a pretext for conformity. I believe that the State will soon be able to take all my work of this sort out of my hands, and then I shall be no better a patriot than my fellow-countrymen. Seen from a lower point of view, the Constitution, with all its faults, is very good; the law and the courts are very respectable; even this State and this American government are, in many respects, very admirable and rare things, to be thankful for, such as a great many have described them; but seen from

3. Muslim.
4. In Greek mythology, Orpheus's singing and playing of the lyre charmed animals and moved even rocks and trees to dance.

a point of view a little higher, they are what I have described them; seen from a higher still, and the highest, who shall say what they are, or that they are worth looking at or thinking of at all?

However, the government does not concern me much, and I shall bestow the fewest possible thoughts on it. It is not many moments that I live under a government, even in this world. If a man is thought-free, fancy-free, imagination-free, that which *is not* never for a long time appearing *to be* to him, unwise rulers or reformers cannot fatally interrupt him.

I know that most men think differently from myself; but those whose lives are by profession devoted to the study of these or kindred subjects, content me as little as any. Statesmen and legislators, standing so completely within the institution, never distinctly and nakedly behold it. They speak of moving society, but have no resting-place without it. They may be men of a certain experience and discrimination, and have no doubt invented ingenious and even useful systems, for which we sincerely thank them; but all their wit and usefulness lie within certain not very wide limits. They are wont to forget that the world is not governed by policy and expediency. Webster[5] never goes behind government, and so cannot speak with authority about it. His words are wisdom to those legislators who contemplate no essential reform in the existing government; but for thinkers, and those who legislate for all time, he never once glances at the subject. I know of those whose serene and wise speculations on this theme would soon reveal the limits of his mind's range and hospitality. Yet, compared with the cheap professions of most reformers, and the still cheaper wisdom and eloquence of politicians in general, his are almost the only sensible and valuable words, and we thank Heaven for him. Comparatively, he is always strong, original, and, above all, practical. Still his quality is not wisdom, but prudence. The lawyer's truth is not Truth, but consistency, or a consistent expediency. Truth is always in harmony with herself, and is not concerned chiefly to reveal the justice that may consist with wrong-doing. He well deserves to be called, as he has been called, the Defender of the Constitution. There are really no blows to be given by him but defensive ones. He is not a leader, but a follower. His leaders are the men of '87.[6] "I have never made an effort," he says, "and never propose to make an effort; I have never countenanced an effort, and never mean to countenance an effort, to disturb the arrangement as originally made, by which the various States came into the Union."[7] Still thinking of the sanction which the Constitution gives to slavery, he says, "Because it was a part of the original compact,—let it stand." Notwithstanding his special acuteness and ability, he is unable to take a fact out of its merely political relations, and behold it as it lies absolutely to be disposed of by the intellect,—what, for instance, it behoves a man to do here in America to-day with regard to slavery, but ventures, or is driven, to make some such desperate answer as the following, while professing to speak absolutely, and as a private man,—from which what new and singular code of social duties might be inferred?—"The manner," says he, "in which the government of those States where slavery exists are to regulate it, is for their own consideration, under their responsi-

5. Daniel Webster (1782–1852), prominent Massachusetts Whig politician of the second quarter of the 19th century.

6. The authors of the U.S. Constitution.

7. From Webster's speech "The Admission of Texas" (December 22, 1845).

bility to their constituents, to the general laws of propriety, humanity, and justice, and to God. Associations formed elsewhere, springing from a feeling of humanity, or any other cause, having nothing whatever to do with it. They have never received any encouragement from me, and they never will."[8]

They who know of no purer sources of truth, who have traced up its stream no higher, stand, and wisely stand, by the Bible and the Constitution, and drink at it there with reverence and humility; but they who behold where it comes trickling into this lake or that pool, gird up their loins once more, and continue their pilgrimage toward its fountain-head.

No man with a genius for legislation has appeared in America. They are rare in the history of the world. There are orators, politicians, and eloquent men, by the thousand; but the speaker has not yet opened his mouth to speak, who is capable of settling the much-vexed questions of the day. We love eloquence for its own sake, and not for any truth which it may utter, or any heroism it may inspire. Our legislators have not yet learned the comparative value of free-trade and of freedom, of union, and of rectitude, to a nation. They have no genius or talent for comparatively humble questions of taxation and finance, commerce and manufactures and agriculture. If we were left solely to the wordy wit of legislators in Congress for our guidance, uncorrected by the seasonable experience and the effectual complaints of the people, America would not long retain her rank among the nations. For eighteen hundred years, though perchance I have no right to say it, the New Testament has been written; yet where is the legislator who has wisdom and practical talent enough to avail himself of the light which it sheds on the science of legislation?

The authority of government, even such as I am willing to submit to,—for I will cheerfully obey those who know and can do better than I, and in many things even those who neither know nor can do so well,—is still an impure one: to be strictly just, it must have the sanction and consent of the governed. It can have no pure right over my person and property but what I concede to it. The progress from an absolute to a limited monarchy, from a limited monarchy to a democracy, is a progress toward a true respect for the individual. Is a democracy, such as we know it, the last improvement possible in government? Is it not possible to take a step further towards recognizing and organizing the rights of man? There will never be a really free and enlightened State, until the State comes to recognize the individual as a higher and independent power, from which all its own power and authority are derived, and treats him accordingly. I please myself with imagining a State at last which can afford to be just to all men, and to treat the individual with respect as a neighbor; which even would not think it inconsistent with its own repose, if a few were to live aloof from it, not meddling with it, nor embraced by it, who fulfilled all the duties of neighbors and fellow-men. A State which bore this kind of fruit, and suffered it to drop off as fast as it ripened, would prepare the way for a still more perfect and glorious State, which also I have imagined, but not yet anywhere seen.

1849, 1866

8. "These extracts have been inserted since the Lecture was read" [Thoreau's note]. He is referring to the quotation beginning "The manner."

WALDEN;

OR,

LIFE IN THE WOODS.

By HENRY D. THOREAU,

AUTHOR OF "A WEEK ON THE CONCORD AND MERRIMACK RIVERS."

I do not propose to write an ode to dejection, but to brag as lustily as chanticleer in the morning, standing on his roost, if only to wake my neighbors up. — Page 92.

BOSTON:

TICKNOR AND FIELDS.

M DCCC LIV.

Walden. Title page of the first edition (1854); the drawing is by Thoreau's sister Sophia.

Walden, or Life in the Woods[1]

> I do not propose to write an ode to dejection, but to brag as lustily as chanticleer in the morning, standing on his roost, if only to wake my neighbors up.

1. Economy

When I wrote the following pages, or rather the bulk of them, I lived alone, in the woods, a mile from any neighbor, in a house which I had built myself, on the shore of Walden Pond, in Concord, Massachusetts, and earned my living by the labor of my hands only. I lived there two years and two months. At present I am a sojourner in civilized life again.

I should not obtrude my affairs so much on the notice of my readers if very particular inquiries had not been made by my townsmen concerning my mode of life, which some would call impertinent, though they do not appear to me at all impertinent, but, considering the circumstances, very natural and pertinent. Some have asked what I got to eat; if I did not feel lonesome; if I was not afraid; and the like. Others have been curious to learn what portion of my income I devoted to charitable purposes; and some, who have large families, how many poor children I maintained. I will therefore ask those of my readers who feel no particular interest in me to pardon me if I undertake to answer some of these questions in this book. In most books, the *I*, or first person, is omitted; in this it will be retained; that, in respect to egotism, is the main difference. We commonly do not remember that it is, after all, always the first person that is speaking. I should not talk so much about myself if there were any body else whom I knew as well. Unfortunately, I am confined to this theme by the narrowness of my experience. Moreover, I, on my side, require of every writer, first or last, a simple and sincere account of his own life, and not merely what he has heard of other men's lives; some such account as he would send to his kindred from a distant land; for if he has lived sincerely, it must have been in a distant land to me. Perhaps these pages are more particularly addressed to poor students. As for the rest of my readers, they will accept such portions as apply to them. I trust that none will stretch the seams in putting on the coat, for it may do good service to him whom it fits.

I would fain say something, not so much concerning the Chinese and Sandwich Islanders[2] as you who read these pages, who are said to live in New England; something about your condition, especially your outward condition or circumstances in this world, in this town, what it is, whether it is necessary that it be as bad as it is, whether it cannot be improved as well as not. I have travelled a good deal in Concord; and every where, in shops, and offices, and fields, the inhabitants have appeared to me to be doing penance in a thousand remarkable ways. What I have heard of Brahmins sitting exposed to four fires and looking in the face of the sun; or hanging suspended, with their

1. Thoreau began writing *Walden* early in 1846, some months after he began living at Walden Pond, and by late 1847, when he moved back into the village of Concord, he had drafted roughly half the book. Between 1852 and 1854 he rewrote the manuscript several times and substantially enlarged it. The text printed here is that of the 1st edition (1854), with a few printer's errors corrected on the basis of Thoreau's set of marked proofs, his corrections in his copy of *Walden*, and scholars' comparisons of the printed book and the manuscript drafts.

2. Hawaiians.

heads downward, over flames; or looking at the heavens over their shoulders "until it becomes impossible for them to resume their natural position, while from the twist of the neck nothing but liquids can pass into the stomach;" or dwelling, chained for life, at the foot of a tree; or measuring with their bodies, like caterpillars, the breadth of vast empires; or standing on one leg on the tops of pillars,—even these forms of conscious penance are hardly more incredible and astonishing than the scenes which I daily witness.[3] The twelve labors of Hercules[4] were trifling in comparison with those which my neighbors have undertaken; for they were only twelve, and had an end; but I could never see that these men slew or captured any monster or finished any labor. They have no friend Iolas to burn with a hot iron the root of the hydra's head, but as soon as one head is crushed, two spring up.

I see young men, my townsmen, whose misfortune it is to have inherited farms, houses, barns, cattle, and farming tools; for these are more easily acquired than got rid of. Better if they had been born in the open pasture and suckled by a wolf,[5] that they might have seen with clearer eyes what field they were called to labor in. Who made them serfs of the soil? Why should they eat their sixty acres, when man is condemned to eat only his peck of dirt? Why should they begin digging their graves as soon as they are born? They have got to live a man's life, pushing all these things before them, and get on as well as they can. How many a poor immortal soul have I met well nigh crushed and smothered under its load, creeping down the road of life, pushing before it a barn seventy-five feet by forty, its Augean stables never cleansed, and one hundred acres of land, tillage, mowing, pasture, and wood-lot! The portionless, who struggle with no such unnecessary inherited encumbrances, find it labor enough to subdue and cultivate a few cubic feet of flesh.

But men labor under a mistake. The better part of the man is soon ploughed into the soil for compost. By a seeming fate, commonly called necessity, they are employed, as it says in an old book, laying up treasures which moth and rust will corrupt and thieves break through and steal.[6] It is a fool's life, as they will find when they get to the end of it, if not before. It is said that Deucalion and Pyrrha created men by throwing stones over their heads behind them:[7]—

> Inde genus durum sumus, experiensque laborum,
> Et documenta damus quâ simus origine nati.[8]

Or, as Raleigh rhymes it in his sonorous way,—

> "From thence our kind hard-hearted is, enduring pain and care,
> Approving that our bodies of a stony nature are."

3. For his information on religious self-torture among high-caste Hindus in India, Thoreau drew on *The History of India* (1817) by James Mill (1773–1836).

4. Son of Zeus and Alcmene, this half-mortal could become a god only by performing twelve labors, each apparently impossible. The second labor, the slaying of the Lernaean hydra, a many-headed sea monster, is referred to just below. (Hercules' friend Iolas helped by searing the stump each time Hercules cut off one of the heads, which otherwise would have regenerated.) The seventh labor, mentioned in the following paragraph, was the cleansing of Augeas's filthy stables in one day, a feat Hercules accomplished by diverting two nearby rivers through the stables.

5. Roman myth tells of how Romulus and Remus, the founders of Rome, were suckled by a wolf.

6. Matthew 6.19.

7. According to Greek mythology, Deucalion and Pyrrha repopulated the earth by throwing stones behind them over their shoulders. The stones thrown by Deucalion turned into men, and the stones thrown by Pyrrha turned into women.

8. From *Metamorphoses*, by the Roman poet Ovid (43 B.C.E.–18 C.E.), and translated by Sir Walter Raleigh (1554?–1618) in his *History of the World* (1614).

So much for a blind obedience to a blundering oracle, throwing the stones over their heads behind them, and not seeing where they fell.

Most men, even in this comparatively free country, through mere ignorance and mistake, are so occupied with the factitious cares and superfluously coarse labors of life that its finer fruits cannot be plucked by them. Their fingers, from excessive toil, are too clumsy and tremble too much for that. Actually, the laboring man has not leisure for a true integrity day by day; he cannot afford to sustain the manliest relations to men; his labor would be depreciated in the market. He has no time to be any thing but a machine. How can he remember well his ignorance—which his growth requires—who has so often to use his knowledge? We should feed and clothe him gratuitously sometimes, and recruit him with our cordials, before we judge of him. The finest qualities of our nature, like the bloom on fruits, can be preserved only by the most delicate handling. Yet we do not treat ourselves nor one another thus tenderly.

Some of you, we all know, are poor, find it hard to live, are sometimes, as it were, gasping for breath. I have no doubt that some of you who read this book are unable to pay for all the dinners which you have actually eaten, or for the coats and shoes which are fast wearing or are already worn out, and have come to this page to spend borrowed or stolen time, robbing your creditors of an hour. It is very evident what mean and sneaking lives many of you live, for my sight has been whetted by experience; always on the limits, trying to get into business and trying to get out of debt, a very ancient slough, called by the Latins, *æs alienum*, another's brass, for some of their coins were made of brass; still living, and dying, and buried by this other's brass; always promising to pay, promising to pay, to-morrow, and dying to-day, insolvent; seeking to curry favor, to get custom, by how many modes, only not state-prison offences; lying, flattering, voting, contracting yourselves into a nutshell of civility, or dilating into an atmosphere of thin and vaporous generosity, that you may persuade your neighbor to let you make his shoes, or his hat, or his coat, or his carriage, or import his groceries for him; making yourselves sick, that you may lay up something against a sick day, something to be tucked away in an old chest, or in a stocking behind the plastering, or, more safely, in the brick bank; no matter where, no matter how much or how little.

I sometimes wonder that we can be so frivolous, I may almost say, as to attend to the gross but somewhat foreign form of servitude called Negro Slavery, there are so many keen and subtle masters that enslave both north and south. It is hard to have a southern overseer; it is worse to have a northern one; but worst of all when you are the slave-driver of yourself. Talk of a divinity in man! Look at the teamster on the highway, wending to market by day or night; does any divinity stir within him? His highest duty to fodder and water his horses! What is his destiny to him compared with the shipping interests? Does not he drive for Squire Make-a-stir?[9] How godlike, how immortal, is he? See how he cowers and sneaks, how vaguely all the day he fears, not being immortal nor divine, but the slave and prisoner of his own opinion of himself, a fame won by his own deeds. Public opinion is a weak tyrant compared with our own private opinion. What a man thinks of himself, that it is which determines, or rather indicates, his fate. Self-emancipation even in the West

9. An allegorical name modeled on those in John Bunyan's *Pilgrim's Progress* (1678, 1684).

Indian provinces of the fancy and imagination,—what Wilberforce[1] is there to bring that about? Think, also, of the ladies of the land weaving toilet cushions against the last day, not to betray too green an interest in their fates! As if you could kill time without injuring eternity.

The mass of men lead lives of quiet desperation. What is called resignation is confirmed desperation. From the desperate city you go into the desperate country, and have to console yourself with the bravery of minks and muskrats. A stereotyped but unconscious despair is concealed even under what are called the games and amusements of mankind. There is no play in them, for this comes after work. But it is a characteristic of wisdom not to do desperate things.

When we consider what, to use the words of the catechism, is the chief end of man,[2] and what are the true necessaries and means of life, it appears as if men had deliberately chosen the common mode of living because they preferred it to any other. Yet they honestly think there is no choice left. But alert and healthy natures remember that the sun rose clear. It is never too late to give up our prejudices. No way of thinking or doing, however ancient, can be trusted without proof. What every body echoes or in silence passes by as true to-day may turn out to be falsehood to-morrow, mere smoke of opinion, which some had trusted for a cloud that would sprinkle fertilizing rain on their fields. What old people say you cannot do you try and find that you can. Old deeds for old people, and new deeds for new. Old people did not know enough once, perchance, to fetch fresh fuel to keep the fire a-going; new people put a little dry wood under a pot, and are whirled round the globe with the speed of birds, in a way to kill old people, as the phrase is. Age is no better, hardly so well, qualified for an instructor as youth, for it has not profited so much as it has lost. One may almost doubt if the wisest man has learned any thing of absolute value by living. Practically, the old have no very important advice to give the young, their own experience has been so partial, and their lives have been such miserable failures, for private reasons, as they must believe; and it may be that they have some faith left which belies that experience, and they are only less young than they were. I have lived some thirty years on this planet, and I have yet to hear the first syllable of valuable or even earnest advice from my seniors. They have told me nothing, and probably cannot tell me any thing, to the purpose. Here is life, an experiment to a great extent untried by me; but it does not avail me that they have tried it. If I have any experience which I think valuable, I am sure to reflect that this my Mentors[3] said nothing about.

One farmer says to me, "You cannot live on vegetable food solely, for it furnishes nothing to make bones with;" and so he religiously devotes a part of his day to supplying his system with the raw material of bones; walking all the while he talks behind his oxen, which, with vegetable-made bones, jerk him and his lumbering plough along in spite of every obstacle. Some things are really necessaries of life in some circles, the most helpless and diseased, which in others are luxuries merely, and in others still are entirely unknown.

1. William Wilberforce (1759–1833), English philanthropist, was instrumental in helping to abolish the slave trade (1807) and end slavery in the British Empire (1833).

2. From the Westminster Shorter Catechism in the *New England Primer*: "What is the chief end of man? Man's chief end is to glorify God and to enjoy him forever."

3. From Mentor, in Homer's *Odyssey*: the friend whom Odysseus entrusted with the education of his son, Telemachus.

The whole ground of human life seems to some to have been gone over by their predecessors, both the heights and the valleys, and all things to have been cared for. According to Evelyn, "the wise Solomon prescribed ordinances for the very distances of trees; and the Roman prætors have decided how often you may go into your neighbor's land to gather the acorns which fall on it without trespass, and what share belongs to that neighbor."[4] Hippocrates[5] has even left directions how we should cut our nails; that is, even with the ends of the fingers, neither shorter nor longer. Undoubtedly the very tedium and ennui which presume to have exhausted the variety and the joys of life are as old as Adam. But man's capacities have never been measured; nor are we to judge of what he can do by any precedents, so little has been tried. Whatever have been thy failures hitherto, "be not afflicted, my child, for who shall assign to thee what thou hast left undone?"[6]

We might try our lives by a thousand simple tests; as, for instance, that the same sun which ripens my beans illumines at once a system of earths like ours. If I had remembered this it would have prevented some mistakes. This was not the light in which I hoed them. The stars are the apexes of what wonderful triangles! What distant and different beings in the various mansions of the universe are contemplating the same one at the same moment! Nature and human life are as various as our several constitutions. Who shall say what prospect life offers to another? Could a greater miracle take place than for us to look through each other's eyes for an instant? We should live in all the ages of the world in an hour; ay, in all the worlds of the ages. History, Poetry, Mythology!—I know of no reading of another's experience so startling and informing as this would be.

The greater part of what my neighbors call good I believe in my soul to be bad, and if I repent of any thing, it is very likely to be my good behavior. What demon possessed me that I behaved so well? You may say the wisest thing you can old man,—you who have lived seventy years, not without honor of a kind,—I hear an irresistible voice which invites me away from all that. One generation abandons the enterprises of another like stranded vessels.

I think that we may safely trust a good deal more than we do. We may waive just so much care of ourselves as we honestly bestow elsewhere. Nature is as well adapted to our weakness as to our strength. The incessant anxiety and strain of some is a well nigh incurable form of disease. We are made to exaggerate the importance of what work we do; and yet how much is not done by us! or, what if we had been taken sick? How vigilant we are! determined not to live by faith if we can avoid it; all the day long on the alert, at night we unwillingly say our prayers and commit ourselves to uncertainties. So thoroughly and sincerely are we compelled to live, reverencing our life, and denying the possibility of change. This is the only way, we say; but there are as many ways as there can be drawn radii from one centre. All change is a miracle to contemplate; but it is a miracle which is taking place every instant. Confucius said, "To know that we know what we know, and that we do not

4. *Silva; or a Discourse of Forest-Trees* (1664), by the English writer John Evelyn (1620–1706), who called for the reforestation of lands cleared for estates. "Prætors": in the Roman Republic, high elected magistrates.

5. Influential Greek physician (460?–377? B.C.E.), who emphasized the importance of doctors making an ethical commitment to the care of their patients (known as the "Hippocratic Oath").

6. From H. H. Wilson's translation of the *Vishnu Purana* (1840), a Hindu religious text.

know what we do not know, this is true knowledge."[7] When one man has reduced a fact of the imagination to be a fact to his understanding, I foresee that all men will at length establish their lives on that basis.

Let us consider for a moment what most of the trouble and anxiety which I have referred to is about, and how much it is necessary that we be troubled, or, at least, careful. It would be some advantage to live a primitive and frontier life, though in the midst of an outward civilization, if only to learn what are the gross necessaries of life and what methods have been taken to obtain them; or even to look over the old day-books of the merchants, to see what it was that men most commonly bought at the stores, what they stored, that is, what are the grossest groceries. For the improvements of ages have had but little influence on the essential laws of man's existence; as our skeletons, probably, are not to be distinguished from those of our ancestors.

By the words *necessary of life*, I mean whatever, of all that man obtains by his own exertions, has been from the first, or from long use has become, so important to human life that few, if any, whether from savageness, or poverty, or philosophy, ever attempt to do without it. To many creatures there is in this sense but one necessary of life, Food. To the bison of the prairie it is a few inches of palatable grass, with water to drink; unless he seeks the Shelter of the forest or the mountain's shadow. None of the brute creation requires more than Food and Shelter. The necessaries of life for man in this climate may, accurately enough, be distributed under the several heads of Food, Shelter, Clothing, and Fuel; for not till we have secured these are we prepared to entertain the true problems of life with freedom and a prospect of success. Man has invented, not only houses, but clothes and cooked food; and possibly from the accidental discovery of the warmth of fire, and the consequent use of it, at first a luxury, arose the present necessity to sit by it. We observe cats and dogs acquiring the same second nature. By proper Shelter and Clothing we legitimately retain our own internal heat; but with an excess of these, or of Fuel, that is, with an external heat greater than our own internal, may not cookery properly be said to begin? Darwin, the naturalist, says of the inhabitants of Tierra del Fuego, that while his own party, who were well clothed and sitting close to a fire, were far from too warm, these naked savages, who were farther off, were observed, to his great surprise, "to be streaming with perspiration at undergoing such a roasting."[8] So, we are told, the New Hollander[9] goes naked with impunity, while the European shivers in his clothes. Is it impossible to combine the hardiness of these savages with the intellectualness of the civilized man? According to Liebig,[1] man's body is a stove, and food the fuel which keeps up the internal combustion in the lungs. In cold weather we eat more, in warm less. The animal heat is the result of a slow combustion, and disease and death take place when this is too rapid; or for want of fuel, or from some defect in the draught, the fire goes out. Of course the vital heat is not to be confounded with fire; but so much for analogy. It appears, therefore, from the above list, that the expression, *animal life*, is nearly synonymous with the expression, *animal heat*; for

7. From *Analects* 2:17, by the Chinese philosopher Confucius (551?–479 B.C.E.).
8. Charles Darwin (1809–1882), *Journal of Researches* (1839).
9. Australian aborigine.
1. Justus, Baron von Liebig (1803–1873), German chemist, author of *Organic Chemistry* (1840).

while Food may be regarded as the Fuel which keeps up the fire within us,—and Fuel serves only to prepare that Food or to increase the warmth of our bodies by addition from without,—Shelter and Clothing also serve only to retain the *heat* thus generated and absorbed.

The grand necessity, then, for our bodies, is to keep warm, to keep the vital heat in us. What pains we accordingly take, not only with our Food, and Clothing, and Shelter, but with our beds, which are our night-clothes, robbing the nests and breasts of birds to prepare this shelter within a shelter, as the mole has its bed of grass and leaves at the end of its burrow! The poor man is wont to complain that this is a cold world; and to cold, no less physical than social, we refer directly a great part of our ails. The summer, in some climates, makes possible to man a sort of Elysian[2] life. Fuel, except to cook his Food, is then unnecessary; the sun is his fire, and many of the fruits are sufficiently cooked by its rays; while Food generally is more various, and more easily obtained, and Clothing and Shelter are wholly or half unnecessary. At the present day, and in this country, as I find by my own experience, a few implements, a knife, an axe, a spade, a wheelbarrow, &c., and for the studious, lamplight, stationery, and access to a few books, rank next to necessaries, and can all be obtained at a trifling cost. Yet some, not wise, go to the other side of the globe, to barbarous and unhealthy regions, and devote themselves to trade for ten or twenty years, in order that they may live,—that is, keep comfortably warm,—and die in New England at last. The luxuriously rich are not simply kept comfortably warm, but unnaturally hot; as I implied before, they are cooked, of course *à la mode*.[3]

Most of the luxuries, and many of the so called comforts of life, are not only not indispensable, but positive hinderances to the elevation of mankind. With respect to luxuries and comforts, the wisest have ever lived a more simple and meager life than the poor. The ancient philosophers, Chinese, Hindoo, Persian, and Greek, were a class than which none has been poorer in outward riches, none so rich in inward. We know not much about them. It is remarkable that *we* know so much of them as we do. The same is true of the more modern reformers and benefactors of their race. None can be an impartial or wise observer of human life but from the vantage ground of what *we* should call voluntary poverty. Of a life of luxury the fruit is luxury, whether in agriculture, or commerce, or literature, or art. There are nowadays professors of philosophy, but not philosophers. Yet it is admirable to profess because it was once admirable to live. To be a philosopher is not merely to have subtle thoughts, nor even to found a school, but so to love wisdom as to live according to its dictates, a life of simplicity, independence, magnanimity, and trust. It is to solve some of the problems of life, not only theoretically, but practically. The success of great scholars and thinkers is commonly a courtier-like success, not kingly, not manly. They make shift to live merely by conformity, practically as their fathers did, and are in no sense the progenitors of a nobler race of men. But why do men degenerate ever? What makes families run out? What is the nature of the luxury which enervates and destroys nations? Are we sure that there is none of it in our own lives? The philosopher is in advance of his age even in the outward form of

2. In Greek mythology, Elysium is the home of the blessed after death.

3. According to the latest fashion (French).

his life. He is not fed, sheltered, clothed, warmed, like his contemporaries. How can a man be a philosopher and not maintain his vital heat by better methods than other men?

When a man is warmed by the several modes which I have described, what does he want next? Surely not more warmth of the same kind, as more and richer food, larger and more splendid houses, finer and more abundant clothing, more numerous incessant and hotter fires, and the like. When he has obtained those things which are necessary to life, there is another alternative than to obtain the superfluities; and that is, to adventure on life now, his vacation from humbler toil having commenced. The soil, it appears, is suited to the seed, for it has sent its radicle downward, and it may now send its shoot upward also with confidence. Why has man rooted himself thus firmly in the earth, but that he may rise in the same proportion into the heavens above?—for the nobler plants are valued for the fruit they bear at last in the air and light, far from the ground, and are not treated like the humbler esculents,[4] which, though they may be biennials, are cultivated only till they have perfected their root, and often cut down at top for this purpose, so that most would not know them in their flowering season.

I do not mean to prescribe rules to strong and valiant natures, who will mind their own affairs whether in heaven or hell, and perchance build more magnificently and spend more lavishly than the richest, without ever impoverishing themselves, not knowing how they live,—if, indeed, there are any such, as has been dreamed; nor to those who find their encouragement and inspiration in precisely the present condition of things, and cherish it with the fondness and enthusiasm of lovers,—and, to some extent, I reckon myself in this number; I do not speak to those who are well employed, in whatever circumstances, and they know whether they are well employed or not;—but mainly to the mass of men who are discontented, and idly complaining of the hardness of their lot or of the times, when they might improve them. There are some who complain most energetically and inconsolably of any, because they are, as they say, doing their duty. I also have in my mind that seemingly wealthy, but most terribly impoverished class of all, who have accumulated dross, but know not how to use it, or get rid of it, and thus have forged their own golden or silver fetters.

If I should attempt to tell how I have desired to spend my life in years past, it would probably surprise those of my readers who are somewhat acquainted with its actual history; it would certainly astonish those who know nothing about it. I will only hint at some of the enterprises which I have cherished.

In any weather, at any hour of the day or night, I have been anxious to improve the nick of time, and notch it on my stick too;[5] to stand on the meeting of two eternities, the past and future, which is precisely the present moment; to toe that line. You will pardon some obscurities, for there are more secrets in my trade than in most men's, and yet not voluntarily kept, but inseparable from its very nature. I would gladly tell all that I know about it, and never paint "No Admittance" on my gate.

4. Edibles.
5. Allusion to Daniel Defoe's *Robinson Crusoe* (1719), a novel Thoreau much admired. Crusoe kept track of time by cutting notches on wood.

I long ago lost a hound, a bay horse, and a turtle-dove,[6] and am still on their trail. Many are the travellers I have spoken concerning them, describing their tracks and what calls they answered to. I have met one or two who had heard the hound, and the tramp of the horse, and even seen the dove disappear behind a cloud, and they seemed as anxious to recover them as if they had lost them themselves.

To anticipate, not the sunrise and the dawn merely, but, if possible, Nature herself! How many mornings, summer and winter, before yet any neighbor was stirring about his business, have I been about mine! No doubt, many of my townsmen have met me returning from this enterprise, farmers starting for Boston in the twilight, or woodchoppers going to their work. It is true, I never assisted the sun materially in his rising, but, doubt not, it was of the last importance only to be present at it.

So many autumn, ay, and winter days, spent outside the town, trying to hear what was in the wind, to hear and carry it express! I well-nigh sunk all my capital in it, and lost my own breath into the bargain, running in the face of it. If it had concerned either of the political parties, depend upon it, it would have appeared in the Gazette with the earliest intelligence.[7] At other times watching from the observatory of some cliff or tree, to telegraph any new arrival; or waiting at evening on the hill-tops for the sky to fall, that I might catch something, though I never caught much, and that, manna-wise,[8] would dissolve again in the sun.

For a long time I was reporter to a journal, of no very wide circulation, whose editor has never yet seen fit to print the bulk of my contributions, and, as is too common with writers, I got only my labor for my pains.[9] However, in this case my pains were their own reward.

For many years I was self-appointed inspector of snow storms and rain storms, and did my duty faithfully; surveyor, if not of highways, then of forest paths and all across-lot routes, keeping them open, and ravines bridged and passable at all seasons, where the public heel had testified to their utility.

I have looked after the wild stock of the town, which give a faithful herdsman a good deal of trouble by leaping fences; and I have had an eye to the unfrequented nooks and corners of the farm; though I did not always know whether Jonas or Solomon worked in a particular field to-day; that was none of my business. I have watered the red huckleberry, the sand cherry and the nettle tree, the red pine and the black ash, the white grape and the yellow violet, which might have withered else in dry seasons.

In short, I went on thus for a long time, I may say it without boasting, faithfully minding my business, till it became more and more evident that my townsmen would not after all admit me into the list of town officers, nor make my place a sinecure with a moderate allowance. My accounts, which I can swear to have kept faithfully, I have, indeed, never got audited, still less accepted, still less paid and settled. However, I have not set my heart on that.

Not long since, a strolling Indian went to sell baskets at the house of a well-known lawyer in my neighborhood. "Do you wish to buy any baskets?"

6. Symbols of elusive ideas, or ideals, whose exact meanings have not been determined.
7. News. "Gazette": newspaper.
8. In Exodus 16, manna is the bread that God rained from heaven so the Israelites could survive in the desert on their way from Egypt to the Promised Land.
9. Thoreau puns on the common usage of *journal* to mean a daily newspaper as well as a diary. Thoreau himself is the negligent or too demanding editor.

he asked. "No, we do not want any," was the reply. "What!" exclaimed the Indian as he went out the gate, "do you mean to starve us?" Having seen his industrious white neighbors so well off,—that the lawyer had only to weave arguments, and by some magic wealth and standing followed, he had said to himself; I will go into business; I will weave baskets; it is a thing which I can do. Thinking that when he had made the baskets he would have done his part, and then it would be the white man's to buy them. He had not discovered that it was necessary for him to make it worth the other's while to buy them, or at least make him think that it was so, or to make something else which it would be worth his while to buy. I too had woven a kind of basket of a delicate texture, but I had not made it worth any one's while to buy them.[1] Yet not the less, in my case, did I think it worth my while to weave them, and instead of studying how to make it worth men's while to buy my baskets, I studied rather how to avoid the necessity of selling them. The life which men praise and regard as successful is but one kind. Why should we exaggerate any one kind at the expense of the others?

Finding that my fellow-citizens were not likely to offer me any room in the court house, or any curacy or living[2] any where else, but I must shift for myself, I turned my face more exclusively than ever to the woods, where I was better known. I determined to go into business at once, and not wait to acquire the usual capital, using such slender means as I had already got. My purpose in going to Walden Pond was not to live cheaply nor to live dearly there, but to transact some private business with the fewest obstacles; to be hindered from accomplishing which for want of a little common sense, a little enterprise and business talent, appeared not so sad as foolish.

I have always endeavored to acquire strict business habits; they are indispensable to every man. If your trade is with the Celestial Empire,[3] then some small counting house on the coast, in some Salem harbor, will be fixture enough. You will export such articles as the country affords, purely native products, much ice and pine timber and a little granite, always in native bottoms. These will be good ventures. To oversee all the details yourself in person; to be at once pilot and captain, and owner and underwriter; to buy and sell and keep the accounts; to read every letter received, and write or read every letter sent; to superintend the discharge of imports night and day; to be upon many parts of the coast almost at the same time;—often the richest freight will be discharged upon a Jersey shore,[4]—to be your own telegraph, unweariedly sweeping the horizon, speaking all passing vessels bound coastwise; to keep up a steady despatch of commodities, for the supply of such a distant and exorbitant market; to keep yourself informed of the state of the markets, prospects of war and peace every where, and anticipate the tendencies of trade and civilization,—taking advantage of the results of all exploring expeditions, using new passages and all improvements in navigation;—charts to be studied, the position of reefs and new lights and buoys to be ascertained, and ever, and ever, the logarithmic tables to be corrected, for by the error of some calculator the vessel often splits upon a rock that should have reached a friendly pier,—there is the untold fate of La

1. A reference to Thoreau's poorly selling first book, *A Week on the Concord and Merrimack Rivers* (1849).
2. A church office with a fixed, steady income.
3. China, from the belief that the Chinese emperors were sons of heaven.
4. I.e., by shipwreck on the way to New York.

Perouse;—universal science to be kept pace with, studying the lives of all great discoverers and navigators, great adventurers and merchants from Hanno[5] and the Phœnicians down to our day; in fine, account of stock to be taken from time to time, to know how you stand. It is a labor to task the faculties of a man,—such problems of profit and loss, of interest, of tare and tret,[6] and gauging of all kinds in it, as demand a universal knowledge.

I have thought that Walden Pond would be a good place for business, not solely on account of the railroad and the ice trade; it offers advantages which it may not be good policy to divulge; it is a good port and a good foundation. No Neva[7] marshes to be filled; though you must every where build on piles of your own driving. It is said that a flood-tide, with a westerly wind, and ice in the Neva, would sweep St. Petersburg from the face of the earth.

As this business was to be entered into without the usual capital, it may not be easy to conjecture where those means, that will still be indispensable to every such undertaking, were to be obtained. As for Clothing, to come at once to the practical part of the question, perhaps we are led oftener by the love of novelty, and a regard for the opinions of men, in procuring it, than by a true utility. Let him who has work to do recollect that the object of clothing is, first, to retain the vital heat, and secondly, in this state of society, to cover nakedness, and he may judge how much of any necessary or important work may be accomplished without adding to his wardrobe. Kings and queens who wear a suit but once, though made by some tailor or dress-maker to their majesties, cannot know the comfort of wearing a suit that fits. They are no better than wooden horses to hang the clean clothes on. Every day our garments become more assimilated to ourselves, receiving the impress of the wearer's character, until we hesitate to lay them aside, without such delay and medical appliances and some such solemnity even as our bodies. No man ever stood the lower in my estimation for having a patch in his clothes; yet I am sure that there is greater anxiety, commonly, to have fashionable, or at least clean and unpatched clothes, than to have a sound conscience. But even if the rent is not mended, perhaps the worst vice betrayed is improvidence. I sometimes try my acquaintances by such tests as this;—who could wear a patch, or two extra seams only, over the knee? Most behave as if they believed that their prospects for life would be ruined if they should do it. It would be easier for them to hobble to town with a broken leg than with a broken pantaloon. Often if an accident happens to a gentleman's legs, they can be mended; but if a similar accident happens to the legs of his pantaloons, there is no help for it; for he considers, not what is truly respectable, but what is respected. We know but few men, a great many coats and breeches. Dress a scarecrow in your last shift, you standing shiftless by, who would not soonest salute the scarecrow? Passing a cornfield the other day, close by a hat and coat on a stake, I recognized the owner of the farm. He was only a little more weather-beaten than when I saw him last. I have heard of a dog that barked at every stranger who approached his master's premises

5. Carthaginian navigator (6th–5th centuries B.C.E.), credited with opening the coast of west Africa to trade. Jean François de Galaup, Comte de la Pérouse (1741–1788), French explorer of the western Pacific.

6. Terms from shipping: "tare" is the deduction to the purchaser for the weight of the container; "tret" is the deduction for any damages.

7. A river in Russia.

with clothes on, but was easily quieted by a naked thief. It is an interesting question how far men would retain their relative rank if they were divested of their clothes. Could you, in such a case, tell surely of any company of civilized men, which belonged to the most respected class? When Madam Pfeiffer, in her adventurous travels round the world, from east to west, had got so near home as Asiatic Russia, she says that she felt the necessity of wearing other than a travelling dress, when she went to meet the authorities, for she "was now in a civilized country, where——people are judged of by their clothes."[8] Even in our democratic New England towns the accidental possession of wealth, and its manifestation in dress and equipage alone, obtain for the possessor almost universal respect. But they who yield such respect, numerous as they are, are so far heathen, and need to have a missionary sent to them. Beside, clothes introduced sewing, a kind of work which you may call endless; a woman's dress, at least, is never done.

A man who has at length found something to do will not need to get a new suit to do it in; for him the old will do, that has lain dusty in the garret for an indeterminate period. Old shoes will serve a hero longer than they have served his valet,—if a hero ever has a valet,—bare feet are older than shoes, and he can make them do. Only they who go to soirées and legislative halls must have new coats, coats to change as often as the man changes in them. But if my jacket and trousers, my hat and shoes, are fit to worship God in, they will do; will they not? Who ever saw his old clothes,—his old coat, actually worn out, resolved into its primitive elements, so that it was not a deed of charity to bestow it on some poor boy, by him perchance to be bestowed on some poorer still, or shall we say richer, who could do with less? I say, beware of all enterprises that require new clothes, and not rather a new wearer of clothes. If there is not a new man, how can the new clothes be made to fit? If you have any enterprise before you, try it in your old clothes. All men want, not something to *do with*, but something to *do*, or rather something to *be*. Perhaps we should never procure a new suit, however ragged or dirty the old, until we have so conducted, so enterprised or sailed in some way, that we feel like new men in the old, and that to retain it would be like keeping new wine in old bottles.[9] Our moulting season, like that of the fowls, must be a crisis in our lives. The loon retires to solitary ponds to spend it. Thus also the snake casts its slough, and the caterpillar its wormy coat, by an internal industry and expansion; for clothes are but our outmost cuticle and mortal coil. Otherwise we shall be found sailing under false colors, and be inevitably cashiered[1] at last by our own opinion, as well as that of mankind.

We don garment after garment, as if we grew like exogenous plants by addition without. Our outside and often thin and fanciful clothes are our epidermis or false skin, which partakes not of our life, and may be stripped off here and there without fatal injury; our thicker garments, constantly worn, are our cellular integument, or cortex; but our shirts are our liber[2] or true bark, which cannot be removed without girdling and so destroying the man. I believe that all races at some seasons wear something equivalent to the shirt. It is desir-

8. Ida Pfeiffer (1797–1858), *A Lady's Voyage round the World* (1852).

9. "Neither do men put new wine into old bottles: else the bottles break, and the wine runneth out, and the bottles perish: but they put new wine into new bottles, and both are preserved" (Matthew 9.17).

1. Fired.

2. Inner bark. "Integument, or cortex": an enveloping inner layer.

able that a man be clad so simply that he can lay his hands on himself in the dark, and that he live in all respects so compactly and preparedly, that, if an enemy take the town, he can, like the old philosopher, walk out the gate empty-handed without anxiety. While one thick garment is, for most purposes, as good as three thin ones, and cheap clothing can be obtained at prices really to suit customers; while a thick coat can be bought for five dollars, which will last as many years, thick pantaloons for two dollars, cowhide boots for a dollar and a half a pair, a summer hat for a quarter of a dollar, and a winter cap for sixty-two and a half cents, or a better be made at home at a nominal cost, where is he so poor that, clad in such a suit, *of his own earning*, there will not be found wise men to do him reverence?

When I ask for a garment of a particular form, my tailoress tells me gravely, "They do not make them so now," not emphasizing the "They" at all, as if she quoted an authority as impersonal as the Fates, and I find it difficult to get made what I want, simply because she cannot believe that I mean what I say, that I am so rash. When I hear this oracular sentence, I am for a moment absorbed in thought, emphasizing to myself each word separately that I may come at the meaning of it, that I may find out by what degree of consanguinity *They* are related to *me*, and what authority they may have in an affair which affects me so nearly; and, finally, I am inclined to answer her with equal mystery, and without any more emphasis of the "they,"—"It is true, they did not make them so recently, but they do now." Of what use this measuring of me if she does not measure my character, but only the breadth of my shoulders, as it were a peg to hang the coat on? We worship not the Graces, nor the Parcæ,[3] but Fashion. She spins and weaves and cuts with full authority. The head monkey at Paris puts on a traveller's cap, and all the monkeys in America do the same. I sometimes despair of getting any thing quite simple and honest done in this world by the help of men. They would have to be passed through a powerful press first, to squeeze their old notions out of them, so that they would not soon get upon their legs again, and then there would be some one in the company with a maggot in his head, hatched from an egg deposited there nobody knows when, for not even fire kills these things, and you would have lost your labor. Nevertheless, we will not forget that some Egyptian wheat is said to have been handed down to us by a mummy.[4]

On the whole, I think that it cannot be maintained that dressing has in this or any country risen to the dignity of an art. At present men make shift to wear what they can get. Like shipwrecked sailors, they put on what they can find on the beach, and at a little distance, whether of space or time, laugh at each other's masquerade. Every generation laughs at the old fashions, but follows religiously the new. We are amused at beholding the costume of Henry VIII, or Queen Elizabeth, as much as if it was that of the King and Queen of the Cannibal Islands. All costume off a man is pitiful or grotesque. It is only the serious eye peering from and the sincere life passed within it, which restrain laughter and consecrate the costume of any people. Let Harlequin[5] be taken with a fit of the colic and his trappings will have to serve that mood too. When the soldier is hit by a cannon ball rags are as becoming as purple.

3. In Roman mythology, the three Fates.
4. Thoreau refers to the popular notion that wheat could be grown from the seeds found in Egyptian tombs.
5. Comic servant in the Italian *commedia dell'arte*, typically dressed in a mask and many-colored tights.

The childish and savage taste of men and women for new patterns keeps how many shaking and squinting through kaleidoscopes that they may discover the particular figure which this generation requires to-day. The manufacturers have learned that this taste is merely whimsical. Of two patterns which differ only by a few threads more or less of a particular color, the one will be sold readily, the other lie on the shelf, though it frequently happens that after the lapse of a season the latter becomes the most fashionable. Comparatively, tattooing is not the hideous custom which it is called. It is not barbarous merely because the printing is skin-deep and unalterable.

I cannot believe that our factory system is the best mode by which men may get clothing. The condition of the operatives is becoming every day more like that of the English; and it cannot be wondered at, since, as far as I have heard or observed, the principal object is, not that mankind may be well and honestly clad, but, unquestionably, that the corporations may be enriched. In the long run men hit only what they aim at. Therefore, though they should fail immediately, they had better aim at something high.

As for a Shelter, I will not deny that this is now a necessary of life, though there are instances of men having done without it for long periods in colder countries than this. Samuel Laing says that "The Laplander in his skin dress, and in a skin bag which he puts over his head and shoulders, will sleep night after night on the snow—in a degree of cold which would extinguish the life of one exposed to it in any woollen clothing." He had seen them asleep thus. Yet he adds, "They are not hardier than other people."[6] But, probably, man did not live long on the earth without discovering the convenience which there is in a house, the domestic comforts, which phrase may have originally signified the satisfactions of the house more than of the family; though these must be extremely partial and occasional in those climates where the house is associated in our thoughts with winter or the rainy season chiefly, and two thirds of the year, except for a parasol, is unnecessary. In our climate, in the summer, it was formerly almost solely a covering at night. In the Indian gazettes a wigwam was the symbol of a day's march, and a row of them cut or painted on the bark of a tree signified that so many times they had camped. Man was not made so large limbed and robust but that he must seek to narrow his world, and wall in a space such as fitted him. He was at first bare and out of doors; but though this was pleasant enough in serene and warm weather, by daylight, the rainy season and the winter, to say nothing of the torrid sun, would perhaps have nipped his race in the bud if he had not made haste to clothe himself with the shelter of a house. Adam and Eve, according to a fable, wore the bower before other clothes. Man wanted a home, a place of warmth, or comfort, first of physical warmth, then the warmth of the affections.

We may imagine a time when, in the infancy of the human race, some enterprising mortal crept into a hollow in a rock for shelter. Every child begins the world again, to some extent, and loves to stay out doors, even in wet and cold. It plays house, as well as horse, having an instinct for it. Who does not remember the interest with which when young he looked at shelving rocks, or any approach to a cave? It was the natural yearning of that portion of our most primitive ancestor which still survived in us. From the cave we have

6. *Journal of a Residence in Norway* (1837), by the English writer Laing (1780–1868).

advanced to roofs of palm leaves, of bark and boughs, of linen woven and stretched, of grass and straw, of boards and shingles, of stones and tiles. At last, we know not what it is to live in the open air, and our lives are domestic in more senses than we think. From the hearth to the field is a great distance. It would be well perhaps if we were to spend more of our days and nights without any obstruction between us and the celestial bodies, if the poet did not speak so much from under a roof, or the saint dwell there so long. Birds do not sing in caves, nor do doves cherish their innocence in dovecots.

However, if one designs to construct a dwelling house, it behooves him to exercise a little Yankee shrewdness, lest after all he find himself in a workhouse, a labyrinth without a clew, a museum, an almshouse, a prison, or a splendid mausoleum instead. Consider first how slight a shelter is absolutely necessary. I have seen Penobscot Indians,[7] in this town, living in tents of thin cotton cloth, while the snow was nearly a foot deep around them, and I thought that they would be glad to have it deeper to keep out the wind. Formerly, when how to get my living honestly, with freedom left for my proper pursuits, was a question which vexed me even more than it does now, for unfortunately I am become somewhat callous, I used to see a large box by the railroad, six feet long by three wide, in which the laborers locked up their tools at night, and it suggested to me that every man who was hard pushed might get such a one for a dollar, and, having bored a few auger holes in it, to admit the air at least, get into it when it rained and at night, and hook down the lid, and so have freedom in his love, and in his soul be free. This did not appear the worst, nor by any means a despicable alternative. You could sit up as late as you pleased, and, whenever you got up, go abroad without any landlord or house-lord dogging you for rent. Many a man is harassed to death to pay the rent of a larger and more luxurious box who would not have frozen to death in such a box as this. I am far from jesting. Economy is a subject which admits of being treated with levity, but it cannot so be disposed of. A comfortable house for a rude and hardy race, that lived mostly out of doors, was once made here almost entirely of such materials as Nature furnished ready to their hands. Gookin, who was superintendent of the Indians subject to the Massachusetts Colony, writing in 1674, says, "The best of their houses are covered very neatly, tight and warm, with barks of trees, slipped from their bodies at those seasons when the sap is up, and made into great flakes, with pressure of weighty timber, when they are green. . . . The meaner sort are covered with mats which they make of a kind of bulrush, and are also indifferently tight and warm, but not so good as the former. . . . Some I have seen, sixty or a hundred feet long and thirty feet broad. . . . I have often lodged in their wigwams, and found them as warm as the best English houses."[8] He adds, that they were commonly carpeted and lined within with well-wrought embroidered mats, and were furnished with various utensils. The Indians had advanced so far as to regulate the effect of the wind by a mat suspended over the hole in the roof and moved by a string. Such a lodge was in the first instance constructed in a day or two at most, and taken down and put up in a few hours; and every family owned one, or its apartment in one.

7. An Algonquin tribe from what is now Maine.
8. Daniel Gookin (1612–1687), *Historical Collections of the Indians in New England* (completed in 1674; first published in 1792).

In the savage state every family owns a shelter as good as the best, and sufficient for its coarser and simpler wants; but I think that I speak within bounds when I say that, though the birds of the air have their nests, and the foxes their holes,[9] and the savages their wigwams, in modern civilized society not more than one half the families own a shelter. In the large towns and cities, where civilization especially prevails, the number of those who own a shelter is a very small fraction of the whole. The rest pay an annual tax for this outside garment of all, become indispensable summer and winter, which would buy a village of Indian wigwams, but now helps to keep them poor as long as they live. I do not mean to insist here on the disadvantage of hiring compared with owning, but it is evident that the savage owns his shelter because it costs so little, while the civilized man hires his commonly because he cannot afford to own it; nor can he, in the long run, any better afford to hire. But, answers one, by merely paying this tax the poor civilized man secures an abode which is a palace compared with the savage's. An annual rent of from twenty-five to a hundred dollars, these are the country rates, entitles him to the benefit of the improvements of centuries, spacious apartments, clean paint and paper, Rumford fireplace,[1] back plastering, Venetian blinds, copper pump, spring lock, a commodious cellar, and many other things. But how happens it that he who is said to enjoy these things is so commonly a *poor* civilized man, while the savage, who has them not, is rich as a savage? If it is asserted that civilization is a real advance in the condition of man,—and I think that it is, though only the wise improve their advantages,—it must be shown that it has produced better dwellings without making them more costly; and the cost of a thing is the amount of what I will call life which is required to be exchanged for it, immediately or in the long run. An average house in this neighborhood costs perhaps eight hundred dollars, and to lay up this sum will take from ten to fifteen years of the laborer's life, even if he is not encumbered with a family;—estimating the pecuniary value of every man's labor at one dollar a day, for if some receive more, others receive less;—so that he must have spent more than half his life commonly before *his* wigwam will be earned. If we suppose him to pay a rent instead, this is but a doubtful choice of evils. Would the savage have been wise to exchange his wigwam for a palace on these terms?

It may be guessed that I reduce almost the whole advantage of holding this superfluous property as a fund in store against the future, so far as the individual is concerned, mainly to the defraying of funeral expenses. But perhaps a man is not required to bury himself. Nevertheless this points to an important distinction between the civilized man and the savage; and, no doubt, they have designs on us for our benefit, in making the life of a civilized people an *institution*, in which the life of the individual is to a great extent absorbed, in order to preserve and perfect that of the race. But I wish to show at what a sacrifice this advantage is at present obtained, and to suggest that we may possibly so live as to secure all the advantage without suffering any of the disadvantage. What mean ye by saying that the poor ye have always with you, or that the fathers have eaten sour grapes, and the children's teeth are set on edge?[2]

9. "The foxes have holes, and the birds of the air have nests; but the Son of man hath not where to lay his head" (Matthew 8.20).

1. Benjamin Thompson, Count Rumford (1753–1814), devised a shelf inside the chimney to prevent smoke from being carried back into a room by downdrafts.

2. Thoreau draws on Jesus' words to his disciples

"As I live, saith the Lord God, ye shall not have occasion any more to use this proverb in Israel."

"Behold all souls are mine; as the soul of the father, so also the soul of the son is mine: the soul that sinneth it shall die."[3]

When I consider my neighbors, the farmers of Concord, who are at least as well off as the other classes, I find that for the most part they have been toiling twenty, thirty, or forty years, that they may become the real owners of their farms, which commonly they have inherited with encumbrances, or else bought with hired money,—and we may regard one third of that toil as the cost of their houses,—but commonly they have not paid for them yet. It is true, the encumbrances sometimes outweigh the value of the farm, so that the farm itself becomes one great encumbrance, and still a man is found to inherit it, being well acquainted with it, as he says. On applying to the assessors, I am surprised to learn that they cannot at once name a dozen in the town who own their farms free and clear. If you would know the history of these homesteads, inquire at the bank where they are mortgaged. The man who has actually paid for his farm with labor on it is so rare that every neighbor can point to him. I doubt if there are three such men in Concord. What has been said of the merchants, that a very large majority, even ninety-seven in a hundred, are sure to fail, is equally true of the farmers. With regard to the merchants, however, one of them says pertinently that a great part of their failures are not genuine pecuniary failures, but merely failures to fulfil their engagements, because it is inconvenient; that is, it is the moral character that breaks down. But this puts an infinitely worse face on the matter, and suggests, beside, that probably not even the other three succeed in saving their souls, but are perchance bankrupt in a worse sense than they who fail honestly. Bankruptcy and repudiation are the spring-boards from which much of our civilization vaults and turns its somersets,[4] but the savage stands on the unelastic plank of famine. Yet the Middlesex Cattle Show goes off here with *éclat* annually, as if all the joints of the agricultural machine were suent.[5]

The farmer is endeavoring to solve the problem of a livelihood by a formula more complicated than the problem itself. To get his shoestrings he speculates in herds of cattle. With consummate skill he has set his trap with a hair spring to catch comfort and independence, and then, as he turned away, got his own leg into it. This is the reason he is poor; and for a similar reason we are all poor in respect to a thousand savage comforts, though surrounded by luxuries. As Chapman[6] sings,—

"The false society of men—
—for earthly greatness
All heavenly comforts rarefies to air."

And when the farmer has got his house, he may not be the richer but the poorer for it, and it be the house that has got him. As I understand it, that was

---

"For ye have the poor always with you; but me ye have not always" (Matthew 26.11) and God's reproof to Ezekiel for employing a self-defeating proverb: "What mean ye, that ye use this proverb concerning the land of Israel, saying, The fathers have eaten sour grapes, and the children's teeth are set on edge?" (Ezekiel 18.2).

3. Ezekiel 18.3–4, which Thoreau abridges to convey his rejection of the idea that the sins of the fathers must be visited on their children.

4. Somersaults.

5. In good working order; broken in. "*Éclat*": brilliance (French).

6. From the play *Caesar and Pompey* 5.2, by the English writer George Chapman (1559?–1634).

a valid objection urged by Momus against the house which Minerva[7] made, that she "had not made it movable, by which means a bad neighborhood might be avoided;" and it may still be urged, for our houses are such unwieldy property that we are often imprisoned rather than housed in them; and the bad neighborhood to be avoided is our own scurvy selves. I know one or two families, at least, in this town, who, for nearly a generation, have been wishing to sell their houses in the outskirts and move into the village, but have not been able to accomplish it, and only death will set them free.

Granted that the *majority* are able at last either to own or hire the modern house with all its improvements. While civilization has been improving our houses, it has not equally improved the men who are to inhabit them. It has created palaces, but it was not so easy to create noblemen and kings. And *if the civilized man's pursuits are no worthier than the savage's, if he is employed the greater part of his life in obtaining gross necessaries and comforts merely, why should he have a better dwelling than the former?*

But how do the poor *minority* fare? Perhaps it will be found, that just in proportion as some have been placed in outward circumstances above the savage, others have been degraded below him. The luxury of one class is counterbalanced by the indigence of another. On the one side is the palace, on the other are the almshouse and "silent poor."[8] The myriads who built the pyramids to be the tombs of the Pharaohs were fed on garlic, and it may be were not decently buried themselves. The mason who finishes the cornice of the palace returns at night perchance to a hut not so good as a wigwam. It is a mistake to suppose that, in a country where the usual evidences of civilization exist, the condition of a very large body of the inhabitants may not be as degraded as that of savages. I refer to the degraded poor, not now to the degraded rich. To know this I should not need to look farther than to the shanties which every where border our railroads, that last improvement in civilization; where I see in my daily walks human beings living in sties, and all winter with an open door, for the sake of light, without any visible, often imaginable, wood pile, and the forms of both old and young are permanently contracted by the long habit of shrinking from cold and misery, and the development of all their limbs and faculties is checked. It certainly is fair to look at that class by whose labor the works which distinguish the generation are accomplished. Such too, to a greater or less extent, is the condition of the operatives of every denomination in England, which is the great workhouse of the world. Or I could refer you to Ireland, which is marked as one of the white or enlightened spots on the map.[9] Contrast the physical condition of the Irish with that of the North American Indian, or the South Sea Islander, or any other savage race before it was degraded by contact with the civilized man. Yet I have no doubt that that people's rulers are as wise as the average of civilized rulers. Their condition only proves what squalidness may consist with civilization. I hardly need refer now to the laborers in our Southern States who produce the staple exports of this country, and are themselves a staple production of the South.[1] But to confine myself to those who are said to be in *moderate* circumstances.

7. In Greek mythology, the goddess of wisdom. Monus was the Greek god of mockery and blame.
8. Poor people who do not want to be identified as needing public charity.
9. Thoreau refers to the habit some mapmakers had of leaving unexplored terrain in a dark color; other cartographers left unexplored areas white.
1. A reference to the domestic slave trade.

Most men appear never to have considered what a house is, and are actually though needlessly poor all their lives because they think that they must have such a one as their neighbors have. As if one were to wear any sort of coat which the tailor might cut out for him, or, gradually leaving off palmleaf hat or cap of woodchuck skin, complain of hard times because he could not afford to buy him a crown! It is possible to invent a house still more convenient and luxurious than we have, which yet all would admit that man could not afford to pay for. Shall we always study to obtain more of these things, and not sometimes to be content with less? Shall the respectable citizen thus gravely teach, by precept and example, the necessity of the young man's providing a certain number of superfluous glow-shoes,[2] and umbrellas, and empty guest chambers for empty guests, before he dies? Why should not our furniture be as simple as the Arab's or the Indian's? When I think of the benefactors of the race, whom we have apotheosized as messengers from heaven, bearers of divine gifts to man, I do not see in my mind any retinue at their heels, any car-load of fashionable furniture. Or what if I were to allow—would it not be a singular allowance?—that our furniture should be more complex than the Arab's, in proportion as we are morally and intellectually his superiors! At present our houses are cluttered and defiled with it, and a good housewife would sweep out the greater part into the dust hole, and not leave her morning's work undone. Morning work! By the blushes of Aurora and the music of Memnon,[3] what should be man's *morning work* in this world? I had three pieces of limestone on my desk, but I was terrified to find that they required to be dusted daily, when the furniture of my mind was all undusted still, and I threw them out the window in disgust. How, then, could I have a furnished house? I would rather sit in the open air, for no dust gathers on the grass, unless where man has broken ground.

It is the luxurious and dissipated who set the fashions which the herd so diligently follow. The traveller who stops at the best houses, so called, soon discovers this, for the publicans presume him to be a Sardanapalus,[4] and if he resigned himself to their tender mercies he would soon be completely emasculated. I think that in the railroad car we are inclined to spend more on luxury than on safety and convenience, and it threatens without attaining these to become no better than a modern drawing room, with its divans, and ottomans, and sunshades, and a hundred other oriental things, which we are taking west with us, invented for the ladies of the harem and the effeminate natives of the Celestial Empire, which Jonathan[5] should be ashamed to know the names of. I would rather sit on a pumpkin and have it all to myself, than be crowded on a velvet cushion. I would rather ride on earth in an ox cart with a free circulation, than go to heaven in the fancy car of an excursion train and breathe a *malaria* all the way.

The very simplicity and nakedness of man's life in the primitive ages imply this advantage at least, that they left him still but a sojourner in nature. When he was refreshed with food and sleep he contemplated his journey again. He dwelt, as it were, in a tent in this world, and was either threading

2. Galoshes.
3. In Roman mythology, the goddess of the dawn and her son. Memnon is associated here with the Egyptian colossus near Thebes that was said to emit musical sounds at dawn.
4. Ruler of Assyria (9th century B.C.E.).
5. A name at first applied comically to New England farmers; then later (as here, or with the name "Brother Jonathan") to the inhabitants of the entire United States.

the valleys, or crossing the plains, or climbing the mountain tops. But lo! men have become the tools of their tools. The man who independently plucked the fruits when he was hungry is become a farmer; and he who stood under a tree for shelter, a housekeeper. We now no longer camp as for a night, but have settled down on earth and forgotten heaven. We have adopted Christianity merely as an improved method of *agri*-culture. We have built for this world a family mansion, and for the next a family tomb. The best works of art are the expression of man's struggle to free himself from this condition, but the effect of our art is merely to make this low state comfortable and that higher state to be forgotten. There is actually no place in this village for a work of *fine* art, if any had come down to us, to stand, for our lives, our houses and streets, furnish no proper pedestal for it. There is not a nail to hang a picture on, nor a shelf to receive the bust of a hero or a saint. When I consider how our houses are built and paid for, or not paid for, and their internal economy managed and sustained, I wonder that the floor does not give way under the visitor while he is admiring the gewgaws upon the mantelpiece, and let him through into the cellar, to some solid and honest though earthy foundation. I cannot but perceive that this so called rich and refined life is a thing jumped at, and I do not get on in the enjoyment of the *fine* arts which adorn it, my attention being wholly occupied with the jump; for I remember that the greatest genuine leap, due to human muscles alone, on record, is that of certain wandering Arabs, who are said to have cleared twenty-five feet on level ground. Without factitious support, man is sure to come to earth again beyond that distance. The first question which I am tempted to put to the proprietor of such great impropriety is, Who bolsters you? Are you one of the ninety-seven who fail? or of the three who succeed? Answer me these questions, and then perhaps I may look at your bawbles and find them ornamental. The cart before the horse is neither beautiful nor useful. Before we can adorn our houses with beautiful objects the walls must be stripped, and our lives must be stripped, and beautiful housekeeping and beautiful living be laid for a foundation: now, a taste for the beautiful is most cultivated out of doors, where there is no house and no housekeeper.

Old Johnson, in his "Wonder-Working Providence," speaking of the first settlers of this town, with whom he was contemporary, tells us that "they burrow themselves in the earth for their first shelter under some hillside, and, casting the soil aloft upon timber, they make a smoky fire against the earth, at the highest side." They did not "provide them houses," says he, "till the earth, by the Lord's blessing, brought forth bread to feed them," and the first year's crop was so light that "they were forced to cut their bread very thin for a long season."[6] The secretary of the Province of New Netherland, writing in Dutch, in 1650, for the information of those who wished to take up land there, states more particularly, that "those in New Netherland, and especially in New England, who have no means to build farm houses at first according to their wishes, dig a square pit in the ground, cellar fashion, six or seven feet deep, as long and as broad as they think proper, case the earth inside with wood all round the wall, and line the wood with the bark of trees or something else to prevent the caving in of the earth; floor this cellar with plank, and wainscot it overhead for a ceiling, raise a roof of spars

6. Edward Johnson (1598–1672), *Wonder-working Providence of Sion's Saviour in New England* (1654).

clear up, and cover the spars with bark or green sods, so that they can live dry and warm in these houses with their entire families for two, three, and four years, it being understood that partitions are run through those cellars which are adapted to the size of the family. The wealthy and principal men in New England, in the beginning of the colonies, commenced their first dwelling houses in this fashion for two reasons; firstly, in order not to waste time in building, and not to want food the next season; secondly, in order not to discourage poor laboring people whom they brought over in numbers from Fatherland. In the course of three or four years, when the country became adapted to agriculture, they built themselves handsome houses, spending on them several thousands."[7]

In this course which our ancestors took there was a show of prudence at least, as if their principle were to satisfy the more pressing wants first. But are the more pressing wants satisfied now? When I think of acquiring for myself one of our luxurious dwellings, I am deterred, for, so to speak, the country is not yet adapted to *human* culture, and we are still forced to cut our *spiritual* bread far thinner than our forefathers did their wheaten. Not that all architectural ornament is to be neglected even in the rudest periods; but let our houses first be lined with beauty, where they come in contact with our lives, like the tenement of the shellfish, and not overlaid with it. But, alas! I have been inside one or two of them, and know what they are lined with.

Though we are not so degenerate but that we might possibly live in a cave or a wigwam or wear skins to-day, it certainly is better to accept the advantages, though so dearly bought, which the invention and industry of mankind offer. In such a neighborhood as this, boards and shingles, lime and bricks, are cheaper and more easily obtained than suitable caves, or whole logs, or bark in sufficient quantities, or even well-tempered clay or flat stones. I speak understandingly on this subject, for I have made myself acquainted with it both theoretically and practically. With a little more wit we might use these materials so as to become richer than the richest now are, and make our civilization a blessing. The civilized man is a more experienced and wiser savage. But to make haste to my own experiment.

Near the end of March, 1845, I borrowed an axe and went down to the woods by Walden Pond, nearest to where I intended to build my house, and began to cut down some tall arrowy white pines, still in their youth, for timber. It is difficult to begin without borrowing, but perhaps it is the most generous course thus to permit your fellow-men to have an interest in your enterprise. The owner of the axe, as he released his hold on it, said that it was the apple of his eye; but I returned it sharper than I received it. It was a pleasant hillside where I worked, covered with pine woods, through which I looked out on the pond, and a small open field in the woods where pines and hickories were springing up. The ice in the pond was not yet dissolved, though there were some open spaces, and it was all dark colored and saturated with water. There were some slight flurries of snow during the days that I worked there; but for the most part when I came out on to the railroad, on my way home, its yellow sand heap stretched away gleaming in the hazy atmosphere, and the rails shone in the spring sun, and I heard the lark and pewee and other birds already come to commence another year with

7. Edmund Bailey O'Callaghan (1797–1880), *Documentary History of the State of New-York* (1851).

us. They were pleasant spring days, in which the winter of man's discontent was thawing as well as the earth, and the life that had lain torpid began to stretch itself. One day, when my axe had come off and I had cut a green hickory for a wedge, driving it with a stone, and had placed the whole to soak in a pond hole in order to swell the wood, I saw a striped snake run into the water, and he lay on the bottom, apparently without inconvenience, as long as I staid there, or more than a quarter of an hour; perhaps because he had not yet fairly come out of the torpid state. It appeared to me that for a like reason men remain in their present low and primitive condition; but if they should feel the influence of the spring of springs arousing them, they would of necessity rise to a higher and more ethereal life. I had previously seen the snakes in frosty mornings in my path with portions of their bodies still numb and inflexible, waiting for the sun to thaw them. On the 1st of April it rained and melted the ice, and in the early part of the day, which was very foggy, I heard a stray goose groping about over the pond and cackling as if lost, or like the spirit of the fog.

So I went on for some days cutting and hewing timber, and also studs and rafters, all with my narrow axe, not having many communicable or scholar-like thoughts, singing to myself,—

Men say they know many things;
But lo! they have taken wings,—
The arts and sciences,
And a thousand appliances;
The wind that blows
Is all that any body knows.[8]

I hewed the main timbers six inches square, most of the studs on two sides only, and the rafters and floor timbers on one side, leaving the rest of the bark on, so that they were just as straight and much stronger than sawed ones. Each stick was carefully mortised or tenoned by its stump, for I had borrowed other tools by this time. My days in the woods were not very long ones; yet I usually carried my dinner of bread and butter, and read the newspaper in which it was wrapped, at noon, sitting amid the green pine boughs which I had cut off, and to my bread was imparted some of their fragrance, for my hands were covered with a thick coat of pitch. Before I had done I was more the friend than the foe of the pine tree, though I had cut down some of them, having become better acquainted with it. Sometimes a rambler in the wood was attracted by the sound of my axe, and we chatted pleasantly over the chips which I had made.

By the middle of April, for I made no haste in my work, but rather made the most of it, my house was framed and ready for the raising. I had already bought the shanty of James Collins, an Irishman who worked on the Fitchburg Railroad, for boards. James Collins' shanty was considered an uncommonly fine one. When I called to see it he was not at home. I walked about the outside, at first unobserved from within, the window was so deep and high. It was of small dimensions, with a peaked cottage roof, and not much else to be seen, the dirt being raised five feet all around as if it were a compost heap. The roof was the soundest part, though a good deal warped and

8. Like other poems in *Walden* not enclosed in quotation marks, this poem is Thoreau's.

made brittle by the sun. Door-sill there was none, but a perennial passage for the hens under the door board. Mrs. C. came to the door and asked me to view it from the inside. The hens were driven in by my approach. It was dark, and had a dirt floor for the most part, dank, clammy, and aguish, only here a board and there a board which would not bear removal. She lighted a lamp to show me the inside of the roof and the walls, and also that the board floor extended under the bed, warning me not to step into the cellar, a sort of dust hole two feet deep. In her own words, they were "good boards overhead, good boards all around, and a good window,"—of two whole squares originally, only the cat had passed out that way lately. There was a stove, a bed, and a place to sit, an infant in the house where it was born, a silk parasol, gilt-framed looking-glass, and a patent new coffee mill nailed to an oak sapling, all told. The bargain was soon concluded, for James had in the mean while returned. I to pay four dollars and twenty-five cents to-night, he to vacate at five to-morrow morning, selling to nobody else meanwhile: I to take possession at six. It were well, he said, to be there early, and anticipate certain indistinct but wholly unjust claims on the score of ground rent and fuel. This he assured me was the only encumbrance. At six I passed him and his family on the road. One large bundle held their all,—bed, coffee-mill, looking-glass, hens,—all but the cat, she took to the woods and became a wild cat, and, as I learned afterward, trod in a trap set for woodchucks, and so became a dead cat at last.

I took down this dwelling the same morning, drawing the nails, and removed it to the pond side by small cartloads, spreading the boards on the grass there to bleach and warp back again in the sun. One early thrush gave me a note or two as I drove along the woodland path. I was informed treacherously by a young Patrick that neighbor Seeley, an Irishman, in the intervals of the carting, transferred the still tolerable, straight, and drivable nails, staples, and spikes to his pocket, and then stood when I came back to pass the time of day, and look freshly up, unconcerned, with spring thoughts, at the devastation; there being a dearth of work, as he said. He was there to represent spectatordom, and help make this seemingly insignificant event one with the removal of the gods of Troy.[9]

I dug my cellar in the side of a hill sloping to the south, where a woodchuck had formerly dug his burrow, down through sumach and blackberry roots, and the lowest stain of vegetation, six feet square by seven deep, to a fine sand where potatoes would not freeze in any winter. The sides were left shelving, and not stoned; but the sun having never shone on them, the sand still keeps its place. It was but two hours' work. I took particular pleasure in this breaking of ground, for in almost all latitudes men dig into the earth for an equable temperature. Under the most splendid house in the city is still to be found the cellar where they store their roots as of old, and long after the superstructure has disappeared posterity remark its dent in the earth. The house is still but a sort of porch at the entrance of a burrow.

At length, in the beginning of May, with the help of some of my acquaintances, rather to improve so good an occasion for neighborliness than from any necessity, I set up the frame of my house. No man was ever more hon-

9. In Virgil's *Aeneid*, book 2, after the fall of Troy, Aeneas escapes with his father and son and his household gods.

ored in the character of his raisers[1] than I. They are destined, I trust, to assist at the raising of loftier structures one day. I began to occupy my house on the 4th of July, as soon as it was boarded and roofed, for the boards were carefully feather-edged and lapped, so that it was perfectly impervious to rain; but before boarding I laid the foundation of a chimney at one end, bringing two cartloads of stones up the hill from the pond in my arms. I built the chimney after my hoeing in the fall, before a fire became necessary for warmth, doing my cooking in the mean while out of doors on the ground, early in the morning: which mode I still think is in some respects more convenient and agreeable than the usual one. When it stormed before my bread was baked, I fixed a few boards over the fire, and sat under them to watch my loaf, and passed some pleasant hours in that way. In those days, when my hands were much employed, I read but little, but the least scraps of paper which lay on the ground, my holder, or table-cloth, afforded me as much entertainment, in fact answered the same purpose as the Iliad.[2]

It would be worth the while to build still more deliberately than I did, considering, for instance, what foundation a door, a window, a cellar, a garret, have in the nature of man, and perchance never raising any superstructure until we found a better reason for it than our temporal necessities even. There is some of the same fitness in a man's building his own house that there is in a bird's building its own nest. Who knows but if men constructed their dwellings with their own hands, and provided food for themselves and families simply and honestly enough, the poetic faculty would be universally developed, as birds universally sing when they are so engaged? But alas! we do like cowbirds and cuckoos, which lay their eggs in nests which other birds have built, and cheer no traveller with their chattering and unmusical notes. Shall we forever resign the pleasure of construction to the carpenter? What does architecture amount to in the experience of the mass of men? I never in all my walks came across a man engaged in so simple and natural an occupation as building his house. We belong to the community. It is not the tailor alone who is the ninth part of a man; it is as much the preacher, and the merchant, and the farmer. Where is this division of labor to end? and what object does it finally serve? No doubt another *may* also think for me; but it is not therefore desirable that he should do so to the exclusion of my thinking for myself.

True, there are architects so called in this country, and I have heard of one at least possessed with the idea of making architectural ornaments have a core of truth, a necessity, and hence a beauty, as if it were a revelation to him.[3] All very well perhaps from his point of view, but only a little better than the common dilettantism. A sentimental reformer in architecture, he began at the cornice, not at the foundation. It was only how to put a core of truth within the ornaments, that every sugar plum in fact might have an almond or caraway seed in it,—though I hold that almonds are most wholesome without the sugar,—and not how the inhabitant, the indweller, might build truly within and without, and let the ornaments take care of themselves. What

1. These "raisers" included Emerson; Alcott; Ellery Channing; two young brothers who had participated in the Brook Farm reform community, Burrill and George William Curtis; and the Concord farmer Edmund Hosmer and his three sons.
2. Greek epic traditionally attributed to Homer.
3. The sculptor Horatio Greenough (1805–1852), who insisted on the importance of function in architectural decoration.

reasonable man ever supposed that ornaments were something outward and in the skin merely,—that the tortoise got his spotted shell, or the shellfish its mother-o'-pearl tints, by such a contract as the inhabitants of Broadway their Trinity Church?[4] But a man has no more to do with the style of architecture of his house than a tortoise with that of its shell: nor need the soldier be so idle as to try to paint the precise *color* of his virtue on his standard. The enemy will find it out. He may turn pale when the trial comes. This man seemed to me to lean over the cornice and timidly whisper his half truth to the rude occupants who really knew it better than he. What of architectural beauty I now see, I know has gradually grown from within outward, out of the necessities and character of the indweller, who is the only builder,—out of some unconscious truthfulness, and nobleness, without ever a thought for the appearance; and whatever additional beauty of this kind is destined to be produced will be preceded by a like unconscious beauty of life. The most interesting dwellings in this country, as the painter knows, are the most unpretending, humble log huts and cottages of the poor commonly; it is the life of the inhabitants whose shells they are, and not any peculiarity in their surfaces merely, which makes them *picturesque;* and equally interesting will be the citizen's suburban box, when his life shall be as simple and as agreeable to the imagination, and there is as little straining after effect in the style of his dwelling. A great proportion of architectural ornaments are literally hollow, and a September gale would strip them off, like borrowed plumes, without injury to the substantials. They can do without *architecture* who have no olives nor wines in the cellar. What if an equal ado were made about the ornaments of style in literature, and the architects of our bibles spent as much time about their cornices as the architects of our churches do? So are made the *belles-lettres* and the *beaux-arts*[5] and their professors. Much it concerns a man, forsooth, how a few sticks are slanted over him or under him, and what colors are daubed upon his box. It would signify somewhat, if, in any earnest sense, *he* slanted them and daubed it; but the spirit having departed out of the tenant, it is of a piece with constructing his own coffin,—the architecture of the grave, and "carpenter" is but another name for "coffin-maker." One man says, in his despair or indifference to life, take up a handful of the earth at your feet, and paint your house that color. Is he thinking of his last and narrow house? Toss up a copper for it as well. What an abundance of leisure he must have! Why do you take up a handful of dirt? Better paint your house your own complexion; let it turn pale or blush for you. An enterprise to improve the style of cottage architecture! When you have got my ornaments ready I will wear them.

Before winter I built a chimney, and shingled the sides of my house, which were already impervious to rain, with imperfect and sappy shingles made of the first slice of the log, whose edges I was obliged to straighten with a plane.

I have thus a tight shingled and plastered house, ten feet wide by fifteen long, and eight-feet posts, with a garret and a closet, a large window on each side, two trap doors, one door at the end, and a brick fireplace opposite. The exact cost of my house, paying the usual price for such materials as I used, but not counting the work, all of which was done by myself, was as follows; and I give the details because very few are able to tell exactly

4. A New York City church built in a Gothic style during the 1840s.

5. Literature and fine arts (French).

what their houses cost, and fewer still, if any, the separate cost of the various materials which compose them:—

Boards,	$8 03½	Mostly shanty boards
Refuse shingles for roof and sides,	4 00	
Laths,	1 25	
Two second-hand windows with glass,	2 43	
One thousand old brick,	4 00	
Two casks of lime,	2 40	That was high
Hair,	0 31	More than I needed
Mantle-tree iron,	0 15	
Nails,	3 90	
Hinges and screws,	0 14	
Latch,	0 10	
Chalk,	0 01	
Transportation,	1 40	I carried a good part on my back
In all,	$28 12½	

These are all the materials excepting the timber stones and sand, which I claimed by squatter's right. I have also a small wood-shed adjoining, made chiefly of the stuff which was left after building the house.

I intend to build me a house which will surpass any on the main street in Concord in grandeur and luxury, as soon as it pleases me as much and will cost me no more than my present one.

I thus found that the student who wishes for a shelter can obtain one for a lifetime at an expense not greater than the rent which he now pays annually. If I seem to boast more than is becoming, my excuse is that I brag for humanity rather than for myself; and my shortcomings and inconsistencies do not affect the truth of my statement. Notwithstanding much cant and hypocrisy,—chaff which I find it difficult to separate from my wheat, but for which I am as sorry as any man,—I will breathe freely and stretch myself in this respect, it is such a relief to both the moral and physical system; and I am resolved that I will not through humility become the devil's attorney. I will endeavor to speak a good word for the truth. At Cambridge College[6] the mere rent of a student's room, which is only a little larger than my own, is thirty dollars each year, though the corporation had the advantage of building thirty-two side by side and under one roof, and the occupant suffers the inconvenience of many and noisy neighbors, and perhaps a residence in the fourth story. I cannot but think that if we had more true wisdom in these respects, not only less education would be needed, because, forsooth, more would already have been acquired, but the pecuniary expense of getting an education would in a great measure vanish. Those conveniences which the student requires at Cambridge or elsewhere cost him or somebody else ten times as great a sacrifice of life as they would with proper management on both sides. Those things for which the most money is demanded are never the things which the student most wants. Tuition, for instance, is an impor-

6. Harvard College.

tant item in the term bill, while for the far more valuable education which he gets by associating with the most cultivated of his contemporaries no charge is made. The mode of founding a college is, commonly, to get up a subscription of dollars and cents, and then following blindly the principles of a division of labor to its extreme, a principle which should never be followed but with circumspection,—to call in a contractor who makes this a subject of speculation, and he employs Irishmen or other operatives actually to lay the foundations, while the students that are to be are said to be fitting themselves for it; and for these oversights successive generations have to pay. I think that it would be *better than this*, for the students, or those who desire to be benefited by it, even to lay the foundation themselves. The student who secures his coveted leisure and retirement by systematically shirking any labor necessary to man obtains but an ignoble and unprofitable leisure, defrauding himself of the experience which alone can make leisure fruitful. "But," says one, "you do not mean that the students should go to work with their hands instead of their heads?" I do not mean that exactly, but I mean something which he might think a good deal like that; I mean that they should not *play* life, or *study* it merely, while the community supports them at this expensive game, but earnestly *live* it from beginning to end. How could youths better learn to live than by at once trying the experiment of living? Methinks this would exercise their minds as much as mathematics. If I wished a boy to know something about the arts and sciences, for instance, I would not pursue the common course, which is merely to send him into the neighborhood of some professor, where any thing is professed and practised but the art of life;—to survey the world through a telescope or a microscope, and never with his natural eye; to study chemistry, and not learn how his bread is made, or mechanics, and not learn how it is earned; to discover new satellites to Neptune, and not detect the motes in his eyes, or to what vagabond he is a satellite himself; or to be devoured by the monsters that swarm all around him, while contemplating the monsters in a drop of vinegar. Which would have advanced the most at the end of the month,—the boy who had made his own jack-knife from the ore which he had dug and smelted, reading as much as would be necessary for this,—or the boy who had attended the lectures on metallurgy at the Institute in the mean while, and had received a Rodgers penknife[7] from his father? Which would be most likely to cut his fingers?—To my astonishment I was informed on leaving college that I had studied navigation!—why, if I had taken one turn down the harbor I should have known more about it. Even the *poor* student studies and is taught only *political* economy, while that economy of living which is synonymous with philosophy is not even sincerely professed in our colleges. The consequence is, that while he is reading Adam Smith, Ricardo, and Say,[8] he runs his father in debt irretrievably.

As with our colleges, so with a hundred "modern improvements"; there is an illusion about them; there is not always a positive advance. The devil goes on exacting compound interest to the last for his early share and numerous succeeding investments in them. Our inventions are wont to be pretty toys, which distract our attention from serious things. They are but improved

7. High-quality knife made by the English firm of Joseph Rodgers and Sons.

8. Three European economists: Adam Smith (1723–1790), David Ricardo (1772–1823), and Jean Baptiste Say (1767–1832).

means to an unimproved end, an end which it was already but too easy to arrive at; as railroads lead to Boston or New York. We are in great haste to construct a magnetic telegraph from Maine to Texas; but Maine and Texas, it may be, have nothing important to communicate. Either is in such a predicament as the man who was earnest to be introduced to a distinguished deaf woman, but when he was presented, and one end of her ear trumpet was put into his hand, had nothing to say. As if the main object were to talk fast and not to talk sensibly. We are eager to tunnel under the Atlantic and bring the old world some weeks nearer to the new; but perchance the first news that will leak through into the broad, flapping American ear will be that the Princess Adelaide[9] has the whooping cough. After all, the man whose horse trots a mile in a minute does not carry the most important messages; he is not an evangelist, nor does he come round eating locusts and wild honey. I doubt if Flying Childers[1] ever carried a peck of corn to mill.

One says to me, "I wonder that you do not lay up money; you love to travel; you might take the cars and go to Fitchburg[2] to-day and see the country." But I am wiser than that. I have learned that the swiftest traveller is he that goes afoot. I say to my friend, Suppose we try who will get there first. The distance is thirty miles; the fare ninety cents. That is almost a day's wages. I remember when wages were sixty cents a day for laborers on this very road. Well, I start now on foot, and get there before night; I have travelled at that rate by the week together. You will in the mean while have earned your fare, and arrive there some time to-morrow, or possibly this evening, if you are lucky enough to get a job in season. Instead of going to Fitchburg, you will be working here the greater part of the day. And so, if the railroad reached round the world, I think that I should keep ahead of you; and as for seeing the country and getting experience of that kind, I should have to cut your acquaintance altogether.

Such is the universal law, which no man can ever outwit, and with regard to the railroad even we may say it is as broad as it is long. To make a railroad round the world available to all mankind is equivalent to grading the whole surface of the planet. Men have an indistinct notion that if they keep up this activity of joint stocks and spades long enough all will at length ride somewhere, in next to no time, and for nothing; but though a crowd rushes to the depot, and the conductor shouts "All aboard!" when the smoke is blown away and the vapor condensed, it will be perceived that a few are riding, but the rest are run over,—and it will be called, and will be, "A melancholy accident." No doubt they can ride at last who shall have earned their fare, that is, if they survive so long, but they will probably have lost their elasticity and desire to travel by that time. This spending of the best part of one's life earning money in order to enjoy a questionable liberty during the least valuable part of it, reminds me of the Englishman who went to India to make a fortune first, in order that he might return to England and live the life of a poet. He should have gone up garret at once. "What!" exclaim a million Irishmen starting up from all the shanties in the land, "is not this railroad which we have built a good thing?" Yes, I answer, *comparatively*

9. Adelaide Louisa Theresa Caroline Amelia (1792–1849), sister of Louis-Philippe, king of France from 1830 to 1848.

1. A famous English racehorse (1714–1741).

2. Village near Concord, Massachusetts.

good, that is, you might have done worse; but I wish, as you are brothers of mine, that you could have spent your time better than digging in this dirt.

Before I finished my house, wishing to earn ten or twelve dollars by some honest and agreeable method, in order to meet my unusual expenses, I planted about two acres and a half of light and sandy soil near it chiefly with beans, but also a small part with potatoes, corn, peas, and turnips. The whole lot contains eleven acres, mostly growing up to pines and hickories, and was sold the preceding season for eight dollars and eight cents an acre. One farmer said that it was "good for nothing but to raise cheeping squirrels on." I put no manure on this land, not being the owner, but merely a squatter, and not expecting to cultivate so much again, and I did not quite hoe it all once. I got out several cords of stumps in ploughing, which supplied me with fuel for a long time, and left small circles of virgin mould, easily distinguishable through the summer by the greater luxuriance of the beans there. The dead and for the most part unmerchantable wood behind my house, and the driftwood from the pond, have supplied the remainder of my fuel. I was obliged to hire a team and a man for the ploughing, though I held the plough myself. My farm outgoes for the first season were, for implements, seed, work, &c., $14 72½. The seed corn was given me. This never costs any thing to speak of, unless you plant more than enough. I got twelve bushels of beans, and eighteen bushels of potatoes, beside some peas and sweet corn. The yellow corn and turnips were too late to come to any thing. My whole income from the farm was

	$23 44.
Deducting the outgoes,	14 72½
there are left,	$ 8 71½,

beside produce consumed and on hand at the time this estimate was made of the value of $4 50,—the amount on hand much more than balancing a little grass which I did not raise. All things considered, that is, considering the importance of a man's soul and of to-day, notwithstanding the short time occupied by my experiment, nay, partly even because of its transient character, I believe that that was doing better than any farmer in Concord did that year.

The next year I did better still, for I spaded up all the land which I required, about a third of an acre, and I learned from the experience of both years, not being in the least awed by many celebrated works on husbandry, Arthur Young[3] among the rest, that if one would live simply and eat only the crop which he raised, and raise no more than he ate, and not exchange it for an insufficient quantity of more luxurious and expensive things, he would need to cultivate only a few rods of ground, and that it would be cheaper to spade up that than to use oxen to plough it, and to select a fresh spot from time to time than to manure the old, and he could do all his necessary farm work as it were with his left hand at odd hours in the summer; and thus he would not be tied to an ox, or horse, or cow, or pig, as at present. I desire to speak impartially on this point, and as one not interested in the success or failure of the

3. Author of *Rural Oeconomy, or Essays on the Practical Parts of Husbandry* (1773).

present economical and social arrangements. I was more independent than any farmer in Concord, for I was not anchored to a house or farm, but could follow the bent of my genius, which is a very crooked one, every moment. Beside being better off than they already, if my house had been burned or my crops had failed, I should have been nearly as well off as before.

I am wont to think that men are not so much the keepers of herds as herds are the keepers of men, the former are so much the freer. Men and oxen exchange work; but if we consider necessary work only, the oxen will be seen to have greatly the advantage, their farm is so much the larger. Man does some of his part of the exchange work in his six weeks of haying, and it is no boy's play. Certainly no nation that lived simply in all respects, that is, no nation of philosophers, would commit so great a blunder as to use the labor of animals. True, there never was and is not likely soon to be a nation of philosophers, nor am I certain it is desirable that there should be. However, *I* should never have broken a horse or bull and taken him to board for any work he might do for me, for fear I should become a horse-man or a herdsman merely; and if society seems to be the gainer by so doing, are we certain that what is one man's gain is not another's loss, and that the stable-boy has equal cause with his master to be satisfied? Granted that some public works would not have been constructed without this aid, and let man share the glory of such with the ox and horse; does it follow that he could not have accomplished works yet more worthy of himself in that case? When men begin to do, not merely unnecessary or artistic, but luxurious and idle work, with their assistance, it is inevitable that a few do all the exchange work with the oxen, or, in other words, become the slaves of the strongest. Man thus not only works for the animal within him, but, for a symbol of this, he works for the animal without him. Though we have many substantial houses of brick or stone, the prosperity of the farmer is still measured by the degree to which the barn overshadows the house. This town is said to have the largest houses for oxen cows and horses hereabouts, and it is not behindhand in its public buildings; but there are very few halls for free worship or free speech in this county. It should not be by their architecture, but why not even by their power of abstract thought, that nations should seek to commemorate themselves? How much more admirable the Bhagvat-Geeta[4] than all the ruins of the East! Towers and temples are the luxury of princes. A simple and independent mind does not toil at the bidding of any prince. Genius is not a retainer to any emperor, nor is its material silver, or gold, or marble, except to a trifling extent. To what end, pray, is so much stone hammered? In Arcadia,[5] when I was there, I did not see any hammering stone. Nations are possessed with an insane ambition to perpetuate the memory of themselves by the amount of hammered stone they leave. What if equal pains were taken to smooth and polish their manners? One piece of good sense would be more memorable than a monument as high as the moon. I love better to see stones in place. The grandeur of Thebes[6] was a vulgar grandeur. More sensible is a rod of stone wall that bounds an honest man's field than a hundred-gated Thebes that has wandered farther from the true end of life. The religion and civilization which are barbaric and heathenish build splendid temples; but

4. A sacred Hindu text.
5. Place epitomizing rustic simplicity and contentment, from a region in Greece.
6. City in ancient Egypt.

what you might call Christianity does not. Most of the stone a nation hammers goes toward its tomb only. It buries itself alive. As for the Pyramids, there is nothing to wonder at in them so much as the fact that so many men could be found degraded enough to spend their lives constructing a tomb for some ambitious booby, whom it would have been wiser and manlier to have drowned in the Nile, and then given his body to the dogs. I might possibly invent some excuse for them and him, but I have no time for it. As for the religion and love of art of the builders, it is much the same all the world over, whether the building be an Egyptian temple or the United States Bank. It costs more than it comes to. The mainspring is vanity, assisted by the love of garlic and bread and butter. Mr. Balcom, a promising young architect, designs it on the back of his Vitruvius,[7] with hard pencil and ruler, and the job is let out to Dobson & Sons, stonecutters. When the thirty centuries begin to look down on it, mankind begin to look up at it. As for your high towers and monuments, there was a crazy fellow once in this town who undertook to dig through to China, and he got so far that, as he said, he heard the Chinese pots and kettles rattle; but I think that I shall not go out of my way to admire the hole which he made. Many are concerned about the monuments of the West and the East,—to know who built them. For my part, I should like to know who in those days did not build them,—who were above such trifling. But to proceed with my statistics.

By surveying, carpentry, and day-labor of various other kinds in the village in the mean while, for I have as many trades as fingers, I had earned $13 34. The expense of food for eight months, namely, from July 4th to March 1st, the time when these estimates were made, though I lived there more than two years,—not counting potatoes, a little green corn, and some peas, which I had raised, nor considering the value of what was on hand at the last date, was

Rice,	01 73½		
Molasses,	1 73	Cheapest form of the saccharine.	
Rye meal,	1 04¾		
Indian meal,	0 99¾	Cheaper than rye.	
Pork,	0 22		
Flour,	0 88	Costs more than Indian meal, both money and trouble.	All experiments which failed.
Sugar,	0 80		
Lard,	0 65		
Apples,	0 25		
Dried apple,	0 22		
Sweet potatoes,	0 10		
One pumpkin,	0 6		
One watermelon,	0 2		
Salt,	0 3		

Yes, I did eat $8 74, all told; but I should not thus unblushingly publish my guilt, if I did not know that most of my readers were equally guilty with

7. Vitruvius Pollio (c. 80–c. 15 B.C.E.), Roman architect during the reigns of Julius Caesar and Augustus, author of *De Architectura*.

myself, and that their deeds would look no better in print. The next year I sometimes caught a mess of fish for my dinner, and once I went so far as to slaughter a woodchuck which ravaged my bean-field,—effect his transmigration, as a Tartar[8] would say,—and devour him, partly for experiment's sake; but though it afforded me a momentary enjoyment, notwithstanding a musky flavor, I saw that the longest use would not make that a good practice, however it might seem to have your woodchucks ready dressed by the village butcher.

Clothing and some incidental expenses within the same dates, though little can be inferred from this item, amounted to

	$8 40¾
Oil and some household utensils,	$2 00

So that all the pecuniary outgoes, excepting for washing and mending, which for the most part were done out of the house, and their bills have not yet been received,—and these are all and more than all the ways by which money necessarily goes out in this part of the world,—were

House,	$28 12½
Farm one year,	14 72½
Food eight months,	8 74
Clothing, &c., eight months,	8 40¾
Oil, &c., eight months,	2 00
In all,	61 99¾

I address myself now to those of my readers who have a living to get. And to meet this I have for farm produce sold

	$23 44
Earned by day-labor,	13 34
In all,	$36 78,

which subtracted from the sum of the outgoes leaves a balance of $25 21¾ on the one side,—this being very nearly the means with which I started, and the measure of expenses to be incurred,—and on the other, beside the leisure and independence and health thus secured, a comfortable house for me as long as I choose to occupy it.

These statistics, however accidental and therefore uninstructive they may appear, as they have a certain completeness, have a certain value also. Nothing was given me of which I have not rendered some account. It appears from the above estimate, that my food alone cost me in money about twenty-seven cents[9] a week. It was, for nearly two years after this, rye and Indian meal without yeast, potatoes, rice, a very little salt pork, molasses, and salt, and my drink water. It was fit that I should live on rice, mainly, who loved so well the philosophy of India. To meet the objections of some inveterate cavillers, I may

8. An inhabitant of Tartary, a broad area of Central Asia, and believer in a form of reincarnation called the transmigration of souls (or metempsychosis).

9. Approximately five dollars in today's currency.

as well state, that if I dined out occasionally, as I always had done, and I trust shall have opportunities to do again, it was frequently to the detriment of my domestic arrangements. But the dining out, being, as I have stated, a constant element, does not in the least affect a comparative statement like this.

I learned from my two years' experience that it would cost incredibly little trouble to obtain one's necessary food, even in this latitude; that a man may use as simple a diet as the animals, and yet retain health and strength. I have made a satisfactory dinner, satisfactory on several accounts, simply off a dish of purslane[1] (*Portulaca oleracea*) which I gathered in my cornfield, boiled and salted. I give the Latin on account of the savoriness of the trivial name. And pray what more can a reasonable man desire, in peaceful times, in ordinary noons, than a sufficient number of ears of green sweet-corn boiled, with the addition of salt? Even the little variety which I used was a yielding to the demands of appetite, and not of health. Yet men have come to such a pass that they frequently starve, not for want of necessaries, but for want of luxuries; and I know a good woman who thinks that her son lost his life because he took to drinking water only.

The reader will perceive that I am treating the subject rather from an economic than a dietetic point of view, and he will not venture to put my abstemiousness to the test unless he has a well-stocked larder.

Bread I at first made of pure Indian meal and salt, genuine hoe-cakes, which I baked before my fire out of doors on a shingle or the end of a stick of timber sawed off in building my house; but it was wont to get smoked and to have a piny flavor. I tried flour also; but have at last found a mixture of rye and Indian meal most convenient and agreeable. In cold weather it was no little amusement to bake several small loaves of this in succession, tending and turning them as carefully as an Egyptian his hatching eggs.[2] They were a real cereal fruit which I ripened, and they had to my senses a fragrance like that of other noble fruits, which I kept in as long as possible by wrapping them in cloths. I made a study of the ancient and indispensable art of bread-making, consulting such authorities as offered, going back to the primitive days and first invention of the unleavened kind, when from the wildness of nuts and meats men first reached the mildness and refinement of this diet, and travelling gradually down in my studies through that accidental souring of the dough which, it is supposed, taught the leavening process, and through the various fermentations thereafter, till I came to "good, sweet, wholesome bread," the staff of life. Leaven, which some deem the soul of bread, the *spiritus* which fills its cellular tissue, which is religiously preserved like the vestal fire,—some precious bottle-full, I suppose, first brought over in the May-flower, did the business for America, and its influence is still rising, swelling, spreading, in cerealian billows over the land,—this seed I regularly and faithfully procured from the village, till at length one morning I forgot the rules, and scalded my yeast; by which accident I discovered that even this was not indispensable,—for my discoveries were not by the synthetic but analytic process,—and I have gladly omitted it since, though most housewives earnestly assured me that safe and wholesome bread without yeast might not be, and elderly people prophesied a speedy decay of the vital forces. Yet I find it not to be an essential ingredient, and after going without it for a year am still

1. A type of greens.

2. Egyptians had devised incubators.

in the land of the living; and I am glad to escape the trivialness of carrying a bottle-full in my pocket, which would sometimes pop and discharge its contents to my discomfiture. It is simpler and more respectable to omit it. Man is an animal who more than any other can adapt himself to all climates and circumstances. Neither did I put any sal soda, or other acid or alkali, into my bread. It would seem that I made it according to the recipe which Marcus Porcius Cato gave about two centuries before Christ. "Panem depsticium sic facito. Manus mortariumque bene lavato. Farinam in mortarium indito, aquæ paulatim addito, subigitoque pulchre. Ubi bene subegeris, defingito, coquitoque sub testu."[3] Which I take to mean—"Make kneaded bread thus. Wash your hands and trough well. Put the meal into the trough, add water gradually, and knead it thoroughly. When you have kneaded it well, mould it, and bake it under a cover," that is, in a baking-kettle. Not a word about leaven. But I did not always use this staff of life. At one time, owing to the emptiness of my purse, I saw none of it for more than a month.

Every New Englander might easily raise all his own breadstuffs in this land of rye and Indian corn, and not depend on distant and fluctuating markets for them. Yet so far are we from simplicity and independence that, in Concord, fresh and sweet meal is rarely sold in the shops, and hominy and corn in a still coarser form are hardly used by any. For the most part the farmer gives to his cattle and hogs the grain of his own producing, and buys flour, which is at least no more wholesome, at a greater cost, at the store. I saw that I could easily raise my bushel or two of rye and Indian corn, for the former will grow on the poorest land, and the latter does not require the best, and grind them in a hand-mill, and so do without rice and pork; and if I must have some concentrated sweet, I found by experiment that I could make a very good molasses either of pumpkins or beets, and I knew that I needed only to set out a few maples to obtain it more easily still, and while these were growing I could use various substitutes beside those which I have named, "For," as the Forefathers sang,—

> "we can make liquor to sweeten our lips
> Of pumpkins and parsnips and walnut-tree chips."[4]

Finally, as for salt, that grossest of groceries, to obtain this might be a fit occasion for a visit to the seashore, or, if I did without it altogether, I should probably drink the less water. I do not learn that the Indians ever troubled themselves to go after it.

Thus I could avoid all trade and barter, so far as my food was concerned, and having a shelter already, it would only remain to get clothing and fuel. The pantaloons which I now wear were woven in a farmer's family,—thank Heaven there is so much virtue still in man; for I think the fall from the farmer to the operative as great and memorable as that from the man to the farmer;—and in a new country fuel is an encumbrance. As for a habitat, if I were not permitted still to squat, I might purchase one acre at the same price for which the land I cultivated was sold—namely, eight dollars and eight cents. But as it was, I considered that I enhanced the value of the land by squatting on it.

3. From *De Agri Cultura*, by the Roman political leader Cato (234–149 B.C.E.), who celebrated the simplicity of country life.

4. From the American historian and engraver John Warner Barber's (1798–1885) *Historical Collections of Massachusetts* (1839).

There is a certain class of unbelievers who sometimes ask me such questions as, if I think that I can live on vegetable food alone; and to strike at the root of the matter at once,—for the root is faith,—I am accustomed to answer such, that I can live on board nails. If they cannot understand that, they cannot understand much that I have to say. For my part, I am glad to hear of experiments of this kind being tried; as that a young man tried for a fortnight to live on hard raw corn on the ear, using his teeth for all mortar. The squirrel tribe tried the same and succeeded. The human race is interested in these experiments, though a few old women who are incapacitated for them, or who own their thirds in mills, may be alarmed.

My furniture, part of which I made myself, and the rest cost me nothing of which I have not rendered an account, consisted of a bed, a table, a desk, three chairs, a looking-glass three inches in diameter, a pair of tongs and andirons, a kettle, a skillet, and a frying-pan, a dipper, a wash-bowl, two knives and forks, three plates, one cup, one spoon, a jug for oil, a jug for molasses, and a japanned[5] lamp. None is so poor that he need sit on a pumpkin. That is shiftlessness. There is a plenty of such chairs as I like best in the village garrets to be had for taking them away. Furniture! Thank God, I can sit and I can stand without the aid of a furniture warehouse. What man but a philosopher would not be ashamed to see his furniture packed in a cart and going up country exposed to the light of heaven and the eyes of men, a beggarly account of empty boxes? That is Spaulding's furniture.[6] I could never tell from inspecting such a load whether it belonged to a so called rich man or a poor one; the owner always seemed poverty-stricken. Indeed, the more you have of such things the poorer you are. Each load looks as if it contained the contents of a dozen shanties; and if one shanty is poor, this is a dozen times as poor. Pray, for what do we *move* ever but to get rid of our furniture, our *exuviæ*;[7] at last to go from this world to another newly furnished, and leave this to be burned? It is the same as if all these traps were buckled to a man's belt, and he could not move over the rough country where our lines are cast without dragging them,—dragging his trap. He was a lucky fox that left his tail in the trap. The muskrat will gnaw his third leg off to be free. No wonder man has lost his elasticity. How often he is at a dead set! "Sir, if I may be so bold, what do you mean by a dead set?" If you are a seer, whenever you meet a man you will see all that he owns, ay, and much that he pretends to disown, behind him, even to his kitchen furniture and all the trumpery which he saves and will not burn, and he will appear to be harnessed to it and making what headway he can. I think that the man is at a dead set who has got through a knot hole or gateway where his sledge load of furniture cannot follow him. I cannot but feel compassion when I hear some trig, compact-looking man, seemingly free, all girded and ready, speak of his "furniture," as whether it is insured or not. "But what shall I do with my furniture?" My gay butterfly is entangled in a spider's web then. Even those who seem for a long while not to have any, if you inquire more narrowly you will find have some stored in somebody's barn. I look upon England to-day as an old gentleman who is travelling with a great deal of baggage, trumpery which has

5. Lacquered with decorative scenes in the Japanese manner.

6. Unidentified.

7. Discarded objects (Latin).

accumulated from long housekeeping, which he has not the courage to burn; great trunk, little trunk, bandbox and bundle. Throw away the first three at least. It would surpass the powers of a well man nowadays to take up his bed and walk, and I should certainly advise a sick one to lay down his bed and run. When I have met an immigrant tottering under a bundle which contained his all,—looking like an enormous wen which had grown out of the nape of his neck,—I have pitied him, not because that was his all, but because he had all *that* to carry. If I have got to drag my trap, I will take care that it be a light one and do not nip me in a vital part. But perchance it would be wisest never to put one's paw into it.

I would observe, by the way, that it costs me nothing for curtains, for I have no gazers to shut out but the sun and moon, and I am willing that they should look in. The moon will not sour milk nor taint meat of mine, nor will the sun injure my furniture or fade my carpet, and if he is sometimes too warm a friend, I find it still better economy to retreat behind some curtain which nature has provided, than to add a single item to the details of housekeeping. A lady once offered me a mat, but as I had no room to spare within the house, nor time to spare within or without to shake it, I declined it, preferring to wipe my feet on the sod before my door. It is best to avoid the beginnings of evil.

Not long since I was present at the auction of a deacon's effects, for his life had not been ineffectual:—

"The evil that men do lives after them."[8]

As usual, a great proportion was trumpery which had begun to accumulate in his father's day. Among the rest was a dried tapeworm. And now, after lying half a century in his garret and other dust holes, these things were not burned; instead of a *bonfire*, or purifying destruction of them, there was an *auction*, or increasing of them.[9] The neighbors eagerly collected to view them, bought them all, and carefully transported them to their garrets and dust holes, to lie there till their estates are settled, when they will start again. When a man dies he kicks the dust.

The customs of some savage nations might, perchance, be profitably imitated by us, for they at least go through the semblance of casting their slough annually; they have the idea of the thing, whether they have the reality or not. Would it not be well if we were to celebrate such a "busk," or "feast of first fruits," as Bartram[1] describes to have been the custom of the Mucclasse Indians? "When a town celebrates the busk," says he, "having previously provided themselves with new clothes, new pots, pans, and other household utensils and furniture, they collect all their worn out clothes and other despicable things, sweep and cleanse their houses, squares, and the whole town, of their filth, which with all the remaining grain and other old provisions they cast together into one common heap, and consume it with fire. After having taken medicine, and fasted for three days, all the fire in the town is extinguished. During this fast they abstain from the gratification of every appetite and passion whatever. A general amnesty is proclaimed; all malefactors may return to their town.—"

8. From Antony's speech to the citizens, in Shakespeare's *Julius Caesar* 3.2.
9. Thoreau puns on the Latin root of *auction*, which means "to increase."
1. William Bartram (1739–1832), *Travels through North and South Carolina* (1791).

"On the fourth morning, the high priest, by rubbing dry wood together, produces new fire in the public square, from whence every habitation in the town is supplied with the new and pure flame."

They then feast on the new corn and fruits and dance and sing for three days, "and the four following days they receive visits and rejoice with their friends from neighboring towns who have in like manner purified and prepared themselves."

The Mexicans also practised a similar purification at the end of every fifty-two years, in the belief that it was time for the world to come to an end.

I have scarcely heard of a truer sacrament, that is, as the dictionary defines it, "outward and visible sign of an inward and spiritual grace," than this, and I have no doubt that they were originally inspired directly from Heaven to do thus, though they have no biblical record of the revelation.

For more than five years I maintained myself thus solely by the labor of my hands, and I found, that by working about six weeks in a year, I could meet all the expenses of living. The whole of my winters, as well as most of my summers, I had free and clear for study. I have thoroughly tried school-keeping, and found that my expenses were in proportion, or rather out of proportion, to my income, for I was obliged to dress and train, not to say think and believe, accordingly, and I lost my time into the bargain. As I did not teach for the good of my fellow-men, but simply for a livelihood, this was a failure. I have tried trade; but I found that it would take ten years to get under way in that, and that then I should probably be on my way to the devil. I was actually afraid that I might by that time be doing what is called a good business. When formerly I was looking about to see what I could do for a living, some sad experience in conforming to the wishes of friends being fresh in my mind to tax my ingenuity, I thought often and seriously of picking huckleberries; that surely I could do, and its small profits might suffice,—for my greatest skill has been to want but little,—so little capital it required, so little distraction from my wonted moods, I foolishly thought. While my acquaintances went unhesitatingly into trade or the professions, I contemplated this occupation as most like theirs; ranging the hills all summer to pick the berries which came in my way, and thereafter carelessly dispose of them; so, to keep the flocks of Admetus.[2] I also dreamed that I might gather the wild herbs, or carry evergreens to such villagers as loved to be reminded of the woods, even to the city, by hay-cart loads. But I have since learned that trade curses every thing it handles; and though you trade in messages from heaven, the whole curse of trade attaches to the business.

As I preferred some things to others, and especially valued my freedom, as I could fare hard and yet succeed well, I did not wish to spend my time in earning rich carpets or other fine furniture, or delicate cookery, or a house in the Grecian or the Gothic style just yet. If there are any to whom it is no interruption to acquire these things, and who know how to use them when acquired, I relinquish to them the pursuit. Some are "industrious," and appear to love labor for its own sake, or perhaps because it keeps them out of worse mischief; to such I have at present nothing to say. Those who would not know what to do with more leisure than they now enjoy, I might

2. Apollo, Greek god of poetry, tended the flocks of Admetus while banished from Olympus.

advise to work twice as hard as they do,—work till they pay for themselves, and get their free papers. For myself I found that the occupation of a day-laborer was the most independent of any, especially as it required only thirty or forty days in a year to support one. The laborer's day ends with the going down of the sun, and he is then free to devote himself to his chosen pursuit, independent of his labor; but his employer, who speculates from month to month, has no respite from one end of the year to the other.

In short, I am convinced, both by faith and experience, that to maintain one's self on this earth is not a hardship but a pastime, if we will live simply and wisely; as the pursuits of the simpler nations are still the sports of the more artificial. It is not necessary that a man should earn his living by the sweat of his brow, unless he sweats easier than I do.

One young man of my acquaintance, who has inherited some acres, told me that he thought he should live as I did, *if he had the means.* I would not have any one adopt *my* mode of living on any account; for, beside that before he has fairly learned it I may have found out another for myself, I desire that there may be as many different persons in the world as possible; but I would have each one be very careful to find out and pursue *his own* way, and not his father's or his mother's or his neighbor's instead. The youth may build or plant or sail, only let him not be hindered from doing that which he tells me he would like to do. It is by a mathematical point only that we are wise, as the sailor or the fugitive slave keeps the polestar in his eye; but that is sufficient guidance for all our life. We may not arrive at our port within a calculable period, but we would preserve the true course.

Undoubtedly, in this case, what is true for one is truer still for a thousand, as a large house is not more expensive than a small one in proportion to its size, since one roof may cover, one cellar underlie, and one wall separate several apartments. But for my part, I preferred the solitary dwelling. Moreover, it will commonly be cheaper to build the whole yourself than to convince another of the advantage of the common wall; and when you have done this, the common partition, to be much cheaper, must be a thin one, and that other may prove a bad neighbor, and also not keep his side in repair. The only coöperation which is commonly possible is exceedingly partial and superficial; and what little true coöperation there is, is as if it were not, being a harmony inaudible to men. If a man has faith he will coöperate with equal faith every where; if he has not faith, he will continue to live like the rest of the world, whatever company he is joined to. To coöperate, in the highest as well as the lowest sense, means *to get our living together.* I heard it proposed lately that two young men should travel together over the world, the one without money, earning his means as he went, before the mast and behind the plough, the other carrying a bill of exchange in his pocket. It was easy to see that they could not long be companions or coöperate, since one would not *operate* at all. They would part at the first interesting crisis in their adventures. Above all, as I have implied, the man who goes alone can start today; but he who travels with another must wait till that other is ready, and it may be a long time before they get off.

But all this is very selfish, I have heard some of my townsmen say. I confess that I have hitherto indulged very little in philanthropic enterprises. I have made some sacrifices to a sense of duty, and among others have sacrificed this pleasure also. There are those who have used all their arts to persuade me to undertake the support of some poor family in the town; and if I had nothing to do,—for the devil finds employment for the idle,—I might try my hand at some such pastime as that. However, when I have thought to indulge myself in this respect, and lay their Heaven under an obligation by maintaining certain poor persons in all respects as comfortably as I maintain myself, and have even ventured so far as to make them the offer, they have one and all unhesitatingly preferred to remain poor. While my townsmen and women are devoted in so many ways to the good of their fellows, I trust that one at least may be spared to other and less humane pursuits. You must have a genius for charity as well as for any thing else. As for Doing-good, that is one of the professions which are full. Moreover, I have tried it fairly, and, strange as it may seem, am satisfied that it does not agree with my constitution. Probably I should not consciously and deliberately forsake my particular calling to do the good which society demands of me, to save the universe from annihilation; and I believe that a like but infinitely greater steadfastness elsewhere is all that now preserves it. But I would not stand between any man and his genius; and to him who does this work, which I decline, with his whole heart and soul and life, I would say, Persevere, even if the world call it doing evil, as it is most likely they will.

I am far from supposing that my case is a peculiar one; no doubt many of my readers would make a similar defence. At doing something,—I will not engage that my neighbors shall pronounce it good,—I do not hesitate to say that I should be a capital fellow to hire; but what that is, it is for my employer to find out. What *good* I do, in the common sense of that word, must be aside from my main path, and for the most part wholly unintended. Men say, practically, Begin where you are and such as you are, without aiming mainly to become of more worth, and with kindness aforethought go about doing good. If I were to preach at all in this strain, I should say rather, Set about being good. As if the sun should stop when he had kindled his fires up to the splendor of a moon or a star of the sixth magnitude, and go about like a Robin Goodfellow,[3] peeping in at every cottage window, inspiring lunatics, and tainting meats, and making darkness visible, instead of steadily increasing his genial heat and beneficence till he is of such brightness that no mortal can look him in the face, and then, and in the mean while too, going about the world in his own orbit, doing it good, or rather, as a truer philosophy has discovered, the world going about him getting good. When Phaeton,[4] wishing to prove his heavenly birth by his beneficence, had the sun's chariot but one day, and drove out of the beaten track, he burned several blocks of houses in the lower streets of heaven, and scorched the surface of the earth, and dried up every spring, and made the great desert of Sahara, till at length Jupiter hurled him headlong to the earth with a thunderbolt, and the sun, through grief at his death, did not shine for a year.

There is no odor so bad as that which arises from goodness tainted. It is human, it is divine, carrion. If I knew for a certainty that a man was coming to my house with the conscious design of doing me good, I should run for my life, as from that dry and parching wind of the African deserts called the

3. Mischievous sprite, known as Puck in Shakespeare's *A Midsummer Night's Dream*.

4. In Greek mythology, the son of Helios. He attempted to drive his father's chariot, the sun.

simoom, which fills the mouth and nose and ears and eyes with dust till you are suffocated, for fear that I should get some of his good done to me,—some of its virus mingled with my blood. No,—in this case I would rather suffer evil the natural way. A man is not a good *man* to me because he will feed me if I should be starving, or warm me if I should be freezing, or pull me out of a ditch if I should ever fall into one. I can find you a Newfoundland dog that will do as much. Philanthropy is not love for one's fellow-man in the broadest sense. Howard[5] was no doubt an exceedingly kind and worthy man in his way, and has his reward; but, comparatively speaking, what are a hundred Howards to *us,* if their philanthropy do not help *us* in our best estate, when we are most worthy to be helped? I never heard of a philanthropic meeting in which it was sincerely proposed to do any good to me, or the like of me.

The Jesuits[6] were quite balked by those Indians who, being burned at the stake, suggested new modes of torture to their tormentors. Being superior to physical suffering, it sometimes chanced that they were superior to any consolation which the missionaries could offer; and the law to do as you would be done by fell with less persuasiveness on the ears of those, who, for their part, did not care how they were done by, who loved their enemies after a new fashion, and came very near freely forgiving them all they did.

Be sure that you give the poor the aid they most need, though it be your example which leaves them far behind. If you give money, spend yourself with it, and do not merely abandon it to them. We make curious mistakes sometimes. Often the poor man is not so cold and hungry as he is dirty and ragged and gross. It is partly his taste, and not merely his misfortune. If you give him money, he will perhaps buy more rags with it. I was wont to pity the clumsy Irish laborers who cut ice on the pond, in such mean and ragged clothes, while I shivered in my more tidy and somewhat more fashionable garments, till, one bitter cold day, one who had slipped into the water came to my house to warm him, and I saw him strip off three pairs of pants and two pairs of stockings ere he got down to the skin, though they were dirty and ragged enough, it is true, and that he could afford to refuse the *extra* garments which I offered him, he had so many *intra* ones. This ducking was the very thing he needed. Then I began to pity myself, and I saw that it would be a greater charity to bestow on me a flannel shirt than a whole slop-shop on him. There are a thousand hacking at the branches of evil to one who is striking at the root, and it may be that he who bestows the largest amount of time and money on the needy is doing the most by his mode of life to produce that misery which he strives in vain to relieve. It is the pious slave-breeder devoting the proceeds of every tenth slave to buy a Sunday's liberty for the rest. Some show their kindness to the poor by employing them in their kitchens. Would they not be kinder if they employed themselves there? You boast of spending a tenth part of your income in charity; may be you should spend the nine tenths so, and done with it. Society recovers only a tenth part of the property then. Is this owing to the generosity of him in whose possession it is found, or to the remissness of the officers of justice?

Philanthropy is almost the only virtue which is sufficiently appreciated by mankind. Nay, it is greatly overrated; and it is our selfishness which

5. John Howard (1726?–1790), English prison reformer.

6. Roman Catholic missionaries of the Society of Jesus who attempted to convert the Indians to Christianity.

overrates it. A robust poor man, one sunny day here in Concord, praised a fellow-townsman to me, because, as he said, he was kind to the poor; meaning himself. The kind uncles and aunts of the race are more esteemed than its true spiritual fathers and mothers. I once heard a reverend lecturer on England, a man of learning and intelligence, after enumerating her scientific, literary, and political worthies, Shakspeare, Bacon, Cromwell, Milton, Newton, and others, speak next of her Christian heroes, whom, as if his profession required it of him, he elevated to a place far above all the rest, as the greatest of the great. They were Penn, Howard, and Mrs. Fry.[7] Every one must feel the falsehood and cant of this. The last were not England's best men and women; only, perhaps, her best philanthropists.

I would not subtract any thing from the praise that is due to philanthropy, but merely demand justice for all who by their lives and works are a blessing to mankind. I do not value chiefly a man's uprightness and benevolence, which are, as it were, his stem and leaves. Those plants of whose greenness withered we make herb tea for the sick, serve but a humble use, and are most employed by quacks. I want the flower and fruit of a man; that some fragrance be wafted over from him to me, and some ripeness flavor our intercourse. His goodness must not be a partial and transitory act, but a constant superfluity, which costs him nothing and of which he is unconscious. This is a charity that hides a multitude of sins. The philanthropist too often surrounds mankind with the remembrance of his own cast-off griefs as an atmosphere, and calls it sympathy. We should impart our courage, and not our despair, our health and ease, and not our disease, and take care that this does not spread by contagion. From what southern plains comes up the voice of wailing? Under what latitudes reside the heathen to whom we would send light? Who is that intemperate and brutal man whom we would redeem? If any thing ail a man, so that he does not perform his functions, if he have a pain in his bowels even,—for that is the seat of sympathy,—he forthwith sets about reforming—the world. Being a microcosm himself, he discovers, and it is a true discovery, and he is the man to make it,—that the world has been eating green apples; to his eyes, in fact, the globe itself is a great green apple, which there is danger awful to think of that the children of men will nibble before it is ripe; and straightway his drastic philanthropy seeks out the Esquimaux and the Patagonian,[8] and embraces the populous Indian and Chinese villages; and thus, by a few years of philanthropic activity, the powers in the mean while using him for their own ends, no doubt, he cures himself of his dyspepsia, the globe acquires a faint blush on one or both of its cheeks, as if it were beginning to be ripe, and life loses its crudity and is once more sweet and wholesome to live. I never dreamed of any enormity greater than I have committed. I never knew, and never shall know, a worse man than myself.

I believe that what so saddens the reformer is not his sympathy with his fellows in distress, but, though he be the holiest son of God, is his private ail. Let this be righted, let the spring come to him, the morning rise over his couch, and he will forsake his generous companions without apology. My excuse for not lecturing against the use of tobacco is, that I never chewed it;

7. Elizabeth Fry (1780–1845), English Quaker and prison reformer. William Penn (1644–1718), Quaker leader and proprietor of Pennsylvania.

8. Inhabitant of Patagonia, in southernmost South America.

that is a penalty which reformed tobacco-chewers have to pay; though there are things enough I have chewed, which I could lecture against. If you should ever be betrayed into any of these philanthropies, do not let your left hand know what your right hand does, for it is not worth knowing. Rescue the drowning and tie your shoe-strings. Take your time, and set about some free labor.

Our manners have been corrupted by communication with the saints. Our hymn-books resound with a melodious cursing of God and enduring him forever. One would say that even the prophets and redeemers had rather consoled the fears than confirmed the hopes of man. There is nowhere recorded a simple and irrepressible satisfaction with the gift of life, any memorable praise of God. All health and success does me good, however far off and withdrawn it may appear; all disease and failure helps to make me sad and does me evil, however much sympathy it may have with me or I with it. If, then, we would indeed restore mankind by truly Indian, botanic, magnetic, or natural means, let us first be as simple and well as Nature ourselves, dispel the clouds which hang over our own brows, and take up a little life into our pores. Do not stay to be an overseer of the poor, but endeavor to become one of the worthies of the world.

I read in the Gulistan, or Flower Garden, of Sheik Sadi of Shiraz, that "They asked a wise man, saying; Of the many celebrated trees which the Most High God has created lofty and umbrageous, they call none azad, or free, excepting the cypress, which bears no fruit; what mystery is there in this? He replied; Each has its appropriate produce, and appointed season, during the continuance of which it is fresh and blooming, and during their absence dry and withered; to neither of which states is the cypress exposed, being always flourishing; and of this nature are the azads, or religious independents.—Fix not thy heart on that which is transitory; for the Dijlah, or Tigris, will continue to flow through Bagdad after the race of caliphs is extinct: if thy hand has plenty, be liberal as the date tree; but if it affords nothing to give away, be an azad, or free man, like the cypress."[9]

Complemental Verses[1]

THE PRETENSIONS OF POVERTY

"Thou dost presume too much, poor needy wretch,
To claim a station in the firmament,
Because thy humble cottage, or thy tub,
Nurses some lazy or pedantic virtue
In the cheap sunshine or by shady springs,
With roots and pot-herbs; where thy right hand,
Tearing those humane passions from the mind,
Upon whose stocks fair blooming virtues flourish,
Degradeth nature, and benumbeth sense,
And, Gorgon-like, turns active men to stone.[2]
We not require the dull society

9. Muslih-ud-Din (Saadi) (1184?–1291), *The Gulistan or Rose Garden.*

1. From *Coelum Britannicum* by the English Cavalier poet Thomas Carew (1595?–1645?). The title is Thoreau's invention.

2. In Greek mythology the Gorgons were three sisters, with snakes for hair and eyes, who turned any beholder into stone.

Of your necessitated temperance,
Or that unnatural stupidity
That knows nor joy nor sorrow; nor your forc'd
Falsely exalted passive fortitude
Above the active. This low abject brood,
That fix their seats in mediocrity,
Become your servile minds; but we advance
Such virtues only as admit excess,
Brave, bounteous acts, regal magnificence,
All-seeing prudence, magnanimity
That knows no bound, and that heroic virtue
For which antiquity hath left no name,
But patterns only, such as Hercules,
Achilles, Theseus. Back to thy loath'd cell;
And when thou seest the new enlightened sphere,
Study to know but what those worthies were."

—T. CAREW

2. *Where I Lived, and What I Lived For*

At a certain season of our life we are accustomed to consider every spot as the possible site of a house. I have thus surveyed the country on every side within a dozen miles of where I live. In imagination I have bought all the farms in succession, for all were to be bought and I knew their price. I walked over each farmer's premises, tasted his wild apples, discoursed on husbandry with him, took his farm at his price, at any price, mortgaging it to him in my mind; even put a higher price on it,—took every thing but a deed of it,—took his word for his deed, for I dearly love to talk,—cultivated it, and him too to some extent, I trust, and withdrew when I had enjoyed it long enough, leaving him to carry it on. This experience entitled me to be regarded as a sort of real-estate broker by my friends. Wherever I sat, there I might live, and the landscape radiated from me accordingly. What is a house but a *sedes*, a seat?—better if a country seat. I discovered many a site for a house not likely to be soon improved, which some might have thought too far from the village, but to my eyes the village was too far from it. Well, there I might live, I said; and there I did live, for an hour, a summer and a winter life; saw how I could let the years run off, buffet the winter through, and see the spring come in. The future inhabitants of this region, wherever they may place their houses, may be sure that they have been anticipated. An afternoon sufficed to lay out the land into orchard woodlot and pasture, and to decide what fine oaks or pines should be left to stand before the door, and whence each blasted tree could be seen to the best advantage; and then I let it lie, fallow perchance, for a man is rich in proportion to the number of things which he can afford to let alone.

My imagination carried me so far that I even had the refusal of several farms,—the refusal was all I wanted,—but I never got my fingers burned by actual possession. The nearest that I came to actual possession was when I bought the Hollowell Place, and had begun to sort my seeds, and collected materials with which to make a wheelbarrow to carry it on or off with; but before the owner gave me a deed of it, his wife—every man has such a wife—changed her mind and wished to keep it, and he offered me ten dollars to release him. Now, to speak the truth, I had but ten cents in the world, and it surpassed my arithmetic to tell, if I was that man who had ten cents, or who had a farm, or ten dollars, or all together. However, I let him keep the ten dollars and the farm too, for I had carried it far enough; or rather, to be generous, I sold him the farm for just what I gave for it, and, as he was not a rich man, made him a present of ten dollars, and still had my ten cents, and seeds, and materials for a wheelbarrow left. I found thus that I had been a rich man without any damage to my poverty. But I retained the landscape, and I have since annually carried off what it yielded without a wheelbarrow. With respect to landscapes,—

> "I am monarch of all I *survey*,
> My right there is none to dispute."[3]

I have frequently seen a poet withdraw, having enjoyed the most valuable part of a farm, while the crusty farmer supposed that he had got a few wild apples only. Why, the owner does not know it for many years when a poet has put his farm in rhyme, the most admirable kind of invisible fence, has fairly impounded it, milked it, skimmed it, and got all the cream, and left the farmer only the skimmed milk.

The real attractions of the Hollowell farm, to me, were; its complete retirement, being about two miles from the village, half a mile from the nearest neighbor, and separated from the highway by a broad field; its bounding on the river, which the owner said protected it by its fogs from frosts in the spring, though that was nothing to me; the gray color and ruinous state of the house and barn, and the dilapidated fences, which put such an interval between me and the last occupant; the hollow and lichen-covered apple trees, gnawed by rabbits, showing what kind of neighbors I should have; but above all, the recollection I had of it from my earliest voyages up the river, when the house was concealed behind a dense grove of red maples, through which I heard the house-dog bark. I was in haste to buy it, before the proprietor finished getting out some rocks, cutting down the hollow apple trees, and grubbing up some young birches which had sprung up in the pasture, or, in short, had made any more of his improvements. To enjoy these advantages I was ready to carry it on; like Atlas,[4] to take the world on my shoulders,—I never heard what compensation he received for that,—and do all those things which had no other motive or excuse but that I might pay for it and be unmolested in my possession of it; for I knew all the while that it would yield the most abundant crop of the kind I wanted if I could only afford to let it alone. But it turned out as I have said.

All that I could say, then, with respect to farming on a large scale, (I have always cultivated a garden,) was, that I had had my seeds ready. Many think that seeds improve with age. I have no doubt that time discriminates between the good and the bad; and when at last I shall plant, I shall be less likely to be disappointed. But I would say to my fellows, once for all, As long

3. William Cowper (1731–1800), "Verses Supposed to Be Written by Alexander Selkirk," with the pun italicized. Selkirk (1676–1721) was Daniel Defoe's model for Robinson Crusoe.

4. A Titan whom Zeus forced to stand on the earth supporting the heavens as punishment for warring against the Olympian gods.

as possible live free and uncommitted. It makes but little difference whether you are committed to a farm or the county jail.

Old Cato, whose "De Re Rusticâ" is my "Cultivator," says, and the only translation I have seen makes sheer nonsense of the passage, "When you think of getting a farm, turn it thus in your mind, not to buy greedily; nor spare your pains to look at it, and do not think it enough to go round it once. The oftener you go there the more it will please you, if it is good."[5] I think I shall not buy greedily, but go round and round it as long as I live, and be buried in it first, that it may please me the more at last.

The present was my next experiment of this kind, which I purpose to describe more at length; for convenience, putting the experience of two years into one. As I have said, I do not propose to write an ode to dejection, but to brag as lustily as chanticleer in the morning, standing on his roost, if only to wake my neighbors up.

When first I took up my abode in the woods, that is, began to spend my nights as well as days there, which, by accident, was on Independence Day, or the fourth of July, 1845, my house was not finished for winter, but was merely a defence against the rain, without plastering or chimney, the walls being of rough weather-stained boards, with wide chinks, which made it cool at night. The upright white hewn studs and freshly planed door and window casings gave it a clean and airy look, especially in the morning, when its timbers were saturated with dew, so that I fancied that by noon some sweet gum would exude from them. To my imagination it retained throughout the day more or less of this auroral character, reminding me of a certain house on a mountain which I had visited the year before. This was an airy and unplastered cabin, fit to entertain a travelling god, and where a goddess might trail her garments. The winds which passed over my dwelling were such as sweep over the ridges of mountains, bearing the broken strains, or celestial parts only, of terrestrial music. The morning wind forever blows, the poem of creation is uninterrupted; but few are the ears that hear it. Olympus[6] is but the outside of the earth every where.

The only house I had been the owner of before, if I except a boat, was a tent, which I used occasionally when making excursions in the summer, and this is still rolled up in my garret; but the boat, after passing from hand to hand, has gone down the stream of time. With this more substantial shelter about me, I had made some progress toward settling in the world. This frame, so slightly clad, was a sort of crystallization around me, and reacted on the builder. It was suggestive somewhat as a picture in outlines. I did not need to go out doors to take the air, for the atmosphere within had lost none of its freshness. It was not so much within doors as behind a door where I sat, even in the rainiest weather. The Harivansa[7] says, "An abode without birds is like a meat without seasoning." Such was not my abode, for I found myself suddenly neighbor to the birds; not by having imprisoned one, but having caged myself near them. I was not only nearer to some of those which commonly frequent the garden and the orchard, but to those wilder and more thrilling songsters of the forest which never, or rarely, serenade a villager,—the wood-thrush,

5. Cato's *De Agri Cultura* 1.1.
6. In Greek mythology, home of the gods.
7. A Hindu epic poem.

the veery, the scarlet tanager, the field-sparrow, the whippoorwill, and many others.

I was seated by the shore of a small pond, about a mile and a half south of the village of Concord and somewhat higher than it, in the midst of an extensive wood between that town and Lincoln, and about two miles south of that our only field known to fame, Concord Battle Ground;[8] but I was so low in the woods that the opposite shore, half a mile off, like the rest, covered with wood, was my most distant horizon. For the first week, whenever I looked out on the pond it impressed me like a tarn[9] high up on the side of a mountain, its bottom far above the surface of other lakes, and, as the sun arose, I saw it throwing off its nightly clothing of mist, and here and there, by degrees, its soft ripples or its smooth reflecting surface was revealed, while the mists, like ghosts, were stealthily withdrawing in every direction into the woods, as at the breaking up of some nocturnal conventicle. The very dew seemed to hang upon the trees later into the day than usual, as on the sides of mountains.

This small lake was of most value as a neighbor in the intervals of a gentle rain storm in August, when, both air and water being perfectly still, but the sky overcast, mid-afternoon had all the serenity of evening, and the wood-thrush sang around, and was heard from shore to shore. A lake like this is never smoother than at such a time; and the clear portion of the air above it being shallow and darkened by clouds, the water, full of light and reflections, becomes a lower heaven itself so much the more important. From a hill top near by, where the wood had been recently cut off, there was a pleasing vista southward across the pond, through a wide indentation in the hills which form the shore there, where their opposite sides sloping toward each other suggested a stream flowing out in that direction through a wooded valley, but stream there was none. That way I looked between and over the near green hills to some distant and higher ones in the horizon, tinged with blue. Indeed, by standing on tiptoe I could catch a glimpse of some of the peaks of the still bluer and more distant mountain ranges in the north-west, those true-blue coins from heaven's own mint, and also of some portion of the village. But in other directions, even from this point, I could not see over or beyond the woods which surrounded me. It is well to have some water in your neighborhood, to give buoyancy to and float the earth. One value even of the smallest well is, that when you look into it you see that earth is not continent but insular. This is as important as that it keeps butter cool. When I looked across the pond from this peak toward the Sudbury meadows, which in time of flood I distinguished elevated perhaps by a mirage in their seething valley, like a coin in a basin, all the earth beyond the pond appeared like a thin crust insulated and floated even by this small sheet of intervening water, and I was reminded that this on which I dwelt was but *dry land*.

Though the view from my door was still more contracted, I did not feel crowded or confined in the least. There was pasture enough for my imagination. The low shrub-oak plateau to which the opposite shore arose, stretched away toward the prairies of the West and the steppes of Tartary,[1] affording ample room for all the roving families of men. "There are none happy in the

8. The site of battle on the first day of the American Revolution, April 19, 1775.

9. A small lake.

1. Grasslands and plains of Asiatic Russia.

world but beings who enjoy freely a vast horizon,"—said Damodara,[2] when his herds required new and larger pastures.

Both place and time were changed, and I dwelt nearer to those parts of the universe and to those eras in history which had most attracted me. Where I lived was as far off as many a region viewed nightly by astronomers. We are wont to imagine rare and delectable places in some remote and more celestial corner of the system, behind the constellation of Cassiopeia's Chair, far from noise and disturbance. I discovered that my house actually had its site in such a withdrawn, but forever new and unprofaned, part of the universe. If it were worth the while to settle in those parts near to the Pleiades or the Hyades, to Aldebaran or Altair,[3] then I was really there, or at an equal remoteness from the life which I had left behind, dwindled and twinkling with as fine a ray to my nearest neighbor, and to be seen only in moonless nights by him. Such was that part of creation where I had squatted;—

> "There was a shepherd that did live,
> And held his thoughts as high
> As were the mounts whereon his flocks
> Did hourly feed him by."[4]

What should we think of the shepherd's life if his flocks always wandered to higher pastures than his thoughts?

Every morning was a cheerful invitation to make my life of equal simplicity, and I may say innocence, with Nature herself. I have been as sincere a worshipper of Aurora as the Greeks. I got up early and bathed in the pond; that was a religious exercise, and one of the best things which I did. They say that characters were engraven on the bathing tub of king Tching-thang to this effect: "Renew thyself completely each day; do it again, and again, and forever again."[5] I can understand that. Morning brings back the heroic ages. I was as much affected by the faint hum of a mosquito making its invisible and unimaginable tour through my apartment at earliest dawn, when I was sitting with door and windows open, as I could be by any trumpet that ever sang of fame. It was Homer's requiem; itself an Iliad and Odyssey in the air, singing its own wrath and wanderings. There was something cosmical about it; a standing advertisement, till forbidden,[6] of the everlasting vigor and fertility of the world. The morning, which is the most memorable season of the day, is the awakening hour. Then there is least somnolence in us; and for an hour, at least, some part of us awakes which slumbers all the rest of the day and night. Little is to be expected of that day, if it can be called a day, to which we are not awakened by our Genius,[7] but by the mechanical nudgings of some servitor, are not awakened by our own newly-acquired force and aspirations from within, accompanied by the undulations of celestial music, instead of factory bells, and a fragrance filling the air—to a higher life than we fell asleep from; and thus the darkness bear its fruit, and prove itself to be

2. Another name for Krishna, the eighth avatar of Vishnu in Hindu mythology; Thoreau translates from a French edition of *Harivansa*.
3. A star in the constellation Aquila. The Pleiades and the Hyades are constellations. Aldebaran, in the constellation Taurus, is one of the brightest stars.
4. Anonymous Jacobean verse set to music in *The Muses Garden* (1611) and probably found by Thoreau in Thomas Evans's *Old Ballads* (1810).
5. Confucius, *The Great Learning*, ch. 1.
6. In newspaper advertisements "TF" signaled to the compositor that an item was to be repeated daily "till forbidden."
7. Personification of the intellect's insights and perceptions.

good, no less than the light. That man who does not believe that each day contains an earlier, more sacred, and auroral hour than he has yet profaned, has despaired of life, and is pursuing a descending and darkening way. After a partial cessation of his sensuous life, the soul of man, or its organs rather, are reinvigorated each day, and his Genius tries again what noble life it can make. All memorable events, I should say, transpire in morning time and in a morning atmosphere. The Vedas[8] say, "All intelligences awake with the morning." Poetry and art, and the fairest and most memorable of the actions of men, date from such an hour. All poets and heroes, like Memnon, are the children of Aurora, and emit their music at sunrise.[9] To him whose elastic and vigorous thought keeps pace with the sun, the day is a perpetual morning. It matters not what the clocks say or the attitudes and labors of men. Morning is when I am awake and there is a dawn in me. Moral reform is the effort to throw off sleep. Why is it that men give so poor an account of their day if they have not been slumbering? They are not such poor calculators. If they had not been overcome with drowsiness they would have performed something. The millions are awake enough for physical labor; but only one in a million is awake enough for effective intellectual exertion, only one in a hundred millions to a poetic or divine life. To be awake is to be alive. I have never yet met a man who was quite awake. How could I have looked him in the face?

We must learn to reawaken and keep ourselves awake, not by mechanical aids, but by an infinite expectation of the dawn, which does not forsake us in our soundest sleep. I know of no more encouraging fact than the unquestionable ability of man to elevate his life by a conscious endeavor. It is something to be able to paint a particular picture, or to carve a statue, and so to make a few objects beautiful; but it is far more glorious to carve and paint the very atmosphere and medium through which we look, which morally we can do. To affect the quality of the day, that is the highest of arts. Every man is tasked to make his life, even in its details, worthy of the contemplation of his most elevated and critical hour. If we refused, or rather used up, such paltry information as we get, the oracles would distinctly inform us how this might be done.

I went to the woods because I wished to live deliberately, to front only the essential facts of life, and see if I could not learn what it had to teach, and not, when I came to die, discover that I had not lived. I did not wish to live what was not life, living is so dear; nor did I wish to practise resignation, unless it was quite necessary. I wanted to live deep and suck out all the marrow of life, to live so sturdily and Spartan[1]-like as to put to rout all that was not life, to cut a broad swath and shave close, to drive life into a corner, and reduce it to its lowest terms, and, if it proved to be mean, why then to get the whole and genuine meanness of it, and publish its meanness to the world; or if it were sublime, to know it by experience, and be able to give a true account of it in my next excursion. For most men, it appears to me, are in a strange uncertainty about it, whether it is of the devil or of God, and have *somewhat hastily* concluded that it is the chief end of man here to "glorify God and enjoy him forever."[2]

8. The Vedas are Hindu scriptures; the quotation has not been located.
9. See p. 999, n. 3.
1. Citizens of Sparta, an ancient Greek city-state, known for their discipline, austerity, and bravery.
2. From the Shorter Catechism in the *New England Primer.*

Still we live meanly, like ants; though the fable tells us that we were long ago changed into men; like pygmies we fight with cranes;[3] it is error upon error, and clout upon clout, and our best virtue has for its occasion a superfluous and evitable wretchedness. Our life is frittered away by detail. An honest man has hardly need to count more than his ten fingers, or in extreme cases he may add his ten toes, and lump the rest. Simplicity, simplicity, simplicity! I say, let your affairs be as two or three, and not a hundred or a thousand; instead of a million count half a dozen, and keep your accounts on your thumb nail. In the midst of this chopping sea of civilized life, such are the clouds and storms and quicksands and thousand-and-one items to be allowed for, that a man has to live, if he would not founder and go to the bottom and not make his port at all, by dead reckoning, and he must be a great calculator indeed who succeeds. Simplify, simplify. Instead of three meals a day, if it be necessary eat but one; instead of a hundred dishes, five; and reduce other things in proportion. Our life is like a German Confederacy,[4] made up of petty states, with its boundary forever fluctuating, so that even a German cannot tell you how it is bounded at any moment. The nation itself, with all its so called internal improvements, which, by the way, are all external and superficial, is just such an unwieldy and overgrown establishment, cluttered with furniture and tripped up by its own traps, ruined by luxury and heedless expense, by want of calculation and a worthy aim, as the million households in the land; and the only cure for it as for them is in a rigid economy, a stern and more than Spartan simplicity of life and elevation of purpose. It lives too fast. Men think that it is essential that the *Nation* have commerce, and export ice, and talk through a telegraph, and ride thirty miles an hour, without a doubt, whether *they* do or not; but whether we should live like baboons or like men, is a little uncertain. If we do not get out sleepers,[5] and forge rails, and devote days and nights to the work, but go to tinkering upon our *lives* to improve *them*, who will build railroads? And if railroads are not built, how shall we get to heaven in season? But if we stay at home and mind our business, who will want railroads? We do not ride on the railroad; it rides upon us. Did you ever think what those sleepers are that underlie the railroad? Each one is a man, an Irish-man, or a Yankee man. The rails are laid on them, and they are covered with sand, and the cars run smoothly over them. They are sound sleepers, I assure you. And every few years a new lot is laid down and run over; so that, if some have the pleasure of riding on a rail, others have the misfortune to be ridden upon. And when they run over a man that is walking in his sleep, a supernumerary sleeper in the wrong position, and wake him up, they suddenly stop the cars, and make a hue and cry about it, as if this were an exception. I am glad to know that it takes a gang of men for every five miles to keep the sleepers down and level in their beds as it is, for this is a sign that they may sometime get up again.

Why should we live with such hurry and waste of life? We are determined to be starved before we are hungry. Men say that a stitch in time saves nine, and so they take a thousand stitches to-day to save nine to-morrow. As for *work*, we haven't any of any consequence. We have the Saint Vitus' dance,[6]

3. In book 3 of the *Iliad*, the Trojans are compared to cranes fighting with pygmies. A story in Greek mythology tells of how Aeacus persuaded Zeus to turn ants into men.

4. Germany was not yet a unified nation.

5. Wooden railroad ties (another pun).

6. Chorea, a severe nervous disorder characterized by jerky motions.

and cannot possibly keep our heads still. If I should only give a few pulls at the parish bell-rope, as for a fire, that is, without setting the bell, there is hardly a man on his farm in the outskirts of Concord, notwithstanding that press of engagements which was his excuse so many times this morning, nor a boy, nor a woman, I might almost say, but would forsake all and follow that sound, not mainly to save property from the flames, but, if we will confess the truth, much more to see it burn, since burn it must, and we, be it known, did not set it on fire,—or to see it put out, and have a hand in it, if that is done as handsomely; yes, even if it were the parish church itself. Hardly a man takes a half hour's nap after dinner, but when he wakes he holds up his head and asks, "What's the news?" as if the rest of mankind had stood his sentinels. Some give directions to be waked every half hour, doubtless for no other purpose; and then, to pay for it, they tell what they have dreamed. After a night's sleep the news is as indispensable as the breakfast. "Pray tell me any thing new that has happened to a man any where on this globe",—and he reads it over his coffee and rolls, that a man had had his eyes gouged out this morning on the Wachito River; never dreaming the while that he lives in the dark unfathomed mammoth cave of this world, and has but the rudiment of an eye himself.[7]

For my part, I could easily do without the post-office. I think that there are very few important communications made through it. To speak critically, I never received more than one or two letters in my life—I wrote this some years ago—that were worth the postage. The penny-post is, commonly, an institution through which you seriously offer a man that penny for his thoughts which is so often safely offered in jest. And I am sure that I never read any memorable news in a newspaper. If we read of one man robbed, or murdered, or killed by accident, or one house burned, or one vessel wrecked, or one steamboat blown up, or one cow run over on the Western Railroad, or one mad dog killed, or one lot of grasshoppers in the winter,—we never need read of another. One is enough. If you are acquainted with the principle, what do you care for a myriad instances and applications? To a philosopher all *news,* as it is called, is gossip, and they who edit and read it are old women over their tea. Yet not a few are greedy after this gossip. There was such a rush, as I hear, the other day at one of the offices to learn the foreign news by the last arrival, that several large squares of plate glass belonging to the establishment were broken by the pressure,—news which I seriously think a ready wit might write a twelvemonth or twelve years beforehand with sufficient accuracy. As for Spain, for instance, if you know how to throw in Don Carlos and the Infanta, and Don Pedro and Seville and Granada, from time to time in the right proportions,—they may have changed the names a little since I saw the papers,—and serve up a bull-fight when other entertainments fail, it will be true to the letter, and give us as good an idea of the exact state or ruin of things in Spain as the most succinct and lucid reports under this head in the newspapers: and as for England, almost the last significant scrap of news from that quarter was the revolution of 1649;[8] and if you have

7. Sightless fish had been found in Kentucky's Mammoth Cave. "Wachito": also spelled "Ouachita," river flowing from Arkansas into the Red River in Louisiana.

8. The year the Puritan Commonwealth, under Oliver Cromwell (1599–1658), temporarily replaced the British monarchy—the culminating event of the English Civil War of 1642–49. During the 1830s and 1840s, King Ferdinand VII of Spain (1784–1833) and his brother Don Carlos (1788–1855) contested for power, and Ferdinand triumphed when his thirteen-year-old daughter,

learned the history of her crops for an average year, you never need attend to that thing again, unless your speculations are of a merely pecuniary character. If one may judge who rarely looks into the newspapers, nothing new does ever happen in foreign parts, a French revolution not excepted.

What news! how much more important to know what that is which was never old! "Kieou-pe-yu (great dignitary of the state of Wei) sent a man to Khoung-tseu to know his news. Khoung-tseu caused the messenger to be seated near him, and questioned him in these terms: What is your master doing? The messenger answered with respect: My master desires to diminish the number of his faults, but he cannot accomplish it. The messenger being gone, the philosopher remarked: What a worthy messenger! What a worthy messenger!"[9] The preacher, instead of vexing the ears of drowsy farmers on their day of rest at the end of the week,—for Sunday is the fit conclusion of an ill-spent week, and not the fresh and brave beginning of a new one,—with this one other draggle-tail of a sermon, should shout with thundering voice,—"Pause! Avast! Why so seeming fast, but deadly slow?"

Shams and delusions are esteemed for soundest truths, while reality is fabulous. If men would steadily observe realities only, and not allow themselves to be deluded, life, to compare it with such things as we know, would be like a fairy tale and the Arabian Nights' Entertainments. If we respected only what is inevitable and has a right to be, music and poetry would resound along the streets. When we are unhurried and wise, we perceive that only great and worthy things have any permanent and absolute existence,—that petty fears and petty pleasures are but the shadow of the reality. This is always exhilarating and sublime. By closing the eyes and slumbering, and consenting to be deceived by shows, men establish and confirm their daily life of routine and habit every where, which still is built on purely illusory foundations. Children, who play life, discern its true law and relations more clearly than men, who fail to live it worthily, but who think that they are wiser by experience, that is, by failure. I have read in a Hindoo book, that "there was a king's son, who, being expelled in infancy from his native city, was brought up by a forester, and, growing up to maturity in that state, imagined himself to belong to the barbarous race with which he lived. One of his father's ministers having discovered him, revealed to him what he was, and the misconception of his character was removed, and he knew himself to be a prince. So soul," continues the Hindoo philosopher, "from the circumstances in which it is placed, mistakes its own character, until the truth is revealed to it by some holy teacher, and then it knows itself to be *Brahme*."[1] I perceive that we inhabitants of New England live this mean life that we do because our vision does not penetrate the surface of things. We think that that *is* which *appears* to be. If a man should walk through this town and see only the reality, where, think you, would the "Mill-dam"[2] go to? If he should give us an account of the realities he beheld there, we should not recognize the place in his description. Look at a meeting-house, or a court-house, or a jail, or a shop, or a dwelling-house, and say what that thing really is before a true gaze, and they

the Infanta, or princess (1830–1904), was crowned Queen Isabella II. In 1362, Don Pedro the Cruel of Seville (1334–1369) and his army killed Abu Said Muhammad VI of Granada.

9. Confucius's *Analects* 14.

1. In the Hindu triad, Brahma is the divine reality in the aspect of creator; Vishnu is the preserver; and Siva, the destroyer.

2. The business center of Concord.

would all go to pieces in your account of them. Men esteem truth remote, in the outskirts of the system, behind the farthest star, before Adam and after the last man. In eternity there is indeed something true and sublime. But all these times and places and occasions are now and here. God himself culminates in the present moment, and will never be more divine in the lapse of all the ages. And we are enabled to apprehend at all what is sublime and noble only by the perpetual instilling and drenching of the reality which surrounds us. The universe constantly and obediently answers to our conceptions; whether we travel fast or slow, the track is laid for us. Let us spend our lives in conceiving them. The poet or the artist never yet had so fair and noble a design but some of his posterity at least could accomplish it.

Let us spend one day as deliberately as Nature, and not be thrown off the track by every nutshell and mosquito's wing that falls on the rails. Let us rise early and fast, or break fast, gently and without perturbation; let company come and let company go, let the bells ring and the children cry,—determined to make a day of it. Why should we knock under and go with the stream? Let us not be upset and overwhelmed in that terrible rapid and whirlpool called a dinner, situated in the meridian shallows. Weather this danger and you are safe, for the rest of the way is down hill. With unrelaxed nerves, with morning vigor, sail by it, looking another way, tied to the mast like Ulysses.[3] If the engine whistles, let it whistle till it is hoarse for its pains. If the bell rings, why should we run? We will consider what kind of music they are like. Let us settle ourselves, and work and wedge our feet downward through the mud and slush of opinion, and prejudice, and tradition, and delusion, and appearance, that alluvion[4] which covers the globe, through Paris and London, through New York and Boston and Concord, through church and state, through poetry and philosophy and religion, till we come to a hard bottom and rocks in place, which we can call *reality*, and say, This is, and no mistake; and then begin, having a *point d'appui*, below freshet and frost and fire, a place where you might found a wall or a state, or set a lamp-post safely, or perhaps a gauge, not a Nilometer,[5] but a Realometer, that future ages might know how deep a freshet of shams and appearances had gathered from time to time. If you stand right fronting and face to face to a fact, you will see the sun glimmer on both its surfaces, as if it were a cimeter, and feel its sweet edge dividing you through the heart and marrow, and so you will happily conclude your mortal career. Be it life or death, we crave only reality. If we are really dying, let us hear the rattle in our throats and feel cold in the extremities; if we are alive, let us go about our business.

Time is but the stream I go a-fishing in. I drink at it; but while I drink I see the sandy bottom and detect how shallow it is. Its thin current slides away, but eternity remains. I would drink deeper; fish in the sky, whose bottom is pebbly with stars. I cannot count one. I know not the first letter of the alphabet. I have always been regretting that I was not as wise as the day I was born. The intellect is a cleaver; it discerns and rifts its way into the secret of things. I do not wish to be any more busy with my hands than is necessary. My head

3. In Homer's *Odyssey*, Ulysses (Odysseus) took such a precaution to keep himself from yielding to the call of the Sirens—sea nymphs whose singing lured men to destruction.

4. Sediment deposited by flowing water along a shore or bank.

5. Gauge used by the ancient Egyptians for measuring the depth of the Nile. "*Point d'appui*": point of support (French).

is hands and feet. I feel all my best faculties concentrated in it. My instinct tells me that my head is an organ for burrowing, as some creatures use their snout and fore-paws, and with it I would mine and burrow my way through these hills. I think that the richest vein is somewhere hereabouts; so by the divining rod and thin rising vapors I judge; and here I will begin to mine.

3. *Reading*

With a little more deliberation in the choice of their pursuits, all men would perhaps become essentially students and observers, for certainly their nature and destiny are interesting to all alike. In accumulating property for ourselves or our posterity, in founding a family or a state, or acquiring fame even, we are mortal; but in dealing with truth we are immortal, and need fear no change nor accident. The oldest Egyptian or Hindoo philosopher raised a corner of the veil from the statue of the divinity;[6] and still the trembling robe remains raised, and I gaze upon as fresh a glory as he did, since it was I in him that was then so bold, and it is he in me that now reviews the vision. No dust has settled on that robe; no time has elapsed since that divinity was revealed. That time which we really improve, or which is improvable, is neither past, present, nor future.

My residence was more favorable, not only to thought, but to serious reading, than a university; and though I was beyond the range of the ordinary circulating library, I had more than ever come within the influence of those books which circulate round the world, whose sentences were first written on bark, and are now merely copied from time to time on to linen paper. Says the poet Mîr Camar Uddîn Mast, "Being seated to run through the region of the spiritual world; I have had this advantage in books. To be intoxicated by a single glass of wine; I have experienced this pleasure when I have drunk the liquor of the esoteric doctrines."[7] I kept Homer's Iliad on my table through the summer, though I looked at his page only now and then. Incessant labor with my hands, at first, for I had my house to finish and my beans to hoe at the same time, made more study impossible. Yet I sustained myself by the prospect of such reading in future. I read one or two shallow books of travel in the intervals of my work, till that employment made me ashamed of myself, and I asked where it was then that *I* lived.

The student may read Homer or Æschylus in the Greek without danger of dissipation or luxuriousness, for it implies that he in some measure emulate their heroes, and consecrate morning hours to their pages. The heroic books, even if printed in the character of our mother tongue, will always be in a language dead to degenerate times; and we must laboriously seek the meaning of each word and line, conjecturing a larger sense than common use permits out of what wisdom and valor and generosity we have. The modern cheap and fertile press, with all its translations, has done little to bring us nearer to the heroic writers of antiquity. They seem as solitary, and the letter in which they are printed as rare and curious, as ever. It is worth the expense

6. Thoreau alludes to the ritual lifting of the veil from the statue of the ancient Egyptian nature goddess, Isis, or the Hindu religion's goddess of creation, Maya, which was believed by those of the respective faiths to provide insights into the mysteries of the universe.

7. Thoreau knew this 18th-century Hindu poet from a French translation in a history of Hindu literature.

of youthful days and costly hours, if you learn only some words of an ancient language, which are raised out of the trivialness of the street, to be perpetual suggestions and provocations. It is not in vain that the farmer remembers and repeats the few Latin words which he has heard. Men sometimes speak as if the study of the classics would at length make way for more modern and practical studies; but the adventurous student will always study classics, in whatever language they may be written and however ancient they may be. For what are the classics but the noblest recorded thoughts of man? They are the only oracles which are not decayed, and there are such answers to the most modern inquiry in them as Delphi and Dodona[8] never gave. We might as well omit to study Nature because she is old. To read well, that is, to read true books in a true spirit, is a noble exercise, and one that will task the reader more than any exercise which the customs of the day esteem. It requires a training such as the athletes underwent, the steady intention almost of the whole life to this object. Books must be read as deliberately and reservedly as they were written. It is not enough even to be able to speak the language of that nation by which they are written, for there is a memorable interval between the spoken and the written language, the language heard and the language read. The one is commonly transitory, a sound, a tongue, a dialect merely, almost brutish, and we learn it unconsciously, like the brutes, of our mothers. The other is the maturity and experience of that; if that is our mother tongue, this is our father tongue, a reserved and select expression, too significant to be heard by the ear, which we must be born again in order to speak. The crowds of men who merely *spoke* the Greek and Latin tongues in the middle ages were not entitled by the accident of birth to *read* the works of genius written in those languages; for these were not written in that Greek or Latin which they knew, but in the select language of literature. They had not learned the nobler dialects of Greece and Rome, but the very materials on which they were written were waste paper to them, and they prized instead a cheap contemporary literature. But when the several nations of Europe had acquired distinct though rude written languages of their own, sufficient for the purposes of their rising literatures, then first learning revived, and scholars were enabled to discern from that remoteness the treasures of antiquity. What the Roman and Grecian multitude could not *hear*, after the lapse of ages a few scholars *read*, and a few scholars only are still reading it.

However much we may admire the orator's occasional bursts of eloquence, the noblest written words are commonly as far behind or above the fleeting spoken language as the firmament with its stars is behind the clouds. *There* are the stars, and they who can may read them. The astronomers forever comment on and observe them. They are not exhalations like our daily colloquies and vaporous breath. What is called eloquence in the forum is commonly found to be rhetoric in the study. The orator yields to the inspiration of a transient occasion, and speaks to the mob before him, to those who can *hear* him; but the writer, whose more equable life is his occasion, and who would be distracted by the event and the crowd which inspire the orator, speaks to the intellect and heart of mankind, to all in any age who can *understand* him.

8. Oracles of ancient Greece.

No wonder that Alexander carried the Iliad with him on his expeditions in a precious casket.[9] A written word is the choicest of relics. It is something at once more intimate with us and more universal than any other work of art. It is the work of art nearest to life itself. It may be translated into every language, and not only be read but actually breathed from all human lips;—not be represented on canvas or in marble only, but be carved out of the breath of life itself. The symbol of an ancient man's thought becomes a modern man's speech. Two thousand summers have imparted to the monuments of Grecian literature, as to her marbles, only a maturer golden and autumnal tint, for they have carried their own serene and celestial atmosphere into all lands to protect them against the corrosion of time. Books are the treasured wealth of the world and the fit inheritance of generations and nations. Books, the oldest and the best, stand naturally and rightfully on the shelves of every cottage. They have no cause of their own to plead, but while they enlighten and sustain the reader his common sense will not refuse them. Their authors are a natural and irresistible aristocracy in every society, and, more than kings or emperors, exert an influence on mankind. When the illiterate and perhaps scornful trader has earned by enterprise and industry his coveted leisure and independence, and is admitted to the circles of wealth and fashion, he turns inevitably at last to those still higher but yet inaccessible circles of intellect and genius, and is sensible only of the imperfection of his culture and the vanity and insufficiency of all his riches, and further proves his good sense by the pains which he takes to secure for his children that intellectual culture whose want he so keenly feels; and thus it is that he becomes the founder of a family.

Those who have not learned to read the ancient classics in the language in which they were written must have a very imperfect knowledge of the history of the human race; for it is remarkable that no transcript of them has ever been made into any modern tongue, unless our civilization itself may be regarded as such a transcript. Homer has never yet been printed in English, nor Æschylus, nor Virgil even,—works as refined, as solidly done, and as beautiful almost as the morning itself; for later writers, say what we will of their genius, have rarely, if ever, equalled the elaborate beauty and finish and the lifelong and heroic literary labors of the ancients. They only talk of forgetting them who never knew them. It will be soon enough to forget them when we have the learning and the genius which will enable us to attend to and appreciate them. That age will be rich indeed when those relics which we call Classics, and the still older and more than classic but even less known Scriptures of the nations, shall have still further accumulated, when the Vaticans shall be filled with Vedas and Zendavestas[1] and Bibles, with Homers and Dantes and Shakspeares, and all the centuries to come shall have successively deposited their trophies in the forum of the world. By such a pile we may hope to scale heaven at last.

The works of the great poets have never yet been read by mankind, for only great poets can read them. They have only been read as the multitude read the stars, at most astrologically, not astronomically. Most men have learned

9. Plutarch (46?–120 C.E.) attests to this in his biography of Alexander the Great of Macedon (356–323 B.C.E.).

1. Scriptures of the ancient Persian religion Zoroastrianism. "Vaticans": i.e., libraries; an allusion to the massive library in the Vatican at Rome.

to read to serve a paltry convenience, as they have learned to cipher in order to keep accounts and not be cheated in trade; but of reading as a noble intellectual exercise they know little or nothing; yet this only is reading, in a high sense, not that which lulls us as a luxury and suffers the nobler faculties to sleep the while, but what we have to stand on tiptoe to read and devote our most alert and wakeful hours to.

I think that having learned our letters we should read the best that is in literature, and not be forever repeating our a b abs, and words of one syllable, in the fourth or fifth classes, sitting on the lowest and foremost form all our lives.[2] Most men are satisfied if they read or hear read, and perchance have been convicted by the wisdom of one good book, the Bible, and for the rest of their lives vegetate and dissipate their faculties in what is called easy reading. There is a work in several volumes in our Circulating Library entitled Little Reading,[3] which I thought referred to a town of that name which I had not been to. There are those who, like cormorants and ostriches, can digest all sorts of this, even after the fullest dinner of meats and vegetables, for they suffer nothing to be wasted. If others are the machines to provide this provender, they are the machines to read it. They read the nine thousandth tale about Zebulon and Sephronia,[4] and how they loved as none had ever loved before, and neither did the course of their true love run smooth,—at any rate, how it did run and stumble, and get up again and go on! how some poor unfortunate got up onto a steeple, who had better never have gone up as far as the belfry; and then, having needlessly got him up there, the happy novelist rings the bell for all the world to come together and hear, O dear! how he did get down again! For my part, I think that they had better metamorphose all such aspiring heroes of universal noveldom into man weathercocks, as they used to put heroes among the constellations, and let them swing round there till they are rusty, and not come down at all to bother honest men with their pranks. The next time the novelist rings the bell I will not stir though the meeting-house burn down. "The Skip of the Tip-Toe-Hop, a Romance of the Middle Ages, by the celebrated author of 'Title-Tol-Tan,' to appear in monthly parts; a great rush; don't all come together." All this they read with saucer eyes, and erect and primitive curiosity, and with unwearied gizzard, whose corrugations even yet need no sharpening, just as some little four-year-old bencher[5] his two-cent gilt-covered edition of Cinderella,—without any improvement, that I can see, in the pronunciation, or accent, or emphasis, or any more skill in extracting or inserting the moral. The result is dulness of sight, a stagnation of the vital circulations, and a general deliquium[6] and sloughing off of all the intellectual faculties. This sort of gingerbread is baked daily and more sedulously than pure wheat or rye-and-Indian in almost every oven, and finds a surer market.

The best books are not read even by those who are called good readers. What does our Concord culture amount to? There is in this town, with a very few exceptions, no taste for the best or for very good books even in English literature, whose words all can read and spell. Even the college-

2. I.e., with the youngest children at the front of a one-room schoolhouse.

3. A book called *Much Instruction from Little Reading* is included in the 1836 *Catalogue of Concord Social Library.*

4. Made-up names, as is the title of the novel mentioned later in the paragraph.

5. A child too young to need a desk.

6. Melting away.

bred and so called liberally educated men here and elsewhere have really little or no acquaintance with the English classics; and as for the recorded wisdom of mankind, the ancient classics and Bibles, which are accessible to all who will know of them, there are the feeblest efforts any where made to become acquainted with them. I know a woodchopper, of middle age, who takes a French paper, not for news as he says, for he is above that, but to "keep himself in practice," he being a Canadian by birth; and when I ask him what he considers the best thing he can do in this world, he says, beside this, to keep up and add to his English. This is about as much as the college bred generally do or aspire to do, and they take an English paper for the purpose. One who has just come from reading perhaps one of the best English books will find how many with whom he can converse about it? Or suppose he comes from reading a Greek or Latin classic in the original, whose praises are familiar even to the so called illiterate; he will find nobody at all to speak to, but must keep silence about it. Indeed, there is hardly the professor in our colleges, who, if he has mastered the difficulties of the language, has proportionally mastered the difficulties of the wit and poetry of a Greek poet, and has any sympathy to impart to the alert and heroic reader; and as for the sacred Scriptures, or Bibles of mankind, who in this town can tell me even their titles? Most men do not know that any nation but the Hebrews have had a scripture. A man, any man, will go considerably out of his way to pick up a silver dollar; but here are golden words, which the wisest men of antiquity have uttered, and whose worth the wise of every succeeding age have assured us of;—and yet we learn to read only as far as Easy Reading, the primers and class-books, and when we leave school, the "Little Reading," and story books, which are for boys and beginners; and our reading, our conversation and thinking, are all on a very low level, worthy only of pygmies and manikens.

I aspire to be acquainted with wiser men than this our Concord soil has produced, whose names are hardly known here. Or shall I hear the name of Plato and never read his book? As if Plato were any townsman and I never saw him,—my next neighbor and I never heard him speak or attended to the wisdom of his words. But how actually is it? His Dialogues, which contain what was immortal in him, lie on the next shelf, and yet I never read them. We are under-bred and low-lived and illiterate; and in this respect I confess I do not make any very broad distinction between the illiterateness of my townsman who cannot read at all, and the illiterateness of him who has learned to read only what is for children and feeble intellects. We should be as good as the worthies of antiquity, but partly by first knowing how good they were. We are a race of tit-men,[7] and soar but little higher in our intellectual flights than the columns of the daily paper.

It is not all books that are as dull as their readers. There are probably words addressed to our condition exactly, which, if we could really hear and understand, would be more salutary than the morning or the spring to our lives, and possibly put a new aspect on the face of things for us. How many a man has dated a new era in his life from the reading of a book. The book exists for us perchance which will explain our miracles and reveal new ones. The at present unutterable things we may find somewhere uttered. These same questions that disturb and puzzle and confound us have in their

7. Small-men; a play on titmouse or titbird.

turn occurred to all the wise men; not one has been omitted; and each has answered them, according to his ability, by his words and his life. Moreover, with wisdom we shall learn liberality. The solitary hired man on a farm in the outskirts of Concord, who has had his second birth and peculiar religious experience, and is driven as he believes into silent gravity and exclusiveness by his faith, may think it is not true; but Zoroaster,[8] thousands of years ago, travelled the same road and had the same experience; but he, being wise, knew it to be universal, and treated his neighbors accordingly, and is even said to have invented and established worship among men. Let him humbly commune with Zoroaster then, and, through the liberalizing influence of all the worthies, with Jesus Christ himself, and let "our church" go by the board.

We boast that we belong to the nineteenth century and are making the most rapid strides of any nation. But consider how little this village does for its own culture. I do not wish to flatter my townsmen, nor to be flattered by them, for that will not advance either of us. We need to be provoked,—goaded like oxen, as we are, into a trot. We have a comparatively decent system of common schools, schools for infants only; but excepting the half-starved Lyceum[9] in the winter, and latterly the puny beginning of a library suggested by the state, no school for ourselves. We spend more on almost any article of bodily aliment or ailment than on our mental aliment. It is time that we had uncommon schools, that we did not leave off our education when we begin to be men and women. It is time that villages were universities, and their elder inhabitants the fellows of universities, with leisure—if they are indeed so well off—to pursue liberal studies the rest of their lives. Shall the world be confined to one Paris or one Oxford forever? Cannot students be boarded here and get a liberal education under the skies of Concord? Can we not hire some Abelard[1] to lecture us? Alas! what with foddering the cattle and tending the store, we are kept from school too long, and our education is sadly neglected. In this country, the village should in some respects take the place of the nobleman of Europe. It should be the patron of the fine arts. It is rich enough. It wants only the magnanimity and refinement. It can spend money enough on such things as farmers and traders value, but it is thought Utopian to propose spending money for things which more intelligent men know to be of far more worth. This town has spent seventeen thousand dollars on a town-house, thank fortune or politics, but probably it will not spend so much on living wit, the true meat to put into that shell, in a hundred years. The one hundred and twenty-five dollars annually subscribed for a Lyceum in the winter is better spent than any other equal sum raised in the town. If we live in the nineteenth century, why should we not enjoy the advantages which the nineteenth century offers? Why should our life be in any respect provincial? If we will read newspapers, why not skip the gossip of Boston and take the best newspaper in the world at once?—not be sucking the pap of "neutral family" papers, or browsing "Olive-Branches"[2] here in New England. Let the reports of all the learned societies come to us, and we will see if they know any thing. Why

8. Persian religious reformer and founder of Zoroastrianism in the 6th century B.C.E.
9. Public lecture hall.
1. Peter Abelard (1079–1142), a great teacher of philosophy and theology in medieval France.
2. Founded in 1836, the *Boston Olive Branch* was a weekly Methodist newspaper. "'Neutral family' papers": those that sought to entertain while avoiding political discussion.

should we leave it to Harper & Brothers and Redding & Co.[3] to select our reading? As the nobleman of cultivated taste surrounds himself with whatever conduces to his culture,—genius—learning—wit—books—paintings—statuary—music—philosophical instruments, and the like; so let the village do,—not stop short at a pedagogue, a parson, a sexton, a parish library, and three selectmen, because our pilgrim forefathers got through a cold winter once on a bleak rock with these. To act collectively is according to the spirit of our institutions; and I am confident that, as our circumstances are more flourishing, our means are greater than the nobleman's. New England can hire all the wise men in the world to come and teach her, and board them round the while, and not be provincial at all. That is the *uncommon* school we want. Instead of noblemen, let us have noble villages of men. If it is necessary, omit one bridge over the river, go round a little there, and throw one arch at least over the darker gulf of ignorance which surrounds us.

4. *Sounds*

But while we are confined to books, though the most select and classic, and read only particular written languages, which are themselves but dialects and provincial, we are in danger of forgetting the language which all things and events speak without metaphor, which alone is copious and standard. Much is published, but little printed. The rays which stream through the shutter will be no longer remembered when the shutter is wholly removed. No method nor discipline can supersede the necessity of being forever on the alert. What is a course of history, or philosophy, or poetry, no matter how well selected, or the best society, or the most admirable routine of life, compared with the discipline of looking always at what is to be seen? Will you be a reader, a student merely, or a seer? Read your fate, see what is before you, and walk on into futurity.

I did not read books the first summer; I hoed beans. Nay, I often did better than this. There were times when I could not afford to sacrifice the bloom of the present moment to any work, whether of the head or hands. I love a broad margin to my life. Sometimes, in a summer morning, having taken my accustomed bath, I sat in my sunny doorway from sunrise till noon, rapt in a revery, amidst the pines and hickories and sumachs, in undisturbed solitude and stillness, while the birds sang around or flitted noiseless through the house, until by the sun falling in at my west window, or the noise of some traveller's wagon on the distant highway, I was reminded of the lapse of time. I grew in those seasons like corn in the night, and they were far better than any work of the hands would have been. They were not time subtracted from my life, but so much over and above my usual allowance. I realized what the Orientals mean by contemplation and the forsaking of works. For the most part, I minded not how the hours went. The day advanced as if to light some work of mine; it was morning, and lo, now it is evening, and nothing memorable is accomplished. Instead of singing like the birds, I silently smiled at my incessant good fortune. As the sparrow had its trill, sitting on the hickory before my door, so had I my chuckle or suppressed warble which he might hear out of my nest. My days were not days of the week, bearing the stamp of any hea-

3. Major publishers and booksellers of New York City and Boston, respectively.

then deity,[4] nor were they minced into hours and fretted by the ticking of a clock; for I lived like the Puri Indians,[5] of whom it is said that "for yesterday, to-day, and to-morrow they have only one word, and they express the variety of meaning by pointing backward for yesterday, forward for to-morrow, and overhead for the passing day." This was sheer idleness to my fellow-townsmen, no doubt; but if the birds and flowers had tried me by their standard, I should not have been found wanting. A man must find his occasions in himself, it is true. The natural day is very calm, and will hardly reprove his indolence.

I had this advantage, at least, in my mode of life, over those who were obliged to look abroad for amusement, to society and the theatre, that my life itself was become my amusement and never ceased to be novel. It was a drama of many scenes and without an end. If we were always indeed getting our living, and regulating our lives according to the last and best mode we had learned, we should never be troubled with ennui. Follow your genius closely enough, and it will not fail to show you a fresh prospect every hour. Housework was a pleasant pastime. When my floor was dirty, I rose early, and, setting all my furniture out of doors on the grass, bed and bedstead making but one budget,[6] dashed water on the floor, and sprinkled white sand from the pond on it, and then with a broom scrubbed it clean and white; and by the time the villagers had broken their fast the morning sun had dried my house sufficiently to allow me to move in again, and my meditations were almost uninterrupted. It was pleasant to see my whole household effects out on the grass, making a little pile like a gypsy's pack, and my three-legged table, from which I did not remove the books and pen and ink, standing amid the pines and hickories. They seemed glad to get out themselves, and as if unwilling to be brought in. I was sometimes tempted to stretch an awning over them and take my seat there. It was worth the while to see the sun shine on these things, and hear the free wind blow on them; so much more interesting most familiar objects look out of doors than in the house. A bird sits on the next bough, life-everlasting grows under the table, and blackberry vines run round its legs; pine cones, chestnut burs, and strawberry leaves are strewn about. It looked as if this was the way these forms came to be transferred to our furniture, to tables, chairs, and bedsteads,—because they once stood in their midst.

My house was on the side of a hill, immediately on the edge of the larger wood, in the midst of a young forest of pitch pines and hickories, and half a dozen rods from the pond, to which a narrow footpath led down the hill. In my front yard grew the strawberry, blackberry, and life-everlasting, johnswort and golden-rod, shrub-oaks and sand-cherry, blueberry and groundnut. Near the end of May, the sand-cherry, *Cerasus pumila*, adorned the sides of the path with its delicate flowers arranged in umbels cylindrically about its short stems, which last, in the fall, weighed down with good sized and handsome cherries, fell over in wreaths like rays on every side. I tasted them out of compliment to Nature, though they were scarcely palatable. The sumach, *Rhus glabra*, grew luxuriantly about the house, pushing up through the embankment which I had made, and growing five or six feet the first

4. Tuesday, Wednesday, Thursday, and Friday all derive from the names of gods of Norse mythology, while Saturday is named for the Roman god Saturn.

5. Brazilian Indians whom Thoreau read about in Ida Pfeiffer's *A Lady's Voyage Round the World* (1852).

6. Collection.

season. Its broad pinnate tropical leaf was pleasant though strange to look on. The large buds, suddenly pushing out late in the spring from dry sticks which had seemed to be dead, developed themselves as by magic into graceful green and tender boughs, an inch in diameter; and sometimes, as I sat at my window, so heedlessly did they grow and tax their weak joints, I heard a fresh and tender bough suddenly fall like a fan to the ground, when there was not a breath of air stirring, broken off by its own weight. In August, the large masses of berries, which, when in flower, had attracted many wild bees, gradually assumed their bright velvety crimson hue, and by their weight again bent down and broke the tender limbs.

As I sit at my window this summer afternoon, hawks are circling about my clearing; the tantivy[7] of wild pigeons, flying by twos and threes athwart my view, or perching restless on the white-pine boughs behind my house, gives a voice to the air; a fishhawk dimples the glassy surface of the pond and brings up a fish; a mink steals out of the marsh before my door and seizes a frog by the shore; the sedge is bending under the weight of the reed-birds flitting hither and thither; and for the last half hour I have heard the rattle of railroad cars, now dying away and then reviving like the beat of a partridge, conveying travellers from Boston to the country. For I did not live so out of the world as that boy, who, as I hear, was put out to a farmer in the east part of the town, but ere long ran away and came home again, quite down at the heel and homesick. He had never seen such a dull and out of-the-way place; the folks were all gone off; why, you couldn't even hear the whistle! I doubt if there is such a place in Massachusetts now:—

"In truth, our village has become a butt
For one of those fleet railroad shafts, and o'er
Our peaceful plain its soothing sound is—Concord."[8]

The Fitchburg railroad touches the pond about a hundred rods south of where I dwell. I usually go to the village along its causeway, and am, as it were, related to society by this link. The men on the freight trains, who go over the whole length of the road, bow to me as to an old acquaintance, they pass me so often, and apparently they take me for an employee; and so I am. I too would fain be a track-repairer somewhere in the orbit of the earth.

The whistle of the locomotive penetrates my woods summer and winter, sounding like the scream of a hawk sailing over some farmer's yard, informing me that many restless city merchants are arriving within the circle of the town, or adventurous country traders from the other side. As they come under one horizon, they shout their warning to get off the track of the other, heard sometimes through the circles of two towns. Here come your groceries, country; your rations, countrymen! Nor is there any man so independent on his farm that he can say them nay. And here's your pay for them! screams the countryman's whistle; timber like long battering rams going twenty miles an hour against the city's walls, and chairs enough to seat all the weary and heavy laden that dwell within them. With such huge and lumbering civility the country hands a chair to the city. All the Indian huckleberry

7. Hurtling.
8. From Ellery Channing's "Walden Spring," published in *The Woodman and Other Poems* (1849). Channing (1817–1901), one of Thoreau's closest friends, published a biography of him in 1873.

hills are stripped, all the cranberry meadows are raked into the city. Up comes the cotton, down goes the woven cloth; up comes the silk, down goes the woollen; up come the books, but down goes the wit that writes them.

When I meet the engine with its train of cars moving off with planetary motion,—or, rather, like a comet, for the beholder knows not if with that velocity and with that direction it will ever revisit this system, since its orbit does not look like a returning curve,—with its steam cloud like a banner streaming behind in golden and silver wreaths, like many a downy cloud which I have seen, high in the heavens, unfolding its masses to the light,—as if this travelling demigod, this cloud-compeller, would ere long take the sunset sky for the livery of his train; when I hear the iron horse make the hills echo with his snort like thunder, shaking the earth with his feet, and breathing fire and smoke from his nostrils, (what kind of winged horse or fiery dragon they will put into the new Mythology I don't know,) it seems as if the earth had got a race now worthy to inhabit it. If all were as it seems, and men made the elements their servants for noble ends! If the cloud that hangs over the engine were the perspiration of heroic deeds, or as beneficent to men as that which floats over the farmer's fields, then the elements and Nature herself would cheerfully accompany men on their errands and be their escort.

I watch the passage of the morning cars with the same feeling that I do the rising of the sun, which is hardly more regular. Their train of clouds stretching far behind and rising higher and higher, going to heaven while the cars are going to Boston, conceals the sun for a minute and casts my distant field into the shade, a celestial train beside which the petty train of cars which hugs the earth is but the barb of the spear. The stabler of the iron horse was up early this winter morning by the light of the stars amid the mountains, to fodder and harness his steed. Fire, too, was awakened thus early to put the vital heat in him and get him off. If the enterprise were as innocent as it is early! If the snow lies deep, they strap on his snow-shoes, and with the giant plow, plow a furrow from the mountains to the seaboard, in which the cars, like a following drill-barrow,[9] sprinkle all the restless men and floating merchandise in the country for seed. All day the fire-steed flies over the country, stopping only that his master may rest, and I am awakened by his tramp and defiant snort at midnight, when in some remote glen in the woods he fronts the elements incased in ice and snow; and he will reach his stall only with the morning star, to start once more on his travels without rest or slumber. Or perchance, at evening, I hear him in his stable blowing off the superfluous energy of the day, that he may calm his nerves and cool his liver and brain for a few hours of iron slumber. If the enterprise were as heroic and commanding as it is protracted and unwearied!

Far through unfrequented woods on the confines of towns, where once only the hunter penetrated by day, in the darkest night dart these bright saloons without the knowledge of their inhabitants; this moment stopping at some brilliant station-house in town or city, where a social crowd is gathered, the next in the Dismal Swamp,[1] scaring the owl and fox. The startings and arrivals of the cars are now the epochs in the village day. They go and come with such regularity and precision, and their whistle can be heard so far, that

9. Machine for planting seeds.
1. The real Dismal Swamp is in southeastern Virginia and northeastern North Carolina.

the farmers set their clocks by them, and thus one well conducted institution regulates a whole country. Have not men improved somewhat in punctuality since the railroad was invented? Do they not talk and think faster in the depot than they did in the stage-office? There is something electrifying in the atmosphere of the former place. I have been astonished at the miracles it has wrought; that some of my neighbors, who, I should have prophesied, once for all, would never get to Boston by so prompt a conveyance, were on hand when the bell rang. To do things "railroad fashion" is now the by-word; and it is worth the while to be warned so often and so sincerely by any power to get off its track. There is no stopping to read the riot act, no firing over the heads of the mob, in this case. We have constructed a fate, an *Atropos*,[2] that never turns aside. (Let that be the name of your engine.) Men are advertised that at a certain hour and minute these bolts will be shot toward particular points of the compass; yet it interferes with no man's business, and the children go to school on the other track. We live the steadier for it. We are all educated thus to be sons of Tell.[3] The air is full of invisible bolts. Every path but your own is the path of fate. Keep on your own track, then.

What recommends commerce to me is its enterprise and bravery. It does not clasp its hands and pray to Jupiter. I see these men every day go about their business with more or less courage and content, doing more even than they suspect, and perchance better employed than they could have consciously devised. I am less affected by their heroism who stood up for half an hour in the front line at Buena Vista,[4] than by the steady and cheerful valor of the men who inhabit the snow-plough for their winter quarters; who have not merely the three-o'-clock in the morning courage,[5] which Bonaparte thought was the rarest, but whose courage does not go to rest so early, who go to sleep only when the storm sleeps or the sinews of their iron steed are frozen. On this morning of the Great Snow, perchance, which is still raging and chilling men's blood, I hear the muffled tone of their engine bell from out the fog bank of their chilled breath, which announces that the cars *are coming*, without long delay, notwithstanding the veto of a New England north-east snow storm, and I behold the ploughmen covered with snow and rime, their heads peering above the mould-board which is turning down other than daisies and the nests of field-mice, like bowlders of the Sierra Nevada,[6] that occupy an outside place in the universe.

Commerce is unexpectedly confident and serene, alert, adventurous, and unwearied. It is very natural in its methods withal, far more so than many fantastic enterprises and sentimental experiments, and hence its singular success. I am refreshed and expanded when the freight train rattles past me, and I smell the stores which go dispensing their odors all the way from Long Wharf to Lake Champlain,[7] reminding me of foreign parts, of coral reefs, and Indian oceans, and tropical climes, and the extent of the globe. I feel more like a citizen of the world at the sight of the palm-leaf which will

2. In Greek mythology, the Fate who cuts the thread of human life.
3. I.e., to live calmly among dangers, like one of the sons of the 13th-century Swiss hero William Tell, who, according to legend, stood still while his father shot an arrow through an apple resting on his head.
4. Battlefield near Saltillo, Mexico, where Zachary Taylor's forces defeated the Mexican army under Santa Anna in 1847.
5. Courage coming forth spontaneously, as when a soldier is awakened suddenly in the dead of night.
6. California mountain range.
7. From Boston Harbor to Lake Champlain, on the New York–Vermont border.

cover so many flaxen New England heads the next summer, the Manilla hemp and cocoa-nut husks, the old junk, gunny bags, scrap iron, and rusty nails. This car-load of torn sails is more legible and interesting now than if they should be wrought into paper and printed books. Who can write so graphically the history of the storms they have weathered as these rents have done? They are proof-sheets which need no correction. Here goes lumber from the Maine woods, which did not go out to sea in the last freshet, risen four dollars on the thousand because of what did go out or was split up; pine, spruce, cedar,—first, second, third and fourth qualities, so lately all of one quality, to wave over the bear, and moose, and caribou. Next rolls Thomaston lime, a prime lot, which will get far among the hills before it gets slacked.[8] These rags in bales, of all hues and qualities, the lowest condition to which cotton and linen descend, the final result of dress,—of patterns which are no no longer cried up, unless it be in Milwaukie, as those splendid articles, English, French, or American prints, ginghams, muslins, &c., gathered from all quarters both of fashion and poverty, going to become paper of one color or a few shades only, on which forsooth will be written tales of real life, high and low, and founded on fact![9] This closed car smells of salt fish, the strong New England and commercial scent, reminding me of the Grand Banks[1] and the fisheries. Who has not seen a salt fish, thoroughly cured for this world, so that nothing can spoil it, and putting the perseverance of the saints to the blush? with which you may sweep or pave the streets, and split your kindlings, and the teamster shelter himself and his lading against sun, wind and rain behind it,—and the trader, as a Concord trader once did, hang it up by his door for a sign when he commences business, until at last his oldest customer cannot tell surely whether it be animal, vegetable, or mineral, and yet it shall be as pure as a snowflake, and if it be put into a pot and boiled, will come out an excellent dun[2] fish for a Saturday's dinner. Next Spanish hides, with the tails still preserving their twist and the angle of elevation they had when the oxen that wore them were careering over the pampas of the Spanish main,[3]—a type of all obstinacy, and evincing how almost hopeless and incurable are all constitutional vices. I confess, that practically speaking, when I have learned a man's real disposition, I have no hopes of changing it for the better or worse in this state of existence. As the Orientals say, "A cur's tail may be warmed, and pressed, and bound round with ligatures, and after a twelve years' labor bestowed upon it, still it will retain its natural form."[4] The only effectual cure for such inveteracies as these tails exhibit is to make glue of them, which I believe is what is usually done with them, and then they will stay put and stick. Here is a hogshead of molasses or of brandy directed to John Smith, Cuttingsville, Vermont, some trader among the Green Mountains, who imports for the farmers near his clearing, and now perchance stands over his bulk-head and thinks of the last arrivals on the coast, how they may affect the price for him, telling his customers this moment, as he has

8. I.e., before the Thomaston, Maine, lime is turned into powder so it could be used for farming.
9. Thoreau parodies conventional titles of popular fiction. "Cried up": praised.
1. Fishing area off the coast of southeastern Newfoundland.
2. Dried codfish, with a pun on "done."
3. An area of grasslands by the northeast coast of South America.
4. From the fable of the lion and the rabbit in Charles Wilkins's translation of *Fables and Proverbs from the Sanskrit* (1787).

told them twenty times before this morning, that he expects some by the next train of prime quality. It is advertised in the Cuttingsville Times.

While these things go up other things come down. Warned by the whizzing sound, I look up from my book and see some tall pine, hewn on far northern hills, which has winged its way over the Green Mountains and the Connecticut,[5] shot like an arrow through the township within ten minutes, and scarce another eye beholds it; going

"to be the mast
Of some great ammiral."[6]

And hark! here comes the cattle-train bearing the cattle of a thousand hills, sheepcots, stables, and cow-yards in the air, drovers with their sticks, and shepherd boys in the midst of their flocks, all but the mountain pastures, whirled along like leaves blown from the mountains by the September gales. The air is filled with the bleating of calves and sheep, and the hustling of oxen, as if a pastoral valley were going by. When the old bell-wether at the head rattles his bell, the mountains do indeed skip like rams and the little hills like lambs.[7] A car-load of drovers, too, in the midst, on a level with their droves now, their vocation gone, but still clinging to their useless sticks as their badge of office. But their dogs, where are they? It is a stampede to them; they are quite thrown out; they have lost the scent. Methinks I hear them barking behind the Peterboro' Hills,[8] or panting up the western slope of the Green Mountains. They will not be in at the death. Their vocation, too, is gone. Their fidelity and sagacity are below par now. They will slink back to their kennels in disgrace, or perchance run wild and strike a league with the wolf and the fox. So is your pastoral life whirled past and away. But the bell rings, and I must get off the track and let the cars go by;—

What's the railroad to me?
I never go to see
Where it ends.
It fills a few hollows,
And makes banks for the swallows,
It sets the sand a-blowing,
And the blackberries a-growing,

but I cross it like a cart-path in the woods. I will not have my eyes put out and my ears spoiled by its smoke and steam and hissing.

Now that the cars are gone by, and all the restless world with them, and the fishes in the pond no longer feel their rumbling, I am more alone than ever. For the rest of the long afternoon, perhaps, my meditations are interrupted only by the faint rattle of a carriage or team along the distant highway.

Sometimes, on Sundays, I heard the bells, the Lincoln, Acton, Bedford, or Concord bell, when the wind was favorable, a faint, sweet, and, as it were, natural melody, worth importing into the wilderness. At a sufficient distance over the woods this sound acquires a certain vibratory hum, as if the

5. The Connecticut River. The Green Mountains run from Vermont into Massachusetts.
6. Milton, *Paradise Lost* 1.293–94.
7. From Psalm 114.4: "The mountains skipped like rams, and the little hills like lambs"; the motivation for skipping is the fear of God, not joy.
8. The Peterborough Hills are in southwestern New Hampshire.

pine needles in the horizon were the strings of a harp which it swept. All sound heard at the greatest possible distance produces one and the same effect, a vibration of the universal lyre, just as the intervening atmosphere makes a distant ridge of earth interesting to our eyes by the azure tint it imparts to it. There came to me in this case a melody which the air had strained, and which had conversed with every leaf and needle of the wood, that portion of the sound which the elements had taken up and modulated and echoed from vale to vale. The echo is, to some extent, an original sound, and therein is the magic and charm of it. It is not merely a repetition of what was worth repeating in the bell, but partly the voice of the wood; the same trivial words and notes sung by a wood-nymph.

At evening, the distant lowing of some cow in the horizon beyond the woods sounded sweet and melodious, and at first I would mistake it for the voices of certain minstrels by whom I was sometimes serenaded, who might be straying over hill and dale; but soon I was not unpleasantly disappointed when it was prolonged into the cheap and natural music of the cow. I do not mean to be satirical, but to express my appreciation of those youths' singing, when I state that I perceived clearly that it was akin to the music of the cow, and they were at length one articulation of Nature.

Regularly at half past seven, in one part of the summer, after the evening train had gone by, the whippoorwills chanted their vespers for half an hour, sitting on a stump by my door, or upon the ridge pole of the house. They would begin to sing almost with as much precision as a clock, within five minutes of a particular time, referred to the setting of the sun, every evening. I had a rare opportunity to become acquainted with their habits. Sometimes I heard four or five at once in different parts of the wood, by accident one a bar behind another, and so near me that I distinguished not only the cluck after each note, but often that singular buzzing sound like a fly in a spider's web, only proportionally louder. Sometimes one would circle round and round me in the woods a few feet distant as if tethered by a string, when probably I was near its eggs. They sang at intervals throughout the night, and were again as musical as ever just before and about dawn.

When other birds are still the screech owls take up the strain, like mourning women their ancient u-lu-lu. Their dismal scream is truly Ben Jonsonian.[9] Wise midnight hags! It is no honest and blunt tu-whit tu-who of the poets, but, without jesting, a most solemn graveyard ditty, the mutual consolations of suicide lovers remembering the pangs and the delights of supernal love in the infernal groves. Yet I love to hear their wailing, their doleful responses, trilled along the wood-side, reminding me sometimes of music and singing birds; as if it were the dark and tearful side of music, the regrets and sighs that would fain be sung. They are the spirits, the low spirits and melancholy forebodings, of fallen souls that once in human shape nightwalked the earth and did the deeds of darkness, now expiating their sins with their wailing hymns or threnodies[1] in the scenery of their transgressions. They give me a new sense of the variety and capacity of that nature which is our common dwelling. *Oh-o-o-o-o that I never had been bor-r-r-r-n!* sighs one on this side of the pond, and circles with the restlessness of despair to

9. Thoreau alludes to "We give thee a shout: Hoo!" in Ben Jonson's *Masque of Queens* (1609) 2.317–18.
1. Dirges.

some new perch on the gray oaks. Then—*that I never had been bor-r-r-r-n!* echoes another on the farther side with tremulous sincerity, and—*bor-r-r-r-n!* comes faintly from far in the Lincoln woods.

I was also serenaded by a hooting owl. Near at hand you could fancy it the most melancholy sound in Nature, as if she meant by this to stereotype and make permanent in her choir the dying moans of a human being,—some poor weak relic of mortality who has left hope behind, and howls like an animal, yet with human sobs, on entering the dark valley, made more awful by a certain gurgling melodiousness,—I find myself beginning with the letters gl when I try to imitate it,—expressive of a mind which has reached the gelatinous mildewy stage in the mortification of all healthy and courageous thought. It reminded me of ghouls and idiots and insane howlings. But now one answers from far woods in a strain made really melodious by distance,—*Hoo hoo hoo, hoorer hoo*; and indeed for the most part it suggested only pleasing associations, whether heard by day or night, summer or winter.

I rejoice that there are owls. Let them do the idiotic and maniacal hooting for men. It is a sound admirably suited to swamps and twilight woods which no day illustrates, suggesting a vast and undeveloped nature which men have not recognized. They represent the stark twilight and unsatisfied thoughts which all have. All day the sun has shone on the surface of some savage swamp, where the double spruce stands hung with usnea lichens, and small hawks circulate above, and the chicadee lisps amid the evergreens, and the partridge and rabbit skulk beneath; but now a more dismal and fitting day dawns, and a different race of creatures awakes to express the meaning of Nature there.

Late in the evening I heard the distant rumbling of wagons over bridges,—a sound heard farther than almost any other at night,—the baying of dogs, and sometimes again the lowing of some disconsolate cow in a distant barn-yard. In the mean while all the shore rang with the trump of bullfrogs, the sturdy spirits of ancient wine-bibbers and wassailers, still unrepentant, trying to sing a catch in their Stygian lake,[2]—if the Walden nymphs will pardon the comparison, for though there are almost no weeds, there are frogs there,—who would fain keep up the hilarious rules of their old festal tables, though their voices have waxed hoarse and solemnly grave, mocking at mirth, and the wine has lost its flavor, and become only liquor to distend their paunches, and sweet intoxication never comes to drown the memory of the past, but mere saturation and waterloggedness and distention. The most aldermanic, with his chin upon a heart-leaf, which serves for a napkin to his drooling chaps, under this northern shore quaffs a deep draught of the once scorned water, and passes round the cup with the ejaculation *tr-r-r-oonk, tr-r-r-oonk, tr-r-r-oonk!* and straightway comes over the water from some distant cove the same password repeated, where the next in seniority and girth has gulped down to his mark; and when this observance has made the circuit of the shores, then ejaculates the master of ceremonies, with satisfaction, *tr-r-r-oonk!* and each in his turn repeats the same down to the least distended, leakiest, and flabbiest paunched, that there be no mistake; and then the bowl goes round again and again, until the sun disperses the morning mist, and only the patriarch is not under the pond, but vainly bellowing *troonk* from time to time, and pausing for a reply.

2. In Greek mythology the Styx is the principal river of the underworld.

I am not sure that I ever heard the sound of cock-crowing from my clearing, and I thought that it might be worth the while to keep a cockerel for his music merely, as a singing bird. The note of this once wild Indian pheasant is certainly the most remarkable of any bird's, and if they could be naturalized without being domesticated, it would soon become the most famous sound in our woods, surpassing the clangor of the goose and the hooting of the owl; and then imagine the cackling of the hens to fill the pauses when their lords' clarions rested! No wonder that man added this bird to his tame stock,—to say nothing of the eggs and drumsticks. To walk in a winter morning in a wood where these birds abounded, their native woods, and hear the wild cockerels crow on the trees, clear and shrill for miles over the resounding earth, drowning the feebler notes of other birds,—think of it! It would put nations on the alert. Who would not be early to rise, and rise earlier and earlier every successive day of his life, till he became unspeakably healthy, wealthy, and wise? This foreign bird's note is celebrated by the poets of all countries along with the notes of their native songsters. All climates agree with brave Chanticleer. He is more indigenous even than the natives. His health is ever good, his lungs are sound, his spirits never flag. Even the sailor on the Atlantic and Pacific is awakened by his voice; but its shrill sound never roused me from my slumbers. I kept neither dog, cat, cow, pig, nor hens, so that you would have said there was a deficiency of domestic sounds; neither the churn, nor the spinning wheel, nor even the singing of the kettle, nor the hissing of the urn, nor children crying, to comfort one. An old-fashioned man would have lost his senses or died of ennui before this. Not even rats in the wall, for they were starved out, or rather were never baited in,—only squirrels on the roof and under the floor, a whippoorwill on the ridge pole, a blue-jay screaming beneath the window, a hare or woodchuck under the house, a screech-owl or a cat-owl behind it, a flock of wild geese or a laughing loon on the pond, and a fox to bark in the night. Not even a lark or an oriole, those mild plantation birds, ever visited my clearing. No cockerels to crow nor hens to cackle in the yard. No yard! but unfenced Nature reaching up to your very sills. A young forest growing up under your windows, and wild sumachs and blackberry vines breaking through into your cellar; sturdy pitch-pines rubbing and creaking against the shingles for want of room, their roots reaching quite under the house. Instead of a scuttle or a blind blown off in the gale,—a pine tree snapped off or torn up by the roots behind your house for fuel. Instead of no path to the front-yard gate in the Great Snow,—no gate,—no front-yard,—and no path to the civilized world!

5. *Solitude*

This is a delicious evening, when the whole body is one sense, and imbibes delight through every pore. I go and come with a strange liberty in Nature, a part of herself. As I walk along the stony shore of the pond in my shirt sleeves, though it is cool as well as cloudy and windy, and I see nothing special to attract me, all the elements are unusually congenial to me. The bullfrogs trump to usher in the night, and the note of the whippoorwill is borne on the rippling wind from over the water. Sympathy with the fluttering alder and poplar leaves almost takes away my breath; yet, like the lake, my serenity is rippled but not ruffled. These small waves raised by the evening wind are as remote from the storm as the smooth reflecting surface. Though it is now dark, the wind still blows and roars in the wood, the waves still dash, and some creatures lull the rest with their notes. The repose is never complete. The wildest animals do not repose, but seek their prey now; the fox, and skunk, and rabbit, now roam the fields and woods without fear. They are Nature's watchmen,—links which connect the days of animated life.

When I return to my house I find that visitors have been there and left their cards, either a bunch of flowers, or a wreath of evergreen, or a name in pencil on a yellow walnut leaf or a chip. They who come rarely to the woods take some little piece of the forest into their hands to play with by the way, which they leave, either intentionally or accidentally. One has peeled a willow wand, woven it into a ring, and dropped it on my table. I could always tell if visitors had called in my absence, either by the bended twigs or grass, or the print of their shoes, and generally of what sex or age or quality they were by some slight trace left, as a flower dropped, or a bunch of grass plucked and thrown away, even as far off as the railroad, half a mile distant, or by the lingering odor of a cigar or pipe. Nay, I was frequently notified of the passage of a traveller along the highway sixty rods off by the scent of his pipe.

There is commonly sufficient space about us. Our horizon is never quite at our elbows. The thick wood is not just at our door, nor the pond, but somewhat is always clearing, familiar and worn by us, appropriated and fenced in some way, and reclaimed from Nature. For what reason have I this vast range and circuit, some square miles of unfrequented forest, for my privacy, abandoned to me by men? My nearest neighbor is a mile distant, and no house is visible from any place but the hill-tops within half a mile of my own. I have my horizon bounded by woods all to myself; a distant view of the railroad where it touches the pond on the one hand, and of the fence which skirts the woodland road on the other. But for the most part it is as solitary where I live as on the prairies. It is as much Asia or Africa as New England. I have, as it were, my own sun and moon and stars, and a little world all to myself. At night there was never a traveller passed my house, or knocked at my door, more than if I were the first or last man; unless it were in the spring, when at long intervals some came from the village to fish for pouts,—they plainly fished much more in the Walden Pond of their own natures, and baited their hooks with darkness,—but they soon retreated, usually with light baskets, and left "the world to darkness and to me,"[3] and the black kernel of the night was never profaned by any human neighborhood. I believe that men are generally still a little afraid of the dark, though the witches are all hung, and Christianity and candles have been introduced.

Yet I experienced sometimes that the most sweet and tender, the most innocent and encouraging society may be found in any natural object, even for the poor misanthrope and most melancholy man. There can be no very black melancholy to him who lives in the midst of Nature and has his senses still. There was never yet such a storm but it was Æolian[4] music to a healthy and innocent ear. Nothing can rightly compel a simple and brave man to a vulgar sadness. While I enjoy the friendship of the seasons I trust

3. From "Elegy Written in a Country Churchyard" (1751), by the English poet Thomas Gray (1716–1771).

4. The Aeolian harp (named for Aeolus, Greek keeper of the winds) was commonly placed in the open air or near an open window so that the wind could cause it to make musical sounds.

that nothing can make life a burden to me. The gentle rain which waters my beans and keeps me in the house to-day is not drear and melancholy, but good for me too. Though it prevents my hoeing them, it is of far more worth than my hoeing. If it should continue so long as to cause the seeds to rot in the ground and destroy the potatoes in the low lands, it would still be good for the grass on the uplands, and, being good for the grass, it would be good for me. Sometimes, when I compare myself with other men, it seems as if I were more favored by the gods than they, beyond any deserts that I am conscious of; as if I had a warrant and surety at their hands which my fellows have not, and were especially guided and guarded. I do not flatter myself, but if it be possible they flatter me. I have never felt lonesome, or in the least oppressed by a sense of solitude, but once, and that was a few weeks after I came to the woods, when, for an hour, I doubted if the near neighborhood of man was not essential to a serene and healthy life. To be alone was something unpleasant. But I was at the same time conscious of a slight insanity in my mood, and seemed to foresee my recovery. In the midst of a gentle rain while these thoughts prevailed, I was suddenly sensible of such sweet and beneficent society in Nature, in the very pattering of the drops, and in every sound and sight around my house, an infinite and unaccountable friendliness all at once like an atmosphere sustaining me, as made the fancied advantages of human neighborhood insignificant, and I have never thought of them since. Every little pine needle expanded and swelled with sympathy and befriended me. I was so distinctly made aware of the presence of something kindred to me, even in scenes which we are accustomed to call wild and dreary, and also that the nearest of blood to me and humanest was not a person nor a villager, that I thought no place could ever be strange to me again.—

"Mourning untimely consumes the sad;
Few are their days in the land of the living,
Beautiful daughter of Toscar."[5]

Some of my pleasantest hours were during the long rain storms in the spring or fall, which confined me to the house for the afternoon as well as the forenoon, soothed by their ceaseless roar and pelting; when an early twilight ushered in a long evening in which many thoughts had time to take root and unfold themselves. In those driving north-east rains which tried the village houses so, when the maids stood ready with mop and pail in front entries to keep the deluge out, I sat behind my door in my little house, which was all entry, and thoroughly enjoyed its protection. In one heavy thunder shower the lightning struck a large pitch-pine across the pond, making a very conspicuous and perfectly regular spiral groove from top to bottom, an inch or more deep, and four or five inches wide, as you would groove a walking-stick. I passed it again the other day, and was struck with awe on looking up and beholding that mark, now more distinct than ever, where a terrific and resistless bolt came down out of the harmless sky eight years ago. Men frequently say to me, "I should think you would feel lonesome down there, and want to be nearer to folks, rainy and snowy days and nights especially." I am tempted to reply to such,—This whole earth which we inhabit

5. From "Croma," in Patrick MacGregor's translation of *The Genuine Remains of Ossian* (1841).

is but a point in space. How far apart, think you, dwell the two most distant inhabitants of yonder star, the breadth of whose disk cannot be appreciated by our instruments? Why should I feel lonely? is not our planet in the Milky Way? This which you put seems to me not to be the most important question. What sort of space is that which separates a man from his fellows and makes him solitary? I have found that no exertion of the legs can bring two minds much nearer to one another. What do we want most to dwell near to? Not to many men surely, the depot, the post-office, the bar-room, the meeting-house, the school-house, the grocery, Beacon Hill, or the Five Points,[6] where men most congregate, but to the perennial source of our life, whence in all our experience we have found that to issue; as the willow stands near the water and sends out its roots in that direction. This will vary with different natures, but this is the place where a wise man will dig his cellar. . . . I one evening overtook one of my townsmen, who has accumulated what is called "a handsome property",—though I never got a *fair* view of it,—on the Walden road, driving a pair of cattle to market, who inquired of me how I could bring my mind to give up so many of the comforts of life. I answered that I was very sure I liked it passably well; I was not joking. And so I went home to my bed, and left him to pick his way through the darkness and the mud to Brighton,—or Bright-town,—which place he would reach some time in the morning.

Any prospect of awakening or coming to life to a dead man makes indifferent all times and places. The place where that may occur is always the same, and indescribably pleasant to all our senses. For the most part we allow only outlying and transient circumstances to make our occasions. They are, in fact, the cause of our distraction. Nearest to all things is that power which fashions their being. *Next* to us the grandest laws are continually being executed. *Next* to us is not the workman whom we have hired, with whom we love so well to talk, but the workman whose work we are.

"How vast and profound is the influence of the subtile powers of Heaven and of Earth!"

"We seek to perceive them, and we do not see them; we seek to hear them, and we do not hear them; identified with the substance of things, they cannot be separated from them."

"They cause that in all the universe men purify and sanctify their hearts, and clothe themselves in their holiday garments to offer sacrifices and oblations to their ancestors. It is an ocean of subtile intelligences. They are every where, above us, on our left, on our right; they environ us on all sides."[7]

We are the subjects of an experiment which is not a little interesting to me. Can we not do without the society of our gossips a little while under these circumstances,—have our own thoughts to cheer us? Confucious says truly, "Virtue does not remain as an abandoned orphan; it must of necessity have neighbors."[8]

With thinking we may be beside ourselves in a sane sense. By a conscious effort of the mind we can stand aloof from actions and their consequences; and all things, good and bad, go by us like a torrent. We are not wholly

6. District in lower Manhattan, notorious in Thoreau's time for its poverty and violence. The State House is on Boston's Beacon Hill.

7. Confucius's *The Doctrine of the Mean* 14.

8. Confucius's *Analects* 4.

involved in Nature. I may be either the drift-wood in the stream, or Indra[9] in the sky looking down on it. I *may* be affected by a theatrical exhibition; on the other hand, I *may not* be affected by an actual event which appears to concern me much more. I only know myself as a human entity; the scene, so to speak, of thoughts and affections; and am sensible of a certain doubleness by which I can stand as remote from myself as from another. However intense my experience, I am conscious of the presence and criticism of a part of me, which, as it were, is not a part of me, but spectator, sharing no experience, but taking note of it; and that is no more I than it is you. When the play, it may be the tragedy, of life is over, the spectator goes his way. It was a kind of fiction, a work of the imagination only, so far as he was concerned. This doubleness may easily make us poor neighbors and friends sometimes.

I find it wholesome to be alone the greater part of the time. To be in company, even with the best, is soon wearisome and dissipating. I love to be alone. I never found the companion that was so companionable as solitude. We are for the most part more lonely when we go abroad among men than when we stay in our chambers. A man thinking or working is always alone, let him be where he will. Solitude is not measured by the miles of space that intervene between a man and his fellows. The really diligent student in one of the crowded hives of Cambridge College is as solitary as a dervish[1] in the desert. The farmer can work alone in the field or the woods all day, hoeing or chopping, and not feel lonesome, because he is employed; but when he comes home at night he cannot sit down in a room alone, at the mercy of his thoughts, but must be where he can "see the folks," and recreate, and as he thinks remunerate himself for his day's solitude; and hence he wonders how the student can sit alone in the house all night and most of the day without ennui and "the blues;" but he does not realize that the student, though in the house, is still at work in *his* field, and chopping in *his* woods, as the farmer in his, and in turn seeks the same recreation and society that the latter does, though it may be a more condensed form of it.

Society is commonly too cheap. We meet at very short intervals, not having had time to acquire any new value for each other. We meet at meals three times a day, and give each other a new taste of that old musty cheese that we are. We have had to agree on a certain set of rules, called etiquette and politeness, to make this frequent meeting tolerable, and that we need not come to open war. We meet at the post-office, and at the sociable, and about the fireside every night; we live thick and are in each other's way, and stumble over one another, and I think that we thus lose some respect for one another. Certainly less frequency would suffice for all important and hearty communications. Consider the girls in a factory,—never alone, hardly in their dreams. It would be better if there were but one inhabitant to a square mile, as where I live. The value of a man is not in his skin, that we should touch him.

I have heard of a man lost in the woods and dying of famine and exhaustion at the foot of a tree, whose loneliness was relieved by the grotesque visions with which, owing to bodily weakness, his diseased imagination surrounded him, and which he believed to be real. So also, owing to bodily and

9. In the Vedas, the Hindu god of the air, associated with rain and thunder.

1. Sufi Muslim who takes religious vows of poverty and austerity.

mental health and strength, we may be continually cheered by a like but more normal and natural society, and come to know that we are never alone.

I have a great deal of company in my house; especially in the morning, when nobody calls. Let me suggest a few comparisons, that some one may convey an idea of my situation. I am no more lonely than the loon in the pond that laughs so loud, or than Walden Pond itself. What company has that lonely lake, I pray? And yet it has not the blue devils, but the blue angels in it, in the azure tint of its waters. The sun is alone, except in thick weather, when there sometimes appear to be two, but one is a mock sun. God is alone,—but the devil, he is far from being alone; he sees a great deal of company; he is legion. I am no more lonely than a single mullein or dandelion in a pasture, or a bean leaf, or sorrel, or a horse-fly, or a humble-bee. I am no more lonely than the Mill Brook, or a weathercock, or the northstar, or the south wind, or an April shower, or a January thaw, or the first spider in a new house.

I have occasional visits in the long winter evenings, when the snow falls fast and the wind howls in the wood, from an old settler and original proprietor, who is reported to have dug Walden Pond, and stoned it, and fringed it with pine woods; who tells me stories of old time and of new eternity; and between us we manage to pass a cheerful evening with social mirth and pleasant views of things, even without apples or cider,—a most wise and humorous friend, whom I love much, who keeps himself more secret than ever did Goffe or Whalley;[2] and though he is thought to be dead, none can show where he is buried. An elderly dame,[3] too, dwells in my neighborhood, invisible to most persons, in whose odorous herb garden I love to stroll sometimes, gathering simples and listening to her fables; for she has a genius of unequalled fertility, and her memory runs back farther than mythology, and she can tell me the original of every fable, and on what fact every one is founded, for the incidents occurred when she was young. A ruddy and lusty old dame, who delights in all weathers and seasons, and is likely to outlive all her children yet.

The indescribable innocence and beneficence of Nature,—of sun and wind and rain, of summer and winter,—such health, such cheer, they afford forever! and such sympathy have they ever with our race, that all Nature would be affected, and the sun's brightness fade, and the winds would sigh humanely, and the clouds rain tears, and the woods shed their leaves and put on mourning in midsummer, if any man should ever for a just cause grieve. Shall I not have intelligence with the earth? Am I not partly leaves and vegetable mould myself?

What is the pill which will keep us well, serene, contented? Not my or thy great-grandfather's, but our great-grandmother Nature's universal, vegetable, botanic medicines, by which she has kept herself young always, outlived so many old Parrs[4] in her day, and fed her health with their decaying fatness. For my panacea, instead of one of those quack vials of a mixture dipped from Acheron[5] and the Dead Sea, which come out of those long shallow black-schooner looking wagons which we sometimes see made to

2. English Puritans who supported the execution of Charles I of England in 1649 and later, when sought as regicides, hid in Connecticut and Massachusetts settlements. "Old settler": some sort of divine creative power.

3. Mother Nature.

4. An Englishman known as Old Tom Parr was said to have been alive during three centuries (1483–1635).

5. In Greek mythology a principal river in Hades.

carry bottles, let me have a draught of undiluted morning air. Morning air! If men will not drink of this at the fountain-head of the day, why, then, we must even bottle up some and sell it in the shops, for the benefit of those who have lost their subscription ticket to morning time in this world. But remember, it will not keep quite till noon-day even in the coolest cellar, but drive out the stopples long ere that and follow westward the steps of Aurora. I am no worshipper of Hygeia, who was the daughter of that old herb-doctor Æsculapius,[6] and who is represented on monuments holding a serpent in one hand, and in the other a cup out of which the serpent sometimes drinks; but rather of Hebe, cupbearer to Jupiter, who was the daughter of Juno and wild lettuce, and who had the power of restoring gods and men to the vigor of youth. She was probably the only thoroughly sound-conditioned, healthy, and robust young lady that ever walked the globe, and wherever she came it was spring.

6. *Visitors*

I think that I love society as much as most, and am ready enough to fasten myself like a bloodsucker for the time to any full-blooded man that comes in my way. I am naturally no hermit, but might possibly sit out the sturdiest frequenter of the bar-room, if my business called me thither.

I had three chairs in my house; one for solitude, two for friendship, three for society. When visitors came in larger and unexpected numbers there was but the third chair for them all, but they generally economized the room by standing up. It is surprising how many great men and women a small house will contain. I have had twenty-five or thirty souls, with their bodies, at once under my roof, and yet we often parted without being aware that we had come very near to one another. Many of our houses, both public and private, with their almost innumerable apartments, their huge halls and their cellars for the storage of wines and other munitions of peace, appear to me extravagantly large for their inhabitants. They are so vast and magnificent that the latter seem to be only vermin which infest them. I am surprised when the herald blows his summons before some Tremont or Astor or Middlesex House,[7] to see come creeping out over the piazza for all inhabitants a ridiculous mouse, which soon again slinks into some hole in the pavement.

One inconvenience I sometimes experienced in so small a house, the difficulty of getting to a sufficient distance from my guest when we began to utter the big thoughts in big words. You want room for your thoughts to get into sailing trim and run a course or two before they make their port. The bullet of your thought must have overcome its lateral and ricochet motion and fallen into its last and steady course before it reaches the ear of the hearer, else it may plough out again through the side of his head. Also, our sentences wanted room to unfold and form their columns in the interval. Individuals, like nations, must have suitable broad and natural boundaries, even a considerable neutral ground, between them. I have found it a singular luxury to talk across the pond to a companion on the opposite side. In my house we were so near that we could not begin to hear,—we could not

6. Roman god of medicine. Hygeia was the Greek goddess of health.

7. Hotels in Boston, New York, and Concord, respectively.

speak low enough to be heard; as when you throw two stones into calm water so near that they break each other's undulations. If we are merely loquacious and loud talkers, then we can afford to stand very near together, cheek by jowl, and feel each other's breath; but if we speak reservedly and thoughtfully, we want to be farther apart, that all animal heat and moisture may have a chance to evaporate. If we would enjoy the most intimate society with that in each of us which is without, or above, being spoken to, we must not only be silent, but commonly so far apart bodily that we cannot possibly hear each other's voice in any case. Referred to this standard, speech is for the convenience of those who are hard of hearing; but there are many fine things which we cannot say if we have to shout. As the conversation began to assume a loftier and grander tone, we gradually shoved our chairs farther apart till they touched the wall in opposite corners, and then commonly there was not room enough.

My "best" room, however, my withdrawing room, always ready for company, on whose carpet the sun rarely fell, was the pine wood behind my house. Thither in summer days, when distinguished guests came, I took them, and a priceless domestic swept the floor and dusted the furniture and kept the things in order.

If one guest came he sometimes partook of my frugal meal, and it was no interruption to conversation to be stirring a hasty-pudding, or watching the rising and maturing of a loaf of bread in the ashes, in the mean while. But if twenty came and sat in my house, there was nothing said about dinner, though there might be bread enough for two, more than if eating were a forsaken habit; but we naturally practised abstinence; and this was never felt to be an offence against hospitality, but the most proper and considerate course. The waste and decay of physical life, which so often needs repair, seemed miraculously retarded in such a case, and the vital vigor stood its ground. I could entertain thus a thousand as well as twenty; and if any ever went away disappointed or hungry from my house when they found me at home, they may depend upon it that I sympathized with them at least. So easy is it, though many housekeepers doubt it, to establish new and better customs in the place of the old. You need not rest your reputation on the dinners you give. For my own part, I was never so effectually deterred from frequenting a man's house, by any kind of Cerberus[8] whatever, as by the parade one made about dining me, which I took to be a very polite and roundabout hint never to trouble him so again. I think I shall never revisit those scenes. I should be proud to have for the motto of my cabin those lines of Spenser which one of my visitors inscribed on a yellow walnut leaf for a card:—

> "Arrivèd there, the little house they fill,
>   Ne looke for entertainment where none was;
> Rest is their feast, and all things at their will:
>   The noblest mind the best contentment has."[9]

When Winslow, afterward governor of the Plymouth Colony, went with a companion on a visit of ceremony to Massassoit on foot through the woods, and arrived tired and hungry at his lodge, they were well received by the

8. In Greek mythology a three-headed dog guarding the entrance of Hades, or Hell.

9. From *The Faerie Queen* (1590) (1.1.35), by the English poet Edmund Spenser (1552?–1599).

king, but nothing was said about eating that day. When the night arrived, to quote their own words,—"He laid us on the bed with himself and his wife, they at the one end and we at the other, it being only plank, laid a foot from the ground, and a thin mat upon them. Two more of his chief men, for want of room, pressed by and upon us; so that we were worse weary of our lodging than of our journey." At one o'clock the next day Massassoit "brought two fishes that he had shot," about thrice as big as a bream; "these being boiled, there were at least forty looked for a share in them. The most ate of them. This meal only we had in two nights and a day; and had not one of us bought a partridge, we had taken our journey fasting." Fearing that they would be light-headed for want of food and also sleep, owing to "the savages' barbarous singing (for they used to sing themselves asleep)" and that they might get home while they had strength to travel, they departed.[1] As for lodging, it is true they were but poorly entertained, though what they found an inconvenience was no doubt intended for an honor; but as far as eating was concerned, I do not see how the Indians could have done better. They had nothing to eat themselves, and they were wiser than to think that apologies could supply the place of food to their guests; so they drew their belts tighter and said nothing about it. Another time when Winslow visited them, it being a season of plenty with them, there was no deficiency in this respect.

As for men, they will hardly fail one any where. I had more visitors while I lived in the woods than at any other period of my life; I mean that I had some. I met several there under more favorable circumstances than I could any where else. But fewer came to see me upon trivial business. In this respect, my company was winnowed by my mere distance from town. I had withdrawn so far within the great ocean of solitude, into which the rivers of society empty, that for the most part, so far as my needs were concerned, only the finest sediment was deposited around me. Beside, there were wafted to me evidences of unexplored and uncultivated continents on the other side.

Who should come to my lodge this morning but a true Homeric or Paphlagonian man,—he had so suitable and poetic a name[2] that I am sorry I cannot print it here,—a Canadian, a wood-chopper and post-maker, who can hole fifty posts in a day, who made his last supper on a woodchuck which his dog caught. He, too, has heard of Homer, and, "if it were not for books," would "not know what to do rainy days," though perhaps he has not read one wholly through for many rainy seasons. Some priest who could pronounce the Greek itself taught him to read his verse in the testament in his native parish far away; and now I must translate to him, while he holds the book, Achilles' reproof to Patroclus for his sad countenance.—"Why are you in tears, Patroclus, like a young girl?"—

> "Or have you alone heard some news from Phthia?
> They say that Menœtius lives yet, son of Actor,
> And Peleus lives, son of Æacus, among the Myrmidons,
> Either of whom having died, we should greatly grieve."[3]

He says, "That's good." He has a great bundle of white-oak bark under his arm for a sick man, gathered this Sunday morning. "I suppose there's no

1. From Edward Winslow's *The English Plantation at Plymouth* (1622). Winslow (1595–1655) was one of the founders of the Plymouth Colony.

2. Alek Therien (1812–1885). Paphlagonia is a mountainous region in Asia Minor.

3. *Iliad*, book 16.

harm in going after such a thing to-day," says he. To him Homer was a great writer, though what his writing was about he did not know. A more simple and natural man it would be hard to find. Vice and disease, which cast such a sombre moral hue over the world, seemed to have hardly any existence for him. He was about twenty-eight years old, and had left Canada and his father's house a dozen years before to work in the States, and earn money to buy a farm with at last, perhaps in his native country. He was cast in the coarsest mould; a stout but sluggish body, yet gracefully carried, with a thick sunburnt neck, dark bushy hair, and dull sleepy blue eyes, which were occasionally lit up with expression. He wore a flat gray cloth cap, a dingy wool-colored greatcoat, and cowhide boots. He was a great consumer of meat, usually carrying his dinner to his work a couple of miles past my house,—for he chopped all summer,—in a tin pail; cold meats, often cold woodchucks, and coffee in a stone bottle which dangled by a string from his belt; and sometimes he offered me a drink. He came along early, crossing my bean-field, though without anxiety or haste to get to his work, such as Yankees exhibit. He wasn't a-going to hurt himself. He didn't care if he only earned his board. Frequently he would leave his dinner in the bushes, when his dog had caught a woodchuck by the way, and go back a mile and a half to dress it and leave it in the cellar of the house where he boarded, after deliberating first for half an hour whether he could not sink it in the pond safely till nightfall,—loving to dwell long upon these themes. He would say, as he went by in the morning, "How thick the pigeons are! If working every day were not my trade, I could get all the meat I should want by hunting,—pigeons, woodchucks, rabbits, partridges,—by gosh! I could get all I should want for a week in one day."

He was a skilful chopper, and indulged in some flourishes and ornaments in his art. He cut his trees level and close to the ground, that the sprouts which came up afterward might be more vigorous and a sled might slide over the stumps; and instead of leaving a whole tree to support his corded wood, he would pare it away to a slender stake or splinter which you could break off with your hand at last.

He interested me because he was so quiet and solitary and so happy withal; a well of good humor and contentment which overflowed at his eyes. His mirth was without alloy. Sometimes I saw him at his work in the woods, felling trees, and he would greet me with a laugh of inexpressible satisfaction, and a salutation in Canadian French, though he spoke English as well. When I approached him he would suspend his work, and with half-suppressed mirth lie along the trunk of a pine which he had felled, and, peeling off the inner bark, roll it up into a ball and chew it while he laughed and talked. Such an exuberance of animal spirits had he that he sometimes tumbled down and rolled on the ground with laughter at any thing which made him think and tickled him. Looking round upon the trees he would exclaim,—"By George! I can enjoy myself well enough here chopping; I want no better sport." Sometimes, when at leisure, he amused himself all day in the woods with a pocket pistol, firing salutes to himself at regular intervals as he walked. In the winter he had a fire by which at noon he warmed his coffee in a kettle; and as he sat on a log to eat his dinner the chicadees would sometimes come round and alight on his arm and peck at the potato in his fingers; and he said that he "liked to have the little *fellers* about him."

In him the animal man chiefly was developed. In physical endurance and contentment he was cousin to the pine and the rock. I asked him once if he was not sometimes tired at night, after working all day; and he answered, with a sincere and serious look, "Gorrappit, I never was tired in my life." But the intellectual and what is called spiritual man in him were slumbering as in an infant. He had been instructed only in that innocent and ineffectual way in which the Catholic priests teach the aborigines, by which the pupil is never educated to the degree of consciousness, but only to the degree of trust and reverence, and a child is not made a man, but kept a child. When Nature made him, she gave him a strong body and contentment for his portion, and propped him on every side with reverence and reliance, that he might live out his threescore years and ten a child. He was so genuine and unsophisticated that no introduction would serve to introduce him, more than if you introduced a woodchuck to your neighbor. He had got to find him out as you did. He would not play any part. Men paid him wages for work, and so helped to feed and clothe him; but he never exchanged opinions with them. He was so simply and naturally humble—if he can be called humble who never aspires—that humility was no distinct quality in him, nor could he conceive of it. Wiser men were demigods to him. If you told him that such a one was coming, he did as if he thought that any thing so grand would expect nothing of himself, but take all the responsibility on itself, and let him be forgotten still. He never heard the sound of praise. He particularly reverenced the writer and the preacher. Their performances were miracles. When I told him that I wrote considerably, he thought for a long time that it was merely the handwriting which I meant, for he could write a remarkably good hand himself. I sometimes found the name of his native parish handsomely written in the snow by the highway, with the proper French accent, and knew that he had passed. I asked him if he ever wished to write his thoughts. He said that he had read and written letters for those who could not, but he never tried to write thoughts,—no, he could not, he could not tell what to put first, it would kill him, and then there was spelling to be attended to at the same time!

I heard that a distinguished wise man and reformer asked him if he did not want the world to be changed; but he answered with a chuckle of surprise in his Canadian accent, not knowing that the question had ever been entertained before, "No, I like it well enough." It would have suggested many things to a philosopher to have dealings with him. To a stranger he appeared to know nothing of things in general; yet I sometimes saw in him a man whom I had not seen before, and I did not know whether he was as wise as Shakspeare or as simply ignorant as a child, whether to suspect him of a fine poetic consciousness or of stupidity. A townsman told me that when he met him sauntering through the village in his small close-fitting cap, and whistling to himself, he reminded him of a prince in disguise.

His only books were an almanac and an arithmetic, in which last he was considerably expert. The former was a sort of cyclopædia to him, which he supposed to contain an abstract of human knowledge, as indeed it does to a considerable extent. I loved to sound him on the various reforms of the day, and he never failed to look at them in the most simple and practical light. He had never heard of such things before. Could he do without factories? I asked. He had worn the home-made Vermont gray, he said, and that was good. Could he dispense with tea and coffee? Did this country afford any beverage beside water? He had soaked hemlock leaves in water and drank it, and thought that was better than water in warm weather. When I asked him if he could do without money, he showed the convenience of money in such a way as to suggest and coincide with the most philosophical accounts of the origin of this institution, and the very derivation of the word *pecunia*.[4] If an ox were his property, and he wished to get needles and thread at the store, he thought it would be inconvenient and impossible soon to go on mortgaging some portion of the creature each time to that amount. He could defend many institutions better than any philosopher, because, in describing them as they concerned him, he gave the true reason for their prevalence, and speculation had not suggested to him any other. At another time, hearing Plato's definition of a man,—a biped without feathers,—and that one exhibited a cock plucked and called it Plato's man, he thought it an important difference that the *knees* bent the wrong way. He would sometimes exclaim, "How I love to talk! By George, I could talk all day!" I asked him once, when I had not seen him for many months, if he had got a new idea this summer. "Good Lord," said he, "a man that has to work as I do, if he does not forget the ideas he has had, he will do well. May be the man you hoe with is inclined to race; then, by gorry, your mind must be there; you think of weeds." He would sometimes ask me first on such occasions, if I had made any improvement. One winter day I asked him if he was always satisfied with himself, wishing to suggest a substitute within him for the priest without, and some higher motive for living. "Satisfied!" said he; "some men are satisfied with one thing, and some with another. One man, perhaps, if he has got enough, will be satisfied to sit all day with his back to the fire and his belly to the table, by George!" Yet I never, by any manœuvring, could get him to take the spiritual view of things; the highest that he appeared to conceive of was a simple expediency, such as you might expect an animal to appreciate; and this, practically, is true of most men. If I suggested any improvement in his mode of life, he merely answered, without expressing any regret, that it was too late. Yet he thoroughly believed in honesty and the like virtues.

There was a certain positive originality, however slight, to be detected in him, and I occasionally observed that he was thinking for himself and expressing his own opinion, a phenomenon so rare that I would any day walk ten miles to observe it, and it amounted to the re-origination of many of the institutions of society. Though he hesitated, and perhaps failed to express himself distinctly, he always had a presentable thought behind. Yet his thinking was so primitive and immersed in his animal life, that, though more promising than a merely learned man's, it rarely ripened to any thing which can be reported. He suggested that there might be men of genius in the lowest grades of life, however permanently humble and illiterate, who take their own view always, or do not pretend to see at all; who are as bottomless even as Walden Pond was thought to be, though they may be dark and muddy.

Many a traveller came out of his way to see me and the inside of my house, and, as an excuse for calling, asked for a glass of water. I told them that I drank at the pond, and pointed thither, offering to lend them a dipper. Far off as I lived, I was not exempted from that annual visitation which occurs,

4. Wealth computed in terms of the number of cattle owned.

methinks, about the first of April, when every body is on the move; and I had my share of good luck, though there were some curious specimens among my visitors. Half-witted men from the almshouse and elsewhere came to see me; but I endeavored to make them exercise all the wit they had, and make their confessions to me; in such cases making wit the theme of our conversation; and so was compensated. Indeed, I found some of them to be wiser than the so called *overseers* of the poor and selectmen of the town, and thought it was time that the tables were turned. With respect to wit, I learned that there was not much difference between the half and the whole. One day, in particular, an inoffensive, simple-minded pauper, whom with others I had often seen used as fencing stuff, standing or setting on a bushel in the fields to keep cattle and himself from straying, visited me, and expressed a wish to live as I did. He told me, with the utmost simplicity and truth, quite superior, or rather *inferior*, to any thing that is called humility, that he was "deficient in intellect." These were his words. The Lord had made him so, yet he supposed the Lord cared as much for him as for another. "I have always been so," said he, "from my childhood; I never had much mind; I was not like other children; I am weak in the head. It was the Lord's will, I suppose." And there he was to prove the truth of his words. He was a metaphysical puzzle to me. I have rarely met a fellow-man on such promising ground,—it was so simple and sincere and so true all that he said. And, true enough, in proportion as he appeared to humble himself was he exalted. I did not know at first but it was the result of a wise policy. It seemed that from such a basis of truth and frankness as the poor weak-headed pauper had laid, our intercourse might go forward to something better than the intercourse of sages.

I had some guests from those not reckoned commonly among the town's poor, but who should be; who are among the world's poor, at any rate; guests who appeal, not to your hospitality, but to your *hospitalality;* who earnestly wish to be helped, and preface their appeal with the information that they are resolved, for one thing, never to help themselves. I require of a visitor that he be not actually starving, though he may have the very best appetite in the world, however he got it. Objects of charity are not guests. Men who did not know when their visit had terminated, though I went about my business again, answering them from greater and greater remoteness. Men of almost every degree of wit called on me in the migrating season. Some who had more wits than they knew what to do with; runaway slaves with plantation manners, who listened from time to time, like the fox in the fable, as if they heard the hounds a-baying on their track, and looked at me beseechingly, as much as to say,—

"O Christian, will you send me back?"

One real runaway slave, among the rest, whom I helped to forward toward the northstar. Men of one idea, like a hen with one chicken, and that a duckling; men of a thousand ideas, and unkempt heads, like those hens which are made to take charge of a hundred chickens, all in pursuit of one bug, a score of them lost in every morning's dew,—and become frizzled and mangy in consequence; men of ideas instead of legs, a sort of intellectual centipede that made you crawl all over. One man proposed a book in which visitors should write their names, as at the White Mountains; but, alas! I have too good a memory to make that necessary.

I could not but notice some of the peculiarities of my visitors. Girls and boys and young women generally seemed glad to be in the woods. They looked in the pond and at the flowers, and improved their time. Men of business, even farmers, thought only of solitude and employment, and of the great distance at which I dwelt from something or other; and though they said that they loved a ramble in the woods occasionally, it was obvious that they did not. Restless committed men, whose time was all taken up in getting a living, or keeping it; ministers who spoke of God as if they enjoyed a monopoly of the subject, who could not bear all kinds of opinions; doctors, lawyers, uneasy housekeepers who pried into my cupboard and bed when I was out,—how came Mrs. —— to know that my sheets were not as clean as hers?—young men who had ceased to be young, and had concluded that it was safest to follow the beaten track of the professions,—all these generally said that it was not possible to do so much good in my position. Ay! there was the rub. The old and infirm and the timid, of whatever age or sex, thought most of sickness, and sudden accident and death; to them life seemed full of danger,—what danger is there if you don't think of any?—and they thought that a prudent man would carefully select the safest position, where Dr. B.[5] might be on hand at a moment's warning. To them the village was literally a *community*, a league for mutual defence, and you would suppose that they would not go a-huckleberrying without a medicine chest. The amount of it is, if a man is alive, there is always *danger* that he may die, though the danger must be allowed to be less in proportion as he is dead-and-alive to begin with. A man sits as many risks as he runs. Finally, there were the self-styled reformers, the greatest bores of all, who thought that I was forever singing,—

> This is the house that I built;
> This is the man that lives in the house that I built;

but they did not know that the third line was,—

> These are the folks that worry the man
> That lives in the house that I built.[6]

I did not fear the hen-harriers,[7] for I kept no chickens; but I feared the men-harriers rather.

I had more cheering visitors than the last. Children come a-berrying, railroad men taking a Sunday morning walk in clean shirts, fishermen and hunters, poets and philosophers, in short, all honest pilgrims, who came out to the woods for freedom's sake, and really left the village behind, I was ready to greet with,—"Welcome, Englishmen! welcome, Englishmen!" for I had had communication with that race.

7. *The Bean-Field*

Meanwhile my beans, the length of whose rows, added together, was seven miles already planted, were impatient to be hoed, for the earliest had grown considerably before the latest were in the ground; indeed they were not easily to be put off. What was the meaning of this so steady and self-respecting,

5. Josiah Bartlett (1796–1878), a Concord physician.
6. Parody of the nursery rhyme "This Is the House That Jack Built."
7. Marsh hawks.

this small Herculean labor, I knew not. I came to love my rows, my beans, though so many more than I wanted. They attached me to the earth, and so I got strength like Antæus.[8] But why should I raise them? Only Heaven knows. This was my curious labor all summer,—to make this portion of the earth's surface, which had yielded only cinquefoil, blackberries, johnswort, and the like, before, sweet wild fruits and pleasant flowers, produce instead this pulse. What shall I learn of beans or beans of me? I cherish them, I hoe them, early and late I have an eye to them; and this is my day's work. It is a fine broad leaf to look on. My auxiliaries are the dews and rains which water this dry soil, and what fertility is in the soil itself, which for the most part is lean and effete. My enemies are worms, cool days, and most of all woodchucks. The last have nibbled for me a quarter of an acre clean. But what right had I to oust johnswort and the rest, and break up their ancient herb garden? Soon, however, the remaining beans will be too tough for them, and go forward to meet new foes.

When I was four years old, as I well remember, I was brought from Boston to this my native town, through these very woods and this field, to the pond. It is one of the oldest scenes stamped on my memory. And now to-night my flute has waked the echoes over that very water. The pines still stand here older than I; or, if some have fallen, I have cooked my supper with their stumps, and a new growth is rising all around, preparing another aspect for new infant eyes. Almost the same johnswort springs from the same perennial root in this pasture, and even I have at length helped to clothe that fabulous landscape of my infant dreams, and one of the results of my presence and influence is seen in these bean leaves, corn blades, and potato vines.

I planted about two acres and a half of upland; and as it was only about fifteen years since the land was cleared, and I myself had got out two or three cords of stumps, I did not give it any manure; but in the course of the summer it appeared by the arrow-heads which I turned up in hoeing, that an extinct nation had anciently dwelt here and planted corn and beans ere white men came to clear the land, and so, to some extent, had exhausted the soil for this very crop.

Before yet any woodchuck or squirrel had run across the road, or the sun had got above the shrub-oaks, while all the dew was on, though the farmers warned me against it,—I would advise you to do all your work if possible while the dew is on,—I began to level the ranks of haughty weeds in my bean-field and throw dust upon their heads. Early in the morning I worked barefooted, dabbling like a plastic artist in the dewy and crumbling sand, but later in the day the sun blistered my feet. There the sun lighted me to hoe beans, pacing slowly backward and forward over that yellow gravelly upland, between the long green rows, fifteen rods, the one end terminating in a shrub oak copse where I could rest in the shade, the other in a blackberry field where the green berries deepened their tints by the time I had made another bout. Removing the weeds, putting fresh soil about the bean stems, and encouraging this weed which I had sown, making the yellow soil express its summer thought in bean leaves and blossoms rather than in wormword and piper and millet grass, making the earth say beans instead of grass,—this was my daily work.

8. In Greek mythology, a giant who drew his strength from the Earth; Hercules strangled him while holding him off the ground.

As I had little aid from horses or cattle, or hired men or boys, or improved implements of husbandry, I was much slower, and became much more intimate with my beans than usual. But labor of the hands, even when pursued to the verge of drudgery, is perhaps never the worst form of idleness. It has a constant and imperishable moral, and to the scholar it yields a classic result. A very *agricola laboriosus* was I to travellers bound westward through Lincoln and Wayland to nobody knows where; they sitting at their ease in gigs,[9] with elbows on knees, and reins loosely hanging in festoons; I the home-staying, laborious native of the soil. But soon my homestead was out of their sight and thought. It was the only open and cultivated field for a great distance on either side of the road; so they made the most of it; and sometimes the man in the field heard more of travellers' gossip and comment than was meant for his ear: "Beans so late! peas so late!"—for I continued to plant when others had begun to hoe,—the ministerial husbandman had not suspected it. "Corn, my boy, for fodder; corn for fodder." "Does he *live* there?" asks the black bonnet of the gray coat; and the hard-featured farmer reins up his grateful dobbin to inquire what you are doing where he sees no manure in the furrow, and recommends a little chip dirt, or any little waste stuff, or it may be ashes or plaster. But here were two acres and a half of furrows, and only a hoe for cart and two hands to draw it,—there being an aversion to other carts and horses,—and chip dirt far away. Fellow-travellers as they rattled by compared it aloud with the fields which they had passed, so that I came to know how I stood in the agricultural world. This was one field not in Mr. Colman's[1] report. And, by the way, who estimates the value of the crop which Nature yields in the still wilder fields unimproved by man? The crop of *English* hay is carefully weighed, the moisture calculated, the silicates and the potash; but in all dells and pond holes in the woods and pastures and swamps grows a rich and various crop only unreaped by man. Mine was, as it were, the connecting link between wild and cultivated fields; as some states are civilized, and others half-civilized, and others savage or barbarous, so my field was, though not in a bad sense, a half-cultivated field. They were beans cheerfully returning to their wild and primitive state that I cultivated, and my hoe played the *Ranz des Vaches*[2] for them.

Near at hand, upon the topmost spray of a birch sings the brown-thrasher or red mavis, as some love to call him—all the morning, glad of your society, that would find out another farmer's field if yours were not here. While you are planting the seed, he cries,—"Drop it, drop it,—cover it up, cover it up,—pull it up, pull it up, pull it up." But this was not corn, and so it was safe from such enemies as he. You may wonder what his rigmarole, his amateur Paganini[3] performances on one string or on twenty, have to do with your planting, and yet prefer it to leached ashes or plaster. It was a cheap sort of top dressing in which I had entire faith.

As I drew a still fresher soil about the rows with my hoe, I disturbed the ashes of unchronicled nations who in primeval years lived under these heavens, and their small implements of war and hunting were brought to the light of this modern day. They lay mingled with other natural stones, some of

9. Light two-wheeled horse-drawn carriage. "*Agricola laboriosus*": hardworking farmer (Latin).
1. Henry Colman (1785–1849), who wrote a series of agricultural surveys for the state of Massachusetts.
2. A Swiss herdsman's song (literally, ranks or rows of cows [French]).
3. Nicolò Paganini (1784–1840), celebrated Italian violinist.

which bore the marks of having been burned by Indian fires, and some by the sun, and also bits of pottery and glass brought hither by the recent cultivators of the soil. When my hoe tinkled against the stones, that music echoed to the woods and the sky, and was an accompaniment to my labor which yielded an instant and immeasurable crop. It was no longer beans that I hoed, nor I that hoed beans; and I remembered with as much pity as pride, if I remembered at all, my acquaintances who had gone to the city to attend the oratorios. The night-hawk circled overhead in the sunny afternoons—for I sometimes made a day of it—like a mote in the eye, or in heaven's eye, falling from time to time with a swoop and a sound as if the heavens were rent, torn at last to very rags and tatters, and yet a seamless cope[4] remained; small imps that fill the air and lay their eggs on the ground on bare sand or rocks on the tops of hills, where few have found them; graceful and slender like ripples caught up from the pond, as leaves are raised by the wind to float in the heavens; such kindredship is in Nature. The hawk is aerial brother of the wave which he sails over and surveys, those his perfect air-inflated wings answering to the elemental unfledged pinions of the sea. Or sometimes I watched a pair of hen-hawks circling high in the sky, alternately soaring and descending, approaching and leaving one another, as if they were the imbodiment of my own thoughts. Or I was attracted by the passage of wild pigeons from this wood to that, with a slight quivering winnowing sound and carrier haste; or from under a rotten stump my hoe turned up a sluggish portentous and outlandish spotted salamander, a trace of Egypt and the Nile, yet our contemporary. When I paused to lean on my hoe, these sounds and sights I heard and saw any where in the row, a part of the inexhaustible entertainment which the country offers.

On gala days the town fires its great guns, which echo like popguns to these woods, and some waifs of martial music occasionally penetrate thus far. To me, away there in my bean-field at the other end of the town, the big guns sounded as if a puff ball had burst; and when there was a military turn-out of which I was ignorant, I have sometimes had a vague sense all the day of some sort of itching and disease in the horizon, as if some eruption would break out there soon, either scarlatina or canker-rash, until at length some more favorable puff of wind, making haste over the fields and up the Wayland road, brought me information of the "trainers."[5] It seemed by the distant hum as if somebody's bees had swarmed, and that the neighbors, according to Virgil's advice, by a faint *tintinnabulum*[6] upon the most sonorous of their domestic utensils, were endeavoring to call them down into the hive again. And when the sound died quite away, and the hum had ceased, and the most favorable breezes told no tale, I knew that they had got the last drone of them all safely into the Middlesex hive, and that now their minds were bent on the honey with which it was smeared.

I felt proud to know that the liberties of Massachusetts and of our fatherland were in such safe keeping; and as I turned to my hoeing again I was filled with an inexpressible confidence, and pursued my labor cheerfully with a calm trust in the future.

When there were several bands of musicians, it sounded as if all the village was a vast bellows, and all the buildings expanded and collapsed alternately

4. Canopy.
5. The local militia. "Scarlatina": scarlet fever. "Canker-rash": a mouth sore.
6. Tinkling (Latin).

with a din. But sometimes it was a really noble and inspiring strain that reached these woods, and the trumpet that sings of fame, and I felt as if I could spit[7] a Mexican with a good relish,—for why should we always stand for trifles?—and looked round for a woodchuck or a skunk to exercise my chivalry upon. These martial strains seemed as far away as Palestine, and reminded me of a march of crusaders in the horizon, with a slight tantivy and tremulous motion of the elm-tree tops which overhang the village. This was one of the *great* days; though the sky had from my clearing only the same everlastingly great look that it wears daily, and I saw no difference in it.

It was a singular experience that long acquaintance which I cultivated with beans, what with planting, and hoeing, and harvesting, and threshing, and picking over, and selling them,—the last was the hardest of all,—I might add eating, for I did taste. I was determined to know beans. When they were growing, I used to hoe from five o'clock in the morning till noon, and commonly spent the rest of the day about other affairs. Consider the intimate and curious acquaintance one makes with various kinds of weeds,—it will bear some iteration in the account, for there was no little iteration in the labor,—disturbing their delicate organizations so ruthlessly, and making such invidious distinction with his hoe, levelling whole ranks of one species, and sedulously cultivating another. That's Roman wormwood,—that's pigweed,—that's sorrel,—that's piper-grass,—have at him, chop him up, turn his roots upward to the sun, don't let him have a fibre in the shade, if you do he'll turn himself t'other side up and be as green as a leek in two days. A long war, not with cranes, but with weeds, those Trojans who had sun and rain and dews on their side. Daily the beans saw me come to their rescue armed with a hoe, and thin the ranks of their enemies, filling up the trenches with weedy dead. Many a lusty crest-waving Hector,[8] that towered a whole foot above his crowding comrades, fell before my weapon and rolled in the dust.

Those summer days which some of my contemporaries devoted to the fine arts in Boston or Rome, and others to contemplation in India, and others to trade in London or New York, I thus, with the other farmers of New England, devoted to husbandry. Not that I wanted beans to eat, for I am by nature a Pythagorean, so far as beans are concerned, whether they mean porridge or voting,[9] and exchanged them for rice; but, perchance, as some must work in fields if only for the sake of tropes and expression, to serve a parable-maker one day. It was on the whole a rare amusement, which, continued too long, might have become a dissipation. Though I gave them no manure, and did not hoe them all at once, I hoed them unusually well as far as I went, and was paid for it in the end, "there being in truth," as Evelyn says, "no compost or lætation whatsoever comparable to this continual motion, repastination, and turning of the mould with the spade." "The earth," he adds elsewhere, "especially if fresh, has a certain magnetism in it, by which it attracts the salt, power, or virtue (call it either) which gives it life, and is the logic of all the labor and stir we keep about it, to sustain us; all dungings and other

7. Bayonet or cook (as on a spit). The Mexican War (1846–48), which Thoreau opposed, began while he was at Walden.

8. In the *Iliad*, a Trojan prince killed by Achilles; popularly associated with bullying and bragging.

9. Beans had been used to keep tally of votes. Pythagoras (6th century B.C.E.), Greek philosopher, opposed the eating of beans. What Thoreau has most in mind is the tendency of beans to cause flatulence.

sordid temperings being but the vicars succedaneous to this improvement." Moreover, this being one of those "worn-out and exhausted lay fields which enjoy their sabbath,"[1] had perchance, as Sir Kenelm Digby thinks likely, attracted "vital spirits" from the air.[2] I harvested twelve bushels of beans.

But to be more particular; for it is complained that Mr. Colman has reported chiefly the expensive experiments of gentlemen farmers; my outgoes were,—

For a hoe,	$0 54	
Ploughing, harrowing, and furrowing,	7 50,	Too much.
Beans for seed,	3 12½	
Potatoes for seed,	1 33	
Peas for seed,	0 40	
Turnip seed,	0 06	
White line for crow fence,	0 02	
Horse cultivator and boy three hours,	1 00	
Horse and cart to get crop,	0 75	
In all,	$14 72½	

My income was, (patrem familias vendacem, non emacem esse oportet,)[3] from

Nine bushels and twelve quarts of beans sold,		$16 94
Five "	large potatoes,	2 50
Nine "	small "	2 25
Grass,		1 00
Stalks,		0 75
In all,		$23 44

Leaving a pecuniary profit, as I have elsewhere said, of $8 71½.

This is the result of my experience in raising beans. Plant the common small white bush bean about the first of June, in rows three feet by eighteen inches apart, being careful to select fresh round and unmixed seed. First look out for worms, and supply vacancies by planting anew. Then look out for woodchucks, if it is an exposed place, for they will nibble off the earliest tender leaves almost clean as they go; and again, when the young tendrils make their appearance, they have notice of it, and will shear them off with both buds and young pods, sitting erect like a squirrel. But above all harvest as early as possible, if you would escape frosts and have a fair and saleable crop; you may save much loss by this means.

This further experience also I gained. I said to myself, I will not plant beans and corn with so much industry another summer, but such seeds, if the seed is not lost, as sincerity, truth, simplicity, faith, innocence, and the like, and see if they will not grow in this soil, even with less toil and manurance,

1. These quotes are from John Evelyn, *Terra: A Philosophical Discourse of Earth* (1729).
2. The quotation from Digby (1603–1665) has not been located.
3. The master should have the habit of selling, not buying (Latin); from Cato's *De Agri Cultura*.

and sustain me, for surely it has not been exhausted for these crops. Alas! I said this to myself; but now another summer is gone, and another, and another, and I am obliged to say to you, Reader, that the seeds which I planted, if indeed they *were* the seeds of those virtues, were wormeaten or had lost their vitality, and so did not come up. Commonly men will only be brave as their fathers were brave, or timid. This generation is very sure to plant corn and beans each new year precisely as the Indians did centuries ago and taught the first settlers to do, as if there were a fate in it. I saw an old man the other day, to my astonishment, making the holes with a hoe for the seventieth time at least, and not for himself to lie down in! But why should not the New Englander try new adventures, and not lay so much stress on his grain, his potato and grass crop, and his orchards?—raise other crops than these? Why concern ourselves so much about our beans for seed, and not be concerned at all about a new generation of men? We should really be fed and cheered if when we met a man we were sure to see that some of the qualities which I have named, which we all prize more than those other productions, but which are for the most part broadcast and floating in the air, had taken root and grown in him. Here comes such a subtile and ineffable quality, for instance, as truth or justice, though the slightest amount or new variety of it, along the road. Our ambassadors should be instructed to send home such seeds as these, and Congress help to distribute them over all the land. We should never stand upon ceremony with sincerity. We should never cheat and insult and banish one another by our meanness, if there were present the kernel of worth and friendliness. We should not meet thus in haste. Most men I do not meet at all, for they seem not to have time; they are busy about their beans. We would not deal with a man thus plodding ever, leaning on a hoe or a spade as a staff between his work, not as a mushroom, but partially risen out of the earth, something more than erect, like swallows alighted and walking on the ground.—

> "And as he spake, his wings would now and then
> Spread, as he meant to fly, then close again,"[4]

so that we should suspect that we might be conversing with an angel. Bread may not always nourish us; but it always does us good, it even takes stiffness out of our joints, and makes us supple and buoyant, when we knew not what ailed us, to recognize any generosity in man or Nature, to share any unmixed and heroic joy.

Ancient poetry and mythology suggest, at least, that husbandry was once a sacred art; but it is pursued with irreverent haste and heedlessness by us, our object being to have large farms and large crops merely. We have no festival, nor procession, nor ceremony, not excepting our Cattle-shows and so called Thanksgivings, by which the farmer expresses a sense of the sacredness of his calling, or is reminded of its sacred origin. It is the premium and the feast which tempt him. He sacrifices not to Ceres and the Terrestrial Jove, but to the infernal Plutus[5] rather. By avarice and selfishness, and a grovelling habit, from which none of us is free, of regarding the soil as property, or the means of acquiring property chiefly, the landscape is

4. From the English poet Francis Quarles's (1592–1644) *The Shepherd's Oracles* (1646), Eclogue 5.

5. Greek god of wealth. Ceres was the Roman goddess of agriculture.

deformed, husbandry is degraded with us, and the farmer leads the meanest of lives. He knows Nature but as a robber. Cato says that the profits of agriculture are particularly pious or just, (*maximeque pius quæstus*,)[6] and according to Varro the old Romans "called the same earth Mother and Ceres, and thought that they who cultivated it led a pious and useful life, and that they alone were left of the race of King Saturn."[7]

We are wont to forget that the sun looks on our cultivated fields and on the prairies and forests without distinction. They all reflect and absorb his rays alike, and the former make but a small part of the glorious picture which he beholds in his daily course. In his view the earth is all equally cultivated like a garden. Therefore we should receive the benefit of his light and heat with a corresponding trust and magnanimity. What though I value the seed of these beans, and harvest that in the fall of the year? This broad field which I have looked at so long looks not to me as the principal cultivator, but away from me to influences more genial to it, which water and make it green. These beans have results which are not harvested by me. Do they not grow for woodchucks partly? The ear of wheat, (in Latin *spica*, obsoletely *speca*, from *spe*, hope,) should not be the only hope of the husbandman; its kernel or grain (*granum*, from *gerendo*, bearing,) is not all that it bears. How, then, can our harvest fail? Shall I not rejoice also at the abundance of the weeds whose seeds are granary of the birds? It matters little comparatively whether the fields fill the farmer's barns. The true husbandman will cease from anxiety, as the squirrels manifest no concern whether the woods will bear chestnuts this year or not, and finish his labor with every day, relinquishing all claim to the produce of his fields, and sacrificing in his mind not only his first but his last fruits also.

8. *The Village*

After hoeing, or perhaps reading and writing, in the forenoon, I usually bathed again in the pond, swimming across one of its coves for a stint, and washed the dust of labor from my person, or smoothed out the last wrinkle which study had made, and for the afternoon was absolutely free. Every day or two I strolled to the village to hear some of the gossip which is incessantly going on there, circulating either from mouth to mouth, or from newspaper to newspaper, and which, taken in homœopathic doses,[8] was really as refreshing in its way as the rustle of leaves and the peeping of frogs. As I walked in the woods to see the birds and squirrels, so I walked in the village to see the men and boys; instead of the wind among the pines I heard the carts rattle. In one direction from my house there was a colony of muskrats in the river meadows; under the grove of elms and buttonwoods in the other horizon was a village of busy men, as curious to me as if they had been prairie dogs, each sitting at the mouth of its burrow, or running over to a neighbor's to gossip. I went there frequently to observe their habits. The village appeared to me a great news room; and on one side, to support it, as once at Redding & Company's on State Street, they kept nuts and raisins, or salt and meal and other groceries. Some

6. Cato's *De Agri Cultura*, Introduction 4. See p. 1014, n. 3.

7. Marcus Terentius Varro (116–27 B.C.E.), *Rerum Rusticarum* 3.1.5.

8. Thoreau alludes to the homeopathic practice of treating diseases with minute doses of the toxin thought to have caused the illness.

have such a vast appetite for the former commodity, that is, the news, and such sound digestive organs, that they can sit forever in public avenues without stirring, and let it simmer and whisper through them like the Etesian winds,[9] or as if inhaling ether, it only producing numbness and insensibility to pain,—otherwise it would often be painful to hear,—without affecting the consciousness. I hardly ever failed, when I rambled through the village, to see a row of such worthies, either sitting on a ladder sunning themselves, with their bodies inclined forward and their eyes glancing along the line this way and that, from time to time, with a voluptuous expression, or else leaning against a barn with their hands in their pockets, like caryatides, as if to prop it up. They, being commonly out of doors, heard whatever was in the wind. These are the coarsest mills, in which all gossip is first rudely digested or cracked up before it is emptied into finer and more delicate hoppers within doors. I observed that the vitals of the village were the grocery, the bar-room, the post-office, and the bank; and, as a necessary part of the machinery, they kept a bell, a big gun, and a fire-engine, at convenient places; and the houses were so arranged as to make the most of mankind, in lanes and fronting one another, so that every traveller had to run the gantlet, and every man, woman, and child might get a lick at him. Of course, those who were stationed nearest to the head of the line, where they could most see and be seen, and have the first blow at him, paid the highest prices for their places; and the few straggling inhabitants in the outskirts, where long gaps in the line began to occur, and the traveller could get over walls or turn aside into cow paths, and so escape, paid a very slight ground or window tax. Signs were hung out on all sides to allure him; some to catch him by the appetite, as the tavern and victualling cellar; some by the fancy, as the dry goods store and the jeweller's; and others by the hair or the feet or the skirts, as the barber, the shoemaker, or the tailor. Besides, there was a still more terrible standing invitation to call at every one of these houses, and company expected about these times. For the most part I escaped wonderfully from these dangers, either by proceeding at once boldly and without deliberation to the goal, as is recommended to those who run the gantlet, or by keeping my thoughts on high things, like Orpheus, who, "loudly singing the praises of the gods to his lyre, drowned the voices of the Sirens, and kept out of danger."[1] Sometimes I bolted suddenly, and nobody could tell my whereabouts, for I did not stand much about gracefulness, and never hesitated at a gap in a fence. I was even accustomed to make an irruption into some houses, where I was well entertained, and after learning the kernels and very last sieveful of news, what had subsided, the prospects of war and peace, and whether the world was likely to hold together much longer, I was let out through the rear avenues, and so escaped to the woods again.

It was very pleasant, when I staid late in town, to launch myself into the night, especially if it was dark and tempestuous, and set sail from some bright village parlor or lecture room, with a bag of rye or Indian meal upon my shoulder, for my snug harbor in the woods, having made all tight without and withdrawn under hatches with a merry crew of thoughts, leaving only my outer man at the helm, or even tying up the helm when it was plain sailing. I had many a genial thought by the cabin fire "as I sailed." I was never cast away nor

9. Summer winds in the Mediterranean.

1. Apparently Thoreau's translation from Sir Francis Bacon's fable collection, *De Sapientia Veterum* (1609).

distressed in any weather, though I encountered some severe storms. It is darker in the woods, even in common nights, than most suppose. I frequently had to look up at the opening between the trees above the path in order to learn my route, and, where there was no cart-path, to feel with my feet the faint track which I had worn, or steer by the known relation of particular trees which I felt with my hands, passing between two pines for instance, not more than eighteen inches apart, in the midst of the woods, invariably, in the darkest night. Sometimes, after coming home thus late in a dark and muggy night, when my feet felt the path which my eyes could not see, dreaming and absent-minded all the way, until I was aroused by having to raise my hand to lift the latch, I have not been able to recall a single step of my walk, and I have thought that perhaps my body would find its way home if its master should forsake it, as the hand finds its way to the mouth without assistance. Several times, when a visitor chanced to stay into evening, and it proved a dark night, I was obliged to conduct him to the cart-path in the rear of the house, and then point out to him the direction he was to pursue, and in keeping which he was to be guided rather by his feet than his eyes. One very dark night I directed thus on their way two young men who had been fishing in the pond. They lived about a mile off through the woods, and were quite used to the route. A day or two after one of them told me that they wandered about the greater part of the night, close by their own premises, and did not get home till toward morning, by which time, as there had been several heavy showers in the mean while, and the leaves were very wet, they were drenched to their skins. I have heard of many going astray even in the village streets, when the darkness was so thick that you could cut it with a knife, as the saying is. Some who live in the outskirts, having come to town a-shopping in their wagons, have been obliged to put up for the night; and gentlemen and ladies making a call have gone half a mile out of their way, feeling the sidewalk only with their feet, and not knowing when they turned. It is a surprising and memorable, as well as valuable experience, to be lost in the woods any time. Often in a snow storm, even by day, one will come out upon a well-known road, and yet find it impossible to tell which way leads to the village. Though he knows that he has travelled it a thousand times, he cannot recognize a feature in it, but it is as strange to him as if it were a road in Siberia. By night, of course, the perplexity is infinitely greater. In our most trivial walks, we are constantly, though unconsciously, steering like pilots by certain well-known beacons and headlands, and if we go beyond our usual course we still carry in our minds the bearing of some neighboring cape; and not till we are completely lost, or turned round,—for a man needs only to be turned round once with his eyes shut in this world to be lost,—do we appreciate the vastness and strangeness of Nature. Every man has to learn the points of compass again as often as he awakes, whether from sleep or any abstraction. Not till we are lost, in other words, not till we have lost the world, do we begin to find ourselves, and realize where we are and the infinite extent of our relations.

One afternoon, near the end of the first summer, when I went to the village to get a shoe from the cobbler's, I was seized and put into jail, because, as I have elsewhere related,[2] I did not pay a tax to, or recognize the authority of, the state which buys and sells men, women, and children, like cattle

2. In "Resistance to Civil Government" (1849), posthumously reprinted as "Civil Disobedience" (1866).

at the door of its senate-house. I had gone down to the woods for other purposes. But, wherever a man goes, men will pursue and paw him with their dirty institutions, and, if they can, constrain him to belong to their desperate odd-fellow society.[3] It is true, I might have resisted forcibly with more or less effect, might have run "amok" against society; but I preferred that society should run "amok" against me, it being the desperate party. However, I was released the next day, obtained my mended shoe, and returned to the woods in season to get my dinner of huckleberries on Fair-Haven Hill. I was never molested by any person but those who represented the state. I had no lock nor bolt but for the desk which held my papers, not even a nail to put over my latch or windows. I never fastened my door night or day, though I was to be absent several days; not even when the next fall I spent a fortnight in the woods of Maine. And yet my house was more respected than if it had been surrounded by a file of soldiers. The tired rambler could rest and warm himself by my fire, the literary amuse himself with the few books on my table, or the curious, by opening my closet door, see what was left of my dinner, and what prospect I had of a supper. Yet, though many people of every class came this way to the pond, I suffered no serious inconvenience from these sources, and I never missed any thing but one small book, a volume of Homer, which perhaps was improperly gilded, and this I trust a soldier of our camp has found by this time. I am convinced, that if all men were to live as simply as I then did, thieving and robbery would be unknown. These take place only in communities where some have got more than is sufficient while others have not enough. The Pope's Homers[4] would soon get properly distributed.—

"Nec bella fuerun
Faginus astabat dum scyphus ante dapes."[5]

"Nor wars did men molest,
When only beechen bowls were in request."

"You who govern public affairs, what need have you to employ punishments? Love virtue, and the people will be virtuous. The virtues of a superior man are like the wind; the virtues of a common man are like the grass; the grass, when the wind passes over it, bends."[6]

9. The Ponds

Sometimes, having had a surfeit of human society and gossip, and worn out all my village friends, I rambled still farther westward than I habitually dwell, into yet more unfrequented parts of the town, "to fresh woods and pastures new,"[7] or, while the sun was setting, made my supper of huckleberries and blueberries on Fair Haven Hill, and laid up a store for several days. The fruits do not yield their true flavor to the purchaser of them, nor to him who raises them for the market. There is but one way to obtain it, yet few take that way. If you would know the flavor of huckleberries, ask

3. The Independent Order of Odd Fellows was a philanthropic fraternal organization.
4. Popular translations of Homer's *Iliad* and *Odyssey* by the English poet Alexander Pope (1688–1744).
5. From *Elegies* 3.11.7–8, by the Roman poet Albius Tibullus (54?–18? B.C.E.).
6. Confucius's *Analects* 12.
7. The last line of John Milton's "Lycidas" (1637).

the cow-boy or the partridge. It is a vulgar error to suppose that you have tasted huckleberries who never plucked them. A huckleberry never reaches Boston; they have not been known there since they grew on her three hills. The ambrosial and essential part of the fruit is lost with the bloom which is rubbed off in the market cart, and they become mere provender. As long as Eternal Justice reigns, not one innocent huckleberry can be transported thither from the country's hills.

Occasionally, after my hoeing was done for the day, I joined some impatient companion who had been fishing on the pond since morning, as silent and motionless as a duck or a floating leaf, and, after practising various kinds of philosophy, had concluded commonly, by the time I arrived, that he belonged to the ancient sect of Cœnobites.[8] There was one older man, an excellent fisher and skilled in all kinds of woodcraft, who was pleased to look upon my house as a building erected for the convenience of fishermen; and I was equally pleased when he sat in my doorway to arrange his lines. Once in a while we sat together on the pond, he at one end of the boat, and I at the other; but not many words passed between us, for he had grown deaf in his later years, but he occasionally hummed a psalm, which harmonized well enough with my philosophy. Our intercourse was thus altogether one of unbroken harmony, far more pleasing to remember than if it had been carried on by speech. When, as was commonly the case, I had none to commune with, I used to raise the echoes by striking with a paddle on the side of my boat, filling the surrounding woods with circling and dilating sound, stirring them up as the keeper of a menagerie his wild beasts, until I elicited a growl from every wooded vale and hill-side.

In warm evenings I frequently sat in the boat playing the flute, and saw the perch, which I seemed to have charmed, hovering around me, and the moon travelling over the ribbed bottom, which was strewed with the wrecks of the forest. Formerly I had come to this pond adventurously, from time to time, in dark summer nights, with a companion, and making a fire close to the water's edge, which we thought attracted the fishes, we caught pouts with a bunch of worms strung on a thread; and when we had done, far in the night, threw the burning brands high into the air like skyrockets, which, coming down into the pond, were quenched with a loud hissing, and we were suddenly groping in total darkness. Through this, whistling a tune, we took our way to the haunts of men again. But now I had made my home by the shore.

Sometimes, after staying in a village parlor till the family had all retired, I have returned to the woods, and, partly with a view to the next day's dinner, spent the hours of midnight fishing from a boat by moonlight, serenaded by owls and foxes, and hearing, from time to time, the creaking note of some unknown bird close at hand. These experiences were very memorable and valuable to me,—anchored in forty feet of water, and twenty or thirty rods from the shore, surrounded sometimes by thousands of small perch and shiners, dimpling the surface with their tails in the moonlight, and communicating by a long flaxen line with mysterious nocturnal fishes which had their dwelling forty feet below, or sometimes dragging sixty feet of line about the pond as I drifted in the gentle night breeze, now and then feeling a slight vibration along it, indicative of some life prowling about its extremity,

8. A monastic religious order. Thoreau puns on the name: "See, no bites."

of dull uncertain blundering purpose there, and slow to make up its mind. At length you slowly raise, pulling hand over hand, some horned pout squeaking and squirming to the upper air. It was very queer, especially in dark nights, when your thoughts had wandered to vast and cosmogonal themes in other spheres, to feel this faint jerk, which came to interrupt your dreams and link you to Nature again. It seemed as if I might next cast my line upward into the air, as well as downward into this element which was scarcely more dense. Thus I caught two fishes as it were with one hook.

The scenery of Walden is on a humble scale, and, though very beautiful, does not approach to grandeur, nor can it much concern one who has not long frequented it or lived by its shore; yet this pond is so remarkable for its depth and purity as to merit a particular description. It is a clear and deep green well, half a mile long and a mile and three quarters in circumference, and contains about sixty-one and a half acres; a perennial spring in the midst of pine and oak woods, without any visible inlet or outlet except by the clouds and evaporation. The surrounding hills rise abruptly from the water to the height of forty to eighty feet, though on the south-east and east they attain to about one hundred and one hundred and fifty feet respectively, within a quarter and a third of a mile. They are exclusively woodland. All our Concord waters have two colors at least, one when viewed at a distance, and another, more proper, close at hand. The first depends more on the light, and follows the sky. In clear weather, in summer, they appear blue at a little distance, especially if agitated, and at a great distance all appear alike. In stormy weather they are sometimes of a dark slate color. The sea, however, is said to be blue one day and green another without any perceptible change in the atmosphere. I have seen our river, when, the landscape being covered with snow, both water and ice were almost as green as grass. Some consider blue "to be the color of pure water, whether liquid or solid."[9] But, looking directly down into our waters from a boat, they are seen to be of very different colors. Walden is blue at one time and green at another, even from the same point of view. Lying between the earth and the heavens, it partakes of the color of both. Viewed from a hill-top it reflects the color of the sky, but near at hand it is of a yellowish tint next the shore where you can see the sand, then a light green, which gradually deepens to a uniform dark green in the body of the pond. In some lights, viewed even from a hill-top, it is of a vivid green next the shore. Some have referred this to the reflection of the verdure; but it is equally green there against the railroad sand-bank, and in the spring, before the leaves are expanded, and it may be simply the result of the prevailing blue mixed with the yellow of the sand. Such is the color of its iris. This is that portion, also, where in the spring, the ice being warmed by the heat of the sun reflected from the bottom, and also transmitted through the earth, melts first and forms a narrow canal about the still frozen middle. Like the rest of our waters, when much agitated, in clear weather, so that the surface of the waves may reflect the sky at the right angle, or because there is more light mixed with it, it appears at a little distance of a darker blue than the sky itself; and at such a time, being on its surface, and looking with divided vision, so as to see the reflection, I have discerned a matchless and indescribable light

9. From *Travels through the Alps of Savoy* (1843), by the Scottish scientist James D. Forbes (1809–1868).

blue, such as watered or changeable silks and sword blades suggest, more cerulean than the sky itself, alternating with the original dark green on the opposite sides of the waves, which last appeared but muddy in comparison. It is a vitreous greenish blue, as I remember it, like those patches of the winter sky seen through cloud vistas in the west before sundown. Yet a single glass of its water held up to the light is as colorless as an equal quantity of air. It is well known that a large plate of glass will have a green tint, owing, as the makers say, to its "body," but a small piece of the same will be colorless. How large a body of Walden water would be required to reflect a green tint I have never proved. The water of our river is black or a very dark brown to one looking directly down on it, and, like that of most ponds, imparts to the body of one bathing in it a yellowish tinge; but this water is of such crystalline purity that the body of the bather appears of an alabaster whiteness, still more unnatural, which, as the limbs are magnified and distorted withal, produces a monstrous effect, making fit studies for a Michael Angelo.[1]

The water is so transparent that the bottom can easily be discerned at the depth of twenty-five or thirty feet. Paddling over it, you may see many feet beneath the surface the schools of perch and shiners, perhaps only an inch long, yet the former easily distinguished by their transverse bars, and you think that they must be ascetic fish that find a subsistence there. Once, in the winter, many years ago, when I had been cutting holes through the ice in order to catch pickerel, as I stepped ashore I tossed my axe back on to the ice, but, as if some evil genius had directed it, it slid four or five rods directly into one of the holes, where the water was twenty-five feet deep. Out of curiosity, I lay down on the ice and looked through the hole, until I saw the axe a little on one side, standing on its head, with its helve erect and gently swaying to and fro with the pulse of the pond; and there it might have stood erect and swaying till in the course of time the handle rotted off, if I had not disturbed it. Making another hole directly over it with an ice chisel which I had, and cutting down the longest birch which I could find in the neighborhood with my knife, I made a slip-noose, which I attached to its end, and, letting it down carefully, passed it over the knob of the handle, and drew it by a line along the birch, and so pulled the axe out again.

The shore is composed of a belt of smooth rounded white stones like paving stones, excepting one or two short sand beaches, and is so steep that in many places a single leap will carry you into water over your head; and were it not for its remarkable transparency, that would be the last to be seen of its bottom till it rose on the opposite side. Some think it is bottomless. It is nowhere muddy, and a casual observer would say that there were no weeds at all in it; and of noticeable plants, except in the little meadows recently overflowed, which do not properly belong to it, a closer scrutiny does not detect a flag nor a bulrush, nor even a lily, yellow or white, but only a few small heart-leaves and potamogetons,[2] and perhaps a water-target or two; all which however a bather might not perceive; and these plants are clean and bright like the element they grow in. The stones extend a rod or two into the water, and then the bottom is pure sand, except in the deepest parts, where there is usually a little sediment, probably from the decay of the leaves which have been

1. Michelangelo Buonarroti (1475–1564), Italian artist, sculptor, and architect.

2. Pondweeds.

wafted on to it so many successive falls, and a bright green weed is brought up on anchors even in midwinter.

We have one other pond just like this, White Pond in Nine Acre Corner, about two and a half miles westerly; but, though I am acquainted with most of the ponds within a dozen miles of this centre, I do not know a third of this pure and well-like character. Successive nations perchance have drank at, admired, and fathomed it, and passed away, and still its water is green and pellucid as ever. Not an intermitting spring! Perhaps on that spring morning when Adam and Eve were driven out of Eden Walden Pond was already in existence, and even then breaking up in a gentle spring rain accompanied with mist and a southerly wind, and covered with myriads of ducks and geese, which had not heard of the fall, when still such pure lakes sufficed them. Even then it had commenced to rise and fall, and had clarified its waters and colored them of the hue they now wear, and obtained a patent of heaven to be the only Walden Pond in the world and distiller of celestial dews. Who knows in how many unremembered nations' literatures this has been the Castalian Fountain?[3] or what nymphs presided over it in the Golden Age? It is a gem of the first water which Concord wears in her coronet.

Yet perchance the first who came to this well have left some trace of their footsteps. I have been surprised to detect encircling the pond, even where a thick wood has just been cut down on the shore, a narrow shelf-like path in the steep hill-side, alternately rising and falling, approaching and receding from the water's edge, as old probably as the race of man here, worn by the feet of aboriginal hunters, and still from time to time unwittingly trodden by the present occupants of the land. This is particularly distinct to one standing on the middle of the pond in winter, just after a light snow has fallen, appearing as a clear undulating white line, unobscured by weeds and twigs, and very obvious a quarter of a mile off in many places where in summer it is hardly distinguishable close at hand. The snow reprints it, as it were, in clear white type alto-relievo.[4] The ornamented grounds of villas which will one day be built here may still preserve some trace of this.

The pond rises and falls, but whether regularly or not, and within what period, nobody knows, though, as usual, many pretend to know. It is commonly higher in the winter and lower in the summer, though not corresponding to the general wet and dryness. I can remember when it was a foot or two lower, and also when it was at least five feet higher, than when I lived by it. There is a narrow sandbar running into it, with very deep water on one side, on which I helped boil a kettle of chowder, some six rods from the main shore, about the year 1824, which it has not been possible to do for twenty-five years; and on the other hand, my friends used to listen with incredulity when I told them, that a few years later I was accustomed to fish from a boat in a secluded cove in the woods, fifteen rods from the only shore they knew, which place was long since converted into a meadow. But the pond has risen steadily for two years, and now, in the summer of '52, is just five feet higher than when I lived there, or as high as it was thirty years ago, and fishing goes on again in the meadow. This makes a difference of level, at the outside, of six or seven feet; and yet the water shed by the surrounding hills is insignificant in amount, and this over-

3. In Greek mythology, a spring on Mount Parnassus, sacred to Apollo and the Muses.

4. High relief (Italian); sculptural term describing a figure raised from a background.

flow must be referred to causes which affect the deep springs. This same summer the pond has begun to fall again. It is remarkable that this fluctuation, whether periodical or not, appears thus to require many years for its accomplishment. I have observed one rise and a part of two falls, and I expect that a dozen or fifteen years hence the water will again be as low as I have ever known it. Flint's Pond, a mile eastward, allowing for the disturbance occasioned by its inlets and outlets, and the smaller intermediate ponds also, sympathize with Walden, and recently attained their greatest height at the same time with the latter. The same is true, as far as my observation goes, of White Pond.

This rise and fall of Walden at long intervals serves this use at least; the water standing at this great height for a year or more, though it makes it difficult to walk round it, kills the shrubs and trees which have sprung up about its edge since the last rise, pitch-pines, birches, alders, aspens, and others, and, falling again, leaves an unobstructed shore; for, unlike many ponds and all waters which are subject to a daily tide, its shore is cleanest when the water is lowest. On the side of the pond next my house, a row of pitch pines fifteen feet high has been killed and tipped over as if by a lever, and thus a stop put to their encroachments; and their size indicates how many years have elapsed since the last rise to this height. By this fluctuation the pond asserts its title to a shore, and thus the *shore* is *shorn*, and the trees cannot hold it by right of possession. These are the lips of the lake on which no beard grows. It licks its chaps from time to time. When the water is at its height, the alders, willows, and maples send forth a mass of fibrous red roots several feet long from all sides of their stems in the water, and to the height of three or four feet from the ground, in the effort to maintain themselves; and I have known the high-blueberry bushes about the shore, which commonly produce no fruit, bear an abundant crop under these circumstances.

Some have been puzzled to tell how the shore became so regularly paved. My townsmen have all heard the tradition, the oldest people tell me that they heard it in their youth, that anciently the Indians were holding a pow-wow upon a hill here, which rose as high into the heavens as the pond now sinks deep into the earth, and they used much profanity, as the story goes, though this vice is one of which the Indians were never guilty, and while they were thus engaged the hill shook and suddenly sank, and only one old squaw, named Walden, escaped, and from her the pond was named. It has been conjectured that when the hill shook these stones rolled down its side and became the present shore. It is very certain, at any rate, that once there was no pond here, and now there is one; and this Indian fable does not in any respect conflict with the account of that ancient settler whom I have mentioned, who remembers so well when he first came here with his divining rod, saw a thin vapor rising from the sward, and the hazel pointed steadily downward, and he concluded to dig a well here. As for the stones, many still think that they are hardly to be accounted for by the action of the waves on these hills; but I observe that the surrounding hills are remarkably full of the same kind of stones, so that they have been obliged to pile them up in walls on both sides of the railroad cut nearest the pond; and, moreover, there are most stones where the shore is most abrupt; so that, unfortunately, it is no longer a mystery to me. I detect the paver.[5] If the name was

5. Glacial movement.

not derived from that of some English locality,—Saffron Walden, for instance,—one might suppose that it was called, originally, *Walled-in* Pond.

The pond was my well ready dug. For four months in the year its water is as cold as it is pure at all times; and I think that it is then as good as any, if not the best, in the town. In the winter, all water which is exposed to the air is colder than springs and wells which are protected from it. The temperature of the pond water which had stood in the room where I sat from five o'clock in the afternoon till noon the next day, the sixth of March, 1846, the thermometer having been up to 65° or 70° some of the time, owing partly to the sun on the roof, was 42°, or one degree colder than the water of one of the coldest wells in the village just drawn. The temperature of the Boiling Spring the same day was 45°, or the warmest of any water tried, though it is the coldest that I know of in summer, when, beside, shallow and stagnant surface water is not mingled with it. Moreover, in summer, Walden never becomes so warm as most water which is exposed to the sun, on account of its depth. In the warmest weather I usually placed a pailful in my cellar, where it became cool in the night, and remained so during the day; though I also resorted to a spring in the neighborhood. It was as good when a week old as the day it was dipped, and had no taste of the pump. Whoever camps for a week in summer by the shore of a pond, needs only bury a pail of water a few feet deep in the shade of his camp to be independent of the luxury of ice.

There have been caught in Walden, pickerel, one weighing seven pounds, to say nothing of another which carried off a reel with great velocity, which the fisherman safely set down at eight pounds because he did not see him, perch and pouts, some of each weighing over two pounds, shiners, chivins or roach, (*Leuciscus pulchellus*,) a very few breams, (*Promotis obesus*,) and a couple of eels, one weighing four pounds,—I am thus particular because the weight of a fish is commonly its only title to fame, and these are the only eels I have heard of here;—also, I have a faint recollection of a little fish some five inches long, with silvery sides and a greenish back, somewhat dace[6]-like in its character, which I mention here chiefly to link my facts to fable. Nevertheless, this pond is not very fertile in fish. Its pickerel, though not abundant, are its chief boast. I have seen at one time lying on the ice pickerel of at least three different kinds; a long and shallow one, steel-colored, most like those caught in the river; a bright golden kind, with greenish reflections and remarkably deep, which is the most common here; and another, golden-colored, and shaped like the last, but peppered on the sides with small dark brown or black spots, intermixed with a few faint blood-red ones, very much like a trout. The specific name *reticulatus* would not apply to this; it should be *guttatus*[7] rather. These are all very firm fish, and weigh more than their size promises. The shiners, pouts, and perch also, and indeed all the fishes which inhabit this pond, are much cleaner, handsomer, and firmer fleshed than those in the river and most other ponds, as the water is purer, and they can easily be distinguished from them. Probably many ichthyologists would make new varieties of some of them. There are also a clean race of frogs and tortoises, and a few muscles in it; muskrats and minks leave their traces about it, and occasionally a travelling mud-turtle visits it. Sometimes, when I pushed off my boat in the morning, I disturbed a great mud-turtle which had secreted

6. Small freshwater fish.

7. Speckled. "*Reticulatus*": netlike.

himself under the boat in the night. Ducks and geese frequent it in the spring and fall, the white-bellied swallows (*Hirundo bicolor*) skim over it, kingfishers dart away from its coves, and the peetweets (*Totanus macularius*) "teter" along its stony shores all summer. I have sometimes disturbed a fishhawk sitting on a white-pine over the water; but I doubt if it is ever profaned by the wing of a gull, like Fair Haven. At most, it tolerates one annual loon. These are all the animals of consequence which frequent it now.

You may see from a boat, in calm weather, near the sandy eastern shore, where the water is eight or ten feet deep, and also in some other parts of the pond, some circular heaps half a dozen feet in diameter by a foot in height, consisting of small stones less than a hen's egg in size, where all around is bare sand. At first you wonder if the Indians could have formed them on the ice for any purpose, and so, when the ice melted, they sank to the bottom; but they are too regular and some of them plainly too fresh for that. They are similar to those found in rivers; but as there are no suckers nor lampreys here, I know not by what fish they could be made. Perhaps they are the nests of the chivin.[8] These lend a pleasing mystery to the bottom.

The shore is irregular enough not to be monotonous. I have in my mind's eye the western indented with deep bays, the bolder northern, and the beautifully scolloped southern shore, where successive capes overlap each other and suggest unexplored coves between. The forest has never so good a setting, nor is so distinctly beautiful, as when seen from the middle of a small lake amid hills which rise from the water's edge; for the water in which it is reflected not only makes the best foreground in such a case, but, with its winding shore, the most natural and agreeable boundary to it. There is no rawness nor imperfection in its edge there, as where the axe has cleared a part, or a cultivated field abuts on it. The trees have ample room to expand on the water side, and each sends forth its most vigorous branch in that direction. There Nature has woven a natural selvage, and the eye rises by just gradations from the low shrubs of the shore to the highest trees. There are few traces of man's hand to be seen. The water laves the shore as it did a thousand years ago.

A lake is the landscape's most beautiful and expressive feature. It is earth's eye; looking into which the beholder measures the depth of his own nature. The fluviatile trees next the shore are the slender eyelashes which fringe it, and the wooded hills and cliffs around are its overhanging brows.

Standing on the smooth sandy beach at the east end of the pond, in a calm September afternoon, when a slight haze makes the opposite shore line indistinct, I have seen whence came the expression, "the glassy surface of a lake." When you invert your head, it looks like a thread of finest gossamer stretched across the valley, and gleaming against the distant pine woods, separating one stratum of the atmosphere from another. You would think that you could walk dry under it to the opposite hills, and that the swallows which skim over might perch on it. Indeed, they sometimes dive below the line, as it were by mistake, and are undeceived. As you look over the pond westward you are obliged to employ both your hands to defend your eyes against the reflected as well as the true sun, for they are equally bright; and if, between the two, you survey its surface critically, it is literally as smooth

8. The chivin is a nest-building fish.

as glass, except where the skater insects, at equal intervals scattered over its whole extent, by their motions in the sun produce the finest imaginable sparkle on it, or, perchance, a duck plumes itself, or, as I have said, a swallow skims so low as to touch it. It may be that in the distance a fish describes an arc of three or four feet in the air, and there is one bright flash where it emerges, and another where it strikes the water; sometimes the whole silvery arc is revealed; or here and there, perhaps, is a thistle-down floating on its surface, which the fishes dart at and so dimple it again. It is like molten glass cooled but not congealed, and the few motes in it are pure and beautiful like the imperfections in glass. You may often detect a yet smoother and darker water, separated from the rest as if by an invisible cobweb, boom of the water nymphs, resting on it. From a hill-top you can see a fish leap in almost any part; for not a pickerel or shiner picks an insect from this smooth surface but it manifestly disturbs the equilibrium of the whole lake. It is wonderful with what elaborateness this simple fact is advertised,—this piscine murder will out,—and from my distant perch I distinguish the circling undulations when they are half a dozen rods in diameter. You can even detect a water-bug (*Gyrinus*) ceaselessly progressing over the smooth surface a quarter of a mile off; for they furrow the water slightly, making a conspicuous ripple bounded by two diverging lines, but the skaters glide over it without rippling it perceptibly. When the surface is considerably agitated there are no skaters nor water-bugs on it, but apparently, in calm days, they leave their havens and adventurously glide forth from the shore by short impulses till they completely cover it. It is a soothing employment, on one of those fine days in the fall when all the warmth of the sun is fully appreciated, to sit on a stump on such a height as this, overlooking the pond, and study the dimpling circles which are incessantly inscribed on its otherwise invisible surface amid the reflected skies and trees. Over this great expanse there is no disturbance but it is thus at once gently smoothed away and assuaged, as, when a vase of water is jarred, the trembling circles seek the shore and all is smooth again. Not a fish can leap or an insect fall on the pond but it is thus reported in circling dimples, in lines of beauty, as it were the constant welling up of its fountain, the gentle pulsing of its life, the heaving of its breast. The thrills of joy and thrills of pain are undistinguishable. How peaceful the phenomena of the lake! Again the works of man shine as in the spring. Ay, every leaf and twig and stone and cobweb sparkles now at mid-afternoon as when covered with dew in a spring morning. Every motion of an oar or an insect produces a flash of light; and if an oar falls, how sweet the echo!

In such a day, in September or October, Walden is a perfect forest mirror, set round with stones as precious to my eye as if fewer or rarer. Nothing so fair, so pure, and at the same time so large, as a lake, perchance, lies on the surface of the earth. Sky water. It needs no fence. Nations come and go without defiling it. It is a mirror which no stone can crack, whose quicksilver will never wear off, whose gilding Nature continually repairs; no storms, no dust, can dim its surface ever fresh;—a mirror in which all impurity presented to it sinks, swept and dusted by the sun's hazy brush,—this the light dust-cloth,—which retains no breath that is breathed on it, but sends its own to float as clouds high above its surface, and be reflected in its bosom still.

A field of water betrays the spirit that is in the air. It is continually receiving new life and motion from above. It is intermediate in its nature between land and sky. On land only the grass and trees wave, but the water itself is rippled by the wind. I see where the breeze dashes across it by the streaks or flakes of light. It is remarkable that we can look down on its surface. We shall, perhaps, look down thus on the surface of air at length, and mark where a still subtler spirit sweeps over it.

The skaters and water-bugs finally disappear in the latter part of October, when the severe frosts have come; and then and in November, usually, in a calm day, there is absolutely nothing to ripple the surface. One November afternoon, in the calm at the end of a rain storm of several days' duration, when the sky was still completely overcast and the air was full of mist, I observed that the pond was remarkably smooth, so that it was difficult to distinguish its surface; though it no longer reflected the bright tints of October, but the sombre November colors of the surrounding hills. Though I passed over it as gently as possible, the slight undulations produced by my boat extended almost as far as I could see, and gave a ribbed appearance to the reflections. But, as I was looking over the surface, I saw here and there at a distance a faint glimmer, as if some skater insects which had escaped the frosts might be collected there, or, perchance, the surface, being so smooth, betrayed where a spring welled up from the bottom. Paddling gently to one of these places, I was surprised to find myself surrounded by myriads of small perch, about five inches long, of a rich bronze color in the green water, sporting there and constantly rising to the surface and dimpling it, sometimes leaving bubbles on it. In such transparent and seemingly bottomless water, reflecting the clouds, I seemed to be floating through the air as in a balloon, and their swimming impressed me as a kind of flight or hovering, as if they were a compact flock of birds passing just beneath my level on the right or left, their fins, like sails, set all around them. There were many such schools in the pond, apparently improving the short season before winter would draw an icy shutter over their broad skylight, sometimes giving to the surface an appearance as if a slight breeze struck it, or a few rain-drops fell there. When I approached carelessly and alarmed them, they made a sudden plash and rippling with their tails, as if one had struck the water with a brushy bough, and instantly took refuge in the depths. At length the wind rose, the mist increased, and the waves began to run, and the perch leaped much higher than before, half out of water, a hundred black points, three inches long, at once above the surface. Even as late as the fifth of December, one year, I saw some dimples on the surface, and thinking it was going to rain hard immediately, the air being full of mist, I made haste to take my place at the oars and row homeward; already the rain seemed rapidly increasing, though I felt none on my cheek, and I anticipated a thorough soaking. But suddenly the dimples ceased, for they were produced by the perch, which the noise of my oars had scared into the depths, and I saw their schools dimly disappearing; so I spent a dry afternoon after all.

An old man who used to frequent this pond nearly sixty years ago, when it was dark with surrounding forests, tells me that in those days he sometimes saw it all alive with ducks and other water fowl, and that there were many eagles about it. He came here a-fishing, and used an old log canoe which he found on the shore. It was made of two white-pine logs dug out and pinned together, and was cut off square at the ends. It was very clumsy, but lasted a great many years before it became water-logged and perhaps sank to the bottom. He did not know whose it was; it belonged to the pond. He used to make a cable for his anchor of strips of hickory bark tied together. An old man, a potter, who lived by the pond before the Revolution, told him once that there was an iron chest at the bottom, and that he had seen it. Sometimes it would come floating up to the shore; but when you went toward it, it would go back into deep water and disappear. I was pleased to hear of the old log canoe, which took the place of an Indian one of the same material but more graceful construction, which perchance had first been a tree on the bank, and then, as it were, fell into the water, to float there for a generation, the most proper vessel for the lake. I remember that when I first looked into these depths there were many large trunks to be seen indistinctly lying on the bottom, which had either been blown over formerly, or left on the ice at the last cutting, when wood was cheaper; but now they have mostly disappeared.

When I first paddled a boat on Walden, it was completely surrounded by thick and lofty pine and oak woods, and in some of its coves grape vines had run over the trees next the water and formed bowers under which a boat could pass. The hills which form its shores are so steep, and the woods on them were then so high, that, as you looked down from the west end, it had the appearance of an amphitheatre for some kind of sylvan spectacle. I have spent many an hour, when I was younger, floating over its surface as the zephyr[9] willed, having paddled my boat to the middle, and lying on my back across the seats, in a summer forenoon, dreaming awake, until I was aroused by the boat touching the sand, and I arose to see what shore my fates had impelled me to; days when idleness was the most attractive and productive industry. Many a forenoon have I stolen away, preferring to spend thus the most valued part of the day; for I was rich, if not in money, in sunny hours and summer days, and spent them lavishly; nor do I regret that I did not waste more of them in the workshop or the teacher's desk. But since I left those shores the woodchoppers have still further laid them waste, and now for many a year there will be no more rambling through the aisles of the wood, with occasional vistas through which you see the water. My Muse may be excused if she is silent henceforth. How can you expect the birds to sing when their groves are cut down?

Now the trunks of trees on the bottom, and the old log canoe, and the dark surrounding woods, are gone, and the villagers, who scarcely know where it lies, instead of going to the pond to bathe or drink, are thinking to bring its water, which should be as sacred as the Ganges[1] at least, to the village in a pipe, to wash their dishes with!—to earn their Walden by the turning of a cock or drawing of a plug! That devilish Iron Horse, whose ear-rending neigh is heard throughout the town, has muddied the Boiling Spring with his foot, and he it is that has browsed off all the woods on Walden shore; that Trojan horse, with a thousand men in his belly, introduced by mercenary Greeks![2] Where is the country's champion, the Moore of Moore Hall, to meet him at the Deep Cut[3] and thrust an avenging lance between the ribs of the bloated pest?

9. The mild west wind.

1. River in northern India, regarded as sacred by the Hindus.

2. The stratagem by which the Greeks entered Troy.

3. A place near Walden Pond where the earth had been cut away for railroad tracks. "Moore of Moore Hall": from "The Dragon of Wantley" in Thomas Percy's *Reliques of Ancient English Poetry* (1765): "But More of More-Hall, with nothing at all, / He slew the dragon of Wantley."

Nevertheless, of all the characters I have known, perhaps Walden wears best, and best preserves its purity. Many men have been likened to it, but few deserve that honor. Though the woodchoppers have laid bare first this shore and then that, and the Irish have built their sties by it, and the railroad has infringed on its border, and the ice-men have skimmed it once, it is itself unchanged, the same water which my youthful eyes fell on; all the change is in me. It has not acquired one permanent wrinkle after all its ripples. It is perennially young, and I may stand and see a swallow dip apparently to pick an insect from its surface as of yore. It struck me again to-night, as if I had not seen it almost daily for more than twenty years,—Why, here is Walden, the same woodland lake that I discovered so many years ago; where a forest was cut down last winter another is springing up by its shore as lustily as ever; the same thought is welling up to its surface that was then; it is the same liquid joy and happiness to itself and its Maker, ay, and it *may* be to me. It is the work of a brave man surely, in whom there was no guile! He rounded this water with his hand, deepened and clarified it in his thought, and in his will bequeathed it to Concord. I see by its face that it is visited by the same reflection; and I can almost say, Walden, is it you?

It is no dream of mine,
To ornament a line;
I cannot come nearer to God and Heaven
Than I live to Walden even.
I am its stony shore,
And the breeze that passes o'er;
In the hollow of my hand
Are its water and its sand,
And its deepest resort
Lies high in my thought.

The cars never pause to look at it; yet I fancy that the engineers and firemen and brakemen, and those passengers who have a season ticket and see it often, are better men for the sight. The engineer does not forget at night, or his nature does not, that he has beheld this vision of serenity and purity once at least during the day. Though seen but once, it helps to wash out State-street and the engine's soot. One proposes that it be called "God's Drop."

I have said that Walden has no visible inlet nor outlet, but it is on the one hand distantly and indirectly related to Flint's Pond, which is more elevated, by a chain of small ponds coming from that quarter, and on the other directly and manifestly to Concord River, which is lower, by a similar chain of ponds through which in some other geological period it may have flowed, and by a little digging, which God forbid, it can be made to flow thither again. If by living thus reserved and austere, like a hermit in the woods, so long, it has acquired such wonderful purity, who would not regret that the comparatively impure waters of Flint's Pond should be mingled with it, or itself should ever go to waste its sweetness in the ocean wave?

Flint's, or Sandy Pond, in Lincoln, our greatest lake and inland sea, lies about a mile east of Walden. It is much larger, being said to contain one hundred and ninety-seven acres, and is more fertile in fish, but it is comparatively shallow, and not remarkably pure. A walk through the woods thither was often my recreation. It was worth the while, if only to feel the wind blow on your cheek freely, and see the waves run, and remember the life of mariners. I went a-chestnutting there in the fall, on windy days, when the nuts were dropping into the water and were washed to my feet; and one day, as I crept along its sedgy shore, the fresh spray blowing in my face, I came upon the mouldering wreck of a boat, the sides gone, and hardly more than the impression of its flat bottom left amid the rushes; yet its model was sharply defined, as if it were a large decayed pad, with its veins. It was as impressive a wreck as one could imagine on the sea-shore, and had as good a moral. It is by this time mere vegetable mould and undistinguishable pond shore, through which rushes and flags have pushed up. I used to admire the ripple marks on the sandy bottom, at the north end of this pond, made firm and hard to the feet of the wader by the pressure of the water, and the rushes which grew in Indian file, in waving lines, corresponding to these marks, rank behind rank, as if the waves had planted them. There also I have found, in considerable quantities, curious balls, composed apparently of fine grass or roots, of pipewort perhaps, from half an inch to four inches in diameter, and perfectly spherical. These wash back and forth in shallow water on a sandy bottom, and are sometimes cast on the shore. They are either solid grass, or have a little sand in the middle. At first you would say that they were formed by the action of the waves, like a pebble; yet the smallest are made of equally coarse materials, half an inch long, and they are produced only at one season of the year. Moreover, the waves, I suspect, do not so much construct as wear down a material which has already acquired consistency. They preserve their form when dry for an indefinite period.

Flint's Pond! Such is the poverty of our nomenclature. What right had the unclean and stupid farmer, whose farm abutted on this sky water, whose shores he has ruthlessly laid bare, to give his name to it? Some skin-flint, who loved better the reflecting surface of a dollar, or a bright cent, in which he could see his own brazen face; who regarded even the wild ducks which settled in it as trespassers; his fingers grown into crooked and horny talons from the long habit of grasping harpy-like;[4]—so it is not named for me. I go not there to see him nor to hear of him; who never *saw* it, who never bathed in it, who never loved it, who never protected it, who never spoke a good word for it, nor thanked God that he had made it. Rather let it be named from the fishes that swim in it, the wild fowl or quadrupeds which frequent it, the wild flowers which grow by its shores, or some wild man or child the thread of whose history is interwoven with its own; not from him who could show no title to it but the deed which a like-minded neighbor or legislature gave him,—him who thought only of its money value; whose presence perchance cursed all the shore; who exhausted the land around it, and would fain have exhausted the waters within it; who regretted only that it was not English hay or cranberry meadow,—there was nothing to redeem it, forsooth, in his eyes,—and would have drained and sold it for the mud at its bottom. It did not turn his mill, and it was no *privilege* to him to behold it. I respect not his labors, his farm where every thing has its price; who would carry the landscape, who would carry his God, to market, if he could get any thing for him;

4. In Greek mythology, the Harpies were monsters with women's heads and birds' bodies who seized and carried off the soul at the moment of death.

who goes to market *for* his god as it is; on whose farm nothing grows free, whose fields bear no crops, whose meadows no flowers, whose trees no fruits, but dollars; who loves not the beauty of his fruits, whose fruits are not ripe for him till they are turned to dollars. Give me the poverty that enjoys true wealth. Farmers are respectable and interesting to me in proportion as they are poor,—poor farmers. A model farm! where the house stands like a fungus in a muck-heap, chambers for men, horses, oxen, and swine, cleansed and uncleansed, all contiguous to one another! Stocked with men! A great grease-spot, redolent of manures and buttermilk! Under a high state of cultivation, being manured with the hearts and brains of men! As if you were to raise your potatoes in the church-yard! Such is a model farm.

No, no; if the fairest features of the landscape are to be named after men, let them be the noblest and worthiest men alone. Let our lakes receive as true names at least as the Icarian Sea, where "still the shore" a "brave attempt resounds."[5]

Goose Pond, of small extent, is on my way to Flint's; Fair-Haven, an expansion of Concord River, said to contain some seventy acres, is a mile southwest; and White Pond, of about forty acres, is a mile and a half beyond Fair-Haven. This is my lake country.[6] These, with Concord River, are my water privileges; and night and day, year in year out, they grind such grist as I carry to them.

Since the woodcutters, and the railroad, and I myself have profaned Walden, perhaps the most attractive, if not the most beautiful, of all our lakes, the gem of the woods, is White Pond;—a poor name from its commonness, whether derived from the remarkable purity of its waters or the color of its sands. In these as in other respects, however, it is a lesser twin of Walden. They are so much alike that you would say they must be connected under ground. It has the same stony shore, and its waters are of the same hue. As at Walden, in sultry dog-day weather, looking down through the woods on some of its bays which are not so deep but that the reflection from the bottom tinges them, its waters are of a misty bluish-green or glaucous color. Many years since I used to go there to collect the sand by cart-loads, to make sand-paper with, and I have continued to visit it ever since. One who frequents it proposes to call it Virid Lake.[7] Perhaps it might be called Yellow-Pine Lake, from the following circumstance. About fifteen years ago you could see the top of a pitch-pine, of the kind called yellow-pine hereabouts, though it is not a distinct species, projecting above the surface in deep water, many rods from the shore. It was even supposed by some that the pond had sunk, and this was one of the primitive forests that formerly stood there. I find that even so long ago as 1792, in a "Topographical Description of the Town of Concord," by one of its citizens, in the Collections of the Massachusetts Historical Society, the author, after speaking of Walden and White Ponds, adds: "In the middle of the latter may be seen, when the water is very low, a tree which appears as if it grew in the place where it now stands, although the roots are fifty feet below the surface of

5. From "Icarus" by the Scottish poet William Drummond of Hawthornden (1585–1649). In Greek mythology, Icarus drowned in the Aegean Sea after flying too near the sun with the waxen wings made by his father, Daedalus.

6. A New England equivalent of the English Lake District associated with Wordsworth and other Romantic-era writers and artists.

7. Green Lake.

the water; the top of this tree is broken off, and at that place measures fourteen inches in diameter."[8] In the spring of '49 I talked with the man who lives nearest the pond in Sudbury, who told me that it was he who got out this tree ten or fifteen years before. As near as he could remember, it stood twelve or fifteen rods from the shore, where the water was thirty or forty feet deep. It was in the winter, and he had been getting out ice in the forenoon, and had resolved that in the afternoon, with the aid of his neighbors, he would take out the old yellow-pine. He sawed a channel in the ice toward the shore, and hauled it over and along and out on to the ice with oxen; but, before he had gone far in his work, he was surprised to find that it was wrong end upward, with the stumps of the branches pointing down, and the small end firmly fastened in the sandy bottom. It was about a foot in diameter at the big end, and he had expected to get a good saw-log, but it was so rotten as to be fit only for fuel, if for that. He had some of it in his shed then. There were marks of an axe and of woodpeckers on the but. He thought that it might have been a dead tree on the shore, but was finally blown over into the pond, and after the top had become waterlogged, while the but-end was still dry and light, had drifted out and sunk wrong end up. His father, eighty years old, could not remember when it was not there. Several pretty large logs may still be seen lying on the bottom, where, owing to the undulation of the surface, they look like huge water snakes in motion.

This pond has rarely been profaned by a boat, for there is little in it to tempt a fisherman. Instead of the white lily, which requires mud, or the common sweet flag, the blue flag (*Iris versicolor*) grows thinly in the pure water, rising from the stony bottom all around the shore, where it is visited by humming birds in June, and the color both of its bluish blades and its flowers, and especially their reflections, are in singular harmony with the glaucous water.

White Pond and Walden are great crystals on the surface of the earth, Lakes of Light. If they were permanently congealed, and small enough to be clutched, they would, perchance, be carried off by slaves, like precious stones, to adorn the heads of emperors; but being liquid, and ample, and secured to us and our successors forever, we disregard them, and run after the diamond of Kohinoor.[9] They are too pure to have a market value; they contain no muck. How much more beautiful than our lives, how much more transparent than our characters, are they! We never learned meanness of them. How much fairer than the pool before the farmer's door, in which his ducks swim! Hither the clean wild ducks come. Nature has no human inhabitant who appreciates her. The birds with their plumage and their notes are in harmony with the flowers, but what youth or maiden conspires with the wild luxuriant beauty of Nature? She flourishes most alone, far from the towns where they reside. Talk of heaven! ye disgrace earth.

10. Baker Farm

Sometimes I rambled to pine groves, standing like temples, or like fleets at sea, full-rigged, with wavy boughs, and rippling with light, so soft and green

8. From "A Topological Description of Concord," a paper presented by William Jones (1772–1813), a student at Harvard, and published in the *Massachusetts Historical Society Collections* (1792).

9. An enormous diamond found in India during the 18th century and added to the British crown jewels in 1850.

and shady that the Druids[1] would have forsaken their oaks to worship in them; or to the cedar wood beyond Flint's Pond, where the trees, covered with hoary blue berries, spiring higher and higher, are fit to stand before Valhalla,[2] and the creeping juniper covers the ground with wreaths full of fruit; or to swamps where the usnea lichen hangs in festoons from the black-spruce trees, and toad-stools, round tables of the swamp gods, cover the ground, and more beautiful fungi adorn the stumps, like butterflies or shells, vegetable winkles; where the swamp-pink and dogwood grow, the red alder-berry glows like eyes of imps, the waxwork grooves and crushes the hardest woods in its folds, and the wild-holly berries make the beholder forget his home with their beauty, and he is dazzled and tempted by nameless other wild forbidden fruits, too fair for mortal taste. Instead of calling on some scholar, I paid many a visit to particular trees, of kinds which are rare in this neighborhood, standing far away in the middle of some pasture, or in the depths of a wood or swamp, or on a hill-top; such as the black-birch, of which we have some handsome specimens two feet in diameter; its cousin the yellow-birch, with its loose golden vest, perfumed like the first; the beech, which has so neat a bole[3] and beautifully lichen-painted, perfect in all its details, of which, excepting scattered specimens, I know but one small grove of sizeable trees left in the township, supposed by some to have been planted by the pigeons that were once baited with beech nuts near by; it is worth the while to see the silver grain sparkle when you split this wood; the bass; the hornbeam; the *Celtis occidentalis*, or false elm, of which we have but one well-grown; some taller mast of a pine, a shingle tree, or a more perfect hemlock than usual, standing like a pagoda in the midst of the woods; and many others I could mention. These were the shrines I visited both summer and winter.

Once it chanced that I stood in the very abutment of a rainbow's arch, which filled the lower stratum of the atmosphere, tinging the grass and leaves around, and dazzling me as if I looked through colored crystal. It was a lake of rainbow light, in which, for a short while, I lived like a dolphin. If it had lasted longer it might have tinged my employments and life. As I walked on the railroad causeway, I used to wonder at the halo of light around my shadow, and would fain fancy myself one of the elect.[4] One who visited me declared that the shadows of some Irishmen before him had no halo about them, that it was only natives that were so distinguished. Benvenuto Cellini tells us in his memoirs, that after a certain terrible dream or vision which he had during his confinement in the castle of St. Angelo, a resplendent light appeared over the shadow of his head at morning and evening, whether he was in Italy or France, and it was particularly conspicuous when the grass was moist with dew.[5] This was probably the same phenomenon to which I have referred, which is especially observed in the morning, but also at other times, and even by moonlight. Though a constant one, it is not commonly noticed, and, in the case of an excitable imagination like Cellini's, it would be basis enough for superstition. Beside, he tells us that he showed it to very few. But are they not indeed distinguished who are conscious that they are regarded at all?

1. Priests of ancient Gaul and Britain to whom the oak was sacred.
2. In Norse mythology, the gigantic hall to which souls of slain heroes go.
3. Trunk.
4. According to Calvinistic theology, the "elect" were those predestined for salvation.
5. In ch. 26 of the *Autobiography* (1558–1662) of Benvenuto Cellini (1500–1571), Italian sculptor and goldsmith.

I set out one afternoon to go a-fishing to Fair-Haven, through the woods, to eke out my scanty fare of vegetables. My way led through Pleasant Meadow, an adjunct of the Baker Farm, that retreat of which a poet has since sung, beginning,—

"Thy entry is a pleasant field,
Which some mossy fruit trees yield
Partly to a ruddy brook,
By gliding musquash undertook,
And mercurial trout,
Darting about."[6]

I thought of living there before I went to Walden. I "hooked" the apples, leaped the brook, and scared the musquash[7] and the trout. It was one of those afternoons which seem indefinitely long before one, in which many events may happen, a large portion of our natural life, though it was already half spent when I started. By the way there came up a shower, which compelled me to stand half an hour under a pine, piling boughs over my head, and wearing my handkerchief for a shed; and when at length I had made one cast over the pickerel-weed, standing up to my middle in water, I found myself suddenly in the shadow of a cloud, and the thunder began to rumble with such emphasis that I could do no more than listen to it. The gods must be proud, thought I, with such forked flashes to rout a poor unarmed fisherman. So I made haste for shelter to the nearest hut, which stood half a mile from any road, but so much the nearer to the pond, and had long been uninhabited:—

"And here a poet builded,
In the completed years,
For behold a trivial cabin
That to destruction steers."

So the Muse fables. But therein, as I found, dwelt now John Field, an Irishman, and his wife, and several children, from the broad-faced boy who assisted his father at his work, and now came running by his side from the bog to escape the rain, to the wrinkled, sibyl[8]-like, cone-headed infant that sat upon its father's knee as in the palaces of nobles, and looked out from its home in the midst of wet and hunger inquisitively upon the stranger, with the privilege of infancy, not knowing but it was the last of a noble line, and the hope and cynosure of the world, instead of John Field's poor starveling brat. There we sat together under that part of the roof which leaked the least, while it showered and thundered without. I had sat there many times of old before the ship was built that floated this family to America. An honest, hardworking, but shiftless man plainly was John Field; and his wife, she too was brave to cook so many successive dinners in the recesses of that lofty stove; with round greasy face and bare breast,[9] still thinking to improve her condition one day; with the never absent mop in one hand, and yet no effects of it visible any where. The chickens, which had also taken shelter here from

6. The poetic excerpts in this chapter are from "Baker Farm," in *The Woodman and Other Poems* (1849), by Ellery Channing (see p. 1041, n. 8).
7. Muskrat.
8. In Greek mythology, Sibyl was granted her wish of living as many years as the number of grains of sand she could hold in one hand. As she aged, she became grotesquely wrinkled.
9. Thoreau suggests that her work clothes overexpose her body.

the rain, stalked about the room like members of the family, too humanized methought to roast well. They stood and looked in my eye or pecked at my shoe significantly. Meanwhile my host told me his story, how hard he worked "bogging" for a neighboring farmer, turning up a meadow with a spade or bog-hoe at the rate of ten dollars an acre and the use of the land with manure for one year, and his little broad-faced son worked cheerfully at his father's side the while, not knowing how poor a bargain the latter had made. I tried to help him with my experience, telling him that he was one of my nearest neighbors, and that I too, who came a-fishing here, and looked like a loafer, was getting my living like himself; that I lived in a tight light and clean house, which hardly cost more than the annual rent of such a ruin as his commonly amounts to; and how, if he chose, he might in a month or two build himself a palace of his own; that I did not use tea, nor coffee, nor butter, nor milk, nor fresh meat, and so did not have to work to get them; again, as I did not work hard, I did not have to eat hard, and it cost me but a trifle for my food; but as he began with tea, and coffee, and butter, and milk, and beef, he had to work hard to pay for them, and when he had worked hard he had to eat hard again to repair the waste of his system,—and so it was as broad as it was long, indeed it was broader than it was long, for he was discontented and wasted his life into the bargain; and yet he had rated it as a gain in coming to America, that here you could get tea, and coffee, and meat every day. But the only true America is that country where you are at liberty to pursue such a mode of life as may enable you to do without these, and where the state does not endeavor to compel you to sustain the slavery and war and other superfluous expenses which directly or indirectly result from the use of such things. For I purposely talked to him as if he were a philosopher, or desired to be one. I should be glad if all the meadows on the earth were left in a wild state, if that were the consequence of men's beginning to redeem themselves. A man will not need to study history to find out what is best for his own culture. But alas! the culture of an Irishman is an enterprise to be undertaken with a sort of moral bog hoe. I told him, that as he worked so hard at bogging, he required thick boots and stout clothing, which yet were soon soiled and worn out, but I wore light shoes and thin clothing, which cost not half so much, though he might think that I was dressed like a gentleman, (which, however, was not the case,) and in an hour or two, without labor, but as a recreation, I could, if I wished, catch as many fish as I should want for two days, or earn enough money to support me a week. If he and his family would live simply, they might all go a-huckleberrying in the summer for their amusement. John heaved a sigh at this, and his wife stared with arms a-kimbo, and both appeared to be wondering if they had capital enough to begin such a course with, or arithmetic enough to carry it through. It was sailing by dead reckoning[1] to them, and they saw not clearly how to make their port so; therefore I suppose they still take life bravely, after their fashion, face to face, giving it tooth and nail, not having skill to split its massive columns with any fine entering wedge, and rout it in detail;—thinking to deal with it roughly, as one should handle a thistle. But they fight at an overwhelming disadvantage,—living, John Field, alas! without arithmetic, and failing so.

1. A way of estimating position without astronomical observation, as by judging direction and distance from a previously determined spot.

"Do you ever fish?" I asked. "Oh yes, I catch a mess now and then when I am lying by; good perch I catch." "What's your bait?" "I catch shiners with fish-worms, and bait the perch with them." "You'd better go now, John," said his wife with glistening and hopeful face; but John demurred.

The shower was now over, and a rainbow above the eastern woods promised a fair evening; so I took my departure. When I had got without I asked for a drink, hoping to get a sight of the well bottom, to complete my survey of the premises; but there, alas! are shallows and quicksands, and rope broken withal, and bucket irrecoverable. Meanwhile the right culinary vessel was selected, water was seemingly distilled, and after consultation and long delay passed out to the thirsty one,—not yet suffered to cool, not yet to settle. Such gruel sustains life here, I thought; so, shutting my eyes, and excluding the motes by a skilfully directed under-current, I drank to genuine hospitality the heartiest draught I could. I am not squeamish in such cases when manners are concerned.

As I was leaving the Irishman's roof after the rain, bending my steps again to the pond, my haste to catch pickerel, wading in retired meadows, in sloughs and bog-holes, in forlorn and savage places, appeared for an instant trivial to me who had been sent to school and college; but as I ran down the hill toward the reddening west, with the rainbow over my shoulder, and some faint tinkling sounds borne to my ear through the cleansed air, from I know not what quarter, my Good Genius seemed to say,—Go fish and hunt far and wide day by day,—farther and wider,—and rest thee by many brooks and hearth-sides without misgiving. Remember thy Creator in the days of thy youth.[2] Rise free from care before the dawn, and seek adventures. Let the noon find thee by other lakes, and the night overtake thee every where at home. There are no larger fields than these, no worthier games than may here be played. Grow wild according to thy nature, like these sedges and brakes, which will never become English hay. Let the thunder rumble; what if it threaten ruin to farmers' crops? that is not its errand to thee. Take shelter under the cloud, while they flee to carts and sheds. Let not to get a living be thy trade, but thy sport. Enjoy the land, but own it not. Through want of enterprise and faith men are where they are, buying and selling, and spending their lives like serfs.

O Baker Farm!

"Landscape where the richest element
Is a little sunshine innocent." . . .
"No one runs to revel
On thy rail-fenced lea." . . .

"Debate with no man hast thou,
  With questions art never perplexed,
As tame at the first sight as now,
  In thy plain russet gabardine dressed." . . .

"Come ye who love,
  And ye who hate,

2. Ecclesiastes 12.1: "Remember now thy Creator in the days of thy youth, while the evil days come not, nor the years draw nigh, when thou shalt say, I have no pleasure in them."

Children of the Holy Dove,
And Guy Faux[3] of the state,
And hang conspiracies
From the tough rafters of the trees!"

Men come tamely home at night only from the next field or street, where their household echoes haunt, and their life pines because it breathes its own breath over again; their shadows morning and evening reach farther than their daily steps. We should come home from far, from adventures, and perils, and discoveries every day, with new experience and character.

Before I had reached the pond some fresh impulse had brought out John Field, with altered mind, letting go "bogging" ere this sunset. But he, poor man, disturbed only a couple of fins while I was catching a fair string, and he said it was his luck; but when we changed seats in the boat luck changed seats too. Poor John Field!—I trust he does not read this, unless he will improve by it,—thinking to live by some derivative old country mode in this primitive new country,—to catch perch with shiners. It is good bait sometimes, I allow. With his horizon all his own, yet he a poor man, born to be poor, with his inherited Irish poverty or poor life, his Adam's grandmother and boggy ways, not to rise in this world, he nor his posterity, till their wading webbed bog-trotting feet get *talaria*[4] to their heels.

11. Higher Laws

As I came home through the woods with my string of fish, trailing my pole, it being now quite dark, I caught a glimpse of a woodchuck stealing across my path, and felt a strange thrill of savage delight, and was strongly tempted to seize and devour him raw; not that I was hungry then, except for that wildness which he represented. Once or twice, however, while I lived at the pond, I found myself ranging the woods, like a half-starved hound, with a strange abandonment, seeking some kind of venison which I might devour, and no morsel could have been too savage for me. The wildest scenes had become unaccountably familiar. I found in myself, and still find, an instinct toward a higher, or, as it is named, spiritual life, as do most men, and another toward a primitive rank and savage one, and I reverence them both. I love the wild not less than the good. The wildness and adventure that are in fishing still recommended it to me. I like sometimes to take rank hold on life and spend my day more as the animals do. Perhaps I have owed to this employment and to hunting, when quite young, my closest acquaintance with Nature. They early introduce us to and detain us in scenery with which otherwise, at that age, we should have little acquaintance. Fishermen, hunters, woodchoppers, and others, spending their lives in the fields and woods, in a peculiar sense a part of Nature themselves, are often in a more favorable mood for observing her, in the intervals of their pursuits, than philosophers or poets even, who approach her with expectation. She is not afraid to exhibit herself to them. The traveller on the prairie is naturally a hunter, on the head waters of the Missouri and Columbia a trapper, and at the Falls of

3. Guy Faux or Fawkes (1570–1606) was an English Catholic conspirator executed after being seized as he was about to explode barrels of gunpowder under the House of Lords.

4. Winged sandals, such as those worn by Hermes in Greek mythology.

St. Mary[5] a fisherman. He who is only a traveller learns things at second-hand and by the halves, and is poor authority. We are most interested when science reports what those men already know practically or instinctively, for that alone is a true *humanity*, or account of human experience.

They mistake who assert that the Yankee has few amusements, because he has not so many public holidays, and men and boys do not play so many games as they do in England, for here the more primitive but solitary amusements of hunting, fishing and the like have not yet given place to the former. Almost every New England boy among my contemporaries shouldered a fowling piece between the ages of ten and fourteen; and his hunting and fishing grounds were not limited like the preserves of an English nobleman, but were more boundless even than those of a savage. No wonder, then, that he did not oftener stay to play on the common. But already a change is taking place, owing, not to an increased humanity, but to an increased scarcity of game, for perhaps the hunter is the greatest friend of the animals hunted, not excepting the Humane Society.

Moreover, when at the pond, I wished sometimes to add fish to my fare for variety. I have actually fished from the same kind of necessity that the first fishers did. Whatever humanity I might conjure up against it was all factitious, and concerned my philosophy more than my feelings. I speak of fishing only now, for I had long felt differently about fowling, and sold my gun before I went to the woods. Not that I am less humane than others, but I did not perceive that my feelings were much affected. I did not pity the fishes nor the worms. This was habit. As for fowling, during the last years that I carried a gun my excuse was that I was studying ornithology, and sought only new or rare birds. But I confess that I am now inclined to think that there is a finer way of studying ornithology than this. It requires so much closer attention to the habits of the birds, that, if for that reason only, I have been willing to omit the gun. Yet notwithstanding the objection on the score of humanity, I am compelled to doubt if equally valuable sports are ever substituted for these; and when some of my friends have asked me anxiously about their boys, whether they should let them hunt, I have answered, yes,—remembering that it was one of the best parts of my education,—*make* them hunters, though sportsmen only at first, if possible, mighty hunters at last, so that they shall not find game large enough for them in this or any vegetable wilderness,—hunters as well as fishers of men.[6] Thus far I am of the opinion of Chaucer's nun, who

> "yave not of the text a pulled hen
> That saith that hunters ben not holy men."[7]

There is a period in the history of the individual, as of the race, when the hunters are the "best men," as the Algonquins[8] called them. We cannot but pity the boy who has never fired a gun; he is no more humane, while his education has been sadly neglected. This was my answer with respect to those youths who were bent on this pursuit, trusting that they would soon outgrow

5. Because the images are progressively more western, this St. Mary's River may be the one in British Columbia.
6. Mark 1.17: "Come ye after me, and I will make you to become fishers of men" (Jesus' words to the fishermen Simon and Andrew).
7. From the Prologue to Chaucer's *The Canterbury Tales*, lines 177–78 (where it is said of the monk, not the nun).
8. American Indian group once widespread in what is now the northeastern United States and southeastern Canada.

it. No humane being, past the thoughtless age of boyhood, will wantonly murder any creature, which holds its life by the same tenure that he does. The hare in its extremity cries like a child. I warn you, mothers, that my sympathies do not always make the usual phil-*anthropic*[9] distinctions.

Such is oftenest the young man's introduction to the forest, and the most original part of himself. He goes thither at first as a hunter and fisher, until at last, if he has the seeds of a better life in him, he distinguishes his proper objects, as a poet or naturalist it may be, and leaves the gun and fish-pole behind. The mass of men are still and always young in this respect. In some countries a hunting parson is no uncommon sight. Such a one might make a good shepherd's dog, but is far from being the Good Shepherd. I have been surprised to consider that the only obvious employment, except wood-chopping, ice-cutting, or the like business, which ever to my knowledge detained at Walden Pond for a whole half day any of my fellow-citizens, whether fathers or children of the town, with just one exception, was fishing. Commonly they did not think that they were lucky, or well paid for their time, unless they got a long string of fish, though they had the opportunity of seeing the pond all the while. They might go there a thousand times before the sediment of fishing would sink to the bottom and leave their purpose pure; but no doubt such a clarifying process would be going on all the while. The governor and his council faintly remember the pond, for they went a-fishing there when they were boys; but now they are too old and dignified to go a-fishing, and so they know it no more forever. Yet even they expect to go to heaven at last. If the legislature regards it, it is chiefly to regulate the number of hooks to be used there; but they know nothing about the hook of hooks with which to angle for the pond itself, impaling the legislature for a bait. Thus, even in civilized communities, the embryo man passes through the hunter stage of development.

I have found repeatedly, of late years, that I cannot fish without falling a little in self-respect. I have tried it again and again. I have skill at it, and, like many of my fellows, a certain instinct for it, which revives from time to time, but always when I have done I feel that it would have been better if I had not fished. I think that I do not mistake. It is a faint intimation, yet so are the first streaks of morning. There is unquestionably this instinct in me which belongs to the lower orders of creation; yet with every year I am less a fisherman, though without more humanity or even wisdom; at present I am no fisherman at all. But I see that if I were to live in a wilderness I should again be tempted to become a fisher and hunter in earnest. Beside, there is something essentially unclean about this diet and all flesh, and I began to see where housework commences, and whence the endeavor, which costs so much, to wear a tidy and respectable appearance each day, to keep the house sweet and free from all ill odors and sights. Having been my own butcher and scullion and cook, as well as the gentleman for whom the dishes were served up, I can speak from an unusually complete experience. The practical objection to animal food in my case was its uncleanness; and, besides, when I had caught and cleaned and cooked and eaten my fish, they seemed not to have fed me essentially. It was insignificant and unnecessary, and cost

9. By emphasizing the Latin derivation of "philanthropic" (*philos*, "to love"; *anthropos*, "man"), Thoreau suggests that his love extends beyond humans.

more than it came to. A little bread or a few potatoes would have done as well, with less trouble and filth. Like many of my contemporaries, I had rarely for many years used animal food, or tea, or coffee, &c.; not so much because of any ill effects which I had traced to them as because they were not agreeable to my imagination. The repugnance to animal food is not the effect of experience, but is an instinct. It appeared more beautiful to live low and fare hard in many respects; and though I never did so, I went far enough to please my imagination. I believe that every man who has ever been earnest to preserve his higher or poetic faculties in the best condition has been particularly inclined to abstain from animal food, and from much food of any kind. It is a significant fact, stated by entomologists, I find it in Kirby and Spence, that "some insects in their perfect state, though furnished with organs of feeding, make no use of them;" and they lay it down as "a general rule, that almost all insects in this state eat much less than in that of larvæ. The voracious caterpillar when transformed into a butterfly," . . "and the gluttonous maggot when become a fly," content themselves with a drop or two of honey or some other sweet liquid.[1] The abdomen under the wings of the butterfly still represents the larva. This is the tid-bit which tempts his insectivorous fate. The gross feeder is a man in the larva state; and there are whole nations in that condition, nations without fancy or imagination, whose vast abdomens betray them.

It is hard to provide and cook so simple and clean a diet as will not offend the imagination; but this, I think, is to be fed when we feed the body; they should both sit down at the same table. Yet perhaps this may be done. The fruits eaten temperately need not make us ashamed of our appetites, nor interrupt the worthiest pursuits. But put an extra condiment into your dish, and it will poison you. It is not worth the while to live by rich cookery. Most men would feel shame if caught preparing with their own hands precisely such a dinner, whether of animal or vegetable food, as is every day prepared for them by others. Yet till this is otherwise we are not civilized, and, if gentlemen and ladies, are not true men and women. This certainly suggests what change is to be made. It may be vain to ask why the imagination will not be reconciled to flesh and fat. I am satisfied that it is not. Is it not a reproach that man is a carnivorous animal? True, he can and does live, in a great measure, by preying on other animals; but this is a miserable way,—as any one who will go to snaring rabbits, or slaughtering lambs, may learn,—and he will be regarded as a benefactor of his race who shall teach man to confine himself to a more innocent and wholesome diet. Whatever my own practice may be, I have no doubt that it is a part of the destiny of the human race, in its gradual improvement, to leave off eating animals, as surely as the savage tribes have left off eating each other when they came in contact with the more civilized.

If one listens to the faintest but constant suggestions of his genius, which are certainly true, he sees not to what extremes, or even insanity, it may lead him; and yet that way, as he grows more resolute and faithful, his road lies. The faintest assured objection which one healthy man feels will at length prevail over the arguments and customs of mankind. No man ever followed his genius till it misled him. Though the result were bodily weakness, yet

1. William Kirby and William Spence, *An Introduction to Entomology* (1815).

perhaps no one can say that the consequences were to be regretted, for these were a life in conformity to higher principles. If the day and the night are such that you greet them with joy, and life emits a fragrance like flowers and sweet-scented herbs, is more elastic, more starry, more immortal,—that is your success. All nature is your congratulation, and you have cause momentarily to bless yourself. The greatest gains and values are farthest from being appreciated. We easily come to doubt if they exist. We soon forget them. They are the highest reality. Perhaps the facts most astounding and most real are never communicated by man to man. The true harvest of my daily life is somewhat as intangible and indescribable as the tints of morning or evening. It is a little star-dust caught, a segment of the rainbow which I have clutched.

Yet, for my part, I was never unusually squeamish; I could sometimes eat a fried rat with a good relish, if it were necessary. I am glad to have drunk water so long, for the same reason that I prefer the natural sky to an opium-eater's heaven. I would fain keep sober always; and there are infinite degrees of drunkenness. I believe that water is the only drink for a wise man; wine is not so noble a liquor; and think of dashing the hopes of a morning with a cup of warm coffee, or of an evening with a dish of tea! Ah, how low I fall when I am tempted by them! Even music may be intoxicating. Such apparently slight causes destroyed Greece and Rome, and will destroy England and America. Of all ebriosity,[2] who does not prefer to be intoxicated by the air he breathes? I have found it to be the most serious objection to coarse labors long continued, that they compelled me to eat and drink coarsely also. But to tell the truth, I find myself at present somewhat less particular in these respects. I carry less religion to the table, ask no blessing; not because I am wiser than I was, but, I am obliged to confess, because, however much it is to be regretted, with years I have grown more coarse and indifferent. Perhaps these questions are entertained only in youth, as most believe of poetry. My practice is "nowhere," my opinion is here. Nevertheless I am far from regarding myself as one of those privileged ones to whom the Ved refers when it says, that "he who has true faith in the Omnipresent Supreme Being may eat all that exists," that is, is not bound to inquire what is his food, or who prepares it; and even in their case it is to be observed, as a Hindoo commentator has remarked, that the Vedant limits this privilege to "the time of distress."[3]

Who has not sometimes derived an inexpressible satisfaction from his food in which appetite had no share? I have been thrilled to think that I owed a mental perception to the commonly gross sense of taste, that I have been inspired through the palate, that some berries which I had eaten on a hill-side had fed my genius. "The soul not being mistress of herself," says Thseng-tseu, "one looks, and one does not see; one listens, and one does not hear; one eats, and one does not know the savor of food."[4] He who distinguishes the true savor of his food can never be a glutton; he who does not cannot be otherwise. A puritan may go to his brown-bread crust with as gross an appetite as ever an alderman to his turtle. Not that food which entereth into the mouth defileth a man, but the appetite with which it is eaten.[5] It is neither the quality nor the quantity, but the devotion to sensual

2. Drunkenness.
3. Rajah Rammohun Roy's translation of the *Vedas* (1832).
4. Confucius's *The Great Learning* 7.
5. Matthew 15.11: "Not that which goeth into the mouth defileth a man; but that which cometh out of the mouth, this defileth a man."

savors; when that which is eaten is not a viand to sustain our animal, or inspire our spiritual life, but food for the worms that possess us. If the hunter has a taste for mud-turtles, muskrats, and other such savage tid-bits, the fine lady indulges a taste for jelly made of a calf's foot, or for sardines from over the sea, and they are even. He goes to the mill-pond, she to her preserve-pot. The wonder is how they, how you and I, can live this slimy beastly life, eating and drinking.

Our whole life is startlingly moral. There is never an instant's truce between virtue and vice. Goodness is the only investment that never fails. In the music of the harp which trembles round the world it is the insisting on this which thrills us. The harp is the travelling patterer for the Universe's Insurance Company, recommending its laws, and our little goodness is all the assessment that we pay. Though the youth at last grows indifferent, the laws of the universe are not indifferent, but are forever on the side of the most sensitive. Listen to every zephyr for some reproof, for it is surely there, and he is unfortunate who does not hear it. We cannot touch a string or move a stop but the charming moral transfixes us. Many an irksome noise, go a long way off, is heard as music, a proud sweet satire on the meanness of our lives.

We are conscious of an animal in us, which awakens in proportion as our higher nature slumbers. It is reptile and sensual, and perhaps cannot be wholly expelled; like the worms which, even in life and health, occupy our bodies. Possibly we may withdraw from it, but never change its nature. I fear that it may enjoy a certain health of its own; that we may be well, yet not pure. The other day I picked up the lower jaw of a hog, with white and sound teeth and tusks, which suggested that there was an animal health and vigor distinct from the spiritual. This creature succeeded by other means than temperance and purity. "That in which men differ from brute beasts," says Mencius, "is a thing very inconsiderable; the common herd lose it very soon; superior men preserve it carefully."[6] Who knows what sort of life would result if we had attained to purity? If I knew so wise a man as could teach me purity I would go to seek him forthwith. "A command over our passions, and over the external senses of the body, and good acts, are declared by the Ved to be indispensable in the mind's approximation to God."[7] Yet the spirit can for the time pervade and control every member and function of the body, and transmute what in form is the grossest sensuality into purity and devotion. The generative energy, which, when we are loose, dissipates and makes us unclean, when we are continent invigorates and inspires us. Chastity is the flowering of man; and what are called Genius, Heroism, Holiness, and the like, are but various fruits which succeed it. Man flows at once to God when the channel of purity is open. By turns our purity inspires and our impurity casts us down. He is blessed who is assured that the animal is dying out in him day by day, and the divine being established. Perhaps there is none but has cause for shame on account of the inferior and brutish nature to which he is allied. I fear that we are such gods or demigods only as fauns and satyrs, the divine allied to beasts, the creatures of appetite, and that, to some extent, our very life is our disgrace.—

6. Mencius (Meng-tzu), Chinese philosopher (372?–289? B.C.E.), *Works* 4.

7. From Roy's translation of the *Vedas*.

"How happy's he who hath due place assigned
To his beasts and disaforested his mind!

• • •

Can use his horse, goat, wolf, and ev'ry beast,
And is not ass himself to all the rest!
Else man not only is the herd of swine,
But he's those devils too which did incline
Them to a headlong rage, and made them worse."[8]

All sensuality is one, though it takes many forms; all purity is one. It is the same whether a man eat, or drink, or cohabit, or sleep sensually. They are but one appetite, and we only need to see a person do any one of these things to know how great a sensualist he is. The impure can neither stand nor sit with purity. When the reptile is attacked at one mouth of his burrow, he shows himself at another. If you would be chaste, you must be temperate. What is chastity? How shall a man know if he is chaste? He shall not know it. We have heard of this virtue, but we know not what it is. We speak conformably to the rumor which we have heard. From exertion come wisdom and purity, from sloth ignorance and sensuality. In the student sensuality is a sluggish habit of mind. An unclean person is universally a slothful one, one who sits by a stove, whom the sun shines on prostrate, who reposes without being fatigued. If you would avoid uncleanness, and all the sins, work earnestly, though it be at cleaning a stable. Nature is hard to be overcome, but she must be overcome. What avails it that you are Christian, if you are not purer than the heathen, if you deny yourself no more, if you are not more religious? I know of many systems of religion esteemed heathenish whose precepts fill the reader with shame, and provoke him to new endeavors, though it be to the performance of rites merely.

I hesitate to say these things, but it is not because of the subject,—I care not how obscene my *words* are,—but because I cannot speak of them without betraying my impurity. We discourse freely without shame of one form of sensuality, and are silent about another. We are so degraded that we cannot speak simply of the necessary functions of human nature. In earlier ages, in some countries, every function was reverently spoken of and regulated by law. Nothing was too trivial for the Hindoo lawgiver, however offensive it may be to modern taste. He teaches how to eat, drink, cohabit, void excrement and urine, and the like, elevating what is mean, and does not falsely excuse himself by calling these things trifles.

Every man is the builder of a temple, called his body, to the god he worships, after a style purely his own, nor can he get off by hammering marble instead. We are all sculptors and painters, and our material is our own flesh and blood and bones. Any nobleness begins at once to refine a man's features, any meanness or sensuality to imbrute them.

John Farmer sat at his door one September evening, after a hard day's work, his mind still running on his labor more or less. Having bathed he sat down to recreate his intellectual man. It was a rather cool evening, and some of his neighbors were apprehending a frost. He had not attended to the train of his thoughts long when he heard some one playing on a flute, and

8. From John Donne (1573–1631), "To Sir Edward Herbert at Iulyers."

that sound harmonized with his mood. Still he thought of his work; but the burden of his thought was, that though this kept running in his head, and he found himself planning and contriving it against his will, yet it concerned him very little. It was no more than the scurf of his skin, which was constantly shuffled off. But the notes of the flute came home to his ears out of a different sphere from that he worked in, and suggested work for certain faculties which slumbered in him. They gently did away with the street, and the village, and the state in which he lived. A voice said to him,—Why do you stay here and live this mean moiling life, when a glorious existence is possible for you? Those same stars twinkle over other fields than these.—But how to come out of this condition and actually migrate thither? All that he could think of was to practise some new austerity, to let his mind descend into his body and redeem it, and treat himself with ever increasing respect.

12. Brute Neighbors

Sometimes I had a companion[9] in my fishing, who came through the village to my house from the other side of the town, and the catching of the dinner was as much a social exercise as the eating of it.

Hermit. I wonder what the world is doing now. I have not heard so much as a locust over the sweet-fern these three hours. The pigeons are all asleep upon their roosts,—no flutter from them. Was that a farmer's noon horn which sounded from beyond the woods just now? The hands are coming in to boiled salt beef and cider and Indian bread. Why will men worry themselves so? He that does not eat need not work. I wonder how much they have reaped. Who would live there where a body can never think for the barking of Bose?[1] And O, the housekeeping! to keep bright the devil's door-knobs, and scour his tubs this bright day! Better not keep a house. Say, some hollow tree; and then for morning calls and dinner-parties! Only a woodpecker tapping. O, they swarm; the sun is too warm there; they are born too far into life for me. I have water from the spring, and a loaf of brown bread on the shelf.—Hark! I hear a rustling of the leaves. Is it some ill-fed village hound yielding to the instinct of the chase? or the lost pig which is said to be in these woods, whose tracks I saw after the rain? It comes on apace; my sumachs and sweet-briars tremble.—Eh, Mr. Poet, is it you? How do you like the world to-day?

Poet. See those clouds; how they hang! That's the greatest thing I have seen to-day. There's nothing like it in old paintings, nothing like it in foreign lands,—unless when we were off the coast of Spain. That's a true Mediterranean sky. I thought, as I have my living to get, and have not eaten to-day, that I might go a-fishing. That's the true industry for poets. It is the only trade I have learned. Come, let's along.

Hermit. I cannot resist. My brown bread will soon be done. I will go with you gladly soon, but I am just concluding a serious meditation. I think that I am near the end of it. Leave me alone, then, for a while. But that we may not be delayed, you shall be digging the bait meanwhile. Angle-worms are rarely to be met with in these parts, where the soil was never fattened with manure; the race is nearly extinct. The sport of digging the bait is nearly

9. Channing, the "Poet" of the following dialog.

1. Common name for a dog.

equal to that of catching the fish, when one's appetite is not too keen; and this you may have all to yourself to-day. I would advise you to set in the spade down yonder among the ground-nuts, where you see the johnswort waving. I think that I may warrant you one worm to every three sods you turn up, if you look well in among the roots of the grass, as if you were weeding. Or, if you choose to go farther, it will not be unwise, for I have found the increase of fair bait to be very nearly as the squares of the distances.

Hermit alone. Let me see; where was I? Methinks I was nearly in this frame of mind; the world lay about at this angle. Shall I go to heaven or a-fishing? If I should soon bring this meditation to an end, would another so sweet occasion be likely to offer? I was as near being resolved into the essence of things as ever I was in my life. I fear my thoughts will not come back to me. If it would do any good, I would whistle for them. When they make us an offer, is it wise to say, We will think of it? My thoughts have left no track, and I cannot find the path again. What was it that I was thinking of? It was a very hazy day. I will just try these three sentences of Con-fut-see;[2] they may fetch that state about again. I know not whether it was the dumps or a budding ecstasy. Mem.[3] There never is but one opportunity of a kind.

Poet. How now, Hermit, is it too soon? I have got just thirteen whole ones, beside several which are imperfect or undersized; but they will do for the smaller fry; they do not cover up the hook so much. Those village worms are quite too large; a shiner may make a meal off one without finding the skewer.

Hermit. Well, then, let's be off. Shall we to the Concord? There's good sport there if the water be not too high.

Why do precisely these objects which we behold make a world? Why has man just these species of animals for his neighbors; as if nothing but a mouse could have filled this crevice? I suspect that Pilpay & Co.[4] have put animals to their best use, for they are all beasts of burden, in a sense, made to carry some portion of our thoughts.

The mice which haunted my house were not the common ones, which are said to have been introduced into the country, but a wild native kind (*Musleucopus*) not found in the village. I sent one to a distinguished naturalist,[5] and it interested him much. When I was building, one of these had its nest underneath the house, and before I had laid the second floor, and swept out the shavings, would come out regularly at lunch time and pick up the crumbs at my feet. It probably had never seen a man before; and it soon became quite familiar, and would run over my shoes and up my clothes. It could readily ascend the sides of the room by short impulses, like a squirrel, which it resembled in its motions. At length, as I leaned with my elbow on the bench one day, it ran up my clothes, and along my sleeve, and round and round the paper which held my dinner, while I kept the latter close, and dodged and played at bo-peep with it; and when at last I held still a piece of cheese between my thumb and finger, it came and nibbled it, sitting in my hand, and afterward cleaned its face and paws, like a fly, and walked away.

2. Confucius.
3. Abbreviation for *memorandum*, used here as a self-reminder.
4. I.e., all tellers of fables. Pilpay, or Bidpai, was credited with authorship of a collection of East Indian fables that Thoreau knew in Charles Wilkins's translation.
5. Louis Agassiz (1807–1873), Swiss-born American naturalist.

A phœbe soon built in my shed, and a robin for protection in a pine which grew against the house. In June the partridge, (*Tetrao umbellus*,) which is so shy a bird, led her brood past my windows, from the woods in the rear to the front of my house, clucking and calling to them like a hen, and in all her behavior proving herself the hen of the woods. The young suddenly disperse on your approach, at a signal from the mother, as if a whirlwind had swept them away, and they so exactly resemble the dried leaves and twigs that many a traveller has placed his foot in the midst of a brood, and heard the whir of the old bird as she flew off, and her anxious calls and mewing, or seen her trail her wings to attract his attention, without suspecting their neighborhood. The parent will sometimes roll and spin round before you in such a dishabille, that you cannot, for a few moments, detect what kind of creature it is. The young squat still and flat, often running their heads under a leaf, and mind only their mother's directions given from a distance, nor will your approach make them run again and betray themselves. You may even tread on them, or have your eyes on them for a minute, without discovering them. I have held them in my open hand at such a time, and still their only care, obedient to their mother and their instinct, was to squat there without fear or trembling. So perfect is this instinct, that once, when I had laid them on the leaves again, and one accidentally fell on its side, it was found with the rest in exactly the same position ten minutes afterward. They are not callow like the young of most birds, but more perfectly developed and precocious even than chickens. The remarkably adult yet innocent expression of their open and serene eyes is very memorable. An intelligence seems reflected in them. They suggest not merely the purity of infancy, but a wisdom clarified by experience. Such an eye was not born when the bird was, but is coeval with the sky it reflects. The woods do not yield another such a gem. The traveller does not often look into such a limpid well. The ignorant or reckless sportsman often shoots the parent at such a time, and leaves these innocents to fall a prey to some prowling beast or bird, or gradually mingle with the decaying leaves which they so much resemble. It is said that when hatched by a hen they will directly disperse on some alarm, and so are lost, for they never hear the mother's call which gathers them again. These were my hens and chickens.

It is remarkable how many creatures live wild and free though secret in the woods, and still sustain themselves in the neighborhood of towns, suspected by hunters only. How retired the otter manages to live here! He grows to be four feet long, as big as a small boy, perhaps without any human being getting a glimpse of him. I formerly saw the raccoon in the woods behind where my house is built, and probably still heard their whinnering at night. Commonly I rested an hour or two in the shade at noon, after planting, and ate my lunch, and read a little by a spring which was the source of a swamp and of a brook, oozing from under Brister's Hill, half a mile from my field. The approach to this was through a succession of descending grassy hollows, full of young pitch-pines, into a larger wood about the swamp. There, in a very secluded and shaded spot, under a spreading white-pine, there was yet a clean firm sward to sit on. I had dug out the spring and made a well of clear gray water, where I could dip up a pailful without roiling it, and thither I went for this purpose almost every day in midsummer, when the pond was warmest. Thither too the wood-cock led her brood, to probe the mud for worms, flying but a foot above them down the bank, while they ran in a troop beneath; but at last, spying me, she would leave her young and circle round and round me, nearer and nearer, till within four or five feet, pretending broken wings and legs, to attract my attention and get off her young, who would already have taken up their march, with faint wiry peep, single file through the swamp, as she directed. Or I heard the peep of the young when I could not see the parent bird. There too the turtle-doves sat over the spring, or fluttered from bough to bough of the soft white-pines over my head; or the red squirrel, coursing down the nearest bough, was particularly familiar and inquisitive. You only need sit still long enough in some attractive spot in the woods that all its inhabitants may exhibit themselves to you by turns.

I was witness to events of a less peaceful character. One day when I went out to my wood-pile, or rather my pile of stumps, I observed two large ants, the one red, the other much larger, nearly half an inch long, and black, fiercely contending with one another. Having once got hold they never let go, but struggled and wrestled and rolled on the chips incessantly. Looking farther, I was surprised to find that the chips were covered with such combatants, that it was not a *duellum*, but a *bellum*, a war between two races of ants, the red always pitted against the black, and frequently two red ones to one black. The legions of these Myrmidons[6] covered all the hills and vales in my wood-yard, and the ground was already strewn with the dead and dying, both red and black. It was the only battle which I have ever witnessed, the only battle-field I ever trod while the battle was raging; internecine war; the red republicans on the one hand, and the black imperialists on the other. On every side they were engaged in deadly combat, yet without any noise that I could hear, and human soldiers never fought so resolutely. I watched a couple that were fast locked in each other's embraces, in a little sunny valley amid the chips, now at noon-day prepared to fight till the sun went down, or life went out. The smaller red champion had fastened himself like a vice to his adversary's front, and through all the tumblings on that field never for an instant ceased to gnaw at one of his feelers near the root, having already caused the other to go by the board; while the stronger black one dashed him from side to side, and, as I saw on looking nearer, had already divested him of several of his members. They fought with more pertinacity than bull-dogs. Neither manifested the least disposition to retreat. It was evident that their battle-cry was Conquer or die. In the mean while there came along a single red ant on the hill-side of this valley, evidently full of excitement, who either had despatched his foe, or had not yet taken part in the battle; probably the latter, for he had lost none of his limbs; whose mother had charged him to return with his shield or upon it.[7] Or perchance he was some Achilles, who had nourished his wrath apart, and had now come to avenge or rescue his Patroclus.[8] He saw this unequal combat from afar,—for the blacks were nearly twice the size of the red,—he drew near with rapid pace till he stood on his guard within half an inch of the combatants; then, watching his opportunity, he sprang upon the black warrior, and commenced his operations near the root of his right fore-leg, leaving the foe to

6. The Myrmidons were warriors who fought against the Trojans.
7. According to legend, Spartan mothers sent their sons into battle with these words.
8. In the *Iliad* Achilles did not join the Greek forces in the Trojan War until after his close friend Patroclus was killed.

select among his own members; and so there were three united for life, as if a new kind of attraction had been invented which put all other locks and cements to shame. I should not have wondered by this time to find that they had their respective musical bands stationed on some eminent chip, and playing their national airs the while, to excite the slow and cheer the dying combatants. I was myself excited somewhat even as if they had been men. The more you think of it, the less the difference. And certainly there is not the fight recorded in Concord history, at least, if in the history of America, that will bear a moment's comparison with this, whether for the numbers engaged in it, or for the patriotism and heroism displayed. For numbers and for carnage it was an Austerlitz or Dresden.[9] Concord Fight! Two killed on the patriots' side, and Luther Blanchard wounded! Why here every ant was a Buttrick,—"Fire! for God's sake fire!"—and thousands shared the fate of Davis and Hosmer.[1] There was not one hireling there. I have no doubt that it was a principle they fought for, as much as our ancestors, and not to avoid a three-penny tax on their tea; and the results of this battle will be as important and memorable to those whom it concerns as those of the battle of Bunker Hill, at least.

I took up the chip on which the three I have particularly described were struggling, carried it into my house, and placed it under a tumbler on my window-sill, in order to see the issue. Holding a microscope[2] to the first-mentioned red ant, I saw that, though he was assiduously gnawing at the near fore-leg of his enemy, having severed his remaining feeler, his own breast was all torn away, exposing what vitals he had there to the jaws of the black warrior, whose breast-plate was apparently too thick for him to pierce; and the dark carbuncles of the sufferer's eyes shone with ferocity such as war only could excite. They struggled half an hour longer under the tumbler, and when I looked again the black soldier had severed the heads of his foes from their bodies, and the still living heads were hanging on either side of him like ghastly trophies at his saddle-bow, still apparently as firmly fastened as ever, and he was endeavoring with feeble struggles, being without feelers and with only the remnant of a leg, and I know not how many other wounds, to divest himself of them; which at length, after half an hour more, he accomplished. I raised the glass, and he went off over the windowsill in that crippled state. Whether he finally survived that combat, and spent the remainder of his days in some Hotel des Invalides,[3] I do not know; but I thought that his industry would not be worth much thereafter. I never learned which party was victorious, nor the cause of the war; but I felt for the rest of that day as if I had had my feelings excited and harrowed by witnessing the struggle, the ferocity and carnage, of a human battle before my door.

Kirby and Spence tell us that the battles of ants have long been celebrated and the date of them recorded, though they say that Huber[4] is the only modern author who appears to have witnessed them. "Æneas Sylvius," say they, "after giving a very circumstantial account of one contested with great obstinacy by a great and small species on the trunk of a pear tree," adds that

9. Important battles (1805, 1813) of the Napoleonic Wars (1799–1815).
1. Isaac Davis and Abner Hosmer were the only two colonists killed at Concord on April 19, 1775; the others named were participants in the battle.
2. Magnifying glass.
3. Old soldiers' home in Paris.
4. François Huber (1750–1831), Swiss entomologist.

"'This action was fought in the pontificate of Eugenius the Fourth, in the presence of Nicholas Pistoriensis, an eminent lawyer, who related the whole history of the battle with the greatest fidelity.' A similar engagement between great and small ants is recorded by Olaus Magnus,[5] in which the small ones, being victorious, are said to have buried the bodies of their own soldiers, but left those of their giant enemies a prey to the birds. This event happened previous to the expulsion of the tyrant Christiern the Second from Sweden." The battle which I witnessed took place in the Presidency of Polk, five years before the passage of Webster's Fugitive-Slave Bill.[6]

Many a village Bose, fit only to course[7] a mud-turtle in a victualling cellar, sported his heavy quarters in the woods, without the knowledge of his master, and ineffectually smelled at old fox burrows and woodchucks' holes; led perchance by some slight cur which nimbly threaded the wood, and might still inspire a natural terror in its denizens;—now far behind his guide, barking like a canine bull toward some small squirrel which had treed itself for scrutiny, then, cantering off, bending the bushes with his weight, imagining that he is on the track of some stray member of the gerbille family. Once I was surprised to see a cat walking along the stony shore of the pond, for they rarely wander so far from home. The surprise was mutual. Nevertheless the most domestic cat, which has lain on a rug all her days, appears quite at home in the woods, and, by her sly and stealthy behavior, proves herself more native there than the regular inhabitants. Once, when berrying, I met with a cat with young kittens in the woods, quite wild, and they all, like their mother, had their backs up and were fiercely spitting at me. A few years before I lived in the woods there was what was called a "winged cat" in one of the farm-houses in Lincoln nearest the pond, Mr. Gilian Baker's. When I called to see her in June, 1842, she was gone a-hunting in the woods, as was her wont, (I am not sure whether it was a male or female, and so use the more common pronoun,) but her mistress told me that she came into the neighborhood a little more than a year before, in April, and was finally taken into their house; that she was of a dark brownish-gray color, with a white spot on her throat, and white feet, and had a large bushy tail like a fox; that in the winter the fur grew thick and flatted out along her sides, forming strips ten or twelve inches long by two and a half wide, and under her chin like a muff, the upper side loose, the under matted like felt, and in the spring these appendages dropped off. They gave me a pair of her "wings," which I keep still. There is no appearance of a membrane about them. Some thought it was part flying-squirrel or some other wild animal, which is not impossible, for, according to naturalists, prolific hybrids have been produced by the union of the marten and domestic cat. This would have been the right kind of cat for me to keep, if I had kept any; for why should not a poet's cat be winged as well as his horse?[8]

In the fall the loon (*Colymbus glacialis*) came, as usual, to moult and bathe in the pond, making the woods ring with his wild laughter before I had risen. At rumor of his arrival all the Mill-dam sportsmen are on the

5. From Kirby and Spence, *Introduction to Entomology* (1846): Æneas Sylvius (1405–1464) was Pope Pius II (1458–64) and Olaus Magnus (1490–1558) was archbishop of Uppsala, Sweden.
6. Thoreau disdained Massachusetts senator Daniel Webster for his support of the Compromise of 1850. James Polk was president from 1845 to 1849.
7. Chase.
8. According to Greek mythology, poets during their flights of inspiration ride on the winged horse Pegasus.

alert, in gigs and on foot, two by two and three by three, with patent rifles and conical balls and spy-glasses. They come rustling through the woods like autumn leaves, at least ten men to one loon. Some station themselves on this side of the pond, some on that, for the poor bird cannot be omnipresent; if he dive here he must come up there. But now the kind October wind rises, rustling the leaves and rippling the surface of the water, so that no loon can be heard or seen, though his foes sweep the pond with spy-glasses, and make the woods resound with their discharges. The waves generously rise and dash angrily, taking sides with all waterfowl, and our sportsmen must beat a retreat to town and shop and unfinished jobs. But they were too often successful. When I went to get a pail of water early in the morning I frequently saw this stately bird sailing out of my cove within a few rods. If I endeavored to overtake him in a boat, in order to see how he would manœuvre, he would dive and be completely lost, so that I did not discover him again, sometimes, till the latter part of the day. But I was more than a match for him on the surface. He commonly went off in a rain.

As I was paddling along the north shore one very calm October afternoon, for such days especially they settle on to the lakes, like the milkweed down, having looked in vain over the pond for a loon, suddenly one, sailing out from the shore toward the middle a few rods in front of me, set up his wild laugh and betrayed himself. I pursued with a paddle and he dived, but when he came up I was nearer than before. He dived again, but I miscalculated the direction he would take, and we were fifty rods apart when he came to the surface this time, for I had helped to widen the interval; and again he laughed long and loud, and with more reason than before. He manœuvred so cunningly that I could not get within half a dozen rods of him. Each time, when he came to the surface, turning his head this way and that, he coolly surveyed the water and the land, and apparently chose his course so that he might come up where there was the widest expanse of water and at the greatest distance from the boat. It was surprising how quickly he made up his mind and put his resolve into execution. He led me at once to the widest part of the pond, and could not be driven from it. While he was thinking one thing in his brain, I was endeavoring to divine his thought in mine. It was a pretty game, played on the smooth surface of the pond, a man against a loon. Suddenly your adversary's checker disappears beneath the board, and the problem is to place yours nearest to where his will appear again. Sometimes he would come up unexpectedly on the opposite side of me, having apparently passed directly under the boat. So long-winded was he and so unweariable, that when he had swum farthest he would immediately plunge again, nevertheless; and then no wit could divine where in the deep pond, beneath the smooth surface, he might be speeding his way like a fish, for he had time and ability to visit the bottom of the pond in its deepest part. It is said that loons have been caught in the New York lakes eighty feet beneath the surface, with hooks set for trout,—though Walden is deeper than that. How surprised must the fishes be to see this ungainly visitor from another sphere speeding his way amid their schools! Yet he appeared to know his course as surely under water as on the surface, and swam much faster there. Once or twice I saw a ripple where he approached the surface, just put his head out to reconnoitre, and instantly dived again. I found that it was as well for me to rest on my oars and wait his reappearing as to endeavor to calculate where he would rise; for again and again, when I was straining my eyes over the surface one way, I would suddenly be startled by his unearthly laugh behind me. But why, after displaying so much cunning, did he invariably betray himself the moment he came up by that loud laugh? Did not his white breast enough betray him? He was indeed a silly loon, I thought. I could commonly hear the plash of the water when he came up, and so also detected him. But after an hour he seemed as fresh as ever, dived as willingly and swam yet farther than at first. It was surprising to see how serenely he sailed off with unruffled breast when he came to the surface, doing all the work with his webbed feet beneath. His usual note was this demoniac laughter, yet somewhat like that of a water-fowl; but occasionally, when he had balked me most successfully and come up a long way off, he uttered a long-drawn unearthly howl, probably more like that of a wolf than any bird; as when a beast puts his muzzle to the ground and deliberately howls. This was his looning,—perhaps the wildest sound that is ever heard here, making the woods ring far and wide. I concluded that he laughed in derision of my efforts, confident of his own resources. Though the sky was by this time overcast, the pond was so smooth that I could see where he broke the surface when I did not hear him. His white breast, the stillness of the air, and the smoothness of the water were all against him. At length, having come up fifty rods off, he uttered one of those prolonged howls, as if calling on the god of loons to aid him, and immediately there came a wind from the east and rippled the surface, and filled the whole air with misty rain, and I was impressed as if it were the prayer of the loon answered, and his god was angry with me; and so I left him disappearing far away on the tumultuous surface.

For hours, in fall days, I watched the ducks cunningly tack and veer and hold the middle of the pond, far from the sportsman; tricks which they will have less need to practise in Louisiana bayous. When compelled to rise they would sometimes circle round and round and over the pond at a considerable height, from which they could easily see to other ponds and the river, like black motes in the sky; and, when I thought they had gone off thither long since, they would settle down by a slanting flight of a quarter of a mile on to a distant part which was left free; but what beside safety they got by sailing in the middle of Walden I do not know, unless they love its water for the same reason that I do.

13. House-Warming

In October I went a-graping to the river meadows, and loaded myself with clusters more precious for their beauty and fragrance than for food. There too I admired, though I did not gather, the cranberries, small waxen gems, pendants of the meadow grass, pearly and red, which the farmer plucks with an ugly rake, leaving the smooth meadow in a snarl, heedlessly measuring them by the bushel and the dollar only, and sells the spoils of the meads to Boston and New York; destined to be *jammed*, to satisfy the tastes of lovers of Nature there. So butchers rake the tongues of bison out of the prairie grass, regardless of the torn and drooping plant. The barberry's brilliant fruit was likewise food for my eyes merely; but I collected a small store of wild apples for coddling, which the proprietor and travellers had overlooked. When chestnuts were ripe I laid up half a bushel for winter. It was very exciting at that season to roam the then boundless chestnut woods of Lincoln,—they now sleep their long sleep under the railroad,—with a bag on my shoulder, and a stick to open burrs with in my hand, for I did not always wait for the frost, amid the rustling of leaves and the loud reproofs of the red-squirrels and the jays, whose half-consumed nuts I sometimes stole, for the burrs which they had selected were sure to contain sound ones. Occasionally I climbed and shook the trees. They grew also behind my house, and one large tree which almost overshadowed it, was, when in flower, a bouquet which scented the whole neighborhood, but the squirrels and the jays got most of its fruit; the last coming in flocks early in the morning and picking the nuts out of the burrs before they fell. I relinquished these trees to them and visited the more distant woods composed wholly of chestnut. These nuts, as far as they went, were a good substitute for bread. Many other substitutes might, perhaps, be found. Digging one day for fish-worms I discovered the ground-nut (*Apios tuberosa*) on its string, the potato of the aborigines, a sort of fabulous fruit, which I had begun to doubt if I had ever dug and eaten in childhood, as I had told, and had not dreamed it. I had often since seen its crimpled red velvety blossom supported by the stems of other plants without knowing it to be the same. Cultivation has well nigh exterminated it. It has a sweetish taste, much like that of a frostbitten potato, and I found it better boiled than roasted. This tuber seemed like a faint promise of Nature to rear her own children and feed them simply here at some future period. In these days of fatted cattle and waving grain-fields, this humble root, which was once the *totem* of an Indian tribe, is quite forgotten, or known only by its flowering vine; but let wild Nature reign here once more, and the tender and luxurious English grains will probably disappear before a myriad of foes, and without the care of man the crow may carry back even the last seeds of corn to the great corn-field of the Indian's God in the south-west, whence he is said to have brought it; but the now almost exterminated ground-nut will perhaps revive and flourish in spite of frosts and wildness, prove itself indigenous, and resume its ancient importance and dignity as the diet of the hunter tribe. Some Indian Ceres or Minerva[9] must have been the inventor and bestower of it; and when the reign of poetry commences here, its leaves and string of nuts may be represented on our works of art.

Already, by the first of September, I had seen two or three small maples turned scarlet across the pond, beneath where the white stems of three aspens diverged, at the point of a promontory, next the water. Ah, many a tale their color told! And gradually from week to week the character of each tree came out, and it admired itself reflected in the smooth mirror of the lake. Each morning the manager of this gallery substituted some new picture, distinguished by more brilliant or harmonious coloring, for the old upon the walls.

The wasps came by thousands to my lodge in October, as to winter quarters, and settled on my windows within and on the walls over-head, sometimes deterring visitors from entering. Each morning, when they were numbed with cold, I swept some of them out, but I did not trouble myself much to get rid of them; I even felt complimented by their regarding my house as a desirable shelter. They never molested me seriously, though they

9. Roman goddesses of agriculture and wisdom, respectively.

bedded with me; and they gradually disappeared, into what crevices I do not know, avoiding winter and unspeakable cold.

Like the wasps, before I finally went into winter quarters in November, I used to resort to the north-east side of Walden, which the sun, reflected from the pitch-pine woods and the stony shore, made the fire-side of the pond; it is so much pleasanter and wholesomer to be warmed by the sun while you can be, than by an artificial fire. I thus warmed myself by the still glowing embers which the summer, like a departed hunter, had left.

When I came to build my chimney I studied masonry. My bricks being second-hand ones required to be cleaned with a trowel, so that I learned more than usual of the qualities of bricks and trowels. The mortar on them was fifty years old, and was said to be still growing harder; but this is one of those sayings which men love to repeat whether they are true or not. Such sayings themselves grow harder and adhere more firmly with age, and it would take many blows with a trowel to clean an old wiseacre of them. Many of the villages of Mesopotamia are built of second-hand bricks of a very good quality, obtained from the ruins of Babylon, and the cement on them is older and probably harder still. However that may be, I was struck by the peculiar toughness of the steel which bore so many violent blows without being worn out. As my bricks had been in a chimney before, though I did not read the name of Nebuchadnezzar[1] on them, I picked out as many fire-place bricks as I could find, to save work and waste, and I filled the spaces between the bricks about the fire-place with stones from the pond shore, and also made my mortar with the white sand from the same place. I lingered most about the fireplace, as the most vital part of the house. Indeed, I worked so deliberately, that though I commenced at the ground in the morning, a course of bricks raised a few inches above the floor served for my pillow at night; yet I did not get a stiff neck for it that I remember; my stiff neck is of older date. I took a poet[2] to board for a fortnight about those times, which caused me to be put to it for room. He brought his own knife, though I had two, and we used to scour them by thrusting them into the earth. He shared with me the labors of cooking. I was pleased to see my work rising so square and solid by degrees, and reflected, that, if it proceeded slowly, it was calculated to endure a long time. The chimney is to some extent an independent structure, standing on the ground and rising through the house to the heavens; even after the house is burned it still stands sometimes, and its importance and independence are apparent. This was toward the end of summer. It was now November.

The north wind had already begun to cool the pond, though it took many weeks of steady blowing to accomplish it, it is so deep. When I began to have a fire at evening, before I plastered my house, the chimney carried smoke particularly well, because of the numerous chinks between the boards. Yet I passed some cheerful evenings in that cool and airy apartment, surrounded by the rough brown boards full of knots, and rafters with the bark on high over-head. My house never pleased my eye so much after it was plastered, though I was obliged to confess that it was more comfortable. Should not every apartment in which man dwells be lofty enough to create some

1. Babylonian king (605–552 B.C.E.), who had his name stamped on the bricks used to build his palace.

2. Ellery Channing.

obscurity over-head, where flickering shadows may play at evening about the rafters? These forms are more agreeable to the fancy and imagination than fresco paintings or other the most expensive furniture. I now first began to inhabit my house, I may say, when I began to use it for warmth as well as shelter. I had got a couple of old fire-dogs to keep the wood from the hearth, and it did me good to see the soot form on the back of the chimney which I had built, and I poked the fire with more right and more satisfaction than usual. My dwelling was small, and I could hardly entertain an echo in it; but it seemed larger for being a single apartment and remote from neighbors. All the attractions of a house were concentrated in one room; it was kitchen, chamber, parlor, and keeping-room; and whatever satisfaction parent or child, master or servant, derive from living in a house, I enjoyed it all. Cato says, the master of a family (*patremfamilias*) must have in his rustic villa "cellam oleariam, vinariam, dolia multa, uti lubeat caritatem expectare, et rei, et virtuti, et gloriæ erit," that is, "an oil and wine cellar, many casks, so that it may be pleasant to expect hard times; it will be for his advantage, and virtue, and glory."[3] I had in my cellar a firkin of potatoes, about two quarts of peas with the weevil in them, and on my shelf a little rice, a jug of molasses, and of rye and Indian meal a peck each.

I sometimes dream of a larger and more populous house, standing in a golden age, of enduring materials, and without ginger-bread work, which shall still consist of only one room, a vast, rude, substantial, primitive hall, without ceiling or plastering, with bare rafters and purlins supporting a sort of lower heaven over one's head,—useful to keep off rain and snow; where the king and queen posts stand out to receive your homage, when you have done reverence to the prostrate Saturn[4] of an older dynasty on stepping over the sill; a cavernous house, wherein you must reach up a torch upon a pole to see the roof; where some may live in the fire-place, some in the recess of a window, and some on settles, some at one end of the hall, some at another, and some aloft on rafters with the spiders, if they choose; a house which you have got into when you have opened the outside door, and the ceremony is over; where the weary traveller may wash, and eat, and converse, and sleep, without further journey; such a shelter as you would be glad to reach in a tempestuous night, containing all the essentials of a house, and nothing for house-keeping; where you can see all the treasures of the house at one view, and every thing hangs upon its peg that a man should use; at once kitchen, pantry, parlor, chamber, store-house, and garret; where you can see so necessary a thing as a barrel or a ladder, so convenient a thing as a cupboard, and hear the pot boil, and pay your respects to the fire that cooks your dinner and the oven that bakes your bread, and the necessary furniture and utensils are the chief ornaments; where the washing is not put out, nor the fire, nor the mistress, and perhaps you are sometimes requested to move from off the trap-door, when the cook would descend into the cellar, and so learn whether the ground is solid or hollow beneath you without stamping. A house whose inside is as open and manifest as a bird's nest, and you cannot go in at the front door and out at the back without seeing

3. Cato's *De Agri Cultura* 3.2.

4. Roman name for the Greek Cronus, chief of the pre-Olympian gods, dethroned by his son Zeus. "Purlins": horizontal beams supporting the rafters. "King posts": central vertical supporting posts connecting to an apex. "Queen posts": vertical posts that run to points some distance below the apex.

some of its inhabitants; where to be a guest is to be presented with the freedom of the house, and not to be carefully excluded from seven eighths of it, shut up in a particular cell, and told to make yourself at home there,—in solitary confinement. Nowadays the host does not admit you to *his* hearth, but has got the mason to build one for yourself somewhere in his alley, and hospitality is the art of *keeping* you at the greatest distance. There is as much secrecy about the cooking as if he had a design to poison you. I am aware that I have been on many a man's premises, and might have been legally ordered off, but I am not aware that I have been in many men's houses. I might visit in my old clothes a king and queen who lived simply in such a house as I have described, if I were going their way; but backing out of a modern palace will be all that I shall desire to learn, if ever I am caught in one.

It would seem as if the very language of our parlors would lose all its nerve and degenerate into *palaver* wholly, our lives pass at such remoteness from its symbols, and its metaphors and tropes are necessarily so far fetched, through slides and dumb-waiters, as it were; in other words, the parlor is so far from the kitchen and workshop. The dinner even is only the parable of a dinner, commonly. As if only the savage dwelt near enough to Nature and Truth to borrow a trope from them. How can the scholar, who dwells away in the North West Territory or the Isle of Man,[5] tell what is parliamentary in the kitchen?

However, only one or two of my guests were ever bold enough to stay and eat a hasty-pudding[6] with me; but when they saw that crisis approaching they beat a hasty retreat rather, as if it would shake the house to its foundations. Nevertheless, it stood through a great many hasty-puddings.

I did not plaster till it was freezing weather. I brought over some whiter and cleaner sand for this purpose from the opposite shore of the pond in a boat, a sort of conveyance which would have tempted me to go much farther if necessary. My house had in the mean while been shingled down to the ground on every side. In lathing I was pleased to be able to send home each nail with a single blow of the hammer, and it was my ambition to transfer the plaster from the board to the wall neatly and rapidly. I remembered the story of a conceited fellow, who, in fine clothes, was wont to lounge about the village once, giving advice to workmen. Venturing one day to substitute deeds for words, he turned up his cuffs, seized a plasterer's board, and having loaded his trowel without mishap, with a complacent look toward the lathing overhead, made a bold gesture thitherward; and straightway, to his complete discomfiture, received the whole contents in his ruffled bosom. I admired anew the economy and convenience of plastering, which so effectually shuts out the cold and takes a handsome finish, and I learned the various casualties to which the plasterer is liable. I was surprised to see how thirsty the bricks were which drank up all the moisture in my plaster before I had smoothed it, and how many pailfuls of water it takes to christen a new hearth. I had the previous winter made a small quantity of lime by burning the shells of the *Unio fluviatilis*,[7] which our river affords, for the sake of the experiment; so that I knew where my materials came from. I might have got

5. Located in the Irish Sea between England and Ireland.
6. Flour or cornmeal stirred into boiling water or milk.
7. Genus and species of a freshwater clam.

good limestone within a mile or two and burned it myself, if I had cared to do so.

The pond had in the mean while skimmed over in the shadiest and shallowest coves, some days or even weeks before the general freezing. The first ice is especially interesting and perfect, being hard, dark, and transparent, and affords the best opportunity that ever offers for examining the bottom where it is shallow; for you can lie at your length on ice only an inch thick, like a skater insect on the surface of the water, and study the bottom at your leisure, only two or three inches distant, like a picture behind a glass, and the water is necessarily always smooth then. There are many furrows in the sand where some creature has travelled about and doubled on its tracks; and, for wrecks, it is strewn with the cases of cadis worms made of minute grains of white quartz. Perhaps these have creased it, for you find some of their cases in the furrows, though they are deep and broad for them to make. But the ice itself is the object of most interest, though you must improve the earliest opportunity to study it. If you examine it closely the morning after it freezes, you find that the greater part of the bubbles, which at first appeared to be within it, are against its under surface, and that more are continually rising from the bottom; while the ice is as yet comparatively solid and dark, that is, you see the water through it. These bubbles are from an eightieth to an eighth of an inch in diameter, very clear and beautiful, and you see your face reflected in them through the ice. There may be thirty or forty of them to a square inch. There are also already within the ice narrow oblong perpendicular bubbles about half an inch long, sharp cones with the apex upward; or oftener, if the ice is quite fresh, minute spherical bubbles one directly above another, like a string of beads. But these within the ice are not so numerous nor obvious as those beneath. I sometimes used to cast on stones to try the strength of the ice, and those which broke through carried in air with them, which formed very large and conspicuous white bubbles beneath. One day when I came to the same place forty-eight hours afterward, I found that those large bubbles were still perfect, though an inch more of ice had formed, as I could see distinctly by the seam in the edge of a cake. But as the last two days had been very warm, like an Indian summer, the ice was not now transparent, showing the dark green color of the water, and the bottom, but opaque and whitish or gray, and though twice as thick was hardly stronger than before, for the air bubbles had greatly expanded under this heat and run together, and lost their regularity; they were no longer one directly over another, but often like silvery coins poured from a bag, one overlapping another, or in thin flakes, as if occupying slight cleavages. The beauty of the ice was gone, and it was too late to study the bottom. Being curious to know what position my great bubbles occupied with regard to the new ice, I broke out a cake containing a middling sized one, and turned it bottom upward. The new ice had formed around and under the bubble, so that it was included between the two ices. It was wholly in the lower ice, but close against the upper, and was flattish, or perhaps slightly lenticular, with a rounded edge, a quarter of an inch deep by four inches in diameter; and I was surprised to find that directly under the bubble the ice was melted with great regularity in the form of a saucer reversed, to the height of five eighths of an inch in the middle, leaving a thin partition there between the water and the bubble, hardly an eighth of an inch thick; and in many places the small bubbles in this partition had burst out downward, and probably there was no ice at all under the largest bubbles, which were a foot in diameter. I inferred that the infinite number of minute bubbles which I had first seen against the under surface of the ice were now frozen in likewise, and that each, in its degree, had operated like a burning glass on the ice beneath to melt and rot it. These are the little air-guns which contribute to make the ice crack and whoop.

At length the winter set in in good earnest, just as I had finished plastering, and the wind began to howl around the house as if it had not had permission to do so till then. Night after night the geese came lumbering in in the dark with a clangor and a whistling of wings, even after the ground was covered with snow, some to alight in Walden, and some flying low over the woods toward Fair Haven, bound for Mexico. Several times, when returning from the village at ten or eleven o'clock at night, I heard the tread of a flock of geese, or else ducks, on the dry leaves in the woods by a pond-hole behind my dwelling, where they had come up to feed, and the faint honk or quack of their leader as they hurried off. In 1845 Walden froze entirely over for the first time on the night of the 22d of December, Flint's and other shallower ponds and the river having been frozen ten days or more; in '46, the 16th; in '49, about the 31st; and in '50, about the 27th of December; in '52, the 5th of January; in '53, the 31st of December. The snow had already covered the ground since the 25th of November, and surrounded me suddenly with the scenery of winter. I withdrew yet farther into my shell, and endeavored to keep a bright fire both within my house and within my breast. My employment out of doors now was to collect the dead wood in the forest, bringing it in my hands or on my shoulders, or sometimes trailing a dead pine tree under each arm to my shed. An old forest fence which had seen its best days was a great haul for me. I sacrificed it to Vulcan, for it was past serving the god Terminus.[8] How much more interesting an event is that man's supper who has just been forth in the snow to hunt, nay, you might say, steal, the fuel to cook it with! His bread and meat are sweet. There are enough fagots and waste wood of all kinds in the forests of most of our towns to support many fires, but which at present warm none, and, some think, hinder the growth of the young wood. There was also the driftwood of the pond. In the course of the summer I had discovered a raft of pitch-pine logs with the bark on, pinned together by the Irish when the railroad was built. This I hauled up partly on the shore. After soaking two years and then lying high six months it was perfectly sound, though waterlogged past drying. I amused myself one winter day with sliding this piecemeal across the pond, nearly half a mile, skating behind with one end of a log fifteen feet long on my shoulder, and the other on the ice; or I tied several logs together with a birch withe, and then, with a longer birch or alder which had a hook at the end, dragged them across. Though completely waterlogged and almost as heavy as lead, they not only burned long, but made a very hot fire; nay, I thought that they burned better for the soaking, as if the pitch, being confined by the water, burned longer as in a lamp.

8. That is, Thoreau burned it (thereby sacrificing it to Vulcan, the god of fire and blacksmith of the Roman gods) rather than using it in a fence (where it would have served Terminus, the Roman god of limits or boundaries).

Gilpin, in his account of the forest borderers of England, says that "the encroachments of trespassers, and the houses and fences thus raised on the borders of the forest," were "considered as great nuisances by the old forest law, and were severely punished under the name of *purprestures*, as tending *ad terrorem ferarum—ad nocumentum forestæ, &c.*,"[9] to the frightening of the game and the detriment of the forest. But I was interested in the preservation of the venison and the vert[1] more than the hunters or wood-choppers, and as much as though I had been the Lord Warden himself; and if any part was burned, though I burned it myself by accident, I grieved with a grief that lasted longer and was more inconsolable than that of the proprietors; nay, I grieved when it was cut down by the proprietors themselves. I would that our farmers when they cut down a forest felt some of that awe which the old Romans did when they came to thin, or let in the light to, a consecrated grove, (*lucum conlucare*), that is, would believe that it is sacred to some god. The Roman made an expiatory offering, and prayed, Whatever god or goddess thou art to whom this grove is sacred, be propitious to me, my family, and children, &c.

It is remarkable what a value is still put upon wood even in this age and in this new country, a value more permanent and universal than that of gold. After all our discoveries and inventions no man will go by a pile of wood. It is as precious to us as it was to our Saxon and Norman ancestors. If they made their bows of it, we make our gun-stocks of it. Michaux, more than thirty years ago, says that the price of wood for fuel in New York and Philadelphia "nearly equals, and sometimes exceeds, that of the best wood in Paris, though this immense capital annually requires more than three hunderd thousand cords, and is surrounded to the distance of three hundred miles by cultivated plains."[2] In this town the price of wood rises almost steadily, and the only question is, how much higher it is to be this year than it was the last. Mechanics and tradesmen who come in person to the forest on no other errand, are sure to attend the wood auction, and even pay a high price for the privilege of gleaning after the wood-chopper. It is now many years that men have resorted to the forest for fuel and the materials of the arts; the New Englander and the New Hollander, the Parisian and the Celt, the farmer and Robinhood, Goody Blake and Harry Gill,[3] in most parts of the world the prince and the peasant, the scholar and the savage, equally require still a few sticks from the forest to warm them and cook their food. Neither could I do without them.

Every man looks at his wood-pile with a kind of affection. I loved to have mine before my window, and the more chips the better to remind me of my pleasing work. I had an old axe which nobody claimed, with which by spells in winter days, on the sunny side of the house, I played about the stumps which I had got out of my bean-field. As my driver prophesied when I was ploughing, they warmed me twice, once while I was splitting them, and again when they were on the fire, so that no fuel could give out more heat. As for the axe, I was advised to get the village blacksmith to "jump" it; but

9. From *Remarks on Forest Scenery* (1782), by the English nature writer William Gilpin (1724–1804).

1. Green vegetation providing cover for deer.

2. From *North American Sylva* (1818), by the French botanist François Andrew Michaux (1746–1802).

3. In Wordsworth's poem "Goody Blake and Harry Gill: A True Story" (1798), Harry Gill seizes old Goody Blake in the act of pulling sticks from his hedge for firewood. God answers her prayer that Harry "never more be warm."

I jumped him, and, putting a hickory helve from the woods into it, made it do. If it was dull, it was at least hung true.

A few pieces of fat pine were a great treasure. It is interesting to remember how much of this food for fire is still concealed in the bowels of the earth. In previous years I had often gone "prospecting" over some bare hill-side, where a pitch-pine wood had formerly stood, and got out the fat pine roots. They are almost indestructible. Stumps thirty or forty years old, at least, will still be sound at the core, though the sapwood has all become vegetable mould, as appears by the scales of the thick bark forming a ring level with the earth four or five inches distant from the heart. With axe and shovel you explore this mine, and follow the marrowy store, yellow as beef tallow, or as if you had struck on a vein of gold, deep into the earth. But commonly I kindled my fire with the dry leaves of the forest, which I had stored up in my shed before the snow came. Green hickory finely split makes the woodchopper's kindlings, when he has a camp in the woods. Once in a while I got a little of this. When the villagers were lighting their fires beyond the horizon, I too gave notice to the various wild inhabitants of Walden vale, by a smoky streamer from my chimney, that I was awake.—

Light-winged Smoke, Icarian bird,
Melting thy pinions in thy upward flight,
Lark without song, and messenger of dawn,
Circling above the hamlets as thy nest;
Or else, departing dream, and shadowy form
Of midnight vision, gathering up thy skirts;
By night star-veiling, and by day
Darkening the light and blotting out the sun;
Go thou my incense upward from this hearth,
And ask the gods to pardon this clear flame.

Hard green wood just cut, though I used but little of that, answered my purpose better than any other. I sometimes left a good fire when I went to take a walk in a winter afternoon; and when I returned, three or four hours afterward, it would be still alive and glowing. My house was not empty though I was gone. It was as if I had left a cheerful housekeeper behind. It was I and Fire that lived there; and commonly my housekeeper proved trustworthy. One day, however, as I was splitting wood, I thought that I would just look in at the window and see if the house was not on fire; it was the only time I remember to have been particularly anxious on this score; so I looked and saw that a spark had caught my bed, and I went in and extinguished it when it had burned a place as big as my hand. But my house occupied so sunny and sheltered a position, and its roof was so low, that I could afford to let the fire go out in the middle of almost any winter day.

The moles nested in my cellar, nibbling every third potato, and making a snug bed even there of some hair left after plastering and of brown paper; for even the wildest animals love comfort and warmth as well as man, and they survive the winter only because they are so careful to secure them. Some of my friends spoke as if I was coming to the woods on purpose to freeze myself. The animal merely makes a bed, which he warms with his body in a sheltered place; but man, having discovered fire, boxes up some air in a spacious apartment, and warms that, instead of robbing himself, makes that his bed, in which he can move about divested of more cumbrous clothing, maintain a kind of summer in the midst of winter, and by means of windows even admit the light, and with a lamp lengthen out the day. Thus he goes a step or two beyond instinct, and saves a little time for the fine arts. Though, when I had been exposed to the rudest blasts a long time, my whole body began to grow torpid, when I reached the genial atmosphere of my house I soon recovered my faculties and prolonged my life. But the most luxuriously housed has little to boast of in this respect, nor need we trouble ourselves to speculate how the human race may be at last destroyed. It would be easy to cut their threads any time with a little sharper blast from the north. We go on dating from Cold Fridays and Great Snows; but a little colder Friday, or greater snow, would put a period to man's existence on the globe.

The next winter I used a small cooking-stove for economy, since I did not own the forest; but it did not keep fire so well as the open fire-place. Cooking was then, for the most part, no longer a poetic, but merely a chemic process. It will soon be forgotten, in these days of stoves, that we used to roast potatoes in the ashes, after the Indian fashion. The stove not only took up room and scented the house, but it concealed the fire, and I felt as if I had lost a companion. You can always see a face in the fire. The laborer, looking into it at evening, purifies his thoughts of the dross and earthiness which they have accumulated during the day. But I could no longer sit and look into the fire, and the pertinent words of a poet recurred to me with new force.—

"Never, bright flame, may be denied to me
Thy dear, life imaging, close sympathy.
What but my hopes shot upward e'er so bright?
What but my fortunes sunk so low in night?

Why art thou banished from our hearth and hall,
Thou who art welcomed and beloved by all?
Was thy existence then too fanciful
For our life's common light, who are so dull?
Did thy bright gleam mysterious converse hold
With our congenial souls? secrets too bold?
Well, we are safe and strong, for now we sit
Beside a hearth where no dim shadows flit,
Where nothing cheers nor saddens, but a fire
Warms feet and hands—nor does to more aspire;
By whose compact utilitarian heap
The present may sit down and go to sleep,
Nor fear the ghosts who from the dim past walked,
And with us by the unequal light of the old wood fire talked."[4]

14. Former Inhabitants; and Winter Visitors

I weathered some merry snow storms, and spent some cheerful winter evenings by my fire-side, while the snow whirled wildly without, and even the hooting of the owl was hushed. For many weeks I met no one in my walks but those who came occasionally to cut wood and sled it to the village. The

4. A slightly altered portion of "The Wood Fire," a poem by Ellen Sturgis Hooper (1816–1848), which appeared in the *Dial* (1840).

elements, however, abetted me in making a path through the deepest snow in the woods, for when I had once gone through the wind blew the oak leaves into my tracks, where they lodged, and by absorbing the rays of the sun melted the snow, and so not only made a dry bed for my feet, but in the night their dark line was my guide. For human society I was obliged to conjure up the former occupants of these woods. Within the memory of many of my townsmen the road near which my house stands resounded with the laugh and gossip of inhabitants, and the woods which border it were notched and dotted here and there with their little gardens and dwellings, though it was then much more shut in by the forest than now. In some places, within my own remembrance, the pines would scrape both sides of a chaise at once, and women and children who were compelled to go this way to Lincoln alone and on foot did it with fear, and often ran a good part of the distance. Though mainly but a humble route to neighboring villages, or for the woodman's team, it once amused the traveller more than now by its variety, and lingered longer in his memory. Where now firm open fields stretch from the village to the woods, it then ran through a maple swamp on a foundation of logs, the remnants of which, doubtless, still underlie the present dusty highway, from the Stratton, now the Alms House, Farm, to Brister's Hill.

East of my bean-field, across the road, lived Cato Ingraham, slave of Duncan Ingraham, Esquire, gentleman of Concord village; who built his slave a house, and gave him permission to live in Walden Woods;—Cato, not Uticensis, but Concordiensis.[5] Some say that he was a Guinea Negro. There are a few who remember his little patch among the walnuts, which he let grow up till he should be old and need them; but a younger and whiter speculator got them at last. He too, however, occupies an equally narrow house at present. Cato's half-obliterated cellar hole still remains, though known to few, being concealed from the traveller by a fringe of pines. It is now filled with the smooth sumach, (*Rhus glabra*,) and one of the earliest species of goldenrod (*Solidago stricta*) grows there luxuriantly.

Here, by the very corner of my field, still nearer to town, Zilpha, a colored woman, had her little house, where she spun linen for the townsfolk, making the Walden Woods ring with her shrill singing, for she had a loud and notable voice. At length, in the war of 1812, her dwelling was set on fire by English soldiers, prisoners on parole, when she was away, and her cat and dog and hens were all burned up together. She led a hard life, and somewhat inhumane. One old frequenter of these woods remembers, that as he passed her house one noon he heard her muttering to herself over her gurgling pot,—"Ye are all bones, bones!" I have seen bricks amid the oak copse there.

Down the road, on the right hand, on Brister's Hill, lived Brister Freeman, "a handy Negro," slave of Squire Cummings once,—there where grow still the apple-trees which Brister planted and tended; large old trees now, but their fruit still wild and ciderish to my taste. Not long since I read his epitaph in the old Lincoln burying-ground, a little on one side, near the unmarked graves of some British grenadiers who fell in the retreat from Concord,—where he is styled "Sippio Brister,"—Scipio Africanus[6] he had some title to be called,—"a man of color," as if he were discolored. It also told me, with star-

5. The grandson of Marcus Porcius Cato, Thoreau's authority on agriculture, was called Cato Uticensis after his death at Utica. Classical names were often given to American slaves.

6. Scipio Africanus (237–183 B.C.E.) was a Roman general who led the invasion of Carthage.

ing emphasis, when he died; which was but an indirect way of informing me that he ever lived. With him dwelt Fenda, his hospitable wife, who told fortunes, yet pleasantly,—large, round, and black, blacker than any of the children of night, such a dusky orb as never rose on Concord before or since.

Farther down the hill, on the left, on the old road in the woods, are marks of some homestead of the Stratton family; whose orchard once covered all the slope of Brister's Hill, but was long since killed out by pitch-pines, excepting a few stumps, whose old roots furnish still the wild stocks of many a thrifty village tree.

Nearer yet to town, you come to Breed's location, on the other side of the way, just on the edge of the wood; ground famous for the pranks of a demon not distinctly named in old mythology, who has acted a prominent and astounding part in our New England life, and deserves, as much as any mythological character, to have his biography written one day; who first comes in the guise of a friend or hired man, and then robs and murders the whole family,—New-England Rum. But history must not yet tell the tragedies enacted here; let time intervene in some measure to assuage and lend an azure tint to them. Here the most indistinct and dubious tradition says that once a tavern stood; the well the same, which tempered the traveller's beverage and refreshed his steed. Here then men saluted one another, and heard and told the news, and went their ways again.

Breed's hut was standing only a dozen years ago, though it had long been unoccupied. It was about the size of mine. It was set on fire by mischievous boys, one Election night, if I do not mistake. I lived on the edge of the village then, and had just lost myself over Davenant's Gondibert, that winter that I labored with a lethargy,—which, by the way, I never knew whether to regard as a family complaint, having an uncle who goes to sleep shaving himself, and is obliged to sprout potatoes in a cellar Sundays, in order to keep awake and keep the Sabbath, or as the consequence of my attempt to read Chalmers' collection of English poetry[7] without skipping. It fairly overcame my Nervii.[8] I had just sunk my head on this when the bells rung fire, and in hot haste the engines rolled that way, led by a straggling troop of men and boys, and I among the foremost, for I had leaped the brook. We thought it was far south over the woods,—we who had run to fires before,—barn, shop, or dwelling-house, or all together. "It's Baker's barn," cried one. "It is the Codman Place," affirmed another. And then fresh sparks went up above the wood, as if the roof fell in, and we all shouted "Concord to the rescue!" Wagons shot past with furious speed and crushing loads, bearing, perchance, among the rest, the agent of the Insurance Company, who was bound to go however far; and ever and anon the engine bell tinkled behind, more slow and sure, and rearmost of all, as it was afterward whispered, came they who set the fire and gave the alarm. Thus we kept on like true idealists, rejecting the evidence of our senses, until at a turn in the road we heard the crackling and actually felt the heat of the fire from over the wall, and realized, alas! that we were there. The very nearness of the fire but cooled our ardor. At first we thought to throw a frog-pond on to it; but concluded to let it burn, it was

7. In 1810, the English critic and anthologist Alexander Chalmers (1759–1834) brought out a twenty-one-volume collection of English poetry. Thoreau refers to William Davenant's *Gondibart: An Heroick Poem* (1672).

8. A tribe that Julius Caesar defeated in Flanders; Thoreau is punning.

so far gone and so worthless. So we stood round our engine, jostled one another, expressed our sentiments through speaking trumpets, or in lower tone referred to the great conflagrations which the world has witnessed, including Bascom's shop, and, between ourselves, we thought that, were we there in season with our "tub," and a full frog-pond by, we could turn that threatened last and universal one into another flood. We finally retreated without doing any mischief,—returned to sleep and Gondibert. But as for Gondibert, I would except that passage in the preface about wit being the soul's powder,—"but most of mankind are strangers to wit, as Indians are to powder."[9]

It chanced that I walked that way across the fields the following night, about the same hour, and hearing a low moaning at this spot, I drew near in the dark, and discovered the only survivor of the family that I know, the heir of both its virtues and its vices, who alone was interested in this burning, lying on his stomach and looking over the cellar wall at the still smouldering cinders beneath, muttering to himself, as is his wont. He had been working far off in the river meadows all day, and had improved the first moments that he could call his own to visit the home of his fathers and his youth. He gazed into the cellar from all sides and points of view by turns, always lying down to it, as if there was some treasure, which he remembered, concealed between the stones, where there was absolutely nothing but a heap of bricks and ashes. The house being gone, he looked at what there was left. He was soothed by the sympathy which my mere presence implied, and showed me, as well as the darkness permitted, where the well was covered up; which, thank Heaven, could never be burned; and he groped long about the wall to find the well-sweep which his father had cut and mounted, feeling for the iron hook or staple by which a burden had been fastened to the heavy end,—all that he could now cling to,—to convince me that it was no common "rider." I felt it, and still remark it almost daily in my walks, for by it hangs the history of a family.

Once more, on the left, where are seen the well and lilac bushes by the wall, in the now open field, lived Nutting and Le Grosse. But to return toward Lincoln.

Farther in the woods than any of these, where the road approaches nearest to the pond, Wyman the potter squatted, and furnished his townsmen with earthen ware, and left descendants to succeed him. Neither were they rich in worldly goods, holding the land by sufferance while they lived; and there often the sheriff came in vain to collect the taxes, and "attached a chip,"[1] for form's sake, as I have read in his accounts, there being nothing else that he could lay his hands on. One day in midsummer, when I was hoeing, a man who was carrying a load of pottery to market stopped his horse against my field and inquired concerning Wyman the younger. He had long ago bought a potter's wheel of him, and wished to know what had become of him. I had read of the potter's clay and wheel in Scripture, but it had never occurred to me that the pots we use were not such as had come down unbroken from those days, or grown on trees like gourds somewhere, and I was pleased to hear that so fictile an art was ever practised in my neighborhood.

9. From "The Author's Preface."

1. Legal act of seizing a worthless item as a way of demonstrating an effort to collect on an unpayable debt.

The last inhabitant of these woods before me was an Irishman, Hugh Quoil, (if I have spelt his name with coil enough,) who occupied Wyman's tenement,—Col. Quoil, he was called. Rumor said that he had been a soldier at Waterloo.[2] If he had lived I should have made him fight his battles over again. His trade here was that of a ditcher. Napoleon went to St. Helena; Quoil came to Walden Woods. All I know of him is tragic. He was a man of manners, like one who had seen the world, and was capable of more civil speech than you could well attend to. He wore a great coat in mid-summer, being affected with the trembling delirium, and his face was the color of carmine. He died in the road at the foot of Brister's Hill shortly after I came to the woods, so that I have not remembered him as a neighbor. Before his house was pulled down, when his comrades avoided it as "an unlucky castle," I visited it. There lay his old clothes curled up by use, as if they were himself, upon his raised plank bed. His pipe lay broken on the hearth, instead of a bowl broken at the fountain. The last could never have been the symbol of his death, for he confessed to me that, though he had heard of Brister's Spring, he had never seen it; and soiled cards, kings of diamonds spades and hearts, were scattered over the floor. One black chicken which the administrator could not catch, black as night and as silent, not even croaking, awaiting Reynard,[3] still went to roost in the next apartment. In the rear there was the dim outline of a garden, which had been planted but had never received its first hoeing, owing to those terrible shaking fits, though it was now harvest time. It was over-run with Roman wormwood and beggar-ticks, which last stuck to my clothes for all fruit. The skin of a woodchuck was freshly stretched upon the back of the house, a trophy of his last Waterloo; but no warm cap or mittens would he want more.

Now only a dent in the earth marks the site of these dwellings, with buried cellar stones, and strawberries, raspberries, thimble-berries, hazel-bushes, and sumachs growing in the sunny sward there; some pitch-pine or gnarled oak occupies what was the chimney nook, and a sweet-scented black-birch, perhaps, waves where the door-stone was. Sometimes the well dent is visible, where once a spring oozed; now dry and tearless grass; or it was covered deep,—not to be discovered till some late day,—with a flat stone under the sod, when the last of the race departed. What a sorrowful act must that be,—the covering up of wells! coincident with the opening of wells of tears. These cellar dents, like deserted fox burrows, old holes, are all that is left where once were the stir and bustle of human life, and "fate, free-will, foreknowledge absolute,"[4] in some form and dialect or other were by turns discussed. But all I can learn of their conclusions amounts to just this, that "Cato and Brister pulled wool;" which is about as edifying as the history of more famous schools of philosophy.

Still grows the vivacious lilac a generation after the door and lintel and the sill are gone, unfolding its sweet-scented flowers each spring, to be plucked by the musing traveller; planted and tended once by children's hands, in front-yard plots,—now standing by wall-sides in retired pastures, and giving place to new-rising forests;—the last of that stirp, sole survivor

2. The Belgian village where Napoleon was defeated by the British in 1815; he was subsequently exiled to the south Atlantic island of St. Helena. "Coil": trouble.

3. Literary name for a fox, from the medieval fable "Reynard the Fox." "Administrator": a person appointed to administer an estate.

4. Milton's *Paradise Lost* 2.560.

of that family. Little did the dusky children think that the puny slip with its two eyes only, which they stuck in the ground in the shadow of the house and daily watered, would root itself so, and outlive them and house itself in the rear that shaded it, and grown man's garden and orchard, and tell their story faintly to the lone wanderer a half century after they had grown up and died,—blossoming as fair, and smelling as sweet, as in that first spring. I mark its still tender, civil, cheerful, lilac colors.

But this small village, germ of something more, why did it fail while Concord keeps its ground? Were there no natural advantages,—no water privileges, forsooth? Ay, the deep Waldon Pond and cool Brister's Spring,—privilege to drink long and healthy draughts at these, all unimproved by these men but to dilute their glass. They were universally a thirsty race. Might not the basket, stable-broom, mat-making, corn-parching, linen-spinning, and pottery business have thrived here, making the wilderness to blossom like the rose, and a numerous posterity have inherited the land of their fathers? The sterile soil would at least have been proof against a low-land degeneracy. Alas! how little does the memory of these human inhabitants enhance the beauty of the landscape! Again, perhaps, Nature will try, with me for a first settler, and my house raised last spring to be the oldest in the hamlet.

I am not aware that any man has ever built on the spot which I occupy. Deliver me from a city built on the site of a more ancient city, whose materials are ruins, whose gardens cemeteries. The soil is blanched and accursed there, and before that becomes necessary the earth itself will be destroyed. With such reminiscences I repeopled the woods and lulled myself asleep.

At this season I seldom had a visitor. When the snow lay deepest no wanderer ventured near my house for a week or fortnight at a time, but there I lived as snug as a meadow mouse, or as cattle and poultry which are said to have survived for a long time buried in drifts, even without food; or like that early settler's family in the town of Sutton, in this state, whose cottage was completely covered by the great snow of 1717 when he was absent, and an Indian found it only by the hole which the chimney's breath made in the drift, and so relieved the family. But no friendly Indian concerned himself about me; nor needed he, for the master of the house was at home. The Great Snow! How cheerful it is to hear of! When the farmers could not get to the woods and swamps with their teams, and were obliged to cut down the shade trees before their houses, and when the crust was harder cut off the trees in the swamps ten feet from the ground, as it appeared the next spring.

In the deepest snows, the path which I used from the highway to my house, about half a mile long, might have been represented by a meandering dotted line, with wide intervals between the dots. For a week of even weather I took exactly the same number of steps, and of the same length, coming and going, stepping deliberately and with the precision of a pair of dividers in my own deep tracks,—to such routine the winter reduces us,—yet often they were filled with heaven's own blue. But no weather interfered fatally with my walks, or rather my going abroad, for I frequently tramped eight or ten miles through the deepest snow to keep an appointment with a beech-tree, or a yellow-birch, or an old acquaintance among the pines; when the ice and snow causing their limbs to droop, and so sharpening their tops, had changed the pines into fir-trees; wading to the tops of the highest hills when the snow was nearly two feet deep on a level, and shaking down another snow-storm on my head at every step; or sometimes creeping and floundering thither on my hands and knees, when the hunters had gone into winter quarters. One afternoon I amused myself by watching a barred owl (*Strix nebulosa*) sitting on one of the lower dead limbs of a white-pine, close to the trunk, in broad daylight, I standing within a rod of him. He could hear me when I moved and cronched the snow with my feet, but could not plainly see me. When I made most noise he would stretch out his neck, and erect his neck feathers, and open his eyes wide; but their lids soon fell again, and he began to nod. I too felt a slumberous influence after watching him half an hour, as he sat thus with his eyes half open, like a cat, winged brother of the cat. There was only a narrow slit left between their lids, by which he preserved a peninsular relation to me; thus, with half-shut eyes, looking out from the land of dreams, and endeavoring to realize me, vague object or mote that interrupted his visions. At length, on some louder noise or my nearer approach, he would grow uneasy and sluggishly turn about on his perch, as if impatient at having his dreams disturbed; and when he launched himself off and flapped through the pines, spreading his wings to unexpected breadth, I could not hear the slightest sound from them. Thus, guided amid the pine boughs rather by a delicate sense of their neighborhood than by sight, feeling his twilight way as it were with his sensitive pinions, he found a new perch, where he might in peace await the dawning of his day.

As I walked over the long causeway made for the railroad through the meadows, I encountered many a blustering and nipping wind, for nowhere has it freer play; and when the frost had smitten me on one cheek, heathen as I was, I turned to it the other also.[5] Nor was it much better by the carriage road from Brister's Hill. For I came to town still, like a friendly Indian, when the contents of the broad open fields were all piled up between the walls of the Walden road, and half an hour sufficed to obliterate the tracks of the last traveller. And when I returned new drifts would have formed, through which I floundered, where the busy north-west wind had been depositing the powdery snow round a sharp angle in the road, and not a rabbit's track, nor even the fine print, the small type, of a deer mouse was to be seen. Yet I rarely failed to find, even in mid-winter, some warm and springy swamp where the grass and the skunk-cabbage still put forth with perennial verdure, and some hardier bird occasionally awaited the return of spring.

Sometimes, notwithstanding the snow, when I returned from my walk at evening I crossed the deep tracks of a woodchopper leading from my door, and found his pile of whittlings on the hearth, and my house filled with the odor of his pipe. Or on a Sunday afternoon, if I chanced to be at home, I heard the cronching of the snow made by the step of a long-headed farmer, who from far through the woods sought my house, to have a social "crack;" one of the few of his vocation who are "men on their farms;"[6] who donned a frock instead of a professor's gown, and is as ready to extract the moral out of church or state as to haul a load of manure from his barn-yard. We talked of rude and simple times, when men sat about large fires in cold

5. Matthew 5.39, Sermon on the Mount: "But I say unto you, That ye resist not evil: but whosoever shall smite thee on thy right cheek, turn to him the other also."

6. A reference to Emerson's classifications of the subdivided condition of humankind in "The American Scholar"; being "Man on the farm" is better than being a farmer. 'Crack": friendly chat.

bracing weather, with clear heads; and when other dessert failed, we tried our teeth on many a nut which wise squirrels have long since abandoned, for those which have the thickest shells are commonly empty.

The one who came from farthest to my lodge, through deepest snows and most dismal tempests, was a poet.[7] A farmer, a hunter, a soldier, a reporter, even a philosopher, may be daunted; but nothing can deter a poet, for he is actuated by pure love. Who can predict his comings and goings? His business calls him out at all hours, even when doctors sleep. We made that small house ring with boisterous mirth and resound with the murmur of much sober talk, making amends then to Walden vale for the long silences. Broadway was still and deserted in comparison. At suitable intervals there were regular salutes of laughter, which might have been referred indifferently to the last uttered or the forth-coming jest. We made many a "bran new" theory of life over a thin dish of gruel, which combined the advantages of conviviality with the clear-headedness which philosophy requires.

I should not forget that during my last winter at the pond there was another welcome visitor, who at one time came through the village, through snow and rain and darkness, till he saw my lamp through the trees, and shared with me some long winter evenings.[8] One of the last of the philosophers,—Connecticut gave him to the world,—he peddled first her wares, afterwards, as he declares, his brains. These he peddles still, prompting God and disgracing man, bearing for fruit his brain only, like the nut its kernel. I think that he must be the man of the most faith of any alive. His words and attitude always suppose a better state of things than other men are acquainted with, and he will be the last man to be disappointed as the ages revolve. He has no venture in the present. But though comparatively disregarded now, when his day comes, laws unsuspected by most will take effect, and masters of families and rulers will come to him for advice.—

"How blind that cannot see serenity!"[9]

A true friend of man; almost the only friend of human progress. An Old Mortality,[1] say rather an Immortality, with unwearied patience and faith making plain the image engraven in men's bodies, the God of whom they are but defaced and leaning monuments. With his hospitable intellect he embraces children, beggars, insane, and scholars, and entertains the thought of all, adding to it commonly some breadth and elegance. I think that he should keep a caravansary on the world's highway, where philosophers of all nations might put up, and on his sign should be printed, "Entertainment for man, but not for his beast. Enter ye that have leisure and a quiet mind, who earnestly seek the right road." He is perhaps the sanest man and has the fewest crotchets of any I chance to know; the same yesterday and to-morrow. Of yore we had sauntered and talked, and effectually put the world behind us; for he was pledged to no institution in it, freeborn, *ingenuus*.[2] Whichever way we turned, it seemed that the heavens and the earth had met together, since he enhanced the beauty of the landscape. A blue-robed man, whose

7. Channing.
8. Bronson Alcott (1799–1888), one of the "raisers" of the cabin.
9. From Thomas Storer's *The Life and Death of Thomas Wolsey, Cardinal* (1599).
1. The title character in Sir Walter Scott's *Old Mortality* (1816) went from churchyard to churchyard clearing away moss and rechiseling half-defaced inscriptions on tombstones.
2. Frank and honest (Latin).

fittest roof is the overarching sky which reflects his serenity. I do not see how he can ever die; Nature cannot spare him.

Having each some shingles of thought well dried, we sat and whittled them, trying our knives, and admiring the clear yellowish grain of the pumpkin pine. We waded so gently and reverently, or we pulled together so smoothly, that the fishes of thought were not scared from the stream, nor feared any angler on the bank, but came and went grandly, like the clouds which float through the western sky, and the mother-o'-pearl flocks which sometimes form and dissolve there. There we worked, revising mythology, rounding a fable here and there, and building castles in the air for which earth offered no worthy foundation. Great Looker! Great Expecter! to converse with whom was a New England Night's Entertainment. Ah! such discourse we had, hermit and philosopher, and the old settler I have spoken of,—we three,—it expanded and racked my little house; I should not dare to say how many pounds' weight there was above the atmospheric pressure on every circular inch; it opened its seams so that they had to be calked with much dulness thereafter to stop the consequent leak;—but I had enough of that kind of oakum already picked.

There was one other[3] with whom I had "solid seasons," long to be remembered, at his house in the village, and who looked in upon me from time to time; but I had no more for society there.

There too, as every where, I sometimes expected the Visitor who never comes.[4] The Vishnu Purana says, "The house-holder is to remain at eventide in his court-yard as long as it takes to milk a cow, or longer if he pleases, to await the arrival of a guest." I often performed this duty of hospitality, waited long enough to milk a whole herd of cows, but did not see the man approaching from the town.

15. Winter Animals

When the ponds were firmly frozen, they afforded not only new and shorter routes to many points, but new views from their surfaces of the familiar landscape around them. When I crossed Flint's Pond, after it was covered with snow, though I had often paddled about and skated over it, it was so unexpectedly wide and so strange that I could think of nothing but Baffin's Bay.[5] The Lincoln hills rose up around me at the extremity of a snowy plain, in which I did not remember to have stood before; and the fishermen, at an indeterminable distance over the ice, moving slowly about with their wolfish dogs, passed for sealers or Esquimaux, or in misty weather loomed like fabulous creatures, and I did not know whether they were giants or pygmies. I took this course when I went to lecture in Lincoln in the evening, travelling in no road and passing no house between my own hut and the lecture room. In Goose Pond, which lay in my way, a colony of muskrats dwelt, and raised their cabins high above the ice, though none could be seen abroad when I crossed it. Walden, being like the rest usually bare of snow, or with only shallow and interrupted drifts on it, was my yard, where I could walk

3. Emerson.

4. Thoreau mixes a quotation from H.H. Wilson's translation of the Sanskrit scripture *Vishnu Purana* (1840) with a folk ballad, "The Children in the Wood": "But never more could see the man / Approaching from the town."

5. Between Greenland and the Canadian islands; now Baffin Bay.

freely when the snow was nearly two feet deep on a level elsewhere and the villagers were confined to their streets. There, far from the village street, and except at very long intervals, from the jingle of sleigh-bells, I slid and skated, as in a vast moose-yard well trodden, over-hung by oak woods and solemn pines bent down with snow or bristling with icicles.

For sounds in winter nights, and often in winter days, I heard the forlorn but melodious note of a hooting owl indefinitely far; such a sound as the frozen earth would yield if struck with a suitable plectrum, the very *lingua vernacula*[6] of Walden Wood, and quite familiar to me at last, though I never saw the bird while it was making it. I seldom opened my door in a winter evening without hearing it; *Hoo hoo hoo, hoorer hoo* sounded sonorously, and the first three syllables accented somewhat like *how der do*; or sometimes *hoo hoo* only. One night in the beginning of winter, before the pond froze over, about nine o'clock, I was startled by the loud honking of a goose, and, stepping to the door, heard the sound of their wings like a tempest in the woods as they flew low over my house. They passed over the pond toward Fair Haven, seemingly deterred from settling by my light, their commodore honking all the while with a regular beat. Suddenly an unmistakable cat-owl from very near me, with the most harsh and tremendous voice I ever heard from any inhabitant of the woods, responded at regular intervals to the goose, as if determined to expose and disgrace this intruder from Hudson's Bay by exhibiting a greater compass and volume of voice in a native, and *boo-hoo* him out of Concord horizon. What do you mean by alarming the citadel at this time of night consecrated to me? Do you think I am ever caught napping at such an hour, and that I have not got lungs and a larynx as well as yourself? *Boo-hoo, boo-hoo, boo-hoo!* It was one of the most thrilling discords I ever heard. And yet, if you had a discriminating ear, there were in it the elements of a concord such as these plains never saw nor heard.

I also heard the whooping of the ice in the pond, my great bed-fellow in that part of Concord, as if it were restless in its bed and would fain turn over, were troubled with flatulency and bad dreams; or I was waked by the cracking of the ground by the frost, as if some one had driven a team against my door, and in the morning would find a crack in the earth a quarter of a mile long and a third of an inch wide.

Sometimes I heard the foxes as they ranged over the snow crust, in moonlight nights, in search of a partridge or other game, barking raggedly and demoniacally like forest dogs, as if laboring with some anxiety, or seeking expression, struggling for light and to be dogs outright and run freely in the streets; for if we take the ages into our account, may there not be a civilization going on among brutes as well as men? They seemed to me to be rudimental, burrowing men, still standing on their defence, awaiting their transformation. Sometimes one came near to my window, attracted by my light, barked a vulpine curse at me, and then retreated.

Usually the red squirrel (*Sciurus Hudsonius*) waked me in the dawn, coursing over the roof and up and down the sides of the house, as if sent out of the woods for this purpose. In the course of the winter I threw out half a bushel of ears of sweet-corn, which had not got ripe, on to the snow crust by my door, and was amused by watching the motions of the various animals which

6. Local dialect (Latin).

were baited by it. In the twilight and the night the rabbits came regularly and made a hearty meal. All day long the red squirrels came and went, and afforded me much entertainment by their manœuvres. One would approach at first warily through the shrub-oaks, running over the snow crust by fits and starts like a leaf blown by the wind, now a few paces this way, with wonderful speed and waste of energy, making inconceivable haste with his "trotters," as if it were for a wager, and now as many paces that way, but never getting on more than half a rod at a time; and then suddenly pausing with a ludicrous expression and a gratuitous somerset,[7] as if all the eyes in the universe were fixed on him,—for all the motions of a squirrel, even in the most solitary recesses of the forest, imply spectators as much as those of a dancing girl,—wasting more time in delay and circumspection than would have sufficed to walk the whole distance,—I never saw one walk,—and then suddenly, before you could say Jack Robinson, he would be in the top of a young pitch-pine, winding up his clock and chiding all imaginary spectators, soliloquizing and talking to all the universe at the same time,—for no reason that I could ever detect, or he himself was aware of, I suspect. At length he would reach the corn, and selecting a suitable ear, frisk about in the same uncertain trigonometrical way to the top-most stick of my wood-pile, before my window, where he looked me in the face, and there sit for hours, supplying himself with a new ear from time to time, nibbling at first voraciously and throwing the half-naked cobs about; till at length he grew more dainty still and played with his food, tasting only the inside of the kernel, and the ear which was held balanced over the stick by one paw, slipped from his careless grasp and fell to the ground, when he would look over at it with a ludicrous expression of uncertainty, as if suspecting that it had life, with a mind not made up whether to get it again, or a new one, or be off; now thinking of corn, then listening to hear what was in the wind. So the little impudent fellow would waste many an ear in a forenoon; till at last, seizing some longer and plumper one, considerably bigger than himself, and skilfully balancing it, he would set out with it to the woods, like a tiger with a buffalo, by the same zig-zag course and frequent pauses, scratching along with it as if it were too heavy for him and falling all the while, making its fall a diagonal between a perpendicular and horizontal, being determined to put it through at any rate;—a singularly frivolous and whimsical fellow;—and so he would get off with it to where he lived, perhaps carry it to the top of a pine tree forty or fifty rods distant, and I would afterwards find the cobs strewn about the woods in various directions.

At length the jays arrive, whose discordant screams were heard long before, as they were warily making their approach an eighth of a mile off, and in a stealthy and sneaking manner they flit from tree to tree, nearer and nearer, and pick up the kernels which the squirrels have dropped. Then, sitting on a pitch-pine bough, they attempt to swallow in their haste a kernel which is too big for their throats and chokes them and after great labor they disgorge it, and spend an hour in the endeavor to crack it by repeated blows with their bills. They were manifestly thieves, and I had not much respect for them; but the squirrels, though at first shy, went to work as if they were taking what was their own.

7. Somersault.

Meanwhile also came the chicadees in flocks, which picking up the crumbs the squirrels had dropped, flew to the nearest twig, and placing them under their claws, hammered away at them with their little bills, as if it were an insect in the bark, till they were sufficiently reduced for their slender throats. A little flock of these tit-mice came daily to pick a dinner out of my wood-pile, or the crumbs at my door, with faint flitting lisping notes, like the tinkling of icicles in the grass, or else with sprightly *day day day* or more rarely, in spring-like days, a wiry summery *phe-be* from the wood-side. They were so familiar that at length one alighted on an armful of wood which I was carrying in, and pecked at the sticks without fear. I once had a sparrow alight upon my shoulder for a moment while I was hoeing in a village garden, and I felt that I was more distinguished by that circumstance than I should have been by any epaulet I could have worn. The squirrels also grew at last to be quite familiar, and occasionally stepped upon my shoe, when that was the nearest way.

When the ground was not yet quite covered, and again near the end of winter, when the snow was melted on my south hill-side and about my wood-pile, the partridges came out of the woods morning and evening to feed there. Whichever side you walk in the woods the partridge bursts away on whirring wings, jarring the snow from the dry leaves and twigs on high, which comes sifting down in the sun-beams like golden dust; for this brave bird is not to be scared by winter. It is frequently covered up by drifts, and, it is said, "sometimes plunges from on wing into the soft snow, where it remains concealed for a day or two."[8] I used to start them in the open land also, where they had come out of the woods at sunset to "bud" the wild apple-trees. They will come regularly every evening to particular trees, where the cunning sportsman lies in wait for them, and the distant orchards next the woods suffer thus not a little. I am glad that the partridge gets fed, at any rate. It is Nature's own bird which lives on buds and diet-drink.[9]

In dark winter mornings, or in short winter afternoons, I sometimes heard a pack of hounds threading all the woods with hounding cry and yelp, unable to resist the instinct of the chase, and the note of the hunting horn at intervals, proving that man was in the rear. The woods ring again, and yet no fox bursts forth on to the open level of the pond, nor following pack pursuing their Actæon.[1] And perhaps at evening I see the hunters returning with a single brush[2] trailing from their sleigh for a trophy, seeking their inn. They tell me that if the fox would remain in the bosom of the frozen earth he would be safe, or if he would run in a straight line away no fox-hound could overtake him; but, having left his pursuers far behind, he stops to rest and listen till they come up, and when he runs he circles round to his old haunts, where the hunters await him. Sometimes, however, he will run upon a wall many rods, and then leap off far to one side, and he appears to know that water will not retain his scent. A hunter told me that he once saw a fox pursued by hounds burst out on to Walden when the ice was covered with shallow puddles, run part way across, and then return to the same shore. Ere long the hounds arrived, but here they lost the scent. Sometimes a pack

8. In a journal entry of 1850, Thoreau attributes the quotation to the ornithologist John James Audubon (1785–1851), but it has not been located.
9. Water.
1. A Greek hunter who saw the goddess Artemis bathing; she transformed him into a stag, and his own dogs killed him.
2. Tail.

hunting by themselves would pass my door, and circle round my house, and yelp and hound without regarding me, as if afflicted by a species of madness, so that nothing could divert them from the pursuit. Thus they circle until they fall upon the recent trail of a fox, for a wise hound will forsake every thing else for this. One day a man came to my hut from Lexington to inquire after his hound that made a large track, and had been hunting for a week by himself. But I fear that he was not the wiser for all I told him, for every time I attempted to answer his questions he interrupted me by asking, "What do you do here?" He had lost a dog, but found a man.

One old hunter who has a dry tongue, who used to come to bathe in Walden once every year when the water was warmest, and at such times looked in upon me, told me, that many years ago he took his gun one afternoon and went out for a cruise in Walden Wood; and as he walked the Wayland road he heard the cry of hounds approaching, and ere long a fox leaped the wall into the road, and as quick as thought leaped the other wall out of the road, and his swift bullet had not touched him. Some way behind came an old hound and her three pups in full pursuit, hunting on their own account, and disappeared again in the woods. Late in the afternoon, as he was resting in the thick woods south of Walden, he heard the voice of the hounds far over toward Fair Haven still pursuing the fox and on they came, their hounding cry which made all the woods ring sounding nearer and nearer, now from Well-Meadow, now from the Baker Farm. For a long time he stood still and listened to their music, so sweet to a hunter's ear, when suddenly the fox appeared, threading the solemn aisles with an easy coursing pace, whose sound was concealed by a sympathetic rustle of the leaves, swift and still, keeping the ground, leaving his pursuers far behind; and, leaping upon a rock amid the woods, he sat erect and listening, with his back to the hunter. For a moment compassion restrained the latter's arm; but that was a short-lived mood, and as quick as thought can follow thought his piece was levelled, and *whang*!—the fox rolling over the rock lay dead on the ground. The hunter still kept his place and listened to the hounds. Still on they came, and now the near woods resounded through all their aisles with their demoniac cry. At length the old hound burst into view with muzzle to the ground, and snapping the air as if possessed, and ran directly to the rock; but spying the dead fox she suddenly ceased her hounding, as if struck dumb with amazement, and walked round and round him in silence; and one by one her pups arrived, and, like their mother, were sobered into silence by the mystery. Then the hunter came forward and stood in their midst, and the mystery was solved. They waited in silence while he skinned the fox, then followed the brush a while, and at length turned off into the woods again. That evening a Weston Squire came to the Concord hunter's cottage to inquire for his hounds, and told how for a week they had been hunting on their own account from Weston woods.[3] The Concord hunter told him what he knew and offered him the skin; but the other declined it and departed. He did not find his hounds that night, but the next day learned that they had crossed the river and put up at a farm-house for the night, whence, having been well fed, they took their departure early in the morning.

3. Thoreau puns on the name of Squire Western, a character in the English novelist Henry Fielding's *Tom Jones* (1749), and Weston, a town near Concord.

The hunter who told me this could remember one Sam Nutting, who used to hunt bears on Fair Haven Ledges, and exchange their skins for rum in Concord village; who told him, even, that he had seen a moose there. Nutting had a famous fox-hound named Burgoyne,—he pronounced it Bugine,—which my informant used to borrow. In the "Wast Book"[4] of an old trader of this town, who was also a captain, town-clerk, and representative, I find the following entry. Jan. 18th, 1742–3, "John Melven Cr. by 1 Grey Fox 0-2-3;" they are not now found here; and in his ledger, Feb. 7th, 1743, Hezekiah Stratton has credit "by 1/2 a Catt skin 0-1-41/2;" of course, a wild-cat, for Stratton was a sergeant in the old French war, and would not have got credit for hunting less noble game. Credit is given for deer skins also, and they were daily sold. One man still preserves the horns of the last deer that was killed in this vicinity, and another has told me the particulars of the hunt in which his uncle was engaged. The hunters were formerly a numerous and merry crew here. I remember well one gaunt Nimrod[5] who would catch up a leaf by the road-side and play a strain on it wilder and more melodious, if my memory serves me, than any hunting horn.

At midnight, when there was a moon, I sometimes met with hounds in my path prowling about the woods, which would skulk out of my way, as if afraid, and stand silent amid the bushes till I had passed.

Squirrels and wild mice disputed for my store of nuts. There were scores of pitch-pines around my house, from one to four inches in diameter, which had been gnawed by mice the previous winter,—a Norwegian winter for them, for the snow lay long and deep, and they were obliged to mix a large proportion of pine bark with their other diet. These trees were alive and apparently flourishing at mid-summer, and many of them had grown a foot, though completely girdled; but after another winter such were without exception dead. It is remarkable that a single mouse should thus be allowed a whole pine tree for its dinner, gnawing round instead of up and down it; but perhaps it is necessary in order to thin these trees, which are wont to grow up densely.

The hares (*Lepus Americanus*) were very familiar. One had her form under my house all winter, separated from me only by the flooring, and she startled me each morning by her hasty departure when I began to stir,—thump, thump, thump, striking her head against the floor timbers in her hurry. They used to come round my door at dusk to nibble the potato parings which I had thrown out, and were so nearly the color of the ground that they could hardly be distinguished when still. Sometimes in the twilight I alternately lost and recovered sight of one sitting motionless under my window. When I opened my door in the evening, off they would go with a squeak and a bounce. Near at hand they only excited my pity. One evening one sat by my door two paces from me, at first trembling with fear, yet unwilling to move; a poor wee thing, lean and bony, with ragged ears and sharp nose, scant tail and slender paws. It looked as if Nature no longer contained the breed of nobler bloods, but stood on her last toes. Its large eyes appeared young and unhealthy, almost dropsical. I took a step, and lo, away it scud with an elastic spring over the snow crust, straightening its body and its limbs into graceful length, and soon put the forest between me

4. A "wast book" or "waste book" is a rough account book where all sorts of entries (sales, expenses, and so on) are made.

5. Hunter; see Genesis 10.9: "He was a mighty hunter before the Lord: wherefore it is said, Even as Nimrod the mighty hunter before the Lord."

and itself,—the wild free venison, asserting its vigor and the dignity of Nature. Not without reason was its slenderness. Such then was its nature. (*Lepus*, *levipes*, light-foot, some think.)

What is a country without rabbits and partridges? They are among the most simple and indigenous animal products; ancient and venerable families known to antiquity as to modern times; of the very hue and substance of Nature, nearest allied to leaves and to the ground,—and to one another; it is either winged or it is legged. It is hardly as if you had seen a wild creature when a rabbit or a partridge bursts away, only a natural one, as much to be expected as rustling leaves. The partridge and the rabbit are still sure to thrive, like true natives of the soil, whatever revolutions occur. If the forest is cut off, the sprouts and bushes which spring up afford them concealment, and they become more numerous than ever. That must be a poor country indeed that does not support a hare. Our woods teem with them both, and around every swamp may be seen the partridge or rabbit walk, beset with twiggy fences and horsehair snares, which some cow-boy tends.

16. The Pond in Winter

After a still winter night I awoke with the impression that some question had been put to me, which I had been endeavoring in vain to answer in my sleep, as what—how—when—where? But there was dawning Nature, in whom all creatures live, looking in at my broad windows with serene and satisfied face, and no question on *her* lips. I awoke to an answered question, to Nature and daylight. The snow lying deep on the earth dotted with young pines, and the very slope of the hill on which my house is placed, seemed to say, Forward! Nature puts no question and answers none which we mortals ask. She has long ago taken her resolution. "O Prince, our eyes contemplate with admiration and transmit to the soul the wonderful and varied spectacle of this universe. The night veils without doubt a part of this glorious creation; but day comes to reveal to us this great work, which extends from earth even into the plains of the ether."[6]

Then to my morning work. First I take an axe and pail and go in search of water, if that be not a dream. After a cold and snowy night it needed a divining rod to find it. Every winter the liquid and trembling surface of the pond, which was so sensitive to every breath, and reflected every light and shadow, becomes solid to the depth of a foot or a foot and a half, so that it will support the heaviest teams, and perchance the snow covers it to an equal depth, and it is not to be distinguished from any level field. Like the marmots in the surrounding hills, it closes its eye-lids and becomes dormant for three months or more. Standing on the snow-covered plain, as if in a pasture amid the hills, I cut my way first through a foot of snow, and then a foot of ice, and open a window under my feet, where, kneeling to drink, I look down into the quiet parlor of the fishes, pervaded by a softened light as through a window of ground glass, with its bright sanded floor the same as in summer; there a perennial waveless serenity reigns as in the amber twilight sky, corresponding to the cool and even temperament of the inhabitants. Heaven is under our feet as well as over our heads.

6. From an appendix to the Hindu epic poem *Mahabharata*, which Thoreau knew in a French translation.

Early in the morning, while all things are crisp with frost, men come with fishing reels and slender lunch, and let down their fine lines through the snowy field to take pickerel and perch; wild men, who instinctively follow other fashions and trust other authorities than their townsmen, and by their goings and comings stitch towns together in parts where else they would be ripped. They sit and eat their luncheon in stout fear-naughts[7] on the dry oak leaves on the shore, as wise in natural lore as the citizen is in artificial. They never consulted with books, and know and can tell much less than they have done. The things which they practise are said not yet to be known. Here is one fishing for pickerel with grown perch for bait. You look into his pail with wonder as into a summer pond, as if he kept summer locked up at home, or knew where she had retreated. How, pray, did he get these in mid-winter? O, he got worms out of rotten logs since the ground froze, and so he caught them. His life itself passes deeper in Nature than the studies of the naturalist penetrate; himself a subject for the naturalist. The latter raises the moss and bark gently with his knife in search of insects; the former lays open logs to their core with his axe, and moss and bark fly far and wide. He gets his living by barking trees. Such a man has some right to fish, and I love to see Nature carried out in him. The perch swallows the grub-worm, the pickerel swallows the perch, and the fisherman swallows the pickerel; and so all the chinks in the scale of being are filled.

When I strolled around the pond in misty weather I was sometimes amused by the primitive mode which some ruder fisherman had adopted. He would perhaps have placed alder branches over the narrow holes in the ice, which were four or five rods apart and an equal distance from the shore, and having fastened the end of the line to a stick to prevent its being pulled through, have passed the slack line over a twig of the alder, a foot or more above the ice, and tied a dry oak leaf to it, which, being pulled down, would show when he had a bite. These alders loomed through the mist at regular intervals as you walked half way round the pond.

Ah, the pickerel of Walden! when I see them lying on the ice, or in the well which the fisherman cuts in the ice, making a little hole to admit the water, I am always surprised by their rare beauty, as if they were fabulous fishes, they are so foreign to the streets, even to the woods, foreign as Arabia to our Concord life. They possess a quite dazzling and transcendent beauty which separates them by a wide interval from the cadaverous cod and haddock whose fame is trumpeted in our streets. They are not green like the pines, nor gray like the stones, nor blue like the sky; but they have, to my eyes, if possible, yet rarer colors, like flowers and precious stones, as if they were the pearls, the animalized *nuclei* or crystals of the Walden water. They, of course, are Walden all over and all through; are themselves small Waldens in the animal kingdom, Waldenses.[8] It is surprising that they are caught here,—that in this deep and capacious spring, far beneath the rattling teams and chaises and tinkling sleighs that travel the Walden road, this great gold and emerald fish swims. I never chanced to see its kind in any market; it would be the cynosure of all eyes there. Easily, with a few convulsive quirks,

7. Dreadnoughts, heavy woolen coats.
8. Thoreau puns on the Waldenses, persecuted religious dissenters of 12th-century France.

they give up their watery ghosts, like a mortal translated before his time to the thin air of heaven.

* * *

As I was desirous to recover the long lost bottom of Walden Pond, I surveyed it carefully, before the ice broke up, early in '46, with compass and chain and sounding line. There have been many stories told about the bottom, or rather no bottom, of this pond, which certainly had no foundation for themselves. It is remarkable how long men will believe in the bottomlessness of a pond without taking the trouble to sound it. I have visited two such Bottomless Ponds in one walk in this neighborhood. Many have believed that Walden reached quite through to the other side of the globe. Some who have lain flat on the ice for a long time, looking down through the illusive medium, perchance with watery eyes into the bargain, and driven to hasty conclusions by the fear of catching cold in their breasts, have seen vast holes "into which a load of hay might be driven," if there were any body to drive it, the undoubted source of the Styx and entrance to the Infernal Regions from these parts. Others have gone down from the village with a 'fifty-six"[9] and a wagon load of inch rope, but yet have failed to find any bottom; for while the "fifty-six" was resting by the way, they were paying out the rope in the vain attempt to fathom their truly immeasurable capacity for marvellousness. But I can assure my readers that Walden has a reasonably tight bottom at a not unreasonable, though at an unusual, depth. I fathomed it easily with a codline and a stone weighing about a pound and a half, and could tell accurately when the stone left the bottom, by having to pull so much harder before the water got underneath to help me. The greatest depth was exactly one hundred and two feet; to which may be added the five feet which it has risen since, making one hundred and seven. This is a remarkable depth for so small an area; yet not an inch of it can be spared by the imagination. What if all ponds were shallow? Would it not react on the minds of men? I am thankful that this pond was made deep and pure for a symbol. While men believe in the infinite some ponds will be thought to be bottomless.

A factory owner, hearing what depth I had found, thought that it could not be true, for, judging from his acquaintance with dams, sand would not lie at so steep an angle. But the deepest ponds are not so deep in proportion to their area as most suppose, and, if drained, would not leave very remarkable valleys. They are not like cups between the hills; for this one, which is so unusually deep for its area, appears in a vertical section through its centre not deeper than a shallow plate. Most ponds, emptied, would leave a meadow no more hollow than we frequently see. William Gilpin,[1] who is so admirable in all that relates to landscapes, and usually so correct, standing at the head of Loch Fyne, in Scotland, which he describes as "a bay of salt water, sixty or seventy fathoms deep, four miles in breadth," and about fifty miles long, surrounded by mountains, observes, "If we could have seen it immediately after the diluvian crash, or whatever convulsion of Nature occasioned it, before the waters gushed in, what a horrid chasm it must have appeared!

9. A fifty-six-pound weight.
1. William Gilpin, *Observations on the Highlands of Scotland* (1808).

> So high as heaved the tumid hills, so low
> Down sunk a hollow bottom, broad, and deep,
> Capacious bed of waters—."[2]

But if, using the shortest diameter of Loch Fyne, we apply these proportions to Walden, which, as we have seen, appears already in a vertical section only like a shallow plate, it will appear four times as shallow. So much for the *increased* horrors of the chasm of Loch Fyne when emptied. No doubt many a smiling valley with its stretching cornfields occupies exactly such a "horrid chasm," from which the waters have receded, though it requires the insight and the far sight of the geologist to convince the unsuspecting inhabitants of this fact. Often an inquisitive eye may detect the shores of a primitive lake in the low horizon hills, and no subsequent elevation of the plain has been necessary to conceal their history. But it is easiest, as they who work on the highways know, to find the hollows by the puddles after a shower. The amount of it is, the imagination, give it the least license, dives deeper and soars higher than Nature goes. So, probably, the depth of the ocean will be found to be very inconsiderable compared with its breadth.

As I sounded through the ice I could determine the shape of the bottom with greater accuracy than is possible in surveying harbors which do not freeze over, and I was surprised at its general regularity. In the deepest part there are several acres more level than almost any field which is exposed to the sun, wind and plough. In one instance, on a line arbitrarily chosen, the depth did not vary more than one foot in thirty rods; and generally, near the middle, I could calculate the variation for each one hundred feet in any direction beforehand within three or four inches. Some are accustomed to speak of deep and dangerous holes even in quiet sandy ponds like this, but the effect of water under these circumstances is to level all inequalities. The regularity of the bottom and its conformity to the shores and the range of the neighboring hills were so perfect that a distant promontory betrayed itself in the soundings quite across the pond, and its direction could be determined by observing the opposite shore. Cape becomes bar, and plain shoal, and valley and gorge deep water and channel.

When I had mapped the pond by the scale of ten rods to an inch, and put down the soundings, more than a hundred in all, I observed this remarkable coincidence. Having noticed that the number indicating the greatest depth was apparently in the centre of the map, I laid a rule on the map lengthwise, and then breadthwise, and found, to my surprise, that the line of greatest length intersected the line of greatest breadth *exactly* at the point of greatest depth, notwithstanding that the middle is so nearly level, the outline of the pond far from regular, and the extreme length and breadth were got by measuring into the coves; and I said to myself, Who knows but this hint would conduct to the deepest part of the ocean as well as of a pond or puddle? Is not this the rule also for the height of mountains, regarded as the opposite of valleys? We know that a hill is not highest at its narrowest part.

Of five coves, three, or all which had been sounded, were observed to have a bar quite across their mouths and deeper water within, so that the bay tended to be an expansion of water within the land not only horizontally

2. Milton's *Paradise Lost* 7.288–90.

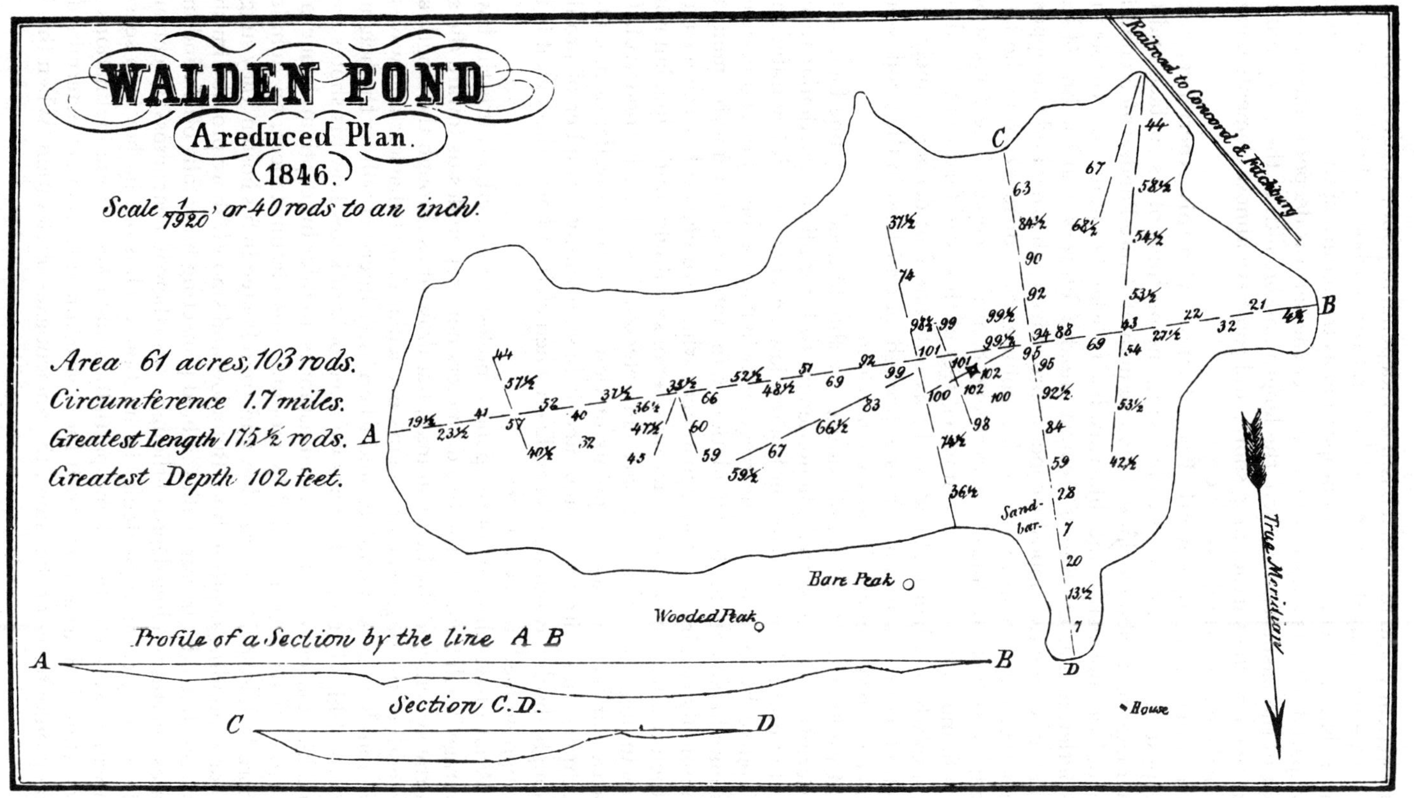
WALDEN POND
A reduced Plan.
1846.
Scale $\frac{1}{1920}$, or 40 rods to an inch.
Area 61 acres, 103 rods.
Circumference 1.7 miles.
Greatest Length 175½ rods.
Greatest Depth 102 feet.
Railroad to Concord & Fitchburg
True Meridian
Sand-bar.
Bare Peak
Wooded Peak
House
Profile of a Section by the line A B
Section C.D.
A
B
C
D

but vertically, and to form a basin or independent pond, the direction of the two capes showing the course of the bar. Every harbor on the sea-coast, also, has its bar at its entrance. In proportion as the mouth of the cove was wider compared with its length, the water over the bar was deeper compared with that in the basin. Given, then, the length and breadth of the cove, and the character of the surrounding shore, and you have almost elements enough to make out a formula for all cases.

In order to see how nearly I could guess, with this experience, at the deepest point in a pond, by observing the outlines of its surface and the character of its shores alone, I made a plan of White Pond, which contains about forty-one acres, and, like this, has no island in it, nor any visible inlet or outlet; and as the line of greatest breadth fell very near the line of least breadth, where two opposite capes approached each other and two opposite bays receded, I ventured to mark a point a short distance from the latter line, but still on the line of greatest length, as the deepest. The deepest part was found to be within one hundred feet of this, still farther in the direction to which I had inclined, and was only one foot deeper, namely, sixty feet. Of course, a stream running through, or an island in the pond, would make the problem much more complicated.

If we knew all the laws of Nature, we should need only one fact, or the description of one actual phenomenon, to infer all the particular results at that point. Now we know only a few laws, and our result is vitiated, not, of course, by any confusion or irregularity in Nature, but by our ignorance of essential elements in the calculation. Our notions of law and harmony are commonly confined to those instances which we detect; but the harmony which results from a far greater number of seemingly conflicting, but really concurring, laws, which we have not detected, is still more wonderful. The particular laws are as our points of view, as, to the traveller, a mountain outline varies with every step, and it has an infinite number of profiles, though absolutely but one form. Even when cleft or bored through it is not comprehended in its entireness.

What I have observed of the pond is no less true in ethics. It is the law of average. Such a rule of the two diameters not only guides us toward the sun in the system and the heart in man, but draw lines through the length and breadth of the aggregate of a man's particular daily behaviors and waves of life into his coves and inlets, and where they intersect will be the height or depth of his character. Perhaps we need only to know how his shores trend and his adjacent country or circumstances, to infer his depth and concealed bottom. If he is surrounded by mountainous circumstances, an Achillean shore,[3] whose peaks overshadow and are reflected in his bosom, they suggest a corresponding depth in him. But a low and smooth shore proves him shallow on that side. In our bodies, a bold projecting brow falls off to and indicates a corresponding depth of thought. Also there is a bar across the entrance of our every cove, or particular inclination; each is our harbor for a season, in which we are detained and partially land-locked. These inclinations are not whimsical usually, but their form, size, and direction are determined by the promontories of the shore, the ancient axes of elevation. When this bar

3. Thessaly, the birthplace of Achilles, is mountainous.

is gradually increased by storms, tides, or currents, or there is a subsidence of the waters, so that it reaches to the surface, that which was at first but an inclination in the shore in which a thought was harbored becomes an individual lake, cut off from the ocean, wherein the thought secures its own conditions, changes, perhaps, from salt to fresh, becomes a sweet sea, dead sea, or a marsh. At the advent of each individual into this life, may we not suppose that such a bar has risen to the surface somewhere? It is true, we are such poor navigators that our thoughts, for the most part, stand off and on upon a harborless coast, are conversant only with the bights[4] of the bays of poesy, or steer for the public ports of entry, and go into the dry docks of science, where they merely refit for this world, and no natural currents concur to individualize them.

As for the inlet or outlet of Walden, I have not discovered any but rain and snow and evaporation, though perhaps, with a thermometer and a line, such places may be found, for where the water flows into the pond it will probably be coldest in summer and warmest in winter. When the ice-men were at work here in '46–7, the cakes sent to the shore were one day rejected by those who were stacking them up there, not being thick enough to lie side by side with the rest; and the cutters thus discovered that the ice over a small space was two or three inches thinner than elsewhere, which made them think that there was an inlet there. They also showed me in another place what they thought was a "leach hole" through which the pond leaked out under a hill into a neighboring meadow, pushing me out on a cake of ice to see it. It was a small cavity under ten feet of water; but I think that I can warrant the pond not to need soldering till they find a worse leak than that. One has suggested, that if such a "leach hole" should be found, its connection with the meadow, if any existed, might be proved by conveying some colored powder or sawdust to the mouth of the hole, and then putting a strainer over the spring in the meadow, which would catch some of the particles carried through by the current.

While I was surveying, the ice, which was sixteen inches thick, undulated under a slight wind like water. It is well known that a level cannot be used on ice. At one rod from the shore its greatest fluctuation, when observed by means of a level on land directed toward a graduated staff on the ice, was three quarters of an inch, though the ice appeared firmly attached to the shore. It was probably greater in the middle. Who knows but if our instruments were delicate enough we might detect an undulation in the crust of the earth? When two legs of my level were on the shore and the third on the ice, and the sights were directed over the latter, a rise or fall of the ice of an almost infinitesimal amount made a difference of several feet on a tree across the pond. When I began to cut holes for sounding, there were three or four inches of water on the ice under a deep snow which had sunk it thus far; but the water began immediately to run into these holes, and continued to run for two days in deep streams, which wore away the ice on every side, and contributed essentially, if not mainly, to dry the surface of the pond; for, as the water ran in, it raised and floated the ice. This was somewhat like cutting a hole in the bottom of a ship to let the water out. When such holes freeze, and a rain

4. Bends or curves.

succeeds, and finally a new freezing forms a fresh smooth ice over all, it is beautifully mottled internally by dark figures, shaped somewhat like a spider's web, what you may call ice rosettes, produced by the channels worn by the water flowing from all sides to a centre. Sometimes, also, when the ice was covered with shallow puddles, I saw a double shadow of myself, one standing on the head of the other, one on the ice, the other on the trees or hill-side.

While yet it is cold January, and snow and ice are thick and solid, the prudent landlord comes from the village to get ice to cool his summer drink; impressively, even pathetically wise, to foresee the heat and thirst of July now in January,—wearing a thick coat and mittens! when so many things are not provided for. It may be that he lays up no treasures in this world which will cool his summer drink in the next.[5] He cuts and saws the solid pond, unroofs the house of fishes, and carts off their very element and air, held fast by chains and stakes like corded wood, through the favoring winter air, to wintry cellars, to underlie the summer there. It looks like solidified azure, as, far off, it is drawn through the streets. These ice-cutters are a merry race, full of jest and sport, and when I went among them they were wont to invite me to saw pit-fashion with them, I standing underneath.

In the winter of '46–7 there came a hundred men of Hyperborean[6] extraction swoop down on to our pond one morning, with many car-loads of ungainly-looking farming tools, sleds, ploughs, drill barrows, turf-knives, spades, saws, rakes, and each man was armed with a double-pointed pike-staff, such as is not described in the New-England Farmer or the Cultivator. I did not know whether they had come to sow a crop of winter rye, or some other kind of grain recently introduced from Iceland. As I saw no manure, I judged that they meant to skim the land, as I had done, thinking the soil was deep and had lain fallow long enough. They said that a gentleman farmer, who was behind the scenes, wanted to double his money, which, as I understood, amounted to half a million already; but in order to cover each one of his dollars with another, he took off the only coat, ay, the skin itself, of Walden Pond in the midst of a hard winter. They went to work at once, ploughing, harrowing, rolling, furrowing, in admirable order, as if they were bent on making this a model farm; but when I was looking sharp to see what kind of seed they dropped into the furrow, a gang of fellows by my side suddenly began to hook up the virgin mould itself, with a peculiar jerk, clean down to the sand, or rather the water,—for it was a very springy soil,—indeed all the *terra firma* there was, and haul it away on sleds, and then I guessed that they must be cutting peat in a bog. So they came and went every day, with a peculiar shriek from the locomotive, from and to some point of the polar regions, as it seemed to me, like a flock of arctic snow-birds. But sometimes Squaw Walden had her revenge, and a hired man, walking behind his team, slipped through a crack in the ground down toward Tartarus, and he who was so brave before suddenly became but the ninth part of a man, almost gave up his animal heat, and was glad to take

5. Thoreau first echoes Jesus' injunction to his disciples not to lay up treasures on earth (Matthew 6.19), then alludes to the rich man in hell who pleads that the beggar Lazarus in heaven be allowed to dip the tip of his finger in water and cool the rich man's tongue (Luke 16.24).

6. In Greek mythology, the Hyperboreans lived far away in the icy north.

refuge in my house, and acknowledged that there was some virtue in a stove; or sometimes the frozen soil took a piece of steel out of a ploughshare, or a plough got set in the furrow and had to be cut out.

To speak literally, a hundred Irishmen, with Yankee overseers, came from Cambridge every day to get out the ice. They divided it into cakes by methods too well known to require description, and these, being sledded to the shore, were rapidly hauled off on to an ice platform, and raised by grappling irons and block and tackle, worked by horses, on to a stack, as surely as so many barrels of flour, and there placed evenly side by side, and row upon row, as if they formed the solid base of an obelisk designed to pierce the clouds. They told me that in a good day they could get out a thousand tons, which was the yield of about one acre. Deep ruts and "cradle holes" were worn in the ice, as on *terra firma*, by the passage of the sleds over the same track, and the horses invariably ate their oats out of cakes of ice hollowed out like buckets. They stacked up the cakes thus in the open air in a pile thirty-five feet high on one side and six or seven rods square, putting hay between the outside layers to exclude the air; for when the wind, though never so cold, finds a passage through, it will wear large cavities, leaving slight supports or studs only here and there, and finally topple it down. At first it looked like a vast blue fort or Valhalla; but when they began to tuck the coarse meadow hay into the crevices, and this became covered with rime and icicles, it looked like a venerable moss-grown and hoary ruin, built of azure-tinted marble, the abode of Winter, that old man we see in the almanac,—his shanty, as if he had a design to estivate[7] with us. They calculated that not twenty-five per cent. of this would reach its destination, and that two or three per cent. would be wasted in the cars. However, a still greater part of this heap had a different destiny from what was intended; for, either because the ice was found not to keep so well as was expected, containing more air than usual, or for some other reason, it never got to market. This heap, made in the winter of '46–7 and estimated to contain ten thousand tons, was finally covered with hay and boards; and though it was unroofed the following July, and a part of it carried off, the rest remaining exposed to the sun, it stood over that summer and the next winter, and was not quite melted till September 1848. Thus the pond recovered the greater part.

Like the water, the Walden ice, seen near at hand, has a green tint, but at a distance is beautifully blue, and you can easily tell it from the white ice of the river, or the merely greenish ice of some ponds, a quarter of a mile off. Sometimes one of those great cakes slips from the ice-man's sled into the village street, and lies there for a week like a great emerald, an object of interest to all passers. I have noticed that a portion of Walden which in the state of water was green will often, when frozen, appear from the same point of view blue. So the hollows about this pond will, sometimes, in the winter, be filled with a greenish water somewhat like its own, but the next day will have frozen blue. Perhaps the blue color of water and ice is due to the light and air they contain, and the most transparent is the bluest. Ice is an interesting subject for contemplation. They told me that they had some in the ice-houses at Fresh Pond five years old which was as good as ever. Why is it that a bucket

7. To pass the summer, especially in a state of dormancy.

of water soon becomes putrid, but frozen remains sweet forever? It is commonly said that this is the difference between the affections and the intellect.

Thus for sixteen days I saw from my window a hundred men at work like busy husbandmen, with teams and horses and apparently all the implements of farming, such a picture as we see on the first page of the almanac; and as often as I looked out I was reminded of the fable of the lark and the reapers, or the parable of the sower,[8] and the like; and now they are all gone, and in thirty days more, probably, I shall look from the same window on the pure sea-green Walden water there, reflecting the clouds and the trees, and sending up its evaporations in solitude, and no traces will appear that a man has ever stood there. Perhaps I shall hear a solitary loon laugh as he dives and plumes himself, or shall see a lonely fisher in his boat, like a floating leaf, beholding his form reflected in the waves, where lately a hundred men securely labored.

Thus it appears that the sweltering inhabitants of Charleston and New Orleans, of Madras and Bombay and Calcutta, drink at my well. In the morning I bathe my intellect in the stupendous and cosmogonal philosophy of the Bhagvat Geeta, since whose composition years of the gods have elapsed, and in comparison with which our modern world and its literature seem puny and trivial; and I doubt if that philosophy is not to be referred to a previous state of existence, so remote is its sublimity from our conceptions. I lay down the book and go to my well for water, and lo! there I meet the servant of the Brahmin, priest of Brahma and Vishnu and Indra, who still sits in his temple on the Ganges reading the Vedas, or dwells at the root of a tree with his crust and water jug. I meet his servant come to draw water for his master, and our buckets as it were grate together in the same well. The pure Walden water is mingled with the sacred water of the Ganges. With favoring winds it is wafted past the site of the fabulous islands of Atlantis and the Hesperides, makes the periplus of Hanno, and, floating by Ternate and Tidore and the mouth of the Persian Gulf, melts in the tropic gales of the Indian seas, and is landed in ports of which Alexander[9] only heard the names.

17. *Spring*

The opening of large tracts by the ice-cutters commonly causes a pond to break up earlier; for the water, agitated by the wind, even in cold weather, wears away the surrounding ice. But such was not the effect on Walden that year, for she had soon got a thick new garment to take the place of the old. This pond never breaks up so soon as the others in this neighborhood, on account both of its greater depth and its having no stream passing through it to melt or wear away the ice. I never knew it to open in the course of a winter, not excepting that of '52–3, which gave the ponds so severe a trial. It commonly opens about the first of April, a week or ten days later than Flint's Pond

8. See Matthew 13.3–43. The fable of the lark and the reapers is from Jean de La Fontaine's (1621–1695) *Fables* 4.22, which Thoreau read in J. Payne Collier, *Old Ballads* (1843).

9. Alexander the Great (356–323 B.C.E.), king of Macedon. Thoreau lists some of the Spice islands in Indonesia mentioned in Milton's *Paradise Lost* 2.639. Atlantis and the Hesperides are mythical islands in the Atlantic. To "make the periplus of Hanno" is to round the western coast of Africa and enter the Indian Ocean (Hanno, the Carthaginian navigator, supposedly made such a voyage in 480 B.C.E.).

and Fair-Haven, beginning to melt on the north side and in the shallower parts where it began to freeze. It indicates better than any water hereabouts the absolute progress of the season, being least affected by transient changes of temperature. A severe cold of a few days' duration in March may very much retard the opening of the former ponds, while the temperature of Walden increases almost uninterruptedly. A thermometer thrust into the middle of Walden on the 6th of March, 1847, stood at 32°, or freezing point; near the shore at 33°; in the middle of Flint's Pond, the same day, at 32½°; at a dozen rods from the shore, in shallow water, under ice a foot thick, at 36°. This difference of three and a half degrees between the temperature of the deep water and the shallow in the latter pond, and the fact that a great proportion of it is comparatively shallow, show why it should break up so much sooner than Walden. The ice in the shallowest part was at this time several inches thinner than in the middle. In mid-winter the middle had been the warmest and the ice thinnest there. So, also, every one who has waded about the shores of a pond in summer must have perceived how much warmer the water is close to the shore, where only three or four inches deep, than a little distance out, and on the surface where it is deep, than near the bottom. In spring the sun not only exerts an influence through the increased temperature of the air and earth, but its heat passes through ice a foot or more thick, and is reflected from the bottom in shallow water, and so also warms the water and melts the under side of the ice, at the same time that it is melting it more directly above, making it uneven, and causing the air bubbles which it contains to extend themselves upward and downward until it is completely honey-combed, and at last disappears suddenly in a single spring rain. Ice has its grain as well as wood, and when a cake begins to rot or "comb," that is, assume the appearance of honey-comb, whatever may be its position, the air cells are at right angles with what was the water surface. Where there is a rock or a log rising near to the surface the ice over it is much thinner, and is frequently quite dissolved by this reflected heat; and I have been told that in the experiment at Cambridge to freeze water in a shallow wooden pond, though the cold air circulated underneath, and so had access to both sides, the reflection of the sun from the bottom more than counterbalanced this advantage. When a warm rain in the middle of the winter melts off the snow-ice from Walden, and leaves a hard dark or transparent ice on the middle, there will be a strip of rotten though thicker white ice, a rod or more wide, about the shores, created by this reflected heat. Also, as I have said, the bubbles themselves within the ice operate as burning glasses to melt the ice beneath.

The phenomena of the year take place every day in a pond on a small scale. Every morning, generally speaking, the shallow water is being warmed more rapidly than the deep, though it may not be made so warm after all, and every evening it is being cooled more rapidly until the morning. The day is an epitome of the year. The night is the winter, the morning and evening are the spring and fall, and the noon is the summer. The cracking and booming of the ice indicate a change of temperature. One pleasant morning after a cold night, February 24th, 1850, having gone to Flint's Pond to spend the day, I noticed with surprise, that when I struck the ice with the head of my axe, it resounded like a gong for many rods around, or as if I had struck on a tight drum-head. The pond began to boom about an hour after sunrise, when it felt the influence of the sun's rays slanted upon it from the hills; it stretched itself and yawned like a waking man with a gradually increasing tumult, which was kept up three or four hours. It took a short siesta at noon, and boomed once more toward night, as the sun was withdrawing his influence. In the right stage of the weather a pond fires its evening gun with great regularity. But in the middle of the day, being full of cracks, and the air also being less elastic, it had completely lost its resonance, and probably fishes and muskrats could not then have been stunned by a blow on it. The fishermen say that the "thundering of the pond" scares the fishes and prevents their biting. The pond does not thunder every evening, and I cannot tell surely when to expect its thundering; but though I may perceive no difference in the weather, it does. Who would have suspected so large and cold and thick-skinned a thing to be so sensitive? Yet it has its law to which it thunders obedience when it should as surely as the buds expand in the spring. The earth is all alive and covered with papillæ. The largest pond is as sensitive to atmospheric changes as the globule of mercury in its tube.

One attraction in coming to the woods to live was that I should have leisure and opportunity to see the spring come in. The ice in the pond at length begins to be honey-combed, and I can set my heel in it as I walk. Fogs and rains and warmer suns are gradually melting the snow; the days have grown sensibly longer; and I see how I shall get through the winter without adding to my wood-pile, for large fires are no longer necessary. I am on the alert for the first signs of spring, to hear the chance note of some arriving bird, or the striped squirrel's chirp, for his stores must be now nearly exhausted, or see the woodchuck venture out of his winter quarters. On the 13th of March, after I had heard the bluebird, song-sparrow, and red-wing, the ice was still nearly a foot thick. As the weather grew warmer, it was not sensibly worn away by the water, nor broken up and floated off as in rivers, but, though it was completely melted for half a rod in width about the shore, the middle was merely honey-combed and saturated with water, so that you could put your foot through it when six inches thick; but by the next day evening, perhaps, after a warm rain followed by fog, it would have wholly disappeared, all gone off with the fog, spirited away. One year I went across the middle only five days before it disappeared entirely. In 1845 Walden was first completely open on the 1st of April; in '46, the 25th of March; in '47, the 8th of April; in '51, the 28th of March; in '52, the 18th of April; in '53, the 23rd of March; in '54, about the 7th of April.

Every incident connected with the breaking up of the rivers and ponds and the settling of the weather is particularly interesting to us who live in a climate of so great extremes. When the warmer days come, they who dwell near the river hear the ice crack at night with a startling whoop as loud as artillery, as if its icy fetters were rent from end to end, and within a few days see it rapidly going out. So the alligator comes out of the mud with quakings of the earth. One old man, who has been a close observer of Nature, and seems as thoroughly wise in regard to all her operations as if she had been put upon the stocks when he was a boy, and he had helped to lay her keel,—who has come to his growth, and can hardly acquire more of natural lore if he should live to the age of Methuselah[1]—told me, and I was surprised to

1. "And the days of Methuselah were nine hundred sixty and nine years: and he died" (Genesis 5.27).

hear him express wonder at any of Nature's operations, for I thought that there were no secrets between them, that one spring day he took his gun and boat, and thought that he would have a little sport with the ducks. There was ice still on the meadows, but it was all gone out of the river, and he dropped down without obstruction from Sudbury, where he lived, to Fair-Haven Pond, which he found, unexpectedly, covered for the most part with a firm field of ice. It was a warm day, and he was surprised to see so great a body of ice remaining. Not seeing any ducks, he hid his boat on the north or back side of an island in the pond, and then concealed himself in the bushes on the south side, to await them. The ice was melted for three or four rods from the shore, and there was a smooth and warm sheet of water, with a muddy bottom, such as the ducks love, within, and he thought it likely that some would be along pretty soon. After he had lain still there about an hour he heard a low and seemingly very distant sound, but singularly grand and impressive, unlike any thing he had ever heard, gradually swelling and increasing as if it would have a universal and memorable ending, a sullen rush and roar, which seemed to him all at once like the sound of a vast body of fowl coming in to settle there, and, seizing his gun, he started up in haste and excited; but he found, to his surprise, that the whole body of the ice had started while he lay there, and drifted in to the shore, and the sound he had heard was made by its edge grating on the shore,—at first gently nibbled and crumbled off, but at length heaving up and scattering its wrecks along the island to a considerable height before it came to a stand still.

At length the sun's rays have attained the right angle, and warm winds blow up mist and rain and melt the snow banks, and the sun dispersing the mist smiles on a checkered landscape of russet and white smoking with incense, through which the traveller picks his way from islet to islet, cheered by the music of a thousand tinkling rills and rivulets whose veins are filled with the blood of winter which they are bearing off.

Few phenomena gave me more delight than to observe the forms which thawing sand and clay assume in flowing down the sides of a deep cut on the railroad through which I passed on my way to the village, a phenomenon not very common on so large a scale, though the number of freshly exposed banks of the right material must have been greatly multiplied since railroads were invented. The material was sand of every degree of fineness and of various rich colors, commonly mixed with a little clay. When the frost comes out in the spring, and even in a thawing day in the winter, the sand begins to flow down the slopes like lava, sometimes bursting out through the snow and overflowing it where no sand was to be seen before. Innumerable little streams overlap and interlace one with another, exhibiting a sort of hybrid product, which obeys half way the law of currents, and half way that of vegetation. As it flows it takes the forms of sappy leaves or vines, making heaps of pulpy sprays a foot or more in depth, and resembling, as you look down on them, the laciniated lobed and imbricated thalluses[2] of some lichens; or you are reminded of coral, of leopards' paws or birds' feet, of brains or lungs or bowels, and excrements of all kinds. It is a truly *grotesque* vegetation, whose forms and color we see imitated in bronze, a sort of architectural foliage

2. Plant shoots or organisms lapped over in regular order like roof tiles. "Laciniated": deeply, irregularly lobed.

more ancient and typical than acanthus, chiccory, ivy, vine, or any vegetable leaves; destined perhaps, under some circumstances, to become a puzzle to future geologists. The whole cut impressed me as if it were a cave with its stalactites laid open to the light. The various shades of the sand are singularly rich and agreeable, embracing the different iron colors, brown, gray, yellowish, and reddish. When the flowing mass reaches the drain at the foot of the bank it spreads out flatter into *strands*, the separate streams losing their semi-cylindrical form and gradually becoming more flat and broad, running together as they are more moist, till they form an almost flat *sand,* still variously and beautifully shaded, but in which you can trace the original forms of vegetation; till at length, in the water itself, they are converted into *banks,* like those formed off the mouths of rivers, and the forms of vegetation are lost in the ripple marks on the bottom.

The whole bank, which is from twenty to forty feet high, is sometimes overlaid with a mass of this kind of foliage, or sandy rupture, for a quarter of a mile on one or both sides, the produce of one spring day. What makes this sand foliage remarkable is its springing into existence thus suddenly. When I see on the one side the inert bank,—for the sun acts on one side first,—and on the other this luxuriant foliage, the creation of an hour, I am affected as if in a peculiar sense I stood in the laboratory of the Artist who made the world and me,—had come to where he was still at work, sporting on this bank, and with excess of energy strewing his fresh designs about. I feel as if I were nearer to the vitals of the globe, for this sandy overflow is something such a foliaceous mass as the vitals of the animal body. You find thus in the very sands an anticipation of the vegetable leaf. No wonder that the earth expresses itself outwardly in leaves, it so labors with the idea inwardly. The atoms have already learned this law, and are pregnant by it. The overhanging leaf sees here its prototype. *Internally,* whether in the globe or animal body, it is a moist thick *lobe,* a word especially applicable to the liver and lungs and the *leaves* of fat. (*λέιβω, labor, lapsus*, to flow or slip downward, a lapsing; *λοβο.*, *globus*, lobe, globe; also lap, flap, and many other words,) *externally* a dry thin *leaf,* even as the *f* and *v* are a pressed and dried *b.* The radicals of lobe are *lb*, the soft mass of the *b* (single lobed, or B, double lobed,) with a liquid *l* behind it pressing it forward. In globe, *glb*, the guttural *g* adds to the meaning the capacity of the throat. The feathers and wings of birds are still drier and thinner leaves. Thus, also, you pass from the lumpish grub in the earth to the airy and fluttering butterfly. The very globe continually transcends and translates itself, and becomes winged in its orbit. Even ice begins with delicate crystal leaves, as if it had flowed into moulds which the fronds of water plants have impressed on the watery mirror. The whole tree itself is but one leaf, and rivers are still vaster leaves whose pulp is intervening earth, and towns and cities are the ova of insects in their axils.

When the sun withdraws the sand ceases to flow, but in the morning the streams will start once more and branch and branch again into a myriad of others. You here see perchance how blood vessels are formed. If you look closely you observe that first there pushes forward from the thawing mass a stream of softened sand with a drop-like point, like the ball of the finger, feeling its way slowly and blindly downward, until at last with more heat and moisture, as the sun gets higher, the moist fluid portion, in its effort to obey the law to which the most inert also yields, separates from the latter and forms for itself a meandering channel or artery within that, in which is seen a little silvery stream glancing like lightning from one stage of pulpy leaves or branches to another, and ever and anon swallowed up in the sand. It is wonderful how rapidly yet perfectly the sand organizes itself as it flows, using the best material its mass affords to form the sharp edges of its channel. Such are the sources of rivers. In the silicious matter which the water deposits is perhaps the bony system, and in the still finer soil and organic matter the fleshy fibre or cellular tissue. What is man but a mass of thawing clay? The ball of the human finger is but a drop congealed. The fingers and toes flow to their extent from the thawing mass of the body. Who knows what the human body would expand and flow out to under a more genial heaven? Is not the hand a spreading *palm* leaf with its lobes and veins? The ear may be regarded, fancifully, as a lichen, *umbilicaria*, on the side of the head, with its lobe or drop. The lip (*labium* from *labor* (?)) laps or lapses from the sides of the cavernous mouth. The nose is a manifest congealed drop or stalactite. The chin is a still larger drop, the confluent dripping of the face. The cheeks are a slide from the brows into the valley of the face, opposed and diffused by the cheek bones. Each rounded lobe of the vegetable leaf, too, is a thick and now loitering drop, larger or smaller; the lobes are the fingers of the leaf; and as many lobes as it has, in so many directions it tends to flow, and more heat or other genial influences would have caused it to flow yet farther.

Thus it seemed that this one hillside illustrated the principle of all the operations of Nature. The Maker of this earth but patented a leaf. What Champollion[3] will decipher this hieroglyphic for us, that we may turn over a new leaf at last? This phenomenon is more exhilarating to me than the luxuriance and fertility of vineyards. True, it is somewhat excrementitious in its character, and there is no end to the heaps of liver, lights[4] and bowels, as if the globe were turned wrong side outward; but this suggests at least that Nature has some bowels, and there again is mother of humanity. This is the frost coming out of the ground; this is Spring. It precedes the green and flowery spring, as mythology precedes regular poetry. I know of nothing more purgative of winter fumes and indigestions. It convinces me that Earth is still in her swaddling clothes, and stretches forth baby fingers on every side. Fresh curls spring from the baldest brow. There is nothing inorganic. These foliaceous heaps lie along the bank like the slag of a furnace, showing that Nature is "in full blast" within. The earth is not a mere fragment of dead history, stratum upon stratum like the leaves of a book, to be studied by geologists and antiquaries chiefly, but living poetry like the leaves of a tree, which precede flowers and fruit,—not a fossil earth, but a living earth; compared with whose great central life all animal and vegetable life is merely parasitic. Its throes will heave our exuviæ from their graves. You may melt your metals and cast them into the most beautiful moulds you can; they will never excite me like the forms which this molten earth flows out into. And not only it, but the institutions upon it, are plastic like clay in the hands of the potter.

3. Jean François Champollion (1790–1832), French archaeologist whose deciphering of the hieroglyphic inscriptions on the Rosetta Stone fueled great popular interest in Egyptology. The stone dates from 196 B.C.E. and was discovered by French soldiers in 1799.

4. Lungs.

Ere long, not only on these banks, but on every hill and plain and in every hollow, the frost comes out of the ground like a dormant quadruped from its burrow, and seeks the sea with music, or migrates to other climes in clouds. Thaw with his gentle persuasion is more powerful than Thor with his hammer. The one melts, the other but breaks in pieces.

When the ground was partially bare of snow, and a few warm days had dried its surface somewhat, it was pleasant to compare the first tender signs of the infant year just peeping forth with the stately beauty of the withered vegetation which had withstood the winter,—life-everlasting, golden-rods, pinweeds, and graceful wild grasses, more obvious and interesting frequently than in summer even, as if their beauty was not ripe till then; even cotton-grass, cat-tails, mulleins, johnswort, hard-hack, meadow-sweet, and other strong stemmed plants, those unexhausted granaries which entertain the earliest birds,—decent weeds,[5] at least, which widowed Nature wears. I am particularly attracted by the arching and sheaf-like top of the wool-grass; it brings back the summer to our winter memories, and is among the forms which art loves to copy, and which, in the vegetable kingdom, have the same relation to types already in the mind of man that astronomy has. It is an antique style older than Greek or Egyptian. Many of the phenomena of Winter are suggestive of an inexpressible tenderness and fragile delicacy. We are accustomed to hear this king described as a rude and boisterous tyrant; but with the gentleness of a lover he adorns the tresses of Summer.

At the approach of spring the red-squirrels got under my house, two at a time, directly under my feet as I sat reading or writing, and kept up the queerest chuckling and chirruping and vocal pirouetting and gurgling sounds that ever were heard; and when I stamped they only chirruped the louder, as if past all fear and respect in their mad pranks, defying humanity to stop them. No you don't—chickaree—chickaree. They were wholly deaf to my arguments, or failed to perceive their force, and fell into a strain of invective that was irresistible.

The first sparrow of spring! The year beginning with younger hope than ever! The faint silvery warblings heard over the partially bare and moist fields from the blue-bird, the song-sparrow, and the red-wing, as if the last flakes of winter tinkled as they fell! What at such a time are histories, chronologies, traditions, and all written revelations? The brooks sing carols and glees to the spring. The marsh-hawk sailing low over the meadow is already seeking the first slimy life that awakes. The sinking sound of melting snow is heard in all dells, and the ice dissolves apace in the ponds. The grass flames up on the hillsides like a spring fire,—"et primitus oritur herba imbribus primoribus evocata,"[6]—as if the earth sent forth an inward heat to greet the returning sun; not yellow but green is the color of its flame;—the symbol of perpetual youth, the grass-blade, like a long green ribbon, streams from the sod into the summer, checked indeed by the frost, but anon pushing on again, lifting its spear of last year's hay with the fresh life below. It grows as steadily as the rill oozes out of the ground. It is almost identical with that, for in the growing days of June, when the rills are dry, the grass blades are their channels, and from year to year the herds drink at this perennial green stream, and the

5. Mourning garments.
6. Varro's *Rerum Rusticarum* 2.2.14; Thoreau goes on to translate.

mower draws from it betimes their winter supply. So our human life but dies down to its roots, and still puts forth its green blade to eternity.

Walden is melting apace. There is a canal two rods wide along the northerly and westerly sides, and wider still at the east end. A great field of ice has cracked off from the main body. I hear a song-sparrow singing from the bushes on the shore,—*olit, olit, olit,—chip, chip, chip, che char,—che wiss, wiss, wiss.* He too is helping to crack it. How handsome the great sweeping curves in the edge of the ice, answering somewhat to those of the shore, but more regular! It is unusually hard, owing to the recent severe but transient cold, and all watered or waved like a palace floor. But the wind slides eastward over its opaque surface in vain, till it reaches the living surface beyond. It is glorious to behold this ribbon of water sparkling in the sun, the bare face of the pond full of glee and youth, as if it spoke the joy of the fishes within it, and of the sands on its shore,—a silvery sheen as from the scales of a *leuciscus*, as it were all one active fish. Such is the contrast between winter and spring. Walden was dead and is alive again. But this spring it broke up more steadily, as I have said.

The change from storm and winter to serene and mild weather, from dark and sluggish hours to bright and elastic ones, is a memorable crisis which all things proclaim. It is seemingly instantaneous at last. Suddenly an influx of light filled my house, though the evening was at hand, and the clouds of winter still overhung it, and the eaves were dripping with sleety rain. I looked out the window, and lo! where yesterday was cold gray ice there lay the transparent pond already calm and full of hope as on a summer evening, reflecting a summer evening sky in its bosom, though none was visible overhead, as if it had intelligence with some remote horizon. I heard a robin in the distance, the first I had heard for many a thousand years, methought, whose note I shall not forget for many a thousand more,—the same sweet and powerful song of yore. O the evening robin, at the end of a New England summer day! If I could ever find the twig he sits upon! I mean *he*; I mean *the twig*. This at least is not the *Turdus migratorius*.[7] The pitch-pines and shrub-oaks about my house, which had so long drooped, suddenly resumed their several characters, looked brighter, greener, and more erect and alive, as if effectually cleansed and restored by the rain. I knew that it would not rain any more. You may tell by looking at any twig of the forest, ay, at your very wood-pile, whether its winter is past or not. As it grew darker, I was startled by the *honking* of geese flying low over the woods, like weary travellers getting in late from southern lakes, and indulging at last in unrestrained complaint and mutual consolation. Standing at my door, I could hear the rush of their wings; when, driving toward my house, they suddenly spied my light, and with hushed clamor wheeled and settled in the pond. So I came in, and shut the door, and passed my first spring night in the woods.

In the morning I watched the geese from the door through the mist, sailing in the middle of the pond, fifty rods off, so large and tumultuous that Walden appeared like an aritifical pond for their amusement. But when I stood on the shore they at once rose up with a great flapping of wings at the signal of their commander, and when they had got into rank circled about

7. American robin.

over my head, twenty-nine of them, and then steered straight to Canada, with a regular *honk* from the leader at intervals, trusting to break their fast in muddier pools. A "plump" of ducks rose at the same time and took the route to the north in the wake of their noisier cousins.

For a week I heard the circling groping clangor of some solitary goose in the foggy mornings, seeking its companion, and still peopling the woods with the sound of a larger life than they could sustain. In April the pigeons were seen again flying express in small flocks, and in due time I heard the martins twittering over my clearing, though it had not seemed that the township contained so many that it could afford me any, and I fancied that they were peculiarly of the ancient race that dwelt in hollow trees ere white men came. In almost all climes the tortoise and the frog are among the precursors and heralds of this season, and birds fly with song and glancing plumage, and plants spring and bloom, and winds blow, to correct this slight oscillation of the poles and preserve the equilibrium of Nature.

As every season seems best to us in its turn, so the coming in of spring is like the creation of Cosmos out of Chaos and the realization of the Golden Age.—

> "Eurus ad Auroram, Nabathæaque regna recessit,
> Persidaque, et radiis juga subdita matutinis."
>
> "The East-Wind withdrew to Aurora and the Nabathæan kingdom,
> And the Persian, and the ridges placed under the morning rays.
>
> • • •
>
> Man was born. Whether that Artificer of things,
> The origin of a better world, made him from the divine seed;
> Or the earth being recent and lately sundered from the high
> Ether, retained some seeds of cognate heaven."[8]

A single gentle rain makes the grass many shades greener. So our prospects brighten on the influx of better thoughts. We should be blessed if we lived in the present always, and took advantage of every accident that befell us, like the grass which confesses the influence of the slightest dew that falls on it; and did not spend our time in atoning for the neglect of past opportunities, which we call doing our duty. We loiter in winter while it is already spring. In a pleasant spring morning all men's sins are forgiven. Such a day is a truce to vice. While such a sun holds out to burn, the vilest sinner may return. Through our own recovered innocence we discern the innocence of our neighbors. You may have known your neighbor yesterday for a thief, a drunkard, or a sensualist, and merely pitied or despised him, and despaired of the world; but the sun shines bright and warm this first spring morning, re-creating the world, and you meet him at some serene work, and see how his exhausted and debauched veins expand with still joy and bless the new day, feel the spring influence with the innocence of infancy, and all his faults are forgotten. There is not only an atmosphere of good will about him, but even a savor of holiness groping for expression, blindly and ineffectually perhaps, like a new-born instinct, and for a short hour the south hill-side

8. Ovid's *Metamorphoses* 1.61–62, 78–81.

echoes to no vulgar jest. You see some innocent fair shoots preparing to burst from his gnarled rind and try another year's life, tender and fresh as the youngest plant. Even he has entered into the joy of his Lord. Why the jailer does not leave open his prison doors,—why the judge does not dismiss his case,—why the preacher does not dismiss his congregation! It is because they do not obey the hint which God gives them, nor accept the pardon which he freely offers to all.

"A return to goodness produced each day in the tranquil and beneficent breath of the morning, causes that in respect to the love of virtue and the hatred of vice, one approaches a little the primitive nature of man, as the sprouts of the forest which has been felled. In like manner the evil which one does in the interval of a day prevents the germs of virtues which began to spring up again from developing themselves and destroys them.

"After the germs of virtue have thus been prevented many times from developing themselves, then the beneficent breath of evening does not suffice to preserve them. As soon as the breath of evening does not suffice longer to preserve them, then the nature of man does not differ much from that of the brute. Men seeing the nature of this man like that of the brute, think that he has never possessed the innate faculty of reason. Are those the true and natural sentiments of man?"[9]

"The Golden Age was first created, which without any avenger
Spontaneously without law cherished fidelity and rectitude.
Punishment and fear were not; nor were threatening words read
On suspended brass; nor did the suppliant crowd fear
The words of their judge; but were safe without an avenger.
Not yet the pine felled on its mountains had descended
To the liquid waves that it might see a foreign world,
And mortals knew no shore but their own.

• • •

There was eternal spring, and placid zephyrs with warm
Blasts soothed the flowers born without seed."[1]

On the 29th of April, as I was fishing from the bank of the river near the Nine-Acre-Corner bridge, standing on the quaking grass and willow roots, where the muskrats lurk, I heard a singular rattling sound, somewhat like that of the sticks which boys play with their fingers, when, looking up, I observed a very slight and graceful hawk, like a night-hawk, alternately soaring like a ripple and tumbling a rod or two over and over, showing the underside of its wings, which gleamed like a satin ribbon in the sun, or like the pearly inside of a shell. This sight reminded me of falconry and what nobleness and poetry are associated with that sport. The Merlin[2] it seemed to me it might be called: but I care not for its name. It was the most ethereal flight I had ever witnessed. It did not simply flutter like a butterfly, nor soar like the larger hawks, but it sported with proud reliance in the fields of air; mounting again and again with its strange chuckle, it repeated its free and beautiful fall, turning over and over like a kite, and then recovering from its

9. Mencius's (Meng-tzu's) *Works* 6.1.
1. Ovid's *Metamorphoses* 1.89–96, 107–08.
2. Small falcon or pigeon hawk.

lofty tumbling, as if it had never set its foot on *terra firma*. It appeared to have no companion in the universe,—sporting there alone,—and to need none but the morning and the ether with which it played. It was not lonely, but made all the earth lonely beneath it. Where was the parent which hatched it, its kindred, and its father in the heavens? The tenant of the air, it seemed related to the earth but by an egg hatched some time in the crevice of a crag;—or was its native nest made in the angle of a cloud, woven of the rainbow's trimmings and the sunset sky, and lined with some soft midsummer haze caught up from earth? Its eyry[3] now some cliffy cloud.

Beside this I got a rare mess of golden and silver and bright cupreous[4] fishes, which looked like a string of jewels. Ah! I have penetrated to those meadows on the morning of many a first spring day, jumping from hummock to hummock, from willow root to willow root, when the wild river valley and the woods were bathed in so pure and bright a light as would have waked the dead, if they had been slumbering in their graves, as some suppose. There needs no stronger proof of immortality. All things must live in such a light. O Death, where was thy sting? O Grave, where was thy victory, then?[5]

Our village life would stagnate if it were not for the unexplored forests and meadows which surround it. We need the tonic of wildness,—to wade sometimes in marshes where the bittern and the meadow-hen lurk, and hear the booming of the snipe; to smell the whispering sedge where only some wilder and more solitary fowl builds her nest, and the mink crawls with its belly close to the ground. At the same time that we are earnest to explore and learn all things, we require that all things be mysterious and unexplorable, that land and sea be infinitely wild, unsurveyed and unfathomed by us because unfathomable. We can never have enough of Nature. We must be refreshed by the sight of inexhaustible vigor, vast and Titanic features, the sea-coast with its wrecks, the wilderness with its living and its decaying trees, the thunder cloud, and the rain which lasts three weeks and produces freshets. We need to witness our own limits transgressed, and some life pasturing freely where we never wander. We are cheered when we observe the vulture feeding on the carrion which disgusts and disheartens us and deriving health and strength from the repast. There was a dead horse in the hollow by the path to my house, which compelled me sometimes to go out of my way, especially in the night when the air was heavy, but the assurance it gave me of the strong appetite and inviolable health of Nature was my compensation for this. I love to see that Nature is so rife with life that myriads can be afforded to be sacrificed and suffered to prey on one another; that tender organizations can be so serenely squashed out of existence like pulp,—tadpoles which herons gobble up, and tortoises and toads run over in the road; and that sometimes it has rained flesh and blood! With the liability to accident, we must see how little account is to be made of it. The impression made on a wise man is that of universal innocence. Poison is not poisonous after all, nor are any wounds fatal. Compassion is a very untenable ground. It must be expeditious. Its pleadings will not bear to be stereotyped.

Early in May, the oaks, hickories, maples, and other trees, just putting out amidst the pine woods around the pond, imparted a brightness like

3. Aerie; bird's nest.
4. Coppery.
5. 1 Corinthians 15.55: "O death, where is thy sting? O grave, where is thy victory?"

sunshine to the landscape, especially in cloudy days, as if the sun were breaking through mists and shining faintly on the hill-sides here and there. On the third or fourth of May I saw a loon in the pond, and during the first week of the month I heard the whippoorwill, the brown-thrasher, the veery, the wood-pewee, the chewink, and other birds. I had heard the woodthrush long before. The phœbe had already come once more and looked in at my door and window, to see if my house was cavern-like enough for her, sustaining herself on humming wings with clinched talons, as if she held by the air, while she surveyed the premises. The sulphur-like pollen of the pitch-pine soon covered the pond and the stones and rotten wood along the shore, so that you could have collected a barrel-ful. This is the "sulphur showers" we hear of. Even in Calidas' drama of Sacontala, we read of "rills dyed yellow with the golden dust of the lotus."[6] And so the seasons went rolling on into summer, as one rambles into higher and higher grass.

Thus was my first year's life in the woods completed; and the second year was similar to it. I finally left Walden September 6th, 1847.

18. Conclusion

To the sick the doctors wisely recommend a change of air and scenery. Thank Heaven, here is not all the world. The buck-eye does not grow in New England, and the mocking-bird is rarely heard here. The wild-goose is more of a cosmopolite than we; he breaks his fast in Canada, takes a luncheon in the Ohio, and plumes himself for the night in a southern bayou. Even the bison, to some extent, keeps pace with the seasons, cropping the pastures of the Colorado only till a greener and sweeter grass awaits him by the Yellowstone. Yet we think that if rail-fences are pulled down, and stone-walls piled up on our farms, bounds are henceforth set to our lives and our fates decided. If you are chosen town-clerk, forsooth, you cannot go to Tierra del Fuego[7] this summer: but you may go to the land of infernal fire nevertheless. The universe is wider than our views of it.

Yet we should oftener look over the tafferel of our craft, like curious passengers, and not make the voyage like stupid sailors picking oakum.[8] The other side of the globe is but the home of our correspondent. Our voyaging is only great-circle sailing, and the doctors prescribe for diseases of the skin merely. One hastens to Southern Africa to chase the giraffe; but surely that is not the game he would be after. How long, pray, would a man hunt giraffes if he could? Snipes and woodcocks also may afford rare sport; but I trust it would be nobler game to shoot one's self.—

"Direct your eye sight inward, and you'll find
A thousand regions in your mind
Yet undiscovered. Travel them, and be
Expert in home-cosmography."[9]

6. Sir William Jones's 18th-century translation of *Sacontalá*, act 5, by Cálidás (5th century), Hindu writer.
7. Thoreau puns on the meaning of the name of the archipelago at the southern tip of South America: land of fire (Spanish).
8. Picking old rope apart so the pieces of hemp could be tarred and used for caulking. "Tafferel": i.e., taffrail; guardrail at a ship's stern.
9. William Habington (1605–1654), "To My Honoured Friend Sir Ed. P. Knight."

What does Africa,—what does the West stand for? Is not our own interior white on the chart? black though it may prove, like the coast, when discovered. Is it the source of the Nile, or the Niger, or the Mississippi, or a North West Passage around this continent, that we would find? Are these the problems which most concern mankind? Is Franklin[1] the only man who is lost, that his wife should be so earnest to find him? Does Mr. Grinnell[2] know where he himself is? Be rather the Mungo Park, the Lewis and Clarke and Frobisher,[3] of your own streams and oceans; explore your own higher latitudes,—with shiploads of preserved meats to support you, if they be necessary; and pile the empty cans sky-high for a sign. Were preserved meats invented to preserve meat merely? Nay, be a Columbus to whole new continents and worlds within you, opening new channels, not of trade, but of thought. Every man is the lord of a realm beside which the earthly empire of the Czar is but a petty state, a hummock left by the ice. Yet some can be patriotic who have no *self*-respect, and sacrifice the greater to the less. They love the soil which makes their graves, but have no sympathy with the spirit which may still animate their clay. Patriotism is a maggot in their heads. What was the meaning of that South-Sea Exploring Expedition,[4] with all its parade and expense, but an indirect recognition of the fact, that there are continents and seas in the moral world, to which every man is an isthmus or an inlet, yet unexplored by him, but that it is easier to sail many thousand miles through cold and storm and cannibals, in a government ship, with five hundred men and boys to assist one, than it is to explore the private sea, the Atlantic and Pacific Ocean of one's being alone.—

> "Erret, et extremos alter scrutetur Iberos.
> Plus habet hic vitæ, plus habet ille viæ."[5]
>
> Let them wander and scrutinize the outlandish Australians.
> I have more of God, they more of the road.

It is not worth the while to go round the world to count the cats in Zanzibar.[6] Yet do this even till you can do better, and you may perhaps find some "Symmes' Hole"[7] by which to get at the inside at last. England and France, Spain and Portugal, Gold Coast and Slave Coast, all front on this private sea; but no bark from them has ventured out of sight of land, though it is without doubt the direct way to India. If you would learn to speak all tongues and conform to the customs of all nations, if you would travel farther than all travellers, be naturalized in all climes, and cause the Sphinx to

1. Sir John Franklin (1785–1847), lost on a British expedition to the Arctic.
2. Henry Grinnell (1799–1874), a rich New York whale-oil merchant from a New Bedford family who sponsored two attempts to rescue Sir Franklin, one in 1850 and another in 1853.
3. I.e., an explorer like Martin Frobisher (1535?–1594), English mariner. Mungo Park (1771–1806), Scottish explorer of Africa. Meriwether Lewis (1774–1809) and William Clark (1770–1838), leaders of the American expedition into the Louisiana Territory (1804–6).
4. The famous expedition to the Pacific Antarctic led by Charles Wilkes (1798–1877) during 1838–42.
5. Thoreau's journal for May 10, 1841, begins: "A good warning to the restless tourists of these days is contained in the last verses of Claudian's 'Old Man of Verona.'" Claudius Claudianus was the last of the Latin classic poets (fl. 395 C.E.) and author of *Epigrammata*, where Thoreau found the passage he loosely translates here.
6. Thoreau had read Charles Pickering's *The Races of Man* (1851), which reports on the domestic cats in Zanzibar.
7. In 1818 Captain John Symmes (1780–1829) theorized that the earth was hollow with openings at both the North and South Poles.

dash her head against a stone,[8] even obey the precept of the old philosopher, and Explore thyself. Herein are demanded the eye and the nerve. Only the defeated and deserters go to the wars, cowards that run away and enlist. Start now on that farthest western way, which does not pause at the Mississippi or the Pacific, nor conduct toward a worn-out China or Japan, but leads on direct a tangent to this sphere, summer and winter, day and night, sun down, moon down, and at last earth down too.

It is said that Mirabeau took to highway robbery "to ascertain what degree of resolution was necessary in order to place one's self in formal opposition to the most sacred laws of society." He declared that "a soldier who fights in the ranks does not require half so much courage as a foot-pad,"—"that honor and religion have never stood in the way of a well-considered and a firm resolve."[9] This was manly, as the world goes; and yet it was idle, if not desperate. A saner man would have found himself often enough "in formal opposition" to what are deemed "the most sacred laws of society," through obedience to yet more sacred laws, and so have tested his resolution without going out of his way. It is not for a man to put himself in such an attitude to society, but to maintain himself in whatever attitude he find himself through obedience to the laws of his being, which will never be one of opposition to a just government, if he should chance to meet with such.

I left the woods for as good a reason as I went there. Perhaps it seemed to me that I had several more lives to live, and could not spare any more time for that one. It is remarkable how easily and insensibly we fall into a particular route, and make a beaten track for ourselves. I had not lived there a week before my feet wore a path from my door to the pond-side; and though it is five or six years since I trod it, it is still quite distinct. It is true, I fear that others may have fallen into it, and so helped to keep it open. The surface of the earth is soft and impressible by the feet of men; and so with the paths which the mind travels. How worn and dusty, then, must be the highways of the world, how deep the ruts of tradition and conformity! I did not wish to take a cabin passage, but rather to go before the mast and on the deck of the world, for there I could best see the moonlight amid the mountains. I do not wish to go below now.

I learned this, at least, by my experiment; that if one advances confidently in the direction of his dreams, and endeavors to live the life which he has imagined, he will meet with a success unexpected in common hours. He will put some things behind, will pass an invisible boundary; new, universal, and more liberal laws will begin to establish themselves around and within him; or the old laws be expanded, and interpreted in his favor in a more liberal sense, and he will live with the license of a higher order of beings. In proportion as he simplifies his life, the laws of the universe will appear less complex, and solitude will not be solitude, nor poverty poverty, nor weakness weakness. If you have built castles in the air, your work need not be lost; that is where they should be. Now put the foundations under them.

8. As the Theban Sphinx did when Oedipus guessed her riddle. Thebes here is the ancient Greek city, not the Egyptian city Thoreau has previously referred to.

9. Thoreau encountered this passage by the French statesman Comte de Mirabeau (1749–1791) in *Harper's* 1 (1850).

It is a ridiculous demand which England and America make, that you shall speak so that they can understand you. Neither men nor toad-stools grow so. As if that were important, and there were not enough to understand you without them. As if Nature could support but one order of understandings, could not sustain birds as well as quadrupeds, flying as well as creeping things, and *hush* and *who*, which Bright[1] can understand, were the best English. As if there were safety in stupidity alone. I fear chiefly lest my expression may not be *extra-vagant*[2] enough, may not wander far enough beyond the narrow limits of my daily experience, so as to be adequate to the truth of which I have been convinced. *Extra vagance!* it depends on how you are yarded. The migrating buffalo, which seeks new pastures in another latitude, is not extravagant like the cow which kicks over the pail, leaps the cow-yard fence, and runs after her calf, in milking time. I desire to speak somewhere *without* bounds; like a man in a waking moment, to men in their waking moments; for I am convinced that I cannot exaggerate enough even to lay the foundation of a true expression. Who that has heard a strain of music feared then lest he should speak extravagantly any more forever? In view of the future or possible, we should live quite laxly and undefined in front, our outlines dim and misty on that side; as our shadows reveal an insensible perspiration toward the sun. The volatile truth of our words should continually betray the inadequacy of the residual statement. Their truth is instantly *translated*; its literal monument alone remains. The words which express our faith and piety are not definite; yet they are significant and fragrant like frankincense to superior natures.

Why level downward to our dullest perception always, and praise that as common sense? The commonest sense is the sense of men asleep, which they express by snoring. Sometimes we are inclined to class those who are once-and-a-half witted with the half-witted, because we appreciate only a third part of their wit. Some would find fault with the morning-red, if they ever got up early enough. "They pretend," as I hear, "that the verses of Kabir have four different senses; illusion, spirit, intellect, and the exoteric doctrine of the Vedas;"[3] but in this part of the world it is considered a ground for complaint if a man's writings admit of more than one interpretation. While England endeavors to cure the potato-rot, will not any endeavor to cure the brain-rot, which prevails so much more widely and fatally?

I do not suppose that I have attained to obscurity, but I should be proud if no more fatal fault were found with my pages on this score than was found with the Walden ice. Southern customers objected to its blue color, which is the evidence of its purity, as if it were muddy, and preferred the Cambridge ice, which is white, but tastes of weeds. The purity men love is like the mists which envelop the earth, and not like the azure ether beyond.

Some are dinning in our ears that we Americans, and moderns generally, are intellectual dwarfs compared with the ancients, or even the Elizabethan men. But what is that to the purpose? A living dog is better than a dead lion.[4] Shall a man go and hang himself because he belongs to the race of

1. Name for an ox.
2. Thoreau provides the hyphen to emphasize the word's Latin roots (*extra*, "outside"; *vagari*, "to wander").
3. M. Garcin de Tassy's *Histoire de la littérature hindoui* (1839).
4. Ecclesiastes 9.4.

pygmies, and not be the biggest pygmy that he can? Let every one mind his own business, and endeavor to be what he was made.

Why should we be in such desperate haste to succeed, and in such desperate enterprises? If a man does not keep pace with his companions, perhaps it is because he hears a different drummer. Let him step to the music which he hears, however measured or far away. It is not important that he should mature as soon as an apple-tree or an oak. Shall he turn his spring into summer? If the condition of things which we were made for is not yet, what were any reality which we can substitute? We will not be shipwrecked on a vain reality. Shall we with pains erect a heaven of blue glass over ourselves, though when it is done we shall be sure to gaze still at the true ethereal heaven far above, as if the former were not?

There was an artist in the city of Kouroo[5] who was disposed to strive after perfection. One day it came into his mind to make a staff. Having considered that in an imperfect work time is an ingredient, but into a perfect work time does not enter, he said to himself, It shall be perfect in all respects, though I should do nothing else in my life. He proceeded instantly to the forest for wood, being resolved that it should not be made of unsuitable material; and as he searched for and rejected stick after stick, his friends gradually deserted him, for they grew old in their works and died, but he grew not older by a moment. His singleness of purpose and resolution, and his elevated piety, endowed him, without his knowledge, with perennial youth. As he made no compromise with Time, Time kept out of his way, and only sighed at a distance because he could not overcome him. Before he had found a stock in all respects suitable the city of Kouroo was a hoary ruin, and he sat on one of its mounds to peel the stick. Before he had given it the proper shape the dynasty of the Candahars was at an end, and with the point of the stick he wrote the name of the last of that race in the sand, and then resumed his work. By the time he had smoothed and polished the staff Kalpa was no longer the pole-star; and ere he had put on the ferule and the head adorned with precious stones, Brahma had awoke and slumbered many times. But why do I stay to mention these things? When the finishing stroke was put to his work, it suddenly expanded before the eyes of the astonished artist into the fairest of all the creations of Brahma. He had made a new system in making a staff, a world with full and fair proportions; in which, though the old cities and dynasties had passed away, fairer and more glorious ones had taken their places. And now he saw by the heap of shavings still fresh at his feet, that, for him and his work, the former lapse of time had been an illusion, and that no more time had elapsed than is required for a single scintillation from the brain of Brahma to fall on and inflame the tinder of a mortal brain. The material was pure, and his art was pure; how could the result be other than wonderful?

No face which we can give to a matter will stead us so well at last as the truth. This alone wears well. For the most part, we are not where we are, but in a false position. Through an infirmity of our natures, we suppose a case, and put ourselves into it, and hence are in two cases at the same time, and it is doubly difficult to get out. In sane moments we regard only the

5. Thoreau in all likelihood invented this fable of artistry, though the reference to "Kouroo" invokes "Kuru," a legendary hero in India.

facts, the case that is. Say what you have to say, not what you ought. Any truth is better than make-believe. Tom Hyde, the tinker, standing on the gallows, was asked if he had any thing to say. "Tell the tailors," said he, "to remember to make a knot in their thread before they take the first stitch."[6] His companion's prayer is forgotten.

However mean your life is, meet it and live it; do not shun it and call it hard names. It is not so bad as you are. It looks poorest when you are richest. The fault-finder will find faults even in paradise. Love your life, poor as it is. You may perhaps have some pleasant, thrilling, glorious hours, even in a poor-house. The setting sun is reflected from the windows of the alms-house as brightly as from the rich man's abode; the snow melts before its door as early in the spring. I do not see but a quiet mind may live as contentedly there, and have as cheering thoughts, as in a palace. The town's poor seem to me often to live the most independent lives of any. May be they are simply great enough to receive without misgiving. Most think that they are above being supported by the town; but it oftener happens that they are not above supporting themselves by dishonest means, which should be more disreputable. Cultivate poverty like a garden herb, like sage. Do not trouble yourself much to get new things, whether clothes or friends. Turn the old; return to them. Things do not change; we change. Sell your clothes and keep your thoughts. God will see that you do not want society. If I were confined to a corner of a garret all my days, like a spider, the world would be just as large to me while I had my thoughts about me. The philosopher said: "From an army of three divisions one can take away its general, and put it in disorder; from the man the most abject and vulgar one cannot take away his thought."[7] Do not seek so anxiously to be developed, to subject yourself to many influences to be played on; it is all dissipation. Humility like darkness reveals the heavenly lights. The shadows of poverty and meanness gather around us, "and lo! creation widens to our view."[8] We are often reminded that if there were bestowed on us the wealth of Crœsus,[9] our aims must still be the same, and our means essentially the same. Moreover, if you are restricted in your range by poverty, if you cannot buy books and newspapers, for instance, you are but confined to the most significant and vital experiences; you are compelled to deal with the material which yields the most sugar and the most starch. It is life near the bone where it is sweetest. You are defended from being a trifler. No man loses ever on a lower level by magnanimity on a higher. Superfluous wealth can buy superfluities only. Money is not required to buy one necessary of the soul.

I live in the angle of a leaden wall, into whose composition was poured a little alloy of bell metal. Often, in the repose of my mid-day, there reaches my ears a confused *tintinnabulum*[1] from without. It is the noise of my contemporaries. My neighbors tell me of their adventures with famous gentlemen and ladies, what notabilities they met at the dinner-table; but I am no more interested in such things than in the contents of the Daily Times. The interest and

6. Presumably a reference to the tailors who will sew Hyde's shroud. Thoreau may have invented this anecdote; scholars have been unable to identify a Tom Hyde who was executed.
7. Confucius's *Analects* 9.25.
8. From the sonnet "To Night" (1828) by the Spanish-born writer Joseph Blanco White (1775–1841), who emigrated to England in 1810.
9. King of Lydia (d. 546 B.C.E.), fabled as the richest man on earth.
1. Tinkling.

the conversation are about costume and manners chiefly; but a goose is a goose still, dress it as you will. They tell me of California and Texas, of England and the Indies, of the Hon. Mr. ——— of Georgia or of Massachusetts, all transient and fleeting phenomena, till I am ready to leap from their court-yard like the Mameluke bey.[2] I delight to come to my bearings,—not walk in procession with pomp and parade, in a conspicuous place, but to walk even with the Builder of the universe, if I may,—not to live in this restless, nervous, bustling, trivial Nineteenth Century, but stand or sit thoughtfully while it goes by. What are men celebrating? They are all on a committee of arrangements, and hourly expect a speech from somebody. God is only the president of the day, and Webster is his orator.[3] I love to weigh, to settle, to gravitate toward that which most strongly and rightfully attracts me;—not hang by the beam of the scale and try to weigh less,—not suppose a case, but take the case that is; to travel the only path I can, and that on which no power can resist me. It affords me no satisfaction to commence to spring an arch before I have got a solid foundation. Let us not play at kittlybenders.[4] There is a solid bottom every where. We read that the traveller asked the boy if the swamp before him had a hard bottom. The boy replied that it had. But presently the traveller's horse sank in up to the girths, and he observed to the boy, "I thought you said that this bog had a hard bottom." "So it has," answered the latter, "but you have not got half way to it yet." So it is with the bogs and quicksands of society; but he is an old boy that knows it. Only what is thought said or done at a certain rare coincidence is good. I would not be one of those who will foolishly drive a nail into mere lath and plastering; such a deed would keep me awake nights. Give me a hammer, and let me feel for the furring.[5] Do not depend on the putty. Drive a nail home and clinch it so faithfully that you can wake up in the night and think of your work with satisfaction,—a work at which you would not be ashamed to invoke the Muse. So will help you God, and so only. Every nail driven should be as another rivet in the machine of the universe, you carrying on the work.

Rather than love, than money, than fame, give me truth. I sat at a table where were rich food and wine in abundance, and obsequious attendance, but sincerity and truth were not; and I went away hungry from the inhospitable board. The hospitality was as cold as the ices. I thought that there was no need of ice to freeze them. They talked to me of the age of the wine and the fame of the vintage; but I thought of an older, a newer, and purer wine, of a more glorious vintage, which they had not got, and could not buy. The style, the house and grounds and "entertainment" pass for nothing with me. I called on the king, but he made me wait in his hall, and conducted like a man incapacitated for hospitality. There was a man in my neighborhood who lived in a hollow tree. His manners were truly regal. I should have done better had I called on him.

2. A famous romantic exploit: in 1811 the Egyptian Mehemet Ali Pasha attempted to massacre the Mameluke caste, but one bey, or officer, escaped by leaping from a wall onto his horse.

3. Political meetings then had "presidents" (because they presided). Thoreau plays on the saying from Islam, "There is no other God than Allah, and Mohammed is his prophet." Thoreau again expresses his contempt for Massachusetts senator Daniel Webster.

4. A game of trying to skate or slide over thin ice without breaking through.

5. Narrow lumber nailed as backing for lath. The first edition reads "furrowing," and one manuscript draft reads "stud."

How long shall we sit in our porticoes practising idle and musty virtues, which any work would make impertinent? As if one were to begin the day with long-suffering, and hire a man to hoe his potatoes; and in the afternoon go forth to practise Christian meekness and charity with goodness aforethought! Consider the China[6] pride and stagnant self-complacency of mankind. This generation reclines a little to congratulate itself on being the last of an illustrious line; and in Boston and London and Paris and Rome, thinking of its long descent, it speaks of its progress in art and science and literature with satisfaction. There are the Records of the Philosophical Societies, and the public Eulogies of *Great Men*! It is the good Adam contemplating his own virtue. "Yes, we have done great deeds, and sung divine songs, which shall never die,"—that is, as long as *we* can remember them. The learned societies and great men of Assyria,[7]—where are they? What youthful philosophers and experimentalists we are! There is not one of my readers who has yet lived a whole human life. These may be but the spring months in the life of the race. If we have had the seven-years' itch,[8] we have not seen the seventeen-year locust yet in Concord. We are acquainted with a mere pellicle[9] of the globe on which we live. Most have not delved six feet beneath the surface, nor leaped as many above it. We know not where we are. Beside, we are sound asleep nearly half our time. Yet we esteem ourselves wise, and have an established order on the surface. Truly, we are deep thinkers, we are ambitious spirits! As I stand over the insect crawling amid the pine needles on the forest floor, and endeavoring to conceal itself from my sight, and ask myself why it will cherish those humble thoughts, and hide its head from me who might perhaps be its benefactor, and impart to its race some cheering information, I am reminded of the greater Benefactor and Intelligence that stands over me the human insect.

There is an incessant influx of novelty into the world, and yet we tolerate incredible dulness. I need only suggest what kind of sermons are still listened to in the most enlightened countries. There are such words as joy and sorrow, but they are only the burden of a psalm, sung with a nasal twang, while we believe in the ordinary and mean. We think that we can change our clothes only. It is said that the British Empire is very large and respectable, and that the United States are a first-rate power. We do not believe that a tide rises and falls behind every man which can float the British Empire like a chip, if he should ever harbor it in his mind. Who knows what sort of seventeen-year locust will next come out of the ground? The government of the world I live in was not framed, like that of Britain, in after-dinner conversations over the wine.

The life in us is like the water in the river. It may rise this year higher than man has ever known it, and flood the parched uplands; even this may be the eventful year, which will drown out all our muskrats. It was not always dry land where we dwell. I see far inland the banks which the stream anciently washed, before science began to record its freshets. Every one has heard the story which has gone the rounds of New England, of a strong and beautiful bug which came out of the dry leaf of an old table of apple-tree wood, which

6. Thoreau and others of the time regarded China as complacent in its isolationism.
7. Ancient empire in western Asia.
8. Painful skin irritation caused by mites.
9. Skin.

had stood in a farmer's kitchen for sixty years, first in Connecticut, and afterward in Massachusetts,—from an egg deposited in the living tree many years earlier still, as appeared by counting the annual layers beyond it; which was heard gnawing out for several weeks, hatched perchance by the heat of an urn.[1] Who does not feel his faith in a resurrection and immortality strengthened by hearing of this? Who knows what beautiful and winged life, whose egg has been buried for ages under many concentric layers of woodenness in the dead dry life of society, deposited at first in the alburnum[2] of the green and living tree, which has been gradually converted into the semblance of its well-seasoned tomb,—heard perchance gnawing out now for years by the astonished family of man, as they sat round the festive board,—may unexpectedly come forth from amidst society's most trivial and handselled furniture, to enjoy its perfect summer life at last!

I do not say that John or Jonathan[3] will realize all this; but such is the character of that morrow which mere lapse of time can never make to dawn. The light which puts out our eyes is darkness to us. Only that day dawns to which we are awake. There is more day to dawn. The sun is but a morning star.

THE END

1854

Slavery in Massachusetts[1]

An Address, Delivered at the Anti-Slavery Celebration at Framingham, July 4th, 1854

I lately attended a meeting of the citizens of Concord, expecting, as one among many, to speak on the subject of slavery in Massachusetts; but I was surprised and disappointed to find that what had called my townsmen together was the destiny of Nebraska, and not of Massachusetts, and that

1. An account of the incident is in Timothy Dwight's *Travels in New England and New York* (1821), vol. 2.
2. Young, soft wood.
3. John Bull or Brother Jonathan, i.e., England or America.

1. Thoreau delivered a shortened version of this essay at Framingham, Massachusetts, on the Fourth of July, 1854. The "Anti-Slavery Celebration" was a massive protest, timed to challenge the self-complacent patriotism of the typical Independence Day celebration. At Framingham, William Lloyd Garrison (1805–1879), the editor of the *Liberator,* publicly burned a copy of the United States Constitution because he believed it condoned slavery; and in the *Liberator* for July 21, 1854, Garrison printed Thoreau's talk as "Slavery in Massachusetts. An Address, Delivered at the Anti-Slavery Celebration at Framingham, July 4th, 1854," the source of the present text.

Behind Thoreau's passionate antislavery speech lay the months-long debate over and the ultimate passage of the Kansas-Nebraska Act, which repealed a key provision of the Missouri Compromise (1820)—the prohibition of slavery in any new states north of 36°30'. The new law, sponsored by Stephen A. Douglas, allowed white inhabitants of a territory not yet a state to decide whether to enter the union as a slave or free state. Thoreau was also angered by two Massachusetts events of national significance: the remanding of the slave Thomas Sims to his Georgia master in 1851 under the Fugitive Slave Law (part of the Compromise of 1850), and the similar remanding of Anthony Burns to Virginia just a month before this speech was given. Both Democratic and Whig newspapers in Massachusetts upheld the return of Sims, but the *Burns* case, coming at the height of the Kansas-Nebraska agitation, helped crystallize public opinion against the Fugitive Slave Law throughout the North. Into his speech Thoreau worked passages written in his journals during both the *Sims* and *Burns* cases.

This speech reached an audience hundreds of times larger than that of *Walden,* which was published in the same year, for Horace Greeley reprinted it in his *New York Tribune* and the *Washington National Anti-Slavery Standard* also reprinted it.

what I had to say would be entirely out of order. I had thought that the house was on fire, and not the prairie; but though several of the citizens of Massachusetts are now in prison for attempting to rescue a slave from her own clutches, not one of the speakers at that meeting expressed regret for it, not one even referred to it.[2] It was only the disposition of some wild lands a thousand miles off, which appeared to concern them. The inhabitants of Concord are not prepared to stand by one of their own bridges,[3] but talk only of taking up a position on the highlands beyond the Yellowstone river. Our Buttricks, and Davises, and Hosmers[4] are retreating thither, and I fear that they will have no Lexington Common between them and the enemy. There is not one slave in Nebraska; there are perhaps a million slaves in Massachusetts.

They who have been bred in the school of politics fail now and always to face the facts. Their measures are half measures and make-shifts, merely. They put off the day of settlement indefinitely, and meanwhile, the debt accumulates. Though the Fugitive Slave Law had not been the subject of discussion on that occasion, it was at length faintly resolved by my townsmen, at an adjourned meeting, as I learn, that the compromise compact of 1820 having been repudiated by one of the parties, 'Therefore, . . . the Fugitive Slave Law must be repealed.' But this is not the reason why an iniquitous law should be repealed. The fact which the politician faces is merely, that there is less honor among thieves than was supposed, and not the fact that they are thieves.

As I had no opportunity to express my thoughts at that meeting, will you allow me to do so here?

Again[5] it happens that the Boston Court House is full of armed men, holding prisoner and trying a MAN, to find out if he is not really a SLAVE. Does any one think that Justice or God awaits Mr. Loring's decision?[6] For him to sit there deciding still, when this question is already decided from eternity to eternity, and the unlettered slave himself, and the multitude around, have long since heard and assented to the decision, is simply to make himself ridiculous. We may be tempted to ask from whom he received his commission, and who he is that received it; what novel statutes he obeys, and what precedents are to him of authority. Such an arbiter's very existence is an impertinence. We do not ask him to make up his mind, but to make up his pack.

I listen to hear the voice of a Governor, Commander-in-Chief of the forces of Massachusetts. I hear only the creaking of crickets and the hum of insects which now fill the summer air. The Governor's exploit is to review the troops on muster days. I have seen him on horseback, with his hat off, listening to a chaplain's prayer. It chances that is all I have ever seen of a Governor. I think that I could manage to get along without one. If *he* is not of the least use to prevent my being kidnapped, pray of what important use is he likely to be to me? When freedom is most endangered, he dwells in the deepest obscurity. A distinguished clergyman told me that he chose the profession

2. Nine men were arrested for participating in the May 25, 1854, attempt to rescue Burns from the Boston courthouse where he was held.

3. Thoreau's audience would have instantly understood his scathing reminder of the bravery of the Revolutionary ancestors of the very Massachusetts citizens who approved of the passage of the Fugitive Slave Law.

4. Isaac Davis and Abner Hosmer were slain at the Battle of Concord on April 19, 1775.

5. I.e., as during the *Sims* case (and others less notorious).

6. U.S. Commissioner Edward G. Loring (1802–1890) heard the *Burns* case and decided it according to the letter of the Fugitive Slave Law.

of a clergyman, because it afforded the most leisure for literary pursuits. I would recommend to him the profession of a Governor.

Three years ago, also, when the Simm's tragedy was acted, I said to myself, there is such an officer, if not such a man, as the Governor of Massachusetts,—what has he been about the last fortnight? Has he had as much as he could do to keep on the fence during this moral earthquake? It seemed to me that no keener satire could have been aimed at, no more cutting insult have been offered to that man, than just what happened—the absence of all inquiry after him in that crisis. The worst and the most I chance to know of him is, that he did not improve that opportunity to make himself known, and worthily known. He could at least have *resigned* himself into fame. It appeared to be forgotten that there was such a man, or such an office. Yet no doubt he was endeavoring to fill the gubernatorial chair all the while. He was no Governor of mine. He did not govern me.

But at last, in the present case, the Governor was heard from. After he and the United States Government had perfectly succeeded in robbing a poor innocent black man of his liberty for life, and, as far as they could, of his Creator's likeness in his breast, he made a speech to his accomplices, at a congratulatory supper!

I have read a recent law of this State, making it penal for 'any officer of the Commonwealth' to 'detain, or aid in the . . . detention,' any where within its limits, 'of any person, for the reason that he is claimed as a fugitive slave.'[7] Also, it was a matter of notoriety that a writ of replevin[8] to take the fugitive out of the custody of the United States Marshal could not be served, for want of sufficient force to aid the officer.

I had thought that the Governor was in some sense the executive officer of the State; that it was his business, as a Governor, to see that the laws of the State were executed; while, as a man, he took care that he did not, by so doing, break the laws of humanity; but when there is any special important use for him, he is useless, or worse than useless, and permits the laws of the State to go unexecuted. Perhaps I do not know what are the duties of a Governor; but if to be a Governor requires to subject one's self to so much ignominy without remedy, if it is to put a restraint upon my manhood, I shall take care never to be Governor of Massachusetts. I have not read far in the statutes of this Commonwealth. It is not profitable reading. They do not always say what is true; and they do not always mean what they say. What I am concerned to know is, that that man's influence and authority were on the side of the slaveholder, and not of the slave—of the guilty, and not of the innocent—of injustice, and not of justice. I never saw him of whom I speak; indeed, I did not know that he was Governor until this event occurred. I heard of him and Anthony Burns at the same time, and thus, undoubtedly, most will hear of him. So far am I from being governed by him. I do not mean that it was any thing to his discredit that I had not heard of him, only that I heard what I did. The worst I shall say of him is, that he proved no better than the majority of his constituents would be likely to prove. In my opinion, he was not equal to the occasion.

7. In response to recent fugitive slave cases, the Massachusetts legislature had passed a personal-liberty law nullifying the Fugitive Slave Law within the commonwealth.

8. A writ requiring the recovery and return of things unlawfully taken; in this case a human being was the "thing."

The whole military force of the State is at the service of a Mr. Suttle,[9] a slaveholder from Virginia, to enable him to catch a man whom he calls his property; but not a soldier is offered to save a citizen of Massachusetts from being kidnapped! Is this what all these soldiers, all this *training* has been for these seventy-nine years past?[1] Have they been trained merely to rob Mexico, and carry back fugitive slaves to their masters?

These very nights, I heard the sound of a drum in our streets. There were men *training* still; and for what? I could with an effort pardon the cockerels of Concord for crowing still, for they, perchance, had not been beaten that morning; but I could not excuse this rub-a-dub of the 'trainers.' The slave was carried back by exactly such as these, i.e., by the soldier, of whom the best you can say in this connection is, that he is a fool made conspicuous by a painted coat.

Three years ago, also, just a week after the authorities of Boston assembled to carry back a perfectly innocent man, and one whom they knew to be innocent, into slavery, the inhabitants of Concord caused the bells to be rung and the cannons to be fired, to celebrate their liberty—and the courage and love of liberty of their ancestors who fought at the bridge. As if *those* three millions had fought for the right to be free themselves, but to hold in slavery three millions others. Now-a-days, men wear a fool's cap, and call it a liberty cap. I do not know but there are some, who, if they were tied to a whipping-post, and could get but one hand free, would use it to ring the bells and fire the cannons, to celebrate *their* liberty. So some of my townsmen took the liberty to ring and fire; that was the extent of their freedom; and when the sound of the bells died away, their liberty died away also; when the powder was all expended, their liberty went off with the smoke.

The joke could be no broader, if the inmates of the prisons were to subscribe for all the powder to be used in such salutes, and hire the jailors to do the firing and ringing for them, while they enjoyed it through the grating.

This is what I thought about my neighbors.

Every humane and intelligent inhabitant of Concord, when he or she heard those bells and those cannons, thought not with pride of the events of the 19th of April, 1775, but with shame of the events of the 12th of April, 1851.[2] But now we have half buried that old shame under a new one.

Massachusetts sat waiting Mr. Loring's decision, as if it could in any way affect her own criminality. Her crime, the most conspicuous and fatal crime of all, was permitting him to be the umpire in such a case. It was really the trial of Massachusetts. Every moment that she hesitated to set this man free—every moment that she now hesitates to atone for her crime, she is convicted. The Commissioner on her case is God; not Edward G. God, but simple God.

I wish my countrymen to consider, that whatever the human law may be, neither an individual nor a nation can ever commit the least act of injustice against the obscurest individual, without having to pay the penalty for it. A

9. Burns's master. Citizens of Boston were shocked by the armed force displayed in the capture, confinement, and remanding of Burns.

1. Since the hallowed battles at Lexington and Concord.

2. On that day, Boston police and federal troops led the fugitive slave Thomas Sims from the Boston courthouse to a ship that took him back to slavery in Georgia.

government which deliberately enacts injustice, and persists in it, will at length ever become the laughing-stock of the world.

Much has been said about American slavery, but I think that we do not even yet realize what slavery is. If I were seriously to propose to Congress to make mankind into sausages, I have no doubt that most of the members would smile at my proposition, and if any believed me to be in earnest, they would think that I proposed something much worse than Congress had ever done. But if any of them will tell me that to make a man into a sausage would be much worse,—would be any worse, than to make him into a slave,—than it was to enact the Fugitive Slave Law, I will accuse him of foolishness, of intellectual incapacity, of making a distinction without a difference. The one is just as reasonable a proposition as the other.

I hear a good deal said about trampling this law under foot. Why, one need not go out of his way to do that. This law rises not to the level of the head or the reason; its natural habitat is in the dirt. It was born and bred, and has its life only in the dust and mire, on a level with the feet, and he who walks with freedom, and does not with Hindoo mercy avoid treading on every venomous reptile, will inevitably tread on it, and so trample it under foot,—and Webster, its maker, with it, like the dirt-bug and its ball.[3]

Recent events will be valuable as a criticism on the administration of justice in our midst, or, rather, as showing what are the true resources of justice in any community. It has come to this, that the friends of liberty, the friends of the slave, have shuddered when they have understood that his fate was left to the legal tribunals of the country to be decided. Free men have no faith that justice will be awarded in such a case; the judge may decide this way or that; it is a kind of accident, at best. It is evident that he is not a competent authority in so important a case. It is no time, then, to be judging according to his precedents, but to establish a precedent for the future. I would much rather trust to the sentiment of the people. In their vote, you would get something of some value, at least, however small; but, in the other case, only the trammelled judgment of an individual, of no significance, be it which way it might.

It is to some extent fatal to the courts, when the people are compelled to go behind them. I do not wish to believe that the courts were made for fair weather, and for very civil cases merely,—but think of leaving it to any court in the land to decide whether more than three millions of people, in this case, a sixth part of a nation, have a right to be freemen or not! But it has been left to the courts of *justice*, so-called—to the Supreme Court of the land—and, as you all know, recognizing no authority but the Constitution, it has decided that the three millions are, and shall continue to be, slaves. Such judges as these are merely the inspectors of a pick-lock and murderer's tools, to tell him whether they are in working order or not, and there they think that their responsibility ends. There was a prior case on the docket, which they, as judges appointed by God, had no right to skip; which having been justly settled, they would have been saved from this humiliation. It was the case of the murderer himself.

3. In Massachusetts, Senator Daniel Webster (1782–1852) was credited with the passage of the Compromise of 1850, of which a major provision was the Fugitive Slave Bill. Thoreau is comparing Webster and the Fugitive Slave Law to a tumblebug and its ball of dung.

The law will never make men free; it is men who have got to make the law free. They are the lovers of law and order, who observe the law when the government breaks it.

Among human beings, the judge whose words seal the fate of a man furthest into eternity, is not he who merely pronounces the verdict of the law, but he, whoever he may be, who, from a love of truth, and unprejudiced by any custom or enactment of men, utters a true opinion or *sentence* concerning him. He it is that *sentences* him. Whoever has discerned truth, has received his commission from a higher source than the chiefest justice in the world, who can discern only law. He finds himself constituted judge of the judge.—Strange that it should be necessary to state such simple truths.

I am more and more convinced that, with reference to any public question, it is more important to know what the country thinks of it, than what the city thinks. The city does not *think* much. On any moral question, I would rather have the opinion of Boxboro' than of Boston and New York put together.[4] When the former speaks, I feel as if somebody *had* spoken, as if *humanity* was yet, and a reasonable being had asserted its rights,—as if some unprejudiced men among the country's hills had at length turned their attention to the subject, and by a few sensible words redeemed the reputation of the race. When, in some obscure country town, the farmers come together to a special town meeting, to express their opinion on some subject which is vexing the land, that, I think, is the true Congress, and the most respectable one that is ever assembled in the United States.

It is evident that there are, in this Commonwealth, at least, two parties, becoming more and more distinct—the party of the city, and the party of the country. I know that the country is mean enough, but I am glad to believe that there is a slight difference in her favor. But as yet, she has few, if any organs, through which to express herself. The editorials which she reads, like the news, come from the sea-board. Let us, the inhabitants of the country, cultivate self-respect. Let us not send to the city for aught more essential than our broadcloths and groceries, or, if we read the opinions of the city, let us entertain opinions of our own.

Among measures to be adopted, I would suggest to make as earnest and vigorous an assault on the Press as has already been made, and with effect, on the Church. The Church has much improved within a few years; but the Press is almost, without exception, corrupt. I believe that, in this country, the press exerts a greater and a more pernicious influence than the Church did in its worst period. We are not a religious people, but we are a nation of politicians. We do not care for the Bible, but we do care for the newspaper. At any meeting of politicians,—like that at Concord the other evening, for instance,—how impertinent it would be to quote from the Bible! how pertinent to quote from a newspaper or from the Constitution! The newspaper is a Bible which we read every morning and every afternoon, standing and sitting, riding and walking. It is a Bible which every man carries in his pocket, which lies on every table and counter, and which the mail, and thousands of missionaries, are continually dispensing. It is, in short, the only book which America has printed, and which America reads. So wide is its influence. The

4. I.e., any obscure country town ruled by democratic town meetings.

editor is a preacher whom you voluntarily support. Your tax is commonly one cent daily, and it costs nothing for pew hire.[5] But how many of these preachers preach the truth? I repeat the testimony of many an intelligent foreigner, as well as my own convictions, when I say, that probably no country was ever ruled by so mean a class of tyrants as, with a few noble exceptions, are the editors of the periodical press in *this* country. And as they live and rule only by their servility, and appealing to the worst, and not the better nature of man, the people who read them are in the condition of the dog that returns to his vomit.

The *Liberator* and the *Commonwealth*[6] were the only papers in Boston, as far as I know, which made themselves heard in condemnation of the cowardice and meanness of the authorities of that city, as exhibited in '51. The other journals, almost without exception, by their manner of referring to and speaking of the Fugitive Slave Law, and the carrying back of the slave Simms, insulted the common sense of the country, at least. And, for the most part, they did this, one would say, because they thought so to secure the approbation of their patrons, not being aware that a sounder sentiment prevailed to any extent in the heart of the Commonwealth. I am told that some of them have improved of late; but they are still eminently time-serving. Such is the character they have won.

But, thank fortune, this preacher can be even more easily reached by the weapons of the reformer than could the recreant priest. The free men of New England have only to refrain from purchasing and reading these sheets, have only to withhold their cents, to kill a score of them at once. One whom I respect told me that he purchased Mitchell's *Citizen* in the cars, and then threw it out the window. But would not his contempt have been more fatally expressed, if he had not bought it?

Are they Americans? are they New Englanders? are they inhabitants of Lexington, and Concord, and Framingham, who read and support the Boston *Post*, *Mail*, *Journal*, *Advertiser*, *Courier*, and *Times*? Are these the Flags of our Union? I am not a newspaper reader, and may omit to name the worst.

Could slavery suggest a more complete servility than some of these journals exhibit? Is there any dust which their conduct does not lick, and make fouler still with its slime? I do not know whether the Boston *Herald* is still in existence, but I remember to have seen it about the streets when Simms was carried off. Did it not act its part well—serve its master faithfully? How could it have gone lower on its belly? How can a man stoop lower than he is low? do more than put his extremities in the place of the head he has? than make his head his lower extremity? When I have taken up this paper with my cuffs turned up, I have heard the gurgling of the sewer through every column. I have felt that I was handling a paper picked out of the public gutters, a leaf from the gospel of the gambling-house, the groggery and the brothel, harmonizing with the gospel of the Merchants' Exchange.

The majority of the men of the North, and of the South, and East, and West, are not men of principle. If they vote, they do not send men to

5. Annual rent for an assigned pew in church.
6. Abolitionist newspapers edited by William Lloyd Garrison (1805–1879) and Franklin Benjamin Sanborn (1831–1917), respectively. Though there was much opposition in Massachusetts to the Fugitive Slave Law, most newspaper editors counseled against violent resistance.

Congress on errands of humanity, but while their brothers and sisters are being scourged and hung for loving liberty, while—I might here insert all that slavery implies and is,—it is the mismanagement of wood and iron and stone and gold which concerns them. Do what you will, O Government! with my wife and children, my mother and brother, my father and sister, I will obey your commands to the letter. It will indeed grieve me if you hurt them, if you deliver them to overseers to be hunted by hounds or to be whipped to death; but nevertheless, I will peaceably pursue my chosen calling on this fair earth, until perchance, one day, when I have put on mourning for them dead, I shall have persuaded you to relent. Such is the attitude, such are the words of Massachusetts.

Rather than do thus, I need not say what match I would touch, what system endeavor to blow up,—but as I love my life, I would side with the light, and let the dark earth roll from under me, calling my mother and my brother to follow.

I would remind my countrymen, that they are to be men first, and Americans only at a late and convenient hour. No matter how valuable law may be to protect your property, even to keep soul and body together, if it do not keep you and humanity together.

I am sorry to say, that I doubt if there is a judge in Massachusetts who is prepared to resign his office, and get his living innocently, whenever it is required of him to pass sentence under a law which is merely contrary to the law of God. I am compelled to see that they put themselves, or rather, are by character, in this respect, exactly on a level with the marine who discharges his musket in any direction he is ordered to. They are just as much tools and as little men. Certainly, they are not the more to be respected, because their master enslaves their understandings and consciences, instead of their bodies.

The judges and lawyers,—simply as such, I mean,—and all men of expediency, try this case by a very low and incompetent standard. They consider, not whether the Fugitive Slave Law is right, but whether it is what they call *constitutional.* Is virtue constitutional, or vice? Is equity constitutional, or iniquity? In important moral and vital questions like this, it is just as impertinent to ask whether a law is constitutional or not, as to ask whether it is profitable or not. They persist in being the servants of the worst of men, and not the servants of humanity. The question is not whether you or your grandfather, seventy years ago, did not enter into an agreement to serve the devil, and that service is not accordingly now due; but whether you will not now, for once and at last, serve God,—in spite of your own past recreancy, or that of your ancestor,—by obeying that eternal and only just CONSTITUTION which He, and not any Jefferson or Adams,[7] has written in your being.

The amount of it is, if the majority vote the devil to be God, the minority will live and behave accordingly, and obey the successful candidate,[8] trusting that some time or other, by some Speaker's casting vote, perhaps, they may reinstate God. This is the highest principle I can get out of or invent for

7. Thoreau appeals to the "higher law" of conscience over the laws and traditions promulgated by Thomas Jefferson, third U.S. president (1801–9), and John Adams, second president (1797–1801).

8. The words "and obey the successful candidate" do not appear in the *Liberator* but are in Thoreau's journal (the source for this passage) and in *A Yankee in Canada, with Anti-Slavery and Reform Papers* (1866).

my neighbors. These men act as if they believed that they could safely slide down hill a little way—or a good way—and would surely come to a place, by and by, where they could begin to slide up again. This is expediency, or choosing that course which offers the slightest obstacles to the feet, that is, a down-hill one. But there is no such thing as accomplishing a righteous reform by the use of 'expediency.' There is no such thing as sliding up hill. In morals, the only sliders are backsliders.

Thus we steadily worship Mammon, both School, and State, and Church, and the Seventh Day curse God with a tintamar[9] from one end of the Union to the other.

Will mankind never learn that policy is not morality—that it never secures any moral right, but considers merely what is expedient? chooses the available candidate, who is invariably the devil,—and what right have his constituents to be surprised, because the devil does not behave like an angel of light? What is wanted is men, not of policy, but of probity—who recognize a higher law than the Constitution, or the decision of the majority. The fate of the country does not depend on how you vote at the polls—the worst man is as strong as the best at that game; it does not depend on what kind of paper you drop into the ballot-box once a year, but on what kind of man you drop from your chamber into the street every morning.

What should concern Massachusetts is not the Nebraska Bill, nor the Fugitive Slave Bill, but her own slaveholding and servility. Let the State dissolve her union with the slaveholder. She may wriggle and hesitate, and ask leave to read the Constitution once more; but she can find no respectable law or precedent which sanctions the continuance of such a Union for an instant.

Let each inhabitant of the State dissolve his union with her, as long as she delays to do her duty.

The events of the past month teach me to distrust Fame. I see that she does not finely discriminate, but coarsely hurrahs. She considers not the simple heroism of an action, but only as it is connected with its apparent consequences. She praises till she is hoarse the easy exploit of the Boston tea party,[1] but will be comparatively silent about the braver and more disinterestedly heroic attack on the Boston Court-House, simply because it was unsuccessful!

Covered with disgrace, the State has sat down coolly to try for their lives and liberties the men who attempted to do its duty for it. And this is called *justice*! They who have shown that they can behave particularly well may perchance be put under bonds for *their good behavior*. They whom truth requires at present to plead guilty, are of all the inhabitants of the State, preëminently innocent. While the Governor, and the Mayor, and countless officers of the Commonwealth, are at large, the champions of liberty are imprisoned.

Only they are guiltless, who commit the crime of contempt of such a Court. It behoves every man to see that his influence is on the side of justice, and let the courts make their own characters. My sympathies in this case are wholly with the accused, and wholly against the accusers and their

9. A general ringing of bells. "Mammon": i.e., materialism, after one of the fallen angels in Milton's *Paradise Lost*.

1. The pre-Revolutionary exploit (Dec. 1773) in which protestors against British taxation disguised themselves (more or less) as Indians, boarded ships in Boston harbor, and dumped tea into the water.

judges. Justice is sweet and musical; but injustice is harsh and discordant. The judge still sits grinding at his organ, but it yields no music, and we hear only the sound of the handle. He believes that all the music resides in the handle, and the crowd toss him their coppers the same as before.

Do you suppose that that Massachusetts which is now doing these things,—which hesitates to crown these men, some of whose lawyers, and even judges, perchance, may be driven to take refuge in some poor quibble, that they may not wholly outrage their instinctive sense of justice,—do you suppose that she is any thing but base and servile? that she is the champion of liberty?

Show me a free State, and a court truly of justice, and I will fight for them, if need be; but show me Massachusetts, and I refuse her my allegiance, and express contempt for her courts.

The effect of a good government is to make life more valuable,—of a bad one, to make it less valuable. We can afford that railroad, and all other merely material stock, should lose some of its value, for that only compels us to live more simply and economically; but suppose that the value of life itself should be diminished! How can we make a less demand on man and nature, how live more economically in respect to virtue and all noble qualities, than we do? I have lived for the last month,—and I think that every man in Massachusetts capable of the sentiment of patriotism must have had a similar experience,—with the sense of having suffered a vast and indefinite loss. I did not know at first what ailed me. At last it occurred to me that what I had lost was a country. I had never respected the Government near to which I had lived, but I had foolishly thought that I might manage to live here, minding my private affairs, and forget it. For my part, my old and worthiest pursuits have lost I cannot say how much of their attraction, and I feel that my investment in life here is worth many per cent. less since Massachusetts last deliberately sent back an innocent man, Anthony Burns, to slavery. I dwelt before, perhaps, in the illusion that my life passed somewhere only *between* heaven and hell, but now I cannot persuade myself that I do not dwell *wholly within* hell. The site of that political organization called Massachusetts is to me morally covered with volcanic *scoriæ*[2] and cinders, such as Milton describes in the infernal regions. If there is any hell more unprincipled than our rulers, and we, the ruled, I feel curious to see it. Life itself being worth less, all things with it, which minister to it, are worth less. Suppose you have a small library, with pictures to adorn the walls—a garden laid out around—and contemplate scientific and literary pursuits, &c., and discover all at once that your villa, with all its contents, is located in hell, and that the justice of the peace has a cloven foot and a forked tail—do not these things suddenly lose their value in your eyes?

I feel that, to some extent, the State has fatally interfered in my lawful business. It has not only interrupted me in my passage through Court street on errands of trade, but it has interrupted me and every man on his onward and upward path, on which he had trusted soon to leave Court street far behind. What right had it to remind me of Court street? I have found that hollow which even I had relied on for solid.

2. Lava (Latin). Thoreau may be alluding to John Milton's description of Satan and the fallen angels by the burning lake of Hell in book I of *Paradise Lost* (1667, 1674).

I am surprised to see men going about their business as if nothing had happened. I say to myself—Unfortunates! they have not heard the news. I am surprised that the man whom I just met on horseback should be so earnest to overtake his newly-bought cows running away—since all property is insecure—and if they do not run away again, they may be taken away from him when he gets them. Fool! does he not know that his seed-corn is worth less this year—that all beneficent harvests fail as you approach the empire of hell? No prudent man will build a stone-house under these circumstances, or engage in any peaceful enterprise which requires a long time to accomplish. Art is as long as ever, but life is more interrupted and less available for a man's proper pursuits. It is not an era of repose. We have used up all our inherited freedom. If we would save our lives, we must fight for them.

I walk toward one of our ponds, but what signifies the beauty of nature when men are base? We walk to lakes to see our serenity reflected in them; when we are not serene, we go not to them. Who can be serene in a country where both the rulers and the ruled are without principle? The remembrance of my country spoils my walk. My thoughts are murder to the State, and involuntarily go plotting against her.

But it chanced the other day that I secured a white water-lily, and a season I had waited for had arrived. It is the emblem of purity. It bursts up so pure and fair to the eye, and so sweet to the scent, as if to show us what purity and sweetness reside in, and can be extracted from, the slime and muck of earth. I think I have plucked the first one that has opened for a mile. What confirmation of our hopes is in the fragrance of this flower! I shall not so soon despair of the world for it, notwithstanding slavery, and the cowardice and want of principle of Northern men. It suggests what kind of laws have prevailed longest and widest, and still prevail, and that the time may come when man's deeds may smell as sweet. Such is the odor which the plant emits. If Nature can compound this fragrance still annually, I shall believe her still young and full of vigor, her integrity and genius unimpaired, and that there is virtue even in man, too, who is fitted to perceive and love it. It reminds me that Nature has been partner to no Missouri Compromise. I scent no compromise in the fragrance of the water-lily. It is not a *Nymphœa Douglassii*.[3] In it, the sweet, and pure, and innocent, are wholly sundered from the obscene and baleful. I do not scent in this the time-serving irresolution of a Massachusetts Governor, nor of a Boston Mayor. So behave that the odor of your actions may enhance the general sweetness of the atmosphere, that when we behold or scent a flower, we may not be reminded how inconsistent your deeds are with it; for all odor is but one form of advertisement of a moral quality, and if fair actions had not been performed, the lily would not smell sweet. The foul slime stands for the sloth and vice of man, the decay of humanity; the fragrant flower that springs from it, for the purity and courage which are immortal.

Slavery and servility have produced no sweet-scented flower annually, to charm the senses of men, for they have no real life: they are merely a decaying and a death, offensive to all healthy nostrils. We do not complain that

3. A pun on the name of the senator from Illinois, Stephen A. Douglas.

they *live*, but that they do not *get buried*. Let the living bury them; even they are good for manure.

1854

From A Plea for Captain John Brown[1]

I trust that you will pardon me for being here. I do not wish to force my thoughts upon you, but I feel forced myself. Little as I know of Captain Brown, I would fain do my part to correct the tone and the statements of the newspapers, and of my countrymen generally, respecting his character and actions. It costs us nothing to be just. We can at least express our sympathy with, and admiration of, him and his companions, and that is what I now propose to do.

First, as to his history. I will endeavor to omit, as much as possible, what you have already read. I need not describe his person to you, for probably most of you have seen and will not soon forget him. I am told that his grandfather, John Brown, was an officer in the Revolution; that he himself was born in Connecticut about the beginning of this century, but early went with his father to Ohio. I heard him say that his father was a contractor who furnished beef to the army there, in the war of 1812; that he accompanied him to the camp, and assisted him in that employment, seeing a good deal of military life, more, perhaps, than if he had been a soldier, for he was often present at the councils of the officers. Especially, he learned by experience how armies are supplied and maintained in the field—a work which, he observed, requires at least as much experience and skill as to lead them in battle. He said that few persons had any conception of the cost, even the pecuniary cost, of firing a single bullet in war. He saw enough, at any rate, to disgust him with a military life; indeed, to excite in him a great abhorrence of it; so much so, that though he was tempted by the offer of some petty office in the army, when he was about eighteen, he not only declined that, but he also refused to train when warned, and was fined for it. He then resolved that he would never have any thing to do with any war, unless it were a war for liberty.

* * *

It was his peculiar doctrine that a man has a perfect right to interfere by force with the slaveholder, in order to rescue the slave. I agree with him. They who are continually shocked by slavery have some right to be shocked by the violent death of the slaveholder, but no others. Such will be more shocked by his life than by his death. I shall not be forward to think him

1. On October 16, 1859, the militant abolitionist John Brown (1800–1859) led twenty-one men, including five African Americans, in an attack on an unguarded federal arsenal at Harpers Ferry in western Virginia in an effort to secure arms for the slave revolt he hoped to inspire. Within two days his group was defeated by American troops and he surrendered. Convicted of treason against the state of Virginia, he was hanged on December 2, 1859. Thoreau had met Brown earlier in the decade when Brown visited Concord, Massachusetts, to raise funds to support armed raids on proslavery settlers in Kansas. Thoreau delivered "A Plea for Captain John Brown" on October 30, 1859, in the Concord Town Hall. The text is taken from *Echoes of Harper's Ferry* (1860), edited by the Scottish-American abolitionist James Redpath (1833–1891).

mistaken in his method who quickest succeeds to liberate the slave. I speak for the slave when I say, that I prefer the philanthropy of Captain Brown to that philanthropy which neither shoots me nor liberates me. At any rate, I do not think it is quite sane for one to spend his whole life in talking or writing about this matter, unless he is continuously inspired, and I have not done so. A man may have other affairs to attend to. I do not wish to kill nor to be killed, but I can foresee circumstances in which both these things would be by me unavoidable. We preserve the so-called peace of our community by deeds of petty violence every day. Look at the policeman's billy and handcuffs! Look at the jail! Look at the gallows! Look at the chaplain of the regiment! We are hoping only to live safely on the outskirts of *this* provisional army. So we defend ourselves and our hen-roosts, and maintain slavery. I know that the mass of my countrymen think that the only righteous use that can be made of Sharpe's rifles[2] and revolvers is to fight duels with them, when we are insulted by other nations, or to hunt Indians, or shoot fugitive slaves with them, or the like. I think that for once the Sharpe's rifles and the revolvers were employed in a righteous cause. The tools were in the hands of one who could use them.

The same indignation that is said to have cleared the temple once will clear it again. The question is not about the weapon, but the spirit in which you use it. No man has appeared in America, as yet, who loved his fellow-man so well, and treated him so tenderly. He lived for him. He took up his life and he laid it down for him. What sort of violence is that which is encouraged, not by soldiers but by peaceable citizens, not so much by laymen as by ministers of the gospel, not so much by the fighting sects as by the Quakers, and not so much by Quaker men as by Quaker women?

This event advertises me that there is such a fact as death—the possibility of a man's dying. It seems as if no man had ever died in America before, for in order to die you must first have lived. I don't believe in the hearses, and palls, and funerals that they have had. There was no death in the case, because there had been no life; they merely rotted or sloughed off, pretty much as they had rotted or sloughed along. No temple's vail was rent, only a hole dug somewhere. Let the dead bury their dead. The best of them fairly ran down like a clock. Franklin—Washington—they were let off without dying; they were merely missing one day. I hear a good many pretend that they are going to die; or that they have died, for aught that I know. Nonsense! I'll defy them to do it. They haven't got life enough in them. They'll deliquesce like fungi, and keep a hundred eulogists mopping the spot where they left off. Only half a dozen or so have died since the world began. Do you think that you are going to die, sir? No! there's no hope of you. You haven't got your lesson yet. You've got to stay after school. We make a needless ado about capital punishment—taking lives, when there is no life to take. *Memento mori!*[3] We don't understand that sublime sentence which some worthy got sculptured on his gravestone once. We've interpreted it in a grovelling and snivelling sense; we've wholly forgotten how to die.

2. Produced by the Sharps Rifle Manufacturing Company of Hartford, Connecticut, which was established by Christian Sharps (1811–1874) in the mid-1850s. (Thoreau gets the spelling wrong.)

3. Reminder of death (Latin).

But be sure you do die, nevertheless. Do your work, and finish it. If you know how to begin, you will know when to end.

These men, in teaching us how to die, have at the same time taught us how to live. If this man's acts and words do not create a revival, it will be the severest possible satire on the acts and words that do. It is the best news that America has ever heard. It has already quickened the feeble pulse of the North, and infused more and more generous blood into her veins and heart, than any number of years of what is called commercial and political prosperity could. How many a man who was lately contemplating suicide has now something to live for!

One writer says that Brown's peculiar monomania made him to be "dreaded by the Missourians as a supernatural being." Sure enough, a hero in the midst of us cowards is always so dreaded. He is just that thing. He shows himself superior to nature. He has a spark of divinity in him.

> "Unless above himself he doth erect himself,
> How poor a thing is man!"[4]

Newspaper editors argue also that it is a proof of his *insanity* that he thought he was appointed to do this work which he did—that he did not suspect himself for a moment! They talk as if it were impossible that a man could be "divinely appointed" in these days to do any work whatever; as if vows and religion were out of date as connected with any man's daily work,—as if the agent to abolish Slavery could only be somebody appointed by the President, or by some political party. They talk as if a man's death were a failure, and his continued life, be it of whatever character, were a success.

When I reflect to what a cause this man devoted himself, and how religiously, and then reflect to what cause his judges and all who condemn him so angrily and fluently devote themselves, I see that they are as far apart as the heavens and earth are asunder.

The amount of it is, our "*leading men*" are a harmless kind of folk, and they know *well enough* that *they* were not divinely appointed, but elected by the votes of their party.

Who is it whose safety requires that Captain Brown be hung? Is it indispensable to any Northern man? Is there no resource but to cast these men also to the Minotaur?[5] If you do not wish it, say so distinctly. While these things are being done, beauty stands veiled and music is a screeching lie. Think of him—of his rare qualities! such a man as it takes ages to make, and ages to understand; no mock hero, nor the representative of any party. A man such as the sun may not rise upon again in this benighted land. To whose making went the costliest material, the finest adamant;[6] sent to be the redeemer of those in captivity; and the only use to which you can put him is to hang him at the end of a rope! You who pretend to care for Christ crucified, consider what you are about to do to him who offered himself to be the saviour of four millions of men.

Any man knows when he is justified, and all the wits in the world cannot enlighten him on that point. The murderer always knows that he is justly

4. From William Wordsworth's *The Excursion* (1814) 4.330–31.
5. In Greek mythology, a monster with the head of a bull and the body of a man; the Minotaur devoured youths brought for sacrifice.
6. Impenetrable or unyielding substance.

punished; but when a government takes the life of a man without the consent of his conscience, it is an audacious government, and is taking a step towards its own dissolution. Is it not possible that an individual may be right and a government wrong? Are laws to be enforced simply because they were made? or declared by any number of men to be good, if they are *not* good? Is there any necessity for a man's being a tool to perform a deed of which his better nature disapproves? Is it the intention of law-makers that *good* men shall be hung ever? Are judges to interpret the law according to the letter, and not the spirit? What right have *you* to enter into a compact with yourself that you *will* do thus or so, against the light within you? Is it for *you* to *make up* your mind—to form any resolution whatever—and not accept the convictions that are forced upon you, and which ever pass your understanding? I do not believe in lawyers, in that mode of attacking or defending a man, because you descend to meet the judge on his own ground, and, in cases of the highest importance, it is of no consequence whether a man breaks a human law or not. Let lawyers decide trivial cases. Business men may arrange that among themselves. If they were the interpreters of the everlasting laws which rightfully bind man, that would be another thing. A counterfeiting law-factory, standing half in a slave land and half in a free! What kind of laws for free men can you expect from that?

I am here to plead his cause with you. I plead not for his life, but for his character—his immortal life; and so it becomes your cause wholly, and is not his in the least. Some eighteen hundred years ago Christ was crucified; this morning, perchance, Captain Brown was hung. These are the two ends of a chain which is not without its links. He is not Old Brown any longer; he is an angel of light.

I see now that it was necessary that the bravest and humanest man in all the country should be hung. Perhaps he saw it himself. I *almost fear* that I may yet hear of his deliverance, doubting if a prolonged life, if *any* life, can do as much good as his death.

"Misguided"! "Garrulous"! "Insane"! "Vindictive"! So ye write in your easy chairs, and thus he wounded responds from the floor of the Armory, clear as a cloudless sky, true as the voice of nature is: "No man sent me here; it was my own prompting and that of my Maker. I acknowledge no master in human form."

And in what a sweet and noble strain he proceeds, addressing his captors, who stand over him: "I think, my friends, you are guilty of a great wrong against God and humanity, and it would be perfectly right for any one to interfere with you so far as to free those you wilfully and wickedly hold in bondage."

And referring to his movement: "It is, in my opinion, the greatest service a man can render to God."

"I pity the poor in bondage that have none to help them; that is why I am here; not to gratify any personal animosity, revenge, or vindictive spirit. It is my sympathy with the oppressed and the wronged, that are as good as you, and as precious in the sight of God."

You don't know your testament when you see it.

"I want you to understand that I respect the rights of the poorest and weakest of colored people, oppressed by the slave power, just as much as I do those of the most wealthy and powerful."

"I wish to say, furthermore, that you had better, all you people at the South, prepare yourselves for a settlement of that question, that must come up for settlement sooner than you are prepared for it. The sooner you are prepared the better. You may dispose of me very easily. I am nearly disposed of now; but this question is still to be settled—this negro question, I mean; the end of that is not yet."

I foresee the time when the painter will paint that scene, no longer going to Rome for a subject; the poet will sing it; the historian record it; and, with the Landing of the Pilgrims and the Declaration of Independence, it will be the ornament of some future national gallery, when at least the present form of Slavery shall be no more here. We shall then be at liberty to weep for Captain Brown. Then, and not till then, we will take our revenge.

1859, 1860

FREDERICK DOUGLASS
1818–1895

In the concluding chapter of his famous autobiography, *Narrative of the Life of Frederick Douglass, An American Slave, Written by Himself* (1845), Douglass describes the moment in 1841 when he first stepped forward to speak at an antislavery convention in Nantucket, Massachusetts. "It was a severe cross," he says, "and I took it up reluctantly." However reluctant he may have been, in the moments following the speech, the twenty-three-year-old fugitive slave "felt a degree of freedom" and, just as important, realized he had discovered his vocation. As he states at the end of the *Narrative*: "From that time until now, I have been engaged in pleading the cause of my brethren—with what success, and with what devotion, I leave those acquainted with my labors to decide." Douglass would continue to plead the cause of African Americans for over fifty years. He published three versions of his autobiography—the *Narrative* (1845), *My Bondage and My Freedom* (1855), *Life and Times of Frederick Douglass* (1881, rev. ed. 1892)—as well as a novella, "The Heroic Slave" (1853), and numerous essays and speeches. He also established and edited three African American newspapers—the *North Star* (1847–51), *Frederick Douglass' Paper* (1851–59), and *Douglass' Monthly* (1859–63)—and edited a fourth, the *New National Era* (1870–73). By the time of his death, Douglass was thought of, in the United States and abroad, as the most influential African American leader of the nineteenth century and as one of the greatest orators of the age. In the manner of Benjamin Franklin, whom he greatly admired, Douglass presented himself as a representative American whose rise to prominence spoke to the promises of the nation's egalitarian ideology. But he also had a clear-eyed understanding of the hurdles that slavery and racism placed in the way of African Americans. Regularly invoking the principles of the Declaration of Independence, Douglass throughout his life challenged the nation to live up to its founding ideals. In "The Lessons of the Hour" (1894), one of his final speeches, Douglass condemned the rise of lynching with the passion and vigor of his early writing, seeing this latest outbreak of violence against black people as a threat to what he had devoted his life to achieving: a multiracial United States offering equal rights and justice for all.

Douglass was born into slavery as Frederick Augustus Washington Bailey in February 1818 at Holme Hill Farm in Talbot County, on the eastern shore of Maryland. His mother was Harriet Bailey; his father was a white man whose identity is still not known, although widely assumed to have been his mother's owner, Aaron Anthony. In 1826, about a year after the death of his mother and shortly after the death of Anthony, Douglass became the property of Thomas Auld and was sent to live with Thomas's brother Hugh Auld and his wife, Sophia, in Baltimore. According to the 1845 *Narrative*, Sophia began to teach Douglass how to read, but Hugh forbade her to continue because, he said, learning "would forever unfit him to be a slave." Nevertheless, as the autobiographies recount, Douglass cleverly found ways to learn how to read and write. During this first residence in Baltimore, Douglass acquired and pored over *The Columbian Orator* (1797), a popular school text, finding its many speeches denouncing oppression applicable to his own situation. He read about abolition as an organized movement in the *Baltimore American* and established a close relationship with the free black Charles Lawson, a lay preacher who became his spiritual mentor and told Douglass that he had been chosen to do "great work."

In 1833, after seven years in Baltimore, Douglass was returned to Thomas Auld's plantation, where he quickly became known for his rebellious attitude and was sent to work on the farm of Edward Covey, a specialist in "slave breaking." The account of his decline and reawakening at Covey's farm, culminating in a hand-to-hand battle between Covey and Douglass in August 1834, is the turning point of the *Narrative*. Following this confrontation, Douglass took on a greater leadership role among the slaves, conducting a Sabbath school at William Freeland's plantation in 1835 and, in 1836, organizing an escape attempt with a group of slaves. For his role in the failed plot, Douglass was briefly jailed in Easton, Maryland. He was then returned to the Aulds in Baltimore, where he learned the caulking trade in the shipyards. Though Hugh Auld kept most of the money Frederick earned, Douglass was able to save enough to develop a feasible plan of escape. In this plan he was helped both financially and emotionally by the free black Anna Murray, to whom he became engaged on September 3, 1838, the very day he boarded a train for New York disguised as a sailor and carrying the borrowed papers of a free black seaman. Douglass withheld information about his mode of escape until the third of his autobiographies, when disclosing it could no longer endanger the lives and plans of other fugitives from Baltimore. Within days of his escape Anna joined him in New York City, and they were married on September 15. They soon left for New Bedford, Massachusetts, where the likelihood of his being captured as a fugitive slave was reduced by his assuming the name "Douglass," which he took from Sir Walter Scott's poem *Lady of the Lake* (1810).

Though Douglass in the *Narrative* emphasizes the splendor of New Bedford compared to towns under slavery, life in New Bedford was not easy for the newly married couple. Douglass was discriminated against when he sought work as a caulker and had to piece together a living doing odd jobs. In 1839 he became a licensed preacher in the African Methodist Episcopal Zion Church; that same year the Douglasses' first child, Rosetta, was born. A son, Lewis, was born the following year, and the other three Douglass children—Frederick, Charles, and Annie—were born in 1842, 1844, and 1849, respectively. Soon after arriving in New Bedford, Douglass subscribed to the abolitionist William Lloyd Garrison's *Liberator*. Garrison was in the audience when Douglass delivered his first antislavery speech, and shortly thereafter he hired Douglass as a speaker in his Massachusetts Anti-Slavery Society. During 1841–43, Douglass delivered his antislavery message on behalf of Garrison's organization in a number of Northern states, and on one occasion in 1843, in Pendleton, Indiana, he was attacked by an anti-abolitionist mob and suffered a broken hand. Douglass began work on his narrative in 1844, and it was published in May 1845 by Garrison's Anti-Slavery Office in Boston. The *Narrative* sold some thirty thousand copies in its first five years, making it a bona fide best seller for the time and helping to establish Douglass as an international spokesperson for freedom and equality. Some earlier slave narratives had been ghostwritten or composed with the help of white editors, but the *Narrative*'s vivid detail and stylistic distinctiveness, combined with the reputation Douglass had earned as an eloquent speaker, left no doubt that Douglass had in fact written his own story in his own words.

Garrison's abolitionist principles—a commitment to an immediate end to slavery, an advocacy of moral persuasion over violence, and a belief that the Constitution was a proslavery document—inspired Douglass in the early to middle 1840s. When he went on an extended speaking tour in Great Britain during 1845–46 (in part to escape the fugitive slave hunters that he feared would track him down after the publication of the *Narrative*), he spoke as a Garrisonian abolitionist. But upon his return to the United States as a free man—British antislavery friends had purchased his freedom for $711 in 1846—Douglass became increasingly suspicious of Garrison, particularly when Garrison attempted to bully him into shutting down his newspaper, the *North Star*, which Douglass founded not in New Bedford, but in Rochester, New York, where Douglass resettled in part to escape the influence of Garrison. In the inaugural issue of December 3, 1847, Douglass declared that in the antislavery and antiracism struggle, African Americans "must be our own representatives and advocates, not exclusively, but peculiarly—not distinct from, but in connection with our white friends." Garrison, who wanted absolute loyalty and control of the movement, began to question Douglass's antislavery politics and even published unsubstantiated rumors in the *Liberator* about Douglass's romantic involvement with Julia Griffiths, a white Englishwoman living in the Douglass home and helping with editorial work on the *North Star*. But along with the personality clashes, there were ideological differences between the two. By 1851, after forming a friendship with the New York abolitionist Gerrit Smith, Douglass formally broke with Garrison, announcing his belief in a more pragmatic political abolitionism that regarded the Constitution as an antislavery document, that saw the value in steadily working toward the goals of antislavery, and that defended the strategic use of black violence as a response to the violence of slavery.

In 1855 Douglass published *My Bondage and My Freedom*, a revised and substantially longer version of his 1845 autobiography. In covering the ten years of his life since the *Narrative*, Douglass wrote about his encounters with racism in the North, his work as an abolitionist, and his break with Garrison. No longer willing to "leave the philosophy" of abolition to Garrison and other white abolitionists, Douglass asserted his intellectual and interpretive independence and also his deeper connections to black moral reformers and abolitionists. It is significant that the second autobiography was introduced not by white abolitionists (as with the *Narrative*) but by the black physician and abolitionist James McCune Smith (1813–1865), who celebrated Douglass as "a Representative American man—a type of his countrymen." Like the *Narrative*, *My Bondage and My Freedom* was widely read, selling eighteen thousand copies during its first two years.

Like all autobiographers, Douglass artistically shaped the facts of his life to underscore the particular truths that he wished to convey at the moment of composition. In the 1845 *Narrative*, he presented himself as relatively isolated from his fellow slaves, describing his fight with Covey as a heroic instance of individual rebellion; in the 1855 *My Bondage and My Freedom*, he depicted the fight as involving several other African Americans who came to his assistance. Similarly, in 1845 Douglass said little about the role of his mother in his life because he wanted to show his white readers how slavery divided mothers and children; in 1855, he celebrated the influence of his grandmother and mother. This new emphasis on the importance of black culture and family to his developing identity as an antislavery leader resonated with the rhetoric of sentiment associated with Harriet Beecher Stowe's *Uncle Tom's*

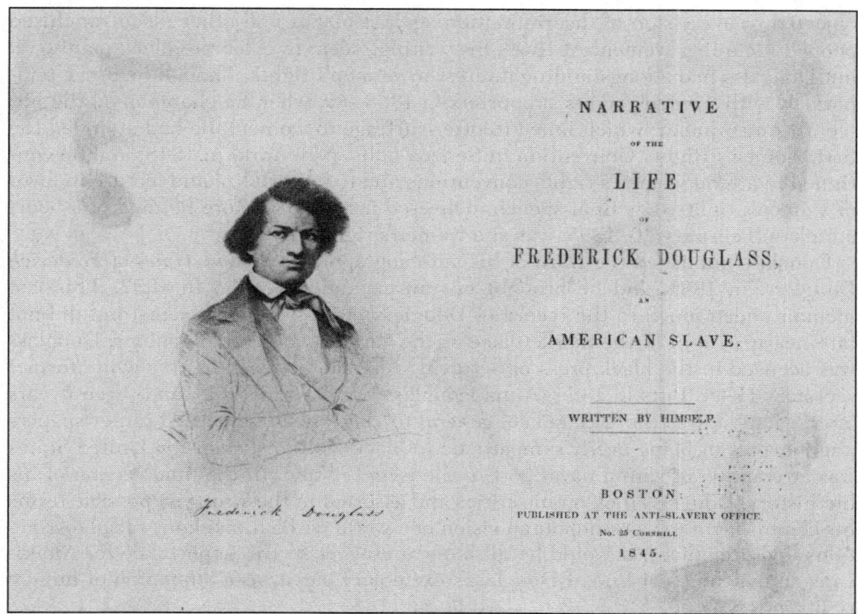
NARRATIVE
OF THE
LIFE
OF
FREDERICK DOUGLASS,
AN
AMERICAN SLAVE.
WRITTEN BY HIMSELF.
BOSTON:
PUBLISHED AT THE ANTI-SLAVERY OFFICE.
No. 25 CORNHILL.
1845.

Douglass's *Narrative*. Frontispiece and title page of the first edition (1845).

Cabin (1852) and other works by popular mid-nineteenth-century women writers; it testified to Douglass's awareness that women were a powerful force within the abolitionist movement. Stowe's influence can also be felt on Douglass's only work of fiction, the novella "The Heroic Slave," which he published in 1853 in *Frederick Douglass' Paper* and in a fund-raising volume for his newspaper. Like Stowe, he represented sympathetic bonds between whites and blacks that could lead to united action against enslavers. Unlike Stowe in *Uncle Tom's Cabin*, he celebrated a dark-skinned man capable of using violence against whites, and showed blacks moving south to the Caribbean instead of north to Canada.

Following the Supreme Court's 1857 ruling in the Dred Scott case, which declared that blacks could never become citizens of the United States, Douglass became more militant in his writing. Though he refused to participate in John Brown's 1859 raid on the federal arsenal at Harpers Ferry, which he regarded as a suicidal action, he was obliged to flee to Canada and thence to England because of his known association with Brown. He returned in May 1860 after receiving news of the death of his daughter Annie. Once the Civil War began, Douglass took an active role in the campaign to make free black men eligible to serve the Union cause; he became a successful recruiter of black soldiers, whose ranks soon included his own sons. Having helped to enlist these men, Douglass subsequently protested directly to President Lincoln over blacks' unequal pay and treatment in the Union army.

After the war, Douglass criticized Lincoln's successors over what he believed was a tardy and unjust Reconstruction policy. He was particularly insistent in calling for the swift passage of the Fifteenth Amendment, guaranteeing suffrage to the newly emancipated male slaves. By the 1870s, Douglass was a significant figure in the Republican Party, taking on such positions as president of the Freedman's Bank, federal marshal, and recorder of deeds for the District of Columbia. Never satisfied with the grudging legal concessions the Civil War yielded, Douglass persistently objected to every sign of discrimination against blacks and other disenfranchised people, including women. At times his writings seem to celebrate black manhood, but Douglass had a longstanding interest in women's rights. Though he broke temporarily with women's rights supporters in 1868–69, when he championed the Fifteenth Amendment (which failed to offer suffrage to women), he had attended the first Women's Rights Convention in Seneca Falls, New York, in 1848, and he continued to attend women's rights conventions and to editorialize and lecture in favor of women's rights. His final speech, delivered just hours before he died of a heart attack on February 20, 1895, was at a women's rights rally.

Douglass published the third of his autobiographies, *Life and Times of Frederick Douglass*, in 1881, and he brought out an expanded version in 1892. This last memoir added much to the record of Douglass's post–Civil War years, but did not fare nearly as well in the marketplace as the earlier two autobiographies. Douglass was accused in the black press of betraying his race by marrying his white former secretary Helen Pitts in 1884 (Anna Douglass had died in 1882), and several years later, when he was the U.S. consul general to Haiti, he was accused in newspapers and journals of being overly sympathetic to black Haitians when the United States was attempting to gain a naval port in the island nation. In the final version of his life history, Douglass took on his critics and asserted in the strongest possible terms his commitment to a cosmopolitan vision of a world without invidious racial distinctions and prejudices. It would be difficult to exaggerate the importance for Americans across the color line of Douglass's exemplary career as a champion of human rights.

Narrative of the Life of Frederick Douglass, An American Slave, Written by Himself[1]

Preface[2]

In the month of August, 1841, I attended an anti-slavery convention in Nantucket, at which it was my happiness to become acquainted with FREDERICK DOUGLASS, the writer of the following Narrative. He was a stranger to nearly every member of that body; but, having recently made his escape from the southern prison-house of bondage, and feeling his curiosity excited to ascertain the principles and measures of the abolitionists,—of whom he had heard a somewhat vague description while he was a slave,—he was induced to give his attendance, on the occasion alluded to, though at that time a resident in New Bedford.[3]

Fortunate, most fortunate occurrence!—fortunate for the millions of his manacled brethren, yet panting for deliverance from their awful thraldom!—fortunate for the cause of negro emancipation, and of universal liberty!—

1. First printed in May 1845 by the Anti-Slavery Office in Boston, the source of the present text. Punctuation and hyphenation have been slightly regularized and a few typographical emendations have also been made.

2. The preface is by William Lloyd Garrison (1805–1879), the most influential white abolitionist at that time. He edited the antislavery newspaper the *Liberator*, which he founded in 1831, and headed the American Anti-Slavery Society, which published Douglass's *Narrative*. Garrison called for immediate emancipation and advocated nonviolent moral persuasion as the best way of achieving social reform. Most slave narratives of the period came with prefaces by white abolitionists attesting to the moral character and literacy of the black author.

3. Douglass escaped from slavery in Maryland in September 1838 and settled in New Bedford, Massachusetts, where he became active among the New Bedford abolitionists.

fortunate for the land of his birth, which he has already done so much to save and bless!—fortunate for a large circle of friends and acquaintances, whose sympathy and affection he has strongly secured by the many sufferings he has endured, by his virtuous traits of character, by his ever-abiding remembrance of those who are in bonds, as being bound with them!—fortunate for the multitudes, in various parts of our republic, whose minds he has enlightened on the subject of slavery, and who have been melted to tears by his pathos, or roused to virtuous indignation by his stirring eloquence against the enslavers of men!—fortunate for himself, as it at once brought him into the field of public usefulness, "gave the world assurance of a MAN," quickened the slumbering energies of his soul, and consecrated him to the great work of breaking the rod of the oppressor, and letting the oppressed go free!

I shall never forget his first speech at the convention—the extraordinary emotion it excited in my own mind—the powerful impression it created upon a crowded auditory,[4] completely taken by surprise—the applause which followed from the beginning to the end of his felicitous remarks. I think I never hated slavery so intensely as at that moment; certainly, my perception of the enormous outrage which is inflicted by it, on the godlike nature of its victims, was rendered far more clear than ever. There stood one, in physical proportion and stature commanding and exact—in intellect richly endowed—in natural eloquence a prodigy—in soul manifestly "created but a little lower than the angels"[5]—yet a slave, ay, a fugitive slave,—trembling for his safety, hardly daring to believe that on the American soil, a single white person could be found who would befriend him at all hazards, for the love of God and humanity! Capable of high attainments as an intellectual and moral being—needing nothing but a comparatively small amount of cultivation to make him an ornament to society and a blessing to his race—by the law of the land, by the voice of the people, by the terms of the slave code, he was only a piece of property, a beast of burden, a chattel[6] personal, nevertheless!

A beloved friend[7] from New Bedford prevailed on Mr. DOUGLASS to address the convention. He came forward to the platform with a hesitancy and embarrassment, necessarily the attendants of a sensitive mind in such a novel position. After apologizing for his ignorance, and reminding the audience that slavery was a poor school for the human intellect and heart, he proceeded to narrate some of the facts in his own history as a slave, and in the course of his speech gave utterance to many noble thoughts and thrilling reflections. As soon as he had taken his seat, filled with hope and admiration, I rose, and declared that PATRICK HENRY,[8] of revolutionary fame, never made a speech more eloquent in the cause of liberty, than the one we had just listened to from the lips of that hunted fugitive. So I believed at that time—such is my belief now. I reminded the audience of the peril which surrounded this self-emancipated young man at the North,—even in Massachusetts, on the soil of the Pilgrim Fathers, among the descendants of

4. Auditorium (archaic).
5. God created people "a little lower than the angels" (Psalms 8.5); Paul declares that Christ was made "a little lower than the angels" (Hebrews 2.7, 9).
6. Property.
7. William C. Coffin (1816–?), a prominent New Bedford abolitionist.
8. U.S. patriot (1736–1799), famous for the words: "I know not what course others may take, but as for me, give me liberty or give me death."

revolutionary sires; and I appealed to them, whether they would ever allow him to be carried back into slavery,—law or no law, constitution or no constitution. The response was unanimous and in thunder-tones—"NO!" "Will you succor and protect him as a brother-man—a resident of the old Bay State."[9] "YES!" shouted the whole mass, with an energy so startling, that the ruthless tyrants south of Mason and Dixon's line[1] might almost have heard the mighty burst of feeling, and recognized it as the pledge of an invincible determination, on the part of those who gave it, never to betray him that wanders, but to hide the outcast, and firmly to abide the consequences.

It was at once deeply impressed upon my mind, that, if Mr. DOUGLASS could be persuaded to consecrate his time and talents to the promotion of the anti-slavery enterprise, a powerful impetus would be given to it, and a stunning blow at the same time inflicted on northern prejudice against a colored complexion. I therefore endeavored to instill hope and courage into his mind, in order that he might dare to engage in a vocation so anomalous and responsible for a person in his situation; and I was seconded in this effort by warm-hearted friends, especially by the late General Agent of the Massachusetts Anti-Slavery Society, Mr. JOHN A. COLLINS, whose judgment in this instance entirely coincided with my own. At first, he could give no encouragement; with unfeigned diffidence, he expressed his conviction that he was not adequate to the performance of so great a task; the path marked out was wholly an untrodden one; he was sincerely apprehensive that he should do more harm than good. After much deliberation, however, he consented to make a trial; and ever since that period, he has acted as a lecturing agent, under the auspices either of the American or the Massachusetts Anti-Slavery Society. In labors he has been most abundant; and his success in combating prejudice, in gaining proselytes, in agitating the public mind, has far surpassed the most sanguine expectations that were raised at the commencement of his brilliant career. He has borne himself with gentleness and meekness, yet with true manliness of character. As a public speaker, he excels in pathos, wit, comparison, imitation, strength of reasoning, and fluency of language. There is in him that union of head and heart, which is indispensable to an enlightenment of the heads and a winning of the hearts of others. May his strength continue to be equal to his day! May he continue to "grow in grace, and in the knowledge of God," that he may be increasingly serviceable in the cause of bleeding humanity, whether at home or abroad!

It is certainly a very remarkable fact, that one of the most efficient advocates of the slave population, now before the public, is a fugitive slave, in the person of FREDERICK DOUGLASS; and that the free colored population of the United States are as ably represented by one of their own number, in the person of CHARLES LENOX REMOND,[2] whose eloquent appeals have extorted the highest applause of multitudes on both sides of the Atlantic. Let the calumniators of the colored race despise themselves for their baseness and illiberality of spirit, and henceforth cease to talk of the natural

9. Massachusetts.
1. Established by the British astronomers and surveyors Charles Mason and Jeremiah Dixon during the 1760s, the line separating Pennsylvania and Maryland came to signify the boundary between slave and free states.
2. A free-born African American (1810–1873) from Massachusetts who was the first black employed in the United States as an antislavery lecturer. He toured with Douglass for the Massachusetts Anti-Slavery Society in 1842.

inferiority of those who require nothing but time and opportunity to attain to the highest point of human excellence.

It may, perhaps, be fairly questioned, whether any other portion of the population of the earth could have endured the privations, sufferings and horrors of slavery, without having become more degraded in the scale of humanity than the slaves of African descent. Nothing has been left undone to cripple their intellects, darken their minds, debase their moral nature, obliterate all traces of their relationship to mankind; and yet how wonderfully they have sustained the mighty load of a most frightful bondage, under which they have been groaning for centuries! To illustrate the effect of slavery on the white man,—to show that he has no powers of endurance, in such a condition, superior to those of his black brother,—DANIEL O'CONNELL,[3] the distinguished advocate of universal emancipation, and the mightiest champion of prostrate but not conquered Ireland, relates the following anecdote in a speech delivered by him in the Conciliation Hall, Dublin, before the Loyal National Repeal Association, March 31, 1845. "No matter," said Mr. O'CONNELL, "under what specious term it may disguise itself, slavery is still hideous. *It has a natural, an inevitable tendency to brutalize every noble faculty of man.* An American sailor, who was cast away on the shore of Africa, where he was kept in slavery for three years, was, at the expiration of that period, found to be imbruted and stultified—he had lost all reasoning power; and having forgotten his native language, could only utter some savage gibberish between Arabic and English, which nobody could understand, and which even he himself found difficulty in pronouncing. So much for the humanizing influence of THE DOMESTIC INSTITUTION!" Admitting this to have been an extraordinary case of mental deterioration, it proves at least that the white slave can sink as low in the scale of humanity as the black one.

Mr. DOUGLASS has very properly chosen to write his own Narrative, in his own style, and according to the best of his ability, rather than to employ some one else. It is, therefore, entirely his own production; and, considering how long and dark was the career he had to run as a slave,—how few have been his opportunities to improve his mind since he broke his iron fetters,—it is, in my judgment, highly creditable to his head and heart. He who can peruse it without a tearful eye, a heaving breast, an afflicted spirit,—without being filled with an unutterable abhorrence of slavery and all its abettors, and animated with a determination to seek the immediate overthrow of that execrable system,—without trembling for the fate of this country in the hands of a righteous God, who is ever on the side of the oppressed, and whose arm is not shortened that it cannot save,—must have a flinty heart, and be qualified to act the part of a trafficker "in slaves and the souls of men."[4] I am confident that it is essentially true in all its statements; that nothing has been set down in malice, nothing exaggerated, nothing drawn from the imagination; that it comes short of the reality, rather than overstates a single fact in regard to SLAVERY AS IT IS.[5] The experience of FREDERICK DOUGLASS, as a slave, was not a peculiar one; his lot was not especially a hard one; his case may be regarded

3. Irish statesman (1775–1847), called the "Liberator," who advocated Irish independence from England.

4. Revelation 18.13.

5. Probably an allusion to Theodore Weld's widely read antislavery compendium *Slavery as It Is* (1839).

as a very fair specimen of the treatment of slaves in Maryland, in which State it is conceded that they are better fed and less cruelly treated than in Georgia, Alabama, or Louisiana. Many have suffered incomparably more, while very few on the plantations have suffered less, than himself. Yet how deplorable was his situation! what terrible chastisements were inflicted upon his person! what still more shocking outrages were perpetrated upon his mind! with all his noble powers and sublime aspirations, how like a brute was he treated, even by those professing to have the same mind in them that was in Christ Jesus! to what dreadful liabilities was he continually subjected! how destitute of friendly counsel and aid, even in his greatest extremities! how heavy was the midnight of woe which shrouded in blackness the last ray of hope, and filled the future with terror and gloom! what longings after freedom took possession of his breast, and how his misery augmented, in proportion as he grew reflective and intelligent,—thus demonstrating that a happy slave is an extinct man! how he thought, reasoned, felt, under the lash of the driver, with the chains upon his limbs! what perils he encountered in his endeavors to escape from his horrible doom! and how signal have been his deliverance and preservation in the midst of a nation of pitiless enemies!

This Narrative contains many affecting incidents, many passages of great eloquence and power; but I think the most thrilling one of them all is the description DOUGLASS gives of his feelings, as he stood soliloquizing respecting his fate, and the chances of his one day being a freeman, on the banks of the Chesapeake Bay—view in the receding vessels as they flew with their white wings before the breeze, and apostrophizing them as animated by the living spirit of freedom. Who can read that passage, and be insensible to its pathos and sublimity? Compressed into it is a whole Alexandrian library[6] of thought, feeling, and sentiment—all that can, all that need be urged, in the form of expostulation, entreaty, rebuke, against that crime of crimes,—making man the property of his fellow-man! O, how accursed is that system, which entombs the godlike mind of man, defaces the divine image, reduces those who by creation were crowned with glory and honor to a level with four-footed beasts, and exalts the dealer in human flesh above all that is called God! Why should its existence be prolonged one hour? Is it not evil, only evil, and that continually? What does its presence imply but the absence of all fear of God, all regard for man, on the part of the people of the United States? Heaven speed its eternal overthrow!

So profoundly ignorant of the nature of slavery are many persons, that they are stubbornly incredulous whenever they read or listen to any recital of the cruelties which are daily inflicted on its victims. They do not deny that the slaves are held as property; but that terrible fact seems to convey to their minds no idea of injustice, exposure to outrage, or savage barbarity. Tell them of cruel scourgings, of mutilations and brandings, of scenes of pollution and blood, of the banishment of all light and knowledge, and they affect to be greatly indignant at such enormous exaggerations, such wholesale misstatements, such abominable libels on the character of the southern planters! As if all these direful outrages were not the natural results of slavery! As if it were less cruel to reduce a human being to the condition of a

6. Alexandria, in Egypt, home of the greatest library in the Greco-Roman world.

thing, than to give him a severe flagellation, or to deprive him of necessary food and clothing! As if whips, chains, thumb-screws, paddles, bloodhounds, overseers, drivers, patrols, were not all indispensable to keep the slaves down, and to give protection to their ruthless oppressors! As if, when the marriage institution is abolished, concubinage, adultery, and incest, must not necessarily abound; when all the rights of humanity are annihilated, any barrier remains to protect the victim from the fury of the spoiler; when absolute power is assumed over life and liberty, it will not be wielded with destructive sway! Skeptics of this character abound in society. In some few instances, their incredulity arises from a want of reflection; but, generally, it indicates a hatred of the light, a desire to shield slavery from the assaults of its foes, a contempt of the colored race, whether bond or free. Such will try to discredit the shocking tales of slaveholding cruelty which are recorded in this truthful Narrative; but they will labor in vain. Mr. DOUGLASS has frankly disclosed the place of his birth, the names of those who claimed ownership in his body and soul, and the names also of those who committed the crimes which he has alleged against them. His statements, therefore, may easily be disproved, if they are untrue.

In the course of his Narrative, he relates two instances of murderous cruelty,—in one of which a planter deliberately shot a slave belonging to a neighboring plantation, who had unintentionally gotten within his lordly domain in quest of fish; and in the other, an overseer blew out the brains of a slave who had fled to a stream of water to escape a bloody scourging. Mr. DOUGLASS states that in neither of these instances was any thing done by way of legal arrest or judicial investigation. The Baltimore American, of March 17, 1845, relates a similar case of atrocity, perpetrated with similar impunity—as follows:—"*Shooting a Slave.*—We learn, upon the authority of a letter from Charles county, Maryland, received by a gentleman of this city, that a young man, named Matthews, a nephew of General Matthews, and whose father, it is believed, holds an office at Washington, killed one of the slaves upon his father's farm by shooting him. The letter states that young Matthews had been left in charge of the farm; that he gave an order to the servant, which was disobeyed, when he proceeded to the house, *obtained a gun, and, returning, shot the servant.* He immediately, the letter continues, fled to his father's residence, where he still remains unmolested."—Let it never be forgotten, that no slaveholder or overseer can be convicted of any outrage perpetrated on the person of a slave, however diabolical it may be, on the testimony of colored witnesses, whether bond or free. By the slave code, they are adjudged to be as incompetent to testify against a white man, as though they were indeed a part of the brute creation. Hence, there is no legal protection in fact, whatever there may be in form, for the slave population; and any amount of cruelty may be inflicted on them with impunity. Is it possible for the human mind to conceive of a more horrible state of society?

The effect of a religious profession on the conduct of southern masters is vividly described in the following Narrative, and shown to be any thing but salutary. In the nature of the case, it must be in the highest degree pernicious. The testimony of Mr. DOUGLASS, on this point, is sustained by a cloud of witnesses, whose veracity is unimpeachable. "A slaveholder's profession of Christianity is a palpable imposture. He is a felon of the highest grade. He is a man-stealer. It is of no importance what you put in the other scale."

Reader! are you with the man-stealers in sympathy and purpose, or on the side of their down-trodden victims? If with the former, then are you the foe of God and man. If with the latter, what are you prepared to do and dare in their behalf? Be faithful, be vigilant, be untiring in your efforts to break every yoke, and let the oppressed go free. Come what may—cost what it may—inscribe on the banner which you unfurl to the breeze, as your religious and political motto—"No Compromise with Slavery! No Union with Slaveholders!"

WM. LLOYD GARRISON

Boston, May 1, 1845.

Letter from Wendell Phillips, Esq.[7]

Boston, *April* 22, 1845.

My Dear Friend:

You remember the old fable of "The Man and the Lion" where the lion complained that he should not be so misrepresented "when the lions wrote history."

I am glad the time has come when the "lions write history." We have been left long enough to gather the character of slavery from the involuntary evidence of the masters. One might, indeed, rest sufficiently satisfied with what, it is evident, must be, in general, the results of such a relation, without seeking farther to find whether they have followed in every instance. Indeed, those who stare at the half-peck of corn a week, and love to count the lashes on the slave's back, are seldom the "stuff" out of which reformers and abolitionists are to be made. I remember that, in 1838, many were waiting for the results of the West India experiment,[8] before they could come into our ranks. Those "results" have come long ago; but, alas! few of that number have come with them, as converts. A man must be disposed to judge of emancipation by other tests than whether it has increased the produce of sugar,—and to hate slavery for other reasons than because it starves men and whips women,—before he is ready to lay the first stone of his anti-slavery life.

I was glad to learn, in your story, how early the most neglected of God's children waken to a sense of their rights, and of the injustice done them. Experience is a keen teacher; and long before you had mastered your A B C, or knew where the "white sails" of the Chesapeake were bound, you began, I see, to gauge the wretchedness of the slave, not by his hunger and want, not by his lashes and toil, but by the cruel and blighting death which gathers over his soul.

In connection with this, there is one circumstance which makes your recollections peculiarly valuable, and renders your early insight the more remarkable. You come from that part of the country where we are told slavery appears with its fairest features. Let us hear, then, what it is at its best estate—-gaze on its bright side, if it has one; and then imagination may task her powers to add dark lines to the picture, as she travels southward

7. A prominent Massachusetts-based abolitionist (1811–1884).
8. On August 1, 1834, England formally abolished slavery in the West Indies; by 1838 slavery had been abolished throughout the British Empire.

to that (for the colored man) Valley of the Shadow of Death,[9] where the Mississippi sweeps along.

Again, we have known you long, and can put the most entire confidence in your truth, candor, and sincerity. Every one who has heard you speak has felt, and, I am confident, every one who reads your book will feel, persuaded that you give them a fair specimen of the whole truth. No one-sided portrait,—no wholesale complaints,—but strict justice done, whenever individual kindliness has neutralized, for a moment, the deadly system with which it was strangely allied. You have been with us, too, some years, and can fairly compare the twilight of rights, which your race enjoy at the North, with that "noon of night" under which they labor south of Mason and Dixon's line. Tell us whether, after all, the half-free colored man of Massachusetts is worse off than the pampered slave of the rice swamps!

In reading your life, no one can say that we have unfairly picked out some rare specimens of cruelty. We know that the bitter drops, which even you have drained from the cup, are no incidental aggravations, no individual ills, but such as must mingle always and necessarily in the lot of every slave. They are the essential ingredients, not the occasional results, of the system.

After all, I shall read your book with trembling for you. Some years ago, when you were beginning to tell me your real name and birthplace, you may remember I stopped you, and preferred to remain ignorant of all. With the exception of a vague description, so I continued, till the other day, when you read me your memoirs. I hardly knew, at the time, whether to thank you or not for the sight of them, when I reflected that it was still dangerous, in Massachusetts, for honest men to tell their names! They say the fathers, in 1776, signed the Declaration of Independence with the halter about their necks. You, too, publish your declaration of freedom with danger compassing you around. In all the broad lands which the Constitution of the United States overshadows, there is no single spot,—however narrow or desolate,—where a fugitive slave can plant himself and say, "I am safe." The whole armory of Northern Law has no shield for you. I am free to say that, in your place, I should throw the MS. into the fire.

You, perhaps, may tell your story in safety, endeared as you are to so many warm hearts by rarer gifts, and a still rare devotion of them to the service of others. But it will be owing only to your labors, and the fearless efforts of those who, trampling the laws and Constitution of the country under their feet, are determined that they will "hide the outcast," and that their hearths shall be, spite of the law, an asylum for the oppressed, if, some time or other, the humblest may stand in our streets, and bear witness in safety against the cruelties which he has been the victim.

Yet it is sad to think, that these very throbbing hearts which welcome your story, and form your best safeguard in telling it, are all beating contrary to the "statute in such case made and provided." Go on, my dear friend, till you, and those who, like you, have been saved, so as by fire, from the dark prison-house, shall stereotype these free, illegal pulses into statutes; and New England, cutting loose from a blood-stained Union, shall glory in being the house of refuge for the oppressed;—till we no longer

9. Psalms 23.4.

merely "*hide* the outcast," or make a merit of standing idly by while he is hunted in our midst; but, consecrating anew the soil of the Pilgrims as an asylum for the oppressed, proclaim our *welcome* to the slave so loudly, that the tones shall reach every hut in the Carolinas, and make the broken-hearted bondman leap up at the thought of old Massachusetts.

God speed the day!

Till then, and ever,

Yours truly,

WENDELL PHILLIPS

FREDERICK DOUGLASS.

Chapter I

I was born in Tuckahoe, near Hillsborough, and about twelve miles from Easton, in Talbot county, Maryland. I have no accurate knowledge of my age, never having seen any authentic record containing it. By far the larger part of the slaves know as little of their ages as horses know of theirs, and it is the wish of most masters within my knowledge to keep their slaves thus ignorant. I do not remember to have ever met a slave who could tell of his birthday. They seldom come nearer to it than planting-time, harvest-time, cherry-time, spring-time, or fall-time. A want of information concerning my own was a source of unhappiness to me even during childhood. The white children could tell their ages. I could not tell why I ought to be deprived of the same privilege. I was not allowed to make any inquiries of my master concerning it. He deemed all such inquiries on the part of a slave improper and impertinent, and evidence of a restless spirit. The nearest estimate I can give makes me now between twenty-seven and twenty-eight years of age. I come to this, from hearing my master say, some time during 1835, I was about seventeen years old.

My mother was named Harriet Bailey. She was the daughter of Isaac and Betsey Bailey, both colored, and quite dark. My mother was of a darker complexion than either my grandmother or grandfather.

My father was a white man. He was admitted to be such by all I ever heard speak of my parentage. The opinion was also whispered that my master was my father; but of the correctness of this opinion, I know nothing; the means of knowing was withheld from me. My mother and I were separated when I was but an infant—before I knew her as my mother. It is a common custom, in the part of Maryland from which I ran away, to part children from their mothers at a very early age. Frequently, before the child has reached its twelfth month, its mother is taken from it, and hired out on some farm a considerable distance off, and the child is placed under the care of an old woman, too old for field labor. For what this separation is done, I do not know, unless it be to hinder the development of the child's affection toward its mother, and to blunt and destroy the natural affection of the mother for the child. This is the inevitable result.

I never saw my mother, to know her as such, more than four or five times in my life; and each of these times was very short in duration, and at night. She was hired[1] by a Mr. Stewart, who lived about twelve miles from my

1. Slaves who were "hired out" had their wages paid to their owners.

home. She made her journeys to see me in the night, travelling the whole distance on foot, after the performance of her day's work. She was a field hand, and a whipping is the penalty of not being in the field at sunrise, unless a slave has special permission from his or her master to the contrary—a permission which they seldom get, and one that gives to him that gives it the proud name of being a kind master. I do not recollect of ever seeing my mother by the light of day. She was with me in the night. She would lie down with me, and get me to sleep, but long before I waked she was gone. Very little communication ever took place between us. Death soon ended what little we could have while she lived, and with it her hardships and suffering. She died when I was about seven years old, on one of my master's farms, near Lee's Mill. I was not allowed to be present during her illness, at her death, or burial. She was gone long before I knew any thing about it. Never having enjoyed, to any considerable extent, her soothing presence, her tender and watchful care, I received the tidings of her death with much the same emotions I should have probably felt at the death of a stranger.

Called thus suddenly away, she left me without the slightest intimation of who my father was. The whisper that my master was my father, may or may not be true; and, true or false, it is of but little consequence to my purpose whilst the fact remains, in all its glaring odiousness, that slaveholders have ordained, and by law established, that the children of slave women shall in all cases follow the condition of their mothers; and this is done too obviously to administer to their own lusts, and make a gratification of their wicked desires profitable as well as pleasurable; for by this cunning arrangement, the slaveholder, in cases not a few, sustains to his slaves the double relation of master and father.

I know of such cases; and it is worthy of remark that such slaves invariably suffer greater hardships, and have more to contend with, than others. They are, in the first place, a constant offence to their mistress. She is ever disposed to find fault with them; they can seldom do any thing to please her; she is never better pleased than when she sees them under the lash, especially when she suspects her husband of showing to his mulatto children favors which he withholds from his black slaves. The master is frequently compelled to sell this class of his slaves, out of deference to the feelings of his white wife; and, cruel as the deed may strike any one to be, for a man to sell his own children to human flesh-mongers, it is often the dictate of humanity for him to do so; for, unless he does this, he must not only whip them himself, but must stand by and see one white son tie up his brother, of but few shades darker complexion than himself, and ply the gory lash to his naked back; and if he lisp one word of disapproval, it is set down to his parental partiality, and only makes a bad matter worse, both for himself and the slave whom he would protect and defend.

Every year brings with it multitudes of this class of slaves. It was doubtless in consequence of a knowledge of this fact, that one great statesman of the south predicted the downfall of slavery by the inevitable laws of population. Whether this prophecy is ever fulfilled or not, it is nevertheless plain that a very different-looking class of people are springing up at the south, and are now held in slavery, from those originally brought to this country from Africa; and if their increase will do no other good, it will do away the force of the argument, that God cursed Ham, and therefore American slavery is right.[2] If the lineal descendants of Ham are alone to be scripturally enslaved, it is certain that slavery at the south must soon become unscriptural; for thousands are ushered into the world, annually, who, like myself, owe their existence to white fathers, and those fathers most frequently their own masters.

I have had two masters. My first master's name was Anthony. I do not remember his first name. He was generally called Captain Anthony—a title which, I presume, he acquired by sailing a craft on the Chesapeake Bay. He was not considered a rich slaveholder. He owned two or three farms, and about thirty slaves. His farms and slaves were under the care of an overseer. The overseer's name was Plummer. Mr. Plummer was a miserable drunkard, a profane swearer, and a savage monster. He always went armed with a cowskin[3] and a heavy cudgel. I have known him to cut and slash the women's heads so horribly, that even master would be enraged at his cruelty, and would threaten to whip him if he did not mind himself. Master, however, was not a humane slaveholder. It required extraordinary barbarity on the part of an overseer to affect him. He was a cruel man, hardened by a long life of slaveholding. He would at times seem to take great pleasure in whipping a slave. I have often been awakened at the dawn of day by the most heart-rending shrieks of an own aunt of mine, whom he used to tie up to a joist, and whip upon her naked back till she was literally covered with blood. No words, no tears, no prayers, from his gory victim, seemed to move his iron heart from its bloody purpose. The louder she screamed, the harder he whipped; and where the blood ran fastest, there he whipped longest. He would whip her to make her scream, and whip her to make her hush; and not until overcome by fatigue, would he cease to swing the blood-clotted cowskin. I remember the first time I ever witnessed this horrible exhibition. I was quite a child, but I well remember it. I never shall forget it whilst I remember any thing. It was the first of a long series of such outrages, of which I was doomed to be a witness and a participant. It struck me with awful force. It was the blood-stained gate, the entrance to the hell of slavery, through which I was about to pass. It was a most terrible spectacle. I wish I could commit to paper the feelings with which I beheld it.

This occurrence took place very soon after I went to live with my old master, and under the following circumstances. Aunt Hester went out one night,—where or for what I do not know,—and happened to be absent when my master desired her presence. He had ordered her not to go out evenings, and warned her that she must never let him catch her in company with a young man, who was paying attention to her, belonging to Colonel Lloyd. The young man's name was Ned Roberts, generally called Lloyd's Ned. Why master was so careful of her, may be safely left to conjecture. She was a woman of noble form, and of graceful proportions, having very few equals, and fewer superiors, in personal appearance, among the colored or white women of our neighborhood.

Aunt Hester had not only disobeyed his orders in going out, but had been found in company with Lloyd's Ned; which circumstance, I found, from

2. Some proslavery writers interpreted Genesis 9.20–27, in which Noah curses his son Ham and condemns him to bondage to his brothers, as a biblical justification of slavery.

3. A whip made of raw cowhide.

what he said while whipping her, was the chief offence. Had he been a man of pure morals himself, he might have been thought interested in protecting the innocence of my aunt; but those who knew him will not suspect him of any such virtue. Before he commenced whipping Aunt Hester, he took her into the kitchen, and stripped her from neck to waist, leaving her neck, shoulders, and back, entirely naked. He then told her to cross her hands, calling her at the same time a d—d b—h. After crossing her hands, he tied them with a strong rope, and led her to a stool under a large hook in the joist, put in for the purpose. He made her get upon the stool, and tied her hands to the hook. She now stood fair for his infernal purpose. Her arms were stretched up at their full length, so that she stood upon the ends of her toes. He then said to her, "Now, you d—d b—h, I'll learn you how to disobey my orders!" and after rolling up his sleeves, he commenced to lay on the heavy cowskin, and soon the warm, red blood (amid heart-rending shrieks from her, and horrid oaths from him) came dripping to the floor. I was so terrified and horror-stricken at the sight, that I hid myself in a closet, and dared not venture out till long after the bloody transaction was over. I expected it would be my turn next. It was all new to me. I had never seen any thing like it before. I had always lived with my grandmother on the outskirts of the plantation, where she was put to raise the children of the younger women. I had therefore been, until now, out of the way of the bloody scenes that often occurred on the plantation.

Chapter II

My master's family consisted of two sons, Andrew and Richard; one daughter, Lucretia, and her husband, Captain Thomas Auld. They lived in one house, upon the home plantation of Colonel Edward Lloyd. My master was Colonel Lloyd's clerk and superintendent. He was what might be called the overseer of the overseers. I spent two years of childhood on this plantation in my old master's family. It was here that I witnessed the bloody transaction recorded in the first chapter; and as I received my first impressions of slavery on this plantation, I will give some description of it, and of slavery as it there existed. The plantation is about twelve miles north of Easton, in Talbot county, and is situated on the border of Miles River. The principal products raised upon it were tobacco, corn, and wheat. These were raised in great abundance; so that, with the products of this and the other farms belonging to him, he was able to keep in almost constant employment a large sloop, in carrying them to market at Baltimore. This sloop was named Sally Lloyd, in honor of one of the colonel's daughters. My master's son-in-law, Captain Auld, was master of the vessel; she was otherwise manned by the colonel's own slaves. Their names were Peter, Isaac, Rich, and Jake. These were esteemed very highly by the other slaves, and looked upon as the privileged ones of the plantation; for it was no small affair, in the eyes of the slaves, to be allowed to see Baltimore.

Colonel Lloyd kept from three to four hundred slaves on his home plantation, and owned a large number more on the neighboring farms belonging to him. The names of the farms nearest to the home plantation were Wye Town and New Design. "Wye Town" was under the overseership of a man named Noah Willis. New Design was under the overseership of a Mr. Townsend.

The overseers of these, and all the rest of the farms, numbering over twenty, received advice and direction from the managers of the home plantation. This was the great business place. It was the seat of government for the whole twenty farms. All disputes among the overseers were settled here. If a slave was convicted of any high misdemeanor, became unmanageable, or evinced a determination to run away, he was brought immediately here, severely whipped, put on board the sloop, carried to Baltimore, and sold to Austin Woolfolk, or some other slave-trader, as a warning to the slaves remaining.

Here, too, the slaves of all the other farms received their monthly allowance of food, and their yearly clothing. The men and women slaves received, as their monthly allowance of food, eight pounds of pork, or its equivalent in fish, and one bushel of corn meal. Their yearly clothing consisted of two coarse linen shirts, one pair of linen trousers, like the shirts, one jacket, one pair of trousers for winter, made of coarse negro cloth, one pair of stockings, and one pair of shoes; the whole of which could not have cost more than seven dollars. The allowance of the slave children was given to their mothers, or the old women having the care of them. The children unable to work in the field had neither shoes, stockings, jackets, nor trousers, given to them; their clothing consisted of two coarse linen shirts per year. When these failed them, they went naked until the next allowance-day. Children from seven to ten years old, of both sexes, almost naked, might be seen at all seasons of the year.

There were no beds given the slaves, unless one coarse blanket be considered such, and none but the men and women had these. This, however, is not considered a very great privation. They find less difficulty from the want of beds, than from the want of time to sleep; for when their day's work in the field is done, the most of them having their washing, mending, and cooking to do, and having few or none of the ordinary facilities for doing either of these, very many of their sleeping hours are consumed in preparing for the field the coming day; and when this is done, old and young, male and female, married and single, drop down side by side, on one common bed,—the cold, damp floor,—each covering himself or herself with their miserable blankets; and here they sleep till they are summoned to the field by the driver's horn. At the sound of this, all must rise, and be off to the field. There must be no halting; every one must be at his or her post; and woe betides them who hear not this morning summons to the field; for if they are not awakened by the sense of hearing, they are by the sense of feeling: no age nor sex finds any favor. Mr. Severe, the overseer, used to stand by the door of the quarter, armed with a large hickory stick and heavy cowskin, ready to whip any one who was so unfortunate as not to hear, or, from any other cause, was prevented from being ready to start for the field at the sound of the horn.

Mr. Severe was rightly named: he was a cruel man. I have seen him whip a woman, causing the blood to run half an hour at the time; and this, too, in the midst of her crying children, pleading for their mother's release. He seemed to take pleasure in manifesting his fiendish barbarity. Added to his cruelty, he was a profane swearer. It was enough to chill the blood and stiffen the hair of an ordinary man to hear him talk. Scarce a sentence escaped him but that was commenced or concluded by some horrid oath. The field was the place to witness his cruelty and profanity. His presence made it both the field of blood and of blasphemy. From the rising till the going down of the sun, he was cursing, raving, cutting, and slashing among the slaves of the field, in the most frightful manner. His career was short. He died very soon after I went to Colonel Lloyd's; and he died as he lived, uttering, with his dying groans, bitter curses and horrid oaths. His death was regarded by the slaves as the result of a merciful providence.

Mr. Severe's place was filled by a Mr. Hopkins. He was a very different man. He was less cruel, less profane, and made less noise, than Mr. Severe. His course was characterized by no extraordinary demonstrations of cruelty. He whipped, but seemed to take no pleasure in it. He was called by the slaves a good overseer.

The home plantation of Colonel Lloyd wore the appearance of a country village. All the mechanical operations for all the farms were performed here. The shoemaking and mending, the blacksmithing, cartwrighting, coopering, weaving, and grain-grinding, were all performed by the slaves on the home plantation. The whole place wore a business-like aspect very unlike the neighboring farms. The number of houses, too, conspired to give it advantage over the neighboring farms. It was called by the slaves the *Great House Farm.* Few privileges were esteemed higher, by the slaves of the out-farms, than that of being selected to do errands at the Great House Farm. It was associated in their minds with greatness. A representative could not be prouder of his election to a seat in the American Congress, than a slave on one of the out-farms would be of his election to do errands at the Great House Farm. They regarded it as evidence of great confidence reposed in them by their overseers; and it was on this account, as well as a constant desire to be out of the field from under the driver's lash, that they esteemed it a high privilege, one worth careful living for. He was called the smartest and most trusty fellow, who had this honor conferred upon him the most frequently. The competitors for this office sought as diligently to please their overseers, as the office-seekers in the political parties seek to please and deceive the people. The same traits of character might be seen in Colonel Lloyd's slaves, as are seen in the slaves of the political parties.

The slaves selected to go to the Great House Farm, for the monthly allowance for themselves and their fellow-slaves, were peculiarly enthusiastic. While on their way, they would make the dense old woods, for miles around, reverberate with their wild songs, revealing at once the highest joy and the deepest sadness. They would compose and sing as they went along, consulting neither time nor tune. The thought that came up, came out—if not in the word, in the sound;—and as frequently in the one as in the other. They would sometimes sing the most pathetic sentiment in the most rapturous tone, and the most rapturous sentiment in the most pathetic tone. Into all of their songs they would manage to weave something of the Great House Farm. Especially would they do this, when leaving home. They would then sing most exultingly the following words:—

> "I am going away to the Great House Farm!
> O, yea! O, yea! O!"

This they would sing, as a chorus, to words which to many would seem unmeaning jargon, but which, nevertheless, were full of meaning to themselves. I have sometimes thought that the mere hearing of those songs would do more to impress some minds with the horrible character of slavery, than the reading of whole volumes of philosophy on the subject could do.

I did not, when a slave, understand the deep meaning of those rude and apparently incoherent songs. I was myself within the circle; so that I neither saw nor heard as those without might see and hear. They told a tale of woe which was then altogether beyond my feeble comprehension; they were tones loud, long, and deep; they breathed the prayer and complaint of souls boiling over with the bitterest anguish. Every tone was a testimony against slavery, and a prayer to God for deliverance from chains. The hearing of those wild notes always depressed my spirit, and filled me with ineffable sadness. I have frequently found myself in tears while hearing them. The mere recurrence to those songs, even now, afflicts me; and while I am writing these lines, an expression of feeling has already found its way down my cheek. To those songs I trace my first glimmering conception of the dehumanizing character of slavery. I can never get rid of that conception. Those songs still follow me, to deepen my hatred of slavery, and quicken my sympathies for my brethren in bonds. If any one wishes to be impressed with the soul-killing effects of slavery, let him go to Colonel Lloyd's plantation, and, on allowance-day, place himself in the deep pine woods, and there let him, in silence, analyze the sounds that shall pass through the chambers of his soul,—and if he is not thus impressed, it will only be because "there is no flesh in his obdurate heart."[4]

I have often been utterly astonished, since I came to the north, to find persons who could speak of the singing, among slaves, as evidence of their contentment and happiness. It is impossible to conceive of a greater mistake. Slaves sing most when they are most unhappy. The songs of the slave represent the sorrows of his heart; and he is relieved by them, only as an aching heart is relieved by its tears. At least, such is my experience. I have often sung to drown my sorrow, but seldom to express my happiness. Crying for joy, and singing for joy, were alike uncommon to me while in the jaws of slavery. The singing of a man cast away upon a desolate island might be as appropriately considered as evidence of contentment and happiness, as the singing of a slave; the songs of the one and of the other are prompted by the same emotion.

Chapter III

Colonel Lloyd kept a large and finely cultivated garden, which afforded almost constant employment for four men, besides the chief gardener, (Mr. M'Durmond.) This garden was probably the greatest attraction of the place. During the summer months, people came from far and near—from Baltimore, Easton, and Annapolis—to see it. It abounded in fruits of almost every description, from the hardy apple of the north to the delicate orange of the south. This garden was not the least source of trouble on the plantation. Its excellent fruit was quite a temptation to the hungry swarms of boys, as well as the older slaves, belonging to the colonel, few of whom had the virtue or the vice to resist it. Scarcely a day passed, during the summer,

4. From William Cowper's popular poem *The Task* (1785).

but that some slave had to take the lash for stealing fruit. The colonel had to resort to all kinds of stratagems to keep his slaves out of the garden. The last and most successful one was that of tarring his fence all around, after which, if a slave was caught with any tar upon his person, it was deemed sufficient proof that he had either been into the garden, or had tried to get in. In either case, he was severely whipped by the chief gardener. This plan worked well; the slaves became as fearful of tar as of the lash. They seemed to realize the impossibility of touching *tar* without being defiled.

The colonel also kept a splendid riding equipage. His stable and carriage-house presented the appearance of some of our large city livery establishments. His horses were of the finest form and noblest blood. His carriage-house contained three splendid coaches, three or four gigs, besides dearborns and barouches[5] of the most fashionable style.

This establishment was under the care of two slaves—old Barney and young Barney—father and son. To attend to this establishment was their sole work. But it was by no means an easy employment; for in nothing was Colonel Lloyd more particular than in the management of his horses. The slightest inattention to these was unpardonable, and was visited upon those, under whose care they were placed, with the severest punishment; no excuse could shield them, if the colonel only suspected any want of attention to his horses—a supposition which he frequently indulged, and one which, of course, made the office of old and young Barney a very trying one. They never knew when they were safe from punishment. They were frequently whipped when least deserving, and escaped whipping when most deserving it. Every thing depended upon the looks of the horses, and the state of Colonel Lloyd's own mind when his horses were brought to him for use. If a horse did not move fast enough, or hold his head high enough, it was owing to some fault of his keepers. It was painful to stand near the stable-door, and hear the various complaints against the keepers when a horse was taken out for use. "This horse has not had proper attention. He has not been sufficiently rubbed and curried, or he has not been properly fed; his food was too wet or too dry; he got it too soon or too late; he was too hot or too cold; he had too much hay, and not enough of grain; or he had too much grain, and not enough of hay; instead of old Barney's attending to the horse, he had very improperly left it to his son." To all these complaints, no matter how unjust, the slave must answer never a word. Colonel Lloyd could not brook any contradiction from a slave. When he spoke, a slave must stand, listen, and tremble; and such was literally the case. I have seen Colonel Lloyd make old Barney, a man between fifty and sixty years of age, uncover his bald head, kneel down upon the cold, damp ground, and receive upon his naked and toil-worn shoulders more than thirty lashes at the time. Colonel Lloyd had three sons—Edward, Murray, and Daniel,—and three sons-in-law, Mr. Winder, Mr. Nicholson, and Mr. Lowndes. All of these lived at the Great House Farm, and enjoyed the luxury of whipping the servants when they pleased, from old Barney down to William Wilkes, the coach-driver. I have seen Winder make one of the house-servants stand off from him a suitable distance to be touched with the end of his whip, and at every stroke raise great ridges upon his back.

5. Different kinds of carriages.

To describe the wealth of Colonel Lloyd would be almost equal to describing the riches of Job.[6] He kept from ten to fifteen house-servants. He was said to own a thousand slaves, and I think this estimate quite within the truth. Colonel Lloyd owned so many that he did not know them when he saw them; nor did all the slaves of the out-farms know him. It is reported of him, that, while riding along the road one day, he met a colored man, and addressed him in the usual manner of speaking to colored people on the public highways of the south: "Well, boy, whom do you belong to?" "To Colonel Lloyd," replied the slave. "Well, does the colonel treat you well?" "No, sir," was the ready reply. "What, does he work you too hard?" "Yes, sir." "Well, don't he give you enough to eat?" "Yes, sir, he gives me enough, such as it is."

The colonel, after ascertaining where the slave belonged, rode on; the man also went on about his business, not dreaming that he had been conversing with his master. He thought, said, and heard nothing more of the matter, until two or three weeks afterwards. The poor man was then informed by his overseer that, for having found fault with his master, he was now to be sold to a Georgia trader. He was immediately chained and handcuffed; and thus, without a moment's warning, he was snatched away, and forever sundered, from his family and friends, by a hand more unrelenting than death. This is the penalty of telling the truth, of telling the simple truth, in answer to a series of plain questions.

It is partly in consequence of such facts, that slaves, when inquired of as to their condition and the character of their masters, almost universally say they are contented, and that their masters are kind. The slaveholders have been known to send in spies among their slaves, to ascertain their views and feelings in regard to their condition. The frequency of this has had the effect to establish among the slaves the maxim, that a still tongue makes a wise head. They suppress the truth rather than take the consequences of telling it, and in so doing prove themselves a part of the human family. If they have any thing to say of their masters, it is generally in their masters' favor, especially when speaking to an untried man. I have been frequently asked, when a slave, if I had a kind master, and do not remember ever to have given a negative answer; nor did I, in pursuing this course, consider myself as uttering what was absolutely false; for I always measured the kindness of my master by the standard of kindness set up among slaveholders around us. Moreover, slaves are like other people, and imbibe prejudices quite common to others. They think their own better than that of others. Many, under the influence of this prejudice, think their own masters are better than the masters of other slaves; and this, too, in some cases, when the very reverse is true. Indeed, it is not uncommon for slaves even to fall out and quarrel among themselves about the relative goodness of their masters, each contending for the superior goodness of his own over that of the others. At the very same time, they mutually execrate their masters when viewed separately. It was so on our plantation. When Colonel Lloyd's slaves met the slaves of Jacob Jepson, they seldom parted without a quarrel about their masters; Colonel Lloyd's slaves contending that he was the richest, and Mr. Jepson's slaves that he was the smartest, and most of a man. Colonel Lloyd's slaves would boast his ability to

6. The biblical figure whose many misfortunes fail to shake his faith in God.

buy and sell Jacob Jepson. Mr. Jepson's slaves would boast his ability to whip Colonel Lloyd. These quarrels would almost always end in a fight between the parties, and those that whipped were supposed to have gained the point at issue. They seemed to think that the greatness of their masters was transferable to themselves. It was considered as being bad enough to be a slave; but to be a poor man's slave was deemed a disgrace indeed!

Chapter IV

Mr. Hopkins remained but a short time in the office of overseer. Why his career was so short, I do not know, but suppose he lacked the necessary severity to suit Colonel Lloyd. Mr. Hopkins was succeeded by Mr. Austin Gore, a man possessing, in an eminent degree, all those traits of character indispensable to what is called a first-rate overseer. Mr. Gore had served Colonel Lloyd, in the capacity of overseer, upon one of the out-farms, and had shown himself worthy of the high station of overseer upon the home or Great House Farm.

Mr. Gore was proud, ambitious, and persevering. He was artful, cruel, and obdurate. He was just the man for such a place, and it was just the place for such a man. It afforded scope for the full exercise of all his powers, and he seemed to be perfectly at home in it. He was one of those who could torture the slightest look, word, or gesture, on the part of the slave, into impudence, and would treat it accordingly. There must be no answering back to him; no explanation was allowed a slave, showing himself to have been wrongfully accused. Mr. Gore acted fully up to the maxim laid down by slaveholders,—"It is better that a dozen slaves suffer under the lash, than that the overseer should be convicted, in the presence of the slaves, of having been at fault." No matter how innocent a slave might be—it availed him nothing, when accused by Mr. Gore of any misdemeanor. To be accused was to be convicted, and to be convicted was to be punished; the one always following the other with immutable certainty. To escape punishment was to escape accusation; and few slaves had the fortune to do either, under the overseership of Mr. Gore. He was just proud enough to demand the most debasing homage of the slave, and quite servile enough to crouch, himself, at the feet of the master. He was ambitious enough to be contented with nothing short of the highest rank of overseers, and persevering enough to reach the height of his ambition. He was cruel enough to inflict the severest punishment, artful enough to descend to the lowest trickery, and obdurate enough to be insensible to the voice of a reproving conscience. He was, of all the overseers, the most dreaded by the slaves. His presence was painful; his eye flashed confusion; and seldom was his sharp, shrill voice heard, without producing horror and trembling in their ranks.

Mr. Gore was a grave man, and, though a young man, he indulged in no jokes, said no funny words, seldom smiled. His words were in perfect keeping with his looks, and his looks were in perfect keeping with his words. Overseers will sometimes indulge in a witty word, even with the slaves; not so with Mr. Gore. He spoke but to command, and commanded but to be obeyed; he dealt sparingly with his words, and bountifully with his whip, never using the former where the latter would answer as well. When he whipped, he seemed to do so from a sense of duty, and feared no consequences. He did nothing reluctantly, no matter how disagreeable; always at his post, never inconsistent. He never promised but to fulfil. He was, in a word, a man of the most inflexible firmness and stone-like coolness.

His savage barbarity was equalled only by the consummate coolness with which he committed the grossest and most savage deeds upon the slaves under his charge. Mr. Gore once undertook to whip one of Colonel Lloyd's slaves, by the name of Demby. He had given Demby but few stripes, when, to get rid of the scourging, he ran and plunged himself into a creek, and stood there at the depth of his shoulders, refusing to come out. Mr. Gore told him that he would give him three calls, and that, if he did not come out at the third call, he would shoot him. The first call was given. Demby made no response, but stood his ground. The second and third calls were given with the same result. Mr. Gore then, without consultation or deliberation with any one, not even giving Demby an additional call, raised his musket to his face, taking deadly aim at his standing victim, and in an instant poor Demby was no more. His mangled body sank out of sight, and blood and brains marked the water where he had stood.

A thrill of horror flashed through every soul upon the plantation, excepting Mr. Gore. He alone seemed cool and collected. He was asked by Colonel Lloyd and my old master, why he resorted to this extraordinary expedient. His reply was, (as well as I can remember,) that Demby had become unmanageable. He was setting a dangerous example to the other slaves,—one which, if suffered to pass without some such demonstration on his part, would finally lead to the total subversion of all rule and order upon the plantation. He argued that if one slave refused to be corrected, and escaped with his life, the other slaves would soon copy the example; the result of which would be, the freedom of the slaves, and the enslavement of the whites. Mr. Gore's defence was satisfactory. He was continued in his station as overseer upon the home plantation. His fame as an overseer went abroad. His horrid crime was not even submitted to judicial investigation. It was committed in the presence of slaves, and they of course could neither institute a suit, nor testify against him; and thus the guilty perpetrator of one of the bloodiest and most foul murders goes unwhipped of justice, and uncensured by the community in which he lives. Mr. Gore lived in St. Michael's, Talbot county, Maryland, when I left there; and if he is still alive, he very probably lives there now; and if so, he is now, as he was then, as highly esteemed and as much respected as though his guilty soul had not been stained with his brother's blood.

I speak advisedly when I say this,—that killing a slave, or any colored person, in Talbot county, Maryland, is not treated as a crime, either by the courts or the community. Mr. Thomas Lanman, of St. Michael's, killed two slaves, one of whom he killed with a hatchet, by knocking his brains out. He used to boast of the commission of the awful and bloody deed. I have heard him do so laughingly, saying, among other things, that he was the only benefactor of his country in the company, and that when others would do as much as he had done, we should be relieved of "the d——d niggers."

The wife of Mr. Giles Hick, living but a short distance from where I used to live, murdered my wife's cousin, a young girl between fifteen and sixteen years of age, mangling her person in the most horrible manner, breaking her nose and breastbone with a stick, so that the poor girl expired in a few hours afterward. She was immediately buried, but had not been in her untimely grave but a few hours before she was taken up and examined by the coroner, who decided that she had come to her death by severe beating. The offence for which this girl was thus murdered was this:—She had been set that night to mind Mrs. Hick's baby, and during the night she fell asleep, and the baby cried. She, having lost her rest for several nights previous, did not hear the crying. They were both in the room with Mrs. Hicks. Mrs. Hicks, finding the girl slow to move, jumped from her bed, seized an oak stick of wood by the fireplace, and with it broke the girl's nose and breastbone, and thus ended her life. I will not say that this most horrid murder produced no sensation in the community. It did produce sensation, but not enough to bring the murderess to punishment. There was a warrant issued for her arrest, but it was never served. Thus she escaped not only punishment, but even the pain of being arraigned before a court for her horrid crime.

Whilst I am detailing bloody deeds which took place during my stay on Colonel Lloyd's plantation, I will briefly narrate another, which occurred about the same time as the murder of Demby by Mr. Gore.

Colonel Lloyd's slaves were in the habit of spending a part of their nights and Sundays in fishing for oysters, and in this way made up the deficiency of their scanty allowance. An old man belonging to Colonel Lloyd, while thus engaged, happened to get beyond the limits of Colonel Lloyd's, and on the premises of Mr. Beal Bondly. At this trespass, Mr. Bondly took offence, and with his musket came down to the shore, and blew its deadly contents into the poor old man.

Mr. Bondly came over to see Colonel Lloyd the next day, whether to pay him for his property, or to justify himself in what he had done, I know not. At any rate, this whole fiendish transaction was soon hushed up. There was very little said about it at all, and nothing done. It was a common saying, even among little white boys, that it was worth a half-cent to kill a "nigger," and a half-cent to bury one.

Chapter V

As to my own treatment while I lived on Colonel Lloyd's plantation, it was very similar to that of the other slave children. I was not old enough to work in the field, and there being little else than field work to do, I had a great deal of leisure time. The most I had to do was to drive up the cows at evening, keep the fowls out of the garden, keep the front yard clean, and run of errands for my old master's daughter, Mrs. Lucretia Auld. The most of my leisure time I spent in helping Master Daniel Lloyd in finding his birds, after he had shot them. My connection with Master Daniel was of some advantage to me. He became quite attached to me, and was a sort of protector of me. He would not allow the older boys to impose upon me, and would divide his cakes with me.

I was seldom whipped by my old master, and suffered little from any thing else than hunger and cold. I suffered much from hunger, but much more from cold. In hottest summer and coldest winter, I was kept almost naked—no shoes, no stockings, no jacket, no trousers, nothing on but a coarse tow linen shirt, reaching only to my knees. I had no bed. I must have perished with cold, but that, the coldest nights, I used to steal a bag which was used for carrying corn to the mill. I would crawl into this bag, and there sleep on the cold, damp, clay floor, with my head in and feet out. My feet have been so cracked with the frost, that the pen with which I am writing might be laid in the gashes.

We were not regularly allowanced. Our food was coarse corn meal boiled. This was called *mush.* It was put into a large wooden tray or trough, and set down upon the ground. The children were then called, like so many pigs, and like so many pigs they would come and devour the mush; some with oyster-shells, others with pieces of shingle, some with naked hands, and none with spoons. He that ate fastest got most; he that was strongest secured the best place; and few left the trough satisfied.

I was probably between seven and eight years old when I left Colonel Lloyd's plantation. I left it with joy. I shall never forget the ecstasy with which I received the intelligence that my old master (Anthony) had determined to let me go to Baltimore, to live with Mr. Hugh Auld, brother to my old master's son-in-law, Captain Thomas Auld. I received this information about three days before my departure. They were three of the happiest days I ever enjoyed. I spent the most part of all these three days in the creek, washing off the plantation scurf, and preparing myself for my departure.

The pride of appearance which this would indicate was not my own. I spent the time in washing, not so much because I wished to, but because Mrs. Lucretia had told me I must get all the dead skin off my feet and knees before I could go to Baltimore; for the people of Baltimore were very cleanly, and would laugh at me if I looked dirty. Besides, she was going to give me a pair of trousers, which I should not put on unless I got all the dirt off me. The thought of owning a pair of trousers was great indeed! It was almost a sufficient motive, not only to make me take off what would be called by pig-drovers the mange, but the skin itself. I went at it in good earnest, working for the first time with the hope of reward.

The ties that ordinarily bind children to their homes were all suspended in my case. I found no severe trial in my departure. My home was charmless; it was not home to me; on parting from it, I could not feel that I was leaving any thing which I could have enjoyed by staying. My mother was dead, my grandmother lived far off, so that I seldom saw her. I had two sisters and one brother, that lived in the same house with me; but the early separation of us from our mother had well nigh blotted the fact of our relationship from our memories. I looked for home elsewhere, and was confident of finding none which I should relish less than the one which I was leaving. If, however, I found in my new home hardship, hunger, whipping, and nakedness, I had the consolation that I should not have escaped any one of them by staying. Having already had more than a taste of them in the house of my old master, and having endured them there, I very naturally inferred my ability to endure them elsewhere, and especially at Baltimore; for I had something of the feeling about Baltimore that is expressed in the proverb, that "being hanged in England is preferable to dying a natural death in Ireland." I had the strongest desire to see Baltimore. Cousin Tom, though not fluent in speech, had inspired me with that desire by his eloquent description of the place. I could never point out any thing at the Great House, no matter how beautiful or powerful, but that he had seen something at Baltimore far exceeding, both in beauty and strength, the object which I pointed out to him. Even the Great House itself, with all its pictures, was far inferior to many buildings in Baltimore. So strong was my desire, that I thought a gratification of it would fully compensate for whatever loss of comforts I should sustain by the exchange. I left without a regret, and with the highest hopes of future happiness.

We sailed out of Miles River for Baltimore on a Saturday morning. I remember only the day of the week, for at that time I had no knowledge of the days of the month, nor the months of the year. On setting sail, I walked aft, and gave to Colonel Lloyd's plantation what I hoped would be the last look. I then placed myself in the bows of the sloop, and there spent the remainder of the day in looking ahead, interesting myself in what was in the distance rather than in things near by or behind.

In the afternoon of that day, we reached Annapolis, the capital of the State. We stopped but a few moments, so that I had no time to go on shore. It was the first large town that I had ever seen, and though it would look small compared with some of our New England factory villages, I thought it a wonderful place for its size—more imposing even than the Great House Farm!

We arrived at Baltimore early on Sunday morning, landing at Smith's Wharf, not far from Bowley's Wharf. We had on board the sloop a large flock of sheep; and after aiding in driving them to the slaughterhouse of Mr. Curtis on Louden Slater's Hill, I was conducted by Rich, one of the hands belonging on board of the sloop, to my new home in Alliciana Street, near Mr. Gardner's ship-yard, on Fells Point.

Mr. and Mrs. Auld were both at home, and met me at the door with their little son Thomas, to take care of whom I had been given. And here I saw what I had never seen before; it was a white face beaming with the most kindly emotions; it was the face of my new mistress, Sophia Auld. I wish I could describe the rapture that flashed through my soul as I beheld it. It was a new and strange sight to me, brightening up my pathway with the light of happiness. Little Thomas was told, there was his Freddy,—and I was told to take care of little Thomas; and thus I entered upon the duties of my new home with the most cheering prospect ahead.

I look upon my departure from Colonel Lloyd's plantation as one of the most interesting events of my life. It is possible, and even quite probable, that but for the mere circumstance of being removed from that plantation to Baltimore, I should have to-day, instead of being here seated by my own table, in the enjoyment of freedom and the happiness of home, writing this Narrative, been confined in the galling chains of slavery. Going to live at Baltimore laid the foundation, and opened the gateway, to all my subsequent prosperity. I have ever regarded it as the first plain manifestation of that kind providence which has ever since attended me, and marked my life with so many favors. I regarded the selection of myself as being somewhat remarkable. There were a number of slave children that might have been sent from the plantation to Baltimore. There were those younger, those older, and those of the same age. I was chosen from among them all, and was the first, last, and only choice.

I may be deemed superstitious, and even egotistical, in regarding this event as a special interposition of divine Providence in my favor. But I should be false to the earliest sentiments of my soul, if I suppressed the opinion. I prefer to be true to myself, even at the hazard of incurring the ridicule of others, rather than to be false, and incur my own abhorrence. From my earliest recollection, I date the entertainment of a deep conviction that slavery would not always be able to hold me within its foul embrace; and in the darkest hours of my career in slavery, this living word of faith and spirit of hope departed not from me, but remained like ministering angels to cheer me through the gloom. This good spirit was from God, and to him I offer thanksgiving and praise.

Chapter VI

My new mistress proved to be all she appeared when I first met her at the door,—a woman of the kindest heart and finest feelings. She had never had a slave under her control previously to myself, and prior to her marriage she had been dependent upon her own industry for a living. She was by trade a weaver; and by constant application to her business, she had been in a good degree preserved from the blighting and dehumanizing effects of slavery. I was utterly astonished at her goodness. I scarcely knew how to behave towards her. She was entirely unlike any other white woman I had ever seen. I could not approach her as I was accustomed to approach other white ladies. My early instruction was all out of place. The crouching servility, usually so acceptable a quality in a slave, did not answer when manifested toward her. Her favor was not gained by it; she seemed to be disturbed by it. She did not deem it impudent or unmannerly for a slave to look her in the face. The meanest slave was put fully at ease in her presence, and none left without feeling better for having seen her. Her face was made of heavenly smiles, and her voice of tranquil music.

But, alas! this kind heart had but a short time to remain such. The fatal poison of irresponsible power was already in her hands, and soon commenced its infernal work. That cheerful eye, under the influence of slavery, soon became red with rage; that voice, made all of sweet accord, changed to one of harsh and horrid discord; and that angelic face gave place to that of a demon.

Very soon after I went to live with Mr. and Mrs. Auld, she very kindly commenced to teach me the A, B, C. After I had learned this, she assisted me in learning to spell words of three or four letters. Just at this point of my progress, Mr. Auld found out what was going on, and at once forbade Mrs. Auld to instruct me further, telling her, among other things, that it was unlawful, as well as unsafe, to teach a slave to read. To use his own words, further, he said, "If you give a nigger an inch, he will take an ell.[7] A nigger should know nothing but to obey his master—to do as he is told to do. Learning would *spoil* the best nigger in the world. Now," said he, "if you teach that nigger (speaking of myself) how to read, there would be no keeping him. It would forever unfit him to be a slave. He would at once become unmanageable, and of no value to his master. As to himself, it could do him no good, but a great deal of harm. It would make him discontented and unhappy." These words sank deep into my heart, stirred up sentiments within that lay slumbering, and called into existence an entirely new train of thought. It was a new and special revelation, explaining dark and mysterious things, with which my youthful understanding had struggled, but struggled in vain. I now

7. Unit of measurement equal to forty-five inches.

understood what had been to me a most perplexing difficulty—to wit, the white man's power to enslave the black man. It was a grand achievement, and I prized it highly. From that moment, I understood the pathway from slavery to freedom. It was just what I wanted, and I got it at a time when I the least expected it. Whilst I was saddened by the thought of losing the aid of my kind mistress, I was gladdened by the invaluable instruction which, by the merest accident, I had gained from my master. Though conscious of the difficulty of learning without a teacher, I set out with high hope, and a fixed purpose, at whatever cost of trouble, to learn how to read. The very decided manner with which he spoke, and strove to impress his wife with the evil consequences of giving me instruction, served to convince me that he was deeply sensible of the truths he was uttering. It gave me the best assurance that I might rely with the utmost confidence on the results which, he said, would flow from teaching me to read. What he most dreaded, that I most desired. What he most loved, that I most hated. That which to him was a great evil, to be carefully shunned, was to me a great good, to be diligently sought; and the argument which he so warmly urged, against my learning to read, only served to inspire me with a desire and determination to learn. In learning to read, I owe almost as much to the bitter opposition of my master, as to the kindly aid of my mistress. I acknowledge the benefit of both.

I had resided but a short time in Baltimore before I observed a marked difference, in the treatment of slaves, from that which I had witnessed in the country. A city slave is almost a freeman, compared with a slave on the plantation. He is much better fed and clothed, and enjoys privileges altogether unknown to the slave on the plantation. There is a vestige of decency, a sense of shame, that does much to curb and check those outbreaks of atrocious cruelty so commonly enacted upon the plantation. He is a desperate slaveholder, who will shock the humanity of his non-slaveholding neighbors with the cries of his lacerated slave. Few are willing to incur the odium attaching to the reputation of being a cruel master; and above all things, they would not be known as not giving a slave enough to eat. Every city slaveholder is anxious to have it known of him, that he feeds his slaves well; and it is due to them to say, that most of them do give their slaves enough to eat. There are, however, some painful exceptions to this rule. Directly opposite to us, on Philpot Street, lived Mr. Thomas Hamilton. He owned two slaves. Their names were Henrietta and Mary. Henrietta was about twenty-two years of age, Mary was about fourteen; and of all the mangled and emaciated creatures I ever looked upon, these two were the most so. His heart must be harder than stone, that could look upon these unmoved. The head, neck, and shoulders of Mary were literally cut to pieces. I have frequently felt her head, and found it nearly covered with festering sores, caused by the lash of her cruel mistress. I do not know that her master ever whipped her, but I have been an eye-witness to the cruelty of Mrs. Hamilton. I used to be in Mr. Hamilton's house nearly every day. Mrs. Hamilton used to sit in a large chair in the middle of the room, with a heavy cowskin always by her side, and scarce an hour passed during the day but was marked by the blood of one of these slaves. The girls seldom passed her without her saying, "Move faster, you *black gip*!" at the same time giving them a blow with the cowskin over the head or shoulders, often drawing the blood. She would then say, "Take that, you *black gip*!"—continuing, "If you don't move faster,

I'll move you!" Added to the cruel lashings to which these slaves were subjected, they were kept nearly half-starved. They seldom knew what it was to eat a full meal. I have seen Mary contending with the pigs for the offal thrown into the street. So much was Mary kicked and cut to pieces, that she was oftener called *"pecked"* than by her name.

Chapter VII

I lived in Master Hugh's family about seven years. During this time, I succeeded in learning to read and write. In accomplishing this, I was compelled to resort to various stratagems. I had no regular teacher. My mistress, who had kindly commenced to instruct me, had, in compliance with the advice and direction of her husband, not only ceased to instruct, but had set her face against my being instructed by any one else. It is due, however, to my mistress to say of her, that she did not adopt this course of treatment immediately. She at first lacked the depravity indispensable to shutting me up in mental darkness. It was at least necessary for her to have some training in the exercise of irresponsible power, to make her equal to the task of treating me as though I were a brute.

My mistress was, as I have said, a kind and tender-hearted woman; and in the simplicity of her soul she commenced, when I first went to live with her, to treat me as she supposed one human being ought to treat another. In entering upon the duties of a slaveholder, she did not seem to perceive that I sustained to her the relation of a mere chattel, and that for her to treat me as a human being was not only wrong, but dangerously so. Slavery proved as injurious to her as it did to me. When I went there, she was a pious, warm, and tender-hearted woman. There was no sorrow or suffering for which she had not a tear. She had bread for the hungry, clothes for the naked, and comfort for every mourner that came within her reach. Slavery soon proved its ability to divest her of these heavenly qualities. Under its influence, the tender heart became stone, and the lamblike disposition gave way to one of tiger-like fierceness. The first step in her downward course was in her ceasing to instruct me. She now commenced to practise her husband's precepts. She finally became even more violent in her opposition than her husband himself. She was not satisfied with simply doing as well as he had commanded; she seemed anxious to do better. Nothing seemed to make her more angry than to see me with a newspaper. She seemed to think that here lay the danger. I have had her rush at me with a face made all up of fury, and snatch from me a newspaper, in a manner that fully revealed her apprehension. She was an apt woman; and a little experience soon demonstrated, to her satisfaction, that education and slavery were incompatible with each other.

From this time I was most narrowly watched. If I was in a separate room any considerable length of time, I was sure to be suspected of having a book, and was at once called to give an account of myself. All this, however, was too late. The first step had been taken. Mistress, in teaching me the alphabet, had given me the *inch*, and no precaution could prevent me from taking the *ell*.

The plan which I adopted, and the one by which I was most successful, was that of making friends of all the little white boys whom I met in the street. As many of these as I could, I converted into teachers. With their kindly aid, obtained at different times and in different places, I finally succeeded in learning to read. When I was sent of errands, I always took my book with me, and by going one part of my errand quickly, I found time to get a lesson before my return. I used also to carry bread with me, enough of which was always in the house, and to which I was always welcome; for I was much better off in this regard than many of the poor white children in our neighborhood. This bread I used to bestow upon the hungry little urchins, who, in return, would give me that more valuable bread of knowledge. I am strongly tempted to give the names of two or three of those little boys, as a testimonial of the gratitude and affection I bear them; but prudence forbids;—not that it would injure me, but it might embarrass them; for it is almost an unpardonable offence to teach slaves to read in this Christian country. It is enough to say of the dear little fellows, that they lived on Philpot Street, very near Durgin and Bailey's shipyard. I used to talk this matter of slavery over with them. I would sometimes say to them, I wished I could be as free as they would be when they got to be men. "You will be free as soon as you are twenty-one, *but I am a slave for life!* Have not I as good a right to be free as you have?" These words used to trouble them; they would express for me the liveliest sympathy, and console me with the hope that something would occur by which I might be free.

I was now about twelve years old, and the thought of being *a slave for life* began to bear heavily upon my heart. Just about this time, I got hold of a book entitled "The Columbian Orator."[8] Every opportunity I got, I used to read this book. Among much of other interesting matter, I found in it a dialogue between a master and his slave. The slave was represented as having run away from his master three times. The dialogue represented the conversation which took place between them, when the slave was retaken the third time. In this dialogue, the whole argument in behalf of slavery was brought forward by the master, all of which was disposed of by the slave. The slave was made to say some very smart as well as impressive things in reply to his master—things which had the desired though unexpected effect; for the conversation resulted in the voluntary emancipation of the slave on the part of the master.

In the same book, I met with one of Sheridan's[9] mighty speeches on and in behalf of Catholic emancipation. These were choice documents to me. I read them over and over again with unabated interest. They gave tongue to interesting thoughts of my own soul, which had frequently flashed through my mind, and died away for want of utterance. The moral which I gained from the dialogue was the power of truth over the conscience of even a slaveholder. What I got from Sheridan was a bold denunciation of slavery, and a powerful vindication of human rights. The reading of these documents enabled me to utter my thoughts, and to meet the arguments brought forward to sustain slavery; but while they relieved me of one difficulty, they brought on another even more painful than the one of which I was relieved. The more I read, the more I was led to abhor and detest my enslavers. I could regard them in no other light than a band of successful robbers, who had left their homes, and gone to Africa, and stolen us from our homes, and in a strange land reduced

8. A popular anthology of pieces for recitation (1797) compiled by the Massachusetts teacher and writer Caleb Bingham (1757–1817).

9. Richard Brinsley Sheridan (1751–1816), Irish dramatist and political leader.

us to slavery. I loathed them as being the meanest as well as the most wicked of men. As I read and contemplated the subject, behold! that very discontentment which Master Hugh had predicted would follow my learning to read had already come, to torment and sting my soul to unutterable anguish. As I writhed under it, I would at times feel that learning to read had been a curse rather than a blessing. It had given me a view of my wretched condition, without the remedy. It opened my eyes to the horrible pit, but to no ladder upon which to get out. In moments of agony, I envied my fellow-slaves for their stupidity. I have often wished myself a beast. I preferred the condition of the meanest reptile to my own. Any thing, no matter what, to get rid of thinking! It was this everlasting thinking of my condition that tormented me. There was no getting rid of it. It was pressed upon me by every object within sight or hearing, animate or inanimate. The silver trump of freedom had roused my soul to eternal wakefulness. Freedom now appeared, to disappear no more forever. It was heard in every sound, and seen in every thing. It was ever present to torment me with a sense of my wretched condition. I saw nothing without seeing it, I heard nothing without hearing it, and felt nothing without feeling it. It looked from every star, it smiled in every calm, breathed in every wind, and moved in every storm.

I often found myself regretting my own existence, and wishing myself dead; and but for the hope of being free, I have no doubt but that I should have killed myself, or done something for which I should have been killed. While in this state of mind, I was eager to hear any one speak of slavery. I was a ready listener. Every little while, I could hear something about the abolitionists. It was some time before I found what the word meant. It was always used in such connections as to make it an interesting word to me. If a slave ran away and succeeded in getting clear, or if a slave killed his master, set fire to a barn, or did any thing very wrong in the mind of a slaveholder, it was spoken of as the fruit of *abolition*. Hearing the word in this connection very often, I set about learning what it meant. The dictionary afforded me little or no help. I found it was "the act of abolishing;" but then I did not know what was to be abolished. Here I was perplexed. I did not dare to ask any one about its meaning, for I was satisfied that it was something they wanted me to know very little about. After a patient waiting, I got one of our city papers, containing an account of the number of petitions from the north, praying for the abolition of slavery in the District of Columbia, and of the slave trade between the States. From this time I understood the words *abolition* and *abolitionist*, and always drew near when that word was spoken, expecting to hear something of importance to myself and fellow-slaves. The light broke in upon me by degrees. I went one day down on the wharf of Mr. Waters; and seeing two Irishmen unloading a scow of stone, I went, unasked, and helped them. When we had finished, one of them came to me and asked me if I were a slave. I told him I was. He asked, "Are ye a slave for life?" I told him that I was. The good Irishman seemed to be deeply affected by the statement. He said to the other that it was a pity so fine a little fellow as myself should be a slave for life. He said it was a shame to hold me. They both advised me to run away to the north; that I should find friends there, and that I should be free. I pretended not to be interested in what they said, and treated them as if I did not understand them; for I feared they might be treacherous. White men have been known to encourage slaves to escape, and then, to get the reward, catch them and return them to their masters. I was afraid that these seemingly good men might use me so; but I nevertheless remembered their advice, and from that time I resolved to run away. I looked forward to a time at which it would be safe for me to escape. I was too young to think of doing so immediately; besides, I wished to learn how to write, as I might have occasion to write my own pass. I consoled myself with the hope that I should one day find a good chance. Meanwhile, I would learn to write.

The idea as to how I might learn to write was suggested to me by being in Durgin and Bailey's ship-yard, and frequently seeing the ship carpenters, after hewing, and getting a piece of timber ready for use, write on the timber the name of that part of the ship for which it was intended. When a piece of timber was intended for the larboard side, it would be marked thus—"L." When a piece was for the starboard side, it would be marked thus—"S." A piece for the larboard side forward, would be marked thus—"L.F." When a piece was for starboard side forward, it would be marked thus—"S.F." For larboard aft, it would be marked thus—"L.A." For starboard aft, it would be marked thus—"S.A." I soon learned the names of these letters, and for what they were intended when placed upon a piece of timber in the ship-yard. I immediately commenced copying them, and in a short time was able to make the four letters named. After that, when I met with any boy who I knew could write, I would tell him I could write as well as he. The next word would be, "I don't believe you. Let me see you try it." I would then make the letters which I had been so fortunate as to learn, and ask him to beat that. In this way I got a good many lessons in writing, which it is quite possible I should never have gotten in any other way. During this time, my copy-book was the board fence, brick wall, and pavement; my pen and ink was a lump of chalk. With these, I learned mainly how to write. I then commenced and continued copying the Italics in Webster's Spelling Book,[1] until I could make them all without looking on the book. By this time, my little Master Thomas had gone to school, and learned how to write, and had written over a number of copy-books. These had been brought home, and shown to some of our near neighbors, and then laid aside. My mistress used to go to class meeting at the Wilk Street meetinghouse every Monday afternoon, and leave me to take care of the house. When left thus, I used to spend the time in writing in the spaces left in Master Thomas's copy-book, copying what he had written. I continued to do this until I could write a hand very similar to that of Master Thomas. Thus, after a long, tedious effort for years, I finally succeeded in learning how to write.

Chapter VIII

In a very short time after I went to live at Baltimore, my old master's youngest son Richard died; and in about three years and six months after his death, my old master, Captain Anthony, died, leaving only his son, Andrew, and daughter, Lucretia, to share his estate. He died while on a visit to see his daughter at Hillsborough. Cut off thus unexpectedly, he left no will as to the disposal of his property. It was therefore necessary to have a valuation

1. *The American Spelling Book* (1783), by Noah Webster (1758–1843).

of the property, that it might be equally divided between Mrs. Lucretia and Master Andrew. I was immediately sent for, to be valued with the other property. Here again my feelings rose up in detestation of slavery. I had now a new conception of my degraded condition. Prior to this, I had become, if not insensible to my lot, at least partly so. I left Baltimore with a young heart overborne with sadness, and a soul full of apprehension. I took passage with Captain Rowe, in the schooner Wild Cat, and, after a sail of about twenty-four hours, I found myself near the place of my birth. I had now been absent from it almost, if not quite, five years. I, however, remembered the place very well. I was only about five years old when I left it, to go and live with my old master on Colonel Lloyd's plantation; so that I was now between ten and eleven years old.

We were all ranked together at the valuation. Men and women, old and young, married and single, were ranked with horses, sheep, and swine. There were horses and men, cattle and women, pigs and children, all holding the same rank in the scale of being, and were all subjected to the same narrow examination. Silvery-headed age and sprightly youth, maids and matrons, had to undergo the same indelicate inspection. At this moment, I saw more clearly than ever the brutalizing effects of slavery upon both slave and slaveholder.

After the valuation, then came the division. I have no language to express the high excitement and deep anxiety which were felt among us poor slaves during this time. Our fate for life was now to be decided. We had no more voice in that decision than the brutes among whom we were ranked. A single word from the white men was enough—against all our wishes, prayers, and entreaties—to sunder forever the dearest friends, dearest kindred, and strongest ties known to human beings. In addition to the pain of separation, there was the horrid dread of falling into the hands of Master Andrew. He was known to us all as being a most cruel wretch,—a common drunkard, who had, by his reckless mismanagement and profligate dissipation, already wasted a large portion of his father's property. We all felt that we might as well be sold at once to the Georgia traders, as to pass into his hands; for we knew that that would be our inevitable condition,—a condition held by us all in the utmost horror and dread.

I suffered more anxiety than most of my fellow-slaves. I had known what it was to be kindly treated; they had known nothing of the kind. They had seen little or nothing of the world. They were in very deed men and women of sorrow, and acquainted with grief. Their backs had been made familiar with the bloody lash, so that they had become callous; mine was yet tender; for while at Baltimore I got few whippings, and few slaves could boast of a kinder master and mistress than myself; and the thought of passing out of their hands into those of Master Andrew—a man who, but a few days before, to give me a sample of his bloody disposition, took my little brother by the throat, threw him on the ground, and with the heel of his boot stamped upon his head till the blood gushed from his nose and ears—was well calculated to make me anxious as to my fate. After he had committed this savage outrage upon my brother, he turned to me, and said that was the way he meant to serve me one of these days,—meaning, I suppose, when I came into his possession.

Thanks to a kind Providence, I fell to the portion of Mrs. Lucretia, and was sent immediately back to Baltimore, to live again in the family of Master

Hugh. Their joy at my return equalled their sorrow at my departure. It was a glad day to me. I had escaped a [fate] worse than lion's jaws. I was absent from Baltimore, for the purpose of valuation and division, just about one month, and it seemed to have been six.

Very soon after my return to Baltimore, my mistress, Lucretia, died, leaving her husband and one child, Amanda; and in a very short time after her death, Master Andrew died. Now all the property of my old master, slaves included, was in the hands of strangers,—strangers who had had nothing to do with accumulating it. Not a slave was left free. All remained slaves, from the youngest to the oldest. If any one thing in my experience, more than another, served to deepen my conviction of the infernal character of slavery, and to fill me with unutterable loathing of slaveholders, it was their base ingratitude to my poor old grandmother. She had served my old master faithfully from youth to old age. She had been the source of all his wealth; she had peopled his plantation with slaves; she had become a great grandmother in his service. She had rocked him in infancy, attended him in childhood, served him through life, and at his death wiped from his icy brow the cold death-sweat, and closed his eyes forever. She was nevertheless left a slave—a slave for life—a slave in the hands of strangers; and in their hands she saw her children, her grandchildren, and her great-grandchildren, divided, like so many sheep, without being gratified with the small privilege of a single word, as to their or her own destiny. And, to cap the climax of their base ingratitude and fiendish barbarity, my grandmother, who was now very old, having outlived my old master and all his children, having seen the beginning and end of all of them, and her present owners finding she was of but little value, her frame already racked with the pains of old age, and complete helplessness fast stealing over her once active limbs, they took her to the woods, built her a little hut, put up a little mud-chimney, and then made her welcome to the privilege of supporting herself there in perfect loneliness; thus virtually turning her out to die! If my poor old grandmother now lives, she lives to suffer in utter loneliness; she lives to remember and mourn over the loss of children, the loss of grandchildren, and the loss of great-grandchildren. They are, in the language of the slave's poet, Whittier,[2]—

"Gone, gone, sold and gone
To the rice swamp dank and lone,
Where the slave-whip ceaseless swings,
Where the noisome insect stings,
Where the fever-demon strews
Poison with the falling dews,
Where the sickly sunbeams glare
Through the hot and misty air:—
  Gone, gone, sold and gone
  To the rice swamp dank and lone,
  From Virginia hills and waters—
  Woe is me, my stolen daughters!"

2. John Greenleaf Whittier (1807–1882), American poet and abolitionist. Douglass quotes from Whittier's antislavery poem "The Farewell: Of a Virginia Slave Mother to Her Daughter Sold into Southern Bondage" (1838).

The hearth is desolate. The children, the unconscious children, who once sang and danced in her presence, are gone. She gropes her way, in the darkness of age, for a drink of water. Instead of the voices of her children, she hears by day the moans of the dove, and by night the screams of the hideous owl. All is gloom. The grave is at the door. And now, when weighed down by the pains and aches of old age, when the head inclines to the feet, when the beginning and ending of human existence meet, and helpless infancy and painful old age combine together—at this time, this most needful time, the time for the exercise of that tenderness and affection which children only can exercise toward a declining parent—my poor old grandmother, the devoted mother of twelve children, is left all alone, in yonder little hut, before a few dim embers. She stands—she sits—she staggers—she falls—she groans—she dies—and there are none of her children or grandchildren present, to wipe from her wrinkled brow the cold sweat of death, or to place beneath the sod her fallen remains. Will not a righteous God visit for these things?

In about two years after the death of Mrs. Lucretia, Master Thomas married his second wife. Her name was Rowena Hamilton. She was the eldest daughter of Mr. William Hamilton. Master now lived in St. Michael's. Not long after his marriage, a misunderstanding took place between himself and Master Hugh; and as a means of punishing his brother, he took me from him to live with himself at St. Michael's. Here I underwent another most painful separation. It, however, was not so severe as the one I dreaded at the division of property; for, during this interval, a great change had taken place in Master Hugh and his once kind and affectionate wife. The influence of brandy upon him, and of slavery upon her, had effected a disastrous change in the characters of both; so that, as far as they were concerned, I thought I had little to lose by the change. But it was not to them that I was attached. It was to those little Baltimore boys that I felt the strongest attachment. I had received many good lessons from them, and was still receiving them, and the thought of leaving them was painful indeed. I was leaving, too, without the hope of ever being allowed to return. Master Thomas had said he would never let me return again. The barrier betwixt himself and brother he considered impassable.

I then had to regret that I did not at least make the attempt to carry out my resolution to run away; for the chances of success are tenfold greater from the city than from the country.

I sailed from Baltimore for St. Michael's in the sloop Amanda, Captain Edward Dodson. On my passage, I paid particular attention to the direction which the steamboats took to go to Philadelphia. I found, instead of going down, on reaching North Point they went up the bay, in a north-easterly direction. I deemed this knowledge of the utmost importance. My determination to run away was again revived. I resolved to wait only so long as the offering of a favorable opportunity. When that came, I was determined to be off.

Chapter IX

I have now reached a period of my life when I can give dates. I left Baltimore, and went to live with Master Thomas Auld, at St. Michael's, in March, 1832. It was now more than seven years since I lived with him in the family of my old master, on Colonel Lloyd's plantation. We of course were now almost entire strangers to each other. He was to me a new master, and I to him a new slave. I was ignorant of his temper and disposition; he was equally so of mine. A very short time, however brought us into full acquaintance with each other. I was made acquainted with his wife not less than with himself. They were well matched, being equally mean and cruel. I was now, for the first time during a space of more than seven years, made to feel the painful gnawings of hunger—a something which I had not experienced before since I left Colonel Lloyd's plantation. It went hard enough with me then, when I could look back to no period at which I had enjoyed a sufficiency. It was tenfold harder after living in Master Hugh's family, where I had always had enough to eat, and of that which was good. I have said Master Thomas was a mean man. He was so. Not to give a slave enough to eat, is regarded as the most aggravated development of meanness even among slaveholders. The rule is, no matter how coarse the food, only let there be enough of it. This is the theory; and in the part of Maryland from which I came, it is the general practice,—though there are many exceptions. Master Thomas gave us enough of neither coarse nor fine food. There were four slaves of us in the kitchen—my sister Eliza, my aunt Priscilla, Henny, and myself; and we were allowed less than half of a bushel of cornmeal per week, and very little else, either in the shape of meat or vegetables. It was not enough for us to subsist upon. We were therefore reduced to the wretched necessity of living at the expense of our neighbors. This we did by begging and stealing, whichever came handy in the time of need, the one being considered as legitimate as the other. A great many times have we poor creatures been nearly perishing with hunger, when food in abundance lay mouldering in the safe and smoke-house,[3] and our pious mistress was aware of the fact; and yet that mistress and her husband would kneel every morning, and pray that God would bless them in basket and store!

Bad as all slaveholders are, we seldom meet one destitute of every element of character commanding respect. My master was one of this rare sort. I do not know of one single noble act ever performed by him. The leading trait in his character was meanness; and if there were any other element in his nature, it was made subject to this. He was mean; and, like most other mean men, he lacked the ability to conceal his meanness. Captain Auld was not born a slaveholder. He had been a poor man, master only of a Bay craft. He came into possession of all his slaves by marriage; and of all men, adopted slaveholders are the worst. He was cruel, but cowardly. He commanded without firmness. In the enforcement of his rules he was at times rigid, and at times lax. At times, he spoke to his slaves with the firmness of Napoleon and the fury of a demon; at other times, he might well be mistaken for an inquirer who had lost his way. He did nothing of himself. He might have passed for a lion, but for his ears.[4] In all things noble which he attempted, his own meanness shone most conspicuous. His airs, words, and actions, were the airs, words, and actions of born slaveholders, and, being assumed, were awkward enough. He was not even a good imitator. He possessed all the disposition to

3. Used both to cure and to store meat and fish. "Safe": a meat safe is a structure for preserving food.

4. The suggestion is that his ears reveal him to be a jackass and thus not as powerful as he pretends.

deceive, but wanted the power. Having no resources within himself, he was compelled to be the copyist of many, and being such, he was forever the victim of inconsistency; and of consequence he was an object of contempt, and was held as such even by his slaves. The luxury of having slaves of his own to wait upon him was something new and unprepared for. He was a slaveholder without the ability to hold slaves. He found himself incapable of managing his slaves either by force, fear, or fraud. We seldom called him "master;" we generally called him "Captain Auld," and were hardly disposed to title him at all. I doubt not that our conduct had much to do with making him appear awkward, and of consequence fretful. Our want of reverence for him must have perplexed him greatly. He wished to have us call him master, but lacked the firmness necessary to command us to do so. His wife used to insist upon our calling him so, but to no purpose. In August, 1832, my master attended a Methodist camp-meeting[5] held in the Bay-side, Talbot county, and there experienced religion. I indulged a faint hope that his conversion would lead him to emancipate his slaves, and that, if he did not do this, it would, at any rate, make him more kind and humane. I was disappointed in both these respects. It neither made him to be humane to his slaves, nor to emancipate them. If it had any effect on his character, it made him more cruel and hateful in all his ways; for I believe him to have been a much worse man after his conversion than before. Prior to his conversion, he relied upon his own depravity to shield and sustain him in his savage barbarity; but after his conversion, he found religious sanction and support for his slaveholding cruelty. He made the greatest pretensions to piety. His house was the house of prayer. He prayed morning, noon, and night. He very soon distinguished himself among his brethren, and was soon made a class-leader and exhorter. His activity in revivals was great, and he proved himself an instrument in the hands of the church in converting many souls. His house was the preachers' home. They used to take great pleasure in coming there to put up; for while he starved us, he stuffed them. We have had three or four preachers there at a time. The names of those who used to come most frequently while I lived there, were Mr. Storks, Mr. Ewery, Mr. Humphry, and Mr. Hickey. I have also seen Mr. George Cookman[6] at our house. We slaves loved Mr. Cookman. We believed him to be a good man. We thought him instrumental in getting Mr. Samuel Harrison, a very rich slaveholder, to emancipate his slaves; and by some means got the impression that he was laboring to effect the emancipation of all the slaves. When he was at our house, we were sure to be called in to prayers. When the others were there, we were sometimes called in and sometimes not. Mr. Cookman took more notice of us than either of the other ministers. He could not come among us with betraying his sympathy for us, and, stupid as we were, we had the sagacity to see it.

While I lived with my master in St. Michael's, there was a white young man, a Mr. Wilson, who proposed to keep a Sabbath school for the instruction of such slaves as might be disposed to learn to read the New Testament. We met but three times, when Mr. West and Mr. Fairbanks, both class-leaders, with many others, came upon us with sticks and other missiles, drove us off,

5. Evangelical religious gathering, usually held outdoors.

6. Prominent English Methodist minister (1800–1841).

and forbade us to meet again. Thus ended our little Sabbath school in the pious town of St. Michael's.

I have said my master found religious sanction for his cruelty. As an example, I will state one of many facts going to prove the charge. I have seen him tie up a lame young woman, and whip her with a heavy cowskin upon her naked shoulders, causing the warm red blood to drip; and, in justification of the bloody deed, he would quote this passage of Scripture—"He that knoweth his master's will, and doeth it not, shall be beaten with many stripes."[7]

Master would keep this lacerated young woman tied up in this horrid situation four or five hours at a time. I have known him to tie her up early in the morning, and whip her before breakfast; leave her, go to his store, return at dinner, and whip her again, cutting her in the places already made raw with his cruel lash. The secret of master's cruelty toward "Henny" is found in the fact of her being almost helpless. When quite a child, she fell into the fire, and burned herself horribly. Her hands were so burnt that she never got the use of them. She could do very little but bear heavy burdens. She was to master a bill of expense; and as he was a mean man, she was a constant offence to him. He seemed desirous of getting the poor girl out of existence. He gave her away once to his sister; but, being a poor gift, she was not disposed to keep her. Finally, my benevolent master, to use his own words, "set her adrift to take care of herself." Here was a recently-converted man, holding on upon the mother, and at the same time turning out her helpless child, to starve and die! Master Thomas was one of the many pious slaveholders who hold slaves for the very charitable purpose of taking care of them.

My master and myself had quite a number of differences. He found me unsuitable to his purpose. My city life, he said, had had a very pernicious effect upon me. It had almost ruined me for every good purpose, and fitted me for every thing which was bad. One of my greatest faults was that of letting his horse run away, and go down to his father-in-law's farm, which was about five miles from St. Michael's. I would then have to go after it. My reason for this kind of carelessness, or carefulness, was, that I could always get something to eat when I went there. Master William Hamilton, my master's father-in-law, always gave his slaves enough to eat. I never left there hungry, no matter how great the need of my speedy return. Master Thomas at length said he would stand it no longer. I had lived with him nine months, during which time he had given me a number of severe whippings, all to no good purpose. He resolved to put me out, as he said, to be broken; and, for this purpose, he let me for one year to a man named Edward Covey. Mr. Covey was a poor man, a farm-renter. He rented the place upon which he lived, as also the hands with which he tilled it. Mr. Covey had acquired a very high reputation for breaking young slaves, and this reputation was of immense value to him. It enabled him to get his farm tilled with much less expense to himself than he could have had it done without such a reputation. Some slaveholders thought it not much loss to allow Mr. Covey to have their slaves one year, for the sake of training to which they were subjected, without any other compensation. He could hire young help with great ease, in consequence of this reputation. Added to the natural good qualities of

7. Luke 12.47.

Mr. Covey, he was a professor of religion—a pious soul—a member and a class-leader in the Methodist church. All of this added weight to his reputation as a "nigger-breaker." I was aware of all the facts, having been made acquainted with them by a young man who had lived there. I nevertheless made the change gladly; for I was sure of getting enough to eat, which is not the smallest consideration to a hungry man.

Chapter X

I left Master Thomas's house, and went to live with Mr. Covey, on the 1st of January, 1833. I was now, for the first time in my life, a field hand. In my new employment, I found myself even more awkward than a country boy appeared to be in a large city. I had been at my new home but one week before Mr. Covey gave me a very severe whipping, cutting my back, causing the blood to run, and raising ridges on my flesh as large as my little finger. The details of this affair are as follows: Mr. Covey sent me, very early in the morning of one of our coldest days in the month of January, to the woods, to get a load of wood. He gave me a team of unbroken oxen. He told me which was the in-hand ox, and which the off-hand one.[8] He then tied the end of a large rope around the horns of the in-hand-ox, and gave me the other end of it, and told me, if the oxen started to run, that I must hold on upon the rope. I had never driven oxen before, and of course I was very awkward. I, however, succeeded in getting to the edge of the woods with little difficulty; but I had got a very few rods into the woods, when the oxen took fright, and started full tilt, carrying the cart against trees, and over stumps, in the most frightful manner. I expected every moment that my brains would be dashed out against the trees. After running thus for a considerable distance, they finally upset the cart, dashing it with great force against a tree, and threw themselves into a dense thicket. How I escaped death, I do not know. There I was, entirely alone, in a thick wood, in a place new to me. My cart was upset and shattered, my oxen were entangled among the young trees, and there was none to help me. After a long spell of effort, I succeeded in getting my cart righted, my oxen disentangled, and again yoked to the cart. I now proceeded with my team to the place where I had, the day before, been chopping wood, and loaded my cart pretty heavily, thinking in this way to tame my oxen. I then proceeded on my way home. I had now consumed one half of the day. I got out of the woods safely, and now felt out of danger. I stopped my oxen to open the woods gate; and just as I did so, before I could get hold of my ox-rope, the oxen again started, rushed through the gate, catching it between the wheel and the body of the cart, tearing it to pieces, and coming within a few inches of crushing me against the gate-post. Thus twice, in one short day, I escaped death by the merest chance. On my return, I told Mr. Covey what had happened, and how it happened. He ordered me to return to the woods again immediately. I did so, and he followed on after me. Just as I got into the woods, he came up and told me to stop my cart, and that he would teach me how to trifle away my time, and break gates. He then went to a large gum-tree, and with his axe cut three large switches, and, after

8. The ox on the right of a pair hitched to a wagon. "In-hand ox": the one to the left.

trimming them up neatly with his pocket-knife, he ordered me to take off my clothes. I made him no answer, but stood with my clothes on. He repeated his order. I still made him no answer, nor did I move to strip myself. Upon this he rushed at me with the fierceness of a tiger, tore off my clothes, and lashed me till he had worn out his switches, cutting me so savagely as to leave the marks visible for a long time after. This whipping was the first of a number just like it, and for similar offences.

I lived with Mr. Covey one year. During the first six months, of that year, scarce a week passed without his whipping me. I was seldom free from a sore back. My awkwardness was almost always his excuse for whipping me. We were worked fully up to the point of endurance. Long before day we were up, our horses fed, and by the first approach of day we were off to the field with our hoes and ploughing teams. Mr. Covey gave us enough to eat, but scarce time to eat it. We were often less than five minutes taking our meals. We were often in the field from the first approach of day till its last lingering ray had left us; and at saving-fodder time, midnight often caught us in the field binding blades.[9]

Covey would be out with us. The way he used to stand it, was this. He would spend the most of his afternoons in bed. He would then come out fresh in the evening, ready to urge us on with his words, example, and frequently with the whip. Mr. Covey was one of the few slaveholders who could and did work with his hands. He was a hard-working man. He knew by himself just what a man or a boy could do. There was no deceiving him. His work went on in his absence almost as well as in his presence; and he had the faculty of making us feel that he was ever present with us. This he did by surprising us. He seldom approached the spot where we were at work openly, if he could do it secretly. He always aimed at taking us by surprise. Such was his cunning, that we used to call him, among ourselves, "the snake." When we were at work in the cornfield, he would sometimes crawl on his hands and knees to avoid detection, and all at once he would rise nearly in our midst, and scream out, "Ha, ha! Come, come! Dash on, dash on!" This being his mode of attack, it was never safe to stop a single minute. His comings were like a thief in the night. He appeared to us as being ever at hand. He was under every tree, behind every stump, in every bush, and at every window, on the plantation. He would sometimes mount his horse, as if bound to St. Michael's, a distance of seven miles, and in half an hour afterwards you would see him coiled up in the corner of the wood-fence, watching every motion of the slaves. He would, for this purpose, leave his horse tied up in the woods. Again, he would sometimes walk up to us, and give us orders as though he was upon the point of starting on a long journey, turn his back upon us, and make as though he was going to the house to get ready; and, before he would get half way thither, he would turn short and crawl into a fence-corner, or behind some tree, and there watch us till the going down of the sun.

Mr. Covey's *forte*[1] consisted in his power to deceive. His life was devoted to planning and perpetrating the grossest deceptions. Every thing he possessed in the shape of learning or religion, he made conform to his disposition to deceive. He seemed to think himself equal to deceiving the Almighty.

9. I.e., of wheat or other plants. "Saving-fodder time": harvest time.

1. Strong point (French).

He would make a short prayer in the morning, and a long prayer at night; and, strange as it may seem, few men would at times appear more devotional than he. The exercises of his family devotions were always commenced with singing; and, as he was a very poor singer himself, the duty of raising the hymn generally came upon me. He would read his hymn, and nod at me to commence. I would at times do so; at others, I would not. My non-compliance would almost always produce much confusion. To show himself independent of me, he would start and stagger through with his hymn in the most discordant manner. In this state of mind, he prayed with more than ordinary spirit. Poor man! such was his disposition, and success at deceiving, I do verily believe that he sometimes deceived himself into the solemn belief, that he was a sincere worshiper of the most high God; and this, too, at a time when he may be said to have been guilty of compelling his woman slave to commit the sin of adultery. The facts in the case are these: Mr. Covey was a poor man; he was just commencing in life; he was only able to buy one slave; and, shocking as is the fact, he bought her, as he said, for *a breeder*. This woman was named Caroline. Mr. Covey bought her from Mr. Thomas Lowe, about six miles from St. Michael's. She was a large, able-bodied woman, about twenty years old. She had already given birth to one child, which proved her to be just what he wanted. After buying her, he hired a married man of Mr. Samuel Harrison, to live with him one year; and him he used to fasten up with her every night! The result was, that, at the end of the year, the miserable woman gave birth to twins. At this result Mr. Covey seemed to be highly pleased, both with the man and the wretched woman. Such was his joy, and that of his wife, that nothing they could do for Caroline during her confinement was too good, or too hard, to be done. The children were regarded as being quite an addition to his wealth.

If at any one time of my life more than another, I was made to drink the bitterest dregs of slavery, that time was during the first six months of my stay with Mr. Covey. We were worked in all weathers. It was never too hot or too cold; it could never rain, blow, hail, or snow, too hard for us to work in the field. Work, work, work, was scarcely more the order of the day than of the night. The longest days were too short for him, and the shortest nights too long for him. I was somewhat unmanageable when I first went there, but a few months of this discipline tamed me. Mr. Covey succeeded in breaking me. I was broken in body, soul, and spirit. My natural elasticity was crushed, my intellect languished, the disposition to read departed, the cheerful spark that lingered about my eye died; the dark night of slavery closed in upon me; and behold a man transformed into a brute!

Sunday was my only leisure time. I spent this in a sort of beast-like stupor, between sleep and wake, under some large tree. At times I would rise up, a flash of energetic freedom would dart through my soul, accompanied with a faint beam of hope, that flickered for a moment, and then vanished. I sank down again, mourning over my wretched condition. I was sometimes prompted to take my life, and that of Covey, but was prevented by a combination of hope and fear. My sufferings on this plantation seem now like a dream rather than a stern reality.

Our house stood within a few rods of the Chesapeake Bay, whose broad bosom was ever white with sails from every quarter of the habitable globe. Those beautiful vessels, robed in purest white, so delightful to the eye of freemen, were to me so many shrouded ghosts, to terrify and torment me with thoughts of my wretched condition. I have often, in the deep stillness of a summer's Sabbath, stood all alone upon the lofty banks of that noble bay, and traced, with saddened heart and tearful eye, the countless number of sails moving off to the mighty ocean. The sight of these always affected me powerfully. My thoughts would compel utterance; and there, with no audience but the Almighty, I would pour out my soul's complaint, in my rude way, with an apostrophe to the moving multitude of ships:—

"You are loosed from your moorings, and are free; I am fast in my chains, and am a slave! You move merrily before the gentle gale, and I sadly before the bloody whip! You are freedom's swift-winged angels, that fly round the world; I am confined in bands of iron! O that I were free! Oh, that I were on one of your gallant decks, and under your protecting wing! Alas! betwixt me and you, the turbid waters roll. Go on, go on. O that I could also go! Could I but swim! If I could fly! O, why was I born a man, of whom to make a brute! The glad ship is gone; she hides in the dim distance. I am left in the hottest hell of unending slavery. O God, save me! God, deliver me! Let me be free! Is there any God? Why am I a slave? I will run away. I will not stand it. Get caught, or get clear, I'll try it. I had as well die with ague as the fever. I have only one life to lose. I had as well be killed running as die standing. Only think of it; one hundred miles straight north, and I am free! Try it? Yes! God helping me, I will. It cannot be that I shall live and die a slave. I will take to the water. This very bay shall yet bear me into freedom. The steamboats steered in a north-east course from North Point. I will do the same; and when I get to the head of the bay, I will turn my canoe adrift, and walk straight through Delaware into Pennsylvania. When I get there, I shall not be required to have a pass; I can travel without being disturbed. Let but the first opportunity offer, and, come what will, I am off. Meanwhile, I will try to bear up under the yoke. I am not the only slave in the world. Why should I fret? I can bear as much as any of them. Besides, I am but a boy, and all boys are bound to some one. It may be that my misery in slavery will only increase my happiness when I get free. There is a better day coming."

Thus I used to think, and thus I used to speak to myself; goaded almost to madness at one moment, and at the next reconciling myself to my wretched lot.

I have already intimated that my condition was much worse, during the first six months of my stay at Mr. Covey's, than in the last six. The circumstances leading to the change in Mr. Covey's course toward me form an epoch in my humble history. You have seen how a man was made a slave; you shall see how a slave was made a man. On one of the hottest days of the month of August, 1833, Bill Smith, William Hughes, a slave named Eli, and myself, were engaged in fanning wheat.[2] Hughes was clearing the fanned wheat from before the fan, Eli was turning, Smith was feeding, and I was carrying wheat to the fan. The work was simple, requiring strength rather than intellect; yet, to one entirely unused to such work, it came very hard. About three o'clock of that day, I broke down; my strength failed me; I was seized with a violent aching of the head, attended with extreme dizziness; I

2. Separating the wheat from the chaff.

trembled in every limb. Finding what was coming, I nerved myself up, feeling it would never do to stop work. I stood as long as I could stagger to the hopper with grain. When I could stand no longer, I fell, and felt as if held down by an immense weight. The fan of course stopped; every one had his own work to do; and no one could do the work of the other, and have his own go on at the same time.

Mr. Covey was at the house, about one hundred yards from the treading-yard where we were fanning. On hearing the fan stop, he left immediately, and came to the spot where we were. He hastily inquired what the matter was. Bill answered that I was sick, and there was no one to bring wheat to the fan. I had by this time crawled away under the side of the post and rail-fence by which the yard was enclosed, hoping to find relief by getting out of the sun. He then asked where I was. He was told by one of the hands. He came to the spot, and, after looking at me awhile, asked me what was the matter. I told him as well as I could, for I scarce had strength to speak. He then gave me a savage kick in the side, and told me to get up. I tried to do so, but fell back in the attempt. He gave me another kick, and again told me to rise. I again tried, and succeeded in gaining my feet; but, stooping to get the tub with which I was feeding the fan, I again staggered and fell. While down in this situation, Mr. Covey took up the hickory slat with which Hughes had been striking off the half-bushel measure, and with it gave me a heavy blow upon the head, making a large wound, and the blood ran freely; and with this again told me to get up. I made no effort to comply, having now made up my mind to let him do his worst. In a short time after receiving this blow, my head grew better. Mr. Covey had now left me to my fate. At this moment I resolved, for the first time, to go to my master, enter a complaint, and ask his protection. In order to do this, I must that afternoon walk seven miles; and this, under the circumstances, was truly a severe undertaking. I was exceedingly feeble; made so as much by the kicks and blows which I received, as by the severe fit of sickness to which I had been subjected. I, however, watched my chance, while Covey was looking in an opposite direction, and started for St. Michael's. I succeeded in getting a considerable distance on my way to the woods, when Covey discovered me, and called after me to come back, threatening what he would do if I did not come. I disregarded both his calls and his threats, and made my way to the woods as fast as my feeble state would allow; and thinking I might be overhauled by him if I kept the road, I walked through the woods, keeping far enough from the road to avoid detection, and near enough to prevent losing my way. I had not gone far before my little strength again failed me. I could go no farther. I fell down, and lay for a considerable time. The blood was yet oozing from the wound on my head. For a time I thought I should bleed to death; and think now that I should have done so, but that the blood so matted my hair as to stop the wound. After lying there about three quarters of an hour, I nerved myself up again, and started on my way, through bogs and briers, barefooted and bareheaded, tearing my feet sometimes at nearly every step; and after a journey of about seven miles, occupying some five hours to perform it, I arrived at master's store. I then presented an appearance enough to affect any but a heart of iron. From the crown of my head to my feet, I was covered with blood. My hair was all clotted with dust and blood; my shirt was stiff with blood. My legs and feet were torn in sundry places with briers and thorns, and were also covered with blood. I suppose I looked like a man who had escaped a den of wild beasts, and barely escaped them. In this state I appeared before my master, humbly entreating him to interpose his authority for my protection. I told him all the circumstances as well as I could, and it seemed, as I spoke, at times to affect him. He would then walk the floor, and seek to justify Covey by saying he expected I deserved it. He asked me what I wanted. I told him, to let me get a new home; that as sure as I lived with Mr. Covey again, I should live with but to die with him; that Covey would surely kill me; he was in a fair way for it. Master Thomas ridiculed the idea that there was any danger of Mr. Covey's killing me, and said that he knew Mr. Covey; that he was a good man, and that he could not think of taking me from him; that, should he do so, he would lose the whole year's wages; that I belonged to Mr. Covey for one year, and that I must go back to him, come what might; and that I must not trouble him with any more stories, or that he would himself *get hold of me*. After threatening me thus, he gave me a very large dose of salts, telling me that I might remain in St. Michael's that night, (it being quite late,) but that I must be off back to Mr. Covey's early in the morning; and that if I did not, he would *get hold of me*, which meant that he would whip me. I remained all night, and, according to his orders, I started off to Covey's in the morning, (Saturday morning), wearied in body and broken in spirit. I got no supper that night, or breakfast that morning. I reached Covey's about nine o'clock; and just as I was getting over the fence that divided Mrs. Kemp's fields from ours, out ran Covey with his cowskin, to give me another whipping. Before he could reach me, I succeeded in getting to the cornfield; and as the corn was very high, it afforded me the means of hiding. He seemed very angry, and searched for me a long time. My behavior was altogether unaccountable. He finally gave up the chase, thinking, I suppose, that I must come home for something to eat; he would give himself no further trouble in looking for me. I spent that day mostly in the woods, having the alternative before me,—to go home and be whipped to death, or stay in the woods and be starved to death. That night, I fell in with Sandy Jenkins, a slave with whom I was somewhat acquainted. Sandy had a free wife[3] who lived about four miles from Mr. Covey's; and it being Saturday, he was on his way to see her. I told him my circumstances, and he very kindly invited me to go home with him. I went home with him, and talked this whole matter over, and got his advice as to what course it was best for me to pursue. I found Sandy an old adviser. He told me, with great solemnity, I must go back to Covey; but that before I went, I must go with him into another part of the woods, where there was a certain *root*, which, if I would take some of it with me, carrying it *always on my right side*, would render it impossible for Mr. Covey, or any other white man, to whip me. He said he had carried it for years; and since he had done so, he had never received a blow, and never expected to while he carried it. I at first rejected the idea, that the simple carrying of a root in my pocket would have any such effect as he had said, and was not disposed to take it; but Sandy impressed the necessity with much earnestness, telling me it could do no harm, if it did no good. To please him, I at length took the root, and, according to his

3. I.e., his wife had been set free and was not legally a slave.

direction, carried it upon my right side. This was Sunday morning. I immediately started for home; and upon entering the yard gate, out came Mr. Covey on his way to meeting. He spoke to me very kindly, bade me drive the pigs from a lot near by, and passed on towards the church. Now, this singular conduct of Mr. Covey really made me begin to think that there was something in the *root* which Sandy had given me; and had it been on any other day than Sunday, I could have attributed the conduct to no other cause then the influence of that root; and as it was, I was half inclined to think the *root* to be something more than I at first had taken it to be. All went well till Monday morning. On this morning, the virtue of the *root* was fully tested. Long before daylight, I was called to go and rub, curry, and feed, the horses. I obeyed, and was glad to obey. But whilst thus engaged, whilst in the act of throwing down some blades from the loft, Mr. Covey entered the stable with a long rope; and just as I was half out of the loft, he caught hold of my legs, and was about tying me. As soon as I found what he was up to, I gave a sudden spring, and as I did so, he holding to my legs, I was brought sprawling on the stable floor. Mr. Covey seemed now to think he had me, and could do what he pleased; but at this moment—from whence came the spirit I don't know—I resolved to fight; and, suiting my action to the resolution, I seized Covey hard by the throat; and as I did so, I rose. He held on to me, and I to him. My resistance was so entirely unexpected, that Covey seemed taken all aback. He trembled like a leaf. This gave me assurance, and I held him uneasy, causing the blood to run where I touched him with the ends of my fingers. Mr. Covey soon called out to Hughes for help. Hughes came, and, while Covey held me, attempted to tie my right hand. While he was in the act of doing so, I watched my chance, and gave him a heavy kick close under the ribs. This kick fairly sickened Hughes, so that he left me in the hands of Mr. Covey. This kick had the effect of not only weakening Hughes, but Covey also. When he saw Hughes bending over with pain, his courage quailed. He asked me if I meant to persist in my resistance. I told him I did, come what might; that he had used me like a brute for six months, and that I was determined to be used so no longer. With that, he strove to drag me to a stick that was lying just out of the stable door. He meant to knock me down. But just as he was leaning over to get the stick, I seized him with both hands by his collar, and brought him by a sudden snatch to the ground. By this time, Bill came. Covey called upon him for assistance. Bill wanted to know what he could do. Covey said, "Take hold of him, take hold of him!" Bill said his master hired him out to work, and not to help to whip me; so he left Covey and myself to fight our own battle out. We were at it for nearly two hours. Covey at length let me go, puffing and blowing at a great rate, saying that if I had not resisted, he would not have whipped me half so much. The truth was, that he had not whipped me at all. I considered him as getting entirely the worst end of the bargain; for he had drawn no blood from me, but I had from him. The whole six months afterwards, that I spent with Mr. Covey, he never laid the weight of his finger upon me in anger. He would occasionally say, he didn't want to get hold of me again. "No," thought I, "you need not; for you will come off worse than you did before."

This battle with Mr. Covey was the turning-point in my career as a slave. It rekindled the few expiring embers of freedom, and revived within me a sense of my own manhood. It recalled the departed self-confidence, and inspired me again with a determination to be free. The gratification afforded by the triumph was a full compensation for whatever else might follow, even death itself. He only can understand the deep satisfaction which I experienced, who has himself repelled by force the bloody arm of slavery. I felt as I never felt before. It was a glorious resurrection, from the tomb of slavery, to the heaven of freedom. My long-crushed spirit rose, cowardice departed, bold defiance took its place; and I now resolved that, however long I might remain a slave in form, the day had passed forever when I could be a slave in fact. I did not hesitate to let it be known of me, that the white man who expected to succeed in whipping, must also succeed in killing me.

From this time I was never again what might be called fairly whipped, though I remained a slave four years afterwards. I had several fights, but was never whipped.

It was for a long time a matter of surprise to me why Mr. Covey did not immediately have me taken by the constable to the whipping-post, and there regularly whipped for the crime of raising my hand against a white man in defence of myself. And the only explanation I can now think of does not entirely satisfy me; but such as it is, I will give it. Mr. Covey enjoyed the most unbounded reputation for being a first-rate overseer and negro-breaker. It was of considerable importance to him. That reputation was at stake; and had he sent me—a boy about sixteen years old—to the public whipping-post, his reputation would have been lost; so, to save his reputation, he suffered me to go unpunished.

My term of actual service to Mr. Edward Covey ended on Christmas day, 1833. The days between Christmas and New Year's day are allowed as holidays; and, accordingly, we were not required to perform any labor, more than to feed and take care of the stock. This time we regarded as our own, by the grace of our masters; and we therefore used or abused it nearly as we pleased. Those of us who had families at a distance, were generally allowed to spend the whole six days in their society. This time, however, was spent in various ways. The staid, sober, thinking and industrious ones of our number would employ themselves in making corn-brooms, mats, horse-collars, and baskets; and another class of us would spend the time hunting opossums, hares, and coons. But by far the larger part engaged in such sports and merriments as playing ball, wrestling, running foot-races, fiddling, dancing, and drinking whisky; and this latter mode of spending the time was by far the most agreeable to the feelings of our master. A slave who would work during the holidays was considered by our masters as scarcely deserving them. He was regarded as one who rejected the favor of his master. It was deemed a disgrace not to get drunk at Christmas; and he was regarded as lazy indeed, who had not provided himself with the necessary means, during the year, to get whisky enough to last him through Christmas.

From what I know of the effect of these holidays upon the slave, I believe them to be among the most effective means in the hands of the slaveholder in keeping down the spirit of insurrection. Were the slaveholders at once to abandon this practice, I have not the slightest doubt it would lead to an immediate insurrection among the slaves. These holidays serve as conductors, or safety-valves, to carry off the rebellious spirit of enslaved humanity. But for these, the slave would be forced up to the wildest desperation; and woe betide the slaveholder, the day he ventures to remove or hinder the operation of those conductors! I warn him that, in such an event, a spirit will go forth in their midst, more to be dreaded than the most appalling earthquake.

The holidays are part and parcel of the gross fraud, wrong, and inhumanity of slavery. They are professedly a custom established by the benevolence of the slaveholders; but I undertake to say, it is the result of selfishness, and one of the grossest frauds committed upon the down-trodden slave. They do not give the slaves this time because they would not like to have their work during its continuance, but because they know it would be unsafe to deprive them of it. This will be seen by the fact, that the slaveholders like to have their slaves spend those days just in such a manner as to make them as glad of their ending as of their beginning. Their object seems to be, to disgust their slaves with freedom, by plunging them into the lowest depths of dissipation. For instance, the slaveholders not only like to see the slave drink of his own accord, but will adopt various plans to make him drunk. One plan is, to make bets on their slaves, as to who can drink the most whisky without getting drunk; and in this way they succeed in getting whole multitudes to drink to excess. Thus, when the slave asks for virtuous freedom, the cunning slaveholder, knowing his ignorance, cheats him with a dose of vicious dissipation, artfully labelled with the name of liberty. The most of us used to drink it down, and the result was just what might be supposed: many of us were led to think that there was little to choose between liberty and slavery. We felt, and very properly too, that we had almost as well be slaves to man as to rum. So, when the holidays ended, we staggered up from the filth of our wallowing, took a long breath, and marched to the field,—feeling, upon the whole, rather glad to go, from what our master had deceived us into a belief was freedom, back to the arms of slavery.

I have said that this mode of treatment is a part of the whole system of fraud and inhumanity of slavery. It is so. The mode here adopted to disgust the slave with freedom, by allowing him to see only the abuse of it, is carried out in other things. For instance, a slave loves molasses; he steals some. His master, in many cases, goes off to town, and buys a large quantity; he returns, takes his whip, and commands the slave to eat the molasses, until the poor fellow is made sick at the very mention of it. The same mode is sometimes adopted to make the slaves refrain from asking for more food than their regular allowance. A slave runs through his allowance, and applies for more. His master is enraged at him; but, not willing to send him off without food, gives him more than is necessary, and compels him to eat it within a given time. Then, if he complains that he cannot eat it, he is said to be satisfied neither full nor fasting, and is whipped for being hard to please! I have an abundance of such illustrations of the same principle, drawn from my own observation, but think the cases I have cited sufficient. The practice is a very common one.

On the first of January, 1834, I left Mr. Covey, and went to live with Mr. William Freeland, who lived about three miles from St. Michael's. I soon found Mr. Freeland a very different man from Mr. Covey. Though not rich, he was what would be called an educated southern gentleman. Mr. Covey, as I have shown, was a well-trained negro-breaker and slave-driver. The former (slaveholder though he was) seemed to possess some regard for honor, some reverence for justice, and some respect for humanity. The latter seemed totally insensible to all such sentiments. Mr. Freeland had many of the faults peculiar to slaveholders, such as being very passionate and fretful; but I must do him the justice to say, that he was exceedingly free from those degrading vices to which Mr. Covey was constantly addicted. The one was open and frank, and we always knew where to find him. The other was a most artful deceiver, and could be understood only by such as were skilful enough to detect his cunningly-devised frauds. Another advantage I gained in my new master was, he made no pretensions to, or profession of, religion; and this, in my opinion, was truly a great advantage. I assert most unhesitatingly, that the religion of the south is a mere covering for the most horrid crimes,—a justifier of the most appalling barbarity,—a sanctifier of the most hateful frauds,—and a dark shelter under which the darkest, foulest, grossest, and most infernal deeds of slaveholders find the strongest protection. Were I to be again reduced to the chains of slavery, next to that enslavement, I should regard being the slave of a religious master the greatest calamity that could befall me. For of all slaveholders with whom I have ever met, religious slaveholders are the worst. I have ever found them the meanest and basest, the most cruel and cowardly, of all others. It was my unhappy lot not only to belong to a religious slaveholder, but to live in a community of such religionists. Very near Mr. Freeland lived the Rev. Daniel Weeden, and in the same neighborhood lived the Rev. Rigby Hopkins. These were members and ministers in the Reformed Methodist Church. Mr. Weeden owned, among others, a woman slave, whose name I have forgotten. This woman's back, for weeks, was kept literally raw, made so by the lash of this merciless, *religious* wretch. He used to hire hands. His maxim was, Behave well or behave ill, it is the duty of a master occasionally to whip a slave, to remind him of his master's authority. Such was his theory, and such his practice.

Mr. Hopkins was even worse than Mr. Weeden. His chief boast was his ability to manage slaves. The peculiar feature of his government was that of whipping slaves in advance of deserving it. He always managed to have one or more of his slaves to whip every Monday morning. He did this to alarm their fears, and strike terror into those who escaped. His plan was to whip for the smallest offences, to prevent the commission of large ones. Mr. Hopkins could always find some excuse for whipping a slave. It would astonish one, unaccustomed to a slaveholding life, to see with what wonderful ease a slaveholder can find things, of which to make occasion to whip a slave. A mere look, word, or motion,—a mistake, accident, or want of power,—are all matters for which a slave may be whipped at any time. Does a slave look dissatisfied? It is said, he has the devil in him, and it must be whipped out. Does he speak loudly when spoken to by his master? Then he is getting high-minded, and should be taken down a button-hole lower. Does he forget to pull off his hat at the approach of a white person? Then he is wanting in reverence, and should be whipped for it. Does he ever venture to vindicate his conduct, when censured for it? Then he is guilty of impudence,—one of the greatest crimes of which a slave can be guilty. Does he ever venture to suggest a different mode of doing things from that pointed out by his master? He is indeed presumptuous, and getting above himself; and nothing less than a flogging will do for him. Does he, while ploughing, break a plough,—or, while hoeing, break a hoe? It is owing to his carelessness, and for it a slave must always be whipped. Mr. Hopkins could always find something of this sort to justify the use of the lash, and he seldom failed to embrace such opportunities. There was not a man in the whole county, with whom the slaves who had the getting their own home, would not prefer to live, rather than with this Rev. Mr. Hopkins. And yet there was not a man any where round, who made higher professions of religion, or was more active in revivals—more attentive to the class, love-feast, prayer and preaching meetings, or more devotional in his family,—that prayed earlier, later, louder, and longer,—than this same reverend slave-driver, Rigby Hopkins.

But to return to Mr. Freeland, and to my experience while in his employment. He, like Mr. Covey, gave us enough to eat; but unlike Mr. Covey, he also gave us sufficient time to take our meals. He worked us hard, but always between sunrise and sunset. He required a good deal of work to be done, but gave us good tools with which to work. His farm was large, but he employed hands enough to work it, and with ease, compared with many of his neighbors. My treatment, while in his employment, was heavenly, compared with what I experienced at the hands of Mr. Edward Covey.

Mr. Freeland was himself the owner of but two slaves. Their names were Henry Harris and John Harris. The rest of his hands he hired. These consisted of myself, Sandy Jenkins[4] and Handy Caldwell. Henry and John were quite intelligent, and in a very little while after I went there, I succeeded in creating in them a strong desire to learn how to read. This desire soon sprang up in the others also. They very soon mustered up some old spelling-books, and nothing would do but that I must keep a Sabbath school. I agreed to do so, and accordingly devoted my Sundays to teaching these my loved fellow-slaves how to read. Neither of them knew his letters when I went there. Some of the slaves of the neighboring farms found what was going on, and also availed themselves of this little opportunity to learn to read. It was understood, among all who came, that there must be as little display about it as possible. It was necessary to keep our religious masters at St. Michael's unacquainted with the fact, that, instead of spending the Sabbath in wrestling, boxing, and drinking whisky, we were trying to learn how to read the will of God; for they had much rather see us engaged in those degrading sports, than to see us behaving like intellectual, moral, and accountable beings. My blood boils as I think of the bloody manner in which Messrs. Wright Fairbanks and Garrison West, both class-leaders, in connection with many others, rushed in upon us with sticks and stones, and broke up our virtuous little Sabbath school, at St. Michael's—all calling themselves Christians! humble followers of the Lord Jesus Christ! But I am again digressing.

I held my Sabbath school at the house of a free colored man, whose name I deem it imprudent to mention; for should it be known, it might embarrass him greatly, though the crime of holding the school was committed ten years ago. I had at one time over forty scholars, and those of the right sort, ardently desiring to learn. They were of all ages, though mostly men and women. I look back to those Sundays with an amount of pleasure not to be

4. This is the same man who gave me the roots to prevent my being whipped by Mr. Covey. He was a "clever soul." We used frequently to talk about the fight with Covey, and as often as we did so, he would claim my success as the result of the roots he gave me. This superstition is very common among the more ignorant slaves. A slave seldom dies but that his death is attributed to trickery [Douglass's note].

expressed. They were great days to my soul. The work of instructing my dear fellow-slaves was the sweetest engagement with which I was ever blessed. We loved each other, and to leave them at the close of the Sabbath was a severe cross indeed. When I think that those precious souls are to-day shut up in the prison-house of slavery, my feelings overcome me, and I am almost ready to ask, "Does a righteous God govern the universe? and for what does he hold the thunders in his right hand, if not to smite the oppressor, and deliver the spoiled out of the hand of the spoiler?" These dear souls came not to Sabbath school because it was popular to do so, nor did I teach them because it was reputable to be thus engaged. Every moment they spent in that school, they were liable to be taken up, and given thirty-nine lashes. They came because they wished to learn. Their minds had been starved by their cruel masters. They had been shut up in mental darkness. I taught them, because it was the delight of my soul to be doing something that looked like bettering the condition of my race. I kept up my school nearly the whole year I lived with Mr. Freeland; and, beside my Sabbath school, I devoted three evenings in the week, during the winter, to teaching the slaves at home. And I have the happiness to know, that several of those who came to Sabbath school learned how to read; and that one, at least, is now free through my agency.

The year passed off smoothly. It seemed only about half as long as the year which preceded it. I went through it without receiving a single blow. I will give Mr. Freeland the credit of being the best master I ever had, *till I became my own master.* For the ease with which I passed the year, I was, however, somewhat indebted to the society of my fellow-slaves. They were noble souls; they not only possessed loving hearts, but brave ones. We were linked and interlinked with each other. I loved them with a love stronger than any thing I have experienced since. It is sometimes said that we slaves do not love and confide in each other. In answer to this assertion, I can say, I never loved any or confided in any people more than my fellow-slaves, and especially those with whom I lived at Mr. Freeland's. I believe we would have died for each other. We never undertook to do any thing, of any importance, without a mutual consultation. We never moved separately. We were one; and as much so by our tempers and dispositions, as by the mutual hardships to which we were necessarily subjected by our condition as slaves.

At the close of the year 1834, Mr. Freeland again hired me of my master, for the year 1835. But, by this time, I began to want to live *upon free land* as well as *with Freeland*; and I was no longer content, therefore, to live with him or any other slaveholder. I began, with the commencement of the year, to prepare myself for a final struggle, which should decide my fate one way or the other. My tendency was upward. I was fast approaching manhood, and year after year had passed, and I was still a slave. These thoughts roused me—I must do something. I therefore resolved that 1835 should not pass without witnessing an attempt, on my part, to secure my liberty. But I was not willing to cherish this determination alone. My fellow-slaves were dear to me. I was anxious to have them participate with me in this, my life-giving determination. I therefore, though with great prudence, commenced early to ascertain their views and feelings in regard to their condition, and to imbue their minds with thoughts of freedom. I bent myself to devising ways and means for our escape, and meanwhile strove, on all fitting occasions, to impress them with the gross fraud and inhumanity of slavery. I went first to Henry, next to John, then to the others. I found, in them all, warm hearts and noble spirits. They were ready to hear, and ready to act when a feasible plan should be proposed. This was what I wanted. I talked to them of our want of manhood, if we submitted to our enslavement without at least one noble effort to be free. We met often, and consulted frequently, and told our hopes and fears, recounted the difficulties, real and imagined, which we should be called on to meet. At times we were almost disposed to give up, and try to content ourselves with our wretched lot; at others, we were firm and unbending in our determination to go. Whenever we suggested any plan, there was shrinking—the odds were fearful. Our path was beset with the greatest obstacles; and if we succeeded in gaining the end of it, our right to be free was yet questionable—we were yet liable to be returned to bondage. We could see no spot, this side of the ocean, where we could be free. We knew nothing about Canada. Our knowledge of the north did not extend farther than New York; and to go there, and be forever harassed with the frightful liability of being returned to slavery—with the certainty of being treated tenfold worse than before—the thought was truly a horrible one, and one which it was not easy to overcome. The case sometimes stood thus: At every gate through which we were to pass, we saw a watchman—at every ferry a guard—on every bridge a sentinel—and in every wood a patrol. We were hemmed in upon every side. Here were the difficulties, real or imagined—the good to be sought, and the evil to be shunned. On the one hand, there stood slavery, a stern reality, glaring frightfully upon us,—its robes already crimsoned with the blood of millions, and even now feasting itself greedily upon our own flesh. On the other hand, away back in the dim distance, under the flickering light of the north star, behind some craggy hill or snow-covered mountain, stood a doubtful freedom—half frozen—beckoning us to come and share its hospitality. This in itself was sometimes enough to stagger us; but when we permitted ourselves to survey the road, we were frequently appalled. Upon either side we saw grim death, assuming the most horrid shapes. Now it was starvation, causing us to eat our own flesh;—now we were contending with the waves, and were drowned;—now we were overtaken, and torn to pieces by the fangs of the terrible bloodhound. We were stung by scorpions, chased by wild beasts, bitten by snakes, and finally, after having nearly reached the desired spot,—after swimming rivers, encountering wild beasts, sleeping in the woods, suffering hunger and nakedness,—we were overtaken by our pursuers, and in our resistance, we were shot dead upon the spot! I say, this picture sometimes appalled us, and made us

> "rather bear those ills we had,
> Than fly to others, that we knew not of."[5]

In coming to a fixed determination to run away, we did more than Patrick Henry, when he resolved upon liberty or death. With us it was a doubtful liberty at most, and almost certain death if we failed. For my part, I should prefer death to hopeless bondage.

Sandy, one of our number, gave up the notion, but still encouraged us. Our company then consisted of Henry Harris, John Harris, Henry Bailey,

5. Shakespeare's *Hamlet* 3.1.81–82.

Charles Roberts, and myself. Henry Bailey was my uncle, and belonged to my master. Charles married my aunt: he belonged to my master's father-in-law, Mr. William Hamilton.

The plan we finally concluded upon was, to get a large canoe belonging to Mr. Hamilton, and upon the Saturday night previous to Easter holidays, paddle directly up the Chesapeake Bay. On our arrival at the head of the bay, a distance of seventy or eighty miles from where we lived, it was our purpose to turn our canoe adrift, and follow the guidance of the north star till we got beyond the limits of Maryland. Our reason for taking the water route was, that we were less liable to be suspected as runaways; we hoped to be regarded as fishermen; whereas, if we should take the land route, we should be subjected to interruptions of almost every kind. Any one having a white face, and being so disposed, could stop us, and subject us to examination.

The week before our intended start, I wrote several protections, one for each of us. As well as I can remember, they were in the following words, to wit:—

> "This is to certify that I, the undersigned, have given the bearer, my servant, full liberty to go to Baltimore, and spend the Easter holidays. Written with mine own hand, etc., 1835.
>
> "William Hamilton,
>
> "Near St. Michael's, in Talbot county, Maryland."

We were not going to Baltimore; but, in going up the bay, we went toward Baltimore, and these protections were only intended to protect us while on the bay.

As the time drew near for our departure, our anxiety became more and more intense. It was truly a matter of life and death with us. The strength of our determination was about to be fully tested. At this time, I was very active in explaining every difficulty, removing every doubt, dispelling every fear, and inspiring all with the firmness indispensable to success in our undertaking; assuring them that half was gained the instant we made the move; we had talked long enough; we were now ready to move; if not now, we never should be; and if we did not intend to move now, we had as well fold our arms, sit down, and acknowledge ourselves fit only to be slaves. This, none of us were prepared to acknowledge. Every man stood firm; and at our last meeting, we pledged ourselves afresh, in the most solemn manner, that, at the time appointed, we would certainly start in pursuit of freedom. This was in the middle of the week, at the end of which we were to be off. We went, as usual, to our several fields of labor, but with bosoms highly agitated with thoughts of our truly hazardous undertaking. We tried to conceal our feelings as much as possible; and I think we succeeded very well.

After a painful waiting, the Saturday morning, whose night was to witness our departure, came. I hailed it with joy, bring what of sadness it might. Friday night was a sleepless one for me. I probably felt more anxious than the rest, because I was, by common consent, at the head of the whole affair. The responsibility of success or failure lay heavily upon me. The glory of the one, and the confusion of the other, were alike mine. The first two hours of that morning were such as I never experienced before, and hope never to again. Early in the morning, we went, as usual, to the field. We were spreading manure; and all at once, while thus engaged, I was overwhelmed with an indescribable feeling, in the fulness of which I turned to Sandy, who was near by, and said, "We are betrayed!" "Well," said he, "that thought has this moment struck me." We said no more. I was never more certain of any thing.

The horn was blown as usual, and we went up from the field to the house for breakfast. I went for the form, more than for want of any thing to eat that morning. Just as I got to the house, in looking out at the lane gate, I saw four white men, with two colored men. The white men were on horseback, and the colored ones were walking behind, as if tied. I watched them a few moments till they got up to our lane gate. Here they halted, and tied the colored men to the gate-post. I was not yet certain as to what the matter was. In a few moments, in rode Mr. Hamilton, with a speed betokening great excitement. He came to the door, and inquired if Master William was in. He was told he was at the barn. Mr. Hamilton, without dismounting, rode up to the barn with extraordinary speed. In a few moments, he and Mr. Freeland returned to the house. By this time, the three constables rode up, and in great haste dismounted, tied their horses, and met Master William and Mr. Hamilton returning from the barn; and after talking awhile, they all walked up to the kitchen door. There was no one in the kitchen but myself and John. Henry and Sandy were up at the barn. Mr. Freeland put his head in at the door, and called me by name, saying, there were some gentlemen at the door who wished to see me. I stepped to the door, and inquired what they wanted. They at once seized me, and, without giving me any satisfaction, tied me—lashing my hands closely together. I insisted upon knowing what the matter was. They at length said, that they had learned I had been in a "scrape," and that I was to be examined before my master; and if their information proved false, I should not be hurt.

In a few moments, they succeeded in tying John. They then turned to Henry, who had by this time returned, and commanded him to cross his hands. "I won't!" said Henry, in a firm tone, indicating his readiness to meet the consequences of his refusal. "Won't you?" said Tom Graham, the constable. "No, I won't!" said Henry, in a still stronger tone. With this, two of the constables pulled out their shining pistols, and swore, by their Creator, that they would make him cross his hands or kill him. Each cocked his pistol, and, with fingers on the trigger, walked up to Henry, saying, at the same time, if he did not cross his hands, they would blow his damned heart out. "Shoot me, shoot me!" said Henry; "you can't kill me but once. Shoot, shoot,—and be damned! *I won't be tied!*" This he said in a tone of loud defiance; and at the same time, with a motion as quick as lightning, he with one single stroke dashed the pistols from the hand of each constable. As he did this, all hands fell upon him, and, after beating him some time, they finally overpowered him, and got him tied.

During the scuffle, I managed, I know not how, to get my pass out, and, without being discovered, put it into the fire. We were all now tied; and just as we were to leave for Easton jail, Betsy Freeland, mother of William Freeland, came to the door with her hands full of biscuits, and divided them between Henry and John. She then delivered herself of a speech, to the following effect:—addressing herself to me, she said, "*You devil! You yellow devil!* it was you that put it into the heads of Henry and John to run away. But for you, you long-legged mulatto devil! Henry nor John would never have thought of such a thing." I made no reply, and was immediately hurried off towards St. Michael's. Just a moment previous to the scuffle with Henry, Mr. Hamilton suggested the propriety of making a search for the protections which he had understood Frederick had written for himself and the rest. But, just at the moment he was about carrying his proposal into effect, his aid was needed in helping to tie Henry; and the excitement attending the scuffle caused them either to forget, or to deem it unsafe, under the circumstances, to search. So we were not yet convicted of the intention to run away.

When we got about half way to St. Michael's, while the constables having us in charge were looking ahead, Henry inquired of me what he should do with his pass. I told him to eat it with his biscuit, and own nothing; and we passed the word around, *"Own nothing;"* and *"Own nothing!"* said we all. Our confidence in each other was unshaken. We were resolved to succeed or fail together, after the calamity had befallen us as much as before. We were now prepared for any thing. We were to be dragged that morning fifteen miles behind horses, and then to be placed in the Easton jail. When we reached St. Michael's, we underwent a sort of examination. We all denied that we ever intended to run away. We did this more to bring out the evidence against us, than from any hope of getting clear of being sold; for, as I have said, we were ready for that. The fact was, we cared but little where we went, so we went together. Our greatest concern was about separation. We dreaded that more than any thing this side of death. We found the evidence against us to be the testimony of one person; our master would not tell who it was; but we came to a unanimous decision among ourselves as to who their informant was. We were sent off to the jail at Easton. When we got there, we were delivered up to the sheriff, Mr. Joseph Graham, and by him placed in jail. Henry, John, and myself, were placed in one room together—Charles, and Henry Bailey, in another. Their object in separating us was to hinder concert.

We had been in jail scarcely twenty minutes, when a swarm of slave traders, and agents for slave traders, flocked into jail to look at us, and to ascertain if we were for sale. Such a set of beings I never saw before! I felt myself surrounded by so many fiends from perdition. A band of pirates never looked more like their father, the devil. They laughed and grinned over us, saying, "Ah, my boys! we have got you, haven't we?" And after taunting us in various ways, they one by one went into an examination of us, with intent to ascertain our value. They would impudently ask us if we would not like to have them for our masters. We would make them no answer, and leave them to find out as best they could. Then they would curse and swear at us, telling us that they could take the devil out of us in a very little while, if we were only in their hands.

While in jail, we found ourselves in much more comfortable quarters than we expected when we went there. We did not get much to eat, nor that which was very good; but we had a good clean room, from the windows of which we could see what was going on in the street, which was very much better than though we had been placed in one of the dark, damp cells. Upon the whole, we got along very well, so far as the jail and its keeper were concerned. Immediately after the holidays were over, contrary to all our expectations, Mr. Hamilton and Mr. Freeland came up to Easton, and took Charles, the two Henrys, and John, out of jail, and carried them home, leaving me alone. I regarded this separation as a final one. It caused me more pain than any thing else in the whole transaction. I was ready for any thing rather than separation. I supposed that they had consulted together, and had decided that, as I was the whole cause of the intention of the others to run away, it was hard to make the innocent suffer with the guilty; and that they had, therefore, concluded to take the others home, and sell me, as a warning to the others that remained. It is due to the noble Henry to say, he seemed almost as reluctant at leaving the prison as at leaving home to come to the prison. But we knew we should, in all probability, be separated, if we were sold; and since he was in their hands, he concluded to go peaceably home.

I was now left to my fate. I was all alone, and within the walls of a stone prison. But a few days before, and I was full of hope. I expected to have been safe in a land of freedom; but now I was covered with gloom, sunk down to the utmost despair. I thought the possibility of freedom was gone. I was kept in this way about one week, at the end of which, Captain Auld, my master, to my surprise and utter astonishment, came up, and took me out, with the intention of sending me, with a gentleman of his acquaintance, into Alabama. But, from some cause or other, he did not send me to Alabama, but concluded to send me back to Baltimore, to live again with his brother Hugh, and to learn a trade.

Thus, after an absence of three years and one month, I was once more permitted to return to my old home at Baltimore. My master sent me away, because there existed against me a very great prejudice in the community, and he feared I might be killed.

In a few weeks after I went to Baltimore, Master Hugh hired me to Mr. William Gardner, an extensive ship-builder, on Fell's Point. I was put there to learn how to calk.[6] It, however, proved a very unfavorable place for the accomplishment of this object. Mr. Gardner was engaged that spring in building two large man-of-war brigs, professedly for the Mexican government. The vessels were to be launched in the July of that year, and in failure thereof, Mr. Gardner was to lose a considerable sum; so that when I entered, all was hurry. There was no time to learn any thing. Every man had to do that which he knew how to do. In entering the ship-yard, my orders from Mr. Gardner were, to do whatever the carpenters commanded me to do. This was placing me at the beck and call of about seventy-five men. I was to regard all these as masters. Their word was to be my law. My situation was a most trying one. At times I needed a dozen pair of hands. I was called a dozen ways in the space of a single minute. Three or four voices would strike my ear at the same moment. It was—"Fred., come help me to cant this timber here."—"Fred., come carry this timber yonder."—"Fred., bring that roller here."—"Fred., go get a fresh can of water."—"Fred., come help saw off the end of this timber."—"Fred., go quick, and get the crowbar."—"Fred., hold on the end of this fall."[7]—"Fred., go to the blacksmith's shop, and get a new punch."—"Hurra, Fred.! run and bring me a cold chisel."—"I say, Fred., bear a hand, and get up a fire as quick as lightning under that steam-box."—"Halloo, nigger! come, turn this grindstone."—"Come, come! move, move! and *bowse*[8] this timber forward."—"I say, darky, blast your eyes, why don't you heat up some pitch?"—"Halloo! halloo! halloo!" (Three voices at the same time.) "Come here!—Go

6. Caulk; to seal a boat's cracks and joints against leakage.
7. Nautical term for the free end of a rope of a tackle or hoisting device.
8. To haul the timber by pulling on the rope.

there!—Hold on where you are! Damn you, if you move, I'll knock your brains out!"

This was my school for eight months; and I might have remained there longer, but for a most horrid fight I had with four of the white apprentices, in which my left eye was nearly knocked out, and I was horribly mangled in other respects. The facts in the case were these: Until a very little while after I went there, white and black ship-carpenters worked side by side, and no one seemed to see any impropriety in it. All hands seemed to be very well satisfied. Many of the black carpenters were freemen. Things seemed to be going on very well. All at once, the white carpenters knocked off, and said they would not work with free colored workmen. Their reason for this, as alleged, was, that if free colored carpenters were encouraged, they would soon take the trade into their own hands, and poor white men would be thrown out of employment. They therefore felt called upon at once to put a stop to it. And, taking advantage of Mr. Gardner's necessities, they broke off, swearing they would work no longer, unless he would discharge his black carpenters. Now, though this did not extend to me in form, it did reach me in fact. My fellow-apprentices very soon began to feel it degrading to them to work with me. They began to put on airs, and talk about the "niggers" taking the country, saying we all ought to be killed; and, being encouraged by the journeymen, they commenced making my condition as hard as they could, by hectoring me around, and sometimes striking me. I, of course, kept the vow I made after the fight with Mr. Covey, and struck back again, regardless of consequences; and while I kept them from combining, I succeeded very well; for I could whip the whole of them, taking them separately. They, however, at length combined, and came upon me, armed with sticks, stones, and heavy handspikes. One came in front with a half brick. There was one at each side of me, and one behind me. While I was attending to those in front, and on either side, the one behind ran up with the handspike, and struck me a heavy blow upon the head. It stunned me. I fell, and with this they all ran upon me, and fell to beating me with their fists. I let them lay on for a while, gathering strength. In an instant, I gave a sudden surge, and rose to my hands and knees. Just as I did that, one of their number gave me, with his heavy boot, a powerful kick in the left eye. My eyeball seemed to have burst. When they saw my eye closed, and badly swollen, they left me. With this I seized the handspike, and for a time pursued them. But here the carpenters interfered, and I thought I might as well give it up. It was impossible to stand my hand against so many. All this took place in sight of not less than fifty white ship-carpenters, and not one interposed a friendly word; but some cried, "Kill the damned nigger! Kill him! kill him! He struck a white person." I found my only chance for life was in flight. I succeeded in getting away without an additional blow, and barely so; for to strike a white man is death by Lynch law,[9]—and that was the law in Mr. Gardner's ship-yard; nor is there much of any other out of Mr. Gardner's ship-yard.

I went directly home, and told the story of my wrongs to Master Hugh; and I am happy to say of him, irreligious as he was, his conduct was heavenly, compared with that of his brother Thomas under similar circumstances. He

9. To be subject to lynching, without benefit of legal procedures.

listened attentively to my narration of the circumstances leading to the savage outrage, and gave many proofs of his strong indignation at it. The heart of my once overkind mistress was again melted into pity. My puffed-out eye and blood-covered face moved her to tears. She took a chair by me, washed the blood from my face, and, with a mother's tenderness, bound up my head, covering the wounded eye with a lean piece of fresh beef. It was almost compensation for my suffering to witness, once more, a manifestation of kindness from this, my once affectionate old mistress. Master Hugh was very much enraged. He gave expression to his feelings by pouring out curses upon the heads of those who did the deed. As soon as I got a little the better of my bruises, he took me with him to Esquire Watson's, on Bond Street, to see what could be done about the matter. Mr. Watson inquired who saw the assault committed. Master Hugh told him it was done in Mr. Gardner's ship-yard, at midday, where there were a large company of men at work. "As to that," he said, "the deed was done, and there was no question as to who did it." His answer was, he could do nothing in the case, unless some white man would come forward and testify. He could issue no warrant on my word. If I had been killed in the presence of a thousand colored people, their testimony combined would have been insufficient to have arrested one of the murderers. Master Hugh, for once, was compelled to say this state of things was too bad. Of course, it was impossible to get any white man to volunteer his testimony in my behalf, and against the white young men. Even those who may have sympathized with me were not prepared to do this. It required a degree of courage unknown to them to do so; for just at that time, the slightest manifestation of humanity toward a colored person was denounced as abolitionism, and that name subjected its bearer to frightful liabilities. The watchwords of the bloody-minded in that region, and in those days, were, "Damn the abolitionists!" and "Damn the niggers!" There was nothing done, and probably nothing would have been done if I had been killed. Such was, and such remains, the state of things in the Christian city of Baltimore.

Master Hugh, finding he could get no redress, refused to let me go back again to Mr. Gardner. He kept me himself, and his wife dressed my wound till I was again restored to health. He then took me into the ship-yard of which he was foreman, in the employment of Mr. Walter Price. There I was immediately set to calking, and very soon learned the art of using my mallet and irons. In the course of one year from the time I left Mr. Gardner's, I was able to command the highest wages given to the most experienced calkers. I was now of some importance to my master. I was bringing him from six to seven dollars per week. I sometimes brought him nine dollars per week: my wages were a dollar and a half a day. After learning how to calk, I sought my own employment, made my own contracts, and collected the money which I earned. My pathway became much more smooth than before; my condition was now much more comfortable. When I could get no calking to do, I did nothing. During these leisure times, those old notions about freedom would steal over me again. When in Mr. Gardner's employment, I was kept in such a perpetual whirl of excitement, I could think of nothing, scarcely, but my life; and in thinking of my life, I almost forgot my liberty. I have observed this in my experience of slavery,—that whenever my condition was improved, instead of its increasing my contentment, it only increased my desire to be free, and set me to thinking of plans to gain my freedom. I have found that, to make a contented slave, it is necessary to make a thoughtless one. It is necessary to darken his moral and mental vision, and, as far as possible, to annihilate the power of reason. He must be able to detect no inconsistencies in slavery; he must be made to feel that slavery is right; and he can be brought to that only when he ceases to be a man.

I was now getting, as I have said, one dollar and fifty cents per day. I contracted for it; I earned it; it was paid to me; it was rightfully my own; yet, upon each returning Saturday night, I was compelled to deliver every cent of that money to Master Hugh. And why? Not because he earned it,—not because he had any hand in earning it,—not because I owed it to him,—nor because he possessed the slightest shadow of a right to it; but solely because he had the power to compel me to give it up. The right of the grim-visaged pirate upon the high seas is exactly the same.

Chapter XI

I now come to that part of my life during which I planned, and finally succeeded in making, my escape from slavery. But before narrating any of the peculiar circumstances, I deem it proper to make known my intention not to state all the facts connected with the transaction.[1] My reasons for pursuing this course may be understood from the following: First, were I to give a minute statement of all the facts, it is not only possible but quite probable, that others would thereby be involved in the most embarrassing difficulties. Secondly, such a statement would most undoubtedly induce greater vigilance on the part of slaveholders than has existed heretofore among them; which would, of course, be the means of guarding a door whereby some dear brother bondman might escape his galling chains. I deeply regret the necessity that impels me to suppress any thing of importance connected with my experience in slavery. It would afford me great pleasure indeed, as well as materially add to the interest of my narrative, were I at liberty to gratify a curiosity, which I know exists in the minds of many, by an accurate statement of all the facts pertaining to my most fortunate escape. But I must deprive myself of this pleasure, and the curious of the gratification which such a statement would afford. I would allow myself to suffer under the greatest imputations which evil-minded men might suggest, rather than exculpate myself, and thereby run the hazard of closing the slightest avenue by which a brother slave might clear himself of the chains and fetters of slavery.

I have never approved of the very public manner in which some of our western friends have conducted what they call the *underground railroad*,[2] but which, I think, by their own declarations, has been made most emphatically the *upperground railroad*. I honor those good men and women for their noble daring, and applaud them for willingly subjecting themselves to bloody persecution, by openly avowing their participation in the escape of slaves. I, however, can see very little good resulting from such a course, either to themselves

1. During this period, many free black men worked as sailors. One of these men loaned Douglass free papers and clothes, enabling Douglass to escape from slavery by train and boat. He described his escape in the third and last of his autobiographies, *Life and Times of Frederick Douglass* (1881; rev. ed. 1892).

2. The network of routes, guides, and safe houses by which many slaves escaped to the North, moving by night from one known stopping place to the next, often the homes of abolitionists.

or the slaves escaping; while, upon the other hand, I see and feel assured that those open declarations are a positive evil to the slaves remaining, who are seeking to escape. They do nothing towards enlightening the slave, whilst they do much towards enlightening the master. They stimulate him to greater watchfulness, and enhance his power to capture his slave. We owe something to the slaves south of the line as well as to those north of it; and in aiding the latter on their way to freedom, we should be careful to do nothing which would be likely to hinder the former from escaping from slavery. I would keep the merciless slaveholder profoundly ignorant of the means of flight adopted by the slave. I would leave him to imagine himself surrounded by myriads of invisible tormentors, ever ready to snatch from his infernal grasp his trembling prey. Let him be left to feel his way in the dark; let darkness commensurate with his crime hover over him; and let him feel that at every step he takes, in pursuit of the flying bondman, he is running the frightful risk of having his hot brains dashed out by an invisible agency. Let us render the tyrant no aid; let us not hold the light by which he can trace the footprints of our flying brother. But enough of this. I will now proceed to the statement of those facts, connected with my escape, for which I am alone responsible, and for which no one can be made to suffer but myself.

In the early part of the year 1838, I became quite restless. I could see no reason why I should, at the end of each week, pour the reward of my toil into the purse of my master. When I carried to him my weekly wages, he would, after counting the money, look me in the face with a robber-like fierceness, and say, "Is this all?" He was satisfied with nothing less than the last cent. He would, however, when I made him six dollars, sometimes give me six cents, to encourage me. It had the opposite effect. I regarded it as a sort of admission of my right to the whole. The fact that he gave me any part of my wages was proof, to my mind, that he believed me entitled to the whole of them. I always felt worse for having received any thing; for I feared that the giving me a few cents would ease his conscience, and make him feel himself to be a pretty honorable sort of robber. My discontent grew upon me. I was ever on the look-out for means of escape; and, finding no direct means, I determined to try to hire my time, with a view of getting money with which to make my escape. In the spring of 1838, when Master Thomas came to Baltimore to purchase his spring goods, I got an opportunity, and applied to him to allow me to hire my time. He unhesitatingly refused my request, and told me this was another stratagem by which to escape. He told me I could go nowhere but that he could get me; and that, in the event of my running away, he should spare no pains in his efforts to catch me. He exhorted me to content myself, and be obedient. He told me, if I would be happy, I must lay out no plans for the future. He said, if I behaved myself properly, he would take care of me. Indeed, he advised me to complete thoughtlessness of the future, and taught me to depend solely upon him for happiness. He seemed to see fully the pressing necessity of setting aside my intellectual nature, in order to [insure] contentment in slavery. But in spite of him, and even in spite of myself, I continued to think, and to think about the injustice of my enslavement, and the means of escape.

About two months after this, I applied to Master Hugh for the privilege of hiring my time. He was not acquainted with the fact that I had applied to Master Thomas, and had been refused. He too, at first, seemed disposed to refuse; but, after some reflection, he granted me the privilege, and proposed the following terms: I was to be allowed all my time, make all contracts with those for whom I worked, and find my own employment; and, in return for this liberty, I was to pay him three dollars at the end of each week; find myself in calking tools, and in board and clothing. My board was two dollars and a half per week. This, with the wear and tear of clothing and calking tools, made my regular expenses about six dollars per week. This amount I was compelled to make up, or relinquish the privilege of hiring my time. Rain or shine, work or no work, at the end of each week the money must be forthcoming, or I must give up my privilege. This arrangement, it will be perceived, was decidedly in my master's favor. It relieved him of all need of looking after me. His money was sure. He received all the benefits of slaveholding without its evils; while I endured all the evils of a slave, and suffered all the care and anxiety of a freeman. I found it a hard bargain. But, hard as it was, I thought it better than the old mode of getting along. It was a step towards freedom to be allowed to bear the responsibilities of a freeman, and I was determined to hold on upon it. I bent myself to the work of making money. I was ready to work at night as well as day, and by the most untiring perseverance and industry, I made enough to meet my expenses, and lay up a little money every week. I went on thus from May till August. Master Hugh then refused to allow me to hire my time longer. The ground for his refusal was a failure on my part, one Saturday night, to pay him for my week's time. This failure was occasioned by my attending a camp meeting about ten miles from Baltimore. During the week, I had entered into an engagement with a number of young friends to start from Baltimore to the camp ground early Saturday evening; and being detained by my employer, I was unable to get down to Master Hugh's without disappointing the company. I knew that Master Hugh was in no special need of the money that night. I therefore decided to go to camp meeting, and upon my return pay him the three dollars. I staid at the camp meeting one day longer than I intended when I left. But as soon as I returned, I called upon him to pay him what he considered his due. I found him very angry; he could scarce restrain his wrath. He said he had a great mind to give me a severe whipping. He wished to know how I dared go out of the city without asking his permission. I told him I hired my time, and while I paid him the price which he asked for it, I did not know that I was bound to ask him when and where I should go. This reply troubled him; and, after reflecting a few moments, he turned to me, and said I should hire my time no longer; that the next thing he should know of, I would be running away. Upon the same plea, he told me to bring my tools and clothing home forthwith. I did so; but instead of seeking work, as I had been accustomed to do previously to hiring my time, I spent the whole week without the performance of a single stroke of work. I did this in retaliation. Saturday night, he called upon me as usual for my week's wages. I told him I had no wages; I had done no work that week. Here we were upon the point of coming to blows. He raved, and swore his determination to get hold of me. I did not allow myself a single word; but was resolved, if he laid the weight of his hand upon me, it should be blow for blow. He did not strike me, but told me that he would find me in constant employment in future. I thought the matter over during the next day, Sunday, and finally resolved upon the third day of September, as the day upon which I would make a second attempt to secure my freedom. I now had three weeks during which to prepare for my journey. Early on Monday morning, before Master Hugh had time to make any engagement for me, I went out and got employment of Mr. Butler, at his ship-yard near the drawbridge, upon what is called the City Block, thus making it unnecessary for him to seek employment for me. At the end of the week, I brought him between eight and nine dollars. He seemed very well pleased, and asked me why I did not do the same the week before. He little knew what my plans were. My object in working steadily was to remove any suspicion he might entertain of my intent to run away; and in this I succeeded admirably. I suppose he thought I was never better satisfied with my condition than at the very time during which I was planning my escape. The second week passed, and again I carried him my full wages; and so well pleased was he, that he gave me twenty-five cents, (quite a large sum for a slaveholder to give a slave), and bade me to make a good use of it. I told him I would.

Things went on without very smoothly indeed, but within there was trouble. It is impossible for me to describe my feelings as the time of my contemplated start drew near. I had a number of warm-hearted friends in Baltimore,—friends that I loved almost as I did my life,—and the thought of being separated from them forever was painful beyond expression. It is my opinion that thousands would escape from slavery, who now remain, but for the strong cords of affection that bind them to their friends. The thought of leaving my friends was decidedly the most painful thought with which I had to contend. The love of them was my tender point, and shook my decision more than all things else. Besides the pain of separation, the dread and apprehension of a failure exceeded what I had experienced at my first attempt. The appalling defeat I then sustained returned to torment me. I felt assured that, if I failed in this attempt, my case would be a hopeless one—it would seal my fate as a slave forever. I could not hope to get off with any thing less than the severest punishment, and being placed beyond the means of escape. It required no very vivid imagination to depict the most frightful scenes through which I should have to pass, in case I failed. The wretchedness of slavery, and the blessedness of freedom, were perpetually before me. It was life and death with me. But I remained firm, and, according to my resolution, on the third day of September, 1838, I left my chains, and succeeded in reaching New York without the slightest interruption of any kind. How I did so,—what means I adopted,—what direction I travelled, and by what mode of conveyance,—I must leave unexplained, for the reasons before mentioned.

I have been frequently asked how I felt when I found myself in a free State. I have never been able to answer the question with any satisfaction to myself. It was a moment of the highest excitement I ever experienced. I suppose I felt as one may imagine the unarmed mariner to feel when he is rescued by a friendly man-of-war from the pursuit of a pirate. In writing to a dear friend, immediately after my arrival at New York, I said I felt like one who had escaped a den of hungry lions. This state of mind, however, very soon subsided; and I was again seized with a feeling of great insecurity and loneliness. I was yet liable to be taken back, and subjected to all the tortures of slavery. This in itself was enough to damp the ardor of my enthusiasm. But the loneliness overcame me. There I was in the midst of thousands, and yet a perfect stranger; without home and without friends, in the midst of thousands of my own brethren—children of a common Father, and yet I dared not to unfold to any one of them my sad condition. I was afraid to speak to any one for fear of speaking to the wrong one, and thereby falling into the hands of money-loving kidnappers, whose business it was to lie in wait for the panting fugitive, as the ferocious beasts of the forest lie in wait for their prey. The motto which I adopted when I started from slavery was this—"Trust no man!" I saw in every white man an enemy, and in almost every colored man cause for distrust. It was a most painful situation; and, to understand it, one must needs experience it, or imagine himself in similar circumstances. Let him be a fugitive slave in a strange land—a land given up to be the hunting-ground for slaveholders—whose inhabitants are legalized kidnappers—where he is every moment subjected to the terrible liability of being seized upon by his fellowmen, as the hideous crocodile seizes upon his prey!—I say, let him place himself in my situation—without home or friends—without money or credit—wanting shelter, and no one to give it—wanting bread, and no money to buy it,—and at the same time let him feel that he is pursued by merciless men-hunters, and in total darkness as to what to do, where to go, or where to stay,—perfectly helpless both as to the means of defence and means of escape,—in the midst of plenty, yet suffering the terrible gnawings of hunger,—in the midst of houses, yet having no home,—among fellow-men, yet feeling as if in the midst of wild beasts, whose greediness to swallow up the trembling and half-famished fugitive is only equalled by that with which the monsters of the deep swallow up the helpless fish upon which they subsist,—I say, let him be placed in this most trying situation,—the situation in which I was placed,—then, and not till then, will he fully appreciate the hardships of, and know how to sympathize with, the toil-worn and whip-scarred fugitive slave.

Thank Heaven, I remained but a short time in this distressed situation. I was relieved from it by the humane hand of MR. DAVID RUGGLES,[3] whose vigilance, kindness, and perseverance, I shall never forget. I am glad of an opportunity to express, as far as words can, the love and gratitude I bear him. Mr. Ruggles is now afflicted with blindness, and is himself in need of the same kind offices which he was once so forward in the performance of toward others. I had been in New York but a few days, when Mr. Ruggles sought me out, and very kindly took me to his boarding-house at the corner of Church and Lespenard Streets. Mr. Ruggles was then very deeply engaged in the memorable *Darg* case,[4] as well as attending to a number of other fugitive slaves; devising ways and means for their successful escape; and, though watched and hemmed in on almost every side, he seemed to be more than a match for his enemies.

Very soon after I went to Mr. Ruggles, he wished to know of me where I wanted to go; as he deemed it unsafe for me to remain in New York. I told him I was a calker, and should like to go where I could get work. I thought of going to Canada; but he decided against it, and in favor of my going to New Bedford, thinking I should be able to get work there at my trade. At

3. A black journalist and abolitionist (1810–1849) who aided Douglass in his escape from Maryland, and in whose house Douglass stayed on his way to New Bedford in 1838.

4. In 1839, Ruggles had been arrested for harboring a fugitive slave from the plantation of John P. Darg of Arkansas.

this time, Anna,[5] my intended wife, came on; for I wrote to her immediately after my arrival at New York, (notwithstanding my homeless, houseless, and helpless condition,) informing her of my successful flight, and wishing her to come on forthwith. In a few days after her arrival, Mr. Ruggles called in the Rev. J.W.C. Pennington,[6] who, in the presence of Mr. Ruggles, Mrs. Michaels, and two or three others, performed the marriage ceremony, and gave us a certificate, of which the following is an exact copy:—

> "This may certify, that I joined together in holy matrimony Frederick Johnson[7] and Anna Murray, as man and wife, in the presence of Mr. David Ruggles and Mrs. Michaels.
>
> "James W. C. Pennington
>
> "*New York, Sept.* 15, 1838."

Upon receiving this certificate, and a five-dollar bill from Mr. Ruggles, I shouldered one part of our baggage, and Anna took up the other, and we set out forthwith to take passage on board of the steamboat John W. Richmond for Newport, on our way to New Bedford. Mr. Ruggles gave me a letter to a Mr. Shaw in Newport, and told me, in case my money did not serve me to New Bedford, to stop in Newport and obtain further assistance; but upon our arrival at Newport, we were so anxious to get to a place of safety, that, notwithstanding we lacked the necessary money to pay our fare, we decided to take seats in the stage, and promise to pay when we got to New Bedford. We were encouraged to do this by two excellent gentlemen, residents of New Bedford, whose names I afterward ascertained to be Joseph Ricketson and William C. Taber. They seemed at once to understand our circumstances, and gave us such assurance of their friendliness as put us fully at ease in their presence. It was good indeed to meet with such friends, at such a time. Upon reaching New Bedford, we were directed to the house of Mr. Nathan Johnson, by whom we were kindly received, and hospitably provided for. Both Mr. and Mrs. Johnson took a deep and lively interest in our welfare. They proved themselves quite worthy of the name of abolitionists. When the stage-driver found us unable to pay our fare, he held on upon our baggage as security for the debt. I had but to mention the fact to Mr. Johnson, and he forthwith advanced the money.

We now began to feel a degree of safety, and to prepare ourselves for the duties and responsibilities of a life of freedom. On the morning after our arrival at New Bedford, while at the breakfast-table, the question arose as to what name I should be called by. The name given me by my mother was, "Frederick Augustus Washington Bailey." I, however, had dispensed with the two middle names long before I left Maryland so that I was generally known by the name of "Frederick Bailey." I started from Baltimore bearing the name of "Stanley." When I got to New York, I again changed my name to "Frederick Johnson," and thought that would be the last change. But when I got to New Bedford, I found it necessary again to change my name. The reason of this

5. She was free [Douglass's note]. Anna Murray Douglass (1813–1882) worked as a domestic in Baltimore and had been a member of the East Baltimore Mental Improvement Society before moving to New York to marry Douglass.

6. Like Douglass, Pennington (1807–1890) escaped from slavery in the eastern shore of Maryland. He became an abolitionist and Presbyterian minister, telling his life history in *The Fugitive Blacksmith* (1850).

7. I had changed my name from Frederick *Bailey* to that of *Johnson* [Douglass's note].

necessity was, that there were so many Johnsons in New Bedford, it was already quite difficult to distinguish between them. I gave Mr. Johnson the privilege of choosing me a name, but told him he must not take from me the name of "Frederick." I must hold on to that, to preserve a sense of my identity. Mr. Johnson had just been reading the "Lady of the Lake," and at once suggested that my name be "Douglass."[8] From that time until now I have been called "Frederick Douglass;" and as I am more widely known by that name than by either of the others, I shall continue to use it as my own.

I was quite disappointed at the general appearance of things in New Bedford. The impression which I had received respecting the character and condition of the people of the north, I found to be singularly erroneous. I had very strangely supposed, while in slavery, that few of the comforts, and scarcely any of the luxuries, of life were enjoyed at the north, compared with what were enjoyed by the slaveholders of the south. I probably came to this conclusion from the fact that northern people owned no slaves. I supposed that they were about upon a level with the non-slaveholding population of the south. I knew *they* were exceedingly poor, and I had been accustomed to regard their poverty as the necessary consequence of their being non-slaveholders. I had somehow imbibed the opinion that, in the absence of slaves, there could be no wealth, and very little refinement. And upon coming to the north, I expected to meet with a rough, hard-handed, and uncultivated population, living in the most Spartanlike simplicity, knowing nothing of the ease, luxury, pomp, and grandeur of southern slaveholders. Such being my conjectures, any one acquainted with the appearance of New Bedford may very readily infer how palpably I must have seen my mistake.

In the afternoon of the day when I reached New Bedford, I visited the wharves, to take a view of the shipping. Here I found myself surrounded with the strongest proofs of wealth. Lying at the wharves, and riding in the stream, I saw many ships of the finest model, in the best order, and of the largest size. Upon the right and left, I was walled in by granite warehouses of the widest dimensions, stowed to their utmost capacity with the necessaries and comforts of life. Added to this, almost every body seemed to be at work, but noiselessly so, compared with what I had been accustomed to in Baltimore. There were no loud songs heard from those engaged in loading and unloading ships. I heard no deep oaths or horrid curses on the laborer. I saw no whipping of men; but all seemed to go smoothly on. Every man appeared to understand his work, and went at it with a sober, yet cheerful earnestness, which betokened the deep interest which he felt in what he was doing, as well as a sense of his own dignity as a man. To me this looked exceedingly strange. From the wharves I strolled around and over the town, gazing with wonder and admiration at the splendid churches, beautiful dwellings, and finely-cultivated gardens; evincing an amount of wealth, comfort, taste, and refinement, such as I had never seen in any part of slaveholding Maryland.

Every thing looked clean, new, and beautiful. I saw few or no dilapidated houses, with poverty-stricken inmates; no half-naked children and barefooted women, such as I had been accustomed to see in Hillsborough,

8. Sir Walter Scott's (1771–1832) poem *Lady of the Lake* (1810), a historical romance set in the Scottish highlands in the 16th century. The plot involves the banishment and redemption of the Scottish hero James of Douglas.

Easton, St. Michael's, and Baltimore. The people looked more able, stronger, healthier, and happier, than those of Maryland. I was for once made glad by a view of extreme wealth, without being saddened by seeing extreme poverty. But the most astonishing as well as the most interesting thing to me was the condition of the colored people, a great many of whom, like myself, had escaped thither as a refuge from the hunters of men. I found many, who had not been seven years out of their chains, living in finer houses, and evidently enjoying more of the comforts of life, than the average of slaveholders in Maryland. I will venture to assert that my friend Mr. Nathan Johnson (of whom I can say with a grateful heart, "I was hungry, and he gave me meat; I was thirsty, and he gave me drink; I was a stranger, and he took me in"[9]) lived in a neater house, dined at a better table; took, paid for, and read, more newspapers; better understood the moral, religious, and political character of the nation,—than nine tenths of the slaveholders in Talbot county Maryland. Yet Mr. Johnson was a working man. His hands were hardened by toil, and not his alone, but those also of Mrs. Johnson. I found the colored people much more spirited than I had supposed they would be. I found among them a determination to protect each other from the blood-thirsty kidnapper, at all hazards. Soon after my arrival, I was told of a circumstance which illustrated their spirit. A colored man and a fugitive slave were on unfriendly terms. The former was heard to threaten the latter with informing his master of his whereabouts. Straightway a meeting was called among the colored people, under the stereotyped notice, "Business of importance!" The betrayer was invited to attend. The people came at the appointed hour, and organized the meeting by appointing a very religious old gentleman as president, who, I believe, made a prayer, after which he addressed the meeting as follows: *"Friends, we have got him here, and I would recommend that you young men just take him outside the door, and kill him!"* With this, a number of them bolted at him; but they were intercepted by some more timid than themselves, and the betrayer escaped their vengeance, and has not been seen in New Bedford since. I believe there have been no more such threats, and should there be hereafter, I doubt not that death would be the consequence.

I found employment, the third day after my arrival, in stowing a sloop with a load of oil. It was new, dirty, and hard work for me; but I went at it with a glad heart and a willing hand. I was now my own master. It was a happy moment, the rapture of which can be understood only by those who have been slaves. It was the first work, the reward of which was to be entirely my own. There was no Master Hugh standing ready, the moment I earned the money, to rob me of it. I worked that day with a pleasure I had never before experienced. I was at work for myself and newly-married wife. It was to me the starting-point of a new existence. When I got through with that job, I went in pursuit of a job of calking; but such was the strength of prejudice against color, among the white calkers, that they refused to work with me, and of course I could get no employment.[1] Finding my trade of no immediate benefit, I threw off my calking habiliments, and prepared myself to do any kind of work I could get to do. Mr. Johnson kindly let me have his wood-horse

9. Cf. Matthew 25.35.
1. I am told that colored persons can now get employment at calking in New Bedford—a result of anti-slavery effort [Douglass's note].

and saw, and I very soon found myself a plenty of work. There was no work too hard—none too dirty. I was ready to saw wood, shovel coal, carry the hod, sweep the chimney, or roll oil casks,—all of which I did for nearly three years in New Bedford, before I became known to the anti-slavery world.

In about four months after I went to New Bedford, there came a young man to me, and inquired if I did not wish to take the "Liberator."[2] I told him I did; but, just having made my escape from slavery, I remarked that I was unable to pay for it then. I, however, finally became a subscriber to it. The paper came, and I read it from week to week with such feelings as it would be quite idle for me to attempt to describe. The paper became my meat and my drink. My soul was set all on fire. Its sympathy for my brethren in bonds—its scathing denunciations of slaveholders—its faithful exposures of slavery—and its powerful attacks upon the upholders of the institution—sent a thrill of joy through my soul, such as I had never felt before!

I had not long been a reader of the "Liberator," before I got a pretty correct idea of the principles, measures and spirit of the anti-slavery reform. I took right hold of the cause. I could do but little; but what I could, I did with a joyful heart, and never felt happier than when in an anti-slavery meeting. I seldom had much to say at the meetings, because what I wanted to say was said so much better by others. But, while attending an anti-slavery convention at Nantucket, on the 11th of August, 1841, I felt strongly moved to speak, and was at the same time much urged to do so by Mr. William C. Coffin, a gentleman who had heard me speak in the colored people's meeting at New Bedford.[3] It was a severe cross, and I took it up reluctantly. The truth was, I felt myself a slave, and the idea of speaking to white people weighed me down. I spoke but a few moments, when I felt a degree of freedom, and said what I desired with considerable ease. From that time until now, I have been engaged in pleading the cause of my brethren—with what success, and with what devotion, I leave those acquainted with my labors to decide.

Appendix

I find, since reading over the foregoing Narrative, that I have, in several instances, spoken in such a tone and manner, respecting religion, as may possibly lead those unacquainted with my religious views to suppose me an opponent of all religion. To remove the liability of such misapprehension, I deem it proper to append the following brief explanation. What I have said respecting and against religion, I mean strictly to apply to the *slaveholding religion* of this land, and with no possible reference to Christianity proper; for, between the Christianity of this land, and the Christianity of Christ, I recognize the widest possible difference—so wide, that to receive the one as good, pure, and holy, is of necessity to reject the other as bad, corrupt, and wicked. To be the friend of the one, is of necessity to be the enemy of the other. I love the pure, peaceable, and impartial Christianity of Christ: I therefore hate the corrupt, slaveholding, women-whipping, cradle-plundering, partial and hypo-

2. The first issue of Garrison's the *Liberator* appeared in January 1831. It became the most widely read abolitionist paper during its thirty-five years of publication.

3. Douglass had become a licensed preacher in the African Methodist Episcopal Zion Church in 1839.

critical Christianity of this land. Indeed, I can see no reason, but the most deceitful one, for calling the religion of this land Christianity. I look upon it as the climax of all misnomers, the boldest of all frauds, and the grossest of all libels. Never was there a clearer case of "stealing the livery of the court of heaven to serve the devil in."[4] I am filled with unutterable loathing when I contemplate the religious pomp and show, together with the horrible inconsistencies, which every where surround me. We have men-stealers for ministers, women-whippers for missionaries, and cradle-plunderers for church members. The man who wields the blood-clotted cowskin during the week fills the pulpit on Sunday, and claims to be a minister of the meek and lowly Jesus. The man who robs me of my earnings at the end of each week meets me as a class-leader on Sunday morning, to show me the way of life, and the path of salvation. He who sells my sister, for purposes of prostitution, stands forth as the pious advocate of purity. He who proclaims it a religious duty to read the Bible denies me the right of learning to read the name of the God who made me. He who is the religious advocate of marriage robs whole millions of its sacred influence, and leaves them to the ravages of wholesale pollution. The warm defender of the sacredness of the family relation is the same that scatters whole families,—sundering husbands and wives, parents and children, sisters and brothers,—leaving the hut vacant, and the hearth desolate. We see the thief preaching against theft, and the adulterer against adultery. We have men sold to build churches, women sold to support the gospel, and babes sold to purchase Bibles for the *poor heathen*! *all for the glory of God and the good of souls*! The slave auctioneer's bell and the church-going bell chime in with each other, and the bitter cries of the heart-broken slave are drowned in the religious shouts of his pious master. Revivals of religion and revivals in the slave-trade go hand in hand together. The slave prison and the church stand near each other. The clanking of fetters and the rattling of chains in the prison, and the pious psalm and solemn prayer in the church, may be heard at the same time. The dealers in the bodies and souls of men erect their stand in the presence of the pulpit, and they mutually help each other. The dealer gives his blood-stained gold to support the pulpit, and the pulpit, in return, covers his infernal business with the garb of Christianity. Here we have religion and robbery the allies of each other—devils dressed in angels' robes, and hell presenting the semblance of paradise.

"Just God! and these are they,
Who minister at thine altar, God of right!
Men who their hands, with prayer and blessing, lay
On Israel's ark of light.[5]

"What! preach, and kidnap men?
Give thanks, and rob thy own afflicted poor?
Talk of thy glorious liberty, and then
Bolt hard the captive's door?

"What! servants of thy own
Merciful Son, who came to seek and save

4. From *The Course of Time* (1827), book 8, 616–18, a popular poem by the Scotsman Robert Pollok (1798–1827).

5. The Holy Ark containing the Torah; by extension, the entire body of law as contained in the Old Testament and Talmud.

The homeless and the outcast, fettering down
The tasked and plundered slave!

"Pilate and Herod[6] friends!
Chief priests and rulers, as of old, combine!
Just God and holy! is that church which lends
Strength to the spoiler thine?"[7]

The Christianity of America is a Christianity, of whose votaries it may be as truly said, as it was of the ancient scribes and Pharisees,[8] "They bind heavy burdens, and grievous to be borne, and lay them on men's shoulders, but they themselves will not move them with one of their fingers. All their works they do for to be seen of men.——They love the uppermost rooms at feasts, and the chief seats in the synagogues, ... and to be called of men, Rabbi, Rabbi.——But woe unto you, scribes and Pharisees, hypocrites! for ye shut up the kingdom of heaven against men; for ye neither go in yourselves, neither suffer ye them that are entering to go in. Ye devour widows' houses, and for a pretence make long prayers; therefore ye shall receive the greater damnation. Ye compass sea and land to make one proselyte, and when he is made, ye make him twofold more the child of hell than yourselves.——Woe unto you, scribes and Pharisees, hypocrites! for ye pay tithe of mint, and anise, and cumin, and have omitted the weightier matters of the law, judgment, mercy, and faith; these ought ye to have done, and not to leave the other undone. Ye blind guides! which strain at a gnat, and swallow a camel. Woe unto you, scribes and Pharisees, hypocrites! for ye make clean the outside of the cup and of the platter; but within, they are full of extortion and excess.——Woe unto you, scribes and Pharisees, hypocrites! for ye are like unto whited sepulchres, which indeed appear beautiful outward, but are within full of dead men's bones, and of all uncleanness. Even so ye also outwardly appear righteous unto men, but within ye are full of hypocrisy and iniquity."[9]

Dark and terrible as is this picture, I hold it to be strictly true of the overwhelming mass of professed Christians in America. They strain at a gnat, and swallow a camel. Could any thing be more true of our churches? They would be shocked at the proposition of fellowshipping a *sheep*-stealer; and at the same time they hug to their communion a *man*-stealer, and brand me with being an infidel, if I find fault with them for it. They attend with Pharisaical strictness to the outward forms of religion, and at the same time neglect the weightier matters of the law, judgment, mercy, and faith. They are always ready to sacrifice, but seldom to show mercy. They are they who are represented as professing to love God whom they have not seen, whilst they hate their brother whom they have seen. They love the heathen on the other side of the globe. They can pray for him, pay money to have the Bible put into his hand, and missionaries to instruct him; while they despise and totally neglect the heathen at their own doors.

6. Herod Antipas, ruler of Galilee, ordered the execution of John the Baptist and participated in the trial of Christ. Pontius Pilate was the Roman authority who condemned Christ to death.

7. From Whittier's antislavery poem "Clerical Oppressors" (1835).

8. Members of a Jewish group that insisted on strict observance of written and oral religious laws. The scribes were the Jewish scholars who taught Jewish law and edited and interpreted the Bible. Christ's denunciation of the scribes and Pharisees is reported in Matthew 23.

9. Cf. Matthew 23.4–28.

Such is, very briefly, my view of the religion of this land; and to avoid any misunderstanding, growing out of the use of general terms, I mean, by the religion of this land, that which is revealed in the words, deeds, and actions, of those bodies, north and south, calling themselves Christian churches, and yet in union with slaveholders. It is against religion, as presented by these bodies, that I have felt it my duty to testify.

I conclude these remarks by copying the following portrait of the religion of the south, (which is, by communion and fellowship, the religion of the north,) which I soberly affirm is "true to the life," and without caricature or the slightest exaggeration. It is said to have been drawn, several years before the present anti-slavery agitation began, by a northern Methodist preacher, who, while residing at the south, had an opportunity to see slaveholding morals, manners, and piety, with his own eyes. "Shall I not visit for these things? saith the Lord. Shall not my soul be avenged on such a nation as this?"[1]

A PARODY[2]

"Come, saints and sinners, hear me tell
How pious priests whip Jack and Nell,
And women buy and children sell,
And preach all sinners down to hell,
  And sing of heavenly union.

"They'll bleat and baa, dona like goats,
Gorge down black sheep, and strain at motes,
Array their backs in fine black coats,
Then seize their negroes by their throats,
  And choke, for heavenly union.

"They'll church you if you sip a dram,
And damn you if you steal a lamb;
Yet rob old Tony, Doll, and Sam,
Of human rights, and bread and ham;
  Kidnapper's heavenly union.

"They'll loudly talk of Christ's reward,
And bind his image with a cord,
And scold, and swing the lash abhorred,
And sell their brother in the Lord
  To handcuffed heavenly union.

"They'll read and sing a sacred song,
And make a prayer both loud and long,
And teach the right and do the wrong,
Hailing the brother, sister throng,
  With words of heavenly union.

"We wonder how such saints can sing,
Or praise the Lord upon the wing,
Who roar, and scold, and whip, and sting,

1. Jeremiah's voicing of God's condemnation of the kingdom of Judah (Jeremiah 5.9).

2. Douglass is parodying "Heavenly Union," a hymn sung in Southern churches at the time.

And to their slaves and mammon cling,
  In guilty conscience union.

"They'll raise tobacco, corn, and rye,
And drive, and thieve, and cheat, and lie,
And lay up treasures in the sky,
By making switch and cowskin fly,
  In hope of heavenly union.

"They'll crack old Tony on the skull,
And preach and roar like Bashan[3] bull,
Or braying ass, of mischief full,
Then seize old Jacob by the wool,
  And pull for heavenly union.

"A roaring, ranting, sleek man-thief,
Who lived on mutton, veal, and beef,
Yet never would afford relief
To needy, sable sons of grief,
  Was big with heavenly union.

"'Love not the world,' the preacher said,
And winked his eye, and shook his head;
He seized on Tom, and Dick, and Ned,
Cut short their meat, and clothes, and bread,
  Yet still loved heavenly union.

"Another preacher whining spoke
Of One whose heart for sinners broke:
He tied old Nanny to an oak,
And drew the blood at every stroke,
  And prayed for heavenly union.

"Two others oped their iron jaws,
And waved their children-stealing paws;
There sat their children in gewgaws;
By stinting negroes' backs and maws,
  They kept up heavenly union.

"All good from Jack another takes,
And entertains their flirts and rakes,
Who dress as sleek as glossy snakes,
And cram their mouths with sweetened cakes;
  And this goes down for union."

Sincerely and earnestly hoping that this little book may do something toward throwing light on the American slave system, and hastening the glad day of deliverance to the millions of my brethren in bonds—faithfully relying upon the power of truth, love, and justice, for success in my humble efforts—and solemnly pledging my self anew to the sacred cause,—I subscribe myself,

FREDERICK DOUGLASS

LYNN, Mass., April 28, 1845.

1845

3. Strong bulls mentioned in the Old Testament.

From My Bondage and My Freedom[1]

Life as a Slave

CHAPTER I. THE AUTHOR'S CHILDHOOD

In Talbot county, Eastern Shore, Maryland, near Easton, the county town of that county, there is a small district of country, thinly populated, and remarkable for nothing that I know of more than for the worn-out, sandy, desert-like appearance of its soil, the general dilapidation of its farms and fences, the indigent and spiritless character of its inhabitants, and the prevalence of ague and fever.

The name of this singularly unpromising and truly famine stricken district is Tuckahoe, a name well known to all Marylanders, black and white. It was given to this section of country probably, at the first, merely in derision; or it may possibly have been applied to it, as I have heard, because some one of its earlier inhabitants had been guilty of the petty meanness of stealing a hoe—or taking a hoe—that did not belong to him. Eastern Shore men usually pronounce the word *took*, as *tuck*; *Took-a-hoe*, therefore, is, in Maryland parlance, *Tuckahoe*. But, whatever may have been its origin—and about this I will not be positive—that name has stuck to the district in question; and it is seldom mentioned but with contempt and derision, on account of the barrenness of its soil, and the ignorance, indolence, and poverty of its people. Decay and ruin are everywhere visible, and the thin population of the place would have quitted it long ago, but for the Choptank river, which runs through it, from which they take abundance of shad and herring, and plenty of ague and fever.

It was in this dull, flat, and unthrifty district, or neighborhood, surrounded by a white population of the lowest order, indolent and drunken to a proverb, and among slaves, who seemed to ask, *"Oh! what's the use?"* every time they lifted a hoe, that I—without any fault of mine—was born, and spent the first years of my childhood.

The reader will pardon so much about the place of my birth, on the score that it is always a fact of some importance to know where a man is born, if, indeed, it be important to know anything about him. In regard to the *time* of my birth, I cannot be as definite as I have been respecting the *place*. Nor, indeed, can I impart much knowledge concerning my parents. Genealogical trees do not flourish among slaves. A person of some consequence here in the north, sometimes designated *father*, is literally abolished in slave law and slave practice. It is only once in a while that an exception is found to this statement. I never met with a slave who could tell me how old he was. Few slave-mothers know anything of the months of the year, nor of the days of the month. They keep no family records, with marriages, births, and deaths. They measure the ages of their children by spring time, winter time, harvest time, planting time, and the like; but these soon become undistinguishable and forgotten. Like other slaves, I cannot tell how old I am. This destitution

1. First published in 1855, the source of the present text. *My Bondage and My Freedom* has two sections, "Life as a Slave" and the shorter "Life as a Freeman." This revised and expanded version of Douglass's life history is more than twice as long as the *Narrative* and is introduced by James McCune Smith (1813–1865), a black physician and abolitionist based in New York City.

was among my earliest troubles. I learned when I grew up, that my master—and this is the case with masters generally—allowed no questions to be put to him, by which a slave might learn his age. Such questions are deemed evidence of impatience, and even of impudent curiosity. From certain events, however, the dates of which I have since learned, I suppose myself to have been born about the year 1817.[2]

The first experience of life with me that I now remember—and I remember it but hazily—began in the family of my grandmother and grandfather, Betsey and Isaac Baily. They were quite advanced in life, and had long lived on the spot where they then resided. They were considered old settlers in the neighborhood, and, from certain circumstances, I infer that my grandmother, especially, was held in high esteem, far higher than is the lot of most colored persons in the slave states. She was a good nurse, and a capital hand at making nets for catching shad and herring; and these nets were in great demand, not only in Tuckahoe, but at Denton and Hillsboro, neighboring villages. She was not only good at making the nets, but was also somewhat famous for her good fortune in taking the fishes referred to. I have known her to be in the water half the day. Grandmother was likewise more provident than most of her neighbors in the preservation of seedling sweet potatoes, and it happened to her—as it will happen to any careful and thrifty person residing in an ignorant and improvident community—to enjoy the reputation of having been born to "good luck." Her "good luck" was owing to the exceeding care which she took in preventing the succulent root from getting bruised in the digging, and in placing it beyond the reach of frost, by actually burying it under the hearth of her cabin during the winter months. In the time of planting sweet potatoes, "Grandmother Betty," as she was familiarly called, was sent for in all directions, simply to place the seedling potatoes in the hills; for superstition had it, that if "Grandmamma Betty but touches them at planting, they will be sure to grow and flourish." This high reputation was full of advantage to her, and to the children around her. Though Tuckahoe had but few of the good things of life, yet of such as it did possess grandmother got a full share, in the way of presents. If good potato crops came after her planting, she was not forgotten by those for whom she planted; and as she was remembered by others, so she remembered the hungry little ones around her.

The dwelling of my grandmother and grandfather had few pretensions. It was a log hut, or cabin, built of clay, wood, and straw. At a distance it resembled—though it was much smaller, less commodious and less substantial—the cabins erected in the western states by the first settlers. To my child's eye, however, it was a noble structure, admirably adapted to promote the comforts and conveniences of its inmates. A few rough, Virginia fence-rails, flung loosely over the rafters above, answered the triple purpose of floors, ceilings, and bedsteads. To be sure, this upper apartment was reached only by a ladder—but what in the world for climbing could be better than a ladder? To me, this ladder was really a high invention, and possessed a sort of charm as I played with delight upon the rounds of it. In this little hut there was a large family of children: I dare not say how many. My grandmother—whether because too old for field service, or because she had

2. It is now known that Douglass was born in February 1818.

so faithfully discharged the duties of her station in early life, I know not—enjoyed the high privilege of living in a cabin, separate from the quarter, with no other burden than her own support, and the necessary care of the little children, imposed. She evidently esteemed it a great fortune to live so. The children were not her own, but her grandchildren—the children of her daughters. She took delight in having them around her, and in attending to their few wants. The practice of separating children from their mothers, and hiring the latter out at distances too great to admit of their meeting, except at long intervals, is a marked feature of the cruelty and barbarity of the slave system. But it is in harmony with the grand aim of slavery, which, always and everywhere, is to reduce man to a level with the brute. It is a successful method of obliterating from the mind and heart of the slave, all just ideas of the sacredness of *the family*, as an institution.

Most of the children, however, in this instance, being the children of my grandmother's daughters, the notions of family, and the reciprocal duties and benefits of the relation, had a better chance of being understood than where children are placed—as they often are—in the hands of strangers, who have no care for them, apart from the wishes of their masters. The daughters of my grandmother were five in number. Their names were JENNY, ESTHER, MILLY, PRISCILLA, and HARRIET. The daughter last named was my mother, of whom the reader shall learn more by-and-by.

Living here, with my dear old grandmother and grandfather, it was a long time before I knew myself to be *a slave*. I knew many other things before I knew that. Grandmother and grandfather were the greatest people in the world to me; and being with them so snugly in their own little cabin—I supposed it be their own—knowing no higher authority over me or the other children than the authority of grandmamma, for a time there was nothing to disturb me; but, as I grew larger and older, I learned by degrees the sad fact, that the "little hut," and the lot on which it stood, belonged not to my dear old grandparents, but to some person who lived a great distance off, and who was called, by grandmother, "OLD MASTER." I further learned the sadder fact, that not only the house and lot, but that grandmother herself, (grandfather was free,) and all the little children around her, belonged to this mysterious personage, called by grandmother, with every mark of reverence, "Old Master." Thus early did clouds and shadows begin to fall upon my path. Once on the track—troubles never come singly—I was not long in finding out another fact, still more grievous to my childish heart. I was told that this "old master," whose name seemed ever to be mentioned with fear and shuddering, only allowed the children to live with grandmother for a limited time, and that in fact as soon as they were big enough, they were promptly taken away, to live with the said "old master." These were distressing revelations indeed; and though I was quite too young to comprehend the full import of the intelligence, and mostly spent my childhood days in gleesome sports with the other children, a shade of disquiet rested upon me.

The absolute power of this distant "old master" had touched my young spirit with but the point of its cold, cruel iron, and left me something to brood over after the play and in moments of repose. Grandmammy was, indeed, at that time, all the world to me; and the thought of being separated from her, in any considerable time, was more than an unwelcome intruder. It was intolerable.

Children have their sorrows as well as men and women; and it would be well to remember this in our dealings with them. SLAVE-children *are* children, and prove no exceptions to the general rule. The liability to be separated from my grandmother, seldom or never to see her again, haunted me. I dreaded the thought of going to live with that mysterious "old master," whose name I never heard mentioned with affection, but always with fear. I look back to this as among the heaviest of my childhood's sorrows. My grandmother! my grandmother! and the little hut, and the joyous circle under her care, but especially *she*, who made us sorry when she left us but for an hour, and glad on her return,—how could I leave her and the good old home?

But the sorrows of childhood, like the pleasures of after life, are transient. It is not even within the power of slavery to write *indelible* sorrow, at a single dash, over the heart of a child.

> "The tear down childhood's cheek that flows,
> Is like the dew-drop on the rose,—
> When next the summer breeze comes by,
> And waves the bush,—the flower is dry."[3]

There is, after all, but little difference in the measure of contentment felt by the slave-child neglected and the slaveholder's child cared for and petted. The spirit of the All Just mercifully holds the balance for the young.

The slaveholder, having nothing to fear from impotent childhood, easily affords to refrain from cruel inflictions; and if cold and hunger do not pierce the tender frame, the first seven or eight years of the slave-boy's life are about as full of sweet content as those of the most favored and petted *white* children of the slaveholder. The slave-boy escapes many troubles which befall and vex his white brother. He seldom has to listen to lectures on propriety of behavior, or on anything else. He is never chided for handling his little knife and fork improperly or awkwardly, for he uses none. He is never reprimanded for soiling the table-cloth, for he takes his meals on the clay floor. He never has the misfortune, in his games or sports, of soiling or tearing his clothes, for he has almost none to soil or tear. He is never expected to act like a nice little gentleman, for he is only a rude little slave. Thus, freed from all restraint, the slave-boy can be, in his life and conduct, a genuine boy, doing whatever his boyish nature suggests; enacting, by turns, all the strange antics and freaks of horses, dogs, pigs, and barn-door fowls, without in any manner compromising his dignity, or incurring reproach of any sort. He literally runs wild; has no pretty little verses to learn in the nursery; no nice little speeches to make for aunts, uncles, or cousins, to show how smart he is; and, if he can only manage to keep out of the way of the heavy feet and fists of the older slave boys, he may trot on, in his joyous and roguish tricks, as happy as any little heathen under the palm trees of Africa. To be sure, he is occasionally reminded, when he stumbles in the path of his master—and this he early learns to avoid—that he is eating his "*white bread*," and that he

3. From Sir Walter Scott's (1771–1832) *Rokeby* (1813), canto IV, stanza II.

will be made to *"see sights"* by-and-by. The threat is soon forgotten; the shadow soon passes, and our sable boy continues to roll in the dust, or play in the mud, as bests suits him, and in the veriest freedom. If he feels uncomfortable, from mud or from dust, the coast is clear; he can plunge into the river or the pond, without the ceremony of undressing or the fear of wetting his clothes; his little tow-linen shirt—for that is all he has on—is easily dried; and it needed ablution as much as did his skin. His food is of the coarsest kind, consisting for the most part of corn-meal mush, which often finds its way from the wooden tray to his mouth in an oyster shell. His days, when the weather is warm, are spent in the pure, open air, and in the bright sunshine. He always sleeps in airy apartments; he seldom has to take powders, or to be paid to swallow pretty little sugar-coated pills, to cleanse his blood, or to quicken his appetite. He eats no candies; gets no lumps of loaf sugar; always relishes his food; cries but little, for nobody cares for his crying; learns to esteem his bruises but slight, because others so esteem them. In a word, he is, for the most part of the first eight years of his life, a spirited, joyous, uproarious, and happy boy, upon whom troubles fall only like water on a duck's back. And such a boy, so far as I can now remember, was the boy whose life in slavery I am now narrating.

CHAPTER II. THE AUTHOR REMOVED FROM HIS FIRST HOME

That mysterious individual referred to in the first chapter as an object of terror among the inhabitants of our little cabin, under the ominous title of "old master," was really a man of some consequence. He owned several farms in Tuckahoe; was the chief clerk and butler on the home plantation of Col. Edward Lloyd; had overseers on his own farms; and gave directions to overseers on the farms belonging to Col. Lloyd. This plantation is situated on Wye river—the river receiving its name, doubtless, from Wales, where the Lloyds originated. They (the Lloyds) are an old and honored family in Maryland, exceedingly wealthy. The home plantation, where they have resided, perhaps for a century or more, is one of the largest, most fertile, and best appointed, in the state.

About this plantation, and about that queer old master—who must be something more than a man, and something worse than an angel—the reader will easily imagine that I was not only curious, but eager, to know all that could be known. Unhappily for me, however, all the information I could get concerning him but increased my great dread of being carried thither—of being separated from and deprived of the protection of my grandmother and grandfather. It was, evidently, a great thing to go to Col. Lloyd's; and I was not without a little curiosity to see the place; but no amount of coaxing could induce in me the wish to remain there. The fact is, such was my dread of leaving the little cabin, that I wished to remain little forever, for I knew the taller I grew the shorter my stay. The old cabin, with its rail floor and rail bedsteads up stairs, and its clay floor down stairs, and its dirt chimney, and windowless sides, and that most curious piece of workmanship of all the rest, the ladder stairway, and the hole curiously dug in front of the fire-place, beneath which grandmammy placed the sweet potatoes to keep them from the frost, was MY HOME—the only home I ever had; and I loved it, and all connected with it. The old fences around it, and the stumps in the edge of the woods near it, and the squirrels that ran, skipped, and played upon them, were objects of interest and affection. There, too, right at the side of the hut, stood the old well, with its stately and skyward-pointing beam, so aptly placed between the limbs of what had once been a tree, and so nicely balanced that I could move it up and down with only one hand, and could get a drink myself without calling for help. Where else in the world could such a well be found, and where could such another home be met with? Nor were these all the attractions of the place. Down in a little valley, not far from grandmammy's cabin, stood Mr. Lee's mill, where the people came often in large numbers to get their corn ground. It was a water-mill; and I never shall be able to tell the many things thought and felt, while I sat on the bank and watched that mill, and the turning of that ponderous wheel. The mill-pond, too, had its charms; and with my pin-hook, and thread line, I could get *nibbles*, if I could catch no fish. But, in all my sports and plays, and in spite of them, there would, occasionally, come the painful foreboding that I was not long to remain there, and that I must soon be called away to the home of old master.

I was A SLAVE—born a slave—and though the fact was incomprehensible to me, it conveyed to my mind a sense of my entire dependence on the will of *somebody* I had never seen; and, from some cause or other, I had been made to fear this somebody above all else on earth. Born for another's benefit, as the *firstling* of the cabin flock I was soon to be selected as a meet offering to the fearful and inexorable *demi-god*, whose huge image on so many occasions haunted my childhood's imagination. When the time of my departure was decided upon, my grandmother, knowing my fears, and in pity for them, kindly kept me ignorant of the dreaded event about to transpire. Up to the morning (a beautiful summer morning) when we were to start, and, indeed, during the whole journey—a journey which, child as I was, I remember as well as if it were yesterday—she kept the sad fact hidden from me. This reserve was necessary; for, could I have known all, I should have given grandmother some trouble in getting me started. As it was, I was helpless, and she—dear woman!—led me along by the hand, resisting, with the reserve and solemnity of a priestess, all my inquiring looks to the last.

The distance from Tuckahoe to Wye river—where my old master lived—was full twelve miles, and the walk was quite a severe test of the endurance of my young legs. The journey would have proved too severe for me, but that my dear old grandmother—blessings on her memory!—afforded occasional relief by "toting" me (as Marylanders have it) on her shoulder. My grandmother, though advanced in years—as was evident from more than one gray hair, which peeped from between the ample and graceful folds of her newly-ironed bandana turban—was yet a woman of power and spirit. She was marvelously straight in figure, elastic, and muscular. I seemed hardly to be a burden to her. She would have "toted" me farther, but that I felt myself too much of a man to allow it, and insisted on walking. Releasing dear grandmamma from carrying me, did not make me altogether independent of her, when we happened to pass through portions of the somber woods which lay between Tuckahoe and Wye river. She often found me increasing the energy of my grip, and holding her clothing, lest something should come out of the woods and eat me up. Several old logs and stumps imposed upon me, and got themselves taken for wild beasts. I could see their legs, eyes, and ears, or

I could see something like eyes, legs, and ears, till I got close enough to them to see that the eyes were knots, washed white with rain, and the legs were broken limbs, and the ears, only ears owing to the point from which they were seen. Thus early I learned that the point from which a thing is viewed is of some importance.

As the day advanced the heat increased; and it was not until the afternoon that we reached the much dreaded end of the journey. I found myself in the midst of a group of children of many colors; black, brown, copper colored, and nearly white. I had not seen so many children before. Great houses loomed up in different directions, and a great many men and women were at work in the fields. All this hurry, noise, and singing was very different from the stillness of Tuckahoe. As a new comer, I was an object of special interest; and, after laughing and yelling around me, and playing all sorts of wild tricks, they (the children) asked me to go out and play with them. This I refused to do, preferring to stay with grandmamma. I could not help feeling that our being there boded no good to me. Grandmamma looked sad. She was soon to lose another object of affection, as she had lost many before. I knew she was unhappy, and the shadow fell from her brow on me, though I knew not the cause.

All suspense, however, must have an end; and the end of mine, in this instance, was at hand. Affectionately patting me on the head, and exhorting me to be a good boy, grandmamma told me to go and play with the little children. "They are kin to you," said she; "go and play with them." Among a number of cousins were Phil, Tom, Steve, and Jerry, Nance and Betty.

Grandmother pointed out my brother PERRY, my sister SARAH, and my sister ELIZA, who stood in the group. I had never seen my brother nor my sisters before; and, though I had sometimes heard of them, and felt a curious interest in them, I really did not understand what they were to me, or I to them. We were brothers and sisters, but what of that? Why should they be attached to me, or I to them? Brothers and sisters we were by blood; but *slavery* had made us strangers. I heard the words brother and sisters, and knew they must mean something; but slavery had robbed these terms of their true meaning. The experience through which I was passing, they had passed through before. They had already been initiated into the mysteries of old master's domicile, and they seemed to look upon me with a certain degree of compassion; but my heart clave to my grandmother. Think it not strange, dear reader, that so little sympathy of feeling existed between us. The conditions of brotherly and sisterly feeling were wanting—we had never nestled and played together. My poor mother, like many other slave-women, had *many children*, but NO FAMILY! The domestic hearth, with its holy lessons and precious endearments, is abolished in the case of a slave-mother and her children. "Little children, love one another,"[4] are words seldom heard in a slave cabin.

CHAPTER III. THE AUTHOR'S PARENTAGE

If the reader will now be kind enough to allow me time to grow bigger, and afford me an opportunity for my experience to become greater, I will tell him

4. Jesus' words in John 13.34: "A new commandment I give unto you, That ye love one another; as I have loved you, that ye also love one another."

something, by-and-by, of slave life, as I saw, felt, and heard it, on Col. Edward Lloyd's plantation, and at the house of old master, where I had now, despite of myself, most suddenly, but not unexpectedly, been dropped. Meanwhile, I will redeem my promise to say something more of my dear mother.

I say nothing of *father*, for he is shrouded in a mystery I have never been able to penetrate. Slavery does away with fathers, as it does away with families. Slavery has no use for either fathers or families, and its laws do not recognize their existence in the social arrangements of the plantation. When they *do* exist, they are not the outgrowths of slavery, but are antagonistic to that system. The order of civilization is reversed here. The name of the child is not expected to be that of its father, and his condition does not necessarily affect that of the child. He may be the slave of Mr. Tilgman; and his child, when born, may be the slave of Mr. Gross. He may be a *freeman;* and yet his child may be a *chattel.* He may be white, glorying in the purity of his Anglo-Saxon blood; and his child may be ranked with the blackest slaves. Indeed, he *may* be, and often *is,* master and father to the same child. He can be father without being a husband, and may sell his child without incurring reproach, if the child be by a woman in whose veins courses one thirty-second part of African blood. My father was a white man, or nearly white. It was sometimes whispered that my master was my father.

But to return, or rather, to begin. My knowledge of my mother is very scanty, but very distinct. Her personal appearance and bearing are ineffaceably stamped upon my memory. She was tall, and finely proportioned; of deep black, glossy complexion; had regular features, and, among the other slaves, was remarkably sedate in her manners. There is in "*Prichard's Natural History of Man*," the head of a figure—on page 157—the features of which so resemble those of my mother, that I often recur to it with something of the feeling which I suppose others experience when looking upon the pictures of dear departed ones.[5]

Yet I cannot say that I was very deeply attached to my mother; certainly not so deeply as I should have been had our relations in childhood been different. We were separated, according to the common custom, when I was but an infant, and, of course, before I knew my mother from any one else.

The germs of affection with which the Almighty, in his wisdom and mercy, arms the helpless infant against the ills and vicissitudes of his lot, had been directed in their growth toward that loving old grandmother, whose gentle hand and kind deportment it was the first effort of my infantile understanding to comprehend and appreciate. Accordingly, the tenderest affection which a beneficent Father allows, as a partial compensation to the mother for the pains and lacerations of her heart, incident to the maternal relation, was, in my case, diverted from its true and natural object, by the envious, greedy, and treacherous hand of slavery. The slave-mother can be spared long enough from the field to endure all the bitterness of a mother's anguish, when it adds another name to a master's ledger, but *not* long enough to receive the joyous reward afforded by the intelligent smiles of her child. I never think of this

5. In chapter 1 of the *Narrative*, Douglass says he can barely recall his mother. Here, in his expanded autobiography, he celebrates her strength by linking her to the Egyptian pharaoh Ramses the Great of the 19th dynasty (1304–1237 B.C.E.), as depicted in James Cowles Pritchard's *Natural History of Man* (1848).

terrible interference of slavery with my infantile affections, and its diverting them from their natural course, without feelings to which I can give no adequate expression.

I do not remember to have seen my mother at my grandmother's at any time. I remember her only in her visits to me at Col. Lloyd's plantation, and in the kitchen of my old master. Her visits to me there were few in number, brief in duration, and mostly made in the night. The pains she took, and the toil she endured, to see me, tells me that a true mother's heart was hers, and that slavery had difficulty in paralyzing it with unmotherly indifference.

My mother was hired out to a Mr. Stewart, who lived about twelve miles from old master's, and, being a field hand, she seldom had leisure, by day, for the performance of the journey. The nights and the distance were both obstacles to her visits. She was obliged to walk, unless chance flung into her way an opportunity to ride; and the latter was sometimes her good luck. But she always had to walk one way or the other. It was a greater luxury than slavery could afford, to allow a black slave-mother a horse or a mule, upon which to travel twenty-four miles, when she could walk the distance. Besides, it is deemed a foolish whim for a slave-mother to manifest concern to see her children, and, in one point of view, the case is made out—she can do nothing for them. She has no control over them; the master is even more than the mother, in all matters touching the fate of her child. Why, then, should she give herself any concern? She has no responsibility. Such is the reasoning, and such the practice. The iron rule of the plantation, always passionately and violently enforced in that neighborhood, makes flogging the penalty of failing to be in the field before sunrise in the morning, unless special permission be given to the absenting slave. "I went to see my child," is no excuse to the ear or heart of the overseer.

One of the visits of my mother to me, while at Col. Lloyd's, I remember very vividly, as affording a bright gleam of a mother's love, and the earnestness of a mother's care.

I had on that day offended "Aunt Katy," (called "Aunt" by way of respect,) the cook of old master's establishment. I do not now remember the nature of my offense in this instance, for my offenses were numerous in that quarter, greatly depending, however, upon the mood of Aunt Katy, as to their heinousness; but she had adopted, that day, her favorite mode of punishing me, namely, making me go without food all day—that is, from after breakfast. The first hour or two after dinner, I succeeded pretty well in keeping up my spirits; but though I made an excellent stand against the foe, and fought bravely during the afternoon, I knew I must be conquered at last, unless I got the accustomed reënforcement of a slice of corn bread, at sundown. Sundown came, but *no bread*, and, in its stead, there came the threat, with a scowl well suited to its terrible import, that she "meant to *starve the life out of me*!" Brandishing her knife, she chopped off the heavy slices for the other children, and put the loaf away, muttering, all the while, her savage designs upon myself. Against this disappointment, for I was expecting that her heart would relent at last, I made an extra effort to maintain my dignity; but when I saw all the other children around me with merry and satisfied faces, I could stand it no longer, I went out behind the house, and cried like a fine fellow! When tired of this, I returned to the kitchen, sat by the fire, and brooded over my hard lot. I was too hungry to sleep. While I sat in the corner, I caught sight of an ear of Indian corn on an upper shelf of the kitchen. I watched my chance, and got it, and, shelling off a few grains, I put it back again. The grains in my hand, I quickly put in some ashes, and covered them with embers, to roast them. All this I did at the risk of getting a brutal thumping, for Aunt Katy could beat, as well as starve me. My corn was not long in roasting, and, with my keen appetite, it did not matter even if the grains were not exactly done. I eagerly pulled them out, and placed them on my stool, in a clever little pile. Just as I began to help myself to my very dry meal, in came my dear mother. And now, dear reader, a scene occurred which was altogether worth beholding, and to me it was instructive as well as interesting. The friendless and hungry boy, in his extremest need—and when he did not dare to look for succor—found himself in the strong, protecting arms of a mother; a mother who was, at the moment (being endowed with high powers of manner as well as matter) more than a match for all his enemies. I shall never forget the indescribable expression of her countenance, when I told her that I had had no food since morning; and that Aunt Katy said she "meant to starve the life out of me." There was pity in her glance at me, and a fiery indignation at Aunt Katy at the same time; and, while she took the corn from me, and gave me a large ginger cake, in its stead, she read Aunt Katy a lecture which she never forgot. My mother threatened her with complaining to old master in my behalf; for the latter, though harsh and cruel himself, at times, did not sanction the meanness, injustice, partiality and oppressions enacted by Aunt Katy in the kitchen. That night I learned the fact, that I was not only a child, but *somebody's* child. The "sweet cake" my mother gave me was in the shape of a heart, with a rich, dark ring glazed upon the edge of it. I was victorious, and well off for the moment; prouder, on my mother's knee, than a king upon his throne. But my triumph was short. I dropped off to sleep, and waked in the morning only to find my mother gone, and myself left at the mercy of the sable virago, dominant in my old master's kitchen, whose fiery wrath was my constant dread.

I do not remember to have seen my mother after this occurrence. Death soon ended the little communication that had existed between us; and with it, I believe, a life—judging from her weary, sad, downcast countenance and mute demeanor—full of heart-felt sorrow. I was not allowed to visit her during any part of her long illness; nor did I see her for a long time before she was taken ill and died. The heartless and ghastly form of *slavery* rises between mother and child, even at the bed of death. The mother, at the verge of the grave, may not gather her children, to impart to them her holy admonitions, and invoke for them her dying benediction. The bondwoman lives as a slave, and is left to die as a beast; often with fewer attentions than are paid to a favorite horse. Scenes of sacred tenderness, around the death-bed, never forgotten, and which often arrest the vicious and confirm the virtuous during life, must be looked for among the free, though they sometimes occur among the slaves. It has been a life-long, standing grief to me, that I knew so little of my mother; and that I was so early separated from her. The counsels of her love must have been beneficial to me. The side view of her face is imaged on my memory, and I take few steps in life, without feeling her presence; but the image is mute, and I have no striking words of her's treasured up.

I learned, after my mother's death, that she could read, and that she was the *only* one of all the slaves and colored people in Tuckahoe who enjoyed that advantage. How she acquired this knowledge, I know not, for Tuckahoe is the last place in the world where she would be apt to find facilities for learning. I can, therefore, fondly and proudly ascribe to her an earnest love of knowledge. That a "field hand" should learn to read, in any slave state, is remarkable; but the achievement of my mother, considering the place, was very extraordinary; and, in view of that fact, I am quite willing, and even happy, to attribute any love of letters I possess, and for which I have got—despite of prejudices—only too much credit, *not* to my admitted Anglo-Saxon paternity, but to the native genius of my sable, unprotected, and uncultivated *mother*—a woman, who belonged to a race whose mental endowments it is, at present, fashionable to hold in disparagement and contempt.

Summoned away to her account, with the impassable gulf of slavery between us during her entire illness, my mother died without leaving me a single intimation of *who* my father was. There was a whisper, that my master was my father; yet it was only a whisper, and I cannot say that I ever gave it credence. Indeed, I now have reason to think he was not; nevertheless, the fact remains, in all its glaring odiousness, that, by the laws of slavery, children, in all cases, are reduced to the condition of their mothers. This arrangement admits of the greatest license to brutal slaveholders, and their profligate sons, brothers, relations and friends, and gives to the pleasure of sin, the additional attraction of profit. A whole volume might be written on this single feature of slavery, as I have observed it.

One might imagine, that the children of such connections, would fare better, in the hands of their masters, than other slaves. The rule is quite the other way; and a very little reflection will satisfy the reader that such is the case. A man who will enslave his own blood, may not be safely relied on for magnanimity. Men do not love those who remind them of their sins—unless they have a mind to repent—and the mulatto child's face is a standing accusation against him who is master and father to the child. What is still worse, perhaps, such a child is a constant offense to the wife. She hates its very presence, and when a slaveholding woman hates, she wants not means to give that hast telling effect. Women—white women, I mean—are IDOLS at the south, not WIVES, for the slave women are preferred in many instances; and if these *idols* but nod, or lift a finger, woe to the poor victim: kicks, cuffs and stripes are sure to follow. Masters are frequently compelled to sell this class of their slaves, out of deference to the feelings of their white wives; and shocking and scandalous as it may seem for a man to sell his own blood to the traffickers in human flesh, it is often an act of humanity toward the slave-child to be thus removed from his merciless tormentors.

It is not within the scope of the design of my simple story, to comment upon every phase of slavery not within my experience as a slave.

But, I may remark, that, if the lineal descendants of Ham are only to be enslaved, according to the scriptures, slavery in this country will soon become an unscriptural institution; for thousands are ushered into the world, annually, who—like myself—owe their existence to white fathers, and, most frequently, to their masters, and master's sons. The slave-woman is at the mercy of the fathers, sons or brothers of her master. The thoughtful know the rest.

After what I have now said of the circumstances of my mother, and my relations to her, the reader will not be surprised, nor be disposed to censure me, when I tell but the simple truth, viz: that I received the tidings of her death with no strong emotions of sorrow for her, and with very little regret for myself on account of her loss. I had to learn the value of my mother long after her death, and by witnessing the devotion of other mothers to their children.

There is not, beneath the sky, an enemy to filial affection so destructive as slavery. It had made my brothers and sisters strangers to me; it converted the mother that bore me, into a myth; it shrouded my father in mystery, and left me without an intelligible beginning in the world.

My mother died when I could not have been more than eight or nine years old, on one of old master's farms in Tuckahoe, in the neighborhood of Hillsborough. Her grave is, as the grave of the dead at sea, unmarked, and without stone or stake.

1855

What to the Slave Is the Fourth of July?

Extract from an Oration, at Rochester, July 5, 1852[1]

Fellow Citizens—Pardon me, and allow me to ask, why am I called upon to speak here to-day? What have I, or those I represent, to do with your national independence? Are the great principles of political freedom and of natural justice, embodied in that Declaration of Independence, extended to us? and am I, therefore, called upon to bring our humble offering to the national altar, and to confess the benefits, and express devout gratitude for the blessings, resulting from your independence to us?

Would to God, both for your sakes and ours, that an affirmative answer could be truthfully returned to these questions! Then would my task be light, and my burden easy and delightful. For who is there so cold that a nation's sympathy could not warm him? Who so obdurate and dead to the claims of gratitude, that would not thankfully acknowledge such priceless benefits? Who so stolid and selfish, that would not give his voice to swell the hallelujahs of a nation's jubilee, when the chains of servitude had been torn from his limbs? I am not that man. In a case like that, the dumb might eloquently speak, and the "lame man leap as an hart."[2]

But, such is not the state of the case. I say it with a sad sense of the disparity between us. I am not included within the pale of this glorious anniversary! Your high independence only reveals the immeasurable distance between us. The blessings in which you this day rejoice, are not enjoyed in common. The rich inheritance of justice, liberty, prosperity, and independence, bequeathed by your fathers, is shared by you, not by me. The sunlight that brought life and healing to you, has brought stripes and death to me. This Fourth of July is *yours*, not *mine*. You may rejoice, *I* must mourn. To drag a man in fetters into the grand illuminated temple of liberty, and call upon him to join you in joyous anthems, were inhuman mockery and sacrilegious irony. Do you mean, citizens, to mock me, by asking me to speak to-day? If so, there is a

1. Douglass delivered this Fourth of July address on July 5, 1852, in Rochester, New York, before a racially mixed audience of approximately six hundred people. Later that year he published it as a pamphlet. He first published the "Extract" (several key pages from the longer work) in the appendix to *My Bondage and My Freedom* (1855), the source of the present text.

2. Deer. The quotation is from Isaiah 35.6.

parallel to your conduct. And let me warn you that it is dangerous to copy the example of a nation whose crimes, towering up to heaven, were thrown down by the breath of the Almighty, burying that nation in irrecoverable ruin! I can to-day take up the plaintive lament of a peeled and woe-smitten people.

"By the rivers of Babylon, there we sat down. Yea! we wept when we remembered Zion. We hanged our harps upon the willows in the midst thereof. For there, they that carried us away captive, required of us a song; and they who wasted us required of us mirth, saying, Sing us one of the songs of Zion. How can we sing the Lord's song in a strange land? If I forget thee, O Jerusalem, let my right hand forget her cunning. If I do not remember thee, let my tongue cleave to the roof of my mouth."[3]

Fellow-citizens, above your national, tumultuous joy, I hear the mournful wail of millions, whose chains, heavy and grievous yesterday, are to-day rendered more intolerable by the jubilant shouts that reach them. If I do forget, if I do not faithfully remember those bleeding children of sorrow this day, "may my right hand forget her cunning, and may my tongue cleave to the roof of my mouth!" To forget them, to pass lightly over their wrongs, and to chime in with the popular theme, would be treason most scandalous and shocking, and would make me a reproach before God and the world. My subject, then, fellow-citizens, is AMERICAN SLAVERY. I shall see this day and its popular characteristics from the slave's point of view. Standing there, identified with the American bondman, making his wrongs mine, I do not hesitate to declare, with all my soul, that the character and conduct of this nation never looked blacker to me than on this Fourth of July. Whether we turn to the declarations of the past, or to the professions of the present, the conduct of the nation seems equally hideous and revolting. America is false to the past, false to the present, and solemnly binds herself to be false to the future. Standing with God and the crushed and bleeding slave on this occasion, I will, in the name of humanity which is outraged, in the name of liberty which is fettered, in the name of the constitution and the bible, which are disregarded and trampled upon, dare to call in question and to denounce, with all the emphasis I can command, everything that serves to perpetuate slavery—the great sin and shame of America! "I will not equivocate; I will not excuse;"[4] I will use the severest language I can command; and yet not one word shall escape me that any man, whose judgment is not blinded by prejudice, or who is not at heart a slaveholder, shall not confess to be right and just.

But I fancy I hear some one of my audience say, it is just in this circumstance that you and your brother abolitionists fail to make a favorable impression on the public mind. Would you argue more, and denounce less, would you persuade more and rebuke less, your cause would be much more likely to succeed. But, I submit, where all is plain there is nothing to be argued. What point in the anti-slavery creed would you have me argue? On what branch of the subject do the people of this country need light? Must I undertake to prove that the slave is a man? That point is conceded already. Nobody doubts it. The slaveholders themselves acknowledge it in the enactment of laws for their government. They acknowledge it when they punish disobedience on the part of the slave. There are seventy-two crimes in the

3. Psalms 137.1–6.
4. From "To the Public," an editorial by William Lloyd Garrison in the inaugural issue of his anti-slavery newspaper *The Liberator* (January 1, 1831).

state of Virginia, which, if committed by a black man, (no matter how ignorant he be,) subject him to the punishment of death; while only two of these same crimes will subject a white man to the like punishment. What is this but the acknowledgment that the slave is a moral, intellectual, and responsible being. The manhood of the slave is conceded. It is admitted in the fact that southern statute books are covered with enactments forbidding, under severe fines and penalties, the teaching of the slave to read or write. When you can point to any such laws, in reference to the beasts of the field, then I may consent to argue the manhood of the slave. When the dogs in your streets, when the fowls of the air, when the cattle on your hills, when the fish of the sea, and the reptiles that crawl, shall be unable to distinguish the slave from a brute, then will I argue with you that the slave is a man!

For the present, it is enough to affirm the equal manhood of the negro race. Is it not astonishing that, while we are plowing, planting, and reaping, using all kinds of mechanical tools, erecting houses, constructing bridges, building ships, working in metals of brass, iron, copper, silver, and gold; that, while we are reading, writing, and cyphering, acting as clerks, merchants, and secretaries, having among us lawyers, doctors, ministers, poets, authors, editors, orators, and teachers; that, while we are engaged in all manner of enterprises common to other men—digging gold in California, capturing the whale in the Pacific, feeding sheep and cattle on the hillside, living, moving, acting, thinking, planning, living in families as husbands, wives, and children, and, above all, confessing and worshiping the christian's God, and looking hopefully for life and immortality beyond the grave,—we are called upon to prove that we are men![5]

Would you have me argue that man is entitled to liberty? that he is the rightful owner of his own body? You have already declared it. Must I argue the wrongfulness of slavery? Is that a question for republicans? Is it to be settled by the rules of logic and argumentation, as a matter beset with great difficulty, involving a doubtful application of the principle of justice, hard to be understood? How should I look to-day in the presence of Americans, dividing and subdividing a discourse, to show that men have a natural right to freedom, speaking of it relatively and positively, negatively and affirmatively? To do so, would be to make myself ridiculous, and to offer an insult to your understanding. There is not a man beneath the canopy of heaven that does not know that slavery is wrong *for him.*

What! am I to argue that it is wrong to make men brutes, to rob them of their liberty, to work them without wages, to keep them ignorant of their relations to their fellow men, to beat them with sticks, to flay their flesh with the lash, to load their limbs with irons, to hunt them with dogs, to sell them at auction, to sunder their families, to knock out their teeth, to burn their flesh, to starve them into obedience and submission to their masters? Must I argue that a system, thus marked with blood and stained with pollution, is wrong? No; I will not. I have better employment for my time and strength than such arguments would imply.

What, then, remains to be argued? Is it that slavery is not divine; that God did not establish it; that our doctors of divinity are mistaken? There is blasphemy in the thought. That which is inhuman cannot be divine. Who

5. As suggested by his reference to women and children, Douglass here uses "men" to mean "human."

can reason on such a proposition! They that can, may; I cannot. The time for such argument is past.

At a time like this, scorching irony, not convincing argument, is needed. Oh! had I the ability, and could I reach the nation's ear, I would to-day pour out a fiery stream of biting ridicule, blasting reproach, withering sarcasm, and stern rebuke. For it is not light that is needed, but fire; it is not the gentle shower, but thunder. We need the storm, the whirlwind, and the earthquake. The feeling of the nation must be quickened; the conscience of the nation must be roused; the propriety of the nation must be startled; the hypocrisy of the nation must be exposed; and its crimes against God and man must be proclaimed and denounced.

What to the American slave is your Fourth of July? I answer, a day that reveals to him, more than all other days in the year, the gross injustice and cruelty to which he is the constant victim. To him, your celebration is a sham; your boasted liberty, an unholy license; your national greatness, swelling vanity; your sounds of rejoicing are empty and heartless; your denunciations of tyrants, brass-fronted impudence; your shouts of liberty and equality, hollow mockery; your prayers and hymns, your sermons and thanksgivings, with all your religious parade and solemnity, are to him mere bombast, fraud, deception, impiety, and hypocrisy—a thin veil to cover up crimes which would disgrace a nation of savages. There is not a nation on the earth guilty of practices more shocking and bloody, than are the people of these United States, at this very hour.

Go where you may, search where you will, roam through all the monarchies and despotisms of the old world, travel through South America, search out every abuse, and when you have found the last, lay your facts by the side of the every-day practices of this nation, and you will say with me, that, for revolting barbarity and shameless hypocrisy, America reigns without a rival.

1852, 1855

The Heroic Slave[1]

Part I

Oh! child of grief, why weepest thou?
Why droops thy sad and mournful brow?
Why is thy look so like despair?
What deep, sad sorrow lingers there?[2]

The State of Virginia is famous in American annals for the multitudinous array of her statesmen and heroes. She has been dignified by some the

1. The "heroic slave" is Madison Washington (b. 1815?), who led a slave revolt on the American ship *Creole* on November 7, 1841. The nineteen slaves aboard the ship, who were being transported from Virginia to Louisiana, took control of the *Creole* and diverted it to the Bahamas, where British authorities freed the slaves. The event created tension between the United States and England that was not resolved until 1853, the year Douglass published his novella, when an Anglo-American claims court awarded compensation to the slaves' former owners. Douglass's novella, his only fictional work, provides a fictional prehistory to the revolt. The novella was serialized in three March 1853 issues of *Frederick Douglass' Paper* and was simultaneously printed in a fund-raising antislavery anthology, *Autographs for Freedom* (1853), edited by Douglass's English friend Julia Griffiths. The text followed here is taken from *Autographs*.

2. The epigraph is by Douglass.

mother of statesmen. History has not been sparing in recording their names, or in blazoning their deeds. Her high position in this respect, has given her an enviable distinction among her sister States. With Virginia for his birthplace, even a man of ordinary parts, on account of the general partiality for her sons, easily rises to eminent stations. Men, not great enough to attract special attention in their native States, have, like a certain distinguished citizen[3] in the State of New York, sighed and repined that they were not born in Virginia. Yet not all the great ones of the Old Dominion have, by the fact of their birth-place, escaped undeserved obscurity. By some strange neglect, *one* of the truest, manliest, and bravest of her children,—one who, in after years, will, I think, command the pen of genius to set his merits forth, holds now no higher place in the records of that grand old Commonwealth than is held by a horse or an ox. Let those account for it who can, but there stands the fact, that a man who loved liberty as well as did Patrick Henry,—who deserved it as much as Thomas Jefferson,—and who fought for it with a valor as high, an arm as strong, and against odds as great, as he who led all the armies of the American colonies through the great war for freedom and independence, lives now only in the chattel[4] records of his native State.

Glimpses of this great character are all that can now be presented. He is brought to view only by a few transient incidents, and these afford but partial satisfaction. Like a guiding star on a stormy night, he is seen through the parted clouds and the howling tempests; or, like the gray peak of a menacing rock on a perilous coast, he is seen by the quivering flash of angry lightning, and he again disappears covered with mystery.

Curiously, earnestly, anxiously we peer into the dark, and wish even for the blinding flash, or the light of northern skies to reveal him. But alas! he is still enveloped in darkness, and we return from the pursuit like a wearied and disheartened mother, (after a tedious and unsuccessful search for a lost child,) who returns weighed down with disappointment and sorrow. Speaking of marks, traces, possibles, and probabilities, we come before our readers.

In the spring of 1835, on a Sabbath morning, within hearing of the solemn peals of the church bells at a distant village, a Northern traveller through the State of Virginia drew up his horse to drink at a sparkling brook, near the edge of a dark pine forest. While his weary and thirsty steed drew in the grateful water, the rider caught the sound of a human voice, apparently engaged in earnest conversation.

Following the direction of the sound, he descried, among the tall pines, the man whose voice had arrested his attention. "To whom can he be speaking?" thought the traveller. "He seems to be alone." The circumstance interested him much, and he became intensely curious to know what thoughts and feelings, or, it might be, high aspirations, guided those rich and mellow accents. Tieing his horse at a short distance from the brook, he

3. Douglass is probably referring to New Yorker Martin Van Buren (1782–1862), eighth president of the United States (1837–41) and in 1848 the presidential candidate of the antislavery Free Soil Party. Van Buren infuriated Douglass when he returned to the fold of the Democratic Party and supported the Compromise of 1850, which included a law requiring Northerners to assist in the capturing of runaway slaves.

4. Slave. The Virginia patriot Henry (1738–1799) was famous for his revolutionary declaration: "Give me liberty or give me death."

stealthily drew near the solitary speaker; and, concealing himself by the side of a huge fallen tree, he distinctly heard the following soliloquy:—

"What, then, is life to me? it is aimless and worthless, and worse than worthless. Those birds, perched on yon swinging boughs, in friendly conclave, sounding forth their merry notes in seeming worship of the rising sun, though liable to the sportsman's fowling-piece, are still my superiors. They *live free*, though they may die slaves. They fly where they list by day, and retire in freedom at night. But what is freedom to me, or I to it? I am a *slave*,—born a slave, an abject slave,—even before I made part of this breathing world, the scourge was platted for my back; the fetters were forged for my limbs. How mean a thing am I. That accursed and crawling snake, that miserable reptile, that has just glided into its slimy home, is freer and better off than I. He escaped my blow, and is safe. But here am I, a man,—yes, *a man*!—with thoughts and wishes, with powers and faculties as far as angel's flight above that hated reptile,—yet he is my superior, and scorns to own me as his master, or to stop to take my blows. When he saw my uplifted arm, he darted beyond my reach, and turned to give me battle. I dare not do as much as that. I neither run nor fight, but do meanly stand, answering each heavy blow of a cruel master with doleful wails and piteous cries. I am galled with irons; but even these are more tolerable than the consciousness, the *galling* consciousness of cowardice and indecision. Can it be that I *dare* not run away? *Perish the thought*, I *dare* do any thing which may be done by another. When that young man struggled with the waves *for life*, and others stood back appalled in helpless horror, did I not plunge in, forgetful of life, to save his? The raging bull from whom all others fled, pale with fright, did I not keep at bay with a single pitchfork? Could a coward do that? *No*,—*no*,—I wrong myself,—I am no coward. *Liberty* I will have, or die in the attempt to gain it. This working that others may live in idleness! This cringing submission to insolence and curses! This living under the constant dread and apprehension of being sold and transferred, like a mere brute, is *too* much for me. I will stand it no longer. What others have done, I will do. These trusty legs, or these sinewy arms shall place me among the free. Tom escaped; so can I. The North Star will not be less kind to me than to him. I will follow it. I will at least make the trial. I have nothing to lose. If I am caught, I shall only be a slave. If I am shot, I shall only lose a life which is a burden and a curse. If I get clear, (as something tells me I shall,) liberty, the inalienable birth-right of every man, precious and priceless, will be mine. My resolution is fixed. *I shall be free*."

At these words the traveller raised his head cautiously and noiselessly, and caught, from his hiding-place, a full view of the unsuspecting speaker. Madison (for that was the name of our hero) was standing erect, a smile of satisfaction rippled upon his expressive countenance, like that which plays upon the face of one who has but just solved a difficult problem, or vanquished a malignant foe; for at that moment he was free, at least in spirit. The future gleamed brightly before him, and his fetters lay broken at his feet. His air was triumphant.

Madison was of manly form. Tall, symmetrical, round, and strong. In his movements he seemed to combine, with the strength of the lion, a lion's elasticity. His torn sleeves disclosed arms like polished iron. His face was "black, but comely."[5] His eye, lit with emotion, kept guard under a brow as dark and as glossy as the raven's wing. His whole appearance betokened Herculean strength; yet there was nothing savage or forbidding in his aspect. A child might play in his arms, or dance on his shoulders. A giant's strength, but not a giant's heart was in him. His broad mouth and nose spoke only of good nature and kindness. But his voice, that unfailing index of the soul, though full and melodious, had that in it which could terrify as well as charm. He was just the man you would choose when hardships were to be endured, or danger to be encountered,—intelligent and brave. He had the head to conceive, and the hand to execute. In a word, he was one to be sought as a friend, but to be dreaded as an enemy.

As our traveller gazed upon him, he almost trembled at the thought of his dangerous intrusion. Still he could not quit the place. He had long desired to sound the mysterious depths of the thoughts and feelings of a slave. He was not, therefore, disposed to allow so providential an opportunity to pass unimproved. He resolved to hear more; so he listened again for those mellow and mournful accents which, he says, made such an impression upon him as can never be erased. He did not have to wait long. There came another gush from the same full fountain; now bitter, and now sweet. Scathing denunciations of the cruelty and injustice of slavery; heart-touching narrations of his own personal suffering, intermingled with prayers to the God of the oppressed for help and deliverance, were followed by presentations of the dangers and difficulties of escape, and formed the burden of his eloquent utterances; but his high resolution clung to him,—for he ended each speech by an emphatic declaration of his purpose to be free. It seemed that the very repetition of this, imparted a glow to his countenance. The hope of freedom seemed to sweeten, for a season, the bitter cup of slavery, and to make it, for a time, tolerable; for when in the very whirlwind of anguish,—when his heart's cord seemed screwed up to snapping tension, hope sprung up and soothed his troubled spirit. Fitfully he would exclaim, "How can I leave her? Poor thing! what can she do when I am gone? Oh! oh! 'tis impossible that I can leave poor Susan!"

A brief pause intervened. Our traveller raised his head, and saw again the sorrow-smitten slave. His eye was fixed upon the ground. The strong man staggered under a heavy load. Recovering himself, he argued thus aloud: "All is uncertain here. To-morrow's sun may not rise before I am sold, and separated from her I love. What, then, could I do for her? I should be in more hopeless slavery, and she no nearer to liberty,—whereas if I were free,—my arms my own,—I might devise the means to rescue her."

This said, Madison cast around a searching glance, as if the thought of being overheard had flashed across his mind. He said no more, but, with measured steps, walked away, and was lost to the eye of our traveller amidst the wildering woods.

Long after Madison had left the ground, Mr. Listwell (our traveller) remained in motionless silence, meditating on the extraordinary revelations to which he had listened. He seemed fastened to the spot, and stood half hoping, half fearing the return of the sable preacher to his solitary temple.

5. Song of Solomon 1.5.

The speech of Madison rung through the chambers of his soul, and vibrated through his entire frame. "Here is indeed a man," thought he, "of rare endowments,—a child of God,—guilty of no crime but the color of his skin,—hiding away from the face of humanity, and pouring out his thoughts and feelings, his hopes and resolutions to the lonely woods; to him those distant church bells have no grateful music. He shuns the church, the altar, and the great congregation of christian worshippers, and wanders away to the gloomy forest, to utter in the vacant air complaints and griefs, which the religion of his times and his country can neither console nor relieve. Goaded almost to madness by the sense of the injustice done him, he resorts hither to give vent to his pent up feelings, and to debate with himself the feasibility of plans, plans of his own invention, for his own deliverance. From this hour I am an abolitionist. I have seen enough and heard enough, and I shall go to my home in Ohio resolved to atone for my past indifference to this ill-starred race, by making such exertions as I shall be able to do, for the speedy emancipation of every slave in the land.

Part II

"The gaudy, blabbing and remorseful day
Is crept into the bosom of the sea;
And now loud-howling wolves arouse the jades
That drag the tragic melancholy night;
Who with their drowsy, slow, and flagging wings
Clip dead men's graves, and from their misty jaws
Breathe foul contagions, darkness in the air."

Shakspeare[6]

Five years after the foregoing singular occurrence, in the winter of 1840, Mr. and Mrs. Listwell sat together by the fireside of their own happy home, in the State of Ohio. The children were all gone to bed. A single lamp burnt brightly on the centre-table. All was still and comfortable within; but the night was cold and dark; a heavy wind sighed and moaned sorrowfully around the house and barn, occasionally bringing against the clattering windows a stray leaf from the large oak trees that embowered their dwelling. It was a night for strange noises and for strange fancies. A whole wilderness of thought might pass through one's mind during such an evening. The smouldering embers, partaking of the spirit of the restless night, became fruitful of varied and fantastic pictures, and revived many bygone scenes and old impressions. The happy pair seemed to sit in silent fascination, gazing on the fire. Suddenly this *reverie* was interrupted by a heavy growl. Ordinarily such an occurrence would have scarcely provoked a single word, or excited the least apprehension. But there are certain seasons when the slightest sound sends a jar through all the subtle chambers of the mind; and such a season was this. The happy pair started up, as if some sudden danger had come upon them. The growl was from their trusty watch-dog.

"What can it mean? certainly no one can be out on such a night as this," said Mrs. Listwell.

"The wind has deceived the dog, my dear; he has mistaken the noise of falling branches, brought down by the wind, for that of the footsteps of

6. *The Second Part of King Henry the Sixth* 4.1.1–7.

persons coming to the house. I have several times to-night thought that I heard the sound of footsteps. I am sure, however, that it was but the wind. Friends would not be likely to come out at such an hour, or such a night; and thieves are too lazy and self-indulgent to expose themselves to this biting frost; but should there be any one about, our brave old Monte, who is on the lookout, will not be slow in sounding the alarm."

Saying this they quietly left the window, whither they had gone to learn the cause of the menacing growl, and re-seated themselves by the fire, as if reluctant to leave the slowly expiring embers, although the hour was late. A few minutes only intervened after resuming their seats, when again their sober meditations were disturbed. Their faithful dog now growled and barked furiously, as if assailed by an advancing foe. Simultaneously the good couple arose, and stood in mute expectation. The contest without seemed fierce and violent. It was, however, soon over,—the barking ceased, for, with true canine instinct, Monte quickly discovered that a friend, not an enemy of the family, was coming to the house, and instead of rushing to repel the supposed intruder, he was now at the door, whimpering and dancing for the admission of himself and his newly made friend.

Mr. Listwell knew by this movement that all was well; he advanced and opened the door, and saw by the light that streamed out into the darkness, a tall man advancing slowly towards the house, with a stick in one hand, and a small bundle in the other. "It is a traveller," thought he, "who has missed his way, and is coming to inquire the road. I am glad we did not go to bed earlier,—I have felt all the evening as if somebody would be here to-night."

The man had now halted a short distance from the door, and looked prepared alike for flight or battle. "Come in, sir, don't be alarmed, you have probably lost your way."

Slightly hesitating, the traveller walked in; not, however, without regarding his host with a scrutinizing glance. "No, sir," said he, "I have come to ask you a greater favor."

Instantly Mr. Listwell exclaimed, (as the recollection of the Virginia forest scene flashed upon him,) "Oh, sir, I know not your name, but I have seen your face, and heard your voice before. I am glad to see you. *I know all.* You are flying for your liberty,—be seated,—be seated,—banish all fear. You are safe under my roof."

This recognition, so unexpected, rather disconcerted and disquieted the noble fugitive. The timidity and suspicion of persons escaping from slavery are easily awakened, and often what is intended to dispel the one, and to allay the other, has precisely the opposite effect. It was so in this case. Quickly observing the unhappy impression made by his words and action, Mr. Listwell assumed a more quiet and inquiring aspect, and finally succeeded in removing the apprehensions which his very natural and generous salutation had aroused.

Thus assured, the stranger said, "Sir, you have rightly guessed, I am, indeed, a fugitive from slavery. My name is Madison,—Madison Washington my mother used to call me. I am on my way to Canada, where I learn that persons of my color are protected in all the rights of men; and my object in calling upon you was, to beg the privilege of resting my weary limbs for the night in your barn. It was my purpose to have continued my journey till morning; but the piercing cold, and the frowning darkness compelled me to seek shelter; and, seeing a light through the lattice of your window, I was encouraged to come here to beg the privilege named. You will do me a great favor by affording me shelter for the night."

"A resting-place, indeed, sir, you shall have; not, however, in my barn, but in the best room of my house. Consider yourself, if you please, under the roof of a friend; for such I am to you, and to all your deeply injured race."

While this introductory conversation was going on, the kind lady had revived the fire, and was diligently preparing supper; for she, not less than her husband, felt for the sorrows of the oppressed and hunted ones of earth, and was always glad of an opportunity to do them a service. A bountiful repast was quickly prepared, and the hungry and toil-worn bondman was cordially invited to partake thereof. Gratefully he acknowledged the favor of his benevolent benefactress; but appeared scarcely to understand what such hospitality could mean. It was the first time in his life that he had met so humane and friendly a greeting at the hands of persons whose color was unlike his own; yet it was impossible for him to doubt the charitableness of his new friends, or the genuineness of the welcome so freely given; and he therefore, with many thanks, took his seat at the table with Mr. and Mrs. Listwell, who, desirous to make him feel at home, took a cup of tea themselves, while urging upon Madison the best that the house could afford.

Supper over, all doubts and apprehensions banished, the three drew around the blazing fire, and a conversation commenced which lasted till long after midnight.

"Now," said Madison to Mr. Listwell, "I was a little surprised and alarmed when I came in, by what you said; do tell me, sir, *why* you thought you had seen my face before, and by what you knew me to be a fugitive from slavery; for I am sure that I never was before in this neighborhood, and I certainly sought to conceal what I supposed to be the manner of a fugitive slave."

Mr. Listwell at once frankly disclosed the secret; describing the place where he first saw him; rehearsing the language which he (Madison) had used; referring to the effect which his manner and speech had made upon him; declaring the resolution he there formed to be an abolitionist; telling how often he had spoken of the circumstance, and the deep concern he had ever since felt to know what had become of him; and whether he had carried out the purpose to make his escape, as in the woods he declared he would do.

"Ever since that morning," said Mr. Listwell, "you have seldom been absent from my mind, and though now I did not dare to hope that I should ever see you again, I have often wished that such might be my fortune; for, from that hour, your face seemed to be daguerreotyped on my memory."

Madison looked quite astonished, and felt amazed at the narration to which he had listened. After recovering himself he said, "I well remember that morning, and the bitter anguish that wrung my heart; I will state the occasion of it. I had, on the previous Saturday, suffered a cruel lashing; had been tied up to the limb of a tree, with my feet chained together, and a heavy iron bar placed between my ankles. Thus suspended, I received on my naked back forty stripes, and was kept in this distressing position three or four hours, and was then let down, only to have my torture increased; for my bleeding back, gashed by the cow-skin, was washed by the overseer with old brine, partly to augment my suffering, and partly, as he said, to prevent inflammation. My crime was that I had stayed longer at the mill, the day previous, than it was thought I ought to have done, which, I assured my master and the overseer, was no fault of mine; but no excuses were allowed. 'Hold your tongue, you impudent rascal,' met my every explanation. Slave-holders are so imperious when their passions are excited, as to construe every word of the slave into insolence. I could do nothing but submit to the agonizing infliction. Smarting still from the wounds, as well as from the consciousness of being whipt for no cause, I took advantage of the absence of my master, who had gone to church, to spend the time in the woods, and brood over my wretched lot. Oh, sir, I remember it well,—and can never forget it."

"But this was five years ago; where have you been since?"

"I will try to tell you," said Madison. "Just four weeks after that Sabbath morning, I gathered up the few rags of clothing I had, and started, as I supposed, for the North and for freedom. I must not stop to describe my feelings on taking this step. It seemed like taking a leap into the dark. The thought of leaving my poor wife and two little children caused me indescribable anguish; but consoling myself with the reflection that once free, I could, possibly, devise ways and means to gain their freedom also, I nerved myself up to make the attempt. I started, but ill-luck attended me; for after being out a whole week, strange to say, I still found myself on my master's grounds; the third night after being out, a season of clouds and rain set in, wholly preventing me from seeing the North Star, which I had trusted as my guide, not dreaming that clouds might intervene between us.

"This circumstance was fatal to my project, for in losing my star, I lost my way; so when I supposed I was far towards the North, and had almost gained my freedom, I discovered myself at the very point from which I had started. It was a severe trial, for I arrived at home in great destitution; my feet were sore, and in travelling in the dark, I had dashed my foot against a stump, and started a nail, and lamed myself. I was wet and cold; one week had exhausted all my stores; and when I landed on my master's plantation, with all my work to do over again,—hungry, tired, lame, and bewildered,—I almost cursed the day that I was born. In this extremity I approached the quarters. I did so stealthily, although in my desperation I hardly cared whether I was discovered or not. Peeping through the rents of the quarters, I saw my fellow-slaves seated by a warm fire, merrily passing away the time, as though their hearts knew no sorrow. Although I envied their seeming contentment, all wretched as I was, I despised the cowardly acquiescence in their own degradation which it implied, and felt a kind of pride and glory in my own desperate lot. I dared not enter the quarters,—for where there is seeming contentment with slavery, there is certain treachery to freedom. I proceeded towards the great house, in the hope of catching a glimpse of my poor wife, whom I knew might be trusted with my secrets even on the scaffold. Just as I reached the fence which divided the field from the garden, I saw a woman in the yard, who in the darkness I took to be my wife; but a nearer approach told me it was not she. I was about to speak; had I done so, I would not have been here this night; for an alarm would have been sounded, and the hunters been put on my track. Here were hunger, cold, thirst, disappointment, and chagrin, confronted only by the dim hope of liberty. I tremble to think of that dreadful hour. To face the deadly cannon's mouth in warm blood unterrified, is, I think, a small achievement, compared with a conflict like this with gaunt starvation. The gnawings of hunger conquers by degrees, till all that a man has he would give in exchange for a single crust of bread. Thank God, I was not quite reduced to this extremity.

"Happily for me, before the fatal moment of utter despair, my good wife made her appearance in the yard. It was she; I knew her step. All was well now. I was, however, afraid to speak, lest I should frighten her. Yet speak I did; and, to my great joy, my voice was known. Our meeting can be more easily imagined than described. For a time hunger, thirst, weariness, and lameness were forgotten. But it was soon necessary for her to return to the house. She being a house-servant, her absence from the kitchen, if discovered, might have excited suspicion. Our parting was like tearing the flesh from my bones; yet it was the part of wisdom for her to go. She left me with the purpose of meeting me at midnight in the very forest where you last saw me. She knew the place well, as one of my melancholy resorts, and could easily find it, though the night was dark.

"I hastened away, therefore, and concealed myself, to await the arrival of my good angel. As I lay there among the leaves, I was strongly tempted to return again to the house of my master and give myself up; but remembering my solemn pledge on that memorable Sunday morning, I was able to linger out the two long hours between ten and midnight. I may well call them long hours. I have endured much hardship; I have encountered many perils; but the anxiety of those two hours, was the bitterest I ever experienced. True to her word, my wife came laden with provisions, and we sat down on the side of a log, at that dark and lonesome hour of the night. I cannot say we talked; our feelings were too great for that; yet we came to an understanding that I should make the woods my home, for if I gave myself up, I should be whipped and sold away; and if I started for the North, I should leave a wife doubly dear to me. We mutually determined, therefore, that I should remain in the vicinity. In the dismal swamps[7] I lived, sir, five long years,—a cave for my home during the day. I wandered about at night with the wolf and the bear,—sustained by the promise that my good Susan would meet me in the pine woods at least once a week. This promise was redeemed, I assure you, to the letter, greatly to my relief. I had partly become contented with my mode of life, and had made up my mind to spend my days there; but the wilderness that sheltered me thus long took fire, and refused longer to be my hiding-place.

"I will not harrow up your feelings by portraying the terrific scene of this awful conflagration. There is nothing to which I can liken it. It was horribly and indescribably grand. The whole world seemed on fire, and it appeared to me that the day of judgment had come; that the burning bowels of the earth had burst forth, and that the end of all things was at hand. Bears and wolves, scorched from their mysterious hiding-places in the earth, and all the wild inhabitants of the untrodden forest, filled with a common dismay, ran forth, yelling, howling, bewildered amidst the smoke and flame. The very heavens seemed to rain down fire through the towering trees; it was by

7. Swamp of over six hundred square miles stretching from Virginia to North Carolina. At the time, it was a refuge for fugitive slaves.

the merest chance that I escaped the devouring element. Running before it, and stopping occasionally to take breath, I looked back to behold its frightful ravages, and to drink in its savage magnificence. It was awful, thrilling, solemn, beyond compare. When aided by the fitful wind, the merciless tempest of fire swept on, sparkling, creaking, cracking, curling, roaring, outdoing in its dreadful splendor a thousand thunderstorms at once. From tree to tree it leaped, swallowing them up in its lurid, baleful glare; and leaving them leafless, limbless, charred, and lifeless behind. The scene was overwhelming, stunning,—nothing was spared,—cattle, tame and wild, herds of swine and of deer, wild beasts of every name and kind,—huge night-birds, bats, and owls, that had retired to their homes in lofty tree-tops to rest, perished in that fiery storm. The long-winged buzzard and croaking raven mingled their dismal cries with those of the countless myriads of small birds that rose up to the skies, and were lost to the sight in clouds of smoke and flame. Oh, I shudder when I think of it! Many a poor wandering fugitive, who, like myself, had sought among wild beasts the mercy denied by our fellow men, saw, in helpless consternation, his dwelling-place and city of refuge reduced to ashes forever. It was this grand conflagration that drove me hither; I ran alike from fire and from slavery."

After a slight pause, (for both speaker and hearers were deeply moved by the above recital,) Mr. Listwell, addressing Madison, said. "If it does not weary you too much, do tell us something of your journeyings since this disastrous burning,—we are deeply interested in everything which can throw light on the hardships of persons escaping from slavery; we could hear you talk all night; are there no incidents that you could relate of your travels hither? or are they such that you do not like to mention them."

"For the most part, sir, my course has been uninterrupted; and, considering the circumstances, at times even pleasant. I have suffered little for want of food; but I need not tell you how I got it. Your moral code may differ from mine, as your customs and usages are different. The fact is, sir, during my flight, I felt myself robbed by society of all my just rights; that I was in an enemy's land, who sought both my life and my liberty. They had transformed me into a brute; made merchandise of my body, and, for all the purposes of my flight, turned day into night,—and guided by my own necessities, and in contempt of their conventionalities, I did not scruple to take bread where I could get it."

"And just there you were right," said Mr. Listwell; "I once had doubts on this point myself, but a conversation with Gerrit Smith,[8] (a man, by the way, that I wish you could see, for he is a devoted friend of your race, and I know he would receive you gladly,) put an end to all my doubts on this point. But do not let me interrupt you."

"I had but one narrow escape during my whole journey," said Madison.

"Do let us hear of it," said Mr. Listwell.

"Two weeks ago," continued Madison, "after travelling all night, I was overtaken by daybreak, in what seemed to me an almost interminable wood. I deemed it unsafe to go farther, and, as usual, I looked around for a suitable

8. The New York antislavery reformer (1797–1874) who helped organize the Liberty Party and was elected to Congress in 1853.

tree in which to spend the day. I liked one with a bushy top, and found one just to my mind. Up I climbed, and hiding myself as well as I could, I, with this strap, (pulling one out of his old coat-pocket,) lashed myself to a bough, and flattered myself that I should get a *good night's* sleep that day; but in this I was soon disappointed. I had scarcely got fastened to my natural hammock, when I heard the voices of a number of persons, apparently approaching the part of the woods where I was. Upon my word, sir, I dreaded more these human voices than I should have done those of wild beasts. I was at a loss to know what to do. If I descended, I should probably be discovered by the men; and if they had dogs I should, doubtless, be *'treed.'* It was an anxious moment, but hardships and dangers have been the accompaniments of my life; and have, perhaps, imparted to me a certain hardness of character, which, to some extent, adapts me to them. In my present predicament, I decided to hold my place in the tree-top, and abide the consequences. But here I must disappoint you; for the men, who were all colored, halted at least a hundred yards from me, and began with their axes, in right good earnest, to attack the trees. The sound of their laughing axes was like the report of as many well-charged pistols. By and by there came down at least a dozen trees with a terrible crash. They leaped upon the fallen trees with an air of victory. I could see no dog with them, and felt myself comparatively safe, though I could not forget the possibility that some freak or fancy might bring the axe a little nearer my dwelling than comported with my safety.

"There was no sleep for me that day, and I wished for night. You may imagine that the thought of having the tree attacked under me was far from agreeable, and that it very easily kept me on the look-out. The day was not without diversion. The men at work seemed to be a gay set; and they would often make the woods resound with that uncontrolled laughter for which we, as a race, are remarkable. I held my place in the tree till sunset,—saw the men put on their jackets to be off. I observed that all left the ground except one, whom I saw sitting on the side of a stump, with his head bowed, and his eyes apparently fixed on the ground. I became interested in him. After sitting in the position to which I have alluded ten or fifteen minutes, he left the stump, walked directly towards the tree in which I was secreted, and halted almost under the same. He stood for a moment and looked around, deliberately and reverently took off his hat, by which I saw that he was a man in the evening of life, slightly bald and quite gray. After laying down his hat carefully, he knelt and prayed aloud, and such a prayer, the most fervent, earnest, and solemn, to which I think I ever listened. After reverently addressing the Almighty, as the all-wise, all-good, and the common Father of all mankind, he besought God for grace, for strength, to bear up under, and to endure, as a good soldier, all the hardships and trials which beset the journey of life, and to enable him to live in a manner which accorded with the gospel of Christ. His soul now broke out in humble supplication for deliverance from bondage. 'O thou,' said he, 'that hearest the raven's cry, take pity on poor me! O deliver me! O deliver me! in mercy, O God, deliver me from the chains and manifold hardships of slavery! With thee, O Father, all things are possible. Thou canst stand and measure the earth. Thou hast beheld and drove asunder the nations,—all power is in thy hand,—thou didst say of old, "I have seen the affliction of my people, and am come to deliver them,"—Oh look down upon our afflictions, and have mercy upon us.' But I cannot repeat his prayer, nor can I give you an idea of its deep pathos. I had given but little attention to religion, and had but little faith in it; yet, as the old man prayed, I felt almost like coming down and kneel by his side, and mingle my broken complaint with his.

"He had already gained my confidence; as how could it be otherwise? I knew enough of religion to know that the man who prays in secret is far more likely to be sincere than he who loves to pray standing in the street, or in the great congregation. When he arose from his knees, like another Zacheus,[9] I came down from the tree. He seemed a little alarmed at first, but I told him my story, and the good man embraced me in his arms, and assured me of his sympathy.

"I was now about out of provisions, and thought I might safely ask him to help me replenish my store. He said he had no money; but if he had, he would freely give it me. I told him I had *one dollar*; it was all the money I had in the world. I gave it to him, and asked him to purchase some crackers and cheese, and to kindly bring me the balance; that I would remain in or near that place, and would come to him on his return, if he would whistle. He was gone only about an hour. Meanwhile, from some cause or other, I know not what, (but as you shall see very wisely,) I changed my place. On his return I started to meet him; but it seemed as if the shadow of approaching danger fell upon my spirit, and checked my progress. In a very few minutes, closely on the heels of the old man, I distinctly saw *fourteen men*, with something like guns in their hands."

"Oh! the old wretch!" exclaimed Mrs. Listwell, "he had betrayed you, had he?"

"I think not," said Madison, "I cannot believe that the old man was to blame. He probably went into a store, asked for the articles for which I sent, and presented the bill I gave him; and it is so unusual for slaves in the country to have money, that fact, doubtless, excited suspicion, and gave rise to inquiry. I can easily believe that the truthfulness of the old man's character compelled him to disclose the facts; and thus were these blood-thirsty men put on my track. Of course I did not present myself; but hugged my hiding-place securely. If discovered and attacked, I resolved to sell my life as dearly as possible.

"After searching about the woods silently for a time, the whole company gathered around the old man; one charged him with lying, and called him an old villain; said he was a thief; charged him with stealing money; said if he did not instantly tell where he got it, they would take the shirt from his old back, and give him thirty-nine lashes.

"'I did *not* steal the money,' said the old man, 'it was given me, as I told you at the store; and if the man who gave it me is not here, it is not my fault.'

"'Hush! you lying old rascal; we'll make you smart for it. You shall not leave this spot until you have told where you got that money.'

"They now took hold of him, and began to strip him; while others went to get sticks with which to beat him. I felt, at the moment, like rushing out in the

9. The tax collector Zacchaeus climbed a tree to view Jesus. After Jesus recognized him and offered his love, Zacchaeus publicly repented for his corruption (Luke 19.1–10).

midst of them; but considering that the old man would be whipped the more for having aided a fugitive slave, and that, perhaps, in the *melée*[1] he might be killed outright, I disobeyed this impulse. They tied him to a tree, and began to whip him. My own flesh crept at every blow, and I seem to hear the old man's piteous cries even now. They laid thirty-nine lashes on his bare back, and were going to repeat that number, when one of the company besought his comrades to desist. 'You'll kill the d—d old scoundrel! You've already whipt a dollar's worth out of him, even if he stole it!' 'O yes,' said another, 'let him down. He'll never tell us another lie, I'll warrant ye!' With this, one of the company untied the old man, and bid him go about his business.

The old man left, but the company remained as much as an hour, scouring the woods. Round and round they went, turning up the underbrush, and peering about like so many bloodhounds. Two or three times they came within six feet of where I lay. I tell you I held my stick with a firmer grasp than I did in coming up to your house tonight. I expected to level one of them at least. Fortunately, however, I eluded their pursuit, and they left me alone in the woods.

"My last dollar was now gone, and you may well suppose I felt the loss of it; but the thought of being once again free to pursue my journey, prevented that depression which a sense of destitution causes; so swinging my little bundle on my back, I caught a glimpse of the *Great Bear*[2] (which ever points the way to my beloved star,) and I started again on my journey. What I lost in money I made up at a hen-roost that same night, upon which I fortunately came."

"But you did'nt eat your food raw? How did you cook it?" said Mrs. Listwell.

"O no, Madam," said Madison, turning to his little bundle;—"I had the means of cooking." Here he took out of his bundle an old-fashioned tinder-box, and taking up a piece of a file, which he brought with him, he struck it with a heavy flint, and brought out at least a dozen sparks at once. "I have had this old box," said he, "more than five years. It is the *only* property saved from the fire in the dismal swamp. It has done me good service. It has given me the means of broiling many a chicken!"

It seemed quite a relief to Mrs. Listwell to know that Madison had, at least, lived upon cooked food. Women have a perfect horror of eating uncooked food.

By this time thoughts of what was best to be done about getting Madison to Canada, began to trouble Mr. Listwell; for the laws of Ohio were very stringent against any one who should aid, or who were found aiding a slave to escape through that State. A citizen, for the simple act of taking a fugitive slave in his carriage, had just been stripped of all his property, and thrown penniless upon the world. Notwithstanding this, Mr. Listwell was determined to see Madison safely on his way to Canada. "Give yourself no uneasiness," said he to Madison, "for if it cost my farm, I shall see you safely out of the States, and on your way to a land of liberty. Thank God that there is *such* a land so near us! You will spend to-morrow with us, and to-morrow night I will take you in my carriage to the Lake. Once upon that, and you are safe."

1. Fight (French).
2. Group of stars commonly called the Big Dipper. An imaginary line running out of the cup of the Big Dipper points to the North Star, which many fugitive slaves used to guide themselves to the North.

"Thank you! thank you," said the fugitive; "I will commit myself to your care."

For the *first* time during *five* years, Madison enjoyed the luxury of resting his limbs on a comfortable bed, and inside a human habitation. Looking at the white sheets, he said to Mr. Listwell, "What, sir! you don't mean that I shall sleep in that bed?"

"Oh yes, oh yes."

After Mr. Listwell left the room, Madison said he really hesitated whether or not he should lie on the floor; for that was *far* more comfortable and inviting than any bed to which he had been used.

We pass over the thoughts and feelings, the hopes and fears, the plans and purposes, that revolved in the mind of Madison during the day that he was secreted at the house of Mr. Listwell. The reader will be content to know that nothing occurred to endanger his liberty, or to excite alarm. Many were the little attentions bestowed upon him in his quiet retreat and hiding-place. In the evening, Mr. Listwell, after treating Madison to a new suit of winter clothes, and replenishing his exhausted purse with five dollars, all in silver, brought out his two-horse wagon, well provided with buffaloes, and silently started off with him to Cleveland. They arrived there without interruption, a few minutes before sunrise the next morning. Fortunately the steamer Admiral lay at the wharf, and was to start for Canada at nine o'clock. Here the last anticipated danger was surmounted. It was feared that just at this point the hunters of men might be on the look-out, and, possibly, pounce upon their victim. Mr. Listwell saw the captain of the boat; cautiously sounded him on the matter of carrying liberty-loving passengers, before he introduced his precious charge. This done, Madison was conducted on board. With usual generosity this true subject of the emancipating queen welcomed Madison, and assured him that he should be safely landed in Canada, free of charge. Madison now felt himself no more a piece of merchandise, but a passenger, and, like any other passenger, going about his business, carrying with him what belonged to him, and nothing which rightfully belonged to anybody else.

Wrapped in his new winter suit, snug and comfortable, a pocket full of silver, safe from his pursuers, embarked for a free country, Madison gave every sign of sincere gratitude, and bade his kind benefactor farewell, with such a grip of the hand as bespoke a heart full of honest manliness, and a soul that knew how to appreciate kindness. It need scarcely be said that Mr. Listwell was deeply moved by the gratitude and friendship he had excited in a nature so noble as that of the fugitive. He went to his home that day with a joy and gratification which knew no bounds. He had done something "to deliver the spoiled out of the hands of the spoiler,"[3] he had given bread to the hungry, and clothes to the naked; he had befriended a man to whom the laws of his country forbade all friendship,—and in proportion to the odds against his righteous deed, was the delightful satisfaction that gladdened his heart. On reaching home, he exclaimed, "*He is safe,—he is safe,—*

3. In Jeremiah 21.12, God declares: "Execute judgment in the morning, and deliver him that is spoiled out of the hand of the oppressor."

he is safe,"—and the cup of his joy was shared by his excellent lady. The following letter was received from Madison a few days after.

"WINDSOR, CANADA WEST, DEC. 16, 1840

My dear Friend,—for such you truly are:—

Madison is out of the woods at last; I nestle in the mane of the British lion, protected by his mighty paw from the talons and the beak of the American eagle. I AM FREE, and breathe an atmosphere too pure for *slaves*, slave-hunters, or slave-holders. My heart is full. As many thanks to you, sir, and to your kind lady, as there are pebbles on the shores of Lake Erie; and may the blessing of God rest upon you both. You will never be forgotten by your profoundly grateful friend,

MADISON WASHINGTON."

Part III

—His head was with his heart,
And that was far away!
Childe Harold.[4]

Just upon the edge of the great road from Petersburg, Virginia, to Richmond, and only about fifteen miles from the latter place, there stands a somewhat ancient and famous public tavern, quite notorious in its better days, as being the grand resort for most of the leading gamblers, horse-racers, cock-fighters, and slave-traders from all the country round about. This old rookery, the nucleus of all sorts of birds, mostly those of ill omen, has, like everything else peculiar to Virginia, lost much of its ancient consequence and splendor; yet it keeps up some appearance of gaiety and high life, and is still frequented, even by respectable travellers, who are unacquainted with its past history and present condition. Its fine old portico looks well at a distance, and gives the building an air of grandeur. A nearer view, however, does little to sustain this pretension. The house is large, and its style imposing, but time and dissipation, unfailing in their results, have made ineffaceable marks upon it, and it must, in the common course of events, soon be numbered with the things that were. The gloomy mantle of ruin is, already, outspread to envelop it, and its remains, even but now remind one of a human skull, after the flesh has mingled with the earth. Old hats and rags fill the places in the upper windows once occupied by large panes of glass, and the moulding boards along the roofing have dropped off from their places, leaving holes and crevices in the rented wall for bats and swallows to build their nests in. The platform of the portico, which fronts the highway is a rickety affair, its planks are loose, and in some places entirely gone, leaving effective mantraps in their stead for nocturnal ramblers. The wooden pillars, which once supported it, but which now hang as encumbrances, are all rotten, and tremble with the touch. A part of the stable, a fine old structure in its day, which has given comfortable shelter to hundreds of the noblest steeds of "the Old Dominion"

4. From *Childe Harold's Pilgrimage* (1818) 4.141, by English poet George Gordon, Lord Byron (1788–1824), with a key change. Byron wrote: "his eyes / Were with his heart—and that was far away."

at once, was blown down many years ago, and never has been, and probably never will be, rebuilt. The doors of the barn are in wretched condition; they will shut with a little human strength to help their worn out hinges, but not otherwise. The side of the great building seen from the road is much discolored in sundry places by slops poured from the upper windows, rendering it unsightly and offensive in other respects. Three or four great dogs, looking as dull and gloomy as the mansion itself, lie stretched out along the door-sills under the portico; and double the number of loafers, some of them completely rum-ripe, and others ripening, dispose themselves like so many sentinels about the front of the house. These latter understand the science of scraping acquaintance to perfection. They know every-body, and almost every-body knows them. Of course, as their title implies, they have no regular employment. They are (to use an expressive phrase) *hangers-on*, or still better, they are what sailors would denominate *holders-on to the slack, in everybody's mess, and in nobody's watch*. They are, however, as good as the newspaper for the events of the day, and they sell their knowledge almost as cheap. Money they seldom have; yet they always have capital the most reliable. They make their way with a succeeding traveller by intelligence gained from a preceding one. All the great names of Virginia they know by heart, and have seen their owners often. The history of the house is folded in their lips, and they rattle off stories in connection with it, equal to the guides at Dryburgh Abbey.[5] He must be a shrewd man, and well skilled in the art of evasion, who gets out of the hands of these fellows without being at the expense of a treat.

It was at this old tavern, while on a second visit to the State of Virginia in 1841, that Mr. Listwell, unacquainted with the fame of the place, turned aside, about sunset, to pass the night. Riding up to the house, he had scarcely dismounted, when one of the half dozen bar-room fraternity met and addressed him in a manner exceedingly bland and accommodating.

"Fine evening, sir."

"Very fine," said Mr. Listwell. "This is a tavern, I believe?"

"O yes, sir, yes; although you may think it looks a little the worse for wear, it was once as good a house as any in Virginy. I make no doubt if ye spend the night here, you'll think it a good house yet; for there aint a more accommodating man in the country than you'll find the landlord."

Listwell. "The most I want is a good bed for myself, and a full manger for my horse. If I get these, I shall be quite satisfied."

Loafer. "Well, I alloys like to hear a gentleman talk for his horse; and just because the horse can't talk for itself. A man that don't care about his beast, and don't look after it when he's travelling, aint much in my eye anyhow. Now, sir, I likes a horse, and I'll guarantee your horse will be taken good care on here. That old stable, for all you see it looks so shabby now, once sheltered the great *Eclipse*, when he run here agin *Batchelor* and *Jumping Jemmy*. Them was fast horses, but he beat 'em both."

Listwell. "Indeed."

Loafer. "Well, I rather reckon you've travelled a right smart distance today, from the look of your horse?"

Listwell. "Forty miles only."

5. Scottish monastery founded in the 12th century.

Loafer. "Well! I'll be darned if that aint a pretty good *only*. Mister, that beast of yours is a singed cat, I warrant you. I never see'd a creature like that that was'nt good on the road. You've come about forty miles, then?"

Listwell. "Yes, yes, and a pretty good pace at that."

Loafer. "You're somewhat in a hurry, then, I make no doubt? I reckon I could guess if I would, what you're going to Richmond for? It would'nt be much of a guess either; for it's rumored hereabouts, that there's to be the greatest sale of niggers at Richmond to-morrow that has taken place there in a long time; and I'll be bound you're a going there to have a hand in it."

Listwell. "Why, you must think, then, that there's money to be made at that business?"

Loafer. "Well, 'pon my honor, sir, I never made any that way myself; but it stands to reason that it's a money making business; for almost all other business in Virginia is dropped to engage in this. One thing is sartain, I never see'd a nigger-buyer yet that had'nt a plenty of money, and he was'nt as free with it as water. I has known one on 'em to treat as high as twenty times in a night; and, ginerally speaking, they's men of edication, and knows all about the government. The fact is, sir, I alloys like to hear 'em talk, bekase I alloys can learn something from them."

Listwell. "What may I call your name, sir?"

Loafer. "Well, now, they calls me Wilkes. I'm known all around by the gentlemen that comes here. They all knows old Wilkes."

Listwell. "Well, Wilkes, you seem to be acquainted here, and I see you have a strong liking for a horse. Be so good as to speak a kind word for mine to the hostler to-night, and you'll not lose anything by it."

Loafer. "Well, sir, I see you don't say much, but you've got an insight into things. It's alloys wise to get the good will of them that's acquainted about a tavern; for a man don't know when he goes into a house what may happen, or how much he may need a friend." Here the loafer gave Mr. Listwell a significant grin, which expressed a sort of triumphant pleasure at having, as he supposed, by his tact succeeded in placing so fine appearing a gentleman under obligations to him.

The pleasure, however, was mutual; for there was something so insinuating in the glance of this loquacious customer, that Mr. Listwell was very glad to get quit of him, and to do so more successfully, he ordered his supper to be brought to him in his private room, private to the eye, but not to the ear. This room was directly over the bar, and the plastering being off, nothing but pine boards and naked laths separated him from the disagreeable company below,—he could easily hear what was said in the bar-room, and was rather glad of the advantage it afforded, for, as you shall see, it furnished him important hints as to the manner and deportment he should assume during his stay at that tavern.

Mr. Listwell says he had got into his room but a few moments, when he heard the officious Wilkes below, in a tone of disappointment, exclaim, "Whar's that gentleman?" Wilkes was evidently expecting to meet with his friend at the bar-room, on his return, and had no doubt of his doing the handsome thing. "He has gone to his room," answered the landlord, "and has ordered his supper to be brought to him."

Here some one shouted out, "Who is he, Wilkes? Where's he going?"

"Well, now, I'll be hanged if I know; but I'm willing to make any man a bet of this old hat agin a five dollar bill, that that gent is as full of money as a dog is of fleas. He's going down to Richmond to buy niggers, I make no doubt. He's no fool, I warrant ye."

"Well, he acts d—d strange," said another, "anyhow. I likes to see a man, when he comes up to a tavern, to come straight into the bar-room, and show that he's a man among men. Nobody was going to bite him."

"Now, I don't blame him a bit for not coming in here. That man knows his business, and means to take care on his money," answered Wilkes.

"Wilkes, you're a fool. You only say that, because you hope to get a few coppers out on him."

"You only measure my corn by your half-bushel, I won't say that you're only mad becase I got the chance of speaking to him first."

"O Wilkes! you're known here. You'll praise up any body that will give you a copper; besides, 't is my opinion that that fellow who took his long slab-sides up stairs, for all the world just like a half-scared woman, afraid to look honest men in the face, is a *Northerner,* and as mean as dishwater."

"Now what will you bet of that," said Wilkes.

The speaker said, "I make no bets with you, 'kase you can get that fellow up stairs there to say anything."

"Well," said Wilkes, "I am willing to bet any man in the company that *that* gentleman is a *nigger*-buyer. He did'nt tell me so right down, but I reckon I knows enough about men to give a pretty clean guess as to what they are arter."

The dispute as to *who* Mr. Listwell was, what his business, where he was going, etc., was kept up with much animation for some time, and more than once threatened a serious disturbance of the peace. Wilkes had his friends as well as his opponents. After this sharp debate, the company amused themselves by drinking whiskey, and telling stories. The latter consisting of quarrels, fights, *rencontres,*[6] and duels, in which distinguished persons of that neighborhood, and frequenters of that house, had been actors. Some of these stories were frightful enough, and were told, too, with a relish which bespoke the pleasure of the parties with the horrid scenes they portrayed. It would not be proper here to give the reader any idea of the vulgarity and dark profanity which rolled, as "a sweet morsel," under these corrupt tongues. A more brutal set of creatures, perhaps, never congregated.

Disgusted, and a little alarmed withal, Mr. Listwell, who was not accustomed to such entertainment, at length retired, but not to sleep. He was *too* much wrought upon by what he had heard to rest quietly, and what snatches of sleep he got, were interrupted by dreams which were anything than pleasant. At eleven o'clock, there seemed to be several hundreds of persons crowding into the house. A loud and confused clamour, cursing and cracking of whips, and the noise of chains startled him from his bed; for a moment he would have given the half of his farm in Ohio to have been at home. This uproar was kept up with undulating course, till near morning. There was loud laughing,—loud singing,—loud cursing,—and yet there

6. Encounters (French).

seemed to be weeping and mourning in the midst of all. Mr. Listwell said he had heard enough during the forepart of the night to convince him that a buyer of men and women stood the best chance of being respected. And he, therefore, thought it best to say nothing which might undo the favorable opinion that had been formed of him in the bar-room by at least one of the fraternity that swarmed about it. While he would not avow himself a purchaser of slaves, he deemed it not prudent to disavow it. He felt that he might, properly, refuse to cast such a pearl before parties which, to him, were worse than swine.[7] To reveal himself, and to impart a knowledge of his real character and sentiments would, to say the least, be imparting intelligence with the certainty of seeing it and himself both abused. Mr. Listwell confesses, that this reasoning did not altogether satisfy his conscience, for, hating slavery as he did, and regarding it to be the immediate duty of every man to cry out against it, "without compromise and without concealment," it was hard for him to admit to himself the possibility of circumstances wherein a man might, properly, hold his tongue on the subject. Having as little of the spirit of a martyr as Erasmus,[8] he concluded, like the latter, that it was wiser to trust the mercy of God for his soul, than the humanity of slave-traders for his body. Bodily fear, not conscientious scruples, prevailed.

In this spirit he rose early in the morning, manifesting no surprise at what he had heard during the night. His quondam[9] friend was soon at his elbow, boring him with all sorts of questions. All, however, directed to find out his character, business, residence, purposes, and destination. With the most perfect appearance of good nature and carelessness, Mr. Listwell evaded these meddlesome inquiries, and turned conversation to general topics, leaving himself and all that specially pertained to him, out of discussion. Disengaging himself from their troublesome companionship, he made his way towards an old bowling-alley, which was connected with the house, and which, like all the rest, was in very bad repair.

On reaching the alley Mr. Listwell saw, for the first time in his life, a slave-gang on their way to market. A sad sight truly. Here were one hundred and thirty human beings,—children of a common Creator—guilty of no crime—men and women, with hearts, minds, and deathless spirits, chained and fettered, and bound for the market, in a christian country,—in a country boasting of its liberty, independence, and high civilization! Humanity converted into merchandise, and linked in iron bands, with no regard to decency or humanity! All sizes, ages, and sexes, mothers, fathers, daughters, brothers, sisters,—all huddled together, on their way to market to be sold and separated from home, and from each other *forever*. And all to fill the pockets of men too lazy to work for an honest living, and who gain their fortune by plundering the helpless, and trafficking in the souls and sinews of men. As he gazed upon this revolting and heart-rending scene, our informant said he almost doubted the existence of a God of justice! And he stood wondering that the earth did not open and swallow up such wickedness.

7. Jesus states to his disciples: "Give not that which is holy unto the dogs, neither cast ye your pearls before swine, lest they trample them under their feet" (Matthew 7.6).

8. Desiderius Erasmus (1466?–1536), Dutch humanist and Roman Catholic priest who attacked the claims of Protestant reformer Martin Luther (1483–1546) that God had predestined some souls for damnation.

9. Former (Latin).

In the midst of these reflections, and while running his eye up and down the fettered ranks, he met the glance of one whose face he thought he had seen before. To be resolved, he moved towards the spot. It was MADISON WASHINGTON! Here was a scene for the pencil! Had Mr. Listwell been confronted by one risen from the dead, he could not have been more appalled. He was completely stunned. A thunderbolt could not have struck him more dumb. He stood, for a few moments, as motionless as one petrified; collecting himself, he at length exclaimed, *"Madison! is that you?"*

The noble fugitive, but little less astonished than himself, answered cheerily, "O yes, sir, they've got me again."

Thoughtless of consequences for the moment, Mr. Listwell ran up to his old friend, placing his hands upon his shoulders, and looked him in the face! Speechless they stood gazing at each other as if to be doubly resolved that there was no mistake about the matter, till Madison motioned his friend away, intimating a fear lest the keepers should find him there, and suspect him of tampering with the slaves.

"They will soon be out to look after us. You can come when they go to breakfast, and I will tell you all."

Pleased with this arrangement, Mr. Listwell passed out of the alley; but only just in time to save himself, for, while near the door, he observed three men making their way to the alley. The thought occurred to him to await their arrival, as the best means of diverting the ever ready suspicions of the guilty.

While the scene between Mr. Listwell and his friend Madison was going on, the other slaves stood as mute spectators,—at a loss to know what all this could mean. As he left, he heard the man chained to Madison ask, "Who is that gentleman?"

"He is a friend of mine. I cannot tell you now. Suffice it to say he is a friend. You shall hear more of him before long, but mark me! whatever shall pass between that gentleman and me, in your hearing, I pray you will say nothing about it. We are all chained here together,—ours is a common lot; and that gentleman is not less *your* friend than *mine*." At these words, all mysterious as they were, the unhappy company gave signs of satisfaction and hope. It seems that Madison, by that mesmeric power which is the invariable accompaniment of genius, had already won the confidence of the gang, and was a sort of general-in-chief among them.

By this time the keepers arrived. A horrid trio, well fitted for their demoniacal work. Their uncombed hair came down over foreheads *"villainously low,"*[1] and with eyes, mouths, and noses to match. "Hallo! hallo!" they growled out as they entered. "Are you all there!"

"All here," said Madison.

"Well, well, that's right! your journey will soon be over. You'll be in Richmond by eleven to-day, and then you'll have an easy time on it."

"I say, gal, what in the devil are you crying about?" said one of them. "I'll give you something to cry about, if you don't mind." This was said to a girl, apparently not more than twelve years old, who had been weeping bitterly. She had, probably, left behind her a loving mother, affectionate sisters,

1. In Shakespeare's *The Tempest*, Caliban refers to "apes / With foreheads villainous low" (4.1.248).

brothers, and friends, and her tears were but the natural expression of her sorrow, and the only solace. But the dealers in human flesh have *no* respect for such sorrow. They look upon it as a protest against their cruel injustice, and they are prompt to punish it.

This is a puzzle not easily solved. *How* came he here? what can I do for him? may I not even now be in some way compromised in this affair? were thoughts that troubled Mr. Listwell, and made him eager for the promised opportunity of speaking to Madison.

The bell now sounded for breakfast, and keepers and drivers, with pistols and bowie-knives gleaming from their belts, hurried in, as if to get the best places. Taking the chance now afforded, Mr. Listwell hastened back to the bowling-alley. Reaching Madison, he said, "Now *do* tell me all about the matter. Do you know me?"

"Oh, yes," said Madison, "I know you well, and shall never forget you nor that cold and dreary night you gave me shelter. I must be short," he continued, "for they'll soon be out again. This, then, is the story in brief. On reaching Canada, and getting over the excitement of making my escape, sir, my thoughts turned to my poor wife, who had well deserved my love by her virtuous fidelity and undying affection for me. I could not bear the thought of leaving her in the cruel jaws of slavery, without making an effort to rescue her. First, I tried to get money to buy her; but oh! the process was *too slow*. I despaired of accomplishing it. She was in all my thoughts by day, and my dreams by night. At times I could almost hear her voice, saying, 'O Madison! Madison! will you then leave me here? can you leave me here to die? No! no! you will come! you will come!' I was wretched. I lost my appetite. I could neither work, eat, nor sleep, till I resolved to hazard my own liberty, to gain that of my wife! But I must be short. Six weeks ago I reached my old master's place. I laid about the neighborhood nearly a week, watching my chance, and, finally, I ventured upon the desperate attempt to reach my poor wife's room by means of a ladder. I reached the window, but the noise in raising it frightened my wife, and she screamed and fainted. I took her in my arms, and was descending the ladder, when the dogs began to bark furiously, and before I could get to the woods the white folks were roused. The cool night air soon restored my wife, and she readily recognized me. We made the best of our way to the woods, but it was now *too* late,—the dogs were after us as though they would have torn us to pieces. It was all over with me now! My old master and his two sons ran out with loaded rifles, and before we were out of gunshot, our ears were assailed with '*Stop! stop! or be shot down.*' Nevertheless we ran on. Seeing that we gave no heed to their calls, they fired, and my poor wife fell by my side dead, while I received but a slight flesh wound. I now became desperate, and stood my ground, and awaited their attack over her dead body. They rushed upon me, with their rifles in hand. I parried their blows, and fought them 'till I was knocked down and overpowered."

"Oh! it was madness to have returned," said Mr. Listwell.

"Sir, I could not be free with the galling thought that my poor wife was still a slave. With her in slavery, my body, not my spirit, was free. I was taken to the house,—chained to a ring-bolt,—my wounds dressed. I was kept there three days. All the slaves, for miles around, were brought to see me. Many slave-holders came with their slaves, using me as proof of the completeness of their power, and of the impossibility of slaves getting away. I was taunted, jeered at, and berated by them, in a manner that pierced me to the soul. Thank God, I was able to smother my rage, and to bear it all with seeming composure. After my wounds were nearly healed, I was taken to a tree and stripped, and I received sixty lashes on my naked back. A few days after, I was sold to a slave-trader, and placed in this gang for the New Orleans market."

"Do you think your master would sell you to me?"

"O no, sir! I was sold on condition of my being taken South. Their motive is revenge."

"Then, then," said Mr. Listwell, "I fear I can do nothing for you. Put your trust in God, and bear your sad lot with the manly fortitude which becomes a man. I shall see you at Richmond, but don't recognize me." Saying this, Mr. Listwell handed Madison ten dollars; said a few words to the other slaves; received their hearty "God bless you," and made his way to the house.

Fearful of exciting suspicion by too long delay, our friend went to the breakfast table, with the air of one who half reproved the greediness of those who rushed in at the sound of the bell. A cup of coffee was all that he could manage. His feelings were too bitter and excited, and his heart was too full with the fate of poor Madison (whom he loved as well as admired) to relish his breakfast; and although he sat long after the company had left the table, he really did little more than change the position of his knife and fork. The strangeness of meeting again one whom he had met on two several occasions before, under extraordinary circumstances, was well calculated to suggest the idea that a supernatural power, a wakeful providence, or an inexorable fate, had linked their destiny together; and that no efforts of his could disentangle him from the mysterious web of circumstances which enfolded him.

On leaving the table, Mr. Listwell nerved himself up and walked firmly into the bar-room. He was at once greeted again by that talkative chatter-box, Mr. Wilkes.

"Them's a likely set of niggers in the alley there," said Wilkes.

"Yes, they're fine looking fellows, one of them I should like to purchase, and for him I would be willing to give a handsome sum."

Turning to one of his comrades, and with a grin of victory, Wilkes said, "Aha, Bill, did you hear that? I told you I know'd that gentleman wanted to buy niggers, and would bid as high as any purchaser in the market."

"Come, come," said Listwell, "don't be too loud in your praise, you are old enough to know that prices rise when purchasers are plenty."

"That's a fact," said Wilkes, "I see you knows the ropes—and there's not a man in old Virginy whom I'd rather help to make a good bargain than you, sir."

Mr. Listwell here threw a dollar at Wilkes, (which the latter caught with a dexterous hand,) saying, "Take that for your kind good will." Wilkes held up the dollar to his right eye, with a grin of victory, and turned to the morose grumbler in the corner who had questioned the liberality of a man of whom he knew nothing.

Mr. Listwell now stood as well with the company as any other occupant of the bar-room.

We pass over the hurry and bustle, the brutal vociferations of the slave-drivers in getting their unhappy gang in motion for Richmond; and we need not narrate every application of the lash to those who faltered in the journey. Mr. Listwell followed the train at a long distance, with a sad heart; and on reaching Richmond, left his horse at a hotel, and made his way to the wharf in the direction of which he saw the slave-coffle driven. He was just in time to see the whole company embark for New Orleans. The thought struck him that, while mixing with the multitude, he might do his friend Madison one last service, and he stept into a hardware store and purchased three strong *files*. These he took with him, and standing near the small boat, which lay in waiting to bear the company by parcels to the side of the brig that lay in the stream, he managed, as Madison passed him, to slip the files into his pocket, and at once darted back among the crowd.

All the company now on board, the imperious voice of the captain sounded, and instantly a dozen hardy seamen were in the rigging, hurrying aloft to unfurl the broad canvas of our Baltimore built American Slaver. The sailors hung about the ropes, like so many black cats, now in the round-tops, now in the cross-trees, now on the yard-arms; all was bluster and activity. Soon the broad fore topsail, the royal and top gallant sail were spread to the breeze. Round went the heavy windlass, clank, clank went the fall-bit,—the anchors weighed,—jibs, mainsails, and topsails hauled to the wind, and the long, low, black slaver, with her cargo of human flesh, careened and moved forward to the sea.

Mr. Listwell stood on the shore, and watched the slaver till the last speck of her upper sails faded from sight, and announced the limit of human vision. "Farewell! farewell! brave and true man! God grant that brighter skies may smile upon your future than have yet looked down upon your thorny pathway."

Saying this to himself, our friend lost no time in completing his business, and in making his way homewards, gladly shaking off from his feet the dust of Old Virginia.

Part IV

Oh, where's the slave so lowly
Condemn'd to chains unholy,
Who could he burst
His bonds at first
Would pine beneath them slowly?
Moore.[2]

——Know ye not
Who would be free, *themselves* must strike the blow.
Childe Harold.[3]

What a world of inconsistency, as well as of wickedness, is suggested by the smooth and gliding phrase, AMERICAN SLAVE TRADE; and how strange and perverse is that moral sentiment which loathes, execrates, and brands as piracy and as deserving of death the carrying away into captivity men, women, and children from the *African coast*; but which is neither shocked nor disturbed by a similar traffic, carried on with the same motives and purposes, and characterized by even *more* odious peculiarities on the coast of our MODEL REPUBLIC. We execrate and hang the wretch guilty of this crime

2. From "Where Is the Slave" (1848), by Irish poet Thomas Moore (1779–1852).

3. Canto 2, stanza 76, of Byron's *Childe Harold's Pilgrimage*.

on the coast of Guinea, while we respect and applaud the guilty participators in this murderous business on the enlightened shores of the Chesapeake. The inconsistency is so flagrant and glaring, that it would seem to cast a doubt on the doctrine of the innate moral sense of mankind.

Just two months after the sailing of the Virginia slave brig, which the reader has seen move off to sea so proudly with her human cargo for the New Orleans market, there chanced to meet, in the Marine Coffee-house at Richmond, a company of *ocean birds*,[4] when the following conversation, which throws some light on the subsequent history, not only of Madison Washington, but of the hundred and thirty human beings with whom we last saw him chained.

"I say, shipmate, you had rather rough weather on your late passage to Orleans?" said Jack Williams, a regular old salt, tauntingly, to a trim, compact, manly looking person, who proved to be the first mate of the slave brig in question.

"Foul play, as well as foul weather," replied the firmly knit personage, evidently but little inclined to enter upon a subject which terminated so ingloriously to the captain and officers of the American slaver.

"Well, betwixt you and me," said Williams, "that whole affair on board of the Creole was miserably and disgracefully managed. Those black rascals got the upper hand of ye altogether; and, in my opinion, the whole disaster was the result of ignorance of the real character of *darkies* in general. With half a dozen *resolute* white men, (I say it not boastingly,) I could have had the rascals in irons in ten minutes, not because I'm so strong, but I know how to manage 'em. With my back against the *caboose*, I could, myself, have flogged a dozen of them; and had I been on board, by every monster of the deep, every black devil of 'em all would have had his neck stretched from the yard-arm. Ye made a mistake in yer manner of fighting 'em. All that is needed in dealing with a set of rebellious *darkies*, is to show that yer not afraid of 'em. For my own part, I would not honor a dozen niggers by pointing a gun at one on 'em,—a good stout whip, or a stiff rope's end, is better than all the guns at Old Point[5] to quell a *nigger* insurrection. Why, sir, to take a gun to a *nigger* is the best way you can select to tell him you are afraid of him, and the best way of inviting his attack."

This speech made quite a sensation among the company, and a part of them indicated solicitude for the answer which might be made to it. Our first mate replied, "Mr. Williams, all that you've now said sounds very well *here* on shore, where, perhaps, you have studied negro character. I do not profess to understand the subject as well as yourself; but it strikes me, you apply the same rule in dissimilar cases. It is quite easy to talk of flogging niggers here on land, where you have the sympathy of the community, and the whole physical force of the government, State and national, at your command; and where, if a negro shall lift his hand against a white man, the whole community, with one accord, are ready to unite in shooting him down. I say, in such circumstances, it's easy to talk of flogging negroes and of negro cowardice; but, sir, I deny that the negro is, naturally, a coward, or that your theory of managing slaves will stand the test of *salt* water. It may

4. Sailors.

5. West Point, the U.S. Military Academy.

do very well for an overseer, a contemptible hireling, to take advantage of fears already in existence, and which his presence has no power to inspire; to swagger about whip in hand, and discourse on the timidity and cowardice of negroes; for they have a smooth sea and a fair wind. It is one thing to manage a company of slaves on a Virginia plantation, and quite another thing to quell an insurrection on the lonely billows of the Atlantic, where every breeze speaks of courage and liberty. For the negro to act cowardly on shore, may be to act wisely; and I've some doubts whether *you*, Mr. Williams, would find it very convenient were you a slave in Algiers, to raise your hand against the bayonets of a whole government."

"By George, shipmate," said Williams, "you're coming rather *too* near. Either I've fallen very low in your estimation, or your notions of negro courage have got up a button-hole too high. Now I more than ever wish I'd been on board of that luckless craft. I'd have given ye practical evidence of the truth of my theory. I don't doubt there's some difference in being at sea. But a nigger's a nigger, on sea or land; and is a coward, find him where you will; a drop of blood from one on 'em will skeer a hundred. A knock on the nose, or a kick on the shin, will tame the wildest *'darkey'* you can fetch me. I say again, and will stand by it, I could, with half a dozen good men, put the whole nineteen on 'em in irons, and have carried them safe to New Orleans too. Mind, I don't blame you, but I do say, and every gentleman here will bear me out in it, that the fault was somewhere, or them niggers would never have got off as they have done. For my part I feel ashamed to have the idea go abroad, that a ship load of slaves can't be safely taken from Richmond to New Orleans. I should like, merely to redeem the character of Virginia sailors, to take charge of a ship load on 'em to-morrow."

Williams went on in this strain, occasionally casting an imploring glance at the company for applause for his wit, and sympathy for his contempt of negro courage. He had, evidently, however, waked up the wrong passenger; for besides being in the right, his opponent carried that in his eye which marked him a man not to be trifled with.

"Well, sir," said the sturdy mate, "you can select your own method for distinguishing yourself;—the path of ambition in this direction is quite open to you in Virginia, and I've no doubt that you will be highly appreciated and compensated for all your valiant achievements in that line; but for myself, while I do not profess to be a giant, I have resolved never to set my foot on the deck of a slave ship, either as officer, or common sailor again; I have got enough of it."

"Indeed! indeed!" exclaimed Williams, derisively.

"Yes, *indeed*," echoed the mate; "but don't misunderstand me. It is not the high value that I set upon my life that makes me say what I have said; yet I'm resolved never to endanger my life again in a cause which my conscience does not approve. I dare say *here* what many men *feel*, but *dare not speak*, that this whole slave-trading business is a disgrace and scandal to Old Virginia."

"Hold! hold on! shipmate," said Williams, "I hardly thought you'd have shown your colors so soon,—I'll be hanged if you're not as good an abolitionist as Garrison[6] himself."

6. William Lloyd Garrison, abolitionist editor of the *Liberator*.

The mate now rose from his chair, manifesting some excitement. "What do you mean, sir," said he, in a commanding tone. "*That man does not live who shall offer me an insult with impunity.*"

The effect of these words was marked; and the company clustered around. Williams, in an apologetic tone, said, "Shipmate! keep your temper. I mean't no insult. We all know that Tom Grant is no coward, and what I said about your being an abolitionist was simply this: you *might* have put down them black mutineers and murderers, but your conscience held you back."

"In that, too," said Grant, "you were mistaken. I did all that any man with equal strength and presence of mind could have done. The fact is, Mr. Williams, you underrate the courage as well as the skill of these negroes, and further, you do not seem to have been correctly informed about the case in hand at all."

"All I know about it is," said Williams, "that on the ninth day after you left Richmond, a dozen or two of the niggers ye had on board, came on deck and took the ship from you;—had her steered into a British port, where, by the by, every woolly head of them went ashore and was free. Now I take this to be a discreditable piece of business, and one demanding explanation."

"There are a great many discreditable things in the world," said Grant. "For a ship to go down under a calm sky is, upon the first flush of it, disgraceful either to sailors or caulkers. But when we learn, that by some mysterious disturbance in nature, the waters parted beneath, and swallowed the ship up, we lose our indignation and disgust in lamentation of the disaster, and in awe of the Power which controls the elements."

"Very true, very true," said Williams, "I should be very glad to have an explanation which would relieve the affair of its present discreditable features. I have desired to see you ever since you got home, and to learn from you a full statement of the facts in the case. To me the whole thing seems unaccountable. I cannot see how a dozen or two of ignorant negroes, not one of whom had ever been to sea before, and all of them were closely ironed, between decks, should be able to get their fetters off, rush out of the hatchway in open daylight, kill two white men, the one the captain and the other their master, and then carry the ship into a British port, where every '*darkey*' of them was set free. There must have been great carelessness, or cowardice somewhere!"

The company which had listened in silence during most of this discussion, now became much excited. One said, I agree with Williams; and several said the thing looks black enough. After the temporary tumultous exclamations had subsided,—

"I see," said Grant, "how you regard this case, and how difficult it will be for me to render our ship's company blameless in your eyes. Nevertheless, I will state the fact precisely as they came under my own observation. Mr. Williams speaks of 'ignorant negroes,' and, as a general rule, they are ignorant; but had he been on board the *Creole* as I was, he would have seen cause to admit that there are exceptions to this general rule. The leader of the mutiny in question was just as shrewd a fellow as ever I met in my life, and was as well fitted to lead in a dangerous enterprise as any one white man in ten thousand. The name of this man, strange to say, (ominous of greatness,) was MADISON WASHINGTON. In the short time he had been on board, he had secured the confidence of every officer. The negroes fairly worshipped him.

His manner and bearing were such, that no one could suspect him of a murderous purpose. The only feeling with which we regarded him was, that he was a powerful, good-disposed negro. He seldom spake to any one, and when he did speak, it was with the utmost propriety. His words were well chosen, and his pronunciation equal to that of any schoolmaster. It was a mystery to us *where* he got his knowledge of language; but as little was said to him, none of us knew the extent of his intelligence and ability till it was too late. It seems he brought three files with him on board, and must have gone to work upon his fetters the first night out; and he must have worked well at that; for on the day of the rising, he got the irons *off eighteen* besides himself.

"The attack began just about twilight in the evening. Apprehending a squall, I had commanded the second mate to order all hands on deck, to take in sail. A few minutes before this I had seen Madison's head above the hatchway, looking out upon the white-capped waves at the leeward. I think I never saw him look more good-natured. I stood just about midship, on the larboard side. The captain was pacing the quarter-deck on the starboard side, in company with Mr. Jameson, the owner of most of the slaves on board. Both were armed. I had just told the men to lay aloft, and was looking to see my orders obeyed, when I heard the discharge of a pistol on the starboard side; and turning suddenly around, the very deck seemed covered with fiends from the pit. The nineteen negroes were all on deck, with their broken fetters in their hands, rushing in all directions. I put my hand quickly in my pocket to draw out my jack-knife; but before I could draw it, I was knocked senseless to the deck. When I came to myself, (which I did in a few minutes, I suppose, for it was yet quite light,) there was not a white man on deck. The sailors were all aloft in the rigging, and dared not come down. Captain Clarke and Mr. Jameson lay stretched on the quarter-deck,—both dying,—while Madison himself stood at the helm unhurt.

"I was completely weakened by the loss of blood, and had not recovered from the stunning blow which felled me to the deck; but it was a little too much for me, even in my prostrate condition, to see our good brig commanded by a *black murderer.* So I called out to the men to come down and take the ship, or die in the attempt. Suiting the action to the word, I started aft. You murderous villain, said I, to the imp at the helm, and rushed upon him to deal him a blow, when he pushed me back with his strong, black arm, as though I had been a boy of twelve. I looked around for the men. They were still in the rigging. Not one had come down. I started towards Madison again. The rascal now told me to stand back. 'Sir,' said he, 'your life is in my hands. I could have killed you a dozen times over during this last half hour, and could kill you now. You call me a *black murderer.* I am not a murderer. God is my witness that LIBERTY, not *malice*, is the motive for this night's work. I have done no more to those dead men yonder, than they would have done to me in like circumstances. We have struck for our freedom, and if a true man's heart be in you, you will honor us for the deed. We have done that which you applaud your fathers for doing, and if we are murderers, *so were they.*'

"I felt little disposition to reply to this impudent speech. By heaven, it disarmed me. The fellow loomed up before me. I forgot his blackness in the dignity of his manner, and the eloquence of his speech. It seemed as if the souls of both the great dead (whose names he bore) had entered him. To the sailors in the rigging he said: 'Men! the battle is over,—your captain is dead. I have complete command of this vessel. All resistance to my authority will be in vain. My men have won their liberty, with no other weapons but their own BROKEN FETTERS. We are nineteen in number. We do not thirst for your blood, we demand only our rightful freedom. Do not flatter yourselves that I am ignorant of chart or compass. I know both. We are now only about sixty miles from Nassau.[7] Come down, and do your duty. Land us in Nassau, and not a hair of your heads shall be hurt.'

"I shouted, *Stay where you are, men,*—when a sturdy black fellow ran at me with a handspike, and would have split my head open, but for the interference of Madison, who darted between me and the blow. 'I know what you are up to,' said the latter to me. 'You want to navigate this brig into a slave port, where you would have us all hanged; but you'll miss it; before this brig shall touch a slave-cursed shore while I am on board, I will myself put a match to the magazine, and blow her, and be blown with her, into a thousand fragments. Now I have saved your life twice within these last twenty minutes,—for, when you lay helpless on deck, my men were about to kill you. I held them in check. And if you now (seeing I am your friend and not your enemy) persist in your resistance to my authority, I give you fair warning, YOU SHALL DIE.'

"Saying this to me, he cast a glance into the rigging where the terror-stricken sailors were clinging, like so many frightened monkeys, and commanded them to come down, in a tone from which there was no appeal; for four men stood by with muskets in hand, ready at the word of command to shoot them down.

"I now became satisfied that resistance was out of the question; that my best policy was to put the brig into Nassau, and secure the assistance of the American consul at that port. I felt sure that the authorities would enable us to secure the murderers, and bring them to trial.

"By this time the apprehended squall had burst upon us. The wind howled furiously,—the ocean was white with foam, which, on account of the darkness, we could see only by the quick flashes of lightning that darted occasionally from the angry sky. All was alarm and confusion. Hideous cries came up from the slave women. Above the roaring billows a succession of heavy thunder rolled along, swelling the terrific din. Owing to the great darkness, and a sudden shift of the wind, we found ourselves in the trough of the sea. When shipping a heavy sea over the starboard bow, the bodies of the captain and Mr. Jameson were washed overboard. For awhile we had dearer interests to look after than slave property. A more savage thunder-gust never swept the ocean. Our brig rolled and creaked as if every bolt would be started, and every thread of oakum would be pressed out of the seams. To the pumps! to the pumps! I cried, but not a sailor would quit his grasp. Fortunately this squall soon passed over, or we must have been food for sharks.

"During all the storm, Madison stood firmly at the helm,—his keen eye fixed upon the binnacle. He was not indifferent to the dreadful hurricane; yet he met it with the equanimity of an old sailor. He was silent but not agitated. The first words he uttered after the storm had slightly subsided, were characteristic of the man. 'Mr. mate, you cannot write the bloody laws of slavery on those restless billows. The ocean, if not the land, is free.' I

7. Capital of the Bahama Islands; under British control until 1973.

confess, gentlemen, I felt myself in the presence of a superior man; one who, had he been a white man, I would have followed willingly and gladly in any honorable enterprise. Our difference of color was the only ground for difference of action. It was not that his principles were wrong in the abstract; for they are the principles of 1776. But I could not bring myself to recognize their application to one whom I deemed my inferior.

"But to my story. What happened now is soon told. Two hours after the frightful tempest had spent itself, we were plump at the wharf in Nassau. I sent two of our men immediately to our consul with a statement of facts, requesting his interference in our behalf. What he did, or whither he did anything, I don't know; but, by order of the authorities, a company of *black* soldiers came on board, for the purpose, as they said, of protecting the property. These impudent rascals, when I called on them to assist me in keeping the slaves on board, sheltered themselves adroitly under their instructions only to protect property,—and said they did not recognize *persons* as *property*. I told them that by the laws of Virginia and the laws of the United States, the slaves on board were as much property as the barrels of flour in the hold. At this the stupid blockheads showed their *ivory*, rolled up their white eyes in horror, as if the idea of putting men on a footing with merchandise were revolting to their humanity. When these instructions were understood among the negroes, it was impossible for us to keep them on board. They deliberately gathered up their baggage before our eyes, and, against our remonstrances, poured through the gangway,—formed themselves into a procession on the wharf,—bid farewell to all on board, and, uttering the wildest shouts of exultation, they marched, amidst the deafening cheers of a multitude of sympathizing spectators, under the triumphant leadership of their heroic chief and deliverer, MADISON WASHINGTON."

1853

Section, Region, Nation, Hemisphere

When the United States achieved its independence in 1783, it was the world's largest republic. Twenty years later, the nation doubled in size with the Louisiana Purchase; and by mid-century it had expanded yet again, making it three times larger than in 1783. National growth was not an orderly process: borders remained uncertain, violent encounters with Native Americans and a war with Mexico (1846–48) could make expansion seem more like invasion, questions about the existence of slavery in the new territories inflamed sectional tensions, and unchecked greed in pursuit of new resources sometimes created social chaos. Nevertheless, ideologies of U.S. nationalism based on the Declaration of Independence and the Constitution crossed the ever-shifting and often nebulous boundaries of sections and regions and helped bring a degree of order and commonality to a widely dispersed people.

But the definition of that nationalism did not go undisputed. Northerners generally conceived of the nation in relation to the values of free institutions and market culture; white Southerners saw it in relation to the preservation of slavery and the plantation culture that slavery sustained. In the West (what we now call the Midwest), far West, and elsewhere, the idea of *nation* was modified by diverse regional values, including frontier individualism, distinctive religious beliefs (such as Mormonism), and the pull of the local (as in vernacular humor). Though commitments to U.S. nationalism helped hold the various regions and sections together, by 1861 the nation had fragmented. Debates over the meaning of the U.S. nation (slave or free, a confederacy of states or a centralized federal order) became violent, and the nation gave way to Civil War.

This grouping of texts samples the rich archive of regional and sectional literatures of the early national and antebellum period. These selections show that concepts of American literature, like concepts of the American nation, had some basis in section and region. The American literary nationalists of the Boston-based *North American Review* who called for a distinctively American literature were not calling for a literature of the plantation South. These writers simply assumed that the Northeast represented "America." This is not to say that the authors who emerged during this time spoke only from particular regional or sectional positions but that those positions were always a recognized constituent of their literary identities. William Cullen Bryant, Washington Irving, and James Fenimore Cooper, for instance, the first group of internationally celebrated U.S. authors, all came from New York, and their regional affiliations had an important place in their writings, even as they moved well beyond the local and the regional to gain wide audiences. Still, it was often the case that writers were valued differently in different parts of the country, and tensions between the sometimes conflicting writings emerging from the free North and the slave South remained an important tension in antebellum literary culture (especially following the publication of *Uncle Tom's Cabin* in 1852). But because nearly all of the major book publishers were located in the North, a popular writer like South Carolina's William Gilmore Simms, whose historical novels often extolled the practice of slavery, gained many readers outside of the South. Ironically, then, Boston, New York, and Philadelphia, both before and after the Civil War, were often the places where regional and sectional literatures came into being. Before the Civil War, any regional or sectional writer might also be a national author; only after the defeat of the South did Simms come to seem an author who could be termed "Southern" in a way that would suggest he was different from a "national" author like Nathaniel Hawthorne. Accordingly, it is in the later years of the nineteenth century rather than the antebellum period that regional writing itself, including New England regional writing, became a distinct American literary practice.

The selections in "Section, Region, Nation, Hemisphere" highlight the tensions between North and South, along with the sheer energy and excitement of the emigration into the western regions of the expanding nation. Several of the selections also help us to understand North-South conflict and westward expansionism in relation to a larger hemispheric context. Put simply, the U.S. nation achieved its independence in the American hemisphere, or the Americas, as one of many nations; inevitably, the place of the United States in the Americas became a central component of U.S. nationalism of the early national and antebellum periods. Up to the time of the Mexican War, southwestern expansionism, inspired by what John O'Sullivan called "Manifest Destiny," meant pushing against and across the borders of Mexican lands. African American writers regularly looked across, and often ventured across, the northern border to Canada, which they regarded as a locale of freedom, even as conflicts on the Northwest border between the United States and England continued into the late 1840s. Looking south, president James Monroe in 1823 enunciated what has become known as the Monroe Doctrine, declaring that the southern Americas should rightly be under U.S., and not European, influence; and in 1854 a committee of Democratic politicians released the Ostend Manifesto, asserting that the United States had the right to annex Cuba from Spain. African American writers such as Martin Delany, James Whitfield, and William Wells Brown, however, increasingly saw Central and South America, and the Caribbean, as a possible home for U.S. blacks, particularly after the Supreme Court's 1857 *Dred Scott* ruling that blacks could never become U.S. citizens. Critics interested in inter-American studies have increasingly argued for the importance of attending to exchange among writers in the American hemisphere, and though this unit is too short to offer examples of such exchanges, it does include the Mexican writer Lorenzo de Zavala, who crossed the border from Mexico into the United States and eventually published his thoughts on the nation to his north.

The first two texts, by Daniel Webster and William Gilmore Simms, can be read as competing cultural manifestos: Webster presents New England as the spiritual foundation and moral center of the nation, whereas Simms, in an American literary nationalist text, attempts to place the South at that center by extolling the "let alone" principles of a states' rights–based confederacy. The Zavala selection looks beyond sectionalism from the perspective of someone who lives in a very different political world. The next three pieces, by Richard Henry Dana Jr., John Louis O'Sullivan, and Francis Parkman Jr., can be read in relation to the excerpts in this anthology from Caroline Kirkland's *A New Home—Who'll Follow?* (1837): all of these texts convey the keen interest of those in the Northeast with the new possibilities of travel, emigration, and continental expansion. Thoreau's insistence on staying at home and Emerson's call for national poets and scholars reflect an awareness of expansionism as well, as does much of Whitman's poetry. Dana and Parkman share the perspective of elite New Englanders on the rough and "uncivilized" (but still appealing) areas that they explore. In his essay on annexation, O'Sullivan makes clear that he regarded emigration as the fulfillment of white Anglo-Saxons' divine right to take the continent; some of the same sense of cultural and racial superiority can be discerned in Dana and Parkman. Resistance to white "Anglo-Saxon" culture led the African American poet James Whitfield to look to the Caribbean for sources of inspiration. His friend Martin Delany, represented in the cluster on "Slavery, Race, and the Making of American Literature," imagined in his serialized novel *Blake* (1859, 1861–62) that blacks of Cuba could unite with blacks of the United States to create a hemispheric black revolution that would put an end to slavery in the Americas once and for all. But Julia Ward Howe, in her 1859 *A Trip to Cuba*, views the island-nation, still under Spanish control, from the perspective of a New England tourist who wouldn't mind the nation going "Yankee."

With the acquisition from Mexico of vast areas of the Southwest after the 1848 Treaty of Guadalupe Hidalgo, politicians and emigrants from the North and South fought in words and in deeds over extending slavery into territories soon to become states. Kansas and Nebraska saw considerable violence during the mid-1850s. Between 1857 and 1859, various votes in Kansas made it a slave state and then a free state, but nothing was decided until 1861, when the free state of Kansas formally entered the Union. The excerpt from Mary Chesnut's diary of March 1861, which concludes this cluster of texts, conveys the tense relations between the sections that would literally explode, only a few weeks later, when South Carolina seceded from the United States and bombarded U.S. Fort Sumter in Charleston Harbor.

DANIEL WEBSTER

Celebrated as one of the greatest orators of his day, Daniel Webster (1782–1852) advocated a nationalism based on his love of New England and his commitment to the Union. Born in Salisbury, New Hampshire, Webster graduated from Dartmouth in 1801 and was admitted to the bar in 1805. He served one term in the U.S. Congress as a representative from New Hampshire (1813–17) before moving to Massachusetts in 1816. In 1822 he was elected to Congress from Massachusetts, and he spent the rest of his life in government as a congressman, senator, or political appointee.

Webster first attained national prominence as a defender of the Union during the controversy in the U.S. Senate on the Tariff of 1828. In response to South Carolina senator Robert Y. Hayne's efforts to lower the tariff by creating alliances between resistant Southerners and Westerners—and thus isolate the Northeast, where a high tariff was favored—Webster warned Hayne against attempting to exacerbate sectional tensions. During a floor debate in the Senate in 1830, Webster delivered his famous "Reply to Hayne," which concluded: "LIBERTY and Union, now and forever, one and inseparable!" Though Webster always opposed slavery, he reluctantly supported the Compromise of 1850, with its toughened Fugitive Slave Act, because he thought the Compromise was the only way to preserve the Union. He said that he supported the Compromise, "not as a Massachusetts man, nor as a northern man, but as an American." Nevertheless, much in his writings suggests that he identified traditional New England values and history with the nation as a whole. In his first speech to gain wide public attention, "First Settlement of New England: A Discourse Delivered at Plymouth, on the 22nd of December, 1820," Webster envisions New England as the birthplace of liberty and union. The text is from *Writings and Speeches of Daniel Webster* (1903).

From First Settlement of New England

Let us rejoice that we behold this day. Let us be thankful that we have lived to see the bright and happy breaking of the auspicious morn, which commences the third century of the history of New England. Auspicious, indeed,—bringing a happiness beyond the common allotment of Providence to men,—full of present joy, and gilding with bright beams the prospect of futurity, is the dawn that awakens us to the commemoration of the landing of the Pilgrims.[1]

Living at an epoch which naturally marks the progress of the history of our native land, we have come hither to celebrate the great event with which that history commenced. For ever honored be this, the place of our fathers' refuge! For ever remembered the day which saw them, weary and distressed, broken in every thing but spirit, poor in all but faith and courage, at last secure from the dangers of wintry seas, and impressing this shore with the first footsteps of civilized man!

It is a noble faculty of our nature which enables us to connect our thoughts, our sympathies, and our happiness with what is distant in place or time; and, looking before and after, to hold communion at once with our ancestors and our posterity. Human and mortal although we are, we are nevertheless not mere insulated beings, without relation to the past or the future. Neither the point of time, nor the spot of earth, in which we physically live, bounds our rational and intellectual enjoyments. We live in the past by a knowledge of its history; and in the future by hope and anticipation. By ascending to an association with our ancestors; by contemplating their example and studying their character; by partaking their sentiments, and imbibing their spirit; by accompanying them in their toils, by sympathizing in their sufferings, and rejoicing in their successes and their triumphs; we seem to belong to their age, and to mingle our own existence with theirs. We become their contemporaries, live the lives which they lived, endure what they endured, and partake in the rewards which they enjoyed.

* * *

We have come to this Rock, to record here our homage for our Pilgrim Fathers; our sympathy in their sufferings; our gratitude for their labors; our admiration of their virtues; our veneration for their piety; and our attachment to those principles of civil and religious liberty, which they encountered the dangers of the ocean, the storms of heaven, the violence of savages, disease, exile, and famine, to enjoy and to establish. And we would leave here, also, for the generations which are rising up rapidly to fill our places, some proof that we have endeavored to transmit the great inheritance unimpaired; that in our estimate of public principles and private virtue, in our veneration of religion and piety, in our devotion to civil and religious liberty, in our regard for whatever advances human knowledge or improves human happiness, we are not altogether unworthy of our origin.

1. English Separatists led by John Carver (c. 1576–1621) and William Bradford (1590–1657), who arrived at Plymouth, Massachusetts, in 1620.

* * *

I deem it my duty on this occasion to suggest, that the land is not yet wholly free from the contamination of a traffic, at which every feeling of humanity must for ever revolt,—I mean the African slave-trade. Neither public sentiment, nor the law, has hitherto been able entirely to put an end to this odious and abominable trade. At the moment when God in his mercy has blessed the Christian world with a universal peace, there is reason to fear, that, to the disgrace of the Christian name and character, new efforts are making for the extension of this trade by subjects and citizens of Christian states, in whose hearts there dwell no sentiments of humanity or of justice, and over whom neither the fear of God nor the fear of man exercises a control. In the sight of our law, the African slave-trader is a pirate and a felon; and in the sight of Heaven, an offender far beyond the ordinary depth of human guilt. There is no brighter page of our history, than that which records the measures which have been adopted by the government at an early day, and at different times since, for the suppression of this traffic; and I would call on all the true sons of New England to cooperate with the laws of man, and the justice of Heaven. If there be, within the extent of our knowledge or influence, any participation in this traffic, let us pledge ourselves here, upon the rock of Plymouth, to extirpate and destroy it. It is not fit that the land of the Pilgrims should bear the shame longer. I hear the sound of the hammer, I see the smoke of the furnaces where manacles and fetters are still forged for human limbs. I see the visages of those who by stealth and at midnight labor in this work of hell, foul and dark, as may become the artificers of such instruments of misery and torture. Let that spot be purified, or let it cease to be of New England. Let it be purified, or let it be set aside from the Christian world; let it be put out of the circle of human sympathies and human regards, and let civilized man henceforth have no communion with it.

* * *

The wealth and population of the country are now so far advanced, as to authorize the expectation of a correct literature and a well formed taste, as well as respectable progress in the abstruse sciences. The country has risen from a state of colonial subjection; it has established an independent government, and is now in the undisturbed enjoyment of peace and political security. The elements of knowledge are universally diffused, and the reading portion of the community is large. Let us hope that the present may be an auspicious era of literature. If, almost on the day of their landing, our ancestors founded schools and endowed colleges, what obligations do not rest upon us, living under circumstances so much more favorable both for providing and for using the means of education? Literature becomes free institutions. It is the graceful ornament of civil liberty, and a happy restraint on the asperities which political controversies sometimes occasion. Just taste is not only an embellishment of society, but it rises almost to the rank of the virtues, and diffuses positive good throughout the whole extent of its influence. There is a connection between right feeling and right principles, and truth in taste is allied with truth in morality. With nothing in our past history to discourage us, and with something in our present condition and prospects to animate us, let us hope, that, as it is our fortune to live in an age when we may behold a wonderful advancement of the country in all its other great interests, we may see also equal progress and success attend the cause of letters.

Finally, let us not forget the religious character of our origin. Our fathers were brought hither by their high veneration for the Christian religion. They journeyed by its light, and labored in its hope. They sought to incorporate its principles with the elements of their society, and to diffuse its influence through all their institutions, civil, political, or literary. Let us cherish these sentiments, and extend this influence still more widely; in the full conviction, that that is the happiest society which partakes in the highest degree of the mild and peaceful spirit of Christianity.

The hours of this day are rapidly flying, and this occasion will soon be passed. Neither we nor our children can expect to behold its return. They are in the distant regions of futurity, they exist only in the all-creating power of God, who shall stand here a hundred years hence, to trace, through us, their descent from the Pilgrims, and to survey, as we have now surveyed, the progress of their country, during the lapse of a century. We would anticipate their concurrence with us in our sentiments of deep regard for our common ancestors. We would anticipate and partake the pleasure with which they will then recount the steps of New England's advancement. On the morning of that day, although it will not disturb us in our repose, the voice of acclamation and gratitude, commencing on the Rock of Plymouth, shall be transmitted through millions of the sons of the Pilgrims, till it lose itself in the murmurs of the Pacific seas.

* * *

WILLIAM GILMORE SIMMS

A poet, novelist, critic, and editor, the South Carolinian William Gilmore Simms (1806–1870) was the most prominent man of letters of the antebellum South. Born in Charleston, Simms received a spotty education before being taken out of school at age twelve to apprentice as an apothecary. He began his literary career in the mid-1820s when he became an editor of the *Album*, a weekly journal published in Charleston; he would later work as an editor at the *Southern Literary Gazette*, the *Charleston City Gazette*, and a number of other journals and newspapers. In 1827 he published his first book, *Lyrical and Other Poems*, but by the mid-1830s he was mainly writing historical novels on the model of Sir Walter Scott. Novels such as *The Yemassee* (1835) and *The Partisan* (1835), both published by Harper & Brothers of New York City, celebrated the role of the South during the colonial and Revolutionary periods. Simms's work had national appeal, even as he increasingly took a states' rights and proslavery position. But by the late 1850s, Simms, a slaveholder himself who had helped publish the influential omnibus collection *The Pro-Slavery Argument* (1852), had lost much of his Northern audience. During the Civil War his plantation was destroyed by fire, and he suffered a number of personal tragedies, including the death of his daughter. He died in Charleston on June 11, 1870.

The text of "Americanism in Literature," which was first published in the January 1845 issue of *Southern and Western Magazine*, is taken from *Views and Reviews in American Literature, History and Fiction* (1845), published in New York City. With its literary nationalist call for a distinctive American literature, "Americanism" bears some resemblance to Ralph Waldo Emerson's "The American Scholar" (1837), though Simms, unlike Emerson, underscores the importance of southern confederacy and states' rights to the possibly glorious future of American literature.

From Americanism in Literature

Europe must cease to taunt us because of our prolonged servility to the imperious genius of the Old World. We must set ourselves free from the tyranny of this genius, and the time has come when we must do so. We have our own national mission to perform—a mission commensurate to the extent of our country,—its resources and possessions,—and the numerous nations, foreign and inferior, all about us, over whom we are required to extend our sway and guardianship. We are now equal to this sway and guardianship. The inferior necessities of our condition have been overcome. The national mind is now free to rise to the consideration of its superior wants and more elevated aims; and individuals, here and there, are starting out from the ranks of the multitude, ready and able to lead out, from the bondage of foreign guidance, the genius which, hitherto, because of its timidity, knew nothing of its own resources, for flight and conquest.

If the time for this movement has not yet arrived, it is certainly very near at hand. This conviction grows out of the fact that we now daily taunt ourselves with our protracted servility to the European. We feel that we are still too humbly imitative, wanting in the courage to strike out boldly, hewing out from our own forests the paths which should lead us to their treasures, and from the giant masses around us the characteristic forms and aspects of native art. This reproach has been hitherto but too much deserved, qualified only by a reference to the circumstances in our condition at which we have been able to glance only for a moment. We have done little that may properly be called our own; and this failure, due to influences which still, in some degree, continue, is one which nothing but a high and stimulating sense of nationality will enable us to remedy. It is so easy, speaking the English language, to draw our inspiration from the mother country, and to seek our audience in her halls and temples, that, but for the passionate appeals of patriotic censure, it may be yet long years before we throw off the patient servility of our dependence. With a daily influx of thousands from foreign shores, seeking to share our political securities and the blessings of the generous skies and rich soil which we possess, Europe sends us her thoughts, her fashions, and her tastes. These have their influence in keeping us in bondage, and we shall require all the activity of our native mind to resist the influence which she thus exercises upon our national institutions and education. * * *

Our orator[1] * * * instances, with effect, the wholesome influences in our government of the "let alone" principle. This, by the way, is an important matter to be understood. Democracy goes into society, with scarcely any farther desire than that men should be protected from one another—left free to the pursuit of happiness, each in the form and manner most agreeable to himself, so long as he does not trespass upon a solitary right of his neighbour. This is the principle. We do not tolerate any interference of government with those employments of its citizens which violate none of the rights of others, and which do not offend against the sense of a christian country. * * * Mr. Meek properly insists upon the value of this "let alone" practice, on the part of government, as vastly promotive of the interests of literature; and particularly dwells upon the advantages, in this regard, which grow out of our system of confederated sovereignties. The very inequalities of things in moral respects, in employments, in climate, soil and circumstance, which we find in these severalties, is at once calculated to provoke the mind in each to exertion, and to endow it with originality. * * * The very divergencies of our paths are favourable to the boldness, the freedom and the flights of the national intellect. We make our own paths—we trace out our own progress—and, just in due degree as we turn aside from the dictation of those great cities, which, among us, are more immediately allied with the marts of Europe, so do we discover marks of the most certain freshness and originality, though coupled with rudeness and irregularity—a harshness which offends and a wilderness which, we are encouraged to believe, it is not beyond the power of time and training to subdue to equable and noble exercises. To any one who looks into the character of our people,—who passes below the surface, and sees in which way the great popular heart beats in the several States of the confederacy,—with what calm, consistent resolve in some—with what impatient heat in others—how cold but how clear in this region,—how fiery, but how clouded in that,—there will be ample promise for the future, not only in the value of the material, but in its exquisite and rich variety. And, even on the surface, how these varieties speak out for themselves, so that it shall not be difficult for a shrewd observer of men to distinguish at a glance, and to declare from what quarter of America the stranger comes,—whether from the banks of the Charles or the Hudson, the Savannah or the Mississippi.

Our orator justly reminds us, while treating of this part of his subject, that, by our compact, the interests of education and literature are left entirely in the control of the States. This vital matter is in our own hands, and nothing but our lachesse[2] or our wilfulness, can possibly lose us the power of moulding the temper of our people in due compliance with our peculiar circumstances, whether moral or physical. We may make our literature what we please if we do not neglect the interests of education. We should confer upon it all the becoming characteristics of our section—our social sympathies, our political temper, and those moral hues and forms

1. Alexander B. Meek (1814–1865), a historian and politician from Alabama. Simms's essay is a response, in part, to Meek's lecture "Americanism in Literature," which he presented to the Phi Kappa and Demosthenean Societies of the University of Georgia on August 8, 1844.
2. Sluggishness.

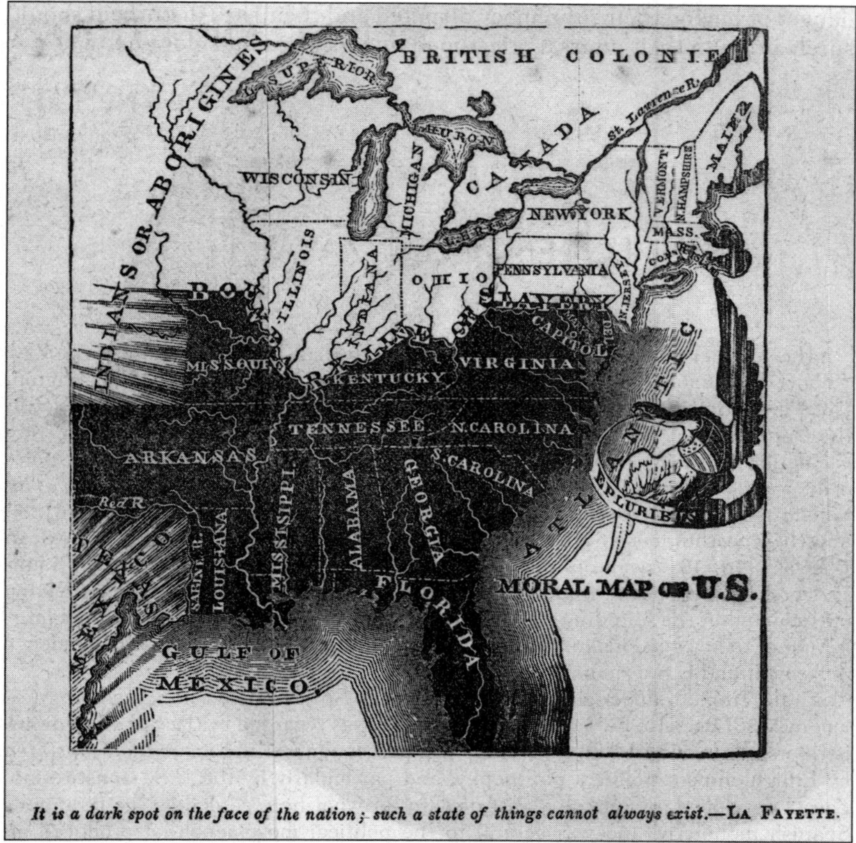

"Moral Map of the U.S.," published in the abolitionist tract *The Legion of Liberty* (1847). Although the map presents an abolitionist perspective on the United States, it nonetheless conveys beliefs about the country that were shared by North and South alike at that time: an increasing concern about the intractability of national division; a sense of the nation's important connections to the larger continent, with the free Canadas to the north and the Mexican territories to the southwest; a view of the West as not "belonging" to a particular country and thus as available to expansionists; and the idea, suggested through the darker shadings south of Florida, that the borders of the nation (perhaps through annexation) could possibly be extended into the Caribbean.

which the intellectual nature so happily imbibes from the aspects which surround us in the natural world. The airy structures of our imagination, born of a like sky and atmosphere with that of Greece, should not shrink from comparison with those of Dodona and Hymettus.[3] Our Olympus rises at our will, and the divine spirits which we summon to make sacred its high abodes, clothed in a political freedom superior to that of Athens, with less

3. Legendary mountain in ancient Greece bearing an image of the Greek god Zeus. Dodona is the Greek town where Zeus's prophetic oracle resided.

danger of having their supremacy disputed and their rites disturbed, should surely bring to their altars a priesthood no less great and glorious.

1845

LORENZO DE ZAVALA

In the summer of 1830, the Mexican political theorist and leader Lorenzo de Zavala (1788–1836) traveled in the United States from New Orleans to Washington, D.C. At the time a political exile, Zavala wanted to observe democracy in practice in the United States, with the hope of inspiring Mexicans in particular to learn from the nation on their northern border. His resulting book, *Viaje a los Estados Unidos del Norte de América* (*Journey to the United States of North America*), which combined travel reportage with political theorizing, was first published in Paris in 1834 and then posthumously in Mexico in 1846, at the beginning of the U.S.-Mexican War of 1846–48. Zavala, initially regarded by the Mexicans as one of their country's great leaders of the 1820s, had been recast by this point as a traitor for having participated in the founding of the Republic of Texas. Zavala's career and his *Journey* point to key tensions in the overlapping histories of the Mexican independence movement and U.S. expansionism.

Zavala, from an upper-class family with ties to Spain, was born in Yucatan, Mexico, in 1788. Because he was Mexican-born, he was regarded by the Spanish administrators of Mexico, at that time a Spanish possession, as inferior to them. Inspired by Enlightenment political philosophy, and particularly by the U.S. Constitution, Zavala developed an anticolonialist disdain for what he regarded as the tyrannous Spanish monarchy, and was central to the political movement that produced an independent Mexico in 1821. He helped to write the first Mexican Constitution. By the late 1820s, however, he had come into conflict with the reactionary military leader General Anastasio Bustamante, and left Mexico, traveling first to the United States in 1830 and then to Paris. During the early 1830s he returned to Texas, then part of Mexico, and worked toward Texas independence, hoping that a new republic on the southwest border of the United States would embody the liberal principles he espoused, including antislavery. After Texas declared its independence in 1836, he helped write the Republic of Texas's constitution, served briefly as the republic's first vice president, and died shortly after resigning. But a decade later Texas, with many settlers from the United States and especially the South, was annexed by the United States, joining the country as a slave state in 1845. Battles in Texas between the United States and Mexico helped initiate the war between the two countries in 1846 that resulted in the United States' annexation of what would become the entire southwestern part of the nation, including California.

In the selection that follows, which is from the conclusion of his 1834 narrative, Zavala suggests that while Mexico has much to learn from the United States, he also sees dangers from the United States, and he conveys his uncertainty about the future of the two nations. As he suggests elsewhere in the text, Zavala hoped that Texas would remain an independent republic but feared its takeover by the United States. The text is taken from Lorenzo de Zavala, *Journey to the United States of North America / Viaje a los Estados Unidos del Norte de América*, ed. John-Michael Rivera, trans. Wallace Woolsey (Houston: Arte Público Press, 2005).

From Journey to the United States of North America

What should be then the consequences of the constant example near at hand presented by the United States of the North to the Mexican nation, young and inexperienced, full of life and desirous of shaking off the remains of its ancient chains? In the narrow circle of continental Europe public right is that of the conservation of certain monarchial principles, the basis of all European political activity. Upon this code, sketched out for the first time in Pillnitz forty years ago,[1] modified several times according to the diverse interests of the high contracting parties, European governments model themselves and change in different ways. In America things are different. Although the monarchial principle is not proscribed, it is evident that the opinion as it can be applied to the emerging republics is almost exclusively democratic. There one finds no interventions nor alliances, no diplomatic maneuvering, no money bags, not a single element with sufficient influence to determine the monarchial form. The only one that exists to some degree is ecclesiastical power, whose weakness is demonstrated by the experience of its fruitless endeavors up to now.

Consequently the influence of the United States upon Mexico will with time be a power of opinion, of teaching by guidance, all the stronger because it is purely moral, founded upon its doctrines and lessons. But there is more. Ten thousand citizens of the United States settle each year in the territory of the Mexican republic, especially in the states of Chihuahua, Coahuila and Texas, Tamaulipas, Nuevo Leon, San Luis Potosi, Durango, Zacatecas, Sonora, Sinaloa, and the Territories of New Mexico and the Californias.[2]

These colonists and businessmen along with their hard work carry with them habits of freedom, economy, industry, their austere and religious ways, their individual independence and their republicanism. What change must these enterprising guests not make in the moral and material existence of the former inhabitants? Carthage was a Carthaginian people, Cadiz a Phoenician people, Marseilles a Greek people for many centuries,[3] because their colonists were from those nations. The Mexican republic then within a few years will come to be molded to a combined regimen of the American system and Spanish customs and traditions.

But it is necessary to distinguish in the Mexican nation that part populated, disciplined, founded, to put it thusly, in the mold of its former mother country,[4] from that part bare of inhabitants, and consequently susceptible to a new population, completely different from the other one. In the first there will exist for many years yet the struggle of opposing principles that have been planted in their institutions, and civil war will be

1. In the 1791 Declaration of Pillnitz, Austrian and Prussian leaders appealed to monarchical rulers throughout Europe to support the monarchy of Louis XVI, under imminent threat from French revolutionaries. Pillnitz is a small town south of what is now Dresden, Germany.
2. Northern Mexican states and territories on the southwest borders of the United States.
3. Marseilles in southeastern France was founded by the ancient Greeks; Carthage, an ancient city in northern Africa, and Cadiz, in southwest Spain, were founded by the peoples of ancient Canaan known as Phoenicians by the Greeks.
4. Spain.

inevitable, while in the second the American, German, Irish, and English colonies are establishing completely free settlements that will prosper peacefully under the influence of their democratic institutions, and even more of their work habits, their ideas and convictions concerning the dignity of man and the respect that is due the law. Thus, while the states of Puehia, Chiapas, Oaxaca, Mexico, Queretaro, Michoacan, and Guanajuato[5] continue in the grip of the military and ecclesiastical arm as a penalty for their prejudices, their ignorance, and their superstition; while in the bosom of these states a few generous and enlightened patriots will make efforts to lift their fellow citizens up to the level of the adopted institutions and will seek to give them lessons in liberty and tolerance; while these opposing elements light the fires of combat among an ardent youth that loves progress and civilization and an ignorant clergy strongly attached to their privileges and income, supported by a few generals and officers of the former Spanish army, without faith, without honor, without patriotism, possessed of a sordid greed and given over to degrading vices; while this is happening in these states, the others will be populated, will become rich, striving to avoid being contaminated by the disastrous things happening to their brothers in the south.

The net result, however, will be the triumph of liberty in these states, and upon the Gothic[6] ashes and the remains of untenable privileges there will be raised up a glorious and enlightened generation that will put into motion all the sources of wealth that abound and will bring into association with the civilized family that indigenous group, until today debased and vilified, and will teach them to think and to hold in esteem their dignity by lifting their thoughts to a higher level.

What barrier can oppose this torrent that was born twenty-four years ago in a small town in the Bagio,[7] obscure in its origins, without direction or channel, destroying everything in its path, today a majestic river that receives pure crystalline waters from other countries that will make fertile the entire Mexican territory? Unsuccessful efforts will oppose a debased generation, heir to Castilian traditions[8] and beliefs and defender without great results of their antisocial doctrines. The American system will obtain a complete though bloody victory.

1834, 1846

5. Zavala here lists Mexican states well south of the United States.

6. A word evoking the architectural style of medieval castles, and hence feudalism and monarchy.

7. Bajío, in central Mexico, north of Mexico City. The war for Mexican independence began here in 1810 when Father Miguel Hidalgo y Costilla (1753–1811) led a group of peasants in an armed revolt against Spanish authorities. Hidalgo was captured and executed in 1811, but the uprising inspired further resistance.

8. Linked to Castile, a region in northern and central Spain which constituted a separate kingdom during the medieval period.

RICHARD HENRY DANA JR.

Born in Cambridge, Massachusetts, Richard Henry Dana Jr. (1815–1882) had a privileged background that gave him entrée into the conventionally successful New England life, the life he mainly chose to follow. His father, Richard Henry Dana, had founded the prestigious literary journal the *North American Review* in 1815, and in 1826 Dana had Ralph Waldo Emerson as his elementary-school teacher. He entered Harvard College in 1831, and after graduating in 1837 (in the same class as Henry David Thoreau), he studied at Harvard's Dane Law School from 1837 to 1840 and was admitted to the bar in 1840. In 1841 he married Sarah Watson, and they had six children, including a son, Richard Henry Dana III, who married Henry Wadsworth Longfellow's daughter Edith. Dana practiced law, served as Abraham Lincoln's U.S. district attorney for Massachusetts during the Civil War, traveled widely, and died in Rome in 1882.

Near the end of his life, Dana stated that he had achieved only one great success, "a boy's work, before I came to the Bar." That work was *Two Years before the Mast,* published in 1840 when Dana was twenty-five. The book emerged from an episode in his life when he diverged from conventional expectations. In 1831 he was suspended from Harvard for protesting against what he believed was unfair punishment administered to a classmate, and during the suspension his vision began to fail. Though he returned to Harvard temporarily, his poor eyesight left him unable to read, and he decided that he might recover his vision through the rigors of a sea voyage. He signed on as an ordinary sailor with the brig *Pilgrim* and in August 1834 sailed from Boston for Cape Horn and the coast of California, returning to Boston in 1836. During the late 1830s he wrote *Two Years,* which was published to wide acclaim in 1840. The book influenced the nautical writings of Herman Melville, who was a great admirer and helped establish Dana as a seaman's lawyer. But the book also had a crucial role in shaping Northerners' understanding of the geographical and cultural landscape of the then remote world of California, where Dana spent 1835–36 gathering and curing steer hides. This selection from the California chapters of *Two Years* comes from the first edition, published by New York's Harper & Brothers in 1840.

From Two Years before the Mast

* * *

The Californians are an idle, thriftless people, and can make nothing for themselves. The country abounds in grapes, yet they buy bad wine made in Boston and brought round by us, at an immense price, and retail it among themselves at a *real*[1] (12½ cents) by the small wine-glass. Their hides too, which they value at two dollars in money, they give for something which costs seventy-five cents in Boston; and buy shoes (as like as not, made of their own hides, which have been carried twice round Cape Horn[2]) at three and four

1. Silver coin of Spanish America. At the time, Mexican and Spanish elites ruled over the Indians in California.
2. Southernmost tip of South America.

dollars, and "chicken-skin" boots at fifteen dollars apiece. Things sell, on an average, at an advance of nearly three hundred per cent upon the Boston prices. This is partly owing to the heavy duties which the government, in their wisdom, with the intent, no doubt, of keeping the silver in the country, has laid upon imports. These duties, and the enormous expenses of so long a voyage, keep all merchants, but those of heavy capital, from engaging in the trade. Nearly two thirds of all the articles imported into the country from round Cape Horn, for the last six years, have been by the single house of Bryant, Sturgis & Co.,[3] to whom our vessel belonged and who have a permanent agent on the coast.

This kind of business was new to us, and we liked it very well for a few days, though we were hard at work every minute from daylight to dark; and sometimes even later.

By being thus continually engaged in transporting passengers with their goods, to and fro, we gained considerable knowledge of the character, dress, and language of the people. The dress of the men was as I have before described it. The women wore gowns of various texture—silks, crape, calicoes, &c.—made after the European style, except that the sleeves were short, leaving the arm bare, and that they were loose about the waist, having no corsets. They wore shoes of kid, or satin; sashes or belts of bright colors; and almost always a necklace and ear-rings. Bonnets they had none. I only saw one on the coast, and that belonged to the wife of an American sea-captain who had settled in San Diego and had imported the chaotic mass of straw and ribbon, as a choice present to his new wife. They wear their hair (which is almost invariably black, or a very dark brown) long in their necks, sometimes loose, and sometimes in long braids; though the married women often do it up on a high comb. Their only protection against the sun and weather is a large mantle which they put over their heads, drawing it close round their faces, when they go out of doors, which is generally only in pleasant weather. When in the house, or sitting out in front of it, which they often do in fine weather, they usually wear a small scarf or neckerchief of a rich pattern. A band, also, about the top of the head, with a cross, star, or other ornament in front, is common. Their complexions are various, depending—as well as their dress and manner—upon their rank; or, in other words, upon the amount of Spanish blood they can lay claim to. Those who are of pure Spanish blood, having never intermarried with the aborigines, have clear brunette complexions, and sometimes, even as fair as those of English women. There are but few of these families in California; being mostly those in official stations, or who, on the expiration of their offices, have settled here upon property which they have acquired; and others who have been banished for state offences. These form the aristocracy; intermarrying, and keeping up an exclusive system in every respect. They can be told by their complexions, dress, manner, and also by their speech; for, calling themselves Castilians, they are very ambitious of speaking the pure Castilian language,[4] which is spoken in a somewhat corrupted dialect by the lower classes. From this upper class, they go down by regular shades, growing more and more dark and muddy, until you come to the pure Indian, who runs about with

3. Pioneering trading firm based in Boston.
4. The standard form of the Spanish language, as spoken in Spain. "Castilians": natives of the former kingdom making up much of Spain.

nothing upon him but a small piece of cloth, kept up by a wide leather strap drawn round his waist. Generally speaking, each person's caste is decided by the quality of the blood, which shows itself, too plainly to be concealed, at first sight. Yet the least drop of Spanish blood, if it be only of quatroon or octoon, is sufficient to raise them from the rank of slaves, and entitle them to a suit of clothes—boots, hat, cloak, spurs, long knife, and all complete, though coarse and dirty as may be,—and to call themselves Españolos,[5] and to hold property, if they can get any.

The fondness for dress among the women is excessive, and is often the ruin of many of them. A present of a fine mantle, or of a necklace or pair of ear-rings, gains the favor of the greater part of them. Nothing is more common than to see a woman living in a house of only two rooms, and the ground for a floor, dressed in spangled satin shoes, silk gown, high comb, and gilt, if not gold ear-rings and necklace. If their husbands do not dress them well enough, they will soon receive presents from others. They used to spend whole days on board our vessel, examining the fine clothes and ornaments, and frequently made purchases at a rate which would have made a semp-stress or waiting-maid in Boston open her eyes.

Next to the love of dress, I was most struck with the fineness of the voices and beauty of the intonations of both sexes. Every common ruffian-looking fellow, with a slouched hat, blanket cloak, dirty under-dress, and soiled leather leggins, appeared to me to be speaking elegant Spanish. It was a pleasure simply to listen to the sound of the language, before I could attach any meaning to it. They have a good deal of the Creole[6] drawl, but it is varied with an occasional extreme rapidity of utterance, in which they seem to skip from consonant to consonant, until, lighting upon a broad, open vowel, they rest upon that to restore the balance of sound. The women carry this peculiarity of speaking to a much greater extreme than the men, who have more evenness and stateliness of utterance. A common bullock-driver, on horseback, delivering a message, seemed to speak like an ambassador at an audience. In fact, they sometimes appeared to me to be a people on whom a curse had fallen, and stripped them of everything but their pride, their manners, and their voices.

* * *

1840

5. Spanish. "Quatroon": one-fourth Spanish blood, or ancestry. "Octoon": one-eighth Spanish blood.
6. The term refers to a person of Spanish descent born in America.

JOHN LOUIS O'SULLIVAN

The son of a naturalized U.S. citizen of Irish ancestry, John O'Sullivan, and an English mother, Mary Rowley, John Louis O'Sullivan (1813–1895) was born off the coast of Gibraltar on a British warship where his mother had taken refuge while her husband was on land doing business. In 1827, after the elder O'Sullivan drowned at sea off the west coast of South America, Mary O'Sullivan moved her family from London to New York City. She enrolled her fourteen-year-old son at Columbia College, where he excelled, graduating in 1831. During the 1830s and 1840s, Louis O'Sullivan was best known as the editor of the *United States Magazine and Democratic Review,* which he founded in Washington, D.C., in 1837 (with the help of a legacy from his father) and then moved to New York City in 1840. This journal linked Jacksonian democratic politics, including expansionism, to the cause of American literary nationalism, publishing works by William Cullen Bryant, Ralph Waldo Emerson, Henry David Thoreau, and many others, along with over twenty stories and sketches by O'Sullivan's good friend Nathaniel Hawthorne. Historians speculate that O'Sullivan may have been the first person to use the term *manifest destiny* to voice the pervasive cultural belief that the United States had a divinely appointed mission to spread its democratic institutions across the North American continent. Though he initially opposed the war with Mexico, his 1845 essay "Annexation," in which he first used the term, helped provide a rationale for the 1846 invasion. He also used the term in the December 27, 1845, *New York Morning News* to argue that the United States should take all of Oregon country from the British "by the right of our manifest destiny to overspread and to possess the whole of the continent." O'Sullivan sold the *Democratic Review* in 1846, and by the late 1840s was arguing that the United States should annex Cuba from Spain. He provided funding for two illegal invasions in the early 1850s, and these unsuccessful ventures depleted his finances. After the outbreak of the Civil War, he accepted money from the Confederacy to travel to Europe and defend its position on states' rights and slavery. O'Sullivan returned to the United States in the early 1870s, and died in obscurity in a New York hotel in 1895. The text of "Annexation" is taken from the July and August 1845 issue of the *United States Magazine and Democratic Review.*

From Annexation

It is time now for opposition to the Annexation of Texas[1] to cease, all further agitation of the waters of bitterness and strife, at least in connexion with this question,—even though it may perhaps be required of us as a necessary condition of the freedom of our institutions, that we must live on for ever in a state of unpausing struggle and excitement upon some subject of party division or other. But, in regard to Texas, enough has now been given to party. It is time for the common duty of Patriotism to the Country to succeed;—or

1. Shortly after O'Sullivan wrote this essay, Texas was admitted to the Union as the twenty-eighth state. This act led to the Mexican-American War (1846–48).

if this claim will not be recognized, it is at least time for common sense to acquiesce with decent grace in the inevitable and the irrevocable.

* * *

Why, were other reasoning wanting, in favor of now elevating this question of the reception of Texas into the Union, out of the lower region of our past party dissensions, up to its proper level of a high and broad nationality, it surely is to be found, found abundantly, in the manner in which other nations[2] have undertaken to intrude themselves into it, between us and the proper parties to the case, in a spirit of hostile interference against us, for the avowed object of thwarting our policy and hampering our power, limiting our greatness and checking the fulfilment of our manifest destiny to overspread the continent allotted by Providence for the free development of our yearly multiplying millions.

* * *

California[3] will, probably, next fall away from the loose adhesion which, in such a country as Mexico, holds a remote province in a slight equivocal kind of dependence on the metropolis. Imbecile and distracted, Mexico never can exert any real governmental authority over such a country. The impotence of the one and the distance of the other, must make the relation one of virtual independence; unless, by stunting the province of all natural growth, and forbidding that immigration which can alone develope its capabilities and fulfil the purposes of its creation, tyranny may retain a military dominion, which is no government in the legitimate sense of the term. In the case of California this is now impossible. The Anglo-Saxon foot is already on its borders. Already the advance guard of the irresistible army of Anglo-Saxon emigration has begun to pour down upon it, armed with the plough and the rifle, and marking its trail with schools and colleges, courts and representative halls, mills and meeting-houses. A population will soon be in actual occupation of California, over which it will be idle for Mexico to dream of dominion. They will necessarily become independent. All this without agency of our government, without responsibility of our people—in the natural flow of events, the spontaneous working of principles, and the adaptation of the tendencies and wants of the human race to the elemental circumstances in the midst of which they find themselves placed.

* * *

1845

2. Around this time there were suspicions that the English and French were plotting to take land in Texas.

3. After the war with Mexico, California entered the Union as the thirty-first state in 1850.

FRANCIS PARKMAN JR.

Born in Boston, Massachusetts, the son of the Unitarian minister Francis Parkman, Francis Parkman Jr. (1823–1893) attended the elite Gideon Thayer private school in Boston (1836–40), and then went to Harvard, graduating in 1844. Like Richard Henry Dana Jr., Parkman was well positioned for a conventional, successful New England life. But soon after entering Harvard's Dane Law School, he withdrew; suffering from eye problems similar to Dana's (but much worse), he decided like Dana that a physical challenge would help improve his health. In 1846 he journeyed into the Wyoming Territory with his cousin Quincy Adams Shaw and spent seven months traveling along the California and Oregon Trail. Upon his return, he did some law work while preparing a manuscript about his travels. He serialized his account in the *Knickerbocker Magazine* from February 1847 to February 1849 and in 1849 published his travel narrative as a book, *The California and Oregon Trail: Being Sketches of Prairie and Rocky Mountain Life*, with the New York firm of George P. Putnam. (Parkman would change the title to *The Oregon Trail* in a revised edition of 1872.) In many ways, Parkman cannot transcend his identity as an invasive New Englander; he writes condescendingly of the Ogillallah and other Indians and laments the passing of the buffalo even as he kills buffalo. But among the impressive achievements of the book is his masterful job of capturing the emigration fever that swept the country around the time of the outbreak of the war with Mexico, and of limning the West as a distinctive region of the expanding nation. Published just a year after gold was discovered in California, the book served as a sort of handbook for the thousands who decided on western emigration. After the publication of *The California and Oregon Trail*, Parkman devoted himself for the next forty years to his nine-volume *France and England in North America* (1865–92), one of the great historical works of the nineteenth century. The selection from *The California and Oregon Trail*, which comes from the book's first chapter, is taken from the first edition of 1849.

From The California and Oregon Trail

* * *

We entered the mouth of the Missouri[1] in a drizzling rain, but the weather soon became clear, and showed distinctly the broad and turbid river, with its eddies, its sand-bars, its ragged islands and forest-covered shores. The Missouri is constantly changing its course; wearing away its banks on one side, while it forms new ones on the other. Its channel is shifting continually. Islands are formed, and then washed away; and while the old forests on one side are undermined and swept off, a young growth springs up from the new soil upon the other. With all these changes, the water is so charged with mud and sand that it is perfectly opaque, and in a few minutes deposits a sedi-

1. Parkman is traveling with his first cousin Quincy A. Shaw (1824–1908); they are on the Missouri River in the spring of 1846.

ment an inch thick in the bottom of a tumbler. The river was now high; but when we descended in the autumn it was fallen very low, and all the secrets of its treacherous shallows were exposed to view. It was frightful to see the dead and broken trees, thick-set as a military abattis,[2] firmly imbedded in the sand, and all pointing down stream, ready to impale any unhappy steamboat that at high water should pass over that dangerous ground.

In five or six days we began to see signs of the great western movement that was then taking place. Parties of emigrants, with their tents and wagons, would be encamped on open spots near the bank, on their way to the common rendezvous at Independence.[3] On a rainy day, near sunset, we reached the landing of this place, which is situated some miles from the river, on the extreme frontier of Missouri. The scene was characteristic, for here were represented at one view the most remarkable features of this wild and enterprising region. On the muddy shore stood some thirty or forty dark slavish-looking Spaniards,[4] gazing stupidly out from beneath their broad hats. They were attached to one of the Santa Fé companies, whose wagons were crowded together on the banks above. In the midst of these, crouching over a smouldering fire, was a group of Indians, belonging to a remote Mexican tribe. One or two French hunters from the mountains, with their long hair and buckskin dresses, were looking at the boat; and seated on a log close at hand were three men, with rifles lying across their knees. The foremost of these, a tall, strong figure, with a clear blue eye and an open, intelligent face, might very well represent that race of restless and intrepid pioneers whose axes and rifles have opened a path from the Alleghanies to the western prairies. He was on his way to Oregon, probably a more congenial field to him than any that now remained on this side the great plains.

Early on the next morning we reached Kanzas,[5] about five hundred miles from the mouth of the Missouri. Here we landed, and leaving our equipments in charge of my good friend Colonel Chick, whose log-house was the substitute for a tavern, we set out in a wagon for Westport,[6] where we hoped to procure mules and horses for the journey.

It was a remarkably fresh and beautiful May morning. The rich and luxuriant woods through which the miserable road conducted us, were lighted by the bright sunshine and enlivened by a multitude of birds. We overtook on the way our late fellow-travellers, the Kanzas Indians, who, adorned with all their finery, were proceeding homeward at a round pace; and whatever they might have seemed on board the boat, they made a very striking and picturesque feature in the forest landscape.

Westport was full of Indians, whose little shaggy ponies were tied by dozens along the houses and fences. Sacs and Foxes, with shaved heads and painted faces, Shawanoes and Delawares, fluttering in calico frocks and turbans, Wyandots dressed like white men, and a few wretched Kanzas wrapped in old blankets, were strolling about the streets, or lounging in and out of the shops and houses.

2. Abatis; trees with sharpened branches tied together and used as a military defense.
3. Town in Missouri.
4. Mexicans.
5. Kansas (archaic spelling). Parkman is at the early site of Kansas City, Missouri.
6. Trading town in Missouri. William Miles "Colonel" Chick (1790–1847) was a leading trader in Westport and one of the founders of what would become Kansas City.

As I stood at the door of the tavern, I saw a remarkable-looking person coming up the street. He had a ruddy face, garnished with the stumps of a bristly red beard and moustache; on one side of his head was a round cap with a knob at the top, such as Scottish laborers sometimes wear: his coat was of a nondescript form, and made of a gray Scotch plaid, with the fringes hanging all about it; he wore pantaloons of coarse homespun, and hob-nailed[7] shoes; and to complete his equipment, a little black pipe was stuck in one corner of his mouth. In this curious attire, I recognized Captain C. of the British army, who, with his brother, and Mr. R. an English gentleman,[8] was bound on a hunting expedition across the continent. I had seen the captain and his companions at St. Louis. They had now been for some time at Westport, making preparations for their departure, and waiting for a reinforcement, since they were too few in number to attempt it alone. They might, it is true, have joined some of the parties of emigrants who were on the point of setting out for Oregon and California; but they professed great disinclination to have any connection with the 'Kentucky fellows.'

* * *

The emigrants for whom our friends professed such contempt, were encamped on the prairie about eight or ten miles distant, to the number of a thousand or more, and new parties were constantly passing out from Independence to join them. They were in great confusion, holding meetings, passing resolutions, and drawing up regulations, but unable to unite in the choice of leaders to conduct them across the prairie. Being at leisure one day, I rode over to Independence. The town was crowded. A multitude of shops had sprung up to furnish the emigrants and Santa Fé traders with necessaries for their journey; and there was an incessant hammering and banging from a dozen blacksmiths' sheds, where the heavy wagons were being repaired, and the horses and oxen shod. The streets were thronged with men, horses, and mules. While I was in the town, a train of emigrant wagons from Illinois passed through, to join the camp on the prairie, and stopped in the principal street. A multitude of healthy children's faces were peeping out from under the covers of the wagons. Here and there a buxom damsel was seated on horseback, holding over her sunburnt face an old umbrella or a parasol, once gaudy enough, but now miserably faded. The men, very sober-looking countrymen, stood about their oxen; and as I passed I noticed three old fellows, who, with their long whips in their hands, were zealously discussing the doctrine of regeneration.[9] The emigrants, however, are not all of this stamp. Among them are some of the vilest outcasts in the country. I have often perplexed myself to divine the various motives that give impulse to this strange migration; but whatever they may be, whether an insane hope of a better condition in life, or a desire of shaking off restraints of law and society, or mere restlessness, certain it is, that multitudes bitterly repent the journey,

7. Large-headed nails used to protect the soles of shoes.
8. Parkman's casual acquaintances: Bill Chandler and his brother Jack, both Irish, and their English leader, William Romaine.
9. Spiritual rebirth or conversion that brings about complete moral reform.

and after they have reached the land of promise, are happy enough to escape from it.

* * *

1849

JAMES M. WHITFIELD

Born free in Exeter, New Hampshire, James M. Whitfield (1822–1871) moved in the late 1830s to Buffalo, New York, where he soon became a leader of Buffalo's African American community. A barber by trade, he participated in black reading societies and helped to organize antislavery protests, where he often recited his poetry. While attending African American conventions in the late 1840s and early 1850s, he met a number of more nationally based African American leaders, including Frederick Douglass and Martin Delany. In 1853 James S. Leavitt of Buffalo published Whitfield's only book of poems, *America and Other Poems*, which was dedicated to Delany. Douglass, for his part, had previously published several of Whitfield's poems in the *North Star* and *Frederick Douglass' Paper*, and he printed a favorable review of *America* in the July 15, 1853, issue of *Frederick Douglass' Paper*. However, around that time Whitfield and Douglass broke on the matter of black emigration. Whitfield accepted Delany's view that blacks should consider emigrating to Central America (see the selection by Delany in the section on "Race, Slavery, and the Making of American Literature"), while Douglass wanted blacks to work for equality and citizenship within the United States. A debate between Whitfield and Douglass's associate editors appeared over several issues of *Frederick Douglass' Paper* and was reprinted in *Arguments, Pro and Con, on the Call for a National Emigration Convention* (1854). Although there is evidence that Whitfield considered emigrating to Haiti in 1859 or 1860, instead he moved to San Francisco in 1861, where he continued to work as a barber and write poetry. At an anniversary celebration of the Emancipation Proclamation in 1867, Whitfield read his poetry to the thousands of attendees at San Francisco's Platt's Hall.

Whitfield's *America* offers a complex view of the United States and of "America" itself, with poems about U.S. leaders, such as the antislavery advocate and sixth president John Quincy Adams, and other poems about black rebels of the Americas, such as Cinque, who led the famous 1839 slave revolt on the Cuban slave ship *Amistad*. The volume also includes an ode on the unfulfilled promises of Fourth of July and the poem printed below on West Indies emancipation, which Whitfield initially read at a First of August celebration in Buffalo in 1849. For many African Americans, England's declaration on August 1, 1834, of the abolition of slavery in the British West Indies (which includes the present-day Caribbean nations of Jamaica, Barbados, Antigua, Guyana, and many others) offered an occasion for mass celebrations in the United States that expressed diasporic longings for black freedom throughout the Americas. The poem is taken from *America* (1853), which is reprinted in *The Works of James M. Whitfield* (2011), ed. Robert S. Levine and Ivy G. Wilson.

Stanzas for the First of August

From bright West Indies' sunny seas,
Comes, borne upon the balmy breeze,
The joyous shout, the gladsome tone,
Long in those bloody isles unknown,
Bearing across the heaving wave
The song of the unfettered slave.

No charging squadrons shook the ground,
When freedom here her claims obtained;
No cannon, with tremendous sound,
The noble patriot's cause maintained:
No furious battle-charger neighed,
No brother fell by brother's blade.

None of those desperate scenes of strife,
Which mark the warrior's proud career,
The awful waste of human life,
Have ever been enacted here;
But truth and justice spoke from heaven,
And slavery's galling chain was riven.

'T was moral force which broke the chain,
That bound eight hundred thousand men;
And when we see it snapped in twain,
Shall we not join in praises then?—
And prayers unto Almighty God,
Who smote to earth the tyrant's rod?

And from those islands of the sea,
The scenes of blood and crime and wrong,
The glorious anthem of the free,
Now swells in mighty chorus strong;
Telling th' oppressed, where'er they roam,
Those islands now are freedom's home.

1853

JULIA WARD HOWE

Best known as the author of "The Battle Hymn of the Republic" (1862), which celebrated the soldiers of the Union army for doing God's redemptive work, the poet Julia Ward Howe (1819–1910) was also an influential leader of the women's suffrage movement. She was born in New York City; in 1841 she traveled to Boston where she met Samuel Gridley Howe (1801–1876), a physician and the head of the Perkins

Institute for the Blind, whom she married in 1843. The Howes shared a passion for reform, but by all accounts their marriage was troubled by Samuel's unwillingness to let his wife participate in public meetings, preferring that she stay at home with their children. She published her first collection of poems, *Passion-Flowers*, in 1854, and her second, *Words for the Hour*, in 1857. The "Battle Hymn of the Republic" was published in the February 1862 issue of the *Atlantic Monthly*, adding to her literary reputation. After the death of her husband in 1876, her advocacy of women's suffrage became her principal vocation. In 1880 she published *Modern Society*, a collection of her addresses on women's rights, and up to the time of her death she had a central role in organizing and leading such organizations as the New England Woman Suffrage Association and the Association for the Advancement of Women.

Howe was a passionate traveler. In 1868 she published *From the Oak to the Olive: A Plain Record of a Pleasant Journey*, which brought together accounts of several European visits from the 1850s and 1860s. In 1859 she traveled to Cuba with her husband and the Boston abolitionist preacher Theodore Parker, sending back reports which were published in the 1859 *Atlantic Monthly* and became the basis of her *A Trip to Cuba*, published by Boston's prestigious firm of Ticknor and Fields in 1860 and the source of the selection below. New Englanders traveling to Cuba during the antebellum period were generally antislavery, and a chapter in *A Trip to Cuba* looks forward to the end of slavery in that country while suggesting that slavery in Cuba is not as cruel as in the United States. Sometimes she even seems to take pleasure in watching slave labor. Aware that Southerners hoped to extend slavery into the southern Americas in one way or another, she disparages the Spanish, another slave power, which at that time had dominion over Cuba. But even as she criticized the Spanish, Howe would have been aware that the president of the United States, James Buchanan, publicly advocated the annexation of Cuba. As is true of other accounts written by Northern travelers, most notably Richard Henry Dana's *To Cuba and Back* (1859), she presents Cuba as having the potential to become more "American" after the overthrow of the Spanish. In the selection below, she even (jokingly) contemplates a Yankee invasion.

From A Trip to Cuba

* * *

I will say that Matanzas[1] is lovely,—with the fair harbor on one hand and the fair hills on the other, sitting like a mother between two beautiful daughters, who looks from one to the other and wonders which she loves best. The air from the water is cool and refreshing, the sky is clear and open, and the country around seems to beckon one to the green bosom of its shades. "Oh, what a relief after Havana!" one says, drawing a full breath, and remembering with a shudder the sickening puffs from its stirring streets, which make you think that Polonius[2] lies unburied in every house, and that you nose him as you *knows* not, as you pass the door and window-gratings. With this

1. City on Cuba's northern coast, approximately fifty miles west of Havana, the nation's capital. At the time Matanzas had numerous sugar plantations and over 100,000 slaves.

2. In Shakespeare's *Hamlet*, Ophelia's father, who is killed by Hamlet; later, when Claudius asks where Polonius's body is, Hamlet tells him, "But indeed, if you find him not this month, you shall nose him as you go up the stairs into the lobby" (4.3.34–36).

exclamation and remembrance, you lower yourself into one of Mr. Ensor's[3] rocking-chairs,—twelve of which, with a rickety table and a piano, four crimson tidies and six white ones, form the furniture of the Ensor drawing-room,—you lean your head on your hand, close your eyes, and wish for a comfortable room with a bed in it. A tolerable room you shall have; but for a bed, only a cot-bedstead with a sacking bottom,—further, nothing. Now, if you are some folks that I know, you will be able to establish very comfortable repose on this slender foundation, Nature having so amply furnished you that you are your own feather-bed, bolster, sofa-cushion, and easy-chair, a moving mass of upholstery, wanting only a frame to be set down in and supported. But if you should be one of Boston's normal skeletons, pinched in every member with dyspepsia, and with the mark of the beast Neuralgia[4] on your forehead, then your skin will have a weary time of it, holding your bones, and you will be fain to entreat with tears the merciful mediation of a mattress.

Now I know very well that those of my readers who intend visiting Cuba will be much more interested in statistics of hotels than in any speculations, poetical or philosophical, with which I might be glad to recompense their patience. Let me tell them, therefore, that the Ensor House is neither better nor worse than other American hotels in Cuba. The rooms are not very bad, the attendance not intolerable, the table[5] almost commendable. The tripe, salt-fish, and plantains were, methought, much as at other places. There were stews of meat, onions, sweet peppers, and *ochra*, which deserve notice. The early coffee was punctual; the tea, for a wonder, black and hot. True, it was served on a bare pine table, with the accompaniment only of a bit of dry bread,—no butter, cake, nor *dulces*.[6] But Mr. Ensor has heard, no doubt, that sweet things are unwholesome, and is determined, at whatever cost to his own feelings, to keep them out of the way of his guests, who are, for the time, his children. Then there is an excellent English servant called John, whom, though the fair Ensor did berate him, we must enumerate among the comforts of the establishment. There is a dark corner about *volantes*,[7] which they are disposed to order for you at a very unreasonable profit; but as there are plenty of livery stables at hand, and street *volantes* passing all the time, it will be your own fault if you pay six dollars where you ought to pay three.

The first thing to be done at Matanzas is to drive out and see the Cumbre, a hill in the neighborhood, and from it the valley of the Yumori. The road is an improvement on those already described;—the ruts being much deeper and the rocks much larger, the jolting is altogether more complete and effective. Still, you remember the doctrine that the *volante* cannot upset, and this blind faith to which you cling carries you through triumphantly. The Cumbre is lofty, the view extensive, and the valley lovely, of a soft, light green, like the early leaves and grass of spring, dotted everywhere with the palms and their dark clusters. It opens far, far down at your feet, and on your left you see the harbor quiet and bright in the afternoon sun, with a cheering display of masts and pennons.[8] You would look and linger long, but that the light will

3. The proprietor of the inn where Howe is staying.
4. Muscle or nerve pains. "Dyspepsia": digestive disorder.
5. I.e., the dinner table and the food served there.
6. Sweets (Spanish).
7. Two-wheeled carriages (Spanish).
8. I.e., streamers, banners.

wane, and you are on your way to Jenks, his sugar-plantation, the only one within convenient distance of the town. Here the people are obviously accustomed to receive visitors, and are decently, not superfluously, civil. The *major-domo*[9] hands you over to a negro who speaks English, and who salutes you at once with, "Good-bye, Sir!" The boiling here is conducted in one huge, open vat. A cup and saucer are brought for you to taste the juice, which is dipped out of the boiling vat for your service. It is very like balm-tea, unduly sweetened; and after a hot sip or so you return the cup with thanks. A loud noise, as of cracking of whips and of hurrahs, guides you to the sugar-mill, where the crushing of the cane goes on in the jolliest fashion. The building is octagonal and open. Its chief feature is a very large horizontal wheel, which turns the smaller ones that grind the cane. This wheel is turned after the following manner. In the centre of the building, and as it were in the second story, stands a stout post, to which are attached, at equal distances, six horizontal bars, which are dragged round by six horses, vehemently flogged by the like number of slaves, male and female. This is really a novel and picturesque sight. Each negro is armed with a short whip, and their attitudes, as they stand, well-balanced on the revolving wheel, are rather striking. Liberal as they were of blows and of objurations to the horses, all their cries and whipping produced scarcely a tenth of the labor so silently performed by the invisible, noiseless slave that works the steam-engine.

* * *

The second thing to be done in Matanzas, if you arrive on Saturday, is to attend military mass at the Cathedral on Sunday morning. This commences at eight o'clock; but the hour previous may be advantageously employed in watching the arrival and arrangement of the female aristocracy of Matanzas. These enter in groups of twos and threes, carrying their prayer-books, and followed by slaves of either sex, who bear the prayer-carpet of their mistresses. The ladies are wonderfully got up, considering the early hour; and their toilettes suggest that they may not have undressed since the ball of the night before. All that hoops, powder, and puffery can do for them has been done; they walk in silk attire, and their hair is what is technically termed dressed. Some of them bring their children, bedizened like dolls, and mimicking mamma's gestures and genuflection in a manner more provoking to sadness than to satire. If the dressing is elaborate, the crossing is also. It does not consist of one simple cross, "*in nomine Patris,*"[1] etc.; they seem to make three or four crosses from forehead to chin, and conclude by kissing the thumb-nail, in honor of what or whom we could not imagine. Entering the middle aisle, which is divided from the rest by a row of seats on either side, they choose their position, and motion to the dark attendant to spread the carpet. Some of them evince considerable strategic skill in the selection of their ground. All being now in readiness, they drop on their knees, spread their flounces,[2] cross themselves, open their books, and look about them. Their attendants retire a little, spread a handkerchief on the ground, and modestly kneel behind them, obviously expecting to be saved with the family. These are neatly,

9. Head steward or butler (Spanish).
1. In the name of the Father (Latin).
2. Decorative materials sewn onto garments.

sometimes handsomely dressed. In this *status* things remain until the music of the regiment is heard. With a martial sound of trumpets it enters the church, and fills the aisles, the officers taking place within the chancel,[3] and a guard of honor of eight soldiers ranging on either side of the officiating priest. And now our devotions begin in good earnest; for, simultaneously with the regiment, the *jeunesse dorée*[4] of Matanzas has made its appearance, and has ranged itself along the two long lines of demarcation which separate the fair penitents from the rest of the congregation. The ladies now spread their flounces again, and their eyes find other occupation than the dreary Latin of their missals. There is, so to speak, a lively and refreshing time between the youths of both sexes, while the band plays its utmost, and *Evangel, Kyrie,* and *Credo* are recited to the music of Trovatore and Traviata.[5] That child of four years old, dressed in white and gold flounces, and white satin boots with heels, handles her veil and uses her eyes like Mamma, eager for notice, and delighted with the gay music and uniforms. The moment comes to elevate the Host,—thump goes the drum, the guard presents arms, and the soldiers, instead of kneeling, bend forward, in a most uncomfortable manner. Another thump, and all that is over; the swords are returned to their sheaths, and soon, the loud music coming to an end, the regiment marches out of church, very much as it marched in, its devotional experiences being known to Heaven alone. Ladies and lovers look their last, the flounces rise in pyramids, the prayer-carpets are rolled up, and with a silken sweep and rush, Youth, Beauty, and Fashion forsake the church, where Piety has hardly been, and go home to breakfast. To that comfortable meal you also betake yourself, musing on the small heads and villainous low foreheads of the Spanish soldiery, and wondering how long it would take a handful of resolute Yankees to knock them all into —— But you are not a Filibuster,[6] you know.

* * *

And here ends our account of Matanzas, our journey thither, stay, and return. Peace rest upon the fair city! May the earthquake and hurricane spare it! May the hateful Spanish government sit lightly on its strong shoulders! May the Filibusters attack it with kisses, and conquer it with loving-kindness! So might it be with the whole Island—*vale*![7]

1860

3. The space around the altar of a church, usually for the officiating clergy.
4. Literally, "gilded youth" (French); the young people of wealth and fashion.
5. Famous operas by the Italian composer Giuseppe Verdi (1813–1901). "*Evangel, Kyrie,* and *Credo*": important Latin prayers in the Roman Catholic liturgy.
6. Name given to those of this era who attempted to mount their own invasions of countries in the southern Americas.
7. A vernacular form of confirmation (Spanish), meaning something like "all night" or "okay."

MARY BOYKIN MILLER CHESNUT

In February 1861, the South Carolinian Mary Boykin Miller Chesnut (1823–1886) began a diary in which she continued to write regularly through February 1865. She returned to this Civil War diary in 1881, and over the next three years revised, edited, rearranged, and expanded the manuscript. The result is a literary masterpiece, one of the richest firsthand accounts that we have of Southern society during the years of the Civil War—an account made all the richer by the fact that it is written from the perspective of a woman who was barred from formal participation in the politics of the Confederacy and the operations of her slave plantation but who nonetheless observed just about everything that was important about her society. The diary presents both an insider's view of the Confederacy and a tough skepticism as well. Chesnut recurrently expresses her hesitations about slavery, about the situation of women in the slave South, and about the South's decision to secede. At the same time, she remains true to her husband, James Chesnut, whom she had married in 1840, at the age of seventeen, and lived with at Mulberry, a slave plantation near Camden, South Carolina. James Chesnut was elected to the U.S. Senate in 1858, and when the South seceded, he became a personal aide to the Confederate's president, Jefferson Davis. Mary Chesnut thus had close relations with (and described in her diary) many of the most prominent men and women of the Confederacy. After the war, James Chesnut worked on restoring their shattered finances and in 1873 was able to build a substantial house in Camden. When he died in 1885, his property was bequeathed to male heirs and Mary Chesnut was left nearly impoverished; she died a year later of a heart condition.

Chesnut's diary, unpublished in her lifetime, appeared in several versions in the twentieth century, culminating in a fully annotated complete version, *Mary Chesnut's Civil War*, ed. C. Vann Woodward, which won the Pulitzer Prize for history in 1981. The text of the selection from Chesnut's diary, an ironically prophetic entry on sectional conflict, is reprinted from this edition with the permission of Yale University Press.

From Mary Chesnut's Civil War

* * *

In the hotel[1] parlor we had a scene.

Mrs. Scott[2] was describing Lincoln, who is of the cleverest Yankee type, she said. "Awfully ugly—even grotesque in appearance, the kind who are always at corner stores, sitting on boxes, whittling sticks. And telling stories as funny as they are vulgar."

Here I interposed to sigh, "But Douglas[3] said one day to Mr. Chesnut, 'Lincoln is the hardest fellow to handle I have ever encountered yet.'" Mr. Scott

1. An unnamed hotel in Montgomery, Alabama, in March 1861.
2. Anne Scott of Alabama was the wife of Charles Lewis Scott (1827–1899), a former Virginia congressman who moved to Alabama and later enlisted as a private in the Confederate Army.
3. Illinois Democratic senator Stephen Douglas (1813–1861) defeated Lincoln in the election of 1858; the two engaged in a series of famous debates on the future of slavery in the United States.

is from California. He said: "Lincoln is an utterly American specimen, coarse, tough, and strong. A good-natured, kindly creature.

"As pleasant-tempered as he is clever. And if this country can be joked and laughed out of its rights, he is the kind-hearted fellow to do it. Now, if there be a war and it pinches the Yankee pocket instead of filling it—"

Here a shrill voice came from the next room (which opened upon the one we were in by folding doors, thrown wide open):

"Yankees are no more mean and stingy than you are. People at the North are as good as people at the South."

The speaker advanced upon us in great wrath. Mrs. Scott apologized and made some smooth, polite remarks, though evidently much embarrassed. But the vinegar face and curly pate refused to receive any concession. She said, "That comes with a very bad grace after what you were saying." And she harangued us loudly for several minutes. Someone in the other room giggled outright. We were quiet as mice.

Nobody wanted to hurt her feelings. She was one against so many. If I were at the North I should expect them to belabor us—and should hold my tongue. We separated because of incompatibility of temper. We are divorced, North from South, because we hated each other so. If we could only separate—a "séparation à l'agréable," as the French say it, and not a horrid fight for divorce.

This poor exile had already been insulted, she said. She was playing "Yankee Doodle" on the piano before breakfast to soothe her wounded spirits. The Judge[4] came in and calmly requested her to leave out the Yankee while she played the Doodle. The Yankee end of it did not suit our climate. Was totally out of place. Had got out of its latitude, &c&c.

* * *

1861

4. The common-law judge Thomas Withers (1804–1866) of Camden, South Carolina, emerged as one of the leaders of the Confederacy; he was Chesnut's uncle.

WALT WHITMAN
1819–1892

Walt Whitman revolutionized American poetry. Responding to Emerson's call in "The Poet" (1842) for an American bard who would address all "the facts of the animal economy, sex, nutriment, gestation, birth," Whitman put the living, breathing, sexual body at the center of much of his poetry, challenging conventions of the day. Responding to Emerson's call for a "metre-making argument," he rejected traditions of poetic scansion and elevated diction, improvising the form that has come to be known as free verse, while adopting a wide-ranging vocabulary opening new possibilities for poetic expression. A poet of democracy, Whitman celebrated the mystical, divine potential of the individual; a poet of the urban, he wrote about the sights, sounds, and energy of the modern metropolis. In his 1855 preface to *Leaves of Grass*, he declared that "the proof of a poet is that his country absorbs him as affectionately as he has absorbed it." On the evidence of his enormous influence on later poets—Hart Crane, Langston Hughes, Robert Lowell, Allen Ginsberg, Adrienne Rich, Cherrie Moraga, and countless others, including Spain's Federico Garcia Lorca and Chile's Pablo Neruda—Whitman not only was affectionately absorbed by his own country but remains a persistent presence in poetry throughout the world.

Whitman was born on May 31, 1819, in West Hills, Long Island (New York), the second of eight surviving children of the Quakers Louisa Van Velsor and Walter Whitman. In 1823, Whitman's father, a farmer turned carpenter, sought to take advantage of a building boom by moving the family to Brooklyn—then a town at the western and most urbanized part of Long Island. Whitman left school when he was eleven, and was soon employed in the printing office of a newspaper; when his family moved east on Long Island in 1833, he remained in Brooklyn on his own. In his midteens he contributed pieces to one of the best Manhattan papers, the *Mirror*, and often crossed the East River on the ferry from Brooklyn to Manhattan to attend debating societies and the theater. He was hired as a compositor in Manhattan in 1835, but two major fires later that year disrupted the printing industry, and he rejoined his family. For five years Whitman taught at country and small-town schools at East Norwich, Long Swamp, and other towns on Long Island, interrupting his teaching to start a newspaper of his own in 1838 and to work briefly on another Long Island paper. By early 1840 he had started the series "Sun-Down Papers from the Desk of a School-Master" for the Jamaica, New York, *Democrat* and was writing poems and fiction. One of his stories prophetically culminated with the dream of writing "a wonderful and ponderous book."

Just before he turned twenty-one Whitman stopped teaching, went back to Manhattan, began work at the literary weekly *New World*, and soon became editor of a Manhattan daily, the *Aurora*. He also began a political career by speaking at Democratic rallies and writing for the *Democratic Review*, the foremost magazine of the Democratic Party. He exulted in the extremes of the city, where street-gang violence was countered by the lectures of Emerson and where even a young editor could get to know the poet William Cullen Bryant, editor of the *Evening Post*. Fired from the *Aurora*, which publicly charged him with laziness, he wrote a temperance novel, *Franklin Evans, or the Inebriate*, for a one-issue extra of the *New World* late in 1842. After three years of various literary and political jobs, he returned to Brooklyn in 1845, becoming a special contributor to the *Long Island Star*, assigned to Manhattan events, including theatrical and musical performances. All through the 1840s he attended operas on his journalist's passes and he would later say that without the "emotions, raptures, uplifts" of opera he could never have written *Leaves of Grass*. Just before he was twenty-seven he took over the editorship of the *Brooklyn Eagle*, writing most of the literary reviews, which included books by Carlyle, Emerson, Melville, Fuller, and Goethe, among others. Like most Democrats, he was able to justify the Mexican War (1846–48) by hailing the great American mission of "peopling the New World with a noble race." Yet at the beginning of 1848 he was fired from the *Eagle* because, like Bryant, he had become a Free-Soiler, opposed to the acquisition of more territory for slavery. Whitman served as a delegate to the Buffalo Free-Soil convention and helped to found the Free-Soil newspaper the *Brooklyn Freeman*. Around this time he began writing poetry in a serious way, experimenting with form and prosody; he published several topical poems in 1850, including "Europe," which would later appear in *Leaves of Grass*.

Whitman's notebook fragments suggest that he began to invent the overall shape of his first volume of poetry during the period 1853–54. On May 15, 1855, he took

Leaves of Grass. Frontispiece and title page of the first edition (1855).

out a copyright for *Leaves of Grass,* and he spent the spring and early summer seeing his book through the press, probably setting some of the type himself. Published in Brooklyn, New York, during the first week of July, the volume, bound in dark green cloth with a sprig of grass in gilt on the cover, contained twelve untitled poems (including the initial version of "Song of Myself") along with an exuberant preface declaring his ambition to be the American bard. In the image of Whitman on the book's frontispiece, which was based on an 1854 daguerreotype, the bearded Whitman—rejecting the conventional suit jacket, buttoned-up shirt, and high collar of the formal studio portrait—stands with one arm akimbo, one hand in a pocket, workingman's hat on slightly cocked head, shirt unbuttoned at the collar, looking directly at the reader. (See the reproduction above.) The image, like the poetry itself, defied convention by aligning the poet with working people. The poems, with their absence of standard verse and stanza patterns (although strongly rhythmic and controlled by numerous poetic devices of repetition and variation), also introduced his use of "catalogs"—journalistic and encyclopedic listings—that were to become a hallmark of his style. Whitman sent out numerous presentation and review copies of his book, receiving an immediate response from Emerson, who greeted him "at the beginning of a great career" (the complete letter is reprinted on p. 348), but otherwise attracting little notice. As weeks passed, Whitman chose to publish a few anonymous reviews himself, praising *Leaves of Grass* in the *American Phrenological Journal,* for instance, as one of "the most glorious triumphs, in the known history of literature." In October he let Horace Greeley's *New York Tribune* print Emerson's private letter of praise, and he put clippings of the letter in presentation copies to Longfellow, among others. Emerson termed Whitman's appropriation of the letter "a strange, rude thing," but he remained interested in meeting the poet. While Whitman was angling for reviews in England and working on expanding his book, Emerson visited him in December of 1855. Thoreau, who admired *Leaves of Grass* but found several of its poems "simply sensual," visited him later in 1856. That year also saw the appearance of the second edition of *Leaves of Grass*, now with thirty-three poems, including "Crossing Brooklyn Ferry" under its initial title "Sundown Poem."

Returning to miscellaneous journalism, Whitman edited the *Brooklyn Times* from 1857 to 1859 and published several pieces in the *Times* affirming his Free-Soiler hopes for a continued national expansion into the western territories that would not entail the expansion of slavery. In the third (1860) edition of *Leaves of Grass*, Whitman began to group his poems thematically. For a section called "Enfans d' Adam," later retitled "Children of Adam," he wrote fifteen poems focused on what he termed the "amative" love of man for woman, in contrast to the "adhesive" love of man for man. Adhesive love figured in forty-five poems in a section titled "Calamus." These two sections in the 1860 edition differ from the sections in the final 1891–92 edition, for in the intervening editions (1867, 1871, 1881) Whitman revised and regrouped some of the poems, as he would with numerous other poems in the expanded editions he would go on to publish.

With the outbreak of the Civil War, Whitman began to visit the wounded and eventually offered his services as a nurse. He started at New-York Hospital, but in early 1863, after visiting with his wounded brother George in an army camp in Virginia, he moved to Washington, D.C., and began to work at the huge open-air military hospitals there. Nursing gave Whitman a profound sense of vocation. As he wrote a friend in 1863: "I am very happy . . . I was never so beloved. I am running over with health, fat, red & sunburnt in face. I tell thee I am just the one to go to our sick boys." But ministering to tens of thousands of maimed and dying young men took its toll. He succinctly voiced his anguish in a notebook entry of 1864: "the dead, the dead, the dead, our dead." During this time he worked on a series of poems that conveyed his evolving view of the war from heroic celebration to despair at the horrifying carnage. He later wrote a chapter in his prose work *Specimen Days* (1882) titled "The Real War Will Never Get in the Books," but to incorporate the "real war" into a book of poetry became one of the dominant impulses of the *Drum-Taps* collection, which he published in 1865. After Lincoln's assassination, Whitman reissued the volume with a sequel including "O Captain! My Captain!" and "When Lilacs Last in the Dooryard Bloom'd," his famous elegy for the murdered president.

As he prepared *Drum-Taps and Sequel* for publication in late 1865, Whitman was also revising *Leaves of Grass* at his desk in the Department of the Interior, where he had obtained a position as clerk. The new secretary of the interior, James Harlan, read the annotated copy and fired Whitman for writing an obscene book, objecting to Whitman's frankness about bodily functions and heterosexual love. Whitman's friend, the poet William O'Connor, found him another clerical position in the attorney general's office; and in his rage at the firing, O'Connor wrote *The Good Gray Poet* (1866), identifying Whitman with Jesus and Harlan with the forces of evil. Whitman continued to rework *Leaves of Grass*, incorporating *Drum-Taps* into it in 1867, and with his friends' help continued to propagandize for its recognition as a landmark in the history of poetry. He also published essays in 1867 and 1868 numbers of the New York periodical *Galaxy*, which he expanded into *Democratic Vistas* (1870), a book conveying his sometimes sharply condemnatory appraisal of postwar democratic culture.

The Washington years came to an abrupt end in 1873 when Whitman suffered a paralytic stroke. His mother died a few months later, and Whitman joined his brother George's household in Camden, New Jersey, to recuperate. During the second year of his illness, the government ceased to hold his clerk job open for him, and he became dependent for a living on occasional publication in newspapers and magazines. The 1867 edition of *Leaves of Grass* had involved much reworking and rearrangement, and the fifth edition (1871) continued that process, adding a new section titled "Passage to India." In 1876 Whitman privately published a prose work, *Memoranda during the War*, and six years later he brought out *Specimen Days*, which has affinities with his early editorial accounts of strolls through the city but is even more intensely personal, the record of representative days in the life of a poet who had lived in the midst of great national events.

During the 1870s and early 1880s, Whitman was increasingly noticed by the leading writers of the time, especially in England. The English poet Algernon Swinburne sent him a poem, the poet laureate Alfred Lord Tennyson sent him an admiring letter, and both Longfellow and Oscar Wilde visited him in Camden. Despite his frail health, Whitman lectured on Thomas Paine in Philadelphia in 1877 and on Abraham Lincoln in New York in 1879 (he would continue to deliver occasional public lectures on Lincoln until 1890). Opposition to his poetry because of its supposed immorality began to dissipate, and readers, having become accustomed over time to Whitman's poetic devices, began to recognize the poet as an artist. Still, in 1881, when the reputable Boston firm of James R. Osgood & Co. printed the sixth edition of *Leaves of Grass*, the Boston district attorney threatened to prosecute on the grounds of obscenity. Ironically, when the Philadelphia firm of Rees Welsh and Company reprinted this edition in 1882, the publicity contributed to Whitman's greatest sales in his lifetime: he earned nearly $1,500 in royalties from that edition (around $25,000 in today's value), compared to the $25 he had earned from the Osgood edition before the publisher withdrew it.

In 1884, the still infirm Whitman moved to a cottage at 328 Mickle Street in Camden, which he purchased for $1,750. A year later friends and admirers, including Mark Twain and John Greenleaf Whittier, presented him with a horse and buggy for local travel. He had another stroke in 1888 and in 1890 made preparations for his death by signing a $4,000 contract for the construction in Camden's Harleigh Cemetery of a granite mausoleum, or what he termed a "burial house," suitable for a national bard. In 1891 he did the final editing of *Complete Prose Works* (1892) and oversaw the preparations of the "deathbed" edition of the now more than three hundred poems in *Leaves of Grass* (1891–92), which was in fact a reissue of the 1881 edition with the addition of two later groups of poems, "Sands at Seventy" and "Good-bye My Fancy." Whitman died in Camden on March 26, 1892, and was buried in Harleigh Cemetery in the mausoleum he had helped design.

Except for the sequence "Live Oak, with Moss" (not published in Whitman's lifetime), all the Whitman poems reprinted here, regardless of when they were first composed and printed, are given in their final form: that of the 1891–92 edition of *Leaves of Grass*.

Preface to *Leaves of Grass* (1855)[1]

America does not repel the past or what it has produced under its forms or amid other politics or the idea of castes or the old religions . . . accepts the lesson with calmness . . . is not so impatient as has been supposed that the slough still sticks to opinions and manners and literature while the life which served its requirements has passed into the new life of the new forms . . . perceives that the corpse is slowly borne from the eating and sleeping rooms of the house . . . perceives that it waits a little while in the door . . . that it

1. The first edition of *Leaves of Grass* contained twelve untitled poems, which were introduced by this manifesto-like preface. The preface was not reprinted in subsequent editions, though some of its ideas were incorporated into future poems. The spellings and ellipses are Whitman's.

was fittest for its days . . . that its action has descended to the stalwart and wellshaped heir who approaches . . . and that he shall be fittest for his days.

The Americans of all nations at any time upon the earth have probably the fullest poetical nature. The United States themselves are essentially the greatest poem. In the history of the earth hitherto the largest and most stirring appear tame and orderly to their ampler largeness and stir. Here at last is something in the doings of man that corresponds with the broadcast doings of the day and night. Here is not merely a nation but a teeming nation of nations. Here is action untied from strings necessarily blind to particulars and details magnificently moving in vast masses. Here is the hospitality which forever indicates heroes. . . . Here are the roughs and beards and space and ruggedness and nonchalance that the soul loves. Here the performance disdaining the trivial unapproached in the tremendous audacity of its crowds and groupings and the push of its perspective spreads with crampless and flowing breadth and showers its prolific and splendid extravagance. One sees it must indeed own the riches of the summer and winter, and need never be bankrupt while corn grows from the ground or the orchards drop apples or the bays contain fish or men beget children upon women.

Other states indicate themselves in their deputies . . . . but the genius of the United States is not best or most in its executives or legislatures, nor in its ambassadors or authors or colleges or churches or parlors, nor even in its newspapers or inventors . . . but always most in the common people. Their manners speech dress friendships—the freshness and candor of their physiognomy—the picturesque looseness of their carriage . . . their deathless attachment to freedom—their aversion to anything indecorous or soft or mean—the practical acknowledgment of the citizens of one state by the citizens of all other states—the fierceness of their roused resentment—their curiosity and welcome of novelty—their self-esteem and wonderful sympathy—their susceptibility to a slight—the air they have of persons who never knew how it felt to stand in the presence of superiors—the fluency of their speech—their delight in music, the sure symptom of manly tenderness and native elegance of soul . . . their good temper and openhandedness—the terrible significance of their elections—the President's taking off his hat to them not they to him—these too are unrhymed poetry. It awaits the gigantic and generous treatment worthy of it.

The largeness of nature or the nation were monstrous without a corresponding largeness and generosity of the spirit of the citizen. Not nature nor swarming states nor streets and steamships nor prosperous business nor farms nor capital nor learning may suffice for the ideal of man . . . nor suffice the poet. No reminiscences may suffice either. A live nation can always cut a deep mark and can have the best authority the cheapest . . . namely from its own soul. This is the sum of the profitable uses of individuals or states and of present action and grandeur and of the subjects of poets.—As if it were necessary to trot back generation after generation to the eastern records! As if the beauty and sacredness of the demonstrable must fall behind that of the mythical! As if men do not make their mark out of any times! As if the opening of the western continent by discovery and what has transpired since in North and South America were less than the small theatre of the antique or the aimless sleepwalking of the middle ages! The pride of the United States leaves the wealth and finesse of the cities and all returns of commerce and agriculture and all the magnitude of geography or shows of exterior victory to enjoy the breed of fullsized men or one fullsized man unconquerable and simple.

The American poets are to enclose old and new for America is the race of races. Of them a bard[2] is to be commensurate with a people. To him the other continents arrive as contributions . . . he gives them reception for their sake and his own sake. His spirit responds to his country's spirit . . . . he incarnates its geography and natural life and rivers and lakes. Mississippi with annual freshets and changing chutes, Missouri and Columbia and Ohio and Saint Lawrence with the falls and beautiful masculine Hudson, do not embouchure[3] where they spend themselves more than they embouchure into him. The blue breadth over the inland sea of Virginia and Maryland and the sea off Massachusetts and Maine and over Manhattan bay and over Champlain and Erie and over Ontario and Huron and Michigan and Superior, and over the Texan and Mexican and Floridian and Cuban seas and over the seas off California and Oregon, is not tallied by the blue breadth of the waters below more than the breadth of above and below is tallied by him. When the long Atlantic coast stretches longer and the Pacific coast stretches longer he easily stretches with them north or south. He spans between them also from east to west and reflects what is between them. On him rise solid growths that offset the growths of pine and cedar and hemlock and liveoak and locust and chestnut and cypress and hickory and limetree and cottonwood and tuliptree and cactus and wildvine and tamarind and persimmon . . . . and tangles as tangled as any canebrake or swamp . . . . and forests coated with transparent ice and icicles hanging from the boughs and crackling in the wind . . . . and sides and peaks of mountains . . . . and pasturage sweet and free as savannah or upland or prairie . . . . with flights and songs and screams that answer those of the wild pigeon and highhold and orchard-oriole and coot and surf-duck and redshouldered-hawk and fish-hawk and white-ibis and indian-hen and cat-owl and water-pheasant and qua-bird and pied-sheldrake and blackbird and mockingbird and buzzard and condor and night-heron and eagle. To him the hereditary countenance descends both mother's and father's. To him enter the essences of the real things and past and present events—of the enormous diversity of temperature and agriculture and mines—the tribes of red aborigines—the weatherbeaten vessels entering new ports or making landings on rocky coasts—the first settlements north or south—the rapid stature and muscle—the haughty defiance of '76, and the war and peace and formation of the constitution . . . . the union always surrounded by blatherers and always calm and impregnable—the perpetual coming of immigrants—the wharf hem'd cities and superior marine—the unsurveyed interior—the loghouses and clearings and wild animals and hunters and trappers . . . . the free commerce—the fisheries and whaling and gold-digging—the endless gestation of new states—the convening of Congress every December, the members duly coming up from all climates and the uttermost parts . . . . the noble character of the young mechanics and of all free American workmen and workwomen . . . . the general ardor and friendliness and enterprise—the perfect equality of the female with the

2. The ideal national poet, usually linked to older heroic or epic traditions.

3. Pour.

male . . . . the large amativeness—the fluid movement of the population—the factories and mercantile life and laborsaving machinery—the Yankee swap—the New-York firemen and the target excursion[4]—the southern plantation life—the character of the northeast and of the northwest and southwest—slavery and the tremulous spreading of hands to protect it, and the stern opposition to it which shall never cease till it ceases or the speaking of tongues and the moving of lips cease. For such the expression of the American poet is to be transcendant and new. It is to be indirect and not direct or descriptive or epic. Its quality goes through these to much more. Let the age and wars of other nations be chanted and their eras and characters be illustrated and that finish the verse. Not so the great psalm of the republic. Here the theme is creative and has vista. Here comes one among the wellbeloved stonecutters and plans with decision and science and sees the solid and beautiful forms of the future where there are now no solid forms.

Of all nations the United States with veins full of poetical stuff most need poets and will doubtless have the greatest and use them the greatest. Their Presidents shall not be their common referee so much as their poets shall. Of all mankind the great poet is the equable man. Not in him but off from him things are grotesque or eccentric or fail of their sanity. Nothing out of its place is good and nothing in its place is bad. He bestows on every object or quality its fit proportions neither more nor less. He is the arbiter of the diverse and he is the key. He is the equalizer of his age and land . . . . he supplies what wants supplying and checks what wants checking. If peace is the routine out of him speaks the spirit of peace, large, rich, thrifty, building vast and populous cities, encouraging agriculture and the arts and commerce—lighting the study of man, the soul, immortality—federal, state or municipal government, marriage, health, freetrade, intertravel by land and sea . . . . nothing too close, nothing too far off . . . the stars not too far off. In war he is the most deadly force of the war. Who recruits him recruits horse and foot . . . he fetches parks of artillery[5] the best that engineer ever knew. If the time becomes slothful and heavy he knows how to arouse it . . . he can make every word he speaks draw blood. Whatever stagnates in the flat of custom or obedience or legislation he never stagnates. Obedience does not master him, he masters it. High up out of reach he stands turning a concentrated light . . . he turns the pivot with his finger . . . he baffles the swiftest runners as he stands and easily overtakes and envelops them. The time straying toward infidelity and confections and persiflage[6] he withholds by his steady faith . . . he spreads out his dishes . . . he offers the sweet firmfibred meat that grows men and women. His brain is the ultimate brain. He is no arguer . . . he is judgment. He judges not as the judge judges but as the sun falling around a helpless thing. As he sees the farthest he has the most faith. His thoughts are the hymns of the praise of things. In the talk on the soul and eternity and God off of his equal plane he is silent. He sees eternity less like a play with a prologue and denouement . . . . he sees eternity in men and women . . . he does not see men and women as dreams or dots. Faith is

4. Shooting contest. "Every December": Before the adoption of the Twentieth Amendment in 1933, Congress convened on the first Monday in December, according to Article 1, Section 4, of the Constitution. "Amativeness": amorousness.

5. I.e., parks full of artillery—from the custom of drilling and parading in civic parks.

6. Bantering talk.

the antiseptic of the soul . . . it pervades the common people and preserves them . . . they never give up believing and expecting and trusting. There is that indescribable freshness and unconsciousness about an illiterate person that humbles and mocks the power of the noblest expressive genius. The poet sees for a certainty how one not a great artist may be just as sacred and perfect as the greatest artist. . . . . . The power to destroy or remould is freely used by him but never the power of attack. What is past is past. If he does not expose superior models and prove himself by every step he takes he is not what is wanted. The presence of the greatest poet conquers . . . not parleying or struggling or any prepared attempts. Now he has passed that way see after him! there is not left any vestige of despair or misanthropy or cunning or exclusiveness or the ignominy of a nativity or color or delusion of hell or the necessity of hell . . . . . . and no man thenceforward shall be degraded for ignorance or weakness or sin.

The greatest poet hardly knows pettiness or triviality. If he breathes into any thing that was before thought small it dilates with the grandeur and life of the universe. He is a seer . . . . he is individual . . . he is complete in himself . . . . the others are as good as he, only he sees it and they do not. He is not one of the chorus . . . . he does not stop for any regulation . . . he is the president of regulation. What the eyesight does to the rest he does to the rest. Who knows the curious mystery of the eyesight? The other senses corroborate themselves, but this is removed from any proof but its own and foreruns the identities of the spiritual world. A single glance of it mocks all the investigations of man and all the instruments and books of the earth and all reasoning. What is marvellous? what is unlikely? what is impossible or baseless or vague? after you have once just opened the space of a peachpit and given audience to far and near and to the sunset and had all things enter with electric swiftness softly and duly without confusion or jostling or jam.

The land and sea, the animals fishes and birds, the sky of heaven and the orbs, the forests mountains and rivers, are not small themes . . . but folks expect of the poet to indicate more than the beauty and dignity which always attach to dumb real objects . . . . they expect him to indicate the path between reality and their souls. Men and women perceive the beauty well enough . . probably as well as he. The passionate tenacity of hunters, woodmen, early risers, cultivators of gardens and orchards and fields, the love of healthy women for the manly form, sea-faring persons, drivers of horses, the passion for light and the open air, all is an old varied sign of the unfailing perception of beauty and of a residence of the poetic in outdoor people. They can never be assisted by poets to perceive . . . some may but they never can. The poetic quality is not marshalled in rhyme or uniformity or abstract addresses to things nor in melancholy complaints or good precepts, but is the life of these and much else and is in the soul. The profit of rhyme is that it drops seeds of a sweeter and more luxuriant rhyme, and of uniformity that it conveys itself into its own roots in the ground out of sight. The rhyme and uniformity of perfect poems show the free growth of metrical laws and bud from them as unerringly and loosely as lilacs or roses on a bush, and take shapes as compact as the shapes of chestnuts and oranges and melons and pears, and shed the perfume impalpable to form. The fluency and ornaments of the finest poems or music or orations or recitations are not independent but dependent. All beauty comes from beautiful blood and a beautiful brain.

If the greatnesses are in conjunction in a man or woman it is enough . . . . the fact will prevail through the universe . . . . but the gaggery[7] and gilt of a million years will not prevail. Who troubles himself about his ornaments or fluency is lost. This is what you shall do: Love the earth and sun and the animals, despise riches, give alms to every one that asks, stand up for the stupid and crazy, devote your income and labor to others, hate tyrants, argue not concerning God, have patience and indulgence toward the people, take off your hat to nothing known or unknown or to any man or number of men, go freely with powerful uneducated persons and with the young and with the mothers of families, read these leaves in the open air every season of every year of your life, reexamine all you have been told at school or church or in any book, dismiss whatever insults your own soul, and your very flesh shall be a great poem and have the richest fluency not only in its words but in the silent lines of its lips and face and between the lashes of your eyes and in every motion and joint of your body. . . . . . . The poet shall not spend his time in unneeded work. He shall know that the ground is always ready ploughed and manured . . . . others may not know it but he shall. He shall go directly to the creation. His trust shall master the trust of everything he touches . . . . and shall master all attachment.

The known universe has one complete lover and that is the greatest poet. He consumes an eternal passion and is indifferent which chance happens and which possible contingency of fortune or misfortune and persuades daily and hourly his delicious pay. What balks or breaks others is fuel for his burning progress to contact and amorous joy. Other proportions of the reception of pleasure dwindle to nothing to his proportions. All expected from heaven or from the highest he is rapport with in the sight of the day-break or a scene of the winter woods or the presence of children playing or with his arm round the neck of a man or woman. His love above all love has leisure and expanse . . . . he leaves room ahead of himself. He is no irresolute or suspicious lover . . . he is sure . . . he scorns intervals. His experience and the showers and thrills are not for nothing. Nothing can jar him . . . . suffering and darkness cannot—death and fear cannot. To him complaint and jealousy and envy are corpses buried and rotten in the earth . . . . he saw them buried. The sea is not surer of the shore or the shore of the sea than he is of the fruition of his love and of all perfection and beauty.

The fruition of beauty is no chance of hit or miss . . . it is inevitable as life . . . . it is exact and plumb as gravitation. From the eyesight proceeds another eyesight and from the hearing proceeds another hearing and from the voice proceeds another voice eternally curious of the harmony of things with man. To these respond perfections not only in the committees that were supposed to stand for the rest but in the rest themselves just the same. These understand the law of perfection in masses and floods . . . that its finish is to each for itself and onward from itself . . . that it is profuse and impartial . . . that there is not a minute of the light or dark nor an acre of the earth or sea without it—nor any direction of the sky nor any trade or employment nor any turn of events. This is the reason that about the proper expression of beauty there is precision and balance . . . one part does not need to be thrust above

7. Falseness.

another. The best singer is not the one who has the most lithe and powerful organ . . . the pleasure of poems is not in them that take the handsomest measure and similes and sound.

Without effort and without exposing in the least how it is done the greatest poet brings the spirit of any or all events and passions and scenes and persons some more and some less to bear on your individual character as you hear or read. To do this well is to compete with the laws that pursue and follow time. What is the purpose must surely be there and the clue of it must be there . . . . and the faintest indication is the indication of the best and then becomes the clearest indication. Past and present and future are not disjoined but joined. The greatest poet forms the consistence of what is to be from what has been and is. He drags the dead out of their coffins and stands them again on their feet . . . . he says to the past, Rise and walk before me that I may realize you. He learns the lesson . . . . he places himself where the future becomes present. The greatest poet does not only dazzle his rays over character and scenes and passions . . . he finally ascends and finishes all . . . he exhibits the pinnacles that no man can tell what they are for or what is beyond . . . . he glows a moment on the extremest verge. He is most wonderful in his last half-hidden smile or frown . . . by that flash of the moment of parting the one that sees it shall be encouraged or terrified afterward for many years. The greatest poet does not moralize or make applications of morals . . . he knows the soul. The soul has that measureless pride which consists in never acknowledging any lessons but its own. But it has sympathy as measureless as its pride and the one balances the other and neither can stretch too far while it stretches in company with the other. The inmost secrets of art sleep with the twain. The greatest poet has lain close betwixt both and they are vital in his style and thoughts.

The art of art, the glory of expression and the sunshine of the light of letters is simplicity. Nothing is better than simplicity . . . . nothing can make up for excess or for the lack of definiteness. To carry on the heave of impulse and pierce intellectual depths and give all subjects their articulations are powers neither common nor very uncommon. But to speak in literature with the perfect rectitude and insousiance of the movements of animals and the unimpeachableness of the sentiment of trees in the woods and grass by the roadside is the flawless triumph of art. If you have looked on him who has achieved it you have looked on one of the masters of the artists of all nations and times. You shall not contemplate the flight of the graygull over the bay or the mettlesome action of the blood horse or the tall leaning of sunflowers on their stalk or the appearance of the sun journeying through heaven or the appearance of the moon afterward with any more satisfaction than you shall contemplate him. The greatest poet has less a marked style and is more the channel of thoughts and things without increase or diminution, and is the free channel of himself. He swears to his art, I will not be meddlesome, I will not have in my writing any elegance or effect or originality to hang in the way between me and the rest like curtains. I will have nothing hang in the way, not the richest curtains. What I tell I tell for precisely what it is. Let who may exalt or startle or fascinate or sooth I will have purposes as health or heat or snow has and be as regardless of observation. What I experience or portray shall go from my composition without a shred of my composition. You shall stand by my side and look in the mirror with me.

The old red blood and stainless gentility of great poets will be proved by their unconstraint. A heroic person walks at his ease through and out of that custom or precedent or authority that suits him not. Of the traits of the brotherhood of writers savans[8] musicians inventors and artists nothing is finer than silent defiance advancing from new free forms. In the need of poems philosophy politics mechanism science behaviour, the craft of art, an appropriate native grand-opera, shipcraft, or any craft, he is greatest forever and forever who contributes the greatest original practical example. The cleanest expression is that which finds no sphere worthy of itself and makes one.

The messages of great poets to each man and woman are, Come to us on equal terms, Only then can you understand us, We are no better than you, What we enclose you enclose, What we enjoy you may enjoy. Did you suppose there could be only one Supreme? We affirm there can be unnumbered Supremes, and that one does not countervail another any more than one eyesight countervails another . . and that men can be good or grand only of the consciousness of their supremacy within them. What do you think is the grandeur of storms and dismemberments and the deadliest battles and wrecks and the wildest fury of the elements and the power of the sea and the motion of nature and of the throes of human desires and dignity and hate and love? It is that something in the soul which says, Rage on, Whirl on, I tread master here and everywhere, Master of the spasms of the sky and of the shatter of the sea, Master of nature and passion and death, And of all terror and all pain.

The American bards shall be marked for generosity and affection and for encouraging competitors . . They shall be kosmos . . without monopoly or secresy . . glad to pass any thing to any one . . . hungry for equals night and day. They shall not be careful of riches and privilege . . . . they shall be riches and privilege . . . . they shall perceive who the most affluent man is. The most affluent man is he that confronts all the shows he sees by equivalents out of the stronger wealth of himself. The American bard shall delineate no class of persons nor one or two out of the strata of interests nor love most nor truth most nor the soul most nor the body most . . . . and not be for the eastern states more than the western or the northern states more than the southern.

Exact science and its practical movements are no checks on the greatest poet but always his encouragement and support. The outset and remembrance are there . . there the arms that lifted him first and brace him best . . . . there he returns after all his goings and comings. The sailor and traveler . . the anatomist chemist astronomer geologist phrenologist spiritualist mathematician historian and lexicographer are not poets, but they are the lawgivers of poets and their construction underlies the structure of every perfect poem. No matter what rises or is uttered they sent the seed of the conception of it . . . of them and by them stand the visible proofs of souls . . . . . always of their fatherstuff must be begotten the sinewy races of bards. If there shall be love and content between the father and the son and if the greatness of the son is the exuding of the greatness of the father there shall

8. Learned persons, scientists.

be love between the poet and the man of demonstrable science. In the beauty of poems are the tuft and final applause of science.

Great is the faith of the flush of knowledge and of the investigation of the depths of qualities and things. Cleaving and circling here swells the soul of the poet yet is president of itself always. The depths are fathomless and therefore calm. The innocence and nakedness are resumed . . . they are neither modest nor immodest. The whole theory of the special and supernatural and all that was twined with it or educed out of it departs as a dream. What has ever happened . . . . what happens and whatever may or shall happen, the vital laws enclose all . . . . they are sufficient for any case and for all cases . . . none to be hurried or retarded . . . . any miracle of affairs or persons inadmissible in the vast clear scheme where every motion and every spear of grass and the frames and spirits of men and women and all that concerns them are unspeakably perfect miracles all referring to all and each distinct and in its place. It is also not consistent with the reality of the soul to admit that there is anything in the known universe more divine than men and women.

Men and women and the earth and all upon it are simply to be taken as they are, and the investigation of their past and present and future shall be unintermitted and shall be done with perfect candor. Upon this basis philosophy speculates ever looking toward the poet, ever regarding the eternal tendencies of all toward happiness never inconsistent with what is clear to the senses and to the soul. For the eternal tendencies of all toward happiness make the only point of sane philosophy. Whatever comprehends less than that . . . whatever is less than the laws of light and of astronomical motion . . . or less than the laws that follow the thief the liar the glutton and the drunkard through this life and doubtless afterward . . . . . . or less than vast stretches of time or the slow formation of density or the patient upheaving of strata—is of no account. Whatever would put God in a poem or system of philosophy as contending against some being or influence is also of no account. Sanity and ensemble characterise the great master . . . spoilt in one principle all is spoilt. The great master has nothing to do with miracles. He sees health for himself in being one of the mass . . . . he sees the hiatus in singular eminence. To the perfect shape comes common ground. To be under the general law is great for that is to correspond with it. The master knows that he is unspeakably great and that all are unspeakably great . . . . that nothing for instance is greater than to conceive children and bring them up well . . . that to be is just as great as to perceive or tell.

In the make of the great masters the idea of political liberty is indispensible. Liberty takes the adherence of heroes wherever men and women exist . . . . but never takes any adherence or welcome from the rest more than from poets. They are the voice and exposition of liberty. They out of ages are worthy the grand idea . . . . to them it is confided and they must sustain it. Nothing has precedence of it and nothing can warp or degrade it. The attitude of great poets is to cheer up slaves and horrify despots. The turn of their necks, the sound of their feet, the motions of their wrists, are full of hazard to the one and hope to the other. Come nigh them awhile and though they neither speak or advise you shall learn the faithful American lesson. Liberty is poorly served by men whose good intent is quelled from one failure or two failures or any number of failures, or from the casual indifference or ingratitude of the people, or from the sharp show of the tushes of power, or the bringing to bear soldiers and cannon or any penal statutes. Liberty relies upon itself, invites no one, promises nothing, sits in calmness and light, is positive and composed, and knows no discouragement. The battle rages with many a loud alarm and frequent advance and retreat . . . . the enemy triumphs . . . . the prison, the handcuffs, the iron necklace and anklet, the scaffold, garrote and leadballs do their work . . . . the cause is asleep . . . . the strong throats are choked with their own blood . . . . the young men drop their eyelashes toward the ground when they pass each other . . . . and is liberty gone out of that place? No never. When liberty goes it is not the first to go nor the second or third to go . . it waits for all the rest to go . . it is the last. . . When the memories of the old martyrs are faded utterly away . . . . when the large names of patriots are laughed at in the public halls from the lips of the orators . . . . when the boys are no more christened after the same but christened after tyrants and traitors instead . . . . when the laws of the free are grudgingly permitted and laws for informers and bloodmoney are sweet to the taste of the people . . . . when I and you walk abroad upon the earth stung with compassion at the sight of numberless brothers answering our equal friendship and calling no man master—and when we are elated with noble joy at the sight of slaves . . . . when the soul retires in the cool communion of the night and surveys its experience and has much extasy over the word and deed that put back a helpless innocent person into the gripe of the gripers or into any cruel inferiority . . . . when those in all parts of these states who could easier realize the true American character but do not yet—when the swarms of cringers, suckers, doughfaces,[9] lice of politics, planners of sly involutions for their own preferment to city offices or state legislatures of the judiciary or congress or the presidency, obtain a response of love and natural deference from the people whether they get the offices or no . . . . when it is better to be a bound booby and rogue in office at a high salary than the poorest free mechanic or farmer with his hat unmoved from his head and firm eyes and a candid and generous heart . . . . and when servility by town or state or the federal government or any oppression on a large scale or small scale can be tried on without its own punishment following duly after in exact proportion against the smallest chance of escape . . . . or rather when all life and all the souls of men and women are discharged from any part of the earth—then only shall the instinct of liberty be discharged from that part of the earth.

As the attributes of the poets of the kosmos concentre in the real body and soul and in the pleasure of things they possess the superiority of genuineness over all fiction and romance. As they emit themselves facts are showered over with light . . . . the daylight is lit with more volatile light . . . . also the deep between the setting and rising sun goes deeper many fold. Each precise object or condition or combination or process exhibits a beauty . . . . the multiplication table its—old age its—the carpenter's trade its—the grand-opera its . . . . the hugehulled cleanshaped New-York clipper at sea under steam or full sail gleams with unmatched beauty . . . . the American circles and large harmonies of government gleam with theirs . . . . and the commonest definite intentions and actions with theirs. The poets of the

9. Pliable politicians. The term was used at the time to refer to Northern politicians who supported Southern proslavery policies.

kosmos advance through all interpositions and coverings and turmoils and strategems to first principles. They are of use . . . . they dissolve poverty from its need and riches from its conceit. You large proprietor they say shall not realize or perceive more than any one else. The owner of the library is not he who holds a legal title to it having bought and paid for it. Any one and every one is owner of the library who can read the same through all the varieties of tongues and subjects and styles, and in whom they enter with ease and take residence and force toward paternity and maternity, and make supple and powerful and rich and large. . . . . These American states strong and healthy and accomplished shall receive no pleasure from violations of natural models and must not permit them. In paintings or mouldings or carvings in mineral or wood, or in the illustrations of books or newspapers, or in any comic or tragic prints, or in the patterns of woven stuffs or any thing to beautify rooms or furniture or costumes, or to put upon cornices or monuments or on the prows or sterns of ships, or to put anywhere before the human eye indoors or out, that which distorts honest shapes or which creates unearthly beings or places or contingencies is a nuisance and revolt. Of the human form especially it is so great it must never be made ridiculous. Of ornaments to a work nothing outre[1] can be allowed . . but those ornaments can be allowed that conform to the perfect facts of the open air and that flow out of the nature of the work and come irrepressibly from it and are necessary to the completion of the work. Most works are most beautiful without ornament . . . Exaggerations will be revenged in human physiology. Clean and vigorous children are jetted and conceived only in those communities where the models of natural forms are public every day. . . . . Great genius and the people of these states must never be demeaned to romances. As soon as histories are properly told there is no more need of romances.

The great poets are also to be known by the absence in them of tricks and by the justification of perfect personal candor. Then folks echo a new cheap joy and a divine voice leaping from their brains: How beautiful is candor! All faults may be forgiven of him who has perfect candor. Henceforth let no man of us lie, for we have seen that openness wins the inner and outer world and that there is no single exception, and that never since our earth gathered itself in a mass have deceit or subterfuge or prevarication attracted its smallest particle or the faintest tinge of a shade—and that through the enveloping wealth and rank of a state or the whole republic of states a sneak or sly person shall be discovered and despised . . . . and that the soul has never been once fooled and never can be fooled . . . . and thrift without the loving nod of the soul is only a fœtid puff . . . . and there never grew up in any of the continents of the globe nor upon any planet or satellite or star, nor upon the asteroids, nor in any part of ethereal space, nor in the midst of density, nor under the fluid wet of the sea, nor in that condition which precedes the birth of babes, nor at any time during the changes of life, nor in that condition that follows what we term death, nor in any stretch of abeyance or action afterward of vitality, nor in any process of formation or reformation anywhere, a being whose instinct hated the truth.

1. Excessive, extravagant; from the French *outré* (outrageous).

Extreme caution or prudence, the soundest organic health, large hope and comparison and fondness for women and children, large alimentiveness[2] and destructiveness and causality, with a perfect sense of the oneness of nature and the propriety of the same spirit applied to human affairs . . these are called up of the float of the brain of the world to be parts of the greatest poet from his birth out of his mother's womb and from her birth out of her mother's. Caution seldom goes far enough. It has been thought that the prudent citizen was the citizen who applied himself to solid gains and did well for himself and his family and completed a lawful life without debt or crime. The greatest poet sees and admits these economies as he sees the economies of food and sleep, but has higher notions of prudence than to think he gives much when he gives a few slight attentions at the latch of the gate. The premises of the prudence of life are not the hospitality of it or the ripeness and harvest of it. Beyond the independence of a little sum laid aside for burial-money, and of a few clapboards around and shingles overhead on a lot of American soil owned, and the easy dollars that supply the year's plain clothing and meals, the melancholy prudence of the abandonment of such a great being as a man is to the toss and pallor of years of moneymaking with all their scorching days and icy nights and all their stifling deceits and underhanded dodgings, or infinitessimals of parlors, or shameless stuffing while others starve . . and all the loss of the bloom and odor of the earth and of the flowers and atmosphere and of the sea and of the true taste of the women and men you pass or have to do with in youth or middle age, and the issuing sickness and desperate revolt at the close of a life without elevation or naivete, and the ghastly chatter of a death without serenity or majesty, is the great fraud upon modern civilization and forethought, blotching the surface and system which civilization undeniably drafts, and moistening with tears the immense features it spreads and spreads with such velocity before the reached kisses of the soul . . . Still the right explanation remains to be made about prudence. The prudence of the mere wealth and respectability of the most esteemed life appears too faint for the eye to observe at all when little and large alike drop quietly aside at the thought of the prudence suitable for immortality. What is wisdom that fills the thinness of a year or seventy or eighty years to wisdom spaced out by ages and coming back at a certain time with strong reinforcements and rich presents and the clear faces of wedding-guests as far as you can look in every direction running gaily toward you? Only the soul is of itself . . . . all else has reference to what ensues. All that a person does or thinks is of consequence. Not a move can a man or woman make that affects him or her in a day or a month or any part of the direct lifetime or the hour of death but the same affects him or her onward afterward through the indirect lifetime. The indirect is always as great and real as the direct. The spirit receives from the body just as much as it gives to the body. Not one name of word or deed . . not of venereal sores or discolorations . . not the privacy of the onanist[3] . . not of the putrid veins of gluttons or rumdrinkers . . . not peculation or cunning or betrayal or murder . . no serpentine poison of those that seduce women . . not the foolish yielding of women . . not prostitution . . not of any depravity of young men . .

2. Love of food.
3. Masturbator; from Onan, son of Judah, who "spilled *it* [his "seed"] on the ground" (Genesis 38.9).

not of the attainment of gain by discreditable means . . not any nastiness of appetite . . not any harshness of officers to men or judges to prisoners or fathers to sons or sons to fathers or of husbands to wives or bosses to their boys . . not of greedy looks or malignant wishes . . . nor any of the wiles practised by people upon themselves . . . ever is or ever can be stamped on the programme but it is duly realized and returned, and that returned in further performances . . . and they returned again. Nor can the push of charity or personal force ever be any thing else than the profoundest reason, whether it brings arguments to hand or no. No specification is necessary . . to add or subtract or divide is in vain. Little or big, learned or unlearned, white or black, legal or illegal, sick or well, from the first inspiration down the windpipe to the last expiration out of it, all that a male or female does that is vigorous and benevolent and clean is so much sure profit to him or her in the unshakable order of the universe and through the whole scope of it forever. If the savage or felon is wise it is well . . . . if the greatest poet or savan is wise it is simply the same . . if the President or chief justice is wise it is the same . . . if the young mechanic or farmer is wise it is no more or less . . if the prostitute is wise it is no more nor less. The interest will come round . . all will come round. All the best actions of war and peace . . . all help given to relatives and strangers and the poor and old and sorrowful and young children and widows and the sick, and to all shunned persons . . all furtherance of fugitives and of the escape of slaves . . all the self-denial that stood steady and aloof on wrecks and saw others take the seats of the boats . . . all offering of substance or life for the good old cause, or for a friend's sake or opinion's sake . . . all pains of enthusiasts scoffed at by their neighbors . . all the vast sweet love and precious suffering of mothers . . . all honest men baffled in strifes recorded or unrecorded . . . . all the grandeur and good of the few ancient nations whose fragments of annals we inherit . . and all the good of the hundreds of far mightier and more ancient nations unknown to us by name or date or location . . . . all that was ever manfully begun, whether it succeeded or no . . . . all that has at any time been well suggested out of the divine heart of man or by the divinity of his mouth or by the shaping of his great hands . . and all that is well thought or done this day on any part of the surface of the globe . . or on any of the wandering stars or fixed stars by those there as we are here . . or that is henceforth to be well thought or done by you whoever you are, or by any one—these singly and wholly inured at their time and inure now and will inure always to the identities from which they sprung or shall spring. . . Did you guess any of them lived only its moment? The world does not so exist . . no parts palpable or impalpable so exist . . . no result exists now without being from its long antecedent result, and that from its antecedent, and so backward without the farthest mentionable spot coming a bit nearer the beginning than any other spot. . . . . Whatever satisfies the soul is truth. The prudence of the greatest poet answers at last the craving and glut of the soul, is not contemptuous of less ways of prudence if they conform to its ways, puts off nothing, permits no let-up for its own case or any case, has no particular sabbath or judgment-day, divides not the living from the dead or the righteous from the unrighteous, is satisfied with the present, matches every thought or act by its correlative, knows no possible forgiveness or deputed atonement . . knows that the young man who composedly periled his life and lost it has done exceeding well for himself, while the man who has not periled his life and retains it to old age in riches and ease has perhaps achieved nothing for himself worth mentioning . . and that only that person has no great prudence to learn who has learnt to prefer real longlived things, and favors body and soul the same, and perceives the indirect assuredly following the direct, and what evil or good he does leaping onward and waiting to meet him again—and who in his spirit in any emergency whatever neither hurries or avoids death.

The direct trial of him who would be the greatest poet is today. If he does not flood himself with the immediate age as with vast oceanic tides . . . . . and if he does not attract his own land body and soul to himself and hang on its neck with incomparable love and plunge his semitic[4] muscle into its merits and demerits . . . and if he be not himself the age transfigured . . . . and if to him is not opened the eternity which gives similitude to all periods and locations and processes and animate and inanimate forms, and which is the bond of time, and rises up from its inconceivable vagueness and infiniteness in the swimming shape of today, and is held by the ductile anchors of life, and makes the present spot the passage from what was to what shall be, and commits itself to the representation of this wave of an hour and this one of the sixty beautiful children of the wave—let him merge in the general run and wait his development. . . . . Still the final test of poems or any character or work remains. The prescient poet projects himself centuries ahead and judges performer or performance after the changes of time. Does it live through them? Does it still hold on untired? Will the same style and the direction of genius to similar points be satisfactory now? Has no new discovery in science or arrival at superior planes of thought and judgment and behaviour fixed him or his so that either can be looked down upon? Have the marches of tens and hundreds and thousands of years made willing detours to the right hand and the left hand for his sake? Is he beloved long and long after he is buried? Does the young man think often of him? and the young woman think often of him? and do the middleaged and the old think of him?

A great poem is for ages and ages in common and for all degrees and complexions and all departments and sects and for a woman as much as a man and a man as much as a woman. A great poem is no finish to a man or woman but rather a beginning. Has any one fancied he could sit at last under some due authority and rest satisfied with explanations and realize and be content and full? To no such terminus does the greatest poet bring . . . he brings neither cessation or sheltered fatness and ease. The touch of him tells in action. Whom he takes he takes with firm sure grasp into live regions previously unattained . . . . thenceforward is no rest . . . . they see the space and ineffable sheen that turn the old spots and lights into dead vacuums. The companion of him beholds the birth and progress of stars and learns one of the meanings. Now there shall be a man cohered out of tumult and chaos . . . . the elder encourages the younger and shows him how . . . they two shall launch off fearlessly together till the new world fits an orbit for itself and looks unabashed on the lesser orbits of the stars and sweeps through the ceaseless rings and shall never be quiet again.

There will soon be no more priests. Their work is done. They may wait awhile . . perhaps a generation or two . . dropping off by degrees. A superior

4. A coinage for penis, derived from the Latin semen (seed).

breed shall take their place . . . . the gangs of kosmos and prophets en masse shall take their place. A new order shall arise and they shall be the priests of man, and every man shall be his own priest. The churches built under their umbrage[5] shall be the churches of men and women. Through the divinity of themselves shall the kosmos and the new breed of poets be interpreters of men and women and of all events and things. They shall find their inspiration in real objects today, symptoms of the past and future . . . . They shall not deign to defend immortality or God or the perfection of things or liberty or the exquisite beauty and reality of the soul. They shall arise in America and be responded to from the remainder of the earth.

The English language befriends the grand American expression . . . . it is brawny enough and limber and full enough. On the tough stock of a race who through all change of circumstance was never without the idea of political liberty, which is the animus of all liberty, it has attracted the terms of daintier and gayer and subtler and more elegant tongues. It is the powerful language of resistance . . . it is the dialect of common sense. It is the speech of the proud and melancholy races and of all who aspire. It is the chosen tongue to express growth faith self-esteem freedom justice equality friendliness amplitude prudence decision and courage. It is the medium that shall well nigh express the inexpressible.

No great literature nor any like style of behaviour or oratory or social intercourse or household arrangements or public institutions or the treatment by bosses of employed people, nor executive detail or detail of the army or navy, nor spirit of legislation or courts or police or tuition or architecture or songs or amusements or the costumes of young men, can long elude the jealous and passionate instinct of American standards. Whether or no the sign appears from the mouths of the people, it throbs a live interrogation in every freeman's and freewoman's heart after that which passes by or this built to remain. Is it uniform with my country? Are its disposals without ignominious distinctions? Is it for the evergrowing communes of brothers and lovers, large, well-united, proud beyond the old models, generous beyond all models? Is it something grown fresh out of the fields or drawn from the sea for use to me today here? I know that what answers for me an American must answer for any individual or nation that serves for a part of my materials. Does this answer? or is it without reference to universal needs? or sprung of the needs of the less developed society of special ranks? or old needs of pleasure overlaid by modern science and forms? Does this acknowledge liberty with audible and absolute acknowledgement, and set slavery at nought for life and death? Will it help breed one goodshaped and wellhung man, and a woman to be his perfect and independent mate? Does it improve manners? Is it for the nursing of the young of the republic? Does it solve[6] readily with the sweet milk of the nipples of the breasts of the mother of many children? Has it too the old ever-fresh forbearance and impartiality? Does it look with the same love on the last born on those hardening toward stature, and on the errant, and on those who disdain all strength of assault outside of their own?

The poems distilled from other poems will probably pass away. The coward will surely pass away. The expectation of the vital and great can only be satisfied by the demeanor of the vital and great. The swarms of the polished

5. Shadow, protection.

6. Dissolve.

deprecating and reflectors and the polite float off and leave no remembrance. America prepares with composure and goodwill for the visitors that have sent word. It is not intellect that is to be their warrant and welcome. The talented, the artist, the ingenious, the editor, the statesman, the erudite . . they are not unappreciated . . they fall in their place and do their work. The soul of the nation also does its work. No disguise can pass on it . . no disguise can conceal from it. It rejects none, it permits all. Only toward as good as itself and toward the like of itself will it advance half-way. An individual is as superb as a nation when he has the qualities which make a superb nation. The soul of the largest and wealthiest and proudest nation may well go half-way to meet that of its poets. The signs are effectual. There is no fear of mistake. If the one is true the other is true. The proof of a poet is that his country absorbs him as affectionately as he has absorbed it.

1855

From Inscriptions[1]

One's-Self I Sing

One's-Self I sing, a simple separate person,
Yet utter the word Democratic, the word En-Masse.

Of physiology from top to toe I sing,
Not physiognomy[2] alone nor brain alone is worthy for the Muse, I
say the Form complete is worthier far,
The Female equally with the Male I sing.

Of Life immense in passion, pulse, and power,
Cheerful, for freest action form'd under the laws divine,
The Modern Man I sing.

1867, 1871

Shut Not Your Doors

Shut not your doors to me proud libraries,
For that which was lacking on all your well-fill'd shelves, yet
needed most, I bring,
Forth from the war emerging, a book I have made,
The words of my book nothing, the drift of it every thing,
A book separate, not link'd with the rest nor felt by the intellect,
But you ye untold latencies will thrill to every page.

1865, 1881

1. This title was first used for the opening poems of *Leaves of Grass* in 1871; in 1881 the number of poems was increased from nine to twenty-four.

2. The practice of judging or interpreting human character from facial features.

Song of Myself[1]

1

I celebrate myself, and sing myself,
And what I assume you shall assume,
For every atom belonging to me as good belongs to you.

I loafe and invite my soul,
I lean and loafe at my ease observing a spear of summer grass.

My tongue, every atom of my blood, form'd from this soil, this air,
Born here of parents born here from parents the same, and their parents the same,
I, now thirty-seven years old in perfect health begin,
Hoping to cease not till death.

Creeds and schools in abeyance,
Retiring back a while sufficed at what they are, but never forgotten,
I harbor for good or bad, I permit to speak at every hazard,
Nature without check with original energy.

2

Houses and rooms are full of perfumes, the shelves are crowded with perfumes,
I breathe the fragrance myself and know it and like it,
The distillation would intoxicate me also, but I shall not let it.

The atmosphere is not a perfume, it has no taste of the distillation, it is odorless,
It is for my mouth forever, I am in love with it,
I will go to the bank by the wood and become undisguised and naked,
I am mad for it to be in contact with me.

The smoke of my own breath,
Echoes, ripples, buzz'd whispers, love-root, silk-thread, crotch and vine,
My respiration and inspiration, the beating of my heart, the passing of blood and air through my lungs,
The sniff of green leaves and dry leaves, and of the shore and dark-color'd sea-rocks, and of hay in the barn,
The sound of the belch'd words of my voice loos'd to the eddies of the wind,
A few light kisses, a few embraces, a reaching around of arms,
The play of shine and shade on the trees as the supple boughs wag,

1. In the 1855 first edition of *Leaves of Grass*, the poem later called "Song of Myself" appeared without a title and without numbered sections or stanzas. For the 1856 edition, Whitman titled it "Poem of Walt Whitman, an American," and in the 1860 edition he titled it "Walt Whitman"; it retained that title in the 1867 and 1871 editions, and in the 1881 edition was named "Song of Myself." Whitman made numerous other changes to the poem from the first 1855 printing to the 1881 final version.

The delight alone or in the rush of the streets, or along the fields and hill-sides,
The feeling of health, the full-noon trill, the song of me rising from bed and meeting the sun.

Have you reckon'd a thousand acres much? have you reckon'd the earth much?
Have you practis'd so long to learn to read?
Have you felt so proud to get at the meaning of poems?

Stop this day and night with me and you shall possess the origin of all poems,
You shall possess the good of the earth and sun, (there are millions of suns left,)
You shall no longer take things at second or third hand, nor look through the eyes of the dead, nor feed on the spectres in books,
You shall not look through my eyes either, nor take things from me,
You shall listen to all sides and filter them from your self.

3

I have heard what the talkers were talking, the talk of the beginning and the end,
But I do not talk of the beginning or the end.

There was never any more inception than there is now,
Nor any more youth or age than there is now,
And will never be any more perfection than there is now,
Nor any more heaven or hell than there is now.

Urge and urge and urge,
Always the procreant urge of the world.

Out of the dimness opposite equals advance, always substance and increase, always sex,
Always a knit of identity, always distinction, always a breed of life.

To elaborate is no avail, learn'd and unlearn'd feel that it is so.

Sure as the most certain sure, plumb in the uprights, well entretied,[2] braced in the beams,
Stout as a horse, affectionate, haughty, electrical,
I and this mystery here we stand.

Clear and sweet is my soul, and clear and sweet is all that is not my soul.

Lack one lacks both, and the unseen is proved by the seen,
Till that becomes unseen and receives proof in its turn.

2. Cross-braced; reinforced.

Showing the best and dividing it from the worst age vexes age,
Knowing the perfect fitness and equanimity of things, while they discuss
I am silent, and go bathe and admire myself.

Welcome is every organ and attribute of me, and of any man hearty and clean,
Not an inch nor a particle of an inch is vile, and none shall be less familiar than the rest.

I am satisfied—I see, dance, laugh, sing;
As the hugging and loving bed-fellow sleeps at my side through the night, and withdraws at the peep of the day with stealthy tread,
Leaving me baskets cover'd with white towels swelling the house with their plenty,
Shall I postpone my acceptation and realization and scream at my eyes,
That they turn from gazing after and down the road,
And forthwith cipher[3] and show me to a cent,
Exactly the value of one and exactly the value of two, and which is ahead?

4

Trippers and askers surround me,
People I meet, the effect upon me of my early life or the ward and city I live in, or the nation,
The latest dates, discoveries, inventions, societies, authors old and new,
My dinner, dress, associates, looks, compliments, dues,
The real or fancied indifference of some man or woman I love,
The sickness of one of my folks or of myself, or ill-doing or loss or lack of money, or depressions or exaltations,
Battles, the horrors of fratricidal war, the fever of doubtful news, the fitful events;
These come to me days and nights and go from me again,
But they are not the Me myself.

Apart from the pulling and hauling stands what I am,
Stands amused, complacent, compassionating, idle, unitary,
Looks down, is erect, or bends an arm on an impalpable certain rest,
Looking with side-curved head curious what will come next,
Both in and out of the game and watching and wondering at it.

Backward I see in my own days where I sweated through fog with linguists and contenders,
I have no mockings or arguments, I witness and wait.

5

I believe in you my soul, the other I am must not abase itself to you,
And you must not be abased to the other.

3. Calculate.

Loafe with me on the grass, loose the stop from your throat,
Not words, not music or rhyme I want, not custom or lecture, not even the best,
Only the lull I like, the hum of your valvèd voice.

I mind how once we lay such a transparent summer morning,
How you settled your head athwart my hips and gently turn'd over upon me,
And parted the shirt from my bosom-bone, and plunged your tongue to my bare-stript heart,
And reach'd till you felt my beard, and reach'd till you held my feet.

Swiftly arose and spread around me the peace and knowledge that pass all the argument of the earth,
And I know that the hand of God is the promise of my own,
And I know that the spirit of God is the brother of my own,
And that all the men ever born are also my brothers, and the women my sisters and lovers,
And that a kelson[4] of the creation is love,
And limitless are leaves stiff or drooping in the fields,
And brown ants in the little wells beneath them,
And mossy scabs of the worm fence,[5] heap'd stones, elder, mullein and poke-weed.

6

A child said *What is the grass?* fetching it to me with full hands;
How could I answer the child? I do not know what it is any more than he.

I guess it must be the flag of my disposition, out of hopeful green stuff woven.

Or I guess it is the handkerchief of the Lord,
A scented gift and remembrancer designedly dropt,
Bearing the owner's name someway in the corners, that we may see and remark, and say *Whose?*

Or I guess the grass is itself a child, the produced babe of the vegetation.

Or I guess it is a uniform hieroglyphic,
And it means, Sprouting alike in broad zones and narrow zones,
Growing among black folks as among white,
Kanuck, Tuckahoe, Congressman, Cuff,[6] I give them the same, I receive them the same.

4. A basic structural unit; a reinforcing timber bolted to the keel (backbone) of a ship.
5. Fence built of interlocking rails in a zigzag pattern.
6. From the African word *cuffee* (name for black male born on a Friday). "Kanuck": French Canadian (now sometimes considered pejorative). "Tuckahoe": Virginian, from eaters of the American Indian food plant Tuckahoe.

And now it seems to me the beautiful uncut hair of graves.

Tenderly will I use you curling grass,
It may be you transpire from the breasts of young men,
It may be if I had known them I would have loved them,
It may be you are from old people, or from offspring taken soon out of their mothers' laps,
And here you are the mothers' laps.

This grass is very dark to be from the white heads of old mothers,
Darker than the colorless beards of old men,
Dark to come from under the faint red roofs of mouths.

O I perceive after all so many uttering tongues,
And I perceive they do not come from the roofs of mouths for nothing.

I wish I could translate the hints about the dead young men and women,
And the hints about old men and mothers, and the offspring taken soon out of their laps.

What do you think has become of the young and old men?
And what do you think has become of the women and children?

They are alive and well somewhere,
The smallest sprout shows there is really no death,
And if ever there was it led forward life, and does not wait at the end to arrest it,
And ceas'd the moment life appear'd.

All goes onward and outward, nothing collapses,
And to die is different from what any one supposed, and luckier.

7

Has any one supposed it lucky to be born?
I hasten to inform him or her it is just as lucky to die, and I know it.

I pass death with the dying and birth with the new-wash'd babe, and am not contain'd between my hat and boots,
And peruse manifold objects, no two alike and every one good,
The earth good and the stars good, and their adjuncts all good.

I am not an earth nor an adjunct of an earth,
I am the mate and companion of people, all just as immortal and fathomless as myself,
(They do not know how immortal, but I know.)

Every kind for itself and its own, for me mine male and female,
For me those that have been boys and that love women,
For me the man that is proud and feels how it stings to be slighted,
For me the sweet-heart and the old maid, for me mothers and the mothers of mothers,

For me lips that have smiled, eyes that have shed tears,
For me children and the begetters of children.

Undrape! you are not guilty to me, nor stale nor discarded,
I see through the broadcloth and gingham whether or no,
And am around, tenacious, acquisitive, tireless, and cannot be shaken away.

8

The little one sleeps in its cradle,
I lift the gauze and look a long time, and silently brush away flies with my hand.

The youngster and the red-faced girl turn aside up the bushy hill,
I peeringly view them from the top.

The suicide sprawls on the bloody floor of the bedroom,
I witness the corpse with its dabbled hair, I note where the pistol has fallen.

The blab of the pave, tires of carts, sluff of boot-soles, talk of the promenaders,
The heavy omnibus, the driver with his interrogating thumb, the clank of the shod horses on the granite floor,
The snow-sleighs, clinking, shouted jokes, pelts of snow-balls,
The hurrahs for popular favorites, the fury of rous'd mobs,
The flap of the curtain'd litter, a sick man inside borne to the hospital,
The meeting of enemies, the sudden oath, the blows and fall,
The excited crowd, the policeman with his star quickly working his passage to the centre of the crowd,
The impassive stones that receive and return so many echoes,
What groans of over-fed or half-starv'd who fall sunstruck or in fits,
What exclamations of women taken suddenly who hurry home and give birth to babes,
What living and buried speech is always vibrating here, what howls restrain'd by decorum,
Arrests of criminals, slights, adulterous offers made, acceptances, rejections with convex lips,
I mind them or the show or resonance of them—I come and I depart.

9

The big doors of the country barn stand open and ready,
The dried grass of the harvest-time loads the slow-drawn wagon,
The clear light plays on the brown gray and green intertinged,
The armfuls are pack'd to the sagging mow.

I am there, I help, I came stretch'd atop of the load,
I felt its soft jolts, one leg reclined on the other,
I jump from the cross-beams and sieze the clover and timothy,
And roll head over heels and tangle my hair full of wisps.

10

Alone far in the wilds and mountains I hunt,
Wandering amazed at my own lightness and glee,
In the late afternoon choosing a safe spot to pass the night,
Kindling a fire and broiling the fresh-kill'd game,
Falling asleep on the gather'd leaves with my dog and gun by my side.

The Yankee clipper is under her sky-sails, she cuts the sparkle and scud,
My eyes settle the land, I bend at her prow or shout joyously from the deck.

The boatmen and clam-diggers arose early and stopt for me,
I tuck'd my trowser-ends in my boots and went and had a good time;
You should have been with us that day round the chowder-kettle.

I saw the marriage of the trapper in the open air in the far west, the bride was a red girl,
Her father and his friends sat near cross-legged and dumbly smoking, they had moccasins to their feet and large thick blankets hanging from their shoulders,
On a bank lounged the trapper, he was drest mostly in skins, his luxuriant beard and curls protected his neck, he held his bride by the hand,
She had long eyelashes, her head was bare, her coarse straight locks descended upon her voluptuous limbs and reach'd to her feet.

The runaway slave came to my house and stopt outside,
I heard his motions crackling the twigs of the woodpile,
Through the swung half-door of the kitchen I saw him limpsy[7] and weak,
And went where he sat on a log and led him in and assured him,
And brought water and fill'd a tub for his sweated body and bruis'd feet,
And gave him a room that enter'd from my own, and gave him some coarse clean clothes,
And remember perfectly well his revolving eyes and his awkwardness,
And remember putting plasters on the galls of his neck and ankles;
He staid with me a week before he was recuperated and pass'd north,
I had him sit next me at table, my fire-lock lean'd in the corner.

11

Twenty-eight young men bathe by the shore,
Twenty-eight young men and all so friendly;
Twenty-eight years of womanly life and all so lonesome.

She owns the fine house by the rise of the bank,
She hides handsome and richly drest aft the blinds of the window.

Which of the young men does she like the best?
Ah the homeliest of them is beautiful to her.

7. Limping or swaying.

Where are you off to, lady? for I see you,
You splash in the water there, yet stay stock still in your room.

Dancing and laughing along the beach came the twenty-ninth bather,
The rest did not see her, but she saw them and loved them.

The beards of the young men glisten'd with wet, it ran from their long hair,
Little streams pass'd over their bodies.

An unseen hand also pass'd over their bodies,
It descended tremblingly from their temples and ribs.

The young men float on their backs, their white bellies bulge to the sun, they do not ask who seizes fast to them,
They do not know who puffs and declines with pendant and bending arch,
They do not think whom they souse with spray.

12

The butcher-boy puts off his killing-clothes, or sharpens his knife at the stall in the market,
I loiter enjoying his repartee and his shuffle and break-down.[8]
Blacksmiths with grimed and hairy chests environ the anvil,
Each has his main-sledge, they are all out, there is a great heat in the fire.

From the cinder-strew'd threshold I follow their movements,
The lithe sheer of their waists plays even with their massive arms,
Overhand the hammers swing, overhand so slow, overhand so sure,
They do not hasten, each man hits in his place.

13

The negro holds firmly the reins of his four horses, the block swags underneath on its tied-over chain,
The negro that drives the long dray of the stone-yard, steady and tall he stands pois'd on one leg on the string-piece,[9]
His blue shirt exposes his ample neck and breast and loosens over his hip-band,
His glance is calm and commanding, he tosses the slouch of his hat away from his forehead,
The sun falls on his crispy hair and mustache, falls on the black of his polish'd and perfect limbs.

8. Dances familiar in popular entertainment and minstrelsy. The "shuffle" involves the sliding of feet across the floor, and the "break-down" is faster and noisier.

9. Long, heavy timber used to keep a load in place.

I behold the picturesque giant and love him, and I do not stop there,
I go with the team also.

In me the caresser of life wherever moving, backward as well as forward sluing,[1]
To niches aside and junior[2] bending, not a person or object missing,
Absorbing all to myself and for this song.

Oxen that rattle the yoke and chain or halt in the leafy shade, what is that you express in your eyes?
It seems to me more than all the print I have read in my life.

My tread scares the wood-drake and wood-duck on my distant and day-long ramble.
They rise together, they slowly circle around.

I believe in those wing'd purposes,
And acknowledge red, yellow, white, playing within me,
And consider green and violet and the tufted crown intentional,
And do not call the tortoise unworthy because she is not something else,
And the jay in the woods never studied the gamut,[3] yet trills pretty well to me,
And the look of the bay mare shames silliness out of me.

14

The wild gander leads his flock through the cool night,
Ya-honk he says, and sounds it down to me like an invitation,
The pert may suppose it meaningless, but I listening close,
Find its purpose and place up there toward the wintry sky.

The sharp-hoof'd moose of the north, the cat on the house-sill, the chickadee, the prairie-dog,
The litter of the grunting sow as they tug at her teats,
The brood of the turkey-hen and she with her half-spread wings,
I see in them and myself the same old law.
The press of my foot to the earth springs a hundred affections,
They scorn the best I can do to relate them.

I am enamour'd of growing out-doors,
Of men that live among cattle or taste of the ocean or woods,
Of the builders and steerers of ships and the wielders of axes and mauls, and the drivers of horses,
I can eat and sleep with them week in and week out.

What is commonest, cheapest, nearest, easiest, is Me,
Me going in for my chances, spending for vast returns,
Adorning myself to bestow myself on the first that will take me,

1. Twisting.
2. Smaller.
3. Notes of the musical scale.

Not asking the sky to come down to my good will,
Scattering it freely forever.

15

The pure contralto sings in the organ loft,
The carpenter dresses his plank, the tongue of his foreplane whistles its wild ascending lisp,
The married and unmarried children ride home to their Thanksgiving dinner,
The pilot seizes the king-pin,[4] he heaves down with a strong arm,
The mate stands braced in the whale-boat, lance and harpoon are ready,
The duck-shooter walks by silent and cautious stretches,
The deacons are ordain'd with cross'd hands at the altar,
The spinning-girl retreats and advances to the hum of the big wheel,
The farmer stops by the bars as he walks on a First-day[5] loafe and looks at the oats and rye,
The lunatic is carried at last to the asylum a confirm'd case,
(He will never sleep any more as he did in the cot in his mother's bed-room;)
The jour printer[6] with gray head and gaunt jaws works at his case,
He turns his quid of tobacco while his eyes blurr with the manuscript;
The malform'd limbs are tied to the surgeon's table,
What is removed drops horribly in a pail;
The quadroon[7] girl is sold at the auction-stand, the drunkard nods by the bar-room stove,
The machinist rolls up his sleeves, the policeman travels his beat, the gate-keeper marks who pass,
The young fellow drives the express-wagon, (I love him, though I do not know him;)
The half-breed straps on his light boots to compete in the race,
The western turkey-shooting draws old and young, some lean on their rifles, some sit on logs,
Out from the crowd steps the marksman, takes his position, levels his piece;
The groups of newly-come immigrants cover the wharf or levee,
As the woolly-pates[8] hoe in the sugar-field, the overseer views them from his saddle,
The bugle calls in the ball-room, the gentlemen run for their partners, the dancers bow to each other,
The youth lies awake in the cedar-roof'd garret and harks to the musical rain,
The Wolverine[9] sets traps on the creek that helps fill the Huron,
The squaw wrapt in her yellow-hemm'd cloth is offering moccasins and bead-bags for sale,

4. The extended spoke of the pilot wheel, used to maintain leverage during storms.
5. Sunday. Whitman frequently uses the numerical Quaker designations for the names of days and months. "Bars": i.e., of a rail fence.
6. I.e., a journeyman printer, or one who has passed an apprenticeship and is fully qualified for all professional work.
7. Term used at the time (often in reference to slaves) to refer to light-complected people thought to be one-fourth black.
8. Black slaves (with stereotypical emphasis on "woolly" hair).
9. Inhabitant of Michigan.

The connoisseur peers along the exhibition-gallery with half-shut eyes
bent sideways,
As the deck-hands make fast the steamboat the plank is thrown for the
shore-going passengers,
The young sister holds out the skein while the elder sister winds it off
in a ball, and stops now and then for the knots,
The one-year wife is recovering and happy having a week ago borne her
first child,
The clean-hair'd Yankee girl works with her sewing-machine or in the
factory or mill,
The paving-man[1] leans on his two-handed rammer, the reporter's lead
flies swiftly over the note-book, the sign-painter is lettering with blue
and gold,
The canal boy trots on the tow-path, the book-keeper counts at his desk,
the shoemaker waxes his thread,
The conductor beats time for the band and all the performers follow him,
The child is baptized, the convert is making his first professions,
The regatta is spread on the bay, the race is begun, (how the white sails
sparkle!)
The drover watching his drove sings out to them that would stray,
The pedler sweats with his pack on his back, (the purchaser higgling
about the odd cent;)
The bride unrumples her white dress, the minute-hand of the clock
moves slowly,
The opium-eater reclines with rigid head and just-open'd lips,
The prostitute draggles her shawl, her bonnet bobs on her tipsy and
pimpled neck,
The crowd laugh at her blackguard oaths, the men jeer and wink to each
other,
(Miserable! I do not laugh at your oaths nor jeer you;)
The President holding a cabinet council is surrounded by the great
Secretaries,
On the piazza walk three matrons stately and friendly with twined arms,
The crew of the fish-smack pack repeated layers of halibut in the hold,
The Missourian crosses the plains toting his wares and his cattle,
As the fare-collector goes through the train he gives notice by the jingling
of loose change,
The floor-men are laying the floor, the tinners are tinning the roof, the
masons are calling for mortar,
In single file each shouldering his hod pass onward the laborers;
Seasons pursuing each other the indescribable crowd is gather'd, it is the
fourth of Seventh-month,[2] (what salutes of cannon and small arms!)
Seasons pursuing each other the plougher ploughs, the mower mows,
and the winter-grain falls in the ground;
Off on the lakes the pike-fisher watches and waits by the hole in the
frozen surface,
The stumps stand thick round the clearing, the squatter strikes deep
with his axe,
Flatboatmen make fast towards dusk near the cotton-wood or pecan-trees,

1. Man building or repairing streets.

2. I.e., the Fourth of July.

Coon-seekers go through the regions of the Red river or through those
drain'd by the Tennessee, or through those of the Arkansas,
Torches shine in the dark that hangs on the Chattahooch or Altamahaw,[3]
Patriarchs sit at supper with sons and grandsons and great-grandsons
around them,
In walls of adobie, in canvas tents, rest hunters and trappers after their
day's sport,
The city sleeps and the country sleeps,
The living sleep for their time, the dead sleep for their time,
The old husband sleeps by his wife and the young husband sleeps by his
wife;
And these tend inward to me, and I tend outward to them,
And such as it is to be of these more or less I am,
And of these one and all I weave the song of myself.

16

I am of old and young, of the foolish as much as the wise,
Regardless of others, ever regardful of others,
Maternal as well as paternal, a child as well as a man,
Stuff'd with the stuff that is coarse and stuff'd with the stuff that is fine,
One of the Nation of many nations, the smallest the same and the largest
the same,
A Southerner soon as a Northerner, a planter nonchalant and hospitable
down by the Oconee[4] I live,
A Yankee bound my own way ready for trade, my joints the limberest joints
on earth and the sternest joints on earth,
A Kentuckian walking the vale of the Elkhorn[5] in my deer-skin leggings, a
Louisianian or Georgian,
A boatman over lakes or bays or along coasts, a Hoosier, Badger, Buckeye;[6]
At home on Kanadian[7] snow-shoes or up in the bush, or with fishermen
off Newfoundland,
At home in the fleet of ice-boats, sailing with the rest and tacking,
At home on the hills of Vermont or in the woods of Maine, or the Texan
ranch,
Comrade of Californians, comrade of free North-Westerners, (loving their
big proportions,)
Comrade of raftsmen and coalmen, comrade of all who shake hands and
welcome to drink and meat,
A learner with the simplest, a teacher of the thoughtfullest,
A novice beginning yet experient of myriads of seasons,
Of every hue and caste am I, of every rank and religion,
A farmer, mechanic, artist, gentleman, sailor, quaker,
Prisoner, fancy-man, rowdy, lawyer, physician, priest.

I resist any thing better than my own diversity,
Breathe the air but leave plenty after me,
And am not stuck up, and am in my place.

3. Georgia rivers.
4. River in central Georgia.
5. River in Nebraska.
6. Inhabitants of Indiana, Wisconsin, and Ohio, respectively.
7. Canadian.

(The moth and the fish-eggs are in their place,
The bright suns I see and the dark suns I cannot see are in their place,
The palpable is in its place and the impalpable is in its place.)

17

These are really the thoughts of all men in all ages and lands, they are
not original with me,
If they are not yours as much as mine they are nothing, or next to nothing,
If they are not the riddle and the untying of the riddle they are nothing,
If they are not just as close as they are distant they are nothing.

This is the grass that grows wherever the land is and the water is,
This the common air that bathes the globe.

18

With music strong I come, with my cornets and my drums,
I play not marches for accepted victors only, I play marches for conquer'd
and slain persons.

Have you heard that it was good to gain the day?
I also say it is good to fall, battles are lost in the same spirit in which they
are won.

I beat and pound for the dead,
I blow through my embouchures[8] my loudest and gayest for them.

Vivas to those who have fail'd!
And to those whose war-vessels sank in the sea!

And to those themselves who sank in the sea!
And to all generals that lost engagements, and all overcome heroes!
And the numberless unknown heroes equal to the greatest heroes known!

19

This is the meal equally set, this the meat for natural hunger,
It is for the wicked just the same as the righteous, I make appointments
with all,
I will not have a single person slighted or left away,
The kept-woman, sponger, thief, are hereby invited,
The heavy-lipp'd slave is invited, the venerealee[9] is invited;
There shall be no difference between them and the rest.

This is the press of a bashful hand, this the float and odor of hair,
This is the touch of my lips to yours, this the murmur of yearning,
This the far-off depth and height reflecting my own face,
This the thoughtful merge of myself, and the outlet again.

8. Mouthpieces of musical instruments such as the cornet.

9. Someone afflicted with a venereal (sexually transmitted) disease.

Do you guess I have some intricate purpose?
Well I have, for the Fourth-month showers have, and the mica on the side of a rock has.

Do you take it I would astonish?
Does the daylight astonish? does the early redstart twittering through the woods?
Do I astonish more than they?

This hour I tell things in confidence,
I might not tell everybody, but I will tell you.

20

Who goes there? hankering, gross, mystical, nude;
How is it I extract strength from the beef I eat?

What is a man anyhow? what am I? what are you?

All I mark as my own you shall offset it with your own,
Else it were time lost listening to me.

I do not snivel that snivel the world over,
That months are vacuums and the ground but wallow and filth.

Whimpering and truckling fold with powders for invalids, conformity goes to the fourth-remov'd,[1]
I wear my hat as I please indoors or out.

Why should I pray? why should I venerate and be ceremonious?

Having pried through the strata, analyzed to a hair, counsel'd with doctors and calculated close,
I find no sweeter fat than sticks to my bones.

In all people I see myself, none more and not one a barley-corn[2] less,
And the good or bad I say of myself I say of them.

I know I am solid and sound,
To me the converging objects of the universe perpetually flow,
All are written to me, and I must get what the writing means.

I know I am deathless,
I know this orbit of mine cannot be swept by a carpenter's compass,
I know I shall not pass like a child's carlacue[3] cut with a burnt stick at night.

1. Those remote in relationship, such as "third cousin, fourth removed." "Fold with powders": a reference to the custom of wrapping a dose of medicine in a piece of paper.
2. The seed or grain of barley, but also a unit of measure equal to about one-third of an inch.
3. Or *curlicue*, a fancy flourish made with a writing implement, here made in the dark with a lighted stick.

I know I am august,
I do not trouble my spirit to vindicate itself or be understood,
I see that the elementary laws never apologize,
(I reckon I behave no prouder than the level I plant my house by, after all.)

I exist as I am, that is enough,
If no other in the world be aware I sit content,
And if each and all be aware I sit content.

One world is aware and by far the largest to me, and that is myself,
And whether I come to my own to-day or in ten thousand or ten million
    years,
I can cheerfully take it now, or with equal cheerfulness I can wait.

My foothold is tenon'd and mortis'd[4] in granite,
I laugh at what you call dissolution,
And I know the amplitude of time.

21

I am the poet of the Body and I am the poet of the Soul,
The pleasures of heaven are with me and the pains of hell are with me,
The first I graft and increase upon myself, the latter I translate into a
    new tongue.

I am the poet of the woman the same as the man,
And I say it is as great to be a woman as to be a man,
And I say there is nothing greater than the mother of men.

I chant the chant of dilation or pride,
We have had ducking and deprecating about enough,
I show that size is only development.

Have you outstript the rest? are you the President?
It is a trifle, they will more than arrive there every one, and still pass on.

I am he that walks with the tender and growing night,
I call to the earth and sea half-held by the night.

Press close bare-bosom'd night—press close magnetic nourishing night!
Night of south winds—night of the large few stars!
Still nodding night—mad naked summer night.

Smile O voluptuous cool-breath'd earth!
Earth of the slumbering and liquid trees!
Earth of departed sunset—earth of the mountains misty-topt!
Earth of the vitreous pour of the full moon just tinged with blue!
Earth of shine and dark mottling the tide of the river!
Earth of the limpid gray of clouds brighter and clearer for my sake!

4. Here, mason's terms for a particular way of joining two stones together. A mortise is a cavity in a stone into which is placed the projection (tenon) from another stone.

Far-swooping elbow'd earth—rich apple-blossom'd earth!
Smile, for your lover comes.

Prodigal, you have given me love—therefore I to you give love!
O unspeakable passionate love.

22

You sea! I resign myself to you also—I guess what you mean,
I behold from the beach your crooked inviting fingers,
I believe you refuse to go back without feeling of me,
We must have a turn together, I undress, hurry me out of sight of the land,
Cushion me soft, rock me in billowy drowse,
Dash me with amorous wet, I can repay you.

Sea of stretch'd ground-swells,
Sea breathing broad and convulsive breaths,
Sea of the brine of life and of unshovell'd yet always-ready graves,
Howler and scooper of storms, capricious and dainty sea,
I am integral with you, I too am of one phase and of all phases.

Partaker of influx and efflux I, extoller of hate and conciliation,
Extoller of amies[5] and those that sleep in each others' arms.

I am he attesting sympathy,
(Shall I make my list of things in the house and skip the house that supports them?)

I am not the poet of goodness only, I do not decline to be the poet of wickedness also.

What blurt is this about virtue and about vice?
Evil propels me and reform of evil propels me, I stand indifferent,
My gait is no fault-finder's or rejecter's gait,
I moisten the roots of all that has grown.

Did you fear some scrofula[6] out of the unflagging pregnancy?
Did you guess the celestial laws are yet to be work'd over and rectified?

I find one side a balance and the antipodal side a balance,
Soft doctrine as steady help as stable doctrine,
Thoughts and deeds of the present our rouse and early start.

This minute that comes to me over the past decillions,[7]
There is no better than it and now.
What behaved well in the past or behaves well to-day is not such a wonder,

5. Friends (French).
6. Form of tuberculosis characterized by swelling of the lymph glands.
7. The number one followed by thirty-three zeroes.

The wonder is always and always how there can be a mean man or an
infidel.

23

Endless unfolding of words of ages!
And mine a word of the modern, the word En-Masse.

A word of the faith that never balks,
Here or henceforward it is all the same to me, I accept Time absolutely.

It alone is without flaw, it alone rounds and completes all,
That mystic baffling wonder alone completes all.

I accept Reality and dare not question it.
Materialism first and last imbuing.

Hurrah for positive science! long live exact demonstration!
Fetch stonecrop mixt with cedar and branches of lilac,
This is the lexicographer, this the chemist, this made a grammar of the
old cartouches,[8]
These mariners put the ship through dangerous unknown seas,
This is the geologist, this works with the scalpel, and this is a
mathematician.

Gentlemen, to you the first honors always!
Your facts are useful, and yet they are not my dwelling,
I but enter by them to an area of my dwelling.

Less the reminders of properties told my words,
And more the reminders they of life untold, and of freedom and extrication,
And make short account of neuters and geldings, and favor men and
women fully equipt,
And beat the gong of revolt, and stop with fugitives and them that plot and
conspire.

24

Walt Whitman, a kosmos, of Manhattan the son,
Turbulent, fleshy, sensual, eating, drinking and breeding,
No sentimentalist, no stander above men and women or apart from them,
No more modest than immodest.

Unscrew the locks from the doors!
Unscrew the doors themselves from their jambs!

Whoever degrades another degrades me,
And whatever is done or said returns at last to me.

8. On tablets of Egyptian hieroglyphics, the ornamental area noting the name of a ruler or deity. "Stone crop": a fleshy-leafed plant.

Through me the afflatus[9] surging and surging, through me the current and index.

I speak the pass-word primeval, I give the sign of democracy,
By God! I will accept nothing which all cannot have their counterpart of on the same terms.

Through me many long dumb voices,
Voices of the interminable generations of prisoners and slaves,
Voices of the diseas'd and despairing and of thieves and dwarfs,
Voices of cycles of preparation and accretion,
And of the threads that connect the stars, and of wombs and of the fatherstuff,
And of the rights of them the others are down upon,
Of the deform'd, trivial, flat, foolish, despised,
Fog in the air, beetles rolling balls of dung.

Through me forbidden voices,
Voices of sexes and lusts, voices veil'd and I remove the veil,
Voices indecent by me clarified and transfigur'd.

I do not press my fingers across my mouth,
I keep as delicate around the bowels as around the head and heart,
Copulation is no more rank to me than death is.

I believe in the flesh and the appetites,
Seeing, hearing, feeling, are miracles, and each part and tag of me is a miracle.

Divine am I inside and out, and I make holy whatever I touch or am touch'd from,
The scent of these arm-pits aroma finer than prayer,
This head more than churches, bibles, and all the creeds.

If I worship one thing more than another it shall be the spread of my own body, or any part of it,
Translucent mould of me it shall be you!
Shaded ledges and rests it shall be you!
Firm masculine colter[1] it shall be you!
Whatever goes to the tilth[2] of me it shall be you!
You my rich blood! your milky stream pale strippings of my life!
Breast that presses against other breasts it shall be you!
My brain it shall be your occult convolutions!
Root of wash'd sweet-flag! timorous pond-snipe! nest of guarded duplicate eggs! it shall be you!
Mix'd tussled hay of head, beard, brawn, it shall be you!
Trickling sap of maple, fibre of manly wheat, it shall be you!
Sun so generous it shall be you!

9. Divine wind or spirit.
1. The blade at the front of a plow.
2. Cultivation or tillage of the soil.

Vapors lighting and shading my face it shall be you!
You sweaty brooks and dews it shall be you!
Winds whose soft-tickling genitals rub against me it shall be you!
Broad muscular fields, branches of live oak, loving lounger in my winding paths, it shall be you!
Hands I have taken, face I have kiss'd, mortal I have ever touch'd, it shall be you.

I dote on myself, there is that lot of me and all so luscious,
Each moment and whatever happens thrills me with joy,
I cannot tell how my ankles bend, nor whence the cause of my faintest wish,
Nor the cause of the friendship I emit, nor the cause of the friendship I take again.

That I walk up my stoop, I pause to consider if it really be,
A morning-glory at my window satisfies me more than the metaphysics of books.

To behold the day-break!
The little light fades the immense and diaphanous shadows,
The air tastes good to my palate.

Hefts[3] of the moving world at innocent gambols silently rising freshly exuding,
Scooting obliquely high and low.

Something I cannot see puts upward libidinous prongs,
Seas of bright juice suffuse heaven.

The earth by the sky staid with, the daily close of their junction,
The heav'd challenge from the east that moment over my head,
The mocking taunt, See then whether you shall be master!

25

Dazzling and tremendous how quick the sun-rise would kill me,
If I could not now and always send sun-rise out of me.

We also ascend dazzling and tremendous as the sun,
We found our own O my soul in the calm and cool of the day-break.

My voice goes after what my eyes cannot reach,
With the twirl of my tongue I encompass worlds and volumes of worlds.

Speech is the twin of my vision, it is unequal to measure itself,
It provokes me forever, it says sarcastically,
Walt you contain enough, why don't you let it out then?

3. Something being heaved or raised upward.

Come now I will not be tantalized, you conceive too much of articulation,
Do you not know O speech how the buds beneath you are folded?
Waiting in gloom, protected by frost,
The dirt receding before my prophetical screams,
I underlying causes to balance them at last,
My knowledge my live parts, it keeping tally with the meaning of all things,
Happiness, (which whoever hears me let him or her set out in search of this day.)

My final merit I refuse you, I refuse putting from me what I really am,
Encompass worlds, but never try to encompass me.
I crowd your sleekest and best by simply looking toward you.

Writing and talk do not prove me,
I carry the plenum[4] of proof and every thing else in my face,
With the hush of my lips I wholly confound the skeptic.

26

Now I will do nothing but listen,
To accrue what I hear into this song, to let sounds contribute toward it.

I hear bravuras of birds, bustle of growing wheat, gossip of flames, clack of sticks cooking my meals,
I hear the sound I love, the sound of the human voice,
I hear all sounds running together, combined, fused or following,
Sounds of the city and sounds out of the city, sounds of the day and night,
Talkative young ones to those that like them, the loud laugh of work-people at their meals,
The angry base of disjointed friendship, the faint tones of the sick,
The judge with hands tight to the desk, his pallid lips pronouncing a death-sentence,
The heave'e'yo of stevedores unlading ships by the wharves, the refrain of the anchor-lifters,
The ring of alarm-bells, the cry of fire, the whirr of swift-streaking engines and hose-carts with premonitory tinkles and color'd lights,
The steam-whistle, the solid roll of the train of approaching cars,
The slow march play'd at the head of the association marching two and two,
(They go to guard some corpse, the flag-tops are draped with black muslin.)

I hear the violoncello ('tis the young man's heart's complaint,)
I hear the key'd cornet, it glides quickly in through my ears,
It shakes mad-sweet pangs through my belly and breast.

I hear the chorus, it is a grand opera,
Ah this indeed is music—this suits me.

4. Fullness.

A tenor large and fresh as the creation fills me,
The orbic flex of his mouth is pouring and filling me full.

I hear the train'd soprano (what work with hers is this?)
The orchestra whirls me wider than Uranus[5] flies,
It wrenches such ardors from me I did not know I possess'd them,
It sails me, I dab with bare feet, they are lick'd by the indolent waves,
I am cut by bitter and angry hail, I lose my breath,
Steep'd amid honey'd morphine, my windpipe throttled in fakes[6] of death,
At length let up again to feel the puzzle of puzzles,
And that we call Being.

27

To be in any form, what is that?
(Round and round we go, all of us, and ever come back thither,)
If nothing lay more develop'd the quahaug[7] in its callous shell were
enough.

Mine is no callous shell,
I have instant conductors all over me whether I pass or stop,
They seize every object and lead it harmlessly through me.

I merely stir, press, feel with my fingers, and am happy,
To touch my person to some one else's is about as much as I can stand.

28

Is this then a touch? quivering me to a new identity,
Flames and ether making a rush for my veins,
Treacherous tip of me reaching and crowding to help them,
My flesh and blood playing out lightning to strike what is hardly different
from myself,
On all sides prurient provokers stiffening my limbs,
Straining the udder of my heart for its withheld drip,
Behaving licentious toward me, taking no denial,
Depriving me of my best as for a purpose,
Unbuttoning my clothes, holding me by the bare waist,
Deluding my confusion with the calm of the sunlight and pasture-fields,
Immodestly sliding the fellow-senses away,
They bribed to swap off with touch and go and graze at the edges of me,
No consideration, no regard for my draining strength or my anger,
Fetching the rest of the herd around to enjoy them a while,
Then all uniting to stand on a headland and worry me.

The sentries desert every other part of me,
They have left me helpless to a red marauder,
They all come to the headland to witness and assist against me.

5. Seventh planet from the sun, thought at the time to be the outermost limit of the solar system.

6. Coils of rope.

7. Edible clam of the Atlantic coast.

I am given up by traitors,
I talk wildly, I have lost my wits, I and nobody else am the greatest traitor,
I went myself first to the headland, my own hands carried me there.

You villain touch! what are you doing? my breath is tight in its throat,
Unclench your floodgates, you are too much for me.

29

Blind loving wrestling touch, sheath'd hooded sharp-tooth'd touch!
Did it make you ache so, leaving me?

Parting track'd by arriving, perpetual payment of perpetual loan,
Rich showering rain, and recompense richer afterward.

Sprouts take and accumulate, stand by the curb prolific and vital,
Landscapes projected masculine, full-sized and golden.

30

All truths wait in all things,
They neither hasten their own delivery nor resist it,
They do not need the obstetric forceps of the surgeon,
The insignificant is as big to me as any,
(What is less or more than a touch?)

Logic and sermons never convince,
The damp of the night drives deeper into my soul.

(Only what proves itself to every man and woman is so,
Only what nobody denies is so.)

A minute and a drop of me settle my brain,
I believe the soggy clods shall become lovers and lamps,
And a compend[8] of compends is the meat of a man or woman,
And a summit and flower there is the feeling they have for each other,
And they are to branch boundlessly out of that lesson until it becomes
omnific,[9]
And until one and all shall delight us, and we them.

31

I believe a leaf of grass is no less than the journey-work of the stars,
And the pismire[1] is equally perfect, and a grain of sand, and the egg of
the wren,
And the tree-toad is a chief-d'œuvre for the highest,

8. I.e., a compendium, where something is reduced to a short, essential summary.

9. All-encompassing.

1. Ant.

And the running blackberry would adorn the parlors of heaven,
And the narrowest hinge in my hand puts to scorn all machinery,
And the cow crunching with depress'd head surpasses any statue,
And a mouse is miracle enough to stagger sextillions of infidels.

I find I incorporate gneiss,[2] coal, long-threaded moss, fruits, grains, esculent roots,
And am stucco'd with quadrupeds and birds all over,
And have distanced what is behind me for good reasons,
But call any thing back again when I desire it.
In vain the speeding or shyness,
In vain the plutonic rocks[3] send their old heat against my approach,
In vain the mastodon retreats beneath its own powder'd bones,
In vain objects stand leagues off and assume manifold shapes,
In vain the ocean settling in hollows and the great monsters lying low,
In vain the buzzard houses herself with the sky,
In vain the snake slides through the creepers and logs,
In vain the elk takes to the inner passes of the woods,
In vain the razor-bill'd auk sails far north to Labrador,
I follow quickly, I ascend to the nest in the fissure of the cliff.

32

I think I could turn and live with animals, they are so placid and self-contain'd,
I stand and look at them long and long.

They do not sweat and whine about their condition,
They do not lie awake in the dark and weep for their sins,
They do not make me sick discussing their duty to God,
Not one is dissatisfied, not one is demented with the mania of owning things,
Not one kneels to another, nor to his kind that lived thousands of years ago,
Not one is respectable or unhappy over the whole earth.

So they show their relations to me and I accept them,
They bring me tokens of myself, they evince them plainly in their possession.

I wonder where they get those tokens,
Did I pass that way huge times ago and negligently drop them?

Myself moving forward then and now and forever,
Gathering and showing more always and with velocity,
Infinite and omnigenous,[4] and the like of these among them,
Not too exclusive toward the reachers of my remembrancers,

2. Metamorphic rock in which minerals are arranged in layers.
3. Rock of igneous (fire-created) or magmatic (molten) origin; from Pluto, ruler of infernal regions.
4. Belonging to every form of life.

Picking out here one that I love, and now go with him on brotherly
 terms.

A gigantic beauty of a stallion, fresh and responsive to my caresses,
Head high in the forehead, wide between the ears,
Limbs glossy and supple, tail dusting the ground,
Eyes full of sparkling wickedness, ears finely cut, flexibly moving.

His nostrils dilate as my heels embrace him,
His well-built limbs tremble with pleasure as we race around and return.

I but use you a minute, then I resign you, stallion,
Why do I need your paces when I myself out-gallop them?
Even as I stand or sit passing faster than you.

33

Space and Time! now I see it is true, what I guess'd at,
What I guess'd when I loaf'd on the grass,
What I guess'd while I lay alone in my bed,
And again as I walk'd the beach under the paling stars of the morning.

My ties and ballasts leave me, my elbows rest in sea-gaps,[5]
I skirt sierras, my palms cover continents,
I am afoot with my vision.

By the city's quadrangular houses—in log huts, camping with lumbermen,
Along the ruts of the turnpike, along the dry gulch and rivulet bed,
Weeding my onion-patch or hoeing rows of carrots and parsnips, crossing
 savannas,[6] trailing in forests,
Prospecting, gold-digging, girdling the trees of a new purchase,
Scorch'd ankle-deep by the hot sand, hauling my boat down the shallow
 river,
Where the panther walks to and fro on a limb overhead, where the buck
 turns furiously at the hunter,
Where the rattlesnake suns his flabby length on a rock, where the otter is
 feeding on fish,
Where the alligator in his tough pimples sleeps by the bayou,
Where the black bear is searching for roots or honey, where the beaver
 pats the mud with his paddle-shaped tail;
Over the growing sugar, over the yellow-flower'd cotton plant, over the rice
 in its low moist field,
Over the sharp-peak'd farm house, with its scallop'd scum and slender
 shoots from the gutters,[7]

Over the western persimmon, over the long-leav'd corn, over the delicate
 blue-flower flax,
Over the white and brown buckwheat, a hummer and buzzer there with
 the rest,

5. Estuaries or bays.
6. Grasslands.
7. Plants growing from soil lodged in house gutters and drain pipes. "Scallop'd scum": rain-washed and sometimes weedy sediment on the roofs of old farmhouses.

Over the dusky green of the rye as it ripples and shades in the breeze;
Scaling mountains, pulling myself cautiously up, holding on by low scragged limbs,
Walking the path worn in the grass and beat through the leaves of the brush,
Where the quail is whistling betwixt the woods and the wheat-lot,
Where the bat flies in the Seventh-month eve, where the great gold-bug[8] drops through the dark,
Where the brook puts out of the roots of the old tree and flows to the meadow,
Where cattle stand and shake away flies with the tremulous shuddering of their hides,
Where the cheese-cloth hangs in the kitchen, where andirons straddle the hearth-slab, where cobwebs fall in festoons from the rafters;
Where trip-hammers crash, where the press is whirling its cylinders,
Wherever the human heart beats with terrible throes under its ribs,
Where the pear-shaped balloon is floating aloft, (floating in it myself and looking composedly down,)
Where the life-car[9] is drawn on the slip-noose, where the heat hatches pale-green eggs in the dented sand,
Where the she-whale swims with her calf and never forsakes it,
Where the steam-ship trails hind-ways its long pennant of smoke,
Where the fin of the shark cuts like a black chip out of the water,
Where the half-burn'd brig is riding on unknown currents,
Where shells grow to her slimy deck, where the dead are corrupting below;
Where the dense-star'd flag is borne at the head of the regiments,
Approaching Manhattan up by the long-stretching island,
Under Niagara, the cataract falling like a veil over my countenance,
Upon a door-step, upon the horse-block of hard wood outside,
Upon the race-course, or enjoying picnics or jigs or a good game of baseball,
At he-festivals, with blackguard gibes, ironical license, bull-dances,[1] drinking, laughter,
At the cider-mill tasting the sweets of the brown mash, sucking the juice through a straw,
At apple-peelings wanting kisses for all the red fruit I find,
At musters, beach-parties, friendly bees,[2] huskings, house-raisings;
Where the mocking-bird sounds his delicious gurgles, cackles, screams, weeps,
Where the hay-rick[3] stands in the barn-yard, where the dry-stalks are scatter'd, where the brood-cow waits in the hovel,
Where the bull advances to do his masculine work, where the stud to the mare, where the cock is treading the hen,
Where the heifers browse, where geese nip their food with short jerks,
Where sun-down shadows lengthen over the limitless and lonesome prairie,

8. Beetle.
9. Watertight compartment for lowering passengers from a ship when emergency evacuation is required.
1. Rowdy backwoods dances for which men took male partners.
2. Gatherings where people work while socializing with their neighbors. "Musters": assemblages of people, particularly gatherings of military troops for drill.
3. Hayrack, from which livestock eat hay.

Where herds of buffalo make a crawling spread of the square miles far
and near,
Where the humming-bird shimmers, where the neck of the long-lived
swan is curving and winding,
Where the laughing-gull scoots by the shore, where she laughs her
near-human laugh,
Where bee-hives range on a gray bench in the garden half hid by the high
weeds,
Where band-neck'd partridges roost in a ring on the ground with their
heads out,
Where burial coaches enter the arch'd gates of a cemetery,
Where winter wolves bark amid wastes of snow and icicled trees,
Where the yellow-crown'd heron comes to the edge of the marsh at night
and feeds upon small crabs,
Where the splash of swimmers and divers cools the warm noon,
Where the katy-did works her chromatic[4] reed on the walnut-tree over
the well,
Through patches of citrons[5] and cucumbers with silver-wired leaves,
Through the salt-lick or orange glade, or under conical firs,
Through the gymnasium, through the curtain'd saloon, through the office
or public hall;
Pleas'd with the native and pleas'd with the foreign, pleas'd with the new
and old,
Pleas'd with the homely woman as well as the handsome,
Pleas'd with the quakeress as she puts off her bonnet and talks melodiously,
Pleas'd with the tune of the choir of the whitewash'd church,
Pleas'd with the earnest words of the sweating Methodist preacher,
impress'd seriously at the camp-meeting;
Looking in at the shop-windows of Broadway the whole forenoon, flatting
the flesh of my nose on the thick plate glass,
Wandering the same afternoon with my face turn'd up to the clouds, or
down a lane or along the beach,
My right and left arms round the sides of two friends, and I in the middle;
Coming home with the silent and dark-cheek'd bush-boy, (behind me he
rides at the drape of the day,)
Far from the settlements studying the print of animals' feet, or the
moccasin print,
By the cot in the hospital reaching lemonade to a feverish patient,
Nigh the coffin'd corpse when all is still, examining with a candle;
Voyaging to every port to dicker and adventure,
Hurrying with the modern crowd as eager and fickle as any,
Hot toward one I hate, ready in my madness to knife him,
Solitary at midnight in my back yard, my thoughts gone from me a long
while,
Walking the old hills of Judæa with the beautiful gentle God by my side,
Speeding through space, speeding through heaven and the stars,
Speeding amid the seven satellites[6] and the broad ring, and the diameter
of eighty thousand miles,
Speeding with tail'd meteors, throwing fire-balls like the rest,

4. Full tonal range.
5. Here, small, hard-skinned watermelons.
6. The then known moons of Saturn.

Carrying the crescent child that carries its own full mother in its belly,[7]
Storming, enjoying, planning, loving, cautioning,
Backing and filling, appearing and disappearing,
I tread day and night such roads.

I visit the orchards of spheres and look at the product,
And look at quintillions ripen'd and look at quintillions green.

I fly those flights of a fluid and swallowing soul,
My course runs below the soundings of plummets.

I help myself to material and immaterial,
No guard can shut me off, no law prevent me.

I anchor my ship for a little while only,
My messengers continually cruise away or bring their returns to me.

I go hunting polar furs and the seal, leaping chasms with a pike-pointed
staff, clinging to topples of brittle and blue.[8]

I ascend to the foretruck,[9]
I take my place late at night in the crow's-nest,
We sail the arctic sea, it is plenty light enough,
Through the clear atmosphere I stretch around on the wonderful beauty,
The enormous masses of ice pass me and I pass them, the scenery is
plain in all directions,
The white-topt mountains show in the distance, I fling out my fancies
toward them,
We are approaching some great battle-field in which we are soon to be
engaged,
We pass the colossal outposts of the encampment, we pass with still feet
and caution,
Or we are entering by the suburbs some vast and ruin'd city,
The blocks and fallen architecture more than all the living cities of the
globe.

I am a free companion, I bivouac by invading watchfires,
I turn the bridegroom out of bed and stay with the bride myself,
I tighten her all night to my thighs and lips.

My voice is the wife's voice, the screech by the rail of the stairs,
They fetch my man's body up dripping and drown'd.

I understand the large hearts of heroes,
The courage of present times and all times,
How the skipper saw the crowded and rudderless wreck of the steam-ship,
and Death chasing it up and down the storm,
How he knuckled tight and gave not back an inch, and was faithful of days
and faithful of nights,

7. A crescent moon, with the full moon also palely visible.
8. Toppled pieces of ice.
9. Highest platform of a foremast.

And chalk'd in large letters on a board, *Be of good cheer, we will not desert you;*
How he follow'd with them and tack'd with them three days and would not give it up,
How he saved the drifting company at last,
How the lank loose-gown'd women look'd when boated from the side of their prepared graves,
How the silent old-faced infants and the lifted sick, and the sharp-lipp'd unshaved men;
All this I swallow, it tastes good, I like it well, it becomes mine,
I am the man, I suffer'd, I was there.[1]

The disdain and calmness of martyrs,
The mother of old, condemn'd for a witch, burnt with dry wood, her children gazing on,
The hounded slave that flags in the race, leans by the fence, blowing, cover'd with sweat,
The twinges that sting like needles his legs and neck, the murderous buckshot and the bullets,
All these I feel or am.

I am the hounded slave, I wince at the bite of the dogs,
Hell and despair are upon me, crack and again crack the marksmen,
I clutch the rails of the fence, my gore dribs, thinn'd with the ooze of my skin,[2]
I fall on the weeds and stones,
The riders spur their unwilling horses, haul close,
Taunt my dizzy ears and beat me violently over the head with whip-stocks.

Agonies are one of my changes of garments,
I do not ask the wounded person how he feels, I myself become the wounded person,
My hurts turn livid upon me as I lean on a cane and observe.

I am the mash'd fireman with breast-bone broken,
Tumbling walls buried me in their debris,
Heat and smoke I inspired, I heard the yelling shouts of my comrades,
I heard the distant click of their picks and shovels,
They have clear'd the beams away, they tenderly lift me forth.

I lie in the night air in my red shirt, the pervading hush is for my sake,
Painless after all I lie exhausted but not so unhappy,
White and beautiful are the faces around me, the heads are bared of their fire-caps,
The kneeling crowd fades with the light of the torches.

Distant and dead resuscitate,
They show as the dial or move as the hands of me, I am the clock myself.

1. Whitman describes the wreck of the *San Francisco,* which sailed from New York on December 22, 1853, bound for South America, and was caught in a storm a day later. The ship drifted helplessly until early January. Over 150 died in the disaster, which was reported widely in the New York papers.

2. Dribbles down, diluted with sweat.

I am an old artillerist, I tell of my fort's bombardment,
I am there again.

Again the long roll of the drummers,
Again the attacking cannon, mortars,
Again to my listening ears the cannon responsive.

I take part, I see and hear the whole,
The cries, curses, roar, the plaudits of well-aim'd shots,
The ambulanza slowly passing trailing its red drip,
Workmen searching after damages, making indispensable repairs,
The fall of grenades through the rent roof, the fan-shaped explosion,
The whizz of limbs, heads, stone, wood, iron, high in the air.

Again gurgles the mouth of my dying general, he furiously waves with
his hand,
He gasps through the clot *Mind not me—mind—the entrenchments.*

34

Now I tell what I knew in Texas in my early youth,
(I tell not the fall of Alamo,[3]
Not one escaped to tell the fall of Alamo,
The hundred and fifty are dumb yet at Alamo,)
'Tis the tale of the murder in cold blood of four hundred and twelve
young men.

Retreating they had form'd in a hollow square with their baggage for
breastworks,
Nine hundred lives out of the surrounding enemy's, nine times their
number, was the price they took in advance,
Their colonel was wounded and their ammunition gone,
They treated for an honorable capitulation, receiv'd writing and seal,
gave up their arms and march'd back prisoners of war.

They were the glory of the race of rangers,
Matchless with horse, rifle, song, supper, courtship,
Large, turbulent, generous, handsome, proud, and affectionate,
Bearded, sunburnt, drest in the free costume of hunters,
Not a single one over thirty years of age.

The second First-day morning they were brought out in squads and
massacred, it was beautiful early summer,
The work commenced about five o'clock and was over by eight.

3. During the Texas Revolution of 1835–36, emigrants from the United States to Texas—at the time part of Mexico—attempted to make Texas into a separate republic. Among battles fought in what is now the state of Texas were the battle of the Alamo—the Alamo fell on March 6, 1836, after a siege by Mexican forces beginning on February 23, when around two hundred men were killed—and the battle of Goliad, when some four hundred secessionist troops were killed after surrendering to the Mexicans on March 19 of the same year.

None obey'd the command to kneel,
Some made a mad and helpless rush, some stood stark and straight,
A few fell at once, shot in the temple or heart, the living and dead lay together,
The maim'd and mangled dug in the dirt, the new-comers saw them there,
Some half-kill'd attempted to crawl away,
These were despatch'd with bayonets or batter'd with the blunts of muskets,
A youth not seventeen years old seiz'd his assassin till two more came to release him,
The three were all torn and cover'd with the boy's blood.

At eleven o'clock began the burning of the bodies;
That is the tale of the murder of the four hundred and twelve young men.

35

Would you hear of an old-time sea-fight?[4]
Would you learn who won by the light of the moon and stars?
List to the yarn, as my grandmother's father the sailor told it to me.

Our foe was no skulk in his ship I tell you, (said he,)
His was the surly English pluck, and there is no tougher or truer, and never was, and never will be;
Along the lower'd eve he came horribly raking us.

We closed with him, the yards entangled, the cannon touch'd,
My captain lash'd fast with his own hands.

We had receiv'd some eighteen pound shots under the water,
On our lower-gun-deck two large pieces had burst at the first fire, killing all around and blowing up overhead.

Fighting at sun-down, fighting at dark,
Ten o'clock at night, the full moon well up, our leaks on the gain, and five feet of water reported,
The master-at-arms loosing the prisoners confined in the after-hold to give them a chance for themselves.

The transit to and from the magazine[5] is now stopt by the sentinels,
They see so many strange faces they do not know whom to trust.

Our frigate takes fire,
The other asks if we demand quarter?
If our colors are struck and the fighting done?

4. The famous Revolutionary War sea battle on September 23, 1779, between the American *Bon-Homme Richard,* commanded by John Paul Jones (1747–1792), and the British *Serapis* off the coast of northern England. When Jones was asked to surrender, he famously declared, "I have not yet begun to fight." He eventually defeated the *Serapis*.

5. Storeroom for ammunition.

Now I laugh content, for I hear the voice of my little captain,
We have not struck, he composedly cries, *we have just begun our part of the fighting.*

Only three guns are in use,
One is directed by the captain himself against the enemy's mainmast,
Two well serv'd with grape and canister[6] silence his musketry and clear his decks.

The tops[7] alone second the fire of this little battery, especially the main-top,
They hold out bravely during the whole of the action.

Not a moment's cease,
The leaks gain fast on the pumps, the fire eats toward the powder-magazine.

One of the pumps has been shot away, it is generally thought we are sinking.

Serene stands the little captain,
He is not hurried, his voice is neither high nor low,
His eyes give more light to us than our battle-lanterns.

Toward twelve there in the beams of the moon they surrender to us.

36

Stretch'd and still lies the midnight,
Two great hulls motionless on the breast of the darkness,
Our vessel riddled and slowly sinking, preparations to pass to the one we have conquer'd,
The captain on the quarter-deck coldly giving his orders through a countenance white as a sheet,
Near by the corpse of the child that serv'd in the cabin,
The dead face of an old salt with long white hair and carefully curl'd whiskers,
The flames spite of all that can be done flickering aloft and below,
The husky voices of the two or three officers yet fit for duty,
Formless stacks of bodies and bodies by themselves, dabs of flesh upon the masts and spars,
Cut of cordage, dangle of rigging, slight shock of the soothe of waves,
Black and impassive guns, litter of powder-parcels, strong scent,
A few large stars overhead, silent and mournful shining,
Delicate sniffs of sea-breeze, smells of sedgy grass and fields by the shore, death-messages given in charge to survivors,
The hiss of the surgeon's knife, the gnawing teeth of his saw,

6. Grapeshot ("grape"), clusters of small iron balls, was packed inside a metal cylinder ("canister") and used to charge a cannon.

7. Platforms enclosing the heads of each mast; here, the sailors manning the tops.

Wheeze, cluck, swash of falling blood, short wild scream, and long, dull,
tapering groan,
These so, these irretrievable.

37

You laggards there on guard! look to your arms!
In at the conquer'd doors they crowd! I am possess'd!
Embody all presences outlaw'd or suffering,
See myself in prison shaped like another man,
And feel the dull unintermitted pain.

For me the keepers of convicts shoulder their carbines and keep
watch,
It is I let out in the morning and barr'd at night.

Not a mutineer walks handcuff'd to jail but I am handcuff'd to him and
walk by his side,
(I am less the jolly one there, and more the silent one with sweat on my
twitching lips.)

Not a youngster is taken for larceny but I go up too, and am tried and
sentenced.

Not a cholera patient lies at the last gasp but I also lie at the last
gasp,
My face is ash-color'd, my sinews gnarl, away from me people retreat.

Askers embody themselves in me and I am embodied in them,
I project my hat, sit shame-faced, and beg.

38

Enough! enough! enough!
Somehow I have been stunn'd. Stand back!
Give me a little time beyond my cuff'd head, slumbers, dreams, gaping,
I discover myself on the verge of a usual mistake.

That I could forget the mockers and insults!
That I could forget the trickling tears and the blows of the bludgeons
and hammers!
That I could look with a separate look on my own crucifixion and bloody
crowning.

I remember now,
I resume the overstaid fraction,
The grave of rock multiplies what has been confided to it, or to any graves,
Corpses rise, gashes heal, fastenings roll from me.

I troop forth replenish'd with supreme power, one of an average unending
procession,
Inland and sea-coast we go, and pass all boundary lines,

Our swift ordinances on their way over the whole earth,
The blossoms we wear in our hats the growth of thousands of years.

Eleves,[8] I salute you! come forward!
Continue your annotations, continue your questionings.

39

The friendly and flowing savage, who is he?
Is he waiting for civilization, or past it and mastering it?

Is he some Southwesterner rais'd out-doors? is he Kanadian?
Is he from the Mississippi country? Iowa, Oregon, California?
The mountains? prairie-life, bush-life? or sailor from the sea?

Wherever he goes men and women accept and desire him,
They desire he should like them, touch them, speak to them, stay with them.

Behavior lawless as snow-flakes, words simple as grass, uncomb'd head, laughter, and naiveté,
Slow-stepping feet, common features, common modes and emanations,
They descend in new forms from the tips of his fingers,
They are wafted with the odor of his body or breath, they fly out of the glance of his eyes.

40

Flaunt of the sunshine I need not your bask—lie over!
You light surfaces only, I force surfaces and depths also.

Earth! you seem to look for something at my hands,
Say, old top-knot,[9] what do you want?

Man or woman, I might tell how I like you, but cannot,
And might tell what it is in me and what it is in you, but cannot,
And might tell that pining I have, that pulse of my nights and days.

Behold, I do not give lectures or a little charity,
When I give I give myself.

You there, impotent, loose in the knees,
Open your scarf'd chops till I blow grit[1] within you,
Spread your palms and lift the flaps of your pockets,
I am not to be denied, I compel, I have stores plenty and to spare,
And any thing I have I bestow.

8. Students (French).
9. An epithet common in frontier humor, deriving from the fact that some Native Americans gathered their hair into tufts at the top of the head. The poet seems to be addressing an older Indian, perhaps picking up on the reference to "the friendly and flowing savage" of the previous stanza.
1. Courage. "Scarf'd chops": lined, worn-down jaw or face.

I do not ask who you are, that is not important to me,
You can do nothing and be nothing but what I will infold you.

To cotton-field drudge or cleaner of privies I lean,
On his right cheek I put the family kiss,
And in my soul I swear I never will deny him.

On women fit for conception I start bigger and nimbler babes,
(This day I am jetting the stuff of far more arrogant republics.)

To any one dying, thither I speed and twist the knob of the door,
Turn the bed-clothes toward the foot of the bed,
Let the physician and the priest go home.

I seize the descending man and raise him with resistless will,
O despairer, here is my neck,
By God, you shall not go down! hang your whole weight upon me.

I dilate you with tremendous breath, I buoy you up,
Every room of the house do I fill with an arm'd force,
Lovers of me, bafflers of graves.

Sleep—I and they keep guard all night,
Not doubt, not decease shall dare to lay finger upon you,
I have embraced you, and henceforth possess you to myself,
And when you rise in the morning you will find what I tell you is so.

41

I am he bringing help for the sick as they pant on their backs,
And for strong upright men I bring yet more needed help.

I heard what was said of the universe,
Heard it and heard it of several thousand years;
It is middling well as far as it goes—but is that all?

Magnifying and applying come I,
Outbidding at the start the old cautious hucksters,
Taking myself the exact dimensions of Jehovah,[2]
Lithographing Kronos, Zeus his son, and Hercules[3] his grandson,
Buying drafts of Osiris, Isis, Belus, Brahma, Buddha,[4]
In my portfolio placing Manito loose, Allah[5] on a leaf, the crucifix
engraved,

2. God of the Jews and Christians.
3. Son of Zeus and the mortal Alcmene, won immortality by performing twelve supposedly impossible feats. Kronos (or Cronus), in Greek mythology, was the Titan who ruled the universe until dethroned by Zeus, his son, the chief of the Olympian gods.
4. The Indian philosopher Siddhartha Gautama (known as the "Buddha"), founder of Buddhism. Osiris was the Egyptian god who annually died and was reborn, symbolizing the fertility of nature. Isis was the Egyptian goddess of fertility and the sister and wife of Osiris. Belus was a legendary god-king of Assyria. Brahma, in Hinduism, is the divine reality in the role of creator.
5. Arabic word for God, the supreme being in Islam. Manito was the nature god of the Algonquian Indians.

With Odin and the hideous-faced Mexitli[6] and every idol and image,
Taking them all for what they are worth and not a cent more,
Admitting they were alive and did the work of their days,
(They bore mites as for unfledg'd birds who have now to rise and fly and sing for themselves,)
Accepting the rough deific sketches to fill out better in myself, bestowing them freely on each man and woman I see,
Discovering as much or more in a framer framing a house,
Putting higher claims for him there with his roll'd-up sleeves driving the mallet and chisel,
Not objecting to special revelations, considering a curl of smoke or a hair on the back of my hand just as curious as any revelation,
Lads ahold of fire-engines and hook-and-ladder ropes no less to me than the gods of the antique wars,
Minding their voices peal through the crash of destruction,
Their brawny limbs passing safe over charr'd laths, their white foreheads whole and unhurt out of the flames;
By the mechanic's wife with her babe at her nipple interceding for every person born,
Three scythes at harvest whizzing in a row from three lusty angels with shirts bagg'd out at their waists,
The snag-tooth'd hostler with red hair redeeming sins past and to come,
Selling all he possesses, traveling on foot to fee lawyers for his brother and sit by him while he is tried for forgery;
What was strewn in the amplest strewing the square rod about me, and not filling the square rod then,
The bull and the bug never worshipp'd half enough,[7]
Dung and dirt more admirable than was dream'd,
The supernatural of no account, myself waiting my time to be one of the supremes,
The day getting ready for me when I shall do as much good as the best, and be as prodigious;
By my life-lumps![8] becoming already a creator,
Putting myself here and now to the ambush'd womb of the shadows.

42

A call in the midst of the crowd,
My own voice, orotund sweeping and final.

Come my children,
Come my boys and girls, my women, household and intimates,
Now the performer launches his nerve, he has pass'd his prelude on the reeds within.

6. An Aztec war god. Odin was the chief Norse god.
7. As Whitman implies, the bull and the bug had been worshiped in earlier religions, the bull in several, the scarab beetle as an Egyptian symbol of the soul.
8. Testicles.

Easily written loose-finger'd chords—I feel the thrum of your climax and close.

My head slues round on my neck,
Music rolls, but not from the organ,
Folks are around me, but they are no household of mine.

Ever the hard unsunk ground,
Ever the eaters and drinkers, ever the upward and downward sun, ever the air and the ceaseless tides,
Ever myself and my neighbors, refreshing, wicked, real,
Ever the old inexplicable query, ever that thorn'd thumb, that breath of itches and thirsts,
Ever the vexer's *hoot! hoot!* till we find where the sly one hides and bring him forth,
Ever love, ever the sobbing liquid of life,
Ever the bandage under the chin, ever the trestles[9] of death.

Here and there with dimes on the eyes[1] walking,
To feed the greed of the belly the brains liberally spooning,
Tickets buying, taking, selling, but in to the feast never once going,
Many sweating, ploughing, thrashing, and then the chaff for payment receiving,
A few idly owning, and they the wheat continually claiming.

This is the city and I am one of the citizens,
Whatever interests the rest interests me, politics, wars, markets, newspapers, schools,
The mayor and councils, banks, tariffs, steamships, factories, stocks, stores, real estate and personal estate.

The little plentiful manikins skipping around in collars and tail'd coats,
I am aware who they are, (they are positively not worms or fleas,)
I acknowledge the duplicates of myself, the weakest and shallowest is deathless with me,
What I do and say the same waits for them,
Every thought that flounders in me the same flounders in them.

I know perfectly well my own egotism,
Know my omnivorous lines and must not write any less,
And would fetch you whoever you are flush with myself.
Not words of routine this song of mine,
But abruptly to question, to leap beyond yet nearer bring;
This printed and bound book—but the printer and the printing-office boy?
The well-taken photographs—but your wife or friend close and solid in your arms?
The black ship mail'd with iron, her mighty guns in her turrets—but the pluck of the captain and engineers?

9. Sawhorses or similar supports holding up a coffin.

1. Coins were placed on eyelids to hold them closed until burial.

In the houses the dishes and fare and furniture—but the host and
 hostess, and the look out of their eyes?
The sky up there—yet here or next door, or across the way?
The saints and sages in history—but you yourself?
Sermons, creeds, theology—but the fathomless human brain,
And what is reason? and what is love? and what is life?

43

I do not despise you priests, all time, the world over,
My faith is the greatest of faiths and the least of faiths,
Enclosing worship ancient and modern and all between ancient and
 modern,
Believing I shall come again upon the earth after five thousand years,
Waiting responses from oracles, honoring the gods, saluting the sun,
Making a fetich of the first rock or stump, powowing with sticks in the
 circle of obis.[2]
Helping the llama or brahmin[3] as he trims the lamps of the idols,
Dancing yet through the streets in a phallic procession, rapt and austere
 in the woods a gymnosophist,[4]
Drinking mead from the skull-cup, to Shastas and Vedas admirant,
 minding the Koran,[5]
Walking the teokallis,[6] spotted with gore from the stone and knife,
 beating the serpent-skin drum,
Accepting the Gospels,[7] accepting him that was crucified, knowing
 assuredly that he is divine,
To the mass kneeling or the puritan's prayer rising, or sitting patiently
 in a pew,
Ranting and frothing in my insane crisis, or waiting dead-like till my spirit
 arouses me,
Looking forth on pavement and land, or outside of pavement and land,
Belonging to the winders of the circuit of circuits.

One of that centripetal and centrifugal gang I turn and talk like a man
 leaving charges before a journey.

Down-hearted doubters dull and excluded,
Frivolous, sullen, moping, angry, affected, disheartenen'd, atheistical,
I know every one of you, I know the sea of torment, doubt, despair and
 unbelief.

How the flukes[8] splash!
How they contort rapid as lightning, with spasms and spouts of blood!

2. Magical charms, such as shells, used in African and West Indian religious practices. "Fetich": i.e., fetish; object of worship.
3. Here, also a Buddhist priest. "Llama": i.e., lama; a Buddhist monk of Tibet or Mongolia.
4. Members of an ancient Hindu ascetic sect.
5. The other worshipers include ancient warriors drinking mead (an alcoholic beverage made of fermented honey) from the skulls of defeated enemies; admiring or wondering readers of the sastras (or shastras or shasters, books of Hindu law) or of the Vedas (the oldest sacred writings of Hinduism); and those attentive to the Koran (the sacred book of Islam, containing Allah's revelations to Muhammad).
6. An ancient Central American temple built on a pyramidal mound.
7. Of the New Testament of the Bible.
8. The flat parts on either side of a whale's tail; here used figuratively.

Be at peace bloody flukes of doubters and sullen mopers,
I take my place among you as much as among any,
The past is the push of you, me, all, precisely the same,
And what is yet untried and afterward is for you, me, all, precisely the same.

I do not know what is untried and afterward,
But I know it will in its turn prove sufficient, and cannot fail.

Each who passes is consider'd, each who stops is consider'd, not a single one can it fail.

It cannot fail the young man who died and was buried,
Nor the young woman who died and was put by his side,
Nor the little child that peep'd in at the door, and then drew back and was never seen again,
Nor the old man who has lived without purpose, and feels it with bitterness worse than gall,
Nor him in the poor house tubercled by rum and the bad disorder,[9]

Nor the numberless slaughter'd and wreck'd, nor the brutish koboo[1] call'd the ordure of humanity,
Nor the sacs merely floating with open mouths for food to slip in,
Nor any thing in the earth, or down in the oldest graves of the earth,
Nor any thing in the myriads of spheres, nor the myriads of myriads that inhabit them,
Nor the present, nor the least wisp that is known.

44

It is time to explain myself—let us stand up.

What is known I strip away,
I launch all men and women forward with me into the Unknown.

The clock indicates the moment—but what does eternity indicate?

We have thus far exhausted trillions of winters and summers,
There are trillions ahead, and trillions ahead of them.

Births have brought us richness and variety,
And other births will bring us richness and variety.

I do not call one greater and one smaller,
That which fills its period and place is equal to any.

Were mankind murderous or jealous upon you, my brother, my sister?
I am sorry for you, they are not murderous or jealous upon me,
All has been gentle with me, I keep no account with lamentation,
(What have I to do with lamentation?)

9. Syphilis.

1. Native of Sumatra.

I am an acme of things accomplish'd, and I an encloser of things to be.

My feet strike an apex of the apices[2] of the stairs,
On every step bunches of ages, and larger bunches between the steps,
All below duly travel'd, and still I mount and mount.

Rise after rise bow the phantoms behind me,
Afar down I see the huge first Nothing, I know I was even there,
I waited unseen and always, and slept through the lethargic mist,
And took my time, and took no hurt from the fetid carbon.[3]

Long I was hugg'd close—long and long.

Immense have been the preparations for me,
Faithful and friendly the arms that have help'd me.

Cycles[4] ferried my cradle, rowing and rowing like cheerful boatmen,
For room to me stars kept aside in their own rings,
They sent influences to look after what was to hold me.

Before I was born out of my mother generations guided me,
My embryo has never been torpid, nothing could overlay it.

For it the nebula cohered to an orb,
The long slow strata piled to rest it on,
Vast vegetables gave it sustenance,
Monstrous sauroids[5] transported it in their mouths and deposited it with
 care.

All forces have been steadily employ'd to complete and delight me,
Now on this spot I stand with my robust soul.

45

O span of youth! ever-push'd elasticity!
O manhood, balanced, florid and full.

My lovers suffocate me,
Crowding my lips, thick in the pores of my skin,
Jostling me through streets and public halls, coming naked to me at night,
Crying by day *Ahoy!* from the rocks of the river, swinging and chirping
 over my head,
Calling my name from flower-beds, vines, tangled underbrush,
Lighting on every moment of my life,
Bussing[6] my body with soft balsamic busses,
Noiselessly passing handfuls out of their hearts and giving them to be
 mine.

2. The highest points (variant plural of *apex*).
3. The "lethargic mist" (line 1154) and "fetid carbon" suggest a time before the appearance of human beings on earth.
4. Centuries.
5. Prehistoric large reptiles or dinosaurs, thought to have carried their eggs in their mouths.
6. Kissing.

Old age superbly rising! O welcome, ineffable grace of dying days!

Every condition promulges[7] not only itself, it promulges what grows after and out of itself,
And the dark hush promulges as much as any.

I open my scuttle[8] at night and see the far-sprinkled systems,
And all I see multiplied as high as I can cipher edge but the rim of the farther systems.

Wider and wider they spread, expanding, always expanding,
Outward and outward and forever outward.

My sun has his sun and round him obediently wheels,
He joins with his partners a group of superior circuit,
And greater sets follow, making specks of the greatest inside them.

There is no stoppage and never can be stoppage,
If I, you, and the worlds, and all beneath or upon their surfaces, were this moment reduced back to a pallid float,[9] it would not avail in the long run,
We should surely bring up again where we now stand,
And surely go as much farther, and then farther and farther.

A few quadrillions of eras, a few octillions of cubic leagues, do not hazard[1] the span or make it impatient,
They are but parts, any thing is but a part.

See ever so far, there is limitless space outside of that,
Count ever so much, there is limitless time around that.

My rendezvous is appointed, it is certain,
The Lord will be there and wait till I come on perfect terms,
The great Camerado, the lover true for whom I pine will be there.

46

I know I have the best of time and space, and was never measured and never will be measured.

I tramp a perpetual journey, (come listen all!)
My signs are a rain-proof coat, good shoes, and a staff cut from the woods,
No friend of mine takes his ease in my chair,
I have no chair, no church, no philosophy,
I lead no man to a dinner-table, library, exchange,[2]
But each man and each woman of you I lead upon a knoll,
My left hand hooking you round the waist,
My right hand pointing to landscapes of continents and the public road.

7. Promulgates, officially announces.
8. Roof hatch.
9. Era before the formation of the solar system.
1. Imperil, make hazardous.
2. Stock exchange.

Not I, not any one else can travel that road for you,
You must travel it for yourself.

It is not far, it is within reach,
Perhaps you have been on it since you were born and did not know,
Perhaps it is everywhere on water and on land.

Shoulder your duds dear son, and I will mine, and let us hasten forth,
Wonderful cities and free nations we shall fetch as we go.

If you tire, give me both burdens, and rest the chuff[3] of your hand on my hip,
And in due time you shall repay the same service to me,
For after we start we never lie by again.

This day before dawn I ascended a hill and look'd at the crowded heaven,
And I said to my spirit *When we become the enfolders of those orbs, and the pleasure and knowledge of every thing in them, shall we be fill'd and satisfied then?*
And my spirit said *No, we but level that lift to pass and continue beyond.*

You are also asking me questions and I hear you,
I answer that I cannot answer, you must find out for yourself.

Sit a while dear son,
Here are biscuits to eat and here is milk to drink,
But as soon as you sleep and renew yourself in sweet clothes, I kiss you with a good-by kiss and open the gate for your egress hence.

Long enough have you dream'd contemptible dreams,
Now I wash the gum from your eyes,
You must habit yourself to the dazzle of the light and of every moment of your life.

Long have you timidly waded holding a plank by the shore,
Now I will you to be a bold swimmer,
To jump off in the midst of the sea, rise again, nod to me, shout, and laughingly dash with your hair.

47

I am the teacher of athletes,
He that by me spreads a wider breast than my own proves the width of my own,
He most honors my style who learns under it to destroy the teacher.

The boy I love, the same becomes a man not through derived power, but in his own right,
Wicked rather than virtuous out of conformity or fear,

3. The fleshy part of the palm.

Fond of his sweetheart, relishing well his steak,
Unrequited love or a slight cutting him worse than sharp steel cuts,
First-rate to ride, to fight, to hit the bull's eye, to sail a skiff, to sing a song or play on the banjo,
Preferring scars and the beard and faces pitted with small-pox over all latherers,
And those well-tann'd to those that keep out of the sun.

I teach straying from me, yet who can stray from me?
I follow you whoever you are from the present hour,
My words itch at your ears till you understand them.

I do not say these things for a dollar or to fill up the time while I wait for a boat,
(It is you talking just as much as myself, I act as the tongue of you,
Tied in your mouth, in mine it begins to be loosen'd.)

I swear I will never again mention love or death inside a house,
And I swear I will never translate myself at all, only to him or her who privately stays with me in the open air.

If you would understand me go to the heights or water-shore,
The nearest gnat is an explanation, and a drop or motion of waves a key,
The maul, the oar, the hand-saw, second my words.

No shutter'd room or school can commune with me,
But roughs and little children better than they.

The young mechanic is closest to me, he knows me well,
The woodman that takes his axe and jug with him shall take me with him all day,
The farm-boy ploughing in the field feels good at the sound of my voice,
In vessels that sail my words sail, I go with fishermen and seamen and love them.

The soldier camp'd or upon the march is mine,
On the night ere the pending battle many seek me, and I do not fail them,
On that solemn night (it may be their last) those that know me seek me.

My face rubs to the hunter's face when he lies down alone in his blanket,
The driver thinking of me does not mind the jolt of his wagon,
The young mother and old mother comprehend me,
The girl and the wife rest the needle a moment and forget where they are,
They and all would resume what I have told them.

48

I have said that the soul is not more than the body,
And I have said that the body is not more than the soul,
And nothing, not God, is greater to one than one's self is,

And whoever walks a furlong without sympathy walks to his own funeral drest in his shroud,
And I or you pocketless of a dime may purchase the pick of the earth,
And to glance with an eye or show a bean in its pod confounds the learning of all times,
And there is no trade or employment but the young man following it may become a hero,
And there is no object so soft but it makes a hub for the wheel'd universe,
And I say to any man or woman, Let your soul stand cool and composed before a million universes.

And I say to mankind, Be not curious about God,
For I who am curious about each am not curious about God,
(No array of terms can say how much I am at peace about God and about death.)

I hear and behold God in every object, yet understand God not in the least,
Nor do I understand who there can be more wonderful than myself.

Why should I wish to see God better than this day?
I see something of God each hour of the twenty-four, and each moment then,
In the faces of men and women I see God, and in my own face in the glass,
I find letters from God dropt in the street, and every one is sign'd by God's name,
And I leave them where they are, for I know that wheresoe'er I go,
Others will punctually come for ever and ever.

49

And as to you Death, and you bitter hug of mortality, it is idle to try to alarm me.

To his work without flinching the accoucheur[4] comes,
I see the elder-hand pressing receiving supporting,
I recline by the sills of the exquisite flexible doors,
And mark the outlet, and mark the relief and escape.

And as to you Corpse I think you are good manure, but that does not offend me,
I smell the white roses sweet-scented and growing,
I reach to the leafy lips, I reach to the polish'd breasts of melons.

And as to you Life I reckon you are the leavings of many deaths,
(No doubt I have died myself ten thousand times before.)

4. Midwife.

I hear you whispering there O stars of heaven,
O suns—O grass of graves—O perpetual transfers and promotions,
If you do not say any thing how can I say any thing?
Of the turbid pool that lies in the autumn forest,
Of the moon that descends the steeps of the soughing twilight,
Toss, sparkles of day and dusk—toss on the black stems that decay in the muck,
Toss to the moaning gibberish of the dry limbs.

I ascend from the moon, I ascend from the night,
I perceive that the ghastly glimmer is noonday sunbeams reflected,
And debouch[5] to the steady and central from the offspring great or small.

50

There is that in me—I do not know what it is—but I know it is in me.

Wrench'd and sweaty—calm and cool then my body becomes,
I sleep—I sleep long.

I do not know it—it is without name—it is a word unsaid,
It is not in any dictionary, utterance, symbol.

Something it swings on more than the earth I swing on,
To it the creation is the friend whose embracing awakes me.

Perhaps I might tell more. Outlines! I plead for my brothers and sisters.
Do you see O my brothers and sisters?
It is not chaos or death—it is form, union, plan—it is eternal life—it is Happiness.

51

The past and present wilt—I have fill'd them, emptied them,
And proceed to fill my next fold of the future.

Listener up there! what have you to confide to me?
Look in my face while I snuff the sidle[6] of evening,
(Talk honestly, no one else hears you, and I stay only a minute longer.)

Do I contradict myself?
Very well then I contradict myself,
(I am large, I contain multitudes.)

I concentrate toward them that are nigh, I wait on the door-slab.

5. Pour forth.
6. To snuff out or extinguish a light, here the last glimmers of evening.

Who has done his day's work? who will soonest be through with his supper?
Who wishes to walk with me?

Will you speak before I am gone? will you prove already too late?

52

The spotted hawk swoops by and accuses me, he complains of my gab
and my loitering.

I too am not a bit tamed, I too am untranslatable.
I sound my barbaric yawp over the roofs of the world.

The last scud of day[7] holds back for me,
It flings my likeness after the rest and true as any on the shadow'd
wilds,
It coaxes me to the vapor and the dusk.

I depart as air, I shake my white locks at the runaway sun,
I effuse my flesh in eddies,[8] and drift it in lacy jags.

I bequeath myself to the dirt to grow from the grass I love,
If you want me again look for me under your boot-soles.

You will hardly know who I am or what I mean,
But I shall be good health to you nevertheless,
And filter and fibre your blood.

Failing to fetch me at first keep encouraged,
Missing me one place search another,
I stop somewhere waiting for you.

1855, 1881

FROM CHILDREN OF ADAM[1]

From Pent-up Aching Rivers

From pent-up aching rivers,
From that of myself without which I were nothing,
From what I am determin'd to make illustrious, even if I stand sole
among men,
From my own voice resonant, singing the phallus,

7. Wind-driven clouds, or the last rays of the sun.
8. Air currents. "Effuse": pour forth.
1. This group of poems first appeared in the 1860 edition of *Leaves of Grass* as *Enfans d'Adam*; later the contents and order were slightly altered until they reached final form in 1871. In a notebook entry Whitman identifies the relationship of this group to the *Calamus* poems: "Theory of a Cluster of Poems the same *to the passion of Woman-Love* as the 'Calamus-Leaves' are to adhesiveness,

Singing the song of procreation,
Singing the need of superb children and therein superb grown people,
Singing the muscular urge and the blending,
Singing the bedfellow's song, (O resistless yearning!
O for any and each the body correlative attracting!
O for you whoever you are your correlative body! O it, more than all else, you delighting!)
From the hungry gnaw that eats me night and day,
From native moments, from bashful pains, singing them,
Seeking something yet unfound though I have diligently sought it many a long year,
Singing the true song of the soul fitful at random,
Renascent with grossest Nature or among animals,
Of that, of them and what goes with them my poems informing,
Of the smell of apples and lemons, of the pairing of birds,
Of the wet of woods, of the lapping of waves,
Of the mad pushes of waves upon the land, I them chanting,
The overture lightly sounding, the strain anticipating,
The welcome nearness, the sight of the perfect body,
The swimmer swimming naked in the bath, or motionless on his back lying and floating,
The female form approaching, I pensive, love-flesh tremulous aching,
The divine list for myself or you or for any one making,
The face, the limbs, the index from head to foot, and what it arouses,
The mystic deliria, the madness amorous, the utter abandonment,
(Hark close and still what I now whisper to you,
I love you, O you entirely possess me,
O that you and I escape from the rest and go utterly off, free and lawless,
Two hawks in the air, two fishes swimming in the sea not more lawless than we;)
The furious storm through me careering, I passionately trembling,
The oath of the inseparableness of two together, of the woman that loves me and whom I love more than my life, that oath swearing,
(O I willingly stake all for you,
O let me be lost if it must be so!
O you and I! what is it to us what the rest do or think?
What is all else to us? only that we enjoy each other and exhaust each other if it must be so;)
From the master, the pilot I yield the vessel to,
The general commanding me, commanding all, from him permission taking,
From time the programme hastening, (I have loiter'd too long as it is,)
From sex, from the warp and from the woof,[2]
From privacy, from frequent repinings alone,
From plenty of persons near and yet the right person not near,

manly love. Full of animal-fire, tender, burning, the tremulous ache, delicious, yet such a torment. The swelling elate and vehement, that will not be denied. Adam, as a central figure and type. One piece presenting a vivid picture (in connection with the spirit) of a fully complete, well-developed man, eld, bearded, swart, fiery, as a more than rival of the youthful type-hero of novels and love poems."

2. Lengthwise ("warp") and crosswise ("woof") threads in a fabric.

From the soft sliding of hands over me and thrusting of fingers through my hair and beard,
From the long sustain'd kiss upon the mouth or bosom,
From the close pressure that makes me or any man drunk, fainting with excess,
From what the divine husband knows, from the work of fatherhood,
From exultation, victory and relief, from the bedfellow's embrace in the night,
From the act-poems of eyes, hands, hips and bosoms,
From the cling of the trembling arm,
From the bending curve and the clinch,
From side by side the pliant coverlet off-throwing,
From the one so unwilling to have me leave, and me just as unwilling to leave,
(Yet a moment O tender waiter, and I return,)
From the hour of shining stars and dropping dews,
From the night a moment I emerging flitting out,
Celebrate you act divine and you children prepared for,
And you stalwart loins.

1860, 1881

A Woman Waits for Me

A woman waits for me, she contains all, nothing is lacking,
Yet all were lacking if sex were lacking, or if the moisture of the right man were lacking.

Sex contains all, bodies, souls,
Meanings, proofs, purities, delicacies, results, promulgations,
Songs, commands, health, pride, the maternal mystery, the seminal milk,
All hopes, benefactions, bestowals, all the passions, loves, beauties, delights of the earth,
All the governments, judges, gods, follow'd persons of the earth,
These are contain'd in sex as parts of itself and justifications of itself.

Without shame the man I like knows and avows the deliciousness of his sex,
Without shame the woman I like knows and avows hers.

Now I will dismiss myself from impassive women,
I will go stay with her who waits for me, and with those women that are warm-blooded and sufficient for me,
I see that they understand me and do not deny me,
I see that they are worthy of me, I will be the robust husband of those women.

They are not one jot less than I am,
They are tann'd in the face by shining suns and blowing winds,
Their flesh has the old divine suppleness and strength,
They know how to swim, row, ride, wrestle, shoot, run, strike, retreat,
advance, resist, defend themselves,
They are ultimate in their own right—they are calm, clear, well possess'd
of themselves.

I draw you close to me, you women,
I cannot let you go, I would do you good,
I am for you, and you are for me, not only for our own sake, but for
others' sakes,
Envelop'd in you sleep greater heroes and bards,
They refuse to awake at the touch of any man but me.

It is I, you women, I make my way,
I am stern, acrid, large, undissuadable, but I love you,
I do not hurt you any more than is necessary for you,
I pour the stuff to start sons and daughters fit for these States, I press
with slow rude muscle,
I brace myself effectually, I listen to no entreaties,
I dare not withdraw till I deposit what has so long accumulated within
me.

Through you I drain the pent-up rivers of myself,
In you I wrap a thousand onward years,
On you I graft the grafts of the best-beloved of me and America,
The drops I distil upon you shall grow fierce and athletic girls, new
artists, musicians, and singers,
The babes I beget upon you are to beget babes in their turn,
I shall demand perfect men and women out of my love-spendings,
I shall expect them to interpenetrate with others, as I and you
interpenetrate now,
I shall count on the fruits of the gushing showers of them, as I count on
the fruits of the gushing showers I give now,
I shall look for loving crops from the birth, life, death, immortality, I
plant so lovingly now.

1856, 1871

Spontaneous Me

Spontaneous me, Nature,
The loving day, the mounting sun, the friend I am happy with,
The arm of my friend hanging idly over my shoulder,
The hillside whiten'd with blossoms of the mountain ash,
The same late in autumn, the hues of red, yellow, drab, purple, and
light and dark green,
The rich coverlet of the grass, animals and birds, the private untrimm'd
bank, the primitive apples, the pebble-stones,

Beautiful dripping fragments, the negligent list of one after another as I
happen to call them to me or think of them,
The real poems, (what we call poems being merely pictures,)
The poems of the privacy of the night, and of men like me,
This poem drooping shy and unseen that I always carry, and that all
men carry,
(Know once for all, avow'd on purpose, wherever are men like me, are
our lusty lurking masculine poems,)
Love-thoughts, love-juice, love-odor, love-yielding, love-climbers, and
the climbing sap,
Arms and hands of love, lips of love, phallic thumb of love, breasts of love,
bellies press'd and glued together with love,
Earth of chaste love, life that is only life after love,
The body of my love, the body of the woman I love, the body of the man,
the body of the earth,
Soft forenoon airs that blow from the south-west,
The hairy wild-bee that murmurs and hankers up and down, that gripes
the full-grown lady-flower, curves upon her with amorous firm legs,
takes his will of her, and holds himself tremulous and tight till he is
satisfied;
The wet of woods through the early hours,
Two sleepers at night lying close together as they sleep, one with an arm
slanting down across and below the waist of the other,
The smell of apples, aromas from crush'd sage-plant, mint, birch-bark,
The boy's longings, the glow and pressure as he confides to me what he
was dreaming,
The dead leaf whirling its spiral whirl and falling still and content to the
ground,
The no-form'd stings that sights, people, objects, sting me with,
The hubb'd sting of myself, stinging me as much as it ever can any one,
The sensitive, orbic, underlapp'd brothers, that only privileged feelers
may be intimate where they are,
The curious roamer the hand roaming all over the body, the bashful
withdrawing of flesh where the fingers soothingly pause and edge
themselves,
The limpid liquid within the young man,
The vex'd corrosion so pensive and so painful,
The torment, the irritable tide that will not be at rest,
The like of the same I feel, the like of the same in others,
The young man that flushes and flushes, and the young woman that
flushes and flushes,
The young man that wakes deep at night, the hot hand seeking to repress
what would master him,
The mystic amorous night, the strange half-welcome pangs, visions,
sweats,
The pulse pounding through palms and trembling encircling fingers, the
young man all color'd, red, ashamed, angry;
The souse upon me of my lover the sea, as I lie willing and naked,
The merriment of the twin babes that crawl over the grass in the sun,
the mother never turning her vigilant eyes from them,
The walnut-trunk, the walnut-husks, and the ripening or ripen'd long-
round walnuts,

The continence of vegetables, birds, animals,
The consequent meanness of me should I skulk or find myself indecent,
    while birds and animals never once skulk or find themselves indecent,
The great chastity of paternity, to match the great chastity of maternity,
The oath of procreation I have sworn, my Adamic and fresh daughters,
The greed that eats me day and night with hungry gnaw, till I saturate
    what shall produce boys to fill my place when I am through,
The wholesome relief, repose, content,
And this bunch pluck'd at random from myself,
It has done its work—I toss it carelessly to fall where it may.

1856, 1867

Once I Pass'd through a Populous City

Once I pass'd through a populous city imprinting my brain for future use
    with its shows, architecture, customs, traditions,
Yet now of all that city I remember only a woman I casually met there
    who detain'd me for love of me,
Day by day and night by night we were together—all else has long been
    forgotten by me,
I remember I say only that woman who passionately clung to me,
Again we wander, we love, we separate again,
Again she holds me by the hand, I must not go,
I see her close beside me with silent lips sad and tremulous.

1860, 1861

Facing West from California's Shores

Facing west from California's shores,
Inquiring, tireless, seeking what is yet unfound,
I, a child, very old, over waves, towards the house of maternity,[1] the land
    of migrations, look afar,
Look off the shores of my Western sea, the circle almost circled;
For starting westward from Hindustan, from the vales of Kashmere,[2]
From Asia, from the north, from the God, the sage, and the hero,
From the south, from the flowery peninsulas and the spice islands,[3]
Long having wander'd since, round the earth having wander'd,
Now I face home again, very pleas'd and joyous,
(But where is what I started for so long ago?
And why is it yet unfound?)

1860, 1867

1. Asia, at the time believed to be the birthplace of civilization.
2. Mountainous region adjacent to India, Pakistan, western China, and Tibet. "Hindustan": India.
3. Indonesia.

From Calamus[1]

Scented Herbage of My Breast

Scented herbage of my breast,
Leaves from you I glean, I write, to be perused best afterwards,
Tomb-leaves, body-leaves growing up above me above death,
Perennial roots, tall leaves, O the winter shall not freeze you delicate leaves,
Every year shall you bloom again, out from where you retired you shall emerge again;
O I do not know whether many passing by will discover you or inhale your faint odor, but I believe a few will;
O slender leaves! O blossoms of my blood! I permit you to tell in your own way of the heart that is under you,
O I do not know what you mean there underneath yourselves, you are not happiness,
You are often more bitter than I can bear, you burn and sting me,
Yet you are beautiful to me you faint tinged roots, you make me think of death,
Death is beautiful from you, (what indeed is finally beautiful except death and love?)
O I think it is not for life I am chanting here my chant of lovers, I think it must be for death,
For how calm, how solemn it grows to ascend to the atmosphere of lovers,
Death or life I am then indifferent, my soul declines to prefer,
(I am not sure but the high soul of lovers welcomes death most,)
Indeed O death, I think now these leaves mean precisely the same as you mean,
Grow up taller sweet leaves that I may see! grow up out of my breast!
Spring away from the conceal'd heart there!
Do not fold yourself so in your pink-tinged roots timid leaves!
Do not remain down there so ashamed, herbage of my breast!
Come I am determin'd to unbare this broad breast of mine, I have long enough stifled and choked;
Emblematic and capricious blades I leave you, now you serve me not,
I will say what I have to say by itself,
I will sound myself and comrades only, I will never again utter a call only their call,
I will raise with it immortal reverberations through the States,
I will give an example to lovers to take permanent shape and will through the States,
Through me shall the words be said to make death exhilarating,
Give me your tone therefore O death, that I may accord with it,

1. The *Calamus* group first appeared in the 3rd edition of *Leaves of Grass* (1860) and was given its final contents and order in 1881. Comparisons with the *Children of Adam* sequence are inevitable; as Whitman remarked in his letters and journals, he saw the first as celebrating "amative" love of men and women and the *Calamus* poems as celebrating "adhesive" love of men for men.

Give me yourself, for I see that you belong to me now above all, and are folded inseparably together, you love and death are,
Nor will I allow you to balk me any more with what I was calling life,
For now it is convey'd to me that you are the purports essential,
That you hide in these shifting forms of life, for reasons, and that they are mainly for you,
That you beyond them come forth to remain, the real reality,
That behind the mask of materials you patiently wait, no matter how long,
That you will one day perhaps take control of all,
That you will perhaps dissipate this entire show of appearance,
That may-be you are what it is all for, but it does not last so very long,
But you will last very long.

1860, 1881

Whoever You Are Holding Me Now in Hand

Whoever you are holding me now in hand,
Without one thing all will be useless,
I give you fair warning before you attempt me further,
I am not what you supposed, but far different.

Who is he that would become my follower?
Who would sign himself a candidate for my affections?

The way is suspicious, the result uncertain, perhaps destructive,
You would have to give up all else, I alone would expect to be your sole and exclusive standard,
Your novitiate would even then be long and exhausting,
The whole past theory of your life and all conformity to the lives around you would have to be abandon'd,
Therefore release me now before troubling yourself any further, let go your hand from my shoulders,
Put me down and depart on your way.

Or else by stealth in some wood for trial,
Or back of a rock in the open air,
(For in any roof'd room of a house I emerge not, nor in company,
And in libraries I lie as one dumb, a gawk, or unborn, or dead,)
But just possibly with you on a high hill, first watching lest any person for miles around approach unawares,
Or possibly with you sailing at sea, or on the beach of the sea or some quiet island,
Here to put your lips upon mine I permit you,
With the comrade's long-dwelling kiss or the new husband's kiss,
For I am the new husband and I am the comrade.

Or if you will, thrusting me beneath your clothing,
Where I may feel the throbs of your heart or rest upon your hip,
Carry me when you go forth over land or sea;

For thus merely touching you is enough, is best,
And thus touching you would I silently sleep and be carried eternally.

But these leaves conning you con at peril,
For these leaves and me you will not understand,
They will elude you at first and still more afterward, I will certainly elude you,
Even while you should think you had unquestionably caught me, behold!
Already you see I have escaped from you.

For it is not for what I have put into it that I have written this book,
Nor is it by reading it you will acquire it,
Nor do those know me best who admire me and vauntingly praise me,
Nor will the candidates for my love (unless at most a very few) prove victorious,
Nor will my poems do good only, they will do just as much evil, perhaps more,
For all is useless without that which you may guess at many times and not hit, that which I hinted at;
Therefore release me and depart on your way.

1860, 1881

Trickle Drops

Trickle drops! my blue veins leaving!
O drops of me! trickle, slow drops,
Candid from me falling, drip, bleeding drops,
From wounds made to free you whence you were prison'd,
From my face, from my forehead and lips,
From my breast, from within where I was conceal'd, press forth red drops, confession drops,
Stain every page, stain every song I sing, every word I say, bloody drops,
Let them know your scarlet heat, let them glisten,
Saturate them with yourself all ashamed and wet,
Glow upon all I have written or shall write, bleeding drops,
Let it all be seen in your light, blushing drops.

1860, 1867

Here the Frailest Leaves of Me

Here the frailest leaves of me and yet my strongest lasting,
Here I shade and hide my thoughts, I myself do not expose them,
And yet they expose me more than all my other poems.

1860, 1871

Crossing Brooklyn Ferry[1]

1

Flood-tide below me! I see you face to face!
Clouds of the west—sun there half an hour high—I see you also face to face.

Crowds of men and women attired in the usual costumes, how curious you are to me!
On the ferry-boats the hundreds and hundreds that cross, returning home, are more curious to me than you suppose,
And you that shall cross from shore to shore years hence are more to me, and more in my meditations, than you might suppose.

2

The impalpable sustenance of me from all things at all hours of the day,
The simple, compact, well-join'd scheme, myself disintegrated, every one disintegrated yet part of the scheme,
The similitudes of the past and those of the future,
The glories strung like beads on my smallest sights and hearings, on the walk in the street and the passage over the river,
The current rushing so swiftly and swimming with me far away,
The others that are to follow me, the ties between me and them,
The certainty of others, the life, love, sight, hearing of others.

Others will enter the gates of the ferry and cross from shore to shore,
Others will watch the run of the flood-tide,
Others will see the shipping of Manhattan north and west, and the heights of Brooklyn to the south and east,
Others will see the islands large and small;
Fifty years hence, others will see them as they cross, the sun half an hour high,
A hundred years hence, or ever so many hundred years hence, others will see them,
Will enjoy the sunset, the pouring-in of the flood-tide, the falling-back to the sea of the ebb-tide.

3

It avails not, time nor place—distance avails not,
I am with you, you men and women of a generation, or ever so many generations hence,
Just as you feel when you look on the river and sky, so I felt,
Just as any of you is one of a living crowd, I was one of a crowd,

1. First published as "Sun-Down Poem" in the 2nd edition of *Leaves of Grass* (1856), where it was the first of a sequence of twelve poems positioned after the *Calamus* section; it was given its final title in 1860.

Just as you are refresh'd by the gladness of the river and the bright flow, I was refresh'd,
Just as you stand and lean on the rail, yet hurry with the swift current, I stood yet was hurried,
Just as you look on the numberless masts of ships and the thick-stemm'd pipes of steamboats, I look'd.

I too many and many a time cross'd the river of old,
Watched the Twelfth-month[2] sea-gulls, saw them high in the air floating with motionless wings, oscillating their bodies,
Saw how the glistening yellow lit up parts of their bodies and left the rest in strong shadow,
Saw the slow-wheeling circles and the gradual edging toward the south,
Saw the reflection of the summer sky in the water,
Had my eyes dazzled by the shimmering track of beams,
Look'd at the fine centrifugal spokes of light round the shape of my head in the sunlit water,
Look'd on the haze on the hills southward and south-westward,
Look'd on the vapor as it flew in fleeces tinged with violet,
Look'd toward the lower bay to notice the vessels arriving,
Saw their approach, saw aboard those that were near me,
Saw the white sails of schooners and sloops, saw the ships at anchor,
The sailors at work in the rigging or out astride the spars,
The round masts, the swinging motion of the hulls, the slender serpentine pennants,
The large and small steamers in motion, the pilots in their pilot-houses,
The white wake left by the passage, the quick tremulous whirl of the wheels,
The flags of all nations, the falling of them at sunset.
The scallop-edged waves in the twilight, the ladled cups, the frolicsome crests and glistening,
The stretch afar growing dimmer and dimmer, the gray walls of the granite storehouses by the docks,
On the river the shadowy group, the big steam-tug closely flank'd on each side by the barges, the hay-boat, the belated lighter,[3]
On the neighboring shore the fires from the foundry chimneys burning high and glaringly into the night,
Casting their flicker of black contrasted with wild red and yellow light over the tops of houses, and down into the clefts of streets.

4

These and all else were to me the same as they are to you,
I loved well those cities, loved well the stately and rapid river,
The men and women I saw were all near to me,
Others the same—others who looked back on me because I look'd forward to them,
(The time will come, though I stop here to-day and to-night.)

2. December.

3. Barge used to load or unload a cargo ship.

5

What is it then between us?
What is the count of the scores or hundreds of years between us?

Whatever it is, it avails not—distance avails not, and place avails not,
I too lived, Brooklyn of ample hills was mine,
I too walk'd the streets of Manhattan island, and bathed in the waters around it,
I too felt the curious abrupt questionings stir within me,
In the day among crowds of people sometimes they came upon me,
In my walks home late at night or as I lay in my bed they came upon me,
I too had been struck from the float forever held in solution,
I too had receiv'd identity by my body,
That I was I knew was of my body, and what I should be I knew I should be of my body.

6

It is not upon you alone the dark patches fall,
The dark threw its patches down upon me also,
The best I had done seem'd to me blank and suspicious,
My great thoughts as I supposed them, were they not in reality meagre?
Nor is it you alone who know what it is to be evil,
I am he who knew what it was to be evil,
I too knitted the old knot of contrariety,
Blabb'd, blush'd, resented, lied, stole, grudg'd,
Had guile, anger, lust, hot wishes I dared not speak,
Was wayward, vain, greedy, shallow, sly, cowardly, malignant,
The wolf, the snake, the hog, not wanting in me,
The cheating look, the frivolous word, the adulterous wish, not wanting,
Refusals, hates, postponements, meanness, laziness, none of these wanting,
Was one with the rest, the days and haps of the rest,
Was call'd by my nighest name by clear loud voices of young men as they saw me approaching or passing,
Felt their arms on my neck as I stood, or the negligent leaning of their flesh against me as I sat,
Saw many I loved in the street or ferry-boat or public assembly, yet never told them a word,
Lived the same life with the rest, the same old laughing, gnawing, leeping,
Play'd the part that still looks back on the actor or actress,
The same old role, the role that is what we make it, as great as we like,
Or as small as we like, or both great and small.

7

Closer yet I approach you,
What thought you have of me now, I had as much of you—I laid in my stores in advance,
I consider'd long and seriously of you before you were born.

Who was to know what should come home to me?
Who knows but I am enjoying this?
Who knows, for all the distance, but I am as good as looking at you now, for all you cannot see me?

8

Ah, what can ever be more stately and admirable to me than mast-hemm'd Manhattan?
River and sunset and scallop-edg'd waves of flood-tide?
The sea-gulls oscillating their bodies, the hay-boat in the twilight, and the belated lighter?
What gods can exceed these that clasp me by the hand, and with voices I love call me promptly and loudly by my nighest name as I approach?
What is more subtle than this which ties me to the woman or man that looks in my face?
Which fuses me into you now, and pours my meaning into you?

We understand then do we not?
What I promis'd without mentioning it, have you not accepted?
What the study could not teach—what the preaching could not accomplish is accomplish'd, is it not?

9

Flow on, river! flow with the flood-tide, and ebb with the ebb-tide!
Frolic on, crested and scallop-edg'd waves!
Gorgeous clouds of the sunset! drench with your splendor me, or the men and women generations after me!
Cross from shore to shore, countless crowds of passengers!
Stand up, tall masts of Mannahatta![4] stand up, beautiful hills of Brooklyn!
Throb, baffled and curious brain! throw out questions and answers!
Suspend here and everywhere, eternal float of solution!
Gaze, loving and thirsting eyes, in the house or street or public assembly!
Sound out, voices of young men! loudly and musically call me by my nighest name!
Live, old life! play the part that looks back on the actor or actress!
Play the old role, the role that is great or small according as one makes it!
Consider, you who peruse me, whether I may not in unknown ways be looking upon you;
Be firm, rail over the river, to support those who lean idly, yet haste with the hasting current;
Fly on, sea-birds! fly sideways, or wheel in large circles high in the air;
Receive the summer sky, you water, and faithfully hold it till all downcast eyes have time to take it from you!
Diverge, fine spokes of light, from the shape of my head, or any one's head, in the sunlit water!

4. Variant of Manhattan.

Come on, ships from the lower bay! pass up or down, white-sail'd schooners, sloops, lighters!
Flaunt away, flags of all nations! be duly lower'd at sunset!
Burn high your fires, foundry chimneys! cast black shadows at nightfall! cast red and yellow light over the tops of the houses!
Appearances, now or henceforth, indicate what you are,
You necessary film, continue to envelop the soul,
About my body for me, and your body for you, be hung our divinest aromas,
Thrive, cities—bring your freight, bring your shows, ample and sufficient rivers,
Expand, being than which none else is perhaps more spiritual,
Keep your places, objects than which none else is more lasting.

You have waited, you always wait, you dumb, beautiful ministers,
We receive you with free sense at last, and are insatiate henceforward,
Not you any more shall be able to foil us, or withhold yourselves from us,
We use you, and do not cast you aside—we plant you permanently within us,
We fathom you not—we love you—there is perfection in you also,
You furnish your parts toward eternity,
Great or small, you furnish your parts toward the soul.

1856, 1881

From Sea-Drift[1]

Out of the Cradle Endlessly Rocking[2]

Out of the cradle endlessly rocking,
Out of the mocking-bird's throat, the musical shuttle,
Out of the Ninth-month midnight,
Over the sterile sands and the fields beyond, where the child leaving his bed wander'd alone, bareheaded, barefoot,
Down from the shower'd halo,
Up from the mystic play of shadows twining and twisting as if they were alive,
Out from the patches of briers and blackberries,
From the memories of the bird that chanted to me,
From your memories sad brother, from the fitful risings and fallings I heard,
From under that yellow half-moon late-risen and swollen as if with tears,
From those beginning notes of yearning and love there in the mist,

1. The *Sea-Drift* section of the 1881 edition of *Leaves of Grass* was made up of two new poems, seven poems from *Sea-Shore Memories* in the 1871 *Passage to India* section, and two poems from the 1876 *Two Rivulets* section.

2. First published as "A Child's Reminiscence" in the *New York Saturday Press* of December 24, 1859, this poem was incorporated into the 1860 *Leaves of Grass* as "A Word Out of the Sea." Whitman continued to revise it until it reached the present form in the *Sea-Drift* section of the 1881 edition. "Out of the Cradle Endlessly Rocking" had been the first of the *Sea-Shore Memories* group.

From the thousand responses of my heart never to cease,
From the myriad thence-arous'd words,
From the word stronger and more delicious than any,
From such as now they start the scene revisiting,
As a flock, twittering, rising, or overhead passing,
Borne hither, ere all eludes me, hurriedly,
A man, yet by these tears a little boy again,
Throwing myself on the sand, confronting the waves,
I, chanter of pains and joys, uniter of here and hereafter,
Taking all hints to use them, but swiftly leaping beyond them,
A reminiscence sing.

Once Paumanok,[3]
When the lilac-scent was in the air and Fifth-month grass was growing,
Up this seashore in some briers,
Two feather'd guests from Alabama, two together,

And their nest, and four light-green eggs spotted with brown,
And every day the he-bird to and fro near at hand,
And every day the she-bird crouch'd on her nest, silent, with bright eyes,
And every day I, a curious boy, never too close, never disturbing them,
Cautiously peering, absorbing, translating.

Shine! shine! shine!
Pour down your warmth, great sun!
While we bask, we two together.

Two together!
Winds blow south, or winds blow north,
Day come white, or night come black,
Home, or rivers and mountains from home,
Singing all time, minding no time,
While we two keep together.

Till of a sudden,
May-be kill'd, unknown to her mate,
One forenoon the she-bird crouch'd not on the nest,
Nor return'd that afternoon, nor the next
Nor ever appear'd again.

And thenceforward all summer in the sound of the sea,
And at night under the full of the moon in calmer weather,
Over the hoarse surging of the sea,
Or flitting from brier to brier by day,
I saw, I heard at intervals the remaining one, the he-bird,
The solitary guest from Alabama.

Blow! blow! blow!
Blow up sea-winds along Paumanok's shore;
I wait and I wait till you blow my mate to me.

3. Long Island.

Yes, when the stars glisten'd,
All night long on the prong of a moss-scallop'd stake,
Down almost amid the slapping waves,
Sat the lone singer wonderful causing tears.

He call'd on his mate,
He pour'd forth the meanings which I of all men know.

Yes my brother I know,
The rest might not, but I have treasur'd every note,
For more than once dimly down to the beach gliding,
Silent, avoiding the moonbeams, blending myself with the shadows,
Recalling now the obscure shapes, the echoes, the sounds and sights
after their sorts,
The white arms out in the breakers tirelessly tossing,
I, with bare feet, a child, the wind wafting my hair,
Listen'd long and long.

Listen'd to keep, to sing, now translating the notes.
Following you my brother.

Soothe! soothe! soothe!
Close on its wave soothes the wave behind,
And again another behind embracing and lapping, every one close,
But my love soothes not me, not me.

Low hangs the moon, it rose late,
It is lagging—O I think it is heavy with love, with love.

O madly the sea pushes upon the land,
With love, with love.

O night! do I not see my love fluttering out among the breakers?
What is that little black thing I see there in the white?

Loud! loud! loud!
Loud I call to you, my love!

High and clear I shoot my voice over the waves,
Surely you must know who is here, is here,
You must know who I am, my love.

Low-hanging moon!
What is that dusky spot in your brown yellow?
O it is the shape, the shape of my mate!
O moon do not keep her from me any longer.

Land! land! O land!
Whichever way I turn, O I think you could give me my mate back again
if you only would,
For I am almost sure I see her dimly whichever way I look.

O rising stars!
Perhaps the one I want so much will rise, will rise with some of you.

O throat! O trembling throat!
Sound clearer through the atmosphere!
Pierce the woods, the earth,
Somewhere listening to catch you must be the one I want.

Shake out carols!
Solitary here, the night's carols!
Carols of lonesome love! death's carols!
Carols under that lagging, yellow, waning moon!
O under that moon where she droops almost down into the sea!
O reckless despairing carols.

But soft! sink low!
Soft! let me just murmur,
And do you wait a moment you husky-nois'd sea,
For somewhere I believe I heard my mate responding to me,
So faint, I must be still, be still to listen,
But not altogether still, for then she might not come immediately to me.

Hither my love!
Here I am! here!
With this just-sustain'd note I announce myself to you,
This gentle call is for you my love, for you.

Do not be decoy'd elsewhere,
That is the whistle of the wind, it is not my voice,
That is the fluttering, the fluttering of the spray,
Those are the shadows of leaves.

O darkness! O in vain!
O I am very sick and sorrowful.

O brown halo in the sky near the moon, drooping upon the sea!
O troubled reflection in the sea!
O throat! O throbbing heart!
And I singing uselessly, uselessly all the night.

O past! O happy life! O songs of joy!
In the air, in the woods, over fields,
Loved! loved! loved! loved! loved!
But my mate no more, no more with me!
We two together no more.

The aria sinking,
All else continuing, the stars shining,
The winds blowing, the notes of the bird continuous echoing,
With angry moans the fierce old mother incessantly moaning,

On the sands of Paumanok's shore gray and rustling,
The yellow half-moon enlarged, sagging down, drooping, the face of the sea almost touching,
The boy ecstatic, with his bare feet the waves, with his hair the atmosphere dallying,
The love in the heart long pent, now loose, now at last tumultuously bursting,
The aria's meaning, the ears, the soul, swiftly depositing,
The strange tears down the cheeks coursing,
The colloquy there, the trio, each uttering,
The undertone, the savage old mother incessantly crying,
To the boy's soul's questions sullenly timing, some drown'd secret hissing,
To the outsetting bard.

Demon or bird! (said the boy's soul,)
Is it indeed toward your mate you sing? or is it really to me?
For I, that was a child, my tongue's use sleeping, now I have heard you,
Now in a moment I know what I am for, I awake,
And already a thousand singers, a thousand songs, clearer, louder and more sorrowful than yours,
A thousand warbling echoes have started to life within me, never to die.

O you singer solitary, singing by yourself, projecting me,
O solitary me listening, never more shall I cease perpetuating you,
Never more shall I escape, never more the reverberations,
Never more the cries of unsatisfied love be absent from me,
Never again leave me to be the peaceful child I was before what there in the night,
By the sea under the yellow and sagging moon,
The messenger there arous'd, the fire, the sweet hell within,
The unknown want, the destiny of me.

O give me the clew! (it lurks in the night here somewhere,)
O if I am to have so much, let me have more!

A word then, (for I will conquer it,)
The word final, superior to all,
Subtle, sent up—what is it?—I listen;
Are you whispering it, and have been all the time, you sea-waves?
Is that it from your liquid rims and wet sands?

Whereto answering, the sea,
Delaying not, hurrying not,
Whisper'd me through the night, and very plainly before daybreak,
Lisp'd to me the low and delicious word death,
And again death, death, death, death,
Hissing melodious, neither like the bird nor like my arous'd child's heart,
But edging near as privately for me rustling at my feet,
Creeping thence steadily up to my ears and laving me softly all over,
Death, death, death, death, death.

Which I do not forget,
But fuse the song of my dusky demon and brother,
That he sang to me in the moonlight on Paumanok's gray beach,
With the thousand responsive songs at random,
My own songs awaked from that hour,
And with them the key, the word up from the waves,
The word of the sweetest song and all songs,
That strong and delicious word which, creeping to my feet,
(Or like some old crone rocking the cradle, swathed in sweet garments, bending aside,)
The sea whisper'd me.

1859, 1881

As I Ebb'd with the Ocean of Life[1]

1

As I ebb'd with the ocean of life,
As I wended the shores I know,
As I walk'd where the ripples continually wash you Paumanok,[2]
Where they rustle up hoarse and sibilant,
Where the fierce old mother endlessly cries for her castaways,
I musing late in the autumn day, gazing off southward,
Held by this electric self out of the pride of which I utter poems,
Was seiz'd by the spirit that trails in the lines underfoot,
The rim, the sediment that stands for all the water and all the land of the globe.

Fascinated, my eyes reverting from the south, dropt, to follow those slender windrows,[3]
Chaff, straw, splinters of wood, weeds, and the sea-gluten,[4]
Scum, scales from shining rocks, leaves of salt-lettuce, left by the tide,
Miles walking, the sound of breaking waves the other side of me,
Paumanok there and then as I thought the old thought of likenesses,
These you presented to me you fish-shaped island,
As I wended the shores I know,
As I walk'd with that electric self seeking types.[5]

2

As I wend to the shores I know not,
As I list to the dirge, the voices of men and women wreck'd,

1. This poem was first published as "Bardic Symbols" in the *Atlantic* of April 1860, minus lines 59–60, which were restored in the 1860 edition of *Leaves of Grass*. Whitman gave it its final title and position as the second poem in *Sea-Drift* in the 1881 edition.

2. Long Island.

3. Rows of waves formed by the wind.

4. Gummy, viscid substance.

5. Types or likenesses of himself, in the debris left by the receding tide.

As I inhale the impalpable breezes that set in upon me,
As the ocean so mysterious rolls toward me closer and closer,
I too but signify at the utmost a little wash'd-up drift,
A few sands and dead leaves to gather,
Gather, and merge myself as part of the sands and drift.

O baffled, balk'd, bent to the very earth,
Oppress'd with myself that I have dared to open my mouth,
Aware now that amid all that blab whose echoes recoil upon me I have not once had the least idea who or what I am,
But that before all my arrogant poems the real Me stands yet untouch'd, untold, altogether unreach'd,
Withdrawn far, mocking me with mock-congratulatory signs and bows,
With peals of distant ironical laughter at every word I have written,
Pointing in silence to these songs, and then to the sand beneath.

I perceive I have not really understood any thing, not a single object, and that no man ever can,
Nature here in sight of the sea taking advantage of me to dart upon me and sting me,
Because I have dared to open my mouth to sing at all.

3

You oceans both, I close with you,
We murmur alike reproachfully rolling sands and drift, knowing not why,
These little shreds indeed standing for you and me and all.
You friable[6] shore with trails of debris,
You fish-shaped island, I take what is underfoot,
What is yours is mine my father.

I too Paumanok,
I too have bubbled up, floated the measureless float, and been wash'd on your shores,
I too am but a trail of drift and debris,
I too leave little wrecks upon you, you fish-shaped island.

I throw myself upon your breast my father,
I cling to you so that you cannot unloose me,
I hold you so firm till you answer me something.

Kiss me my father,
Touch me with your lips as I touch those I love,
Breathe to me while I hold you close the secret of the murmuring I envy.

4

Ebb, ocean of life, (the flow will return,)
Cease not your moaning you fierce old mother,

6. Crumbling.

Endlessly cry for your castaways, but fear not, deny not me,
Rustle not up so hoarse and angry against my feet as I touch you or gather from you.

I mean tenderly by you and all,
I gather for myself and for this phantom looking down where we lead, and following me and mine.
Me and mine, loose windrows, little corpses,
Froth, snowy white, and bubbles,
(See, from my dead lips the ooze exuding at last,
See, the prismatic colors glistening and rolling,)
Tufts of straw, sands, fragments,
Buoy'd hither from many moods, one contradicting another,
From the storm, the long calm, the darkness, the swell,
Musing, pondering, a breath, a briny tear, a dab of liquid or soil,
Up just as much out of fathomless workings fermented and thrown,
A limp blossom or two, torn, just as much over waves floating, drifted at random,
Just as much for us that sobbing dirge of Nature,
Just as much whence we come that blare of the cloud-trumpets,
We, capricious, brought hither we know not whence, spread out before you,
You up there walking or sitting,
Whoever you are, we too lie in drifts at your feet.

1860, 1881

From By the Roadside[1]

When I Heard the Learn'd Astronomer

When I heard the learn'd astronomer,
When the proofs, the figures, were ranged in columns before me,
When I was shown the charts and diagrams, to add, divide, and measure them,
When I sitting heard the astronomer where he lectured with much applause in the lecture-room,
How soon unaccountable I became tired and sick,
Till rising and gliding out I wander'd off by myself,
In the mystical moist night-air, and from time to time,
Look'd up in perfect silence at the stars.

1865

1. *By the Roadside* is the 1881 section title for around two dozen short poems of roadside observation, most of which first appeared in the 1860 edition of *Leaves of Grass*.

The Dalliance of the Eagles

Skirting the river road, (my forenoon walk, my rest,)
Skyward in air a sudden muffled sound, the dalliance of the eagles,
The rushing amorous contact high in space together,
The clinching interlocking claws, a living, fierce, gyrating wheel,
Four beating wings, two beaks, a swirling mass tight grappling,
In tumbling turning clustering loops, straight downward falling,
Till o'er the river pois'd, the twain yet one, a moment's lull,
A motionless still balance in the air, then parting, talons loosing,
Upward again on slow-firm pinions slanting, their separate diverse flight,
She hers, he his, pursuing.

1880, 1881

From Drum-Taps[1]

Beat! Beat! Drums!

Beat! beat! drums!—blow! bugles! blow!
Through the windows—through doors—burst like a ruthless force,
Into the solemn church, and scatter the congregation,
Into the school where the scholar is studying;
Leave not the bridegroom quiet—no happiness must he have now with his bride,
Nor the peaceful farmer any peace, ploughing his field or gathering his grain,
So fierce you whirr and pound you drums—so shrill you bugles blow.

Beat! beat! drums!—blow! bugles! blow!
Over the traffic of cities—over the rumble of wheels in the streets;
Are beds prepared for sleepers at night in the houses? no sleepers must sleep in those beds,
No bargainers' bargains by day—no brokers or speculators—would they continue?
Would the talkers be talking? would the singer attempt to sing?

1. The contents of the original *Drum-Taps* (first printed in 1865 as a little book) differed considerably from the contents of the *Drum-Taps* section finally arrived at in the 1881 *Leaves of Grass.* In the final arrangement the poetic purpose shifts throughout, roughly reflecting the chronology of the Civil War and the chronology of the composition of the poems. Whitman's initial aim was propagandistic. Indeed, "Beat! Beat! Drums!" served as a kind of recruiting poem when it was first printed in September 1861 issues of *Harper's Weekly* and the *New York Leader,* having been composed after the Southern victory at the first battle of Bull Run. The dominant impulse of most of the later poems is realistic—a determination to record the war the way it was, and in the best of the poems the realism is achieved through elaborate technical subtleties. The stages of Whitman's own attitudes toward the war are well stated in the epigraph he gave the *Drum-Taps* group in 1871 and then inserted parenthetically into "The Wound Dresser" in the 1881 edition: "Arous'd and angry, I'd thought to beat the alarum, and urge relentless war, / But soon my fingers fail'd me, my face droop'd and I resign'd myself / To sit by the wounded and soothe them, or silently watch the dead."

Would the lawyer rise in the court to state his case before the judge?
Then rattle quicker, heavier drums—you bugles wilder blow.

Beat! beat! drums!—blow! bugles! blow!
Make no parley—stop for no expostulation,
Mind not the timid—mind not the weeper or prayer,
Mind not the old man beseeching the young man,
Let not the child's voice be heard, nor the mother's entreaties,
Make even the trestles to shake the dead where they lie awaiting the hearses,
So strong you thump O terrible drums—so loud you bugles blow.

1861, 1867

Cavalry Crossing a Ford

A line in long array where they wind betwixt green islands,
They take a serpentine course, their arms flash in the sun—hark to the musical clank,
Behold the silvery river, in it the splashing horses loitering stop to drink,
Behold the brown-faced men, each group, each person a picture, the negligent rest on the saddles,
Some emerge on the opposite bank, others are just entering the ford—while,
Scarlet and blue and snowy white,
The guidon flags[1] flutter gayly in the wind.

1865, 1871

Vigil Strange I Kept on the Field One Night

Vigil strange I kept on the field one night;
When you my son and my comrade dropt at my side that day,
One look I but gave which your dear eyes return'd with a look I shall never forget,
One touch of your hand to mine O boy, reach'd up as you lay on the ground,
Then onward I sped in the battle, the even-contested battle,
Till late in the night reliev'd to the place at last again I made my way,
Found you in death so cold dear comrade, found your body son of responding kisses, (never again on earth responding,)
Bared your face in the starlight, curious the scene, cool blew the moderate night-wind,
Long there and then in vigil I stood, dimly around me the battle-field spreading,
Vigil wondrous and vigil sweet there in the fragrant silent night,
But not a tear fell, not even a long-drawn sigh, long, long I gazed,

1. Small military flags carried by soldiers for signaling and identification at a distance.

Then on the earth partially reclining sat by your side leaning my chin in my hands,
Passing sweet hours, immortal and mystic hours with you dearest comrade—not a tear, not a word,
Vigil of silence, love and death, vigil for you my son and my soldier,
As onward silently stars aloft, eastward new ones upward stole,
Vigil final for you brave boy, (I could not save you, swift was your death,
I faithfully loved you and cared for you living, I think we shall surely meet again,)
Till at latest lingering of the night, indeed just as the dawn appear'd,
My comrade I wrapt in his blanket, envelop'd well his form,
Folded the blanket well, tucking it carefully over head and carefully under feet,
And there and then and bathed by the rising sun, my son in his grave, in his rude-dug grave I deposited,
Ending my vigil strange with that, vigil of night and battle-field dim,
Vigil for boy of responding kisses, (never again on earth responding,)
Vigil for comrade swiftly slain, vigil I never forget, how as day brighten'd,
I rose from the chill ground and folded my soldier well in his blanket,
And buried him where he fell.

1865, 1867

A March in the Ranks Hard-Prest, and the Road Unknown

A march in the ranks hard-prest, and the Road Unknown,
A route through a heavy wood with muffled steps in the darkness,
Our army foil'd with loss severe, and the sullen remnant retreating,
Till after midnight glimmer upon us the lights of a dim-lighted building,
We come to an open space in the woods, and halt by the dim-lighted building,
'Tis a large old church at the crossing roads, now an impromptu hospital,
Entering but for a minute I see a sight beyond all the pictures and poems ever made,
Shadows of deepest, deepest black, just lit by moving candles and lamps,
And by one great pitchy torch stationary with wild red flame and clouds of smoke,
By these, crowds, groups of forms vaguely I see on the floor some in the pews laid down,
At my feet more distinctly a soldier, a mere lad, in danger of bleeding to death, (he is shot in the abdomen,)
I stanch the blood temporarily, (the youngster's face is white as a lily,)
Then before I depart I sweep my eyes o'er the scene fain to absorb it all,
Faces, varieties, postures beyond description, most in obscurity, some of them dead,
Surgeons operating, attendants holding lights, the smell of ether, the odor of blood,
The crowd, O the crowd of the bloody forms, the yard outside also fill'd,
Some on the bare ground, some on planks or stretchers, some in the death-spasm sweating,

An occasional scream or cry, the doctor's shouted orders or calls,
The glisten of the little steel instruments catching the glint of the torches,
These I resume as I chant, I see again the forms, I smell the odor,
Then hear outside the orders given, *Fall in, my men, fall in;*
But first I bend to the dying lad, his eyes open, a half-smile gives he me,
Then the eyes close, calmly close, and I speed forth to the darkness,
Resuming, marching, ever in darkness marching, on in the ranks,
The unknown road still marching.

1865, 1867

A Sight in Camp in the Daybreak Gray and Dim

A sight in camp in the daybreak gray and dim,
As from my tent I emerge so early sleepless,
As slow I walk in the cool fresh air the path near by the hospital tent,
Three forms I see on stretchers lying, brought out there untended lying,
Over each the blanket spread, ample brownish woolen blanket,
Gray and heavy blanket, folding, covering all.

Curious I halt and silent stand,
Then with light fingers I from the face of the nearest the first just lift the blanket;
Who are you elderly man so gaunt and grim, with well-gray'd hair, and flesh all sunken about the eyes?
Who are you my dear comrade?
Then to the second I step—and who are you my child and darling?

Who are you sweet boy with cheeks yet blooming?

Then to the third—a face nor child nor old, very calm, as of beautiful yellow-white ivory;
Young man I think I know you—I think this face is the face of the Christ himself,
Dead and divine and brother of all, and here again he lies.

1865, 1867

As Toilsome I Wander'd Virginia's Woods

As toilsome I wander'd Virginia's woods,
To the music of rustling leaves kick'd by my feet, (for 'twas autumn,)
I mark'd at the foot of a tree the grave of a soldier;
Mortally wounded he and buried on the retreat, (easily all could I understand,)
The halt of a mid-day hour, when up! no time to lose—yet this sign left,
On a tablet scrawl'd and nail'd on the tree by the grave,
Bold, cautious, true, and my loving comrade.

Long, long I muse, then on my way go wandering,
Many a changeful season to follow, and many a scene of life,
Yet at times through changeful season and scene, abrupt, alone, or in the crowded street,
Comes before me the unknown soldier's grave, comes the inscription rude in Virginia's woods,
Bold, cautious, true, and my loving comrade.

1865, 1867

The Wound-Dresser

1

An old man bending I come among new faces,
Years looking backward resuming in answer to children,
Come tell us old man, as from young men and maidens that love me,
(Arous'd and angry, I'd thought to beat the alarum, and urge relentless war,
But soon my fingers fail'd me, my face droop'd and I resign'd myself,
To sit by the wounded and soothe them, or silently watch the dead;)
Years hence of these scenes, of these furious passions, these chances,
Of unsurpass'd heroes, (was one side so brave? the other was equally brave;)
Now be witness again, paint the mightiest armies of earth,
Of those armies so rapid so wondrous what saw you to tell us?
What stays with you latest and deepest? of curious panics,
Of hard-fought engagements or sieges tremendous what deepest remains?

2

O maidens and young men I love and that love me,
What you ask of my days those the strangest and sudden your talking recalls,
Soldier alert I arrive after a long march cover'd with sweat and dust,
In the nick of time I come, plunge in the fight, loudly shout in the rush of successful charge,
Enter the captur'd works[1]—yet lo, like a swift-running river they fade,
Pass and are gone they fade—I dwell not on soldiers' perils or soldiers' joys,
(Both I remember well—many the hardships, few the joys, yet I was content.)

But in silence in dreams' projections,
While the world of gain and appearance and mirth goes on,
So soon what is over forgotten, and waves wash the imprints off the sand,
With hinged knees returning I enter the doors, (while for you up there,
Whoever you are, follow without noise and be of strong heart.)

1. Fortified earthworks.

Bearing the bandages, water and sponge,
Straight and swift to my wounded I go,
Where they lie on the ground after the battle brought in,
Where their priceless blood reddens the grass the ground,
Or to the rows of the hospital tent, or under the roof'd hospital,

To the long rows of cots up and down each side I return,
To each and all one after another I draw near, not one do I miss,
An attendant follows holding a tray, he carries a refuse pail,
Soon to be fill'd with clotted rags and blood, emptied, and fill'd again.

I onward go, I stop,
With hinged knees and steady hand to dress wounds,
I am firm with each, the pangs are sharp yet unavoidable,
One turns to me his appealing eyes—poor boy! I never knew you,
Yet I think I could not refuse this moment to die for you, if that would
save you.

3

On, on I go, (open doors of time! open hospital doors!)
The crush'd head I dress, (poor crazed hand tear not the bandage away,)
The neck of the cavalry-man with the bullet through and through I
examine,
Hard the breathing rattles, quite glazed already the eye, yet life struggles
hard,
(Come sweet death! be persuaded O beautiful death!
In mercy come quickly.)

From the stump of the arm, the amputated hand,
I undo the clotted lint, remove the slough, wash off the matter and blood,
Back on his pillow the soldier bends with curv'd neck and side-falling head,
His eyes are closed, his face is pale, he dares not look on the bloody stump,
And has not yet look'd on it.

I dress a wound in the side, deep, deep,
But a day or two more, for see the frame all wasted and sinking,
And the yellow-blue countenance see.

I dress the perforated shoulder, the foot with the bullet-wound,
Cleanse the one with a gnawing and putrid gangrene, so sickening, so
offensive,
While the attendant stands behind aside me holding the tray and pail.

I am faithful, I do not give out,
The fractur'd thigh, the knee, the wound in the abdomen,
These and more I dress with impassive hand, (yet deep in my breast a fire,
a burning flame.)

4

Thus in silence in dreams' projections,
Returning, resuming, I thread my way through the hospitals,
The hurt and wounded I pacify with soothing hand,
I sit by the restless all the dark night, some are so young,
Some suffer so much, I recall the experience sweet and sad,
(Many a soldier's loving arms about this neck have cross'd and rested,
Many a soldier's kiss dwells on these bearded lips.)

1865, 1881

Reconciliation

Word over all, beautiful as the sky,
Beautiful that war and all its deeds of carnage must in time be utterly lost,
That the hands of the sisters Death and Night incessantly softly wash again, and ever again, this soil'd world;
For my enemy is dead, a man divine as myself is dead,
I look where he lies white-faced and still in the coffin—I draw near,
Bend down and touch lightly with my lips the white face in the coffin.

1865–66, 1881

As I Lay with My Head in Your Lap Camerado

As I lay with my head in your lap camerado,
The confession I made I resume, what I said to you and the open air I resume,
I know I am restless and make others so,
I know my words are weapons full of danger, full of death,
For I confront peace, security, and all the settled laws, to unsettle them,
I am more resolute because all have denied me than I could ever have been had all accepted me,
I heed not and have never heeded either experience, cautions, majorities, nor ridicule,
And the threat of what is call'd hell is little or nothing to me,
And the lure of what is call'd heaven is little or nothing to me;
Dear camerado! I confess I have urged you onward with me, and still urge you, without the least idea what is our destination,
Or whether we shall be victorious, or utterly quell'd and defeated.

1865–66, 1881

Spirit Whose Work Is Done

(Washington City, 1865.)

Spirit whose work is done—spirit of dreadful hours!
Ere departing fade from my eyes your forests of bayonets;
Spirit of gloomiest fears and doubts, (yet onward ever unfaltering pressing,)
Spirit of many a solemn day and many a savage scene—electric spirit,
That with muttering voice through the war now closed, like a tireless
    phantom flitted,
Rousing the land with breath of flame, while you beat and beat the drum,
Now as the sound of the drum, hollow and harsh to the last, reverberates
    round me,
As your ranks, your immortal ranks, return, return from the battles,
As the muskets of the young men yet lean over their shoulders,
As I look on the bayonets bristling over their shoulders,
As those slanted bayonets, whole forests of them appearing in the
    distance, approach and pass on, returning homeward,
Moving with steady motion, swaying to and fro to the right and left,
Evenly lightly rising and falling while the steps keep time;
Spirit of hours I knew, all hectic red one day, but pale as death next day,
Touch my mouth ere you depart, press my lips close,
Leave me your pulses of rage—bequeath them to me—fill me with
    currents convulsive,
Let them scorch and blister out of my chants when you are gone,
Let them identify you to the future in these songs.

1865–66, 1881

From Memories of President Lincoln[1]

When Lilacs Last in the Dooryard Bloom'd

1

When lilacs last in the dooryard bloom'd,
And the great star[2] early droop'd in the western sky in the night,
I mourn'd, and yet shall mourn with ever-returning spring.

Ever-returning spring, trinity sure to me you bring,
Lilac blooming perennial and drooping star in the west,
And thought of him I love.

1. Composed in the months following Lincoln's assassination on April 14, 1865, this elegy was printed in the fall of that year as an appendix to the recently published *Drum-Taps* volume. In the 1881 edition of *Leaves of Grass* it and three shorter poems were joined to make up the section *Memories of President Lincoln*.

2. Literally Venus, although it becomes associated with Lincoln himself.

2

O powerful western fallen star!
O shades of night—O moody, tearful night!
O great star disappear'd—O the black murk that hides the star!
O cruel hands that hold me powerless—O helpless soul of me!
O harsh surrounding cloud that will not free my soul.

3

In the dooryard fronting an old farm-house near the white-wash'd palings,
Stands the lilac-bush tall-growing with heart-shaped leaves of rich green,
With many a pointed blossom rising delicate, with the perfume strong I love,
With every leaf a miracle—and from this bush in the dooryard,
With delicate-color'd blossoms and heart-shaped leaves of rich green,
A sprig with its flower I break.

4

In the swamp in secluded recesses,
A shy and hidden bird is warbling a song.

Solitary the thrush,
The hermit withdrawn to himself, avoiding the settlements,
Sings by himself a song.
Song of the bleeding throat,
Death's outlet song of life, (for well dear brother I know,
If thou wast not granted to sing thou would'st surely die.)

5

Over the breast of the spring, the land, amid cities,
Amid lanes and through old woods, where lately the violets peep'd from the ground, spotting the gray debris,
Amid the grass in the fields each side of the lanes, passing the endless grass,
Passing the yellow-spear'd wheat, every grain from its shroud in the dark-brown fields uprisen,
Passing the apple-tree blows[3] of white and pink in the orchards,
Carrying a corpse to where it shall rest in the grave,
Night and day journeys a coffin.[4]

6

Coffin that passes through lanes and streets,
Through day and night with the great cloud darkening the land,
With the pomp of the inloop'd flags with the cities draped in black,
With the show of the States themselves as of crape-veil'd women standing,

3. Blossoms.
4. The train carrying Lincoln's body for burial traveled from Washington, D.C., to Springfield, Illinois.

With processions long and winding and the flambeaus[5] of the night,
With the countless torches lit, with the silent sea of faces and the unbared heads,
With the waiting depot, the arriving coffin, and the sombre faces,
With dirges through the night, with the thousand voices rising strong and solemn,
With all the mournful voices of the dirges pour'd around the coffin,
The dim-lit churches and the shuddering organs—where amid these you journey,
With the tolling tolling bells' perpetual clang,
Here, coffin that slowly passes,
I give you my sprig of lilac.

7

(Nor for you, for one alone,
Blossoms and branches green to coffins all I bring,
For fresh as the morning, thus would I chant a song for you O sane and sacred death.

All over bouquets of roses,
O death, I cover you over with roses and early lilies,
But mostly and now the lilac that blooms the first,
Copious I break, I break the sprigs from the bushes,
With loaded arms I come, pouring for you,
For you and the coffins all of you O death.)

8

O western orb sailing the heaven,
Now I know what you must have meant as a month since I walk'd,
As I walk'd in silence the transparent shadowy night,
As I saw you had something to tell as you bent to me night after night,
As you droop'd from the sky low down as if to my side, (while the other stars all look'd on,)
As we wander'd together the solemn night, (for something I know not what kept me from sleep,)
As the night advanced, and I saw on the rim of the west how full you were of woe,
As I stood on the rising ground in the breeze in the cool transparent night,
As I watch'd where you pass'd and was lost in the netherward black of the night,
As my soul in its trouble dissatisfied sank, as where you sad orb,
Concluded, dropt in the night, and was gone.

9

Sing on there in the swamp,
O singer bashful and tender, I hear your notes, I hear your call,
I hear, I come presently, I understand you,

5. Torches.

But a moment I linger, for the lustrous star has detain'd me,
The star my departing comrade holds and detains me.

10

O how shall I warble myself for the dead one there I loved?
And how shall I deck my song for the large sweet soul that has gone?
And what shall my perfume be for the grave of him I love?

Sea-winds blown from east and west,
Blown from the Eastern sea and blown from the Western sea, till there on the prairies meeting,
These and with these and the breath of my chant,
I'll perfume the grave of him I love.

11

O what shall I hang on the chamber walls?
And what shall the pictures be that I hang on the walls,
To adorn the burial-house of him I love?

Pictures of growing spring and farms and homes,
With the Fourth-month[6] eve at sundown, and the gray smoke lucid and bright,
With floods of the yellow gold of the gorgeous, indolent, sinking sun, burning, expanding the air,
With the fresh sweet herbage under foot, and the pale green leaves of the trees prolific,
In the distance the flowing glaze, the breast of the river, with a wind-dapple here and there,
With ranging hills on the banks, with many a line against the sky, and shadows,
And the city at hand with dwellings so dense, and stacks of chimneys,
And all the scenes of life and the workshops, and the workmen homeward returning.

12

Lo, body and soul—this land,
My own Manhattan with spires, and the sparkling and hurrying tides, and the ships,
The varied and ample land, the South and the North in the light, Ohio's shores and flashing Missouri,
And ever the far-spreading prairies cover'd with grass and corn.

Lo, the most excellent sun so calm and haughty,
The violet and purple morn with just-felt breezes,
The gentle soft-born measureless light,
The miracle spreading bathing all, the fulfill'd noon,

6. April.

The coming eve delicious, the welcome night and the stars,
Over my cities shining all, enveloping man and land.

13

Sing on, sing on you gray-brown bird,
Sing from the swamps, the recesses, pour your chant from the bushes,
Limitless out of the dusk, out of the cedars and pines.

Sing on dearest brother, warble your reedy song,
Loud human song, with voice of uttermost woe.

O liquid and free and tender!
O wild and loose to my soul!—O wondrous singer!
You only I hear—yet the star holds me, (but will soon depart,)
Yet the lilac with mastering odor holds me.

14

Now while I sat in the day and look'd forth,
In the close of the day with its light and the fields of spring, and the
farmers preparing their crops,
In the large unconscious scenery of my land with its lakes and forests,
In the heavenly aerial beauty, (after the perturb'd winds and the storms,)
Under the arching heavens of the afternoon swift passing, and the voices
of children and women,
The many-moving sea-tides, and I saw the ships how they sail'd,
And the summer approaching with richness, and the fields all busy with
labor,
And the infinite separate houses, how they all went on, each with its
meals and minutia of daily usages,
And the streets how their throbbings throbb'd, and the cities pent—lo,
then and there,
Falling upon them all and among them all, enveloping me with the rest,
Appear'd the cloud, appear'd the long black trail,
And I knew death, its thought, and the sacred knowledge of death.

Then with the knowledge of death as walking one side of me,
And the thought of death close-walking the other side of me,
And I in the middle as with companions, and as holding the hands of
companions,
I fled forth to the hiding receiving night that talks not,
Down to the shores of the water, the path by the swamp in the dimness,
To the solemn shadowy cedars and ghostly pines so still.

And the singer so shy to the rest receiv'd me,
The gray-brown bird I know receiv'd us comrades three,
And he sang the carol of death, and a verse for him I love.

From deep secluded recesses,
From the fragrant cedars and the ghostly pines so still,
Came the carol of the bird.

And the charm of the carol rapt me,
As I held as if by their hands my comrades in the night,
And the voice of my spirit tallied the song of the bird.

Come lovely and soothing death,
Undulate round the world, serenely arriving, arriving,
In the day, in the night, to all, to each,
Sooner or later delicate death.

Prais'd be the fathomless universe,
For life and joy, and for objects and knowledge curious,
And for love, sweet love—but praise! praise! praise!
For the sure-enwinding arms of cool-enfolding death.

Dark mother always gliding near with soft feet,
Have none chanted for thee a chant of fullest welcome?
Then I chant it for thee, I glorify thee above all,
I bring thee a song that when thou must indeed come, come unfalteringly.

Approach strong deliveress,
When it is so, when thou hast taken them I joyously sing the dead,
Lost in the loving floating ocean of thee,
Laved in the flood of thy bliss O death.

From me to thee glad serenades,
Dances for thee I propose saluting thee, adornments and feastings for thee,
And the sights of the open landscape and the high-spread sky are fitting,
And life and the fields, and the huge and thoughtful night.

The night in silence under many a star,
The ocean shore and the husky whispering wave whose voice I know,
And the soul turning to thee O vast and well-veil'd death,
And the body gratefully nestling close to thee.

Over the tree-tops I float thee a song,
Over the rising and sinking waves, over the myriad fields and the prairies wide,
Over the dense-pack'd cities all and the teeming wharves and ways,
I float this carol with joy, with joy to thee O death.

15

To the tally of my soul,
Loud and strong kept up the gray-brown bird,
With pure deliberate notes spreading filling the night.

Loud in the pines and cedars dim,
Clear in the freshness moist and the swamp-perfume,
And I with my comrades there in the night.

While my sight that was bound in my eyes unclosed,
As to long panoramas of visions.

And I saw askant[7] the armies,
I saw as in noiseless dreams hundreds of battle-flags,
Borne through the smoke of the battles and pierc'd with missiles I saw them,
And carried hither and yon through the smoke, and torn and bloody,
And at last but a few shreds left on the staffs, (and all in silence,)
And the staffs all splinter'd and broken.

I saw battle-corpses, myriads of them,
And the white skeletons of young men, I saw them,
I saw the debris and debris of all the slain soldiers of the war,
But I saw they were not as was thought,
They themselves were fully at rest, they suffer'd not,
The living remain'd and suffer'd, the mother suffer'd,
And the wife and the child and the musing comrade suffer'd,
And the armies that remain'd suffer'd.

16

Passing the visions, passing the night,
Passing, unloosing the hold of my comrades' hands,
Passing the song of the hermit bird and the tallying song of my soul,
Victorious song, death's outlet song, yet varying ever-altering song,
As low and wailing, yet clear the notes, rising and falling, flooding the night,
Sadly sinking and fainting, as warning and warning, and yet again bursting with joy,
Covering the earth and filling the spread of the heaven,
As that powerful psalm in the night I heard from recesses,
Passing, I leave thee lilac with heart-shaped leaves,
I leave thee there in the door-yard, blooming, returning with spring.

I cease from my song for thee,
From my gaze on thee in the west, fronting the west, communing with thee,
O comrade lustrous with silver face in the night.

Yet each to keep and all, retrievements out of the night,
The song, the wondrous chant of the gray-brown bird,
And the tallying chant, the echo arous'd in my soul,
With the lustrous and drooping star with the countenance full of woe,
With the holders holding my hand nearing the call of the bird,
Comrades mine and I in the midst, and their memory ever to keep, for the dead I loved so well,
For the sweetest, wisest soul of all my days and lands—and this for his dear sake,
Lilac and star and bird twined with the chant of my soul,
There in the fragrant pines and the cedars dusk and dim.

1865–66, 1881

7. Sideways, aslant.

From Whispers of Heavenly Death

A Noiseless Patient Spider

A noiseless patient spider,
I mark'd where on a little promontory it stood isolated,
Mark'd how to explore the vacant vast surrounding,
It launch'd forth filament, filament, filament, out of itself,
Ever unreeling them, ever tirelessly speeding them.

And you O my soul where you stand,
Surrounded, detached, in measureless oceans of space,
Ceaselessly musing, venturing, throwing, seeking the spheres to connect
them,
Till the bridge you will need be form'd, till the ductile[1] anchor hold,
Till the gossamer thread you fling catch somewhere, O my soul.

1868, 1881

Letter to Ralph Waldo Emerson[1]

Brooklyn, August, 1856.

Here are thirty-two Poems, which I send you, dear Friend and Master, not having found how I could satisfy myself with sending any usual acknowledgment of your letter. The first edition, on which you mailed me that till now unanswered letter, was twelve poems—I printed a thousand copies, and they readily sold; these thirty-two Poems I stereotype,[2] to print several thousand copies of. I much enjoy making poems. Other work I have set for myself to do, to meet people and The States face to face, to confront them with an American rude tongue; but the work of my life is making poems. I keep on till I make a hundred, and then several hundred—perhaps a thousand. The way is clear to me. A few years, and the average annual call for my Poems is ten or twenty thousand copies—more, quite likely. Why should I hurry or compromise? In poems or in speeches I say the word or two that has got to be said, adhere to the body, step with the countless common footsteps, and remind every man and woman of something.

1. Capable of being fashioned into a new form.

1. In July 21, 1855, Emerson sent Whitman a letter praising the first edition of *Leaves of Grass* (see p. 348). Having already "allowed" the *New York Tribune* to print the letter in a November issue, Whitman embellished the spine of the 1856 edition of *Leaves of Grass* with these words lettered in gold taken from the letter: "I Greet You at the / Beginning of A / Great Career / R.W. Emerson." In the back of the 1856 edition Whitman reprinted Emerson's letter in full and followed it by this "Letter to Ralph Waldo Emerson," dated Brooklyn, August 1856. Emerson's annoyance at Whitman's unauthorized use of his letter has obscured the extraordinary virtues of Whitman's 1856 "reply," which can be read, in part, as a preface to the 1856 edition, despite its placement at the back of the volume.

2. A printer's term before it became metaphorical, to stereotype was to make a mold of standing type, which could then be reused, while later printings could be made from the stereotyped plates. To go to the cost of stereotyping was evidence of optimism that future printings would be needed. In all likelihood, Whitman exaggerates press runs and sales here. The rarity of the 1856 edition of *Leaves of Grass*, for instance, argues against a publication run of several thousand copies.

Master, I am a man who has perfect faith. Master, we have not come through centuries, caste, heroisms, fables, to halt in this land today. Or I think it is to collect a ten-fold impetus that any halt is made. As nature, inexorable, onward, resistless, impassive amid the threats and screams of disputants, so America. Let all defer. Let all attend respectfully the leisure of These States, their politics, poems, literature, manners, and their free-handed modes of training their own offspring. Their own comes, just matured, certain, numerous and capable enough, with egotistical tongues, with sinewed wrists, seizing openly what belongs to them. They resume Personality, too long left out of mind. Their shadows are projected in employments, in books, in the cities, in trade; their feet are on the flights of the steps of the Capitol; they dilate, a large brawnier, more candid, more democratic, lawless, positive native to The States, sweet-bodied, completer, dauntless, flowing, masterful, beard-faced, new race of men.

Swiftly, on limitless foundations, the United States too are founding a literature. It is all as well done, in my opinion, as could be practicable. Each element here is in condition. Every day I go among the people of Manhattan Island, Brooklyn, and other cities, and among the young men, to discover the spirit of them, and to refresh myself. These are to be attended to; I am myself more drawn here than to those authors, publishers, importations, reprints, and so forth. I pass coolly through those, understanding them perfectly well, and that they do the indispensable service, outside of men like me, which nothing else could do. In poems, the young men of The States shall be represented, for they out-rival the best of the rest of the earth.

The lists of ready-made literature which America inherits by the mighty inheritance of the English language—all the rich repertoire of traditions, poems, histories, metaphysics, plays, classics, translations, have made, and still continue, magnificent preparations for that other plainly significant literature, to be our own, to be electric, fresh, lusty, to express the full-sized body, male and female—to give the modern meanings of things, to grow up beautiful, lasting, commensurate with America, with all the passions of home, with the inimitable sympathies of having been boys and girls together, and of parents who were with our parents.

What else can happen The States,[3] even in their own despite? That huge English flow, so sweet, so undeniable, has done incalculable good here, and is to be spoken of for its own sake with generous praise and with gratitude. Yet the price The States have had to lie under for the same has not been a small price. Payment prevails; a nation can never take the issues of the needs of other nations for nothing. America, grandest of lands in the theory of its politics, in popular reading, in hospitality, breadth, animal beauty, cities, ships, machines, money, credit, collapses quick as lightning at the repeated, admonishing, stern words. Where are any mental expressions from you, beyond what you have copied or stolen? Where the born throngs of poets, literats, orators, you promised? Will you but tag after other nations? They struggled long for their literature, painfully working their way, some with deficient languages, some with priest-craft, some in the endeavor just to live—yet achieved for their times, works, poems, perhaps the only solid consolation left to them through ages afterward of shame and decay. You are young, have

3. Presumably, "to The States."

the perfectest of dialects, a free press, a free government, the world forwarding its best to be with you. As justice has been strictly done to you, from this hour do strict justice to yourself. Strangle the singers who will not sing you loud and strong. Open the doors of The West. Call for new great masters to comprehend new arts, new perfections, new wants. Submit to the most robust bard till he remedy your barrenness. Then you will not need to adopt the heirs of others; you will have true heirs, begotten of yourself, blooded with your own blood.

With composure I see such propositions, seeing more and more every day of the answers that serve. Expressions do not yet serve, for sufficient reasons; but that is getting ready, beyond what the earth has hitherto known, to take home the expressions when they come, and to identify them with the populace of The States, which is the schooling cheaply procured by any outlay any number of years. Such schooling The States extract from the swarms of reprints, and from the current authors and editors. Such service and extract are done after enormous, reckless, free modes, characteristic of The States. Here are to be attained results never elsewhere thought possible; the modes are very grand too. The instincts of the American people are all perfect, and tend to make heroes. It is a rare thing in a man here to understand The States.

All current nourishments to literature serve. Of authors and editors I do not know how many there are in The States, but there are thousands, each one building his or her step to the stairs by which giants shall mount. Of the twenty-four modern mammoth two-double, three-double, and four-double cylinder presses now in the world, printing by steam, twenty-one of them are in These States. The twelve thousand large and small shops for dispensing books and newspapers—the same number of public libraries, any one of which has all the reading wanted to equip a man or woman for American reading—the three thousand different newspapers, the nutriment of the imperfect ones coming in just as usefully as any—the story papers, various, full of strong-flavored romances, widely circulated—the one cent and two-cent journals—the political ones, no matter what side—the weeklies in the country—the sporting and pictorial papers—the monthly magazines, with plentiful imported feed—the sentimental novels, numberless copies of them—the low-priced flaring tales, adventures, biographies—all are prophetic; all waft rapidly on. I see that they swell wide, for reasons. I am not troubled at the movement of them, but greatly pleased. I see plying shuttles, the active ephemeral myriads of books also, faithfully weaving the garments of a generation of men, and a generation of women, they do not perceive or know. What a progress popular reading and writing has made in fifty years! What a progress fifty years hence! The time is at hand when inherent literature will be a main part of These States, as general and real as steam-power, iron, corn, beef, fish. First-rate American persons are to be supplied. Our perennial materials for fresh thoughts, histories, poems, music, orations, religions, recitations, amusements, will then not be disregarded, any more than our perennial fields, mines, rivers, seas. Certain things are established, and are immovable; in those things millions of years stand justified. The mothers and fathers of whom modern centuries have come, have not existed for nothing; they too had brains and hearts. Of course all literature, in all nations and years, will share marked attributes in common, as we all, of all ages, share the common human attributes. America is to be kept coarse and broad. What is to be done is to withdraw from precedents, and be directed to men and women—also to The States in their federalness; for the union of the parts of the body is not more necessary to their life than the union of These States is to their life.

A profound person can easily know more of the people than they know of themselves. Always waiting untold in the souls of the armies of common people, is stuff better than anything that can possibly appear in the leadership of the same. That gives final verdicts. In every department of These States, he who travels with a coterie, or with selected persons, or with imitators, or with infidels, or with the owners of slaves, or with that which is ashamed of the body of a man, or with that which is ashamed of the body of a woman, or with any thing less than the bravest and the openest, travels straight for the slopes of dissolution. The genius of all foreign literature is clipped and cut small, compared to our genius, and is essentially insulting to our usages, and to the organic compacts of These States. Old forms, old poems, majestic and proper in their own lands here in this land are exiles; the air here is very strong. Much that stands well and has a little enough place provided for it in the small scales of European kingdoms, empires, and the like, here stands haggard, dwarfed, ludicrous, or has no place little enough provided for it. Authorities, poems, models, laws, names, imported into America, are useful to America today to destroy them, and so move disencumbered to great works, great days.

Just so long, in our country or any country, as no revolutionists advance, and are backed by the people, sweeping off the swarms of routine representatives, officers in power, book-makers, teachers, ecclesiastics; politicians, just so long, I perceive, do they who are in power fairly represent that country, and remain of use, probably of very great use. To supersede them, when it is the pleasure of These States, full provision is made; and I say the time has arrived to use it with a strong hand. Here also the souls of the armies have not only overtaken the souls of the officers, but passed on, and left the souls of the officers behind out of sight many weeks' journey; and the souls of the armies now go en-masse without officers. Here also formulas, glosses, blanks, minutiæ, are choking the throats of the spokesmen to death. Those things most listened for, certainly those are the things least said. There is not a single History of the World. There is not one of America, or of the organic compacts of These States, or of Washington, or of Jefferson, nor of Language, nor any Dictionary of the English Language. There is no great author; every one has demeaned himself to some etiquette or some impotence. There is no manhood or life-power in poems; there are shoats and geldings more like. Or literature will be dressed up, a fine gentleman, distasteful to our instincts, foreign to our soil. Its neck bends right and left wherever it goes. Its costumes and jewelry prove how little it knows Nature. Its flesh is soft; it shows less and less of the indefinable hard something that is Nature. Where is any thing but the shaved Nature of synods and schools? Where is a savage and luxuriant man? Where is an overseer? In lives, in poems, in codes of law, in Congress, in tuitions, theatres, conversations, argumentations, not a single head lifts itself clean out, with proof that it is their master, and has subordinated them to itself, and is ready to try their superiors. None believes in These States, boldly illustrating them in himself. Not a man faces round at the rest with terrible negative voice, refusing all terms to be bought off from his own eye-sight, or from the soul that he is, or from friendship, or from the body that he is, or from the soil and sea. To creeds, literature, art, the army, the navy, the executive, life is hardly proposed, but the sick and dying are proposed to cure the sick and dying. The churches are one vast lie; the people do not believe them, and they do not believe themselves; the priests are continually telling what they know well enough is not so, and keeping back what they know is so. The spectacle is a pitiful one. I think there can never be again upon the festive earth more bad-disordered persons deliberately taking seats, as of late in These States, at the heads of the public tables—such corpses' eyes for judges—such a rascal and thief in the Presidency.[4]

Up to the present, as helps best, the people, like a lot of large boys, have no determined tastes, are quite unaware of the grandeur of themselves, and of their destiny, and of their immense strides—accept with voracity whatever is presented them in novels, histories, newspapers, poems, schools, lectures, every thing. Pretty soon, through these and other means, their development makes the fibre that is capable of itself, and will assume determined tastes. The young men will be clear what they want, and will have it. They will follow none except him whose spirit leads them in the like spirit with themselves. Any such man will be welcome as the flowers of May. Others will be put out without ceremony. How much is there anyhow, to the young men of These States, in a parcel of helpless dandies, who can neither fight, work, shoot, ride, run, command—some of them devout, some quite insane, some castrated—all second-hand, or third, fourth, or fifth hand—waited upon by waiters, putting not this land first, but always other lands first, talking of art, doing the most ridiculous things for fear of being called ridiculous, smirking and skipping along, continually taking off their hats—no one behaving, dressing, writing, talking, loving, out of any natural and manly tastes of his own, but each one looking cautiously to see how the rest behave, dress, write, talk, love—pressing the noses of dead books upon themselves and upon their country—favoring no poets, philosophs, literats here, but dog-like danglers at the heels of the poets, philosophs, literats of enemies' lands—favoring mental expressions, models of gentlemen and ladies, social habitudes in These States, to grow up in sneaking defiance of the popular substratums of The States? Of course they and the likes of them can never justify the strong poems of America. Of course no feed of theirs is to stop and be made welcome to muscle the bodies, male and female, for Manhattan Island, Brooklyn, Boston, Worcester, Hartford, Portland, Montreal, Detroit, Buffalo, Cleaveland, Milwaukee, St. Louis, Indianapolis, Chicago, Cincinnati, Iowa City, Philadelphia, Baltimore, Raleigh, Savannah, Charleston, Mobile, New Orleans, Galveston, Brownsville, San Francisco, Havana, and a thousand equal cities, present and to come. Of course what they and the likes of them have been used for, draws toward its close, after which they will all be discharged, and not one of them will ever be heard of any more.

America, having duly conceived, bears out of herself offspring of her own to do the workmanship wanted. To freedom, to strength, to poems, to personal greatness, it is never permitted to rest, not a generation or part of a generation. To be ripe beyond further increase is to prepare to die. The architects of These States laid their foundations, and passed to further spheres.

4. The proslavery sympathizer Franklin Pierce (U.S. president 1853–57).

What they laid is a work done; as much more remains. Now are needed other architects, whose duty is not less difficult, but perhaps more difficult. Each age forever needs architects. America is not finished, perhaps never will be; now America is a divine true sketch. There are Thirty-Two States sketched—the population thirty millions. In a few years there will be Fifty States. Again in a few years there will be A Hundred States, the population hundreds of millions, the freshest and freest of men. Of course such men stand to nothing less than the freshest and freest expression.

Poets here, literats here, are to rest on organic different bases from other countries; not a class set apart, circling only in the circle of themselves, modest and pretty, desperately scratching for rhymes, pallid with white paper, shut off, aware of the old pictures and traditions of the race, but unaware of the actual race around them—not breeding in and in among each other till they all have the scrofula. Lands of ensemble, bards of ensemble! Walking freely out from the old traditions, as our politics has walked out, American poets and literats recognize nothing behind them superior to what is present with them—recognize with joy the sturdy living forms of men and women of These States, the divinity of sex, the perfect eligibility of the female with the male, all The States, liberty and equality, real articles, the different trades, mechanics, the young fellows of Manhattan Island, customs, instincts, slang, Wisconsin, Georgia, the noble Southern heart, the hot blood, the spirit that will be nothing less than master, the filibuster[5] spirit, the Western man, native-born perceptions, the eye for forms, the perfect models of made things, the wild smack of freedom, California, money, electric-telegraphs, free-trade, iron and the iron mines—recognize without demur those splendid resistless black poems, the steam-ships of the sea-board states, and those other resistless splendid poems, the locomotives, followed through the interior states by trains of rail-road cars.

A word remains to be said, as of one ever present, not yet permitted to be acknowledged, discarded or made dumb by literature, and the results apparent. To the lack of an avowed, empowered, unabashed development of sex, (the only salvation for the same,) and to the fact of speakers and writers fraudulently assuming as always dead what every one knows to be always alive, is attributable the remarkable non-personality and indistinctness of modern productions in books, art, talk; also that in the scanned lives of men and women most of them appear to have been for some time past of the neuter gender; and also the stinging fact that in orthodox society today, if the dresses were changed, the men might easily pass for women and the women for men.

Infidelism usurps most with fœtid polite face; among the rest infidelism about sex. By silence or obedience the pens of savans, poets, historians, biographers, and the rest, have long connived at the filthy law, and books enslaved to it, that what makes the manhood of a man, that sex, womanhood, maternity, desires, lusty animations, organs, acts, are unmentionable and to be ashamed of, to be driven to skulk out of literature with whatever belongs to them. This filthy law has to be repealed—it stands in the way of great reforms. Of women just as much as men, it is the interest that there should not be infidelism about sex, but perfect faith. Women in These States

5. During the 1850s, *filibuster* referred to those who led privately funded armed expeditions against Cuba, Mexico, and countries in Central and South America.

approach the day of that organic equality with men, without which, I see, men cannot have organic equality among themselves. This empty dish, gallantry, will then be filled with something. This tepid wash, this diluted deferential love, as in songs, fictions, and so forth, is enough to make a man vomit; as to manly friendship, everywhere observed in The States, there is not the first breath of it to be observed in print. I say that the body of a man or woman, the main matter, is so far quite unexpressed in poems; but that the body is to be expressed, and sex is. Of bards for These States, if it come to a question, it is whether they shall celebrate in poems the eternal decency of the amativeness of Nature, the motherhood of all, or whether they shall be the bards of the fashionable delusion of the inherent nastiness of sex, and of the feeble and querulous modesty of deprivation. This is important in poems, because the whole of the other expressions of a nation are but flanges out of its great poems. To me, henceforth, that theory of any thing, no matter what, stagnates in its vitals, cowardly and rotten, while it cannot publicly accept, and publicly name, with specific words, the things on which all existence, all souls, all realization, all decency, all health, all that is worth being here for, all of woman and of man, all beauty, all purity, all sweetness, all friendship, all strength, all life, all immortality depend. The courageous soul, for a year or two to come, may be proved by faith in sex, and by disdaining concessions.

To poets and literats—to every woman and man, today or any day, the conditions of the present, needs, dangers, prejudices, and the like, are the perfect conditions on which we are here, and the conditions for wording the future with undissuadable words. These States, receivers of the stamina of past ages and lands, initiate the outlines of repayment a thousand fold. They fetch the American great masters, waited for by old words and new, who accept evil as well as good, ignorance as well as erudition, black as soon as white, foreign-born materials as well as home-born, reject none, force discrepancies into range, surround the whole, concentrate them on present periods and places, show the application to each and any one's body and soul, and show the true use of precedents. Always America will be agitated and turbulent. This day it is taking shape, not to be less so, but to be more so, stormily, capriciously, on native principles, with such vast proportions of parts! As for me, I love screaming, wrestling, boiling-hot days.

Of course, we shall have a national character, an identity. As it ought to be, and as soon as it ought to be, it will be. That, with much else, takes care of itself, is a result, and the cause of greater results. With Ohio, Illinois, Missouri, Oregon—with the states around the Mexican sea—with cheerfully welcomed immigrants from Europe, Asia, Africa—with Connecticut, Vermont, New Hampshire, Rhode Island—with all varied interests, facts, beliefs, parties, genesis—there is being fused a determined character, fit for the broadest use for the freewomen and freemen of The States, accomplished and to be accomplished, without any exception whatever—each indeed free, each idiomatic, as becomes live states and men, but each adhering to one enclosing general form of politics, manners, talk, personal style, as the plenteous varieties of the race adhere to one physical form. Such character is the brain and spine to all, including literature, including poems. Such character, strong, limber, just, open-mouthed, American-blooded, full of pride, full of ease, of passionate friendliness, is to stand compact upon that vast basis of the supremacy of Individuality—that new moral American continent without which, I see, the physical continent remained incomplete, may-be a carcass, a bloat—that newer America, answering face to face with The States, with ever-satisfying and ever-unsurveyable seas and shores.

Those shores you found. I say you have led The States there—have led Me there. I say that none has ever done, or ever can do, a greater deed for The States, than your deed. Others may line out the lines, build cities, work mines, break up farms; it is yours to have been the original true Captain who put to sea, intuitive, positive, rendering the first report, to be told less by any report, and more by the mariners of a thousand bays, in each tack of their arriving and departing, many years after you.

Receive, dear Master, these statements and assurances through me, for all the young men, and for an earnest that we know none before you, but the best following you; and that we demand to take your name into our keeping, and that we understand what you have indicated, and find the same indicated in ourselves, and that we will stick to it and enlarge upon it through These States.

WALT WHITMAN.

1856

Live Oak, with Moss[1]

I.

Not the heat flames up and consumes,
Not the sea-waves hurry in and out,
Not the air, delicious and dry, the air of the ripe summer, bears lightly along white down-balls of myriads of seeds, wafted, sailing gracefully, to drop where they may,
Not these—O none of these, more than the flames of me, consuming, burning for his love whom I love—O none, more than I, hurrying in and out;
Does the tide hurry, seeking something, and never give up?—O I, the same, to seek my life-long lover;
O nor down-balls, nor perfumes, nor the high rain-emitting clouds, are borne through the open air, more than my copious soul is borne through the open air, wafted in all directions, for friendship, for love.—

II.

I saw in Louisiana a live-oak growing,
All alone stood it, and the moss hung down from the branches,

1. The *Live Oak, with Moss* sequence, composed in the late 1850s, is Whitman's most direct and coherent narrative of "manly love." Whitman included all twelve of the *Live Oak* poems in the forty-five-poem *Calamus* section of the 1860 edition of *Leaves of Grass*, but reordered the sequence in a way that obscured the narrative progression. Fredson Bowers first printed the original sequence in *Studies in Bibliography* (1953) from the manuscript in the Valentine Collection from the Library of Clifton Waller Barrett at the University of Virginia; its first textbook appearance was the 4th edition (1994) of this anthology. On scholarly debate about whether Whitman intended to publish these poems as a sequence, see Robert J. Scholnick in *Walt Whitman Quarterly Review* (2004).

Without any companion it grew there, glistening out joyous leaves of dark green,
And its look, rude, unbending, lusty, made me think of myself;
But I wondered how it could utter joyous leaves, standing alone there without its friend, its lover—For I knew I could not;
And I plucked a twig with a certain number of leaves upon it, and twined around it a little moss, and brought it away—And I have placed it in sight in my room,
It is not needed to remind me as of my friends, (for I believe lately I think of little else than of them,)
Yet it remains to me a curious token—I write these pieces, and name them after it,
For all that, and though the live oak glistens there in Louisiana, solitary in a wide flat space, uttering joyous leaves all its life, without a friend, a lover, near—I know very well I could not.

III.

When I heard at the close of the day how I had been praised in the Capitol, still it was not a happy night for me that followed;
Nor when I caroused—Nor when my favorite plans were accomplished—was I really happy,
But that day I rose at dawn from the bed of perfect health, electric, inhaling sweet breath,
When I saw the full moon in the west grow pale and disappear in the morning light,
When I wandered alone over the beach, and undressing, bathed, laughing with the waters, and saw the sun rise,
And when I thought how my friend, my lover, was coming, then O I was happy;
Each breath tasted sweeter—and all that day my food nourished me more—And the beautiful day passed well,
And the next came with equal joy—And with the next, at evening, came my friend,
And that night, while all was still, I heard the waters roll slowly continually up the shores,
I heard the hissing rustle of the liquid and sands, as directed to me, whispering to congratulate me,—For the friend I love lay sleeping by my side,
In the stillness his face was inclined towards me, while the moon's clear beams shone,
And his arm lay lightly over my breast—And that night I was happy.

IV.

This moment as I sit alone, yearning and pensive, it seems to me there are other men, in other lands, yearning and pensive.
It seems to me I can look over and behold them, in Germany, France, Spain—Or far away in China, India, or Russia—talking other dialects,
And it seems to me if I could know those men I should love them as I love men in my own lands,

It seems to me they are as wise, beautiful, benevolent, as any in my own lands;
O I think we should be brethren—I think I should be happy with them.

V.

Long I thought that knowledge alone would suffice me—O if I could but obtain knowledge!
Then the Land of the Prairies engrossed me—the south savannas engrossed me—For them I would live—I would be their orator;
Then I met the examples of old and new heroes—I heard of warriors, sailors, and all dauntless persons—And it seemed to me I too had it in me to be as dauntless as any, and would be so;
And then to finish all, it came to me to strike up the songs of the New World—And then I believed my life must be spent in singing;
But now take notice, Land of the prairies, Land of the south savannas, Ohio's land,
Take notice, you Kanuck woods—and you, Lake Huron—and all that with you roll toward Niagara—and you Niagara also,
And you, Californian mountains—that you all find some one else that he be your singer of songs,
For I can be your singer of songs no longer—I have ceased to enjoy them.
I have found him who loves me, as I him, in perfect love,
With the rest I dispense—I sever from all that I thought would suffice me, for it does not—it is now empty and tasteless to me,
I heed knowledge, and the grandeur of The States, and the examples of heroes, no more,
I am indifferent to my own songs—I am to go with him I love, and he is to go with me,
It is to be enough for each of us that we are together—We never separate again.—

VI.

What think you I have taken my pen to record?
Not the battle-ship, perfect-model'd, majestic, that I saw to day arrive in the offing, under full sail,
Nor the splendors of the past day—nor the splendors of the night that envelopes me—Nor the glory and growth of the great city spread around me,
But the two men I saw to-day on the pier, parting the parting of dear friends.
The one to remain hung on the other's neck and passionately kissed him—while the one to depart tightly prest the one to remain in his arms.

VII.

You bards of ages hence! when you refer to me, mind not so much my poems,
Nor speak of me that I prophesied of The States and led them the way of their glories,

But come, I will inform you who I was underneath that impassive exterior—I will tell you what to say of me,
Publish my name and hang up my picture as that of the tenderest lover,
The friend, the lover's portrait, of whom his friend, his lover, was fondest,
Who was not proud of his songs, but of the measureless ocean of love within him—and freely poured it forth,
Who often walked lonesome walks thinking of his dearest friends, his lovers,
Who pensive, away from one he loved, often lay sleepless and dissatisfied at night,
Who, dreading lest the one he loved might after all be indifferent to him, felt the sick feeling—O sick! sick!
Whose happiest days were those, far away through fields, in woods, on hills, he and another, wandering hand in hand, they twain, apart from other men.
Who ever, as he sauntered the streets, curved with his arm the manly shoulder of his friend—while the curving arm of his friend rested upon him also.

VIII.

Hours continuing long, sore and heavy-hearted,
Hours of the dusk, when I withdraw to a lonesome and unfrequented spot, seating myself, leaning my face in my hands,
Hours sleepless, deep in the night, when I go forth, speeding swiftly the country roads, or through the city streets, or pacing miles and miles, stifling plaintive cries,
Hours discouraged, distracted,—For he, the one I cannot content myself without—soon I saw him content himself without me,
Hours when I am forgotten—(O weeks and months are passing, but I believe I am never to forget!)
Sullen and suffering hours—(I am ashamed—but it is useless—I am what I am;)
Hours of torment—I wonder if other men ever have the like, out of the like feelings?
Is there even one other like me—distracted—his friend, his lover, lost to him?
Is he too as I am now? Does he still rise in the morning, dejected, thinking who is lost to him?
And at night, awaking, think who is lost?
Does he too harbor his friendship silent and endless? Harbor his anguish and passion?
Does some stray reminder, or the casual mention of a name, bring the fit back upon him, taciturn and depressed?
Does he see himself reflected in me? In these hours does he see the face of his hours reflected?

IX.

I dreamed in a dream of a city where all the men were like brothers,
O I saw them tenderly love each other—I often saw them, in numbers, walking hand in hand;

I dreamed that was the city of robust friends—Nothing was greater there than manly love—it led the rest,
It was seen every hour in the actions of the men of that city, and in all their looks and words.—

X.

O you whom I often and silently come where you are, that I may be with you,
As I walk by your side, or sit near, or remain in the same room with you,
Little you know the subtle electric fire that for your sake is playing within me.—

XI.

Earth! Though you look so impassive, ample and spheric there—I now suspect that is not all,
I now suspect there is something terrible in you, ready to break forth,
For an athlete loves me,—and I him—But toward him there is something fierce and terrible in me,
I dare not tell it in words—not even in these songs.

XII.

To the young man, many things to absorb, to engraft, to develop, I teach, that he be my eleve,[2]
But if through him speed not the blood of friendship, hot and red—If he be not silently selected by lovers, and do not silently select lovers—of what use were it for him to seek to become eleve of mine?

1858–59 1953

From Democratic Vistas[1]

* * *

Once, before the war, (Alas! I dare not say how many times the mood has come!) I, too, was fill'd with doubt and gloom. A foreigner, an acute and good man, had impressively said to me, that day—putting in form, indeed, my own observations: "I have travel'd much in the United States, and watch'd their politicians, and listen'd to the speeches of the candidates, and read the journals, and gone into the public houses, and heard the unguarded talk of men. And I have found your vaunted America honeycomb'd from top to toe with infidelism, even to itself and its own programme. I have mark'd the brazen hell-faces of secession and slavery gazing defiantly from all the windows and doorways. I have everywhere found, primarily, thieves and scalliwags arrang-

2. Student (French).

1. First published in 1871, *Democratic Vistas* drew on two essays, "Democracy" and "Personalism," that Whitman had previously published in the *New York Galaxy* of 1867 and 1868. The text is taken from Whitman's revised version in *Complete Prose Works* (1892).

ing the nominations to offices, and sometimes filling the offices themselves. I have found the north just as full of bad stuff as the south. Of the holders of public office in the Nation or the States or their municipalities, I have found that not one in a hundred has been chosen by any spontaneous selection of the outsiders, the people, but all have been nominated and put through by little or large caucuses of the politicians, and have got in by corrupt rings and electioneering, not capacity or desert. I have noticed how the millions of sturdy farmers and mechanics are thus the helpless supple-jacks[2] of comparatively few politicians. And I have noticed more and more, the alarming spectacle of parties usurping the government, and openly and shamelessly wielding it for party purposes."

Sad, serious, deep truths. Yet are there other, still deeper, amply confronting, dominating truths. Over those politicians and great and little rings, and over all their insolence and wiles, and over the powerfulest parties, looms a power, too sluggish maybe, but ever holding decisions and decrees in hand, ready, with stern process, to execute them as soon as plainly needed—and at times, indeed, summarily crushing to atoms the mightiest parties, even in the hour of their pride.

In saner hours far different are the amounts of these things from what, at first sight, they appear. Though it is no doubt important who is elected governor, mayor, or legislator (and full of dismay when incompetent or vile ones get elected, as they sometimes do), there are other, quieter contingencies, infinitely more important. Shams, &c., will always be the show, like ocean's scum; enough, if waters deep and clear make up the rest. Enough, that while the piled embroider'd shoddy gaud and fraud spreads to the superficial eye, the hidden warp and weft are genuine, and will wear forever. Enough, in short, that the race, the land which could raise such as the late rebellion, could also put it down.

The average man of a land at last only is important. He, in these States, remains immortal owner and boss, deriving good uses, somehow, out of any sort of servant in office, even the basest; (certain universal requisites, and their settled regularity and protection, being first secured,) a nation like ours, in a sort of geological formation state, trying continually new experiments, choosing new delegations, is not served by the best men only, but sometimes more by those that provoke it—by the combats they arouse. Thus national rage, fury, discussion, &c., better than content. Thus, also, the warning signals, invaluable for after times.

What is more dramatic than the spectacle we have seen repeated, and doubtless long shall see—the popular judgment taking the successful candidates on trial in the offices—standing off, as it were, and observing them and their doings for a while, and always giving, finally, the fit, exactly due reward? I think, after all, the sublimest part of political history, and its culmination, is currently issuing from the American people. I know nothing grander, better exercise, better digestion, more positive proof of the past, the triumphant result of faith in human kind, than a well-contested American national election.

2. Pliant walking sticks.

Then still the thought returns, (like the thread-passage in overtures,) giving the key and echo to these pages. When I pass to and fro, different latitudes, different seasons, beholding the crowds of the great cities, New York, Boston, Philadelphia, Cincinnati, Chicago, St. Louis, San Francisco, New Orleans, Baltimore—when I mix with these interminable swarms of alert, turbulent, good-natured, independent citizens, mechanics, clerks, young persons—at the idea of this mass of men, so fresh and free, so loving and so proud, a singular awe falls upon me. I feel, with dejection and amazement, that among our geniuses and talented writers or speakers, few or none have yet really spoken to this people, created a single image-making work for them, or absorb'd the central spirit and the idiosyncrasies which are theirs—and which, thus, in highest ranges, so far remain entirely uncelebrated, unexpress'd.

Dominion strong is the body's; dominion stronger is the mind's. What has fill'd, and fills to-day our intellect, our fancy, furnishing the standards therein, is yet foreign. The great poems, Shakspere[3] included, are poisonous to the idea of the pride and dignity of the common people, the life blood of democracy. The models of our literature, as we get it from other lands, ultramarine,[4] have had their birth in courts, and bask'd and grown in castle sunshine; all smells of princes' favors. Of workers of a certain sort, we have indeed, plenty, contributing after their kind; many elegant, many learn'd, all complacent. But touch'd by the national test, or tried by the standards of democratic personality, they wither to ashes. I say I have not seen a single writer, artist, lecturer, or what not, that has confronted the voiceless but ever erect and active, pervading, underlying will and typic aspiration of the land, in a spirit kindred to itself. Do you call those genteel little creatures American poets? Do you term that perpetual, pistareen,[5] paste-pot work, American art, American drama, taste, verse? I think I hear, echoed as from some mountain-top afar in the west, the scornful laugh of the Genius of these States.

Democracy, in silence, biding its time, ponders its own ideals, not of literature and art only—not of men only, but of women. The idea of the women of America, (extricated from this daze, this fossil and unhealthy air which hangs about the word *lady*,) develop'd, raised to become the robust equals, workers, and, it may be, even practical and political deciders with the men—greater than man, we may admit, through their divine maternity, always their towering, emblematical attribute—but great, at any rate, as man, in all departments; or, rather, capable of being so, soon as they realize it, and can bring themselves to give up toys and fictions, and launch forth, as men do, amid real, independent, stormy life.

Then, as towards our thought's finalé, (and, in that, over-arching the true scholar's lesson,) we have to say there can be no complete or epical presentation of democracy in the aggregate, or anything like it, at this day, because its doctrines will only be effectually incarnated in any one branch, when, in all, their spirit is at the root and centre. Far, far, indeed, stretch, in distance, our

3. I.e., Shakespeare (19th-century variant spelling).

4. Beyond the sea.

5. Of little worth.

Vistas! How much is still to be disentangled, freed! How long it takes to make this American world see that it is, in itself, the final authority and reliance!

Did you, too, O friend, suppose democracy was only for elections, for politics, and for a party name? I say democracy is only of use there that it may pass on and come to its flower and fruits in manners, in the highest forms of interaction between men, and their beliefs—in religion, literature, colleges, and schools—democracy in all public and private life, and in the army and navy.[6] I have intimated that, as a paramount scheme, it has yet few or no full realizers and believers. I do not see, either, that it owes any serious thanks to noted propagandists or champions, or has been essentially help'd, though often harm'd, by them. It has been and is carried on by all the moral forces, and by trade, finance, machinery, intercommunications, and, in fact, by all the developments of history, and can no more be stopp'd than the tides, or the earth in its orbit. Doubtless, also, it resides, crude and latent, well down in the hearts of the fair average of the American-born people, mainly in the agricultural regions. But it is not yet, there or anywhere, the fully-receiv'd, the fervid, the absolute faith.

I submit, therefore, that the fruition of democracy, on aught like a grand scale, resides altogether in the future. As, under any profound and comprehensive view of the gorgeous-composite feudal world, we see in it, through the long ages and cycles of ages, the results of a deep, integral, human and divine principle, or fountain, from which issued laws, ecclesia, manners, institutes, costumes, personalities, poems, (hitherto unequall'd,) faithfully partaking of their source, and indeed only arising either to betoken it, or to furnish parts of that varied-flowing display, whose centre was one and absolute—so, long ages hence, shall the due historian or critic make at least an equal retrospect, an equal history for the democratic principle. It too must be adorn'd, credited with its results—then, when it, with imperial power, through amplest time, has dominated mankind—has been the source and test of all the moral, esthetic, social, political, and religious expressions and institutes of the civilized world—has begotten them in spirit and in form, and has carried them to its own unprecedented heights—has had, (it is possible,) monastics and ascetics, more numerous, more devout than the monks and priests of all previous creeds—has sway'd the ages with a breadth and rectitude tallying Nature's own—has fashion'd, systematized, and triumphantly finish'd and carried out, in its own interest, and with unparallel'd success, a new earth and a new man.

Thus we presume to write, as it were, upon things that exist not, and travel by maps yet unmade, and a blank. But the throes of birth are upon us; and we have something of this advantage in seasons of strong formations, doubts, suspense—for then the afflatus of such themes haply may fall upon us, more or less; and then, hot from surrounding war and revolution, our speech, though without polish'd coherence, and a failure by the standard called criticism, comes forth, real at least as the lightnings.

6. The whole present system of the officering and personnel of the army and navy of these States, and the spirit and letter of their trebly aristocratic rules and regulations, is a monstrous exotic, a nuisance and revolt, and belong here just as much as orders of nobility, or the Pope's council of cardinals. I say if the present theory of our army and navy is sensible and true, then the rest of America is an unmitigated fraud [Whitman's note].

And may-be we, these days, have, too, our own reward—(for there are yet some, in all lands, worthy to be so encouraged.) Though not for us the joy of entering at the last the conquer'd city—not ours the chance ever to see with our own eyes the peerless power and splendid *eclat*[7] of the democratic principle, arriv'd at meridian, filling the world with effulgence and majesty far beyond those of past history's kings, or all dynastic sway—there is yet, to whoever is eligible among us, the prophetic vision, the joy of being toss'd in the brave turmoil of these times—the promulgation and the path, obedient, lowly reverent to the voice, the gesture of the god, or holy ghost, which others see not, hear not—with the proud consciousness that amid whatever clouds, seductions, or heart-wearying postponements, we have never deserted, never despair'd, never abandon'd the faith.

* * *

1871, 1892

7. Brilliant success. (French).

HERMAN MELVILLE
1819–1891

Herman Melville was born in New York City in 1819, the third of eight children of Allan Melvill, a dry-goods merchant, and Maria Gansevoort, daughter of American Revolutionary hero General Peter Gansevoort. Melville's father incurred massive debt before dying suddenly and in delirium in 1832, and his wife and children, then living in Albany, became dependent on the Gansevoorts. Taken out of school when he was twelve, Melville (the *e* was added in the 1830s) held a succession of jobs: at a bank, at his brother Gansevoort's fur-cap store in Albany, at his uncle Thomas Melvill's farm in Pittsfield, Massachusetts, and at a country school near Pittsfield. In 1839 he voyaged to and from Liverpool as a cabin boy, but uncertainties about employment continued on his return. At age twenty-one, in January 1841, he sailed on a whaler for the South Seas. After over a year at sea, Melville and a shipmate, Toby Greene, jumped ship at the Marquesas Islands, approximately one thousand miles northeast of Tahiti, and for a few weeks in the summer of 1842 the two lived among the supposedly cannibalistic islanders of Tapai Valley. Picked up by an Australian whaler less than a month after he deserted, Melville signed on as an ordinary seaman with the naval frigate *United States*, cruised the Pacific, and arrived at Boston in October 1844.

Melville was twenty-five; he later said that from that year he dated the beginning of his life. He apparently did not look for a job after his discharge from the navy; he stayed with his brothers in New York City and began writing *Typee*, which drew on his experiences in the Marquesas. The book, published in 1846 in England and the United States, made a great sensation, capturing the imagination of readers with its combination of anthropological novelty and adventure. Shortly after its publication, Melville began writing a second novel, *Omoo*, which also drew on his experiences in the South Sea islands. Published in 1847, it was another best seller. Three days after his twenty-eighth birthday and in the flush of his success, Melville married Elizabeth Knapp Shaw on August 4, 1847. Her father, Lemuel Shaw, the chief justice of the Massachusetts Supreme Court, had been a school friend of Alan Melvill's. After the marriage Shaw provided several advances against his daughter's inheritance, allowing Melville to establish himself in Manhattan with his bride, his younger brother Allan, Allan's wife, his mother, his four sisters, and his new manuscript. But instead of supplying his publisher with yet another commercially promising tale of a Polynesian adventure, Melville attempted to elevate the travel-narrative genre to the level of spiritual and political allegory. In this third novel, *Mardi*, which was published in April 1849, Melville presented travel (as he would in *Moby-Dick*) as a philosophical journey. It is his longest novel and remains a difficult text for most readers. When first published, it sold poorly and received generally unfavorable reviews. After the birth of his first son, Malcolm, in 1849, Melville, seeking to regain his reputation, rapidly wrote the more accessible *Redburn* (1849), which drew on his travels to Liverpool, and *White-Jacket* (1850), based on his experiences on the man-of-war *United States*. Both novels were received enthusiastically in England and America.

In a buoyant mood, Melville began his whaling novel, *Moby-Dick*. Like *Mardi*, *Moby-Dick* was an enormously ambitious undertaking. There is compelling textual and biographical evidence that Melville wrote the book in stages, radically altering his conception of the novel from a relatively straightforward whaling narrative to something that aspired to be a "Gospels in this century" (as he termed the novel in an 1851 letter to Nathaniel Hawthorne). While composing the novel, Melville came under the spell of Shakespeare, Milton, Emerson, and numerous other writers. Melville was also inspired by his new literary friendship with Hawthorne, whom he had met at an August 1850 picnic in Pittsfield, Massachusetts. Immediately after their meeting, he read Hawthorne's *Mosses from an Old Manse* (1846) and wrote a belated review in which he expressed his thoughts about the challenges facing American writers. Convinced that the day had come when American writers could rival Shakespeare, Melville, in praising Hawthorne's achievements, honored what he believed infused the book he was writing: dark "Shakespearean" truths about human nature and the universe that, "in this world of lies," can be told only "covertly" and "by snatches."

As he continued to work on *Moby-Dick* and struggle with his finances, Melville late in 1850 moved his family to a farm near Pittsfield, where he was able to keep up his friendship with Hawthorne, who was living in nearby Lenox. In May 1851, Melville borrowed $2,050 from an old acquaintance; and as he anticipated doing final work on the galleys of *Moby-Dick*, he painfully defined his literary-economic dilemma to Hawthorne: "What I feel most moved to write, that is banned,—it will not pay. Yet, altogether, write the other way I cannot. So the product is a final hash, and all my books are botches." When *Moby-Dick* was published in late 1851, a reviewer for the *London Britannia* declared it "a most extraordinary work"; and a reviewer in the *New York Tribune* proclaimed that it was "the best production which has yet come from that seething brain, and . . . it gives us a higher opinion of the author's originality and power than even the favorite and fragrant first-fruits of his genius, the never-to-be-forgotten *Typee*." Still, there were a number of negative reviews from critics unhappy with the novel's length, philosophical abstractness, and mixing of genres, and the novel quickly vanished from the literary scene without bringing Melville the critical admiration that he had expected. (For more on *Moby-Dick*, see p. 1440.)

But Melville was not totally discouraged. Shortly after publishing *Moby-Dick*, he began *Pierre*, thinking he could express the agonies of the growth of a human psyche in a domestic novel focusing on the romantic, ethical, and intellectual perplexities attending Pierre Glendinning's coming into manhood. As he worked on this novel, reviews of *Moby-Dick* continued to appear. Disturbed by the mixed and sometimes hostile responses (the January 1852 *Southern Quarterly Review*, for instance, said a "writ de lunatic" was justified against Melville and his characters), Melville folded into his novel-in-progress a satirical account of the U.S. literary scene in which the timid and genteel succeed and the boldly adventurous fail. With its depictions of clerical hypocrisy, family dishonesty, and seemingly incestuous sexuality, Melville's wildly inventive and parodic novel was greeted—by those who bothered to take notice of it—as the work of a maniac, and it further hurt his chances for a commercially successful literary career. The novel, published in 1852, was widely denounced as immoral, and one *Pierre*-inspired account of the author was captioned: "HERMAN MELVILLE CRAZY." In a panic, family and friends attempted to get Melville a government job, but nothing came of their efforts.

Melville stayed on at the Pittsfield farm with his expanding household (his second son, Stanwix, was born in 1851, and two daughters, Elizabeth and Frances, were born in 1853 and 1855) and began a new career as a writer of short stories and novellas for two major American monthlies, *Harper's* and *Putnam's*. Paid at modest rates for fiction that was published anonymously, Melville, in works like "Bartleby, the Scrivener," "The Paradise of Bachelors and the Tartarus of Maids," and "Benito Cereno," took on such vexing issues of antebellum culture as racial and gender inequities, the social transformations caused by emerging industrial capitalism, and slavery. Some critics regard these works as among Melville's most socially progressive writings; others argue that Melville's choice of topical subjects should not obscure his metaphysical interest in the situation of individuals who exist, as the narrator of "Bartleby" puts it, "alone, absolutely alone in the universe. A bit of wreck in the mid Atlantic." In these enigmatic fictions, Melville seems more intent on exploring and engaging the ideological discourses of his time than on arguing for any particular reforms. For instance, although there may be no shrewder investigation of white racism and the evils of slavery than "Benito Cereno" (1855), which partly entraps readers in the stereotypical racist assumptions of the sea captain Amasa Delano, the novella is not an obvious attack on slavery as such, and it was ignored by the abolitionist press.

In 1855 Melville published *Israel Potter*, a tale of the American Revolution which had been serialized in *Putnam's*; and in 1856 he collected his stories in a volume titled *The Piazza Tales*. One year later he published *The Confidence-Man*, an indictment of the selfishness and duplicities of his contemporary world in the form of a metaphysical satire, allegory, and low comedy set on a Mississippi steamship. The novel went almost unread in the United States; in England the reviews were admiring but sales were disappointing. Deeply depressed by his struggles as a writer, Melville took an extended trip to Europe and the Levant, from October 1856 to May 1857, with funds supplied by his father-in-law, who hoped that the trip would lighten Melville's mood. But in England Melville confessed to Hawthorne (at the time U.S. consul at Liverpool) that he did not expect to enjoy his travels because "the spirit of adventure" had gone out of him. Upon his return he told a Gansevoort relative that he was "not going to write any more at the present." Instead, he lectured for small fees in eastern and midwestern states on "Statues in Rome" (1857), "The South Sea" (1858), and "Travel" (1859).

After the death of Judge Shaw in 1861, the Melvilles inherited funds that eased their economic pressures, and by October 1863 they were living in Manhattan. In 1864 Melville and his brother Allan made a trip to the Virginia battlefields looking for a Gansevoort cousin and (as Allan put it) hoping to "have opportunities to see that they may describe." Some of those opportunities proved fruitful for *Battle-Pieces* (1866), Melville's volume of Civil War poems, which was barely noticed by reviewers. Highly allusive, tightly formal, and marked by a seemingly Olympian detachment, *Battle-Pieces* is now regarded by many critics, along with Whitman's *Drum-Taps* (1865), as among the best volumes of poetry to have come out of the war. In the same year that he published *Battle-Pieces*, Melville at last obtained a political job as a deputy inspector of customs in New York City. When he had time to write, he worked mostly on his poetry.

These were dreary years for Melville. His job was dull and paid poorly, he had little ability to manage finances, and he was prone to anger and depression. His wife's half-brothers even considered him a danger to their sister, and by early 1867 Elizabeth may have begun to believe that he was insane. Her loyalty to him and her horror of gossip, however, kept her from acting on her minister's suggestion that she seek refuge with her family in Boston. Adding to the misery of the period, Malcolm killed himself late in 1867 at the age of eighteen. In the aftermath of the suicide, Melville began working on a poem about a diverse group of American and European pilgrims—and tourists—who talked their way through some of the same Palestinian scenes he had visited in 1857. This poem, *Clarel*, grew to eighteen thousand lines and appeared in 1876, paid for by a bequest from Elizabeth's uncle Peter Gansevoort. Addressing the conflict between religious faith and Darwinian skepticism that obsessed English contemporaries such as Matthew Arnold, the poem found few readers during the nineteenth century and remains one of Melville's understudied works.

A series of legacies came to the Melvilles in their last years, allowing Melville to retire from the customhouse at the beginning of 1886. During the late 1880s Melville and his wife drew closer together, in part out of their grief at the death of their second son, Stanwix, who was found dead in a San Francisco hotel in 1886. Around that time Melville once again began to devote himself to writing and publishing. He put together two volumes of poems, which he published with his own funds. In the mid-1880s a poem he was working on about a British sailor led him to compose a fictional narrative that was left nearly finished at Melville's death as *Billy Budd, Sailor,* his final study of the tense and ambiguous conflicts between the individual and various forms of authority.

Famously known during the 1840s as the "man who lived among the cannibals," Melville was neglected in the post–Civil War literary world. Shortly before his death in 1891, however, a revival of interest began, especially in England. The true Melville revival, however, took off with essays published on the occasion of Melville's centennial in 1919 and was given added momentum by the posthumous publication of *Billy Budd* in 1924. In one of the most curious phenomena of American literary history, the neglected Melville suddenly came to be regarded in the rarefied company of Shakespeare as a writer who, as Melville said of Shakespeare and Hawthorne, had mastered "the great Art of Telling the Truth" through the dazzling plentitude and sly indirections of his language.

Hawthorne and His Mosses

By a Virginian Spending July in Vermont[1]

A papered chamber in a fine old farm-house—a mile from any other dwelling, and dipped to the eaves in foliage—surrounded by mountains, old woods, and Indian ponds,—this, surely, is the place to write of Hawthorne. Some charm is in this northern air, for love and duty seem both impelling

1. Adopting the persona of a Virginian, perhaps to suggest the national appeal of Hawthorne, Melville wrote this review-essay of Hawthorne's *Mosses from an Old Manse* (1846) shortly after meeting Hawthorne at a picnic in the Massachusetts Berkshire Mountains on August 5, 1850. The review first appeared anonymously in the *New York Literary World* on August 17 and 25, 1850. The text is taken from the Northwestern-Newberry edition of the Writings of Herman Melville, *The Piazza Tales and Other Prose Pieces, 1839–1860* (1987).

to the task. A man of a deep and noble nature has seized me in this seclusion. His wild, witch voice rings through me; or, in softer cadences, I seem to hear it in the songs of the hill-side birds, that sing in the larch trees at my window.

Would that all excellent books were foundlings, without father or mother, that so it might be, we could glorify them, without including their ostensible authors. Nor would any true man take exception to this;—least of all, he who writes,—"When the Artist rises high enough to achieve the Beautiful, the symbol by which he makes it perceptible to mortal senses becomes of little value in his eyes, while his spirit possesses itself in the enjoyment of the reality."[2]

But more than this. I know not what would be the right name to put on the title-page of an excellent book, but this I feel, that the names of all fine authors are fictitious ones, far more so than that of Junius,[3]—simply standing, as they do, for the mystical, ever-eluding Spirit of all Beauty, which ubiquitously possesses men of genius. Purely imaginative as this fancy may appear, it nevertheless seems to receive some warranty from the fact, that on a personal interview no great author has ever come up to the idea of his reader. But that dust of which our bodies are composed, how can it fitly express the nobler intelligences among us? With reverence be it spoken, that not even in the case of one deemed more than man, not even in our Saviour, did his visible frame betoken anything of the augustness of the nature within. Else, how could those Jewish eyewitnesses fail to see heaven in his glance.

It is curious, how a man may travel along a country road, and yet miss the grandest, or sweetest of prospects, by reason of an intervening hedge, so like all other hedges, as in no way to hint of the wide landscape beyond. So has it been with me concerning the enchanting landscape in the soul of this Hawthorne, this most excellent Man of Mosses. His "Old Manse" has been written now four years, but I never read it till a day or two since. I had seen it in the book-stores—heard of it often—even had it recommended to me by a tasteful friend, as a rare, quiet book, perhaps too deserving of popularity to be popular. But there are so many books called "excellent", and so much unpopular merit, that amid the thick stir of other things, the hint of my tasteful friend was disregarded; and for four years the Mosses on the old Manse never refreshed me with their perennial green. It may be, however, that all this while, the book, like wine, was only improving in flavor and body. At any rate, it so chanced that this long procrastination eventuated in a happy result. At breakfast the other day, a mountain girl, a cousin of mine, who for the last two weeks has every morning helped me to strawberries and raspberries,—which, like the roses and pearls in the fairy-tale, seemed to fall into the saucer from those strawberry-beds her cheeks,—this delightful creature, this charming Cherry says to me—"I see you spend your mornings in the hay-mow; and yesterday I found there 'Dwight's Travels in New England'.[4] Now I have something far better than that,—something

2. The conclusion of Hawthorne's "The Artist and the Beautiful," which appeared in *Mosses*. Throughout the review-essay, Melville quotes from and praises a number of the tales and sketches in the volume.

3. The pen name of an English political writer who attacked King George III and his ministers in a series of letters published in the London *Public Advertiser* from 1769 to 1772. "Junius" has never been authoritatively identified.

4. Timothy Dwight's four-volume *Travels in New-England and New-York* (1821–22).

more congenial to our summer on these hills.[5] Take these raspberries, and then I will give you some moss."—"Moss!" said I.—"Yes, and you must take it to the barn with you, and good-bye to 'Dwight'".

With that she left me, and soon returned with a volume, verdantly bound, and garnished with a curious frontispiece in green,—nothing less, than a fragment of real moss cunningly pressed to a fly-leaf.—"Why this," said I spilling my raspberries, "this is the 'Mosses from an Old Manse'". "Yes" said cousin Cherry "yes, it is that flowery Hawthorne."—"Hawthorne and Mosses" said I "no more: it is morning: it is July in the country: and I am off for the barn".

Stretched on that new mown clover, the hill-side breeze blowing over me through the wide barn door, and soothed by the hum of the bees in the meadows around, how magically stole over me this Mossy Man! and how amply, how bountifully, did he redeem that delicious promise to his guests in the Old Manse, of whom it is written—"Others could give them pleasure, or amusement, or instruction—these could be picked up anywhere—but it was for me to give them rest. Rest, in a life of trouble! What better could be done for weary and world-worn spirits? what better could be done for anybody, who came within our magic circle, than to throw the spell of a magic spirit over him?"[6]—So all that day, half-buried in the new clover, I watched this Hawthorne's "Assyrian dawn, and Paphian sunset and moonrise, from the summit of our Eastern Hill."[7]

The soft ravishments of the man spun me round about in a web of dreams, and when the book was closed, when the spell was over, this wizard "dismissed me with but misty reminiscences, as if I had been dreaming of him".[8]

What a mild moonlight of contemplative humor bathes that Old Manse!—the rich and rare distilment of a spicy and slowly-oozing heart. No rollicking rudeness, no gross fun fed on fat dinners, and bred in the lees[9] of wine,—but a humor so spiritually gentle, so high, so deep, and yet so richly relishable, that it were hardly inappropriate in an angel. It is the very religion of mirth; for nothing so human but it may be advanced to that. The orchard of the Old Manse seems the visible type of the fine mind that has described it. Those twisted, and contorted old trees, "that stretch out their crooked branches, and take such hold of the imagination, that we remember them as humorists, and odd-fellows." And then, as surrounded by these grotesque forms, and hushed in the noon-day repose of this Hawthorne's spell, how aptly might the still fall of his ruddy thoughts into your soul be symbolized by "the thump of a great apple, in the stillest afternoon, falling without a breath of wind, from the mere necessity of perfect ripeness"! For no less ripe than ruddy are the apples of the thoughts and fancies in this sweet Man of Mosses.

5. In fact, Melville's aunt Mary Melvill gave him the book two weeks before he met Hawthorne.

6. From Hawthorne's introductory essay, "The Old Manse."

7. Also from "The Old Manse," in Hawthorne's description of the "little nook of a study": "It was here that Emerson wrote 'Nature'; for he was then an inhabitant of the Manse, and used to watch the Assyrian dawn and the Paphian sunset and moonrise, from the summit of our eastern hill." (With his references to ancient cities, Hawthorne paraphrases a passage from "Beauty" in *Nature* [1836].)

8. A rephrasing of a passage in "The Old Manse": "what better could be done for anybody, who came within our magic circle, than to throw the spell of a tranquil spirit over him? And when it had wrought its full effect, then we dismissed him, with but misty reminiscences, as if he had been dreaming of us."

9. Yeasty sediment from fermentation.

"Buds and Bird-voices"—What a delicious thing is that!—"Will the world ever be so decayed, that Spring may not renew its greenness?"—And the "Fire-Worship". Was ever the hearth so glorified into an altar before? The mere title of that piece is better than any common work in fifty folio volumes. How exquisite is this:—"Nor did it lessen the charm of his soft, familiar courtesy and helpfulness, that the mighty spirit, were opportunity offered him, would run riot through the peaceful house, wrap its inmates in his terrible embrace, and leave nothing of them save their whitened bones. This possibility of mad destruction only made his domestic kindness the more beautiful and touching. It was so sweet of him, being endowed with such power, to dwell, day after day, and one long, lonesome night after another, on the dusky hearth, only now and then betraying his wild nature, by thrusting his red tongue out of the chimney-top! True, he had done much mischief in the world, and was pretty certain to do more, but his warm heart atoned for all. He was kindly to the race of man."

But he has still other apples, not quite so ruddy, though full as ripe;—apples, that have been left to wither on the tree, after the pleasant autumn gathering is past. The sketch of "The Old Apple Dealer" is conceived in the subtlest spirit of sadness; he whose "subdued and nerveless boyhood prefigured his abortive prime, which, likewise, contained within itself the prophecy and image of his lean and torpid age". Such touches as are in this piece can not proceed from any common heart. They argue such a depth of tenderness, such a boundless sympathy with all forms of being, such an omnipresent love, that we must needs say, that this Hawthorne is here almost alone in his generation,—at least, in the artistic manifestation of these things. Still more. Such touches as these,—and many, very many similar ones, all through his chapters—furnish clews, whereby we enter a little way into the intricate, profound heart where they originated. And we see, that suffering, some time or other and in some shape or other,—this only can enable any man to depict it in others. All over him Hawthorne's melancholy rests like an Indian Summer, which though bathing a whole country in one softness, still reveals the distinctive hue of every towering hill, and each far-winding vale.

But it is the least part of genius that attracts admiration. Where Hawthorne is known, he seems to be deemed a pleasant writer, with a pleasant style,—a sequestered, harmless man, from whom any deep and weighty thing would hardly be anticipated:—a man who means no meanings. But there is no man, in whom humor and love, like mountain peaks, soar to such a rapt height, as to receive the irradiations of the upper skies;—there is no man in whom humor and love are developed in that high form called genius; no such man can exist without also possessing, as the indispensable complement of these, a great, deep intellect, which drops down into the universe like a plummet. Or, love and humor are only the eyes, through which such an intellect views this world. The great beauty in such a mind is but the product of its strength. What, to all readers, can be more charming than the piece entitled "Monsieur du Miroir"; and to a reader at all capable of fully fathoming it, what, at the same time, can possess more mystical depth of meaning?—Yes, there he sits, and looks at me,—this "shape of mystery", this "identical Monsieur du Miroir".—"Methinks I should tremble now, were his wizard power of gliding through all impediments in search of me, to place him suddenly before my eyes".

How profound, nay appalling, is the moral evolved by the "Earth's Holocaust"; where—beginning with the hollow follies and affectations of the world,—all vanities and empty theories and forms, are, one after another, and by an admirably graduated, growing comprehensiveness, thrown into the allegorical fire, till, at length, nothing is left but the all-engendering heart of man; which remaining still unconsumed, the great conflagration is nought.

Of a piece with this, is the "Intelligence Office", a wondrous symbolizing of the secret workings in men's souls. There are other sketches, still more charged with ponderous import.

"The Christmas Banquet", and "The Bosom Serpent" would be fine subjects for a curious and elaborate analysis, touching the conjectural parts of the mind that produced them. For spite of all the Indian-summer sunlight on the hither side of Hawthorne's soul, the other side—like the dark half of the physical sphere—is shrouded in a blackness, ten times black. But this darkness but gives more effect to the ever-moving dawn, that forever advances through it, and circumnavigates his world. Whether Hawthorne has simply availed himself of this mystical blackness as a means to the wondrous effects he makes it to produce in his lights and shades; or whether there really lurks in him, perhaps unknown to himself, a touch of Puritanic gloom,—this, I cannot altogether tell. Certain it is, however, that this great power of blackness in him derives its force from its appeals to that Calvinistic sense of Innate Depravity and Original Sin,[1] from whose visitations, in some shape or other, no deeply thinking mind is always and wholly free. For, in certain moods, no man can weigh this world, without throwing in something, somehow like Original Sin, to strike the uneven balance. At all events, perhaps no writer has ever wielded this terrific thought with greater terror than this same harmless Hawthorne. Still more: this black conceit pervades him, through and through. You may be witched by his sunlight,—transported by the bright gildings in the skies he builds over you;—but there is the blackness of darkness beyond; and even his bright gildings but fringe, and play upon the edges of thunder-clouds.—In one word, the world is mistaken in this Nathaniel Hawthorne. He himself must often have smiled at its absurd misconception of him. He is immeasurably deeper than the plummet of the mere critic. For it is not the brain that can test such a man; it is only the heart. You cannot come to know greatness by inspecting it; there is no glimpse to be caught of it, except by intuition; you need not ring it, you but touch it, and you find it is gold.

Now it is that blackness in Hawthorne, of which I have spoken, that so fixes and fascinates me. It may be, nevertheless, that it is too largely developed in him. Perhaps he does not give us a ray of his light for every shade of his dark. But however this may be, this blackness it is that furnishes the infinite obscure of his back-ground,—that back-ground, against which Shakespeare plays his grandest conceits, the things that have made for Shakespeare his loftiest, but most circumscribed renown, as the profoundest of thinkers. For by philosophers Shakespeare is not adored as the great man

1. Key doctrines of John Calvin (1509–1564), the influential French theologian of the Protestant Reformation, who interpreted Adam and Eve's eating of the forbidden fruit in the Garden of Eden as the original sin that revealed innate human depravity.

of tragedy and comedy.—"Off with his head! so much for Buckingham!"[2] this sort of rant, interlined by another hand, brings down the house,—those mistaken souls, who dream of Shakespeare as a mere man of Richard-the-Third humps, and Macbeth daggers. But it is those deep far-away things in him; those occasional flashings-forth of the intuitive Truth in him; those short, quick probings at the very axis of reality;—these are the things that make Shakespeare, Shakespeare. Through the mouths of the dark characters of Hamlet, Timon, Lear, and Iago, he craftily says, or sometimes insinuates the things, which we feel to be so terrifically true, that it were all but madness for any good man, in his own proper character, to utter, or even hint of them. Tormented into desperation, Lear the frantic King tears off the mask, and speaks the sane madness of vital truth. But, as I before said, it is the least part of genius that attracts admiration. And so, much of the blind, unbridled admiration that has been heaped upon Shakespeare, has been lavished upon the least part of him. And few of his endless commentators and critics seem to have remembered, or even perceived, that the immediate products of a great mind are not so great, as that undeveloped, (and sometimes undevelopable) yet dimly-discernable greatness, to which these immediate products are but the infallible indices. In Shakespeare's tomb lies infinitely more than Shakspeare ever wrote. And if I magnify Shakespeare, it is not so much for what he did do, as for what he did not do, or refrained from doing. For in this world of lies, Truth is forced to fly like a scared white doe in the woodlands; and only by cunning glimpses will she reveal herself, as in Shakespeare and other masters of the great Art of Telling the Truth,—even though it be covertly, and by snatches.

But if this view of the all-popular Shakespeare be seldom taken by his readers, and if very few who extol him, have ever read him deeply, or, perhaps, only have seen him on the tricky stage, (which alone made, and is still making him his mere mob renown)—if few men have time, or patience, or palate, for the spiritual truth as it is in that great genius;—it is, then, no matter of surprise that in a contemporaneous age, Nathaniel Hawthorne is a man, as yet, almost utterly mistaken among men. Here and there, in some quiet arm-chair in the noisy town, or some deep nook among the noiseless mountains, he may be appreciated for something of what he is. But unlike Shakespeare, who was forced to the contrary course by circumstances, Hawthorne (either from simple disinclination, or else from inaptitude) refrains from all the popularizing noise and show of broad farce, and blood-besmeared tragedy; content with the still, rich utterances of a great intellect in repose, and which sends few thoughts into circulation, except they be arterialized at his large warm lungs, and expanded in his honest heart.

Nor need you fix upon that blackness in him, if it suit you not. Nor, indeed, will all readers discern it, for it is, mostly, insinuated to those who may best understand it, and account for it; it is not obtruded upon every one alike.

Some may start to read of Shakespeare and Hawthorne on the same page. They may say, that if an illustration were needed, a lesser light might have sufficed to elucidate this Hawthorne, this small man of yesterday. But I am not, willingly, one of those, who, as touching Shakespeare at least, exemplify

2. The line is from Shakespeare's *Richard III*, as revised by the English dramatist Colley Cibber (1671–1757) in his 1700 edition of the play.

the maxim of Rochefoucault,[3] that "we exalt the reputation of some, in order to depress that of others";—who, to teach all noble-souled aspirants that there is no hope for them, pronounce Shakespeare absolutely unapproachable. But Shakespeare has been approached. There are minds that have gone as far as Shakespeare into the universe. And hardly a mortal man, who, at some time or other, has not felt as great thoughts in him as any you will find in Hamlet. We must not inferentially malign mankind for the sake of any one man, whoever he may be. This is too cheap a purchase of contentment for conscious mediocrity to make. Besides, this absolute and unconditional adoration of Shakespeare has grown to be a part of our Anglo Saxon superstitions. The Thirty Nine articles[4] are now Forty. Intolerance has come to exist in this matter. You must believe in Shakespeare's unapproachability, or quit the country. But what sort of a belief is this for an American, a man who is bound to carry republican progressiveness into Literature, as well as into Life? Believe me, my friends, that Shakespeares are this day being born on the banks of the Ohio. And the day will come, when you shall say who reads a book by an Englishman that is a modern?[5] The great mistake seems to be, that even with those Americans who look forward to the coming of a great literary genius among us, they somehow fancy he will come in the costume of Queen Elizabeth's day,—be a writer of dramas founded upon old English history, or the tales of Boccaccio.[6] Whereas, great geniuses are parts of the times; they themselves are the times; and possess a correspondent coloring. It is of a piece with the Jews, who while their Shiloh[7] was meekly walking in their streets, were still praying for his magnificent coming; looking for him in a chariot, who was already among them on an ass. Nor must we forget, that, in his own life-time, Shakespeare was not Shakespeare, but only Master William Shakespeare of the shrewd, thriving, business firm of Condell, Shakespeare & Co., proprietors of the Globe Theatre in London; and by a courtly author, of the name of Greene,[8] was hooted at, as an "upstart crow" beautified "with other birds' feathers". For, mark it well, imitation is often the first charge brought against real originality. Why this is so, there is not space to set forth here. You must have plenty of sea-room to tell the Truth in; especially, when it seems to have an aspect of newness, as America did in 1492, though it was then just as old, and perhaps older than Asia, only those sagacious philosophers, the common sailors, had never seen it before; swearing it was all water and moonshine there.

Now, I do not say that Nathaniel of Salem is a greater than William of Avon, or as great. But the difference between the two men is by no means immeasurable. Not a very great deal more, and Nathaniel were verily William.

This, too, I mean, that if Shakespeare has not been equalled, he is sure to be surpassed, and surpassed by an American born now or yet to be born. For it will never do for us who in most other things out-do as well as out-brag

3. François de la Rochefoucauld (1613–1680), French moralist.
4. Doctrines of the Church of England; here, any national set of beliefs.
5. Reference to a famous insult by Sydney Smith, a Scottish critic, in the *Edinburgh Review* (January 1820): "In the four quarters of the globe, who reads an American book? Or goes to an American play? Or looks at an American picture or statue?"
6. Giovanni Boccaccio (1313–1375), Italian author of *The Decameron* (1353).
7. Messiah.
8. Robert Greene (1558?–1592) made these slurs against Shakespeare in *Groatsworth of Witte Bought with a Million of Repentance* (1592).

the world, it will not do for us to fold our hands and say, In the highest department advance there is none. Nor will it at all do to say, that the world is getting grey and grizzled now, and has lost that fresh charm which she wore of old, and by virtue of which the great poets of past times made themselves what we esteem them to be. Not so. The world is as young today, as when it was created; and this Vermont morning dew is as wet to my feet, as Eden's dew to Adam's. Nor has Nature been all over ransacked by our progenitors, so that no new charms and mysteries remain for this latter generation to find. Far from it. The trillionth part has not yet been said; and all that has been said, but multiplies the avenues to what remains to be said. It is not so much paucity, as superabundance of material that seems to incapacitate modern authors.

Let America then prize and cherish her writers; yea, let her glorify them. They are not so many in number, as to exhaust her good-will. And while she has good kith and kin of her own, to take to her bosom, let her not lavish her embraces upon the household of an alien. For believe it or not England, after all, is, in many things, an alien to us. China has more bowels of real love for us than she. But even were there no Hawthorne, no Emerson, no Whittier, no Irving, no Bryant, no Dana, no Cooper, no Willis[9] (not the author of the "Dashes", but the author of the "Belfry Pigeon")—were there none of these, and others of like calibre among us, nevertheless, let America first praise mediocrity even, in her own children, before she praises (for everywhere, merit demands acknowledgment from every one) the best excellence in the children of any other land. Let her own authors, I say, have the priority of appreciation. I was much pleased with a hot-headed Carolina cousin of mine, who once said,—"If there were no other American to stand by, in Literature,—why, then, I would stand by Pop Emmons[1] and his 'Fredoniad,' and till a better epic came along, swear it was not very far behind the Iliad." Take away the words, and in spirit he was sound.

Not that American genius needs patronage in order to expand. For that explosive sort of stuff will expand though screwed up in a vice, and burst it, though it were triple steel. It is for the nation's sake, and not for her authors' sake, that I would have America be heedful of the increasing greatness among her writers. For how great the shame, if other nations should be before her, in crowning her heroes of the pen. But this is almost the case now. American authors have received more just and discriminating praise (however loftily and ridiculously given, in certain cases) even from some Englishmen, than from their own countrymen. There are hardly five critics in America; and several of them are asleep. As for patronage, it is the American author who now patronizes his country, and not his country him. And if at times some among them appeal to the people for more recognition, it is not always with selfish motives, but patriotic ones.

It is true, that but few of them as yet have evinced that decided originality which merits great praise. But that graceful writer,[2] who perhaps of all Americans has received the most plaudits from his own country for his

9. The New York writer and editor Nathaniel Parker Willis (1806–1867), author of *Dashes at Life with a Free Pencil* (1845) and the poem "The Belfry Pigeon" (1831).

1. Richard Emmons (1788–1840) wrote the four-volume *Fredoniad; or, Independence Preserved—an Epic Poem of the War of 1812*. Melville's reference to Emmons as "Pop" may have been a matter of confusion, as "Pop" Emmons was the nickname of Richard Emmons's brother, the orator William Emmons.

2. Washington Irving.

productions,—that very popular and amiable writer, however good, and self-reliant in many things, perhaps owes his chief reputation to the self-acknowledged imitation of a foreign model, and to the studied avoidance of all topics but smooth ones. But it is better to fail in originality, than to succeed in imitation. He who has never failed somewhere, that man can not be great. Failure is the true test of greatness. And if it be said, that continual success is a proof that a man wisely knows his powers,—it is only to be added, that, in that case, he knows them to be small. Let us believe it, then, once for all, that there is no hope for us in these smooth pleasing writers that know their powers. Without malice, but to speak the plain fact, they but furnish an appendix to Goldsmith,[3] and other English authors. And we want no American Goldsmiths; nay, we want no American Miltons. It were the vilest thing you could say of a true American author, that he were an American Tompkins.[4] Call him an American, and have done; for you can not say a nobler thing of him.—But it is not meant that all American writers should studiously cleave to nationality in their writings; only this, no American writer should write like an Englishman, or a Frenchman; let him write like a man, for then he will be sure to write like an American. Let us away with this Bostonian leaven of literary flunkeyism towards England. If either must play the flunkey in this thing, let England do it, not us. And the time is not far off when circumstances may force her to it. While we are rapidly preparing for that political supremacy among the nations, which prophetically awaits us at the close of the present century; in a literary point of view, we are deplorably unprepared for it; and we seem studious to remain so. Hitherto, reasons might have existed why this should be; but no good reason exists now. And all that is requisite to amendment in this matter, is simply this: that, while freely acknowledging all excellence, everywhere, we should refrain from unduly lauding foreign writers and, at the same time, duly recognize the meritorious writers that are our own;—those writers, who breathe that unshackled, democratic spirit of Christianity in all things, which now takes the practical lead in this world, though at the same time led by ourselves—us Americans. Let us boldly contemn all imitation, though it comes to us graceful and fragrant as the morning; and foster all originality, though, at first, it be crabbed and ugly as our own pine knots. And if any of our authors fail, or seem to fail, then, in the words of my enthusiastic Carolina cousin, let us clap him on the shoulder, and back him against all Europe for his second round. The truth is, that in our point of view, this matter of a national literature has come to such a pass with us, that in some sense we must turn bullies, else the day is lost, or superiority so far beyond us, that we can hardly say it will ever be ours.

And now, my countrymen, as an excellent author, of your own flesh and blood,—an unimitating, and, perhaps, in his way, an inimitable man—whom better can I commend to you, in the first place, than Nathaniel Hawthorne. He is one of the new, and far better generation of your writers. The smell of your beeches and hemlocks is upon him; your own broad praries are in his soul; and if you travel away inland into his deep and noble nature, you will

3. Oliver Goldsmith (1728–1774), British poet, playwright, and novelist known for the clarity of his style and gentle wit. Irving was often called the American Goldsmith.

4. Briticism for *anybody* (that is, an American Milton or an American equivalent of any British author one can name).

hear the far roar of his Niagara. Give not over to future generations the glad duty of acknowledging him for what he is. Take that joy to your self, in your own generation; and so shall he feel those grateful impulses in him, that may possibly prompt him to the full flower of some still greater achievement in your eyes. And by confessing him, you thereby confess others; you brace the whole brotherhood. For genius, all over the world, stands hand in hand, and one shock of recognition runs the whole circle round.

In treating of Hawthorne, or rather of Hawthorne in his writings (for I never saw the man; and in the chances of a quiet plantation life, remote from his haunts, perhaps never shall) in treating of his works, I say, I have thus far omitted all mention of his "Twice Told Tales", and "Scarlet Letter".[5] Both are excellent; but full of such manifold, strange and diffusive beauties, that time would all but fail me, to point the half of them out. But there are things in those two books, which, had they been written in England a century ago, Nathaniel Hawthorne had utterly displaced many of the bright names we now revere on authority. But I am content to leave Hawthorne to himself, and to the infallible finding of posterity; and however great may be the praise I have bestowed upon him, I feel, that in so doing, I have more served and honored myself, than him. For, at bottom, great excellence is praise enough to itself; but the feeling of a sincere and appreciative love and admiration towards it, this is relieved by utterance; and warm, honest praise ever leaves a pleasant flavor in the mouth; and it is an honorable thing to confess to what is honorable in others.

But I cannot leave my subject yet. No man can read a fine author, and relish him to his very bones, while he reads, without subsequently fancying to himself some ideal image of the man and his mind. And if you rightly look for it, you will almost always find that the author himself has somewhere furnished you with his own picture.—For poets (whether in prose or verse), being painters of Nature, are like their brethren of the pencil, the true portrait-painters, who, in the multitude of likenesses to be sketched, do not invariably omit their own; and in all high instances, they paint them without any vanity, though, at times, with a lurking something, that would take several pages to properly define.

I submit it, then, to those best acquainted with the man personally, whether the following is not Nathaniel Hawthorne;—and to himself, whether something involved in it does not express the temper of his mind,—that lasting temper of all true, candid men—a seeker, not a finder yet;—

> "A man now entered, in neglected attire, with the aspect of a thinker, but somewhat too rough-hewn and brawny for a scholar. His face was full of sturdy vigor, with some finer and keener attribute beneath; though harsh at first, it was tempered with the glow of a large, warm heart, which had force enough to heat his powerful intellect through and through. He advanced to the Intelligencer, and looked at him with a glance of such stern sincerity, that perhaps few secrets were beyond its scope.
>
> "'I seek for Truth', said he."[6]

• • • • •

5. Published in 1837 and 1850, respectively.

6. From Hawthorne's "The Intelligence Office."

Twenty four hours have elapsed since writing the foregoing. I have just returned from the hay mow, charged more and more with love and admiration of Hawthorne. For I have just been gleaning through the Mosses, picking up many things here and there that had previously escaped me. And I found that but to glean after this man, is better than to be in at the harvest of others. To be frank (though, perhaps, rather foolish) notwithstanding what I wrote yesterday of these Mosses, I had not then culled them all; but had, nevertheless, been sufficiently sensible of the subtle essence, in them, as to write as I did. To what infinite height of loving wonder and admiration I may yet be borne, when by repeatedly banquetting on these Mosses, I shall have thoroughly incorporated their whole stuff into my being,—that, I can not tell. But already I feel that this Hawthorne has dropped germinous seeds into my soul. He expands and deepens down, the more I contemplate him; and further, and further, shoots his strong New-England roots into the hot soil of my Southern soul.

By careful reference to the "Table of Contents", I now find, that I have gone through all the sketches; but that when I yesterday wrote, I had not at all read two particular pieces, to which I now desire to call special attention,—"A Select Party", and "Young Goodman Brown". Here, be it said to all those whom this poor fugitive scrawl of mine may tempt to the perusal of the "Mosses," that they must on no account suffer themselves to be trifled with, disappointed, or deceived by the triviality of many of the titles to these Sketches. For in more than one instance, the title utterly belies the piece. It is as if rustic demijohns containing the very best and costliest of Falernian and Tokay,[7] were labelled "Cider", "Perry," and "Elderberry wine". The truth seems to be, that like many other geniuses, this Man of Mosses takes great delight in hoodwinking the world,—at least, with respect to himself. Personally, I doubt not, that he rather prefers to be generally esteemed but a so-so sort of author; being willing to reserve the thorough and acute appreciation of what he is, to that party most qualified to judge—that is, to himself. Besides, at the bottom of their natures, men like Hawthorne, in many things, deem the plaudits of the public such strong presumptive evidence of mediocrity in the object of them, that it would in some degree render them doubtful of their own powers, did they hear much and vociferous braying concerning them in the public pastures. True, I have been braying myself (if you please to be witty enough, to have it so) but then I claim to be the first that has so brayed in this particular matter; and therefore, while pleading guilty to the charge still claim all the merit due to originality.

But with whatever motive, playful or profound, Nathaniel Hawthorne has chosen to entitle his pieces in the manner he has, it is certain, that some of them are directly calculated to deceive—egregiously deceive, the superficial skimmer of pages. To be downright and candid once more, let me cheerfully say, that two of these titles did dolefully dupe no less an eagle-eyed reader than myself; and that, too, after I had been impressed with a sense of the great depth and breadth of this American man. "Who in the name of thunder" (as the country-people say in this neighborhood) "who in the name of thunder", would anticipate any marvel in a piece entitled "Young Goodman Brown"? You would of course suppose that it was a simple little

7. Renowned wines from Italy and Hungary, respectively.

tale, intended as a supplement to "Goody Two Shoes".[8] Whereas, it is deep as Dante; nor can you finish it, without addressing the author in his own words—"It is yours to penetrate, in every bosom, the deep mystery of sin". And with Young Goodman, too, in allegorical pursuit of his Puritan wife, you cry out in your anguish,—

> "'Faith!' shouted Goodman Brown, in a voice of agony and desperation; and the echoes of the forest mocked him, crying—'Faith! Faith!' as if bewildered wretches were seeking her all through the wilderness."

Now this same piece, entitled "Young Goodman Brown", is one of the two that I had not all read yesterday; and I allude to it now, because it is, in itself, such a strong positive illustration of that blackness in Hawthorne, which I had assumed from the mere occasional shadows of it, as revealed in several of the other sketches. But had I previously perused "Young Goodman Brown", I should have been at no pains to draw the conclusion, which I came to, at a time, when I was ignorant that the book contained one such direct and unqualified manifestation of it.

The other piece of the two referred to, is entitled "A Select Party", which, in my first simplicity upon originally taking hold of the book, I fancied must treat of some pumpkin-pie party in Old Salem, or some chowder party on Cape Cod. Whereas, by all the gods of Peedee! it is the sweetest and sublimest thing that has been written since Spencer[9] wrote. Nay, there is nothing in Spencer that surpasses it, perhaps, nothing that equals it. And the test is this: read any canto in "The Faery Queen", and then read "A Select Party", and decide which pleases you the most,—that is, if you are qualified to judge. Do not be frightened at this; for when Spencer was alive, he was thought of very much as Hawthorne is now,—was generally accounted just such a "gentle" harmless man. It may be, that to common eyes, the sublimity of Hawthorne seems lost in his sweetness,—as perhaps in this same "Select Party" of his; for whom, he has builded so august a dome of sunset clouds, and served them on richer plate, than Belshazzar's when he banquetted his lords in Babylon.[1]

But my chief business now, is to point out a particular page in this piece, having reference to an honored guest, who under the name of "The Master Genius" but in the guise of "a young man of poor attire, with no insignia of rank or acknowledged eminence", is introduced to the Man of Fancy, who is the giver of the feast. Now the page having reference to this "Master Genius", so happily expresses much of what I yesterday wrote, touching the coming of the literary Shiloh of America, that I cannot but be charmed by the coincidence; especially, when it shows such a parity of ideas, at least in this one point, between a man like Hawthorne and a man like me.

And here, let me throw out another conceit of mine touching this American Shiloh, or "Master Genius", as Hawthorne calls him. May it not be, that this commanding mind has not been, is not, and never will be, individually developed in any one man? And would it, indeed, appear so unreasonable to

8. The popular children's story "The History of Goody Two-Shoes," which is thought to have been written by Oliver Goldsmith, was first published in 1765.
9. The English poet Edmund Spenser (1552?–1599). The Peedee is a river in the Carolinas.
1. Daniel 5.1: "Belshazzar the king made a great feast to a thousand of his lords, and drank wine before the thousand."

suppose, that this great fullness and overflowing may be, or may be destined to be, shared by a plurality of men of genius? Surely, to take the very greatest example on record, Shakespeare cannot be regarded as in himself the concretion of all the genius of his time; nor as so immeasurably beyond Marlow, Webster, Ford, Beaumont, Jonson,[2] that those great men can be said to share none of his power? For one, I conceive that there were dramatists in Elizabeth's day, between whom and Shakespeare the distance was by no means great. Let anyone, hitherto little acquainted with those neglected old authors, for the first time read them thoroughly, or even read Charles Lamb's Specimens of them, and he will be amazed at the wondrous ability of those Anaks[3] of men, and shocked at this renewed example of the fact, that Fortune has more to do with fame than merit,—though, without merit, lasting fame there can be none.

Nevertheless, it would argue too illy of my country were this maxim to hold good concerning Nathaniel Hawthorne, a man, who already, in some few minds, has shed "such a light, as never illuminates the earth, save when a great heart burns as the household fire of a grand intellect."

The words are his,—in the "Select Party"; and they are a magnificent setting to a coincident sentiment of my own, but ramblingly expressed yesterday, in reference to himself. Gainsay it who will, as I now write, I am Posterity speaking by proxy—and after times will make it more than good, when I declare—that the American, who up to the present day, has evinced, in Literature, the largest brain with the largest heart, that man is Nathaniel Hawthorne. Moreover, that whatever Nathaniel Hawthorne may hereafter write, "The Mosses from an Old Manse" will be ultimately accounted his masterpiece. For there is a sure, though a secret sign in some works which prove the culmination of the powers (only the developable ones, however) that produced them. But I am by no means desirous of the glory of a prophet. I pray Heaven that Hawthorne may *yet* prove me an impostor in this prediction. Especially, as I somehow cling to the strange fancy, that, in all men, hiddenly reside certain wondrous, occult properties—as in some plants and minerals—which by some happy but very rare accident (as bronze was discovered by the melting of the iron and brass in the burning of Corinth)[4] may chance to be called forth here on earth; not entirely waiting for their better discovery in the more congenial, blessed atmosphere of heaven.

Once more—for it is hard to be finite upon an infinite subject, and all subjects are infinite. By some people, this entire scrawl of mine may be esteemed altogether unnecessary, inasmuch, "as years ago" (they may say) "we found out the rich and rare stuff in this Hawthorne, whom you now parade forth, as if only *yourself* were the discoverer of this Portuguese diamond in our Literature".—But even granting all this; and adding to it, the assumption that the books of Hawthorne have sold by the five-thousand,—what does that signify?—They should be sold by the hundred-thousand; and read by the million; and admired by every one who is capable of admiration.

1850

2. English dramatists: Christopher Marlowe (1564–1593), John Webster (1580?–1634), John Ford (1586–c. 1640), Francis Beaumont (1584?–1616), and Ben Jonson (1572–1637).
3. Giants (Joshua 11.21). Lamb (1775–1834), editor of *Specimens of the English Dramatic Poets Who Lived about the Time of Shakespeare* (1808).
4. Wealthy and powerful city of ancient Greece, burned by the Romans in 146 B.C.E.

Moby-Dick Most people know that the first chapter of *Moby-Dick* begins with "Call me Ishmael," and any scanner of cartoons in magazines and newspapers knows that the one-legged captain cries out to other ships, "Hast seen the white whale?" Upon its publication late in 1851 the book delighted many readers in England (where it was called *The Whale*) and the United States and inspired a few young men to go to sea on whale ships; but in the following decades it was almost never mentioned in print. In England late in the century it emerged as a cult favorite among people from several overlapping groups—pre-Raphaelite writers and painters, second-generation admirers of the Romantic poet Percy Shelley, members of the workingman's movement, Fabian socialists, sexual reformers, and people who had lived in outposts of the British Empire. On the hundredth anniversary of Melville's birth, in 1919, English admirers of *Moby-Dick* celebrated the book in influential magazines, and Viola Meynell's fervent tribute in her introduction to the 1920 reprinting in the Oxford World's Classics evoked other tributes from old admirers and new readers. By the time the American Raymond Weaver published his biography *Herman Melville: Mariner and Mystic* (1921), the Melville revival in England was an achieved fact. Literary Americans scrambled to catch up with the British admirers; and in the years after World War II, when American literature at last became part of the college curriculum in English departments, *Moby-Dick* was acknowledged as a classic. Yet its length has limited its appearance in survey courses. Conditioned to assign all of a work or none of it, some teachers choose to ignore *Moby-Dick*, contrary to the spirit of Melville, who was an omnivorous sampler of books as well as a profound and patient reader. The chapters reprinted here are designed to introduce readers to the novel's main characters, plot, narrative style, thematic concerns, and inimitable prose.

The novel begins when its narrator decides to go to sea on a whaling ship. Whaling, a major industry that provided valuable oil for lamps before kerosene became available, was a dangerous calling. At Nantucket, Ishmael signs on with the *Pequod* eager for adventure, but is soon surprised to learn that Captain Ahab is dedicating the voyage to his vengeful pursuit of Moby Dick, the enormous sperm whale, legendary in the whale fishery, which had bitten off one of his legs. In the course of the narrative, Melville explores a remarkable range of bodily and mental states as Ishmael becomes the tragic dramatist who evokes the mystery of Ahab's obsessions and confronts his own versions of the ultimate cosmic puzzles that had tormented his captain. The selections are taken from the Northwestern-Newberry edition of the Writings of Herman Melville, *Moby-Dick; or, The Whale* (1988).

From Moby-Dick

Chapter I

LOOMINGS

Call me Ishmael.[1] Some years ago—never mind how long precisely—having little or no money in my purse, and nothing particular to interest me on shore, I thought I would sail about a little and see the watery part of the world. It is a way I have of driving off the spleen, and regulating the circula-

1. The name of the first-person narrator implies that he is an outcast. In the Bible, Ishmael is the oldest son of the patriarch Abraham, by the Egyptian Hagar, servant to his then barren wife, Sarah. During Hagar's pregnancy, an angel reveals that she is pregnant with Ishmael, who will be "a wild man," whose "hand will be against every man, and every man's hand against him" (Genesis 16.12). After Sarah bears Isaac, she prevails on Abraham to send Hagar and Ishmael into the wilderness.

tion. Whenever I find myself growing grim about the mouth; whenever it is a damp, drizzly November in my soul; whenever I find myself involuntarily pausing before coffin warehouses, and bringing up the rear of every funeral I meet; and especially whenever my hypos[2] get such an upper hand of me, that it requires a strong moral principle to prevent me from deliberately stepping into the street, and methodically knocking people's hats off—then, I account it high time to get to sea as soon as I can. This is my substitute for pistol and ball. With a philosophical flourish Cato[3] throws himself upon his sword; I quietly take to the ship. There is nothing surprising in this. If they but knew it, almost all men in their degree, some time or other, cherish very nearly the same feelings towards the ocean with me.

There now is your insular city of the Manhattoes, belted round by wharves as Indian isles by coral reefs—commerce surrounds it with her surf. Right and left, the streets take you waterward. Its extreme down-town is the Battery,[4] where that noble mole is washed by waves, and cooled by breezes, which a few hours previous were out of sight of land. Look at the crowds of water-gazers there.

Circumambulate the city of a dreamy Sabbath afternoon. Go from Corlears Hook to Coenties Slip, and from thence, by Whitehall, northward.[5] What do you see?—Posted like silent sentinels all around the town, stand thousands upon thousands of mortal men fixed in ocean reveries. Some leaning against the spiles;[6] some seated upon the pier-heads; some looking over the bulwarks of ships from China; some high aloft in the rigging, as if striving to get a still better seaward peep. But these are all landsmen; of week days pent up in lath and plaster—tied to counters, nailed to benches, clinched to desks. How then is this? Are the green fields gone? What do they here?

But look! here come more crowds, pacing straight for the water, and seemingly bound for a dive. Strange! Nothing will content them but the extremest limit of the land; loitering under the shady lee of yonder warehouses will not suffice. No. They must get just as nigh the water as they possibly can without falling in. And there they stand—miles of them—leagues. Inlanders all, they come from lanes and alleys, streets and avenues—north, east, south, and west. Yet here they all unite. Tell me, does the magnetic virtue of the needles of the compasses of all those ships attract them thither?

Once more. Say, you are in the country; in some high land of lakes. Take almost any path you please, and ten to one it carries you down in a dale, and leaves you there by a pool in the stream. There is magic in it. Let the most absent-minded of men be plunged in his deepest reveries—stand that man on his legs, set his feet a-going, and he will infallibly lead you to water, if water there be in all that region. Should you ever be athirst in the great American desert, try this experiment, if your caravan happen to be supplied with a metaphysical professor. Yes, as every one knows, meditation and water are wedded for ever.

2. Hypochondrias (slang); here, more like anxieties or depression.
3. Marcus Porcius Cato (95–46 B.C.E.), Roman statesman, committed suicide rather than be taken captive by Caesar.
4. At the southern tip of Manhattan, formerly the site of a fort.
5. Melville directs the reader on a tour of streets in lower Manhattan with extensive views of the wharves and the Hudson River.
6. Large support posts.

But here is an artist. He desires to paint you the dreamiest, shadiest, quietest, most enchanting bit of romantic landscape in all the valley of the Saco.[7] What is the chief element he employs? There stand his trees, each with a hollow trunk, as if a hermit and a crucifix were within; and here sleeps his meadow, and there sleep his cattle; and up from yonder cottage goes a sleepy smoke. Deep into distant woodlands winds a mazy way, reaching to overlapping spurs of mountains bathed in their hill-side blue. But though the picture lies thus tranced, and though this pine-tree shakes down its sighs like leaves upon this shepherd's head, yet all were vain, unless the shepherd's eye were fixed upon the magic stream before him. Go visit the Prairies in June, when for scores on scores of miles you wade knee-deep among Tiger-lilies—what is the one charm wanting?—Water—there is not a drop of water there! Were Niagara but a cataract of sand, would you travel your thousand miles to see it? Why did the poor poet of Tennessee, upon suddenly receiving two handfuls of silver, deliberate whether to buy him a coat, which he sadly needed, or invest his money in a pedestrian trip to Rockaway Beach?[8] Why is almost every robust healthy boy with a robust healthy soul in him, at some time or other crazy to go to sea? Why upon your first voyage as a passenger, did you yourself feel such a mystical vibration, when first told that you and your ship were now out of sight of land? Why did the old Persians hold the sea holy? Why did the Greeks give it a separate deity, and make him the own brother of Jove?[9] Surely all this is not without meaning. And still deeper the meaning of that story of Narcissus,[1] who because he could not grasp the tormenting, mild image he saw in the fountain, plunged into it and was drowned. But that same image, we ourselves see in all rivers and oceans. It is the image of the ungraspable phantom of life; and this is the key to it all.

Now, when I say that I am in the habit of going to sea whenever I begin to grow hazy about the eyes, and begin to be over conscious of my lungs, I do not mean to have it inferred that I ever go to sea as a passenger. For to go as a passenger you must needs have a purse, and a purse is but a rag unless you have something in it. Besides, passengers get sea-sick—grow quarrelsome—don't sleep of nights—do not enjoy themselves much, as a general thing;—no, I never go as a passenger; nor, though I am something of a salt, do I ever go to sea as a Commodore, or a Captain, or a Cook. I abandon the glory and distinction of such offices to those who like them. For my part, I abominate all honorable respectable toils, trials, and tribulations of every kind whatsoever. It is quite as much as I can do to take care of myself, without taking care of ships, barques, brigs, schooners, and what not. And as for going as cook,— though I confess there is considerable glory in that, a cook being a sort of officer on ship-board—yet, somehow, I never fancied broiling fowls;—though once broiled, judiciously buttered, and judgmatically salted and peppered, there is no one who will speak more respectfully, not to say reverentially, of a broiled fowl than I will. It is out of the idolatrous dotings of the old Egyptians upon broiled ibis and roasted river horse,[2] that you see the mummies of those creatures in their huge bake-houses the pyramids.

7. In southern New Hampshire.
8. On the southern coast of Long Island. "Poor poet of Tennessee": probably Melville's invention.
9. I.e., Poseidon, in Greek mythology (Neptune, in Roman mythology).
1. In Book 3 of Ovid's *Metamorphoses*, Narcissus falls in love with his own reflection in the water (but does not plunge into it and drown).
2. Hippopotamus.

No, when I go to sea, I go as a simple sailor, right before the mast, plumb down into the forecastle, aloft there to the royal mast-head. True, they rather order me about some, and make me jump from spar to spar, like a grasshopper in a May meadow. And at first, this sort of thing is unpleasant enough. It touches one's sense of honor, particularly if you come of an old established family in the land, the Van Rensselaers, or Randolphs, or Hardicanutes.[3] And more than all, if just previous to putting your hand into the tar-pot, you have been lording it as a country schoolmaster, making the tallest boys stand in awe of you. The transition is a keen one, I assure you, from a schoolmaster to a sailor, and requires a strong decoction of Seneca[4] and the Stoics to enable you to grin and bear it. But even this wears off in time.

What of it, if some old hunks[5] of a sea-captain orders me to get a broom and sweep down the decks? What does that indignity amount to, weighed, I mean, in the scales of the New Testament? Do you think the archangel Gabriel thinks anything the less of me, because I promptly and respectfully obey that old hunks in that particular instance? Who aint a slave? Tell me that. Well, then, however the old sea-captains may order me about—however they may thump and punch me about, I have the satisfaction of knowing that it is all right; that everybody else is one way or other served in much the same way—either in a physical or metaphysical point of view, that is; and so the universal thump is passed round, and all hands should rub each other's shoulder-blades, and be content.

Again, I always go to sea as a sailor, because they make a point of paying me for my trouble, whereas they never pay passengers a single penny that I ever heard of. On the contrary, passengers themselves must pay. And there is all the difference in the world between paying and being paid. The act of paying is perhaps the most uncomfortable infliction that the two orchard thieves entailed upon us. But *being paid*,—what will compare with it? The urbane activity with which a man receives money is really marvellous, considering that we so earnestly believe money to be the root of all earthly ills, and that on no account can a monied man enter heaven. Ah! how cheerfully we consign ourselves to perdition!

Finally, I always go to sea as a sailor, because of the wholesome exercise and pure air of the forecastle deck. For as in this world, head winds are far more prevalent than winds from astern (that is, if you never violate the Pythagorean[6] maxim), so for the most part the Commodore on the quarter-deck gets his atmosphere at second hand from the sailors on the forecastle. He thinks he breathes it first; but not so. In much the same way do the commonalty lead their leaders in many other things, at the same time that the leaders little suspect it. But wherefore it was that after having repeatedly smelt the sea as a merchant sailor, I should now take it into my head to go on a whaling voyage; this the invisible police officer of the Fates, who has the constant surveillance of me, and secretly dogs me, and influences me in some

3. Danish rulers of England. Melville's mother was a descendant of the Van Rensselaers, the dominant Dutch family in colonial New York and the early republic. The Randolphs included many eminent Virginians (among them Thomas Jefferson).

4. Lucius Annaeus Seneca (ca. 4 B.C.E.–65 C.E.), Roman adherent of Stoicism, the belief that people should calmly accept all events as ordained by fate.

5. Bully, grouch.

6. The Greek philosopher Pythagoras (6th century B.C.E.) advised against eating beans because they cause flatulence. Melville jokes about the location of the tiny toilets on the sides of whale ships—toward the front, while the captain's quarters are at the back.

unaccountable way—he can better answer than any one else. And, doubtless, my going on this whaling voyage, formed part of the grand programme of Providence that was drawn up a long time ago. It came in as a sort of brief interlude and solo between more extensive performances. I take it that this part of the bill must have run something like this:

"*Grand Contested Election for the Presidency of the United States.*
"WHALING VOYAGE BY ONE ISHMAEL.
"BLOODY BATTLE IN AFFGHANISTAN."

Though I cannot tell why it was exactly that those stage managers, the Fates, put me down for this shabby part of a whaling voyage, when others were set down for magnificent parts in high tragedies, and short and easy parts in genteel comedies, and jolly parts in farces—though I cannot tell why this was exactly; yet, now that I recall all the circumstances, I think I can see a little into the springs and motives which being cunningly presented to me under various disguises, induced me to set about performing the part I did, besides cajoling me into the delusion that it was a choice resulting from my own unbiased freewill and discriminating judgment.

Chief among these motives was the overwhelming idea of the great whale himself. Such a portentous and mysterious monster roused all my curiosity. Then the wild and distant seas where he rolled his island bulk; the undeliverable, nameless perils of the whale; these, with all the attending marvels of a thousand Patagonian[7] sights and sounds, helped to sway me to my wish. With other men, perhaps, such things would not have been inducements; but as for me, I am tormented with an everlasting itch for things remote. I love to sail forbidden seas, and land on barbarous coasts. Not ignoring what is good, I am quick to perceive a horror, and could still be social with it—would they let me—since it is but well to be on friendly terms with all the inmates of the place one lodges in.

By reason of these things, then, the whaling voyage was welcome; the great flood-gates of the wonder-world swung open, and in the wild conceits that swayed me to my purpose, two and two there floated into my inmost soul, endless processions of the whale, and, midmost of them all, one grand hooded phantom, like a snow hill in the air.

* * *

Chapter 3

THE SPOUTER-INN[8]

Entering that gable-ended Spouter-Inn, you found yourself in a wide, low, straggling entry with old-fashioned wainscots, reminding one of the bulwarks of some condemned old craft. On one side hung a very large oil-painting so thoroughly besmoked, and every way defaced, that in the unequal cross-lights by which you viewed it, it was only by diligent study and a series of systematic visits to it, and careful inquiry of the neighbors, that you could any way arrive at an understanding of its purpose. Such unaccountable

7. Patagonia is the southernmost region of South America.

8. Ishmael has journeyed from New York to the coastal town of New Bedford, Massachusetts, and is entering an inn that, according to the sign, is run by Peter Coffin.

masses of shades and shadows, that at first you almost thought some ambitious young artist, in the time of the New England hags,[9] had endeavored to delineate chaos bewitched. But by dint of much and earnest contemplation, and oft repeated ponderings, and especially by throwing open the little window towards the back of the entry, you at last came to the conclusion that such an idea, however wild, might not be altogether unwarranted.

But what most puzzled and confounded you was a long, limber, portentous, black mass of something hovering in the centre of the picture over three blue, dim, perpendicular lines floating in a nameless yeast. A boggy, soggy, squitchy[1] picture truly, enough to drive a nervous man distracted. Yet was there a sort of indefinite, half-attained, unimaginable sublimity about it that fairly froze you to it, till you involuntarily took an oath with yourself to find out what that marvellous painting meant. Ever and anon a bright, but, alas, deceptive idea would dart you through.—It's the Black Sea in a midnight gale.—It's the unnatural combat of the four primal elements.—It's a blasted heath.—It's a Hyperborean[2] winter scene.—It's the breaking-up of the ice-bound stream of Time. But at last all these fancies yielded to that one portentous something in the picture's midst. *That* once found out, and all the rest were plain. But stop; does it not bear a faint resemblance to a gigantic fish? even the great leviathan[3] himself?

In fact, the artist's design seemed this: a final theory of my own, partly based upon the aggregated opinions of many aged persons with whom I conversed upon the subject. The picture represents a Cape-Horner[4] in a great hurricane; the half-foundered ship weltering there with its three dismantled masts alone visible; and an exasperated whale, purposing to spring clean over the craft, is in the enormous act of impaling himself upon the three mastheads.

The opposite wall of this entry was hung all over with a heathenish array of monstrous clubs and spears. Some were thickly set with glittering teeth resembling ivory saws; others were tufted with knots of human hair; and one was sickle-shaped, with a vast handle, sweeping round like the segment made in the new-mown grass by a long-armed mower. You shuddered as you gazed, and wondered what monstrous cannibal and savage could ever have gone a death-harvesting with such a hacking, horrifying implement. Mixed with these were rusty old whaling lances and harpoons all broken and deformed. Some were storied weapons. With this once long lance, now wildly elbowed, fifty years ago did Nathan Swain kill fifteen whales between a sunrise and a sunset. And that harpoon—so like a corkscrew now—was flung in Javan seas, and run away with by a whale, years afterwards slain off the Cape of Blanco.[5] The original iron entered nigh the tail, and, like a restless needle sojourning in the body of a man, travelled full forty feet, and at last was found imbedded in the hump.

Crossing this dusky entry, and on through yon low-arched way—cut through what in old times must have been a great central chimney with fireplaces all

9. Vernacular reference to women accused of witchcraft in 17th-century Salem.
1. Sloppy, dirty.
2. Mythical land of perpetual sunshine and natural abundance.
3. In the Bible, a sea monster; in *Moby-Dick*, one of Melville's terms for a whale.
4. Person from a small Chilean island at the southern extremity of South America.
5. Off the Peruvian coast of South America. The Javan Seas are waters in the East Indies.

round—you enter the public room. A still duskier place is this, with such low ponderous beams above, and such old wrinkled planks beneath, that you would almost fancy you trod some old craft's cockpits, especially of such a howling night, when this corner-anchored old ark rocked so furiously. On one side stood a long, low, shelf-like table covered with cracked glass cases, filled with dusty rarities gathered from this wide world's remotest nooks. Projecting from the further angle of the room stands a dark-looking den—the bar—a rude attempt at a right whale's head. Be that how it may, there stands the vast arched bone of the whale's jaw, so wide, a coach might almost drive beneath it. Within are shabby shelves, ranged round with old decanters, bottles, flasks; and in those jaws of swift destruction, like another cursed Jonah[6] (by which name indeed they called him), bustles a little withered old man, who, for their money, dearly sells the sailors deliriums and death.

Abominable are the tumblers into which he pours his poison. Though true cylinders without—within, the villanous green goggling glasses deceitfully tapered downwards to a cheating bottom. Parallel meridians rudely pecked into the glass, surround these footpads' goblets. Fill to *this* mark, and your charge is but a penny; to *this* a penny more; and so on to the full glass—the Cape Horn measure,[7] which you may gulph down for a shilling.

Upon entering the place I found a number of young seamen gathered about a table, examining by a dim light divers specimens of *skrimshander.*[8] I sought the landlord, and telling him I desired to be accommodated with a room, received for answer that his house was full—not a bed unoccupied. "But avast," he added, tapping his forehead, "you haint no objections to sharing a harpooneer's blanket, have ye? I s'pose you are goin' a whalin', so you'd better get used to that sort of thing."

I told him that I never liked to sleep two in a bed; that if I should ever do so, it would depend upon who the harpooneer might be, and that if he (the landlord) really had no other place for me, and the harpooneer was not decidedly objectionable, why rather than wander further about a strange town on so bitter a night, I would put up with the half of any decent man's blanket.

"I thought so. All right; take a seat. Supper?—you want supper? Supper 'll be ready directly."

I sat down on an old wooden settle, carved all over like a bench on the Battery. At one end a ruminating tar[9] was still further adorning it with his jack-knife, stooping over and diligently working away at the space between his legs. He was trying his hand at a ship under full sail, but he didn't make much headway, I thought.

At last some four or five of us were summoned to our meal in an adjoining room. It was cold as Iceland—no fire at all—the landlord said he couldn't afford it. Nothing but two dismal tallow candles, each in a winding sheet. We were fain to button up our monkey jackets,[1] and hold to our lips cups of scalding tea with our half frozen fingers. But the fare was of the most substantial kind—not only meat and potatoes, but dumplings; good heavens!

6. Hebrew prophet who is swallowed by a "great fish" when he disobeys God. Jonah repents after being vomited by the fish, and God shows his mercy (see Jonah 1–2).
7. The full glass.
8. I.e., scrimshaw—delicate carvings in whale ivory, often highlighted by black pigment. "Gulph": obsolete form of "gulp."
9. Sailor.
1. Tight-fitting coats.

dumplings for supper! One young fellow in a green box coat, addressed himself to these dumplings in a most direful manner.

"My boy," said the landlord, "you'll have the nightmare to a dead sartainty."

"Landlord," I whispered, "that aint the harpooneer, is it?"

"Oh, no," said he, looking a sort of diabolically funny, "the harpooner is a dark complexioned chap. He never eats dumplings, he don't—he eats nothing but steaks, and likes 'em rare."

"The devil he does," says I. "Where is that harpooneer? Is he here?"

"He'll be here afore long," was the answer.

I could not help it, but I began to feel suspicious of this "dark complexioned" harpooneer. At any rate, I made up my mind that if it so turned out that we should sleep together, he must undress and get into bed before I did.

Supper over, the company went back to the bar-room, when, knowing not what else to do with myself, I resolved to spend the rest of the evening as a looker on.

Presently a rioting noise was heard without. Starting up, the landlord cried, "That's the Grampus's crew. I seed her reported in the offing this morning; a four years' voyage, and a full ship. Hurrah, boys; now we'll have the latest news from the Feegees."[2]

A tramping of sea boots was heard in the entry; the door was flung open, and in rolled a wild set of mariners enough. Enveloped in their shaggy watch coats, and with their heads muffled in woollen comforters, all bedarned and ragged, and their beards stiff with icicles, they seemed an eruption of bears from Labrador.[3] They had just landed from their boat, and this was the first house they entered. No wonder, then, that they made a straight wake for the whale's mouth—the bar—when the wrinkled little old Jonah, there officiating, soon poured them out brimmers all round. One complained of a bad cold in his head, upon which Jonah mixed him a pitch-like potion of gin and molasses, which he swore was a sovereign cure for all colds and catarrhs whatsoever, never mind of how long standing, or whether caught off the coast of Labrador, or on the weather side of an ice-island.

The liquor soon mounted into their heads, as it generally does even with the arrantest topers[4] newly landed from sea, and they began capering about most obstreperously.

I observed, however, that one of them held somewhat aloof, and though he seemed desirous not to spoil the hilarity of his shipmates by his own sober face, yet upon the whole he refrained from making as much noise as the rest. This man interested me at once; and since the sea-gods had ordained that he should soon become my shipmate (though but a sleeping-partner one, so far as this narrative is concerned), I will here venture upon a little description of him. He stood full six feet in height, with noble shoulders, and a chest like a coffer-dam.[5] I have seldom seen such brawn in a man. His face was deeply brown and burnt, making his white teeth dazzling by the contrast; while in the deep shadows of his eyes floated some reminiscences that did not seem to give him much joy. His voice at once announced that he was a Southerner, and from his fine stature, I thought he must be one of those tall mountaineers from the Alleganian Ridge in Virginia. When the revelry of his companions

2. The Fiji Islands, in the southwest Pacific.
3. Region of Newfoundland, Canada.
4. Drinkers.
5. Watertight repair box on ship.

had mounted to its height, this man slipped away unobserved, and I saw no more of him till he became my comrade on the sea. In a few minutes, however, he was missed by his shipmates, and being, it seems, for some reason a huge favorite with them, they raised a cry of "Bulkington! Bulkington! where's Bulkington?" and darted out of the house in pursuit of him.

It was now about nine o'clock, and the room seeming almost supernaturally quiet after these orgies, I began to congratulate myself upon a little plan that had occurred to me just previous to the entrance of the seamen.

No man prefers to sleep two in a bed. In fact, you would a good deal rather not sleep with your own brother. I don't know how it is, but people like to be private when they are sleeping. And when it comes to sleeping with an unknown stranger, in a strange inn, in a strange town, and that stranger a harpooneer, then your objections indefinitely multiply. Nor was there any earthly reason why I as a sailor should sleep two in a bed, more than anybody else; for sailors no more sleep two in a bed at sea, than bachelor Kings do ashore. To be sure they all sleep together in one apartment, but you have your own hammock, and cover yourself with your own blanket, and sleep in your own skin.

The more I pondered over this harpooneer, the more I abominated the thought of sleeping with him. It was fair to presume that being a harpooneer, his linen or woollen, as the case might be, would not be of the tidiest, certainly none of the finest. I began to twitch all over. Besides, it was getting late, and any decent harpooneer ought to be home and going bedwards. Suppose now, he should tumble in upon me at midnight—how could I tell from what vile hole he had been coming?

"Landlord! I've changed my mind about that harpooneer.—I shan't sleep with him. I'll try the bench here."

"Just as you please; I'm sorry I cant spare ye a table-cloth for a mattress, and it's a plaguy rough board here"—feeling of the knots and notches. "But wait a bit, Skrimshander; I've got a carpenter's plane there in the bar—wait, I say, and I'll make ye snug enough." So saying he procured the plane; and with his old silk handkerchief first dusting the bench, vigorously set to planing away at my bed, the while grinning like an ape. The shavings flew right and left; till at last the plane-iron came bump against an indestructible knot. The landlord was near spraining his wrist, and I told him for heaven's sake to quit—the bed was soft enough to suit me, and I did not know how all the planing in the world could make eider down of a pine plank. So gathering up the shavings with another grin, and throwing them into the great stove in the middle of the room, he went about his business, and left me in a brown study.[6]

I now took the measure of the bench, and found that it was a foot too short; but that could be mended with a chair. But it was a foot too narrow, and the other bench in the room was about four inches higher than the planed one—so there was no yoking them. I then placed the first bench lengthwise along the only clear space against the wall, leaving a little interval between, for my back to settle down in. But I soon found that there came such a draught of cold air over me from under the sill of the window, that this plan would never do at all, especially as another current from the rickety door met the one from the window, and both together formed a series of

6. Meditative state.

small whirlwinds in the immediate vicinity of the spot where I had thought to spend the night.

The devil fetch that harpooneer, thought I, but stop, couldn't I steal a march on him—bolt his door inside, and jump into his bed, not to be wakened by the most violent knockings? It seemed no bad idea; but upon second thoughts I dismissed it. For who could tell but what the next morning, so soon as I popped out of the room, the harpooneer might be standing in the entry, all ready to knock me down!

Still, looking round me again, and seeing no possible chance of spending a sufferable night unless in some other person's bed, I began to think that after all I might be cherishing unwarrantable prejudices against this unknown harpooneer. Thinks I, I'll wait awhile; he must be dropping in before long. I'll have a good look at him then, and perhaps we may become jolly good bedfellows after all—there's no telling.

But though the other boarders kept coming in by ones, twos, and threes, and going to bed, yet no sign of my harpooneer.

"Landlord!" said I, "what sort of a chap is he—does he always keep such late hours?" It was now hard upon twelve o'clock.

The landlord chuckled again with his lean chuckle, and seemed to be mightily tickled at something beyond my comprehension. "No," he answered, "generally he's an airley bird—airley to bed and airley to rise—yes, he's the bird what catches the worm.—But to-night he went out a peddling, you see, and I don't see what on airth keeps him so late, unless, may be, he can't sell his head."

"Can't sell his head?—What sort of a bamboozling story is this you are telling me?" getting into a towering rage. "Do you pretend to say, landlord, that this harpooneer is actually engaged this blessed Saturday night, or rather Sunday morning, in peddling his head around this town?"

"That's precisely it," said the landlord, "and I told him he couldn't sell it here, the market's overstocked."

"With what?" shouted I.

"With heads to be sure; ain't there too many heads in the world?"

"I tell you what it is, landlord," said I, quite calmly, "you'd better stop spinning that yarn to me—I'm not green."

"May be not," taking out a stick and whittling a toothpick, "but I raything guess you'll be done *brown*[7] if that ere harpooneer hears you a slanderin' his head."

"I'll break it for him," said I, now flying into a passion again at this unaccountable farrago of the landlord's.

"It's broke a'ready," said he.

"Broke," said I—"*broke*, do you mean?"

"Sartain, and that's the very reason he can't sell it, I guess."

"Landlord," said I, going up to him as cool as Mt. Hecla in a snow storm,[8]—"landlord, stop whittling. You and I must understand one another, and that too without delay. I come to your house and want a bed; you tell me you can only give me half a one; that the other half belongs to a certain harpooneer. And about this harpooneer, whom I have not yet seen, you persist in telling

7. Overcooked, punished.

8. I.e., calm on the outside, furious on the inside. Mount Hecla, in Iceland, was known for its volcanic activity.

me the most mystifying and exasperating stories, tending to beget in me an uncomfortable feeling towards the man whom you design for my bedfellow—a sort of connexion, landlord, which is an intimate and confidential one in the highest degree. I now demand of you to speak out and tell me who and what this harpooneer is, and whether I shall be in all respects safe to spend the night with him. And in the first place, you will be so good as to unsay that story about selling his head, which if true I take to be good evidence that this harpooneer is stark mad, and I've no idea of sleeping with a madman; and you, sir, *you* I mean, landlord, *you*, sir, by trying to induce me to do so knowingly, would thereby render yourself liable to a criminal prosecution."

"Wall," said the landlord, fetching a long breath, "that's a purty long sarmon for a chap that rips a little now and then. But be easy, be easy, this here harpooneer I have been tellin' you of has just arrived from the south seas, where he bought up a lot of 'balmed New Zealand heads (great curios, you know), and he's sold all on 'em but one, and that one he's trying to sell to-night, cause to-morrow's Sunday, and it would not do to be sellin' human heads about the streets when folks is goin' to churches. He wanted to, last Sunday, but I stopped him just as he was goin' out of the door with four heads strung on a string, for all the airth like a string of inions."

This account cleared up the otherwise unaccountable mystery, and showed that the landlord, after all, had had no idea of fooling me—but at the same time what could I think of a harpooneer who stayed out of a Saturday night clean into the holy Sabbath, engaged in such a cannibal business as selling the heads of dead idolators?

"Depend upon it, landlord, that harpooneer is a dangerous man."

"He pays reg'lar," was the rejoinder. "But come, it's getting dreadful late, you had better be turning flukes—it's a nice bed: Sal and me slept in that ere bed the night we were spliced.[9] There's plenty room for two to kick about in that bed; it's an almighty big bed that. Why, afore we give it up, Sal used to put our Sam and little Johnny in the foot of it. But I got a dreaming and sprawling about one night, and somehow, Sam got pitched on the floor, and came near breaking his arm. Arter that, Sal said it wouldn't do. Come along here, I'll give ye a glim[1] in a jiffy;" and so saying he lighted a candle and held it towards me, offering to lead the way. But I stood irresolute; when looking at a clock in the corner, he exclaimed "I vum[2] it's Sunday—you won't see that harpooneer to-night; he's come to anchor somewhere—come along then; *do* come; *won't* ye come?"

I considered the matter a moment, and then up stairs we went, and I was ushered into a small room, cold as a clam, and furnished, sure enough, with a prodigious bed, almost big enough indeed for any four harpooneers to sleep abreast.

"There," said the landlord, placing the candle on a crazy old sea chest that did double duty as a wash-stand and centre table; "there, make yourself comfortable now, and good night to ye." I turned round from eyeing the bed, but he had disappeared.

Folding back the counterpane, I stooped over the bed. Though none of the most elegant, it yet stood the scrutiny tolerably well. I then glanced round the

9. Married. "Flukes": parts of an anchor.
1. Light.
2. Vow.

room; and besides the bedstead and centre table, could see no other furniture belonging to the place, but a rude shelf, the four walls, and a papered fire-board representing a man striking[3] a whale. Of things not properly belonging to the room, there was a hammock lashed up, and thrown upon the floor in one corner; also a large seaman's bag, containing the harpooneer's wardrobe no doubt, in lieu of a land trunk. Likewise, there was a parcel of outlandish bone fish hooks on the shelf over the fire-place, and a tall harpoon standing at the head of the bed.

But what is this on the chest? I took it up, and held it close to the light, and felt it, and smelt it, and tried every way possible to arrive at some satisfactory conclusion concerning it. I can compare it to nothing but a large door mat, ornamented at the edges with little tinkling tags something like the stained porcupine quills round an Indian moccasin. There was a hole or slit in the middle of this mat, the same as in South American ponchos. But could it be possible that any sober harpooneer would get into a door mat, and parade the streets of any Christian town in that sort of guise? I put it on, to try it, and it weighed me down like a hamper, being uncommonly shaggy and thick, and I thought a little damp, as though this mysterious harpooneer had been wearing it of a rainy day. I went up in it to a bit of glass stuck against the wall, and I never saw such a sight in my life. I tore myself out of it in such a hurry that I gave myself a kink in the neck.

I sat down on the side of the bed, and commenced thinking about this head-peddling harpooneer, and his door mat. After thinking some time on the bed-side, I got up and took off my monkey jacket, and then stood in the middle of the room thinking. I then took off my coat, and thought a little more in my shirt sleeves. But beginning to feel very cold now, half undressed as I was, and remembering what the landlord said about the harpooneer's not coming home at all that night, it being so very late, I made no more ado, but jumped out of my pantaloons and boots, and then blowing out the light tumbled into bed, and commended myself to the care of heaven.

Whether that mattress was stuffed with corn-cobs or broken crockery, there is no telling, but I rolled about a good deal, and could not sleep for a long time. At last I slid off into a light doze, and had pretty nearly made a good offing towards the land of Nod, when I heard a heavy footfall in the passage, and saw a glimmer of light come into the room from under the door.

Lord save me, thinks I, that must be the harpooneer, the infernal head-peddler. But I lay perfectly still, and resolved not to say a word till spoken to. Holding a light in one hand, and that identical New Zealand head in the other, the stranger entered the room, and without looking towards the bed, placed his candle a good way off from me on the floor in one corner, and then began working away at the knotted cords of the large bag I before spoke of as being in the room. I was all eagerness to see his face, but he kept it averted for some time while employed in unlacing the bag's mouth. This accomplished, however, he turned round—when, good heavens! what a sight! Such a face! It was of a dark, purplish, yellow color, here and there stuck over with large, blackish looking squares. Yes, it's just as I thought, he's a terrible bedfellow; he's been in a fight, got dreadfully cut, and here he is, just from the surgeon. But at that moment he chanced to turn his face so towards the light, that

3. Harpooning. "Fireboard": covering for a fireplace when not in use.

I plainly saw they could not be sticking-plasters at all, those black squares on his cheeks. They were stains of some sort or other. At first I knew not what to make of this; but soon an inkling of the truth occurred to me. I remembered a story of a white man—a whaleman too—who, falling among the cannibals, had been tattooed by them. I concluded that this harpooneer, in the course of his distant voyages, must have met with a similar adventure. And what is it, thought I, after all! It's only his outside; a man can be honest in any sort of skin. But then, what to make of his unearthly complexion, that part of it, I mean, lying round about, and completely independent of the squares of tattooing. To be sure, it might be nothing but a good coat of tropical tanning; but I never heard of a hot sun's tanning a white man into a purplish yellow one. However, I had never been in the South Seas; and perhaps the sun there produced these extraordinary effects upon the skin. Now, while all these ideas were passing through me like lightning, this harpooneer never noticed me at all. But, after some difficulty having opened his bag, he commenced fumbling in it, and presently pulled out a sort of tomahawk, and a seal-skin wallet with the hair on. Placing these on the old chest in the middle of the room, he then took the New Zealand head—a ghastly thing enough—and crammed it down into the bag. He now took off his hat—a new beaver hat—when I came nigh singing out with fresh surprise. There was no hair on his head—none to speak of at least—nothing but a small scalp-knot twisted up on his forehead. His bald purplish head now looked for all the world like a mildewed skull. Had not the stranger stood between me and the door, I would have bolted out of it quicker than ever I bolted a dinner.

Even as it was, I thought something of slipping out of the window, but it was the second floor back. I am no coward, but what to make of this head-peddling purple rascal altogether passed my comprehension. Ignorance is the parent of fear, and being completely nonplussed and confounded about the stranger, I confess I was now as much afraid of him as if it was the devil himself who had thus broken into my room at the dead of night. In fact, I was so afraid of him that I was not game enough just then to address him, and demand a satisfactory answer concerning what seemed inexplicable in him.

Meanwhile, he continued the business of undressing, and at last showed his chest and arms. As I live, these covered parts of him were checkered with the same squares as his face; his back, too, was all over the same dark squares; he seemed to have been in a Thirty Years' War, and just escaped from it with a sticking-plaster shirt.[4] Still more, his very legs were marked, as if a parcel of dark green frogs were running up the trunks of young palms. It was now quite plain that he must be some abominable savage or other shipped aboard of a whaleman in the South Seas, and so landed in this Christian country. I quaked to think of it. A peddler of heads too—perhaps the heads of his own brothers. He might take a fancy to mine—heavens look at that tomahawk!

But there was no time for shuddering, for now the savage went about something that completely fascinated my attention, and convinced me that he must indeed be a heathen. Going to his heavy grego, or wrapall, or dread-

4. Covered with bandages, as if wounded during the 1618–48 European war fought mainly in Germany.

naught,[5] which he had previously hung on a chair, he fumbled in the pockets, and produced at length a curious little deformed image with a hunch on its back, and exactly the color of a three days' old Congo baby. Remembering the embalmed head, at first I almost thought that this black manikin was a real baby preserved in some similar manner. But seeing that it was not at all limber, and that it glistened a good deal like polished ebony, I concluded that it must be nothing but a wooden idol, which indeed it proved to be. For now the savage goes up to the empty fire-place, and removing the papered fire-board, sets up this little hunchbacked image, like a tenpin, between the andirons. The chimney jambs and all the bricks inside were very sooty, so that I thought this fire-place made a very appropriate little shrine or chapel for his Congo idol.

I now screwed my eyes hard towards the half hidden image, feeling but ill at ease meantime—to see what was next to follow. First he takes about a double handful of shavings out of his grego pocket, and places them carefully before the idol; then laying a bit of ship biscuit on top and applying the flame from the lamp, he kindled the shavings into a sacrificial blaze. Presently, after many hasty snatches into the fire, and still hastier withdrawals of his fingers (whereby he seemed to be scorching them badly), he at last succeeded in drawing out the biscuit; then blowing off the heat and ashes a little, he made a polite offer of it to the little negro. But the little devil did not seem to fancy such dry sort of fare at all; he never moved his lips. All these strange antics were accompanied by still stranger guttural noises from the devotee, who seemed to be praying in a sing-song or else singing some pagan psalmody or other, during which his face twitched about in the most unnatural manner. At last extinguishing the fire, he took the idol up very unceremoniously, and bagged it again in his grego pocket as carelessly as if he were a sportsman bagging a dead woodcock.

All these queer proceedings increased my uncomfortableness, and seeing him now exhibiting strong symptoms of concluding his business operations, and jumping into bed with me, I thought it was high time, now or never, before the light was put out, to break the spell in which I had so long been bound.

But the interval I spent in deliberating what to say, was a fatal one. Taking up his tomahawk from the table, he examined the head of it for an instant, and then holding it to the light, with his mouth at the handle, he puffed out great clouds of tobacco smoke. The next moment the light was extinguished, and this wild cannibal, tomahawk between his teeth, sprang into bed with me. I sang out, I could not help it now; and giving a sudden grunt of astonishment he began feeling me.

Stammering out something, I knew not what, I rolled away from him against the wall, and then conjured him, whoever or whatever he might be, to keep quiet, and let me get up and light the lamp again. But his guttural responses satisfied me at once that he but ill comprehended my meaning.

"Who-e debel you?"—he at last said—"you no speak-e, dam-me, I kill-e." And so saying the lighted tomahawk began flourishing about me in the dark.

"Landlord, for God's sake, Peter Coffin!" shouted I. "Landlord! Watch! Coffin! Angels! save me!"

5. Types of heavy overcoats.

"Speak-e! tell-ee me who-ee be, or dam-me, I kill-e!" again growled the cannibal, while his horrid flourishings of the tomahawk scattered the hot tobacco ashes about me till I thought my linen would get on fire. But thank heaven, at that moment the landlord came into the room light in hand, and leaping from the bed I ran up to him.

"Don't be afraid now," said he, grinning again. "Queequeg here wouldn't harm a hair of your head."

"Stop your grinning," shouted I, "and why didn't you tell me that that infernal harpooneer was a cannibal?"

"I thought ye know'd it;—didn't I tell ye, he was a peddlin' heads around town?—but turn flukes again and go to sleep. Queequeg, look here—you sabbee me, I sabbee you—this man sleepe you—you sabbee?"—

"Me sabbee plenty"—grunted Queequeg, puffing away at his pipe and sitting up in bed.

"You gettee in," he added, motioning to me with his tomahawk, and throwing the clothes to one side. He really did this in not only a civil but a really kind and charitable way. I stood looking at him a moment. For all his tattooings he was on the whole a clean, comely looking cannibal. What's all this fuss I have been making about, thought I to myself—the man's a human being just as I am: he has just as much reason to fear me, as I have to be afraid of him. Better sleep with a sober cannibal than a drunken Christian.

"Landlord," said I, "tell him to stash his tomahawk there, or pipe, or whatever you call it; tell him to stop smoking, in short, and I will turn in with him. But I don't fancy having a man smoking in bed with me. It's dangerous. Besides, I aint insured."

This being told to Queequeg, he at once complied, and again politely motioned me to get into bed—rolling over to one side as much as to say—I wont touch a leg of ye.

"Good night, landlord," said I, "you may go."

I turned in, and never slept better in my life.

* * *

Chapter 28

AHAB[6]

For several days after leaving Nantucket, nothing above hatches was seen of Captain Ahab. The mates regularly relieved each other at the watches, and for aught that could be seen to the contrary, they seemed to be the only commanders of the ship; only they sometimes issued from the cabin with orders so sudden and peremptory, that after all it was plain they but commanded vicariously. Yes, their supreme lord and dictator was there, though hitherto unseen by any eyes not permitted to penetrate into the now sacred retreat of the cabin.

6. Ishmael and Queequeg have signed on for a three-year voyage with the Nantucket whaler the *Pequod*, which is under the command of Captain Ahab, who lost part of a leg in an earlier effort to kill the whale called Moby Dick. Characters appearing in the selections reprinted here include the following: the chief mate is Starbuck, a Quaker and native of Nantucket; the second mate is Stubb, from Cape Cod; and the third mate is Flask, from the village of Gay Head on Martha's Vineyard. Queequeg is one of the ship's three main harpooners; the others are Tashtego, an Indian from Martha's Vineyard, and Daggoo, from Africa. The name *Ahab* is ominous; 1 Kings 16.28–22.40 traces the wicked reign of the idolatrous King Ahab and his wife, Jezebel.

Every time I ascended to the deck from my watches below, I instantly gazed aft to mark if any strange face were visible; for my first vague disquietude touching the unknown captain, now in the seclusion of the sea, became almost a perturbation. This was strangely heightened at times by the ragged Elijah's[7] diabolical incoherences uninvitedly recurring to me, with a subtle energy I could not have before conceived of. But poorly could I withstand them, much as in other moods I was almost ready to smile at the solemn whimsicalities of that outlandish prophet of the wharves. But whatever it was of apprehensiveness or uneasiness—to call it so—which I felt, yet whenever I came to look about me in the ship, it seemed against all warranty to cherish such emotions. For though the harpooneers, with the great body of the crew, were a far more barbaric, heathenish, and motley set than any of the tame merchant-ship companies which my previous experiences had made me acquainted with, still I ascribed this—and rightly ascribed it—to the fierce uniqueness of the very nature of that wild Scandinavian vocation in which I had so abandonedly embarked. But it was especially the aspect of the three chief officers of the ship, the mates, which was most forcibly calculated to allay these colorless misgivings, and induce confidence and cheerfulness in every presentment of the voyage. Three better, more likely sea-officers and men, each in his own different way, could not readily be found, and they were every one of them Americans; a Nantucketer, a Vineyarder, a Cape man. Now, it being Christmas when the ship shot from out her harbor, for a space we had biting Polar weather, though all the time running away from it to the southward; and by every degree and minute of latitude which we sailed, gradually leaving that merciless winter and all its intolerable weather behind us. It was one of those less lowering,[8] but still grey and gloomy enough mornings of the transition, when with a fair wind the ship was rushing through the water with a vindictive sort of leaping and melancholy rapidity, that as I mounted to the deck at the call of the forenoon watch, so soon as I levelled my glance towards the taffrail,[9] foreboding shivers ran over me. Reality outran apprehension; Captain Ahab stood upon his quarter-deck.

There seemed no sign of common bodily illness about him, nor of the recovery from any. He looked like a man cut away from the stake, when the fire has overrunningly wasted all the limbs without consuming them, or taking away one particle from their compacted aged robustness. His whole high, broad form, seemed made of solid bronze, and shaped in an unalterable mould, like Cellini's cast Perseus.[1] Threading its way out from among his grey hairs, and continuing right down one side of his tawny scorched face and neck, till it disappeared in his clothing, you saw a slender rod-like mark, lividly whitish. It resembled that perpendicular seam sometimes made in the straight, lofty trunk of a great tree, when the upper lightning tearingly darts down it, and without wrenching a single twig, peels and grooves out the bark from top to bottom, ere running off into the soil, leaving the tree still greenly alive, but branded. Whether that mark was born with him, or whether it was the scar

7. Introduced in chapter 19 of the novel as a shabbily appareled and pockmarked stranger who prophesies a dire fate for Ahab. In 1 Kings 21.23–24, the prophet Elijah foretells that "the dogs shall eat Jezebel by the walls of Jezreel."
8. Threatening.
9. Rail at the back of the ship.

1. From engravings Melville knew the bronze statue by the Italian sculptor Benevenuto Cellini (1500–1571) in the Loggia of the Signoria in Florence: the trimphant Perseus (the son of Zeus) holds aloft the newly severed head of Medusa, one of the snake-haired Gorgons whose eyes turned anyone who looked at them into stone.

left by some desperate wound, no one could certainly say. By some tacit consent, throughout the voyage little or no allusion was made to it, especially by the mates. But once Tashtego's senior, an old Gay-Head Indian among the crew, superstitiously asserted that not till he was full forty years old did Ahab become that way branded, and then it came upon him, not in the fury of any mortal fray, but in an elemental strife at sea. Yet, this wild hint seemed inferentially negatived, by what a grey Manxman[2] insinuated, an old sepulchral man, who, having never before sailed out of Nantucket, had never ere this laid eye upon wild Ahab. Nevertheless, the old sea-traditions, the immemorial credulities, popularly invested this old Manxman with preternatural powers of discernment. So that no white sailor seriously contradicted him when he said that if ever Captain Ahab should be tranquilly laid out—which might hardly come to pass, so he muttered—then, whoever should do that last office for the dead, would find a birth-mark on him from crown to sole.

So powerfully did the whole grim aspect of Ahab affect me, and the livid brand which streaked it, that for the first few moments I hardly noted that not a little of this overbearing grimness was owing to the barbaric white leg upon which he partly stood. It had previously come to me that this ivory leg had at sea been fashioned from the polished bone of the sperm whale's jaw. "Aye, he was dismasted off Japan," said the old Gay-Head Indian once; "but like his dismasted craft, he shipped another mast without coming home for it. He has a quiver of 'em."

I was struck with the singular posture he maintained. Upon each side of the Pequod's quarter deck, and pretty close to the mizen shrouds, there was an auger hole, bored about half an inch or so, into the plank. His bone leg steadied in that hole; one arm elevated, and holding by a shroud; Captain Ahab stood erect, looking straight out beyond the ship's ever-pitching prow. There was an infinity of firmest fortitude, a determinate, unsurrenderable wilfulness, in the fixed and fearless, forward dedication of that glance. Not a word he spoke; nor did his officers say aught to him; though by all their minutest gestures and expressions, they plainly showed the uneasy, if not painful, consciousness of being under a troubled master-eye. And not only that, but moody stricken Ahab stood before them with a crucifixion in his face; in all the nameless regal overbearing dignity of some mighty woe.

Ere long, from his first visit in the air, he withdrew into his cabin. But after that morning, he was every day visible to the crew; either standing in his pivot-hole, or seated upon an ivory stool he had; or heavily walking the deck. As the sky grew less gloomy; indeed, began to grow a little genial, he became still less and less a recluse; as if, when the ship had sailed from home, nothing but the dead wintry bleakness of the sea had then kept him so secluded. And, by and by, it came to pass, that he was almost continually in the air; but, as yet, for all that he said, or perceptibly did, on the at last sunny deck, he seemed as unnecessary there as another mast. But the Pequod was only making a passage now; not regularly cruising; nearly all whaling preparatives needing supervision the mates were fully competent to, so that there was little or nothing, out of himself, to employ or excite Ahab, now; and thus chase away, for that one interval, the clouds that layer upon layer were piled upon his brow, as ever all clouds choose the loftiest peaks to pile themselves upon.

2. Someone from the Isle of Man, in the Irish Sea.

Nevertheless, ere long, the warm, warbling persuasiveness of the pleasant, holiday weather we came to, seemed gradually to charm him from his mood. For, as when the red-cheeked, dancing girls, April and May, trip home to the wintry, misanthropic woods; even the barest, ruggedest, most thunder-cloven old oak will at least send forth some few green sprouts, to welcome such glad-hearted visitants; so Ahab did, in the end, a little respond to the playful allurings of that girlish air. More than once did he put forth the faint blossom of a look, which, in any other man, would have soon flowered out in a smile.

* * *

Chapter 36

THE QUARTER-DECK

(Enter Ahab: Then, all.)

It was not a great while after the affair of the pipe,[3] that one morning shortly after breakfast, Ahab, as was his wont, ascended the cabin-gangway to the deck. There most sea-captains usually walk at that hour, as country gentlemen, after the same meal, take a few turns in the garden.

Soon his steady, ivory stride was heard, as to and fro he paced his old rounds, upon planks so familiar to his tread, that they were all over dented, like geological stones, with the peculiar mark of his walk. Did you fixedly gaze, too, upon that ribbed and dented brow; there also, you would see still stranger foot-prints—the foot-prints of his one unsleeping, ever-pacing thought.

But on the occasion in question, those dents looked deeper, even as his nervous step that morning left a deeper mark. And, so full of his thought was Ahab, that at every uniform turn that he made, now at the main-mast and now at the binnacle, you could almost see that thought turn in him as he turned, and pace in him as he paced; so completely possessing him, indeed, that it all but seemed the inward mould of every outer movement.

"D'ye mark him, Flask?" whispered Stubb; "the chick that's in him pecks the shell. T'will soon be out."

The hours wore on;—Ahab now shut up within his cabin; anon, pacing the deck, with the same intense bigotry of purpose in his aspect.

It drew near the close of day. Suddenly he came to a halt by the bulwarks, and inserting his bone leg into the auger-hole there, and with one hand grasping a shroud, he ordered Starbuck to send everybody aft.

"Sir!" said the mate, astonished at an order seldom or never given on ship-board except in some extraordinary case.

"Send everybody aft," repeated Ahab. "Mast-heads, there! come down!"

When the entire ship's company were assembled, and with curious and not wholly unapprehensive faces, were eyeing him, for he looked not unlike the weather horizon when a storm is coming up, Ahab, after rapidly glancing over the bulwarks, and then darting his eyes among the crew, started from his stand-point; and as though not a soul were nigh him resumed his heavy turns upon the deck. With bent head and half-slouched hat he continued to pace, unmindful of the wondering whispering among the men; till Stubb

3. In chapter 30, Ahab angrily throws his still lit pipe overboard when he is no longer soothed by smoking it.

cautiously whispered to Flask, that Ahab must have summoned them there for the purpose of witnessing a pedestrian feat. But this did not last long. Vehemently pausing, he cried:—

"What do ye do when ye see a whale, men?"

"Sing out for him!" was the impulsive rejoinder from a score of clubbed voices.

"Good!" cried Ahab, with a wild approval in his tones; observing the hearty animation into which his unexpected question had so magnetically thrown them.

"And what do ye next, men?"

"Lower away, and after him!"

"And what tune is it ye pull to, men?"

"A dead whale or a stove[4] boat!"

More and more strangely and fiercely glad and approving, grew the countenance of the old man at every shout; while the mariners began to gaze curiously at each other, as if marvelling how it was that they themselves became so excited at such seemingly purposeless questions.

But, they were all eagerness again, as Ahab, now half-revolving in his pivot-hole, with one hand reaching high up a shroud, and tightly, almost convulsively grasping it, addressed them thus:—

"All ye mast-headers have before now heard me give orders about a white whale. Look ye! d'ye see this Spanish ounce of gold?"—holding up a broad bright coin to the sun—"it is a sixteen dollar piece, men,—a doubloon. D'ye see it? Mr. Starbuck, hand me yon top-maul."

While the mate was getting the hammer, Ahab, without speaking, was slowly rubbing the gold piece against the skirts of his jacket, as if to heighten its lustre, and without using any words was meanwhile lowly humming to himself, producing a sound so strangely muffled and inarticulate that it seemed the mechanical humming of the wheels of his vitality in him.

Receiving the top-maul from Starbuck, he advanced towards the mainmast with the hammer uplifted in one hand, exhibiting the gold with the other, and with a high raised voice exclaiming: "Whosoever of ye raises me a white-headed whale with a wrinkled brow and a crooked jaw; whosoever of ye raises me that white-headed whale, with three holes punctured in his starboard fluke—look ye, whosoever of ye raises me that same white whale, he shall have this gold ounce, my boys!"

"Huzza! huzza!" cried the seamen, as with swinging tarpaulins they hailed the act of nailing the gold to the mast.

"It's a white whale, I say," resumed Ahab, as he threw down the top-maul; "a white whale. Skin your eyes for him, men; look sharp for white water; if ye see but a bubble, sing out."

All this while Tashtego, Daggoo, and Queequeg had looked on with even more intense interest and surprise than the rest, and at the mention of the wrinkled brow and crooked jaw they had started as if each was separately touched by some specific recollection.

"Captain Ahab," said Tashtego, "that white whale must be the same that some call Moby Dick."

4. Wrecked; crushed inward.

"Moby Dick?" shouted Ahab. "Do ye know the white whale then, Tash?"

"Does he fan-tail a little curious, sir, before he goes down?" said the Gay-Header deliberately.

"And has he a curious spout, too," said Daggoo, "very bushy, even for a parmacetty,[5] and mighty quick, Captain Ahab?"

"And he have one, two, tree—oh! good many iron in him hide, too, Captain," cried Queequeg disjointedly, "all twiske-tee be-twisk, like him—him—" faltering hard for a word, and screwing his hand round and round as though uncorking a bottle—"like him—him—"

"Corkscrew!" cried Ahab, "aye, Queequeg, the harpoons lie all twisted and wrenched in him; aye, Daggoo, his spout is a big one, like a whole shock of wheat, and white as a pile of our Nantucket wool after the great annual sheep-shearing; aye, Tashtego, and he fan-tails like a split jib[6] in a squall. Death and devils! men, it is Moby Dick ye have seen—Moby Dick—Moby Dick!"

"Captain Ahab," said Starbuck, who, with Stubb and Flask, had thus far been eyeing his superior with increasing surprise, but at last seemed struck with a thought which somewhat explained all the wonder. "Captain Ahab, I have heard of Moby Dick—but it was not Moby Dick that took off thy leg?"

"Who told thee that?" cried Ahab; then pausing, "Aye, Starbuck; aye, my hearties all round; it was Moby Dick that dismasted me; Moby Dick that brought me to this dead stump I stand on now. Aye, aye," he shouted with a terrific, loud, animal sob, like that of a heart-stricken moose; "Aye, aye! it was that accursed white whale that razeed me; made a poor pegging lubber[7] of me for ever and a day!" Then tossing both arms, with measureless imprecations he shouted out: "Aye, aye! and I'll chase him round Good Hope, and round the Horn, and round the Norway Maelstrom,[8] and round perdition's flames before I give him up. And this is what ye have shipped for, men! to chase that white whale on both sides of land,[9] and over all sides of earth, till he spouts black blood and rolls fin out. What say ye, men, will ye splice hands on it, now? I think ye do look brave."

"Aye, aye!" shouted the harpooneers and seamen, running closer to the excited old man: "A sharp eye for the White Whale; a sharp lance for Moby Dick!"

"God bless ye," he seemed to half sob and half shout. "God bless ye, men. Steward! go draw the great measure of grog.[1] But what's this long face about, Mr. Starbuck; wilt thou not chase the white whale? art not game for Moby Dick?"

"I am game for his crooked jaw, and for the jaws of Death too, Captain Ahab, if it fairly comes in the way of the business we follow; but I came here to hunt whales, not my commander's vengeance. How many barrels will thy vengeance yield thee even if thou gettest it, Captain Ahab? it will not fetch thee much in our Nantucket market."

"Nantucket market! Hoot! But come closer, Starbuck; thou requirest a little lower layer. If money's to be the measurer, man, and the accountants have computed their great counting-house the globe, by girdling it with guineas,

5. Sperm whale.
6. Torn sail.
7. Limping landman. "Razeed": cut down in height.
8. Tidal whirlpool off Norway.
9. I.e., in both the Atlantic and Pacific sides of the Americas.
1. Watered-down rum.

one to every three parts of an inch; then, let me tell thee, that my vengeance will fetch a great premium *here*!"

"He smites his chest," whispered Stubb, "what's that for? methinks it rings most vast, but hollow."

"Vengeance on a dumb brute!" cried Starbuck, "that simply smote thee from blindest instinct! Madness! To be enraged with a dumb thing, Captain Ahab, seems blasphemous."

"Hark ye yet again,—the little lower layer. All visible objects, man, are but as pasteboard masks. But in each event—in the living act, the undoubted deed—there, some unknown but still reasoning thing puts forth the mouldings of its features from behind the unreasoning mask. If man will strike, strike through the mask! How can the prisoner reach outside except by thrusting through the wall? To me, the white whale is that wall, shoved near to me. Sometimes I think there's naught beyond. But 'tis enough. He tasks me; he heaps me; I see in him outrageous strength, with an inscrutable malice sinewing it. That inscrutable thing is chiefly what I hate; and be the white whale agent, or be the white whale principal, I will wreak that hate upon him. Talk not to me of blasphemy, man; I'd strike the sun if it insulted me. For could the sun do that, then could I do the other; since there is ever a sort of fair play herein, jealousy presiding over all creations. But not my master, man, is even that fair play. Who's over me? Truth hath no confines. Take off thine eye! more intolerable than fiends' glarings is a doltish stare! So, so; thou reddenest and palest; my heat has melted thee to anger-glow. But look ye, Starbuck, what is said in heat, that thing unsays itself. There are men from whom warm words are small indignity. I meant not to incense thee. Let it go. Look! see yonder Turkish cheeks of spotted tawn[2]—living, breathing pictures painted by the sun. The Pagan leopards—the unrecking and unworshipping things, that live; and seek, and give no reasons for the torrid life they feel! The crew, man, the crew! Are they not one and all with Ahab, in this matter of the whale? See Stubb! he laughs! See yonder Chilian! he snorts to think of it. Stand up amid the general hurricane, thy one tost sapling cannot, Starbuck! And what is it? Reckon it. 'Tis but to help strike a fin; no wondrous feat for Starbuck. What is it more? From this one poor hunt, then, the best lance out of all Nantucket, surely he will not hang back, when every foremast-hand has clutched a whetstone? Ah! constrainings seize thee; I see! the billow lifts thee! Speak, but speak!—Aye, aye! thy silence, then, *that* voices thee. *(Aside)* Something shot from my dilated nostrils, he has inhaled it in his lungs. Starbuck now is mine; cannot oppose me now, without rebellion."

"God keep me!—keep us all!" murmured Starbuck, lowly.

But in his joy at the enchanted, tacit acquiescence of the mate, Ahab did not hear his foreboding invocation; nor yet the low laugh from the hold; nor yet the presaging vibrations of the winds in the cordage; nor yet the hollow flap of the sails against the masts, as for a moment their hearts sank in. For again Starbuck's downcast eyes lighted up with the stubbornness of life; the subterranean laugh died away; the winds blew on; the sails filled out; the ship heaved and rolled as before. Ah, ye admonitions and warnings! why stay ye not when ye come? But rather are ye predictions than warnings, ye shadows!

2. Tan.

Yet not so much predictions from without, as verifications of the foregoing things within. For with little external to constrain us, the innermost necessities in our being, these still drive us on.

"The measure! the measure!" cried Ahab.

Receiving the brimming pewter, and turning to the harpooneers, he ordered them to produce their weapons. Then ranging them before him near the capstan, with their harpoons in their hands, while his three mates stood at his side with their lances, and the rest of the ship's company formed a circle round the group; he stood for an instant searchingly eyeing every man of his crew. But those wild eyes met his, as the bloodshot eyes of the prairie wolves meet the eye of their leader, ere he rushes on at their head in the trail of the bison; but, alas! only to fall into the hidden snare of the Indian.

"Drink and pass!" he cried, handing the heavy charged flagon to the nearest seaman. "The crew alone now drink. Round with it, round! Short draughts—long swallows, men; 'tis hot as Satan's hoof. So, so; it goes round excellently. It spiralizes in ye; forks out at the serpent-snapping eye. Well done; almost drained. That way it went, this way it comes. Hand it me—here's a hollow! Men, ye seem the years; so brimming life is gulped and gone. Steward, refill!

"Attend now, my braves. I have mustered ye all round this capstan; and ye mates, flank me with your lances; and ye harpooneers, stand there with your irons; and ye, stout mariners, ring me in, that I may in some sort revive a noble custom of my fisherman fathers before me. O men, you will yet see that——Ha! boy, come back? bad pennies come not sooner. Hand it me. Why, now, this pewter had run brimming again, wert not thou St. Vitus' imp[3]—away, thou ague!

"Advance, ye mates! Cross your lances full before me. Well done! Let me touch the axis." So saying, with extended arm, he grasped the three level, radiating lances at their crossed centre; while so doing, suddenly and nervously twitched them; meanwhile, glancing intently from Starbuck to Stubb; from Stubb to Flask. It seemed as though, by some nameless, interior volition, he would fain have shocked into them the same fiery emotion accumulated within the Leyden jar[4] of his own magnetic life. The three mates quailed before his strong, sustained, and mystic aspect. Stubb and Flask looked sideways from him; the honest eye of Starbuck fell downright.

"In vain!" cried Ahab; "but, maybe, 'tis well. For did ye three but once take the full-forced shock, then mine own electric thing, *that* had perhaps expired from out me. Perchance, too, it would have dropped ye dead. Perchance ye need it not. Down lances! And now, ye mates, I do appoint ye three cup-bearers to my three pagan kinsmen there—yon three most honorable gentlemen and noblemen, my valiant harpooneers. Disdain the task? What, when the great Pope washes the feet of beggars, using his tiara for ewer? Oh, my sweet cardinals! your own condescension, *that* shall bend ye to it. I do not order ye; ye will it. Cut your seizings[5] and draw the poles, ye harpooneers!"

3. Saint Vitus's dance is a spasmodic muscular jerking, now known as the neuromuscular disorder chorea. Ahab blames the steward for spilling some of the rum.

4. In early experiments with electric circuits, a glass jar lined with tinfoil with a conducting rod passing through an isolated stopper.

5. Ropes.

Silently obeying the order, the three harpooneers now stood with the detached iron part of their harpoons, some three feet long, held, barbs up, before him.

"Stab me not with that keen steel! Cant them; cant them over! know ye not the goblet end? Turn up the socket! So, so; now, ye cup-bearers, advance. The irons! take them; hold them while I fill!" Forthwith, slowly going from one officer to the other, he brimmed the harpoon sockets with the fiery waters from the pewter.

"Now, three to three, ye stand. Commend the murderous chalices![6] Bestow them, ye who are now made parties to this indissoluble league. Ha! Starbuck! but the deed is done! Yon ratifying sun now waits to sit upon it. Drink, ye harpooneers! drink and swear, ye men that man the deathful whaleboat's bow—Death to Moby Dick! God hunt us all, if we do not hunt Moby Dick to his death!" The long, barbed steel goblets were lifted; and to cries and maledictions against the white whale, the spirits were simultaneously quaffed down with a hiss. Starbuck paled, and turned, and shivered. Once more, and finally, the replenished pewter went the rounds among the frantic crew; when, waving his free hand to them, they all dispersed; and Ahab retired within his cabin.

* * *

Chapter 41

MOBY DICK

I, Ishmael, was one of that crew; my shouts had gone up with the rest; my oath had been welded with theirs; and stronger I shouted, and more did I hammer and clinch my oath, because of the dread in my soul. A wild, mystical, sympathetical feeling was in me; Ahab's quenchless feud seemed mine. With greedy ears I learned the history of that murderous monster against whom I and all the others had taken our oaths of violence and revenge.

For some time past, though at intervals only, the unaccompanied, secluded White Whale had haunted those uncivilized seas mostly frequented by the Sperm Whale fishermen. But not all of them knew of his existence; only a few of them, comparatively, had knowingly seen him; while the number who as yet had actually and knowingly given battle to him, was small indeed. For, owing to the large number of whale-cruisers; the disorderly way they were sprinkled over the entire watery circumference, many of them adventurously pushing their quest along solitary latitudes, so as seldom or never for a whole twelvemonth or more on a stretch, to encounter a single news-telling sail of any sort; the inordinate length of each separate voyage; the irregularity of the times of sailing from home; all these, with other circumstances, direct and indirect, long obstructed the spread through the whole world-wide whaling-fleet of the special individualizing tidings concerning Moby Dick. It was hardly to be doubted, that several vessels reported to have encountered, at such or such a time, or on such or such a meridian, a Sperm Whale of uncommon magnitude and malignity, which whale, after doing great mischief to his assailants, had completely escaped them; to some minds it was

6. Echo of Shakespeare's *Macbeth* 1.7.10–12: "this even-handed justice / Commends the ingredients of our poison'd chalice / To our own lips."

not an unfair presumption, I say, that the whale in question must have been no other than Moby Dick. Yet as of late the Sperm Whale fishery had been marked by various and not unfrequent instances of great ferocity, cunning, and malice in the monster attacked; therefore it was, that those who by accident ignorantly gave battle to Moby Dick; such hunters, perhaps, for the most part, were content to ascribe the peculiar terror he bred, more, as it were, to the perils of the Sperm Whale fishery at large, than to the individual cause. In that way, mostly, the disastrous encounter between Ahab and the whale had hitherto been popularly regarded.

And as for those who, previously hearing of the White Whale, by chance caught sight of him; in the beginning of the thing they had every one of them, almost, as boldly and fearlessly lowered for him, as for any other whale of that species. But at length, such calamities did ensue in these assaults—not restricted to sprained wrists and ancles, broken limbs, or devouring amputations—but fatal to the last degree of fatality; those repeated disastrous repulses, all accumulating and piling their terrors upon Moby Dick; those things had gone far to shake the fortitude of many brave hunters, to whom the story of the White Whale had eventually come.

Nor did wild rumors of all sorts fail to exaggerate, and still the more horrify the true histories of these deadly encounters. For not only do fabulous rumors naturally grow out of the very body of all surprising terrible events,—as the smitten tree gives birth to its fungi; but, in maritime life, far more than in that of terra firma, wild rumors abound, wherever there is any adequate reality for them to cling to. And as the sea surpasses the land in this matter, so the whale fishery surpasses every other sort of maritime life, in the wonderfulness and fearfulness of the rumors which sometimes circulate there. For not only are whalemen as a body unexempt from that ignorance and superstitiousness hereditary to all sailors; but of all sailors, they are by all odds the most directly brought into contact with whatever is appallingly astonishing in the sea; face to face they not only eye its greatest marvels, but, hand to jaw, give battle to them. Alone, in such remotest waters, that though you sailed a thousand miles, and passed a thousand shores, you would not come to any chiselled hearthstone, or aught hospitable beneath that part of the sun; in such latitudes and longitudes, pursuing too such a calling as he does, the whaleman is wrapped by influences all tending to make his fancy pregnant with many a mighty birth.

No wonder, then, that ever gathering volume from the mere transit over the widest watery spaces, the outblown rumors of the White Whale did in the end incorporate with themselves all manner of morbid hints, and half-formed fœtal suggestions of supernatural agencies, which eventually invested Moby Dick with new terrors unborrowed from anything that visibly appears. So that in many cases such a panic did he finally strike, that few who by those rumors, at least, had heard of the White Whale, few of those hunters were willing to encounter the perils of his jaw.

But there were still other and more vital practical influences at work. Not even at the present day has the original prestige of the Sperm Whale, as fearfully distinguished from all other species of the leviathan, died out of the minds of the whalemen as a body. There are those this day among them, who, though intelligent and courageous enough in offering battle to the Greenland or Right whale, would perhaps—either from professional inexperience, or incompetency, or timidity, decline a contest with the Sperm Whale; at any rate, there are plenty of whalemen, especially among those whaling nations not sailing under the American flag, who have never hostilely encountered the Sperm Whale, but whose sole knowledge of the leviathan is restricted to the ignoble monster primitively pursued in the North; seated on their hatches, these men will hearken with a childish fireside interest and awe, to the wild, strange tales of Southern whaling. Nor is the pre-eminent tremendousness of the great Sperm Whale anywhere more feelingly comprehended, than on board of those prows which stem him.

And as if the now tested reality of his might had in former legendary times thrown its shadow before it; we find some book naturalists—Olassen and Povelsen[7]—declaring the Sperm Whale not only to be a consternation to every other creature in the sea, but also to be so incredibly ferocious as continually to be athirst for human blood. Nor even down to so late a time as Cuvier's,[8] were these or almost similar impressions effaced. For in his Natural History, the Baron himself affirms that at sight of the Sperm Whale, all fish (sharks included) are "struck with the most lively terror," and "often in the precipitancy of their flight dash themselves against the rocks with such violence as to cause instantaneous death." And however the general experiences in the fishery may amend such reports as these; yet in their full terribleness, even to the bloodthirsty item of Povelsen, the superstitious belief in them is, in some vicissitudes of their vocation, revived in the minds of the hunters.

So that overawed by the rumors and portents concerning him, not a few of the fishermen recalled, in reference to Moby Dick, the earlier days of the Sperm Whale fishery, when it was oftentimes hard to induce long practised Right whalemen to embark in the perils of this new and daring warfare; such men protesting that although other leviathans might be hopefully pursued, yet to chase and point lance at such an apparition as the Sperm Whale was not for mortal man. That to attempt it, would be inevitably to be torn into a quick eternity. On this head, there are some remarkable documents that may be consulted.

Nevertheless, some there were, who even in the face of these things were ready to give chase to Moby Dick; and a still greater number who, chancing only to hear of him distantly and vaguely, without the specific details of any certain calamity, and without superstitious accompaniments, were sufficiently hardy not to flee from the battle if offered.

One of the wild suggestings referred to, as at last coming to be linked with the White Whale in the minds of the superstitiously inclined, was the unearthly conceit that Moby Dick was ubiquitous; that he had actually been encountered in opposite latitudes at one and the same instant of time.

Nor, credulous as such minds must have been, was this conceit altogether without some faint show of superstitious probability. For as the secrets of the currents in the seas have never yet been divulged, even to the most erudite research; so the hidden ways of the Sperm Whale when beneath the surface

7. What he knew of Olafsen and Povelsen, the authors of *Travels in Iceland* (1805)—even the misspelling of Olafsen's name—Melville picked up secondhand from one of his major sources, Thomas Beale's *Natural History of the Sperm Whale* (1839).

8. Melville's information from Frederick Cuvier's *Natural History of Whales* (1836) also came from Beale's *Natural History*.

remain, in great part, unaccountable to his pursuers; and from time to time have originated the most curious and contradictory speculations regarding them, especially concerning the mystic modes whereby, after sounding to a great depth, he transports himself with such vast swiftness to the most widely distant points.

It is a thing well known to both American and English whale-ships, and as well a thing placed upon authoritative record years ago by Scoresby, that some whales have been captured far north in the Pacific, in whose bodies have been found the barbs of harpoons darted in the Greenland seas.[9] Nor is it to be gainsaid, that in some of these instances it has been declared that the interval of time between the two assaults could not have exceeded very many days. Hence, by inference, it has been believed by some whalemen, that the Nor' West Passage,[1] so long a problem to man, was never a problem to the whale. So that here, in the real living experience of living men, the prodigies related in old times of the inland Strella mountain in Portugal (near whose top there was said to be a lake in which the wrecks of ships floated up to the surface); and that still more wonderful story of the Arethusa fountain near Syracuse (whose waters were believed to have come from the Holy Land by an underground passage);[2] these fabulous narrations are almost fully equalled by the realities of the whaleman.

Forced into familiarity, then, with such prodigies as these; and knowing that after repeated, intrepid assaults, the White Whale had escaped alive; it cannot be much matter of surprise that some whalemen should go still further in their superstitions; declaring Moby Dick not only ubiquitous, but immortal (for immortality is but ubiquity in time); that though groves of spears should be planted in his flanks, he would still swim away unharmed; or if indeed he should ever be made to spout thick blood, such a sight would be but a ghastly deception; for again in unensanguined billows hundreds of leagues away, his unsullied jet would once more be seen.

But even stripped of these supernatural surmisings, there was enough in the earthly make and incontestable character of the monster to strike the imagination with unwonted power. For, it was not so much his uncommon bulk that so much distinguished him from other sperm whales, but, as was elsewhere thrown out—a peculiar snow-white wrinkled forehead, and a high, pyramidical white hump. These were his prominent features; the tokens whereby, even in the limitless, uncharted seas, he revealed his identity, at a long distance, to those who knew him.

The rest of his body was so streaked, and spotted, and marbled with the same shrouded hue, that, in the end, he had gained his distinctive appellation of the White Whale; a name, indeed, literally justified by his vivid aspect, when seen gliding at high noon through a dark blue sea, leaving a milky-way wake of creamy foam, all spangled with golden gleamings.

Nor was it his unwonted magnitude, nor his remarkable hue, nor yet his deformed lower jaw, that so much invested the whale with natural terror, as

9. Reports of transpolar passages of whales are in vol. 1 of William Scoresby Jr.'s *An Account of the Arctic Regions* (1820).

1. The hoped-for navigable connection between the Atlantic and Pacific Oceans in the Arctic.

2. It is not known how Melville learned of this legend, current in the 17th century. In Greek mythology the nymph Arethusa, fleeing a river god in Greece (not the Holy Land), was saved by being transformed into a current of water that flowed beneath the sea floor and emerged as a fountain on the island of Ortygia near ancient Syracuse.

that unexampled, intelligent malignity which, according to specific accounts, he had over and over again evinced in his assaults. More than all, his treacherous retreats struck more of dismay than perhaps aught else. For, when swimming before his exulting pursuers, with every apparent symptom of alarm, he had several times been known to turn round suddenly, and, bearing down upon them, either stave their boats to splinters, or drive them back in consternation to their ship.

Already several fatalities had attended his chase. But though similar disasters, however little bruited ashore, were by no means unusual in the fishery; yet, in most instances, such seemed the White Whale's infernal aforethought of ferocity, that every dismembering or death that he caused, was not wholly regarded as having been inflicted by an unintelligent agent.

Judge, then, to what pitches of inflamed, distracted fury the minds of his more desperate hunters were impelled, when amid the chips of chewed boats, and the sinking limbs of torn comrades, they swam out of the white curds of the whale's direful wrath into the serene, exasperating sunlight, that smiled on, as if at a birth or a bridal.

His three boats stove around him, and oars and men both whirling in the eddies; one captain, seizing the line-knife from his broken prow, had dashed at the whale, as an Arkansas duellist at his foe, blindly seeking with a six inch blade to reach the fathom-deep life of the whale. That captain was Ahab. And then it was, that suddenly sweeping his sickle-shaped lower jaw beneath him, Moby Dick had reaped away Ahab's leg, as a mower a blade of grass in the field. No turbaned Turk,[3] no hired Venetian or Malay, could have smote him with more seeming malice. Small reason was there to doubt, then, that ever since that almost fatal encounter, Ahab had cherished a wild vindictiveness against the whale, all the more fell for that in his frantic morbidness he at last came to identify with him, not only all his bodily woes, but all his intellectual and spiritual exasperations. The White Whale swam before him as the monomaniac incarnation of all those malicious agencies which some deep men feel eating in them, till they are left living on with half a heart and half a lung. That intangible malignity which has been from the beginning; to whose dominion even the modern Christians ascribe one-half of the worlds; which the ancient Ophites[4] of the east reverenced in their statue devil;—Ahab did not fall down and worship it like them; but deliriously transferring its idea to the abhorred white whale, he pitted himself, all mutilated, against it. All that most maddens and torments; all that stirs up the lees of things; all truth with malice in it; all that cracks the sinews and cakes the brain; all the subtle demonisms of life and thought; all evil, to crazy Ahab, were visibly personified, and made practically assailable in Moby Dick. He piled upon the whale's white hump the sum of all the general rage and hate felt by his whole race from Adam down; and then, as if his chest had been a mortar, he burst his hot heart's shell upon it.

It is not probable that this monomania in him took its instant rise at the precise time of his bodily dismemberment. Then, in darting at the monster, knife in hand, he had but given loose to a sudden, passionate, corporal ani-

3. An echo of Shakespeare's *Othello* 5.2.352: "a malignant and a turban'd Turk."

4. A serpent-worshiping Christian sect of the 2nd century C.E.

mosity; and when he received the stroke that tore him, he probably but felt the agonizing bodily laceration, but nothing more. Yet, when by this collision forced to turn towards home, and for long months of days and weeks, Ahab and anguish lay stretched together in one hammock, rounding in mid winter that dreary, howling Patagonian Cape; then it was, that his torn body and gashed soul bled into one another; and so interfusing, made him mad. That it was only then, on the homeward voyage, after the encounter, that the final monomania seized him, seems all but certain from the fact that, at intervals during the passage, he was a raving lunatic; and, though unlimbed of a leg, yet such vital strength yet lurked in his Egyptian chest, and was moreover intensified by his delirium, that his mates were forced to lace him fast, even there, as he sailed, raving in his hammock. In a strait-jacket, he swung to the mad rockings of the gales. And, when running into more sufferable latitudes, the ship, with mild stun'sails spread, floated across the tranquil tropics, and, to all appearances, the old man's delirium seemed left behind him with the Cape Horn swells, and he came forth from his dark den into the blessed light and air; even then, when he bore that firm, collected front, however pale, and issued his calm orders once again; and his mates thanked God the direful madness was now gone; even then, Ahab, in his hidden self, raved on. Human madness is oftentimes a cunning and most feline thing. When you think it fled, it may have but become transfigured into some still subtler form. Ahab's full lunacy subsided not, but deepeningly contracted; like the unabated Hudson, when that noble Northman flows narrowly, but unfathomably through the Highland gorge.[5] But, as in his narrow-flowing monomania, not one jot of Ahab's broad madness had been left behind; so in that broad madness, not one jot of his great natural intellect had perished. That before living agent, now became the living instrument. If such a furious trope may stand, his special lunacy stormed his general sanity, and carried it, and turned all its concentred cannon upon its own mad mark; so that far from having lost his strength, Ahab, to that one end, did now possess a thousand fold more potency than ever he had sanely brought to bear upon any one reasonable object.

This is much; yet Ahab's larger, darker, deeper part remains unhinted. But vain to popularize profundities, and all truth is profound. Winding far down from within the very heart of this spiked Hotel de Cluny where we here stand—however grand and wonderful, now quit it;—and take your way, ye nobler, sadder souls, to those vast Roman halls of Thermes,[6] where far beneath the fantastic towers of man's upper earth, his root of grandeur, his whole awful essence sits in bearded state; an antique buried beneath antiquities, and throned on torsoes! So with a broken throne, the great gods mock that captive king; so like a Caryatid,[7] he patient sits, upholding on his frozen brow the piled entablatures of ages. Wind ye down there, ye prouder, sadder souls! question that proud, sad king! A family likeness! aye, he did beget ye, ye young exiled royalties; and from your grim sire only will the old State-secret come.

5. The Hudson River at its narrowest point, flowing through the Catskill Mountains.
6. Baths (French). The Hotel de Cluny is a medieval building in the Paris Latin Quarter, built above two-thousand-year-old Roman ruins.
7. Structural column sculpted into a female form.

Now, in his heart, Ahab had some glimpse of this, namely: all my means are sane, my motive and my object mad. Yet without power to kill, or change, or shun the fact; he likewise knew that to mankind he did long dissemble; in some sort, did still. But that thing of his dissembling was only subject to his perceptibility, not to his will determinate. Nevertheless, so well did he succeed in that dissembling, that when with ivory leg he stepped ashore at last, no Nantucketer thought him otherwise than but naturally grieved, and that to the quick, with the terrible casualty which had overtaken him.

The report of his undeniable delirium at sea was likewise popularly ascribed to a kindred cause. And so too, all the added moodiness which always afterwards, to the very day of sailing in the Pequod on the present voyage, sat brooding on his brow. Nor is it so very unlikely, that far from distrusting his fitness for another whaling voyage, on account of such dark symptoms, the calculating people of that prudent isle were inclined to harbor the conceit, that for those very reasons he was all the better qualified and set on edge, for a pursuit so full of rage and wildness as the bloody hunt of whales. Gnawed within and scorched without, with the infixed, unrelenting fangs of some incurable idea; such an one, could he be found, would seem the very man to dart his iron and lift his lance against the most appalling of all brutes. Or, if for any reason thought to be corporeally incapacitated for that, yet such an one would seem superlatively competent to cheer and howl on his underlings to the attack. But be all this as it may, certain it is, that with the mad secret of his unabated rage bolted up and keyed in him, Ahab had purposely sailed upon the present voyage with the one only and all-engrossing object of hunting the White Whale. Had any one of his old acquaintances on shore but half dreamed of what was lurking in him then, how soon would their aghast and righteous souls have wrenched the ship from such a fiendish man! They were bent on profitable cruises, the profit to be counted down in dollars from the mint. He was intent on an audacious, immitigable, and supernatural revenge.

Here, then, was this grey-headed, ungodly old man, chasing with curses a Job's whale[8] round the world, at the head of a crew, too, chiefly made up of mongrel renegades, and castaways, and cannibals—morally enfeebled also, by the incompetence of mere unaided virtue or right-mindedness in Starbuck, the invulnerable jollity of indifference and recklessness in Stubb, and the pervading mediocrity in Flask. Such a crew, so officered, seemed specially picked and packed by some infernal fatality to help him to his monomaniac revenge. How it was that they so aboundingly responded to the old man's ire—by what evil magic their souls were possessed, that at times his hate seemed almost theirs; the White Whale as much their insufferable foe as his; how all this came to be—what the White Whale was to them, or how to their unconscious understandings, also, in some dim, unsuspected way, he might have seemed the gliding great demon of the seas of life,—all this to explain, would be to dive deeper than Ishmael can go. The subterranean miner that works in us all, how can one tell whither leads his shaft by the ever shifting, muffled sound of his pick? Who does not feel the irresistible arm drag? What skiff in tow of a seventy-four can stand still? For one, I gave myself up to the

8. See Job 41.1: "Canst thou draw out leviathan with an hook? or his tongue with a cord which thou lettest down?"

abandonment of the time and the place; but while yet all a-rush to encounter the whale, could see naught in that brute but the deadliest ill.

Chapter 42

THE WHITENESS OF THE WHALE

What the white whale was to Ahab, has been hinted; what, at times, he was to me, as yet remains unsaid.

Aside from those more obvious considerations touching Moby Dick, which could not but occasionally awaken in any man's soul some alarm, there was another thought, or rather vague, nameless horror concerning him, which at times by its intensity completely overpowered all the rest; and yet so mystical and well nigh ineffable was it, that I almost despair of putting it in a comprehensible form. It was the whiteness of the whale that above all things appalled me. But how can I hope to explain myself here; and yet, in some dim, random way, explain myself I must, else all these chapters might be naught.

Though in many natural objects, whiteness refiningly enhances beauty, as if imparting some special virtue of its own, as in marbles, japonicas,[9] and pearls; and though various nations have in some way recognised a certain royal pre-eminence in this hue; even the barbaric, grand old kings of Pegu placing the title "Lord of the White Elephants" above all their other magniloquent ascriptions of dominion; and the modern kings of Siam unfurling the same snow-white quadruped in the royal standard; and the Hanoverian flag bearing the one figure of a snow-white charger; and the great Austrian Empire,[1] Cæsarian heir to overlording Rome, having for the imperial color the same imperial hue; and though this pre-eminence in it applies to the human race itself, giving the white man ideal mastership over every dusky tribe;[2] and though, besides all this, whiteness has been even made significant of gladness, for among the Romans a white stone marked a joyful day; and though in other mortal sympathies and symbolizings, this same hue is made the emblem of many touching, noble things—the innocence of brides, the benignity of age; though among the Red Men of America the giving of the white belt of wampum was the deepest pledge of honor; though in many climes, whiteness typifies the majesty of Justice in the ermine of the Judge, and contributes to the daily state of kings and queens drawn by milk-white steeds; though even in the higher mysteries of the most august religions it has been made the symbol of the divine spotlessness and power; by the Persian fire worshippers, the white forked flame being held the holiest on the altar; and in the Greek mythologies, Great Jove himself being made incarnate in a snow-white bull;[3] and though to the noble Iroquois, the midwinter sacrifice of the sacred White Dog was by far the holiest festival of their theology, that spotless, faithful creature being held the purest envoy they could send to the Great Spirit with the annual tidings of their own fidelity; and though directly from the Latin word for white, all Christian

9. Made from the typically hard black substance of Japonica acid. Melville's meaning is unclear here.

1. I.e., The Holy Roman Empire, claiming succession from the Roman Caesars. Pegu is in lower Burma.

2. Conventional statement of white supremacy, at odds with attitudes toward race exemplified elsewhere in the book and in Melville's other writings.

3. The shape in which the king of the Greek gods carried away the Princess Europa.

priests derive the name of one part of their sacred vesture, the alb or tunic, worn beneath the cassock; and though among the holy pomps of the Romish faith, white is specially employed in the celebration of the Passion of our Lord; though in the Vision of St. John,[4] white robes are given to the redeemed, and the four-and-twenty elders stand clothed in white before the great white throne, and the Holy One that sitteth there white like wool; yet for all these accumulated associations, with whatever is sweet, and honorable, and sublime, there yet lurks an elusive something in the innermost idea of this hue, which strikes more of panic to the soul than that redness which affrights in blood.

This elusive quality it is, which causes the thought of whiteness, when divorced from more kindly associations, and coupled with any object terrible in itself, to heighten that terror to the furthest bounds. Witness the white bear of the poles, and the white shark of the tropics; what but their smooth, flaky whiteness makes them the transcendent horrors they are? That ghastly whiteness it is which imparts such an abhorrent mildness, even more loathsome than terrific, to the dumb gloating of their aspect. So that not the fierce-fanged tiger in his heraldic coat can so stagger courage as the white-shrouded bear or shark.[5]

Bethink thee of the albatross: whence come those clouds of spiritual wonderment and pale dread, in which that white phantom sails in all imaginations? Not Coleridge first threw that spell; but God's great, unflattering laureate, Nature.[6]

4. Revelation 7.9: "After this I beheld, and, lo, a great multitude, which no man could number, of all nations and kindreds, and people, and tongues, stood before the throne, and before the Lamb, clothed with white robes and palms in their hands."

5. With reference to the Polar bear, it may possibly be urged by him who would fain go still deeper into this matter, that it is not the whiteness, separately regarded, which heightens the intolerable hideousness of that brute; for, analysed, that heightened hideousness, it might be said, only arises from the circumstance, that the irresponsible ferociousness of the creature stands invested in the fleece of celestial innocence and love; and hence, by bringing together two such opposite emotions in our minds, the Polar bear frightens us with so unnatural a contrast. But even assuming all this to be true; yet, were it not for the whiteness, you would not have that intensified terror.

As for the white shark, the white gliding ghostliness of repose in that creature, when beheld in his ordinary moods, strangely tallies with the same quality in the Polar quadruped. This peculiarity is most vividly hit by the French in the name they bestow upon that fish. The Romish mass for the dead begins with "Requiem eternam" (eternal rest), whence *Requiem* denominating the mass itself, and any other funereal music. Now, in allusion to the white, silent stillness of death in this shark, and the mild deadliness of his habits, the French call him *Requin* [Melville's note].

6. I remember the first albatross I ever saw. It was during a prolonged gale, in waters hard upon the Antarctic seas. From my forenoon watch below, I ascended to the overclouded deck; and there, dashed upon the main hatches, I saw a regal, feathery thing of unspotted whiteness, and with a hooked, Roman bill sublime. At intervals, it arched forth its vast archangel wings, as if to embrace some holy ark. Wondrous flutterings and throbbings shook it. Though bodily unharmed, it uttered cries, as some king's ghost in supernatural distress. Through its inexpressible, strange eyes, methought I peeped to secrets which took hold of God. As Abraham before the angels, I bowed myself; the white thing was so white, its wings so wide, and in those for ever exiled waters, I had lost the miserable warping memories of traditions and of towns. Long I gazed at that prodigy of plumage. I cannot tell, can only hint, the things that darted through me then. But at last I awoke, and turning, asked a sailor what bird was this. A goney, he replied. Goney! I never had heard that name before; is it conceivable that this glorious thing is utterly unknown to men ashore! never! But some time after, I learned that goney was some seaman's name for albatross. So that by no possibility could Coleridge's wild Rhyme have had aught to do with those mystical impressions which were mine, when I saw that bird upon our deck. For neither had I then read the Rhyme, nor knew the bird to be an albatross. Yet, in saying this, I do but indirectly burnish a little brighter the noble merit of the poem and the poet.

I assert, then, that in the wondrous bodily whiteness of the bird chiefly lurks the secret of the spell; a truth the more evinced in this, that by a solecism of terms there are birds called grey albatrosses; and these I have frequently seen, but never with such emotions as when I beheld the Antarctic fowl.

But how had the mystic thing been caught? Whisper it not, and I will tell; with a treacherous hook and line, as the fowl floated on the sea. At

Most famous in our Western annals and Indian traditions is that of the White Steed of the Praries: a magnificent milk-white charger, large-eyed, small-headed, bluff-chested, and with the dignity of a thousand monarchs in his lofty, overscorning carriage. He was the elected Xerxes[7] of vast herds of wild horses, whose pastures in those days were only fenced by the Rocky Mountains and the Alleghanies. At their flaming head he westward trooped it like that chosen star[8] which every evening leads on the hosts of light. The flashing cascade of his mane, the curving comet of his tail, invested him with housings more resplendent than gold and silver-beaters could have furnished him. A most imperial and archangelical apparition of that unfallen, western world, which to the eyes of the old trappers and hunters revived the glories of those primeval times when Adam walked majestic as a god, bluff-bowed[9] and fearless as this mighty steed. Whether marching amid his aides and marshals in the van of countless cohorts that endlessly streamed it over the plains, like an Ohio; or whether with his circumambient subjects browsing all around at the horizon, the White Steed gallopingly reviewed them with warm nostrils reddening through his cool milkiness; in whatever aspect he presented himself, always to the bravest Indians he was the object of trembling reverence and awe. Nor can it be questioned from what stands on legendary record of this noble horse, that it was his spiritual whiteness chiefly, which so clothed him with divineness; and that this divineness had that in it which, though commanding worship, at the same time enforced a certain nameless terror.

But there are other instances where this whiteness loses all that accessory and strange glory which invests it in the White Steed and Albatross.

What is it that in the Albino man so peculiarly repels and often shocks the eye, as that sometimes he is loathed by his own kith and kin? It is that whiteness which invests him, a thing expressed by the name he bears. The Albino is as well made as other men—has no substantive deformity—and yet this mere aspect of all-pervading whiteness makes him more strangely hideous than the ugliest abortion. Why should this be so?

Nor, in quite other aspects, does Nature in her least palpable but not the less malicious agencies, fail to enlist among her forces this crowning attribute of the terrible. From its snowy aspect, the gauntleted ghost of the Southern Seas has been denominated the White Squall. Nor, in some historic instances, has the art of human malice omitted so potent an auxiliary. How wildly it heightens the effect of that passage in Froissart,[1] when, masked in the snowy symbol of their faction, the desperate White Hoods of Ghent murder their bailiff in the market-place!

Nor, in some things, does the common, hereditary experience of all mankind fail to bear witness to the supernaturalism of this hue. It cannot well be doubted, that the one visible quality in the aspect of the dead which most appals the gazer, is the marble pallor lingering there; as if indeed that

last the Captain made a postman of it; tying a lettered, leathern tally round its neck, with the ship's time and place; and then letting it escape. But I doubt not, that leathern tally, meant for man, was taken off in Heaven, when the white fowl flew to join the wing-folding, the invoking, and adoring cherubim! [Melville's note]. Melville refers to English poet Samuel Taylor Coleridge's *The Rime of the Ancient Mariner* (1798).

7. Persian military leader who led large armies against the Greeks in the 5th century B.C.E.

8. I.e., the planet Venus.

9. With a full and square chest.

1. A 1379 murder described in *Chronicles of England, France, and Spain* by French poet and historian Sir John Froissart (1337–1410).

pallor were as much the badge of consternation in the other world, as of mortal trepidation here. And from that pallor of the dead, we borrow the expressive hue of the shroud in which we wrap them. Nor even in our superstitions do we fail to throw the same snowy mantle round our phantoms; all ghosts rising in a milk-white fog—Yea, while these terrors seize us, let us add, that even the king of terrors, when personified by the evangelist, rides on his pallid horse.

Therefore, in his other moods, symbolize whatever grand or gracious thing he will by whiteness, no man can deny that in its profoundest idealized significance it calls up a peculiar apparition to the soul.

But though without dissent this point be fixed, how is mortal man to account for it? To analyse it, would seem impossible. Can we, then, by the citation of some of those instances wherein this thing of whiteness—though for the time either wholly or in great part stripped of all direct associations calculated to impart to it aught fearful, but, nevertheless, is found to exert over us the same sorcery, however modified;—can we thus hope to light upon some chance clue to conduct us to the hidden cause we seek?

Let us try. But in a matter like this, subtlety appeals to subtlety, and without imagination no man can follow another into these halls. And though, doubtless, some at least of the imaginative impressions about to be presented may have been shared by most men, yet few perhaps were entirely conscious of them at the time, and therefore may not be able to recall them now.

Why to the man of untutored ideality, who happens to be but loosely acquainted with the peculiar character of the day, does the bare mention of Whitsuntide[2] marshal in the fancy such long, dreary, speechless processions of slow-pacing pilgrims, down-cast and hooded with new-fallen snow? Or, to the unread, unsophisticated Protestant of the Middle American States,[3] why does the passing mention of a White Friar or a White Nun, evoke such an eyeless statue in the soul?

Or what is there apart from the traditions of dungeoned warriors and kings (which will not wholly account for it) that makes the White Tower[4] of London tell so much more strongly on the imagination of an untravelled American, than those other storied structures, its neighbors—the Byward Tower, or even the Bloody? And those sublimer towers, the White Mountains of New Hampshire, whence, in peculiar moods, comes that gigantic ghostliness over the soul at the bare mention of that name, while the thought of Virginia's Blue Ridge[5] is full of a soft, dewy, distant dreaminess? Or why, irrespective of all latitudes and longitudes, does the name of the White Sea exert such a spectralness over the fancy, while that of the Yellow Sea[6] lulls us with mortal thoughts of long lacquered mild afternoons on the waves, followed by the gaudiest and yet sleepiest of sunsets? Or, to choose a wholly unsubstantial instance, purely addressed to the fancy, why, in reading the old fairy tales of Central Europe, does "the tall pale man" of the Hartz forests, whose changeless pallor unrustlingly glides through the green of the groves—

2. The week beginning with Whitsunday (Pentacost), the seventh Sunday after Easter, when converts are baptized in white robes.
3. I.e., the Midatlantic States (New York, New Jersey, Pennsylvania, Delaware, Maryland).
4. One of the cluster of thirteen towers on the Thames, formerly whitewashed inside and out.
5. The Blue Ridge Mountains.
6. Between China and Korea. The White Sea is off the north coast of Russia.

why is this phantom more terrible than all the whooping imps of the Blocksburg?[7]

Nor is it, altogether, the remembrance of her cathedral-toppling earthquakes; nor the stampedoes of her frantic seas; nor the tearlessness of arid skies that never rain; nor the sight of her wide field of leaning spires, wrenched cope-stones, and crosses all adroop (like canted yards of anchored fleets); and her suburban avenues of house-walls lying over upon each other, as a tossed pack of cards;—it is not these things alone which make tearless Lima, the strangest, saddest city thou can'st see. For Lima has taken the white veil; and there is a higher horror in this whiteness of her woe. Old as Pizarro,[8] this whiteness keeps her ruins for ever new; admits not the cheerful greenness of complete decay; spreads over her broken ramparts the rigid pallor of an apoplexy that fixes its own distortions.

I know that, to the common apprehension, this phenomenon of whiteness is not confessed to be the prime agent in exaggerating the terror of objects otherwise terrible; nor to the unimaginative mind is there aught of terror in those appearances whose awfulness to another mind almost solely consists in this one phenomenon, especially when exhibited under any form at all approaching to muteness or universality. What I mean by these two statements may perhaps be respectively elucidated by the following examples.

First: The mariner, when drawing nigh the coasts of foreign lands, if by night he hear the roar of breakers, starts to vigilance, and feels just enough of trepidation to sharpen all his faculties; but under precisely similar circumstances, let him be called from his hammock to view his ship sailing through a midnight sea of milky whiteness—as if from encircling headlands shoals of combed white bears were swimming round him, then he feels a silent, superstitious dread; the shrouded phantom of the whitened waters is horrible to him as a real ghost; in vain the lead assures him he is still off soundings; heart and helm they both go down; he never rests till blue water is under him again. Yet where is the mariner who will tell thee, "Sir, it was not so much the fear of striking hidden rocks, as the fear of that hideous whiteness that so stirred me?"

Second: To the native Indian of Peru, the continual sight of the snowhowdahed Andes conveys naught of dread, except, perhaps, in the mere fancying of the eternal frosted desolateness reigning at such vast altitudes, and the natural conceit of what a fearfulness it would be to lose oneself in such inhuman solitudes. Much the same is it with the backwoodsman of the West, who with comparative indifference views an unbounded prairie sheeted with driven snow, no shadow of tree or twig to break the fixed trance of whiteness. Not so the sailor, beholding the scenery of the Antarctic seas; where at times, by some infernal trick of legerdemain in the powers of frost and air, he, shivering and half shipwrecked, instead of rainbows speaking hope and solace to his misery, views what seems a boundless church-yard grinning upon him with its lean ice monuments and splintered crosses.

7. I.e., Brocken, highest peak in the Harz forests in central Germany, which were the haunting ground of such folklore figures as the "pale man."

8. Francisco Pizarro (1470–1541), Spanish conqueror of Peru, who founded Lima in 1535. Lima has an annual rainfall of less than two inches, limiting vegetation. Still visible to Melville when he visited Lima in 1844 were the effects of the earthquake that destroyed the city a century before, in 1746.

But thou sayest, methinks this white-lead chapter about whiteness is but a white flag hung out from a craven soul; thou surrenderest to a hypo, Ishmael.

Tell me, why this strong young colt, foaled in some peaceful valley of Vermont, far removed from all beasts of prey—why is it that upon the sunniest day, if you but shake a fresh buffalo robe behind him, so that he cannot even see it, but only smells its wild animal muskiness—why will he start, snort, and with bursting eyes paw the ground in phrensies of affright? There is no remembrance in him of any gorings of wild creatures in his green northern home, so that the strange muskiness he smells cannot recall to him anything associated with the experience of former perils; for what knows he, this New England colt, of the black bisons of distant Oregon?

No: but here thou beholdest even in a dumb brute, the instinct of the knowledge of the demonism in the world. Though thousands of miles from Oregon, still when he smells that savage musk, the rending, goring bison herds are as present as to the deserted wild foal of the prairies, which this instant they may be trampling into dust.

Thus, then, the muffled rollings of a milky sea; the bleak rustlings of the festooned frosts of mountains; the desolate shiftings of the windrowed snows of prairies; all these, to Ishmael, are as the shaking of that buffalo robe to the frightened colt!

Though neither knows where lie the nameless things of which the mystic sign gives forth such hints; yet with me, as with the colt, somewhere those things must exist. Though in many of its aspects this visible world seems formed in love, the invisible spheres were formed in fright.

But not yet have we solved the incantation of this whiteness, and learned why it appeals with such power to the soul; and more strange and far more portentous—why, as we have seen, it is at once the most meaning symbol of spiritual things, nay, the very veil of the Christian's Deity; and yet should be as it is, the intensifying agent in things the most appalling to mankind.

Is it that by its indefiniteness it shadows forth the heartless voids and immensities of the universe, and thus stabs us from behind with the thought of annihilation, when beholding the white depths of the milky way? Or is it, that as in essence whiteness is not so much a color as the visible absence of color, and at the same time the concrete of all colors; is it for these reasons that there is such a dumb blankness, full of meaning, in a wide landscape of snows—a colorless, all-color of atheism from which we shrink? And when we consider that other theory of the natural philosophers, that all other earthly hues—every stately or lovely emblazoning—the sweet tinges of sunset skies and woods; yea, and the gilded velvets of butterflies, and the butterfly cheeks of young girls; all these are but subtile deceits, not actually inherent in substances, but only laid on from without; so that all deified Nature absolutely paints like the harlot, whose allurements cover nothing but the charnel-house within; and when we proceed further, and consider that the mystical cosmetic which produces every one of her hues, the great principle of light, for ever remains white or colorless in itself, and if operating without medium upon matter, would touch all objects, even tulips and roses, with its own blank tinge—pondering all this, the palsied universe lies before us a leper; and like wilful travellers in Lapland,[9] who refuse to wear

9. Vast region of northern Europe largely within the Arctic Circle.

colored and coloring glasses upon their eyes, so the wretched infidel gazes himself blind at the monumental white shroud that wraps all the prospect around him. And of all these things the Albino whale was the symbol. Wonder ye then at the fiery hunt?

* * *

Chapter 135

THE CHASE—THIRD DAY[1]

The morning of the third day dawned fair and fresh, and once more the solitary night-man at the fore-mast-head was relieved by crowds of the daylight look-outs, who dotted every mast and almost every spar.

"D'ye see him?" cried Ahab; but the whale was not yet in sight.

"In his infallible wake, though; but follow that wake, that's all. Helm there; steady, as thou goest, and hast been going. What a lovely day again! were it a new-made world, and made for a summer-house to the angels, and this morning the first of its throwing open to them, a fairer day could not dawn upon that world. Here's food for thought, had Ahab time to think; but Ahab never thinks; he only feels, feels, feels; *that's* tingling enough for mortal man! to think's audacity. God only has that right and privilege. Thinking is, or ought to be, a coolness and a calmness; and our poor hearts throb, and our poor brains beat too much for that. And yet, I've sometimes thought my brain was very calm—frozen calm, this old skull cracks so, like a glass in which the contents turn to ice, and shiver it. And still this hair is growing now; this moment growing, and heat must breed it; but no, it's like that sort of common grass that will grow anywhere, between the earthy clefts of Greenland ice or in Vesuvius lava. How the wild winds blow it; they whip it about me as the torn shreds of split sails lash the tossed ship they cling to. A vile wind that has no doubt blown ere this through prison corridors and cells, and wards of hospitals, and ventilated them, and now comes blowing hither as innocent as fleeces. Out upon it!—it's tainted. Were I the wind, I'd blow no more on such a wicked, miserable world. I'd crawl somewhere to a cave, and slink there. And yet, 'tis a noble and heroic thing, the wind! who ever conquered it? In every fight it has the last and bitterest blow. Run tilting at it, and you but run through it. Ha! a coward wind that strikes stark naked men, but will not stand to receive a single blow. Even Ahab is a braver thing—a nobler thing than *that*. Would now the wind but had a body; but all the things that most exasperate and outrage mortal man, all these things are bodiless, but only bodiless as objects, not as agents. There's a most special, a most cunning, oh, a most malicious difference! And yet, I say again, and swear it now, that there's something all glorious and gracious in the wind. These warm Trade Winds, at least, that in the clear heavens blow straight on, in strong and steadfast, vigorous mildness; and veer not from their mark, however the baser currents of the sea may turn and tack, and mightiest Mississippies of the land swift and swerve about, uncertain where to go at last. And by the eternal Poles! these same Trades that so directly blow my good ship on these Trades, or something like them—something so unchangeable,

1. The *Pequod* has been pursuing Moby Dick in the Pacific Ocean east of Japan.

and full as strong, blow my keeled soul along! To it! Aloft there! What d'ye see?"

"Nothing, sir."

"Nothing! and noon at hand! The doubloon goes a-begging! See the sun! Aye, aye, it must be so. I've oversailed him. How, got the start? Aye he's chasing *me* now; not I, *him*—that's bad; I might have known it, too. Fool! the lines—the harpoons he's towing. Aye, aye, I have run him by last night. About! about! Come down, all of ye, but the regular look outs! Man the braces!"

Steering as she had done, the wind had been somewhat on the Pequod's quarter, so that now being pointed in the reverse direction, the braced ship sailed hard upon the breeze as she rechurned the cream in her own white wake.

"Against the wind he now steers for the open jaw," murmured Starbuck to himself, as he coiled the new-hauled main-brace upon the rail. "God keep us, but already my bones feel damp within me, and from the inside wet my flesh. I misdoubt me that I disobey my God in obeying him!"

"Stand by to sway me up!" cried Ahab, advancing to the hempen basket. "We should meet him soon."

"Aye, aye, sir," and straightway Starbuck did Ahab's bidding, and once more Ahab swung on high.

A whole hour now passed; gold-beaten out to ages. Time itself now held long breaths with keen suspense. But at last, some three points off the weather bow, Ahab descried the spout again, and instantly from the three mast-heads three shrieks went up as if the tongues of fire had voiced it.

"Forehead to forehead I meet thee, this third time, Moby Dick! On deck there!—brace sharper up; crowd her into the wind's eye. He's too far off to lower yet, Mr. Starbuck. The sails shake! Stand over that helmsman with a top-maul! So, so; he travels fast, and I must down. But let me have one more good round look aloft here at the sea; there's time for that. An old, old sight, and yet somehow so young; aye, and not changed a wink since I first saw it, a boy, from the sand-hills of Nantucket! The same!—the same!—the same to Noah as to me. There's a soft shower to leeward. Such lovely leewardings! They must lead somewhere—to something else than common land, more palmy than the palms. Leeward! the white whale goes that way; look to windward, then; the better if the bitterer quarter. But good bye, good bye, old mast-head! What's this?—green? aye, tiny mosses in these warped cracks. No such green weather stains on Ahab's head! There's the difference now between man's old age and matter's. But aye, old mast, we both grow old together; sound in our hulls, though, are we not, my ship? Aye, minus a leg, that's all. By heaven this dead wood has the better of my live flesh every way. I can't compare with it; and I've known some ships made of dead trees outlast the lives of men made of the most vital stuff of vital fathers. What's that he said? he should still go before me, my pilot; and yet to be seen again? But where? Will I have eyes at the bottom of the sea, supposing I descend those endless stairs? and all night I've been sailing from him, wherever he did sink to. Aye, aye, like many more thou told'st direful truth as touching thyself, O Parsee; but, Ahab, there thy shot fell short. Good by, mast-head—keep a good eye upon the whale, the while I'm gone. We'll talk to-morrow, nay, to-night, when the white whale lies down there, tied by head and tail."

He gave the word; and still gazing round him, was steadily lowered through the cloven blue air to the deck.

In due time the boats were lowered; but as standing in his shallop's stern, Ahab just hovered upon the point of the descent, he waved to the mate,—who held one of the tackle-ropes on deck—and bade him pause.

"Starbuck!"

"Sir?"

"For the third time my soul's ship starts upon this voyage, Starbuck."

"Aye, sir, thou wilt have it so."

"Some ships sail from their ports, and ever afterwards are missing, Starbuck!"

"Truth, sir: saddest truth."

"Some men die at ebb tide; some at low water; some at the full of the flood;—and I feel now like a billow that's all one crested comb, Starbuck. I am old;—shake hands with me, man."

Their hands met; their eyes fastened; Starbuck's tears the glue.

"Oh, my captain, my captain!—noble heart—go not—go not!—see, it's a brave man that weeps; how great the agony of the persuasion then!"

"Lower away!"—cried Ahab, tossing the mate's arm from him. "Stand by the crew!"

In an instant the boat was pulling round close under the stern.

"The sharks! the sharks!" cried a voice from the low cabin-window there; "O master, my master, come back!"

But Ahab heard nothing; for his own voice was high-lifted then; and the boat leaped on.

Yet the voice spake true; for scarce had he pushed from the ship, when numbers of sharks, seemingly rising from out the dark waters beneath the hull, maliciously snapped at the blades of the oars, every time they dipped in the water; and in this way accompanied the boat with their bites. It is a thing not uncommonly happening to the whale-boats in those swarming seas; the sharks at times apparently following them in the same prescient way that vultures hover over the banners of marching regiments in the east. But these were the first sharks that had been observed by the Pequod since the White Whale had been first descried; and whether it was that Ahab's crew were all such tiger-yellow barbarians, and therefore their flesh more musky to the senses of the sharks—a matter sometimes well known to affect them,—however it was, they seemed to follow that one boat without molesting the others.

"Heart of wrought steel!" murmured Starbuck gazing over the side and following with his eyes the receding boat—"canst thou yet ring boldly to that sight?—lowering thy keel among ravening sharks, and followed by them, open-mouthed to the chase; and this the critical third day?—For when three days flow together in one continuous intense pursuit; be sure the first is the morning, the second the noon, and the third the evening and the end of that thing—be that end what it may. Oh! my God! what is this that shoots through me, and leaves me so deadly calm, yet expectant,—fixed at the top of a shudder! Future things swim before me, as in empty outlines and skeletons; all the past is somehow grown dim. Mary, girl! thou fadest in pale glories behind me; boy! I seem to see but thy eyes grown wondrous blue. Strangest problems of life seem clearing; but clouds sweep between—Is my journey's end coming? My legs feel faint; like his who has footed it all day. Feel thy heart,—beats it yet?—Stir thyself, Starbuck!—stave it off—move, move! speak aloud!—Mast-head there! See ye my boy's hand on the hill?—Crazed;—aloft there!—keep thy keenest eye upon the boats:—mark well the whale!—Ho! again!—drive off that hawk! see! he pecks—he tears the vane"—pointing to the red flag flying at the main-truck—"Ha! he soars away with it!—Where's the old man now? sees't thou that sight, oh Ahab!—shudder, shudder!"

The boats had not gone very far, when by a signal from the mast-heads—a downward pointed arm, Ahab knew that the whale had sounded; but intending to be near him at the next rising, he held on his way a little sideways from the vessel; the becharmed crew maintaining the profoundest silence, as the head-beat waves hammered and hammered against the opposing bow.

"Drive, drive in your nails, oh ye waves! to their uttermost heads drive them in! ye but strike a thing without a lid; and no coffin and no hearse can be mine:—and hemp only can kill me! Ha! ha!"

Suddenly the waters around them slowly swelled in broad circles; then quickly upheaved, as if sideways sliding from a submerged berg of ice, swiftly rising to the surface. A low rumbling sound was heard; a subterraneous hum; and then all held their breaths; as bedraggled with trailing ropes, and harpoons, and lances, a vast form shot lengthwise, but obliquely from the sea. Shrouded in a thin drooping veil of mist, it hovered for a moment in the rainbowed air; and then fell swamping back into the deep. Crushed thirty feet upwards, the waters flashed for an instant like heaps of fountains, then brokenly sank in a shower of flakes, leaving the circling surface creamed like new milk round the marble trunk of the whale.

"Give way!" cried Ahab to the oarsmen, and the boats darted forward to the attack; but maddened by yesterday's fresh irons that corroded in him, Moby Dick seemed combinedly possessed by all the angels that fell from heaven. The wide tiers of welded tendons overspreading his broad white forehead, beneath the transparent skin, looked knitted together; as head on, he came churning his tail among the boats; and once more flailed them apart; spilling out the irons and lances from the two mates' boats, and dashing in one side of the upper part of their bows, but leaving Ahab's almost without a scar.

While Daggoo and Tashtego were stopping the strained planks; and as the whale swimming out from them, turned, and showed one entire flank as he shot by them again; at that moment a quick cry went up. Lashed round and round to the fish's back; pinioned in the turns upon turns in which, during the past night, the whale had reeled the involutions of the lines around him, the half torn body of the Parsee[2] was seen; his sable raiment frayed to shreds; his distended eyes turned full upon old Ahab.

The harpoon dropped from his hand.

"Befooled, befooled!"—drawing in a long lean breath—"Aye, Parsee! I see thee again.—Aye, and thou goest before; and this, *this* then is the hearse that thou didst promise. But I hold thee to the last letter of thy word. Where is the

2. Fedallah, the leader of a crew of five whale hunters Ahab had secreted in the hold of the *Pequod*, first appears in chapter 50. Called "the Parsee" (i.e., the Persian), Fedallah has ambiguous links to Asian geographies and religions, especially to Manichaeism, which conceives of the world as a perpetual conflict between the equally forceful powers of good and evil.

second hearse?[3] Away, mates, to the ship! those boats are useless now; repair them if ye can in time, and return to me; if not, Ahab is enough to die— Down, men! the first thing that but offers to jump from this boat I stand in, that thing I harpoon. Ye are not other men, but my arms and my legs; and so obey me.—Where's the whale? gone down again?"

But he looked too nigh the boat; for as if bent upon escaping with the corpse he bore, and as if the particular place of the last encounter had been but a stage in his leeward voyage, Moby Dick was now again steadily swimming forward; and had almost passed the ship,—which thus far had been sailing in the contrary direction to him, though for the present her headway had been stopped. He seemed swimming with his utmost velocity, and now only intent upon pursuing his own straight path in the sea.

"Oh! Ahab," cried Starbuck, "not too late is it, even now, the third day; to desist. See! Moby Dick seeks thee not. It is thou, thou, that madly seekest him!"

Setting sail to the rising wind, the lonely boat was swiftly impelled to leeward, by both oars and canvas. And at last when Ahab was sliding by the vessel, so near as plainly to distinguish Starbuck's face as he leaned over the rail, he hailed him to turn the vessel about, and follow him, not too swiftly, at a judicious interval. Glancing upwards, he saw Tashtego, Queequeg, and Daggoo, eagerly mounting to the three mast-heads; while the oarsmen were rocking in the two staved boats which had but just been hoisted to the side and were busily at work in repairing them. One after the other, through the port-holes, as he sped, he also caught flying glimpses of Stubb and Flask, busying themselves on deck among bundles of new irons and lances. As he saw all this; as he heard the hammers in the broken boats; far other hammers seemed driving a nail into his heart. But he rallied. And now marking that the vane or flag was gone from the main-mast-head, he shouted to Tashtego, who had just gained that perch, to descend again for another flag, and a hammer and nails, and so nail it to the mast.

Whether fagged by the three days' running chase, and the resistance to his swimming in the knotted hamper he bore; or whether it was some latent deceitfulness and malice in him: whichever was true, the White Whale's way now began to abate, as it seemed, from the boat so rapidly nearing him once more; though indeed the whale's last start had not been so long a one as before. And still as Ahab glided over the waves the unpitying sharks accompanied him; and so pertinaciously stuck to the boat; and so continually bit at the plying oars, that the blades became jagged and crunched, and left small splinters in the sea, at almost every dip.

"Heed them not! those teeth but give new rowlocks to your oars. Pull on! 'tis the better rest, the shark's jaw than the yielding water."

"But at every bite, sir, the thin blades grow smaller and smaller!"

"They will last long enough! pull on!—But who can tell"—he muttered— "whether these sharks swim to feast on the whale or on Ahab?—But pull on! Aye, all alive, now—we near him. The helm! take the helm; let me

3. Before the chase, Fedallah had prophesied to Ahab: "ere thou couldst die on this voyage, two hearses must verily be seen by thee on the sea; the first not made by mortal hands; and the visible wood of the last one must be grown in America." He also declared that "I shall go before thee thy pilot," and "Hemp only can kill thee" (chapter 117).

pass,"—and so saying, two of the oarsmen helped him forward to the bows of the still flying boat.

At length as the craft was cast to one side, and ran ranging along with the White Whale's flank, he seemed strangely oblivious of its advance—as the whale sometimes will—and Ahab was fairly within the smoky mountain mist, which, thrown off from the whale's spout, curled round his great, Monadnock[4] hump; he was even thus close to him; when, with body arched back, and both arms lengthwise high-lifted to the poise, he darted his fierce iron, and his far fiercer curse into the hated whale. As both steel and curse sank to the socket, as if sucked into a morass, Moby Dick sideways writhed; spasmodically rolled his nigh flank against the bow, and, without staving a hole in it, so suddenly canted the boat over, that had it not been for the elevated part of the gunwale to which he then clung, Ahab would once more have been tossed into the sea. As it was, three of the oarsmen—who foreknew not the precise instant of the dart, and were therefore unprepared for its effects—these were flung out; but so fell, that, in an instant two of them clutched the gunwale again, and rising to its level on a combing wave, hurled themselves bodily inboard again; the third man helplessly dropping astern, but still afloat and swimming.

Almost simultaneously, with a mighty volition of ungraduated, instantaneous swiftness, the White Whale darted through the weltering sea. But when Ahab cried out to the steersman to take new turns with the line, and hold it so; and commanded the crew to turn round on their seats, and tow the boat up to the mark; the moment the treacherous line felt that double strain and tug, it snapped in the empty air!

"What breaks in me? Some sinew cracks!—'tis whole again; oars! oars! Burst in upon him!"

Hearing the tremendous rush of the sea-crashing boat, the whale wheeled round to present his blank forehead at bay; but in that evolution, catching sight of the nearing black hull of the ship; seemingly seeing in it the source of all his persecutions; bethinking it—it may be—a larger and nobler foe; of a sudden, he bore down upon its advancing prow, smiting his jaws amid fiery showers of foam.

Ahab staggered; his hand smote his forehead. "I grow blind; hands! stretch out before me that I may yet grope my way. Is't night?"

"The whale! The ship!" cried the cringing oarsmen.

"Oars! oars! Slope downwards to thy depths, O sea, that ere it be for ever too late, Ahab may slide this last, last time upon his mark! I see: the ship! the ship! Dash on, my men! Will ye not save my ship?"

But as the oarsmen violently forced their boat through the sledge-hammering seas, the before whale-smitten bow-ends of two planks burst through, and in an instant almost, the temporarily disabled boat lay nearly level with the waves; its half-wading, splashing crew, trying hard to stop the gap and bale out the pouring water.

Meantime, for that one beholding instant, Tashtego's mast-head hammer remained suspended in his hand; and the red flag, half-wrapping him as with a plaid, then streamed itself straight out from him, as his own forward-

4. Mountain in southern New Hampshire.

flowing heart; while Starbuck and Stubb, standing upon the bowsprit beneath, caught sight of the down-coming monster just as soon as he.

"The whale, the whale! Up helm, up helm! Oh, all ye sweet powers of air, now hug me close! Let not Starbuck die, if die he must, in a woman's fainting fit. Up helm, I say—ye fools, the jaw! the jaw! Is this the end of all my bursting prayers? all my life-long fidelities? Oh, Ahab, Ahab, lo, thy work. Steady! helmsman, steady. Nay, nay! Up helm again! He turns to meet us! Oh, his unappeasable brow drives on towards one, whose duty tells him he cannot depart. My God, stand by me now!"

"Stand not by me, but stand under me, whoever you are that will now help Stubb; for Stubb, too, sticks here. I grin at thee, thou grinning whale! Who ever helped Stubb, or kept Stubb awake, but Stubb's own unwinking eye? And now poor Stubb goes to bed upon a mattrass that is all too soft; would it were stuffed with brushwood! I grin at thee, thou grinning whale! Look ye, sun, moon, and stars! I call ye assassins of as good a fellow as ever spouted up his ghost. For all that, I would yet ring glasses with ye, would ye but hand the cup! Oh, oh! oh, oh! thou grinning whale, but there'll be plenty of gulping soon! Why fly ye not, O Ahab! For me, off shoes and jacket to it; let Stubb die in his drawers! A most mouldy and over salted death, though;—cherries! cherries! cherries! oh, Flask, for one red cherry ere we die!"

"Cherries? I only wish that we were where they grow. Oh, Stubb, I hope my poor mother's drawn my part-pay ere this; if not, few coppers will now come to her, for the voyage is up."

From the ship's bows, nearly all the seamen now hung inactive; hammers, bits of plank, lances, and harpoons, mechanically retained in their hands, just as they had darted from their various employments; all their enchanted eyes intent upon the whale, which from side to side strangely vibrating his predestinating head, sent a broad band of overspreading semi-circular foam before him as he rushed. Retribution, swift vengeance, eternal malice were in his whole aspect, and spite of all that mortal man could do, the solid white buttress of his forehead smote the ship's starboard bow, till men and timbers reeled. Some fell flat upon their faces. Like dislodged trucks,[5] the heads of the harpooneers aloft shook on their bull-like necks. Through the breach, they heard the waters pour, as mountain torrents down a flume.

"The ship! The hearse!—the second hearse!" cried Ahab from the boat; "its wood could only be American!"

Diving beneath the settling ship, the whale ran quivering along its keel; but turning under water, swiftly shot to the surface again, far off the other bow, but within a few yards of Ahab's boat, where, for a time, he lay quiescent.

"I turn my body from the sun. What ho, Tashtego! let me hear thy hammer. Oh! ye three unsurrendered spires of mine; thou uncracked keel; and only god-bullied hull; thou firm deck, and haughty helm, and Pole-pointed prow,—death-glorious ship! must ye then perish, and without me? Am I cut off from the last fond pride of meanest shipwrecked captains? Oh, lonely death on lonely life! Oh, now I feel my topmost greatness lies in my topmost grief. Ho, ho! from all your furthest bounds, pour ye now in, ye bold billows of my whole foregone life, and top this one piled comber of my death! Towards thee I roll, thou all-destroying but unconquering whale; to the last

5. Wooden caps at the top of mastheads.

I grapple with thee; from hell's heart I stab at thee; for hate's sake I spit my last breath at thee. Sink all coffins and all hearses to one common pool! and since neither can be mine, let me then tow to pieces, while still chasing thee, though tied to thee, thou damned whale! *Thus*, I give up the spear!"

The harpoon was darted; the stricken whale flew forward; with igniting velocity the line ran through the groove;—ran foul. Ahab stooped to clear it; he did clear it; but the flying turn caught him round the neck, and voicelessly as Turkish mutes bowstring their victim, he was shot out of the boat, ere the crew knew he was gone. Next instant, the heavy eye-splice in the rope's final end flew out of the stark-empty tub, knocked down an oarsman, and smiting the sea, disappeared in its depths.

For an instant, the tranced boat's crew stood still; then turned. "The ship? Great God, where is the ship?" Soon they through dim, bewildering mediums saw her sidelong fading phantom, as in the gaseous Fata Morgana;[6] only the uppermost masts out of water; while fixed by infatuation, or fidelity, or fate, to their once lofty perches, the pagan harpooneers still maintained their sinking lookouts on the sea. And now, concentric circles seized the lone boat itself, and all its crew, and each floating oar, and every lance-pole, and spinning, animate and inanimate, all round and round in one vortex, carried the smallest chip of the Pequod out of sight.

But as the last whelmings intermixingly poured themselves over the sunken head of the Indian at the mainmast, leaving a few inches of the erect spar yet visible, together with long streaming yards of the flag, which calmly undulated, with ironical coincidings, over the destroying billows they almost touched;—at that instant, a red arm and a hammer hovered backwardly uplifted in the open air, in the act of nailing the flag faster and yet faster to the subsiding spar. A sky-hawk that tauntingly had followed the main-truck downwards from its natural home among the stars, pecking at the flag, and incommoding Tashtego there; this bird now chanced to intercept its broad fluttering wing between the hammer and the wood; and simultaneously feeling that etherial thrill, the submerged savage beneath, in his death-grasp, kept his hammer frozen there; and so the bird of heaven, with archangelic shrieks, and his imperial beak thrust upwards, and his whole captive form folded in the flag of Ahab, went down with his ship, which, like Satan, would not sink to hell till she had dragged a living part of heaven along with her, and helmeted herself with it.

Now small fowls flew screaming over the yet yawning gulf; a sullen white surf beat against its steep sides; then all collapsed, and the great shroud of the sea rolled on as it rolled five thousand years ago.[7]

Epilogue

"And I only am escaped alone to tell thee."

Job.[8]

The drama's done. Why then here does any one step forth?—Because one did survive the wreck.

6. Mirage; from the Italian for Morgan la Fay, sorceress sister of King Arthur in Celtic legends.
7. At the time of Noah's flood.
8. Job 1.14–19, the words with which each of four messengers concludes his terrible news about the loss of Job's animals, servants, and children.

It so chanced, that after the Parsee's disappearance, I was he whom the Fates ordained to take the place of Ahab's bowsman, when that bowsman assumed the vacant post; the same, who, when on the last day the three men were tossed from out the rocking boat, was dropped astern. So, floating on the margin of the ensuing scene, and in full sight of it, when the half-spent suction of the sunk ship reached me, I was then, but slowly, drawn towards the closing vortex. When I reached it, it had subsided to a creamy pool. Round and round, then, and ever contracting towards the button-like black bubble at the axis of that slowly wheeling circle, like another Ixion[9] *I did revolve. Till, gaining that vital centre, the black bubble upward burst; and now, liberated by reason of its cunning spring, and, owing to its great buoyancy, rising with great force, the coffin life-buoy shot lengthwise from the sea, fell over, and floated by my side. Buoyed up by that coffin, for almost one whole day and night, I floated on a soft and dirge-like main. The unharming sharks, they glided by as if with padlocks on their mouths; the savage sea-hawks sailed with sheathed beaks. On the second day, a sail drew near, nearer, and picked me up at last. It was the devious-cruising Rachel,*[1] *that in her retracing search after her missing children, only found another orphan.*

FINIS

1851

Bartleby, the Scrivener[1]

A Story of Wall-Street

I am a rather elderly man. The nature of my avocations for the last thirty years has brought me into more than ordinary contact with what would seem an interesting and somewhat singular set of men, of whom as yet nothing that I know of has ever been written:—I mean the law-copyists or scriveners. I have known very many of them, professionally and privately, and if I pleased, could relate divers histories, at which good-natured gentlemen might smile, and sentimental souls might weep. But I waive the biographies of all other scriveners for a few passages in the life of Bartleby, who was a scrivener the strangest I ever saw or heard of. While of other law-copyists I might write the complete life, of Bartleby nothing of that sort can be done. I believe that no materials exist for a full and satisfactory biography of this man. It is an irreparable loss to literature. Bartleby was one of those beings of whom nothing is ascertainable, except from the original sources, and in his case those are very small. What my own astonished eyes saw of Bartleby, *that* is all I know of him, except, indeed, one vague report which will appear in the sequel.

9. In Greek mythology, Zeus punished Ixion for attempting to seduce his wife; he chained Ixion to a fiery revolving wheel in the underworld.

1. In chapter 128, Ahab refuses to help the captain of the *Rachel*, who is searching for his son lost at sea.

1. The text of *Bartleby, the Scrivener* is from the first printing in the November and December 1853 issues of *Putnam's Monthly Magazine*. "Scrivener": copyist or writer; in this story employed to make multiple copies of legal documents with pen and ink.

Ere introducing the scrivener, as he first appeared to me, it is fit I make some mention of myself, my *employées*, my business, my chambers, and general surroundings; because some such description is indispensable to an adequate understanding of the chief character about to be presented.

Imprimis:[2] I am a man who, from his youth upwards, has been filled with a profound conviction that the easiest way of life is the best. Hence, though I belong to a profession proverbially energetic and nervous, even to turbulence, at times, yet nothing of that sort have I ever suffered to invade my peace. I am one of those unambitious lawyers who never addresses a jury, or in any way draws down public applause; but in the cool tranquillity of a snug retreat, do a snug business among rich men's bonds and mortgages and title-deeds. All who know me, consider me an eminently *safe* man. The late John Jacob Astor,[3] a personage little given to poetic enthusiasm, had no hesitation in pronouncing my first grand point to be prudence; my next, method. I do not speak it in vanity, but simply record the fact, that I was not unemployed in my profession by the late John Jacob Astor; a name which, I admit, I love to repeat, for it hath a rounded and orbicular sound to it, and rings like unto bullion. I will freely add, that I was not insensible to the late John Jacob Astor's good opinion.

Some time prior to the period at which this little history begins, my avocations had been largely increased. The good old office, now extinct in the State of New-York, of a Master in Chancery, had been conferred upon me. It was not a very arduous office, but very pleasantly remunerative. I seldom lose my temper; much more seldom indulge in dangerous indignation at wrongs and outrages; but I must be permitted to be rash here and declare, that I consider the sudden and violent abrogation of the office of Master in Chancery, by the new Constitution,[4] as a——premature act; inasmuch as I had counted upon a life-lease of the profits, whereas I only received those of a few short years. But this is by the way.

My chambers were up stairs at No.—Wall-street. At one end they looked upon the white wall of the interior of a spacious sky-light shaft, penetrating the building from top to bottom. This view might have been considered rather tame than otherwise, deficient in what landscape painters call "life." But if so, the view from the other end of my chambers offered, at least, a contrast, if nothing more. In that direction my windows commanded an unobstructed view of a lofty brick wall, black by age and everlasting shade; which wall required no spy-glass to bring out its lurking beauties, but for the benefit of all near-sighted spectators, was pushed up to within ten feet of my window panes. Owing to the great height of the surrounding buildings, and my chambers being on the second floor, the interval between this wall and mine not a little resembled a huge square cistern.

At the period just preceding the advent of Bartleby, I had two persons as copyists in my employment, and a promising lad as an office-boy. First, Turkey; second, Nippers; third, Ginger Nut. These may seem names, the like of which are not usually found in the Directory. In truth they were nicknames, mutually conferred upon each other by my three clerks, and were

2. In the first place (Latin).
3. Astor (1763–1848), a New Yorker, had made one of the largest fortunes of his era, first in fur trading and then in real estate and finance.
4. New York had adopted a "new Constitution" in 1846. *Chancery*: cases involving equity law that do not require a jury.

Wall Street, viewed from the corner of Broad Street, New York City, c. 1846.

deemed expressive of their respective persons or characters. Turkey was a short, pursy[5] Englishman of about my own age, that is, somewhere not far from sixty. In the morning, one might say, his face was of a fine florid hue, but after twelve o'clock, meridian—his dinner hour—it blazed like a grate full of Christmas coals; and continued blazing—but, as it were, with a gradual wane—till 6 o'clock, P.M. or thereabouts, after which I saw no more of the proprietor of the face, which gaining its meridian with the sun, seemed to set with it, to rise, culminate, and decline the following day, with the like regularity and undiminished glory. There are many singular coincidences I have known in the course of my life, not the least among which was the fact, that exactly when Turkey displayed his fullest beams from his red and radiant countenance, just then, too, at that critical moment, began the daily period when I considered his business capacities as seriously disturbed for the remainder of the twenty-four hours. Not that he was absolutely idle, or averse to business then; far from it. The difficulty was, he was apt to be altogether too energetic. There was a strange, inflamed, flurried, flighty recklessness of activity about him. He would be incautious in dipping his pen into his inkstand. All his blots upon my documents, were dropped there after twelve o'clock, meridian. Indeed, not only would he be reckless and sadly given to making blots in the afternoon, but some days he went further, and was rather noisy. At such times, too, his face flamed with augmented blazonry, as if cannel coal had been heaped on anthracite.[6] He made an unpleasant racket with his chair; spilled his sand-box;[7] in mending his pens, impatiently split them all to pieces, and threw them on the floor in

5. Shortwinded from obesity.
6. The combination of "cannal coal," which burns quickly, and "anthracite," which burns slowly, produces a high, bright flame.
7. Sand for blotting ink.

a sudden passion; stood up and leaned over his table, boxing his papers about in a most indecorous manner, very sad to behold in an elderly man like him. Nevertheless, as he was in many ways a most valuable person to me, and all the time before twelve o'clock, meridian, was the quickest, steadiest creature too, accomplishing a great deal of work in a style not easy to be matched—for these reasons, I was willing to overlook his eccentricities, though indeed, occasionally, I remonstrated with him. I did this very gently, however, because, though the civilest, nay, the blandest and most reverential of men in the morning, yet in the afternoon he was disposed, upon provocation, to be slightly rash with his tongue, in fact, insolent. Now, valuing his morning services as I did, and resolved not to lose them; yet, at the same time made uncomfortable by his inflamed ways after twelve o'clock; and being a man of peace, unwilling by my admonitions to call forth unseemly retorts from him; I took upon me, one Saturday noon (he was always worse on Saturdays), to hint to him, very kindly, that perhaps now that he was growing old, it might be well to abridge his labors; in short, he need not come to my chambers after twelve o'clock, but, dinner over, had best go home to his lodgings and rest himself till tea-time. But no; he insisted upon his afternoon devotions. His countenance became intolerably fervid, as he oratorically assured me—gesticulating with a long ruler at the other end of the room—that if his services in the morning were useful, how indispensable, then, in the afternoon?

"With submission, sir," said Turkey on this occasion, "I consider myself your right-hand man. In the morning I but marshal and deploy my columns; but in the afternoon I put myself at their head, and gallantly charge the foe, thus!"—and he made a violent thrust with the ruler.

"But the blots, Turkey," intimated I.

"True,—but, with submission, sir, behold these hairs! I am getting old. Surely, sir, a blot or two of a warm afternoon is not to be severely urged against gray hairs. Old age—even if it blot the page—is honorable. With submission, sir, we *both* are getting old."

This appeal to my fellow-feeling was hardly to be resisted. At all events, I saw that go he would not. So I made up my mind to let him stay, resolving, nevertheless, to see to it, that during the afternoon he had to do with my less important papers.

Nippers, the second on my list, was a whiskered, sallow, and, upon the whole, rather piratical-looking young man of about five and twenty. I always deemed him the victim of two evil powers—ambition and indigestion. The ambition was evinced by a certain impatience of the duties of a mere copyist, an unwarrantable usurpation of strictly professional affairs, such as the original drawing up of legal documents. The indigestion seemed betokened in an occasional nervous testiness and grinning irritability, causing the teeth to audibly grind together over mistakes committed in copying; unnecessary maledictions, hissed, rather than spoken, in the heat of business; and especially by a continual discontent with the height of the table where he worked. Though of a very ingenious mechanical turn, Nippers could never get this table to suit him. He put chips under it, blocks of various sorts, bits of pasteboard, and at last went so far as to attempt an exquisite adjustment by final pieces of folded blotting paper. But no invention would answer. If, for the sake of easing his back, he brought the table lid at a sharp angle well up towards his chin, and wrote there like a man using the steep roof of a Dutch house for his desk:—then he declared that it stopped the circulation in his arms. If now he lowered the table to his waistbands, and stooped over it in writing, then there was a sore aching in his back. In short, the truth of the matter was, Nippers knew not what he wanted. Or, if he wanted any thing, it was to be rid of a scrivener's table altogether. Among the manifestations of his diseased ambition was a fondness he had for receiving visits from certain ambiguous-looking fellows in seedy coats, whom he called his clients. Indeed I was aware that not only was he, at times, considerable of a ward-politician, but he occasionally did a little business at the Justices' courts, and was not unknown on the steps of the Tombs.[8] I have good reason to believe, however, that one individual who called upon him at my chambers, and who, with a grand air, he insisted was his client, was no other than a dun, and the alleged title-deed, a bill. But with all his failings, and the annoyances he caused me, Nippers, like his compatriot Turkey, was a very useful man to me; wrote a neat, swift hand; and, when he chose, was not deficient in a gentlemanly sort of deportment. Added to this, he always dressed in a gentlemanly sort of way; and so, incidentally, reflected credit upon my chambers. Whereas with respect to Turkey, I had much ado to keep him from being a reproach to me. His clothes were apt to look oily and smell of eating-houses. He wore his pantaloons very loose and baggy in summer. His coats were execrable; his hat not to be handled. But while the hat was a thing of indifference to me, inasmuch as his natural civility and deference, as a dependent Englishman, always led him to doff it the moment he entered the room, yet his coat was another matter. Concerning his coats, I reasoned with him; but with no effect. The truth was, I suppose, that a man with so small an income, could not afford to sport such a lustrous face and a lustrous coat at one and the same time. As Nippers once observed, Turkey's money went chiefly for red ink. One winter day I presented Turkey with a highly-respectable looking coat of my own, a padded gray coat, of a most comfortable warmth, and which buttoned straight up from the knee to the neck. I thought Turkey would appreciate the favor, and abate his rashness and obstreperousness of afternoons. But no. I verily believe that buttoning himself up in so downy and blanket-like a coat had a pernicious effect upon him; upon the same principle that too much oats are bad for horses. In fact, precisely as a rash, restive horse is said to feel his oats, so Turkey felt his coat. It made him insolent. He was a man whom prosperity harmed.

Though concerning the self-indulgent habits of Turkey I had my own private surmises, yet touching Nippers I was well persuaded that whatever might be his faults in other respects, he was, at least, a temperate young man. But indeed, nature herself seemed to have been his vintner, and at his birth charged him so thoroughly with an irritable, brandy-like disposition, that all subsequent potations were needless. When I consider how, amid the stillness of my chambers, Nippers would sometimes impatiently rise from his seat, and stooping over his table, spread his arms wide apart, seize the whole desk, and move it, and jerk it, with a grim, grinding motion on the floor, as if the table were a perverse voluntary agent, intent on thwarting and

8. The New York City prison, built in 1839 in the spirit of the Egyptian revival architecture of the time.

vexing him; I plainly perceive that for Nippers, brandy and water were altogether superfluous.

It was fortunate for me that, owing to its peculiar cause—indigestion—the irritability and consequent nervousness of Nippers, were mainly observable in the morning, while in the afternoon he was comparatively mild. So that Turkey's paroxysms only coming on about twelve o'clock, I never had to do with their eccentricities at one time. Their fits relieved each other like guards. When Nippers' was on, Turkey's was off; and *vice versa*. This was a good natural arrangement under the circumstances.

Ginger Nut, the third on my list, was a lad some twelve years old. His father was a carman,[9] ambitious of seeing his son on the bench instead of a cart, before he died. So he sent him to my office as student at law, errand boy, and cleaner and sweeper, at the rate of one dollar a week. He had a little desk to himself, but he did not use it much. Upon inspection, the drawer exhibited a great array of the shells of various sorts of nuts. Indeed, to this quick-witted youth the whole noble science of the law was contained in a nut-shell. Not the least among the employments of Ginger Nut, as well as one which he discharged with the most alacrity, was his duty as cake and apple purveyor for Turkey and Nippers. Copying law papers being proverbially a dry, husky sort of business, my two scriveners were fain to moisten their mouths very often with Spitzenbergs[1] to be had at the numerous stalls nigh the Custom House and Post Office. Also, they sent Ginger Nut very frequently for that peculiar cake—small, flat, round, and very spicy—after which he had been named by them. Of a cold morning when business was but dull, Turkey would gobble up scores of these cakes, as if they were mere wafers—indeed they sell them at the rate of six or eight for a penny—the scrape of his pen blending with the crunching of the crisp particles in his mouth. Of all the fiery afternoon blunders and flurried rashnesses of Turkey, was his once moistening a ginger-cake between his lips, and clapping it on to a mortgage for a seal.[2] I came within an ace of dismissing him then. But he mollified me by making an oriental bow, and saying—"With submission, sir, it was generous of me to find you in stationery on my own account."

Now my original business—that of a conveyancer and title hunter,[3] and drawer-up of recondite documents of all sorts—was considerably increased by receiving the master's office. There was now great work for scriveners. Not only must I push the clerks already with me, but I must have additional help. In answer to my advertisement, a motionless young man one morning, stood upon my office threshold, the door being open, for it was summer. I can see that figure now—pallidly neat, pitiably respectable, incurably forlorn! It was Bartleby.

After a few words touching his qualifications, I engaged him, glad to have among my corps of copyists a man of so singularly sedate an aspect, which I thought might operate beneficially upon the flighty temper of Turkey, and the fiery one of Nippers.

9. Driver, teamster.
1. Red-and-yellow New York apples.
2. The narrator is playing on the resemblance between thin cookies and wax wafers used for sealing documents.
3. Someone who checks records to be sure there are no encumbrances on the title of property to be transferred. "Conveyancer": someone who draws up deeds for transferring title to property.

I should have stated before that ground glass folding-doors divided my premises into two parts, one of which was occupied by my scriveners, the other by myself. According to my humor I threw open these doors, or closed them. I resolved to assign Bartleby a corner by the folding-doors, but on my side of them, so as to have this quiet man within easy call, in case any trifling thing was to be done. I placed his desk close up to a small side-window in that part of the room, a window which originally had afforded a lateral view of certain grimy back-yards and bricks, but which, owing to subsequent erections, commanded at present no view at all, though it gave some light. Within three feet of the panes was a wall, and the light came down from far above, between two lofty buildings, as from a very small opening in a dome. Still further to a satisfactory arrangement, I procured a high green folding screen, which might entirely isolate Bartleby from my sight, though not remove him from my voice. And thus, in a manner, privacy and society were conjoined.

At first Bartleby did an extraordinary quantity of writing. As if long famishing for something to copy, he seemed to gorge himself on my documents. There was no pause for digestion. He ran a day and night line, copying by sun-light and by candle-light. I should have been quite delighted with his application, had he been cheerfully industrious. But he wrote on silently, palely, mechanically.

It is, of course, an indispensable part of a scrivener's business to verify the accuracy of his copy, word by word. Where there are two or more scriveners in an office, they assist each other in this examination, one reading from the copy, the other holding the original. It is a very dull, wearisome, and lethargic affair. I can readily imagine that to some sanguine temperaments it would be altogether intolerable. For example, I cannot credit that the mettlesome poet Byron would have contentedly sat down with Bartleby to examine a law document of, say five hundred pages, closely written in a crimpy hand.

Now and then, in the haste of business, it had been my habit to assist in comparing some brief document myself, calling Turkey or Nippers for this purpose. One object I had in placing Bartleby so handy to me behind the screen, was to avail myself of his services on such trivial occasions. It was on the third day, I think, of his being with me, and before any necessity had arisen for having his own writing examined, that, being much hurried to complete a small affair I had in hand, I abruptly called to Bartleby. In my haste and natural expectancy of instant compliance, I sat with my head bent over the original on my desk, and my right hand sideways, and somewhat nervously extended with the copy, so that immediately upon emerging from his retreat, Bartleby might snatch it and proceed to business without the least delay.

In this very attitude did I sit when I called to him, rapidly stating what it was I wanted him to do—namely, to examine a small paper with me. Imagine my surprise, nay, my consternation, when without moving from his privacy, Bartleby in a singularly mild, firm voice, replied, "I would prefer not to."

I sat awhile in perfect silence, rallying my stunned faculties. Immediately it occurred to me that my ears had deceived me, or Bartleby had entirely misunderstood my meaning. I repeated my request in the clearest tone I could assume. But in quite as clear a one came the previous reply, "I would prefer not to."

"Prefer not to," echoed I, rising in high excitement, and crossing the room with a stride. "What do you mean? Are you moon-struck? I want you to help me compare this sheet here—take it," and I thrust it towards him.

"I would prefer not to," said he.

I looked at him steadfastly. His face was leanly composed; his gray eye dimly calm. Not a wrinkle of agitation rippled him. Had there been the least uneasiness, anger, impatience or impertinence in his manner; in other words, had there been any thing ordinarily human about him, doubtless I should have violently dismissed him from the premises. But as it was, I should have as soon thought of turning my pale plaster-of-paris bust of Cicero[4] out of doors. I stood gazing at him awhile, as he went on with his own writing, and then reseated myself at my desk. This is very strange, thought I. What had one best do? But my business hurried me. I concluded to forget the matter for the present, reserving it for my future leisure. So calling Nippers from the other room, the paper was speedily examined.

A few days after this, Bartleby concluded four lengthy documents, being quadruplicates of a week's testimony taken before me in my High Court of Chancery. It became necessary to examine them. It was an important suit, and great accuracy was imperative. Having all things arranged I called Turkey, Nippers and Ginger Nut from the next room, meaning to place the four copies in the hands of my four clerks, while I should read from the original. Accordingly Turkey, Nippers and Ginger Nut had taken their seats in a row, each with his document in hand, when I called to Bartleby to join this interesting group.

"Bartleby! quick, I am waiting."

I heard a slow scrape of his chair legs on the uncarpeted floor, and soon he appeared standing at the entrance of his hermitage.

"What is wanted?" said he mildly.

"The copies, the copies," said I hurriedly. "We are going to examine them. There"—and I held towards him the fourth quadruplicate.

"I would prefer not to," he said, and gently disappeared behind the screen.

For a few moments I was turned into a pillar of salt,[5] standing at the head of my seated column of clerks. Recovering myself, I advanced towards the screen, and demanded the reason for such extraordinary conduct.

"*Why* do you refuse?"

"I would prefer not to."

With any other man I should have flown outright into a dreadful passion, scorned all further words, and thrust him ignominiously from my presence. But there was something about Bartleby that not only strangely disarmed me, but in a wonderful manner touched and disconcerted me. I began to reason with him.

"These are your own copies we are about to examine. It is labor saving to you, because one examination will answer for your four papers. It is common usage. Every copyist is bound to help examine his copy. Is it not so? Will you not speak? Answer!"

"I prefer not to," he replied in a flute-like tone. It seemed to me that while I had been addressing him, he carefully revolved every statement that I made;

4. Roman orator and statesman (106–42 B.C.E.).
5. The punishment of Lot's disobedient wife (Genesis 19.26).

fully comprehended the meaning; could not gainsay the irresistible conclusion; but, at the same time, some paramount consideration prevailed with him to reply as he did.

"You are decided, then, not to comply with my request—a request made according to common usage and common sense?"

He briefly gave me to understand that on that point my judgment was sound. Yes: his decision was irreversible.

It is not seldom the case that when a man is browbeaten in some unprecedented and violently unreasonable way, he begins to stagger in his own plainest faith. He begins, as it were, vaguely to surmise that, wonderful as it may be, all the justice and all the reason is on the other side. Accordingly, if any disinterested persons are present, he turns to them for some reinforcement for his own faltering mind.

"Turkey," said I, "what do you think of this? Am I not right?"

"With submission, sir," said Turkey, with his blandest tone, "I think that you are."

"Nippers," said I, "what do *you* think of it?"

"I think I should kick him out of the office."

(The reader of nice perceptions will here perceive that, it being morning, Turkey's answer is couched in polite and tranquil terms, but Nippers replies in ill-tempered ones. Or, to repeat a previous sentence, Nippers's ugly mood was on duty, and Turkey's off.)

"Ginger Nut," said I, willing to enlist the smallest suffrage in my behalf, "what do *you* think of it?"

"I think, sir, he's a little *luny*," replied Ginger Nut, with a grin.

"You hear what they say," said I, turning towards the screen, "come forth and do your duty."

But he vouchsafed no reply. I pondered a moment in sore perplexity. But once more business hurried me. I determined again to postpone the consideration of this dilemma to my future leisure. With a little trouble we made out to examine the papers without Bartleby, though at every page or two, Turkey deferentially dropped his opinion that this proceeding was quite out of the common; while Nippers, twitching in his chair with a dyspeptic nervousness, ground out between his set teeth occasional hissing maledictions against the stubborn oaf behind the screen. And for his (Nippers's) part, this was the first and the last time he would do another man's business without pay.

Meanwhile Bartleby sat in his hermitage, oblivious to every thing but his own peculiar business there.

Some days passed, the scrivener being employed upon another lengthy work. His late remarkable conduct led me to regard his ways narrowly. I observed that he never went to dinner; indeed that he never went any where. As yet I had never of my personal knowledge known him to be outside of my office. He was a perpetual sentry in the corner. At about eleven o'clock though, in the morning, I noticed that Ginger Nut would advance toward the opening in Bartleby's screen, as if silently beckoned thither by a gesture invisible to me where I sat. The boy would then leave the office jingling a few pence, and reappear with a handful of ginger-nuts which he delivered in the hermitage, receiving two of the cakes for his trouble.

He lives, then, on ginger-nuts, thought I; never eats a dinner, properly speaking; he must be a vegetarian then; but no; he never eats even vegetables, he eats nothing but ginger-nuts. My mind then ran on in reveries concerning the probable effects upon the human constitution of living entirely on ginger-nuts. Ginger-nuts are so called because they contain ginger as one of their peculiar constituents, and the final flavoring one. Now what was ginger? A hot, spicy thing. Was Bartleby hot and spicy? Not at all. Ginger, then, had no effect upon Bartleby. Probably he preferred it should have none.

Nothing so aggravates an earnest person as a passive resistance. If the individual so resisted be of a not inhumane temper, and the resisting one perfectly harmless in his passivity; then, in the better moods of the former, he will endeavor charitably to construe to his imagination what proves impossible to be solved by his judgment. Even so, for the most part, I regarded Bartleby and his ways. Poor fellow! thought I, he means no mischief; it is plain he intends no insolence; his aspect sufficiently evinces that his eccentricities are involuntary. He is useful to me. I can get along with him. If I turn him away, the chances are he will fall in with some less indulgent employer, and then he will be rudely treated, and perhaps driven forth miserably to starve. Yes. Here I can cheaply purchase a delicious self-approval. To befriend Bartleby; to humor him in his strange wilfulness, will cost me little or nothing, while I lay up in my soul what will eventually prove a sweet morsel for my conscience. But this mood was not invariable with me. The passiveness of Bartleby sometimes irritated me. I felt strangely goaded on to encounter him in new opposition, to elicit some angry spark from him answerable to my own. But indeed I might as well have essayed to strike fire with my knuckles against a bit of Windsor soap.[6] But one afternoon the evil impulse in me mastered me, and the following little scene ensued:

"Bartleby," said I, "when those papers are all copied, I will compare them with you."

"I would prefer not to."

"How? Surely you do not mean to persist in that mulish vagary?"

No answer.

I threw open the folding-doors near by, and turning upon Turkey and Nippers, exclaimed in an excited manner—

"He says, a second time, he won't examine his papers. What do you think of it, Turkey?"

It was afternoon, be it remembered. Turkey sat glowing like a brass boiler, his bald head steaming, his hands reeling among his blotted papers.

"Think of it?" roared Turkey; "I think I'll just step behind his screen, and black his eyes for him!"

So saying, Turkey rose to his feet and threw his arms into a pugilistic position. He was hurrying away to make good his promise, when I detained him, alarmed at the effect of incautiously rousing Turkey's combativeness after dinner.

"Sit down, Turkey," said I, "and hear what Nippers has to say. What do you think of it, Nippers? Would I not be justified in immediately dismissing Bartleby?"

"Excuse me, that is for you to decide, sir. I think his conduct quite unusual, and indeed unjust, as regards Turkey and myself. But it may only be a passing whim."

6. Brown hand soap.

"Ah," exclaimed I, "you have strangely changed your mind then—you speak very gently of him now."

"All beer," cried Turkey; "gentleness is effects of beer—Nippers and I dined together to-day. You see how gentle *I* am, sir. Shall I go and black his eyes?"

"You refer to Bartleby, I suppose. No, not to-day, Turkey," I replied; "pray, put up your fists."

I closed the doors, and again advanced towards Bartleby. I felt additional incentives tempting me to my fate. I burned to be rebelled against again. I remembered that Bartleby never left the office.

"Bartleby," said I, "Ginger Nut is away; just step round to the Post Office, won't you? (it was but a three minutes' walk,) and see if there is any thing for me."

"I would prefer not to."

"You *will* not?"

"I *prefer* not."

I staggered to my desk, and sat there in a deep study. My blind inveteracy returned. Was there any other thing in which I could procure myself to be ignominiously repulsed by this lean, penniless wight?—my hired clerk? What added thing is there, perfectly reasonable, that he will be sure to refuse to do?

"Bartleby!"

No answer.

"Bartleby," in a louder tone.

No answer.

"Bartleby," I roared.

Like a very ghost, agreeably to the laws of magical invocation, at the third summons, he appeared at the entrance of his hermitage.

"Go to the next room, and tell Nippers to come to me."

"I prefer not to," he respectfully and slowly said, and mildly disappeared.

"Very good, Bartleby," said I, in a quiet sort of serenely severe self-possessed tone, intimating the unalterable purpose of some terrible retribution very close at hand. At the moment I half intended something of the kind. But upon the whole, as it was drawing towards my dinner-hour, I thought it best to put on my hat and walk home for the day, suffering much from perplexity and distress of mind.

Shall I acknowledge it? The conclusion of this whole business was, that it soon became a fixed fact of my chambers, that a pale young scrivener, by the name of Bartleby, had a desk there; that he copied for me at the usual rate of four cents a folio (one hundred words); but he was permanently exempt from examining the work done by him, that duty being transferred to Turkey and Nippers, out of compliment doubtless to their superior acuteness; moreover, said Bartleby was never on any account to be dispatched on the most trivial errand of any sort; and that even if entreated to take upon him such a matter, it was generally understood that he would prefer not to—in other words, that he would refuse point-blank.

As days passed on, I became considerably reconciled to Bartleby. His steadiness, his freedom from all dissipation, his incessant industry (except when he chose to throw himself into a standing revery behind his screen), his great stillness, his unalterableness of demeanor under all circumstances, made him a valuable acquisition. One prime thing was this,—*he was always there*;—first in the morning, continually through the day, and the last at night. I had a singular confidence in his honesty. I felt my most precious papers perfectly safe in his hands. Sometimes to be sure I could not, for the very soul of me, avoid falling into sudden spasmodic passions with him. For it was exceeding difficult to bear in mind all the time those strange peculiarities, privileges, and unheard of exemptions, forming the tacit stipulations on Bartleby's part under which he remained in my office. Now and then, in the eagerness of dispatching pressing business, I would inadvertently summon Bartleby, in a short, rapid tone, to put his finger, say, on the incipient tie of a bit of red tape with which I was about compressing some papers. Of course, from behind the screen the usual answer, "I prefer not to," was sure to come; and then, how could a human creature with common infirmities of our nature, refrain from bitterly exclaiming upon such perverseness—such unreasonableness. However, every added repulse of this sort which I received only tended to lessen the probability of my repeating the inadvertence.

Here it must be said, that according to the customs of most legal gentlemen occupying chambers in densely-populated law buildings, there were several keys to my door. One was kept by a woman residing in the attic, which person weekly scrubbed and daily swept and dusted my apartments. Another was kept by Turkey for convenience sake. The third I sometimes carried in my own pocket. The fourth I knew not who had.

Now, one Sunday morning I happened to go to Trinity Church, to hear a celebrated preacher, and finding myself rather early on the ground, I thought I would walk round to my chambers for a while. Luckily I had my key with me; but upon applying it to the lock, I found it resisted by something inserted from the inside. Quite surprised, I called out; when to my consternation a key was turned from within; and thrusting his lean visage at me, and holding the door ajar, the apparition of Bartleby appeared, in his shirt sleeves, and otherwise in a strangely tattered dishabille, saying quietly that he was sorry, but he was deeply engaged just then, and—preferred not admitting me at present. In a brief word or two, he moreover added, that perhaps I had better walk round the block two or three times, and by that time he would probably have concluded his affairs.

Now, the utterly unsurmised appearance of Bartleby, tenanting my law-chambers of a Sunday morning, with his cadaverously gentlemanly *nonchalance*, yet withal firm and self-possessed, had such a strange effect upon me, that incontinently I slunk away from my own door, and did as desired. But not without sundry twinges of impotent rebellion against the mild effrontery of this unaccountable scrivener. Indeed, it was his wonderful mildness chiefly, which not only disarmed me, but unmanned me, as it were. For I consider that one, for the time, is a sort of unmanned when he tranquilly permits his hired clerk to dictate to him, and order him away from his own premises. Furthermore, I was full of uneasiness as to what Bartleby could possibly be doing in my office in his shirt sleeves, and in an otherwise dismantled condition of a Sunday morning. Was any thing amiss going on? Nay, that was out of the question. It was not to be thought of for a moment that Bartleby was an immoral person. But what could he be doing there?—copying? Nay again, whatever might be his eccentricities, Bartleby was an eminently decorous person. He would be the last man to sit down to his desk in any state approaching to nudity. Besides, it was Sunday; and there was something about Bartleby that forbade the supposition that he would by any secular occupation violate the proprieties of the day.

Nevertheless, my mind was not pacified; and full of a restless curiosity, at last I returned to the door. Without hindrance I inserted my key, opened it, and entered. Bartleby was not to be seen. I looked round anxiously, peeped behind his screen; but it was very plain that he was gone. Upon more closely examining the place, I surmised that for an indefinite period Bartleby must have ate, dressed, and slept in my office, and that too without plate, mirror, or bed. The cushioned seat of a ricketty old sofa in one corner bore the faint impress of a lean, reclining form. Rolled away under his desk, I found a blanket; under the empty grate, a blacking box and brush; on a chair, a tin basin, with soap and a ragged towel; in a newspaper a few crumbs of ginger-nuts and a morsel of cheese. Yes, thought I, it is evident enough that Bartleby has been making his home here, keeping bachelor's hall all by himself. Immediately then the thought came sweeping across me, What miserable friendlessness and loneliness are here revealed! His poverty is great; but his solitude, how horrible! Think of it. Of a Sunday, Wall-street is deserted as Petra;[7] and every night of every day it is an emptiness. This building too, which of week-days hums with industry and life, at nightfall echoes with sheer vacancy, and all through Sunday is forlorn. And here Bartleby makes his home; sole spectator of a solitude which he has seen all populous—a sort of innocent and transformed Marius[8] brooding among the ruins of Carthage!

For the first time in my life a feeling of overpowering stinging melancholy seized me. Before, I had never experienced aught but a not-unpleasing sadness. The bond of a common humanity now drew me irresistibly to gloom. A fraternal melancholy! For both I and Bartleby were sons of Adam. I remembered the bright silks and sparkling faces I had seen that day, in gala trim, swan-like sailing down the Mississippi of Broadway; and I contrasted them with the pallid copyist, and thought to myself, Ah, happiness courts the light, so we deem the world is gay; but misery hides aloof, so we deem that misery there is none. These sad fancyings—chimeras, doubtless, of a sick and silly brain—led on to other and more special thoughts, concerning the eccentricities of Bartleby. Presentiments of strange discoveries hovered round me. The scrivener's pale form appeared to me laid out, among uncaring strangers, in its shivering winding sheet.

Suddenly I was attracted by Bartleby's closed desk, the key in open sight left in the lock.

I mean no mischief, seek the gratification of no heartless curiosity, thought I; besides, the desk is mine, and its contents too, so I will make bold to look within. Every thing was methodically arranged, the papers smoothly placed. The pigeon holes were deep, and removing the files of documents, I groped into their recesses. Presently I felt something there, and dragged it out. It was an old bandanna handkerchief, heavy and knotted. I opened it, and saw it was a saving's bank.

7. Ancient city whose ruins are in Jordan, on a slope of Mount Hor.

8. Gaius Marius (157–86 B.C.E.), Roman general who returned to power after exile.

I now recalled all the quiet mysteries which I had noted in the man. I remembered that he never spoke but to answer; that though at intervals he had considerable time to himself, yet I had never seen him reading—no, not even a newspaper; that for long periods he would stand looking out, at his pale window behind the screen, upon the dead brick wall; I was quite sure he never visited any refectory or eating house; while his pale face clearly indicated that he never drank beer like Turkey, or tea and coffee even, like other men; that he never went any where in particular that I could learn; never went out for a walk, unless indeed that was the case at present; that he had declined telling who he was, or whence he came, or whether he had any relatives in the world; that though so thin and pale, he never complained of ill health. And more than all, I remembered a certain unconscious air of pallid—how shall I call it?—of pallid haughtiness, say, or rather an austere reserve about him, which had positively awed me into my tame compliance with his eccentricities, when I had feared to ask him to do the slightest incidental thing for me, even though I might know, from his long-continued motionlessness, that behind his screen he must be standing in one of those dead-wall reveries of his.

Revolving all these things, and coupling them with the recently discovered fact that he made my office his constant abiding place and home, and not forgetful of his morbid moodiness; revolving all these things, a prudential feeling began to steal over me. My first emotions had been those of pure melancholy and sincerest pity; but just in proportion as the forlornness of Bartleby grew and grew to my imagination, did that same melancholy merge into fear, that pity into repulsion. So true it is, and so terrible too, that up to a certain point the thought or sight of misery enlists our best affections; but, in certain special cases, beyond that point it does not. They err who would assert that invariably this is owing to the inherent selfishness of the human heart. It rather proceeds from a certain hopelessness of remedying excessive and organic ill. To a sensitive being, pity is not seldom pain. And when at last it is perceived that such pity cannot lead to effectual succor, common sense bids the soul be rid of it. What I saw that morning persuaded me that the scrivener was the victim of innate and incurable disorder. I might give alms to his body; but his body did not pain him; it was his soul that suffered, and his soul I could not reach.

I did not accomplish the purpose of going to Trinity Church that morning. Somehow, the things I had seen disqualified me for the time from church-going. I walked homeward, thinking what I would do with Bartleby. Finally, I resolved upon this;—I would put certain calm questions to him the next morning, touching his history, &c., and if he declined to answer them openly and unreservedly (and I supposed he would prefer not), then to give him a twenty dollar bill over and above whatever I might owe him, and tell him his services were no longer required; but that if in any other way I could assist him, I would be happy to do so, especially if he desired to return to his native place, wherever that might be, I would willingly help to defray the expenses. Moreover, if, after reaching home, he found himself at any time in want of aid, a letter from him would be sure of a reply.

The next morning came.

"Bartleby," said I, gently calling to him behind his screen.

No reply.

"Bartleby," said I, in a still gentler tone, "come here; I am not going to ask you to do any thing you would prefer not to do—I simply wish to speak to you."

Upon this he noiselessly slid into view.

"Will you tell me, Bartleby, where you were born?"

"I would prefer not to."

"Will you tell me *any thing* about yourself?"

"I would prefer not to."

"But what reasonable objection can you have to speak to me? I feel friendly towards you."

He did not look at me while I spoke, but kept his glance fixed upon my bust of Cicero, which as I then sat, was directly behind me, some six inches above my head.

"What is your answer, Bartleby?" said I, after waiting a considerable time for a reply, during which his countenance remained immovable, only there was the faintest conceivable tremor of the white attenuated mouth.

"At present I prefer to give no answer," he said, and retired into his hermitage.

It was rather weak in me I confess, but his manner on this occasion nettled me. Not only did there seem to lurk in it a certain calm disdain, but his perverseness seemed ungrateful, considering the undeniable good usage and indulgence he had received from me.

Again I sat ruminating what I should do. Mortified as I was at his behavior, and resolved as I had been to dismiss him when I entered my office, nevertheless I strangely felt something superstitious knocking at my heart, and forbidding me to carry out my purpose, and denouncing me for a villain if I dared to breathe one bitter word against this forlornest of mankind. At last, familiarly drawing my chair behind his screen, I sat down and said: "Bartleby, never mind then about revealing your history; but let me entreat you, as a friend, to comply as far as may be with the usages of this office. Say now you will help to examine papers to-morrow or next day: in short, say now that in a day or two you will begin to be a little reasonable:—say so, Bartleby."

"At present I would prefer not to be a little reasonable," was his mildly cadaverous reply.

Just then the folding-doors opened, and Nippers approached. He seemed suffering from an unusually bad night's rest, induced by severer indigestion than common. He overheard those final words of Bartleby.

"*Prefer not*, eh?" gritted Nippers—"I'd *prefer* him, if I were you, sir," addressing me—"I'd *prefer* him; I'd give him preferences, the stubborn mule! What is it, sir, pray, that he *prefers* not to do now?"

Bartleby moved not a limb.

"Mr. Nippers," said I, "I'd prefer that you would withdraw for the present."

Somehow, of late I had got into the way of involuntarily using this word "prefer" upon all sorts of not exactly suitable occasions. And I trembled to think that my contact with the scrivener had already and seriously affected me in a mental way. And what further and deeper aberration might it not yet produce? This apprehension had not been without efficacy in determining me to summary means.

As Nippers, looking very sour and sulky, was departing, Turkey blandly and deferentially approached.

"With submission, sir," said he, "yesterday I was thinking about Bartleby here, and I think that if he would but prefer to take a quart of good ale every day, it would do much towards mending him, and enabling him to assist in examining his papers."

"So you have got the word too," said I, slightly excited.

"With submission, what word, sir," asked Turkey, respectfully crowding himself into the contracted space behind the screen, and by so doing, making me jostle the scrivener. "What word, sir?"

"I would prefer to be left alone here," said Bartleby, as if offended at being mobbed in his privacy.

"*That's* the word, Turkey," said I—"*that's* it."

"Oh, *prefer*? oh yes—queer word. I never use it myself. But, sir, as I was saying, if he would but prefer—"

"Turkey," interrupted I, "you will please withdraw."

"Oh certainly, sir, if you prefer that I should."

As he opened the folding-door to retire, Nippers at his desk caught a glimpse of me, and asked whether I would prefer to have a certain paper copied on blue paper or white. He did not in the least roguishly accent the word prefer. It was plain that it involuntarily rolled from his tongue. I thought to myself, surely I must get rid of a demented man, who already has in some degree turned the tongues, if not the heads of myself and clerks. But I thought it prudent not to break the dismission at once.

The next day I noticed that Bartleby did nothing but stand at his window in his dead-wall revery. Upon asking him why he did not write, he said that he had decided upon doing no more writing.

"Why, how now? what next?" exclaimed I, "do no more writing?"

"No more."

"And what is the reason?"

"Do you not see the reason for yourself," he indifferently replied.

I looked steadfastly at him, and perceived that his eyes looked dull and glazed. Instantly it occurred to me, that his unexampled diligence in copying by his dim window for the first few weeks of his stay with me might have temporarily impaired his vision.

I was touched. I said something in condolence with him. I hinted that of course he did wisely in abstaining from writing for a while; and urged him to embrace that opportunity of taking wholesome exercise in the open air. This, however, he did not do. A few days after this, my other clerks being absent, and being in a great hurry to dispatch certain letters by the mail, I thought that, having nothing else earthly to do, Bartleby would surely be less inflexible than usual, and carry these letters to the post-office. But he blankly declined. So, much to my inconvenience, I went myself.

Still added days went by. Whether Bartleby's eyes improved or not, I could not say. To all appearance, I thought they did. But when I asked him if they did, he vouchsafed no answer. At all events, he would do no copying. At last, in reply to my urgings, he informed me that he had permanently given up copying.

"What!" exclaimed I; "suppose your eyes should get entirely well—better than ever before—would you not copy then?"

"I have given up copying," he answered, and slid aside.

He remained as ever, a fixture in my chamber. Nay—if that were possible—he became still more of a fixture than before. What was to be done? He would do nothing in the office: why should he stay there? In plain fact, he had now become a millstone to me, not only useless as a necklace, but afflictive to bear. Yet I was sorry for him. I speak less than truth when I say that, on his own account, he occasioned me uneasiness. If he would but have named a single relative or friend, I would instantly have written, and urged their taking the poor fellow away to some convenient retreat. But he seemed alone, absolutely alone in the universe. A bit of wreck in the mid Atlantic. At length, necessities connected with my business tyrannized over all other considerations. Decently as I could, I told Bartleby that in six days' time he must unconditionally leave the office. I warned him to take measures, in the interval, for procuring some other abode. I offered to assist him in this endeavor, if he himself would but take the first step towards a removal. "And when you finally quit me, Bartleby," added I, "I shall see that you go not away entirely unprovided. Six days from this hour, remember."

At the expiration of that period, I peeped behind the screen, and lo! Bartleby was there.

I buttoned up my coat, balanced myself; advanced slowly towards him, touched his shoulder, and said, "The time has come; you must quit this place; I am sorry for you; here is money; but you must go."

"I would prefer not," he replied, with his back still towards me.

"You *must*."

He remained silent.

Now I had an unbounded confidence in this man's common honesty. He had frequently restored to me sixpences and shillings carelessly dropped upon the floor, for I am apt to be very reckless in such shirt-button affairs. The proceeding then which followed will not be deemed extraordinary.

"Bartleby," said I, "I owe you twelve dollars on account; here are thirty-two; the odd twenty are yours.—Will you take it?" and I handed the bills towards him.

But he made no motion.

"I will leave them here then," putting them under a weight on the table. Then taking my hat and cane and going to the door I tranquilly turned and added—"After you have removed your things from these offices, Bartleby, you will of course lock the door—since every one is now gone for the day but you—and if you please, slip your key underneath the mat, so that I may have it in the morning. I shall not see you again; so good-bye to you. If hereafter in your new place of abode I can be of any service to you, do not fail to advise me by letter. Good-bye, Bartleby, and fare you well."

But he answered not a word; like the last column of some ruined temple, he remained standing mute and solitary in the middle of the otherwise deserted room.

As I walked home in a pensive mood, my vanity got the better of my pity. I could not but highly plume myself on my masterly management in getting rid of Bartleby. Masterly I call it, and such it must appear to any dispassionate thinker. The beauty of my procedure seemed to consist in its perfect quietness. There was no vulgar bullying, no bravado of any sort, no choleric hectoring, and striding to and fro across the apartment, jerking out vehement commands for Bartleby to bundle himself off with his beggarly traps. Nothing of the kind. Without loudly bidding Bartleby depart—as an inferior genius might have done—I *assumed* the ground that depart he must; and upon that assumption built all I had to say. The more I thought over my procedure, the more I was charmed with it. Nevertheless, next morning, upon awakening, I had my doubts,—I had somehow slept off the fumes of vanity. One of the coolest and wisest hours a man has, is just after he awakes in the morning. My procedure seemed as sagacious as ever,—but only in theory. How it would prove in practice—there was the rub. It was truly a beautiful thought to have assumed Bartleby's departure; but, after all, that assumption was simply my own, and none of Bartleby's. The great point was, not whether I had assumed that he would quit me, but whether he would prefer so to do. He was more a man of preferences than assumptions.

After breakfast, I walked down town, arguing the probabilities *pro* and *con*. One moment I thought it would prove a miserable failure, and Bartleby would be found all alive at my office as usual; the next moment it seemed certain that I should see his chair empty. And so I kept veering about. At the corner of Broadway and Canal-street, I saw quite an excited group of people standing in earnest conversation.

"I'll take odds he doesn't," said a voice as I passed.

"Doesn't go?—done!" said I, "put up your money."

I was instinctively putting my hand in my pocket to produce my own, when I remembered that this was an election day. The words I had overheard bore no reference to Bartleby, but to the success or non-success of some candidate for the mayoralty. In my intent frame of mind, I had, as it were, imagined that all Broadway shared in my excitement, and were debating the same question with me. I passed on, very thankful that the uproar of the street screened my momentary absent-mindedness.

As I had intended, I was earlier than usual at my office door. I stood listening for a moment. All was still. He must be gone. I tried the knob. The door was locked. Yes, my procedure had worked to a charm; he indeed must be vanished. Yet a certain melancholy mixed with this: I was almost sorry for my brilliant success. I was fumbling under the door mat for the key, which Bartleby was to have left there for me, when accidentally my knee knocked against a panel, producing a summoning sound, and in response a voice came to me from within—"Not yet; I am occupied."

It was Bartleby.

I was thunderstruck. For an instant I stood like the man who, pipe in mouth, was killed one cloudless afternoon long ago in Virginia, by summer lightning; at his own warm open window he was killed, and remained leaning out there upon the dreamy afternoon, till some one touched him, when he fell.

"Not gone!" I murmured at last. But again obeying that wondrous ascendancy which the inscrutable scrivener had over me, and from which ascendancy, for all my chafing, I could not completely escape, I slowly went down stairs and out into the street, and while walking round the block, considered what I should next do in this unheard-of perplexity. Turn the man out by an actual thrusting I could not; to drive him away by calling him hard names would not do; calling in the police was an unpleasant idea; and yet, permit him to enjoy his cadaverous triumph over me,—this too I could not think of.

What was to be done? or, if nothing could be done, was there any thing further that I could *assume* in the matter? Yes, as before I had prospectively assumed that Bartleby would depart, so now I might retrospectively assume that departed he was. In the legitimate carrying out of this assumption, I might enter my office in a great hurry, and pretending not to see Bartleby at all, walk straight against him as if he were air. Such a proceeding would in a singular degree have the appearance of a home-thrust. It was hardly possible that Bartleby could withstand such an application of the doctrine of assumptions. But upon second thoughts the success of the plan seemed rather dubious. I resolved to argue the matter over with him again.

"Bartleby," said I, entering the office, with a quietly severe expression, "I am seriously displeased. I am pained, Bartleby. I had thought better of you. I had imagined you of such a gentlemanly organization, that in any delicate dilemma a slight hint would suffice—in short, an assumption. But it appears I am deceived. Why," I added, unaffectedly starting, "you have not even touched that money yet," pointing to it, just where I had left it the evening previous.

He answered nothing.

"Will you, or will you not, quit me?" I now demanded in a sudden passion, advancing close to him.

"I would prefer *not* to quit you," he replied, gently emphasizing the *not*.

"What earthly right have you to stay here? Do you pay any rent? Do you pay my taxes? Or is this property yours?"

He answered nothing.

"Are you ready to go on and write now? Are your eyes recovered? Could you copy a small paper for me this morning? or help examine a few lines? or step round to the post-office? In a word, will you do any thing at all, to give a coloring to your refusal to depart the premises?"

He silently retired into his hermitage.

I was now in such a state of nervous resentment that I thought it but prudent to check myself at present from further demonstrations. Bartleby and I were alone. I remembered the tragedy of the unfortunate Adams and the still more unfortunate Colt in the solitary office of the latter; and how poor Colt, being dreadfully incensed by Adams,[9] and imprudently permitting himself to get wildly excited, was at unawares hurried into his fatal act—an act which certainly no man could possibly deplore more than the actor himself. Often it had occurred to me in my ponderings upon the subject, that had that altercation taken place in the public street, or at a private residence, it would not have terminated as it did. It was the circumstance of being alone in a solitary office, up stairs, of a building entirely unhallowed by humanizing domestic associations—an uncarpeted office, doubtless, of a dusty, haggard sort of appearance;—this it must have been, which greatly helped to enhance the irritable desperation of the hapless Colt.

9. Notorious murder case that occurred while Melville was in the South Seas. In 1841 Samuel Adams, a printer, called on John C. Colt (brother of the inventor of the revolver) at Broadway and Chambers Street in lower Manhattan to collect a debt. Colt murdered Adams with a hatchet and crated the corpse for shipment to New Orleans. The body was found, and Colt was soon arrested. Despite his pleas of self-defense Colt was convicted the next year, amid continuing newspaper publicity, and stabbed himself to death just before he was to be hanged. The setting of "Bartleby" is not far from the scene of the murder.

But when this old Adam of resentment rose in me and tempted me concerning Bartleby, I grappled him and threw him. How? Why, simply by recalling the divine injunction: "A new commandment give I unto you, that ye love one another."[1] Yes, this it was that saved me. Aside from higher considerations, charity often operates as a vastly wise and prudent principle—a great safeguard to its possessor. Men have committed murder for jealousy's sake, and anger's sake, and hatred's sake, and selfishness' sake, and spiritual pride's sake; but no man that ever I heard of, ever committed a diabolical murder for sweet charity's sake. Mere self-interest, then, if no better motive can be enlisted, should, especially with high-tempered men, prompt all beings to charity and philanthropy. At any rate, upon the occasion in question, I strove to drown my exasperated feelings towards the scrivener by benevolently constructing his conduct. Poor fellow, poor fellow! thought I, he don't mean any thing; and besides, he has seen hard times, and ought to be indulged.

I endeavored also immediately to occupy myself, and at the same time to comfort my despondency. I tried to fancy that in the course of the morning, at such time as might prove agreeable to him, Bartleby, of his own free accord, would emerge from his hermitage, and take up some decided line of march in the direction of the door. But no. Half-past twelve o'clock came; Turkey began to glow in the face, overturn his inkstand, and become generally obstreperous; Nippers abated down into quietude and courtesy; Ginger Nut munched his noon apple; and Bartleby remained standing at his window in one of his profoundest dead-wall reveries. Will it be credited? Ought I to acknowledge it? That afternoon I left the office without saying one further word to him.

Some days now passed, during which, at leisure intervals I looked a little into "Edwards on the Will," and "Priestley on Necessity."[2] Under the circumstances, those books induced a salutary feeling. Gradually I slid into the persuasion that these troubles of mine touching the scrivener, had been all predestinated from eternity, and Bartleby was billeted upon me for some mysterious purpose of an all-wise Providence, which it was not for a mere mortal like me to fathom. Yes, Bartleby, stay there behind your screen, thought I; I shall persecute you no more; you are harmless and noiseless as any of these old chairs; in short, I never feel so private as when I know you are here. At last I see it, I feel it; I penetrate to the predestinated purpose of my life. I am content. Others may have loftier parts to enact; but my mission in this world, Bartleby, is to furnish you with office-room for such period as you may see fit to remain.

I believe that this wise and blessed frame of mind would have continued with me, had it not been for the unsolicited and uncharitable remarks obtruded upon me by my professional friends who visited the rooms. But thus it often is, that the constant friction of illiberal minds wears out at last the best resolves of the more generous. Though to be sure, when I reflected upon it, it was not strange that people entering my office should be struck

1. John 13.34.

2. *Freedom of the Will*, by colonial minister Jonathan Edwards (1703–1754), and *Doctrine of Philosophical Necessity Illustrated*, by English theologian and scientist Joseph Priestley (1733–1804). Both concluded that the will is not free, though from different perspectives. Whereas Edwards believed that God before the beginning of time had decided who should be saved and who should be damned (the Calvinist doctrine of predestination), Priestley rejected Calvinism and believed that benevolent divine forces in the material universe constrained individual free will in order to guide humankind towards a higher perfection.

by the peculiar aspect of the unaccountable Bartleby, and so be tempted to throw out some sinister observations concerning him. Sometimes an attorney having business with me, and calling at my office, and finding no one but the scrivener there, would undertake to obtain some sort of precise information from him touching my whereabouts; but without heeding his idle talk, Bartleby would remain standing immovable in the middle of the room. So after contemplating him in that position for a time, the attorney would depart, no wiser than he came.

Also, when a Reference[3] was going on, and the room full of lawyers and witnesses and business was driving fast; some deeply occupied legal gentleman present, seeing Bartleby wholly unemployed, would request him to run round to his (the legal gentleman's) office and fetch some papers for him. Thereupon, Bartleby would tranquilly decline, and yet remain idle as before. Then the lawyer would give a great stare, and turn to me. And what could I say? At last I was made aware that all through the circle of my professional acquaintance, a whisper of wonder was running round, having reference to the strange creature I kept at my office. This worried me very much. And as the idea came upon me of his possibly turning out a long-lived man, and keep occupying my chambers, and denying my authority; and perplexing my visitors; and scandalizing my professional reputation; and casting a general gloom over the premises; keeping soul and body together to the last upon his savings (for doubtless he spent but half a dime a day), and in the end perhaps outlive me, and claim possession of my office by right of his perpetual occupancy: as all these dark anticipations crowded upon me more and more, and my friends continually intruded their relentless remarks upon the apparition in my room; a great change was wrought in me. I resolved to gather all my faculties together, and for ever rid me of this intolerable incubus.

Ere revolving any complicated project, however, adapted to this end, I first simply suggested to Bartleby the propriety of his permanent departure. In a calm and serious tone, I commended the idea to his careful and mature consideration. But having taken three days to meditate upon it, he apprised me that his original determination remained the same; in short, that he still preferred to abide with me.

What shall I do? I now said to myself, buttoning up my coat to the last button. What shall I do? what ought I to do? what does conscience say I *should* do with this man, or rather ghost. Rid myself of him, I must; go, he shall. But how? You will not thrust him, the poor, pale, passive mortal,—you will not thrust such a helpless creature out of your door? you will not dishonor yourself by such cruelty? No, I will not, I cannot do that. Rather would I let him live and die here, and then mason up his remains in the wall. What then will you do? For all your coaxing, he will not budge. Bribes he leaves under your own paper-weight on your table; in short, it is quite plain that he prefers to cling to you.

Then something severe, something unusual must be done. What! surely you will not have him collared by a constable, and commit his innocent pallor to the common jail? And upon what ground could you procure such a thing to be done?—a vagrant, is he? What! he a vagrant, a wanderer, who refuses to budge? It is because he will *not* be a vagrant, then, that you seek to

3. The act of referring a disputed matter to referees.

count him *as* a vagrant. That is too absurd. No visible means of support: there I have him. Wrong again: for indubitably he *does* support himself, and that is the only unanswerable proof that any man can show of his possessing the means so to do. No more then. Since he will not quit me, I must quit him. I will change my offices; I will move elsewhere; and give him fair notice, that if I find him on my new premises I will then proceed against him as a common trespasser.

Acting accordingly, next day I thus addressed him: "I find these chambers too far from the City Hall; the air is unwholesome. In a word, I propose to remove my offices next week, and shall no longer require your services. I tell you this now, in order that you may seek another place."

He made no reply, and nothing more was said.

On the appointed day I engaged carts and men, proceeded to my chambers, and having but little furniture, every thing was removed in a few hours. Throughout, the scrivener remained standing behind the screen, which I directed to be removed the last thing. It was withdrawn; and being folded up like a huge folio, left him the motionless occupant of a naked room. I stood in the entry watching him a moment, while something from within me upbraided me.

I re-entered, with my hand in my pocket—and—and my heart in my mouth.

"Good-bye, Bartleby; I am going—good-bye, and God some way bless you; and take that," slipping something in his hand. But it dropped upon the floor, and then,—strange to say—I tore myself from him whom I had so longed to be rid of.

Established in my new quarters, for a day or two I kept the door locked, and started at every footfall in the passages. When I returned to my rooms after any little absence, I would pause at the threshold for an instant, and attentively listen, ere applying my key. But these fears were needless. Bartleby never came nigh me.

I thought all was going well, when a perturbed looking stranger visited me, inquiring whether I was the person who had recently occupied rooms at No.—Wall-street.

Full of forebodings, I replied that I was.

"Then sir," said the stranger, who proved a lawyer, "you are responsible for the man you left there. He refuses to do any copying; he refuses to do any thing; he says he prefers not to; and he refuses to quit the premises."

"I am very sorry, sir," said I, with assumed tranquillity, but an inward tremor, "but, really, the man you allude to is nothing to me—he is no relation or apprentice of mine, that you should hold me responsible for him."

"In mercy's name, who is he?"

"I certainly cannot inform you. I know nothing about him. Formerly I employed him as a copyist; but he has done nothing for me now for some time past."

"I shall settle him then,—good morning, sir."

Several days passed, and I heard nothing more; and though I often felt a charitable prompting to call at the place and see poor Bartleby, yet a certain squeamishness of I know not what withheld me.

All is over with him, by this time, thought I at last, when through another week no further intelligence reached me. But coming to my room the day after, I found several persons waiting at my door in a high state of nervous excitement.

"That's the man—here he comes," cried the foremost one, whom I recognized as the lawyer who had previously called upon me alone.

"You must take him away, sir, at once," cried a portly person among them, advancing upon me, and whom I knew to be the landlord of No.—Wall-street. "These gentlemen, my tenants, cannot stand it any longer; Mr. B——" pointing to the lawyer, "has turned him out of his room, and he now persists in haunting the building generally, sitting upon the banisters of the stairs by day, and sleeping in the entry by night. Every body is concerned; clients are leaving the offices; some fears are entertained of a mob; something you must do, and that without delay."

Aghast at this torrent, I fell back before it, and would fain have locked myself in my new quarters. In vain I persisted that Bartleby was nothing to me—no more than to any one else. In vain:—I was the last person known to have any thing to do with him, and they held me to the terrible account. Fearful then of being exposed in the papers (as one person present obscurely threatened) I considered the matter, and at length said, that if the lawyer would give me a confidential interview with the scrivener, in his (the lawyer's) own room, I would that afternoon strive my best to rid them of the nuisance they complained of.

Going up stairs to my old haunt, there was Bartleby silently sitting upon the banister at the landing.

"What are you doing here, Bartleby?" said I.

"Sitting upon the banister," he mildly replied.

I motioned him into the lawyer's room, who then left us.

"Bartleby," said I, "are you aware that you are the cause of great tribulation to me, by persisting in occupying the entry after being dismissed from the office?"

No answer.

"Now one of two things must take place. Either you must do something, or something must be done to you. Now what sort of business would you like to engage in? Would you like to re-engage in copying for some one?"

"No; I would prefer not to make any change."

"Would you like a clerkship in a dry-goods store?"

"There is too much confinement about that. No, I would not like a clerkship; but I am not particular."

"Too much confinement," I cried, "why you keep yourself confined all the time!"

"I would prefer not to take a clerkship," he rejoined, as if to settle that little item at once.

"How would a bar-tender's business suit you? There is no trying of the eyesight in that."

"I would not like it at all; though, as I said before, I am not particular."

His unwonted wordiness inspirited me. I returned to the charge.

"Well then, would you like to travel through the country collecting bills for the merchants? That would improve your health."

"No, I would prefer to be doing something else."

"How then would going as a companion to Europe, to entertain some young gentleman with your conversation,—how would that suit you?"

"Not at all. It does not strike me that there is any thing definite about that. I like to be stationary. But I am not particular."

"Stationary you shall be then," I cried, now losing all patience, and for the first time in all my exasperating connection with him fairly flying into a passion. "If you do not go away from these premises before night, I shall feel bound—indeed I *am* bound—to—to—to quit the premises myself!" I rather absurdly concluded, knowing not with what possible threat to try to frighten his immobility into compliance. Despairing of all further efforts, I was precipitately leaving him, when a final thought occurred to me—one which had not been wholly unindulged before.

"Bartleby," said I, in the kindest tone I could assume under such exciting circumstances, "will you go home with me now—not to my office, but my dwelling—and remain there till we can conclude upon some convenient arrangement for you at our leisure? Come, let us start now, right away."

"No: at present I would prefer not to make any change at all."

I answered nothing; but effectually dodging every one by the suddenness and rapidity of my flight, rushed from the building, ran up Wall-street towards Broadway, and jumping into the first omnibus was soon removed from pursuit. As soon as tranquillity returned I distinctly perceived that I had now done all that I possibly could, both in respect to the demands of the landlord and his tenants, and with regard to my own desire and sense of duty, to benefit Bartleby, and shield him from rude persecution. I now strove to be entirely care-free and quiescent; and my conscience justified me in the attempt; though indeed it was not so successful as I could have wished. So fearful was I of being again hunted out by the incensed landlord and his exasperated tenants, that, surrendering my business to Nippers, for a few days I drove about the upper part of the town and through the suburbs, in my rockaway; crossed over to Jersey City and Hoboken, and paid fugitive visits to Manhattanville and Astoria.[4] In fact I almost lived in my rockaway for the time.

When again I entered my office, lo, a note from the landlord lay upon the desk. I opened it with trembling hands. It informed me that the writer had sent to the police, and had Bartleby removed to the Tombs as a vagrant. Moreover, since I knew more about him than any one else, he wished me to appear at that place, and make a suitable statement of the facts. These tidings had a conflicting effect upon me. At first I was indignant; but at last almost approved. The landlord's energetic, summary disposition, had led him to adopt a procedure which I do not think I would have decided upon myself; and yet as a last resort, under such peculiar circumstances, it seemed the only plan.

As I afterwards learned, the poor scrivener, when told that he must be conducted to the Tombs, offered not the slightest obstacle, but in his pale unmoving way, silently acquiesced.

Some of the compassionate and curious bystanders joined the party; and headed by one of the constables arm in arm with Bartleby, the silent pro-

4. The narrator crossed the Hudson River to Jersey City and Hoboken, then drove far up Manhattan Island to the community of Manhattanville (Grant's Tomb is in what was Manhattanville), and finally crossed the East River to Astoria, on Long Island. "Rockaway": light open-sided carriage.

cession filed its way through all the noise, and heat, and joy of the roaring thoroughfares at noon.

The same day I received the note I went to the Tombs, or to speak more properly, the Halls of Justice. Seeking the right officer, I stated the purpose of my call, and was informed that the individual I described was indeed within. I then assured the functionary that Bartleby was a perfectly honest man, and greatly to be compassionated, however unaccountably eccentric. I narrated all I knew, and closed by suggesting the idea of letting him remain in as indulgent confinement as possible till something less harsh might be done—though indeed I hardly knew what. At all events, if nothing else could be decided upon, the alms-house must receive him. I then begged to have an interview.

Being under no disgraceful charge, and quite serene and harmless in all his ways, they had permitted him freely to wander about the prison, and especially in the inclosed grass-platted yards thereof. And so I found him there, standing all alone in the quietest of the yards, his face towards a high wall, while all around, from the narrow slits of the jail windows, I thought I saw peering out upon him the eyes of murderers and thieves.

"Bartleby!"

"I know you," he said, without looking round,—"and I want nothing to say to you."

"It was not I that brought you here, Bartleby," said I, keenly pained at his implied suspicion. "And to you, this should not be so vile a place. Nothing reproachful attaches to you by being here. And see, it is not so sad a place as one might think. Look, there is the sky, and here is the grass."

"I know where I am," he replied, but would say nothing more, and so I left him.

As I entered the corridor again, a broad meat-like man, in an apron, accosted me, and jerking his thumb over his shoulder said—"Is that your friend?"

"Yes."

"Does he want to starve? If he does, let him live on the prison fare, that's all."

"Who are you?" asked I, not knowing what to make of such an unofficially speaking person in such a place.

"I am the grub-man. Such gentlemen as have friends here, hire me to provide them with something good to eat."

"Is this so?" said I, turning to the turnkey.

He said it was.

"Well then," said I, slipping some silver into the grub-man's hands (for so they called him). "I want you to give particular attention to my friend there; let him have the best dinner you can get. And you must be as polite to him as possible."

"Introduce me, will you?" said the grub-man, looking at me with an expression which seemed to say he was all impatience for an opportunity to give a specimen of his breeding.

Thinking it would prove of benefit to the scrivener, I acquiesced; and asking the grub-man his name, went up with him to Bartleby.

"Bartleby, this is Mr. Cutlets; you will find him very useful to you."

"Your sarvant, sir, your sarvant," said the grub-man, making a low salutation behind his apron. "Hope you find it pleasant here, sir;—spacious grounds—cool apartments, sir—hope you'll stay with us some time—try to make it agreeable. May Mrs. Cutlets and I have the pleasure of your company to dinner, sir, in Mrs. Cutlets' private room?"

"I prefer not to dine to-day," said Bartleby, turning away. "It would disagree with me; I am unused to dinners." So saying he slowly moved to the other side of the inclosure, and took up a position fronting the dead-wall.

"How's this?" said the grub-man, addressing me with a stare of astonishment. "He's odd, aint he?"

"I think he is a little deranged," said I, sadly.

"Deranged? deranged is it? Well now, upon my word, I thought that friend of yourn was a gentleman forger; they are always pale and genteel-like, them forgers. I can't help pity 'em—can't help it, sir. Did you know Monroe Edwards?"[5] he added touchingly, and paused. Then, laying his hand pityingly on my shoulder, sighed, "he died of consumption at Sing-Sing.[6] So you weren't acquainted with Monroe?"

"No, I was never socially acquainted with any forgers. But I cannot stop longer. Look to my friend yonder. You will not lose by it. I will see you again."

Some few days after this, I again obtained admission to the Tombs, and went through the corridors in quest of Bartleby; but without finding him.

"I saw him coming from his cell not long ago," said a turnkey, "may be he's gone to loiter in the yards."

So I went in that direction.

"Are you looking for the silent man?" said another turnkey passing me. "Yonder he lies—sleeping in the yard there. 'Tis not twenty minutes since I saw him lie down."

The yard was entirely quiet. It was not accessible to the common prisoners. The surrounding walls, of amazing thickness, kept off all sounds behind them. The Egyptian character of the masonry weighed upon me with its gloom. But a soft imprisoned turf grew under foot. The heart of the eternal pyramids, it seemed, wherein, by some strange magic, through the clefts, grass-seed, dropped by birds, had sprung.

Strangely huddled at the base of the wall, his knees drawn up, and lying on his side, his head touching the cold stones, I saw the wasted Bartleby. But nothing stirred. I paused; then went close up to him; stooped over, and saw that his dim eyes were open; otherwise he seemed profoundly sleeping. Something prompted me to touch him. I felt his hand, when a tingling shiver ran up my arm and down my spine to my feet.

The round face of the grub-man peered upon me now. "His dinner is ready. Won't he dine to-day, either? Or does he live without dining?"

"Lives without dining," said I, and closed the eyes.

"Eh!—He's asleep, aint he?"

"With kings and counsellors,"[7] murmured I.

There would seem little need for proceeding further in this history. Imagination will readily supply the meagre recital of poor Bartleby's inter-

5. The much-publicized trial of Colonel Edwards (1808–1847), accused of swindling two firms, was held in New York City in 1842 and ended in his conviction.

6. Prison at Ossining, New York, approximately thirty-five miles north of lower Manhattan.

7. Job 3.14.

ment. But ere parting with the reader, let me say, that if this little narrative has sufficiently interested him, to awaken curiosity as to who Bartleby was, and what manner of life he led prior to the present narrator's making his acquaintance, I can only reply, that in such curiosity I fully share, but am wholly unable to gratify it. Yet here I hardly know whether I should divulge one little item of rumor, which came to my ear a few months after the scrivener's decease. Upon what basis it rested, I could never ascertain; and hence, how true it is I cannot now tell. But inasmuch as this vague report has not been without a certain strange suggestive interest to me, however sad, it may prove the same with some others; and so I will briefly mention it. The report was this: that Bartleby had been a subordinate clerk in the Dead Letter Office at Washington, from which he had been suddenly removed by a change in the administration. When I think over this rumor, I cannot adequately express the emotions which seize me. Dead letters! does it not sound like dead men? Conceive a man by nature and misfortune prone to a pallid hopelessness, can any business seem more fitted to heighten it than that of continually handling these dead letters, and assorting them for the flames? For by the cart-load they are annually burned. Sometimes from out the folded paper the pale clerk takes a ring:—the finger it was meant for, perhaps, moulders in the grave; a bank-note sent in swiftest charity:—he whom it would relieve, nor eats nor hungers any more; pardon for those who died despairing; hope for those who died unhoping; good tidings for those who died stifled by unrelieved calamities. On errands of life, these letters speed to death.

Ah Bartleby! Ah humanity!

1853

The Paradise of Bachelors and the Tartarus of Maids[1]

I. The Paradise of Bachelors

It lies not far from Temple-Bar.[2]

Going to it, by the usual way, is like stealing from a heated plain into some cool, deep glen, shady among harboring hills.

Sick with the din and soiled with the mud of Fleet Street—where the Benedick tradesmen are hurrying by, with ledger-lines ruled along their brows, thinking upon rise of bread and fall of babies—you adroitly turn a mystic corner—not a street—glide down a dim, monastic way, flanked

1. The text is from the first publication in *Harper's New Monthly Magazine* (April 1855). As the full-title running heads in *Harper's* emphasized, this is a single story, each part of which—the "Paradise" of Part One and the "Tartarus" (the lowest region of the underworld in Greek mythology) of Part Two—yields its significance in the light of the other. The story derives from two episodes in Melville's life. In December 1849, after weeks of trying to find an English publisher for his novel *White-Jacket* (1850), Melville was feted by several acquaintances from the London literary and legal community at Elm Court, Temple (a London building housing law offices and societies). A little more than a year later, in December 1851, Melville traveled around five miles from his home in Pittsfield to purchase a sleigh-load of paper from Carson's Mill in Dalton, Massachusetts. What he saw there can be surmised by the second half of the story.

2. Ornate stone gateway between Fleet Street and the Strand in London, built by the architect Christopher Wren (1632–1723) in 1670. The Strand runs along the north bank of the Thames. Fleet Street had many literary associations for Melville, particularly with 18th-century writers, and was becoming an area for newspaper and publishing offices.

by dark, sedate, and solemn piles, and still wending on, give the whole care-worn world the slip, and, disentangled, stand beneath the quiet cloisters of the Paradise of Bachelors.[3]

Sweet are the oases in Sahara; charming the isle-groves of August prairies; delectable pure faith amidst a thousand perfidies: but sweeter, still more charming, most delectable the dreamy Paradise of Bachelors, found in the stony heart of stunning London.

In mild meditation pace the cloisters; take your pleasure, sip your leisure, in the garden waterward; go linger in the ancient library; go worship in the sculptured chapel;[4] but little have you seen, just nothing do you know, not the sweet kernel have you tasted, till you dine among the banded Bachelors, and see their convivial eyes and glasses sparkle. Not dine in bustling commons, during term-time, in the hall; but tranquilly, by private hint, at a private table; some fine Templar's[5] hospitably invited guest.

Templar? That's a romantic name. Let me see. Brian de Bois Gilbert[6] was a Templar, I believe. Do we understand you to insinuate that those famous Templars still survive in modern London? May the ring of their armed heels be heard, and the rattle of their shields, as in mailed prayer the monk-knights kneel before the consecrated Host? Surely a monk-knight were a curious sight picking his way along the Strand, his gleaming corselet and snowy surcoat[7] spattered by an omnibus. Long-bearded, too, according to his order's rule; his face furry as a pard's;[8] how would the grim ghost look among the crop-haired, close-shaven citizens? We know indeed—sad history recounts it—that a moral blight tainted at last this sacred Brotherhood. Though no sworded foe might outskill them in the fence, yet the worm of luxury crawled beneath their guard, gnawing the core of knightly troth, nibbling the monastic vow, till at last the monk's austerity relaxed to wassailing,[9] and the sworn knights-bachelors grew to be but hypocrites and rakes.

But for all this, quite unprepared were we to learn that Knights-Templars (if at all in being) were so entirely secularized as to be reduced from carving out immortal fame in glorious battling for the Holy Land, to the carving of roast-mutton at a dinner-board. Like Anacreon,[1] do these degenerate Templars now think it sweeter far to fall in banquet than in war? Or, indeed, how can there be any survival of that famous order? Templars in modern London! Templars in their red-cross mantles smoking cigars at the Divan![2] Templars crowded in a railway train, till, stacked with steel helmet, spear, and shield, the whole train looks like one elongated locomotive!

No. The genuine Templar is long since departed. Go view the wondrous tombs in the Temple Church;[3] see there the rigidly-haughty forms stretched

3. These cloisters are the four Inns of Court, inhabited by lawyers and legal students. This passage echoes the opening of Irving's "London Antiques" in *The Sketch Book*. "Benedick": married men, especially newly married men who have resisted the state of matrimony; from Benedick, who at the end of Shakespeare's *Much Ado about Nothing* surrenders his cherished bachelorhood.

4. The chapel is "sculptured" with grotesque figures on columns but primarily by effigies of knights lying prone on the floor.

5. Order of Catholic soldier-monks established in the 12th century to protect pilgrims on their way to the Holy Land. Henry I introduced the order to England; after it grew corrupt, it was dissolved in 1312.

6. I.e., Brian de Bois-Guilbert, evil Knight Templar in Sir Walter Scott's *Ivanhoe* (1819).

7. Outercoat, over armor. "Corselet": body armor, such as a breastplate.

8. Leopard.

9. Drinking, carousing.

1. Greek poet (563?–478? B.C.E.) known for songs celebrating wine and love.

2. Muslim council chamber.

3. The great Round Church, or Temple Church, was constructed in 1185 and belonged to two of the Inns of Court, the Inner Temple and the Middle Temple.

out, with crossed arms upon their stilly hearts, in everlasting and undreaming rest. Like the years before the flood, the bold Knights-Templars are no more. Nevertheless, the name remains, and the nominal society, and the ancient grounds, and some of the ancient edifices. But the iron heel is changed to a boot of patent-leather; the long two-handed sword to a one-handed quill, the monk-giver of gratuitous ghostly counsel now counsels for a fee; the defender of the sarcophagus (if in good practice with his weapon) now has more than one case to defend; the vowed opener and clearer of all highways leading to the Holy Sepulchre, now has it in particular charge to check, to clog, to hinder, and embarrass all the courts and avenues of Law; the knight-combatant of the Saracen, breasting spear-points at Acre, now fights law-points in Westminster Hall.[4] The helmet is a wig. Struck by Time's enchanter's wand, the Templar is to-day a Lawyer.

But, like many others tumbled from proud glory's height—like the apple, hard on the bough but mellow on the ground—the Templar's fall has but made him all the finer fellow.

I dare say those old warrior-priests were but gruff and grouty at the best; cased in Birmingham[5] hardware, how could their crimped arms give yours or mine a hearty shake? Their proud, ambitious, monkish souls clasped shut, like horn-book missals; their very faces clapped in bomb-shells;[6] what sort of genial men were these? But best of comrades, most affable of hosts, capital diner is the modern Templar. His wit and wine are both of sparkling brands.

The church and cloisters, courts and vaults, lanes and passages, banquet-halls, refectories, libraries, terraces, gardens, broad walks, domicils, and dessert-rooms, covering a very large space of ground, and all grouped in central neighborhood, and quite sequestered from the old city's surrounding din; and every thing about the place being kept in most bachelor-like particularity, no part of London offers to a quiet wight so agreeable a refuge.

The Temple is, indeed, a city by itself. A city with all the best appurtenances, as the above enumeration shows. A city with a park to it, and flower-beds, and a river-side—the Thames flowing by as openly, in one part, as by Eden's primal garden flowed the mild Euphrates.[7] In what is now the Temple Garden the old Crusaders used to exercise their steeds and lances; the modern Templars now lounge on the benches beneath the trees, and, switching their patent-leather boots, in gay discourse exercise at repartee.

Long lines of stately portraits in the banquet halls, show what great men of mark—famous nobles, judges, and Lord Chancellors—have in their time been Templars. But all Templars are not known to universal fame; though, if the having warm hearts and warmer welcomes, full minds and fuller cellars, and giving good advice and glorious dinners, spiced with

4. A vestibule of the new houses of Parliament, part of the ancient Palace of Westminster founded by the Anglo-Saxon kings, used in Melville's time as a law court. The Holy Sepulchre is the Roman Catholic church at the supposed site of Jesus' tomb in Jerusalem. "Saracen": Muslim. "Acre": seaport of Palestine, long held by Christians during the Crusades.

5. I.e., made in Birmingham, a west-central English industrial city (in facetious anachronism). "Grouty": sullen, cross.

6. Armored helmets. "Missals": devotional books of parchment mounted on a board with a handle; here, made with covers protected by a thin layer of horn.

7. River in southwest Asia that some believed had nourished the Garden of Eden.

rare divertisements of fun and fancy, merit immortal mention, set down, ye muses, the names of R.F.C.[8] and his imperial brother.

Though to be a Templar, in the one true sense, you must needs be a lawyer, or a student at the law, and be ceremoniously enrolled as member of the order, yet as many such, though Templars, do not reside within the Temple's precincts, though they may have their offices there, just so, on the other hand, there are many residents of the hoary old domicils who are not admitted Templars. If being, say, a lounging gentleman and bachelor, or a quiet, unmarried, literary man, charmed with the soft seclusion of the spot, you much desire to pitch your shady tent among the rest in this serene encampment, then you must make some special friend among the order, and procure him to rent, in his name but at your charge, whatever vacant chamber you may find to suit.

Thus, I suppose, did Dr. Johnson,[9] that nominal Benedick and widower but virtual bachelor, when for a space he resided here. So, too, did that undoubted bachelor and rare good soul, Charles Lamb.[1] And hundreds more, of sterling spirits, Brethren of the Order of Celibacy, from time to time have dined, and slept, and tabernacled here. Indeed, the place is all a honeycomb of offices and domicils. Like any cheese, it is quite perforated through and through in all directions with the snug cells of bachelors. Dear, delightful spot! Ah! when I bethink me of the sweet hours there passed, enjoying such genial hospitalities beneath those time-honored roofs, my heart only finds due utterance through poetry; and, with a sigh, I softly sing, "Carry me back to old Virginny!"[2]

Such then, at large, is the Paradise of Bachelors. And such I found it one pleasant afternoon in the smiling month of May, when, sallying from my hotel in Trafalgar Square, I went to keep my dinner-appointment with that fine Barrister, Bachelor, and Bencher,[3] R.F.C. (he *is* the first and second, and *should be* the third; I hereby nominate him), whose card I kept fast pinched between my gloved forefinger and thumb, and every now and then snatched still another look at the pleasant address inscribed beneath the name, "No.—, Elm Court, Temple."

At the core he was a right bluff, care-free, right comfortable, and most companionable Englishman. If on a first acquaintance he seemed reserved, quite icy in his air—patience; this Champagne will thaw. And if it never do, better frozen Champagne than liquid vinegar.

There were nine gentlemen, all bachelors, at the dinner. One was from "No.—, King's Bench Walk, Temple;" a second, third, and fourth, and fifth, from various courts or passages christened with some similarly rich resounding syllables. It was indeed a sort of Senate of the Bachelors, sent to this dinner from widely-scattered districts, to represent the general celibacy of the Temple. Nay it was, by representation, a Grand Parliament of the best Bachelors in universal London; several of those present being from distant

8. Robert Francis Cooke, who entertained in Elm Court, Temple, on December 19, 1849. On the twenty-first Melville called on a Mr. Cleaves in the Temple and visited the library.
9. Samuel Johnson (1709–1784), English writer and lexicographer.
1. English essayist (1775–1834).
2. From a song of the same title by Edwin P. Christy (1847), not the still-familiar song with the line "old Virginny, the state where I was born."
3. Judge. Trafalgar Square contains the column and statue erected in 1843 in honor of Lord Nelson's naval victory at Trafalgar in 1805 against the combined French and Spanish fleets.

quarters of the town, noted immemorial seats of lawyers and un-married men—Lincoln's Inn, Furnival's Inn; and one gentleman, upon whom I looked with a sort of collateral awe, hailed from the spot where Lord Verulam[4] once abode a bachelor—Gray's Inn.

The apartment was well up toward heaven. I know not how many strange old stairs I climbed to get to it. But a good dinner, with famous company, should be well earned. No doubt our host had his dining-room so high with a view to secure the prior exercise necessary to the due relishing and digesting of it.

The furniture was wonderfully unpretending, old, and snug. No new shining mahogany, sticky with undried varnish; no uncomfortably luxurious ottomans, and sofas too fine to use, vexed you in this sedate apartment. It is a thing which every sensible American should learn from every sensible Englishman, that glare and glitter, gimcracks and gewgaws, are not indispensable to domestic solacement. The American Benedick snatches, down-town, a tough chop in a gilded show-box; the English bachelor leisurely dines at home on that incomparable South Down of his, off a plain deal board.[5]

The ceiling of the room was low. Who wants to dine under the dome of St. Peter's?[6] High ceilings! If that is your demand, and the higher the better, and you be so very tall, then go dine out with the topping giraffe in the open air.

In good time the nine gentlemen sat down to nine covers, and soon were fairly under way.

If I remember right, ox-tail soup inaugurated the affair. Of a rich russet hue, its agreeable flavor dissipated my first confounding of its main ingredient with teamster's gads and the rawhides of ushers.[7] (By way of interlude, we here drank a little claret.) Neptune's was the next tribute rendered—turbot[8] coming second; snowwhite, flaky, and just gelatinous enough, not too turtleish in its unctuousness.

(At this point we refreshed ourselves with a glass of sherry.) After these light skirmishers had vanished, the heavy artillery of the feast marched in, led by that well-known English generalissimo, roast beef. For aids-de-camp we had a saddle of mutton, a fat turkey, a chicken-pie, and endless other savory things; while for avant-couriers came nine silver flagons of humming[9] ale. This heavy ordnance[1] having departed on the track of the light skirmishers, a picked brigade of game-fowl encamped upon the board, their campfires lit by the ruddiest of decanters.

Tarts and puddings followed, with innumerable niceties; then cheese and crackers. (By way of ceremony, simply, only to keep up good old fashions, we here each drank a glass of good old port.)

4. Francis Bacon (1561–1626), English writer and statesman. Lincoln's Inn is one of the Inns of Court. Furnival's Inn, a Gothic building, was formerly an Inn of Chancery, which was destroyed after Melville saw it.

5. Wooden platter. "South Down": or Southdown, an English breed of sheep, i.e., mutton.

6. The basilica in Vatican City whose dome was constructed under the direction of Michelangelo. The Inns of Court are between the smaller-domed St. Paul's and the Thames.

7. Assistant schoolteachers (especially old thick-skinned ones). "Gads": goads (whips made from oxtails).

8. European flatfish, in tribute to the god of the sea, Neptune.

9. Still effervescent. "Aids-de-camp": i.e., aides-de-camp; military aides. "Avant-couriers": i.e., avant-coureurs or avant-courriers; forerunners.

1. Artillery.

The cloth was now removed; and like Blucher's[2] army coming in at the death on the field of Waterloo, in marched a fresh detachment of bottles, dusty with their hurried march.

All these manœuvrings of the forces were superintended by a surprising old field-marshal (I can not school myself to call him by the inglorious name of waiter), with snowy hair and napkin, and a head like Socrates.[3] Amidst all the hilarity of the feast, intent on important business, he disdained to smile. Venerable man!

I have above endeavored to give some slight schedule of the general plan of operations. But any one knows that a good, genial dinner is a sort of pell-mell, indiscriminate affair, quite baffling to detail in all particulars. Thus, I spoke of taking a glass of claret, and a glass of sherry, and a glass of port, and a mug of ale—all at certain specific periods and times. But those were merely the state bumpers,[4] so to speak. Innumerable impromptu glasses were drained between the periods of those grand imposing ones.

The nine bachelors seemed to have the most tender concern for each other's health. All the time, in flowing wine, they most earnestly expressed their sincerest wishes for the entire well-being and lasting hygiene of the gentlemen on the right and on the left. I noticed that when one of these kind bachelors desired a little more wine (just for his stomach's sake, like Timothy[5]), he would not help himself to it unless some other bachelor would join him. It seemed held something indelicate, selfish, and unfraternal, to be seen taking a lonely, unparticipated glass. Meantime, as the wine ran apace, the spirits of the company grew more and more to perfect genialness and unconstraint. They related all sort of pleasant stories. Choice experiences in their private lives were now brought out, like choice brands of Moselle or Rhenish,[6] only kept for particular company. One told us how mellowly he lived when a student at Oxford; with various spicy anecdotes of most frank-hearted noble lords, his liberal companions. Another bachelor, a gray-headed man, with a sunny face, who, by his own account, embraced every opportunity of leisure to cross over into the Low Countries,[7] on sudden tours of inspection of the fine old Flemish architecture there—this learned, white-haired, sunny-faced old bachelor, excelled in his descriptions of the elaborate splendors of those old guild-halls, town-halls, and stadthold-houses, to be seen in the land of the ancient Flemings. A third was a great frequenter of the British Museum, and knew all about scores of wonderful antiquities, of Oriental manuscripts, and costly books without a duplicate. A fourth had lately returned from a trip to Old Granada, and, of course, was full of Saracenic scenery. A fifth had a funny case in law to tell. A sixth was erudite in wines. A seventh had a strange characteristic anecdote of the private life of the Iron Duke,[8] never printed, and never before announced in any public or private company. An

2. Gebhard von Blucher (1742–1819), leader of Prussian troops that helped in the defeat of Napoleon at Waterloo in 1815.
3. Greek philosopher (470?–399 B.C.E.).
4. Any large glass or mug with bulging sides, meant to be filled to the brim for drinking toasts.
5. Paul's *prescription in* 1 Timothy 5.23: "Drink no longer water, but use a little wine for thy stomach's sake and thine often infirmities."
6. Wines from the Moselle or Rhenish River regions of Germany.
7. The Netherlands, Belgium, and Luxembourg, but the context suggests that Melville knew the bawdy play on "Low Countries" in, for instance, Shakespeare's *A Comedy of Errors* (3.2), in which a kitchen maid is described according to the geography of Europe.
8. I.e., the duke of Wellington (1769–1852), victor over Napoleon at Waterloo (1815).

eighth had lately been amusing his evenings, now and then, with translating a comic poem of Pulci's.[9] He quoted for us the more amusing passages.

And so the evening slipped along, the hours told, not by a water-clock, like King Alfred's, but a wine-chronometer.[1] Meantime the table seemed a sort of Epsom Heath;[2] a regular ring, where the decanters galloped round. For fear one decanter should not with sufficient speed reach his destination, another was sent express after him to hurry him; and then a third to hurry the second; and so on with a fourth and fifth. And throughout all this nothing loud, nothing unmannerly, nothing turbulent. I am quite sure, from the scrupulous gravity and austerity of his air, that had Socrates, the field-marshal, perceived aught of indecorum in the company he served, he would have forthwith departed without giving warning. I afterward learned that, during the repast, an invalid bachelor in an adjoining chamber enjoyed his first sound refreshing slumber in three long, weary weeks.

It was the very perfection of quiet absorption of good living, good drinking, good feeling, and good talk. We were a band of brothers. Comfort—fraternal, household comfort, was the grand trait of the affair. Also, you could plainly see that these easy-hearted men had no wives or children to give an anxious thought. Almost all of them were travelers, too; for bachelors alone can travel freely, and without any twinges of their consciences touching desertion of the fireside.

The thing called pain, the bugbear styled trouble—those two legends seemed preposterous to their bachelor imaginations. How could men of liberal sense, ripe scholarship in the world, and capacious philosophical and convivial understandings—how could they suffer themselves to be imposed upon by such monkish fables? Pain! Trouble! As well talk of Catholic miracles. No such thing.—Pass the sherry, Sir.—Pooh, pooh! Can't be!—The port, Sir, if you please. Nonsense; don't tell me so.—The decanter stops with you, Sir, I believe.

And so it went.

Not long after the cloth was drawn our host glanced significantly upon Socrates, who, solemnly stepping to a stand, returned with an immense convolved horn, a regular Jericho horn,[3] mounted with polished silver, and otherwise chased and curiously enriched; not omitting two life-like goat's heads, with four more horns of solid silver, projecting from opposite sides of the mouth of the noble main horn.

Not having heard that our host was a performer on the bugle, I was surprised to see him lift this horn from the table, as if he were about to blow an inspiring blast. But I was relieved from this and set quite right as touching the purposes of the horn, by his now inserting his thumb and forefinger into its mouth; whereupon a slight aroma was stirred up, and my nostrils were greeted with the smell of some choice Rappee.[4] It was a mull[5] of snuff. It went the rounds. Capital idea this, thought I, of taking snuff about this

9. Luigi Pulci (1432–1484), Florentine poet.
1. Alfred the Great (849–899), king of Wessex, England, was thought to have designed a clock that measured time by the flow of water. This fictional clock, or chronometer, would measure time by the flow of wine.
2. Racetrack in Epsom, Surrey, where the Derby has been run since 1780.
3. In Joshua 6.1–20, seven priests circled Jericho making long blasts with rams' horns until on the seventh day "the walls fell flat" and Joshua took the city.
4. A strong, dark snuff.
5. A small, usually ornate box with an apparatus for pulverizing tobacco into snuff.

juncture. This goodly fashion must be introduced among my countrymen at home, further ruminated I.

The remarkable decorum of the nine bachelors—a decorum not to be affected by any quantity of wine—a decorum unassailable by any degree of mirthfulness—this was again set in a forcible light to me, by now observing that, though they took snuff very freely, yet not a man so far violated the proprieties, or so far molested the invalid bachelor in the adjoining room as to indulge himself in a sneeze. The snuff was snuffed silently, as if it had been some fine innoxious[6] powder brushed off the wings of butterflies.

But fine though they be, bachelors' dinners, like bachelors' lives, can not endure forever. The time came for breaking up. One by one the bachelors took their hats, and two by two, and arm-in-arm they descended, still conversing, to the flagging of the court; some going to their neighboring chambers to turn over the Decameron[7] ere retiring for the night; some to smoke a cigar, promenading in the garden on the cool river-side; some to make for the street, call a hack, and be driven snugly to their distant lodgings.

I was the last lingerer.

"Well," said my smiling host, "what do you think of the Temple here, and the sort of life we bachelors make out to live in it?"

"Sir," said I, with a burst of admiring candor—"Sir, this is the very Paradise of Bachelors!"

II. The Tartarus of Maids

It lies not far from Woedolor Mountain in New England. Turning to the east, right out from among bright farms and sunny meadows, nodding in early June with odorous grasses, you enter ascendingly among bleak hills. These gradually close in upon a dusky pass, which, from the violent Gulf Stream of air unceasingly diving between its cloven walls of haggard rock, as well as from the tradition of a crazy spinster's hut having long ago stood somewhere hereabouts, is called the Mad Maid's Bellows'-pipe.

Winding along at the bottom of the gorge is a dangerously narrow wheel-road, occupying the bed of a former torrent. Following this road to its highest point, you stand as within a Dantean gateway.[8] From the steepness of the walls here, their strangely ebon hue, and the sudden contraction of the gorge, this particular point is called the Black Notch. The ravine now expandingly descends into a great, purple, hopper-shaped hollow, far sunk among many Plutonian,[9] shaggy-wooded mountains. By the country people this hollow is called the Devil's Dungeon. Sounds of torrents fall on all sides upon the ear. These rapid waters unite at last in one turbid brick-colored stream, boiling through a flume among enormous boulders. They call this strange-colored torrent Blood River. Gaining a dark precipice it wheels suddenly to the west, and makes one maniac spring of sixty feet into the arms of a stunted wood of gray-haired pines, between which it thence eddies on its further way down to the invisible lowlands.

6. Harmless.
7. Bawdy tales by the Italian writer Giovanni Boccaccio (1313–1375).
8. Such as the entrance to hell the Italian poet Dante (1265–1321) describes in the *Inferno*; over it is written: "Abandon hope, all ye who enter here." The contrast is with the beautiful Wren gateway, Temple Bar.
9. Ruled by the god of the underworld. "Hopper-shaped": funnel-shaped.

Conspicuously crowning a rocky bluff high to one side, at the cataract's verge, is the ruin of an old saw-mill, built in those primitive times when vast pines and hemlocks superabounded throughout the neighboring region. The black-mossed bulk of those immense, rough-hewn, and spike-knotted logs, here and there tumbled all together, in long abandonment and decay, or left in solitary, perilous projection over the cataract's gloomy brink, impart to this rude wooden ruin not only much of the aspect of one of rough-quarried stone, but also a sort of feudal, Rhineland, and Thurmberg[1] look, derived from the pinnacled wildness of the neighboring scenery.

Not far from the bottom of the Dungeon stands a large whitewashed building, relieved, like some great whited sepulchre,[2] against the sullen background of mountain-side firs, and other hardy evergreens, inaccessibly rising in grim terraces for some two thousand feet.

The building is a paper-mill.

Having embarked on a large scale in the seedsman's business (so extensively and broadcast, indeed, that at length my seeds were distributed through all the Eastern and Northern States, and even fell into the far soil of Missouri and the Carolinas), the demand for paper at my place became so great, that the expenditure soon amounted to a most important item in the general account. It need hardly be hinted how paper comes into use with seedsmen, as envelopes. These are mostly made of yellowish paper, folded square; and when filled, are all but flat, and being stamped, and superscribed with the nature of the seeds contained, assume not a little the appearance of business-letters ready for the mail. Of these small envelopes I used an incredible quantity—several hundreds of thousands in a year. For a time I had purchased my paper from the wholesale dealers in a neighboring town. For economy's sake, and partly for the adventure of the trip, I now resolved to cross the mountains, some sixty miles, and order my future paper at the Devil's Dungeon paper-mill.

The sleighing being uncommonly fine toward the end of January, and promising to hold so for no small period, in spite of the bitter cold I started one gray Friday noon in my pung,[3] well fitted with buffalo and wolf robes; and, spending one night on the road, next noon came in sight of Woedolor Mountain.

The far summit fairly smoked with frost; white vapors curled up from its white-wooded top, as from a chimney. The intense congelation made the whole country look like one petrifaction. The steel shoes of my pung craunched and gritted over the vitreous, chippy snow, as if it had been broken glass. The forests here and there skirting the route, feeling the same all-stiffening influence, their inmost fibres penetrated with the cold, strangely groaned—not in the swaying branches merely, but likewise in the vertical trunk—as the fitful gusts remorselessly swept through them. Brittle with excessive frost, many colossal tough-grained maples, snapped in twain like pipe-stems, cumbered the unfeeling earth.

Flaked all over with frozen sweat, white as a milky ram, his nostrils at each breath sending forth two horn-shaped shoots of heated respiration, Black, my

1. A 14th-century castle on the Rhine River in Germany.
2. A recollection of Jesus' description of the Scribes and Pharisees as "whited sepulchres, which indeed appear beautiful outward, but are within full of dead men's bones, and of all uncleanness" (Matthew 23.27).
3. Boxlike one-horse sleigh.

good horse, but six years old, started at a sudden turn, where, right across the track—not ten minutes fallen—an old distorted hemlock lay, darkly undulatory as an anaconda.

Gaining the Bellows'-pipe, the violent blast, dead from behind, all but shoved my high-backed pung up-hill. The gust shrieked through the shivered pass, as if laden with lost spirits bound to the unhappy world. Ere gaining the summit, Black, my horse, as if exasperated by the cutting wind, slung out with his strong hind legs, tore the light pung straight up-hill, and sweeping grazingly through the narrow notch, sped downward madly past the ruined saw-mill. Into the Devil's Dungeon horse and cataract rushed together.

With might and main, quitting my seat and robes, and standing backward, with one foot braced against the dash-board, I rasped and churned the bit, and stopped him just in time to avoid collision, at a turn, with the bleak nozzle of a rock, couchant[4] like a lion in the way—a road-side rock.

At first I could not discover the paper-mill.

The whole hollow gleamed with the white, except, here and there, where a pinnacle of granite showed one wind-swept angle bare. The mountains stood pinned in shrouds—a pass of Alpine corpses. Where stands the mill? Suddenly a whirling, humming sound broke upon my ear. I looked, and there, like an arrested avalanche, lay the large whitewashed factory. It was subordinately surrounded by a cluster of other and smaller buildings, some of which, from their cheap, blank air, great length, gregarious windows, and comfortless expression, no doubt were boarding-houses of the operatives.[5] A snow-white hamlet amidst the snows. Various rude, irregular squares and courts resulted from the somewhat picturesque clusterings of these buildings, owing to the broken, rocky nature of the ground, which forbade all method in their relative arrangement. Several narrow lanes and alleys, too, partly blocked with snow fallen from the roof, cut up the hamlet in all directions.

When, turning from the traveled highway, jingling with bells of numerous farmers—who, availing themselves of the fine sleighing, were dragging their wood to market—and frequently diversified with swift cutters dashing from inn to inn of the scattered villages—when, I say, turning from that bustling main-road, I by degrees wound into the Mad Maid's Bellows'-pipe, and saw the grim Black Notch beyond, then something latent, as well as something obvious in the time and scene, strangely brought back to my mind my first sight of dark and grimy Temple-Bar. And when Black, my horse, went darting through the Notch, perilously grazing its rocky wall, I remembered being in a runaway London omnibus, which in much the same sort of style, though by no means at an equal rate, dashed through the ancient arch of Wren.[6] Though the two objects did by no means completely correspond, yet this partial inadequacy but served to tinge the similitude not less with the vividness than the disorder of a dream. So that, when upon reining up at the protruding rock I at last caught sight of the quaint groupings of the factory-buildings, and with the traveled highway and the Notch behind, found myself all alone, silently and privily stealing through deep-cloven passages into this sequestered spot, and saw the long, high-gabled main factory edifice, with a rude tower—for hoisting[7] heavy boxes—at one end, standing

4. Crouching.
5. Factory workers.
6. At Temple Bar (see n. 8, p. 1516).
7. I.e., with a pulley fastening to the outhanging structure.

among its crowded outbuildings and boarding-houses, as the Temple Church amidst the surrounding offices and dormitories, and when the marvelous retirement of this mysterious mountain nook fastened its whole spell upon me, then, what memory lacked, all tributary imagination furnished, and I said to myself, "This is the very counterpart of the Paradise of Bachelors, but snowed upon, and frost-painted to a sepulchre."

Dismounting, and warily picking my way down the dangerous declivity—horse and man both sliding now and then upon the icy ledges—at length I drove, or the blast drove me, into the largest square, before one side of the main edifice. Piercingly and shrilly the shotted blast blew by the corner; and redly and demoniacally boiled Blood River at one side. A long woodpile, of many scores of cords, all glittering in mail of crusted ice, stood crosswise in the square. A row of horse-posts, their north sides plastered with adhesive snow, flanked the factory wall. The bleak frost packed and paved the square as with some ringing metal.

The inverted similitude recurred—"The sweet, tranquil Temple-garden, with the Thames bordering its green beds," strangely meditated I.

But where are the gay bachelors?

Then, as I and my horse stood shivering in the wind-spray, a girl ran from a neighboring dormitory door, and throwing her thin apron over her bare head, made for the opposite building.

"One moment, my girl; is there no shed hereabouts which I may drive into?"

Pausing, she turned upon me a face pale with work, and blue with cold; an eye supernatural with unrelated misery.

"Nay," faltered I, "I mistook you. Go on; I want nothing."

Leading my horse close to the door from which she had come, I knocked. Another pale, blue girl appeared, shivering in the doorway as, to prevent the blast, she jealously held the door ajar.

"Nay, I mistake again. In God's name shut the door. But hold, is there no man about?"

That moment a dark-complexioned well-wrapped personage passed, making for the factory door, and spying him coming, the girl rapidly closed the other one.

"Is there no horse-shed here, Sir?"

"Yonder, to the wood-shed," he replied, and disappeared inside the factory.

With much ado I managed to wedge in horse and pung between the scattered piles of wood all sawn and split. Then, blanketing my horse, and piling my buffalo on the blanket's top, tucking in its edges well around the breast-hand and breeching, so that the wind might not strip him bare, I tied him fast, and ran lamely for the factory door, stiff with frost, and cumbered with my driver's dreadnaught.[8]

Immediately I found myself standing in a spacious place, intolerably lighted by long rows of windows, focusing inward the snowy scene without.

At rows of blank-looking counters sat rows of blank-looking girls, with blank, white folders in the blank hands, all blankly folding blank paper.

8. Thick woolen coat.

In one corner stood some huge frame of ponderous iron, with a vertical thing like a piston periodically rising and falling upon a heavy wooden block. Before it—its tame minister—stood a tall girl, feeding the iron animal with half-quires[9] of rose-hued note paper, which, at every downward dab of the piston-like machine, received in the corner the impress of a wreath of roses. I looked from the rosy paper to the pallid cheek, but said nothing.

Seated before a long apparatus, strung with long, slender strings like any harp, another girl was feeding it with foolscap sheets,[1] which, so soon as they curiously traveled from her on the cords, were withdrawn at the opposite end of the machine by a second girl. They came to the first girl blank; they went to the second girl ruled.

I looked upon the first girl's brow, and saw it was young and fair; I looked upon the second girl's brow, and saw it was ruled and wrinkled. Then, as I still looked, the two—for some small variety to the monotony—changed places; and where had stood the young, fair brow, now stood the ruled and wrinkled one.

Perched high upon a narrow platform, and still higher upon a high stool crowning it, sat another figure serving some other iron animal; while below the platform sat her mate in some sort of reciprocal attendance.

Not a syllable was breathed. Nothing was heard but the low, steady, overruling hum of the iron animals. The human voice was banished from the spot. Machinery—that vaunted slave of humanity—here stood menially served by human beings, who served mutely and cringingly as the slave serves the Sultan. The girls did not so much seem accessory wheels to the general machinery as mere cogs to the wheels.

All this scene around me was instantaneously taken in at one sweeping glance—even before I had proceeded to unwind the heavy fur tippet[2] from around my neck. But as soon as this fell from me the dark-complexioned man, standing close by, raised a sudden cry, and seizing my arm, dragged me out into the open air, and without pausing for a word instantly caught up some congealed snow and began rubbing both my cheeks.

"Two white spots like the whites of your eyes," he said; "man, your cheeks are frozen."

"That may well be," muttered I, "'tis some wonder the frost of the Devil's Dungeon strikes in no deeper. Rub away."

Soon a horrible, tearing pain caught at my reviving cheeks. Two gaunt blood-hounds, one on each side, seemed mumbling them. I seemed Actæon.[3]

Presently, when all was over, I re-entered the factory, made known my business, concluded it satisfactorily, and then begged to be conducted throughout the place to view it.

"Cupid is the boy for that," said the dark-complexioned man. "Cupid!" and by this odd fancy-name calling a dimpled, red-cheeked, spirited-looking, forward little fellow, who was rather impudently, I thought, gliding about among the passive-looking girls—like a gold fish through hueless waves—yet doing nothing in particular that I could see, the man bade him lead the stranger through the edifice.

9. Twelve sheets of paper.
1. Writing paper, usually about thirteen by seventeen inches.
2. Muffler.
3. In Greek mythology, the hunter who watched Diana (Artemis) bathing and was punished by being turned into a stag that was then torn apart by his own dogs.

"Come first and see the water-wheel," said this lively lad, with the air of boyishly-brisk importance.

Quitting the folding-room, we crossed some damp, cold boards, and stood beneath a great wet shed, incessantly showering with foam, like the green barnacled bow of some East India-man[4] in a gale. Round and round here went the enormous revolutions of the dark colossal water-wheel, grim with its one immutable purpose.

"This sets our whole machinery a-going, Sir; in every part of all these buildings; where the girls work and all."

I looked, and saw that the turbid waters of Blood River had not changed their hue by coming under the use of man.

"You make only blank paper; no printing of any sort, I suppose? All blank paper, don't you?"

"Certainly; what else should a paper-factory make?"

The lad here looked at me as if suspicious of my common-sense.

"Oh, to be sure!" said I, confused and stammering; "it only struck me as so strange that red waters should turn out pale chee—paper, I mean."

He took me up a wet and rickety stair to a great light room, furnished with no visible thing but rude, manger-like receptacles running all round its sides; and up to these mangers, like so many mares haltered to the rack, stood rows of girls. Before each was vertically thrust up a long, glittering scythe, immovably fixed at bottom to the manger-edge. The curve of the scythe, and its having no snath[5] to it, made it look exactly like a sword. To and fro, across the sharp edge, the girls forever dragged long strips of rags, washed white, picked from baskets at one side; thus ripping asunder every seam, and converting the tatters almost into lint. The air swam with the fine, poisonous particles, which from all sides darted, subtilely, as motes in sunbeams, into the lungs.

"This is the rag-room," coughed the boy.

"You find it rather stifling here," coughed I, in answer; "but the girls don't cough."

"Oh, they are used to it."

"Where do you get such hosts of rags?" picking up a handful from a basket.

"Some from the country round about; some from far over sea—Leghorn[6] and London."

"'Tis not unlikely, then," murmured I, "that among these heaps of rags there may be some old shirts, gathered from the dormitories of the Paradise of Bachelors. But the buttons are all dropped off. Pray, my lad, do you ever find any bachelor's buttons hereabouts?"

"None grow in this part of the country. The Devil's Dungeon is no place for flowers."

"Oh! you mean the *flowers* so called—the Bachelor's Buttons?"

"And was not that what you asked about? Or did you mean the gold bosom-buttons of our boss, Old Bach,[7] as our whispering girls all call him?"

"The man, then, I saw below is a bachelor, is he?"

"Oh, yes, he's a Bach."

4. Enormous, many-sailed ship in the East India Company's fleet.
5. Curved handle.
6. Livorno, port on the northwestern coast of Italy.
7. Pronounced *batch*.

"The edges of those swords, they are turned outward from the girls, if I see right; but their rags and fingers fly so, I can not distinctly see."

"Turned outward."

Yes, murmured I to myself; I see it now; turned outward; and each erected sword is so borne, edge-outward, before each girl. If my reading fails me not, just so, of old, condemned state-prisoners went from the hall of judgment to their doom: an officer before, bearing a sword, its edge turned outward, in significance of their fatal sentence. So, through consumptive pallors[8] of this blank, raggy life, go these white girls to death.

"Those scythes look very sharp," again turning toward the boy.

"Yes; they have to keep them so. Look!"

That moment two of the girls, dropping their rags, plied each a whetstone up and down the sword-blade. My unaccustomed blood curdled at the sharp shriek of the tormented steel.

Their own executioners; themselves whetting the very swords that slay them; meditated I.

"What makes those girls so sheet-white, my lad?"

"Why"—with a roguish twinkle, pure ignorant drollery, not knowing heartlessness—"I suppose the handling of such white bits of sheets all the time makes them so sheety."

"Let us leave the rag-room now, my lad."

More tragical and more inscrutably mysterious than any mystic sight, human or machine, throughout the factory, was the strange innocence of cruel-heartedness in this usage-hardened boy.

"And now," said he, cheerily, "I suppose you want to see our great machine, which cost us twelve thousand dollars only last autumn. That's the machine that makes the paper, too. This way, Sir."

Following him, I crossed a large, bespattered place, with two great round vats in it, full of a white, wet, woolly-looking stuff, not unlike the albuminous part of an egg, soft-boiled.

"There," said Cupid, tapping the vats carelessly, "these are the first beginnings of the paper; this white pulp you see. Look how it swims bubbling round and round, moved by the paddle here. From hence it pours from both vats into that one common channel yonder; and so goes, mixed up and leisurely, to the great machine. And now for that."

He led me into a room, stifling with a strange, blood-like, abdominal heat, as if here, true enough, were being finally developed the germinous particles lately seen.

Before me, rolled out like some long Eastern manuscript, lay stretched one continuous length of iron frame-work—multitudinous and mystical, with all sorts of rollers, wheels, and cylinders, in slowly-measured and unceasing motion.

"Here first comes the pulp now," said Cupid, pointing to the nighest end of the machine. "See; first it pours out and spreads itself upon this wide, sloping board; and then—look—slides, thin and quivering, beneath the first roller there. Follow on now, and see it as it slides from under that to the next cylinder. There; see how it has become just a very little less pulpy now. One step

8. I.e., the paleness characteristic of tuberculosis.

more, and it grows still more to some slight consistence. Sill another cylinder, and it is so knitted—though as yet mere dragon-fly wing—that it forms an air-bridge here, like a suspended cobweb, between two more separated rollers; and flowing over the last one, and under again, and doubling about there out of sight for a minute among all those mixed cylinders you indistinctly see, it reappears here, looking now at last a little less like pulp and more like paper, but still quite delicate and defective yet awhile. But—a little further onward, Sir, if you please—here now, at this further point, it puts on something of a real look, as if it might turn out to be something you might possibly handle in the end. But it's not yet done, Sir. Good way to travel yet, and plenty more of cylinders must roll it."

"Bless my soul!" said I, amazed at the elongation, interminable convolutions, and deliberate slowness of the machine; "it must take a long time for the pulp to pass from end to end, and come out paper."

"Oh! not so long," smiled the precocious lad, with a superior and patronizing air; "only nine minutes. But look; you may try it for yourself. Have you a bit of paper? Ah! here's a bit on the floor. Now mark that with any word you please, and let me dab it on here, and we'll see how long before it comes out at the other end."

"Well, let me see," said I, taking out my pencil; "come, I'll mark it with your name."

Bidding me take out my watch, Cupid adroitly dropped the inscribed slip on an exposed part of the incipient mass.

Instantly my eye marked the second-hand on my dial-plate.

Slowly I followed the slip, inch by inch; sometimes pausing for full half a minute as it disappeared beneath inscrutable groups of the lower cylinders, but only gradually to emerge again; and so, on, and on, and on—inch by inch; now in open sight, sliding along like a freckle on the quivering sheet; and then again wholly vanished; and so, on, and on, and on—inch by inch; all the time the main sheet growing more and more to final firmness—when, suddenly, I saw a sort of paper-fall, not wholly unlike a water-fall; a scissory sound smote my ear, as of some cord being snapped; and down dropped an unfolded sheet of perfect foolscap, with my "Cupid" half faded out of it, and still moist and warm.

My travels were at an end, for here was the end of the machine.

"Well, how long was it?" said Cupid.

"Nine minutes to a second," replied I, watch in hand.

"I told you so."

For a moment a curious emotion filled me, not wholly unlike that which one might experience at the fulfillment of some mysterious prophecy. But how absurd, thought I again; the thing is a mere machine, the essence of which is unvarying punctuality and precision.

Previously absorbed by the wheels and cylinders, my attention was now directed to a sad-looking woman standing by.

"That is rather an elderly person so silently tending the machine-end here. She would not seem wholly used to it either."

"Oh," knowingly whispered Cupid, through the din, "she only came last week. She was a nurse formerly. But the business is poor in these parts, and she's left it. But look at the paper she is piling there."

"Ay, foolscap," handling the piles of moist, warm sheets, which continually were being delivered into the woman's waiting hands. "Don't you turn out any thing but foolscap at this machine?"

"Oh, sometimes, but not often, we turn out finer work—creamlaid and royal sheets, we call them. But foolscap being in chief demand, we turn out foolscap most."

It was very curious. Looking at that blank paper continually dropping, dropping, dropping, my mind ran on in wonderings of those strange uses to which those thousand sheets eventually would be put. All sorts of writings would be writ on those now vacant things—sermons, lawyers' briefs, physicians' prescriptions, love-letters, marriage certificates, bills of divorce, registers of births, death-warrants, and so on, without end. Then, recurring back to them as they here lay all blank, I could not but bethink me of that celebrated comparison of John Locke, who, in demonstration of his theory that man had no innate ideas, compared the human mind at birth to a sheet of blank paper;[9] something destined to be scribbled on, but what sort of characters no soul might tell.

Pacing slowly to and fro along the involved machine, still humming with its play, I was struck as well by the inevitability as the evolvement-power in all its motions.

"Does that thin cobweb there," said I, pointing to the sheet in its more imperfect stage, "does that never tear or break? It is marvelous fragile, and yet this machine it passes through is so mighty."

"It never is known to tear a hair's point."

"Does it never stop—get clogged?"

"No. It *must* go. The machinery makes it go just *so*; just that very way, and at that very pace you there plainly *see* it go. The pulp can't help going."

Something of awe now stole over me, as I gazed upon this inflexible iron animal. Always, more or less, machinery of this ponderous, elaborate sort strikes, in some moods, strange dread into the human heart, as some living, panting Behemoth might. But what made the thing I saw so specially terrible to me was the metallic necessity, the unbudging fatality which governed it. Though, here and there, I could not follow the thin, gauzy vail of pulp in the course of its more mysterious or entirely invisible advance, yet it was indubitable that, at those points where it eluded me, it still marched on in unvarying docility to the autocratic cunning of the machine. A fascination fastened on me. I stood spellbound and wandering in my soul. Before my eyes—there, passing in slow procession along the wheeling cylinders, I seemed to see, glued to the pallid incipience of the pulp, the yet more pallid faces of all the pallid girls, I had eyed that heavy day. Slowly, mournfully, beseechingly, yet unresistingly, they gleamed along, their agony dimly outlined on the imperfect paper, like the print of the tormented face on the handkerchief of Saint Veronica.[1]

"Halloa! the heat of the room is too much for you," cried Cupid, staring at me.

9. Locke (1632–1704), English philosopher, compared the mind of a newborn to a *tabula rasa* (Latin), or blank slate, in *Essay Concerning Human Understanding* (1690).

1. Legendary woman who wiped the bleeding face of Jesus as he carried the cross to Calvary and then found that the handkerchief was imprinted with the image of his face.

"No—I am rather chill, if any thing."

"Come out, Sir—out—out," and, with the protecting air of a careful father, the precocious lad hurried me outside.

In a few moments, feeling revived a little, I went into the folding-room—the first room I had entered, and where the desk for transacting business stood, surrounded by the blank counters and blank girls engaged at them.

"Cupid here has led me a strange tour," said I to the dark-complexioned man before mentioned, whom I had ere this discovered not only to be an old bachelor, but also the principal proprietor. "Yours is a most wonderful factory. Your great machine is a miracle of inscrutable intricacy."

"Yes, all our visitors think it so. But we don't have many. We are in a very out-of-the-way corner here. Few inhabitants, too. Most of our girls come from far-off villages."

"The girls," echoed I, glancing round at their silent forms. "Why is it, Sir, that in most factories, female operatives, of whatever age, are indiscriminately called girls, never women?"

"Oh! as to that—why, I suppose, the fact of their being generally unmarried—that's the reason, I should think. But it never struck me before. For our factory here, we will not have married women; they are apt to be off-and-on too much. We want none but steady workers: twelve hours to the day, day after day, through the three hundred and sixty-five days, excepting Sundays, Thanksgiving, and Fastdays. That's our rule. And so, having no married women, what females we have are rightly enough called girls."

"Then these are all maids," said I, while some pained homage to their pale virginity made me involuntarily bow.

"All maids."

Again the strange emotion filled me.

"Your cheeks look whitish yet, Sir," said the man, gazing at me narrowly. "You must be careful going home. Do they pain you at all now? It's a bad sign, if they do."

"No doubt, Sir," answered I, "when once I have got out of the Devil's Dungeon, I shall feel them mending."

"Ah, yes; the winter air in valleys, or gorges, or any sunken place, is far colder and more bitter than elsewhere. You would hardly believe it now, but it is colder here than at the top of Woedolor Mountain."

"I dare say it is, Sir. But time presses me; I must depart."

With that, remuffling myself in dread-naught and tippet, thrusting my hands into my huge seal-skin mittens, I sallied out into the nipping air, and found poor Black, my horse, all cringing and doubled up with the cold.

Soon, wrapped in furs and meditations, I ascended from the Devil's Dungeon.

At the Black Notch I paused, and once more bethought me of Temple-Bar. Then, shooting through the pass, all alone with inscrutable nature, I exclaimed—Oh! Paradise of Bachelors! and oh! Tartarus of Maids!

1855

Benito Cereno[1]

In the year 1799, Captain Amasa Delano, of Duxbury, in Massachusetts, commanding a large sealer and general trader, lay at anchor, with a valuable cargo, in the harbor of St. Maria—a small, desert, uninhabited island toward the southern extremity of the long coast of Chili. There he had touched for water.

On the second day, not long after dawn, while lying in his berth, his mate came below, informing him that a strange sail was coming into the bay. Ships were then not so plenty in those waters as now. He rose, dressed, and went on deck.

The morning was one peculiar to that coast. Everything was mute and calm; everything gray. The sea, though undulated into long roods of swells, seemed fixed, and was sleeked at the surface like waved lead that has cooled and set in the smelter's mold. The sky seemed a gray surtout.[2] Flights of troubled gray fowl, kith and kin with flights of troubled gray vapors among which they were mixed, skimmed low and fitfully over the waters, as swallows over meadows before storms. Shadows present, foreshadowing deeper shadows to come.

To Captain Delano's surprise, the stranger, viewed through the glass,[3] showed no colors; though to do so upon entering a haven, however uninhabited in its shores, where but a single other ship might be lying, was the custom among peaceful seamen of all nations. Considering the lawlessness and loneliness of the spot, and the sort of stories, at that day, associated with those seas, Captain Delano's surprise might have deepened into some uneasiness had he not been a person of a singularly undistrustful good nature, not liable, except on extraordinary and repeated incentives, and hardly then, to indulge in personal alarms, any way involving the imputation of malign evil in man. Whether, in view of what humanity is capable, such a trait implies, along with a benevolent heart, more than ordinary quickness and accuracy of intellectual perception, may be left to the wise to determine.

But whatever misgivings might have obtruded on first seeing the stranger, would almost, in any seaman's mind, have been dissipated by observing that, the ship, in navigating into the harbor, was drawing too near the land; a sunken reef making out off her bow. This seemed to prove her a stranger, indeed, not only to the sealer, but the island; consequently, she could be no wonted freebooter[4] on that ocean. With no small interest, Captain Delano continued to watch her—a proceeding not much facilitated by the vapors partly mantling the hull, through which the far matin light from her cabin streamed equivocally enough; much like the sun—by this time hemisphered on the rim of the horizon, and apparently, in company with the strange ship, entering the harbor—which, wimpled by the same low, creeping clouds,

1. This text is based on the first printing, in *Putnam's Monthly* for October, November, and December 1855, but it also incorporates the many small revisions Melville made for its 1856 republication in *The Piazza Tales.* Melville based his plot on a few narrative pages in ch. 18 of Captain Amasa Delano's *Narrative of Voyages and Travels in the Northern and Southern Hemispheres* (1817). Melville's "deposition" near the end of *Benito Cereno* is roughly half from Delano's much longer section of documents, half his own writing. (A later relative of the real Delano [1763–1823] was Franklin Delano Roosevelt.)

2. Long overcoat.

3. Spyglass or telescope.

4. Pirate.

showed not unlike a Lima intriguante's one sinister eye peering across the Plaza from the Indian loop-hole of her dusk *saya-y-manta*.[5]

It might have been but a deception of the vapors, but, the longer the stranger was watched, the more singular appeared her maneuvers. Ere long it seemed hard to decide whether she meant to come in or no—what she wanted, or what she was about. The wind, which had breezed up a little during the night, was now extremely light and baffling, which the more increased the apparent uncertainty of her movements.

Surmising, at last, that it might be a ship in distress, Captain Delano ordered his whale-boat to be dropped, and, much to the wary opposition of his mate, prepared to board her, and, at the least, pilot her in. On the night previous, a fishing-party of the seamen had gone a long distance to some detached rocks out of sight from the sealer, and, an hour or two before daybreak, had returned, having met with no small success. Presuming that the stranger might have been long off soundings, the good captain put several baskets of the fish, for presents, into his boat, and so pulled away. From her continuing too near the sunken reef, deeming her in danger, calling to his men, he made all haste to apprise those on board of their situation. But, some time ere the boat came up, the wind, light though it was, having shifted, had headed the vessel off, as well as partly broken the vapors from about her.

Upon gaining a less remote view, the ship, when made signally visible on the verge of the leaden-hued swells, with the shreds of fog here and there raggedly furring her, appeared like a white-washed monastery after a thunderstorm, seen perched upon some dun cliff among the Pyrenees. But it was no purely fanciful resemblance which now, for a moment, almost led Captain Delano to think that nothing less than a ship-load of monks was before him. Peering over the bulwarks were what really seemed, in the hazy distance, throngs of dark cowls; while, fitfully revealed through the open port-holes, other dark moving figures were dimly descried, as of Black Friars[6] pacing the cloisters.

Upon a still nigher approach, this appearance was modified, and the true character of the vessel was plain—a Spanish merchantman of the first class; carrying negro slaves, amongst other valuable freight, from one colonial port to another. A very large, and, in its time, a very fine vessel, such as in those days were at intervals encountered along that main; sometimes superseded Acapulco treasure-ships, or retired frigates of the Spanish king's navy, which, like superannuated Italian palaces, still, under a decline of masters, preserved signs of former state.

As the whale-boat drew more and more nigh, the cause of the peculiar pipe-clayed[7] aspect of the stranger was seen in the slovenly neglect pervading her. The spars, ropes, and great part of the bulwarks, looked woolly, from long unacquaintance with the scraper, tar, and the brush. Her keel seemed laid, her ribs put together, and she launched, from Ezekiel's Valley of Dry Bones.[8]

5. Skirt-and-cloak combination, the shawl part of which could be drawn about the face so that little more than an eye would show. "Matin": early morning. "Wimpled": veiled.

6. Dominicans; an order of monks who wore black robes, including hoods.

7. Whitened.

8. Ezekiel 37.1.

In the present business in which she was engaged, the ship's general model and rig appeared to have undergone no material change from their original war-like and Froissart pattern.[9] However, no guns were seen.

The tops were large, and were railed about with what had once been octagonal net-work, all now in sad disrepair. These tops hung overhead like three ruinous aviaries, in one of which was seen perched, on a ratlin, a white noddy,[1] strange fowl, so called from its lethargic, somnambulistic character, being frequently caught by hand at sea. Battered and mouldy, the castellated forecastle seemed some ancient turret, long ago taken by assault, and then left to decay. Toward the stern, two high-raised quarter galleries—the balustrades here and there covered with dry, tindery sea-moss—opening out from the unoccupied state-cabin, whose dead lights, for all the mild weather, were hermetically closed and calked—these tenantless balconies hung over the sea as if it were the grand Venetian canal. But the principal relic of faded grandeur was the ample oval of the shield-like stern-piece, intricately carved with the arms of Castile and Leon,[2] medallioned about by groups of mythological or symbolical devices; uppermost and central of which was a dark satyr in a mask, holding his foot on the prostrate neck of a writhing figure, likewise masked.

Whether the ship had a figure-head, or only a plain beak, was not quite certain, owing to canvas wrapped about that part, either to protect it while undergoing a re-furbishing, or else decently to hide its decay. Rudely painted or chalked, as in a sailor freak, along the forward side of a sort of pedestal below the canvas, was the sentence, "*Seguid vuestro jefe,*" (follow your leader); while upon the tarnished head-boards, near by, appeared, in stately capitals, once gilt, the ship's name, "SAN DOMINICK," each letter streakingly corroded with tricklings of copper-spike rust; while, like mourning weeds, dark festoons of sea-grass slimily swept to and fro over the name, with every hearse-like roll of the hull.

As at last the boat was hooked from the bow along toward the gangway amidship, its keel, while yet some inches separated from the hull, harshly grated as on a sunken coral reef. It proved a huge bunch of conglobated barnacles adhering below the water to the side like a wen;[3] a token of baffling airs and long calms passed somewhere in those seas.

Climbing the side, the visitor was at once surrounded by a clamorous throng of whites and blacks, but the latter outnumbering the former more than could have been expected, negro transportation-ship as the stranger in port was. But, in one language, and as with one voice, all poured out a common tale of suffering; in which the negresses, of whom there were not a few, exceeded the others in their dolorous vehemence. The scurvy, together with a fever, had swept off a great part of their number, more especially the Spaniards. Off Cape Horn,[4] they had narrowly escaped shipwreck; then, for days together, they had lain tranced without wind; their provisions were low; their water next to none; their lips that moment were baked.

9. Medieval; from Jean Froissart (1337–1410), historian of wars of England and France.
1. Seabird, usually black or brown. "Ratlin": small rope attached to the shrouds of a ship and forming a step of a rope ladder.
2. Old kingdoms of Spain; the arms would include a castle for Castile and a lion for León.
3. Cyst. "Conglobated": ball-like.
4. At the southern tip of South America.

While Captain Delano was thus made the mark of all eager tongues, his one eager glance took in all the faces, with every other object about him.

Always upon first boarding a large and populous ship at sea, especially a foreign one, with a nondescript crew such as Lascars or Manilla men,[5] the impression varies in a peculiar way from that produced by first entering a strange house with strange inmates in a strange land. Both house and ship, the one by its walls and blinds, the other by its high bulwarks like ramparts, hoard from view their interiors till the last moment; but in the case of the ship there is this addition; that the living spectacle it contains, upon its sudden and complete disclosure, has, in contrast with the blank ocean which zones it, something of the effect of enchantment. The ship seems unreal; these strange costumes, gestures, and faces, but a shadowy tableau just emerged from the deep, which directly must receive back what it gave.

Perhaps it was some such influence as above is attempted to be described, which, in Captain Delano's mind, hightened whatever, upon a staid scrutiny, might have seemed unusual; especially the conspicuous figures of four elderly grizzled negroes, their heads like black, doddered willow tops, who, in venerable contrast to the tumult below them, were couched sphynx-like, one on the starboard cat-head,[6] another on the larboard, and the remaining pair face to face on the opposite bulwarks above the main-chains. They each had bits of unstranded old junk in their hands, and, with a sort of stoical self-content, were picking the junk into oakum,[7] a small heap of which lay by their sides. They accompanied the task with a continuous, low, monotonous chant; droning and druling[8] away like so many gray-headed bag-pipers playing a funeral march.

The quarter-deck rose into an ample elevated poop, upon the forward verge of which, lifted, like the oakum-pickers, some eight feet above the general throng, sat along in a row, separated by regular spaces, the cross-legged figures of six other blacks; each with a rusty hatchet in his hand, which, with a bit of brick and a rag, he was engaged like a scullion in scouring; while between each two was a small stack of hatchets, their rusted edges turned forward awaiting a like operation. Though occasionally the four oakum-pickers would briefly address some person or persons in the crowd below, yet the six hatchet-polishers neither spoke to others, nor breathed a whisper among themselves, but sat intent upon their task, except at intervals, when, with the peculiar love in negroes of uniting industry with pastime, two and two they sideways clashed their hatchets together, like cymbals, with a barbarous din. All six, unlike the generality, had the raw aspect of unsophisticated Africans.

But that first comprehensive glance which took in those ten figures, with scores less conspicuous, rested but an instant upon them, as, impatient of the hubbub of voices, the visitor turned in quest of whomsoever it might be that commanded the ship.

But as if not unwilling to let nature make known her own case among his suffering charge, or else in despair of restraining it for the time, the Spanish

5. From East India or the Philippines, respectively.
6. Projecting piece of timber near the bow (to which the anchor is hoisted and secured).
7. Loose fiber from pieces of rope, used as waterproof sealant. "Old junk": worn-out rope.
8. Moaning.

captain, a gentlemanly, reserved-looking, and rather young man to a stranger's eye, dressed with singular richness, but bearing plain traces of recent sleepless cares and disquietudes, stood passively by, leaning against the main-mast, at one moment casting a dreary, spiritless look upon his excited people, at the next an unhappy glance toward his visitor. By his side stood a black of small stature, in whose rude face, as occasionally, like a shepherd's dog, he mutely turned it up into the Spaniard's, sorrow and affection were equally blended.

Struggling through the throng, the American advanced to the Spaniard, assuring him of his sympathies, and offering to render whatever assistance might be in his power. To which the Spaniard returned, for the present, but grave and ceremonious acknowledgments, his national formality dusked by the saturnine mood of ill health.

But losing no time in mere compliments, Captain Delano returning to the gangway, had his baskets of fish brought up; and as the wind still continued light, so that some hours at least must elapse ere the ship could be brought to the anchorage, he bade his men return to the sealer, and fetch back as much water as the whale-boat could carry, with whatever soft bread the steward might have, all the remaining pumpkins on board, with a box of sugar, and a dozen of his private bottles of cider.

Not many minutes after the boat's pushing off, to the vexation of all, the wind entirely died away, and the tide turning, began drifting back the ship helplessly seaward. But trusting this would not long last, Captain Delano sought with good hopes to cheer up the strangers, feeling no small satisfaction that, with persons in their condition he could—thanks to his frequent voyages along the Spanish main[9]—converse with some freedom in their native tongue.

While left alone with them, he was not long in observing some things tending to heighten his first impressions; but surprise was lost in pity, both for the Spaniards and blacks, alike evidently reduced from scarcity of water and provisions; while long-continued suffering seemed to have brought out the less good-natured qualities of the negroes, besides, at the same time, impairing the Spaniard's authority over them. But, under the circumstances, precisely this condition of things was to have been anticipated. In armies, navies, cities, or families, in nature herself, nothing more relaxes good order than misery. Still, Captain Delano was not without the idea, that had Benito Cereno been a man of greater energy, misrule would hardly have come to the present pass. But the debility, constitutional or induced by the hardships, bodily and mental, of the Spanish captain, was too obvious to be overlooked. A prey to settled dejection, as if long mocked with hope he would not now indulge it, even when it had ceased to be a mock, the prospect of that day or evening at furthest, lying at anchor, with plenty of water for his people, and a brother captain to counsel and befriend, seemed in no perceptible degree to encourage him. His mind appeared unstrung, if not still more seriously affected. Shut up in these oaken walls, chained to one dull round of command, whose unconditionality cloyed him, like some hypochondriac abbot he moved slowly about, at times suddenly pausing, starting, or staring, biting his

9. Sometimes used for the Caribbean Sea, but here the Atlantic and Pacific coasts of South America (mainland as opposed to islands).

lip, biting his finger-nail, flushing, paling, twitching his beard, with other symptoms of an absent or moody mind. This distempered spirit was lodged, as before hinted, in as distempered a frame. He was rather tall, but seemed never to have been robust, and now with nervous suffering was almost worn to a skeleton. A tendency to some pulmonary complaint appeared to have been lately confirmed. His voice was like that of one with lungs half gone, hoarsely suppressed, a husky whisper. No wonder that, as in this state he tottered about, his private servant apprehensively followed him. Sometimes the negro gave his master his arm, or took his handkerchief out of his pocket for him; performing these and similar offices with that affectionate zeal which transmutes into something filial or fraternal acts in themselves but menial; and which has gained for the negro the repute of making the most pleasing body servant in the world; one, too, whom a master need be on no stiffly superior terms with, but may treat with familiar trust; less a servant than a devoted companion.

Marking the noisy indocility of the blacks in general, as well as what seemed the sullen inefficiency of the whites, it was not without humane satisfaction that Captain Delano witnessed the steady good conduct of Babo.

But the good conduct of Babo, hardly more than the ill-behavior of others, seemed to withdraw the half-lunatic Don Benito from his cloudy langour. Not that such precisely was the impression made by the Spaniard on the mind of his visitor. The Spaniard's individual unrest was, for the present, but noted as a conspicuous feature in the ship's general affliction. Still, Captain Delano was not a little concerned at what he could not help taking for the time to be Don Benito's unfriendly indifference towards himself. The Spaniard's manner, too, conveyed a sort of sour and gloomy disdain, which he seemed at no pains to disguise. But this the American in charity ascribed to the harassing effects of sickness, since, in former instances, he had noted that there are peculiar natures on whom prolonged physical suffering seems to cancel every social instinct of kindness; as if forced to black bread themselves, they deemed it but equity that each person coming nigh them should, indirectly, by some slight or affront, be made to partake of their fare.

But ere long Captain Delano bethought him that, indulgent as he was at the first, in judging the Spaniard, he might not, after all, have exercised charity enough. At bottom it was Don Benito's reserve which displeased him; but the same reserve was shown towards all but his faithful personal attendant. Even the formal reports which, according to sea-usage, were, at stated times, made to him by some petty underling, either a white, mulatto or black, he hardly had patience enough to listen to, without betraying contemptuous aversion. His manner upon such occasions was, in its degree, not unlike that which might be supposed to have been his imperial countryman's, Charles V.,[1] just previous to the anchoritish retirement of that monarch from the throne.

This splenetic disrelish of his place was evinced in almost every function pertaining to it. Proud as he was moody, he condescended to no personal mandate. Whatever special orders were necessary, their delivery was delegated to his body-servant, who in turn transferred them to their ultimate destination, through runners, alert Spanish boys or slave boys, like pages or

1. King of Spain and Holy Roman emperor (1500–1558) who spent his last years in a monastery (without, however, relinquishing all political power and material possessions).

pilot-fish[2] within easy call continually hovering round Don Benito. So that to have beheld this undemonstrative invalid gliding about, apathetic and mute, no landsman could have dreamed that in him was lodged a dictatorship beyond which, while at sea, there was no earthly appeal.

Thus, the Spaniard, regarded in his reserve, seemed as the involuntary victim of mental disorder. But, in fact, his reserve might, in some degree, have proceeded from design. If so, then here was evinced the unhealthy climax of that icy though conscientious policy, more or less adopted by all commanders of large ships, which, except in signal emergencies, obliterates alike the manifestation of sway with every trace of sociality; transforming the man into a block, or rather into a loaded cannon, which, until there is call for thunder, has nothing to say.

Viewing him in this light, it seemed but a natural token of the perverse habit induced by a long course of such hard self-restraint, that, notwithstanding the present condition of his ship, the Spaniard should still persist in a demeanor, which, however harmless, or, it may be, appropriate, in a well appointed vessel, such as the San Dominick might have been at the outset of the voyage, was anything but judicious now. But the Spaniard perhaps thought that it was with captains as with gods: reserve, under all events, must still be their cue. But more probably this appearance of slumbering dominion might have been but an attempted disguise to conscious imbecility—not deep policy, but shallow device. But be all this as it might, whether Don Benito's manner was designed or not, the more Captain Delano noted its pervading reserve, the less he felt uneasiness at any particular manifestation of that reserve towards himself.

Neither were his thoughts taken up by the captain alone. Wonted to the quiet orderliness of the sealer's comfortable family of a crew, the noisy confusion of the San Dominick's suffering host repeatedly challenged his eye. Some prominent breaches not only of discipline but of decency were observed. These Captain Delano could not but ascribe, in the main, to the absence of those subordinate deck-officers to whom, along with higher duties, is entrusted what may be styled the police department of a populous ship. True, the old oakum-pickers appeared at times to act the part of monitorial constables to their countrymen, the blacks; but though occasionally succeeding in allaying trifling outbreaks now and then between man and man, they could do little or nothing toward establishing general quiet. The San Dominick was in the condition of a transatlantic emigrant ship, among whose multitude of living freight are some individuals, doubtless, as little troublesome as crates and bales; but the friendly remonstrances of such with their ruder companions are of not so much avail as the unfriendly arm of the mate. What the San Dominick wanted was, what the emigrant ship has, stern superior officers. But on these decks not so much as a fourth mate was to be seen.

The visitor's curiosity was roused to learn the particulars of those mishaps which had brought about such absenteeism, with its consequences; because, though deriving some inkling of the voyage from the wails which at the first moment had greeted him, yet of the details no clear understand-

2. Fish often swimming in the company of a shark, therefore thought to pilot it.

ing had been had. The best account would, doubtless, be given by the captain. Yet at first the visitor was loth to ask it, unwilling to provoke some distant rebuff. But plucking up courage, he at last accosted Don Benito, renewing the expression of his benevolent interest, adding, that did he (Captain Delano) but know the particulars of the ship's misfortunes, he would, perhaps, be better able in the end to relieve them. Would Don Benito favor him with the whole story?

Don Benito faltered; then, like some somnambulist suddenly interfered with, vacantly stared at his visitor, and ended by looking down on the deck. He maintained this posture so long, that Captain Delano, almost equally disconcerted, and involuntarily almost as rude, turned suddenly from him, walking forward to accost one of the Spanish seamen for the desired information. But he had hardly gone five paces, when with a sort of eagerness Don Benito invited him back, regretting his momentary absence of mind, and professing readiness to gratify him.

While most part of the story was being given, the two captains stood on the after part of the main-deck, a privileged spot, no one being near but the servant.

"It is now a hundred and ninety days," began the Spaniard, in his husky whisper, "that this ship, well officered and well manned, with several cabin passengers—some fifty Spaniards in all—sailed from Buenos Ayres bound to Lima, with a general cargo, hardware, Paraguay tea and the like—and," pointing forward, "that parcel of negroes, now not more than a hundred and fifty, as you see, but then numbering over three hundred souls. Off Cape Horn we had heavy gales. In one moment, by night, three of my best officers, with fifteen sailors, were lost, with the main-yard; the spar snapping under them in the slings, as they sought, with heavers,[3] to beat down the icy sail. To lighten the hull, the heavier sacks of mata were thrown into the sea, with most of the water-pipes[4] lashed on deck at the time. And this last necessity it was, combined with the prolonged detentions afterwards experienced, which eventually brought about our chief causes of suffering. When——"

Here there was a sudden fainting attack of his cough, brought on, no doubt, by his mental distress. His servant sustained him, and drawing a cordial from his pocket placed it to his lips. He a little revived. But unwilling to leave him unsupported while yet imperfectly restored, the black with one arm still encircled his master, at the same time keeping his eye fixed on his face, as if to watch for the first sign of complete restoration, or relapse, as the event might prove.

The Spaniard proceeded, but brokenly and obscurely, as one in a dream.

—"Oh, my God! rather than pass through what I have, with joy I would have hailed the most terrible gales; but——"

His cough returned and with increased violence; this subsiding, with reddened lips and closed eyes he fell heavily against his supporter.

"His mind wanders. He was thinking of the plague that followed the gales," plaintively sighed the servant; "my poor, poor master!" wringing one hand, and with the other wiping the mouth. "But be patient, Señor," again turning to Captain Delano, "these fits do not last long; master will soon be himself."

3. Bars, most often used as levers.

4. Kegs of water. "Mata": Brazilian cotton.

Don Benito reviving, went on; but as this portion of the story was very brokenly delivered, the substance only will here be set down.

It appeared that after the ship had been many days tossed in storms off the Cape, the scurvy broke out, carrying off numbers of the whites and blacks. When at last they had worked round into the Pacific, their spars and sails were so damaged, and so inadequately handled by the surviving mariners, most of whom were become invalids, that, unable to lay her northerly course by the wind, which was powerful, the unmanageable ship for successive days and nights was blown northwestward, where the breeze suddenly deserted her, in unknown waters, to sultry calms. The absence of the water-pipes now proved as fatal to life as before their presence had menaced it. Induced, or at least aggravated, by the less than scanty allowance of water, a malignant fever followed the scurvy; with the excessive heat of the lengthened calm, making such short work of it as to sweep away, as by billows, whole families of the Africans, and a yet larger number, proportionably, of the Spaniards, including, by a luckless fatality, every remaining officer on board. Consequently, in the smart west winds eventually following the calm, the already rent sails having to be simply dropped, not furled, at need, had been gradually reduced to the beggar's rags they were now. To procure substitutes for his lost sailors, as well as supplies of water and sails, the captain at the earliest opportunity had made for Baldivia, the southernmost civilized port of Chili and South America; but upon nearing the coast the thick weather had prevented him from so much as sighting that harbor. Since which period, almost without a crew, and almost without canvas and almost without water, and at intervals giving its added dead to the sea, the San Dominick had been battle-dored[5] about by contrary winds, inveigled by currents, or grown weedy in calms. Like a man lost in woods, more than once she had doubled upon her own track.

"But throughout these calamities," huskily continued Don Benito, painfully turning in the half embrace of his servant, "I have to thank those negroes you see, who, though to your inexperienced eyes appearing unruly, have, indeed, conducted themselves with less of restlessness than even their owner could have thought possible under such circumstances."

Here he again fell faintly back. Again his mind wandered: but he rallied, and less obscurely proceeded.

"Yes, their owner was quite right in assuring me that no fetters would be needed with his blacks; so that while, as is wont in this transportation, those negroes have always remained upon deck—not thrust below, as in the Guineamen[6]—they have, also, from the beginning, been freely permitted to range within given bounds at their pleasure."

Once more the faintness returned—his mind roved—but, recovering, he resumed:

"But it is Babo here to whom, under God, I owe not only my own preservation, but likewise to him, chiefly, the merit is due, of pacifying his more ignorant brethren, when at intervals tempted to murmurings."

"Ah, master," sighed the black, bowing his face, "don't speak of me; Babo is nothing; what Babo has done was but duty."

5. Tossed back and forth, as a shuttlecock is hit back and forth by a pair of battledores (or paddles).

6. Ships transporting slaves from Guinea in West Africa.

"Faithful fellow!" cried Capt. Delano. "Don Benito, I envy you such a friend; slave I cannot call him."

As master and man stood before him, the black upholding the white, Captain Delano could not but bethink him of the beauty of that relationship which could present such a spectacle of fidelity on the one hand and confidence on the other. The scene was hightened by the contrast in dress, denoting their relative positions. The Spaniard wore a loose Chili jacket of dark velvet; white small clothes and stockings, with silver buckles at the knee and instep; a high-crowned sombrero, of fine grass; a slender sword, silver mounted, hung from a knot in his sash; the last being an almost invariable adjunct, more for ornament than utility, of a South American gentleman's dress to this hour. Excepting when his occasional nervous contortions brought about disarray, there was a certain precision in his attire, curiously at variance with the unsightly disorder around; especially in the belittered Ghetto, forward of the main-mast, wholly occupied by the blacks.

The servant wore nothing but wide trowsers, apparently, from their coarseness and patches, made out of some old topsail; they were clean, and confined at the waist by a bit of unstranded rope, which, with his composed, deprecatory air at times, made him look something like a begging friar of St. Francis.

However unsuitable for the time and place, at least in the blunt-thinking American's eyes, and however strangely surviving in the midst of all his afflictions, the toilette of Don Benito might not, in fashion at least, have gone beyond the style of the day among South Americans of his class. Though on the present voyage sailing from Buenos Ayres, he had avowed himself a native and resident of Chili, whose inhabitants had not so generally adopted the plain coat and once plebeian pantaloons; but, with a becoming modification, adhered to their provincial costume, picturesque as any in the world. Still, relatively to the pale history of the voyage, and his own pale face, there seemed something so incongruous in the Spaniard's apparel, as almost to suggest the image of an invalid courtier tottering about London streets in the time of the plague.

The portion of the narrative which, perhaps, most excited interest, as well as some surprise, considering the latitudes in question, was the long calms spoken of, and more particularly the ship's so long drifting about. Without communicating the opinion, of course, the American could not but impute at least part of the detentions both to clumsy seamanship and faulty navigation. Eying Don Benito's small, yellow hands, he easily inferred that the young captain had not got into command at the hawse-hole,[7] but the cabin-window; and if so, why wonder at incompetence, in youth, sickness, and gentility united?

But drowning criticism in compassion, after a fresh repetition of his sympathies, Captain Delano having heard out his story, not only engaged, as in the first place, to see Don Benito and his people supplied in their immediate bodily needs, but, also, now further promised to assist him in procuring a large permanent supply of water, as well as some sails and rigging; and, though it would involve no small embarrassment to himself, yet he would spare three of his best seamen for temporary deck officers; so that without

7. Metal-lined hole in the bow of a ship, through which a cable passes; the expression here means to begin a career as an ordinary seaman and not as an officer.

delay the ship might proceed to Conception,[8] there fully to refit for Lima, her destined port.

Such generosity was not without its effect, even upon the invalid. His face lighted up; eager and hectic, he met the honest glance of his visitor. With gratitude he seemed overcome.

"This excitement is bad for master," whispered the servant, taking his arm, and with soothing words gently drawing him aside.

When Don Benito returned, the American was pained to observe that his hopefulness, like the sudden kindling in his cheek, was but febrile and transient.

Ere long, with a joyless mien, looking up towards the poop, the host invited his guest to accompany him there, for the benefit of what little breath of wind might be stirring.

As during the telling of the story, Captain Delano had once or twice started at the occasional cymballing of the hatchet-polishers, wondering why such an interruption should be allowed, especially in that part of the ship, and in the ears of an invalid; and moreover, as the hatchets had anything but an attractive look, and the handlers of them still less so, it was, therefore, to tell the truth, not without some lurking reluctance, or even shrinking, it may be, that Captain Delano, with apparent complaisance, acquiesced in his host's invitation. The more so, since with an untimely caprice of punctilio, rendered distressing by his cadaverous aspect, Don Benito, with Castilian bows, solemnly insisted upon his guest's preceding him up the ladder leading to the elevation; where, one on each side of the last step, sat for armorial supporters and sentries two of the ominous file. Gingerly enough stepped good Captain Delano between them, and in the instant of leaving them behind, like one running the gauntlet, he felt an apprehensive twitch in the calves of his legs.

But when, facing about, he saw the whole file, like so many organ-grinders, still stupidly intent on their work, unmindful of everything beside, he could not but smile at his late fidgety panic.

Presently, while standing with his host, looking forward upon the decks below, he was struck by one of those instances of insubordination previously alluded to. Three black boys, with two Spanish boys, were sitting together on the hatches, scraping a rude wooden platter, in which some scanty mess had recently been cooked. Suddenly, one of the black boys, enraged at a word dropped by one of his white companions, seized a knife, and though called to forbear by one of the oakum-pickers, struck the lad over the head, inflicting a gash from which blood flowed.

In amazement, Captain Delano inquired what this meant. To which the pale Don Benito dully muttered, that it was merely the sport of the lad.

"Pretty serious sport, truly," rejoined Captain Delano. "Had such a thing happened on board the Bachelor's Delight, instant punishment would have followed."

At these words the Spaniard turned upon the American one of his sudden, staring, half-lunatic looks; then relapsing into his torpor, answered, "Doubtless, doubtless, Señor."

8. Concepción, Chile.

Is it, thought Captain Delano, that this hapless man is one of those paper captains I've known, who by policy wink at what by power they cannot put down? I know no sadder sight than a commander who has little of command but the name.

"I should think, Don Benito," he now said, glancing towards the oakum-picker who had sought to interfere with the boys, "that you would find it advantageous to keep all your blacks employed, especially the younger ones, no matter at what useless task, and no matter what happens to the ship. Why, even with my little band, I find such a course indispensable. I once kept a crew on my quarter-deck thrumming[9] mats for my cabin, when, for three days, I had given up my ship—mats, men, and all—for a speedy loss, owing to the violence of a gale, in which we could do nothing but helplessly drive before it."

"Doubtless, doubtless," muttered Don Benito.

"But," continued Captain Delano, again glancing upon the oakum-pickers and then at the hatchet-polishers, near by. "I see you keep some at least of your host employed."

"Yes," was again the vacant response.

"Those old men there, shaking their pows[1] from their pulpits," continued Captain Delano, pointing to the oakum-pickers, "seem to act the part of old dominies to the rest, little heeded as their admonitions are at times. Is this voluntary on their part, Don Benito, or have you appointed them shepherds to your flock of black sheep?"

"What posts they fill, I appointed them," rejoined the Spaniard, in an acrid tone, as if resenting some supposed satiric reflection.

"And these others, these Ashantee[2] conjurors here," continued Captain Delano, rather uneasily eying the brandished steel of the hatchet-polishers, where in spots it had been brought to a shine, "this seems a curious business they are at, Don Benito?"

"In the gales we met," answered the Spaniard, "what of our general cargo was not thrown overboard was much damaged by the brine. Since coming into calm weather, I have had several cases of knives and hatchets daily brought up for overhauling and cleaning."

"A prudent idea, Don Benito. You are part owner of ship and cargo, I presume; but not of the slaves, perhaps?"

"I am owner of all you see," impatiently returned Don Benito, "except the main company of blacks, who belonged to my late friend, Alexandro Aranda."

As he mentioned this name, his air was heart-broken; his knees shook: his servant supported him.

Thinking he divined the cause of such unusual emotion, to confirm his surmise, Captain Delano, after a pause, said "And may I ask, Don Benito, whether—since awhile ago you spoke of some cabin passengers—the friend, whose loss so afflicts you at the outset of the voyage accompanied his blacks?"

"Yes."

"But died of the fever?"

"Died of the fever.—Oh, could I but—"

9. To "thrum" is to insert pieces of rope yarn into canvas, thus making a rough surface or mat (usually for keeping ropes from chafing against wood or metal).

1. Heads.

2. West African peoples.

Again quivering, the Spaniard paused.

"Pardon me," said Captain Delano lowly, "but I think that, by a sympathetic experience, I conjecture, Don Benito, what it is that gives the keener edge to your grief. It was once my hard fortune to lose at sea a dear friend, my own brother, then supercargo.[3] Assured of the welfare of his spirit, its departure I could have borne like a man; but that honest eye, that honest hand—both of which had so often met mine—and that warm heart; all, all—like scraps to the dogs—to throw all to the sharks! It was then I vowed never to have for fellow-voyager a man I loved, unless, unbeknown to him, I had provided every requisite, in case of a fatality, for embalming his mortal part for interment on shore. Were your friend's remains now on board this ship, Don Benito, not thus strangely would the mention of his name affect you."

"On board this ship?" echoed the Spaniard. Then, with horrified gestures, as directed against some specter, he unconsciously fell into the ready arms of his attendant, who, with a silent appeal toward Captain Delano, seemed beseeching him not again to broach a theme so unspeakably distressing to his master.

This poor fellow now, thought the pained American, is the victim of that sad superstition which associates goblins with the deserted body of man, as ghosts with an abandoned house. How unlike are we made! What to me, in like case, would have been a solemn satisfaction, the bare suggestion, even, terrifies the Spaniard into this trance. Poor Alexandro Aranda! what would you say could you here see your friend—who, on former voyages, when you for months were left behind, has, I dare say, often longed, and longed, for one peep at you—now transported with terror at the least thought of having you anyway nigh him.

At this moment, with a dreary graveyard toll, betokening a flaw, the ship's forecastle bell, smote by one of the grizzled oakum-pickers, proclaimed ten o'clock through the leaden calm; when Captain Delano's attention was caught by the moving figure of a gigantic black, emerging from the general crowd below, and slowly advancing towards the elevated poop. An iron collar was about his neck, from which depended a chain, thrice wound round his body; the terminating links padlocked together at a broad band of iron, his girdle.

"How like a mute Atufal moves," murmured the servant.

The black mounted the steps of the poop, and, like a brave prisoner, brought up to receive sentence, stood in unquailing muteness before Don Benito, now recovered from his attack.

At the first glimpse of his approach, Don Benito had started, a resentful shadow swept over his face; and, as with the sudden memory of bootless rage, his white lips glued together.

This is some mulish mutineer, thought Captain Delano, surveying, not without a mixture of admiration, the colossal form of the negro.

"See, he waits your question, master," said the servant.

Thus reminded, Don Benito, nervously averting his glance, as if shunning, by anticipation, some rebellious response, in a disconcerted voice, thus spoke:—

"Atufal, will you ask my pardon now?"

The black was silent.

3. The officer responsible for the commercial affairs of the ship's voyage.

"Again, master," murmured the servant, with bitter upbraiding eying his countryman, "Again, master; he will bend to master yet."

"Answer," said Don Benito, still averting his glance, "say but the one word *pardon*, and your chains shall be off."

Upon this, the black, slowly raising both arms, let them lifelessly fall, his links clanking, his head bowed; as much as to say, "no, I am content."

"Go," said Don Benito, with inkept and unknown emotion.

Deliberately as he had come, the black obeyed.

"Excuse me, Don Benito," said Captain Delano, "but this scene surprises me; what means it, pray?"

"It means that that negro alone, of all the band, has given me peculiar cause of offense. I have put him in chains; I——"

Here he paused; his hand to his head, as if there were a swimming there, or a sudden bewilderment of memory had come over him; but meeting his servant's kindly glance seemed reassured, and proceeded:—

"I could not scourge such a form. But I told him he must ask my pardon. As yet he has not. At my command, every two hours he stands before me."

"And how long has this been?"

"Some sixty days."

"And obedient in all else? And respectful?"

"Yes."

"Upon my conscience, then," exclaimed Captain Delano, impulsively, "he has a royal spirit in him, this fellow."

"He may have some right to it," bitterly returned Don Benito, "he says he was king in his own land."

"Yes," said the servant, entering a word, "those slits in Atufal's ears once held wedges of gold; but poor Babo here, in his own land, was only a poor slave; a black man's slave was Babo, who now is the white's."

Somewhat annoyed by these conversational familiarities, Captain Delano turned curiously upon the attendant, then glanced inquiringly at his master; but, as if long wonted to these little informalities, neither master nor man seemed to understand him.

"What, pray, was Atufal's offense, Don Benito?" asked Captain Delano; "if it was not something very serious, take a fool's advice, and, in view of his general docility, as well as in some natural respect for his spirit, remit him his penalty."

"No, no, master never will do that," here murmured the servant to himself, "proud Atufal must first ask master's pardon. The slave there carries the padlock, but master here carries the key."

His attention thus directed, Captain Delano now noticed for the first time that, suspended by a slender silken cord, from Don Benito's neck hung a key. At once, from the servant's muttered syllables divining the key's purpose, he smiled and said:—"So, Don Benito—padlock and key—significant symbols, truly."

Biting his lip, Don Benito faltered.

Though the remark of Captain Delano, a man of such native simplicity as to be incapable of satire or irony, had been dropped in playful allusion to the Spaniard's singularly evidenced lordship over the black; yet the hypochondriac seemed in some way to have taken it as a malicious reflection upon his confessed inability thus far to break down, at least, on a verbal summons, the entrenched will of the slave. Deploring this supposed misconception, yet despairing of correcting it, Captain Delano shifted the subject; but finding his companion more than ever withdrawn, as if still sourly digesting the lees of the presumed affront above-mentioned, by-and-by Captain Delano likewise became less talkative, oppressed, against his own will, by what seemed the secret vindictiveness of the morbidly sensitive Spaniard. But the good sailor himself, of a quite contrary disposition, refrained, on his part, alike from the appearance as from the feeling of resentment, and if silent, was only so from contagion.

Presently the Spaniard, assisted by his servant, somewhat discourteously crossed over from his guest; a procedure which, sensibly enough, might have been allowed to pass for idle caprice of ill-humor, had not master and man, lingering round the corner of the elevated skylight, began whispering together in low voices. This was unpleasing. And more: the moody air of the Spaniard, which at times had not been without a sort of valetudinarian stateliness, now seemed anything but dignified; while the menial familiarity of the servant lost its original charm of simple-hearted attachment.

In his embarrassment, the visitor turned his face to the other side of the ship. By so doing, his glance accidentally fell on a young Spanish sailor, a coil of rope in his hand, just stepped from the deck to the first round of the mizzen-rigging. Perhaps the man would not have been particularly noticed, were it not that, during his ascent to one of the yards, he, with a sort of covert intentness, kept his eye fixed on Captain Delano, from whom, presently, it passed, as if by a natural sequence, to the two whisperers.

His own attention thus redirected to that quarter, Captain Delano gave a slight start. From something in Don Benito's manner just then, it seemed as if the visitor had, at least partly, been the subject of the withdrawn consultation going on—a conjecture as little agreeable to the guest as it was little flattering to the host.

The singular alternations of courtesy and ill-breeding in the Spanish captain were unaccountable, except on one of two suppositions—innocent lunacy, or wicked imposture.

But the first idea, though it might naturally have occurred to an indifferent observer, and, in some respect, had not hitherto been wholly a stranger to Captain Delano's mind, yet, now that, in an incipient way, he began to regard the stranger's conduct something in the light of an intentional affront, of course the idea of lunacy was virtually vacated. But if not a lunatic, what then? Under the circumstances, would a gentleman, nay, any honest boor, act the part now acted by his host? The man was an impostor. Some low-born adventurer, masquerading as an oceanic grandee; yet so ignorant of the first requisites of mere gentlemanhood as to be betrayed into the present remarkable indecorum. That strange ceremoniousness, too, at other times evinced, seemed not uncharacteristic of one playing a part above his real level. Benito Cereno—Don Benito Cereno—a sounding name. One, too, at that period, not unknown, in the surname, to supercargoes and sea captains trading along the Spanish Main, as belonging to one of the most enterprising and extensive mercantile families in all those provinces; several members of it having titles; a sort of Castilian Rothschild,[4] with a noble brother, or cousin, in every great trading town of South

4. Renowned German banking family.

America. The alleged Don Benito was in early manhood, about twenty-nine or thirty. To assume a sort of roving cadetship[5] in the maritime affairs of such a house, what more likely scheme for a young knave of talent and spirit? But the Spaniard was a pale invalid. Never mind. For even to the degree of simulating mortal disease, the craft of some tricksters had been known to attain. To think that, under the aspect of infantile weakness, the most savage energies might be couched—those velvets of the Spaniard but the silky paw to his fangs.

From no train of thought did these fancies come; not from within, but from without; suddenly, too, and in one throng, like hoar frost; yet as soon to vanish as the mild sun of Captain Delano's good-nature regained its meridian.

Glancing over once more towards his host—whose side-face, revealed above the skylight, was now turned towards him—he was struck by the profile, whose clearness of cut was refined by the thinness incident to ill-health, as well as ennobled about the chin by the beard. Away with suspicion. He was a true off-shoot of a true hidalgo[6] Cereno.

Relieved by these and other better thoughts, the visitor, lightly humming a tune, now began indifferently pacing the poop, so as not to betray to Don Benito that he had at all mistrusted incivility, much less duplicity; for such mistrust would yet be proved illusory, and by the event; though, for the present, the circumstance which had provoked that distrust remained unexplained. But when that little mystery should have been cleared up, Captain Delano thought he might extremely regret it, did he allow Don Benito to become aware that he had indulged in ungenerous surmises. In short, to the Spaniard's black-letter text, it was best, for awhile, to leave open margin.[7]

Presently, his pale face twitching and overcast, the Spaniard, still supported by his attendant, moved over towards his guest, when, with even more than his usual embarrassment, and a strange sort of intriguing intonation in his husky whisper, the following conversation began:—

"Señor, may I ask how long you have lain at this isle?"

"Oh, but a day or two, Don Benito."

"And from what port are you last?"

"Canton."[8]

"And there, Señor, you exchanged your seal-skins for teas and silks, I think you said?"

"Yes. Silks, mostly."

"And the balance you took in specie,[9] perhaps?"

Captain Delano, fidgeting a little, answered—

"Yes; some silver; not a very great deal, though."

"Ah—well. May I ask how many men have you, Señor?"

Captain Delano slightly started, but answered—

"About five-and-twenty, all told."

5. Position of on-the-job training for a post of authority, appropriate for a younger or youngest son of an aristocratic family.
6. Spanish nobleman.
7. Without the elucidatory comments then often printed in margins as a gloss on the main text rather than printed at the bottom of the page as footnotes. Delano is deciding to reserve judgment. "Black-letter text": books printed in early type imitative of medieval script.
8. A port in China.
9. Coin, typically gold or silver.

"And at present, Señor, all on board, I suppose?"

"All on board, Don Benito," replied the Captain, now with satisfaction.

"And will be to-night, Señor?"

At this last question, following so many pertinacious ones, for the soul of him Captain Delano could not but look very earnestly at the questioner, who, instead of meeting the glance, with every token of craven discomposure dropped his eyes to the deck; presenting an unworthy contrast to his servant, who, just then, was kneeling at his feet, adjusting a loose shoe-buckle; his disengaged face meantime, with humble curiosity, turned openly up into his master's downcast one.

The Spaniard, still with a guilty shuffle, repeated his question:—

"And—and will be to-night, Señor?"

"Yes, for aught I know," returned Captain Delano,—"but nay," rallying himself into fearless truth, "some of them talked of going off on another fishing party about midnight."

"Your ships generally go—go more or less armed, I believe, Señor?"

"Oh, a six-pounder or two, in case of emergency," was the intrepidly indifferent reply, "with a small stock of muskets, sealing-spears, and cutlasses, you know."

As he thus responded, Captain Delano again glanced at Don Benito, but the latter's eyes were averted; while abruptly and awkwardly shifting the subject, he made some peevish allusion to the calm, and then, without apology, once more, with his attendant, withdrew to the opposite bulwarks, where the whispering was resumed.

At this moment, and ere Captain Delano could cast a cool thought upon what had just passed, the young Spanish sailor before mentioned was seen descending from the rigging. In act of stooping over to spring inboard to the deck, his voluminous, unconfined frock, or shirt, of coarse woollen, much spotted with tar, opened out far down the chest, revealing a soiled under garment of what seemed the finest linen, edged, about the neck, with a narrow blue ribbon, sadly faded and worn. At this moment the young sailor's eye was again fixed on the whisperers, and Captain Delano thought he observed a lurking significance in it, as if silent signs of some Freemason[1] sort had that instant been interchanged.

This once more impelled his own glance in the direction of Don Benito, and, as before, he could not but infer that himself formed the subject of the conference. He paused. The sound of the hatchet-polishing fell on his ears. He cast another swift side-look at the two. They had the air of conspirators. In connection with the late questionings and the incident of the young sailor, these things now begat such return of involuntary suspicion, that the singular guilelessness of the American could not endure it. Plucking up a gay and humorous expression, he crossed over to the two rapidly, saying:—"Ha, Don Benito, your black here seems high in your trust; a sort of privy-counselor, in fact."

Upon this, the servant looked up with a good-natured grin, but the master started as from a venomous bite. It was a moment or two before the Span-

1. A fraternal association founded early in the 18th century in Europe, characterized by local lodges whose members recognized each other by secret signs. It was politically active in New York in Melville's youth, associated in the public mind with atheism and revolution.

iard sufficiently recovered himself to reply; which he did, at last, with cold constraint:—"Yes, Señor, I have trust in Babo."

Here Babo, changing his previous grin of mere animal humor into an intelligent smile, not ungratefully eyed his master.

Finding that the Spaniard now stood silent and reserved, as if involuntarily, or purposely giving hint that his guest's proximity was inconvenient just then, Captain Delano, unwilling to appear uncivil even to incivility itself, made some trivial remark and moved off; again and again turning over in his mind the mysterious demeanor of Don Benito Cereno.

He had descended from the poop, and, wrapped in thought, was passing near a dark hatchway, leading down into the steerage, when, perceiving motion there, he looked to see what moved. The same instant there was a sparkle in the shadowy hatchway, and he saw one of the Spanish sailors prowling there hurriedly placing his hand in the bosom of his frock, as if hiding something. Before the man could have been certain who it was that was passing, he slunk below out of sight. But enough was seen of him to make it sure that he was the same young sailor before noticed in the rigging.

What was that which so sparkled? thought Captain Delano. It was no lamp—no match—no live coal. Could it have been a jewel? But how come sailors with jewels?—or with silk-trimmed under-shirts either? Has he been robbing the trunks of the dead cabin passengers? But if so, he would hardly wear one of the stolen articles on board ship here. Ah, ah—if now that was, indeed, a secret sign I saw passing between this suspicious fellow and his captain awhile since; if I could only be certain that in my uneasiness my senses did not deceive me, then—

Here, passing from one suspicious thing to another, his mind revolved the strange questions put to him concerning his ship.

By a curious coincidence, as each point was recalled, the black wizards of Ashantee would strike up with their hatchets, as in ominous comment on the white stranger's thoughts. Pressed by such enigmas and portents, it would have been almost against nature, had not, even into the least distrustful heart, some ugly misgivings obtruded.

Observing the ship now helplessly fallen into a current, with enchanted sails, drifting with increased rapidity seaward; and noting that, from a lately intercepted projection of the land, the sealer was hidden, the stout mariner began to quake at thoughts which he barely durst confess to himself. Above all, he began to feel a ghostly dread of Don Benito. And yet when he roused himself, dilated his chest, felt himself strong on his legs, and coolly considered it—what did all these phantoms amount to?

Had the Spaniard any sinister scheme, it must have reference not so much to him (Captain Delano) as to his ship (the Bachelor's Delight). Hence the present drifting away of the one ship from the other, instead of favoring any such possible scheme, was, for the time at least, opposed to it. Clearly any suspicion, combining such contradictions, must need be delusive. Beside, was it not absurd to think of a vessel in distress—a vessel by sickness almost dismanned of her crew—a vessel whose inmates were parched for water—was it not a thousand times absurd that such a craft should, at present, be of a piratical character; or her commander, either for himself or those under him, cherish any desire but for speedy relief and refreshment? But then, might not general distress, and thirst in particular, be affected? And might not that same undiminished Spanish crew, alleged to have perished off to a remnant, be at that very moment lurking in the hold? On heart-broken pretense of entreating a cup of cold water, fiends in human form had got into lonely dwellings, nor retired until a dark deed had been done. And among the Malay pirates, it was no unusual thing to lure ships after them into their treacherous harbors, or entice boarders from a declared enemy at sea, by the spectacle of thinly manned or vacant decks, beneath which prowled a hundred spears with yellow arms ready to upthrust them through the mats. Not that Captain Delano had entirely credited such things. He had heard of them—and now, as stories, they recurred. The present destination of the ship was the anchorage. There she would be near his own vessel. Upon gaining that vicinity, might not the San Dominick, like a slumbering volcano, suddenly let loose energies now hid?

He recalled the Spaniard's manner while telling his story. There was a gloomy hesitancy and subterfuge about it. It was just the manner of one making up his tale for evil purposes, as he goes. But if that story was not true, what was the truth? That the ship had unlawfully come into the Spaniard's possession? But in many of its details, especially in reference to the more calamitous parts, such as the fatalities among the seamen, the consequent prolonged beating about, the past sufferings from obstinate calms, and still continued suffering from thirst; in all these points, as well as others, Don Benito's story had corroborated not only the wailing ejaculations of the indiscriminate multitude, white and black, but likewise—what seemed impossible to be counterfeit—by the very expression and play of every human feature, which Captain Delano saw. If Don Benito's story was throughout an invention, then every soul on board, down to the youngest negress, was his carefully drilled recruit in the plot: an incredible inference. And yet, if there was ground for mistrusting his veracity, that inference was a legitimate one.

But those questions of the Spaniard. There, indeed, one might pause. Did they not seem put with much the same object with which the burglar or assassin, by day-time, reconnoitres the walls of a house? But, with ill purposes, to solicit such information openly of the chief person endangered, and so, in effect, setting him on his guard; how unlikely a procedure was that? Absurd, then, to suppose that those questions had been prompted by evil designs. Thus, the same conduct, which, in this instance, had raised the alarm, served to dispel it. In short, scarce any suspicion or uneasiness, however apparently reasonable at the time, which was not now, with equal apparent reason, dismissed.

At last he began to laugh at his former forebodings; and laugh at the strange ship for, in its aspect someway siding with them, as it were; and laugh, too, at the odd-looking blacks, particularly those old scissors-grinders, the Ashantees; and those bed-ridden old knitting-women, the oakum-pickers; and almost at the dark Spaniard himself, the central hobglobin of all.

For the rest, whatever in a serious way seemed enigmatical, was now good-naturedly explained away by the thought that, for the most part, the poor invalid scarcely knew what he was about; either sulking in black vapors, or putting idle questions without sense or object. Evidently, for the present, the man was not fit to be entrusted with the ship. On some benevolent plea withdrawing the command from him, Captain Delano would yet have to send her to Conception, in charge of his second mate, a worthy person and good navigator—a plan not more convenient for the San Dominick than for Don Benito; for, relieved from all anxiety, keeping wholly to his cabin, the sick man, under the good nursing of his servant, would probably, by the end of the passage, be in a measure restored to health, and with that he should also be restored to authority.

Such were the American's thoughts. They were tranquilizing. There was a difference between the idea of Don Benito's darkly pre-ordaining Captain Delano's fate, and Captain Delano's lightly arranging Don Benito's. Nevertheless, it was not without something of relief that the good seaman presently perceived his whale-boat in the distance. Its absence had been prolonged by unexpected detention at the sealer's side, as well as its returning trip lengthened by the continual recession of the goal.

The advancing speck was observed by the blacks. Their shouts attracted the attention of Don Benito, who, with a return of courtesy, approaching Captain Delano, expressed satisfaction at the coming of some supplies, slight and temporary as they must necessarily prove.

Captain Delano responded; but while doing so, his attention was drawn to something passing on the deck below: among the crowd climbing the landward bulwarks, anxiously watching the coming boat, two blacks, to all appearances accidentally incommoded by one of the sailors, violently pushed him aside, which the sailor someway resenting, they dashed him to the deck, despite the earnest cries of the oakum-pickers.

"Don Benito," said Captain Delano quickly, "do you see what is going on there? Look!"

But, seized by his cough, the Spaniard staggered, with both hands to his face, on the point of falling. Captain Delano would have supported him, but the servant was more alert, who, with one hand sustaining his master, with the other applied the cordial. Don Benito restored, the black withdrew his support, slipping aside a little, but dutifully remaining within call of a whisper. Such discretion was here evinced as quite wiped away, in the visitor's eyes, any blemish of impropriety which might have attached to the attendant, from the indecorous conferences before mentioned; showing, too, that if the servant were to blame, it might be more the master's fault than his own, since when left to himself he could conduct thus well.

His glance called away from the spectacle of disorder to the more pleasing one before him, Captain Delano could not avoid again congratulating his host upon possessing such a servant, who, though perhaps a little too forward now and then, must upon the whole be invaluable to one in the invalid's situation.

"Tell me, Don Benito," he added, with a smile—"I should like to have your man here myself—what will you take for him? Would fifty doubloons be any object?"

"Master wouldn't part with Babo for a thousand doubloons," murmured the black, overhearing the offer, and taking it in earnest, and, with the strange vanity of a faithful slave appreciated by his master, scorning to hear so paltry a valuation put upon him by a stranger. But Don Benito, apparently hardly yet completely restored, and again interrupted by his cough, made but some broken reply.

Soon his physical distress became so great, affecting his mind, too, apparently, that, as if to screen the sad spectacle, the servant gently conducted his master below.

Left to himself, the American, to while away the time till his boat should arrive, would have pleasantly accosted some one of the few Spanish seamen he saw; but recalling something that Don Benito had said touching their ill conduct, he refrained, as a ship-master indisposed to countenance cowardice or unfaithfulness in seamen.

While, with these thoughts, standing with eye directed forward towards that handful of sailors, suddenly he thought that one or two of them returned the glance and with a sort of meaning. He rubbed his eyes, and looked again; but again seemed to see the same thing. Under a new form, but more obscure than any previous one, the old suspicions recurred, but, in the absence of Don Benito, with less of panic than before. Despite the bad account given of the sailors, Captain Delano resolved forthwith to accost one of them. Descending the poop, he made his way through the blacks, his movement drawing a queer cry from the oakum-pickers, prompted by whom, the negroes, twitching each other aside, divided before him; but, as if curious to see what was the object of this deliberate visit to their Ghetto, closing in behind, in tolerable order, followed the white stranger up. His progress thus proclaimed as by mounted kings-at-arms, and escorted as by a Caffre[2] guard of honor, Captain Delano, assuming a good humored, off-handed air, continued to advance; now and then saying a blithe word to the negroes, and his eye curiously surveying the white faces, here and there sparsely mixed in with the blacks, like stray white pawns venturously involved in the ranks of the chess-men opposed.

While thinking which of them to select for his purpose, he chanced to observe a sailor seated on the deck engaged in tarring the strap of a large block, with a circle of blacks squatted round him inquisitively eying the process.

The mean employment of the man was in contrast with something superior in his figure. His hand, black with continually thrusting it into the tar-pot held for him by a negro, seemed not naturally allied to his face, a face which would have been a very fine one but for its haggardness. Whether this haggardness had aught to do with criminality, could not be determined; since, as intense heat and cold, though unlike, produce like sensations, so innocence and guilt, when, through casual association with mental pain, stamping any visible impress, use one seal—a hacked one.

Not again that this reflection occurred to Captain Delano at the time, charitable man as he was. Rather another idea. Because observing so singular a haggardness combined with a dark eye, averted as in trouble and shame, and then again recalling Don Benito's confessed ill opinion of his crew, insensibly he was operated upon by certain general notions, which, while disconnecting pain and abashment from virtue, invariably link them with vice.

If, indeed, there be any wickedness on board this ship, thought Captain Delano, be sure that man there has fouled his hand in it, even as now he fouls it in the pitch. I don't like to accost him. I will speak to this other, this old Jack here on the windlass.[3]

2. Many 19th-century travelers to southern Africa referred admiringly to the Caffre tribe or tribes.

3. Mechanical device used for hoisting heavy objects or hauling up the anchor chain. "Jack": sailor.

He advanced to an old Barcelona tar, in ragged red breeches and dirty night-cap, cheeks trenched and bronzed, whiskers dense as thorn hedges. Seated between two sleepy-looking Africans, this mariner, like his younger shipmate, was employed upon some rigging—splicing a cable—the sleepy-looking blacks performing the inferior function of holding the outer parts of the ropes for him.

Upon Captain Delano's approach, the man at once hung his head below its previous level; the one necessary for business. It appeared as if he desired to be thought absorbed, with more than common fidelity, in his task. Being addressed, he glanced up, but with what seemed a furtive, diffident air, which sat strangely enough on his weather-beaten visage, much as if a grizzly bear, instead of growling and biting, should simper and cast sheep's eyes. He was asked several questions concerning the voyage, questions purposely referring to several particulars in Don Benito's narrative, not previously corroborated by those impulsive cries greeting the visitor on first coming on board. The questions were briefly answered, confirming all that remained to be confirmed of the story. The negroes about the windlass joined in with the old sailor, but, as they became talkative, he by degrees became mute, and at length quite glum, seemed morosely unwilling to answer more questions, and yet, all the while, this ursine air was somehow mixed with his sheepish one.

Despairing of getting into unembarrassed talk with such a centaur, Captain Delano, after glancing round for a more promising countenance, but seeing none, spoke pleasantly to the blacks to make way for him; and so, amid various grins and grimaces, returned to the poop, feeling a little strange at first, he could hardly tell why, but upon the whole with regained confidence in Benito Cereno.

How plainly, thought he, did that old whiskerando yonder betray a consciousness of ill-desert. No doubt, when he saw me coming, he dreaded lest I, apprised by his Captain of the crew's general misbehavior, came with sharp words for him, and so down with his head. And yet—and yet, now that I think of it, that very old fellow, if I err not, was one of those who seemed so earnestly eying me here awhile since. Ah, these currents spin one's head round almost as much as they do the ship. Ha, there now's a pleasant sort of sunny sight; quite sociable, too.

His attention had been drawn to a slumbering negress, partly disclosed through the lace-work of some rigging, lying, with youthful limbs carelessly disposed, under the lee of the bulwarks, like a doe in the shade of a woodland rock. Sprawling at her lapped breasts was her wide-awake fawn, stark naked, its black little body half lifted from the deck, crosswise with its dam's; its hands, like two paws, clambering upon her; its mouth and nose ineffectually rooting to get at the mark; and meantime giving a vexatious half-grunt, blending with the composed snore of the negress.

The uncommon vigor of the child at length roused the mother. She started up, at distance facing Captain Delano. But as if not at all concerned at the attitude in which she had been caught, delightedly she caught the child up, with maternal transports, covering it with kisses.

There's naked nature, now; pure tenderness and love, thought Captain Delano, well pleased.

This incident prompted him to remark the other negresses more particularly than before. He was gratified with their manners; like most uncivilized women, they seemed at once tender of heart and tough of constitution; equally ready to die for their infants or fight for them. Unsophisticated as leopardesses; loving as doves. Ah! thought Captain Delano, these perhaps are some of the very women whom Ledyard[4] saw in Africa, and gave such a noble account of.

These natural sights somehow insensibly deepened his confidence and ease. At last he looked to see how his boat was getting on; but it was still pretty remote. He turned to see if Don Benito had returned; but he had not.

To change the scene, as well as to please himself with a leisurely observation of the coming boat, stepping over into the mizzen-chains he clambered his way into the starboard quarter-gallery;[5] one of those abandoned Venetian-looking water-balconies previously mentioned; retreats cut off from the deck. As his foot pressed the half-damp, half-dry sea-mosses matting the place, and a chance phantom cats-paw[6]—an islet of breeze, unheralded, unfollowed—as this ghostly cats-paw came fanning his cheek, as his glance fell upon the row of small, round dead-lights, all closed like coppered eyes of the coffined, and the state-cabin door, once connecting with the gallery, even as the dead-lights had once looked out upon it, but now calked fast like a sarcophagus lid, to a purple-black, tarred-over panel, threshold, and post; and he bethought him of the time, when that state-cabin and this state-balcony had heard the voices of the Spanish king's officers, and the forms of the Lima viceroy's daughters had perhaps leaned where he stood—as these and other images flitted through his mind, as the cats-paw through the calm, gradually he felt rising a dreamy inquietude, like that of one who alone on the prairie feels unrest from the repose of the noon.

He leaned against the carved balustrade, again looking off toward his boat; but found his eye falling upon the ribboned grass, trailing along the ship's water-line, straight as a border of green box; and parterres[7] of sea-weed, broad ovals and crescents, floating nigh and far, with what seemed long formal alleys between, crossing the terraces of swells, and sweeping round as if leading to the grottoes below. And overhanging all was the balustrade by his arm, which, partly stained with pitch and partly embossed with moss, seemed the charred ruin of some summer-house in a grand garden long running to waste.

Trying to break one charm, he was but becharmed anew. Though upon the wide sea, he seemed in some far inland country; prisoner in some deserted château, left to stare at empty grounds, and peer out at vague roads, where never wagon or wayfarer passed.

But these enchantments were a little disenchanted as his eye fell on the corroded main-chains. Of an ancient style, massy and rusty in link, shackle and bolt, they seemed even more fit for the ship's present business than the one for which she had been built.

4. John Ledyard (1751–1789), American traveler, whose comment appeared in *Proceedings of the Association for Promoting the Discovery of the Interior Parts of Africa* (1790). In the *Putnam's* serialization, Melville attributed the passage to the Scottish traveler Mungo Park, who quoted it from Ledyard in his *Travels in the Interior of Africa* (1799); in *The Piazza Tales* Ledyard's name is properly restored.

5. Balcony or platform projecting from the stern of a ship.

6. Patch of open water visibly stirred by a puff of wind; also, the wind that produces a cat's-paw.

7. Ornamental arrangements, as of flower beds.

Presently he thought something moved nigh the chains. He rubbed his eyes, and looked hard. Groves of rigging were about the chains; and there, peering from behind a great stay, like an Indian from behind a hemlock, a Spanish sailor, a marlingspike[8] in his hand, was seen, who made what seemed an imperfect gesture towards the balcony, but immediately, as if alarmed by some advancing step along the deck within, vanished into the recesses of the hempen forest, like a poacher.

What meant this? Something the man had sought to communicate, unbeknown to any one, even to his captain. Did the secret involve aught unfavorable to his captain? Were those previous misgivings of Captain Delano's about to be verified? Or, in his haunted mood at the moment, had some random, unintentional motion of the man, while busy with the stay, as if repairing it, been mistaken for a significant beckoning?

Not unbewildered, again he gazed off for his boat. But it was temporarily hidden by a rocky spur of the isle. As with some eagerness he bent forward, watching for the first shooting view of its beak, the balustrade gave way before him like charcoal. Had he not clutched an outreaching rope he would have fallen into the sea. The crash, though feeble, and the fall, though hollow, of the rotten fragments, must have been overheard. He glanced up. With sober curiosity peering down upon him was one of the old oakum-pickers, slipped from his perch to an outside boom; while below the old negro, and, invisible to him, reconnoitering from a port-hole like a fox from the mouth of its den, crouched the Spanish sailor again. From something suddenly suggested by the man's air, the mad idea now darted into Captain Delano's mind, that Don Benito's plea of indisposition, in withdrawing below, was but a pretense: that he was engaged there maturing his plot, of which the sailor, by some means gaining an inkling, had a mind to warn the stranger against; incited, it may be, by gratitude for a kind word on first boarding the ship. Was it from foreseeing some possible interference like this, that Don Benito had, beforehand, given such a bad character of his sailors, while praising the negroes; though, indeed, the former seemed as docile as the latter the contrary? The whites, too, by nature, were the shrewder race. A man with some evil design, would he not be likely to speak well of that stupidity which was blind to his depravity, and malign that intelligence from which it might not be hidden? Not unlikely, perhaps. But if the whites had dark secrets concerning Don Benito, could then Don Benito be any way in complicity with the blacks? But they were too stupid. Besides, who ever heard of a white so far a renegade as to apostatize[9] from his very species almost, by leaguing in against it with negroes? These difficulties recalled former ones. Lost in their mazes, Captain Delano, who had now regained the deck, was uneasily advancing along it, when he observed a new face; an aged sailor seated cross-legged near the main hatchway. His skin was shrunk up with wrinkles like a pelican's empty pouch; his hair frosted; his countenance grave and composed. His hands were full of ropes, which he was working into a large knot. Some blacks were about him obligingly dipping the strands for him, here and there, as the exigencies of the operation demanded.

8. Pointed iron tool used to separate and splice strands of rope.

9. To deny or renounce (typically said of religious faith).

Captain Delano crossed over to him, and stood in silence surveying the knot; his mind, by a not uncongenial transition, passing from its own entanglements to those of the hemp. For intricacy such a knot he had never seen in an American ship, or indeed any other. The old man looked like an Egyptian priest, making gordian knots for the temple of Ammon.[1] The knot seemed a combination of double-bowline-knot, treble-crown-knot, back-handed-well-knot, knot-in-and-out-knot, and jamming-knot.

At last, puzzled to comprehend the meaning of such a knot, Captain Delano addressed the knotter:—

"What are you knotting there, my man?"

"The knot," was the brief reply, without looking up.

"So it seems; but what is it for?"

"For some one else to undo," muttered back the old man, plying his fingers harder than ever, the knot being now nearly completed.

While Captain Delano stood watching him, suddenly the old man threw the knot towards him, saying in broken English,—the first heard in the ship,—something to this effect—"Undo it, cut it, quick." It was said lowly, but with such condensation of rapidity, that the long, slow words in Spanish, which had preceded and followed, almost operated as covers to the brief English between.

For a moment, knot in hand, and knot in head, Captain Delano stood mute; while, without further heeding him, the old man was now intent upon other ropes. Presently there was a slight stir behind Captain Delano. Turning, he saw the chained negro, Atufal, standing quietly there. The next moment the old sailor rose, muttering, and, followed by his subordinate negroes, removed to the forward part of the ship, where in the crowd he disappeared.

An elderly negro, in a clout[2] like an infant's, and with a pepper and salt head, and a kind of attorney air, now approached Captain Delano. In tolerable Spanish, and with a good-natured, knowing wink, he informed him that the old knotter was simple-witted, but harmless; often playing his odd tricks. The negro concluded by begging the knot, for of course the stranger would not care to be troubled with it. Unconsciously, it was handed to him. With a sort of congé,[3] the negro received it, and turning his back, ferreted into it like a detective Custom House officer after smuggled laces. Soon, with some African word, equivalent to pshaw, he tossed the knot overboard.

All this is very queer now, thought Captain Delano, with a qualmish sort of emotion; but as one feeling incipient sea-sickness, he strove, by ignoring the symptoms, to get rid of the malady. Once more he looked off for his boat. To his delight, it was now again in view, leaving the rocky spur astern.

The sensation here experienced, after at first relieving his uneasiness, with unforeseen efficacy, soon began to remove it. The less distant sight of that well-known boat—showing it, not as before, half blended with the haze, but with outline defined, so that its individuality, like a man's, was manifest; that

1. In Egypt the oracle of Jupiter Ammon predicted to Alexander the Great (356–323 B.C.E.) that he would conquer the world. Later in Phrygia (in north-central Asia Minor), where the former King Gordius had foretold that whoever would untie his intricate knot would become master of Asia, Alexander cut the knot with his sword.

2. Diaper; small piece of cloth.

3. Leave taking, signaled by a low bow.

boat, Rover by name, which, though now in strange seas, had often pressed the beach of Captain Delano's home, and, brought to its threshold for repairs, had familiarly lain there, as a Newfoundland dog; the sight of that household boat evoked a thousand trustful associations, which, contrasted with previous suspicions, filled him not only with lightsome confidence, but somehow with half humorous self-reproaches at his former lack of it.

"What, I, Amasa Delano—Jack of the Beach, as they called me when a lad—I, Amasa; the same that, duck-satchel in hand, used to paddle along the waterside to the school-house made from the old hulk;—I, little Jack of the Beach, that used to go berrying with cousin Nat and the rest; I to be murdered here at the ends of the earth, on board a haunted pirate-ship by a horrible Spaniard?—Too nonsensical to think of! Who would murder Amasa Delano? His conscience is clean. There is some one above. Fie, fie, Jack of the Beach! you are a child indeed; a child of the second childhood, old boy; you are beginning to dote and drule, I'm afraid."

Light of heart and foot, he stepped aft, and there was met by Don Benito's servant, who, with a pleasing expression, responsive to his own present feelings, informed him that his master had recovered from the effects of his coughing fit, and had just ordered him to go present his compliments to his good guest, Don Amasa, and say that he (Don Benito) would soon have the happiness to rejoin him.

There now, do you mark that? again thought Captain Delano, walking the poop. What a donkey I was. This kind gentleman who here sends me his kind compliments, he, but ten minutes ago, dark-lantern in hand, was dodging round some old grind-stone in the hold, sharpening a hatchet for me, I thought. Well, well; these long calms have a morbid effect on the mind, I've often heard, though I never believed it before. Ha! glancing towards the boat; there's Rover; good dog; a white bone in her mouth. A pretty big bone though, seems to me.—What? Yes, she has fallen afoul of the bubbling tide-rip there. It sets her the other way, too, for the time. Patience.

It was now about noon, though, from the grayness of everything, it seemed to be getting towards dusk.

The calm was confirmed. In the far distance, away from the influence of land, the leaden ocean seemed laid out and leaded up, its course finished, soul gone, defunct. But the current from landward, where the ship was, increased; silently sweeping her further and further towards the tranced waters beyond.

Still, from his knowledge of those latitudes, cherishing hopes of a breeze, and a fair and fresh one, at any moment, Captain Delano, despite present prospects, buoyantly counted upon bringing the San Dominick safely to anchor ere night. The distance swept over was nothing; since, with a good wind, ten minutes' sailing would retrace more than sixty minutes' drifting. Meantime, one moment turning to mark "Rover" fighting the tide-rip, and the next to see Don Benito approaching, he continued walking the poop.

Gradually he felt a vexation arising from the delay of his boat; this soon merged into uneasiness; and at last, his eye falling continually, as from a stage-box into the pit, upon the strange crowd before and below him, and by and by recognising there the face—now composed to indifference—of the Spanish sailor who had seemed to beckon from the main chains, something of his old trepidations returned.

Ah, thought he—gravely enough—this is like the ague:[4] because it went off, it follows not that it won't come back.

Though ashamed of the relapse, he could not altogether subdue it; and so, exerting his good nature to the utmost, insensibly he came to a compromise.

Yes, this is a strange craft; a strange history, too, and strange folks on board. But—nothing more.

By way of keeping his mind out of mischief till the boat should arrive, he tried to occupy it with turning over and over, in a purely speculative sort of way, some lesser peculiarities of the captain and crew. Among others, four curious points recurred.

First, the affair of the Spanish lad assailed with a knife by the slave boy; an act winked at by Don Benito. Second, the tyranny in Don Benito's treatment of Atufal, the black; as if a child should lead a bull of the Nile by the ring in his nose. Third, the trampling of the sailor by the two negroes; a piece of insolence passed over without so much as a reprimand. Fourth, the cringing submission to their master of all the ship's underlings, mostly blacks; as if by the least inadvertence they feared to draw down his despotic displeasure.

Coupling these points, they seemed somewhat contradictory. But what then, thought Captain Delano, glancing towards his now nearing boat,—what then? Why, Don Benito is a very capricious commander. But he is not the first of the sort I have seen; though it's true he rather exceeds any other. But as a nation—continued he in his reveries—these Spaniards are all an odd set; the very word Spaniard has a curious, conspirator, Guy-Fawkish[5] twang to it. And yet, I dare say, Spaniards in the main are as good folks as any in Duxbury, Massachusetts. Ah good! At last "Rover" has come.

As, with its welcome freight, the boat touched the side, the oakum-pickers, with venerable gestures, sought to restrain the blacks, who, at the sight of three gurried[6] water-casks in its bottom, and a pile of wilted pumpkins in its bow, hung over the bulwarks in disorderly raptures.

Don Benito with his servant now appeared; his coming, perhaps, hastened by hearing the noise. Of him Captain Delano sought permission to serve out the water, so that all might share alike, and none injure themselves by unfair excess. But sensible, and, on Don Benito's account, kind as this offer was, it was received with what seemed impatience; as if aware that he lacked energy as a commander, Don Benito, with the true jealousy of weakness, resented as an affront any interference. So, at least, Captain Delano inferred.

In another moment the casks were being hoisted in, when some of the eager negroes accidentally jostled Captain Delano, where he stood by the gangway; so that, unmindful of Don Benito, yielding to the impulse of the moment, with good-natured authority he bade the blacks stand back; to enforce his words making use of a half-mirthful, half-menacing gesture. Instantly the blacks paused, just where they were, each negro and negress suspended in his or her posture, exactly as the word had found them—for a few seconds continuing so—while, as between the responsive posts of a telegraph, an unknown syllable ran from man to man among the perched oakum-

4. Fever with chills.
5. Guy Fawkes (1570–1606), Catholic conspirator executed for plotting to blow up the House of Lords.
6. Coated with slime, from "gurry," fish offal.

pickers. While the visitor's attention was fixed by this scene, suddenly the hatchet-polishers half rose, and a rapid cry came from Don Benito.

Thinking that at the signal of the Spaniard he was about to be massacred, Captain Delano would have sprung for his boat, but paused, as the oakum-pickers, dropping down into the crowd with earnest exclamations, forced every white and every negro back, at the same moment, with gestures friendly and familiar, almost jocose, bidding him, in substance, not be a fool. Simultaneously the hatchet-polishers resumed their seats, quietly as so many tailors, and at once, as if nothing had happened, the work of hoisting in the casks was resumed, whites and blacks singing at the tackle.

Captain Delano glanced towards Don Benito. As he saw his meager form in the act of recovering itself from reclining in the servant's arms, into which the agitated invalid had fallen, he could not but marvel at the panic by which himself had been surprised on the darting supposition that such a commander, who upon a legitimate occasion, so trivial, too, as it now appeared, could lose all self-command, was, with energetic iniquity, going to bring about his murder.

The casks being on deck, Captain Delano was handed a number of jars and cups by one of the steward's aids, who, in the name of his captain, entreated him to do as he had proposed: dole out the water. He complied, with republican impartiality as to this republican element, which always seeks one level, serving the oldest white no better than the youngest black; excepting, indeed, poor Don Benito, whose condition, if not rank, demanded an extra allowance. To him, in the first place, Captain Delano presented a fair pitcher of the fluid; but, thirsting as he was for it, the Spaniard quaffed not a drop until after several grave bows and salutes. A reciprocation of courtesies which the sight-loving Africans hailed with clapping of hands.

Two of the less wilted pumpkins being reserved for the cabin table, the residue were minced up on the spot for the general regalement. But the soft bread, sugar, and bottled cider, Captain Delano would have given the whites alone, and in chief Don Benito; but the latter objected; which disinterestedness not a little pleased the American; and so mouthfuls all around were given alike to whites and blacks; excepting one bottle of cider, which Babo insisted upon setting aside for his master.

Here it may be observed that as, on the first visit of the boat, the American had not permitted his men to board the ship, neither did he now; being unwilling to add to the confusion of the decks.

Not uninfluenced by the peculiar good humor at present prevailing, and for the time oblivious of any but benevolent thoughts, Captain Delano, who from recent indications counted upon a breeze within an hour or two at furthest, dispatched the boat back to the sealer with orders for all the hands that could be spared immediately to set about rafting casks to the watering-place and filling them. Likewise he bade word be carried to his chief officer, that if against present expectation the ship was not brought to anchor by sunset, he need be under no concern, for as there was to be a full moon that night, he (Captain Delano) would remain on board ready to play the pilot, come the wind soon or late.

As the two Captains stood together, observing the departing boat—the servant as it happened having just spied a spot on his master's velvet sleeve, and silently engaged rubbing it out—the American expressed his regrets that the San Dominick had no boats; none, at least, but the unseaworthy old hulk of the long-boat,[7] which, warped as a camel's skeleton in the desert, and almost as bleached, lay pot-wise inverted amidships, one side a little tipped, furnishing a subterraneous sort of den for family groups of the blacks, mostly women and small children; who, squatting on old mats below, or perched above in the dark dome, on the elevated seats, were descried, some distance within, like a social circle of bats, sheltering in some friendly cave; at intervals, ebon flights of naked boys and girls, three or four years old, darting in and out of the den's mouth.

"Had you three or four boats now, Don Benito," said Captain Delano, "I think that, by tugging at the oars, your negroes here might help along matters some.—Did you sail from port without boats, Don Benito?"

"They were stove in the gales, Señor."

"That was bad. Many men, too, you lost then. Boats and men.—Those must have been hard gales, Don Benito."

"Past all speech," cringed the Spaniard.

"Tell me, Don Benito," continued his companion with increased interest, "tell me, were these gales immediately off the pitch of Cape Horn?"

"Cape Horn?—who spoke of Cape Horn?"

"Yourself did, when giving me an account of your voyage," answered Captain Delano with almost equal astonishment at this eating of his own words, even as he ever seemed eating his own heart, on the part of the Spaniard. "You yourself, Don Benito, spoke of Cape Horn," he emphatically repeated.

The Spaniard turned, in a sort of stooping posture, pausing an instant, as one about to make a plunging exchange of elements, as from air to water.

At this moment a messenger-boy, a white, hurried by, in the regular performance of his function carrying the last expired half hour forward to the forecastle, from the cabin time-piece, to have it struck at the ship's large bell.

"Master," said the servant, discontinuing his work on the coat sleeve, and addressing the rapt Spaniard with a sort of timid apprehensiveness, as one charged with a duty, the discharge of which, it was foreseen, would prove irksome to the very person who had imposed it, and for whose benefit it was intended, "master told me never mind where he was, or how engaged, always to remind him, to a minute, when shaving-time comes. Miguel has gone to strike the half-hour afternoon. It is *now*, master. Will master go into the cuddy?"[8]

"Ah—yes," answered the Spaniard, starting, somewhat as from dreams into realities; then turning upon Captain Delano, he said that ere long he would resume the conversation.

"Then if master means to talk more to Don Amasa," said the servant, "why not let Don Amasa sit by master in the cuddy, and master can talk, and Don Amasa can listen, while Babo here lathers and strops."

"Yes," said Captain Delano, not unpleased with this sociable plan, "yes, Don Benito, unless you had rather not, I will go with you."

"Be it so, Señor."

As the three passed aft, the American could not but think it another strange instance of his host's capriciousness, this being shaved with such

7. The largest rowboat stowed on the deck of a large ship.

8. Small cabin on the deck of a ship or boat.

uncommon punctuality in the middle of the day. But he deemed it more than likely that the servant's anxious fidelity had something to do with the matter; inasmuch as the timely interruption served to rally his master from the mood which had evidently been coming upon him.

The place called the cuddy was a light deck-cabin formed by the poop, a sort of attic to the large cabin below. Part of it had formerly been the quarters of the officers; but since their death all the partitionings had been thrown down, and the whole interior converted into one spacious and airy marine hall; for absence of fine furniture and picturesque disarray, of odd appurtenances, somewhat answering to the wide, cluttered hall of some eccentric bachelor-squire in the country, who hangs his shooting-jacket and tobacco-pouch on deer antlers, and keeps his fishing-rod, tongs, and walking-stick in the same corner.

The similitude was hightened, if not originally suggested, by glimpses of the surrounding sea; since, in one aspect, the country and the ocean seem cousins-german.[9]

The floor of the cuddy was matted. Overhead, four or five old muskets were stuck into horizontal holes along the beams. On one side was a claw-footed old table lashed to the deck; a thumbed missal on it, and over it a small, meager crucifix attached to the bulkhead. Under the table lay a dented cutlass or two, with a hacked harpoon, among some melancholy old rigging, like a heap of poor friars' girdles.[1] There were also two long, sharp-ribbed settees of malacca cane, black with age, and uncomfortable to look at as inquisitors' racks, with a large, misshapen arm-chair, which, furnished with a rude barber's crutch[2] at the back, working with a screw, seemed some grotesque engine of torment. A flag locker was in one corner, open, exposing various colored bunting, some rolled up, others half unrolled, still others tumbled. Opposite was a cumbrous washstand, of black mahogany, all of one block, with a pedestal, like a font, and over it a railed shelf, containing combs, brushes, and other implements of the toilet. A torn hammock of stained grass swung near; the sheets tossed, and the pillow wrinkled up like a brow, as if whoever slept here slept but illy, with alternate visitations of sad thoughts and bad dreams.

The further extremity of the cuddy, overhanging the ship's stern, was pierced with three openings, windows or port holes, according as men or cannon might peer, socially or unsocially, out of them. At present neither men nor cannon were seen, though huge ring-bolts and other rusty iron fixtures of the wood-work hinted of twenty-four-pounders.

Glancing towards the hammock as he entered, Captain Delano said, "You sleep here, Don Benito?"

"Yes, Señor, since we got into mild weather."

"This seems a sort of dormitory, sitting-room, sail-loft, chapel, armory, and private closet all together, Don Benito," added Captain Delano, looking round.

"Yes, Señor; events have not been favorable to much order in my arrangements."

9. First cousins.
1. Rope belts.
2. Headrest.

Here the servant, napkin on arm, made a motion as if waiting his master's good pleasure. Don Benito signified his readiness, when, seating him in the malacca arm-chair, and for the guest's convenience drawing opposite it one of the settees, the servant commenced operations by throwing back his master's collar and loosening his cravat.

There is something in the negro which, in a peculiar way, fits him for avocations about one's person. Most negroes are natural valets and hairdressers; taking to the comb and brush congenially as to the castinets, and flourishing them apparently with almost equal satisfaction. There is, too, a smooth tact about them in this employment, with a marvelous, noiseless, gliding briskness, not ungraceful in its way, singularly pleasing to behold, and still more so to be the manipulated subject of. And above all is the great gift of good humor. Not the mere grin or laugh is here meant. Those were unsuitable. But a certain easy cheerfulness, harmonious in every glance and gesture; as though God had set the whole negro to some pleasant tune.

When to all this is added the docility arising from the unaspiring contentment of a limited mind, and that susceptibility of blind attachment sometimes inhering in indisputable inferiors, one readily perceives why those hypochondriacs, Johnson and Byron—it may be something like the hypochondriac, Benito Cereno—took to their hearts, almost to the exclusion of the entire white race, their serving men, the negroes, Barber and Fletcher.[3] But if there be that in the negro which exempts him from the inflicted sourness of the morbid or cynical mind, how, in his most prepossessing aspects, must he appear to a benevolent one? When at ease with respect to exterior things, Captain Delano's nature was not only benign, but familiarly and humorously so. At home, he had often taken rare satisfaction in sitting in his door, watching some free man of color at his work or play. If on a voyage he chanced to have a black sailor, invariably he was on chatty, and half-gamesome terms with him. In fact, like most men of a good, blithe heart, Captain Delano took to negroes, not philanthropically, but genially, just as other men to Newfoundland dogs.

Hitherto the circumstances in which he found the San Dominick had repressed the tendency. But in the cuddy, relieved from his former uneasiness, and, for various reasons, more sociably inclined than at any previous period of the day, and seeing the colored servant, napkin on arm, so debonair about his master, in a business so familiar as that of shaving, too, all his old weakness for negroes returned.

Among other things, he was amused with an odd instance of the African love of bright colors and fine shows, in the black's informally taking from the flag-locker a great piece of bunting of all hues, and lavishly tucking it under his master's chin for an apron.

The mode of shaving among the Spaniards is a little different from what it is with other nations. They have a basin, specifically called a barber's basin, which on one side is scooped out, so as accurately to receive the chin, against which it is closely held in lathering; which is done, not with a brush, but with soap dipped in the water of the basin and rubbed on the face.

3. William Fletcher, valet of Lord Byron (1788–1824), was a white Englishman, here confused with an American black servant of Edward Trelawny who accompanied Byron on some journeys. Frank Barber worked for the English writer Samuel Johnson (1709–1784) for three decades; at his death in 1784 Johnson left Barber a large annuity.

In the present instance salt-water was used for lack of better; and the parts lathered were only the upper lip, and low down under the throat, all the rest being cultivated beard.

The preliminaries being somewhat novel to Captain Delano, he sat curiously eying them, so that no conversation took place, nor for the present did Don Benito appear disposed to renew any.

Setting down his basin, the negro searched among the razors, as for the sharpest, and having found it, gave it an additional edge by expertly strapping it on the firm, smooth, oily skin of his open palm; he then made a gesture as if to begin, but midway stood suspended for an instant, one hand elevating the razor, the other professionally dabbling among the bubbling suds on the Spaniard's lank neck. Not unaffected by the close sight of the gleaming steel, Don Benito nervously shuddered, his usual ghastliness was hightened by the lather, which lather, again, was intensified in its hue by the contrasting sootiness of the negro's body. Altogether the scene was somewhat peculiar, at least to Captain Delano, nor, as he saw the two thus postured, could he resist the vagary, that in the black he saw a headsman, and in the white, a man at the block. But this was one of those antic conceits, appearing and vanishing in a breath, from which, perhaps, the best regulated mind is not always free.

Meantime the agitation of the Spaniard had a little loosened the bunting from around him, so that one broad fold swept curtain-like over the chair-arm to the floor, revealing, amid a profusion of armorial bars and ground-colors—black, blue, and yellow—a closed castle in a blood-red field diagonal with a lion rampant in a white.

"The castle and the lion," exclaimed Captain Delano—"why, Don Benito, this is the flag of Spain you use here. It's well it's only I, and not the King, that sees this," he added with a smile, "but"—turning towards the black,—"it's all one, I suppose, so the colors be gay;" which playful remark did not fail somewhat to tickle the negro.

"Now, master," he said, readjusting the flag, and pressing the head gently further back into the crotch of the chair; "now master," and the steel glanced nigh the throat.

Again Don Benito faintly shuddered.

"You must not shake so, master.—See, Don Amasa, master always shakes when I shave him. And yet master knows I never yet have drawn blood, though it's true, if master will shake so, I may some of these times. Now master," he continued. "And now, Don Amasa, please go on with your talk about the gale, and all that, master can hear, and between times master can answer."

"Ah yes, these gales," said Captain Delano; "but the more I think of your voyage, Don Benito, the more I wonder, not at the gales, terrible as they must have been, but at the disastrous interval following them. For here, by your account, have you been these two months and more getting from Cape Horn to St. Maria, a distance which I myself, with a good wind, have sailed in a few days. True, you had calms, and long ones, but to be becalmed for two months, that is, at least, unusual. Why, Don Benito, had almost any other gentleman told me such a story, I should have been half disposed to a little incredulity."

Here an involuntary expression came over the Spaniard, similar to that just before on the deck, and whether it was the start he gave, or a sudden gawky roll of the hull in the calm, or a momentary unsteadiness of the servant's hand; however it was, just then the razor drew blood, spots of which stained the creamy lather under the throat; immediately the black barber drew back his steel, and remaining in his professional attitude, back to Captain Delano, and face to Don Benito, held up the trickling razor, saying, with a sort of half humorous sorrow, "See, master,—you shook so—here's Babo's first blood."

No sword drawn before James the First of England, no assassination in that timid King's presence,[4] could have produced a more terrified aspect than was now presented by Don Benito.

Poor fellow, thought Captain Delano, so nervous he can't even bear the sight of barber's blood; and this unstrung, sick man, is it credible that I should have imagined he meant to spill all my blood, who can't endure the sight of one little drop of his own? Surely, Amasa Delano, you have been beside yourself this day. Tell it not when you get home, sappy Amasa. Well, well, he looks like a murderer, doesn't he? More like as if himself were to be done for. Well, well, this day's experience shall be a good lesson.

Meantime, while these things were running through the honest seaman's mind, the servant had taken the napkin from his arm, and to Don Benito had said—"But answer Don Amasa, please, master, while I wipe this ugly stuff off the razor, and strop it again."

As he said the words, his face was turned half round, so as to be alike visible to the Spaniard and the American, and seemed by its expression to hint, that he was desirous, by getting his master to go on with the conversation, considerately to withdraw his attention from the recent annoying accident. As if glad to snatch the offered relief, Don Benito resumed, rehearsing to Captain Delano, that not only were the calms of unusual duration, but the ship had fallen in with obstinate currents; and other things he added, some of which were but repetitions of former statements, to explain how it came to pass that the passage from Cape Horn to St. Maria had been so exceedingly long, now and then mingling with his words, incidental praises, less qualified than before, to the blacks, for their general good conduct.

These particulars were not given consecutively, the servant at convenient times using his razor, and so, between the intervals of shaving, the story and panegyric went on with more than usual huskiness.

To Captain Delano's imagination, now again not wholly at rest, there was something so hollow in the Spaniard's manner, with apparently some reciprocal hollowness in the servant's dusky comment of silence, that the idea flashed across him, that possibly master and man, for some unknown purpose, were acting out, both in word and deed, nay, to the very tremor of Don Benito's limbs, some juggling play before him. Neither did the suspicion of collusion lack apparent support, from the fact of those whispered conferences before mentioned. But then, what could be the object of enacting this play of the barber before him? At last, regarding the notion as a whimsy, insensibly suggested, perhaps, by the theatrical aspect of Don Benito in his harlequin ensign,[5] Captain Delano speedily banished it.

4. James I (1566–1625), king of Great Britain and Ireland (r. 1604–25), who lived in terror of assassination by Catholics, especially after the Gunpowder Plot (1605) and the assassination of King Henry IV of France in 1610.
5. Colorful Spanish flag.

The shaving over, the servant bestirred himself with a small bottle of scented waters, pouring a few drops on the head, and then diligently rubbing; the vehemence of the exercise causing the muscles of his face to twitch rather strangely.

His next operation was with comb, scissors and brush; going round and round, smoothing a curl here, clipping an unruly whisker-hair there, giving a graceful sweep to the temple-lock, with other impromptu touches evincing the hand of a master; while, like any resigned gentleman in barber's hands, Don Benito bore all, much less uneasily, at least, than he had done the razoring; indeed, he sat so pale and rigid now, that the negro seemed a Nubian[6] sculptor finishing off a white statue-head.

All being over at last, the standard of Spain removed, tumbled up, and tossed back into the flag-locker, the negro's warm breath blowing away any stray hair which might have lodged down his master's neck; collar and cravat readjusted; a speck of lint whisked off the velvet lapel; all this being done; backing off a little space, and pausing with an expression of subdued self-complacency, the servant for a moment surveyed his master, as, in toilet at least, the creature of his own tasteful hands.

Captain Delano playfully complimented him upon his achievement; at the same time congratulating Don Benito.

But neither sweet waters, nor shampooing, nor fidelity, nor sociality, delighted the Spaniard. Seeing him relapsing into forbidding gloom, and still remaining seated, Captain Delano, thinking that his presence was undesired just then, withdrew, on pretense of seeing whether, as he had prophecied, any signs of a breeze were visible.

Walking forward to the mainmast, he stood awhile thinking over the scene, and not without some undefined misgivings, when he heard a noise near the cuddy, and turning, saw the negro, his hand to his cheek. Advancing, Captain Delano perceived that the cheek was bleeding. He was about to ask the cause, when the negro's wailing soliloquy enlightened him.

"Ah, when will master get better from his sickness; only the sour heart that sour sickness breeds made him serve Babo so; cutting Babo with the razor, because, only by accident, Babo had given master one little scratch; and for the first time in so many a day, too. Ah, ah, ah," holding his hand to his face.

Is it possible, thought Captain Delano; was it to wreak in private his Spanish spite against this poor friend of his, that Don Benito, by his sullen manner, impelled me to withdraw? Ah, this slavery breeds ugly passions in man—Poor fellow!

He was about to speak in sympathy to the negro, but with a timid reluctance he now reëntered the cuddy.

Presently master and man came forth; Don Benito leaning on his servant as if nothing had happened.

But a sort of love-quarrel, after all, thought Captain Delano.

He accosted Don Benito, and they slowly walked together. They had gone but a few paces, when the steward—a tall, rajah-looking mulatto, orientally set off with a pagoda turban formed by three or four Madras handkerchiefs

6. Native of Nubia in East Africa, now part of Sudan.

wound about his head, tier on tier—approaching with a saalam,[7] announced lunch in the cabin.

On their way thither, the two Captains were preceded by the mulatto, who, turning round as he advanced, with continual smiles and bows, ushered them on, a display of elegance which quite completed the insignificance of the small bare-headed Babo, who, as if not unconscious of inferiority, eyed askance the graceful steward. But in part, Captain Delano imputed his jealous watchfulness to that peculiar feeling which the full-blooded African entertains for the adulterated one. As for the steward, his manner, if not bespeaking much dignity of self-respect, yet evidenced his extreme desire to please; which is doubly meritorious, as at once Christian and Chesterfieldian.[8]

Captain Delano observed with interest that while the complexion of the mulatto was hybrid, his physiognomy was European; classically so.

"Don Benito," whispered he, "I am glad to see this usher-of the-golden-rod[9] of yours; the sight refutes an ugly remark once made to me by a Barbadoes planter; that when a mulatto has a regular European face, look out for him; he is a devil. But see, your steward here has features more regular than King George's of England; and yet there he nods, and bows, and smiles; a king, indeed—the king of kind hearts and polite fellows. What a pleasant voice he has, too?"

"He has, Señor."

"But, tell me, has he not, so far as you have known him, always proved a good, worthy fellow?" said Captain Delano, pausing, while with a final genuflexion the steward disappeared into the cabin; "come, for the reason just mentioned, I am curious to know."

"Francesco is a good man," a sort of sluggishly responded Don Benito, like a phlegmatic appreciator, who would neither find fault nor flatter.

"Ah, I thought so. For it were strange indeed, and not very creditable to us white-skins, if a little of our blood mixed with the African's, should, far from improving the latter's quality, have the sad effect of pouring vitriolic acid into black broth; improving the hue, perhaps, but not the wholesomeness."

"Doubtless, doubtless, Señor, but"—glancing at Babo—"not to speak of negroes, your planter's remark I have heard applied to the Spanish and Indian intermixtures in our provinces. But I know nothing about the matter," he listlessly added.

And here they entered the cabin.

The lunch was a frugal one. Some of Captain Delano's fresh fish and pumpkins, biscuit and salt beef, the reserved bottle of cider, and the San Dominick's last bottle of Canary.[1]

As they entered, Francesco, with two or three colored aids, was hovering over the table giving the last adjustments. Upon perceiving their master they withdrew, Francesco making a smiling congé, and the Spaniard, without condescending to notice it, fastidiously remarking to his companion that he relished not superfluous attendance.

7. Literally, "health" (Arabic); a Muslim ceremonial greeting.
8. In his popular *Letters to His Son on the Art of Becoming a Man of the World and a Gentleman* (1747), Philip Stanhope, the fourth earl of Chesterfield (1694–1773), advocated a worldly code at variance with Jesus' absolute morality.
9. In this English usage, "usher" means an attendant charged with walking ceremoniously before a person of rank; certain ushers were known by the color of the rod or scepter they traditionally carried.
1. I.e., wine from the Canary Islands.

Without companions, host and guest sat down, like a childless married couple, at opposite ends of the table, Don Benito waving Captain Delano to his place, and, weak as he was, insisting upon that gentleman being seated before himself.

The negro placed a rug under Don Benito's feet, and a cushion behind his back, and then stood behind, not his master's chair, but Captain Delano's. At first, this a little surprised the latter. But it was soon evident that, in taking his position, the black was still true to his master; since by facing him he could the more readily anticipate his slightest want.

"This is an uncommonly intelligent fellow of yours, Don Benito," whispered Captain Delano across the table.

"You say true, Señor."

During the repast, the guest again reverted to parts of Don Benito's story, begging further particulars here and there. He inquired how it was that the scurvy and fever should have committed such wholesale havoc upon the whites, while destroying less than half of the blacks. As if this question reproduced the whole scene of plague before the Spaniard's eyes, miserably reminding him of his solitude in a cabin where before he had had so many friends and officers round him, his hand shook, his face became hueless, broken words escaped; but directly the sane memory of the past seemed replaced by insane terrors of the present. With starting eyes he stared before him at vacancy. For nothing was to be seen but the hand of his servant pushing the Canary over towards him. At length a few sips served partially to restore him. He made random reference to the different constitution of races, enabling one to offer more resistance to certain maladies than another. The thought was new to his companion.

Presently Captain Delano, intending to say something to his host concerning the pecuniary part of the business he had undertaken for him, especially—since he was strictly accountable to his owners—with reference to the new suit of sails, and other things of that sort; and naturally preferring to conduct such affairs in private, was desirous that the servant should withdraw; imagining that Don Benito for a few minutes could dispense with his attendance. He, however, waited awhile; thinking that, as the conversation proceeded, Don Benito, without being prompted, would perceive the propriety of the step.

But it was otherwise. At last catching his host's eye, Captain Delano, with a slight backward gesture of his thumb, whispered, "Don Benito, pardon me, but there is an interference with the full expression of what I have to say to you."

Upon this the Spaniard changed countenance; which was imputed to his resenting the hint, as in some way a reflection upon his servant. After a moment's pause, he assured his guest that the black's remaining with them could be of no disservice; because since losing his officers he had made Babo (whose original office, it now appeared, had been captain of the slaves) not only his constant attendant and companion, but in all things his confidant.

After this, nothing more could be said; though, indeed, Captain Delano could hardly avoid some little tinge of irritation upon being left ungratified in so inconsiderable a wish, by one, too, for whom he intended such solid services. But it is only his querulousness, thought he; and so filling his glass he proceeded to business.

The price of the sails and other matters was fixed upon. But while this was being done, the American observed that, though his original offer of assistance had been hailed with hectic animation, yet now when it was reduced to a business transaction, indifference and apathy were betrayed. Don Benito, in fact, appeared to submit to hearing the details more out of regard to common propriety, than from any impression that weighty benefit to himself and his voyage was involved.

Soon, his manner became still more reserved. The effort was vain to seek to draw him into social talk. Gnawed by his splenetic mood, he sat twitching his beard, while to little purpose the hand of his servant, mute as that on the wall, slowly pushed over the Canary.

Lunch being over, they sat down on the cushioned transom; the servant placing a pillow behind his master. The long continuance of the calm had now affected the atmosphere. Don Benito sighed heavily, as if for breath.

"Why not adjourn to the cuddy," said Captain Delano; "there is more air there." But the host sat silent and motionless.

Meantime his servant knelt before him, with a large fan of feathers. And Francesco coming in on tiptoes, handed the negro a little cup of aromatic waters, with which at intervals he chafed his master's brow; smoothing the hair along the temples as a nurse does a child's. He spoke no word. He only rested his eye on his master's, as if, amid all Don Benito's distress, a little to refresh his spirit by the silent sight of fidelity.

Presently the ship's bell sounded two o'clock; and through the cabin-windows a slight rippling of the sea was discerned; and from the desired direction.

"There," exclaimed Captain Delano, "I told you so, Don Benito, look!"

He had risen to his feet, speaking in a very animated tone, with a view the more to rouse his companion. But though the crimson curtain of the stern-window near him that moment fluttered against his pale cheek, Don Benito seemed to have even less welcome for the breeze than the calm.

Poor fellow, thought Captain Delano, bitter experience has taught him that one ripple does not make a wind, any more than one swallow a summer. But he is mistaken for once. I will get his ship in for him, and prove it.

Briefly alluding to his weak condition, he urged his host to remain quietly where he was, since he (Captain Delano) would with pleasure take upon himself the responsibility of making the best use of the wind.

Upon gaining the deck, Captain Delano started at the unexpected figure of Atufal, monumentally fixed at the threshold, like one of those sculptured porters of black marble guarding the porches of Egyptian tombs.

But this time the start was, perhaps, purely physical. Atufal's presence, singularly attesting docility even in sullenness, was contrasted with that of the hatchet-polishers, who in patience evinced their industry; while both spectacles showed, that lax as Don Benito's general authority might be, still, whenever he chose to exert it, no man so savage or colossal but must, more or less, bow.

Snatching a trumpet which hung from the bulwarks, with a free step Captain Delano advanced to the forward edge of the poop, issuing his orders in his best Spanish. The few sailors and many negroes, all equally pleased, obediently set about heading the ship towards the harbor.

While giving some directions about setting a lower stu'n'-sail, suddenly Captain Delano heard a voice faithfully repeating his orders. Turning, he saw Babo, now for the time acting, under the pilot, his original part of captain of the slaves. This assistance proved valuable. Tattered sails and warped yards were soon brought into some trim. And no brace or halyard was pulled but to the blithe songs of the inspirited negroes.

Good fellows, thought Captain Delano, a little training would make fine sailors of them. Why see, the very women pull and sing too. These must be some of those Ashantee negresses that make such capital soldiers, I've heard. But who's at the helm. I must have a good hand there.

He went to see.

The San Dominick steered with a cumbrous tiller, with large horizontal pullies attached. At each pully-end stood a subordinate black, and between them, at the tiller-head, the responsible post, a Spanish seaman, whose countenance evinced his due share in the general hopefulness and confidence at the coming of the breeze.

He proved the same man who had behaved with so shame-faced an air on the windlass.

"Ah—it is you, my man," exclaimed Captain Delano—"well, no more sheep's-eyes now;—look straightforward and keep the ship so. Good hand, I trust? And want to get into the harbor, don't you?"

The man assented with an inward chuckle, grasping the tiller-head firmly. Upon this, unperceived by the American, the two blacks eyed the sailor intently.

Finding all right at the helm, the pilot went forward to the forecastle, to see how matters stood there.

The ship now had way enough to breast the current. With the approach of evening, the breeze would be sure to freshen.

Having done all that was needed for the present, Captain Delano, giving his last orders to the sailors, turned aft to report affairs to Don Benito in the cabin; perhaps additionally incited to rejoin him by the hope of snatching a moment's private chat while the servant was engaged upon deck.

From opposite sides, there were, beneath the poop, two approaches to the cabin; one further forward than the other, and consequently communicating with a longer passage. Marking the servant still above, Captain Delano, taking the nighest entrance—the one last named, and at whose porch Atufal still stood—hurried on his way, till, arrived at the cabin threshold, he paused an instant, a little to recover from his eagerness. Then, with the words of his intended business upon his lips, he entered. As he advanced toward the seated Spaniard, he heard another footstep, keeping time with his. From the opposite door, a salver in hand, the servant was likewise advancing.

"Confound the faithful fellow," thought Captain Delano; "what a vexatious coincidence."

Possibly, the vexation might have been something different, were it not for the brisk confidence inspired by the breeze. But even as it was, he felt a slight twinge, from a sudden indefinite association in his mind of Babo with Atufal.

"Don Benito," said he, "I give you joy; the breeze will hold, and will increase. By the way, your tall man and time-piece, Atufal, stands without. By your order, of course?"

Don Benito recoiled, as if at some bland satirical touch, delivered with such adroit garnish of apparent good-breeding as to present no handle for retort.

He is like one flayed alive, thought Captain Delano; where may one touch him without causing a shrink?

The servant moved before his master, adjusting a cushion; recalled to civility, the Spaniard stiffly replied: "You are right. The slave appears where you saw him, according to my command; which is, that if at the given hour I am below, he must take his stand and abide my coming."

"Ah now, pardon me, but that is treating the poor fellow like an ex-king indeed. Ah, Don Benito," smiling, "for all the license you permit in some things, I fear lest, at bottom, you are a bitter hard master."

Again Don Benito shrank; and this time, as the good sailor thought, from a genuine twinge of his conscience.

Again conversation became constrained. In vain Captain Delano called attention to the now perceptible motion of the keel gently cleaving the sea; with lack-lustre eye, Don Benito returned words few and reserved.

By-and-by, the wind having steadily risen, and still blowing right into the harbor, bore the San Dominick swiftly on. Rounding a point of land, the sealer at distance came into open view.

Meantime Captain Delano had again repaired to the deck, remaining there some time. Having at last altered the ship's course, so as to give the reef a wide berth, he returned for a few moments below.

I will cheer up my poor friend, this time, thought he.

"Better and better, Don Benito," he cried as he blithely reëntered; "there will soon be an end to your cares, at least for awhile. For when, after a long, sad voyage, you know, the anchor drops into the haven, all its vast weight seems lifted from the captain's heart. We are getting on famously, Don Benito. My ship is in sight. Look through this side-light here; there she is; all a-taunt-o! The Bachelor's Delight, my good friend. Ah, how this wind braces one up. Come, you must take a cup of coffee with me this evening. My old steward will give you as fine a cup as ever any sultan tasted. What say you, Don Benito, will you?"

At first, the Spaniard glanced feverishly up, casting a longing look towards the sealer, while with mute concern his servant gazed into his face. Suddenly the old ague of coldness returned, and dropping back to his cushions he was silent.

"You do not answer. Come, all day you have been my host; would you have hospitality all on one side?"

"I cannot go," was the response.

"What? it will not fatigue you. The ships will lie together as near as they can, without swinging foul. It will be little more than stepping from deck to deck; which is but as from room to room. Come, come, you must not refuse me."

"I cannot go," decisively and repulsively repeated Don Benito.

Renouncing all but the last appearance of courtesy, with a sort of cadaverous sullenness, and biting his thin nails to the quick, he glanced, almost glared, at his guest; as if impatient that a stranger's presence should interfere with the full indulgence of his morbid hour. Meantime the sound of the parted waters came more and more gurglingly and merrily in at the windows;

as reproaching him for his dark spleen; as telling him that, sulk as he might, and go mad with it, nature cared not a jot; since, whose fault was it, pray?

But the foul mood was now at its depth, as the fair wind at its hight.

There was something in the man so far beyond any mere unsociality or sourness previously evinced, that even the forbearing good-nature of his guest could no longer endure it. Wholly at a loss to account for such demeanor, and deeming sickness with eccentricity, however extreme, no adequate excuse, well satisfied, too, that nothing in his own conduct could justify it, Captain Delano's pride began to be roused. Himself became reserved. But all seemed one to the Spaniard. Quitting him, therefore, Captain Delano once more went to the deck.

The ship was now within less than two miles of the sealer. The whale-boat was seen darting over the interval.

To be brief, the two vessels, thanks to the pilot's skill, ere long in neighborly style lay anchored together.

Before returning to his own vessel, Captain Delano had intended communicating to Don Benito the smaller details of the proposed services to be rendered. But, as it was, unwilling anew to subject himself to rebuffs, he resolved, now that he had seen the San Dominick safely moored, immediately to quit her, without further allusion to hospitality or business. Indefinitely postponing his ulterior plans, he would regulate his future actions according to future circumstances. His boat was ready to receive him; but his host still tarried below. Well, thought Captain Delano, if he has little breeding, the more need to show mine. He descended to the cabin to bid a ceremonious, and, it may be, tacitly rebukeful adieu. But to his great satisfaction, Don Benito, as if he began to feel the weight of that treatment with which his slighted guest had, not indecorously, retaliated upon him, now supported by his servant, rose to his feet, and grasping Captain Delano's hand, stood tremulous; too much agitated to speak. But the good augury hence drawn was suddenly dashed, by his resuming all his previous reserve, with augmented gloom, as, with half-averted eyes, he silently reseated himself on his cushions. With a corresponding return of his own chilled feelings, Captain Delano bowed and withdrew.

He was hardly midway in the narrow corridor, dim as a tunnel, leading from the cabin to the stairs, when a sound, as of the tolling for execution in some jail-yard, fell on his ears. It was the echo of the ship's flawed bell, striking the hour, drearily reverberated in this subterranean vault. Instantly, by a fatality not to be withstood, his mind, responsive to the portent, swarmed with superstitious suspicions. He paused. In images far swifter than these sentences, the minutest details of all his former distrusts swept through him.

Hitherto, credulous good-nature had been too ready to furnish excuses for reasonable fears. Why was the Spaniard, so superfluously punctilious at times, now heedless of common propriety in not accompanying to the side his departing guest? Did indisposition forbid? Indisposition had not forbidden more irksome exertion that day. His last equivocal demeanor recurred. He had risen to his feet, grasped his guest's hand, motioned toward his hat; then, in an instant, all was eclipsed in sinister muteness and gloom. Did this imply one brief, repentent relenting at the final moment, from some iniquitous plot, followed by remorseless return to it? His last glance seemed to express a calamitous, yet acquiescent farewell to Captain Delano forever. Why decline the invitation to visit the sealer that evening? Or was the Spaniard less hardened than the Jew, who refrained not from supping at the board of him whom the same night he meant to betray?[2] What imported all those day-long enigmas and contradictions, except they were intended to mystify, preliminary to some stealthy blow? Atufal, the pretended rebel, but punctual shadow, that moment lurked by the threshold without. He seemed a sentry, and more. Who, by his own confession, had stationed him there? Was the negro now lying in wait?

The Spaniard behind—his creature before: to rush from darkness to light was the involuntary choice.

The next moment, with clenched jaw and hand, he passed Atufal, and stood unharmed in the light. As he saw his trim ship lying peacefully at anchor, and almost within ordinary call; as he saw his household boat, with familiar faces in it, patiently rising and falling on the short waves by the San Dominick's side; and then, glancing about the decks where he stood, saw the oakum-pickers still gravely plying their fingers; and heard the low, buzzing whistle and industrious hum of the hatchet-polishers, still bestirring themselves over their endless occupation; and more than all, as he saw the benign aspect of nature, taking her innocent repose in the evening; the screened sun in the quiet camp of the west shining out like the mild light from Abraham's tent,[3] as charmed eye and ear took in all these, with the chained figure of the black, clenched jaw and hand relaxed. Once again he smiled at the phantoms which had mocked him, and felt something like a tinge of remorse, that, by harboring them even for a moment, he should, by implication, have betrayed an atheist doubt of the ever-watchful Providence above.

There was a few minutes' delay, while, in obedience to his orders, the boat was being hooked along to the gangway. During this interval, a sort of saddened satisfaction stole over Captain Delano, at thinking of the kindly offices he had that day discharged for a stranger. Ah, thought he, after good actions one's conscience is never ungrateful, however much so the benefited party may be.

Presently, his foot, in the first act of descent into the boat, pressed the first round of the side-ladder, his face presented inward upon the deck. In the same moment, he heard his name courteously sounded; and, to his pleased surprise, saw Don Benito advancing—an unwonted energy in his air, as if, at the last moment, intent upon making amends for his recent discourtesy. With instinctive good feeling, Captain Delano, withdrawing his foot, turned and reciprocally advanced. As he did so, the Spaniard's nervous eagerness increased, but his vital energy failed; so that, the better to support him, the servant, placing his master's hand on his naked shoulder, and gently holding it there, formed himself into a sort of crutch.

When the two captains met, the Spaniard again fervently took the hand of the American, at the same time casting an earnest glance into his eyes, but, as before, too much overcome to speak.

2. Judas Iscariot, who betrayed Christ after the Last Supper (Matthew 26).

3. The biblical patriarch Abraham, who pitched his tent in many places during his westward journey from Ur of the Chaldees to Canaan, on to Egypt, and then back to Canaan.

I have done him wrong, self-reproachfully thought Captain Delano; his apparent coldness has deceived me; in no instance has he meant to offend.

Meantime, as if fearful that the continuance of the scene might too much unstring his master, the servant seemed anxious to terminate it. And so, still presenting himself as a crutch, and walking between the two captains, he advanced with them towards the gangway; while still, as if full of kindly contrition, Don Benito would not let go the hand of Captain Delano, but retained it in his, across the black's body.

Soon they were standing by the side, looking over into the boat, whose crew turned up their curious eyes. Waiting a moment for the Spaniard to relinquish his hold, the now embarrassed Captain Delano lifted his foot, to overstep the threshold of the open gangway; but still Don Benito would not let go his hand. And yet, with an agitated tone, he said, "I can go no further; here I must bid you adieu. Adieu, my dear, dear Don Amasa. Go—go!" suddenly tearing his hand loose, "go, and God guard you better than me, my best friend."

Not unaffected, Captain Delano would now have lingered; but catching the meekly admonitory eye of the servant, with a hasty farewell he descended into his boat, followed by the continual adieus of Don Benito, standing rooted in the gangway.

Seating himself in the stern, Captain Delano, making a last salute, ordered the boat shoved off. The crew had their oars on end. The bowsman pushed the boat a sufficient distance for the oars to be lengthwise dropped. The instant that was done, Don Benito sprang over the bulwarks, falling at the feet of Captain Delano; at the same time, calling towards his ship, but in tones so frenzied, that none in the boat could understand him. But, as if not equally obtuse, three sailors, from three different and distant parts of the ship, splashed into the sea, swimming after their captain, as if intent upon his rescue.

The dismayed officer of the boat eagerly asked what this meant. To which, Captain Delano, turning a disdainful smile upon the unaccountable Spaniard, answered that, for his part, he neither knew nor cared; but it seemed as if Don Benito had taken it into his head to produce the impression among his people that the boat wanted to kidnap him. "Or else—give way for your lives," he wildly added, starting at a clattering hubbub in the ship, above which rang the tocsin of the hatchet-polishers; and seizing Don Benito by the throat he added, "this plotting pirate means murder!" Here, in apparent verification of the words, the servant, a dagger in his hand, was seen on the rail overhead, poised in the act of leaping, as if with desperate fidelity to befriend his master to the last; while, seemingly to aid the black, the three white sailors were trying to clamber into the hampered bow. Meantime, the whole host of negroes, as if inflamed at the sight of their jeopardized captain, impended in one sooty avalanche over the bulwarks.

All this, with what preceded, and what followed, occurred with such involutions of rapidity, that past, present, and future seemed one.

Seeing the negro coming, Captain Delano had flung the Spaniard aside, almost in the very act of clutching him, and, by the unconscious recoil, shifting his place, with arms thrown up, so promptly grappled the servant in his descent, that with dagger presented at Captain Delano's heart, the black seemed of purpose to have leaped there as to his mark. But the weapon was wrenched away, and the assailant dashed down into the bottom of the boat, which now, with disentangled oars, began to speed through the sea.

At this juncture, the left hand of Captain Delano, on one side, again clutched the half-reclined Don Benito, heedless that he was in a speechless faint, while his right foot, on the other side, ground the prostrate negro; and his right arm pressed for added speed on the after oar, his eye bent forward, encouraging his men to their utmost.

But here, the officer of the boat, who had at last succeeded in beating off the towing sailors, and was now, with face turned aft, assisting the bowsman at his oar, suddenly called to Captain Delano, to see what the black was about; while a Portuguese oarsman shouted to him to give heed to what the Spaniard was saying.

Glancing down at his feet, Captain Delano saw the freed hand of the servant aiming with a second dagger—a small one, before concealed in his wool—with this he was snakishly writhing up from the boat's bottom, at the heart of his master, his countenance lividly vindictive, expressing the centred purpose of his soul, while the Spaniard, half-choked, was vainly shrinking away, with husky words, incoherent to all but the Portuguese.

That moment, across the long-benighted mind of Captain Delano, a flash of revelation swept, illuminating in unanticipated clearness, his host's whole mysterious demeanor, with every enigmatic event of the day, as well as the entire past voyage of the San Dominick. He smote Babo's hand down, but his own heart smote him harder. With infinite pity he withdrew his hold from Don Benito. Not Captain Delano, but Don Benito, the black, in leaping into the boat, had intended to stab.

Both the black's hands were held, as, glancing up towards the San Dominick, Captain Delano, now with scales dropped from his eyes, saw the negroes, not in misrule, not in tumult, not as if frantically concerned for Don Benito, but with mask torn away, flourishing hatchets and knives, in ferocious piratical revolt. Like delirious black dervishes, the six Ashantees danced on the poop. Prevented by their foes from springing into the water, the Spanish boys were hurrying up to the topmost spars, while such of the few Spanish sailors, not already in the sea, less alert, were descried, helplessly mixed in, on deck, with the blacks.

Meantime Captain Delano hailed his own vessel, ordering the ports up, and the guns run out. But by this time the cable of the San Dominick had been cut; and the fag-end, in lashing out, whipped away the canvas shroud about the beak, suddenly revealing, as the bleached hull swung round towards the open ocean, death for the figure-head, in a human skeleton; chalky comment on the chalked words below, *"Follow your leader."*

At the sight, Don Benito, covering his face, wailed out: "'Tis he, Aranda! my murdered, unburied friend!"

Upon reaching the sealer, calling for ropes, Captain Delano bound the negro, who made no resistance, and had him hoisted to the deck. He would then have assisted the now almost helpless Don Benito up the side; but Don Benito, wan as he was, refused to move, or be moved, until the negro should have been first put below out of view. When, presently assured that it was done, he no more shrank from the ascent.

The boat was immediately dispatched back to pick up the three swimming sailors. Meantime, the guns were in readiness, though, owing to the San

Dominick having glided somewhat astern of the sealer, only the aftermost one could be brought to bear. With this, they fired six times; thinking to cripple the fugitive ship by bringing down her spars. But only a few inconsiderable ropes were shot away. Soon the ship was beyond the guns' range, steering broad out of the bay; the blacks thickly clustering round the bowsprit,[4] one moment with taunting cries towards the whites, the next with upthrown gestures hailing the now dusky moors of ocean—cawing crows escaped from the hand of the fowler.

The first impulse was to slip the cables and give chase. But, upon second thoughts, to pursue with whale-boat and yawl seemed more promising.

Upon inquiring of Don Benito what fire arms they had on board the San Dominick, Captain Delano was answered that they had none that could be used; because, in the earlier stages of the mutiny, a cabin-passenger, since dead, had secretly put out of order the locks of what few muskets there were. But with all his remaining strength, Don Benito entreated the American not to give chase, either with ship or boat; for the negroes had already proved themselves such desperadoes, that, in case of a present assault, nothing but a total massacre of the whites could be looked for. But, regarding this warning as coming from one whose spirit had been crushed by misery, the American did not give up his design.

The boats were got ready and armed. Captain Delano ordered his men into them. He was going himself when Don Benito grasped his arm.

"What! have you saved my life, señor, and are you now going to throw away your own?"

The officers also, for reasons connected with their interests and those of the voyage, and a duty owing to the owners, strongly objected against their commander's going. Weighing their remonstrances a moment, Captain Delano felt bound to remain; appointing his chief mate—an athletic and resolute man, who had been a privateer's-man[5]—to head the party. The more to encourage the sailors, they were told, that the Spanish captain considered his ship good as lost; that she and her cargo, including some gold and silver, were worth more than a thousand doubloons. Take her, and no small part should be theirs. The sailors replied with a shout.

The fugitives had now almost gained an offing. It was nearly night; but the moon was rising. After hard, prolonged pulling, the boats came up on the ship's quarters, at a suitable distance laying upon their oars to discharge their muskets. Having no bullets to return, the negroes sent their yells. But, upon the second volley, Indian-like, they hurtled their hatchets. One took off a sailor's fingers. Another struck the whale-boat's bow, cutting off the rope there, and remaining stuck in the gunwale like a woodman's axe. Snatching it, quivering from its lodgment, the mate hurled it back. The returned gauntlet now stuck in the ship's broken quarter-gallery, and so remained.

The negroes giving too hot a reception, the whites kept a more respectful distance. Hovering now just out of reach of the hurtling hatchets, they, with a view to the close encounter which must soon come, sought to decoy the blacks into entirely disarming themselves of their most murderous weapons

4. The large spar, such as the pole for a mast, extending from the foremost part of the ship.

5. Had served on a privateer—a ship commissioned by a government to prey on the shipping of other countries.

in a hand-to-hand fight, by foolishly flinging them, as missiles, short of the mark, into the sea. But ere long perceiving the stratagem, the negroes desisted, though not before many of them had to replace their lost hatchets with hand-spikes; an exchange which, as counted upon, proved in the end favorable to the assailants.

Meantime, with a strong wind, the ship still clove the water; the boats alternately falling behind, and pulling up, to discharge fresh volleys.

The fire was mostly directed towards the stern, since there, chiefly, the negroes, at present, were clustering. But to kill or maim the negroes was not the object. To take them, with the ship, was the object. To do it, the ship must be boarded; which could not be done by boats while she was sailing so fast.

A thought now struck the mate. Observing the Spanish boys still aloft, high as they could get, he called to them to descend to the yards, and cut adrift the sails. It was done. About this time, owing to causes hereafter to be shown, two Spaniards, in the dress of sailors and conspicuously showing themselves, were killed; not by volleys, but by deliberate marksman's shots; while, as it afterwards appeared, by one of the general discharges, Atufal, the black, and the Spaniard at the helm likewise were killed. What now, with the loss of the sails, and loss of leaders, the ship became unmanageable to the negroes.

With creaking masts, she came heavily round to the wind; the prow slowly swinging, into view of the boats, its skeleton gleaming in the horizontal moonlight, and casting a gigantic ribbed shadow upon the water. One extended arm of the ghost seemed beckoning the whites to avenge it.

"Follow your leader!" cried the mate; and, one on each bow, the boats boarded. Sealing-spears and cutlasses crossed hatchets and hand-spikes. Huddled upon the long-boat amidships, the negresses raised a wailing chant, whose chorus was the clash of the steel.

For a time, the attack wavered; the negroes wedging themselves to beat it back; the half-repelled sailors, as yet unable to gain a footing, fighting as troopers in the saddle, one leg sideways flung over the bulwarks, and one without, plying their cutlasses like carters' whips. But in vain. They were almost overborne, when, rallying themselves into a squad as one man, with a huzza, they sprang inboard; where, entangled, they involuntarily separated again. For a few breaths' space, there was a vague, muffled, inner sound, as of submerged sword-fish rushing hither and thither through shoals of black-fish. Soon, in a reunited band, and joined by the Spanish seamen, the whites came to the surface, irresistibly driving the negroes toward the stern. But a barricade of casks and sacks, from side to side, had been thrown up by the mainmast. Here the negroes faced about, and though scorning peace or truce, yet fain would have had respite. But, without pause, overleaping the barrier, the unflagging sailors again closed. Exhausted, the blacks now fought in despair. Their red tongues lolled, wolf-like, from their black mouths. But the pale sailors' teeth were set; not a word was spoken; and, in five minutes more, the ship was won.

Nearly a score of the negroes were killed. Exclusive of those by the balls,[6] many were mangled; their wounds—mostly inflicted by the long-edged

6. Those killed by musketballs.

sealing-spears—resembling those shaven ones of the English at Preston Pans, made by the poled scythes of the Highlanders.[7] On the other side, none were killed, though several were wounded; some severely, including the mate. The surviving negroes were temporarily secured, and the ship, towed back into the harbor at midnight, once more lay anchored.

Omitting the incidents and arrangements ensuing, suffice it that, after two days spent in refitting, the ships sailed in company for Conception, in Chili, and thence for Lima, in Peru; where, before the vice-regal courts, the whole affair, from the beginning, underwent investigation.

Though, midway on the passage, the ill-fated Spaniard, relaxed from constraint, showed some signs of regaining health with free-will; yet, agreeably to his own foreboding, shortly before arriving at Lima, he relapsed, finally becoming so reduced as to be carried ashore in arms. Hearing of his story and plight, one of the many religious institutions of the City of Kings opened an hospitable refuge to him, where both physician and priest were his nurses, and a member of the order volunteered to be his one special guardian and consoler, by night and by day.

The following extracts, translated from one of the official Spanish documents, will it is hoped, shed light on the preceding narrative, as well as, in the first place, reveal the true port of departure and true history of the San Dominick's voyage, down to the time of her touching at the island of St. Maria.

But, ere the extracts come, it may be well to preface them with a remark.

The document selected, from among many others, for partial translation, contains the deposition of Benito Cereno; the first taken in the case. Some disclosures therein were, at the time, held dubious for both learned and natural reasons. The tribunal inclined to the opinion that the deponent, not undisturbed in his mind by recent events, raved of some things which could never have happened. But subsequent depositions of the surviving sailors, bearing out the revelations of their captain in several of the strangest particulars, gave credence to the rest. So that the tribunal, in its final decision, rested its capital sentences upon statements which, had they lacked confirmation, it would have deemed it but duty to reject.

I, DON JOSE DE ABOS AND PADILLA, His Majesty's Notary for the Royal Revenue, and Register of this Province, and Notary Public of the Holy Crusade of this Bishopric, etc.

Do certify and declare, as much as is requisite in law, that, in the criminal cause commenced the twenty-fourth of the month of September, in the year seventeen hundred and ninety-nine, against the negroes of the ship San Dominick, the following declaration before me was made.

Declaration of the first witness, DON BENITO CERENO

The same day, and month, and year, His Honor, Doctor Juan Martinez de Rozas, Councilor of the Royal Audience of this Kingdom, and learned in the law of this Intendency, ordered the captain of the ship San Dominick,

7. At the battle of Preston Pans (in East Lothian, Scotland) during 1745, Prince Charles Edward, grandson of James II, led Scottish Highlanders armed with scythes fastened to poles to victory over the royal forces.

Don Benito Cereno, to appear; which he did in his litter, attended by the monk Infelez; of whom he received the oath, which he took by God, our Lord, and a sign of the Cross; under which he promised to tell the truth of whatever he should know and should be asked;—and being interrogated agreeably to the tenor of the act commencing the process, he said, that on the twentieth of May last, he set sail with his ship from the port of Valparaiso, bound to that of Callao; loaded with the produce of the country beside thirty cases of hardware and one hundred and sixty blacks, of both sexes, mostly belonging to Don Alexandro Aranda, gentleman, of the city of Mendoza;[8] that the crew of the ship consisted of thirty-six men, beside the persons who went as passengers; that the negroes were in part as follows:

[*Here, in the original, follows a list of some fifty names, descriptions, and ages, compiled from certain recovered documents of Aranda's, and also from recollections of the deponent, from which portions only are extracted.*]

—One, from about eighteen to nineteen years, named José, and this was the man that waited upon his master, Don Alexandro, and who speaks well the Spanish, having served him four or five years; * * * a mulatto, named Francisco, the cabin steward, of a good person and voice, having sung in the Valparaiso churches, native of the province of Buenos Ayres, aged about thirty-five years. * * * A smart negro, named Dago, who had been for many years a grave-digger among the Spaniards, aged forty-six years. * * * Four old negroes, born in Africa, from sixty to seventy, but sound, calkers by trade, whose names are as follows:—the first was named Muri, and he was killed (as was also his son named Diamelo); the second, Nacta; the third, Yola, likewise killed; the fourth, Ghofan; and six full-grown negroes, aged from thirty to forty-five, all raw, and born among the Ashantees—Matiluqui, Yan, Lecbe, Mapenda, Yambaio, Akim; four of whom were killed; * * * a powerful negro named Atufal, who, being supposed to have been a chief in Africa, his owners set great store by him. * * * And a small negro of Senegal, but some years among the Spaniards, aged about thirty, which negro's name was Babo; * * * that he does not remember the names of the others, but that still expecting the residue of Don Alexandro's papers will be found, will then take due account of them all, and remit to the court; * * * and thirty-nine women and children of all ages.

[*The catalogue over, the deposition goes on:*]

* * * That all the negroes slept upon deck, as is customary in this navigation, and none wore fetters, because the owner, his friend Aranda, told him that they were all tractable; * * * that on the seventh day after leaving port, at three o'clock in the morning, all the Spaniards being asleep except the two officers on the watch, who were the boatswain, Juan Robles, and the carpenter, Juan Bautista Gayete, and the helmsman and his boy, the negroes revolted suddenly, wounded dangerously the boatswain and the carpenter,

8. City in Argentina. "Intendency": court district. "Litter": seat or chair in which a person can be carried. Callao is a city in Peru; Valparaiso is in Chile.

and successively killed eighteen men of those who were sleeping upon deck, some with hand-spikes and hatchets, and others by throwing them alive overboard, after tying them; that of the Spaniards upon deck, they left about seven, as he thinks, alive and tied, to manœuvre the ship, and three or four more who hid themselves, remained also alive. Although in the act of revolt the negroes made themselves masters of the hatchway, six or seven wounded went through it to the cockpit, without any hindrance on their part; that during the act of revolt, the mate and another person, whose name he does not recollect, attempted to come up through the hatchway, but being quickly wounded, were obliged to return to the cabin; that the deponent resolved at break of day to come up the companionway, where the negro Babo was, being the ringleader, and Atufal, who assisted him, and having spoken to them, exhorted them to cease committing such atrocities, asking them, at the same time, what they wanted and intended to do, offering, himself, to obey their commands; that, notwithstanding this, they threw, in his presence, three men, alive and tied, overboard; that they told the deponent to come up, and that they would not kill him; which having done, the negro Babo asked him whether there were in those seas any negro countries where they might be carried, and he answered them, No; that the negro Babo afterwards told him to carry them to Senegal, or to the neighboring islands of St. Nicholas; and he answered, that this was impossible, on account of the great distance, the necessity involved of rounding Cape Horn, the bad condition of the vessel, the want of provisions, sails, and water; but that the negro Babo replied to him he must carry them in any way; that they would do and conform themselves to everything the deponent should require as to eating and drinking; that after a long conference, being absolutely compelled to please them, for they threatened him to kill all the whites if they were not, at all events, carried to Senegal, he told them that what was most wanting for the voyage was water; that they would go near the coast to take it, and thence they would proceed on their course; that the negro Babo agreed to it; and the deponent steered towards the intermediate ports, hoping to meet some Spanish or foreign vessel that would save them; that within ten or eleven days they saw the land, and continued their course by it in the vicinity of Nasca; that the deponent observed that the negroes were now restless and mutinous, because he did not effect the taking in of water, the negro Babo having required, with threats, that it should be done, without fail, the following day; he told him he saw plainly that the coast was steep, and the rivers designated in the maps were not to be found, with other reasons suitable to the circumstances; that the best way would be to go to the island of Santa Maria, where they might water easily, it being a solitary island, as the foreigners did; that the deponent did not go to Pisco, that was near, nor make any other port of the coast, because the negro Babo had intimated to him several times, that he would kill all the whites the very moment he should perceive any city, town, or settlement of any kind on the shores to which they should be carried; that having determined to go to the island of Santa Maria, as the deponent had planned, for the purpose of trying whether, on the passage or near the island itself, they could find any vessel that should favor them, or whether he could escape from it in a boat to the neighboring coast of Arruco;[9] to

9. I.e., Arica, Chile. Nasca and Pisco are both in Peru.

adopt the necessary means he immediately changed his course, steering for the island; that the negroes Babo and Atufal held daily conferences, in which they discussed what was necessary for their design of returning to Senegal, whether they were to kill all the Spaniards, and particularly the deponent; that eight days after parting from the coast of Nasca, the deponent being on the watch a little after day-break, and soon after the negroes had their meeting, the negro Babo came to the place where the deponent was, and told him that he had determined to kill his master, Don Alexandro Aranda, both because he and his companions could not otherwise be sure of their liberty, and that, to keep the seamen in subjection, he wanted to prepare a warning of what road they should be made to take did they or any of them oppose him; and that, by means of the death of Don Alexandro, that warning would best be given; but, that what this last meant, the deponent did not at the time comprehend, nor could not, further than that the death of Don Alexandro was intended; and moreover, the negro Babo proposed to the deponent to call the mate Raneds, who was sleeping in the cabin, before the thing was done, for fear, as the deponent understood it, that the mate, who was a good navigator, should be killed with Don Alexandro and the rest; that the deponent, who was the friend, from youth, of Don Alexandro, prayed and conjured, but all was useless; for the negro Babo answered him that the thing could not be prevented, and that all the Spaniards risked their death if they should attempt to frustrate his will in this matter or any other; that, in this conflict, the deponent called the mate, Raneds, who was forced to go apart, and immediately the negro Babo commanded the Ashantee Martinqui and the Ashantee Lecbe to go and commit the murder; that those two went down with hatchets to the berth of Don Alexandro; that, yet half alive and mangled, they dragged him on deck; that they were going to throw him overboard in that state, but the negro Babo stopped them, bidding the murder be completed on the deck before him, which was done, when, by his orders, the body was carried below, forward; that nothing more was seen of it by the deponent for three days; * * * that Don Alonzo Sidonia, an old man, long resident at Valparaiso, and lately appointed to a civil office in Peru, whither he had taken passage, was at the time sleeping in the berth opposite Don Alexandro's; that, awakening at his cries, surprised by them, and at the sight of the negroes with their bloody hatchets in their hands, he threw himself into the sea through a window which was near him, and was drowned, without it being in the power of the deponent to assist or take him up; * * * that, a short time after killing Aranda, they brought upon deck his german-cousin, of middle-age, Don Francisco Masa, of Mendoza, and the young Don Joaquin, Marques de Aramboalaza, then lately from Spain, with his Spanish servant Ponce, and the three young clerks of Aranda, José Morairi, Lorenzo Bargas, and Hermenegildo Gandix, all of Cadiz; that Don Joaquin and Hermenegildo Gandix, the negro Babo for purposes hereafter to appear, preserved alive; but Don Francisco Masa, José Morairi, and Lorenzo Bargas, with Ponce the servant, beside the boatswain, Juan Robles, the boatswain's mates, Manuel Viscaya and Roderigo Hurta, and four of the sailors, the negro Babo ordered to be thrown alive into the sea, although they made no resistance, nor begged for anything else but mercy; that the boatswain, Juan Robles, who knew how to swim, kept the longest above water, making acts of contrition, and, in the last words he uttered, charged this deponent to cause mass to be said for his soul to our Lady of Succor; * * * that, during the three days which followed, the deponent, uncertain what fate had befallen the remains of Don Alexandro, frequently asked the negro Babo where they were, and if still on board, whether they were to be preserved for interment ashore, entreating him so to order it; that the negro Babo answered nothing till the fourth day, when at sunrise, the deponent coming on deck, the negro Babo showed him a skeleton, which had been substituted for the ship's proper figure-head, the image of Christopher Colon, the discoverer of the New World; that the negro Babo asked him whose skeleton that was, and whether, from its whiteness, he should not think it a white's; that, upon his covering his face, the negro Babo, coming close, said words to this effect: "Keep faith with the blacks from here to Senegal, or you shall in spirit, as now in body, follow your leader," pointing to the prow; * * * that the same morning the negro Babo took by succession each Spaniard forward, and asked him whose skeleton that was, and whether, from its whiteness, he should not think it a white's; that each Spaniard covered his face; that then to each the negro Babo repeated the words in the first place said to the deponent; * * * that they (the Spaniards), being then assembled aft, the negro Babo harangued them, saying that he had now done all; that the deponent (as navigator for the negroes) might pursue his course, warning him and all of them that they should, soul and body, go the way of Don Alexandro if he saw them (the Spaniards) speak or plot anything against them (the negroes)—a threat which was repeated every day; that, before the events last mentioned, they had tied the cook to throw him overboard, for it is not known what thing they heard him speak, but finally the negro Babo spared his life, at the request of the deponent; that a few days after, the deponent, endeavoring not to omit any means to preserve the lives of the remaining whites, spoke to the negroes peace and tranquillity, and agreed to draw up a paper, signed by the deponent and the sailors who could write, as also by the negro Babo, for himself and all the blacks, in which the deponent obliged himself to carry them to Senegal, and they not to kill any more, and he formally to make over to them the ship, with the cargo, with which they were for that time satisfied and quieted. * * * But the next day, the more surely to guard against the sailors' escape, the negro Babo commanded all the boats to be destroyed but the long-boat, which was unseaworthy, and another, a cutter in good condition, which, knowing it would yet be wanted for towing the water casks, he had lowered down into the hold.

* * * * *

[*Various particulars of the prolonged and perplexed navigation ensuing here follow, with incidents of a calamitous calm, from which portion one passage is extracted, to wit:*]

—That on the fifth day of the calm, all on board suffering much from the heat, and want of water, and five having died in fits, and mad, the negroes became irritable, and for a chance gesture, which they deemed suspicious—though it was harmless—made by the mate, Raneds, to the deponent, in the act of handing a quadrant, they killed him; but that for this they afterwards were sorry, the mate being the only remaining navigator on board, except the deponent.

* * * * *

—That omitting other events, which daily happened, and which can only serve uselessly to recall past misfortunes and conflicts, after seventy-three days' navigation, reckoned from the time they sailed from Nasca, during which they navigated under a scanty allowance of water, and were afflicted with the calms before mentioned, they at last arrived at the island of Santa Maria, on the seventeenth of the month of August, at about six o'clock in the afternoon, at which hour they cast anchor very near the American ship, Bachelor's Delight, which lay in the same bay, commanded by the generous Captain Amasa Delano; but at six o'clock in the morning, they had already descried the port, and the negroes became uneasy, as soon as at distance they saw the ship, not having expected to see one there; that the negro Babo pacified them, assuring them that no fear need be had; that straightway he ordered the figure on the bow to be covered with canvas, as for repairs, and had the decks a little set in order; that for a time the negro Babo and the negro Atufal conferred; that the negro Atufal was for sailing away, but the negro Babo would not, and, by himself, cast about what to do; that at last he came to the deponent, proposing to him to say and do all that the deponent declares to have said and done to the American captain; * * * * * * that the negro Babo warned him that if he varied in the least, or uttered any word, or gave any look that should give the least intimation of the past events or present state, he would instantly kill him, with all his companions, showing a dagger, which he carried hid, saying something which, as he understood it, meant that that dagger would be alert as his eye; that the negro Babo then announced the plan to all his companions, which pleased them; that he then, the better to disguise the truth, devised many expedients, in some of them uniting deceit and defense; that of this sort was the device of the six Ashantees before named, who were his bravoes;[1] that them he stationed on the break of the poop, as if to clean certain hatchets (in cases, which were part of the cargo), but in reality to use them, and distribute them at need, and at a given word he told them that, among other devices, was the device of presenting Atufal, his right-hand man, as chained, though in a moment the chains could be dropped; that in every particular he informed the deponent what part he was expected to enact in every device, and what story he was to tell on every occasion, always threatening him with instant death if he varied in the least; that, conscious that many of the negroes would be turbulent, the negro Babo appointed the four aged negroes, who were calkers, to keep what domestic order they could on the decks; that again and again he harangued the Spaniards and his companions, informing them of his intent, and of his devices, and of the invented story that this deponent was to tell, charging them lest any of them varied from that story; that these arrangements were made and matured during the interval of two or three hours, between their first sighting the ship and the arrival on board of Captain Amasa Delano; that this happened about half-past seven o'clock in the morning, Captain

1. Henchmen.

Amasa Delano coming in his boat, and all gladly receiving him; that the deponent, as well as he could force himself, acting then the part of principal owner, and a free captain of the ship, told Captain Amasa Delano, when called upon, that he came from Buenos Ayres, bound to Lima, with three hundred negroes; that off Cape Horn, and in a subsequent fever, many negroes had died; that also, by similar casualties, all the sea officers and the greatest part of the crew had died.

* * * * *

[*And so the deposition goes on, circumstantially recounting the fictitious story dictated to the deponent by Babo, and through the deponent imposed upon Captain Delano; and also recounting the friendly offers of Captain Delano, with other things, but all of which is here omitted. After the fictitious story, etc., the deposition proceeds:*]

—that the generous Captain Amasa Delano remained on board all the day, till he left the ship anchored at six o'clock in the evening, deponent speaking to him always of his pretended misfortunes, under the forementioned principles, without having had it in his power to tell a single word, or give him the least hint, that he might know the truth and state of things; because the negro Babo, performing the office of an officious servant with all the appearance of submission of the humble slave, did not leave the deponent one moment; that this was in order to observe the deponent's actions and words, for the negro Babo understands well the Spanish; and besides, there were thereabout some others who were constantly on the watch, and likewise understood the Spanish; * * * that upon one occasion, while deponent was standing on the deck conversing with Amasa Delano, by a secret sign the negro Babo drew him (the deponent) aside, the act appearing as if originating with the deponent; that then, he being drawn aside, the negro Babo proposed to him to gain from Amasa Delano full particulars about his ship, and crew, and arms; that the deponent asked "For what?" that the negro Babo answered he might conceive; that, grieved at the prospect of what might overtake the generous Captain Amasa Delano, the deponent at first refused to ask the desired questions, and used every argument to induce the negro Babo to give up this new design; that the negro Babo showed the point of his dagger; that, after the information had been obtained, the negro Babo again drew him aside, telling him that that very night he (the deponent) would be captain of two ships, instead of one, for that, great part of the American's ship's crew being to be absent fishing, the six Ashantees, without any one else, would easily take it; that at this time he said other things to the same purpose; that no entreaties availed; that, before Amasa Delano's coming on board, no hint had been given touching the capture of the American ship; that to prevent this project the deponent was powerless; * * * —that in some things his memory is confused, he cannot distinctly recall every event; * * * —that as soon as they had cast anchor at six of the clock in the evening, as has before been stated, the American Captain took leave to return to his vessel; that upon a sudden impulse, which the deponent believes to have come from God and his angels, he, after the farewell had been said, followed the generous Captain Amasa Delano as far as the gunwale, where he stayed, under pretense of taking leave, until Amasa Delano should have been seated in his boat; that on shoving off, the deponent sprang from the gunwale into the boat, and fell into it, he knows not how, God guarding him; that—

* * * * *

[*Here, in the original, follows the account of what further happened at the escape, and how the San Dominick was retaken, and of the passage to the coast; including in the recital many expressions of "eternal gratitude" to the "generous Captain Amasa Delano." The deposition then proceeds with recapitulatory remarks, and a partial renumeration of the negroes, making record of their individual part in the past events, with a view to furnishing, according to command of the court, the data whereon to found the criminal sentences to be pronounced. From this portion is the following:*]

—That he believes that all the negroes, though not in the first place knowing to the design of revolt, when it was accomplished, approved it. * * * That the negro, José, eighteen years old, and in the personal service of Don Alexandro, was the one who communicated the information to the negro Babo, about the state of things in the cabin, before the revolt; that this is known, because, in the preceding midnight, he used to come from his berth, which was under his master's, in the cabin, to the deck where the ringleader and his associates were, and had secret conversations with the negro Babo, in which he was several times seen by the mate; that, one night, the mate drove him away twice; * * that this same negro José, was the one who, without being commanded to do so by the negro Babo, as Lecbe and Martinqui were, stabbed his master, Don Alexandro, after he had been dragged half-lifeless to the deck; * * that the mulatto steward, Francisco, was of the first band of revolters, that he was, in all things, the creature and tool of the negro Babo; that, to make his court, he, just before a repast in the cabin, proposed, to the negro Babo, poisoning a dish for the generous Captain Amasa Delano; this is known and believed, because the negroes have said it; but that the negro Babo, having another design, forbade Francisco; * * that the Ashantee Lecbe was one of the worst of them; for that, on the day the ship was retaken, he assisted in the defense of her, with a hatchet in each hand, one of which he wounded, in the breast, the chief mate of Amasa Delano, in the first act of boarding; this all knew; that, in sight of the deponent, Lecbe struck, with a hatchet, Don Francisco Masa when, by the negro Babo's orders, he was carrying him to throw him overboard, alive; beside participating in the murder, before mentioned, of Don Alexandro Aranda, and others of the cabin-passengers; that, owing to the fury with which the Ashantees fought in the engagement with the boats, but this Lecbe and Yau survived; that Yau was bad as Lecbe; that Yau was the man who, by Babo's command, willingly prepared the skeleton of Don Alexandro, in a way the negroes afterwards told the deponent, but which he, so long as reason is left him, can never divulge; that Yau and Lecbe were the two who, in a calm by night, riveted the skeleton to the bow; this also the negroes told him; that the negro Babo was he who traced the inscription below it; that the negro Babo was the plotter from first to last; he ordered every murder, and was the helm and keel of the revolt; that Atufal was his lieutenant in all; but Atufal, with his own hand, committed no murder; nor did the negro Babo; * * that Atufal was shot, being killed in the fight with the boats, ere boarding; * * that the negresses, of age, were knowing to the revolt and testified themselves satisfied at the death of their master, Don Alexandro; that, had the negroes not restrained them, they would have tortured to death, instead of simply killing, the Spaniards slain by command of the negro Babo; that the negresses used their utmost influence to have the deponent made away with; that, in the various acts of murder, they sang songs and danced—not gaily, but solemnly; and before the engagement with the boats, as well as during the action, they sang melancholy songs to the negroes, and that this melancholy tone was more inflaming than a different one would have been, and was so intended; that all this is believed, because the negroes have said it.

—that of the thirty-six men of the crew exclusive of the passengers, (all of whom are now dead), which the deponent had knowledge of, six only remained alive, with four cabin-boys and ship-boys, not included with the crew; * * —that the negroes broke an arm of one of the cabin-boys and gave him strokes with hatchets.

[*Then follow various random disclosures referring to various periods of time. The following are extracted:*]

—That during the presence of Captain Amasa Delano on board, some attempts were made by the sailors, and one by Hermenegildo Gandix, to convey hints to him of the true state of affairs; but that these attempts were ineffectual, owing to fear of incurring death, and furthermore owing to the devices which offered contradictions to the true state of affairs; as well as owing to the generosity and piety of Amasa Delano incapable of sounding such wickedness; * * * that Luys Galgo, a sailor about sixty years of age, and formerly of the king's navy, was one of those who sought to convey tokens to Captain Amasa Delano; but his intent, though undiscovered, being suspected, he was, on a pretense, made to retire out of sight, and at last into the hold, and there was made away with. This the negroes have since said; * * * that one of the ship-boys feeling, from Captain Amasa Delano's presence, some hopes of release, and not having enough prudence, dropped some chance-word respecting his expectations, which being overheard and understood by a slave-boy with whom he was eating at the time, the latter struck him on the head with a knife, inflicting a bad wound, but of which the boy is now healing; that likewise, not long before the ship was brought to anchor, one of the seamen, steering at the time, endangered himself by letting the blacks remark some expression in his countenance, arising from a cause similar to the above; but this sailor, by his heedful after conduct, escaped; * * * that these statements are made to show the court that from the beginning to the end of the revolt, it was impossible for the deponent and his men to act otherwise than they did; * * * —that the third clerk, Hermenegildo Gandix, who before had been forced to live among the seamen, wearing a seaman's habit, and in all respects appearing to be one for the time; he, Gandix, was killed by a musket-ball fired through a mistake from the boats before boarding; having in his fright run up the mizzen-rigging, calling to the boats—"don't board," lest upon their boarding the negroes should kill him; that this inducing the Americans to believe he some way favored the cause of the negroes, they fired two balls at him, so that he fell wounded from the rigging, and was drowned in the sea; * * * —that the young Don Joaquin, Marques de Arambaolaza, like Hermenegildo Gandix, the third clerk, was degraded to the office and appearance of a common seaman; that upon one occasion when Don Joaquin shrank, the negro Babo commanded the Ashantee Lecbe to take tar and heat it, and pour it upon Don Joaquin's hands; * * * —that Don Joaquin was killed owing to another mistake of the Americans, but one impossible to be avoided, as upon the approach of the boats, Don Joaquin, with a hatchet tied edge out and upright to his hand, was made by the negroes to appear on the bulwarks; whereupon, seen with arms in his hands and in a questionable attitude, he was shot for a renegade seaman; * * * —that on the person of Don Joaquin was found secreted a jewel, which, by papers that were discovered, proved to have been meant for the shrine of our Lady of Mercy in Lima; a votive offering, beforehand prepared and guarded, to attest his gratitude, when he should have landed in Peru, his last destination, for the safe conclusion of his entire voyage from Spain; * * * —that the jewel, with the other effects of the late Don Joaquin, is in the custody of the brethren of the Hospital de Sacerdotes, awaiting the disposition of the honorable court; * * * —that, owing to the condition of the deponent, as well as the haste in which the boats departed for the attack, the Americans were not forewarned that there were, among the apparent crew, a passenger and one of the clerks disguised by the negro Babo; * * * —that, beside the negroes killed in the action, some were killed after the capture and re-anchoring at night, when shackled to the ring-bolts on deck; that these deaths were committed by the sailors, ere they could be prevented. That so soon as informed of it, Captain Amasa Delano used all his authority, and, in particular with his own hand, struck down Martinez Gola, who, having found a razor in the pocket of an old jacket of his, which one of the shackled negroes had on, was aiming it at the negro's throat; that the noble Captain Amasa Delano also wrenched from the hand of Bartholomew Barlo, a dagger secreted at the time of the massacre of the whites, with which he was in the act of stabbing a shackled negro, who, the same day, with another negro, had thrown him down and jumped upon him; * * * —that, for all the events, befalling through so long a time, during which the ship was in the hands of the negro Babo, he cannot here give account; but that, what he had said is the most substantial of what occurs to him at present, and is the truth under the oath which he has taken; which declaration he affirmed and ratified, after hearing it read to him.

He said that he is twenty-nine years of age, and broken in body and mind; that when finally dismissed by the court, he shall not return home to Chili, but betake himself to the monastery on Mount Agonia without; and signed with his honor, and crossed himself, and, for the time, departed as he came, in his litter, with the monk Infelez, to the Hospital de Sacerdotes.

BENITO CERENO.

DOCTOR ROZAS.

If the Deposition have served as the key to fit into the lock of the complications which precede it, then, as a vault whose door has been flung back, the San Dominick's hull lies open to-day.

Hitherto the nature of this narrative, besides rendering the intricacies in the beginning unavoidable, has more or less required that many things, instead of being set down in the order of occurrence, should be retrospectively, or irregularly given; this last is the case with the following passages, which will conclude the account:

During the long, mild voyage to Lima, there was, as before hinted, a period during which the sufferer a little recovered his health, or, at least in some degree, his tranquillity. Ere the decided relapse which came, the two captains had many cordial conversations—their fraternal unreserve in singular contrast with former withdrawments.

Again and again, it was repeated, how hard it had been to enact the part forced on the Spaniard by Babo.

"Ah, my dear friend," Don Benito once said, "at those very times when you thought me so morose and ungrateful, nay, when, as you now admit, you half thought me plotting your murder, at those very times my heart was frozen; I could not look at you, thinking of what, both on board this ship and your own, hung, from other hands, over my kind benefactor. And as God lives, Don Amasa, I know not whether desire for my own safety alone could have nerved me to that leap into your boat, had it not been for the thought that, did you, unenlightened, return to your ship, you, my best friend, with all who might be with you, stolen upon, that night, in your hammocks, would never in this world have wakened again. Do but think how you walked this deck, how you sat in this cabin, every inch of ground mined into honeycombs under you. Had I dropped the least hint, made the least advance towards an understanding between us, death, explosive death—yours as mine—would have ended the scene."

"True, true," cried Captain Delano, starting, "you saved my life, Don Benito, more than I yours; saved it, too, against my knowledge and will."

"Nay, my friend," rejoined the Spaniard, courteous even to the point of religion, "God charmed your life, but you saved mine. To think of some things you did—those smilings and chattings, rash pointings and gesturings. For less than these, they slew my mate, Raneds; but you had the Prince of Heaven's safe conduct through all ambuscades."

"Yes, all is owing to Providence, I know; but the temper of my mind that morning was more than commonly pleasant, while the sight of so much suffering, more apparent than real, added to my good nature, compassion, and charity, happily interweaving the three. Had it been otherwise, doubtless, as you hint, some of my interferences might have ended unhappily enough. Besides, those feelings I spoke of enabled me to get the better of momentary distrust, at times when acuteness might have cost me my life, without saving another's. Only at the end did my suspicions get the better of me, and you know how wide of the mark they then proved."

"Wide, indeed," said Don Benito, sadly; "you were with me all day; stood with me, sat with me, talked with me, looked at me, ate with me, drank with me; and yet, your last act was to clutch for a monster, not only an innocent man, but the most pitiable of all men. To such degree may malign machinations and deceptions impose. So far may even the best man err, in judging the conduct of one with the recesses of whose condition he is not acquainted. But you were forced to it; and you were in time undeceived. Would that, in both respects, it was so ever, and with all men."

"You generalize, Don Benito; and mournfully enough. But the past is passed; why moralize upon it? Forget it. See, yon bright sun has forgotten it all, and the blue sea, and the blue sky; these have turned over new leaves."

"Because they have no memory," he dejectedly replied; "because they are not human."

"But these mild trades[2] that now fan your cheek, do they not come with a human-like healing to you? Warm friends, steadfast friends are the trades."

"With their steadfastness they but waft me to my tomb, señor," was the foreboding response.

"You are saved," cried Captain Delano, more and more astonished and pained; "you are saved; what has cast such a shadow upon you?"

"The negro."

There was silence, while the moody man sat, slowly and unconsciously gathering his mantle about him, as if it were a pall.

There was no more conversation that day.

But if the Spaniard's melancholy sometimes ended in muteness upon topics like the above, there were others upon which he never spoke at all; on which, indeed, all his old reserves were piled. Pass over the worst, and, only to elucidate, let an item or two of these be cited. The dress so precise and costly, worn by him on the day whose events have been narrated, had not willingly been put on. And that silver-mounted sword, apparent symbol of despotic command, was not, indeed, a sword, but the ghost of one. The scabbard, artificially stiffened, was empty.

As for the black—whose brain, not body, had schemed and led the revolt, with the plot—his slight frame, inadequate to that which it held, had at once yielded to the superior muscular strength of his captor, in the boat. Seeing all was over, he uttered no sound, and could not be forced to. His aspect seemed to say, since I cannot do deeds, I will not speak words. Put in irons in the hold, with the rest, he was carried to Lima. During the passage Don Benito did not visit him. Nor then, nor at any time after, would he look at him. Before the tribunal he refused. When pressed by the judges he fainted. On the testimony of the sailors alone rested the legal identity of Babo.

Some months after, dragged to the gibbet at the tail of a mule, the black met his voiceless end. The body was burned to ashes; but for many days, the head, that hive of subtlety, fixed on a pole in the Plaza, met, unabashed, the gaze of the whites; and across the Plaza looked towards St. Bartholomew's church, in whose vaults slept then, as now, the recovered bones of Aranda; and across the Rimac bridge looked towards the monastery, on Mount Agonia without; where, three months after being dismissed by the court, Benito Cereno, borne on the bier, did, indeed, follow his leader.

1855, 1856

2. Trade winds; here, dependable winds blowing from southeast to northwest.

From Battle-Pieces[1]

The Portent

(1859)[2]

Hanging from the beam,
Slowly swaying (such the law),
Gaunt the shadow on your green,
Shenandoah!
The cut is on the crown[3]
(Lo, John Brown),
And the stabs shall heal no more.

Hidden in the cap[4]
Is the anguish none can draw;
So your future veils its face,
Shenandoah!
But the streaming beard is shown
(Weird John Brown),
The meteor of the war.

1866

The March into Virginia

Ending in the First Manassas (July, 1861)[1]

Did all the lets[2] and bars appear
To every just or larger end,
Whence should come the trust and cheer?
Youth must its ignorant impulse lend—
Age finds place in the rear.
All wars are boyish, and are fought by boys,
The champions and enthusiasts of the state:
Turbid ardors and vain joys
Not barrenly abate—
Stimulants to the power mature,
Preparatives of fate.

1. *Battle-Pieces and Aspects of the War* was published by the Harpers in 1866, the source of the present texts.
2. On October 16, 1859, John Brown (1800–1859) led twenty-one men, including five African Americans, in an attack on an unguarded federal arsenal at Harpers Ferry in western Virginia in an effort to secure arms for the slave revolt he hoped to inspire. Within two days his group was defeated by a force of American troops. Convicted of treason against the state of Virginia, he was hanged in the Shenandoah Valley, at Charlestown, Virginia, on December 2, 1859. Melville takes Brown's raid as a portent of the Civil War.
3. Brown received a head wound when captured.
4. Hood placed over the head at the time of execution.
1. Confederate forces routed the Union Army in July 1861 at Manassas, Virginia (a railroad junction some thirty miles from Washington). The first battle at Manassas, also known as the Battle of Bull Run, was the earliest major engagement of the Civil War.
2. Obstacles.

Who here forecasteth the event?
What heart but spurns at precedent
And warnings of the wise,
Contemned foreclosures of surprise?
The banners play, the bugles call,
The air is blue and prodigal.
    No berrying party, pleasure-wooed,
No picnic party in the May,
Ever went less loth than they
    Into that leafy neighborhood.
In Bacchic[3] glee they file toward Fate,
Moloch's[4] uninitiate;
Expectancy, and glad surmise
Of battle's unknown mysteries.
All they feel is this: 'tis glory,
A rapture sharp, though transitory,
Yet lasting in belaureled story.
So they gayly go to fight,
Chatting left and laughing right.

But some who this blithe mood present,
  As on in lightsome files they fare,
Shall die experienced ere three days are spent—
  Perish, enlightened by the vollied glare;
Or shame survive, and, like to adamant,
  The throe of Second Manassas[5] share.

1866

Shiloh[1]

A Requiem

(April, 1862)

Skimming lightly, wheeling still,
  The swallows fly low
Over the field in clouded days,
  The forest-field of Shiloh—
Over the field where April rain
Solaced the parched ones stretched in pain
Through the pause of night
That followed the Sunday fight
  Around the church of Shiloh—

3. Bacchus was the Roman god of wine.
4. Old Testament deity to whom children were burnt in sacrifice (see Leviticus 20.2–5). Melville probably had in mind Milton's *Paradise Lost* 1.392ff., the description of "Moloch, horrid King besmear'd with blood / Of human sacrifice, and parents tears."
5. In August 1862, Robert E. Lee and "Stonewall" Jackson defeated the Union Army once again.
1. The site of a Confederate victory over Union forces in western Tennessee, in early April 1862, which made clear to the North that the war was going to go on for quite a while. The battle, in which over 23,000 were killed or wounded, was fought near the Shiloh Baptist Church.

The church so lone, the log-built one,
That echoed to many a parting groan
And natural prayer
Of dying foemen mingled there—
Foemen at morn, but friends at eve—
Fame or country least their care:
(What like a bullet can undeceive!)
But now they lie low,
While over them the swallows skim,
And all is hushed at Shiloh.

1866

The House-top

A Night Piece (*July, 1863*)[1]

No sleep. The sultriness pervades the air
And binds the brain—a dense oppression, such
As tawny tigers feel in matted shades,
Vexing their blood and making apt for ravage.
Beneath the stars the roofy desert spreads
Vacant as Libya. All is hushed near by.
Yet fitfully from far breaks a mixed surf
Of muffled sound, the Atheist roar of riot.
Yonder, where parching Sirius[2] set in drought,
Balefully glares red Arson—there—and there.
The Town is taken by its rats—ship-rats
And rats of the wharves. All civil charms
And priestly spells which late held hearts in awe—
Fear-bound, subjected to a better sway
Than sway of self; these like a dream dissolve,
And man rebounds whole æons back in nature.[3]
Hail to the low dull rumble, dull and dead,
And ponderous drag that shakes the wall.
Wise Draco[4] comes, deep in the midnight roll
Of black artillery; he comes, though late;
In code corroborating Calvin's[5] creed
And cynic tyrannies of honest kings;
He comes, nor parlies; and the Town, redeemed,

1. In July 1863, New York City mobs composed largely of Irish immigrants rioted against the new draft laws, destroying property and attacking free blacks (their economic competitors) in their rage at being required to fight for the abolition of slavery.

2. The dog star associated with the miserable "dog days" in which the riots occurred.

3. "I dare not write the horrible and inconceivable atrocities committed," says Froissart, in alluding to the remarkable sedition in France during his time. The like may be hinted of some proceedings of the draft-rioters [Melville's note]. French historian and poet Jean Froissart (c. 1337–1410?) described the violent suppression of a peasant uprising of 1358. During the three-day riot of July 1863, which resulted in the deaths of over a hundred people, black men were tortured and lynched and the Colored Orphanage Asylum was burned to the ground.

4. An Athenian who in 621 B.C.E. set forth laws that became proverbial for their harshness.

5. John Calvin (1509–1564), French theologian, believed every human being was born guilty of Original Sin, the consequence of God's curse when Adam and Eve disobeyed Him in Eden.

Gives thanks devout; nor, being thankful, heeds
The grimy slur on the Republic's faith implied,
Which holds that Man is naturally good,
And—more—is Nature's Roman, never to be scourged.[6]

1866

From John Marr and Other Sailors[1]

The Maldive Shark

About the Shark, phlegmatical one,
Pale sot of the Maldive sea,[2]
The sleek little pilot-fish,[3] azure and slim,
How alert in attendance be.
From his saw-pit of mouth, from his charnel of maw
They have nothing of harm to dread,
But liquidly glide on his ghastly flank
Or before his Gorgonian[4] head;
Or lurk in the port of serrated teeth
In white triple tiers of glittering gates,
And there find a haven when peril's abroad,
An asylum in jaws of the Fates!
They are friends; and friendly they guide him to prey,
Yet never partake of the treat—
Eyes and brains to the dotard lethargic and dull,
Pale ravener of horrible meat.

1888

From Timoleon, Etc.[1]

Monody[2]

To have known him, to have loved him
   After loneness long;
And then to be estranged in life,
   And neither in the wrong;

6. Acts 22.25: "And as they bound him with thongs, Paul said unto the centurion that stood by, Is it lawful for you to scourge a man that is a Roman, and uncondemned?"
1. Published in New York by the De Vinne Press in 1888, with a run of twenty-five copies. Melville paid for the publication.
2. The Maldive Islands lie off the southern tip of India. Sot: scourge (archaic).
3. Small fish that accompany the shark and seem to guide it.
4. In Greek mythology, the Gorgons were three sisters, with snakes for hair, whose glance could turn beholders into stone.
1. Published in New York by the Caxton Press in 1891. Like *John Marr*, the book was privately published with a run of twenty-five copies.
2. In Greek pastoral poetry, a monody was typically a poem that lamented the death of a fellow poet. Some critics believe that Melville's monody is about Nathaniel Hawthorne, who died in 1864.

And now for death to set his seal—
  Ease me, a little ease, my song!

By wintry hills his hermit-mound
  The sheeted snow-drifts drape,
And houseless there the snow-bird flits
  Beneath the fir-trees' crape:
Glazed now with ice the cloistral vine
  That hid the shyest grape.

1891

Billy Budd, Sailor[1]

(*An Inside Narrative*)

DEDICATED
TO
JACK CHASE
ENGLISHMAN
Wherever that great heart may now be
Here on Earth or harbored in Paradise
Captain of the Maintop
in the year 1843
in the U.S. Frigate
United States[2]

1

In the time before steamships, or then more frequently than now, a stroller along the docks of any considerable seaport would occasionally have his attention arrested by a group of bronzed mariners, man-of-war's men or merchant sailors in holiday attire, ashore on liberty. In certain instances they would flank, or like a bodyguard quite surround, some superior figure of their own class, moving along with them like Aldebaran[3] among the lesser lights of his constellation. That signal object was the "Handsome Sailor" of the less prosaic time alike of the military and merchant navies. With no perceptible trace of the vainglorious about him, rather with the offhand unaffectedness of natural regality, he seemed to accept the spontaneous homage of his shipmates.

1. Melville may have begun *Billy Budd* while he was still at the New York customhouse, but serious work on it began early in 1886, just after his retirement, and continued until his death in September 1891. It remained unpublished until 1924, when Raymond Weaver transcribed the manuscript for the Constable edition of Melville's works. The manuscript presented many difficulties, and Weaver did not surmount all of them; notably, he printed a discarded passage from a late chapter as a preface, having misread a query of Elizabeth Melville's. The standard edition of the story, based on a careful study and fresh transcription of the manuscript, is that of Harrison Hayford and Merton M. Sealts Jr., first published in 1962. The Hayford-Sealts text is reprinted here, and the editors' explanatory notes have been drawn on for some of the footnotes to this reprinting.

2. In *White-Jacket* (1850), a novel drawn from his experiences on the navy ship *The United States*, Melville made his actual shipmate Jack Chase into a major character.

3. Brightest star in the constellation Taurus, the Bull, where it forms the animal's eye.

A somewhat remarkable instance recurs to me. In Liverpool, now half a century ago, I saw under the shadow of the great dingy street-wall of Prince's Dock (an obstruction long since removed) a common sailor so intensely black that he must needs have been a native African of the unadulterate blood of Ham[4]—a symmetric figure much above the average height. The two ends of a gay silk handkerchief thrown loose about the neck danced upon the displayed ebony of his chest, in his ears were big hoops of gold, and a Highland bonnet with a tartan band set off his shapely head. It was a hot noon in July; and his face, lustrous with perspiration, beamed with barbaric good humor. In jovial sallies right and left, his white teeth flashing into view, he rollicked along, the center of a company of his shipmates. These were made up of such an assortment of tribes and complexions as would have well fitted them to be marched up by Anacharsis Cloots[5] before the bar of the first French Assembly as Representatives of the Human Race. At each spontaneous tribute rendered by the wayfarers to this black pagod[6] of a fellow—the tribute of a pause and stare, and less frequently an exclamation—the motley retinue showed that they took that sort of pride in the evoker of it which the Assyrian priests doubtless showed for their grand sculptured Bull when the faithful prostrated themselves.

To return. If in some cases a bit of a nautical Murat[7] in setting forth his person ashore, the Handsome Sailor of the period in question evinced nothing of the dandified Billy-be-Dam, an amusing character all but extinct now, but occasionally to be encountered, and in a form yet more amusing than the original, at the tiller of the boats on the tempestuous Erie Canal or, more likely, vaporing in the groggeries along the towpath.[8] Invariably a proficient in his perilous calling, he was also more or less of a mighty boxer or wrestler. It was strength and beauty. Tales of his prowess were recited. Ashore he was the champion; afloat the spokesman; on every suitable occasion always foremost. Close-reefing topsails in a gale, there he was, astride the weather yardarm-end, foot in the Flemish horse as stirrup, both hands tugging at the earing as at a bridle, in very much the attitude of young Alexander curbing the fiery Bucephalus. A superb figure, tossed up as by the horns of Taurus[9] against the thunderous sky, cheerily hallooing to the strenuous file along the spar.

The moral nature was seldom out of keeping with the physical make. Indeed, except as toned by the former, the comeliness and power, always attractive in masculine conjunction, hardly could have drawn the sort of hon-

4. Noah's son, who was cursed by his father for mocking him (Genesis 9.22–25). That curse was traditionally understood by white Europeans and Americans as having made Ham's descendants black. During the nineteenth century, proslavery writers regularly adduced the story of the curse as a way of justifying slavery; but as is evident from his presentation of the highly admired black sailor, Melville's use of the biblical reference is ironic.

5. Melville knew of the Prussian-born Baron de Cloots (1755–1794) from Thomas Carlyle's *The French Revolution*, pt. 2, bk. 1, ch. 10. In 1790, Cloots had brought before the French National Assembly men of different nations, classes, and ethnicities to display the variety and unity of humankind.

6. An idol.

7. I.e., a dandy, like Joachim Murat (1767?–1815), whom Napoleon made king of Naples.

8. A joke, there being little danger from tempests on the man-made canal.

9. Alexander the Great (356–323 B.C.E.) tamed the fierce horse Bucephalus ("bull-head"), thereby fulfilling the prophecy of an oracle. The horns of Taurus are in the constellation.

est homage the Handsome Sailor in some examples received from his less gifted associates.

Such a cynosure, at least in aspect, and something such too in nature, though with important variations made apparent as the story proceeds, was welkin-eyed Billy Budd—or Baby Budd, as more familiarly, under circumstances hereafter to be given, he at last came to be called—aged twenty-one, a foretopman[1] of the British fleet toward the close of the last decade of the eighteenth century. It was not very long prior to the time of the narration that follows that he had entered the King's service, having been impressed on the Narrow Seas from a homeward-bound English merchantman into a seventy-four outward bound, H.M.S. *Bellipotent*;[2] which ship, as was not unusual in those hurried days, having been obliged to put to sea short of her proper complement of men. Plump upon Billy at first sight in the gangway the boarding officer, Lieutenant Ratcliffe, pounced, even before the merchantman's crew was formally mustered on the quarter-deck for his deliberate inspection. And him only he elected. For whether it was because the other men when ranged before him showed to ill advantage after Billy, or whether he had some scruples in view of the merchantman's being rather short-handed, however it might be, the officer contented himself with his first spontaneous choice. To the surprise of the ship's company, though much to the lieutenant's satisfaction, Billy made no demur. But, indeed, any demur would have been as idle as the protest of a goldfinch popped into a cage.

Noting this uncomplaining acquiescence, all but cheerful, one might say, the shipmaster[3] turned a surprised glance of silent reproach at the sailor. The shipmaster was one of those worthy mortals found in every vocation, even the humbler ones—the sort of person whom everybody agrees in calling "a respectable man." And—nor so strange to report as it may appear to be—though a ploughman of the troubled waters, lifelong contending with the intractable elements, there was nothing this honest soul at heart loved better than simple peace and quiet. For the rest, he was fifty or thereabouts, a little inclined to corpulence, a prepossessing face, unwhiskered, and of an agreeable color—a rather full face, humanely intelligent in expression. On a fair day with a fair wind and all going well, a certain musical chime in his voice seemed to be the veritable unobstructed outcome of the innermost man. He had much prudence, much conscientiousness, and there were occasions when these virtues were the cause of overmuch disquietude in him. On a passage, so long as his craft was in any proximity to land, no sleep for Captain Graveling. He took to heart those serious responsibilities not so heavily borne by some shipmasters.

Now while Billy Budd was down in the forecastle getting his kit together, the *Bellipotent*'s lieutenant, burly and bluff, nowise disconcerted by Captain Graveling's omitting to proffer the customary hospitalities on an occasion so unwelcome to him, an omission simply caused by preoccupation of thought, unceremoniously invited himself into the cabin, and also to a flask from

1. Crewman assigned to the top of a ship's forward mast. "Welkin-eyed": blue, like the heavens.
2. Meaning "powerful in war" (derived from Latin); through most of the composition the name of the ship was the *Indomitable* but Melville eventually decided on *Bellipotent*. "Impressed": i.e., taken into naval service by force. "Narrow Seas": the English Channel and St. George's Channel. "Seventy-four": i.e., warship armed with 74 cannons.
3. Captain.

the spirit locker, a receptacle which his experienced eye instantly discovered. In fact he was one of those sea dogs in whom all the hardship and peril of naval life in the great prolonged wars of his time never impaired the natural instinct for sensuous enjoyment. His duty he always faithfully did; but duty is sometimes a dry obligation, and he was for irrigating its aridity, whensoever possible, with a fertilizing decoction of strong waters. For the cabin's proprietor there was nothing left but to play the part of the enforced host with whatever grace and alacrity were practicable. As necessary adjuncts to the flask, he silently placed tumbler and water jug before the irrepressible guest. But excusing himself from partaking just then, he dismally watched the unembarrassed officer deliberately diluting his grog a little, then tossing it off in three swallows, pushing the empty tumbler away, yet not so far as to be beyond easy reach, at the same time settling himself in his seat and smacking his lips with high satisfaction, looking straight at the host.

These proceedings over, the master broke the silence; and there lurked a rueful reproach in the tone of his voice: "Lieutenant, you are going to take my best man from me, the jewel of 'em."

"Yes, I know," rejoined the other, immediately drawing back the tumbler preliminary to a replenishing. "Yes, I know. Sorry."

"Beg pardon, but you don't understand, Lieutenant. See here, now. Before I shipped that young fellow, my forecastle was a rat-pit of quarrels. It was black times, I tell you, aboard the *Rights* here. I was worried to that degree my pipe had no comfort for me. But Billy came; and it was like a Catholic priest striking peace in an Irish shindy.[4] Not that he preached to them or said or did anything in particular; but a virtue went out of him, sugaring the sour ones. They took to him like hornets to treacle; all but the buffer of the gang, the big shaggy chap with the fire-red whiskers. He indeed, out of envy, perhaps, of the newcomer, and thinking such a "sweet and pleasant fellow," as he mockingly designated him to the others, could hardly have the spirit of a gamecock, must needs bestir himself in trying to get up an ugly row with him. Billy forebore with him and reasoned with him in a pleasant way—he is something like myself, Lieutenant, to whom aught like a quarrel is hateful—but nothing served. So, in the second dogwatch one day, the Red Whiskers in presence of the others, under pretense of showing Billy just whence a sirloin steak was cut—for the fellow had once been a butcher—insultingly gave him a dig under the ribs. Quick as lightning Billy let fly his arm. I dare say he never meant to do quite as much as he did, but anyhow he gave the burly fool a terrible drubbing. It took about half a minute, I should think. And, lord bless you, the lubber was astonished at the celerity. And will you believe it, Lieutenant, the Red Whiskers now really loves Billy—loves him, or is the biggest hypocrite that ever I heard of. But they all love him. Some of 'em do his washing, darn his old trousers for him; the carpenter is at odd times making a pretty little chest of drawers for him. Anybody will do anything for Billy Budd; and it's the happy family here. But now, Lieutenant, if that young fellow goes—I know how it will be aboard the *Rights*. Not again very soon shall I, coming up from dinner, lean over the capstan smoking a quiet pipe—no, not very soon again, I think. Ay, Lieutenant, you are going to

4. Brawl.

take away the jewel of 'em; you are going to take away my peacemaker!" And with that the good soul had really some ado in checking a rising sob.

"Well," said the lieutenant, who had listened with amused interest to all this and now was waxing merry with his tipple; "well, blessed are the peacemakers, especially the fighting peacemakers. And such are the seventy-four beauties some of which you see poking their noses out of the portholes of yonder warship lying to for me," pointing through the cabin window at the *Bellipotent*. "But courage! Don't look so downhearted, man. Why, I pledge you in advance the royal approbation. Rest assured that His Majesty will be delighted to know that in a time when his hardtack[5] is not sought for by sailors with such avidity as should be, a time also when some shipmasters privily resent the borrowing from them a tar or two for the service; His Majesty, I say, will be delighted to learn that *one* shipmaster at least cheerfully surrenders to the King the flower of his flock, a sailor who with equal loyalty makes no dissent.—But where's my beauty? Ah," looking through the cabin's open door "here he comes; and, by Jove, lugging along his chest—Apollo with his portmanteau!—My man," stepping out to him, "you can't take that big box aboard a warship. The boxes there are mostly shot boxes. Put your duds in a bag, lad. Boot and saddle for the cavalryman, bag and hammock for the man-of-war's man."

The transfer from chest to bag was made. And, after seeing his man into the cutter and then following him down, the lieutenant pushed off from the *Rights-of-Man*. That was the merchant ship's name, though by her master and crew abbreviated in sailor fashion into the *Rights*. The hardheaded Dundee owner was a staunch admirer of Thomas Paine, whose book in rejoinder to Burke's arraignment of the French Revolution had then been published for some time and had gone everywhere.[6] In christening his vessel after the title of Paine's volume the man of Dundee was something like his contemporary shipowner, Stephen Girard of Philadelphia, whose sympathies, alike with his native land and its liberal philosophers, he evinced by naming his ships after Voltaire, Diderot,[7] and so forth.

But now, when the boat swept under the merchantman's stern, and officer and oarsmen were noting—some bitterly and others with a grin—the name emblazoned there; just then it was that the new recruit jumped up from the bow where the coxswain[8] had directed him to sit, and waving hat to his silent shipmates sorrowfully looking over at him from the taffrail, bade the lads a genial good-bye. Then, making a salutation as to the ship herself, "And good-bye to you too, old *Rights-of-Man*."

"Down, sir!" roared the lieutenant, instantly assuming all the rigor of his rank, though with difficulty repressing a smile.

To be sure, Billy's action was a terrible breach of naval decorum. But in that decorum he had never been instructed; in consideration of which the lieutenant would hardly have been so energetic in reproof but for the concluding farewell to the ship. This he rather took as meant to convey a

5. Large, hard biscuit.

6. *The Rights of Man* (1791), by the English-born Thomas Paine (1737–1809), was a response to *Reflections on the Revolution in France* (1790) by the English statesman Edmund Burke (1729–1797). Burke's book made a classic case for the priority of social institutions, Paine's book for the primacy of natural human rights. "Dundee": i.e., from the seaport of Dundee, Scotland.

7. French philosophers Denis Diderot (1713–1784) and Voltaire (1694–1778). Girard (1750–1831), a well-known shipowner and merchant.

8. Steersman of the boat.

covert sally on the new recruit's part, a sly slur at impressment in general, and that of himself in especial. And yet, more likely, if satire it was in effect, it was hardly so by intention, for Billy, though happily endowed with the gaiety of high health, youth, and a free heart, was yet by no means of a satirical turn. The will to it and the sinister dexterity were alike wanting. To deal in double meanings and insinuations of any sort was quite foreign to his nature.

As to his enforced enlistment, that he seemed to take pretty much as he was wont to take any vicissitude of weather. Like the animals, though no philosopher, he was, without knowing it, practically a fatalist. And it may be that he rather liked this adventurous turn in his affairs, which promised an opening into novel scenes and martial excitements.

Aboard the *Bellipotent* our merchant sailor was forthwith rated as an able seaman and assigned to the starboard watch of the foretop.[9] He was soon at home in the service, not at all disliked for his unpretentious good looks and a sort of genial happy-go-lucky air. No merrier man in his mess:[1] in marked contrast to certain other individuals included like himself among the impressed portion of the ship's company; for these when not actively employed were sometimes, and more particularly in the last dogwatch[2] when the drawing near of twilight induced revery, apt to fall into a saddish mood which in some partook of sullenness. But they were not so young as our foretopman, and no few of them must have known a hearth of some sort, others may have had wives and children left, too probably, in uncertain circumstances, and hardly any but must have had acknowledged kith and kin, while for Billy, as will shortly be seen, his entire family was practically invested in himself.

2

Though our new-made foretopman was well received in the top and on the gun decks, hardly here was he that cynosure he had previously been among those minor ship's companies of the merchant marine, with which companies only had he hitherto consorted.

He was young; and despite his all but fully developed frame, in aspect looked even younger than he really was, owing to a lingering adolescent expression in the as yet smooth face all but feminine in purity of natural complexion but where, thanks to his seagoing, the lily was quite suppressed and the rose had some ado visibly to flush through the tan.

To one essentially such a novice in the complexities of factitious life, the abrupt transition from his former and simpler sphere to the ampler and more knowing world of a great warship; this might well have abashed him had there been any conceit or vanity in his composition. Among her miscellaneous multitude, the *Bellipotent* mustered several individuals who however inferior in grade were of no common natural stamp, sailors more signally susceptive of that air which continuous martial discipline and repeated presence in battle can in some degree impart even to the average man. As the Handsome Sailor, Billy Budd's position aboard the seventy-four was some-

9. Platform at the head of the foremast.
1. Group of sailors assigned to eat together.
2. From 6 to 8 P.M.

thing analogous to that of a rustic beauty transplanted from the provinces and brought into competition with the highborn dames of the court. But this change of circumstances he scarce noted. As little did he observe that something about him provoked an ambiguous smile in one or two harder faces among the bluejackets. Nor less unaware was he of the peculiar favorable effect his person and demeanor had upon the more intelligent gentlemen of the quarter-deck. Nor could this well have been otherwise. Cast in a mold peculiar to the finest physical examples of those Englishmen in whom the Saxon strain would seem not at all to partake of any Norman or other admixture, he showed in face that humane look of reposeful good nature which the Greek sculptor in some instances gave to his heroic strong man, Hercules. But this again was subtly modified by another and pervasive quality. The ear, small and shapely, the arch of the foot, the curve in mouth and nostril, even the indurated hand dyed to the orange-tawny of the toucan's bill, a hand telling alike of the halyards and tar bucket; but, above all, something in the mobile expression, and every chance attitude and movement, something suggestive of a mother eminently favored by Love and the Graces; all this strangely indicated a lineage in direct contradiction to his lot. The mysteriousness here became less mysterious through a matter of fact elicited when Billy at the capstan was being formally mustered into the service. Asked by the officer, a small, brisk little gentleman as it chanced, among other questions, his place of birth, he replied, "Please, sir, I don't know."

"Don't know where you were born? Who was your father?"

"God knows, sir."

Struck by the straightforward simplicity of these replies, the officer next asked, "Do you know anything about your beginning?"

"No, sir. But I have heard that I was found in a pretty silk-lined basket hanging one morning from the knocker of a good man's door in Bristol."[3]

"*Found*, say you? Well," throwing back his head and looking up and down the new recruit; "well, it turns out to have been a pretty good find. Hope they'll find some more like you, my man; the fleet sadly needs them."

Yes, Billy Budd was a foundling, a presumable by-blow,[4] and, evidently, no ignoble one. Noble descent was as evident in him as in a blood horse.

For the rest, with little or no sharpness of faculty or any trace of the wisdom of the serpent, nor yet quite a dove, he possessed that kind and degree of intelligence going along with the unconventional rectitude of a sound human creature, one to whom not yet has been proffered the questionable apple of knowledge. He was illiterate; he could not read, but he could sing, and like the illiterate nightingale was sometimes the composer of his own song.

Of self-consciousness he seemed to have little or none, or about as much as we may reasonably impute to a dog of Saint Bernard's breed.

Habitually living with the elements and knowing little more of the land than as a beach, or, rather, that portion of the terraqueous globe providentially set apart for dance-houses, doxies, and tapsters,[5] in short what sailors call a "fiddler's green," his simple nature remained unsophisticated by those moral obliquities which are not in every case incompatible with that manufacturable thing known as respectability. But are sailors, frequenters of fiddlers'

3. Seaport in the Bristol Channel in southwest England.

4. Child born out of wedlock.

5. Bartenders. "Doxies": prostitutes.

greens, without vices? No; but less often than with landsmen do their vices, so called, partake of crookedness of heart, seeming less to proceed from viciousness than exuberance of vitality after long constraint: frank manifestations in accordance with natural law. By his original constitution aided by the co-operating influences of his lot, Billy in many respects was little more than a sort of upright barbarian, much such perhaps as Adam presumably might have been ere the urbane Serpent wriggled himself into his company.

And here be it submitted that apparently going to corroborate the doctrine of man's Fall, a doctrine now popularly ignored, it is observable that where certain virtues pristine and unadulterate peculiarly characterize anybody in the external uniform of civilization, they will upon scrutiny seem not to be derived from custom or convention, but rather to be out of keeping with these, as if indeed exceptionally transmitted from a period prior to Cain's city[6] and citified man. The character marked by such qualities has to an unvitiated taste an untampered-with flavor like that of berries, while the man thoroughly civilized, even in a fair specimen of the breed, has to the same moral palate a questionable smack as of a compounded wine. To any stray inheritor of these primitive qualities found, like Caspar Hauser,[7] wandering dazed in any Christian capital of our time, the good-natured poet's famous invocation, near two thousand years ago, of the good rustic out of his latitude in the Rome of the Caesars, still appropriately holds:

> Honest and poor, faithful in word and thought,
> What hath thee, Fabian, to the city brought?[8]

Though our Handsome Sailor had as much of masculine beauty as one can expect anywhere to see; nevertheless, like the beautiful woman in one of Hawthorne's minor tales,[9] there was just one thing amiss in him. No visible blemish indeed, as with the lady; no, but an occasional liability to a vocal defect. Though in the hour of elemental uproar or peril he was everything that a sailor should be, yet under sudden provocation of strong heart-feeling his voice, otherwise singularly musical, as if expressive of the harmony within, was apt to develop an organic hesitancy, in fact more or less of a stutter or even worse. In this particular Billy was a striking instance that the arch interferer, the envious marplot of Eden,[1] still has more or less to do with every human consignment to this planet of Earth. In every case, one way or another he is sure to slip in his little card, as much as to remind us—I too have a hand here.

The avowal of such an imperfection in the Handsome Sailor should be evidence not alone that he is not presented as a conventional hero, but also that the story in which he is the main figure is no romance.

6. After slaying his brother, Abel, the accursed Cain "went out from the presence of the Lord" and "builded a city" (Genesis 4.16–17).
7. Found wandering in Nuremberg in 1828, Hauser (1812?–1833) claimed to have spent his childhood in a darkened cell.
8. The Roman poet Martial (1st century C.E.), *Epigrams* 1.4.1–2.
9. Hawthorne's story "The Birthmark" (1843). "Minor": shorter.
1. Satan.

3

At the time of Billy Budd's arbitrary enlistment into the *Bellipotent* that ship was on her way to join the Mediterranean fleet. No long time elapsed before the junction was effected. As one of that fleet the seventy-four participated in its movements, though at times on account of her superior sailing qualities, in the absence of frigates, dispatched on separate duty as a scout and at times on less temporary service. But with all this the story has little concernment, restricted as it is to the inner life of one particular ship and the career of an individual sailor.

It was the summer of 1797. In the April of that year had occurred the commotion at Spithead followed in May by a second and yet more serious outbreak in the fleet at the Nore.[2] The latter is known, and without exaggeration in the epithet, as "the Great Mutiny." It was indeed a demonstration more menacing to England than the contemporary manifestoes and conquering and proselyting armies of the French Directory.[3] To the British Empire the Nore Mutiny was what a strike in the fire brigade would be to London threatened by general arson. In a crisis when the kingdom might well have anticipated the famous signal that some years later published along the naval line of battle what it was that upon occasion England expected of Englishmen; *that* was the time when at the mastheads of the three-deckers and seventy-fours moored in her own roadstead[4]—a fleet the right arm of a Power then all but the sole free conservative one of the Old World—the bluejackets, to be numbered by thousands, ran up with huzzas the British colors with the union and cross wiped out; by that cancellation transmuting the flag of founded law and freedom defined, into the enemy's red meteor of unbridled and unbounded revolt. Reasonable discontent growing out of practical grievances in the fleet had been ignited into irrational combustion as by live cinders blown across the Channel from France in flames.[5]

The event converted into irony for a time those spirited strains of Dibdin[6]—as a song-writer no mean auxiliary to the English government at that European conjuncture—strains celebrating, among other things, the patriotic devotion of the British tar: "And as for my life, 'tis the King's!"

Such an episode in the Island's grand naval story her naval historians naturally abridge, one of them (William James)[7] candidly acknowledging that fain would he pass it over did not "impartiality forbid fastidiousness." And yet his mention is less a narration than a reference, having to do hardly at all with details. Nor are these readily to be found in the libraries. Like some other events in every age befalling states everywhere, including America, the Great Mutiny was of such character that national pride along with views of policy would fain shade it off into the historical background. Such events cannot be ignored, but there is a considerate way of historically treating

2. At the mouth of the Thames. Spithead is a protected anchorage in the English Channel in the south of England.
3. Body of five which held executive power in France from 1795 to 1799. Though Melville here restricts the term to the Nore mutiny, the "Great Mutiny" was the term generally applied to a series of mutinies in the spring of 1797 at various locations.
4. Protected anchorage. "Famous signal": the message of Lord Horatio Nelson (1758–1805) to his fleet just before the Battle of Trafalgar (1805): "England expects that every man will do his duty."
5. Especially during the Reign of Terror (1793–94) and its aftermath.
6. Charles Dibdin (1745–1814), English playwright and songwriter.
7. English historian (d. 1827), author of *Naval History of Great Britain*.

them. If a well-constituted individual refrains from blazoning aught amiss or calamitous in his family, a nation in the like circumstance may without reproach be equally discreet.

Though after parleyings between government and the ring-leaders, and concessions by the former as to some glaring abuses, the first uprising—that at Spithead—with difficulty was put down, or matters for the time pacified; yet at the Nore the unforeseen renewal of insurrection on a yet larger scale, and emphasized in the conferences that ensued by demands deemed by the authorities not only inadmissible but aggressively insolent, indicated—if the Red Flag[8] did not sufficiently do so—what was the spirit animating the men. Final suppression, however, there was; but only made possible perhaps by the unswerving loyalty of the marine corps and a voluntary resumption of loyalty among influential sections of the crews.

To some extent the Nore Mutiny may be regarded as analogous to the distempering irruption of contagious fever in a frame constitutionally sound, and which anon throws it off.

At all events, of these thousands of mutineers were some of the tars who not so very long afterwards—whether wholly prompted thereto by patriotism, or pugnacious instinct, or by both—helped to win a coronet for Nelson at the Nile, and the naval crown of crowns for him at Trafalgar.[9] To the mutineers, those battles and especially Trafalgar were a plenary absolution and a grand one. For all that goes to make up scenic naval display and heroic magnificence in arms, those battles, especially Trafalgar, stand unmatched in human annals.

4

In this matter of writing, resolve as one may to keep to the main road, some bypaths have an enticement not readily to be withstood. I am going to err into such a bypath. If the reader will keep me company I shall be glad. At the least, we can promise ourselves that pleasure which is wickedly said to be in sinning, for a literary sin the divergence will be.

Very likely it is no new remark that the inventions of our time have at last brought about a change in sea warfare in degree corresponding to the revolution in all warfare effected by the original introduction from China into Europe of gunpowder. The first European firearm, a clumsy contrivance, was, as is well known, scouted by no few of the knights as a base implement, good enough peradventure for weavers too craven to stand up crossing steel with steel in frank fight. But as ashore knightly valor, though shorn of its blazonry, did not cease with the knights, neither on the seas—though nowadays in encounters there a certain kind of displayed gallantry be fallen out of date as hardly applicable under changed circumstances—did the nobler qualities of such naval magnates as Don John of Austria, Doria, Van Tromp, Jean Bart, the long line of British admirals, and the American Decaturs[1] of 1812 become obsolete with their wooden walls.

8. Traditional banner of revolution.

9. Nelson defeated the French at the Bay of Aboukir near the mouth of the Nile in 1798, then died during his victory at Trafalgar in 1805.

1. Stephen Decatur (1779–1820) fought against the British in the War of 1812. Don John of Austria (1547–1578), commander for the Holy League at the Battle of Lepanto (1571). Andrea Doria (1468–1560), leader of the Genoese fleet against the Turks. Maarten Tromp (1597–1653)

Nevertheless, to anybody who can hold the Present at its worth without being inappreciative of the Past, it may be forgiven, if to such an one the solitary old hulk at Portsmouth, Nelson's *Victory*, seems to float there, not alone as the decaying monument of a fame incorruptible, but also as a poetic reproach, softened by its picturesqueness, to the *Monitors*[2] and yet mightier hulls of the European ironclads. And this not altogether because such craft are unsightly, unavoidably lacking the symmetry and grand lines of the old battleships, but equally for other reasons.

There are some, perhaps, who while not altogether inaccessible to that poetic reproach just alluded to, may yet on behalf of the new order be disposed to parry it; and this to the extent of iconoclasm, if need be. For example, prompted by the sight of the star inserted in the *Victory*'s quarter-deck designating the spot where the Great Sailor fell, these martial utilitarians may suggest considerations implying that Nelson's ornate publication of his person in battle was not only unnecessary, but not military, nay, savored of foolhardiness and vanity.[3] They may add, too, that at Trafalgar it was in effect nothing less than a challenge to death; and death came; and that but for his bravado the victorious admiral might possibly have survived the battle, and so, instead of having his sagacious dying injunctions overruled by his immediate successor in command, he himself when the contest was decided might have brought his shattered fleet to anchor, a proceeding which might have averted the deplorable loss of life by shipwreck in the elemental tempest that followed the martial one.

Well, should we set aside the more than disputable point whether for various reasons it was possible to anchor the fleet, then plausibly enough the Benthamites[4] of war may urge the above. But the *might-have-been* is but boggy ground to build on. And, certainly, in foresight as to the larger issue of an encounter, and anxious preparations for it—buoying the deadly way and mapping it out, as at Copenhagen[5]—few commanders have been so painstakingly cirumspect as this same reckless declarer of his person in fight.

Personal prudence, even when dictated by quite other than selfish considerations, surely is no special virtue in a military man; while an excessive love of glory, impassioning a less burning impulse, the honest sense of duty, is the first. If the name *Wellington*[6] is not so much of a trumpet to the blood as the simpler name *Nelson*, the reason for this may perhaps be inferred from the above. Alfred in his funeral ode[7] on the victor of Waterloo ventures not to call him the greatest soldier of all time, though in the same ode he invokes Nelson as "the greatest sailor since our world began."

At Trafalgar Nelson on the brink of opening the fight sat down and wrote his last brief will and testament. If under the presentiment of the most magnificent of all victories to be crowned by his own glorious death, a sort

led the Dutch fleet against the Spanish. Jean Bart (1650–1702) commanded French privateers against the Dutch and British.

2. The Union ironclad *Monitor* engaged the Confederate ironclad *Virginia* in 1862 in the harbor of Hampton Roads, Virginia. "*Victory*": Horatio Nelson's flagship at the Battle of Trafalgar.

3. Nelson's uniform, with its many glittering medallions, may have made him an easy target for French riflemen.

4. Those who weigh decisions in terms of utility, from Jeremy Bentham (1748–1832), English philosopher, expounder of Utilitarianism.

5. In 1801 the Danes thought they had thwarted Nelson by removing the buoys near Copenhagen, but he took soundings and replaced the markers so he could navigate.

6. Arthur Wellesley, first duke of Wellington (1769–1852), British general in the Napoleonic Wars, who defeated Napoleon at Waterloo (1815).

7. Alfred, Lord Tennyson (1809–1892), "Ode on the Death of the Duke of Wellington" (1852).

of priestly motive led him to dress his person in the jewelled vouchers of his own shining deeds; if thus to have adorned himself for the altar and the sacrifice were indeed vainglory, then affectation and fustian is each more heroic line in the great epics and dramas, since in such lines the poet but embodies in verse those exaltations of sentiment that a nature like Nelson, the opportunity being given, vitalizes into acts.

5

Yes, the outbreak at the Nore was put down. But not every grievance was redressed. If the contractors, for example, were no longer permitted to ply some practices peculiar to their tribe everywhere, such as providing shoddy cloth, rations not sound, or false in the measure; not the less impressment, for one thing, went on. By custom sanctioned for centuries, and judicially maintained by a Lord Chancellor as late as Mansfield,[8] that mode of manning the fleet, a mode now fallen into a sort of abeyance but never formally renounced, it was not practicable to give up in those years. Its abrogation would have crippled the indispensable fleet, one wholly under canvas, no steam power, its innumerable sails and thousands of cannon, everything in short, worked by muscle alone; a fleet the more insatiate in demand for men, because then multiplying its ships of all grades against contingencies present and to come of the convulsed Continent.

Discontent foreran the Two Mutinies,[9] and more or less it lurkingly survived them. Hence it was not unreasonable to apprehend some return of trouble sporadic or general. One instance of such apprehensions: In the same year with this story, Nelson, then Rear Admiral Sir Horatio, being with the fleet off the Spanish coast, was directed by the admiral in command to shift his pennant from the *Captain* to the *Theseus*;[1] and for this reason: that the latter ship having newly arrived on the station from home, where it had taken part in the Great Mutiny, danger was apprehended from the temper of the men; and it was thought that an officer like Nelson was the one, not indeed to terrorize the crew into base subjection, but to win them, by force of his mere presence and heroic personality, back to an allegiance if not as enthusiastic as his own yet as true.

So it was that for a time, on more than one quarter-deck, anxiety did exist. At sea, precautionary vigilance was strained against relapse. At short notice an engagement might come on. When it did, the lieutenants assigned to batteries felt it incumbent on them, in some instances, to stand with drawn swords behind the men working the guns.

6

But on board the seventy-four in which Billy now swung his hammock, very little in the manner of the men and nothing obvious in the demeanor of the officers would have suggested to an ordinary observer that the Great Mutiny

8. William Murray, earl of Mansfield (1705–1793), lord chief justice of Britain.
9. At Spithead and the Nore.
1. I.e., to take command of the *Theseus* as his flagship.

was a recent event. In their general bearing and conduct the commissioned officers of a warship naturally take their tone from the commander, that is if he have that ascendancy of character that ought to be his.

Captain the Honorable Edward Fairfax Vere, to give his full title, was a bachelor of forty or thereabouts, a sailor of distinction even in a time prolific of renowned seamen. Though allied to the higher nobility, his advancement had not been altogether owing to influences connected with that circumstance. He had seen much service, been in various engagements, always acquitting himself as an officer mindful of the welfare of his men, but never tolerating an infraction of discipline; thoroughly versed in the science of his profession, and intrepid to the verge of temerity, though never injudiciously so. For his gallantry in the West Indian waters as flag lieutenant under Rodney in that admiral's crowning victory over De Grasse,[2] he was made a post captain.

Ashore, in the garb of a civilian, scarce anyone would have taken him for a sailor, more especially that he never garnished unprofessional talk with nautical terms, and grave in his bearing, evinced little appreciation of mere humor. It was not out of keeping with these traits that on a passage when nothing demanded his paramount action, he was the most undemonstrative of men. Any landsman observing this gentleman not conspicuous by his stature and wearing no pronounced insignia, emerging from his cabin to the open deck, and noting the silent deference of the officers retiring to leeward, might have taken him for the King's guest, a civilian aboard the King's ship, some highly honorable discreet envoy on his way to an important post. But in fact this unobtrusiveness of demeanor may have proceeded from a certain unaffected modesty of manhood sometimes accompanying a resolute nature, a modesty evinced at all times not calling for pronounced action, which shown in any rank of life suggests a virtue aristocratic in kind. As with some others engaged in various departments of the world's more heroic activities, Captain Vere though practical enough upon occasion would at times betray a certain dreaminess of mood. Standing alone on the weather side of the quarter-deck, one hand holding by the rigging, he would absently gaze off at the blank sea. At the presentation to him then of some minor matter interrupting the current of his thoughts, he would show more or less irascibility; but instantly he would control it.

In the navy he was popularly known by the appellation "Starry Vere." How such a designation happened to fall upon one who whatever his sterling qualities was without any brilliant ones, was in this wise: A favorite kinsman, Lord Denton, a freehearted fellow, had been the first to meet and congratulate him upon his return to England from his West Indian cruise; and but the day previous turning over a copy of Andrew Marvell's[3] poems had lighted, not for the first time, however, upon the lines entitled "Appleton House," the name of one of the seats of their common ancestor, a hero in the German wars of the seventeenth century, in which poem occur the lines:

2. The British admiral George Brydges, Baron Rodney (1719–1792), defeated the French admiral François de Grasse (1723–1788) off Dominica in 1782.

3. The English poet (1621–1678) wrote "Upon Appleton House, to My Lord Fairfax" around 1650.

This 'tis to have been from the first
In a domestic heaven nursed,
Under the discipline severe
Of Fairfax and the starry Vere.[4]

And so, upon embracing his cousin fresh from Rodney's great victory wherein he had played so gallant a part, brimming over with just family pride in the sailor of their house, he exuberantly exclaimed, "Give ye joy, Ed; give ye joy, my starry Vere!" This got currency, and the novel prefix serving in familiar parlance readily to distinguish the *Bellipotent*'s captain from another Vere his senior, a distant relative, an officer of like rank in the navy, it remained permanently attached to the surname.

7

In view of the part that the commander of the *Bellipotent* plays in scenes shortly to follow, it may be well to fill out that sketch of him outlined in the previous chapter.

Aside from his qualities as a sea officer Captain Vere was an exceptional character. Unlike no few of England's renowned sailors, long and arduous service with signal devotion to it had not resulted in absorbing and *salting* the entire man. He had a marked leaning toward everything intellectual. He loved books, never going to sea without a newly replenished library, compact but of the best. The isolated leisure, in some cases so wearisome, falling at intervals to commanders even during a war cruise, never was tedious to Captain Vere. With nothing of that literary taste which less heeds the thing conveyed than the vehicle, his bias was toward those books to which every serious mind of superior order occupying any active post of authority in the world naturally inclines: books treating of actual men and events no matter of what era—history, biography, and unconventional writers like Montaigne,[5] who, free from cant and convention, honestly and in the spirit of common sense philosophize upon realities. In this line of reading he found confirmation of his own more reserved thoughts—confirmation which he had vainly sought in social converse, so that as touching most fundamental topics, there had got to be established in him some positive convictions which he forefelt would abide in him essentially unmodified so long as his intelligent part remained unimpaired. In view of the troubled period in which his lot was cast, this was well for him. His settled convictions were as a dike against those invading waters of novel opinion social, political, and otherwise, which carried away as in a torrent no few minds in those days, minds by nature not inferior to his own. While other members of that aristocracy to which by birth he belonged were incensed at the innovators mainly because their theories were inimical to the privileged classes, Captain Vere disinterestedly opposed them not alone because they seemed to him insusceptible of embodiment in lasting institutions, but at war with the peace of the world and the true welfare of mankind.

With minds less stored than his and less earnest, some officers of his rank, with whom at times he would necessarily consort, found him lacking

4. Anne Vere (d. 1665), wife of Lord Fairfax (1612–1671), owner of Appleton House.

5. Michel de Montaigne (1533–1592), influential French essayist.

in the companionable quality, a dry and bookish gentleman, as they deemed. Upon any chance withdrawal from their company one would be apt to say to another something like this: "Vere is a noble fellow, Starry Vere. 'Spite the gazettes,[6] Sir Horatio" (meaning him who became Lord Nelson) "is at bottom scarce a better seaman or fighter. But between you and me now, don't you think there is a queer streak of the pedantic running through him? Yes, like the King's yarn[7] in a coil of navy rope?"

Some apparent ground there was for this sort of confidential criticism; since not only did the captain's discourse never fall into the jocosely familiar, but in illustrating of any point touching the stirring personages and events of the time he would be as apt to cite some historic character or incident of antiquity as he would be to cite from the moderns. He seemed unmindful of the circumstance that to his bluff company such remote allusions, however pertinent they might really be, were altogether alien to men whose reading was mainly confined to the journals. But considerateness in such matters is not easy to natures constituted like Captain Vere's. Their honesty prescribes to them directness, sometimes far-reaching like that of a migratory fowl that in its flight never heeds when it crosses a frontier.

8

The lieutenants and other commissioned gentlemen forming Captain Vere's staff it is not necessary here to particularize, nor needs it to make any mention of any of the warrant officers. But among the petty officers[8] was one who, having much to do with the story, may as well be forthwith introduced. His portrait I essay, but shall never hit it. This was John Claggart, the master-at-arms. But that sea title may to landsmen seem somewhat equivocal. Originally, doubtless, that petty officer's function was the instruction of the men in the use of arms, sword or cutlass. But very long ago, owing to the advance in gunnery making hand-to-hand encounters less frequent and giving to niter and sulphur the pre-eminence over steel, that function ceased; the master-at-arms of a great warship becoming a sort of chief of police charged among other matters with the duty of preserving order on the populous lower gun decks.

Claggart was a man about five-and-thirty, somewhat spare and tall, yet of no ill figure upon the whole. His hand was too small and shapely to have been accustomed to hard toil. The face was a notable one, the features all except the chin cleanly cut as those on a Greek medallion; yet the chin, beardless as Tecumseh's, had something of strange protuberant broadness in its make that recalled the prints of the Reverend Dr. Titus Oates, the historic deponent with the clerical drawl in the time of Charles II and the fraud of the alleged Popish Plot.[9] It served Claggart in his office that his eye could cast a tutoring glance. His brow was of the sort phrenologically[1] associated

6. Newspapers, or possibly the official publications of the British navy listing ranks, honors, etc.
7. Distinctive thread identifying the rope as property of the British navy.
8. Lesser officers appointed to their functions by the commander.
9. Oates (1649–1705), a convicted perjurer, accused Catholics of attempting to assassinate Protestants and burn London in what was termed the "Popish Plot" (1678). Tecumseh (1768?–1813), Shawnee chief, who in an effort to unite the Indian tribes against U.S. whites, sided with the British in the War of 1812 and was defeated at Tippecanoe by William Henry Harrison.
1. According to the pseudoscience of phrenology, in which contours of the skull were thought to indicate character.

with more than average intellect; silken jet curls partly clustering over it, making a foil to the pallor below, a pallor tinged with a faint shade of amber akin to the hue of time-tinted marbles of old. This complexion, singularly contrasting with the red or deeply bronzed visages of the sailors, and in part the result of his official seclusion from the sunlight, though it was not exactly displeasing, nevertheless seemed to hint of something defective or abnormal in the constitution and blood. But his general aspect and manner were so suggestive of an education and career incongruous with his naval function that when not actively engaged in it he looked like a man of high quality, social and moral, who for reasons of his own was keeping incog.[2] Nothing was known of his former life. It might be that he was an Englishman; and yet there lurked a bit of accent in his speech suggesting that possibly he was not such by birth, but through naturalization in early childhood. Among certain grizzled sea gossips of the gun decks and forecastle went a rumor perdue that the master-at-arms was a *chevalier* who had volunteered into the King's navy by way of compounding for some mysterious swindle whereof he had been arraigned at the King's Bench.[3] The fact that nobody could substantiate this report was, of course, nothing against its secret currency. Such a rumor once started on the gun decks in reference to almost anyone below the rank of a commissioned officer would, during the period assigned to this narrative, have seemed not altogether wanting in credibility to the tarry old wiseacres of a man-of-war crew. And indeed a man of Claggart's accomplishments, without prior nautical experience entering the navy at mature life, as he did, and necessarily allotted at the start to the lowest grade in it; a man too who never made allusion to his previous life ashore; these were circumstances which in the dearth of exact knowledge as to his true antecedents opened to the invidious a vague field for unfavorable surmise.

But the sailors' dogwatch gossip concerning him derived a vague plausibility from the fact that now for some period the British navy could so little afford to be squeamish in the matter of keeping up the muster rolls, that not only were press gangs[4] notoriously abroad both afloat and ashore, but there was little or no secret about another matter, namely, that the London police were at liberty to capture any able-bodied suspect, any questionable fellow at large, and summarily ship him to the dockyard or fleet. Furthermore, even among voluntary enlistments there were instances where the motive thereto partook neither of patriotic impulse nor yet of a random desire to experience a bit of sea life and martial adventure. Insolvent debtors of minor grade, together with the promiscuous lame ducks of morality, found in the navy a convenient and secure refuge, secure because, once enlisted aboard a King's ship, they were as much in sanctuary as the transgressor of the Middle Ages harboring himself under the shadow of the altar. Such sanctioned irregularities, which for obvious reasons the government would hardly think to parade at the time and which consequently, and as affecting the least influential class of mankind, have all but dropped into oblivion, lend color to something for the truth whereof I do not vouch, and hence have some scruple in stating;

2. Short for incognito; with concealed identity.
3. I.e., in a court of law. "Rumor perdue": secretive rumor. "*Chevalier*": knight (French); though the suggestion here is conman or swindler.
4. Gangs charged with rounding up men for ships. "Muster rolls": register of officers and men in a ship's company.

something I remember having seen in print though the book I cannot recall; but the same thing was personally communicated to me now more than forty years ago by an old pensioner in a cocked hat with whom I had a most interesting talk on the terrace at Greenwich, a Baltimore Negro, a Trafalgar man.[5] It was to this effect: In the case of a warship short of hands whose speedy sailing was imperative, the deficient quota, in lack of any other way of making it good, would be eked out by drafts culled direct from the jails. For reasons previously suggested it would not perhaps be easy at the present day directly to prove or disprove the allegation. But allowed as a verity, how significant would it be of England's straits at the time confronted by those wars which like a flight of harpies rose shrieking from the din and dust of the fallen Bastille.[6] That era appears measurably clear to us who look back at it, and but read of it. But to the grandfathers of us graybeards, the more thoughtful of them, the genius of it presented an aspect like that of Camoëns' Spirit of the Cape,[7] an eclipsing menace mysterious and prodigious. Not America was exempt from apprehension. At the height of Napoleon's unexampled conquests, there were Americans who had fought at Bunker Hill[8] who looked forward to the possibility that the Atlantic might prove no barrier against the ultimate schemes of this French portentous upstart from the revolutionary chaos who seemed in act of fulfilling judgment prefigured in the Apocalypse.[9]

But the less credence was to be given to the gun-deck talk touching Claggart, seeing that no man holding his office in a man-of-war can ever hope to be popular with the crew. Besides, in derogatory comments upon anyone against whom they have a grudge, or for any reason or no reason mislike, sailors are much like landsmen: they are apt to exaggerate or romance it.

About as much was really known to the *Bellipotent*'s tars of the master-at-arms' career before entering the service as an astronomer knows about a comet's travels prior to its first observable appearance in the sky. The verdict of the sea quidnuncs[1] has been cited only by way of showing what sort of moral impression the man made upon rude uncultivated natures whose conceptions of human wickedness were necessarily of the narrowest, limited to ideas of vulgar rascality—a thief among the swinging hammocks during a night watch, or the man-brokers and land-sharks of the seaports.

It was no gossip, however, but fact that though, as before hinted, Claggart upon his entrance into the navy was, as a novice, assigned to the least honorable section of a man-of-war's crew, embracing the drudgery, he did not long remain there. The superior capacity he immediately evinced, his constitutional sobriety, an ingratiating deference to superiors, together with a peculiar ferreting genius manifested on a singular occasion; all this, capped by a certain austere patriotism, abruptly advanced him to the position of master-at-arms.

5. A veteran of the Battle of Trafalgar. Greenwich is a district of London known for dockyards and the Royal Naval Hospital.
6. A 14th-century fortress in Paris, in use as a prison when citizens demolished it on July 14, 1789, at the start of the French Revolution. "Harpies": rapacious female creatures in mythology.
7. In the *Lusiads* (1572), an epic poem by the Portuguese Luiz de Camoëns (1524–1580), the spirit menaces Vasco da Gama as he rounds the Cape of Good Hope on his way to India.
8. Boston, Massachusetts, on June 17, 1775, where the British defeated the colonists.
9. I.e., the Book of Revelation.
1. Busybodies.

Of this maritime chief of police the ship's corporals, so called, were the immediate subordinates, and compliant ones; and this, as is to be noted in some business departments ashore, almost to a degree inconsistent with entire moral volition. His place put various converging wires of underground influence under the chief's control, capable when astutely worked through his understrappers of operating to the mysterious discomfort, if nothing worse, of any of the sea commonalty.

9

Life in the foretop well agreed with Billy Budd. There, when not actually engaged on the yards yet higher aloft, the topmen, who as such had been picked out for youth and activity, constituted an aerial club lounging at ease against the smaller stun'sails rolled up into cushions, spinning yarns like the lazy gods, and frequently amused with what was going on in the busy world of the decks below. No wonder then that a young fellow of Billy's disposition was well content in such society. Giving no cause of offense to anybody, he was always alert at a call. So in the merchant service it had been with him. But now such a punctiliousness in duty was shown that his topmates would sometimes good-naturedly laugh at him for it. This heightened alacrity had its cause, namely, the impression made upon him by the first formal gangway-punishment he had ever witnessed, which befell the day following his impressment. It had been incurred by a little fellow, young, a novice after-guardsman[2] absent from his assigned post when the ship was being put about; a dereliction resulting in a rather serious hitch to that maneuver, one demanding instantaneous promptitude in letting go and making fast. When Billy saw the culprit's naked back under the scourge, gridironed with red welts and worse, when he marked the dire expression in the liberated man's face as with his woolen shirt flung over him by the executioner he rushed forward from the spot to bury himself in the crowd, Billy was horrified. He resolved that never through remissness would he make himself liable to such a visitation or do or omit aught that might merit even verbal reproof. What then was his surprise and concern when ultimately he found himself getting into petty trouble occasionally about such matters as the stowage of his bag or something amiss in his hammock, matters under the police oversight of the ship's corporals of the lower decks, and which brought down on him a vague threat from one of them.

So heedful in all things as he was, how could this be? He could not understand it, and it more than vexed him. When he spoke to his young topmates about it they were either lightly incredulous or found something comical in his unconcealed anxiety. "Is it your bag, Billy?" said one. "Well, sew yourself up in it, bully boy, and then you'll be sure to know if anybody meddles with it."

Now there was a veteran aboard who because his years began to disqualify him for more active work had been recently assigned duty as mainmastman in his watch, looking to the gear belayed at the rail roundabout that great spar near the deck.[3] At off-times the foretopman had picked up

2. Crew member responsible for the sails at the rear of the ship.
3. Charged with duty pertaining to the mainmast but only from the mainyard to the deck, not higher.

some acquaintance with him, and now in his trouble it occurred to him that he might be the sort of person to go to for wise counsel. He was an old Dansker[4] long anglicized in the service, of few words, many wrinkles, and some honorable scars. His wizened face, time-tinted and weather-stained to the complexion of an antique parchment, was here and there peppered blue by the chance explosion of a gun cartridge in action.

He was an *Agamemnon* man, some two years prior to the time of this story having served under Nelson when still captain in that ship immortal in naval memory, which dismantled and in part broken up to her bare ribs is seen a grand skeleton in Haden's etching.[5] As one of a boarding party from the *Agamemnon* he had received a cut slantwise along one temple and cheek leaving a long pale scar like a streak of dawn's light falling athwart the dark visage. It was on account of that scar and the affair in which it was known that he had received it, as well as from his blue-peppered complexion, that the Dansker went among the *Bellipotent*'s crew by the name of "Board-Her-in-the-Smoke."

Now the first time that his small weasel eyes happened to light on Billy Budd, a certain grim internal merriment set all his ancient wrinkles into antic play. Was it that his eccentric unsentimental old sapience, primitive in its kind, saw or thought it saw something which in contrast with the warship's environment looked oddly incongruous in the Handsome Sailor? But after slyly studying him at intervals, the old Merlin's[6] equivocal merriment was modified; for now when the twain would meet, it would start in his face a quizzing sort of look, but it would be but momentary and sometimes replaced by an expression of speculative query as to what might eventually befall a nature like that, dropped into a world not without some mantraps and against whose subtleties simple courage lacking experience and address, and without any touch of defensive ugliness, is of little avail; and where such innocence as man is capable of does yet in a moral emergency not always sharpen the faculties or enlighten the will.

However it was, the Dansker in his ascetic way rather took to Billy. Nor was this only because of certain philosophic interest in such a character. There was another cause. While the old man's eccentricities, sometimes bordering on the ursine,[7] repelled the juniors, Billy, undeterred thereby, revering him as a salt hero, would make advances, never passing the old *Agamemnon* man without a salutation marked by that respect which is seldom lost on the aged, however crabbed at times or whatever their station in life.

There was a vein of dry humor, or what not, in the mastman; and, whether in freak of patriarchal irony touching Billy's youth and athletic frame, or for some other and more recondite reason, from the first in addressing him he always substituted *Baby* for Billy, the Dansker in fact being the originator of the name by which the foretopman eventually became known aboard ship.

Well then, in his mysterious little difficulty going in quest of the wrinkled one, Billy found him off duty in a dogwatch ruminating by himself, seated on a shot box of the upper gun deck, now and then surveying with a

4. Dane.
5. *Breaking Up of the "Agamemnon"* (1870) by English artist Sir Francis Seymour Haden (1818–1910).
6. Wizard or prophet, from the character in Arthurian legends.
7. Bearlike.

somewhat cynical regard certain of the more swaggering promenaders there. Billy recounted his trouble, again wondering how it all happened. The salt seer attentively listened, accompanying the foretopman's recital with queer twitchings of his wrinkles and problematical little sparkles of his small ferret eyes. Making an end of his story, the foretopman asked, "And now, Dansker, do tell me what you think of it."

The old man, shoving up the front of his tarpaulin and deliberately rubbing the long slant scar at the point where it entered the thin hair, laconically said, "Baby Budd, *Jemmy Legs*" (meaning the master-at-arms) "is down on you."

"Jemmy Legs!" ejaculated Billy, his welkin eyes expanding. "What for? Why, he calls me 'the sweet and pleasant young fellow,' they tell me."

"Does he so?" grinned the grizzled one; then said, "Ay, Baby lad, a sweet voice has Jemmy Legs."

"No, not always. But to me he has. I seldom pass him but there comes a pleasant word."

"And that's because he's down upon you, Baby Budd."

Such reiteration, along with the manner of it, incomprehensible to a novice, disturbed Billy almost as much as the mystery for which he had sought explanation. Something less unpleasingly oracular he tried to extract; but the old sea Chiron, thinking perhaps that for the nonce he had sufficiently instructed his young Achilles,[8] pursed his lips, gathered all his wrinkles together, and would commit himself to nothing further.

Years, and those experiences which befall certain shrewder men subordinated lifelong to the will of superiors, all this had developed in the Dansker the pithy guarded cynicism that was his leading characteristic.

10

The next day an incident served to confirm Billy Budd in his incredulity as to the Dansker's strange summing up of the case submitted. The ship at noon, going large before the wind, was rolling on her course,[9] and he below at dinner and engaged in some sportful talk with the members of his mess, chanced in a sudden lurch to spill the entire contents of his soup pan upon the new-scrubbed deck. Claggart, the master-at-arms, official rattan[1] in hand, happened to be passing along the battery in a bay of which the mess was lodged, and the greasy liquid streamed just across his path. Stepping over it, he was proceeding on his way without comment, since the matter was nothing to take notice of under the circumstances, when he happened to observe who it was that had done the spilling. His countenance changed. Pausing, he was about to ejaculate something hasty at the sailor, but checked himself, and pointing down to the streaming soup, playfully tapped him from behind with his rattan, saying in a low musical voice peculiar to him at times, "Handsomely done, my lad! And handsome is as handsome did it, too!" And with that passed on. Not noted by Billy as not coming within his view was the involuntary smile, or rather grimace, that accompanied Claggart's equivocal words. Aridly it drew down the thin corners of his shapely

8. In Greek mythology, the centaur Chiron tutored Achilles.
9. With the wind behind it, the ship was making good time.
1. Cane.

mouth. But everybody taking his remark as meant for humorous, and at which therefore as coming from a superior they were bound to laugh "with counterfeited glee,"[2] acted accordingly; and Billy, tickled, it may be, by the allusion to his being the Handsome Sailor, merrily joined in; then addressing his messmates exclaimed, "There now, who says that Jemmy Legs is down on me!"

"And who said he was, Beauty?" demanded one Donald with some surprise. Whereat the foretopman looked a little foolish, recalling that it was only one person, Board-Her-in-the-Smoke, who had suggested what to him was the smoky idea that this master-at-arms was in any peculiar way hostile to him. Meantime that functionary, resuming his path, must have momentarily worn some expression less guarded than that of the bitter smile, usurping the face from the heart—some distorting expression perhaps, for a drummer-boy heedlessly frolicking along from the opposite direction and chancing to come into light collision with his person was strangely disconcerted by his aspect. Nor was the impression lessened when the official, impetuously giving him a sharp cut with the rattan, vehemently exclaimed, "Look where you go!"

11

What was the matter with the master-at-arms? And, be the matter what it might, how could it have direct relation to Billy Budd, with whom prior to the affair of the spilled soup he had never come into any special contact official or otherwise? What indeed could the trouble have to do with one so little inclined to give offense as the merchant-ship's "peacemaker," even him who in Claggart's own phrase was "the sweet and pleasant young fellow"? Yes, why should Jemmy Legs, to borrow the Dansker's expression, be "down" on the Handsome Sailor? But, at heart and not for nothing, as the late chance encounter may indicate to the discerning, down on him, secretly down on him, he assuredly was.

Now to invent something touching the more private career of Claggart, something involving Billy Budd, of which something the latter should be wholly ignorant, some romantic incident implying that Claggart's knowledge of the young bluejacket began at some period anterior to catching sight of him on board the seventy-four—all this, not so difficult to do, might avail in a way more or less interesting to account for whatever of enigma may appear to lurk in the case. But in fact there was nothing of the sort. And yet the cause necessarily to be assumed as the sole one assignable is in its very realism as much charged with that prime element of Radcliffian[3] romance, the mysterious, as any that the ingenuity of the author of *The Mysteries of Udolpho* could devise. For what can more partake of the mysterious than an antipathy spontaneous and profound such as is evoked in certain exceptional mortals by the mere aspect of some other mortal, however harmless he may be, if not called forth by this very harmlessness itself?

2. In *The Deserted Village* (1770) by English writer Oliver Goldsmith (1730–1774), the students laugh at the jokes of the tyrannical schoolmaster, but only "with counterfeited glee."

3. Ann Radcliffe (1764–1823), English author of *The Mysteries of Udolpho* (1794) and other Gothic fiction.

Now there can exist no irritating juxtaposition of dissimilar personalities comparable to that which is possible aboard a great warship fully manned and at sea. There, every day among all ranks, almost every man comes into more or less of contact with almost every other man. Wholly there to avoid even the sight of an aggravating object one must needs give it Jonah's toss[4] or jump overboard himself. Imagine how all this might eventually operate on some peculiar human creature the direct reverse of a saint!

But for the adequate comprehending of Claggart by a normal nature these hints are insufficient. To pass from a normal nature to him one must cross "the deadly space between." And this is best done by indirection.

Long ago an honest scholar, my senior, said to me in reference to one who like himself is now no more, a man so unimpeachably respectable that against him nothing was ever openly said though among the few something was whispered, "Yes, X—— is a nut not to be cracked by the tap of a lady's fan. You are aware that I am the adherent of no organized religion, much less of any philosophy built into a system. Well, for all that, I think that to try and get into X——, enter his labyrinth and get out again, without a clue derived from some source other than what is known as 'knowledge of the world'—that were hardly possible, at least for me."

"Why," said I, "X——, however singular a study to some, is yet human, and knowledge of the world assuredly implies the knowledge of human nature, and in most of its varieties."

"Yes, but a superficial knowledge of it, serving ordinary purposes. But for anything deeper, I am not certain whether to know the world and to know human nature be not two distinct branches of knowledge, which while they may coexist in the same heart, yet either may exist with little or nothing of the other. Nay, in an average man of the world, his constant rubbing with it blunts that finer spiritual insight indispensable to the understanding of the essential in certain exceptional characters, whether evil ones or good. In a matter of some importance I have seen a girl wind an old lawyer about her little finger. Nor was it the dotage of senile love. Nothing of the sort. But he knew law better than he knew the girl's heart. Coke and Blackstone[5] hardly shed so much light into obscure spiritual places as the Hebrew prophets. And who were they? Mostly recluses."

At the time, my inexperience was such that I did not quite see the drift of all this. It may be that I see it now. And, indeed, if that lexicon which is based on Holy Writ were any longer popular, one might with less difficulty define and denominate certain phenomenal men. As it is, one must turn to some authority not liable to the charge of being tinctured with the biblical element.

In a list of definitions included in the authentic translation of Plato, a list attributed to him, occurs this: "Natural Depravity: a depravity according to nature," a definition which, though savoring of Calvinism, by no means involves Calvin's[6] dogma as to total mankind. Evidently its intent makes it applicable but to individuals. Not many are the examples of this depravity which the gallows and jail supply. At any rate, for notable instances, since

4. In Jonah 1.15, sailors toss Jonah overboard to rid themselves of a man whom God sought to punish by raising a storm at sea.
5. Sir Edward Coke (1552–1634) and Sir William Blackstone (1723–1780), British jurists.
6. French theologian (1509–1564) who regarded all human beings as depraved, a consequence of the Fall. Melville found the Plato quotation in the Bohn edition, vol. 6 (1854).

these have no vulgar alloy of the brute in them, but invariably are dominated by intellectuality, one must go elsewhere. Civilization, especially if of the austerer sort, is auspicious to it. It folds itself in the mantle of respectability. It has its certain negative virtues serving as silent auxiliaries. It never allows wine to get within its guard. It is not going too far to say that it is without vices or small sins. There is a phenomenal pride in it that excludes them. It is never mercenary or avaricious. In short, the depravity here meant partakes nothing of the sordid or sensual. It is serious, but free from acerbity. Though no flatterer of mankind it never speaks ill of it.

But the thing which in eminent instances signalizes so exceptional a nature is this: Though the man's even temper and discreet bearing would seem to intimate a mind peculiarly subject to the law of reason, not the less in heart he would seem to riot in complete exemption from that law, having apparently little to do with reason further than to employ it as an ambidexter implement for effecting the irrational. That is to say: Toward the accomplishment of an aim which in wantonness of atrocity would seem to partake of the insane, he will direct a cool judgment sagacious and sound. These men are madmen, and of the most dangerous sort, for their lunacy is not continuous, but occasional, evoked by some special object; it is protectively secretive, which is as much as to say it is self-contained, so that when, moreover, most active it is to the average mind not distinguishable from sanity, and for the reason above suggested: that whatever its aims may be—and the aim is never declared—the method and the outward proceeding are always perfectly rational.

Now something such an one was Claggart, in whom was the mania of an evil nature, not engendered by vicious training or corrupting books or licentious living, but born with him and innate, in short "a depravity according to nature."

Dark sayings are these, some will say. But why? Is it because they somewhat savor of Holy Writ in its phrase "mystery of iniquity"?[7] If they do, such savor was far enough from being intended, for little will it commend these pages to many a reader of today.

The point of the present story turning on the hidden nature of the master-at-arms has necessitated this chapter. With an added hint or two in connection with the incident at the mess, the resumed narrative must be left to vindicate, as it may, its own credibility.

12

That Claggart's figure was not amiss, and his face, save the chin, well molded, has already been said. Of these favorable points he seemed not insensible, for he was not only neat but careful in his dress. But the form of Billy Budd was heroic; and if his face was without the intellectual look of the pallid Claggart's, not the less was it lit, like his, from within, though from a different source. The bonfire in his heart made luminous the rose-tan in his cheek.

7. "For the mystery of iniquity doth already work" (2 Thessalonians 2.7).

In view of the marked contrast between the persons of the twain, it is more than probable that when the master-at-arms in the scene last given applied to the sailor the proverb "Handsome is as handsome does," he there let escape an ironic inkling, not caught by the young sailors who heard it, as to what it was that had first moved him against Billy, namely, his significant personal beauty.

Now envy and antipathy, passions irreconcilable in reason, nevertheless in fact may spring conjoined like Chang and Eng[8] in one birth. Is Envy then such a monster? Well, though many an arraigned mortal has in hopes of mitigated penalty pleaded guilty to horrible actions, did ever anybody seriously confess to envy? Something there is in it universally felt to be more shameful than even felonious crime. And not only does everybody disown it, but the better sort are inclined to incredulity when it is in earnest imputed to an intelligent man. But since its lodgment is in the heart not the brain, no degree of intellect supplies a guarantee against it. But Claggart's was no vulgar form of the passion. Nor, as directed toward Billy Budd, did it partake of that streak of apprehensive jealousy that marred Saul's visage perturbedly brooding on the comely young David.[9] Claggart's envy struck deeper. If askance he eyed the good looks, cheery health, and frank enjoyment of young life in Billy Budd, it was because these went along with a nature that, as Claggart magnetically felt, had in its simplicity never willed malice or experienced the reactionary bite of that serpent. To him, the spirit lodged within Billy, and looking out from his welkin eyes as from windows, that ineffability it was which made the dimple in his dyed cheek, suppled his joints, and dancing in his yellow curls made him pre-eminently the Handsome Sailor. One person excepted, the master-at-arms was perhaps the only man in the ship intellectually capable of adequately appreciating the moral phenomenon presented in Billy Budd. And the insight but intensified his passion, which assuming various secret forms within him, at times assumed that of cynic disdain, disdain of innocence—to be nothing more than innocent! Yet in an aesthetic way he saw the charm of it, the courageous free-and-easy temper of it, and fain would have shared it, but he despaired of it.

With no power to annul the elemental evil in him, though readily enough he could hide it; apprehending the good, but powerless to be it; a nature like Claggart's, surcharged with energy as such natures almost invariably are, what recourse is left to it but to recoil upon itself and, like the scorpion for which the Creator alone is responsible, act out to the end the part allotted it.

13

Passion, and passion in its profoundest, is not a thing demanding a palatial stage whereon to play its part. Down among the groundlings,[1] among the beggars and rakers of the garbage, profound passion is enacted. And the circumstances that provoke it, however trivial or mean, are no measure of

8. Siamese twins (1811–1874), exhibited in the United States by the circus showman P. T. Barnum (1810–1874).

9. 1 Samuel 16.18. Saul, the first king of Israel, was jealous of his eventual successor, the "comely" David.

1. Spectators in the pit, the cheapest area of a theater.

its power. In the present instance the stage is a scrubbed gun deck, and one of the external provocations a man-of-war's man's spilled soup.

Now when the master-at-arms noticed whence came that greasy fluid streaming before his feet, he must have taken it—to some extent wilfully, perhaps—not for the mere accident it assuredly was, but for the sly escape of a spontaneous feeling on Billy's part more or less answering to the antipathy on his own. In effect a foolish demonstration, he must have thought, and very harmless, like the futile kick of a heifer, which yet were the heifer a shod stallion would not be so harmless. Even so was it that into the gall of Claggart's envy he infused the vitriol of his contempt. But the incident confirmed to him certain telltale reports purveyed to his ear by "Squeak," one of his more cunning corporals, a grizzled little man, so nicknamed by the sailors on account of his squeaky voice and sharp visage ferreting about the dark corners of the lower decks after interlopers, satirically suggesting to them the idea of a rat in a cellar.

From his chief's employing him as an implicit tool in laying little traps for the worriment of the foretopman—for it was from the master-at-arms that the petty persecutions heretofore adverted to had proceeded—the corporal, having naturally enough concluded that his master could have no love for the sailor, made it his business, faithful understrapper that he was, to foment the ill blood by perverting to his chief certain innocent frolics of the good-natured foretopman, besides inventing for his mouth sundry contumelious epithets he claimed to have overheard him let fall. The master-at-arms never suspected the veracity of these reports, more especially as to the epithets, for he well knew how secretly unpopular may become a master-at-arms, at least a master-at-arms of those days, zealous in his function, and how the bluejackets shoot at him in private their raillery and wit; the nickname by which he goes among them (Jemmy Legs) implying under the form of merriment their cherished disrespect and dislike. But in view of the greediness of hate for pabulum[2] it hardly needed a purveyor to feed Claggart's passion.

An uncommon prudence is habitual with the subtler depravity, for it has everything to hide. And in case of an injury but suspected, its secretiveness voluntarily cuts it off from enlightenment or disillusion; and, not unreluctantly, action is taken upon surmise as upon certainty. And the retaliation is apt to be in monstrous disproportion to the supposed offense; for when in anybody was revenge in its exactions aught else but an inordinate usurer? But how with Claggart's conscience? For though consciences are unlike as foreheads, every intelligence, not excluding the scriptural devils who "believe and tremble,"[3] has one. But Claggart's conscience being but the lawyer to his will, made ogres of trifles, probably arguing that the motive imputed to Billy in spilling the soup just when he did, together with the epithets alleged, these, if nothing more, made a strong case against him; nay, justified animosity into a sort of retributive righteousness. The Pharisee is the Guy Fawkes[4] prowling in the hid chambers underlying some natures like Claggart's. And they can really form no conception of an unreciprocated malice. Probably

2. Nourishment.

3. "Thou believest that there is one God; thou doest well: the devils also believe, and tremble" (James 2.19).

4. The Pharisee (the self-righteous hypocrite) is the Guy Fawkes (the treacherous terrorist); references to the conspirators against Jesus (as in Matthew 22.15) and to the Catholic who conspired to blow up the Houses of Parliament in 1605.

the master-at-arms' clandestine persecution of Billy was started to try the temper of the man; but it had not developed any quality in him that enmity could make official use of or even pervert into plausible self-justification; so that the occurrence at the mess, petty if it were, was a welcome one to that peculiar conscience assigned to be the private mentor of Claggart; and, for the rest, not improbably it put him upon new experiments.

14

Not many days after the last incident narrated, something befell Billy Budd that more graveled him than aught that had previously occurred.

It was a warm night for the latitude; and the foretopman, whose watch at the time was properly below, was dozing on the uppermost deck whither he had ascended from his hot hammock, one of hundreds suspended so closely wedged together over a lower gun deck that there was little or no swing to them. He lay as in the shadow of a hillside, stretched under the lee[5] of the booms, a piled ridge of spare spars amidships between foremast and mainmast among which the ship's largest boat, the launch, was stowed. Alongside of three other slumberers from below, he lay near that end of the booms which approaches the foremast; his station aloft on duty as a foretopman being just over the deck-station of the forecastlemen, entitling him according to usage to make himself more or less at home in that neighborhood.

Presently he was stirred into semiconsciousness by somebody, who must have previously sounded the sleep of the others, touching his shoulder, and then, as the foretopman raised his head, breathing into his ear in a quick whisper, "Slip into the lee forechains,[6] Billy; there is something in the wind. Don't speak. Quick, I will meet you there," and disappearing.

Now Billy, like sundry other essentially good-natured ones, had some of the weaknesses inseparable from essential good nature; and among these was a reluctance, almost an incapacity of plumply saying *no* to an abrupt proposition not obviously absurd on the face of it, nor obviously unfriendly, nor iniquitous. And being of warm blood, he had not the phlegm tacitly to negative any proposition by unresponsive inaction. Like his sense of fear, his apprehension as to aught outside of the honest and natural was seldom very quick. Besides, upon the present occasion, the drowse from his sleep still hung upon him.

However it was, he mechanically rose and, sleepily wondering what could be in the wind, betook himself to the designated place, a narrow platform, one of six, outside of the high bulwarks and screened by the great deadeyes and multiple columned lanyards of the shrouds and backstays;[7] and, in a great warship of that time, of dimensions commensurate to the hull's magnitude; a tarry balcony in short, overhanging the sea, and so secluded that one mariner of the *Bellipotent*, a Nonconformist old tar of a serious turn, made it even in daytime his private oratory.[8]

5. Shelter (away from the wind).
6. A hidden platform (as explained two paragraphs below).
7. Heavy ropes that support the masts, extending from the mastheads to the sides of the ship. "Deadeyes": wooden blocks with holes through which ropes are run. "Lanyards": short ropes passing through deadeyes and used to extend shrouds, the ropes giving lateral support to the masts.
8. Prayer room. "Nonconformist": Protestant dissenter, refusing the religious policies and practices of the Church of England.

In this retired nook the stranger soon joined Billy Budd. There was no moon as yet; a haze obscured the starlight. He could not distinctly see the stranger's face. Yet from something in the outline and carriage, Billy took him, and correctly, for one of the afterguard.

"Hist! Billy," said the man, in the same quick cautionary whisper as before. "You were impressed, weren't you? Well, so was I"; and he paused, as to mark the effect. But Billy, not knowing exactly what to make of this, said nothing. Then the other: "We are not the only impressed ones, Billy. There's a gang of us.—Couldn't you—help—at a pinch?"

"What do you mean?" demanded Billy, here thoroughly shaking off his drowse.

"Hist, hist!" the hurried whisper now growing husky. "See here," and the man held up two small objects faintly twinkling in the night-light; "see, they are yours, Billy, if you'll only——"

But Billy broke in, and in his resentful eagerness to deliver himself his vocal infirmity somewhat intruded. "D—d—damme, I don't know what you are d—d—driving at, or what you mean, but you had better g—g—go where you belong!" For the moment the fellow, as confounded, did not stir; and Billy, springing to his feet, said, "If you d—don't start, I'll t—t—toss you back over the r—rail!" There was no mistaking this, and the mysterious emissary decamped, disappearing in the direction of the mainmast in the shadow of the booms.

"Hallo, what's the matter?" here came growling from a forecastleman awakened from his deck-doze by Billy's raised voice. And as the foretopman reappeared and was recognized by him: "Ah, Beauty, is it you? Well, something must have been the matter, for you st—st—stuttered."

"Oh," rejoined Billy, now mastering the impediment, "I found an afterguardsman in our part of the ship here, and I bid him be off where he belongs."

"And is that all you did about it, Foretopman?" gruffly demanded another, an irascible old fellow of brick-colored visage and hair who was known to his associate forecastlemen as "Red Pepper." "Such sneaks I should like to marry to the gunner's daughter!"—by that expression meaning that he would like to subject them to disciplinary castigation over a gun.

However, Billy's rendering of the matter satisfactorily accounted to these inquirers for the brief commotion, since of all the sections of a ship's company the forecastlemen, veterans for the most part and bigoted in their sea prejudices, are the most jealous in resenting territorial encroachments, especially on the part of any of the afterguard, of whom they have but a sorry opinion—chiefly landsmen, never going aloft except to reef or furl the mainsail, and in no wise competent to handle a marlinspike or turn in a deadeye, say.

15

This incident sorely puzzled Billy Budd. It was an entirely new experience, the first time in his life that he had ever been personally approached in underhand intriguing fashion. Prior to this encounter he had known nothing of the afterguardsman, the two men being stationed wide apart, one forward and aloft during his watch, the other on deck and aft.

What could it mean? And could they really be guineas,[9] those two glittering objects the interloper had held up to his (Billy's) eyes? Where could the fellow get guineas? Why, even spare buttons are not so plentiful at sea. The more he turned the matter over, the more he was nonplussed, and made uneasy and discomfited. In his disgustful recoil from an overture which, though he but ill comprehended, he instinctively knew must involve evil of some sort, Billy Budd was like a young horse fresh from the pasture suddenly inhaling a vile whiff from some chemical factory, and by repeated snortings trying to get it out of his nostrils and lungs. This frame of mind barred all desire of holding further parley with the fellow, even were it but for the purpose of gaining some enlightenment as to his design in approaching him. And yet he was not without natural curiosity to see how such a visitor in the dark would look in broad day.

He espied him the following afternoon in his first dogwatch below, one of the smokers on that forward part of the upper gun deck[1] allotted to the pipe. He recognized him by his general cut and build more than by his round freckled face and glassy eyes of pale blue, veiled with lashes all but white. And yet Billy was a bit uncertain whether indeed it were he—yonder chap about his own age chatting and laughing in freehearted way, leaning against a gun; a genial young fellow enough to look at, and something of a rattlebrain, to all appearance. Rather chubby too for a sailor, even an afterguardsman. In short, the last man in the world, one would think, to be overburdened with thoughts, especially those perilous thoughts that must needs belong to a conspirator in any serious project, or even to the underling of such a conspirator.

Although Billy was not aware of it, the fellow, with a side-long watchful glance, had perceived Billy first, and then noting that Billy was looking at him, thereupon nodded a familiar sort of friendly recognition as to an old acquaintance, without interrupting the talk he was engaged in with the group of smokers. A day or two afterwards, chancing in the evening promenade on a gun deck to pass Billy, he offered a flying word of good-fellowship, as it were, which by its unexpectedness, and equivocalness under the circumstances, so embarrassed Billy that he knew not how to respond to it, and let it go unnoticed.

Billy was now left more at a loss than before. The ineffectual speculations into which he was led were so disturbingly alien to him that he did his best to smother them. It never entered his mind that here was a matter which, from its extreme questionableness, it was his duty as a loyal bluejacket to report in the proper quarter. And, probably, had such a step been suggested to him, he would have been deterred from taking it by the thought, one of novice magnanimity, that it would savor overmuch of the dirty work of a telltale. He kept the thing to himself. Yet upon one occasion he could not forbear a little disburdening himself to the old Dansker, tempted thereto perhaps by the influence of a balmy night when the ship lay becalmed; the twain, silent for the most part, sitting together on deck, their heads propped against the bulwarks. But it was only a partial and anonymous account that Billy gave, the unfounded scruples above referred to preventing full disclo-

9. Gold coins worth a little more than one British pound.

1. The only place where the crew was permitted to smoke.

sure to anybody. Upon hearing Billy's version, the sage Dansker seemed to divine more than he was told; and after a little meditation, during which his wrinkles were pursed as into a point, quite effacing for the time that quizzing expression his face sometimes wore: "Didn't I say so, Baby Budd?"

"Say what?" demanded Billy.

"Why, *Jemmy Legs* is *down* on you."

"And what," rejoined Billy in amazement, "has *Jemmy Legs* to do with that cracked afterguardsman?"

"Ho, it was an afterguardsman, then. A cat's-paw, a cat's-paw!" And with that exclamation, whether it had reference to a light puff of air just then coming over the calm sea, or a subtler relation to the afterguardsman, there is no telling, the old Merlin gave a twisting wrench with his black teeth at his plug of tobacco, vouchsafing no reply to Billy's impetuous question, though now repeated, for it was his wont to relapse into grim silence when interrogated in skeptical sort as to any of his sententious oracles, not always very clear ones, rather partaking of that obscurity which invests most Delphic[2] deliverances from any quarter.

Long experience had very likely brought this old man to that bitter prudence which never interferes in aught and never gives advice.

16

Yes, despite the Dansker's pithy insistence as to the master-at-arms being at the bottom of these strange experiences of Billy on board the *Bellipotent*, the young sailor was ready to ascribe them to almost anybody but the man who, to use Billy's own expression, "always had a pleasant word for him." This is to be wondered at. Yet not so much to be wondered at. In certain matters, some sailors even in mature life remain unsophisticated enough. But a young seafarer of the disposition of our athletic foretopman is much of a child-man. And yet a child's utter innocence is but its blank ignorance, and the innocence more or less wanes as intelligence waxes. But in Billy Budd intelligence, such as it was, had advanced while yet his simple-mindedness remained for the most part unaffected. Experience is a teacher indeed; yet did Billy's years make his experience small. Besides, he had none of that intuitive knowledge of the bad which in natures not good or incompletely so foreruns experience, and therefore may pertain, as in some instances it too clearly does pertain, even to youth.

And what could Billy know of man except of man as a mere sailor? And the old-fashioned sailor, the veritable man before the mast, the sailor from boyhood up, he, though indeed of the same species as a landsman, is in some respects singularly distinct from him. The sailor is frankness, the landsman is finesse. Life is not a game with the sailor, demanding the long head[3]—no intricate game of chess where few moves are made in straightforwardness and ends are attained by indirection, an oblique, tedious, barren game hardly worth that poor candle burnt out in playing it.

Yes, as a class, sailors are in character a juvenile race. Even their deviations are marked by juvenility, this more especially holding true with the sailors

2. In Greek mythology, the prophecies of the oracle at Delphi, Greece, were renowned for their terseness and ambiguity.
3. Foresight, wisdom.

of Billy's time. Then too, certain things which apply to all sailors do more pointedly operate here and there upon the junior one. Every sailor, too, is accustomed to obey orders without debating them; his life afloat is externally ruled for him; he is not brought into that promiscuous commerce with mankind where unobstructed free agency on equal terms—equal superficially, at least—soon teaches one that unless upon occasion he exercise a distrust keen in proportion to the fairness of the appearance, some foul turn may be served him. A ruled undemonstrative distrustfulness is so habitual, not with businessmen so much as with men who know their kind in less shallow relations than business, namely, certain men of the world, that they come at last to employ it all but unconsciously; and some of them would very likely feel real surprise at being charged with it as one of their general characteristics.

17

But after the little matter at the mess Billy Budd no more found himself in strange trouble at times about his hammock or his clothes bag or what not. As to that smile that occasionally sunned him, and the pleasant passing word, these were, if not more frequent, yet if anything more pronounced than before.

But for all that, there were certain other demonstrations now. When Claggart's unobserved glance happened to light on belted Billy rolling along the upper gun deck in the leisure of the second dogwatch, exchanging passing broadsides of fun with other young promenaders in the crowd, that glance would follow the cheerful sea Hyperion[4] with a settled meditative and melancholy expression, his eyes strangely suffused with incipient feverish tears. Then would Claggart look like the man of sorrows.[5] Yes, and sometimes the melancholy expression would have in it a touch of soft yearning, as if Claggart could even have loved Billy but for fate and ban. But this was an evanescence, and quickly repented of, as it were, by an immitigable look, pinching and shriveling the visage into the momentary semblance of a wrinkled walnut. But sometimes catching sight in advance of the foretopman coming in his direction, he would, upon their nearing, step aside a little to let him pass, dwelling upon Billy for the moment with the glittering dental satire of a Guise.[6] But upon any abrupt unforeseen encounter a red light would flash forth from his eye like a spark from an anvil in a dusk smithy. That quick, fierce light was a strange one, darted from orbs which in repose were of a color nearest approaching a deeper violet, the softest of shades.

Though some of these caprices of the pit could not but be observed by their object, yet were they beyond the construing of such a nature. And the thews[7] of Billy were hardly compatible with that sort of sensitive spiritual organization which in some cases instinctively conveys to ignorant innocence an admonition of the proximity of the malign. He thought the master-at-arms acted in a manner rather queer at times. That was all. But the occasional

4. Another name for Apollo, Greek god of the sun who was also the god of manly beauty.
5. In Isaiah 53.3, the Lord's servant is termed "a man of sorrows, and acquainted with grief."
6. A 16th- and 17th-century French noble family known for its bloody treacheries and smiling hypocrisies. Henri de Guise (1550–1588) was one of those responsible for the massacre of French Huguenots that began on Saint Bartholomew's Day (August 24, 1572).
7. Muscles.

frank air and pleasant word went for what they purported to be, the young sailor never having heard as yet of the "too fair-spoken man."

Had the foretopman been conscious of having done or said anything to provoke the ill will of the official, it would have been different with him, and his sight might have been purged if not sharpened. As it was, innocence was his blinder.

So was it with him in yet another matter. Two minor officers, the armorer and captain of the hold,[8] with whom he had never exchanged a word, his position in the ship not bringing him into contact with them, these men now for the first began to cast upon Billy, when they chanced to encounter him, that peculiar glance which evidences that the man from whom it comes has been some way tampered with, and to the prejudice of him upon whom the glance lights. Never did it occur to Billy as a thing to be noted or a thing suspicious, though he well knew the fact, that the armorer and captain of the hold, with the ship's yeoman, apothecary, and others of that grade, were by naval usage messmates of the master-at-arms, men with ears convenient to his confidential tongue.

But the general popularity that came from our Handsome Sailor's manly forwardness upon occasion and irresistible good nature, indicating no mental superiority tending to excite an invidious feeling, this good will on the part of most of his shipmates made him the less to concern himself about such mute aspects toward him as those whereto allusion has just been made, aspects he could not so fathom as to infer their whole import.

As to the afterguardsman, though Billy for reasons already given necessarily saw little of him, yet when the two did happen to meet, invariably came the fellow's offhand cheerful recognition, sometimes accompanied by a passing pleasant word or two. Whatever that equivocal young person's original design may really have been, or the design of which he might have been the deputy, certain it was from his manner upon these occasions that he had wholly dropped it.

It was as if his precocity of crookedness (and every vulgar villain is precocious) had for once deceived him, and the man he had sought to entrap as a simpleton had through his very simplicity ignominiously baffled him.

But shrewd ones may opine that it was hardly possible for Billy to refrain from going up to the afterguardsman and bluntly demanding to know his purpose in the initial interview so abruptly closed in the forechains. Shrewd ones may also think it but natural in Billy to set about sounding some of the other impressed men of the ship in order to discover what basis, if any, there was for the emissary's obscure suggestions as to plotting disaffection aboard. Yes, shrewd ones may so think. But something more, or rather something else than mere shrewdness is perhaps needful for the due understanding of such a character as Billy Budd's.

As to Claggart, the monomania in the man—if that indeed it were—as involuntarily disclosed by starts in the manifestations detailed, yet in general covered over by his self-contained and rational demeanor; this, like a subterranean fire, was eating its way deeper and deeper in him. Something decisive must come of it.

8. Petty officers in charge of caring for arms ("armorer") and of supervising the interior of a vessel in the lower decks ("captain of the hold").

18

After the mysterious interview in the forechains, the one so abruptly ended there by Billy, nothing especially germane to the story occurred until the events now about to be narrated.

Elsewhere it has been said that in the lack of frigates (of course better sailers than line-of-battle ships) in the English squadron up the Straits at that period, the *Bellipotent* 74 was occasionally employed not only as an available substitute for a scout, but at times on detached service of more important kind. This was not alone because of her sailing qualities, not common in a ship of her rate, but quite as much, probably, that the character of her commander, it was thought, specially adapted him for any duty where under unforeseen difficulties a prompt initiative might have to be taken in some matter demanding knowledge and ability in addition to those qualities implied in good seamanship. It was on an expedition of the latter sort, a somewhat distant one, and when the *Bellipotent* was almost at her furthest remove from the fleet, that in the latter part of an afternoon watch she unexpectedly came in sight of a ship of the enemy. It proved to be a frigate. The latter, perceiving through the glass that the weight of men and metal would be heavily against her, invoking her light heels crowded sail to get away. After a chase urged almost against hope and lasting until about the middle of the first dogwatch, she signally succeeded in effecting her escape.

Not long after the pursuit had been given up, and ere the excitement incident thereto had altogether waned away, the master-at-arms, ascending from his cavernous sphere, made his appearance cap in hand by the mainmast respectfully waiting the notice of Captain Vere, then solitary walking the weather side of the quarter-deck, doubtless somewhat chafed at the failure of the pursuit. The spot where Claggart stood was the place allotted to men of lesser grades seeking some more particular interview either with the officer of the deck or the captain himself. But from the latter it was not often that a sailor or petty officer of those days would seek a hearing; only some exceptional cause would, according to established custom, have warranted that.

Presently, just as the commander, absorbed in his reflections, was on the point of turning aft in his promenade, he became sensible of Claggart's presence, and saw the doffed cap held in deferential expectancy. Here be it said that Captain Vere's personal knowledge of this petty officer had only begun at the time of the ship's last sailing from home, Claggart then for the first, in transfer from a ship detained for repairs, supplying on board the *Bellipotent* the place of a previous master-at-arms disabled and ashore.

No sooner did the commander observe who it was that now deferentially stood awaiting his notice than a peculiar expression came over him. It was not unlike that which uncontrollably will flit across the countenance of one at unawares encountering a person who, though known to him indeed, has hardly been long enough known for thorough knowledge, but something in whose aspect nevertheless now for the first provokes a vaguely repellent distaste. But coming to a stand and resuming much of his wonted official manner, save that a sort of impatience lurked in the intonation of the opening word, he said "Well? What is it, Master-at-arms?"

With the air of a subordinate grieved at the necessity of being a messenger of ill tidings, and while conscientiously determined to be frank yet equally resolved upon shunning overstatement, Claggart at this invitation, or rather summons to disburden, spoke up. What he said, conveyed in the language of no uneducated man, was to the effect following, if not altogether in these words, namely, that during the chase and preparations for the possible encounter he had seen enough to convince him that at least one sailor aboard was a dangerous character in a ship mustering some who not only had taken a guilty part in the late serious troubles, but others also who, like the man in question, had entered His Majesty's service under another form than enlistment.

At this point Captain Vere with some impatience interrupted him: "Be direct, man; say *impressed men.*"

Claggart made a gesture of subservience, and proceeded. Quite lately he (Claggart) had begun to suspect that on the gun decks some sort of movement prompted by the sailor in question was covertly going on, but he had not thought himself warranted in reporting the suspicion so long as it remained indistinct. But from what he had that afternoon observed in the man referred to, the suspicion of something clandestine going on had advanced to a point less removed from certainty. He deeply felt, he added, the serious responsibility assumed in making a report involving such possible consequences to the individual mainly concerned, besides tending to augment those natural anxieties which every naval commander must feel in view of extraordinary outbreaks so recent as those which, he sorrowfully said it, it needed not to name.

Now at the first broaching of the matter Captain Vere, taken by surprise, could not wholly dissemble his disquietude. But as Claggart went on, the former's aspect changed into restiveness under something in the testifier's manner in giving his testimony. However, he refrained from interrupting him. And Claggart, continuing, concluded with this: "God forbid, your honor, that the *Bellipotent*'s should be the experience of the—"

"Never mind that!" here peremptorily broke in the superior, his face altering with anger, instinctively divining the ship that the other was about to name, one in which the Nore Mutiny had assumed a singularly tragical character that for a time jeopardized the life of its commander. Under the circumstances he was indignant at the purposed allusion. When the commissioned officers themselves were on all occasions very heedful how they referred to the recent events in the fleet, for a petty officer unnecessarily to allude to them in the presence of his captain, this struck him as a most immodest presumption. Besides, to his quick sense of self-respect it even looked under the circumstances something like an attempt to alarm him. Nor at first was he without some surprise that one who so far as he had hitherto come under his notice had shown considerable tact in his function should in this particular evince such lack of it.

But these thoughts and kindred dubious ones flitting across his mind were suddenly replaced by an intuitional surmise which, though as yet obscure in form, served practically to affect his reception of the ill tidings. Certain it is that, long versed in everything pertaining to the complicated gun-deck life, which like every other form of life has its secret mines and dubious side, the side popularly disclaimed, Captain Vere did not permit himself to be unduly disturbed by the general tenor of his subordinate's report.

Furthermore, if in view of recent events prompt action should be taken at the first palpable sign of recurring insubordination, for all that, not judicious would it be, he thought, to keep the idea of lingering disaffection alive by undue forwardness in crediting an informer, even if his own subordinate and charged among other things with police surveillance of the crew. This feeling would not perhaps have so prevailed with him were it not that upon a prior occasion the patriotic zeal officially evinced by Claggart had somewhat irritated him as appearing rather supersensible and strained. Furthermore, something even in the official's self-possessed and somewhat ostentatious manner in making his specifications strangely reminded him of a bandsman, a perjurous witness in a capital case before a court-martial ashore of which when a lieutenant he (Captain Vere) had been a member.

Now the peremptory check given to Claggart in the matter of the arrested allusion was quickly followed up by this: "You say that there is at least one dangerous man aboard. Name him."

"William Budd, a foretopman, your honor."

"William Budd!" repeated Captain Vere with unfeigned astonishment. "And mean you the man that Lieutenant Ratcliffe took from the merchantman not very long ago, the young fellow who seems to be so popular with the men—Billy, the Handsome Sailor, as they call him?"

"The same, your honor; but for all his youth and good looks, a deep one. Not for nothing does he insinuate himself into the good will of his shipmates, since at the least they will at a pinch say—all hands will—a good word for him, and at all hazards. Did Lieutenant Ratcliffe happen to tell your honor of that adroit fling of Budd's, jumping up in the cutter's bow under the merchantman's stern when he was being taken off? It is even masked by that sort of good-humored air that at heart he resents his impressment. You have but noted his fair cheek. A mantrap may be under the ruddy-tipped daisies."

Now the Handsome Sailor as a signal figure among the crew had naturally enough attracted the captain's attention from the first. Though in general not very demonstrative to his officers, he had congratulated Lieutenant Ratcliffe upon his good fortune in lighting on such a fine specimen of the *genus homo*,[9] who in the nude might have posed for a statue of young Adam before the Fall. As to Billy's adieu to the ship *Rights-of-Man*, which the boarding lieutenant had indeed reported to him, but, in a deferential way, more as a good story than aught else, Captain Vere, though mistakenly understanding it as a satiric sally, had but thought so much the better of the impressed man for it; as a military sailor, admiring the spirit that could take an arbitrary enlistment so merrily and sensibly. The foretopman's conduct, too, so far as it had fallen under the captain's notice, had confirmed the first happy augury, while the new recruit's qualities as a "sailor-man" seemed to be such that he had thought of recommending him to the executive officer for promotion to a place that would more frequently bring him under his own observation, namely, the captaincy of the mizzentop,[1] replacing there in the starboard watch a man not so young whom partly for that reason he deemed less fitted for the post. Be it parenthesized here that since the mizzentopmen have not to handle such breadths of heavy canvas as the lower sails on the mainmast and foremast, a young man if of the right stuff not only seems best adapted to duty there, but in fact is generally selected for the captaincy of that top, and

9. Human race.

1. The watch assigned to the rear mast.

the company under him are light hands and often but striplings. In sum, Captain Vere had from the beginning deemed Billy Budd to be what in the naval parlance of the time was called a "King's bargain": that is to say, for His Britannic Majesty's navy a capital investment at small outlay or none at all.

After a brief pause, during which the reminiscences above mentioned passed vividly through his mind and he weighed the import of Claggart's last suggestion conveyed in the phrase "mantrap under the daisies," and the more he weighed it the less reliance he felt in the informer's good faith, suddenly he turned upon him and in a low voice demanded: "Do you come to me, Master-at-arms, with so foggy a tale? As to Budd, cite me an act or spoken word of his confirmatory of what you in general charge against him. Stay," drawing nearer to him; "heed what you speak. Just now, and in a case like this, there is a yardarm-end[2] for the false witness."

"Ah, your honor!" sighed Claggart, mildly shaking his shapely head as in sad deprecation of such unmerited severity of tone. Then, bridling—erecting himself as in virtuous self-assertion—he circumstantially alleged certain words and acts which collectively, if credited, led to presumptions mortally inculpating Budd. And for some of these averments, he added, substantiating proof was not far.

With gray eyes impatient and distrustful essaying to fathom to the bottom Claggart's calm violet ones, Captain Vere again heard him out; then for the moment stood ruminating. The mood he evinced, Claggart—himself for the time liberated from the other's scrutiny—steadily regarded with a look difficult to render: a look curious of the operation of his tactics, a look such as might have been that of the spokesman of the envious children of Jacob deceptively imposing upon the troubled patriarch the blood-dyed coat of young Joseph.[3]

Though something exceptional in the moral quality of Captain Vere made him, in earnest encounter with a fellow man, a veritable touchstone of that man's essential nature, yet now as to Claggart and what was really going on in him his feeling partook less of intuitional conviction than of strong suspicion clogged by strange dubieties. The perplexity he evinced proceeded less from aught touching the man informed against—as Claggart doubtless opined—than from considerations how best to act in regard to the informer. At first, indeed, he was naturally for summoning that substantiation of his allegations which Claggart said was at hand. But such a proceeding would result in the matter at once getting abroad, which in the present stage of it, he thought, might undesirably affect the ship's company. If Claggart was a false witness—that closed the affair. And therefore, before trying the accusation, he would first practically test the accuser; and he thought this could be done in a quiet, undemonstrative way.

The measure he determined upon involved a shifting of the scene, a transfer to a place less exposed to observation than the broad quarter-deck. For although the few gun-room officers there at the time had, in due observance of naval etiquette, withdrawn to leeward the moment Captain Vere had begun his promenade on the deck's weather side; and though during the

2. Used for hangings.

3. In Genesis 37.31–33, Joseph's brothers sell him into bondage and then stain his coat with blood in an effort to convince their father, Jacob, that their brother is dead.

colloquy with Claggart they of course ventured not to diminish the distance; and though throughout the interview Captain Vere's voice was far from high, and Claggart's silvery and low; and the wind in the cordage and the wash of the sea helped the more to put them beyond earshot; nevertheless, the interview's continuance already had attracted observation from some topmen aloft and other sailors in the waist or further forward.

Having determined upon his measures, Captain Vere forthwith took action. Abruptly turning to Claggart, he asked, "Master-at-arms, is it now Budd's watch aloft?"

"No, your honor."

Whereupon, "Mr. Wilkes!" summoning the nearest midshipman. "Tell Albert to come to me." Albert was the captain's hammock-boy, a sort of sea valet in whose discretion and fidelity his master had much confidence. The lad appeared.

"You know Budd, the foretopman?"

"I do, sir."

"Go find him. It is his watch off. Manage to tell him out of earshot that he is wanted aft. Contrive it that he speaks to nobody. Keep him in talk yourself. And not till you get well aft here, not till then let him know that the place where he is wanted is my cabin. You understand. Go.—Master-at-arms, show yourself on the decks below, and when you think it time for Albert to be coming with his man, stand by quietly to follow the sailor in."

19

Now when the foretopman found himself in the cabin, closeted there, as it were, with the captain and Claggart, he was surprised enough. But it was a surprise unaccompanied by apprehension or distrust. To an immature nature essentially honest and humane, forewarning intimations of subtler danger from one's kind come tardily if at all. The only thing that took shape in the young sailor's mind was this: Yes, the captain, I have always thought, looks kindly upon me. Wonder if he's going to make me his coxswain. I should like that. And may be now he is going to ask the master-at-arms about me.

"Shut the door there, sentry," said the commander; "stand without, and let nobody come in.—Now, Master-at-arms, tell this man to his face what you told of him to me," and stood prepared to scrutinize the mutually confronting visages.

With the measured step and calm collected air of an asylum physician approaching in the public hall some patient beginning to show indications of a coming paroxysm, Claggart deliberately advanced within short range of Billy and, mesmerically looking him in the eye, briefly recapitulated the accusation.

Not at first did Billy take it in. When he did, the rose-tan of his cheek looked struck as by white leprosy. He stood like one impaled and gagged. Meanwhile the accuser's eyes, removing not as yet from the blue dilated ones, underwent a phenomenal change, their wonted rich violet color blurring into a muddy purple. Those lights of human intelligence, losing human expression, were gelidly protruding like the alien eyes of certain uncatalogued creatures of the deep. The first mesmeristic glance was one of serpent fascination; the last was as the paralyzing lurch of the torpedo fish.

"Speak, man!" said Captain Vere to the transfixed one, struck by his aspect even more than by Claggart's. "Speak! Defend yourself!" Which appeal caused but a strange dumb gesturing and gurgling in Billy; amazement at such an accusation so suddenly sprung on inexperienced nonage; this, and, it may be, horror of the accuser's eyes, serving to bring out his lurking defect and in this instance for the time intensifying it into a convulsed tongue-tie; while the intent head and entire form straining forward in an agony of ineffectual eagerness to obey the injunction to speak and defend himself, gave an expression to the face like that of a condemned vestal priestess in the moment of being buried alive, and in the first struggle against suffocation.[4]

Though at the time Captain Vere was quite ignorant of Billy's liability to vocal impediment, he now immediately divined it, since vividly Billy's aspect recalled to him that of a bright young schoolmate of his whom he had once seen struck by much the same startling impotence in the act of eagerly rising in the class to be foremost in response to a testing question put to it by the master. Going close up to the young sailor, and laying a soothing hand on his shoulder, he said, "There is no hurry, my boy. Take your time, take your time." Contrary to the effect intended, these words so fatherly in tone, doubtless touching Billy's heart to the quick, prompted yet more violent efforts at utterance—efforts soon ending for the time in confirming the paralysis, and bringing to his face an expression which was as a crucifixion to behold. The next instant, quick as the flame from a discharged cannon at night, his right arm shot out, and Claggart dropped to the deck. Whether intentionally or but owing to the young athlete's superior height, the blow had taken effect full upon the forehead, so shapely and intellectual-looking a feature in the master-at-arms; so that the body fell over lengthwise, like a heavy plank tilted from erectness. A gasp or two, and he lay motionless.

"Fated boy," breathed Captain Vere in tone so low as to be almost a whisper, "what have you done! But here, help me."

The twain raised the felled one from the loins up into a sitting position. The spare form flexibly acquiesced, but inertly. It was like handling a dead snake. They lowered it back. Regaining erectness, Captain Vere with one hand covering his face stood to all appearance as impassive as the object at his feet. Was he absorbed in taking in all the bearings of the event and what was best not only now at once to be done, but also in the sequel? Slowly he uncovered his face; and the effect was as if the moon emerging from eclipse should reappear with quite another aspect than that which had gone into hiding. The father in him, manifested towards Billy thus far in the scene, was replaced by the military disciplinarian. In his official tone he bade the foretopman retire to a stateroom aft (pointing it out), and there remain till thence summoned. This order Billy in silence mechanically obeyed. Then going to the cabin door where it opened on the quarter-deck, Captain Vere said to the sentry without, "Tell somebody to send Albert here." When the lad appeared, his master so contrived it that he should not catch sight of the prone one. "Albert," he said to him, "tell the surgeon I wish to see him. You need not come back till called."

When the surgeon entered—a self-poised character of that grave sense and experience that hardly anything could take him aback—Captain Vere

4. The punishment of unchaste priestesses of the Roman goddess of the hearth, Vesta.

advanced to meet him, thus unconsciously intercepting his view of Claggart, and, interrupting the other's wonted ceremonious salutation, said, "Nay. Tell me how it is with yonder man," directing his attention to the prostrate one.

The surgeon looked, and for all his self-command somewhat started at the abrupt revelation. On Claggart's always pallid complexion, thick black blood was now oozing from nostril and ear. To the gazer's professional eye it was unmistakably no living man that he saw.

"Is it so, then?" said Captain Vere, intently watching him. "I thought it. But verify it." Whereupon the customary tests confirmed the surgeon's first glance, who now, looking up in unfeigned concern, cast a look of intense inquisitiveness upon his superior. But Captain Vere, with one hand to his brow, was standing motionless. Suddenly, catching the surgeon's arm convulsively, he exclaimed, pointing down to the body, "It is the divine judgment on Ananias![5] Look!"

Disturbed by the excited manner he had never before observed in the *Bellipotent*'s captain, and as yet wholly ignorant of the affair, the prudent surgeon nevertheless held his peace, only again looking an earnest interrogatory as to what it was that had resulted in such a tragedy.

But Captain Vere was now again motionless, standing absorbed in thought. Again starting, he vehemently exclaimed, "Struck dead by an angel of God! Yet the angel must hang!"

At these passionate interjections, mere incoherences to the listener as yet unapprised of the antecedents, the surgeon was profoundly discomposed. But now, as recollecting himself, Captain Vere in less passionate tone briefly related the circumstances leading up to the event. "But come; we must dispatch," he added. "Help me to remove him" (meaning the body) "to yonder compartment," designating one opposite that where the foretopman remained immured. Anew disturbed by a request that, as implying a desire for secrecy, seemed unaccountably strange to him, there was nothing for the subordinate to do but comply.

"Go now," said Captain Vere with something of his wonted manner. "Go now. I presently shall call a drumhead court.[6] Tell the lieutenants what has happened, and tell Mr. Mordant" (meaning the captain of marines),[7] "and charge them to keep the matter to themselves."

20

Full of disquietude and misgiving, the surgeon left the cabin. Was Captain Vere suddenly affected in his mind, or was it but a transient excitement, brought about by so strange and extraordinary a tragedy? As to the drumhead court, it struck the surgeon as impolitic, if nothing more. The thing to do, he thought, was to place Billy Budd in confinement, and in a way dictated by usage, and postpone further action in so extraordinary a case to such time as they should rejoin the squadron, and then refer it to the admiral. He recalled the unwonted agitation of Captain Vere and his excited exclamations, so at variance with his normal manner. Was he unhinged?

5. In Acts 5.3–5, Ananias falls dead when the apostle Peter reveals he has lied to God.
6. An emergency court (from the custom of using a drum for a table in an impromptu military or naval trial).
7. Captain of the soldiers stationed on shipboard.

But assuming that he is, it is not so susceptible of proof. What then can the surgeon do? No more trying situation is conceivable than that of an officer subordinate under a captain whom he suspects to be not mad, indeed, but yet not quite unaffected in his intellects. To argue his order to him would be insolence. To resist him would be mutiny.

In obedience to Captain Vere, he communicated what had happened to the lieutenants and captain of marines, saying nothing as to the captain's state. They fully shared his own surprise and concern. Like him too, they seemed to think that such a matter should be referred to the admiral.

21

Who in the rainbow can draw the line where the violet tint ends and the orange tint begins? Distinctly we see the difference of the colors, but where exactly does the one first blendingly enter into the other? So with sanity and insanity. In pronounced cases there is no question about them. But in some supposed cases, in various degrees supposedly less pronounced, to draw the exact line of demarcation few will undertake, though for a fee becoming considerate some professional experts will. There is nothing namable but that some men will, or undertake to, do it for pay.

Whether Captain Vere, as the surgeon professionally and privately surmised, was really the sudden victim of any degree of aberration, every one must determine for himself by such light as this narrative may afford.

That the unhappy event which has been narrated could not have happened at a worse juncture was but too true. For it was close on the heel of the suppressed insurrections, an aftertime very critical to naval authority, demanding from every English sea commander two qualities not readily interfusable—prudence and rigor. Moreover, there was something crucial in the case.

In the jugglery of circumstances preceding and attending the event on board the *Bellipotent*, and in the light of that martial code whereby it was formally to be judged, innocence and guilt personified in Claggart and Budd in effect changed places. In a legal view the apparent victim of the tragedy was he who had sought to victimize a man blameless; and the indisputable deed of the latter, navally regarded, constituted the most heinous of military crimes. Yet more. The essential right and wrong involved in the matter, the clearer that might be, so much the worse for the responsibility of a loyal sea commander, inasmuch as he was not authorized to determine the matter on that primitive basis.

Small wonder then that the *Bellipotent*'s captain, though in general a man of rapid decision, felt that circumspectness not less than promptitude was necessary. Until he could decide upon his course, and in each detail; and not only so, but until the concluding measure was upon the point of being enacted, he deemed it advisable, in view of all the circumstances, to guard as much as possible against publicity. Here he may or may not have erred. Certain it is, however, that subsequently in the confidential talk of more than one or two gun rooms and cabins he was not a little criticized by some officers, a fact imputed by his friends and vehemently by his cousin Jack Denton to professional jealousy of Starry Vere. Some imaginative ground for invidious comment there was. The maintenance of secrecy in the matter, the confining all knowledge of it for a time to the place where the homicide occurred, the quarter-deck cabin; in these particulars lurked some resemblance to the policy adopted in those tragedies of the palace which have occurred more than once in the capital founded by Peter the Barbarian.[8]

The case indeed was such that fain would the *Bellipotent*'s captain have deferred taking any action whatever respecting it further than to keep the foretopman a close prisoner till the ship rejoined the squadron and then submitting the matter to the judgment of his admiral.

But a true military officer is in one particular like a true monk. Not with more of self-abnegation will the latter keep his vows of monastic obedience than the former his vows of allegiance to martial duty.

Feeling that unless quick action was taken on it, the deed of the foretopman, so soon as it should be known on the gun decks, would tend to awaken any slumbering embers of the Nore among the crew, a sense of the urgency of the case overruled in Captain Vere every other consideration. But though a conscientious disciplinarian, he was no lover of authority for mere authority's sake. Very far was he from embracing opportunities for monopolizing to himself the perils of moral responsibility, none at least that could properly be referred to an official superior or shared with him by his official equals or even subordinates. So thinking, he was glad it would not be at variance with usage to turn the matter over to a summary court of his own officers, reserving to himself, as the one on whom the ultimate accountability would rest, the right of maintaining a supervision of it, or formally or informally interposing at need. Accordingly a drumhead court was summarily convened, he electing the individuals composing it: the first lieutenant, the captain of marines, and the sailing master.[9]

In associating an officer of marines with the sea lieutenant and the sailing master in a case having to do with a sailor, the commander perhaps deviated from general custom. He was prompted thereto by the circumstance that he took that soldier to be a judicious person, thoughtful, and not altogether incapable of grappling with a difficult case unprecedented in his prior experience. Yet even as to him he was not without some latent misgiving, for withal he was an extremely good-natured man, an enjoyer of his dinner, a sound sleeper, and inclined to obesity—a man who though he would always maintain his manhood in battle might not prove altogether reliable in a moral dilemma involving aught of the tragic. As to the first lieutenant and the sailing master, Captain Vere could not but be aware that though honest natures, of approved gallantry upon occasion, their intelligence was mostly confined to the matter of active seamanship and the fighting demands of their profession.

The court was held in the same cabin where the unfortunate affair had taken place. This cabin, the commander's, embraced the entire area under the poop deck. Aft, and on either side, was a small stateroom, the one now temporarily a jail and the other a dead-house, and a yet smaller compartment, leaving a space between expanding forward into a goodly oblong of length coinciding with the ship's beam.[1] A skylight of moderate dimension was over-

8. Peter the Great (1672–1725), czar of Russia.
9. Officer charged with navigating the ship.
1. The maximum width of the ship.

head, and at each end of the oblong space were two sashed porthole windows easily convertible back into embrasures for short carronades.[2]

All being quickly in readiness, Billy Budd was arraigned, Captain Vere necessarily appearing as the sole witness in the case, and as such temporarily sinking his rank, though singularly maintaining it in a matter apparently trivial, namely, that he testified from the ship's weather side, with that object having caused the court to sit on the lee side.[3] Concisely he narrated all that had led up to the catastrophe, omitting nothing in Claggart's accusation and deposing as to the manner in which the prisoner had received it. At this testimony the three officers glanced with no little surprise at Billy Budd, the last man they would have suspected either of the mutinous design alleged by Claggart or the undeniable deed he himself had done. The first lieutenant, taking judicial primacy and turning toward the prisoner, said, "Captain Vere has spoken. Is it or is it not as Captain Vere says?"

In response came syllables not so much impeded in the utterance as might have been anticipated. They were these: "Captain Vere tells the truth. It is just as Captain Vere says, but it is not as the master-at-arms said. I have eaten the King's bread and I am true to the King."

"I believe you, my man," said the witness, his voice indicating a suppressed emotion not otherwise betrayed.

"God will bless you for that, your honor!" not without stammering said Billy, and all but broke down. But immediately he was recalled to self-control by another question, to which with the same emotional difficulty of utterance he said, "No, there was no malice between us. I never bore malice against the master-at-arms. I am sorry that he is dead. I did not mean to kill him. Could I have used my tongue I would not have struck him. But he foully lied to my face and in presence of my captain, and I had to say something, and I could only say it with a blow, God help me!"

In the impulsive aboveboard manner of the frank one the court saw confirmed all that was implied in words that just previously had perplexed them, coming as they did from the testifier to the tragedy and promptly following Billy's impassioned disclaimer of mutinous intent—Captain Vere's words, "I believe you, my man."

Next it was asked of him whether he knew of or suspected aught savoring of incipient trouble (meaning mutiny, though the explicit term was avoided) going on in any section of the ship's company.

The reply lingered. This was naturally imputed by the court to the same vocal embarrassment which had retarded or obstructed previous answers. But in main it was otherwise here, the question immediately recalling to Billy's mind the interview with the afterguardsman in the forechains. But an innate repugnance to playing a part at all approaching that of an informer against one's own shipmates—the same erring sense of uninstructed honor which had stood in the way of his reporting the matter at the time, though as a loyal man-of-war's man it was incumbent on him, and failure so to do, if charged against him and proven, would have subjected him to the heaviest of penalties; this, with the blind feeling now his that nothing really was being hatched, prevailed with him. When the answer came it was a negative.

2. Light iron cannons (from Carron, Scotland, where they were first made).

3. Vere testifies from the side from which the wind is blowing, so he looms higher than the officers.

"One question more," said the officer of marines, now first speaking and with a troubled earnestness. "You tell us that what the master-at-arms said against you was a lie. Now why should he have so lied, so maliciously lied, since you declare there was no malice between you?"

At that question, unintentionally touching on a spiritual sphere wholly obscure to Billy's thoughts, he was nonplussed, evincing a confusion indeed that some observers, such as can readily be imagined, would have construed into involuntary evidence of hidden guilt. Nevertheless, he strove some way to answer, but all at once relinquished the vain endeavor, at the same time turning an appealing glance towards Captain Vere as deeming him his best helper and friend. Captain Vere, who had been seated for a time, rose to his feet, addressing the interrogator. "The question you put to him comes naturally enough. But how can he rightly answer it?—or anybody else, unless indeed it be he who lies within there," designating the compartment where lay the corpse. "But the prone one there will not rise to our summons. In effect, though, as it seems to me, the point you make is hardly material. Quite aside from any conceivable motive actuating the master-at-arms, and irrespective of the provocation to the blow, a martial court must needs in the present case confine its attention to the blow's consequence, which consequence justly is to be deemed not otherwise than as the striker's deed."

This utterance, the full significance of which it was not at all likely that Billy took in, nevertheless caused him to turn a wistful interrogative look toward the speaker, a look in its dumb expressiveness not unlike that which a dog of generous breed might turn upon his master, seeking in his face some elucidation of a previous gesture ambiguous to the canine intelligence. Nor was the same utterance without marked effect upon the three officers, more especially the soldier. Couched in it seemed to them a meaning unanticipated, involving a prejudgment on the speaker's part. It served to augment a mental disturbance previously evident enough.

The soldier once more spoke, in a tone of suggestive dubiety addressing at once his associates and Captain Vere: "Nobody is present—none of the ship's company, I mean—who might shed lateral light, if any is to be had, upon what remains mysterious in this matter."

"That is thoughtfully put," said Captain Vere; "I see your drift. Ay, there is a mystery; but, to use a scriptural phrase, it is a 'mystery of iniquity,' a matter for psychologic theologians to discuss. But what has a military court to do with it? Not to add that for us any possible investigation of it is cut off by the lasting tongue-tie of—him—in yonder," again designating the mortuary stateroom. "The prisoner's deed—with that alone we have to do."

To this, and particularly the closing reiteration, the marine soldier, knowing not how aptly to reply, sadly abstained from saying aught. The first lieutenant, who at the outset had not unnaturally assumed primacy in the court, now overrulingly instructed by a glance from Captain Vere, a glance more effective than words, resumed that primacy. Turning to the prisoner, "Budd," he said, and scarce in equable tones, "Budd, if you have aught further to say for yourself, say it now."

Upon this the young sailor turned another quick glance toward Captain Vere; then, as taking a hint from that aspect, a hint confirming his own instinct that silence was now best, replied to the lieutenant, "I have said all, sir."

The marine—the same who had been the sentinel without the cabin door at the time that the foretopman, followed by the master-at-arms, entered it—he, standing by the sailor throughout these judicial proceedings, was now directed to take him back to the after compartment originally assigned to the prisoner and his custodian. As the twain disappeared from view, the three officers, as partially liberated from some inward constraint associated with Billy's mere presence, simultaneously stirred in their seats. They exchanged looks of troubled indecision, yet feeling that decide they must and without long delay. For Captain Vere, he for the time stood—unconsciously with his back toward them, apparently in one of his absent fits—gazing out from a sashed porthole to windward upon the monotonous blank of the twilight sea. But the court's silence continuing, broken only at moments by brief consultations, in low earnest tones, this served to arouse him and energize him. Turning, he to-and-fro paced the cabin athwart; in the returning ascent to windward climbing the slant deck in the ship's lee roll,[4] without knowing it symbolizing thus in his action a mind resolute to surmount difficulties even if against primitive instincts strong as the wind and the sea. Presently he came to a stand before the three. After scanning their faces he stood less as mustering his thoughts for expression than as one inly deliberating how best to put them to well-meaning men not intellectually mature, men with whom it was necessary to demonstrate certain principles that were axioms to himself. Similar impatience as to talking is perhaps one reason that deters some minds from addressing any popular assemblies.

When speak he did, something, both in the substance of what he said and his manner of saying it, showed the influence of unshared studies modifying and tempering the practical training of an active career. This, along with his phraseology, now and then was suggestive of the grounds whereon rested that imputation of a certain pedantry socially alleged against him by certain naval men of wholly practical cast, captains who nevertheless would frankly concede that His Majesty's navy mustered no more efficient officer of their grade than Starry Vere.

What he said was to this effect: "Hitherto I have been but the witness, little more; and I should hardly think now to take another tone, that of your coadjutor for the time, did I not perceive in you—at the crisis too—a troubled hesitancy, proceeding, I doubt not, from the clash of military duty with moral scruple—scruple vitalized by compassion. For the compassion, how can I otherwise than share it? But, mindful of paramount obligations, I strive against scruples that may tend to enervate decision. Not, gentlemen, that I hide from myself that the case is an exceptional one. Speculatively regarded, it well might be referred to a jury of casuists.[5] But for us here, acting not as casuists or moralists, it is a case practical, and under martial law practically to be dealt with.

"But your scruples: do they move as in a dusk? Challenge them. Make them advance and declare themselves. Come now; do they import something like this: If, mindless of palliating circumstances, we are bound to regard the death of the master-at-arms as the prisoner's deed, then does that deed constitute a capital crime whereof the penalty is a mortal one. But in

4. I.e., climbing as the ship rolled away from the wind.

5. Those who resolve matters of right and wrong by hairsplitting arguments.

natural justice is nothing but the prisoner's overt act to be considered? How can we adjudge to summary and shameful death a fellow creature innocent before God, and whom we feel to be so?—Does that state it aright? You sign sad assent. Well, I too feel that, the full force of that. It is Nature. But do these buttons that we wear attest that our allegiance is to Nature? No, to the King. Though the ocean, which is inviolate Nature primeval, though this be the element where we move and have our being as sailors, yet as the King's officers lies our duty in a sphere correspondingly natural? So little is that true, that in receiving our commissions we in the most important regards ceased to be natural free agents. When war is declared are we the commissioned fighters previously consulted? We fight at command. If our judgments approve the war, that is but coincidence. So in other particulars. So now. For suppose condemnation to follow these present proceedings. Would it be so much we ourselves that would condemn as it would be martial law operating through us? For that law and the rigor of it, we are not responsible. Our vowed responsibility is in this: That however pitilessly that law may operate in any instances, we nevertheless adhere to it and administer it.

"But the exceptional in the matter moves the hearts within you. Even so too is mine moved. But let not warm hearts betray heads that should be cool. Ashore in a criminal case, will an upright judge allow himself off the bench to be waylaid by some tender kinswoman of the accused seeking to touch him with her tearful plea? Well, the heart here, sometimes the feminine in man, is as that piteous woman, and hard though it be, she must here be ruled out."

He paused, earnestly studying them for a moment; then resumed.

"But something in your aspect seems to urge that it is not solely the heart that moves in you, but also the conscience, the private conscience. But tell me whether or not, occupying the position we do, private conscience should not yield to that imperial one formulated in the code under which alone we officially proceed?"

Here the three men moved in their seats, less convinced than agitated by the course of an argument troubling but the more the spontaneous conflict within.

Perceiving which, the speaker paused for a moment; then abruptly changing his tone, went on.

"To steady us a bit, let us recur to the facts.—In wartime at sea a man-of-war's man strikes his superior in grade, and the blow kills. Apart from its effect the blow itself is, according to the Articles of War, a capital crime. Furthermore—"

"Ay, sir," emotionally broke in the officer of marines, "in one sense it was. But surely Budd purposed neither mutiny nor homicide."

"Surely not, my good man. And before a court less arbitrary and more merciful than a martial one, that plea would largely extenuate. At the Last Assizes[6] it shall acquit. But how here? We proceed under the law of the Mutiny Act. In feature no child can resemble his father more than that Act resembles in spirit the thing from which it derives—War. In His Majesty's service—in this ship, indeed—there are Englishmen forced to fight for the

6. The Last Judgment.

King against their will. Against their conscience, for aught we know. Though as their fellow creatures some of us may appreciate their position, yet as navy officers what reck we of it? Still less recks the enemy. Our impressed men he would fain cut down in the same swath with our volunteers. As regards the enemy's naval conscripts, some of whom may even share our own abhorrence of the regicidal French Directory, it is the same on our side. War looks but to the frontage, the appearance. And the Mutiny Act, War's child, takes after the father. Budd's intent or non-intent is nothing to the purpose.

"But while, put to it by those anxieties in you which I cannot but respect, I only repeat myself—while thus strangely we prolong proceedings that should be summary—the enemy may be sighted and an engagement result. We must do; and one of two things must we do—condemn or let go."

"Can we not convict and yet mitigate the penalty?" asked the sailing master, here speaking, and falteringly, for the first.

"Gentlemen, were that clearly lawful for us under the circumstances, consider the consequences of such clemency. The people" (meaning the ship's company) "have native sense; most of them are familiar with our naval usage and tradition; and how would they take it? Even could you explain to them—which our official position forbids—they, long molded by arbitrary discipline, have not that kind of intelligent responsiveness that might qualify them to comprehend and discriminate. No, to the people the foretopman's deed, however it be worded in the announcement, will be plain homicide committed in a flagrant act of mutiny. What penalty for that should follow, they know. But it does not follow. *Why*? they will ruminate. You know what sailors are. Will they not revert to the recent outbreak at the Nore? Ay. They know the well-founded alarm—the panic it struck throughout England. Your clement sentence they would account pusillanimous. They would think that we flinch, that we are afraid of them—afraid of practicing a lawful rigor singularly demanded at this juncture, lest it should provoke new troubles. What shame to us such a conjecture on their part, and how deadly to discipline. You see then, whither, prompted by duty and the law, I steadfastly drive. But I beseech you, my friends, do not take me amiss. I feel as you do for this unfortunate boy. But did he know our hearts, I take him to be of that generous nature that he would feel even for us on whom in this military necessity so heavy a compulsion is laid."

With that, crossing the deck he resumed his place by the sashed porthole, tacitly leaving the three to come to a decision. On the cabin's opposite side the troubled court sat silent. Loyal lieges, plain and practical, though at bottom they dissented from some points Captain Vere had put to them, they were without the faculty, hardly had the inclination, to gainsay one whom they felt to be an earnest man, one too not less their superior in mind than in naval rank. But it is not improbable that even such of his words as were not without influence over them, less came home to them than his closing appeal to their instinct as sea officers: in the forethought he threw out as to the practical consequences to discipline, considering the unconfirmed tone of the fleet at the time, should a man-of-war's man's violent killing at sea of a superior in grade be allowed to pass for aught else than a capital crime demanding prompt infliction of the penalty.

Not unlikely they were brought to something more or less akin to that harassed frame of mind which in the year 1842 actuated the commander of the U.S. brig-of-war *Somers* to resolve, under the so-called Articles of War, Articles modeled upon the English Mutiny Act, to resolve upon the execution at sea of a midshipman and two sailors as mutineers designing the seizure of the brig. Which resolution was carried out though in a time of peace and within not many days' sail of home. An act vindicated by a naval court of inquiry subsequently convened ashore. History, and here cited without comment. True, the circumstances on board the *Somers* were different from those on board the *Bellipotent*. But the urgency felt, well-warranted or otherwise, was much the same.

Says a writer[7] whom few know, "Forty years after a battle it is easy for a noncombatant to reason about how it ought to have been fought. It is another thing personally and under fire to have to direct the fighting while involved in the obscuring smoke of it. Much so with respect to other emergencies involving considerations both practical and moral, and when it is imperative promptly to act. The greater the fog the more it imperils the steamer, and speed is put on though at the hazard of running somebody down. Little ween the snug card players in the cabin of the responsibilities of the sleepless man on the bridge."

In brief, Billy Budd was formally convicted and sentenced to be hung at the yardarm in the early morning watch, it being now night. Otherwise, as is customary in such cases, the sentence would forthwith have been carried out. In wartime on the field or in the fleet, a mortal punishment decreed by a drumhead court—on the field sometimes decreed by but a nod from the general—follows without delay on the heel of conviction, without appeal.

22

It was Captain Vere himself who of his own motion communicated the finding of the court to the prisoner, for that purpose going to the compartment where he was in custody and bidding the marine there to withdraw for the time.

Beyond the communication of the sentence, what took place at this interview was never known. But in view of the character of the twain briefly closeted in that stateroom, each radically sharing in the rarer qualities of our nature—so rare indeed as to be all but incredible to average minds however much cultivated—some conjectures may be ventured.

It would have been in consonance with the spirit of Captain Vere should he on this occasion have concealed nothing from the condemned one—should he indeed have frankly disclosed to him the part he himself had played in bringing about the decision, at the same time revealing his actuating motives. On Billy's side it is not improbable that such a confession would have been received in much the same spirit that prompted it. Not without a sort of joy, indeed, he might have appreciated the brave opinion of him implied in his captain's making such a confidant of him. Nor, as to the sentence itself, could he have been insensible that it was imparted to

7. An ironic reference to Melville himself. Melville had a long-standing interest in the *Somers* case. His cousin Guert Gansevoort (1812–1868) had been first lieutenant of the ship and had presided over the ship's court that found the three sailors guilty and condemned them to hang. Melville had earlier written about the case in *White-Jacket*.

him as to one not afraid to die. Even more may have been. Captain Vere in end may have developed the passion sometimes latent under an exterior stoical or indifferent. He was old enough to have been Billy's father. The austere devotee of military duty, letting himself melt back into what remains primeval in our formalized humanity, may in end have caught Billy to his heart, even as Abraham may have caught young Isaac on the brink of resolutely offering him up in obedience to the exacting behest.[8] But there is no telling the sacrament, seldom if in any case revealed to the gadding world, wherever under circumstances at all akin to those here attempted to be set forth two of great Nature's nobler order embrace. There is privacy at the time, inviolable to the survivor; and holy oblivion, the sequel to each diviner magnanimity, providentially covers all at last.

The first to encounter Captain Vere in act of leaving the compartment was the senior lieutenant. The face he beheld, for the moment one expressive of the agony of the strong, was to that officer, though a man of fifty, a startling revelation. That the condemned one suffered less than he who mainly had effected the condemnation was apparently indicated by the former's exclamation in the scene soon perforce to be touched upon.

23

Of a series of incidents within a brief term rapidly following each other, the adequate narration may take up a term less brief, especially if explanation or comment here and there seem requisite to the better understanding of such incidents. Between the entrance into the cabin of him who never left it alive, and him who when he did leave it left it as one condemned to die; between this and the closeted interview just given, less than an hour and a half had elapsed. It was an interval long enough, however, to awaken speculations among no few of the ship's company as to what it was that could be detaining in the cabin the master-at-arms and the sailor; for a rumor that both of them had been seen to enter it and neither of them had been seen to emerge, this rumor had got abroad upon the gun decks and in the tops, the people of a great warship being in one respect like villagers, taking microscopic note of every outward movement or non-movement going on. When therefore, in weather not at all tempestuous, all hands were called in the second dogwatch, a summons under such circumstances not usual in those hours, the crew were not wholly unprepared for some announcement extraordinary, one having connection too with the continued absence of the two men from their wonted haunts.

There was a moderate sea at the time; and the moon, newly risen and near to being at its full, silvered the white spar deck wherever not blotted by the clear-cut shadows horizontally thrown of fixtures and moving men. On either side the quarter-deck the marine guard under arms was drawn up; and Captain Vere, standing in his place surrounded by all the wardroom officers,[9] addressed his men. In so doing, his manner showed neither more nor less than that properly pertaining to his supreme position aboard his own ship. In

8. In Genesis 22.1–18, God commands Abraham to sacrifice his son, Isaac, and then withdraws the command at the last minute when it is clear that Abraham is willing to obey.

9. The commissioned (higher-ranking) officers.

clear terms and concise he told them what had taken place in the cabin: that the master-at-arms was dead, that he who had killed him had been already tried by a summary court and condemned to death, and that the execution would take place in the early morning watch. The word *mutiny* was not named in what he said. He refrained too from making the occasion an opportunity for any preachment as to the maintenance of discipline, thinking perhaps that under existing circumstances in the navy the consequence of violating discipline should be made to speak for itself.

Their captain's announcement was listened to by the throng of standing sailors in a dumbness like that of a seated congregation of believers in hell listening to the clergyman's announcement of his Calvinistic text.

At the close, however, a confused murmur went up. It began to wax. All but instantly, then, at a sign, it was pierced and suppressed by shrill whistles of the boatswain and his mates. The word was given to about ship.

To be prepared for burial Claggart's body was delivered to certain petty officers of his mess. And here, not to clog the sequel with lateral matters, it may be added that at a suitable hour, the master-at-arms was committed to the sea with every funeral honor properly belonging to his naval grade.

In this proceeding as in every public one growing out of the tragedy strict adherence to usage was observed. Nor in any point could it have been at all deviated from, either with respect to Claggart or Billy Budd, without begetting undesirable speculations in the ship's company, sailors, and more particularly men-of-war's men, being of all men the greatest sticklers for usage. For similar cause, all communication between Captain Vere and the condemned one ended with the closeted interview already given, the latter being now surrendered to the ordinary routine preliminary to the end. His transfer under guard from the captain's quarters was effected without unusual precautions—at least no visible ones. If possible, not to let the men so much as surmise that their officers anticipate aught amiss from them is the tacit rule in a military ship. And the more that some sort of trouble should really be apprehended, the more do the officers keep that apprehension to themselves, though not the less unostentatious vigilance may be augmented. In the present instance, the sentry placed over the prisoner had strict orders to let no one have communication with him but the chaplain. And certain unobtrusive measures were taken absolutely to insure this point.

24

In a seventy-four of the old order the deck known as the upper gun deck was the one covered over by the spar deck, which last, though not without its armament, was for the most part exposed to the weather. In general it was at all hours free from hammocks; those of the crew swinging on the lower gun deck and berth deck, the latter being not only a dormitory but also the place for the stowing of the sailors' bags, and on both sides lined with the large chests or movable pantries of the many messes of the men.

On the starboard side of the *Bellipotent*'s upper gun deck, behold Billy Budd under sentry lying prone in irons in one of the bays formed by the regular spacing of the guns comprising the batteries on either side. All these pieces were of the heavier caliber of that period. Mounted on lumbering wooden carriages, they were hampered with cumbersome harness of breeching and strong side-tackles for running them out. Guns and carriages, together with the long rammers and shorter linstocks[1] lodged in loops overhead—all these, as customary, were painted black; and the heavy hempen breechings, tarred to the same tint, wore the like livery of the undertakers. In contrast with the funereal hue of these surroundings, the prone sailor's exterior apparel, white jumper and white duck trousers, each more or less soiled, dimly glimmered in the obscure light of the bay like a patch of discolored snow in early April lingering at some upland cave's black mouth. In effect he is already in his shroud, or the garments that shall serve him in lieu of one. Over him but scarce illuminating him, two battle lanterns swing from two massive beams of the deck above. Fed with the oil supplied by the war contractors (whose gains, honest or otherwise, are in every land an anticipated portion of the harvest of death), with flickering splashes of dirty yellow light they pollute the pale moonshine all but ineffectually struggling in obstructed flecks through the open ports from which the tampioned[2] cannon protrude. Other lanterns at intervals serve but to bring out somewhat the obscurer bays which, like small confessionals or side-chapels in a cathedral, branch from the long dim-vistaed broad aisle between the two batteries of that covered tier.

Such was the deck where now lay the Handsome Sailor. Through the rose-tan of his complexion no pallor could have shown. It would have taken days of sequestration from the winds and the sun to have brought about the effacement of that. But the skeleton in the cheekbone at the point of its angle was just beginning delicately to be defined under the warm-tinted skin. In fervid hearts self-contained, some brief experiences devour our human tissue as secret fire in a ship's hold consumes cotton in the bale.

But now lying between the two guns, as nipped in the vice of fate, Billy's agony, mainly proceeding from a generous young heart's virgin experience of the diabolical incarnate and effective in some men—the tension of that agony was over now. It survived not the something healing in the closeted interview with Captain Vere. Without movement, he lay as in a trance, that adolescent expression previously noted as his taking on something akin to the look of a slumbering child in the cradle when the warm hearth-glow of the still chamber at night plays on the dimples that at whiles mysteriously form in the cheek, silently coming and going there. For now and then in the gyved[3] one's trance a serene happy light born of some wandering reminiscence or dream would diffuse itself over his face, and then wane away only anew to return.

The chaplain, coming to see him and finding him thus, and perceiving no sign that he was conscious of his presence, attentively regarded him for a space, then slipping aside, withdrew for the time, peradventure feeling that even he, the minister of Christ though receiving his stipend from Mars,[4] had no consolation to proffer which could result in a peace transcending that which he beheld. But in the small hours he came again. And the prisoner, now awake to his surroundings, noticed his approach, and civilly, all but cheerfully, welcomed him. But it was to little purpose that in the interview

1. Fork-tipped staffs to hold a lighted match for firing cannon. "Rammers": rods for ramming home the charge of a gun.

2. Covered or plugged.

3. Shackled.

4. Roman god of war.

following, the good man sought to bring Billy Budd to some godly understanding that he must die, and at dawn. True, Billy himself freely referred to his death as a thing close at hand; but it was something in the way that children will refer to death in general, who yet among their other sports will play a funeral with hearse and mourners.

Not that like children Billy was incapable of conceiving what death really is. No, but he was wholly without irrational fear of it, a fear more prevalent in highly civilized communities than those so-called barbarous ones which in all respects stand nearer to unadulterate Nature. And, as elsewhere said, a barbarian Billy radically was—as much so, for all the costume, as his countrymen the British captives, living trophies, made to march in the Roman triumph of Germanicus.[5] Quite as much so as those later barbarians, young men probably, and picked specimens among the earlier British converts to Christianity, at least nominally such, taken to Rome (as today converts from lesser isles of the sea may be taken to London), of whom the Pope[6] of that time, admiring the strangeness of their personal beauty so unlike the Italian stamp, their clear ruddy complexion and curled flaxen locks, exclaimed, "Angles" (meaning *English*, the modern derivative), "Angles, do you call them? And is it because they look so like angels?" Had it been later in time, one would think that the Pope had in mind Fra Angelico's seraphs, some of whom, plucking apples in gardens of the Hesperides,[7] have the faint rosebud complexion of the more beautiful English girls.

If in vain the good chaplain sought to impress the young barbarian with ideas of death akin to those conveyed in the skull, dial, and crossbones on old tombstones, equally futile to all appearance were his efforts to bring home to him the thought of salvation and a Savior. Billy listened, but less out of awe or reverence, perhaps, than from a certain natural politeness, doubtless at bottom regarding all that in much the same way that most mariners of his class take any discourse abstract or out of the common tone of the workaday world. And this sailor way of taking clerical discourse is not wholly unlike the way in which the primer of Christianity, full of transcendent miracles, was received long ago on tropic isles by any superior *savage*, so called—a Tahitian, say, of Captain Cook's time[8] or shortly after that time. Out of a natural courtesy he received, but did not appropriate. It was like a gift placed in the palm of an outreached hand upon which the fingers do not close.

But the *Bellipotent*'s chaplain was a discreet man possessing the good sense of a good heart. So he insisted not in his vocation here. At the instance of Captain Vere, a lieutenant had apprised him of pretty much everything as to Billy; and since he felt that innocence was even a better thing than religion wherewith to go to Judgment, he reluctantly withdrew; but in his emotion not without first performing an act strange enough in an Englishman, and under the circumstances yet more so in any regular priest. Stooping over, he kissed on the fair cheek his fellow man, a felon in martial law, one

5. Germanicus Caesar (15 B.C.E.–19 C.E.), Roman general who fought Germanic tribes and was given an elaborate triumphal procession when he returned to Rome (17 C.E.).
6. Pope Gregory (540?–604).
7. In Greek mythology, islands where golden apples grew (guarded by a dragon). In Florence during 1857 Melville saw paintings by Giovanni da Fiesole (Fra Angelico) (1387–1455).
8. The English explorer James Cook (1728–1779) first visited Tahiti in 1769.

whom though on the confines of death he felt he could never convert to a dogma; nor for all that did he fear for his future.

Marvel not that having been made acquainted with the young sailor's essential innocence the worthy man lifted not a finger to avert the doom of such a martyr to martial discipline. So to do would not only have been as idle as invoking the desert, but would also have been an audacious transgression of the bounds of his function, one as exactly prescribed to him by military law as that of the boatswain or any other naval officer. Bluntly put, a chaplain is the minister of the Prince of Peace serving in the host of the God of War—Mars. As such, he is as incongruous as a musket would be on the altar at Christmas. Why, then, is he there? Because he indirectly subserves the purpose attested by the cannon; because too he lends the sanction of the religion of the meek to that which practically is the abrogation of everything but brute Force.

25

The night so luminous on the spar deck, but otherwise on the cavernous ones below, levels so like the tiered galleries in a coal mine—the luminous night passed away. But like the prophet in the chariot disappearing in heaven and dropping his mantle to Elisha,[9] the withdrawing night transferred its pale robe to the breaking day. A meek, shy light appeared in the East, where stretched a diaphanous fleece of white furrowed vapor. That light slowly waxed. Suddenly *eight bells* was struck aft, responded to by one louder metallic stroke from forward. It was four o'clock in the morning. Instantly the silver whistles were heard summoning all hands to witness punishment. Up through the great hatchways rimmed with racks of heavy shot the watch below came pouring, overspreading with the watch already on deck the space between the mainmast and foremast including that occupied by the capacious launch and the black booms tiered on either side of it, boat and booms making a summit of observation for the powder-boys and younger tars. A different group comprising one watch of topmen leaned over the rail of that sea balcony, no small one in a seventy-four, looking down on the crowd below. Man or boy, none spake but in whisper, and few spake at all. Captain Vere—as before, the central figure among the assembled commissioned officers—stood nigh the break of the poop deck facing forward. Just below him on the quarter-deck the marines in full equipment were drawn up much as at the scene of the promulgated sentence.

At sea in the old time, the execution by halter[1] of a military sailor was generally from the foreyard. In the present instance, for special reasons the mainyard was assigned. Under an arm of that yard the prisoner was presently brought up, the chaplain attending him. It was noted at the time, and remarked upon afterwards, that in this final scene the good man evinced little or nothing of the perfunctory. Brief speech indeed he had with the condemned one, but the genuine Gospel was less on his tongue than in his aspect and manner towards him. The final preparations personal to the latter being speedily brought to an end by two boatswain's mates, the

9. When the prophet Elijah is transported to heaven, he drops his cloak, which is picked up by his disciple Elisha (2 Kings 2.9–15).

1. Hangman's noose.

consummation impended. Billy stood facing aft. At the penultimate moment, his words, his only ones, words wholly unobstructed in the utterance, were these: "God bless Captain Vere!" Syllables so unanticipated coming from one with the ignominious hemp about his neck—a conventional felon's benediction directed aft towards the quarters of honor; syllables too delivered in the clear melody of a singing bird on the point of launching from the twig—had a phenomenal effect, not unenhanced by the rare personal beauty of the young sailor, spiritualized now through late experiences so poignantly profound.

Without volition, as it were, as if indeed the ship's populace were but the vehicles of some vocal current electric, with one voice from alow and aloft came a resonant sympathetic echo: "God bless Captain Vere!" And yet at that instant Billy alone must have been in their hearts, even as in their eyes.

At the pronounced words and the spontaneous echo that voluminously rebounded them, Captain Vere, either through stoic self-control or a sort of momentary paralysis induced by emotional shock, stood erectly rigid as a musket in the ship-armorer's rack.

The hull, deliberately recovering from the periodic roll to leeward, was just regaining an even keel when the last signal, a preconcerted dumb one, was given. At the same moment it chanced that the vapory fleece hanging low in the East was shot through with a soft glory as of the fleece of the Lamb of God seen in mystical vision,[2] and simultaneously therewith, watched by the wedged mass of upturned faces, Billy ascended; and, ascending, took the full rose of the dawn.

In the pinioned figure arrived at the yard-end, to the wonder of all no motion was apparent, none save that created by the slow roll of the hull in moderate weather, so majestic in a great ship ponderously cannoned.

26

When some days afterwards, in reference to the singularity just mentioned, the purser,[3] a rather ruddy, rotund person more accurate as an accountant than profound as a philosopher, said at mess to the surgeon, "What testimony to the force lodged in will power," the latter, saturnine, spare, and tall, one in whom a discreet causticity went along with a manner less genial than polite, replied, "Your pardon, Mr. Purser. In a hanging scientifically conducted—and under special orders I myself directed how Budd's was to be effected—any movement following the completed suspension and originating in the body suspended, such movement indicates mechanical spasm in the muscular system. Hence the absence of that is no more attributable to will power, as you call it, than to horsepower—begging your pardon."

"But this muscular spasm you speak of, is not that in a degree more or less invariable in these cases?"

"Assuredly so, Mr. Purser."

"How then, my good sir, do you account for its absence in this instance?"

"Mr. Purser, it is clear that your sense of the singularity in this matter equals not mine. You account for it by what you call will power—a term not

2. As in Revelation 1.14.

3. Paymaster.

yet included in the lexicon of science. For me, I do not, with my present knowledge, pretend to account for it at all. Even should we assume the hypothesis that at the first touch of the halyards the action of Budd's heart, intensified by extraordinary emotion at its climax, abruptly stopped—much like a watch when in carelessly winding it up you strain at the finish, thus snapping the chain—even under that hypothesis how account for the phenomenon that followed?"

"You admit, then, that the absence of spasmodic movement was phenomenal."

"It was phenomenal, Mr. Purser, in the sense that it was an appearance the cause of which is not immediately to be assigned."

"But tell me, my dear sir," pertinaciously continued the other, "was the man's death effected by the halter, or was it a species of euthanasia?"[4]

"*Euthanasia*, Mr. Purser, is something like your *will power*: I doubt its authenticity as a scientific term—begging your pardon again. It is at once imaginative and metaphysical—in short, Greek.—But," abruptly changing his tone, "there is a case in the sick bay that I do not care to leave to my assistants. Beg your pardon, but excuse me." And rising from the mess he formally withdrew.

27

The silence at the moment of execution and for a moment or two continuing thereafter, a silence but emphasized by the regular wash of the sea against the hull or the flutter of a sail caused by the helmsman's eyes being tempted astray, this emphasized silence was gradually disturbed by a sound not easily to be verbally rendered. Whoever has heard the freshet-wave of a torrent suddenly swelled by pouring showers in tropical mountains, showers not shared by the plain; whoever has heard the first muffled murmur of its sloping advance through precipitous woods may form some conception of the sound now heard. The seeming remoteness of its source was because of its murmurous indistinctness, since it came from close by, even from the men massed on the ship's open deck. Being inarticulate, it was dubious in significance further than it seemed to indicate some capricious revulsion of thought or feeling such as mobs ashore are liable to, in the present instance possibly implying a sullen revocation on the men's part of their involuntary echoing of Billy's benediction. But ere the murmur had time to wax into clamor it was met by a strategic command, the more telling that it came with abrupt unexpectedness: "Pipe down the starboard watch, Boatswain, and see that they go."

Shrill as the shriek of the sea hawk, the silver whistles of the boatswain and his mates pierced that ominous low sound, dissipating it; and yielding to the mechanism of discipline the throng was thinned by one-half. For the remainder, most of them were set to temporary employments connected with trimming the yards and so forth, business readily to be got up to serve occasion by any officer of the deck.

4. Melville uses the term as he found it in the works of the German philosopher Arthur Schopenhauer (1788–1860), where it means "an easy death, not ushered in by disease, and free from all pain and struggle."

Now each proceeding that follows a mortal sentence pronounced at sea by a drumhead court is characterized by promptitude not perceptibly merging into hurry, though bordering that. The hammock, the one which had been Billy's bed when alive, having already been ballasted with shot and otherwise prepared to serve for his canvas coffin, the last offices of the sea undertakers, the sailmaker's mates, were now speedily completed. When everything was in readiness a second call for all hands, made necessary by the strategic movement before mentioned, was sounded, now to witness burial.

The details of this closing formality it needs not to give. But when the tilted plank let slide its freight into the sea, a second strange human murmur was heard, blended now with another inarticulate sound proceeding from certain larger seafowl who, their attention having been attracted by the peculiar commotion in the water resulting from the heavy sloped dive of the shotted hammock into the sea, flew screaming to the spot. So near the hull did they come, that the stridor or bony creak of their gaunt double-jointed pinions was audible. As the ship under light airs passed on, leaving the burial spot astern, they still kept circling it low down with the moving shadow of their outstretched wings and the croaked requiem of their cries.

Upon sailors as superstitious as those of the age preceding ours, men-of-war's men too who had just beheld the prodigy of repose in the form suspended in air, and now foundering in the deeps; to such mariners the action of the seafowl, though dictated by mere animal greed for prey, was big with no prosaic significance. An uncertain movement began among them, in which some encroachment was made. It was tolerated but for a moment. For suddenly the drum beat to quarters, which familiar sound happening at least twice every day, had upon the present occasion a signal peremptoriness in it. True martial discipline long continued superinduces in average man a sort of impulse whose operation at the official word of command much resembles in its promptitude the effect of an instinct.

The drumbeat dissolved the multitude, distributing most of them along the batteries of the two covered gun decks. There, as wonted, the guns' crews stood by their respective cannon erect and silent. In due course the first officer, sword under arm and standing in his place on the quarter-deck, formally received the successive reports of the sworded lieutenants commanding the sections of batteries below; the last of which reports being made, the summed report he delivered with the customary salute to the commander. All this occupied time, which in the present case was the object in beating to quarters at an hour prior to the customary one. That such variance from usage was authorized by an officer like Captain Vere, a martinet as some deemed him, was evidence of the necessity for unusual action implied in what he deemed to be temporarily the mood of his men. "With mankind," he would say, "forms, measured forms, are everything; and that is the import couched in the story of Orpheus with his lyre spellbinding the wild denizens of the wood."[5] And this he once applied to the disruption of forms going on across the Channel and the consequences thereof.

At this unwonted muster at quarters, all proceeded as at the regular hour. The band on the quarter-deck played a sacred air, after which the chaplain went through the customary morning service. That done, the drum beat the

5. In Greek mythology, Orpheus's music was so powerful that it held wild beasts spellbound.

retreat; and toned by music and religious rites subserving the discipline and purposes of war, the men in their wonted orderly manner dispersed to the places allotted them when not at the guns.

And now it was full day. The fleece of low-hanging vapor had vanished, licked up by the sun that late had so glorified it. And the circumambient air in the clearness of its serenity was like smooth white marble in the polished block not yet removed from the marble-dealer's yard.

28

The symmetry of form attainable in pure fiction cannot so readily be achieved in a narration essentially having less to do with fable than with fact. Truth uncompromisingly told will always have its ragged edges; hence the conclusion of such a narration is apt to be less finished than an architectural finial.[6]

How it fared with the Handsome Sailor during the year of the Great Mutiny has been faithfully given. But though properly the story ends with his life, something in way of sequel will not be amiss. Three brief chapters will suffice.

In the general rechristening under the Directory of the craft originally forming the navy of the French monarchy, the *St. Louis* line-of-battle ship was named the *Athée* (the *Atheist*). Such a name, like some other substituted ones in the Revolutionary fleet, while proclaiming the infidel audacity of the ruling power, was yet, though not so intended to be, the aptest name, if one consider it, ever given to a warship; far more so indeed than the *Devastation*, the *Erebus* (the *Hell*), and similar names bestowed upon fighting ships.

On the return passage to the English fleet from the detached cruise during which occurred the events already recorded, the *Bellipotent* fell in with the *Athée*. An engagement ensued, during which Captain Vere, in the act of putting his ship alongside the enemy with a view of throwing his boarders across her bulwarks, was hit by a musket ball from a porthole of the enemy's main cabin. More than disabled, he dropped to the deck and was carried below to the same cockpit where some of his men already lay. The senior lieutenant took command. Under him the enemy was finally captured, and though much crippled was by rare good fortune successfully taken into Gibraltar, an English port not very distant from the scene of the fight. There, Captain Vere with the rest of the wounded was put ashore. He lingered for some days, but the end came. Unhappily he was cut off too early for the Nile and Trafalgar.[7] The spirit that 'spite its philosophic austerity may yet have indulged in the most secret of all passions, ambition, never attained to the fulness of fame.

Not long before death, while lying under the influence of that magical drug[8] which, soothing the physical frame, mysteriously operates on the subtler element in man, he was heard to murmur words inexplicable to his attendant: "Billy Budd, Billy Budd." That these were not the accents of remorse would seem clear from what the attendant said to the *Bellipotent*'s senior officer of marines, who, as the most reluctant to condemn of the members of

6. An ornament that forms the top of a post, pillar, or other architectural feature.
7. Vere died before the battles of the Nile (1798) and Trafalgar (1805).
8. Probably opium.

the drumhead court, too well knew, though here he kept the knowledge to himself, who Billy Budd was.

29

Some few weeks after the execution, among other matters under the head of "News from the Mediterranean," there appeared in a naval chronicle of the time, an authorized weekly publication, an account of the affair. It was doubtless for the most part written in good faith, though the medium, partly rumor, through which the facts must have reached the writer served to deflect and in part falsify them. The account was as follows:

"On the tenth of the last month a deplorable occurrence took place on board H.M.S. *Bellipotent*. John Claggart, the ship's master-at-arms, discovering that some sort of plot was incipient among an inferior section of the ship's company, and that the ringleader was one William Budd; he, Claggart, in the act of arraigning the man before the captain, was vindictively stabbed to the heart by the suddenly drawn sheath knife of Budd.

"The deed and the implement employed sufficiently suggest that though mustered into the service under an English name the assassin was no Englishman, but one of those aliens adopting English cognomens whom the present extraordinary necessities of the service have caused to be admitted into it in considerable numbers.

"The enormity of the crime and the extreme depravity of the criminal appear the greater in view of the character of the victim, a middle-aged man respectable and discreet, belonging to that minor official grade, the petty officers, upon whom, as none know better than the commissioned gentlemen, the efficiency of His Majesty's navy so largely depends. His function was a responsible one, at once onerous and thankless; and his fidelity in it the greater because of his strong patriotic impulse. In this instance as in so many other instances in these days, the character of this unfortunate man signally refutes, if refutation were needed, that peevish saying attributed to the late Dr. Johnson, that patriotism is the last refuge of a scoundrel.[9]

"The criminal paid the penalty of his crime. The promptitude of the punishment has proved salutary. Nothing amiss is now apprehended aboard H.M.S. *Bellipotent*."

The above, appearing in a publication now long ago superannuated and forgotten, is all that hitherto has stood in human record to attest what manner of men respectively were John Claggart and Billy Budd.

30

Everything is for a term venerated in navies. Any tangible object associated with some striking incident of the service is converted into a monument. The spar from which the foretopman was suspended was for some few years kept trace of by the bluejackets. Their knowledges followed it from ship to dockyard and again from dockyard to ship, still pursuing it even when at last reduced to a mere dockyard boom. To them a chip of it was as a piece of the

9. Reported by James Boswell in his *Life of Johnson* (1791) as a statement made by the English writer Samuel Johnson on April 7, 1775.

Cross. Ignorant though they were of the secret facts of the tragedy, and not thinking but that the penalty was somehow unavoidably inflicted from the naval point of view, for all that, they instinctively felt that Billy was a sort of man as incapable of mutiny as of wilful murder. They recalled the fresh young image of the Handsome Sailor, that face never deformed by a sneer or subtler vile freak of the heart within. This impression of him was doubtless deepened by the fact that he was gone, and in a measure mysteriously gone. On the gun decks of the *Bellipotent* the general estimate of his nature and its unconscious simplicity eventually found rude utterance from another foretopman, one of his own watch, gifted, as some sailors are, with an artless *poetic* temperament. The tarry hand made some lines which, after circulating among the shipboard crews for a while, finally got rudely printed at Portsmouth as a ballad. The title given to it was the sailor's.

BILLY IN THE DARBIES[1]

Good of the chaplain to enter Lone Bay
And down on his marrowbones[2] here and pray
For the likes just o'me, Billy Budd.—But, look:
Through the port comes the moonshine astray!
It tips the guard's cutlass and silvers this nook;
But 'twill die in the dawning of Billy's last day.
A jewel-block they'll make of me tomorrow,
Pendant pearl from the yardarm-end
Like the eardrop I gave to Bristol Molly—
O, 'tis me, not the sentence they'll suspend.
Ay, ay, all is up; and I must up too,
Early in the morning, aloft from alow.
On an empty stomach now never it would do.
They'll give me a nibble—bit o'biscuit ere I go.
Sure, a messmate will reach me the last parting cup;
But, turning heads away from the hoist and the belay,[3]
Heaven knows who will have the running of me up!
No pipe to those halyards.—But aren't it all sham?
A blur's in my eyes; it is dreaming that I am.
A hatchet to my hawser? All adrift to go?
The drum roll to grog, and Billy never know?
But Donald he has promised to stand by the plank;
So I'll shake a friendly hand ere I sink.
But—no! It is dead then I'll be, come to think.
I remember Taff the Welshman when he sank.
And his cheek it was like the budding pink.
But me they'll lash in hammock, drop me deep.
Fathoms down, fathoms down, how I'll dream fast asleep.
I feel it stealing now. Sentry, are you there?
Just ease these darbies at the wrist,
And roll me over fair!
I am sleepy, and the oozy weeds about me twist.

1886?–91 1924, 1962

1. Handcuffs or chains (archaic).
2. Knees.
3. Securing of the hoisted body.

FRANCES ELLEN WATKINS HARPER
1825–1911

Frances Ellen Watkins Harper was the most popular African American poet of the nineteenth century. The author of nine volumes of poetry, four novels, several short stories, and numerous essays and letters, she was also a strikingly effective lecturer, known for her ability to extemporize on such topics as antislavery, temperance, and black uplift. Born in Baltimore, Maryland, then a slave state, to free black parents who died when she was young, Harper was raised by her uncle William J. Watkins, a prominent educator, minister, and abolitionist. She taught school in Ohio and Pennsylvania, writing poetry in her spare time (she may have published a volume, *Forest Leaves*, in 1845, but no copies survive). In the early 1850s she left teaching to lecture for the Maine Anti-Slavery Society and other antislavery organizations. She also worked with the African American abolitionist William Still (1821–1902) to help fugitive slaves escape to Canada through the linked networks of sympathizers, known as the Underground Railroad, who offered refuge to fugitives as they traveled north. During this time she began publishing poems in antislavery periodicals and newspapers, bringing out *Poems on Miscellaneous Subjects* in 1854. Prefaced by the abolitionist William Lloyd Garrison, the collection included several poetic responses to Stowe's *Uncle Tom's Cabin* (a novel Harper greatly admired), along with poems on temperance, biblical stories, and the black experience in slavery. During its first four years in print, *Poems* sold approximately twelve thousand copies; she revised and enlarged it in 1857, and it was reprinted twenty times thereafter during her lifetime.

In her best poems of the antebellum period, such as "Bury Me in a Free Land" (1858), Harper wrote about the slaves' suffering with lyrical intensity; but she also conveyed the sense of blacks' powerful resistance to slavery, along with her hopes for an egalitarian, multiracial America. In her intriguing short story "The Two Offers" (1859), one of the first published short stories by an African American, Harper presents female characters whose conversations and lives illustrate the possibility that women can achieve happiness without marriage. The story also spoke to Harper's concerns (shared by a number of women reformers) about the threat that intemperance posed to women. Perhaps in an effort to convey a feminist vision that was not limited by race, Harper, who published the story in an African American journal, kept the racial identities of the characters unclear.

With the exception of "Learning to Read," the selections printed here draw from Harper's work during the antebellum period, when she was known as Frances Ellen Watkins, but she remained an actively publishing author and lecturer until around 1900. Though primarily motivated by her literary and political passions, Harper also needed to keep up with her writing and lecturing out of financial necessity. In 1860 she married Fenton Harper, a widower with three children, and when he died in 1864, virtually bankrupt, she took on the responsibility of supporting Fenton Harper's children, along with their own child, Mary. Harper worked as a paid lecturer for several reform organizations, even as she continued to publish her poetry, including *Moses: A Story of the Nile* (1869), a long poem in blank verse; *Poems* (1871), which sold approximately 50,000 copies over several printings; and *Sketches of Southern Life* (1872), poems that have at their center the feisty former slave Aunt Chloe. That volume, more than any of her other collections published after the Civil War, was informed by Harper's optimism that blacks could rise in the culture and become fully integrated into national life. Between 1869 and 1882, Harper serialized three novels in the *Christian Recorder*, the journal of the African Methodist Episcopal Church—*Minnie's Sacrifice* (1869), *Sowing and Reaping* (1876–77), and *Trial and Triumph* (1888–89). Her best-known work, in addition to her 1854 and 1871 poetry collections, is the 1892 novel *Iola Leroy; or, Shadows Uplifted*, a historical novel tracing the efforts of the light-skinned mulatta Iola Leroy as she attempts to reunite members of her formerly enslaved family after the Civil War. Crucially, at a key point near the end of the novel, Iola rejects the marriage proposal of a white doctor, who wants her to pass as white, choosing to remain close to her family and devote herself to the uplift of her race. In her fiercely determined feminism and race consciousness, Iola Leroy exemplified her author's commitment to black community. After the publication of *Iola Leroy*, Harper published five additional volumes of poetry; she also remained politically active, continuing her work for the Women's Christian Temperance Union and helping to found the National Association of Colored Women in 1896. She died of heart disease in Philadelphia on February 22, 1911.

Eliza Harris[1]

Like a fawn from the arrow, startled and wild,
A woman swept by us, bearing a child;
In her eye was the night of a settled despair,
And her brow was o'ershaded with anguish and care.

She was nearing the river—in reaching the brink,
She heeded no danger, she paused not to think!
For she is a mother—her child is a slave—
And she'll give him his freedom, or find him a grave!

'Twas a vision to haunt us, that innocent face—
So pale in its aspect, so fair in its grace;
As the tramp of the horse and the bay of the hound,
With the fetters that gall, were trailing the ground!

She was nerved by despair, and strengthen'd by woe,
As she leap'd o'er the chasms that yawn'd from below;
Death howl'd in the tempest, and rav'd in the blast,
But she heard not the sound till the danger was past.

Oh! how shall I speak of my proud country's shame?
Of the stains on her glory, how give them their name?
How say that her banner in mockery waves—
Her "star-spangled banner"—o'er millions of slaves?

How say that the lawless may torture and chase
A woman whose crime is the hue of her face?
How the depths of the forest may echo around
With the shrieks of despair, and the bay of the hound?

1. The text is from *Poems on Miscellaneous Subjects* (Boston, 1854). Earlier versions appeared in December 1853 issues of *Frederick Douglass' Paper* and the *Liberator*. In chap. 7 of Harriet Beecher Stowe's *Uncle Tom's Cabin* (1852), the slave Eliza Harris escapes to the North with her son by crossing the icy Ohio River (see p. 818).

With her step on the ice, and her arm on her child,
The danger was fearful, the pathway was wild;
But, aided by Heaven, she gained a free shore,
Where the friends of humanity open'd their door.

So fragile and lovely, so fearfully pale,
Like a lily that bends to the breath of the gale,
Save the heave of her breast, and the sway of her hair,
You'd have thought her a statue of fear and despair.

In agony close to her bosom she press'd
The life of her heart, the child of her breast:—
Oh! love from its tenderness gathering might,
Had strengthen'd her soul for the dangers of flight.

But she's free!—yes, free from the land where the slave
From the hand of oppression must rest in the grave;
Where bondage and torture, where scourges and chains
Have plac'd on our banner indelible stains.

The bloodhounds have miss'd the scent of her way;
The hunter is rifled and foil'd of his prey;
Fierce jargon and cursing, with clanking of chains,
Make sounds of strange discord on Liberty's plains.

With the rapture of love and fullness of bliss,
She plac'd on his brow a mother's fond kiss:—
Oh! poverty, danger and death she can brave,
For the child of her love is no longer a slave!

1853, 1854

The Slave Mother[1]

Heard you that shriek? It rose
  So wildly on the air,
It seem'd as if a burden'd heart
  Was breaking in despair.

Saw you those hands so sadly clasped—
  The bowed and feeble head—
The shuddering of that fragile form—
  That look of grief and dread?

Saw you the sad, imploring eye?
  Its every glance was pain,
As if a storm of agony
  Were sweeping through the brain.

1. The text is from *Poems* (1854).

She is a mother pale with fear,
   Her boy clings to her side,
And in her kyrtle[2] vainly tries
   His trembling form to hide.

He is not hers, although she bore
   For him a mother's pains;
He is not hers, although her blood
   Is coursing through his veins!

He is not hers, for cruel hands
   May rudely tear apart
The only wreath of household love
   That binds her breaking heart.

His love has been a joyous light
   That o'er her pathway smiled,
A fountain gushing ever new,
   Amid life's desert wild.

His lightest word has been a tone
   Of music round her heart,
Their lives a streamlet blent in one—
   Oh, Father! must they part?

They tear him from her circling arms,
   Her last and fond embrace:—
Oh! never more may her sad eyes
   Gaze on his mournful face.

No marvel, then, these bitter shrieks
   Disturb the listening air;
She is a mother, and her heart
   Is breaking in despair.

1854

Ethiopia[1]

Yes! Ethiopia yet shall stretch
   Her bleeding hands abroad;
Her cry of agony shall reach
   The burning throne of God.[2]

The tyrant's yoke from off her neck,
   His fetters from her soul,

2. Loose gown.

1. The text is from *Poems* (1854). In the 19th century the term *Ethiopia* was often used to designate Africa and Africans or people of African descent.

2. Allusion to Psalms 68.31: "Princes shall come out of Egypt; Ethiopia shall soon stretch out her hands unto God."

The mighty hand of God shall break,
And spurn the base control.

Redeemed from dust and freed from chains,
Her sons shall lift their eyes;
From cloud-capt hills and verdant plains
Shall shouts of triumph rise.

Upon her dark, despairing brow,
Shall play a smile of peace;
For God shall bend unto her wo,
And bid her sorrows cease.

'Neath sheltering vines and stately palms
Shall laughing children play,
And aged sires with joyous psalms
Shall gladden every day.

Secure by night, and blest by day,
Shall pass her happy hours;
Nor human tigers hunt for prey
Within her peaceful bowers.

Then, Ethiopia! stretch, oh! stretch
Thy bleeding hands abroad;
Thy cry of agony shall reach
And find redress from God.

1854

The Tennessee Hero[1]

"He had heard his comrades plotting to obtain their liberty, and rather than betray them he received 750 lashes and died."

He stood before the savage throng,
The base and coward crew;
A tameless light flashed from his eye,
His heart beat firm and true.

He was the hero of his band,
The noblest of them all;
Though fetters galled his weary limbs,
His spirit spurned their thrall.

And towered, in its manly might,
Above the murderous crew.
Oh! liberty had nerved his heart,
And every pulse beat true.

1. The text is from *Poems on Miscellaneous Subjects* (Philadelphia, 1857).

"Now tell us," said the savage troop,
"And life thy gain shall be!
Who are the men that plotting, say—
'They must and will be free!'"

Oh, could you have seen the hero then,
As his lofty soul arose,
And his dauntless eyes defiance flashed
On his mean and craven foes!

"I know the men who would be free;
They are the heroes of your land;
But death and torture I defy,
Ere I betray that band.

"And what! oh, what is life to me,
Beneath your base control?
Nay ! do your worst. Ye have no chains
To bind my free-born soul."

They brought the hateful lash and scourge,
With murder in each eye.
But a solemn vow was on his lips—
He had resolved to die.

Yes, rather than betray his trust,
He'd meet a death of pain;
'T was sweeter far to meet it thus
Than wear a treason stain!

Like storms of wrath, of hate and pain,
The blows rained thick and fast;
But the monarch soul kept true
Till the gates of life were past.

And the martyr spirit fled
To the throne of God on high,
And showed his gaping wounds
Before the unslumbering eye.

1857

Bury Me in a Free Land[1]

You may make my grave wherever you will,
In a lowly vale or a lofty hill;
You may make it among earth's humblest graves,
But not in a land where men are slaves.

1. The text is from the November 20, 1858, issue of the *Anti-Slavery Bugle*, published in Salem, Ohio.

I could not sleep if around my grave
  I heard the steps of a trembling slave;
His shadow above my silent tomb
  Would make it a place of fearful gloom.

I could not rest if I heard the tread
  Of a coffle-gang to the shambles[2] led,
And the mother's shriek of wild despair
  Rise like a curse on the trembling air.

I could not rest if I heard the lash
  Drinking her blood at each fearful gash,
And I saw her babes torn from her breast
  Like trembling doves from their parent nest.

I'd shudder and start, if I heard the bay
  Of the bloodhounds seizing their human prey;
If I heard the captive plead in vain
  As they tightened afresh his galling[3] chain.

If I saw young girls, from their mothers' arms
  Bartered and sold for their youthful charms
My eye would flash with a mournful flame,
  My death paled cheek grow red with shame.

I would sleep, dear friends, where bloated might
  Can rob no man of his dearest right;
My rest shall be calm in any grave
  Where none calls his brother a slave.

I ask no monument proud and high
  To arrest the gaze of passers by;
All that my spirit yearning craves,
  Is—bury me not in the land of slaves.

1858

Learning to Read[1]

Very soon the Yankee teachers
  Came down and set up school;
But, oh! how the Rebs[2] did hate it,—
  It was agin' their rule.

Our masters always tried to hide
  Book learning from our eyes;

2. Slaughterhouse. "Coffle-gang": chained slaves.
3. Chafing.
1. The text is from *Sketches from Southern Life* (1872). This is one of six poems in the volume in the voice of the former slave Aunt Chloe.
2. Rebels; Southerners are here linked to the Rebel or Confederate forces that fought during the Civil War.

Knowledge did'nt agree with slavery—
'Twould make us all too wise.

But some of us would try to steal
A little from the book,
And put the words together,
And learn by hook or crook.

I remember Uncle Caldwell,
Who took pot liquor[3] fat
And greased the pages of his book,
And hid it in his hat.

And had his master ever seen
The leaves upon his head,
He'd have thought them greasy papers,
But nothing to be read.

And there was Mr. Turner's Ben,
Who heard the children spell,
And picked the words right up by heart,
And learned to read 'em well.

Well, the Northern folks kept sending
The Yankee teachers down;
And they stood right up and helped us,
Though Rebs did sneer and frown.

And, I longed to read my Bible,
For precious words it said;
But when I begun to learn it,
Folks just shook their heads,

And said there is no use trying,
Oh! Chloe, you're too late;
But as I was rising sixty,
I had no time to wait.

So I got a pair of glasses,
And straight to work I went,
And never stopped till I could read
The hymns and Testament.

Then I got a little cabin
A place to call my own—
And I felt as independent
As the queen upon her throne.

1872

3. The liquid left after cooking meat and vegetables together.

The Two Offers[1]

"What is the matter with you, Laura, this morning? I have been watching you this hour, and in that time you have commenced a half dozen letters and torn them all up. What matter of such grave moment is puzzling your dear little head, that you do not know how to decide?"

"Well, it is an important matter: I have two offers for marriage, and I do not know which to choose."

"I should accept neither, or to say the least, not at present."

"Why not?"

"Because I think a woman who is undecided between two offers, has not love enough for either to make a choice; and in that very hesitation, indecision, she has a reason to pause and seriously reflect, lest her marriage, instead of being an affinity of souls or a union of hearts, should only be a mere matter of bargain and sale, or an affair of convenience and selfish interest."

"But I consider them both very good offers, just such as many a girl would gladly receive. But to tell you the truth, I do not think that I regard either as a woman should the man she chooses for her husband. But then if I refuse, there is the risk of being an old maid, and that is not to be thought of."

"Well, suppose there is, is that the most dreadful fate that can befall a woman? Is there not more intense wretchedness in an ill-assorted marriage—more utter loneliness in a loveless home, than in the lot of the old maid who accepts her earthly mission as a gift from God, and strives to walk the path of life with earnest and unfaltering steps?"

"Oh! what a little preacher you are. I really believe that you were cut out for an old maid; that when nature formed you, she put in a double portion of intellect to make up for a deficiency of love; and yet you are kind and affectionate. But I do not think that you know anything of the grand, overmastering passion, or the deep necessity of woman's heart for loving."

"Do you think so?" resumed the first speaker; and bending over her work she quietly applied herself to the knitting that had lain neglected by her side, during this brief conversation; but as she did so, a shadow flitted over her pale and intellectual brow, a mist gathered in her eyes, and a slight quivering of the lips, revealed a depth of feeling to which her companion was a stranger.

But before I proceed with my story, let me give you a slight history of the speakers. They were cousins, who had met life under different auspices. Laura Lagrange, was the only daughter of rich and indulgent parents, who had spared no pains to make her an accomplished lady. Her cousin, Janette Alston, was the child of parents, rich only in goodness and affection. Her father had been unfortunate in business, and dying before he could retrieve his fortunes, left his business in an embarrassed state. His widow was unacquainted with his business affairs, and when the estate was settled, hungry creditors had brought their claims and the lawyers had received their fees, she found herself homeless and almost penniless, and she who had been sheltered in the warm clasp of loving arms, found them too powerless to shield her from the pitiless pelting storms of adversity. Year after year she struggled

1. The text is from the serialized first publication in the September and October 1859 issues of the *Anglo-African Magazine*.

with poverty and wrestled with want, till her toil-worn hands became too feeble to hold the shattered chords of existence, and her tear-dimmed eyes grew heavy with the slumber of death. Her daughter had watched over her with untiring devotion, had closed her eyes in death, and gone out into the busy, restless world, missing a precious tone from the voices of earth, a beloved step from the paths of life. Too self reliant to depend on the charity of relations, she endeavored to support herself by her own exertions, and she had succeeded. Her path for a while was marked with struggle and trial, but instead of uselessly repining, she met them bravely, and her life became not a thing of ease and indulgence, but of conquest, victory, and accomplishments. At the time when this conversation took place, the deep trials of her life had passed away. The achievements of her genius had won her a position in the literary world, where she shone as one of its bright particular stars. And with her fame came a competence of worldly means, which gave her leisure for improvement, and the riper development of her rare talents. And she, that pale intellectual woman, whose genius gave life and vivacity to the social circle, and whose presence threw a halo of beauty and grace around the charmed atmosphere in which she moved, had at one period of her life, known the mystic and solemn strength of an all-absorbing love. Years faded into the misty past, had seen the kindling of her eye, the quick flushing of her cheek, and the wild throbbing of her heart, at tones of a voice long since hushed to the stillness of death. Deeply, wildly, passionately, she had loved. Her whole life seemed like the pouring out of rich, warm and gushing affections. This love quickened her talents, inspired her genius, and threw over her life a tender and spiritual earnestness. And then came a fearful shock, a mournful waking from that "dream of beauty and delight." A shadow fell around her path; it came between her and the object of her heart's worship; first a few cold words, estrangement, and then a painful separation; the old story of woman's pride—digging the sepulchre of her happiness, and then a new-made grave, and her path over it to the spirit world; and thus faded out from that young heart her bright, brief and saddened dream of life. Faint and spirit-broken, she turned from the scenes associated with the memory of the loved and lost. She tried to break the chain of sad associations that bound her to the mournful past; and so, pressing back the bitter sobs from her almost breaking heart, like the dying dolphin, whose beauty is born of its death anguish,[2] her genius gathered strength from suffering and wonderous power and brilliancy from the agony she hid within the desolate chambers of her soul. Men hailed her as one of earth's strangely gifted children, and wreathed the garlands of fame for her brow, when it was throbbing with a wild and fearful unrest. They breathed her name with applause, when through the lonely halls of her stricken spirit, was an earnest cry for peace, a deep yearning for sympathy and heart-support.

But life, with its stern realities, met her; its solemn responsibilities confronted her, and turning, with an earnest and shattered spirit, to life's duties and trials, she found a calmness and strength that she had only imagined in her dreams of poetry and song. We will now pass over a period of ten years, and the cousins have met again. In that calm and lovely woman, in whose eyes is a depth of tenderness, tempering the flashes of her genius, whose

2. The ancient Greeks revered the dolphin and believed that it gave off beautiful colors at its death.

looks and tones are full of sympathy and love, we recognize the once smitten and stricken Janette Alston. The bloom of her girlhood had given way to a higher type of spiritual beauty, as if some unseen hand had been polishing and refining the temple in which her lovely spirit found its habitation; and this had been the fact. Her inner life had grown beautiful, and it was this that was constantly developing the outer. Never, in the early flush of womanhood, when an absorbing love had lit up her eyes and glowed in her life, had she appeared so interesting as when, with a countenance which seemed overshadowed with a spiritual light, she bent over the death-bed of a young woman, just lingering at the shadowy gates of the unseen land.

"Has he come?" faintly but eagerly exclaimed the dying woman. "Oh! how I have longed for his coming, and even in death he forgets me."

"Oh, do not say so, dear Laura, some accident may have detained him," said Janette to her cousin; for on that bed, from whence she will never rise, lies the once-beautiful and light-hearted Laura Lagrange, the brightness of whose eyes has long since been dimmed with tears, and whose voice had become like a harp whose every chord is tuned to sadness—whose faintest thrill and loudest vibrations are but the variations of agony. A heavy hand was laid upon her once warm and bounding heart, and a voice came whispering through her soul, that she must die. But, to her, the tidings was a message of deliverance—a voice, hushing her wild sorrows to the calmness of resignation and hope. Life had grown so weary upon her head—the future looked so hopeless—she had no wish to tread again the track where thorns had pierced her feet, and clouds overcast her sky; and she hailed the coming of death's angel as the footsteps of a welcome friend. And yet, earth had one object so very dear to her weary heart. It was her absent and recreant husband; for, since that conversation, she had accepted one of her offers, and become a wife. But, before she married, she learned that great lesson of human experience and woman's life, to love the man who bowed at her shrine, a willing worshipper. He had a pleasing address, raven hair, flashing eyes, a voice of thrilling sweetness, and lips of persuasive eloquence; and being well versed in the ways of the world, he won his way to her heart, and she became his bride, and he was proud of his prize. Vain and superficial in his character, he looked upon marriage not as a divine sacrament for the soul's development and human progression, but as the title-deed that gave him possession of the woman he thought he loved. But alas for her, the laxity of his principles had rendered him unworthy of the deep and undying devotion of a pure-hearted woman; but, for awhile, he hid from her his true character, and she blindly loved him, and for a short period was happy in the consciousness of being beloved; though sometimes a vague unrest would fill her soul, when, overflowing with a sense of the good, the beautiful, and the true, she would turn to him, but find no response to the deep yearnings of her soul—no appreciation of life's highest realities—its solemn grandeur and significant importance. Their souls never met, and soon she found a void in her bosom, that his earth-born love could not fill. He did not satisfy the wants of her mental and moral nature—between him and her there was no affinity of minds, no intercommunion of souls.

Talk as you will of woman's deep capacity for loving, of the strength of her affectional nature. I do not deny it; but will the mere possession of any human love, fully satisfy all the demands of her whole being? You may paint her in poetry or fiction, as a frail vine, clinging to her brother man for support, and dying when deprived of it; and all this may sound well enough to please the imaginations of school-girls, or love-lorn maidens. But woman—the true woman—if you would render her happy, it needs more than the mere development of her affectional nature. Her conscience should be enlightened, her faith in the true and right established, and scope given to her Heaven-endowed and God-given faculties. The true aim of female education should be, not a development of one or two, but all the faculties of the human soul, because no perfect womanhood is developed by imperfect culture. Intense love is often akin to intense suffering, and to trust the whole wealth of a woman's nature on the frail bark of human love, may often be like trusting a cargo of gold and precious gems, to a bark that has never battled with the storm, or buffetted the waves. Is it any wonder, then, that so many life-barks go down, paving the ocean of time with precious hearts and wasted hopes? that so many float around us, shattered and dismasted wrecks? that so many are stranded on the shoals of existence, mournful beacons and solemn warnings for the thoughtless, to whom marriage is a careless and hasty rushing together of the affections? Alas that an institution so fraught with good for humanity should be so perverted, and that state of life, which should be filled with happiness, become so replete with misery. And this was the fate of Laura Lagrange. For a brief period after her marriage her life seemed like a bright and beautiful dream, full of hope and radiant with joy. And then there came a change—he found other attractions that lay beyond the pale of home influences. The gambling saloon had power to win him from her side, he had lived in an element of unhealthy and unhallowed excitements, and the society of a loving wife, the pleasures of a well-regulated home, were enjoyments too tame for one who had vitiated his tastes by the pleasures of sin. There were charmed houses of vice, built upon dead men's loves, where, amid a flow of song, laughter, wine, and careless mirth, he would spend hour after hour, forgetting the cheek that was paling through his neglect, heedless of the tear-dimmed eyes, peering anxiously into the darkness, waiting, or watching his return.

The influence of old associations was upon him. In early life, home had been to him a place of ceilings and walls, not a true home, built upon goodness, love and truth. It was a place where velvet carpets hushed his tread, where images of loveliness and beauty invoked into being by painter's art and sculptor's skill, pleased the eye and gratified the taste, where magnificence surrounded his way and costly clothing adorned his person; but it was not the place for the true culture and right development of his soul. His father had been too much engrossed in making money, and his mother in spending it, in striving to maintain a fashionable position in society, and shining in the eyes of the world, to give the proper direction to the character of their wayward and impulsive son. His mother put beautiful robes upon his body, but left ugly scars upon his soul; she pampered his appetite, but starved his spirit. Every mother should be a true artist, who knows how to weave into her child's life images of grace and beauty, the true poet capable of writing on the soul of childhood the harmony of love and truth, and teaching it how to produce the grandest of all poems—the poetry of a true and noble life. But in his home, a love for the good, the true and right, had been sacrificed at the shrine of frivolity and fashion. That parental authority which should have been preserved as a string of precious pearls, unbroken and unscattered, was simply the administration of chance. At one time obedience was enforced by authority, at another time by flattery and promises, and just as often it was not enforced at all. His early associations were formed as chance directed, and from his want of home-training, his character received a bias, his life a shade, which ran through every avenue of his existence, and darkened all his future hours. Oh, if we would trace the history of all the crimes that have o'ershadowed this sin-shrouded and sorrow-darkened world of ours, how many might be seen arising from the wrong home influences, or the weakening of the home ties. Home should always be the best school for the affections, the birthplace of high resolves, and the altar upon which lofty aspirations are kindled, from whence the soul may go forth strengthened, to act its part aright in the great drama of life, with conscience enlightened, affections cultivated, and reason and judgment dominant. But alas for the young wife. Her husband had not been blessed with such a home. When he entered the arena of life, the voices from home did not linger around his path as angels of guidance about his steps; they were not like so many messages to invite him to deeds of high and holy worth. The memory of no sainted mother arose between him and deeds of darkness; the earnest prayers of no father arrested him in his downward course: and before a year of his married life had waned, his young wife had learned to wait and mourn his frequent and uncalled-for absence. More than once had she seen him come home from his midnight haunts, the bright intelligence of his eye displaced by the drunkard's stare, and his manly gait changed to the inebriate's stagger; and she was beginning to know the bitter agony that is compressed in the mournful words, a drunkard's wife. And then there came a bright but brief episode in her experience; the angel of life gave to her existence a deeper meaning and loftier significance: she sheltered in the warm clasp of her loving arms, a dear babe, a precious child, whose love filled every chamber of her heart, and felt the fount of maternal love gushing so new within her soul. That child was hers. How overshadowing was the love with which she bent over its helplessness, how much it helped to fill the void and chasms in her soul. How many lonely hours were beguiled by its winsome ways, its answering smiles and fond caresses. How exquisite and solemn was the feeling that thrilled her heart when she clasped the tiny hands together and taught her dear child to call God "Our Father."

What a blessing was that child. The father paused in his headlong career, awed by the strange beauty and precocious intellect of his child; and the mother's life had a better expression through her ministrations of love. And then there came hours of bitter anguish, shading the sunlight of her home and hushing the music of her heart. The angel of death bent over the couch of her child and beaconed it away. Closer and closer the mother strained her child to her wildly heaving breast, and struggled with the heavy hand that lay upon its heart. Love and agony contended with death, and the language of the mother's heart was,

"Oh, Death, away! that innocent is mine;
  I cannot spare him from my arms
To lay him, Death, in thine.

I am a mother, Death; I gave that darling birth
I could not bear his lifeless limbs
Should moulder in the earth."

But death was stronger than love and mightier than agony and won the child for the land of crystal founts and deathless flowers, and the poor, stricken mother sat down beneath the shadow of her mighty grief, feeling as if a great light had gone out from her soul, and that the sunshine had suddenly faded around her path. She turned in her deep anguish to the father of her child, the loved and cherished dead. For awhile his words were kind and tender, his heart seemed subdued, and his tenderness fell upon her worn and weary heart like rain on perishing flowers, or cooling waters to lips all parched with thirst and scorched with fever; but the change was evanescent, the influence of unhallowed associations and evil habits had vitiated and poisoned the springs of his existence. They had bound him in their meshes, and he lacked the moral strength to break his fetters, and stand erect in all the strength and dignity of a true manhood, making life's highest excellence his ideal, and striving to gain it.

And yet moments of deep contrition would sweep over him, when he would resolve to abandon the wine-cup forever, when he was ready to forswear the handling of another card, and he would try to break away from the associations that he felt were working his ruin; but when the hour of temptation came his strength was weakness, his earnest purposes were cobwebs, his well-meant resolutions ropes of sand, and thus passed year after year of the married life of Laura Lagrange. She tried to hide her agony from the public gaze, to smile when her heart was almost breaking. But year after year her voice grew fainter and sadder, her once light and bounding step grew slower and faltering. Year after year she wrestled with agony, and strove with despair, till the quick eyes of her brother read, in the paling of her cheek and the dimning eye, the secret anguish of her worn and weary spirit. On that wan, sad face, he saw the death-tokens, and he knew the dark wing of the mystic angel swept coldly around her path. "Laura," said her brother to her one day, "you are not well, and I think you need our mother's tender care and nursing. You are daily losing strength, and if you will go I will accompany you." At first, she hesitated, she shrank almost instinctively from presenting that pale sad face to the loved ones at home. That face was such a tell-tale; it told of heart-sickness, of hope deferred, and the mournful story of unrequited love. But then a deep yearning for home sympathy woke within her a passionate longing for love's kind words, for tenderness and heart-support, and she resolved to seek the home of her childhood, and lay her weary head upon her mother's bosom, to be folded again in her loving arms, to lay that poor, bruised and aching heart where it might beat and throb closely to the loved ones at home. A kind welcome awaited her. All that love and tenderness could devise was done to bring the bloom to her cheek and the light to her eye; but it was all in vain; her's was a disease that no medicine could cure, no earthly balm would heal. It was a slow wasting of the vital forces, the sickness of the soul. The unkindness and neglect of her husband, lay like a leaden weight upon her heart, and slowly oozed away its life-drops. And where was he that had won her love, and then cast it aside as a useless thing, who rifled her heart of its wealth and spread bitter ashes upon its broken altars? He was lingering away from her when the death-damps were gathering on her brow, when his name was trembling on her lips! lingering away! when she was watching his coming, though the death films were gathering before her eyes, and earthly things were fading from her vision. "I think I hear him now," said the dying woman, "surely that is his step;" but the sound died away in the distance. Again she started from an uneasy slumber, "that is his voice! I am so glad he has come." Tears gathered in the eyes of the sad watchers by that dying bed, for they knew that she was deceived. He had not returned. For her sake they wished his coming. Slowly the hours waned away, and then came the sad, soul-sickening thought that she was forgotten, forgotten in the last hour of human need, forgotten when the spirit, about to be dissolved, paused for the last time on the threshold of existence, a weary watcher at the gates of death. "He has forgotten me," again she faintly murmured, and the last tears she would ever shed on earth sprung to her mournful eyes, and clasping her hands together in silent anguish, a few broken sentences issued from her pale and quivering lips. They were prayers for strength and earnest pleading for him who had desolated her young life, by turning its sunshine to shadows, its smiles to tears. "He has forgotten me," she murmured again, "but I can bear it, the bitterness of death is passed, and soon I hope to exchange the shadows of death for the brightness of eternity, the rugged paths of life for the golden streets of glory, and the care and turmoils of earth for the peace and rest of heaven." Her voice grew fainter and fainter, they saw the shadows that never deceive flit over her pale and faded face, and knew that the death angel waited to soothe their weary one to rest, to calm the throbbing of her bosom and cool the fever of her brain. And amid the silent hush of their grief the freed spirit, refined through suffering, and brought into divine harmony through the spirit of the living Christ, passed over the dark waters of death as on a bridge of light, over whose radiant arches hovering angels bent. They parted the dark locks from her marble brow, closed the waxen lids over the once bright and laughing eye, and left her to the dreamless slumber of the grave. Her cousin turned from that death-bed a sadder and wiser woman. She resolved more earnestly than ever to make the world better by her example, gladder by her presence, and to kindle the fires of her genius on the altars of universal love and truth. She had a higher and better object in all her writings than the mere acquisition of gold, or acquirement of fame. She felt that she had a high and holy mission on the battle-field of existence, that life was not given her to be frittered away in nonsense, or wasted away in trifling pursuits. She would willingly espouse an unpopular cause but not an unrighteous one. In her the down-trodden slave found an earnest advocate; the flying fugitive remembered her kindness as he stepped cautiously through our Republic, to gain his freedom in a monarchial land,[3] having broken the chains on which the rust of centuries had gathered. Little children learned to name her with affection, the poor called her blessed, as she broke her bread to the pale lips of hunger. Her life was like a beautiful story, only it was clothed with the dignity of reality and invested with the sublimity of truth. True, she was an old maid, no husband brightened her life with his love, or shaded it with his neglect. No children nestling lovingly in her arms called her mother. No one appended Mrs. to her name; she was indeed an old maid,

3. Canada.

not vainly striving to keep up an appearance of girlishness, when departed was written on her youth. Not vainly pining at her loneliness and isolation: the world was full of warm, loving hearts, and her own beat in unison with them. Neither was she always sentimentally sighing for something to love, objects of affection were all around her, and the world was not so wealthy in love that it had no use for her's; in blessing others she made a life and benediction, and as old age descended peacefully and gently upon her, she had learned one of life's most precious lessons, that true happiness consists not so much in the fruition of our wishes as in the regulation of desires and the full development and right culture of our whole natures.

1859

EMILY DICKINSON
1830–1886

Emily Dickinson is recognized as one of the greatest American poets, a poet who continues to exert an enormous influence on the way writers think about the possibilities of poetic craft and vocation. Little known in her own lifetime, she was first publicized in almost mythic terms as a reclusive, eccentric, death-obsessed spinster who wrote in fits and starts as the spirit moved her—the image of the woman poet at her oddest. As with all myths, this one has some truth to it, but the reality is more interesting and complicated. Though she lived in her parents' homes for all but a year of her life, she was acutely aware of current events and drew on them for some of her poetry. Her dazzlingly complex lyrics—compressed statements abounding in startling imagery and marked by an extraordinary vocabulary—explore a wide range of subjects: psychic pain and joy, the relationship of self to nature, the intensely spiritual, and the intensely ordinary. Her poems about death confront its grim reality with honesty, humor, curiosity, and above all a refusal to be comforted. In her poems about religion, she expressed piety and hostility, and she was fully capable of moving within the same poem from religious consolation to a rejection of doctrinal piety and a querying of God's plans for the universe. Her many love poems seem to have emerged in part from close relationships with at least one woman and several men. It is sometimes possible to extract autobiography from her poems, but she was not a confessional poet; rather, she used personae—first-person speakers—to dramatize the various situations, moods, and perspectives she explored in her lyrics. Though each of her poems is individually short, when collected in one volume her nearly eighteen hundred surviving poems (she probably wrote hundreds more that were lost) have the feel of an epic produced by a person who devoted much of her life to her art.

Emily Elizabeth Dickinson was born on December 10, 1830, in Amherst, Massachusetts, the second child of Emily Norcross Dickinson and Edward Dickinson. Economically, politically, and intellectually, the Dickinsons were among Amherst's most prominent families. Edward Dickinson, a lawyer, served as a state representative and a state senator. He helped found Amherst College as a Calvinist alternative to the more liberal Harvard and Yale, and was its treasurer for thirty-six years. During his term in the U.S. House of Representatives (1853–54), Emily visited him in Washington,

D.C., and stayed briefly in Philadelphia on her way home, but travel of any kind was unusual for her. She lived most of her life in the spacious Dickinson family house in Amherst called the Homestead. Among her closest friends and lifelong allies were her brother, Austin, a year and a half older than she, and her younger sister, Lavinia. In 1856, when her brother married Emily's close friend Susan Gilbert, the couple moved into what was called the Evergreens, a house next door to the Homestead, built for the newlyweds by Edward Dickinson. Neither Emily nor Lavinia married. The two women stayed with their parents, as was typical of unmarried middle- and upper-class women of the time. New England in this period had many more women than men in these groups, owing to the male population exodus during the California Gold Rush years (1849 and after) and the carnage of the Civil War. For Dickinson, home was a place of "Infinite power."

Dickinson attended Amherst Academy from 1840 through 1846, and then boarded at Mount Holyoke Female Seminary—located in South Hadley, some ten miles from Amherst—for less than a year, never completing the three-year course of study. The school, presided over by the devoutly Calvinist Mary Lyon, was especially interested in the students' religious development, and hoped that those needing to support themselves or their families would become missionaries. Students were regularly queried as to whether they "professed faith," had "hope," or were resigned to "no hope"; Dickinson remained adamantly among the small group of "no hopes." Arguably, her assertion of no hope was a matter of defiance, a refusal to capitulate to the demands of orthodoxy. A year after leaving Mount Holyoke, Dickinson, in a letter to a friend, described her failure to convert with darkly comic glee: "*I* am one of the lingering *bad* ones," she said. But she went on to assert that it was her very "failure" to conform to the conventional expectations of her evangelical culture that helped liberate her to think on her own—to "pause," as she put it, "and ponder, and ponder."

Once back at home, Dickinson embarked on a lifelong course of reading. Her deepest literary debts were to the Bible and classic English authors, such as Shakespeare and Milton. Through the national magazines the family subscribed to and books ordered from Boston, she encountered the full range of the English and American literature of her time, including among Americans Longfellow, Holmes, Lowell, Hawthorne, and Emerson. She read the novels of Charles Dickens as they appeared and knew the poems of Robert Browning and the poet laureate Tennyson. But the English contemporaries who mattered most to her were the Brontë sisters, George Eliot, and above all, as an example of a successful contemporary woman poet, Elizabeth Barrett Browning. Poem 627, reprinted here, suggests that Browning may have helped awaken Dickinson to her vocation when she was still "a somber Girl."

No one has persuasively traced the precise stages of Dickinson's artistic growth from this supposedly "somber Girl" to the young woman who, within a few years of her return from Mount Holyoke, began writing a new kind of poetry, with its distinctive voice, style, and transformation of traditional form. She found a paradoxical poetic freedom within the confines of the meter of the "fourteener"—seven-beat lines usually broken into stanzas alternating four and three beats—familiar to her from earliest childhood. This is the form of nursery rhymes, ballads, church hymns, and some classic English poetry—strongly rhythmical, easy to memorize and recite. But Dickinson veered sharply from this form's expectations. If Walt Whitman at this time was heeding Emerson's call for a "metre-making argument" by turning to an open form—as though rules did not exist—Dickinson made use of this and other familiar forms only to break their rules. She used dashes and syntactical fragments to convey her pursuit of a truth that could best be communicated indirectly; these fragments dispensed with prosy verbiage and went directly to the core. Her use of enjambment (the syntactical technique of running past the conventional stopping place of a line or a stanza break) forced her reader to learn where to pause to collect the sense before reading on, often creating dizzying ambiguities. She multiplied aural possibilities by making use of what later critics termed "off" or "slant" rhymes that, as with her metrical and syntactical experimentations, contributed to the expressive power of her poetry. In short, poetic forms thought to be simple, predictable, and safe were altered irrevocably by Dickinson's language experiments with the lyric. Along with its opposite, free verse, the compressed lyric flaunting its refusal to conform became a hallmark of modernist poetry in the twentieth century.

Writing about religion, science, music, nature, books, and contemporary events both national and local, Dickinson often presented her poetic ideas as terse, striking definitions or propositions, or dramatic narrative scenes, in a highly abstracted moment, or setting, often at the boundaries between life and death. The result was a poetry that, as is typical of the lyric tradition, focused on the speaker's response to a situation rather than the details of the situation itself. Her "nature" poems offer precise observations that are often as much about psychological and spiritual matters as about the specifics of nature. The sight of a familiar bird—the robin—in the poem beginning "A bird came down the walk" leads to a statement about nature's strangeness rather than the expected statement about friendly animals. Whitman generally seems intoxicated by his ability to appropriate nature for his own purposes; Dickinson's nature is much more resistant to human schemes, and the poet's experiences of nature range from a sense of its hostility to an ability to become an "Inebriate of Air" and "Debauchee of Dew." Openly expressive of sexual and romantic longings, her personae reject conventional gender roles. In one of her most famous poems, for instance, she imagines herself as a "Loaded Gun" with "the power to kill."

Dickinson's private letters, in particular three drafts of letters to an unidentified "Master," and dozens of love poems have convinced biographers that she fell in love a number of times; candidates include Benjamin Newton, a law clerk in her father's office; one or more married men; and, Susan Gilbert Dickinson, the friend who became her sister-in-law. The exact nature of any of these relationships is hard to determine, in part because Dickinson's letters and poems could just as easily be taken as poetic meditations on desire as writings directed to specific people. On the evidence of the approximately five hundred letters that Dickinson wrote Susan, many of which contained drafts or copies of her latest poems, that relationship melded love, friendship, intellectual exchange, and art. (See their letters on a Dickinson poem on p. 1700.) One of the men she was involved with was Samuel Bowles, editor of the Springfield *Republican*, whom Dickinson described (in a letter to Bowles himself) as having "the most triumphant face out of paradise"; another was the Reverend Charles Wadsworth, whom she met in Philadelphia in 1855 and who visited her in Amherst in 1860. Evidence suggests that she was upset by his decision to move to San Francisco in 1862, but none of her letters to Wadsworth survive.

Knowing her powers as a poet, Dickinson wanted to be published, but only around a dozen poems appeared during her lifetime. She sent many poems to Bowles, perhaps hoping he would publish them in the *Republican*. Although he did publish a few, he also edited them into more conventional shape. She also sent poems to editor Josiah Holland at *Scribner's*, who chose not to publish her. She sent four poems to Thomas Wentworth Higginson, a contributing editor at the *Atlantic Monthly*, after he printed "Letter to a Young Contributor" in the April 1862 issue. Her cover letter of April 15, 1862, asked him, "Are you too deeply occupied to say if my Verse is alive?" (See two Dickinson letters to Higginson on pp. 1703–04.) Higginson, like other editors, saw her formal innovations as imperfections. But he remained intrigued by Dickinson and in 1869 invited her to visit him in Boston. When she refused, he visited her in 1870. He would eventually become one of the editors of her posthumously published poetry.

But if Dickinson sought publication, she also regarded it as "the Auction / Of the Mind of Man," as she put it in poem 788; at the very least, she was unwilling to submit to the changes, which she called "surgery," imposed on her poems by editors. Some critics have argued that Dickinson's letters constituted a form of publication, for Dickinson included poems in many of her letters. Even more intriguing, beginning around 1858 Dickinson began to record her poems on white, unlined paper, in some cases marking moments of textual revision, and then folded and stacked the sheets and sewed groups of them together in what are called fascicles. She created thirty such fascicles, ranging in length from sixteen to twenty-four pages; and there is considerable evidence that she worked diligently at the groupings, thinking about chronology, subject matter, and specific thematic orderings within each. These fascicles were left for others to discover after her death, neatly stacked in a drawer. It can be speculated that Dickinson, realizing that her unconventional poetry would not be published in her own lifetime as written, became a sort of self-publisher. Critics remain uncertain, however, about just how self-conscious her arrangements were and argue over what is lost and gained by considering individual poems in the context of their fascicle placement. There is also debate about whether the posthumous publication of Dickinson's manuscript poetry violates the visual look of the poems—their inconsistent dashes and even some of the designs that Dickinson added to particular poems. The selections printed here include a photographic reproduction of poem 269, which can be compared to the now-standard printed version, also included here.

Dickinson's final decades were marked by health problems and a succession of losses. Beginning in the early 1860s she suffered from eye pain. She consulted with an ophthalmologist in Boston in 1864 and remained concerned about losing her vision. In 1874 her father died in a Boston hotel room after taking an injection of morphine for his pain, and one year later her mother had a stroke and would remain bedridden until her death in 1882. Her beloved eight-year-old nephew, Gilbert, died of typhoid fever in 1883, next door at the Evergreens; and in 1885, her close friend from childhood, Helen Hunt Jackson, who had asked to be Dickinson's literary executor, died suddenly in San Francisco. Dickinson's seclusion late in life may have been a response to her grief at these losses or a concern for her own health, but ultimately a focus on the supposed eccentricity of her desire for privacy draws attention away from the huge number of poems she wrote—she may well have secluded herself so that she could follow her vocation. Emily Dickinson died on May 15, 1886, perhaps from a kidney disorder called "Bright's Disease," the official diagnosis, but just as likely from hypertension.

In 1881 the astronomer David Todd, with his young wife, Mabel Loomis Todd, arrived in Amherst to direct the Amherst College Observatory. The next year, Austin Dickinson and Mabel Todd began an affair that lasted until Austin's death in 1895. Despite this turn of events, Mabel Todd and Emily Dickinson established a friendship without actually meeting (Todd saw Dickinson once, in her coffin), and Todd decided that the poet was "in many respects a genius." Soon after Dickinson's death, Mabel Todd (at Emily's sister Lavinia's invitation) painstakingly transcribed many of her poems. The subsequent preservation and publication of her poetry and letters were initiated and carried forth by Todd. She persuaded Higginson to help her see a posthumous collection of poems into print in 1890 and a second volume of poems in 1891; she went on to publish a collection of Dickinson's letters in 1894 and a third volume of poems in 1896. In the 1890s some critics reacted patronizingly toward what they saw as verse that violated the laws of meter, and even Todd and Higginson edited some of the poems to make them more conventional. The three volumes were popular, going through more than ten printings and selling over ten thousand copies. During the 1890s, Susan Dickinson and her daughter, Martha Dickinson Bianchi, also published a few of Dickinson's poems in journals such as *The Century*. By 1900 or so, however, Dickinson's work had fallen out of favor, and had Martha Dickinson Bianchi not resumed publication of her aunt's poetry in 1914 (she published eight volumes of Dickinson's work between 1914 and 1937), Dickinson's writings might never have achieved the audience they have today. Taken together, the editorial labors of Todd, Higginson, Susan Dickinson, and Bianchi set in motion the critical and textual work that would help establish Dickinson as one of the great American poets. They also made her poetry available to the American modernists, poets such as

Hart Crane and Marianne Moore; Dickinson and Whitman are the nineteenth-century poets who exerted the greatest influence on American poetry to come.

The texts of the poems, and the numbering, are from R.W. Franklin's one-volume edition, *The Poems of Emily Dickinson: Reading Edition* (1999), which draws on his three-volume variorum, *The Poems of Emily Dickinson* (1998). Bracketed numbers refer to the numbering of Thomas Johnson's *The Poems of Emily Dickinson* (1955), for many years the standard edition. The dating of Dickinson's poetry remains uncertain, though Franklin is more accurate than Johnson. The date following each poem corresponds to Franklin's estimate of Dickinson's first finished draft; if the poem was published in Dickinson's lifetime, that date is supplied as well.

39

[49]

I never lost as much but twice -
And that was in the sod.
Twice have I stood a beggar
Before the door of God!

Angels - twice descending
Reimbursed my store -
Burglar! Banker - Father!
I am poor once more!

1858

112[1]

[67]

Success is counted sweetest
By those who ne'er succeed.
To comprehend a nectar
Requires sorest need.

Not one of all the purple Host
Who took the Flag[2] today
Can tell the definition
So clear of Victory

As he defeated - dying -
On whose forbidden ear
The distant strains of triumph
Burst agonized and clear!

1859, 1864

1. Dickinson published a version of this poem in the *Brooklyn Daily Union*, April 27, 1864, and it was republished in *A Masque of Poets* (1878), edited by her friend Helen Hunt Jackson. When it was printed in *Masque*, most reviewers thought it was by Emerson.
2. Triumphed.

122[1]

[*130*]

These are the days when Birds come back -
A very few - a Bird or two -
To take a backward look.

These are the days when skies resume
The old - old sophistries[2] of June -
A blue and gold mistake.

Oh fraud that cannot cheat the Bee.
Almost thy plausibility
Induces my belief,

Till ranks of seeds their witness bear -
And softly thro' the altered air
Hurries a timid leaf.

Oh sacrament of summer days,
Oh Last Communion[3] in the Haze -
Permit a child to join -

Thy sacred emblems to partake -
Thy consecrated bread to take
And thine immortal wine!

1859, 1864

123

[*131*]

Besides the Autumn poets sing
A few prosaic days
A little this side of the snow
And that side of the Haze -

A few incisive mornings -
A few Ascetic eves -
Gone - Mr Bryant's "Golden Rod" -
And Mr Thomson's "sheaves."[1]

1. Dickinson published a version of this poem in the *Drum Beat*, March 11, 1864.
2. Deceptively subtle reasonings.
3. The end of summer is compared to the death of Christ commemorated by the Christian sacrament of Communion.
1. English poet James Thomson (1700–1748) published *The Seasons* (1730, 1748) in four parts, the last of which was "Autumn." In "Summer," he describes farmers using sheaves of hay for protection against storms. Dickinson also alludes to William Cullen Bryant's "The Death of the Flowers" (1832).

Still, is the bustle in the Brook -
Sealed are the spicy valves -
Mesmeric fingers[2] softly touch
The eyes of many Elves -

Perhaps a squirrel may remain -
My sentiments to share -
Grant me, Oh Lord, a sunny mind -
Thy windy will to bear!

1859

124[1]

[*216*]

Safe in their Alabaster[2] Chambers -
Untouched by Morning -
And untouched by noon -
Sleep the meek members of the Resurrection,
Rafter of Satin and Roof of Stone -

Grand go the Years,
In the Crescent above them -
Worlds scoop their Arcs -
And Firmaments - row -
Diadems - drop -
And Doges[3] - surrender -
Soundless as Dots,
On a Disc of Snow.[4]

1859, 1862

146

[*148*]

All overgrown by cunning moss,
All interspersed with weed,
The little cage of "Currer Bell"[1]
In quiet "Haworth"[2] laid.

This Bird - observing others
When frosts too sharp became

2. Mesmerists (or hypnotists) of the time put their fingers on a person's eyelids to induce sleep.
1. Dickinson published a version of this poem in the *Springfield Daily Republican*, March 1, 1862.
2. Translucent, white chalky material.
3. Chief magistrates in the republics of Venice and Genoa from the 11th through the 16th centuries.
4. For Dickinson's other versions of this poem, see pp. 1700–03.
1. Pseudonym of English writer Charlotte Brontë (1816–1855).
2. Brontë's Yorkshire parsonage home.

Retire to other latitudes -
Quietly did the same -

But differed in returning -
Since Yorkshire hills are green -
Yet not in all the nests I meet -
Can Nightingale be seen -

1860

194

[*1072*]

Title divine, is mine.
The Wife without the Sign -
Acute Degree conferred on me -
Empress of Calvary[1] -
Royal, all but the Crown -
Betrothed, without the Swoon
God gives us Women -
When You hold Garnet to Garnet -
Gold - to Gold -
Born - Bridalled - Shrouded -
In a Day -
Tri Victory -
"My Husband" - Women say
Stroking the Melody -
Is this the way -

1861

202

[*185*]

"Faith" is a fine invention
For Gentlemen who *see*!
But Microscopes are prudent
In an Emergency!

1861

1. The hill outside of Jerusalem where Jesus was crucified (Luke 23.33).

207

[*214*]

I taste a liquor never brewed -
From Tankards scooped in Pearl -
Not all the Frankfort Berries
Yield such an Alcohol!

Inebriate of air - am I -
And Debauchee of Dew -
Reeling - thro' endless summer days -
From inns of molten Blue -

When "Landlords" turn the drunken Bee
Out of the Foxglove's door -
When Butterflies - renounce their "drams" -
I shall but drink the more!

Till Seraphs[1] swing their snowy Hats -
And Saints - to windows run -
To see the little Tippler
Leaning against the - Sun!

1861

225

[*199*]

I'm "wife" - I've finished that -
That other state -
I'm Czar - I'm "Woman" now -
It's safer so -

How odd the Girl's life looks
Behind this soft Eclipse -
I think that Earth feels so
To folks in Heaven - now -

This being comfort - then
That other kind - was pain -
But Why compare?
I'm "Wife"! Stop there!

1861

1. Angels.

236

[324]

Some keep the Sabbath going to Church -
I keep it, staying at Home -
With a Bobolink for a Chorister -
And an Orchard, for a Dome -

Some keep the Sabbath in Surplice[1]
I, just wear my Wings -
And instead of tolling the Bell, for Church,
Our little Sexton[2] - sings.

God preaches, a noted Clergyman -
And the sermon is never long,
So instead of getting to Heaven, at last -
I'm going, all along.

1861

256

[285]

The Robin's my Criterion for Tune -
Because I grow - where Robins do -
But, were I Cuckoo born -
I'd swear by him -
The ode familiar - rules the Noon -
The Buttercup's, my whim for Bloom -
Because, we're Orchard sprung -
But, were I Britain born,
I'd Daisies spurn -

None but the Nut - October fit -
Because - through dropping it,
The Seasons flit - I'm taught -
Without the Snow's Tableau
Winter, were lie - to me -
Because I see - New Englandly -
The Queen, discerns like me -
Provincially -

1861

1. Open-sleeved ceremonial robe worn by clergymen.

2. Church custodian.

259

[287]

A Clock stopped -
Not the Mantel's -
Geneva's[1] farthest skill
Cant put the puppet bowing -
That just now dangled still -

An awe came on the Trinket!
The Figures hunched - with pain -
Then quivered out of Decimals -
Into Degreeless noon -

It will not stir for Doctor's -
This Pendulum of snow -
The Shopman importunes it -
While cool - concernless No -

Nods from the Gilded pointers -
Nods from the Seconds slim -
Decades of Arrogance between
The Dial life -
And Him -

1861

260

[288]

I'm Nobody! Who are you?
Are you - Nobody - too?
Then there's a pair of us!
Dont tell! they'd advertise - you know!

How dreary - to be - Somebody!
How public - like a Frog -
To tell one's name - the livelong June -
To an admiring Bog!

1861

1. A city in Switzerland famous for its clocks.

269

[249]

Wild nights - Wild nights!
Were I with thee
Wild nights should be
Our luxury!

Futile - the winds -
To a Heart in port -
Done with the Compass -
Done with the Chart!

Rowing in Eden -
Ah - the Sea!
Might I but moor - tonight -
In thee!

1861

279

[664]

Of all the Souls that stand create -
I have Elected - One -
When Sense from Spirit - files away -
And Subterfuge - is done -
When that which is - and that which was -
Apart - intrinsic - stand -
And this brief Drama in the flesh -
Is shifted - like a Sand -
When Figures show their royal Front -
And Mists - are carved away,
Behold the Atom - I preferred -
To all the lists[1] of Clay!

1862

1. Arts, cunning (archaic).

Wild Nights - Wild Nights!
Were I with Thee
Wild Nights should be
Our Luxury!

Futile - the winds -
To a Heart in port -
Done with the Compass -
Done with the Chart!

Rowing in Eden -
Ah! the Sea!
Might I but moor -
Tonight -
In Thee!

Poem 269 [249] of Fascicle 11, from vol. 1 of *The Manuscript Books of Emily Dickinson* (1981), ed. R. W. Franklin, reproduced with the permission of Harvard University Press. Dickinson's handwriting, which changed over the years, can be dated by comparison with her letters.

320

[258]

There's a certain Slant of light,
Winter Afternoons -
That oppresses, like the Heft
Of Cathedral Tunes -

Heavenly Hurt, it gives us -
We can find no scar,
But internal difference -
Where the Meanings, are -

None may teach it - Any -
'Tis the Seal Despair -
An imperial affliction
Sent us of the Air -

When it comes, the Landscape listens -
Shadows - hold their breath -
When it goes, 'tis like the Distance
On the look of Death -

1862

339

[*241*]

I like a look of Agony,
Because I know it's true -
Men do not sham Convulsion,
Nor simulate, a Throe -

The eyes glaze once - and that is Death -
Impossible to feign
The Beads opon the Forehead
By homely Anguish strung.

1862

340

[280]

I felt a Funeral, in my Brain,
And Mourners to and fro
Kept treading - treading - till it seemed
That Sense was breaking through -

And when they all were seated,
A Service, like a Drum -
Kept beating - beating - till I thought
My mind was going numb -

And then I heard them lift a Box
And creak across my Soul
With those same Boots of Lead, again,
Then Space - began to toll,

As all the Heavens were a Bell,
And Being, but an Ear,
And I, and Silence, some strange Race
Wrecked, solitary, here -

And then a Plank in Reason, broke,
And I dropped down, and down -
And hit a World, at every plunge,
And Finished knowing - then -

1862

347

[348]

I dreaded that first Robin, so,
But He is mastered, now,
I'm some accustomed to Him grown,
He hurts a little, though -

I thought if I could only live
Till that first Shout got by -
Not all Pianos in the Woods
Had power to mangle me -

I dared not meet the Daffodils -
For fear their Yellow Gown
Would pierce me with a fashion
So foreign to my own -

I wished the Grass would hurry -
So when 'twas time to see -
He'd be too tall, the tallest one
Could stretch to look at me -

I could not bear the Bees should come,
I wished they'd stay away
In those dim countries where they go,
What word had they, for me?

They're here, though; not a creature failed -
No Blossom stayed away
In gentle deference to me -
The Queen of Calvary[1] -

Each one salutes me, as he goes,
And I, my childish Plumes,
Lift, in bereaved acknowledgement
Of their unthinking Drums -

1862

348

[505]

I would not paint - a picture -
I'd rather be the One
It's bright impossibility
To dwell - delicious - on -
And wonder how the fingers feel
Whose rare - celestial - stir -
Evokes so sweet a torment -
Such sumptuous - Despair -

I would not talk, like Cornets -
I'd rather be the One
Raised softly to the Ceilings -
And out, and easy on -
Through Villages of Ether -
Myself endued Balloon
By but a lip of Metal -
The pier to my Pontoon[1] -

Nor would I be a Poet -
It's finer - Own the Ear -
Enamored - impotent - content -
The License to revere,
A privilege so awful
What would the Dower be,
Had I the Art to stun myself
With Bolts - of Melody!

1862

1. Hill on which Jesus was crucified (Luke 23.33).
1. Floating structure or boat.

353

[508]

I'm ceded - I've stopped being Their's -
The name They dropped opon my face
With water, in the country church
Is finished using, now,
And They can put it with my Dolls,
My childhood, and the string of spools,
I've finished threading - too -

Baptized, before, without the choice,
But this time, consciously, Of Grace -
Unto supremest name -
Called to my Full - The Crescent dropped -
Existence's whole Arc, filled up,
With one - small Diadem -

My second Rank - too small the first -
Crowned - Crowing - on my Father's breast -
A half unconscious Queen -
But this time - Adequate - Erect,
With Will to choose,
Or to reject,
And I choose, just a Crown -

1862

355

[510]

It was not Death, for I stood up,
And all the Dead, lie down -
It was not Night, for all the Bells
Put out their Tongues, for Noon.

It was not Frost, for on my Flesh
I felt Siroccos[1] - crawl -
Nor Fire - for just my marble feet
Could keep a Chancel,[2] cool -

And yet, it tasted, like them all,
The Figures I have seen
Set orderly, for Burial,
Reminded me, of mine -

As if my life were shaven,
And fitted to a frame,

1. Hot winds from North Africa.
2. The part of the church that contains the choir and sanctuary.

And could not breathe without a key,
And 'twas like Midnight, some -

When everything that ticked - has stopped -
And space stares - all around -
Or Grisly frosts - first Autumn morns,
Repeal the Beating Ground -

But, most, like Chaos - Stopless - cool -
Without a Chance, or spar -
Or even a Report of Land -
To justify - Despair.

1862

359

[328]

A Bird, came down the Walk -
He did not know I saw -
He bit an Angle Worm in halves
And ate the fellow, raw,

And then, he drank a Dew
From a convenient Grass -
And then hopped sidewise to the Wall
To let a Beetle pass -

He glanced with rapid eyes,
That hurried all abroad -
They looked like frightened Beads, I thought,
He stirred his Velvet Head. -

Like one in danger, Cautious,
I offered him a Crumb,
And he unrolled his feathers,
And rowed him softer Home -

Than Oars divide the Ocean,
Too silver for a seam,
Or Butterflies, off Banks of Noon,
Leap, plashless[1] as they swim.

1862

1. Splashless.

365

[338]

I know that He exists.
Somewhere - in silence -
He has hid his rare life
From our gross eyes.

'Tis an instant's play-
'Tis a fond Ambush -
Just to make Bliss
Earn her own surprise!

But - should the play
Prove piercing earnest -
Should the glee - glaze -
In Death's - stiff - stare -

Would not the fun
Look too expensive!
Would not the jest -
Have crawled too far!

1862

372

[*341*]

After great pain, a formal feeling comes -
The Nerves sit ceremonious, like Tombs -
The stiff Heart questions 'was it He, that bore,'
And 'Yesterday, or Centuries before'?

The Feet, mechanical, go round -
A Wooden way
Of Ground, or Air, or Ought -
Regardless grown,
A Quartz contentment, like a stone -

This is the Hour of Lead -
Remembered, if outlived,
As Freezing persons, recollect the Snow -
First - Chill - then Stupor - then the letting go -

1862

373

[*501*]

This World is not conclusion.
A Species stands beyond -
Invisible, as Music -
But positive, as Sound -
It beckons, and it baffles -
Philosophy, dont know -
And through a Riddle, at the last -
Sagacity, must go -
To guess it, puzzles scholars -
To gain it, Men have borne
Contempt of Generations
And Crucifixion, shown -
Faith slips - and laughs, and rallies -
Blushes, if any see -
Plucks at a twig of Evidence -
And asks a Vane, the way -
Much Gesture, from the Pulpit -
Strong Hallelujahs roll -
Narcotics cannot still the Tooth
That nibbles at the soul -

1862

381

[*326*]

I cannot dance opon[1] my Toes -
No Man instructed me -
But oftentimes, among my mind,
A Glee possesseth me,

That had I Ballet Knowledge -
Would put itself abroad
In Pirouette to blanch a Troupe -
Or lay a Prima,[2] mad,

And though I had no Gown of Gauze -
No Ringlet, to my Hair,
Nor hopped for Audiences - like Birds -
One Claw opon the air -

Nor tossed my shape in Eider[3] Balls,
Nor rolled on wheels of snow

1. Upon.
2. Principal female dancer in a ballet company
3. Down or soft feathers.

Till I was out of sight, in sound,
The House encore me so -

Nor any know I know the Art
I mention - easy - Here -
Nor any Placard boast me -
It's full as Opera -

1862

395

[*336*]

The face I carry with me - last -
When I go out of Time -
To take my Rank - by - in the West -
That face - will just be thine -

I'll hand it to the Angel -
That - Sir - was my Degree -
In Kingdoms - you have heard the Raised -
Refer to - possibly.

He'll take it - scan it - step aside -
Return - with such a crown
As Gabriel - never capered at -
And beg me put it on -

And then - he'll turn me round and round -
To an admiring sky -
As One that bore her Master's name -
Sufficient Royalty!

1862

407

[*670*]

One need not be a Chamber - to be Haunted -
One need not be a House -
The Brain has Corridors - surpassing
Material Place -

Far safer, of a midnight meeting
External Ghost
Than it's interior confronting -
That cooler Host -

Far safer, through an Abbey gallop,
The Stones a'chase -
Than unarmed, one's a'self encounter -
In lonesome Place -

Ourself behind ourself, concealed -
Should startle most -
Assassin hid in our Apartment
Be Horror's least -

The Body - borrows a Revolver -
He bolts the Door -
O'erlooking a superior spectre -
Or More -

1862

409

[303]

The Soul selects her own Society -
Then - shuts the Door -
To her divine Majority -
Present no more -

Unmoved - she notes the Chariots - pausing -
At her low Gate -
Unmoved - an Emperor be kneeling
Opon her Mat -

I've known her - from an ample nation -
Choose One -
Then - close the Valves of her attention -
Like Stone -

1862

411

[528]

Mine - by the Right of the White Election!
Mine - by the Royal Seal!
Mine - by the sign in the Scarlet prison -
Bars - cannot conceal!

Mine - here - in Vision - and in Veto!
Mine - by the Grave's Repeal -
Titled - Confirmed -
Delirious Charter!
Mine - long as Ages steal!

1862

446

[*448*]

This was a Poet -
It is That
Distills amazing sense
From Ordinary Meanings -
And Attar[1] so immense

From the familiar species
That perished by the Door -
We wonder it was not Ourselves
Arrested it - before -

Of Pictures, the Discloser -
The Poet - it is He -
Entitles Us - by Contrast -
To ceaseless Poverty -

Of Portion - so unconscious -
The Robbing - could not harm -
Himself - to Him - a Fortune -
Exterior - to Time -

1862

448

[*449*]

I died for Beauty - but was scarce
Adjusted in the Tomb
When One who died for Truth, was lain
In an adjoining Room -

He questioned softly "Why I failed"?
"For Beauty", I replied -
"And I - for Truth - Themself are One -
We Bretheren, are", He said -

And so, as Kinsmen, met a Night -
We talked between the Rooms -
Until the Moss had reached our lips -
And covered up - Our names -

1862

1. Fragrance.

466

[657]

I dwell in Possibility -
A fairer House than Prose -
More numerous of Windows -
Superior - for Doors -

Of Chambers as the Cedars -
Impregnable of eye -
And for an everlasting Roof
The Gambrels[1] of the Sky -

Of Visitors - the fairest -
For Occupation - This -
The spreading wide my narrow Hands
To gather Paradise -

1862

475

[488]

Myself was formed - a Carpenter -
An unpretending time
My Plane, and I, together wrought
Before a Builder came -

To measure our attainments -
Had we the Art of Boards
Sufficiently developed - He'd hire us
At Halves -

My Tools took Human - Faces -
The Bench, where we had toiled -
Against the Man, persuaded -
We - Temples build - I said -

1862

1. Sloped roofs.

477

[*315*]

He fumbles at your Soul
As Players at the Keys -
Before they drop full Music on -
He stuns you by Degrees -

Prepares your brittle nature
For the etherial Blow
By fainter Hammers - further heard -
Then nearer - Then so - slow -

Your Breath - has time to straighten -
Your Brain - to bubble cool -
Deals One - imperial Thunderbolt -
That scalps your naked soul -

When Winds hold Forests in their Paws -
The Universe - is still -

1862

479

[*712*]

Because I could not stop for Death -
He kindly stopped for me -
The Carriage held but just Ourselves -
And Immortality.

We slowly drove - He knew no haste
And I had put away
My labor and my leisure too,
For His Civility -

We passed the School, where Children strove
At Recess - in the Ring -
We passed the Fields of Gazing Grain -
We passed the Setting Sun -

Or rather - He passed Us -
The Dews drew quivering and Chill -
For only Gossamer,[1] my Gown -
My Tippet - only Tulle[2] -

1. Delicate, light fabric.
2. Thin silk. "Tippet": scarf for covering neck and shoulders.

We paused before a House that seemed
A Swelling of the Ground -
The Roof was scarcely visible -
The Cornice[3] - in the Ground -

Since then - 'tis Centuries - and yet
Feels shorter than the Day
I first surmised the Horses' Heads
Were toward Eternity -

1862

519

[*441*]

This is my letter to the World
That never wrote to Me -
The simple News that Nature told -
With tender Majesty

Her Message is committed
To Hands I cannot see -
For love of Her - Sweet - countrymen -
Judge tenderly - of Me

1863

576

[*305*]

The difference between Despair
And Fear, is like the One
Between the instant of a Wreck
And when the Wreck has been -
The Mind is smooth -
No motion - Contented as the Eye
Opon the Forehead of a Bust -
That knows it cannot see -

1863

3. Decorative molding beneath a roof.

588

[536]

The Heart asks Pleasure - first -
And then - excuse from Pain -
And then - those little Anodynes[1]
That deaden suffering -

And then - to go to sleep -
And then - if it should be
The will of it's Inquisitor
The privilege to die -

1863

591

[465]

I heard a Fly buzz - when I died -
The Stillness in the Room
Was like the Stillness in the Air -
Between the Heaves of Storm -

The Eyes around - had wrung them dry -
And Breaths were gathering firm
For that last Onset - when the King
Be witnessed - in the Room -

I willed my Keepsakes - Signed away
What portion of me be
Assignable - and then it was
There interposed a Fly -

With Blue - uncertain - stumbling Buzz -
Between the light - and me -
And then the Windows failed - and then
I could not see to see -

1863

1. Drugs or medicines that relieve pain.

598

[632]

The Brain - is wider than the Sky -
For - put them side by side -
The one the other will contain
With ease - and You - beside -

The Brain is deeper than the sea -
For - hold them - Blue to Blue -
The one the other will absorb -
As Sponges - Buckets - do -

The Brain is just the weight of God -
For - Heft them - Pound for Pound -
And they will differ - if they do -
As Syllable from Sound -

1863

600[1]

[312]

Her - last Poems -
Poets ended -
Silver - perished - with her Tongue -
Not on Record - bubbled Other -
Flute - or Woman - so divine -

Not unto it's Summer Morning -
Robin - uttered half the Tune
Gushed too full for the adoring -
From the Anglo-Florentine -

Late - the Praise - 'Tis dull - Conferring
On the Head too High - to Crown -
Diadem - or Ducal showing -
Be it's Grave - sufficient Sign -

Nought - that We - No Poet's Kinsman -
Suffocate - with easy Wo -
What - and if Ourself a Bridegroom -
Put Her down - in Italy?

1863

1. The overall poem is a tribute to English poet Elizabeth Barrett Browning (1806–1861), who moved to Italy and lived in Florence after marrying the poet Robert Browning (1812–1889) in 1848.

620

[435]

Much Madness is divinest Sense -
To a discerning Eye -
Much Sense - the starkest Madness -
'Tis the Majority
In this, as all, prevail -
Assent - and you are sane -
Demur - you're straightway dangerous -
And handled with a Chain -

1863

627

[593]

I think I was enchanted
When first a sombre Girl -
I read that Foreign Lady[1] -
The Dark - felt beautiful -

And whether it was noon at night -
Or only Heaven - at noon -
For very Lunacy of Light
I had not power to tell -

The Bees - became as Butterflies -
The Butterflies - as Swans -
Approached - and spurned the narrow Grass -
And just the meanest Tunes

That Nature murmured to herself
To keep herself in Cheer -
I took for Giants - practising
Titanic Opera -

The Days - To Mighty Metres stept -
The Homeliest - adorned
As if unto a Jubilee
'Twere suddenly confirmed -

I could not have defined the change -
Conversion of the Mind
Like Sanctifying in the Soul -
Is witnessed - not explained -

1. Probably Elizabeth Barrett Browning.

'Twas a Divine Insanity -
The Danger to be sane
Should I again experience -
'Tis Antidote to turn -

To Tomes of Solid Witchcraft -
Magicians be asleep -
But Magic - hath an element
Like Deity - to keep -

1863

648

[547]

I've seen a Dying Eye
Run round and round a Room -
In search of Something - as it seemed -
Then Cloudier become -
And then - obscure with Fog -
And then - be soldered down
Without disclosing what it be
'Twere blessed to have seen -

1863

656

[520]

I started Early - Took my Dog -
And visited the Sea -
The Mermaids in the Basement
Came out to look at me -

And Frigates - in the Upper Floor
Extended Hempen Hands -
Presuming Me to be a Mouse -
Aground - opon the Sands -

But no Man moved Me - till the Tide
Went past my simple Shoe -
And past my Apron - and my Belt
And past my Boddice - too -

And made as He would eat me up -
As wholly as a Dew
Opon a Dandelion's Sleeve -
And then - I started - too -

And He - He followed - close behind -
I felt His Silver Heel
Opon my Ancle - Then My Shoes
Would overflow with Pearl -

Until We met the Solid Town -
No One He seemed to know -
And bowing - with a Mighty look -
At me - The Sea withdrew -

1863

675

[*154*]

What Soft - Cherubic Creatures -
These Gentlewomen are -
One would as soon assault a Plush -
Or violate a Star -

Such Dimity[1] Convictions -
A Horror so refined
Of freckled Human Nature -
Of Deity - Ashamed -

It's such a common - Glory -
A Fisherman's - Degree -
Redemption - Brittle Lady -
Be so - ashamed of Thee -

1863

706

[*640*]

I cannot live with You -
It would be Life -
And Life is over there -
Behind the Shelf

The Sexton keeps the key to -
Putting up
Our Life - His Porcelain -
Like a Cup -

1. Thin cotton fabric.

Discarded of the Housewife -
Quaint - or Broke -
A newer Sevres[1] pleases -
Old Ones crack -

I could not die - with You -
For One must wait
To shut the Other's Gaze down -
You - could not -

And I - Could I stand by
And see You - freeze -
Without my Right of Frost -
Death's privilege?

Nor could I rise - with You -
Because Your Face
Would put out Jesus' -
That New Grace

Glow plain - and foreign
On my homesick eye -
Except that You than He
Shone closer by -

They'd judge Us - How -
For You - served Heaven - You know,
Or sought to -
I could not -

Because You saturated sight -
And I had no more eyes
For sordid excellence
As Paradise

And were You lost, I would be -
Though my name
Rang loudest
On the Heavenly fame -

And were You - saved -
And I - condemned to be
Where You were not
That self - were Hell to me -

1. Porcelain china (French), usually elaborately decorated.

So we must meet apart -
You there - I - here -
With just the Door ajar
That Oceans are - and Prayer -
And that White Sustenance -
Despair -

1863

760

[650]

Pain - has an Element of Blank -
It cannot recollect
When it begun - Or if there were
A time when it was not -

It has no Future - but itself -
It's Infinite contain
It's Past - enlightened to perceive
New Periods - Of Pain.

1863

764

[754]

My Life had stood - a Loaded Gun -
In Corners - till a Day
The Owner passed - identified -
And carried Me away -

And now We roam in Sovreign Woods -
And now We hunt the Doe -
And every time I speak for Him
The Mountains straight reply -

And do I smile, such cordial light
Opon the Valley glow -
It is as a Vesuvian[1] face
Had let it's pleasure through

And when at Night - Our good Day done -
I guard My Master's Head -
'Tis better than the Eider Duck's
Deep Pillow - to have shared -

1. Reference to Mount Vesuvius, the volcano in southern Italy that destroyed Pompeii (79 C.E.).

To foe of His - I'm deadly foe -
None stir the second time -
On whom I lay a Yellow Eye -
Or an emphatic Thumb -

Though I than He - may longer live
He longer must - than I -
For I have but the power to kill,
Without - the power to die -

1863

788

[709]

Publication - is the Auction
Of the Mind of Man -
Poverty - be justifying
For so foul a thing

Possibly - but We - would rather
From Our Garret go
White - unto the White Creator -
Than invest - Our Snow -

Thought belong to Him who gave it -
Then - to Him Who bear
It's Corporeal illustration - sell
The Royal Air -

In the Parcel - Be the Merchant
Of the Heavenly Grace -
But reduce no Human Spirit
To Disgrace of Price -

1863

817

[822]

This Consciousness that is aware
Of Neighbors and the Sun
Will be the one aware of Death
And that itself alone

Is traversing the interval
Experience between

And most profound experiment
Appointed unto Men -

How adequate unto itself
It's properties shall be
Itself unto itself and None
Shall make discovery -

Adventure most unto itself
The Soul condemned to be -
Attended by a single Hound
It's own identity.

1864

857

[732]

She rose to His Requirement - dropt
The Playthings of Her Life
To take the honorable Work
Of Woman, and of Wife -

If ought She missed in Her new Day,
Of Amplitude, or Awe -
Or first Prospective - or the Gold
In using, wear away,

It lay unmentioned - as the Sea
Develope Pearl, and Weed,
But only to Himself - be known
The Fathoms they abide -

1864

935

[*1540*]

As imperceptibly as Grief
The Summer lapsed away -
Too imperceptible at last
To seem like Perfidy -
A Quietness distilled
As Twilight long begun,
Or Nature spending with herself
Sequestered Afternoon -
The Dusk drew earlier in -

The Morning foreign shone -
A courteous, yet harrowing Grace,
As Guest, that would be gone -
And thus, without a Wing
Or service of a Keel
Our Summer made her light escape
Into the Beautiful -

1865

1096[1]

[986]

A narrow Fellow in the Grass
Occasionally rides -
You may have met him? Did you not
His notice instant is -

The Grass divides as with a Comb -
A spotted Shaft is seen,
And then it closes at your Feet
And opens further on -

He likes a Boggy Acre -
A Floor too cool for Corn -
But when a Boy and Barefoot
I more than once at Noon

Have passed I thought a Whip Lash
Unbraiding in the Sun
When stooping to secure it
It wrinkled And was gone -

Several of Nature's People
I know and they know me
I feel for them a transport
Of Cordiality

But never met this Fellow
Attended or alone
Without a tighter Breathing
And Zero at the Bone.

1865, 1866

1. Dickinson published a version of this poem in the *Springfield Daily Republican*, February 14, 1866.

1108

[*1078*]

The Bustle in a House
The Morning after Death
Is solemnest of industries
Enacted opon Earth -

The Sweeping up the Heart
And putting Love away
We shall not want to use again
Until Eternity -

1865

1163

[*1138*]

A Spider sewed at Night
Without a Light
Opon an Arc of White -

If Ruff it was of Dame
Or Shroud of Gnome
Himself himself inform -

Of Immortality
His strategy
Was physiognomy[1] -

1869

1243

[*1126*]

Shall I take thee, the Poet said
To the propounded word?
Be stationed with the Candidates
Till I have finer tried -

The Poet searched Philology
And was about to ring
For the suspended Candidate
There came unsummoned in -

1. The art of interpreting inner character from the body or face.

That portion of the Vision
The Word applied to fill
Not unto nomination
The Cherubim reveal -

1872

1263

[*1129*]

Tell all the truth but tell it slant -
Success in Circuit lies
Too bright for our infirm Delight
The Truth's superb surprise
As Lightning to the Children eased
With explanation kind
The Truth must dazzle gradually
Or every man be blind -

1872

1353

[*1247*]

To pile like Thunder to it's close
Then crumble grand away
While everything created hid
This - would be Poetry -

Or Love - the two coeval come -
We both and neither prove -
Experience either and consume -
For none see God and live -

1875

1454

[*1397*]

It sounded as if the Streets were running -
And then the Streets stood still -
Eclipse - was all we could see at the Window,
And Awe - was all we could feel -

By and by - the boldest stole out of his Covert
To see if Time was there -

Nature was in an Opal[1] Apron,
Mixing fresher Air.

1877

1489

[*1463*]

A Route of Evanescence,
With a revolving Wheel -
A Resonance of Emerald
A Rush of Cochineal[1] -
And every Blossom on the Bush
Adjusts it's tumbled Head -
The Mail from Tunis[2] - probably,
An easy Morning's Ride -

1879

1577

[*1545*]

The Bible is an antique Volume -
Written by faded Men
At the suggestion of Holy Spectres -
Subjects - Bethlehem -
Eden - the ancient Homestead -
Satan - the Brigadier -
Judas - the Great Defaulter -
David - the Troubadour -
Sin - a distinguished Precipice
Others must resist -
Boys that "believe" are very lonesome -
Other Boys are "lost" -
Had but the Tale a warbling Teller -
All the Boys would come -
Orpheu's Sermon[1] captivated -
It did not condemn -

1882

1. An iridescent semiprecious gem.
1. Red dye.
2. City on the northern coast of Africa.
1. In Greek mythology, Orpheus played music that would transfix wild beasts and still rivers.

1593

[*1587*]

He ate and drank the precious Words -
His Spirit grew robust -
He knew no more that he was poor,
Nor that his frame was Dust -
He danced along the dingy Days
And this Bequest of Wings
Was but a Book - What Liberty
A loosened Spirit brings -

1882

1665

[*1581*]

The farthest Thunder that I heard
Was nearer than the Sky
And rumbles still, though torrid Noons
Have lain their Missiles by -
The Lightning that preceded it
Struck no one but myself -
But I would not exchange the Bolt
For all the rest of Life -
Indebtedness to Oxygen
The Happy may repay,
But not the obligation
To Electricity -
It founds the Homes and decks the Days
And every clamor bright
Is but the gleam concomitant
Of that waylaying Light -
The Thought is quiet as a Flake -
A Crash without a Sound,
How Life's reverberation
It's Explanation found -

1884

1668

[*1624*]

Apparently with no surprise
To any happy Flower
The Frost beheads it at it's play -
In accidental power -

The blonde Assassin passes on -
The Sun proceeds unmoved
To measure off another Day
For an Approving God -

1884

1675

[*1601*]

Of God we ask one favor, that we may be forgiven -
For what, he is presumed to know -
The Crime, from us, is hidden -
Immured the whole of Life
Within a magic Prison
We reprimand the Happiness
That too competes with Heaven -

1885

1715[1]

[*1651*]

A word made Flesh is seldom
And tremblingly partook
Nor then perhaps reported
But have I not mistook
Each one of us has tasted
With ecstasies of stealth
The very food debated
To our specific strength -

A word that breathes distinctly
Has not the power to die
Cohesive as the Spirit
It may expire if He -

"Made Flesh and dwelt among us"[2]
Could condescension be
Like this consent of Language
This loved Philology

1. The poem was transcribed by Susan Dickinson and there is no surviving manuscript; the dating is even more uncertain than that of other Dickinson poems.
2. John 1.14.

1773[1]

[*1732*]

My life closed twice before it's close;
It yet remains to see
If Immortality unveil
A third event to me,

So huge, so hopeless to conceive
As these that twice befell.
Parting is all we know of heaven,
And all we need of hell.

Letter Exchange with Susan Gilbert Dickinson on Poem 124 [216][1]

The Sleeping[2]

Safe in their alabaster chambers,
Untouched by morning,
  And untouched by noon,
Sleep the meek members of the Resurrection,
  Rafter of satin, and roof of stone.

Light laughs the breeze
In her castle above them,
  Babbles the bee in a stolid ear,
Pipe the sweet birds in ignorant cadences:
  Ah! What sagacity perished here!
Pelham Hill, June, 1861.

Emily Dickinson to Susan Gilbert Dickinson

Safe in their Alabaster Chambers,
Untouched by Morning -
And untouched by Noon -
Lie the meek members of
the Resurrection -
Rafter of Satin - and Roof of
Stone -

1. Transcribed by Mabel Loomis Todd; there is no surviving manuscript. As with poem 1715, it is hard to determine a probable date of composition.

1. Dickinson exchanged hundreds of letters with her friend and sister-in-law Susan Huntington Gilbert Dickinson (1850–1913). who married Emily's brother, Austin in 1856. The letters and poems printed here are from *Open Me Carefully: Emily Dickinson's Intimate Letters of Susan Huntington Dickinson* (1998), ed. Ellen Louise Hart and Martha Nell Smith, reprinted with the permission of Paris Press. The letters, which in manuscript appear to be letter-poems, were probably all written in 1861. Their focus is on Dickinson's poem 124 [216], which exists in multiple versions.

2. This version of poem 124 was published in the Springfield *Republican* on March 1, 1862. Dickinson had sent Susan a manuscript version of this poem sometime between 1859 and 1861, but the manuscript is not extant, nor is Susan's initial letter of response, which had criticized the second stanza.

Grand go the Years - in the
Crescent - above them -
Worlds scoop their Arcs -
And Firmaments - row -
Diadems - drop - and Doges -
Surrender -
Soundless as dots - on a
Disc of Snow -

Perhaps this verse would
please you better - Sue -
Emily'

Susan Gilbert Dickinson to Emily Dickinson

I am not suited
dear Emily with the second
verse - It is remarkable as the
chain lightening that blinds us
hot nights in the Southern sky
but it does not go with the
ghostly shimmer of the first verse
as well as the other one - It just
occurs to me that the first verse
is complete in itself it needs
no other, and can't be coupled -
Strange things always go alone - as
there is only one Gabriel and one
Sun - You never made a peer
for that verse,[3] and I guess you[r]
kingdom doesn't hold one - I
always go to the fire and get warm
after thinking of it, but I never
can again - The flowers are sweet
and bright and look as if they
would kiss one - ah, they expect
a humming-bird - Thanks for
them of course - and not thanks
only recognition either - Did it
ever occur to you that is all there
is here after all - "Lord that I
may receive my sight"[4] -
Susan is tired making bibs for
her bird - her ring-dove[5] - he will
paint my cheeks when I am old
to pay me -

Sue -

3. Susan refers to Dickinson's poem 285 [673], which calls life on earth "but a filament" of the "diviner thing" that "smites the Tinder in the Sun" and "hinders Gabriel's wing."
4. In Luke 18.41–43, the blind man's faith in Jesus brings him sight.
5. Susan's son, Ned, who was born on July 19, 1861. Susan is imagining her grown son repaying all her attention by caring for her in old age.

Emily Dickinson to Susan Gilbert Dickinson

Is this, frostier?

Springs - shake the Sills -
But - the Echoes - stiffen -
Hoar - is the Window - and
numb - the Door -
Tribes of Eclipse - in Tents
of Marble -
Staples of Ages - have
buckled - there[6] -

Dear Sue -
Your praise is good -
to me - because I know
it knows - and suppose -
it means -
Could I make you and
Austin - proud - sometime - a
great way off - 'twould give
me taller feet -
Here is a crumb - for the
"Ring dove" - and a spray'
for his Nest, a little while
ago - just - "Sue" -
Emily'

From Fascicle 10[7]

Safe in their Alabaster chambers -
Untouched by Morning -
And untouched by Noon -
Lie the meek members of the Resurrection -
Rafter of Satin - and Roof of Stone!

Grand go the Years - in the Crescent - above them -
Worlds scoop their Arcs -
And Firmaments - row -
Diadems - drop - and Doges - surrender -
Soundless as dots - on a Disc of snow -

Springs - shake the sills -
But - the Echoes - stiffen -
Hoar - is the window -

6. Dickinson incorporated this stanza into a new version of the poem, which she bound into Fascicle 10.

7. Dickinson wrote out a complete record of her attempts with poem 124 [216], as influenced by her exchanges with Susan Dickinson, and bound it into Fascicle 10. She first wrote a ten-line version of the entire poem and then beneath that version wrote two versions of a six-line stanza that she was considering as a substitution for the five-line second stanza. The fascicle version of poem 124 [216] suggests that many Dickinson poems were always in progress. The source here is *The Poems of Emily Dickinson: Variorum Edition* (1998), ed. R.W. Franklin, reprinted with the permission of Harvard University Press.

And - numb - the door -
Tribes - of Eclipse - in Tents - of Marble -
Staples - of Ages - have buckled - there -

Springs - shake the seals -
But the silence - stiffens -
Frosts unhook - in the Northern Zones -
Icicles - crawl from polar Caverns -
Midnights in Marble -
Refutes - the Suns -

Letters to Thomas Wentworth Higginson[1]

15 April 1862

Mr Higginson,

Are you too deeply occupied to say if my Verse is alive?[2]

The Mind is so near itself – it cannot see, distinctly – and I have none to ask –

Should you think it breathed – and had you the leisure to tell me, I should feel quick gratitude –

If I make the mistake – that you dared to tell me – would give me sincerer honor – toward you –

I enclose my name – asking you, if you please – Sir – to tell me what is true?

That you will not betray me – it is needless to ask – since Honor is it's own pawn –[3]

25 April 1862

Mr Higginson,

Your kindness claimed earlier gratitude – but I was ill – and write today, from my pillow:

Thank you for the surgery – it was not so painful as I supposed. I bring you others – as you ask – though they might not differ –

While my thought is undressed – I can make the distinction, but when I put them in the Gown – they look alike, and numb.

You asked how old I was? I made no verse – but one or two – until this winter – Sir –

1. Dickinson first wrote Higginson (1823–1911) on April 15, 1862, responding to his article "Letter to a Young Contributor," which he published in the *Atlantic Monthly* earlier in the month. A contributing editor at the magazine, and for the past decade a radical abolitionist, Higginson, who had trained at Harvard Divinity School, had recently resigned his ministry. As an editor, he was intrigued by Dickinson's poetry, but he never offered to publish her work. In her letter of April 25, 1862, Dickinson refers to the editorial "surgery" he did on the poems she sent him. Over the next twenty-four years, she sent him many letters (including one just before she died) and nearly 100 poems. He visited her twice at her Amherst home, in 1870 and 1873. When he helped to publish the first two volumes of her posthumously published poems, Higginson edited the poems, giving them more conventional rhyme and meter. Both letters are taken from *Emily Dickinson: Selected Letters* (1971), ed. Thomas H. Johnson.

2. Dickinson sent four poems with the letter, including 124 [216], "Safe in their Alabaster Chambers."

3. Instead of signing the letter, Dickinson enclosed a card with her signature.

I had a terror – since September – I could tell to none – and so I sing, as the Boy does by the Burying Ground – because I am afraid – You inquire my Books – For Poets – I have Keats – and Mr and Mrs Browning. For Prose – Mr Ruskin - Sir Thomas Browne – and the Revelations.[4] I went to school – but in your manner of the phrase – had no education. When a little Girl, I had a friend, who taught me Immortality – but venturing too near, himself – he never returned – Soon after, my Tutor, died[5] – and for several years, my Lexicon – was my only companion – Then I found one more – but he was not contented I be his scholar – so he left the Land.[6]

You ask of my Companions Hills – Sir – and the Sundown – and a Dog – large as myself, that my Father bought me – They are better than Beings – because they know – but do not tell – and the noise in the Pool, at Noon – excels my Piano. I have a Brother and Sister – My Mother does not care for thought – and Father, too busy with his Briefs[7] – to notice what we do – He buys me many Books – but begs me not to read them – because he fears they joggle the Mind. They are religious – except me – and address an Eclipse, every morning – whom they call their "Father." But I fear my story fatigues you – I would like to learn – Could you tell me how to grow – or is it unconveyed – like Melody – or Witchcraft?

You speak of Mr Whitman – I never read his Book[8] – but was told that he was disgraceful –

I read Miss Prescott's "Circumstance,"[9] but it followed me, in the Dark – so I avoided her –

Two Editors of Journals[1] came to my Father's House, this winter – and asked me for my Mind – and when I asked them "Why," they said I was penurious – and they, would use it for the World –

I could not weigh myself – Myself –

My size felt small – to me – I read your Chapters in the Atlantic – and experienced honor for you – I was sure you would not reject a confiding question –

Is this – Sir – what you asked me to tell you?

Your friend,
E – Dickinson.

4. Revelation is the concluding prophetic book of the New Testament. Dickinson refers to the English poets John Keats (1795–1821), Elizabeth Barrett Browning, and Robert Browning; the English art critic and social theorist John Ruskin (1819–1900); and the English physician and writer Sir Thomas Browne (1605–1682).
5. The friend and tutor was probably Benjamin Franklin Newton (1821–1853), who had studied law in her father's office during the 1840s.
6. Dickinson's friend the Reverend Charles Wadsworth (1814–1882) had recently accepted a pastorate in California.
7. Legal statements.
8. The third edition of Whitman's *Leaves of Grass* was published in 1860.
9. Harriet Prescott Spofford's (1835–1921) short story "Circumstance" had appeared in the May 1860 *Atlantic*.
1. Possibly Samuel Bowles (1826–1878) and J. G. Holland (1819–1881), who were both associated with the *Springfield Daily Republican*.

REBECCA HARDING DAVIS
1831–1910

The author of over five hundred published works, including short stories, essays, sketches, novels, and children's writings, Rebecca Harding Davis is best known today for the pioneering realism of her first published story, "Life in the Iron-Mills." The story was a sensation when it appeared in the 1861 *Atlantic Monthly*, and while Davis's subsequent work never equaled it in power, her career was marked by success with both the highbrow readers of the *Atlantic* and the mass audiences that enjoyed her writings in the popular magazines and newspapers of the day.

Rebecca Harding was born in 1831 in Washington, Pennsylvania, her mother's hometown, and then taken to Florence, Alabama, where her father, a book-loving English emigrant, was in business. In 1836 the family moved to Wheeling, Virginia, a jumping-off place for the West as well as a prosperous manufacturing center, located in an anomalous fingerlike part of a slave state that reached far north between the free states of Ohio and Pennsylvania. Rebecca Harding at fourteen returned to her Pennsylvania birthplace, living with an aunt while attending a female seminary. After graduating as valedictorian in 1848, she returned to her family in Wheeling. By her late twenties she had read English reform novels such as those by Charles Kingsley and Elizabeth Gaskell and had begun to publish anonymous reviews of new books in local newspapers. During the election year 1860, she wrote "Life in the Iron-Mills," apparently the first story she completed, and sent it to the *Atlantic Monthly*, the most prestigious magazine in the country, published in Boston under the editorship of James T. Fields. The story appeared anonymously (by custom and by Harding's request) the month the Civil War broke out and Wheeling became capital of the new free state of West Virginia. With the author's name an open secret, the story's strength was recognized by many readers, including Emily Dickinson. Buoyed by Fields's enthusiastic request for additional contributions, Harding began a serialized novel in the October 1861 *Atlantic*—"A Story of Today"—which offered, in one of the characters' words, "a glimpse of the underlife in America." In the voice of her narrator, Harding offered a manifesto of realism before there was a literary movement so identified: "You want something . . . to lift you out of this crowded, tobacco-stained commonplace, to kindle and chafe and glow in you. I want you to dig into this commonplace, this vulgar American life, and see what is in it. Sometimes I think it has a raw and awful significance that we do not see." This work, which Fields published in book form as *Margret Howth* (1862), further explored the dire effects of industrial capitalism, while addressing as well, through her portrayal of the black woman Lois Yare, the racial injustice that helped bring about the Civil War.

As a literary celebrity, Harding journeyed to Boston in 1862 and was welcomed by the literary establishment. She met Oliver Wendell Holmes and Nathaniel Hawthorne (whose fiction had inspired her own work), and became good friends with Annie Fields, her hostess. She had received a fan letter from an apprentice lawyer in Philadelphia, L. Clarke Davis, a man literary enough himself to have a connection with *Peterson's Magazine*, one of the leading magazines of the day. She met him on her way home from Boston, and they married in 1863. She continued her career as a magazine writer even after her three children were born, creating an extensive body of work that alternated between formula romance and social realism. In the best of her later novels, *Waiting for the Verdict* (1868), Davis addressed the continuing injustices facing African Americans in the postemancipation United States. She also addressed questions of gender, and in *Earthen Pitchers* (1873–74) and the short story "The Wife's Story" (1864) paid particular attention to conflicts between motherhood and career aspirations, as she and many other women of her generation were experiencing them.

In 1892 Davis received favorable critical attention for a collection of short stories, *Silhouettes of American Life*. But well before her death in 1910, she had been overshadowed, first by the success of her husband as an editor and then by the astonishing success of her son, Richard Harding Davis (1864–1916), who became the most glamorous journalist and one of the most popular writers of his generation. Concerned that he might sacrifice his talent for money as perhaps she thought she herself had done, in 1890 she warned him about "beginning to do hack work for money . . . the beginning of decadence both in work and reputation for you. I know by my own and a thousand other people."

"Life in the Iron-Mills" remains a landmark in the development of literary realism in nineteenth-century America. The story achieved a renewed popularity—and brought Rebecca Harding Davis back into a prominent place in literary history—through its republication in 1972 in a Feminist Press volume edited by the fiction writer and essayist Tillie Olson. In "Life in the Iron-Mills," Davis compels her middle-class readers to confront the underside of American industrial prosperity, particularly the exploitation of immigrant laborers, while refusing to provide easy answers to the social problems she so powerfully represents.

Life in the Iron-Mills[1]

"Is this the end?
O Life, as futile, then, as frail!
What hope of answer or redress?"[2]

A cloudy day: do you know what that is in a town of iron-works?[3] The sky sank down before dawn, muddy, flat, immovable. The air is thick, clammy with the breath of crowded human beings. It stifles me. I open the window, and, looking out, can scarcely see through the rain the grocer's shop opposite, where a crowd of drunken Irishmen are puffing Lynchburg tobacco[4] in their pipes. I can detect the scent through all the foul smells ranging loose in the air.

The idiosyncrasy of this town is smoke. It rolls sullenly in slow folds from the great chimneys of the iron-foundries, and settles down in black, slimy pools on the muddy streets. Smoke on the wharves, smoke on the dingy boats, on the yellow river,—clinging in a coating of greasy soot to the house-front, the two faded poplars, the faces of the passers-by. The long train of mules, dragging masses of pig-iron[5] through the narrow street, have a foul vapor hanging to their reeking sides. Here, inside, is a little broken figure of an angel pointing upward from the mantel-shelf; but even its wings are covered with smoke, clotted and black. Smoke everywhere! A dirty canary chirps

1. The text is that of the first printing in the *Atlantic Monthly* (April 1861), except for two paragraphs on page 1725, the source of which is *Atlantic Tales* (1865).
2. Adapted from Alfred, Lord Tennyson's *In Memoriam A.H.H.* (1850), 12.4: "'Is this the end of all my care?' . . . 'Is this the end? Is this the end?'" and from 56.7: "O Life as futile, then, as frail / O for thy voice to soothe and bless! / What hope of answer, or redress? / Behind the veil, behind the veil."
3. The town is not named, but is based on Harding's hometown, Wheeling, Virginia (now West Virginia), on the banks of the Ohio River.
4. A low-cost tobacco from south-central Virginia.
5. Oblong blocks of iron, hardened after being poured from a smelting furnace.

desolately in a cage beside me. Its dream of green fields and sunshine is a very old dream,—almost worn out, I think.

From the back-window I can see a narrow brick-yard sloping down to the river-side, strewed with rain-butts[6] and tubs. The river, dull and tawny-colored, (*la belle rivière!*)[7] drags itself sluggishly along, tired of the heavy weight of boats and coal-barges. What wonder? When I was a child, I used to fancy a look of weary, dumb appeal upon the face of the negro-like river slavishly bearing its burden day after day. Something of the same idle notion comes to me to-day, when from the street-window I look on the slow stream of human life creeping past, night and morning, to the great mills. Masses of men, with dull, besotted faces bent to the ground, sharpened here and there by pain or cunning; skin and muscle and flesh begrimed with smoke and ashes; stooping all night over boiling caldrons of metal, laired by day in dens of drunkenness and infamy; breathing from infancy to death an air saturated with fog and grease and soot, vileness for soul and body. What do you make of a case like that, amateur psychologist? You call it an altogether serious thing to be alive: to these men it is a drunken jest, a joke,—horrible to angels perhaps, to them commonplace enough. My fancy about the river was an idle one: it is no type of such a life. What if it be stagnant and slimy here? It knows that beyond there waits for it odorous sunlight,—quaint old gardens, dusky with soft, green foliage of apple-trees, and flushing crimson with roses,—air, and fields, and mountains. The future of the Welsh puddler[8] passing just now is not so pleasant. To be stowed away, after his grimy work is done, in a hole in the muddy graveyard, and after that,——*not* air, nor green fields, nor curious roses.

Can you see how foggy the day is? As I stand here, idly tapping the window-pane, and looking out through the rain at the dirty back-yard and the coal-boats below, fragments of an old story float up before me,—a story of this house into which I happened to come to-day. You may think it a tiresome story enough, as foggy as the day, sharpened by no sudden flashes of pain or pleasure.—I know: only the outline of a dull life, that long since, with thousands of dull lives like its own, was vainly lived and lost: thousands of them,—massed, vile, slimy lives, like those of the torpid lizards in yonder stagnant water-butt.—Lost? There is a curious point for you to settle, my friend, who study psychology in a lazy, *dilettante* way. Stop a moment. I am going to be honest. This is what I want you to do. I want you to hide your disgust, take no heed to your clean clothes, and come right down with me,—here, into the thickest of the fog and mud and foul effluvia. I want you to hear this story. There is a secret down here, in this nightmare fog, that has lain dumb for centuries: I want to make it a real thing to you. You, Egoist, or Pantheist, or Arminian, busy in making straight paths[9] for your feet on the hills, do not see it clearly,—this terrible question which men here have gone mad and died trying to answer. I dare not put this secret into words. I

6. Large casks used to catch rainwater for household and industrial use.
7. The beautiful river (French).
8. Worker who stirs iron oxide into a molten vat of pig iron to make wrought iron or steel.
9. Echoes Hebrews 12.13: "And make straight paths for your feet, lest that which is lame be turned out of the way; but let it rather be healed." "Egoist": one acting only according to self-interest. "Pantheist": one who identifies the deity with nature. "Arminian": follower of theologian Jacobus Arminius (1560–1607), who argued that salvation was freely available to all through good works.

told you it was dumb. These men, going by with drunken faces and brains full of unawakened power, do not ask it of Society or of God. Their lives ask it; their deaths ask it. There is no reply. I will tell you plainly that I have a great hope; and I bring it to you to be tested. It is this: that this terrible dumb question is its own reply; that it is not the sentence of death we think it, but, from the very extremity of its darkness, the most solemn prophecy which the world has known of the Hope to come. I dare make my meaning no clearer, but will only tell my story. It will, perhaps, seem to you as foul and dark as this thick vapor about us, and as pregnant with death; but if your eyes are free as mine are to look deeper, no perfume-tinted dawn will be so fair with promise of the day that shall surely come.

My story is very simple,—only what I remember of the life of one of these men,—a furnace-tender in one of Kirby & John's rolling-mills,—Hugh Wolfe. You know the mills? They took the great order for the lower Virginia railroads there last winter; run usually with about a thousand men. I cannot tell why I choose the half-forgotten story of this Wolfe more than that of myriads of these furnace-hands. Perhaps because there is a secret, underlying sympathy between that story and this day with its impure fog and thwarted sunshine,—or perhaps simply for the reason that this house is the one where the Wolfes lived. There were the father and son,—both hands, as I said, in one of Kirby & John's mills for making railroad-iron,—and Deborah, their cousin, a picker[1] in some of the cotton-mills. The house was rented then to half a dozen families. The Wolfes had two of the cellar-rooms. The old man, like many of the puddlers and feeders[2] of the mills, was Welsh,—had spent half of his life in the Cornish tin-mines. You may pick the Welsh emigrants, Cornish miners, out of the throng passing the windows, any day. They are a trifle more filthy; their muscles are not so brawny; they stoop more. When they are drunk, they neither yell, nor shout, nor stagger, but skulk along like beaten hounds. A pure, unmixed blood, I fancy: shows itself in the slight angular bodies and sharply-cut facial lines. It is nearly thirty years since the Wolfes lived here. Their lives were like those of their class: incessant labor, sleeping in kennel-like rooms, eating rank pork and molasses, drinking—God and the distillers only know what; with an occasional night in jail, to atone for some drunken excess. Is that all of their lives?—of the portion given to them and these their duplicates swarming the streets to-day?—nothing beneath?—all? So many a political reformer will tell you,—and many a private reformer, too, who has gone among them with a heart tender with Christ's charity, and come out outraged, hardened.

One rainy night, about eleven o'clock, a crowd of half-clothed women stopped outside of the cellar-door. They were going home from the cotton-mill.

"Good-night, Deb," said one, a mulatto, steadying herself against the gas-post. She needed the post to steady her. So did more than one of them.

"Dah's a ball to Miss Potts' to-night. Ye'd best come."

"Inteet, Deb, if hur'll come, hur'll hef fun," said a shrill Welsh voice in the crowd.

1. Worker in a cotton mill who operates the machine that separates cotton fibers.

2. Worker who feeds molten metal into the casting form while the iron is hardening.

Two or three dirty hands were thrust out to catch the gown of the woman, who was groping for the latch of the door.

"No."

"No? Where's Kit Small, then?"

"Begorra! on the spools.[3] Alleys behint, though we helped her, we dud. An wid ye! Let Deb alone! It's ondacent frettin' a quite body. Be the powers, an' we'll have a night of it! there'll be lashin's o' drink,—the Vargent[4] be blessed and praised for 't!"

They went on, the mulatto inclining for a moment to show fight, and drag the woman Wolfe off with them; but, being pacified, she staggered away.

Deborah groped her way into the cellar, and, after considerable stumbling, kindled a match, and lighted a tallow dip, that sent a yellow glimmer over the room. It was low, damp,—the earthen floor covered with a green, slimy moss,—a fetid air smothering the breath. Old Wolfe lay asleep on a heap of straw, wrapped in a torn horse-blanket. He was a pale, meek little man, with a white face and red rabbit-eyes. The woman Deborah was like him; only her face was even more ghastly, her lips bluer, her eyes more watery. She wore a faded cotton gown and a slouching bonnet. When she walked, one could see that she was deformed, almost a hunchback. She trod softly, so as not to waken him, and went through into the room beyond. There she found by the half-extinguished fire an iron saucepan filled with cold boiled potatoes, which she put upon a broken chair with a pint-cup of ale. Placing the old candlestick beside this dainty repast, she untied her bonnet, which hung limp and wet over her face, and prepared to eat her supper. It was the first food that had touched her lips since morning. There was enough of it, however: there is not always. She was hungry,—one could see that easily enough,—and not drunk, as most of her companions would have been found at this hour. She did not drink, this woman,—her face told that, too,—nothing stronger than ale. Perhaps the weak, flaccid wretch had some stimulant in her pale life to keep her up,—some love or hope, it might be, or urgent need. When that stimulant was gone, she would take to whiskey. Man cannot live by work alone. While she was skinning the potatoes, and munching them, a noise behind her made her stop.

"Janey!" she called, lifting the candle and peering into the darkness. "Janey, are you there?"

A heap of ragged coats was heaved up, and the face of a young girl emerged, staring sleepily at the woman.

"Deborah," she said, at last, "I'm here the night."

"Yes, child. Hur's welcome," she said, quietly eating on.

The girl's face was haggard and sickly; her eyes were heavy with sleep and hunger: real Milesian[5] eyes they were, dark, delicate blue, glooming out from black shadows with a pitiful fright.

"I was alone," she said, timidly.

"Where's the father?" asked Deborah, holding out a potato, which the girl greedily seized.

3. Spindles in the mill on which the cotton is stretched and wound by the spinning machine. "Begorra!": a stereotypically Irish form of "By God!"

4. The Virgin Mary.

5. Reference to the legendary Miletus, an ancient city on the Aegean whose people were thought by some to be the ancestors of the Irish.

"He's beyant,—wid Haley,—in the stone house." (Did you ever hear the word *jail* from an Irish mouth?) "I came here. Hugh told me never to stay me-lone."

"Hugh?"

"Yes."

A vexed frown crossed her face. The girl saw it, and added quickly,—

"I have not seen Hugh the day, Deb. The old man says his watch[6] lasts till the mornin'."

The woman sprang up, and hastily began to arrange some bread and flitch[7] in a tin pail, and to pour her own measure of ale into a bottle. Tying on her bonnet, she blew out the candle.

"Lay ye down, Janey dear," she said, gently, covering her with the old rags. "Hur can eat the potatoes, if hur's hungry."

"Where are ye goin', Deb? The rain's sharp."

"To the mill, with Hugh's supper."

"Let him bide till th' morn. Sit ye down."

"No, no,"—sharply pushing her off. "The boy'll starve."

She hurried from the cellar, while the child wearily coiled herself up for sleep. The rain was falling heavily, as the woman, pail in hand, emerged from the mouth of the alley, and turned down the narrow street, that stretched out, long and black, miles before her. Here and there a flicker of gas lighted an uncertain space of muddy footwalk and gutter; the long rows of houses, except an occasional lager-bier shop, were closed; now and then she met a band of millhands skulking to or from their work.

Not many even of the inhabitants of a manufacturing town know the vast machinery of system by which the bodies of workmen are governed, that goes on unceasingly from year to year. The hands of each mill are divided into watches that relieve each other as regularly as the sentinels of an army. By night and day the work goes on, the unsleeping engines groan and shriek, the fiery pools of metal boil and surge. Only for a day in the week, in half-courtesy to public censure, the fires are partially veiled; but as soon as the clock strikes midnight, the great furnaces break forth with renewed fury, the clamor begins with fresh, breathless vigor, the engines sob and shriek like "gods in pain."

As Deborah hurried down through the heavy rain, the noise of these thousand engines sounded through the sleep and shadow of the city like far-off thunder. The mill to which she was going lay on the river, a mile below the city-limits. It was far, and she was weak, aching from standing twelve hours at the spools. Yet it was her almost nightly walk to take this man his supper, though at every square she sat down to rest, and she knew she should receive small word of thanks.

Perhaps, if she had possessed an artist's eye, the picturesque oddity of the scene might have made her step stagger less, and the path seem shorter; but to her the mills were only "summat deilish[8] to look at by night."

The road leading to the mills had been quarried from the solid rock, which rose abrupt and bare on one side of the cinder-covered road, while the river, sluggish and black, crept past on the other. The mills for rolling[9] iron

6. Work shift.
7. Salt pork.
8. Devilish.
9. Process of producing sheet metal.

are simply immense tent-like roofs, covering acres of ground, open on every side. Beneath these roofs Deborah looked in on a city of fires, that burned hot and fiercely in the night. Fire in every horrible form: pits of flame waving in the wind; liquid metal-flames writhing in tortuous streams through the sand; wide caldrons filled with boiling fire, over which bent ghastly wretches stirring the strange brewing; and through all, crowds of half-clad men, looking like revengeful ghosts in the red light, hurried, throwing masses of glittering fire. It was like a street in Hell. Even Deborah muttered, as she crept through, " 'T looks like t' Devil's place!" It did,—in more ways than one.

She found the man she was looking for, at last, heaping coal on a furnace. He had not time to eat his supper; so she went behind the furnace, and waited. Only a few men were with him, and they noticed her only by a "Hyur comes t' hunchback, Wolfe."

Deborah was stupid with sleep; her back pained her sharply; and her teeth chattered with cold, with the rain that soaked her clothes and dripped from her at every step. She stood, however, patiently holding the pail, and waiting.

"Hout, woman! ye look like a drowned cat. Come near to the fire,"—said one of the men, approaching to scrape away the ashes.

She shook her head. Wolfe had forgotten her. He turned, hearing the man, and came closer.

"I did no' think; gi' me my supper, woman."

She watched him eat with a painful eagerness. With a woman's quick instinct, she saw that he was not hungry,—was eating to please her. Her pale, watery eyes began to gather a strange light.

"Is't good, Hugh? T' ale was a bit sour, I feared."

"No, good enough." He hesitated a moment. "Ye 're tired, poor lass! Bide here till I go. Lay down there on that heap of ash, and go to sleep."

He threw her an old coat for a pillow, and turned to his work. The heap was the refuse of the burnt iron, and was not a hard bed; the half-smothered warmth, too, penetrated her limbs, dulling their pain and cold shiver.

Miserable enough she looked, lying there on the ashes like a limp, dirty rag,—yet not an unfitting figure to crown the scene of hopeless discomfort and veiled crime: more fitting, if one looked deeper into the heart of things,—at her thwarted woman's form, her colorless life, her waking stupor that smothered pain and hunger,—even more fit to be a type of her class. Deeper yet if one could look, was there nothing worth reading in this wet, faded thing, halfcovered with ashes? no story of a soul filled with groping passionate love, heroic unselfishness, fierce jealousy? of years of weary trying to please the one human being whom she loved, to gain one look of real heart-kindness from him? If anything like this were hidden beneath the pale, bleared eyes, and dull, washed-out-looking face, no one had ever taken the trouble to read its faint signs: not the half-clothed furnace-tender, Wolfe, certainly. Yet he was kind to her: it was his nature to be kind, even to the very rats that swarmed in the cellar: kind to her in just the same way. She knew that. And it might be that very knowledge had given to her face its apathy and vacancy more than her low, torpid life. One sees that dead, vacant look steal sometimes over the rarest, finest of women's faces,—in the very midst, it may be, of their warmest summer's day; and then one can guess at the secret of intolerable solitude that lies hid beneath the delicate laces and brilliant smile. There was no warmth, no brilliancy, no summer for this woman; so the stupor and vacancy had time to gnaw into her face perpetually. She was young, too, though no one guessed it; so the gnawing was the fiercer.

She lay quiet in the dark corner, listening, through the monotonous din and uncertain glare of the works, to the dull plash of the rain in the far distance,—shrinking back whenever the man Wolfe happened to look towards her. She knew, in spite of all his kindness, that there was that in her face and form which made him loathe the sight of her. She felt by instinct, although she could not comprehend it, the finer nature of the man, which made him among his fellow-workmen something unique, set apart. She knew, that, down under all the vileness and coarseness of his life, there was a groping passion for whatever was beautiful and pure,—that his soul sickened with disgust at her deformity, even when his words were kindest. Through this dull consciousness, which never left her, came, like a sting, the recollection of the dark blue eyes and lithe figure of the little Irish girl she had left in the cellar. The recollection struck through even her stupid intellect with a vivid glow of beauty and of grace. Little Janey, timid, helpless, clinging to Hugh as her only friend: that was the sharp thought, the bitter thought, that drove into the glazed eyes a fierce light of pain. You laugh at it? Are pain and jealousy less savage realities down here in this place I am taking you to than in your own house or your own heart,—your heart, which they clutch at sometimes? The note is the same, I fancy, be the octave high or low.

If you could go into this mill where Deborah lay, and drag out from the hearts of these men the terrible tragedy of their lives, taking it as a symptom of the disease of their class, no ghost Horror would terrify you more. A reality of soul-starvation, of living death, that meets you every day under the besotted faces on the street,—I can paint nothing of this, only give you the outside outlines of a night, a crisis in the life of one man: whatever muddy depth of soul-history lies beneath you can read according to the eyes God has given you.

Wolfe, while Deborah watched him as a spaniel its master, bent over the furnace with his iron pole, unconscious of her scrutiny, only stopping to receive orders. Physically, Nature had promised the man but little. He had already lost the strength and instinct vigor of a man, his muscles were thin, his nerves weak, his face (a meek, woman's face) haggard, yellow with consumption. In the mill he was known as one of the girl-men: "Molly Wolfe" was his *sobriquet*.[1] He was never seen in the cockpit, did not own a terrier,[2] drank but seldom; when he did, desperately. He fought sometimes, but was always thrashed, pommelled to a jelly. The man was game enough, when his blood was up: but he was no favorite in the mill; he had the taint of school-learning on him,—not to a dangerous extent, only a quarter or so in the free-school in fact, but enough to ruin him as a good hand in a fight.

For other reasons, too, he was not popular. Not one of themselves, they felt that, though outwardly as filthy and ash-covered; silent, with foreign thoughts and longings breaking out through his quietness in innumerable curious ways: this one, for instance. In the neighboring furnace-buildings lay great

1. Nickname.
2. Dogs bred to hunt. "Cockpit": where fighting cocks are set against each other until one is severely injured or killed.

heaps of the refuse from the ore after the pig-metal is run. *Korl* we call it here: a light, porous substance, of a delicate, waxen, flesh-colored tinge. Out of the blocks of this korl, Wolfe, in his off-hours from the furnace, had a habit of chipping and moulding figures,—hideous, fantastic enough, but sometimes strangely beautiful: even the mill-men saw that, while they jeered at him. It was a curious fancy in the man, almost a passion. The few hours for rest he spent hewing and hacking with his blunt knife, never speaking, until his watch came again,—working at one figure for months, and, when it was finished, breaking it to pieces perhaps, in a fit of disappointment. A morbid, gloomy man, untaught, unled, left to feed his soul in grossness and crime, and hard, grinding labor.

I want you to come down and look at this Wolfe, standing there among the lowest of his kind, and see him just as he is, that you may judge him justly when you hear the story of this night. I want you to look back, as he does every day, at his birth in vice, his starved infancy; to remember the heavy years he has groped through as boy and man,—the slow, heavy years of constant, hot work. So long ago he began, that he thinks sometimes he has worked there for ages. There is no hope that it will ever end. Think that God put into this man's soul a fierce thirst for beauty,—to know it, to create it; to *be*—something, he knows not what,—other than he is. There are moments when a passing cloud, the sun glinting on the purple thistles, a kindly smile, a child's face, will rouse him to a passion of pain,—when his nature starts up with a mad cry of rage against God, man, whoever it is that has forced this vile, slimy life upon him. With all this groping, this mad desire, a great blind intellect stumbling through wrong, a loving poet's heart, the man was by habit only a coarse, vulgar laborer, familiar with sights and words you would blush to name. Be just: when I tell you about this night, see him as he is. Be just,—not like man's law, which seizes on one isolated fact, but like God's judging angel, whose clear, sad eye saw all the countless cankering days of this man's life, all the countless nights, when, sick with starving, his soul fainted in him, before it judged him for this night, the saddest of all.

I called this night the crisis of his life. If it was, it stole on him unawares. These great turning-days of life cast no shadow before, slip by unconsciously. Only a trifle, a little turn of the rudder, and the ship goes to heaven or hell.

Wolfe, while Deborah watched him, dug into the furnace of melting iron with his pole, dully thinking only how many rails the lump would yield. It was late,—nearly Sunday morning; another hour, and the heavy work would be done,—only the furnaces to replenish and cover for the next day. The workmen were growing more noisy, shouting, as they had to do, to be heard over the deep clamor of the mills. Suddenly they grew less boisterous,—at the far end, entirely silent. Something unusual had happened. After a moment, the silence came nearer; the men stopped their jeers and drunken choruses. Deborah, stupidly lifting up her head, saw the cause of the quiet. A group of five or six men were slowly approaching, stopping to examine each furnace as they came. Visitors often came to see the mills after night: except by growing less noisy, the men took no notice of them. The furnace where Wolfe worked was near the bounds of the works; they halted there hot and tired: a walk over one of these great foundries is no trifling task. The woman, drawing out of sight, turned over to sleep. Wolfe, seeing them stop, suddenly roused from his indifferent stupor, and watched them keenly. He knew some of them: the overseer, Clarke,—a son of Kirby, one of the mill-owners,—and a Doctor May, one of the town-physicians. The other two were strangers. Wolfe came closer. He seized eagerly every chance that brought him into contact with this mysterious class that shone down on him perpetually with the glamour of another order of being. What made the difference between them? That was the mystery of his life. He had a vague notion that perhaps to-night he could find it out. One of the strangers sat down on a pile of bricks, and beckoned young Kirby to his side.

"This *is* hot, with a vengeance. A match, please?"—lighting his cigar. "But the walk is worth the trouble. If it were not that you must have heard it so often, Kirby, I would tell you that your works look like Dante's Inferno."[3]

Kirby laughed.

"Yes. Yonder is Farinata himself[4] in the burning tomb,"—pointing to some figure in the shimmering shadows.

"Judging from some of the faces of your men," said the other, "they bid fair to try the reality of Dante's vision, some day."

Young Kirby looked curiously around, as if seeing the faces of his hands for the first time.

"They're bad enough, that's true. A desperate set, I fancy. Eh, Clarke?"

The overseer did not hear him. He was talking of net profits just then,—giving, in fact, a schedule of the annual business of the firm to a sharp peering little Yankee, who jotted down notes on a paper laid on the crown of his hat: a reporter for one of the city-papers, getting up a series of reviews of the leading manufactories. The other gentlemen had accompanied them merely for amusement. They were silent until the notes were finished, drying their feet at the furnaces, and sheltering their faces from the intolerable heat. At last the overseer concluded with—

"I believe that is a pretty fair estimate, Captain."

"Here, some of you men!" said Kirby, "bring up those boards. We may as well sit down, gentlemen, until the rain is over. It cannot last much longer at this rate."

"Pig-metal,"—mumbled the reporter,—"um!—coal facilities,—um!—hands employed, twelve hundred,—bitumen,—um!—all right, I believe, Mr. Clarke;—sinking-fund,—what did you say was your sinking-fund?"[5]

"Twelve hundred hands?" said the stranger, the young man who had first spoken. "Do you control their votes, Kirby?"

"Control? No." The young man smiled complacently. "But my father brought seven hundred votes to the polls for his candidate last November. No force-work, you understand,—only a speech or two, a hint to form themselves into a society, and a bit of red and blue bunting to make them a flag. The Invincible Roughs,—I believe that is their name. I forget the motto: 'Our country's hope,' I think."

There was a laugh. The young man talking to Kirby sat with an amused light in his cool gray eye, surveying critically the half-clothed figures of the puddlers, and the slow swing of their brawny muscles. He was a stranger in

3. *Hell*, the first part of *The Divine Comedy* by the Italian poet Dante Alighieri (1265–1321).

4. In Canto 10 of the *Inferno*, Farinata degli Uberti is one of the heretics, a leader of the Florentine faction opposed to Dante's own family.

5. Fund accumulated to pay off a corporate debt.

the city,—spending a couple of months in the borders of a Slave State,[6] to study the institutions of the South,—a brother-in-law of Kirby's,—Mitchell. He was an amateur gymnast,—hence his anatomical eye; a patron, in a *blasé* way, of the prize-ring; a man who sucked the essence out of a science or philosophy in an indifferent, gentlemanly way; who took Kant, Novalis, Humboldt,[7] for what they were worth in his own scales; accepting all, despising nothing, in heaven, earth, or hell, but one-idead men; with a temper yielding and brilliant as summer water, until his Self was touched, when it was ice, though brilliant still. Such men are not rare in the States.

As he knocked the ashes from his cigar, Wolfe caught with a quick pleasure the contour of the white hand, the blood-glow of a red ring he wore. His voice, too, and that of Kirby's, touched him like music,—low, even, with chording cadences. About this man Mitchell hung the impalpable atmosphere belonging to the thoroughbred gentleman. Wolfe, scraping away the ashes beside him, was conscious of it, did obeisance to it with his artist sense, unconscious that he did so.

The rain did not cease. Clarke and the reporter left the mills; the others, comfortably seated near the furnace, lingered, smoking and talking in a desultory way. Greek would not have been more unintelligible to the furnace-tenders, whose presence they soon forgot entirely. Kirby drew out a newspaper from his pocket and read aloud some article, which they discussed eagerly. At every sentence, Wolfe listened more and more like a dumb, hopeless animal, with a duller, more stolid look creeping over his face, glancing now and then at Mitchell, marking acutely every smallest sign of refinement, then back to himself, seeing as in a mirror his filthy body, his more stained soul.

Never! He had no words for such a thought, but he knew now, in all the sharpness of the bitter certainty, that between them there was a great gulf[8] never to be passed. Never!

The bell of the mills rang for midnight. Sunday morning had dawned. Whatever hidden message lay in the tolling bells floated past these men unknown. Yet it was there. Veiled in the solemn music ushering the risen Saviour was a key-note to solve the darkest secrets of a world gone wrong,—even this social riddle which the brain of the grimy puddler grappled with madly to-night.

The men began to withdraw the metal from the caldrons. The mills were deserted on Sundays, except by the hands who fed the fires, and those who had no lodgings and slept usually on the ash-heaps. The three strangers sat still during the next hour, watching the men cover the furnaces, laughing now and then at some jest of Kirby's.

"Do you know," said Mitchell, "I like this view of the works better than when the glare was fiercest? These heavy shadows and the amphitheatre of smothered fires are ghostly, unreal. One could fancy these red smouldering

6. The story was written and set a few years before the northwest area of the slave state of Virginia broke off to become the free state of West Virginia (1863).

7. Alexander von Humboldt (1769–1859), German naturalist and explorer of South America and Asia. Immanuel Kant (1724–1804), German philosopher. Novalis, pseudonym of the German poet Friedrich von Hardenberg (1772–1801).

8. Words Jesus assigns to Abraham in the parable of the beggar Lazarus and the rich man (Luke 16.26): "And beside all this between us and you there is a great gulf fixed"—the gulf between heaven, where Lazarus has found comfort, and hell, where the rich man is suffering.

lights to be the half-shut eyes of wild beasts, and the spectral figures their victims in the den."

Kirby laughed. "You are fanciful. Come, let us get out of the den. The spectral figures, as you call them, are a little too real for me to fancy a close proximity in the darkness,—unarmed, too."

The others rose, buttoning their overcoats, and lighting cigars.

"Raining, still," said Doctor May, "and hard. Where did we leave the coach, Mitchell?"

"At the other side of the works.—Kirby, what's that?"

Mitchell started back, half-frightened, as, suddenly turning a corner, the white figure of a woman faced him in the darkness,—a woman, white, of giant proportions, crouching on the ground, her arms flung out in some wild gesture of warning.

"Stop! Make that fire burn there!" cried Kirby, stopping short.

The flame burst out, flashing the gaunt figure into bold relief.

Mitchell drew a long breath.

"I thought it was alive," he said, going up curiously.

The others followed.

"Not marble, eh?" asked Kirby, touching it.

One of the lower overseers stopped.

"Korl, Sir."

"Who did it?"

"Can't say. Some of the hands; chipped it out in off-hours."

"Chipped to some purpose, I should say. What a flesh-tint the stuff has! Do you see, Mitchell?"

"I see."

He had stepped aside where the light fell boldest on the figure, looking at it in silence. There was not one line of beauty or grace in it: a nude woman's form, muscular, grown coarse with labor, the powerful limbs instinct with some one poignant longing. One idea: there it was in the tense, rigid muscles, the clutching hands, the wild, eager face, like that of a starving wolf's. Kirby and Doctor May walked around it, critical, curious. Mitchell stood aloof, silent. The figure touched him strangely.

"Not badly done," said Doctor May. "Where did the fellow learn that sweep of the muscles in the arm and hand? Look at them! They are groping,—do you see?—clutching: the peculiar action of a man dying of thirst."

"They have ample facilities for studying anatomy," sneered Kirby, glancing at the half-naked figures.

"Look," continued the Doctor, "at this bony wrist, and the strained sinews of the instep! A working-woman,—the very type of her class."

"God forbid!" muttered Mitchell.

"Why?" demanded May. "What does the fellow intend by the figure? I cannot catch the meaning."

"Ask him," said the other, dryly. "There he stands,"—pointing to Wolfe, who stood with a group of men, leaning on his ash-rake.

The Doctor beckoned him with the affable smile which kind-hearted men put on, when talking to these people.

"Mr. Mitchell has picked you out as the man who did this,—I'm sure I don't know why. But what did you mean by it?"

"She be hungry."

Wolfe's eyes answered Mitchell, not the Doctor.

"Oh-h! But what a mistake you have made, my fine fellow! You have given no sign of starvation to the body. It is strong,—terribly strong. It has the mad, half-despairing gesture of drowning."

Wolfe stammered, glanced appealingly at Mitchell, who saw the soul of the thing, he knew. But the cool, probing eyes were turned on himself now,—mocking, cruel, relentless.

"Not hungry for meat," the furnace-tender said at last.

"What then? Whiskey?" jeered Kirby, with a coarse laugh.

Wolfe was silent a moment, thinking.

"I dunno," he said, with a bewildered look. "It mebbe. Summat to make her live, I think,—like you. Whiskey ull do it, in a way."

The young man laughed again. Mitchell flashed a look of disgust somewhere,—not at Wolfe.

"May," he broke out impatiently, "are you blind? Look at that woman's face! It asks questions of God, and says, 'I have a right to know.' Good God, how hungry it is!"

They looked a moment; then May turned to the mill-owner:—

"Have you many such hands as this? What are you going to do with them? Keep them at puddling iron?"

Kirby shrugged his shoulders. Mitchell's look had irritated him.

"*Ce n'est pas mon affaire.*[9] I have no fancy for nursing infant geniuses. I suppose there are some stray gleams of mind and soul among these wretches. The Lord will take care of his own; or else they can work out their own salvation. I have heard you call our American system a ladder which any man can scale. Do you doubt it? Or perhaps you want to banish all social ladders, and put us all on a flat table-land,—eh, May?"

The Doctor looked vexed, puzzled. Some terrible problem lay hid in this woman's face, and troubled these men. Kirby waited for an answer, and, receiving none, went on, warming with his subject.

"I tell you, there's something wrong that no talk of '*Liberté*' or '*Egalité*'[1] will do away. If I had the making of men, these men who do the lowest part of the world's work should be machines,—nothing more,—hands. It would be kindness. God help them! What are taste, reason, to creatures who must live such lives as that?" He pointed to Deborah, sleeping on the ash-heap. "So many nerves to sting them to pain. What if God had put your brain, with all its agony of touch, into your fingers, and bid you work and strike with that?"

"You think you could govern the world better?" laughed the Doctor.

"I do not think at all."

"That is true philosophy. Drift with the stream, because you cannot dive deep enough to find bottom, eh?"

"Exactly," rejoined Kirby. "I do not think. I wash my hands of all social problems,—slavery, caste, white or black. My duty to my operatives has a narrow limit,—the pay-hour on Saturday night. Outside of that, if they cut korl, or cut each other's throats, (the more popular amusement of the two,) I am not responsible."

9. It's none of my business (French).
1. "Liberty" and "Equality," slogans of the French Revolution.

The Doctor sighed,—a good honest sigh, from the depths of his stomach. "God help us! Who is responsible?"

"Not I, I tell you," said Kirby, testily. "What has the man who pays them money to do with their souls' concerns, more than the grocer or butcher who takes it?"

"And yet," said Mitchell's cynical voice, "look at her! How hungry she is!"

Kirby tapped his boot with his cane. No one spoke. Only the dumb face of the rough image looking into their faces with the awful question, "What shall we do to be saved?"[2] Only Wolfe's face, with its heavy weight of brain, its weak, uncertain mouth, its desperate eyes, out of which looked the soul of his class,—only Wolfe's face turned towards Kirby's. Mitchell laughed,—a cool, musical laugh.

"Money has spoken!" he said, seating himself lightly on a stone with the air of an amused spectator at a play. "Are you answered?"—turning to Wolfe his clear, magnetic face.

Bright and deep and cold as Arctic air, the soul of the man lay tranquil beneath. He looked at the furnace-tender as he had looked at a rare mosaic in the morning; only the man was the more amusing study of the two.

"Are you answered? Why, May, look at him! '*De profundis clamavi.*'[3] Or, to quote in English, 'Hungry and thirsty, his soul faints in him.' And so Money sends back its answer into the depths through you, Kirby! Very clear the answer, too!—I think I remember reading the same words somewhere:—washing your hands in Eau de Cologne, and saying, 'I am innocent of the blood of this man. See ye to it!'"[4]

Kirby flushed angrily.

"You quote Scripture freely."

"Do I not quote correctly? I think I remember another line, which may amend my meaning? 'Inasmuch as ye did it unto one of the least of these, ye did it unto me.' Deist?[5] Bless you, man, I was raised on the milk of the Word. Now, Doctor, the pocket of the world having uttered its voice, what has the heart to say? You are a philanthropist, in a small way,—*n'est ce pas?*[6] Here, boy, this gentleman can show you how to cut korl better,—or your destiny. Go on, May!"

"I think a mocking devil possesses you to-night," rejoined the Doctor, seriously.

He went to Wolfe and put his hand kindly on his arm. Something of a vague idea possessed the Doctor's brain that much good was to be done here by a friendly word or two: a latent genius to be warmed into life by a waited-for sunbeam. Here it was: he had brought it. So he went on complacently:—

"Do you know, boy, you have it in you to be a great sculptor, a great man?—do you understand?" (talking down to the capacity of his hearer: it

2. The keeper of the prison in Philippi implored Paul and Silas, after an earthquake had opened the prison doors and released the prisoners' bonds, "Sirs, what must I do to be saved?" (Acts 16.30).

3. The Latin version of Psalm 130.1: "Out of the depths have I cried unto thee, O Lord."

4. The Roman governor Pontius Pilate yielded to the mob's demand that Jesus be crucified but renounced responsibility for it: "When Pilate saw that he could prevail nothing, but that rather a tumult was made, he took water, and washed his hands before the multitude, saying, I am innocent of the blood of this just person: see ye to it" (Matthew 27.24).

5. One who believes in a God who created the world but thereafter leaves it alone. What Jesus says in Matthew 25.40: "Verily I say unto you, Inasmuch as ye have done it unto one of the least of these my brethren, ye have done it unto me."

6. Aren't you? (French).

is a way people have with children, and men like Wolfe,)—"to live a better, stronger life than I, or Mr. Kirby here? A man may make himself anything he chooses. God has given you stronger powers than many men,—me, for instance."

May stopped, heated, glowing with his own magnanimity. And it was magnanimous. The puddler had drunk in every word, looking through the Doctor's flurry, and generous heat, and self-approval, into his will, with those slow, absorbing eyes of his.

"Make yourself what you will. It is your right."

"I know," quietly. "Will you help me?"

Mitchell laughed again. The Doctor turned now, in a passion,—

"You know, Mitchell, I have not the means. You know, if I had, it is in my heart to take this boy and educate him for"—

"The glory of God, and the glory of John May."

May did not speak for a moment; then, controlled, he said,—

"Why should one be raised, when myriads are left?—I have not the money, boy," to Wolfe, shortly.

"Money?" He said it over slowly, as one repeats the guessed answer to a riddle, doubtfully. "That is it? Money?"

"Yes, money,—that is it," said Mitchell, rising, and drawing his furred coat about him. "You've found the cure for all the world's diseases.—Come, May, find your good-humor, and come home. This damp wind chills my very bones. Come and preach your Saint-Simonian doctrines[7] to-morrow to Kirby's hands. Let them have a clear idea of the rights of the soul, and I'll venture next week they'll strike for higher wages. That will be the end of it."

"Will you send the coach-driver to this side of the mills?" asked Kirby, turning to Wolfe.

He spoke kindly: it was his habit to do so. Deborah, seeing the puddler go, crept after him. The three men waited outside. Doctor May walked up and down, chafed. Suddenly he stopped.

"Go back, Mitchell! You say the pocket and the heart of the world speak without meaning to these people. What has its head to say? Taste, culture, refinement? Go!"

Mitchell was leaning against a brick wall. He turned his head indolently, and looked into the mills. There hung about the place a thick, unclean odor. The slightest motion of his hand marked that he perceived it, and his insufferable disgust. That was all. May said nothing, only quickened his angry tramp.

"Besides," added Mitchell, giving a corollary to his answer, "it would be of no use. I am not one of them."

"You do not mean"—said May, facing him.

"Yes, I mean just that. Reform is born of need, not pity. No vital movement of the people's has worked down, for good or evil; fermented, instead, carried up the heaving, cloggy mass. Think back through history, and you will know it. What will this lowest deep—thieves, Magdalens, negroes—do with the light filtered through ponderous Church creeds, Baconian theories,

7. Doctrines of Henri de Saint-Simon (1760–1825), founder of French socialism.

Goethe schemes?[8] Some day, out of their bitter need will be thrown up their own light-bringer,—their Jean Paul, their Cromwell,[9] their Messiah."

"Bah!" was the Doctor's inward criticism. However, in practice, he adopted the theory; for, when, night and morning, afterwards, he prayed that power might be given these degraded souls to rise, he glowed at heart, recognizing an accomplished duty.

Wolfe and the woman had stood in the shadow of the works as the coach drove off. The Doctor had held out his hand in a frank, generous way, telling him to "take care of himself, and to remember it was his right to rise." Mitchell had simply touched his hat, as to an equal, with a quiet look of thorough recognition. Kirby had thrown Deborah some money, which she found, and clutched eagerly enough. They were gone now, all of them. The man sat down on the cinder-road, looking up into the murky sky.

"'T be late, Hugh. Wunnot hur come?"

He shook his head doggedly, and the woman crouched out of his sight against the wall. Do you remember rare moments when a sudden light flashed over yourself, your world, God? when you stood on a mountain-peak, seeing your life as it might have been, as it is? one quick instant, when custom lost its force and every-day usage? when your friend, wife, brother, stood in a new light? your soul was bared, and the grave,—a foretaste of the nakedness of the Judgment-Day? So it came before him, his life, that night. The slow tides of pain he had borne gathered themselves up and surged against his soul. His squalid daily life, the brutal coarseness eating into his brain, as the ashes into his skin: before, these things had been a dull aching into his consciousness; to-night, they were reality. He griped the filthy red shirt that clung, stiff with soot, about him, and tore it savagely from his arm. The flesh beneath was muddy with grease and ashes,—and the heart beneath that! And the soul? God knows.

Then flashed before his vivid poetic sense the man who had left him,—the pure face, the delicate, sinewy limbs, in harmony with all he knew of beauty or truth. In his cloudy fancy he had pictured a Something like this. He had found it in this Mitchell, even when he idly scoffed at his pain: a Man all-knowing, all-seeing, crowned by Nature, reigning,—the keen glance of his eye falling like a sceptre on other men. And yet his instinct taught him that he too—He! He looked at himself with sudden loathing, sick, wrung his hands with a cry, and then was silent. With all the phantoms of his heated, ignorant fancy, Wolfe had not been vague in his ambitions. They were practical, slowly built up before him out of his knowledge of what he could do. Through years he had day by day made this hope a real thing to himself,—a clear, projected figure of himself, as he might become.

Able to speak, to know what was best, to raise these men and women working at his side up with him: sometimes he forgot this defined hope in the frantic anguish to escape,—only to escape,—out of the wet, the pain, the ashes,

8. Abstract or fanciful theories such as those the English essayist and statesman Francis Bacon (1561–1624) advanced in his *New Atlantis* (1627), or the visionary faith in technological progress revealed by the German writer Johann Wolfgang von Goethe (1749–1832) in *Wilhelm Meister's Travels* (1821–29). "Magdalens": whores; from Mary Magdalene, out of whom Jesus cast seven devils (Mark 16.9).

9. Oliver Cromwell (1599–1658), English military, political, and religious leader. Jean Paul Richter (1763–1825), German novelist, author of *The Titan* (1803).

somewhere, anywhere,—only for one moment of free air on a hillside, to lie down and let his sick soul throb itself out in the sunshine. But to-night he panted for life. The savage strength of his nature was roused; his cry was fierce to God for justice.

"Look at me!" he said to Deborah, with a low, bitter laugh, striking his puny chest savagely. "What am I worth, Deb? Is it my fault that I am no better? My fault? My fault?"

He stopped, stung with a sudden remorse, seeing her hunchback shape writhing with sobs. For Deborah was crying thankless tears, according to the fashion of women.

"God forgi' me, woman! Things go harder wi' you nor me. It's a worse share."

He got up and helped her to rise; and they went doggedly down the muddy street, side by side.

"It's all wrong," he muttered, slowly,—"all wrong! I dunnot understan'. But it'll end some day."

"Come home, Hugh!" she said, coaxingly; for he had stopped, looking around bewildered.

"Home,—and back to the mill!" He went on saying this over to himself, as if he would mutter down every pain in this dull despair.

She followed him through the fog, her blue lips chattering with cold. They reached the cellar at last. Old Wolfe had been drinking since she went out, and had crept nearer the door. The girl Janey slept heavily in the corner. He went up to her, touching softly the worn white arm with his fingers. Some bitterer thought stung him, as he stood there. He wiped the drops from his forehead, and went into the room beyond, livid, trembling. A hope, trifling, perhaps, but very dear, had died just then out of the poor puddler's life, as he looked at the sleeping, innocent girl,—some plan for the future, in which she had borne a part. He gave it up that moment, then and forever. Only a trifle, perhaps, to us: his face grew a shade paler,—that was all. But, somehow, the man's soul, as God and the angels looked down on it, never was the same afterwards.

Deborah followed him into the inner room. She carried a candle, which she placed on the floor, closing the door after her. She had seen the look on his face, as he turned away: her own grew deadly. Yet, as she came up to him, her eyes glowed. He was seated on an old chest, quiet, holding his face in his hands.

"Hugh!" she said, softly.

He did not speak.

"Hugh, did hur hear what the man said,—him with the clear voice? Did hur hear? Money, money,—that it wud do all?"

He pushed her away,—gently, but he was worn out; her rasping tone fretted him.

"Hugh!"

The candle flared a pale yellow light over the cobwebbed brick walls, and the woman standing there. He looked at her. She was young, in deadly earnest; her faded eyes, and wet, ragged figure caught from their frantic eagerness a power akin to beauty.

"Hugh, it is true! Money ull do it! Oh, Hugh, boy, listen till me! He said it true! It is money!"

"I know. Go back! I do not want you here."

"Hugh, it is t' last time. I'll never worrit hur again."

There were tears in her voice now, but she choked them back.

"Hear till me only to-night! If one of t' witch people wud come, them we heard of t' home, and gif hur all hur wants, what then? Say, Hugh!"

"What do you mean?"

"I mean money."

Her whisper shrilled through his brain.

"If one of t' witch dwarfs wud come from t' lane moors to-night, and gif hur money, to go out,—*out*, I say,—out, lad, where t' sun shines, and t' heath grows, and t' ladies walk in silken gownds, and God stays all t' time,—where t' man lives that talked to us to-night,—Hugh knows,—Hugh could walk there like a king!"

He thought the woman mad, tried to check her, but she went on, fierce in her eager haste.

"If *I* were t' witch dwarf, if I had t' money, wud hur thank me? Wud hur take me out o' this place wid hur and Janey? I wud not come into the gran' house hur wud build, to vex hur wid t' hunch,—only at night, when t' shadows were dark, stand far off to see hur."

Mad? Yes! Are many of us mad in this way?

"Poor Deb! poor Deb!" he said, soothingly.

"It is here," she said, suddenly, jerking into his hand a small roll. "I took it! I did it! Me, me!—not hur! I shall be hanged, I shall be burnt in hell, if anybody knows I took it! Out of his pocket, as he leaned against t' bricks. Hur knows?"

She thrust it into his hand, and then, her errand done, began to gather chips together to make a fire, choking down hysteric sobs.

"Has it come to this?"

That was all he said. The Welsh Wolfe blood was honest. The roll was a small green pocket-book containing one or two gold pieces, and a check for an incredible amount, as it seemed to the poor puddler. He laid it down, hiding his face again in his hands.

"Hugh, don't be angry wud me! It's only poor Deb,—hur knows?"

He took the long skinny fingers kindly in his.

"Angry? God help me, no! Let me sleep. I am tired."

He threw himself heavily down on the wooden bench, stunned with pain and weariness. She brought some old rags to cover him.

It was late on Sunday evening before he awoke. I tell God's truth, when I say he had then no thought of keeping this money. Deborah had hid it in his pocket. He found it there. She watched him eagerly, as he took it out.

"I must gif it to him," he said, reading her face.

"Hur knows," she said with a bitter sigh of disappointment. "But it is hur right to keep it."

His right! The word struck him. Doctor May had used the same. He washed himself, and went out to find this man Mitchell. His right! Why did this chance word cling to him so obstinately? Do you hear the fierce devils whisper in his ear, as he went slowly down the darkening street?

The evening came on, slow and calm. He seated himself at the end of an alley leading into one of the larger streets. His brain was clear to-night, keen, intent, mastering. It would not start back, cowardly, from any hellish temptation, but meet it face to face. Therefore the great temptation of his life came to him veiled by no sophistry,[1] but bold, defiant, owning its own vile name, trusting to one bold blow for victory.

He did not deceive himself. Theft! That was it. At first the word sickened him; then he grappled with it. Sitting there on a broken cart-wheel, the fading day, the noisy groups, the church-bells' tolling passed before him like a panorama,[2] while the sharp struggle went on within. This money! He took it out, and looked at it. If he gave it back, what then? He was going to be cool about it.

People going by to church saw only a sickly mill-boy watching them quietly at the alley's mouth. They did not know that he was mad, or they would not have gone by so quietly: mad with hunger; stretching out his hands to the world, that had given so much to them, for leave to live the life God meant him to live. His soul within him was smothering to death; he wanted so much, thought so much, and *knew*—nothing. There was nothing of which he was certain, except the mill and things there. Of God and heaven he had heard so little, that they were to him what fairy-land is to a child: something real, but not here; very far off. His brain, greedy, dwarfed, full of thwarted energy and unused powers, questioned these men and women going by, coldly, bitterly, that night. Was it not his right to live as they,—a pure life, a good, true-hearted life, full of beauty and kind words? He only wanted to know how to use the strength within him. His heart warmed, as he thought of it. He suffered himself to think of it longer. If he took the money?

Then he saw himself as he might be, strong, helpful, kindly. The night crept on, as this one image slowly evolved itself from the crowd of other thoughts and stood triumphant. He looked at it. As he might be! What wonder, if it blinded him to delirium,—the madness that underlies all revolution, all progress, and all fall?

You laugh at the shallow temptation? You see the error underlying its argument so clearly,—that to him a true life was one of full development rather than self-restraint? that he was deaf to the higher tone in a cry of voluntary suffering for truth's sake than in the fullest flow of spontaneous harmony? I do not plead his cause. I only want to show you the mote in my brother's eye: then you can see clearly to take it out.[3]

The money,—there it lay on his knee, a little blotted slip of paper, nothing in itself; used to raise him out of the pit, something straight from God's hand. A thief! Well, what was it to be a thief? He met the question at last, face to face, wiping the clammy drops of sweat from his forehead. God made this money—the fresh air, too—for his children's use. He never made the difference between poor and rich. The Something who looked down on him that moment through the cool gray sky had a kindly face, he knew,—loved his children alike. Oh, he knew that!

1. Subtly deceptive argumentation or reasoning.
2. Continuous scenes painted on a huge canvas and unrolled before audiences; attending a panorama was a popular mid-19th-century recreation.
3. Jesus' words in the Sermon on the Mount (Matthew 7.3–4): "And why beholdest thou the mote that is in thy brother's eye, but considerest not the beam that is in thine own eye? Or how wilt thou say to thy brother, Let me pull out the mote out of thine eye; and behold, a beam is in thine own eye?" (Here a mote is a speck of dust and a beam is the large timber used to support a roof.)

There were times when the soft floods of color in the crimson and purple flames, or the clear depth of amber in the water below the bridge, had somehow given him a glimpse of another world than this,—of an infinite depth of beauty and of quiet somewhere,—somewhere,—a depth of quiet and rest and love. Looking up now, it became strangely real. The sun had sunk quite below the hills, but his last rays struck upward, touching the zenith. The fog had risen, and the town and river were steeped in its thick, gray damp; but overhead, the sun-touched smoke-clouds opened like a cleft ocean,—shifting, rolling seas of crimson mist, waves of billowy silver veined with blood-scarlet, inner depths unfathomable of glancing light. Wolfe's artist-eye grew drunk with color. The gates of that other world! Fading, flashing before him now! What, in that world of Beauty, Content, and Right, were the petty laws, the mine and thine, of mill—owners and mill hands?

A consciousness of power stirred within him. He stood up. A man,—he thought, stretching out his hands,—free to work, to live, to love! Free! His right! He folded the scrap of paper in his hand. As his nervous fingers took it in, limp and blotted, so his soul took in the mean temptation, lapped it in fancied rights, in dreams of improved existences, drifting and endless as the cloud—seas of color. Clutching it, as if the tightness of his hold would strengthen his sense of possession, he went aimlessly down the street. It was his watch at the mill. He need not go, need never go again, thank God!—shaking off the thought with unspeakable loathing.

Shall I go over the history of the hours of that night? how the man wandered from one to another of his old haunts, with a half-consciousness of bidding them farewell,—lanes and alleys and back-yards where the mill-hands lodged,—noting, with a new eagerness, the filth and drunkenness, the pig-pens, the ash-heaps covered with potato-skins, the bloated, pimpled women at the doors,—with a new disgust, a new sense of sudden triumph, and, under all, a new, vague dread, unknown before, smothered down, kept under, but still there? It left him but once during the night, when, for the second time in his life, he entered a church. It was a sombre Gothic pile, where the stained light lost itself in far-retreating arches; built to meet the requirements and sympathies of a far other class than Wolfe's. Yet it touched, moved him uncontrollably. The distances, the shadows, the still, marble figures, the mass of silent kneeling worshippers, the mysterious music, thrilled, lifted his soul with a wonderful pain. Wolfe forgot himself, forgot the new life he was going to live, the mean terror gnawing underneath. The voice of the speaker strengthened the charm; it was clear, feeling, full, strong. An old man, who had lived much, suffered much; whose brain was keenly alive, dominant; whose heart was summer-warm with charity. He taught it to-night. He held up Humanity in its grand total; showed the great world-cancer to his people. Who could show it better? He was a Christian reformer; he had studied the age thoroughly; his outlook at man had been free, world-wide, over all time. His faith stood sublime upon the Rock of Ages; his fiery zeal guided vast schemes by which the Gospel was to be preached to all nations. How did he preach it to-night? In burning, light-laden words he painted Jesus, the incarnate Life, Love, the universal Man: words that became reality in the lives of these people,—that lived again in beautiful words and actions, trifling, but heroic. Sin, as he defined it, was a real foe to them; their trials, temptations, were his. His words passed far over the furnace-tender's grasp, toned to suit another class of culture; they sounded in his ears a very pleasant song in an unknown tongue. He meant to cure this world-cancer with a steady eye that had never glared with hunger, and a hand that neither poverty nor strychnine-whiskey[4] had taught to shake. In this morbid, distorted heart of the Welsh puddler he had failed.

Eighteen centuries ago, the Master of this man tried reform in the streets of a city as crowded and vile as this, and did not fail. His disciple, showing Him to-night to cultured hearers, showing the clearness of the God-power acting through Him, shrank back from one coarse fact; that in birth and habit the man Christ was thrown up from the lowest of the people: his flesh, their flesh; their blood, his blood; tempted like them, to brutalize day by day; to lie, to steal: the actual slime and want of their hourly life, and the winepress he trod alone.

Yet, is there no meaning in this perpetually covered truth? If the son of the carpenter had stood in the church that night, as he stood with the fishermen and harlots by the sea of Galilee, before His Father and their Father, despised and rejected of men, without a place to lay His head, wounded for their iniquities, bruised for their transgressions, would not that hungry mill-boy at least, in the back seat, have "known the man"? That Jesus did not stand there.[5]

Wolfe rose at last, and turned from the church down the street. He looked up; the night had come on foggy, damp; the golden mists had vanished, and the sky lay dull and ash-colored. He wandered again aimlessly down the street, idly wondering what had become of the cloud-sea of crimson and scarlet. The trial-day of this man's life was over, and he had lost the victory. What followed was mere drifting circumstance,—a quicker walking over the path,—that was all. Do you want to hear the end of it? You wish me to make a tragic story out of it? Why, in the police-reports of the morning paper you can find a dozen such tragedies: hints of shipwrecks unlike any that ever befell on the high seas; hints that here a power was lost to heaven,—that there a soul went down where no tide can ebb or flow. Commonplace enough the hints are,—jocose sometimes, done up in rhyme.

Doctor May, a month after the night I have told you of, was reading to his wife at breakfast from this fourth column of the morning-paper: an unusual thing,—these police-reports not being, in general, choice reading for ladies; but it was only one item he read.

"Oh, my dear! You remember that man I told you of, that we saw at Kirby's mill?—that was arrested for robbing Mitchell? Here he is; just listen:—'Circuit Court. Judge Day. Hugh Wolfe, operative in Kirby & John's Loudon Mills. Charge, grand larceny. Sentence, nineteen years hard labor in penitentiary.'—Scoundrel! Serves him right! After all our kindness that night! Picking Mitchell's pocket at the very time!"

His wife said something about the ingratitude of that kind of people, and then they began to talk of something else.

4. Whiskey full of impurities, sometimes poisonous.

5. This paragraph and the previous one are taken from the 1865 collection, *Atlantic Tales*, where the author was allowed to insert this in place of the passage censored from her manuscript. See Janice Milner Lasseter in the Davis entry in "Selected Bibliographies."

Nineteen years! How easy that was to read! What a simple word for Judge Day to utter! Nineteen years! Half a lifetime!

Hugh Wolfe sat on the window-ledge of his cell, looking out. His ankles were ironed. Not usual in such cases; but he had made two desperate efforts to escape. "Well," as Haley, the jailer, said, "small blame to him! Nineteen years' inprisonment was not a pleasant thing to look forward to." Haley was very good-natured about it, though Wolfe had fought him savagely.

"When he was first caught," the jailer said afterwards, in telling the story, "before the trial, the fellow was cut down at once,—laid there on that pallet like a dead man, with his hands over his eyes. Never saw a man so cut down in my life. Time of the trial, too, came the queerest dodge[6] of any customer I ever had. Would choose no lawyer. Judge gave him one, of course. Gibson it was. He tried to prove the fellow crazy; but it wouldn't go. Thing was plain as daylight: money found on him. 'T was a hard sentence,—all the law allows; but it was for 'xample's sake. These mill-hands are gettin' onbearable. When the sentence was read, he just looked up, and said the money was his by rights, and that all the world had gone wrong. That night, after the trial, a gentleman came to see him here, name of Mitchell,—him as he stole from. Talked to him for an hour. Thought he came for curiosity, like. After he was gone, thought Wolfe was remarkable quiet, and went into his cell. Found him very low; bed all bloody. Doctor said he had been bleeding at the lungs. He was as weak as a cat; yet if ye'll b'lieve me, he tried to get a-past me and get out. I just carried him like a baby, and threw him on the pallet. Three days after, he tried it again: that time reached the wall. Lord help you! he fought like a tiger,—giv' some terrible blows. Fightin' for life, you see; for he can't live long, shut up in the stone crib down yonder. Got a death-cough now. 'T took two of us to bring him down that day; so I just put the irons on his feet. There he sits, in there. Goin' to-morrow, with a batch more of 'em. That woman, hunchback, tried with him,—you remember?—she's only got three years. 'Complice. But *she's* a woman, you know. He's been quiet ever since I put on irons: giv' up, I suppose. Looks white, sick-lookin'. It acts different on 'em, bein' sentenced. Most of 'em gets reckless, devilish—like. Some prays awful, and sings them vile songs of the mills, all in a breath. That woman, now, she's desper't'. Been beggin' to see Hugh, as she calls him, for three days. I'm a-goin' to let her in. She don't go with him. Here she is in this next cell. I'm a-goin' now to let her in."

He let her in. Wolfe did not see her. She crept into a corner of the cell, and stood watching him. He was scratching the iron bars of the window with a piece of tin which he had picked up, with an idle, uncertain, vacant stare, just as a child or idiot would do.

"Tryin' to get out, old boy?" laughed Haley. "Them irons will need a crowbar beside your tin, before you can open 'em."

Wolfe laughed, too, in a senseless way.

"I think I'll get out," he said.

"I believe his brain's touched," said Haley, when he came out.

The puddler scraped away with the tin for half an hour. Still Deborah did not speak. At last she ventured nearer, and touched his arm.

6. Trick, stratagem.

"Blood?" she said, looking at some spots on his coat with a shudder.

He looked up at her. "Why, Deb!" he said, smiling,—such a bright, boyish smile, that it went to poor Deborah's heart directly, and she sobbed and cried out loud.

"Oh, Hugh, lad! Hugh! dunnot look at me, when it wur my fault! To think I brought hur to it! And I loved hur so! Oh lad, I dud!"

The confession, even in this wretch, came with the woman's blush through the sharp cry.

He did not seem to hear her,—scraping away diligently at the bars with the bit of tin.

Was he going mad? She peered closely into his face. Something she saw there made her draw suddenly back,—something which Haley had not seen, that lay beneath the pinched, vacant look it had caught since the trial, or the curious gray shadow that rested on it. That gray shadow,—yes, she knew what that meant. She had often seen it creeping over women's faces for months, who died at last of slow hunger or consumption. That meant death, distant, lingering: but this—Whatever it was the woman saw, or thought she saw, used as she was to crime and misery, seemed to make her sick with a new horror. Forgetting her fear of him, she caught his shoulders, and looked keenly, steadily, into his eyes.

"Hugh!" she cried, in a desperate whisper,—"oh, boy, not that! for God's sake, not *that*!"

The vacant laugh went off his face, and he answered her in a muttered word or two that drove her away. Yet the words were kindly enough. Sitting there on his pallet, she cried silently a hopeless sort of tears, but did not speak again. The man looked up furtively at her now and then. Whatever his own trouble was, her distress vexed him with a momentary sting.

It was market-day. The narrow window of the jail looked down directly on the carts and wagons drawn up in a long line, where they had unloaded. He could see, too, and hear distinctly the clink of money as it changed hands, the busy crowd of whites and blacks shoving, pushing one another, and the chaffering and swearing at the stalls. Somehow, the sound, more than anything else had done, wakened him up,—made the whole real to him. He was done with the world and the business of it. He let the tin fall, and looked out, pressing his face close to the rusty bars. How they crowded and pushed! And he,—he should never walk that pavement again! There came Neff Sanders, one of the feeders at the mill, with a basket on his arm. Sure enough, Neff was married the other week. He whistled, hoping he would look up; but he did not. He wondered if Neff remembered he was there,—if any of the boys thought of him up there, and thought that he never was to go down that old cinder-road again. Never again! He had not quite understood it before; but now he did. Not for days or years, but never!—that was it.

How clear the light fell on that stall in front of the market! and how like a picture it was, the dark-green heaps of corn, and the crimson beets, and golden melons! There was another with game: how the light flickered on that pheasant's breast, with the purplish blood dripping over the brown feathers! He could see the red shining of the drops, it was so near. In one minute he could be down there. It was just a step. So easy, as it seemed, so natural to go! Yet it could never be—not in all the thousands of years to come—that he should put his foot on that street again! He thought of himself with a sorrowful pity, as of some one else. There was a dog down in the market, walking after his master with such a stately, grave look!—only a dog, yet he could go backwards and forwards just as he pleased: he had good luck! Why, the very vilest cur, yelping there in the gutter, had not lived his life, had been free to act out whatever thought God had put into his brain; while he—No, he would not think of that! He tried to put the thought away, and to listen to a dispute between a countryman and a woman about some meat; but it would come back. He, what had he done to bear this?

Then came the sudden picture of what might have been, and now. He knew what it was to be in the penitentiary,—how it went with men there. He knew how in these long years he should slowly die, but not until soul and body had become corrupt and rotten,—how, when he came out, if he lived to come, even the lowest of the mill-hands would jeer him,—how his hands would be weak, and his brain senseless and stupid. He believed he was almost that now. He put his hand to his head, with a puzzled, weary look. It ached, his head, with thinking. He tried to quiet himself. It was only right, perhaps; he had done wrong. But was there right or wrong for such as he? What was right? And who had ever taught him? He thrust the whole matter away. A dark, cold quiet crept through his brain. It was all wrong; but let it be! It was nothing to him more than the others. Let it be!

The door grated, as Haley opened it.

"Come, my woman! Must lock up for t' night. Come, stir yerself!"

She went up and took Hugh's hand.

"Good—night, Deb," he said, carelessly.

She had not hoped he would say more; but the tired pain on her mouth just then was bitterer than death. She took his passive hand and kissed it.

"Hur'll never see Deb again!" she ventured, her lips growing colder and more bloodless.

What did she say that for? Did he not know it? Yet he would not be impatient with poor old Deb. She had trouble of her own, as well as he.

"No, never again," he said, trying to be cheerful.

She stood just a moment, looking at him. Do you laugh at her, standing there, with her hunchback, her rags, her bleared, withered face, and the great despised love tugging at her heart?

"Come, you!" called Haley, impatiently.

She did not move.

"Hugh!" she whispered.

It was to be her last word. What was it?

"Hugh, boy, not THAT!"

He did not answer. She wrung her hands, trying to be silent, looking in his face in an agony of entreaty. He smiled again, kindly.

"It is best, Deb. I cannot bear to be hurted any more."

"Hur knows," she said, humbly.

"Tell my father good-bye; and—and kiss little Janey."

She nodded, saying nothing, looked in his face again, and went out of the door. As she went, she staggered.

"Drinkin' to-day?" broke out Haley, pushing her before him. "Where the Devil did you get it? Here, in with ye!" and he shoved her into her cell, next to Wolfe's, and shut the door.

Along the wall of her cell there was a crack low down by the floor, through which she could see the light from Wolfe's. She had discovered it days before. She hurried in now, and, kneeling down by it, listened, hoping to hear some sound. Nothing but the rasping of the tin on the bars. He was at his old amusement again. Something in the noise jarred on her ear, for she shivered as she heard it. Hugh rasped away at the bars. A dull old bit of tin, not fit to cut korl with.

He looked out of the window again. People were leaving the market now. A tall mulatto girl, following her mistress, her basket on her head, crossed the street just below, and looked up. She was laughing; but, when she caught sight of the haggard face peering out through the bars, suddenly grew grave, and hurried by. A free, firm step, a clear-cut olive face, with a scarlet turban tied on one side, dark, shining eyes, and on the head the basket poised, filled with fruit and flowers, under which the scarlet turban and bright eyes looked out half-shadowed. The picture caught his eye. It was good to see a face like that. He would try to-morrow, and cut one like it. *To-morrow*! He threw down the tin, trembling, and covered his face with his hands. When he looked up again, the daylight was gone.

Deborah, crouching near by on the other side of the wall, heard no noise. He sat on the side of the low pallet, thinking. Whatever was the mystery which the woman had seen on his face, it came out now slowly, in the dark there, and became fixed,—a something never seen on his face before. The evening was darkening fast. The market had been over for an hour; the rumbling of the carts over the pavement grew more infrequent: he listened to each, as it passed, because he thought it was to be for the last time. For the same reason, it was, I suppose, that he strained his eyes to catch a glimpse of each passer-by, wondering who they were, what kind of homes they were going to, if they had children,—listening eagerly to every chance word in the street, as if—(God be merciful to the man! what strange fancy was this?)—as if he never should hear human voices again.

It was quite dark at last. The street was a lonely one. The last passenger, he thought, was gone. No,—there was a quick step: Joe Hill, lighting the lamps. Joe was a good old chap; never passed a fellow without some joke or other. He remembered once seeing the place where he lived with his wife. "Granny Hill" the boys called her. Bedridden she was; but so kind as Joe was to her! kept the room so clean!—and the old woman, when he was there, was laughing at "some of t' lad's foolishness." The step was far down the street; but he could see him place the ladder, run up, and light the gas. A longing seized him to be spoken to once more.

"Joe!" he called, out of the grating. "Good-bye, Joe!"

The old man stopped a moment, listening uncertainly; then hurried on. The prisoner thrust his hand out of the window, and called again, louder; but Joe was too far down the street. It was a little thing; but it hurt him,—this disappointment.

"Good-bye, Joe!" he called, sorrowfully enough.

"Be quiet!" said one of the jailers, passing the door, striking on it with his club.

Oh, that was the last, was it?

There was an inexpressible bitterness on his face, as he lay down on the bed, taking the bit of tin, which he had rasped to a tolerable degree of sharpness, in his hand,—to play with, it may be. He bared his arms, looking intently at their corded veins and sinews. Deborah, listening in the next cell, heard a slight clicking sound, often repeated. She shut her lips tightly, that she might not scream; the cold drops of sweat broke over her, in her dumb agony.

"Hur knows best," she muttered at last, fiercely clutching the boards where she lay.

If she could have seen Wolfe, there was nothing about him to frighten her. He lay quite still, his arms outstretched, looking at the pearly stream of moonlight coming into the window. I think in that one hour that came then he lived back over all the years that had gone before. I think that all the low, vile life, all his wrongs, all his starved hopes, came then, and stung him with a farewell poison that made him sick unto death. He made neither moan nor cry, only turned his worn face now and then to the pure light, that seemed so far off, as one that said, "How long, O Lord? how long?"

The hour was over at last. The moon, passing over her nightly path, slowly came nearer, and threw the light across his bed on his feet. He watched it steadily, as it crept up, inch by inch, slowly. It seemed to him to carry with it a great silence. He had been so hot and tired there always in the mills! The years had been so fierce and cruel! There was coming now quiet and coolness and sleep. His tense limbs relaxed, and settled in a calm languor. The blood ran fainter and slow from his heart. He did not think now with a savage anger of what might be and was not; he was conscious only of deep stillness creeping over him. At first he saw a sea of faces: the mill-men,—women he had known, drunken and bloated,—Janey's timid and pitiful—poor old Debs: then they floated together like a mist, and faded away, leaving only the clear, pearly moonlight.

Whether, as the pure light crept up the stretched-out figure, it brought with it calm and peace, who shall say? His dumb soul was alone with God in judgment. A Voice may have spoken for it from far-off Calvary, "Father, forgive them, for they know not what they do!"[7] Who dare say? Fainter and fainter the heart rose and fell, slower and slower the moon floated from behind a cloud, until, when at last its full tide of white splendor swept over the cell, it seemed to wrap and fold into a deeper stillness the dead figure that never should move again. Silence deeper than the Night! Nothing that moved, save the black, nauseous stream of blood dripping slowly from the pallet to the floor!

There was outcry and crowd enough in the cell the next day. The coroner and his jury, the local editors, Kirby himself, and boys with their hands thrust knowingly into their pockets and heads on one side, jammed into the corners. Coming and going all day. Only one woman. She came late, and outstayed them all. A Quaker, or Friend, as they call themselves. I think this woman was known by that name in heaven. A homely body, coarsely dressed in gray and white. Deborah (for Haley had let her in) took notice of her. She watched them all—sitting on the end of the pallet, holding his head in her arms—with the ferocity of a watch-dog, if any of them touched the body. There was no meekness, no sorrow, in her face; the stuff out of which mur-

7. Luke 23.34: "Father, forgive them: for they know not what they do" (Jesus' words on the cross). Calvary was the site of the Crucifixion.

derers are made, instead. All the time Haley and the woman were laying straight the limbs and cleaning the cell, Deborah sat still, keenly watching the Quaker's face. Of all the crowd there that day, this woman alone had not spoken to her,—only once or twice had put some cordial to her lips. After they all were gone, the woman, in the same still, gentle way, brought a vase of wood-leaves and berries, and placed it by the pallet, then opened the narrow window. The fresh air blew in, and swept the woody fragrance over the dead face. Deborah looked up with a quick wonder.

"Did hur know my boy wud like it? Did hur know Hugh?"

"I know Hugh now."

The white fingers passed in a slow, pitiful way over the dead, worn face. There was a heavy shadow in the quiet eyes.

"Did hur know where they'll bury Hugh?" said Deborah in a shrill tone, catching her arm.

This had been the question hanging on her lips all day.

"In t' town-yard? Under t' mud and ash? T' lad 'll smother, woman! He wur born in t' lane moor, where t' air is frick[8] and strong. Take hur out, for God's sake, take hur out where t' air blows!"

The Quaker hesitated, but only for a moment. She put her strong arm around Deborah and led her to the window.

"Thee sees the hills, friend, over the river? Thee sees how the light lies warm there, and the winds of God blow all the day? I live there,—where the blue smoke is, by the trees. Look at me." She turned Deborah's face to her own, clear and earnest. "Thee will believe me? I will take Hugh and bury him there to-morrow."

Deborah did not doubt her. As the evening wore on, she leaned against the iron bars, looking at the hills that rose far off, through the thick sodden clouds, like a bright, unattainable calm. As she looked, a shadow of their solemn repose fell on her face; its fierce discontent faded into a pitiful, humble quiet. Slow, solemn tears gathered in her eyes: the poor weak eyes turned so hopelessly to the place where Hugh was to rest, the grave heights looking higher and brighter and more solemn than ever before. The Quaker watched her keenly. She came to her at last, and touched her arm.

"When thee comes back," she said, in a low, sorrowful tone, like one who speaks from a strong heart deeply moved with remorse or pity, "thee shall begin thy life again,—there on the hills. I came too late; but not for thee,—by God's help, it may be."

Not too late. Three years after, the Quaker began her work. I end my story here. At evening-time it was light. There is no need to tire you with the long years of sunshine, and fresh air, and slow, patient Christ-love, needed to make healthy and hopeful this impure body and soul. There is a homely pine house, on one of these hills, whose windows overlook broad, wooded slopes and clover-crimsoned meadows,—niched into the very place where the light is warmest, the air freest. It is the Friends'[9] meeting-house. Once a week they sit there, in their grave, earnest way, waiting for the Spirit of Love to speak, opening their simple hearts to receive His words. There is a woman, old, deformed, who takes a humble place among them: waiting like them: in

8. Fresh.

9. Quakers.

her gray dress, her worn face, pure and meek, turned now and then to the sky. A woman much loved by these silent, restful people; more silent than they, more humble, more loving. Waiting: with her eyes turned to hills higher and purer than these on which she lives,—dim and far off now, but to be reached some day. There may be in her heart some latent hope to meet there the love denied her here,—that she shall find him whom she lost, and that then she will not be all-unworthy. Who blames her? Something is lost in the passage of every soul from one eternity to the other,—something pure and beautiful, which might have been and was not: a hope, a talent, a love, over which the soul mourns, like Esau deprived of his birthright.[1] What blame to the meek Quaker, if she took her lost hope to make the hills of heaven more fair?

Nothing remains to tell that the poor Welsh puddler once lived, but this figure of the mill-woman cut in korl. I have it here in a corner of my library. I keep it hid behind a curtain,—it is such a rough, ungainly thing. Yet there are about it touches, grand sweeps of outline, that show a master's hand. Sometimes,—to-night, for instance,—the curtain is accidentally drawn back, and I see a bare arm stretched out imploringly in the darkness, and an eager, wolfish face watching mine: a wan, woful face, through which the spirit of the dead korl-cutter looks out, with its thwarted life, its mighty hunger, its unfinished work. Its pale, vague lips seem to tremble with a terrible question. "Is this the End?" they say,—"nothing beyond?—no more?" Why, you tell me you have seen that look in the eyes of dumb brutes,—horses dying under the lash. I know.

The deep of the night is passing while I write. The gas-light wakens from the shadows here and there the objects which lie scattered through the room: only faintly, though; for they belong to the open sunlight. As I glance at them, they each recall some task or pleasure of the coming day. A half-moulded child's head; Aphrodite;[2] a bough of forest-leaves; music; work; homely fragments, in which lie the secrets of all eternal truth and beauty. Prophetic all! Only this dumb, woful face seems to belong to and end with the night. I turn to look at it. Has the power of its desperate need commanded the darkness away? While the room is yet steeped in heavy shadow, a cool, gray light suddenly touches its head like a blessing hand, and its groping arm points through the broken cloud to the far East, where, in the flickering, nebulous crimson, God has set the promise of the Dawn.

1861, 1865

1. Genesis 25 and 27 tell the story of Jacob's depriving his elder twin brother, Esau, of his birthright.

2. Venus, the goddess of love.

LOUISA MAY ALCOTT
1832–1888

The author of the perennially popular novel *Little Women* (1868–69), Louisa May Alcott was the second of four daughters of the philosopher-teacher Amos Bronson Alcott and Abigail May Alcott. Born in Germantown, near Philadelphia, on November 29, 1832, she grew up in Boston and Concord and lived among the leading Massachusetts cultural figures of the time. Margaret Fuller taught in her father's school in Boston (which folded in 1839 after controversies over sex education and admitting black children); Ralph Waldo Emerson introduced her to Goethe's writings and encouraged her to borrow books from his library; Thoreau gave her informal lessons about the natural world, and later hosted her and her father while he was living at Walden Pond; Hawthorne for several years lived nearby. Her maternal uncle, Samuel May, was a leading Boston abolitionist, and she came to know William Lloyd Garrison, Theodore Parker, and other prominent abolitionists, joining with them in 1854 when they attempted to prevent the return of the fugitive slave Anthony Burns to Virginia. In "Recollections of My Childhood" (1888), Alcott gloried in having shared in the struggle "which put an end to a great wrong."

During Louisa May Alcott's youth, her father was well known and controversial, regarded by some as a great philosopher but by others as a half-crazed mystic, particularly after the first installment of his abstruse "Orphic Sayings" appeared in the 1840 *Dial*, the journal published by the informal group known as "transcendentalists." As an educator, he observed his first two daughters closely and took hundreds of pages of notes on their behavior. He believed self-contradictorily in a child's natural goodness and in the importance of instilling traits in a child that his Puritan ancestors would have approved, such as self-denial and self-criticism. When Louisa was two years old, he gave her an apple with instructions not to eat it; she ate the apple, while her older sister, to whom Bronson had given the same instructions, dutifully left it alone, an outcome that he interpreted as a sign of his second daughter's overly willful nature. Over time, Louisa, while remaining deeply attached to her father, increasingly resented his efforts to stifle her independence, and much of her writing would deal with young women struggling to express and value their individuality. Her mother more warmly encouraged her reading and writing. With her sisters, she wrote and staged plays for family entertainment. She kept a regular journal, wrote stories from a very early age, and was enamored of Sir Walter Scott's historical novels, John Bunyan's *Pilgrim's Progress*, and Charles Dickens's novels (which she read as they were being serialized), as well as works by Goethe, Hawthorne, the Brontës, and many other writers.

In 1843, when Louisa May Alcott was ten, her father founded Fruitlands, a vegetarian reform community near Concord that banned money and regarded participants as members of one large family. He moved his family there, but after several months of hardship in which, according to his wife's view, the men did nothing but think and the women did all the hard physical work, Abigail threatened to leave with her children, even if this meant severing her ties with her husband. He reluctantly gave up on the project early in 1844 and moved the family back to Concord. (Alcott would later satirize the community in her short story "Transcendental Wild Oats" [1873]). Because Bronson had invested all of his money in Fruitlands, for years afterward the Alcotts lived in poverty. After several years in Concord they moved to Boston, where Abigail tried to support the family by becoming a social worker—one of the earliest practitioners of this profession—and then by running an employment agency, while Bronson attempted to make money through holding "conversations" (symposia in which participants paid a small fee) on various philosophical topics. The family moved constantly in attempts to find rental situations they could afford. Writing about these years of economic struggle in her 1888 "Recollections," Alcott maintained that as a sixteen-year-old she made the following declaration: "I will do something by-and-by. Don't care what, teach, sew, act, write, anything to help the family; I'll be rich and famous and happy before I die, see if I won't."

Alcott did teach and sew; she also worked as a governess and took on other short-term jobs. But mainly she attempted to make money through her writing. Her first story, "The Rival Painters," for which she was paid the modest sum of five dollars, appeared in an 1852 issue of a weekly newspaper called the *Olive Branch*, while a collection of childrens' stories, *Flower Fables*, originally written for Emerson's daughter Ellen during the 1840s, was published in 1854, earning a total of thirty-five dollars. Although it would be some years before Alcott learned to demand proper payment for her work, she was gaining a reputation with her early publications. In 1860 her story "A Modern Cinderella" appeared in the *Atlantic Monthly*, the most prestigious literary magazine of the time.

Shortly before the Civil War, Alcott's younger sister Lizzie died of the aftereffects of scarlet fever, which Louisa managed to fight off. Her beloved neighbor Henry David Thoreau died in 1862. She was struggling with a novel, *Moods*, which she would eventually publish in 1864, but at this time her chief ambition was to contribute to the Civil War effort. Shortly after writing in her journal "I long to be a man; but as I can't fight, I will content myself with working for those who can," she volunteered for the nursing corps. Beginning in December 1862, she worked at the unsanitary and poorly run Union Hotel Hospital in Washington, D.C., overseeing amputations and comforting the many men who were dying. The work took its toll, and by late January of 1863 she was suffering from typhoid pneumonia and had to give up nursing. Although she survived the disease, she was badly damaged by the poisonous treatment—huge doses of mercury, at that time the normal therapy for many diseases—which left her with permanent fatigue and neuralgia over the remaining twenty-five years of her life.

Despite her health problems, Alcott began to write again after she recovered from pneumonia. In 1863 she published sketches about her hospital experience in the *Boston Commonwealth*, working with the persona of a feisty, ironic nurse named Tribulation Periwinkle, and the pieces were published as *Hospital Sketches* later in the year. She also published several short stories about the Civil War, including two, "M.L." and "My Contraband," about interracial sexuality. ("M.L." points to the possibility of love across the color line; "My Contraband" offers suggestions about such a possibility, while underscoring the hard truths of the sexual violation of black women on slave plantations.) Eager for money and desirous of experimenting with fiction that would allow her to write unconventionally, in a Gothic mode, about such topics as incest, suicide, drug addiction, sexual passion, and the supernatural, she began publishing melodramatic sensation stories under the name of A. M. Barnard, earning $100 (around $1200 in today's currency) for each story. Those stories, discovered by the critic Madeleine Stern during the 1980s and 1990s, helped transform critics' understanding of Alcott, who for over a century was known mainly as the author of *Little Women* (though Alcott does write about her surrogate Jo's turn to sensation fiction in *Little Women*).

In 1867 Alcott was offered the editorship of a children's magazine, *Mercury Museum*, and at the same time she was solicited by the editor Thomas Niles of Roberts Brothers to write a novel for girls. She was not initially enthusiastic about the novel, and Niles found the first twelve chapters dull. But his nieces loved what they read. Accordingly, Niles urged Alcott to persevere, and she wrote 400 manuscript pages during June and July of 1868. Part 1 of *Little Women*, appearing later in the year, quickly sold out its first printing; Part II appeared in 1869, and the novel has never gone out of print. A semiautobiographical story of her girlhood and young womanhood, the novel, which sanitized some of the misery of the Alcotts' poverty, brought together the four differently imperfect but sympathetic March sisters and their adored mother in a family portrait that focused on the girls' struggles and triumphs as three of the four (one dies tragically) grow into young womanhood. More adventurously, the novel explored questions of gender and power, focusing on Jo's dissatisfaction with the constraints of girlhood and her efforts to become a successful writer. There is an appealing neighbor, Laurie, who seems a likely candidate to marry Jo, but she declines his offer. By the end of the novel the successful author Jo chooses to marry the more fatherly Professor Bhaer, temporarily giving up writing to have children and assist her husband in running a school for boys. In Alcott's later novel *Jo's Boys* (1886), however, Jo resumes writing and helps to make the school coeducational.

The novel's success allowed Alcott to pay off her family's debts and support her mother and father. She published *An Old-Fashioned Girl* in 1870, *Little Men* in 1872, and *Work* (one of the finest nineteenth-century novels about women and labor) in 1873. As the physical act of writing became increasingly painful, she tried learning to write with her left hand. In 1874 she confided to her journal: "When I had youth I had no money; now that I have the money I have no time; and when I get the time, if I ever do, I shall have no health to enjoy life." Still, she continued to push on with her writing, returning to the mode of sensation fiction with the novel *A Modern Mephistopheles*, published in 1877 in Roberts Brothers' "No Name Series" (novels published anonymously by famous writers). By the late 1870s Alcott had become almost too ill to write, though she labored on with *Jo's Boys* and several other projects. Her beloved mother, Abigail, died in 1877; two years later, her youngest sister, May (the prototype for Amy in *Little Women*), died in childbirth in Paris, and Louisa adopted the child, Louisa May Nierker, in 1880. Three years later, her father suffered a paralytic stroke, and for a while Alcott was caring for her father and the young Louisa. In 1886, suffering from pain and exhaustion, she was admitted to Dr. Rhoda Lawrence's nursing home in West Roxbury, Massachusetts. She died on March 6, 1888, two days after the death of her father.

In recent decades much of Alcott's writing has been put back into print, allowing readers to appreciate the wide range of her children's fiction, her realistic novels and short stories, and her slyly comic melodramas and sensation fiction. Jo March's goals were not only to be independent and to help those she loved, but also to produce a literary work of enduring merit that "went to the hearts of those who read it." Alcott achieved that goal as the author of *Little Women* and many other works published during her approximately forty-year career as a writer.

My Contraband[1]

Doctor Franck came in as I sat sewing up the rents in an old shirt, that Tom might go tidily to his grave. New shirts were needed for the living, and there was no wife or mother to "dress him handsome when he went to meet the Lord," as one woman said, describing the fine funeral she had pinched[2] herself to give her son.

1. The story first appeared as "The Brothers" in the November 1863 *Atlantic Monthly*. Alcott objected to the title, which editor James T. Fields had insisted on, and she reprinted the story with her preferred title, along with other editorial changes, in *Hospital Sketches and Camp and Fireside Stories* (1869), the source of the text printed here. "Contraband": during the Civil War, the term referred to a slave who escaped to the Union side, or was taken by Union forces, and then was granted his or her freedom. The word also means "prohibited," which adds resonance to a title that could also refer to Nurse Dane's prohibited or forbidden thoughts.

"Miss Dane, I'm in a quandary," began the Doctor, with that expression of countenance which says as plainly as words, "I want to ask a favor, but I wish you'd save me the trouble."

"Can I help you out of it?"

"Faith! I don't like to propose it, but you certainly can, if you please."

"Then name it, I beg."

"You see a Reb[3] has just been brought in crazy with typhoid; a bad case every way; a drunken, rascally little captain somebody took the trouble to capture, but whom nobody wants to take the trouble to cure. The wards are full, the ladies worked to death, and willing to be for our own boys, but rather slow to risk their lives for a Reb. Now, you've had the fever,[4] you like queer patients, your mate will see to your ward for a while, and I will find you a good attendant. The fellow won't last long, I fancy; but he can't die without some sort of care, you know. I've put him in the fourth story of the west wing, away from the rest. It is airy, quiet, and comfortable there. I'm on that ward, and will do my best for you in every way. Now, then, will you go?"

"Of course I will, out of perversity, if not common charity; for some of these people think that because I'm an abolitionist I am also a heathen, and I should rather like to show them that, though I cannot quite love my enemies, I am willing to take care of them."

"Very good; I thought you'd go; and speaking of abolition reminds me that you can have a contraband for servant, if you like. It is that fine mulatto fellow who was found burying his rebel master after the fight, and, being badly cut over the head, our boys brought him along. Will you have him?"

"By all means,—for I'll stand to my guns on that point, as on the other; these black boys are far more faithful and handy than some of the white scamps given me to serve, instead of being served by. But is this man well enough?"

"Yes, for that sort of work, and I think you'll like him. He must have been a handsome fellow before he got his face slashed; not much darker than myself; his master's son, I dare say, and the white blood makes him rather high and haughty about some things. He was in a bad way when he came in, but vowed he'd die in the street rather than turn in with the black fellows below; so I put him up in the west wing, to be out of the way, and he's seen to the captain all the morning. When can you go up?"

"As soon as Tom is laid out, Skinner moved, Haywood washed, Marble dressed, Charley rubbed, Downs taken up, Upham laid down, and the whole forty fed."

We both laughed, though the Doctor was on his way to the dead-house and I held a shroud on my lap. But in a hospital one learns that cheerfulness is one's salvation; for, in an atmosphere of suffering and death, heaviness of heart would soon paralyze usefulness of hand, if the blessed gift of smiles had been denied us.

In an hour I took possession of my new charge, finding a dissipated-looking boy of nineteen or twenty raving in the solitary little room, with no one near him but the contraband in the room adjoining. Feeling decidedly more interest in the black man than in the white, yet remembering the Doctor's hint of

2. Scrimped.

3. Short for "Rebel," term used by the Union side to describe Confederate soldiers.

4. I.e., to have immunities through antibodies.

his being "high and haughty," I glanced furtively at him as I scattered chloride of lime about the room to purify the air, and settled matters to suit myself. I had seen many contrabands, but never one so attractive as this. All colored men are called "boys," even if their heads are white; this boy was five-and-twenty at least, strong-limbed and manly, and had the look of one who never had been cowed by abuse or worn with oppressive labor. He sat on his bed doing nothing; no book, no pipe, no pen or paper anywhere appeared, yet anything less indolent or listless than his attitude and expression I never saw. Erect he sat, with a hand on either knee, and eyes fixed on the bare wall opposite, so rapt in some absorbing thought as to be unconscious of my presence, though the door stood wide open and my movements were by no means noiseless. His face was half averted, but I instantly approved the Doctor's taste, for the profile which I saw possessed all the attributes of comeliness belonging to his mixed race. He was more quadroon[5] than mulatto, with Saxon features, Spanish complexion darkened by exposure, color in lips and cheek, waving hair, and an eye full of the passionate melancholy which in such men always seems to utter a mute protest against the broken law that doomed them at their birth. What could he be thinking of? The sick boy cursed and raved, I rustled to and fro, steps passed the door, bells rang, and the steady rumble of army-wagons came up from the street, still he never stirred. I had seen colored people in what they call "the black sulks," when, for days, they neither smiled nor spoke, and scarcely ate. But this was something more than that; for the man was not dully brooding over some small grievance; he seemed to see an all-absorbing fact or fancy recorded on the wall, which was a blank to me. I wondered if it were some deep wrong or sorrow, kept alive by memory and impotent regret; if he mourned for the dead master to whom he had been faithful to the end; or if the liberty now his were robbed of half its sweetness by the knowledge that some one near and dear to him still languished in the hell from which he had escaped. My heart quite warmed to him at that idea; I wanted to know and comfort him; and, following the impulse of the moment, I went in and touched him on the shoulder.

In an instant the man vanished and the slave appeared. Freedom was too new a boon to have wrought its blessed changes yet; and as he started up, with his hand at his temple, and an obsequious "Yes, Missis," any romance that had gathered round him fled away, leaving the saddest of all sad facts in living guise before me. Not only did the manhood seem to die out of him, but the comeliness that first attracted me; for, as he turned, I saw the ghastly wound that had laid open cheek and forehead. Being partly healed, it was no longer bandaged, but held together with strips of that transparent plaster which I never see without a shiver, and swift recollections of the scenes with which it is associated in my mind. Part of his black hair had been shorn away, and one eye was nearly closed; pain so distorted, and the cruel sabre-cut so marred that portion of his face, that, when I saw it, I felt as if a fine medal had been suddenly reversed, showing me a far more striking type of human suffering and wrong than Michael Angelo's bronze prisoner.[6] By one of those inexplicable processes that often teach us how little we understand

5. One-fourth black; a term used at the time to refer to a light-complected person of mixed racial ancestry.

ourselves, my purpose was suddenly changed; and, though I went in to offer comfort as a friend, I merely gave an order as a mistress.

"Will you open these windows? this man needs more air."

He obeyed at once, and, as he slowly urged up the unruly sash, the handsome profile was again turned toward me, and again I was possessed by my first impression so strongly that I involuntarily said,—

"Thank you."

Perhaps it was fancy, but I thought that in the look of mingled surprise and something like reproach which he gave me, there was also a trace of grateful pleasure. But he said, in that tone of spiritless humility these poor souls learn so soon,—

"I isn't a white man, Missis, I'se a contraband."

"Yes, I know it; but a contraband is a free man, and I heartily congratulate you."

He liked that; his face shone, he squared his shoulders, lifted his head, and looked me full in the eye with a brisk,—

"Thank ye, Missis; anything more to do fer yer?"

"Doctor Franck thought you would help me with this man, as there are many patients and few nurses or attendants. Have you had the fever?"

"No, Missis."

"They should have thought of that when they put him here; wounds and fevers should not be together. I'll try to get you moved."

He laughed a sudden laugh: if he had been a white man, I should have called it scornful; as he was a few shades darker than myself, I suppose it must be considered an insolent, or at least an unmannerly one.

"It don't matter, Missis. I'd rather be up here with the fever than down with those niggers; and there isn't no other place fer me."

Poor fellow! that was true. No ward in all the hospital would take him in to lie side by side with the most miserable white wreck there. Like the bat in Æsop's fable,[7] he belonged to neither race; and the pride of one and the helplessness of the other, kept him hovering alone in the twilight a great sin has brought to overshadow the whole land.

"You shall stay, then; for I would far rather have you than my lazy Jack. But are you well and strong enough?"

"I guess I'll do, Missis."

He spoke with a passive sort of acquiescence,—as if it did not much matter if he were not able, and no one would particularly rejoice if he were.

"Yes, I think you will. By what name shall I call you?"

"Bob, Missis."

Every woman has her pet whim; one of mine was to teach the men self-respect by treating them respectfully. Tom, Dick, and Harry would pass, when lads rejoiced in those familiar abbreviations; but to address men often old enough to be my father in that style did not suit my old-fashioned ideas of propriety. This "Bob" would never do; I should have found it as easy to call

6. "The Rebellious Slave," a sculpture by the Italian artist Michelangelo Buonarroti (1475–1564).

7. In a fable by the ancient Greek storyteller Aesop (c. 620–564 B.C.E.), during a war between birds and mammals, the bat takes turns fighting on either side and ends up an outcast.

the chaplain "Gus" as my tragical-looking contraband by a title so strongly associated with the tail of a kite.[8]

"What is your other name?" I asked. "I like to call my attendants by their last names rather than by their first."

"I'se got no other, Missis; we has our masters' names, or do without. Mine's dead, and I won't have anything of his 'bout me."

"Well, I'll call you Robert, then, and you may fill this pitcher for me, if you will be so kind."

He went; but, through all the tame obedience years of servitude had taught him, I could see that the proud spirit his father gave him was not yet subdued, for the look and gesture with which he repudiated his master's name were a more effective declaration of independence than any Fourth-of-July orator could have prepared.

We spent a curious week together. Robert seldom left his room, except upon my errands; and I was a prisoner all day, often all night, by the bedside of the rebel. The fever burned itself rapidly away, for there seemed little vitality to feed it in the feeble frame of this old young man, whose life had been none of the most righteous, judging from the revelations made by his unconscious lips; since more than once Robert authoritatively silenced him, when my gentler hushings were of no avail, and blasphemous wanderings or ribald camp-songs made my cheeks burn and Robert's face assume an aspect of disgust. The captain was a gentleman in the world's eye, but the contraband was the gentleman in mine;—I was a fanatic, and that accounts for such depravity of taste, I hope. I never asked Robert of himself, feeling that somewhere there was a spot still too sore to bear the lightest touch; but, from his language, manner, and intelligence, I inferred that his color had procured for him the few advantages within the reach of a quick-witted, kindly-treated slave. Silent, grave, and thoughtful, but most serviceable, was my contraband; glad of the books I brought him, faithful in the performance of the duties I assigned to him, grateful for the friendliness I could not but feel and show toward him. Often I longed to ask what purpose was so visibly altering his aspect with such daily deepening gloom. But I never dared, and no one else had either time or desire to pry into the past of this specimen of one branch of the chivalrous "F. F. Vs."[9]

On the seventh night, Dr. Franck suggested that it would be well for some one, besides the general watchman of the ward, to be with the captain, as it might be his last. Although the greater part of the two preceding nights had been spent there, of course I offered to remain,—for there is a strange fascination in these scenes, which renders one careless of fatigue and unconscious of fear until the crisis is past.

"Give him water as long as he can drink, and if he drops into a natural sleep, it may save him. I'll look in at midnight, when some change will probably take place. Nothing but sleep or a miracle will keep him now. Good-night."

Away went the Doctor; and, devouring a whole mouthful of grapes, I lowered the lamp, wet the captain's head, and sat down on a hard stool to begin

8. The "bob" or weight on the kite tail provides balance.

9. First Families of Virginia (typically wealthy landowners, and usually descended from early settlers of the colony).

my watch. The captain lay with his hot, haggard face turned toward me, filling the air with his poisonous breath, and feebly muttering, with lips and tongue so parched that the sanest speech would have been difficult to understand. Robert was stretched on his bed in the inner room, the door of which stood ajar, that a fresh draught from his open window might carry the fever-fumes away through mine. I could just see a long, dark figure, with the lighter outline of a face, and, having little else to do just then, I fell to thinking of this curious contraband, who evidently prized his freedom highly, yet seemed in no haste to enjoy it. Dr. Franck had offered to send him on to safer quarters, but he had said, "No, thank yer, sir, not yet," and then had gone away to fall into one of those black moods of his, which began to disturb me, because I had no power to lighten them. As I sat listening to the clocks from the steeples all about us, I amused myself with planning Robert's future, as I often did my own, and had dealt out to him a generous hand of trumps wherewith to play this game of life which hitherto had gone so cruelly against him, when a harsh choked voice called,—

"Lucy!"

It was the captain, and some new terror seemed to have gifted him with momentary strength.

"Yes, here's Lucy," I answered, hoping that by following the fancy I might quiet him,—for his face was damp with the clammy moisture, and his frame shaken with the nervous tremor that so often precedes death. His dull eye fixed upon me, dilating with a bewildered look of incredulity and wrath, till he broke out fiercely,—

"That's a lie! she's dead,—and so's Bob, damn him!"

Finding speech a failure, I began to sing the quiet tune that had often soothed delirium like this; but hardly had the line,—

"See gentle patience smile on pain,"[1]

passed my lips, when he clutched me by the wrist, whispering like one in mortal fear,—

"Hush! she used to sing that way to Bob, but she never would to me. I swore I'd whip the devil out of her, and I did; but you know before she cut her throat she said she'd haunt me, and there she is!"

He pointed behind me with an aspect of such pale dismay, that I involuntarily glanced over my shoulder and started as if I had seen a veritable ghost; for, peering from the gloom of that inner room, I saw a shadowy face, with dark hair all about it, and a glimpse of scarlet at the throat. An instant showed me that it was only Robert leaning from his bed's foot, wrapped in a gray army-blanket, with his red shirt just visible above it, and his long hair disordered by sleep. But what a strange expression was on his face! The unmarred side was toward me, fixed and motionless as when I first observed it,—less absorbed now, but more intent. His eye glittered, his lips were apart like one who listened with every sense, and his whole aspect reminded me of a hound to which some wind had brought the scent of unsuspected prey.

1. From the song "See, Gentle Patience Smiles on Pain" (1835), words by the English poet Anne Steele (1716–1778) and arranged by Henry Kemble Oliver (1800–1885), from *The Boston Academy's Collection of Church Music* (1836).

"Do you know him, Robert? Does he mean you?"

"Laws, no, Missis; they all own half-a-dozen Bobs: but hearin' my name woke me; that's all."

He spoke quite naturally, and lay down again, while I returned to my charge, thinking that this paroxysm was probably his last. But by another hour I perceived a hopeful change; for the tremor had subsided, the cold dew was gone, his breathing was more regular, and Sleep, the healer, had descended to save or take him gently away. Doctor Franck looked in at midnight, bade me keep all cool and quiet, and not fail to administer a certain draught as soon as the captain woke. Very much relieved, I laid my head on my arms, uncomfortably folded on the little table, and fancied I was about to perform one of the feats which practice renders possible,—"sleeping with one eye open," as we say: a half-and-half doze, for all senses sleep but that of hearing; the faintest murmur, sigh, or motion will break it, and give one back one's wits much brightened by the brief permission to "stand at ease." On this night the experiment was a failure, for previous vigils, confinement, and much care had rendered naps a dangerous indulgence. Having roused half-a-dozen times in an hour to find all quiet, I dropped my heavy head on my arms, and, drowsily resolving to look up again in fifteen minutes, fell fast asleep.

The striking of a deep-voiced clock awoke me with a start. "That is one," thought I; but, to my dismay, two more strokes followed, and in remorseful haste I sprang up to see what harm my long oblivion had done. A strong hand put me back into my seat, and held me there. It was Robert. The instant my eye met his my heart began to beat, and all along my nerves tingled that electric flash which foretells a danger that we cannot see. He was very pale, his mouth grim, and both eyes full of somber fire; for even the wounded one was open now, all the more sinister for the deep scar above and below. But his touch was steady, his voice quiet, as he said,—

"Sit still, Missis; I won't hurt yer, nor scare yer, ef I can help it, but yer waked too soon."

"Let me go, Robert,—the captain is stirring,—I must give him something."

"No, Missis, yer can't stir an inch. Look here!"

Holding me with one hand, with the other he took up the glass in which I had left the draught, and showed me it was empty.

"Has he taken it?" I asked, more and more bewildered.

"I flung it out o' winder, Missis; he'll have to do without."

"But why, Robert? why did you do it?"

"'Kase I hate him!"

Impossible to doubt the truth of that; his whole face showed it, as he spoke through his set teeth, and launched a fiery glance at the unconscious captain. I could only hold my breath and stare blankly at him, wondering what mad act was coming next. I suppose I shook and turned white, as women have a foolish habit of doing when sudden danger daunts them; for Robert released my arm, sat down upon the bedside just in front of me, and said, with the ominous quietude that made me cold to see and hear,—

"Don't yer be frightened, Missis; don't try to run away, fer the door's locked and the key in my pocket; don't yer cry out, fer yer'd have to scream a long while, with my hand on yer mouth, 'efore yer was heard. Be still, an' I'll tell yer what I'm gwine to do."

"Lord help us! he has taken the fever in some sudden, violent way, and is out of his head. I must humor him till some one comes"; in pursuance of which swift determination, I tried to say, quite composedly,—

"I will be still and hear you; but open the window. Why did you shut it?"

"I'm sorry I can't do it, Missis; but yer'd jump out, or call, if I did, an' I'm not ready yet. I shut it to make yer sleep, an' heat would do it quicker'n anything else I could do."

The captain moved, and feebly muttered "Water!" Instinctively I rose to give it to him, but the heavy hand came down upon my shoulder, and in the same decided tone Robert said,—

"The water went with the physic;[2] let him call."

"Do let me go to him! he'll die without care!"

"I mean he shall;—don't yer meddle, ef yer please, Missis."

In spite of his quiet tone and respectful manner, I saw murder in his eyes, and turned faint with fear; yet the fear excited me, and, hardly knowing what I did, I seized the hands that had seized me, crying,—

"No, no; you shall not kill him! It is base to hurt a helpless man. Why do you hate him? He is not your master."

"He's my brother."

I felt that answer from head to foot, and seemed to fathom what was coming, with a prescience vague, but unmistakable. One appeal was left to me, and I made it.

"Robert, tell me what it means? Do not commit a crime and make me accessory to it. There is a better way of righting wrong than by violence;—let me help you find it."

My voice trembled as I spoke, and I heard the frightened flutter of my heart; so did he, and if any little act of mine had ever won affection or respect from him, the memory of it served me then. He looked down, and seemed to put some question to himself; whatever it was, the answer was in my favor, for when his eyes rose again, they were gloomy, but not desperate.

"I *will* tell yer, Missis; but mind, this makes no difference; the boy is mine. I'll give the Lord a chance to take him fust: if He don't, I shall."

"Oh, no! remember he is your brother."

An unwise speech; I felt it as it passed my lips, for a black frown gathered on Robert's face, and his strong hands closed with an ugly sort of grip. But he did not touch the poor soul gasping there behind him, and seemed content to let the slow suffocation of that stifling room end his frail life.

"I'm not like to forgit dat, Missis, when I've been thinkin' of it all this week. I knew him when they fetched him in, an' would 'a' done it long 'fore this, but I wanted to ask where Lucy was; he knows,—he told to-night,—an' now he's done for."

"Who is Lucy?" I asked hurriedly, intent on keeping his mind busy with any thought but murder.

With one of the swift transitions of a mixed temperament like this, at my question Robert's deep eyes filled, the clenched hands were spread before his face, and all I heard were the broken words,—

"My wife,—he took her——"

2. Medicine.

In that instant every thought of fear was swallowed up in burning indignation for the wrong, and a perfect passion of pity for the desperate man so tempted to avenge an injury for which there seemed no redress but this. He was no longer slave or contraband, no drop of black blood marred him in my sight, but an infinite compassion yearned to save, to help, to comfort him. Words seemed so powerless I offered none, only put my hand on his poor head, wounded, homeless, bowed down with grief for which I had no cure, and softly smoothed the long, neglected hair, pitifully wondering the while where was the wife who must have loved this tender-hearted man so well.

The captain moaned again, and faintly whispered, "Air!" but I never stirred. God forgive me! just then I hated him as only a woman thinking of a sister woman's wrong could hate. Robert looked up; his eyes were dry again, his mouth grim. I saw that, said, "Tell me more," and he did; for sympathy is a gift the poorest may give, the proudest stoop to receive.

"Yer see, Missis, his father,—I might say ours, ef I warn't ashamed of both of 'em,—his father died two years ago, an' left us all to Marster Ned,—that's him here, eighteen then. He always hated me, I looked so like old Marster: he don't,—only the light skin an' hair. Old Marster was kind to all of us, me 'specially, an' bought Lucy off the next plantation down there in South Car'lina, when he found I liked her. I married her, all I could;[3] it warn't much, but we was true to one another till Marster Ned come home a year after an' made hell fer both of us. He sent my old mother to be used up in his rice-swamp in Georgy; he found me with my pretty Lucy, an' though young Miss cried, an' I prayed to him on my knees, an' Lucy run away, he wouldn't have no mercy; he brought her back, an'—took her."

"Oh, what did you do?" I cried, hot with helpless pain and passion.

How the man's outraged heart sent the blood flaming up into his face and deepened the tones of his impetuous voice, as he stretched his arm across the bed, saying, with a terribly expressive gesture,—

"I half murdered him, an' to-night I'll finish."

"Yes, yes,—but go on now; what came next?"

He gave me a look that showed no white man could have felt a deeper degradation in remembering and confessing these last acts of brotherly oppression.

"They whipped me till I couldn't stand, an' then they sold me further South. Yer thought I was a white man once,—look here!"

With a sudden wrench he tore the shirt from neck to waist, and on his strong, brown shoulders showed me furrows deeply ploughed, wounds which, though healed, were ghastlier to me than any in that house. I could not speak to him, and, with the pathetic dignity a great grief lends the humblest sufferer, he ended his brief tragedy by simply saying,—

"That's all, Missis. I'se never seen her since, an' now I never shall in this world,—maybe not in t'other."

"But, Robert, why think her dead? The captain was wandering when he said those sad things; perhaps he will retract them when he is sane. Don't despair; don't give up yet."

3. Southern states did not recognize slave marriages as having legal standing.

"No, Missis, I'spect he's right; she was too proud to bear that long. It's like her to kill herself. I told her to, if there was no other way; an' she always minded me, Lucy did. My poor girl! Oh, it warn't right! No, by God, it warn't!"

As the memory of this bitter wrong, this double bereavement, burned in his sore heart, the devil that lurks in every strong man's blood leaped up; he put his hand upon his brother's throat, and, watching the white face before him, muttered low between his teeth,—

"I'm lettin' him go too easy; there's no pain in this; we a'n't even yet. I wish he knew me. Marster Ned! it's Bob; where's Lucy?"

From the captain's lips there came a long faint sigh, and nothing but a flutter of the eyelids showed that he still lived. A strange stillness filled the room as the elder brother held the younger's life suspended in his hand, while wavering between a dim hope and a deadly hate. In the whirl of thoughts that went on in my brain, only one was clear enough to act upon. I must prevent murder, if I could,—but how? What could I do up there alone, locked in with a dying man and a lunatic?—for any mind yielded utterly to any unrighteous impulse is mad while the impulse rules it. Strength I had not, nor much courage, neither time nor wit for stratagem, and chance only could bring me help before it was too late. But one weapon I possessed,—a tongue,—often a woman's best defence; and sympathy, stronger than fear, gave me power to use it. What I said Heaven only knows, but surely Heaven helped me; words burned on my lips, tears streamed from my eyes, and some good angel prompted me to use the one name that had power to arrest my hearer's hand and touch his heart. For at that moment I heartily believed that Lucy lived, and this earnest faith roused in him a like belief.

He listened with the lowering look of one in whom brute instinct was sovereign for the time,—a look that makes the noblest countenance base. He was but a man,—a poor, untaught, outcast, outraged man. Life had few joys for him; the world offered him no honors, no success, no home, no love. What future would this crime mar? and why should he deny himself that sweet, yet bitter morsel called revenge? How many white men, with all New England's freedom, culture, Christianity, would not have felt as he felt then? Should I have reproached him for a human anguish, a human longing for redress, all now left him from the ruin of his few poor hopes? Who had taught him that self-control, self-sacrifice, are attributes that make men masters of the earth, and lift them nearer heaven? Should I have urged the beauty of forgiveness, the duty of devout submission? He had no religion, for he was no saintly "Uncle Tom,"[4] and Slavery's black shadow seemed to darken all the world to him, and shut out God. Should I have warned him of penalties, of judgments, and the potency of law? What did he know of justice, or the mercy that should temper that stern virtue, when every law, human and divine, had been broken on his hearthstone? Should I have tried to touch him by appeals to filial duty, to brotherly love? How had his appeals been answered? What memories had father and brother stored up in his heart to plead for either now? No,—all these influences, these associations, would have proved worse than useless, had I been calm enough to try them. I was not; but instinct, subtler than reason, showed me the one safe clue by which to lead this troubled soul from the labyrinth in which it groped and nearly

4. Reference to the black Christian hero of Harriet Beecher Stowe's novel *Uncle Tom's Cabin* (1852).

fell. When I paused, breathless, Robert turned to me, asking, as if human assurances could strengthen his faith in Divine Omnipotence,—

"Do you believe, if I let Marster Ned live, the Lord will give me back my Lucy?"

"As surely as there is a Lord, you will find her here or in the beautiful hereafter, where there is no black or white, no master and no slave."

He took his hand from his brother's throat, lifted his eyes from my face to the wintry sky beyond, as if searching for that blessed country, happier even than the happy North. Alas, it was the darkest hour before the dawn!—there was no star above, no light below but the pale glimmer of the lamp that showed the brother who had made him desolate. Like a blind man who believes there is a sun, yet cannot see it, he shook his head, let his arms drop nervelessly upon his knees, and sat there dumbly asking that question which many a soul whose faith is firmer fixed than his has asked in hours less dark than this,—"Where is God?" I saw the tide had turned, and strenuously tried to keep this rudderless life-boat from slipping back into the whirlpool wherein it had been so nearly lost.

"I have listened to you, Robert; now hear me, and heed what I say, because my heart is full of pity for you, full of hope for your future, and a desire to help you now. I want you to go away from here, from the temptation of this place, and the sad thoughts that haunt it. You have conquered yourself once, and I honor you for it, because, the harder the battle, the more glorious the victory; but it is safer to put a greater distance between you and this man. I will write you letters, give you money, and send you to good old Massachusetts to begin your new life a freeman,—yes, and a happy man; for when the captain is himself again, I will learn where Lucy is, and move heaven and earth to find and give her back to you. Will you do this, Robert?"

Slowly, very slowly, the answer came; for the purpose of a week, perhaps a year, was hard to relinquish in an hour.

"Yes, Missis, I will."

"Good! Now you are the man I thought you, and I'll work for you with all my heart. You need sleep, my poor fellow; go, and try to forget. The captain is alive, and as yet you are spared that sin. No, don't look there; I'll care for him. Come, Robert, for Lucy's sake."

Thank Heaven for the immortality of love! for when all other means of salvation failed, a spark of this vital fire softened the man's iron will, until a woman's hand could bend it. He let me take from him the key, let me draw him gently away, and lead him to the solitude which now was the most healing balm I could bestow. Once in his little room, he fell down on his bed and lay there, as if spent with the sharpest conflict of his life. I slipped the bolt across his door, and unlocked my own, flung up the window, steadied myself with a breath of air, then rushed to Doctor Franck. He came; and till dawn we worked together, saving one brother's life, and taking earnest thought how best to secure the other's liberty. When the sun came up as blithely as if it shone only upon happy homes, the Doctor went to Robert. For an hour I heard the murmur of their voices; once I caught the sound of heavy sobs, and for a time a reverent hush, as if in the silence that good man were ministering to soul as well as body. When he departed he took Robert with him, pausing to tell me he should get him off as soon as possible, but not before we met again.

Nothing more was seen of them all day; another surgeon came to see the captain, and another attendant came to fill the empty place. I tried to rest, but could not, with the thought of poor Lucy tugging at my heart, and was soon back at my post again, anxiously hoping that my contraband had not been too hastily spirited away. Just as night fell there came a tap, and, opening, I saw Robert literally "clothed, and in his right mind."[5] The Doctor had replaced the ragged suit with tidy garments, and no trace of that tempestuous night remained but deeper lines upon the forehead, and the docile look of a repentant child. He did not cross the threshold, did not offer me his hand,—only took off his cap, saying, with a traitorous falter in his voice,—

"God bless yer, Missis! I'm gwine."

I put out both my hands, and held his fast.

"Good-by, Robert! Keep up good heart, and when I come home to Massachusetts we'll meet in a happier place than this. Are you quite ready, quite comfortable for your journey?"

"Yes, Missis, yes; the Doctor's fixed everything; I'se gwine with a friend of his; my papers are all right, an' I'm as happy as I can be till I find"—

He stopped there; then went on, with a glance into the room,—

"I'm glad I didn't do it, an' I thank yer, Missis, fer hinderin' me,—thank yer hearty; but I'm afraid I hate him jest the same."

Of course he did; and so did I; for these faulty hearts of ours cannot turn perfect in a night, but need frost and fire, wind and rain, to ripen and make them ready for the great harvest-home. Wishing to divert his mind, I put my poor mite[6] into his hand, and, remembering the magic of a certain little book, I gave him mine, on whose dark cover whitely shone the Virgin Mother and the Child, the grand history of whose life the book contained. The money went into Robert's pocket with a grateful murmur, the book into his bosom, with a long look and a tremulous—

"I never saw *my* baby, Missis."

I broke down then; and though my eyes were too dim to see, I felt the touch of lips upon my hands, heard the sound of departing feet, and knew my contraband was gone.

When one feels an intense dislike, the less one says about the subject of it the better; therefore I shall merely record that the captain lived,—in time was exchanged;[7] and that, whoever the other party was, I am convinced the Government got the best of the bargain. But long before this occurred, I had fulfilled my promise to Robert; for as soon as my patient recovered strength of memory enough to make his answer trustworthy, I asked, without any circumlocution,—

"Captain Fairfax, where is Lucy?"

And too feeble to be angry, surprised, or insincere, he straightway answered,—

"Dead, Miss Dane."

"And she killed herself when you sold Bob?"

"How the devil did you know that?" he muttered, with an expression half-remorseful, half-amazed; but I was satisfied, and said no more.

5. Refers to a follower of Jesus who had formerly been wild and demonical; see Mark 5.15.

6. Small amount of money.

7. The "exchange" would have been for a captured Union officer.

Of course this went to Robert, waiting far away there in a lonely home,—waiting, working, hoping for his Lucy. It almost broke my heart to do it; but delay was weak, deceit was wicked; so I sent the heavy tidings, and very soon the answer came,—only three lines; but I felt that the sustaining power of the man's life was gone.

"I tort I'd never see her any more; I'm glad to know she's out of trouble. I thank yer, Missis; an' if they let us, I'll fight fer yer till I'm killed, which I hope will be 'fore long."

Six months later he had his wish, and kept his word.

Every one knows the story of the attack on Fort Wagner; but we should not tire yet of recalling how our Fifty-Fourth,[8] spent with three sleepless nights, a day's fast, and a march under the July sun, stormed the fort as night fell, facing death in many shapes, following their brave leaders through a fiery rain of shot and shell, fighting valiantly for "God and Governor Andrew,"—how the regiment that went into action seven hundred strong, came out having had nearly half its number captured, killed, or wounded, leaving their young commander to be buried, like a chief of earlier times, with his body-guard around him, faithful to the death. Surely, the insult turns to honor, and the wide grave needs no monument but the heroism that consecrates it in our sight; surely, the hearts that held him nearest, see through their tears a noble victory in the seeming sad defeat; and surely, God's benediction was bestowed, when this loyal soul answered, as Death called the roll, "Lord, here am I, with the brothers Thou hast given me!"

The future must show how well that fight was fought; for though Fort Wagner once defied us, public prejudice is down; and through the cannon-smoke of that black night, the manhood of the colored race shines before many eyes that would not see, rings in many ears that would not hear, wins many hearts that would not hitherto believe.

When the news came that we were needed, there was none so glad as I to leave teaching contrabands, the new work I had taken up, and go to nurse "our boys," as my dusky flock so proudly called the wounded of the Fifty-Fourth. Feeling more satisfaction, as I assumed my big apron and turned up my cuffs, than if dressing for the President's levee,[9] I fell to work in Hospital No. 10 at Beaufort.[1] The scene was most familiar, and yet strange; for only dark faces looked up at me from the pallets so thickly laid along the floor, and I missed the sharp accent of my Yankee boys in the slower, softer voices calling cheerily to one another, or answering my questions with a stout, "We'll never give it up, Missis, till the last Reb's dead," or, "If our people's free, we can afford to die."

Passing from bed to bed, intent on making one pair of hands do the work of three, at least, I gradually washed, fed, and bandaged my way down the long line of sable heroes, and coming to the very last, found that he was my contraband. So old, so worn, so deathly weak and wan, I never should have known him but for the deep scar on his cheek. That side lay uppermost, and

8. The Fifty-Fourth Massachusetts Voluntary Infantry, a black regiment led by the white captain Robert Gould Shaw (1837–1863), made a valiant but failed attack on Fort Wagner, near Charleston, South Carolina, in July 1863. Shaw and a number of the black soldiers were killed during the battle. The first black troops were organized with the help of abolitionist John Albion Andrew (1818–1867), governor of Massachusetts.

9. A formal reception.

1. City in South Carolina located on Port Royal Island.

caught my eye at once; but even then I doubted, such an awful change had come upon him, when, turning to the ticket just above his head, I saw the name, "Robert Dane." That both assured and touched me, for, remembering that he had no name, I knew that he had taken mine. I longed for him to speak to me, to tell how he had fared since I lost sight of him, and let me perform some little service for him in return for many he had done for me; but he seemed asleep; and as I stood re-living that strange night again, a bright lad, who lay next him softly waving an old fan across both beds, looked up and said,—

"I guess you know him, Missis?"

"You are right. Do you?"

"As much as any one was able to, Missis."

"Why do you say 'was,' as if the man were dead and gone?"

"I s'pose because I know he'll have to go. He's got a bad jab in the breast, an' is bleedin' inside, the Doctor says. He don't suffer any, only gets weaker 'n' weaker every minute. I've been fannin' him this long while, an' he's talked a little; but he don't know me now, so he's most gone, I guess."

There was so much sorrow and affection in the boy's face, that I remembered something, and asked, with redoubled interest,—

"Are you the one that brought him off? I was told about a boy who nearly lost his life in saving that of his mate."

I dare say the young fellow blushed, as any modest lad might have done; I could not see it, but I heard the chuckle of satisfaction that escaped him, as he glanced from his shattered arm and bandaged side to the pale figure opposite.

"Lord, Missis, that's nothin'; we boys always stan' by one another, an' I warn't goin' to leave him to be tormented any more by them cussed Rebs. He's been a slave once, though he don't look half so much like it as me, an' I was born in Boston."

He did not; for the speaker was as black as the ace of spades,—being a sturdy specimen, the knave of clubs would perhaps be a fitter representative,—but the dark freeman looked at the white slave with the pitiful, yet puzzled expression I have so often seen on the faces of our wisest men, when this tangled question of Slavery presented itself, asking to be cut or patiently undone.

"Tell me what you know of this man; for, even if he were awake, he is too weak to talk."

"I never saw him till I joined the regiment, an' no one 'peared to have got much out of him. He was a shut-up sort of feller, an' didn't seem to care for anything but gettin' at the Rebs. Some say he was the fust man of us that enlisted; I know he fretted till we were off, an' when we pitched into old Wagner, he fought like the devil."

"Were you with him when he was wounded? How was it?"

"Yes, Missis. There was somethin' queer about it; for he 'peared to know the chap that killed him, an' the chap knew him. I don't dare to ask, but I rather guess one owned the other some time; for, when they clinched, the chap sung out, 'Bob!' an' Dane, 'Marster Ned!'—then they went at it."

I sat down suddenly, for the old anger and compassion struggled in my heart, and I both longed and feared to hear what was to follow.

"You see, when the Colonel,—Lord keep an' send him back to us!—it a'n't certain yet, you know, Missis, though it's two days ago we lost him,—well, when the Colonel shouted, 'Rush on, boys, rush on!' Dane tore away as if he was goin' to take the fort alone; I was next him, an' kept close as we went through the ditch an' up the wall. Hi! warn't that a rusher!" and the boy flung up his well arm with a whoop, as if the mere memory of that stirring moment came over him in a gust of irrepressible excitement.

"Were you afraid?" I said, asking the question women often put, and receiving the answer they seldom fail to get.

"No, Missis!"—emphasis on the "Missis"—"I never thought of anything but the damn' Rebs, that scalp, slash, an' cut our ears off, when they git us. I was bound to let daylight into one of 'em at least, an' I did. Hope he liked it!"

"It is evident that you did. Now go on about Robert, for I should be at work."

"He was one of the fust up; I was just behind, an' though the whole thing happened in a minute, I remember how it was, for all I was yellin' an' knockin' round like mad. Just where we were, some sort of an officer was wavin' his sword an' cheerin' on his men; Dane saw him by a big flash that come by; he flung away his gun, give a leap, an' went at that feller as if he was Jeff, Beauregard, an' Lee, all in one.[2] I scrabbled after as quick as I could, but was only up in time to see him git the sword straight through him an' drop into the ditch. You needn't ask what I did next, Missis, for I don't quite know myself; all I'm clear about is, that I managed somehow to pitch that Reb into the fort as dead as Moses, git hold of Dane, an' bring him off. Poor old feller! we said we went in to live or die; he said he went in to die, an' he's done it."

I had been intently watching the excited speaker; but as he regretfully added those last words I turned again, and Robert's eyes met mine,—those melancholy eyes, so full of an intelligence that proved he had heard, remembered, and reflected with that preternatural power which often outlives all other faculties. He knew me, yet gave no greeting; was glad to see a woman's face, yet had no smile wherewith to welcome it; felt that he was dying, yet uttered no farewell. He was too far across the river to return or linger now; departing thought, strength, breath, were spent in one grateful look, one murmur of submission to the last pang he could ever feel. His lips moved, and, bending to them, a whisper chilled my cheek, as it shaped the broken words,—

"I'd 'a' done it,—but it's better so,—I'm satisfied."

Ah! well he might be,—for, as he turned his face from the shadow of the life that was, the sunshine of the life to be touched it with a beautiful content, and in the drawing of a breath my contraband found wife and home, eternal liberty and God.

1863 1869

2. Political and military leaders of the Confederacy: Jefferson Davis (1808–1889) was president of the Confederate States of America (1861–65), and P. G. T. Beauregard (1818–1893) and Robert E. Lee (1807–1870) were his key military commanders.

From Little Women[1]

From Part Second

Chapter IV

LITERARY LESSONS[2]

Fortune suddenly smiled upon Jo, and dropped a good-luck penny in her path. Not a golden penny, exactly, but I doubt if half a million would have given more real happiness than did the little sum that came to her in this wise.

Every few weeks she would shut herself up in her room, put on her scribbling suit, and "fall into a vortex," as she expressed it, writing away at her novel with all her heart and soul, for till that was finished she could find no peace. Her "scribbling suit" consisted of a black pinafore on which she could wipe her pen at will, and a cap of the same material, adorned with a cheerful red bow, into which she bundled her hair when the decks were cleared for action. This cap was a beacon to the inquiring eyes of her family, who, during these periods, kept their distance, merely popping in their heads semi-occasionally, to ask, with interest, "Does genius burn, Jo?" They did not always venture even to ask this question, but took an observation of the cap, and judged accordingly. If this expressive article of dress was drawn low upon the forehead, it was a sign that hard work was going on; in exciting moments it was pushed rakishly askew, and when despair seized the author it was plucked wholly off, and cast upon the floor. At such times the intruder silently withdrew; and not until the red bow was seen gaily erect upon the gifted brow, did any one dare address Jo.

She did not think herself a genius by any means; but when the writing fit came on, she gave herself up to it with entire abandon, and led a blissful life, unconscious of want, care, or bad weather, while she sat safe and happy in an imaginary world, full of friends almost as real and dear to her as any in the flesh. Sleep forsook her eyes, meals stood untasted, day and night were all too short to enjoy the happiness which blessed her only at such times, and made these hours worth living, even if they bore no other fruit. The divine afflatus[3] usually lasted a week or two, and then she emerged from her "vortex" hungry, sleepy, cross, or despondent.

She was just recovering from one of these attacks when she was prevailed upon to escort Miss Crocker[4] to a lecture, and in return for her virtue was rewarded with a new idea. It was a People's Course,[5]—the lecture on the Pyramids,—and Jo rather wondered at the choice of such a subject for such an audience, but took it for granted that some great social evil would be remedied, or some great want supplied by unfolding the glories of the Pharaohs, to an audience whose thoughts were busy with the price of coal and

1. Alcott published *Little Women; or, Meg, Jo, Beth and Amy* in 1868, and a sequel, Part Second, in 1869; the selection here is taken from the 1869 printing. Subsequent printings linked the two parts as one complete novel.
2. At this point in the novel, Jo March, the impetuous and literary second daughter, has decided to devote herself to her writing, as Alcott did, in large part to make money for her impoverished family. In the first part of the novel, Jo at age sixteen had placed tales and sketches at a newspaper, the *Spread Eagle*, but she's initially paid nothing for her work and then earns a dollar a column. Now in her early twenties, she lives with her three sisters, father, and mother (affectionately known as "Marmee") in a town resembling Concord, Massachusetts.
3. Inspiration.
4. A neighbor and minor character.
5. A series of free public lectures.

"Jo in a vortex." From the 1869 first printing of *Little Women*, Part Second.

flour, and whose lives were spent in trying to solve harder riddles than that of the Sphinx.[6]

They were early; and while Miss Crocker set the heel of her stocking, Jo amused herself by examining the faces of the people who occupied the seat with them. On her left were two matrons with massive foreheads, and bonnets to match, discussing Woman's Rights and making tatting.[7] Beyond sat a pair of humble lovers artlessly holding each other by the hand, a somber spinster eating peppermints out of a paper bag, and an old gentleman taking his preparatory nap behind a yellow bandanna. On her right, her only neighbor was a studious-looking lad absorbed in a newspaper.

It was a pictorial sheet, and Jo examined the work of art nearest her, idly wondering what unfortuitous concatenation of circumstances needed the melodramatic illustration of an Indian in full war costume, tumbling over a precipice with a wolf at his throat, while two infuriated young gentlemen, with unnaturally small feet and big eyes, were stabbing each other close by, and a dishevelled female was flying away in the background, with her mouth wide open. Pausing to turn a page, the lad saw her looking, and, with boyish

6. In Greek mythology, a winged monster with a lion's body and head of a woman, who challenged those entering the city of Thebes with a riddle; she killed those who answered incorrectly. When Oedipus answered correctly, the Sphinx was so distraught that she killed herself, much to the delight of the Theban people, who named Oedipus king.

7. Needlework with handmade lace.

good-nature, offered half his paper, saying, bluntly, "Want to read it? That's a first-rate story."

Jo accepted it with a smile, for she had never outgrown her liking for lads, and soon found herself involved in the usual labyrinth of love, mystery, and murder, for the story belonged to that class of light literature in which the passions have a holiday, and when the author's invention fails, a grand catastrophe clears the stage of one-half the *dramatis personæ*,[8] leaving the other half to exult over their downfall.

"Prime, isn't it?" asked the boy, as her eye went down the last paragraph of her portion.

"I guess you and I could do most as well as that if we tried," returned Jo, amused at his admiration of the trash.

"I should think I was a pretty lucky chap if I could. She makes a good living out of such stories, they say;" and he pointed to the name of Mrs. S. L. A. N. G. Northbury,[9] under the title of the tale.

"Do you know her?" asked Jo, with sudden interest.

"No; but I read all her pieces, and I know a fellow that works in the office where this paper is printed."

"Do you say she makes a good living out of stories like this?" and Jo looked more respectfully at the agitated group and thickly-sprinkled exclamation points that adorned the page.

"Guess she does! she knows just what folks like, and gets paid well for writing it."

Here the lecture began, but Jo heard very little of it, for while Professor Sands was prosing away about Belzoni,[1] Cheops, scarabei, and hieroglyphics, she was covertly taking down the address of the paper, and boldly resolving to try for the hundred dollar prize offered in its columns for a sensational story. By the time the lecture ended, and the audience awoke, she had built up a splendid fortune for herself (not the first founded upon paper), and was already deep in the concoction of her story, being unable to decide whether the duel should come before the elopement or after the murder.

She said nothing of her plan at home, but fell to work next day, much to the disquiet of her mother, who always looked a little anxious when "genius took to burning." Jo had never tried this style before, contenting herself with very mild romances for the "Spread Eagle." Her theatrical experience and miscellaneous reading were of service now, for they gave her some idea of dramatic effect, and supplied plot, language, and costumes. Her story was as full of desperation and despair as her limited acquaintance with those uncomfortable emotions enabled her to make it, and, having located it in Lisbon, she wound up with an earthquake, as a striking and appropriate *denouement*.[2] The manuscript was privately dispatched, accompanied by a note, modestly saying that if the tale didn't get the prize, which the writer

8. Characters in a dramatic work (Latin).

9. A parodic reworking of the name of the writer Mrs. E. D. E. N. Southworth (1819–1899), author of *The Hidden Hand* (1859) and other popular novels.

1. The Venetian explorer Giovanni Battista Belzoni (1778–1823) was best known for his study of Egyptology. He explored Cheops, a pyramid built between 2589 and 2566 B.C.E., and studied the Egyptian writing system of hieroglyphics and the use of beetle images (scarabei) for seals and decorations.

2. Final outcome (French). In 1755, an earthquake had devastated Lisbon, the capital of Portugal, killing over sixty thousand people.

hardly dared expect, she would be very glad to receive any sum it might be considered worth.

Six weeks is a long time to wait, and a still longer time for a girl to keep a secret; but Jo did both, and was just beginning to give up all hope of ever seeing her manuscript again, when a letter arrived which almost took her breath away; for, on opening it, a check for a hundred dollars fell into her lap.[3] For a minute she stared at it as if it had been a snake, then she read her letter, and began to cry. If the amiable gentleman who wrote that kindly note could have known what intense happiness he was giving a fellow-creature, I think he would devote his leisure hours, if he has any, to that amusement; for Jo valued the letter more than the money, because it was encouraging; and after years of effort it was *so* pleasant to find that she had learned to do *something*, though it was only to write a sensation story.

A prouder young woman was seldom seen than she, when, having composed herself, she electrified the family by appearing before them with the letter in one hand, the check in the other, announcing that she had won the prize! Of course there was a great jubilee, and when the story came every one read and praised it; though after her father had told her that the language was good, the romance fresh and hearty, and the tragedy quite thrilling, he shook his head, and said in his unworldly way,—

"You can do better than this, Jo. Aim at the highest, and never mind the money."

"*I* think the money is the best part of it. What *will* you do with such a fortune?" asked Amy, regarding the magic slip of paper with a reverential eye.

"Send Beth and mother to the sea-side for a month or two," answered Jo promptly.

"Oh, how splendid! No, I can't do it, dear, it would be so selfish," cried Beth, who had clapped her thin hands, and taken a long breath, as if pining for fresh ocean breezes; then stopped herself, and motioned away the check which her sister waved before her.

"Ah, but you shall go, I've set my heart on it; that's what I tried for, and that's why I succeeded. I never get on when I think of myself alone, so it will help me to work for you, don't you see. Besides, Marmee needs the change, and she won't leave you, so you *must* go. Won't it be fun to see you come home plump and rosy again? Hurrah for Dr. Jo, who always cures her patients!"

To the sea-side they went, after much discussion; and though Beth didn't come home as plump and rosy as could be desired, she was much better, while Mrs. March declared she felt ten years younger; so Jo was satisfied with the investment of her prize-money, and fell to work with a cheery spirit, bent on earning more of those delightful checks. She did earn several that year, and began to feel herself a power in the house; for by the magic of a pen, her "rubbish" turned into comforts for them all. "The Duke's Daughter" paid the butcher's bill, "A Phantom Hand" put down a new carpet, and "The Curse of the Coventrys" proved the blessing of the Marches in the way of groceries and gowns.

3. In 1863 Alcott won $100 for her own sensation story, "Pauline's Passion and Punishment," which was published in *Frank Leslie's Illustrated Newspaper.* Over the next four years, Alcott published a number of such stories.

Wealth is certainly a most desirable thing, but poverty has its sunny side, and one of the sweet uses of adversity, is the genuine satisfaction which comes from hearty work of head or hand; and to the inspiration of necessity, we owe half the wise, beautiful, and useful blessings of the world. Jo enjoyed a taste of this satisfaction, and ceased to envy richer girls, taking great comfort in the knowledge that she could supply her own wants, and need ask no one for a penny.

Little notice was taken of her stories, but they found a market; and, encouraged by this fact, she resolved to make a bold stroke for fame and fortune. Having copied her novel for the fourth time, read it to all her confidential friends, and submitted it with fear and trembling to three publishers, she at last disposed of it, on condition that she would cut it down one-third, and omit all the parts which she particularly admired.

"Now I must either bundle it back into my tin-kitchen, to mould, pay for printing it myself, or chop it up to suit purchasers, and get what I can for it. Fame is a very good thing to have in the house, but cash is more convenient; so I wish to take the sense of the meeting on this important subject," said Jo, calling a family council.

"Don't spoil your book, my girl, for there is more in it than you know, and the idea is well worked out. Let it wait and ripen," was her father's advice; and he practiced as he preached, having waited patiently thirty years for fruit of his own to ripen, and being in no haste to gather it, even now, when it was sweet and mellow.

"It seems to me that Jo will profit more by making the trial than by waiting," said Mrs. March. "Criticism is the best test of such work, for it will show her both unsuspected merits and faults, and help her to do better next time. We are too partial; but the praise and blame of outsiders will prove useful, even if she gets but little money."

"Yes," said Jo, knitting her brows, "that's just it; I've been fussing over the thing so long, I really don't know whether it's good, bad, or indifferent. It will be a great help to have cool, impartial persons take a look at it, and tell me what they think of it."

"I wouldn't leave out a word of it; you'll spoil it if you do, for the interest of the story is more in the minds than in the actions of the people, and it will be all a muddle if you don't explain as you go on," said Meg, who firmly believed that this book was the most remarkable novel ever written.

"But Mr. Allen says, 'Leave out the explanations, make it brief and dramatic, and let the characters tell the story,'" interrupted Jo, turning to the publisher's note.

"Do as he tells you; he knows what will sell, and we don't. Make a good, popular book, and get as much money as you can. By and by, when you've got a name, you can afford to digress, and have philosophical and metaphysical people in your novels," said Amy, who took a strictly practical view of the subject.

"Well," said Jo, laughing, "if my people *are* 'philosophical and metaphysical,' it isn't my fault, for I know nothing about such things, except what I hear father say, sometimes. If I've got some of his wise ideas jumbled up with my romance, so much the better for me. Now, Beth, what do you say?"

"I should so like to see it printed *soon*," was all Beth said, and smiled in saying it; but there was an unconscious emphasis on the last word, and a wistful look in the eyes that never lost their child-like candor, which chilled Jo's heart, for a minute, with a foreboding fear, and decided her to make her little venture "soon."[4]

So, with Spartan firmness, the young authoress laid her first-born on her table, and chopped it up as ruthlessly as any ogre. In the hope of pleasing every one, she took every one's advice; and, like the old man and his donkey in the fable, suited nobody.[5]

Her father liked the metaphysical streak which had unconsciously got into it, so that was allowed to remain, though she had her doubts about it. Her mother thought that there *was* a trifle too much description; out, therefore, it nearly all came, and with it many necessary links in the story. Meg admired the tragedy; so Jo piled up the agony to suit her, while Amy objected to the fun, and, with the best intentions in life, Jo quenched the sprightly scenes which relieved the sombre character of the story. Then, to complete the ruin, she cut it down one-third, and confidingly sent the poor little romance, like a picked robin, out into the big, busy world, to try its fate.

Well, it was printed, and she got three hundred dollars for it; likewise plenty of praise and blame both so much greater than she expected, that she was thrown into a state of bewilderment, from which it took her some time to recover.

"You said, mother, that criticism would help me; but how can it, when it's so contradictory that I don't know whether I have written a promising book, or broken all the ten commandments," cried poor Jo, turning over a heap of notices, the perusal of which filled her with pride and joy one minute—wrath and dire dismay the next. "This man says 'An exquisite book, full of truth, beauty, and earnestness; all is sweet, pure, and healthy,'" continued the perplexed authoress. "The next, 'The theory of the book is bad,—full of morbid fancies, spiritualistic ideas, and unnatural characters.' Now, as I had no theory of any kind, don't believe in spiritualism,[6] and copied my characters from life, I don't see how this critic *can* be right. Another says, 'It's one of the best American novels which has appeared for years' (I know better than that); and the next asserts that 'though it is original, and written with great force and feeling, it is a dangerous book.' 'Tisn't! Some make fun of it, some over-praise, and nearly all insist that I had a deep theory to expound, when I only wrote it for the pleasure and the money. I wish I'd printed it whole, or not at all, for I do hate to be so horridly misjudged."

Her family and friends administered comfort and commendation liberally; yet it was a hard time for sensitive, high-spirited Jo, who meant so well, and had apparently done so ill. But it did her good, for those whose opinion had real value, gave her the criticism which is an author's best education; and when the first soreness was over, she could laugh at her poor little book, yet believe in it still, and feel herself the wiser and stronger for the buffeting she had received.

4. The third sister, Beth, like Alcott's sister, Lizzie, eventually dies of the lingering effects of scarlet fever.
5. In the fable by the Greek storyteller Aesop, a father and his son are criticized by passers-by for the different ways they ride their donkey; trying to please their critics, they inadvertently drown the donkey. Alcott published her novel *Moods* in 1864, after cutting ten chapters to please her editor. She restored a number of the cut chapters and made other major changes in a revised version that she published in 1881.
6. A belief that the living can communicate with the spirits of the dead, usually through a medium.

"Not being a genius, like Keats,[7] it won't kill me," she said stoutly; "and I've got the joke on my side, after all; for the parts that were taken straight out of real life, are denounced as impossible and absurd, and the scenes that I made up out of my own silly head, are pronounced 'charmingly natural, tender, and true.' So I'll comfort myself with that; and, when I'm ready, I'll up again and take another."

1869

7. The English Romantic poet John Keats (1797–1821), who, according to his poet-friend Percy Bysshe Shelley (1792–1822), died at a young age in part because of critics' attacks on his poem *Endymion* (1818).

Selected Bibliographies

Reference Works

For basic information on writers and writings of this period, see Philip W. Leininger's 1995 updating of James D. Hart's *Oxford Companion to American Literature*; and the four-volume *Oxford Encyclopedia of American Literature* (2004), edited by Jay Parini. The entries on authors in the 1999 *American National Biography* are mostly excellent; each *ANB* entry on a writer concludes with a brief guide to his or her surviving papers, to major editions, and to the most reliable biographies. Gale's multivolume *Dictionary of Literary Biography* is also worth consulting. Richard M. Ludwig and Clifford A. Nault Jr.'s *Annals of American Literature: 1602–1983* (1983) and Daniel S. Burt's *The Chronology of American Literature* (2004) provide useful timelines and detailed year-by-year listings of publications in the United States.

For scholarship and criticism on writers in this anthology, the best bibliographical resource is the annual *American Literary Scholarship*; many research libraries have access to both the print and the online versions. Before the latest *ALS* comes out, students may consult the articles, reviews, and advertisements in journals such as *American Literature, American Literary History, ESQ: A Journal of the American Renaissance, African American Review, Studies in American Indian Literature, Legacy: A Journal of American Women Writers*, and *Nineteenth-Century Literature*. Also invaluable is the annual *MLA International Bibliography*, which, like *ALS*, is available both in print and online versions. Clarence Gohdes and Sanford E. Marovitz's *Bibliographical Guide to the Literature of the U.S.A.* (1984) remains useful, especially to students interested in the history of scholarship and criticism. On developments in the field, see Caroline F. Levander and Robert S. Levine's *A Companion to American Literary Studies* (2011) and Russ Castronovo's *The Oxford Handbook to Nineteenth-Century American Literature* (2011).

The Web has revolutionized bibliographical, textual, historical, and critical studies in American literature. While it is important to keep in mind that some websites are considerably more reliable than others, and that archives can be short-lived, one can still recognize the crucial importance of digital archives for American literary scholarship in the twenty-first century. The best overview site on American literature is Donna M. Campbell's *American Authors, Timelines, Literary Movements* <wsu.edu/~campbelld/>. This digital archive makes available just about all of the main websites devoted to American authors, while providing information on chronologies and literary history. Also useful is *PAL: Perspectives in American Literature—A Research and Reference Guide* <www.csustan.edu/english/reuben/pal/table.html>. The Library of Congress's *American Memory* archive <loc.gov/index.html> provides images and rare texts, as does the New York Public Library's Schomburg Center for Research in Black Culture <nypl.org/locations/schomburg>. Other sites worth consulting are Northeastern University's archive on nineteenth-century American women writers <scribblingwomen.org/>; the University of North Carolina's archive on slave narratives <docsouth.unc.edu/neh/index.html>; and the Wright American Fiction archive, 1851–75 <letrs.indiana.edu/web/w/wright2/>, which makes available nearly three thousand full texts. Finally, many hard-to-find texts relating to U.S. literary, cultural, and political history can be found in the *Making of America* archive being developed jointly at Cornell University and the University of Michigan <hti.umich.edu/m/moagrp/> and <cdl.library.cornell.edu/moa/>.

Histories

The *Literary History of the United States* (1948, 1974), edited by Robert E. Spiller et al., includes some still useful guides to writers and topics. The *Columbia Literary History of the United States* (1988), under the general editorship of Emory Elliott, is an excellent one-volume history. Greil Marcus and Werner Sollors's provocative *A New Literary History of America* (2009) offers short, punchy essays on authors, texts, cultural events, and literary movements. Sacvan Bercovitch is general editor of the *Cambridge History of American Literature*, now the best resource for a comprehensive literary historical overview. Volume 2, *1820–1865* (1994), consists of monograph-length sections by four contributors: Michael Davitt Bell on "Conditions of Literary Vocation," Eric J. Sundquist on "The Literature of Expansion and Race," Barbara L. Packer on "The Transcendentalists," and Jonathan Arac on "Narrative Forms"; and Volume 4, *Nineteenth-Century Poetry: 1800–1910* (2004), consists of monograph-length sections by two contributors: Barbara Packer on "American Verse Traditions, 1800–1855," and Shira Wolosky on "Poetry and Public Discourse, 1820–1910." *The Cambridge History of the American Novel* (2011), edited by Leonard Cassuto et al., includes up-to-date essays on antebellum novelists; see also Shirley Samuels's *A Companion to American Fiction, 1780–1865* (2004). Also useful is *The Columbia History of the American Novel* (1991), under the general editorship of Emory Elliott; and Gregg Crane's *The Cambridge Introduction to the Nineteenth-Century American Novel* (2007).

Eric L. Haralson's *Encyclopedia of American Poetry: The Nineteenth Century* (1998) is a companion to John Hollander's two-volume anthology, *American Poetry: The Nineteenth Century* (1993). On drama see the *Cambridge History of American Theatre: Beginnings to 1870*, edited by Don B. Wilmeth and Christopher Bigsby (1998). The *Oxford Companion to African American Literature* (1997) is edited by William L. Andrews, Frances Smith Foster, and Trudier Harris, with a foreword by Henry Louis Gates Jr.; see also Blyden Jackson's *A History of Afro-American Literature: The Long Beginnings, 1746–1895* (1989), Audrey A. Fisch's *The Cambridge Companion to the Afri-*

can American Slave Narrative (2007), and Gene Andrew Jarrett's *A Companion to African American Literature* (2010). Other useful works are the volumes of Frank Luther Mott's *History of American Magazines* (1938, 1968), Mott's *American Journalism: A History of Newspapers in the United States* (1950), Edward E. Chielens's *American Literary Magazines: The Eighteenth and Nineteenth Centuries* (1986), Louis D. Rubin Jr.'s *The History of Southern Literature* (1985, 1990), Joseph M. Flora and Lucinda H. MacKethan's *The Companion to Southern Literature: Themes, Genres, Places, People, Movements, and Motifs* (2002), Cathy Davidson and Linda Wagner-Martin's *Oxford Companion to Women's Writing in the United States* (1995), and Denise D. Knight's *Nineteenth-Century American Women Writers: A Bio-Bibliographical Critical Source Book* (1997). On Transcendentalism, see Charles Capper and Conrad Edick Wright's *Transient and Permanent: The Transcendentalist Movement and Its Contexts* (1999), Joel Myerson's *Transcendentalism: A Reader* (2000), Philip F. Gura's *American Transcendentalism: A History* (2007), and Myerson, Sandra Harbert Petrulionis, and Laura Dassow Walls's *The Oxford Handbook of Transcendentalism* (2010). Also useful are Bruce Burgett and Glenn Hendler's *Keywords for American Cultural Studies* (2007) and Karen Halttunen's *A Companion to American Cultural History* (2008).

Literary Criticism

For a sampling of classic works in the field, see D. H. Lawrence's *Studies in Classic American Literature* (1923), F. O. Matthiessen's *American Renaissance: Art and Expression in the Age of Emerson and Whitman* (1941), Richard Chase's *The American Novel and Its Tradition* (1957), Leslie A. Fiedler's *Love and Death in the American Novel* (1960), Leo Marx's *The Machine in the Garden: Technology and the Pastoral Ideal in America* (1964), and Richard Poirier's *A World Elsewhere: The Place of Style in American Literature* (1966). Other influential works include Lawrence Buell's *Literary Transcendentalism: Style and Vision in the American Renaissance* (1973), Richard Slotkin's *Regeneration through Violence: The Mythology of the American Frontier, 1600–1860* (1973), Michael Davitt Bell's *The Development of American Romance: The Sacrifice of Relation* (1980), Annette Kolodny's *The Land before Her: Fantasy and Experience of the American Frontiers, 1630–1860* (1984), Jane Tompkins's *Sensational Designs: The Cultural Work of American Fiction, 1790–1860* (1985), Buell's *New England Literary Culture: From Revolution through Renaissance* (1986), George Dekker's *The American Historical Romance* (1988), Larry J. Reynolds's *European Revolutions and the American Renaissance* (1988), David S. Reynolds's *Beneath the American Renaissance: The Subversive Imagination in the Age of Emerson and Melville* (1989), Robert S. Levine's *Conspiracy and Romance: Studies in Brockden Brown, Cooper, Hawthorne, and Melville* (1989), David Leverenz's *Manhood and the American Renaissance* (1989), Nicholas Bromell's *By the Sweat of the Brow: Literature and Labor in Antebellum America* (1993), Priscilla Wald's *Constituting Americans: Cultural Anxiety and Narrative Form* (1995), Nina Baym's *American Women Writers and the Work of History, 1790–1860* (1995), Teresa A. Goddu's *Gothic America: Narrative, History, and Nation* (1997), Mary

Loeffelholz's, *From School to Salon: Reading Nineteenth-Century American Women's Poetry* (2004), Max Cavitch's *American Elegy: The Poetry of Mourning from the Puritans to Whitman* (2007), Christopher Castiglia's *Interior States: Institutional Consciousness and the Inner Life of Democracy in the Antebellum United States* (2008), and Paul Gilmore's *Aesthetic Materialism: Electricity and American Romanticism* (2008).

Discussions of the early national and antebellum literary marketplace can be found in William Charvat's *The Profession of Authorship in America, 1800–1870* (1968), Michael T. Gilmore's *American Romanticism and the Marketplace* (1985), Susan Coultrap-McQuin's *Doing Literary Business: American Women Writers in the Nineteenth Century* (1990), Michael Winship's *American Literary Publishing in the Mid-Nineteenth Century* (1995), Meredith L. McGill's *American Literature and the Culture of Reprinting, 1834–1853* (2003), and Trish Loughran's *The Republic in Print: Print Culture in the Age of U.S. Nation-Building, 1770–1870* (2007). On connections between law and literature, see Robert A. Ferguson's *Law and Letters in American Culture* (1984), Brook Thomas's *Cross-Examinations of Law and Literature: Cooper, Hawthorne, Stowe, and Melville* (1987) and *Civic Myths: A Law-and-Literature Approach to Citizenship* (2007), and Gregg D. Crane's *Race, Citizenship, and Law in American Literature* (2002). For discussions of transatlantic and hemispheric perspectives, see Robert Weisbuch's *Atlantic Double-Cross: American Literature and British Influence in the Age of Emerson* (1986), Paul Giles's *Transatlantic Insurrections: British Culture and the Formation of American Literature, 1730–1860* (2001), Anna Brickhouse's *Transamerican Literary Relations and the Nineteenth-Century Public Sphere* (2004), Gretchen Murphy's *Hemispheric Imaginings: The Monroe Doctrine and Narratives of U.S. Empire* (2005), Leonard Tennenhouse's *The Importance of Feeling English: American Literature and the British Diaspora, 1750–1850* (2007), Meredith L. McGill's *The Traffic in Poems: Nineteenth-Century Poetry and Transatlantic Exchange* (2008), and Caroline F. Levander and Robert S. Levine's *Hemispheric American Studies* (2008). Questions of empire and imperialism have been taken up by a number of critics; see, for example, John Carlos Rowe's *Literary Culture and U.S. Imperialism: From the Revolution to World War II* (2000), Amy Kaplan's *The Anarchy of Empire in the Making of U.S. Culture* (2002), and Laura Doyle's *Freedom's Empire: Race and the Rise of the Novel in Atlantic Modernity, 1640–1940* (2008).

Much recent criticism has been inspired by work on gender and race and the recovery of neglected writings by women, African Americans, and Native Americans. Nina Baym's *Women's Fiction: A Guide to Novels by and about Women in America, 1820–1870* (1978, 1993 with a new preface) and Mary Kelley's *Private Woman, Public Stage: Literary Domesticity in Nineteenth-Century America* (1984) have been especially influential. On the sometimes overlapping concerns of domesticity, sentimentalism, and sympathy in nineteenth-century U.S. writing, see Gillian Brown's *Domestic Individualism: Imagining Self in Nineteenth-Century America* (1990), Baym's *Feminism and American Literary History* (1992), Lora Romero's *Home Fronts: Domesticity and Its Critics in the Antebellum United States* (1997), Elizabeth Young's *Disarming the Nation: Women's Writing and the American Civil War* (1999), Glenn Hendler's *Public Sentiments: Structures of Feeling in Nineteenth-Century American Literature* (2001), Cindy Weinstein's *Family, Kinship, and Sympathy in Nineteenth-Century American Literature* (2004), Melissa J. Homestead's *American Women Authors and Literary Property, 1822–1869* (2005), and Elizabeth Barnes's *Love's Whipping Boy: Violence and Sentimentality in the American Imagination* (2011). Key works in the study of race and slavery in antebellum writing include Houston A. Baker Jr.'s *The Journey Back: Issues in Black Literature and Criticism* (1980), Henry Louis Gates Jr.'s *Figures in Black: Words, Signs, and the "Racial Self"* (1987), William L. Andrews's *To Tell a Free Story: The First Century of Afro-American Autobiography, 1760–1865* (1986), Dana D. Nelson's *The Word in Black and White: Reading "Race" in American Literature, 1638–1867* (1992), Karen Sánchez-Eppler's *Touching Liberty: Abolition, Feminism, and the Politics of the Body* (1993), Eric J. Sundquist's *To Wake the Nations: Race in the Making of American Literature* (1993), John Ernest's *Resistance and Reformation in Nineteenth-Century American Literature* (1995), Carla L. Peterson's *"Doers of the Word": African-American Women Speakers and Writers in the North (1830–1880)* (1995), Russ Castronovo's *Fathering the Nation: American Genealogies of Slavery and Freedom* (1995), Leonard Cassuto's *The Inhuman Race: The Racial Grotesque in American Literature and Culture* (1997), Rafia Zafar's *African Americans Write American Literature, 1760–1870* (1997), Dickson D. Bruce Jr.'s *The Origins of African American Literature, 1680–1865* (2001), Susan M. Ryan's *The Grammar of Good Intentions: Race and the Antebellum Culture of Benevolence* (2003), Maurice S. Lee's *Slavery, Philosophy, and American Literature, 1830–1860* (2005), Caroline F. Levander's *Cradle of Liberty: Race, the Child, and National Belonging from Thomas Jefferson to W. E. B. Du Bois* (2006), Robert S. Levine's *Dislocating Race and Nation: Episodes in Nineteenth-Century American Literary Nationalism* (2008), Ian Frederick Finseth's *Shades of Green: Visions of Nature in the Literature of American Slavery, 1770–1860* (2009), and John Ernest's *Chaotic Justice: Rethinking African American Literary History* (2009). For important critical work in Native American studies, see Lucy Maddox's *Removals: Nineteenth-Century American Indian Literature and the Politics of Indian Affairs* (1991), Arnold Krupat's *Ethnocriticism: Ethnography, History, Literature* (1992), Helen Carr's *Inventing the American Primitive: Politics, Gender and the Representation of Native American Literary Traditions, 1789–1936* (1996), Cheryl Walker's *Indian Nation: Native American Literature and Nineteenth-Century Nationalisms* (1997), John M. Coward's *The Newspaper Indian: Native American Identity in the Press, 1820–90* (1999), Neil Schmitz's *White Robe's Dilemma: Tribal History in American Literature* (2001), Maureen Konkle's *Writing American Indian Nations: Native Intellectuals and the Politics of Historiography, 1827–1863* (2004), Daniel Justice's *Our Fire Survives the Storm: A Cherokee Literary History* (2006), Krupat's *All That Remains: Varieties of Indigenous Expression* (2009), and Scott Richard Lyons's *X-Marks: Native Signatures of Assent* (2010).

AMERICAN LITERATURE 1820–1865

Louisa May Alcott

Some of Alcott's work never went out of print, and much of the rest has been republished. Madeleine B. Stern has played a pioneering role in the recovery of Alcott's larger canon, including the sensation fiction that Alcott published anonymously. Key editions include Stern's *Behind a Mask: The Unknown Thrillers of Louisa May Alcott* (1975); Elaine Showalter's *Alternative Alcott* (1988); Daniel Shealy, Stern, and Joel Myerson's *Louisa May Alcott: Selected Fiction* (1990) and *Freaks of Genius: Unknown Thrillers of Louisa May Alcott* (1991); Elizabeth Lennox Keyser's *Whispers in the Dark: The Fiction of Louisa May Alcott* (1993); Shealy's *Louisa May Alcott's Fairy Tales and Fantasy Stories* (1992); Sarah Elbert's *Louisa May Alcott on Race, Sex, and Slavery* (1997); Stern's *Louisa May Alcott Unmasked: Collected Thrillers* (1995) and *Louisa May Alcott: From Blood and Thunder to Hearth and Home* (1998); Keyser's *The Portable Louisa May Alcott* (2000); and Stern's *L. M. Alcott: Signature of Reform* (2002). The Library of America's *Little Women, Little Men, Jo's Boys*, edited by Showalter, was published in 2005; and the Norton Critical Edition of *Little Women*, edited by Anne K. Phillips and Gregory Eiselein, appeared in 2003. Stern's edition of *A Modern Mephistopheles* (1877) appeared in 1987; Joy S. Kasson's edition of *Work* (1873) appeared in 1994; and Elbert's edition of *Moods* (1864; revised 1882) appeared in 1991. Myerson and Daniel Shealy, with Stern as associate, edited *The Selected Letters of Louisa May Alcott* (1987) and *The Journals of Louisa May Alcott* (1989); and Shealy edited *Literary Women Abroad: The Alcott Sisters' Letters from Europe, 1870–1871* (2008). Ednah D. Cheney's *Louisa May Alcott: Her Life, Letters, and Journals* (1889) was reprinted in 1980. Stern's important biography, *Louisa May Alcott* (1950, 1978), was republished in 1996 in a revised edition, *Louisa May Alcott: A Biography*. Two excellent recent biographies are John Matteson's *Eden's Outcasts: The Story of Louisa May Alcott and Her Father* (2007) and Harriet Reisen's *Louisa May Alcott: The Woman behind Little Women* (2009). For primary texts bearing on biography, see Shealy's *Alcott in Her Own Time: A Biographical Chronicle of Her Life, Drawn from Recollections, Interviews, and Memoirs* (2005).

On critical reception, see Beverly Lyon Clark's *Louisa May Alcott: The Contemporary Reviews* (2004). An excellent resource for Alcott's most famous novel is Janice M. Alberghene and Clark's *Little Women and the Feminist Imagination: Criticism, Controversy, Personal Essays* (1999). Also useful is Eiselein and Phillips's *The Louisa May Alcott Encyclopedia* (2001). Important critical work includes Stern's *Critical Essays on Louisa May Alcott* (1984), Sarah Elbert's *A Hunger for Home: Louisa May Alcott and "Little Women"* (1987), Keyser's *Whispers in the Dark: The Fiction of Louisa May Alcott* (1993), Anne E. Boyd's *Writing for Immortality: Women and the Emergence of High Literary Culture in America* (2004), Susan S. Williams's *Reclaiming Authorship: Literary Women in America, 1850–1900* (2006), and Michelle Ann Abate's *Tomboys: A Literary and Cultural History* (2008).

William Apess

Barry O'Connell's *On Our Own Ground: The Complete Writings of William Apess, a Pequot* (1992) is the indispensable starting point for a study of Apess. O'Connell's *A Son of the Forest and Other Writings* (1997), a selection from Apess' work, has an updated introduction that provides some new material. Arnold Krupat has chapters on Apess in *The Voice in the Margin* (1989) and *Ethnocriticism* (1992); more recently he has considered "William Apess as Public Intellectual" in *All That Remains* (2009). Berndt Peyer's chapter on Apess in *The Tutor'd Mind* (1997) is valuable, as are the reflections of Hilary Wyss in "Captivity and Conversion: William Apess, Mary Jemison, and Narratives of Racial Identity," *American Indian Quarterly* (1999). Maureen Konkle has a chapter on Apess in her *Writing Indian Nations* (2004), and Robert Warrior offers a "Eulogy" for William Apess in his *The People and the Word: Reading Native Nonfiction* (2005). Michael Elliott's "Indians, Incorporated," *American Literary History* (2007), is also worth consulting. Most recent—and extremely interesting—is Lisa Brooks's chapter, "Regenerating the Village Dish: William Apess and the Mashpee Woodland Revolt," in her book *The Common Pot: The Recovery of Native Space in the Northeast* (2008).

William Wells Brown

The standard biography is William Edward Farrison's *William Wells Brown: Author and Reformer* (1969). For a generous sampling of speeches and letters by Brown, see the five-volume *The Black Abolitionist Papers*, edited by Peter C. Ripley et al. (1985–92). A useful bibliography is Curtis W. Ellison's *William Wells Brown and Martin R. Delany: A Reference Guide* (2000). Robert S. Levine's edition of *Clotel* (2000; revised 2nd edition 2011) provides a sampling of the many primary documents that Brown drew on for his novel; see also Christopher Mulvey's *Clotel, by William Wells Brown: An Electronic Scholarly Edition*

(2006). There are two Brown readers: Paula Garrett and Hollis Robbins's *Works of William Wells Brown: Using His "Strong, Manly Voice"* (2006) and Ezra Greenspan's *William Wells Brown: A Reader* (2008). Illuminating discussions of Brown's writings can be found in William L. Andrews's *To Tell a Free Story: The First Century of Afro-American Autobiography* (1986), Ann duCille's *The Coupling Convention: Sex, Text, and Tradition in Black Women's Fiction* (1993), John Ernest's *Resistance and Reformation in Nineteenth-Century African-American Literature* (1995), Russ Castronovo's *Fathering the Nation: American Genealogies of Slavery and Freedom* (1995), Paul Gilmore's *The Genuine Article: Race, Mass Culture, and American Literary Manhood* (2001), M. Guilia Fabi's *Passing and the Rise of the African American Novel* (2001), and Trish Loughran's *The Republic in Print: Print Culture in the Age of U.S. Nation Building* (2007).

William Cullen Bryant

William Cullen Bryant II and Thomas G. Voss edited *The Letters of William Cullen Bryant* (1975–92) in six volumes. Earlier biographies are superseded by Albert F. McLean's *William Cullen Bryant* (1989). Bryant's poetry has not been edited according to modern standards, but the edition of his *Poetical Works* (1878) published at his death is a useful starting point. His newspaper writing had been buried in the files of the *New York Evening Post* until William Cullen Bryant II republished selected editorials in *Power for Sanity* (1994). For a good collection of Bryant's major writings, see Frank Gado and Nicholas B. Stevens's *William Cullen Bryant: An American Voice* (2006). An excellent recent study is Gilbert H. Muller's *William Cullen Bryant: Author of America* (2008). Bernard Duffey's *Poetry in America: Expression and Its Values in the Times of Bryant, Whitman, and Pound* (1978) remains provocative.

Lydia Maria Child

The best selection of primary writings is *A Lydia Maria Child Reader* (1997), edited by Carolyn L. Karcher, who also edited *Hobomok and Other Writings on Indians* (1986). Reprints of individual works include *History of the Condition of Women, in Various Ages and Nations* (1972); *The American Frugal Housewife* (1985); *An Appeal in Favor of That Class of Americans Called Africans* (1996), edited by Carolyn L. Karcher; *A Romance of the Republic* (1997), edited by Dana D. Nelson; and *Letters from New-York* (1998), edited by Bruce Mills. An excellent work of scholarship is *Lydia Maria Child, Selected Letters, 1817–1880* (1982), edited by Milton Meltzer and Patricia G. Holland, with Francine Krasno. All earlier biographies are superseded by Carolyn L. Karcher's *The First Woman in the Republic: A Cultural Biography of Lydia Maria Child* (1994), though Deborah Pickman Clifford's *Crusader for Freedom: A Life of Lydia Maria Child* (1992) remains useful. On Child in the reform context of her times, see Bruce Mills's *Cultural Reformations: Lydia Maria Child and the Literature of Reform* (1994); and for recent critical work, see the Lydia Maria Child special issue of *ESQ: A Journal of the American Renaissance* 56.1 (2010).

James Fenimore Cooper

James Franklin Beard was editor-in-chief of a long-planned and, after 1979, fast-appearing edition, *The Writings of James Fenimore Cooper*, published by the State University of New York. Excellent volumes of *The Pioneers* and *The Last of the Mohicans*, and many of Cooper's other works, have already appeared as part of an edition with forty-eight proposed volumes. Beard also edited the indispensable six-volume *Letters and Journals of James Fenimore Cooper* (1960–68). Wayne Franklin's biography should become standard; see the first volume, *James Fenimore Cooper: The Early Years* (2007). For good overviews, see James Grossman's *James Fenimore Cooper* (1949) and Robert Emmet Long's *James Fenimore Cooper* (1990). Essential background is in Alan Taylor's *William Cooper's Town: Power and Persuasion on the Frontier of the Early American Republic* (1995), a biography of Cooper's father.

Critical reception is surveyed in George Dekker and John P. McWilliams's *Fenimore Cooper: The Critical Heritage* (1973). For collections of essays, see Robert Clark's *James Fenimore Cooper: New Critical Essays* (1985), W. M. Verhoeven's *James Fenimore Cooper: New Historical and Literary Contexts* (1993), and Leland S. Person's *Historical Guide to James Fenimore Cooper* (2006). Useful critical work includes McWilliams's *Political Justice in a Republic: James Fenimore Cooper's America* (1972), H. Daniel Peck's *A World by Itself: The Pastoral Moment in Cooper's Fiction* (1977), Wayne Franklin's *The New World of James Fenimore Cooper* (1982), James D. Wallace's *Early Cooper and His Audience* (1986), Charles Hansford Adams's *"The Guardian of the Law": Authority and Identity in James Fenimore Cooper* (1990), and Geoffrey Rans's *Cooper's Leatherstocking Series, A Secular Reading* (1991). For up-to-date scholarship, see the essays in *Literature in the Early Republic: Annual Studies on Cooper and His Contemporaries* (2009–present), edited by Matthew Wynn Sivils and Jeffrey Walker.

Rebecca Harding Davis

In 1972, Tillie Olson's Feminist Press edition of *Life in the Iron Mills*, accompanied by Olson's "A Biographical Interpretation," helped to revive Davis's critical reputation. Up to that time, Davis had mainly been known through writings about her son, the author-celebrity Richard Harding Davis. Rebecca Harding Davis published an autobiographical volume, *Bits of Gossip*, in 1904. Useful critical studies include Sharon M. Harris's *Rebecca Harding Davis and American Realism* (1991), Jane Atteridge Rose's *Rebecca Harding Davis* (1993), Jean Pfaelzer's *Parlor Radical: Rebecca Harding Davis and the Origins of American Social Realism* (1996), and William Dow's *Narrating Class in American Fiction* (2009). A groundbreaking article is Janice Milner Lasseter's "The Censored and Uncensored Literary Lives of *Life in the Iron-Mills*," *Legacy* 20 (2003): 175–89. Davis's 1862 novel *Margret Howth* is available in a 1990 edition with an afterword by Jean Fagan Yellin. Cecelia Tichi edited a cultural edition of *Life in the Iron-Mills* (1998). There are three excellent collections of Davis's writings: Jean Pfaelzer's *A Rebecca Harding Davis Reader* (1995), Janice Milner Lasseter and Sharon M. Harris's *Rebecca Harding Davis: Writing Cultural Autobiography* (2001), and Harris and Robin L. Cadwallader's *Rebecca Harding Davis's Stories of the Civil War Era: Selected Writings from the Borderlands* (2010).

Emily Dickinson

Three volumes of *The Poems of Emily Dickinson* (1955) were edited by Thomas H. Johnson; and Johnson and Theodora Ward edited three companion volumes of *The Letters of Emily Dickinson* (1958). R. W. Franklin's *The Manuscript Books of Emily Dickinson* (1981) provides, in two volumes, facsimile reproductions of the poems Dickinson left at her death in fascicles. R. W. Franklin's three-volume *Poems of Emily Dickinson: Variorum Edition* (1998) augments and updates Johnson's three-volume *Poems*. In 1999 Franklin published the one-volume *The Poems of Emily Dickinson: Reading Edition*. Important biographies include Richard B. Sewall's *The Life of Emily Dickinson* (1974), Cynthia Griffin Wolff's *Emily Dickinson* (1986), Alfred Habegger's *My Wars Are Laid Away in Books: The Life of Emily Dickinson* (2001), Brenda Wineapple's *White Heat: The Friendship of Emily Dickinson and Thomas Wentworth Higginson* (2008), and Lyndall Gordon's *Lives Like Loaded Guns: Emily Dickinson and Her Family's Feuds* (2010). Jay Leyda's *The Years and Hours of Emily Dickinson* (1960) provides two volumes of documents, such as excerpts from family letters. Additional documents can be found in Polly Longsworth's *The World of Emily Dickinson* (1990) and Ellen Louise Hart and Martha Nell Smith's *Open Me Carefully: Emily Dickinson's Intimate Letters to Susan Huntington Dickinson* (1998).

Research tools include Joseph Duchac's *The Poems of Emily Dickinson: An Annotated Guide to Commentary Published in English, 1890–1977* (1979), and the continuation (published in 1993) covering 1978–89; Karen Dandurand's *Dickinson Scholarship: An Annotated Bibliography 1969–1985* (1988), and the treasure trove compiled by Willis J. Buckingham (drawing on Mabel Loomis Todd's scrapbooks), *Emily Dickinson's Reception in the 1890s* (1989). Also useful are Jane Donahue Eberwein's *An Emily Dickinson Encyclopedia* (1998) and Sharon Leiter's *Critical Companion to Emily Dickinson: A Literary Reference to Her Life and Work* (2007). The *Dickinson Electronic Archives* <emilydickinson.org>, directed by Martha Nell Smith with Ellen Louise Hart, Lara Vetter, and Marta Werner, offer access to Dickinson's manuscripts, out-of-print volumes about Dickinson, and never-before-published writings by various family members. Another valuable research tool is Martha Nell Smith and Lara Vetter's *Emily Dickinson's Correspondences: A Born-Digital Textual Inquiry* (2008).

Edited collections of critical essays provide an excellent introduction to Dickinson studies. See Susan Juhasz's *Feminist Critics Read Emily Dickinson* (1983); Judith Farr's *Emily Dickinson: A Collection of Critical Essays* (1996); Gudrun Grabher, Roland Hagenbüchle, and Cristanne Miller's *The Emily Dickinson Handbook* (1998, 2006); Wendy Martin's *The Cambridge Companion to Emily Dickinson* (2002); Vivian R. Pollak's *A Historical Guide to Emily Dickinson* (2004); Martha Nell Smith and Mary Loeffelholz's *A Companion to Emily Dickinson* (2008); and Jane Donahue Eberwein and Cindy MacKenzie's *Reading Emily Dickinson's Letters: Critical Essays* (2009). Important studies include Paula Bennett's *Emily Dickinson: Woman Poet* (1990), Judith Farr's *The Passion of Emily Dickinson* (1992), Martha Nell Smith's *Rowing in Eden: Rereading Emily Dickinson* (1992), Sharon Cameron's *Choosing Not Choosing: Dickinson's Fascicles* (1993), Domhnall Mitchell's *Emily Dickinson: Monarch of Perception* (2000), Eleanor Elson Heginbotham's *Reading the Fascicles of Emily Dickinson* (2003), and Virginia Walker Jackson's *Dickinson's Misery: A Theory of Lyric Reading* (2005). For a lively engagement with Dickinson's poetry from a celebrated close reader, see Helen Vendler's *Dickinson: Poems and Commentaries* (2010).

Frederick Douglass

The definitive edition of Douglass's writings is under the editorship of John Blassingame and John R. McKivigan; six volumes have appeared since 1979. The Library of America's *Frederick Douglass: Autobiographies*, edited by Henry Louis Gates Jr., contains *Narrative of the Life of Frederick Douglass, An American Slave, Written by Himself* (1845), *My Bondage and My Freedom* (1855), and *Life and Times of Frederick Douglass* (1892). William L. Andrews's *The Oxford Frederick Douglass Reader* (1996) offers an excellent selection and a perceptive introduction. Philip S. Foner edited *The Life and Writings of Frederick Douglass* in five volumes (1950–75). In addition, Andrews and William S. McFeely have edited a Norton Critical Edition of the *Narrative* (1997).

The standard biography is William S. McFeely's *Frederick Douglass* (1991), but it should be supplemented by Benjamin Quarles's *Frederick Douglass* (1948), Dickson J. Preston's *Young Frederick Douglass* (1980), David W. Blight's *Frederick Douglass's Civil War* (1989), Maria Diedrich's *Love Across the Color Lines: Ottilie Assing and Frederick Douglass* (1999), and John Stauffer's *Giants: The Parallel Lives of Frederick Douglass and Abraham Lincoln* (2008). Waldo E. Martin Jr.'s *The Mind of Frederick Douglass* (1984) offers a full-scale intellectual history and remains among the best books in Douglass studies.

Important essays on Douglass can be found in Eric J. Sundquist's *Frederick Douglass: New Literary and Historical Essays* (1990), William L. Andrews's *Critical Essays on Frederick Douglass* (1991), Bill E. Lawson and Frank M. Kirkland's *Frederick Douglass: A Critical Reader* (1999), Robert S. Levine and Samuel Otter's *Frederick Douglass and Herman Melville: Essays in Relation* (2008), and Maurice S. Lee's *The Cambridge Companion to Frederick Douglass* 2009). A useful reference work is *The Frederick Douglass Encyclopedia* (2010), edited by Julius E. Thompson, James L. Conyers Jr., and Nancy J. Dawson. Valuable critical studies include Houston A. Baker Jr.'s *Blues, Ideology, and Afro-American Literature* (1984), William L. Andrews's *To Tell a Free Story: The First Century of Afro-American Autobiography, 1760–1865* (1986), Eric J. Sundquist's *To Wake the Nations: Race in the Making of American Literature* (1993), John Ernest's *Resistance and Reformation in Nineteenth-Century African-American Literature* (1995), Robert S. Levine's *Martin Delany, Frederick Douglass, and the Politics of Representative Identity* (1997), Maggie M. Sale's *The Slumbering Volcano: American Slave Ship Revolts and the Production of Rebellious Masculinity* (1997), Maurice O. Wallace's *Constructing the Black Masculine: Identity and Ideality in African American Men's Literature and Culture, 1775–1995* (2002), William Jeremiah Moses's *Creative Conflict in African American Thought: Frederick Douglass, Alexander Crummell, Booker T. Washington, W. E. B. Du Bois, and Marcus Garvey* (2004), James Colaiaco's *Frederick Douglass and the Fourth of July* (2006), and Robert B. Stepto's *A Home Elsewhere: Rereading African American Classics in the Age of Obama* (2010).

Ralph Waldo Emerson

An outstanding achievement in Emerson scholarship is the edition of *Journals and Miscellaneous Notebooks*, 16 vols. (1960–82), edited by William H. Gilman et al. For a one-volume introduction to the journals, see Joel Porte's *Emerson in His Journals* (1982); a fuller selection is available in the Library of America's two-volume *Selected Journals* (2010), edited by Lawrence Rosenwald. Stephen E. Whicher, Robert E. Spiller, and Wallace E. Williams edited *The Early Lectures of Ralph Waldo Emerson*, 3 vols. (1959–72); Ronald A. Bosco and Joel Myerson edited *The Later Lectures of Ralph Waldo Emerson, 1843–1871* (2001). The *Complete Sermons of Ralph Waldo Emerson* (1989) is available in four volumes, under the editorship of Albert J. von Frank. Merton M. Sealts Jr. and Alfred R. Ferguson edited *"Nature": Origin, Growth, Meaning* (1969), which Sealts updated and revised (1979). Ralph L. Rusk and Eleanor M. Tilton edited the ten-volume *Letters* (1939, 1990–95); a welcome distillation is Joel Myerson's *Selected Letters of Ralph Waldo Emerson* (1997). Len Gougeon and Myerson edited *Emerson's Antislavery Writings* (1995); Joel Porte edited the Library of America's *Emerson: Essays and Lectures* (1993); and Kenneth S. Sachs edited *Political Writings / Emerson* (2008).

The most detailed biography is still Ralph L. Rusk's *The Life of Ralph Waldo Emerson* (1949), but see also Gay Wilson Allen's *Waldo Emerson* (1981) and especially Robert D. Richardson's *Emerson: The Mind on Fire* (1995). Phyllis Cole's *Mary Moody Emerson and the Origins of Transcendentalism: A Family History* (1998) explores the crucial influence of Emerson's aunt on his life and thought. Albert J. von Frank compiled *An Emerson Chronology* (1993); Joel Myerson edited *Emerson and Thoreau: The Contemporary Reviews* (1992) and prepared *Ralph Waldo Emerson: A Descriptive Bibliography* (1982); and Robert E. Burkholder edited *Ralph Waldo Emerson: An Annotated Bibliography of Criticism, 1980–1991* (1994).

For critical essays, see Burkholder and Myerson's *Critical Essays on Ralph Waldo Emerson* (1983), Lawrence Buell's *Ralph Waldo Emerson: A Collection of Critical Essays* (1993), Myerson's *A Historical Guide to Ralph Waldo Emerson* (1999), Ronald A. Bosco and Myerson's *Emerson Bicentennial Essays* (2006), Arthur S. Lothstein and Michael Brodrick's *New Morning: Emerson in the Twenty-first*

Century (2008), John Lysaker and William Rossi's *Emerson and Thoreau: Figures of Friendship* (2010), and Branka Arsić and Cary Wolfe's *The Other Emerson* (2010). Joel Porte and Saundra Morris edited both the *Cambridge Companion to Ralph Waldo Emerson* (1999) and the Norton Critical Edition of *Ralph Waldo Emerson: Prose and Poetry* (2001). Important critical studies include Len Gougeon's *Virtue's Hero: Emerson, Antislavery, and Reform* (1990), Christopher Newfield's *The Emerson Effect: Individualism and Submission in America* (1996), Eduardo Cadava's *Emerson and the Climates of History* (1997), Lawrence Buell's *Emerson* (2003), Kris Fresonke's *West of Emerson: The Design of Manifest Destiny* (2003), Joel Porte's *Consciousness and Culture: Emerson and Thoreau Reviewed* (2004), Randall Fuller's *Emerson's Ghosts: Literature, Politics, and the Making of Americanists* (2007), Neil Dolan's *Emerson's Liberalism* (2009), and Branka Arsić's *On Leaving: A Reading in Emerson* (2010).

Fanny Fern (Sarah Willis Parton)
The fullest selection of Fern's work is *Ruth Hall and Other Writings* (1986), edited by Joyce W. Warren (1986), who also wrote a biography, *Fanny Fern: An Independent Woman* (1992). Shedding light on Fern and her milieu is Thomas N. Baker's 1999 book on Fern's brother, *Sentiment and Celebrity: Nathaniel Parker Willis and the Trials of Literary Fame.* Good critical discussions can be found in Mary Kelley's *Private Woman, Public Stage: Literary Domesticity in Nineteenth-Century America* (1984), Susan K. Harris's *Nineteenth-Century American Women's Novels: Interpretive Strategies* (1990), Nina Baym's *Woman's Fiction: A Guide to Novels by and about Women in America, 1820–70* (1978, 1993), Nancy A. Walker's *Fanny Fern* (1993), Nicole Tonkovich's *Domesticity with a Difference: The Nonfiction of Catharine Beecher, Sarah J. Hale, Fanny Fern, and Margaret Fuller* (1997), Melissa J. Homestead's *American Women Authors and Literary Property, 1822–1869* (2005), and Laura Laffrado's *Uncommon Women: Gender and Representation in Nineteenth-Century U.S. Women's Writing* (2009).

Margaret Fuller
There are substantial collections of Fuller's writings: Bell Gale Chevigny's *The Woman and the Myth: Margaret Fuller's Life and Writings* (1976, 1994), Larry J. Reynolds and Susan Belasco Smith's *"These Sad but Glorious Days": Dispatches from Europe 1846–1850* (1992), Jeffrey Steele's *The Essential Margaret Fuller* (1992), Mary Kelley's *The Portable Margaret Fuller* (1994), and Judith Mattson Bean and Joel Myerson's *Margaret Fuller, Critic: Writings for the New-York Tribune, 1844–1846* (2000). Robert N. Hudspeth's edition of Fuller's *Letters* is complete in six volumes (1983–94). Susan Belasco Smith edited *Summer on the Lakes in 1843* (1990), and Larry J. Reynolds edited a Norton Critical Edition of *Woman in the Nineteenth Century* (1997). Madeleine B. Stern's pioneering *The Life of Margaret Fuller* (1942, 1991) should be supplemented by Joseph J. Deiss's *The Roman Years of Margaret Fuller* (1969) and Eve Kornfeld's *Margaret Fuller: A Brief Biography with Documents* (1997). The standard biography is now Charles Capper's *Margaret Fuller: An American Romantic Life*, vol. 1: *The Private Years* (1994), and vol. 2: *The Public Years* (2002); but see also Meg McGavran's *Margaret Fuller, Wandering Pilgrim* (2008). Myerson edited *Fuller in Her Own Time: A Biographical Chronicle of Her Life, Drawn from Recollections, Interviews, and Memoirs* (2008). Important criticism includes Christina Zwarg's *Feminist Conversations: Fuller, Emerson, and the Play of Reading* (1995), Jeffrey Steele's *Transfiguring America: Myth, Ideology, Mourning in Margaret Fuller's Writing* (2001), Bruce Mills's *Poe, Fuller, and the Mesmeric Arts* (2006), and Charles Capper and Cristina Giorcelli's edited collection, *Margaret Fuller: Transatlantic Crossings in a Revolutionary Age* (2007).

Frances Ellen Watkins Harper
The best introduction to Harper is Frances Smith Foster's *A Brighter Day Coming: A Frances Watkins Harper Reader* (1990). Maryemma Graham edited Harper's *Complete Poems* (1988), and Foster edited *Three Rediscovered Novels by Frances E. W. Harper* (2000) and Harper's *Iola Leroy* (1988). On the racial dynamics of "The Two Offers," see Gene Andrew Jarrett's *African American Literature beyond Race* (2006). Good critical commentary on Harper can be found in Hazel V. Carby's *Reconstructing Womanhood: The Emergence of the Afro-American Woman Novelist* (1987), Joan R. Sherman's *Invisible Poets: Afro-Americans of the Nineteenth Century* (1989), Foster's *Written by Herself: Literary Production of Early African-American Women Writers* (1993), Carla L. Peterson's *"Doers of the Word": African-American Women Speakers and Writers in the North (1830–1880)* (1995), John Ernest's *Resistance and Reformation in Nineteenth-Century African-American Literature* (1995), and Janet Sinclair Gray's *Race and Time: American Women's Poetics from Antislavery to Racial Modernity* (2004). For a biographical overview, see Melba Joyce Boyd's *Discovered Legacy: Politics and Poetics in the Life of Frances E. W. Harper, 1825–1911* (1994).

Nathaniel Hawthorne
The Centenary Edition of the Works of Nathaniel Hawthorne (1962–97), published by the

Ohio State University Press, is now complete and offers a comprehensive scholarly edition of Hawthorne's letters, journals, children's writings, romances, stories and sketches, and nonfiction. For a good selection from the voluminous notebooks, see Robert Milder and Randall Fuller's *The Business of Reflection: Hawthorne in His Notebooks* (2009). An excellent recent biography is Brenda Wineapple's *Hawthorne: A Life* (2003); this should be supplemented with James Mellow's *Nathaniel Hawthorne in His Times* (1980) and T. Walter Herbert's *Dearest Beloved: The Hawthornes and the Making of the Middle-Class Family* (1993). Also useful is Ronald A. Bosco and Jillmarie Murphy's *Hawthorne in His Own Time: A Biographical Chronicle of His Life, Drawn from Recollections, Interviews, and Memoirs* (2007).

John L. Idol and Buford Jones edited *Hawthorne: The Contemporary Reviews* (1994); see also B. Bernard Cohen's *The Recognition of Nathaniel Hawthorne* (1969), J. Donald Crowley's *Hawthorne: The Critical Heritage* (1970), and Gary Scharnhorst's *Nathaniel Hawthorne: An Annotated Bibliography of Comment and Criticism before 1900* (1988). For critical essays see Michael J. Colacurcio's *New Essays on "The Scarlet Letter"* (1985), Millicent Bell's *New Essays on Hawthorne's Major Tales* (1993), Claudia D. Johnson's *Understanding "The Scarlet Letter": A Student Casebook to Issues, Sources, and Historical Documents* (1995), John L. Idol Jr. and Melissa Ponder's *Hawthorne and Women: Engendering and Expanding the Hawthorne Tradition* (1999), Larry J. Reynolds's *A Historical Guide to Nathaniel Hawthorne* (2001), Richard H. Millington's *The Cambridge Companion to Nathaniel Hawthorne* (2004), Bell's *Hawthorne and the Real: Bicentennial Essays* (2005), and Jana L. Argersinger and Leland S. Person's *Hawthorne and Melville: Writing a Relationship* (2008). Person's Norton Critical Edition of *The Scarlet Letter and Other Writings* (2005) collects a wide range of primary and secondary texts; see also James McIntosh's Norton Critical Edition of *Nathaniel Hawthorne's Tales* (1987) and Robert S. Levine's Norton Critical Edition of *The House of the Seven Gables* (2006).

The scholarship on Hawthorne is rich and voluminous. A good starting point is Leland S. Person's *The Cambridge Introduction to Nathaniel Hawthorne* (2007). Important studies include Frederick Crews's *The Sins of the Fathers: Hawthorne's Psychological Themes* (1966), Michael Davitt Bell's *Hawthorne and the Historical Romance of New England* (1971), Nina Baym's *The Shape of Hawthorne's Career* (1976), Michael J. Colacurcio's *The Province of Piety: Moral History in Hawthorne's Early Tales* (1984), Richard Brodhead's *The School of Hawthorne* (1986), Baym's *The Scarlet Letter: A Reading* (1986), Gordon Hutner's *Secrets and Sympathy: Forms of Disclosure in Hawthorne's Novels* (1988), Sacvan Bercovitch's *The Office of the Scarlet Letter* (1991), Joel Pfister's *The Production of Personal Life: Class, Gender, and the Psychological in Hawthorne's Fiction* (1991), Richard H. Millington's *Practicing Romance: Narrative Form and Cultural Engagement in Hawthorne's Fiction* (1992), Samuel Chase Coale's *Mesmerism and Hawthorne* (1998), Clark Davis's *Hawthorne's Shyness: Ethics, Politics, and the Question of Engagement* (2005), and Larry J. Reynolds's *Devils and Rebels: The Making of Hawthorne's Damned Politics* (2008).

Washington Irving

The Complete Works of Washington Irving (1969–), organized under the editorship of Henry A. Pochmann, was continued by Herbert L. Kleinfield, then by Richard Dilworth Rust. The introductory essays to this edition provide an excellent history of Irving's career. Three volumes of Irving's writings are available in the Library of America series: *History, Tales, and Sketches* (1983), *Bracebridge Hall; Tales of a Traveller; The Alhambra* (1991), and *Three Western Narratives* (2004). The standard biographies are Stanley T. Williams's *Life of Washington Irving* (1935) and William L. Hedges's *Washington Irving: An American Study 1802–1832* (1965), though these need to be supplemented by Andrew Burstein's *The Original Knickerbocker: The Life of Washington Irving* (2007) and Brian Jay Jones's *Washington Irving: An American Original* (2008). On reception and critical debate, see Andrew B. Myers's *A Century of Commentary on the Works of Washington Irving* (1976), Edwin and Ralph M. Aderman's *Critical Essays on Washington Irving* (1990), and James Tuttleton's *Washington Irving: The Critical Reaction* (1993). An important study is Jeffrey Rubin-Dorsky's *Adrift in the Old World: The Psychological Pilgrimage of Washington Irving* (1988).

Harriet Jacobs

Jean Fagin Yellin's pioneering edition of *Incidents in the Life of a Slave Girl* (1987), with biography, interpretation, and annotation, has been reissued (2000) with Harriet's brother John S. Jacobs's 1861 "A True Tale of Slavery." Frances Smith Foster and Nellie Y. McKay edited a Norton Critical Edition of *Incidents* (2001). Yellin's *Harriet Jacobs: A Life* (2004) should remain the standard biography for some time to come. An essential resource is the two-volume *The Harriet Jacobs Family Papers* (2008), edited by Yellin et al. For critical discussion, see Rafia Zafar and Deborah M. Garfield's edited collection, *Harriet Jacobs and "Incidents in the Life of a Slave Girl": New Critical Essays* (1996). Additional commentary may be found in Valerie Smith's *Self-Discovery and Authority in Afro-American Narrative* (1987), Karen Sánchez-Eppler's *Touching Liberty: Abolition, Feminism, and the Politics of the Body* (1993), Frances Smith Foster's *Written by Herself: Literary Production by African American Women, 1746–1892* (1993), Jennifer Fleischner's *Mastering Slavery: Memory, Family, and Identity in Women's Slave Narratives* (1996), and Carla Kaplan's *The Erotics of Talk: Women's Writing and Feminist Paradigms* (1996). On Lydia Maria Child's editing of *Incidents*, see Carolyn L. Karcher's *Lydia Maria Child: A Cultural Biography* (1994) and Bruce Mills's *Cultural Reformations: Lydia Maria Child and the Literature of Reform* (1994).

Caroline Stansbury Kirkland
William S. Osborne's *Caroline M. Kirkland* (1972) was pioneering, as was Annette Kolodny's chapter on Kirkland in *The Land before Her: Fantasy and Experience of the American Frontiers, 1630–1860* (1984). For recent work, see Erika M. Kreger's "A Bibliography of Works by and about Caroline Kirkland," in *Tulsa Studies in Women's Literature* 17 (1999): 299–350; and Elizabeth C. Barnes's "The Politics of Vision in Caroline Kirkland's Frontier Fiction," in *Legacy* 20 (2003): 62–75. For an excellent edition with a useful introduction, see Sandra A. Zagarell's *A New Home—Who'll Follow? or, Glimpses of Western Life* (1990).

Abraham Lincoln
The most comprehensive collection is *The Collected Works of Abraham Lincoln* (1953), 9 vols., edited by Roy P. Basler et al. The best introductions to Lincoln as a writer are Andrew Delbanco's *The Portable Abraham Lincoln* (1992) and Fred Kaplan's *Lincoln: The Biography of a Writer* (2008). Books on Lincoln constitute a library in themselves. For a sampling, see Steven B. Oates's *With Malice toward None: The Life of Abraham Lincoln* (1977), James M. McPherson's *Abraham Lincoln and the Second American Revolution* (1990), Garry Wills's *Lincoln at Gettysburg: The Words That Remade America* (1992), Harry V. Jaffa's *A New Birth of Freedom: Abraham Lincoln and the Coming of the Civil War* (2000), John Channing Briggs's *Lincoln's Speeches Reconsidered* (2005), and John Stauffer's *Giants: The Parallel Lives of Frederick Douglass and Abraham Lincoln* (2008). Excellent recent edited collections include Harold Holzer's *The Lincoln Anthology: Great Writers on His Life and Legacy from 1860 to Now* (2008), Eric Foner's *Our Lincoln: New Perspectives on Lincoln and His World* (2008), and Henry Louis Gates Jr.'s *Lincoln on Race and Slavery* (2009).

Henry Wadsworth Longfellow
The fullest biography is still the two-volume *Life of Henry Wadsworth Longfellow* (1886–87), written and edited by the poet's brother, Samuel Longfellow; this should be supplemented by Charles C. Calhoun's *Longfellow: A Rediscovered Life* (2003). Andrew Hilen's *The Letters of Henry Wadsworth Longfellow* (1966–82) is invaluable, revealing much that Samuel Longfellow suppressed. Lawrence Buell edited *Selected Poems* (1988), and J. D. McClatchy edited the Library of America's *Henry Wadsworth Longfellow: Poems and Other Writings* (2000). Still useful are Edward Wagenknecht's edition of *Mrs. Longfellow: Selected Letters and Journals of Fanny Appleton Longfellow (1817–1861)* (1956), Newton Arvin's *Longfellow* (1963), and Wagenknecht's *Henry Wadsworth Longfellow, His Poetry and Prose* (1986). Important discussions of Longfellow and the literary marketplace may be found in William Charvat's *The Profession of Authorship in America, 1800–1870* (1968) and Christopher Irmscher's provocative *Longfellow Redux* (2006). For good introductions to Longfellow as a poet, see Dana Gioia, "Longfellow in the Aftermath of Modernism," in *The Columbia History of American Poetry* (1993), and Robert L. Gale's *A Henry Wadsworth Longfellow Companion* (2003).

Herman Melville
The Northwestern-Newberry Edition of *The Writings of Herman Melville* (1968–), edited by Harrison Hayford, Hershel Parker, and G. Thomas Tanselle, is standard. The Parker-Hayford revised and updated Norton Critical Edition of *Moby-Dick* (2001) contains much new documentary information. Dan McCall has a Norton Critical Edition of *Melville's Short Novels* (2002). Parker and Mark Niemayer have edited a Norton Critical Edition of *The Confidence-Man* (2nd edition, 2006). Jay Leyda's monumental compilation of documents, *The Melville Log* (1951; reprinted 1969, with a supplement), is being expanded by Parker. Parker's magisterial *Herman Melville: A Biography, 1819–1851* (1996) and *Herman Melville: A Biography, 1851–1891* (2002) provide a wealth of new information about Melville and his family. For a good shorter life, see Andrew Delbanco's *Melville: His World and Work* (2005). Stanton Garner's *The Civil War World of Herman Melville* (1993) remains of great value, and the "Historical Notes" in the Northwestern-Newberry volumes contain essential biographical, historical, and textual scholarship. Nineteenth-century biographical accounts are reprinted and analyzed in Merton M. Sealts Jr.'s *The Early Lives of Melville* (1974). Sealts's *Melville's Reading* (1988), primarily a list of books known to have been in Melville's possession, should be supplemented by Mary K. Bercaw's *Melville's Sources* (1987). Brian Higgins and Parker compiled *Herman Melville: The*

Contemporary Reviews (1995). Basic research tools are Higgins's *Herman Melville: An Annotated Bibliography, 1846–1930* (1979) and *Herman Melville: A Reference Guide, 1931–1960* (1987). See also Gail H. Coffler's *Melville's Allusions to Religion: A Comprehensive Index and Glossary* (2002).

Edited collections of critical essays and reviews provide excellent introductions to a range of Melville criticism; see John Bryant's *A Companion to Melville Studies* (1986), Robert Milder's *Critical Essays on Melville's "Billy Budd, Sailor"* (1989), Robert Burkholder's *Critical Essays on Herman Melville's "Benito Cereno"* (1992), Brian Higgins and Hershel Parker's *Critical Essays on Herman Melville's "Moby-Dick"* (1992), Myra Jehlen's *Herman Melville: A Collection of Critical Essays* (1994), John Bryant and Robert Milder's *Melville's Evermoving Dawn: Centennial Essays* (1997), Robert S. Levine's *The Cambridge Companion to Herman Melville* (1998), Donald Yannella's *New Essays on "Billy Budd"* (2002), Giles Gunn's *A Historical Guide to Herman Melville* (2005), Wyn Kelly's *A Companion to Herman Melville* (2006), John Bryant, Mary K. Bercaw, and Timothy Marr's *Ungraspable Phantom: Essays on Moby-Dick* (2006), Robert S. Levine and Samuel Otter's *Frederick Douglass and Herman Melville: Essays in Relation* (2008), Jana L. Argersinger and Leland S. Person's *Hawthorne and Melville: Writing a Relationship* (2008), and Samuel Otter and Geoffrey Sanborn's *Melville and Aesthetics* (2011). Visually stunning and illuminating are Robert K. Wallace's *Melville and Turner: Spheres of Love and Fright* (1992) and Elizabeth A. Schultz's *Unpainted to the Last: "Moby-Dick" and Twentieth-Century American Art* (1995). Among the most influential recent works in Melville studies are Wai-chee Dimock's *Empire for Liberty: Melville and the Poetics of Individualism* (1989), John Bryant's *Melville and Repose: The Rhetoric of Humor in the American Renaissance* (1993), Wyn Kelley's *Melville's City* (1996), Elizabeth Renker's *Strike through the Mask: Herman Melville and the Scene of Writing* (1996), Samuel Otter's *Melville's Anatomies* (1999), Robert Milder's *Exiled Royalties: Melville and the Life We Imagine* (2006), Hershel Parker's *Melville: The Making of the Poet* (2008), and Sterling Stuckey's *African Culture and Melville's Art: The Creative Process in "Benito Cereno" and "Moby-Dick"* (2009). A good starting point is Kelley's *Herman Melville: An Introduction* (2008).

Edgar Allan Poe

There is no complete modern scholarly edition of Poe, although there are a number of facsimile reprints of early editions as well as modern volumes of the poems edited by Floyd Stovall (1965) and Thomas O. Mabbott (1969). Burton R. Pollin continued Mabbott's long-projected edition of the *Collected Writings*; the first volume appeared in 1981. Patrick F. Quinn's Library of America *Edgar Allan Poe: Poetry and Tales* (1984) is an excellent one-volume collection; and G. R. Thompson's Library of America *Edgar Allan Poe: Essays and Revisions* (1984) makes many elusive documents readily available. See also G. R. Thompson's Norton Critical Edition of *The Selected Writings of Edgar Allan Poe* (2004) and Stuart Levine and Susan F. Levine's *Edgar Allan Poe, Critical Theory: The Major Documents* (2009). John W. Ostrom edited *The Letters of Edgar Allan Poe* (1966). Partly because of forgeries and calumnies by Poe's literary executor, Rufus Griswold, Poe biography has remained enmeshed in legends. John Carl Miller's *Building Poe Biography* (1977) lucidly traces the gradual emergence of knowledge about Poe. The best recent biography is Kenneth Silverman's *Edgar A. Poe* (1991), but that should be supplemented by Dwight Thomas and David K. Jackson's essential *The Poe Log: A Documentary Life of Edgar Allan Poe, 1809–1849* (1987) and Benjamin Franklin Fisher's *Poe in His Own Time: A Biographical Chronicle of His Life, Drawn from Recollections, Interviews, and Memoirs* (2010). J. R. Hammond's *An Edgar Allan Poe Chronology* (1998) is also useful. Two good handbooks are Frederick S. Frank and Anthony Magistrale's *The Poe Encyclopedia* (1997) and Dawn B. Sova's *Critical Companion to Edgar Allan Poe* (2007). Elizabeth Wiley prepared a *Concordance to the Poetry of Edgar Allan Poe* (1989).

Poe's early reputation is traced in Eric Carlson's *The Recognition of Edgar Allan Poe* (1966) and Jean Alexander's *Affidavits of Genius: Edgar Allan Poe and the French Critics, 1847–1924* (1971). Modern collections of criticism, such as I. M. Walker's *Edgar Allan Poe: The Critical Heritage* (1986), are largely superseded by Graham Clarke's four-volume *Edgar Allan Poe: Critical Assessments* (1991). Valuable recent collections include Kenneth Silverman's *New Essays on Poe's Major Tales* (1993), Shawn Rosenheim and Stephen Rachman's *The American Face of Edgar Allan Poe* (1995), Eric W. Carlson's *A Companion to Poe Studies* (1996), J. Gerald Kennedy's *A Historical Guide to Edgar Allan Poe* (2001), Kennedy and Liliane Weissberg's *Romancing the Shadow: Poe and Race* (2001), and Kevin J. Hayes's *The Cambridge Companion to Edgar Allan Poe* (2002). Recent studies include Jonathan Elmer's *Reading at the Social Limit: Affect, Mass Culture, and Edgar Allan Poe* (1995), Terence Whalen's *Edgar Allan Poe and the Masses: The Political Economy of Literature in Antebellum America* (1999), Meredith L. McGill's *American Literature and the Culture of Reprinting, 1834–1853* (2003), Scott Peeples's *The Afterlife of Edgar Allan Poe* (2004), Eliza Richards's *Gender and the Politics of Reception in Poe's Circle* (2004), Richard Kopley's *Edgar Allan Poe and the Dupin Mysteries* (2008), and Douglas Anderson's *Pictures of Ascent in the Fiction of Edgar Allan Poe* (2009). For good short introductions, see Benjamin F. Fisher's *The Cambridge Introduction to Edgar Allan Poe* (2008) and Kevin J. Hayes's *Edgar Allan Poe* (2009). Daniel Hoffman's *Poe Poe Poe Poe Poe Poe Poe* (1972) continues to entertain and instruct.

Jane Johnston Schoolcraft
The indispensable work is *The Sound the Stars Make Rushing through the Sky: The Writings of Jane Johnston Schoolcraft* (2007), edited by Robert Dale Parker. Parker's introduction and notes provide a wealth of valuable information. Broad biographical background is provided by Elizabeth Hambleton and Elizabeth W. Stoutamire, who edited *The John Johnston Family of Sault Ste. Marie* (1992). Mary Loeffelholz provides useful critical insights in *From School to Salon: Reading Nineteenth-Century American Women's Poetry* (2004), and Lavonne Brown Ruoff's "Early Native American Women Authors: Jane Johnston Schoolcraft, Sarah Winnemucca, S. Alice Callahan, E. Pauline Johnson, and Zitkala-Sa," in *Nineteenth-Century American Women Writers: A Critical Reader*, edited by Karen Kilcup (1998), offers a brief treatment.

Catharine Maria Sedgwick
Mary Kelley's 1987 edition of *Hope Leslie; or, Early Times in the Massachusetts* (1987) helped to stimulate new interest in Sedgwick. Other editions of Sedgwick's novels include *A New-England Tale; or, Sketches of New England Character and Manners* (1995), edited by Victoria Clements, and *The Linwoods* (2002), edited by Maria Karafilis. Mary E. Dewey's essential *Life and Letters of Catharine Maria Sedgwick* (1871) should be reprinted; it may be supplemented by *The Power of Her Sympathy: The Autobiography and Journal of Catharine Maria Sedgwick* (1993), edited by Mary Kelley. Excellent discussions of Sedgwick can be found in Christopher Castiglia's *Bound and Determined: Captivity, Culture-Crossing, and White Womanhood from Mary Rowlandson to Patty Hearst* (1996), Philip Gould's *Covenant and Republic: Historical Romance and the Politics of Puritanism* (1996), Melissa J. Homestead's *American Women Authors and Literary Property, 1822–69* (2005), and Ivy Schweitzer's *Perfecting Friendship: Politics and Affiliation in Early American Literature* (2006). See also Lucinda L. Damon-Bach and Victoria Clements's edited collection, *Catharine Maria Sedgwick: Critical Perspectives* (2003).

Lydia Howard Huntley Sigourney
The best introduction to Sigourney is Gary Kelly's comprehensive *Lydia Sigourney: Selected Poetry and Prose* (2008). See also Annie Finch's "The Sentimental Poetess in the World: Metaphor and Subject in Lydia Sigourney's Nature Poetry," *Legacy* 5 (1988): 3–18; and Mary G. DeJong's "Profile of Lydia Sigourney," *Legacy* 5 (1988): 35–43. Particularly useful are the chapters on Sigourney in Cheryl Walker's *The Nightingale's Burden: Women Poets and American Culture before 1900* (1982), Nina Baym's *American Women Writers and the Work of History* (1995), and Mary Loeffelholz's *From School to Salon: Reading Nineteenth-Century American Women's Poetry* (2004). Sigourney's autobiographical *Letters of Life* (1867) was reprinted in 1980. Gordon Sherman Haight's *Mrs. Sigourney, the Sweet Singer of Hartford* (1930) is informative but dated.

Harriet Beecher Stowe
The Writings of Harriet Beecher Stowe (1896, 1967), in sixteen volumes, though not complete, is comprehensive enough to represent Stowe's literary range. The Library of America's volume contains *Uncle Tom's Cabin, The Minister's Wooing*, and *Oldtown Folks* (1982). Elizabeth Ammons edited a Norton Critical Edition of *Uncle Tom's Cabin* (1994; 2nd edition 2010), and Joan D. Hedrick edited *The Oxford Harriet Beecher Stowe Reader* (1999). Stowe's second antislavery novel, *Dred: A Tale of the Great Dismal Swamp* (1856), is available in an edition edited by Robert S. Levine (2006). Bibliographical resources include Margaret Holbrook Hildreth's *Harriet Beecher Stowe: A Bibliography* (1976) and Jean Ashton's *Harriet Beecher Stowe: A Reference Guide* (1977).

Joan D. Hedrick's *Harriet Beecher Stowe: A Life* (1994) is the standard biography. Two earlier biographies focusing on Stowe's religious ideas remain useful: Robert Forrest Wilson's *Crusader in Crinoline* (1941) and Charles H. Foster's *The Rungless Ladder: Harriet Beecher Stowe and New England Puritanism* (1954, 1970). A good family biography is Milton Rugoff's *The Beechers: An American Family* (1981), which should be supplemented by Barbara A. White's *The Beecher Sisters* (2003). See also Susan Belasco's *Stowe in Her Own Time: A Biographical Chronicle of Her Life, Drawn from Recollections, Interviews, and Memoirs* (2009). Thomas R. Gossett's *"Uncle Tom's Cabin" and American Culture* (1985) is invaluable; see also Sarah Meer's *Uncle Tom Mania: Slavery, Minstrelsy, and Transatlantic Culture in the 1850s* (2005). Useful collections of critical essays include Elizabeth Ammons's *Critical Essays on Harriet Beecher Stowe* (1980); Eric Sundquist's *New Essays on "Uncle Tom's Cabin"* (1986); Mason L. Lowance Jr., Ellen E.

Wesbrook, and R. C. De Prospo's *The Stowe Debate: Rhetorical Strategies in "Uncle Tom's Cabin"* (1994); Cindy Weinstein's *The Cambridge Companion to Harriet Beecher Stowe* (2004); and Ammons's *Harriet Beecher Stowe's Uncle Tom's Cabin: A Casebook* (2007).

Specialized critical studies dealing wholly or in part with Stowe include Edwin Bruce Kirkham's *The Building of "Uncle Tom's Cabin"* (1977), Gillian Brown's *Domestic Individualism: Imagining Self in Nineteenth-Century America* (1992), Marianne Noble's *The Masochistic Pleasures of Sentimental Literature* (2000), and Susan M. Ryan's *The Grammar of Good Intentions: Race and the Antebellum Culture of Benevolence* (2003). Stephen Railton has developed a superb website, *Uncle Tom's Cabin and American Culture* <iath.virginia.edu/utc/>.

Henry David Thoreau

The Princeton Edition of Thoreau's writings (1971–) is standard. Of the volumes published so far, *Walden* (1971), edited by J. Lyndon Shanley, should be supplemented by Shanley's *The Making of "Walden"* (1957, 1966) and Jeffrey S. Cramer's *Walden: A Fully Annotated Edition* (2004). See also the Norton Critical Edition edited by William Rossi (3rd edition 2008). The Princeton Edition of Thoreau's writings includes the journals (1981–); for an excellent selection, see *I to Myself: An Annotated Selection from the Journal of Henry D. Thoreau* (2007), edited by Cramer. The bulk of Thoreau's letters can be found in Carl Bode and Walter Harding's *Correspondence of Henry David Thoreau* (1958), supplemented by Kenneth W. Cameron's *Companion to Thoreau's Correspondence* (1964). The Library of America has made available *Collected Essays and Poems* (2001), edited by Elizabeth Hall Witherell. Raymond R. Borst compiled *The Thoreau Log: A Documentary Life of Henry David Thoreau, 1817–1862* (1992); see also Richard Schneider's *Henry David Thoreau: A Documentary Volume* (2004). The most reliable narrative biography is still Walter Harding's *The Days of Henry Thoreau: A Biography* (1965); for an excellent intellectual biography, see Robert D. Richardson's *Henry Thoreau: A Life of the Mind* (1986).

Walter Harding's *Thoreau Handbook* (1959) was revised by Harding and Michael Meyer (1980). Essential is Robert Sattelmeyer's *Thoreau's Reading: A Study in Intellectual History with Bibliographical Catalogue* (1988). Gary Scharnhorst compiled *Henry David Thoreau: An Annotated Bibliography of Comment and Criticism before 1900* (1992). Thoreau's reputation is surveyed in Michael Meyer's *Several More Lives to Live: Thoreau's Political Reputation in America* (1977), Joel Myerson's *Emerson and Thoreau: The Contemporary Reviews* (1992), and Scharnhorst's *Henry David Thoreau: A Case Study in Canonization* (1993). Good collections of critical essays include Myerson's *The Cambridge Companion to Henry David Thoreau* (1995), William E. Cain's *A Historical Guide to Henry David Thoreau* (2000), Sandra Harbert Petrulionis and Laura Dassow Walls's *More Day to Dawn: Thoreau's "Walden" for the Twenty-first Century* (2007), Jack Turner's *A Political Companion to Henry David Thoreau* (2009), and John T. Lysaker and William Rossi's *Emerson and Thoreau: Figures of Friendship* (2010). Three critical books related by their interest in Thoreau's compositional process and literary professionalism are Stephen Adams and Donald Ross Jr.'s *Revising Mythologies: The Composition of Thoreau's Major Works* (1988), Steven Fink's *Prophet in the Marketplace: Thoreau's Development as a Professional Writer* (1992), and Robert Milder's *Reimagining Thoreau* (1995). Lawrence Buell's *The Environmental Imagination* (1995), which has a major section on Thoreau, is a classic in a new field of study; see also Robert F. Sayre's *Thoreau and the American Indians* (1977) and Walls's *Seeing New Worlds: Henry David Thoreau and Nineteenth-Century Natural Science* (1995). Recent critical work includes Alan D. Hodder's *Thoreau's Ecstatic Witness* (2001), Joel Porte's *Consciousness and Culture: Emerson and Thoreau Reviewed* (2004), David M. Robinson's *Natural Life: Thoreau's Worldly Transcendentalism* (2004), and Sharon Mariotti's *Thoreau's Democratic Withdrawal: Alienation, Participation, and Modernity* (2010). For an illuminating new perspective on Walden Pond, see Elise Virginia Lemire's *Black Walden: Slavery and Its Aftermath in Concord, Massachusetts* (2009).

Walt Whitman

The study of Whitman has been revolutionized by the *Walt Whitman Hypertext Archive* <whitman.archive.org>, directed by Kenneth M. Price and Ed Folsom. Before going to the printed sources listed below, students should explore this huge and superbly organized archive, which includes a lengthy and reliable biographical essay by Folsom and Price, all the known contemporary reviews, all the known photographs, the various editions of *Leaves of Grass* and other of Whitman's writings, and a current bibliography of scholarship and criticism.

The Collected Writings of Walt Whitman was under the general editorship of Gay Wilson Allen; part of this edition is *Walt Whitman: The Correspondence* (1961–69), a six-volume set with two supplements (1990–91), edited by Edwin H. Miller. Essential, in three volumes, is *"Leaves of Grass": A Textual Vario-*

rum of the Printed Poems (1980), edited by Sculley Bradley, Harold W. Blodgett, Arthur Golden, and William White; see also Michael Moon's Norton Critical Edition of *Leaves of Grass* (2002). Important documents can be found in *Notebooks and Unpublished Prose Manuscripts* (1984), edited by Edward P. Grier in six volumes. The first volume of Whitman's *Journalism*, edited by Herbert Bergman, Douglas A. Noverr, and Edward J. Recchia, appeared in 1998. For Whitman's temperance novel, *Franklin Evans, or The Inebriate: A Tale of the Times* (1842), see Christopher Castiglia and Glenn Hendler's informative edition (2007); and Ed Folsom has edited a new facsimile edition (2010) of Whitman's 1870 *Democratic Vistas*. Valuable editions of documentary materials include Joel Myerson's *Whitman in His Own Time: A Biographical Chronicle of His Life, Drawn from Recollections, Memoirs, and Interviews, Friends and Associates* (1991, rev. 2000), and Myerson's *Walt Whitman: A Documentary Volume* (2000). The last of nine volumes of Horace Traubel's *With Walt Whitman in Camden*, edited by Jeanne Chapman and Robert Macisaac, appeared in 1996; an excellent starting place is Gary Schmidgall's *Intimate with Walt: Selections from Whitman's Conversations with Horace Traubel, 1888–1892* (2001).

The standard biography is still Gay Wilson Allen's *The Solitary Singer* (1967). It should be supplemented by Justin Kaplan's *Walt Whitman: A Life* (1980), David S. Reynolds's *Walt Whitman's America: A Cultural Biography* (1995), Gary Schmidgall's *Walt Whitman: A Gay Life* (1998), Jerome Loving's *Walt Whitman: The Song of Himself* (1999), and Ed Folsom and Kenneth M. Price's *Re-scripting Walt Whitman: An Introduction to His Life and Work* (2005). On the Civil War period, see Roy Morris Jr.'s *The Better Angel: Walt Whitman in the Civil War* (2000), and Ted Genoways's *Walt Whitman and the Civil War* (2009); and for a good biographical and critical overview, see M. Jimmie Killingsworth's *The Cambridge Introduction to Walt Whitman* (2007).

On Whitman's critical reception, see Graham Clarke's four-volume *Walt Whitman: Critical Assessments* (1996) and Kenneth M. Price's *Walt Whitman: The Contemporary Reviews* (1996). Valuable collections of critical essays include Robert K. Martin's *The Continuing Presence of Walt Whitman: The Life after the Life* (1992); Gay Wilson Allen and Ed Folsom's *Walt Whitman and the World* (1995); Ezra Greenspan's *The Cambridge Companion to Walt Whitman* (1995); Betsy Erkkila and Jay Grossman's *Breaking Bounds: Whitman and American Cultural Studies* (1996); David S. Reynolds's *A Historical Guide to Walt Whitman* (2000); Donald D. Kummings's *A Companion to Walt Whitman* (2006); Susan Belasco, Ed Folsom, and Kenneth M. Price's *Leaves of Grass: The Sesquicentennial Essays* (2007); and David Haven Blake and Michael Robertson's *Walt Whitman: Where the Future Becomes Present* (2008). Important critical work includes Betsy Erkkila's *Whitman the Political Poet* (1989), Kenneth M. Price's *Whitman and Tradition* (1990), Michael Moon's *Disseminating Whitman: Revision and Corporeality in "Leaves of Grass"* (1991), Ezra Greenspan's *Walt Whitman and the American Reader* (1991), Ed Folsom's *Walt Whitman's Native Representations* (1994), Martin Klammer's *Whitman, Slavery, and the Emergence of "Leaves of Grass"* (1995), Vivian R. Pollack's *The Erotic Whitman* (2000), Jay Grossman's *Reconstituting the American Renaissance: Emerson, Whitman, and the Poetics of Representation* (2003), M. Wynn Thomas's *Transatlantic Connections: Whitman U.S., Whitman U.K.* (2005), David Haven Blake's *Walt Whitman and the Culture of American Celebrity* (2006), Michael Robertson's *Worshipping Whitman: The Whitman Disciples* (2008), and Edward Whitley's *American Bards: Walt Whitman and Other Unlikely Candidates for National Poet* (2010). Kenneth M. Price's *To Walt Whitman, America* (2004) traces Whitman's continuing impact on U.S. literary culture.

John Greenleaf Whittier

Brenda Wineapple has edited a recent collection of Whittier's *Selected Poems* (2004), but see also Robert Penn Warren's *John Greenleaf Whittier's Poetry: An Appraisal and a Selection* (1971). An interesting collection of Whittier's nonfiction is Edwin Harrison Cady and Harry Hayden Clark's *Whittier on Writers and Writing: The Uncollected Critical Writings* (1971). Samuel T. Pickard's *Life and Letters of John Greenleaf Whittier* (1894) was superseded by *John Greenleaf Whittier: Friend of Man* (1949), John B. Pickard's *John Greenleaf Whittier: An Introduction and Interpretation* (1961), Pickard's three-volume *Letters of John Greenleaf Whittier* (1975), and Roland H. Woodwell's *John Greenleaf Whittier: A Biography* (1985). For a bibliographical guide, see Albert J. von Frank's *Whittier: A Comprehensive Annotated Bibliography* (1976). Pickard edited a collection of criticism, *Memorabilia of John Greenleaf Whittier* (1968), but even more useful is Jayne K. Kribbs's *Critical Essays on John Greenleaf Whittier* (1980).

PERMISSIONS ACKNOWLEDGMENTS

IMAGE CREDITS

P. 11: The Library Company of Philadelphia; p. 17: Library of Congress; p. 79: American Antiquarian Society; p. 87: Granger Collection; p. 132: Old Sturbridge Village Museum; p. 216: Cranch, Christopher Pearse, 1813–92. Illustrations of the New Philosophy: drawings, [ca. 1837–39] (MS Am 1506). Houghton Library, Harvard University; p. 359: Library of Congress; p. 453: Library of Congress; p. 629: Library of Congress; p. 741: Bettmann/Corbis; p. 797: Bettmann/Corbis; p. 800: Bettmann/Corbis; p. 958: Image courtesy of Documenting the American South, The University of North Carolina at Chapel Hill Libraries; p. 980: Brown University Archives; p. 1173: NYPL Digital Gallery; p. 1291: Library Company of Philadelphia; p. 1312: Library of Congress; p. 1485: NYPL Digital Gallery; p. 1671: Fascicle 11; Wild nights-Wild nights! The Manuscript of Books of Emily Dickinson edited by R. W. Franklin. Vol.1, 1981. The Houghton Library/New York Public Library; p. 1751: Louisa May Alcott Collection, Hale Library Special Collections, Kansas State University.

COLOR INSERT CREDITS

Page C1: National Gallery of Art Washington; p. C2 (top): New York Public Library/Art Resource; (bottom): Smithsonian American Art Museum, Art Resource; p. C3 (both): New York Historical Society, Bridgeman Art Library; p. C4: Granger Collection; p. C5: The Detroit Institute of Arts, Bridgeman Art Library; p. C6: Ohio Historical Society; p. C7: National Gallery of Art Washington, Gift of Mrs. Huttleston Rogers; p. C8: Butler Institute of American Art/Bridgeman Art Library.

TEXT CREDITS

Mary Chesnut: From MARY CHESTNUT'S CIVIL WAR, ed. by C. Vann Woodward. Copyright © 1981 by C. Vann Woodward, Sally Bland Metts, Barbara G. Carpenter, Sally Bland Johnson and Katherine W. Herbert. Used by permission of the publisher, Yale University Press.

Emily Dickinson: Poems by Emily Dickinson are reprinted by permission of the publishers and the Trustees of Amherst College from THE POEMS OF EMILY DICKINSON: READING EDITION, Ralph W. Franklin, ed., Cambridge, Mass.: The Belknap Press of Harvard University Press. Copyright © 1998 by the President and Fellows of Harvard College. Copyright © 1951, 1955, 1979, 1983 by the President and Fellows of Harvard College. Correspondence with T. W. Higginson and Letter #238 by Emily Dickinson to Susan Huntington Gilbert Dickinson, Summer 1861, are reprinted by permission of the publishers from THE LETTERS OF EMILY DICKINSON, ed. by Thomas H. Johnson, L238, Cambridge, Mass.: The Belknap Press of Harvard University Press. Copyright © 1958, 1986 by the President and Fellows of Harvard College. Copyright 1914, 1924, 1932, 1942 by Martha Dickinson Bianchi; 1952 by Alfred Leete Hampson; 1960 by Mary L Hampson. Letter exchange with Susan Huntington Gilbert Dickinson on poem #124 from the Manuscript Division at Houghton Library, Harvard University, is reprinted with permission from OPEN ME CAREFULLY: EMILY DICKINSON'S INTIMATE LETTERS TO SUSAN HUNTINGTON DICKINSON, copyright © 1998 Ellen Louise Hart and Martha Nell Smith. Published by Paris Press.

Herman Melville: From THE PIAZZA TALES AND OTHER PROSE PIECES 1839–1860, ed. by Harrison Hayford et al. Copyright © 1987 by Northwestern University Press and The Newberry Library. From MOBY DICK, OR, THE WHALE, ed. by Harrison Hayford et al. Copyright © 1988 by Northwestern University Press and The Newberry Library. Reprinted by permission of the publisher, Northwestern University Press. BILLY BUDD, SAILOR, reading text, ed. by H. Hayford and M. M. Sealts, Jr. is reprinted by permission of the publisher, The University of Chicago Press. Copyright © 1962 by The University of Chicago. All rights reserved.

Jane Johnston Schoolcraft: "Moowis, the Indian Coquette" and "The Little Spirit, or Boy-Man" from THE SOUND THE STARS MAKE RUSHING THROUGH THE SKY, ed. by Robert Dale Parker (2006). Copyright © 2006 by the University of Pennsylvania Press. Reprinted with permission of the University of Pennsylvania Press.

Lorenzo de Zavala: From JOURNEY TO THE UNITED STATES OF NORTH AMERICA, tr. Wallace Woolsey, ed. John-Michael Rivera. Reprinted with permission from the publisher. Copyright © 2005 Arte Publico Press—University of Houston.

Index